GOOD Sp🏐rts

Home Team

by Sue Briggs-Pattison
and Bev Harvey
illustrated by Helen Jones

PiCTURE WiNDOW BOOKS
Minneapolis, Minnesota

Editor: Jill Kalz
Page Production: Melissa Kes
Creative Director: Keith Griffin
Editorial Director: Carol Jones

First American edition published in 2006 by
Picture Window Books
5115 Excelsior Boulevard
Suite 232
Minneapolis, MN 55416
877-845-8392
www.picturewindowbooks.com

First published in Australia by
Blake Education Pty Ltd
ACN 074 266 023
Locked Bag 2022
Glebe NSW 2037
Ph: (02) 9518 4222; Fax: (02) 9518 4333
E-mail: mail@blake.com.au
www.askblake.com.au
Text copyright © 2000 Bev Harvey and Sue Briggs-Pattison
Illustrations copyright © 2000 Blake Education
Illustrated by Helen Jones

Printed in the United States of America.

Library of Congress Cataloging-in-Publication Data
Briggs-Pattison, Sue.
Home team / by Sue Briggs-Pattison & Bev Harvey ; illustrated by
Helen Jones.
p. cm. — (Read-it! chapter books. Sports)
Summary: Emma has grown to hate netball because she thinks the coach
and other girls dislike her, but everything changes when she switches to a
new school and team.
ISBN 1-4048-1667-4 (hardcover)
[1. Netball—Fiction. 2. Sportsmanship—Fiction.] I. Harvey, Bev. II. Jones, Helen,
1953– ill. III. Title. IV. Series.
PZ7.B7647Hom 2005
[E]—dc22   2005027159

Table of Contents

Chapter 1
I Hate Netball

My name is Emma, and I live in Australia. Netball is the most popular women's sport here. It's kind of like basketball. Everybody loves netball—except me. I hate it. Last year, things were OK. But this year, I'm on a new team, and things are definitely not OK!

I can catch, I can throw, and I can play
defense. What I like doing most is shooting.
Last year, everyone took turns playing in
the goal circle.

This year, I have to play Wing Defense all of the time. I have to try to stop the other team's Wing Attack from passing to their shooters. I feel like I'm always a step behind. The Wing Attack is always so fast.

The position I really want to play is Goal Attack, "GA" for short. GA is right in the middle of the action, and you get to shoot!

Lisa, the captain of the team, plays GA, so I don't have a chance. This team just doesn't feel right. The other girls all stick together. None of my old friends are here.

My grandma says, "Think about how you feel. Then you will find out why you feel that way." Well, I know how I feel about netball!

9

Chapter 2
Begging and Yelling

I've tried everything to get out of playing. I've begged. I've yelled. I've cried. I even tried talking to Mom about how I feel. This time I'm going to tell her that the coach doesn't want me on the team.

"Mom, can I please quit netball?" I ask.

"No. I've spent a fortune on your uniform and fees. You'll have to finish the season," Mom says.

"But I hate it," I complain.

"Well, it's too late now. You'll be letting the team down if you quit," Mom says.

"How was I supposed to know the coach was rotten, and the girls on the team didn't want me? They're always laughing at me. They think I'm hopeless. And I always have to play Wing Defense!" I cry.

"Darling, they do want you. You're a good netballer," Mom says.

"How would you know?" I yell and stomp off to my bedroom.

"What's your problem, Sis?" a voice asks.

That's my brother, Monty. He keeps an
eye on me. My grandma lives with us, too.
I'm lucky I have Grandma. She's just like a
sister, only better. She knows more!

14

When I get upset, I sit in the dark and stare at the stars through the window above my bed. I can see a dark shape in the tree. It's my opossum! She's not really my pet, but I like to talk to her. She always listens.

At our first training session this season, the coach tripped me. She said it was an accident. I scraped my knee. There was blood everywhere, so I sat out and missed training. Then, because we had eight players the next Saturday, the coach didn't put me in at all!

As if the coach isn't bad enough, Lisa is worse. After I tripped, she came over and whispered, "You know, Emma, you're not good enough to play netball on my team."

Then she walked off. Her hips wiggled in her netball skirt. She thinks she owns the place.

Chapter 3

She Was Here First

Lisa and the other girls on the team have been friends forever. Why won't they be my friends?

What's wrong with me?

Am I too tall?

Am I boring?

Why won't they at least give me a chance?

My grandma says I'm better than they are anyway.

I like lying in my bedroom at night in the dark. It's so peaceful. And I talk to my special friend.

She scurries through the branches and stops on the tree beside my house. She loves that tree. It's her favorite. She doesn't live there, though. She lives in our attic. She's always waking us up, running through the attic, above the ceiling. But Grandma never wakes up.

Mom says she should plug up all the holes so that my opossum can't get in. She's right. My opossum doesn't belong in the attic. She belongs in the trees.

My oldest brother, Tom, wants to catch her.
He's always complaining about the noise.
I don't think it's fair.

My opossum was here first. It's her place, too.
She's got just as much right to be here as
we do.

Chapter 4
The Way Out

"Well, Emma, it's all set," my mom says.

"What is, Mom?" I ask.

"Last night, the boss from the factory called and offered me a job. A full-time job!" Mom says.

"Wow! That's great," I say.

"More money, more food, more clothes, and more fun," Mom says.

Mom continues, "The factory is just down the road from the Bagshot Primary School. It's a lovely school, a small school. How would you feel about changing schools? I could drop you off in the morning and pick you up after school. Think about it."

"That means I'll have to leave my friends and my teacher and my, my ... netball team!" I say.

Yes! This is sounding good! I won't have to put up with those netball girls anymore!

"OK, Mom," I say. "I don't have to think about it. I'll try it, just as long as I can still go to the same high school as Monty."

But then Mom gives me the worst news! She has signed me up for the Bagshot netball team. They didn't have enough players, so my mom said that I'd play.

My heart feels like it's sinking in my stomach one minute and sticking in my throat the next minute.

What if the new girls don't like me?

What if they think I am too tall or too slow or too hopeless?

Chapter 5
Practice Makes Perfect

It's times like this that I'm glad my cousins are always hanging around. With my four brothers and a few of my cousins, we have enough people to play half-court netball in our backyard.

I line up to play Wing Defense like I always do. Then my cousin Leah has the best idea ever.

"Emma, why don't you go in the goal circle? You'll be good at defending. You're tall," she says.

Leah is older than me. She knows how to play really well.

So, here I am, playing defense and loving it. Yes, you heard me. I am loving it! Jenny is so confused by my defense, she can't throw one goal. If I time it just right, I can get the rebounds.

At half time, we all change positions. I'm on attack. I race to catch the ball and land just inside the goal circle. Leah leaps up like a pro, so I have to aim and throw high as she tries to block the ball.

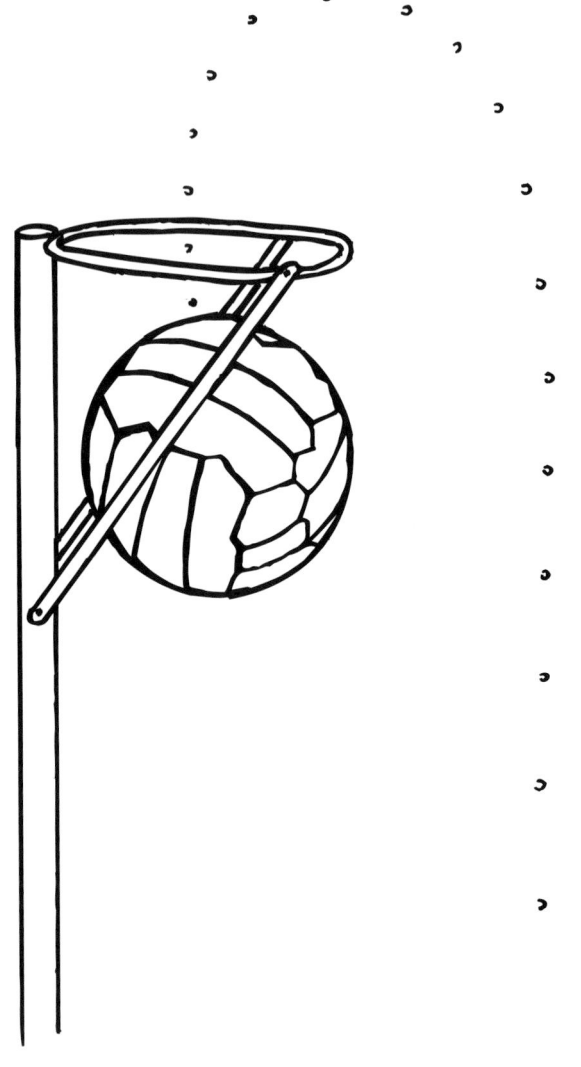

The ball makes it. A GOAL! It hardly even touches the ring! Everyone says it was a great shot.

Leah says I should be a goalie. She says that if I practice, I could be really good.

You know what? I think I just might.

Chapter 6

Where's Home?

Last night my opossum was really noisy. Mom has had enough. I can hear her up in the attic banging away, trying to fix the many holes.

My brother Tom says he's going to make a trap. He says he's going to find some forest far away from here and dump her. No way will I let him!

My opossum needs a home just as much as we do. This is her home. Maybe she doesn't belong in our attic, but she does belong in our trees. She must feel so unwanted. I know that feeling.

That gives me a brilliant idea! I will build her a home. She can have her own home in the trees instead of having to find shelter in our attic. I hope Monty will help me.

Chapter 7
Teaming Up with Bagshot

It's my first training session with my new team. I wish I could calm my nerves. I know Grandma says to "take notice of my feelings," but if I take any more notice of these feelings, I'll throw up!

Be cool, Emma.

Be confident, Emma.

Get it right, Emma.

Oh no, here comes the coach!

"Hi, Emma. We're so lucky you've joined us. If it wasn't for you, we wouldn't have a team," my new coach says.

"Gee, thanks," I say.

"Now, tell me, where do you like to play? What's your best position?" she asks.

Hey! No one ever asked me that before.

What do I say? I know the position I really want. I know how I feel.

"I think I'm good in the goals, either defense or attack," I say.

"Great, just what we need: a versatile player," Coach says.

What does the word "versatile" mean? I'll ask Grandma later.

I train well. I feel like I am good enough for the team. Every time I get the ball, they yell, "Em-ma! Em-ma! Em-ma!" It makes me feel good. I think the girls like me. I already know everyone's name.

Coach doesn't know where she'll put me on Saturday. She keeps saying how great it is that I'm so versatile.

I wish I had my dictionary. I'm dying to know what "versatile" means.

I don't want to get too excited just yet, but my new school is great. The kids are really friendly, and everyone's making me feel right at home. All of the girls play netball at lunchtime. And guess what? I'm one of them!

This afternoon, Monty and I finished my
opossum's house. We hung it in her
favorite tree.

Chapter 8

VERSATILE:

able to do or to be used for many different things

I love being versatile, and it feels great to be part of a team—a team that wants me, that is. I feel like I'm part of their family. Everyone says hello. Everyone's happy to see me.

Today is our first real game together. I plan to be versatile, just like the dictionary says.

One quarter, I play Goal Defense, and then I play Wing Defense. Best of all, for the last two quarters, I play Goal Shooter.

Wow! Me, a Goal Shooter! The Goal Attack shoots more goals than I do, but my team eventually wins.

Grandma and the rest of my family all
cheer and jump up and down. It sure feels
good! Mom says that it was just a matter
of finding the right spot for me, with the
right group.

Chapter 9

Coming Home

It's been so quiet. Where is she? I haven't seen my opossum for two nights. I hope Tom hasn't caught her.

I shine my flashlight up and down her tree
looking for her. I stop at the wooden box
we made. Monty put it in just the right
spot. Still nothing.

Then, just as the batteries in my flashlight start to run out, I see something. I strain my eyes. What is it? Yes! There she is. In the moonlight are her two little eyes shining down at me. She's inside the box!

What's this? Another pair of eyes? Two pairs of eyes! They both disappear back inside the box.

I'm so excited. I want to wake up Grandma
to tell her the news. But nothing ever
wakes Grandma.

My opossum has not only found a friend, but she has found a home as well!

Luckily, it is just the right size—for two!

Glossary

accident—an unfortunate event

confident—sure of oneself

fortune—a lot of money

netball—a team game that resembles basketball; goals are made by throwing a ball through a ring at the top of a pole

opossum—a little, furry night animal

scraped—took off the skin

scurries—moves quickly with little steps

Technical Terms

coach—the person responsible for training the team

defense—trying to stop the other team from scoring

position—each player's job on the team

rebounds—when someone gets the ball after it misses the ring and bounces back

season—the length of the competition

shoot—to throw for a goal

Wing Attack—position that tries to get the ball to the players on her team who score the goals

Wing Defense—position that tries to stop the opposing team's Wing Attack

Netball Court

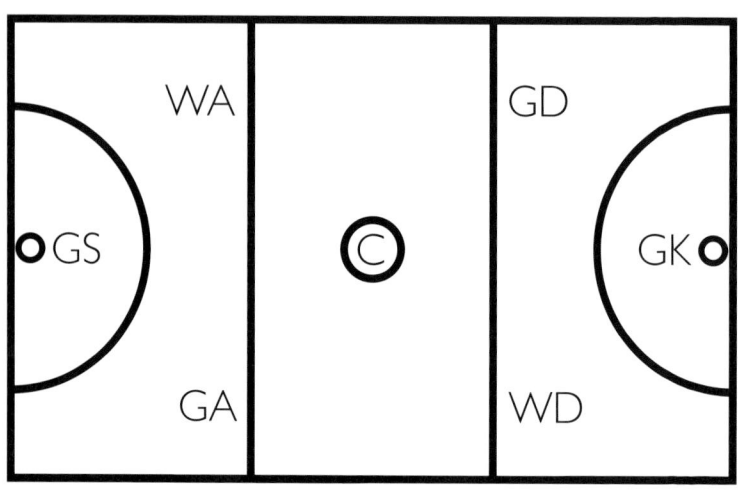

Equipment

lettered vest

team uniform

tennis shoes

netball

Basic Rules

- Players must not move with the ball.

- The ball must not be held for more than three seconds at a time.

- Each player has her own area in which to move.

- The game begins with the center pass.

- The court is divided into thirds, and the ball must be touched in each third. The ball cannot be thrown the length of the court without being touched.

GS — Goal Shooter

GA — Goal Attack

WA — Wing Attack

C — Center

WD — Wing Defense

GD — Goal Defense

GK — Goal Keeper

Training Tips

Pivot

When holding the ball, one foot must stay firmly in one spot. The other foot can move, so the player can turn on the spot.

Passes

- One-handed shoulder pass
- Overhead pass
- Bounce pass

If passing to someone on the move, pass the ball into the space ahead of the moving player.

Practice passing the ball in pairs. Slowly increase the pace.

Shooting a Goal

The ball should be released from as high of a position as possible.

Defending

Practice shadowing in pairs.

Footwork and Movement

Practice running and then stopping on the spot.

Practice rapid changes in speed.

When stopping quickly or landing from a jump, bend the knees to cushion the impact on the ankles.

Before throwing the ball, make sure the body is in a balanced position.

Practice moving forward and catching the ball.

Look for More
Read-it!
Chapter Books

Dash! Crash! Splash! 1-4048-1662-3

Horsing Around 1-4048-1666-6

Let Toby Lane Play Goalie 1-4048-1668-2

The Marathon Runner 1-4048-1669-0

The Super Electrics 1-4048-1663-1

Tennis Balls and Rotten Shrimp 1-4048-1664-X

Tomorrow's Olympian 1-4048-1665-8

Looking for a specific title?
A complete list of *Read-it!* Chapter Books
is available on our Web site:

www.picturewindowbooks.com

Pokémon BLACK VERSION 2

Pokémon WHITE VERSION 2

The Official National Pokédex & Guide:
Volume 2

The Ultimate PC Boxes

◀◀ 001-030 ▶▶

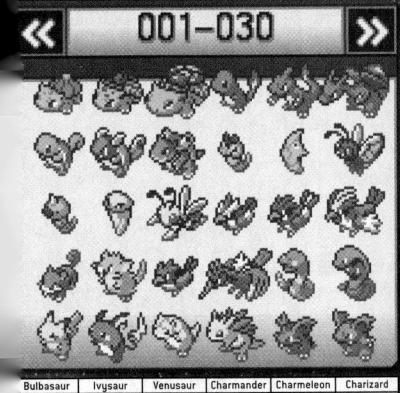

Bulbasaur	Ivysaur	Venusaur	Charmander	Charmeleon	Charizard
Squirtle	Wartortle	Blastoise	Caterpie	Metapod	Butterfree
Weedle	Kakuna	Beedrill	Pidgey	Pidgeotto	Pidgeot
Rattata	Raticate	Spearow	Fearow	Ekans	Arbok
Pikachu	Raichu	Sandshrew	Sandslash	Nidoran ♀	Nidorina

◀◀ 031-060 ▶▶

Nidoqueen	Nidoran ♂	Nidorino	Nidoking	Clefairy	Clefable
Vulpix	Ninetales	Jigglypuff	Wigglytuff	Zubat	Golbat
Oddish	Gloom	Vileplume	Paras	Parasect	Venonat
Venomoth	Diglett	Dugtrio	Meowth	Persian	Psyduck
Golduck	Mankey	Primeape	Growlithe	Arcanine	Poliwag

◀◀ 061-090 ▶▶

Poliwhirl	Poliwrath	Abra	Kadabra	Alakazam	Machop
Machoke	Machamp	Bellsprout	Weepinbell	Victreebel	Tentacool
Tentacruel	Geodude	Graveler	Golem	Ponyta	Rapidash
Slowpoke	Slowbro	Magnemite	Magneton	Farfetch'd	Doduo
Dodrio	Seel	Dewgong	Grimer	Muk	Shellder

◀◀ 181-210 ▶▶

Ampharos	Bellossom	Marill	Azumarill	Sudowoodo	Politoed
Hoppip	Skiploom	Jumpluff	Aipom	Sunkern	Sunflora
Yanma	Wooper	Quagsire	Espeon	Umbreon	Murkrow
Slowking	Misdreavus	Unown	Wobbuffet	Girafarig	Pineco
Forretress	Dunsparce	Gligar	Steelix	Snubbull	Granbull

◀◀ 211-240 ▶▶

Qwilfish	Scizor	Shuckle	Heracross	Sneasel	Teddiursa
Ursaring	Slugma	Magcargo	Swinub	Piloswine	Corsola
Remoraid	Octillery	Delibird	Mantine	Skarmory	Houndour
Houndoom	Kingdra	Phanpy	Donphan	Porygon2	Stantler
Smeargle	Tyrogue	Hitmontop	Smoochum	Elekid	Magby

◀◀ 241-270 ▶▶

Miltank	Blissey	Raikou	Entei	Suicune	Larvitar
Pupitar	Tyranitar	Lugia	Ho-Oh	Celebi	Treecko
Grovyle	Sceptile	Torchic	Combusken	Blaziken	Mudkip
Marshtomp	Swampert	Poochyena	Mightyena	Zigzagoon	Linoone
Wurmple	Silcoon	Beautifly	Cascoon	Dustox	Lotad

◀◀ 361-390 ▶▶

Snorunt	Glalie	Spheal	Sealeo	Walrein	Clamperl
Huntail	Gorebyss	Relicanth	Luvdisc	Bagon	Shelgon
Salamence	Beldum	Metang	Metagross	Regirock	Regice
Registeel	Latias	Latios	Kyogre	Groudon	Rayquaza
Jirachi	Deoxys Normal Forme	Turtwig	Grotle	Torterra	Chimchar

◀◀ 391-420 ▶▶

Monferno	Infernape	Piplup	Prinplup	Empoleon	Starly
Staravia	Staraptor	Bidoof	Bibarel	Kricketot	Kricketune
Shinx	Luxio	Luxray	Budew	Roserade	Cranidos
Rampardos	Shieldon	Bastiodon	Burmy Plant Cloak	Wormadam Plant Cloak	Mothim
Combee	Vespiquen	Pachirisu	Buizel	Floatzel	Cherubi

◀◀ 421-450 ▶▶

Cherrim	Shellos West Sea	Gastrodon West Sea	Ambipom	Drifloon	Drifblim
Buneary	Lopunny	Mismagius	Honchkrow	Glameow	Purugly
Chingling	Stunky	Skuntank	Bronzor	Bronzong	Bonsly
Mime Jr.	Happiny	Chatot	Spiritomb	Gible	Gabite
Garchomp	Munchlax	Riolu	Lucario	Hippopotas	Hippowdon

◀◀ 541-570 ▶▶

Swadloon	Leavanny	Venipede	Whirlipede	Scolipede	Cottonee
Whimsicott	Petilil	Lilligant	Basculin Red-Striped Form	Sandile	Krokorok
Krookodile	Darumaka	Darmanitan	Maractus	Dwebble	Crustle
Scraggy	Scrafty	Sigilyph	Yamask	Cofagrigus	Tirtouga
Carracosta	Archen	Archeops	Trubbish	Garbodor	Zorua

◀◀ 571-600 ▶▶

Zoroark	Minccino	Cinccino	Gothita	Gothorita	Gothitelle
Solosis	Duosion	Reuniclus	Ducklett	Swanna	Vanillite
Vanillish	Vanilluxe	Deerling Spring Form	Sawsbuck Spring Form	Emolga	Karrablast
Escavalier	Foongus	Amoonguss	Frillish ♂	Jellicent ♂	Alomomola
Joltik	Galvantula	Ferroseed	Ferrothorn	Klink	Klang

◀◀ 601-630 ▶▶

Klinklang	Tynamo	Eelektrik	Eelektross	Elgyem	Beheeyem
Litwick	Lampent	Chandelure	Axew	Fraxure	Haxorus
Cubchoo	Beartic	Cryogonal	Shelmet	Accelgor	Stunfisk
Mienfoo	Mienshao	Druddigon	Golett	Golurk	Pawniard
Bisharp	Bouffalant	Rufflet	Braviary	Vullaby	Mandibuzz

● To complete the National Pokédex, you'll need to register 636 species of Pokémon. There are thirteen species that are not counted toward this—Mew, Celebi, Jirachi, Deoxys, Phione, Manaphy, Darkrai, Shaymin, Arceus, Victini, Keldeo, Meloetta, and Genesect. You do not need to place every Pokémon in the PC Boxes like below, either. Black Kyurem and White Kyurem cannot be stored in the same Box.

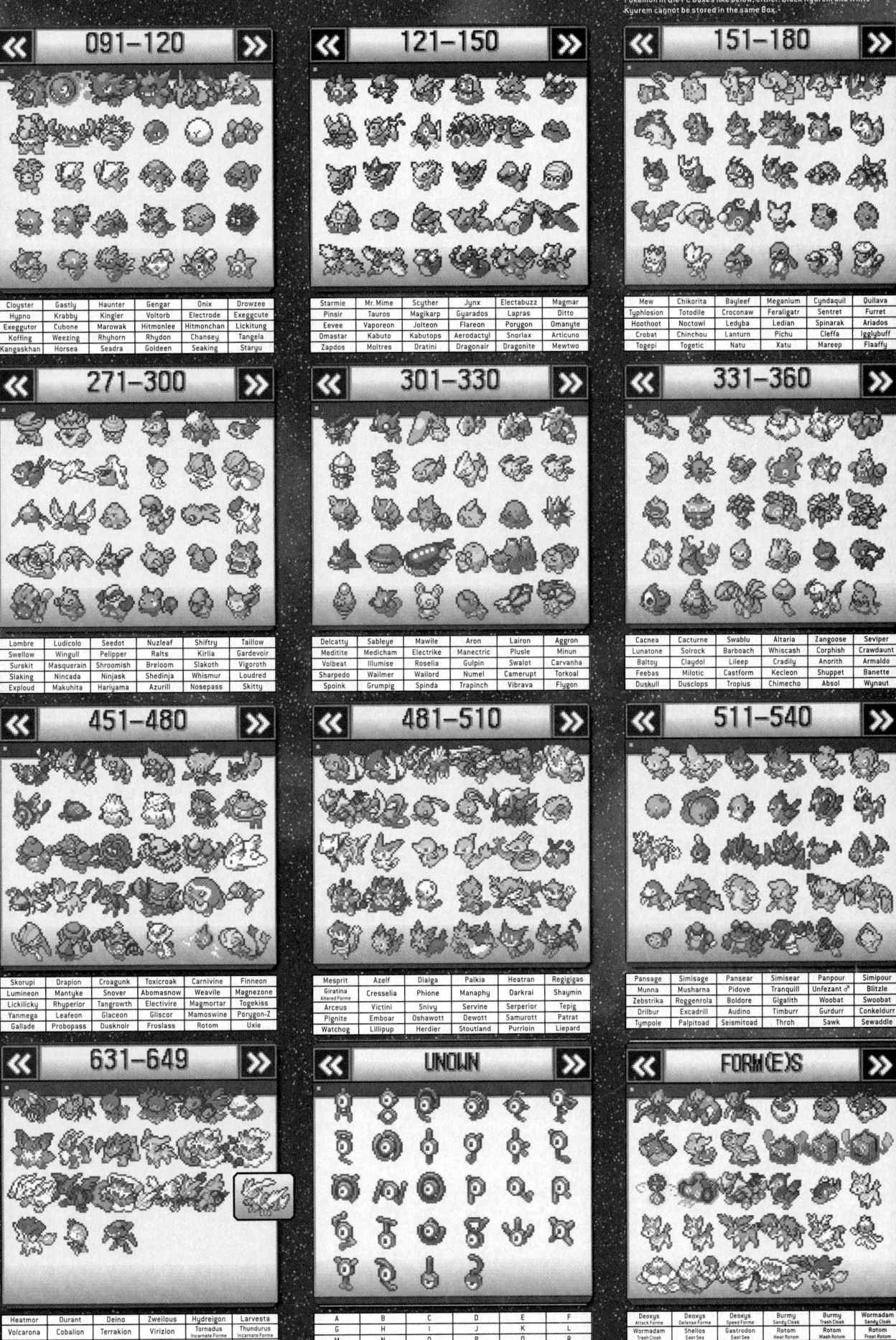

091–120

Cloyster	Gastly	Haunter	Gengar	Onix	Drowzee
Hypno	Krabby	Kingler	Voltorb	Electrode	Exeggcute
Exeggutor	Cubone	Marowak	Hitmonlee	Hitmonchan	Lickitung
Koffing	Weezing	Rhyhorn	Rhydon	Chansey	Tangela
Kangaskhan	Horsea	Seadra	Goldeen	Seaking	Staryu

121–150

Starmie	Mr. Mime	Scyther	Jynx	Electabuzz	Magmar
Pinsir	Tauros	Magikarp	Gyarados	Lapras	Ditto
Eevee	Vaporeon	Jolteon	Flareon	Porygon	Omanyte
Omastar	Kabuto	Kabutops	Aerodactyl	Snorlax	Articuno
Zapdos	Moltres	Dratini	Dragonair	Dragonite	Mewtwo

151–180

Mew	Chikorita	Bayleef	Meganium	Cyndaquil	Quilava
Typhlosion	Totodile	Croconaw	Feraligatr	Sentret	Furret
Hoothoot	Noctowl	Ledyba	Ledian	Spinarak	Ariados
Crobat	Chinchou	Lanturn	Pichu	Cleffa	Igglybuff
Togepi	Togetic	Natu	Xatu	Mareep	Flaaffy

271–300

Lombre	Ludicolo	Seedot	Nuzleaf	Shiftry	Taillow
Swellow	Wingull	Pelipper	Ralts	Kirlia	Gardevoir
Surskit	Masquerain	Shroomish	Breloom	Slakoth	Vigoroth
Slaking	Nincada	Ninjask	Shedinja	Whismur	Loudred
Exploud	Makuhita	Hariyama	Azurill	Nosepass	Skitty

301–330

Delcatty	Sableye	Mawile	Aron	Lairon	Aggron
Meditite	Medicham	Electrike	Manectric	Plusle	Minun
Volbeat	Illumise	Roselia	Gulpin	Swalot	Carvanha
Sharpedo	Wailmer	Wailord	Numel	Camerupt	Torkoal
Spoink	Grumpig	Spinda	Trapinch	Vibrava	Flygon

331–360

Cacnea	Cacturne	Swablu	Altaria	Zangoose	Seviper
Lunatone	Solrock	Barboach	Whiscash	Corphish	Crawdaunt
Baltoy	Claydol	Lileep	Cradily	Anorith	Armaldo
Feebas	Milotic	Castform	Kecleon	Shuppet	Banette
Duskull	Dusclops	Tropius	Chimecho	Absol	Wynaut

451–480

Skorupi	Drapion	Croagunk	Toxicroak	Carnivine	Finneon
Lumineon	Mantyke	Snover	Abomasnow	Weavile	Magnezone
Lickilicky	Rhyperior	Tangrowth	Electivire	Magmortar	Togekiss
Yanmega	Leafeon	Glaceon	Gliscor	Mamoswine	Porygon-Z
Gallade	Probopass	Dusknoir	Froslass	Rotom	Uxie

481–510

Mesprit	Azelf	Dialga	Palkia	Heatran	Regigigas
Giratina Altered Forme	Cresselia	Phione	Manaphy	Darkrai	Shaymin
Arceus	Victini	Snivy	Servine	Serperior	Tepig
Pignite	Emboar	Oshawott	Dewott	Samurott	Patrat
Watchog	Lillipup	Herdier	Stoutland	Purrloin	Liepard

511–540

Pansage	Simisage	Pansear	Simisear	Panpour	Simipour
Munna	Musharna	Pidove	Tranquill	Unfezant ♂	Blitzle
Zebstrika	Roggenrola	Boldore	Gigalith	Woobat	Swoobat
Drilbur	Excadrill	Audino	Timburr	Gurdurr	Conkeldurr
Tympole	Palpitoad	Seismitoad	Throh	Sawk	Sewaddle

631–649

Heatmor	Durant	Deino	Zweilous	Hydreigon	Larvesta
Volcarona	Cobalion	Terrakion	Virizion	Tornadus Incarnate Forme	Thundurus Incarnate Forme
Reshiram	Zekrom	Landorus Incarnate Forme	Kyurem	Kyurem Black Kyurem	Kyurem White Kyurem
Keldeo Ordinary Form	Meloetta	Genesect			

UNOWN

A	B	C	D	E	F
G	H	I	J	K	L
M	N	O	P	Q	R
S	T	U	V	W	X
Y	Z	!	?		

FORM(E)S

Deoxys Attack Forme	Deoxys Defense Forme	Deoxys Speed Forme	Burmy Trash Cloak	Burmy Sandy Cloak	Wormadam Sandy Cloak
Wormadam Trash Cloak	Shellos East Sea	Gastrodon East Sea	Rotom Heat Rotom	Rotom Wash Rotom	Rotom Frost Rotom
Rotom Fan Rotom	Rotom Mow Rotom	Giratina Origin Forme	Unfezant ♀	Basculin Blue-Striped Form	Deerling Summer Form
Deerling Autumn Form	Deerling Winter Form	Sawsbuck Summer Form	Sawsbuck Autumn Form	Sawsbuck Winter Form	Frillish ♀
Jellicent ♀	Tornadus Therian Forme	Thundurus Therian Forme	Landorus Therian Forme	Keldeo Resolute Form	

Unova Region Map

You can fly to the places marked with a bird Pokémon icon.

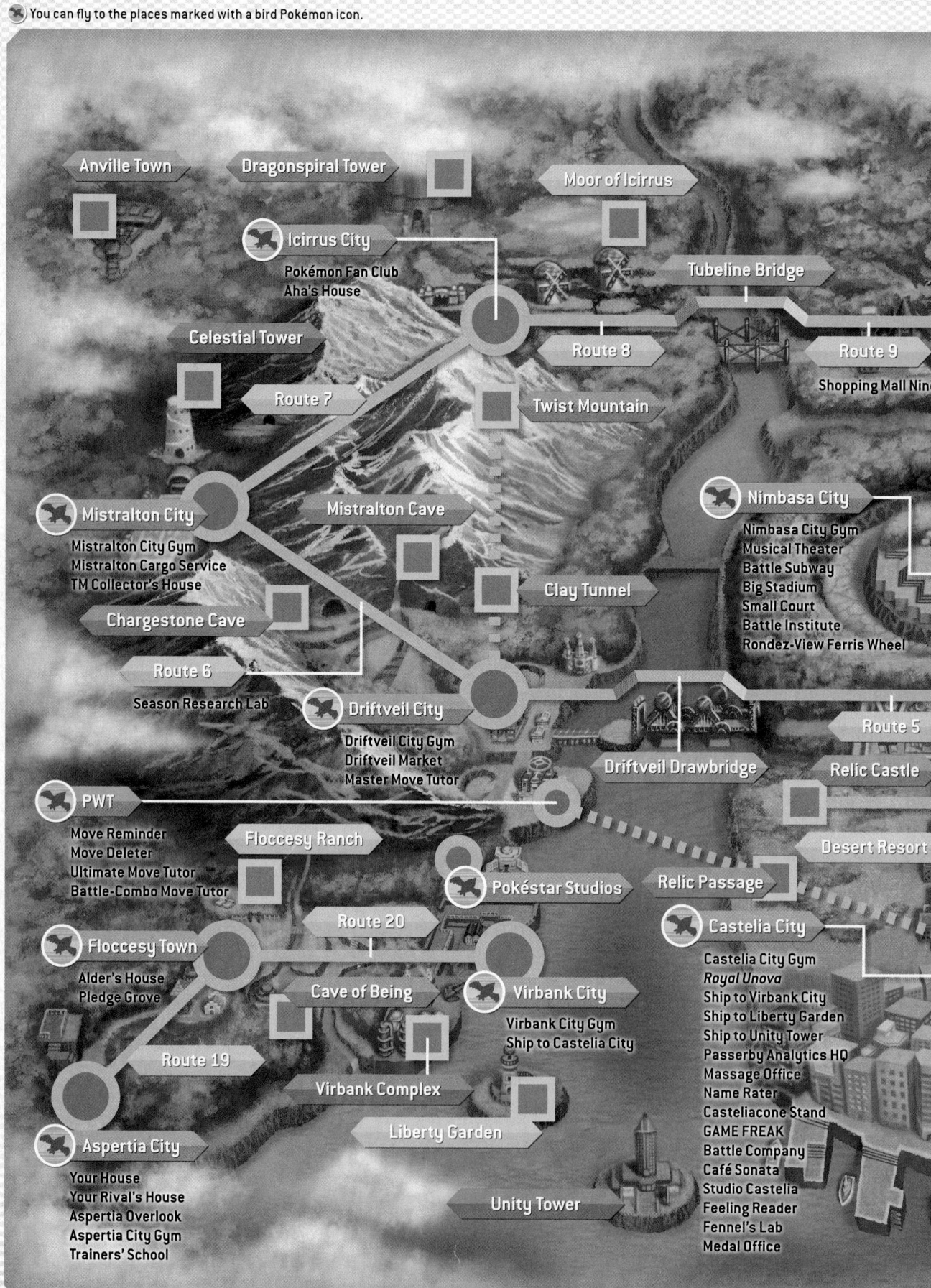

Anville Town

Dragonspiral Tower

Moor of Icirrus

Icirrus City
Pokémon Fan Club
Aha's House

Tubeline Bridge

Celestial Tower

Route 8

Route 9
Shopping Mall Nine

Route 7

Twist Mountain

Mistralton City
Mistralton City Gym
Mistralton Cargo Service
TM Collector's House

Mistralton Cave

Nimbasa City
Nimbasa City Gym
Musical Theater
Battle Subway
Big Stadium
Small Court
Battle Institute
Rondez-View Ferris Wheel

Clay Tunnel

Chargestone Cave

Route 6
Season Research Lab

Driftveil City
Driftveil City Gym
Driftveil Market
Master Move Tutor

Route 5

Driftveil Drawbridge

Relic Castle

PWT
Move Reminder
Move Deleter
Ultimate Move Tutor
Battle-Combo Move Tutor

Floccesy Ranch

Pokéstar Studios

Relic Passage

Desert Resort

Route 20

Castelia City
Castelia City Gym
Royal Unova
Ship to Virbank City
Ship to Liberty Garden
Ship to Unity Tower
Passerby Analytics HQ
Massage Office
Name Rater
Casteliacone Stand
GAME FREAK
Battle Company
Café Sonata
Studio Castelia
Feeling Reader
Fennel's Lab
Medal Office

Floccesy Town
Alder's House
Pledge Grove

Cave of Being

Virbank City
Virbank City Gym
Ship to Castelia City

Route 19

Virbank Complex

Aspertia City
Your House
Your Rival's House
Aspertia Overlook
Aspertia City Gym
Trainers' School

Liberty Garden

Unity Tower

This is the map of the Unova region, where your adventure awaits. All of the cities, towns, routes, caves, and other important places are shown. Make good use of it to complete the National Pokédex.

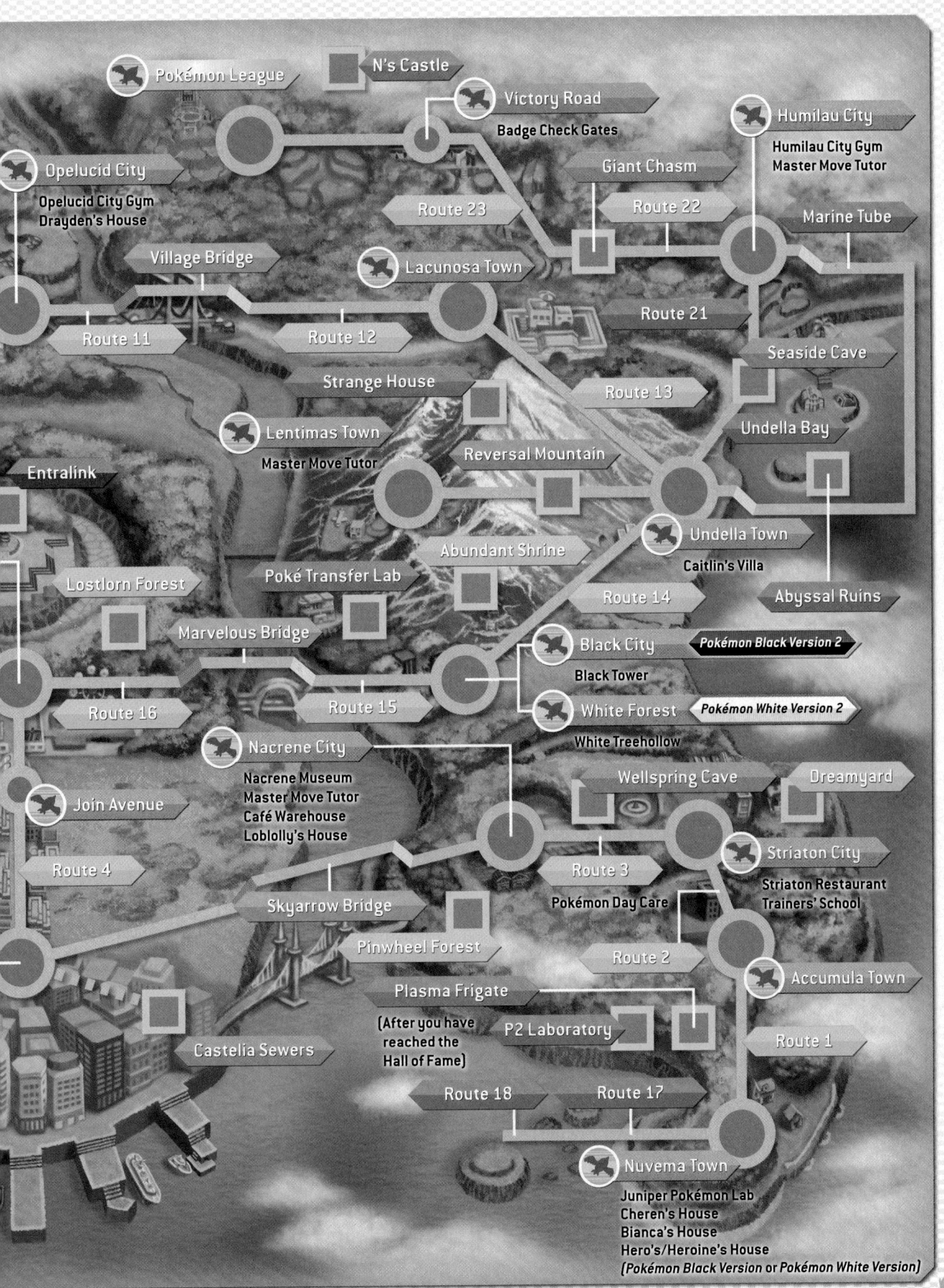

Pokémon League

N's Castle

Victory Road

Badge Check Gates

Humilau City

Humilau City Gym
Master Move Tutor

Opelucid City

Opelucid City Gym
Drayden's House

Giant Chasm

Route 23

Route 22

Marine Tube

Village Bridge

Lacunosa Town

Route 21

Route 11

Route 12

Seaside Cave

Strange House

Route 13

Undella Bay

Lentimas Town

Master Move Tutor

Reversal Mountain

Entralink

Abundant Shrine

Undella Town

Caitlin's Villa

Abyssal Ruins

Poké Transfer Lab

Route 14

Lostlorn Forest

Black City

Pokémon Black Version 2

Marvelous Bridge

Black Tower

White Forest

Pokémon White Version 2

Route 16

Route 15

White Treehollow

Nacrene City

Nacrene Museum
Master Move Tutor
Café Warehouse
Loblolly's House

Wellspring Cave

Dreamyard

Join Avenue

Striaton City

Striaton Restaurant
Trainers' School

Route 4

Route 3

Pokémon Day Care

Skyarrow Bridge

Route 2

Pinwheel Forest

Accumula Town

Plasma Frigate

(After you have
reached the
Hall of Fame)

P2 Laboratory

Route 1

Castelia Sewers

Route 18

Route 17

Nuvema Town

Juniper Pokémon Lab
Cheren's House
Bianca's House
Hero's/Heroine's House
(Pokémon Black Version or Pokémon White Version)

Pokémon Black Version 2 & Pokémon White Version 2 : The Official National Pokédex & Guide

National Pokédex

CONTENTS

Bonus! Get a Special Gothorita with the Shadow Tag Hidden Ability

Find the special password in the book and enter it in the Pokémon Global Link to get a Gothorita with the Shadow Tag Hidden Ability. Shadow Tag prevents the opponent from fleeing. Stop the opponent in its tracks and attack it with powerful moves like Psyshock and Future Sight.

Lv. 32

Gothorita ♂
Psychic

Gothorita's Moves

Move	Psyshock	Psychic
Move	Flatter	Dark
Move	Future Sight	Psychic
Move	Mirror Coat	Psychic

◆ Mirror Coat is normally learned as an Egg Move.   ◆ *Pokémon Black Version* and *Pokémon White Version* are not eligible to participate in this promotion.

National Pokédex

National Pokédex Guide

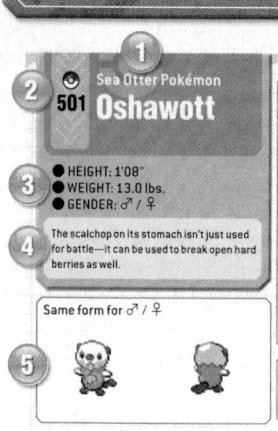

(1) Sea Otter Pokémon
501 Oshawott **(2)**

- HEIGHT: 1'08" **(3)**
- WEIGHT: 13.0 lbs.
- GENDER: ♂ / ♀

The scalchop on its stomach isn't just used for battle—it can be used to break open hard berries as well. **(4)**

Same form for ♂ / ♀

 **(5)**

Pokémon AR Marker **(14)**

TYPE	Water	**(8)**
ABILITY		**(9)**
● Torrent		
HIDDEN ABILITY		**(10)**

STATS **(11)**
- HP
- Attack
- Defense
- Sp. Atk
- Sp. Def
- Speed

EGG GROUPS **(12)**
Field

ITEMS SOMETIMES HELD **(6)**
● None

EVOLUTION **(7)**

Oshawott — Lv. 17 → Dewott — Lv. 36 → Samurott

HOW TO OBTAIN **(13)**

Pokémon Black Version 2	Get from Bianca at the start of the adventure
Pokémon White Version 2	Get from Bianca at the start of the adventure

HOW TO OBTAIN FROM OTHER GAMES

LEVEL-UP AND LEARNED MOVES **(15)**

	Name	Type	Kind	Pow.	Acc.	PP	Range	Long	DA
	Tackle	Normal	Physical	50	100	35	Normal	—	○
5	Tail Whip	Normal	Status	—	100	30	Many Others	—	—
11	Water Gun	Water	Special	40	100	25	Normal	—	○
13	Water Sport	Water	Status	—	—	15	Both Sides	—	—
13	Focus Energy	Normal	Status	—	—	30	Self	—	—
17	Razor Shell	Water	Physical	75	95	10	Normal	—	○
19	Fury Cutter	Bug	Physical	20	95	20	Normal	—	○
23	Water Pulse	Water	Special	60	100	20	Normal	○	—
25	Revenge	Fighting	Physical	60	100	10	Normal	—	○
29	Aqua Jet	Water	Physical	40	100	20	Normal	—	○
31	Encore	Normal	Status	—	100	5	Normal	—	—
35	Aqua Tail	Water	Physical	90	90	10	Normal	—	○
37	Retaliate	Normal	Physical	70	100	5	Normal	—	○
41	Swords Dance	Normal	Status	—	—	30	Self	—	—
43	Hydro Pump	Water	Special	120	80	5	Normal	—	○

TM & HM MOVES **(16)**

	Name	Type	Kind	Pow.	Acc.	PP	Range	Long	DA
TM06	Toxic	Poison	Status	—	90	10	Normal	—	—
TM07	Hail	Ice	Status	—	—	10	Both Sides	—	—
TM10	Hidden Power	Normal	Special	—	100	15	Normal	—	—
TM12	Taunt	Dark	Status	—	100	20	Normal	—	—
TM13	Ice Beam	Ice	Special	95	100	10	Normal	—	○
TM14	Blizzard	Ice	Special	120	70	5	Many Others	—	—
TM17	Protect	Normal	Status	—	—	10	Self	—	—
TM18	Rain Dance	Water	Status	—	—	5	Both Sides	—	—
TM21	Frustration	Normal	Physical	—	100	20	Normal	—	○
TM27	Return	Normal	Physical	—	100	20	Normal	—	○
TM28	Dig	Ground	Physical	80	100	10	Normal	—	○
TM32	Double Team	Normal	Status	—	—	15	Self	—	—
TM40	Aerial Ace	Flying	Physical	60	—	20	Normal	○	○
TM42	Facade	Normal	Physical	70	100	20	Normal	—	○
TM44	Rest	Psychic	Status	—	—	10	Self	—	—
TM45	Attract	Normal	Status	—	100	15	Normal	—	—
TM48	Round	Normal	Special	60	100	15	Normal	—	—
TM54	False Swipe	Normal	Physical	40	100	40	Normal	—	○
TM55	Scald	Water	Special	80	100	15	Normal	—	○
TM56	Fling	Dark	Physical	—	100	10	Normal	—	○
TM67	Retaliate	Normal	Physical	70	100	5	Normal	—	○
TM75	Swords Dance	Normal	Status	—	—	30	Self	—	—
TM81	X-Scissor	Bug	Physical	80	100	15	Normal	—	○
TM86	Grass Knot	Grass	Special	—	100	20	Normal	—	○
TM87	Swagger	Normal	Status	—	90	15	Normal	—	—
TM90	Substitute	Normal	Status	—	—	10	Self	—	—
TM94	Rock Smash	Fighting	Physical	40	100	15	Normal	—	○
HM01	Cut	Normal	Physical	50	95	30	Normal	—	○
HM03	Surf	Water	Special	95	100	15	Adjacent	—	○
HM05	Waterfall	Water	Physical	80	100	15	Normal	—	○
HM06	Dive	Water	Physical	80	100	10	Normal	—	○

MOVES TAUGHT BY PEOPLE **(17)**

Name	Type	Kind	Pow.	Acc.	PP	Range	Long	DA
Pledge	Water	Special	50	100	10	Normal	—	—

MOVES TAUGHT BY MOVE TUTORS FOR SHARDS **(18)**

Name	Type	Kind	Pow.	Acc.	PP	Range	Long	DA
	Normal	Physical	60	100	40	Normal	—	○
Icy Wind	Ice	Special	55	95	15	Many Others	—	—
Iron Tail	Steel	Physical	100	75	15	Normal	—	○
Aqua Tail	Water	Physical	90	90	10	Normal	—	○
Snore	Normal	Special	40	100	15	Normal	—	○
Helping Hand	Normal	Status	—	—	20	1 Ally	—	—
Sleep Talk	Normal	Status	—	—	10	Self	—	—

EGG MOVES **(19)**

Name	Type	Kind	Pow.	Acc.	PP	Range	Long	DA
	Normal	Status	—	—	20	Self	—	—
Detect	Fighting	Status	—	—	5	Self	—	—
Air Slash	Flying	Special	75	95	20	Normal	○	—
Assurance	Dark	Physical	50	100	10	Normal	—	○
Brine	Water	Special	65	100	10	Normal	—	○
Night Slash	Dark	Physical	70	100	15	Normal	—	○
Trump Card	Normal	Special	—	—	5	Normal	—	—
Screech	Normal	Status	—	85	40	Normal	—	—

---

1 Pokémon Category

The Pokémon's category tells you what kind of features it has.

2 National Pokédex Number

The National Pokédex number of the Pokémon. After entering the Hall of Fame, Cedric Juniper will upgrade your Unova Pokédex to the National Pokédex.

3 Height, Weight, and Gender

The height and weight of the Pokémon, as well as which genders, if any, the Pokémon has.

> There are still many, many Pokémon in this world.
>
> Sometimes Pokémon attack each other for food.
>
> Sometimes they help one another. They protect each other's places.
>
> I'd be happy if you think about things like that while looking at the Pokédex.

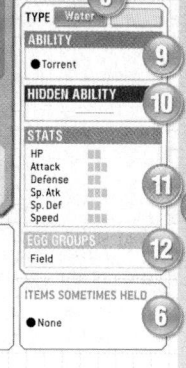

The Authority in the Field of Pokémon Research, Professor Cedric Juniper

4 Pokédex Entry

This is the summary of the Pokémon's characteristics given in the Pokédex. The content is the same for both *Pokémon Black Version 2* and *Pokémon White Version 2*.

5 In-Game Form

Here you can see how the Pokémon looks from both the front and the back. If the male and female have different appearances, they will be shown here. If the Pokémon can change Formes, each Forme will be shown here, too.

6 Items It May Be Holding When Encountered in the Wild

Some wild Pokémon will have a held item. The type of item that the Pokémon may be holding is shown. If you use a Poké Ball to catch that Pokémon when they have a held item, you will also receive the item.

7 Evolution

If the Pokémon evolves, this shows the course of evolution for the Pokémon as well as any conditions governing its evolution. For example, if it says "Lv. 17," that means the Pokémon will evolve when it reaches Level 17.

8 Type

The Pokémon's type. Some Pokémon have two types.

9 Abilities

The Pokémon's Ability. If two Abilities are listed, each individual Pokémon will have one of the two.

10 Hidden Ability

Some Pokémon have Hidden Abilities. Obtaining Pokémon with Hidden Abilities requires that you fulfill certain conditions, such as catching the Pokémon in a Hidden Grotto, or befriending the Pokémon over the Pokémon Global Link (p. 420).

11 Stat Levels

The levels of the Pokémon's stats are listed here. The stat levels are calculated by comparing the stat to the stats of other Pokémon in the National Pokédex. There are ten stat levels. The first five levels will be displayed in green, while stat levels of six to ten will be shown in red.

12 Egg Groups

The Egg Group the Pokémon belongs to. When two Egg Groups are listed, the Pokémon belongs to both (p. 369).

13 Main Ways to Add Pokémon to the National Pokédex

The main methods for adding Pokémon to the National Pokédex are shown. The areas listed correspond with the area names in the *Pokémon Black Version 2* and *Pokémon White Version 2*: The Official Pokémon Unova Strategy Guide. If the Pokémon needs to be transferred over from another game via Link Trade or by using the Poké Transfer, the game in which the Pokémon can be caught, and how to catch it, are shown.

14 Nintendo 3DS Download Software— *Pokédex 3D Pro* Pokémon AR Marker

The Pokémon AR Marker for the Nintendo 3DS download software—*Pokédex 3D Pro*—is shown here. Using the AR Viewer, point the Nintendo 3DS Camera at a Pokémon AR Marker to make the Pokémon appear as if it's in the real world.

15 Level-Up Moves

A list of the moves the Pokémon can learn by leveling up. Moves shown in red are new moves that have been newly added since the previous titles—*Pokémon Black Version* and *Pokémon White Version*. When the level at which the move is learned has changed, it will be shown in blue.

16 TM & HM Moves

A list of the moves the Pokémon can learn by using a TM or an HM. TMs and HMs do not go away once used, so they can be used to teach Pokémon moves as many times as you like. Moves that have been newly added since the previous titles—*Pokémon Black Version* and *Pokémon White Version*—will be shown in red.

17 Moves Taught by People

A list of moves that people can teach Pokémon. There are a total of seven different moves that people can teach to Pokémon. There are three ultimate moves, three battle-combo moves, and one other move that is the strongest Dragon-type move.

18 Moves That Can Be Learned by Giving Shards to the Master Move Tutor

A list of the moves that can be learned by giving Shards to the master Move Tutor. The master Move Tutor in Driftveil City will teach moves to Pokémon if you give him Red Shards. The master Move Tutor in Lentimas Town will teach moves to Pokémon if you give him Blue Shards. The master Move Tutor in Humilau City will teach moves to Pokémon if you give him Yellow Shards. The master Move Tutor in Nacrene City will teach moves to Pokémon if you give him Green Shards.

19 Egg Moves

These moves are occasionally learned by the Pokémon upon hatching from an Egg as long as they are known by the male Pokémon you left at the Pokémon Day Care (p. 367).

Move List Guide

Lv. ....The level at which the move can be learned

No. ....The TM or HM's number

Type ....The move's type

Kind ....Whether the move is a physical, special, or status move

Physical Move:	Does more damage the higher the Attack stat is.
Special Move:	Does more damage the higher the Sp. Atk stat is.
Status Move:	Changes stats or inflicts status conditions on the target(s).

Pow. ....The move's attack power

Acc. ....The move's accuracy

PP ....How many times the move can be used

Range ....The number and range of targets the move can affect

Long ....Whether the move is a long-range move that can affect faraway targets during a Triple Battle

DA ....Whether the move is a direct attack that makes direct contact with the target

Range Guide

■ **Normal:** The move affects the selected target. If the move is used by a Pokémon in the middle position during a Triple Battle, the move can target any of the other five Pokémon (including allies). If the move is used by a Pokémon in the left or right position, the move can target any of the three surrounding Pokémon (including its ally).

■ **Many Others:** The move affects multiple Pokémon at the same time. If the move is used by a Pokémon in the middle position during a Triple Battle, the move will affect all three opposing Pokémon. If the move is used by a Pokémon in the left or right position, the move will affect two opposing Pokémon.

■ **1 Random:** The move affects one of the opposing Pokémon at random.

■ **Adjacent:** The move affects the surrounding Pokémon at the same time. If the move is used by a Pokémon in the middle position during a Triple Battle, the move will affect the other five Pokémon (including allies) simultaneously. If the move is used by a Pokémon in the left or right position, the move will affect the three surrounding Pokémon (including its ally) simultaneously.

■ **1 Ally:** This move affects an adjacent ally. It has no effect in a Single Battle.

■ **Self/Ally:** The move affects the user or one of its allies at random. (In a Single Battle, it affects only the user.)

■ **Self:** The move affects only the user.

■ **Your Party:** The move affects your entire party, including Pokémon who are still in their Poké Balls.

■ **Other Side:** The move affects all Pokémon on the opponent's side of the field. Since the move affects the field, the move's effects continue even if the Pokémon are swapped out (except for moves that only work for one turn).

■ **Your Side:** The move affects all Pokémon on your side of the field. Since the move affects the field, the move's effects continue even if the Pokémon are swapped out (except for moves that only work for one turn).

■ **Both Sides:** The move affects all Pokémon on the field, regardless of which side they are on. Since the move affects the field, the move's effects continue even if the Pokémon are swapped out.

■ **Varies:** The move is influenced by things like the opposing Pokémon's move or the user's type, so the range is not fixed.

001 Bulbasaur

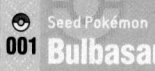

Seed Pokémon

001 Bulbasaur

- HEIGHT: 2'04"
- WEIGHT: 15.2 lbs.
- GENDER: ♂ / ♀

For some time after its birth, it grows by gaining nourishment from the seed on its back.

Same form for ♂ / ♀

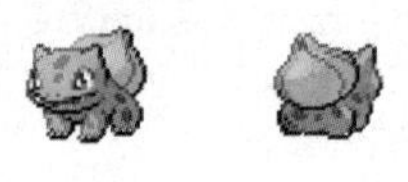

TYPE Grass Poison

ABILITY

- Overgrow

HIDDEN ABILITY

- Chlorophyll

STATS

HP
Attack
Defense
Sp. Atk
Sp. Def
Speed

EGG GROUPS

Monster/Grass

ITEMS SOMETIMES HELD

- None

EVOLUTION

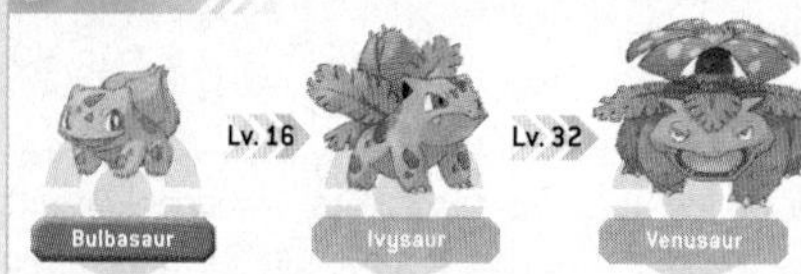

HOW TO OBTAIN

Pokémon Black Version 2	Link Trade or Poké Transfer
Pokémon White Version 2	Link Trade or Poké Transfer

HOW TO OBTAIN FROM OTHER GAMES

Pokémon HeartGold Version	Receive from Professor Oak in Pallet Town [after defeating Red]
Pokémon SoulSilver Version	Receive from Professor Oak in Pallet Town [after defeating Red]

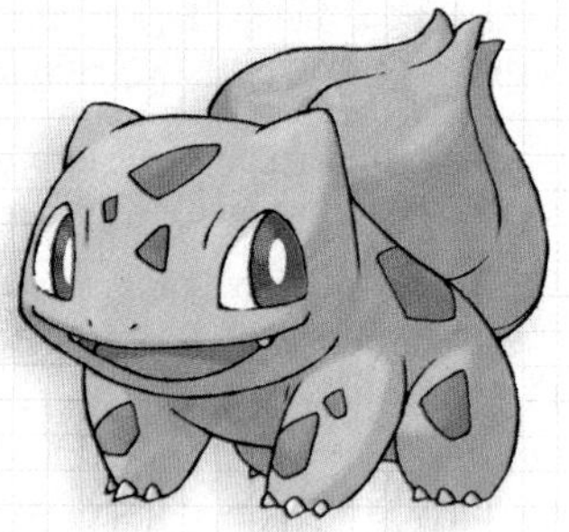

LEVEL-UP AND LEARNED MOVES

Lv.	Name	Type	Kind	Pow.	Acc.	PP	Range	Long	DA
1	Tackle	Normal	Physical	50	100	35	Normal	—	○
3	Growl	Normal	Status	—	100	40	Many Others	—	—
7	Leech Seed	Grass	Status	—	90	10	Normal	—	—
9	Vine Whip	Grass	Physical	35	100	15	Normal	—	○
13	PoisonPowder	Poison	Status	—	75	35	Normal	—	—
13	Sleep Powder	Grass	Status	—	75	15	Normal	—	—
15	Take Down	Normal	Physical	90	85	20	Normal	—	○
19	Razor Leaf	Grass	Physical	55	95	25	Many Others	—	—
21	Sweet Scent	Normal	Status	—	100	20	Many Others	—	—
25	Growth	Normal	Status	—	—	40	Self	—	—
27	Double-Edge	Normal	Physical	120	100	15	Normal	—	○
31	Worry Seed	Grass	Status	—	100	10	Normal	—	—
33	Synthesis	Grass	Status	—	—	5	Self	—	—
37	Seed Bomb	Grass	Physical	80	100	15	Normal	—	—

TM & HM MOVES

Lv.	Name	Type	Kind	Pow.	Acc.	PP	Range	Long	DA
TM06	Toxic	Poison	Status	—	90	10	Normal	—	—
TM09	Venoshock	Poison	Special	65	100	10	Normal	—	—
TM10	Hidden Power	Normal	Special	—	100	15	Normal	—	—
TM11	Sunny Day	Fire	Status	—	—	5	Both Sides	—	—
TM16	Light Screen	Psychic	Status	—	—	30	Your Side	—	—
TM17	Protect	Normal	Status	—	—	10	Self	—	—
TM20	Safeguard	Normal	Status	—	—	25	Your Side	—	—
TM21	Frustration	Normal	Physical	—	100	20	Normal	—	○
TM22	SolarBeam	Grass	Special	120	100	10	Normal	—	—
TM27	Return	Normal	Physical	—	100	20	Normal	—	○
TM32	Double Team	Normal	Status	—	—	15	Self	—	—
TM36	Sludge Bomb	Poison	Special	90	100	10	Normal	—	—
TM42	Facade	Normal	Physical	70	100	20	Normal	—	○
TM44	Rest	Psychic	Status	—	—	10	Self	—	—
TM45	Attract	Normal	Status	—	100	15	Normal	—	—
TM48	Round	Normal	Special	60	100	15	Normal	—	—
TM49	Echoed Voice	Normal	Special	40	100	15	Normal	—	—
TM53	Energy Ball	Grass	Special	80	100	10	Normal	—	—
TM70	Flash	Normal	Status	—	100	20	Normal	—	—
TM75	Swords Dance	Normal	Status	—	—	30	Self	—	—
TM86	Grass Knot	Grass	Special	—	100	20	Normal	—	○
TM87	Swagger	Normal	Status	—	90	15	Normal	—	—
TM90	Substitute	Normal	Status	—	—	10	Self	—	—
TM94	Rock Smash	Fighting	Physical	40	100	15	Normal	—	○
HM01	Cut	Normal	Physical	50	95	30	Normal	—	○
HM04	Strength	Normal	Physical	80	100	15	Normal	—	○

MOVES TAUGHT BY PEOPLE

Name	Type	Kind	Pow.	Acc.	PP	Range	Long	DA
Grass Pledge	Grass	Special	50	100	10	Normal	—	—

MOVES TAUGHT BY MOVE TUTORS FOR SHARDS

Name	Type	Kind	Pow.	Acc.	PP	Range	Long	DA
Seed Bomb	Grass	Physical	80	100	15	Normal	—	—
Bind	Normal	Physical	15	85	20	Normal	—	○
Snore	Normal	Special	40	100	15	Normal	—	—
Knock Off	Dark	Physical	20	100	20	Normal	—	○
Synthesis	Grass	Status	—	—	5	Self	—	—
Giga Drain	Grass	Special	75	100	10	Normal	—	—
Worry Seed	Grass	Status	—	100	10	Normal	—	—
Sleep Talk	Normal	Status	—	—	10	Self	—	—

EGG MOVES

Name	Type	Kind	Pow.	Acc.	PP	Range	Long	DA
Skull Bash	Normal	Physical	100	100	15	Normal	—	○
Charm	Normal	Status	—	100	20	Normal	—	—
Petal Dance	Grass	Special	120	100	10	1 Random	—	○
Magical Leaf	Grass	Special	60	—	20	Normal	—	—
GrassWhistle	Grass	Status	—	55	15	Normal	—	—
Curse	Ghost	Status	—	—	10	Varies	—	—
Ingrain	Grass	Status	—	—	20	Self	—	—
Nature Power	Normal	Status	—	—	20	Varies	—	—
Amnesia	Psychic	Status	—	—	20	Self	—	—
Leaf Storm	Grass	Special	140	90	5	Normal	—	—
Power Whip	Grass	Physical	120	85	10	Normal	—	○
Sludge	Poison	Special	65	100	20	Normal	—	—
Endure	Normal	Status	—	—	10	Self	—	—
Giga Drain	Grass	Special	75	100	10	Normal	—	—

Pokémon AR Marker

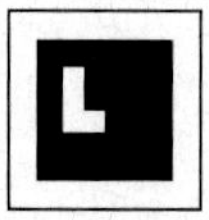

002 Ivysaur

Seed Pokémon

002 Ivysaur

- HEIGHT: 3'03"
- WEIGHT: 28.7 lbs.
- GENDER: ♂ / ♀

When the bud on its back starts swelling, a sweet aroma wafts to indicate the flower's coming bloom.

Same form for ♂ / ♀

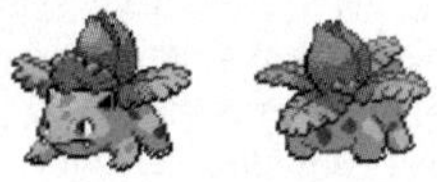

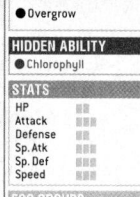

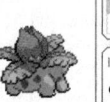

TYPE Grass Poison

ABILITY

- Overgrow

HIDDEN ABILITY

- Chlorophyll

STATS

HP
Attack
Defense
Sp. Atk
Sp. Def
Speed

EGG GROUPS

Monster/Grass

ITEMS SOMETIMES HELD

- None

EVOLUTION

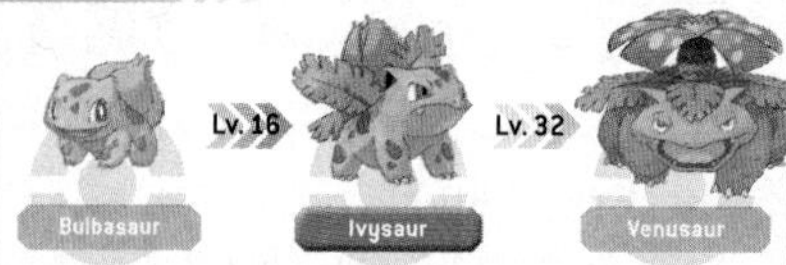

HOW TO OBTAIN

Pokémon Black Version 2	Level up a Bulbasaur you obtain via Link Trade or Poké Transfer to Lv. 16
Pokémon White Version 2	Level up a Bulbasaur you obtain via Link Trade or Poké Transfer to Lv. 16

HOW TO OBTAIN FROM OTHER GAMES

—
—

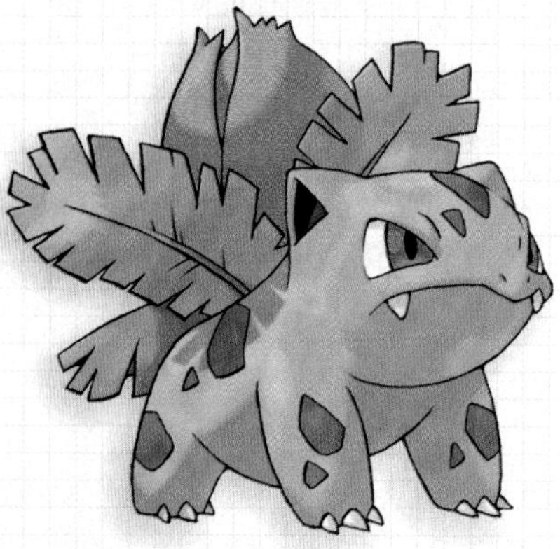

LEVEL-UP AND LEARNED MOVES

Lv.	Name	Type	Kind	Pow.	Acc.	PP	Range	Long	DA
1	Tackle	Normal	Physical	50	100	35	Normal	—	○
1	Growl	Normal	Status	—	100	40	Many Others	—	—
1	Leech Seed	Grass	Status	—	90	10	Normal	—	—
3	Growl	Normal	Status	—	100	40	Many Others	—	—
7	Leech Seed	Grass	Status	—	90	10	Normal	—	—
9	Vine Whip	Grass	Physical	35	100	15	Normal	—	○
13	PoisonPowder	Poison	Status	—	75	35	Normal	—	—
13	Sleep Powder	Grass	Status	—	75	15	Normal	—	—
15	Take Down	Normal	Physical	90	85	20	Normal	—	○
20	Razor Leaf	Grass	Physical	55	95	25	Many Others	—	—
23	Sweet Scent	Normal	Status	—	100	20	Many Others	—	—
28	Growth	Normal	Status	—	—	40	Self	—	—
31	Double-Edge	Normal	Physical	120	100	15	Normal	—	○
36	Worry Seed	Grass	Status	—	100	10	Normal	—	—
39	Synthesis	Grass	Status	—	—	5	Self	—	—
44	SolarBeam	Grass	Special	120	100	10	Normal	—	—

TM & HM MOVES

Lv.	Name	Type	Kind	Pow.	Acc.	PP	Range	Long	DA
TM06	Toxic	Poison	Status	—	90	10	Normal	—	—
TM09	Venoshock	Poison	Special	65	100	10	Normal	—	—
TM10	Hidden Power	Normal	Special	—	100	15	Normal	—	—
TM11	Sunny Day	Fire	Status	—	—	5	Both Sides	—	—
TM16	Light Screen	Psychic	Status	—	—	30	Your Side	—	—
TM17	Protect	Normal	Status	—	—	10	Self	—	—
TM20	Safeguard	Normal	Status	—	—	25	Your Side	—	—
TM21	Frustration	Normal	Physical	—	100	20	Normal	—	○
TM22	SolarBeam	Grass	Special	120	100	10	Normal	—	—
TM27	Return	Normal	Physical	—	100	20	Normal	—	○
TM32	Double Team	Normal	Status	—	—	15	Self	—	—
TM36	Sludge Bomb	Poison	Special	90	100	10	Normal	—	—
TM42	Facade	Normal	Physical	70	100	20	Normal	—	○
TM44	Rest	Psychic	Status	—	—	10	Self	—	—
TM45	Attract	Normal	Status	—	100	15	Normal	—	—
TM48	Round	Normal	Special	60	100	15	Normal	—	—
TM49	Echoed Voice	Normal	Special	40	100	15	Normal	—	—
TM53	Energy Ball	Grass	Special	80	100	10	Normal	—	—
TM70	Flash	Normal	Status	—	100	20	Normal	—	—
TM75	Swords Dance	Normal	Status	—	—	30	Self	—	—
TM86	Grass Knot	Grass	Special	—	100	20	Normal	—	○
TM87	Swagger	Normal	Status	—	90	15	Normal	—	—
TM90	Substitute	Normal	Status	—	—	10	Self	—	—
TM94	Rock Smash	Fighting	Physical	40	100	15	Normal	—	○
HM01	Cut	Normal	Physical	50	95	30	Normal	—	○
HM04	Strength	Normal	Physical	80	100	15	Normal	—	○

MOVES TAUGHT BY PEOPLE

Name	Type	Kind	Pow.	Acc.	PP	Range	Long	DA
Grass Pledge	Grass	Special	50	100	10	Normal	—	—

MOVES TAUGHT BY MOVE TUTORS FOR SHARDS

Name	Type	Kind	Pow.	Acc.	PP	Range	Long	DA
Seed Bomb	Grass	Physical	80	100	15	Normal	—	—
Bind	Normal	Physical	15	85	20	Normal	—	○
Snore	Normal	Special	40	100	15	Normal	—	—
Knock Off	Dark	Physical	20	100	20	Normal	—	○
Synthesis	Grass	Status	—	—	5	Self	—	—
Giga Drain	Grass	Special	75	100	10	Normal	—	—
Worry Seed	Grass	Status	—	100	10	Normal	—	—
Sleep Talk	Normal	Status	—	—	10	Self	—	—

Pokémon AR Marker

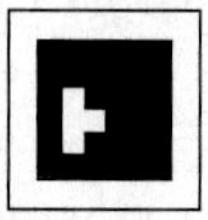

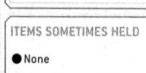

003 Venusaur

Seed Pokémon

- HEIGHT: 6'07"
- WEIGHT: 220.5 lbs.
- GENDER: ♂ / ♀

After a rainy day, the flower on its back smells stronger. The scent attracts other Pokémon.

♂ ♀

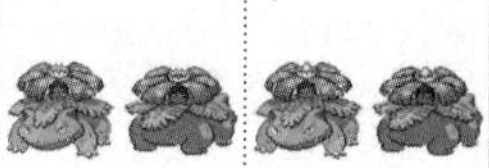

TYPE: Grass / Poison

ABILITY
- Overgrow

HIDDEN ABILITY
- Chlorophyll

STATS
HP
Attack
Defense
Sp. Atk
Sp. Def
Speed

EGG GROUPS
Monster/Grass

ITEMS SOMETIMES HELD
- None

EVOLUTION

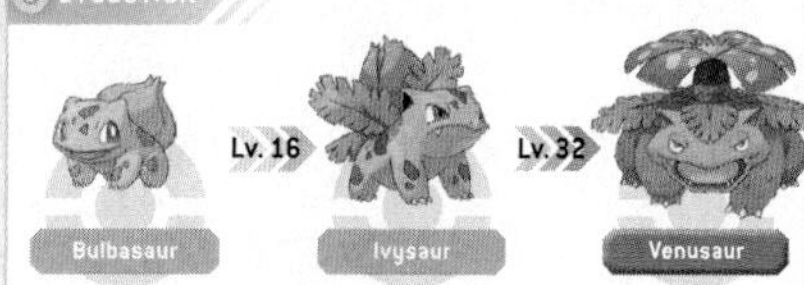
Lv. 16
Lv. 32
Bulbasaur
Ivysaur
Venusaur

HOW TO OBTAIN

Pokémon Black Version 2	Level up an Ivysaur you obtain via Link Trade or Poké Transfer to Lv. 32
Pokémon White Version 2	Level up an Ivysaur you obtain via Link Trade or Poké Transfer to Lv. 32

HOW TO OBTAIN FROM OTHER GAMES

—

—

LEVEL-UP AND LEARNED MOVES

Lv.	Name	Type	Kind	Pow.	Acc.	PP	Range	Long	DA
1	Tackle	Normal	Physical	50	100	35	Normal	—	○
1	Growl	Normal	Status	—	100	40	Many Others	—	—
1	Leech Seed	Grass	Status	—	90	10	Normal	—	—
1	Vine Whip	Grass	Physical	35	100	15	Normal	—	○
3	Growl	Normal	Status	—	100	40	Many Others	—	—
7	Leech Seed	Grass	Status	—	90	10	Normal	—	—
9	Vine Whip	Grass	Physical	35	100	15	Normal	—	○
13	PoisonPowder	Poison	Status	—	75	35	Normal	—	—
13	Sleep Powder	Grass	Status	—	75	15	Normal	—	—
15	Take Down	Normal	Physical	90	85	20	Normal	—	○
20	Razor Leaf	Grass	Physical	55	95	25	Many Others	—	—
23	Sweet Scent	Normal	Status	—	100	20	Many Others	—	—
28	Growth	Normal	Status	—	—	40	Self	—	—
31	Double-Edge	Normal	Physical	120	100	15	Normal	—	○
32	Petal Dance	Grass	Special	120	100	10	1 Random	—	○
39	Worry Seed	Grass	Status	—	100	10	Normal	—	—
45	Synthesis	Grass	Status	—	—	5	Self	—	—
53	SolarBeam	Grass	Special	120	100	10	Normal	—	—

TM & HM MOVES

Lv.	Name	Type	Kind	Pow.	Acc.	PP	Range	Long	DA
TM05	Roar	Normal	Status	—	100	20	Normal	—	—
TM06	Toxic	Poison	Status	—	90	10	Normal	—	—
TM09	Venoshock	Poison	Special	65	100	10	Normal	—	—
TM10	Hidden Power	Normal	Special	—	100	15	Normal	—	—
TM11	Sunny Day	Fire	Status	—	—	5	Both Sides	—	—
TM15	Hyper Beam	Normal	Special	150	90	5	Normal	—	—
TM16	Light Screen	Psychic	Status	—	—	30	Your Side	—	—
TM17	Protect	Normal	Status	—	—	10	Self	—	—
TM20	Safeguard	Normal	Status	—	—	25	Your Side	—	—
TM21	Frustration	Normal	Physical	—	100	20	Normal	—	○
TM22	SolarBeam	Grass	Special	120	100	10	Normal	—	—
TM26	Earthquake	Ground	Physical	100	100	10	Adjacent	—	—
TM27	Return	Normal	Physical	—	100	20	Normal	—	○
TM32	Double Team	Normal	Status	—	—	15	Self	—	—
TM36	Sludge Bomb	Poison	Special	90	100	10	Normal	—	—
TM42	Facade	Normal	Physical	70	100	20	Normal	—	○
TM44	Rest	Psychic	Status	—	—	10	Self	—	—
TM45	Attract	Normal	Status	—	100	15	Normal	—	—
TM48	Round	Normal	Special	60	100	15	Normal	—	—
TM49	Echoed Voice	Normal	Special	40	100	15	Normal	—	—
TM53	Energy Ball	Grass	Special	80	100	10	Normal	—	—
TM68	Giga Impact	Normal	Physical	150	90	5	Normal	—	○
TM70	Flash	Normal	Status	—	100	20	Normal	—	—
TM75	Swords Dance	Normal	Status	—	—	30	Self	—	—
TM78	Bulldoze	Ground	Physical	60	100	20	Adjacent	—	—
TM86	Grass Knot	Grass	Special	—	100	20	Normal	—	○
TM87	Swagger	Normal	Status	—	90	15	Normal	—	—
TM90	Substitute	Normal	Status	—	—	10	Self	—	—
TM94	Rock Smash	Fighting	Physical	40	100	15	Normal	—	○
HM01	Cut	Normal	Physical	50	95	30	Normal	—	○
HM04	Strength	Normal	Physical	80	100	15	Normal	—	○

MOVES TAUGHT BY PEOPLE

Name	Type	Kind	Pow.	Acc.	PP	Range	Long	DA
Grass Pledge	Grass	Special	50	100	10	Normal	—	—
Frenzy Plant	Grass	Special	150	90	5	Normal	—	—

MOVES TAUGHT BY MOVE TUTORS FOR SHARDS

Name	Type	Kind	Pow.	Acc.	PP	Range	Long	DA
Seed Bomb	Grass	Physical	80	100	15	Normal	—	—
Block	Normal	Status	—	—	5	Normal	—	—
Bind	Normal	Physical	15	85	20	Normal	—	○
Snore	Normal	Special	40	100	15	Normal	—	—
Knock Off	Dark	Physical	20	100	20	Normal	—	○
Synthesis	Grass	Status	—	—	5	Self	—	—
Giga Drain	Grass	Special	75	100	10	Normal	—	—
Worry Seed	Grass	Status	—	100	10	Normal	—	—
Outrage	Dragon	Physical	120	100	10	1 Random	—	○
Sleep Talk	Normal	Status	—	—	10	Self	—	—

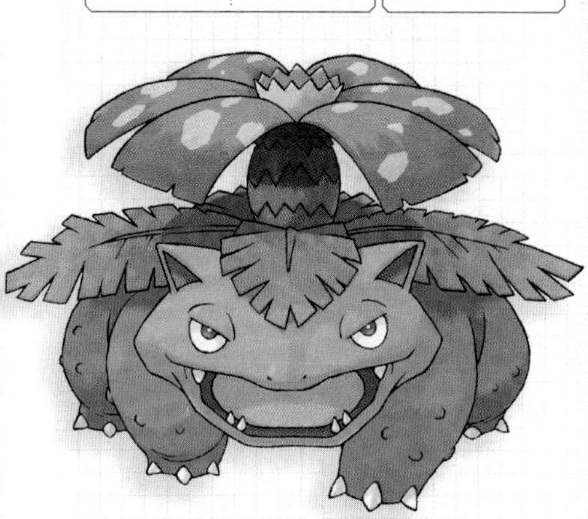

Pokémon AR Marker

004 Charmander

Lizard Pokémon

- HEIGHT: 2'00"
- WEIGHT: 14.3 lbs.
- GENDER: ♂ / ♀

The fire on the tip of its tail is a measure of its life. If healthy, its tail burns intensely.

Same form for ♂ / ♀

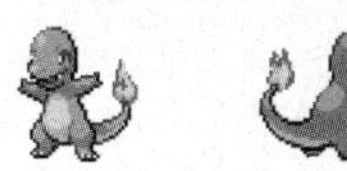

TYPE: Fire

ABILITY
- Blaze

HIDDEN ABILITY
- Solar Power

STATS
HP
Attack
Defense
Sp. Atk
Sp. Def
Speed

EGG GROUPS
Monster/Dragon

ITEMS SOMETIMES HELD
- None

EVOLUTION

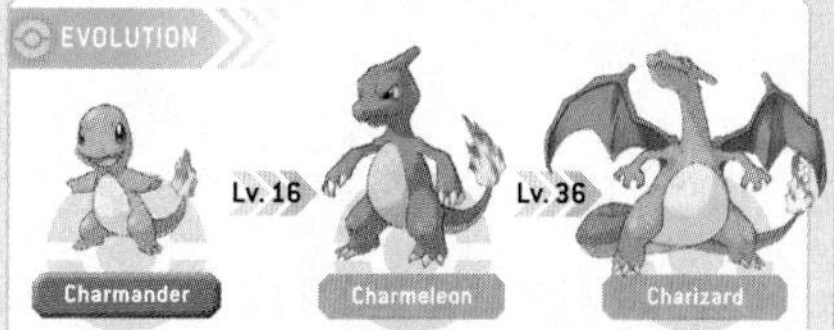
Lv. 16
Lv. 36
Charmander
Charmeleon
Charizard

HOW TO OBTAIN

Pokémon Black Version 2	Link Trade or Poké Transfer
Pokémon White Version 2	Link Trade or Poké Transfer

HOW TO OBTAIN FROM OTHER GAMES

Pokémon HeartGold Version	Receive from Professor Oak in Pallet Town (after defeating Red)
Pokémon SoulSilver Version	Receive from Professor Oak in Pallet Town (after defeating Red)

LEVEL-UP AND LEARNED MOVES

Lv.	Name	Type	Kind	Pow.	Acc.	PP	Range	Long	DA
1	Scratch	Normal	Physical	40	100	35	Normal	—	○
1	Growl	Normal	Status	—	100	40	Many Others	—	—
7	Ember	Fire	Special	40	100	25	Normal	—	—
10	SmokeScreen	Normal	Status	—	100	20	Normal	—	—
16	Dragon Rage	Dragon	Special	—	100	10	Normal	—	—
19	Scary Face	Normal	Status	—	100	10	Normal	—	—
25	Fire Fang	Fire	Physical	65	95	15	Normal	—	○
28	Flame Burst	Fire	Special	70	100	15	Normal	—	—
34	Slash	Normal	Physical	70	100	20	Normal	—	○
37	Flamethrower	Fire	Special	95	100	15	Normal	—	—
43	Fire Spin	Fire	Special	35	85	15	Normal	—	—
46	Inferno	Fire	Special	100	50	5	Normal	—	—

TM & HM MOVES

Lv.	Name	Type	Kind	Pow.	Acc.	PP	Range	Long	DA
TM01	Hone Claws	Dark	Status	—	—	15	Self	—	—
TM02	Dragon Claw	Dragon	Physical	80	100	15	Normal	—	○
TM06	Toxic	Poison	Status	—	90	10	Normal	—	—
TM10	Hidden Power	Normal	Special	—	100	15	Normal	—	—
TM11	Sunny Day	Fire	Status	—	—	5	Both Sides	—	—
TM17	Protect	Normal	Status	—	—	10	Self	—	—
TM21	Frustration	Normal	Physical	—	100	20	Normal	—	○
TM27	Return	Normal	Physical	—	100	20	Normal	—	○
TM28	Dig	Ground	Physical	80	100	10	Normal	—	○
TM31	Brick Break	Fighting	Physical	75	100	15	Normal	—	○
TM32	Double Team	Normal	Status	—	—	15	Self	—	—
TM35	Flamethrower	Fire	Special	95	100	15	Normal	—	—
TM38	Fire Blast	Fire	Special	120	85	5	Normal	—	—
TM39	Rock Tomb	Rock	Physical	50	80	10	Normal	—	—
TM40	Aerial Ace	Flying	Physical	60	—	20	Normal	○	○
TM42	Facade	Normal	Physical	70	100	20	Normal	—	○
TM43	Flame Charge	Fire	Physical	50	100	20	Normal	—	○
TM44	Rest	Psychic	Status	—	—	10	Self	—	—
TM45	Attract	Normal	Status	—	100	15	Normal	—	—
TM48	Round	Normal	Special	60	100	15	Normal	—	—
TM49	Echoed Voice	Normal	Special	40	100	15	Normal	—	—
TM50	Overheat	Fire	Special	140	90	5	Normal	—	—
TM56	Fling	Dark	Physical	—	100	10	Normal	—	—
TM59	Incinerate	Fire	Special	30	100	15	Many Others	—	—
TM61	Will-O-Wisp	Fire	Status	—	75	15	Normal	—	—
TM65	Shadow Claw	Ghost	Physical	70	100	15	Normal	—	○
TM75	Swords Dance	Normal	Status	—	—	30	Self	—	—
TM80	Rock Slide	Rock	Physical	75	90	10	Many Others	—	—
TM87	Swagger	Normal	Status	—	90	15	Normal	—	—
TM90	Substitute	Normal	Status	—	—	10	Self	—	—
TM94	Rock Smash	Fighting	Physical	40	100	15	Normal	—	○
HM01	Cut	Normal	Physical	50	95	30	Normal	—	○
HM04	Strength	Normal	Physical	80	100	15	Normal	—	○

MOVES TAUGHT BY PEOPLE

Name	Type	Kind	Pow.	Acc.	PP	Range	Long	DA
Fire Pledge	Fire	Special	50	100	10	Normal	—	—

MOVES TAUGHT BY MOVE TUTORS FOR SHARDS

Name	Type	Kind	Pow.	Acc.	PP	Range	Long	DA
Fire Punch	Fire	Physical	75	100	15	Normal	—	○
ThunderPunch	Electric	Physical	75	100	15	Normal	—	○
Iron Tail	Steel	Physical	100	75	15	Normal	—	○
Snore	Normal	Special	40	100	15	Normal	—	—
Heat Wave	Fire	Special	100	90	10	Many Others	—	—
Outrage	Dragon	Physical	120	100	10	1 Random	—	○
Sleep Talk	Normal	Status	—	—	10	Self	—	—

EGG MOVES

Name	Type	Kind	Pow.	Acc.	PP	Range	Long	DA
Belly Drum	Normal	Status	—	—	10	Self	—	—
AncientPower	Rock	Special	60	100	5	Normal	—	—
Bite	Dark	Physical	60	100	25	Normal	—	○
Outrage	Dragon	Physical	120	100	10	1 Random	—	○
Beat Up	Dark	Physical	—	100	10	Normal	—	—
Dragon Dance	Dragon	Status	—	—	20	Self	—	—
Crunch	Dark	Physical	80	100	15	Normal	—	○
Dragon Rush	Dragon	Physical	100	75	10	Normal	—	○
Metal Claw	Steel	Physical	50	95	35	Normal	—	○
Flare Blitz	Fire	Physical	120	100	15	Normal	—	○
Counter	Fighting	Physical	—	100	20	Varies	—	○
Dragon Pulse	Dragon	Special	90	100	10	Normal	○	—
Focus Punch	Fighting	Physical	150	100	20	Normal	—	○

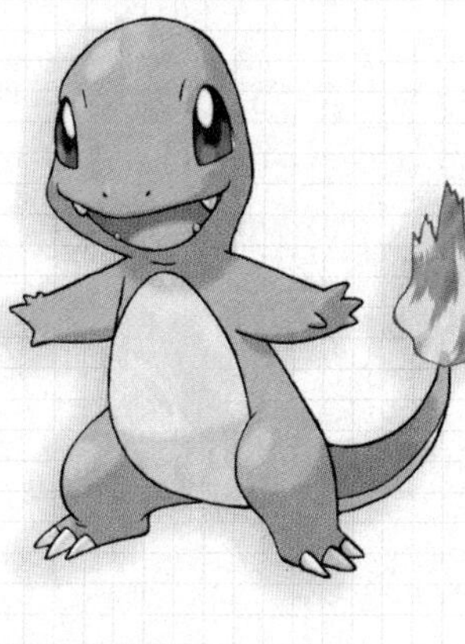

Pokémon AR Marker

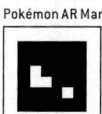

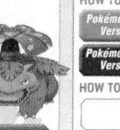

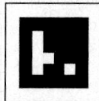

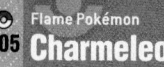

Flame Pokémon

005 Charmeleon

● HEIGHT: 3'07"
● WEIGHT: 41.9 lbs.
● GENDER: ♂ / ♀

In the rocky mountains where Charmeleon live, their fiery tails shine at night like stars.

Same form for ♂ / ♀

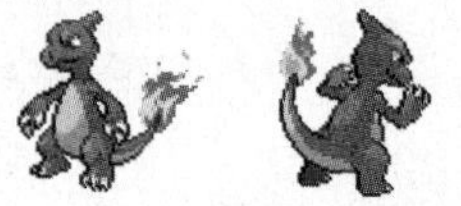

TYPE Fire

ABILITY
● Blaze

HIDDEN ABILITY
● Solar Power

STATS
HP
Attack
Defense
Sp. Atk
Sp. Def
Speed

EGG GROUPS
Monster/Dragon

ITEMS SOMETIMES HELD
● None

EVOLUTION

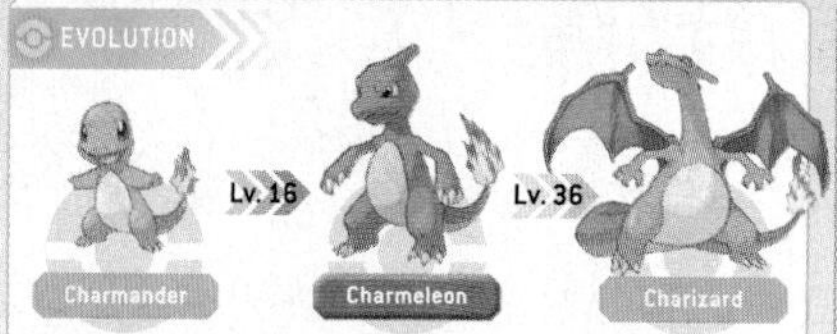

HOW TO OBTAIN

Pokémon Black Version 2	Level up a Charmander you obtain via Link Trade or Poké Transfer to Lv. 16
Pokémon White Version 2	Level up a Charmander you obtain via Link Trade or Poké Transfer to Lv. 16

HOW TO OBTAIN FROM OTHER GAMES

—

—

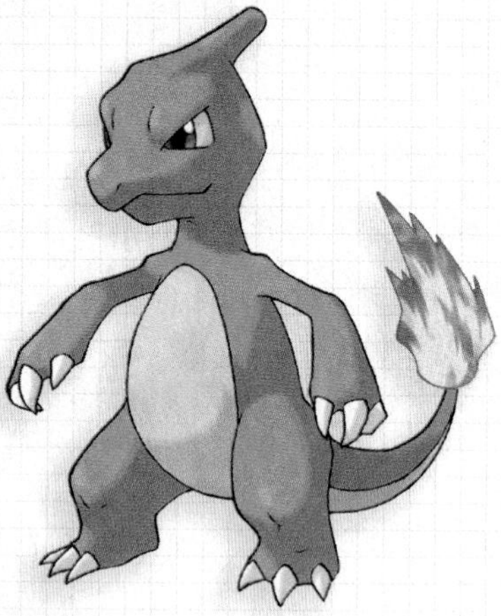

Pokémon AR Marker

LEVEL-UP AND LEARNED MOVES

Lv.	Name	Type	Kind	Pow.	Acc.	PP	Range	Long	DA
1	Scratch	Normal	Physical	40	100	35	Normal	—	○
1	Growl	Normal	Status	—	100	40	Many Others	—	—
1	Ember	Fire	Special	40	100	25	Normal	—	—
7	Ember	Fire	Special	40	100	25	Normal	—	—
10	SmokeScreen	Normal	Status	—	100	20	Normal	—	—
17	Dragon Rage	Dragon	Special	—	100	10	Normal	—	—
21	Scary Face	Normal	Status	—	100	10	Normal	—	—
28	Fire Fang	Fire	Physical	65	95	15	Normal	—	○
32	Flame Burst	Fire	Special	70	100	15	Normal	—	—
39	Slash	Normal	Physical	70	100	20	Normal	—	○
43	Flamethrower	Fire	Special	95	100	15	Normal	—	—
50	Fire Spin	Fire	Special	35	85	15	Normal	—	—
54	Inferno	Fire	Special	100	50	5	Normal	—	—

TM & HM MOVES

Lv.	Name	Type	Kind	Pow.	Acc.	PP	Range	Long	DA
TM01	Hone Claws	Dark	Status	—	—	15	Self	—	—
TM02	Dragon Claw	Dragon	Physical	80	100	15	Normal	—	○
TM06	Toxic	Poison	Status	—	90	10	Normal	—	—
TM10	Hidden Power	Normal	Special	—	100	15	Normal	—	—
TM11	Sunny Day	Fire	Status	—	—	5	Both Sides	—	—
TM17	Protect	Normal	Status	—	—	10	Self	—	—
TM21	Frustration	Normal	Physical	—	100	20	Normal	—	○
TM27	Return	Normal	Physical	—	100	20	Normal	—	○
TM28	Dig	Ground	Physical	80	100	10	Normal	—	○
TM31	Brick Break	Fighting	Physical	75	100	15	Normal	—	○
TM32	Double Team	Normal	Status	—	—	15	Self	—	—
TM35	Flamethrower	Fire	Special	95	100	15	Normal	—	—
TM38	Fire Blast	Fire	Special	120	85	5	Normal	—	—
TM39	Rock Tomb	Rock	Physical	50	80	10	Normal	—	—
TM40	Aerial Ace	Flying	Physical	60	—	20	Normal	○	○
TM42	Facade	Normal	Physical	70	100	20	Normal	—	○
TM43	Flame Charge	Fire	Physical	50	100	20	Normal	—	○
TM44	Rest	Psychic	Status	—	—	10	Self	—	—
TM45	Attract	Normal	Status	—	100	15	Normal	—	—
TM48	Round	Normal	Special	60	100	15	Normal	—	—
TM49	Echoed Voice	Normal	Special	40	100	15	Normal	—	—
TM50	Overheat	Fire	Special	140	90	5	Normal	—	—
TM56	Fling	Dark	Physical	—	100	10	Normal	—	—
TM59	Incinerate	Fire	Special	30	100	15	Many Others	—	—
TM61	Will-O-Wisp	Fire	Status	—	75	15	Normal	—	—
TM65	Shadow Claw	Ghost	Physical	70	100	15	Normal	—	○
TM75	Swords Dance	Normal	Status	—	—	30	Self	—	—
TM80	Rock Slide	Rock	Physical	75	90	10	Many Others	—	—
TM87	Swagger	Normal	Status	—	90	15	Normal	—	—
TM90	Substitute	Normal	Status	—	—	10	Self	—	—
TM94	Rock Smash	Fighting	Physical	40	100	15	Normal	—	○
HM01	Cut	Normal	Physical	50	95	30	Normal	—	○
HM04	Strength	Normal	Physical	80	100	15	Normal	—	○

MOVES TAUGHT BY PEOPLE

Name	Type	Kind	Pow.	Acc.	PP	Range	Long	DA
Fire Pledge	Fire	Special	50	100	10	Normal	—	—

MOVES TAUGHT BY MOVE TUTORS FOR SHARDS

Name	Type	Kind	Pow.	Acc.	PP	Range	Long	DA
Fire Punch	Fire	Physical	75	100	15	Normal	—	○
ThunderPunch	Electric	Physical	75	100	15	Normal	—	○
Iron Tail	Steel	Physical	100	75	15	Normal	—	○
Snore	Normal	Special	40	100	15	Normal	—	—
Heat Wave	Fire	Special	100	90	10	Many Others	—	—
Outrage	Dragon	Physical	120	100	10	1 Random	—	○
Sleep Talk	Normal	Status	—	—	10	Self	—	—

Flame Pokémon

006 Charizard

● HEIGHT: 5'07"
● WEIGHT: 199.5 lbs.
● GENDER: ♂ / ♀

It is said that Charizard's fire burns hotter if it has experienced harsh battles.

Same form for ♂ / ♀

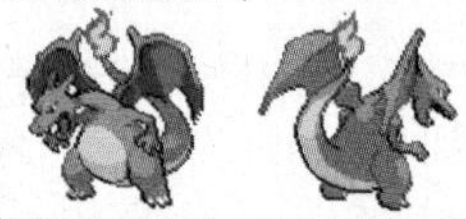

TYPE Fire Flying

ABILITY
● Blaze

HIDDEN ABILITY
● Solar Power

STATS
HP
Attack
Defense
Sp. Atk
Sp. Def
Speed

EGG GROUPS
Monster/Dragon

ITEMS SOMETIMES HELD
● None

EVOLUTION

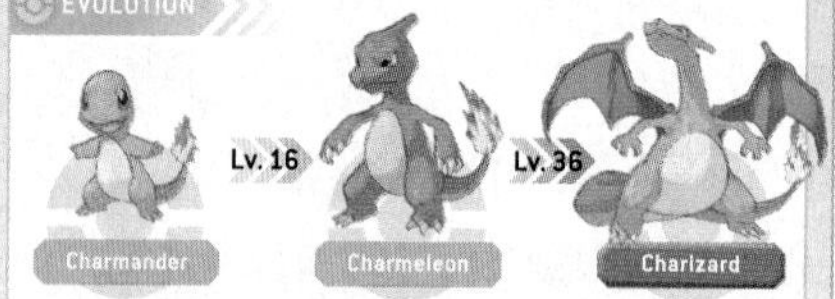

HOW TO OBTAIN

Pokémon Black Version 2	Level up a Charmeleon you obtain via Link Trade or Poké Transfer to Lv. 36
Pokémon White Version 2	Level up a Charmeleon you obtain via Link Trade or Poké Transfer to Lv. 36

HOW TO OBTAIN FROM OTHER GAMES

—

—

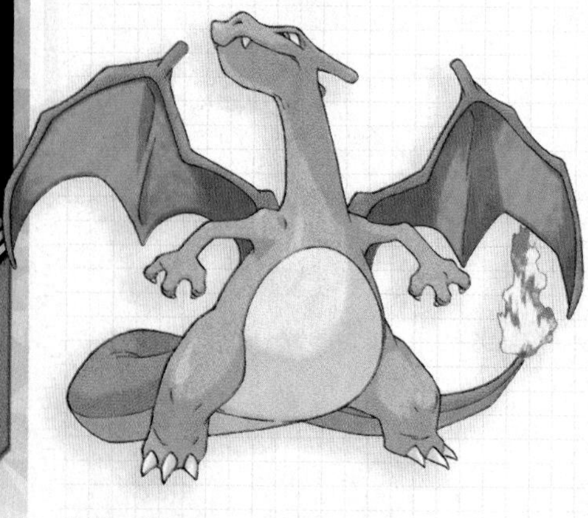

Pokémon AR Marker

LEVEL-UP AND LEARNED MOVES

Lv.	Name	Type	Kind	Pow.	Acc.	PP	Range	Long	DA
1	Dragon Claw	Dragon	Physical	80	100	15	Normal	—	○
1	Shadow Claw	Ghost	Physical	70	100	15	Normal	—	○
1	Air Slash	Flying	Special	75	95	20	Normal	○	—
1	Scratch	Normal	Physical	40	100	35	Normal	—	○
1	Growl	Normal	Status	—	100	40	Many Others	—	—
1	Ember	Fire	Special	40	100	25	Normal	—	—
1	SmokeScreen	Normal	Status	—	100	20	Normal	—	—
7	Ember	Fire	Special	40	100	25	Normal	—	—
10	SmokeScreen	Normal	Status	—	100	20	Normal	—	—
17	Dragon Rage	Dragon	Special	—	100	10	Normal	—	—
21	Scary Face	Normal	Status	—	100	10	Normal	—	—
28	Fire Fang	Fire	Physical	65	95	15	Normal	—	○
32	Flame Burst	Fire	Special	70	100	15	Normal	—	—
36	Wing Attack	Flying	Physical	60	100	35	Normal	○	○
41	Slash	Normal	Physical	70	100	20	Normal	—	○
47	Flamethrower	Fire	Special	95	100	15	Normal	—	—
56	Fire Spin	Fire	Special	35	85	15	Normal	—	—
62	Inferno	Fire	Special	100	50	5	Normal	—	—
71	Heat Wave	Fire	Special	100	90	10	Many Others	—	—
77	Flare Blitz	Fire	Physical	120	100	15	Normal	—	○

TM & HM MOVES

Lv.	Name	Type	Kind	Pow.	Acc.	PP	Range	Long	DA
TM01	Hone Claws	Dark	Status	—	—	15	Self	—	—
TM02	Dragon Claw	Dragon	Physical	80	100	15	Normal	—	○
TM05	Roar	Normal	Status	—	100	20	Normal	—	—
TM06	Toxic	Poison	Status	—	90	10	Normal	—	—
TM10	Hidden Power	Normal	Special	—	100	15	Normal	—	—
TM11	Sunny Day	Fire	Status	—	—	5	Both Sides	—	—
TM15	Hyper Beam	Normal	Special	150	90	5	Normal	—	—
TM17	Protect	Normal	Status	—	—	10	Self	—	—
TM21	Frustration	Normal	Physical	—	100	20	Normal	—	○
TM22	SolarBeam	Grass	Special	120	100	10	Normal	—	—
TM26	Earthquake	Ground	Physical	100	100	10	Adjacent	—	—
TM27	Return	Normal	Physical	—	100	20	Normal	—	○
TM28	Dig	Ground	Physical	80	100	10	Normal	—	○
TM31	Brick Break	Fighting	Physical	75	100	15	Normal	—	○
TM32	Double Team	Normal	Status	—	—	15	Self	—	—
TM35	Flamethrower	Fire	Special	95	100	15	Normal	—	—
TM38	Fire Blast	Fire	Special	120	85	5	Normal	—	—
TM39	Rock Tomb	Rock	Physical	50	80	10	Normal	—	—
TM40	Aerial Ace	Flying	Physical	60	—	20	Normal	○	○
TM42	Facade	Normal	Physical	70	100	20	Normal	—	○
TM43	Flame Charge	Fire	Physical	50	100	20	Normal	—	○
TM44	Rest	Psychic	Status	—	—	10	Self	—	—
TM45	Attract	Normal	Status	—	100	15	Normal	—	—
TM48	Round	Normal	Special	60	100	15	Normal	—	—
TM49	Echoed Voice	Normal	Special	40	100	15	Normal	—	—
TM50	Overheat	Fire	Special	140	90	5	Normal	—	—
TM52	Focus Blast	Fighting	Special	120	70	5	Normal	—	—
TM56	Fling	Dark	Physical	—	100	10	Normal	—	—
TM58	Sky Drop	Flying	Physical	60	100	10	Normal	○	○
TM59	Incinerate	Fire	Special	30	100	15	Many Others	—	—
TM61	Will-O-Wisp	Fire	Status	—	75	15	Normal	—	—
TM65	Shadow Claw	Ghost	Physical	70	100	15	Normal	—	○
TM68	Giga Impact	Normal	Physical	150	90	5	Normal	—	○
TM75	Swords Dance	Normal	Status	—	—	30	Self	—	—
TM78	Bulldoze	Ground	Physical	60	100	20	Adjacent	—	—
TM80	Rock Slide	Rock	Physical	75	90	10	Many Others	—	—
TM82	Dragon Tail	Dragon	Physical	60	90	10	Normal	—	○
TM87	Swagger	Normal	Status	—	90	15	Normal	—	—
TM90	Substitute	Normal	Status	—	—	10	Self	—	—
TM94	Rock Smash	Fighting	Physical	40	100	15	Normal	—	○
HM01	Cut	Normal	Physical	50	95	30	Normal	—	○
HM02	Fly	Flying	Physical	90	95	15	Normal	○	○
HM04	Strength	Normal	Physical	80	100	15	Normal	—	○

MOVES TAUGHT BY PEOPLE

Name	Type	Kind	Pow.	Acc.	PP	Range	Long	DA
Fire Pledge	Fire	Special	50	100	10	Normal	—	—
Blast Burn	Fire	Special	150	90	5	Normal	—	—

MOVES TAUGHT BY MOVE TUTORS FOR SHARDS

Name	Type	Kind	Pow.	Acc.	PP	Range	Long	DA
Fire Punch	Fire	Physical	75	100	15	Normal	—	○
ThunderPunch	Electric	Physical	75	100	15	Normal	—	○
Iron Tail	Steel	Physical	100	75	15	Normal	—	○
Dragon Pulse	Dragon	Special	90	100	10	Normal	○	—
Snore	Normal	Special	40	100	15	Normal	—	—
Roost	Flying	Status	—	—	10	Self	—	—
Heat Wave	Fire	Special	100	90	10	Many Others	—	—
Tailwind	Flying	Status	—	—	30	Your Side	—	—
Outrage	Dragon	Physical	120	100	10	1 Random	—	○
Sleep Talk	Normal	Status	—	—	10	Self	—	—

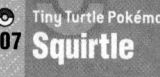

007 Squirtle

Tiny Turtle Pokémon

- HEIGHT: 1'08"
- WEIGHT: 19.8 lbs.
- GENDER: ♂ / ♀

It shelters itself in its shell, then strikes back with spouts of water at every opportunity.

TYPE: Water

ABILITY
- Torrent

HIDDEN ABILITY
- Rain Dish

STATS
HP
Attack
Defense
Sp. Atk
Sp. Def
Speed

EGG GROUPS
Monster/Water

ITEMS SOMETIMES HELD
- None

Same form for ♂ / ♀

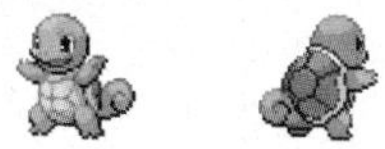

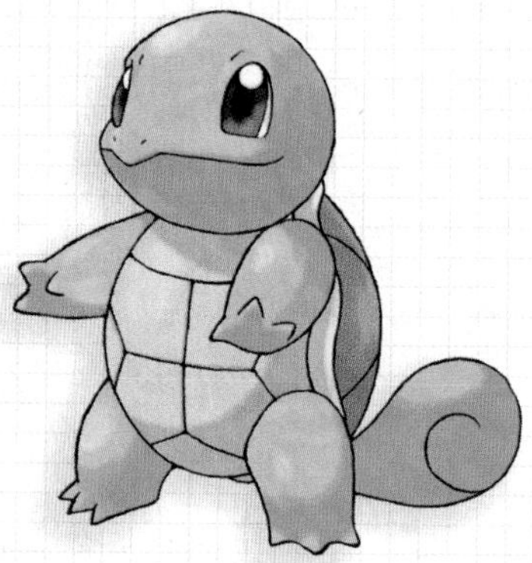

Pokémon AR Marker

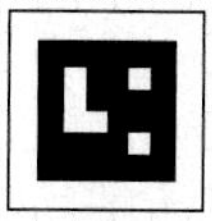

EVOLUTION

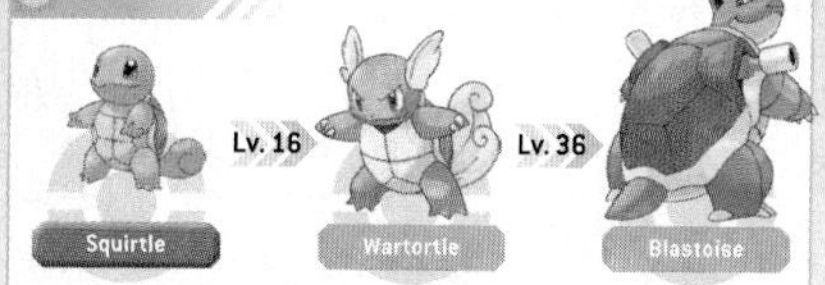

HOW TO OBTAIN

Pokémon Black Version 2	Link Trade or Poké Transfer
Pokémon White Version 2	Link Trade or Poké Transfer

HOW TO OBTAIN FROM OTHER GAMES

Pokémon HeartGold Version	Receive from Professor Oak in Pallet Town (after defeating Red)
Pokémon SoulSilver Version	Receive from Professor Oak in Pallet Town (after defeating Red)

LEVEL-UP AND LEARNED MOVES

Lv.	Name	Type	Kind	Pow.	Acc.	PP	Range	Long	DA
1	Tackle	Normal	Physical	50	100	35	Normal	—	○
4	Tail Whip	Normal	Status	—	100	30	Many Others	—	—
7	Bubble	Water	Special	20	100	30	Many Others	—	—
10	Withdraw	Water	Status	—	—	40	Self	—	—
13	Water Gun	Water	Special	40	100	25	Normal	—	—
16	Bite	Dark	Physical	60	100	25	Normal	—	○
19	Rapid Spin	Normal	Physical	20	100	40	Normal	—	○
22	Protect	Normal	Status	—	—	10	Self	—	—
25	Water Pulse	Water	Special	60	100	20	Normal	○	—
28	Aqua Tail	Water	Physical	90	90	10	Normal	—	○
31	Skull Bash	Normal	Physical	100	100	15	Normal	—	○
34	Iron Defense	Steel	Status	—	—	15	Self	—	—
37	Rain Dance	Water	Status	—	—	5	Both Sides	—	—
40	Hydro Pump	Water	Special	120	80	5	Normal	—	—

TM & HM MOVES

Lv.	Name	Type	Kind	Pow.	Acc.	PP	Range	Long	DA
TM06	Toxic	Poison	Status	—	90	10	Normal	—	—
TM07	Hail	Ice	Status	—	—	10	Both Sides	—	—
TM10	Hidden Power	Normal	Special	—	100	15	Normal	—	—
TM13	Ice Beam	Ice	Special	95	100	10	Normal	—	—
TM14	Blizzard	Ice	Special	120	70	5	Many Others	—	—
TM17	Protect	Normal	Status	—	—	10	Self	—	—
TM18	Rain Dance	Water	Status	—	—	5	Both Sides	—	—
TM21	Frustration	Normal	Physical	—	100	20	Normal	—	○
TM27	Return	Normal	Physical	—	100	20	Normal	—	○
TM28	Dig	Ground	Physical	80	100	10	Normal	—	○
TM31	Brick Break	Fighting	Physical	75	100	15	Normal	—	○
TM32	Double Team	Normal	Status	—	—	15	Self	—	—
TM39	Rock Tomb	Rock	Physical	50	80	10	Normal	—	—
TM42	Facade	Normal	Physical	70	100	20	Normal	—	○
TM44	Rest	Psychic	Status	—	—	10	Self	—	—
TM45	Attract	Normal	Status	—	100	15	Normal	—	—
TM48	Round	Normal	Special	60	100	15	Normal	—	—
TM55	Scald	Water	Special	80	100	15	Normal	—	—
TM56	Fling	Dark	Physical	—	100	10	Normal	—	—
TM74	Gyro Ball	Steel	Physical	—	100	5	Normal	—	○
TM87	Swagger	Normal	Status	—	90	15	Normal	—	—
TM90	Substitute	Normal	Status	—	—	10	Self	—	—
TM94	Rock Smash	Fighting	Physical	40	100	15	Normal	—	○
HM03	Surf	Water	Special	95	100	15	Adjacent	—	—
HM04	Strength	Normal	Physical	80	100	15	Normal	—	○
HM05	Waterfall	Water	Physical	80	100	15	Normal	—	○
HM06	Dive	Water	Physical	80	100	10	Normal	—	○

MOVES TAUGHT BY PEOPLE

Name	Type	Kind	Pow.	Acc.	PP	Range	Long	DA
Water Pledge	Water	Special	50	100	10	Normal	—	—

MOVES TAUGHT BY MOVE TUTORS FOR SHARDS

Name	Type	Kind	Pow.	Acc.	PP	Range	Long	DA
Ice Punch	Ice	Physical	75	100	15	Normal	—	○
Iron Defense	Steel	Status	—	—	15	Self	—	—
Icy Wind	Ice	Special	55	95	15	Many Others	—	—
Iron Tail	Steel	Physical	100	75	15	Normal	—	○
Aqua Tail	Water	Physical	90	90	10	Normal	—	○
Zen Headbutt	Psychic	Physical	80	90	15	Normal	—	○
Snore	Normal	Special	40	100	15	Normal	—	—
Sleep Talk	Normal	Status	—	—	10	Self	—	—

EGG MOVES

Name	Type	Kind	Pow.	Acc.	PP	Range	Long	DA
Mirror Coat	Psychic	Special	—	100	20	Varies	—	—
Haze	Ice	Status	—	—	30	Both Sides	—	—
Mist	Ice	Status	—	—	30	Your Side	—	—
Foresight	Normal	Status	—	—	40	Normal	—	—
Flail	Normal	Physical	—	100	15	Normal	—	○
Refresh	Normal	Status	—	—	20	Self	—	—
Mud Sport	Ground	Status	—	—	15	Both Sides	—	—
Yawn	Normal	Status	—	—	10	Normal	—	—
Muddy Water	Water	Special	95	85	10	Many Others	—	—
Fake Out	Normal	Physical	40	100	10	Normal	—	○
Aqua Ring	Water	Status	—	—	20	Self	—	—
Aqua Jet	Water	Physical	40	100	20	Normal	—	○
Water Spout	Water	Special	150	100	5	Many Others	—	—
Brine	Water	Special	65	100	10	Normal	—	—

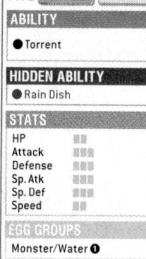

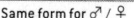

008 Wartortle

Turtle Pokémon

- HEIGHT: 3'03"
- WEIGHT: 49.6 lbs.
- GENDER: ♂ / ♀

It is said to live 10,000 years. Its furry tail is popular as a symbol of longevity.

TYPE: Water

ABILITY
- Torrent

HIDDEN ABILITY
- Rain Dish

STATS
HP
Attack
Defense
Sp. Atk
Sp. Def
Speed

EGG GROUPS
Monster/Water

ITEMS SOMETIMES HELD
- None

Same form for ♂ / ♀

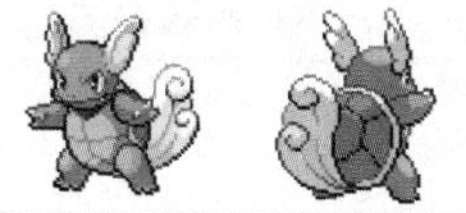

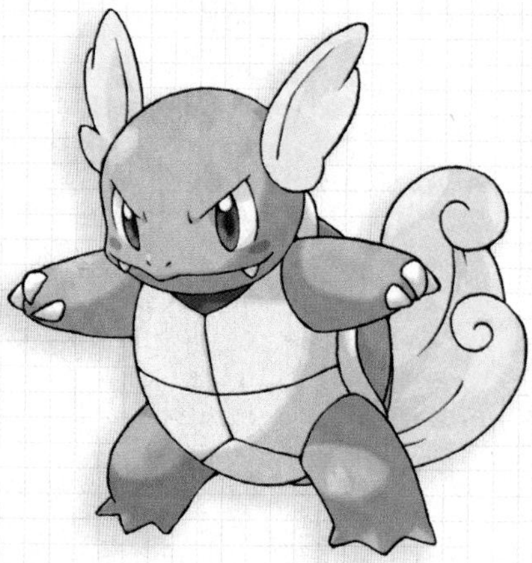

Pokémon AR Marker

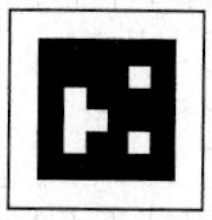

Find this Pokémon's weaknesses in the back of the book

EVOLUTION

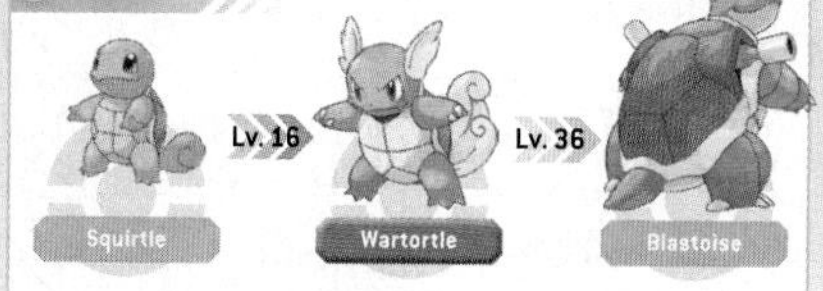

HOW TO OBTAIN

Pokémon Black Version 2	Level up a Squirtle you obtain via Link Trade or Poké Transfer to Lv. 16
Pokémon White Version 2	Level up a Squirtle you obtain via Link Trade or Poké Transfer to Lv. 16

HOW TO OBTAIN FROM OTHER GAMES

—

—

LEVEL-UP AND LEARNED MOVES

Lv.	Name	Type	Kind	Pow.	Acc.	PP	Range	Long	DA
1	Tackle	Normal	Physical	50	100	35	Normal	—	○
1	Tail Whip	Normal	Status	—	100	30	Many Others	—	—
1	Bubble	Water	Special	20	100	30	Many Others	—	—
4	Tail Whip	Normal	Status	—	100	30	Many Others	—	—
7	Bubble	Water	Special	20	100	30	Many Others	—	—
10	Withdraw	Water	Status	—	—	40	Self	—	—
13	Water Gun	Water	Special	40	100	25	Normal	—	—
16	Bite	Dark	Physical	60	100	25	Normal	—	○
20	Rapid Spin	Normal	Physical	20	100	40	Normal	—	○
24	Protect	Normal	Status	—	—	10	Self	—	—
28	Water Pulse	Water	Special	60	100	20	Normal	○	—
32	Aqua Tail	Water	Physical	90	90	10	Normal	—	○
36	Skull Bash	Normal	Physical	100	100	15	Normal	—	○
40	Iron Defense	Steel	Status	—	—	15	Self	—	—
44	Rain Dance	Water	Status	—	—	5	Both Sides	—	—
48	Hydro Pump	Water	Special	120	80	5	Normal	—	—

TM & HM MOVES

Lv.	Name	Type	Kind	Pow.	Acc.	PP	Range	Long	DA
TM06	Toxic	Poison	Status	—	90	10	Normal	—	—
TM07	Hail	Ice	Status	—	—	10	Both Sides	—	—
TM10	Hidden Power	Normal	Special	—	100	15	Normal	—	—
TM13	Ice Beam	Ice	Special	95	100	10	Normal	—	—
TM14	Blizzard	Ice	Special	120	70	5	Many Others	—	—
TM17	Protect	Normal	Status	—	—	10	Self	—	—
TM18	Rain Dance	Water	Status	—	—	5	Both Sides	—	—
TM21	Frustration	Normal	Physical	—	100	20	Normal	—	○
TM27	Return	Normal	Physical	—	100	20	Normal	—	○
TM28	Dig	Ground	Physical	80	100	10	Normal	—	○
TM31	Brick Break	Fighting	Physical	75	100	15	Normal	—	○
TM32	Double Team	Normal	Status	—	—	15	Self	—	—
TM39	Rock Tomb	Rock	Physical	50	80	10	Normal	—	—
TM42	Facade	Normal	Physical	70	100	20	Normal	—	○
TM44	Rest	Psychic	Status	—	—	10	Self	—	—
TM45	Attract	Normal	Status	—	100	15	Normal	—	—
TM48	Round	Normal	Special	60	100	15	Normal	—	—
TM55	Scald	Water	Special	80	100	15	Normal	—	—
TM56	Fling	Dark	Physical	—	100	10	Normal	—	—
TM74	Gyro Ball	Steel	Physical	—	100	5	Normal	—	○
TM87	Swagger	Normal	Status	—	90	15	Normal	—	—
TM90	Substitute	Normal	Status	—	—	10	Self	—	—
TM94	Rock Smash	Fighting	Physical	40	100	15	Normal	—	○
HM03	Surf	Water	Special	95	100	15	Adjacent	—	—
HM04	Strength	Normal	Physical	80	100	15	Normal	—	○
HM05	Waterfall	Water	Physical	80	100	15	Normal	—	○
HM06	Dive	Water	Physical	80	100	10	Normal	—	○

MOVES TAUGHT BY PEOPLE

Name	Type	Kind	Pow.	Acc.	PP	Range	Long	DA
Water Pledge	Water	Special	50	100	10	Normal	—	—

MOVES TAUGHT BY MOVE TUTORS FOR SHARDS

Name	Type	Kind	Pow.	Acc.	PP	Range	Long	DA
Ice Punch	Ice	Physical	75	100	15	Normal	—	○
Iron Defense	Steel	Status	—	—	15	Self	—	—
Icy Wind	Ice	Special	55	95	15	Many Others	—	—
Iron Tail	Steel	Physical	100	75	15	Normal	—	○
Aqua Tail	Water	Physical	90	90	10	Normal	—	○
Zen Headbutt	Psychic	Physical	80	90	15	Normal	—	○
Snore	Normal	Special	40	100	15	Normal	—	—
Sleep Talk	Normal	Status	—	—	10	Self	—	—

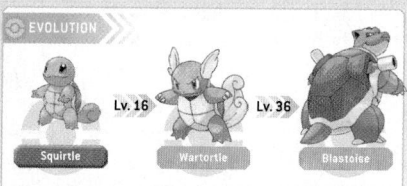

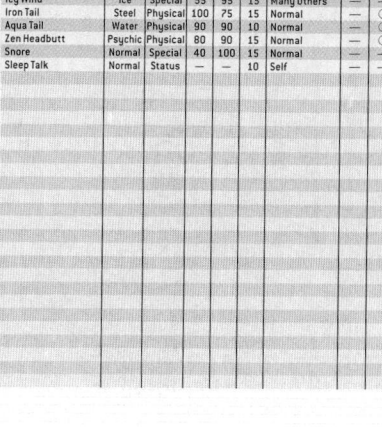

009 Blastoise
Shellfish Pokémon

TYPE Water

ABILITY
- Torrent

HIDDEN ABILITY
- Rain Dish

- HEIGHT: 5'03"
- WEIGHT: 188.5 lbs.
- GENDER: ♂ / ♀

The jets of water it spouts from the rocket cannons on its shell can punch through thick steel.

STATS
HP
Attack
Defense
Sp. Atk
Sp. Def
Speed

EGG GROUPS
Monster/Water ❶

ITEMS SOMETIMES HELD
- None

Same form for ♂ / ♀

Pokémon AR Marker

EVOLUTION
Squirtle → Lv. 16 → Wartortle → Lv. 36 → Blastoise

HOW TO OBTAIN
Pokémon Black Version 2	Level up a Wartortle you obtain via Link Trade or Poké Transfer to Lv. 36
Pokémon White Version 2	Level up a Wartortle you obtain via Link Trade or Poké Transfer to Lv. 36

HOW TO OBTAIN FROM OTHER GAMES

LEVEL-UP AND LEARNED MOVES
Lv.	Name	Type	Kind	Pow.	Acc.	PP	Range	Long	DA
1	Flash Cannon	Steel	Special	80	100	10	Normal	—	—
1	Tackle	Normal	Physical	50	100	35	Normal	—	○
1	Tail Whip	Normal	Status	—	100	30	Many Others	—	—
1	Bubble	Water	Special	20	100	30	Many Others	—	—
1	Withdraw	Water	Status	—	—	40	Self	—	—
4	Tail Whip	Normal	Status	—	100	30	Many Others	—	—
7	Bubble	Water	Special	20	100	30	Many Others	—	—
10	Withdraw	Water	Status	—	—	40	Self	—	—
13	Water Gun	Water	Special	40	100	25	Normal	—	—
16	Bite	Dark	Physical	60	100	25	Normal	—	○
20	Rapid Spin	Normal	Physical	20	100	40	Normal	—	○
24	Protect	Normal	Status	—	—	10	Self	—	—
28	Water Pulse	Water	Special	60	100	20	Normal	○	○
32	Aqua Tail	Water	Physical	90	90	10	Normal	—	○
39	Skull Bash	Normal	Physical	100	100	15	Normal	—	○
46	Iron Defense	Steel	Status	—	—	15	Self	—	—
53	Rain Dance	Water	Status	—	—	5	Both Sides	—	—
60	Hydro Pump	Water	Special	120	80	5	Normal	—	—

TM & HM MOVES
Lv.	Name	Type	Kind	Pow.	Acc.	PP	Range	Long	DA
TM05	Roar	Normal	Status	—	100	20	Normal	—	—
TM06	Toxic	Poison	Status	—	90	10	Normal	—	—
TM07	Hail	Ice	Status	—	—	10	Both Sides	—	—
TM10	Hidden Power	Normal	Special	—	100	15	Normal	—	—
TM13	Ice Beam	Ice	Special	95	100	10	Normal	—	—
TM14	Blizzard	Ice	Special	120	70	5	Many Others	—	—
TM15	Hyper Beam	Normal	Special	150	90	5	Normal	—	—
TM17	Protect	Normal	Status	—	—	10	Self	—	—
TM18	Rain Dance	Water	Status	—	—	5	Both Sides	—	—
TM21	Frustration	Normal	Physical	—	100	20	Normal	—	○
TM23	Smack Down	Rock	Physical	50	100	15	Normal	—	○
TM26	Earthquake	Ground	Physical	100	100	10	Adjacent	—	—
TM27	Return	Normal	Physical	—	100	20	Normal	—	○
TM28	Dig	Ground	Physical	80	100	10	Normal	—	○
TM31	Brick Break	Fighting	Physical	75	100	15	Normal	—	○
TM32	Double Team	Normal	Status	—	—	15	Self	—	—
TM39	Rock Tomb	Rock	Physical	50	80	10	Normal	—	○
TM42	Facade	Normal	Physical	70	100	20	Normal	—	○
TM44	Rest	Psychic	Status	—	—	10	Self	—	—
TM45	Attract	Normal	Status	—	100	15	Normal	—	—
TM48	Round	Normal	Special	60	100	15	Normal	—	—
TM52	Focus Blast	Fighting	Special	120	70	5	Normal	—	—
TM55	Scald	Water	Special	80	100	15	Normal	—	—
TM56	Fling	Dark	Physical	—	100	10	Normal	—	—
TM68	Giga Impact	Normal	Physical	150	90	5	Normal	—	○
TM74	Gyro Ball	Steel	Physical	—	100	5	Normal	—	○
TM78	Bulldoze	Ground	Physical	60	100	20	Adjacent	—	—
TM80	Rock Slide	Rock	Physical	75	90	10	Many Others	—	—
TM82	Dragon Tail	Dragon	Physical	60	90	10	Normal	—	○
TM87	Swagger	Normal	Status	—	90	15	Normal	—	—
TM90	Substitute	Normal	Status	—	—	10	Self	—	—
TM91	Flash Cannon	Steel	Special	80	100	10	Normal	—	—
TM94	Rock Smash	Fighting	Physical	40	100	15	Normal	—	○
HM03	Surf	Water	Special	95	100	15	Adjacent	—	—
HM04	Strength	Normal	Physical	80	100	15	Normal	—	—
HM05	Waterfall	Water	Physical	80	100	15	Normal	—	○
HM06	Dive	Water	Physical	80	100	10	Normal	—	○

MOVES TAUGHT BY PEOPLE
Name	Type	Kind	Pow.	Acc.	PP	Range	Long	DA
Water Pledge	Water	Special	50	100	10	Normal	—	—
Hydro Cannon	Water	Special	150	90	5	Normal	—	—

MOVES TAUGHT BY MOVE TUTORS FOR SHARDS
Name	Type	Kind	Pow.	Acc.	PP	Range	Long	DA
Signal Beam	Bug	Special	75	100	15	Normal	—	—
Ice Punch	Ice	Physical	75	100	15	Normal	—	○
Iron Defense	Steel	Status	—	—	15	Self	—	—
Icy Wind	Ice	Special	55	95	15	Many Others	—	—
Iron Tail	Steel	Physical	100	75	15	Normal	—	○
Aqua Tail	Water	Physical	90	90	10	Normal	—	○
Zen Headbutt	Psychic	Physical	80	90	15	Normal	—	○
Snore	Normal	Special	40	100	15	Normal	—	—
Outrage	Dragon	Physical	120	100	10	1 Random	—	○
Sleep Talk	Normal	Status	—	—	10	Self	—	—

  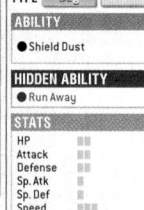

010 Caterpie
Worm Pokémon

TYPE Bug

ABILITY
- Shield Dust

HIDDEN ABILITY
- Run Away

- HEIGHT: 1'00"
- WEIGHT: 6.4 lbs.
- GENDER: ♂ / ♀

It releases a stench from its red antenna to repel enemies. It grows by molting repeatedly.

STATS
HP
Attack
Defense
Sp. Atk
Sp. Def
Speed

EGG GROUPS
Bug

ITEMS SOMETIMES HELD
- None

Same form for ♂ / ♀

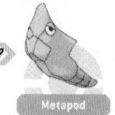 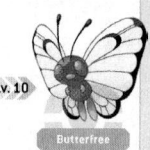

Pokémon AR Marker

EVOLUTION
Caterpie → Lv. 7 → Metapod → Lv. 10 → Butterfree

HOW TO OBTAIN
Pokémon Black Version 2	Link Trade or Poké Transfer
Pokémon White Version 2	Catch a Butterfree, leave it at the Pokémon Day Care, and hatch the Egg that is found

HOW TO OBTAIN FROM OTHER GAMES
Pokémon White Version	Catch a Metapod or Butterfree, leave it at the Pokémon Day Care, and hatch the Egg that is found

LEVEL-UP AND LEARNED MOVES
Lv.	Name	Type	Kind	Pow.	Acc.	PP	Range	Long	DA
1	Tackle	Normal	Physical	50	100	35	Normal	—	—
1	String Shot	Bug	Status	—	95	40	Many Others	—	—
15	Bug Bite	Bug	Physical	60	100	20	Normal	—	—

TM & HM MOVES
Lv.	Name	Type	Kind	Pow.	Acc.	PP	Range	Long	DA

MOVES TAUGHT BY PEOPLE
Name	Type	Kind	Pow.	Acc.	PP	Range	Long	DA

MOVES TAUGHT BY MOVE TUTORS FOR SHARDS
Name	Type	Kind	Pow.	Acc.	PP	Range	Long	DA
Bug Bite	Bug	Physical	60	100	20	Normal	—	○
Electroweb	Electric	Special	55	95	15	Many Others	—	—
Snore	Normal	Special	40	100	15	Normal	—	—

EGG MOVES
Name	Type	Kind	Pow.	Acc.	PP	Range	Long	DA

Cocoon Pokémon
011 Metapod

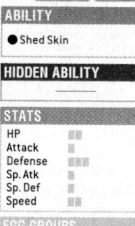

- HEIGHT: 2'04"
- WEIGHT: 21.8 lbs.
- GENDER: ♂ / ♀

A steel-hard shell protects its tender body. It quietly endures hardships while awaiting evolution.

Same form for ♂ / ♀

TYPE Bug

ABILITY
- Shed Skin

HIDDEN ABILITY
—

STATS
- HP
- Attack
- Defense
- Sp. Atk
- Sp. Def
- Speed

EGG GROUPS
Bug

ITEMS SOMETIMES HELD
- None

EVOLUTION

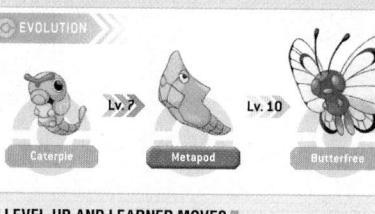

| Caterpie | Lv. 7 → Metapod | Lv. 10 → Butterfree |

HOW TO OBTAIN

| Pokémon Black Version 2 | Link Trade or Poké Transfer |
| Pokémon White Version 2 | Level up Caterpie to Lv. 7 |

HOW TO OBTAIN FROM OTHER GAMES

| Pokémon White Version | Route 12 |

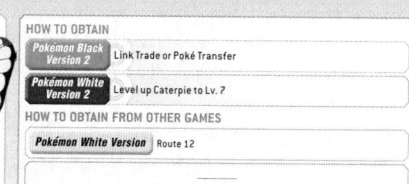

LEVEL-UP AND LEARNED MOVES

Lv.	Name	Type	Kind	Pow.	Acc.	PP	Range	Long	DA
1	Harden	Normal	Status	—	—	30	Self	—	—
7	Harden	Normal	Status	—	—	30	Self	—	—

TM & HM MOVES

Lv.	Name	Type	Kind	Pow.	Acc.	PP	Range	Long	DA

MOVES TAUGHT BY PEOPLE

Name	Type	Kind	Pow.	Acc.	PP	Range	Long	DA

MOVES TAUGHT BY MOVE TUTORS FOR SHARDS

Name	Type	Kind	Pow.	Acc.	PP	Range	Long	DA
Bug Bite	Bug	Physical	60	100	20	Normal	—	○
Iron Defense	Steel	Status	—	—	15	Self	—	—
Electroweb	Electric	Special	55	95	15	Many Others	—	—

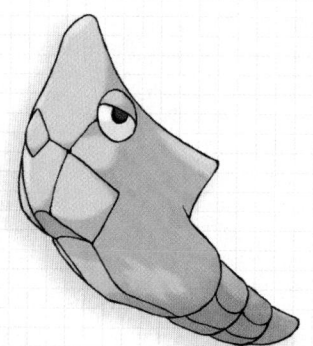

Pokémon AR Marker

011 | Metapod

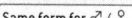

Butterfly Pokémon
012 Butterfree

- HEIGHT: 3'07"
- WEIGHT: 70.5 lbs.
- GENDER: ♂ / ♀

It loves the honey of flowers and can locate flower patches that have even tiny amounts of pollen.

♂ ♀

TYPE Bug Flying

ABILITY
- Compoundeyes

HIDDEN ABILITY
- Tinted Lens

STATS
- HP
- Attack
- Defense
- Sp. Atk
- Sp. Def
- Speed

EGG GROUPS
Bug

ITEMS SOMETIMES HELD
- SilverPowder

EVOLUTION

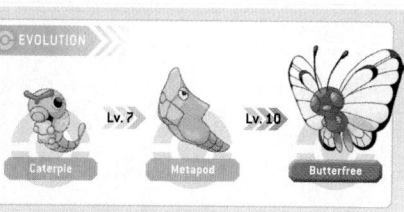

| Caterpie | Lv. 7 → Metapod | Lv. 10 → Butterfree |

HOW TO OBTAIN

| Pokémon Black Version 2 | Link Trade or Poké Transfer |
| Pokémon White Version 2 | Pinwheel Forest interior (Hidden Grotto) |

HOW TO OBTAIN FROM OTHER GAMES

| Pokémon White Version | Route 12 (rustling grass) |

LEVEL-UP AND LEARNED MOVES

Lv.	Name	Type	Kind	Pow.	Acc.	PP	Range	Long	DA
1	Confusion	Psychic	Special	50	100	25	Normal	—	—
10	Confusion	Psychic	Special	50	100	25	Normal	—	—
12	PoisonPowder	Poison	Status	—	75	35	Normal	—	—
12	Stun Spore	Grass	Status	—	75	30	Normal	—	—
12	Sleep Powder	Grass	Status	—	75	15	Normal	—	—
16	Gust	Flying	Special	40	100	35	Normal	○	—
18	Supersonic	Normal	Status	—	55	20	Normal	—	—
22	Whirlwind	Normal	Status	—	100	20	Normal	—	—
24	Psybeam	Psychic	Special	65	100	20	Normal	—	—
28	Silver Wind	Bug	Special	60	100	5	Normal	—	—
30	Tailwind	Flying	Status	—	—	30	Your Side	—	—
34	Rage Powder	Bug	Status	—	—	20	Self	—	—
36	Safeguard	Normal	Status	—	—	25	Your Side	—	—
40	Captivate	Normal	Status	—	100	20	Many Others	—	—
42	Bug Buzz	Bug	Special	90	100	10	Normal	—	—
46	Quiver Dance	Bug	Status	—	—	20	Self	—	—

TM & HM MOVES

Lv.	Name	Type	Kind	Pow.	Acc.	PP	Range	Long	DA
TM06	Toxic	Poison	Status	—	90	10	Normal	—	—
TM09	Venoshock	Poison	Special	65	100	10	Normal	—	—
TM10	Hidden Power	Normal	Special	—	100	15	Normal	—	—
TM11	Sunny Day	Fire	Status	—	—	5	Both Sides	—	—
TM15	Hyper Beam	Normal	Special	150	90	5	Normal	—	—
TM17	Protect	Normal	Status	—	—	10	Self	—	—
TM18	Rain Dance	Water	Status	—	—	5	Both Sides	—	—
TM20	Safeguard	Normal	Status	—	—	25	Your Side	—	—
TM21	Frustration	Normal	Physical	—	100	20	Normal	—	○
TM22	SolarBeam	Grass	Special	120	100	10	Normal	—	—
TM27	Return	Normal	Physical	—	100	20	Normal	—	○
TM29	Psychic	Psychic	Special	90	100	10	Normal	—	—
TM30	Shadow Ball	Ghost	Special	80	100	15	Normal	—	—
TM32	Double Team	Normal	Status	—	—	15	Self	—	—
TM40	Aerial Ace	Flying	Physical	60	—	20	Normal	○	○
TM42	Facade	Normal	Physical	70	100	20	Normal	—	—
TM44	Rest	Psychic	Status	—	—	10	Self	—	—
TM45	Attract	Normal	Status	—	100	15	Normal	—	—
TM46	Thief	Dark	Physical	40	100	10	Normal	—	—
TM48	Round	Normal	Special	60	100	15	Normal	—	—
TM53	Energy Ball	Grass	Special	80	100	10	Normal	—	—
TM62	Acrobatics	Flying	Physical	55	100	15	Normal	○	○
TM68	Giga Impact	Normal	Physical	150	90	5	Normal	—	—
TM70	Flash	Normal	Status	—	100	20	Normal	—	—
TM76	Struggle Bug	Bug	Special	30	100	20	Many Others	—	—
TM77	Psych Up	Normal	Status	—	—	10	Self	—	—
TM85	Dream Eater	Psychic	Special	100	100	15	Normal	—	—
TM87	Swagger	Normal	Status	—	90	15	Normal	—	—
TM89	U-turn	Bug	Physical	70	100	20	Normal	—	—
TM90	Substitute	Normal	Status	—	—	10	Self	—	—

MOVES TAUGHT BY PEOPLE

Name	Type	Kind	Pow.	Acc.	PP	Range	Long	DA

MOVES TAUGHT BY MOVE TUTORS FOR SHARDS

Name	Type	Kind	Pow.	Acc.	PP	Range	Long	DA
Bug Bite	Bug	Physical	60	100	20	Normal	—	○
Signal Beam	Bug	Special	75	100	15	Normal	—	—
Electroweb	Electric	Special	55	95	15	Many Others	—	—
Snore	Normal	Special	40	100	15	Normal	—	—
Roost	Flying	Status	—	—	10	Self	—	—
Giga Drain	Grass	Special	75	100	10	Normal	—	—
Tailwind	Flying	Status	—	—	30	Your Side	—	—
Sleep Talk	Normal	Status	—	—	10	Self	—	—
Skill Swap	Psychic	Status	—	—	10	Normal	—	—

Pokémon AR Marker

012 | Butterfree

Hairy Bug Pokémon
013 Weedle

- HEIGHT: 1'00"
- WEIGHT: 7.1 lbs.
- GENDER: ♂ / ♀

It eats its weight in leaves every day. It fends off attackers with the needle on its head.

Same form for ♂ / ♀

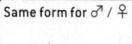

TYPE	Bug	Poison

ABILITY
- Shield Dust

HIDDEN ABILITY
- Run Away

STATS
- HP
- Attack
- Defense
- Sp. Atk
- Sp. Def
- Speed

EGG GROUPS
Bug

ITEMS SOMETIMES HELD
- None

EVOLUTION

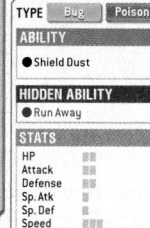

Weedle — Lv. 7 — Kakuna — Lv. 10 — Beedrill

HOW TO OBTAIN

Pokémon Black Version 2	Catch a Beedrill, leave it at the Pokémon Day Care, and hatch the Egg that is found
Pokémon White Version 2	Link Trade or Poké Transfer

HOW TO OBTAIN FROM OTHER GAMES

Pokémon Black Version	Catch a Kakuna or Beedrill, leave it at the Pokémon Day Care, and hatch the Egg that is found

LEVEL-UP AND LEARNED MOVES

Lv.	Name	Type	Kind	Pow.	Acc.	PP	Range	Long	DA
1	Poison Sting	Poison	Physical	15	100	35	Normal	—	—
1	String Shot	Bug	Status	—	95	40	Many Others	—	—
15	Bug Bite	Bug	Physical	60	100	20	Normal	—	○

TM & HM MOVES

Lv.	Name	Type	Kind	Pow.	Acc.	PP	Range	Long	DA

MOVES TAUGHT BY PEOPLE

Name	Type	Kind	Pow.	Acc.	PP	Range	Long	DA

MOVES TAUGHT BY MOVE TUTORS FOR SHARDS

Name	Type	Kind	Pow.	Acc.	PP	Range	Long	DA
Bug Bite	Bug	Physical	60	100	20	Normal	—	○
Electroweb	Electric	Special	55	95	15	Many Others	—	—

EGG MOVES

Name	Type	Kind	Pow.	Acc.	PP	Range	Long	DA

Pokémon AR Marker

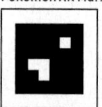

Cocoon Pokémon
014 Kakuna

- HEIGHT: 2'00"
- WEIGHT: 22.0 lbs.
- GENDER: ♂ / ♀

While awaiting evolution, it hides from predators under leaves and in nooks of branches.

Same form for ♂ / ♀

TYPE	Bug	Poison

ABILITY
- Shed Skin

HIDDEN ABILITY

STATS
- HP
- Attack
- Defense
- Sp. Atk
- Sp. Def
- Speed

EGG GROUPS
Bug

ITEMS SOMETIMES HELD
- None

EVOLUTION

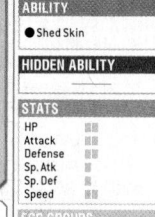

Weedle — Lv. 7 — Kakuna — Lv. 10 — Beedrill

HOW TO OBTAIN

Pokémon Black Version 2	Level up Weedle to Lv. 7
Pokémon White Version 2	Link Trade or Poké Transfer

HOW TO OBTAIN FROM OTHER GAMES

Pokémon Black Version	Route 12

LEVEL-UP AND LEARNED MOVES

Lv.	Name	Type	Kind	Pow.	Acc.	PP	Range	Long	DA
1	Harden	Normal	Status	—	—	30	Self	—	—
7	Harden	Normal	Status	—	—	30	Self	—	—

TM & HM MOVES

Lv.	Name	Type	Kind	Pow.	Acc.	PP	Range	Long	DA

MOVES TAUGHT BY PEOPLE

Name	Type	Kind	Pow.	Acc.	PP	Range	Long	DA

MOVES TAUGHT BY MOVE TUTORS FOR SHARDS

Name	Type	Kind	Pow.	Acc.	PP	Range	Long	DA
Bug Bite	Bug	Physical	60	100	20	Normal	—	○
Iron Defense	Steel	Status	—	—	15	Self	—	—
Electroweb	Electric	Special	55	95	15	Many Others	—	—

Pokémon AR Marker

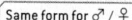

015 Beedrill!
Poison Bee Pokémon

TYPE Bug / Poison

ABILITY
- Swarm

HIDDEN ABILITY
- Sniper

STATS
- HP
- Attack
- Defense
- Sp. Atk
- Sp. Def
- Speed

EGG GROUPS
Bug

ITEMS SOMETIMES HELD
- Poison Barb

- HEIGHT: 3'03"
- WEIGHT: 65.0 lbs.
- GENDER: ♂ / ♀

Its best attack involves flying around at high speed, striking with poison needles, then flying off.

Same form for ♂ / ♀

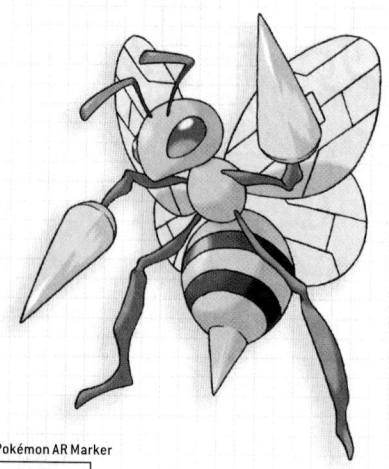

Pokémon AR Marker

EVOLUTION
Weedle — Lv. 7 — Kakuna — Lv. 10 — Beedrill

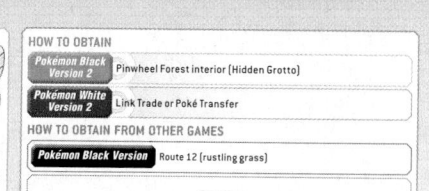

HOW TO OBTAIN
Pokémon Black Version 2 — Pinwheel Forest interior (Hidden Grotto)
Pokémon White Version 2 — Link Trade or Poké Transfer

HOW TO OBTAIN FROM OTHER GAMES
Pokémon Black Version — Route 12 (rustling grass)

LEVEL-UP AND LEARNED MOVES

Lv.	Name	Type	Kind	Pow.	Acc.	PP	Range	Long	DA
1	Fury Attack	Normal	Physical	15	85	20	Normal	—	—
10	Fury Attack	Normal	Physical	15	85	20	Normal	—	○
13	Focus Energy	Normal	Status	—	—	30	Self	—	○
16	Twineedle	Bug	Physical	25	100	20	Normal	—	—
19	Rage	Normal	Physical	20	100	20	Normal	—	—
22	Pursuit	Dark	Physical	40	100	20	Normal	—	○
25	Pin Missile	Bug	Physical	14	85	20	Normal	—	—
28	Toxic Spikes	Poison	Status	—	—	20	Other Side	—	—
31	Agility	Psychic	Status	—	—	30	Self	—	○
34	Assurance	Dark	Physical	50	100	10	Normal	—	○
37	Poison Jab	Poison	Physical	80	100	20	Normal	—	○
40	Endeavor	Normal	Physical	—	100	5	Normal	—	○

TM & HM MOVES

Lv.	Name	Type	Kind	Pow.	Acc.	PP	Range	Long	DA
TM06	Toxic	Poison	Status	—	90	10	Normal	—	—
TM09	Venoshock	Poison	Special	65	100	10	Normal	—	—
TM10	Hidden Power	Normal	Special	—	100	15	Normal	—	—
TM11	Sunny Day	Fire	Status	—	—	5	Both Sides	—	—
TM15	Hyper Beam	Normal	Special	150	90	5	Normal	—	—
TM17	Protect	Normal	Status	—	—	10	Self	—	—
TM21	Frustration	Normal	Physical	—	100	20	Normal	—	○
TM22	SolarBeam	Grass	Special	120	100	10	Normal	—	—
TM27	Return	Normal	Physical	—	100	20	Normal	—	○
TM31	Brick Break	Fighting	Physical	75	100	15	Normal	—	—
TM32	Double Team	Normal	Status	—	—	15	Self	—	—
TM36	Sludge Bomb	Poison	Special	90	100	10	Normal	—	—
TM40	Aerial Ace	Flying	Physical	60	—	20	Normal	—	○
TM42	Facade	Normal	Physical	70	100	20	Normal	—	○
TM44	Rest	Psychic	Status	—	—	10	Self	—	—
TM45	Attract	Normal	Status	—	100	15	Normal	—	—
TM46	Thief	Dark	Physical	40	100	10	Normal	—	○
TM48	Round	Normal	Special	60	100	15	Normal	—	—
TM54	False Swipe	Normal	Physical	40	100	40	Normal	—	○
TM62	Acrobatics	Flying	Physical	55	100	15	Normal	—	○
TM66	Payback	Dark	Physical	50	100	10	Normal	○	○
TM68	Giga Impact	Normal	Physical	150	90	5	Normal	—	—
TM70	Flash	Normal	Status	—	100	20	Normal	—	—
TM75	Swords Dance	Normal	Status	—	—	30	Self	—	—
TM76	Struggle Bug	Bug	Special	30	100	20	Many Others	—	—
TM81	X-Scissor	Bug	Physical	80	100	15	Normal	—	○
TM84	Poison Jab	Poison	Physical	80	100	20	Normal	—	○
TM87	Swagger	Normal	Status	—	90	15	Normal	—	—
TM89	U-turn	Bug	Physical	70	100	20	Normal	—	○
TM90	Substitute	Normal	Status	—	—	10	Self	—	—
TM94	Rock Smash	Fighting	Physical	40	100	15	Normal	—	—
HM01	Cut	Normal	Physical	50	95	30	Normal	—	○

MOVES TAUGHT BY PEOPLE

Name	Type	Kind	Pow.	Acc.	PP	Range	Long	DA

MOVES TAUGHT BY MOVE TUTORS FOR SHARDS

Name	Type	Kind	Pow.	Acc.	PP	Range	Long	DA
Bug Bite	Bug	Physical	60	100	20	Normal	—	○
Drill Run	Ground	Physical	80	95	10	Normal	—	○
Electroweb	Electric	Special	55	95	15	Many Others	—	○
Snore	Normal	Special	40	100	15	Normal	—	—
Knock Off	Dark	Physical	20	100	20	Normal	—	○
Roost	Flying	Status	—	—	10	Self	—	—
Giga Drain	Grass	Special	75	100	10	Normal	—	—
Tailwind	Flying	Status	—	—	30	Your Side	—	—
Endeavor	Normal	Physical	—	100	5	Normal	—	○
Sleep Talk	Normal	Status	—	—	10	Self	—	—

016 Pidgey
Tiny Bird Pokémon

TYPE Normal / Flying

ABILITIES
- Keen Eye
- Tangled Feet

HIDDEN ABILITY
- Big Pecks

STATS
- HP
- Attack
- Defense
- Sp. Atk
- Sp. Def
- Speed

EGG GROUPS
Flying

ITEMS SOMETIMES HELD
- None

- HEIGHT: 1'00"
- WEIGHT: 4.0 lbs.
- GENDER: ♂ / ♀

It is docile and prefers to avoid conflict. If disturbed, however, it can ferociously strike back.

Same form for ♂ / ♀

Pokémon AR Marker
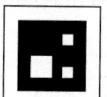

EVOLUTION
Pidgey — Lv. 18 — Pidgeotto — Lv. 36 — Pidgeot

HOW TO OBTAIN
Pokémon Black Version 2 — Link Trade or Poké Transfer
Pokémon White Version 2 — Link Trade or Poké Transfer

HOW TO OBTAIN FROM OTHER GAMES
Pokémon HeartGold Version — Route 29 (morning and afternoon only)
Pokémon SoulSilver Version — Route 29 (morning and afternoon only)

LEVEL-UP AND LEARNED MOVES

Lv.	Name	Type	Kind	Pow.	Acc.	PP	Range	Long	DA
1	Tackle	Normal	Physical	50	100	35	Normal	—	—
5	Sand-Attack	Ground	Status	—	100	15	Normal	—	—
9	Gust	Flying	Special	40	100	35	Normal	—	—
13	Quick Attack	Normal	Physical	40	100	30	Normal	—	—
17	Whirlwind	Normal	Status	—	100	20	Normal	—	—
21	Twister	Dragon	Special	40	100	20	Many Others	—	—
25	FeatherDance	Flying	Status	—	100	15	Normal	—	—
29	Agility	Psychic	Status	—	—	30	Self	—	○
33	Wing Attack	Flying	Physical	60	100	35	Normal	—	○
37	Roost	Flying	Status	—	—	10	Self	—	—
41	Tailwind	Flying	Status	—	—	30	Your Side	—	—
45	Mirror Move	Flying	Status	—	—	20	Normal	—	—
49	Air Slash	Flying	Special	75	95	20	Normal	○	○
53	Hurricane	Flying	Special	120	70	10	Normal	—	○

TM & HM MOVES

Lv.	Name	Type	Kind	Pow.	Acc.	PP	Range	Long	DA
TM06	Toxic	Poison	Status	—	90	10	Normal	—	—
TM10	Hidden Power	Normal	Special	—	100	15	Normal	—	—
TM11	Sunny Day	Fire	Status	—	—	5	Both Sides	—	—
TM17	Protect	Normal	Status	—	—	10	Self	—	—
TM18	Rain Dance	Water	Status	—	—	5	Both Sides	—	—
TM21	Frustration	Normal	Physical	—	100	20	Normal	—	○
TM27	Return	Normal	Physical	—	100	20	Normal	—	○
TM32	Double Team	Normal	Status	—	—	15	Self	—	—
TM40	Aerial Ace	Flying	Physical	60	—	20	Normal	—	○
TM42	Facade	Normal	Physical	70	100	20	Normal	—	○
TM44	Rest	Psychic	Status	—	—	10	Self	—	—
TM45	Attract	Normal	Status	—	100	15	Normal	—	—
TM46	Thief	Dark	Physical	40	100	10	Normal	—	○
TM48	Round	Normal	Special	60	100	15	Normal	—	—
TM83	Work Up	Normal	Status	—	—	30	Self	—	—
TM87	Swagger	Normal	Status	—	90	15	Normal	—	—
TM88	Pluck	Flying	Physical	60	100	20	Normal	—	○
TM89	U-turn	Bug	Physical	70	100	20	Normal	—	○
TM90	Substitute	Normal	Status	—	—	10	Self	—	—
HM02	Fly	Flying	Physical	90	95	15	Normal	○	○

MOVES TAUGHT BY PEOPLE

Name	Type	Kind	Pow.	Acc.	PP	Range	Long	DA

MOVES TAUGHT BY MOVE TUTORS FOR SHARDS

Name	Type	Kind	Pow.	Acc.	PP	Range	Long	DA
Uproar	Normal	Special	90	100	10	1 Random	—	—
Snore	Normal	Special	40	100	15	Normal	—	—
Roost	Flying	Status	—	—	10	Self	—	—
Heat Wave	Fire	Special	100	90	10	Many Others	—	—
Tailwind	Flying	Status	—	—	30	Your Side	—	—
Sleep Talk	Normal	Status	—	—	10	Self	—	—

EGG MOVES

Name	Type	Kind	Pow.	Acc.	PP	Range	Long	DA
Pursuit	Dark	Physical	40	100	20	Normal	—	○
Faint Attack	Dark	Physical	60	—	20	Normal	—	—
Foresight	Normal	Status	—	—	40	Normal	—	○
Steel Wing	Steel	Physical	70	90	25	Normal	—	—
Air Cutter	Flying	Special	55	95	25	Many Others	—	—
Air Slash	Flying	Special	75	95	20	Normal	○	○
Brave Bird	Flying	Physical	120	100	15	Normal	○	○
Uproar	Normal	Special	90	100	10	1 Random	—	—
Defog	Flying	Status	—	—	15	Normal	—	—

017 Pidgeotto
Bird Pokémon

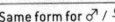

TYPE Normal | Flying

ABILITIES
- Keen Eye
- Tangled Feet

HIDDEN ABILITY
- Big Pecks

STATS

HP	▓▓▓
Attack	▓▓▓
Defense	▓▓▓
Sp. Atk	▓▓
Sp. Def	▓▓
Speed	▓▓▓

EGG GROUPS
Flying

ITEMS SOMETIMES HELD
- None

- HEIGHT: 3'07"
- WEIGHT: 66.1 lbs.
- GENDER: ♂ / ♀

It flies over its wide territory in search of prey, downing it with its highly developed claws.

Same form for ♂ / ♀

Pokémon AR Marker

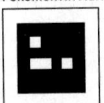

EVOLUTION

Pidgey — Lv. 18 → Pidgeotto — Lv. 36 → Pidgeot

HOW TO OBTAIN

Pokémon Black Version 2	Link Trade or Poké Transfer
Pokémon White Version 2	Link Trade or Poké Transfer

HOW TO OBTAIN FROM OTHER GAMES

Pokémon HeartGold Version	Route 43 (morning and afternoon only)
Pokémon SoulSilver Version	Route 43 (morning and afternoon only)

LEVEL-UP AND LEARNED MOVES

Lv.	Name	Type	Kind	Pow.	Acc.	PP	Range	Long	DA
1	Tackle	Normal	Physical	50	100	35	Normal	—	—
1	Sand-Attack	Ground	Status	—	100	15	Normal	—	—
1	Gust	Flying	Special	40	100	35	Normal	○	—
5	Sand-Attack	Ground	Status	—	100	15	Normal	—	—
9	Gust	Flying	Special	40	100	35	Normal	○	—
13	Quick Attack	Normal	Physical	40	100	30	Normal	—	○
17	Whirlwind	Normal	Status	—	100	20	Normal	—	—
22	Twister	Dragon	Special	40	100	15	Many Others	—	—
27	FeatherDance	Flying	Status	—	100	15	Normal	—	—
32	Agility	Psychic	Status	—	—	30	Self	—	—
37	Wing Attack	Flying	Physical	60	100	35	Normal	○	—
42	Roost	Flying	Status	—	—	10	Self	—	—
47	Tailwind	Flying	Status	—	—	30	Your Side	—	—
52	Mirror Move	Flying	Status	—	—	20	Normal	—	—
57	Air Slash	Flying	Special	75	95	20	Normal	○	—
62	Hurricane	Flying	Special	120	70	10	Normal	○	—

TM & HM MOVES

Lv.	Name	Type	Kind	Pow.	Acc.	PP	Range	Long	DA
TM06	Toxic	Poison	Status	—	90	10	Normal	—	—
TM10	Hidden Power	Normal	Special	—	100	15	Normal	—	—
TM11	Sunny Day	Fire	Status	—	—	5	Both Sides	—	—
TM17	Protect	Normal	Status	—	—	10	Self	—	—
TM18	Rain Dance	Water	Status	—	—	5	Both Sides	—	—
TM21	Frustration	Normal	Physical	—	100	20	Normal	—	○
TM27	Return	Normal	Physical	—	100	20	Normal	—	○
TM32	Double Team	Normal	Status	—	—	15	Self	—	—
TM40	Aerial Ace	Flying	Physical	60	—	20	Normal	—	—
TM42	Facade	Normal	Physical	70	100	20	Normal	—	○
TM44	Rest	Psychic	Status	—	—	10	Self	—	—
TM45	Attract	Normal	Status	—	100	15	Normal	—	—
TM46	Thief	Dark	Physical	40	100	10	Normal	—	—
TM48	Round	Normal	Special	60	100	15	Normal	—	—
TM83	Work Up	Normal	Status	—	—	30	Self	—	—
TM87	Swagger	Normal	Status	—	90	15	Normal	—	—
TM88	Pluck	Flying	Physical	60	100	20	Normal	—	○
TM89	U-turn	Bug	Physical	70	100	20	Normal	—	○
TM90	Substitute	Normal	Status	—	—	10	Self	—	—
HM02	Fly	Flying	Physical	90	95	15	Normal	○	—

MOVES TAUGHT BY PEOPLE

Name	Type	Kind	Pow.	Acc.	PP	Range	Long	DA

MOVES TAUGHT BY MOVE TUTORS FOR SHARDS

Name	Type	Kind	Pow.	Acc.	PP	Range	Long	DA
Uproar	Normal	Special	90	100	10	1 Random	—	—
Snore	Normal	Special	40	100	15	Normal	—	—
Roost	Flying	Status	—	—	10	Self	—	—
Heat Wave	Fire	Special	100	90	10	Many Others	—	—
Tailwind	Flying	Status	—	—	30	Your Side	—	—
Sleep Talk	Normal	Status	—	—	10	Self	—	—

---

018 Pidgeot
Bird Pokémon

TYPE Normal | Flying

ABILITIES
- Keen Eye
- Tangled Feet

HIDDEN ABILITY
- Big Pecks

STATS

HP	▓▓▓
Attack	▓▓▓
Defense	▓▓▓
Sp. Atk	▓▓▓
Sp. Def	▓▓
Speed	▓▓▓▓

EGG GROUPS
Flying

ITEMS SOMETIMES HELD
- None

- HEIGHT: 4'11"
- WEIGHT: 87.1 lbs.
- GENDER: ♂ / ♀

By flapping its wings with all its might, Pidgeot can make a gust of wind capable of bending tall trees.

Same form for ♂ / ♀

  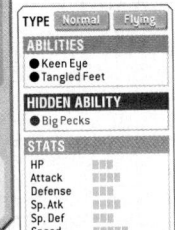

Pokémon AR Marker

EVOLUTION

Pidgey — Lv. 18 → Pidgeotto — Lv. 36 → Pidgeot

HOW TO OBTAIN

Pokémon Black Version 2	Level up a Pidgeotto you obtain via Link Trade or Poké Transfer to Lv. 36
Pokémon White Version 2	Level up a Pidgeotto you obtain via Link Trade or Poké Transfer to Lv. 36

HOW TO OBTAIN FROM OTHER GAMES

	—
	—

LEVEL-UP AND LEARNED MOVES

Lv.	Name	Type	Kind	Pow.	Acc.	PP	Range	Long	DA
1	Tackle	Normal	Physical	50	100	35	Normal	—	—
1	Sand-Attack	Normal	Status	—	100	15	Normal	—	—
1	Gust	Flying	Special	40	100	35	Normal	○	—
1	Quick Attack	Normal	Physical	40	100	30	Normal	—	○
5	Sand-Attack	Ground	Status	—	100	15	Normal	—	—
9	Gust	Flying	Special	40	100	35	Normal	○	—
13	Quick Attack	Normal	Physical	40	100	30	Normal	—	○
17	Whirlwind	Normal	Status	—	100	20	Normal	—	—
22	Twister	Dragon	Special	40	100	15	Many Others	—	—
27	FeatherDance	Flying	Status	—	100	15	Normal	—	—
32	Agility	Psychic	Status	—	—	30	Self	—	—
38	Wing Attack	Flying	Physical	60	100	35	Normal	○	—
44	Roost	Flying	Status	—	—	10	Self	—	—
50	Tailwind	Flying	Status	—	—	30	Your Side	—	—
56	Mirror Move	Flying	Status	—	—	20	Normal	—	—
62	Air Slash	Flying	Special	75	95	20	Normal	○	—
68	Hurricane	Flying	Special	120	70	10	Normal	○	—

TM & HM MOVES

Lv.	Name	Type	Kind	Pow.	Acc.	PP	Range	Long	DA
TM06	Toxic	Poison	Status	—	90	10	Normal	—	—
TM10	Hidden Power	Normal	Special	—	100	15	Normal	—	—
TM11	Sunny Day	Fire	Status	—	—	5	Both Sides	—	—
TM15	Hyper Beam	Normal	Special	150	90	5	Normal	—	—
TM17	Protect	Normal	Status	—	—	10	Self	—	—
TM18	Rain Dance	Water	Status	—	—	5	Both Sides	—	—
TM21	Frustration	Normal	Physical	—	100	20	Normal	—	○
TM27	Return	Normal	Physical	—	100	20	Normal	—	○
TM32	Double Team	Normal	Status	—	—	15	Self	—	—
TM40	Aerial Ace	Flying	Physical	60	—	20	Normal	—	—
TM42	Facade	Normal	Physical	70	100	20	Normal	—	○
TM44	Rest	Psychic	Status	—	—	10	Self	—	—
TM45	Attract	Normal	Status	—	100	15	Normal	—	—
TM46	Thief	Dark	Physical	40	100	10	Normal	—	—
TM48	Round	Normal	Special	60	100	15	Normal	—	—
TM68	Giga Impact	Normal	Physical	150	90	5	Normal	—	○
TM83	Work Up	Normal	Status	—	—	30	Self	—	—
TM87	Swagger	Normal	Status	—	90	15	Normal	—	—
TM88	Pluck	Flying	Physical	60	100	20	Normal	—	○
TM89	U-turn	Bug	Physical	70	100	20	Normal	—	○
TM90	Substitute	Normal	Status	—	—	10	Self	—	—
HM02	Fly	Flying	Physical	90	95	15	Normal	○	—

MOVES TAUGHT BY PEOPLE

Name	Type	Kind	Pow.	Acc.	PP	Range	Long	DA

MOVES TAUGHT BY MOVE TUTORS FOR SHARDS

Name	Type	Kind	Pow.	Acc.	PP	Range	Long	DA
Uproar	Normal	Special	90	100	10	1 Random	—	—
Snore	Normal	Special	40	100	15	Normal	—	—
Roost	Flying	Status	—	—	10	Self	—	—
Sky Attack	Flying	Physical	140	90	5	Normal	○	—
Heat Wave	Fire	Special	100	90	10	Many Others	—	—
Tailwind	Flying	Status	—	—	30	Your Side	—	—
Sleep Talk	Normal	Status	—	—	10	Self	—	—

019 Rattata

Mouse Pokémon

- HEIGHT: 1'00"
- WEIGHT: 7.7 lbs.
- GENDER: ♂ / ♀

It searches for food all day. It gnaws on hard objects to wear down its fangs, which grow constantly during its lifetime.

♂ ♀

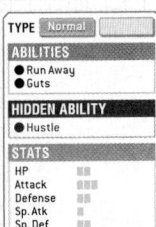

TYPE: Normal

ABILITIES
- Run Away
- Guts

HIDDEN ABILITY
- Hustle

STATS
HP
Attack
Defense
Sp. Atk
Sp. Def
Speed

EGG GROUPS
Field

ITEMS SOMETIMES HELD
- None

EVOLUTION

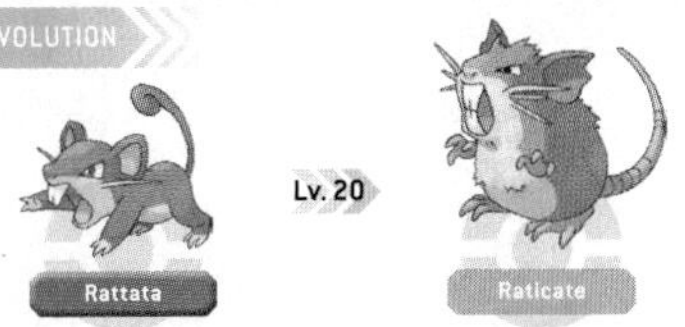

HOW TO OBTAIN

Pokémon Black Version 2: ❶ Castelia Sewers ❷ Castelia City empty lot

Pokémon White Version 2: ❶ Castelia Sewers ❷ Castelia City empty lot

HOW TO OBTAIN FROM OTHER GAMES

—

—

Pokémon AR Marker

LEVEL-UP AND LEARNED MOVES

Lv.	Name	Type	Kind	Pow.	Acc.	PP	Range	Long	DA
1	Tackle	Normal	Physical	50	100	35	Normal	—	○
1	Tail Whip	Normal	Status	—	100	30	Many Others	—	—
4	Quick Attack	Normal	Physical	40	100	30	Normal	—	○
7	Focus Energy	Normal	Status	—	—	30	Self	—	—
10	Bite	Dark	Physical	60	100	25	Normal	—	○
13	Pursuit	Dark	Physical	40	100	20	Normal	—	○
16	Hyper Fang	Normal	Physical	80	90	15	Normal	—	○
19	Sucker Punch	Dark	Physical	80	100	5	Normal	—	○
22	Crunch	Dark	Physical	80	100	15	Normal	—	○
25	Assurance	Dark	Physical	50	100	10	Normal	—	○
28	Super Fang	Normal	Physical	—	90	10	Normal	—	○
31	Double-Edge	Normal	Physical	120	100	15	Normal	—	○
34	Endeavor	Normal	Physical	—	100	5	Normal	—	○

TM & HM MOVES

Lv.	Name	Type	Kind	Pow.	Acc.	PP	Range	Long	DA
TM06	Toxic	Poison	Status	—	90	10	Normal	—	—
TM10	Hidden Power	Normal	Special	—	100	15	Normal	—	—
TM11	Sunny Day	Fire	Status	—	—	5	Both Sides	—	—
TM12	Taunt	Dark	Status	—	100	20	Normal	—	—
TM13	Ice Beam	Ice	Special	95	100	10	Normal	—	—
TM14	Blizzard	Ice	Special	120	70	5	Many Others	—	—
TM17	Protect	Normal	Status	—	—	10	Self	—	—
TM18	Rain Dance	Water	Status	—	—	5	Both Sides	—	—
TM21	Frustration	Normal	Physical	—	100	20	Normal	—	○
TM24	Thunderbolt	Electric	Special	95	100	15	Normal	—	—
TM25	Thunder	Electric	Special	120	70	10	Normal	—	—
TM27	Return	Normal	Physical	—	100	20	Normal	—	○
TM28	Dig	Ground	Physical	80	100	10	Normal	—	○
TM30	Shadow Ball	Ghost	Special	80	100	15	Normal	—	—
TM32	Double Team	Normal	Status	—	—	15	Self	—	—
TM42	Facade	Normal	Physical	70	100	20	Normal	—	○
TM44	Rest	Psychic	Status	—	—	10	Self	—	—
TM45	Attract	Normal	Status	—	100	15	Normal	—	—
TM46	Thief	Dark	Physical	40	100	10	Normal	—	○
TM48	Round	Normal	Special	60	100	15	Normal	—	—
TM57	Charge Beam	Electric	Special	50	90	10	Normal	—	—
TM67	Retaliate	Normal	Physical	70	100	5	Normal	—	○
TM73	Thunder Wave	Electric	Status	—	100	20	Normal	—	—
TM83	Work Up	Normal	Status	—	—	30	Self	—	—
TM86	Grass Knot	Grass	Special	—	100	20	Normal	—	○
TM87	Swagger	Normal	Status	—	90	15	Normal	—	—
TM88	Pluck	Flying	Physical	60	100	20	Normal	○	○
TM89	U-turn	Bug	Physical	70	100	20	Normal	—	○
TM90	Substitute	Normal	Status	—	—	10	Self	—	—
TM93	Wild Charge	Electric	Physical	90	100	15	Normal	—	○
TM94	Rock Smash	Fighting	Physical	40	100	15	Normal	—	○
HM01	Cut	Normal	Physical	50	95	30	Normal	—	○

MOVES TAUGHT BY PEOPLE

Name	Type	Kind	Pow.	Acc.	PP	Range	Long	DA

MOVES TAUGHT BY MOVE TUTORS FOR SHARDS

Name	Type	Kind	Pow.	Acc.	PP	Range	Long	DA
Covet	Normal	Physical	60	100	40	Normal	—	○
Super Fang	Normal	Physical	—	90	10	Normal	—	○
Uproar	Normal	Special	90	100	10	1 Random	—	—
Last Resort	Normal	Physical	140	100	5	Normal	—	○
Icy Wind	Ice	Special	55	95	15	Many Others	—	—
Iron Tail	Steel	Physical	100	75	15	Normal	—	○
Zen Headbutt	Psychic	Physical	80	90	15	Normal	—	○
Snore	Normal	Special	40	100	15	Normal	—	—
Endeavor	Normal	Physical	—	100	5	Normal	—	○
Sleep Talk	Normal	Status	—	—	10	Self	—	—

EGG MOVES

Name	Type	Kind	Pow.	Acc.	PP	Range	Long	DA
Screech	Normal	Status	—	85	40	Normal	—	—
Flame Wheel	Fire	Physical	60	100	25	Normal	—	○
Fury Swipes	Normal	Physical	18	80	15	Normal	—	○
Bite	Dark	Physical	60	100	25	Normal	—	○
Counter	Fighting	Physical	—	100	20	Varies	—	○
Reversal	Fighting	Physical	—	100	15	Normal	—	○
Uproar	Normal	Special	90	100	10	1 Random	—	—
Last Resort	Normal	Physical	140	100	5	Normal	—	○
Me First	Normal	Status	—	—	20	Varies	—	—
Revenge	Fighting	Physical	60	100	10	Normal	—	○
Final Gambit	Fighting	Special	—	100	5	Normal	—	○

020 Raticate

Mouse Pokémon

- HEIGHT: 2'04"
- WEIGHT: 40.8 lbs.
- GENDER: ♂ / ♀

With its long fangs, this surprisingly violent Pokémon can gnaw away even thick concrete with ease.

♂ ♀

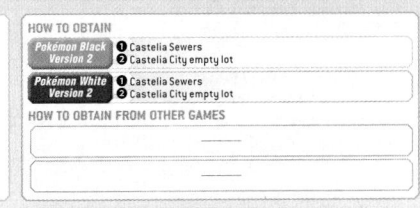

TYPE: Normal

ABILITIES
- Run Away
- Guts

HIDDEN ABILITY
- Hustle

STATS
HP
Attack
Defense
Sp. Atk
Sp. Def
Speed

EGG GROUPS
Field

ITEMS SOMETIMES HELD
- None

EVOLUTION

HOW TO OBTAIN

Pokémon Black Version 2: ❶ Relic Passage middle ❷ Strange House entrance

Pokémon White Version 2: ❶ Relic Passage middle ❷ Strange House entrance

HOW TO OBTAIN FROM OTHER GAMES

—

—

Pokémon AR Marker

LEVEL-UP AND LEARNED MOVES

Lv.	Name	Type	Kind	Pow.	Acc.	PP	Range	Long	DA
1	Swords Dance	Normal	Status	—	—	30	Self	—	—
1	Tackle	Normal	Physical	50	100	35	Normal	—	○
1	Tail Whip	Normal	Status	—	100	30	Many Others	—	—
1	Quick Attack	Normal	Physical	40	100	30	Normal	—	○
1	Focus Energy	Normal	Status	—	—	30	Self	—	—
4	Quick Attack	Normal	Physical	40	100	30	Normal	—	○
7	Focus Energy	Normal	Status	—	—	30	Self	—	—
10	Bite	Dark	Physical	60	100	25	Normal	—	○
13	Pursuit	Dark	Physical	40	100	20	Normal	—	○
16	Hyper Fang	Normal	Physical	80	90	15	Normal	—	○
19	Sucker Punch	Dark	Physical	80	100	5	Normal	—	○
20	Scary Face	Normal	Status	—	100	10	Normal	—	—
24	Crunch	Dark	Physical	80	100	15	Normal	—	○
29	Assurance	Dark	Physical	50	100	10	Normal	—	○
34	Super Fang	Normal	Physical	—	90	10	Normal	—	○
39	Double-Edge	Normal	Physical	120	100	15	Normal	—	○
44	Endeavor	Normal	Physical	—	100	5	Normal	—	○

TM & HM MOVES

Lv.	Name	Type	Kind	Pow.	Acc.	PP	Range	Long	DA
TM05	Roar	Normal	Status	—	100	20	Normal	—	—
TM06	Toxic	Poison	Status	—	90	10	Normal	—	—
TM10	Hidden Power	Normal	Special	—	100	15	Normal	—	—
TM11	Sunny Day	Fire	Status	—	—	5	Both Sides	—	—
TM12	Taunt	Dark	Status	—	100	20	Normal	—	—
TM13	Ice Beam	Ice	Special	95	100	10	Normal	—	—
TM14	Blizzard	Ice	Special	120	70	5	Many Others	—	—
TM15	Hyper Beam	Normal	Special	150	90	5	Normal	—	—
TM17	Protect	Normal	Status	—	—	10	Self	—	—
TM18	Rain Dance	Water	Status	—	—	5	Both Sides	—	—
TM21	Frustration	Normal	Physical	—	100	20	Normal	—	○
TM24	Thunderbolt	Electric	Special	95	100	15	Normal	—	—
TM25	Thunder	Electric	Special	120	70	10	Normal	—	—
TM27	Return	Normal	Physical	—	100	20	Normal	—	○
TM28	Dig	Ground	Physical	80	100	10	Normal	—	○
TM30	Shadow Ball	Ghost	Special	80	100	15	Normal	—	—
TM32	Double Team	Normal	Status	—	—	15	Self	—	—
TM42	Facade	Normal	Physical	70	100	20	Normal	—	○
TM44	Rest	Psychic	Status	—	—	10	Self	—	—
TM45	Attract	Normal	Status	—	100	15	Normal	—	—
TM46	Thief	Dark	Physical	40	100	10	Normal	—	○
TM48	Round	Normal	Special	60	100	15	Normal	—	—
TM57	Charge Beam	Electric	Special	50	90	10	Normal	—	—
TM67	Retaliate	Normal	Physical	70	100	5	Normal	—	○
TM68	Giga Impact	Normal	Physical	150	90	5	Normal	—	○
TM73	Thunder Wave	Electric	Status	—	100	20	Normal	—	—
TM75	Swords Dance	Normal	Status	—	—	30	Self	—	—
TM83	Work Up	Normal	Status	—	—	30	Self	—	—
TM86	Grass Knot	Grass	Special	—	100	20	Normal	—	○
TM87	Swagger	Normal	Status	—	90	15	Normal	—	—
TM88	Pluck	Flying	Physical	60	100	20	Normal	○	○
TM89	U-turn	Bug	Physical	70	100	20	Normal	—	○
TM90	Substitute	Normal	Status	—	—	10	Self	—	—
TM93	Wild Charge	Electric	Physical	90	100	15	Normal	—	○
TM94	Rock Smash	Fighting	Physical	40	100	15	Normal	—	○
HM01	Cut	Normal	Physical	50	95	30	Normal	—	○
HM04	Strength	Normal	Physical	80	100	15	Normal	—	○

MOVES TAUGHT BY PEOPLE

Name	Type	Kind	Pow.	Acc.	PP	Range	Long	DA

MOVES TAUGHT BY MOVE TUTORS FOR SHARDS

Name	Type	Kind	Pow.	Acc.	PP	Range	Long	DA
Covet	Normal	Physical	60	100	40	Normal	—	○
Super Fang	Normal	Physical	—	90	10	Normal	—	○
Uproar	Normal	Special	90	100	10	1 Random	—	—
Last Resort	Normal	Physical	140	100	5	Normal	—	○
Icy Wind	Ice	Special	55	95	15	Many Others	—	—
Iron Tail	Steel	Physical	100	75	15	Normal	—	○
Zen Headbutt	Psychic	Physical	80	90	15	Normal	—	○
Snore	Normal	Special	40	100	15	Normal	—	—
Endeavor	Normal	Physical	—	100	5	Normal	—	○
Sleep Talk	Normal	Status	—	—	10	Self	—	—

Tiny Bird Pokémon
021 Spearow

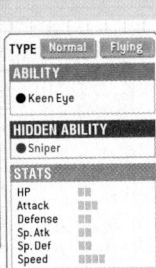

TYPE Normal Flying

ABILITY
- Keen Eye

HIDDEN ABILITY
- Sniper

STATS
- HP
- Attack
- Defense
- Sp. Atk
- Sp. Def
- Speed

EGG GROUPS
Flying

ITEMS SOMETIMES HELD
- None

- HEIGHT: 1'00"
- WEIGHT: 4.4 lbs.
- GENDER: ♂ / ♀

It flaps its small wings busily to fly. Using its beak, it searches in grass for prey.

Same form for ♂ / ♀

Pokémon AR Marker

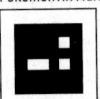

● EVOLUTION

Spearow — Lv. 20 — Fearow

HOW TO OBTAIN
Pokémon Black Version 2	Catch a Fearow, leave it at the Pokémon Day Care, and hatch the Egg that is found
Pokémon White Version 2	Catch a Fearow, leave it at the Pokémon Day Care, and hatch the Egg that is found

HOW TO OBTAIN FROM OTHER GAMES
Pokémon HeartGold Version	Route 33 (morning and afternoon only)
Pokémon SoulSilver Version	Route 33 (morning and afternoon only)

LEVEL-UP AND LEARNED MOVES
Lv.	Name	Type	Kind	Pow.	Acc.	PP	Range	Long	DA
1	Peck	Flying	Physical	35	100	35	Normal		
1	Growl	Normal	Status	—	100	40	Many Others		
5	Leer	Normal	Status	—	100	30	Many Others		
9	Fury Attack	Normal	Physical	15	85	20	Normal		
13	Pursuit	Dark	Physical	40	100	20	Normal		
17	Aerial Ace	Flying	Physical	60	—	20	Normal		○
21	Mirror Move	Flying	Status	—	—	20	Self		
25	Agility	Psychic	Status	—	—	30	Self		
29	Assurance	Dark	Physical	50	100	10	Normal		○
33	Roost	Flying	Status	—	—	10	Self		
37	Drill Peck	Flying	Physical	80	100	20	Normal		

TM & HM MOVES
Lv.	Name	Type	Kind	Pow.	Acc.	PP	Range	Long	DA
TM06	Toxic	Poison	Status	—	90	10	Normal		—
TM10	Hidden Power	Normal	Special	—	100	15	Normal		—
TM11	Sunny Day	Fire	Status	—	—	5	Both Sides		—
TM17	Protect	Normal	Status	—	—	10	Self		—
TM18	Rain Dance	Water	Status	—	—	5	Both Sides		—
TM21	Frustration	Normal	Physical	—	100	20	Normal		○
TM27	Return	Normal	Physical	—	100	20	Normal		○
TM32	Double Team	Normal	Status	—	—	15	Self		—
TM40	Aerial Ace	Flying	Physical	60	—	20	Normal	○	○
TM42	Facade	Normal	Physical	70	100	20	Normal		○
TM44	Rest	Psychic	Status	—	—	10	Self		—
TM45	Attract	Normal	Status	—	100	15	Normal		—
TM46	Thief	Dark	Physical	40	100	10	Normal		○
TM48	Round	Normal	Special	60	100	15	Normal		—
TM49	Echoed Voice	Normal	Special	40	100	15	Normal		—
TM54	False Swipe	Normal	Physical	40	100	40	Normal		○
TM83	Work Up	Normal	Status	—	—	30	Self		—
TM87	Swagger	Normal	Status	—	90	15	Normal		—
TM88	Pluck	Flying	Physical	60	100	20	Normal	○	○
TM89	U-turn	Bug	Physical	70	100	20	Normal		○
TM90	Substitute	Normal	Status	—	—	10	Self		—
HM02	Fly	Flying	Physical	90	95	15	Normal		○

● MOVES TAUGHT BY PEOPLE
Name	Type	Kind	Pow.	Acc.	PP	Range	Long	DA

● MOVES TAUGHT BY MOVE TUTORS FOR SHARDS
Name	Type	Kind	Pow.	Acc.	PP	Range	Long	DA
Drill Run	Ground	Physical	80	95	10	Normal	—	○
Uproar	Normal	Special	90	100	10	1 Random		
Snore	Normal	Special	40	100	15	Normal		
Roost	Flying	Status	—	—	5	Self		
Sky Attack	Flying	Physical	140	90	5	Normal	○	
Heat Wave	Fire	Special	100	90	10	Many Others		○
Tailwind	Flying	Status	—	—	30	Your Side		
Sleep Talk	Normal	Status	—	—	10	Self		

● EGG MOVES
Name	Type	Kind	Pow.	Acc.	PP	Range	Long	DA
Faint Attack	Dark	Physical	60	—	20	Normal	—	—
Scary Face	Normal	Status	—	100	10	Normal	—	—
Quick Attack	Normal	Physical	40	100	30	Normal	—	○
Tri Attack	Normal	Special	80	100	10	Normal	—	—
Astonish	Ghost	Physical	30	100	15	Normal	○	○
Sky Attack	Flying	Physical	140	90	5	Normal	—	—
Whirlwind	Normal	Status	—	—	20	Normal	—	—
Uproar	Normal	Special	90	100	10	1 Random	—	—
FeatherDance	Flying	Status	—	100	15	Normal	—	—
Steel Wing	Steel	Physical	70	90	25	Normal	—	○
Razor Wind	Normal	Special	80	100	10	Many Others	—	—

Beak Pokémon
022 Fearow

TYPE Normal Flying

ABILITY
- Keen Eye

HIDDEN ABILITY
- Sniper

STATS
- HP
- Attack
- Defense
- Sp. Atk
- Sp. Def
- Speed

EGG GROUPS
Flying

ITEMS SOMETIMES HELD
- Sharp Beak

- HEIGHT: 3'11"
- WEIGHT: 83.8 lbs.
- GENDER: ♂ / ♀

It has the stamina to fly all day on its broad wings. It fights by using its sharp beak.

Same form for ♂ / ♀

Pokémon AR Marker

● EVOLUTION

Spearow — Lv. 20 — Fearow

HOW TO OBTAIN
Pokémon Black Version 2	Route 15 (mass outbreak)
Pokémon White Version 2	Route 15 (mass outbreak)

HOW TO OBTAIN FROM OTHER GAMES

LEVEL-UP AND LEARNED MOVES
Lv.	Name	Type	Kind	Pow.	Acc.	PP	Range	Long	DA
1	Pluck	Flying	Physical	60	100	20	Normal	○	○
1	Peck	Flying	Physical	35	100	35	Normal		
1	Growl	Normal	Status	—	100	40	Many Others		
1	Leer	Normal	Status	—	100	30	Many Others		
9	Fury Attack	Normal	Physical	15	85	20	Normal		
5	Leer	Normal	Status	—	100	30	Many Others		
9	Fury Attack	Normal	Physical	15	85	20	Normal		
13	Pursuit	Dark	Physical	40	100	20	Normal		
17	Aerial Ace	Flying	Physical	60	—	20	Normal		○
23	Mirror Move	Flying	Status	—	—	20	Self		
29	Agility	Psychic	Status	—	—	30	Self		
35	Assurance	Dark	Physical	50	100	10	Normal		○
41	Roost	Flying	Status	—	—	10	Self		
47	Drill Peck	Flying	Physical	80	100	20	Normal		
53	Drill Run	Ground	Physical	80	95	10	Normal		○

TM & HM MOVES
Lv.	Name	Type	Kind	Pow.	Acc.	PP	Range	Long	DA
TM06	Toxic	Poison	Status	—	90	10	Normal		—
TM10	Hidden Power	Normal	Special	—	100	15	Normal		—
TM11	Sunny Day	Fire	Status	—	—	5	Both Sides		—
TM15	Hyper Beam	Normal	Special	150	90	5	Normal		—
TM17	Protect	Normal	Status	—	—	10	Self		—
TM18	Rain Dance	Water	Status	—	—	5	Both Sides		—
TM21	Frustration	Normal	Physical	—	100	20	Normal		○
TM27	Return	Normal	Physical	—	100	20	Normal		○
TM32	Double Team	Normal	Status	—	—	15	Self		—
TM40	Aerial Ace	Flying	Physical	60	—	20	Normal	○	○
TM42	Facade	Normal	Physical	70	100	20	Normal		○
TM44	Rest	Psychic	Status	—	—	10	Self		—
TM45	Attract	Normal	Status	—	100	15	Normal		—
TM46	Thief	Dark	Physical	40	100	10	Normal		○
TM48	Round	Normal	Special	60	100	15	Normal		—
TM49	Echoed Voice	Normal	Special	40	100	15	Normal		—
TM54	False Swipe	Normal	Physical	40	100	40	Normal		○
TM68	Giga Impact	Normal	Physical	150	90	5	Normal		—
TM83	Work Up	Normal	Status	—	—	30	Self		—
TM87	Swagger	Normal	Status	—	90	15	Normal		—
TM88	Pluck	Flying	Physical	60	100	20	Normal	○	○
TM89	U-turn	Bug	Physical	70	100	20	Normal		○
TM90	Substitute	Normal	Status	—	—	10	Self		—
HM02	Fly	Flying	Physical	90	95	15	Normal	○	○

● MOVES TAUGHT BY PEOPLE
Name	Type	Kind	Pow.	Acc.	PP	Range	Long	DA

● MOVES TAUGHT BY MOVE TUTORS FOR SHARDS
Name	Type	Kind	Pow.	Acc.	PP	Range	Long	DA
Drill Run	Ground	Physical	80	95	10	Normal	—	○
Uproar	Normal	Special	90	100	10	1 Random		
Snore	Normal	Special	40	100	15	Normal		
Roost	Flying	Status	—	—	5	Self		
Sky Attack	Flying	Physical	140	90	5	Normal	○	
Heat Wave	Fire	Special	100	90	10	Many Others		○
Tailwind	Flying	Status	—	—	30	Your Side		
Sleep Talk	Normal	Status	—	—	10	Self		

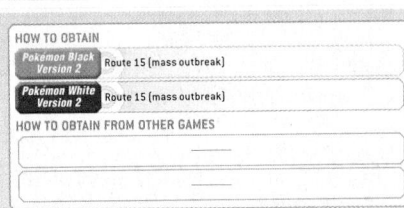

Snake Pokémon
023 Ekans

- HEIGHT: 6'07"
- WEIGHT: 15.2 lbs.
- GENDER: ♂ / ♀

It sneaks through grass without making a sound and strikes unsuspecting prey from behind.

Same form for ♂ / ♀

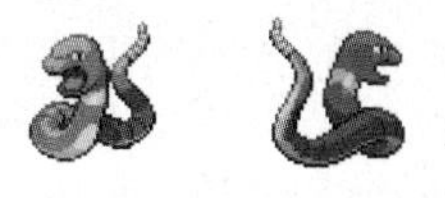

TYPE Poison

ABILITIES
- Intimidate
- Shed Skin

HIDDEN ABILITY
—

STATS
HP
Attack
Defense
Sp. Atk
Sp. Def
Speed

EGG GROUPS
Field/Dragon

ITEMS SOMETIMES HELD
- None

EVOLUTION

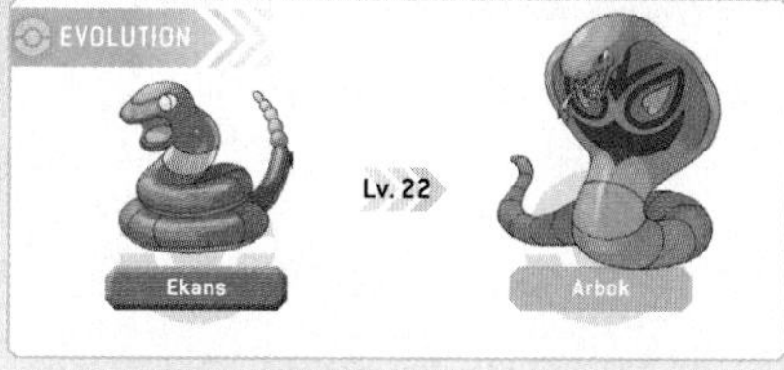

HOW TO OBTAIN

Pokémon Black Version 2	Link Trade or Poké Transfer
Pokémon White Version 2	Link Trade or Poké Transfer

HOW TO OBTAIN FROM OTHER GAMES

Pokémon HeartGold Version	Goldenrod Game Corner prize (700 Coins)
Pokémon SoulSilver Version	Route 32

LEVEL-UP AND LEARNED MOVES

Lv.	Name	Type	Kind	Pow.	Acc.	PP	Range	Long	DA
1	Wrap	Normal	Physical	15	90	20	Normal	—	○
1	Leer	Normal	Status	—	100	30	Many Others	—	—
4	Poison Sting	Poison	Physical	15	100	35	Normal	—	—
9	Bite	Dark	Physical	60	100	25	Normal	—	○
12	Glare	Normal	Status	—	90	30	Normal	—	—
17	Screech	Normal	Status	—	85	40	Normal	—	—
20	Acid	Poison	Special	40	100	30	Many Others	—	—
25	Stockpile	Normal	Status	—	—	20	Self	—	—
25	Swallow	Normal	Status	—	—	10	Self	—	—
25	Spit Up	Normal	Special	—	100	10	Normal	—	—
28	Acid Spray	Poison	Special	40	100	20	Normal	—	—
33	Mud Bomb	Ground	Special	65	85	10	Normal	—	—
36	Gastro Acid	Poison	Status	—	100	10	Normal	—	—
41	Haze	Ice	Status	—	—	30	Both Sides	—	—
44	Coil	Poison	Status	—	—	20	Self	—	—
49	Gunk Shot	Poison	Physical	120	70	5	Normal	—	—

TM & HM MOVES

Lv.	Name	Type	Kind	Pow.	Acc.	PP	Range	Long	DA
TM06	Toxic	Poison	Status	—	90	10	Normal	—	—
TM09	Venoshock	Poison	Special	65	100	10	Normal	—	—
TM10	Hidden Power	Normal	Special	—	100	15	Normal	—	—
TM11	Sunny Day	Fire	Status	—	—	5	Both Sides	—	—
TM17	Protect	Normal	Status	—	—	10	Self	—	—
TM18	Rain Dance	Water	Status	—	—	5	Both Sides	—	—
TM21	Frustration	Normal	Physical	—	100	20	Normal	—	○
TM26	Earthquake	Ground	Physical	100	100	10	Adjacent	—	—
TM27	Return	Normal	Physical	—	100	20	Normal	—	○
TM28	Dig	Ground	Physical	80	100	10	Normal	—	○
TM32	Double Team	Normal	Status	—	—	15	Self	—	—
TM34	Sludge Wave	Poison	Special	95	100	10	Adjacent	—	—
TM36	Sludge Bomb	Poison	Special	90	100	10	Normal	—	—
TM39	Rock Tomb	Rock	Physical	50	80	10	Normal	—	—
TM41	Torment	Dark	Status	—	100	15	Normal	—	—
TM42	Facade	Normal	Physical	70	100	20	Normal	—	○
TM44	Rest	Psychic	Status	—	—	10	Self	—	—
TM45	Attract	Normal	Status	—	100	15	Normal	—	—
TM46	Thief	Dark	Physical	40	100	10	Normal	—	○
TM48	Round	Normal	Special	60	100	15	Normal	—	—
TM66	Payback	Dark	Physical	50	100	10	Normal	—	○
TM78	Bulldoze	Ground	Physical	60	100	20	Adjacent	—	—
TM80	Rock Slide	Rock	Physical	75	90	10	Many Others	—	—
TM84	Poison Jab	Poison	Physical	80	100	20	Normal	—	○
TM87	Swagger	Normal	Status	—	90	15	Normal	—	—
TM90	Substitute	Normal	Status	—	—	10	Self	—	—
HM04	Strength	Normal	Physical	80	100	15	Normal	—	○

MOVES TAUGHT BY PEOPLE

Name	Type	Kind	Pow.	Acc.	PP	Range	Long	DA

MOVES TAUGHT BY MOVE TUTORS FOR SHARDS

Name	Type	Kind	Pow.	Acc.	PP	Range	Long	DA
Seed Bomb	Grass	Physical	80	100	15	Normal	—	—
Gunk Shot	Poison	Physical	120	70	5	Normal	—	—
Iron Tail	Steel	Physical	100	75	15	Normal	—	○
Aqua Tail	Water	Physical	90	90	10	Normal	—	○
Dark Pulse	Dark	Special	80	100	15	Normal	○	—
Bind	Normal	Physical	15	85	20	Normal	—	○
Snore	Normal	Special	40	100	15	Normal	—	—
Giga Drain	Grass	Special	75	100	10	Normal	—	—
Gastro Acid	Poison	Status	—	100	10	Normal	—	—
Spite	Ghost	Status	—	100	10	Normal	—	—
Sleep Talk	Normal	Status	—	—	10	Self	—	—
Snatch	Dark	Status	—	—	10	Self	—	—

EGG MOVES

Name	Type	Kind	Pow.	Acc.	PP	Range	Long	DA
Pursuit	Dark	Physical	40	100	20	Normal	—	○
Slam	Normal	Physical	80	75	20	Normal	—	○
Spite	Ghost	Status	—	100	10	Normal	—	—
Beat Up	Dark	Physical	—	100	10	Normal	—	—
Poison Fang	Poison	Physical	50	100	15	Normal	—	○
Scary Face	Normal	Status	—	100	10	Normal	—	—
Poison Tail	Poison	Physical	50	100	25	Normal	—	○
Disable	Normal	Status	—	100	20	Normal	—	—
Switcheroo	Dark	Status	—	100	10	Normal	—	—
Iron Tail	Steel	Physical	100	75	15	Normal	—	○
Sucker Punch	Dark	Physical	80	100	5	Normal	—	○
Snatch	Dark	Status	—	—	10	Self	—	—

Pokémon AR Marker

023 Ekans

Cobra Pokémon
024 Arbok

- HEIGHT: 11'06"
- WEIGHT: 143.3 lbs.
- GENDER: ♂ / ♀

The pattern on its belly is for intimidation. It constricts foes while they are frozen in fear.

Same form for ♂ / ♀

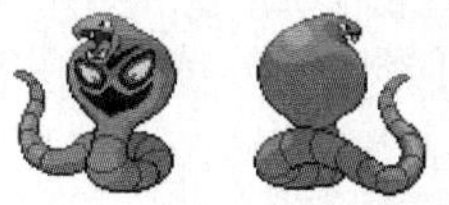

TYPE Poison

ABILITIES
- Intimidate
- Shed Skin

HIDDEN ABILITY
—

STATS
HP
Attack
Defense
Sp. Atk
Sp. Def
Speed

EGG GROUPS
Field/Dragon

ITEMS SOMETIMES HELD
- None

EVOLUTION

HOW TO OBTAIN

Pokémon Black Version 2	Link Trade or Poké Transfer
Pokémon White Version 2	Link Trade or Poké Transfer

HOW TO OBTAIN FROM OTHER GAMES

Pokémon SoulSilver Version	Route 27
	—

LEVEL-UP AND LEARNED MOVES

Lv.	Name	Type	Kind	Pow.	Acc.	PP	Range	Long	DA
1	Ice Fang	Ice	Physical	65	95	15	Normal	—	○
1	Thunder Fang	Electric	Physical	65	95	15	Normal	—	○
1	Fire Fang	Fire	Physical	65	95	15	Normal	—	○
1	Wrap	Normal	Physical	15	90	20	Normal	—	○
1	Leer	Normal	Status	—	100	30	Many Others	—	—
1	Poison Sting	Poison	Physical	15	100	35	Normal	—	—
1	Bite	Dark	Physical	60	100	25	Normal	—	○
4	Poison Sting	Poison	Physical	15	100	35	Normal	—	—
9	Bite	Dark	Physical	60	100	25	Normal	—	○
12	Glare	Normal	Status	—	90	30	Normal	—	—
17	Screech	Normal	Status	—	85	40	Normal	—	—
20	Acid	Poison	Special	40	100	30	Many Others	—	—
22	Crunch	Dark	Physical	80	100	15	Normal	—	○
27	Stockpile	Normal	Status	—	—	20	Self	—	—
27	Swallow	Normal	Status	—	—	10	Self	—	—
27	Spit Up	Normal	Special	—	100	10	Normal	—	—
32	Acid Spray	Poison	Special	40	100	20	Normal	—	—
39	Mud Bomb	Ground	Special	65	85	10	Normal	—	—
44	Gastro Acid	Poison	Status	—	100	10	Normal	—	—
51	Haze	Ice	Status	—	—	30	Both Sides	—	—
56	Coil	Poison	Status	—	—	20	Self	—	—
63	Gunk Shot	Poison	Physical	120	70	5	Normal	—	—

TM & HM MOVES

Lv.	Name	Type	Kind	Pow.	Acc.	PP	Range	Long	DA
TM06	Toxic	Poison	Status	—	90	10	Normal	—	—
TM09	Venoshock	Poison	Special	65	100	10	Normal	—	—
TM10	Hidden Power	Normal	Special	—	100	15	Normal	—	—
TM11	Sunny Day	Fire	Status	—	—	5	Both Sides	—	—
TM15	Hyper Beam	Normal	Special	150	90	5	Normal	—	—
TM17	Protect	Normal	Status	—	—	10	Self	—	—
TM18	Rain Dance	Water	Status	—	—	5	Both Sides	—	—
TM21	Frustration	Normal	Physical	—	100	20	Normal	—	○
TM26	Earthquake	Ground	Physical	100	100	10	Adjacent	—	—
TM27	Return	Normal	Physical	—	100	20	Normal	—	○
TM28	Dig	Ground	Physical	80	100	10	Normal	—	○
TM32	Double Team	Normal	Status	—	—	15	Self	—	—
TM34	Sludge Wave	Poison	Special	95	100	10	Adjacent	—	—
TM36	Sludge Bomb	Poison	Special	90	100	10	Normal	—	—
TM39	Rock Tomb	Rock	Physical	50	80	10	Normal	—	—
TM41	Torment	Dark	Status	—	100	15	Normal	—	—
TM42	Facade	Normal	Physical	70	100	20	Normal	—	○
TM44	Rest	Psychic	Status	—	—	10	Self	—	—
TM45	Attract	Normal	Status	—	100	15	Normal	—	—
TM46	Thief	Dark	Physical	40	100	10	Normal	—	○
TM48	Round	Normal	Special	60	100	15	Normal	—	—
TM66	Payback	Dark	Physical	50	100	10	Normal	—	○
TM68	Giga Impact	Normal	Physical	150	90	5	Normal	—	○
TM78	Bulldoze	Ground	Physical	60	100	20	Adjacent	—	—
TM80	Rock Slide	Rock	Physical	75	90	10	Many Others	—	—
TM82	Dragon Tail	Dragon	Physical	60	90	10	Normal	—	○
TM84	Poison Jab	Poison	Physical	80	100	20	Normal	—	○
TM87	Swagger	Normal	Status	—	90	15	Normal	—	—
TM90	Substitute	Normal	Status	—	—	10	Self	—	—
HM04	Strength	Normal	Physical	80	100	15	Normal	—	○

MOVES TAUGHT BY PEOPLE

Name	Type	Kind	Pow.	Acc.	PP	Range	Long	DA

MOVES TAUGHT BY MOVE TUTORS FOR SHARDS

Name	Type	Kind	Pow.	Acc.	PP	Range	Long	DA
Seed Bomb	Grass	Physical	80	100	15	Normal	—	—
Gunk Shot	Poison	Physical	120	70	5	Normal	—	—
Iron Tail	Steel	Physical	100	75	15	Normal	—	○
Aqua Tail	Water	Physical	90	90	10	Normal	—	○
Dark Pulse	Dark	Special	80	100	15	Normal	○	—
Bind	Normal	Physical	15	85	20	Normal	—	○
Snore	Normal	Special	40	100	15	Normal	—	—
Giga Drain	Grass	Special	75	100	10	Normal	—	—
Gastro Acid	Poison	Status	—	100	10	Normal	—	—
Spite	Ghost	Status	—	100	10	Normal	—	—
Sleep Talk	Normal	Status	—	—	10	Self	—	—
Snatch	Dark	Status	—	—	10	Self	—	—

Pokémon AR Marker

024 Arbok

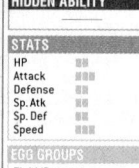

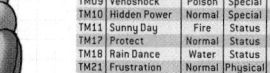

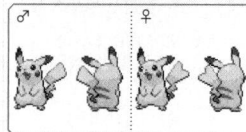
Pikachu | 025

025 Pikachu

Mouse Pokémon

TYPE Electric

ABILITY
● Static

HIDDEN ABILITY
● Lightningrod

● HEIGHT: 1'04"
● WEIGHT: 13.2 lbs.
● GENDER: ♂ / ♀

It occasionally uses an electric shock to recharge a fellow Pikachu that is in a weakened state.

STATS
HP
Attack
Defense
Sp. Atk
Sp. Def
Speed

EGG GROUPS
Field/Fairy

ITEMS SOMETIMES HELD
● None

♂   ♀

Pokémon AR Marker

EVOLUTION

Pichu → Level up with high friendship → Pikachu → Use Thunderstone → Raichu

→ p. 99

HOW TO OBTAIN

| Pokémon Black Version 2 | Link Trade or Poké Transfer |
| Pokémon White Version 2 | Link Trade or Poké Transfer |

HOW TO OBTAIN FROM OTHER GAMES

| Pokémon HeartGold Version | Viridian Forest |
| Pokémon SoulSilver Version | Viridian Forest |

LEVEL-UP AND LEARNED MOVES

Lv.	Name	Type	Kind	Pow.	Acc.	PP	Range	Long	DA
1	Growl	Normal	Status	—	100	40	Many Others	—	—
1	ThunderShock	Electric	Special	40	100	30	Normal	—	—
5	Tail Whip	Normal	Status	—	100	30	Many Others	—	—
10	Thunder Wave	Electric	Status	—	100	20	Normal	—	—
13	Quick Attack	Normal	Physical	40	100	30	Normal	—	○
18	Electro Ball	Electric	Special	—	100	10	Normal	—	○
21	Double Team	Normal	Status	—	—	15	Self	—	—
26	Slam	Normal	Physical	80	75	20	Normal	—	○
29	Thunderbolt	Electric	Special	95	100	15	Normal	—	—
34	Feint	Normal	Physical	30	100	10	Normal	—	○
37	Agility	Psychic	Status	—	—	30	Self	—	—
42	Discharge	Electric	Special	80	100	15	Adjacent	—	—
45	Light Screen	Psychic	Status	—	—	30	Your Side	—	—
50	Thunder	Electric	Special	120	70	10	Normal	—	—

TM & HM MOVES

Lv.	Name	Type	Kind	Pow.	Acc.	PP	Range	Long	DA
TM06	Toxic	Poison	Status	—	90	10	Normal	—	—
TM10	Hidden Power	Normal	Special	—	100	15	Normal	—	—
TM16	Light Screen	Psychic	Status	—	—	30	Your Side	—	—
TM17	Protect	Normal	Status	—	—	10	Self	—	—
TM18	Rain Dance	Water	Status	—	—	5	Both Sides	—	—
TM21	Frustration	Normal	Physical	—	100	20	Normal	—	○
TM24	Thunderbolt	Electric	Special	95	100	15	Normal	—	—
TM25	Thunder	Electric	Special	120	70	10	Normal	—	—
TM27	Return	Normal	Physical	—	100	20	Normal	—	○
TM28	Dig	Ground	Physical	80	100	10	Normal	—	○
TM31	Brick Break	Fighting	Physical	75	100	15	Normal	—	○
TM32	Double Team	Normal	Status	—	—	15	Self	—	—
TM42	Facade	Normal	Physical	70	100	20	Normal	—	○
TM44	Rest	Psychic	Status	—	—	10	Self	—	—
TM45	Attract	Normal	Status	—	100	15	Normal	—	—
TM48	Round	Normal	Special	60	100	15	Normal	—	—
TM49	Echoed Voice	Normal	Special	40	100	15	Normal	—	—
TM56	Fling	Dark	Physical	—	100	10	Normal	—	○
TM57	Charge Beam	Electric	Special	50	90	10	Normal	—	—
TM70	Flash	Normal	Status	—	100	20	Normal	—	—
TM72	Volt Switch	Electric	Special	70	100	20	Normal	—	—
TM73	Thunder Wave	Electric	Status	—	100	20	Normal	—	—
TM86	Grass Knot	Grass	Special	—	100	20	Normal	—	○
TM87	Swagger	Normal	Status	—	90	15	Normal	—	—
TM90	Substitute	Normal	Status	—	—	10	Self	—	—
TM93	Wild Charge	Electric	Physical	90	100	15	Normal	—	○
TM94	Rock Smash	Fighting	Physical	40	100	15	Normal	—	○
HM04	Strength	Normal	Physical	80	100	15	Normal	—	○

MOVES TAUGHT BY PEOPLE

Name	Type	Kind	Pow.	Acc.	PP	Range	Long	DA

MOVES TAUGHT BY MOVE TUTORS FOR SHARDS

Name	Type	Kind	Pow.	Acc.	PP	Range	Long	DA
Covet	Normal	Physical	60	100	40	Normal	—	○
Signal Beam	Bug	Special	75	100	15	Normal	—	○
ThunderPunch	Electric	Physical	75	100	15	Normal	—	○
Magnet Rise	Electric	Status	—	—	10	Self	—	—
Iron Tail	Steel	Physical	100	75	15	Normal	—	○
Snore	Normal	Special	40	100	15	Normal	—	—
Knock Off	Dark	Physical	20	100	20	Normal	—	○
Helping Hand	Normal	Status	—	—	20	1 Ally	—	—
Sleep Talk	Normal	Status	—	—	10	Self	—	—

 ...

026 Raichu
Mouse Pokémon

TYPE Electric

ABILITY
● Static

HIDDEN ABILITY
● Lightningrod

● HEIGHT: 2'07"
● WEIGHT: 66.1 lbs.
● GENDER: ♂ / ♀

Its tail discharges electricity into the ground, protecting it from getting shocked.

STATS
HP
Attack
Defense
Sp. Atk
Sp. Def
Speed

EGG GROUPS
Field/Fairy

ITEMS SOMETIMES HELD
● None

♂   ♀

Raichu | 026

Pokémon AR Marker

EVOLUTION

Pichu → Level up with high friendship → Pikachu → Use Thunderstone → Raichu

→ p. 99

HOW TO OBTAIN

| Pokémon Black Version 2 | Use Thunderstone on a Pikachu you obtain via Link Trade or Poké Transfer |
| Pokémon White Version 2 | Use Thunderstone on a Pikachu you obtain via Link Trade or Poké Transfer |

HOW TO OBTAIN FROM OTHER GAMES

| — |
| — |

LEVEL-UP AND LEARNED MOVES

Lv.	Name	Type	Kind	Pow.	Acc.	PP	Range	Long	DA
1	ThunderShock	Electric	Special	40	100	30	Normal	—	—
1	Tail Whip	Normal	Status	—	100	30	Many Others	—	—
1	Quick Attack	Normal	Physical	40	100	30	Normal	—	○
1	Thunderbolt	Electric	Special	95	100	15	Normal	—	—

TM & HM MOVES

Lv.	Name	Type	Kind	Pow.	Acc.	PP	Range	Long	DA
TM06	Toxic	Poison	Status	—	90	10	Normal	—	—
TM10	Hidden Power	Normal	Special	—	100	15	Normal	—	—
TM15	Hyper Beam	Normal	Special	150	90	5	Normal	—	—
TM16	Light Screen	Psychic	Status	—	—	30	Your Side	—	—
TM17	Protect	Normal	Status	—	—	10	Self	—	—
TM18	Rain Dance	Water	Status	—	—	5	Both Sides	—	—
TM21	Frustration	Normal	Physical	—	100	20	Normal	—	○
TM24	Thunderbolt	Electric	Special	95	100	15	Normal	—	—
TM25	Thunder	Electric	Special	120	70	10	Normal	—	—
TM27	Return	Normal	Physical	—	100	20	Normal	—	○
TM28	Dig	Ground	Physical	80	100	10	Normal	—	○
TM31	Brick Break	Fighting	Physical	75	100	15	Normal	—	○
TM32	Double Team	Normal	Status	—	—	15	Self	—	—
TM42	Facade	Normal	Physical	70	100	20	Normal	—	○
TM44	Rest	Psychic	Status	—	—	10	Self	—	—
TM45	Attract	Normal	Status	—	100	15	Normal	—	—
TM46	Thief	Dark	Physical	40	100	10	Normal	—	○
TM48	Round	Normal	Special	60	100	15	Normal	—	—
TM49	Echoed Voice	Normal	Special	40	100	15	Normal	—	—
TM52	Focus Blast	Fighting	Special	120	70	5	Normal	—	—
TM56	Fling	Dark	Physical	—	100	10	Normal	—	○
TM57	Charge Beam	Electric	Special	50	90	10	Normal	—	—
TM68	Giga Impact	Normal	Physical	150	90	5	Normal	—	○
TM70	Flash	Normal	Status	—	100	20	Normal	—	—
TM72	Volt Switch	Electric	Special	70	100	20	Normal	—	—
TM73	Thunder Wave	Electric	Status	—	100	20	Normal	—	—
TM86	Grass Knot	Grass	Special	—	100	20	Normal	—	○
TM87	Swagger	Normal	Status	—	90	15	Normal	—	—
TM90	Substitute	Normal	Status	—	—	10	Self	—	—
TM93	Wild Charge	Electric	Physical	90	100	15	Normal	—	○
TM94	Rock Smash	Fighting	Physical	40	100	15	Normal	—	○
HM04	Strength	Normal	Physical	80	100	15	Normal	—	○

MOVES TAUGHT BY PEOPLE

Name	Type	Kind	Pow.	Acc.	PP	Range	Long	DA

MOVES TAUGHT BY MOVE TUTORS FOR SHARDS

Name	Type	Kind	Pow.	Acc.	PP	Range	Long	DA
Covet	Normal	Physical	60	100	40	Normal	—	○
Signal Beam	Bug	Special	75	100	15	Normal	—	○
ThunderPunch	Electric	Physical	75	100	15	Normal	—	○
Magnet Rise	Electric	Status	—	—	10	Self	—	—
Iron Tail	Steel	Physical	100	75	15	Normal	—	○
Snore	Normal	Special	40	100	15	Normal	—	—
Knock Off	Dark	Physical	20	100	20	Normal	—	○
Helping Hand	Normal	Status	—	—	20	1 Ally	—	—
Sleep Talk	Normal	Status	—	—	10	Self	—	—

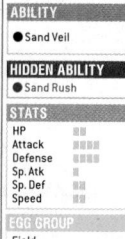

Mouse Pokémon

027 Sandshrew

TYPE Ground

ABILITY
- Sand Veil

HIDDEN ABILITY
- Sand Rush

STATS
HP
Attack
Defense
Sp. Atk
Sp. Def
Speed

EGG GROUP
Field

- HEIGHT: 2'00"
- WEIGHT: 26.5 lbs.
- GENDER: ♂ / ♀

It digs deep burrows to live in. When in danger, it rolls up its body to withstand attacks.

Same form for ♂ / ♀

ITEMS SOMETIMES HELD
- Quick Claw

EVOLUTION

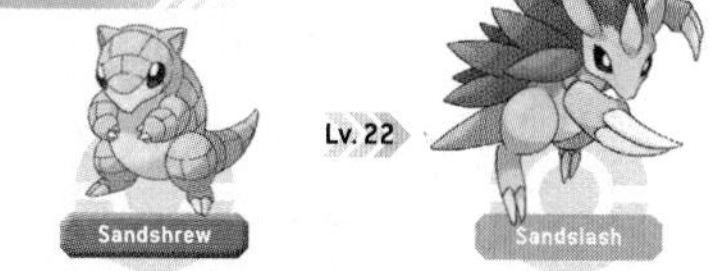

HOW TO OBTAIN

Pokémon Black Version 2	❶ Desert Resort entrance ❷ Relic Castle 1F
Pokémon White Version 2	❶ Desert Resort entrance ❷ Relic Castle 1F

HOW TO OBTAIN FROM OTHER GAMES

—

—

Pokémon AR Marker

LEVEL-UP AND LEARNED MOVES

Lv.	Name	Type	Kind	Pow.	Acc.	PP	Range	Long	DA
1	Scratch	Normal	Physical	40	100	35	Normal	—	○
1	Defense Curl	Normal	Status	—	—	40	Self	—	—
3	Sand-Attack	Ground	Status	—	100	15	Normal	—	—
5	Poison Sting	Poison	Physical	15	100	35	Normal	—	—
7	Rollout	Rock	Physical	30	90	20	Normal	—	○
9	Rapid Spin	Normal	Physical	20	100	40	Normal	—	○
11	Swift	Normal	Special	60	—	20	Many Others	—	—
14	Fury Cutter	Bug	Physical	20	95	20	Normal	—	○
17	Magnitude	Ground	Physical	—	100	30	Adjacent	—	—
20	Fury Swipes	Normal	Physical	18	80	15	Normal	—	○
23	Sand Tomb	Ground	Physical	35	85	15	Normal	—	—
26	Slash	Normal	Physical	70	100	20	Normal	—	○
30	Dig	Ground	Physical	80	100	10	Normal	—	○
34	Gyro Ball	Steel	Physical	—	100	5	Normal	—	○
38	Swords Dance	Normal	Status	—	—	30	Self	—	—
42	Sandstorm	Rock	Status	—	—	10	Both Sides	—	—
46	Earthquake	Ground	Physical	100	100	10	Adjacent	—	—

TM & HM MOVES

Lv.	Name	Type	Kind	Pow.	Acc.	PP	Range	Long	DA
TM01	Hone Claws	Dark	Status	—	—	15	Self	—	—
TM06	Toxic	Poison	Status	—	90	10	Normal	—	—
TM10	Hidden Power	Normal	Special	—	100	15	Normal	—	—
TM11	Sunny Day	Fire	Status	—	—	5	Both Sides	—	—
TM17	Protect	Normal	Status	—	—	10	Self	—	—
TM20	Safeguard	Normal	Status	—	—	25	Your Side	—	—
TM21	Frustration	Normal	Physical	—	100	20	Normal	—	○
TM26	Earthquake	Ground	Physical	100	100	10	Adjacent	—	—
TM27	Return	Normal	Physical	—	100	20	Normal	—	○
TM28	Dig	Ground	Physical	80	100	10	Normal	—	○
TM31	Brick Break	Fighting	Physical	75	100	15	Normal	—	○
TM32	Double Team	Normal	Status	—	—	15	Self	—	—
TM37	Sandstorm	Rock	Status	—	—	10	Both Sides	—	—
TM39	Rock Tomb	Rock	Physical	50	80	10	Normal	—	—
TM40	Aerial Ace	Flying	Physical	60	—	20	Normal	○	○
TM42	Facade	Normal	Physical	70	100	20	Normal	—	○
TM44	Rest	Psychic	Status	—	—	10	Self	—	—
TM45	Attract	Normal	Status	—	100	15	Normal	—	—
TM46	Thief	Dark	Physical	40	100	10	Normal	—	○
TM48	Round	Normal	Special	60	100	15	Normal	—	—
TM56	Fling	Dark	Physical	—	100	10	Normal	—	—
TM65	Shadow Claw	Ghost	Physical	70	100	15	Normal	—	○
TM74	Gyro Ball	Steel	Physical	—	100	5	Normal	—	○
TM75	Swords Dance	Normal	Status	—	—	30	Self	—	—
TM78	Bulldoze	Ground	Physical	60	100	20	Adjacent	—	—
TM80	Rock Slide	Rock	Physical	75	90	10	Many Others	—	—
TM81	X-Scissor	Bug	Physical	80	100	15	Normal	—	○
TM84	Poison Jab	Poison	Physical	80	100	20	Normal	—	○
TM87	Swagger	Normal	Status	—	90	15	Normal	—	—
TM90	Substitute	Normal	Status	—	—	10	Self	—	—
TM94	Rock Smash	Fighting	Physical	40	100	15	Normal	—	○
HM01	Cut	Normal	Physical	50	95	30	Normal	—	○
HM04	Strength	Normal	Physical	80	100	15	Normal	—	○

MOVES TAUGHT BY PEOPLE

Name	Type	Kind	Pow.	Acc.	PP	Range	Long	DA

MOVES TAUGHT BY MOVE TUTORS FOR SHARDS

Name	Type	Kind	Pow.	Acc.	PP	Range	Long	DA
Covet	Normal	Physical	60	100	40	Normal	—	○
Super Fang	Normal	Physical	—	90	10	Normal	—	○
Iron Tail	Steel	Physical	100	75	15	Normal	—	○
Earth Power	Ground	Special	90	100	10	Normal	—	—
Snore	Normal	Special	40	100	15	Normal	—	—
Knock Off	Dark	Physical	20	100	20	Normal	—	○
Stealth Rock	Rock	Status	—	—	20	Other Side	—	—
Sleep Talk	Normal	Status	—	—	10	Self	—	—

EGG MOVES

Name	Type	Kind	Pow.	Acc.	PP	Range	Long	DA
Flail	Normal	Physical	—	100	15	Normal	—	○
Counter	Fighting	Physical	—	100	20	Varies	—	○
Rapid Spin	Normal	Physical	20	100	40	Normal	—	○
Metal Claw	Steel	Physical	50	95	35	Normal	—	○
Crush Claw	Normal	Physical	75	95	10	Normal	—	○
Night Slash	Dark	Physical	70	100	15	Normal	—	○
Mud Shot	Ground	Special	55	95	15	Normal	—	—
Endure	Normal	Status	—	—	10	Self	—	—
Chip Away	Normal	Physical	70	100	20	Normal	—	○
Rock Climb	Normal	Physical	90	85	20	Normal	—	○

Mouse Pokémon

028 Sandslash

TYPE Ground

ABILITY
- Sand Veil

HIDDEN ABILITY
- Sand Rush

STATS
HP
Attack
Defense
Sp. Atk
Sp. Def
Speed

EGG GROUP
Field

- HEIGHT: 3'03"
- WEIGHT: 65.0 lbs.
- GENDER: ♂ / ♀

The spikes on its body are made up of its hardened hide. It rolls up and attacks foes with its spikes.

Same form for ♂ / ♀

ITEMS SOMETIMES HELD
- Quick Claw

EVOLUTION

HOW TO OBTAIN

Pokémon Black Version 2	❶ Relic Castle lowest floor passageways ①②④⑤ ❷ Route 15
Pokémon White Version 2	❶ Relic Castle lowest floor passageways ①②④⑤ ❷ Route 15

HOW TO OBTAIN FROM OTHER GAMES

—

—

Pokémon AR Marker

LEVEL-UP AND LEARNED MOVES

Lv.	Name	Type	Kind	Pow.	Acc.	PP	Range	Long	DA
1	Scratch	Normal	Physical	40	100	35	Normal	—	○
1	Defense Curl	Normal	Status	—	—	40	Self	—	—
1	Sand-Attack	Ground	Status	—	100	15	Normal	—	—
1	Poison Sting	Poison	Physical	15	100	35	Normal	—	—
3	Sand-Attack	Ground	Status	—	100	15	Normal	—	—
5	Poison Sting	Poison	Physical	15	100	35	Normal	—	—
7	Rollout	Rock	Physical	30	90	20	Normal	—	○
9	Rapid Spin	Normal	Physical	20	100	40	Normal	—	○
11	Swift	Normal	Special	60	—	20	Many Others	—	—
14	Fury Cutter	Bug	Physical	20	95	20	Normal	—	○
17	Magnitude	Ground	Physical	—	100	30	Adjacent	—	—
20	Fury Swipes	Normal	Physical	18	80	15	Normal	—	○
22	Crush Claw	Normal	Physical	75	95	10	Normal	—	○
23	Sand Tomb	Ground	Physical	35	85	15	Normal	—	—
26	Slash	Normal	Physical	70	100	20	Normal	—	○
30	Dig	Ground	Physical	80	100	10	Normal	—	○
34	Gyro Ball	Steel	Physical	—	100	5	Normal	—	○
38	Swords Dance	Normal	Status	—	—	30	Self	—	—
42	Sandstorm	Rock	Status	—	—	10	Both Sides	—	—
46	Earthquake	Ground	Physical	100	100	10	Adjacent	—	—

TM & HM MOVES

Lv.	Name	Type	Kind	Pow.	Acc.	PP	Range	Long	DA
TM01	Hone Claws	Dark	Status	—	—	15	Self	—	—
TM06	Toxic	Poison	Status	—	90	10	Normal	—	—
TM10	Hidden Power	Normal	Special	—	100	15	Normal	—	—
TM11	Sunny Day	Fire	Status	—	—	5	Both Sides	—	—
TM15	Hyper Beam	Normal	Special	150	90	5	Normal	—	—
TM17	Protect	Normal	Status	—	—	10	Self	—	—
TM20	Safeguard	Normal	Status	—	—	25	Your Side	—	—
TM21	Frustration	Normal	Physical	—	100	20	Normal	—	○
TM26	Earthquake	Ground	Physical	100	100	10	Adjacent	—	—
TM27	Return	Normal	Physical	—	100	20	Normal	—	○
TM28	Dig	Ground	Physical	80	100	10	Normal	—	○
TM31	Brick Break	Fighting	Physical	75	100	15	Normal	—	○
TM32	Double Team	Normal	Status	—	—	15	Self	—	—
TM37	Sandstorm	Rock	Status	—	—	10	Both Sides	—	—
TM39	Rock Tomb	Rock	Physical	50	80	10	Normal	—	—
TM40	Aerial Ace	Flying	Physical	60	—	20	Normal	○	○
TM42	Facade	Normal	Physical	70	100	20	Normal	—	○
TM44	Rest	Psychic	Status	—	—	10	Self	—	—
TM45	Attract	Normal	Status	—	100	15	Normal	—	—
TM46	Thief	Dark	Physical	40	100	10	Normal	—	○
TM48	Round	Normal	Special	60	100	15	Normal	—	—
TM52	Focus Blast	Fighting	Special	120	70	5	Normal	—	—
TM56	Fling	Dark	Physical	—	100	10	Normal	—	—
TM65	Shadow Claw	Ghost	Physical	70	100	15	Normal	—	○
TM68	Giga Impact	Normal	Physical	150	90	5	Normal	—	○
TM71	Stone Edge	Rock	Physical	100	80	5	Normal	—	—
TM74	Gyro Ball	Steel	Physical	—	100	5	Normal	—	○
TM75	Swords Dance	Normal	Status	—	—	30	Self	—	—
TM78	Bulldoze	Ground	Physical	60	100	20	Adjacent	—	—
TM80	Rock Slide	Rock	Physical	75	90	10	Many Others	—	—
TM81	X-Scissor	Bug	Physical	80	100	15	Normal	—	○
TM84	Poison Jab	Poison	Physical	80	100	20	Normal	—	○
TM87	Swagger	Normal	Status	—	90	15	Normal	—	—
TM90	Substitute	Normal	Status	—	—	10	Self	—	—
TM94	Rock Smash	Fighting	Physical	40	100	15	Normal	—	○
HM01	Cut	Normal	Physical	50	95	30	Normal	—	○
HM04	Strength	Normal	Physical	80	100	15	Normal	—	○

MOVES TAUGHT BY PEOPLE

Name	Type	Kind	Pow.	Acc.	PP	Range	Long	DA

MOVES TAUGHT BY MOVE TUTORS FOR SHARDS

Name	Type	Kind	Pow.	Acc.	PP	Range	Long	DA
Covet	Normal	Physical	60	100	40	Normal	—	○
Super Fang	Normal	Physical	—	90	10	Normal	—	○
Iron Tail	Steel	Physical	100	75	15	Normal	—	○
Earth Power	Ground	Special	90	100	10	Normal	—	—
Snore	Normal	Special	40	100	15	Normal	—	—
Knock Off	Dark	Physical	20	100	20	Normal	—	○
Stealth Rock	Rock	Status	—	—	20	Other Side	—	—
Sleep Talk	Normal	Status	—	—	10	Self	—	—

029 Nidoran ♀
Poison Pin Pokémon

TYPE Poison

ABILITIES
- Poison Point
- Rivalry

HIDDEN ABILITY
- Hustle

- HEIGHT: 1'04"
- WEIGHT: 15.4 lbs.
- GENDER: ♀

While it does not prefer to fight, even one drop of the poison it secretes from barbs can be fatal.

STATS
HP	
Attack	
Defense	
Sp. Atk	
Sp. Def	
Speed	

EGG GROUPS
Monster/Field

ITEMS SOMETIMES HELD
- None

 ♀

Pokémon AR Marker

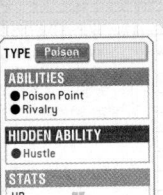

EVOLUTION

Nidoran ♀ → (Lv. 16) → Nidorina → (Use Moon Stone) → Nidoqueen

HOW TO OBTAIN
Pokémon Black Version 2	Route 2 (Hidden Grotto)
Pokémon White Version 2	Route 2 (Hidden Grotto)

HOW TO OBTAIN FROM OTHER GAMES

LEVEL-UP AND LEARNED MOVES
Lv.	Name	Type	Kind	Pow.	Acc.	PP	Range	Long	DA
1	Growl	Normal	Status	—	100	40	Many Others	—	○
1	Scratch	Normal	Physical	40	100	35	Normal	—	○
7	Tail Whip	Normal	Status	—	100	30	Many Others	—	○
9	Double Kick	Fighting	Physical	30	100	30	Normal	—	○
13	Poison Sting	Poison	Physical	15	100	35	Normal	—	○
19	Fury Swipes	Normal	Physical	18	80	15	Normal	—	○
21	Bite	Dark	Physical	60	100	25	Normal	—	○
25	Helping Hand	Normal	Status	—	—	20	1 Ally	—	○
31	Toxic Spikes	Poison	Status	—	—	20	Other Side	—	—
33	Flatter	Dark	Status	—	100	15	Normal	—	○
37	Crunch	Dark	Physical	80	100	15	Normal	—	○
43	Captivate	Normal	Status	—	100	20	Many Others	—	○
45	Poison Fang	Poison	Physical	50	100	15	Normal	—	○

TM & HM MOVES
Lv.	Name	Type	Kind	Pow.	Acc.	PP	Range	Long	DA
TM01	Hone Claws	Dark	Status	—	—	15	Self	—	—
TM06	Toxic	Poison	Status	—	90	10	Normal	—	○
TM09	Venoshock	Poison	Special	65	100	10	Normal	—	○
TM10	Hidden Power	Normal	Special	—	100	15	Normal	—	○
TM11	Sunny Day	Fire	Status	—	—	5	Both Sides	—	—
TM13	Ice Beam	Ice	Special	95	100	10	Normal	—	○
TM14	Blizzard	Ice	Special	120	70	5	Many Others	—	○
TM17	Protect	Normal	Status	—	—	10	Self	—	—
TM18	Rain Dance	Water	Status	—	—	5	Both Sides	—	—
TM21	Frustration	Normal	Physical	—	100	20	Normal	—	○
TM24	Thunderbolt	Electric	Special	95	100	15	Normal	—	○
TM25	Thunder	Electric	Special	120	70	10	Normal	—	○
TM27	Return	Normal	Physical	—	100	20	Normal	—	○
TM28	Dig	Ground	Physical	80	100	10	Normal	—	○
TM32	Double Team	Normal	Status	—	—	15	Self	—	—
TM36	Sludge Bomb	Poison	Special	90	100	10	Normal	—	○
TM40	Aerial Ace	Flying	Physical	60	—	20	Normal	○	○
TM42	Facade	Normal	Physical	70	100	20	Normal	—	○
TM44	Rest	Psychic	Status	—	—	10	Self	—	—
TM45	Attract	Normal	Status	—	100	15	Normal	—	○
TM46	Thief	Dark	Physical	40	100	10	Normal	—	○
TM48	Round	Normal	Special	60	100	15	Normal	—	○
TM65	Shadow Claw	Ghost	Physical	70	100	15	Normal	—	○
TM84	Poison Jab	Poison	Physical	80	100	20	Normal	—	○
TM87	Swagger	Normal	Status	—	90	15	Normal	—	○
TM90	Substitute	Normal	Status	—	—	10	Self	—	—
TM94	Rock Smash	Fighting	Physical	40	100	15	Normal	—	○
HM01	Cut	Normal	Physical	50	95	30	Normal	—	○
HM04	Strength	Normal	Physical	80	100	15	Normal	—	○

MOVES TAUGHT BY PEOPLE
Name	Type	Kind	Pow.	Acc.	PP	Range	Long	DA

MOVES TAUGHT BY MOVE TUTORS FOR SHARDS
Name	Type	Kind	Pow.	Acc.	PP	Range	Long	DA
Super Fang	Normal	Physical	—	90	10	Normal	—	○
Iron Tail	Steel	Physical	100	75	15	Normal	—	○
Snore	Normal	Special	40	100	15	Normal	—	○
Helping Hand	Normal	Status	—	—	20	1 Ally	—	—
Sleep Talk	Normal	Status	—	—	10	Self	—	—

EGG MOVES
Name	Type	Kind	Pow.	Acc.	PP	Range	Long	DA
Supersonic	Normal	Status	—	55	20	Normal	—	—
Disable	Normal	Status	—	100	20	Normal	—	—
Take Down	Normal	Physical	90	85	20	Normal	—	○
Focus Energy	Normal	Status	—	—	30	Self	—	—
Charm	Normal	Status	—	100	20	Normal	—	○
Counter	Fighting	Physical	—	100	20	Varies	—	○
Beat Up	Dark	Physical	—	100	10	Normal	—	○
Pursuit	Dark	Physical	40	100	20	Normal	—	○
Skull Bash	Normal	Physical	100	100	15	Normal	—	○
Iron Tail	Steel	Physical	100	75	15	Normal	—	○
Poison Tail	Poison	Physical	50	100	25	Normal	—	○
Endure	Normal	Status	—	—	10	Self	—	—
Chip Away	Normal	Physical	70	100	20	Normal	—	○

---

030 Nidorina
Poison Pin Pokémon

TYPE Poison

ABILITIES
- Poison Point
- Rivalry

HIDDEN ABILITY
- Hustle

- HEIGHT: 2'07"
- WEIGHT: 44.1 lbs.
- GENDER: ♀

When it senses danger, it raises all the barbs on its body. These barbs grow slower than Nidorino's.

STATS
HP	
Attack	
Defense	
Sp. Atk	
Sp. Def	
Speed	

EGG GROUPS
No Egg has ever been discovered

ITEMS SOMETIMES HELD
- None

 ♀

Pokémon AR Marker

EVOLUTION

Nidoran ♀ → (Lv. 16) → Nidorina → (Use Moon Stone) → Nidoqueen

HOW TO OBTAIN
Pokémon Black Version 2	Level up Nidoran ♀ to Lv. 16
Pokémon White Version 2	Level up Nidoran ♀ to Lv. 16

HOW TO OBTAIN FROM OTHER GAMES

LEVEL-UP AND LEARNED MOVES
Lv.	Name	Type	Kind	Pow.	Acc.	PP	Range	Long	DA
1	Growl	Normal	Status	—	100	40	Many Others	—	○
1	Scratch	Normal	Physical	40	100	35	Normal	—	○
7	Tail Whip	Normal	Status	—	100	30	Many Others	—	○
9	Double Kick	Fighting	Physical	30	100	30	Normal	—	○
13	Poison Sting	Poison	Physical	15	100	35	Normal	—	○
20	Fury Swipes	Normal	Physical	18	80	15	Normal	—	○
23	Bite	Dark	Physical	60	100	25	Normal	—	○
28	Helping Hand	Normal	Status	—	—	20	1 Ally	—	—
35	Toxic Spikes	Poison	Status	—	—	20	Other Side	—	—
38	Flatter	Dark	Status	—	100	15	Normal	—	○
43	Crunch	Dark	Physical	80	100	15	Normal	—	○
50	Captivate	Normal	Status	—	100	20	Many Others	—	○
58	Poison Fang	Poison	Physical	50	100	15	Normal	—	○

TM & HM MOVES
Lv.	Name	Type	Kind	Pow.	Acc.	PP	Range	Long	DA
TM01	Hone Claws	Dark	Status	—	—	15	Self	—	—
TM06	Toxic	Poison	Status	—	90	10	Normal	—	○
TM09	Venoshock	Poison	Special	65	100	10	Normal	—	○
TM10	Hidden Power	Normal	Special	—	100	15	Normal	—	○
TM11	Sunny Day	Fire	Status	—	—	5	Both Sides	—	—
TM13	Ice Beam	Ice	Special	95	100	10	Normal	—	○
TM14	Blizzard	Ice	Special	120	70	5	Many Others	—	○
TM17	Protect	Normal	Status	—	—	10	Self	—	—
TM18	Rain Dance	Water	Status	—	—	5	Both Sides	—	—
TM21	Frustration	Normal	Physical	—	100	20	Normal	—	○
TM24	Thunderbolt	Electric	Special	95	100	15	Normal	—	○
TM25	Thunder	Electric	Special	120	70	10	Normal	—	○
TM27	Return	Normal	Physical	—	100	20	Normal	—	○
TM28	Dig	Ground	Physical	80	100	10	Normal	—	○
TM32	Double Team	Normal	Status	—	—	15	Self	—	—
TM36	Sludge Bomb	Poison	Special	90	100	10	Normal	—	○
TM40	Aerial Ace	Flying	Physical	60	—	20	Normal	○	○
TM42	Facade	Normal	Physical	70	100	20	Normal	—	○
TM44	Rest	Psychic	Status	—	—	10	Self	—	—
TM45	Attract	Normal	Status	—	100	15	Normal	—	○
TM46	Thief	Dark	Physical	40	100	10	Normal	—	○
TM48	Round	Normal	Special	60	100	15	Normal	—	○
TM49	Echoed Voice	Normal	Special	40	100	15	Normal	—	○
TM65	Shadow Claw	Ghost	Physical	70	100	15	Normal	—	○
TM84	Poison Jab	Poison	Physical	80	100	20	Normal	—	○
TM87	Swagger	Normal	Status	—	90	15	Normal	—	○
TM90	Substitute	Normal	Status	—	—	10	Self	—	—
TM94	Rock Smash	Fighting	Physical	40	100	15	Normal	—	○
HM01	Cut	Normal	Physical	50	95	30	Normal	—	○
HM04	Strength	Normal	Physical	80	100	15	Normal	—	○

MOVES TAUGHT BY PEOPLE
Name	Type	Kind	Pow.	Acc.	PP	Range	Long	DA

MOVES TAUGHT BY MOVE TUTORS FOR SHARDS
Name	Type	Kind	Pow.	Acc.	PP	Range	Long	DA
Super Fang	Normal	Physical	—	90	10	Normal	—	○
Iron Tail	Steel	Physical	100	75	15	Normal	—	○
Snore	Normal	Special	40	100	15	Normal	—	○
Helping Hand	Normal	Status	—	—	20	1 Ally	—	—
Sleep Talk	Normal	Status	—	—	10	Self	—	—

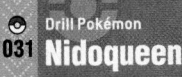

031 Nidoqueen

Drill Pokémon

● HEIGHT: 4'03"
● WEIGHT: 132.3 lbs.
● GENDER: ♀

Its entire body is armored with hard scales. It will protect the young in its burrow with its life.

TYPE Poison / Ground

ABILITIES
● Poison Point
● Rivalry

HIDDEN ABILITY
● Sheer Force

STATS
HP
Attack
Defense
Sp. Atk
Sp. Def
Speed

EGG GROUPS
No Egg has ever been discovered

ITEMS SOMETIMES HELD
● None

♀

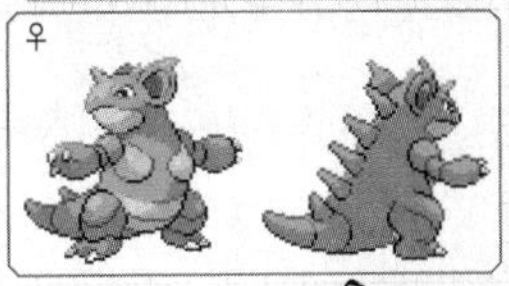

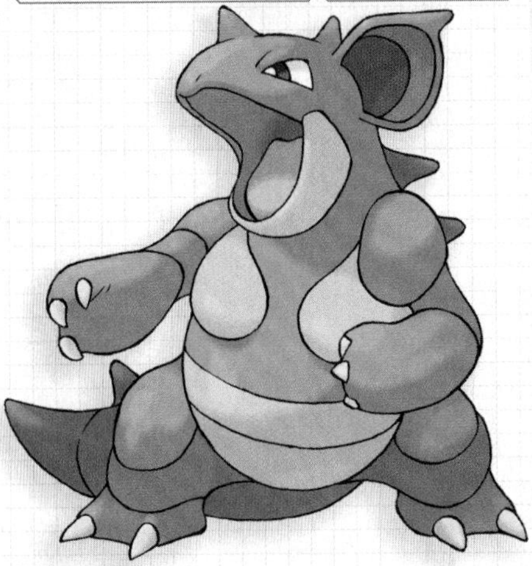

Pokémon AR Marker

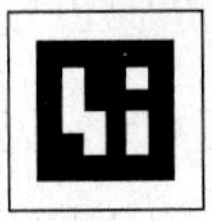

EVOLUTION

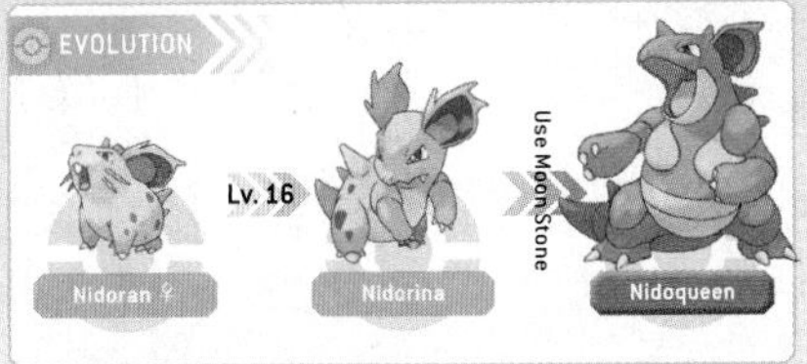

HOW TO OBTAIN

Pokémon Black Version 2	Use Moon Stone on Nidorina
Pokémon White Version 2	Use Moon Stone on Nidorina

HOW TO OBTAIN FROM OTHER GAMES

——

——

LEVEL-UP AND LEARNED MOVES

Lv.	Name	Type	Kind	Pow.	Acc.	PP	Range	Long	DA
1	Scratch	Normal	Physical	40	100	35	Normal	—	○
1	Tail Whip	Normal	Status	—	100	30	Many Others	—	—
1	Double Kick	Fighting	Physical	30	100	30	Normal	—	○
1	Poison Sting	Poison	Physical	15	100	35	Normal	—	—
23	Chip Away	Normal	Physical	70	100	20	Normal	—	○
35	Body Slam	Normal	Physical	85	100	15	Normal	—	○
43	Earth Power	Ground	Special	90	100	10	Normal	—	—
58	Superpower	Fighting	Physical	120	100	5	Normal	—	○

TM & HM MOVES

Lv.	Name	Type	Kind	Pow.	Acc.	PP	Range	Long	DA
TM01	Hone Claws	Dark	Status	—	—	15	Self	—	—
TM05	Roar	Normal	Status	—	100	20	Normal	—	—
TM06	Toxic	Poison	Status	—	90	10	Normal	—	—
TM09	Venoshock	Poison	Special	65	100	10	Normal	—	—
TM10	Hidden Power	Normal	Special	—	100	15	Normal	—	—
TM11	Sunny Day	Fire	Status	—	—	5	Both Sides	—	—
TM12	Taunt	Dark	Status	—	100	20	Normal	—	—
TM13	Ice Beam	Ice	Special	95	100	10	Normal	—	—
TM14	Blizzard	Ice	Special	120	70	5	Many Others	—	—
TM15	Hyper Beam	Normal	Special	150	90	5	Normal	—	—
TM17	Protect	Normal	Status	—	—	10	Self	—	—
TM18	Rain Dance	Water	Status	—	—	5	Both Sides	—	—
TM21	Frustration	Normal	Physical	—	100	20	Normal	—	○
TM23	Smack Down	Rock	Physical	50	100	15	Normal	—	—
TM24	Thunderbolt	Electric	Special	95	100	15	Normal	—	—
TM25	Thunder	Electric	Special	120	70	10	Normal	—	—
TM26	Earthquake	Ground	Physical	100	100	10	Adjacent	—	—
TM27	Return	Normal	Physical	—	100	20	Normal	—	○
TM28	Dig	Ground	Physical	80	100	10	Normal	—	○
TM30	Shadow Ball	Ghost	Special	80	100	15	Normal	—	—
TM31	Brick Break	Fighting	Physical	75	100	15	Normal	—	○
TM32	Double Team	Normal	Status	—	—	15	Self	—	—
TM34	Sludge Wave	Poison	Special	95	100	10	Adjacent	—	—
TM35	Flamethrower	Fire	Special	95	100	15	Normal	—	—
TM36	Sludge Bomb	Poison	Special	90	100	10	Normal	—	—
TM37	Sandstorm	Rock	Status	—	—	10	Both Sides	—	—
TM38	Fire Blast	Fire	Special	120	85	5	Normal	—	—
TM39	Rock Tomb	Rock	Physical	50	80	10	Normal	—	—
TM40	Aerial Ace	Flying	Physical	60	—	20	Normal	○	○
TM41	Torment	Dark	Status	—	100	15	Normal	—	—
TM42	Facade	Normal	Physical	70	100	20	Normal	—	○
TM44	Rest	Psychic	Status	—	—	10	Self	—	—
TM45	Attract	Normal	Status	—	100	15	Normal	—	—
TM46	Thief	Dark	Physical	40	100	10	Normal	—	○
TM48	Round	Normal	Special	60	100	15	Normal	—	—
TM49	Echoed Voice	Normal	Special	40	100	15	Normal	—	—
TM52	Focus Blast	Fighting	Special	120	70	5	Normal	—	—
TM56	Fling	Dark	Physical	—	100	10	Normal	—	—
TM59	Incinerate	Fire	Special	30	100	15	Many Others	—	—
TM60	Quash	Dark	Status	—	100	15	Normal	—	—
TM65	Shadow Claw	Ghost	Physical	70	100	15	Normal	—	○
TM68	Giga Impact	Normal	Physical	150	90	5	Normal	—	○
TM71	Stone Edge	Rock	Physical	100	80	5	Normal	—	—
TM78	Bulldoze	Ground	Physical	60	100	20	Adjacent	—	—
TM80	Rock Slide	Rock	Physical	75	90	10	Many Others	—	—
TM82	Dragon Tail	Dragon	Physical	60	90	10	Normal	—	○
TM84	Poison Jab	Poison	Physical	80	100	20	Normal	—	○
TM87	Swagger	Normal	Status	—	90	15	Normal	—	—
TM90	Substitute	Normal	Status	—	—	10	Self	—	—
TM94	Rock Smash	Fighting	Physical	40	100	15	Normal	—	○
HM01	Cut	Normal	Physical	50	95	30	Normal	—	○
HM03	Surf	Water	Special	95	100	15	Adjacent	—	—
HM04	Strength	Normal	Physical	80	100	15	Normal	—	○

MOVES TAUGHT BY PEOPLE

Name	Type	Kind	Pow.	Acc.	PP	Range	Long	DA

MOVES TAUGHT BY MOVE TUTORS FOR SHARDS

Name	Type	Kind	Pow.	Acc.	PP	Range	Long	DA
Super Fang	Normal	Physical	—	90	10	Normal	—	○
Uproar	Normal	Special	90	100	10	1 Random	—	—
Fire Punch	Fire	Physical	75	100	15	Normal	—	○
ThunderPunch	Electric	Physical	75	100	15	Normal	—	○
Ice Punch	Ice	Physical	75	100	15	Normal	—	○
Icy Wind	Ice	Special	55	95	15	Many Others	—	—
Iron Tail	Steel	Physical	100	75	15	Normal	—	○
Aqua Tail	Water	Physical	90	90	10	Normal	—	○
Earth Power	Ground	Special	90	100	10	Normal	—	—
Superpower	Fighting	Physical	120	100	5	Normal	—	○
Dragon Pulse	Dragon	Special	90	100	10	Normal	○	—
Snore	Normal	Special	40	100	15	Normal	—	—
Helping Hand	Normal	Status	—	—	20	1 Ally	—	—
Stealth Rock	Rock	Status	—	—	20	Other Side	—	—
Outrage	Dragon	Physical	120	100	10	1 Random	—	○
Sleep Talk	Normal	Status	—	—	10	Self	—	—

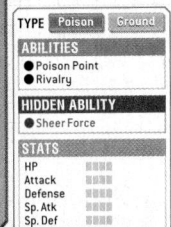

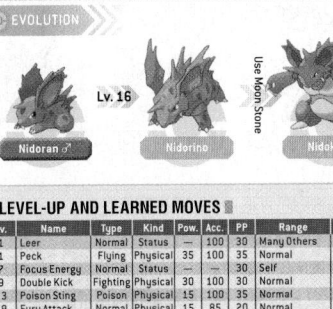

032 Nidoran ♂

Poison Pin Pokémon

● HEIGHT: 1'08"
● WEIGHT: 19.8 lbs.
● GENDER: ♂

It scans its surroundings by raising its ears out of the grass. Its toxic horn is for protection.

TYPE Poison

ABILITIES
● Poison Point
● Rivalry

HIDDEN ABILITY
● Hustle

STATS
HP
Attack
Defense
Sp. Atk
Sp. Def
Speed

EGG GROUPS
Monster/Field

ITEMS SOMETIMES HELD
● None

♂

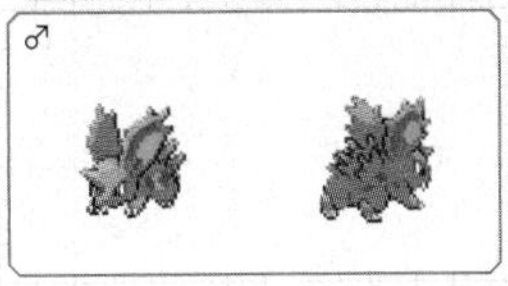

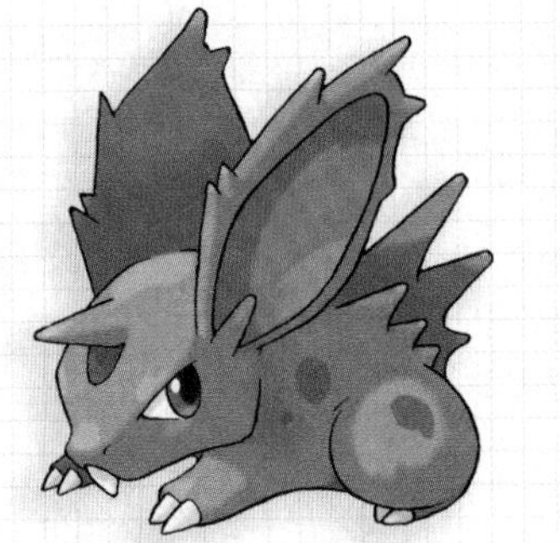

Pokémon AR Marker

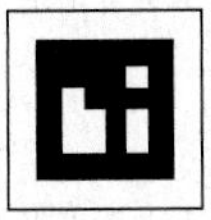

EVOLUTION

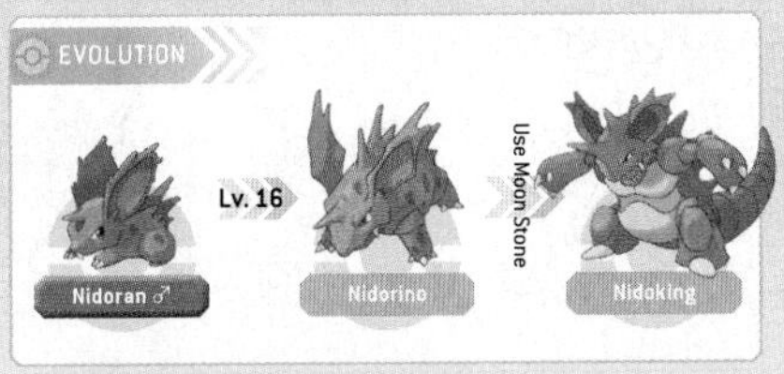

HOW TO OBTAIN

Pokémon Black Version 2	Route 2 (Hidden Grotto)
Pokémon White Version 2	Route 2 (Hidden Grotto)

HOW TO OBTAIN FROM OTHER GAMES

——

——

LEVEL-UP AND LEARNED MOVES

Lv.	Name	Type	Kind	Pow.	Acc.	PP	Range	Long	DA
1	Leer	Normal	Status	—	100	30	Many Others	—	—
1	Peck	Flying	Physical	35	100	35	Normal	○	○
7	Focus Energy	Normal	Status	—	—	30	Self	—	—
9	Double Kick	Fighting	Physical	30	100	30	Normal	—	○
13	Poison Sting	Poison	Physical	15	100	35	Normal	—	—
19	Fury Attack	Normal	Physical	15	85	20	Normal	—	○
21	Horn Attack	Normal	Physical	65	100	25	Normal	—	○
25	Helping Hand	Normal	Status	—	—	20	1 Ally	—	—
31	Toxic Spikes	Poison	Status	—	—	20	Other Side	—	—
33	Flatter	Dark	Status	—	100	15	Normal	—	—
37	Poison Jab	Poison	Physical	80	100	20	Normal	—	○
43	Captivate	Normal	Status	—	100	20	Many Others	—	—
45	Horn Drill	Normal	Physical	—	30	5	Normal	—	○

TM & HM MOVES

Lv.	Name	Type	Kind	Pow.	Acc.	PP	Range	Long	DA
TM01	Hone Claws	Dark	Status	—	—	15	Self	—	—
TM06	Toxic	Poison	Status	—	90	10	Normal	—	—
TM09	Venoshock	Poison	Special	65	100	10	Normal	—	—
TM10	Hidden Power	Normal	Special	—	100	15	Normal	—	—
TM11	Sunny Day	Fire	Status	—	—	5	Both Sides	—	—
TM13	Ice Beam	Ice	Special	95	100	10	Normal	—	—
TM14	Blizzard	Ice	Special	120	70	5	Many Others	—	—
TM17	Protect	Normal	Status	—	—	10	Self	—	—
TM18	Rain Dance	Water	Status	—	—	5	Both Sides	—	—
TM21	Frustration	Normal	Physical	—	100	20	Normal	—	○
TM24	Thunderbolt	Electric	Special	95	100	15	Normal	—	—
TM25	Thunder	Electric	Special	120	70	10	Normal	—	—
TM27	Return	Normal	Physical	—	100	20	Normal	—	○
TM28	Dig	Ground	Physical	80	100	10	Normal	—	○
TM32	Double Team	Normal	Status	—	—	15	Self	—	—
TM36	Sludge Bomb	Poison	Special	90	100	10	Normal	—	—
TM42	Facade	Normal	Physical	70	100	20	Normal	—	○
TM44	Rest	Psychic	Status	—	—	10	Self	—	—
TM45	Attract	Normal	Status	—	100	15	Normal	—	—
TM46	Thief	Dark	Physical	40	100	10	Normal	—	○
TM48	Round	Normal	Special	60	100	15	Normal	—	—
TM49	Echoed Voice	Normal	Special	40	100	15	Normal	—	—
TM65	Shadow Claw	Ghost	Physical	70	100	15	Normal	—	○
TM84	Poison Jab	Poison	Physical	80	100	20	Normal	—	○
TM87	Swagger	Normal	Status	—	90	15	Normal	—	—
TM90	Substitute	Normal	Status	—	—	10	Self	—	—
TM94	Rock Smash	Fighting	Physical	40	100	15	Normal	—	○
HM01	Cut	Normal	Physical	50	95	30	Normal	—	○
HM04	Strength	Normal	Physical	80	100	15	Normal	—	○

MOVES TAUGHT BY PEOPLE

Name	Type	Kind	Pow.	Acc.	PP	Range	Long	DA

MOVES TAUGHT BY MOVE TUTORS FOR SHARDS

Name	Type	Kind	Pow.	Acc.	PP	Range	Long	DA
Drill Run	Ground	Physical	80	95	10	Normal	—	○
Super Fang	Normal	Physical	—	90	10	Normal	—	○
Iron Tail	Steel	Physical	100	75	15	Normal	—	○
Snore	Normal	Special	40	100	15	Normal	—	—
Helping Hand	Normal	Status	—	—	20	1 Ally	—	—
Sleep Talk	Normal	Status	—	—	10	Self	—	—

EGG MOVES

Name	Type	Kind	Pow.	Acc.	PP	Range	Long	DA
Counter	Fighting	Physical	—	100	20	Varies	—	○
Disable	Normal	Status	—	100	20	Normal	—	—
Supersonic	Normal	Status	—	55	20	Normal	—	—
Take Down	Normal	Physical	90	85	20	Normal	—	○
Amnesia	Psychic	Status	—	—	20	Self	—	—
Confusion	Psychic	Special	50	100	25	Normal	—	—
Beat Up	Dark	Physical	—	100	10	Normal	—	—
Sucker Punch	Dark	Physical	80	100	5	Normal	—	○
Head Smash	Rock	Physical	150	80	5	Normal	—	○
Iron Tail	Steel	Physical	100	75	15	Normal	—	○
Poison Tail	Poison	Physical	50	100	25	Normal	—	○
Endure	Normal	Status	—	—	10	Self	—	—
Chip Away	Normal	Physical	70	100	20	Normal	—	○

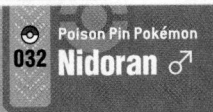

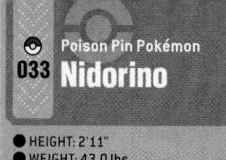

Poison Pin Pokémon

033 Nidorino

● HEIGHT: 2'11"
● WEIGHT: 43.0 lbs.
● GENDER: ♂

It has a violent disposition and stabs foes with its horn, which oozes poison upon impact.

♂

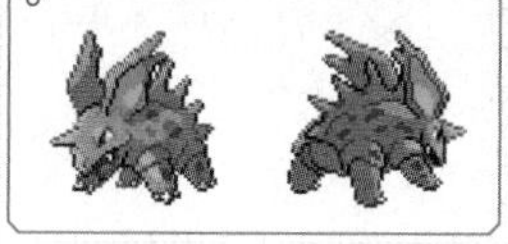

TYPE: Poison

ABILITIES
● Poison Point
● Rivalry

HIDDEN ABILITY
● Hustle

STATS
HP
Attack
Defense
Sp. Atk
Sp. Def
Speed

EGG GROUPS
Monster/Field

ITEMS SOMETIMES HELD
● None

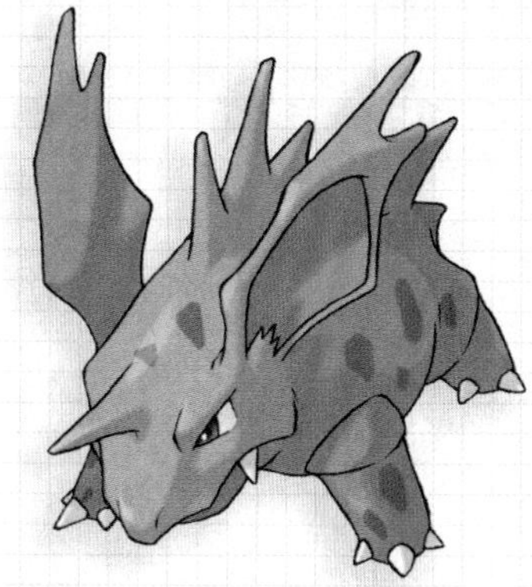

Pokémon AR Marker

EVOLUTION

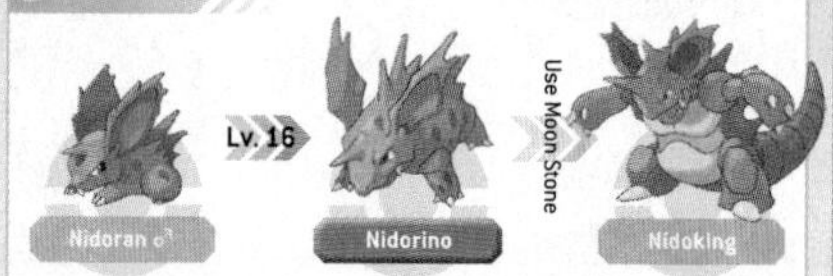

HOW TO OBTAIN

Pokémon Black Version 2	Level up Nidoran ♂ to Lv. 16
Pokémon White Version 2	Level up Nidoran ♂ to Lv. 16

HOW TO OBTAIN FROM OTHER GAMES

—
—

LEVEL-UP AND LEARNED MOVES

Lv.	Name	Type	Kind	Pow.	Acc.	PP	Range	Long	DA
1	Leer	Normal	Status	—	100	30	Many Others	—	—
1	Peck	Flying	Physical	35	100	35	Normal	○	○
7	Focus Energy	Normal	Status	—	—	30	Self	—	—
9	Double Kick	Fighting	Physical	30	100	30	Normal	—	○
13	Poison Sting	Poison	Physical	15	100	35	Normal	—	—
20	Fury Attack	Normal	Physical	15	85	20	Normal	—	○
23	Horn Attack	Normal	Physical	65	100	25	Normal	—	○
28	Helping Hand	Normal	Status	—	—	20	1 Ally	—	—
35	Toxic Spikes	Poison	Status	—	—	20	Other Side	—	—
38	Flatter	Dark	Status	—	100	15	Normal	—	—
43	Poison Jab	Poison	Physical	80	100	20	Normal	—	○
50	Captivate	Normal	Status	—	100	20	Many Others	—	—
58	Horn Drill	Normal	Physical	—	30	5	Normal	—	○

TM & HM MOVES

Lv.	Name	Type	Kind	Pow.	Acc.	PP	Range	Long	DA
TM01	Hone Claws	Dark	Status	—	—	15	Self	—	—
TM06	Toxic	Poison	Status	—	90	10	Normal	—	—
TM09	Venoshock	Poison	Special	65	100	10	Normal	—	—
TM10	Hidden Power	Normal	Special	—	100	15	Normal	—	—
TM11	Sunny Day	Fire	Status	—	—	5	Both Sides	—	—
TM13	Ice Beam	Ice	Special	95	100	10	Normal	—	—
TM14	Blizzard	Ice	Special	120	70	5	Many Others	—	—
TM17	Protect	Normal	Status	—	—	10	Self	—	—
TM18	Rain Dance	Water	Status	—	—	5	Both Sides	—	—
TM21	Frustration	Normal	Physical	—	100	20	Normal	—	○
TM24	Thunderbolt	Electric	Special	95	100	15	Normal	—	—
TM25	Thunder	Electric	Special	120	70	10	Normal	—	—
TM27	Return	Normal	Physical	—	100	20	Normal	—	○
TM28	Dig	Ground	Physical	80	100	10	Normal	—	○
TM32	Double Team	Normal	Status	—	—	15	Self	—	—
TM36	Sludge Bomb	Poison	Special	90	100	10	Normal	—	—
TM42	Facade	Normal	Physical	70	100	20	Normal	—	○
TM44	Rest	Psychic	Status	—	—	10	Self	—	—
TM45	Attract	Normal	Status	—	100	15	Normal	—	—
TM46	Thief	Dark	Physical	40	100	10	Normal	—	○
TM48	Round	Normal	Special	60	100	15	Normal	—	—
TM49	Echoed Voice	Normal	Special	40	100	15	Normal	—	—
TM65	Shadow Claw	Ghost	Physical	70	100	15	Normal	—	○
TM84	Poison Jab	Poison	Physical	80	100	20	Normal	—	○
TM87	Swagger	Normal	Status	—	90	15	Normal	—	—
TM90	Substitute	Normal	Status	—	—	10	Self	—	—
TM94	Rock Smash	Fighting	Physical	40	100	15	Normal	—	○
HM01	Cut	Normal	Physical	50	95	30	Normal	—	○
HM04	Strength	Normal	Physical	80	100	15	Normal	—	○

MOVES TAUGHT BY PEOPLE

Name	Type	Kind	Pow.	Acc.	PP	Range	Long	DA

MOVES TAUGHT BY MOVE TUTORS FOR SHARDS

Name	Type	Kind	Pow.	Acc.	PP	Range	Long	DA
Drill Run	Ground	Physical	80	95	10	Normal	—	○
Super Fang	Normal	Physical	—	90	10	Normal	—	○
Iron Tail	Steel	Physical	100	75	15	Normal	—	○
Snore	Normal	Special	40	100	15	Normal	—	—
Helping Hand	Normal	Status	—	—	20	1 Ally	—	—
Sleep Talk	Normal	Status	—	—	10	Self	—	—

Drill Pokémon

034 Nidoking

● HEIGHT: 4'07"
● WEIGHT: 136.7 lbs.
● GENDER: ♂

One swing of its mighty tail can snap a telephone pole as if it were a matchstick.

♂

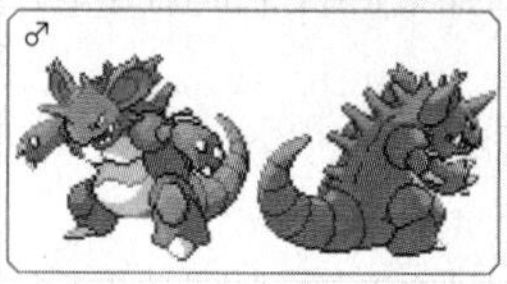

TYPE: Poison / Ground

ABILITIES
● Poison Point
● Rivalry

HIDDEN ABILITY
● Sheer Force

STATS
HP
Attack
Defense
Sp. Atk
Sp. Def
Speed

EGG GROUPS
Monster/Field

ITEMS SOMETIMES HELD
● None

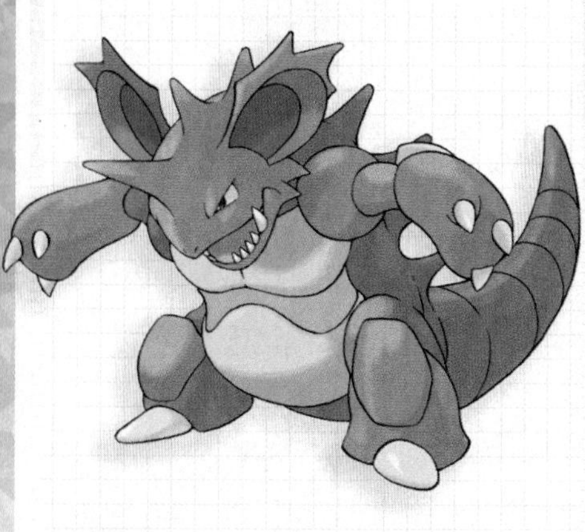

Pokémon AR Marker

EVOLUTION

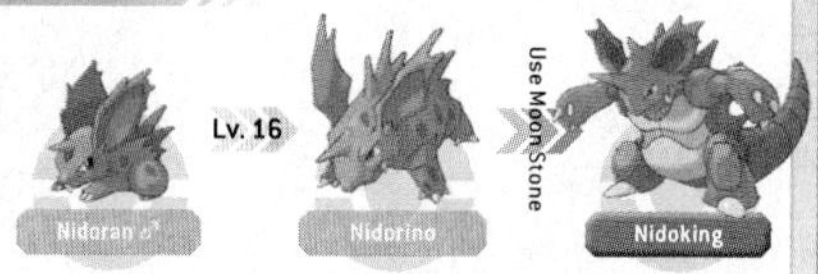

HOW TO OBTAIN

Pokémon Black Version 2	Use Moon Stone on Nidorino
Pokémon White Version 2	Use Moon Stone on Nidorino

HOW TO OBTAIN FROM OTHER GAMES

—
—

LEVEL-UP AND LEARNED MOVES

Lv.	Name	Type	Kind	Pow.	Acc.	PP	Range	Long	DA
1	Peck	Flying	Physical	35	100	35	Normal	○	○
1	Focus Energy	Normal	Status	—	—	30	Self	—	—
1	Double Kick	Fighting	Physical	30	100	30	Normal	—	○
1	Poison Sting	Poison	Physical	15	100	35	Normal	—	—
23	Chip Away	Normal	Physical	70	100	20	Normal	—	○
35	Thrash	Normal	Physical	120	100	10	1 Random	—	○
43	Earth Power	Ground	Special	90	100	10	Normal	—	—
58	Megahorn	Bug	Physical	120	85	10	Normal	—	○

TM & HM MOVES

Lv.	Name	Type	Kind	Pow.	Acc.	PP	Range	Long	DA
TM01	Hone Claws	Dark	Status	—	—	15	Self	—	—
TM05	Roar	Normal	Status	—	100	20	Normal	—	—
TM06	Toxic	Poison	Status	—	90	10	Normal	—	—
TM09	Venoshock	Poison	Special	65	100	10	Normal	—	—
TM10	Hidden Power	Normal	Special	—	100	15	Normal	—	—
TM11	Sunny Day	Fire	Status	—	—	5	Both Sides	—	—
TM12	Taunt	Dark	Status	—	100	20	Normal	—	—
TM13	Ice Beam	Ice	Special	95	100	10	Normal	—	—
TM14	Blizzard	Ice	Special	120	70	5	Many Others	—	—
TM15	Hyper Beam	Normal	Special	150	90	5	Normal	—	—
TM17	Protect	Normal	Status	—	—	10	Self	—	—
TM18	Rain Dance	Water	Status	—	—	5	Both Sides	—	—
TM21	Frustration	Normal	Physical	—	100	20	Normal	—	○
TM23	Smack Down	Rock	Physical	50	100	15	Normal	—	—
TM24	Thunderbolt	Electric	Special	95	100	15	Normal	—	—
TM25	Thunder	Electric	Special	120	70	10	Normal	—	—
TM26	Earthquake	Ground	Physical	100	100	10	Adjacent	—	—
TM27	Return	Normal	Physical	—	100	20	Normal	—	○
TM28	Dig	Ground	Physical	80	100	10	Normal	—	○
TM30	Shadow Ball	Ghost	Special	80	100	15	Normal	—	—
TM31	Brick Break	Fighting	Physical	75	100	15	Normal	—	○
TM32	Double Team	Normal	Status	—	—	15	Self	—	—
TM34	Sludge Wave	Poison	Special	95	100	10	Adjacent	—	—
TM35	Flamethrower	Fire	Special	95	100	15	Normal	—	—
TM36	Sludge Bomb	Poison	Special	90	100	10	Normal	—	—
TM37	Sandstorm	Rock	Status	—	—	10	Both Sides	—	—
TM38	Fire Blast	Fire	Special	120	85	5	Normal	—	—
TM39	Rock Tomb	Rock	Physical	50	80	10	Normal	—	—
TM41	Torment	Dark	Status	—	100	15	Normal	—	—
TM42	Facade	Normal	Physical	70	100	20	Normal	—	○
TM44	Rest	Psychic	Status	—	—	10	Self	—	—
TM45	Attract	Normal	Status	—	100	15	Normal	—	—
TM46	Thief	Dark	Physical	40	100	10	Normal	—	○
TM48	Round	Normal	Special	60	100	15	Normal	—	—
TM49	Echoed Voice	Normal	Special	40	100	15	Normal	—	—
TM52	Focus Blast	Fighting	Special	120	70	5	Normal	—	—
TM56	Fling	Dark	Physical	—	100	10	Normal	—	—
TM59	Incinerate	Fire	Special	30	100	15	Many Others	—	—
TM60	Quash	Dark	Status	—	100	15	Normal	—	—
TM65	Shadow Claw	Ghost	Physical	70	100	15	Normal	—	○
TM68	Giga Impact	Normal	Physical	150	90	5	Normal	—	○
TM71	Stone Edge	Rock	Physical	100	80	5	Normal	—	—
TM78	Bulldoze	Ground	Physical	60	100	20	Adjacent	—	—
TM80	Rock Slide	Rock	Physical	75	90	10	Many Others	—	—
TM82	Dragon Tail	Dragon	Physical	60	90	10	Normal	—	○
TM84	Poison Jab	Poison	Physical	80	100	20	Normal	—	○
TM87	Swagger	Normal	Status	—	90	15	Normal	—	—
TM90	Substitute	Normal	Status	—	—	10	Self	—	—
TM94	Rock Smash	Fighting	Physical	40	100	15	Normal	—	○
HM01	Cut	Normal	Physical	50	95	30	Normal	—	○
HM03	Surf	Water	Special	95	100	15	Adjacent	—	—
HM04	Strength	Normal	Physical	80	100	15	Normal	—	○

MOVES TAUGHT BY PEOPLE

Name	Type	Kind	Pow.	Acc.	PP	Range	Long	DA

MOVES TAUGHT BY MOVE TUTORS FOR SHARDS

Name	Type	Kind	Pow.	Acc.	PP	Range	Long	DA
Drill Run	Ground	Physical	80	95	10	Normal	—	○
Super Fang	Normal	Physical	—	90	10	Normal	—	○
Uproar	Normal	Special	90	100	10	1 Random	—	—
Fire Punch	Fire	Physical	75	100	15	Normal	—	○
ThunderPunch	Electric	Physical	75	100	15	Normal	—	○
Ice Punch	Ice	Physical	75	100	15	Normal	—	○
Icy Wind	Ice	Special	55	95	15	Many Others	—	—
Iron Tail	Steel	Physical	100	75	15	Normal	—	○
Aqua Tail	Water	Physical	90	90	10	Normal	—	○
Earth Power	Ground	Special	90	100	10	Normal	—	—
Superpower	Fighting	Physical	120	100	5	Normal	—	○
Dragon Pulse	Dragon	Special	90	100	10	Normal	○	—
Snore	Normal	Special	40	100	15	Normal	—	—
Helping Hand	Normal	Status	—	—	20	1 Ally	—	—
Stealth Rock	Rock	Status	—	—	20	Other Side	—	—
Outrage	Dragon	Physical	120	100	10	1 Random	—	○
Sleep Talk	Normal	Status	—	—	10	Self	—	—

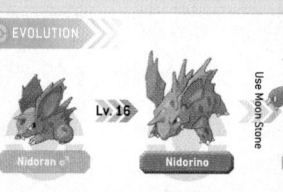

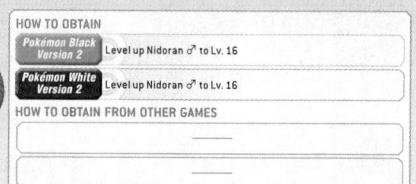

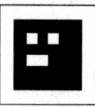

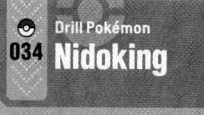

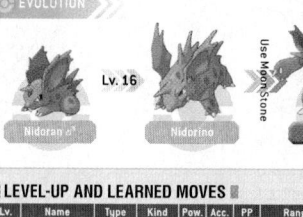

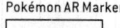

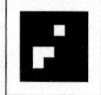

Fairy Pokémon
035 Clefairy

- HEIGHT: 2'00"
- WEIGHT: 16.5 lbs.
- GENDER: ♂ / ♀

On nights with a full moon, Clefairy gather from all over and dance. Bathing in moonlight makes them float.

TYPE Normal

ABILITIES
- Cute Charm
- Magic Guard

HIDDEN ABILITY
- Friend Guard

STATS
- HP
- Attack
- Defense
- Sp. Atk
- Sp. Def
- Speed

EGG GROUPS
Fairy

ITEMS SOMETIMES HELD
- Leppa Berry
- Comet Shard
- Moon Stone

Same form for ♂ / ♀

Pokémon AR Marker
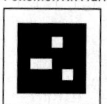

EVOLUTION

Cleffa → (Level up with high friendship) → Clefairy → (Use Moon Stone) → Clefable

➡ p. 100

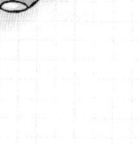

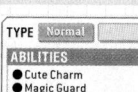

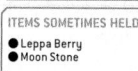

HOW TO OBTAIN

| Pokémon Black Version 2 | ❶ Giant Chasm caves ❷ Giant Chasm crater forest |
| Pokémon White Version 2 | ❶ Giant Chasm caves ❷ Giant Chasm crater forest |

HOW TO OBTAIN FROM OTHER GAMES

LEVEL-UP AND LEARNED MOVES

Lv.	Name	Type	Kind	Pow.	Acc.	PP	Range	Long	DA
1	Pound	Normal	Physical	40	100	35	Normal	—	○
1	Growl	Normal	Status	—	100	40	Many Others	—	—
4	Encore	Normal	Status	—	100	5	Normal	—	—
7	Sing	Normal	Status	—	55	15	Normal	—	—
10	DoubleSlap	Normal	Physical	15	85	10	Normal	—	○
13	Defense Curl	Normal	Status	—	—	40	Self	—	—
16	Follow Me	Normal	Status	—	—	20	Self	—	—
19	Bestow	Normal	Status	—	—	15	Normal	—	—
22	Wake-Up Slap	Fighting	Physical	60	100	10	Normal	—	○
25	Minimize	Normal	Status	—	—	20	Self	—	—
28	Stored Power	Psychic	Special	20	100	10	Normal	—	—
31	Metronome	Normal	Status	—	—	10	Self	—	—
34	Cosmic Power	Psychic	Status	—	—	20	Self	—	—
37	Lucky Chant	Normal	Status	—	—	30	Your Side	—	—
40	Body Slam	Normal	Physical	85	100	15	Normal	—	○
43	Moonlight	Normal	Status	—	—	5	Self	—	—
46	Light Screen	Psychic	Status	—	—	30	Your Side	—	—
49	Gravity	Psychic	Status	—	—	5	Both Sides	—	—
52	Meteor Mash	Steel	Physical	100	85	10	Normal	—	○
55	Healing Wish	Psychic	Status	—	—	10	Self	—	—
58	After You	Normal	Status	—	—	15	Normal	—	—

TM & HM MOVES

Lv.	Name	Type	Kind	Pow.	Acc.	PP	Range	Long	DA
TM03	Psyshock	Psychic	Special	80	100	10	Normal	—	—
TM04	Calm Mind	Psychic	Status	—	—	20	Self	—	—
TM06	Toxic	Poison	Status	—	90	10	Normal	—	—
TM10	Hidden Power	Normal	Special	—	100	15	Normal	—	—
TM11	Sunny Day	Fire	Status	—	—	5	Both Sides	—	—
TM13	Ice Beam	Ice	Special	95	100	10	Normal	—	—
TM14	Blizzard	Ice	Special	120	70	5	Many Others	—	—
TM16	Light Screen	Psychic	Status	—	—	30	Your Side	—	—
TM17	Protect	Normal	Status	—	—	10	Self	—	—
TM18	Rain Dance	Water	Status	—	—	5	Both Sides	—	—
TM19	Telekinesis	Psychic	Status	—	—	15	Normal	—	—
TM20	Safeguard	Normal	Status	—	—	25	Your Side	—	—
TM21	Frustration	Normal	Physical	—	100	20	Normal	—	○
TM22	SolarBeam	Grass	Special	120	100	10	Normal	—	—
TM24	Thunderbolt	Electric	Special	95	100	15	Normal	—	—
TM25	Thunder	Electric	Special	120	70	10	Normal	—	—
TM27	Return	Normal	Physical	—	100	20	Normal	—	○
TM28	Dig	Ground	Physical	80	100	10	Normal	—	○
TM29	Psychic	Psychic	Special	90	100	10	Normal	—	—
TM30	Shadow Ball	Ghost	Special	80	100	15	Normal	—	—
TM31	Brick Break	Fighting	Physical	75	100	15	Normal	—	○
TM32	Double Team	Normal	Status	—	—	15	Self	—	—
TM33	Reflect	Psychic	Status	—	—	20	Your Side	—	—
TM35	Flamethrower	Fire	Special	95	100	15	Normal	—	—
TM38	Fire Blast	Fire	Special	120	85	5	Normal	—	—
TM42	Facade	Normal	Physical	70	100	20	Normal	—	○
TM44	Rest	Psychic	Status	—	—	10	Self	—	—
TM45	Attract	Normal	Status	—	100	15	Normal	—	—
TM48	Round	Normal	Special	60	100	15	Normal	—	—
TM49	Echoed Voice	Normal	Special	40	100	15	Normal	—	—
TM56	Fling	Dark	Physical	—	100	10	Normal	—	○
TM57	Charge Beam	Electric	Special	50	90	10	Normal	—	—

Lv.	Name	Type	Kind	Pow.	Acc.	PP	Range	Long	DA
TM59	Incinerate	Fire	Special	30	100	15	Many Others	—	—
TM67	Retaliate	Normal	Physical	70	100	5	Normal	—	○
TM70	Flash	Normal	Status	—	100	20	Normal	—	—
TM73	Thunder Wave	Electric	Status	—	100	20	Normal	—	—
TM77	Psych Up	Normal	Status	—	—	10	Self	—	—
TM83	Work Up	Normal	Status	—	—	30	Self	—	—
TM85	Dream Eater	Psychic	Special	100	100	15	Normal	—	—
TM86	Grass Knot	Grass	Special	—	100	20	Normal	—	○
TM87	Swagger	Normal	Status	—	90	15	Normal	—	—
TM90	Substitute	Normal	Status	—	—	10	Self	—	—
TM94	Rock Smash	Fighting	Physical	40	100	15	Normal	—	○
HM04	Strength	Normal	Physical	80	100	15	Normal	—	○

MOVES TAUGHT BY PEOPLE

Name	Type	Kind	Pow.	Acc.	PP	Range	Long	DA

MOVES TAUGHT BY MOVE TUTORS FOR SHARDS

Name	Type	Kind	Pow.	Acc.	PP	Range	Long	DA
Covet	Normal	Physical	60	100	40	Normal	—	○
Bounce	Flying	Physical	85	85	5	Normal	○	○
Signal Beam	Bug	Special	75	100	15	Normal	—	—
Fire Punch	Fire	Physical	75	100	15	Normal	—	○
ThunderPunch	Electric	Physical	75	100	15	Normal	—	○
Ice Punch	Ice	Physical	75	100	15	Normal	—	○
Last Resort	Normal	Physical	140	100	5	Normal	—	○
Magic Coat	Psychic	Status	—	—	15	Self	—	—
Hyper Voice	Normal	Special	90	100	10	Many Others	—	—
Icy Wind	Ice	Special	55	95	15	Many Others	—	—
Iron Tail	Steel	Physical	100	75	15	Normal	—	○
Zen Headbutt	Psychic	Physical	80	90	15	Normal	—	○
Gravity	Psychic	Status	—	—	5	Both Sides	—	—
Snore	Normal	Special	40	100	15	Normal	—	—
Heal Bell	Normal	Status	—	—	5	Your Party	—	—
Knock Off	Dark	Physical	20	100	20	Normal	—	○
Role Play	Psychic	Status	—	—	10	Normal	—	—
Drain Punch	Fighting	Physical	75	100	10	Normal	—	○
Helping Hand	Normal	Status	—	—	20	1 Ally	—	—
After You	Normal	Status	—	—	15	Normal	—	—
Wonder Room	Psychic	Status	—	—	10	Both Sides	—	—
Recycle	Normal	Status	—	—	10	Self	—	—
Trick	Psychic	Status	—	100	10	Normal	—	—
Stealth Rock	Rock	Status	—	—	20	Other Side	—	—
Endeavor	Normal	Physical	—	100	5	Normal	—	○
Sleep Talk	Normal	Status	—	—	10	Self	—	—
Snatch	Dark	Status	—	—	10	Self	—	—

Fairy Pokémon
036 Clefable

- HEIGHT: 4'03"
- WEIGHT: 88.2 lbs.
- GENDER: ♂ / ♀

Their ears are sensitive enough to hear a pin drop from over a mile away, so they're usually found in quiet places.

TYPE Normal

ABILITIES
- Cute Charm
- Magic Guard

HIDDEN ABILITY
- Unaware

STATS
- HP
- Attack
- Defense
- Sp. Atk
- Sp. Def
- Speed

EGG GROUPS
Fairy

ITEMS SOMETIMES HELD
- Leppa Berry
- Moon Stone

Same form for ♂ / ♀

Pokémon AR Marker

EVOLUTION

Cleffa → (Level up with high friendship) → Clefairy → (Use Moon Stone) → Clefable

➡ p. 100

HOW TO OBTAIN

| Pokémon Black Version 2 | ❶ Giant Chasm crater entrance (rustling grass) ❷ Giant Chasm crater forest (rustling grass) |
| Pokémon White Version 2 | ❶ Giant Chasm crater entrance (rustling grass) ❷ Giant Chasm crater forest (rustling grass) |

HOW TO OBTAIN FROM OTHER GAMES

LEVEL-UP AND LEARNED MOVES

Lv.	Name	Type	Kind	Pow.	Acc.	PP	Range	Long	DA
1	Sing	Normal	Status	—	55	15	Normal	—	—
1	DoubleSlap	Normal	Physical	15	85	10	Normal	—	○
1	Minimize	Normal	Status	—	—	20	Self	—	—
1	Metronome	Normal	Status	—	—	10	Self	—	—

TM & HM MOVES

Lv.	Name	Type	Kind	Pow.	Acc.	PP	Range	Long	DA
TM03	Psyshock	Psychic	Special	80	100	10	Normal	—	—
TM04	Calm Mind	Psychic	Status	—	—	20	Self	—	—
TM06	Toxic	Poison	Status	—	90	10	Normal	—	—
TM10	Hidden Power	Normal	Special	—	100	15	Normal	—	—
TM11	Sunny Day	Fire	Status	—	—	5	Both Sides	—	—
TM13	Ice Beam	Ice	Special	95	100	10	Normal	—	—
TM14	Blizzard	Ice	Special	120	70	5	Many Others	—	—
TM15	Hyper Beam	Normal	Special	150	90	5	Normal	—	—
TM16	Light Screen	Psychic	Status	—	—	30	Your Side	—	—
TM17	Protect	Normal	Status	—	—	10	Self	—	—
TM18	Rain Dance	Water	Status	—	—	5	Both Sides	—	—
TM19	Telekinesis	Psychic	Status	—	—	15	Normal	—	—
TM20	Safeguard	Normal	Status	—	—	25	Your Side	—	—
TM21	Frustration	Normal	Physical	—	100	20	Normal	—	○
TM22	SolarBeam	Grass	Special	120	100	10	Normal	—	—
TM24	Thunderbolt	Electric	Special	95	100	15	Normal	—	—
TM25	Thunder	Electric	Special	120	70	10	Normal	—	—
TM27	Return	Normal	Physical	—	100	20	Normal	—	○
TM28	Dig	Ground	Physical	80	100	10	Normal	—	○
TM29	Psychic	Psychic	Special	90	100	10	Normal	—	—
TM30	Shadow Ball	Ghost	Special	80	100	15	Normal	—	—
TM31	Brick Break	Fighting	Physical	75	100	15	Normal	—	○
TM32	Double Team	Normal	Status	—	—	15	Self	—	—
TM33	Reflect	Psychic	Status	—	—	20	Your Side	—	—
TM35	Flamethrower	Fire	Special	95	100	15	Normal	—	—
TM38	Fire Blast	Fire	Special	120	85	5	Normal	—	—
TM42	Facade	Normal	Physical	70	100	20	Normal	—	○
TM44	Rest	Psychic	Status	—	—	10	Self	—	—
TM45	Attract	Normal	Status	—	100	15	Normal	—	—
TM48	Round	Normal	Special	60	100	15	Normal	—	—
TM49	Echoed Voice	Normal	Special	40	100	15	Normal	—	—
TM52	Focus Blast	Fighting	Special	120	70	5	Normal	—	—
TM56	Fling	Dark	Physical	—	100	10	Normal	—	○
TM57	Charge Beam	Electric	Special	50	90	10	Normal	—	—
TM59	Incinerate	Fire	Special	30	100	15	Many Others	—	—
TM67	Retaliate	Normal	Physical	70	100	5	Normal	—	○
TM68	Giga Impact	Normal	Physical	150	90	5	Normal	—	○
TM70	Flash	Normal	Status	—	100	20	Normal	—	—
TM73	Thunder Wave	Electric	Status	—	100	20	Normal	—	—
TM77	Psych Up	Normal	Status	—	—	10	Self	—	—
TM83	Work Up	Normal	Status	—	—	30	Self	—	—
TM85	Dream Eater	Psychic	Special	100	100	15	Normal	—	—
TM86	Grass Knot	Grass	Special	—	100	20	Normal	—	○
TM87	Swagger	Normal	Status	—	90	15	Normal	—	—
TM90	Substitute	Normal	Status	—	—	10	Self	—	—
TM94	Rock Smash	Fighting	Physical	40	100	15	Normal	—	○
HM04	Strength	Normal	Physical	80	100	15	Normal	—	○

MOVES TAUGHT BY PEOPLE

Name	Type	Kind	Pow.	Acc.	PP	Range	Long	DA

MOVES TAUGHT BY MOVE TUTORS FOR SHARDS

Name	Type	Kind	Pow.	Acc.	PP	Range	Long	DA
Covet	Normal	Physical	60	100	40	Normal	—	○
Bounce	Flying	Physical	85	85	5	Normal	○	○
Signal Beam	Bug	Special	75	100	15	Normal	—	—
Fire Punch	Fire	Physical	75	100	15	Normal	—	○
ThunderPunch	Electric	Physical	75	100	15	Normal	—	○
Ice Punch	Ice	Physical	75	100	15	Normal	—	○
Last Resort	Normal	Physical	140	100	5	Normal	—	○
Magic Coat	Psychic	Status	—	—	15	Self	—	—
Hyper Voice	Normal	Special	90	100	10	Many Others	—	—
Icy Wind	Ice	Special	55	95	15	Many Others	—	—
Iron Tail	Steel	Physical	100	75	15	Normal	—	○
Zen Headbutt	Psychic	Physical	80	90	15	Normal	—	○
Gravity	Psychic	Status	—	—	5	Both Sides	—	—
Snore	Normal	Special	40	100	15	Normal	—	—
Heal Bell	Normal	Status	—	—	5	Your Party	—	—
Knock Off	Dark	Physical	20	100	20	Normal	—	○
Role Play	Psychic	Status	—	—	10	Normal	—	—
Drain Punch	Fighting	Physical	75	100	10	Normal	—	○
Helping Hand	Normal	Status	—	—	20	1 Ally	—	—
After You	Normal	Status	—	—	15	Normal	—	—
Wonder Room	Psychic	Status	—	—	10	Both Sides	—	—
Recycle	Normal	Status	—	—	10	Self	—	—
Trick	Psychic	Status	—	100	10	Normal	—	—
Stealth Rock	Rock	Status	—	—	20	Other Side	—	—
Endeavor	Normal	Physical	—	100	5	Normal	—	○
Sleep Talk	Normal	Status	—	—	10	Self	—	—
Snatch	Dark	Status	—	—	10	Self	—	—

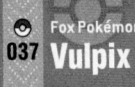

NATIONAL POKÉDEX

037 Vulpix

037 Vulpix

Fox Pokémon

- HEIGHT: 2'00"
- WEIGHT: 21.8 lbs.
- GENDER: ♂ / ♀

As each tail grows, its fur becomes more lustrous. When held, it feels slightly warm.

Same form for ♂ / ♀

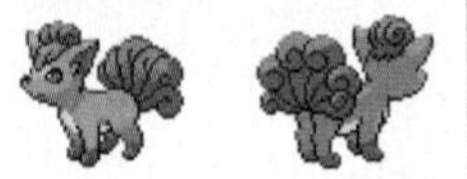

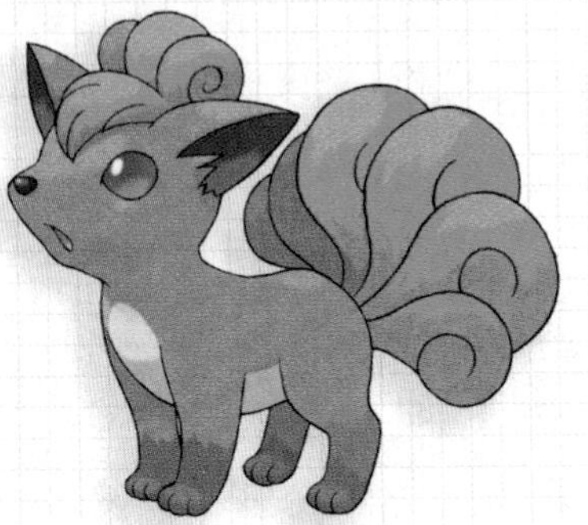

Pokémon AR Marker

TYPE: Fire

ABILITY
- Flash Fire

HIDDEN ABILITY
- Drought

STATS
HP
Attack
Defense
Sp. Atk
Sp. Def
Speed

EGG GROUPS
Field

ITEMS SOMETIMES HELD
- Rawst Berry

EVOLUTION

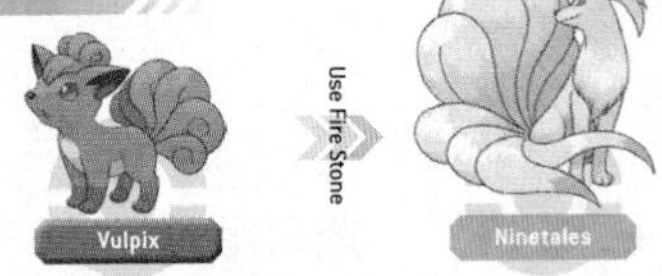

HOW TO OBTAIN

Pokémon Black Version 2	❶ Abundant Shrine ❷ Abundant Shrine (Hidden Grotto)
Pokémon White Version 2	❶ Abundant Shrine ❷ Abundant Shrine (Hidden Grotto)

HOW TO OBTAIN FROM OTHER GAMES

—

—

LEVEL-UP AND LEARNED MOVES

Lv.	Name	Type	Kind	Pow.	Acc.	PP	Range	Long	DA
1	Ember	Fire	Special	40	100	25	Normal	—	—
4	Tail Whip	Normal	Status	—	100	30	Many Others	—	—
7	Roar	Normal	Status	—	100	20	Normal	—	—
10	Quick Attack	Normal	Physical	40	100	30	Normal	—	○
12	Fire Spin	Fire	Special	35	85	15	Normal	—	—
15	Confuse Ray	Ghost	Status	—	100	10	Normal	—	—
18	Imprison	Psychic	Status	—	—	10	Self	—	—
20	Faint Attack	Dark	Physical	60	—	20	Normal	—	○
23	Flame Burst	Fire	Special	70	100	15	Normal	—	—
26	Will-O-Wisp	Fire	Status	—	75	15	Normal	—	—
28	Hex	Ghost	Special	50	100	10	Normal	—	—
31	Payback	Dark	Physical	50	100	10	Normal	—	○
34	Flamethrower	Fire	Special	95	100	15	Normal	—	—
36	Safeguard	Normal	Status	—	—	25	Your Side	—	—
39	Extrasensory	Psychic	Special	80	100	30	Normal	—	—
42	Fire Blast	Fire	Special	120	85	5	Normal	—	—
44	Grudge	Ghost	Status	—	—	5	Self	—	—
47	Captivate	Normal	Status	—	100	20	Many Others	—	—
50	Inferno	Fire	Special	100	50	5	Normal	—	—

TM & HM MOVES

Lv.	Name	Type	Kind	Pow.	Acc.	PP	Range	Long	DA
TM05	Roar	Normal	Status	—	100	20	Normal	—	—
TM06	Toxic	Poison	Status	—	90	10	Normal	—	—
TM10	Hidden Power	Normal	Special	—	100	15	Normal	—	—
TM11	Sunny Day	Fire	Status	—	—	5	Both Sides	—	—
TM17	Protect	Normal	Status	—	—	10	Self	—	—
TM20	Safeguard	Normal	Status	—	—	25	Your Side	—	—
TM21	Frustration	Normal	Physical	—	100	20	Normal	—	○
TM27	Return	Normal	Physical	—	100	20	Normal	—	○
TM28	Dig	Ground	Physical	80	100	10	Normal	—	○
TM32	Double Team	Normal	Status	—	—	15	Self	—	—
TM35	Flamethrower	Fire	Special	95	100	15	Normal	—	—
TM38	Fire Blast	Fire	Special	120	85	5	Normal	—	—
TM42	Facade	Normal	Physical	70	100	20	Normal	—	○
TM43	Flame Charge	Fire	Physical	50	100	20	Normal	—	○
TM44	Rest	Psychic	Status	—	—	10	Self	—	—
TM45	Attract	Normal	Status	—	100	15	Normal	—	—
TM48	Round	Normal	Special	60	100	15	Normal	—	—
TM50	Overheat	Fire	Special	140	90	5	Normal	—	—
TM53	Energy Ball	Grass	Special	80	100	10	Normal	—	—
TM59	Incinerate	Fire	Special	30	100	15	Many Others	—	—
TM61	Will-O-Wisp	Fire	Status	—	75	15	Normal	—	—
TM66	Payback	Dark	Physical	50	100	10	Normal	—	○
TM77	Psych Up	Normal	Status	—	—	10	Normal	—	—
TM87	Swagger	Normal	Status	—	90	15	Normal	—	—
TM90	Substitute	Normal	Status	—	—	10	Self	—	—

MOVES TAUGHT BY PEOPLE

Name	Type	Kind	Pow.	Acc.	PP	Range	Long	DA

MOVES TAUGHT BY MOVE TUTORS FOR SHARDS

Name	Type	Kind	Pow.	Acc.	PP	Range	Long	DA
Covet	Normal	Physical	60	100	40	Normal	—	○
Iron Tail	Steel	Physical	100	75	15	Normal	—	○
Zen Headbutt	Psychic	Physical	80	90	15	Normal	—	○
Foul Play	Dark	Physical	95	100	15	Normal	—	○
Dark Pulse	Dark	Special	80	100	15	Normal	○	—
Snore	Normal	Special	40	100	15	Normal	—	—
Role Play	Psychic	Status	—	—	10	Normal	—	—
Heat Wave	Fire	Special	100	90	10	Many Others	—	—
Pain Split	Normal	Status	—	—	20	Normal	—	—
Spite	Ghost	Status	—	100	10	Normal	—	—
Sleep Talk	Normal	Status	—	—	10	Self	—	—

EGG MOVES

Name	Type	Kind	Pow.	Acc.	PP	Range	Long	DA
Faint Attack	Dark	Physical	60	—	20	Normal	—	○
Hypnosis	Psychic	Status	—	60	20	Normal	—	—
Flail	Normal	Physical	—	100	15	Normal	—	○
Spite	Ghost	Status	—	100	10	Normal	—	—
Disable	Normal	Status	—	100	20	Normal	—	—
Howl	Normal	Status	—	—	40	Self	—	—
Heat Wave	Fire	Special	100	90	10	Many Others	—	—
Flare Blitz	Fire	Physical	120	100	15	Normal	—	○
Extrasensory	Psychic	Special	80	100	30	Normal	—	—
Power Swap	Psychic	Status	—	—	10	Normal	—	—
Secret Power	Normal	Physical	70	100	20	Normal	—	—
Hex	Ghost	Special	50	100	10	Normal	—	—
Tail Slap	Normal	Physical	25	85	10	Normal	—	○

038 Ninetales

038 Ninetales

Fox Pokémon

- HEIGHT: 3'07"
- WEIGHT: 43.9 lbs.
- GENDER: ♂ / ♀

Each of its nine tails is imbued with supernatural power, and it can live for a thousand years.

Same form for ♂ / ♀

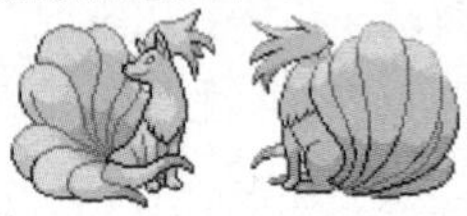

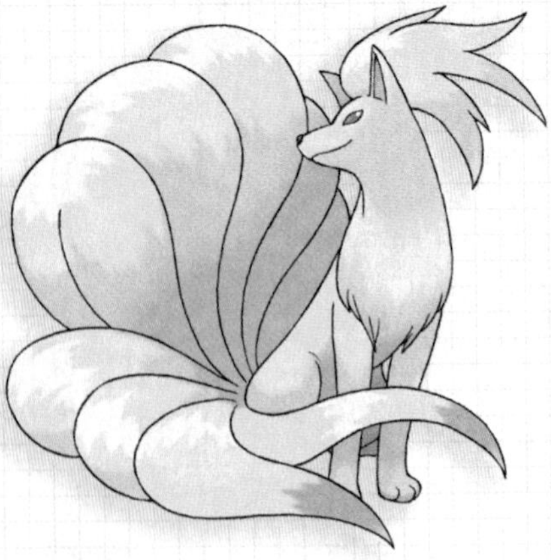

Pokémon AR Marker

TYPE: Fire

ABILITY
- Flash Fire

HIDDEN ABILITY
- Drought

STATS
HP
Attack
Defense
Sp. Atk
Sp. Def
Speed

EGG GROUPS
Field

ITEMS SOMETIMES HELD
- Rawst Berry

EVOLUTION

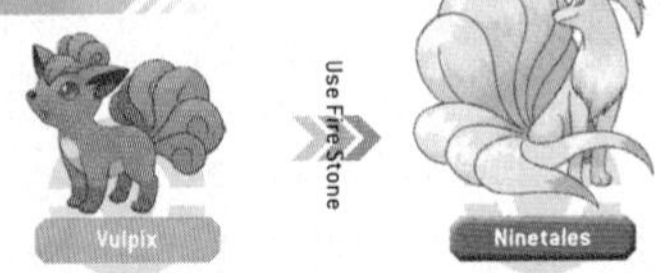

HOW TO OBTAIN

Pokémon Black Version 2	Abundant Shrine (rustling grass)
Pokémon White Version 2	Abundant Shrine (rustling grass)

HOW TO OBTAIN FROM OTHER GAMES

—

—

LEVEL-UP AND LEARNED MOVES

Lv.	Name	Type	Kind	Pow.	Acc.	PP	Range	Long	DA
1	Nasty Plot	Dark	Status	—	—	20	Self	—	—
1	Ember	Fire	Special	40	100	25	Normal	—	—
1	Quick Attack	Normal	Physical	40	100	30	Normal	—	○
1	Confuse Ray	Ghost	Status	—	100	10	Normal	—	—
1	Safeguard	Normal	Status	—	—	25	Your Side	—	—

TM & HM MOVES

Lv.	Name	Type	Kind	Pow.	Acc.	PP	Range	Long	DA
TM03	Psyshock	Psychic	Special	80	100	10	Normal	—	—
TM04	Calm Mind	Psychic	Status	—	—	20	Self	—	—
TM05	Roar	Normal	Status	—	100	20	Normal	—	—
TM06	Toxic	Poison	Status	—	90	10	Normal	—	—
TM10	Hidden Power	Normal	Special	—	100	15	Normal	—	—
TM11	Sunny Day	Fire	Status	—	—	5	Both Sides	—	—
TM15	Hyper Beam	Normal	Special	150	90	5	Normal	—	—
TM17	Protect	Normal	Status	—	—	10	Self	—	—
TM20	Safeguard	Normal	Status	—	—	25	Your Side	—	—
TM21	Frustration	Normal	Physical	—	100	20	Normal	—	○
TM22	SolarBeam	Grass	Special	120	100	10	Normal	—	—
TM27	Return	Normal	Physical	—	100	20	Normal	—	○
TM28	Dig	Ground	Physical	80	100	10	Normal	—	○
TM32	Double Team	Normal	Status	—	—	15	Self	—	—
TM35	Flamethrower	Fire	Special	95	100	15	Normal	—	—
TM38	Fire Blast	Fire	Special	120	85	5	Normal	—	—
TM42	Facade	Normal	Physical	70	100	20	Normal	—	○
TM43	Flame Charge	Fire	Physical	50	100	20	Normal	—	○
TM44	Rest	Psychic	Status	—	—	10	Self	—	—
TM45	Attract	Normal	Status	—	100	15	Normal	—	—
TM48	Round	Normal	Special	60	100	15	Normal	—	—
TM50	Overheat	Fire	Special	140	90	5	Normal	—	—
TM53	Energy Ball	Grass	Special	80	100	10	Normal	—	—
TM59	Incinerate	Fire	Special	30	100	15	Many Others	—	—
TM61	Will-O-Wisp	Fire	Status	—	75	15	Normal	—	—
TM66	Payback	Dark	Physical	50	100	10	Normal	—	○
TM68	Giga Impact	Normal	Physical	150	90	5	Normal	—	○
TM77	Psych Up	Normal	Status	—	—	10	Normal	—	—
TM85	Dream Eater	Psychic	Special	100	100	15	Normal	—	—
TM87	Swagger	Normal	Status	—	90	15	Normal	—	—
TM90	Substitute	Normal	Status	—	—	10	Self	—	—

MOVES TAUGHT BY PEOPLE

Name	Type	Kind	Pow.	Acc.	PP	Range	Long	DA

MOVES TAUGHT BY MOVE TUTORS FOR SHARDS

Name	Type	Kind	Pow.	Acc.	PP	Range	Long	DA
Covet	Normal	Physical	60	100	40	Normal	—	○
Iron Tail	Steel	Physical	100	75	15	Normal	—	○
Zen Headbutt	Psychic	Physical	80	90	15	Normal	—	○
Foul Play	Dark	Physical	95	100	15	Normal	—	○
Dark Pulse	Dark	Special	80	100	15	Normal	○	—
Snore	Normal	Special	40	100	15	Normal	—	—
Role Play	Psychic	Status	—	—	10	Normal	—	—
Heat Wave	Fire	Special	100	90	10	Many Others	—	—
Pain Split	Normal	Status	—	—	20	Normal	—	—
Spite	Ghost	Status	—	100	10	Normal	—	—
Sleep Talk	Normal	Status	—	—	10	Self	—	—

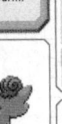

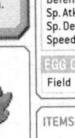

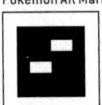

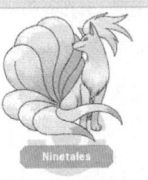

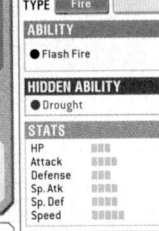

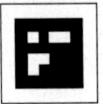

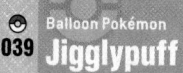

Balloon Pokémon

039 Jigglypuff

- HEIGHT: 1'08"
- WEIGHT: 12.1 lbs.
- GENDER: ♂ / ♀

Looking into its cute, round eyes makes it start singing a song so pleasant that listeners can't help but fall asleep.

Same form for ♂ / ♀

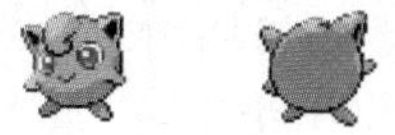

TYPE: Normal

ABILITY
- Cute Charm

HIDDEN ABILITY
- Friend Guard

STATS
- HP
- Attack
- Defense
- Sp. Atk
- Sp. Def
- Speed

EGG GROUPS
Fairy

ITEMS SOMETIMES HELD
- None

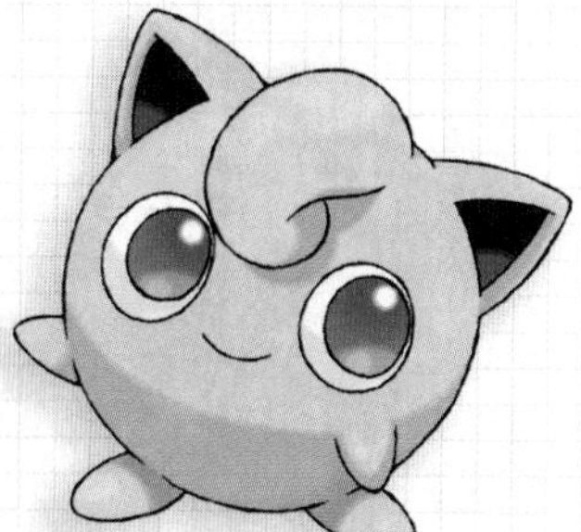

Pokémon AR Marker

EVOLUTION

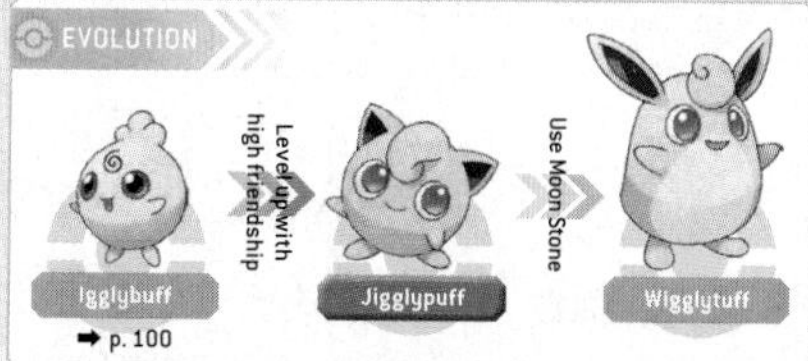
Igglybuff
Level up with high friendship
Jigglypuff
Use Moon Stone
Wigglytuff

➡ p. 100

HOW TO OBTAIN

- Pokémon Black Version 2: ❶ Dreamyard ❷ Route 2
- Pokémon White Version 2: ❶ Dreamyard ❷ Route 2

HOW TO OBTAIN FROM OTHER GAMES

—

—

LEVEL-UP AND LEARNED MOVES

Lv.	Name	Type	Kind	Pow.	Acc.	PP	Range	Long	DA
1	Sing	Normal	Status	—	55	15	Normal	—	—
5	Defense Curl	Normal	Status	—	—	40	Self	—	—
9	Pound	Normal	Physical	40	100	35	Normal	—	○
13	Disable	Normal	Status	—	100	20	Normal	—	—
17	Round	Normal	Special	60	100	15	Normal	—	—
21	Rollout	Rock	Physical	30	90	20	Normal	—	○
25	DoubleSlap	Normal	Physical	15	85	10	Normal	—	○
29	Rest	Psychic	Status	—	—	10	Self	—	—
33	Body Slam	Normal	Physical	85	100	15	Normal	—	○
37	Gyro Ball	Steel	Physical	—	100	5	Normal	—	○
41	Wake-Up Slap	Fighting	Physical	60	100	10	Normal	—	○
45	Mimic	Normal	Status	—	—	10	Normal	—	—
49	Hyper Voice	Normal	Special	90	100	10	Many Others	—	—
53	Double-Edge	Normal	Physical	120	100	15	Normal	—	○

TM & HM MOVES

Lv.	Name	Type	Kind	Pow.	Acc.	PP	Range	Long	DA
TM06	Toxic	Poison	Status	—	90	10	Normal	—	—
TM10	Hidden Power	Normal	Special	—	100	15	Normal	—	—
TM11	Sunny Day	Fire	Status	—	—	5	Both Sides	—	—
TM13	Ice Beam	Ice	Special	95	100	10	Normal	—	—
TM14	Blizzard	Ice	Special	120	70	5	Many Others	—	—
TM16	Light Screen	Psychic	Status	—	—	30	Your Side	—	—
TM17	Protect	Normal	Status	—	—	10	Self	—	—
TM18	Rain Dance	Water	Status	—	—	5	Both Sides	—	—
TM20	Safeguard	Normal	Status	—	—	25	Your Side	—	—
TM21	Frustration	Normal	Physical	—	100	20	Normal	—	○
TM22	SolarBeam	Grass	Special	120	100	10	Normal	—	—
TM24	Thunderbolt	Electric	Special	95	100	15	Normal	—	—
TM25	Thunder	Electric	Special	120	70	10	Normal	—	—
TM27	Return	Normal	Physical	—	100	20	Normal	—	○
TM28	Dig	Ground	Physical	80	100	10	Normal	—	○
TM29	Psychic	Psychic	Special	90	100	10	Normal	—	—
TM30	Shadow Ball	Ghost	Special	80	100	15	Normal	—	—
TM31	Brick Break	Fighting	Physical	75	100	15	Normal	—	○
TM32	Double Team	Normal	Status	—	—	15	Self	—	—
TM33	Reflect	Psychic	Status	—	—	20	Your Side	—	—
TM35	Flamethrower	Fire	Special	95	100	15	Normal	—	—
TM38	Fire Blast	Fire	Special	120	85	5	Normal	—	—
TM42	Facade	Normal	Physical	70	100	20	Normal	—	○
TM44	Rest	Psychic	Status	—	—	10	Self	—	—
TM45	Attract	Normal	Status	—	100	15	Normal	—	—
TM48	Round	Normal	Special	60	100	15	Normal	—	—
TM49	Echoed Voice	Normal	Special	40	100	15	Normal	—	—
TM56	Fling	Dark	Physical	—	100	10	Normal	—	—
TM57	Charge Beam	Electric	Special	50	90	10	Normal	—	—
TM59	Incinerate	Fire	Special	30	100	15	Many Others	—	—
TM67	Retaliate	Normal	Physical	70	100	5	Normal	—	○
TM70	Flash	Normal	Status	—	100	20	Normal	—	—
TM73	Thunder Wave	Electric	Status	—	100	20	Normal	—	—
TM74	Gyro Ball	Steel	Physical	—	100	5	Normal	—	○
TM77	Psych Up	Normal	Status	—	—	10	Normal	—	—
TM83	Work Up	Normal	Status	—	—	30	Self	—	—
TM85	Dream Eater	Psychic	Special	100	100	15	Normal	—	—
TM86	Grass Knot	Grass	Special	—	100	20	Normal	—	○
TM87	Swagger	Normal	Status	—	90	15	Normal	—	—
TM90	Substitute	Normal	Status	—	—	10	Self	—	—
TM93	Wild Charge	Electric	Physical	90	100	15	Normal	—	○
HM04	Strength	Normal	Physical	80	100	15	Normal	—	○

MOVES TAUGHT BY PEOPLE

Name	Type	Kind	Pow.	Acc.	PP	Range	Long	DA

MOVES TAUGHT BY MOVE TUTORS FOR SHARDS

Name	Type	Kind	Pow.	Acc.	PP	Range	Long	DA
Covet	Normal	Physical	60	100	40	Normal	—	○
Bounce	Flying	Physical	85	85	5	Normal	○	○
Fire Punch	Fire	Physical	75	100	15	Normal	—	○
ThunderPunch	Electric	Physical	75	100	15	Normal	—	○
Ice Punch	Ice	Physical	75	100	15	Normal	—	○
Last Resort	Normal	Physical	140	100	5	Normal	—	○
Magic Coat	Psychic	Status	—	—	15	Self	—	—
Hyper Voice	Normal	Special	90	100	10	Many Others	—	—
Icy Wind	Ice	Special	55	95	15	Many Others	—	—
Gravity	Psychic	Status	—	—	5	Both Sides	—	—
Snore	Normal	Special	40	100	15	Normal	—	—
Heal Bell	Normal	Status	—	—	5	Your Party	—	—
Knock Off	Dark	Physical	20	100	20	Normal	—	○
Role Play	Psychic	Status	—	—	10	Normal	—	—
Drain Punch	Fighting	Physical	75	100	10	Normal	—	○
Pain Split	Normal	Status	—	—	20	Normal	—	—
Helping Hand	Normal	Status	—	—	20	1 Ally	—	—
Recycle	Normal	Status	—	—	10	Self	—	—
Stealth Rock	Rock	Status	—	—	20	Other Side	—	—
Endeavor	Normal	Physical	—	100	5	Normal	—	○
Sleep Talk	Normal	Status	—	—	10	Self	—	—
Snatch	Dark	Status	—	—	10	Self	—	—

Balloon Pokémon

040 Wigglytuff

- HEIGHT: 3'03"
- WEIGHT: 26.5 lbs.
- GENDER: ♂ / ♀

Its fine fur feels so pleasant, those who accidentally touch it cannot take their hands away.

Same form for ♂ / ♀

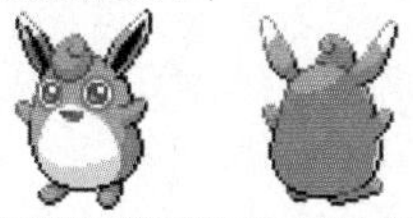

TYPE: Normal

ABILITY
- Cute Charm

HIDDEN ABILITY
- Frisk

STATS
- HP
- Attack
- Defense
- Sp. Atk
- Sp. Def
- Speed

EGG GROUPS
Fairy

ITEMS SOMETIMES HELD
- None

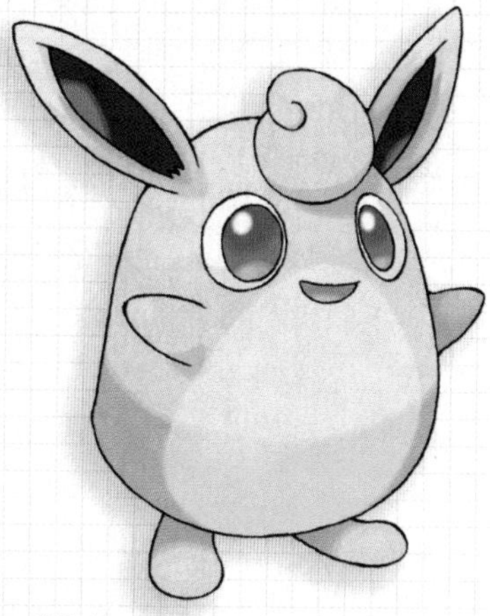

Pokémon AR Marker

EVOLUTION

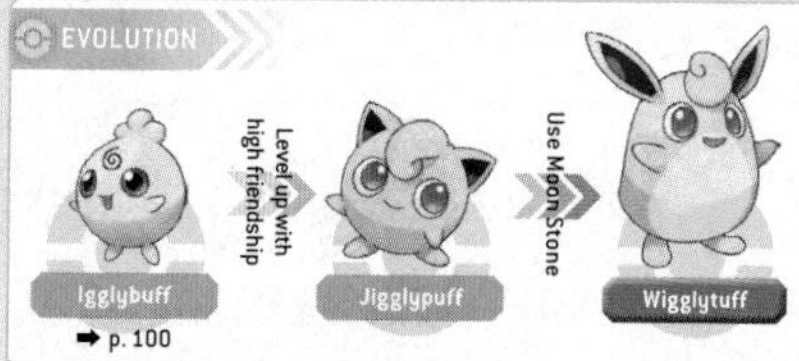
Igglybuff
Level up with high friendship
Jigglypuff
Use Moon Stone
Wigglytuff

➡ p. 100

HOW TO OBTAIN

- Pokémon Black Version 2: ❶ Dreamyard (rustling grass) ❷ Route 2 (rustling grass)
- Pokémon White Version 2: ❶ Dreamyard (rustling grass) ❷ Route 2 (rustling grass)

HOW TO OBTAIN FROM OTHER GAMES

—

—

LEVEL-UP AND LEARNED MOVES

Lv.	Name	Type	Kind	Pow.	Acc.	PP	Range	Long	DA
1	Sing	Normal	Status	—	55	15	Normal	—	—
1	Disable	Normal	Status	—	100	20	Normal	—	—
1	Defense Curl	Normal	Status	—	—	40	Self	—	—
1	DoubleSlap	Normal	Physical	15	85	10	Normal	—	○

TM & HM MOVES

Lv.	Name	Type	Kind	Pow.	Acc.	PP	Range	Long	DA
TM06	Toxic	Poison	Status	—	90	10	Normal	—	—
TM10	Hidden Power	Normal	Special	—	100	15	Normal	—	—
TM11	Sunny Day	Fire	Status	—	—	5	Both Sides	—	—
TM13	Ice Beam	Ice	Special	95	100	10	Normal	—	—
TM14	Blizzard	Ice	Special	120	70	5	Many Others	—	—
TM15	Hyper Beam	Normal	Special	150	90	5	Normal	—	—
TM16	Light Screen	Psychic	Status	—	—	30	Your Side	—	—
TM17	Protect	Normal	Status	—	—	10	Self	—	—
TM18	Rain Dance	Water	Status	—	—	5	Both Sides	—	—
TM20	Safeguard	Normal	Status	—	—	25	Your Side	—	—
TM21	Frustration	Normal	Physical	—	100	20	Normal	—	○
TM22	SolarBeam	Grass	Special	120	100	10	Normal	—	—
TM24	Thunderbolt	Electric	Special	95	100	15	Normal	—	—
TM25	Thunder	Electric	Special	120	70	10	Normal	—	—
TM27	Return	Normal	Physical	—	100	20	Normal	—	○
TM28	Dig	Ground	Physical	80	100	10	Normal	—	○
TM29	Psychic	Psychic	Special	90	100	10	Normal	—	—
TM30	Shadow Ball	Ghost	Special	80	100	15	Normal	—	—
TM31	Brick Break	Fighting	Physical	75	100	15	Normal	—	○
TM32	Double Team	Normal	Status	—	—	15	Self	—	—
TM33	Reflect	Psychic	Status	—	—	20	Your Side	—	—
TM35	Flamethrower	Fire	Special	95	100	15	Normal	—	—
TM38	Fire Blast	Fire	Special	120	85	5	Normal	—	—
TM42	Facade	Normal	Physical	70	100	20	Normal	—	○
TM44	Rest	Psychic	Status	—	—	10	Self	—	—
TM45	Attract	Normal	Status	—	100	15	Normal	—	—
TM48	Round	Normal	Special	60	100	15	Normal	—	—
TM49	Echoed Voice	Normal	Special	40	100	15	Normal	—	—
TM52	Focus Blast	Fighting	Special	120	70	5	Normal	—	—
TM56	Fling	Dark	Physical	—	100	10	Normal	—	—
TM57	Charge Beam	Electric	Special	50	90	10	Normal	—	—
TM59	Incinerate	Fire	Special	30	100	15	Many Others	—	—
TM67	Retaliate	Normal	Physical	70	100	5	Normal	—	○
TM68	Giga Impact	Normal	Physical	150	90	5	Normal	—	○
TM70	Flash	Normal	Status	—	100	20	Normal	—	—
TM73	Thunder Wave	Electric	Status	—	100	20	Normal	—	—
TM74	Gyro Ball	Steel	Physical	—	100	5	Normal	—	○
TM77	Psych Up	Normal	Status	—	—	10	Normal	—	—
TM83	Work Up	Normal	Status	—	—	30	Self	—	—
TM85	Dream Eater	Psychic	Special	100	100	15	Normal	—	—
TM86	Grass Knot	Grass	Special	—	100	20	Normal	—	○
TM87	Swagger	Normal	Status	—	90	15	Normal	—	—
TM90	Substitute	Normal	Status	—	—	10	Self	—	—
TM93	Wild Charge	Electric	Physical	90	100	15	Normal	—	○
HM04	Strength	Normal	Physical	80	100	15	Normal	—	○

MOVES TAUGHT BY PEOPLE

Name	Type	Kind	Pow.	Acc.	PP	Range	Long	DA

MOVES TAUGHT BY MOVE TUTORS FOR SHARDS

Name	Type	Kind	Pow.	Acc.	PP	Range	Long	DA
Covet	Normal	Physical	60	100	40	Normal	—	○
Bounce	Flying	Physical	85	85	5	Normal	○	○
Fire Punch	Fire	Physical	75	100	15	Normal	—	○
ThunderPunch	Electric	Physical	75	100	15	Normal	—	○
Ice Punch	Ice	Physical	75	100	15	Normal	—	○
Last Resort	Normal	Physical	140	100	5	Normal	—	○
Magic Coat	Psychic	Status	—	—	15	Self	—	—
Hyper Voice	Normal	Special	90	100	10	Many Others	—	—
Icy Wind	Ice	Special	55	95	15	Many Others	—	—
Gravity	Psychic	Status	—	—	5	Both Sides	—	—
Snore	Normal	Special	40	100	15	Normal	—	—
Heal Bell	Normal	Status	—	—	5	Your Party	—	—
Knock Off	Dark	Physical	20	100	20	Normal	—	○
Role Play	Psychic	Status	—	—	10	Normal	—	—
Drain Punch	Fighting	Physical	75	100	10	Normal	—	○
Pain Split	Normal	Status	—	—	20	Normal	—	—
Helping Hand	Normal	Status	—	—	20	1 Ally	—	—
Magic Room	Psychic	Status	—	—	10	Both Sides	—	—
Recycle	Normal	Status	—	—	10	Self	—	—
Stealth Rock	Rock	Status	—	—	20	Other Side	—	—
Endeavor	Normal	Physical	—	100	5	Normal	—	○
Sleep Talk	Normal	Status	—	—	10	Self	—	—
Snatch	Dark	Status	—	—	10	Self	—	—

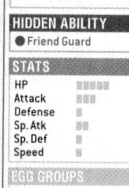

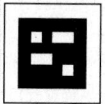

041 Zubat
Bat Pokémon

TYPE Poison | Flying

ABILITY
- Inner Focus

HIDDEN ABILITY
- Infiltrator

- HEIGHT: 2'07"
- WEIGHT: 16.5 lbs.
- GENDER: ♂/♀

It does not need eyes, because it emits ultrasonic waves to check its surroundings while it flies.

STATS
- HP
- Attack
- Defense
- Sp. Atk
- Sp. Def
- Speed

EGG GROUPS
Flying

ITEMS SOMETIMES HELD
- None

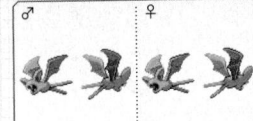

Pokémon AR Marker

EVOLUTION

Zubat → Golbat (Lv. 22) → Crobat (Level up with high friendship)

➡ p. 98

HOW TO OBTAIN
| Pokémon Black Version 2 | Castelia Sewers |
| Pokémon White Version 2 | Castelia Sewers |

HOW TO OBTAIN FROM OTHER GAMES
—

LEVEL-UP AND LEARNED MOVES

Lv.	Name	Type	Kind	Pow.	Acc.	PP	Range	Long	DA
1	Leech Life	Bug	Physical	20	100	15	Normal	—	○
4	Supersonic	Normal	Status	—	55	20	Normal	—	—
8	Astonish	Ghost	Physical	30	100	15	Normal	—	○
12	Bite	Dark	Physical	60	100	25	Normal	—	○
15	Wing Attack	Flying	Physical	60	100	35	Normal	○	○
19	Confuse Ray	Ghost	Status	—	100	10	Normal	—	—
23	Swift	Normal	Special	60	—	20	Many Others	—	—
26	Air Cutter	Flying	Special	55	95	25	Many Others	—	—
30	Acrobatics	Flying	Physical	55	100	15	Normal	○	○
34	Mean Look	Normal	Status	—	—	5	Normal	—	—
37	Poison Fang	Poison	Physical	50	100	15	Normal	—	○
41	Haze	Ice	Status	—	—	30	Both Sides	—	—
45	Air Slash	Flying	Special	75	95	20	Normal	○	—

TM & HM MOVES

Lv.	Name	Type	Kind	Pow.	Acc.	PP	Range	Long	DA
TM06	Toxic	Poison	Status	—	90	10	Normal	—	—
TM09	Venoshock	Poison	Special	65	100	10	Normal	—	—
TM10	Hidden Power	Normal	Special	—	100	15	Normal	—	—
TM11	Sunny Day	Fire	Status	—	—	5	Both Sides	—	—
TM12	Taunt	Dark	Status	—	100	20	Normal	—	—
TM17	Protect	Normal	Status	—	—	10	Self	—	—
TM18	Rain Dance	Water	Status	—	—	5	Both Sides	—	—
TM21	Frustration	Normal	Physical	—	100	20	Normal	—	○
TM27	Return	Normal	Physical	—	100	20	Normal	—	○
TM30	Shadow Ball	Ghost	Special	80	100	15	Normal	—	—
TM32	Double Team	Normal	Status	—	—	15	Self	—	—
TM36	Sludge Bomb	Poison	Special	90	100	10	Normal	—	—
TM40	Aerial Ace	Flying	Physical	60	—	20	Normal	○	○
TM41	Torment	Dark	Status	—	100	15	Normal	—	—
TM42	Facade	Normal	Physical	70	100	20	Normal	—	○
TM44	Rest	Psychic	Status	—	—	10	Self	—	—
TM45	Attract	Normal	Status	—	100	15	Normal	—	—
TM46	Thief	Dark	Physical	40	100	10	Normal	—	○
TM48	Round	Normal	Special	60	100	15	Normal	—	—
TM62	Acrobatics	Flying	Physical	55	100	15	Normal	○	○
TM66	Payback	Dark	Physical	50	100	10	Normal	—	○
TM87	Swagger	Normal	Status	—	90	15	Normal	—	—
TM88	Pluck	Flying	Physical	60	100	20	Normal	○	○
TM89	U-turn	Bug	Physical	70	100	20	Normal	—	○
TM90	Substitute	Normal	Status	—	—	10	Self	—	—
HM02	Fly	Flying	Physical	90	95	15	Normal	○	○

MOVES TAUGHT BY PEOPLE

Name	Type	Kind	Pow.	Acc.	PP	Range	Long	DA

MOVES TAUGHT BY MOVE TUTORS FOR SHARDS

Name	Type	Kind	Pow.	Acc.	PP	Range	Long	DA
Super Fang	Normal	Physical	—	90	10	Normal	—	○
Uproar	Normal	Special	90	100	10	1 Random	—	—
Zen Headbutt	Psychic	Physical	80	90	15	Normal	—	○
Snore	Normal	Special	40	100	15	Normal	—	—
Roost	Flying	Status	—	—	10	Self	—	—
Heat Wave	Fire	Special	100	90	10	Many Others	—	—
Giga Drain	Grass	Special	75	100	10	Normal	—	—
Tailwind	Flying	Status	—	—	30	Your Side	—	—
Sleep Talk	Normal	Status	—	—	10	Self	—	—
Snatch	Dark	Status	—	—	10	Self	—	—

EGG MOVES

Name	Type	Kind	Pow.	Acc.	PP	Range	Long	DA
Quick Attack	Normal	Physical	40	100	30	Normal	—	○
Pursuit	Dark	Physical	40	100	20	Normal	—	○
Faint Attack	Dark	Physical	60	—	20	Normal	—	—
Gust	Flying	Special	40	100	35	Normal	—	—
Whirlwind	Normal	Status	—	100	20	Normal	—	—
Curse	Ghost	Status	—	—	10	Varies	—	—
Nasty Plot	Dark	Status	—	—	20	Self	—	—
Hypnosis	Psychic	Status	—	60	20	Normal	—	—
Zen Headbutt	Psychic	Physical	80	90	15	Normal	—	○
Brave Bird	Flying	Physical	120	100	15	Normal	○	○
Giga Drain	Grass	Special	75	100	10	Normal	—	—
Steel Wing	Steel	Physical	70	90	25	Normal	—	○
Defog	Flying	Status	—	—	15	Normal	—	—

---

042 Golbat
Bat Pokémon

TYPE Poison | Flying

ABILITY
- Inner Focus

HIDDEN ABILITY
- Infiltrator

- HEIGHT: 5'03"
- WEIGHT: 121.3 lbs.
- GENDER: ♂/♀

Flitting around in the dead of night, it sinks its fangs into its prey and drains a nearly fatal amount of blood.

STATS
- HP
- Attack
- Defense
- Sp. Atk
- Sp. Def
- Speed

EGG GROUPS
Flying

ITEMS SOMETIMES HELD
- None

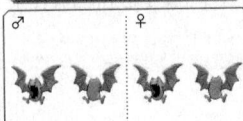

Pokémon AR Marker

EVOLUTION

Zubat → Golbat (Lv. 22) → Crobat (Level up with high friendship)

➡ p. 98

HOW TO OBTAIN
| Pokémon Black Version 2 | ❶ Celestial Tower 4F ❷ Strange House entrance |
| Pokémon White Version 2 | ❶ Celestial Tower 4F ❷ Strange House entrance |

HOW TO OBTAIN FROM OTHER GAMES
—

LEVEL-UP AND LEARNED MOVES

Lv.	Name	Type	Kind	Pow.	Acc.	PP	Range	Long	DA
1	Screech	Normal	Status	—	85	40	Normal	—	○
1	Leech Life	Bug	Physical	20	100	15	Normal	—	○
1	Supersonic	Normal	Status	—	55	20	Normal	—	—
1	Astonish	Ghost	Physical	30	100	15	Normal	—	○
4	Supersonic	Normal	Status	—	55	20	Normal	—	—
8	Astonish	Ghost	Physical	30	100	15	Normal	—	○
12	Bite	Dark	Physical	60	100	25	Normal	—	○
15	Wing Attack	Flying	Physical	60	100	35	Normal	○	○
19	Confuse Ray	Ghost	Status	—	100	10	Normal	—	—
24	Swift	Normal	Special	60	—	20	Many Others	—	—
28	Air Cutter	Flying	Special	55	95	25	Many Others	—	—
33	Acrobatics	Flying	Physical	55	100	15	Normal	○	○
38	Mean Look	Normal	Status	—	—	5	Normal	—	—
42	Poison Fang	Poison	Physical	50	100	15	Normal	—	○
47	Haze	Ice	Status	—	—	30	Both Sides	—	—
52	Air Slash	Flying	Special	75	95	20	Normal	○	—

TM & HM MOVES

Lv.	Name	Type	Kind	Pow.	Acc.	PP	Range	Long	DA
TM06	Toxic	Poison	Status	—	90	10	Normal	—	—
TM09	Venoshock	Poison	Special	65	100	10	Normal	—	—
TM10	Hidden Power	Normal	Special	—	100	15	Normal	—	—
TM11	Sunny Day	Fire	Status	—	—	5	Both Sides	—	—
TM12	Taunt	Dark	Status	—	100	20	Normal	—	—
TM15	Hyper Beam	Normal	Special	150	90	5	Normal	—	—
TM17	Protect	Normal	Status	—	—	10	Self	—	—
TM18	Rain Dance	Water	Status	—	—	5	Both Sides	—	—
TM21	Frustration	Normal	Physical	—	100	20	Normal	—	○
TM27	Return	Normal	Physical	—	100	20	Normal	—	○
TM30	Shadow Ball	Ghost	Special	80	100	15	Normal	—	—
TM32	Double Team	Normal	Status	—	—	15	Self	—	—
TM36	Sludge Bomb	Poison	Special	90	100	10	Normal	—	—
TM40	Aerial Ace	Flying	Physical	60	—	20	Normal	○	○
TM41	Torment	Dark	Status	—	100	15	Normal	—	—
TM42	Facade	Normal	Physical	70	100	20	Normal	—	○
TM44	Rest	Psychic	Status	—	—	10	Self	—	—
TM45	Attract	Normal	Status	—	100	15	Normal	—	—
TM46	Thief	Dark	Physical	40	100	10	Normal	—	○
TM48	Round	Normal	Special	60	100	15	Normal	—	—
TM62	Acrobatics	Flying	Physical	55	100	15	Normal	○	○
TM66	Payback	Dark	Physical	50	100	10	Normal	—	○
TM68	Giga Impact	Normal	Physical	150	90	5	Normal	—	○
TM87	Swagger	Normal	Status	—	90	15	Normal	—	—
TM88	Pluck	Flying	Physical	60	100	20	Normal	○	○
TM89	U-turn	Bug	Physical	70	100	20	Normal	—	○
TM90	Substitute	Normal	Status	—	—	10	Self	—	○
HM02	Fly	Flying	Physical	90	95	15	Normal	○	○

MOVES TAUGHT BY PEOPLE

Name	Type	Kind	Pow.	Acc.	PP	Range	Long	DA

MOVES TAUGHT BY MOVE TUTORS FOR SHARDS

Name	Type	Kind	Pow.	Acc.	PP	Range	Long	DA
Super Fang	Normal	Physical	—	90	10	Normal	—	○
Uproar	Normal	Special	90	100	10	1 Random	—	—
Zen Headbutt	Psychic	Physical	80	90	15	Normal	—	○
Snore	Normal	Special	40	100	15	Normal	—	—
Roost	Flying	Status	—	—	10	Self	—	—
Heat Wave	Fire	Special	100	90	10	Many Others	—	—
Giga Drain	Grass	Special	75	100	10	Normal	—	—
Tailwind	Flying	Status	—	—	30	Your Side	—	—
Sleep Talk	Normal	Status	—	—	10	Self	—	—
Snatch	Dark	Status	—	—	10	Self	—	—

043 Oddish

Weed Pokémon

TYPE Grass | Poison

ABILITY
- Chlorophyll

HIDDEN ABILITY
- Run Away

- **HEIGHT:** 1'08"
- **WEIGHT:** 11.9 lbs.
- **GENDER:** ♂ / ♀

It often plants its root feet in the ground during the day and sows seeds as it walks about at night.

Same form for ♂ / ♀

STATS
- HP
- Attack
- Defense
- Sp. Atk
- Sp. Def
- Speed

EGG GROUPS
Grass

ITEMS SOMETIMES HELD
- None

Pokémon AR Marker

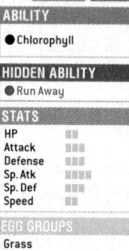

EVOLUTION

Oddish → (Lv. 21) → Gloom
→ (Use Leaf Stone) → Vileplume
→ (Use Sun Stone) → Bellossom
→ p. 104

HOW TO OBTAIN

Pokémon Black Version 2	Link Trade or Poké Transfer
Pokémon White Version 2	Link Trade or Poké Transfer

HOW TO OBTAIN FROM OTHER GAMES

Pokémon HeartGold Version	Ilex Forest (night only)
Pokémon SoulSilver Version	Ilex Forest (night only)

LEVEL-UP AND LEARNED MOVES

Lv.	Name	Type	Kind	Pow.	Acc.	PP	Range	Long	DA
1	Absorb	Grass	Special	20	100	25	Normal	—	—
5	Sweet Scent	Normal	Status	—	100	20	Many Others	—	—
9	Acid	Poison	Special	40	100	30	Many Others	—	—
13	PoisonPowder	Poison	Status	—	75	35	Normal	—	—
15	Stun Spore	Grass	Status	—	75	30	Normal	—	—
17	Sleep Powder	Grass	Status	—	75	15	Normal	—	—
21	Mega Drain	Grass	Special	40	100	15	Normal	—	—
25	Lucky Chant	Normal	Status	—	—	30	Your Side	—	—
29	Natural Gift	Normal	Physical	—	100	15	Normal	—	—
33	Moonlight	Normal	Status	—	—	5	Self	—	—
37	Giga Drain	Grass	Special	75	100	10	Normal	—	—
41	Petal Dance	Grass	Special	120	100	10	1 Random	—	○

TM & HM MOVES

Lv.	Name	Type	Kind	Pow.	Acc.	PP	Range	Long	DA
TM06	Toxic	Poison	Status	—	90	10	Normal	—	—
TM09	Venoshock	Poison	Special	65	100	10	Normal	—	—
TM10	Hidden Power	Normal	Special	—	100	15	Normal	—	—
TM11	Sunny Day	Fire	Status	—	—	5	Both Sides	—	—
TM17	Protect	Normal	Status	—	—	10	Self	—	—
TM21	Frustration	Normal	Physical	—	100	20	Normal	—	○
TM22	SolarBeam	Grass	Special	120	100	10	Normal	—	—
TM27	Return	Normal	Physical	—	100	20	Normal	—	○
TM32	Double Team	Normal	Status	—	—	15	Self	—	—
TM36	Sludge Bomb	Poison	Special	90	100	10	Normal	—	—
TM42	Facade	Normal	Physical	70	100	20	Normal	—	○
TM44	Rest	Psychic	Status	—	—	10	Self	—	—
TM45	Attract	Normal	Status	—	100	15	Normal	—	—
TM48	Round	Normal	Special	60	100	15	Normal	—	—
TM53	Energy Ball	Grass	Special	80	100	10	Normal	—	—
TM70	Flash	Normal	Status	—	100	20	Normal	—	—
TM75	Swords Dance	Normal	Status	—	—	30	Self	—	—
TM86	Grass Knot	Grass	Special	—	100	20	Normal	—	○
TM87	Swagger	Normal	Status	—	90	15	Normal	—	—
TM90	Substitute	Normal	Status	—	—	10	Self	—	—
HM01	Cut	Normal	Physical	50	95	30	Normal	—	○

MOVES TAUGHT BY PEOPLE

Name	Type	Kind	Pow.	Acc.	PP	Range	Long	DA

MOVES TAUGHT BY MOVE TUTORS FOR SHARDS

Name	Type	Kind	Pow.	Acc.	PP	Range	Long	DA
Seed Bomb	Grass	Physical	80	100	15	Normal	—	—
Snore	Normal	Special	40	100	15	Normal	—	—
Synthesis	Grass	Status	—	—	5	Self	—	—
Giga Drain	Grass	Special	75	100	10	Normal	—	—
Worry Seed	Grass	Status	—	100	10	Normal	—	—
Gastro Acid	Poison	Status	—	100	10	Normal	—	—
After You	Normal	Status	—	—	15	Normal	—	—
Sleep Talk	Normal	Status	—	—	10	Self	—	—

EGG MOVES

Name	Type	Kind	Pow.	Acc.	PP	Range	Long	DA
Razor Leaf	Grass	Physical	55	95	25	Many Others	—	—
Flail	Normal	Physical	—	100	15	Normal	—	○
Synthesis	Grass	Status	—	—	5	Self	—	—
Charm	Normal	Status	—	100	20	Normal	—	—
Ingrain	Grass	Status	—	—	20	Self	—	—
Tickle	Normal	Status	—	100	20	Normal	—	—
Teeter Dance	Normal	Status	—	100	20	Adjacent	—	—
Secret Power	Normal	Physical	70	100	20	Normal	—	—
Nature Power	Normal	Status	—	—	20	Varies	—	—
After You	Normal	Status	—	—	15	Normal	—	—

044 Gloom

Weed Pokémon

TYPE Grass | Poison

ABILITY
- Chlorophyll

HIDDEN ABILITY
- Stench

- **HEIGHT:** 2'07"
- **WEIGHT:** 19.0 lbs.
- **GENDER:** ♂ / ♀

The honey it drools from its mouth smells so atrocious, it can curl noses more than a mile away.

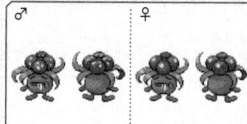
♂   ♀

STATS
- HP
- Attack
- Defense
- Sp. Atk
- Sp. Def
- Speed

EGG GROUPS
Grass ❶❷❸

ITEMS SOMETIMES HELD
- None

Pokémon AR Marker

EVOLUTION

Oddish → (Lv. 21) → Gloom
→ (Use Leaf Stone) → Vileplume
→ (Use Sun Stone) → Bellossom
→ p. 104

HOW TO OBTAIN

Pokémon Black Version 2	Link Trade or Poké Transfer
Pokémon White Version 2	Link Trade or Poké Transfer

HOW TO OBTAIN FROM OTHER GAMES

Pokémon HeartGold Version	Route 48
Pokémon SoulSilver Version	Route 48

LEVEL-UP AND LEARNED MOVES

Lv.	Name	Type	Kind	Pow.	Acc.	PP	Range	Long	DA
1	Absorb	Grass	Special	20	100	25	Normal	—	—
1	Sweet Scent	Normal	Status	—	100	20	Many Others	—	—
1	Acid	Poison	Special	40	100	30	Many Others	—	—
5	Sweet Scent	Normal	Status	—	100	20	Many Others	—	—
9	Acid	Poison	Special	40	100	30	Many Others	—	—
13	PoisonPowder	Poison	Status	—	75	35	Normal	—	—
15	Stun Spore	Grass	Status	—	75	30	Normal	—	—
17	Sleep Powder	Grass	Status	—	75	15	Normal	—	—
23	Mega Drain	Grass	Special	40	100	15	Normal	—	—
29	Lucky Chant	Normal	Status	—	—	30	Your Side	—	—
35	Natural Gift	Normal	Physical	—	100	15	Normal	—	—
41	Moonlight	Normal	Status	—	—	5	Self	—	—
47	Giga Drain	Grass	Special	75	100	10	Normal	—	—
53	Petal Dance	Grass	Special	120	100	10	1 Random	—	○

TM & HM MOVES

Lv.	Name	Type	Kind	Pow.	Acc.	PP	Range	Long	DA
TM06	Toxic	Poison	Status	—	90	10	Normal	—	—
TM09	Venoshock	Poison	Special	65	100	10	Normal	—	—
TM10	Hidden Power	Normal	Special	—	100	15	Normal	—	—
TM11	Sunny Day	Fire	Status	—	—	5	Both Sides	—	—
TM17	Protect	Normal	Status	—	—	10	Self	—	—
TM21	Frustration	Normal	Physical	—	100	20	Normal	—	○
TM22	SolarBeam	Grass	Special	120	100	10	Normal	—	—
TM27	Return	Normal	Physical	—	100	20	Normal	—	○
TM32	Double Team	Normal	Status	—	—	15	Self	—	—
TM36	Sludge Bomb	Poison	Special	90	100	10	Normal	—	—
TM42	Facade	Normal	Physical	70	100	20	Normal	—	○
TM44	Rest	Psychic	Status	—	—	10	Self	—	—
TM45	Attract	Normal	Status	—	100	15	Normal	—	—
TM48	Round	Normal	Special	60	100	15	Normal	—	—
TM53	Energy Ball	Grass	Special	80	100	10	Normal	—	—
TM56	Fling	Dark	Physical	—	100	10	Normal	—	—
TM70	Flash	Normal	Status	—	100	20	Normal	—	—
TM75	Swords Dance	Normal	Status	—	—	30	Self	—	—
TM86	Grass Knot	Grass	Special	—	100	20	Normal	—	○
TM87	Swagger	Normal	Status	—	90	15	Normal	—	—
TM90	Substitute	Normal	Status	—	—	10	Self	—	—
HM01	Cut	Normal	Physical	50	95	30	Normal	—	○

MOVES TAUGHT BY PEOPLE

Name	Type	Kind	Pow.	Acc.	PP	Range	Long	DA

MOVES TAUGHT BY MOVE TUTORS FOR SHARDS

Name	Type	Kind	Pow.	Acc.	PP	Range	Long	DA
Seed Bomb	Grass	Physical	80	100	15	Normal	—	—
Snore	Normal	Special	40	100	15	Normal	—	—
Synthesis	Grass	Status	—	—	5	Self	—	—
Giga Drain	Grass	Special	75	100	10	Normal	—	—
Drain Punch	Fighting	Physical	75	100	10	Normal	—	○
Worry Seed	Grass	Status	—	100	10	Normal	—	—
Gastro Acid	Poison	Status	—	100	10	Normal	—	—
After You	Normal	Status	—	—	15	Normal	—	—
Sleep Talk	Normal	Status	—	—	10	Self	—	—

045 Vileplume
Flower Pokémon

TYPE: Grass / Poison

ABILITY
- Chlorophyll

HIDDEN ABILITY
- Effect Spore

- **HEIGHT:** 3'11"
- **WEIGHT:** 41.0 lbs.
- **GENDER:** ♂ / ♀

Its petals are the largest in the world. As it walks, it scatters extremely allergenic pollen.

STATS
HP	▪▪▪
Attack	▪▪▪
Defense	▪▪▪
Sp. Atk	▪▪▪▪
Sp. Def	▪▪▪▪
Speed	▪▪▪

EGG GROUPS
Grass

ITEMS SOMETIMES HELD
- None

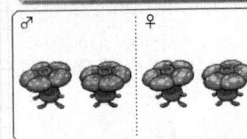

♂ / ♀

EVOLUTION
Oddish → Lv. 21 → Gloom → Use Leaf Stone → Vileplume
Gloom → Use Sun Stone → Bellossom → p. 104

HOW TO OBTAIN
Pokémon Black Version 2	Use Leaf Stone on a Gloom you obtain via Link Trade or Poké Transfer
Pokémon White Version 2	Use Leaf Stone on a Gloom you obtain via Link Trade or Poké Transfer

HOW TO OBTAIN FROM OTHER GAMES

LEVEL-UP AND LEARNED MOVES
Lv.	Name	Type	Kind	Pow.	Acc.	PP	Range	Long	DA
1	Mega Drain	Grass	Special	40	100	15	Normal	—	—
1	Aromatherapy	Grass	Status	—	—	5	Your Party	—	—
1	Stun Spore	Grass	Status	—	75	30	Normal	—	—
1	PoisonPowder	Poison	Status	—	75	35	Normal	—	—
53	Petal Dance	Grass	Special	120	100	10	1 Random	—	○
65	SolarBeam	Grass	Special	120	100	10	Normal	—	—

TM & HM MOVES
Lv.	Name	Type	Kind	Pow.	Acc.	PP	Range	Long	DA
TM06	Toxic	Poison	Status	—	90	10	Normal	—	—
TM09	Venoshock	Poison	Special	65	100	10	Normal	—	—
TM10	Hidden Power	Normal	Special	—	100	15	Normal	—	—
TM11	Sunny Day	Fire	Status	—	—	5	Both Sides	—	—
TM15	Hyper Beam	Normal	Special	150	90	5	Normal	—	—
TM17	Protect	Normal	Status	—	—	10	Self	—	—
TM21	Frustration	Normal	Physical	—	100	20	Normal	—	○
TM22	SolarBeam	Grass	Special	120	100	10	Normal	—	—
TM27	Return	Normal	Physical	—	100	20	Normal	—	○
TM32	Double Team	Normal	Status	—	—	15	Self	—	—
TM36	Sludge Bomb	Poison	Special	90	100	10	Normal	—	—
TM42	Facade	Normal	Physical	70	100	20	Normal	—	○
TM44	Rest	Psychic	Status	—	—	10	Self	—	—
TM45	Attract	Normal	Status	—	100	15	Normal	—	—
TM48	Round	Normal	Special	60	100	15	Normal	—	—
TM53	Energy Ball	Grass	Special	80	100	10	Normal	—	—
TM56	Fling	Dark	Physical	—	100	10	Normal	—	○
TM68	Giga Impact	Normal	Physical	150	90	5	Normal	—	○
TM70	Flash	Normal	Status	—	100	20	Normal	—	—
TM75	Swords Dance	Normal	Status	—	—	30	Self	—	—
TM86	Grass Knot	Grass	Special	—	100	20	Normal	—	—
TM87	Swagger	Normal	Status	—	90	15	Normal	—	—
TM90	Substitute	Normal	Status	—	—	10	Self	—	○
HM01	Cut	Normal	Physical	50	95	30	Normal	—	○

MOVES TAUGHT BY PEOPLE
Name	Type	Kind	Pow.	Acc.	PP	Range	Long	DA

MOVES TAUGHT BY MOVE TUTORS FOR SHARDS
Name	Type	Kind	Pow.	Acc.	PP	Range	Long	DA
Seed Bomb	Grass	Physical	80	100	15	Normal	—	—
Snore	Normal	Special	40	100	15	Normal	—	—
Synthesis	Grass	Status	—	—	5	Self	—	—
Giga Drain	Grass	Special	75	100	10	Normal	—	—
Drain Punch	Fighting	Physical	75	100	10	Normal	—	○
Worry Seed	Grass	Status	—	100	10	Normal	—	—
Gastro Acid	Poison	Status	—	100	10	Normal	—	—
After You	Normal	Status	—	—	15	Normal	—	—
Sleep Talk	Normal	Status	—	—	10	Self	—	—

Pokémon AR Marker

046 Paras
Mushroom Pokémon

TYPE: Bug / Grass

ABILITIES
- Effect Spore
- Dry Skin

HIDDEN ABILITY
- Effect Spore

- **HEIGHT:** 1'00"
- **WEIGHT:** 11.9 lbs.
- **GENDER:** ♂ / ♀

Mushrooms named tochukaso grow on its back. They grow along with the host Paras.

STATS
HP	▪▪
Attack	▪▪▪
Defense	▪▪▪
Sp. Atk	▪▪
Sp. Def	▪▪
Speed	▪▪

EGG GROUPS
Bug/Grass

ITEMS SOMETIMES HELD
- None

Same form for ♂ / ♀

EVOLUTION
 Paras → Lv. 24 → Parasect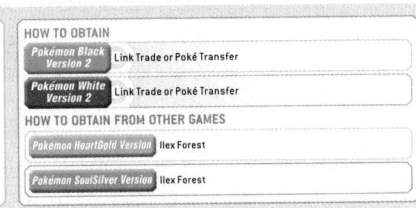

HOW TO OBTAIN
Pokémon Black Version 2	Link Trade or Poké Transfer
Pokémon White Version 2	Link Trade or Poké Transfer

HOW TO OBTAIN FROM OTHER GAMES
Pokémon HeartGold Version	Ilex Forest
Pokémon SoulSilver Version	Ilex Forest

LEVEL-UP AND LEARNED MOVES
Lv.	Name	Type	Kind	Pow.	Acc.	PP	Range	Long	DA
1	Scratch	Normal	Physical	40	100	35	Normal	—	○
6	Stun Spore	Grass	Status	—	75	30	Normal	—	—
6	PoisonPowder	Poison	Status	—	75	35	Normal	—	—
11	Leech Life	Bug	Physical	20	100	15	Normal	—	○
17	Fury Cutter	Bug	Physical	20	95	20	Normal	—	○
22	Spore	Grass	Status	—	100	15	Normal	—	—
27	Slash	Normal	Physical	70	100	20	Normal	—	○
33	Growth	Normal	Status	—	—	40	Self	—	—
38	Giga Drain	Grass	Special	75	100	10	Normal	—	—
43	Aromatherapy	Grass	Status	—	—	5	Your Party	—	—
49	Rage Powder	Bug	Status	—	—	20	Self	—	—
54	X-Scissor	Bug	Physical	80	100	15	Normal	—	○

TM & HM MOVES
Lv.	Name	Type	Kind	Pow.	Acc.	PP	Range	Long	DA
TM01	Hone Claws	Dark	Status	—	—	15	Self	—	—
TM06	Toxic	Poison	Status	—	90	10	Normal	—	—
TM09	Venoshock	Poison	Special	65	100	10	Normal	—	—
TM10	Hidden Power	Normal	Special	—	100	15	Normal	—	—
TM11	Sunny Day	Fire	Status	—	—	5	Both Sides	—	—
TM16	Light Screen	Psychic	Status	—	—	30	Your Side	—	—
TM17	Protect	Normal	Status	—	—	10	Self	—	—
TM21	Frustration	Normal	Physical	—	100	20	Normal	—	○
TM22	SolarBeam	Grass	Special	120	100	10	Normal	—	—
TM27	Return	Normal	Physical	—	100	20	Normal	—	○
TM28	Dig	Ground	Physical	80	100	10	Normal	—	○
TM31	Brick Break	Fighting	Physical	75	100	15	Normal	—	○
TM32	Double Team	Normal	Status	—	—	15	Self	—	—
TM36	Sludge Bomb	Poison	Special	90	100	10	Normal	—	—
TM40	Aerial Ace	Flying	Physical	60	—	20	Normal	○	○
TM42	Facade	Normal	Physical	70	100	20	Normal	—	○
TM44	Rest	Psychic	Status	—	—	10	Self	—	—
TM45	Attract	Normal	Status	—	100	15	Normal	—	—
TM46	Thief	Dark	Physical	40	100	10	Normal	—	○
TM48	Round	Normal	Special	60	100	15	Normal	—	—
TM53	Energy Ball	Grass	Special	80	100	10	Normal	—	—
TM54	False Swipe	Normal	Physical	40	100	40	Normal	—	○
TM70	Flash	Normal	Status	—	100	20	Normal	—	—
TM75	Swords Dance	Normal	Status	—	—	30	Self	—	—
TM76	Struggle Bug	Bug	Special	30	100	20	Many Others	—	—
TM81	X-Scissor	Bug	Physical	80	100	15	Normal	—	○
TM86	Grass Knot	Grass	Special	—	100	20	Normal	—	—
TM87	Swagger	Normal	Status	—	90	15	Normal	—	—
TM90	Substitute	Normal	Status	—	—	10	Self	—	○
TM94	Rock Smash	Fighting	Physical	40	100	15	Normal	—	○
HM01	Cut	Normal	Physical	50	95	30	Normal	—	○

MOVES TAUGHT BY PEOPLE
Name	Type	Kind	Pow.	Acc.	PP	Range	Long	DA

MOVES TAUGHT BY MOVE TUTORS FOR SHARDS
Name	Type	Kind	Pow.	Acc.	PP	Range	Long	DA
Bug Bite	Bug	Physical	60	100	20	Normal	—	○
Seed Bomb	Grass	Physical	80	100	15	Normal	—	—
Snore	Normal	Special	40	100	15	Normal	—	—
Knock Off	Dark	Physical	20	100	20	Normal	—	○
Synthesis	Grass	Status	—	—	5	Self	—	—
Giga Drain	Grass	Special	75	100	10	Normal	—	—
Worry Seed	Grass	Status	—	100	10	Normal	—	—
After You	Normal	Status	—	—	15	Normal	—	—
Sleep Talk	Normal	Status	—	—	10	Self	—	—

EGG MOVES
Name	Type	Kind	Pow.	Acc.	PP	Range	Long	DA
Screech	Normal	Status	—	85	40	Normal	—	—
Counter	Fighting	Physical	—	100	20	Varies	—	○
Psybeam	Psychic	Special	65	100	20	Normal	—	—
Flail	Normal	Physical	—	100	15	Normal	—	○
Sweet Scent	Normal	Status	—	100	20	Many Others	—	—
Pursuit	Dark	Physical	40	100	20	Normal	—	○
Metal Claw	Steel	Physical	50	95	35	Normal	—	○
Bug Bite	Bug	Physical	60	100	20	Normal	—	○
Cross Poison	Poison	Physical	70	100	20	Normal	—	○
Agility	Psychic	Status	—	—	30	Self	—	—
Endure	Normal	Status	—	—	10	Self	—	—
Natural Gift	Normal	Physical	—	100	15	Normal	—	—
Leech Seed	Grass	Status	—	90	10	Normal	—	—

Pokémon AR Marker

Mushroom Pokémon

047 Parasect

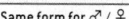

TYPE Bug Grass

ABILITIES
- Effect Spore
- Dry Skin

HIDDEN ABILITY

—

- HEIGHT: 3'03"
- WEIGHT: 65.0 lbs.
- GENDER: ♂ / ♀

A mushroom grown larger than the host's body controls Parasect. It scatters poisonous spores.

STATS

HP
Attack
Defense
Sp. Atk
Sp. Def
Speed

EGG GROUPS

Bug/Grass

ITEMS SOMETIMES HELD
- None

Same form for ♂ / ♀

EVOLUTION

HOW TO OBTAIN

Pokémon Black Version 2	Link Trade or Poké Transfer
Pokémon White Version 2	Link Trade or Poké Transfer

HOW TO OBTAIN FROM OTHER GAMES

Pokémon HeartGold Version	Cerulean Cave
Pokémon SoulSilver Version	Cerulean Cave

Pokémon AR Marker

LEVEL-UP AND LEARNED MOVES

Lv.	Name	Type	Kind	Pow.	Acc.	PP	Range	Long	DA
1	Cross Poison	Poison	Physical	70	100	20	Normal	—	○
1	Scratch	Normal	Physical	40	100	35	Normal	—	○
1	Stun Spore	Grass	Status	—	75	30	Normal	—	—
1	PoisonPowder	Poison	Status	—	75	35	Normal	—	—
1	Leech Life	Bug	Physical	20	100	15	Normal	—	○
6	Stun Spore	Grass	Status	—	75	30	Normal	—	—
6	PoisonPowder	Poison	Status	—	75	35	Normal	—	—
11	Leech Life	Bug	Physical	20	100	15	Normal	—	○
17	Fury Cutter	Bug	Physical	20	95	20	Normal	—	○
22	Spore	Grass	Status	—	100	15	Normal	—	—
29	Slash	Normal	Physical	70	100	20	Normal	—	○
37	Growth	Normal	Status	—	—	40	Self	—	—
44	Giga Drain	Grass	Special	75	100	10	Normal	—	—
51	Aromatherapy	Grass	Status	—	—	5	Your Party	—	—
59	Rage Powder	Bug	Status	—	—	20	Self	—	—
66	X-Scissor	Bug	Physical	80	100	15	Normal	—	○

TM & HM MOVES

Lv.	Name	Type	Kind	Pow.	Acc.	PP	Range	Long	DA
TM01	Hone Claws	Dark	Status	—	—	15	Self	—	—
TM06	Toxic	Poison	Status	—	90	10	Normal	—	—
TM09	Venoshock	Poison	Special	65	100	10	Normal	—	—
TM10	Hidden Power	Normal	Special	—	100	15	Normal	—	—
TM11	Sunny Day	Fire	Status	—	—	5	Both Sides	—	—
TM15	Hyper Beam	Normal	Special	150	90	5	Normal	—	—
TM16	Light Screen	Psychic	Status	—	—	30	Your Side	—	—
TM17	Protect	Normal	Status	—	—	10	Self	—	—
TM21	Frustration	Normal	Physical	—	100	20	Normal	—	○
TM22	SolarBeam	Grass	Special	120	100	10	Normal	—	—
TM27	Return	Normal	Physical	—	100	20	Normal	—	○
TM28	Dig	Ground	Physical	80	100	10	Normal	—	○
TM31	Brick Break	Fighting	Physical	75	100	15	Normal	—	○
TM32	Double Team	Normal	Status	—	—	15	Self	—	—
TM36	Sludge Bomb	Poison	Special	90	100	10	Normal	—	—
TM40	Aerial Ace	Flying	Physical	60	—	20	Normal	○	○
TM42	Facade	Normal	Physical	70	100	20	Normal	—	○
TM44	Rest	Psychic	Status	—	—	10	Self	—	—
TM45	Attract	Normal	Status	—	100	15	Normal	—	—
TM46	Thief	Dark	Physical	40	100	10	Normal	—	○
TM48	Round	Normal	Special	60	100	15	Normal	—	—
TM53	Energy Ball	Grass	Special	80	100	10	Normal	—	—
TM54	False Swipe	Normal	Physical	40	100	40	Normal	—	○
TM68	Giga Impact	Normal	Physical	150	90	5	Normal	—	○
TM70	Flash	Normal	Status	—	100	20	Normal	—	—
TM75	Swords Dance	Normal	Status	—	—	30	Self	—	—
TM76	Struggle Bug	Bug	Special	30	100	20	Many Others	—	—
TM81	X-Scissor	Bug	Physical	80	100	15	Normal	—	○
TM86	Grass Knot	Grass	Special	—	100	20	Normal	—	○
TM87	Swagger	Normal	Status	—	90	15	Normal	—	—
TM90	Substitute	Normal	Status	—	—	10	Self	—	—
TM94	Rock Smash	Fighting	Physical	40	100	15	Normal	—	○
HM01	Cut	Normal	Physical	50	95	30	Normal	—	○

MOVES TAUGHT BY PEOPLE

Name	Type	Kind	Pow.	Acc.	PP	Range	Long	DA

MOVES TAUGHT BY MOVE TUTORS FOR SHARDS

Name	Type	Kind	Pow.	Acc.	PP	Range	Long	DA
Bug Bite	Bug	Physical	60	100	20	Normal	—	○
Seed Bomb	Grass	Physical	80	100	15	Normal	—	—
Snore	Normal	Special	40	100	15	Normal	—	—
Knock Off	Dark	Physical	20	100	20	Normal	—	○
Synthesis	Grass	Status	—	—	5	Self	—	—
Giga Drain	Grass	Special	75	100	10	Normal	—	—
Worry Seed	Grass	Status	—	100	10	Normal	—	—
After You	Normal	Status	—	—	15	Normal	—	—
Sleep Talk	Normal	Status	—	—	10	Self	—	—

Insect Pokémon

048 Venonat

TYPE Bug Poison

ABILITIES
- Compoundeyes
- Tinted Lens

HIDDEN ABILITY
- Run Away

- HEIGHT: 3'03"
- WEIGHT: 66.1 lbs.
- GENDER: ♂ / ♀

Its big eyes are actually clusters of tiny eyes. At night, its kind is drawn by light.

STATS

HP
Attack
Defense
Sp. Atk
Sp. Def
Speed

EGG GROUPS

Bug

ITEMS SOMETIMES HELD
- None

Same form for ♂ / ♀

EVOLUTION

HOW TO OBTAIN

Pokémon Black Version 2	Route 3 (Hidden Grotto)
Pokémon White Version 2	Route 3 (Hidden Grotto)

HOW TO OBTAIN FROM OTHER GAMES

—

—

Pokémon AR Marker

LEVEL-UP AND LEARNED MOVES

Lv.	Name	Type	Kind	Pow.	Acc.	PP	Range	Long	DA
1	Tackle	Normal	Physical	50	100	35	Normal	—	○
1	Disable	Normal	Status	—	100	20	Normal	—	—
1	Foresight	Normal	Status	—	—	40	Normal	—	—
5	Supersonic	Normal	Status	—	55	20	Normal	—	—
11	Confusion	Psychic	Special	50	100	25	Normal	—	—
13	PoisonPowder	Poison	Status	—	75	35	Normal	—	—
17	Leech Life	Bug	Physical	20	100	15	Normal	—	○
23	Stun Spore	Grass	Status	—	75	30	Normal	—	—
25	Psybeam	Psychic	Special	65	100	20	Normal	—	—
29	Sleep Powder	Grass	Status	—	75	15	Normal	—	—
35	Signal Beam	Bug	Special	75	100	15	Normal	—	—
37	Zen Headbutt	Psychic	Physical	80	90	15	Normal	—	○
41	Poison Fang	Poison	Physical	50	100	15	Normal	—	○
47	Psychic	Psychic	Special	90	100	10	Normal	—	—

TM & HM MOVES

Lv.	Name	Type	Kind	Pow.	Acc.	PP	Range	Long	DA
TM06	Toxic	Poison	Status	—	90	10	Normal	—	—
TM09	Venoshock	Poison	Special	65	100	10	Normal	—	—
TM10	Hidden Power	Normal	Special	—	100	15	Normal	—	—
TM11	Sunny Day	Fire	Status	—	—	5	Both Sides	—	—
TM17	Protect	Normal	Status	—	—	10	Self	—	—
TM21	Frustration	Normal	Physical	—	100	20	Normal	—	○
TM22	SolarBeam	Grass	Special	120	100	10	Normal	—	—
TM27	Return	Normal	Physical	—	100	20	Normal	—	○
TM29	Psychic	Psychic	Special	90	100	10	Normal	—	—
TM32	Double Team	Normal	Status	—	—	15	Self	—	—
TM36	Sludge Bomb	Poison	Special	90	100	10	Normal	—	—
TM42	Facade	Normal	Physical	70	100	20	Normal	—	○
TM44	Rest	Psychic	Status	—	—	10	Self	—	—
TM45	Attract	Normal	Status	—	100	15	Normal	—	—
TM46	Thief	Dark	Physical	40	100	10	Normal	—	○
TM48	Round	Normal	Special	60	100	15	Normal	—	—
TM70	Flash	Normal	Status	—	100	20	Normal	—	—
TM76	Struggle Bug	Bug	Special	30	100	20	Many Others	—	—
TM87	Swagger	Normal	Status	—	90	15	Normal	—	—
TM90	Substitute	Normal	Status	—	—	10	Self	—	—

MOVES TAUGHT BY PEOPLE

Name	Type	Kind	Pow.	Acc.	PP	Range	Long	DA

MOVES TAUGHT BY MOVE TUTORS FOR SHARDS

Name	Type	Kind	Pow.	Acc.	PP	Range	Long	DA
Bug Bite	Bug	Physical	60	100	20	Normal	—	○
Signal Beam	Bug	Special	75	100	15	Normal	—	—
Zen Headbutt	Psychic	Physical	80	90	15	Normal	—	○
Snore	Normal	Special	40	100	15	Normal	—	—
Giga Drain	Grass	Special	75	100	10	Normal	—	—
Sleep Talk	Normal	Status	—	—	10	Self	—	—
Skill Swap	Psychic	Status	—	—	10	Normal	—	—

EGG MOVES

Name	Type	Kind	Pow.	Acc.	PP	Range	Long	DA
Baton Pass	Normal	Status	—	—	40	Self	—	—
Screech	Normal	Status	—	85	40	Normal	—	—
Giga Drain	Grass	Special	75	100	10	Normal	—	—
Signal Beam	Bug	Special	75	100	15	Normal	—	—
Agility	Psychic	Status	—	—	30	Self	—	—
Morning Sun	Normal	Status	—	—	5	Self	—	—
Toxic Spikes	Poison	Status	—	—	20	Other Side	—	—
Bug Bite	Bug	Physical	60	100	20	Normal	—	○
Secret Power	Normal	Physical	70	100	20	Normal	—	—
Skill Swap	Psychic	Status	—	—	10	Normal	—	—
Rage Powder	Bug	Status	—	—	20	Self	—	—

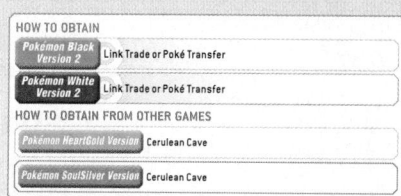

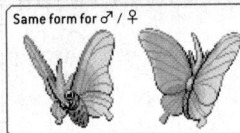

Poison Moth Pokémon
049 Venomoth

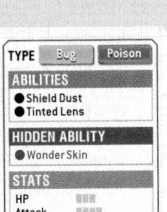

- **TYPE** Bug | Poison
- **HEIGHT:** 4'11"
- **WEIGHT:** 27.6 lbs.
- **GENDER:** ♂ / ♀

ABILITIES
- Shield Dust
- Tinted Lens

HIDDEN ABILITY
- Wonder Skin

It flutters its wings to scatter dustlike scales. The scales leach toxins if they contact skin.

STATS
- HP
- Attack
- Defense
- Sp. Atk
- Sp. Def
- Speed

Same form for ♂ / ♀

EGG GROUPS
- Bug

ITEMS SOMETIMES HELD
- None

EVOLUTION

Venonat → Lv. 31 → Venomoth

HOW TO OBTAIN

Pokémon Black Version 2	Level up Venonat to Lv. 31
Pokémon White Version 2	Level up Venonat to Lv. 31

HOW TO OBTAIN FROM OTHER GAMES

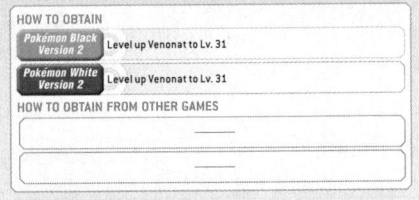

LEVEL-UP AND LEARNED MOVES

Lv.	Name	Type	Kind	Pow.	Acc.	PP	Range	Long	DA
1	Silver Wind	Bug	Special	60	100	5	Normal	—	
1	Tackle	Normal	Physical	50	100	35	Normal	—	○
1	Disable	Normal	Status	—	100	20	Normal	—	
1	Foresight	Normal	Status	—	—	40	Normal	—	
1	Supersonic	Normal	Status	—	55	20	Normal	—	
5	Supersonic	Normal	Status	—	55	20	Normal	—	
11	Confusion	Psychic	Special	50	100	25	Normal	—	
13	PoisonPowder	Poison	Status	—	75	35	Normal	—	
17	Leech Life	Bug	Physical	20	100	15	Normal	—	○
23	Stun Spore	Grass	Status	—	75	30	Normal	—	
25	Psybeam	Psychic	Special	65	100	20	Normal	—	
29	Sleep Powder	Grass	Status	—	75	15	Normal	—	
31	Gust	Flying	Special	40	100	35	Normal	○	
37	Signal Beam	Bug	Special	75	100	15	Normal	—	
41	Zen Headbutt	Psychic	Physical	80	90	15	Normal	—	○
47	Poison Fang	Poison	Physical	50	100	15	Normal	—	○
55	Psychic	Psychic	Special	90	100	10	Normal	—	
59	Bug Buzz	Bug	Special	90	100	10	Normal	—	
63	Quiver Dance	Bug	Status	—	—	20	Self	—	

TM & HM MOVES

Lv.	Name	Type	Kind	Pow.	Acc.	PP	Range	Long	DA
TM06	Toxic	Poison	Status	—	90	10	Normal	—	
TM09	Venoshock	Poison	Special	65	100	10	Normal	—	
TM10	Hidden Power	Normal	Special	—	100	15	Normal	—	
TM11	Sunny Day	Fire	Status	—	—	5	Both Sides	—	
TM15	Hyper Beam	Normal	Special	150	90	5	Normal	—	
TM17	Protect	Normal	Status	—	—	10	Self	—	
TM21	Frustration	Normal	Physical	—	100	20	Normal	—	○
TM22	SolarBeam	Grass	Special	120	100	10	Normal	—	
TM27	Return	Normal	Physical	—	100	20	Normal	—	○
TM29	Psychic	Psychic	Special	90	100	10	Normal	—	
TM32	Double Team	Normal	Status	—	—	15	Self	—	
TM36	Sludge Bomb	Poison	Special	90	100	10	Normal	—	
TM40	Aerial Ace	Flying	Physical	60	—	20	Normal	○	○
TM42	Facade	Normal	Physical	70	100	20	Normal	—	○
TM44	Rest	Psychic	Status	—	—	10	Self	—	
TM45	Attract	Normal	Status	—	100	15	Normal	—	
TM46	Thief	Dark	Physical	40	100	10	Normal	—	○
TM48	Round	Normal	Special	60	100	15	Normal	—	
TM53	Energy Ball	Grass	Special	80	100	10	Normal	—	
TM62	Acrobatics	Flying	Physical	55	100	15	Normal	○	○
TM68	Giga Impact	Normal	Physical	150	90	5	Normal	—	○
TM70	Flash	Normal	Status	—	100	20	Normal	—	
TM76	Struggle Bug	Bug	Special	30	100	20	Many Others	—	
TM87	Swagger	Normal	Status	—	90	15	Normal	—	
TM89	U-turn	Bug	Physical	70	100	20	Normal	—	○
TM90	Substitute	Normal	Status	—	—	10	Self	—	

MOVES TAUGHT BY PEOPLE

Name	Type	Kind	Pow.	Acc.	PP	Range	Long	DA

MOVES TAUGHT BY MOVE TUTORS FOR SHARDS

Name	Type	Kind	Pow.	Acc.	PP	Range	Long	DA
Bug Bite	Bug	Physical	60	100	20	Normal	—	○
Signal Beam	Bug	Special	75	100	15	Normal	—	
Zen Headbutt	Psychic	Physical	80	90	15	Normal	—	○
Snore	Normal	Special	40	100	15	Normal	—	
Roost	Flying	Status	—	—	10	Self	—	
Giga Drain	Grass	Special	75	100	10	Normal	—	
Tailwind	Flying	Status	—	—	30	Your Side	—	
Sleep Talk	Normal	Status	—	—	10	Self	—	
Skill Swap	Psychic	Status	—	—	10	Normal	—	

Pokémon AR Marker

Mole Pokémon
050 Diglett

- **TYPE** Ground
- **HEIGHT:** 0'08"
- **WEIGHT:** 1.8 lbs.
- **GENDER:** ♂ / ♀

ABILITIES
- Sand Veil
- Arena Trap

HIDDEN ABILITY
- Sand Force

A Pokémon that lives underground. Because of its dark habitat, it is repelled by bright sunlight.

STATS
- HP
- Attack
- Defense
- Sp. Atk
- Sp. Def
- Speed

Same form for ♂ / ♀

EGG GROUPS
- Field

ITEMS SOMETIMES HELD
- None

EVOLUTION

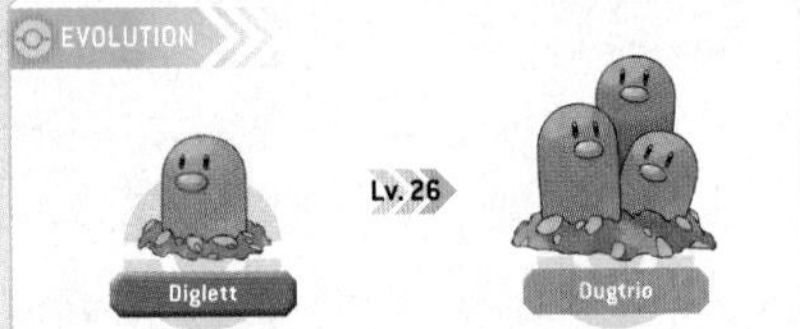

Diglett → Lv. 26 → Dugtrio

HOW TO OBTAIN

Pokémon Black Version 2	Link Trade or Poké Transfer
Pokémon White Version 2	Link Trade or Poké Transfer

HOW TO OBTAIN FROM OTHER GAMES

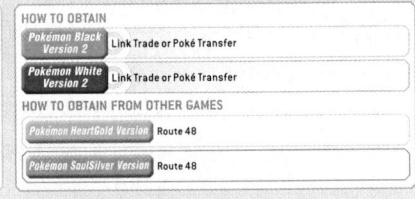

Pokémon HeartGold Version	Route 48
Pokémon SoulSilver Version	Route 48

LEVEL-UP AND LEARNED MOVES

Lv.	Name	Type	Kind	Pow.	Acc.	PP	Range	Long	DA
1	Scratch	Normal	Physical	40	100	35	Normal	—	○
1	Sand-Attack	Ground	Status	—	100	15	Normal	—	
4	Growl	Normal	Status	—	100	40	Many Others	—	
7	Astonish	Ghost	Physical	30	100	15	Normal	—	○
12	Mud-Slap	Ground	Special	20	100	10	Normal	—	
15	Magnitude	Ground	Physical	—	100	30	Adjacent	—	
18	Bulldoze	Ground	Physical	60	100	20	Adjacent	—	
23	Sucker Punch	Dark	Physical	80	100	5	Normal	—	○
26	Mud Bomb	Ground	Special	65	85	10	Normal	—	
29	Earth Power	Ground	Special	90	100	10	Normal	—	
34	Dig	Ground	Physical	80	100	10	Normal	—	○
37	Slash	Normal	Physical	70	100	20	Normal	—	○
40	Earthquake	Ground	Physical	100	100	10	Adjacent	—	
45	Fissure	Ground	Physical	—	30	5	Normal	—	

TM & HM MOVES

Lv.	Name	Type	Kind	Pow.	Acc.	PP	Range	Long	DA
TM01	Hone Claws	Dark	Status	—	—	15	Self	—	
TM06	Toxic	Poison	Status	—	90	10	Normal	—	
TM10	Hidden Power	Normal	Special	—	100	15	Normal	—	
TM11	Sunny Day	Fire	Status	—	—	5	Both Sides	—	
TM17	Protect	Normal	Status	—	—	10	Self	—	
TM21	Frustration	Normal	Physical	—	100	20	Normal	—	○
TM26	Earthquake	Ground	Physical	100	100	10	Adjacent	—	
TM27	Return	Normal	Physical	—	100	20	Normal	—	○
TM28	Dig	Ground	Physical	80	100	10	Normal	—	○
TM32	Double Team	Normal	Status	—	—	15	Self	—	
TM36	Sludge Bomb	Poison	Special	90	100	10	Normal	—	
TM37	Sandstorm	Rock	Status	—	—	10	Both Sides	—	
TM39	Rock Tomb	Rock	Physical	50	80	10	Normal	—	
TM40	Aerial Ace	Flying	Physical	60	—	20	Normal	○	○
TM42	Facade	Normal	Physical	70	100	20	Normal	—	○
TM44	Rest	Psychic	Status	—	—	10	Self	—	
TM45	Attract	Normal	Status	—	100	15	Normal	—	
TM46	Thief	Dark	Physical	40	100	10	Normal	—	○
TM48	Round	Normal	Special	60	100	15	Normal	—	
TM49	Echoed Voice	Normal	Special	40	100	15	Normal	—	
TM65	Shadow Claw	Ghost	Physical	70	100	15	Normal	—	○
TM78	Bulldoze	Ground	Physical	60	100	20	Adjacent	—	
TM80	Rock Slide	Rock	Physical	75	90	10	Many Others	—	
TM87	Swagger	Normal	Status	—	90	15	Normal	—	
TM90	Substitute	Normal	Status	—	—	10	Self	—	
TM94	Rock Smash	Fighting	Physical	40	100	15	Normal	—	○
HM01	Cut	Normal	Physical	50	95	30	Normal	—	○

MOVES TAUGHT BY PEOPLE

Name	Type	Kind	Pow.	Acc.	PP	Range	Long	DA

MOVES TAUGHT BY MOVE TUTORS FOR SHARDS

Name	Type	Kind	Pow.	Acc.	PP	Range	Long	DA
Uproar	Normal	Special	90	100	10	1 Random	—	
Earth Power	Ground	Special	90	100	10	Normal	—	
Snore	Normal	Special	40	100	15	Normal	—	
Stealth Rock	Rock	Status	—	—	20	Other Side	—	
Sleep Talk	Normal	Status	—	—	10	Self	—	

EGG MOVES

Name	Type	Kind	Pow.	Acc.	PP	Range	Long	DA
Faint Attack	Dark	Physical	60	—	20	Normal	—	○
Screech	Normal	Status	—	85	40	Normal	—	
AncientPower	Rock	Special	60	100	5	Normal	—	
Pursuit	Dark	Physical	40	100	20	Normal	—	○
Beat Up	Dark	Physical	—	100	10	Normal	—	○
Uproar	Normal	Special	90	100	10	1 Random	—	
Mud Bomb	Ground	Special	65	85	10	Normal	—	
Astonish	Ghost	Physical	30	100	15	Normal	—	○
Reversal	Fighting	Physical	—	100	15	Normal	—	○
Headbutt	Normal	Physical	70	100	15	Normal	—	○
Endure	Normal	Status	—	—	10	Self	—	
Final Gambit	Fighting	Special	—	100	5	Normal	—	
Memento	Dark	Status	—	100	10	Normal	—	

Pokémon AR Marker

Mole Pokémon

051 Dugtrio

TYPE

ABILITIES
- Sand Veil
- Arena Trap

HIDDEN ABILITY
- Sand Force

STATS
HP
Attack
Defense
Sp. Atk
Sp. Def
Speed

EGG GROUPS
Field

- HEIGHT: 2'04"
- WEIGHT: 73.4 lbs.
- GENDER: ♂ / ♀

Its three heads move alternately, driving it through tough soil to depths of over 60 miles.

Same form for ♂ / ♀

ITEMS SOMETIMES HELD
- None

EVOLUTION

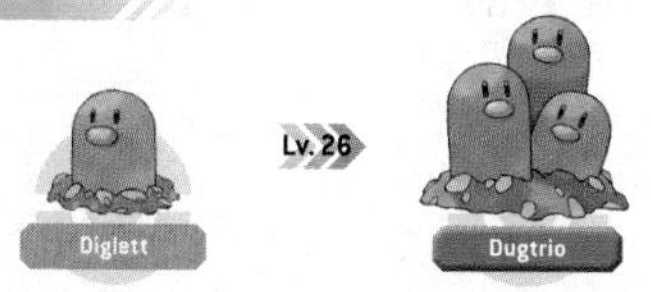
Diglett
Lv. 26
Dugtrio

HOW TO OBTAIN

Pokémon Black Version 2	Link Trade or Poké Transfer
Pokémon White Version 2	Link Trade or Poké Transfer

HOW TO OBTAIN FROM OTHER GAMES

Pokémon HeartGold Version	DIGLETT's Cave
Pokémon SoulSilver Version	DIGLETT's Cave

Pokémon AR Marker

LEVEL-UP AND LEARNED MOVES

Lv.	Name	Type	Kind	Pow.	Acc.	PP	Range	Long	DA
1	Night Slash	Dark	Physical	70	100	15	Normal	—	○
1	Tri Attack	Normal	Special	80	100	10	Normal	—	—
1	Scratch	Normal	Physical	40	100	35	Normal	—	○
1	Sand-Attack	Ground	Status	—	100	15	Normal	—	—
1	Growl	Normal	Status	—	100	40	Many Others	—	—
4	Growl	Normal	Status	—	100	40	Many Others	—	—
7	Astonish	Ghost	Physical	30	100	15	Normal	—	○
12	Mud-Slap	Ground	Special	20	100	10	Normal	—	—
15	Magnitude	Ground	Physical	—	100	30	Adjacent	—	—
18	Bulldoze	Ground	Physical	60	100	20	Adjacent	—	—
23	Sucker Punch	Dark	Physical	80	100	5	Normal	—	○
26	Sand Tomb	Ground	Physical	35	85	15	Normal	—	—
28	Mud Bomb	Ground	Special	65	85	10	Normal	—	—
33	Earth Power	Ground	Special	90	100	10	Normal	—	—
40	Dig	Ground	Physical	80	100	10	Normal	—	○
45	Slash	Normal	Physical	70	100	20	Normal	—	○
50	Earthquake	Ground	Physical	100	100	10	Adjacent	—	—
57	Fissure	Ground	Physical	—	30	5	Normal	—	—

TM & HM MOVES

Lv.	Name	Type	Kind	Pow.	Acc.	PP	Range	Long	DA
TM01	Hone Claws	Dark	Status	—	—	15	Self	—	—
TM06	Toxic	Poison	Status	—	90	10	Normal	—	—
TM10	Hidden Power	Normal	Special	—	100	15	Normal	—	—
TM11	Sunny Day	Fire	Status	—	—	5	Both Sides	—	—
TM15	Hyper Beam	Normal	Special	150	90	5	Normal	—	—
TM17	Protect	Normal	Status	—	—	10	Self	—	—
TM21	Frustration	Normal	Physical	—	100	20	Normal	—	○
TM26	Earthquake	Ground	Physical	100	100	10	Adjacent	—	—
TM27	Return	Normal	Physical	—	100	20	Normal	—	○
TM28	Dig	Ground	Physical	80	100	10	Normal	—	○
TM32	Double Team	Normal	Status	—	—	15	Self	—	—
TM34	Sludge Wave	Poison	Special	95	100	10	Adjacent	—	—
TM36	Sludge Bomb	Poison	Special	90	100	10	Normal	—	—
TM37	Sandstorm	Rock	Status	—	—	10	Both Sides	—	—
TM39	Rock Tomb	Rock	Physical	50	80	10	Normal	—	—
TM40	Aerial Ace	Flying	Physical	60	—	20	Normal	○	○
TM42	Facade	Normal	Physical	70	100	20	Normal	—	○
TM44	Rest	Psychic	Status	—	—	10	Self	—	—
TM45	Attract	Normal	Status	—	100	15	Normal	—	—
TM46	Thief	Dark	Physical	40	100	10	Normal	—	○
TM48	Round	Normal	Special	60	100	15	Normal	—	—
TM49	Echoed Voice	Normal	Special	40	100	15	Normal	—	—
TM65	Shadow Claw	Ghost	Physical	70	100	15	Normal	—	○
TM68	Giga Impact	Normal	Physical	150	90	5	Normal	—	○
TM71	Stone Edge	Rock	Physical	100	80	5	Normal	—	—
TM78	Bulldoze	Ground	Physical	60	100	20	Adjacent	—	—
TM80	Rock Slide	Rock	Physical	75	90	10	Many Others	—	—
TM87	Swagger	Normal	Status	—	90	15	Normal	—	—
TM90	Substitute	Normal	Status	—	—	10	Self	—	—
TM94	Rock Smash	Fighting	Physical	40	100	15	Normal	—	○
HM01	Cut	Normal	Physical	50	95	30	Normal	—	○

MOVES TAUGHT BY PEOPLE

Name	Type	Kind	Pow.	Acc.	PP	Range	Long	DA

MOVES TAUGHT BY MOVE TUTORS FOR SHARDS

Name	Type	Kind	Pow.	Acc.	PP	Range	Long	DA
Uproar	Normal	Special	90	100	10	1 Random	—	—
Earth Power	Ground	Special	90	100	10	Normal	—	—
Snore	Normal	Special	40	100	15	Normal	—	—
Stealth Rock	Rock	Status	—	—	20	Other Side	—	—
Sleep Talk	Normal	Status	—	—	10	Self	—	—

Scratch Cat Pokémon

052 Meowth

TYPE

ABILITIES
- Pickup
- Technician

HIDDEN ABILITY
- Unnerve

STATS
HP
Attack
Defense
Sp. Atk
Sp. Def
Speed

EGG GROUPS
Field

- HEIGHT: 1'04"
- WEIGHT: 9.3 lbs.
- GENDER: ♂ / ♀

It is nocturnal in nature. If it spots something shiny, its eyes glitter brightly.

Same form for ♂ / ♀

ITEMS SOMETIMES HELD
- None

EVOLUTION

Meowth
Lv. 28
Persian

HOW TO OBTAIN

Pokémon Black Version 2	If your character is a boy, trade Pokémon during a date with Yancy (first time)
Pokémon White Version 2	If your character is a boy, trade Pokémon during a date with Yancy (first time)

HOW TO OBTAIN FROM OTHER GAMES

Pokémon SoulSilver Version	Route 38
Pokémon Platinum Version	Pokémon Mansion on Route 212 (after obtaining the National Pokédex, talk to Mr. Backlot)

Pokémon AR Marker

LEVEL-UP AND LEARNED MOVES

Lv.	Name	Type	Kind	Pow.	Acc.	PP	Range	Long	DA
1	Scratch	Normal	Physical	40	100	35	Normal	—	○
1	Growl	Normal	Status	—	100	40	Many Others	—	—
6	Bite	Dark	Physical	60	100	25	Normal	—	○
9	Fake Out	Normal	Physical	40	100	10	Normal	—	○
14	Fury Swipes	Normal	Physical	18	80	15	Normal	—	○
17	Screech	Normal	Status	—	85	40	Normal	—	—
22	Faint Attack	Dark	Physical	60	—	20	Normal	—	○
25	Taunt	Dark	Status	—	100	20	Normal	—	—
30	Pay Day	Normal	Physical	40	100	20	Normal	—	—
33	Slash	Normal	Physical	70	100	20	Normal	—	○
38	Nasty Plot	Dark	Status	—	—	20	Self	—	—
41	Assurance	Dark	Physical	50	100	10	Normal	—	○
46	Captivate	Normal	Status	—	100	20	Many Others	—	—
49	Night Slash	Dark	Physical	70	100	15	Normal	—	○
54	Feint	Normal	Physical	30	100	10	Normal	—	—

TM & HM MOVES

Lv.	Name	Type	Kind	Pow.	Acc.	PP	Range	Long	DA
TM01	Hone Claws	Dark	Status	—	—	15	Self	—	—
TM06	Toxic	Poison	Status	—	90	10	Normal	—	—
TM10	Hidden Power	Normal	Special	—	100	15	Normal	—	—
TM11	Sunny Day	Fire	Status	—	—	5	Both Sides	—	—
TM12	Taunt	Dark	Status	—	100	20	Normal	—	—
TM17	Protect	Normal	Status	—	—	10	Self	—	—
TM18	Rain Dance	Water	Status	—	—	5	Both Sides	—	—
TM21	Frustration	Normal	Physical	—	100	20	Normal	—	○
TM24	Thunderbolt	Electric	Special	95	100	15	Normal	—	—
TM25	Thunder	Electric	Special	120	70	10	Normal	—	—
TM27	Return	Normal	Physical	—	100	20	Normal	—	○
TM28	Dig	Ground	Physical	80	100	10	Normal	—	○
TM30	Shadow Ball	Ghost	Special	80	100	15	Normal	—	—
TM32	Double Team	Normal	Status	—	—	15	Self	—	—
TM40	Aerial Ace	Flying	Physical	60	—	20	Normal	○	○
TM41	Torment	Dark	Status	—	100	15	Normal	—	—
TM42	Facade	Normal	Physical	70	100	20	Normal	—	○
TM44	Rest	Psychic	Status	—	—	10	Self	—	—
TM45	Attract	Normal	Status	—	100	15	Normal	—	—
TM46	Thief	Dark	Physical	40	100	10	Normal	—	○
TM48	Round	Normal	Special	60	100	15	Normal	—	—
TM49	Echoed Voice	Normal	Special	40	100	15	Normal	—	—
TM65	Shadow Claw	Ghost	Physical	70	100	15	Normal	—	○
TM66	Payback	Dark	Physical	50	100	10	Normal	—	○
TM67	Retaliate	Normal	Physical	70	100	5	Normal	—	○
TM70	Flash	Normal	Status	—	100	20	Normal	—	—
TM77	Psych Up	Normal	Status	—	—	10	Normal	—	—
TM83	Work Up	Normal	Status	—	—	30	Self	—	—
TM85	Dream Eater	Psychic	Special	100	100	15	Normal	—	—
TM87	Swagger	Normal	Status	—	90	15	Normal	—	—
TM89	U-turn	Bug	Physical	70	100	20	Normal	—	○
TM90	Substitute	Normal	Status	—	—	10	Self	—	—
HM01	Cut	Normal	Physical	50	95	30	Normal	—	○

MOVES TAUGHT BY PEOPLE

Name	Type	Kind	Pow.	Acc.	PP	Range	Long	DA

MOVES TAUGHT BY MOVE TUTORS FOR SHARDS

Name	Type	Kind	Pow.	Acc.	PP	Range	Long	DA
Covet	Normal	Physical	60	100	40	Normal	—	○
Uproar	Normal	Special	90	100	10	1 Random	—	—
Seed Bomb	Grass	Physical	80	100	15	Normal	—	—
Gunk Shot	Poison	Physical	120	70	5	Normal	—	—
Last Resort	Normal	Physical	140	100	5	Normal	—	○
Hyper Voice	Normal	Special	90	100	10	Many Others	—	—
Icy Wind	Ice	Special	55	95	15	Many Others	—	—
Iron Tail	Steel	Physical	100	75	15	Normal	—	○
Foul Play	Dark	Physical	95	100	15	Normal	—	○
Dark Pulse	Dark	Special	80	100	15	Normal	○	—
Snore	Normal	Special	40	100	15	Normal	—	—
Knock Off	Dark	Physical	20	100	20	Normal	—	○
Spite	Ghost	Status	—	100	10	Normal	—	—
Sleep Talk	Normal	Status	—	—	10	Self	—	—
Snatch	Dark	Status	—	—	10	Self	—	—

EGG MOVES

Name	Type	Kind	Pow.	Acc.	PP	Range	Long	DA
Spite	Ghost	Status	—	100	10	Normal	—	—
Charm	Normal	Status	—	100	20	Normal	—	—
Hypnosis	Psychic	Status	—	60	20	Normal	—	—
Amnesia	Psychic	Status	—	—	20	Self	—	—
Assist	Normal	Status	—	—	20	Self	—	—
Odor Sleuth	Normal	Status	—	—	40	Normal	—	—
Flail	Normal	Physical	—	100	15	Normal	—	○
Last Resort	Normal	Physical	140	100	5	Normal	—	○
Punishment	Dark	Physical	—	100	5	Normal	—	○
Tail Whip	Normal	Status	—	100	30	Many Others	—	—
Snatch	Dark	Status	—	—	10	Self	—	—
Iron Tail	Steel	Physical	100	75	15	Normal	—	○
Foul Play	Dark	Physical	95	100	15	Normal	—	○

053 Persian

Classy Cat Pokémon

- HEIGHT: 3'03"
- WEIGHT: 70.5 lbs.
- GENDER: ♂ / ♀

A very haughty Pokémon. Among fans, the size of the jewel in its forehead is a topic of much talk.

Same form for ♂ / ♀

TYPE Normal

ABILITIES
- Limber
- Technician

HIDDEN ABILITY
- Unnerve

STATS
HP
Attack
Defense
Sp. Atk
Sp. Def
Speed

EGG GROUPS
Field

ITEMS SOMETIMES HELD
- None

EVOLUTION

HOW TO OBTAIN

Pokémon Black Version 2	If your character is a boy, level up the Meowth you receive from Yancy to Lv. 28
Pokémon White Version 2	If your character is a boy, level up the Meowth you receive from Yancy to Lv. 28

HOW TO OBTAIN FROM OTHER GAMES

Pokémon SoulSilver Version	Route 7
	—

Pokémon AR Marker

LEVEL-UP AND LEARNED MOVES

Lv.	Name	Type	Kind	Pow.	Acc.	PP	Range	Long	DA
1	Switcheroo	Dark	Status	—	100	10	Normal	—	—
1	Scratch	Normal	Physical	40	100	35	Normal	—	○
1	Growl	Normal	Status	—	100	40	Many Others	—	—
1	Bite	Dark	Physical	60	100	25	Normal	—	○
1	Fake Out	Normal	Physical	40	100	10	Normal	—	○
6	Bite	Dark	Physical	60	100	25	Normal	—	○
9	Fake Out	Normal	Physical	40	100	10	Normal	—	○
14	Fury Swipes	Normal	Physical	18	80	15	Normal	—	○
17	Screech	Normal	Status	—	85	40	Normal	—	—
22	Faint Attack	Dark	Physical	60	—	20	Normal	—	○
25	Taunt	Dark	Status	—	100	20	Normal	—	—
28	Swift	Normal	Special	60	—	20	Many Others	—	—
32	Power Gem	Rock	Special	70	100	20	Normal	—	—
37	Slash	Normal	Physical	70	100	20	Normal	—	○
44	Nasty Plot	Dark	Status	—	—	20	Self	—	—
49	Assurance	Dark	Physical	50	100	10	Normal	—	○
56	Captivate	Normal	Status	—	100	20	Many Others	—	—
61	Night Slash	Dark	Physical	70	100	15	Normal	—	○
68	Feint	Normal	Physical	30	100	10	Normal	—	—

TM & HM MOVES

Lv.	Name	Type	Kind	Pow.	Acc.	PP	Range	Long	DA
TM01	Hone Claws	Dark	Status	—	—	15	Self	—	—
TM05	Roar	Normal	Status	—	100	20	Normal	—	—
TM06	Toxic	Poison	Status	—	90	10	Normal	—	—
TM10	Hidden Power	Normal	Special	—	100	15	Normal	—	—
TM11	Sunny Day	Fire	Status	—	—	5	Both Sides	—	—
TM12	Taunt	Dark	Status	—	100	20	Normal	—	—
TM15	Hyper Beam	Normal	Special	150	90	5	Normal	—	—
TM17	Protect	Normal	Status	—	—	10	Self	—	—
TM18	Rain Dance	Water	Status	—	—	5	Both Sides	—	—
TM21	Frustration	Normal	Physical	—	100	20	Normal	—	○
TM24	Thunderbolt	Electric	Special	95	100	15	Normal	—	—
TM25	Thunder	Electric	Special	120	70	10	Normal	—	—
TM27	Return	Normal	Physical	—	100	20	Normal	—	○
TM28	Dig	Ground	Physical	80	100	10	Normal	—	○
TM30	Shadow Ball	Ghost	Special	80	100	15	Normal	—	—
TM32	Double Team	Normal	Status	—	—	15	Self	—	—
TM40	Aerial Ace	Flying	Physical	60	—	20	Normal	○	○
TM41	Torment	Dark	Status	—	100	15	Normal	—	—
TM42	Facade	Normal	Physical	70	100	20	Normal	—	○
TM44	Rest	Psychic	Status	—	—	10	Self	—	—
TM45	Attract	Normal	Status	—	100	15	Normal	—	—
TM46	Thief	Dark	Physical	40	100	10	Normal	—	○
TM48	Round	Normal	Special	60	100	15	Normal	—	—
TM49	Echoed Voice	Normal	Special	40	100	15	Normal	—	—
TM63	Embargo	Dark	Status	—	100	15	Normal	—	—
TM65	Shadow Claw	Ghost	Physical	70	100	15	Normal	—	○
TM66	Payback	Dark	Physical	50	100	10	Normal	—	○
TM67	Retaliate	Normal	Physical	70	100	5	Normal	—	○
TM68	Giga Impact	Normal	Physical	150	90	5	Normal	—	○
TM70	Flash	Normal	Status	—	100	20	Normal	—	—
TM77	Psych Up	Normal	Status	—	—	10	Normal	—	—
TM83	Work Up	Normal	Status	—	—	30	Self	—	—
TM85	Dream Eater	Psychic	Special	100	100	15	Normal	—	—
TM87	Swagger	Normal	Status	—	90	15	Normal	—	—
TM89	U-turn	Bug	Physical	70	100	20	Normal	—	○
TM90	Substitute	Normal	Status	—	—	10	Self	—	—
HM01	Cut	Normal	Physical	50	95	30	Normal	—	○

MOVES TAUGHT BY PEOPLE

Name	Type	Kind	Pow.	Acc.	PP	Range	Long	DA

MOVES TAUGHT BY MOVE TUTORS FOR SHARDS

Name	Type	Kind	Pow.	Acc.	PP	Range	Long	DA
Covet	Normal	Physical	60	100	40	Normal	—	○
Uproar	Normal	Special	90	100	10	1 Random	—	—
Seed Bomb	Grass	Physical	80	100	15	Normal	—	—
Gunk Shot	Poison	Physical	120	70	5	Normal	—	—
Last Resort	Normal	Physical	140	100	5	Normal	—	○
Hyper Voice	Normal	Special	90	100	10	Many Others	—	—
Icy Wind	Ice	Special	55	95	15	Many Others	—	—
Iron Tail	Steel	Physical	100	75	15	Normal	—	○
Foul Play	Dark	Physical	95	100	15	Normal	—	○
Dark Pulse	Dark	Special	80	100	15	Normal	○	—
Snore	Normal	Special	40	100	15	Normal	—	—
Knock Off	Dark	Physical	20	100	20	Normal	—	○
Spite	Ghost	Status	—	100	10	Normal	—	—
Sleep Talk	Normal	Status	—	—	10	Self	—	—
Snatch	Dark	Status	—	—	10	Self	—	—

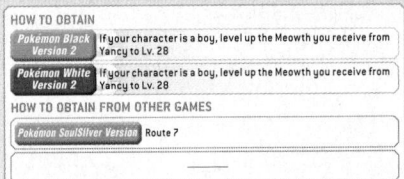

054 Psyduck

Duck Pokémon

- HEIGHT: 2'07"
- WEIGHT: 43.2 lbs.
- GENDER: ♂ / ♀

When headaches stimulate its brain cells, which are usually inactive, it can use a mysterious power.

Same form for ♂ / ♀

TYPE Water

ABILITIES
- Damp
- Cloud Nine

HIDDEN ABILITY
- Swift Swim

STATS
HP
Attack
Defense
Sp. Atk
Sp. Def
Speed

EGG GROUPS
Water 1/Field

ITEMS SOMETIMES HELD
- None

EVOLUTION

HOW TO OBTAIN

Pokémon Black Version 2	Floccesy Ranch
Pokémon White Version 2	Floccesy Ranch

HOW TO OBTAIN FROM OTHER GAMES

—
—

Pokémon AR Marker

LEVEL-UP AND LEARNED MOVES

Lv.	Name	Type	Kind	Pow.	Acc.	PP	Range	Long	DA
1	Water Sport	Water	Status	—	—	15	Both Sides	—	—
1	Scratch	Normal	Physical	40	100	35	Normal	—	○
4	Tail Whip	Normal	Status	—	100	30	Many Others	—	—
8	Water Gun	Water	Special	40	100	25	Normal	—	—
11	Disable	Normal	Status	—	100	20	Normal	—	—
15	Confusion	Psychic	Special	50	100	25	Normal	—	—
18	Water Pulse	Water	Special	60	100	20	Normal	○	—
22	Fury Swipes	Normal	Physical	18	80	15	Normal	—	○
25	Screech	Normal	Status	—	85	40	Normal	—	—
29	Zen Headbutt	Psychic	Physical	80	90	15	Normal	—	○
32	Aqua Tail	Water	Physical	90	90	10	Normal	—	○
36	Soak	Water	Status	—	100	20	Normal	—	—
39	Psych Up	Normal	Status	—	—	10	Normal	—	—
43	Amnesia	Psychic	Status	—	—	20	Self	—	—
46	Hydro Pump	Water	Special	120	80	5	Normal	—	—
50	Wonder Room	Psychic	Status	—	—	10	Both Sides	—	—

TM & HM MOVES

Lv.	Name	Type	Kind	Pow.	Acc.	PP	Range	Long	DA
TM01	Hone Claws	Dark	Status	—	—	15	Self	—	—
TM03	Psyshock	Psychic	Special	80	100	10	Normal	—	—
TM04	Calm Mind	Psychic	Status	—	—	20	Self	—	—
TM06	Toxic	Poison	Status	—	90	10	Normal	—	—
TM07	Hail	Ice	Status	—	—	10	Both Sides	—	—
TM10	Hidden Power	Normal	Special	—	100	15	Normal	—	—
TM13	Ice Beam	Ice	Special	95	100	10	Normal	—	—
TM14	Blizzard	Ice	Special	120	70	5	Many Others	—	—
TM16	Light Screen	Psychic	Status	—	—	30	Your Side	—	—
TM17	Protect	Normal	Status	—	—	10	Self	—	—
TM18	Rain Dance	Water	Status	—	—	5	Both Sides	—	—
TM19	Telekinesis	Psychic	Status	—	—	15	Normal	—	—
TM21	Frustration	Normal	Physical	—	100	20	Normal	—	○
TM27	Return	Normal	Physical	—	100	20	Normal	—	○
TM28	Dig	Ground	Physical	80	100	10	Normal	—	○
TM29	Psychic	Psychic	Special	90	100	10	Normal	—	—
TM31	Brick Break	Fighting	Physical	75	100	15	Normal	—	○
TM32	Double Team	Normal	Status	—	—	15	Self	—	—
TM40	Aerial Ace	Flying	Physical	60	—	20	Normal	○	○
TM42	Facade	Normal	Physical	70	100	20	Normal	—	○
TM44	Rest	Psychic	Status	—	—	10	Self	—	—
TM45	Attract	Normal	Status	—	100	15	Normal	—	—
TM48	Round	Normal	Special	60	100	15	Normal	—	—
TM55	Scald	Water	Special	80	100	15	Normal	—	—
TM56	Fling	Dark	Physical	—	100	10	Normal	—	—
TM65	Shadow Claw	Ghost	Physical	70	100	15	Normal	—	○
TM70	Flash	Normal	Status	—	100	20	Normal	—	—
TM77	Psych Up	Normal	Status	—	—	10	Normal	—	—
TM87	Swagger	Normal	Status	—	90	15	Normal	—	—
TM90	Substitute	Normal	Status	—	—	10	Self	—	—
TM94	Rock Smash	Fighting	Physical	40	100	15	Normal	—	○
HM03	Surf	Water	Special	95	100	15	Adjacent	—	—
HM04	Strength	Normal	Physical	80	100	15	Normal	—	○
HM05	Waterfall	Water	Physical	80	100	15	Normal	—	○
HM06	Dive	Water	Physical	80	100	10	Normal	—	○

MOVES TAUGHT BY PEOPLE

Name	Type	Kind	Pow.	Acc.	PP	Range	Long	DA

MOVES TAUGHT BY MOVE TUTORS FOR SHARDS

Name	Type	Kind	Pow.	Acc.	PP	Range	Long	DA
Signal Beam	Bug	Special	75	100	15	Normal	—	—
Ice Punch	Ice	Physical	75	100	15	Normal	—	○
Icy Wind	Ice	Special	55	95	15	Many Others	—	—
Iron Tail	Steel	Physical	100	75	15	Normal	—	○
Aqua Tail	Water	Physical	90	90	10	Normal	—	○
Zen Headbutt	Psychic	Physical	80	90	15	Normal	—	○
Snore	Normal	Special	40	100	15	Normal	—	—
Role Play	Psychic	Status	—	—	10	Normal	—	—
Worry Seed	Grass	Status	—	100	10	Normal	—	—
Wonder Room	Psychic	Status	—	—	10	Both Sides	—	—
Sleep Talk	Normal	Status	—	—	10	Self	—	—

EGG MOVES

Name	Type	Kind	Pow.	Acc.	PP	Range	Long	DA
Hypnosis	Psychic	Status	—	60	20	Normal	—	—
Psybeam	Psychic	Special	65	100	20	Normal	—	—
Foresight	Normal	Status	—	—	40	Normal	—	—
Future Sight	Psychic	Special	100	100	10	Normal	—	—
Cross Chop	Fighting	Physical	100	80	5	Normal	—	○
Refresh	Normal	Status	—	—	20	Self	—	—
Confuse Ray	Ghost	Status	—	100	10	Normal	—	—
Yawn	Normal	Status	—	—	10	Normal	—	—
Mud Bomb	Ground	Special	65	85	10	Normal	—	—
Encore	Normal	Status	—	100	5	Normal	—	—
Secret Power	Normal	Physical	70	100	20	Normal	—	—
Sleep Talk	Normal	Status	—	—	10	Self	—	—
Synchronoise	Psychic	Special	70	100	15	Adjacent	—	—

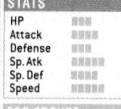

055 Golduck
Duck Pokémon

- **HEIGHT:** 5'07"
- **WEIGHT:** 168.9 lbs.
- **GENDER:** ♂ / ♀

When its forehead shines mysteriously, Golduck can use the full extent of its power.

Same form for ♂ / ♀

Pokémon AR Marker

TYPE: Water

ABILITIES
- Damp
- Cloud Nine

HIDDEN ABILITY
- Swift Swim

STATS
- HP
- Attack
- Defense
- Sp. Atk
- Sp. Def
- Speed

EGG GROUPS
Water ❶ / Field

ITEMS SOMETIMES HELD
- None

EVOLUTION

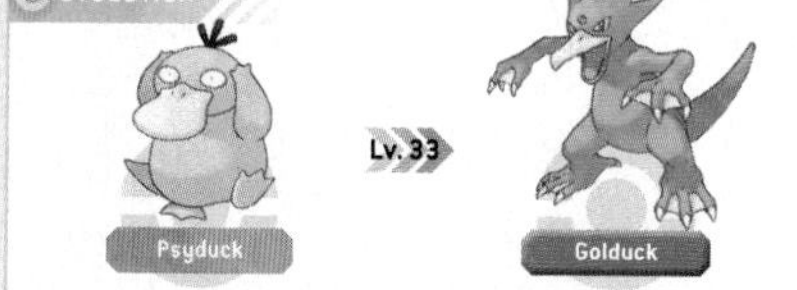

Psyduck → Lv. 33 → Golduck

HOW TO OBTAIN

Pokémon Black Version 2	❶ Route 14 ❷ Village Bridge
Pokémon White Version 2	❶ Route 14 ❷ Village Bridge

HOW TO OBTAIN FROM OTHER GAMES

LEVEL-UP AND LEARNED MOVES

Lv.	Name	Type	Kind	Pow.	Acc.	PP	Range	Long	DA
1	Aqua Jet	Water	Physical	40	100	20	Normal	—	—
1	Water Sport	Water	Status	—	—	15	Both Sides	—	—
1	Scratch	Normal	Physical	40	100	35	Normal	—	○
1	Tail Whip	Normal	Status	—	100	30	Many Others	—	—
1	Water Gun	Water	Special	40	100	25	Normal	—	—
4	Tail Whip	Normal	Status	—	100	30	Many Others	—	—
8	Water Gun	Water	Special	40	100	25	Normal	—	—
11	Disable	Normal	Status	—	100	20	Normal	—	—
15	Confusion	Psychic	Special	50	100	25	Normal	—	—
18	Water Pulse	Water	Special	60	100	20	Normal	○	—
22	Fury Swipes	Normal	Physical	18	80	15	Normal	—	○
25	Screech	Normal	Status	—	85	40	Normal	—	—
29	Zen Headbutt	Psychic	Physical	80	90	15	Normal	—	○
32	Aqua Tail	Water	Physical	90	90	10	Normal	—	○
38	Soak	Water	Status	—	100	20	Normal	—	—
43	Psych Up	Normal	Status	—	—	10	Normal	—	—
49	Amnesia	Psychic	Status	—	—	20	Self	—	—
54	Hydro Pump	Water	Special	120	80	5	Normal	—	—
60	Wonder Room	Psychic	Status	—	—	10	Both Sides	—	—

TM & HM MOVES

Lv.	Name	Type	Kind	Pow.	Acc.	PP	Range	Long	DA
TM01	Hone Claws	Dark	Status	—	—	15	Self	—	—
TM03	Psyshock	Psychic	Special	80	100	10	Normal	—	—
TM04	Calm Mind	Psychic	Status	—	—	20	Self	—	—
TM06	Toxic	Poison	Status	—	90	10	Normal	—	—
TM07	Hail	Ice	Status	—	—	10	Both Sides	—	—
TM10	Hidden Power	Normal	Special	—	100	15	Normal	—	—
TM13	Ice Beam	Ice	Special	95	100	10	Normal	—	—
TM14	Blizzard	Ice	Special	120	70	5	Many Others	—	—
TM15	Hyper Beam	Normal	Special	150	90	5	Normal	—	—
TM16	Light Screen	Psychic	Status	—	—	30	Your Side	—	—
TM17	Protect	Normal	Status	—	—	10	Self	—	—
TM18	Rain Dance	Water	Status	—	—	5	Both Sides	—	—
TM19	Telekinesis	Psychic	Status	—	—	15	Normal	—	—
TM21	Frustration	Normal	Physical	—	100	20	Normal	—	○
TM27	Return	Normal	Physical	—	100	20	Normal	—	○
TM28	Dig	Ground	Physical	80	100	10	Normal	—	—
TM29	Psychic	Psychic	Special	90	100	10	Normal	—	—
TM31	Brick Break	Fighting	Physical	75	100	15	Normal	—	—
TM32	Double Team	Normal	Status	—	—	15	Self	—	—
TM40	Aerial Ace	Flying	Physical	60	—	20	Normal	○	—
TM42	Facade	Normal	Physical	70	100	20	Normal	—	—
TM44	Rest	Psychic	Status	—	—	10	Self	—	—
TM45	Attract	Normal	Status	—	100	15	Normal	—	—
TM47	Low Sweep	Fighting	Physical	60	100	20	Normal	—	○
TM48	Round	Normal	Special	60	100	15	Normal	—	—
TM52	Focus Blast	Fighting	Special	120	70	5	Normal	—	—
TM55	Scald	Water	Special	80	100	15	Normal	—	—
TM56	Fling	Dark	Physical	—	100	10	Normal	—	○
TM65	Shadow Claw	Ghost	Physical	70	100	15	Normal	—	○
TM68	Giga Impact	Normal	Physical	150	90	5	Normal	—	—
TM70	Flash	Normal	Status	—	100	20	Normal	—	—
TM77	Psych Up	Normal	Status	—	—	10	Normal	—	—
TM87	Swagger	Normal	Status	—	90	15	Normal	—	—
TM90	Substitute	Normal	Status	—	—	10	Self	—	—

Lv.	Name	Type	Kind	Pow.	Acc.	PP	Range	Long	DA
TM94	Rock Smash	Fighting	Physical	40	100	15	Normal	—	○
HM03	Surf	Water	Special	95	100	15	Adjacent	—	—
HM04	Strength	Normal	Physical	80	100	15	Normal	—	○
HM05	Waterfall	Water	Physical	80	100	15	Normal	—	○
HM06	Dive	Water	Physical	80	100	10	Normal	—	—

MOVES TAUGHT BY PEOPLE

Name	Type	Kind	Pow.	Acc.	PP	Range	Long	DA

MOVES TAUGHT BY MOVE TUTORS FOR SHARDS

Name	Type	Kind	Pow.	Acc.	PP	Range	Long	DA
Signal Beam	Bug	Special	75	100	15	Normal	—	—
Low Kick	Fighting	Physical	—	100	20	Normal	—	○
Ice Punch	Ice	Physical	75	100	15	Normal	—	○
Icy Wind	Ice	Special	55	95	15	Many Others	—	—
Iron Tail	Steel	Physical	100	75	15	Normal	—	○
Aqua Tail	Water	Physical	90	90	10	Normal	—	○
Zen Headbutt	Psychic	Physical	80	90	15	Normal	—	○
Snore	Normal	Special	40	100	15	Normal	—	—
Role Play	Psychic	Status	—	—	10	Normal	—	—
Worry Seed	Grass	Status	—	100	10	Normal	—	—
Wonder Room	Psychic	Status	—	—	10	Both Sides	—	—
Sleep Talk	Normal	Status	—	—	10	Self	—	—

056 Mankey
Pig Monkey Pokémon

- **HEIGHT:** 1'08"
- **WEIGHT:** 61.7 lbs.
- **GENDER:** ♂ / ♀

It lives in treetop colonies. If one becomes enraged, the whole colony rampages for no reason.

Same form for ♂ / ♀

Pokémon AR Marker

TYPE: Fighting

ABILITIES
- Vital Spirit
- Anger Point

HIDDEN ABILITY
- Defiant

STATS
- HP
- Attack
- Defense
- Sp. Atk
- Sp. Def
- Speed

EGG GROUPS
Field

ITEMS SOMETIMES HELD
- None

EVOLUTION

Mankey → Lv. 28 → Primeape

HOW TO OBTAIN

Pokémon Black Version 2	If your character is a girl, trade Pokémon during a date with Curtis (first time)
Pokémon White Version 2	If your character is a girl, trade Pokémon during a date with Curtis (first time)

HOW TO OBTAIN FROM OTHER GAMES

Pokémon Black Version	Route 15 (mass outbreak)
Pokémon White Version	Route 15 (mass outbreak)

LEVEL-UP AND LEARNED MOVES

Lv.	Name	Type	Kind	Pow.	Acc.	PP	Range	Long	DA
1	Covet	Normal	Physical	60	100	40	Normal	—	○
1	Scratch	Normal	Physical	40	100	35	Normal	—	○
1	Low Kick	Fighting	Physical	—	100	20	Normal	—	○
1	Leer	Normal	Status	—	100	30	Many Others	—	—
1	Focus Energy	Normal	Status	—	—	30	Self	—	—
9	Fury Swipes	Normal	Physical	18	80	15	Normal	—	○
13	Karate Chop	Fighting	Physical	50	100	25	Normal	—	—
17	Seismic Toss	Fighting	Physical	—	100	20	Normal	—	—
21	Screech	Normal	Status	—	85	40	Normal	—	—
25	Assurance	Dark	Physical	50	100	10	Normal	—	—
33	Swagger	Normal	Status	—	90	15	Normal	—	—
37	Cross Chop	Fighting	Physical	100	80	5	Normal	—	—
41	Thrash	Normal	Physical	120	100	10	1 Random	—	—
45	Punishment	Dark	Physical	—	100	5	Normal	—	—
49	Close Combat	Fighting	Physical	120	100	5	Normal	—	—
53	Final Gambit	Fighting	Special	—	100	5	Normal	—	—

TM & HM MOVES

Lv.	Name	Type	Kind	Pow.	Acc.	PP	Range	Long	DA
TM01	Hone Claws	Dark	Status	—	—	15	Self	—	—
TM06	Toxic	Poison	Status	—	90	10	Normal	—	—
TM08	Bulk Up	Fighting	Status	—	—	20	Self	—	—
TM10	Hidden Power	Normal	Special	—	100	15	Normal	—	—
TM11	Sunny Day	Fire	Status	—	—	5	Both Sides	—	—
TM12	Taunt	Dark	Status	—	100	20	Normal	—	—
TM17	Protect	Normal	Status	—	—	10	Self	—	—
TM18	Rain Dance	Water	Status	—	—	5	Both Sides	—	—
TM21	Frustration	Normal	Physical	—	100	20	Normal	—	○
TM23	Smack Down	Rock	Physical	50	100	15	Normal	—	—
TM24	Thunderbolt	Electric	Special	95	100	15	Normal	—	—
TM25	Thunder	Electric	Special	120	70	10	Normal	—	—
TM26	Earthquake	Ground	Physical	100	100	10	Adjacent	—	—
TM27	Return	Normal	Physical	—	100	20	Normal	—	○
TM28	Dig	Ground	Physical	80	100	10	Normal	—	—
TM31	Brick Break	Fighting	Physical	75	100	15	Normal	—	—
TM32	Double Team	Normal	Status	—	—	15	Self	—	—
TM39	Rock Tomb	Rock	Physical	50	80	10	Normal	—	—
TM40	Aerial Ace	Flying	Physical	60	—	20	Normal	○	—
TM42	Facade	Normal	Physical	70	100	20	Normal	—	—
TM44	Rest	Psychic	Status	—	—	10	Self	—	—
TM45	Attract	Normal	Status	—	100	15	Normal	—	—
TM46	Thief	Dark	Physical	40	100	10	Normal	—	○
TM47	Low Sweep	Fighting	Physical	60	100	20	Normal	—	○
TM48	Round	Normal	Special	60	100	15	Normal	—	—
TM50	Overheat	Fire	Special	140	90	5	Normal	—	—
TM52	Focus Blast	Fighting	Special	120	70	5	Normal	—	—
TM56	Fling	Dark	Physical	—	100	10	Normal	—	○
TM62	Acrobatics	Flying	Physical	55	100	15	Normal	—	○
TM66	Payback	Dark	Physical	50	100	10	Normal	—	○
TM67	Retaliate	Normal	Physical	70	100	5	Normal	—	—
TM78	Bulldoze	Ground	Physical	60	100	20	Adjacent	—	—
TM80	Rock Slide	Rock	Physical	75	90	10	Many Others	—	—
TM83	Work Up	Normal	Status	—	—	30	Self	—	—
TM84	Poison Jab	Poison	Physical	80	100	20	Normal	—	—
TM87	Swagger	Normal	Status	—	90	15	Normal	—	—
TM89	U-turn	Bug	Physical	70	100	20	Normal	—	—

Lv.	Name	Type	Kind	Pow.	Acc.	PP	Range	Long	DA
TM90	Substitute	Normal	Status	—	—	10	Self	—	—
TM94	Rock Smash	Fighting	Physical	40	100	15	Normal	—	○
HM04	Strength	Normal	Physical	80	100	15	Normal	—	○

MOVES TAUGHT BY PEOPLE

Name	Type	Kind	Pow.	Acc.	PP	Range	Long	DA

MOVES TAUGHT BY MOVE TUTORS FOR SHARDS

Name	Type	Kind	Pow.	Acc.	PP	Range	Long	DA
Covet	Normal	Physical	60	100	40	Normal	—	○
Uproar	Normal	Special	90	100	10	1 Random	—	—
Seed Bomb	Grass	Physical	80	100	15	Normal	—	—
Dual Chop	Dragon	Physical	40	90	15	Normal	—	—
Low Kick	Fighting	Physical	—	100	20	Normal	—	○
Gunk Shot	Poison	Physical	120	70	5	Normal	—	—
Fire Punch	Fire	Physical	75	100	15	Normal	—	○
ThunderPunch	Electric	Physical	75	100	15	Normal	—	○
Ice Punch	Ice	Physical	75	100	15	Normal	—	○
Iron Tail	Steel	Physical	100	75	15	Normal	—	○
Role Play	Psychic	Status	—	—	10	1 Ally	—	—
Helping Hand	Normal	Status	—	—	20	1 Ally	—	—
Spite	Ghost	Status	—	100	10	Normal	—	—
Outrage	Dragon	Physical	120	100	10	1 Random	—	—
Endeavor	Normal	Physical	—	100	5	Normal	—	—
Sleep Talk	Normal	Status	—	—	10	Self	—	—

EGG MOVES

Name	Type	Kind	Pow.	Acc.	PP	Range	Long	DA
Foresight	Normal	Status	—	—	40	Normal	—	—
Meditate	Psychic	Status	—	—	40	Self	—	—
Counter	Fighting	Physical	—	100	20	Varies	—	—
Reversal	Fighting	Physical	—	100	15	Normal	—	—
Beat Up	Dark	Physical	—	100	10	Normal	—	○
Revenge	Fighting	Physical	60	100	10	Normal	—	—
SmellingSalt	Normal	Physical	60	100	10	Normal	—	—
Close Combat	Fighting	Physical	120	100	5	Normal	—	—
Encore	Normal	Status	—	100	5	Normal	—	—
Focus Punch	Fighting	Physical	150	100	20	Normal	—	—
Sleep Talk	Normal	Status	—	—	10	Self	—	—

Pig Monkey Pokémon

057 Primeape

- HEIGHT: 3'03"
- WEIGHT: 70.5 lbs.
- GENDER: ♂ / ♀

It grows angry if you see its eyes and gets angrier if you run. If you beat it, it gets even madder.

Same form for ♂ / ♀

TYPE Fighting

ABILITIES
- Vital Spirit
- Anger Point

HIDDEN ABILITY
- Defiant

STATS
HP
Attack
Defense
Sp. Atk
Sp. Def
Speed

EGG GROUPS
Field

ITEMS SOMETIMES HELD
- None

Pokémon AR Marker

EVOLUTION

HOW TO OBTAIN

Pokémon Black Version 2	If your character is a girl, level up the Mankey you receive from Curtis to Lv. 28
Pokémon White Version 2	If your character is a girl, level up the Mankey you receive from Curtis to Lv. 28

HOW TO OBTAIN FROM OTHER GAMES

Pokémon HeartGold Version	Cerulean Cave
Pokémon Platinum Version	Occasionally appears on Route 225 (use Poké Radar for a better chance)

LEVEL-UP AND LEARNED MOVES

Lv.	Name	Type	Kind	Pow.	Acc.	PP	Range	Long	DA
1	Fling	Dark	Physical	—	100	10	Normal	—	—
1	Scratch	Normal	Physical	40	100	35	Normal	—	○
1	Low Kick	Fighting	Physical	—	100	20	Normal	—	○
1	Leer	Normal	Status	—	100	30	Many Others	—	—
1	Focus Energy	Normal	Status	—	—	30	Self	—	—
9	Fury Swipes	Normal	Physical	18	80	15	Normal	—	○
13	Karate Chop	Fighting	Physical	50	100	25	Normal	—	○
17	Seismic Toss	Fighting	Physical	—	100	20	Normal	—	○
21	Screech	Normal	Status	—	85	40	Normal	—	—
25	Assurance	Dark	Physical	50	100	10	Normal	—	○
28	Rage	Normal	Physical	20	100	20	Normal	—	○
35	Swagger	Normal	Status	—	90	15	Normal	—	—
41	Cross Chop	Fighting	Physical	100	80	5	Normal	—	○
47	Thrash	Normal	Physical	120	100	10	1 Random	—	○
53	Punishment	Dark	Physical	—	100	5	Normal	—	○
59	Close Combat	Fighting	Physical	120	100	5	Normal	—	○
63	Final Gambit	Fighting	Special	—	100	5	Normal	—	○

TM & HM MOVES

Lv.	Name	Type	Kind	Pow.	Acc.	PP	Range	Long	DA
TM01	Hone Claws	Dark	Status	—	—	15	Self	—	—
TM06	Toxic	Poison	Status	—	90	10	Normal	—	—
TM08	Bulk Up	Fighting	Status	—	—	20	Self	—	—
TM10	Hidden Power	Normal	Special	—	100	15	Normal	—	—
TM11	Sunny Day	Fire	Status	—	—	5	Both Sides	—	—
TM12	Taunt	Dark	Status	—	100	20	Normal	—	—
TM15	Hyper Beam	Normal	Special	150	90	5	Normal	—	—
TM17	Protect	Normal	Status	—	—	10	Self	—	—
TM18	Rain Dance	Water	Status	—	—	5	Both Sides	—	—
TM21	Frustration	Normal	Physical	—	100	20	Normal	—	○
TM23	Smack Down	Rock	Physical	50	100	15	Normal	—	—
TM24	Thunderbolt	Electric	Special	95	100	15	Normal	—	—
TM25	Thunder	Electric	Special	120	70	10	Normal	—	—
TM26	Earthquake	Ground	Physical	100	100	10	Adjacent	—	—
TM27	Return	Normal	Physical	—	100	20	Normal	—	○
TM28	Dig	Ground	Physical	80	100	10	Normal	—	○
TM31	Brick Break	Fighting	Physical	75	100	15	Normal	—	○
TM32	Double Team	Normal	Status	—	—	15	Self	—	—
TM39	Rock Tomb	Rock	Physical	50	80	10	Normal	—	—
TM40	Aerial Ace	Flying	Physical	60	—	20	Normal	○	○
TM42	Facade	Normal	Physical	70	100	20	Normal	—	○
TM44	Rest	Psychic	Status	—	—	10	Self	—	—
TM45	Attract	Normal	Status	—	100	15	Normal	—	—
TM46	Thief	Dark	Physical	40	100	10	Normal	—	○
TM47	Low Sweep	Fighting	Physical	60	100	20	Normal	—	○
TM48	Round	Normal	Special	60	100	15	Normal	—	—
TM50	Overheat	Fire	Special	140	90	5	Normal	—	—
TM52	Focus Blast	Fighting	Special	120	70	5	Normal	—	—
TM56	Fling	Dark	Physical	—	100	10	Normal	—	—
TM62	Acrobatics	Flying	Physical	55	100	15	Normal	○	○
TM66	Payback	Dark	Physical	50	100	10	Normal	—	○
TM67	Retaliate	Normal	Physical	70	100	5	Normal	—	○
TM68	Giga Impact	Normal	Physical	150	90	5	Normal	—	○
TM71	Stone Edge	Rock	Physical	100	80	5	Normal	—	—
TM78	Bulldoze	Ground	Physical	60	100	20	Adjacent	—	—
TM80	Rock Slide	Rock	Physical	75	90	10	Many Others	—	—
TM83	Work Up	Normal	Status	—	—	30	Self	—	—
TM84	Poison Jab	Poison	Physical	80	100	20	Normal	—	○
TM87	Swagger	Normal	Status	—	90	15	Normal	—	—
TM89	U-turn	Bug	Physical	70	100	20	Normal	—	○
TM90	Substitute	Normal	Status	—	—	10	Self	—	—
TM94	Rock Smash	Fighting	Physical	40	100	15	Normal	—	○
HM04	Strength	Normal	Physical	80	100	15	Normal	—	○

MOVES TAUGHT BY PEOPLE

Name	Type	Kind	Pow.	Acc.	PP	Range	Long	DA

MOVES TAUGHT BY MOVE TUTORS FOR SHARDS

Name	Type	Kind	Pow.	Acc.	PP	Range	Long	DA
Covet	Normal	Physical	60	100	40	Normal	—	○
Uproar	Normal	Special	90	100	10	1 Random	—	—
Seed Bomb	Grass	Physical	80	100	15	Normal	—	—
Dual Chop	Dragon	Physical	40	90	15	Normal	—	○
Low Kick	Fighting	Physical	—	100	20	Normal	—	○
Gunk Shot	Poison	Physical	120	70	5	Normal	—	—
Fire Punch	Fire	Physical	75	100	15	Normal	—	○
ThunderPunch	Electric	Physical	75	100	15	Normal	—	○
Ice Punch	Ice	Physical	75	100	15	Normal	—	○
Iron Tail	Steel	Physical	100	75	15	Normal	—	○
Role Play	Psychic	Status	—	—	10	Normal	—	—
Helping Hand	Normal	Status	—	—	20	1 Ally	—	—
Spite	Ghost	Status	—	100	10	Normal	—	—
Outrage	Dragon	Physical	120	100	10	1 Random	—	○
Endeavor	Normal	Physical	—	100	5	Normal	—	○
Sleep Talk	Normal	Status	—	—	10	Self	—	—

Puppy Pokémon

058 Growlithe

- HEIGHT: 2'04"
- WEIGHT: 41.9 lbs.
- GENDER: ♂ / ♀

Extremely loyal to its Trainer, it will bark at those who approach the Trainer unexpectedly and run them out of town.

Same form for ♂ / ♀

TYPE Fire

ABILITIES
- Intimidate
- Flash Fire

HIDDEN ABILITY
- Justified

STATS
HP
Attack
Defense
Sp. Atk
Sp. Def
Speed

EGG GROUPS
Field

ITEMS SOMETIMES HELD
- Rawst Berry

Pokémon AR Marker

EVOLUTION

HOW TO OBTAIN

Pokémon Black Version 2	Virbank Complex Interior
Pokémon White Version 2	Virbank Complex Interior

HOW TO OBTAIN FROM OTHER GAMES

—
—

LEVEL-UP AND LEARNED MOVES

Lv.	Name	Type	Kind	Pow.	Acc.	PP	Range	Long	DA
1	Bite	Dark	Physical	60	100	25	Normal	—	○
1	Roar	Normal	Status	—	100	20	Normal	—	—
6	Ember	Fire	Special	40	100	25	Normal	—	—
8	Leer	Normal	Status	—	100	30	Many Others	—	—
10	Odor Sleuth	Normal	Status	—	—	40	Normal	—	—
12	Helping Hand	Normal	Status	—	—	20	1 Ally	—	—
17	Flame Wheel	Fire	Physical	60	100	25	Normal	—	○
19	Reversal	Fighting	Physical	—	100	15	Normal	—	○
21	Fire Fang	Fire	Physical	65	95	15	Normal	—	○
23	Take Down	Normal	Physical	90	85	20	Normal	—	○
28	Flame Burst	Fire	Special	70	100	15	Normal	—	—
30	Agility	Psychic	Status	—	—	30	Self	—	—
32	Retaliate	Normal	Physical	70	100	5	Normal	—	○
34	Flamethrower	Fire	Special	95	100	15	Normal	—	—
39	Crunch	Dark	Physical	80	100	15	Normal	—	○
41	Heat Wave	Fire	Special	100	90	10	Many Others	—	—
43	Outrage	Dragon	Physical	120	100	10	1 Random	—	○
45	Flare Blitz	Fire	Physical	120	100	15	Normal	—	○

TM & HM MOVES

Lv.	Name	Type	Kind	Pow.	Acc.	PP	Range	Long	DA
TM05	Roar	Normal	Status	—	100	20	Normal	—	—
TM06	Toxic	Poison	Status	—	90	10	Normal	—	—
TM10	Hidden Power	Normal	Special	—	100	15	Normal	—	—
TM11	Sunny Day	Fire	Status	—	—	5	Both Sides	—	—
TM17	Protect	Normal	Status	—	—	10	Self	—	—
TM20	Safeguard	Normal	Status	—	—	25	Your Side	—	—
TM21	Frustration	Normal	Physical	—	100	20	Normal	—	○
TM27	Return	Normal	Physical	—	100	20	Normal	—	○
TM28	Dig	Ground	Physical	80	100	10	Normal	—	○
TM32	Double Team	Normal	Status	—	—	15	Self	—	—
TM35	Flamethrower	Fire	Special	95	100	15	Normal	—	—
TM38	Fire Blast	Fire	Special	120	85	5	Normal	—	—
TM40	Aerial Ace	Flying	Physical	60	—	20	Normal	○	○
TM42	Facade	Normal	Physical	70	100	20	Normal	—	○
TM43	Flame Charge	Fire	Physical	50	100	20	Normal	—	○
TM44	Rest	Psychic	Status	—	—	10	Self	—	—
TM45	Attract	Normal	Status	—	100	15	Normal	—	—
TM46	Thief	Dark	Physical	40	100	10	Normal	—	○
TM48	Round	Normal	Special	60	100	15	Normal	—	—
TM50	Overheat	Fire	Special	140	90	5	Normal	—	—
TM59	Incinerate	Fire	Special	30	100	15	Many Others	—	—
TM61	Will-O-Wisp	Fire	Status	—	75	15	Normal	—	—
TM67	Retaliate	Normal	Physical	70	100	5	Normal	—	○
TM87	Swagger	Normal	Status	—	90	15	Normal	—	—
TM90	Substitute	Normal	Status	—	—	10	Self	—	—
TM93	Wild Charge	Electric	Physical	90	100	15	Normal	—	○
TM94	Rock Smash	Fighting	Physical	40	100	15	Normal	—	○
TM95	Snarl	Dark	Special	55	95	15	Many Others	—	—
HM04	Strength	Normal	Physical	80	100	15	Normal	—	○

MOVES TAUGHT BY PEOPLE

Name	Type	Kind	Pow.	Acc.	PP	Range	Long	DA

MOVES TAUGHT BY MOVE TUTORS FOR SHARDS

Name	Type	Kind	Pow.	Acc.	PP	Range	Long	DA
Covet	Normal	Physical	60	100	40	Normal	—	○
Iron Tail	Steel	Physical	100	75	15	Normal	—	○
Snore	Normal	Special	40	100	15	Normal	—	—
Heat Wave	Fire	Special	100	90	10	Many Others	—	—
Helping Hand	Normal	Status	—	—	20	1 Ally	—	—
Outrage	Dragon	Physical	120	100	10	1 Random	—	○
Sleep Talk	Normal	Status	—	—	10	Self	—	—

EGG MOVES

Name	Type	Kind	Pow.	Acc.	PP	Range	Long	DA
Body Slam	Normal	Physical	85	100	15	Normal	—	○
Crunch	Dark	Physical	80	100	15	Normal	—	○
Thrash	Normal	Physical	120	100	10	1 Random	—	○
Fire Spin	Fire	Special	35	85	15	Normal	—	—
Howl	Normal	Status	—	—	40	Self	—	—
Heat Wave	Fire	Special	100	90	10	Many Others	—	—
Double-Edge	Normal	Physical	120	100	15	Normal	—	○
Flare Blitz	Fire	Physical	120	100	15	Normal	—	○
Morning Sun	Normal	Status	—	—	5	Self	—	—
Covet	Normal	Physical	60	100	40	Normal	—	○
Iron Tail	Steel	Physical	100	75	15	Normal	—	○
Double Kick	Fighting	Physical	30	100	30	Normal	—	○
Close Combat	Fighting	Physical	120	100	5	Normal	—	○

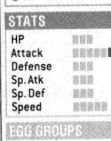

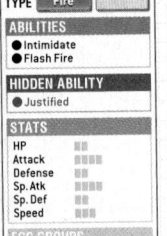

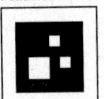

059 Arcanine
Legendary Pokémon

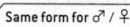

TYPE Fire

ABILITIES
- Intimidate
- Flash Fire

HIDDEN ABILITY
- Justified

- HEIGHT: 6'03"
- WEIGHT: 341.7 lbs.
- GENDER: ♂ / ♀

The sight of it running over 6,200 miles in a single day and night has captivated many people.

STATS
- HP
- Attack
- Defense
- Sp. Atk
- Sp. Def
- Speed

EGG GROUPS
Field

ITEMS SOMETIMES HELD
- None

Same form for ♂ / ♀

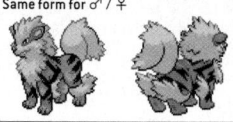

EVOLUTION

Growlithe → Arcanine (Use Fire Stone)

HOW TO OBTAIN
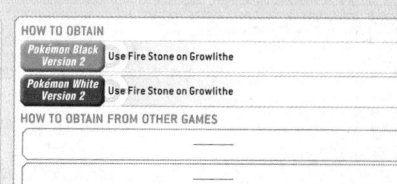

Pokémon Black Version 2	Use Fire Stone on Growlithe
Pokémon White Version 2	Use Fire Stone on Growlithe

HOW TO OBTAIN FROM OTHER GAMES
——

LEVEL-UP AND LEARNED MOVES

Lv.	Name	Type	Kind	Pow.	Acc.	PP	Range	Long	DA
1	Thunder Fang	Electric	Physical	65	95	15	Normal	—	○
1	Bite	Dark	Physical	60	100	25	Normal	—	○
1	Roar	Normal	Status	—	100	20	Normal	—	—
1	Odor Sleuth	Normal	Status	—	—	40	Normal	—	—
1	Fire Fang	Fire	Physical	65	95	15	Normal	—	○
34	ExtremeSpeed	Normal	Physical	80	100	5	Normal	—	—

TM & HM MOVES

Lv.	Name	Type	Kind	Pow.	Acc.	PP	Range	Long	DA
TM05	Roar	Normal	Status	—	100	20	Normal	—	—
TM06	Toxic	Poison	Status	—	90	10	Normal	—	—
TM10	Hidden Power	Normal	Special	—	100	15	Normal	—	—
TM11	Sunny Day	Fire	Status	—	—	5	Both Sides	—	—
TM15	Hyper Beam	Normal	Special	150	90	5	Normal	—	—
TM17	Protect	Normal	Status	—	—	10	Self	—	—
TM20	Safeguard	Normal	Status	—	—	25	Your Side	—	—
TM21	Frustration	Normal	Physical	—	100	20	Normal	—	○
TM22	SolarBeam	Grass	Special	120	100	10	Normal	—	—
TM27	Return	Normal	Physical	—	100	20	Normal	—	○
TM28	Dig	Ground	Physical	80	100	10	Normal	—	○
TM32	Double Team	Normal	Status	—	—	15	Self	—	—
TM35	Flamethrower	Fire	Special	95	100	15	Normal	—	—
TM38	Fire Blast	Fire	Special	120	85	5	Normal	—	—
TM40	Aerial Ace	Flying	Physical	60	—	20	Normal	○	○
TM42	Facade	Normal	Physical	70	100	20	Normal	—	○
TM43	Flame Charge	Fire	Physical	50	100	20	Normal	—	○
TM44	Rest	Psychic	Status	—	—	10	Self	—	—
TM45	Attract	Normal	Status	—	100	15	Normal	—	—
TM46	Thief	Dark	Physical	40	100	10	Normal	—	○
TM48	Round	Normal	Special	60	100	15	Normal	—	—
TM50	Overheat	Fire	Special	140	90	5	Normal	—	—
TM59	Incinerate	Fire	Special	30	100	15	Many Others	—	—
TM61	Will-O-Wisp	Fire	Status	—	75	15	Normal	—	—
TM67	Retaliate	Normal	Physical	70	100	5	Normal	—	○
TM68	Giga Impact	Normal	Physical	150	90	5	Normal	—	○
TM78	Bulldoze	Ground	Physical	60	100	20	Adjacent	—	○
TM87	Swagger	Normal	Status	—	90	15	Normal	—	—
TM90	Substitute	Normal	Status	—	—	10	Self	—	—
TM93	Wild Charge	Electric	Physical	90	100	15	Normal	—	○
TM94	Rock Smash	Fighting	Physical	40	100	15	Normal	—	○
TM95	Snarl	Dark	Special	55	95	15	Many Others	—	—
HM04	Strength	Normal	Physical	80	100	15	Normal	—	○

MOVES TAUGHT BY PEOPLE

Name	Type	Kind	Pow.	Acc.	PP	Range	Long	DA

MOVES TAUGHT BY MOVE TUTORS FOR SHARDS

Name	Type	Kind	Pow.	Acc.	PP	Range	Long	DA
Covet	Normal	Physical	60	100	40	Normal	—	○
Iron Head	Steel	Physical	80	100	15	Normal	—	○
Iron Tail	Steel	Physical	100	75	15	Normal	—	○
Dragon Pulse	Dragon	Special	90	100	10	Normal	○	—
Snore	Normal	Special	40	100	15	Normal	—	—
Heat Wave	Fire	Special	100	90	10	Many Others	—	—
Helping Hand	Normal	Status	—	—	20	1 Ally	—	—
Outrage	Dragon	Physical	120	100	10	1 Random	—	○
Sleep Talk	Normal	Status	—	—	10	Self	—	—

Pokémon AR Marker

---

060 Poliwag
Tadpole Pokémon

TYPE Water

ABILITIES
- Water Absorb
- Damp

HIDDEN ABILITY
- Swift Swim

- HEIGHT: 2'00"
- WEIGHT: 27.3 lbs.
- GENDER: ♂ / ♀

Its skin is so thin, its internal organs are visible. It has trouble walking on its newly grown feet.

STATS
- HP
- Attack
- Defense
- Sp. Atk
- Sp. Def
- Speed

EGG GROUPS
Water ①

ITEMS SOMETIMES HELD
- None

Same form for ♂ / ♀

EVOLUTION

 Poliwag → Poliwhirl (Lv. 25) → Poliwrath (Use Water Stone) / Politoed (Have it hold King's Rock and Link Trade it)

→ p. 106

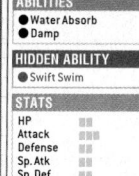

HOW TO OBTAIN
Pokémon Black Version 2	❶ Route 19 (Super Rod) ❷ Route 20 (Super Rod)
Pokémon White Version 2	❶ Route 19 (Super Rod) ❷ Route 20 (Super Rod)

HOW TO OBTAIN FROM OTHER GAMES
——

LEVEL-UP AND LEARNED MOVES

Lv.	Name	Type	Kind	Pow.	Acc.	PP	Range	Long	DA
1	Water Sport	Water	Status	—	—	15	Both Sides	—	—
5	Bubble	Water	Special	20	100	30	Many Others	—	—
8	Hypnosis	Psychic	Status	—	60	20	Normal	—	—
11	Water Gun	Water	Special	40	100	25	Normal	—	—
15	DoubleSlap	Normal	Physical	15	85	10	Normal	—	—
18	Rain Dance	Water	Status	—	—	5	Both Sides	—	—
21	Body Slam	Normal	Physical	85	100	15	Normal	—	○
25	BubbleBeam	Water	Special	65	100	20	Normal	—	—
28	Mud Shot	Ground	Special	55	95	15	Normal	—	—
31	Belly Drum	Normal	Status	—	—	10	Self	—	—
35	Wake-Up Slap	Fighting	Physical	60	100	10	Normal	—	○
39	Hydro Pump	Water	Special	120	80	5	Normal	—	—
41	Mud Bomb	Ground	Special	65	85	10	Normal	—	—

TM & HM MOVES

Lv.	Name	Type	Kind	Pow.	Acc.	PP	Range	Long	DA
TM06	Toxic	Poison	Status	—	90	10	Normal	—	—
TM07	Hail	Ice	Status	—	—	10	Both Sides	—	—
TM10	Hidden Power	Normal	Special	—	100	15	Normal	—	—
TM13	Ice Beam	Ice	Special	95	100	10	Normal	—	—
TM14	Blizzard	Ice	Special	120	70	5	Many Others	—	—
TM17	Protect	Normal	Status	—	—	10	Self	—	—
TM18	Rain Dance	Water	Status	—	—	5	Both Sides	—	—
TM21	Frustration	Normal	Physical	—	100	20	Normal	—	○
TM27	Return	Normal	Physical	—	100	20	Normal	—	○
TM28	Dig	Ground	Physical	80	100	10	Normal	—	○
TM29	Psychic	Psychic	Special	90	100	10	Normal	—	—
TM32	Double Team	Normal	Status	—	—	15	Self	—	—
TM42	Facade	Normal	Physical	70	100	20	Normal	—	○
TM44	Rest	Psychic	Status	—	—	10	Self	—	—
TM45	Attract	Normal	Status	—	100	15	Normal	—	—
TM46	Thief	Dark	Physical	40	100	10	Normal	—	○
TM48	Round	Normal	Special	60	100	15	Normal	—	—
TM55	Scald	Water	Special	80	100	15	Normal	—	—
TM87	Swagger	Normal	Status	—	90	15	Normal	—	—
TM90	Substitute	Normal	Status	—	—	10	Self	—	—
HM03	Surf	Water	Special	95	100	15	Adjacent	—	—
HM05	Waterfall	Water	Physical	80	100	15	Normal	—	○
HM06	Dive	Water	Physical	80	100	10	Normal	—	○

MOVES TAUGHT BY PEOPLE

Name	Type	Kind	Pow.	Acc.	PP	Range	Long	DA

MOVES TAUGHT BY MOVE TUTORS FOR SHARDS

Name	Type	Kind	Pow.	Acc.	PP	Range	Long	DA
Icy Wind	Ice	Special	55	95	15	Many Others	—	—
Snore	Normal	Special	40	100	15	Normal	—	—
Helping Hand	Normal	Status	—	—	20	1 Ally	—	—
Endeavor	Normal	Physical	—	100	5	Normal	—	○
Sleep Talk	Normal	Status	—	—	10	Self	—	—

EGG MOVES

Name	Type	Kind	Pow.	Acc.	PP	Range	Long	DA
Mist	Ice	Status	—	—	30	Your Side	—	—
Splash	Normal	Status	—	—	40	Self	—	—
BubbleBeam	Water	Special	65	100	20	Normal	—	—
Haze	Ice	Status	—	—	30	Both Sides	—	—
Mind Reader	Normal	Status	—	—	5	Normal	—	—
Water Sport	Water	Status	—	—	15	Both Sides	—	—
Ice Ball	Ice	Physical	30	90	20	Normal	—	○
Mud Shot	Ground	Special	55	95	15	Normal	—	—
Refresh	Normal	Status	—	—	20	Self	—	—
Endeavor	Normal	Physical	—	100	5	Normal	—	○
Encore	Normal	Status	—	100	5	Normal	—	—
Endure	Normal	Status	—	—	10	Self	—	—
Water Pulse	Water	Special	60	100	20	Normal	○	—

Pokémon AR Marker

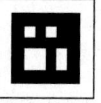

43

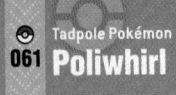

Tadpole Pokémon

061 Poliwhirl

- HEIGHT: 3'03"
- WEIGHT: 44.1 lbs.
- GENDER: ♂ / ♀

The spiral pattern on its belly subtly undulates. Staring at it gradually causes drowsiness.

Same form for ♂ / ♀

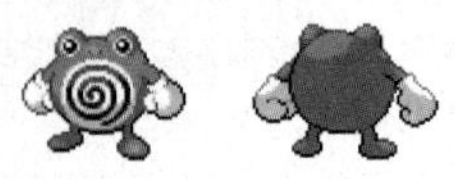

TYPE Water

ABILITIES
- Water Absorb
- Damp

HIDDEN ABILITY
- Swift Swim

STATS
HP
Attack
Defense
Sp. Atk
Sp. Def
Speed

EGG GROUPS
Water ❶

ITEMS SOMETIMES HELD
- King's Rock

EVOLUTION

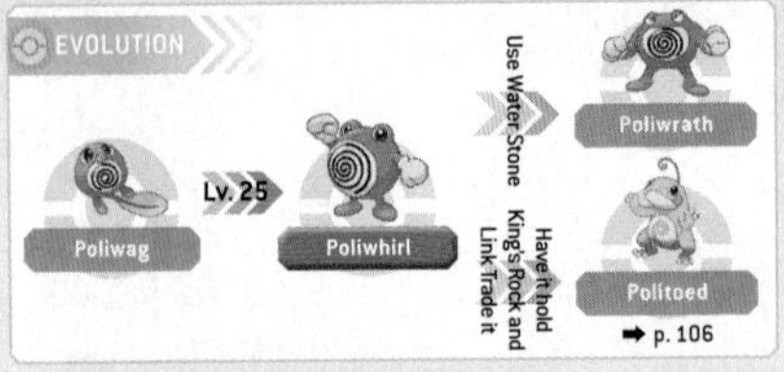

Poliwag
Lv. 25
Poliwhirl
Use Water Stone
Poliwrath
Have it hold King's Rock and Link Trade it
Politoed

➡ p. 106

HOW TO OBTAIN

Pokémon Black Version 2	❶ Route 19 (Super Rod/ripples in water) ❷ Route 20 (Super Rod/ripples in water)
Pokémon White Version 2	❶ Route 19 (Super Rod/ripples in water) ❷ Route 20 (Super Rod/ripples in water)

HOW TO OBTAIN FROM OTHER GAMES

—

—

LEVEL-UP AND LEARNED MOVES

Lv.	Name	Type	Kind	Pow.	Acc.	PP	Range	Long	DA
1	Water Sport	Water	Status	—	—	15	Both Sides	—	—
1	Bubble	Water	Special	20	100	30	Many Others	—	—
1	Hypnosis	Psychic	Status	—	60	20	Normal	—	—
5	Bubble	Water	Special	20	100	30	Many Others	—	—
8	Hypnosis	Psychic	Status	—	60	20	Normal	—	—
11	Water Gun	Water	Special	40	100	25	Normal	—	—
15	DoubleSlap	Normal	Physical	15	85	10	Normal	—	○
18	Rain Dance	Water	Status	—	—	5	Both Sides	—	—
21	Body Slam	Normal	Physical	85	100	15	Normal	—	○
27	BubbleBeam	Water	Special	65	100	20	Normal	—	—
32	Mud Shot	Ground	Special	55	95	15	Normal	—	—
37	Belly Drum	Normal	Status	—	—	10	Self	—	—
43	Wake-Up Slap	Fighting	Physical	60	100	10	Normal	—	○
48	Hydro Pump	Water	Special	120	80	5	Normal	—	—
53	Mud Bomb	Ground	Special	65	85	10	Normal	—	—

TM & HM MOVES

Lv.	Name	Type	Kind	Pow.	Acc.	PP	Range	Long	DA
TM06	Toxic	Poison	Status	—	90	10	Normal	—	—
TM07	Hail	Ice	Status	—	—	10	Both Sides	—	—
TM10	Hidden Power	Normal	Special	—	100	15	Normal	—	—
TM13	Ice Beam	Ice	Special	95	100	10	Normal	—	—
TM14	Blizzard	Ice	Special	120	70	5	Many Others	—	—
TM17	Protect	Normal	Status	—	—	10	Self	—	—
TM18	Rain Dance	Water	Status	—	—	5	Both Sides	—	—
TM21	Frustration	Normal	Physical	—	100	20	Normal	—	○
TM26	Earthquake	Ground	Physical	100	100	10	Adjacent	—	—
TM27	Return	Normal	Physical	—	100	20	Normal	—	○
TM28	Dig	Ground	Physical	80	100	10	Normal	—	○
TM29	Psychic	Psychic	Special	90	100	10	Normal	—	—
TM31	Brick Break	Fighting	Physical	75	100	15	Normal	—	○
TM32	Double Team	Normal	Status	—	—	15	Self	—	—
TM42	Facade	Normal	Physical	70	100	20	Normal	—	○
TM44	Rest	Psychic	Status	—	—	10	Self	—	—
TM45	Attract	Normal	Status	—	100	15	Normal	—	—
TM46	Thief	Dark	Physical	40	100	10	Normal	—	○
TM48	Round	Normal	Special	60	100	15	Normal	—	—
TM55	Scald	Water	Special	80	100	15	Normal	—	—
TM56	Fling	Dark	Physical	—	100	10	Normal	—	—
TM78	Bulldoze	Ground	Physical	60	100	20	Adjacent	—	—
TM87	Swagger	Normal	Status	—	90	15	Normal	—	—
TM90	Substitute	Normal	Status	—	—	10	Self	—	—
TM94	Rock Smash	Fighting	Physical	40	100	15	Normal	—	○
HM03	Surf	Water	Special	95	100	15	Adjacent	—	—
HM04	Strength	Normal	Physical	80	100	15	Normal	—	○
HM05	Waterfall	Water	Physical	80	100	15	Normal	—	○
HM06	Dive	Water	Physical	80	100	10	Normal	—	○

MOVES TAUGHT BY PEOPLE

Name	Type	Kind	Pow.	Acc.	PP	Range	Long	DA

MOVES TAUGHT BY MOVE TUTORS FOR SHARDS

Name	Type	Kind	Pow.	Acc.	PP	Range	Long	DA
Ice Punch	Ice	Physical	75	100	15	Normal	—	○
Icy Wind	Ice	Special	55	95	15	Many Others	—	—
Snore	Normal	Special	40	100	15	Normal	—	—
Helping Hand	Normal	Status	—	—	20	1 Ally	—	—
Endeavor	Normal	Physical	—	100	5	Normal	—	○
Sleep Talk	Normal	Status	—	—	10	Self	—	—

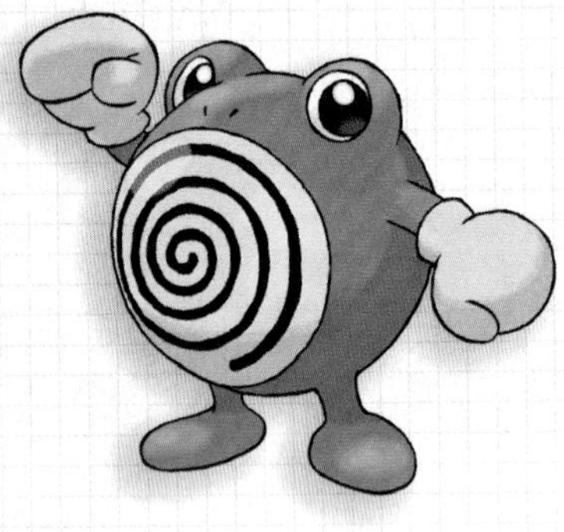

Pokémon AR Marker

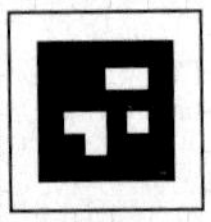

Tadpole Pokémon

062 Poliwrath

- HEIGHT: 4'03"
- WEIGHT: 119.0 lbs.
- GENDER: ♂ / ♀

With its extremely tough muscles, it can keep swimming in the Pacific Ocean without resting.

Same form for ♂ / ♀

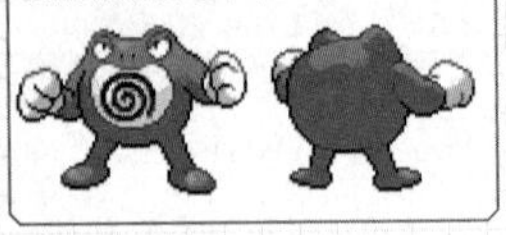

TYPE Water Fighting

ABILITIES
- Water Absorb
- Damp

HIDDEN ABILITY
- Swift Swim

STATS
HP
Attack
Defense
Sp. Atk
Sp. Def
Speed

EGG GROUPS
Water ❶

ITEMS SOMETIMES HELD
- King's Rock

EVOLUTION

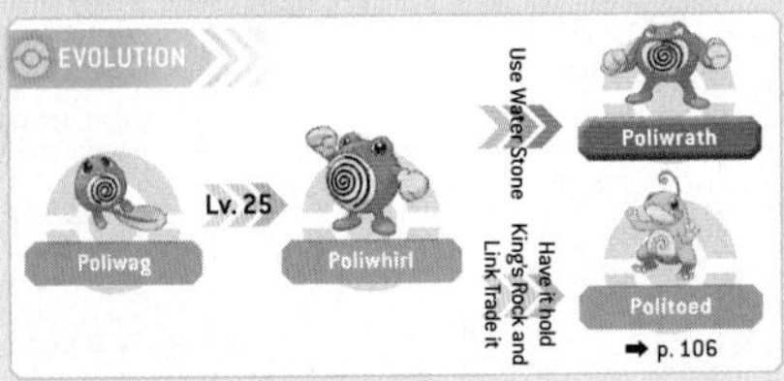

Poliwag
Lv. 25
Poliwhirl
Use Water Stone
Poliwrath
Have it hold King's Rock and Link Trade it
Politoed

➡ p. 106

HOW TO OBTAIN

Pokémon Black Version 2	❶ Relic Passage middle (Super Rod/ripples in water) ❷ Giant Chasm caves (Super Rod/ripples in water)
Pokémon White Version 2	❶ Relic Passage middle (Super Rod/ripples in water) ❷ Giant Chasm caves (Super Rod/ripples in water)

HOW TO OBTAIN FROM OTHER GAMES

—

—

LEVEL-UP AND LEARNED MOVES

Lv.	Name	Type	Kind	Pow.	Acc.	PP	Range	Long	DA
1	BubbleBeam	Water	Special	65	100	20	Normal	—	—
1	Hypnosis	Psychic	Status	—	60	20	Normal	—	—
1	DoubleSlap	Normal	Physical	15	85	10	Normal	—	○
1	Submission	Fighting	Physical	80	80	25	Normal	—	○
32	DynamicPunch	Fighting	Physical	100	50	5	Normal	—	○
43	Mind Reader	Normal	Status	—	—	5	Normal	—	—
53	Circle Throw	Fighting	Physical	60	90	10	Normal	—	○

TM & HM MOVES

Lv.	Name	Type	Kind	Pow.	Acc.	PP	Range	Long	DA
TM06	Toxic	Poison	Status	—	90	10	Normal	—	—
TM07	Hail	Ice	Status	—	—	10	Both Sides	—	—
TM08	Bulk Up	Fighting	Status	—	—	20	Self	—	—
TM10	Hidden Power	Normal	Special	—	100	15	Normal	—	—
TM13	Ice Beam	Ice	Special	95	100	10	Normal	—	—
TM14	Blizzard	Ice	Special	120	70	5	Many Others	—	—
TM15	Hyper Beam	Normal	Special	150	90	5	Normal	—	—
TM17	Protect	Normal	Status	—	—	10	Self	—	—
TM18	Rain Dance	Water	Status	—	—	5	Both Sides	—	—
TM21	Frustration	Normal	Physical	—	100	20	Normal	—	○
TM26	Earthquake	Ground	Physical	100	100	10	Adjacent	—	—
TM27	Return	Normal	Physical	—	100	20	Normal	—	○
TM28	Dig	Ground	Physical	80	100	10	Normal	—	○
TM29	Psychic	Psychic	Special	90	100	10	Normal	—	—
TM31	Brick Break	Fighting	Physical	75	100	15	Normal	—	○
TM32	Double Team	Normal	Status	—	—	15	Self	—	—
TM39	Rock Tomb	Rock	Physical	50	80	10	Normal	—	—
TM42	Facade	Normal	Physical	70	100	20	Normal	—	○
TM44	Rest	Psychic	Status	—	—	10	Self	—	—
TM45	Attract	Normal	Status	—	100	15	Normal	—	—
TM46	Thief	Dark	Physical	40	100	10	Normal	—	○
TM47	Low Sweep	Fighting	Physical	60	100	20	Normal	—	○
TM48	Round	Normal	Special	60	100	15	Normal	—	—
TM52	Focus Blast	Fighting	Special	120	70	5	Normal	—	—
TM55	Scald	Water	Special	80	100	15	Normal	—	—
TM56	Fling	Dark	Physical	—	100	10	Normal	—	—
TM66	Payback	Dark	Physical	50	100	10	Normal	—	○
TM68	Giga Impact	Normal	Physical	150	90	5	Normal	—	○
TM78	Bulldoze	Ground	Physical	60	100	20	Adjacent	—	—
TM80	Rock Slide	Rock	Physical	75	90	10	Many Others	—	—
TM83	Work Up	Normal	Status	—	—	30	Self	—	—
TM84	Poison Jab	Poison	Physical	80	100	20	Normal	—	○
TM87	Swagger	Normal	Status	—	90	15	Normal	—	—
TM90	Substitute	Normal	Status	—	—	10	Self	—	—
TM94	Rock Smash	Fighting	Physical	40	100	15	Normal	—	○
HM03	Surf	Water	Special	95	100	15	Adjacent	—	—
HM04	Strength	Normal	Physical	80	100	15	Normal	—	○
HM05	Waterfall	Water	Physical	80	100	15	Normal	—	○
HM06	Dive	Water	Physical	80	100	10	Normal	—	○

MOVES TAUGHT BY PEOPLE

Name	Type	Kind	Pow.	Acc.	PP	Range	Long	DA

MOVES TAUGHT BY MOVE TUTORS FOR SHARDS

Name	Type	Kind	Pow.	Acc.	PP	Range	Long	DA
Ice Punch	Ice	Physical	75	100	15	Normal	—	○
Icy Wind	Ice	Special	55	95	15	Many Others	—	—
Snore	Normal	Special	40	100	15	Normal	—	—
Helping Hand	Normal	Status	—	—	20	1 Ally	—	—
Endeavor	Normal	Physical	—	100	5	Normal	—	○
Sleep Talk	Normal	Status	—	—	10	Self	—	—

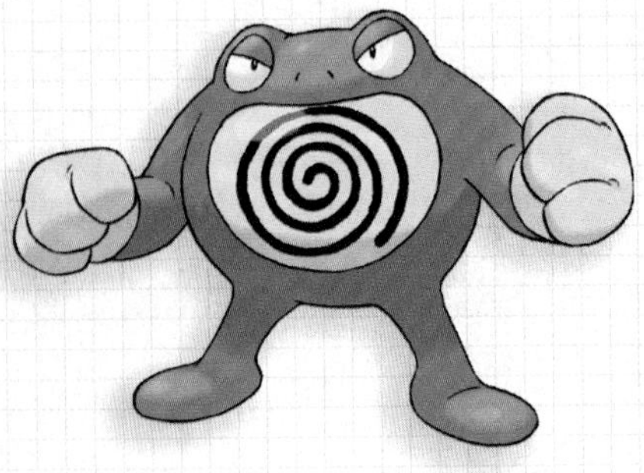

Pokémon AR Marker

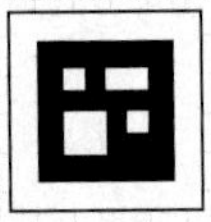

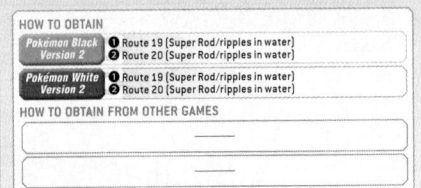

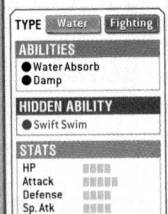

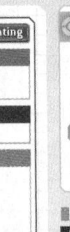

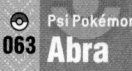

Psi Pokémon

063 Abra

TYPE Psychic

ABILITIES
- Synchronize
- Inner Focus

HIDDEN ABILITY
- Magic Guard

- HEIGHT: 2'11"
- WEIGHT: 43.0 lbs.
- GENDER: ♂ / ♀

Using its psychic power is such a strain on its brain that it needs to sleep for 18 hours a day.

STATS
HP
Attack
Defense
Sp. Atk
Sp. Def
Speed

EGG GROUPS
Human-Like

Same form for ♂ / ♀

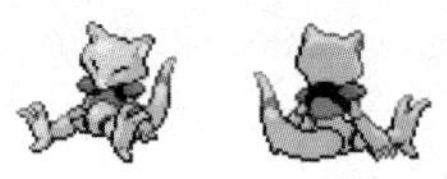

ITEMS SOMETIMES HELD
- None

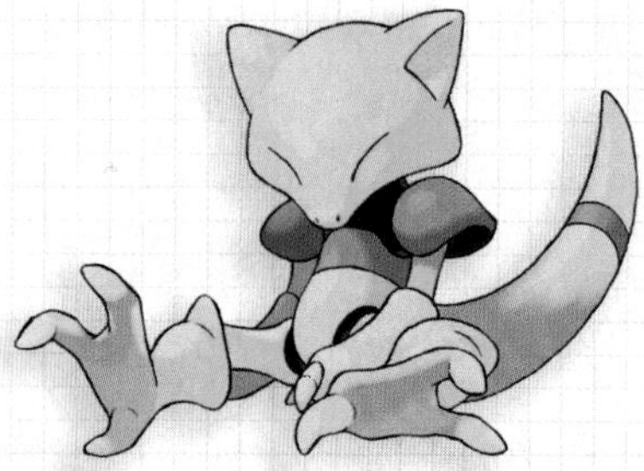

Pokémon AR Marker

EVOLUTION

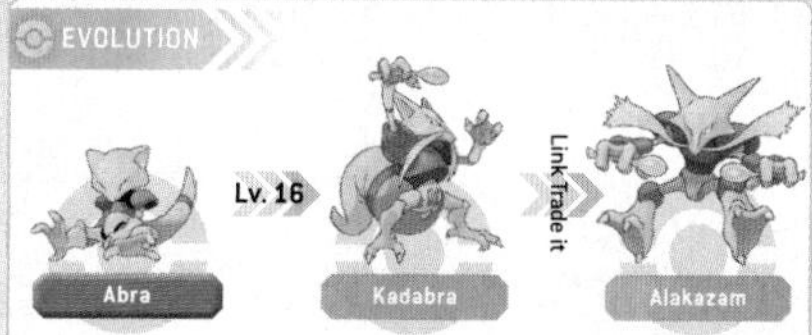
Abra
Lv. 16
Kadabra
Link Trade it
Alakazam

HOW TO OBTAIN

Pokémon Black Version 2	Catch an Alakazam, leave it at the Pokémon Day Care, and hatch the Egg that is found
Pokémon White Version 2	Catch an Alakazam, leave it at the Pokémon Day Care, and hatch the Egg that is found

HOW TO OBTAIN FROM OTHER GAMES

Pokémon HeartGold Version	Route 34
Pokémon SoulSilver Version	Route 34

LEVEL-UP AND LEARNED MOVES

Lv.	Name	Type	Kind	Pow.	Acc.	PP	Range	Long	DA
1	Teleport	Psychic	Status	—	—	20	Self	—	—

TM & HM MOVES

Lv.	Name	Type	Kind	Pow.	Acc.	PP	Range	Long	DA
TM03	Psyshock	Psychic	Special	80	100	10	Normal	—	—
TM04	Calm Mind	Psychic	Status	—	—	20	Self	—	—
TM06	Toxic	Poison	Status	—	90	10	Normal	—	—
TM10	Hidden Power	Normal	Special	—	100	15	Normal	—	—
TM11	Sunny Day	Fire	Status	—	—	5	Both Sides	—	—
TM12	Taunt	Dark	Status	—	100	20	Normal	—	—
TM16	Light Screen	Psychic	Status	—	—	30	Your Side	—	—
TM17	Protect	Normal	Status	—	—	10	Self	—	—
TM18	Rain Dance	Water	Status	—	—	5	Both Sides	—	—
TM19	Telekinesis	Psychic	Status	—	—	15	Normal	—	—
TM20	Safeguard	Normal	Status	—	—	25	Your Side	—	—
TM21	Frustration	Normal	Physical	—	100	20	Normal	—	○
TM27	Return	Normal	Physical	—	100	20	Normal	—	○
TM29	Psychic	Psychic	Special	90	100	10	Normal	—	—
TM30	Shadow Ball	Ghost	Special	80	100	15	Normal	—	—
TM32	Double Team	Normal	Status	—	—	15	Self	—	—
TM33	Reflect	Psychic	Status	—	—	20	Your Side	—	—
TM41	Torment	Dark	Status	—	100	15	Normal	—	—
TM42	Facade	Normal	Physical	70	100	20	Normal	—	○
TM44	Rest	Psychic	Status	—	—	10	Self	—	—
TM45	Attract	Normal	Status	—	100	15	Normal	—	—
TM46	Thief	Dark	Physical	40	100	10	Normal	—	○
TM48	Round	Normal	Special	60	100	15	Normal	—	—
TM51	Ally Switch	Psychic	Status	—	—	15	Self	—	—
TM53	Energy Ball	Grass	Special	80	100	10	Normal	—	—
TM56	Fling	Dark	Physical	—	100	10	Normal	—	—
TM57	Charge Beam	Electric	Special	50	90	10	Normal	—	—
TM63	Embargo	Dark	Status	—	100	15	Normal	—	—
TM70	Flash	Normal	Status	—	100	20	Normal	—	—
TM73	Thunder Wave	Electric	Status	—	100	20	Normal	—	—
TM77	Psych Up	Normal	Status	—	—	10	Normal	—	—
TM85	Dream Eater	Psychic	Special	100	100	15	Normal	—	—
TM86	Grass Knot	Grass	Special	—	100	20	Normal	—	○
TM87	Swagger	Normal	Status	—	90	15	Normal	—	—
TM90	Substitute	Normal	Status	—	—	10	Self	—	—
TM92	Trick Room	Psychic	Status	—	—	5	Both Sides	—	—

MOVES TAUGHT BY PEOPLE

Name	Type	Kind	Pow.	Acc.	PP	Range	Long	DA

MOVES TAUGHT BY MOVE TUTORS FOR SHARDS

Name	Type	Kind	Pow.	Acc.	PP	Range	Long	DA
Signal Beam	Bug	Special	75	100	15	Normal	—	—
Fire Punch	Fire	Physical	75	100	15	Normal	—	○
ThunderPunch	Electric	Physical	75	100	15	Normal	—	○
Ice Punch	Ice	Physical	75	100	15	Normal	—	○
Magic Coat	Psychic	Status	—	—	15	Self	—	—
Iron Tail	Steel	Physical	100	75	15	Normal	—	○
Zen Headbutt	Psychic	Physical	80	90	15	Normal	—	○
Foul Play	Dark	Physical	95	100	15	Normal	—	○
Gravity	Psychic	Status	—	—	5	Both Sides	—	—
Snore	Normal	Special	40	100	15	Normal	—	—
Knock Off	Dark	Physical	20	100	20	Normal	—	○
Role Play	Psychic	Status	—	—	10	Normal	—	—
Drain Punch	Fighting	Physical	75	100	10	Normal	—	○
Magic Room	Psychic	Status	—	—	10	Both Sides	—	—
Wonder Room	Psychic	Status	—	—	10	Both Sides	—	—
Recycle	Normal	Status	—	—	10	Self	—	—
Trick	Psychic	Status	—	100	10	Normal	—	—
Sleep Talk	Normal	Status	—	—	10	Self	—	—
Skill Swap	Psychic	Status	—	—	10	Normal	—	—
Snatch	Dark	Status	—	—	10	Self	—	—

EGG MOVES

Name	Type	Kind	Pow.	Acc.	PP	Range	Long	DA
Encore	Normal	Status	—	100	5	Normal	—	—
Barrier	Psychic	Status	—	—	30	Self	—	—
Knock Off	Dark	Physical	20	100	20	Normal	—	○
Fire Punch	Fire	Physical	75	100	15	Normal	—	○
ThunderPunch	Electric	Physical	75	100	15	Normal	—	○
Ice Punch	Ice	Physical	75	100	15	Normal	—	○
Power Trick	Psychic	Status	—	—	10	Self	—	—
Guard Swap	Psychic	Status	—	—	10	Normal	—	—
Skill Swap	Psychic	Status	—	—	10	Normal	—	—
Guard Split	Psychic	Status	—	—	10	Normal	—	—

Psi Pokémon

064 Kadabra

TYPE Psychic

ABILITIES
- Synchronize
- Inner Focus

HIDDEN ABILITY
- Magic Guard

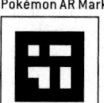

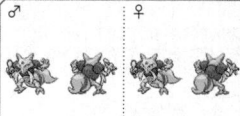

- HEIGHT: 4'03"
- WEIGHT: 124.6 lbs.
- GENDER: ♂ / ♀

It stares at its silver spoon to focus its mind. It emits more alpha waves while doing so.

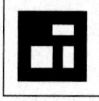

STATS
HP
Attack
Defense
Sp. Atk
Sp. Def
Speed

EGG GROUPS
Human-Like

♂ ♀

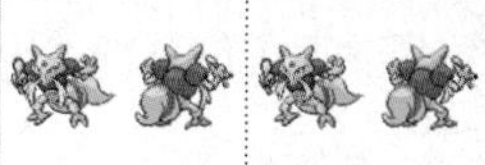

ITEMS SOMETIMES HELD
- None

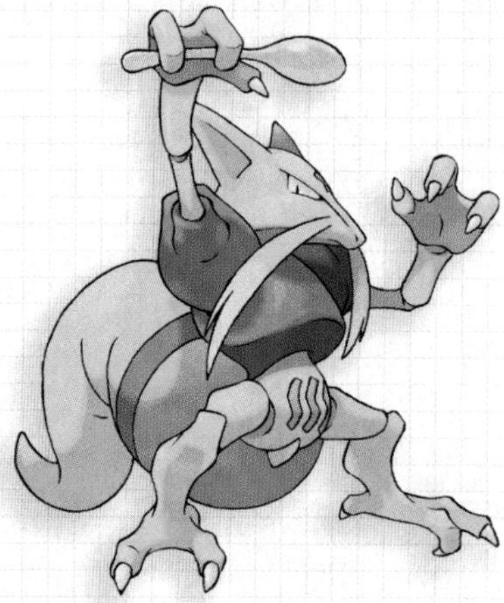

Pokémon AR Marker

EVOLUTION

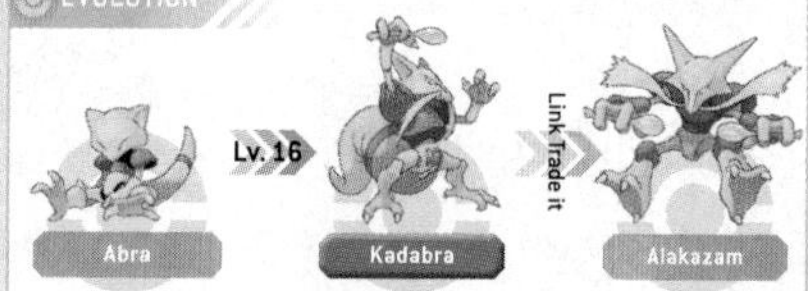
Abra
Lv. 16
Kadabra
Link Trade it
Alakazam

HOW TO OBTAIN

Pokémon Black Version 2	Level up Abra to Lv. 16
Pokémon White Version 2	Level up Abra to Lv. 16

HOW TO OBTAIN FROM OTHER GAMES

—
—

LEVEL-UP AND LEARNED MOVES

Lv.	Name	Type	Kind	Pow.	Acc.	PP	Range	Long	DA
1	Teleport	Psychic	Status	—	—	20	Self	—	—
1	Kinesis	Psychic	Status	—	80	15	Normal	—	—
1	Confusion	Psychic	Special	50	100	25	Normal	—	—
16	Confusion	Psychic	Special	50	100	25	Normal	—	—
18	Disable	Normal	Status	—	100	20	Normal	—	—
22	Miracle Eye	Psychic	Status	—	—	40	Normal	—	—
24	Ally Switch	Psychic	Status	—	—	15	Self	—	—
28	Psybeam	Psychic	Special	65	100	20	Normal	—	—
30	Reflect	Psychic	Status	—	—	20	Your Side	—	—
34	Telekinesis	Psychic	Status	—	—	15	Normal	—	—
36	Recover	Normal	Status	—	—	10	Self	—	—
40	Psycho Cut	Psychic	Physical	70	100	20	Normal	—	—
42	Role Play	Psychic	Status	—	—	10	Normal	—	—
46	Psychic	Psychic	Special	90	100	10	Normal	—	—
48	Future Sight	Psychic	Special	100	100	10	Normal	—	—
52	Trick	Psychic	Status	—	100	10	Normal	—	—

TM & HM MOVES

Lv.	Name	Type	Kind	Pow.	Acc.	PP	Range	Long	DA
TM03	Psyshock	Psychic	Special	80	100	10	Normal	—	—
TM04	Calm Mind	Psychic	Status	—	—	20	Self	—	—
TM06	Toxic	Poison	Status	—	90	10	Normal	—	—
TM10	Hidden Power	Normal	Special	—	100	15	Normal	—	—
TM11	Sunny Day	Fire	Status	—	—	5	Both Sides	—	—
TM12	Taunt	Dark	Status	—	100	20	Normal	—	—
TM16	Light Screen	Psychic	Status	—	—	30	Your Side	—	—
TM17	Protect	Normal	Status	—	—	10	Self	—	—
TM18	Rain Dance	Water	Status	—	—	5	Both Sides	—	—
TM19	Telekinesis	Psychic	Status	—	—	15	Normal	—	—
TM20	Safeguard	Normal	Status	—	—	25	Your Side	—	—
TM21	Frustration	Normal	Physical	—	100	20	Normal	—	○
TM27	Return	Normal	Physical	—	100	20	Normal	—	○
TM29	Psychic	Psychic	Special	90	100	10	Normal	—	—
TM30	Shadow Ball	Ghost	Special	80	100	15	Normal	—	—
TM32	Double Team	Normal	Status	—	—	15	Self	—	—
TM33	Reflect	Psychic	Status	—	—	20	Your Side	—	—
TM41	Torment	Dark	Status	—	100	15	Normal	—	—
TM42	Facade	Normal	Physical	70	100	20	Normal	—	○
TM44	Rest	Psychic	Status	—	—	10	Self	—	—
TM45	Attract	Normal	Status	—	100	15	Normal	—	—
TM46	Thief	Dark	Physical	40	100	10	Normal	—	○
TM48	Round	Normal	Special	60	100	15	Normal	—	—
TM51	Ally Switch	Psychic	Status	—	—	15	Self	—	—
TM53	Energy Ball	Grass	Special	80	100	10	Normal	—	—
TM56	Fling	Dark	Physical	—	100	10	Normal	—	—
TM57	Charge Beam	Electric	Special	50	90	10	Normal	—	—
TM63	Embargo	Dark	Status	—	100	15	Normal	—	—
TM70	Flash	Normal	Status	—	100	20	Normal	—	—
TM73	Thunder Wave	Electric	Status	—	100	20	Normal	—	—
TM77	Psych Up	Normal	Status	—	—	10	Normal	—	—
TM85	Dream Eater	Psychic	Special	100	100	15	Normal	—	—
TM86	Grass Knot	Grass	Special	—	100	20	Normal	—	○
TM87	Swagger	Normal	Status	—	90	15	Normal	—	—
TM90	Substitute	Normal	Status	—	—	10	Self	—	—
TM92	Trick Room	Psychic	Status	—	—	5	Both Sides	—	—

MOVES TAUGHT BY PEOPLE

Name	Type	Kind	Pow.	Acc.	PP	Range	Long	DA

MOVES TAUGHT BY MOVE TUTORS FOR SHARDS

Name	Type	Kind	Pow.	Acc.	PP	Range	Long	DA
Signal Beam	Bug	Special	75	100	15	Normal	—	—
Fire Punch	Fire	Physical	75	100	15	Normal	—	○
ThunderPunch	Electric	Physical	75	100	15	Normal	—	○
Ice Punch	Ice	Physical	75	100	15	Normal	—	○
Magic Coat	Psychic	Status	—	—	15	Self	—	—
Iron Tail	Steel	Physical	100	75	15	Normal	—	○
Zen Headbutt	Psychic	Physical	80	90	15	Normal	—	○
Foul Play	Dark	Physical	95	100	15	Normal	—	○
Gravity	Psychic	Status	—	—	5	Both Sides	—	—
Snore	Normal	Special	40	100	15	Normal	—	—
Knock Off	Dark	Physical	20	100	20	Normal	—	○
Role Play	Psychic	Status	—	—	10	Normal	—	—
Drain Punch	Fighting	Physical	75	100	10	Normal	—	○
Magic Room	Psychic	Status	—	—	10	Both Sides	—	—
Wonder Room	Psychic	Status	—	—	10	Both Sides	—	—
Recycle	Normal	Status	—	—	10	Self	—	—
Trick	Psychic	Status	—	100	10	Normal	—	—
Sleep Talk	Normal	Status	—	—	10	Self	—	—
Skill Swap	Psychic	Status	—	—	10	Normal	—	—
Snatch	Dark	Status	—	—	10	Self	—	—

065 Alakazam

Psi Pokémon

TYPE Psychic

- HEIGHT: 4'11"
- WEIGHT: 105.8 lbs.
- GENDER: ♂ / ♀

The spoons clutched in its hands are said to have been created by its psychic powers.

ABILITIES
- Synchronize
- Inner Focus

HIDDEN ABILITY
- Magic Guard

STATS
- HP
- Attack
- Defense
- Sp. Atk
- Sp. Def
- Speed

EGG GROUPS
Human-Like

ITEMS SOMETIMES HELD
- None

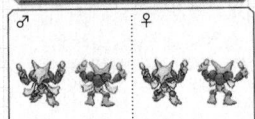

EVOLUTION

Abra — Lv. 16 → Kadabra — Link Trade it → Alakazam

HOW TO OBTAIN

Pokémon Black Version 2	Trade Hippowdon for it in a house in Accumula Town
Pokémon White Version 2	Trade Hippowdon for it in a house in Accumula Town

HOW TO OBTAIN FROM OTHER GAMES
— — —

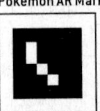

Pokémon AR Marker

LEVEL-UP AND LEARNED MOVES

Lv.	Name	Type	Kind	Pow.	Acc.	PP	Range	Long	DA
1	Teleport	Psychic	Status	—	—	20	Self	—	—
1	Kinesis	Psychic	Status	—	80	15	Normal	—	—
1	Confusion	Psychic	Special	50	100	25	Normal	—	—
16	Confusion	Psychic	Special	50	100	25	Normal	—	—
18	Disable	Normal	Status	—	100	20	Normal	—	—
22	Miracle Eye	Psychic	Status	—	—	40	Normal	—	—
24	Ally Switch	Psychic	Status	—	—	15	Self	—	—
28	Psybeam	Psychic	Special	65	100	20	Normal	—	—
30	Reflect	Psychic	Status	—	—	20	Your Side	—	—
34	Telekinesis	Psychic	Status	—	—	15	Normal	—	—
36	Recover	Normal	Status	—	—	10	Self	—	—
40	Psycho Cut	Psychic	Physical	70	100	20	Normal	—	—
42	Calm Mind	Psychic	Status	—	—	20	Self	—	—
46	Psychic	Psychic	Special	90	100	10	Normal	—	—
48	Future Sight	Psychic	Special	100	100	10	Normal	—	—
52	Trick	Psychic	Status	—	100	10	Normal	—	—

TM & HM MOVES

Lv.	Name	Type	Kind	Pow.	Acc.	PP	Range	Long	DA
TM03	Psyshock	Psychic	Special	80	100	10	Normal	—	—
TM04	Calm Mind	Psychic	Status	—	—	20	Self	—	—
TM06	Toxic	Poison	Status	—	90	10	Normal	—	—
TM10	Hidden Power	Normal	Special	—	100	15	Normal	—	—
TM11	Sunny Day	Fire	Status	—	—	5	Both Sides	—	—
TM12	Taunt	Dark	Status	—	100	20	Normal	—	—
TM15	Hyper Beam	Normal	Special	150	90	5	Normal	—	—
TM16	Light Screen	Psychic	Status	—	—	30	Your Side	—	—
TM17	Protect	Normal	Status	—	—	10	Self	—	—
TM18	Rain Dance	Water	Status	—	—	5	Both Sides	—	—
TM19	Telekinesis	Psychic	Status	—	—	15	Normal	—	—
TM20	Safeguard	Normal	Status	—	—	25	Your Side	—	—
TM21	Frustration	Normal	Physical	—	100	20	Normal	—	○
TM27	Return	Normal	Physical	—	100	20	Normal	—	○
TM29	Psychic	Psychic	Special	90	100	10	Normal	—	—
TM30	Shadow Ball	Ghost	Special	80	100	15	Normal	—	—
TM32	Double Team	Normal	Status	—	—	15	Self	—	—
TM33	Reflect	Psychic	Status	—	—	20	Your Side	—	—
TM41	Torment	Dark	Status	—	100	15	Normal	—	—
TM42	Facade	Normal	Physical	70	100	20	Normal	—	—
TM44	Rest	Psychic	Status	—	—	10	Self	—	—
TM45	Attract	Normal	Status	—	100	15	Normal	—	—
TM46	Thief	Dark	Physical	40	100	10	Normal	—	○
TM48	Round	Normal	Special	60	100	15	Normal	—	—
TM51	Ally Switch	Psychic	Status	—	—	15	Self	—	—
TM52	Focus Blast	Fighting	Special	120	70	5	Normal	—	—
TM53	Energy Ball	Grass	Special	80	100	10	Normal	—	—
TM56	Fling	Dark	Physical	—	100	10	Normal	—	○
TM57	Charge Beam	Electric	Special	50	90	10	Normal	—	—
TM63	Embargo	Dark	Status	—	100	15	Normal	—	—
TM68	Giga Impact	Normal	Physical	150	90	5	Normal	—	—
TM70	Flash	Normal	Status	—	100	20	Normal	—	—
TM73	Thunder Wave	Electric	Status	—	100	20	Normal	—	—
TM77	Psych Up	Normal	Status	—	—	10	Self	—	—
TM85	Dream Eater	Psychic	Special	100	100	15	Normal	—	—
TM86	Grass Knot	Grass	Special	—	100	20	Normal	—	○
TM87	Swagger	Normal	Status	—	90	15	Normal	—	—

Lv.	Name	Type	Kind	Pow.	Acc.	PP	Range	Long	DA
TM90	Substitute	Normal	Status	—	—	10	Self	—	—
TM92	Trick Room	Psychic	Status	—	—	5	Both Sides	—	—

MOVES TAUGHT BY PEOPLE

Name	Type	Kind	Pow.	Acc.	PP	Range	Long	DA

MOVES TAUGHT BY MOVE TUTORS FOR SHARDS

Name	Type	Kind	Pow.	Acc.	PP	Range	Long	DA
Signal Beam	Bug	Special	75	100	15	Normal	—	○
Fire Punch	Fire	Physical	75	100	15	Normal	—	○
ThunderPunch	Electric	Physical	75	100	15	Normal	—	○
Ice Punch	Ice	Physical	75	100	15	Normal	—	○
Magic Coat	Psychic	Status	—	—	15	Self	—	—
Iron Tail	Steel	Physical	100	75	15	Normal	—	○
Zen Headbutt	Psychic	Physical	80	90	15	Normal	—	○
Foul Play	Dark	Physical	95	100	15	Normal	—	○
Gravity	Psychic	Status	—	—	5	Both Sides	—	—
Snore	Normal	Special	40	100	15	Normal	—	—
Knock Off	Dark	Physical	20	100	20	Normal	—	○
Role Play	Psychic	Status	—	—	10	Normal	—	—
Drain Punch	Fighting	Physical	75	100	10	Normal	—	○
Magic Room	Psychic	Status	—	—	10	Both Sides	—	—
Wonder Room	Psychic	Status	—	—	10	Both Sides	—	—
Recycle	Normal	Status	—	—	10	Self	—	—
Trick	Psychic	Status	—	100	10	Normal	—	—
Sleep Talk	Normal	Status	—	—	10	Self	—	—
Skill Swap	Psychic	Status	—	—	10	Normal	—	—
Snatch	Dark	Status	—	—	10	Self	—	—

066 Machop

Superpower Pokémon

TYPE Fighting

- HEIGHT: 2'07"
- WEIGHT: 43.0 lbs.
- GENDER: ♂ / ♀

Though small in stature, it is powerful enough to easily heft and throw a number of Geodude at once.

ABILITIES
- Guts
- No Guard

HIDDEN ABILITY
- Steadfast

STATS
- HP
- Attack
- Defense
- Sp. Atk
- Sp. Def
- Speed

EGG GROUPS
Human-Like

ITEMS SOMETIMES HELD
- None

Same form for ♂ / ♀

EVOLUTION

Machop — Lv. 28 → Machoke — Link Trade it → Machamp

HOW TO OBTAIN

Pokémon Black Version 2	Link Trade or Poké Transfer
Pokémon White Version 2	Link Trade or Poké Transfer

HOW TO OBTAIN FROM OTHER GAMES

Pokémon HeartGold Version	Mt. Mortar
Pokémon SoulSilver Version	Mt. Mortar

Pokémon AR Marker

LEVEL-UP AND LEARNED MOVES

Lv.	Name	Type	Kind	Pow.	Acc.	PP	Range	Long	DA
1	Low Kick	Fighting	Physical	—	100	20	Normal	—	○
1	Leer	Normal	Status	—	100	30	Many Others	—	—
7	Focus Energy	Normal	Status	—	—	30	Self	—	—
10	Karate Chop	Fighting	Physical	50	100	25	Normal	—	○
13	Low Sweep	Fighting	Physical	60	100	20	Normal	—	○
19	Foresight	Normal	Status	—	—	40	Normal	—	—
22	Seismic Toss	Fighting	Physical	—	100	20	Normal	—	○
25	Revenge	Fighting	Physical	60	100	10	Normal	—	○
31	Vital Throw	Fighting	Physical	70	—	10	Normal	—	○
34	Submission	Fighting	Physical	80	80	25	Normal	—	○
37	Wake-Up Slap	Fighting	Physical	60	100	10	Normal	—	○
43	Cross Chop	Fighting	Physical	100	80	5	Normal	—	○
46	Scary Face	Normal	Status	—	100	10	Normal	—	—
49	DynamicPunch	Fighting	Physical	100	50	5	Normal	—	○

TM & HM MOVES

Lv.	Name	Type	Kind	Pow.	Acc.	PP	Range	Long	DA
TM06	Toxic	Poison	Status	—	90	10	Normal	—	—
TM08	Bulk Up	Fighting	Status	—	—	20	Self	—	—
TM10	Hidden Power	Normal	Special	—	100	15	Normal	—	—
TM11	Sunny Day	Fire	Status	—	—	5	Both Sides	—	—
TM16	Light Screen	Psychic	Status	—	—	30	Your Side	—	—
TM17	Protect	Normal	Status	—	—	10	Self	—	—
TM18	Rain Dance	Water	Status	—	—	5	Both Sides	—	—
TM21	Frustration	Normal	Physical	—	100	20	Normal	—	○
TM23	Smack Down	Rock	Physical	50	100	15	Normal	—	—
TM26	Earthquake	Ground	Physical	100	100	10	Adjacent	—	—
TM27	Return	Normal	Physical	—	100	20	Normal	—	○
TM28	Dig	Ground	Physical	80	100	10	Normal	—	—
TM31	Brick Break	Fighting	Physical	75	100	15	Normal	—	—
TM32	Double Team	Normal	Status	—	—	15	Self	—	—
TM35	Flamethrower	Fire	Special	95	100	15	Normal	—	—
TM38	Fire Blast	Fire	Special	120	85	5	Normal	—	—
TM39	Rock Tomb	Rock	Physical	50	80	10	Normal	—	—
TM42	Facade	Normal	Physical	70	100	20	Normal	—	—
TM44	Rest	Psychic	Status	—	—	10	Self	—	—
TM45	Attract	Normal	Status	—	100	15	Normal	—	—
TM47	Low Sweep	Fighting	Physical	60	100	20	Normal	—	○
TM48	Round	Normal	Special	60	100	15	Normal	—	—
TM52	Focus Blast	Fighting	Special	120	70	5	Normal	—	—
TM56	Fling	Dark	Physical	—	100	10	Normal	—	○
TM59	Incinerate	Fire	Special	30	100	15	Many Others	—	—
TM66	Payback	Dark	Physical	50	100	10	Normal	—	○
TM67	Retaliate	Normal	Physical	70	100	5	Normal	—	—
TM78	Bulldoze	Ground	Physical	60	100	20	Adjacent	—	—
TM80	Rock Slide	Rock	Physical	75	90	10	Many Others	—	—
TM83	Work Up	Normal	Status	—	—	30	Self	—	—
TM84	Poison Jab	Poison	Physical	80	100	20	Normal	—	○
TM87	Swagger	Normal	Status	—	90	15	Normal	—	—
TM90	Substitute	Normal	Status	—	—	10	Self	—	—
TM94	Rock Smash	Fighting	Physical	40	100	15	Normal	—	○
HM04	Strength	Normal	Physical	80	100	15	Normal	—	—

MOVES TAUGHT BY PEOPLE

Name	Type	Kind	Pow.	Acc.	PP	Range	Long	DA

MOVES TAUGHT BY MOVE TUTORS FOR SHARDS

Name	Type	Kind	Pow.	Acc.	PP	Range	Long	DA
Dual Chop	Dragon	Physical	40	90	15	Normal	—	○
Low Kick	Fighting	Physical	—	100	20	Normal	—	○
Fire Punch	Fire	Physical	75	100	15	Normal	—	○
ThunderPunch	Electric	Physical	75	100	15	Normal	—	○
Ice Punch	Ice	Physical	75	100	15	Normal	—	○
Superpower	Fighting	Physical	120	100	5	Normal	—	○
Snore	Normal	Special	40	100	15	Normal	—	—
Knock Off	Dark	Physical	20	100	20	Normal	—	○
Role Play	Psychic	Status	—	—	10	Normal	—	—
Helping Hand	Normal	Status	—	—	20	1 Ally	—	—
Sleep Talk	Normal	Status	—	—	10	Self	—	—

EGG MOVES

Name	Type	Kind	Pow.	Acc.	PP	Range	Long	DA
Meditate	Psychic	Status	—	—	40	Self	—	—
Rolling Kick	Fighting	Physical	60	85	15	Normal	—	○
Encore	Normal	Status	—	100	5	Normal	—	—
SmellingSalt	Normal	Physical	60	100	10	Normal	—	—
Counter	Fighting	Physical	—	100	20	Varies	—	○
Close Combat	Fighting	Physical	120	100	5	Normal	—	○
Fire Punch	Fire	Physical	75	100	15	Normal	—	○
ThunderPunch	Electric	Physical	75	100	15	Normal	—	○
Ice Punch	Ice	Physical	75	100	15	Normal	—	○
Bullet Punch	Steel	Physical	40	100	30	Normal	—	○
Power Trick	Psychic	Status	—	—	10	Self	—	—
Heavy Slam	Steel	Physical	—	100	10	Normal	—	—
Knock Off	Dark	Physical	20	100	20	Normal	—	○
Tickle	Normal	Status	—	100	20	Normal	—	—

Superpower Pokémon

067 Machoke

- HEIGHT: 4'11"
- WEIGHT: 155.4 lbs.
- GENDER: ♂ / ♀

It happily carries heavy cargo to toughen up. It willingly does hard work for people.

Same form for ♂ / ♀

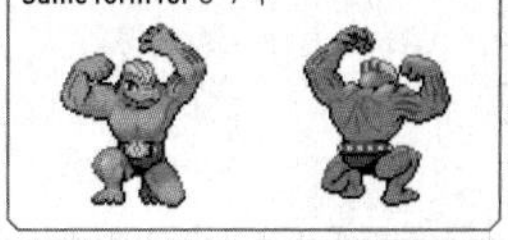

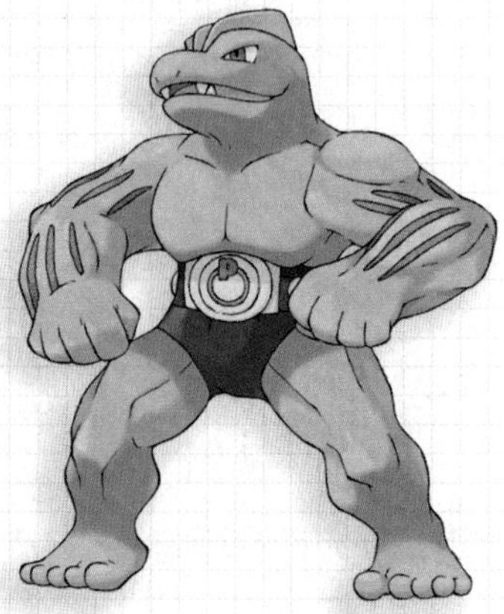

Pokémon AR Marker

TYPE Fighting

ABILITIES
- Guts
- No Guard

HIDDEN ABILITY
- Steadfast

STATS
HP
Attack
Defense
Sp. Atk
Sp. Def
Speed

EGG GROUPS
Human-Like

ITEMS SOMETIMES HELD
- None

EVOLUTION

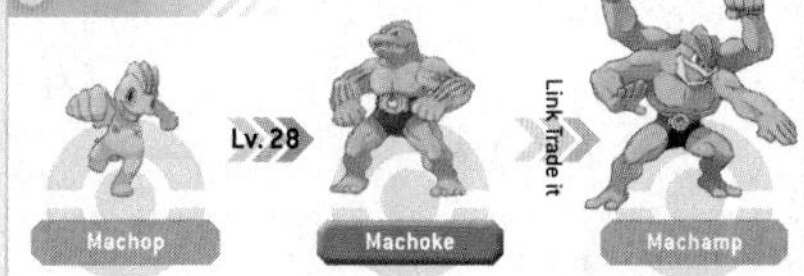

HOW TO OBTAIN

Pokémon Black Version 2	Link Trade or Poké Transfer
Pokémon White Version 2	Link Trade or Poké Transfer

HOW TO OBTAIN FROM OTHER GAMES

Pokémon HeartGold Version	Cliff Cave
Pokémon SoulSilver Version	Cliff Cave

LEVEL-UP AND LEARNED MOVES

Lv.	Name	Type	Kind	Pow.	Acc.	PP	Range	Long	DA
1	Low Kick	Fighting	Physical	—	100	20	Normal	—	○
1	Leer	Normal	Status	—	100	30	Many Others	—	—
1	Focus Energy	Normal	Status	—	—	30	Self	—	—
1	Karate Chop	Fighting	Physical	50	100	25	Normal	—	○
7	Focus Energy	Normal	Status	—	—	30	Self	—	—
10	Karate Chop	Fighting	Physical	50	100	25	Normal	—	○
13	Low Sweep	Fighting	Physical	60	100	20	Normal	—	○
19	Foresight	Normal	Status	—	—	40	Normal	—	—
22	Seismic Toss	Fighting	Physical	—	100	20	Normal	—	○
25	Revenge	Fighting	Physical	60	100	10	Normal	—	○
32	Vital Throw	Fighting	Physical	70	—	10	Normal	—	○
36	Submission	Fighting	Physical	80	80	25	Normal	—	○
40	Wake-Up Slap	Fighting	Physical	60	100	10	Normal	—	○
44	Cross Chop	Fighting	Physical	100	80	5	Normal	—	○
51	Scary Face	Normal	Status	—	100	10	Normal	—	—
55	DynamicPunch	Fighting	Physical	100	50	5	Normal	—	○

TM & HM MOVES

Lv.	Name	Type	Kind	Pow.	Acc.	PP	Range	Long	DA
TM06	Toxic	Poison	Status	—	90	10	Normal	—	—
TM08	Bulk Up	Fighting	Status	—	—	20	Self	—	—
TM10	Hidden Power	Normal	Special	—	100	15	Normal	—	—
TM11	Sunny Day	Fire	Status	—	—	5	Both Sides	—	—
TM16	Light Screen	Psychic	Status	—	—	30	Your Side	—	—
TM17	Protect	Normal	Status	—	—	10	Self	—	—
TM18	Rain Dance	Water	Status	—	—	5	Both Sides	—	—
TM21	Frustration	Normal	Physical	—	100	20	Normal	—	○
TM23	Smack Down	Rock	Physical	50	100	15	Normal	—	—
TM26	Earthquake	Ground	Physical	100	100	10	Adjacent	—	—
TM27	Return	Normal	Physical	—	100	20	Normal	—	○
TM28	Dig	Ground	Physical	80	100	10	Normal	—	○
TM31	Brick Break	Fighting	Physical	75	100	15	Normal	—	○
TM32	Double Team	Normal	Status	—	—	15	Self	—	—
TM35	Flamethrower	Fire	Special	95	100	15	Normal	—	—
TM38	Fire Blast	Fire	Special	120	85	5	Normal	—	—
TM39	Rock Tomb	Rock	Physical	50	80	10	Normal	—	—
TM42	Facade	Normal	Physical	70	100	20	Normal	—	○
TM44	Rest	Psychic	Status	—	—	10	Self	—	—
TM45	Attract	Normal	Status	—	100	15	Normal	—	—
TM46	Thief	Dark	Physical	40	100	10	Normal	—	○
TM47	Low Sweep	Fighting	Physical	60	100	20	Normal	—	○
TM48	Round	Normal	Special	60	100	15	Normal	—	—
TM52	Focus Blast	Fighting	Special	120	70	5	Normal	—	—
TM56	Fling	Dark	Physical	—	100	10	Normal	—	—
TM59	Incinerate	Fire	Special	30	100	15	Many Others	—	—
TM66	Payback	Dark	Physical	50	100	10	Normal	—	○
TM67	Retaliate	Normal	Physical	70	100	5	Normal	—	○
TM78	Bulldoze	Ground	Physical	60	100	20	Adjacent	—	—
TM80	Rock Slide	Rock	Physical	75	90	10	Many Others	—	—
TM83	Work Up	Normal	Status	—	—	30	Self	—	—
TM84	Poison Jab	Poison	Physical	80	100	20	Normal	—	○
TM87	Swagger	Normal	Status	—	90	15	Normal	—	—
TM90	Substitute	Normal	Status	—	—	10	Self	—	—
TM94	Rock Smash	Fighting	Physical	40	100	15	Normal	—	○
HM04	Strength	Normal	Physical	80	100	15	Normal	—	○

MOVES TAUGHT BY PEOPLE

Name	Type	Kind	Pow.	Acc.	PP	Range	Long	DA

MOVES TAUGHT BY MOVE TUTORS FOR SHARDS

Name	Type	Kind	Pow.	Acc.	PP	Range	Long	DA
Dual Chop	Dragon	Physical	40	90	15	Normal	—	○
Low Kick	Fighting	Physical	—	100	20	Normal	—	○
Fire Punch	Fire	Physical	75	100	15	Normal	—	○
ThunderPunch	Electric	Physical	75	100	15	Normal	—	○
Ice Punch	Ice	Physical	75	100	15	Normal	—	○
Superpower	Fighting	Physical	120	100	5	Normal	—	○
Snore	Normal	Special	40	100	15	Normal	—	—
Knock Off	Dark	Physical	20	100	20	Normal	—	○
Role Play	Psychic	Status	—	—	10	Normal	—	—
Helping Hand	Normal	Status	—	—	20	1 Ally	—	—
Sleep Talk	Normal	Status	—	—	10	Self	—	—

Superpower Pokémon

068 Machamp

- HEIGHT: 5'03"
- WEIGHT: 286.6 lbs.
- GENDER: ♂ / ♀

Its four muscled arms slam foes with powerful punches and chops at blinding speed.

Same form for ♂ / ♀

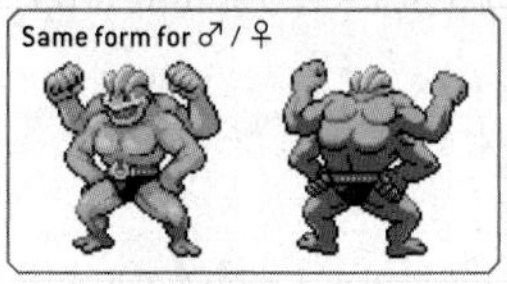

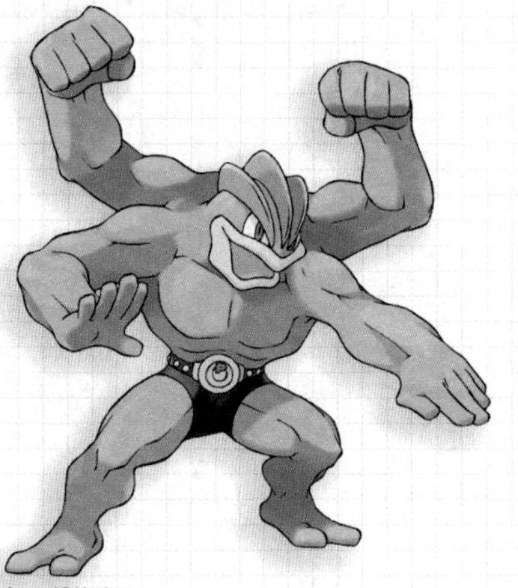

Pokémon AR Marker

TYPE Fighting

ABILITIES
- Guts
- No Guard

HIDDEN ABILITY
- Steadfast

STATS
HP
Attack
Defense
Sp. Atk
Sp. Def
Speed

EGG GROUPS
Human-Like

ITEMS SOMETIMES HELD
- None

EVOLUTION

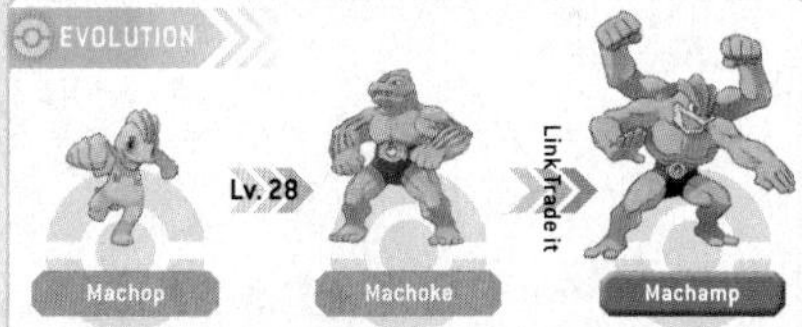

HOW TO OBTAIN

Pokémon Black Version 2	Have Machoke sent to you via Link Trade to receive Machamp
Pokémon White Version 2	Have Machoke sent to you via Link Trade to receive Machamp

HOW TO OBTAIN FROM OTHER GAMES

—
—

LEVEL-UP AND LEARNED MOVES

Lv.	Name	Type	Kind	Pow.	Acc.	PP	Range	Long	DA
1	Wide Guard	Rock	Status	—	—	10	Your Side	—	—
1	Low Kick	Fighting	Physical	—	100	20	Normal	—	○
1	Leer	Normal	Status	—	100	30	Many Others	—	—
1	Focus Energy	Normal	Status	—	—	30	Self	—	—
1	Karate Chop	Fighting	Physical	50	100	25	Normal	—	○
7	Focus Energy	Normal	Status	—	—	30	Self	—	—
10	Karate Chop	Fighting	Physical	50	100	25	Normal	—	○
13	Low Sweep	Fighting	Physical	60	100	20	Normal	—	○
19	Foresight	Normal	Status	—	—	40	Normal	—	—
22	Seismic Toss	Fighting	Physical	—	100	20	Normal	—	○
25	Revenge	Fighting	Physical	60	100	10	Normal	—	○
32	Vital Throw	Fighting	Physical	70	—	10	Normal	—	○
36	Submission	Fighting	Physical	80	80	25	Normal	—	○
40	Wake-Up Slap	Fighting	Physical	60	100	10	Normal	—	○
44	Cross Chop	Fighting	Physical	100	80	5	Normal	—	○
51	Scary Face	Normal	Status	—	100	10	Normal	—	—
55	DynamicPunch	Fighting	Physical	100	50	5	Normal	—	○

TM & HM MOVES

Lv.	Name	Type	Kind	Pow.	Acc.	PP	Range	Long	DA
TM06	Toxic	Poison	Status	—	90	10	Normal	—	—
TM08	Bulk Up	Fighting	Status	—	—	20	Self	—	—
TM10	Hidden Power	Normal	Special	—	100	15	Normal	—	—
TM11	Sunny Day	Fire	Status	—	—	5	Both Sides	—	—
TM15	Hyper Beam	Normal	Special	150	90	5	Normal	—	—
TM16	Light Screen	Psychic	Status	—	—	30	Your Side	—	—
TM17	Protect	Normal	Status	—	—	10	Self	—	—
TM18	Rain Dance	Water	Status	—	—	5	Both Sides	—	—
TM21	Frustration	Normal	Physical	—	100	20	Normal	—	○
TM23	Smack Down	Rock	Physical	50	100	15	Normal	—	—
TM26	Earthquake	Ground	Physical	100	100	10	Adjacent	—	—
TM27	Return	Normal	Physical	—	100	20	Normal	—	○
TM28	Dig	Ground	Physical	80	100	10	Normal	—	○
TM31	Brick Break	Fighting	Physical	75	100	15	Normal	—	○
TM32	Double Team	Normal	Status	—	—	15	Self	—	—
TM35	Flamethrower	Fire	Special	95	100	15	Normal	—	—
TM38	Fire Blast	Fire	Special	120	85	5	Normal	—	—
TM39	Rock Tomb	Rock	Physical	50	80	10	Normal	—	—
TM42	Facade	Normal	Physical	70	100	20	Normal	—	○
TM44	Rest	Psychic	Status	—	—	10	Self	—	—
TM45	Attract	Normal	Status	—	100	15	Normal	—	—
TM46	Thief	Dark	Physical	40	100	10	Normal	—	○
TM47	Low Sweep	Fighting	Physical	60	100	20	Normal	—	○
TM48	Round	Normal	Special	60	100	15	Normal	—	—
TM52	Focus Blast	Fighting	Special	120	70	5	Normal	—	—
TM56	Fling	Dark	Physical	—	100	10	Normal	—	—
TM59	Incinerate	Fire	Special	30	100	15	Many Others	—	—
TM66	Payback	Dark	Physical	50	100	10	Normal	—	○
TM67	Retaliate	Normal	Physical	70	100	5	Normal	—	○
TM68	Giga Impact	Normal	Physical	150	90	5	Normal	—	○
TM71	Stone Edge	Rock	Physical	100	80	5	Normal	—	—
TM78	Bulldoze	Ground	Physical	60	100	20	Adjacent	—	—
TM80	Rock Slide	Rock	Physical	75	90	10	Many Others	—	—
TM83	Work Up	Normal	Status	—	—	30	Self	—	—
TM84	Poison Jab	Poison	Physical	80	100	20	Normal	—	○
TM87	Swagger	Normal	Status	—	90	15	Normal	—	—
TM90	Substitute	Normal	Status	—	—	10	Self	—	—
TM94	Rock Smash	Fighting	Physical	40	100	15	Normal	—	○
HM04	Strength	Normal	Physical	80	100	15	Normal	—	○

MOVES TAUGHT BY PEOPLE

Name	Type	Kind	Pow.	Acc.	PP	Range	Long	DA

MOVES TAUGHT BY MOVE TUTORS FOR SHARDS

Name	Type	Kind	Pow.	Acc.	PP	Range	Long	DA
Dual Chop	Dragon	Physical	40	90	15	Normal	—	○
Low Kick	Fighting	Physical	—	100	20	Normal	—	○
Fire Punch	Fire	Physical	75	100	15	Normal	—	○
ThunderPunch	Electric	Physical	75	100	15	Normal	—	○
Ice Punch	Ice	Physical	75	100	15	Normal	—	○
Superpower	Fighting	Physical	120	100	5	Normal	—	○
Snore	Normal	Special	40	100	15	Normal	—	—
Knock Off	Dark	Physical	20	100	20	Normal	—	○
Role Play	Psychic	Status	—	—	10	Normal	—	—
Helping Hand	Normal	Status	—	—	20	1 Ally	—	—
Sleep Talk	Normal	Status	—	—	10	Self	—	—

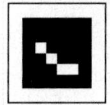

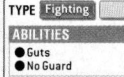

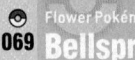

069 Bellsprout

Flower Pokémon

- HEIGHT: 2'04"
- WEIGHT: 8.8 lbs.
- GENDER: ♂ / ♀

It prefers hot and humid environments. It is quick at capturing prey with its vines.

Same form for ♂ / ♀

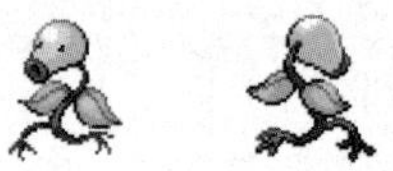

TYPE Grass Poison

ABILITY
- Chlorophyll

HIDDEN ABILITY
- Gluttony

STATS
HP
Attack
Defense
Sp. Atk
Sp. Def
Speed

EGG GROUPS
Grass

ITEMS SOMETIMES HELD
- None

EVOLUTION

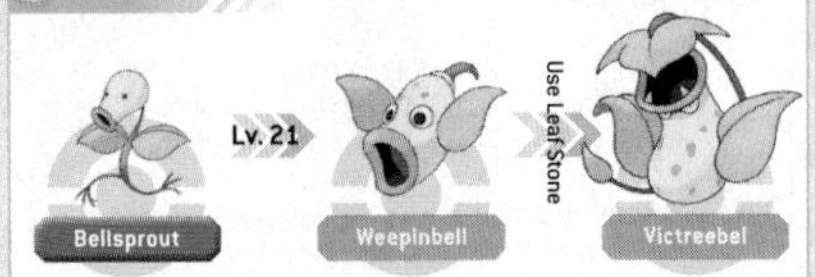
Lv. 21
Use Leaf Stone
Bellsprout
Weepinbell
Victreebel

HOW TO OBTAIN

Pokémon Black Version 2	Link Trade or Poké Transfer
Pokémon White Version 2	Link Trade or Poké Transfer

HOW TO OBTAIN FROM OTHER GAMES

Pokémon HeartGold Version	Route 31
Pokémon SoulSilver Version	Route 31

LEVEL-UP AND LEARNED MOVES

Lv.	Name	Type	Kind	Pow.	Acc.	PP	Range	Long	DA
1	Vine Whip	Grass	Physical	35	100	15	Normal	—	○
7	Growth	Normal	Status	—	—	40	Self	—	—
11	Wrap	Normal	Physical	15	90	20	Normal	—	○
13	Sleep Powder	Grass	Status	—	75	15	Normal	—	—
15	PoisonPowder	Poison	Status	—	75	35	Normal	—	—
17	Stun Spore	Grass	Status	—	75	30	Normal	—	—
23	Acid	Poison	Special	40	100	30	Many Others	—	—
27	Knock Off	Dark	Physical	20	100	20	Normal	—	○
29	Sweet Scent	Normal	Status	—	100	20	Many Others	—	—
35	Gastro Acid	Poison	Status	—	100	10	Normal	—	—
39	Razor Leaf	Grass	Physical	55	95	25	Many Others	—	—
41	Slam	Normal	Physical	80	75	20	Normal	—	○
47	Wring Out	Normal	Special	—	100	5	Normal	—	○

TM & HM MOVES

Lv.	Name	Type	Kind	Pow.	Acc.	PP	Range	Long	DA
TM06	Toxic	Poison	Status	—	90	10	Normal	—	—
TM09	Venoshock	Poison	Special	65	100	10	Normal	—	—
TM10	Hidden Power	Normal	Special	—	100	15	Normal	—	—
TM11	Sunny Day	Fire	Status	—	—	5	Both Sides	—	—
TM17	Protect	Normal	Status	—	—	10	Self	—	—
TM21	Frustration	Normal	Physical	—	100	20	Normal	—	○
TM22	SolarBeam	Grass	Special	120	100	10	Normal	—	—
TM27	Return	Normal	Physical	—	100	20	Normal	—	○
TM32	Double Team	Normal	Status	—	—	15	Self	—	—
TM33	Reflect	Psychic	Status	—	—	20	Your Side	—	—
TM36	Sludge Bomb	Poison	Special	90	100	10	Normal	—	—
TM42	Facade	Normal	Physical	70	100	20	Normal	—	○
TM44	Rest	Psychic	Status	—	—	10	Self	—	—
TM45	Attract	Normal	Status	—	100	15	Normal	—	—
TM46	Thief	Dark	Physical	40	100	10	Normal	—	○
TM48	Round	Normal	Special	60	100	15	Normal	—	—
TM53	Energy Ball	Grass	Special	80	100	10	Normal	—	—
TM70	Flash	Normal	Status	—	100	20	Normal	—	—
TM75	Swords Dance	Normal	Status	—	—	30	Self	—	—
TM86	Grass Knot	Grass	Special	—	100	20	Normal	—	○
TM87	Swagger	Normal	Status	—	90	15	Normal	—	—
TM90	Substitute	Normal	Status	—	—	10	Self	—	—
HM01	Cut	Normal	Physical	50	95	30	Normal	—	○

MOVES TAUGHT BY PEOPLE

Name	Type	Kind	Pow.	Acc.	PP	Range	Long	DA

MOVES TAUGHT BY MOVE TUTORS FOR SHARDS

Name	Type	Kind	Pow.	Acc.	PP	Range	Long	DA
Seed Bomb	Grass	Physical	80	100	15	Normal	—	—
Bind	Normal	Physical	15	85	20	Normal	—	○
Snore	Normal	Special	40	100	15	Normal	—	—
Knock Off	Dark	Physical	20	100	20	Normal	—	○
Synthesis	Grass	Status	—	—	5	Self	—	—
Giga Drain	Grass	Special	75	100	10	Normal	—	—
Worry Seed	Grass	Status	—	100	10	Normal	—	—
Gastro Acid	Poison	Status	—	100	10	Normal	—	—
Sleep Talk	Normal	Status	—	—	10	Self	—	—

EGG MOVES

Name	Type	Kind	Pow.	Acc.	PP	Range	Long	DA
Encore	Normal	Status	—	100	5	Normal	—	—
Synthesis	Grass	Status	—	—	5	Self	—	—
Leech Life	Bug	Physical	20	100	15	Normal	—	○
Ingrain	Grass	Status	—	—	20	Self	—	—
Magical Leaf	Grass	Special	60	—	20	Normal	—	—
Worry Seed	Grass	Status	—	100	10	Normal	—	—
Tickle	Normal	Status	—	100	20	Normal	—	—
Weather Ball	Normal	Special	50	100	10	Normal	—	—
Bullet Seed	Grass	Physical	25	100	30	Normal	—	—
Natural Gift	Normal	Physical	—	100	15	Normal	—	—
Giga Drain	Grass	Special	75	100	10	Normal	—	—
Clear Smog	Poison	Special	50	—	15	Normal	—	—
Power Whip	Grass	Physical	120	85	10	Normal	—	○

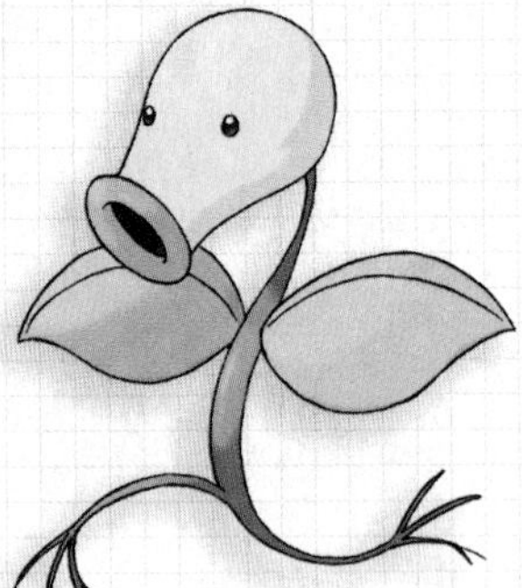

Pokémon AR Marker

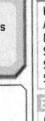

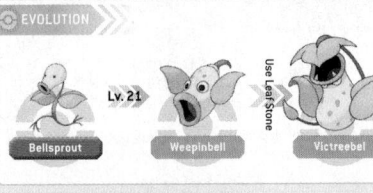

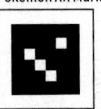

070 Weepinbell

Flycatcher Pokémon

- HEIGHT: 3'03"
- WEIGHT: 14.1 lbs.
- GENDER: ♂ / ♀

A Pokémon that appears to be a plant. It captures unwary prey by dousing them with a toxic powder.

Same form for ♂ / ♀

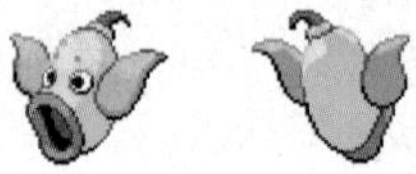

TYPE Grass Poison

ABILITY
- Chlorophyll

HIDDEN ABILITY
- Gluttony

STATS
HP
Attack
Defense
Sp. Atk
Sp. Def
Speed

EGG GROUPS
Grass

ITEMS SOMETIMES HELD
- None

EVOLUTION

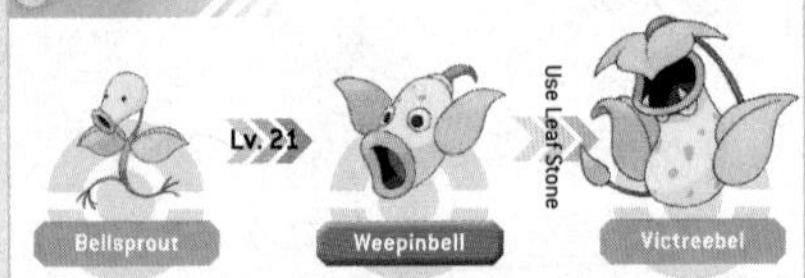
Lv. 21
Use Leaf Stone
Bellsprout
Weepinbell
Victreebel

HOW TO OBTAIN

Pokémon Black Version 2	Link Trade or Poké Transfer
Pokémon White Version 2	Link Trade or Poké Transfer

HOW TO OBTAIN FROM OTHER GAMES

Pokémon HeartGold Version	Route 44
Pokémon SoulSilver Version	Route 44

LEVEL-UP AND LEARNED MOVES

Lv.	Name	Type	Kind	Pow.	Acc.	PP	Range	Long	DA
1	Vine Whip	Grass	Physical	35	100	15	Normal	—	○
1	Growth	Normal	Status	—	—	40	Self	—	—
1	Wrap	Normal	Physical	15	90	20	Normal	—	○
7	Growth	Normal	Status	—	—	40	Self	—	—
11	Wrap	Normal	Physical	15	90	20	Normal	—	○
13	Sleep Powder	Grass	Status	—	75	15	Normal	—	—
15	PoisonPowder	Poison	Status	—	75	35	Normal	—	—
17	Stun Spore	Grass	Status	—	75	30	Normal	—	—
23	Acid	Poison	Special	40	100	30	Many Others	—	—
27	Knock Off	Dark	Physical	20	100	20	Normal	—	○
29	Sweet Scent	Normal	Status	—	100	20	Many Others	—	—
35	Gastro Acid	Poison	Status	—	100	10	Normal	—	—
39	Razor Leaf	Grass	Physical	55	95	25	Many Others	—	—
41	Slam	Normal	Physical	80	75	20	Normal	—	○
47	Wring Out	Normal	Special	—	100	5	Normal	—	○

TM & HM MOVES

Lv.	Name	Type	Kind	Pow.	Acc.	PP	Range	Long	DA
TM06	Toxic	Poison	Status	—	90	10	Normal	—	—
TM09	Venoshock	Poison	Special	65	100	10	Normal	—	—
TM10	Hidden Power	Normal	Special	—	100	15	Normal	—	—
TM11	Sunny Day	Fire	Status	—	—	5	Both Sides	—	—
TM17	Protect	Normal	Status	—	—	10	Self	—	—
TM21	Frustration	Normal	Physical	—	100	20	Normal	—	○
TM22	SolarBeam	Grass	Special	120	100	10	Normal	—	—
TM27	Return	Normal	Physical	—	100	20	Normal	—	○
TM32	Double Team	Normal	Status	—	—	15	Self	—	—
TM33	Reflect	Psychic	Status	—	—	20	Your Side	—	—
TM36	Sludge Bomb	Poison	Special	90	100	10	Normal	—	—
TM42	Facade	Normal	Physical	70	100	20	Normal	—	○
TM44	Rest	Psychic	Status	—	—	10	Self	—	—
TM45	Attract	Normal	Status	—	100	15	Normal	—	—
TM46	Thief	Dark	Physical	40	100	10	Normal	—	○
TM48	Round	Normal	Special	60	100	15	Normal	—	—
TM53	Energy Ball	Grass	Special	80	100	10	Normal	—	—
TM70	Flash	Normal	Status	—	100	20	Normal	—	—
TM75	Swords Dance	Normal	Status	—	—	30	Self	—	—
TM86	Grass Knot	Grass	Special	—	100	20	Normal	—	○
TM87	Swagger	Normal	Status	—	90	15	Normal	—	—
TM90	Substitute	Normal	Status	—	—	10	Self	—	—
HM01	Cut	Normal	Physical	50	95	30	Normal	—	○

MOVES TAUGHT BY PEOPLE

Name	Type	Kind	Pow.	Acc.	PP	Range	Long	DA

MOVES TAUGHT BY MOVE TUTORS FOR SHARDS

Name	Type	Kind	Pow.	Acc.	PP	Range	Long	DA
Bug Bite	Bug	Physical	60	100	20	Normal	—	○
Seed Bomb	Grass	Physical	80	100	15	Normal	—	—
Bind	Normal	Physical	15	85	20	Normal	—	○
Snore	Normal	Special	40	100	15	Normal	—	—
Knock Off	Dark	Physical	20	100	20	Normal	—	○
Synthesis	Grass	Status	—	—	5	Self	—	—
Giga Drain	Grass	Special	75	100	10	Normal	—	—
Worry Seed	Grass	Status	—	100	10	Normal	—	—
Gastro Acid	Poison	Status	—	100	10	Normal	—	—
Sleep Talk	Normal	Status	—	—	10	Self	—	—

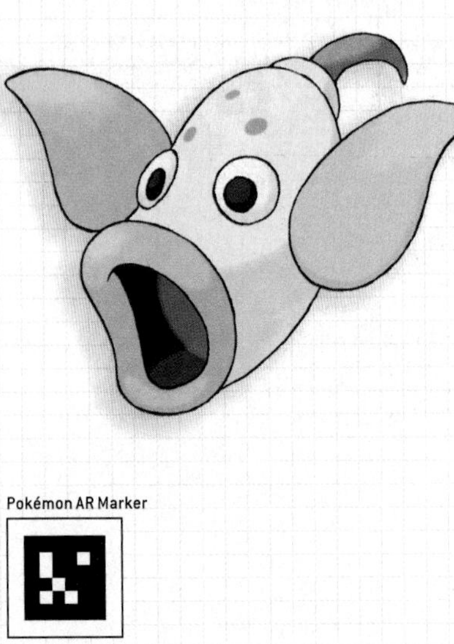

Pokémon AR Marker

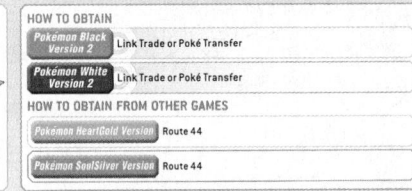

071 Victreebel
Flycatcher Pokémon

TYPE Grass Poison

ABILITY
● Chlorophyll

HIDDEN ABILITY
● Gluttony

● HEIGHT: 5'07"
● WEIGHT: 34.2 lbs.
● GENDER: ♂ / ♀

It pools in its mouth with a honey-like scent, which is really an acid that dissolves anything.

STATS
HP	
Attack	
Defense	
Sp. Atk	
Sp. Def	
Speed	

EGG GROUPS
Grass

ITEMS SOMETIMES HELD
● None

Same form for ♂ / ♀

EVOLUTION
Bellsprout → Lv. 21 → Weepinbell → Use Leaf Stone → Victreebel

HOW TO OBTAIN
Pokémon Black Version 2	Use Leaf Stone on a Weepinbell you obtain via Link Trade or Poké Transfer
Pokémon White Version 2	Use Leaf Stone on a Weepinbell you obtain via Link Trade or Poké Transfer

HOW TO OBTAIN FROM OTHER GAMES
————
————

LEVEL-UP AND LEARNED MOVES
Lv.	Name	Type	Kind	Pow.	Acc.	PP	Range	Long	DA
1	Stockpile	Normal	Status	—	—	20	Self	—	—
1	Swallow	Normal	Status	—	—	10	Self	—	—
1	Spit Up	Normal	Special	—	100	10	Normal	—	—
1	Vine Whip	Grass	Physical	35	100	15	Normal	—	○
1	Sleep Powder	Grass	Status	—	75	15	Normal	—	—
1	Sweet Scent	Normal	Status	—	100	20	Many Others	—	—
1	Razor Leaf	Grass	Physical	55	95	25	Many Others	—	—
27	Leaf Tornado	Grass	Special	65	90	10	Normal	—	—
47	Leaf Storm	Grass	Special	140	90	5	Normal	—	—
47	Leaf Blade	Grass	Physical	90	100	15	Normal	—	○

TM & HM MOVES
Lv.	Name	Type	Kind	Pow.	Acc.	PP	Range	Long	DA
TM06	Toxic	Poison	Status	—	90	10	Normal	—	—
TM09	Venoshock	Poison	Special	65	100	10	Normal	—	—
TM10	Hidden Power	Normal	Special	—	100	15	Normal	—	—
TM11	Sunny Day	Fire	Status	—	—	5	Both Sides	—	—
TM15	Hyper Beam	Normal	Special	150	90	5	Normal	—	—
TM17	Protect	Normal	Status	—	—	10	Self	—	—
TM21	Frustration	Normal	Physical	—	100	20	Normal	—	○
TM22	SolarBeam	Grass	Special	120	100	10	Normal	—	—
TM27	Return	Normal	Physical	—	100	20	Normal	—	○
TM32	Double Team	Normal	Status	—	—	15	Self	—	—
TM33	Reflect	Psychic	Status	—	—	20	Your Side	—	—
TM36	Sludge Bomb	Poison	Special	90	100	10	Normal	—	—
TM42	Facade	Normal	Physical	70	100	20	Normal	—	—
TM44	Rest	Psychic	Status	—	—	10	Self	—	—
TM45	Attract	Normal	Status	—	100	15	Normal	—	—
TM46	Thief	Dark	Physical	40	100	10	Normal	—	○
TM48	Round	Normal	Special	60	100	15	Normal	—	—
TM53	Energy Ball	Grass	Special	80	100	10	Normal	—	—
TM68	Giga Impact	Normal	Physical	150	90	5	Normal	—	○
TM70	Flash	Normal	Status	—	100	20	Normal	—	—
TM75	Swords Dance	Normal	Status	—	—	30	Self	—	—
TM86	Grass Knot	Grass	Special	—	100	20	Normal	—	○
TM87	Swagger	Normal	Status	—	90	15	Normal	—	—
TM90	Substitute	Normal	Status	—	—	10	Self	—	—
HM01	Cut	Normal	Physical	50	95	30	Normal	—	○

MOVES TAUGHT BY PEOPLE
Name	Type	Kind	Pow.	Acc.	PP	Range	Long	DA

MOVES TAUGHT BY MOVE TUTORS FOR SHARDS
Name	Type	Kind	Pow.	Acc.	PP	Range	Long	DA
Bug Bite	Bug	Physical	60	100	20	Normal	—	○
Seed Bomb	Grass	Physical	80	100	15	Normal	—	○
Bind	Normal	Physical	15	85	20	Normal	—	—
Snore	Normal	Special	40	100	15	Normal	—	—
Knock Off	Dark	Physical	20	100	20	Normal	—	○
Synthesis	Grass	Status	—	—	5	Self	—	—
Giga Drain	Grass	Special	75	100	10	Normal	—	—
Worry Seed	Grass	Status	—	100	10	Normal	—	—
Gastro Acid	Poison	Status	—	100	10	Normal	—	—
Sleep Talk	Normal	Status	—	—	10	Self	—	—

Pokémon AR Marker

---

072 Tentacool
Jellyfish Pokémon

TYPE Water Poison

ABILITIES
● Clear Body
● Liquid Ooze

HIDDEN ABILITY
● Rain Dish

● HEIGHT: 2'11"
● WEIGHT: 100.3 lbs.
● GENDER: ♂ / ♀

Because its body is almost entirely composed of water, it shrivels up if it is washed ashore.

STATS
HP	
Attack	
Defense	
Sp. Atk	
Sp. Def	
Speed	

EGG GROUPS
Water ❸

ITEMS SOMETIMES HELD
● None

Same form for ♂ / ♀

EVOLUTION
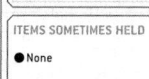
Tentacool → Lv. 30 → Tentacruel

HOW TO OBTAIN
Pokémon Black Version 2	Link Trade or Poké Transfer
Pokémon White Version 2	Link Trade or Poké Transfer

HOW TO OBTAIN FROM OTHER GAMES
Pokémon HeartGold Version	New Bark Town (water surface)
Pokémon SoulSilver Version	New Bark Town (water surface)

LEVEL-UP AND LEARNED MOVES
Lv.	Name	Type	Kind	Pow.	Acc.	PP	Range	Long	DA
1	Poison Sting	Poison	Physical	15	100	35	Normal	—	—
5	Supersonic	Normal	Status	—	55	20	Normal	—	—
8	Constrict	Normal	Physical	10	100	35	Normal	—	—
12	Acid	Poison	Special	40	100	30	Many Others	—	—
15	Toxic Spikes	Poison	Status	—	—	20	Other Side	—	—
19	BubbleBeam	Water	Special	65	100	20	Normal	—	—
22	Wrap	Normal	Physical	15	90	20	Normal	—	—
26	Acid Spray	Poison	Special	40	100	20	Normal	—	—
29	Barrier	Psychic	Status	—	—	30	Self	—	—
33	Water Pulse	Water	Special	60	100	20	Normal	○	—
36	Poison Jab	Poison	Physical	80	100	20	Normal	—	○
40	Screech	Normal	Status	—	85	40	Normal	—	—
43	Hex	Ghost	Special	50	100	10	Normal	—	—
47	Hydro Pump	Water	Special	120	80	5	Normal	—	—
50	Sludge Wave	Poison	Special	95	100	10	Adjacent	—	—
54	Wring Out	Normal	Special	—	100	5	Normal	—	—

TM & HM MOVES
Lv.	Name	Type	Kind	Pow.	Acc.	PP	Range	Long	DA
TM06	Toxic	Poison	Status	—	90	10	Normal	—	—
TM07	Hail	Ice	Status	—	—	10	Both Sides	—	—
TM09	Venoshock	Poison	Special	65	100	10	Normal	—	—
TM10	Hidden Power	Normal	Special	—	100	15	Normal	—	—
TM13	Ice Beam	Ice	Special	95	100	10	Normal	—	—
TM14	Blizzard	Ice	Special	120	70	5	Many Others	—	—
TM17	Protect	Normal	Status	—	—	10	Self	—	—
TM18	Rain Dance	Water	Status	—	—	5	Both Sides	—	—
TM20	Safeguard	Normal	Status	—	—	25	Your Side	—	—
TM21	Frustration	Normal	Physical	—	100	20	Normal	—	○
TM27	Return	Normal	Physical	—	100	20	Normal	—	○
TM32	Double Team	Normal	Status	—	—	15	Self	—	—
TM34	Sludge Wave	Poison	Special	95	100	10	Adjacent	—	—
TM36	Sludge Bomb	Poison	Special	90	100	10	Normal	—	—
TM42	Facade	Normal	Physical	70	100	20	Normal	—	—
TM44	Rest	Psychic	Status	—	—	10	Self	—	—
TM45	Attract	Normal	Status	—	100	15	Normal	—	—
TM46	Thief	Dark	Physical	40	100	10	Normal	—	○
TM48	Round	Normal	Special	60	100	15	Normal	—	—
TM55	Scald	Water	Special	80	100	15	Normal	—	—
TM66	Payback	Dark	Physical	50	100	10	Normal	—	○
TM75	Swords Dance	Normal	Status	—	—	30	Self	—	—
TM84	Poison Jab	Poison	Physical	80	100	20	Normal	—	○
TM87	Swagger	Normal	Status	—	90	15	Normal	—	—
TM90	Substitute	Normal	Status	—	—	10	Self	—	—
HM01	Cut	Normal	Physical	50	95	30	Normal	—	○
HM03	Surf	Water	Special	95	100	15	Adjacent	—	—
HM05	Waterfall	Water	Physical	80	100	15	Normal	—	○
HM06	Dive	Water	Physical	80	100	10	Normal	—	—

MOVES TAUGHT BY PEOPLE
Name	Type	Kind	Pow.	Acc.	PP	Range	Long	DA

MOVES TAUGHT BY MOVE TUTORS FOR SHARDS
Name	Type	Kind	Pow.	Acc.	PP	Range	Long	DA
Magic Coat	Psychic	Status	—	—	15	Self	—	—
Icy Wind	Ice	Special	55	95	15	Many Others	—	—
Bind	Normal	Physical	15	85	20	Normal	—	○
Snore	Normal	Special	40	100	15	Normal	—	—
Knock Off	Dark	Physical	20	100	20	Normal	—	○
Giga Drain	Grass	Special	75	100	10	Normal	—	—
Sleep Talk	Normal	Status	—	—	10	Self	—	—

EGG MOVES
Name	Type	Kind	Pow.	Acc.	PP	Range	Long	DA
Aurora Beam	Ice	Special	65	100	20	Normal	—	—
Mirror Coat	Psychic	Special	—	100	20	Varies	—	—
Rapid Spin	Normal	Physical	20	100	40	Normal	—	○
Haze	Ice	Status	—	—	30	Both Sides	—	—
Confuse Ray	Ghost	Status	—	100	10	Normal	—	—
Knock Off	Dark	Physical	20	100	20	Normal	—	○
Acupressure	Normal	Status	—	—	30	Self/Ally	—	—
Muddy Water	Water	Special	95	85	10	Many Others	—	—
Bubble	Water	Special	20	100	30	Many Others	—	—
Aqua Ring	Water	Status	—	—	20	Self	—	—
Tickle	Normal	Status	—	100	20	Normal	—	—

Pokémon AR Marker

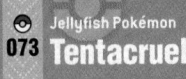

Jellyfish Pokémon

073 Tentacruel

- HEIGHT: 5'03"
- WEIGHT: 121.3 lbs.
- GENDER: ♂ / ♀

It extends its 80 tentacles to form an encircling poisonous net that is difficult to escape.

Same form for ♂ / ♀

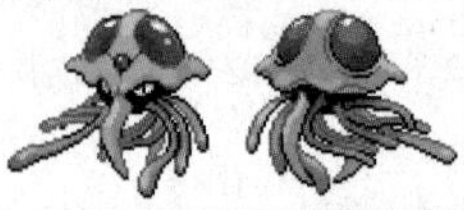

TYPE Water Poison

ABILITIES
- Clear Body
- Liquid Ooze

HIDDEN ABILITY
- Rain Dish

STATS
HP
Attack
Defense
Sp. Atk
Sp. Def
Speed

EGG GROUPS
Water ❸

ITEMS SOMETIMES HELD
- None

EVOLUTION

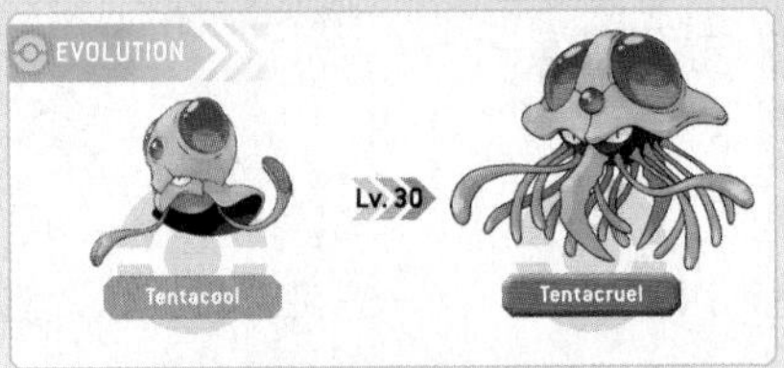

HOW TO OBTAIN

Pokémon Black Version 2	Link Trade or Poké Transfer
Pokémon White Version 2	Link Trade or Poké Transfer

HOW TO OBTAIN FROM OTHER GAMES

Pokémon HeartGold Version	New Bark Town (water surface)
Pokémon SoulSilver Version	New Bark Town (water surface)

LEVEL-UP AND LEARNED MOVES

Lv.	Name	Type	Kind	Pow.	Acc.	PP	Range	Long	DA
1	Poison Sting	Poison	Physical	15	100	35	Normal	—	—
1	Supersonic	Normal	Status	—	55	20	Normal	—	—
1	Constrict	Normal	Physical	10	100	35	Normal	—	○
5	Supersonic	Normal	Status	—	55	20	Normal	—	—
8	Constrict	Normal	Physical	10	100	35	Normal	—	○
12	Acid	Poison	Special	40	100	30	Many Others	—	—
15	Toxic Spikes	Poison	Status	—	—	20	Other Side	—	—
19	BubbleBeam	Water	Special	65	100	20	Normal	—	—
22	Wrap	Normal	Physical	15	90	20	Normal	—	○
26	Acid Spray	Poison	Special	40	100	20	Normal	—	—
29	Barrier	Psychic	Status	—	—	30	Self	—	—
34	Water Pulse	Water	Special	60	100	20	Normal	○	—
38	Poison Jab	Poison	Physical	80	100	20	Normal	—	○
43	Screech	Normal	Status	—	85	40	Normal	—	—
47	Hex	Ghost	Special	50	100	10	Normal	—	—
52	Hydro Pump	Water	Special	120	80	5	Normal	—	—
56	Sludge Wave	Poison	Special	95	100	10	Adjacent	—	—
61	Wring Out	Normal	Special	—	100	5	Normal	—	○

TM & HM MOVES

Lv.	Name	Type	Kind	Pow.	Acc.	PP	Range	Long	DA
TM06	Toxic	Poison	Status	—	90	10	Normal	—	—
TM07	Hail	Ice	Status	—	—	10	Both Sides	—	—
TM09	Venoshock	Poison	Special	65	100	10	Normal	—	—
TM10	Hidden Power	Normal	Special	—	100	15	Normal	—	—
TM13	Ice Beam	Ice	Special	95	100	10	Normal	—	—
TM14	Blizzard	Ice	Special	120	70	5	Many Others	—	—
TM15	Hyper Beam	Normal	Special	150	90	5	Normal	—	—
TM17	Protect	Normal	Status	—	—	10	Self	—	—
TM18	Rain Dance	Water	Status	—	—	5	Both Sides	—	—
TM20	Safeguard	Normal	Status	—	—	25	Your Side	—	—
TM21	Frustration	Normal	Physical	—	100	20	Normal	—	○
TM27	Return	Normal	Physical	—	100	20	Normal	—	○
TM32	Double Team	Normal	Status	—	—	15	Self	—	—
TM34	Sludge Wave	Poison	Special	95	100	10	Adjacent	—	—
TM36	Sludge Bomb	Poison	Special	90	100	10	Normal	—	—
TM42	Facade	Normal	Physical	70	100	20	Normal	—	○
TM44	Rest	Psychic	Status	—	—	10	Self	—	—
TM45	Attract	Normal	Status	—	100	15	Normal	—	—
TM46	Thief	Dark	Physical	40	100	10	Normal	—	○
TM48	Round	Normal	Special	60	100	15	Normal	—	—
TM55	Scald	Water	Special	80	100	15	Normal	—	—
TM66	Payback	Dark	Physical	50	100	10	Normal	—	○
TM68	Giga Impact	Normal	Physical	150	90	5	Normal	—	○
TM75	Swords Dance	Normal	Status	—	—	30	Self	—	—
TM84	Poison Jab	Poison	Physical	80	100	20	Normal	—	○
TM87	Swagger	Normal	Status	—	90	15	Normal	—	—
TM90	Substitute	Normal	Status	—	—	10	Self	—	—
HM01	Cut	Normal	Physical	50	95	30	Normal	—	○
HM03	Surf	Water	Special	95	100	15	Adjacent	—	—
HM05	Waterfall	Water	Physical	80	100	15	Normal	—	○
HM06	Dive	Water	Physical	80	100	10	Normal	—	○

MOVES TAUGHT BY PEOPLE

Name	Type	Kind	Pow.	Acc.	PP	Range	Long	DA

MOVES TAUGHT BY MOVE TUTORS FOR SHARDS

Name	Type	Kind	Pow.	Acc.	PP	Range	Long	DA
Magic Coat	Psychic	Status	—	—	15	Self	—	—
Icy Wind	Ice	Special	55	95	15	Many Others	—	—
Bind	Normal	Physical	15	85	20	Normal	—	○
Snore	Normal	Special	40	100	15	Normal	—	—
Knock Off	Dark	Physical	20	100	20	Normal	—	○
Giga Drain	Grass	Special	75	100	10	Normal	—	—
Sleep Talk	Normal	Status	—	—	10	Self	—	—

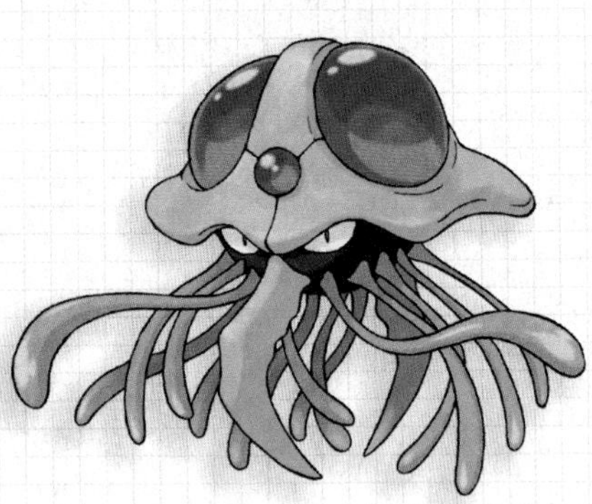

Pokémon AR Marker

Rock Pokémon

074 Geodude

- HEIGHT: 1'04"
- WEIGHT: 44.1 lbs.
- GENDER: ♂ / ♀

At rest, it looks just like a rock. Carelessly stepping on it will make it swing its fists angrily.

Same form for ♂ / ♀

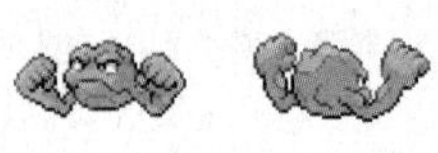

TYPE Rock Ground

ABILITIES
- Rock Head
- Sturdy

HIDDEN ABILITY
- Sand Veil

STATS
HP
Attack
Defense
Sp. Atk
Sp. Def
Speed

EGG GROUPS
Mineral

ITEMS SOMETIMES HELD
- None

EVOLUTION

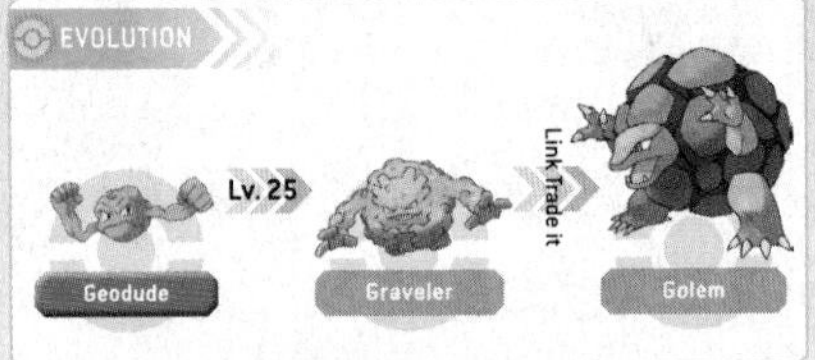

HOW TO OBTAIN

Pokémon Black Version 2	Link Trade or Poké Transfer
Pokémon White Version 2	Link Trade or Poké Transfer

HOW TO OBTAIN FROM OTHER GAMES

Pokémon HeartGold Version	Union Cave
Pokémon SoulSilver Version	Union Cave

LEVEL-UP AND LEARNED MOVES

Lv.	Name	Type	Kind	Pow.	Acc.	PP	Range	Long	DA
1	Tackle	Normal	Physical	50	100	35	Normal	—	○
1	Defense Curl	Normal	Status	—	—	40	Self	—	—
4	Mud Sport	Ground	Status	—	—	15	Both Sides	—	—
8	Rock Polish	Rock	Status	—	—	20	Self	—	—
11	Rock Throw	Rock	Physical	50	90	15	Normal	—	—
15	Magnitude	Ground	Physical	—	100	30	Adjacent	—	—
18	Rollout	Rock	Physical	30	90	20	Normal	—	○
22	Rock Blast	Rock	Physical	25	90	10	Normal	—	—
25	Smack Down	Rock	Physical	50	100	15	Normal	—	—
29	Selfdestruct	Normal	Physical	200	100	5	Adjacent	—	—
32	Bulldoze	Ground	Physical	60	100	20	Adjacent	—	—
36	Stealth Rock	Rock	Status	—	—	20	Other Side	—	—
39	Earthquake	Ground	Physical	100	100	10	Adjacent	—	—
43	Explosion	Normal	Physical	250	100	5	Adjacent	—	—
46	Double-Edge	Normal	Physical	120	100	15	Normal	—	○
50	Stone Edge	Rock	Physical	100	80	5	Normal	—	—

TM & HM MOVES

Lv.	Name	Type	Kind	Pow.	Acc.	PP	Range	Long	DA
TM06	Toxic	Poison	Status	—	90	10	Normal	—	—
TM10	Hidden Power	Normal	Special	—	100	15	Normal	—	—
TM11	Sunny Day	Fire	Status	—	—	5	Both Sides	—	—
TM17	Protect	Normal	Status	—	—	10	Self	—	—
TM21	Frustration	Normal	Physical	—	100	20	Normal	—	○
TM23	Smack Down	Rock	Physical	50	100	15	Normal	—	—
TM26	Earthquake	Ground	Physical	100	100	10	Adjacent	—	—
TM27	Return	Normal	Physical	—	100	20	Normal	—	○
TM28	Dig	Ground	Physical	80	100	10	Normal	—	○
TM31	Brick Break	Fighting	Physical	75	100	15	Normal	—	○
TM32	Double Team	Normal	Status	—	—	15	Self	—	—
TM35	Flamethrower	Fire	Special	95	100	15	Normal	—	—
TM37	Sandstorm	Rock	Status	—	—	10	Both Sides	—	—
TM38	Fire Blast	Fire	Special	120	85	5	Normal	—	—
TM39	Rock Tomb	Rock	Physical	50	80	10	Normal	—	—
TM42	Facade	Normal	Physical	70	100	20	Normal	—	○
TM44	Rest	Psychic	Status	—	—	10	Self	—	—
TM45	Attract	Normal	Status	—	100	15	Normal	—	—
TM48	Round	Normal	Special	60	100	15	Normal	—	—
TM56	Fling	Dark	Physical	—	100	10	Normal	—	—
TM59	Incinerate	Fire	Special	30	100	15	Many Others	—	—
TM64	Explosion	Normal	Physical	250	100	5	Adjacent	—	—
TM69	Rock Polish	Rock	Status	—	—	20	Self	—	—
TM71	Stone Edge	Rock	Physical	100	80	5	Normal	—	—
TM74	Gyro Ball	Steel	Physical	—	100	5	Normal	—	○
TM78	Bulldoze	Ground	Physical	60	100	20	Adjacent	—	—
TM80	Rock Slide	Rock	Physical	75	90	10	Many Others	—	—
TM87	Swagger	Normal	Status	—	90	15	Normal	—	—
TM90	Substitute	Normal	Status	—	—	10	Self	—	—
TM94	Rock Smash	Fighting	Physical	40	100	15	Normal	—	○
HM04	Strength	Normal	Physical	80	100	15	Normal	—	○

MOVES TAUGHT BY PEOPLE

Name	Type	Kind	Pow.	Acc.	PP	Range	Long	DA

MOVES TAUGHT BY MOVE TUTORS FOR SHARDS

Name	Type	Kind	Pow.	Acc.	PP	Range	Long	DA
Fire Punch	Fire	Physical	75	100	15	Normal	—	○
ThunderPunch	Electric	Physical	75	100	15	Normal	—	○
Iron Defense	Steel	Status	—	—	15	Self	—	—
Block	Normal	Status	—	—	5	Normal	—	—
Earth Power	Ground	Special	90	100	10	Normal	—	—
Superpower	Fighting	Physical	120	100	5	Normal	—	○
Snore	Normal	Special	40	100	15	Normal	—	—
Stealth Rock	Rock	Status	—	—	20	Other Side	—	—
Sleep Talk	Normal	Status	—	—	10	Self	—	—

EGG MOVES

Name	Type	Kind	Pow.	Acc.	PP	Range	Long	DA
Mega Punch	Normal	Physical	80	85	20	Normal	—	○
Block	Normal	Status	—	—	5	Normal	—	—
Hammer Arm	Fighting	Physical	100	90	10	Normal	—	○
Flail	Normal	Physical	—	100	15	Normal	—	○
Curse	Ghost	Status	—	—	10	Varies	—	—
Focus Punch	Fighting	Physical	150	100	20	Normal	—	○
Rock Climb	Normal	Physical	90	85	20	Normal	—	○
Endure	Normal	Status	—	—	10	Self	—	—
Autotomize	Steel	Status	—	—	15	Self	—	—

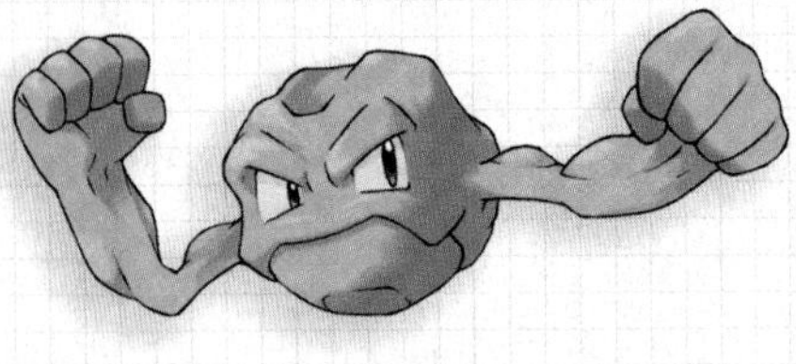

Pokémon AR Marker

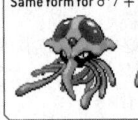

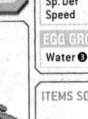

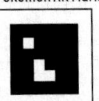

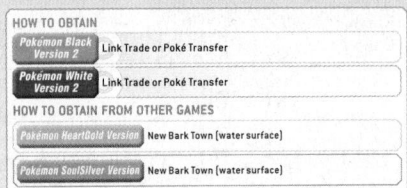

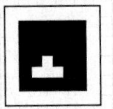

Rock Pokémon

075 Graveler

- HEIGHT: 3'03"
- WEIGHT: 231.5 lbs.
- GENDER: ♂ / ♀

It rolls on mountain paths to move. Once it builds momentum, no Pokémon can stop it without difficulty.

Same form for ♂ / ♀

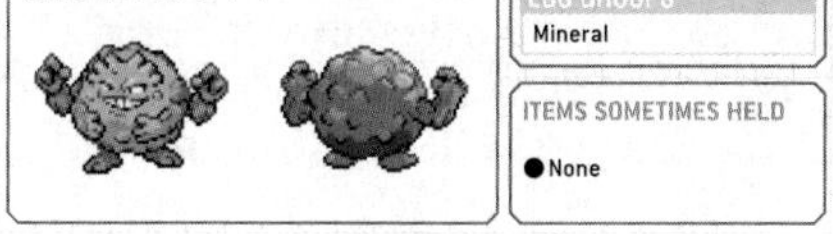

TYPE: Rock, Ground

ABILITIES
- Rock Head
- Sturdy

HIDDEN ABILITY
- Sand Veil

STATS
HP
Attack
Defense
Sp. Atk
Sp. Def
Speed

EGG GROUPS
Mineral

ITEMS SOMETIMES HELD
- None

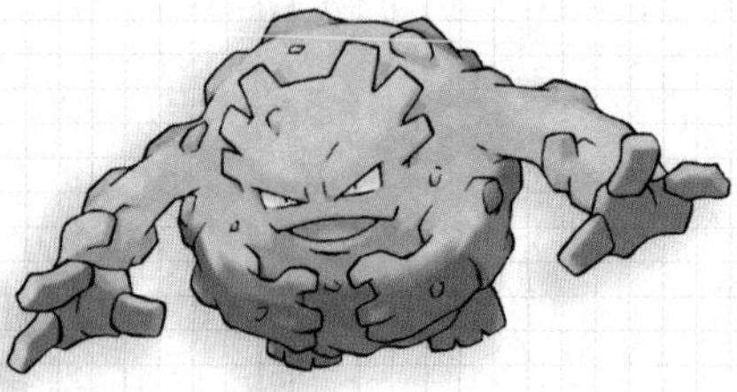

Pokémon AR Marker

EVOLUTION

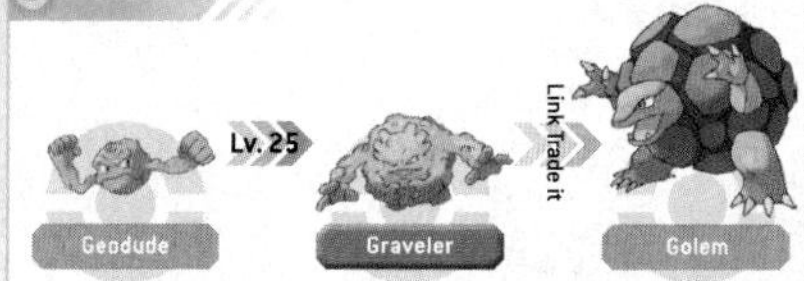

HOW TO OBTAIN

Pokémon Black Version 2	Link Trade or Poké Transfer
Pokémon White Version 2	Link Trade or Poké Transfer

HOW TO OBTAIN FROM OTHER GAMES

Pokémon Black Version	Challenger's Cave 1F
Pokémon White Version	Challenger's Cave 1F

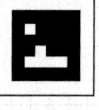

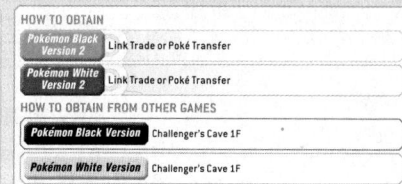

LEVEL-UP AND LEARNED MOVES

Lv.	Name	Type	Kind	Pow.	Acc.	PP	Range	Long	DA
1	Tackle	Normal	Physical	50	100	35	Normal	—	○
1	Defense Curl	Normal	Status	—	—	40	Self	—	—
1	Mud Sport	Ground	Status	—	—	15	Both Sides	—	—
1	Rock Polish	Rock	Status	—	—	20	Self	—	—
4	Mud Sport	Ground	Status	—	—	15	Both Sides	—	—
8	Rock Polish	Rock	Status	—	—	20	Self	—	—
11	Rock Throw	Rock	Physical	50	90	15	Normal	—	—
15	Magnitude	Ground	Physical	—	100	30	Adjacent	—	—
18	Rollout	Rock	Physical	30	90	20	Normal	—	○
22	Rock Blast	Rock	Physical	25	90	10	Normal	—	—
27	Smack Down	Rock	Physical	50	100	15	Normal	—	—
31	Selfdestruct	Normal	Physical	200	100	5	Adjacent	—	—
36	Bulldoze	Ground	Physical	60	100	20	Adjacent	—	—
42	Stealth Rock	Rock	Status	—	—	20	Other Side	—	—
47	Earthquake	Ground	Physical	100	100	10	Adjacent	—	—
53	Explosion	Normal	Physical	250	100	5	Adjacent	—	—
58	Double-Edge	Normal	Physical	120	100	15	Normal	—	○
64	Stone Edge	Rock	Physical	100	80	5	Normal	—	—

TM & HM MOVES

Lv.	Name	Type	Kind	Pow.	Acc.	PP	Range	Long	DA
TM06	Toxic	Poison	Status	—	90	10	Normal	—	—
TM10	Hidden Power	Normal	Special	—	100	15	Normal	—	—
TM11	Sunny Day	Fire	Status	—	—	5	Both Sides	—	—
TM17	Protect	Normal	Status	—	—	10	Self	—	—
TM21	Frustration	Normal	Physical	—	100	20	Normal	—	○
TM23	Smack Down	Rock	Physical	50	100	15	Normal	—	—
TM26	Earthquake	Ground	Physical	100	100	10	Adjacent	—	—
TM27	Return	Normal	Physical	—	100	20	Normal	—	○
TM28	Dig	Ground	Physical	80	100	10	Normal	—	○
TM31	Brick Break	Fighting	Physical	75	100	15	Normal	—	○
TM32	Double Team	Normal	Status	—	—	15	Self	—	—
TM35	Flamethrower	Fire	Special	95	100	15	Normal	—	—
TM37	Sandstorm	Rock	Status	—	—	10	Both Sides	—	—
TM38	Fire Blast	Fire	Special	120	85	5	Normal	—	—
TM39	Rock Tomb	Rock	Physical	50	80	10	Normal	—	—
TM42	Facade	Normal	Physical	70	100	20	Normal	—	○
TM44	Rest	Psychic	Status	—	—	10	Self	—	—
TM45	Attract	Normal	Status	—	100	15	Normal	—	—
TM48	Round	Normal	Special	60	100	15	Normal	—	—
TM56	Fling	Dark	Physical	—	100	10	Normal	—	—
TM59	Incinerate	Fire	Special	30	100	15	Many Others	—	—
TM64	Explosion	Normal	Physical	250	100	5	Adjacent	—	—
TM69	Rock Polish	Rock	Status	—	—	20	Self	—	—
TM71	Stone Edge	Rock	Physical	100	80	5	Normal	—	—
TM74	Gyro Ball	Steel	Physical	—	100	5	Normal	—	○
TM78	Bulldoze	Ground	Physical	60	100	20	Adjacent	—	—
TM80	Rock Slide	Rock	Physical	75	90	10	Many Others	—	—
TM87	Swagger	Normal	Status	—	90	15	Normal	—	—
TM90	Substitute	Normal	Status	—	—	10	Self	—	—
TM94	Rock Smash	Fighting	Physical	40	100	15	Normal	—	○
HM04	Strength	Normal	Physical	80	100	15	Normal	—	○

MOVES TAUGHT BY PEOPLE

Name	Type	Kind	Pow.	Acc.	PP	Range	Long	DA

MOVES TAUGHT BY MOVE TUTORS FOR SHARDS

Name	Type	Kind	Pow.	Acc.	PP	Range	Long	DA
Fire Punch	Fire	Physical	75	100	15	Normal	—	○
ThunderPunch	Electric	Physical	75	100	15	Normal	—	○
Iron Defense	Steel	Status	—	—	15	Self	—	—
Block	Normal	Status	—	—	5	Normal	—	—
Earth Power	Ground	Special	90	100	10	Normal	—	—
Superpower	Fighting	Physical	120	100	5	Normal	—	○
Snore	Normal	Special	40	100	15	Normal	—	—
Stealth Rock	Rock	Status	—	—	20	Other Side	—	—
Sleep Talk	Normal	Status	—	—	10	Self	—	—

Megaton Pokémon

076 Golem

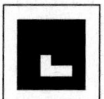

- HEIGHT: 4'07"
- WEIGHT: 661.4 lbs.
- GENDER: ♂ / ♀

Even dynamite can't harm its hard, boulder-like body. It sheds its hide just once a year.

Same form for ♂ / ♀

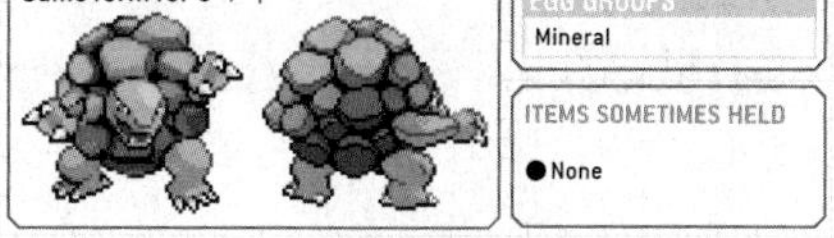

TYPE: Rock, Ground

ABILITIES
- Rock Head
- Sturdy

HIDDEN ABILITY
- Sand Veil

STATS
HP
Attack
Defense
Sp. Atk
Sp. Def
Speed

EGG GROUPS
Mineral

ITEMS SOMETIMES HELD
- None

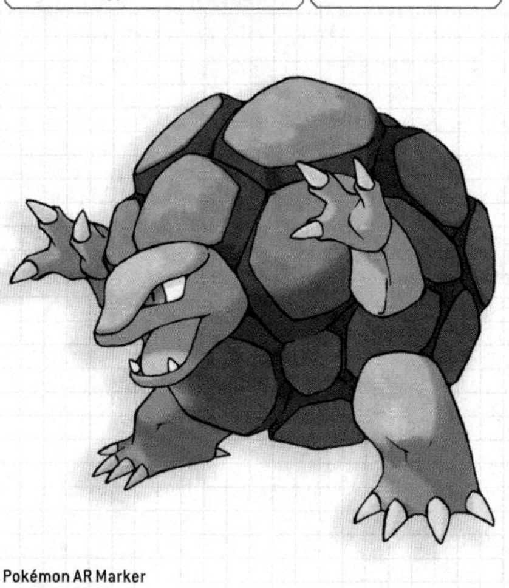

Pokémon AR Marker

EVOLUTION

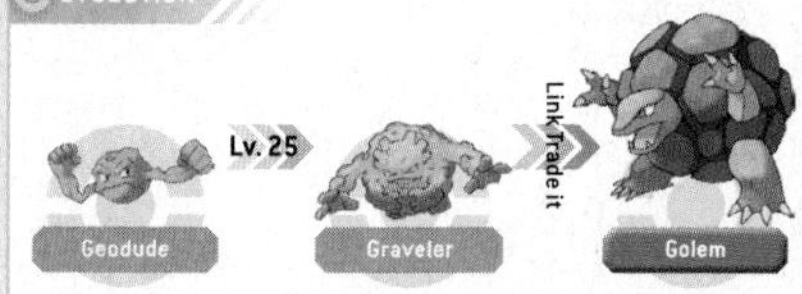

HOW TO OBTAIN

Pokémon Black Version 2	Have Graveler sent to you via Link Trade to receive Golem
Pokémon White Version 2	Have Graveler sent to you via Link Trade to receive Golem

HOW TO OBTAIN FROM OTHER GAMES

—

—

LEVEL-UP AND LEARNED MOVES

Lv.	Name	Type	Kind	Pow.	Acc.	PP	Range	Long	DA
1	Tackle	Normal	Physical	50	100	35	Normal	—	○
1	Defense Curl	Normal	Status	—	—	40	Self	—	—
1	Mud Sport	Ground	Status	—	—	15	Both Sides	—	—
1	Rock Polish	Rock	Status	—	—	20	Self	—	—
4	Mud Sport	Ground	Status	—	—	15	Both Sides	—	—
8	Rock Polish	Rock	Status	—	—	20	Self	—	—
11	Rock Throw	Rock	Physical	50	90	15	Normal	—	—
15	Magnitude	Ground	Physical	—	100	30	Adjacent	—	—
18	Steamroller	Bug	Physical	65	100	20	Normal	—	○
22	Rock Blast	Rock	Physical	25	90	10	Normal	—	—
27	Smack Down	Rock	Physical	50	100	15	Normal	—	—
31	Selfdestruct	Normal	Physical	200	100	5	Adjacent	—	—
36	Bulldoze	Ground	Physical	60	100	20	Adjacent	—	—
42	Stealth Rock	Rock	Status	—	—	20	Other Side	—	—
47	Earthquake	Ground	Physical	100	100	10	Adjacent	—	—
53	Explosion	Normal	Physical	250	100	5	Adjacent	—	—
58	Double-Edge	Normal	Physical	120	100	15	Normal	—	○
64	Stone Edge	Rock	Physical	100	80	5	Normal	—	—
69	Heavy Slam	Steel	Physical	—	100	10	Normal	—	○

TM & HM MOVES

Lv.	Name	Type	Kind	Pow.	Acc.	PP	Range	Long	DA
TM05	Roar	Normal	Status	—	100	20	Normal	—	—
TM06	Toxic	Poison	Status	—	90	10	Normal	—	—
TM10	Hidden Power	Normal	Special	—	100	15	Normal	—	—
TM11	Sunny Day	Fire	Status	—	—	5	Both Sides	—	—
TM15	Hyper Beam	Normal	Special	150	90	5	Normal	—	—
TM17	Protect	Normal	Status	—	—	10	Self	—	—
TM21	Frustration	Normal	Physical	—	100	20	Normal	—	○
TM23	Smack Down	Rock	Physical	50	100	15	Normal	—	—
TM26	Earthquake	Ground	Physical	100	100	10	Adjacent	—	—
TM27	Return	Normal	Physical	—	100	20	Normal	—	○
TM28	Dig	Ground	Physical	80	100	10	Normal	—	○
TM31	Brick Break	Fighting	Physical	75	100	15	Normal	—	○
TM32	Double Team	Normal	Status	—	—	15	Self	—	—
TM35	Flamethrower	Fire	Special	95	100	15	Normal	—	—
TM37	Sandstorm	Rock	Status	—	—	10	Both Sides	—	—
TM38	Fire Blast	Fire	Special	120	85	5	Normal	—	—
TM39	Rock Tomb	Rock	Physical	50	80	10	Normal	—	—
TM42	Facade	Normal	Physical	70	100	20	Normal	—	○
TM44	Rest	Psychic	Status	—	—	10	Self	—	—
TM45	Attract	Normal	Status	—	100	15	Normal	—	—
TM48	Round	Normal	Special	60	100	15	Normal	—	—
TM52	Focus Blast	Fighting	Special	120	70	5	Normal	—	—
TM56	Fling	Dark	Physical	—	100	10	Normal	—	—
TM59	Incinerate	Fire	Special	30	100	15	Many Others	—	—
TM64	Explosion	Normal	Physical	250	100	5	Adjacent	—	—
TM68	Giga Impact	Normal	Physical	150	90	5	Normal	—	○
TM69	Rock Polish	Rock	Status	—	—	20	Self	—	—
TM71	Stone Edge	Rock	Physical	100	80	5	Normal	—	—
TM74	Gyro Ball	Steel	Physical	—	100	5	Normal	—	○
TM78	Bulldoze	Ground	Physical	60	100	20	Adjacent	—	—
TM80	Rock Slide	Rock	Physical	75	90	10	Many Others	—	—
TM87	Swagger	Normal	Status	—	90	15	Normal	—	—
TM90	Substitute	Normal	Status	—	—	10	Self	—	—
TM94	Rock Smash	Fighting	Physical	40	100	15	Normal	—	○
HM04	Strength	Normal	Physical	80	100	15	Normal	—	○

MOVES TAUGHT BY PEOPLE

Name	Type	Kind	Pow.	Acc.	PP	Range	Long	DA

MOVES TAUGHT BY MOVE TUTORS FOR SHARDS

Name	Type	Kind	Pow.	Acc.	PP	Range	Long	DA
Iron Head	Steel	Physical	80	100	15	Normal	—	○
Fire Punch	Fire	Physical	75	100	15	Normal	—	○
ThunderPunch	Electric	Physical	75	100	15	Normal	—	○
Iron Defense	Steel	Status	—	—	15	Self	—	—
Block	Normal	Status	—	—	5	Normal	—	—
Earth Power	Ground	Special	90	100	10	Normal	—	—
Superpower	Fighting	Physical	120	100	5	Normal	—	○
Snore	Normal	Special	40	100	15	Normal	—	—
Stealth Rock	Rock	Status	—	—	20	Other Side	—	—
Sleep Talk	Normal	Status	—	—	10	Self	—	—

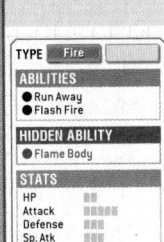

Fire Horse Pokémon
077 Ponyta

- HEIGHT: 3'03"
- WEIGHT: 66.1 lbs.
- GENDER: ♂/♀

As a newborn, it can barely stand. However, through galloping, its legs are made tougher and faster.

TYPE Fire

ABILITIES
- Run Away
- Flash Fire

HIDDEN ABILITY
- Flame Body

STATS
- HP
- Attack
- Defense
- Sp. Atk
- Sp. Def
- Speed

EGG GROUPS
Field

ITEMS SOMETIMES HELD
- None

Same form for ♂ / ♀
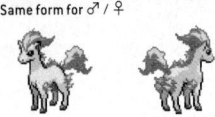

Pokémon AR Marker

EVOLUTION

Ponyta → Lv. 40 → Rapidash

HOW TO OBTAIN
| Pokémon Black Version 2 | Link Trade or Poké Transfer |
| Pokémon White Version 2 | Link Trade or Poké Transfer |

HOW TO OBTAIN FROM OTHER GAMES
| Pokémon HeartGold Version | Route 26 |
| Pokémon SoulSilver Version | Route 26 |

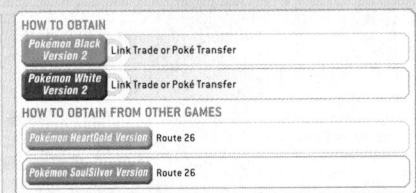

LEVEL-UP AND LEARNED MOVES
Lv.	Name	Type	Kind	Pow.	Acc.	PP	Range	Long	DA
1	Growl	Normal	Status	—	100	40	Many Others	—	—
1	Tackle	Normal	Physical	50	100	35	Normal	—	○
4	Tail Whip	Normal	Status	—	100	30	Many Others	—	—
9	Ember	Fire	Special	40	100	25	Normal	—	○
13	Flame Wheel	Fire	Physical	60	100	25	Normal	—	○
17	Stomp	Normal	Physical	65	100	20	Normal	—	○
21	Flame Charge	Fire	Physical	50	100	20	Normal	—	○
25	Fire Spin	Fire	Special	35	85	15	Normal	—	—
29	Take Down	Normal	Physical	90	85	20	Normal	—	○
33	Inferno	Fire	Special	100	50	5	Normal	—	○
37	Agility	Psychic	Status	—	—	30	Self	—	—
41	Fire Blast	Fire	Special	120	85	5	Normal	—	—
45	Bounce	Flying	Physical	85	85	5	Normal	○	○
49	Flare Blitz	Fire	Physical	120	100	15	Normal	—	○

TM & HM MOVES
Lv.	Name	Type	Kind	Pow.	Acc.	PP	Range	Long	DA
TM06	Toxic	Poison	Status	—	90	10	Normal	—	—
TM10	Hidden Power	Normal	Special	—	100	15	Normal	—	○
TM11	Sunny Day	Fire	Status	—	—	5	Both Sides	—	—
TM17	Protect	Normal	Status	—	—	10	Self	—	—
TM21	Frustration	Normal	Physical	—	100	20	Normal	—	○
TM22	SolarBeam	Grass	Special	120	100	10	Normal	—	—
TM27	Return	Normal	Physical	—	100	20	Normal	—	○
TM32	Double Team	Normal	Status	—	—	15	Self	—	—
TM35	Flamethrower	Fire	Special	95	100	15	Normal	—	—
TM38	Fire Blast	Fire	Special	120	85	5	Normal	—	—
TM42	Facade	Normal	Physical	70	100	20	Normal	—	○
TM43	Flame Charge	Fire	Physical	50	100	20	Normal	—	○
TM44	Rest	Psychic	Status	—	—	10	Self	—	—
TM45	Attract	Normal	Status	—	100	15	Normal	—	—
TM48	Round	Normal	Special	60	100	15	Normal	—	—
TM49	Echoed Voice	Normal	Special	40	100	15	Normal	—	—
TM50	Overheat	Fire	Special	140	90	5	Normal	—	—
TM59	Incinerate	Fire	Special	30	100	15	Many Others	—	—
TM61	Will-O-Wisp	Fire	Status	—	75	15	Normal	—	—
TM87	Swagger	Normal	Status	—	90	15	Normal	—	—
TM90	Substitute	Normal	Status	—	—	10	Self	—	—
TM93	Wild Charge	Electric	Physical	90	100	15	Normal	—	○
HM04	Strength	Normal	Physical	80	100	15	Normal	—	○

MOVES TAUGHT BY PEOPLE
Name	Type	Kind	Pow.	Acc.	PP	Range	Long	DA

MOVES TAUGHT BY MOVE TUTORS FOR SHARDS
Name	Type	Kind	Pow.	Acc.	PP	Range	Long	DA
Bounce	Flying	Physical	85	85	5	Normal	○	○
Low Kick	Fighting	Physical	—	100	20	Normal	—	○
Iron Tail	Steel	Physical	100	75	15	Normal	—	○
Snore	Normal	Special	40	100	15	Normal	—	—
Heat Wave	Fire	Special	100	90	10	Many Others	—	—
Sleep Talk	Normal	Status	—	—	10	Self	—	—

EGG MOVES
Name	Type	Kind	Pow.	Acc.	PP	Range	Long	DA
Flame Wheel	Fire	Physical	60	100	25	Normal	—	○
Thrash	Normal	Physical	120	100	10	1 Random	—	○
Double Kick	Fighting	Physical	30	100	30	Normal	—	○
Hypnosis	Psychic	Status	—	60	20	Normal	—	—
Charm	Normal	Status	—	100	20	Normal	—	—
Double-Edge	Normal	Physical	120	100	15	Normal	—	○
Horn Drill	Normal	Physical	—	30	5	Normal	—	○
Morning Sun	Normal	Status	—	—	5	Self	—	—
Low Kick	Fighting	Physical	—	100	20	Normal	—	○
Captivate	Normal	Status	—	100	20	Many Others	—	—

Fire Horse Pokémon
078 Rapidash

- HEIGHT: 5'07"
- WEIGHT: 209.4 lbs.
- GENDER: ♂/♀

When at an all-out gallop, its blazing mane sparkles, enhancing its beautiful appearance.

TYPE Fire

ABILITIES
- Run Away
- Flash Fire

HIDDEN ABILITY
- Flame Body

STATS
- HP
- Attack
- Defense
- Sp. Atk
- Sp. Def
- Speed

EGG GROUPS
Field

ITEMS SOMETIMES HELD
- None

Same form for ♂ / ♀

Pokémon AR Marker

EVOLUTION
Ponyta → Lv. 40 → Rapidash

HOW TO OBTAIN
| Pokémon Black Version 2 | Link Trade or Poké Transfer |
| Pokémon White Version 2 | Link Trade or Poké Transfer |

HOW TO OBTAIN FROM OTHER GAMES
| Pokémon Black Version | Route 12 |
| Pokémon White Version | Route 12 |

LEVEL-UP AND LEARNED MOVES
Lv.	Name	Type	Kind	Pow.	Acc.	PP	Range	Long	DA
1	Poison Jab	Poison	Physical	80	100	20	Normal	—	○
1	Megahorn	Bug	Physical	120	85	10	Normal	—	○
1	Growl	Normal	Status	—	100	40	Many Others	—	—
1	Quick Attack	Normal	Physical	40	100	30	Normal	—	○
1	Tail Whip	Normal	Status	—	100	30	Many Others	—	—
1	Ember	Fire	Special	40	100	25	Normal	—	○
4	Tail Whip	Normal	Status	—	100	30	Many Others	—	—
9	Ember	Fire	Special	40	100	25	Normal	—	○
13	Flame Wheel	Fire	Physical	60	100	25	Normal	—	○
17	Stomp	Normal	Physical	65	100	20	Normal	—	○
21	Flame Charge	Fire	Physical	50	100	20	Normal	—	○
25	Fire Spin	Fire	Special	35	85	15	Normal	—	—
29	Take Down	Normal	Physical	90	85	20	Normal	—	○
33	Inferno	Fire	Special	100	50	5	Normal	—	○
37	Agility	Psychic	Status	—	—	30	Self	—	—
40	Fury Attack	Normal	Physical	15	85	20	Normal	—	○
41	Fire Blast	Fire	Special	120	85	5	Normal	—	—
45	Bounce	Flying	Physical	85	85	5	Normal	○	○
49	Flare Blitz	Fire	Physical	120	100	15	Normal	—	○

TM & HM MOVES
Lv.	Name	Type	Kind	Pow.	Acc.	PP	Range	Long	DA
TM06	Toxic	Poison	Status	—	90	10	Normal	—	—
TM10	Hidden Power	Normal	Special	—	100	15	Normal	—	○
TM11	Sunny Day	Fire	Status	—	—	5	Both Sides	—	—
TM15	Hyper Beam	Normal	Special	150	90	5	Normal	—	—
TM17	Protect	Normal	Status	—	—	10	Self	—	—
TM21	Frustration	Normal	Physical	—	100	20	Normal	—	○
TM22	SolarBeam	Grass	Special	120	100	10	Normal	—	—
TM27	Return	Normal	Physical	—	100	20	Normal	—	○
TM32	Double Team	Normal	Status	—	—	15	Self	—	—
TM35	Flamethrower	Fire	Special	95	100	15	Normal	—	—
TM38	Fire Blast	Fire	Special	120	85	5	Normal	—	—
TM42	Facade	Normal	Physical	70	100	20	Normal	—	○
TM43	Flame Charge	Fire	Physical	50	100	20	Normal	—	○
TM44	Rest	Psychic	Status	—	—	10	Self	—	—
TM45	Attract	Normal	Status	—	100	15	Normal	—	—
TM48	Round	Normal	Special	60	100	15	Normal	—	—
TM49	Echoed Voice	Normal	Special	40	100	15	Normal	—	—
TM50	Overheat	Fire	Special	140	90	5	Normal	—	—
TM59	Incinerate	Fire	Special	30	100	15	Many Others	—	—
TM61	Will-O-Wisp	Fire	Status	—	75	15	Normal	—	—
TM68	Giga Impact	Normal	Physical	150	90	5	Normal	—	○
TM84	Poison Jab	Poison	Physical	80	100	20	Normal	—	○
TM87	Swagger	Normal	Status	—	90	15	Normal	—	—
TM90	Substitute	Normal	Status	—	—	10	Self	—	—
TM93	Wild Charge	Electric	Physical	90	100	15	Normal	—	○
HM04	Strength	Normal	Physical	80	100	15	Normal	—	○

MOVES TAUGHT BY PEOPLE
Name	Type	Kind	Pow.	Acc.	PP	Range	Long	DA

MOVES TAUGHT BY MOVE TUTORS FOR SHARDS
Name	Type	Kind	Pow.	Acc.	PP	Range	Long	DA
Drill Run	Ground	Physical	80	95	10	Normal	—	○
Bounce	Flying	Physical	85	85	5	Normal	○	○
Low Kick	Fighting	Physical	—	100	20	Normal	—	○
Iron Tail	Steel	Physical	100	75	15	Normal	—	○
Snore	Normal	Special	40	100	15	Normal	—	—
Heat Wave	Fire	Special	100	90	10	Many Others	—	—
Sleep Talk	Normal	Status	—	—	10	Self	—	—

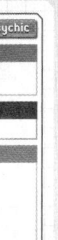

Dopey Pokémon
079 Slowpoke

- HEIGHT: 3'11"
- WEIGHT: 79.4 lbs.
- GENDER: ♂ / ♀

Although slow, it is skilled at fishing with its tail. It does not feel pain if its tail is bitten.

Same form for ♂ / ♀

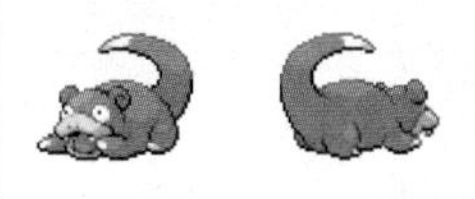

TYPE: Water / Psychic

ABILITIES
- Oblivious
- Own Tempo

HIDDEN ABILITY
- Regenerator

STATS
HP
Attack
Defense
Sp. Atk
Sp. Def
Speed

EGG GROUPS
Monster/Water ❶

ITEMS SOMETIMES HELD
- Lagging Tail

EVOLUTION

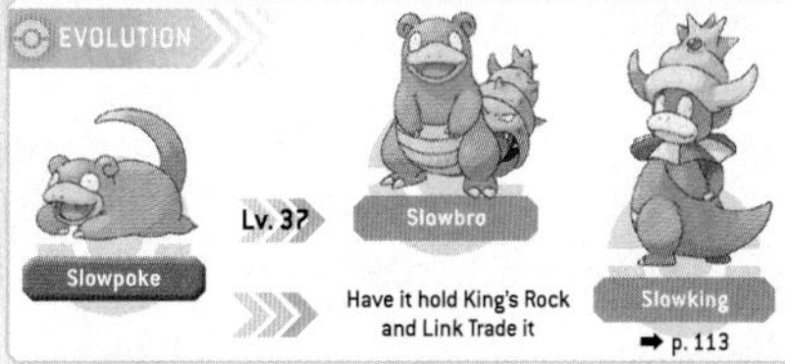
Slowpoke
Lv. 37
Slowbro
Have it hold King's Rock and Link Trade it
Slowking

➡ p. 113

HOW TO OBTAIN

Pokémon Black Version 2	Abundant Shrine (mass outbreak)
Pokémon White Version 2	Abundant Shrine (mass outbreak)

HOW TO OBTAIN FROM OTHER GAMES

—

—

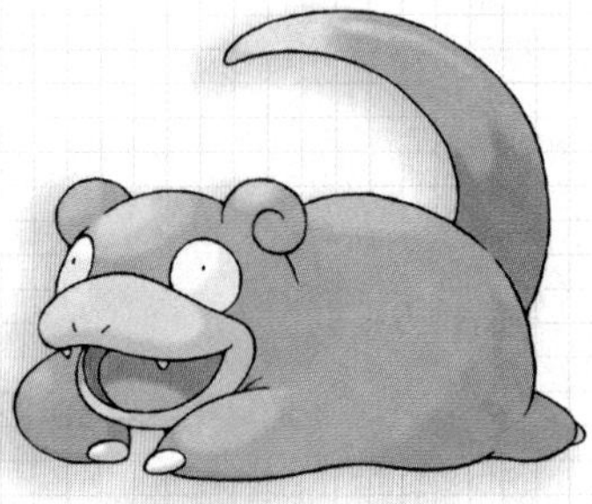

Pokémon AR Marker

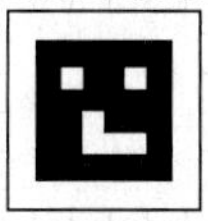

LEVEL-UP AND LEARNED MOVES

Lv.	Name	Type	Kind	Pow.	Acc.	PP	Range	Long	DA
1	Curse	Ghost	Status	—	—	10	Varies	—	—
1	Yawn	Normal	Status	—	—	10	Normal	—	—
1	Tackle	Normal	Physical	50	100	35	Normal	—	○
5	Growl	Normal	Status	—	100	40	Many Others	—	—
9	Water Gun	Water	Special	40	100	25	Normal	—	—
14	Confusion	Psychic	Special	50	100	25	Normal	—	—
19	Disable	Normal	Status	—	100	20	Normal	—	—
23	Headbutt	Normal	Physical	70	100	15	Normal	—	○
28	Water Pulse	Water	Special	60	100	20	Normal	○	—
32	Zen Headbutt	Psychic	Physical	80	90	15	Normal	—	○
36	Slack Off	Normal	Status	—	—	10	Self	—	—
41	Amnesia	Psychic	Status	—	—	20	Self	—	—
45	Psychic	Psychic	Special	90	100	10	Normal	—	—
49	Rain Dance	Water	Status	—	—	5	Both Sides	—	—
54	Psych Up	Normal	Status	—	—	10	Normal	—	—
58	Heal Pulse	Psychic	Status	—	—	10	Normal	○	—

TM & HM MOVES

Lv.	Name	Type	Kind	Pow.	Acc.	PP	Range	Long	DA
TM03	Psyshock	Psychic	Special	80	100	10	Normal	—	—
TM04	Calm Mind	Psychic	Status	—	—	20	Self	—	—
TM06	Toxic	Poison	Status	—	90	10	Normal	—	—
TM07	Hail	Ice	Status	—	—	10	Both Sides	—	—
TM10	Hidden Power	Normal	Special	—	100	15	Normal	—	—
TM11	Sunny Day	Fire	Status	—	—	5	Both Sides	—	—
TM13	Ice Beam	Ice	Special	95	100	10	Normal	—	—
TM14	Blizzard	Ice	Special	120	70	5	Many Others	—	—
TM16	Light Screen	Psychic	Status	—	—	30	Your Side	—	—
TM17	Protect	Normal	Status	—	—	10	Self	—	—
TM18	Rain Dance	Water	Status	—	—	5	Both Sides	—	—
TM19	Telekinesis	Psychic	Status	—	—	15	Normal	—	—
TM20	Safeguard	Normal	Status	—	—	25	Your Side	—	—
TM21	Frustration	Normal	Physical	—	100	20	Normal	—	○
TM26	Earthquake	Ground	Physical	100	100	10	Adjacent	—	—
TM27	Return	Normal	Physical	—	100	20	Normal	—	○
TM28	Dig	Ground	Physical	80	100	10	Normal	—	○
TM29	Psychic	Psychic	Special	90	100	10	Normal	—	—
TM30	Shadow Ball	Ghost	Special	80	100	15	Normal	—	—
TM32	Double Team	Normal	Status	—	—	15	Self	—	—
TM35	Flamethrower	Fire	Special	95	100	15	Normal	—	—
TM38	Fire Blast	Fire	Special	120	85	5	Normal	—	—
TM42	Facade	Normal	Physical	70	100	20	Normal	—	○
TM44	Rest	Psychic	Status	—	—	10	Self	—	—
TM45	Attract	Normal	Status	—	100	15	Normal	—	—
TM48	Round	Normal	Special	60	100	15	Normal	—	—
TM49	Echoed Voice	Normal	Special	40	100	15	Normal	—	—
TM55	Scald	Water	Special	80	100	15	Normal	—	—
TM59	Incinerate	Fire	Special	30	100	15	Many Others	—	—
TM70	Flash	Normal	Status	—	100	20	Normal	—	—
TM73	Thunder Wave	Electric	Status	—	100	20	Normal	—	—
TM77	Psych Up	Normal	Status	—	—	10	Normal	—	—
TM78	Bulldoze	Ground	Physical	60	100	20	Adjacent	—	—
TM85	Dream Eater	Psychic	Special	100	100	15	Normal	—	—
TM86	Grass Knot	Grass	Special	—	100	20	Normal	—	○
TM87	Swagger	Normal	Status	—	90	15	Normal	—	—
TM90	Substitute	Normal	Status	—	—	10	Self	—	—
TM92	Trick Room	Psychic	Status	—	—	5	Both Sides	—	—
HM03	Surf	Water	Special	95	100	15	Adjacent	—	—
HM04	Strength	Normal	Physical	80	100	15	Normal	—	○
HM06	Dive	Water	Physical	80	100	10	Normal	—	○

MOVES TAUGHT BY PEOPLE

Name	Type	Kind	Pow.	Acc.	PP	Range	Long	DA

MOVES TAUGHT BY MOVE TUTORS FOR SHARDS

Name	Type	Kind	Pow.	Acc.	PP	Range	Long	DA
Signal Beam	Bug	Special	75	100	15	Normal	—	—
Magic Coat	Psychic	Status	—	—	15	Self	—	—
Block	Normal	Status	—	—	5	Normal	—	—
Icy Wind	Ice	Special	55	95	15	Many Others	—	—
Iron Tail	Steel	Physical	100	75	15	Normal	—	○
Aqua Tail	Water	Physical	90	90	10	Normal	—	○
Zen Headbutt	Psychic	Physical	80	90	15	Normal	—	○
Snore	Normal	Special	40	100	15	Normal	—	—
After You	Normal	Status	—	—	15	Normal	—	—
Wonder Room	Psychic	Status	—	—	10	Both Sides	—	—
Recycle	Normal	Status	—	—	10	Self	—	—
Trick	Psychic	Status	—	100	10	Normal	—	—
Sleep Talk	Normal	Status	—	—	10	Self	—	—
Skill Swap	Psychic	Status	—	—	10	Normal	—	—

EGG MOVES

Name	Type	Kind	Pow.	Acc.	PP	Range	Long	DA
Belly Drum	Normal	Status	—	—	10	Self	—	—
Future Sight	Psychic	Special	100	100	10	Normal	—	—
Stomp	Normal	Physical	65	100	20	Normal	—	○
Mud Sport	Ground	Status	—	—	15	Both Sides	—	—
Sleep Talk	Normal	Status	—	—	10	Self	—	—
Snore	Normal	Special	40	100	15	Normal	—	—
Me First	Normal	Status	—	—	20	Varies	—	—
Block	Normal	Status	—	—	5	Normal	—	—
Zen Headbutt	Psychic	Physical	80	90	15	Normal	—	○
Wonder Room	Psychic	Status	—	—	10	Both Sides	—	—

Hermit Crab Pokémon
080 Slowbro

- HEIGHT: 5'03"
- WEIGHT: 173.1 lbs.
- GENDER: ♂ / ♀

Though usually dim witted, it seems to become inspired if the Shellder on its tail bites down.

Same form for ♂ / ♀

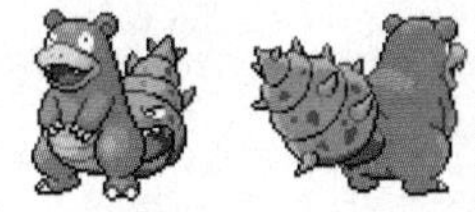

TYPE: Water / Psychic

ABILITIES
- Oblivious
- Own Tempo

HIDDEN ABILITY
- Regenerator

STATS
HP
Attack
Defense
Sp. Atk
Sp. Def
Speed

EGG GROUPS
Monster/Water ❶

ITEMS SOMETIMES HELD
- None

EVOLUTION

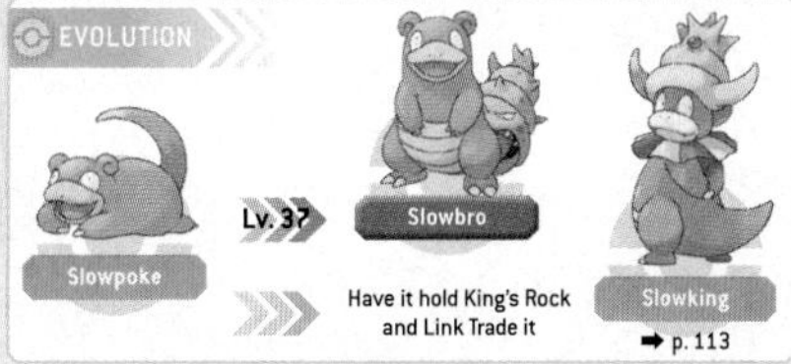
Slowpoke
Lv. 37
Slowbro
Have it hold King's Rock and Link Trade it
Slowking

➡ p. 113

HOW TO OBTAIN

Pokémon Black Version 2	Level up Slowpoke to Lv. 37
Pokémon White Version 2	Level up Slowpoke to Lv. 37

HOW TO OBTAIN FROM OTHER GAMES

—

—

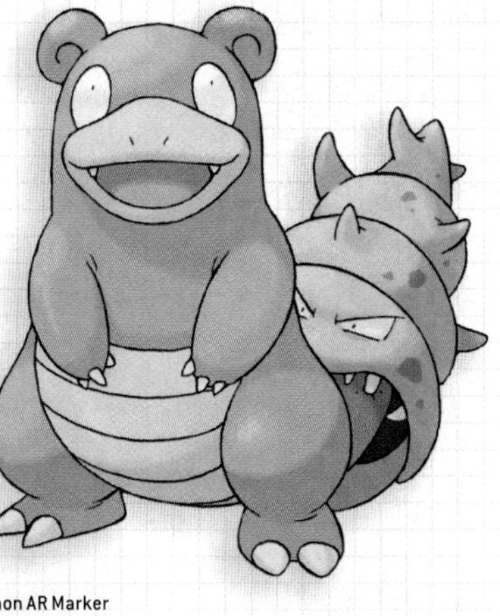

Pokémon AR Marker

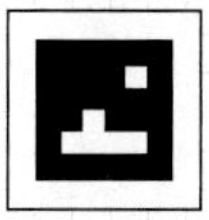

LEVEL-UP AND LEARNED MOVES

Lv.	Name	Type	Kind	Pow.	Acc.	PP	Range	Long	DA
1	Curse	Ghost	Status	—	—	10	Varies	—	—
1	Yawn	Normal	Status	—	—	10	Normal	—	—
1	Tackle	Normal	Physical	50	100	35	Normal	—	○
1	Growl	Normal	Status	—	100	40	Many Others	—	—
5	Growl	Normal	Status	—	100	40	Many Others	—	—
9	Water Gun	Water	Special	40	100	25	Normal	—	—
14	Confusion	Psychic	Special	50	100	25	Normal	—	—
19	Disable	Normal	Status	—	100	20	Normal	—	—
23	Headbutt	Normal	Physical	70	100	15	Normal	—	○
28	Water Pulse	Water	Special	60	100	20	Normal	○	—
32	Zen Headbutt	Psychic	Physical	80	90	15	Normal	—	○
36	Slack Off	Normal	Status	—	—	10	Self	—	—
37	Withdraw	Water	Status	—	—	40	Self	—	—
43	Amnesia	Psychic	Status	—	—	20	Self	—	—
49	Psychic	Psychic	Special	90	100	10	Normal	—	—
55	Rain Dance	Water	Status	—	—	5	Both Sides	—	—
62	Psych Up	Normal	Status	—	—	10	Normal	—	—
68	Heal Pulse	Psychic	Status	—	—	10	Normal	○	—

TM & HM MOVES

Lv.	Name	Type	Kind	Pow.	Acc.	PP	Range	Long	DA
TM03	Psyshock	Psychic	Special	80	100	10	Normal	—	—
TM04	Calm Mind	Psychic	Status	—	—	20	Self	—	—
TM06	Toxic	Poison	Status	—	90	10	Normal	—	—
TM07	Hail	Ice	Status	—	—	10	Both Sides	—	—
TM10	Hidden Power	Normal	Special	—	100	15	Normal	—	—
TM11	Sunny Day	Fire	Status	—	—	5	Both Sides	—	—
TM13	Ice Beam	Ice	Special	95	100	10	Normal	—	—
TM14	Blizzard	Ice	Special	120	70	5	Many Others	—	—
TM15	Hyper Beam	Normal	Special	150	90	5	Normal	—	—
TM16	Light Screen	Psychic	Status	—	—	30	Your Side	—	—
TM17	Protect	Normal	Status	—	—	10	Self	—	—
TM18	Rain Dance	Water	Status	—	—	5	Both Sides	—	—
TM19	Telekinesis	Psychic	Status	—	—	15	Normal	—	—
TM20	Safeguard	Normal	Status	—	—	25	Your Side	—	—
TM21	Frustration	Normal	Physical	—	100	20	Normal	—	○
TM26	Earthquake	Ground	Physical	100	100	10	Adjacent	—	—
TM27	Return	Normal	Physical	—	100	20	Normal	—	○
TM28	Dig	Ground	Physical	80	100	10	Normal	—	○
TM29	Psychic	Psychic	Special	90	100	10	Normal	—	—
TM30	Shadow Ball	Ghost	Special	80	100	15	Normal	—	—
TM31	Brick Break	Fighting	Physical	75	100	15	Normal	—	○
TM32	Double Team	Normal	Status	—	—	15	Self	—	—
TM35	Flamethrower	Fire	Special	95	100	15	Normal	—	—
TM38	Fire Blast	Fire	Special	120	85	5	Normal	—	—
TM40	Aerial Ace	Flying	Physical	60	—	20	Normal	○	○
TM42	Facade	Normal	Physical	70	100	20	Normal	—	○
TM44	Rest	Psychic	Status	—	—	10	Self	—	—
TM45	Attract	Normal	Status	—	100	15	Normal	—	—
TM48	Round	Normal	Special	60	100	15	Normal	—	—
TM49	Echoed Voice	Normal	Special	40	100	15	Normal	—	—
TM52	Focus Blast	Fighting	Special	120	70	5	Normal	—	—
TM55	Scald	Water	Special	80	100	15	Normal	—	—
TM56	Fling	Dark	Physical	—	100	10	Normal	—	—
TM59	Incinerate	Fire	Special	30	100	15	Many Others	—	—
TM68	Giga Impact	Normal	Physical	150	90	5	Normal	—	○
TM70	Flash	Normal	Status	—	100	20	Normal	—	—
TM73	Thunder Wave	Electric	Status	—	100	20	Normal	—	—
TM77	Psych Up	Normal	Status	—	—	10	Normal	—	—
TM78	Bulldoze	Ground	Physical	60	100	20	Adjacent	—	—
TM85	Dream Eater	Psychic	Special	100	100	15	Normal	—	—
TM86	Grass Knot	Grass	Special	—	100	20	Normal	—	○
TM87	Swagger	Normal	Status	—	90	15	Normal	—	—
TM90	Substitute	Normal	Status	—	—	10	Self	—	—
TM92	Trick Room	Psychic	Status	—	—	5	Both Sides	—	—
TM94	Rock Smash	Fighting	Physical	40	100	15	Normal	—	○
HM03	Surf	Water	Special	95	100	15	Adjacent	—	—
HM04	Strength	Normal	Physical	80	100	15	Normal	—	○
HM06	Dive	Water	Physical	80	100	10	Normal	—	○

MOVES TAUGHT BY PEOPLE

Name	Type	Kind	Pow.	Acc.	PP	Range	Long	DA

MOVES TAUGHT BY MOVE TUTORS FOR SHARDS

Name	Type	Kind	Pow.	Acc.	PP	Range	Long	DA
Signal Beam	Bug	Special	75	100	15	Normal	—	—
Ice Punch	Ice	Physical	75	100	15	Normal	—	○
Iron Defense	Steel	Status	—	—	15	Self	—	—
Magic Coat	Psychic	Status	—	—	15	Self	—	—
Block	Normal	Status	—	—	5	Normal	—	—
Icy Wind	Ice	Special	55	95	15	Many Others	—	—
Iron Tail	Steel	Physical	100	75	15	Normal	—	○
Aqua Tail	Water	Physical	90	90	10	Normal	—	○
Zen Headbutt	Psychic	Physical	80	90	15	Normal	—	○
Foul Play	Dark	Physical	95	100	15	Normal	—	○
Snore	Normal	Special	40	100	15	Normal	—	—
Drain Punch	Fighting	Physical	75	100	10	Normal	—	○
After You	Normal	Status	—	—	15	Normal	—	—
Wonder Room	Psychic	Status	—	—	10	Both Sides	—	—
Recycle	Normal	Status	—	—	10	Self	—	—
Trick	Psychic	Status	—	100	10	Normal	—	—
Sleep Talk	Normal	Status	—	—	10	Self	—	—
Skill Swap	Psychic	Status	—	—	10	Normal	—	—

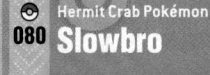

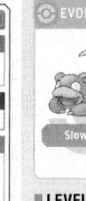

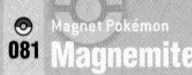

Magnet Pokémon

081 Magnemite

- HEIGHT: 1'00"
- WEIGHT: 13.2 lbs.
- GENDER: Unknown

The electromagnetic waves emitted by the units at the sides of its head expel antigravity, which allows it to float.

Gender unknown

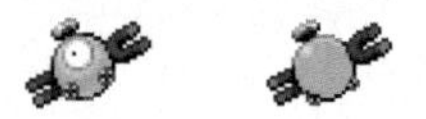

TYPE Electric Steel

ABILITIES
- Magnet Pull
- Sturdy

HIDDEN ABILITY
- Analytic

STATS
HP
Attack
Defense
Sp. Atk
Sp. Def
Speed

EGG GROUPS
Mineral

ITEMS SOMETIMES HELD
- Metal Coat

EVOLUTION

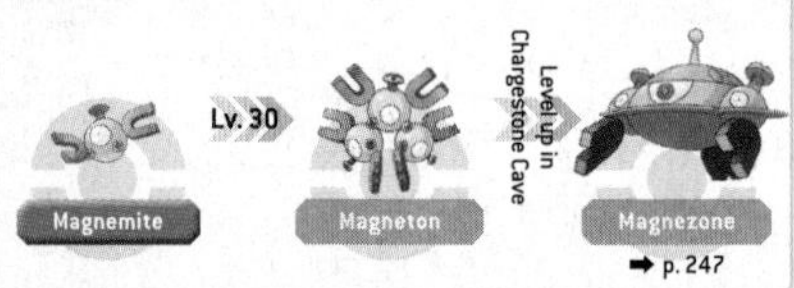
Magnemite
Lv. 30
Magneton
Level up in Chargestone Cave
Magnezone

➡ p. 247

HOW TO OBTAIN

Pokémon Black Version 2	❶ Virbank Complex entrance ❷ Virbank Complex interior
Pokémon White Version 2	❶ Virbank Complex entrance ❷ Virbank Complex interior

HOW TO OBTAIN FROM OTHER GAMES

—

—

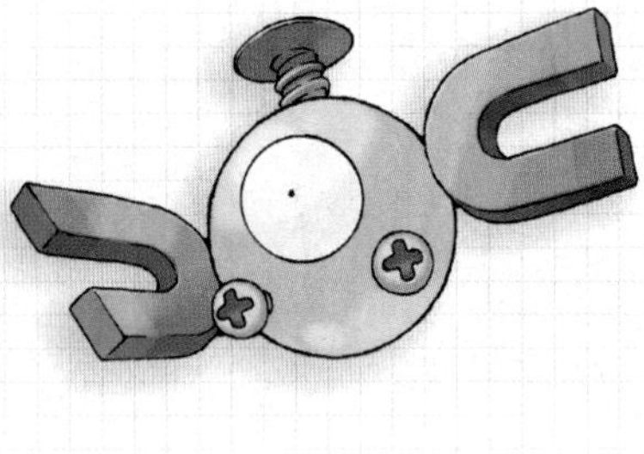

LEVEL-UP AND LEARNED MOVES

Lv.	Name	Type	Kind	Pow.	Acc.	PP	Range	Long	DA
1	Tackle	Normal	Physical	50	100	35	Normal	—	○
4	Supersonic	Normal	Status	—	55	20	Normal	—	—
7	ThunderShock	Electric	Special	40	100	30	Normal	—	—
11	SonicBoom	Normal	Special	—	90	20	Normal	—	—
15	Thunder Wave	Electric	Status	—	100	20	Normal	—	—
18	Magnet Bomb	Steel	Physical	60	—	20	Normal	—	—
21	Spark	Electric	Physical	65	100	20	Normal	—	○
25	Mirror Shot	Steel	Special	65	85	10	Normal	—	—
29	Metal Sound	Steel	Status	—	85	40	Normal	—	—
32	Electro Ball	Electric	Special	—	100	10	Normal	—	—
35	Flash Cannon	Steel	Special	80	100	10	Normal	—	—
39	Screech	Normal	Status	—	85	40	Normal	—	—
43	Discharge	Electric	Special	80	100	15	Adjacent	—	—
46	Lock-On	Normal	Status	—	—	5	Normal	—	—
49	Magnet Rise	Electric	Status	—	—	10	Self	—	—
53	Gyro Ball	Steel	Physical	—	100	5	Normal	—	○
57	Zap Cannon	Electric	Special	120	50	5	Normal	—	—

TM & HM MOVES

Lv.	Name	Type	Kind	Pow.	Acc.	PP	Range	Long	DA
TM06	Toxic	Poison	Status	—	90	10	Normal	—	—
TM10	Hidden Power	Normal	Special	—	100	15	Normal	—	—
TM11	Sunny Day	Fire	Status	—	—	5	Both Sides	—	—
TM16	Light Screen	Psychic	Status	—	—	30	Your Side	—	—
TM17	Protect	Normal	Status	—	—	10	Self	—	—
TM18	Rain Dance	Water	Status	—	—	5	Both Sides	—	—
TM21	Frustration	Normal	Physical	—	100	20	Normal	—	○
TM24	Thunderbolt	Electric	Special	95	100	15	Normal	—	—
TM25	Thunder	Electric	Special	120	70	10	Normal	—	—
TM27	Return	Normal	Physical	—	100	20	Normal	—	○
TM32	Double Team	Normal	Status	—	—	15	Self	—	—
TM33	Reflect	Psychic	Status	—	—	20	Your Side	—	—
TM42	Facade	Normal	Physical	70	100	20	Normal	—	○
TM44	Rest	Psychic	Status	—	—	10	Self	—	—
TM48	Round	Normal	Special	60	100	15	Normal	—	—
TM57	Charge Beam	Electric	Special	50	90	10	Normal	—	—
TM64	Explosion	Normal	Physical	250	100	5	Adjacent	—	—
TM70	Flash	Normal	Status	—	100	20	Normal	—	—
TM72	Volt Switch	Electric	Special	70	100	20	Normal	—	—
TM73	Thunder Wave	Electric	Status	—	100	20	Normal	—	—
TM74	Gyro Ball	Steel	Physical	—	100	5	Normal	—	○
TM77	Psych Up	Normal	Status	—	—	10	Normal	—	—
TM87	Swagger	Normal	Status	—	90	15	Normal	—	—
TM90	Substitute	Normal	Status	—	—	10	Self	—	—
TM91	Flash Cannon	Steel	Special	80	100	10	Normal	—	—
TM93	Wild Charge	Electric	Physical	90	100	15	Normal	—	○

MOVES TAUGHT BY PEOPLE

Name	Type	Kind	Pow.	Acc.	PP	Range	Long	DA

MOVES TAUGHT BY MOVE TUTORS FOR SHARDS

Name	Type	Kind	Pow.	Acc.	PP	Range	Long	DA
Signal Beam	Bug	Special	75	100	15	Normal	—	—
Iron Defense	Steel	Status	—	—	15	Self	—	—
Magnet Rise	Electric	Status	—	—	10	Self	—	—
Magic Coat	Psychic	Status	—	—	15	Self	—	—
Electroweb	Electric	Special	55	95	15	Many Others	—	—
Gravity	Psychic	Status	—	—	5	Both Sides	—	—
Snore	Normal	Special	40	100	15	Normal	—	—
Recycle	Normal	Status	—	—	10	Self	—	—
Sleep Talk	Normal	Status	—	—	10	Self	—	—

EGG MOVES

Name	Type	Kind	Pow.	Acc.	PP	Range	Long	DA

Pokémon AR Marker

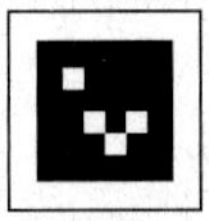

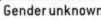

Magnet Pokémon

082 Magneton

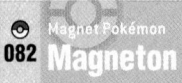

- HEIGHT: 3'03"
- WEIGHT: 132.3 lbs.
- GENDER: Unknown

The stronger electromagnetic waves from the three linked Magnemite are enough to dry out surrounding moisture.

Gender unknown

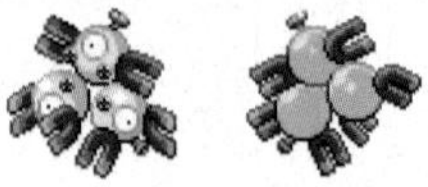

TYPE Electric Steel

ABILITIES
- Magnet Pull
- Sturdy

HIDDEN ABILITY
- Analytic

STATS
HP
Attack
Defense
Sp. Atk
Sp. Def
Speed

EGG GROUPS
Mineral

ITEMS SOMETIMES HELD
- Metal Coat

EVOLUTION

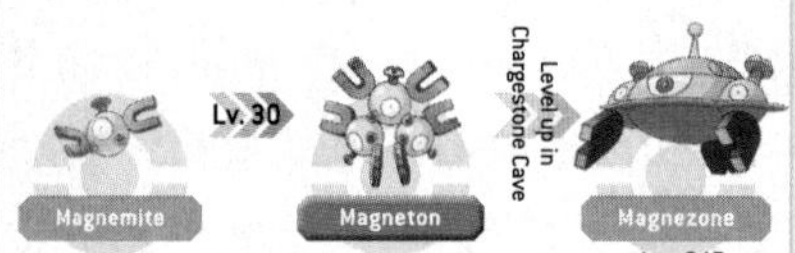
Magnemite
Lv. 30
Magneton
Level up in Chargestone Cave
Magnezone

➡ p. 247

HOW TO OBTAIN

Pokémon Black Version 2	P2 Laboratory
Pokémon White Version 2	P2 Laboratory

HOW TO OBTAIN FROM OTHER GAMES

—

—

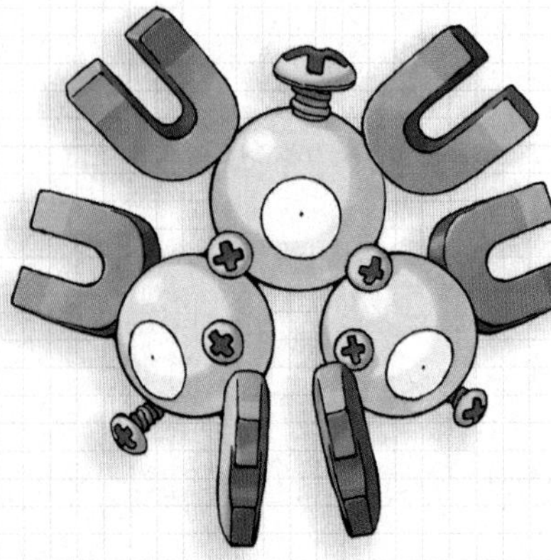

LEVEL-UP AND LEARNED MOVES

Lv.	Name	Type	Kind	Pow.	Acc.	PP	Range	Long	DA
1	Tri Attack	Normal	Special	80	100	10	Normal	—	—
1	Tackle	Normal	Physical	50	100	35	Normal	—	○
1	Supersonic	Normal	Status	—	55	20	Normal	—	—
1	ThunderShock	Electric	Special	40	100	30	Normal	—	—
1	SonicBoom	Normal	Special	—	90	20	Normal	—	—
4	Supersonic	Normal	Status	—	55	20	Normal	—	—
7	ThunderShock	Electric	Special	40	100	30	Normal	—	—
11	SonicBoom	Normal	Special	—	90	20	Normal	—	—
15	Thunder Wave	Electric	Status	—	100	20	Normal	—	—
18	Magnet Bomb	Steel	Physical	60	—	20	Normal	—	—
21	Spark	Electric	Physical	65	100	20	Normal	—	○
25	Mirror Shot	Steel	Special	65	85	10	Normal	—	—
29	Metal Sound	Steel	Status	—	85	40	Normal	—	—
34	Electro Ball	Electric	Special	—	100	10	Normal	—	—
39	Flash Cannon	Steel	Special	80	100	10	Normal	—	—
45	Screech	Normal	Status	—	85	40	Normal	—	—
51	Discharge	Electric	Special	80	100	15	Adjacent	—	—
56	Lock-On	Normal	Status	—	—	5	Normal	—	—
62	Magnet Rise	Electric	Status	—	—	10	Self	—	—
67	Gyro Ball	Steel	Physical	—	100	5	Normal	—	○
73	Zap Cannon	Electric	Special	120	50	5	Normal	—	—

TM & HM MOVES

Lv.	Name	Type	Kind	Pow.	Acc.	PP	Range	Long	DA
TM06	Toxic	Poison	Status	—	90	10	Normal	—	—
TM10	Hidden Power	Normal	Special	—	100	15	Normal	—	—
TM11	Sunny Day	Fire	Status	—	—	5	Both Sides	—	—
TM15	Hyper Beam	Normal	Special	150	90	5	Normal	—	—
TM16	Light Screen	Psychic	Status	—	—	30	Your Side	—	—
TM17	Protect	Normal	Status	—	—	10	Self	—	—
TM18	Rain Dance	Water	Status	—	—	5	Both Sides	—	—
TM21	Frustration	Normal	Physical	—	100	20	Normal	—	○
TM24	Thunderbolt	Electric	Special	95	100	15	Normal	—	—
TM25	Thunder	Electric	Special	120	70	10	Normal	—	—
TM27	Return	Normal	Physical	—	100	20	Normal	—	○
TM32	Double Team	Normal	Status	—	—	15	Self	—	—
TM33	Reflect	Psychic	Status	—	—	20	Your Side	—	—
TM42	Facade	Normal	Physical	70	100	20	Normal	—	○
TM44	Rest	Psychic	Status	—	—	10	Self	—	—
TM48	Round	Normal	Special	60	100	15	Normal	—	—
TM57	Charge Beam	Electric	Special	50	90	10	Normal	—	—
TM64	Explosion	Normal	Physical	250	100	5	Adjacent	—	—
TM68	Giga Impact	Normal	Physical	150	90	5	Normal	—	○
TM70	Flash	Normal	Status	—	100	20	Normal	—	—
TM72	Volt Switch	Electric	Special	70	100	20	Normal	—	—
TM73	Thunder Wave	Electric	Status	—	100	20	Normal	—	—
TM74	Gyro Ball	Steel	Physical	—	100	5	Normal	—	○
TM77	Psych Up	Normal	Status	—	—	10	Normal	—	—
TM87	Swagger	Normal	Status	—	90	15	Normal	—	—
TM90	Substitute	Normal	Status	—	—	10	Self	—	—
TM91	Flash Cannon	Steel	Special	80	100	10	Normal	—	—
TM93	Wild Charge	Electric	Physical	90	100	15	Normal	—	○

MOVES TAUGHT BY PEOPLE

Name	Type	Kind	Pow.	Acc.	PP	Range	Long	DA

MOVES TAUGHT BY MOVE TUTORS FOR SHARDS

Name	Type	Kind	Pow.	Acc.	PP	Range	Long	DA
Signal Beam	Bug	Special	75	100	15	Normal	—	—
Iron Defense	Steel	Status	—	—	15	Self	—	—
Magnet Rise	Electric	Status	—	—	10	Self	—	—
Magic Coat	Psychic	Status	—	—	15	Self	—	—
Electroweb	Electric	Special	55	95	15	Many Others	—	—
Gravity	Psychic	Status	—	—	5	Both Sides	—	—
Snore	Normal	Special	40	100	15	Normal	—	—
Recycle	Normal	Status	—	—	10	Self	—	—
Sleep Talk	Normal	Status	—	—	10	Self	—	—

Pokémon AR Marker

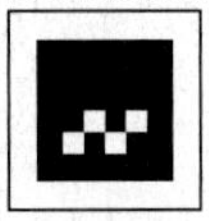

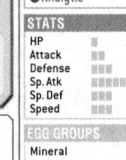

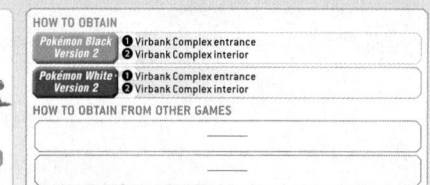

083 Farfetch'd
Wild Duck Pokémon

TYPE Normal Flying

ABILITIES
● Keen Eye
● Inner Focus

HIDDEN ABILITY
● Defiant

● HEIGHT: 2'07"
● WEIGHT: 33.1 lbs.
● GENDER: ♂ / ♀

It can't live without the stalk it holds. That's why it defends the stalk from attackers with its life.

STATS
HP
Attack
Defense
Sp. Atk
Sp. Def
Speed

EGG GROUPS
Flying/Field

ITEMS SOMETIMES HELD
● Stick

Same form for ♂ / ♀

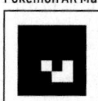

Pokémon AR Marker

EVOLUTION
Does not evolve

HOW TO OBTAIN

Pokémon Black Version 2	Route 1 (mass outbreak)
Pokémon White Version 2	Route 1 (mass outbreak)

HOW TO OBTAIN FROM OTHER GAMES

LEVEL-UP AND LEARNED MOVES

Lv.	Name	Type	Kind	Pow.	Acc.	PP	Range	Long	DA
1	Poison Jab	Poison	Physical	80	100	20	Normal	—	—
1	Peck	Flying	Physical	35	100	35	Normal	○	○
1	Sand-Attack	Ground	Status	—	100	15	Normal	—	○
1	Leer	Normal	Status	—	100	30	Many Others	—	○
1	Fury Cutter	Bug	Physical	20	95	20	Normal	—	○
7	Fury Attack	Normal	Physical	15	85	20	Normal	—	○
9	Knock Off	Dark	Physical	20	100	20	Normal	—	○
13	Aerial Ace	Flying	Physical	60	—	20	Normal	○	○
19	Slash	Normal	Physical	70	100	20	Normal	—	○
21	Air Cutter	Flying	Special	55	95	25	Many Others	○	—
25	Swords Dance	Normal	Status	—	—	30	Self	—	○
31	Agility	Psychic	Status	—	—	30	Self	—	○
33	Night Slash	Dark	Physical	70	100	15	Normal	—	○
37	Acrobatics	Flying	Physical	55	100	15	Normal	○	○
43	Feint	Normal	Physical	30	100	10	Normal	—	—
45	False Swipe	Normal	Physical	40	100	40	Normal	—	○
49	Air Slash	Flying	Special	75	95	20	Normal	○	—
55	Brave Bird	Flying	Physical	120	100	15	Normal	○	○

TM & HM MOVES

Lv.	Name	Type	Kind	Pow.	Acc.	PP	Range	Long	DA
TM06	Toxic	Poison	Status	—	90	10	Normal	—	—
TM10	Hidden Power	Normal	Special	—	100	15	Normal	—	—
TM11	Sunny Day	Fire	Status	—	—	5	Both Sides	—	—
TM17	Protect	Normal	Status	—	—	10	Self	—	—
TM21	Frustration	Normal	Physical	—	100	20	Normal	—	○
TM27	Return	Normal	Physical	—	100	20	Normal	—	○
TM32	Double Team	Normal	Status	—	—	15	Self	—	—
TM40	Aerial Ace	Flying	Physical	60	—	20	Normal	○	○
TM42	Facade	Normal	Physical	70	100	20	Normal	—	○
TM44	Rest	Psychic	Status	—	—	10	Self	—	—
TM45	Attract	Normal	Status	—	100	15	Normal	—	○
TM46	Thief	Dark	Physical	40	100	10	Normal	—	○
TM48	Round	Normal	Special	60	100	15	Normal	—	—
TM54	False Swipe	Normal	Physical	40	100	40	Normal	—	○
TM62	Acrobatics	Flying	Physical	55	100	15	Normal	○	○
TM67	Retaliate	Normal	Physical	70	100	5	Normal	—	—
TM75	Swords Dance	Normal	Status	—	—	30	Self	—	○
TM77	Psych Up	Normal	Status	—	—	10	Normal	—	—
TM83	Work Up	Normal	Status	—	—	30	Self	—	—
TM84	Poison Jab	Poison	Physical	80	100	20	Normal	—	—
TM87	Swagger	Normal	Status	—	90	15	Normal	—	○
TM88	Pluck	Flying	Physical	60	100	20	Normal	○	○
TM89	U-turn	Bug	Physical	70	100	20	Normal	—	○
TM90	Substitute	Normal	Status	—	—	10	Self	—	—
HM01	Cut	Normal	Physical	50	95	30	Normal	—	○
HM02	Fly	Flying	Physical	90	95	15	Normal	○	—

MOVES TAUGHT BY PEOPLE

Name	Type	Kind	Pow.	Acc.	PP	Range	Long	DA

MOVES TAUGHT BY MOVE TUTORS FOR SHARDS

Name	Type	Kind	Pow.	Acc.	PP	Range	Long	DA
Covet	Normal	Physical	60	100	40	Normal	—	○
Uproar	Normal	Special	90	100	10	1 Random	—	—
Last Resort	Normal	Physical	140	100	5	Normal	—	○
Iron Tail	Steel	Physical	100	75	15	Normal	—	○
Snore	Normal	Special	40	100	15	Normal	—	—
Knock Off	Dark	Physical	20	100	20	Normal	—	○
Roost	Flying	Status	—	—	10	Self	—	—
Sky Attack	Flying	Physical	140	90	5	Normal	○	—
Heat Wave	Fire	Special	100	90	10	Many Others	—	—
Tailwind	Flying	Status	—	—	30	Your Side	—	—
Helping Hand	Normal	Status	—	—	20	1 Ally	—	—
Sleep Talk	Normal	Status	—	—	10	Self	—	—

EGG MOVES

Name	Type	Kind	Pow.	Acc.	PP	Range	Long	DA
Steel Wing	Steel	Physical	70	90	25	Normal	—	○
Foresight	Normal	Status	—	—	40	Normal	—	—
Mirror Move	Flying	Status	—	—	20	Normal	—	—
Gust	Flying	Special	40	100	35	Normal	○	—
Quick Attack	Normal	Physical	40	100	30	Normal	—	○
Flail	Normal	Physical	—	100	15	Normal	—	○
FeatherDance	Flying	Status	—	100	15	Normal	—	—
Curse	Ghost	Status	—	—	10	Varies	—	—
Covet	Normal	Physical	60	100	40	Normal	—	○
Mud-Slap	Ground	Special	20	100	10	Normal	—	○
Night Slash	Dark	Physical	70	100	15	Normal	—	○
Leaf Blade	Grass	Physical	90	100	15	Normal	—	○
Revenge	Fighting	Physical	60	100	10	Normal	—	○
Roost	Flying	Status	—	—	10	Self	—	—
Trump Card	Normal	Special	—	—	5	Normal	—	○

---

084 Doduo
Twin Bird Pokémon

TYPE Normal Flying

ABILITIES
● Run Away
● Early Bird

HIDDEN ABILITY
● Tangled Feet

● HEIGHT: 4'07"
● WEIGHT: 86.4 lbs.
● GENDER: ♂ / ♀

The brains in its two heads appear to communicate emotions to each other with a telepathic power.

STATS
HP
Attack
Defense
Sp. Atk
Sp. Def
Speed

EGG GROUPS
Flying

ITEMS SOMETIMES HELD
● Sharp Beak

♂   ♀
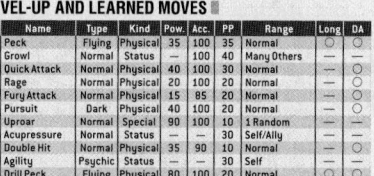

Pokémon AR Marker

EVOLUTION

Doduo — Lv. 31 → Dodrio

HOW TO OBTAIN

Pokémon Black Version 2	Route 12 (mass outbreak)
Pokémon White Version 2	Route 12 (mass outbreak)

HOW TO OBTAIN FROM OTHER GAMES

LEVEL-UP AND LEARNED MOVES

Lv.	Name	Type	Kind	Pow.	Acc.	PP	Range	Long	DA
1	Peck	Flying	Physical	35	100	35	Normal	○	○
1	Growl	Normal	Status	—	100	40	Many Others	—	○
5	Quick Attack	Normal	Physical	40	100	30	Normal	—	○
10	Rage	Normal	Physical	20	100	20	Normal	—	—
14	Fury Attack	Normal	Physical	15	85	20	Normal	—	○
19	Pursuit	Dark	Physical	40	100	20	Normal	—	○
23	Uproar	Normal	Special	90	100	10	1 Random	—	—
28	Acupressure	Normal	Status	—	—	30	Self/Ally	—	—
32	Double Hit	Normal	Physical	35	90	10	Normal	—	○
37	Agility	Psychic	Status	—	—	30	Self	—	○
41	Drill Peck	Flying	Physical	80	100	20	Normal	○	○
46	Endeavor	Normal	Physical	—	100	5	Normal	—	○
50	Thrash	Normal	Physical	120	100	10	1 Random	—	○

TM & HM MOVES

Lv.	Name	Type	Kind	Pow.	Acc.	PP	Range	Long	DA
TM06	Toxic	Poison	Status	—	90	10	Normal	—	—
TM10	Hidden Power	Normal	Special	—	100	15	Normal	—	—
TM11	Sunny Day	Fire	Status	—	—	5	Both Sides	—	—
TM17	Protect	Normal	Status	—	—	10	Self	—	—
TM21	Frustration	Normal	Physical	—	100	20	Normal	—	○
TM27	Return	Normal	Physical	—	100	20	Normal	—	○
TM32	Double Team	Normal	Status	—	—	15	Self	—	—
TM40	Aerial Ace	Flying	Physical	60	—	20	Normal	○	○
TM42	Facade	Normal	Physical	70	100	20	Normal	—	○
TM44	Rest	Psychic	Status	—	—	10	Self	—	—
TM45	Attract	Normal	Status	—	100	15	Normal	—	○
TM46	Thief	Dark	Physical	40	100	10	Normal	—	○
TM48	Round	Normal	Special	60	100	15	Normal	—	—
TM49	Echoed Voice	Normal	Special	40	100	15	Normal	—	—
TM83	Work Up	Normal	Status	—	—	30	Self	—	—
TM87	Swagger	Normal	Status	—	90	15	Normal	—	○
TM88	Pluck	Flying	Physical	60	100	20	Normal	○	○
TM90	Substitute	Normal	Status	—	—	10	Self	—	—
HM02	Fly	Flying	Physical	90	95	15	Normal	○	—

MOVES TAUGHT BY PEOPLE

Name	Type	Kind	Pow.	Acc.	PP	Range	Long	DA

MOVES TAUGHT BY MOVE TUTORS FOR SHARDS

Name	Type	Kind	Pow.	Acc.	PP	Range	Long	DA
Uproar	Normal	Special	90	100	10	1 Random	—	—
Snore	Normal	Special	40	100	15	Normal	—	—
Knock Off	Dark	Physical	20	100	20	Normal	—	○
Roost	Flying	Status	—	—	10	Self	—	—
Endeavor	Normal	Physical	—	100	5	Normal	—	○
Sleep Talk	Normal	Status	—	—	10	Self	—	—

EGG MOVES

Name	Type	Kind	Pow.	Acc.	PP	Range	Long	DA
Quick Attack	Normal	Physical	40	100	30	Normal	—	○
Supersonic	Normal	Status	—	55	20	Normal	—	—
Haze	Ice	Status	—	—	30	Both Sides	—	—
Faint Attack	Dark	Physical	60	—	20	Normal	—	○
Flail	Normal	Physical	—	100	15	Normal	—	○
Endeavor	Normal	Physical	—	100	5	Normal	—	○
Mirror Move	Flying	Status	—	—	20	Normal	—	—
Brave Bird	Flying	Physical	120	100	15	Normal	○	○
Natural Gift	Normal	Physical	—	100	15	Normal	—	—
Assurance	Dark	Physical	50	100	10	Normal	—	○

55

Triple Bird Pokémon

085 Dodrio

TYPE: Normal / Flying

ABILITIES
- Run Away
- Early Bird

HIDDEN ABILITY
- Tangled Feet

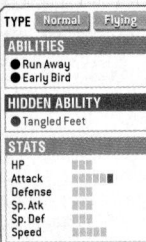

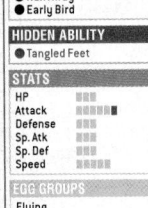

- HEIGHT: 5'11"
- WEIGHT: 187.8 lbs.
- GENDER: ♂ / ♀

When Doduo evolves into this odd breed, one of its heads splits into two. It runs at nearly 40 mph.

STATS
HP
Attack
Defense
Sp. Atk
Sp. Def
Speed

EGG GROUPS
Flying

♂ ♀

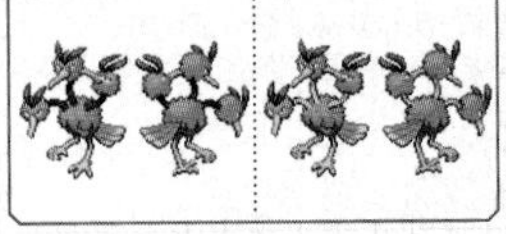

ITEMS SOMETIMES HELD
- None

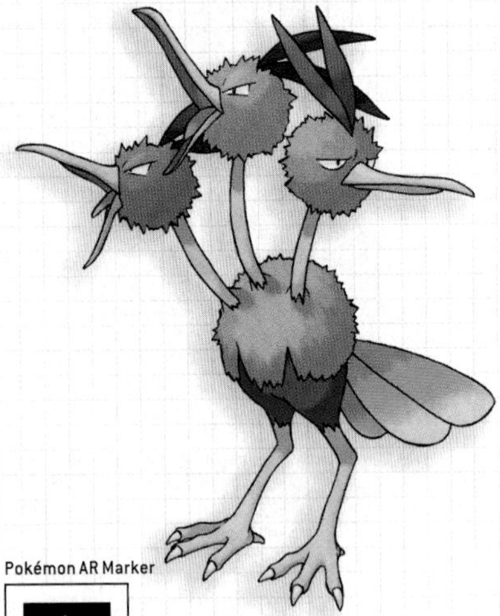

Pokémon AR Marker

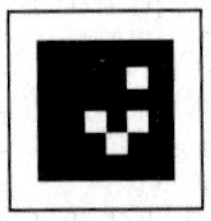

EVOLUTION

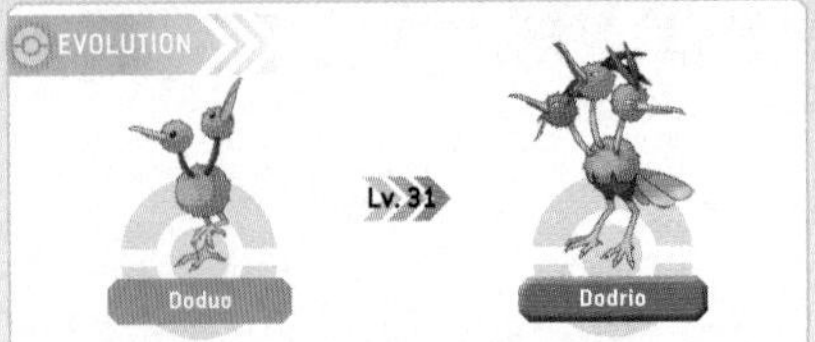
Doduo
Lv. 31
Dodrio

HOW TO OBTAIN

Pokémon Black Version 2	Level up Doduo to Lv. 31
Pokémon White Version 2	Level up Doduo to Lv. 31

HOW TO OBTAIN FROM OTHER GAMES

—

—

LEVEL-UP AND LEARNED MOVES

Lv.	Name	Type	Kind	Pow.	Acc.	PP	Range	Long	DA
1	Pluck	Flying	Physical	60	100	20	Normal	○	○
1	Peck	Flying	Physical	35	100	35	Normal	○	○
1	Growl	Normal	Status	—	100	40	Many Others	—	—
1	Quick Attack	Normal	Physical	40	100	30	Normal	—	○
1	Rage	Normal	Physical	20	100	20	Normal	—	○
5	Quick Attack	Normal	Physical	40	100	30	Normal	—	○
10	Rage	Normal	Physical	20	100	20	Normal	—	○
14	Fury Attack	Normal	Physical	15	85	20	Normal	—	○
19	Pursuit	Dark	Physical	40	100	20	Normal	—	○
23	Uproar	Normal	Special	90	100	10	1 Random	—	—
28	Acupressure	Normal	Status	—	—	30	Self/Ally	—	—
34	Tri Attack	Normal	Special	80	100	10	Normal	—	—
41	Agility	Psychic	Status	—	—	30	Self	—	—
47	Drill Peck	Flying	Physical	80	100	20	Normal	○	○
54	Endeavor	Normal	Physical	—	100	5	Normal	—	○
60	Thrash	Normal	Physical	120	100	10	1 Random	—	○

TM & HM MOVES

Lv.	Name	Type	Kind	Pow.	Acc.	PP	Range	Long	DA
TM06	Toxic	Poison	Status	—	90	10	Normal	—	—
TM10	Hidden Power	Normal	Special	—	100	15	Normal	—	—
TM11	Sunny Day	Fire	Status	—	—	5	Both Sides	—	—
TM12	Taunt	Dark	Status	—	100	20	Normal	—	—
TM15	Hyper Beam	Normal	Special	150	90	5	Normal	—	—
TM17	Protect	Normal	Status	—	—	10	Self	—	—
TM21	Frustration	Normal	Physical	—	100	20	Normal	—	○
TM27	Return	Normal	Physical	—	100	20	Normal	—	○
TM32	Double Team	Normal	Status	—	—	15	Self	—	—
TM40	Aerial Ace	Flying	Physical	60	—	20	Normal	○	○
TM41	Torment	Dark	Status	—	100	15	Normal	—	—
TM42	Facade	Normal	Physical	70	100	20	Normal	—	○
TM44	Rest	Psychic	Status	—	—	10	Self	—	—
TM45	Attract	Normal	Status	—	100	15	Normal	—	—
TM46	Thief	Dark	Physical	40	100	10	Normal	—	○
TM48	Round	Normal	Special	60	100	15	Normal	—	—
TM49	Echoed Voice	Normal	Special	40	100	15	Normal	—	—
TM66	Payback	Dark	Physical	50	100	10	Normal	—	○
TM68	Giga Impact	Normal	Physical	150	90	5	Normal	—	○
TM83	Work Up	Normal	Status	—	—	30	Self	—	—
TM87	Swagger	Normal	Status	—	90	15	Normal	—	—
TM88	Pluck	Flying	Physical	60	100	20	Normal	○	○
TM90	Substitute	Normal	Status	—	—	10	Self	—	—
HM02	Fly	Flying	Physical	90	95	15	Normal	○	○

MOVES TAUGHT BY PEOPLE

Name	Type	Kind	Pow.	Acc.	PP	Range	Long	DA

MOVES TAUGHT BY MOVE TUTORS FOR SHARDS

Name	Type	Kind	Pow.	Acc.	PP	Range	Long	DA
Uproar	Normal	Special	90	100	10	1 Random	—	—
Snore	Normal	Special	40	100	15	Normal	—	—
Knock Off	Dark	Physical	20	100	20	Normal	—	○
Roost	Flying	Status	—	—	10	Self	—	—
Sky Attack	Flying	Physical	140	90	5	Normal	○	—
Endeavor	Normal	Physical	—	100	5	Normal	—	○
Sleep Talk	Normal	Status	—	—	10	Self	—	—

Sea Lion Pokémon

086 Seel

TYPE: Water

ABILITIES
- Thick Fat
- Hydration

HIDDEN ABILITY
- Ice Body

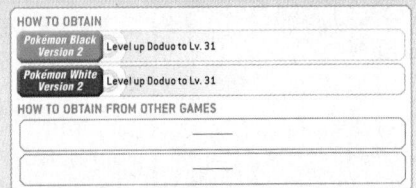

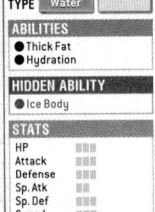

- HEIGHT: 3'07"
- WEIGHT: 198.4 lbs.
- GENDER: ♂ / ♀

The colder it gets, the better it feels. It joyfully swims around oceans so cold that they are filled with floating ice.

STATS
HP
Attack
Defense
Sp. Atk
Sp. Def
Speed

EGG GROUPS
Water ❶/Field

Same form for ♂ / ♀

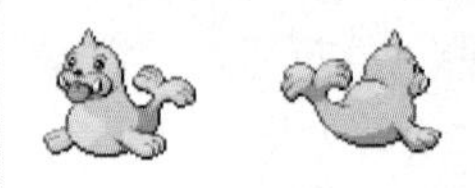

ITEMS SOMETIMES HELD
- None

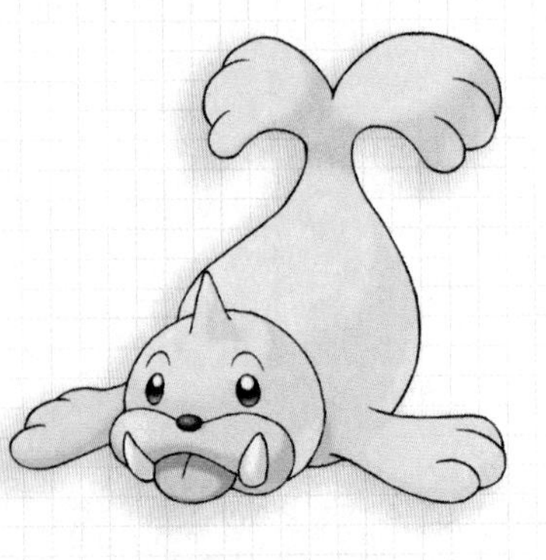

Pokémon AR Marker

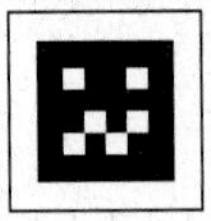

EVOLUTION

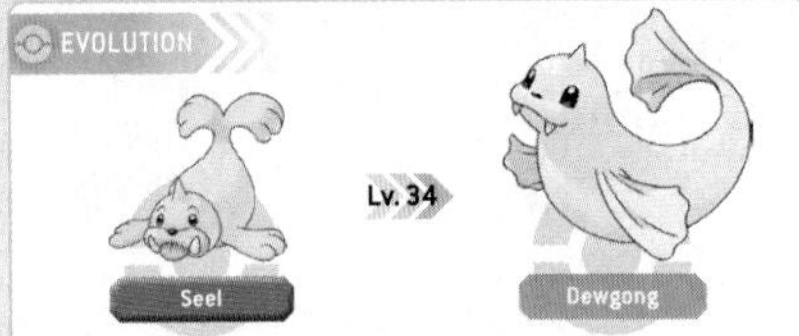
Seel
Lv. 34
Dewgong

HOW TO OBTAIN

Pokémon Black Version 2	❶ Seaside Cave 1F ❷ Giant Chasm caves (water surface)
Pokémon White Version 2	❶ Seaside Cave 1F ❷ Giant Chasm caves (water surface)

HOW TO OBTAIN FROM OTHER GAMES

—

—

LEVEL-UP AND LEARNED MOVES

Lv.	Name	Type	Kind	Pow.	Acc.	PP	Range	Long	DA
1	Headbutt	Normal	Physical	70	100	15	Normal	—	○
3	Growl	Normal	Status	—	100	40	Many Others	—	—
7	Water Sport	Water	Status	—	—	15	Both Sides	—	—
11	Icy Wind	Ice	Special	55	95	15	Many Others	—	—
13	Encore	Normal	Status	—	100	5	Normal	—	—
17	Ice Shard	Ice	Physical	40	100	30	Normal	—	—
21	Rest	Psychic	Status	—	—	10	Self	—	—
23	Aqua Ring	Water	Status	—	—	20	Self	—	—
27	Aurora Beam	Ice	Special	65	100	20	Normal	—	—
31	Aqua Jet	Water	Physical	40	100	20	Normal	—	○
33	Brine	Water	Special	65	100	10	Normal	—	—
37	Take Down	Normal	Physical	90	85	20	Normal	—	○
41	Dive	Water	Physical	80	100	10	Normal	—	○
43	Aqua Tail	Water	Physical	90	90	10	Normal	—	○
47	Ice Beam	Ice	Special	95	100	10	Normal	—	—
51	Safeguard	Normal	Status	—	—	25	Your Side	—	—
53	Hail	Ice	Status	—	—	10	Both Sides	—	—

TM & HM MOVES

Lv.	Name	Type	Kind	Pow.	Acc.	PP	Range	Long	DA
TM06	Toxic	Poison	Status	—	90	10	Normal	—	—
TM07	Hail	Ice	Status	—	—	10	Both Sides	—	—
TM10	Hidden Power	Normal	Special	—	100	15	Normal	—	—
TM13	Ice Beam	Ice	Special	95	100	10	Normal	—	—
TM14	Blizzard	Ice	Special	120	70	5	Many Others	—	—
TM17	Protect	Normal	Status	—	—	10	Self	—	—
TM18	Rain Dance	Water	Status	—	—	5	Both Sides	—	—
TM20	Safeguard	Normal	Status	—	—	25	Your Side	—	—
TM21	Frustration	Normal	Physical	—	100	20	Normal	—	○
TM27	Return	Normal	Physical	—	100	20	Normal	—	○
TM32	Double Team	Normal	Status	—	—	15	Self	—	—
TM42	Facade	Normal	Physical	70	100	20	Normal	—	○
TM44	Rest	Psychic	Status	—	—	10	Self	—	—
TM45	Attract	Normal	Status	—	100	15	Normal	—	—
TM46	Thief	Dark	Physical	40	100	10	Normal	—	○
TM48	Round	Normal	Special	60	100	15	Normal	—	—
TM49	Echoed Voice	Normal	Special	40	100	15	Normal	—	—
TM56	Fling	Dark	Physical	—	100	10	Normal	—	—
TM87	Swagger	Normal	Status	—	90	15	Normal	—	—
TM90	Substitute	Normal	Status	—	—	10	Self	—	—
HM03	Surf	Water	Special	95	100	15	Adjacent	—	—
HM05	Waterfall	Water	Physical	80	100	15	Normal	—	○
HM06	Dive	Water	Physical	80	100	10	Normal	—	○

MOVES TAUGHT BY PEOPLE

Name	Type	Kind	Pow.	Acc.	PP	Range	Long	DA

MOVES TAUGHT BY MOVE TUTORS FOR SHARDS

Name	Type	Kind	Pow.	Acc.	PP	Range	Long	DA
Drill Run	Ground	Physical	80	95	10	Normal	—	○
Signal Beam	Bug	Special	75	100	15	Normal	—	—
Icy Wind	Ice	Special	55	95	15	Many Others	—	—
Iron Tail	Steel	Physical	100	75	15	Normal	—	○
Aqua Tail	Water	Physical	90	90	10	Normal	—	○
Snore	Normal	Special	40	100	15	Normal	—	—
Sleep Talk	Normal	Status	—	—	10	Self	—	—

EGG MOVES

Name	Type	Kind	Pow.	Acc.	PP	Range	Long	DA
Lick	Ghost	Physical	20	100	30	Normal	—	○
Perish Song	Normal	Status	—	—	5	Adjacent	○	—
Disable	Normal	Status	—	100	20	Normal	—	—
Horn Drill	Normal	Physical	—	30	5	Normal	—	○
Slam	Normal	Physical	80	75	20	Normal	—	○
Encore	Normal	Status	—	100	5	Normal	—	—
Fake Out	Normal	Physical	40	100	10	Normal	—	○
Icicle Spear	Ice	Physical	25	100	30	Normal	—	—
Signal Beam	Bug	Special	75	100	15	Normal	—	—
Stockpile	Normal	Status	—	—	20	Self	—	—
Swallow	Normal	Status	—	—	10	Self	—	—
Spit Up	Normal	Special	—	100	10	Normal	—	—
Water Pulse	Water	Special	60	100	20	Normal	○	—
Iron Tail	Steel	Physical	100	75	15	Normal	—	○
Sleep Talk	Normal	Status	—	—	10	Self	—	—

087 Dewgong

Sea Lion Pokémon

- HEIGHT: 5'07"
- WEIGHT: 264.6 lbs.
- GENDER: ♂ / ♀

Its streamlined body has low resistance, and it swims around cold oceans at a speed of eight knots.

Same form for ♂ / ♀

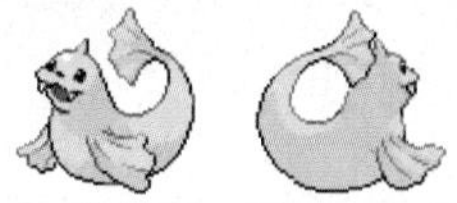

TYPE: Water / Ice

ABILITIES
- Thick Fat
- Hydration

HIDDEN ABILITY
- Ice Body

STATS
HP
Attack
Defense
Sp. Atk
Sp. Def
Speed

EGG GROUPS
Water ❶/Field

ITEMS SOMETIMES HELD
- None

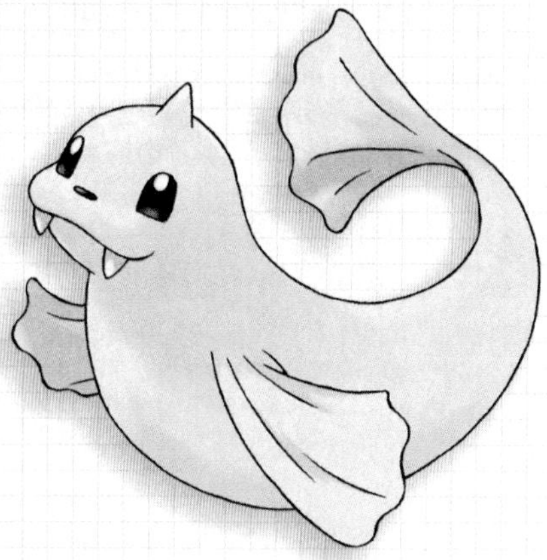

Pokémon AR Marker

EVOLUTION

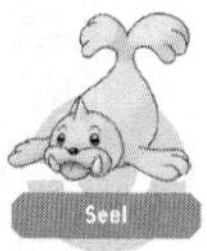

Lv. 34

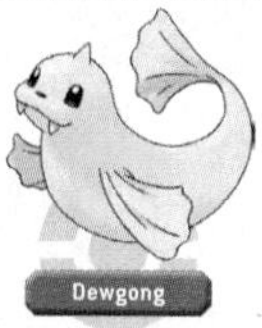

HOW TO OBTAIN

- Pokémon Black Version 2: ❶ Seaside Cave 1F (ripples in water) ❷ Giant Chasm caves (ripples in water)
- Pokémon White Version 2: ❶ Seaside Cave 1F (ripples in water) ❷ Giant Chasm caves (ripples in water)

HOW TO OBTAIN FROM OTHER GAMES

—

—

LEVEL-UP AND LEARNED MOVES

Lv.	Name	Type	Kind	Pow.	Acc.	PP	Range	Long	DA
1	Headbutt	Normal	Physical	70	100	15	Normal	—	○
1	Growl	Normal	Status	—	100	40	Many Others	—	—
1	Signal Beam	Bug	Special	75	100	15	Normal	—	—
1	Icy Wind	Ice	Special	55	95	15	Many Others	—	—
3	Growl	Normal	Status	—	100	40	Many Others	—	—
7	Signal Beam	Bug	Special	75	100	15	Normal	—	—
11	Icy Wind	Ice	Special	55	95	15	Many Others	—	—
13	Encore	Normal	Status	—	100	5	Normal	—	—
17	Ice Shard	Ice	Physical	40	100	30	Normal	—	—
21	Rest	Psychic	Status	—	—	10	Self	—	—
23	Aqua Ring	Water	Status	—	—	20	Self	—	—
27	Aurora Beam	Ice	Special	65	100	20	Normal	—	—
31	Aqua Jet	Water	Physical	40	100	20	Normal	—	○
33	Brine	Water	Special	65	100	10	Normal	—	—
34	Sheer Cold	Ice	Special	—	30	5	Normal	—	—
39	Take Down	Normal	Physical	90	85	20	Normal	—	○
45	Dive	Water	Physical	80	100	10	Normal	—	○
49	Aqua Tail	Water	Physical	90	90	10	Normal	—	○
55	Ice Beam	Ice	Special	95	100	10	Normal	—	—
61	Safeguard	Normal	Status	—	—	25	Your Side	—	—
65	Hail	Ice	Status	—	—	10	Both Sides	—	—

TM & HM MOVES

Lv.	Name	Type	Kind	Pow.	Acc.	PP	Range	Long	DA
TM06	Toxic	Poison	Status	—	90	10	Normal	—	—
TM07	Hail	Ice	Status	—	—	10	Both Sides	—	—
TM10	Hidden Power	Normal	Special	—	100	15	Normal	—	—
TM13	Ice Beam	Ice	Special	95	100	10	Normal	—	—
TM14	Blizzard	Ice	Special	120	70	5	Many Others	—	—
TM15	Hyper Beam	Normal	Special	150	90	5	Normal	—	—
TM17	Protect	Normal	Status	—	—	10	Self	—	—
TM18	Rain Dance	Water	Status	—	—	5	Both Sides	—	—
TM20	Safeguard	Normal	Status	—	—	25	Your Side	—	—
TM21	Frustration	Normal	Physical	—	100	20	Normal	—	○
TM27	Return	Normal	Physical	—	100	20	Normal	—	○
TM32	Double Team	Normal	Status	—	—	15	Self	—	—
TM42	Facade	Normal	Physical	70	100	20	Normal	—	○
TM44	Rest	Psychic	Status	—	—	10	Self	—	—
TM45	Attract	Normal	Status	—	100	15	Normal	—	—
TM46	Thief	Dark	Physical	40	100	10	Normal	—	○
TM48	Round	Normal	Special	60	100	15	Normal	—	—
TM49	Echoed Voice	Normal	Special	40	100	15	Normal	—	—
TM56	Fling	Dark	Physical	—	100	10	Normal	—	—
TM68	Giga Impact	Normal	Physical	150	90	5	Normal	—	○
TM79	Frost Breath	Ice	Special	40	90	10	Normal	—	—
TM87	Swagger	Normal	Status	—	90	15	Normal	—	—
TM90	Substitute	Normal	Status	—	—	10	Self	—	—
HM03	Surf	Water	Special	95	100	15	Adjacent	—	—
HM05	Waterfall	Water	Physical	80	100	15	Normal	—	○
HM06	Dive	Water	Physical	80	100	10	Normal	—	○

MOVES TAUGHT BY PEOPLE

Name	Type	Kind	Pow.	Acc.	PP	Range	Long	DA

MOVES TAUGHT BY MOVE TUTORS FOR SHARDS

Name	Type	Kind	Pow.	Acc.	PP	Range	Long	DA
Drill Run	Ground	Physical	80	95	10	Normal	—	○
Signal Beam	Bug	Special	75	100	15	Normal	—	—
Icy Wind	Ice	Special	55	95	15	Many Others	—	—
Iron Tail	Steel	Physical	100	75	15	Normal	—	○
Aqua Tail	Water	Physical	90	90	10	Normal	—	○
Snore	Normal	Special	40	100	15	Normal	—	—
Sleep Talk	Normal	Status	—	—	10	Self	—	—

088 Grimer

Sludge Pokémon

- HEIGHT: 2'11"
- WEIGHT: 66.1 lbs.
- GENDER: ♂ / ♀

Born from sludge, these Pokémon now gather in polluted places and increase the bacteria in their bodies.

Same form for ♂ / ♀

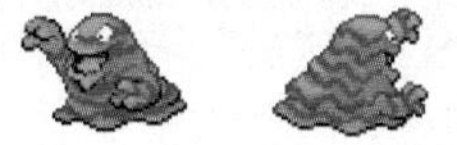

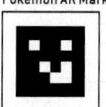

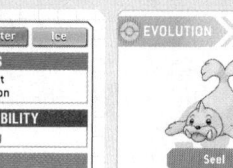

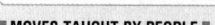

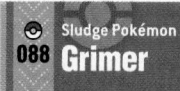

TYPE: Poison

ABILITIES
- Stench
- Sticky Hold

HIDDEN ABILITY
- Poison Touch

STATS
HP
Attack
Defense
Sp. Atk
Sp. Def
Speed

EGG GROUPS
Amorphous

ITEMS SOMETIMES HELD
- Black Sludge

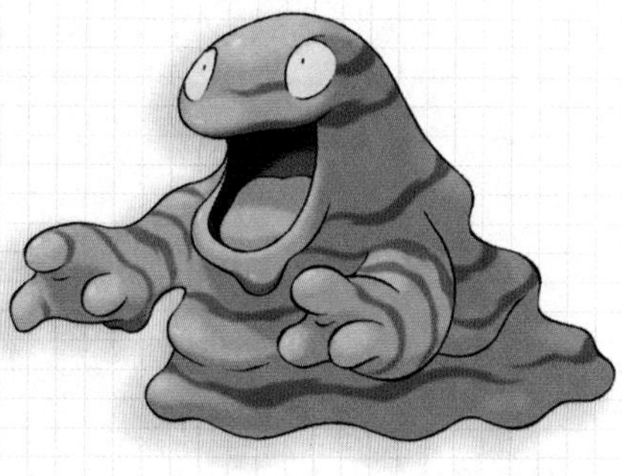

Pokémon AR Marker

EVOLUTION

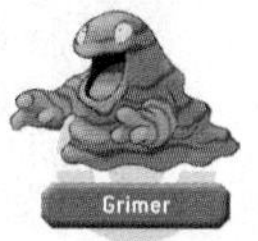

Lv. 38

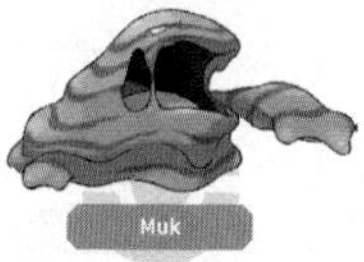

HOW TO OBTAIN

- Pokémon Black Version 2: ❶ Castelia Sewers ❷ Giant Chasm caves (water surface—spring and summer only)
- Pokémon White Version 2: ❶ Castelia Sewers ❷ Giant Chasm caves (water surface—spring and summer only)

HOW TO OBTAIN FROM OTHER GAMES

—

—

LEVEL-UP AND LEARNED MOVES

Lv.	Name	Type	Kind	Pow.	Acc.	PP	Range	Long	DA
1	Pound	Normal	Physical	40	100	35	Normal	—	○
1	Poison Gas	Poison	Status	—	80	40	Many Others	—	—
4	Harden	Normal	Status	—	—	30	Self	—	—
7	Mud-Slap	Ground	Special	20	100	10	Normal	—	—
12	Disable	Normal	Status	—	100	20	Normal	—	—
15	Sludge	Poison	Special	65	100	20	Normal	—	—
18	Minimize	Normal	Status	—	—	20	Self	—	—
21	Mud Bomb	Ground	Special	65	85	10	Normal	—	—
26	Sludge Bomb	Poison	Special	90	100	10	Normal	—	—
29	Fling	Dark	Physical	—	100	10	Normal	—	—
32	Screech	Normal	Status	—	85	40	Normal	—	—
37	Sludge Wave	Poison	Special	95	100	10	Adjacent	—	—
40	Acid Armor	Poison	Status	—	—	40	Self	—	—
43	Gunk Shot	Poison	Physical	120	70	5	Normal	—	—
48	Memento	Dark	Status	—	100	10	Normal	—	—

TM & HM MOVES

Lv.	Name	Type	Kind	Pow.	Acc.	PP	Range	Long	DA
TM06	Toxic	Poison	Status	—	90	10	Normal	—	—
TM09	Venoshock	Poison	Special	65	100	10	Normal	—	—
TM10	Hidden Power	Normal	Special	—	100	15	Normal	—	—
TM11	Sunny Day	Fire	Status	—	—	5	Both Sides	—	—
TM12	Taunt	Dark	Status	—	100	20	Normal	—	—
TM17	Protect	Normal	Status	—	—	10	Self	—	—
TM18	Rain Dance	Water	Status	—	—	5	Both Sides	—	—
TM21	Frustration	Normal	Physical	—	100	20	Normal	—	○
TM24	Thunderbolt	Electric	Special	95	100	15	Normal	—	—
TM25	Thunder	Electric	Special	120	70	10	Normal	—	—
TM27	Return	Normal	Physical	—	100	20	Normal	—	○
TM28	Dig	Ground	Physical	80	100	10	Normal	—	○
TM30	Shadow Ball	Ghost	Special	80	100	15	Normal	—	—
TM32	Double Team	Normal	Status	—	—	15	Self	—	—
TM34	Sludge Wave	Poison	Special	95	100	10	Adjacent	—	—
TM35	Flamethrower	Fire	Special	95	100	15	Normal	—	—
TM36	Sludge Bomb	Poison	Special	90	100	10	Normal	—	—
TM38	Fire Blast	Fire	Special	120	85	5	Normal	—	—
TM39	Rock Tomb	Rock	Physical	50	80	10	Normal	—	—
TM41	Torment	Dark	Status	—	100	15	Normal	—	—
TM42	Facade	Normal	Physical	70	100	20	Normal	—	○
TM44	Rest	Psychic	Status	—	—	10	Self	—	—
TM45	Attract	Normal	Status	—	100	15	Normal	—	—
TM46	Thief	Dark	Physical	40	100	10	Normal	—	○
TM48	Round	Normal	Special	60	100	15	Normal	—	—
TM56	Fling	Dark	Physical	—	100	10	Normal	—	—
TM59	Incinerate	Fire	Special	30	100	15	Many Others	—	—
TM64	Explosion	Normal	Physical	250	100	5	Adjacent	—	—
TM66	Payback	Dark	Physical	50	100	10	Normal	—	○
TM80	Rock Slide	Rock	Physical	75	90	10	Many Others	—	—
TM84	Poison Jab	Poison	Physical	80	100	20	Normal	—	○
TM87	Swagger	Normal	Status	—	90	15	Normal	—	—
TM90	Substitute	Normal	Status	—	—	10	Self	—	—
HM04	Strength	Normal	Physical	80	100	15	Normal	—	○

MOVES TAUGHT BY PEOPLE

Name	Type	Kind	Pow.	Acc.	PP	Range	Long	DA

MOVES TAUGHT BY MOVE TUTORS FOR SHARDS

Name	Type	Kind	Pow.	Acc.	PP	Range	Long	DA
Gunk Shot	Poison	Physical	120	70	5	Normal	—	—
Fire Punch	Fire	Physical	75	100	15	Normal	—	○
ThunderPunch	Electric	Physical	75	100	15	Normal	—	○
Ice Punch	Ice	Physical	75	100	15	Normal	—	○
Snore	Normal	Special	40	100	15	Normal	—	—
Giga Drain	Grass	Special	75	100	10	Normal	—	—
Pain Split	Normal	Status	—	—	20	Normal	—	—
Sleep Talk	Normal	Status	—	—	10	Self	—	—

EGG MOVES

Name	Type	Kind	Pow.	Acc.	PP	Range	Long	DA
Haze	Ice	Status	—	—	30	Both Sides	—	—
Mean Look	Normal	Status	—	—	5	Normal	—	—
Lick	Ghost	Physical	20	100	30	Normal	—	○
Imprison	Psychic	Status	—	—	10	Self	—	—
Curse	Ghost	Status	—	—	10	Varies	—	—
Shadow Punch	Ghost	Physical	60	—	20	Normal	—	○
Shadow Sneak	Ghost	Physical	40	100	30	Normal	—	○
Stockpile	Normal	Status	—	—	20	Self	—	—
Swallow	Normal	Status	—	—	10	Self	—	—
Spit Up	Normal	Special	—	100	10	Normal	—	—
Scary Face	Normal	Status	—	100	10	Normal	—	—
Acid Spray	Poison	Special	40	100	20	Normal	—	—

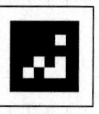

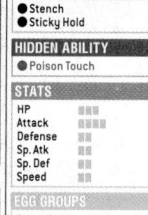

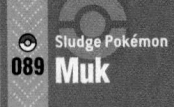

089 Muk

Sludge Pokémon

TYPE Poison

ABILITIES
- Stench
- Sticky Hold

HIDDEN ABILITY
- Poison Touch

- HEIGHT: 3'11"
- WEIGHT: 66.1 lbs.
- GENDER: ♂ / ♀

It's so stinky! Muk's body contains toxic elements, and any plant will wilt when it passes by.

STATS
HP
Attack
Defense
Sp. Atk
Sp. Def
Speed

Same form for ♂ / ♀

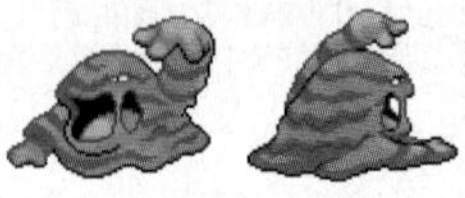

EGG GROUPS
Amorphous

ITEMS SOMETIMES HELD
- Black Sludge
- Toxic Orb

EVOLUTION

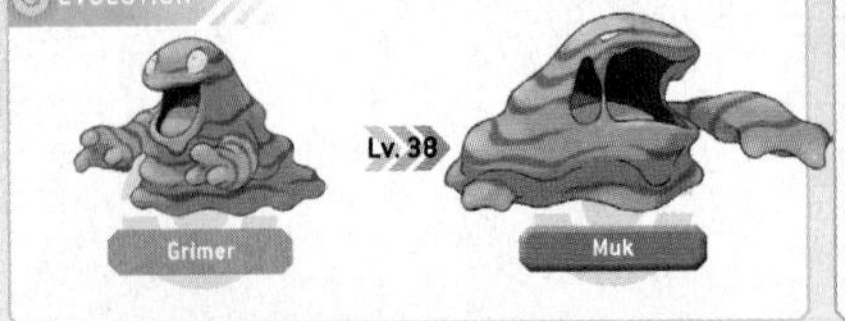

HOW TO OBTAIN

Pokémon Black Version 2	❶ Castelia Sewers (ripples in water—spring and summer only) ❷ Route 9
Pokémon White Version 2	❶ Castelia Sewers (ripples in water—spring and summer only) ❷ Route 9

HOW TO OBTAIN FROM OTHER GAMES

—

—

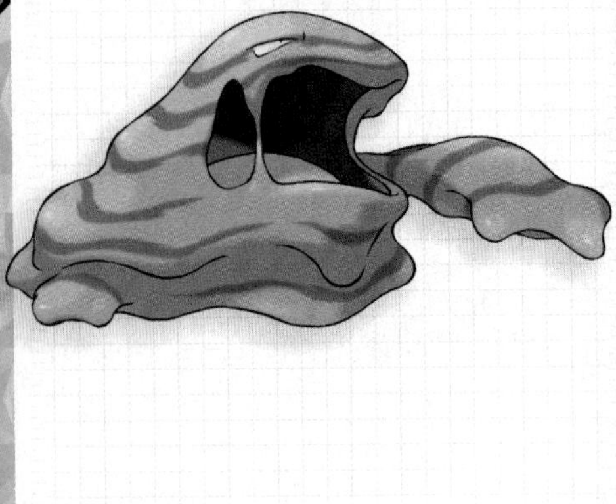

LEVEL-UP AND LEARNED MOVES

Lv.	Name	Type	Kind	Pow.	Acc.	PP	Range	Long	DA
1	Pound	Normal	Physical	40	100	35	Normal	—	○
1	Poison Gas	Poison	Status	—	80	40	Many Others	—	—
1	Harden	Normal	Status	—	—	30	Self	—	—
1	Mud-Slap	Ground	Special	20	100	10	Normal	—	—
4	Harden	Normal	Status	—	—	30	Self	—	—
7	Mud-Slap	Ground	Special	20	100	10	Normal	—	—
12	Disable	Normal	Status	—	100	20	Normal	—	—
15	Sludge	Poison	Special	65	100	20	Normal	—	—
18	Minimize	Normal	Status	—	—	20	Self	—	—
21	Mud Bomb	Ground	Special	65	85	10	Normal	—	—
26	Sludge Bomb	Poison	Special	90	100	10	Normal	—	—
29	Fling	Dark	Physical	—	100	10	Normal	—	—
32	Screech	Normal	Status	—	85	40	Normal	—	—
37	Sludge Wave	Poison	Special	95	100	10	Adjacent	—	—
43	Acid Armor	Poison	Status	—	—	40	Self	—	—
49	Gunk Shot	Poison	Physical	120	70	5	Normal	—	—
57	Memento	Dark	Status	—	100	10	Normal	—	—

TM & HM MOVES

Lv.	Name	Type	Kind	Pow.	Acc.	PP	Range	Long	DA
TM06	Toxic	Poison	Status	—	90	10	Normal	—	—
TM09	Venoshock	Poison	Special	65	100	10	Normal	—	—
TM10	Hidden Power	Normal	Special	—	100	15	Normal	—	—
TM11	Sunny Day	Fire	Status	—	—	5	Both Sides	—	—
TM12	Taunt	Dark	Status	—	100	20	Normal	—	—
TM15	Hyper Beam	Normal	Special	150	90	5	Normal	—	—
TM17	Protect	Normal	Status	—	—	10	Self	—	—
TM18	Rain Dance	Water	Status	—	—	5	Both Sides	—	—
TM21	Frustration	Normal	Physical	—	100	20	Normal	—	○
TM24	Thunderbolt	Electric	Special	95	100	15	Normal	—	—
TM25	Thunder	Electric	Special	120	70	10	Normal	—	—
TM27	Return	Normal	Physical	—	100	20	Normal	—	○
TM28	Dig	Ground	Physical	80	100	10	Normal	—	○
TM30	Shadow Ball	Ghost	Special	80	100	15	Normal	—	—
TM31	Brick Break	Fighting	Physical	75	100	15	Normal	—	○
TM32	Double Team	Normal	Status	—	—	15	Self	—	—
TM34	Sludge Wave	Poison	Special	95	100	10	Adjacent	—	—
TM35	Flamethrower	Fire	Special	95	100	15	Normal	—	—
TM36	Sludge Bomb	Poison	Special	90	100	10	Normal	—	—
TM38	Fire Blast	Fire	Special	120	85	5	Normal	—	—
TM39	Rock Tomb	Rock	Physical	50	80	10	Normal	—	—
TM41	Torment	Dark	Status	—	100	15	Normal	—	—
TM42	Facade	Normal	Physical	70	100	20	Normal	—	○
TM44	Rest	Psychic	Status	—	—	10	Self	—	—
TM45	Attract	Normal	Status	—	100	15	Normal	—	—
TM46	Thief	Dark	Physical	40	100	10	Normal	—	○
TM48	Round	Normal	Special	60	100	15	Normal	—	—
TM52	Focus Blast	Fighting	Special	120	70	5	Normal	—	—
TM56	Fling	Dark	Physical	—	100	10	Normal	—	—
TM59	Incinerate	Fire	Special	30	100	15	Many Others	—	—
TM64	Explosion	Normal	Physical	250	100	5	Adjacent	—	—
TM66	Payback	Dark	Physical	50	100	10	Normal	—	○
TM68	Giga Impact	Normal	Physical	150	90	5	Normal	—	○
TM80	Rock Slide	Rock	Physical	75	90	10	Many Others	—	—
TM84	Poison Jab	Poison	Physical	80	100	20	Normal	—	○
TM87	Swagger	Normal	Status	—	90	15	Normal	—	—
TM90	Substitute	Normal	Status	—	—	10	Self	—	—
TM94	Rock Smash	Fighting	Physical	40	100	15	Normal	—	○
HM04	Strength	Normal	Physical	80	100	15	Normal	—	○

MOVES TAUGHT BY PEOPLE

Name	Type	Kind	Pow.	Acc.	PP	Range	Long	DA

MOVES TAUGHT BY MOVE TUTORS FOR SHARDS

Name	Type	Kind	Pow.	Acc.	PP	Range	Long	DA
Gunk Shot	Poison	Physical	120	70	5	Normal	—	—
Fire Punch	Fire	Physical	75	100	15	Normal	—	○
ThunderPunch	Electric	Physical	75	100	15	Normal	—	○
Ice Punch	Ice	Physical	75	100	15	Normal	—	○
Block	Normal	Status	—	—	5	Normal	—	—
Dark Pulse	Dark	Special	80	100	15	Normal	○	—
Snore	Normal	Special	40	100	15	Normal	—	—
Giga Drain	Grass	Special	75	100	10	Normal	—	—
Pain Split	Normal	Status	—	—	20	Normal	—	—
Sleep Talk	Normal	Status	—	—	10	Self	—	—

Pokémon AR Marker

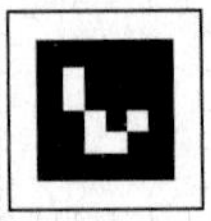

090 Shellder

Bivalve Pokémon

TYPE Water

ABILITIES
- Shell Armor
- Skill Link

HIDDEN ABILITY
- Overcoat

- HEIGHT: 1'00"
- WEIGHT: 8.8 lbs.
- GENDER: ♂ / ♀

It swims backward by opening and closing its two shells. Its large tongue is always kept hanging out.

STATS
HP
Attack
Defense
Sp. Atk
Sp. Def
Speed

Same form for ♂ / ♀

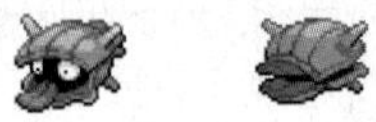

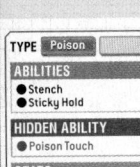

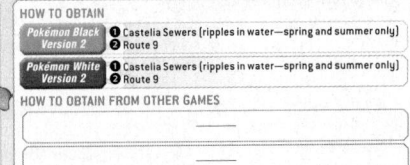

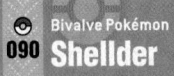

EGG GROUPS
Water ❸

ITEMS SOMETIMES HELD
- Pearl
- Big Pearl

EVOLUTION

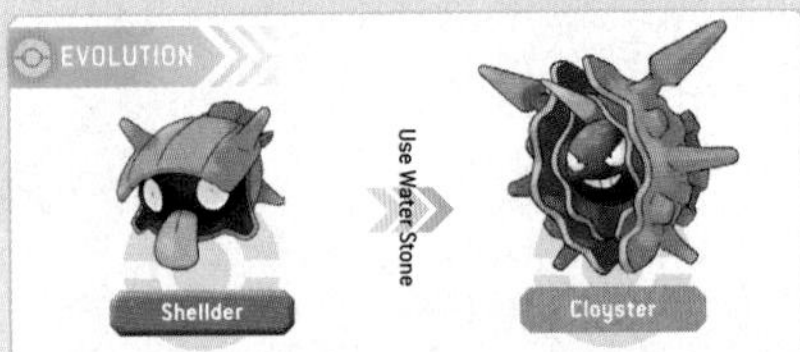

HOW TO OBTAIN

Pokémon Black Version 2	❶ Undella Town (Super Rod) ❷ Humilau City (Super Rod)
Pokémon White Version 2	❶ Undella Town (Super Rod) ❷ Humilau City (Super Rod)

HOW TO OBTAIN FROM OTHER GAMES

—

—

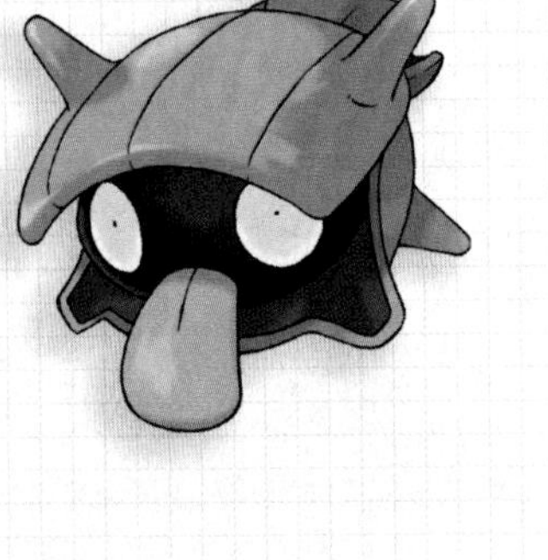

LEVEL-UP AND LEARNED MOVES

Lv.	Name	Type	Kind	Pow.	Acc.	PP	Range	Long	DA
1	Tackle	Normal	Physical	50	100	35	Normal	—	○
4	Withdraw	Water	Status	—	—	40	Self	—	—
8	Supersonic	Normal	Status	—	55	20	Normal	—	—
13	Icicle Spear	Ice	Physical	25	100	30	Normal	—	—
16	Protect	Normal	Status	—	—	10	Self	—	—
20	Leer	Normal	Status	—	100	30	Many Others	—	—
25	Clamp	Water	Physical	35	85	15	Normal	—	○
28	Ice Shard	Ice	Physical	40	100	30	Normal	—	—
32	Razor Shell	Water	Physical	75	95	10	Normal	—	○
37	Aurora Beam	Ice	Special	65	100	20	Normal	—	—
40	Whirlpool	Water	Special	35	85	15	Normal	—	—
44	Brine	Water	Special	65	100	10	Normal	—	—
49	Iron Defense	Steel	Status	—	—	15	Self	—	—
52	Ice Beam	Ice	Special	95	100	10	Normal	—	—
56	Shell Smash	Normal	Status	—	—	15	Self	—	—
61	Hydro Pump	Water	Special	120	80	5	Normal	—	—

TM & HM MOVES

Lv.	Name	Type	Kind	Pow.	Acc.	PP	Range	Long	DA
TM06	Toxic	Poison	Status	—	90	10	Normal	—	—
TM07	Hail	Ice	Status	—	—	10	Both Sides	—	—
TM10	Hidden Power	Normal	Special	—	100	15	Normal	—	—
TM13	Ice Beam	Ice	Special	95	100	10	Normal	—	—
TM14	Blizzard	Ice	Special	120	70	5	Many Others	—	—
TM17	Protect	Normal	Status	—	—	10	Self	—	—
TM18	Rain Dance	Water	Status	—	—	5	Both Sides	—	—
TM21	Frustration	Normal	Physical	—	100	20	Normal	—	○
TM27	Return	Normal	Physical	—	100	20	Normal	—	○
TM32	Double Team	Normal	Status	—	—	15	Self	—	—
TM42	Facade	Normal	Physical	70	100	20	Normal	—	○
TM44	Rest	Psychic	Status	—	—	10	Self	—	—
TM45	Attract	Normal	Status	—	100	15	Normal	—	—
TM48	Round	Normal	Special	60	100	15	Normal	—	—
TM64	Explosion	Normal	Physical	250	100	5	Adjacent	—	—
TM66	Payback	Dark	Physical	50	100	10	Normal	—	○
TM87	Swagger	Normal	Status	—	90	15	Normal	—	—
TM90	Substitute	Normal	Status	—	—	10	Self	—	—
HM03	Surf	Water	Special	95	100	15	Adjacent	—	—
HM06	Dive	Water	Physical	80	100	10	Normal	—	○

MOVES TAUGHT BY PEOPLE

Name	Type	Kind	Pow.	Acc.	PP	Range	Long	DA

MOVES TAUGHT BY MOVE TUTORS FOR SHARDS

Name	Type	Kind	Pow.	Acc.	PP	Range	Long	DA
Iron Defense	Steel	Status	—	—	15	Self	—	—
Icy Wind	Ice	Special	55	95	15	Many Others	—	—
Snore	Normal	Special	40	100	15	Normal	—	—
Sleep Talk	Normal	Status	—	—	10	Self	—	—

EGG MOVES

Name	Type	Kind	Pow.	Acc.	PP	Range	Long	DA
BubbleBeam	Water	Special	65	100	20	Normal	—	—
Take Down	Normal	Physical	90	85	20	Normal	—	○
Barrier	Psychic	Status	—	—	30	Self	—	—
Rapid Spin	Normal	Physical	20	100	40	Normal	—	○
Screech	Normal	Status	—	85	40	Normal	—	—
Icicle Spear	Ice	Physical	25	100	30	Normal	—	—
Mud Shot	Ground	Special	55	95	15	Normal	—	—
Rock Blast	Rock	Physical	25	90	10	Normal	—	—
Water Pulse	Water	Special	60	100	20	Normal	○	—
Aqua Ring	Water	Status	—	—	20	Self	—	—
Avalanche	Ice	Physical	60	100	10	Normal	—	○
Twineedle	Bug	Physical	25	100	20	Normal	—	—

Pokémon AR Marker

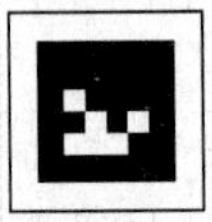

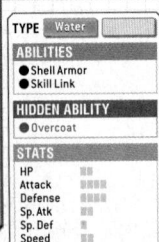

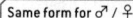

Bivalve Pokémon

091 Cloyster

- HEIGHT: 4'11'
- WEIGHT: 292.1 lbs.
- GENDER: ♂ / ♀

It fights by keeping its shell tightly shut for protection and by shooting spikes to repel foes.

Same form for ♂ / ♀

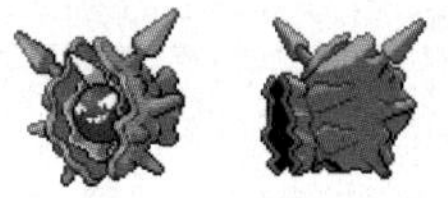

TYPE: Water / Ice

ABILITIES
- Shell Armor
- Skill Link

HIDDEN ABILITY
- Overcoat

STATS
HP
Attack
Defense
Sp. Atk
Sp. Def
Speed

EGG GROUPS
Water ❸

ITEMS SOMETIMES HELD
- Pearl
- Big Pearl

EVOLUTION

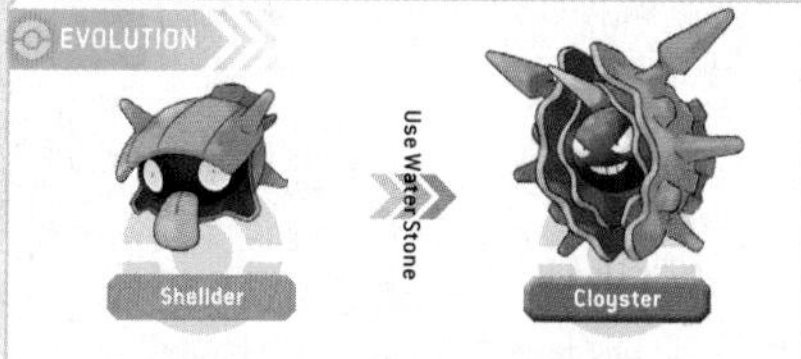
Shellder
Use Water Stone
Cloyster

HOW TO OBTAIN

Pokémon Black Version 2: ❶ Undella Town (Super Rod/ripples in water) ❷ Humilau City (Super Rod/ripples in water)

Pokémon White Version 2: ❶ Undella Town (Super Rod/ripples in water) ❷ Humilau City (Super Rod/ripples in water)

HOW TO OBTAIN FROM OTHER GAMES

—

—

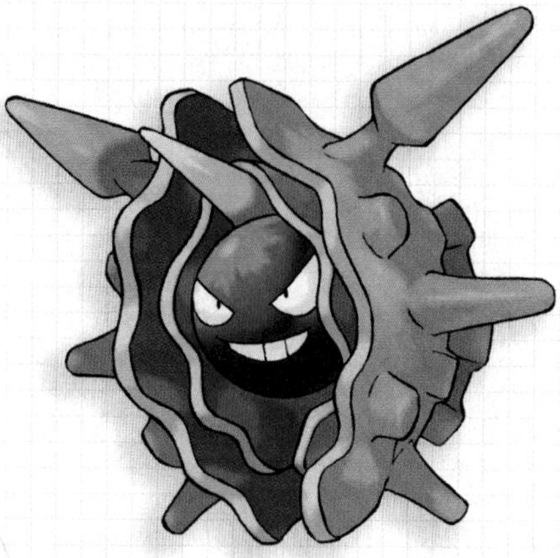

Pokémon AR Marker

LEVEL-UP AND LEARNED MOVES

Lv.	Name	Type	Kind	Pow.	Acc.	PP	Range	Long	DA
1	Toxic Spikes	Poison	Status	—	—	20	Other Side	—	—
1	Withdraw	Water	Status	—	—	40	Self	—	—
1	Supersonic	Normal	Status	—	55	20	Normal	—	—
1	Protect	Normal	Status	—	—	10	Self	—	—
1	Aurora Beam	Ice	Special	65	100	20	Normal	—	—
13	Spike Cannon	Normal	Physical	20	100	15	Normal	—	—
28	Spikes	Ground	Status	—	—	20	Other Side	—	—
52	Icicle Crash	Ice	Physical	85	90	10	Normal	—	—

TM & HM MOVES

Lv.	Name	Type	Kind	Pow.	Acc.	PP	Range	Long	DA
TM06	Toxic	Poison	Status	—	90	10	Normal	—	—
TM07	Hail	Ice	Status	—	—	10	Both Sides	—	—
TM10	Hidden Power	Normal	Special	—	100	15	Normal	—	—
TM13	Ice Beam	Ice	Special	95	100	10	Normal	—	—
TM14	Blizzard	Ice	Special	120	70	5	Many Others	—	—
TM15	Hyper Beam	Normal	Special	150	90	5	Normal	—	—
TM17	Protect	Normal	Status	—	—	10	Self	—	—
TM18	Rain Dance	Water	Status	—	—	5	Both Sides	—	—
TM21	Frustration	Normal	Physical	—	100	20	Normal	—	○
TM27	Return	Normal	Physical	—	100	20	Normal	—	○
TM32	Double Team	Normal	Status	—	—	15	Self	—	—
TM41	Torment	Dark	Status	—	100	15	Normal	—	—
TM42	Facade	Normal	Physical	70	100	20	Normal	—	○
TM44	Rest	Psychic	Status	—	—	10	Self	—	—
TM45	Attract	Normal	Status	—	100	15	Normal	—	—
TM48	Round	Normal	Special	60	100	15	Normal	—	—
TM64	Explosion	Normal	Physical	250	100	5	Adjacent	—	—
TM66	Payback	Dark	Physical	50	100	10	Normal	—	○
TM68	Giga Impact	Normal	Physical	150	90	5	Normal	—	○
TM79	Frost Breath	Ice	Special	40	90	10	Normal	—	—
TM84	Poison Jab	Poison	Physical	80	100	20	Normal	—	○
TM87	Swagger	Normal	Status	—	90	15	Normal	—	—
TM90	Substitute	Normal	Status	—	—	10	Self	—	—
HM03	Surf	Water	Special	95	100	15	Adjacent	—	—
HM06	Dive	Water	Physical	80	100	10	Normal	—	○

MOVES TAUGHT BY PEOPLE

Name	Type	Kind	Pow.	Acc.	PP	Range	Long	DA

MOVES TAUGHT BY MOVE TUTORS FOR SHARDS

Name	Type	Kind	Pow.	Acc.	PP	Range	Long	DA
Signal Beam	Bug	Special	75	100	15	Normal	—	—
Iron Defense	Steel	Status	—	—	15	Self	—	—
Icy Wind	Ice	Special	55	95	15	Many Others	—	—
Snore	Normal	Special	40	100	15	Normal	—	—
Sleep Talk	Normal	Status	—	—	10	Self	—	—

Gas Pokémon

092 Gastly

- HEIGHT: 4'03"
- WEIGHT: 0.2 lbs.
- GENDER: ♂ / ♀

Born from gases, anyone would faint if engulfed by its gaseous body, which contains poison.

Same form for ♂ / ♀

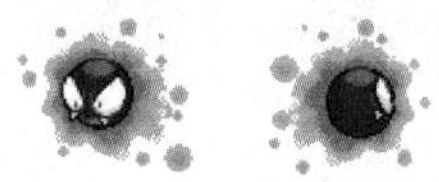

TYPE: Ghost / Poison

ABILITY
- Levitate

HIDDEN ABILITY
—

STATS
HP
Attack
Defense
Sp. Atk
Sp. Def
Speed

EGG GROUPS
Amorphous

ITEMS SOMETIMES HELD
- None

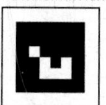

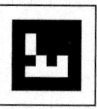

EVOLUTION

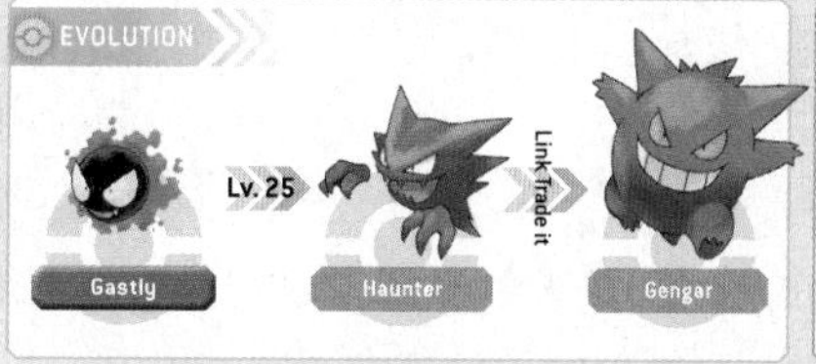
Gastly
Lv. 25
Haunter
Link Trade it
Gengar

HOW TO OBTAIN

Pokémon Black Version 2: Link Trade or Poké Transfer

Pokémon White Version 2: Link Trade or Poké Transfer

HOW TO OBTAIN FROM OTHER GAMES

Pokémon HeartGold Version: Sprout Tower (night only)

Pokémon SoulSilver Version: Sprout Tower (night only)

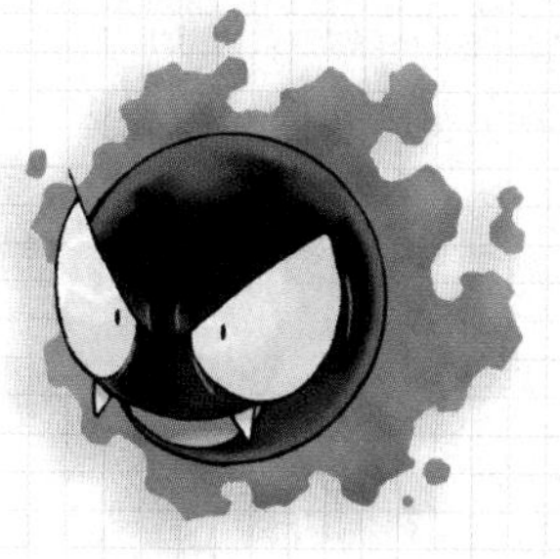

Pokémon AR Marker

LEVEL-UP AND LEARNED MOVES

Lv.	Name	Type	Kind	Pow.	Acc.	PP	Range	Long	DA
1	Hypnosis	Psychic	Status	—	60	20	Normal	—	—
1	Lick	Ghost	Physical	20	100	30	Normal	—	○
5	Spite	Ghost	Status	—	100	10	Normal	—	—
8	Mean Look	Normal	Status	—	—	5	Normal	—	—
12	Curse	Ghost	Status	—	—	10	Varies	—	—
15	Night Shade	Ghost	Special	—	100	15	Normal	—	—
19	Confuse Ray	Ghost	Status	—	100	10	Normal	—	—
22	Sucker Punch	Dark	Physical	80	100	5	Normal	—	○
26	Payback	Dark	Physical	50	100	10	Normal	—	○
29	Shadow Ball	Ghost	Special	80	100	15	Normal	—	—
33	Dream Eater	Psychic	Special	100	100	15	Normal	—	—
36	Dark Pulse	Dark	Special	80	100	15	Normal	○	—
40	Destiny Bond	Ghost	Status	—	—	5	Self	—	—
43	Hex	Ghost	Special	50	100	10	Normal	—	—
47	Nightmare	Ghost	Status	—	100	15	Normal	—	—

TM & HM MOVES

Lv.	Name	Type	Kind	Pow.	Acc.	PP	Range	Long	DA
TM06	Toxic	Poison	Status	—	90	10	Normal	—	—
TM09	Venoshock	Poison	Special	65	100	10	Normal	—	—
TM10	Hidden Power	Normal	Special	—	100	15	Normal	—	—
TM11	Sunny Day	Fire	Status	—	—	5	Both Sides	—	—
TM12	Taunt	Dark	Status	—	100	20	Normal	—	—
TM17	Protect	Normal	Status	—	—	10	Self	—	—
TM18	Rain Dance	Water	Status	—	—	5	Both Sides	—	—
TM19	Telekinesis	Psychic	Status	—	—	15	Normal	—	—
TM21	Frustration	Normal	Physical	—	100	20	Normal	—	○
TM24	Thunderbolt	Electric	Special	95	100	15	Normal	—	—
TM27	Return	Normal	Physical	—	100	20	Normal	—	○
TM29	Psychic	Psychic	Special	90	100	10	Normal	—	—
TM30	Shadow Ball	Ghost	Special	80	100	15	Normal	—	—
TM32	Double Team	Normal	Status	—	—	15	Self	—	—
TM36	Sludge Bomb	Poison	Special	90	100	10	Normal	—	—
TM41	Torment	Dark	Status	—	100	15	Normal	—	—
TM42	Facade	Normal	Physical	70	100	20	Normal	—	○
TM44	Rest	Psychic	Status	—	—	10	Self	—	—
TM45	Attract	Normal	Status	—	100	15	Normal	—	—
TM46	Thief	Dark	Physical	40	100	10	Normal	—	○
TM48	Round	Normal	Special	60	100	15	Normal	—	—
TM53	Energy Ball	Grass	Special	80	100	10	Normal	—	—
TM61	Will-O-Wisp	Fire	Status	—	75	15	Normal	—	—
TM63	Embargo	Dark	Status	—	100	15	Normal	—	—
TM64	Explosion	Normal	Physical	250	100	5	Adjacent	—	—
TM66	Payback	Dark	Physical	50	100	10	Normal	—	○
TM77	Psych Up	Normal	Status	—	—	10	Normal	—	—
TM85	Dream Eater	Psychic	Special	100	100	15	Normal	—	—
TM87	Swagger	Normal	Status	—	90	15	Normal	—	—
TM90	Substitute	Normal	Status	—	—	10	Self	—	—
TM92	Trick Room	Psychic	Status	—	—	5	Both Sides	—	—

MOVES TAUGHT BY PEOPLE

Name	Type	Kind	Pow.	Acc.	PP	Range	Long	DA

MOVES TAUGHT BY MOVE TUTORS FOR SHARDS

Name	Type	Kind	Pow.	Acc.	PP	Range	Long	DA
Uproar	Normal	Special	90	100	10	1 Random	—	—
Fire Punch	Fire	Physical	75	100	15	Normal	—	○
ThunderPunch	Electric	Physical	75	100	15	Normal	—	○
Ice Punch	Ice	Physical	75	100	15	Normal	—	○
Icy Wind	Ice	Special	55	95	15	Many Others	—	—
Foul Play	Dark	Physical	95	100	15	Normal	—	○
Dark Pulse	Dark	Special	80	100	15	Normal	○	—
Snore	Normal	Special	40	100	15	Normal	—	—
Knock Off	Dark	Physical	20	100	20	Normal	—	○
Giga Drain	Grass	Special	75	100	10	Normal	—	—
Pain Split	Normal	Status	—	—	20	Normal	—	—
Wonder Room	Psychic	Status	—	—	10	Both Sides	—	—
Spite	Ghost	Status	—	100	10	Normal	—	—
Trick	Psychic	Status	—	100	10	Normal	—	—
Sleep Talk	Normal	Status	—	—	10	Self	—	—
Skill Swap	Psychic	Status	—	—	10	Normal	—	—
Snatch	Dark	Status	—	—	10	Self	—	—

EGG MOVES

Name	Type	Kind	Pow.	Acc.	PP	Range	Long	DA
Psywave	Psychic	Special	—	80	15	Normal	—	—
Perish Song	Normal	Status	—	—	5	Adjacent	○	—
Haze	Ice	Status	—	—	30	Both Sides	—	—
Astonish	Ghost	Physical	30	100	15	Normal	—	○
Grudge	Ghost	Status	—	—	5	Self	—	—
Fire Punch	Fire	Physical	75	100	15	Normal	—	○
Ice Punch	Ice	Physical	75	100	15	Normal	—	○
ThunderPunch	Electric	Physical	75	100	15	Normal	—	○
Disable	Normal	Status	—	100	20	Normal	—	—
Scary Face	Normal	Status	—	100	10	Normal	—	—
Clear Smog	Poison	Special	50	—	15	Normal	—	—
Smog	Poison	Special	20	70	20	Normal	—	—

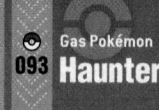

093 Haunter

Gas Pokémon

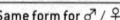

093 Haunter

● HEIGHT: 5'03"
● WEIGHT: 0.2 lbs.
● GENDER: ♂ / ♀

It likes to lurk in the dark and tap shoulders with a gaseous hand. Its touch causes endless shuddering.

Same form for ♂ / ♀

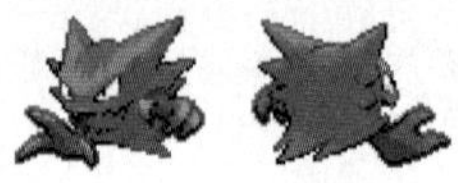

TYPE Ghost Poison

ABILITY

● Levitate

HIDDEN ABILITY

—

STATS

HP
Attack
Defense
Sp. Atk
Sp. Def
Speed

EGG GROUPS

Amorphous

ITEMS SOMETIMES HELD

● None

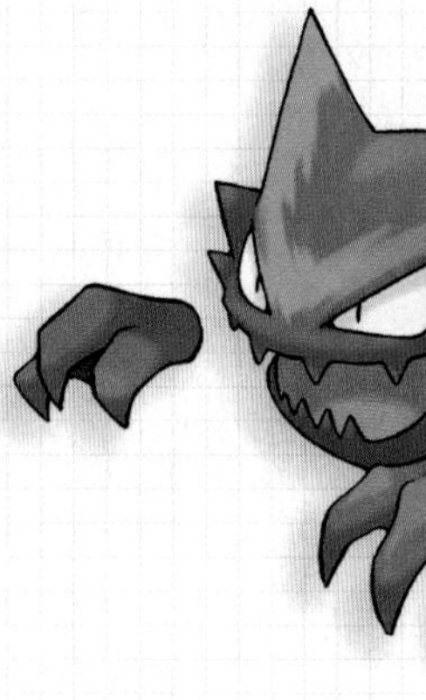

Pokémon AR Marker

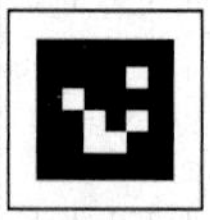

EVOLUTION

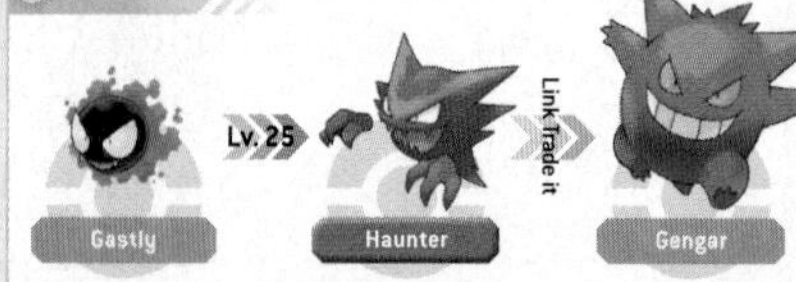

HOW TO OBTAIN

Pokémon Black Version 2	Link Trade or Poké Transfer
Pokémon White Version 2	Link Trade or Poké Transfer

HOW TO OBTAIN FROM OTHER GAMES

Pokémon HeartGold Version	Safari Zone Forest Area (night only)
Pokémon SoulSilver Version	Safari Zone Forest Area (night only)

LEVEL-UP AND LEARNED MOVES

Lv.	Name	Type	Kind	Pow.	Acc.	PP	Range	Long	DA
1	Hypnosis	Psychic	Status	—	60	20	Normal	—	—
1	Lick	Ghost	Physical	20	100	30	Normal	—	○
1	Spite	Ghost	Status	—	100	10	Normal	—	—
5	Spite	Ghost	Status	—	100	10	Normal	—	—
8	Mean Look	Normal	Status	—	—	5	Normal	—	—
12	Curse	Ghost	Status	—	—	10	Varies	—	—
15	Night Shade	Ghost	Special	—	100	15	Normal	—	—
19	Confuse Ray	Ghost	Status	—	100	10	Normal	—	—
22	Sucker Punch	Dark	Physical	80	100	5	Normal	—	○
25	Shadow Punch	Ghost	Physical	60	—	20	Normal	—	○
28	Payback	Dark	Physical	50	100	10	Normal	—	○
33	Shadow Ball	Ghost	Special	80	100	15	Normal	—	—
39	Dream Eater	Psychic	Special	100	100	15	Normal	—	—
44	Dark Pulse	Dark	Special	80	100	15	Normal	○	—
50	Destiny Bond	Ghost	Status	—	—	5	Self	—	—
55	Hex	Ghost	Special	50	100	10	Normal	—	—
61	Nightmare	Ghost	Status	—	100	15	Normal	—	—

TM & HM MOVES

Lv.	Name	Type	Kind	Pow.	Acc.	PP	Range	Long	DA
TM06	Toxic	Poison	Status	—	90	10	Normal	—	—
TM09	Venoshock	Poison	Special	65	100	10	Normal	—	—
TM10	Hidden Power	Normal	Special	—	100	15	Normal	—	—
TM11	Sunny Day	Fire	Status	—	—	5	Both Sides	—	—
TM12	Taunt	Dark	Status	—	100	20	Normal	—	—
TM17	Protect	Normal	Status	—	—	10	Self	—	—
TM18	Rain Dance	Water	Status	—	—	5	Both Sides	—	—
TM19	Telekinesis	Psychic	Status	—	—	15	Normal	—	—
TM21	Frustration	Normal	Physical	—	100	20	Normal	—	○
TM24	Thunderbolt	Electric	Special	95	100	15	Normal	—	—
TM27	Return	Normal	Physical	—	100	20	Normal	—	○
TM29	Psychic	Psychic	Special	90	100	10	Normal	—	—
TM30	Shadow Ball	Ghost	Special	80	100	15	Normal	—	—
TM32	Double Team	Normal	Status	—	—	15	Self	—	—
TM36	Sludge Bomb	Poison	Special	90	100	10	Normal	—	—
TM41	Torment	Dark	Status	—	100	15	Normal	—	—
TM42	Facade	Normal	Physical	70	100	20	Normal	—	○
TM44	Rest	Psychic	Status	—	—	10	Self	—	—
TM45	Attract	Normal	Status	—	100	15	Normal	—	—
TM46	Thief	Dark	Physical	40	100	10	Normal	—	○
TM48	Round	Normal	Special	60	100	15	Normal	—	—
TM53	Energy Ball	Grass	Special	80	100	10	Normal	—	—
TM56	Fling	Dark	Physical	—	100	10	Normal	—	—
TM61	Will-O-Wisp	Fire	Status	—	75	15	Normal	—	—
TM63	Embargo	Dark	Status	—	100	15	Normal	—	—
TM64	Explosion	Normal	Physical	250	100	5	Adjacent	—	—
TM65	Shadow Claw	Ghost	Physical	70	100	15	Normal	—	○
TM66	Payback	Dark	Physical	50	100	10	Normal	—	○
TM77	Psych Up	Normal	Status	—	—	10	Normal	—	—
TM84	Poison Jab	Poison	Physical	80	100	20	Normal	—	○
TM85	Dream Eater	Psychic	Special	100	100	15	Normal	—	—
TM87	Swagger	Normal	Status	—	90	15	Normal	—	—
TM90	Substitute	Normal	Status	—	—	10	Self	—	—
TM92	Trick Room	Psychic	Status	—	—	5	Both Sides	—	—

MOVES TAUGHT BY PEOPLE

Name	Type	Kind	Pow.	Acc.	PP	Range	Long	DA

MOVES TAUGHT BY MOVE TUTORS FOR SHARDS

Name	Type	Kind	Pow.	Acc.	PP	Range	Long	DA
Uproar	Normal	Special	90	100	10	1 Random	—	—
Fire Punch	Fire	Physical	75	100	15	Normal	—	○
ThunderPunch	Electric	Physical	75	100	15	Normal	—	○
Ice Punch	Ice	Physical	75	100	15	Normal	—	○
Icy Wind	Ice	Special	55	95	15	Many Others	—	—
Foul Play	Dark	Physical	95	100	15	Normal	—	○
Dark Pulse	Dark	Special	80	100	15	Normal	○	—
Snore	Normal	Special	40	100	15	Normal	—	—
Knock Off	Dark	Physical	20	100	20	Normal	—	○
Giga Drain	Grass	Special	75	100	10	Normal	—	—
Pain Split	Normal	Status	—	—	20	Normal	—	—
Wonder Room	Psychic	Status	—	—	10	Both Sides	—	—
Spite	Ghost	Status	—	100	10	Normal	—	—
Trick	Psychic	Status	—	100	10	Normal	—	—
Sleep Talk	Normal	Status	—	—	10	Self	—	—
Skill Swap	Psychic	Status	—	—	10	Normal	—	—
Snatch	Dark	Status	—	—	10	Self	—	—

094 Gengar

Shadow Pokémon

094 Gengar

● HEIGHT: 4'11"
● WEIGHT: 89.3 lbs.
● GENDER: ♂ / ♀

The leer that floats in darkness belongs to a Gengar delighting in casting curses on people.

Same form for ♂ / ♀

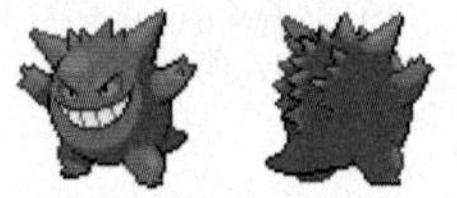

TYPE Ghost Poison

ABILITY

● Levitate

HIDDEN ABILITY

—

STATS

HP
Attack
Defense
Sp. Atk
Sp. Def
Speed

EGG GROUPS

Amorphous

ITEMS SOMETIMES HELD

● None

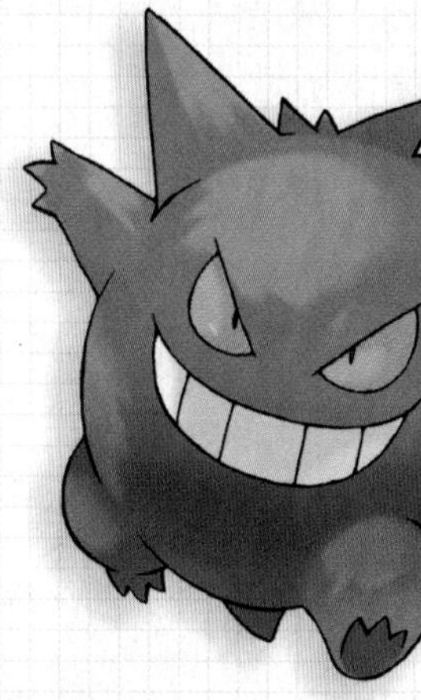

Pokémon AR Marker

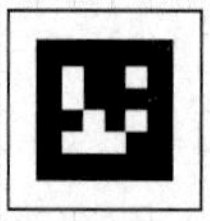

EVOLUTION

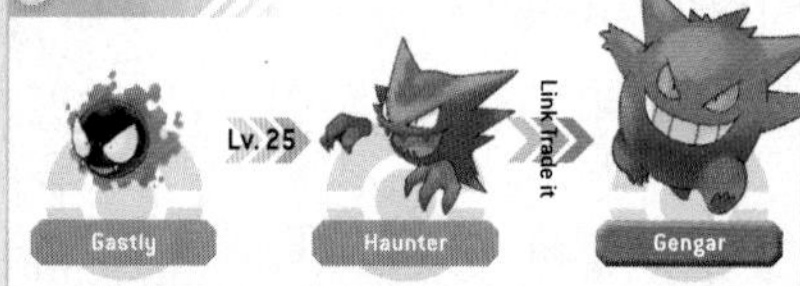

HOW TO OBTAIN

Pokémon Black Version 2	Have Haunter sent to you via Link Trade to receive Gengar
Pokémon White Version 2	Have Haunter sent to you via Link Trade to receive Gengar

HOW TO OBTAIN FROM OTHER GAMES

—

—

LEVEL-UP AND LEARNED MOVES

Lv.	Name	Type	Kind	Pow.	Acc.	PP	Range	Long	DA
1	Hypnosis	Psychic	Status	—	60	20	Normal	—	—
1	Lick	Ghost	Physical	20	100	30	Normal	—	○
1	Spite	Ghost	Status	—	100	10	Normal	—	—
5	Spite	Ghost	Status	—	100	10	Normal	—	—
8	Mean Look	Normal	Status	—	—	5	Normal	—	—
12	Curse	Ghost	Status	—	—	10	Varies	—	—
15	Night Shade	Ghost	Special	—	100	15	Normal	—	—
19	Confuse Ray	Ghost	Status	—	100	10	Normal	—	—
22	Sucker Punch	Dark	Physical	80	100	5	Normal	—	○
25	Shadow Punch	Ghost	Physical	60	—	20	Normal	—	○
28	Payback	Dark	Physical	50	100	10	Normal	—	○
33	Shadow Ball	Ghost	Special	80	100	15	Normal	—	—
39	Dream Eater	Psychic	Special	100	100	15	Normal	—	—
44	Dark Pulse	Dark	Special	80	100	15	Normal	○	—
50	Destiny Bond	Ghost	Status	—	—	5	Self	—	—
55	Hex	Ghost	Special	50	100	10	Normal	—	—
61	Nightmare	Ghost	Status	—	100	15	Normal	—	—

TM & HM MOVES

Lv.	Name	Type	Kind	Pow.	Acc.	PP	Range	Long	DA
TM06	Toxic	Poison	Status	—	90	10	Normal	—	—
TM09	Venoshock	Poison	Special	65	100	10	Normal	—	—
TM10	Hidden Power	Normal	Special	—	100	15	Normal	—	—
TM11	Sunny Day	Fire	Status	—	—	5	Both Sides	—	—
TM12	Taunt	Dark	Status	—	100	20	Normal	—	—
TM15	Hyper Beam	Normal	Special	150	90	5	Normal	—	—
TM17	Protect	Normal	Status	—	—	10	Self	—	—
TM18	Rain Dance	Water	Status	—	—	5	Both Sides	—	—
TM19	Telekinesis	Psychic	Status	—	—	15	Normal	—	—
TM21	Frustration	Normal	Physical	—	100	20	Normal	—	○
TM24	Thunderbolt	Electric	Special	95	100	15	Normal	—	—
TM25	Thunder	Electric	Special	120	70	10	Normal	—	—
TM27	Return	Normal	Physical	—	100	20	Normal	—	○
TM29	Psychic	Psychic	Special	90	100	10	Normal	—	—
TM30	Shadow Ball	Ghost	Special	80	100	15	Normal	—	—
TM31	Brick Break	Fighting	Physical	75	100	15	Normal	—	○
TM32	Double Team	Normal	Status	—	—	15	Self	—	—
TM36	Sludge Bomb	Poison	Special	90	100	10	Normal	—	—
TM41	Torment	Dark	Status	—	100	15	Normal	—	—
TM42	Facade	Normal	Physical	70	100	20	Normal	—	○
TM44	Rest	Psychic	Status	—	—	10	Self	—	—
TM45	Attract	Normal	Status	—	100	15	Normal	—	—
TM46	Thief	Dark	Physical	40	100	10	Normal	—	○
TM48	Round	Normal	Special	60	100	15	Normal	—	—
TM52	Focus Blast	Fighting	Special	120	70	5	Normal	—	—
TM53	Energy Ball	Grass	Special	80	100	10	Normal	—	—
TM56	Fling	Dark	Physical	—	100	10	Normal	—	—
TM61	Will-O-Wisp	Fire	Status	—	75	15	Normal	—	—
TM63	Embargo	Dark	Status	—	100	15	Normal	—	—
TM64	Explosion	Normal	Physical	250	100	5	Adjacent	—	—
TM65	Shadow Claw	Ghost	Physical	70	100	15	Normal	—	○
TM66	Payback	Dark	Physical	50	100	10	Normal	—	○
TM68	Giga Impact	Normal	Physical	150	90	5	Normal	—	○
TM77	Psych Up	Normal	Status	—	—	10	Normal	—	—
TM84	Poison Jab	Poison	Physical	80	100	20	Normal	—	○
TM85	Dream Eater	Psychic	Special	100	100	15	Normal	—	—
TM87	Swagger	Normal	Status	—	90	15	Normal	—	—
TM90	Substitute	Normal	Status	—	—	10	Self	—	—
TM92	Trick Room	Psychic	Status	—	—	5	Both Sides	—	—
TM94	Rock Smash	Fighting	Physical	40	100	15	Normal	—	○
HM04	Strength	Normal	Physical	80	100	15	Normal	—	○

MOVES TAUGHT BY PEOPLE

Name	Type	Kind	Pow.	Acc.	PP	Range	Long	DA

MOVES TAUGHT BY MOVE TUTORS FOR SHARDS

Name	Type	Kind	Pow.	Acc.	PP	Range	Long	DA
Uproar	Normal	Special	90	100	10	1 Random	—	—
Fire Punch	Fire	Physical	75	100	15	Normal	—	○
ThunderPunch	Electric	Physical	75	100	15	Normal	—	○
Ice Punch	Ice	Physical	75	100	15	Normal	—	○
Icy Wind	Ice	Special	55	95	15	Many Others	—	—
Foul Play	Dark	Physical	95	100	15	Normal	—	○
Dark Pulse	Dark	Special	80	100	15	Normal	○	—
Snore	Normal	Special	40	100	15	Normal	—	—
Knock Off	Dark	Physical	20	100	20	Normal	—	○
Role Play	Psychic	Status	—	—	10	Normal	—	—
Giga Drain	Grass	Special	75	100	10	Normal	—	—
Drain Punch	Fighting	Physical	75	100	10	Normal	—	○
Pain Split	Normal	Status	—	—	20	Normal	—	—
Wonder Room	Psychic	Status	—	—	10	Both Sides	—	—
Spite	Ghost	Status	—	100	10	Normal	—	—
Trick	Psychic	Status	—	100	10	Normal	—	—
Sleep Talk	Normal	Status	—	—	10	Self	—	—
Skill Swap	Psychic	Status	—	—	10	Normal	—	—
Snatch	Dark	Status	—	—	10	Self	—	—

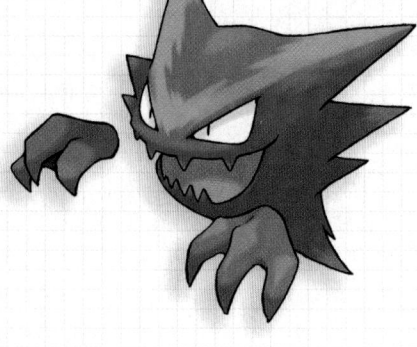

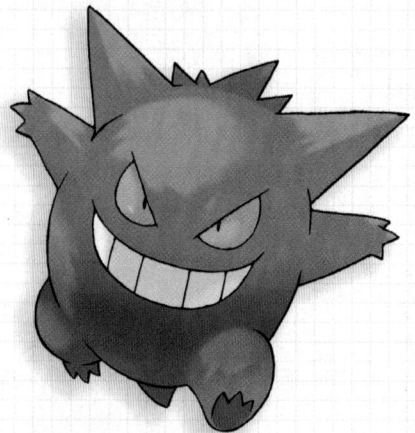

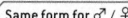

095 Onix

Rock Snake Pokémon

- HEIGHT: 28'10"
- WEIGHT: 463.0 lbs.
- GENDER: ♂ / ♀

Opening its large mouth, it ingests massive amounts of soil and creates long tunnels.

Same form for ♂ / ♀

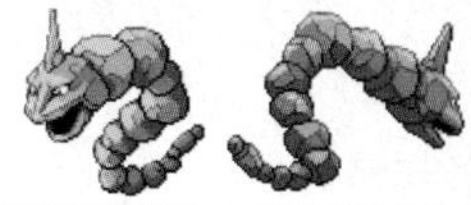

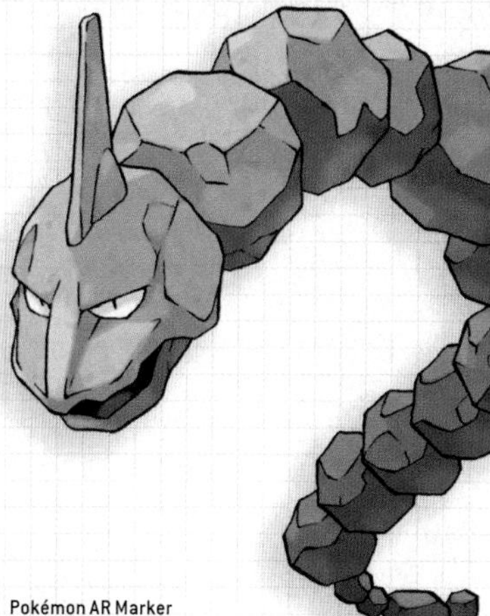

Pokémon AR Marker

TYPE Rock Ground

ABILITIES
- Rock Head
- Sturdy

HIDDEN ABILITY
- Weak Armor

STATS
HP
Attack
Defense
Sp. Atk
Sp. Def
Speed

EGG GROUPS
Mineral

ITEMS SOMETIMES HELD
- None

EVOLUTION

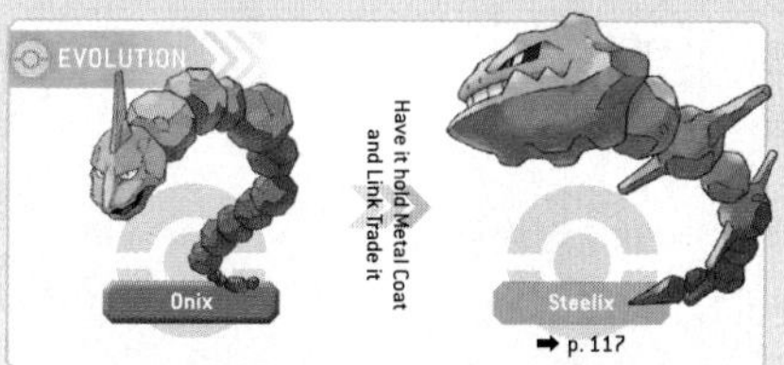
Onix
Have it hold Metal Coat and Link Trade it
Steelix

➡ p. 117

HOW TO OBTAIN

Pokémon Black Version 2	❶ Relic Passage Driftveil City exit ❷ Victory Road caves 2F
Pokémon White Version 2	❶ Relic Passage Driftveil City exit ❷ Victory Road caves 2F

HOW TO OBTAIN FROM OTHER GAMES

—

—

LEVEL-UP AND LEARNED MOVES

Lv.	Name	Type	Kind	Pow.	Acc.	PP	Range	Long	DA
1	Mud Sport	Ground	Status	—	—	15	Both Sides	—	—
1	Tackle	Normal	Physical	50	100	35	Normal	—	○
1	Harden	Normal	Status	—	—	30	Self	—	—
1	Bind	Normal	Physical	15	85	20	Normal	—	○
4	Curse	Ghost	Status	—	—	10	Varies	—	—
7	Rock Throw	Rock	Physical	50	90	15	Normal	—	—
10	Rage	Normal	Physical	20	100	20	Normal	—	○
13	Rock Tomb	Rock	Physical	50	80	10	Normal	—	—
16	Stealth Rock	Rock	Status	—	—	20	Other Side	—	—
19	Rock Polish	Rock	Status	—	—	20	Self	—	—
22	Smack Down	Rock	Physical	50	100	15	Normal	—	—
25	DragonBreath	Dragon	Special	60	100	20	Normal	—	—
28	Slam	Normal	Physical	80	75	20	Normal	—	○
31	Screech	Normal	Status	—	85	40	Normal	—	—
34	Rock Slide	Rock	Physical	75	90	10	Many Others	—	—
37	Sand Tomb	Ground	Physical	35	85	15	Normal	—	—
40	Iron Tail	Steel	Physical	100	75	15	Normal	—	○
43	Dig	Ground	Physical	80	100	10	Normal	—	○
46	Stone Edge	Rock	Physical	100	80	5	Normal	—	—
49	Double-Edge	Normal	Physical	120	100	15	Normal	—	○
52	Sandstorm	Rock	Status	—	—	10	Both Sides	—	—

TM & HM MOVES

Lv.	Name	Type	Kind	Pow.	Acc.	PP	Range	Long	DA
TM05	Roar	Normal	Status	—	100	20	Normal	—	—
TM06	Toxic	Poison	Status	—	90	10	Normal	—	—
TM10	Hidden Power	Normal	Special	—	100	15	Normal	—	—
TM11	Sunny Day	Fire	Status	—	—	5	Both Sides	—	—
TM12	Taunt	Dark	Status	—	100	20	Normal	—	—
TM17	Protect	Normal	Status	—	—	10	Self	—	—
TM21	Frustration	Normal	Physical	—	100	20	Normal	—	○
TM23	Smack Down	Rock	Physical	50	100	15	Normal	—	—
TM26	Earthquake	Ground	Physical	100	100	10	Adjacent	—	—
TM27	Return	Normal	Physical	—	100	20	Normal	—	○
TM28	Dig	Ground	Physical	80	100	10	Normal	—	○
TM32	Double Team	Normal	Status	—	—	15	Self	—	—
TM37	Sandstorm	Rock	Status	—	—	10	Both Sides	—	—
TM39	Rock Tomb	Rock	Physical	50	80	10	Normal	—	—
TM41	Torment	Dark	Status	—	100	15	Normal	—	—
TM42	Facade	Normal	Physical	70	100	20	Normal	—	○
TM44	Rest	Psychic	Status	—	—	10	Self	—	—
TM45	Attract	Normal	Status	—	100	15	Normal	—	—
TM48	Round	Normal	Special	60	100	15	Normal	—	—
TM64	Explosion	Normal	Physical	250	100	5	Adjacent	—	—
TM66	Payback	Dark	Physical	50	100	10	Normal	—	○
TM69	Rock Polish	Rock	Status	—	—	20	Self	—	—
TM71	Stone Edge	Rock	Physical	100	80	5	Normal	—	—
TM74	Gyro Ball	Steel	Physical	—	100	5	Normal	—	○
TM77	Psych Up	Normal	Status	—	—	10	Normal	—	—
TM78	Bulldoze	Ground	Physical	60	100	20	Adjacent	—	—
TM80	Rock Slide	Rock	Physical	75	90	10	Many Others	—	—
TM82	Dragon Tail	Dragon	Physical	60	90	10	Normal	—	○
TM87	Swagger	Normal	Status	—	90	15	Normal	—	—
TM90	Substitute	Normal	Status	—	—	10	Self	—	—
TM91	Flash Cannon	Steel	Special	80	100	10	Normal	—	—
TM94	Rock Smash	Fighting	Physical	40	100	15	Normal	—	○
HM04	Strength	Normal	Physical	80	100	15	Normal	—	○

MOVES TAUGHT BY PEOPLE

Name	Type	Kind	Pow.	Acc.	PP	Range	Long	DA

MOVES TAUGHT BY MOVE TUTORS FOR SHARDS

Name	Type	Kind	Pow.	Acc.	PP	Range	Long	DA
Iron Head	Steel	Physical	80	100	15	Normal	—	○
Block	Normal	Status	—	—	5	Normal	—	—
Iron Tail	Steel	Physical	100	75	15	Normal	—	○
Earth Power	Ground	Special	90	100	10	Normal	—	—
Dragon Pulse	Dragon	Special	90	100	10	Normal	○	—
Bind	Normal	Physical	15	85	20	Normal	—	○
Snore	Normal	Special	40	100	15	Normal	—	—
Stealth Rock	Rock	Status	—	—	20	Other Side	—	—
Sleep Talk	Normal	Status	—	—	10	Self	—	—

EGG MOVES

Name	Type	Kind	Pow.	Acc.	PP	Range	Long	DA
Flail	Normal	Physical	—	100	15	Normal	—	○
Block	Normal	Status	—	—	5	Normal	—	—
Defense Curl	Normal	Status	—	—	40	Self	—	—
Rollout	Rock	Physical	30	90	20	Normal	—	○
Rock Blast	Rock	Physical	25	90	10	Normal	—	—
Rock Climb	Normal	Physical	90	85	20	Normal	—	○
Heavy Slam	Steel	Physical	—	100	10	Normal	—	○
Stealth Rock	Rock	Status	—	—	20	Other Side	—	—

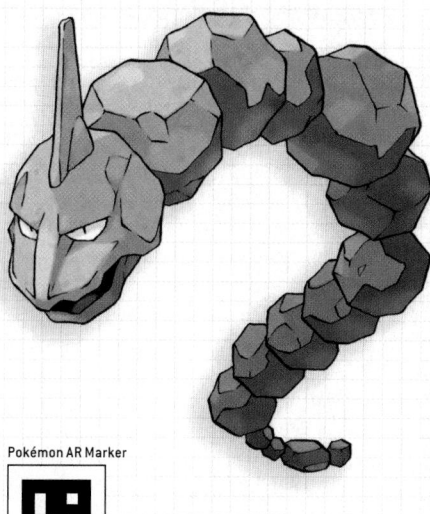

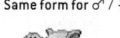

096 Drowzee

Hypnosis Pokémon

- HEIGHT: 3'03"
- WEIGHT: 71.4 lbs.
- GENDER: ♂ / ♀

It can tell what people are dreaming by sniffing with its big nose. It loves fun dreams.

Same form for ♂ / ♀

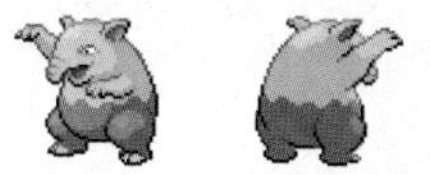

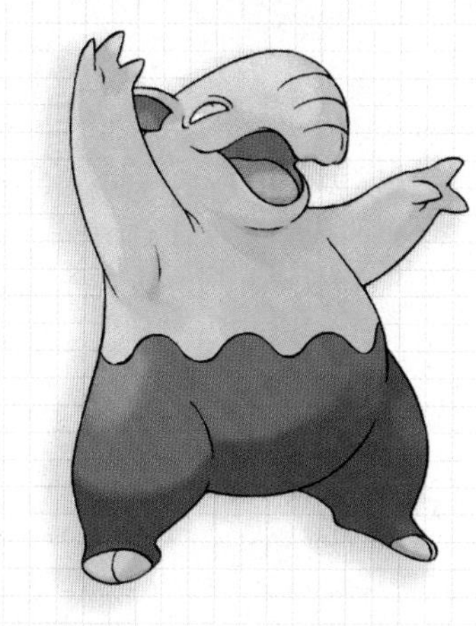

Pokémon AR Marker

TYPE Psychic

ABILITIES
- Insomnia
- Forewarn

HIDDEN ABILITY
- Inner Focus

STATS
HP
Attack
Defense
Sp. Atk
Sp. Def
Speed

EGG GROUPS
Human-Like

ITEMS SOMETIMES HELD
- None

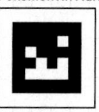

EVOLUTION

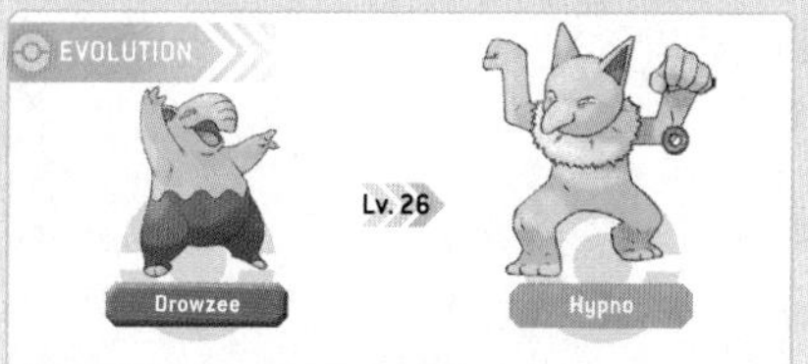
Drowzee
Lv. 26
Hypno

HOW TO OBTAIN

Pokémon Black Version 2	Catch a Hypno, leave it at the Pokémon Day Care, and hatch the Egg that is found
Pokémon White Version 2	Catch a Hypno, leave it at the Pokémon Day Care, and hatch the Egg that is found

HOW TO OBTAIN FROM OTHER GAMES

Pokémon HeartGold Version	Route 34
Pokémon SoulSilver Version	Route 34

LEVEL-UP AND LEARNED MOVES

Lv.	Name	Type	Kind	Pow.	Acc.	PP	Range	Long	DA
1	Pound	Normal	Physical	40	100	35	Normal	—	○
1	Hypnosis	Psychic	Status	—	60	20	Normal	—	—
5	Disable	Normal	Status	—	100	20	Normal	—	—
9	Confusion	Psychic	Special	50	100	25	Normal	—	—
13	Headbutt	Normal	Physical	70	100	15	Normal	—	○
17	Poison Gas	Poison	Status	—	80	40	Many Others	—	—
21	Meditate	Psychic	Status	—	—	40	Self	—	—
25	Psybeam	Psychic	Special	65	100	20	Normal	—	—
29	Headbutt	Normal	Physical	70	100	15	Normal	—	○
33	Psych Up	Normal	Status	—	—	10	Normal	—	—
37	Synchronoise	Psychic	Special	70	100	15	Adjacent	—	—
41	Zen Headbutt	Psychic	Physical	80	90	15	Normal	—	○
45	Swagger	Normal	Status	—	90	15	Normal	—	—
49	Psychic	Psychic	Special	90	100	10	Normal	—	—
53	Nasty Plot	Dark	Status	—	—	20	Self	—	—
57	Psyshock	Psychic	Special	80	100	10	Normal	—	—
61	Future Sight	Psychic	Special	100	100	10	Normal	—	—

TM & HM MOVES

Lv.	Name	Type	Kind	Pow.	Acc.	PP	Range	Long	DA
TM03	Psyshock	Psychic	Special	80	100	10	Normal	—	—
TM04	Calm Mind	Psychic	Status	—	—	20	Self	—	—
TM06	Toxic	Poison	Status	—	90	10	Normal	—	—
TM10	Hidden Power	Normal	Special	—	100	15	Normal	—	—
TM11	Sunny Day	Fire	Status	—	—	5	Both Sides	—	—
TM12	Taunt	Dark	Status	—	100	20	Normal	—	—
TM16	Light Screen	Psychic	Status	—	—	30	Your Side	—	—
TM17	Protect	Normal	Status	—	—	10	Self	—	—
TM18	Rain Dance	Water	Status	—	—	5	Both Sides	—	—
TM19	Telekinesis	Psychic	Status	—	—	15	Normal	—	—
TM20	Safeguard	Normal	Status	—	—	25	Your Side	—	—
TM21	Frustration	Normal	Physical	—	100	20	Normal	—	○
TM27	Return	Normal	Physical	—	100	20	Normal	—	○
TM29	Psychic	Psychic	Special	90	100	10	Normal	—	—
TM30	Shadow Ball	Ghost	Special	80	100	15	Normal	—	—
TM31	Brick Break	Fighting	Physical	75	100	15	Normal	—	○
TM32	Double Team	Normal	Status	—	—	15	Self	—	—
TM33	Reflect	Psychic	Status	—	—	20	Your Side	—	—
TM41	Torment	Dark	Status	—	100	15	Normal	—	—
TM42	Facade	Normal	Physical	70	100	20	Normal	—	○
TM44	Rest	Psychic	Status	—	—	10	Self	—	—
TM45	Attract	Normal	Status	—	100	15	Normal	—	—
TM46	Thief	Dark	Physical	40	100	10	Normal	—	○
TM47	Low Sweep	Fighting	Physical	60	100	20	Normal	—	○
TM48	Round	Normal	Special	60	100	15	Normal	—	—
TM56	Fling	Dark	Physical	—	100	10	Normal	—	—
TM70	Flash	Normal	Status	—	100	20	Normal	—	—
TM73	Thunder Wave	Electric	Status	—	100	20	Normal	—	—
TM77	Psych Up	Normal	Status	—	—	10	Normal	—	—
TM85	Dream Eater	Psychic	Special	100	100	15	Normal	—	—
TM86	Grass Knot	Grass	Special	—	100	20	Normal	—	○
TM87	Swagger	Normal	Status	—	90	15	Normal	—	—
TM90	Substitute	Normal	Status	—	—	10	Self	—	—
TM92	Trick Room	Psychic	Status	—	—	5	Both Sides	—	—

MOVES TAUGHT BY PEOPLE

Name	Type	Kind	Pow.	Acc.	PP	Range	Long	DA

MOVES TAUGHT BY MOVE TUTORS FOR SHARDS

Name	Type	Kind	Pow.	Acc.	PP	Range	Long	DA
Signal Beam	Bug	Special	75	100	15	Normal	—	—
Low Kick	Fighting	Physical	—	100	20	Normal	—	○
Fire Punch	Fire	Physical	75	100	15	Normal	—	○
ThunderPunch	Electric	Physical	75	100	15	Normal	—	○
Ice Punch	Ice	Physical	75	100	15	Normal	—	○
Magic Coat	Psychic	Status	—	—	15	Self	—	—
Zen Headbutt	Psychic	Physical	80	90	15	Normal	—	○
Foul Play	Dark	Physical	95	100	15	Normal	—	○
Role Play	Psychic	Status	—	—	10	Normal	—	—
Drain Punch	Fighting	Physical	75	100	10	Normal	—	○
Magic Room	Psychic	Status	—	—	10	Both Sides	—	—
Recycle	Normal	Status	—	—	10	Self	—	—
Trick	Psychic	Status	—	100	10	Normal	—	—
Sleep Talk	Normal	Status	—	—	10	Self	—	—
Skill Swap	Psychic	Status	—	—	10	Normal	—	—
Snatch	Dark	Status	—	—	10	Self	—	—

EGG MOVES

Name	Type	Kind	Pow.	Acc.	PP	Range	Long	DA
Barrier	Psychic	Status	—	—	30	Self	—	—
Assist	Normal	Status	—	—	20	Self	—	—
Role Play	Psychic	Status	—	—	10	Normal	—	—
Fire Punch	Fire	Physical	75	100	15	Normal	—	○
ThunderPunch	Electric	Physical	75	100	15	Normal	—	○
Ice Punch	Ice	Physical	75	100	15	Normal	—	○
Nasty Plot	Dark	Status	—	—	20	Self	—	—
Flatter	Dark	Status	—	100	15	Normal	—	—
Psycho Cut	Psychic	Physical	70	100	20	Normal	—	—
Guard Swap	Psychic	Status	—	—	10	Normal	—	—
Secret Power	Normal	Physical	70	100	20	Normal	—	—
Skill Swap	Psychic	Status	—	—	10	Normal	—	—

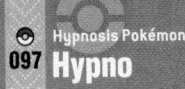

097 Hypno
Hypnosis Pokémon

- HEIGHT: 5'03"
- WEIGHT: 166.7 lbs.
- GENDER: ♂ / ♀

Seeing its swinging pendulum can induce sleep in three seconds, even in someone who just woke up.

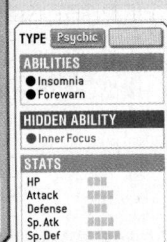

TYPE Psychic

ABILITIES
- Insomnia
- Forewarn

HIDDEN ABILITY
- Inner Focus

STATS
HP
Attack
Defense
Sp. Atk
Sp. Def
Speed

EGG GROUPS
Human-Like

ITEMS SOMETIMES HELD
- None

♂ ♀

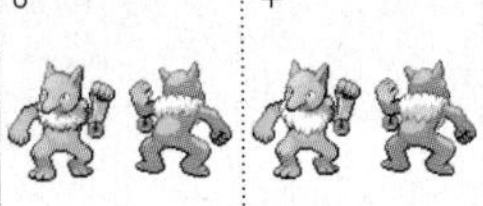

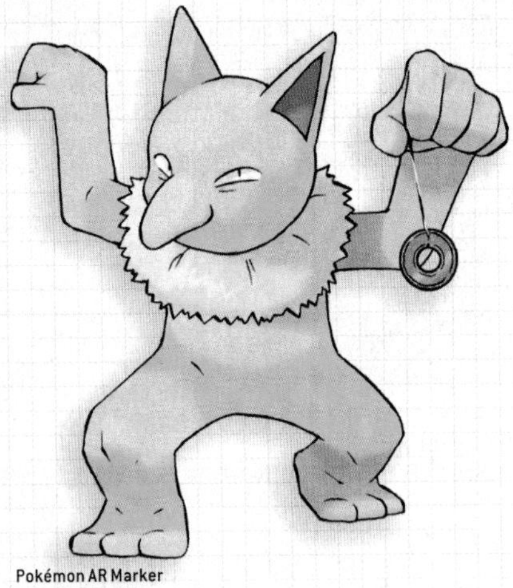

Pokémon AR Marker

EVOLUTION

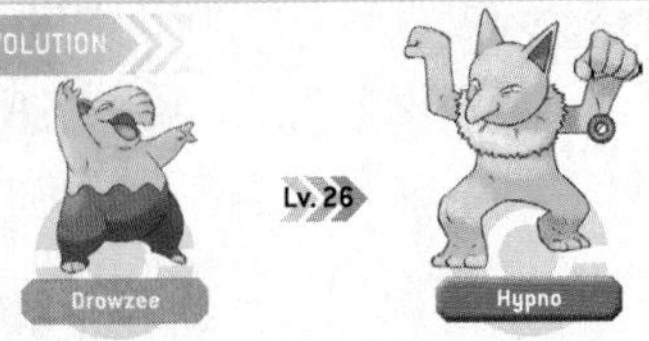
Drowzee
Lv. 26
Hypno

HOW TO OBTAIN

Pokémon Black Version 2	Dreamyard (mass outbreak)
Pokémon White Version 2	Dreamyard (mass outbreak)

HOW TO OBTAIN FROM OTHER GAMES

—

—

LEVEL-UP AND LEARNED MOVES

Lv.	Name	Type	Kind	Pow.	Acc.	PP	Range	Long	DA
1	Nightmare	Ghost	Status	—	100	15	Normal	—	—
1	Switcheroo	Dark	Status	—	100	10	Normal	—	—
1	Pound	Normal	Physical	40	100	35	Normal	—	○
1	Hypnosis	Psychic	Status	—	60	20	Normal	—	—
1	Disable	Normal	Status	—	100	20	Normal	—	—
1	Confusion	Psychic	Special	50	100	25	Normal	—	—
5	Disable	Normal	Status	—	100	20	Normal	—	—
9	Confusion	Psychic	Special	50	100	25	Normal	—	—
13	Headbutt	Normal	Physical	70	100	15	Normal	—	○
17	Poison Gas	Poison	Status	—	80	40	Many Others	—	—
21	Meditate	Psychic	Status	—	—	40	Self	—	—
25	Psybeam	Psychic	Special	65	100	20	Normal	—	—
29	Headbutt	Normal	Physical	70	100	15	Normal	—	○
33	Psych Up	Normal	Status	—	—	10	Normal	—	—
37	Synchronoise	Psychic	Special	70	100	15	Adjacent	—	—
41	Zen Headbutt	Psychic	Physical	80	90	15	Normal	—	○
45	Swagger	Normal	Status	—	90	15	Normal	—	—
49	Psychic	Psychic	Special	90	100	10	Normal	—	—
53	Nasty Plot	Dark	Status	—	—	20	Self	—	—
57	Psyshock	Psychic	Special	80	100	10	Normal	—	—
61	Future Sight	Psychic	Special	100	100	10	Normal	—	—

TM & HM MOVES

Lv.	Name	Type	Kind	Pow.	Acc.	PP	Range	Long	DA
TM03	Psyshock	Psychic	Special	80	100	10	Normal	—	—
TM04	Calm Mind	Psychic	Status	—	—	20	Self	—	—
TM06	Toxic	Poison	Status	—	90	10	Normal	—	—
TM10	Hidden Power	Normal	Special	—	100	15	Normal	—	—
TM11	Sunny Day	Fire	Status	—	—	5	Both Sides	—	—
TM12	Taunt	Dark	Status	—	100	20	Normal	—	—
TM15	Hyper Beam	Normal	Special	150	90	5	Normal	—	—
TM16	Light Screen	Psychic	Status	—	—	30	Your Side	—	—
TM17	Protect	Normal	Status	—	—	10	Self	—	—
TM18	Rain Dance	Water	Status	—	—	5	Both Sides	—	—
TM19	Telekinesis	Psychic	Status	—	—	15	Normal	—	—
TM20	Safeguard	Normal	Status	—	—	25	Your Side	—	—
TM21	Frustration	Normal	Physical	—	100	20	Normal	—	○
TM27	Return	Normal	Physical	—	100	20	Normal	—	○
TM29	Psychic	Psychic	Special	90	100	10	Normal	—	—
TM30	Shadow Ball	Ghost	Special	80	100	15	Normal	—	—
TM31	Brick Break	Fighting	Physical	75	100	15	Normal	—	○
TM32	Double Team	Normal	Status	—	—	15	Self	—	—
TM33	Reflect	Psychic	Status	—	—	20	Your Side	—	—
TM41	Torment	Dark	Status	—	100	15	Normal	—	—
TM42	Facade	Normal	Physical	70	100	20	Normal	—	○
TM44	Rest	Psychic	Status	—	—	10	Self	—	—
TM45	Attract	Normal	Status	—	100	15	Normal	—	—
TM46	Thief	Dark	Physical	40	100	10	Normal	—	○
TM47	Low Sweep	Fighting	Physical	60	100	20	Normal	—	○
TM48	Round	Normal	Special	60	100	15	Normal	—	—
TM52	Focus Blast	Fighting	Special	120	70	5	Normal	—	—
TM56	Fling	Dark	Physical	—	100	10	Normal	—	—
TM68	Giga Impact	Normal	Physical	150	90	5	Normal	—	○
TM70	Flash	Normal	Status	—	100	20	Normal	—	—
TM73	Thunder Wave	Electric	Status	—	100	20	Normal	—	—
TM77	Psych Up	Normal	Status	—	—	10	Normal	—	—
TM85	Dream Eater	Psychic	Special	100	100	15	Normal	—	—
TM86	Grass Knot	Grass	Special	—	100	20	Normal	—	○
TM87	Swagger	Normal	Status	—	90	15	Normal	—	—
TM90	Substitute	Normal	Status	—	—	10	Self	—	—
TM92	Trick Room	Psychic	Status	—	—	5	Both Sides	—	—

MOVES TAUGHT BY PEOPLE

Name	Type	Kind	Pow.	Acc.	PP	Range	Long	DA

MOVES TAUGHT BY MOVE TUTORS FOR SHARDS

Name	Type	Kind	Pow.	Acc.	PP	Range	Long	DA
Signal Beam	Bug	Special	75	100	15	Normal	—	—
Low Kick	Fighting	Physical	—	100	20	Normal	—	○
Fire Punch	Fire	Physical	75	100	15	Normal	—	○
ThunderPunch	Electric	Physical	75	100	15	Normal	—	○
Ice Punch	Ice	Physical	75	100	15	Normal	—	○
Magic Coat	Psychic	Status	—	—	15	Self	—	—
Zen Headbutt	Psychic	Physical	80	90	15	Normal	—	○
Foul Play	Dark	Physical	95	100	15	Normal	—	○
Role Play	Psychic	Status	—	—	10	Normal	—	—
Drain Punch	Fighting	Physical	75	100	10	Normal	—	○
Magic Room	Psychic	Status	—	—	10	Both Sides	—	—
Recycle	Normal	Status	—	—	10	Self	—	—
Trick	Psychic	Status	—	100	10	Normal	—	—
Sleep Talk	Normal	Status	—	—	10	Self	—	—
Skill Swap	Psychic	Status	—	—	10	Normal	—	—
Snatch	Dark	Status	—	—	10	Self	—	—

098 Krabby
River Crab Pokémon

- HEIGHT: 1'04"
- WEIGHT: 14.3 lbs.
- GENDER: ♂ / ♀

It lives in burrows dug on sandy beaches. Its pincers fully grow back if they are broken in battle.

TYPE Water

ABILITIES
- Hyper Cutter
- Shell Armor

HIDDEN ABILITY
- Sheer Force

STATS
HP
Attack
Defense
Sp. Atk
Sp. Def
Speed

EGG GROUPS
Water ❸

ITEMS SOMETIMES HELD
- None

Same form for ♂ / ♀

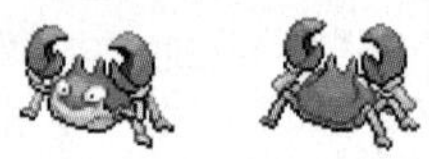

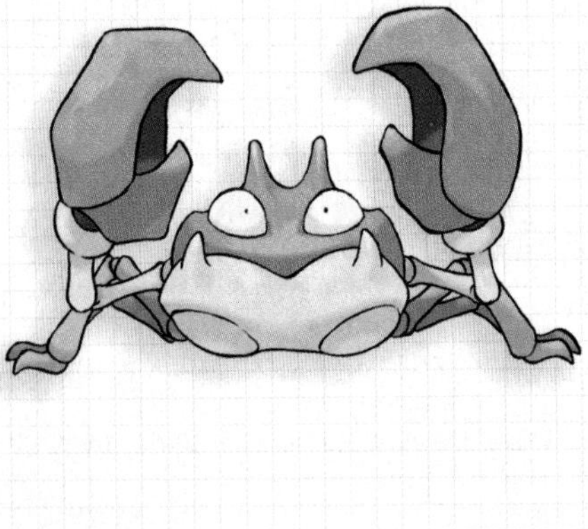

Pokémon AR Marker

EVOLUTION

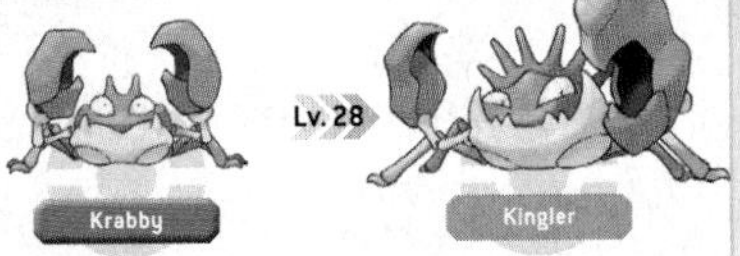
Krabby
Lv. 28
Kingler

HOW TO OBTAIN

Pokémon Black Version 2	❶ Virbank City (Super Rod) ❷ Virbank Complex (Super Rod)
Pokémon White Version 2	❶ Virbank City (Super Rod) ❷ Virbank Complex (Super Rod)

HOW TO OBTAIN FROM OTHER GAMES

—

—

LEVEL-UP AND LEARNED MOVES

Lv.	Name	Type	Kind	Pow.	Acc.	PP	Range	Long	DA
1	Mud Sport	Ground	Status	—	—	15	Both Sides	—	—
1	Bubble	Water	Special	20	100	30	Many Others	—	—
5	ViceGrip	Normal	Physical	55	100	30	Normal	—	○
9	Leer	Normal	Status	—	100	30	Many Others	—	—
11	Harden	Normal	Status	—	—	30	Self	—	—
15	BubbleBeam	Water	Special	65	100	20	Normal	—	—
19	Mud Shot	Ground	Special	55	95	15	Normal	—	—
21	Metal Claw	Steel	Physical	50	95	35	Normal	—	○
25	Stomp	Normal	Physical	65	100	20	Normal	—	○
29	Protect	Normal	Status	—	—	10	Self	—	—
31	Guillotine	Normal	Physical	—	30	5	Normal	—	○
35	Slam	Normal	Physical	80	75	20	Normal	—	○
39	Brine	Water	Special	65	100	10	Normal	—	—
41	Crabhammer	Water	Physical	90	90	10	Normal	—	○
45	Flail	Normal	Physical	—	100	15	Normal	—	○

TM & HM MOVES

Lv.	Name	Type	Kind	Pow.	Acc.	PP	Range	Long	DA
TM01	Hone Claws	Dark	Status	—	—	15	Self	—	—
TM06	Toxic	Poison	Status	—	90	10	Normal	—	—
TM07	Hail	Ice	Status	—	—	10	Both Sides	—	—
TM10	Hidden Power	Normal	Special	—	100	15	Normal	—	—
TM13	Ice Beam	Ice	Special	95	100	10	Normal	—	—
TM14	Blizzard	Ice	Special	120	70	5	Many Others	—	—
TM17	Protect	Normal	Status	—	—	10	Self	—	—
TM18	Rain Dance	Water	Status	—	—	5	Both Sides	—	—
TM21	Frustration	Normal	Physical	—	100	20	Normal	—	○
TM27	Return	Normal	Physical	—	100	20	Normal	—	○
TM28	Dig	Ground	Physical	80	100	10	Normal	—	○
TM31	Brick Break	Fighting	Physical	75	100	15	Normal	—	○
TM32	Double Team	Normal	Status	—	—	15	Self	—	—
TM39	Rock Tomb	Rock	Physical	50	80	10	Normal	—	—
TM42	Facade	Normal	Physical	70	100	20	Normal	—	○
TM44	Rest	Psychic	Status	—	—	10	Self	—	—
TM45	Attract	Normal	Status	—	100	15	Normal	—	—
TM46	Thief	Dark	Physical	40	100	10	Normal	—	○
TM48	Round	Normal	Special	60	100	15	Normal	—	—
TM54	False Swipe	Normal	Physical	40	100	40	Normal	—	○
TM55	Scald	Water	Special	80	100	15	Normal	—	—
TM56	Fling	Dark	Physical	—	100	10	Normal	—	—
TM75	Swords Dance	Normal	Status	—	—	30	Self	—	—
TM80	Rock Slide	Rock	Physical	75	90	10	Many Others	—	—
TM81	X-Scissor	Bug	Physical	80	100	15	Normal	—	○
TM87	Swagger	Normal	Status	—	90	15	Normal	—	—
TM90	Substitute	Normal	Status	—	—	10	Self	—	—
TM94	Rock Smash	Fighting	Physical	40	100	15	Normal	—	○
HM01	Cut	Normal	Physical	50	95	30	Normal	—	○
HM03	Surf	Water	Special	95	100	15	Adjacent	—	—
HM04	Strength	Normal	Physical	80	100	15	Normal	—	○
HM06	Dive	Water	Physical	80	100	10	Normal	—	○

MOVES TAUGHT BY PEOPLE

Name	Type	Kind	Pow.	Acc.	PP	Range	Long	DA

MOVES TAUGHT BY MOVE TUTORS FOR SHARDS

Name	Type	Kind	Pow.	Acc.	PP	Range	Long	DA
Iron Defense	Steel	Status	—	—	15	Self	—	—
Icy Wind	Ice	Special	55	95	15	Many Others	—	—
Superpower	Fighting	Physical	120	100	5	Normal	—	○
Snore	Normal	Special	40	100	15	Normal	—	—
Knock Off	Dark	Physical	20	100	20	Normal	—	○
Sleep Talk	Normal	Status	—	—	10	Self	—	—

EGG MOVES

Name	Type	Kind	Pow.	Acc.	PP	Range	Long	DA
Haze	Ice	Status	—	—	30	Both Sides	—	—
Amnesia	Psychic	Status	—	—	20	Self	—	—
Flail	Normal	Physical	—	100	15	Normal	—	○
Slam	Normal	Physical	80	75	20	Normal	—	○
Knock Off	Dark	Physical	20	100	20	Normal	—	○
Tickle	Normal	Status	—	100	20	Normal	—	—
AncientPower	Rock	Special	60	100	5	Normal	—	—
Agility	Psychic	Status	—	—	30	Self	—	—
Endure	Normal	Status	—	—	10	Self	—	—
Chip Away	Normal	Physical	70	100	20	Normal	—	○
Bide	Normal	Physical	—	—	10	Self	—	○

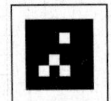

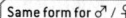

099 Kingler

Pincer Pokémon

- HEIGHT: 4'03"
- WEIGHT: 132.3 lbs.
- GENDER: ♂ / ♀

The larger pincer has 10,000-horsepower strength. However, it is so heavy, it is difficult to aim.

Same form for ♂ / ♀

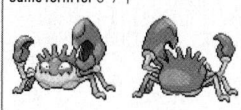

TYPE Water

ABILITIES
- Hyper Cutter
- Shell Armor

HIDDEN ABILITY
- Sheer Force

STATS
HP
Attack
Defense
Sp. Atk
Sp. Def
Speed

EGG GROUPS
Water 3

ITEMS SOMETIMES HELD
- None

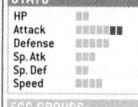

EVOLUTION

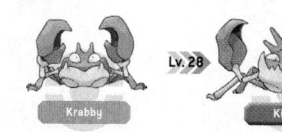

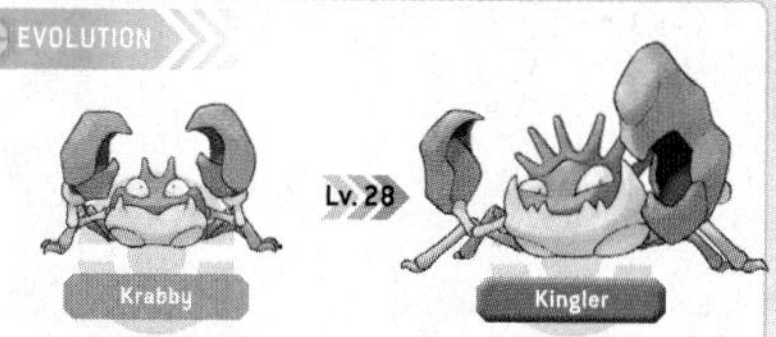

Krabby
Lv. 28
Kingler

HOW TO OBTAIN

Pokémon Black Version 2	1 Virbank City (Super Rod/ripples in water) 2 Virbank Complex (Super Rod/ripples in water)
Pokémon White Version 2	1 Virbank City (Super Rod/ripples in water) 2 Virbank Complex (Super Rod/ripples in water)

HOW TO OBTAIN FROM OTHER GAMES

———

———

Pokémon AR Marker

LEVEL-UP AND LEARNED MOVES

Lv.	Name	Type	Kind	Pow.	Acc.	PP	Range	Long	DA
1	Wide Guard	Rock	Status	—	—	10	Your Side	—	—
1	Mud Sport	Ground	Status	—	—	15	Both Sides	—	—
1	Bubble	Water	Special	20	100	30	Many Others	—	—
1	ViceGrip	Normal	Physical	55	100	30	Normal	—	○
1	Leer	Normal	Status	—	100	30	Many Others	—	—
5	ViceGrip	Normal	Physical	55	100	30	Normal	—	○
9	Leer	Normal	Status	—	100	30	Many Others	—	—
11	Harden	Normal	Status	—	—	30	Self	—	—
15	BubbleBeam	Water	Special	65	100	20	Normal	—	—
19	Mud Shot	Ground	Special	55	95	15	Normal	—	—
21	Metal Claw	Steel	Physical	50	95	35	Normal	—	○
25	Stomp	Normal	Physical	65	100	20	Normal	—	○
32	Protect	Normal	Status	—	—	10	Self	—	—
37	Guillotine	Normal	Physical	—	30	5	Normal	—	○
44	Slam	Normal	Physical	80	75	20	Normal	—	○
51	Brine	Water	Special	65	100	10	Normal	—	—
56	Crabhammer	Water	Physical	90	90	10	Normal	—	○
63	Flail	Normal	Physical	—	100	15	Normal	—	○

TM & HM MOVES

Lv.	Name	Type	Kind	Pow.	Acc.	PP	Range	Long	DA
TM01	Hone Claws	Dark	Status	—	—	15	Self	—	—
TM06	Toxic	Poison	Status	—	90	10	Normal	—	—
TM07	Hail	Ice	Status	—	—	10	Both Sides	—	—
TM10	Hidden Power	Normal	Special	—	100	15	Normal	—	—
TM13	Ice Beam	Ice	Special	95	100	10	Normal	—	—
TM14	Blizzard	Ice	Special	120	70	5	Many Others	—	—
TM15	Hyper Beam	Normal	Special	150	90	5	Normal	—	—
TM17	Protect	Normal	Status	—	—	10	Self	—	—
TM18	Rain Dance	Water	Status	—	—	5	Both Sides	—	—
TM21	Frustration	Normal	Physical	—	100	20	Normal	—	○
TM27	Return	Normal	Physical	—	100	20	Normal	—	○
TM28	Dig	Ground	Physical	80	100	10	Normal	—	○
TM31	Brick Break	Fighting	Physical	75	100	15	Normal	—	○
TM32	Double Team	Normal	Status	—	—	15	Self	—	—
TM39	Rock Tomb	Rock	Physical	50	80	10	Normal	—	—
TM42	Facade	Normal	Physical	70	100	20	Normal	—	○
TM44	Rest	Psychic	Status	—	—	10	Self	—	—
TM45	Attract	Normal	Status	—	100	15	Normal	—	—
TM46	Thief	Dark	Physical	40	100	10	Normal	—	○
TM48	Round	Normal	Special	60	100	15	Normal	—	—
TM54	False Swipe	Normal	Physical	40	100	40	Normal	—	○
TM55	Scald	Water	Special	80	100	15	Normal	—	—
TM56	Fling	Dark	Physical	—	100	10	Normal	—	—
TM60	Quash	Dark	Status	—	100	15	Normal	—	—
TM68	Giga Impact	Normal	Physical	150	90	5	Normal	—	○
TM75	Swords Dance	Normal	Status	—	—	30	Self	—	—
TM80	Rock Slide	Rock	Physical	75	90	10	Many Others	—	—
TM81	X-Scissor	Bug	Physical	80	100	15	Normal	—	○
TM87	Swagger	Normal	Status	—	90	15	Normal	—	—
TM90	Substitute	Normal	Status	—	—	10	Self	—	—
TM94	Rock Smash	Fighting	Physical	40	100	15	Normal	—	○
HM01	Cut	Normal	Physical	50	95	30	Normal	—	○
HM03	Surf	Water	Special	95	100	15	Adjacent	—	—
HM04	Strength	Normal	Physical	80	100	15	Normal	—	○
HM06	Dive	Water	Physical	80	100	10	Normal	—	○

MOVES TAUGHT BY PEOPLE

Name	Type	Kind	Pow.	Acc.	PP	Range	Long	DA

MOVES TAUGHT BY MOVE TUTORS FOR SHARDS

Name	Type	Kind	Pow.	Acc.	PP	Range	Long	DA
Iron Defense	Steel	Status	—	—	15	Self	—	—
Icy Wind	Ice	Special	55	95	15	Many Others	—	—
Superpower	Fighting	Physical	120	100	5	Normal	—	○
Snore	Normal	Special	40	100	15	Normal	—	—
Knock Off	Dark	Physical	20	100	20	Normal	—	○
Sleep Talk	Normal	Status	—	—	10	Self	—	—

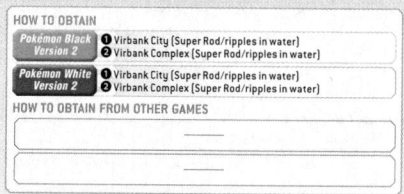

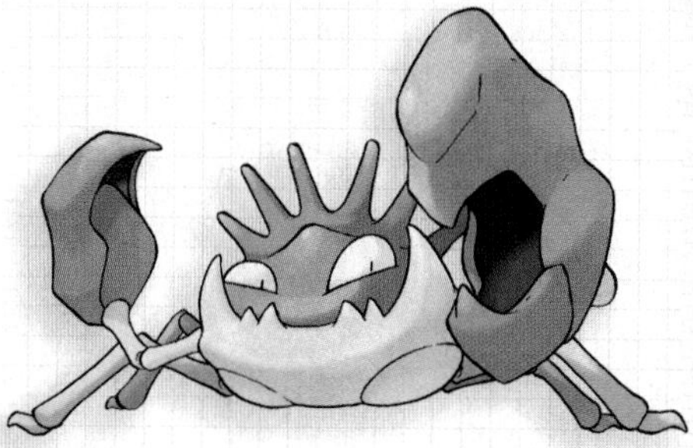

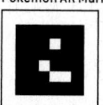

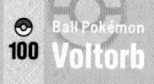

100 Voltorb

Ball Pokémon

- HEIGHT: 1'08"
- WEIGHT: 22.9 lbs.
- GENDER: Unknown

It looks just like a Poké Ball. It is dangerous because it may electrocute or explode on contact.

Gender unknown

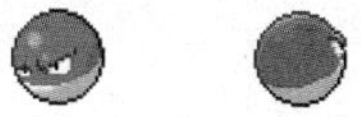

TYPE Electric

ABILITY ABILITIES
- Soundproof
- Static

HIDDEN ABILITY
- Aftermath

STATS
HP
Attack
Defense
Sp. Atk
Sp. Def
Speed

EGG GROUPS
Mineral

ITEMS SOMETIMES HELD
- None

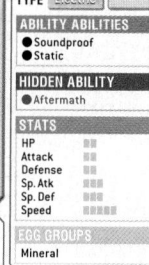

EVOLUTION

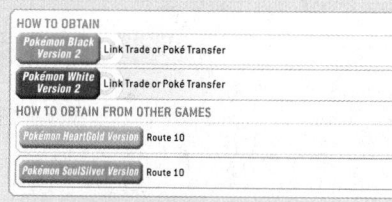

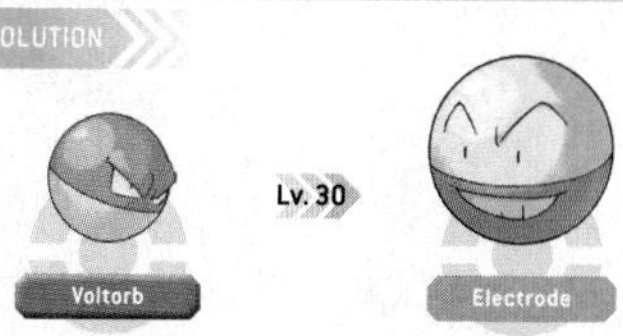

Voltorb
Lv. 30
Electrode

HOW TO OBTAIN

Pokémon Black Version 2	Link Trade or Poké Transfer
Pokémon White Version 2	Link Trade or Poké Transfer

HOW TO OBTAIN FROM OTHER GAMES

Pokémon HeartGold Version	Route 10
Pokémon SoulSilver Version	Route 10

Pokémon AR Marker

LEVEL-UP AND LEARNED MOVES

Lv.	Name	Type	Kind	Pow.	Acc.	PP	Range	Long	DA
1	Charge	Electric	Status	—	—	20	Self	—	—
5	Tackle	Normal	Physical	50	100	35	Normal	—	○
8	SonicBoom	Normal	Special	—	90	20	Normal	—	—
12	Spark	Electric	Physical	65	100	20	Normal	—	○
15	Rollout	Rock	Physical	30	90	20	Normal	—	○
19	Screech	Normal	Status	—	85	40	Normal	—	—
22	Charge Beam	Electric	Special	50	90	10	Normal	—	—
26	Light Screen	Psychic	Status	—	—	30	Your Side	—	—
29	Electro Ball	Electric	Special	—	100	10	Normal	—	—
33	Selfdestruct	Normal	Physical	200	100	5	Adjacent	—	—
36	Swift	Normal	Special	60	—	20	Many Others	—	—
40	Magnet Rise	Electric	Status	—	—	10	Self	—	—
43	Gyro Ball	Steel	Physical	—	100	5	Normal	—	○
47	Explosion	Normal	Physical	250	100	5	Adjacent	—	—
50	Mirror Coat	Psychic	Special	—	100	20	Varies	—	—

TM & HM MOVES

Lv.	Name	Type	Kind	Pow.	Acc.	PP	Range	Long	DA
TM06	Toxic	Poison	Status	—	90	10	Normal	—	—
TM10	Hidden Power	Normal	Special	—	100	15	Normal	—	—
TM12	Taunt	Dark	Status	—	100	20	Normal	—	—
TM16	Light Screen	Psychic	Status	—	—	30	Your Side	—	—
TM17	Protect	Normal	Status	—	—	10	Self	—	—
TM18	Rain Dance	Water	Status	—	—	5	Both Sides	—	—
TM21	Frustration	Normal	Physical	—	100	20	Normal	—	○
TM24	Thunderbolt	Electric	Special	95	100	15	Normal	—	—
TM25	Thunder	Electric	Special	120	70	10	Normal	—	—
TM27	Return	Normal	Physical	—	100	20	Normal	—	○
TM32	Double Team	Normal	Status	—	—	15	Self	—	—
TM41	Torment	Dark	Status	—	100	15	Normal	—	—
TM42	Facade	Normal	Physical	70	100	20	Normal	—	○
TM44	Rest	Psychic	Status	—	—	10	Self	—	—
TM46	Thief	Dark	Physical	40	100	10	Normal	—	○
TM48	Round	Normal	Special	60	100	15	Normal	—	—
TM57	Charge Beam	Electric	Special	50	90	10	Normal	—	—
TM64	Explosion	Normal	Physical	250	100	5	Adjacent	—	—
TM70	Flash	Normal	Status	—	100	20	Normal	—	—
TM72	Volt Switch	Electric	Special	70	100	20	Normal	—	—
TM73	Thunder Wave	Electric	Status	—	100	20	Normal	—	—
TM74	Gyro Ball	Steel	Physical	—	100	5	Normal	—	○
TM87	Swagger	Normal	Status	—	90	15	Normal	—	—
TM90	Substitute	Normal	Status	—	—	10	Self	—	—
TM93	Wild Charge	Electric	Physical	90	100	15	Normal	—	○

MOVES TAUGHT BY PEOPLE

Name	Type	Kind	Pow.	Acc.	PP	Range	Long	DA

MOVES TAUGHT BY MOVE TUTORS FOR SHARDS

Name	Type	Kind	Pow.	Acc.	PP	Range	Long	DA
Signal Beam	Bug	Special	75	100	15	Normal	—	—
Magnet Rise	Electric	Status	—	—	10	Self	—	—
Magic Coat	Psychic	Status	—	—	15	Self	—	—
Foul Play	Dark	Physical	95	100	15	Normal	—	○
Snore	Normal	Special	40	100	15	Normal	—	—
Sleep Talk	Normal	Status	—	—	10	Self	—	—

EGG MOVES

Name	Type	Kind	Pow.	Acc.	PP	Range	Long	DA

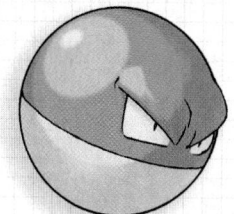

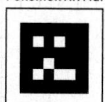

Ball Pokémon

101 Electrode

- HEIGHT: 3'11"
- WEIGHT: 146.8 lbs.
- GENDER: Unknown

It is known to drift on winds if it is bloated to bursting with stored electricity.

Gender unknown

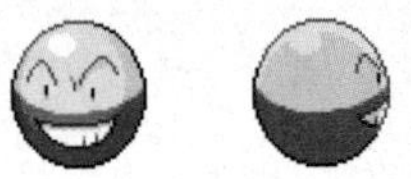

TYPE Electric

ABILITIES
- Soundproof
- Static

HIDDEN ABILITY
- Aftermath

STATS

HP
Attack
Defense
Sp. Atk
Sp. Def
Speed

EGG GROUPS

Mineral

ITEMS SOMETIMES HELD
- None

EVOLUTION

HOW TO OBTAIN

Pokémon Black Version 2	Link Trade or Poké Transfer
Pokémon White Version 2	Link Trade or Poké Transfer

HOW TO OBTAIN FROM OTHER GAMES

Pokémon HeartGold Version	Team Rocket's HQ
Pokémon SoulSilver Version	Team Rocket's HQ

Pokémon AR Marker

LEVEL-UP AND LEARNED MOVES

Lv.	Name	Type	Kind	Pow.	Acc.	PP	Range	Long	DA
1	Charge	Electric	Status	—	—	20	Self	—	—
1	Tackle	Normal	Physical	50	100	35	Normal	—	○
1	SonicBoom	Normal	Special	—	90	20	Normal	—	—
1	Spark	Electric	Physical	65	100	20	Normal	—	○
5	Tackle	Normal	Physical	50	100	35	Normal	—	○
8	SonicBoom	Normal	Special	—	90	20	Normal	—	—
12	Spark	Electric	Physical	65	100	20	Normal	—	○
15	Rollout	Rock	Physical	30	90	20	Normal	—	○
19	Screech	Normal	Status	—	85	40	Normal	—	—
22	Charge Beam	Electric	Special	50	90	10	Normal	—	—
26	Light Screen	Psychic	Status	—	—	30	Your Side	—	—
29	Electro Ball	Electric	Special	—	100	10	Normal	—	—
35	Selfdestruct	Normal	Physical	200	100	5	Adjacent	—	—
40	Swift	Normal	Special	60	—	20	Many Others	—	—
46	Magnet Rise	Electric	Status	—	—	10	Self	—	—
51	Gyro Ball	Steel	Physical	—	100	5	Normal	—	○
57	Explosion	Normal	Physical	250	100	5	Adjacent	—	—
62	Mirror Coat	Psychic	Special	—	100	20	Varies	—	—

TM & HM MOVES

Lv.	Name	Type	Kind	Pow.	Acc.	PP	Range	Long	DA
TM06	Toxic	Poison	Status	—	90	10	Normal	—	—
TM10	Hidden Power	Normal	Special	—	100	15	Normal	—	—
TM12	Taunt	Dark	Status	—	100	20	Normal	—	—
TM15	Hyper Beam	Normal	Special	150	90	5	Normal	—	—
TM16	Light Screen	Psychic	Status	—	—	30	Your Side	—	—
TM17	Protect	Normal	Status	—	—	10	Self	—	—
TM18	Rain Dance	Water	Status	—	—	5	Both Sides	—	—
TM21	Frustration	Normal	Physical	—	100	20	Normal	—	○
TM24	Thunderbolt	Electric	Special	95	100	15	Normal	—	—
TM25	Thunder	Electric	Special	120	70	10	Normal	—	—
TM27	Return	Normal	Physical	—	100	20	Normal	—	○
TM32	Double Team	Normal	Status	—	—	15	Self	—	—
TM41	Torment	Dark	Status	—	100	15	Normal	—	—
TM42	Facade	Normal	Physical	70	100	20	Normal	—	○
TM44	Rest	Psychic	Status	—	—	10	Self	—	—
TM46	Thief	Dark	Physical	40	100	10	Normal	—	○
TM48	Round	Normal	Special	60	100	15	Normal	—	—
TM57	Charge Beam	Electric	Special	50	90	10	Normal	—	—
TM64	Explosion	Normal	Physical	250	100	5	Adjacent	—	—
TM68	Giga Impact	Normal	Physical	150	90	5	Normal	—	○
TM70	Flash	Normal	Status	—	100	20	Normal	—	—
TM72	Volt Switch	Electric	Special	70	100	20	Normal	—	—
TM73	Thunder Wave	Electric	Status	—	100	20	Normal	—	—
TM74	Gyro Ball	Steel	Physical	—	100	5	Normal	—	○
TM87	Swagger	Normal	Status	—	90	15	Normal	—	—
TM90	Substitute	Normal	Status	—	—	10	Self	—	—
TM93	Wild Charge	Electric	Physical	90	100	15	Normal	—	○

MOVES TAUGHT BY PEOPLE

Name	Type	Kind	Pow.	Acc.	PP	Range	Long	DA

MOVES TAUGHT BY MOVE TUTORS FOR SHARDS

Name	Type	Kind	Pow.	Acc.	PP	Range	Long	DA
Signal Beam	Bug	Special	75	100	15	Normal	—	—
Magnet Rise	Electric	Status	—	—	10	Self	—	—
Magic Coat	Psychic	Status	—	—	15	Self	—	—
Foul Play	Dark	Physical	95	100	15	Normal	—	○
Snore	Normal	Special	40	100	15	Normal	—	—
Sleep Talk	Normal	Status	—	—	10	Self	—	—

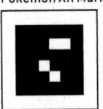

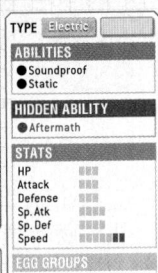

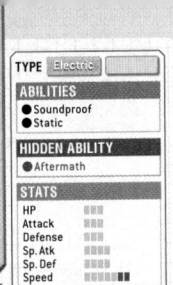

Egg Pokémon

102 Exeggcute

- HEIGHT: 1'04"
- WEIGHT: 5.5 lbs.
- GENDER: ♂ / ♀

Its six eggs converse using telepathy. They can quickly gather if they become separated.

Same form for ♂ / ♀

TYPE Grass Psychic

ABILITY
- Chlorophyll

HIDDEN ABILITY
- Harvest

STATS

HP
Attack
Defense
Sp. Atk
Sp. Def
Speed

EGG GROUPS

Grass

ITEMS SOMETIMES HELD
- None

EVOLUTION

HOW TO OBTAIN

Pokémon Black Version 2	Link Trade or Poké Transfer
Pokémon White Version 2	Link Trade or Poké Transfer

HOW TO OBTAIN FROM OTHER GAMES

Pokémon Black Version	Route 18 (mass outbreak)
Pokémon White Version	Route 18 (mass outbreak)

Pokémon AR Marker

LEVEL-UP AND LEARNED MOVES

Lv.	Name	Type	Kind	Pow.	Acc.	PP	Range	Long	DA
1	Barrage	Normal	Physical	15	85	20	Normal	—	—
1	Uproar	Normal	Special	90	100	10	1 Random	—	—
1	Hypnosis	Psychic	Status	—	60	20	Normal	—	—
7	Reflect	Psychic	Status	—	—	20	Your Side	—	—
11	Leech Seed	Grass	Status	—	90	10	Normal	—	—
17	Bullet Seed	Grass	Physical	25	100	30	Normal	—	—
19	Stun Spore	Grass	Status	—	75	30	Normal	—	—
21	PoisonPowder	Poison	Status	—	75	35	Normal	—	—
23	Sleep Powder	Grass	Status	—	75	15	Normal	—	—
27	Confusion	Psychic	Special	50	100	25	Normal	—	—
33	Worry Seed	Grass	Status	—	100	10	Normal	—	—
37	Natural Gift	Normal	Physical	—	100	15	Normal	—	—
43	SolarBeam	Grass	Special	120	100	10	Normal	—	—
47	Extrasensory	Psychic	Special	80	100	30	Normal	—	—
53	Bestow	Normal	Status	—	—	15	Normal	—	—

TM & HM MOVES

Lv.	Name	Type	Kind	Pow.	Acc.	PP	Range	Long	DA
TM06	Toxic	Poison	Status	—	90	10	Normal	—	—
TM10	Hidden Power	Normal	Special	—	100	15	Normal	—	—
TM11	Sunny Day	Fire	Status	—	—	5	Both Sides	—	—
TM16	Light Screen	Psychic	Status	—	—	30	Your Side	—	—
TM17	Protect	Normal	Status	—	—	10	Self	—	—
TM19	Telekinesis	Psychic	Status	—	—	15	Normal	—	—
TM21	Frustration	Normal	Physical	—	100	20	Normal	—	○
TM22	SolarBeam	Grass	Special	120	100	10	Normal	—	—
TM27	Return	Normal	Physical	—	100	20	Normal	—	○
TM29	Psychic	Psychic	Special	90	100	10	Normal	—	—
TM32	Double Team	Normal	Status	—	—	15	Self	—	—
TM33	Reflect	Psychic	Status	—	—	20	Your Side	—	—
TM36	Sludge Bomb	Poison	Special	90	100	10	Normal	—	—
TM42	Facade	Normal	Physical	70	100	20	Normal	—	○
TM44	Rest	Psychic	Status	—	—	10	Self	—	—
TM45	Attract	Normal	Status	—	100	15	Normal	—	—
TM46	Thief	Dark	Physical	40	100	10	Normal	—	○
TM48	Round	Normal	Special	60	100	15	Normal	—	—
TM53	Energy Ball	Grass	Special	80	100	10	Normal	—	—
TM64	Explosion	Normal	Physical	250	100	5	Adjacent	—	—
TM70	Flash	Normal	Status	—	100	20	Normal	—	—
TM75	Swords Dance	Normal	Status	—	—	30	Self	—	—
TM77	Psych Up	Normal	Status	—	—	10	Normal	—	—
TM85	Dream Eater	Psychic	Special	100	100	15	Normal	—	—
TM86	Grass Knot	Grass	Special	—	100	20	Normal	—	○
TM87	Swagger	Normal	Status	—	90	15	Normal	—	—
TM90	Substitute	Normal	Status	—	—	10	Self	—	—
TM92	Trick Room	Psychic	Status	—	—	5	Both Sides	—	—
HM04	Strength	Normal	Physical	80	100	15	Normal	—	○

MOVES TAUGHT BY PEOPLE

Name	Type	Kind	Pow.	Acc.	PP	Range	Long	DA

MOVES TAUGHT BY MOVE TUTORS FOR SHARDS

Name	Type	Kind	Pow.	Acc.	PP	Range	Long	DA
Uproar	Normal	Special	90	100	10	1 Random	—	—
Seed Bomb	Grass	Physical	80	100	15	Normal	—	—
Block	Normal	Status	—	—	5	Normal	—	—
Gravity	Psychic	Status	—	—	5	Both Sides	—	—
Snore	Normal	Special	40	100	15	Normal	—	—
Synthesis	Grass	Status	—	—	5	Self	—	—
Giga Drain	Grass	Special	75	100	10	Normal	—	—
Worry Seed	Grass	Status	—	100	10	Normal	—	—
Sleep Talk	Normal	Status	—	—	10	Self	—	—
Skill Swap	Psychic	Status	—	—	10	Normal	—	—

EGG MOVES

Name	Type	Kind	Pow.	Acc.	PP	Range	Long	DA
Synthesis	Grass	Status	—	—	5	Self	—	—
Moonlight	Normal	Status	—	—	5	Self	—	—
AncientPower	Rock	Special	60	100	5	Normal	—	—
Ingrain	Grass	Status	—	—	20	Self	—	—
Curse	Ghost	Status	—	—	10	Varies	—	—
Nature Power	Normal	Status	—	—	20	Varies	—	—
Lucky Chant	Normal	Status	—	—	30	Your Side	—	—
Leaf Storm	Grass	Special	140	90	5	Normal	—	—
Power Swap	Psychic	Status	—	—	10	Normal	—	—
Giga Drain	Grass	Special	75	100	10	Normal	—	—
Skill Swap	Psychic	Status	—	—	10	Normal	—	—
Natural Gift	Normal	Physical	—	100	15	Normal	—	—
Block	Normal	Status	—	—	5	Normal	—	—

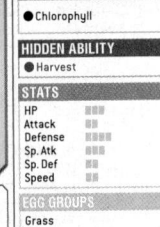

Coconut Pokémon
103 Exeggutor

TYPE: Grass / Psychic

ABILITY
- Chlorophyll

HIDDEN ABILITY
- Harvest

- HEIGHT: 6'07"
- WEIGHT: 264.6 lbs.
- GENDER: ♂ / ♀

It is called "The Walking Jungle." If a head grows too big, it falls off and becomes an Exeggcute.

STATS
HP
Attack
Defense
Sp. Atk
Sp. Def
Speed

Same form for ♂ / ♀

EGG GROUPS
Grass

ITEMS SOMETIMES HELD
- None

Pokémon AR Marker

EVOLUTION

HOW TO OBTAIN

Pokémon Black Version 2	Use Leaf Stone on an Exeggcute you obtain via Link Trade or Poké Transfer
Pokémon White Version 2	Use Leaf Stone on an Exeggcute you obtain via Link Trade or Poké Transfer

HOW TO OBTAIN FROM OTHER GAMES

—

—

LEVEL-UP AND LEARNED MOVES

Lv.	Name	Type	Kind	Pow.	Acc.	PP	Range	Long	DA
1	Seed Bomb	Grass	Physical	80	100	15	Normal	—	—
1	Barrage	Normal	Physical	15	85	20	Normal	—	—
1	Hypnosis	Psychic	Status	—	60	20	Normal	—	—
1	Confusion	Psychic	Special	50	100	25	Normal	—	—
1	Stomp	Normal	Physical	65	100	20	Normal	—	○
17	Psyshock	Psychic	Special	80	100	10	Normal	—	—
27	Egg Bomb	Normal	Physical	100	75	10	Normal	—	—
37	Wood Hammer	Grass	Physical	120	100	15	Normal	—	○
47	Leaf Storm	Grass	Special	140	90	5	Normal	—	—

TM & HM MOVES

Lv.	Name	Type	Kind	Pow.	Acc.	PP	Range	Long	DA
TM03	Psyshock	Psychic	Special	80	100	10	Normal	—	—
TM06	Toxic	Poison	Status	—	90	10	Normal	—	—
TM10	Hidden Power	Normal	Special	—	100	15	Normal	—	—
TM11	Sunny Day	Fire	Status	—	—	5	Both Sides	—	—
TM15	Hyper Beam	Normal	Special	150	90	5	Normal	—	—
TM16	Light Screen	Psychic	Status	—	—	30	Your Side	—	—
TM17	Protect	Normal	Status	—	—	10	Self	—	—
TM19	Telekinesis	Psychic	Status	—	—	15	Normal	—	—
TM21	Frustration	Normal	Physical	—	100	20	Normal	—	○
TM22	SolarBeam	Grass	Special	120	100	10	Normal	—	—
TM27	Return	Normal	Physical	—	100	20	Normal	—	○
TM29	Psychic	Psychic	Special	90	100	10	Normal	—	—
TM32	Double Team	Normal	Status	—	—	15	Self	—	—
TM33	Reflect	Psychic	Status	—	—	20	Your Side	—	—
TM36	Sludge Bomb	Poison	Special	90	100	10	Normal	—	—
TM42	Facade	Normal	Physical	70	100	20	Normal	—	○
TM44	Rest	Psychic	Status	—	—	10	Self	—	—
TM45	Attract	Normal	Status	—	100	15	Normal	—	—
TM46	Thief	Dark	Physical	40	100	10	Normal	—	○
TM48	Round	Normal	Special	60	100	15	Normal	—	—
TM53	Energy Ball	Grass	Special	80	100	10	Normal	—	—
TM64	Explosion	Normal	Physical	250	100	5	Adjacent	—	—
TM68	Giga Impact	Normal	Physical	150	90	5	Normal	—	○
TM70	Flash	Normal	Status	—	100	20	Normal	—	—
TM75	Swords Dance	Normal	Status	—	—	30	Self	—	—
TM77	Psych Up	Normal	Status	—	—	10	Normal	—	—
TM85	Dream Eater	Psychic	Special	100	100	15	Normal	—	—
TM86	Grass Knot	Grass	Special	—	100	20	Normal	—	○
TM87	Swagger	Normal	Status	—	90	15	Normal	—	—
TM90	Substitute	Normal	Status	—	—	10	Self	—	—
TM92	Trick Room	Psychic	Status	—	—	5	Both Sides	—	—
HM04	Strength	Normal	Physical	80	100	15	Normal	—	○

MOVES TAUGHT BY PEOPLE

Name	Type	Kind	Pow.	Acc.	PP	Range	Long	DA

MOVES TAUGHT BY MOVE TUTORS FOR SHARDS

Name	Type	Kind	Pow.	Acc.	PP	Range	Long	DA
Seed Bomb	Grass	Physical	80	100	15	Normal	—	—
Low Kick	Fighting	Physical	—	100	20	Normal	—	○
Block	Normal	Status	—	—	5	Normal	—	—
Zen Headbutt	Psychic	Physical	80	90	15	Normal	—	○
Gravity	Psychic	Status	—	—	5	Both Sides	—	—
Snore	Normal	Special	40	100	15	Normal	—	—
Synthesis	Grass	Status	—	—	5	Self	—	—
Giga Drain	Grass	Special	75	100	10	Normal	—	—
Worry Seed	Grass	Status	—	100	10	Normal	—	—
Sleep Talk	Normal	Status	—	—	10	Self	—	—
Skill Swap	Psychic	Status	—	—	10	Normal	—	—

Lonely Pokémon
104 Cubone

TYPE: Ground

ABILITIES
- Rock Head
- Lightningrod

HIDDEN ABILITY
- Battle Armor

- HEIGHT: 1'04"
- WEIGHT: 14.3 lbs.
- GENDER: ♂ / ♀

When it thinks of its dead mother, it cries. Its crying makes the skull it wears rattle hollowly.

STATS
HP
Attack
Defense
Sp. Atk
Sp. Def
Speed

Same form for ♂ / ♀

EGG GROUPS
Monster

ITEMS SOMETIMES HELD
- None

Pokémon AR Marker

EVOLUTION

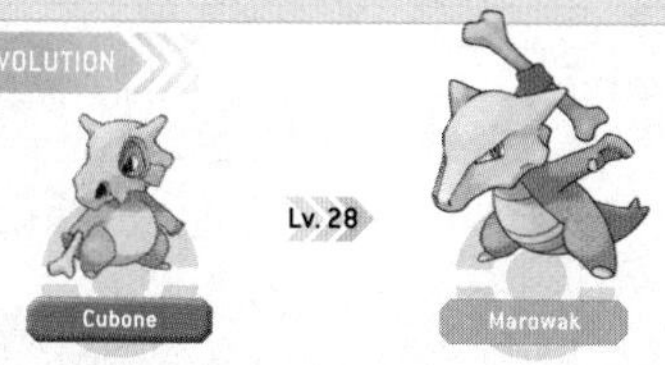

HOW TO OBTAIN

Pokémon Black Version 2	Link Trade or Poké Transfer
Pokémon White Version 2	Link Trade or Poké Transfer

HOW TO OBTAIN FROM OTHER GAMES

Pokémon HeartGold Version	Safari Zone Desert Area (morning and afternoon only)
Pokémon SoulSilver Version	Safari Zone Desert Area (morning and afternoon only)

LEVEL-UP AND LEARNED MOVES

Lv.	Name	Type	Kind	Pow.	Acc.	PP	Range	Long	DA
1	Growl	Normal	Status	—	100	40	Many Others	—	—
3	Tail Whip	Normal	Status	—	100	30	Many Others	—	—
7	Bone Club	Ground	Physical	65	85	20	Normal	—	—
11	Headbutt	Normal	Physical	70	100	15	Normal	—	○
13	Leer	Normal	Status	—	100	30	Many Others	—	—
17	Focus Energy	Normal	Status	—	—	30	Self	—	—
21	Bonemerang	Ground	Physical	50	90	10	Normal	—	—
23	Rage	Normal	Physical	20	100	20	Normal	—	○
27	False Swipe	Normal	Physical	40	100	40	Normal	—	○
31	Thrash	Normal	Physical	120	100	10	1 Random	—	○
33	Fling	Dark	Physical	—	100	10	Normal	—	—
37	Bone Rush	Ground	Physical	25	90	10	Normal	—	—
41	Endeavor	Normal	Physical	—	100	5	Normal	—	○
43	Double-Edge	Normal	Physical	120	100	15	Normal	—	○
47	Retaliate	Normal	Physical	70	100	5	Normal	—	○

TM & HM MOVES

Lv.	Name	Type	Kind	Pow.	Acc.	PP	Range	Long	DA
TM06	Toxic	Poison	Status	—	90	10	Normal	—	—
TM10	Hidden Power	Normal	Special	—	100	15	Normal	—	—
TM11	Sunny Day	Fire	Status	—	—	5	Both Sides	—	—
TM13	Ice Beam	Ice	Special	95	100	10	Normal	—	—
TM14	Blizzard	Ice	Special	120	70	5	Many Others	—	—
TM17	Protect	Normal	Status	—	—	10	Self	—	—
TM21	Frustration	Normal	Physical	—	100	20	Normal	—	○
TM23	Smack Down	Rock	Physical	50	100	15	Normal	—	—
TM26	Earthquake	Ground	Physical	100	100	10	Adjacent	—	—
TM27	Return	Normal	Physical	—	100	20	Normal	—	○
TM28	Dig	Ground	Physical	80	100	10	Normal	—	○
TM31	Brick Break	Fighting	Physical	75	100	15	Normal	—	○
TM32	Double Team	Normal	Status	—	—	15	Self	—	—
TM35	Flamethrower	Fire	Special	95	100	15	Normal	—	—
TM37	Sandstorm	Rock	Status	—	—	10	Both Sides	—	—
TM38	Fire Blast	Fire	Special	120	85	5	Normal	—	—
TM39	Rock Tomb	Rock	Physical	50	80	10	Normal	—	—
TM40	Aerial Ace	Flying	Physical	60	—	20	Normal	○	○
TM42	Facade	Normal	Physical	70	100	20	Normal	—	○
TM44	Rest	Psychic	Status	—	—	10	Self	—	—
TM45	Attract	Normal	Status	—	100	15	Normal	—	—
TM46	Thief	Dark	Physical	40	100	10	Normal	—	○
TM48	Round	Normal	Special	60	100	15	Normal	—	—
TM49	Echoed Voice	Normal	Special	40	100	15	Normal	—	—
TM54	False Swipe	Normal	Physical	40	100	40	Normal	—	○
TM56	Fling	Dark	Physical	—	100	10	Normal	—	—
TM59	Incinerate	Fire	Special	30	100	15	Many Others	—	—
TM67	Retaliate	Normal	Physical	70	100	5	Normal	—	○
TM75	Swords Dance	Normal	Status	—	—	30	Self	—	—
TM78	Bulldoze	Ground	Physical	60	100	20	Adjacent	—	—
TM80	Rock Slide	Rock	Physical	75	90	10	Many Others	—	—
TM87	Swagger	Normal	Status	—	90	15	Normal	—	—
TM90	Substitute	Normal	Status	—	—	10	Self	—	—
TM94	Rock Smash	Fighting	Physical	40	100	15	Normal	—	○
HM04	Strength	Normal	Physical	80	100	15	Normal	—	○

MOVES TAUGHT BY PEOPLE

Name	Type	Kind	Pow.	Acc.	PP	Range	Long	DA

MOVES TAUGHT BY MOVE TUTORS FOR SHARDS

Name	Type	Kind	Pow.	Acc.	PP	Range	Long	DA
Iron Head	Steel	Physical	80	100	15	Normal	—	○
Uproar	Normal	Special	90	100	10	1 Random	—	—
Low Kick	Fighting	Physical	—	100	20	Normal	—	○
Fire Punch	Fire	Physical	75	100	15	Normal	—	○
ThunderPunch	Electric	Physical	75	100	15	Normal	—	○
Iron Defense	Steel	Status	—	—	15	Self	—	—
Icy Wind	Ice	Special	55	95	15	Many Others	—	—
Iron Tail	Steel	Physical	100	75	15	Normal	—	○
Earth Power	Ground	Special	90	100	10	Normal	—	—
Snore	Normal	Special	40	100	15	Normal	—	—
Knock Off	Dark	Physical	20	100	20	Normal	—	○
Stealth Rock	Rock	Status	—	—	20	Other Side	—	—
Endeavor	Normal	Physical	—	100	5	Normal	—	○
Sleep Talk	Normal	Status	—	—	10	Self	—	—

EGG MOVES

Name	Type	Kind	Pow.	Acc.	PP	Range	Long	DA
AncientPower	Rock	Special	60	100	5	Normal	—	—
Belly Drum	Normal	Status	—	—	10	Self	—	—
Screech	Normal	Status	—	85	40	Normal	—	—
Skull Bash	Normal	Physical	100	100	15	Normal	—	○
Perish Song	Normal	Status	—	—	5	Adjacent	○	—
Double Kick	Fighting	Physical	30	100	30	Normal	—	○
Iron Head	Steel	Physical	80	100	15	Normal	—	○
Detect	Fighting	Status	—	—	5	Self	—	—
Endure	Normal	Status	—	—	10	Self	—	—
Chip Away	Normal	Physical	70	100	20	Normal	—	○

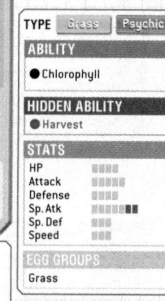

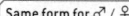

Bone Keeper Pokémon
105 Marowak

- HEIGHT: 3'03"
- WEIGHT: 99.2 lbs.
- GENDER: ♂ / ♀

From its birth, this savage Pokémon constantly holds bones. It is skilled in using them as weapons.

Same form for ♂ / ♀

Pokémon AR Marker

TYPE Ground

ABILITIES
- Rock Head
- Lightningrod

HIDDEN ABILITY
- Battle Armor

STATS
- HP
- Attack
- Defense
- Sp. Atk
- Sp. Def
- Speed

EGG GROUPS
Monster

ITEMS SOMETIMES HELD
- None

EVOLUTION

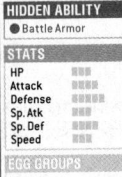

Cubone → Lv. 28 → Marowak

HOW TO OBTAIN

Pokémon Black Version 2	Link Trade or Poké Transfer
Pokémon White Version 2	Link Trade or Poké Transfer

HOW TO OBTAIN FROM OTHER GAMES

Pokémon Black Version	Route 15
Pokémon White Version	Route 15

LEVEL-UP AND LEARNED MOVES

Lv.	Name	Type	Kind	Pow.	Acc.	PP	Range	Long	DA
1	Growl	Normal	Status	—	100	40	Many Others	—	—
1	Tail Whip	Normal	Status	—	100	30	Many Others	—	—
1	Bone Club	Ground	Physical	65	85	20	Normal	—	—
1	Headbutt	Normal	Physical	70	100	15	Normal	—	○
3	Tail Whip	Normal	Status	—	100	30	Many Others	—	—
7	Bone Club	Ground	Physical	65	85	20	Normal	—	—
11	Headbutt	Normal	Physical	70	100	15	Normal	—	○
13	Leer	Normal	Status	—	100	30	Many Others	—	—
17	Focus Energy	Normal	Status	—	—	30	Self	—	—
21	Bonemerang	Ground	Physical	50	90	10	Normal	—	○
23	Rage	Normal	Physical	20	100	20	Normal	—	—
27	False Swipe	Normal	Physical	40	100	40	Normal	—	○
33	Thrash	Normal	Physical	120	100	10	1 Random	—	—
37	Fling	Dark	Physical	—	100	10	Normal	—	○
43	Bone Rush	Ground	Physical	25	90	10	Normal	—	—
49	Endeavor	Normal	Physical	—	100	5	Normal	—	—
53	Double-Edge	Normal	Physical	120	100	15	Normal	—	—
59	Retaliate	Normal	Physical	70	100	5	Normal	—	—

TM & HM MOVES

Lv.	Name	Type	Kind	Pow.	Acc.	PP	Range	Long	DA
TM06	Toxic	Poison	Status	—	90	10	Normal	—	—
TM10	Hidden Power	Normal	Special	—	100	15	Normal	—	—
TM11	Sunny Day	Fire	Status	—	—	5	Both Sides	—	—
TM13	Ice Beam	Ice	Special	95	100	10	Normal	—	—
TM14	Blizzard	Ice	Special	120	70	5	Many Others	—	—
TM15	Hyper Beam	Normal	Special	150	90	5	Normal	—	—
TM17	Protect	Normal	Status	—	—	10	Self	—	—
TM21	Frustration	Normal	Physical	—	100	20	Normal	—	○
TM23	Smack Down	Rock	Physical	50	100	15	Normal	—	—
TM26	Earthquake	Ground	Physical	100	100	10	Adjacent	—	—
TM27	Return	Normal	Physical	—	100	20	Normal	—	○
TM28	Dig	Ground	Physical	80	100	10	Normal	—	○
TM31	Brick Break	Fighting	Physical	75	100	15	Normal	—	—
TM32	Double Team	Normal	Status	—	—	15	Self	—	—
TM35	Flamethrower	Fire	Special	95	100	15	Normal	—	—
TM37	Sandstorm	Rock	Status	—	—	10	Both Sides	—	—
TM38	Fire Blast	Fire	Special	120	85	5	Normal	—	—
TM39	Rock Tomb	Rock	Physical	50	80	10	Normal	—	—
TM40	Aerial Ace	Flying	Physical	60	—	20	Normal	○	○
TM42	Facade	Normal	Physical	70	100	20	Normal	—	—
TM44	Rest	Psychic	Status	—	—	10	Self	—	—
TM45	Attract	Normal	Status	—	100	15	Normal	—	—
TM46	Thief	Dark	Physical	40	100	10	Normal	—	○
TM48	Round	Normal	Special	60	100	15	Normal	—	—
TM49	Echoed Voice	Normal	Special	40	100	15	Normal	—	—
TM52	Focus Blast	Fighting	Special	120	70	5	Normal	—	—
TM54	False Swipe	Normal	Physical	40	100	40	Normal	—	○
TM56	Fling	Dark	Physical	—	100	10	Normal	—	○
TM59	Incinerate	Fire	Special	30	100	15	Many Others	—	—
TM67	Retaliate	Normal	Physical	70	100	5	Normal	—	—
TM68	Giga Impact	Normal	Physical	150	90	5	Normal	—	—
TM71	Stone Edge	Rock	Physical	100	80	5	Normal	—	—
TM75	Swords Dance	Normal	Status	—	—	30	Self	—	—
TM78	Bulldoze	Ground	Physical	60	100	20	Adjacent	—	—
TM80	Rock Slide	Rock	Physical	75	90	10	Many Others	—	—

Lv.	Name	Type	Kind	Pow.	Acc.	PP	Range	Long	DA
TM87	Swagger	Normal	Status	—	90	15	Normal	—	—
TM90	Substitute	Normal	Status	—	—	10	Self	—	—
TM94	Rock Smash	Fighting	Physical	40	100	15	Normal	—	○
HM04	Strength	Normal	Physical	80	100	15	Normal	—	○

MOVES TAUGHT BY PEOPLE

Name	Type	Kind	Pow.	Acc.	PP	Range	Long	DA

MOVES TAUGHT BY MOVE TUTORS FOR SHARDS

Name	Type	Kind	Pow.	Acc.	PP	Range	Long	DA
Iron Head	Steel	Physical	80	100	15	Normal	—	○
Uproar	Normal	Special	90	100	10	1 Random	—	—
Low Kick	Fighting	Physical	—	100	20	Normal	—	○
Fire Punch	Fire	Physical	75	100	15	Normal	—	○
ThunderPunch	Electric	Physical	75	100	15	Normal	—	○
Iron Defense	Steel	Status	—	—	15	Self	—	—
Icy Wind	Ice	Special	55	95	15	Many Others	—	—
Iron Tail	Steel	Physical	100	75	15	Normal	—	○
Earth Power	Ground	Special	90	100	10	Normal	—	—
Snore	Normal	Special	40	100	15	Normal	—	—
Knock Off	Dark	Physical	20	100	20	Normal	—	○
Stealth Rock	Rock	Status	—	—	20	Other Side	—	—
Outrage	Dragon	Physical	120	100	10	1 Random	—	○
Endeavor	Normal	Physical	—	100	5	Normal	—	—
Sleep Talk	Normal	Status	—	—	10	Self	—	—

Kicking Pokémon
106 Hitmonlee

- HEIGHT: 4'11"
- WEIGHT: 109.8 lbs.
- GENDER: ♂ / ♀

Its legs can stretch double. First-time foes are startled by its extensible reach.

Same form for ♂ / ♀

Pokémon AR Marker

TYPE Fighting

ABILITY ABILITIES
- Limber
- Reckless

HIDDEN ABILITY
- Unburden

STATS
- HP
- Attack
- Defense
- Sp. Atk
- Sp. Def
- Speed

EGG GROUPS
Human-Like

ITEMS SOMETIMES HELD
- None

EVOLUTION

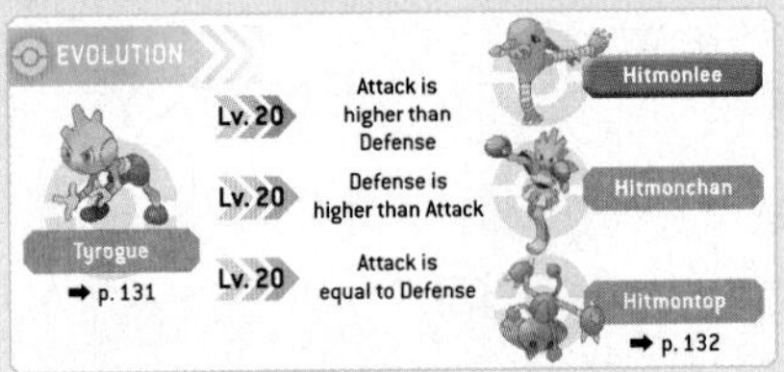

Tyrogue → p. 131

- Lv. 20 — Attack is higher than Defense → Hitmonlee
- Lv. 20 — Defense is higher than Attack → Hitmonchan
- Lv. 20 — Attack is equal to Defense → Hitmontop → p. 132

HOW TO OBTAIN

Pokémon Black Version 2	Level up Tyrogue to Lv. 20 while its Attack is higher than its Defense
Pokémon White Version 2	Level up Tyrogue to Lv. 20 while its Attack is higher than its Defense

HOW TO OBTAIN FROM OTHER GAMES

—	
—	

LEVEL-UP AND LEARNED MOVES

Lv.	Name	Type	Kind	Pow.	Acc.	PP	Range	Long	DA
1	Revenge	Fighting	Physical	60	100	10	Normal	—	○
1	Double Kick	Fighting	Physical	30	100	30	Normal	—	—
5	Meditate	Psychic	Status	—	—	40	Self	—	—
9	Rolling Kick	Fighting	Physical	60	85	15	Normal	—	—
13	Jump Kick	Fighting	Physical	100	95	10	Normal	—	—
17	Brick Break	Fighting	Physical	75	100	15	Normal	—	—
21	Focus Energy	Normal	Status	—	—	30	Self	—	—
25	Feint	Normal	Physical	30	100	10	Normal	—	—
29	Hi Jump Kick	Fighting	Physical	130	90	10	Normal	—	—
33	Mind Reader	Normal	Status	—	—	5	Normal	—	—
37	Foresight	Normal	Status	—	—	40	Normal	—	—
41	Wide Guard	Rock	Status	—	—	10	Your Side	—	—
45	Blaze Kick	Fire	Physical	85	90	10	Normal	—	—
49	Endure	Normal	Status	—	—	10	Self	—	—
53	Mega Kick	Normal	Physical	120	75	5	Normal	—	—
57	Close Combat	Fighting	Physical	120	100	5	Normal	—	—
61	Reversal	Fighting	Physical	—	100	15	Normal	—	—

TM & HM MOVES

Lv.	Name	Type	Kind	Pow.	Acc.	PP	Range	Long	DA
TM06	Toxic	Poison	Status	—	90	10	Normal	—	—
TM08	Bulk Up	Fighting	Status	—	—	20	Self	—	—
TM10	Hidden Power	Normal	Special	—	100	15	Normal	—	—
TM11	Sunny Day	Fire	Status	—	—	5	Both Sides	—	—
TM17	Protect	Normal	Status	—	—	10	Both Sides	—	—
TM18	Rain Dance	Water	Status	—	—	5	Both Sides	—	—
TM21	Frustration	Normal	Physical	—	100	20	Normal	—	○
TM26	Earthquake	Ground	Physical	100	100	10	Adjacent	—	—
TM27	Return	Normal	Physical	—	100	20	Normal	—	○
TM31	Brick Break	Fighting	Physical	75	100	15	Normal	—	—
TM32	Double Team	Normal	Status	—	—	15	Self	—	—
TM39	Rock Tomb	Rock	Physical	50	80	10	Normal	—	—
TM42	Facade	Normal	Physical	70	100	20	Normal	—	—
TM44	Rest	Psychic	Status	—	—	10	Self	—	—
TM45	Attract	Normal	Status	—	100	15	Normal	—	—
TM46	Thief	Dark	Physical	40	100	10	Normal	—	○
TM47	Low Sweep	Fighting	Physical	60	100	20	Normal	—	—
TM48	Round	Normal	Special	60	100	15	Normal	—	—
TM52	Focus Blast	Fighting	Special	120	70	5	Normal	—	—
TM56	Fling	Dark	Physical	—	100	10	Normal	—	○
TM67	Retaliate	Normal	Physical	70	100	5	Normal	—	—
TM71	Stone Edge	Rock	Physical	100	80	5	Normal	—	—
TM78	Bulldoze	Ground	Physical	60	100	20	Adjacent	—	—
TM80	Rock Slide	Rock	Physical	75	90	10	Many Others	—	—
TM83	Work Up	Normal	Status	—	—	30	Self	—	—
TM84	Poison Jab	Poison	Physical	80	100	20	Normal	—	—
TM87	Swagger	Normal	Status	—	90	15	Normal	—	—
TM90	Substitute	Normal	Status	—	—	10	Self	—	—
TM94	Rock Smash	Fighting	Physical	40	100	15	Normal	—	○
HM04	Strength	Normal	Physical	80	100	15	Normal	—	○

MOVES TAUGHT BY PEOPLE

Name	Type	Kind	Pow.	Acc.	PP	Range	Long	DA

MOVES TAUGHT BY MOVE TUTORS FOR SHARDS

Name	Type	Kind	Pow.	Acc.	PP	Range	Long	DA
Covet	Normal	Physical	60	100	40	Normal	—	○
Bounce	Flying	Physical	85	85	5	Normal	○	○
Low Kick	Fighting	Physical	—	100	20	Normal	—	○
Superpower	Fighting	Physical	120	100	5	Normal	—	—
Snore	Normal	Special	40	100	15	Normal	—	—
Knock Off	Dark	Physical	20	100	20	Normal	—	○
Role Play	Psychic	Status	—	—	10	Normal	—	—
Helping Hand	Normal	Status	—	—	20	1 Ally	—	—
Sleep Talk	Normal	Status	—	—	10	Self	—	—

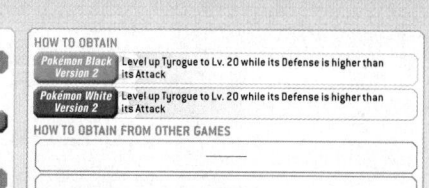

107 Hitmonchan

Punching Pokémon

TYPE: Fighting

ABILITIES
- Keen Eye
- Iron Fist

HIDDEN ABILITY
- Inner Focus

STATS
- HP
- Attack
- Defense
- Sp. Atk
- Sp. Def
- Speed

EGG GROUPS
Human-Like

ITEMS SOMETIMES HELD
- None

- HEIGHT: 4'07"
- WEIGHT: 110.7 lbs.
- GENDER: ♂

The arm-twisting punches it throws pulverize even concrete. It rests after three minutes of fighting.

♂

Pokémon AR Marker

EVOLUTION

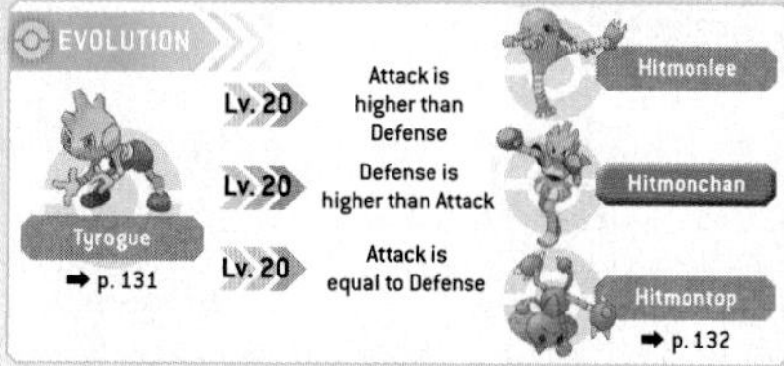
Tyrogue
→ p. 131
Lv. 20
Attack is higher than Defense
Hitmonlee
Lv. 20
Defense is higher than Attack
Hitmonchan
Lv. 20
Attack is equal to Defense
Hitmontop
→ p. 132

HOW TO OBTAIN

Pokémon Black Version 2	Level up Tyrogue to Lv. 20 while its Defense is higher than its Attack
Pokémon White Version 2	Level up Tyrogue to Lv. 20 while its Defense is higher than its Attack

HOW TO OBTAIN FROM OTHER GAMES

—

—

LEVEL-UP AND LEARNED MOVES

Lv.	Name	Type	Kind	Pow.	Acc.	PP	Range	Long	DA
1	Revenge	Fighting	Physical	60	100	10	Normal	—	○
1	Comet Punch	Normal	Physical	18	85	15	Normal	—	○
6	Agility	Psychic	Status	—	—	30	Self	—	—
11	Pursuit	Dark	Physical	40	100	20	Normal	—	○
16	Mach Punch	Fighting	Physical	40	100	30	Normal	—	○
16	Bullet Punch	Steel	Physical	40	100	30	Normal	—	○
21	Feint	Normal	Physical	30	100	10	Normal	—	—
26	Vacuum Wave	Fighting	Special	40	100	30	Normal	—	—
31	Quick Guard	Fighting	Status	—	—	15	Your Side	—	—
36	ThunderPunch	Electric	Physical	75	100	15	Normal	—	○
36	Ice Punch	Ice	Physical	75	100	15	Normal	—	○
36	Fire Punch	Fire	Physical	75	100	15	Normal	—	○
41	Sky Uppercut	Fighting	Physical	85	90	15	Normal	—	○
46	Mega Punch	Normal	Physical	80	85	20	Normal	—	○
51	Detect	Fighting	Status	—	—	5	Self	—	—
56	Focus Punch	Fighting	Physical	150	100	20	Normal	—	○
61	Counter	Fighting	Physical	—	100	20	Varies	—	○
66	Close Combat	Fighting	Physical	120	100	5	Normal	—	○

TM & HM MOVES

Lv.	Name	Type	Kind	Pow.	Acc.	PP	Range	Long	DA
TM06	Toxic	Poison	Status	—	90	10	Normal	—	—
TM08	Bulk Up	Fighting	Status	—	—	20	Self	—	—
TM10	Hidden Power	Normal	Special	—	100	15	Normal	—	—
TM11	Sunny Day	Fire	Status	—	—	5	Both Sides	—	—
TM17	Protect	Normal	Status	—	—	10	Self	—	—
TM18	Rain Dance	Water	Status	—	—	5	Both Sides	—	—
TM21	Frustration	Normal	Physical	—	100	20	Normal	—	○
TM26	Earthquake	Ground	Physical	100	100	10	Adjacent	—	—
TM27	Return	Normal	Physical	—	100	20	Normal	—	○
TM31	Brick Break	Fighting	Physical	75	100	15	Normal	—	○
TM32	Double Team	Normal	Status	—	—	15	Self	—	—
TM39	Rock Tomb	Rock	Physical	50	80	10	Normal	—	—
TM42	Facade	Normal	Physical	70	100	20	Normal	—	○
TM44	Rest	Psychic	Status	—	—	10	Self	—	—
TM45	Attract	Normal	Status	—	100	15	Normal	—	—
TM46	Thief	Dark	Physical	40	100	10	Normal	—	○
TM47	Low Sweep	Fighting	Physical	60	100	20	Normal	—	○
TM48	Round	Normal	Special	60	100	15	Normal	—	—
TM52	Focus Blast	Fighting	Special	120	70	5	Normal	—	—
TM56	Fling	Dark	Physical	—	100	10	Normal	—	—
TM67	Retaliate	Normal	Physical	70	100	5	Normal	—	○
TM71	Stone Edge	Rock	Physical	100	80	5	Normal	—	—
TM78	Bulldoze	Ground	Physical	60	100	20	Adjacent	—	—
TM80	Rock Slide	Rock	Physical	75	90	10	Many Others	—	—
TM83	Work Up	Normal	Status	—	—	30	Self	—	—
TM87	Swagger	Normal	Status	—	90	15	Normal	—	—
TM90	Substitute	Normal	Status	—	—	10	Self	—	—
TM94	Rock Smash	Fighting	Physical	40	100	15	Normal	—	○
HM04	Strength	Normal	Physical	80	100	15	Normal	—	○

MOVES TAUGHT BY PEOPLE

Name	Type	Kind	Pow.	Acc.	PP	Range	Long	DA

MOVES TAUGHT BY MOVE TUTORS FOR SHARDS

Name	Type	Kind	Pow.	Acc.	PP	Range	Long	DA
Covet	Normal	Physical	60	100	40	Normal	—	○
Low Kick	Fighting	Physical	—	100	20	Normal	—	○
Fire Punch	Fire	Physical	75	100	15	Normal	—	○
ThunderPunch	Electric	Physical	75	100	15	Normal	—	○
Ice Punch	Ice	Physical	75	100	15	Normal	—	○
Snore	Normal	Special	40	100	15	Normal	—	—
Role Play	Psychic	Status	—	—	10	Normal	—	—
Drain Punch	Fighting	Physical	75	100	10	Normal	—	○
Helping Hand	Normal	Status	—	—	20	1 Ally	—	—
Sleep Talk	Normal	Status	—	—	10	Self	—	—

108 Lickitung

Licking Pokémon

TYPE: Normal

ABILITIES
- Own Tempo
- Oblivious

HIDDEN ABILITY
- Cloud Nine

STATS
- HP
- Attack
- Defense
- Sp. Atk
- Sp. Def
- Speed

EGG GROUPS
Monster

ITEMS SOMETIMES HELD
- Lagging Tail

- HEIGHT: 3'11"
- WEIGHT: 144.4 lbs.
- GENDER: ♂ / ♀

Being licked by its long, saliva-covered tongue leaves a tingling sensation. Extending its tongue retracts its tail.

Same form for ♂ / ♀

Pokémon AR Marker

EVOLUTION

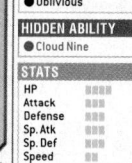

Lickitung
Level up Lickitung to Lv. 33 and teach it Rollout or level it up after it knows Rollout
Lickilicky
→ p. 247

HOW TO OBTAIN

Pokémon Black Version 2	Route 2
Pokémon White Version 2	Route 2

HOW TO OBTAIN FROM OTHER GAMES

—

—

LEVEL-UP AND LEARNED MOVES

Lv.	Name	Type	Kind	Pow.	Acc.	PP	Range	Long	DA
1	Lick	Ghost	Physical	20	100	30	Normal	—	○
5	Supersonic	Normal	Status	—	55	20	Normal	—	—
9	Defense Curl	Normal	Status	—	—	40	Self	—	—
13	Knock Off	Dark	Physical	20	100	20	Normal	—	○
17	Wrap	Normal	Physical	15	90	20	Normal	—	○
21	Stomp	Normal	Physical	65	100	20	Normal	—	○
25	Disable	Normal	Status	—	100	20	Normal	—	—
29	Slam	Normal	Physical	80	75	20	Normal	—	○
33	Rollout	Rock	Physical	30	90	20	Normal	—	○
37	Chip Away	Normal	Physical	70	100	20	Normal	—	○
41	Me First	Normal	Status	—	—	20	Varies	—	—
45	Refresh	Normal	Status	—	—	20	Self	—	—
49	Screech	Normal	Status	—	85	40	Normal	—	—
53	Power Whip	Grass	Physical	120	85	10	Normal	—	○
57	Wring Out	Normal	Special	—	100	5	Normal	—	○

TM & HM MOVES

Lv.	Name	Type	Kind	Pow.	Acc.	PP	Range	Long	DA
TM06	Toxic	Poison	Status	—	90	10	Normal	—	—
TM10	Hidden Power	Normal	Special	—	100	15	Normal	—	—
TM11	Sunny Day	Fire	Status	—	—	5	Both Sides	—	—
TM13	Ice Beam	Ice	Special	95	100	10	Normal	—	—
TM14	Blizzard	Ice	Special	120	70	5	Many Others	—	—
TM15	Hyper Beam	Normal	Special	150	90	5	Normal	—	—
TM17	Protect	Normal	Status	—	—	10	Self	—	—
TM18	Rain Dance	Water	Status	—	—	5	Both Sides	—	—
TM21	Frustration	Normal	Physical	—	100	20	Normal	—	○
TM22	SolarBeam	Grass	Special	120	100	10	Normal	—	—
TM24	Thunderbolt	Electric	Special	95	100	15	Normal	—	—
TM25	Thunder	Electric	Special	120	70	10	Normal	—	—
TM26	Earthquake	Ground	Physical	100	100	10	Adjacent	—	—
TM27	Return	Normal	Physical	—	100	20	Normal	—	○
TM28	Dig	Ground	Physical	80	100	10	Normal	—	○
TM30	Shadow Ball	Ghost	Special	80	100	15	Normal	—	—
TM31	Brick Break	Fighting	Physical	75	100	15	Normal	—	○
TM32	Double Team	Normal	Status	—	—	15	Self	—	—
TM35	Flamethrower	Fire	Special	95	100	15	Normal	—	—
TM37	Sandstorm	Rock	Status	—	—	10	Both Sides	—	—
TM38	Fire Blast	Fire	Special	120	85	5	Normal	—	—
TM39	Rock Tomb	Rock	Physical	50	80	10	Normal	—	—
TM42	Facade	Normal	Physical	70	100	20	Normal	—	○
TM44	Rest	Psychic	Status	—	—	10	Self	—	—
TM45	Attract	Normal	Status	—	100	15	Normal	—	—
TM46	Thief	Dark	Physical	40	100	10	Normal	—	○
TM48	Round	Normal	Special	60	100	15	Normal	—	—
TM56	Fling	Dark	Physical	—	100	10	Normal	—	—
TM59	Incinerate	Fire	Special	30	100	15	Many Others	—	—
TM67	Retaliate	Normal	Physical	70	100	5	Normal	—	○
TM68	Giga Impact	Normal	Physical	150	90	5	Normal	—	○
TM75	Swords Dance	Normal	Status	—	—	30	Self	—	—
TM77	Psych Up	Normal	Status	—	—	10	Normal	—	—
TM78	Bulldoze	Ground	Physical	60	100	20	Adjacent	—	—
TM80	Rock Slide	Rock	Physical	75	90	10	Many Others	—	—
TM82	Dragon Tail	Dragon	Physical	60	90	10	Normal	—	○
TM83	Work Up	Normal	Status	—	—	30	Self	—	—
TM85	Dream Eater	Psychic	Special	100	100	15	Normal	—	—
TM87	Swagger	Normal	Status	—	90	15	Normal	—	—
TM90	Substitute	Normal	Status	—	—	10	Self	—	—
TM94	Rock Smash	Fighting	Physical	40	100	15	Normal	—	○
HM01	Cut	Normal	Physical	50	95	30	Normal	—	○
HM03	Surf	Water	Special	95	100	15	Adjacent	—	—
HM04	Strength	Normal	Physical	80	100	15	Normal	—	○

MOVES TAUGHT BY PEOPLE

Name	Type	Kind	Pow.	Acc.	PP	Range	Long	DA

MOVES TAUGHT BY MOVE TUTORS FOR SHARDS

Name	Type	Kind	Pow.	Acc.	PP	Range	Long	DA
Fire Punch	Fire	Physical	75	100	15	Normal	—	○
ThunderPunch	Electric	Physical	75	100	15	Normal	—	○
Ice Punch	Ice	Physical	75	100	15	Normal	—	○
Icy Wind	Ice	Special	55	95	15	Many Others	—	—
Iron Tail	Steel	Physical	100	75	15	Normal	—	○
Aqua Tail	Water	Physical	90	90	10	Normal	—	○
Zen Headbutt	Psychic	Physical	80	90	15	Normal	—	○
Bind	Normal	Physical	15	85	20	Normal	—	○
Snore	Normal	Special	40	100	15	Normal	—	—
Knock Off	Dark	Physical	20	100	20	Normal	—	○
Sleep Talk	Normal	Status	—	—	10	Self	—	—

EGG MOVES

Name	Type	Kind	Pow.	Acc.	PP	Range	Long	DA
Belly Drum	Normal	Status	—	—	10	Self	—	—
Magnitude	Ground	Physical	—	100	30	Adjacent	—	—
Body Slam	Normal	Physical	85	100	15	Normal	—	○
Curse	Ghost	Status	—	—	10	Varies	—	—
SmellingSalt	Normal	Physical	60	100	10	Normal	—	○
Sleep Talk	Normal	Status	—	—	10	Self	—	—
Snore	Normal	Special	40	100	15	Normal	—	—
Amnesia	Psychic	Status	—	—	20	Self	—	—
Hammer Arm	Fighting	Physical	100	90	10	Normal	—	○
Muddy Water	Water	Special	95	85	10	Many Others	—	—
Zen Headbutt	Psychic	Physical	80	90	15	Normal	—	○

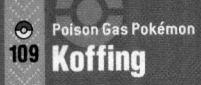

109 Koffing

Poison Gas Pokémon

- HEIGHT: 2'00"
- WEIGHT: 146.8 lbs.
- GENDER: Unknown

Toxic gas is held within its thin, balloon-shaped body, so it can cause massive explosions.

TYPE: Poison

ABILITY
- Levitate

HIDDEN ABILITY
—

STATS
HP
Attack
Defense
Sp. Atk
Sp. Def
Speed

EGG GROUPS
Amorphous

Gender unknown

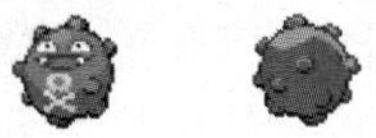

ITEMS SOMETIMES HELD
- Smoke Ball

EVOLUTION

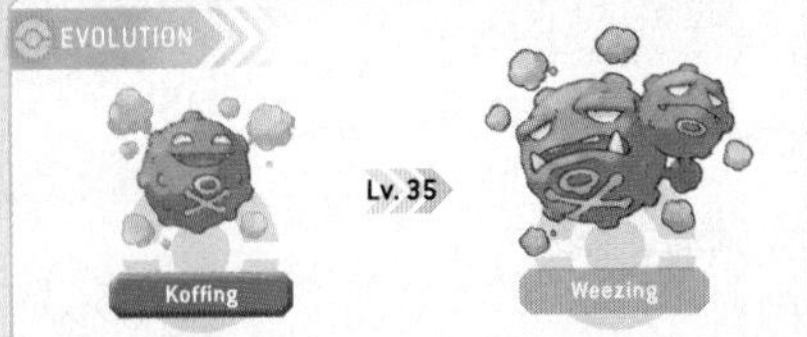

HOW TO OBTAIN

Pokémon Black Version 2	Virbank Complex interior
Pokémon White Version 2	Virbank Complex interior

HOW TO OBTAIN FROM OTHER GAMES

—
—

LEVEL-UP AND LEARNED MOVES

Lv.	Name	Type	Kind	Pow.	Acc.	PP	Range	Long	DA
1	Poison Gas	Poison	Status	—	80	40	Many Others	—	—
1	Tackle	Normal	Physical	50	100	35	Normal	—	○
4	Smog	Poison	Special	20	70	20	Normal	—	—
7	SmokeScreen	Normal	Status	—	100	20	Normal	—	—
12	Assurance	Dark	Physical	50	100	10	Normal	—	○
15	Clear Smog	Poison	Special	50	—	15	Normal	—	—
18	Sludge	Poison	Special	65	100	20	Normal	—	—
23	Selfdestruct	Normal	Physical	200	100	5	Adjacent	—	—
26	Haze	Ice	Status	—	—	30	Both Sides	—	—
29	Gyro Ball	Steel	Physical	—	100	5	Normal	—	○
34	Sludge Bomb	Poison	Special	90	100	10	Normal	—	—
37	Explosion	Normal	Physical	250	100	5	Adjacent	—	—
40	Destiny Bond	Ghost	Status	—	—	5	Self	—	—
45	Memento	Dark	Status	—	100	10	Normal	—	—

TM & HM MOVES

Lv.	Name	Type	Kind	Pow.	Acc.	PP	Range	Long	DA
TM06	Toxic	Poison	Status	—	90	10	Normal	—	—
TM09	Venoshock	Poison	Special	65	100	10	Normal	—	—
TM10	Hidden Power	Normal	Special	—	100	15	Normal	—	—
TM11	Sunny Day	Fire	Status	—	—	5	Both Sides	—	—
TM12	Taunt	Dark	Status	—	100	20	Normal	—	—
TM17	Protect	Normal	Status	—	—	10	Self	—	—
TM18	Rain Dance	Water	Status	—	—	5	Both Sides	—	—
TM21	Frustration	Normal	Physical	—	100	20	Normal	—	○
TM24	Thunderbolt	Electric	Special	95	100	15	Normal	—	—
TM25	Thunder	Electric	Special	120	70	10	Normal	—	—
TM27	Return	Normal	Physical	—	100	20	Normal	—	○
TM30	Shadow Ball	Ghost	Special	80	100	15	Normal	—	—
TM32	Double Team	Normal	Status	—	—	15	Self	—	—
TM35	Flamethrower	Fire	Special	95	100	15	Normal	—	—
TM36	Sludge Bomb	Poison	Special	90	100	10	Normal	—	—
TM38	Fire Blast	Fire	Special	120	85	5	Normal	—	—
TM41	Torment	Dark	Status	—	100	15	Normal	—	—
TM42	Facade	Normal	Physical	70	100	20	Normal	—	○
TM44	Rest	Psychic	Status	—	—	10	Self	—	—
TM45	Attract	Normal	Status	—	100	15	Normal	—	—
TM46	Thief	Dark	Physical	40	100	10	Normal	—	○
TM48	Round	Normal	Special	60	100	15	Normal	—	—
TM59	Incinerate	Fire	Special	30	100	15	Many Others	—	—
TM61	Will-O-Wisp	Fire	Status	—	75	15	Normal	—	—
TM64	Explosion	Normal	Physical	250	100	5	Adjacent	—	—
TM66	Payback	Dark	Physical	50	100	10	Normal	—	○
TM70	Flash	Normal	Status	—	100	20	Normal	—	—
TM74	Gyro Ball	Steel	Physical	—	100	5	Normal	—	○
TM87	Swagger	Normal	Status	—	90	15	Normal	—	—
TM90	Substitute	Normal	Status	—	—	10	Self	—	—

MOVES TAUGHT BY PEOPLE

Name	Type	Kind	Pow.	Acc.	PP	Range	Long	DA

MOVES TAUGHT BY MOVE TUTORS FOR SHARDS

Name	Type	Kind	Pow.	Acc.	PP	Range	Long	DA
Uproar	Normal	Special	90	100	10	1 Random	—	—
Dark Pulse	Dark	Special	80	100	15	Normal	○	—
Snore	Normal	Special	40	100	15	Normal	—	—
Pain Split	Normal	Status	—	—	20	Normal	—	—
Spite	Ghost	Status	—	100	10	Normal	—	—
Sleep Talk	Normal	Status	—	—	10	Self	—	—

EGG MOVES

Name	Type	Kind	Pow.	Acc.	PP	Range	Long	DA
Screech	Normal	Status	—	85	40	Normal	—	—
Psywave	Psychic	Special	—	80	15	Normal	—	—
Psybeam	Psychic	Special	65	100	20	Normal	—	—
Destiny Bond	Ghost	Status	—	—	5	Self	—	—
Pain Split	Normal	Status	—	—	20	Normal	—	—
Grudge	Ghost	Status	—	—	5	Self	—	—
Spite	Ghost	Status	—	100	10	Normal	—	—
Curse	Ghost	Status	—	—	10	Varies	—	—
Stockpile	Normal	Status	—	—	20	Self	—	—
Swallow	Normal	Status	—	—	10	Self	—	—
Spit Up	Normal	Special	—	100	10	Normal	—	—

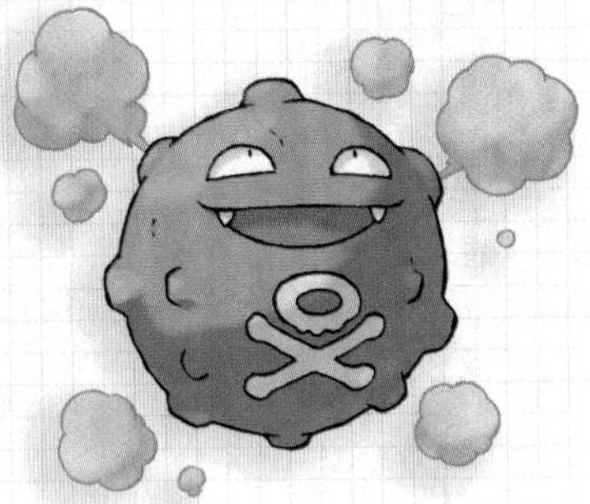

Pokémon AR Marker

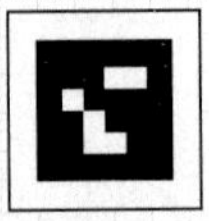

110 Weezing

Poison Gas Pokémon

- HEIGHT: 3'11"
- WEIGHT: 20.9 lbs.
- GENDER: ♂ / ♀

Inhaling toxic fumes from trash and mixing them inside its body lets it spread an even fouler stench.

TYPE: Poison

ABILITY
- Levitate

HIDDEN ABILITY
—

STATS
HP
Attack
Defense
Sp. Atk
Sp. Def
Speed

EGG GROUPS
Amorphous

Same form for ♂ / ♀

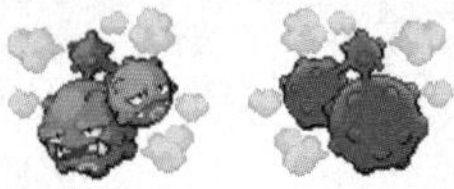

ITEMS SOMETIMES HELD
- Smoke Ball

EVOLUTION

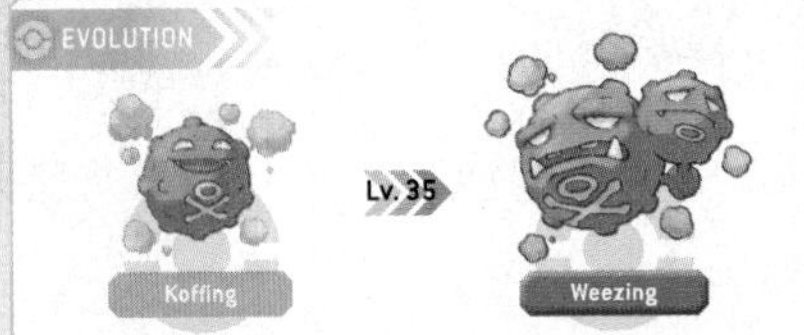

HOW TO OBTAIN

Pokémon Black Version 2	P2 Laboratory
Pokémon White Version 2	P2 Laboratory

HOW TO OBTAIN FROM OTHER GAMES

—
—

LEVEL-UP AND LEARNED MOVES

Lv.	Name	Type	Kind	Pow.	Acc.	PP	Range	Long	DA
1	Poison Gas	Poison	Status	—	80	40	Many Others	—	—
1	Tackle	Normal	Physical	50	100	35	Normal	—	○
1	Smog	Poison	Special	20	70	20	Normal	—	—
1	SmokeScreen	Normal	Status	—	100	20	Normal	—	—
4	Smog	Poison	Special	20	70	20	Normal	—	—
7	SmokeScreen	Normal	Status	—	100	20	Normal	—	—
12	Assurance	Dark	Physical	50	100	10	Normal	—	○
15	Clear Smog	Poison	Special	50	—	15	Normal	—	—
18	Sludge	Poison	Special	65	100	20	Normal	—	—
23	Selfdestruct	Normal	Physical	200	100	5	Adjacent	—	—
26	Haze	Ice	Status	—	—	30	Both Sides	—	—
29	Double Hit	Normal	Physical	35	90	10	Normal	—	○
34	Sludge Bomb	Poison	Special	90	100	10	Normal	—	—
40	Explosion	Normal	Physical	250	100	5	Adjacent	—	—
46	Destiny Bond	Ghost	Status	—	—	5	Self	—	—
54	Memento	Dark	Status	—	100	10	Normal	—	—

TM & HM MOVES

Lv.	Name	Type	Kind	Pow.	Acc.	PP	Range	Long	DA
TM06	Toxic	Poison	Status	—	90	10	Normal	—	—
TM09	Venoshock	Poison	Special	65	100	10	Normal	—	—
TM10	Hidden Power	Normal	Special	—	100	15	Normal	—	—
TM11	Sunny Day	Fire	Status	—	—	5	Both Sides	—	—
TM12	Taunt	Dark	Status	—	100	20	Normal	—	—
TM15	Hyper Beam	Normal	Special	150	90	5	Normal	—	—
TM17	Protect	Normal	Status	—	—	10	Self	—	—
TM18	Rain Dance	Water	Status	—	—	5	Both Sides	—	—
TM21	Frustration	Normal	Physical	—	100	20	Normal	—	○
TM24	Thunderbolt	Electric	Special	95	100	15	Normal	—	—
TM25	Thunder	Electric	Special	120	70	10	Normal	—	—
TM27	Return	Normal	Physical	—	100	20	Normal	—	○
TM30	Shadow Ball	Ghost	Special	80	100	15	Normal	—	—
TM32	Double Team	Normal	Status	—	—	15	Self	—	—
TM35	Flamethrower	Fire	Special	95	100	15	Normal	—	—
TM36	Sludge Bomb	Poison	Special	90	100	10	Normal	—	—
TM38	Fire Blast	Fire	Special	120	85	5	Normal	—	—
TM41	Torment	Dark	Status	—	100	15	Normal	—	—
TM42	Facade	Normal	Physical	70	100	20	Normal	—	○
TM44	Rest	Psychic	Status	—	—	10	Self	—	—
TM45	Attract	Normal	Status	—	100	15	Normal	—	—
TM46	Thief	Dark	Physical	40	100	10	Normal	—	○
TM48	Round	Normal	Special	60	100	15	Normal	—	—
TM59	Incinerate	Fire	Special	30	100	15	Many Others	—	—
TM61	Will-O-Wisp	Fire	Status	—	75	15	Normal	—	—
TM64	Explosion	Normal	Physical	250	100	5	Adjacent	—	—
TM66	Payback	Dark	Physical	50	100	10	Normal	—	○
TM68	Giga Impact	Normal	Physical	150	90	5	Normal	—	○
TM70	Flash	Normal	Status	—	100	20	Normal	—	—
TM74	Gyro Ball	Steel	Physical	—	100	5	Normal	—	○
TM87	Swagger	Normal	Status	—	90	15	Normal	—	—
TM90	Substitute	Normal	Status	—	—	10	Self	—	—

MOVES TAUGHT BY PEOPLE

Name	Type	Kind	Pow.	Acc.	PP	Range	Long	DA

MOVES TAUGHT BY MOVE TUTORS FOR SHARDS

Name	Type	Kind	Pow.	Acc.	PP	Range	Long	DA
Uproar	Normal	Special	90	100	10	1 Random	—	—
Dark Pulse	Dark	Special	80	100	15	Normal	○	—
Snore	Normal	Special	40	100	15	Normal	—	—
Pain Split	Normal	Status	—	—	20	Normal	—	—
Spite	Ghost	Status	—	100	10	Normal	—	—
Sleep Talk	Normal	Status	—	—	10	Self	—	—

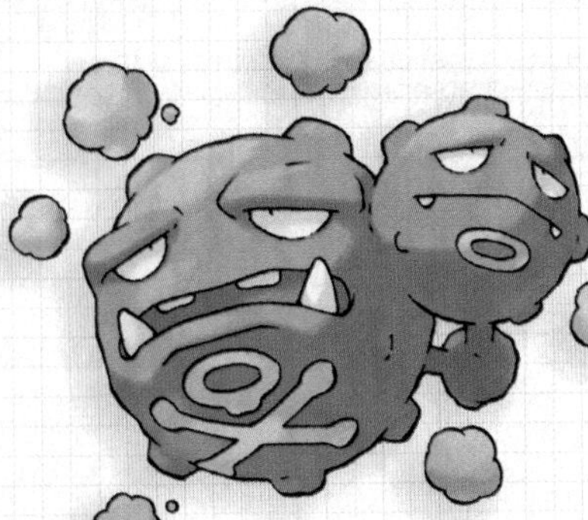

Pokémon AR Marker

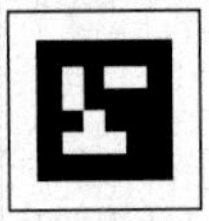

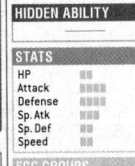

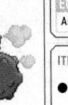

Spikes Pokémon

111 Rhyhorn

- HEIGHT: 3'03"
- WEIGHT: 253.5 lbs.
- GENDER: ♂ / ♀

Its powerful tackles can destroy anything. However, it is too slow witted to help people work.

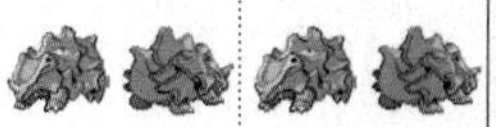

TYPE: Ground / Rock

ABILITY ABILITIES
- Lightningrod
- Rock Head

HIDDEN ABILITY
- Reckless

STATS
HP
Attack
Defense
Sp. Atk
Sp. Def
Speed

EGG GROUPS
Monster/Field

ITEMS SOMETIMES HELD
- None

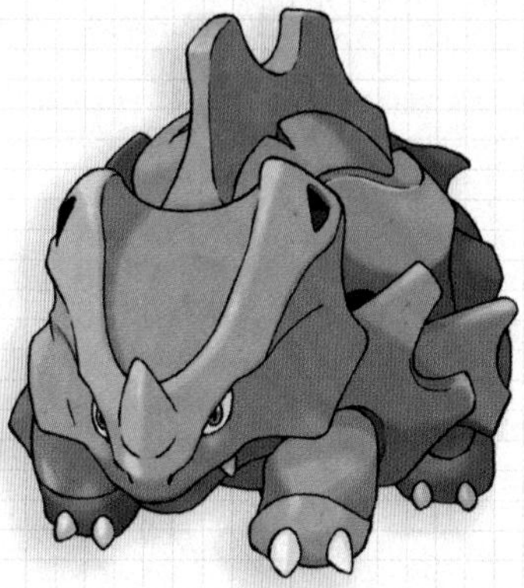

Pokémon AR Marker

EVOLUTION

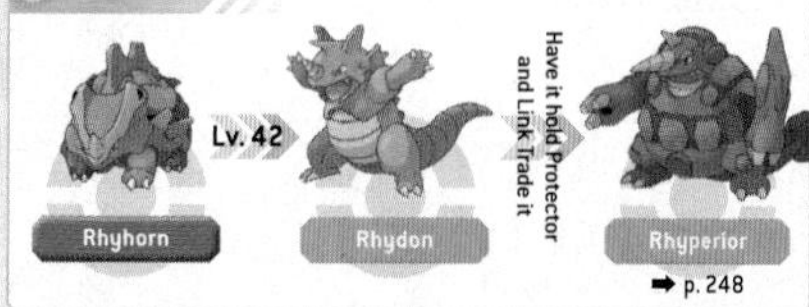

Rhyhorn
Lv. 42
Rhydon
Have it hold Protector and Link Trade it
Rhyperior

➡ p. 248

HOW TO OBTAIN

Pokémon Black Version 2	Trade Pokémon during a date with Yancy or Curtis
Pokémon White Version 2	Trade Pokémon during a date with Yancy or Curtis (fifth t

HOW TO OBTAIN FROM OTHER GAMES

Pokémon HeartGold Version	Victory Road
Pokémon SoulSilver Version	Victory Road

LEVEL-UP AND LEARNED MOVES

Lv.	Name	Type	Kind	Pow.	Acc.	PP	Range	Long	DA
1	Horn Attack	Normal	Physical	65	100	25	Normal	—	○
1	Tail Whip	Normal	Status	—	100	30	Many Others	—	—
8	Stomp	Normal	Physical	65	100	20	Normal	—	○
12	Fury Attack	Normal	Physical	15	85	20	Normal	—	○
19	Scary Face	Normal	Status	—	100	10	Normal	—	—
23	Rock Blast	Rock	Physical	25	90	10	Normal	—	—
30	Bulldoze	Ground	Physical	60	100	20	Adjacent	—	—
34	Chip Away	Normal	Physical	70	100	20	Normal	—	○
41	Take Down	Normal	Physical	90	85	20	Normal	—	○
45	Drill Run	Ground	Physical	80	95	10	Normal	—	○
52	Stone Edge	Rock	Physical	100	80	5	Normal	—	—
56	Earthquake	Ground	Physical	100	100	10	Adjacent	—	—
63	Horn Drill	Normal	Physical	—	30	5	Normal	—	○
67	Megahorn	Bug	Physical	120	85	10	Normal	—	○

TM & HM MOVES

Lv.	Name	Type	Kind	Pow.	Acc.	PP	Range	Long	DA
TM05	Roar	Normal	Status	—	100	20	Normal	—	—
TM06	Toxic	Poison	Status	—	90	10	Normal	—	—
TM10	Hidden Power	Normal	Special	—	100	15	Normal	—	—
TM11	Sunny Day	Fire	Status	—	—	5	Both Sides	—	—
TM13	Ice Beam	Ice	Special	95	100	10	Normal	—	—
TM14	Blizzard	Ice	Special	120	70	5	Many Others	—	—
TM17	Protect	Normal	Status	—	—	10	Self	—	—
TM18	Rain Dance	Water	Status	—	—	5	Both Sides	—	—
TM21	Frustration	Normal	Physical	—	100	20	Normal	—	○
TM24	Thunderbolt	Electric	Special	95	100	15	Normal	—	—
TM25	Thunder	Electric	Special	120	70	10	Normal	—	—
TM26	Earthquake	Ground	Physical	100	100	10	Adjacent	—	—
TM27	Return	Normal	Physical	—	100	20	Normal	—	○
TM28	Dig	Ground	Physical	80	100	10	Normal	—	○
TM32	Double Team	Normal	Status	—	—	15	Self	—	—
TM35	Flamethrower	Fire	Special	95	100	15	Normal	—	—
TM37	Sandstorm	Rock	Status	—	—	10	Both Sides	—	—
TM38	Fire Blast	Fire	Special	120	85	5	Normal	—	—
TM39	Rock Tomb	Rock	Physical	50	80	10	Normal	—	—
TM42	Facade	Normal	Physical	70	100	20	Normal	—	○
TM44	Rest	Psychic	Status	—	—	10	Self	—	—
TM45	Attract	Normal	Status	—	100	15	Normal	—	—
TM46	Thief	Dark	Physical	40	100	10	Normal	—	○
TM48	Round	Normal	Special	60	100	15	Normal	—	—
TM59	Incinerate	Fire	Special	30	100	15	Many Others	—	—
TM66	Payback	Dark	Physical	50	100	10	Normal	—	○
TM69	Rock Polish	Rock	Status	—	—	20	Self	—	—
TM71	Stone Edge	Rock	Physical	100	80	5	Normal	—	—
TM75	Swords Dance	Normal	Status	—	—	30	Self	—	—
TM78	Bulldoze	Ground	Physical	60	100	20	Adjacent	—	—
TM80	Rock Slide	Rock	Physical	75	90	10	Many Others	—	—
TM84	Poison Jab	Poison	Physical	80	100	20	Normal	—	○
TM87	Swagger	Normal	Status	—	90	15	Normal	—	—
TM90	Substitute	Normal	Status	—	—	10	Self	—	—
TM94	Rock Smash	Fighting	Physical	40	100	15	Normal	—	○
HM04	Strength	Normal	Physical	80	100	15	Normal	—	○

MOVES TAUGHT BY PEOPLE

Name	Type	Kind	Pow.	Acc.	PP	Range	Long	DA

MOVES TAUGHT BY MOVE TUTORS FOR SHARDS

Name	Type	Kind	Pow.	Acc.	PP	Range	Long	DA
Drill Run	Ground	Physical	80	95	10	Normal	—	○
Uproar	Normal	Special	90	100	10	1 Random	—	—
Icy Wind	Ice	Special	55	95	15	Many Others	—	—
Iron Tail	Steel	Physical	100	75	15	Normal	—	○
Aqua Tail	Water	Physical	90	90	10	Normal	—	○
Earth Power	Ground	Special	90	100	10	Normal	—	—
Superpower	Fighting	Physical	120	100	5	Normal	—	○
Dragon Pulse	Dragon	Special	90	100	10	Normal	○	—
Snore	Normal	Special	40	100	15	Normal	—	—
Spite	Ghost	Status	—	100	10	Normal	—	—
Stealth Rock	Rock	Status	—	—	20	Other Side	—	—
Endeavor	Normal	Physical	—	100	5	Normal	—	○
Sleep Talk	Normal	Status	—	—	10	Self	—	—

EGG MOVES

Name	Type	Kind	Pow.	Acc.	PP	Range	Long	DA
Crunch	Dark	Physical	80	100	15	Normal	—	○
Reversal	Fighting	Physical	—	100	15	Normal	—	○
Counter	Fighting	Physical	—	100	20	Varies	—	○
Magnitude	Ground	Physical	—	100	30	Adjacent	—	—
Curse	Ghost	Status	—	—	10	Varies	—	—
Crush Claw	Normal	Physical	75	95	10	Normal	—	○
Dragon Rush	Dragon	Physical	100	75	10	Normal	—	○
Ice Fang	Ice	Physical	65	95	15	Normal	—	○
Fire Fang	Fire	Physical	65	95	15	Normal	—	○
Thunder Fang	Electric	Physical	65	95	15	Normal	—	○
Skull Bash	Normal	Physical	100	100	15	Normal	—	○
Iron Tail	Steel	Physical	100	75	15	Normal	—	○
Rock Climb	Normal	Physical	90	85	20	Normal	—	○

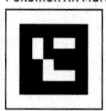

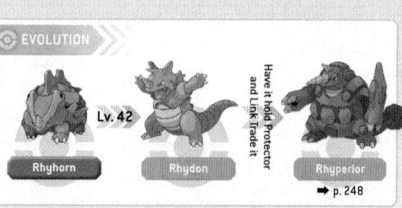

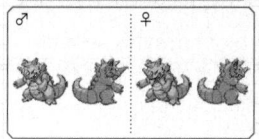

Drill Pokémon

112 Rhydon

- HEIGHT: 6'03"
- WEIGHT: 264.6 lbs.
- GENDER: ♂ / ♀

Standing on its hind legs freed its forelegs and made it smarter. It is very forgetful, however.

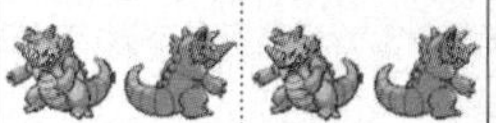

TYPE: Ground / Rock

ABILITIES
- Lightningrod
- Rock Head

HIDDEN ABILITY
- Reckless

STATS
HP
Attack
Defense
Sp. Atk
Sp. Def
Speed

EGG GROUPS
Monster/Field

ITEMS SOMETIMES HELD
- None

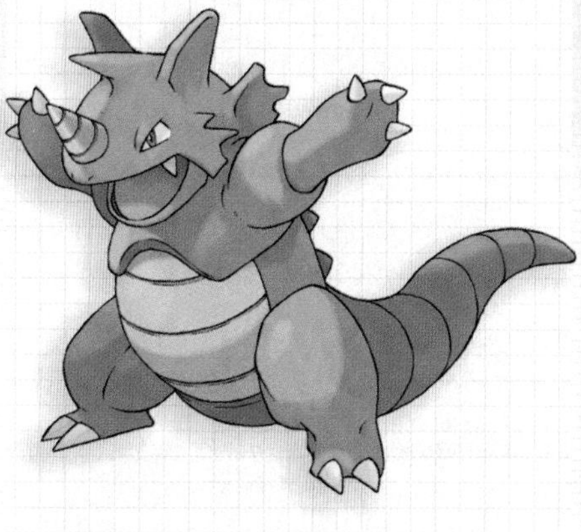

Pokémon AR Marker

EVOLUTION

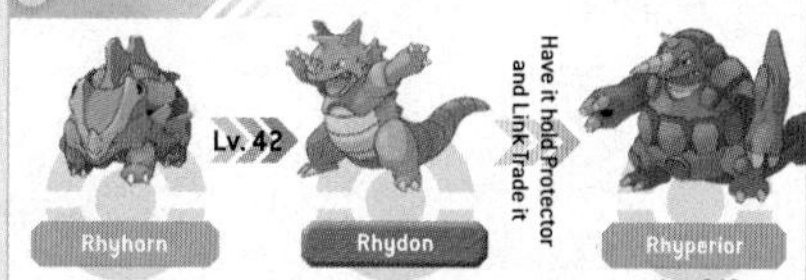

Rhyhorn
Lv. 42
Rhydon
Have it hold Protector and Link Trade it
Rhyperior

➡ p. 248

HOW TO OBTAIN

Pokémon Black Version 2	Level up the Rhyhorn you receive from Yancy or Curtis to Lv. 42
Pokémon White Version 2	Level up the Rhyhorn you receive from Yancy or Curtis to Lv. 42

HOW TO OBTAIN FROM OTHER GAMES

Pokémon Platinum Version	Victory Road 1F
	—

LEVEL-UP AND LEARNED MOVES

Lv.	Name	Type	Kind	Pow.	Acc.	PP	Range	Long	DA
1	Horn Attack	Normal	Physical	65	100	25	Normal	—	○
1	Tail Whip	Normal	Status	—	100	30	Many Others	—	—
1	Stomp	Normal	Physical	65	100	20	Normal	—	○
1	Fury Attack	Normal	Physical	15	85	20	Normal	—	○
9	Stomp	Normal	Physical	65	100	20	Normal	—	○
12	Fury Attack	Normal	Physical	15	85	20	Normal	—	○
19	Scary Face	Normal	Status	—	100	10	Normal	—	—
23	Rock Blast	Rock	Physical	25	90	10	Normal	—	—
30	Bulldoze	Ground	Physical	60	100	20	Adjacent	—	—
34	Chip Away	Normal	Physical	70	100	20	Normal	—	○
41	Take Down	Normal	Physical	90	85	20	Normal	—	○
42	Hammer Arm	Fighting	Physical	100	90	10	Normal	—	○
47	Drill Run	Ground	Physical	80	95	10	Normal	—	○
56	Stone Edge	Rock	Physical	100	80	5	Normal	—	—
62	Earthquake	Ground	Physical	100	100	10	Adjacent	—	—
71	Horn Drill	Normal	Physical	—	30	5	Normal	—	○
77	Megahorn	Bug	Physical	120	85	10	Normal	—	○

TM & HM MOVES

Lv.	Name	Type	Kind	Pow.	Acc.	PP	Range	Long	DA
TM05	Roar	Normal	Status	—	100	20	Normal	—	—
TM06	Toxic	Poison	Status	—	90	10	Normal	—	—
TM10	Hidden Power	Normal	Special	—	100	15	Normal	—	—
TM11	Sunny Day	Fire	Status	—	—	5	Both Sides	—	—
TM13	Ice Beam	Ice	Special	95	100	10	Normal	—	—
TM14	Blizzard	Ice	Special	120	70	5	Many Others	—	—
TM15	Hyper Beam	Normal	Special	150	90	5	Normal	—	—
TM17	Protect	Normal	Status	—	—	10	Self	—	—
TM18	Rain Dance	Water	Status	—	—	5	Both Sides	—	—
TM21	Frustration	Normal	Physical	—	100	20	Normal	—	○
TM23	Smack Down	Rock	Physical	50	100	15	Normal	—	—
TM24	Thunderbolt	Electric	Special	95	100	15	Normal	—	—
TM25	Thunder	Electric	Special	120	70	10	Normal	—	—
TM26	Earthquake	Ground	Physical	100	100	10	Adjacent	—	—
TM27	Return	Normal	Physical	—	100	20	Normal	—	○
TM28	Dig	Ground	Physical	80	100	10	Normal	—	○
TM31	Brick Break	Fighting	Physical	75	100	15	Normal	—	○
TM32	Double Team	Normal	Status	—	—	15	Self	—	—
TM35	Flamethrower	Fire	Special	95	100	15	Normal	—	—
TM37	Sandstorm	Rock	Status	—	—	10	Both Sides	—	—
TM38	Fire Blast	Fire	Special	120	85	5	Normal	—	—
TM39	Rock Tomb	Rock	Physical	50	80	10	Normal	—	—
TM42	Facade	Normal	Physical	70	100	20	Normal	—	○
TM44	Rest	Psychic	Status	—	—	10	Self	—	—
TM45	Attract	Normal	Status	—	100	15	Normal	—	—
TM46	Thief	Dark	Physical	40	100	10	Normal	—	○
TM48	Round	Normal	Special	60	100	15	Normal	—	—
TM52	Focus Blast	Fighting	Special	120	70	5	Normal	—	—
TM56	Fling	Dark	Physical	—	100	10	Normal	—	—
TM59	Incinerate	Fire	Special	30	100	15	Many Others	—	—
TM65	Shadow Claw	Ghost	Physical	70	100	15	Normal	—	○
TM66	Payback	Dark	Physical	50	100	10	Normal	—	○
TM68	Giga Impact	Normal	Physical	150	90	5	Normal	—	○
TM69	Rock Polish	Rock	Status	—	—	20	Self	—	—
TM71	Stone Edge	Rock	Physical	100	80	5	Normal	—	—
TM75	Swords Dance	Normal	Status	—	—	30	Self	—	—
TM78	Bulldoze	Ground	Physical	60	100	20	Adjacent	—	—
TM80	Rock Slide	Rock	Physical	75	90	10	Many Others	—	—
TM82	Dragon Tail	Dragon	Physical	60	90	10	Normal	—	○
TM84	Poison Jab	Poison	Physical	80	100	20	Normal	—	○
TM87	Swagger	Normal	Status	—	90	15	Normal	—	—
TM90	Substitute	Normal	Status	—	—	10	Self	—	—
TM94	Rock Smash	Fighting	Physical	40	100	15	Normal	—	○
HM01	Cut	Normal	Physical	50	95	30	Normal	—	○
HM03	Surf	Water	Special	95	100	15	Adjacent	—	—
HM04	Strength	Normal	Physical	80	100	15	Normal	—	○

MOVES TAUGHT BY PEOPLE

Name	Type	Kind	Pow.	Acc.	PP	Range	Long	DA

MOVES TAUGHT BY MOVE TUTORS FOR SHARDS

Name	Type	Kind	Pow.	Acc.	PP	Range	Long	DA
Drill Run	Ground	Physical	80	95	10	Normal	—	○
Uproar	Normal	Special	90	100	10	1 Random	—	—
Fire Punch	Fire	Physical	75	100	15	Normal	—	○
ThunderPunch	Electric	Physical	75	100	15	Normal	—	○
Ice Punch	Ice	Physical	75	100	15	Normal	—	○
Block	Normal	Status	—	—	5	Normal	—	—
Icy Wind	Ice	Special	55	95	15	Many Others	—	—
Iron Tail	Steel	Physical	100	75	15	Normal	—	○
Aqua Tail	Water	Physical	90	90	10	Normal	—	○
Earth Power	Ground	Special	90	100	10	Normal	—	—
Superpower	Fighting	Physical	120	100	5	Normal	—	○
Dragon Pulse	Dragon	Special	90	100	10	Normal	○	—
Snore	Normal	Special	40	100	15	Normal	—	—
Spite	Ghost	Status	—	100	10	Normal	—	—
Stealth Rock	Rock	Status	—	—	20	Other Side	—	—
Outrage	Dragon	Physical	120	100	10	1 Random	—	○
Endeavor	Normal	Physical	—	100	5	Normal	—	○
Sleep Talk	Normal	Status	—	—	10	Self	—	—

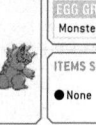

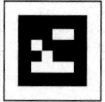

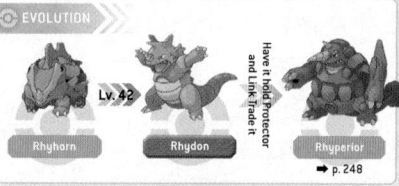

...on
...ey

highly nutritious
injured Pokémon

TYPE Normal

ABILITIES
- Natural Cure
- Serene Grace

HIDDEN ABILITY
- Healer

STATS
HP
Attack
Defense
Sp. Atk
Sp. Def
Speed

EGG GROUPS
Fairy

♀

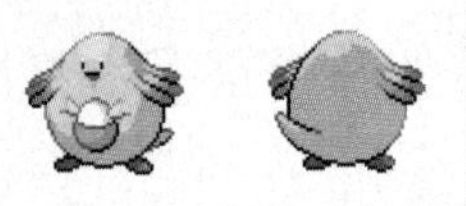

ITEMS SOMETIMES HELD
- None

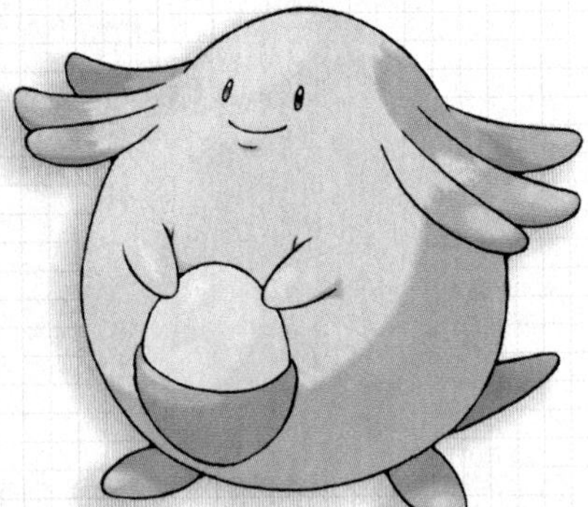

Pokémon AR Marker

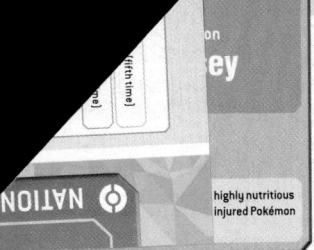

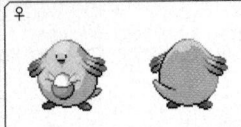

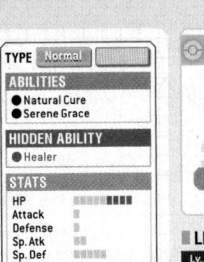

EVOLUTION

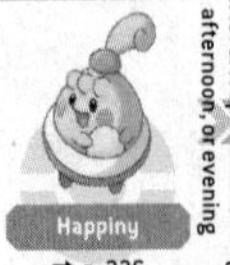

Happiny
➡ p. 236

Have it hold Oval Stone, then level it up in the morning, afternoon, or evening

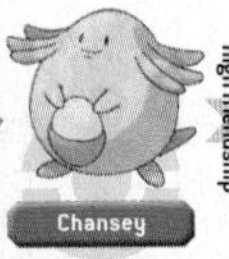

Chansey

Level up with high friendship

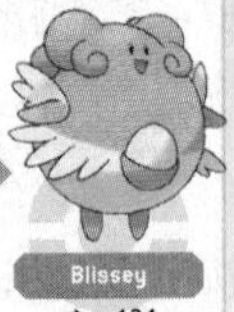

Blissey
➡ p. 134

HOW TO OBTAIN

Pokémon Black Version 2	Have Happiny hold Oval Stone, then level it up in the morning, afternoon, or evening
Pokémon White Version 2	Have Happiny hold Oval Stone, then level it up in the morning, afternoon, or evening

HOW TO OBTAIN FROM OTHER GAMES

—

—

LEVEL-UP AND LEARNED MOVES

Lv.	Name	Type	Kind	Pow.	Acc.	PP	Range	Long	DA
1	Defense Curl	Normal	Status	—	—	40	Self	—	—
1	Pound	Normal	Physical	40	100	35	Normal	—	○
1	Growl	Normal	Status	—	100	40	Many Others	—	—
5	Tail Whip	Normal	Status	—	100	30	Many Others	—	—
9	Refresh	Normal	Status	—	—	20	Self	—	—
12	DoubleSlap	Normal	Physical	15	85	10	Normal	—	○
16	Softboiled	Normal	Status	—	—	10	Self	—	—
20	Bestow	Normal	Status	—	—	15	Normal	—	—
23	Minimize	Normal	Status	—	—	20	Self	—	—
27	Take Down	Normal	Physical	90	85	20	Normal	—	○
31	Sing	Normal	Status	—	55	15	Normal	—	—
34	Fling	Dark	Physical	—	100	10	Normal	—	—
38	Heal Pulse	Psychic	Status	—	—	10	Normal	○	—
42	Egg Bomb	Normal	Physical	100	75	10	Normal	—	—
46	Light Screen	Psychic	Status	—	—	30	Your Side	—	—
50	Healing Wish	Psychic	Status	—	—	10	Self	—	—
54	Double-Edge	Normal	Physical	120	100	15	Normal	—	○

TM & HM MOVES

Lv.	Name	Type	Kind	Pow.	Acc.	PP	Range	Long	DA
TM04	Calm Mind	Psychic	Status	—	—	20	Self	—	—
TM06	Toxic	Poison	Status	—	90	10	Normal	—	—
TM07	Hail	Ice	Status	—	—	10	Both Sides	—	—
TM10	Hidden Power	Normal	Special	—	100	15	Normal	—	—
TM11	Sunny Day	Fire	Status	—	—	5	Both Sides	—	—
TM13	Ice Beam	Ice	Special	95	100	10	Normal	—	—
TM14	Blizzard	Ice	Special	120	70	5	Many Others	—	—
TM15	Hyper Beam	Normal	Special	150	90	5	Normal	—	—
TM16	Light Screen	Psychic	Status	—	—	30	Your Side	—	—
TM17	Protect	Normal	Status	—	—	10	Self	—	—
TM18	Rain Dance	Water	Status	—	—	5	Both Sides	—	—
TM20	Safeguard	Normal	Status	—	—	25	Your Side	—	—
TM21	Frustration	Normal	Physical	—	100	20	Normal	—	○
TM22	SolarBeam	Grass	Special	120	100	10	Normal	—	—
TM24	Thunderbolt	Electric	Special	95	100	15	Normal	—	—
TM25	Thunder	Electric	Special	120	70	10	Normal	—	—
TM26	Earthquake	Ground	Physical	100	100	10	Adjacent	—	—
TM27	Return	Normal	Physical	—	100	20	Normal	—	○
TM29	Psychic	Psychic	Special	90	100	10	Normal	—	—
TM30	Shadow Ball	Ghost	Special	80	100	15	Normal	—	—
TM31	Brick Break	Fighting	Physical	75	100	15	Normal	—	○
TM32	Double Team	Normal	Status	—	—	15	Self	—	—
TM35	Flamethrower	Fire	Special	95	100	15	Normal	—	—
TM37	Sandstorm	Rock	Status	—	—	10	Both Sides	—	—
TM38	Fire Blast	Fire	Special	120	85	5	Normal	—	—
TM39	Rock Tomb	Rock	Physical	50	80	10	Normal	—	—
TM42	Facade	Normal	Physical	70	100	20	Normal	—	○
TM44	Rest	Psychic	Status	—	—	10	Self	—	—
TM45	Attract	Normal	Status	—	100	15	Normal	—	—
TM48	Round	Normal	Special	60	100	15	Normal	—	—
TM49	Echoed Voice	Normal	Special	40	100	15	Normal	—	—
TM56	Fling	Dark	Physical	—	100	10	Normal	—	—
TM57	Charge Beam	Electric	Special	50	90	10	Normal	—	—
TM59	Incinerate	Fire	Special	30	100	15	Many Others	—	—
TM67	Retaliate	Normal	Physical	70	100	5	Normal	—	○
TM68	Giga Impact	Normal	Physical	150	90	5	Normal	—	○
TM70	Flash	Normal	Status	—	100	20	Normal	—	—
TM73	Thunder Wave	Electric	Status	—	100	20	Normal	—	—
TM77	Psych Up	Normal	Status	—	—	10	Normal	—	—
TM78	Bulldoze	Ground	Physical	60	100	20	Adjacent	—	—
TM80	Rock Slide	Rock	Physical	75	90	10	Many Others	—	—
TM83	Work Up	Normal	Status	—	—	30	Self	—	—
TM85	Dream Eater	Psychic	Special	100	100	15	Normal	—	—
TM86	Grass Knot	Grass	Special	—	100	20	Normal	—	○
TM87	Swagger	Normal	Status	—	90	15	Normal	—	—
TM90	Substitute	Normal	Status	—	—	10	Self	—	—
TM93	Wild Charge	Electric	Physical	90	100	15	Normal	—	○
TM94	Rock Smash	Fighting	Physical	40	100	15	Normal	—	○
HM04	Strength	Normal	Physical	80	100	15	Normal	—	○

MOVES TAUGHT BY PEOPLE

Name	Type	Kind	Pow.	Acc.	PP	Range	Long	DA

MOVES TAUGHT BY MOVE TUTORS FOR SHARDS

Name	Type	Kind	Pow.	Acc.	PP	Range	Long	DA
Covet	Normal	Physical	60	100	40	Normal	—	○
Fire Punch	Fire	Physical	75	100	15	Normal	—	○
ThunderPunch	Electric	Physical	75	100	15	Normal	—	○
Ice Punch	Ice	Physical	75	100	15	Normal	—	○
Last Resort	Normal	Physical	140	100	5	Normal	—	○
Hyper Voice	Normal	Special	90	100	10	Many Others	—	—
Icy Wind	Ice	Special	55	95	15	Many Others	—	—
Iron Tail	Steel	Physical	100	75	15	Normal	—	○
Zen Headbutt	Psychic	Physical	80	90	15	Normal	—	○
Gravity	Psychic	Status	—	—	5	Both Sides	—	—
Snore	Normal	Special	40	100	15	Normal	—	—
Heal Bell	Normal	Status	—	—	5	Your Party	—	—
Drain Punch	Fighting	Physical	75	100	10	Normal	—	○
Helping Hand	Normal	Status	—	—	20	1 Ally	—	—
Recycle	Normal	Status	—	—	10	Self	—	—
Stealth Rock	Rock	Status	—	—	20	Other Side	—	—
Endeavor	Normal	Physical	—	100	5	Normal	—	○
Sleep Talk	Normal	Status	—	—	10	Self	—	—
Skill Swap	Psychic	Status	—	—	10	Normal	—	—
Snatch	Dark	Status	—	—	10	Self	—	—

EGG MOVES

Name	Type	Kind	Pow.	Acc.	PP	Range	Long	DA
Present	Normal	Physical	—	90	15	Normal	—	—
Metronome	Normal	Status	—	—	10	Self	—	—
Heal Bell	Normal	Status	—	—	5	Your Party	—	—
Aromatherapy	Grass	Status	—	—	5	Your Party	—	—
Counter	Fighting	Physical	—	100	20	Varies	—	○
Helping Hand	Normal	Status	—	—	20	1 Ally	—	—
Gravity	Psychic	Status	—	—	5	Both Sides	—	—
Mud Bomb	Ground	Special	65	85	10	Normal	—	—
Natural Gift	Normal	Physical	—	100	15	Normal	—	—
Endure	Normal	Status	—	—	10	Self	—	—

Vine Pokémon

114 Tangela

- HEIGHT: 3'03"
- WEIGHT: 77.2 lbs.
- GENDER: ♂ / ♀

Many writhing vines cover it, so its true identity remains unknown. The blue vines grow its whole life long.

TYPE Grass

ABILITIES
- Chlorophyll
- Leaf Guard

HIDDEN ABILITY
- Regenerator

STATS
HP
Attack
Defense
Sp. Atk
Sp. Def
Speed

EGG GROUPS
Grass

Same form for ♂ / ♀

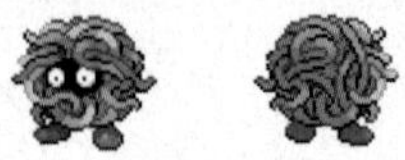

ITEMS SOMETIMES HELD
- None

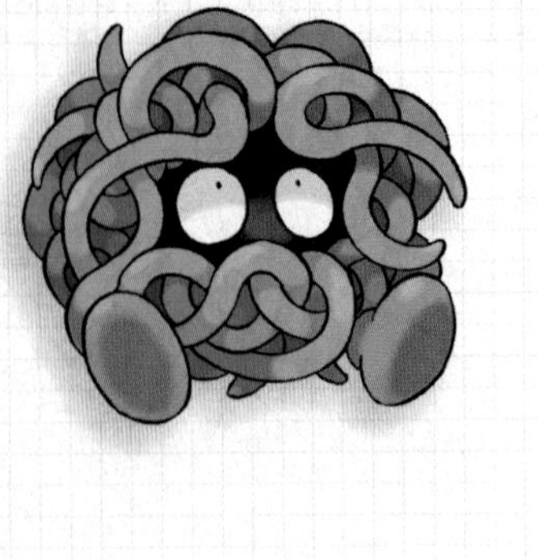

Pokémon AR Marker

EVOLUTION

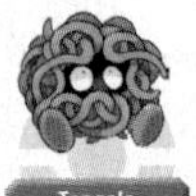

Tangela

Level up Tangela to Lv. 40 and teach it AncientPower or level it up after it knows AncientPower

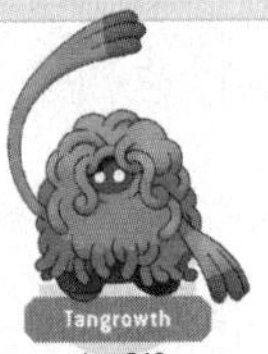

Tangrowth
➡ p. 248

HOW TO OBTAIN

Pokémon Black Version 2	❶ Route 13 ❷ Giant Chasm entrance
Pokémon White Version 2	❶ Route 13 ❷ Giant Chasm entrance

HOW TO OBTAIN FROM OTHER GAMES

—

—

LEVEL-UP AND LEARNED MOVES

Lv.	Name	Type	Kind	Pow.	Acc.	PP	Range	Long	DA
1	Ingrain	Grass	Status	—	—	20	Self	—	—
1	Constrict	Normal	Physical	10	100	35	Normal	—	○
4	Sleep Powder	Grass	Status	—	75	15	Normal	—	—
7	Vine Whip	Grass	Physical	35	100	15	Normal	—	○
10	Absorb	Grass	Special	20	100	25	Normal	—	—
14	PoisonPowder	Poison	Status	—	75	35	Normal	—	—
17	Bind	Normal	Physical	15	85	20	Normal	—	○
20	Growth	Normal	Status	—	—	40	Self	—	—
23	Mega Drain	Grass	Special	40	100	15	Normal	—	—
27	Knock Off	Dark	Physical	20	100	20	Normal	—	○
30	Stun Spore	Grass	Status	—	75	30	Normal	—	—
33	Natural Gift	Normal	Physical	—	100	15	Normal	—	—
36	Giga Drain	Grass	Special	75	100	10	Normal	—	—
40	AncientPower	Rock	Special	60	100	5	Normal	—	—
43	Slam	Normal	Physical	80	75	20	Normal	—	○
46	Tickle	Normal	Status	—	100	20	Normal	—	—
49	Wring Out	Normal	Special	—	100	5	Normal	—	○
53	Power Whip	Grass	Physical	120	85	10	Normal	—	○

TM & HM MOVES

Lv.	Name	Type	Kind	Pow.	Acc.	PP	Range	Long	DA
TM06	Toxic	Poison	Status	—	90	10	Normal	—	—
TM10	Hidden Power	Normal	Special	—	100	15	Normal	—	—
TM11	Sunny Day	Fire	Status	—	—	5	Both Sides	—	—
TM15	Hyper Beam	Normal	Special	150	90	5	Normal	—	—
TM17	Protect	Normal	Status	—	—	10	Self	—	—
TM21	Frustration	Normal	Physical	—	100	20	Normal	—	○
TM22	SolarBeam	Grass	Special	120	100	10	Normal	—	—
TM27	Return	Normal	Physical	—	100	20	Normal	—	○
TM32	Double Team	Normal	Status	—	—	15	Self	—	—
TM33	Reflect	Psychic	Status	—	—	20	Your Side	—	—
TM36	Sludge Bomb	Poison	Special	90	100	10	Normal	—	—
TM42	Facade	Normal	Physical	70	100	20	Normal	—	○
TM44	Rest	Psychic	Status	—	—	10	Self	—	—
TM45	Attract	Normal	Status	—	100	15	Normal	—	—
TM46	Thief	Dark	Physical	40	100	10	Normal	—	○
TM48	Round	Normal	Special	60	100	15	Normal	—	—
TM53	Energy Ball	Grass	Special	80	100	10	Normal	—	—
TM68	Giga Impact	Normal	Physical	150	90	5	Normal	—	○
TM70	Flash	Normal	Status	—	100	20	Normal	—	—
TM75	Swords Dance	Normal	Status	—	—	30	Self	—	—
TM77	Psych Up	Normal	Status	—	—	10	Normal	—	—
TM86	Grass Knot	Grass	Special	—	100	20	Normal	—	○
TM87	Swagger	Normal	Status	—	90	15	Normal	—	—
TM90	Substitute	Normal	Status	—	—	10	Self	—	—
TM94	Rock Smash	Fighting	Physical	40	100	15	Normal	—	○
HM01	Cut	Normal	Physical	50	95	30	Normal	—	○

MOVES TAUGHT BY PEOPLE

Name	Type	Kind	Pow.	Acc.	PP	Range	Long	DA

MOVES TAUGHT BY MOVE TUTORS FOR SHARDS

Name	Type	Kind	Pow.	Acc.	PP	Range	Long	DA
Seed Bomb	Grass	Physical	80	100	15	Normal	—	—
Bind	Normal	Physical	15	85	20	Normal	—	○
Snore	Normal	Special	40	100	15	Normal	—	—
Knock Off	Dark	Physical	20	100	20	Normal	—	○
Synthesis	Grass	Status	—	—	5	Self	—	—
Giga Drain	Grass	Special	75	100	10	Normal	—	—
Pain Split	Normal	Status	—	—	20	Normal	—	—
Worry Seed	Grass	Status	—	100	10	Normal	—	—
Endeavor	Normal	Physical	—	100	5	Normal	—	○
Sleep Talk	Normal	Status	—	—	10	Self	—	—

EGG MOVES

Name	Type	Kind	Pow.	Acc.	PP	Range	Long	DA
Flail	Normal	Physical	—	100	15	Normal	—	○
Confusion	Psychic	Special	50	100	25	Normal	—	—
Mega Drain	Grass	Special	40	100	15	Normal	—	—
Amnesia	Psychic	Status	—	—	20	Self	—	—
Leech Seed	Grass	Status	—	90	10	Normal	—	—
Nature Power	Normal	Status	—	—	20	Varies	—	—
Endeavor	Normal	Physical	—	100	5	Normal	—	○
Leaf Storm	Grass	Special	140	90	5	Normal	—	—
Power Swap	Psychic	Status	—	—	10	Normal	—	—
Giga Drain	Grass	Special	75	100	10	Normal	—	—
Rage Powder	Bug	Status	—	—	20	Self	—	—
Natural Gift	Normal	Physical	—	100	15	Normal	—	—

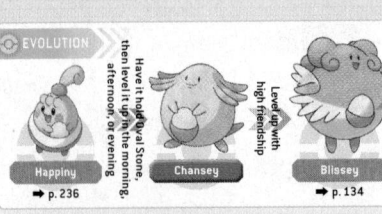

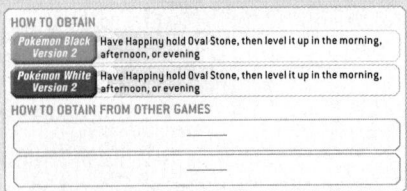

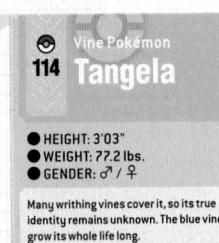

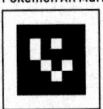

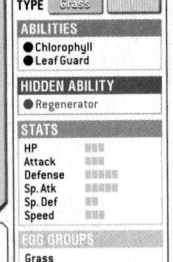

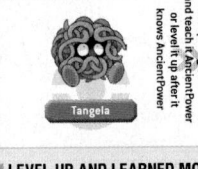

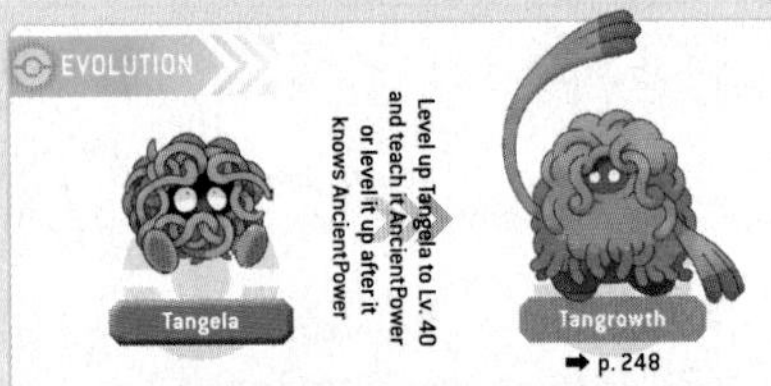

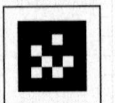

Parent Pokémon

115 Kangaskhan

- HEIGHT: 7'03"
- WEIGHT: 176.4 lbs.
- GENDER: ♂ / ♀

It raises its offspring in its belly pouch. It lets the baby out to play only when it feels safe.

Same form for ♂ / ♀

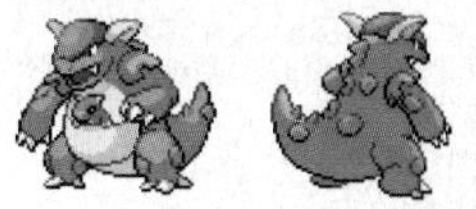

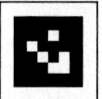

TYPE Normal

ABILITIES
- Early Bird
- Scrappy

HIDDEN ABILITY
- Inner Focus

STATS
HP
Attack
Defense
Sp. Atk
Sp. Def
Speed

EGG GROUPS
Monster

ITEMS SOMETIMES HELD
- None

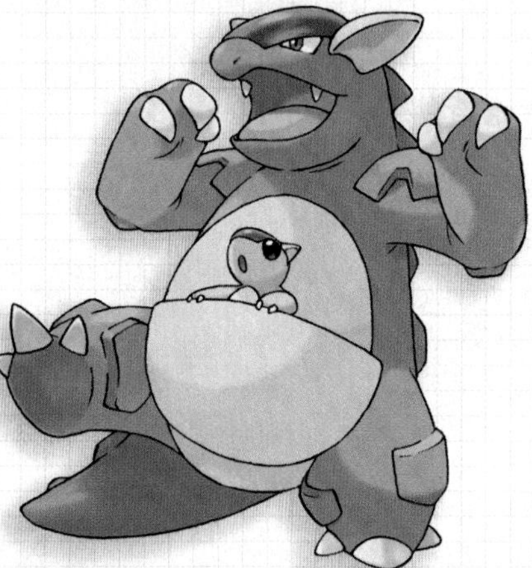

Pokémon AR Marker

EVOLUTION

Does not evolve

HOW TO OBTAIN

Pokémon Black Version 2	Link Trade or Poké Transfer
Pokémon White Version 2	Link Trade or Poké Transfer

HOW TO OBTAIN FROM OTHER GAMES

Pokémon Black Version	Route 15
Pokémon White Version	Route 15

LEVEL-UP AND LEARNED MOVES

Lv.	Name	Type	Kind	Pow.	Acc.	PP	Range	Long	DA
1	Comet Punch	Normal	Physical	18	85	15	Normal	—	○
1	Leer	Normal	Status	—	100	30	Many Others	—	—
7	Fake Out	Normal	Physical	40	100	10	Normal	—	○
10	Tail Whip	Normal	Status	—	100	30	Many Others	—	—
13	Bite	Dark	Physical	60	100	25	Normal	—	○
19	Double Hit	Normal	Physical	35	90	10	Normal	—	○
22	Rage	Normal	Physical	20	100	20	Normal	—	○
25	Mega Punch	Normal	Physical	80	85	20	Normal	—	○
31	Chip Away	Normal	Physical	70	100	20	Normal	—	○
34	Dizzy Punch	Normal	Physical	70	100	10	Normal	—	○
37	Crunch	Dark	Physical	80	100	15	Normal	—	○
43	Endure	Normal	Status	—	—	10	Self	—	—
46	Outrage	Dragon	Physical	120	100	10	1 Random	—	○
49	Sucker Punch	Dark	Physical	80	100	5	Normal	—	○
55	Reversal	Fighting	Physical	—	100	15	Normal	—	○

TM & HM MOVES

Lv.	Name	Type	Kind	Pow.	Acc.	PP	Range	Long	DA
TM05	Roar	Normal	Status	—	100	20	Normal	—	—
TM06	Toxic	Poison	Status	—	90	10	Normal	—	—
TM07	Hail	Ice	Status	—	—	10	Both Sides	—	—
TM10	Hidden Power	Normal	Special	—	100	15	Normal	—	—
TM11	Sunny Day	Fire	Status	—	—	5	Both Sides	—	—
TM13	Ice Beam	Ice	Special	95	100	10	Normal	—	—
TM14	Blizzard	Ice	Special	120	70	5	Many Others	—	—
TM15	Hyper Beam	Normal	Special	150	90	5	Normal	—	—
TM17	Protect	Normal	Status	—	—	10	Self	—	—
TM18	Rain Dance	Water	Status	—	—	5	Both Sides	—	—
TM20	Safeguard	Normal	Status	—	—	25	Your Side	—	—
TM21	Frustration	Normal	Physical	—	100	20	Normal	—	○
TM22	SolarBeam	Grass	Special	120	100	10	Normal	—	—
TM24	Thunderbolt	Electric	Special	95	100	15	Normal	—	—
TM25	Thunder	Electric	Special	120	70	10	Normal	—	—
TM26	Earthquake	Ground	Physical	100	100	10	Adjacent	—	—
TM27	Return	Normal	Physical	—	100	20	Normal	—	○
TM28	Dig	Ground	Physical	80	100	10	Normal	—	○
TM30	Shadow Ball	Ghost	Special	80	100	15	Normal	—	—
TM31	Brick Break	Fighting	Physical	75	100	15	Normal	—	○
TM32	Double Team	Normal	Status	—	—	15	Self	—	—
TM35	Flamethrower	Fire	Special	95	100	15	Normal	—	—
TM37	Sandstorm	Rock	Status	—	—	10	Both Sides	—	—
TM38	Fire Blast	Fire	Special	120	85	5	Normal	—	—
TM39	Rock Tomb	Rock	Physical	50	80	10	Normal	—	—
TM40	Aerial Ace	Flying	Physical	60	—	20	Normal	○	○
TM42	Facade	Normal	Physical	70	100	20	Normal	—	○
TM44	Rest	Psychic	Status	—	—	10	Self	—	—
TM45	Attract	Normal	Status	—	100	15	Normal	—	—
TM46	Thief	Dark	Physical	40	100	10	Normal	—	○
TM48	Round	Normal	Special	60	100	15	Normal	—	—
TM52	Focus Blast	Fighting	Special	120	70	5	Normal	—	—
TM56	Fling	Dark	Physical	—	100	10	Normal	—	—
TM59	Incinerate	Fire	Special	30	100	15	Many Others	—	—
TM65	Shadow Claw	Ghost	Physical	70	100	15	Normal	—	○
TM67	Retaliate	Normal	Physical	70	100	5	Normal	—	○
TM68	Giga Impact	Normal	Physical	150	90	5	Normal	—	○
TM78	Bulldoze	Ground	Physical	60	100	20	Adjacent	—	—
TM80	Rock Slide	Rock	Physical	75	90	10	Many Others	—	—
TM83	Work Up	Normal	Status	—	—	30	Self	—	—
TM87	Swagger	Normal	Status	—	90	15	Normal	—	—
TM90	Substitute	Normal	Status	—	—	10	Self	—	—
TM94	Rock Smash	Fighting	Physical	40	100	15	Normal	—	○
HM01	Cut	Normal	Physical	50	95	30	Normal	—	○
HM03	Surf	Water	Special	95	100	15	Adjacent	—	—
HM04	Strength	Normal	Physical	80	100	15	Normal	—	○

MOVES TAUGHT BY PEOPLE

Name	Type	Kind	Pow.	Acc.	PP	Range	Long	DA

MOVES TAUGHT BY MOVE TUTORS FOR SHARDS

Name	Type	Kind	Pow.	Acc.	PP	Range	Long	DA
Covet	Normal	Physical	60	100	40	Normal	—	○
Uproar	Normal	Special	90	100	10	1 Random	—	—
Low Kick	Fighting	Physical	—	100	20	Normal	—	○
Fire Punch	Fire	Physical	75	100	15	Normal	—	○
ThunderPunch	Electric	Physical	75	100	15	Normal	—	○
Ice Punch	Ice	Physical	75	100	15	Normal	—	○
Icy Wind	Ice	Special	55	95	15	Many Others	—	—
Iron Tail	Steel	Physical	100	75	15	Normal	—	○
Aqua Tail	Water	Physical	90	90	10	Normal	—	○
Snore	Normal	Special	40	100	15	Normal	—	—
Drain Punch	Fighting	Physical	75	100	10	Normal	—	○
Helping Hand	Normal	Status	—	—	20	1 Ally	—	—
Spite	Ghost	Status	—	100	10	Normal	—	—
Outrage	Dragon	Physical	120	100	10	1 Random	—	○
Endeavor	Normal	Physical	—	100	5	Normal	—	○
Sleep Talk	Normal	Status	—	—	10	Self	—	—

EGG MOVES

Name	Type	Kind	Pow.	Acc.	PP	Range	Long	DA
Stomp	Normal	Physical	65	100	20	Normal	—	○
Foresight	Normal	Status	—	—	40	Normal	—	—
Focus Energy	Normal	Status	—	—	30	Self	—	—
Disable	Normal	Status	—	100	20	Normal	—	—
Counter	Fighting	Physical	—	100	20	Varies	—	○
Crush Claw	Normal	Physical	75	95	10	Normal	—	○
Double-Edge	Normal	Physical	120	100	15	Normal	—	○
Endeavor	Normal	Physical	—	100	5	Normal	—	○
Hammer Arm	Fighting	Physical	100	90	10	Normal	—	○
Focus Punch	Fighting	Physical	150	100	20	Normal	—	○
Trump Card	Normal	Special	—	—	5	Normal	—	○
Uproar	Normal	Special	90	100	10	1 Random	—	—
Circle Throw	Fighting	Physical	60	90	10	Normal	—	○

Dragon Pokémon

116 Horsea

- HEIGHT: 1'04"
- WEIGHT: 17.6 lbs.
- GENDER: ♂ / ♀

It makes its nest in the shade of corals. If it senses danger, it spits murky ink and flees.

Same form for ♂ / ♀

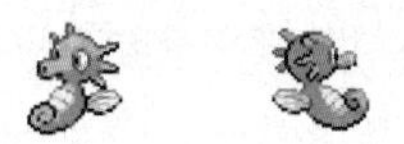

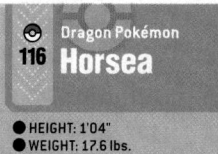

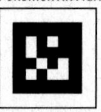

TYPE Water

ABILITIES
- Swift Swim
- Sniper

HIDDEN ABILITY
- Damp

STATS
HP
Attack
Defense
Sp. Atk
Sp. Def
Speed

EGG GROUPS
Water ❶ /Dragon

ITEMS SOMETIMES HELD
- Dragon Scale

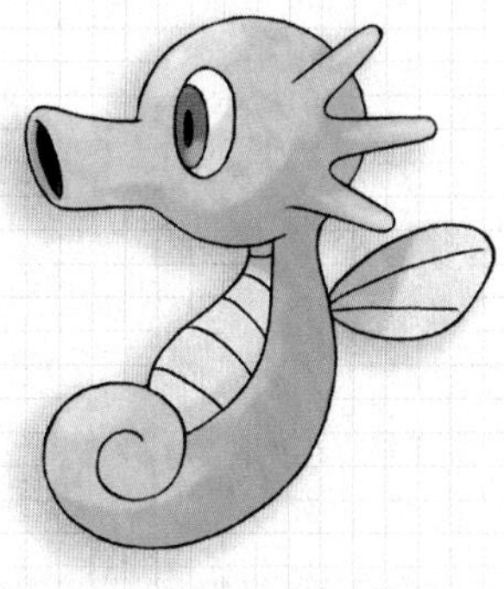

Pokémon AR Marker

EVOLUTION

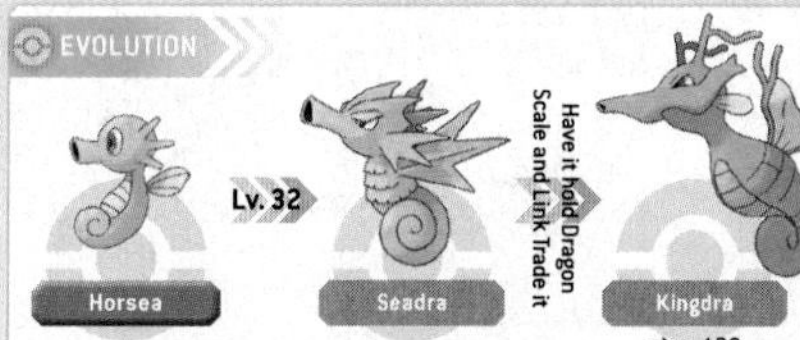
Horsea
Lv. 32
Seadra
Have it hold Dragon Scale and Link Trade it
Kingdra

➡ p. 128

HOW TO OBTAIN

Pokémon Black Version 2	❶ Route 17 (Super Rod) ❷ Route 18 (Super Rod)
Pokémon White Version 2	❶ Route 17 (Super Rod) ❷ Route 18 (Super Rod)

HOW TO OBTAIN FROM OTHER GAMES

——

——

LEVEL-UP AND LEARNED MOVES

Lv.	Name	Type	Kind	Pow.	Acc.	PP	Range	Long	DA
1	Bubble	Water	Special	20	100	30	Many Others	—	—
4	SmokeScreen	Normal	Status	—	100	20	Normal	—	—
8	Leer	Normal	Status	—	100	30	Many Others	—	—
11	Water Gun	Water	Special	40	100	25	Normal	—	—
14	Focus Energy	Normal	Status	—	—	30	Self	—	—
18	BubbleBeam	Water	Special	65	100	20	Normal	—	—
23	Agility	Psychic	Status	—	—	30	Self	—	—
26	Twister	Dragon	Special	40	100	20	Many Others	—	—
30	Brine	Water	Special	65	100	10	Normal	—	—
35	Hydro Pump	Water	Special	120	80	5	Normal	—	—
38	Dragon Dance	Dragon	Status	—	—	20	Self	—	—
42	Dragon Pulse	Dragon	Special	90	100	10	Normal	○	—

TM & HM MOVES

Lv.	Name	Type	Kind	Pow.	Acc.	PP	Range	Long	DA
TM06	Toxic	Poison	Status	—	90	10	Normal	—	—
TM07	Hail	Ice	Status	—	—	10	Both Sides	—	—
TM10	Hidden Power	Normal	Special	—	100	15	Normal	—	—
TM13	Ice Beam	Ice	Special	95	100	10	Normal	—	—
TM14	Blizzard	Ice	Special	120	70	5	Many Others	—	—
TM17	Protect	Normal	Status	—	—	10	Self	—	—
TM18	Rain Dance	Water	Status	—	—	5	Both Sides	—	—
TM21	Frustration	Normal	Physical	—	100	20	Normal	—	○
TM27	Return	Normal	Physical	—	100	20	Normal	—	○
TM32	Double Team	Normal	Status	—	—	15	Self	—	—
TM42	Facade	Normal	Physical	70	100	20	Normal	—	○
TM44	Rest	Psychic	Status	—	—	10	Self	—	—
TM45	Attract	Normal	Status	—	100	15	Normal	—	—
TM48	Round	Normal	Special	60	100	15	Normal	—	—
TM55	Scald	Water	Special	80	100	15	Normal	—	—
TM87	Swagger	Normal	Status	—	90	15	Normal	—	—
TM90	Substitute	Normal	Status	—	—	10	Self	—	—
TM91	Flash Cannon	Steel	Special	80	100	10	Normal	—	—
HM03	Surf	Water	Special	95	100	15	Adjacent	—	—
HM05	Waterfall	Water	Physical	80	100	15	Normal	—	○
HM06	Dive	Water	Physical	80	100	10	Normal	—	○

MOVES TAUGHT BY PEOPLE

Name	Type	Kind	Pow.	Acc.	PP	Range	Long	DA

MOVES TAUGHT BY MOVE TUTORS FOR SHARDS

Name	Type	Kind	Pow.	Acc.	PP	Range	Long	DA
Bounce	Flying	Physical	85	85	5	Normal	○	○
Signal Beam	Bug	Special	75	100	15	Normal	—	—
Icy Wind	Ice	Special	55	95	15	Many Others	—	—
Dragon Pulse	Dragon	Special	90	100	10	Normal	○	—
Snore	Normal	Special	40	100	15	Normal	—	—
Outrage	Dragon	Physical	120	100	10	1 Random	—	○
Sleep Talk	Normal	Status	—	—	10	Self	—	—

EGG MOVES

Name	Type	Kind	Pow.	Acc.	PP	Range	Long	DA
Flail	Normal	Physical	—	100	15	Normal	—	○
Aurora Beam	Ice	Special	65	100	20	Normal	—	—
Octazooka	Water	Special	65	85	10	Normal	—	—
Disable	Normal	Status	—	100	20	Normal	—	—
Splash	Normal	Status	—	—	40	Self	—	—
Dragon Rage	Dragon	Special	—	100	10	Normal	—	—
DragonBreath	Dragon	Special	60	100	20	Normal	—	—
Signal Beam	Bug	Special	75	100	15	Normal	—	—
Razor Wind	Normal	Special	80	100	10	Many Others	—	—
Muddy Water	Water	Special	95	85	10	Many Others	—	—
Water Pulse	Water	Special	60	100	20	Normal	○	—
Clear Smog	Poison	Special	50	—	15	Normal	—	—
Outrage	Dragon	Physical	120	100	10	1 Random	—	○

117 Seadra
Dragon Pokémon

TYPE Water

ABILITIES
● Poison Point
● Sniper

HIDDEN ABILITY
● Damp

● HEIGHT: 3'11"
● WEIGHT: 55.1 lbs.
● GENDER: ♂ / ♀

Its spines provide protection. Its fins and bones are prized as traditional-medicine ingredients.

Same form for ♂ ♀

STATS
HP	
Attack	
Defense	
Sp. Atk	
Sp. Def	
Speed	

EGG GROUPS
Water ❶ /Dragon

ITEMS SOMETIMES HELD
● Dragon Scale

Pokémon AR Marker

EVOLUTION

Horsea → Lv. 32 → Seadra → Kingdra

Have it hold Dragon Scale and Link Trade it

➡ p. 128

HOW TO OBTAIN

Pokémon Black Version 2	❶ Route 17 (Super Rod/ripples in water) ❷ Route 18 (Super Rod/ripples in water)
Pokémon White Version 2	❶ Route 17 (Super Rod/ripples in water) ❷ Route 18 (Super Rod/ripples in water)

HOW TO OBTAIN FROM OTHER GAMES

LEVEL-UP AND LEARNED MOVES

Lv.	Name	Type	Kind	Pow.	Acc.	PP	Range	Long	DA
1	Bubble	Water	Special	20	100	30	Many Others	—	—
1	SmokeScreen	Normal	Status	—	100	20	Normal	—	—
1	Leer	Normal	Status	—	100	30	Many Others	—	—
1	Water Gun	Water	Special	40	100	25	Normal	—	—
4	SmokeScreen	Normal	Status	—	100	20	Normal	—	—
8	Leer	Normal	Status	—	100	30	Many Others	—	—
11	Water Gun	Water	Special	40	100	25	Normal	—	—
14	Focus Energy	Normal	Status	—	—	30	Self	—	—
18	BubbleBeam	Water	Special	65	100	20	Normal	—	—
23	Agility	Psychic	Status	—	—	30	Self	—	—
26	Twister	Dragon	Special	40	100	20	Many Others	—	—
30	Brine	Water	Special	65	100	10	Normal	—	—
40	Hydro Pump	Water	Special	120	80	5	Normal	—	—
48	Dragon Dance	Dragon	Status	—	—	20	Self	—	—
57	Dragon Pulse	Dragon	Special	90	100	10	Normal	○	—

TM & HM MOVES

Lv.	Name	Type	Kind	Pow.	Acc.	PP	Range	Long	DA
TM06	Toxic	Poison	Status	—	90	10	Normal	—	—
TM07	Hail	Ice	Status	—	—	10	Both Sides	—	—
TM10	Hidden Power	Normal	Special	—	100	15	Normal	—	—
TM13	Ice Beam	Ice	Special	95	100	10	Normal	—	—
TM14	Blizzard	Ice	Special	120	70	5	Many Others	—	—
TM15	Hyper Beam	Normal	Special	150	90	5	Normal	—	—
TM17	Protect	Normal	Status	—	—	10	Self	—	—
TM18	Rain Dance	Water	Status	—	—	5	Both Sides	—	—
TM21	Frustration	Normal	Physical	—	100	20	Normal	—	○
TM27	Return	Normal	Physical	—	100	20	Normal	—	○
TM32	Double Team	Normal	Status	—	—	15	Self	—	—
TM42	Facade	Normal	Physical	70	100	20	Normal	—	—
TM44	Rest	Psychic	Status	—	—	10	Self	—	—
TM45	Attract	Normal	Status	—	100	15	Normal	—	—
TM48	Round	Normal	Special	60	100	15	Normal	—	—
TM55	Scald	Water	Special	80	100	15	Normal	—	—
TM68	Giga Impact	Normal	Physical	150	90	5	Normal	—	—
TM87	Swagger	Normal	Status	—	90	15	Normal	—	—
TM90	Substitute	Normal	Status	—	—	10	Self	—	—
TM91	Flash Cannon	Steel	Special	80	100	10	Normal	—	—
HM03	Surf	Water	Special	95	100	15	Adjacent	—	—
HM05	Waterfall	Water	Physical	80	100	15	Normal	—	○
HM06	Dive	Water	Physical	80	100	10	Normal	—	○

MOVES TAUGHT BY PEOPLE

Name	Type	Kind	Pow.	Acc.	PP	Range	Long	DA

MOVES TAUGHT BY MOVE TUTORS FOR SHARDS

Name	Type	Kind	Pow.	Acc.	PP	Range	Long	DA
Bounce	Flying	Physical	85	85	5	Normal	○	—
Signal Beam	Bug	Special	75	100	15	Normal	—	—
Icy Wind	Ice	Special	55	95	15	Many Others	—	—
Dragon Pulse	Dragon	Special	90	100	10	Normal	○	—
Snore	Normal	Special	40	100	15	Normal	—	—
Outrage	Dragon	Physical	120	100	10	1 Random	—	○
Sleep Talk	Normal	Status	—	—	10	Self	—	—

118 Goldeen
Goldfish Pokémon

TYPE Water

ABILITIES
● Swift Swim
● Water Veil

HIDDEN ABILITY
● Lightningrod

● HEIGHT: 2'00"
● WEIGHT: 33.1 lbs.
● GENDER: ♂ / ♀

Though it appears very elegant when swimming with fins unfurled, it can jab powerfully with its horn.

♂   ♀

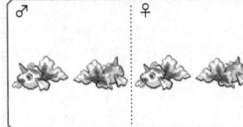

STATS
HP	
Attack	
Defense	
Sp. Atk	
Sp. Def	
Speed	

EGG GROUPS
Water ❷

ITEMS SOMETIMES HELD
● None

Pokémon AR Marker

EVOLUTION

Goldeen → Lv. 33 → Seaking

HOW TO OBTAIN

Pokémon Black Version 2	❶ Aspertia City (Super Rod) ❷ Route 14 (Super Rod)
Pokémon White Version 2	❶ Aspertia City (Super Rod) ❷ Route 14 (Super Rod)

HOW TO OBTAIN FROM OTHER GAMES

LEVEL-UP AND LEARNED MOVES

Lv.	Name	Type	Kind	Pow.	Acc.	PP	Range	Long	DA
1	Peck	Flying	Physical	35	100	35	Normal	○	—
1	Tail Whip	Normal	Status	—	100	30	Many Others	—	—
1	Water Sport	Water	Status	—	—	15	Both Sides	—	—
7	Supersonic	Normal	Status	—	55	20	Normal	—	—
11	Horn Attack	Normal	Physical	65	100	25	Normal	—	—
17	Water Pulse	Water	Special	60	100	20	Normal	○	—
21	Flail	Normal	Physical	—	100	15	Normal	—	—
27	Aqua Ring	Water	Status	—	—	20	Self	—	—
31	Fury Attack	Normal	Physical	15	85	20	Normal	—	—
37	Waterfall	Water	Physical	80	100	15	Normal	—	○
41	Horn Drill	Normal	Physical	—	30	5	Normal	—	—
47	Agility	Psychic	Status	—	—	30	Self	—	—
51	Soak	Water	Status	—	100	20	Normal	—	—
57	Megahorn	Bug	Physical	120	85	10	Normal	—	—

TM & HM MOVES

Lv.	Name	Type	Kind	Pow.	Acc.	PP	Range	Long	DA
TM06	Toxic	Poison	Status	—	90	10	Normal	—	—
TM07	Hail	Ice	Status	—	—	10	Both Sides	—	—
TM10	Hidden Power	Normal	Special	—	100	15	Normal	—	—
TM13	Ice Beam	Ice	Special	95	100	10	Normal	—	—
TM14	Blizzard	Ice	Special	120	70	5	Many Others	—	—
TM17	Protect	Normal	Status	—	—	10	Self	—	—
TM18	Rain Dance	Water	Status	—	—	5	Both Sides	—	—
TM21	Frustration	Normal	Physical	—	100	20	Normal	—	○
TM27	Return	Normal	Physical	—	100	20	Normal	—	○
TM32	Double Team	Normal	Status	—	—	15	Self	—	—
TM42	Facade	Normal	Physical	70	100	20	Normal	—	—
TM44	Rest	Psychic	Status	—	—	10	Self	—	—
TM45	Attract	Normal	Status	—	100	15	Normal	—	—
TM48	Round	Normal	Special	60	100	15	Normal	—	—
TM55	Scald	Water	Special	80	100	15	Normal	—	—
TM84	Poison Jab	Poison	Physical	80	100	20	Normal	—	—
TM87	Swagger	Normal	Status	—	90	15	Normal	—	—
TM90	Substitute	Normal	Status	—	—	10	Self	—	—
HM03	Surf	Water	Special	95	100	15	Adjacent	—	—
HM05	Waterfall	Water	Physical	80	100	15	Normal	—	○
HM06	Dive	Water	Physical	80	100	10	Normal	—	○

MOVES TAUGHT BY PEOPLE

Name	Type	Kind	Pow.	Acc.	PP	Range	Long	DA

MOVES TAUGHT BY MOVE TUTORS FOR SHARDS

Name	Type	Kind	Pow.	Acc.	PP	Range	Long	DA
Drill Run	Ground	Physical	80	95	10	Normal	—	○
Bounce	Flying	Physical	85	85	5	Normal	○	○
Signal Beam	Bug	Special	75	100	15	Normal	—	—
Icy Wind	Ice	Special	55	95	15	Many Others	—	—
Aqua Tail	Water	Physical	90	90	10	Normal	—	○
Snore	Normal	Special	40	100	15	Normal	—	—
Knock Off	Dark	Physical	20	100	20	Normal	—	○
Sleep Talk	Normal	Status	—	—	10	Self	—	—

EGG MOVES

Name	Type	Kind	Pow.	Acc.	PP	Range	Long	DA
Psybeam	Psychic	Special	65	100	20	Normal	—	—
Haze	Ice	Status	—	—	30	Both Sides	—	—
Hydro Pump	Water	Special	120	80	5	Normal	—	—
Sleep Talk	Normal	Status	—	—	10	Self	—	—
Mud Sport	Ground	Status	—	—	15	Both Sides	—	—
Mud-Slap	Ground	Special	20	100	10	Normal	—	—
Aqua Tail	Water	Physical	90	90	10	Normal	—	○
Body Slam	Normal	Physical	85	100	15	Normal	—	—
Mud Shot	Ground	Special	55	95	15	Normal	—	—
Skull Bash	Normal	Physical	100	100	15	Normal	—	—
Signal Beam	Bug	Special	75	100	15	Normal	—	—

119 Seaking
Goldfish Pokémon

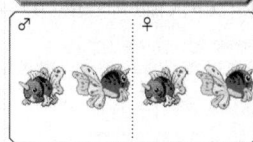

- HEIGHT: 4'03"
- WEIGHT: 86.0 lbs.
- GENDER: ♂ / ♀

In autumn, its body becomes more fatty in preparing to propose to a mate. It takes on beautiful colors.

TYPE	Water	

ABILITIES
- Swift Swim
- Water Veil

HIDDEN ABILITY
- Lightningrod

STATS
- HP
- Attack
- Defense
- Sp. Atk
- Sp. Def
- Speed

EGG GROUPS
- Water ❷

ITEMS SOMETIMES HELD
- None

 EVOLUTION

Goldeen → Lv. 33 → Seaking

HOW TO OBTAIN

Pokémon Black Version 2	❶ Aspertia City (Super Rod/ripples in water)
	❷ Route 14 (Super Rod/ripples in water)
Pokémon White Version 2	❶ Aspertia City (Super Rod/ripples in water)
	❷ Route 14 (Super Rod/ripples in water)

HOW TO OBTAIN FROM OTHER GAMES
| — |
| — |

LEVEL-UP AND LEARNED MOVES

Lv.	Name	Type	Kind	Pow.	Acc.	PP	Range	Long	DA
1	Poison Jab	Poison	Physical	80	100	20	Normal	—	○
1	Peck	Flying	Physical	35	100	35	Normal	○	○
1	Tail Whip	Normal	Status	—	100	30	Many Others	—	—
1	Water Sport	Water	Status	—	—	15	Both Sides	—	—
1	Supersonic	Normal	Status	—	55	20	Normal	—	—
7	Supersonic	Normal	Status	—	55	20	Normal	—	—
11	Horn Attack	Normal	Physical	65	100	25	Normal	—	—
17	Water Pulse	Water	Special	60	100	20	Normal	○	○
21	Flail	Normal	Physical	—	100	15	Normal	—	—
27	Aqua Ring	Water	Status	—	—	20	Self	—	—
31	Fury Attack	Normal	Physical	15	85	20	Normal	—	—
40	Waterfall	Water	Physical	80	100	15	Normal	—	○
47	Horn Drill	Normal	Physical	—	30	5	Normal	—	—
56	Agility	Psychic	Status	—	—	30	Self	—	—
63	Soak	Water	Status	—	100	20	Normal	—	—
72	Megahorn	Bug	Physical	120	85	10	Normal	—	—

TM & HM MOVES

Lv.	Name	Type	Kind	Pow.	Acc.	PP	Range	Long	DA
TM06	Toxic	Poison	Status	—	90	10	Normal	—	—
TM07	Hail	Ice	Status	—	—	10	Both Sides	—	—
TM10	Hidden Power	Normal	Special	—	100	15	Normal	—	—
TM13	Ice Beam	Ice	Special	95	100	10	Normal	—	—
TM14	Blizzard	Ice	Special	120	70	5	Many Others	—	—
TM15	Hyper Beam	Normal	Special	150	90	5	Normal	—	—
TM17	Protect	Normal	Status	—	—	10	Self	—	—
TM18	Rain Dance	Water	Status	—	—	5	Both Sides	—	—
TM21	Frustration	Normal	Physical	—	100	20	Normal	—	○
TM27	Return	Normal	Physical	—	100	20	Normal	—	○
TM32	Double Team	Normal	Status	—	—	15	Self	—	—
TM42	Facade	Normal	Physical	70	100	20	Normal	—	—
TM44	Rest	Psychic	Status	—	—	10	Self	—	—
TM45	Attract	Normal	Status	—	100	15	Normal	—	—
TM48	Round	Normal	Special	60	100	15	Normal	—	—
TM55	Scald	Water	Special	80	100	15	Normal	—	—
TM68	Giga Impact	Normal	Physical	150	90	5	Normal	—	—
TM84	Poison Jab	Poison	Physical	80	100	20	Normal	—	—
TM87	Swagger	Normal	Status	—	90	15	Normal	—	—
TM90	Substitute	Normal	Status	—	—	10	Self	—	—
HM03	Surf	Water	Special	95	100	15	Adjacent	—	—
HM05	Waterfall	Water	Physical	80	100	15	Normal	—	—
HM06	Dive	Water	Physical	80	100	10	Normal	—	—

MOVES TAUGHT BY PEOPLE

Name	Type	Kind	Pow.	Acc.	PP	Range	Long	DA

MOVES TAUGHT BY MOVE TUTORS FOR SHARDS

Name	Type	Kind	Pow.	Acc.	PP	Range	Long	DA
Drill Run	Ground	Physical	80	95	10	Normal	—	○
Bounce	Flying	Physical	85	85	5	Normal	○	○
Signal Beam	Bug	Special	75	100	15	Normal	—	—
Icy Wind	Ice	Special	55	95	15	Many Others	—	—
Aqua Tail	Water	Physical	90	90	10	Normal	—	○
Snore	Normal	Special	40	100	15	Normal	—	—
Knock Off	Dark	Physical	20	100	20	Normal	—	○
Sleep Talk	Normal	Status	—	—	10	Self	—	—

Pokémon AR Marker

---

120 Staryu
Star Shape Pokémon

- HEIGHT: 2'07"
- WEIGHT: 76.1 lbs.
- GENDER: Unknown

As long as its red core remains, it can regenerate its body instantly, even if it's torn apart.

TYPE	Water	

ABILITIES
- Illuminate
- Natural Cure

HIDDEN ABILITY
- Analytic

STATS
- HP
- Attack
- Defense
- Sp. Atk
- Sp. Def
- Speed

EGG GROUPS
- Water ❸

ITEMS SOMETIMES HELD
- Stardust
- Star Piece

Same form for ♂ / ♀

 EVOLUTION

Staryu → Use Water Stone → Starmie

HOW TO OBTAIN

Pokémon Black Version 2	❶ Undella Town (water surface)
	❷ Humilau City (water surface)
Pokémon White Version 2	❶ Undella Town (water surface)
	❷ Humilau City (water surface)

HOW TO OBTAIN FROM OTHER GAMES
| — |
| — |

LEVEL-UP AND LEARNED MOVES

Lv.	Name	Type	Kind	Pow.	Acc.	PP	Range	Long	DA
1	Tackle	Normal	Physical	50	100	35	Normal	—	—
1	Harden	Normal	Status	—	—	30	Self	—	—
6	Water Gun	Water	Special	40	100	25	Normal	—	—
10	Rapid Spin	Normal	Physical	20	100	40	Normal	—	—
12	Recover	Normal	Status	—	—	10	Self	—	—
15	Camouflage	Normal	Status	—	—	20	Self	—	—
18	Swift	Normal	Special	60	—	20	Many Others	—	—
22	BubbleBeam	Water	Special	65	100	20	Normal	—	—
25	Minimize	Normal	Status	—	—	20	Self	—	—
30	Gyro Ball	Steel	Physical	—	100	5	Normal	—	○
33	Light Screen	Psychic	Status	—	—	30	Your Side	—	—
36	Brine	Water	Special	65	100	10	Normal	—	—
40	Reflect Type	Normal	Status	—	—	15	Normal	—	—
43	Power Gem	Rock	Special	70	100	20	Normal	—	—
48	Cosmic Power	Psychic	Status	—	—	20	Self	—	—
52	Hydro Pump	Water	Special	120	80	5	Normal	—	—

TM & HM MOVES

Lv.	Name	Type	Kind	Pow.	Acc.	PP	Range	Long	DA
TM06	Toxic	Poison	Status	—	90	10	Normal	—	—
TM07	Hail	Ice	Status	—	—	10	Both Sides	—	—
TM10	Hidden Power	Normal	Special	—	100	15	Normal	—	—
TM13	Ice Beam	Ice	Special	95	100	10	Normal	—	—
TM14	Blizzard	Ice	Special	120	70	5	Many Others	—	—
TM16	Light Screen	Psychic	Status	—	—	30	Your Side	—	—
TM17	Protect	Normal	Status	—	—	10	Self	—	—
TM18	Rain Dance	Water	Status	—	—	5	Both Sides	—	—
TM21	Frustration	Normal	Physical	—	100	20	Normal	—	○
TM24	Thunderbolt	Electric	Special	95	100	15	Normal	—	—
TM25	Thunder	Electric	Special	120	70	10	Normal	—	—
TM27	Return	Normal	Physical	—	100	20	Normal	—	○
TM29	Psychic	Psychic	Special	90	100	10	Normal	—	—
TM32	Double Team	Normal	Status	—	—	15	Self	—	—
TM33	Reflect	Psychic	Status	—	—	20	Your Side	—	—
TM42	Facade	Normal	Physical	70	100	20	Normal	—	—
TM44	Rest	Psychic	Status	—	—	10	Self	—	—
TM48	Round	Normal	Special	60	100	15	Normal	—	—
TM55	Scald	Water	Special	80	100	15	Normal	—	—
TM70	Flash	Normal	Status	—	100	20	Normal	—	—
TM73	Thunder Wave	Electric	Status	—	100	20	Normal	—	—
TM74	Gyro Ball	Steel	Physical	—	100	5	Normal	—	○
TM77	Psych Up	Normal	Status	—	—	10	Self	—	—
TM87	Swagger	Normal	Status	—	90	15	Normal	—	—
TM90	Substitute	Normal	Status	—	—	10	Self	—	—
TM91	Flash Cannon	Steel	Special	80	100	10	Normal	—	—
HM03	Surf	Water	Special	95	100	15	Adjacent	—	—
HM05	Waterfall	Water	Physical	80	100	15	Normal	—	—
HM06	Dive	Water	Physical	80	100	10	Normal	—	—

MOVES TAUGHT BY PEOPLE

Name	Type	Kind	Pow.	Acc.	PP	Range	Long	DA

MOVES TAUGHT BY MOVE TUTORS FOR SHARDS

Name	Type	Kind	Pow.	Acc.	PP	Range	Long	DA
Signal Beam	Bug	Special	75	100	15	Normal	—	—
Magic Coat	Psychic	Status	—	—	15	Self	—	—
Icy Wind	Ice	Special	55	95	15	Many Others	—	—
Gravity	Psychic	Status	—	—	5	Both Sides	—	—
Snore	Normal	Special	40	100	15	Normal	—	—
Pain Split	Normal	Status	—	—	20	Normal	—	—
Recycle	Normal	Status	—	—	10	Self	—	—
Sleep Talk	Normal	Status	—	—	10	Self	—	—

EGG MOVES

Name	Type	Kind	Pow.	Acc.	PP	Range	Long	DA

Pokémon AR Marker

121 Starmie

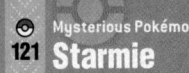

Mysterious Pokémon

- HEIGHT: 3'07"
- WEIGHT: 176.4 lbs.
- GENDER: Unknown

It's core shines in many colors and sends radio signals into space to communicate with something.

TYPE Water Psychic

ABILITIES
- Illuminate
- Natural Cure

HIDDEN ABILITY
- Analytic

STATS
- HP
- Attack
- Defense
- Sp. Atk
- Sp. Def
- Speed

EGG GROUPS
Water 3

Gender unknown

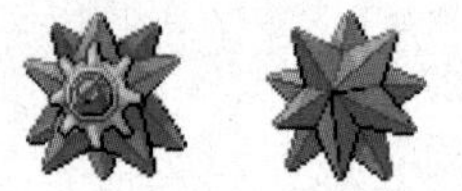

ITEMS SOMETIMES HELD
- Stardust
- Star Piece

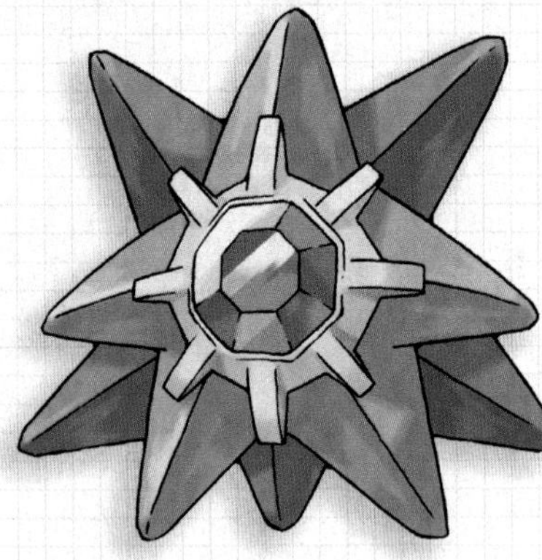

Pokémon AR Marker

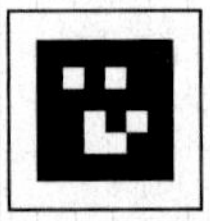

EVOLUTION

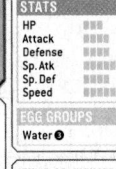

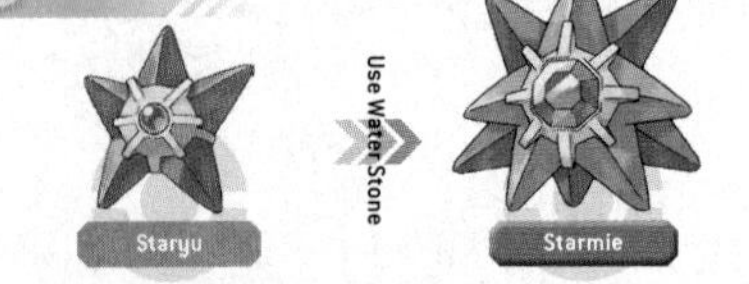
Staryu
Use Water Stone
Starmie

HOW TO OBTAIN

Pokémon Black Version 2	1 Undella Town (ripples in water) 2 Humilau City (ripples in water)
Pokémon White Version 2	1 Undella Town (ripples in water) 2 Humilau City (ripples in water)

HOW TO OBTAIN FROM OTHER GAMES

—

—

LEVEL-UP AND LEARNED MOVES

Lv.	Name	Type	Kind	Pow.	Acc.	PP	Range	Long	DA
1	Water Gun	Water	Special	40	100	25	Normal	—	—
1	Rapid Spin	Normal	Physical	20	100	40	Normal	—	○
1	Recover	Normal	Status	—	—	10	Self	—	—
1	Swift	Normal	Special	60	—	20	Many Others	—	—
22	Confuse Ray	Ghost	Status	—	100	10	Normal	—	—

TM & HM MOVES

Lv.	Name	Type	Kind	Pow.	Acc.	PP	Range	Long	DA
TM03	Psyshock	Psychic	Special	80	100	10	Normal	—	—
TM06	Toxic	Poison	Status	—	90	10	Normal	—	—
TM07	Hail	Ice	Status	—	—	10	Both Sides	—	—
TM10	Hidden Power	Normal	Special	—	100	15	Normal	—	—
TM13	Ice Beam	Ice	Special	95	100	10	Normal	—	—
TM14	Blizzard	Ice	Special	120	70	5	Many Others	—	—
TM15	Hyper Beam	Normal	Special	150	90	5	Normal	—	—
TM16	Light Screen	Psychic	Status	—	—	30	Your Side	—	—
TM17	Protect	Normal	Status	—	—	10	Self	—	—
TM18	Rain Dance	Water	Status	—	—	5	Both Sides	—	—
TM19	Telekinesis	Psychic	Status	—	—	15	Normal	—	—
TM21	Frustration	Normal	Physical	—	100	20	Normal	—	○
TM24	Thunderbolt	Electric	Special	95	100	15	Normal	—	—
TM25	Thunder	Electric	Special	120	70	10	Normal	—	—
TM27	Return	Normal	Physical	—	100	20	Normal	—	○
TM29	Psychic	Psychic	Special	90	100	10	Normal	—	—
TM32	Double Team	Normal	Status	—	—	15	Self	—	—
TM33	Reflect	Psychic	Status	—	—	20	Your Side	—	—
TM42	Facade	Normal	Physical	70	100	20	Normal	—	○
TM44	Rest	Psychic	Status	—	—	10	Self	—	—
TM48	Round	Normal	Special	60	100	15	Normal	—	—
TM55	Scald	Water	Special	80	100	15	Normal	—	—
TM68	Giga Impact	Normal	Physical	150	90	5	Normal	—	○
TM70	Flash	Normal	Status	—	100	20	Normal	—	—
TM73	Thunder Wave	Electric	Status	—	100	20	Normal	—	—
TM74	Gyro Ball	Steel	Physical	—	100	5	Normal	—	○
TM77	Psych Up	Normal	Status	—	—	10	Normal	—	—
TM85	Dream Eater	Psychic	Special	100	100	15	Normal	—	—
TM86	Grass Knot	Grass	Special	—	100	20	Normal	—	○
TM87	Swagger	Normal	Status	—	90	15	Normal	—	—
TM90	Substitute	Normal	Status	—	—	10	Self	—	—
TM91	Flash Cannon	Steel	Special	80	100	10	Normal	—	—
TM92	Trick Room	Psychic	Status	—	—	5	Both Sides	—	—
HM03	Surf	Water	Special	95	100	15	Adjacent	—	—
HM05	Waterfall	Water	Physical	80	100	15	Normal	—	○
HM06	Dive	Water	Physical	80	100	10	Normal	—	○

MOVES TAUGHT BY PEOPLE

Name	Type	Kind	Pow.	Acc.	PP	Range	Long	DA

MOVES TAUGHT BY MOVE TUTORS FOR SHARDS

Name	Type	Kind	Pow.	Acc.	PP	Range	Long	DA
Signal Beam	Bug	Special	75	100	15	Normal	—	—
Magic Coat	Psychic	Status	—	—	15	Self	—	—
Icy Wind	Ice	Special	55	95	15	Many Others	—	—
Gravity	Psychic	Status	—	—	5	Both Sides	—	—
Snore	Normal	Special	40	100	15	Normal	—	—
Pain Split	Normal	Status	—	—	20	Normal	—	—
Wonder Room	Psychic	Status	—	—	10	Both Sides	—	—
Recycle	Normal	Status	—	—	10	Self	—	—
Trick	Psychic	Status	—	100	10	Normal	—	—
Sleep Talk	Normal	Status	—	—	10	Self	—	—
Skill Swap	Psychic	Status	—	—	10	Normal	—	—

122 Mr. Mime

Barrier Pokémon

- HEIGHT: 4'03"
- WEIGHT: 120.1 lbs.
- GENDER: ♂ / ♀

It shapes an invisible wall in midair by minutely vibrating its fingertips to stop molecules in the air.

TYPE Psychic

ABILITIES
- Soundproof
- Filter

HIDDEN ABILITY
- Technician

STATS
- HP
- Attack
- Defense
- Sp. Atk
- Sp. Def
- Speed

EGG GROUPS
Human-Like

Same form for ♂ / ♀

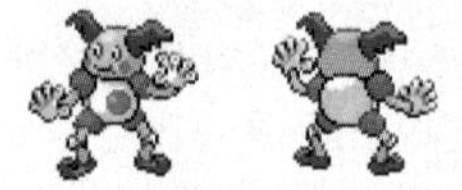

ITEMS SOMETIMES HELD
- None

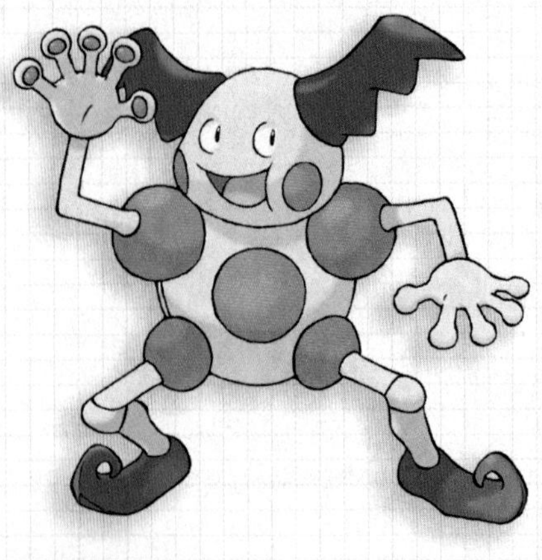

Pokémon AR Marker

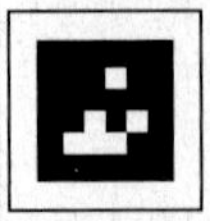

EVOLUTION

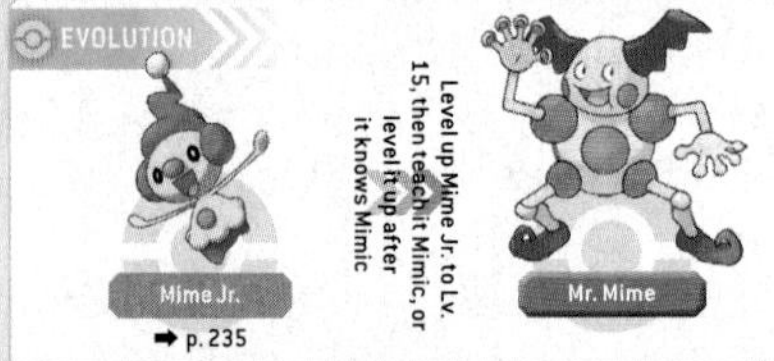
Mime Jr.
Level up Mime Jr. to Lv. 15, then teach it Mimic, or level it up after it knows Mimic
Mr. Mime

➡ p. 235

HOW TO OBTAIN

Pokémon Black Version 2	Link Trade or Poké Transfer
Pokémon White Version 2	Route 20 (mass outbreak)

HOW TO OBTAIN FROM OTHER GAMES

Pokémon Diamond Version	Route 218
Pokémon Platinum Version	Route 218

LEVEL-UP AND LEARNED MOVES

Lv.	Name	Type	Kind	Pow.	Acc.	PP	Range	Long	DA
1	Magical Leaf	Grass	Special	60	—	20	Normal	—	—
1	Quick Guard	Fighting	Status	—	—	15	Your Side	—	—
1	Wide Guard	Rock	Status	—	—	10	Your Side	—	—
1	Power Swap	Psychic	Status	—	—	10	Normal	—	—
1	Guard Swap	Psychic	Status	—	—	10	Normal	—	—
1	Barrier	Psychic	Status	—	—	30	Self	—	—
1	Confusion	Psychic	Special	50	100	25	Normal	—	—
4	Copycat	Normal	Status	—	—	20	Self	—	—
8	Meditate	Psychic	Status	—	—	40	Self	—	—
11	DoubleSlap	Normal	Physical	15	85	10	Normal	—	○
15	Mimic	Normal	Status	—	—	10	Normal	—	—
15	Psywave	Psychic	Special	—	80	15	Normal	—	—
18	Encore	Normal	Status	—	100	5	Normal	—	—
22	Light Screen	Psychic	Status	—	—	30	Your Side	—	—
22	Reflect	Psychic	Status	—	—	20	Your Side	—	—
25	Psybeam	Psychic	Special	65	100	20	Normal	—	—
29	Substitute	Normal	Status	—	—	10	Self	—	—
32	Recycle	Normal	Status	—	—	10	Self	—	—
36	Trick	Psychic	Status	—	100	10	Normal	—	—
39	Psychic	Psychic	Special	90	100	10	Normal	—	—
43	Role Play	Psychic	Status	—	—	10	Normal	—	—
46	Baton Pass	Normal	Status	—	—	40	Self	—	—
50	Safeguard	Normal	Status	—	—	25	Your Side	—	—

TM & HM MOVES

Lv.	Name	Type	Kind	Pow.	Acc.	PP	Range	Long	DA
TM03	Psyshock	Psychic	Special	80	100	10	Normal	—	—
TM04	Calm Mind	Psychic	Status	—	—	20	Self	—	—
TM06	Toxic	Poison	Status	—	90	10	Normal	—	—
TM10	Hidden Power	Normal	Special	—	100	15	Normal	—	—
TM11	Sunny Day	Fire	Status	—	—	5	Both Sides	—	—
TM12	Taunt	Dark	Status	—	100	20	Normal	—	—
TM15	Hyper Beam	Normal	Special	150	90	5	Normal	—	—
TM16	Light Screen	Psychic	Status	—	—	30	Your Side	—	—
TM17	Protect	Normal	Status	—	—	10	Self	—	—
TM18	Rain Dance	Water	Status	—	—	5	Both Sides	—	—
TM19	Telekinesis	Psychic	Status	—	—	15	Normal	—	—
TM20	Safeguard	Normal	Status	—	—	25	Your Side	—	—
TM21	Frustration	Normal	Physical	—	100	20	Normal	—	○
TM22	SolarBeam	Grass	Special	120	100	10	Normal	—	—
TM24	Thunderbolt	Electric	Special	95	100	15	Normal	—	—
TM25	Thunder	Electric	Special	120	70	10	Normal	—	—
TM27	Return	Normal	Physical	—	100	20	Normal	—	○
TM29	Psychic	Psychic	Special	90	100	10	Normal	—	—
TM30	Shadow Ball	Ghost	Special	80	100	15	Normal	—	—
TM31	Brick Break	Fighting	Physical	75	100	15	Normal	—	○
TM32	Double Team	Normal	Status	—	—	15	Self	—	—
TM33	Reflect	Psychic	Status	—	—	20	Your Side	—	—
TM40	Aerial Ace	Flying	Physical	60	—	20	Normal	○	○
TM41	Torment	Dark	Status	—	100	15	Normal	—	—
TM42	Facade	Normal	Physical	70	100	20	Normal	—	○
TM44	Rest	Psychic	Status	—	—	10	Self	—	—
TM45	Attract	Normal	Status	—	100	15	Normal	—	—
TM46	Thief	Dark	Physical	40	100	10	Normal	—	○
TM48	Round	Normal	Special	60	100	15	Normal	—	—
TM52	Focus Blast	Fighting	Special	120	70	5	Normal	—	—
TM53	Energy Ball	Grass	Special	80	100	10	Normal	—	—
TM56	Fling	Dark	Physical	—	100	10	Normal	—	—
TM57	Charge Beam	Electric	Special	50	90	10	Normal	—	—
TM66	Payback	Dark	Physical	50	100	10	Normal	—	○
TM68	Giga Impact	Normal	Physical	150	90	5	Normal	—	○
TM70	Flash	Normal	Status	—	100	20	Normal	—	—
TM73	Thunder Wave	Electric	Status	—	100	20	Normal	—	—
TM77	Psych Up	Normal	Status	—	—	10	Normal	—	—
TM85	Dream Eater	Psychic	Special	100	100	15	Normal	—	—
TM86	Grass Knot	Grass	Special	—	100	20	Normal	—	○
TM87	Swagger	Normal	Status	—	90	15	Normal	—	—
TM90	Substitute	Normal	Status	—	—	10	Self	—	—
TM92	Trick Room	Psychic	Status	—	—	5	Both Sides	—	—

MOVES TAUGHT BY PEOPLE

Name	Type	Kind	Pow.	Acc.	PP	Range	Long	DA

MOVES TAUGHT BY MOVE TUTORS FOR SHARDS

Name	Type	Kind	Pow.	Acc.	PP	Range	Long	DA
Covet	Normal	Physical	60	100	40	Normal	—	○
Signal Beam	Bug	Special	75	100	15	Normal	—	—
Fire Punch	Fire	Physical	75	100	15	Normal	—	○
ThunderPunch	Electric	Physical	75	100	15	Normal	—	○
Ice Punch	Ice	Physical	75	100	15	Normal	—	○
Iron Defense	Steel	Status	—	—	15	Self	—	—
Magic Coat	Psychic	Status	—	—	15	Self	—	—
Icy Wind	Ice	Special	55	95	15	Many Others	—	—
Zen Headbutt	Psychic	Physical	80	90	15	Normal	—	○
Foul Play	Dark	Physical	95	100	15	Normal	—	○
Snore	Normal	Special	40	100	15	Normal	—	—
Role Play	Psychic	Status	—	—	10	Normal	—	—
Drain Punch	Fighting	Physical	75	100	10	Normal	—	○
Helping Hand	Normal	Status	—	—	20	1 Ally	—	—
Magic Room	Psychic	Status	—	—	10	Both Sides	—	—
Wonder Room	Psychic	Status	—	—	10	Both Sides	—	—
Recycle	Normal	Status	—	—	10	Self	—	—
Trick	Psychic	Status	—	100	10	Normal	—	—
Sleep Talk	Normal	Status	—	—	10	Self	—	—
Skill Swap	Psychic	Status	—	—	10	Normal	—	—
Snatch	Dark	Status	—	—	10	Self	—	—

EGG MOVES

Name	Type	Kind	Pow.	Acc.	PP	Range	Long	DA
Future Sight	Psychic	Special	100	100	10	Normal	—	—
Hypnosis	Psychic	Status	—	60	20	Normal	—	—
Mimic	Normal	Status	—	—	10	Normal	—	—
Fake Out	Normal	Physical	40	100	10	Normal	—	○
Trick	Psychic	Status	—	100	10	Normal	—	—
Confuse Ray	Ghost	Status	—	100	10	Normal	—	—
Wake-Up Slap	Fighting	Physical	60	100	10	Normal	—	○
Teeter Dance	Normal	Status	—	100	20	Adjacent	—	—
Nasty Plot	Dark	Status	—	—	20	Self	—	—
Power Split	Psychic	Status	—	—	10	Normal	—	—
Magic Room	Psychic	Status	—	—	10	Both Sides	—	—
Icy Wind	Ice	Special	55	95	15	Many Others	—	—

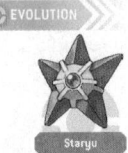

123 Mantis Pokémon

Scyther

TYPE Bug Flying

ABILITIES
- Swarm
- Technician

HIDDEN ABILITY
- Steadfast

STATS
HP
Attack
Defense
Sp. Atk
Sp. Def
Speed

EGG GROUPS
Bug

ITEMS SOMETIMES HELD
- None

- HEIGHT: 4'11"
- WEIGHT: 123.5 lbs.
- GENDER: ♂ / ♀

The sharp scythes on its forearms become increasingly sharp by cutting through hard objects.

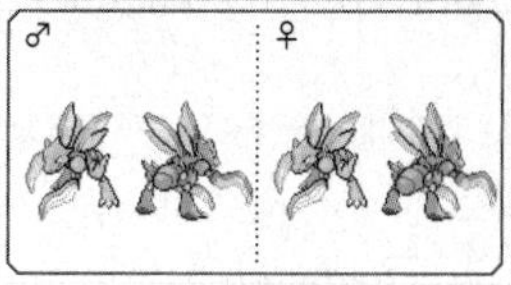

♂
♀

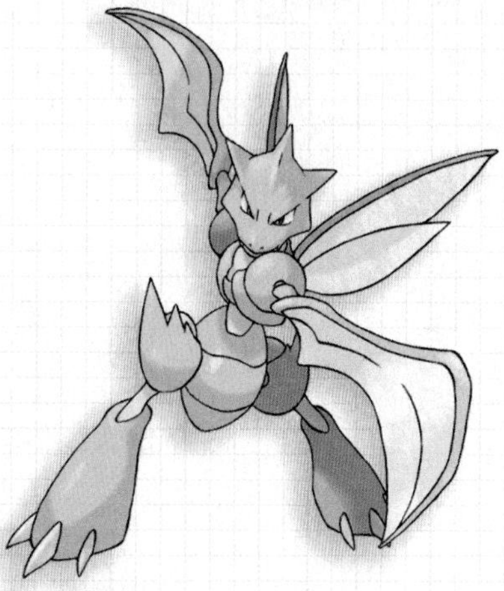

Pokémon AR Marker

EVOLUTION

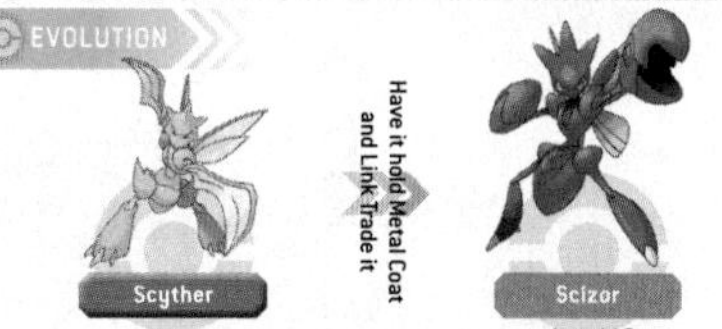

Scyther
Have it hold Metal Coat and Link Trade it
Scizor

➡ p. 119

HOW TO OBTAIN

Pokémon Black Version 2	Link Trade or Poké Transfer
Pokémon White Version 2	Link Trade or Poké Transfer

HOW TO OBTAIN FROM OTHER GAMES

Pokémon Diamond Version	Route 229
Pokémon Platinum Version	Route 210

LEVEL-UP AND LEARNED MOVES

Lv.	Name	Type	Kind	Pow.	Acc.	PP	Range	Long	DA
1	Vacuum Wave	Fighting	Special	40	100	30	Normal	—	—
1	Quick Attack	Normal	Physical	40	100	30	Normal	—	○
1	Leer	Normal	Status	—	100	30	Many Others	—	—
5	Focus Energy	Normal	Status	—	—	30	Self	—	—
9	Pursuit	Dark	Physical	40	100	20	Normal	—	○
13	False Swipe	Normal	Physical	40	100	40	Normal	—	○
17	Agility	Psychic	Status	—	—	30	Self	—	—
21	Wing Attack	Flying	Physical	60	100	35	Normal	○	○
25	Fury Cutter	Bug	Physical	20	95	20	Normal	—	○
29	Slash	Normal	Physical	70	100	20	Normal	—	○
33	Razor Wind	Normal	Special	80	100	10	Many Others	—	—
37	Double Team	Normal	Status	—	—	15	Self	—	—
41	X-Scissor	Bug	Physical	80	100	15	Normal	—	○
45	Night Slash	Dark	Physical	70	100	15	Normal	—	○
49	Double Hit	Normal	Physical	35	90	10	Normal	—	○
53	Air Slash	Flying	Special	75	95	20	Normal	○	—
57	Swords Dance	Normal	Status	—	—	30	Self	—	—
61	Feint	Normal	Physical	30	100	10	Normal	—	—

TM & HM MOVES

Lv.	Name	Type	Kind	Pow.	Acc.	PP	Range	Long	DA
TM06	Toxic	Poison	Status	—	90	10	Normal	—	—
TM10	Hidden Power	Normal	Special	—	100	15	Normal	—	—
TM11	Sunny Day	Fire	Status	—	—	5	Both Sides	—	—
TM15	Hyper Beam	Normal	Special	150	90	5	Normal	—	—
TM16	Light Screen	Psychic	Status	—	—	30	Your Side	—	—
TM17	Protect	Normal	Status	—	—	10	Self	—	—
TM18	Rain Dance	Water	Status	—	—	5	Both Sides	—	—
TM20	Safeguard	Normal	Status	—	—	25	Your Side	—	—
TM21	Frustration	Normal	Physical	—	100	20	Normal	—	○
TM27	Return	Normal	Physical	—	100	20	Normal	—	○
TM31	Brick Break	Fighting	Physical	75	100	15	Normal	—	○
TM32	Double Team	Normal	Status	—	—	15	Self	—	—
TM40	Aerial Ace	Flying	Physical	60	—	20	Normal	○	○
TM42	Facade	Normal	Physical	70	100	20	Normal	—	○
TM44	Rest	Psychic	Status	—	—	10	Self	—	—
TM45	Attract	Normal	Status	—	100	15	Normal	—	—
TM46	Thief	Dark	Physical	40	100	10	Normal	—	○
TM48	Round	Normal	Special	60	100	15	Normal	—	—
TM54	False Swipe	Normal	Physical	40	100	40	Normal	—	○
TM68	Giga Impact	Normal	Physical	150	90	5	Normal	—	○
TM75	Swords Dance	Normal	Status	—	—	30	Self	—	—
TM76	Struggle Bug	Bug	Special	30	100	20	Many Others	—	—
TM81	X-Scissor	Bug	Physical	80	100	15	Normal	—	○
TM87	Swagger	Normal	Status	—	90	15	Normal	—	—
TM89	U-turn	Bug	Physical	70	100	20	Normal	—	○
TM90	Substitute	Normal	Status	—	—	10	Self	—	—
TM94	Rock Smash	Fighting	Physical	40	100	15	Normal	—	○
HM01	Cut	Normal	Physical	50	95	30	Normal	—	○

MOVES TAUGHT BY PEOPLE

Name	Type	Kind	Pow.	Acc.	PP	Range	Long	DA

MOVES TAUGHT BY MOVE TUTORS FOR SHARDS

Name	Type	Kind	Pow.	Acc.	PP	Range	Long	DA
Bug Bite	Bug	Physical	60	100	20	Normal	—	○
Snore	Normal	Special	40	100	15	Normal	—	—
Knock Off	Dark	Physical	20	100	20	Normal	—	○
Roost	Flying	Status	—	—	10	Self	—	—
Tailwind	Flying	Status	—	—	30	Your Side	—	—
Sleep Talk	Normal	Status	—	—	10	Self	—	—

EGG MOVES

Name	Type	Kind	Pow.	Acc.	PP	Range	Long	DA
Counter	Fighting	Physical	—	100	20	Varies	—	○
Baton Pass	Normal	Status	—	—	40	Self	—	—
Razor Wind	Normal	Special	80	100	10	Many Others	—	—
Reversal	Fighting	Physical	—	100	15	Normal	—	○
Endure	Normal	Status	—	—	10	Self	—	—
Silver Wind	Bug	Special	60	100	5	Normal	—	—
Bug Buzz	Bug	Special	90	100	10	Normal	—	—
Night Slash	Dark	Physical	70	100	15	Normal	—	○
Defog	Flying	Status	—	—	15	Normal	—	—
Steel Wing	Steel	Physical	70	90	25	Normal	—	○

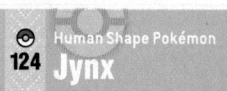

124 Human Shape Pokémon

Jynx

TYPE Ice Psychic

ABILITIES
- Oblivious
- Forewarn

HIDDEN ABILITY
- Dry Skin

STATS
HP
Attack
Defense
Sp. Atk
Sp. Def
Speed

EGG GROUPS
Human-Like

ITEMS SOMETIMES HELD
- None

- HEIGHT: 4'07"
- WEIGHT: 89.5 lbs.
- GENDER: ♀

Its cries sound like human speech. However, it is impossible to tell what it is trying to say.

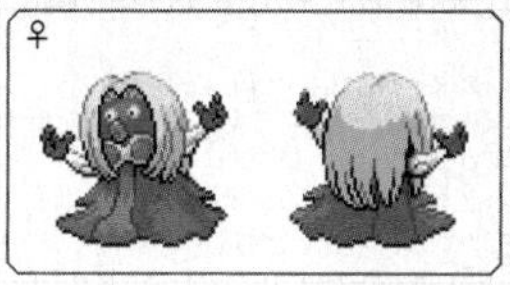

♀

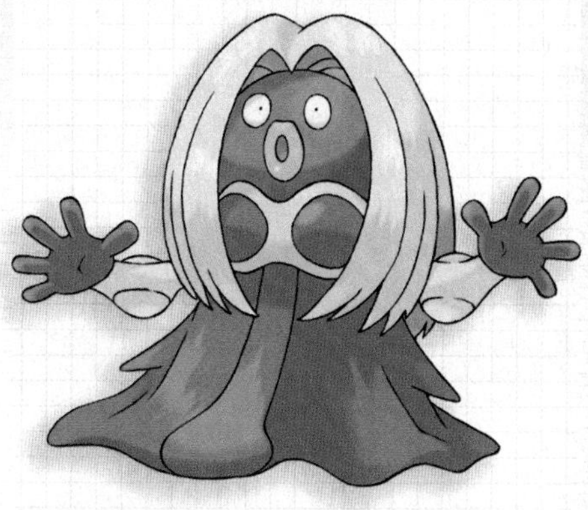

Pokémon AR Marker

EVOLUTION

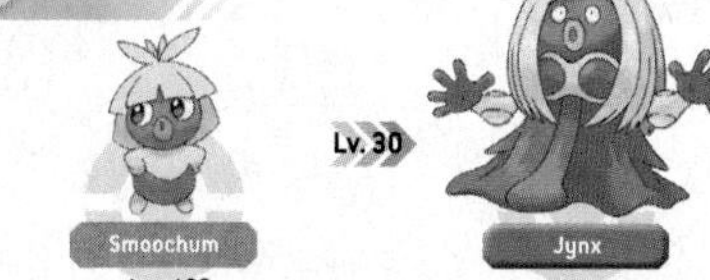

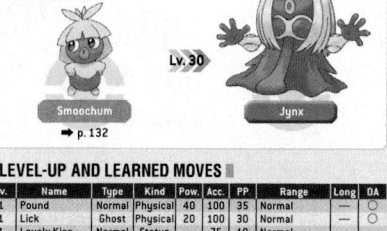

Smoochum
Lv. 30
Jynx

➡ p. 132

HOW TO OBTAIN

Pokémon Black Version 2	Link Trade or Poké Transfer
Pokémon White Version 2	Link Trade or Poké Transfer

HOW TO OBTAIN FROM OTHER GAMES

Pokémon Black Version	Giant Chasm caves
Pokémon White Version	Giant Chasm caves

LEVEL-UP AND LEARNED MOVES

Lv.	Name	Type	Kind	Pow.	Acc.	PP	Range	Long	DA
1	Pound	Normal	Physical	40	100	35	Normal	—	○
1	Lick	Ghost	Physical	20	100	30	Normal	—	○
1	Lovely Kiss	Normal	Status	—	75	10	Normal	—	—
1	Powder Snow	Ice	Special	40	100	25	Many Others	—	—
5	Lick	Ghost	Physical	20	100	30	Normal	—	○
8	Lovely Kiss	Normal	Status	—	75	10	Normal	—	—
11	Powder Snow	Ice	Special	40	100	25	Many Others	—	—
15	DoubleSlap	Normal	Physical	15	85	10	Normal	—	○
18	Ice Punch	Ice	Physical	75	100	15	Normal	—	○
21	Heart Stamp	Psychic	Physical	60	100	25	Normal	—	○
25	Mean Look	Normal	Status	—	—	5	Normal	—	—
28	Fake Tears	Dark	Status	—	100	20	Normal	—	—
33	Wake-Up Slap	Fighting	Physical	60	100	10	Normal	—	○
39	Avalanche	Ice	Physical	60	100	10	Normal	—	○
44	Body Slam	Normal	Physical	85	100	15	Normal	—	○
49	Wring Out	Normal	Special	—	100	5	Normal	—	○
55	Perish Song	Normal	Status	—	—	5	Adjacent	○	—
60	Blizzard	Ice	Special	120	70	5	Many Others	—	—

TM & HM MOVES

Lv.	Name	Type	Kind	Pow.	Acc.	PP	Range	Long	DA
TM03	Psyshock	Psychic	Special	80	100	10	Normal	—	—
TM04	Calm Mind	Psychic	Status	—	—	20	Self	—	—
TM06	Toxic	Poison	Status	—	90	10	Normal	—	—
TM07	Hail	Ice	Status	—	—	10	Both Sides	—	—
TM10	Hidden Power	Normal	Special	—	100	15	Normal	—	—
TM12	Taunt	Dark	Status	—	100	20	Normal	—	—
TM13	Ice Beam	Ice	Special	95	100	10	Normal	—	—
TM14	Blizzard	Ice	Special	120	70	5	Many Others	—	—
TM15	Hyper Beam	Normal	Special	150	90	5	Normal	—	—
TM16	Light Screen	Psychic	Status	—	—	30	Your Side	—	—
TM17	Protect	Normal	Status	—	—	10	Self	—	—
TM18	Rain Dance	Water	Status	—	—	5	Both Sides	—	—
TM19	Telekinesis	Psychic	Status	—	—	15	Normal	—	—
TM21	Frustration	Normal	Physical	—	100	20	Normal	—	○
TM27	Return	Normal	Physical	—	100	20	Normal	—	○
TM29	Psychic	Psychic	Special	90	100	10	Normal	—	—
TM30	Shadow Ball	Ghost	Special	80	100	15	Normal	—	—
TM31	Brick Break	Fighting	Physical	75	100	15	Normal	—	○
TM32	Double Team	Normal	Status	—	—	15	Self	—	—
TM33	Reflect	Psychic	Status	—	—	20	Your Side	—	—
TM41	Torment	Dark	Status	—	100	15	Normal	—	—
TM42	Facade	Normal	Physical	70	100	20	Normal	—	○
TM44	Rest	Psychic	Status	—	—	10	Self	—	—
TM45	Attract	Normal	Status	—	100	15	Normal	—	—
TM46	Thief	Dark	Physical	40	100	10	Normal	—	○
TM48	Round	Normal	Special	60	100	15	Normal	—	—
TM49	Echoed Voice	Normal	Special	40	100	15	Normal	—	—
TM52	Focus Blast	Fighting	Special	120	70	5	Normal	—	—
TM53	Energy Ball	Grass	Special	80	100	10	Normal	—	—
TM56	Fling	Dark	Physical	—	100	10	Normal	—	—
TM66	Payback	Dark	Physical	50	100	10	Normal	—	○
TM68	Giga Impact	Normal	Physical	150	90	5	Normal	—	○
TM70	Flash	Normal	Status	—	100	20	Normal	—	—
TM77	Psych Up	Normal	Status	—	—	10	Normal	—	—
TM79	Frost Breath	Ice	Special	40	90	10	Normal	—	—
TM85	Dream Eater	Psychic	Special	100	100	15	Normal	—	—
TM86	Grass Knot	Grass	Special	—	100	20	Normal	—	○
TM87	Swagger	Normal	Status	—	90	15	Normal	—	—
TM90	Substitute	Normal	Status	—	—	10	Self	—	—
TM92	Trick Room	Psychic	Status	—	—	5	Both Sides	—	—

MOVES TAUGHT BY PEOPLE

Name	Type	Kind	Pow.	Acc.	PP	Range	Long	DA

MOVES TAUGHT BY MOVE TUTORS FOR SHARDS

Name	Type	Kind	Pow.	Acc.	PP	Range	Long	DA
Covet	Normal	Physical	60	100	40	Normal	—	○
Signal Beam	Bug	Special	75	100	15	Normal	—	—
Ice Punch	Ice	Physical	75	100	15	Normal	—	○
Magic Coat	Psychic	Status	—	—	15	Self	—	—
Hyper Voice	Normal	Special	90	100	10	Many Others	—	—
Icy Wind	Ice	Special	55	95	15	Many Others	—	—
Zen Headbutt	Psychic	Physical	80	90	15	Normal	—	○
Snore	Normal	Special	40	100	15	Normal	—	—
Heal Bell	Normal	Status	—	—	5	Your Party	—	—
Role Play	Psychic	Status	—	—	10	Normal	—	—
Drain Punch	Fighting	Physical	75	100	10	Normal	—	○
Helping Hand	Normal	Status	—	—	20	1 Ally	—	—
Magic Room	Psychic	Status	—	—	10	Both Sides	—	—
Recycle	Normal	Status	—	—	10	Self	—	—
Trick	Psychic	Status	—	100	10	Normal	—	—
Sleep Talk	Normal	Status	—	—	10	Self	—	—
Skill Swap	Psychic	Status	—	—	10	Normal	—	—

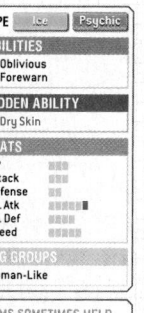

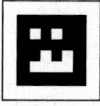

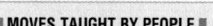

Electric Pokémon
125 Electabuzz

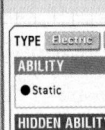

- HEIGHT: 3'07"
- WEIGHT: 66.1 lbs.
- GENDER: ♂ / ♀

Research is progressing on storing lightning in Electabuzz so this energy can be used at any time.

Same form for ♂ / ♀

Pokémon AR Marker

TYPE: Electric

ABILITY
- Static

HIDDEN ABILITY
- Vital Spirit

STATS
- HP
- Attack
- Defense
- Sp. Atk
- Sp. Def
- Speed

EGG GROUPS
- Human-Like

ITEMS SOMETIMES HELD
- None

EVOLUTION

Have it hold Electirizer and Link Trade it

Elekid	Electabuzz	Electivire
→ p. 133		→ p. 249

HOW TO OBTAIN

Pokémon Black Version 2	Link Trade or Poké Transfer
Pokémon White Version 2	Level up Elekid to Lv. 30

HOW TO OBTAIN FROM OTHER GAMES

Pokémon HeartGold Version	Route 10
Pokémon SoulSilver Version	Route 10

LEVEL-UP AND LEARNED MOVES

Lv.	Name	Type	Kind	Pow.	Acc.	PP	Range	Long	DA
1	Quick Attack	Normal	Physical	40	100	30	Normal	—	○
1	Leer	Normal	Status	—	100	30	Many Others	—	—
1	ThunderShock	Electric	Special	40	100	30	Normal	—	—
5	ThunderShock	Electric	Special	40	100	30	Normal	—	—
8	Low Kick	Fighting	Physical	—	100	20	Normal	—	○
12	Swift	Normal	Special	60	—	20	Many Others	—	—
15	Shock Wave	Electric	Special	60	—	20	Normal	—	—
19	Thunder Wave	Electric	Status	—	100	20	Normal	—	—
22	Electro Ball	Electric	Special	—	100	10	Normal	—	○
26	Light Screen	Psychic	Status	—	—	30	Your Side	—	—
29	ThunderPunch	Electric	Physical	75	100	15	Normal	—	○
36	Discharge	Electric	Special	80	100	15	Adjacent	—	—
42	Screech	Normal	Status	—	85	40	Normal	—	—
49	Thunderbolt	Electric	Special	95	100	15	Normal	—	—
55	Thunder	Electric	Special	120	70	10	Normal	—	—

TM & HM MOVES

Lv.	Name	Type	Kind	Pow.	Acc.	PP	Range	Long	DA
TM06	Toxic	Poison	Status	—	90	10	Normal	—	—
TM10	Hidden Power	Normal	Special	—	100	15	Normal	—	—
TM15	Hyper Beam	Normal	Special	150	90	5	Normal	—	—
TM16	Light Screen	Psychic	Status	—	—	30	Your Side	—	—
TM17	Protect	Normal	Status	—	—	10	Self	—	—
TM18	Rain Dance	Water	Status	—	—	5	Both Sides	—	—
TM21	Frustration	Normal	Physical	—	100	20	Normal	—	○
TM24	Thunderbolt	Electric	Special	95	100	15	Normal	—	—
TM25	Thunder	Electric	Special	120	70	10	Normal	—	—
TM27	Return	Normal	Physical	—	100	20	Normal	—	○
TM29	Psychic	Psychic	Special	90	100	10	Normal	—	—
TM31	Brick Break	Fighting	Physical	75	100	15	Normal	—	○
TM32	Double Team	Normal	Status	—	—	15	Self	—	—
TM42	Facade	Normal	Physical	70	100	20	Normal	—	○
TM44	Rest	Psychic	Status	—	—	10	Self	—	—
TM45	Attract	Normal	Status	—	100	15	Normal	—	—
TM46	Thief	Dark	Physical	40	100	10	Normal	—	○
TM48	Round	Normal	Special	60	100	15	Normal	—	—
TM52	Focus Blast	Fighting	Special	120	70	5	Normal	—	—
TM56	Fling	Dark	Physical	—	100	10	Normal	—	○
TM57	Charge Beam	Electric	Special	50	90	10	Normal	—	—
TM68	Giga Impact	Normal	Physical	150	90	5	Normal	—	○
TM70	Flash	Normal	Status	—	100	20	Normal	—	—
TM72	Volt Switch	Electric	Special	70	100	20	Normal	—	—
TM73	Thunder Wave	Electric	Status	—	100	20	Normal	—	—
TM87	Swagger	Normal	Status	—	90	15	Normal	—	—
TM90	Substitute	Normal	Status	—	—	10	Self	—	—
TM93	Wild Charge	Electric	Physical	90	100	15	Normal	—	○
TM94	Rock Smash	Fighting	Physical	40	100	15	Normal	—	○
HM04	Strength	Normal	Physical	80	100	15	Normal	—	○

MOVES TAUGHT BY PEOPLE

Name	Type	Kind	Pow.	Acc.	PP	Range	Long	DA

MOVES TAUGHT BY MOVE TUTORS FOR SHARDS

Name	Type	Kind	Pow.	Acc.	PP	Range	Long	DA
Covet	Normal	Physical	60	100	40	Normal	—	○
Signal Beam	Bug	Special	75	100	15	Normal	—	—
Dual Chop	Dragon	Physical	40	90	15	Normal	—	○
Low Kick	Fighting	Physical	—	100	20	Normal	—	○
Fire Punch	Fire	Physical	75	100	15	Normal	—	○
ThunderPunch	Electric	Physical	75	100	15	Normal	—	○
Ice Punch	Ice	Physical	75	100	15	Normal	—	○
Magnet Rise	Electric	Status	—	—	10	Self	—	—
Electroweb	Electric	Special	55	95	15	Many Others	—	—
Iron Tail	Steel	Physical	100	75	15	Normal	—	○
Snore	Normal	Special	40	100	15	Normal	—	—
Helping Hand	Normal	Status	—	—	20	1 Ally	—	—
Sleep Talk	Normal	Status	—	—	10	Self	—	—

Spitfire Pokémon
126 Magmar

- HEIGHT: 4'03"
- WEIGHT: 98.1 lbs.
- GENDER: ♂ / ♀

The scorching fire exhaled by Magmar forms heat waves around its body, making it hard to see the Pokémon clearly.

Same form for ♂ / ♀

Pokémon AR Marker

TYPE: Fire

ABILITY
- Flame Body

HIDDEN ABILITY
- Vital Spirit

STATS
- HP
- Attack
- Defense
- Sp. Atk
- Sp. Def
- Speed

EGG GROUPS
- Human-Like

ITEMS SOMETIMES HELD
- None

EVOLUTION

Have it hold Magmarizer and Link Trade it

Magby	Magmar	Magmortar
→ p. 133		→ p. 249

HOW TO OBTAIN

Pokémon Black Version 2	Level up Magby to Lv. 30
Pokémon White Version 2	Link Trade or Poké Transfer

HOW TO OBTAIN FROM OTHER GAMES

Pokémon HeartGold Version	Burned Tower B1F
Pokémon SoulSilver Version	Burned Tower B1F

LEVEL-UP AND LEARNED MOVES

Lv.	Name	Type	Kind	Pow.	Acc.	PP	Range	Long	DA
1	Smog	Poison	Special	20	70	20	Normal	—	—
1	Leer	Normal	Status	—	100	30	Many Others	—	—
1	Ember	Fire	Special	40	100	25	Normal	—	—
5	Ember	Fire	Special	40	100	25	Normal	—	—
8	SmokeScreen	Normal	Status	—	100	20	Normal	—	—
12	Faint Attack	Dark	Physical	60	—	20	Normal	—	○
15	Fire Spin	Fire	Special	35	85	15	Normal	—	—
19	Clear Smog	Poison	Special	50	—	15	Normal	—	—
22	Flame Burst	Fire	Special	70	100	15	Normal	—	—
26	Confuse Ray	Ghost	Status	—	100	10	Normal	—	—
29	Fire Punch	Fire	Physical	75	100	15	Normal	—	○
36	Lava Plume	Fire	Special	80	100	15	Adjacent	—	—
42	Sunny Day	Fire	Status	—	—	5	Both Sides	—	—
49	Flamethrower	Fire	Special	95	100	15	Normal	—	—
55	Fire Blast	Fire	Special	120	85	5	Normal	—	—

TM & HM MOVES

Lv.	Name	Type	Kind	Pow.	Acc.	PP	Range	Long	DA
TM06	Toxic	Poison	Status	—	90	10	Normal	—	—
TM10	Hidden Power	Normal	Special	—	100	15	Normal	—	—
TM11	Sunny Day	Fire	Status	—	—	5	Both Sides	—	—
TM15	Hyper Beam	Normal	Special	150	90	5	Normal	—	—
TM17	Protect	Normal	Status	—	—	10	Self	—	—
TM21	Frustration	Normal	Physical	—	100	20	Normal	—	○
TM27	Return	Normal	Physical	—	100	20	Normal	—	○
TM29	Psychic	Psychic	Special	90	100	10	Normal	—	—
TM31	Brick Break	Fighting	Physical	75	100	15	Normal	—	○
TM32	Double Team	Normal	Status	—	—	15	Self	—	—
TM35	Flamethrower	Fire	Special	95	100	15	Normal	—	—
TM38	Fire Blast	Fire	Special	120	85	5	Normal	—	—
TM42	Facade	Normal	Physical	70	100	20	Normal	—	○
TM43	Flame Charge	Fire	Physical	50	100	20	Normal	—	○
TM44	Rest	Psychic	Status	—	—	10	Self	—	—
TM45	Attract	Normal	Status	—	100	15	Normal	—	—
TM46	Thief	Dark	Physical	40	100	10	Normal	—	○
TM48	Round	Normal	Special	60	100	15	Normal	—	—
TM50	Overheat	Fire	Special	140	90	5	Normal	—	—
TM52	Focus Blast	Fighting	Special	120	70	5	Normal	—	—
TM56	Fling	Dark	Physical	—	100	10	Normal	—	○
TM59	Incinerate	Fire	Special	30	100	15	Many Others	—	—
TM61	Will-O-Wisp	Fire	Status	—	75	15	Normal	—	—
TM68	Giga Impact	Normal	Physical	150	90	5	Normal	—	○
TM87	Swagger	Normal	Status	—	90	15	Normal	—	—
TM90	Substitute	Normal	Status	—	—	10	Self	—	—
TM94	Rock Smash	Fighting	Physical	40	100	15	Normal	—	○
HM04	Strength	Normal	Physical	80	100	15	Normal	—	○

MOVES TAUGHT BY PEOPLE

Name	Type	Kind	Pow.	Acc.	PP	Range	Long	DA

MOVES TAUGHT BY MOVE TUTORS FOR SHARDS

Name	Type	Kind	Pow.	Acc.	PP	Range	Long	DA
Covet	Normal	Physical	60	100	40	Normal	—	○
Dual Chop	Dragon	Physical	40	90	15	Normal	—	○
Low Kick	Fighting	Physical	—	100	20	Normal	—	○
Fire Punch	Fire	Physical	75	100	15	Normal	—	○
ThunderPunch	Electric	Physical	75	100	15	Normal	—	○
Iron Tail	Steel	Physical	100	75	15	Normal	—	○
Snore	Normal	Special	40	100	15	Normal	—	—
Heat Wave	Fire	Special	100	90	10	Many Others	—	—
Helping Hand	Normal	Status	—	—	20	1 Ally	—	—
Sleep Talk	Normal	Status	—	—	10	Self	—	—

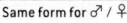

Stag Beetle Pokémon

127 Pinsir

- HEIGHT: 4'11"
- WEIGHT: 121.3 lbs.
- GENDER: ♂ / ♀

It grips prey with its powerful pincers and will not let go until the prey is torn in half.

Same form for ♂ / ♀

Pokémon AR Marker

TYPE Bug

ABILITIES
- Hyper Cutter
- Mold Breaker

HIDDEN ABILITY
- Moxie

STATS

HP	■■■
Attack	■■■■■■■
Defense	■■■■
Sp. Atk	■■■
Sp. Def	■■■
Speed	■■■■■

EGG GROUPS

Bug

ITEMS SOMETIMES HELD
- None

EVOLUTION

Does not evolve

HOW TO OBTAIN

Pokémon Black Version 2	Lostlorn Forest (Hidden Grotto)
Pokémon White Version 2	❶ Lostlorn Forest ❷ Route 12

HOW TO OBTAIN FROM OTHER GAMES

—

—

LEVEL-UP AND LEARNED MOVES

Lv.	Name	Type	Kind	Pow.	Acc.	PP	Range	Long	DA
1	ViceGrip	Normal	Physical	55	100	30	Normal	—	○
1	Focus Energy	Normal	Status	—	—	30	Self	—	—
4	Bind	Normal	Physical	15	85	20	Normal	—	○
8	Seismic Toss	Fighting	Physical	—	100	20	Normal	—	○
11	Harden	Normal	Status	—	—	30	Self	—	—
15	Revenge	Fighting	Physical	60	100	10	Normal	—	○
18	Brick Break	Fighting	Physical	75	100	15	Normal	—	○
22	Vital Throw	Fighting	Physical	70	—	10	Normal	—	○
26	Submission	Fighting	Physical	80	80	25	Normal	—	○
29	X-Scissor	Bug	Physical	80	100	15	Normal	—	○
33	Storm Throw	Fighting	Physical	40	100	10	Normal	—	○
36	Thrash	Normal	Physical	120	100	10	1 Random	—	○
40	Swords Dance	Normal	Status	—	—	30	Self	—	—
43	Superpower	Fighting	Physical	120	100	5	Normal	—	○
47	Guillotine	Normal	Physical	—	30	5	Normal	—	○

TM & HM MOVES

Lv.	Name	Type	Kind	Pow.	Acc.	PP	Range	Long	DA
TM06	Toxic	Poison	Status	—	90	10	Normal	—	—
TM08	Bulk Up	Fighting	Status	—	—	20	Self	—	—
TM10	Hidden Power	Normal	Special	—	100	15	Normal	—	—
TM11	Sunny Day	Fire	Status	—	—	5	Both Sides	—	—
TM15	Hyper Beam	Normal	Special	150	90	5	Normal	—	—
TM17	Protect	Normal	Status	—	—	10	Self	—	—
TM18	Rain Dance	Water	Status	—	—	5	Both Sides	—	—
TM21	Frustration	Normal	Physical	—	100	20	Normal	—	○
TM23	Smack Down	Rock	Physical	50	100	15	Normal	—	—
TM26	Earthquake	Ground	Physical	100	100	10	Adjacent	—	—
TM27	Return	Normal	Physical	—	100	20	Normal	—	○
TM28	Dig	Ground	Physical	80	100	10	Normal	—	○
TM31	Brick Break	Fighting	Physical	75	100	15	Normal	—	○
TM32	Double Team	Normal	Status	—	—	15	Self	—	—
TM39	Rock Tomb	Rock	Physical	50	80	10	Normal	—	—
TM42	Facade	Normal	Physical	70	100	20	Normal	—	○
TM44	Rest	Psychic	Status	—	—	10	Self	—	—
TM45	Attract	Normal	Status	—	100	15	Normal	—	—
TM46	Thief	Dark	Physical	40	100	10	Normal	—	○
TM48	Round	Normal	Special	60	100	15	Normal	—	—
TM52	Focus Blast	Fighting	Special	120	70	5	Normal	—	—
TM54	False Swipe	Normal	Physical	40	100	40	Normal	—	○
TM56	Fling	Dark	Physical	—	100	10	Normal	—	—
TM68	Giga Impact	Normal	Physical	150	90	5	Normal	—	○
TM71	Stone Edge	Rock	Physical	100	80	5	Normal	—	—
TM75	Swords Dance	Normal	Status	—	—	30	Self	—	—
TM76	Struggle Bug	Bug	Special	30	100	20	Many Others	—	—
TM78	Bulldoze	Ground	Physical	60	100	20	Adjacent	—	—
TM80	Rock Slide	Rock	Physical	75	90	10	Many Others	—	—
TM81	X-Scissor	Bug	Physical	80	100	15	Normal	—	○
TM87	Swagger	Normal	Status	—	90	15	Normal	—	—
TM90	Substitute	Normal	Status	—	—	10	Self	—	—
TM94	Rock Smash	Fighting	Physical	40	100	15	Normal	—	○
HM01	Cut	Normal	Physical	50	95	30	Normal	—	○
HM04	Strength	Normal	Physical	80	100	15	Normal	—	○

MOVES TAUGHT BY PEOPLE

Name	Type	Kind	Pow.	Acc.	PP	Range	Long	DA

MOVES TAUGHT BY MOVE TUTORS FOR SHARDS

Name	Type	Kind	Pow.	Acc.	PP	Range	Long	DA
Bug Bite	Bug	Physical	60	100	20	Normal	—	○
Iron Defense	Steel	Status	—	—	15	Self	—	—
Superpower	Fighting	Physical	120	100	5	Normal	—	○
Bind	Normal	Physical	15	85	20	Normal	—	○
Snore	Normal	Special	40	100	15	Normal	—	—
Knock Off	Dark	Physical	20	100	20	Normal	—	○
Stealth Rock	Rock	Status	—	—	20	Other Side	—	—
Sleep Talk	Normal	Status	—	—	10	Self	—	—

EGG MOVES

Name	Type	Kind	Pow.	Acc.	PP	Range	Long	DA
Fury Attack	Normal	Physical	15	85	20	Normal	—	○
Flail	Normal	Physical	—	100	15	Normal	—	○
Faint Attack	Dark	Physical	60	—	20	Normal	—	○
Quick Attack	Normal	Physical	40	100	30	Normal	—	○
Close Combat	Fighting	Physical	120	100	5	Normal	—	○
Feint	Normal	Physical	30	100	10	Normal	—	—
Me First	Normal	Status	—	—	20	Varies	—	—
Bug Bite	Bug	Physical	60	100	20	Normal	—	○
Superpower	Fighting	Physical	120	100	5	Normal	—	○

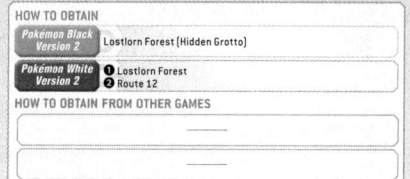

Wild Bull Pokémon

128 Tauros

- HEIGHT: 4'07"
- WEIGHT: 194.9 lbs.
- GENDER: ♂

Once it takes aim at its foe, it makes a headlong charge. It is famous for its violent nature.

♂

Pokémon AR Marker

TYPE Normal

ABILITIES
- Intimidate
- Anger Point

HIDDEN ABILITY
- Sheer Force

STATS

HP	■■■
Attack	■■■■■
Defense	■■■■
Sp. Atk	■■
Sp. Def	■■■
Speed	■■■■■■

EGG GROUPS

Field

ITEMS SOMETIMES HELD
- None

EVOLUTION

Does not evolve

HOW TO OBTAIN

Pokémon Black Version 2	Link Trade or Poké Transfer
Pokémon White Version 2	Link Trade or Poké Transfer

HOW TO OBTAIN FROM OTHER GAMES

Pokémon HeartGold Version	Route 38
Pokémon SoulSilver Version	Route 38

LEVEL-UP AND LEARNED MOVES

Lv.	Name	Type	Kind	Pow.	Acc.	PP	Range	Long	DA
1	Tackle	Normal	Physical	50	100	35	Normal	—	○
3	Tail Whip	Normal	Status	—	100	30	Many Others	—	—
5	Rage	Normal	Physical	20	100	20	Normal	—	○
8	Horn Attack	Normal	Physical	65	100	25	Normal	—	○
11	Scary Face	Normal	Status	—	100	10	Normal	—	—
15	Pursuit	Dark	Physical	40	100	20	Normal	—	○
19	Rest	Psychic	Status	—	—	10	Self	—	—
24	Payback	Dark	Physical	50	100	10	Normal	—	○
29	Work Up	Normal	Status	—	—	30	Self	—	—
35	Zen Headbutt	Psychic	Physical	80	90	15	Normal	—	○
41	Take Down	Normal	Physical	90	85	20	Normal	—	○
48	Swagger	Normal	Status	—	90	15	Normal	—	—
55	Thrash	Normal	Physical	120	100	10	1 Random	—	○
63	Giga Impact	Normal	Physical	150	90	5	Normal	—	○

TM & HM MOVES

Lv.	Name	Type	Kind	Pow.	Acc.	PP	Range	Long	DA
TM06	Toxic	Poison	Status	—	90	10	Normal	—	—
TM10	Hidden Power	Normal	Special	—	100	15	Normal	—	—
TM11	Sunny Day	Fire	Status	—	—	5	Both Sides	—	—
TM13	Ice Beam	Ice	Special	95	100	10	Normal	—	—
TM14	Blizzard	Ice	Special	120	70	5	Many Others	—	—
TM15	Hyper Beam	Normal	Special	150	90	5	Normal	—	—
TM17	Protect	Normal	Status	—	—	10	Self	—	—
TM18	Rain Dance	Water	Status	—	—	5	Both Sides	—	—
TM21	Frustration	Normal	Physical	—	100	20	Normal	—	○
TM22	SolarBeam	Grass	Special	120	100	10	Normal	—	—
TM24	Thunderbolt	Electric	Special	95	100	15	Normal	—	—
TM25	Thunder	Electric	Special	120	70	10	Normal	—	—
TM26	Earthquake	Ground	Physical	100	100	10	Adjacent	—	—
TM27	Return	Normal	Physical	—	100	20	Normal	—	○
TM32	Double Team	Normal	Status	—	—	15	Self	—	—
TM35	Flamethrower	Fire	Special	95	100	15	Normal	—	—
TM37	Sandstorm	Rock	Status	—	—	10	Both Sides	—	—
TM38	Fire Blast	Fire	Special	120	85	5	Normal	—	—
TM39	Rock Tomb	Rock	Physical	50	80	10	Normal	—	—
TM42	Facade	Normal	Physical	70	100	20	Normal	—	○
TM44	Rest	Psychic	Status	—	—	10	Self	—	—
TM45	Attract	Normal	Status	—	100	15	Normal	—	—
TM48	Round	Normal	Special	60	100	15	Normal	—	—
TM59	Incinerate	Fire	Special	30	100	15	Many Others	—	—
TM66	Payback	Dark	Physical	50	100	10	Normal	—	○
TM67	Retaliate	Normal	Physical	70	100	5	Normal	—	○
TM68	Giga Impact	Normal	Physical	150	90	5	Normal	—	○
TM71	Stone Edge	Rock	Physical	100	80	5	Normal	—	—
TM78	Bulldoze	Ground	Physical	60	100	20	Adjacent	—	—
TM80	Rock Slide	Rock	Physical	75	90	10	Many Others	—	—
TM83	Work Up	Normal	Status	—	—	30	Self	—	—
TM87	Swagger	Normal	Status	—	90	15	Normal	—	—
TM90	Substitute	Normal	Status	—	—	10	Self	—	—
TM93	Wild Charge	Electric	Physical	90	100	15	Normal	—	○
TM94	Rock Smash	Fighting	Physical	40	100	15	Normal	—	○
HM03	Surf	Water	Special	95	100	15	Adjacent	—	—
HM04	Strength	Normal	Physical	80	100	15	Normal	—	○

MOVES TAUGHT BY PEOPLE

Name	Type	Kind	Pow.	Acc.	PP	Range	Long	DA

MOVES TAUGHT BY MOVE TUTORS FOR SHARDS

Name	Type	Kind	Pow.	Acc.	PP	Range	Long	DA
Iron Head	Steel	Physical	80	100	15	Normal	—	○
Uproar	Normal	Special	90	100	10	1 Random	—	—
Icy Wind	Ice	Special	55	95	15	Many Others	—	—
Iron Tail	Steel	Physical	100	75	15	Normal	—	○
Zen Headbutt	Psychic	Physical	80	90	15	Normal	—	○
Snore	Normal	Special	40	100	15	Normal	—	—
Role Play	Psychic	Status	—	—	10	Normal	—	—
Helping Hand	Normal	Status	—	—	20	1 Ally	—	—
Spite	Ghost	Status	—	100	10	Normal	—	—
Outrage	Dragon	Physical	120	100	10	1 Random	—	○
Endeavor	Normal	Physical	—	100	5	Normal	—	○
Sleep Talk	Normal	Status	—	—	10	Self	—	—

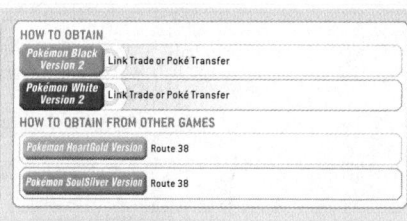

Fish Pokémon
129 Magikarp

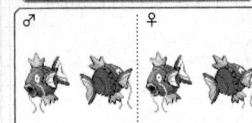

TYPE Water

ABILITY
● Swift Swim

HIDDEN ABILITY
● Rattled

● HEIGHT: 2'11"
● WEIGHT: 22.0 lbs.
● GENDER: ♂ / ♀

A Magikarp living for many years can leap a mountain using Splash. The move remains useless, though.

STATS
HP
Attack
Defense
Sp. Atk
Sp. Def
Speed

EGG GROUPS
Water ❷/Dragon

ITEMS SOMETIMES HELD
● None

EVOLUTION

Magikarp — Lv. 20 → Gyarados

HOW TO OBTAIN

| Pokémon Black Version 2 | ❶ Nature Preserve (Super Rod) ❷ Buy from the man on Marvelous Bridge for 500 in prize money |
| Pokémon White Version 2 | ❶ Nature Preserve (Super Rod) ❷ Buy from the man on Marvelous Bridge for 500 in prize money |

HOW TO OBTAIN FROM OTHER GAMES

LEVEL-UP AND LEARNED MOVES

Lv.	Name	Type	Kind	Pow.	Acc.	PP	Range	Long	DA
1	Splash	Normal	Status	—	—	40	Self	—	
15	Tackle	Normal	Physical	50	100	35	Normal	—	○
30	Flail	Normal	Physical	—	100	15	Normal	—	○

TM & HM MOVES

Lv.	Name	Type	Kind	Pow.	Acc.	PP	Range	Long	DA

MOVES TAUGHT BY PEOPLE

Name	Type	Kind	Pow.	Acc.	PP	Range	Long	DA

MOVES TAUGHT BY MOVE TUTORS FOR SHARDS

Name	Type	Kind	Pow.	Acc.	PP	Range	Long	DA
Bounce	Flying	Physical	85	85	5	Normal	○	○

EGG MOVES

Name	Type	Kind	Pow.	Acc.	PP	Range	Long	DA

Pokémon AR Marker

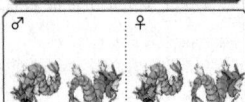

Atrocious Pokémon
130 Gyarados

TYPE Water Flying

ABILITY
● Intimidate

HIDDEN ABILITY
● Moxie

● HEIGHT: 21'04"
● WEIGHT: 518.1 lbs.
● GENDER: ♂ / ♀

Once it begins to rampage, a Gyarados will burn everything down, even in a harsh storm.

STATS
HP
Attack
Defense
Sp. Atk
Sp. Def
Speed

EGG GROUPS
Water ❷/Dragon

ITEMS SOMETIMES HELD
● None

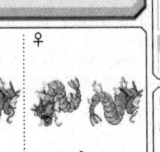

EVOLUTION

Magikarp — Lv. 20 → Gyarados

HOW TO OBTAIN

| Pokémon Black Version 2 | Nature Preserve (Super Rod/ripples in water) |
| Pokémon White Version 2 | Nature Preserve (Super Rod/ripples in water) |

HOW TO OBTAIN FROM OTHER GAMES

LEVEL-UP AND LEARNED MOVES

Lv.	Name	Type	Kind	Pow.	Acc.	PP	Range	Long	DA
1	Thrash	Normal	Physical	120	100	10	1 Random	—	○
20	Bite	Dark	Physical	60	100	25	Normal	—	○
23	Dragon Rage	Dragon	Special	—	100	10	Normal	—	
26	Leer	Normal	Status	—	100	30	Many Others	—	
29	Twister	Dragon	Special	40	100	20	Many Others	—	○
32	Ice Fang	Ice	Physical	65	95	15	Normal	—	○
35	Aqua Tail	Water	Physical	90	90	10	Normal	—	○
38	Rain Dance	Water	Status	—	—	5	Both Sides	—	
41	Hydro Pump	Water	Special	120	80	5	Normal	—	
44	Dragon Dance	Dragon	Status	—	—	20	Self	—	
47	Hyper Beam	Normal	Special	150	90	5	Normal	—	

TM & HM MOVES

Lv.	Name	Type	Kind	Pow.	Acc.	PP	Range	Long	DA
TM05	Roar	Normal	Status	—	100	20	Normal	—	—
TM06	Toxic	Poison	Status	—	90	10	Normal	—	—
TM07	Hail	Ice	Status	—	—	10	Both Sides	—	—
TM10	Hidden Power	Normal	Special	—	100	15	Normal	—	—
TM12	Taunt	Dark	Status	—	100	20	Normal	—	—
TM13	Ice Beam	Ice	Special	95	100	10	Normal	—	—
TM14	Blizzard	Ice	Special	120	70	5	Many Others	—	—
TM15	Hyper Beam	Normal	Special	150	90	5	Normal	—	—
TM17	Protect	Normal	Status	—	—	10	Self	—	—
TM18	Rain Dance	Water	Status	—	—	5	Both Sides	—	—
TM21	Frustration	Normal	Physical	—	100	20	Normal	—	○
TM24	Thunderbolt	Electric	Special	95	100	15	Normal	—	—
TM25	Thunder	Electric	Special	120	70	10	Normal	—	—
TM26	Earthquake	Ground	Physical	100	100	10	Adjacent	—	—
TM27	Return	Normal	Physical	—	100	20	Normal	—	○
TM32	Double Team	Normal	Status	—	—	15	Self	—	—
TM35	Flamethrower	Fire	Special	95	100	15	Normal	—	—
TM37	Sandstorm	Rock	Status	—	—	10	Both Sides	—	—
TM38	Fire Blast	Fire	Special	120	85	5	Normal	—	—
TM41	Torment	Dark	Status	—	100	15	Normal	—	—
TM42	Facade	Normal	Physical	70	100	20	Normal	—	○
TM44	Rest	Psychic	Status	—	—	10	Self	—	—
TM45	Attract	Normal	Status	—	100	15	Normal	—	—
TM48	Round	Normal	Special	60	100	15	Normal	—	—
TM55	Scald	Water	Special	80	100	15	Normal	—	—
TM59	Incinerate	Fire	Special	30	100	15	Many Others	—	—
TM66	Payback	Dark	Physical	50	100	10	Normal	—	—
TM68	Giga Impact	Normal	Physical	150	90	5	Normal	—	—
TM71	Stone Edge	Rock	Physical	100	80	5	Normal	—	—
TM73	Thunder Wave	Electric	Status	—	100	20	Normal	—	—
TM78	Bulldoze	Ground	Physical	60	100	20	Adjacent	—	—
TM82	Dragon Tail	Dragon	Physical	60	90	10	Normal	—	—
TM87	Swagger	Normal	Status	—	90	15	Normal	—	—
TM90	Substitute	Normal	Status	—	—	10	Self	—	—
TM94	Rock Smash	Fighting	Physical	40	100	15	Normal	—	○
HM03	Surf	Water	Special	95	100	15	Adjacent	—	—
HM04	Strength	Normal	Physical	80	100	15	Normal	—	—
HM05	Waterfall	Water	Physical	80	100	15	Normal	—	—
HM06	Dive	Water	Physical	80	100	10	Normal	—	—

MOVES TAUGHT BY PEOPLE

Name	Type	Kind	Pow.	Acc.	PP	Range	Long	DA

MOVES TAUGHT BY MOVE TUTORS FOR SHARDS

Name	Type	Kind	Pow.	Acc.	PP	Range	Long	DA
Bounce	Flying	Physical	85	85	5	Normal	○	○
Iron Head	Steel	Physical	80	100	15	Normal	—	○
Uproar	Normal	Special	90	100	10	1 Random	—	—
Icy Wind	Ice	Special	55	95	15	Many Others	—	—
Iron Tail	Steel	Physical	100	75	15	Normal	—	○
Aqua Tail	Water	Physical	90	90	10	Normal	—	○
Dragon Pulse	Dragon	Special	90	100	10	Normal	○	—
Dark Pulse	Dark	Special	80	100	15	Normal	○	—
Snore	Normal	Special	40	100	15	Normal	—	○
Spite	Ghost	Status	—	100	10	Normal	—	—
Outrage	Dragon	Physical	120	100	10	1 Random	—	○
Sleep Talk	Normal	Status	—	—	10	Self	—	—

Pokémon AR Marker

131 Lapras
Transport Pokémon

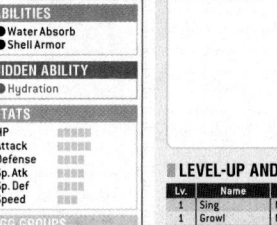

- HEIGHT: 8'02"
- WEIGHT: 485.0 lbs.
- GENDER: ♂ / ♀

Able to understand human speech and very intelligent, it loves to swim in the sea with people on its back.

Same form for ♂ / ♀

TYPE Water Ice

ABILITIES
- Water Absorb
- Shell Armor

HIDDEN ABILITY
- Hydration

STATS
- HP
- Attack
- Defense
- Sp. Atk
- Sp. Def
- Speed

EGG GROUPS
Monster/Water ❶

ITEMS SOMETIMES HELD
- None

EVOLUTION
Does not evolve

HOW TO OBTAIN
Pokémon Black Version 2 — Village Bridge (ripples in water)
Pokémon White Version 2 — Village Bridge (ripples in water)
HOW TO OBTAIN FROM OTHER GAMES
———
———

LEVEL-UP AND LEARNED MOVES

Lv.	Name	Type	Kind	Pow.	Acc.	PP	Range	Long	DA
1	Sing	Normal	Status	—	55	15	Normal	—	—
1	Growl	Normal	Status	—	100	40	Many Others	—	—
1	Water Gun	Water	Special	40	100	25	Normal	—	—
4	Mist	Ice	Status	—	—	30	Your Side	—	—
7	Confuse Ray	Ghost	Status	—	100	10	Normal	—	—
10	Ice Shard	Ice	Physical	40	100	30	Normal	—	—
14	Water Pulse	Water	Special	60	100	20	Normal	—	○
18	Body Slam	Normal	Physical	85	100	15	Normal	—	○
22	Rain Dance	Water	Status	—	—	5	Both Sides	—	—
27	Perish Song	Normal	Status	—	—	5	Adjacent	○	—
32	Ice Beam	Ice	Special	95	100	10	Normal	—	○
37	Brine	Water	Special	65	100	10	Normal	—	—
43	Safeguard	Normal	Status	—	—	25	Your Side	—	—
49	Hydro Pump	Water	Special	120	80	5	Normal	—	—
55	Sheer Cold	Ice	Special	—	30	5	Normal	—	—

TM & HM MOVES

Lv.	Name	Type	Kind	Pow.	Acc.	PP	Range	Long	DA
TM05	Roar	Normal	Status	—	100	20	Normal	—	—
TM06	Toxic	Poison	Status	—	90	10	Normal	—	—
TM07	Hail	Ice	Status	—	—	10	Both Sides	—	—
TM10	Hidden Power	Normal	Special	—	100	15	Normal	—	—
TM13	Ice Beam	Ice	Special	95	100	10	Normal	—	○
TM14	Blizzard	Ice	Special	120	70	5	Many Others	—	—
TM15	Hyper Beam	Normal	Special	150	90	5	Normal	—	—
TM17	Protect	Normal	Status	—	—	10	Self	—	—
TM18	Rain Dance	Water	Status	—	—	5	Both Sides	—	—
TM20	Safeguard	Normal	Status	—	—	25	Your Side	—	—
TM21	Frustration	Normal	Physical	—	100	20	Normal	—	○
TM24	Thunderbolt	Electric	Special	95	100	15	Normal	—	○
TM25	Thunder	Electric	Special	120	70	10	Normal	—	—
TM27	Return	Normal	Physical	—	100	20	Normal	—	○
TM29	Psychic	Psychic	Special	90	100	10	Normal	—	○
TM32	Double Team	Normal	Status	—	—	15	Self	—	—
TM42	Facade	Normal	Physical	70	100	20	Normal	—	○
TM44	Rest	Psychic	Status	—	—	10	Self	—	—
TM45	Attract	Normal	Status	—	100	15	Normal	—	—
TM48	Round	Normal	Special	60	100	15	Normal	—	—
TM49	Echoed Voice	Normal	Special	40	100	15	Normal	—	—
TM68	Giga Impact	Normal	Physical	150	90	5	Normal	—	○
TM78	Bulldoze	Ground	Physical	60	100	20	Adjacent	—	—
TM79	Frost Breath	Ice	Special	40	90	10	Normal	—	—
TM85	Dream Eater	Psychic	Special	100	100	15	Normal	—	—
TM87	Swagger	Normal	Status	—	90	15	Normal	—	—
TM90	Substitute	Normal	Status	—	—	10	Self	—	—
TM94	Rock Smash	Fighting	Physical	40	100	15	Normal	—	○
HM03	Surf	Water	Special	95	100	15	Adjacent	—	—
HM04	Strength	Normal	Physical	80	100	15	Normal	—	○
HM05	Waterfall	Water	Physical	80	100	15	Normal	—	—
HM06	Dive	Water	Physical	80	100	10	Normal	—	—

MOVES TAUGHT BY PEOPLE

Name	Type	Kind	Pow.	Acc.	PP	Range	Long	DA

MOVES TAUGHT BY MOVE TUTORS FOR SHARDS

Name	Type	Kind	Pow.	Acc.	PP	Range	Long	DA
Drill Run	Ground	Physical	80	95	10	Normal	—	—
Signal Beam	Bug	Special	75	100	15	Normal	—	—
Iron Head	Steel	Physical	80	100	15	Normal	—	○
Block	Normal	Status	—	—	5	Normal	—	—
Hyper Voice	Normal	Special	90	100	10	Many Others	—	—
Icy Wind	Ice	Special	55	95	15	Many Others	—	—
Iron Tail	Steel	Physical	100	75	15	Normal	—	○
Aqua Tail	Water	Physical	90	90	10	Normal	—	○
Zen Headbutt	Psychic	Physical	80	90	15	Normal	—	○
Dragon Pulse	Dragon	Special	90	100	10	Normal	○	—
Snore	Normal	Special	40	100	15	Normal	—	—
Heal Bell	Normal	Status	—	—	5	Your Party	—	—
Outrage	Dragon	Physical	120	100	10	1 Random	—	○
Sleep Talk	Normal	Status	—	—	10	Self	—	—

EGG MOVES

Name	Type	Kind	Pow.	Acc.	PP	Range	Long	DA
Foresight	Normal	Status	—	—	40	Normal	—	—
Tickle	Normal	Status	—	100	20	Normal	—	—
Refresh	Normal	Status	—	—	20	Self	—	—
Dragon Dance	Dragon	Status	—	—	20	Self	—	—
Curse	Ghost	Status	—	—	10	Varies	—	—
Sleep Talk	Normal	Status	—	—	10	Self	—	—
Horn Drill	Normal	Physical	—	30	5	Normal	—	—
AncientPower	Rock	Special	60	100	5	Normal	—	○
Whirlpool	Water	Special	35	85	15	Normal	—	—
Fissure	Ground	Physical	—	30	5	Normal	—	—
Dragon Pulse	Dragon	Special	90	100	10	Normal	○	—
Avalanche	Ice	Physical	60	100	10	Normal	—	○
Future Sight	Psychic	Special	100	100	10	Normal	—	—

Pokémon AR Marker

---

132 Ditto
Transform Pokémon

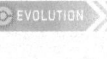

- HEIGHT: 1'00"
- WEIGHT: 8.8 lbs.
- GENDER: Unknown

It can reconstitute its entire cellular structure to change into what it sees, but it returns to normal when it relaxes.

Gender unknown

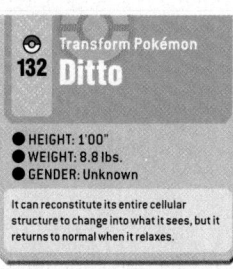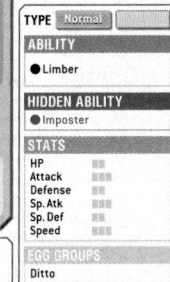

TYPE Normal

ABILITY
- Limber

HIDDEN ABILITY
- Imposter

STATS
- HP
- Attack
- Defense
- Sp. Atk
- Sp. Def
- Speed

EGG GROUPS
Ditto

ITEMS SOMETIMES HELD
- Quick Powder
- Metal Powder

EVOLUTION
Does not evolve

HOW TO OBTAIN
Pokémon Black Version 2 — ❶ Giant Chasm crater forest ❷ Giant Chasm (Hidden Grotto)
Pokémon White Version 2 — ❶ Giant Chasm crater forest ❷ Giant Chasm (Hidden Grotto)
HOW TO OBTAIN FROM OTHER GAMES
———
———

LEVEL-UP AND LEARNED MOVES

Lv.	Name	Type	Kind	Pow.	Acc.	PP	Range	Long	DA
1	Transform	Normal	Status	-	-	10	Normal	—	—

TM & HM MOVES

Lv.	Name	Type	Kind	Pow.	Acc.	PP	Range	Long	DA

MOVES TAUGHT BY PEOPLE

Name	Type	Kind	Pow.	Acc.	PP	Range	Long	DA

MOVES TAUGHT BY MOVE TUTORS FOR SHARDS

Name	Type	Kind	Pow.	Acc.	PP	Range	Long	DA

Pokémon AR Marker
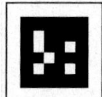

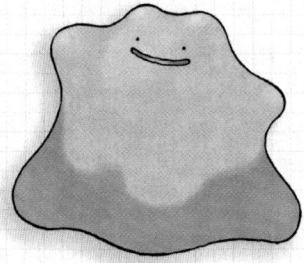

133 Eevee

Evolution Pokémon

- HEIGHT: 1'00"
- WEIGHT: 14.3 lbs.
- GENDER: ♂ / ♀

Thanks to its unstable genetic makeup, this special Pokémon conceals many different possible evolutions.

Same form for ♂ / ♀

Pokémon AR Marker

TYPE Normal

ABILITIES
- Run Away
- Adaptability

HIDDEN ABILITY
- Anticipation

STATS

HP
Attack
Defense
Sp. Atk
Sp. Def
Speed

EGG GROUPS

Field

ITEMS SOMETIMES HELD

- None

EVOLUTION

Eevee

Vaporeon — Use Water Stone on Eevee

Jolteon — Use Thunderstone on Eevee

Flareon — Use Fire Stone on Eevee

Espeon ➡ p. 111 — Level up Eevee with high friendship in the morning, afternoon, or evening

Umbreon ➡ p. 112 — Level up Eevee with high friendship at night or late night

Leafeon ➡ p. 251 — Level up Eevee around the moss-covered rock in Pinwheel Forest

Glaceon ➡ p. 251 — Level up Eevee around the ice-covered rock in Twist Mountain

HOW TO OBTAIN

Pokémon Black Version 2	❶ Castelia City empty lot ❷ Receive from Amanita in Castelia City
Pokémon White Version 2	❶ Castelia City empty lot ❷ Receive from Amanita in Castelia City

HOW TO OBTAIN FROM OTHER GAMES

—

—

LEVEL-UP AND LEARNED MOVES

Lv.	Name	Type	Kind	Pow.	Acc.	PP	Range	Long	DA
1	Helping Hand	Normal	Status	—	—	20	1 Ally	—	—
1	Tackle	Normal	Physical	50	100	35	Normal	—	○
1	Tail Whip	Normal	Status	—	100	30	Many Others	—	—
5	Sand-Attack	Ground	Status	—	100	15	Normal	—	—
9	Growl	Normal	Status	—	100	40	Many Others	—	—
13	Quick Attack	Normal	Physical	40	100	30	Normal	—	○
17	Bite	Dark	Physical	60	100	25	Normal	—	○
21	Covet	Normal	Physical	60	100	40	Normal	—	○
25	Take Down	Normal	Physical	90	85	20	Normal	—	○
29	Charm	Normal	Status	—	100	20	Normal	—	—
33	Baton Pass	Normal	Status	—	—	40	Self	—	—
37	Double-Edge	Normal	Physical	120	100	15	Normal	—	○
41	Last Resort	Normal	Physical	140	100	5	Normal	—	○
45	Trump Card	Normal	Special	—	—	5	Normal	—	○

TM & HM MOVES

Lv.	Name	Type	Kind	Pow.	Acc.	PP	Range	Long	DA
TM06	Toxic	Poison	Status	—	90	10	Normal	—	—
TM10	Hidden Power	Normal	Special	—	100	15	Normal	—	—
TM11	Sunny Day	Fire	Status	—	—	5	Both Sides	—	—
TM17	Protect	Normal	Status	—	—	10	Self	—	—
TM18	Rain Dance	Water	Status	—	—	5	Both Sides	—	—
TM21	Frustration	Normal	Physical	—	100	20	Normal	—	○
TM27	Return	Normal	Physical	—	100	20	Normal	—	○
TM28	Dig	Ground	Physical	80	100	10	Normal	—	○
TM30	Shadow Ball	Ghost	Special	80	100	15	Normal	—	—
TM32	Double Team	Normal	Status	—	—	15	Self	—	—
TM42	Facade	Normal	Physical	70	100	20	Normal	—	○
TM44	Rest	Psychic	Status	—	—	10	Self	—	—
TM45	Attract	Normal	Status	—	100	15	Normal	—	—
TM48	Round	Normal	Special	60	100	15	Normal	—	—
TM49	Echoed Voice	Normal	Special	40	100	15	Normal	—	—
TM67	Retaliate	Normal	Physical	70	100	5	Normal	—	○
TM83	Work Up	Normal	Status	—	—	30	Self	—	—
TM87	Swagger	Normal	Status	—	90	15	Normal	—	—
TM90	Substitute	Normal	Status	—	—	10	Self	—	—

MOVES TAUGHT BY PEOPLE

Name	Type	Kind	Pow.	Acc.	PP	Range	Long	DA

MOVES TAUGHT BY MOVE TUTORS FOR SHARDS

Name	Type	Kind	Pow.	Acc.	PP	Range	Long	DA
Covet	Normal	Physical	60	100	40	Normal	—	○
Last Resort	Normal	Physical	140	100	5	Normal	—	○
Hyper Voice	Normal	Special	90	100	10	Many Others	—	—
Iron Tail	Steel	Physical	100	75	15	Normal	—	○
Snore	Normal	Special	40	100	15	Normal	—	—
Heal Bell	Normal	Status	—	—	5	Your Party	—	—
Helping Hand	Normal	Status	—	—	20	1 Ally	—	—
Sleep Talk	Normal	Status	—	—	10	Self	—	—

EGG MOVES

Name	Type	Kind	Pow.	Acc.	PP	Range	Long	DA
Charm	Normal	Status	—	100	20	Normal	—	—
Flail	Normal	Physical	—	100	15	Normal	—	○
Endure	Normal	Status	—	—	10	Self	—	—
Curse	Ghost	Status	—	—	10	Varies	—	—
Tickle	Normal	Status	—	100	20	Normal	—	—
Wish	Normal	Status	—	—	10	Self	—	—
Yawn	Normal	Status	—	—	10	Normal	—	—
Fake Tears	Dark	Status	—	100	20	Normal	—	—
Covet	Normal	Physical	60	100	40	Normal	—	○
Detect	Fighting	Status	—	—	5	Self	—	—
Natural Gift	Normal	Physical	—	100	15	Normal	—	—
Stored Power	Psychic	Special	20	100	10	Normal	—	—
Synchronoise	Psychic	Special	70	100	15	Adjacent	—	—

134 Vaporeon

Bubble Jet Pokémon

- HEIGHT: 3'03"
- WEIGHT: 63.9 lbs.
- GENDER: ♂ / ♀

Its cell composition is similar to water molecules. As a result, it can't be seen when it melts away into water.

Same form for ♂ / ♀

Pokémon AR Marker

TYPE Water

ABILITY
- Water Absorb

HIDDEN ABILITY
- Hydration

STATS

HP
Attack
Defense
Sp. Atk
Sp. Def
Speed

EGG GROUPS

Field

ITEMS SOMETIMES HELD

- None

EVOLUTION

Eevee

Vaporeon — Use Water Stone on Eevee

Jolteon — Use Thunderstone on Eevee

Flareon — Use Fire Stone on Eevee

Espeon ➡ p. 111 — Level up Eevee with high friendship in the morning, afternoon, or evening

Umbreon ➡ p. 112 — Level up Eevee with high friendship at night or late night

Leafeon ➡ p. 251 — Level up Eevee around the moss-covered rock in Pinwheel Forest

Glaceon ➡ p. 251 — Level up Eevee around the ice-covered rock in Twist Mountain

HOW TO OBTAIN

Pokémon Black Version 2	Use Water Stone on Eevee
Pokémon White Version 2	Use Water Stone on Eevee

HOW TO OBTAIN FROM OTHER GAMES

—

—

LEVEL-UP AND LEARNED MOVES

Lv.	Name	Type	Kind	Pow.	Acc.	PP	Range	Long	DA
1	Helping Hand	Normal	Status	—	—	20	1 Ally	—	—
1	Tackle	Normal	Physical	50	100	35	Normal	—	○
1	Tail Whip	Normal	Status	—	100	30	Many Others	—	—
5	Sand-Attack	Ground	Status	—	100	15	Normal	—	—
9	Water Gun	Water	Special	40	100	25	Normal	—	—
13	Quick Attack	Normal	Physical	40	100	30	Normal	—	○
17	Water Pulse	Water	Special	60	100	20	Normal	○	—
21	Aurora Beam	Ice	Special	65	100	20	Normal	—	—
25	Aqua Ring	Water	Status	—	—	20	Self	—	—
29	Acid Armor	Poison	Status	—	—	40	Self	—	—
33	Haze	Ice	Status	—	—	30	Both Sides	—	—
37	Muddy Water	Water	Special	95	85	10	Many Others	—	—
41	Last Resort	Normal	Physical	140	100	5	Normal	—	○
45	Hydro Pump	Water	Special	120	80	5	Normal	—	—

TM & HM MOVES

Lv.	Name	Type	Kind	Pow.	Acc.	PP	Range	Long	DA
TM05	Roar	Normal	Status	—	100	20	Normal	—	—
TM06	Toxic	Poison	Status	—	90	10	Normal	—	—
TM07	Hail	Ice	Status	—	—	10	Both Sides	—	—
TM10	Hidden Power	Normal	Special	—	100	15	Normal	—	—
TM11	Sunny Day	Fire	Status	—	—	5	Both Sides	—	—
TM13	Ice Beam	Ice	Special	95	100	10	Normal	—	—
TM14	Blizzard	Ice	Special	120	70	5	Many Others	—	—
TM15	Hyper Beam	Normal	Special	150	90	5	Normal	—	—
TM17	Protect	Normal	Status	—	—	10	Self	—	—
TM18	Rain Dance	Water	Status	—	—	5	Both Sides	—	—
TM21	Frustration	Normal	Physical	—	100	20	Normal	—	○
TM27	Return	Normal	Physical	—	100	20	Normal	—	○
TM28	Dig	Ground	Physical	80	100	10	Normal	—	○
TM30	Shadow Ball	Ghost	Special	80	100	15	Normal	—	—
TM32	Double Team	Normal	Status	—	—	15	Self	—	—
TM42	Facade	Normal	Physical	70	100	20	Normal	—	○
TM44	Rest	Psychic	Status	—	—	10	Self	—	—
TM45	Attract	Normal	Status	—	100	15	Normal	—	—
TM48	Round	Normal	Special	60	100	15	Normal	—	—
TM49	Echoed Voice	Normal	Special	40	100	15	Normal	—	—
TM55	Scald	Water	Special	80	100	15	Normal	—	—
TM67	Retaliate	Normal	Physical	70	100	5	Normal	—	○
TM68	Giga Impact	Normal	Physical	150	90	5	Normal	—	○
TM83	Work Up	Normal	Status	—	—	30	Self	—	—
TM87	Swagger	Normal	Status	—	90	15	Normal	—	—
TM90	Substitute	Normal	Status	—	—	10	Self	—	—
TM94	Rock Smash	Fighting	Physical	40	100	15	Normal	—	○
HM03	Surf	Water	Special	95	100	15	Adjacent	—	—
HM04	Strength	Normal	Physical	80	100	15	Normal	—	○
HM05	Waterfall	Water	Physical	80	100	15	Normal	—	○
HM06	Dive	Water	Physical	80	100	10	Normal	—	○

MOVES TAUGHT BY PEOPLE

Name	Type	Kind	Pow.	Acc.	PP	Range	Long	DA

MOVES TAUGHT BY MOVE TUTORS FOR SHARDS

Name	Type	Kind	Pow.	Acc.	PP	Range	Long	DA
Covet	Normal	Physical	60	100	40	Normal	—	○
Signal Beam	Bug	Special	75	100	15	Normal	—	—
Last Resort	Normal	Physical	140	100	5	Normal	—	○
Hyper Voice	Normal	Special	90	100	10	Many Others	—	—
Icy Wind	Ice	Special	55	95	15	Many Others	—	—
Iron Tail	Steel	Physical	100	75	15	Normal	—	○
Aqua Tail	Water	Physical	90	90	10	Normal	—	○
Snore	Normal	Special	40	100	15	Normal	—	—
Heal Bell	Normal	Status	—	—	5	Your Party	—	—
Helping Hand	Normal	Status	—	—	20	1 Ally	—	—
Sleep Talk	Normal	Status	—	—	10	Self	—	—

135 Jolteon

Lightning Pokémon

- HEIGHT: 2'07"
- WEIGHT: 54.0 lbs.
- GENDER: ♂ / ♀

By storing electricity in its body, it can shoot its bristlelike fur like a barrage of missiles.

Same form for ♂ / ♀

Pokémon AR Marker

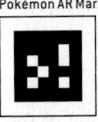

TYPE Electric

ABILITY
- Volt Absorb

HIDDEN ABILITY
- Quick Feet

STATS
HP
Attack
Defense
Sp. Atk
Sp. Def
Speed

EGG GROUPS
Field

ITEMS SOMETIMES HELD
- None

EVOLUTION
- Eevee
- Vaporeon: Use Water Stone on Eevee
- Jolteon: Use Thunderstone on Eevee
- Flareon: Use Fire Stone on Eevee
- Espeon ➡ p. 111: Level up Eevee with high friendship in the morning, afternoon, or evening
- Umbreon ➡ p. 112: Level up Eevee with high friendship at night or late night
- Leafeon ➡ p. 251: Level up Eevee around the moss-covered rock in Pinwheel Forest
- Glaceon ➡ p. 251: Level up Eevee around the ice-covered rock in Twist Mountain

HOW TO OBTAIN

Pokémon Black Version 2	Use Thunderstone on Eevee
Pokémon White Version 2	Use Thunderstone on Eevee

HOW TO OBTAIN FROM OTHER GAMES

—	
—	

LEVEL-UP AND LEARNED MOVES

Lv.	Name	Type	Kind	Pow.	Acc.	PP	Range	Long	DA
1	Helping Hand	Normal	Status	—	—	20	1 Ally	—	—
1	Tackle	Normal	Physical	50	100	35	Normal	—	○
1	Tail Whip	Normal	Status	—	100	30	Many Others	—	—
5	Sand-Attack	Ground	Status	—	100	15	Normal	—	—
9	ThunderShock	Electric	Special	40	100	30	Normal	—	—
13	Quick Attack	Normal	Physical	40	100	30	Normal	—	○
17	Double Kick	Fighting	Physical	30	100	30	Normal	—	○
21	Thunder Fang	Electric	Physical	65	95	15	Normal	—	○
25	Pin Missile	Bug	Physical	14	85	20	Normal	—	—
29	Agility	Psychic	Status	—	—	30	Self	—	—
33	Thunder Wave	Electric	Status	—	100	20	Normal	—	—
37	Discharge	Electric	Special	80	100	15	Adjacent	—	—
41	Last Resort	Normal	Physical	140	100	5	Normal	—	○
45	Thunder	Electric	Special	120	70	10	Normal	—	—

TM & HM MOVES

Lv.	Name	Type	Kind	Pow.	Acc.	PP	Range	Long	DA
TM05	Roar	Normal	Status	—	100	20	Normal	—	—
TM06	Toxic	Poison	Status	—	90	10	Normal	—	—
TM10	Hidden Power	Normal	Special	—	100	15	Normal	—	—
TM11	Sunny Day	Fire	Status	—	—	5	Both Sides	—	—
TM15	Hyper Beam	Normal	Special	150	90	5	Normal	—	—
TM16	Light Screen	Psychic	Status	—	—	30	Your Side	—	—
TM17	Protect	Normal	Status	—	—	10	Self	—	—
TM18	Rain Dance	Water	Status	—	—	5	Both Sides	—	—
TM21	Frustration	Normal	Physical	—	100	20	Normal	—	○
TM24	Thunderbolt	Electric	Special	95	100	15	Normal	—	—
TM25	Thunder	Electric	Special	120	70	10	Normal	—	—
TM27	Return	Normal	Physical	—	100	20	Normal	—	○
TM28	Dig	Ground	Physical	80	100	10	Normal	—	○
TM30	Shadow Ball	Ghost	Special	80	100	15	Normal	—	—
TM32	Double Team	Normal	Status	—	—	15	Self	—	—
TM42	Facade	Normal	Physical	70	100	20	Normal	—	○
TM44	Rest	Psychic	Status	—	—	10	Self	—	—
TM45	Attract	Normal	Status	—	100	15	Normal	—	—
TM48	Round	Normal	Special	60	100	15	Normal	—	—
TM49	Echoed Voice	Normal	Special	40	100	15	Normal	—	—
TM57	Charge Beam	Electric	Special	50	90	10	Normal	—	—
TM67	Retaliate	Normal	Physical	70	100	5	Normal	—	○
TM68	Giga Impact	Normal	Physical	150	90	5	Normal	—	○
TM70	Flash	Normal	Status	—	100	20	Normal	—	—
TM72	Volt Switch	Electric	Special	70	100	20	Normal	—	—
TM73	Thunder Wave	Electric	Status	—	100	20	Normal	—	—
TM83	Work Up	Normal	Status	—	—	30	Self	—	—
TM87	Swagger	Normal	Status	—	90	15	Normal	—	—
TM90	Substitute	Normal	Status	—	—	10	Self	—	—
TM93	Wild Charge	Electric	Physical	90	100	15	Normal	—	○
TM94	Rock Smash	Fighting	Physical	40	100	15	Normal	—	○
HM04	Strength	Normal	Physical	80	100	15	Normal	—	○

MOVES TAUGHT BY PEOPLE

Name	Type	Kind	Pow.	Acc.	PP	Range	Long	DA

MOVES TAUGHT BY MOVE TUTORS FOR SHARDS

Name	Type	Kind	Pow.	Acc.	PP	Range	Long	DA
Covet	Normal	Physical	60	100	40	Normal	—	○
Signal Beam	Bug	Special	75	100	15	Normal	—	—
Last Resort	Normal	Physical	140	100	5	Normal	—	○
Magnet Rise	Electric	Status	—	—	10	Self	—	—
Hyper Voice	Normal	Special	90	100	10	Many Others	—	—
Iron Tail	Steel	Physical	100	75	15	Normal	—	○
Snore	Normal	Special	40	100	15	Normal	—	—
Heal Bell	Normal	Status	—	—	5	Your Party	—	—
Helping Hand	Normal	Status	—	—	20	1 Ally	—	—
Sleep Talk	Normal	Status	—	—	10	Self	—	—

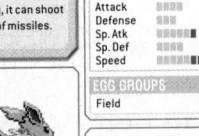

136 Flareon

Flame Pokémon

- HEIGHT: 2'11"
- WEIGHT: 55.1 lbs.
- GENDER: ♂ / ♀

Inhaled air is carried to its flame sac, heated, and exhaled as fire that reaches over 3,000 degrees F.

Same form for ♂ / ♀

Pokémon AR Marker

TYPE Fire

ABILITY
- Flash Fire

HIDDEN ABILITY
- Guts

STATS
HP
Attack
Defense
Sp. Atk
Sp. Def
Speed

EGG GROUPS
Field

ITEMS SOMETIMES HELD
- None

EVOLUTION
- Eevee
- Vaporeon: Use Water Stone on Eevee
- Jolteon: Use Thunderstone on Eevee
- Flareon: Use Fire Stone on Eevee
- Espeon ➡ p. 111: Level up Eevee with high friendship in the morning, afternoon, or evening
- Umbreon ➡ p. 112: Level up Eevee with high friendship at night or late night
- Leafeon ➡ p. 251: Level up Eevee around the moss-covered rock in Pinwheel Forest
- Glaceon ➡ p. 251: Level up Eevee around the ice-covered rock in Twist Mountain

HOW TO OBTAIN

Pokémon Black Version 2	Use Fire Stone on Eevee
Pokémon White Version 2	Use Fire Stone on Eevee

HOW TO OBTAIN FROM OTHER GAMES

—	
—	

LEVEL-UP AND LEARNED MOVES

Lv.	Name	Type	Kind	Pow.	Acc.	PP	Range	Long	DA
1	Helping Hand	Normal	Status	—	—	20	1 Ally	—	—
1	Tackle	Normal	Physical	50	100	35	Normal	—	○
1	Tail Whip	Normal	Status	—	100	30	Many Others	—	—
5	Sand-Attack	Ground	Status	—	100	15	Normal	—	—
9	Ember	Fire	Special	40	100	25	Normal	—	—
13	Quick Attack	Normal	Physical	40	100	30	Normal	—	○
17	Bite	Dark	Physical	60	100	25	Normal	—	○
21	Fire Fang	Fire	Physical	65	95	15	Normal	—	○
25	Fire Spin	Fire	Special	35	85	15	Normal	—	—
29	Scary Face	Normal	Status	—	100	10	Normal	—	—
33	Smog	Poison	Special	20	70	20	Normal	—	—
37	Lava Plume	Fire	Special	80	100	15	Adjacent	—	—
41	Last Resort	Normal	Physical	140	100	5	Normal	—	○
45	Fire Blast	Fire	Special	120	85	5	Normal	—	—

TM & HM MOVES

Lv.	Name	Type	Kind	Pow.	Acc.	PP	Range	Long	DA
TM05	Roar	Normal	Status	—	100	20	Normal	—	—
TM06	Toxic	Poison	Status	—	90	10	Normal	—	—
TM10	Hidden Power	Normal	Special	—	100	15	Normal	—	—
TM11	Sunny Day	Fire	Status	—	—	5	Both Sides	—	—
TM15	Hyper Beam	Normal	Special	150	90	5	Normal	—	—
TM17	Protect	Normal	Status	—	—	10	Self	—	—
TM18	Rain Dance	Water	Status	—	—	5	Both Sides	—	—
TM21	Frustration	Normal	Physical	—	100	20	Normal	—	○
TM27	Return	Normal	Physical	—	100	20	Normal	—	○
TM28	Dig	Ground	Physical	80	100	10	Normal	—	○
TM30	Shadow Ball	Ghost	Special	80	100	15	Normal	—	—
TM32	Double Team	Normal	Status	—	—	15	Self	—	—
TM35	Flamethrower	Fire	Special	95	100	15	Normal	—	—
TM38	Fire Blast	Fire	Special	120	85	5	Normal	—	—
TM42	Facade	Normal	Physical	70	100	20	Normal	—	○
TM43	Flame Charge	Fire	Physical	50	100	20	Normal	—	○
TM44	Rest	Psychic	Status	—	—	10	Self	—	—
TM45	Attract	Normal	Status	—	100	15	Normal	—	—
TM48	Round	Normal	Special	60	100	15	Normal	—	—
TM49	Echoed Voice	Normal	Special	40	100	15	Normal	—	—
TM50	Overheat	Fire	Special	140	90	5	Normal	—	—
TM59	Incinerate	Fire	Special	30	100	15	Many Others	—	—
TM61	Will-O-Wisp	Fire	Status	—	75	15	Normal	—	—
TM67	Retaliate	Normal	Physical	70	100	5	Normal	—	○
TM68	Giga Impact	Normal	Physical	150	90	5	Normal	—	○
TM83	Work Up	Normal	Status	—	—	30	Self	—	—
TM87	Swagger	Normal	Status	—	90	15	Normal	—	—
TM90	Substitute	Normal	Status	—	—	10	Self	—	—
TM94	Rock Smash	Fighting	Physical	40	100	15	Normal	—	○
HM04	Strength	Normal	Physical	80	100	15	Normal	—	○

MOVES TAUGHT BY PEOPLE

Name	Type	Kind	Pow.	Acc.	PP	Range	Long	DA

MOVES TAUGHT BY MOVE TUTORS FOR SHARDS

Name	Type	Kind	Pow.	Acc.	PP	Range	Long	DA
Covet	Normal	Physical	60	100	40	Normal	—	○
Last Resort	Normal	Physical	140	100	5	Normal	—	○
Hyper Voice	Normal	Special	90	100	10	Many Others	—	—
Iron Tail	Steel	Physical	100	75	15	Normal	—	○
Superpower	Fighting	Physical	120	100	5	Normal	—	○
Snore	Normal	Special	40	100	15	Normal	—	—
Heal Bell	Normal	Status	—	—	5	Your Party	—	—
Heat Wave	Fire	Special	100	90	10	Many Others	—	—
Helping Hand	Normal	Status	—	—	20	1 Ally	—	—
Sleep Talk	Normal	Status	—	—	10	Self	—	—

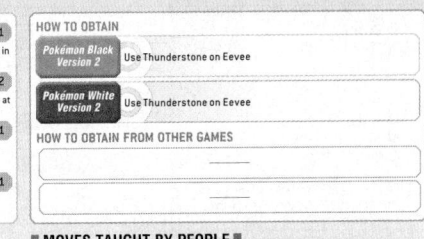

137 Porygon

Virtual Pokémon

- HEIGHT: 2'07"
- WEIGHT: 80.5 lbs.
- GENDER: Unknown

A man-made Pokémon created using advanced scientific means. It can move freely in cyberspace.

TYPE Normal

ABILITIES
- Trace
- Download

HIDDEN ABILITY
- Analytic

STATS
HP
Attack
Defense
Sp. Atk
Sp. Def
Speed

EGG GROUPS
Mineral

ITEMS SOMETIMES HELD
- None

Gender unknown

Pokémon AR Marker

EVOLUTION

Porygon
Have it hold Up-Grade and Link Trade it
Porygon2
Have it hold Dubious Disc and Link Trade it
Porygon-Z

➡ p. 130
➡ p. 253

HOW TO OBTAIN

Pokémon Black Version 2	Link Trade or Poké Transfer
Pokémon White Version 2	Link Trade or Poké Transfer

HOW TO OBTAIN FROM OTHER GAMES

Pokémon Platinum Version	Receive from a man in a house in Veilstone City
—	

LEVEL-UP AND LEARNED MOVES

Lv.	Name	Type	Kind	Pow.	Acc.	PP	Range	Long	DA
1	Conversion 2	Normal	Status	—	—	30	Normal	—	—
1	Tackle	Normal	Physical	50	100	35	Normal	—	○
1	Conversion	Normal	Status	—	—	30	Self	—	—
1	Sharpen	Normal	Status	—	—	30	Self	—	—
7	Psybeam	Psychic	Special	65	100	20	Normal	—	—
12	Agility	Psychic	Status	—	—	30	Self	—	—
18	Recover	Normal	Status	—	—	10	Self	—	—
23	Magnet Rise	Electric	Status	—	—	10	Self	—	—
29	Signal Beam	Bug	Special	75	100	15	Normal	—	—
34	Recycle	Normal	Status	—	—	10	Self	—	—
40	Discharge	Electric	Special	80	100	15	Adjacent	—	—
45	Lock—On	Normal	Status	—	—	5	Normal	—	—
51	Tri Attack	Normal	Special	80	100	10	Normal	—	—
56	Magic Coat	Psychic	Status	—	—	15	Self	—	—
62	Zap Cannon	Electric	Special	120	50	5	Normal	—	—

TM & HM MOVES

Lv.	Name	Type	Kind	Pow.	Acc.	PP	Range	Long	DA
TM03	Psyshock	Psychic	Special	80	100	10	Normal	—	—
TM06	Toxic	Poison	Status	—	90	10	Normal	—	—
TM10	Hidden Power	Normal	Special	—	100	15	Normal	—	—
TM11	Sunny Day	Fire	Status	—	—	5	Both Sides	—	—
TM13	Ice Beam	Ice	Special	95	100	10	Normal	—	—
TM14	Blizzard	Ice	Special	120	70	5	Many Others	—	—
TM15	Hyper Beam	Normal	Special	150	90	5	Normal	—	—
TM17	Protect	Normal	Status	—	—	10	Self	—	—
TM18	Rain Dance	Water	Status	—	—	5	Both Sides	—	—
TM21	Frustration	Normal	Physical	—	100	20	Normal	—	○
TM22	SolarBeam	Grass	Special	120	100	10	Normal	—	—
TM24	Thunderbolt	Electric	Special	95	100	15	Normal	—	—
TM25	Thunder	Electric	Special	120	70	10	Normal	—	—
TM27	Return	Normal	Physical	—	100	20	Normal	—	○
TM29	Psychic	Psychic	Special	90	100	10	Normal	—	—
TM30	Shadow Ball	Ghost	Special	80	100	15	Normal	—	—
TM32	Double Team	Normal	Status	—	—	15	Self	—	—
TM40	Aerial Ace	Flying	Physical	60	—	20	Normal	○	○
TM42	Facade	Normal	Physical	70	100	20	Normal	—	○
TM44	Rest	Psychic	Status	—	—	10	Self	—	—
TM46	Thief	Dark	Physical	40	100	10	Normal	—	○
TM48	Round	Normal	Special	60	100	15	Normal	—	—
TM57	Charge Beam	Electric	Special	50	90	10	Normal	—	—
TM68	Giga Impact	Normal	Physical	150	90	5	Normal	—	○
TM70	Flash	Normal	Status	—	100	20	Normal	—	—
TM73	Thunder Wave	Electric	Status	—	100	20	Normal	—	—
TM77	Psych Up	Normal	Status	—	—	10	Normal	—	—
TM85	Dream Eater	Psychic	Special	100	100	15	Normal	—	—
TM87	Swagger	Normal	Status	—	90	15	Normal	—	—
TM90	Substitute	Normal	Status	—	—	10	Self	—	—
TM92	Trick Room	Psychic	Status	—	—	5	Both Sides	—	—

MOVES TAUGHT BY PEOPLE

Name	Type	Kind	Pow.	Acc.	PP	Range	Long	DA

MOVES TAUGHT BY MOVE TUTORS FOR SHARDS

Name	Type	Kind	Pow.	Acc.	PP	Range	Long	DA
Signal Beam	Bug	Special	75	100	15	Normal	—	—
Last Resort	Normal	Physical	140	100	5	Normal	—	○
Magnet Rise	Electric	Status	—	—	10	Self	—	—
Magic Coat	Psychic	Status	—	—	15	Self	—	—
Electroweb	Electric	Special	55	95	15	Many Others	—	—
Icy Wind	Ice	Special	55	95	15	Many Others	—	—
Iron Tail	Steel	Physical	100	75	15	Normal	—	○
Zen Headbutt	Psychic	Physical	80	90	15	Normal	—	○
Foul Play	Dark	Physical	95	100	15	Normal	—	○
Gravity	Psychic	Status	—	—	5	Both Sides	—	—
Snore	Normal	Special	40	100	15	Normal	—	—
Pain Split	Normal	Status	—	—	20	Normal	—	—
Wonder Room	Psychic	Status	—	—	10	Both Sides	—	—
Recycle	Normal	Status	—	—	10	Self	—	—
Trick	Psychic	Status	—	100	10	Normal	—	—
Sleep Talk	Normal	Status	—	—	10	Self	—	—

EGG MOVES

Name	Type	Kind	Pow.	Acc.	PP	Range	Long	DA

138 Omanyte

Spiral Pokémon

- HEIGHT: 1'04"
- WEIGHT: 16.5 lbs.
- GENDER: ♂ / ♀

A Pokémon that was resurrected from a fossil using modern science. It swam in ancient seas.

TYPE Rock Water

ABILITIES
- Swift Swim
- Shell Armor

HIDDEN ABILITY
- Weak Armor

STATS
HP
Attack
Defense
Sp. Atk
Sp. Def
Speed

EGG GROUPS
Water 1 / Water 3

ITEMS SOMETIMES HELD
- None

Same form for ♂ / ♀

Pokémon AR Marker

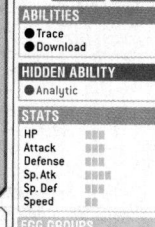

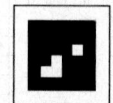

EVOLUTION

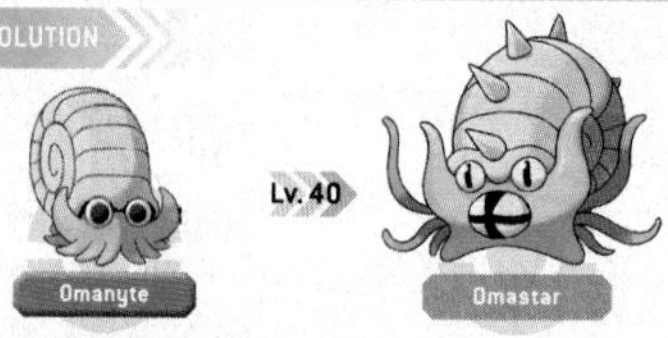
Omanyte
Lv. 40
Omastar

HOW TO OBTAIN

Pokémon Black Version 2	Get the Helix Fossil in Twist Mountain and have it restored at the Nacrene Museum
Pokémon White Version 2	Get the Helix Fossil in Twist Mountain and have it restored at the Nacrene Museum

HOW TO OBTAIN FROM OTHER GAMES

—	
—	

LEVEL-UP AND LEARNED MOVES

Lv.	Name	Type	Kind	Pow.	Acc.	PP	Range	Long	DA
1	Constrict	Normal	Physical	10	100	35	Normal	—	○
1	Withdraw	Water	Status	—	—	40	Self	—	—
7	Bite	Dark	Physical	60	100	25	Normal	—	○
10	Water Gun	Water	Special	40	100	25	Normal	—	—
16	Rollout	Rock	Physical	30	90	20	Normal	—	○
19	Leer	Normal	Status	—	100	30	Many Others	—	—
25	Mud Shot	Ground	Special	55	95	15	Normal	—	—
28	Brine	Water	Special	65	100	10	Normal	—	—
34	Protect	Normal	Status	—	—	10	Self	—	—
37	AncientPower	Rock	Special	60	100	5	Normal	—	—
43	Tickle	Normal	Status	—	100	20	Normal	—	—
46	Rock Blast	Rock	Physical	25	90	10	Normal	—	—
52	Shell Smash	Normal	Status	—	—	15	Self	—	—
55	Hydro Pump	Water	Special	120	80	5	Normal	—	—

TM & HM MOVES

Lv.	Name	Type	Kind	Pow.	Acc.	PP	Range	Long	DA
TM06	Toxic	Poison	Status	—	90	10	Normal	—	—
TM07	Hail	Ice	Status	—	—	10	Both Sides	—	—
TM10	Hidden Power	Normal	Special	—	100	15	Normal	—	—
TM13	Ice Beam	Ice	Special	95	100	10	Normal	—	—
TM14	Blizzard	Ice	Special	120	70	5	Many Others	—	—
TM17	Protect	Normal	Status	—	—	10	Self	—	—
TM18	Rain Dance	Water	Status	—	—	5	Both Sides	—	—
TM21	Frustration	Normal	Physical	—	100	20	Normal	—	○
TM23	Smack Down	Rock	Physical	50	100	15	Normal	—	—
TM27	Return	Normal	Physical	—	100	20	Normal	—	○
TM32	Double Team	Normal	Status	—	—	15	Self	—	—
TM37	Sandstorm	Rock	Status	—	—	10	Both Sides	—	—
TM39	Rock Tomb	Rock	Physical	50	80	10	Normal	—	—
TM42	Facade	Normal	Physical	70	100	20	Normal	—	○
TM44	Rest	Psychic	Status	—	—	10	Self	—	—
TM45	Attract	Normal	Status	—	100	15	Normal	—	—
TM46	Thief	Dark	Physical	40	100	10	Normal	—	○
TM48	Round	Normal	Special	60	100	15	Normal	—	—
TM55	Scald	Water	Special	80	100	15	Normal	—	—
TM69	Rock Polish	Rock	Status	—	—	20	Self	—	—
TM74	Gyro Ball	Steel	Physical	—	100	5	Normal	—	○
TM80	Rock Slide	Rock	Physical	75	90	10	Many Others	—	—
TM87	Swagger	Normal	Status	—	90	15	Normal	—	—
TM90	Substitute	Normal	Status	—	—	10	Self	—	—
TM94	Rock Smash	Fighting	Physical	40	100	15	Normal	—	○
HM03	Surf	Water	Special	95	100	15	Adjacent	—	—
HM05	Waterfall	Water	Physical	80	100	15	Normal	—	○
HM06	Dive	Water	Physical	80	100	10	Normal	—	○

MOVES TAUGHT BY PEOPLE

Name	Type	Kind	Pow.	Acc.	PP	Range	Long	DA

MOVES TAUGHT BY MOVE TUTORS FOR SHARDS

Name	Type	Kind	Pow.	Acc.	PP	Range	Long	DA
Iron Defense	Steel	Status	—	—	15	Self	—	—
Icy Wind	Ice	Special	55	95	15	Many Others	—	—
Earth Power	Ground	Special	90	100	10	Normal	—	—
Bind	Normal	Physical	15	85	20	Normal	—	○
Snore	Normal	Special	40	100	15	Normal	—	—
Knock Off	Dark	Physical	20	100	20	Normal	—	○
Stealth Rock	Rock	Status	—	—	20	Other Side	—	—
Sleep Talk	Normal	Status	—	—	10	Self	—	—

EGG MOVES

Name	Type	Kind	Pow.	Acc.	PP	Range	Long	DA
BubbleBeam	Water	Special	65	100	20	Normal	—	—
Aurora Beam	Ice	Special	65	100	20	Normal	—	—
Slam	Normal	Physical	80	75	20	Normal	—	○
Supersonic	Normal	Status	—	55	20	Normal	—	—
Haze	Ice	Status	—	—	30	Both Sides	—	—
Spikes	Ground	Status	—	—	20	Other Side	—	—
Knock Off	Dark	Physical	20	100	20	Normal	—	○
Wring Out	Normal	Special	—	100	5	Normal	—	○
Toxic Spikes	Poison	Status	—	—	20	Other Side	—	—
Muddy Water	Water	Special	95	85	10	Many Others	—	—
Bide	Normal	Physical	—	—	10	Self	—	○
Water Pulse	Water	Special	60	100	20	Normal	○	—
Whirlpool	Water	Special	35	85	15	Normal	—	—

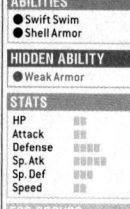

139 Omastar

Spiral Pokémon

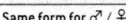

TYPE Rock / Water

ABILITIES
- Swift Swim
- Shell Armor

HIDDEN ABILITY
- Weak Armor

- HEIGHT: 3'03"
- WEIGHT: 77.2 lbs.
- GENDER: ♂ / ♀

It is thought that this Pokémon became extinct because its spiral shell grew too large.

STATS
- HP
- Attack
- Defense
- Sp. Atk
- Sp. Def
- Speed

EGG GROUPS
Water ① / Water ③

ITEMS SOMETIMES HELD
- None

Same form for ♂ / ♀

Pokémon AR Marker

EVOLUTION

 Omanyte — Lv. 40 → 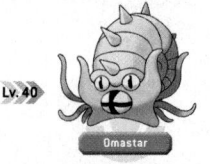 Omastar

HOW TO OBTAIN

Pokémon Black Version 2	Level up Omanyte to Lv. 40
Pokémon White Version 2	Level up Omanyte to Lv. 40

HOW TO OBTAIN FROM OTHER GAMES

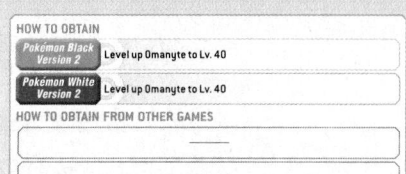

LEVEL-UP AND LEARNED MOVES

Lv.	Name	Type	Kind	Pow.	Acc.	PP	Range	Long	DA
1	Constrict	Normal	Physical	10	100	35	Normal	—	○
1	Withdraw	Water	Status	—	—	40	Self	—	—
1	Bite	Dark	Physical	60	100	25	Normal	—	○
7	Bite	Dark	Physical	60	100	25	Normal	—	○
10	Water Gun	Water	Special	40	100	25	Normal	—	—
16	Rollout	Rock	Physical	30	90	20	Normal	—	○
19	Leer	Normal	Status	—	100	30	Many Others	—	—
25	Mud Shot	Ground	Special	55	95	15	Normal	—	—
28	Brine	Water	Special	65	100	10	Normal	—	—
34	Protect	Normal	Status	—	—	10	Self	—	—
37	AncientPower	Rock	Special	60	100	5	Normal	—	—
40	Spike Cannon	Normal	Physical	20	100	15	Normal	—	—
48	Tickle	Normal	Status	—	100	20	Normal	—	—
56	Rock Blast	Rock	Physical	25	90	10	Normal	—	○
67	Shell Smash	Normal	Status	—	—	15	Self	—	—
75	Hydro Pump	Water	Special	120	80	5	Normal	—	—

TM & HM MOVES

Lv.	Name	Type	Kind	Pow.	Acc.	PP	Range	Long	DA
TM06	Toxic	Poison	Status	—	90	10	Normal	—	—
TM07	Hail	Ice	Status	—	—	10	Both Sides	—	—
TM10	Hidden Power	Normal	Special	—	100	15	Normal	—	—
TM13	Ice Beam	Ice	Special	95	100	10	Normal	—	—
TM14	Blizzard	Ice	Special	120	70	5	Many Others	—	—
TM15	Hyper Beam	Normal	Special	150	90	5	Normal	—	—
TM17	Protect	Normal	Status	—	—	10	Self	—	—
TM18	Rain Dance	Water	Status	—	—	5	Both Sides	—	—
TM21	Frustration	Normal	Physical	—	100	20	Normal	—	○
TM23	Smack Down	Rock	Physical	50	100	15	Normal	—	○
TM27	Return	Normal	Physical	—	100	20	Normal	—	○
TM32	Double Team	Normal	Status	—	—	15	Self	—	—
TM37	Sandstorm	Rock	Status	—	—	10	Both Sides	—	—
TM39	Rock Tomb	Rock	Physical	50	80	10	Normal	—	○
TM42	Facade	Normal	Physical	70	100	20	Normal	—	○
TM44	Rest	Psychic	Status	—	—	10	Self	—	—
TM45	Attract	Normal	Status	—	100	15	Normal	—	—
TM46	Thief	Dark	Physical	40	100	10	Normal	—	○
TM48	Round	Normal	Special	60	100	15	Normal	—	—
TM55	Scald	Water	Special	80	100	15	Normal	—	—
TM68	Giga Impact	Normal	Physical	150	90	5	Normal	—	○
TM69	Rock Polish	Rock	Status	—	—	20	Self	—	—
TM71	Stone Edge	Rock	Physical	100	80	5	Normal	—	○
TM74	Gyro Ball	Steel	Physical	—	100	5	Normal	—	○
TM80	Rock Slide	Rock	Physical	75	90	10	Many Others	—	○
TM87	Swagger	Normal	Status	—	90	15	Normal	—	—
TM90	Substitute	Normal	Status	—	—	10	Self	—	—
TM94	Rock Smash	Fighting	Physical	40	100	15	Normal	—	○
HM03	Surf	Water	Special	95	100	15	Adjacent	—	—
HM05	Waterfall	Water	Physical	80	100	15	Normal	—	○
HM06	Dive	Water	Physical	80	100	10	Normal	—	○

MOVES TAUGHT BY PEOPLE

Name	Type	Kind	Pow.	Acc.	PP	Range	Long	DA

MOVES TAUGHT BY MOVE TUTORS FOR SHARDS

Name	Type	Kind	Pow.	Acc.	PP	Range	Long	DA
Iron Defense	Steel	Status	—	—	15	Self	—	—
Icy Wind	Ice	Special	55	95	15	Many Others	—	—
Earth Power	Ground	Special	90	100	10	Normal	—	—
Bind	Normal	Physical	15	85	20	Normal	—	○
Snore	Normal	Special	40	100	15	Normal	—	○
Knock Off	Dark	Physical	20	100	20	Normal	—	○
Stealth Rock	Rock	Status	—	—	20	Other Side	—	—
Sleep Talk	Normal	Status	—	—	10	Self	—	—

---

140 Kabuto

Shellfish Pokémon

TYPE Rock / Water

ABILITIES
- Swift Swim
- Battle Armor

HIDDEN ABILITY
- Weak Armor

- HEIGHT: 1'08"
- WEIGHT: 25.4 lbs.
- GENDER: ♂ / ♀

It is thought to have inhabited beaches 300 million years ago. It is protected by a stiff shell.

STATS
- HP
- Attack
- Defense
- Sp. Atk
- Sp. Def
- Speed

EGG GROUPS
Water ① / Water ③

ITEMS SOMETIMES HELD
- None

Same form for ♂ / ♀

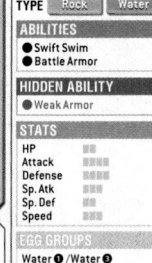

Pokémon AR Marker

EVOLUTION

 Kabuto — Lv. 40 →  Kabutops

HOW TO OBTAIN

Pokémon Black Version 2	Get the Dome Fossil in Twist Mountain and have it restored at the Nacrene Museum
Pokémon White Version 2	Get the Dome Fossil in Twist Mountain and have it restored at the Nacrene Museum

HOW TO OBTAIN FROM OTHER GAMES

LEVEL-UP AND LEARNED MOVES

Lv.	Name	Type	Kind	Pow.	Acc.	PP	Range	Long	DA
1	Scratch	Normal	Physical	40	100	35	Normal	—	○
1	Harden	Normal	Status	—	—	30	Self	—	—
6	Absorb	Grass	Special	20	100	25	Normal	—	—
11	Leer	Normal	Status	—	100	30	Many Others	—	—
16	Mud Shot	Ground	Special	55	95	15	Normal	—	—
21	Sand-Attack	Ground	Status	—	100	15	Normal	—	—
26	Endure	Normal	Status	—	—	10	Self	—	—
31	Aqua Jet	Water	Physical	40	100	20	Normal	—	○
36	Mega Drain	Grass	Special	40	100	15	Normal	—	—
41	Metal Sound	Steel	Status	—	85	40	Normal	—	—
46	AncientPower	Rock	Special	60	100	5	Normal	—	—
51	Wring Out	Normal	Special	—	100	5	Normal	—	○

TM & HM MOVES

Lv.	Name	Type	Kind	Pow.	Acc.	PP	Range	Long	DA
TM01	Hone Claws	Dark	Status	—	—	15	Self	—	—
TM06	Toxic	Poison	Status	—	90	10	Normal	—	—
TM07	Hail	Ice	Status	—	—	10	Both Sides	—	—
TM10	Hidden Power	Normal	Special	—	100	15	Normal	—	—
TM13	Ice Beam	Ice	Special	95	100	10	Normal	—	—
TM14	Blizzard	Ice	Special	120	70	5	Many Others	—	—
TM17	Protect	Normal	Status	—	—	10	Self	—	—
TM18	Rain Dance	Water	Status	—	—	5	Both Sides	—	—
TM21	Frustration	Normal	Physical	—	100	20	Normal	—	○
TM23	Smack Down	Rock	Physical	50	100	15	Normal	—	○
TM27	Return	Normal	Physical	—	100	20	Normal	—	○
TM28	Dig	Ground	Physical	80	100	10	Normal	—	○
TM32	Double Team	Normal	Status	—	—	15	Self	—	—
TM37	Sandstorm	Rock	Status	—	—	10	Both Sides	—	—
TM39	Rock Tomb	Rock	Physical	50	80	10	Normal	—	○
TM42	Facade	Normal	Physical	70	100	20	Normal	—	○
TM44	Rest	Psychic	Status	—	—	10	Self	—	—
TM45	Attract	Normal	Status	—	100	15	Normal	—	—
TM46	Thief	Dark	Physical	40	100	10	Normal	—	○
TM48	Round	Normal	Special	60	100	15	Normal	—	—
TM55	Scald	Water	Special	80	100	15	Normal	—	—
TM69	Rock Polish	Rock	Status	—	—	20	Self	—	—
TM80	Rock Slide	Rock	Physical	75	90	10	Many Others	—	○
TM87	Swagger	Normal	Status	—	90	15	Normal	—	—
TM90	Substitute	Normal	Status	—	—	10	Self	—	—
TM94	Rock Smash	Fighting	Physical	40	100	15	Normal	—	○
HM03	Surf	Water	Special	95	100	15	Adjacent	—	—
HM05	Waterfall	Water	Physical	80	100	15	Normal	—	○

MOVES TAUGHT BY PEOPLE

Name	Type	Kind	Pow.	Acc.	PP	Range	Long	DA

MOVES TAUGHT BY MOVE TUTORS FOR SHARDS

Name	Type	Kind	Pow.	Acc.	PP	Range	Long	DA
Iron Defense	Steel	Status	—	—	15	Self	—	—
Icy Wind	Ice	Special	55	95	15	Many Others	—	—
Earth Power	Ground	Special	90	100	10	Normal	—	—
Snore	Normal	Special	40	100	15	Normal	—	○
Knock Off	Dark	Physical	20	100	20	Normal	—	○
Giga Drain	Grass	Special	75	100	10	Normal	—	—
Stealth Rock	Rock	Status	—	—	20	Other Side	—	—
Sleep Talk	Normal	Status	—	—	10	Self	—	—

EGG MOVES

Name	Type	Kind	Pow.	Acc.	PP	Range	Long	DA
BubbleBeam	Water	Special	65	100	20	Normal	—	—
Aurora Beam	Ice	Special	65	100	20	Normal	—	○
Rapid Spin	Normal	Physical	20	100	40	Normal	—	○
Flail	Normal	Physical	—	100	15	Normal	—	○
Knock Off	Dark	Physical	20	100	20	Normal	—	○
Confuse Ray	Ghost	Status	—	100	10	Normal	—	—
Mud Shot	Ground	Special	55	95	15	Normal	—	—
Icy Wind	Ice	Special	55	95	15	Many Others	—	—
Screech	Normal	Status	—	85	40	Normal	—	—
Giga Drain	Grass	Special	75	100	10	Normal	—	—
Foresight	Normal	Status	—	—	40	Normal	—	—

Shellfish Pokémon

141 Kabutops

- HEIGHT: 4'03"
- WEIGHT: 89.3 lbs.
- GENDER: ♂ / ♀

It is thought that this Pokémon came onto land because its prey adapted to life on land.

TYPE: Rock / Water

ABILITIES
- Swift Swim
- Battle Armor

HIDDEN ABILITY
- Weak Armor

STATS
HP
Attack
Defense
Sp. Atk
Sp. Def
Speed

EGG GROUPS
Water 1 / Water 3

Same form for ♂ / ♀

ITEMS SOMETIMES HELD
- None

EVOLUTION

HOW TO OBTAIN

Pokémon Black Version 2	Level up Kabuto to Lv. 40
Pokémon White Version 2	Level up Kabuto to Lv. 40

HOW TO OBTAIN FROM OTHER GAMES

—

—

Pokémon AR Marker

LEVEL-UP AND LEARNED MOVES

Lv.	Name	Type	Kind	Pow.	Acc.	PP	Range	Long	DA
1	Feint	Normal	Physical	30	100	10	Normal	—	—
1	Scratch	Normal	Physical	40	100	35	Normal	—	○
1	Harden	Normal	Status	—	—	30	Self	—	—
1	Absorb	Grass	Special	20	100	25	Normal	—	—
1	Leer	Normal	Status	—	100	30	Many Others	—	—
6	Absorb	Grass	Special	20	100	25	Normal	—	—
11	Leer	Normal	Status	—	100	30	Many Others	—	—
16	Mud Shot	Ground	Special	55	95	15	Normal	—	—
21	Sand-Attack	Ground	Status	—	100	15	Normal	—	—
26	Endure	Normal	Status	—	—	10	Self	—	—
31	Aqua Jet	Water	Physical	40	100	20	Normal	—	○
36	Mega Drain	Grass	Special	40	100	15	Normal	—	—
40	Slash	Normal	Physical	70	100	20	Normal	—	○
45	Metal Sound	Steel	Status	—	85	40	Normal	—	—
54	AncientPower	Rock	Special	60	100	5	Normal	—	—
63	Wring Out	Normal	Special	—	100	5	Normal	—	○
72	Night Slash	Dark	Physical	70	100	15	Normal	—	○

TM & HM MOVES

Lv.	Name	Type	Kind	Pow.	Acc.	PP	Range	Long	DA
TM01	Hone Claws	Dark	Status	—	—	15	Self	—	—
TM06	Toxic	Poison	Status	—	90	10	Normal	—	—
TM07	Hail	Ice	Status	—	—	10	Both Sides	—	—
TM10	Hidden Power	Normal	Special	—	100	15	Normal	—	—
TM13	Ice Beam	Ice	Special	95	100	10	Normal	—	—
TM14	Blizzard	Ice	Special	120	70	5	Many Others	—	—
TM15	Hyper Beam	Normal	Special	150	90	5	Normal	—	—
TM17	Protect	Normal	Status	—	—	10	Self	—	—
TM18	Rain Dance	Water	Status	—	—	5	Both Sides	—	—
TM21	Frustration	Normal	Physical	—	100	20	Normal	—	○
TM23	Smack Down	Rock	Physical	50	100	15	Normal	—	—
TM27	Return	Normal	Physical	—	100	20	Normal	—	○
TM28	Dig	Ground	Physical	80	100	10	Normal	—	○
TM31	Brick Break	Fighting	Physical	75	100	15	Normal	—	○
TM32	Double Team	Normal	Status	—	—	15	Self	—	—
TM37	Sandstorm	Rock	Status	—	—	10	Both Sides	—	—
TM39	Rock Tomb	Rock	Physical	50	80	10	Normal	—	—
TM40	Aerial Ace	Flying	Physical	60	—	20	Normal	○	○
TM42	Facade	Normal	Physical	70	100	20	Normal	—	○
TM44	Rest	Psychic	Status	—	—	10	Self	—	—
TM45	Attract	Normal	Status	—	100	15	Normal	—	—
TM46	Thief	Dark	Physical	40	100	10	Normal	—	○
TM48	Round	Normal	Special	60	100	15	Normal	—	—
TM55	Scald	Water	Special	80	100	15	Normal	—	—
TM68	Giga Impact	Normal	Physical	150	90	5	Normal	—	○
TM69	Rock Polish	Rock	Status	—	—	20	Self	—	—
TM71	Stone Edge	Rock	Physical	100	80	5	Normal	—	—
TM75	Swords Dance	Normal	Status	—	—	30	Self	—	—
TM80	Rock Slide	Rock	Physical	75	90	10	Many Others	—	—
TM81	X-Scissor	Bug	Physical	80	100	15	Normal	—	○
TM87	Swagger	Normal	Status	—	90	15	Normal	—	—
TM90	Substitute	Normal	Status	—	—	10	Self	—	—
TM94	Rock Smash	Fighting	Physical	40	100	15	Normal	—	○
HM01	Cut	Normal	Physical	50	95	30	Normal	—	○
HM03	Surf	Water	Special	95	100	15	Adjacent	—	—
HM05	Waterfall	Water	Physical	80	100	15	Normal	—	○
HM06	Dive	Water	Physical	80	100	10	Normal	—	○

MOVES TAUGHT BY PEOPLE

Name	Type	Kind	Pow.	Acc.	PP	Range	Long	DA

MOVES TAUGHT BY MOVE TUTORS FOR SHARDS

Name	Type	Kind	Pow.	Acc.	PP	Range	Long	DA
Low Kick	Fighting	Physical	—	100	20	Normal	—	○
Iron Defense	Steel	Status	—	—	15	Self	—	—
Icy Wind	Ice	Special	55	95	15	Many Others	—	—
Aqua Tail	Water	Physical	90	90	10	Normal	—	○
Earth Power	Ground	Special	90	100	10	Normal	—	—
Superpower	Fighting	Physical	120	100	5	Normal	—	○
Snore	Normal	Special	40	100	15	Normal	—	—
Knock Off	Dark	Physical	20	100	20	Normal	—	○
Giga Drain	Grass	Special	75	100	10	Normal	—	—
Stealth Rock	Rock	Status	—	—	20	Other Side	—	—
Sleep Talk	Normal	Status	—	—	10	Self	—	—

Fossil Pokémon

142 Aerodactyl

- HEIGHT: 5'11"
- WEIGHT: 130.1 lbs.
- GENDER: ♂ / ♀

A Pokémon that roamed the skies in the dinosaur era. Its teeth are like saw blades.

TYPE: Rock / Flying

ABILITIES
- Rock Head
- Pressure

HIDDEN ABILITY
- Unnerve

STATS
HP
Attack
Defense
Sp. Atk
Sp. Def
Speed

EGG GROUPS
Flying

Same form for ♂ / ♀

ITEMS SOMETIMES HELD
- None

EVOLUTION

Does not evolve

HOW TO OBTAIN

Pokémon Black Version 2	Get the Old Amber in Twist Mountain and have it restored at the Nacrene Museum
Pokémon White Version 2	Get the Old Amber in Twist Mountain and have it restored at the Nacrene Museum

HOW TO OBTAIN FROM OTHER GAMES

—

—

Pokémon AR Marker

LEVEL-UP AND LEARNED MOVES

Lv.	Name	Type	Kind	Pow.	Acc.	PP	Range	Long	DA
1	Ice Fang	Ice	Physical	65	95	15	Normal	—	○
1	Fire Fang	Fire	Physical	65	95	15	Normal	—	○
1	Thunder Fang	Electric	Physical	65	95	15	Normal	—	○
1	Wing Attack	Flying	Physical	60	100	35	Normal	○	○
1	Supersonic	Normal	Status	—	55	20	Normal	—	—
1	Bite	Dark	Physical	60	100	25	Normal	—	○
1	Scary Face	Normal	Status	—	100	10	Normal	—	—
9	Roar	Normal	Status	—	100	20	Normal	—	—
17	Agility	Psychic	Status	—	—	30	Self	—	—
25	AncientPower	Rock	Special	60	100	5	Normal	—	—
33	Crunch	Dark	Physical	80	100	15	Normal	—	○
41	Take Down	Normal	Physical	90	85	20	Normal	—	○
49	Sky Drop	Flying	Physical	60	100	10	Normal	○	○
57	Iron Head	Steel	Physical	80	100	15	Normal	—	○
65	Hyper Beam	Normal	Special	150	90	5	Normal	—	—
73	Rock Slide	Rock	Physical	75	90	10	Many Others	—	—
81	Giga Impact	Normal	Physical	150	90	5	Normal	—	○

TM & HM MOVES

Lv.	Name	Type	Kind	Pow.	Acc.	PP	Range	Long	DA
TM01	Hone Claws	Dark	Status	—	—	15	Self	—	—
TM02	Dragon Claw	Dragon	Physical	80	100	15	Normal	—	○
TM05	Roar	Normal	Status	—	100	20	Normal	—	—
TM06	Toxic	Poison	Status	—	90	10	Normal	—	—
TM10	Hidden Power	Normal	Special	—	100	15	Normal	—	—
TM11	Sunny Day	Fire	Status	—	—	5	Both Sides	—	—
TM12	Taunt	Dark	Status	—	100	20	Normal	—	—
TM15	Hyper Beam	Normal	Special	150	90	5	Normal	—	—
TM17	Protect	Normal	Status	—	—	10	Self	—	—
TM18	Rain Dance	Water	Status	—	—	5	Both Sides	—	—
TM21	Frustration	Normal	Physical	—	100	20	Normal	—	○
TM23	Smack Down	Rock	Physical	50	100	15	Normal	—	—
TM26	Earthquake	Ground	Physical	100	100	10	Adjacent	—	—
TM27	Return	Normal	Physical	—	100	20	Normal	—	○
TM32	Double Team	Normal	Status	—	—	15	Self	—	—
TM35	Flamethrower	Fire	Special	95	100	15	Normal	—	—
TM37	Sandstorm	Rock	Status	—	—	10	Both Sides	—	—
TM38	Fire Blast	Fire	Special	120	85	5	Normal	—	—
TM39	Rock Tomb	Rock	Physical	50	80	10	Normal	—	—
TM40	Aerial Ace	Flying	Physical	60	—	20	Normal	○	○
TM41	Torment	Dark	Status	—	100	15	Normal	—	—
TM42	Facade	Normal	Physical	70	100	20	Normal	—	○
TM44	Rest	Psychic	Status	—	—	10	Self	—	—
TM45	Attract	Normal	Status	—	100	15	Normal	—	—
TM46	Thief	Dark	Physical	40	100	10	Normal	—	○
TM48	Round	Normal	Special	60	100	15	Normal	—	—
TM58	Sky Drop	Flying	Physical	60	100	10	Normal	○	○
TM59	Incinerate	Fire	Special	30	100	15	Many Others	—	—
TM66	Payback	Dark	Physical	50	100	10	Normal	—	○
TM68	Giga Impact	Normal	Physical	150	90	5	Normal	—	○
TM69	Rock Polish	Rock	Status	—	—	20	Self	—	—
TM71	Stone Edge	Rock	Physical	100	80	5	Normal	—	—
TM78	Bulldoze	Ground	Physical	60	100	20	Adjacent	—	—
TM80	Rock Slide	Rock	Physical	75	90	10	Many Others	—	—
TM87	Swagger	Normal	Status	—	90	15	Normal	—	—
TM90	Substitute	Normal	Status	—	—	10	Self	—	—
TM94	Rock Smash	Fighting	Physical	40	100	15	Normal	—	○
HM02	Fly	Flying	Physical	90	95	15	Normal	○	○
HM04	Strength	Normal	Physical	80	100	15	Normal	—	○

MOVES TAUGHT BY PEOPLE

Name	Type	Kind	Pow.	Acc.	PP	Range	Long	DA

MOVES TAUGHT BY MOVE TUTORS FOR SHARDS

Name	Type	Kind	Pow.	Acc.	PP	Range	Long	DA
Iron Head	Steel	Physical	80	100	15	Normal	—	○
Iron Tail	Steel	Physical	100	75	15	Normal	—	○
Aqua Tail	Water	Physical	90	90	10	Normal	—	○
Earth Power	Ground	Special	90	100	10	Normal	—	—
Dragon Pulse	Dragon	Special	90	100	10	Normal	○	—
Snore	Normal	Special	40	100	15	Normal	—	—
Roost	Flying	Status	—	—	10	Self	—	—
Sky Attack	Flying	Physical	140	90	5	Normal	○	—
Heat Wave	Fire	Special	100	90	10	Many Others	—	—
Tailwind	Flying	Status	—	—	30	Your Side	—	—
Stealth Rock	Rock	Status	—	—	20	Other Side	—	—
Sleep Talk	Normal	Status	—	—	10	Self	—	—

EGG MOVES

Name	Type	Kind	Pow.	Acc.	PP	Range	Long	DA
Whirlwind	Normal	Status	—	100	20	Normal	—	—
Pursuit	Dark	Physical	40	100	20	Normal	—	○
Foresight	Normal	Status	—	—	40	Normal	—	—
Steel Wing	Steel	Physical	70	90	25	Normal	—	○
DragonBreath	Dragon	Special	60	100	20	Normal	—	—
Curse	Ghost	Status	—	—	10	Varies	—	—
Assurance	Dark	Physical	50	100	10	Normal	—	○
Roost	Flying	Status	—	—	10	Self	—	—
Tailwind	Flying	Status	—	—	30	Your Side	—	—

Sleeping Pokémon

143 Snorlax

- HEIGHT: 6'11"
- WEIGHT: 1,014.1 lbs.
- GENDER: ♂ / ♀

When its belly is full, it becomes too lethargic to even lift a finger, so it is safe to bounce on its belly.

Same form for ♂ / ♀

TYPE Normal

ABILITIES
- Immunity
- Thick Fat

HIDDEN ABILITY
- Gluttony

STATS
HP
Attack
Defense
Sp. Atk
Sp. Def
Speed

EGG GROUPS
Monster

ITEMS SOMETIMES HELD
- None

Pokémon AR Marker

EVOLUTION

Munchlax

➡ p. 239

Level up with high friendship

Snorlax

HOW TO OBTAIN

Pokémon Black Version 2	Trade Pokémon during a date with Yancy or Curtis (ninth time)
Pokémon White Version 2	Trade Pokémon during a date with Yancy or Curtis (ninth time)

HOW TO OBTAIN FROM OTHER GAMES

Pokémon HeartGold Version	Wake up the sleeping Snorlax on Route 11 by tuning the radio to the Poké Flute
Pokémon SoulSilver Version	Wake up the sleeping Snorlax on Route 11 by tuning the radio to the Poké Flute

LEVEL-UP AND LEARNED MOVES

Lv.	Name	Type	Kind	Pow.	Acc.	PP	Range	Long	DA
1	Tackle	Normal	Physical	50	100	35	Normal	—	○
4	Defense Curl	Normal	Status	—	—	40	Self	—	—
9	Amnesia	Psychic	Status	—	—	20	Self	—	—
12	Lick	Ghost	Physical	20	100	30	Normal	—	○
17	Belly Drum	Normal	Status	—	—	10	Self	—	—
20	Yawn	Normal	Status	—	—	10	Normal	—	—
25	Chip Away	Normal	Physical	70	100	20	Normal	—	○
28	Rest	Psychic	Status	—	—	10	Self	—	—
28	Snore	Normal	Special	40	100	15	Normal	—	—
33	Sleep Talk	Normal	Status	—	—	10	Self	—	—
36	Body Slam	Normal	Physical	85	100	15	Normal	—	○
41	Block	Normal	Status	—	—	5	Normal	—	—
44	Rollout	Rock	Physical	30	90	20	Normal	—	○
49	Crunch	Dark	Physical	80	100	15	Normal	—	○
52	Heavy Slam	Steel	Physical	—	100	10	Normal	—	○
57	Giga Impact	Normal	Physical	150	90	5	Normal	—	○

TM & HM MOVES

Lv.	Name	Type	Kind	Pow.	Acc.	PP	Range	Long	DA
TM06	Toxic	Poison	Status	—	90	10	Normal	—	—
TM10	Hidden Power	Normal	Special	—	100	15	Normal	—	—
TM11	Sunny Day	Fire	Status	—	—	5	Both Sides	—	—
TM13	Ice Beam	Ice	Special	95	100	10	Normal	—	—
TM14	Blizzard	Ice	Special	120	70	5	Many Others	—	—
TM15	Hyper Beam	Normal	Special	150	90	5	Normal	—	—
TM17	Protect	Normal	Status	—	—	10	Self	—	—
TM18	Rain Dance	Water	Status	—	—	5	Both Sides	—	—
TM21	Frustration	Normal	Physical	—	100	20	Normal	—	○
TM22	SolarBeam	Grass	Special	120	100	10	Normal	—	—
TM23	Smack Down	Rock	Physical	50	100	15	Normal	—	—
TM24	Thunderbolt	Electric	Special	95	100	15	Normal	—	—
TM25	Thunder	Electric	Special	120	70	10	Normal	—	—
TM26	Earthquake	Ground	Physical	100	100	10	Adjacent	—	—
TM27	Return	Normal	Physical	—	100	20	Normal	—	○
TM29	Psychic	Psychic	Special	90	100	10	Normal	—	—
TM30	Shadow Ball	Ghost	Special	80	100	15	Normal	—	—
TM31	Brick Break	Fighting	Physical	75	100	15	Normal	—	○
TM32	Double Team	Normal	Status	—	—	15	Self	—	—
TM35	Flamethrower	Fire	Special	95	100	15	Normal	—	—
TM37	Sandstorm	Rock	Status	—	—	10	Both Sides	—	—
TM38	Fire Blast	Fire	Special	120	85	5	Normal	—	—
TM39	Rock Tomb	Rock	Physical	50	80	10	Normal	—	—
TM42	Facade	Normal	Physical	70	100	20	Normal	—	○
TM44	Rest	Psychic	Status	—	—	10	Self	—	—
TM45	Attract	Normal	Status	—	100	15	Normal	—	—
TM48	Round	Normal	Special	60	100	15	Normal	—	—
TM52	Focus Blast	Fighting	Special	120	70	5	Normal	—	—
TM56	Fling	Dark	Physical	—	100	10	Normal	—	—
TM59	Incinerate	Fire	Special	30	100	15	Many Others	—	—
TM67	Retaliate	Normal	Physical	70	100	5	Normal	—	○
TM68	Giga Impact	Normal	Physical	150	90	5	Normal	—	○
TM78	Bulldoze	Ground	Physical	60	100	20	Adjacent	—	—
TM80	Rock Slide	Rock	Physical	75	90	10	Many Others	—	—
TM83	Work Up	Normal	Status	—	—	30	Self	—	—
TM87	Swagger	Normal	Status	—	90	15	Normal	—	—
TM90	Substitute	Normal	Status	—	—	10	Self	—	—
TM93	Wild Charge	Electric	Physical	90	100	15	Normal	—	○
TM94	Rock Smash	Fighting	Physical	40	100	15	Normal	—	○
HM03	Surf	Water	Special	95	100	15	Adjacent	—	—
HM04	Strength	Normal	Physical	80	100	15	Normal	—	○

MOVES TAUGHT BY PEOPLE

Name	Type	Kind	Pow.	Acc.	PP	Range	Long	DA

MOVES TAUGHT BY MOVE TUTORS FOR SHARDS

Name	Type	Kind	Pow.	Acc.	PP	Range	Long	DA
Covet	Normal	Physical	60	100	40	Normal	—	○
Iron Head	Steel	Physical	80	100	15	Normal	—	○
Seed Bomb	Grass	Physical	80	100	15	Normal	—	—
Gunk Shot	Poison	Physical	120	70	5	Normal	—	—
Fire Punch	Fire	Physical	75	100	15	Normal	—	○
ThunderPunch	Electric	Physical	75	100	15	Normal	—	○
Ice Punch	Ice	Physical	75	100	15	Normal	—	○
Last Resort	Normal	Physical	140	100	5	Normal	—	○
Block	Normal	Status	—	—	5	Normal	—	—
Hyper Voice	Normal	Special	90	100	10	Many Others	—	—
Icy Wind	Ice	Special	55	95	15	Many Others	—	—
Zen Headbutt	Psychic	Physical	80	90	15	Normal	—	○
Superpower	Fighting	Physical	120	100	5	Normal	—	○
Snore	Normal	Special	40	100	15	Normal	—	—
After You	Normal	Status	—	—	15	Normal	—	—
Recycle	Normal	Status	—	—	10	Self	—	—
Outrage	Dragon	Physical	120	100	10	1 Random	—	○
Sleep Talk	Normal	Status	—	—	10	Self	—	—

EGG MOVES

Name	Type	Kind	Pow.	Acc.	PP	Range	Long	DA
Lick	Ghost	Physical	20	100	30	Normal	—	○
Charm	Normal	Status	—	100	20	Normal	—	—
Double-Edge	Normal	Physical	120	100	15	Normal	—	○
Curse	Ghost	Status	—	—	10	Varies	—	—
Fissure	Ground	Physical	—	30	5	Normal	—	—
Whirlwind	Normal	Status	—	100	20	Normal	—	—
Pursuit	Dark	Physical	40	100	20	Normal	—	○
Counter	Fighting	Physical	—	100	20	Varies	—	○
Natural Gift	Normal	Physical	—	100	15	Normal	—	—
After You	Normal	Status	—	—	15	Normal	—	—

Freeze Pokémon

144 Articuno

- HEIGHT: 5'07"
- WEIGHT: 122.1 lbs.
- GENDER: Unknown

A legendary bird Pokémon. It can create blizzards by freezing moisture in the air.

Gender unknown

TYPE Ice / Flying

ABILITY
- Pressure

HIDDEN ABILITY
—

STATS
HP
Attack
Defense
Sp. Atk
Sp. Def
Speed

EGG GROUPS
No Egg has ever been discovered

ITEMS SOMETIMES HELD
- None

Pokémon AR Marker

EVOLUTION

Does not evolve

HOW TO OBTAIN

Pokémon Black Version 2	Link Trade or Poké Transfer
Pokémon White Version 2	Link Trade or Poké Transfer

HOW TO OBTAIN FROM OTHER GAMES

Pokémon HeartGold Version	Seafoam Islands
Pokémon SoulSilver Version	Seafoam Islands

LEVEL-UP AND LEARNED MOVES

Lv.	Name	Type	Kind	Pow.	Acc.	PP	Range	Long	DA
1	Gust	Flying	Special	40	100	35	Normal	○	—
1	Powder Snow	Ice	Special	40	100	25	Many Others	—	—
8	Mist	Ice	Status	—	—	30	Your Side	—	—
15	Ice Shard	Ice	Physical	40	100	30	Normal	—	—
22	Mind Reader	Normal	Status	—	—	5	Normal	—	—
29	AncientPower	Rock	Special	60	100	5	Normal	—	—
36	Agility	Psychic	Status	—	—	30	Self	—	—
43	Ice Beam	Ice	Special	95	100	10	Normal	—	—
50	Reflect	Psychic	Status	—	—	20	Your Side	—	—
57	Roost	Flying	Status	—	—	10	Self	—	—
64	Tailwind	Flying	Status	—	—	30	Your Side	—	—
71	Blizzard	Ice	Special	120	70	5	Many Others	—	—
78	Sheer Cold	Ice	Special	—	30	5	Normal	—	—
85	Hail	Ice	Status	—	—	10	Both Sides	—	—
92	Hurricane	Flying	Special	120	70	10	Normal	○	—

TM & HM MOVES

Lv.	Name	Type	Kind	Pow.	Acc.	PP	Range	Long	DA
TM05	Roar	Normal	Status	-	100	20	Normal	-	-
TM06	Toxic	Poison	Status	-	90	10	Normal	-	-
TM07	Hail	Ice	Status	-	-	10	Both Sides	-	-
TM10	Hidden Power	Normal	Special	-	100	15	Normal	-	-
TM11	Sunny Day	Fire	Status	-	-	5	Both Sides	-	-
TM13	Ice Beam	Ice	Special	95	100	10	Normal	-	-
TM14	Blizzard	Ice	Special	120	70	5	Many Others	-	-
TM15	Hyper Beam	Normal	Special	150	90	5	Normal	-	-
TM17	Protect	Normal	Status	-	-	10	Self	-	-
TM18	Rain Dance	Water	Status	-	-	5	Both Sides	-	-
TM21	Frustration	Normal	Physical	-	100	20	Normal	-	○
TM27	Return	Normal	Physical	-	100	20	Normal	-	○
TM32	Double Team	Normal	Status	-	-	15	Self	-	-
TM33	Reflect	Psychic	Status	-	-	20	Your Side	-	-
TM37	Sandstorm	Rock	Status	-	-	10	Both Sides	-	-
TM40	Aerial Ace	Flying	Physical	60	-	20	Normal	○	○
TM42	Facade	Normal	Physical	70	100	20	Normal	-	○
TM44	Rest	Psychic	Status	-	-	10	Self	-	-
TM48	Round	Normal	Special	60	100	15	Normal	-	-
TM58	Sky Drop	Flying	Physical	60	100	10	Normal	○	○
TM68	Giga Impact	Normal	Physical	150	90	5	Normal	-	○
TM79	Frost Breath	Ice	Special	40	90	10	Normal	-	-
TM87	Swagger	Normal	Status	-	90	15	Normal	-	-
TM88	Pluck	Flying	Physical	60	100	20	Normal	○	○
TM89	U-turn	Bug	Physical	70	100	20	Normal	-	○
TM90	Substitute	Normal	Status	-	-	10	Self	-	-
TM94	Rock Smash	Fighting	Physical	40	100	15	Normal	-	○
HM02	Fly	Flying	Physical	90	95	15	Normal	○	○

MOVES TAUGHT BY PEOPLE

Name	Type	Kind	Pow.	Acc.	PP	Range	Long	DA

MOVES TAUGHT BY MOVE TUTORS FOR SHARDS

Name	Type	Kind	Pow.	Acc.	PP	Range	Long	DA
Signal Beam	Bug	Special	75	100	15	Normal	—	—
Icy Wind	Ice	Special	55	95	15	Many Others	—	—
Snore	Normal	Special	40	100	15	Normal	—	—
Roost	Flying	Status	—	—	10	Self	—	—
Sky Attack	Flying	Physical	140	90	5	Normal	○	—
Tailwind	Flying	Status	—	—	30	Your Side	—	—
Sleep Talk	Normal	Status	—	—	10	Self	—	—

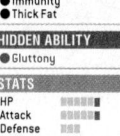

 Electric Pokémon

145 Zapdos

TYPE Electric Flying

ABILITY
● Pressure

HIDDEN ABILITY

● HEIGHT: 5'03"
● WEIGHT: 116.0 lbs.
● GENDER: Unknown

A legendary Pokémon that is said to live in thunderclouds. It freely controls lightning bolts.

STATS
HP	
Attack	
Defense	
Sp. Atk	
Sp. Def	
Speed	

EGG GROUPS
No Egg has ever been discovered

ITEMS SOMETIMES HELD
● None

Gender unknown

EVOLUTION

Does not evolve

HOW TO OBTAIN
Pokémon Black Version 2	Link Trade or Poké Transfer
Pokémon White Version 2	Link Trade or Poké Transfer

HOW TO OBTAIN FROM OTHER GAMES
Pokémon HeartGold Version	Route 10 (after collecting all eight Kanto Gym Badges)
Pokémon SoulSilver Version	Route 10 (after collecting all eight Kanto Gym Badges)

LEVEL-UP AND LEARNED MOVES
Lv.	Name	Type	Kind	Pow.	Acc.	PP	Range	Long	DA
1	Peck	Flying	Physical	35	100	35	Normal	○	○
1	ThunderShock	Electric	Special	40	100	30	Normal	—	—
8	Thunder Wave	Electric	Status	—	100	20	Normal	—	—
15	Detect	Fighting	Status	—	—	5	Self	—	—
22	Pluck	Flying	Physical	60	100	20	Normal	○	○
29	AncientPower	Rock	Special	60	100	5	Normal	—	—
36	Charge	Electric	Status	—	—	20	Self	—	—
43	Agility	Psychic	Status	—	—	30	Self	—	—
50	Discharge	Electric	Special	80	100	15	Adjacent	—	—
57	Roost	Flying	Status	—	—	10	Self	—	—
64	Light Screen	Psychic	Status	—	—	30	Your Side	—	—
71	Drill Peck	Flying	Physical	80	100	20	Normal	○	○
78	Thunder	Electric	Special	120	70	10	Normal	—	—
85	Rain Dance	Water	Status	—	—	5	Both Sides	—	—
92	Zap Cannon	Electric	Special	120	50	5	Normal	—	—

MOVES TAUGHT BY PEOPLE
Name	Type	Kind	Pow.	Acc.	PP	Range	Long	DA

MOVES TAUGHT BY MOVE TUTORS FOR SHARDS
Name	Type	Kind	Pow.	Acc.	PP	Range	Long	DA
Signal Beam	Bug	Special	75	100	15	Normal	—	—
Snore	Normal	Special	40	100	15	Normal	—	—
Roost	Flying	Status	—	—	10	Self	—	—
Sky Attack	Flying	Physical	140	90	5	Normal	○	—
Heat Wave	Fire	Special	100	90	10	Many Others	—	—
Tailwind	Flying	Status	—	—	30	Your Side	—	—
Sleep Talk	Normal	Status	—	—	10	Self	—	—

TM & HM MOVES
Lv.	Name	Type	Kind	Pow.	Acc.	PP	Range	Long	DA
TM05	Roar	Normal	Status	—	100	20	Normal	—	—
TM06	Toxic	Poison	Status	—	90	10	Normal	—	—
TM10	Hidden Power	Normal	Special	—	100	15	Normal	—	—
TM11	Sunny Day	Fire	Status	—	—	5	Both Sides	—	—
TM15	Hyper Beam	Normal	Special	150	90	5	Normal	—	—
TM16	Light Screen	Psychic	Status	—	—	30	Your Side	—	—
TM17	Protect	Normal	Status	—	—	10	Self	—	—
TM18	Rain Dance	Water	Status	—	—	5	Both Sides	—	—
TM21	Frustration	Normal	Physical	—	100	20	Normal	—	—
TM24	Thunderbolt	Electric	Special	95	100	15	Normal	—	—
TM25	Thunder	Electric	Special	120	70	10	Normal	—	—
TM27	Return	Normal	Physical	—	100	20	Normal	—	○
TM32	Double Team	Normal	Status	—	—	15	Self	—	—
TM37	Sandstorm	Rock	Status	—	—	10	Both Sides	—	—
TM40	Aerial Ace	Flying	Physical	60	—	20	Normal	○	○
TM42	Facade	Normal	Physical	70	100	20	Normal	—	—
TM44	Rest	Psychic	Status	—	—	10	Self	—	—
TM48	Round	Normal	Special	60	100	15	Normal	—	—
TM57	Charge Beam	Electric	Special	50	90	10	Normal	—	—
TM58	Sky Drop	Flying	Physical	60	100	10	Normal	○	○
TM68	Giga Impact	Normal	Physical	150	90	5	Normal	—	—
TM70	Flash	Normal	Status	—	100	20	Normal	—	—
TM72	Volt Switch	Electric	Special	70	100	20	Normal	—	—
TM73	Thunder Wave	Electric	Status	—	100	20	Normal	—	—
TM87	Swagger	Normal	Status	—	90	15	Normal	—	—
TM88	Pluck	Flying	Physical	60	100	20	Normal	○	○
TM89	U-turn	Bug	Physical	70	100	20	Normal	—	○
TM90	Substitute	Normal	Status	—	—	10	Self	—	—
TM93	Wild Charge	Electric	Physical	90	100	15	Normal	—	—
TM94	Rock Smash	Fighting	Physical	40	100	15	Normal	○	○
HM02	Fly	Flying	Physical	90	95	15	Normal	—	—

Pokémon AR Marker

 Flame Pokémon

146 Moltres

TYPE Fire Flying

ABILITY
● Pressure

HIDDEN ABILITY

● HEIGHT: 6'07"
● WEIGHT: 132.3 lbs.
● GENDER: Unknown

One of the legendary bird Pokémon. It is said that its appearance indicates the coming of spring.

STATS
HP	
Attack	
Defense	
Sp. Atk	
Sp. Def	
Speed	

EGG GROUPS
No Egg has ever been discovered

ITEMS SOMETIMES HELD
● None

Gender unknown

EVOLUTION

Does not evolve

HOW TO OBTAIN
Pokémon Black Version 2	Link Trade or Poké Transfer
Pokémon White Version 2	Link Trade or Poké Transfer

HOW TO OBTAIN FROM OTHER GAMES
Pokémon HeartGold Version	Mt. Silver
Pokémon SoulSilver Version	Mt. Silver

LEVEL-UP AND LEARNED MOVES
Lv.	Name	Type	Kind	Pow.	Acc.	PP	Range	Long	DA
1	Wing Attack	Flying	Physical	60	100	35	Normal	○	○
1	Ember	Fire	Special	40	100	25	Normal	—	—
8	Fire Spin	Fire	Special	35	85	15	Normal	—	—
15	Agility	Psychic	Status	—	—	30	Self	—	—
22	Endure	Normal	Status	—	—	10	Self	—	—
29	AncientPower	Rock	Special	60	100	5	Normal	—	—
36	Flamethrower	Fire	Special	95	100	15	Normal	—	—
43	Safeguard	Normal	Status	—	—	25	Your Side	—	—
50	Air Slash	Flying	Special	75	95	20	Normal	—	—
57	Roost	Flying	Status	—	—	10	Self	—	—
64	Heat Wave	Fire	Special	100	90	10	Many Others	—	—
71	SolarBeam	Grass	Special	120	100	10	Normal	—	—
78	Sky Attack	Flying	Physical	140	90	5	Normal	○	—
85	Sunny Day	Fire	Status	—	—	5	Both Sides	—	—
92	Hurricane	Flying	Special	120	70	10	Normal	—	—

MOVES TAUGHT BY PEOPLE
Name	Type	Kind	Pow.	Acc.	PP	Range	Long	DA

MOVES TAUGHT BY MOVE TUTORS FOR SHARDS
Name	Type	Kind	Pow.	Acc.	PP	Range	Long	DA
Snore	Normal	Special	40	100	15	Normal	—	—
Roost	Flying	Status	—	—	10	Self	—	—
Sky Attack	Flying	Physical	140	90	5	Normal	○	—
Heat Wave	Fire	Special	100	90	10	Many Others	—	—
Tailwind	Flying	Status	—	—	30	Your Side	—	—
Sleep Talk	Normal	Status	—	—	10	Self	—	—

TM & HM MOVES
Lv.	Name	Type	Kind	Pow.	Acc.	PP	Range	Long	DA
TM05	Roar	Normal	Status	—	100	20	Normal	—	—
TM06	Toxic	Poison	Status	—	90	10	Normal	—	—
TM10	Hidden Power	Normal	Special	—	100	15	Normal	—	—
TM11	Sunny Day	Fire	Status	—	—	5	Both Sides	—	—
TM15	Hyper Beam	Normal	Special	150	90	5	Normal	—	—
TM17	Protect	Normal	Status	—	—	10	Self	—	—
TM18	Rain Dance	Water	Status	—	—	5	Both Sides	—	—
TM20	Safeguard	Normal	Status	—	—	25	Your Side	—	—
TM21	Frustration	Normal	Physical	—	100	20	Normal	—	○
TM22	SolarBeam	Grass	Special	120	100	10	Normal	—	—
TM27	Return	Normal	Physical	—	100	20	Normal	—	○
TM32	Double Team	Normal	Status	—	—	15	Self	—	—
TM35	Flamethrower	Fire	Special	95	100	15	Normal	—	—
TM37	Sandstorm	Rock	Status	—	—	10	Both Sides	—	—
TM38	Fire Blast	Fire	Special	120	85	5	Normal	—	—
TM40	Aerial Ace	Flying	Physical	60	—	20	Normal	○	○
TM42	Facade	Normal	Physical	70	100	20	Normal	—	—
TM43	Flame Charge	Fire	Physical	50	100	20	Normal	—	—
TM44	Rest	Psychic	Status	—	—	10	Self	—	—
TM48	Round	Normal	Special	60	100	15	Normal	—	—
TM50	Overheat	Fire	Special	140	90	5	Normal	—	—
TM58	Sky Drop	Flying	Physical	60	100	10	Normal	○	○
TM59	Incinerate	Fire	Special	30	100	15	Many Others	—	—
TM61	Will-O-Wisp	Fire	Status	—	75	15	Normal	—	—
TM68	Giga Impact	Normal	Physical	150	90	5	Normal	—	—
TM87	Swagger	Normal	Status	—	90	15	Normal	—	—
TM88	Pluck	Flying	Physical	60	100	20	Normal	○	○
TM89	U-turn	Bug	Physical	70	100	20	Normal	—	○
TM90	Substitute	Normal	Status	—	—	10	Self	—	—
TM94	Rock Smash	Fighting	Physical	40	100	15	Normal	○	○
HM02	Fly	Flying	Physical	90	95	15	Normal	—	—

Pokémon AR Marker

Dratini

Dragon Pokémon
147 **Dratini**

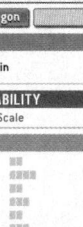

- HEIGHT: 5'11"
- WEIGHT: 7.3 lbs.
- GENDER: ♂/♀

It is called the "Mirage Pokémon" because so few have seen it. Its shed skin has been found.

Same form for ♂/♀

TYPE Dragon

ABILITY
- Shed Skin

HIDDEN ABILITY
- Marvel Scale

STATS
HP	
Attack	
Defense	
Sp. Atk	
Sp. Def	
Speed	

EGG GROUPS
Water ❶/Dragon

ITEMS SOMETIMES HELD
- Dragon Scale

Pokémon AR Marker

EVOLUTION

Dratini — Lv. 30 → Dragonair — Lv. 55 → Dragonite

HOW TO OBTAIN

| Pokémon Black Version 2 | Dragonspiral Tower 1F outside (Super Rod) |
| Pokémon White Version 2 | Dragonspiral Tower 1F outside (Super Rod) |

HOW TO OBTAIN FROM OTHER GAMES
| ——— |
| ——— |

LEVEL-UP AND LEARNED MOVES

Lv.	Name	Type	Kind	Pow.	Acc.	PP	Range	Long	DA
1	Wrap	Normal	Physical	15	90	20	Normal	—	—
1	Leer	Normal	Status	—	100	30	Many Others	—	—
5	Thunder Wave	Electric	Status	—	100	20	Normal	—	—
11	Twister	Dragon	Special	40	100	20	Many Others	—	—
15	Dragon Rage	Dragon	Special	—	100	10	Normal	—	—
21	Slam	Normal	Physical	80	75	20	Normal	—	○
25	Agility	Psychic	Status	—	—	30	Self	—	—
31	Dragon Tail	Dragon	Physical	60	90	10	Normal	—	○
35	Aqua Tail	Water	Physical	90	90	10	Normal	—	○
41	Dragon Rush	Dragon	Physical	100	75	10	Normal	—	○
45	Safeguard	Normal	Status	—	—	25	Your Side	—	—
51	Dragon Dance	Dragon	Status	—	—	20	Self	—	—
55	Outrage	Dragon	Physical	120	100	10	1 Random	—	○
61	Hyper Beam	Normal	Special	150	90	5	Normal	—	—

TM & HM MOVES

Lv.	Name	Type	Kind	Pow.	Acc.	PP	Range	Long	DA
TM06	Toxic	Poison	Status	—	90	10	Normal	—	—
TM07	Hail	Ice	Status	—	—	10	Both Sides	—	—
TM10	Hidden Power	Normal	Special	—	100	15	Normal	—	—
TM11	Sunny Day	Fire	Status	—	—	5	Both Sides	—	—
TM13	Ice Beam	Ice	Special	95	100	10	Normal	—	—
TM14	Blizzard	Ice	Special	120	70	5	Many Others	—	—
TM15	Hyper Beam	Normal	Special	150	90	5	Normal	—	—
TM16	Light Screen	Psychic	Status	—	—	30	Your Side	—	—
TM17	Protect	Normal	Status	—	—	10	Self	—	—
TM18	Rain Dance	Water	Status	—	—	5	Both Sides	—	—
TM20	Safeguard	Normal	Status	—	—	25	Your Side	—	—
TM21	Frustration	Normal	Physical	—	100	20	Normal	—	○
TM24	Thunderbolt	Electric	Special	95	100	15	Normal	—	—
TM25	Thunder	Electric	Special	120	70	10	Normal	—	—
TM27	Return	Normal	Physical	—	100	20	Normal	—	○
TM32	Double Team	Normal	Status	—	—	15	Self	—	—
TM35	Flamethrower	Fire	Special	95	100	15	Normal	—	—
TM38	Fire Blast	Fire	Special	120	85	5	Normal	—	—
TM42	Facade	Normal	Physical	70	100	20	Normal	—	—
TM44	Rest	Psychic	Status	—	—	10	Self	—	—
TM45	Attract	Normal	Status	—	100	15	Normal	—	—
TM48	Round	Normal	Special	60	100	15	Normal	—	—
TM59	Incinerate	Fire	Special	30	100	15	Many Others	—	—
TM73	Thunder Wave	Electric	Status	—	100	20	Normal	—	—
TM82	Dragon Tail	Dragon	Physical	60	90	10	Normal	—	○
TM87	Swagger	Normal	Status	—	90	15	Normal	—	—
TM90	Substitute	Normal	Status	—	—	10	Self	—	—
HM03	Surf	Water	Special	95	100	15	Adjacent	—	—
HM05	Waterfall	Water	Physical	80	100	15	Normal	—	○

MOVES TAUGHT BY PEOPLE

Name	Type	Kind	Pow.	Acc.	PP	Range	Long	DA
Draco Meteor	Dragon	Special	140	90	5	Normal	—	—

MOVES TAUGHT BY MOVE TUTORS FOR SHARDS

Name	Type	Kind	Pow.	Acc.	PP	Range	Long	DA
Icy Wind	Ice	Special	55	95	15	Many Others	—	—
Iron Tail	Steel	Physical	100	75	15	Normal	—	○
Aqua Tail	Water	Physical	90	90	10	Normal	—	○
Dragon Pulse	Dragon	Special	90	100	10	Normal	○	—
Bind	Normal	Physical	15	85	20	Normal	—	—
Snore	Normal	Special	40	100	15	Normal	—	—
Outrage	Dragon	Physical	120	100	10	1 Random	—	○
Sleep Talk	Normal	Status	—	—	10	Self	—	—

EGG MOVES

Name	Type	Kind	Pow.	Acc.	PP	Range	Long	DA
Mist	Ice	Status	—	—	30	Your Side	—	—
Haze	Ice	Status	—	—	30	Both Sides	—	—
Supersonic	Normal	Status	—	55	20	Normal	—	—
DragonBreath	Dragon	Special	60	100	20	Normal	—	—
Dragon Dance	Dragon	Status	—	—	20	Self	—	—
Dragon Rush	Dragon	Physical	100	75	10	Normal	—	○
ExtremeSpeed	Normal	Physical	80	100	5	Normal	—	○
Water Pulse	Water	Special	60	100	20	Normal	○	○
Aqua Jet	Water	Physical	40	100	20	Normal	—	○
Dragon Pulse	Dragon	Special	90	100	10	Normal	○	—
Iron Tail	Steel	Physical	100	75	15	Normal	—	○

Dragonair

Dragon Pokémon
148 **Dragonair**

- HEIGHT: 13'01"
- WEIGHT: 36.4 lbs.
- GENDER: ♂/♀

If its body takes on an aura, the weather changes instantly. It is said to live in seas and lakes.

Same form for ♂/♀

TYPE Dragon

ABILITY
- Shed Skin

HIDDEN ABILITY
- Marvel Scale

STATS
HP	
Attack	
Defense	
Sp. Atk	
Sp. Def	
Speed	

EGG GROUPS
Water ❶/Dragon

ITEMS SOMETIMES HELD
- Dragon Scale

Pokémon AR Marker

EVOLUTION

Dratini — Lv. 30 → Dragonair — Lv. 55 → Dragonite

HOW TO OBTAIN

| Pokémon Black Version 2 | Dragonspiral Tower 1F outside (Super Rod/ripples in water) |
| Pokémon White Version 2 | Dragonspiral Tower 1F outside (Super Rod/ripples in water) |

HOW TO OBTAIN FROM OTHER GAMES
| ——— |
| ——— |

LEVEL-UP AND LEARNED MOVES

Lv.	Name	Type	Kind	Pow.	Acc.	PP	Range	Long	DA
1	Wrap	Normal	Physical	15	90	20	Normal	—	○
1	Leer	Normal	Status	—	100	30	Many Others	—	—
1	Thunder Wave	Normal	Status	—	100	20	Normal	—	—
1	Twister	Dragon	Special	40	100	20	Many Others	—	—
5	Thunder Wave	Electric	Status	—	100	20	Normal	—	—
11	Twister	Dragon	Special	40	100	20	Many Others	—	—
15	Dragon Rage	Dragon	Special	—	100	10	Normal	—	—
21	Slam	Normal	Physical	80	75	20	Normal	—	○
25	Agility	Psychic	Status	—	—	30	Self	—	—
33	Dragon Tail	Dragon	Physical	60	90	10	Normal	—	○
39	Aqua Tail	Water	Physical	90	90	10	Normal	—	○
47	Dragon Rush	Dragon	Physical	100	75	10	Normal	—	○
53	Safeguard	Normal	Status	—	—	25	Your Side	—	—
61	Dragon Dance	Dragon	Status	—	—	20	Self	—	—
67	Outrage	Dragon	Physical	120	100	10	1 Random	—	○
75	Hyper Beam	Normal	Special	150	90	5	Normal	—	—

TM & HM MOVES

Lv.	Name	Type	Kind	Pow.	Acc.	PP	Range	Long	DA
TM06	Toxic	Poison	Status	—	90	10	Normal	—	—
TM07	Hail	Ice	Status	—	—	10	Both Sides	—	—
TM10	Hidden Power	Normal	Special	—	100	15	Normal	—	—
TM11	Sunny Day	Fire	Status	—	—	5	Both Sides	—	—
TM13	Ice Beam	Ice	Special	95	100	10	Normal	—	—
TM14	Blizzard	Ice	Special	120	70	5	Many Others	—	—
TM15	Hyper Beam	Normal	Special	150	90	5	Normal	—	—
TM16	Light Screen	Psychic	Status	—	—	30	Your Side	—	—
TM17	Protect	Normal	Status	—	—	10	Self	—	—
TM18	Rain Dance	Water	Status	—	—	5	Both Sides	—	—
TM20	Safeguard	Normal	Status	—	—	25	Your Side	—	—
TM21	Frustration	Normal	Physical	—	100	20	Normal	—	○
TM24	Thunderbolt	Electric	Special	95	100	15	Normal	—	—
TM25	Thunder	Electric	Special	120	70	10	Normal	—	—
TM27	Return	Normal	Physical	—	100	20	Normal	—	○
TM32	Double Team	Normal	Status	—	—	15	Self	—	—
TM35	Flamethrower	Fire	Special	95	100	15	Normal	—	—
TM38	Fire Blast	Fire	Special	120	85	5	Normal	—	—
TM42	Facade	Normal	Physical	70	100	20	Normal	—	—
TM44	Rest	Psychic	Status	—	—	10	Self	—	—
TM45	Attract	Normal	Status	—	100	15	Normal	—	—
TM48	Round	Normal	Special	60	100	15	Normal	—	—
TM59	Incinerate	Fire	Special	30	100	15	Many Others	—	—
TM73	Thunder Wave	Electric	Status	—	100	20	Normal	—	—
TM82	Dragon Tail	Dragon	Physical	60	90	10	Normal	—	○
TM87	Swagger	Normal	Status	—	90	15	Normal	—	—
TM90	Substitute	Normal	Status	—	—	10	Self	—	—
HM03	Surf	Water	Special	95	100	15	Adjacent	—	—
HM05	Waterfall	Water	Physical	80	100	15	Normal	—	○

MOVES TAUGHT BY PEOPLE

Name	Type	Kind	Pow.	Acc.	PP	Range	Long	DA
Draco Meteor	Dragon	Special	140	90	5	Normal	—	—

MOVES TAUGHT BY MOVE TUTORS FOR SHARDS

Name	Type	Kind	Pow.	Acc.	PP	Range	Long	DA
Icy Wind	Ice	Special	55	95	15	Many Others	—	—
Iron Tail	Steel	Physical	100	75	15	Normal	—	○
Aqua Tail	Water	Physical	90	90	10	Normal	—	○
Dragon Pulse	Dragon	Special	90	100	10	Normal	○	—
Bind	Normal	Physical	15	85	20	Normal	—	—
Snore	Normal	Special	40	100	15	Normal	—	—
Outrage	Dragon	Physical	120	100	10	1 Random	—	○
Sleep Talk	Normal	Status	—	—	10	Self	—	—

 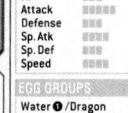 

Dragon Pokémon
149 Dragonite

TYPE Dragon / Flying

ABILITY
● Inner Focus

HIDDEN ABILITY
● Multiscale

● HEIGHT: 7'03"
● WEIGHT: 463.0 lbs.
● GENDER: ♂ / ♀

It is said to make its home somewhere in the sea. It guides crews of shipwrecks to shore.

STATS
HP
Attack
Defense
Sp. Atk
Sp. Def
Speed

EGG GROUPS
Water ❶/Dragon

ITEMS SOMETIMES HELD
● Dragon Scale

Same form for ♂ / ♀

EVOLUTION

Dratini — Lv. 30 → Dragonair — Lv. 55 → Dragonite

HOW TO OBTAIN

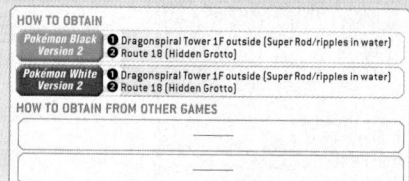

Pokémon Black Version 2	❶ Dragonspiral Tower 1F outside (Super Rod/ripples in water) ❷ Route 18 (Hidden Grotto)
Pokémon White Version 2	❶ Dragonspiral Tower 1F outside (Super Rod/ripples in water) ❷ Route 18 (Hidden Grotto)

HOW TO OBTAIN FROM OTHER GAMES

—
—

LEVEL-UP AND LEARNED MOVES

Lv.	Name	Type	Kind	Pow.	Acc.	PP	Range	Long	DA
1	Fire Punch	Fire	Physical	75	100	15	Normal	—	○
1	ThunderPunch	Electric	Physical	75	100	15	Normal	—	○
1	Roost	Flying	Status	—	—	10	Self	—	
1	Wrap	Normal	Physical	15	90	20	Normal	—	
1	Leer	Normal	Status	—	100	30	Many Others	—	
1	Thunder Wave	Electric	Status	—	100	20	Normal	—	
1	Twister	Dragon	Special	40	100	20	Many Others	—	
5	Thunder Wave	Electric	Status	—	100	20	Normal	—	
11	Twister	Dragon	Special	40	100	20	Many Others	—	
15	Dragon Rage	Dragon	Special	—	100	10	Normal	—	
21	Slam	Normal	Physical	80	75	20	Normal	—	
25	Agility	Psychic	Status	—	—	30	Self	—	
33	Dragon Tail	Dragon	Physical	60	90	10	Normal	—	
39	Aqua Tail	Water	Physical	90	90	10	Normal	—	
47	Dragon Rush	Dragon	Physical	100	75	10	Normal	—	○
53	Safeguard	Normal	Status	—	—	25	Your Side	—	
55	Wing Attack	Flying	Physical	60	100	35	Normal	○	
61	Dragon Dance	Dragon	Status	—	—	20	Self	—	
67	Outrage	Dragon	Physical	120	100	10	1 Random	—	○
75	Hyper Beam	Normal	Special	150	90	5	Normal	—	
81	Hurricane	Flying	Special	120	70	10	Normal	—	

TM & HM MOVES

Lv.	Name	Type	Kind	Pow.	Acc.	PP	Range	Long	DA
TM01	Hone Claws	Dark	Status	—	—	15	Self	—	
TM02	Dragon Claw	Dragon	Physical	80	100	15	Normal	—	○
TM05	Roar	Normal	Status	—	100	20	Normal	—	
TM06	Toxic	Poison	Status	—	90	10	Normal	—	
TM07	Hail	Ice	Status	—	—	10	Both Sides	—	
TM10	Hidden Power	Normal	Special	—	100	15	Normal	—	
TM11	Sunny Day	Fire	Status	—	—	5	Both Sides	—	
TM13	Ice Beam	Ice	Special	95	100	10	Normal	—	
TM14	Blizzard	Ice	Special	120	70	5	Many Others	—	
TM15	Hyper Beam	Normal	Special	150	90	5	Normal	—	
TM16	Light Screen	Psychic	Status	—	—	30	Your Side	—	
TM17	Protect	Normal	Status	—	—	10	Self	—	
TM18	Rain Dance	Water	Status	—	—	5	Both Sides	—	
TM20	Safeguard	Normal	Status	—	—	25	Your Side	—	
TM21	Frustration	Normal	Physical	—	100	20	Normal	—	
TM24	Thunderbolt	Electric	Special	95	100	15	Normal	—	
TM25	Thunder	Electric	Special	120	70	10	Normal	—	
TM26	Earthquake	Ground	Physical	100	100	10	Adjacent	—	
TM27	Return	Normal	Physical	—	100	20	Normal	—	
TM31	Brick Break	Fighting	Physical	75	100	15	Normal	—	
TM32	Double Team	Normal	Status	—	—	15	Self	—	
TM35	Flamethrower	Fire	Special	95	100	15	Normal	—	
TM37	Sandstorm	Rock	Status	—	—	10	Both Sides	—	
TM38	Fire Blast	Fire	Special	120	85	5	Normal	—	
TM39	Rock Tomb	Rock	Physical	50	80	10	Normal	—	
TM40	Aerial Ace	Flying	Physical	60	—	20	Normal	○	○
TM42	Facade	Normal	Physical	70	100	20	Normal	—	
TM44	Rest	Psychic	Status	—	—	10	Self	—	
TM45	Attract	Normal	Status	—	100	15	Normal	—	
TM48	Round	Normal	Special	60	100	15	Normal	—	
TM52	Focus Blast	Fighting	Special	120	70	5	Normal	—	
TM56	Fling	Dark	Physical	—	100	10	Normal	—	

Lv.	Name	Type	Kind	Pow.	Acc.	PP	Range	Long	DA
TM58	Sky Drop	Flying	Physical	60	100	10	Normal	—	○
TM59	Incinerate	Fire	Special	30	100	15	Many Others	—	
TM68	Giga Impact	Normal	Physical	150	90	5	Normal	—	
TM71	Stone Edge	Rock	Physical	100	80	5	Normal	—	
TM73	Thunder Wave	Electric	Status	—	100	20	Normal	—	
TM78	Bulldoze	Ground	Physical	60	100	20	Adjacent	—	
TM80	Rock Slide	Rock	Physical	75	90	10	Many Others	—	
TM82	Dragon Tail	Dragon	Physical	60	90	10	Normal	—	○
TM87	Swagger	Normal	Status	—	90	15	Normal	—	
TM90	Substitute	Normal	Status	—	—	10	Self	—	
TM94	Rock Smash	Fighting	Physical	40	100	15	Normal	—	
HM01	Cut	Normal	Physical	50	95	30	Normal	—	
HM02	Fly	Flying	Physical	90	95	15	Normal	—	○
HM03	Surf	Water	Special	95	100	15	Adjacent	—	
HM04	Strength	Normal	Physical	80	100	15	Normal	—	
HM05	Waterfall	Water	Physical	80	100	15	Normal	—	
HM06	Dive	Water	Physical	80	100	10	Normal	—	

MOVES TAUGHT BY PEOPLE

Name	Type	Kind	Pow.	Acc.	PP	Range	Long	DA
Draco Meteor	Dragon	Special	140	90	5	Normal	—	

MOVES TAUGHT BY MOVE TUTORS FOR SHARDS

Name	Type	Kind	Pow.	Acc.	PP	Range	Long	DA
Iron Head	Steel	Physical	80	100	15	Normal	—	○
Fire Punch	Fire	Physical	75	100	15	Normal	—	○
ThunderPunch	Electric	Physical	75	100	15	Normal	—	○
Ice Punch	Ice	Physical	75	100	15	Normal	—	○
Icy Wind	Ice	Special	55	95	15	Many Others	—	
Iron Tail	Steel	Physical	100	75	15	Normal	—	○
Aqua Tail	Water	Physical	90	90	10	Normal	—	○
Superpower	Fighting	Physical	120	100	5	Normal	—	
Dragon Pulse	Dragon	Special	90	100	10	Normal	—	
Bind	Normal	Physical	15	85	20	Normal	—	
Snore	Normal	Special	40	100	15	Normal	—	
Roost	Flying	Status	—	—	10	Self	—	
Heat Wave	Fire	Special	100	90	10	Many Others	—	
Tailwind	Flying	Status	—	—	30	Your Side	—	
Outrage	Dragon	Physical	120	100	10	1 Random	—	○
Sleep Talk	Normal	Status	—	—	10	Self	—	

Pokémon AR Marker

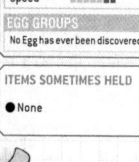

Genetic Pokémon
150 Mewtwo

TYPE Psychic

ABILITY
● Pressure

HIDDEN ABILITY

● HEIGHT: 6'07"
● WEIGHT: 269.0 lbs.
● GENDER: Unknown

A Pokémon created by recombining Mew's genes. It's said to have the most savage heart among Pokémon.

STATS
HP
Attack
Defense
Sp. Atk
Sp. Def
Speed

EGG GROUPS
No Egg has ever been discovered

ITEMS SOMETIMES HELD
● None

Gender unknown

EVOLUTION

Does not evolve

HOW TO OBTAIN

Pokémon Black Version 2	Link Trade or Poké Transfer
Pokémon White Version 2	Link Trade or Poké Transfer

HOW TO OBTAIN FROM OTHER GAMES

Pokémon HeartGold Version	Cerulean Cave
Pokémon SoulSilver Version	Cerulean Cave

LEVEL-UP AND LEARNED MOVES

Lv.	Name	Type	Kind	Pow.	Acc.	PP	Range	Long	DA
1	Confusion	Psychic	Special	50	100	25	Normal	—	
1	Disable	Normal	Status	—	100	20	Normal	—	
1	Barrier	Psychic	Status	—	—	30	Self	—	
8	Swift	Normal	Special	60	—	20	Many Others	—	
15	Future Sight	Psychic	Special	100	100	10	Normal	—	
22	Psych Up	Normal	Status	—	—	10	Normal	—	
29	Miracle Eye	Psychic	Status	—	—	40	Normal	—	
36	Mist	Ice	Status	—	—	30	Your Side	—	
43	Psycho Cut	Psychic	Physical	70	100	20	Normal	—	○
50	Amnesia	Psychic	Status	—	—	20	Self	—	
57	Power Swap	Psychic	Status	—	—	10	Normal	—	
57	Guard Swap	Psychic	Status	—	—	10	Normal	—	
64	Psychic	Psychic	Special	90	100	10	Normal	—	
71	Me First	Normal	Status	—	—	20	Varies	—	
79	Recover	Normal	Status	—	—	10	Self	—	
86	Safeguard	Normal	Status	—	—	25	Your Side	—	
93	Aura Sphere	Fighting	Special	90	—	20	Normal	—	
100	Psystrike	Psychic	Special	100	100	10	Normal	—	

TM & HM MOVES

Lv.	Name	Type	Kind	Pow.	Acc.	PP	Range	Long	DA
TM03	Psyshock	Psychic	Special	80	100	10	Normal	—	
TM04	Calm Mind	Psychic	Status	—	—	20	Self	—	
TM06	Toxic	Poison	Status	—	90	10	Normal	—	
TM07	Hail	Ice	Status	—	—	10	Both Sides	—	
TM08	Bulk Up	Fighting	Status	—	—	20	Self	—	
TM10	Hidden Power	Normal	Special	—	100	15	Normal	—	
TM11	Sunny Day	Fire	Status	—	—	5	Both Sides	—	
TM12	Taunt	Dark	Status	—	100	20	Normal	—	
TM13	Ice Beam	Ice	Special	95	100	10	Normal	—	
TM14	Blizzard	Ice	Special	120	70	5	Many Others	—	
TM15	Hyper Beam	Normal	Special	150	90	5	Normal	—	
TM16	Light Screen	Psychic	Status	—	—	30	Your Side	—	
TM17	Protect	Normal	Status	—	—	10	Self	—	
TM18	Rain Dance	Water	Status	—	—	5	Both Sides	—	
TM19	Telekinesis	Psychic	Status	—	—	15	Normal	—	
TM20	Safeguard	Normal	Status	—	—	25	Your Side	—	
TM21	Frustration	Normal	Physical	—	100	20	Normal	—	
TM22	SolarBeam	Grass	Special	120	100	10	Normal	—	
TM24	Thunderbolt	Electric	Special	95	100	15	Normal	—	
TM25	Thunder	Electric	Special	120	70	10	Normal	—	
TM26	Earthquake	Ground	Physical	100	100	10	Adjacent	—	
TM27	Return	Normal	Physical	—	100	20	Normal	—	
TM29	Psychic	Psychic	Special	90	100	10	Normal	—	
TM30	Shadow Ball	Ghost	Special	80	100	15	Normal	—	
TM31	Brick Break	Fighting	Physical	75	100	15	Normal	—	
TM32	Double Team	Normal	Status	—	—	15	Self	—	
TM33	Reflect	Psychic	Status	—	—	20	Your Side	—	
TM35	Flamethrower	Fire	Special	95	100	15	Normal	—	
TM37	Sandstorm	Rock	Status	—	—	10	Both Sides	—	
TM38	Fire Blast	Fire	Special	120	85	5	Normal	—	
TM39	Rock Tomb	Rock	Physical	50	80	10	Normal	—	
TM40	Aerial Ace	Flying	Physical	60	—	20	Normal	○	
TM41	Torment	Dark	Status	—	100	15	Normal	—	
TM42	Facade	Normal	Physical	70	100	20	Normal	—	
TM44	Rest	Psychic	Status	—	—	10	Self	—	

Lv.	Name	Type	Kind	Pow.	Acc.	PP	Range	Long	DA
TM47	Low Sweep	Fighting	Physical	60	100	20	Normal	—	
TM48	Round	Normal	Special	60	100	15	Normal	—	
TM52	Focus Blast	Fighting	Special	120	70	5	Normal	—	
TM53	Energy Ball	Grass	Special	80	100	10	Normal	—	
TM56	Fling	Dark	Physical	—	100	10	Normal	—	
TM57	Charge Beam	Electric	Special	50	90	10	Normal	—	
TM59	Incinerate	Fire	Special	30	100	15	Many Others	—	
TM61	Will-O-Wisp	Fire	Status	—	75	15	Normal	—	
TM63	Embargo	Dark	Status	—	100	15	Normal	—	
TM68	Giga Impact	Normal	Physical	150	90	5	Normal	—	
TM70	Flash	Normal	Status	—	100	20	Normal	—	
TM71	Stone Edge	Rock	Physical	100	80	5	Normal	—	
TM73	Thunder Wave	Electric	Status	—	100	20	Normal	—	
TM77	Psych Up	Normal	Status	—	—	10	Normal	—	
TM78	Bulldoze	Ground	Physical	60	100	20	Adjacent	—	
TM80	Rock Slide	Rock	Physical	75	90	10	Many Others	—	
TM84	Poison Jab	Poison	Physical	80	100	20	Normal	—	
TM85	Dream Eater	Psychic	Special	100	100	15	Normal	—	
TM86	Grass Knot	Grass	Special	—	100	20	Normal	—	
TM87	Swagger	Normal	Status	—	90	15	Normal	—	
TM90	Substitute	Normal	Status	—	—	10	Self	—	
TM92	Trick Room	Psychic	Status	—	—	5	Both Sides	—	
TM94	Rock Smash	Fighting	Physical	40	100	15	Normal	—	
HM04	Strength	Normal	Physical	80	100	15	Normal	—	

MOVES TAUGHT BY PEOPLE

Name	Type	Kind	Pow.	Acc.	PP	Range	Long	DA

MOVES TAUGHT BY MOVE TUTORS FOR SHARDS

Name	Type	Kind	Pow.	Acc.	PP	Range	Long	DA
Signal Beam	Bug	Special	75	100	15	Normal	—	
Low Kick	Fighting	Physical	—	100	20	Normal	—	○
Fire Punch	Fire	Physical	75	100	15	Normal	—	○
ThunderPunch	Electric	Physical	75	100	15	Normal	—	○
Ice Punch	Ice	Physical	75	100	15	Normal	—	○
Magic Coat	Psychic	Status	—	—	15	Self	—	
Icy Wind	Ice	Special	55	95	15	Many Others	—	
Iron Tail	Steel	Physical	100	75	15	Normal	—	○
Aqua Tail	Water	Physical	90	90	10	Normal	—	○
Zen Headbutt	Psychic	Physical	80	90	15	Normal	—	○
Foul Play	Dark	Physical	95	100	15	Normal	—	○
Gravity	Psychic	Status	—	—	5	Both Sides	—	
Snore	Normal	Special	40	100	15	Normal	—	
Role Play	Psychic	Status	—	—	10	Normal	—	
Drain Punch	Fighting	Physical	75	100	10	Normal	—	○
Magic Room	Psychic	Status	—	—	10	Both Sides	—	
Wonder Room	Psychic	Status	—	—	10	Both Sides	—	
Recycle	Normal	Status	—	—	10	Self	—	
Trick	Psychic	Status	—	100	10	Normal	—	
Sleep Talk	Normal	Status	—	—	10	Self	—	
Skill Swap	Psychic	Status	—	—	10	Normal	—	
Snatch	Dark	Status	—	—	10	Self	—	

Pokémon AR Marker

151 Mew
New Species Pokémon

TYPE Psychic

ABILITY
● Synchronize

HIDDEN ABILITY
—

- HEIGHT: 1'04"
- WEIGHT: 8.8 lbs.
- GENDER: Unknown

Because it can use all kinds of moves, many scientists believe Mew to be the ancestor of Pokémon.

STATS
HP	
Attack	
Defense	
Sp. Atk	
Sp. Def	
Speed	

EGG GROUPS
No Egg has ever been discovered

Gender unknown

EVOLUTION

Does not evolve

HOW TO OBTAIN
Only available through special distribution events. Check www.pokemon.com for the latest information on how to catch this Pokémon.

LEVEL-UP AND LEARNED MOVES
Lv.	Name	Type	Kind	Pow.	Acc.	PP	Range	Long	DA
1	Pound	Normal	Physical	40	100	35	Normal	—	—
1	Reflect Type	Normal	Status	—	—	10	Normal	—	—
1	Transform	Normal	Status	—	—	10	Normal	—	—
10	Mega Punch	Normal	Physical	80	85	20	Normal	—	○
20	Metronome	Normal	Status	—	—	10	Self	—	—
30	Psychic	Psychic	Special	90	100	10	Normal	—	—
40	Barrier	Psychic	Status	—	—	30	Self	—	—
50	AncientPower	Rock	Special	60	100	5	Normal	—	—
60	Amnesia	Psychic	Status	—	—	20	Self	—	—
70	Me First	Normal	Status	—	—	20	Varies	—	—
80	Baton Pass	Normal	Status	—	—	40	Self	—	—
90	Nasty Plot	Dark	Status	—	—	20	Self	—	—
100	Aura Sphere	Fighting	Special	90	—	20	Normal	○	—

TM & HM MOVES
Lv.	Name	Type	Kind	Pow.	Acc.	PP	Range	Long	DA

Mew can learn every TM and HM.

MOVES TAUGHT BY PEOPLE
Name	Type	Kind	Pow.	Acc.	PP	Range	Long	DA

MOVES TAUGHT BY MOVE TUTORS FOR SHARDS
Name	Type	Kind	Pow.	Acc.	PP	Range	Long	DA

Mew can learn every move that Move Tutors will teach in exchange for Shards.

Pokémon AR Marker

---

152 Chikorita
Leaf Pokémon

TYPE Grass

ABILITY
● Overgrow

HIDDEN ABILITY
—

- HEIGHT: 2'11"
- WEIGHT: 14.1 lbs.
- GENDER: ♂ / ♀

It uses the leaf on its head to determine the temperature and humidity. It loves to sunbathe.

STATS
HP	
Attack	
Defense	
Sp. Atk	
Sp. Def	
Speed	

EGG GROUPS
Monster/Grass

ITEMS SOMETIMES HELD
● None

Same form for ♂ / ♀

EVOLUTION

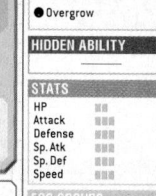 Chikorita → Lv. 16 → Bayleef 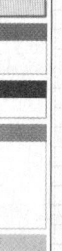 → Lv. 32 → Meganium

HOW TO OBTAIN
Pokémon Black Version 2	Link Trade or Poké Transfer
Pokémon White Version 2	Link Trade or Poké Transfer

HOW TO OBTAIN FROM OTHER GAMES
Pokémon HeartGold Version	Get from Professor Elm at the start of the adventure
Pokémon SoulSilver Version	Get from Professor Elm at the start of the adventure

LEVEL-UP AND LEARNED MOVES
Lv.	Name	Type	Kind	Pow.	Acc.	PP	Range	Long	DA
1	Tackle	Normal	Physical	50	100	35	Normal	—	—
1	Growl	Normal	Status	—	100	40	Many Others	—	—
6	Razor Leaf	Grass	Physical	55	95	25	Many Others	—	—
9	PoisonPowder	Poison	Status	—	75	35	Normal	—	—
12	Synthesis	Grass	Status	—	—	5	Self	—	—
17	Reflect	Psychic	Status	—	—	20	Your Side	—	—
20	Magical Leaf	Grass	Special	60	—	20	Normal	—	—
23	Natural Gift	Normal	Physical	—	100	15	Normal	—	—
28	Sweet Scent	Normal	Status	—	100	20	Many Others	—	—
31	Light Screen	Psychic	Status	—	—	30	Your Side	—	—
34	Body Slam	Normal	Physical	85	100	15	Normal	—	○
39	Safeguard	Normal	Status	—	—	25	Your Side	—	—
42	Aromatherapy	Grass	Status	—	—	5	Your Party	—	—
45	SolarBeam	Grass	Special	120	100	10	Normal	—	—

TM & HM MOVES
Lv.	Name	Type	Kind	Pow.	Acc.	PP	Range	Long	DA
TM06	Toxic	Poison	Status	—	90	10	Normal	—	—
TM10	Hidden Power	Normal	Special	—	100	15	Normal	—	—
TM11	Sunny Day	Fire	Status	—	—	5	Both Sides	—	—
TM16	Light Screen	Psychic	Status	—	—	30	Your Side	—	—
TM17	Protect	Normal	Status	—	—	10	Self	—	—
TM20	Safeguard	Normal	Status	—	—	25	Your Side	—	—
TM21	Frustration	Normal	Physical	—	100	20	Normal	—	○
TM22	SolarBeam	Grass	Special	120	100	10	Normal	—	—
TM27	Return	Normal	Physical	—	100	20	Normal	—	○
TM32	Double Team	Normal	Status	—	—	15	Self	—	—
TM33	Reflect	Psychic	Status	—	—	20	Your Side	—	—
TM42	Facade	Normal	Physical	70	100	20	Normal	—	○
TM44	Rest	Psychic	Status	—	—	10	Self	—	—
TM45	Attract	Normal	Status	—	100	15	Normal	—	—
TM48	Round	Normal	Special	60	100	15	Normal	—	—
TM49	Echoed Voice	Normal	Special	40	100	15	Normal	—	—
TM53	Energy Ball	Grass	Special	80	100	10	Normal	—	—
TM70	Flash	Normal	Status	—	100	20	Normal	—	—
TM75	Swords Dance	Normal	Status	—	—	30	Self	—	—
TM86	Grass Knot	Grass	Special	—	100	20	Normal	—	○
TM87	Swagger	Normal	Status	—	90	15	Normal	—	—
TM90	Substitute	Normal	Status	—	—	10	Self	—	—
HM01	Cut	Normal	Physical	50	95	30	Normal	—	○

MOVES TAUGHT BY PEOPLE
Name	Type	Kind	Pow.	Acc.	PP	Range	Long	DA
Grass Pledge	Grass	Special	50	100	10	Normal	—	—

MOVES TAUGHT BY MOVE TUTORS FOR SHARDS
Name	Type	Kind	Pow.	Acc.	PP	Range	Long	DA
Seed Bomb	Grass	Physical	80	100	15	Normal	—	—
Magic Coat	Psychic	Status	—	—	15	Self	—	—
Iron Tail	Steel	Physical	100	75	15	Normal	—	○
Snore	Normal	Special	40	100	15	Normal	—	—
Synthesis	Grass	Status	—	—	5	Self	—	—
Giga Drain	Grass	Special	75	100	10	Normal	—	—
Worry Seed	Grass	Status	—	100	10	Normal	—	—
Sleep Talk	Normal	Status	—	—	10	Self	—	—

EGG MOVES
Name	Type	Kind	Pow.	Acc.	PP	Range	Long	DA
Vine Whip	Grass	Physical	35	100	15	Normal	—	○
Leech Seed	Grass	Status	—	90	10	Normal	—	—
Counter	Fighting	Physical	—	100	20	Varies	—	○
AncientPower	Rock	Special	60	100	5	Normal	—	—
Flail	Normal	Physical	—	100	15	Normal	—	○
Nature Power	Normal	Status	—	—	20	Varies	—	—
Ingrain	Grass	Status	—	—	20	Self	—	—
Grasswhistle	Grass	Status	—	55	15	Normal	—	—
Leaf Storm	Grass	Special	140	90	5	Normal	—	—
Aromatherapy	Grass	Status	—	—	5	Your Party	—	—
Wring Out	Normal	Special	—	100	5	Normal	—	○
Body Slam	Normal	Physical	85	100	15	Normal	—	○
Refresh	Normal	Status	—	—	20	Self	—	—
Heal Pulse	Psychic	Status	—	—	10	Normal	○	—

Pokémon AR Marker

Leaf Pokémon

153 Bayleef

● HEIGHT: 3'11"
● WEIGHT: 34.8 lbs.
● GENDER: ♂ / ♀

The buds that ring its neck give off a spicy aroma that perks people up.

Same form for ♂ / ♀

TYPE: Grass

ABILITY
● Overgrow

HIDDEN ABILITY
—

STATS
HP
Attack
Defense
Sp. Atk
Sp. Def
Speed

EGG GROUPS
Monster/Grass

ITEMS SOMETIMES HELD
● None

EVOLUTION

HOW TO OBTAIN

Pokémon Black Version 2	Level up a Chikorita you obtain via Link Trade or Poké Transfer to Lv. 16
Pokémon White Version 2	Level up a Chikorita you obtain via Link Trade or Poké Transfer to Lv. 16

HOW TO OBTAIN FROM OTHER GAMES

—

—

LEVEL-UP AND LEARNED MOVES

Lv.	Name	Type	Kind	Pow.	Acc.	PP	Range	Long	DA
1	Tackle	Normal	Physical	50	100	35	Normal	—	○
1	Growl	Normal	Status	—	100	40	Many Others	—	—
1	Razor Leaf	Grass	Physical	55	95	25	Many Others	—	—
1	PoisonPowder	Poison	Status	—	75	35	Normal	—	—
6	Razor Leaf	Grass	Physical	55	95	25	Many Others	—	—
9	PoisonPowder	Poison	Status	—	75	35	Normal	—	—
12	Synthesis	Grass	Status	—	—	5	Self	—	—
18	Reflect	Psychic	Status	—	—	20	Your Side	—	—
22	Magical Leaf	Grass	Special	60	—	20	Normal	—	—
26	Natural Gift	Normal	Physical	—	100	15	Normal	—	—
32	Sweet Scent	Normal	Status	—	100	20	Many Others	—	—
36	Light Screen	Psychic	Status	—	—	30	Your Side	—	—
40	Body Slam	Normal	Physical	85	100	15	Normal	—	○
46	Safeguard	Normal	Status	—	—	25	Your Side	—	—
50	Aromatherapy	Grass	Status	—	—	5	Your Party	—	—
54	SolarBeam	Grass	Special	120	100	10	Normal	—	—

TM & HM MOVES

Lv.	Name	Type	Kind	Pow.	Acc.	PP	Range	Long	DA
TM06	Toxic	Poison	Status	—	90	10	Normal	—	—
TM10	Hidden Power	Normal	Special	—	100	15	Normal	—	—
TM11	Sunny Day	Fire	Status	—	—	5	Both Sides	—	—
TM16	Light Screen	Psychic	Status	—	—	30	Your Side	—	—
TM17	Protect	Normal	Status	—	—	10	Self	—	—
TM20	Safeguard	Normal	Status	—	—	25	Your Side	—	—
TM21	Frustration	Normal	Physical	—	100	20	Normal	—	○
TM22	SolarBeam	Grass	Special	120	100	10	Normal	—	—
TM27	Return	Normal	Physical	—	100	20	Normal	—	○
TM32	Double Team	Normal	Status	—	—	15	Self	—	—
TM33	Reflect	Psychic	Status	—	—	20	Your Side	—	—
TM42	Facade	Normal	Physical	70	100	20	Normal	—	○
TM44	Rest	Psychic	Status	—	—	10	Self	—	—
TM45	Attract	Normal	Status	—	100	15	Normal	—	—
TM48	Round	Normal	Special	60	100	15	Normal	—	—
TM49	Echoed Voice	Normal	Special	40	100	15	Normal	—	—
TM53	Energy Ball	Grass	Special	80	100	10	Normal	—	—
TM70	Flash	Normal	Status	—	100	20	Normal	—	—
TM75	Swords Dance	Normal	Status	—	—	30	Self	—	—
TM86	Grass Knot	Grass	Special	—	100	20	Normal	—	○
TM87	Swagger	Normal	Status	—	90	15	Normal	—	—
TM90	Substitute	Normal	Status	—	—	10	Self	—	—
TM94	Rock Smash	Fighting	Physical	40	100	15	Normal	—	○
HM01	Cut	Normal	Physical	50	95	30	Normal	—	○
HM04	Strength	Normal	Physical	80	100	15	Normal	—	○

MOVES TAUGHT BY PEOPLE

Name	Type	Kind	Pow.	Acc.	PP	Range	Long	DA
Grass Pledge	Grass	Special	50	100	10	Normal	—	—

MOVES TAUGHT BY MOVE TUTORS FOR SHARDS

Name	Type	Kind	Pow.	Acc.	PP	Range	Long	DA
Seed Bomb	Grass	Physical	80	100	15	Normal	—	—
Magic Coat	Psychic	Status	—	—	15	Self	—	—
Iron Tail	Steel	Physical	100	75	15	Normal	—	○
Snore	Normal	Special	40	100	15	Normal	—	—
Synthesis	Grass	Status	—	—	5	Self	—	—
Giga Drain	Grass	Special	75	100	10	Normal	—	—
Worry Seed	Grass	Status	—	100	10	Normal	—	—
Sleep Talk	Normal	Status	—	—	10	Self	—	—

Pokémon AR Marker

Herb Pokémon

154 Meganium

● HEIGHT: 5'11"
● WEIGHT: 221.6 lbs.
● GENDER: ♂ / ♀

Its breath has the fantastic ability to revive dead plants and flowers.

♂ ♀

TYPE: Grass

ABILITY
● Overgrow

HIDDEN ABILITY
—

STATS
HP
Attack
Defense
Sp. Atk
Sp. Def
Speed

EGG GROUPS
Monster/Grass

ITEMS SOMETIMES HELD
● None

EVOLUTION

HOW TO OBTAIN

Pokémon Black Version 2	Level up a Bayleef you obtain via Link Trade or Poké Transfer to Lv. 32
Pokémon White Version 2	Level up a Bayleef you obtain via Link Trade or Poké Transfer to Lv. 32

HOW TO OBTAIN FROM OTHER GAMES

—

—

LEVEL-UP AND LEARNED MOVES

Lv.	Name	Type	Kind	Pow.	Acc.	PP	Range	Long	DA
1	Tackle	Normal	Physical	50	100	35	Normal	—	○
1	Growl	Normal	Status	—	100	40	Many Others	—	—
1	Razor Leaf	Grass	Physical	55	95	25	Many Others	—	—
1	PoisonPowder	Poison	Status	—	75	35	Normal	—	—
6	Razor Leaf	Grass	Physical	55	95	25	Many Others	—	—
9	PoisonPowder	Poison	Status	—	75	35	Normal	—	—
12	Synthesis	Grass	Status	—	—	5	Self	—	—
18	Reflect	Psychic	Status	—	—	20	Your Side	—	—
22	Magical Leaf	Grass	Special	60	—	20	Normal	—	—
26	Natural Gift	Normal	Physical	—	100	15	Normal	—	—
32	Petal Dance	Grass	Special	120	100	10	1 Random	—	○
34	Sweet Scent	Normal	Status	—	100	20	Many Others	—	—
40	Light Screen	Psychic	Status	—	—	30	Your Side	—	—
46	Body Slam	Normal	Physical	85	100	15	Normal	—	○
54	Safeguard	Normal	Status	—	—	25	Your Side	—	—
60	Aromatherapy	Grass	Status	—	—	5	Your Party	—	—
66	SolarBeam	Grass	Special	120	100	10	Normal	—	—

TM & HM MOVES

Lv.	Name	Type	Kind	Pow.	Acc.	PP	Range	Long	DA
TM06	Toxic	Poison	Status	—	90	10	Normal	—	—
TM10	Hidden Power	Normal	Special	—	100	15	Normal	—	—
TM11	Sunny Day	Fire	Status	—	—	5	Both Sides	—	—
TM15	Hyper Beam	Normal	Special	150	90	5	Normal	—	—
TM16	Light Screen	Psychic	Status	—	—	30	Your Side	—	—
TM17	Protect	Normal	Status	—	—	10	Self	—	—
TM20	Safeguard	Normal	Status	—	—	25	Your Side	—	—
TM21	Frustration	Normal	Physical	—	100	20	Normal	—	○
TM22	SolarBeam	Grass	Special	120	100	10	Normal	—	—
TM26	Earthquake	Ground	Physical	100	100	10	Adjacent	—	—
TM27	Return	Normal	Physical	—	100	20	Normal	—	○
TM32	Double Team	Normal	Status	—	—	15	Self	—	—
TM33	Reflect	Psychic	Status	—	—	20	Your Side	—	—
TM42	Facade	Normal	Physical	70	100	20	Normal	—	○
TM44	Rest	Psychic	Status	—	—	10	Self	—	—
TM45	Attract	Normal	Status	—	100	15	Normal	—	—
TM48	Round	Normal	Special	60	100	15	Normal	—	—
TM49	Echoed Voice	Normal	Special	40	100	15	Normal	—	—
TM53	Energy Ball	Grass	Special	80	100	10	Normal	—	—
TM68	Giga Impact	Normal	Physical	150	90	5	Normal	—	○
TM70	Flash	Normal	Status	—	100	20	Normal	—	—
TM75	Swords Dance	Normal	Status	—	—	30	Self	—	—
TM78	Bulldoze	Ground	Physical	60	100	20	Adjacent	—	—
TM82	Dragon Tail	Dragon	Physical	60	90	10	Normal	—	○
TM86	Grass Knot	Grass	Special	—	100	20	Normal	—	○
TM87	Swagger	Normal	Status	—	90	15	Normal	—	—
TM90	Substitute	Normal	Status	—	—	10	Self	—	—
TM94	Rock Smash	Fighting	Physical	40	100	15	Normal	—	○
HM01	Cut	Normal	Physical	50	95	30	Normal	—	○
HM04	Strength	Normal	Physical	80	100	15	Normal	—	○

MOVES TAUGHT BY PEOPLE

Name	Type	Kind	Pow.	Acc.	PP	Range	Long	DA
Grass Pledge	Grass	Special	50	100	10	Normal	—	—
Frenzy Plant	Grass	Special	150	90	5	Normal	—	—

MOVES TAUGHT BY MOVE TUTORS FOR SHARDS

Name	Type	Kind	Pow.	Acc.	PP	Range	Long	DA
Seed Bomb	Grass	Physical	80	100	15	Normal	—	—
Magic Coat	Psychic	Status	—	—	15	Self	—	—
Iron Tail	Steel	Physical	100	75	15	Normal	—	○
Snore	Normal	Special	40	100	15	Normal	—	—
Synthesis	Grass	Status	—	—	5	Self	—	—
Giga Drain	Grass	Special	75	100	10	Normal	—	—
Worry Seed	Grass	Status	—	100	10	Normal	—	—
Outrage	Dragon	Physical	120	100	10	1 Random	—	○
Sleep Talk	Normal	Status	—	—	10	Self	—	—

Pokémon AR Marker

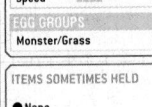

155 Cyndaquil — Fire Mouse Pokémon

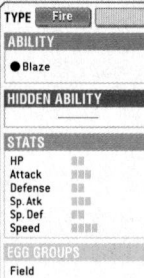

- **TYPE:** Fire
- **ABILITY:** Blaze
- **HIDDEN ABILITY:** —

- HEIGHT: 1'08"
- WEIGHT: 17.4 lbs.
- GENDER: ♂ / ♀

It has a timid nature. If it is startled, the flames on its back burn more vigorously.

STATS
- HP
- Attack
- Defense
- Sp. Atk
- Sp. Def
- Speed

EGG GROUPS: Field

ITEMS SOMETIMES HELD: None

Same form for ♂ / ♀

Pokémon AR Marker
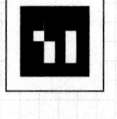

EVOLUTION

Cyndaquil → (Lv. 14) Quilava → (Lv. 36) Typhlosion

HOW TO OBTAIN
Pokémon Black Version 2	Link Trade or Poké Transfer
Pokémon White Version 2	Link Trade or Poké Transfer

HOW TO OBTAIN FROM OTHER GAMES
Pokémon HeartGold Version	Get from Professor Elm at the start of the adventure
Pokémon SoulSilver Version	Get from Professor Elm at the start of the adventure

LEVEL-UP AND LEARNED MOVES
Lv.	Name	Type	Kind	Pow.	Acc.	PP	Range	Long	DA
1	Tackle	Normal	Physical	50	100	35	Normal	—	○
1	Leer	Normal	Status	—	100	30	Many Others	—	—
6	SmokeScreen	Normal	Status	—	100	20	Normal	—	—
10	Ember	Fire	Special	40	100	25	Normal	—	—
13	Quick Attack	Normal	Physical	40	100	30	Normal	—	○
19	Flame Wheel	Fire	Physical	60	100	25	Normal	—	○
22	Defense Curl	Normal	Status	—	—	40	Self	—	—
28	Flame Charge	Fire	Physical	50	100	20	Normal	—	○
31	Swift	Normal	Special	60	—	20	Many Others	—	—
37	Lava Plume	Fire	Special	80	100	15	Adjacent	—	—
40	Flamethrower	Fire	Special	95	100	15	Normal	—	—
46	Inferno	Fire	Special	100	50	5	Normal	—	—
49	Rollout	Rock	Physical	30	90	20	Normal	—	○
55	Double-Edge	Normal	Physical	120	100	15	Normal	—	○
58	Eruption	Fire	Special	150	100	5	Many Others	—	—

TM & HM MOVES
Lv.	Name	Type	Kind	Pow.	Acc.	PP	Range	Long	DA
TM06	Toxic	Poison	Status	—	90	10	Normal	—	—
TM10	Hidden Power	Normal	Special	—	100	15	Normal	—	—
TM11	Sunny Day	Fire	Status	—	—	5	Both Sides	—	—
TM17	Protect	Normal	Status	—	—	10	Self	—	—
TM21	Frustration	Normal	Physical	—	100	20	Normal	—	○
TM27	Return	Normal	Physical	—	100	20	Normal	—	○
TM28	Dig	Ground	Physical	80	100	10	Normal	—	○
TM32	Double Team	Normal	Status	—	—	15	Self	—	—
TM35	Flamethrower	Fire	Special	95	100	15	Normal	—	—
TM38	Fire Blast	Fire	Special	120	85	5	Normal	—	—
TM40	Aerial Ace	Flying	Physical	60	—	20	Normal	○	○
TM42	Facade	Normal	Physical	70	100	20	Normal	—	○
TM43	Flame Charge	Fire	Physical	50	100	20	Normal	—	○
TM44	Rest	Psychic	Status	—	—	10	Self	—	—
TM45	Attract	Normal	Status	—	100	15	Normal	—	—
TM48	Round	Normal	Special	60	100	15	Normal	—	—
TM50	Overheat	Fire	Special	140	90	5	Normal	—	—
TM59	Incinerate	Fire	Special	30	100	15	Many Others	—	—
TM61	Will-O-Wisp	Fire	Status	—	75	15	Normal	—	—
TM87	Swagger	Normal	Status	—	90	15	Normal	—	—
TM90	Substitute	Normal	Status	—	—	10	Self	—	—
TM93	Wild Charge	Electric	Physical	90	100	15	Normal	—	○
HM01	Cut	Normal	Physical	50	95	30	Normal	—	—

MOVES TAUGHT BY PEOPLE
Name	Type	Kind	Pow.	Acc.	PP	Range	Long	DA
Fire Pledge	Fire	Special	50	100	10	Normal	—	—

MOVES TAUGHT BY MOVE TUTORS FOR SHARDS
Name	Type	Kind	Pow.	Acc.	PP	Range	Long	DA
Covet	Normal	Physical	60	100	40	Normal	—	○
Snore	Normal	Special	40	100	15	Normal	—	—
Heat Wave	Fire	Special	100	90	10	Many Others	—	—
Sleep Talk	Normal	Status	—	—	10	Self	—	—

EGG MOVES
Name	Type	Kind	Pow.	Acc.	PP	Range	Long	DA
Fury Swipes	Normal	Physical	18	80	15	Normal	—	○
Quick Attack	Normal	Physical	40	100	30	Normal	—	○
Reversal	Fighting	Physical	—	100	15	Normal	—	○
Thrash	Normal	Physical	120	100	10	1 Random	—	○
Foresight	Normal	Status	—	—	40	Normal	—	—
Covet	Normal	Physical	60	100	40	Normal	—	○
Howl	Normal	Status	—	—	40	Self	—	—
Crush Claw	Normal	Physical	75	95	10	Normal	—	○
Double-Edge	Normal	Physical	120	100	15	Normal	—	○
Double Kick	Fighting	Physical	30	100	30	Normal	—	○
Flare Blitz	Fire	Physical	120	100	15	Normal	—	○
Extrasensory	Psychic	Special	80	100	30	Normal	—	—
Nature Power	Normal	Status	—	—	20	Varies	—	—
Flame Burst	Fire	Special	70	100	15	Normal	—	—

---

156 Quilava — Volcano Pokémon

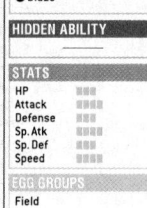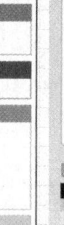

- **TYPE:** Fire
- **ABILITY:** Blaze
- **HIDDEN ABILITY:** —

- HEIGHT: 2'11"
- WEIGHT: 41.9 lbs.
- GENDER: ♂ / ♀

It intimidates foes with the heat of its flames. The fire burns more strongly when it readies to fight.

STATS
- HP
- Attack
- Defense
- Sp. Atk
- Sp. Def
- Speed

EGG GROUPS: Field

ITEMS SOMETIMES HELD: None

Same form for ♂ / ♀

Pokémon AR Marker

EVOLUTION
Cyndaquil → (Lv. 14) Quilava → (Lv. 36) Typhlosion

HOW TO OBTAIN
Pokémon Black Version 2	Get Cyndaquil with Link Trade or Poké Transfer, then level it up to Lv. 14
Pokémon White Version 2	Get Cyndaquil with Link Trade or Poké Transfer, then level it up to Lv. 14

HOW TO OBTAIN FROM OTHER GAMES
—	
—	

LEVEL-UP AND LEARNED MOVES
Lv.	Name	Type	Kind	Pow.	Acc.	PP	Range	Long	DA
1	Tackle	Normal	Physical	50	100	35	Normal	—	○
1	Leer	Normal	Status	—	100	30	Many Others	—	—
1	SmokeScreen	Normal	Status	—	100	20	Normal	—	—
6	SmokeScreen	Normal	Status	—	100	20	Normal	—	—
10	Ember	Fire	Special	40	100	25	Normal	—	—
13	Quick Attack	Normal	Physical	40	100	30	Normal	—	○
20	Flame Wheel	Fire	Physical	60	100	25	Normal	—	○
24	Defense Curl	Normal	Status	—	—	40	Self	—	—
31	Swift	Normal	Special	60	—	20	Many Others	—	—
35	Flame Charge	Fire	Physical	50	100	20	Normal	—	○
42	Lava Plume	Fire	Special	80	100	15	Adjacent	—	—
46	Flamethrower	Fire	Special	95	100	15	Normal	—	—
53	Inferno	Fire	Special	100	50	5	Normal	—	—
57	Rollout	Rock	Physical	30	90	20	Normal	—	○
64	Double-Edge	Normal	Physical	120	100	15	Normal	—	○
68	Eruption	Fire	Special	150	100	5	Many Others	—	—

TM & HM MOVES
Lv.	Name	Type	Kind	Pow.	Acc.	PP	Range	Long	DA
TM05	Roar	Normal	Status	—	100	20	Normal	—	—
TM06	Toxic	Poison	Status	—	90	10	Normal	—	—
TM10	Hidden Power	Normal	Special	—	100	15	Normal	—	—
TM11	Sunny Day	Fire	Status	—	—	5	Both Sides	—	—
TM17	Protect	Normal	Status	—	—	10	Self	—	—
TM21	Frustration	Normal	Physical	—	100	20	Normal	—	○
TM27	Return	Normal	Physical	—	100	20	Normal	—	○
TM28	Dig	Ground	Physical	80	100	10	Normal	—	○
TM31	Brick Break	Fighting	Physical	75	100	15	Normal	—	○
TM32	Double Team	Normal	Status	—	—	15	Self	—	—
TM35	Flamethrower	Fire	Special	95	100	15	Normal	—	—
TM38	Fire Blast	Fire	Special	120	85	5	Normal	—	—
TM40	Aerial Ace	Flying	Physical	60	—	20	Normal	○	○
TM42	Facade	Normal	Physical	70	100	20	Normal	—	○
TM43	Flame Charge	Fire	Physical	50	100	20	Normal	—	○
TM44	Rest	Psychic	Status	—	—	10	Self	—	—
TM45	Attract	Normal	Status	—	100	15	Normal	—	—
TM48	Round	Normal	Special	60	100	15	Normal	—	—
TM50	Overheat	Fire	Special	140	90	5	Normal	—	—
TM59	Incinerate	Fire	Special	30	100	15	Many Others	—	—
TM61	Will-O-Wisp	Fire	Status	—	75	15	Normal	—	—
TM87	Swagger	Normal	Status	—	90	15	Normal	—	—
TM90	Substitute	Normal	Status	—	—	10	Self	—	—
TM93	Wild Charge	Electric	Physical	90	100	15	Normal	—	○
TM94	Rock Smash	Fighting	Physical	40	100	15	Normal	—	○
HM01	Cut	Normal	Physical	50	95	30	Normal	—	—
HM04	Strength	Normal	Physical	80	100	15	Normal	—	○

MOVES TAUGHT BY PEOPLE
Name	Type	Kind	Pow.	Acc.	PP	Range	Long	DA
Fire Pledge	Fire	Special	50	100	10	Normal	—	—

MOVES TAUGHT BY MOVE TUTORS FOR SHARDS
Name	Type	Kind	Pow.	Acc.	PP	Range	Long	DA
Covet	Normal	Physical	60	100	40	Normal	—	○
Snore	Normal	Special	40	100	15	Normal	—	—
Heat Wave	Fire	Special	100	90	10	Many Others	—	—
Sleep Talk	Normal	Status	—	—	10	Self	—	—

157 Typhlosion

157 Typhlosion

Volcano Pokémon

TYPE: Fire

ABILITY
- Blaze

HIDDEN ABILITY
—

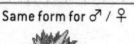

- HEIGHT: 5'07"
- WEIGHT: 175.3 lbs.
- GENDER: ♂ / ♀

STATS
HP
Attack
Defense
Sp. Atk
Sp. Def
Speed

It attacks using blasts of fire. It creates heat shimmers with intense fire to hide itself.

EGG GROUPS
Field

Same form for ♂ / ♀

ITEMS SOMETIMES HELD
- None

Pokémon AR Marker

EVOLUTION

Cyndaquil
Lv. 14
Quilava
Lv. 36
Typhlosion

HOW TO OBTAIN

Pokémon Black Version 2	Get Quilava with Link Trade or Poké Transfer, then level it up to Lv. 36
Pokémon White Version 2	Get Quilava with Link Trade or Poké Transfer, then level it up to Lv. 36

HOW TO OBTAIN FROM OTHER GAMES

—

—

LEVEL-UP AND LEARNED MOVES

Lv.	Name	Type	Kind	Pow.	Acc.	PP	Range	Long	DA
1	Gyro Ball	Steel	Physical	—	100	5	Normal	—	○
1	Tackle	Normal	Physical	50	100	35	Normal	—	○
1	Leer	Normal	Status	—	100	30	Many Others	—	—
1	SmokeScreen	Normal	Status	—	100	20	Normal	—	—
1	Ember	Fire	Special	40	100	25	Normal	—	—
6	SmokeScreen	Normal	Status	—	100	20	Normal	—	—
10	Ember	Fire	Special	40	100	25	Normal	—	—
13	Quick Attack	Normal	Physical	40	100	30	Normal	—	○
20	Flame Wheel	Fire	Physical	60	100	25	Normal	—	○
24	Defense Curl	Normal	Status	—	—	40	Self	—	—
31	Swift	Normal	Special	60	—	20	Many Others	—	—
35	Flame Charge	Fire	Physical	50	100	20	Normal	—	○
43	Lava Plume	Fire	Special	80	100	15	Adjacent	—	—
48	Flamethrower	Fire	Special	95	100	15	Normal	—	—
56	Inferno	Fire	Special	100	50	5	Normal	—	—
61	Rollout	Rock	Physical	30	90	20	Normal	—	○
69	Double-Edge	Normal	Physical	120	100	15	Normal	—	○
74	Eruption	Fire	Special	150	100	5	Many Others	—	—

TM & HM MOVES

Lv.	Name	Type	Kind	Pow.	Acc.	PP	Range	Long	DA
TM05	Roar	Normal	Status	—	100	20	Normal	—	—
TM06	Toxic	Poison	Status	—	90	10	Normal	—	—
TM10	Hidden Power	Normal	Special	—	100	15	Normal	—	—
TM11	Sunny Day	Fire	Status	—	—	5	Both Sides	—	—
TM15	Hyper Beam	Normal	Special	150	90	5	Normal	—	—
TM17	Protect	Normal	Status	—	—	10	Self	—	—
TM21	Frustration	Normal	Physical	—	100	20	Normal	—	○
TM22	SolarBeam	Grass	Special	120	100	10	Normal	—	—
TM26	Earthquake	Ground	Physical	100	100	10	Adjacent	—	—
TM27	Return	Normal	Physical	—	100	20	Normal	—	○
TM28	Dig	Ground	Physical	80	100	10	Normal	—	○
TM31	Brick Break	Fighting	Physical	75	100	15	Normal	—	○
TM32	Double Team	Normal	Status	—	—	15	Self	—	—
TM35	Flamethrower	Fire	Special	95	100	15	Normal	—	—
TM38	Fire Blast	Fire	Special	120	85	5	Normal	—	—
TM39	Rock Tomb	Rock	Physical	50	80	10	Normal	—	—
TM40	Aerial Ace	Flying	Physical	60	—	20	Normal	○	○
TM42	Facade	Normal	Physical	70	100	20	Normal	—	○
TM43	Flame Charge	Fire	Physical	50	100	20	Normal	—	○
TM44	Rest	Psychic	Status	—	—	10	Self	—	—
TM45	Attract	Normal	Status	—	100	15	Normal	—	—
TM48	Round	Normal	Special	60	100	15	Normal	—	—
TM50	Overheat	Fire	Special	140	90	5	Normal	—	—
TM52	Focus Blast	Fighting	Special	120	70	5	Normal	—	—
TM56	Fling	Dark	Physical	—	100	10	Normal	—	—
TM59	Incinerate	Fire	Special	30	100	15	Many Others	—	—
TM61	Will-O-Wisp	Fire	Status	—	75	15	Normal	—	—
TM65	Shadow Claw	Ghost	Physical	70	100	15	Normal	—	○
TM68	Giga Impact	Normal	Physical	150	90	5	Normal	—	○
TM74	Gyro Ball	Steel	Physical	—	100	5	Normal	—	○
TM78	Bulldoze	Ground	Physical	60	100	20	Adjacent	—	—
TM80	Rock Slide	Rock	Physical	75	90	10	Many Others	—	—
TM87	Swagger	Normal	Status	—	90	15	Normal	—	—
TM90	Substitute	Normal	Status	—	—	10	Self	—	—
TM93	Wild Charge	Electric	Physical	90	100	15	Normal	—	○
TM94	Rock Smash	Fighting	Physical	40	100	15	Normal	—	○
HM01	Cut	Normal	Physical	50	95	30	Normal	—	○
HM04	Strength	Normal	Physical	80	100	15	Normal	—	○

MOVES TAUGHT BY PEOPLE

Name	Type	Kind	Pow.	Acc.	PP	Range	Long	DA
Fire Pledge	Fire	Special	50	100	10	Normal	—	—
Blast Burn	Fire	Special	150	90	5	Normal	—	—

MOVES TAUGHT BY MOVE TUTORS FOR SHARDS

Name	Type	Kind	Pow.	Acc.	PP	Range	Long	DA
Covet	Normal	Physical	60	100	40	Normal	—	○
Low Kick	Fighting	Physical	—	100	20	Normal	—	○
Fire Punch	Fire	Physical	75	100	15	Normal	—	○
ThunderPunch	Electric	Physical	75	100	15	Normal	—	○
Snore	Normal	Special	40	100	15	Normal	—	—
Heat Wave	Fire	Special	100	90	10	Many Others	—	—
Sleep Talk	Normal	Status	—	—	10	Self	—	—

158 Totodile

158 Totodile

Big Jaw Pokémon

TYPE: Water

ABILITY
- Torrent

HIDDEN ABILITY
—

- HEIGHT: 2'00"
- WEIGHT: 20.9 lbs.
- GENDER: ♂ / ♀

STATS
HP
Attack
Defense
Sp. Atk
Sp. Def
Speed

It has the habit of biting anything with its developed jaws. Even its Trainer needs to be careful.

EGG GROUPS
Monster/Water ❶

Same form for ♂ / ♀

ITEMS SOMETIMES HELD
- None

Pokémon AR Marker

EVOLUTION

Totodile
Lv. 18
Croconaw
Lv. 30
Feraligatr

HOW TO OBTAIN

Pokémon Black Version 2	Link Trade or Poké Transfer
Pokémon White Version 2	Link Trade or Poké Transfer

HOW TO OBTAIN FROM OTHER GAMES

Pokémon HeartGold Version	Get from Professor Elm at the start of the adventure
Pokémon SoulSilver Version	Get from Professor Elm at the start of the adventure

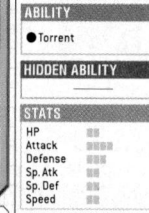

LEVEL-UP AND LEARNED MOVES

Lv.	Name	Type	Kind	Pow.	Acc.	PP	Range	Long	DA
1	Scratch	Normal	Physical	40	100	35	Normal	—	○
1	Leer	Normal	Status	—	100	30	Many Others	—	—
6	Water Gun	Water	Special	40	100	25	Normal	—	—
8	Rage	Normal	Physical	20	100	20	Normal	—	○
13	Bite	Dark	Physical	60	100	25	Normal	—	○
15	Scary Face	Normal	Status	—	100	10	Normal	—	—
20	Ice Fang	Ice	Physical	65	95	15	Normal	—	○
22	Flail	Normal	Physical	—	100	15	Normal	—	○
27	Crunch	Dark	Physical	80	100	15	Normal	—	○
29	Chip Away	Normal	Physical	70	100	20	Normal	—	○
34	Slash	Normal	Physical	70	100	20	Normal	—	○
36	Screech	Normal	Status	—	85	40	Normal	—	—
41	Thrash	Normal	Physical	120	100	10	1 Random	—	○
43	Aqua Tail	Water	Physical	90	90	10	Normal	—	○
48	Superpower	Fighting	Physical	120	100	5	Normal	—	○
50	Hydro Pump	Water	Special	120	80	5	Normal	—	—

TM & HM MOVES

Lv.	Name	Type	Kind	Pow.	Acc.	PP	Range	Long	DA
TM01	Hone Claws	Dark	Status	—	—	15	Self	—	—
TM02	Dragon Claw	Dragon	Physical	80	100	15	Normal	—	○
TM06	Toxic	Poison	Status	—	90	10	Normal	—	—
TM07	Hail	Ice	Status	—	—	10	Both Sides	—	—
TM10	Hidden Power	Normal	Special	—	100	15	Normal	—	—
TM13	Ice Beam	Ice	Special	95	100	10	Normal	—	—
TM14	Blizzard	Ice	Special	120	70	5	Many Others	—	—
TM17	Protect	Normal	Status	—	—	10	Self	—	—
TM18	Rain Dance	Water	Status	—	—	5	Both Sides	—	—
TM21	Frustration	Normal	Physical	—	100	20	Normal	—	○
TM27	Return	Normal	Physical	—	100	20	Normal	—	○
TM28	Dig	Ground	Physical	80	100	10	Normal	—	○
TM31	Brick Break	Fighting	Physical	75	100	15	Normal	—	○
TM32	Double Team	Normal	Status	—	—	15	Self	—	—
TM39	Rock Tomb	Rock	Physical	50	80	10	Normal	—	—
TM40	Aerial Ace	Flying	Physical	60	—	20	Normal	○	○
TM42	Facade	Normal	Physical	70	100	20	Normal	—	○
TM44	Rest	Psychic	Status	—	—	10	Self	—	—
TM45	Attract	Normal	Status	—	100	15	Normal	—	—
TM48	Round	Normal	Special	60	100	15	Normal	—	—
TM55	Scald	Water	Special	80	100	15	Normal	—	—
TM56	Fling	Dark	Physical	—	100	10	Normal	—	—
TM65	Shadow Claw	Ghost	Physical	70	100	15	Normal	—	○
TM75	Swords Dance	Normal	Status	—	—	30	Self	—	—
TM80	Rock Slide	Rock	Physical	75	90	10	Many Others	—	—
TM87	Swagger	Normal	Status	—	90	15	Normal	—	—
TM90	Substitute	Normal	Status	—	—	10	Self	—	—
HM01	Cut	Normal	Physical	50	95	30	Normal	—	○
HM03	Surf	Water	Special	95	100	15	Adjacent	—	—
HM05	Waterfall	Water	Physical	80	100	15	Normal	—	○
HM06	Dive	Water	Physical	80	100	10	Normal	—	○

MOVES TAUGHT BY PEOPLE

Name	Type	Kind	Pow.	Acc.	PP	Range	Long	DA
Water Pledge	Water	Special	50	100	10	Normal	—	—

MOVES TAUGHT BY MOVE TUTORS FOR SHARDS

Name	Type	Kind	Pow.	Acc.	PP	Range	Long	DA
Uproar	Normal	Special	90	100	10	1 Random	—	—
Low Kick	Fighting	Physical	—	100	20	Normal	—	○
Ice Punch	Ice	Physical	75	100	15	Normal	—	○
Block	Normal	Status	—	—	5	Normal	—	—
Icy Wind	Ice	Special	55	95	15	Many Others	—	—
Iron Tail	Steel	Physical	100	75	15	Normal	—	○
Aqua Tail	Water	Physical	90	90	10	Normal	—	○
Superpower	Fighting	Physical	120	100	5	Normal	—	○
Snore	Normal	Special	40	100	15	Normal	—	—
Spite	Ghost	Status	—	100	10	Normal	—	—
Sleep Talk	Normal	Status	—	—	10	Self	—	—

EGG MOVES

Name	Type	Kind	Pow.	Acc.	PP	Range	Long	DA
Crunch	Dark	Physical	80	100	15	Normal	—	○
Thrash	Normal	Physical	120	100	10	1 Random	—	○
Hydro Pump	Water	Special	120	80	5	Normal	—	—
AncientPower	Rock	Special	60	100	5	Normal	—	—
Mud Sport	Ground	Status	—	—	15	Both Sides	—	—
Water Sport	Water	Status	—	—	15	Both Sides	—	—
Ice Punch	Ice	Physical	75	100	15	Normal	—	○
Metal Claw	Steel	Physical	50	95	35	Normal	—	○
Dragon Dance	Dragon	Status	—	—	20	Self	—	—
Aqua Jet	Water	Physical	40	100	20	Normal	—	○
Fake Tears	Dark	Status	—	100	20	Normal	—	—
Block	Normal	Status	—	—	5	Normal	—	—
Water Pulse	Water	Special	60	100	20	Normal	○	—

159 Croconaw

Big Jaw Pokémon

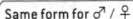

- HEIGHT: 3'07"
- WEIGHT: 55.1 lbs.
- GENDER: ♂ / ♀

Once it bites down, it won't let go until it loses its fangs. New fangs quickly grow into place.

Same form for ♂ / ♀

Pokémon AR Marker

TYPE Water

ABILITY
- Torrent

HIDDEN ABILITY
—

STATS
HP
Attack
Defense
Sp. Atk
Sp. Def
Speed

EGG GROUPS
Monster/Water

ITEMS SOMETIMES HELD
- None

EVOLUTION

HOW TO OBTAIN

Pokémon Black Version 2	Level up a Totodile you obtain via Link Trade or Poké Transfer to Lv. 18
Pokémon White Version 2	Level up a Totodile you obtain via Link Trade or Poké Transfer to Lv. 18

HOW TO OBTAIN FROM OTHER GAMES

—

—

LEVEL-UP AND LEARNED MOVES

Lv.	Name	Type	Kind	Pow.	Acc.	PP	Range	Long	DA
1	Scratch	Normal	Physical	40	100	35	Normal	—	○
1	Leer	Normal	Status	—	100	30	Many Others	—	—
1	Water Gun	Water	Special	40	100	25	Normal	—	—
6	Water Gun	Water	Special	40	100	25	Normal	—	—
8	Rage	Normal	Physical	20	100	20	Normal	—	○
13	Bite	Dark	Physical	60	100	25	Normal	—	○
15	Scary Face	Normal	Status	—	100	10	Normal	—	—
21	Ice Fang	Ice	Physical	65	95	15	Normal	—	○
24	Flail	Normal	Physical	—	100	15	Normal	—	○
30	Crunch	Dark	Physical	80	100	15	Normal	—	○
33	Chip Away	Normal	Physical	70	100	20	Normal	—	○
39	Slash	Normal	Physical	70	100	20	Normal	—	○
42	Screech	Normal	Status	—	85	40	Normal	—	—
48	Thrash	Normal	Physical	120	100	10	1 Random	—	○
51	Aqua Tail	Water	Physical	90	90	10	Normal	—	○
57	Superpower	Fighting	Physical	120	100	5	Normal	—	○
60	Hydro Pump	Water	Special	120	80	5	Normal	—	—

TM & HM MOVES

Lv.	Name	Type	Kind	Pow.	Acc.	PP	Range	Long	DA
TM01	Hone Claws	Dark	Status	—	—	15	Self	—	—
TM02	Dragon Claw	Dragon	Physical	80	100	15	Normal	—	○
TM05	Roar	Normal	Status	—	100	20	Normal	—	—
TM06	Toxic	Poison	Status	—	90	10	Normal	—	—
TM07	Hail	Ice	Status	—	—	10	Both Sides	—	—
TM10	Hidden Power	Normal	Special	—	100	15	Normal	—	—
TM13	Ice Beam	Ice	Special	95	100	10	Normal	—	—
TM14	Blizzard	Ice	Special	120	70	5	Many Others	—	—
TM17	Protect	Normal	Status	—	—	10	Self	—	—
TM18	Rain Dance	Water	Status	—	—	5	Both Sides	—	—
TM21	Frustration	Normal	Physical	—	100	20	Normal	—	○
TM27	Return	Normal	Physical	—	100	20	Normal	—	○
TM28	Dig	Ground	Physical	80	100	10	Normal	—	○
TM31	Brick Break	Fighting	Physical	75	100	15	Normal	—	○
TM32	Double Team	Normal	Status	—	—	15	Self	—	—
TM39	Rock Tomb	Rock	Physical	50	80	10	Normal	—	—
TM40	Aerial Ace	Flying	Physical	60	—	20	Normal	○	○
TM42	Facade	Normal	Physical	70	100	20	Normal	—	○
TM44	Rest	Psychic	Status	—	—	10	Self	—	—
TM45	Attract	Normal	Status	—	100	15	Normal	—	—
TM48	Round	Normal	Special	60	100	15	Normal	—	—
TM55	Scald	Water	Special	80	100	15	Normal	—	—
TM56	Fling	Dark	Physical	—	100	10	Normal	—	—
TM65	Shadow Claw	Ghost	Physical	70	100	15	Normal	—	○
TM75	Swords Dance	Normal	Status	—	—	30	Self	—	—
TM80	Rock Slide	Rock	Physical	75	90	10	Many Others	—	—
TM87	Swagger	Normal	Status	—	90	15	Normal	—	—
TM90	Substitute	Normal	Status	—	—	10	Self	—	—
TM94	Rock Smash	Fighting	Physical	40	100	15	Normal	—	○
HM01	Cut	Normal	Physical	50	95	30	Normal	—	○
HM03	Surf	Water	Special	95	100	15	Adjacent	—	—
HM04	Strength	Normal	Physical	80	100	15	Normal	—	○
HM05	Waterfall	Water	Physical	80	100	15	Normal	—	○
HM06	Dive	Water	Physical	80	100	10	Normal	—	○

MOVES TAUGHT BY PEOPLE

Name	Type	Kind	Pow.	Acc.	PP	Range	Long	DA
Water Pledge	Water	Special	50	100	10	Normal	—	—

MOVES TAUGHT BY MOVE TUTORS FOR SHARDS

Name	Type	Kind	Pow.	Acc.	PP	Range	Long	DA
Uproar	Normal	Special	90	100	10	1 Random	—	—
Low Kick	Fighting	Physical	—	100	20	Normal	—	○
Ice Punch	Ice	Physical	75	100	15	Normal	—	○
Block	Normal	Status	—	—	5	Normal	—	—
Icy Wind	Ice	Special	55	95	15	Many Others	—	—
Iron Tail	Steel	Physical	100	75	15	Normal	—	○
Aqua Tail	Water	Physical	90	90	10	Normal	—	○
Superpower	Fighting	Physical	120	100	5	Normal	—	○
Snore	Normal	Special	40	100	15	Normal	—	—
Spite	Ghost	Status	—	100	10	Normal	—	—
Sleep Talk	Normal	Status	—	—	10	Self	—	—

160 Feraligatr

Big Jaw Pokémon

- HEIGHT: 7'07"
- WEIGHT: 195.8 lbs.
- GENDER: ♂ / ♀

It usually moves slowly, but it goes at blinding speed when it attacks and bites prey.

Same form for ♂ / ♀

Pokémon AR Marker

TYPE Water

ABILITY
- Torrent

HIDDEN ABILITY
—

STATS
HP
Attack
Defense
Sp. Atk
Sp. Def
Speed

EGG GROUPS
Monster/Water

ITEMS SOMETIMES HELD
- None

EVOLUTION

HOW TO OBTAIN

Pokémon Black Version 2	Level up a Croconaw you obtain via Link Trade or Poké Transfer to Lv. 30
Pokémon White Version 2	Level up a Croconaw you obtain via Link Trade or Poké Transfer to Lv. 30

HOW TO OBTAIN FROM OTHER GAMES

—

—

LEVEL-UP AND LEARNED MOVES

Lv.	Name	Type	Kind	Pow.	Acc.	PP	Range	Long	DA
1	Scratch	Normal	Physical	40	100	35	Normal	—	○
1	Leer	Normal	Status	—	100	30	Many Others	—	—
1	Water Gun	Water	Special	40	100	25	Normal	—	—
1	Rage	Normal	Physical	20	100	20	Normal	—	○
6	Water Gun	Water	Special	40	100	25	Normal	—	—
8	Rage	Normal	Physical	20	100	20	Normal	—	○
13	Bite	Dark	Physical	60	100	25	Normal	—	○
15	Scary Face	Normal	Status	—	100	10	Normal	—	—
21	Ice Fang	Ice	Physical	65	95	15	Normal	—	○
24	Flail	Normal	Physical	—	100	15	Normal	—	○
30	Agility	Psychic	Status	—	—	30	Self	—	—
32	Crunch	Dark	Physical	80	100	15	Normal	—	○
37	Chip Away	Normal	Physical	70	100	20	Normal	—	○
45	Slash	Normal	Physical	70	100	20	Normal	—	○
50	Screech	Normal	Status	—	85	40	Normal	—	—
58	Thrash	Normal	Physical	120	100	10	1 Random	—	○
63	Aqua Tail	Water	Physical	90	90	10	Normal	—	○
71	Superpower	Fighting	Physical	120	100	5	Normal	—	○
76	Hydro Pump	Water	Special	120	80	5	Normal	—	—

TM & HM MOVES

Lv.	Name	Type	Kind	Pow.	Acc.	PP	Range	Long	DA
TM01	Hone Claws	Dark	Status	—	—	15	Self	—	—
TM02	Dragon Claw	Dragon	Physical	80	100	15	Normal	—	○
TM05	Roar	Normal	Status	—	100	20	Normal	—	—
TM06	Toxic	Poison	Status	—	90	10	Normal	—	—
TM07	Hail	Ice	Status	—	—	10	Both Sides	—	—
TM10	Hidden Power	Normal	Special	—	100	15	Normal	—	—
TM13	Ice Beam	Ice	Special	95	100	10	Normal	—	—
TM14	Blizzard	Ice	Special	120	70	5	Many Others	—	—
TM15	Hyper Beam	Normal	Special	150	90	5	Normal	—	—
TM17	Protect	Normal	Status	—	—	10	Self	—	—
TM18	Rain Dance	Water	Status	—	—	5	Both Sides	—	—
TM21	Frustration	Normal	Physical	—	100	20	Normal	—	○
TM26	Earthquake	Ground	Physical	100	100	10	Adjacent	—	—
TM27	Return	Normal	Physical	—	100	20	Normal	—	○
TM28	Dig	Ground	Physical	80	100	10	Normal	—	○
TM31	Brick Break	Fighting	Physical	75	100	15	Normal	—	○
TM32	Double Team	Normal	Status	—	—	15	Self	—	—
TM39	Rock Tomb	Rock	Physical	50	80	10	Normal	—	—
TM40	Aerial Ace	Flying	Physical	60	—	20	Normal	○	○
TM42	Facade	Normal	Physical	70	100	20	Normal	—	○
TM44	Rest	Psychic	Status	—	—	10	Self	—	—
TM45	Attract	Normal	Status	—	100	15	Normal	—	—
TM48	Round	Normal	Special	60	100	15	Normal	—	—
TM52	Focus Blast	Fighting	Special	120	70	5	Normal	—	—
TM55	Scald	Water	Special	80	100	15	Normal	—	—
TM56	Fling	Dark	Physical	—	100	10	Normal	—	—
TM65	Shadow Claw	Ghost	Physical	70	100	15	Normal	—	○
TM68	Giga Impact	Normal	Physical	150	90	5	Normal	—	○
TM75	Swords Dance	Normal	Status	—	—	30	Self	—	—
TM78	Bulldoze	Ground	Physical	60	100	20	Adjacent	—	—
TM80	Rock Slide	Rock	Physical	75	90	10	Many Others	—	—
TM82	Dragon Tail	Dragon	Physical	60	90	10	Normal	—	○
TM87	Swagger	Normal	Status	—	90	15	Normal	—	—
TM90	Substitute	Normal	Status	—	—	10	Self	—	—
TM94	Rock Smash	Fighting	Physical	40	100	15	Normal	—	○
HM01	Cut	Normal	Physical	50	95	30	Normal	—	○
HM03	Surf	Water	Special	95	100	15	Adjacent	—	—
HM04	Strength	Normal	Physical	80	100	15	Normal	—	○
HM05	Waterfall	Water	Physical	80	100	15	Normal	—	○
HM06	Dive	Water	Physical	80	100	10	Normal	—	○

MOVES TAUGHT BY PEOPLE

Name	Type	Kind	Pow.	Acc.	PP	Range	Long	DA
Water Pledge	Water	Special	50	100	10	Normal	—	—
Hydro Cannon	Water	Special	150	90	5	Normal	—	—

MOVES TAUGHT BY MOVE TUTORS FOR SHARDS

Name	Type	Kind	Pow.	Acc.	PP	Range	Long	DA
Uproar	Normal	Special	90	100	10	1 Random	—	—
Low Kick	Fighting	Physical	—	100	20	Normal	—	○
Ice Punch	Ice	Physical	75	100	15	Normal	—	○
Block	Normal	Status	—	—	5	Normal	—	—
Icy Wind	Ice	Special	55	95	15	Many Others	—	—
Iron Tail	Steel	Physical	100	75	15	Normal	—	○
Aqua Tail	Water	Physical	90	90	10	Normal	—	○
Superpower	Fighting	Physical	120	100	5	Normal	—	○
Dragon Pulse	Dragon	Special	90	100	10	Normal	○	—
Snore	Normal	Special	40	100	15	Normal	—	—
Spite	Ghost	Status	—	100	10	Normal	—	—
Outrage	Dragon	Physical	120	100	10	1 Random	—	○
Sleep Talk	Normal	Status	—	—	10	Self	—	—

161 Sentret

161 Sentret
Scout Pokémon

- HEIGHT: 2'07"
- WEIGHT: 13.2 lbs.
- GENDER: ♂ / ♀

It has a very nervous nature. It stands up high on its tail so it can scan wide areas.

TYPE Normal

ABILITIES
- Run Away
- Keen Eye

HIDDEN ABILITY
- Frisk

STATS
HP
Attack
Defense
Sp. Atk
Sp. Def
Speed

EGG GROUPS
Field

Same form for ♂ / ♀

ITEMS SOMETIMES HELD
- None

EVOLUTION

HOW TO OBTAIN

Pokémon Black Version 2	Catch a Furret, leave it at the Pokémon Day Care, and hatch the Egg that is found
Pokémon White Version 2	Catch a Furret, leave it at the Pokémon Day Care, and hatch the Egg that is found

HOW TO OBTAIN FROM OTHER GAMES

Pokémon Black Version	Route 7 (mass outbreak)
Pokémon White Version	Route 7 (mass outbreak)

LEVEL-UP AND LEARNED MOVES

Lv.	Name	Type	Kind	Pow.	Acc.	PP	Range	Long	DA
1	Scratch	Normal	Physical	40	100	35	Normal	—	○
1	Foresight	Normal	Status	—	—	40	Normal	—	—
4	Defense Curl	Normal	Status	—	—	40	Self	—	—
7	Quick Attack	Normal	Physical	40	100	30	Normal	—	○
13	Fury Swipes	Normal	Physical	18	80	15	Normal	—	○
16	Helping Hand	Normal	Status	—	—	20	1 Ally	—	—
19	Follow Me	Normal	Status	—	—	20	Self	—	—
25	Slam	Normal	Physical	80	75	20	Normal	—	○
28	Rest	Psychic	Status	—	—	10	Self	—	—
31	Sucker Punch	Dark	Physical	80	100	5	Normal	—	○
36	Amnesia	Psychic	Status	—	—	20	Self	—	—
39	Baton Pass	Normal	Status	—	—	40	Self	—	—
42	Me First	Normal	Status	—	—	20	Varies	—	—
47	Hyper Voice	Normal	Special	90	100	10	Many Others	—	—

MOVES TAUGHT BY PEOPLE

Name	Type	Kind	Pow.	Acc.	PP	Range	Long	DA

MOVES TAUGHT BY MOVE TUTORS FOR SHARDS

Name	Type	Kind	Pow.	Acc.	PP	Range	Long	DA
Covet	Normal	Physical	60	100	40	Normal	—	○
Super Fang	Normal	Physical	—	90	10	Normal	—	○
Uproar	Normal	Special	90	100	10	1 Random	—	—
Fire Punch	Fire	Physical	75	100	15	Normal	—	○
ThunderPunch	Electric	Physical	75	100	15	Normal	—	○
Ice Punch	Ice	Physical	75	100	15	Normal	—	○
Last Resort	Normal	Physical	140	100	5	Normal	—	○
Hyper Voice	Normal	Special	90	100	10	Many Others	—	—
Iron Tail	Steel	Physical	100	75	15	Normal	—	○
Aqua Tail	Water	Physical	90	90	10	Normal	—	○
Snore	Normal	Special	40	100	15	Normal	—	—
Knock Off	Dark	Physical	20	100	20	Normal	—	○
Helping Hand	Normal	Status	—	—	20	1 Ally	—	—
Trick	Psychic	Status	—	100	10	Normal	—	—
Sleep Talk	Normal	Status	—	—	10	Self	—	—

TM & HM MOVES

Lv.	Name	Type	Kind	Pow.	Acc.	PP	Range	Long	DA
TM01	Hone Claws	Dark	Status	—	—	15	Self	—	—
TM06	Toxic	Poison	Status	—	90	10	Normal	—	—
TM10	Hidden Power	Normal	Special	—	100	15	Normal	—	—
TM11	Sunny Day	Fire	Status	—	—	5	Both Sides	—	—
TM13	Ice Beam	Ice	Special	95	100	10	Normal	—	—
TM17	Protect	Normal	Status	—	—	10	Self	—	—
TM18	Rain Dance	Water	Status	—	—	5	Both Sides	—	—
TM21	Frustration	Normal	Physical	—	100	20	Normal	—	○
TM22	SolarBeam	Grass	Special	120	100	10	Normal	—	—
TM24	Thunderbolt	Electric	Special	95	100	15	Normal	—	—
TM27	Return	Normal	Physical	—	100	20	Normal	—	○
TM28	Dig	Ground	Physical	80	100	10	Normal	—	○
TM30	Shadow Ball	Ghost	Special	80	100	15	Normal	—	—
TM31	Brick Break	Fighting	Physical	75	100	15	Normal	—	○
TM32	Double Team	Normal	Status	—	—	15	Self	—	—
TM35	Flamethrower	Fire	Special	95	100	15	Normal	—	—
TM42	Facade	Normal	Physical	70	100	20	Normal	—	○
TM44	Rest	Psychic	Status	—	—	10	Self	—	—
TM45	Attract	Normal	Status	—	100	15	Normal	—	—
TM46	Thief	Dark	Physical	40	100	10	Normal	—	○
TM48	Round	Normal	Special	60	100	15	Normal	—	—
TM49	Echoed Voice	Normal	Special	40	100	15	Normal	—	—
TM56	Fling	Dark	Physical	—	100	10	Normal	—	—
TM57	Charge Beam	Electric	Special	50	90	10	Normal	—	—
TM65	Shadow Claw	Ghost	Physical	70	100	15	Normal	—	○
TM67	Retaliate	Normal	Physical	70	100	5	Normal	—	○
TM83	Work Up	Normal	Status	—	—	30	Self	—	—
TM86	Grass Knot	Grass	Special	—	100	20	Normal	—	○
TM87	Swagger	Normal	Status	—	90	15	Normal	—	—
TM89	U-turn	Bug	Physical	70	100	20	Normal	—	○
TM90	Substitute	Normal	Status	—	—	10	Self	—	—
HM01	Cut	Normal	Physical	50	95	30	Normal	—	○
HM03	Surf	Water	Special	95	100	15	Adjacent	—	—

EGG MOVES

Name	Type	Kind	Pow.	Acc.	PP	Range	Long	DA
Double-Edge	Normal	Physical	120	100	15	Normal	—	○
Pursuit	Dark	Physical	40	100	20	Normal	—	○
Slash	Normal	Physical	70	100	20	Normal	—	○
Focus Energy	Normal	Status	—	—	30	Self	—	—
Reversal	Fighting	Physical	—	100	15	Normal	—	○
Trick	Psychic	Status	—	100	10	Normal	—	—
Assist	Normal	Status	—	—	20	Self	—	—
Last Resort	Normal	Physical	140	100	5	Normal	—	○
Charm	Normal	Status	—	100	20	Normal	—	—
Covet	Normal	Physical	60	100	40	Normal	—	○
Natural Gift	Normal	Physical	—	100	15	Normal	—	—
Iron Tail	Steel	Physical	100	75	15	Normal	—	○

Pokémon AR Marker

162 Furret

162 Furret
Long Body Pokémon

- HEIGHT: 5'11"
- WEIGHT: 71.6 lbs.
- GENDER: ♂ / ♀

The mother puts its offspring to sleep by curling up around them. It corners foes with speed.

TYPE Normal

ABILITIES
- Run Away
- Keen Eye

HIDDEN ABILITY
- Frisk

STATS
HP
Attack
Defense
Sp. Atk
Sp. Def
Speed

EGG GROUPS
Field

Same form for ♂ / ♀

ITEMS SOMETIMES HELD
- Oran Berry
- Sitrus Berry

EVOLUTION

HOW TO OBTAIN

Pokémon Black Version 2	Route 7 (mass outbreak)
Pokémon White Version 2	Route 7 (mass outbreak)

HOW TO OBTAIN FROM OTHER GAMES

—

—

LEVEL-UP AND LEARNED MOVES

Lv.	Name	Type	Kind	Pow.	Acc.	PP	Range	Long	DA
1	Scratch	Normal	Physical	40	100	35	Normal	—	○
1	Foresight	Normal	Status	—	—	40	Normal	—	—
1	Defense Curl	Normal	Status	—	—	40	Self	—	—
1	Quick Attack	Normal	Physical	40	100	30	Normal	—	○
4	Defense Curl	Normal	Status	—	—	40	Self	—	—
7	Quick Attack	Normal	Physical	40	100	30	Normal	—	○
13	Fury Swipes	Normal	Physical	18	80	15	Normal	—	○
17	Helping Hand	Normal	Status	—	—	20	1 Ally	—	—
21	Follow Me	Normal	Status	—	—	20	Self	—	—
28	Slam	Normal	Physical	80	75	20	Normal	—	○
32	Rest	Psychic	Status	—	—	10	Self	—	—
36	Sucker Punch	Dark	Physical	80	100	5	Normal	—	○
42	Amnesia	Psychic	Status	—	—	20	Self	—	—
46	Baton Pass	Normal	Status	—	—	40	Self	—	—
50	Me First	Normal	Status	—	—	20	Varies	—	—
56	Hyper Voice	Normal	Special	90	100	10	Many Others	—	—

TM & HM MOVES

Lv.	Name	Type	Kind	Pow.	Acc.	PP	Range	Long	DA
TM01	Hone Claws	Dark	Status	—	—	15	Self	—	—
TM06	Toxic	Poison	Status	—	90	10	Normal	—	—
TM10	Hidden Power	Normal	Special	—	100	15	Normal	—	—
TM11	Sunny Day	Fire	Status	—	—	5	Both Sides	—	—
TM13	Ice Beam	Ice	Special	95	100	10	Normal	—	—
TM14	Blizzard	Ice	Special	120	70	5	Many Others	—	—
TM15	Hyper Beam	Normal	Special	150	90	5	Normal	—	—
TM17	Protect	Normal	Status	—	—	10	Self	—	—
TM18	Rain Dance	Water	Status	—	—	5	Both Sides	—	—
TM21	Frustration	Normal	Physical	—	100	20	Normal	—	○
TM22	SolarBeam	Grass	Special	120	100	10	Normal	—	—
TM24	Thunderbolt	Electric	Special	95	100	15	Normal	—	—
TM25	Thunder	Electric	Special	120	70	10	Normal	—	—
TM27	Return	Normal	Physical	—	100	20	Normal	—	○
TM28	Dig	Ground	Physical	80	100	10	Normal	—	○
TM30	Shadow Ball	Ghost	Special	80	100	15	Normal	—	—
TM31	Brick Break	Fighting	Physical	75	100	15	Normal	—	○
TM32	Double Team	Normal	Status	—	—	15	Self	—	—
TM35	Flamethrower	Fire	Special	95	100	15	Normal	—	—
TM42	Facade	Normal	Physical	70	100	20	Normal	—	○
TM44	Rest	Psychic	Status	—	—	10	Self	—	—
TM45	Attract	Normal	Status	—	100	15	Normal	—	—
TM46	Thief	Dark	Physical	40	100	10	Normal	—	○
TM48	Round	Normal	Special	60	100	15	Normal	—	—
TM49	Echoed Voice	Normal	Special	40	100	15	Normal	—	—
TM52	Focus Blast	Fighting	Special	120	70	5	Normal	—	—
TM56	Fling	Dark	Physical	—	100	10	Normal	—	—
TM57	Charge Beam	Electric	Special	50	90	10	Normal	—	—
TM65	Shadow Claw	Ghost	Physical	70	100	15	Normal	—	○
TM67	Retaliate	Normal	Physical	70	100	5	Normal	—	○
TM68	Giga Impact	Normal	Physical	150	90	5	Normal	—	○
TM83	Work Up	Normal	Status	—	—	30	Self	—	—
TM86	Grass Knot	Grass	Special	—	100	20	Normal	—	○
TM87	Swagger	Normal	Status	—	90	15	Normal	—	—
TM89	U-turn	Bug	Physical	70	100	20	Normal	—	○
TM90	Substitute	Normal	Status	—	—	10	Self	—	—
TM94	Rock Smash	Fighting	Physical	40	100	15	Normal	—	○

Lv.	Name	Type	Kind	Pow.	Acc.	PP	Range	Long	DA
HM01	Cut	Normal	Physical	50	95	30	Normal	—	○
HM03	Surf	Water	Special	95	100	15	Adjacent	—	—
HM04	Strength	Normal	Physical	80	100	15	Normal	—	○

MOVES TAUGHT BY PEOPLE

Name	Type	Kind	Pow.	Acc.	PP	Range	Long	DA

MOVES TAUGHT BY MOVE TUTORS FOR SHARDS

Name	Type	Kind	Pow.	Acc.	PP	Range	Long	DA
Covet	Normal	Physical	60	100	40	Normal	—	○
Super Fang	Normal	Physical	—	90	10	Normal	—	○
Uproar	Normal	Special	90	100	10	1 Random	—	—
Fire Punch	Fire	Physical	75	100	15	Normal	—	○
ThunderPunch	Electric	Physical	75	100	15	Normal	—	○
Ice Punch	Ice	Physical	75	100	15	Normal	—	○
Last Resort	Normal	Physical	140	100	5	Normal	—	○
Hyper Voice	Normal	Special	90	100	10	Many Others	—	—
Iron Tail	Steel	Physical	100	75	15	Normal	—	○
Aqua Tail	Water	Physical	90	90	10	Normal	—	○
Snore	Normal	Special	40	100	15	Normal	—	—
Knock Off	Dark	Physical	20	100	20	Normal	—	○
Helping Hand	Normal	Status	—	—	20	1 Ally	—	—
Trick	Psychic	Status	—	100	10	Normal	—	—
Sleep Talk	Normal	Status	—	—	10	Self	—	—

Pokémon AR Marker

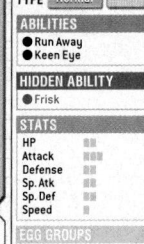

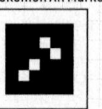

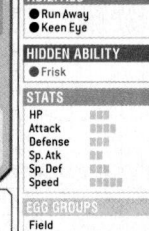

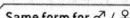

Owl Pokémon

163 Hoothoot

- HEIGHT: 2'04"
- WEIGHT: 46.7 lbs.
- GENDER: ♂ / ♀

It marks time precisely. Some countries consider it to be a wise friend, versed in the world's ways.

Same form for ♂ / ♀

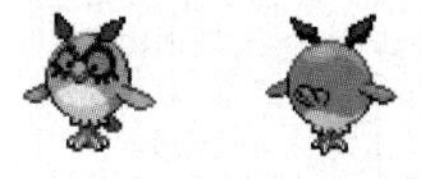

TYPE Normal Flying

ABILITIES
- Insomnia
- Keen Eye

HIDDEN ABILITY
- Tinted Lens

STATS
HP
Attack
Defense
Sp. Atk
Sp. Def
Speed

EGG GROUPS
Flying

ITEMS SOMETIMES HELD
- None

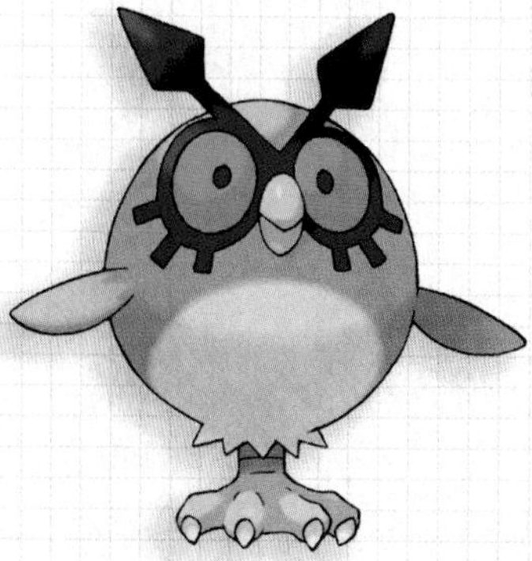

Pokémon AR Marker

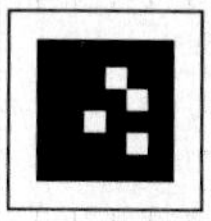

EVOLUTION

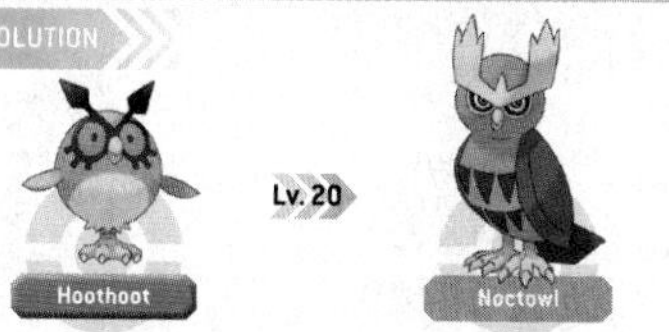

HOW TO OBTAIN

Pokémon Black Version 2	Catch a Noctowl, leave it at the Pokémon Day Care, and hatch the Egg that is found
Pokémon White Version 2	Catch a Noctowl, leave it at the Pokémon Day Care, and hatch the Egg that is found

HOW TO OBTAIN FROM OTHER GAMES

Pokémon HeartGold Version	Route 29 (night only)
Pokémon SoulSilver Version	Route 29 (night only)

LEVEL-UP AND LEARNED MOVES

Lv.	Name	Type	Kind	Pow.	Acc.	PP	Range	Long	DA
1	Tackle	Normal	Physical	50	100	35	Normal	—	○
1	Growl	Normal	Status	—	100	40	Many Others	—	—
1	Foresight	Normal	Status	—	—	40	Normal	—	—
5	Hypnosis	Psychic	Status	—	60	20	Normal	—	—
9	Peck	Flying	Physical	35	100	35	Normal	○	○
13	Uproar	Normal	Special	90	100	10	1 Random	—	—
17	Reflect	Psychic	Status	—	—	20	Your Side	—	—
21	Confusion	Psychic	Special	50	100	25	Normal	—	—
25	Echoed Voice	Normal	Special	40	100	15	Normal	—	—
29	Take Down	Normal	Physical	90	85	20	Normal	—	○
33	Air Slash	Flying	Special	75	95	20	Normal	○	—
37	Zen Headbutt	Psychic	Physical	80	90	15	Normal	—	○
41	Synchronoise	Psychic	Special	70	100	15	Adjacent	—	—
45	Extrasensory	Psychic	Special	80	100	30	Normal	—	—
49	Psycho Shift	Psychic	Status	—	90	10	Normal	—	—
53	Roost	Flying	Status	—	—	10	Self	—	—
57	Dream Eater	Psychic	Special	100	100	15	Normal	—	—

TM & HM MOVES

Lv.	Name	Type	Kind	Pow.	Acc.	PP	Range	Long	DA
TM06	Toxic	Poison	Status	—	90	10	Normal	—	—
TM10	Hidden Power	Normal	Special	—	100	15	Normal	—	—
TM11	Sunny Day	Fire	Status	—	—	5	Both Sides	—	—
TM17	Protect	Normal	Status	—	—	10	Self	—	—
TM18	Rain Dance	Water	Status	—	—	5	Both Sides	—	—
TM21	Frustration	Normal	Physical	—	100	20	Normal	—	○
TM27	Return	Normal	Physical	—	100	20	Normal	—	○
TM29	Psychic	Psychic	Special	90	100	10	Normal	—	—
TM30	Shadow Ball	Ghost	Special	80	100	15	Normal	—	—
TM32	Double Team	Normal	Status	—	—	15	Self	—	—
TM33	Reflect	Psychic	Status	—	—	20	Your Side	—	—
TM40	Aerial Ace	Flying	Physical	60	—	20	Normal	○	○
TM42	Facade	Normal	Physical	70	100	20	Normal	—	○
TM44	Rest	Psychic	Status	—	—	10	Self	—	—
TM45	Attract	Normal	Status	—	100	15	Normal	—	—
TM46	Thief	Dark	Physical	40	100	10	Normal	—	○
TM48	Round	Normal	Special	60	100	15	Normal	—	—
TM49	Echoed Voice	Normal	Special	40	100	15	Normal	—	—
TM77	Psych Up	Normal	Status	—	—	10	Normal	—	—
TM83	Work Up	Normal	Status	—	—	30	Self	—	—
TM85	Dream Eater	Psychic	Special	100	100	15	Normal	—	—
TM87	Swagger	Normal	Status	—	90	15	Normal	—	—
TM88	Pluck	Flying	Physical	60	100	20	Normal	○	○
TM90	Substitute	Normal	Status	—	—	10	Self	—	—
HM02	Fly	Flying	Physical	90	95	15	Normal	○	○

MOVES TAUGHT BY PEOPLE

Name	Type	Kind	Pow.	Acc.	PP	Range	Long	DA

MOVES TAUGHT BY MOVE TUTORS FOR SHARDS

Name	Type	Kind	Pow.	Acc.	PP	Range	Long	DA
Uproar	Normal	Special	90	100	10	1 Random	—	—
Magic Coat	Psychic	Status	—	—	15	Self	—	—
Hyper Voice	Normal	Special	90	100	10	Many Others	—	—
Zen Headbutt	Psychic	Physical	80	90	15	Normal	—	○
Roost	Flying	Status	—	—	10	Self	—	—
Sky Attack	Flying	Physical	140	90	5	Normal	○	—
Heat Wave	Fire	Special	100	90	10	Many Others	—	—
Tailwind	Flying	Status	—	—	30	Your Side	—	—
Recycle	Normal	Status	—	—	10	Self	—	—
Sleep Talk	Normal	Status	—	—	10	Self	—	—

EGG MOVES

Name	Type	Kind	Pow.	Acc.	PP	Range	Long	DA
Mirror Move	Flying	Status	—	—	20	Normal	—	—
Supersonic	Normal	Status	—	55	20	Normal	—	—
Faint Attack	Dark	Physical	60	—	20	Normal	—	○
Wing Attack	Flying	Physical	60	100	35	Normal	○	○
Whirlwind	Normal	Status	—	100	20	Normal	—	—
Sky Attack	Flying	Physical	140	90	5	Normal	○	—
FeatherDance	Flying	Status	—	100	15	Normal	—	—
Agility	Psychic	Status	—	—	30	Self	—	—
Night Shade	Ghost	Special	—	100	15	Normal	—	—
Defog	Flying	Status	—	—	15	Normal	—	—

Owl Pokémon

164 Noctowl

- HEIGHT: 5'03"
- WEIGHT: 89.9 lbs.
- GENDER: ♂ / ♀

Its eyes are specially developed to enable it to see clearly even in murky darkness and minimal light.

Same form for ♂ / ♀

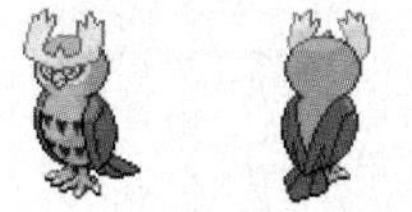

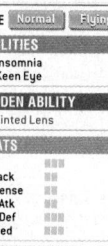

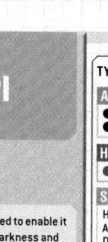

TYPE Normal Flying

ABILITIES
- Insomnia
- Keen Eye

HIDDEN ABILITY
- Tinted Lens

STATS
HP
Attack
Defense
Sp. Atk
Sp. Def
Speed

EGG GROUPS
Flying

ITEMS SOMETIMES HELD
- None

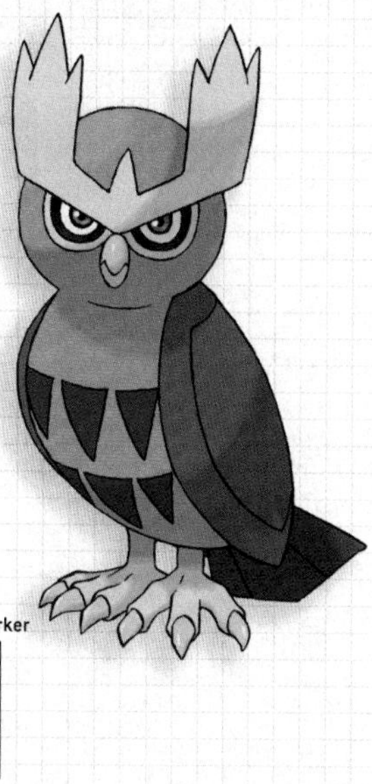

Pokémon AR Marker

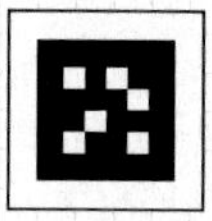

EVOLUTION

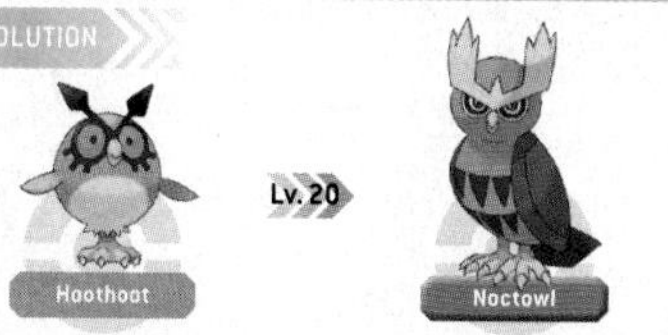

HOW TO OBTAIN

Pokémon Black Version 2	Nature Preserve
Pokémon White Version 2	Nature Preserve

HOW TO OBTAIN FROM OTHER GAMES

	—
	—

LEVEL-UP AND LEARNED MOVES

Lv.	Name	Type	Kind	Pow.	Acc.	PP	Range	Long	DA
1	Sky Attack	Flying	Physical	140	90	5	Normal	○	—
1	Tackle	Normal	Physical	50	100	35	Normal	—	○
1	Growl	Normal	Status	—	100	40	Many Others	—	—
1	Foresight	Normal	Status	—	—	40	Normal	—	—
1	Hypnosis	Psychic	Status	—	60	20	Normal	—	—
5	Hypnosis	Psychic	Status	—	60	20	Normal	—	—
9	Peck	Flying	Physical	35	100	35	Normal	○	○
13	Uproar	Normal	Special	90	100	10	1 Random	—	—
17	Reflect	Psychic	Status	—	—	20	Your Side	—	—
22	Confusion	Psychic	Special	50	100	25	Normal	—	—
27	Echoed Voice	Normal	Special	40	100	15	Normal	—	—
32	Take Down	Normal	Physical	90	85	20	Normal	—	○
37	Air Slash	Flying	Special	75	95	20	Normal	○	—
42	Zen Headbutt	Psychic	Physical	80	90	15	Normal	—	○
47	Synchronoise	Psychic	Special	70	100	15	Adjacent	—	—
52	Extrasensory	Psychic	Special	80	100	30	Normal	—	—
57	Psycho Shift	Psychic	Status	—	90	10	Normal	—	—
62	Roost	Flying	Status	—	—	10	Self	—	—
67	Dream Eater	Psychic	Special	100	100	15	Normal	—	—

TM & HM MOVES

Lv.	Name	Type	Kind	Pow.	Acc.	PP	Range	Long	DA
TM06	Toxic	Poison	Status	—	90	10	Normal	—	—
TM10	Hidden Power	Normal	Special	—	100	15	Normal	—	—
TM11	Sunny Day	Fire	Status	—	—	5	Both Sides	—	—
TM15	Hyper Beam	Normal	Special	150	90	5	Normal	—	—
TM17	Protect	Normal	Status	—	—	10	Self	—	—
TM18	Rain Dance	Water	Status	—	—	5	Both Sides	—	—
TM21	Frustration	Normal	Physical	—	100	20	Normal	—	○
TM27	Return	Normal	Physical	—	100	20	Normal	—	○
TM29	Psychic	Psychic	Special	90	100	10	Normal	—	—
TM30	Shadow Ball	Ghost	Special	80	100	15	Normal	—	—
TM32	Double Team	Normal	Status	—	—	15	Self	—	—
TM33	Reflect	Psychic	Status	—	—	20	Your Side	—	—
TM40	Aerial Ace	Flying	Physical	60	—	20	Normal	○	○
TM42	Facade	Normal	Physical	70	100	20	Normal	—	○
TM44	Rest	Psychic	Status	—	—	10	Self	—	—
TM45	Attract	Normal	Status	—	100	15	Normal	—	—
TM46	Thief	Dark	Physical	40	100	10	Normal	—	○
TM48	Round	Normal	Special	60	100	15	Normal	—	—
TM49	Echoed Voice	Normal	Special	40	100	15	Normal	—	—
TM68	Giga Impact	Normal	Physical	150	90	5	Normal	—	○
TM77	Psych Up	Normal	Status	—	—	10	Normal	—	—
TM83	Work Up	Normal	Status	—	—	30	Self	—	—
TM85	Dream Eater	Psychic	Special	100	100	15	Normal	—	—
TM87	Swagger	Normal	Status	—	90	15	Normal	—	—
TM88	Pluck	Flying	Physical	60	100	20	Normal	○	○
TM90	Substitute	Normal	Status	—	—	10	Self	—	—
HM02	Fly	Flying	Physical	90	95	15	Normal	○	○

MOVES TAUGHT BY PEOPLE

Name	Type	Kind	Pow.	Acc.	PP	Range	Long	DA

MOVES TAUGHT BY MOVE TUTORS FOR SHARDS

Name	Type	Kind	Pow.	Acc.	PP	Range	Long	DA
Uproar	Normal	Special	90	100	10	1 Random	—	—
Magic Coat	Psychic	Status	—	—	15	Self	—	—
Hyper Voice	Normal	Special	90	100	10	Many Others	—	—
Zen Headbutt	Psychic	Physical	80	90	15	Normal	—	○
Roost	Flying	Status	—	—	10	Self	—	—
Sky Attack	Flying	Physical	140	90	5	Normal	○	—
Heat Wave	Fire	Special	100	90	10	Many Others	—	—
Tailwind	Flying	Status	—	—	30	Your Side	—	—
Recycle	Normal	Status	—	—	10	Self	—	—
Sleep Talk	Normal	Status	—	—	10	Self	—	—

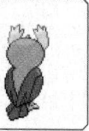

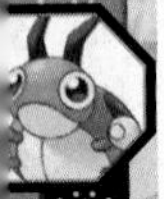

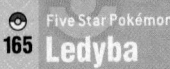

165 Ledyba

Five Star Pokémon

- HEIGHT: 3'03"
- WEIGHT: 23.8 lbs.
- GENDER: ♂ / ♀

It is so timid, it can't move if it isn't with a swarm of others. It conveys its feelings with scent.

♂ ♀

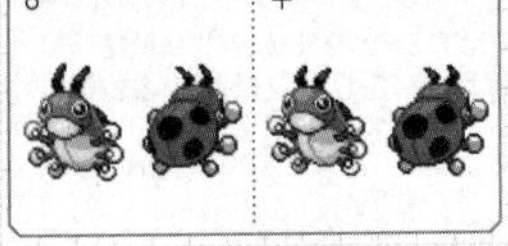

TYPE: Bug / Flying

ABILITIES
- Swarm
- Early Bird

HIDDEN ABILITY
- Rattled

STATS

HP	■■
Attack	■
Defense	■■
Sp. Atk	■■
Sp. Def	■■■■
Speed	■■■

EGG GROUPS

Bug

ITEMS SOMETIMES HELD
- None

EVOLUTION

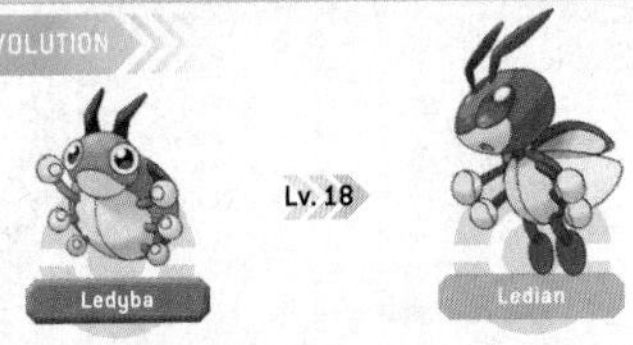

HOW TO OBTAIN

Pokémon Black Version 2	Link Trade or Poké Transfer
Pokémon White Version 2	Catch a Ledian, leave it at the Pokémon Day Care, and hatch the Egg that is found

HOW TO OBTAIN FROM OTHER GAMES

Pokémon SoulSilver Version	Route 30 (morning only)
	—

LEVEL-UP AND LEARNED MOVES

Lv.	Name	Type	Kind	Pow.	Acc.	PP	Range	Long	DA
1	Tackle	Normal	Physical	50	100	35	Normal	—	○
6	Supersonic	Normal	Status	—	55	20	Normal	—	—
9	Comet Punch	Normal	Physical	18	85	15	Normal	—	○
14	Light Screen	Psychic	Status	—	—	30	Your Side	—	—
14	Reflect	Psychic	Status	—	—	20	Your Side	—	—
14	Safeguard	Normal	Status	—	—	25	Your Side	—	—
17	Mach Punch	Fighting	Physical	40	100	30	Normal	—	○
22	Baton Pass	Normal	Status	—	—	40	Self	—	—
25	Silver Wind	Bug	Special	60	100	5	Normal	—	—
30	Agility	Psychic	Status	—	—	30	Self	—	—
33	Swift	Normal	Special	60	—	20	Many Others	—	—
38	Double-Edge	Normal	Physical	120	100	15	Normal	—	○
41	Bug Buzz	Bug	Special	90	100	10	Normal	—	—

TM & HM MOVES

Lv.	Name	Type	Kind	Pow.	Acc.	PP	Range	Long	DA
TM06	Toxic	Poison	Status	—	90	10	Normal	—	—
TM10	Hidden Power	Normal	Special	—	100	15	Normal	—	—
TM11	Sunny Day	Fire	Status	—	—	5	Both Sides	—	—
TM16	Light Screen	Psychic	Status	—	—	30	Your Side	—	—
TM17	Protect	Normal	Status	—	—	10	Self	—	—
TM20	Safeguard	Normal	Status	—	—	25	Your Side	—	—
TM21	Frustration	Normal	Physical	—	100	20	Normal	—	○
TM22	SolarBeam	Grass	Special	120	100	10	Normal	—	—
TM27	Return	Normal	Physical	—	100	20	Normal	—	○
TM28	Dig	Ground	Physical	80	100	10	Normal	—	○
TM31	Brick Break	Fighting	Physical	75	100	15	Normal	—	○
TM32	Double Team	Normal	Status	—	—	15	Self	—	—
TM33	Reflect	Psychic	Status	—	—	20	Your Side	—	—
TM40	Aerial Ace	Flying	Physical	60	—	20	Normal	○	○
TM42	Facade	Normal	Physical	70	100	20	Normal	—	○
TM44	Rest	Psychic	Status	—	—	10	Self	—	—
TM45	Attract	Normal	Status	—	100	15	Normal	—	—
TM46	Thief	Dark	Physical	40	100	10	Normal	—	○
TM48	Round	Normal	Special	60	100	15	Normal	—	—
TM56	Fling	Dark	Physical	—	100	10	Normal	—	—
TM62	Acrobatics	Flying	Physical	55	100	15	Normal	○	○
TM70	Flash	Normal	Status	—	100	20	Normal	—	—
TM75	Swords Dance	Normal	Status	—	—	30	Self	—	—
TM76	Struggle Bug	Bug	Special	30	100	20	Many Others	—	—
TM87	Swagger	Normal	Status	—	90	15	Normal	—	—
TM89	U-turn	Bug	Physical	70	100	20	Normal	—	○
TM90	Substitute	Normal	Status	—	—	10	Self	—	—

MOVES TAUGHT BY PEOPLE

Name	Type	Kind	Pow.	Acc.	PP	Range	Long	DA

MOVES TAUGHT BY MOVE TUTORS FOR SHARDS

Name	Type	Kind	Pow.	Acc.	PP	Range	Long	DA
Bug Bite	Bug	Physical	60	100	20	Normal	—	○
Uproar	Normal	Special	90	100	10	1 Random	—	—
ThunderPunch	Electric	Physical	75	100	15	Normal	—	○
Ice Punch	Ice	Physical	75	100	15	Normal	—	○
Snore	Normal	Special	40	100	15	Normal	—	—
Knock Off	Dark	Physical	20	100	20	Normal	—	○
Roost	Flying	Status	—	—	10	Self	—	—
Giga Drain	Grass	Special	75	100	10	Normal	—	—
Drain Punch	Fighting	Physical	75	100	10	Normal	—	○
Tailwind	Flying	Status	—	—	30	Your Side	—	—
Sleep Talk	Normal	Status	—	—	10	Self	—	—

EGG MOVES

Name	Type	Kind	Pow.	Acc.	PP	Range	Long	DA
Psybeam	Psychic	Special	65	100	20	Normal	—	—
Bide	Normal	Physical	—	—	10	Self	—	○
Silver Wind	Bug	Special	60	100	5	Normal	—	—
Bug Buzz	Bug	Special	90	100	10	Normal	—	—
Screech	Normal	Status	—	85	40	Normal	—	—
Encore	Normal	Status	—	100	5	Normal	—	—
Knock Off	Dark	Physical	20	100	20	Normal	—	○
Bug Bite	Bug	Physical	60	100	20	Normal	—	○
Focus Punch	Fighting	Physical	150	100	20	Normal	—	○
Drain Punch	Fighting	Physical	75	100	10	Normal	—	○
Dizzy Punch	Normal	Physical	70	100	10	Normal	—	○

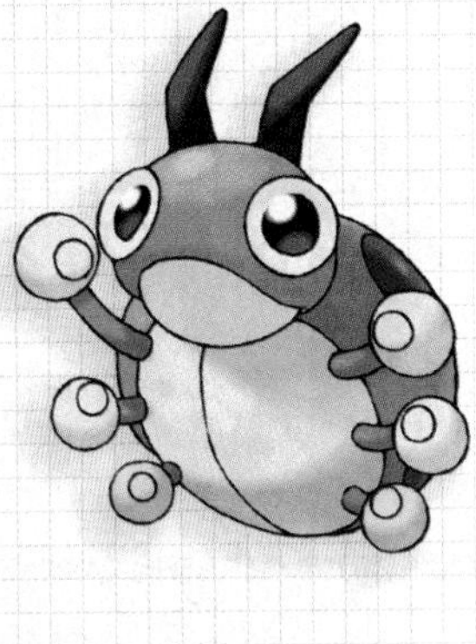

Pokémon AR Marker

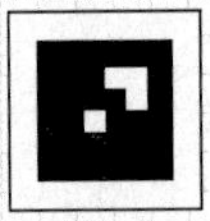

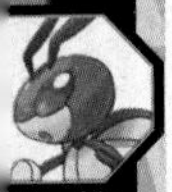

166 Ledian

Five Star Pokémon

- HEIGHT: 4'07"
- WEIGHT: 78.5 lbs.
- GENDER: ♂ / ♀

It uses starlight as energy. When more stars appear at night, the patterns on its back grow larger.

♂ ♀

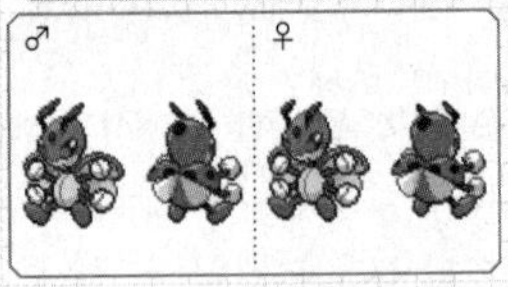

TYPE: Bug / Flying

ABILITIES
- Swarm
- Early Bird

HIDDEN ABILITY
- Iron Fist

STATS

HP	■■
Attack	■■
Defense	■■
Sp. Atk	■■■
Sp. Def	■■■■■
Speed	■■■■■

EGG GROUPS

Bug

ITEMS SOMETIMES HELD
- None

EVOLUTION

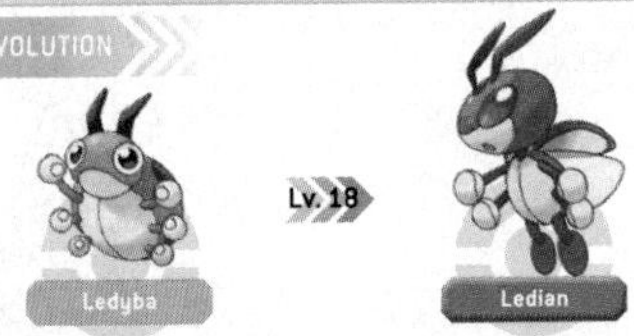

HOW TO OBTAIN

Pokémon Black Version 2	Link Trade or Poké Transfer
Pokémon White Version 2	Route 22 (mass outbreak)

HOW TO OBTAIN FROM OTHER GAMES

Pokémon Black Version	Dreamyard basement (after finishing the main story—dark grass)
Pokémon White Version	Dreamyard basement (after finishing the main story—dark grass)

LEVEL-UP AND LEARNED MOVES

Lv.	Name	Type	Kind	Pow.	Acc.	PP	Range	Long	DA
1	Tackle	Normal	Physical	50	100	35	Normal	—	○
1	Supersonic	Normal	Status	—	55	20	Normal	—	—
1	Comet Punch	Normal	Physical	18	85	15	Normal	—	○
6	Supersonic	Normal	Status	—	55	20	Normal	—	—
9	Comet Punch	Normal	Physical	18	85	15	Normal	—	○
14	Light Screen	Psychic	Status	—	—	30	Your Side	—	—
14	Reflect	Psychic	Status	—	—	20	Your Side	—	—
14	Safeguard	Normal	Status	—	—	25	Your Side	—	—
17	Mach Punch	Fighting	Physical	40	100	30	Normal	—	○
24	Baton Pass	Normal	Status	—	—	40	Self	—	—
29	Silver Wind	Bug	Special	60	100	5	Normal	—	—
36	Agility	Psychic	Status	—	—	30	Self	—	—
41	Swift	Normal	Special	60	—	20	Many Others	—	—
48	Double-Edge	Normal	Physical	120	100	15	Normal	—	○
53	Bug Buzz	Bug	Special	90	100	10	Normal	—	—

TM & HM MOVES

Lv.	Name	Type	Kind	Pow.	Acc.	PP	Range	Long	DA
TM06	Toxic	Poison	Status	—	90	10	Normal	—	—
TM10	Hidden Power	Normal	Special	—	100	15	Normal	—	—
TM11	Sunny Day	Fire	Status	—	—	5	Both Sides	—	—
TM15	Hyper Beam	Normal	Special	150	90	5	Normal	—	—
TM16	Light Screen	Psychic	Status	—	—	30	Your Side	—	—
TM17	Protect	Normal	Status	—	—	10	Self	—	—
TM20	Safeguard	Normal	Status	—	—	25	Your Side	—	—
TM21	Frustration	Normal	Physical	—	100	20	Normal	—	○
TM22	SolarBeam	Grass	Special	120	100	10	Normal	—	—
TM27	Return	Normal	Physical	—	100	20	Normal	—	○
TM28	Dig	Ground	Physical	80	100	10	Normal	—	○
TM31	Brick Break	Fighting	Physical	75	100	15	Normal	—	○
TM32	Double Team	Normal	Status	—	—	15	Self	—	—
TM33	Reflect	Psychic	Status	—	—	20	Your Side	—	—
TM40	Aerial Ace	Flying	Physical	60	—	20	Normal	○	○
TM42	Facade	Normal	Physical	70	100	20	Normal	—	○
TM44	Rest	Psychic	Status	—	—	10	Self	—	—
TM45	Attract	Normal	Status	—	100	15	Normal	—	—
TM46	Thief	Dark	Physical	40	100	10	Normal	—	○
TM48	Round	Normal	Special	60	100	15	Normal	—	—
TM52	Focus Blast	Fighting	Special	120	70	5	Normal	—	—
TM56	Fling	Dark	Physical	—	100	10	Normal	—	—
TM62	Acrobatics	Flying	Physical	55	100	15	Normal	○	○
TM68	Giga Impact	Normal	Physical	150	90	5	Normal	—	○
TM70	Flash	Normal	Status	—	100	20	Normal	—	—
TM75	Swords Dance	Normal	Status	—	—	30	Self	—	—
TM76	Struggle Bug	Bug	Special	30	100	20	Many Others	—	—
TM87	Swagger	Normal	Status	—	90	15	Normal	—	—
TM89	U-turn	Bug	Physical	70	100	20	Normal	—	○
TM90	Substitute	Normal	Status	—	—	10	Self	—	—
TM94	Rock Smash	Fighting	Physical	40	100	15	Normal	—	○
HM04	Strength	Normal	Physical	80	100	15	Normal	—	○

MOVES TAUGHT BY PEOPLE

Name	Type	Kind	Pow.	Acc.	PP	Range	Long	DA

MOVES TAUGHT BY MOVE TUTORS FOR SHARDS

Name	Type	Kind	Pow.	Acc.	PP	Range	Long	DA
Bug Bite	Bug	Physical	60	100	20	Normal	—	○
Uproar	Normal	Special	90	100	10	1 Random	—	—
ThunderPunch	Electric	Physical	75	100	15	Normal	—	○
Ice Punch	Ice	Physical	75	100	15	Normal	—	○
Snore	Normal	Special	40	100	15	Normal	—	—
Knock Off	Dark	Physical	20	100	20	Normal	—	○
Roost	Flying	Status	—	—	10	Self	—	—
Giga Drain	Grass	Special	75	100	10	Normal	—	—
Drain Punch	Fighting	Physical	75	100	10	Normal	—	○
Tailwind	Flying	Status	—	—	30	Your Side	—	—
Sleep Talk	Normal	Status	—	—	10	Self	—	—

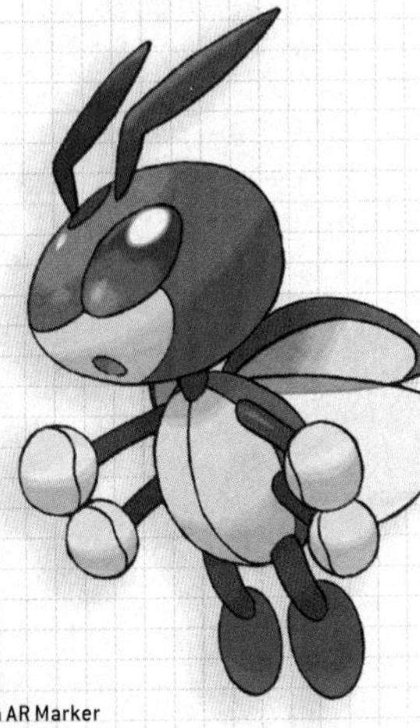

Pokémon AR Marker

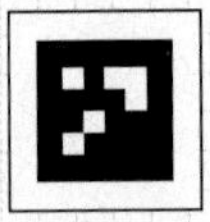

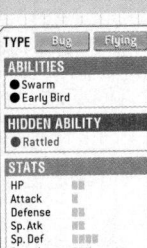

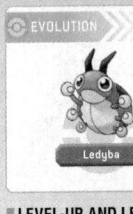

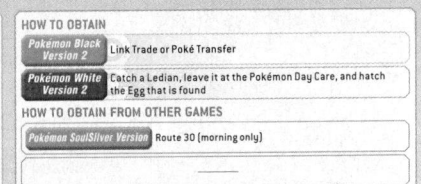

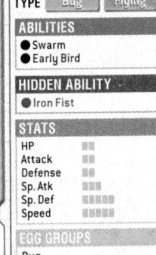

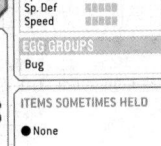

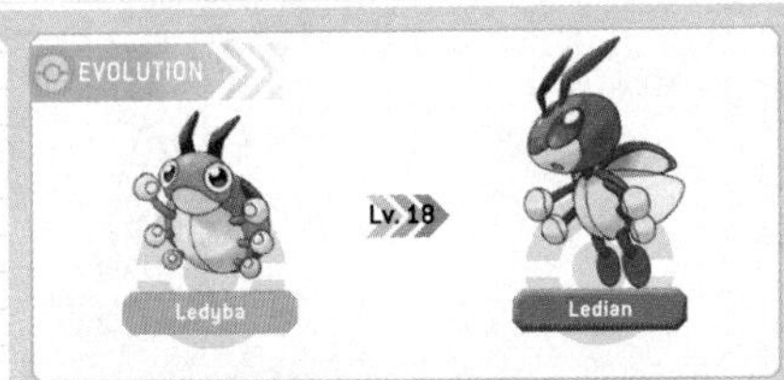

167 Spinarak — String Spit Pokémon

TYPE: Bug / Poison

ABILITIES
- Swarm
- Insomnia

HIDDEN ABILITY
- Sniper

- HEIGHT: 1'08"
- WEIGHT: 18.7 lbs.
- GENDER: ♂ / ♀

It sets a trap by spinning a web with thin but strong silk. It waits motionlessly for prey to arrive.

STATS
- HP
- Attack
- Defense
- Sp. Atk
- Sp. Def
- Speed

EGG GROUPS
Bug

ITEMS SOMETIMES HELD
- None

Same form for ♂ / ♀

Pokémon AR Marker

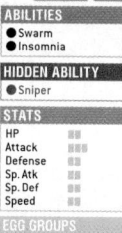

EVOLUTION

Spinarak → Lv. 22 → Ariados

HOW TO OBTAIN

Pokémon Black Version 2	Catch an Ariados, leave it at the Pokémon Day Care, and hatch the Egg that is found
Pokémon White Version 2	Link Trade or Poké Transfer

HOW TO OBTAIN FROM OTHER GAMES

Pokémon HeartGold Version	Route 30 (night only)

LEVEL-UP AND LEARNED MOVES

Lv.	Name	Type	Kind	Pow.	Acc.	PP	Range	Long	DA
1	Poison Sting	Poison	Physical	15	100	35	Normal	—	—
1	String Shot	Bug	Status	—	95	40	Many Others	—	—
5	Scary Face	Normal	Status	—	100	10	Normal	—	—
8	Constrict	Normal	Physical	10	100	35	Normal	—	○
12	Leech Life	Bug	Physical	20	100	15	Normal	—	—
15	Night Shade	Ghost	Special	—	100	15	Normal	—	—
19	Shadow Sneak	Ghost	Physical	40	100	30	Normal	—	—
22	Fury Swipes	Normal	Physical	18	80	15	Normal	—	—
26	Sucker Punch	Dark	Physical	80	100	5	Normal	—	—
29	Spider Web	Bug	Status	—	—	10	Normal	—	—
33	Agility	Psychic	Status	—	—	30	Self	—	—
36	Pin Missile	Bug	Physical	14	85	20	Normal	—	—
40	Psychic	Psychic	Special	90	100	10	Normal	—	—
43	Poison Jab	Poison	Physical	80	100	20	Normal	—	○
47	Cross Poison	Poison	Physical	70	100	20	Normal	—	—

TM & HM MOVES

Lv.	Name	Type	Kind	Pow.	Acc.	PP	Range	Long	DA
TM01	Hone Claws	Dark	Status	—	—	15	Self	—	—
TM06	Toxic	Poison	Status	—	90	10	Normal	—	—
TM09	Venoshock	Poison	Special	65	100	10	Normal	—	—
TM10	Hidden Power	Normal	Special	—	100	15	Normal	—	—
TM11	Sunny Day	Fire	Status	—	—	5	Both Sides	—	—
TM17	Protect	Normal	Status	—	—	10	Self	—	—
TM21	Frustration	Normal	Physical	—	100	20	Normal	—	○
TM22	SolarBeam	Grass	Special	120	100	10	Normal	—	—
TM27	Return	Normal	Physical	—	100	20	Normal	—	○
TM28	Dig	Ground	Physical	80	100	10	Normal	—	—
TM29	Psychic	Psychic	Special	90	100	10	Normal	—	—
TM32	Double Team	Normal	Status	—	—	15	Self	—	—
TM36	Sludge Bomb	Poison	Special	90	100	10	Normal	—	—
TM42	Facade	Normal	Physical	70	100	20	Normal	—	○
TM44	Rest	Psychic	Status	—	—	10	Self	—	—
TM45	Attract	Normal	Status	—	100	15	Normal	—	—
TM46	Thief	Dark	Physical	40	100	10	Normal	—	—
TM48	Round	Normal	Special	60	100	15	Normal	—	—
TM70	Flash	Normal	Status	—	100	20	Normal	—	—
TM76	Struggle Bug	Bug	Special	30	100	20	Many Others	—	—
TM81	X-Scissor	Bug	Physical	80	100	15	Normal	—	—
TM84	Poison Jab	Poison	Physical	80	100	20	Normal	—	○
TM87	Swagger	Normal	Status	—	90	15	Normal	—	—
TM90	Substitute	Normal	Status	—	—	10	Self	—	—

MOVES TAUGHT BY PEOPLE

Name	Type	Kind	Pow.	Acc.	PP	Range	Long	DA

MOVES TAUGHT BY MOVE TUTORS FOR SHARDS

Name	Type	Kind	Pow.	Acc.	PP	Range	Long	DA
Bug Bite	Bug	Physical	60	100	20	Normal	—	○
Bounce	Flying	Physical	85	85	5	Normal	○	○
Signal Beam	Bug	Special	75	100	15	Normal	—	—
Electroweb	Electric	Special	55	95	15	Many Others	—	—
Foul Play	Dark	Physical	95	100	15	Normal	—	○
Giga Drain	Grass	Special	75	100	10	Normal	—	—
Sleep Talk	Normal	Status	—	—	10	Self	—	—

EGG MOVES

Name	Type	Kind	Pow.	Acc.	PP	Range	Long	DA
Psybeam	Psychic	Special	65	100	20	Normal	—	—
Disable	Normal	Status	—	100	20	Normal	—	—
SonicBoom	Normal	Special	—	90	20	Normal	—	—
Baton Pass	Normal	Status	—	—	40	Self	—	—
Pursuit	Dark	Physical	40	100	20	Normal	—	○
Signal Beam	Bug	Special	75	100	15	Normal	—	—
Toxic Spikes	Poison	Status	—	—	20	Other Side	—	—
Twineedle	Bug	Physical	25	100	20	Normal	—	—
Electroweb	Electric	Special	55	95	15	Many Others	—	—
Rage Powder	Bug	Status	—	—	20	Self	—	—
Night Slash	Dark	Physical	70	100	15	Normal	—	○

---

168 Ariados — Long Leg Pokémon

TYPE: Bug / Poison

ABILITIES
- Swarm
- Insomnia

HIDDEN ABILITY
- Sniper

- HEIGHT: 3'07"
- WEIGHT: 73.9 lbs.
- GENDER: ♂ / ♀

It attaches silk to its prey and sets it free. Later, it tracks the silk to the prey and its friends.

STATS
- HP
- Attack
- Defense
- Sp. Atk
- Sp. Def
- Speed

EGG GROUPS
Bug

ITEMS SOMETIMES HELD
- None

Same form for ♂ / ♀

Pokémon AR Marker

EVOLUTION

Spinarak → Lv. 22 → Ariados

HOW TO OBTAIN

Pokémon Black Version 2	Route 22 (mass outbreak)
Pokémon White Version 2	Link Trade or Poké Transfer

HOW TO OBTAIN FROM OTHER GAMES

Pokémon Black Version	Dreamyard basement (after finishing the main story—dark grass)
Pokémon White Version	Dreamyard basement (after finishing the main story—dark grass)

LEVEL-UP AND LEARNED MOVES

Lv.	Name	Type	Kind	Pow.	Acc.	PP	Range	Long	DA
1	Bug Bite	Bug	Physical	60	100	20	Normal	—	○
1	Poison Sting	Poison	Physical	15	100	35	Normal	—	—
1	String Shot	Bug	Status	—	95	40	Many Others	—	—
1	Scary Face	Normal	Status	—	100	10	Normal	—	—
1	Constrict	Normal	Physical	10	100	35	Normal	—	○
5	Scary Face	Normal	Status	—	100	10	Normal	—	—
8	Constrict	Normal	Physical	10	100	35	Normal	—	○
12	Leech Life	Bug	Physical	20	100	15	Normal	—	—
15	Night Shade	Ghost	Special	—	100	15	Normal	—	—
19	Shadow Sneak	Ghost	Physical	40	100	30	Normal	—	—
23	Fury Swipes	Normal	Physical	18	80	15	Normal	—	—
28	Sucker Punch	Dark	Physical	80	100	5	Normal	—	—
32	Spider Web	Bug	Status	—	—	10	Normal	—	—
37	Agility	Psychic	Status	—	—	30	Self	—	—
41	Pin Missile	Bug	Physical	14	85	20	Normal	—	—
46	Psychic	Psychic	Special	90	100	10	Normal	—	—
50	Poison Jab	Poison	Physical	80	100	20	Normal	—	○
55	Cross Poison	Poison	Physical	70	100	20	Normal	—	—

TM & HM MOVES

Lv.	Name	Type	Kind	Pow.	Acc.	PP	Range	Long	DA
TM01	Hone Claws	Dark	Status	—	—	15	Self	—	—
TM06	Toxic	Poison	Status	—	90	10	Normal	—	—
TM09	Venoshock	Poison	Special	65	100	10	Normal	—	—
TM10	Hidden Power	Normal	Special	—	100	15	Normal	—	—
TM11	Sunny Day	Fire	Status	—	—	5	Both Sides	—	—
TM15	Hyper Beam	Normal	Special	150	90	5	Normal	—	—
TM17	Protect	Normal	Status	—	—	10	Self	—	—
TM21	Frustration	Normal	Physical	—	100	20	Normal	—	○
TM22	SolarBeam	Grass	Special	120	100	10	Normal	—	—
TM27	Return	Normal	Physical	—	100	20	Normal	—	○
TM28	Dig	Ground	Physical	80	100	10	Normal	—	—
TM29	Psychic	Psychic	Special	90	100	10	Normal	—	—
TM32	Double Team	Normal	Status	—	—	15	Self	—	—
TM36	Sludge Bomb	Poison	Special	90	100	10	Normal	—	—
TM42	Facade	Normal	Physical	70	100	20	Normal	—	○
TM44	Rest	Psychic	Status	—	—	10	Self	—	—
TM45	Attract	Normal	Status	—	100	15	Normal	—	—
TM46	Thief	Dark	Physical	40	100	10	Normal	—	—
TM48	Round	Normal	Special	60	100	15	Normal	—	—
TM68	Giga Impact	Normal	Physical	150	90	5	Normal	—	—
TM70	Flash	Normal	Status	—	100	20	Normal	—	—
TM76	Struggle Bug	Bug	Special	30	100	20	Many Others	—	—
TM81	X-Scissor	Bug	Physical	80	100	15	Normal	—	—
TM84	Poison Jab	Poison	Physical	80	100	20	Normal	—	○
TM87	Swagger	Normal	Status	—	90	15	Normal	—	—
TM90	Substitute	Normal	Status	—	—	10	Self	—	—

MOVES TAUGHT BY PEOPLE

Name	Type	Kind	Pow.	Acc.	PP	Range	Long	DA

MOVES TAUGHT BY MOVE TUTORS FOR SHARDS

Name	Type	Kind	Pow.	Acc.	PP	Range	Long	DA
Bug Bite	Bug	Physical	60	100	20	Normal	—	○
Bounce	Flying	Physical	85	85	5	Normal	○	○
Signal Beam	Bug	Special	75	100	15	Normal	—	—
Electroweb	Electric	Special	55	95	15	Many Others	—	—
Foul Play	Dark	Physical	95	100	15	Normal	—	○
Giga Drain	Grass	Special	75	100	10	Normal	—	—
Sleep Talk	Normal	Status	—	—	10	Self	—	—

169 Crobat

Bat Pokémon

- HEIGHT: 5'11"
- WEIGHT: 165.3 lbs.
- GENDER: ♂ / ♀

Having four wings allows it to fly more quickly and quietly so it can sneak up on prey without its noticing.

Same form for ♂ / ♀

TYPE Poison Flying

ABILITY
- Inner Focus

HIDDEN ABILITY
- Infiltrator

STATS
HP
Attack
Defense
Sp. Atk
Sp. Def
Speed

EGG GROUPS
Flying

ITEMS SOMETIMES HELD
- None

EVOLUTION

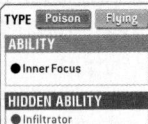

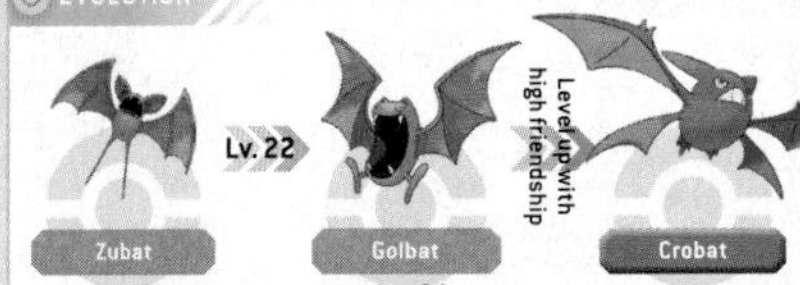
Lv. 22
Level up with high friendship
Zubat
Golbat
Crobat
➡ p. 34
➡ p. 34

HOW TO OBTAIN

Pokémon Black Version 2	Dreamyard outside (rustling grass)
Pokémon White Version 2	Dreamyard outside (rustling grass)

HOW TO OBTAIN FROM OTHER GAMES

———

———

LEVEL-UP AND LEARNED MOVES

Lv.	Name	Type	Kind	Pow.	Acc.	PP	Range	Long	DA
1	Cross Poison	Poison	Physical	70	100	20	Normal	—	○
1	Screech	Normal	Status	—	85	40	Normal	—	—
1	Leech Life	Bug	Physical	20	100	15	Normal	—	○
1	Supersonic	Normal	Status	—	55	20	Normal	—	—
1	Astonish	Ghost	Physical	30	100	15	Normal	—	○
4	Supersonic	Normal	Status	—	55	20	Normal	—	—
8	Astonish	Ghost	Physical	30	100	15	Normal	—	○
12	Bite	Dark	Physical	60	100	25	Normal	—	○
15	Wing Attack	Flying	Physical	60	100	35	Normal	○	○
19	Confuse Ray	Ghost	Status	—	100	10	Normal	—	—
24	Swift	Normal	Special	60	—	20	Many Others	—	—
28	Air Cutter	Flying	Special	55	95	25	Many Others	—	—
33	Acrobatics	Flying	Physical	55	100	15	Normal	○	○
38	Mean Look	Normal	Status	—	—	5	Normal	—	—
42	Poison Fang	Poison	Physical	50	100	15	Normal	—	○
47	Haze	Ice	Status	—	—	30	Both Sides	—	—
52	Air Slash	Flying	Special	75	95	20	Normal	○	—

TM & HM MOVES

Lv.	Name	Type	Kind	Pow.	Acc.	PP	Range	Long	DA
TM06	Toxic	Poison	Status	—	90	10	Normal	—	—
TM09	Venoshock	Poison	Special	65	100	10	Normal	—	—
TM10	Hidden Power	Normal	Special	—	100	15	Normal	—	—
TM11	Sunny Day	Fire	Status	—	—	5	Both Sides	—	—
TM12	Taunt	Dark	Status	—	100	20	Normal	—	—
TM15	Hyper Beam	Normal	Special	150	90	5	Normal	—	—
TM17	Protect	Normal	Status	—	—	10	Self	—	—
TM18	Rain Dance	Water	Status	—	—	5	Both Sides	—	—
TM21	Frustration	Normal	Physical	—	100	20	Normal	—	○
TM27	Return	Normal	Physical	—	100	20	Normal	—	○
TM30	Shadow Ball	Ghost	Special	80	100	15	Normal	—	—
TM32	Double Team	Normal	Status	—	—	15	Self	—	—
TM36	Sludge Bomb	Poison	Special	90	100	10	Normal	—	—
TM40	Aerial Ace	Flying	Physical	60	—	20	Normal	○	○
TM41	Torment	Dark	Status	—	100	15	Normal	—	—
TM42	Facade	Normal	Physical	70	100	20	Normal	—	○
TM44	Rest	Psychic	Status	—	—	10	Self	—	—
TM45	Attract	Normal	Status	—	100	15	Normal	—	—
TM46	Thief	Dark	Physical	40	100	10	Normal	—	○
TM48	Round	Normal	Special	60	100	15	Normal	—	—
TM62	Acrobatics	Flying	Physical	55	100	15	Normal	○	○
TM66	Payback	Dark	Physical	50	100	10	Normal	—	○
TM68	Giga Impact	Normal	Physical	150	90	5	Normal	—	○
TM81	X-Scissor	Bug	Physical	80	100	15	Normal	—	○
TM87	Swagger	Normal	Status	—	90	15	Normal	—	—
TM88	Pluck	Flying	Physical	60	100	20	Normal	○	○
TM89	U-turn	Bug	Physical	70	100	20	Normal	—	○
TM90	Substitute	Normal	Status	—	—	10	Self	—	—
HM02	Fly	Flying	Physical	90	95	15	Normal	○	○

MOVES TAUGHT BY PEOPLE

Name	Type	Kind	Pow.	Acc.	PP	Range	Long	DA

MOVES TAUGHT BY MOVE TUTORS FOR SHARDS

Name	Type	Kind	Pow.	Acc.	PP	Range	Long	DA
Super Fang	Normal	Physical	—	90	10	Normal	—	○
Uproar	Normal	Special	90	100	10	1 Random	—	—
Zen Headbutt	Psychic	Physical	80	90	15	Normal	—	○
Dark Pulse	Dark	Special	80	100	15	Normal	○	—
Snore	Normal	Special	40	100	15	Normal	—	—
Roost	Flying	Status	—	—	10	Self	—	—
Sky Attack	Flying	Physical	140	90	5	Normal	○	—
Heat Wave	Fire	Special	100	90	10	Many Others	—	—
Giga Drain	Grass	Special	75	100	10	Normal	—	—
Tailwind	Flying	Status	—	—	30	Your Side	—	—
Sleep Talk	Normal	Status	—	—	10	Self	—	—
Snatch	Dark	Status	—	—	10	Self	—	—

Pokémon AR Marker

170 Chinchou

Angler Pokémon

- HEIGHT: 1'08"
- WEIGHT: 26.5 lbs.
- GENDER: ♂ / ♀

It discharges positive and negative electricity from its antenna tips to shock its foes.

Same form for ♂ / ♀

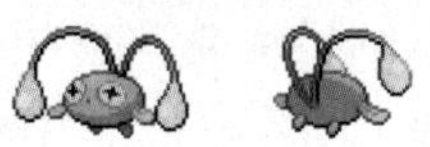

TYPE Water Electric

ABILITIES
- Volt Absorb
- Illuminate

HIDDEN ABILITY
- Water Absorb

STATS
HP
Attack
Defense
Sp. Atk
Sp. Def
Speed

EGG GROUPS
Water ❷

ITEMS SOMETIMES HELD
- DeepSeaScale

EVOLUTION

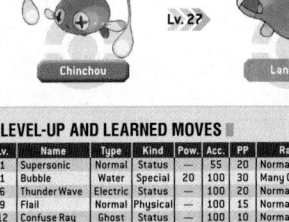

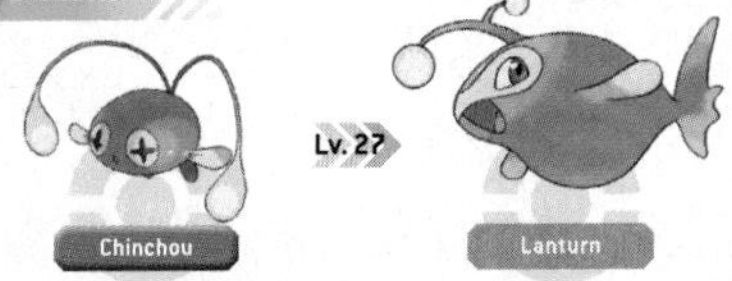
Lv. 27
Chinchou
Lanturn

HOW TO OBTAIN

Pokémon Black Version 2	Undella Bay (Super Rod)
Pokémon White Version 2	Undella Bay (Super Rod)

HOW TO OBTAIN FROM OTHER GAMES

———

———

LEVEL-UP AND LEARNED MOVES

Lv.	Name	Type	Kind	Pow.	Acc.	PP	Range	Long	DA
1	Supersonic	Normal	Status	—	55	20	Normal	—	—
1	Bubble	Water	Special	20	100	30	Many Others	—	—
6	Thunder Wave	Electric	Status	—	100	20	Normal	—	—
9	Flail	Normal	Physical	—	100	15	Normal	—	○
12	Confuse Ray	Ghost	Status	—	100	10	Normal	—	—
17	Water Gun	Water	Special	40	100	25	Normal	—	—
20	Spark	Electric	Physical	65	100	20	Normal	—	○
23	Take Down	Normal	Physical	90	85	20	Normal	—	○
28	Electro Ball	Electric	Special	—	100	10	Normal	—	—
31	BubbleBeam	Water	Special	65	100	20	Normal	—	—
34	Signal Beam	Bug	Special	75	100	15	Normal	—	—
39	Discharge	Electric	Special	80	100	15	Adjacent	—	—
42	Aqua Ring	Water	Status	—	—	20	Self	—	—
45	Hydro Pump	Water	Special	120	80	5	Normal	—	—
50	Charge	Electric	Status	—	—	20	Self	—	—

TM & HM MOVES

Lv.	Name	Type	Kind	Pow.	Acc.	PP	Range	Long	DA
TM06	Toxic	Poison	Status	—	90	10	Normal	—	—
TM07	Hail	Ice	Status	—	—	10	Both Sides	—	—
TM10	Hidden Power	Normal	Special	—	100	15	Normal	—	—
TM13	Ice Beam	Ice	Special	95	100	10	Normal	—	—
TM14	Blizzard	Ice	Special	120	70	5	Many Others	—	—
TM17	Protect	Normal	Status	—	—	10	Self	—	—
TM18	Rain Dance	Water	Status	—	—	5	Both Sides	—	—
TM21	Frustration	Normal	Physical	—	100	20	Normal	—	○
TM24	Thunderbolt	Electric	Special	95	100	15	Normal	—	—
TM25	Thunder	Electric	Special	120	70	10	Normal	—	—
TM27	Return	Normal	Physical	—	100	20	Normal	—	○
TM32	Double Team	Normal	Status	—	—	15	Self	—	—
TM42	Facade	Normal	Physical	70	100	20	Normal	—	○
TM44	Rest	Psychic	Status	—	—	10	Self	—	—
TM45	Attract	Normal	Status	—	100	15	Normal	—	—
TM48	Round	Normal	Special	60	100	15	Normal	—	—
TM55	Scald	Water	Special	80	100	15	Normal	—	—
TM57	Charge Beam	Electric	Special	50	90	10	Normal	—	—
TM70	Flash	Normal	Status	—	100	20	Normal	—	—
TM72	Volt Switch	Electric	Special	70	100	20	Normal	—	—
TM73	Thunder Wave	Electric	Status	—	100	20	Normal	—	—
TM87	Swagger	Normal	Status	—	90	15	Normal	—	—
TM90	Substitute	Normal	Status	—	—	10	Self	—	—
TM93	Wild Charge	Electric	Physical	90	100	15	Normal	—	○
HM03	Surf	Water	Special	95	100	15	Adjacent	—	—
HM05	Waterfall	Water	Physical	80	100	15	Normal	—	○
HM06	Dive	Water	Physical	80	100	10	Normal	—	○

MOVES TAUGHT BY PEOPLE

Name	Type	Kind	Pow.	Acc.	PP	Range	Long	DA

MOVES TAUGHT BY MOVE TUTORS FOR SHARDS

Name	Type	Kind	Pow.	Acc.	PP	Range	Long	DA
Bounce	Flying	Physical	85	85	5	Normal	○	○
Signal Beam	Bug	Special	75	100	15	Normal	—	—
Icy Wind	Ice	Special	55	95	15	Many Others	—	—
Snore	Normal	Special	40	100	15	Normal	—	—
Heal Bell	Normal	Status	—	—	5	Your Party	—	—
Sleep Talk	Normal	Status	—	—	10	Self	—	—

EGG MOVES

Name	Type	Kind	Pow.	Acc.	PP	Range	Long	DA
Flail	Normal	Physical	—	100	15	Normal	—	○
Screech	Normal	Status	—	85	40	Normal	—	—
Amnesia	Psychic	Status	—	—	20	Self	—	—
Psybeam	Psychic	Special	65	100	20	Normal	—	—
Whirlpool	Water	Special	35	85	15	Normal	—	—
Agility	Psychic	Status	—	—	30	Self	—	—
Mist	Ice	Status	—	—	30	Your Side	—	—
Shock Wave	Electric	Special	60	—	20	Normal	—	—
Brine	Water	Special	65	100	10	Normal	—	—
Water Pulse	Water	Special	60	100	20	Normal	○	—

Pokémon AR Marker

171 Lanturn

Light Pokémon

- HEIGHT: 3'11"
- WEIGHT: 49.6 lbs.
- GENDER: ♂ / ♀

Lanturn's light can shine up from great depths. It is nicknamed "The Deep-Sea Star."

Same form for ♂ / ♀

ITEMS SOMETIMES HELD
- DeepSeaScale

TYPE Water Electric

ABILITIES
- Volt Absorb
- Illuminate

HIDDEN ABILITY
- Water Absorb

STATS
HP	▪▪▪
Attack	▪▪
Defense	▪▪▪
Sp. Atk	▪▪▪
Sp. Def	▪▪▪
Speed	▪▪

EGG GROUPS
Water ❷

◆ EVOLUTION

Chinchou → Lv. 27 → Lanturn

HOW TO OBTAIN

Pokémon Black Version 2	Undella Bay (Super Rod/ripples in water)
Pokémon White Version 2	Undella Bay (Super Rod/ripples in water)

HOW TO OBTAIN FROM OTHER GAMES

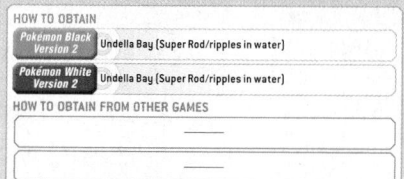

LEVEL-UP AND LEARNED MOVES

Lv.	Name	Type	Kind	Pow.	Acc.	PP	Range	Long	DA
1	Bubble	Water	Special	20	100	30	Many Others	—	—
1	Supersonic	Normal	Status	—	55	20	Normal	—	—
1	Thunder Wave	Electric	Status	—	100	20	Normal	—	—
6	Thunder Wave	Electric	Status	—	100	20	Normal	—	—
9	Flail	Normal	Physical	—	100	15	Normal	—	○
12	Water Gun	Water	Special	40	100	25	Normal	—	—
17	Confuse Ray	Ghost	Status	—	100	10	Normal	—	—
20	Spark	Electric	Physical	65	100	20	Normal	—	—
23	Take Down	Normal	Physical	90	85	20	Normal	—	○
27	Stockpile	Normal	Status	—	—	20	Self	—	—
27	Swallow	Normal	Status	—	—	10	Self	—	—
27	Spit Up	Normal	Special	—	100	10	Normal	—	—
30	Electro Ball	Electric	Special	—	100	10	Normal	—	—
35	BubbleBeam	Water	Special	65	100	20	Normal	—	—
40	Signal Beam	Bug	Special	75	100	15	Normal	—	—
47	Discharge	Electric	Special	80	100	15	Adjacent	—	—
52	Aqua Ring	Water	Status	—	—	20	Self	—	—
57	Hydro Pump	Water	Special	120	80	5	Normal	—	—
64	Charge	Electric	Status	—	—	20	Self	—	—

TM & HM MOVES

Lv.	Name	Type	Kind	Pow.	Acc.	PP	Range	Long	DA
TM06	Toxic	Poison	Status	—	90	10	Normal	—	—
TM07	Hail	Ice	Status	—	—	10	Both Sides	—	—
TM10	Hidden Power	Normal	Special	—	100	15	Normal	—	—
TM13	Ice Beam	Ice	Special	95	100	10	Normal	—	—
TM14	Blizzard	Ice	Special	120	70	5	Many Others	—	—
TM15	Hyper Beam	Normal	Special	150	90	5	Normal	—	—
TM17	Protect	Normal	Status	—	—	10	Self	—	—
TM18	Rain Dance	Water	Status	—	—	5	Both Sides	—	—
TM21	Frustration	Normal	Physical	—	100	20	Normal	—	○
TM24	Thunderbolt	Electric	Special	95	100	15	Normal	—	—
TM25	Thunder	Electric	Special	120	70	10	Normal	—	—
TM27	Return	Normal	Physical	—	100	20	Normal	—	○
TM32	Double Team	Normal	Status	—	—	15	Self	—	—
TM42	Facade	Normal	Physical	70	100	20	Normal	—	—
TM44	Rest	Psychic	Status	—	—	10	Self	—	—
TM45	Attract	Normal	Status	—	100	15	Normal	—	—
TM48	Round	Normal	Special	60	100	15	Normal	—	—
TM55	Scald	Water	Special	80	100	15	Normal	—	—
TM57	Charge Beam	Electric	Special	50	90	10	Normal	—	—
TM68	Giga Impact	Normal	Physical	150	90	5	Normal	—	○
TM70	Flash	Normal	Status	—	100	20	Normal	—	—
TM72	Volt Switch	Electric	Special	70	100	20	Normal	—	—
TM73	Thunder Wave	Electric	Status	—	100	20	Normal	—	—
TM87	Swagger	Normal	Status	—	90	15	Normal	—	—
TM90	Substitute	Normal	Status	—	—	10	Self	—	—
TM93	Wild Charge	Electric	Physical	90	100	15	Adjacent	—	○
HM03	Surf	Water	Special	95	100	15	Many Others	—	—
HM05	Waterfall	Water	Physical	80	100	15	Normal	—	○
HM06	Dive	Water	Physical	80	100	10	Normal	—	○

MOVES TAUGHT BY PEOPLE

Name	Type	Kind	Pow.	Acc.	PP	Range	Long	DA

MOVES TAUGHT BY MOVE TUTORS FOR SHARDS

Name	Type	Kind	Pow.	Acc.	PP	Range	Long	DA
Bounce	Flying	Physical	85	85	5	Normal	○	—
Signal Beam	Bug	Special	75	100	15	Normal	—	—
Icy Wind	Ice	Special	55	95	15	Many Others	—	—
Aqua Tail	Water	Physical	90	90	10	Normal	—	○
Snore	Normal	Special	40	100	15	Normal	—	—
Heal Bell	Normal	Status	—	—	5	Your Party	—	—
Sleep Talk	Normal	Status	—	—	10	Self	—	—

Pokémon AR Marker

---

172 Pichu

Tiny Mouse Pokémon

- HEIGHT: 1'00"
- WEIGHT: 4.4 lbs.
- GENDER: ♂ / ♀

The electric sacs in its cheeks are small. If even a little electricity leaks, it becomes shocked.

Same form for ♂ / ♀

ITEMS SOMETIMES HELD
- None

TYPE Electric

ABILITY
- Static

HIDDEN ABILITY
- Lightningrod

STATS
HP	▪▪
Attack	▪▪
Defense	▪
Sp. Atk	▪▪
Sp. Def	▪▪
Speed	▪▪▪

EGG GROUPS
No Egg has ever been discovered

◆ EVOLUTION

Pichu → (Level up with high friendship) → Pikachu → (Use Thunderstone) → Raichu

➡ p. 26   ➡ p. 26

HOW TO OBTAIN

Pokémon Black Version 2	Link Trade or Poké Transfer
Pokémon White Version 2	Link Trade or Poké Transfer

HOW TO OBTAIN FROM OTHER GAMES

Pokémon Platinum Version	Pokémon Mansion on Route 212

LEVEL-UP AND LEARNED MOVES

Lv.	Name	Type	Kind	Pow.	Acc.	PP	Range	Long	DA
1	ThunderShock	Electric	Special	40	100	30	Normal	—	—
1	Charm	Normal	Status	—	100	20	Normal	—	—
5	Tail Whip	Normal	Status	—	100	30	Many Others	—	—
10	Thunder Wave	Electric	Status	—	100	20	Normal	—	—
13	Sweet Kiss	Normal	Status	—	75	10	Normal	—	—
18	Nasty Plot	Dark	Status	—	—	20	Self	—	—

TM & HM MOVES

Lv.	Name	Type	Kind	Pow.	Acc.	PP	Range	Long	DA
TM06	Toxic	Poison	Status	—	90	10	Normal	—	—
TM10	Hidden Power	Normal	Special	—	100	15	Normal	—	—
TM16	Light Screen	Psychic	Status	—	—	30	Your Side	—	—
TM17	Protect	Normal	Status	—	—	10	Self	—	—
TM18	Rain Dance	Water	Status	—	—	5	Both Sides	—	—
TM21	Frustration	Normal	Physical	—	100	20	Normal	—	○
TM24	Thunderbolt	Electric	Special	95	100	15	Normal	—	—
TM25	Thunder	Electric	Special	120	70	10	Normal	—	—
TM27	Return	Normal	Physical	—	100	20	Normal	—	—
TM32	Double Team	Normal	Status	—	—	15	Self	—	—
TM42	Facade	Normal	Physical	70	100	20	Normal	—	—
TM44	Rest	Psychic	Status	—	—	10	Self	—	—
TM45	Attract	Normal	Status	—	100	15	Normal	—	—
TM48	Round	Normal	Special	60	100	15	Normal	—	—
TM49	Echoed Voice	Normal	Special	40	100	15	Normal	—	—
TM56	Fling	Dark	Physical	—	100	10	Normal	—	—
TM57	Charge Beam	Electric	Special	50	90	10	Normal	—	—
TM70	Flash	Normal	Status	—	100	20	Normal	—	—
TM72	Volt Switch	Electric	Special	70	100	20	Normal	—	—
TM73	Thunder Wave	Electric	Status	—	100	20	Normal	—	—
TM86	Grass Knot	Grass	Special	—	100	20	Normal	—	—
TM87	Swagger	Normal	Status	—	90	15	Normal	—	—
TM90	Substitute	Normal	Status	—	—	10	Self	—	—
TM93	Wild Charge	Electric	Physical	90	100	15	Normal	—	○

MOVES TAUGHT BY PEOPLE

Name	Type	Kind	Pow.	Acc.	PP	Range	Long	DA

MOVES TAUGHT BY MOVE TUTORS FOR SHARDS

Name	Type	Kind	Pow.	Acc.	PP	Range	Long	DA
Covet	Normal	Physical	60	100	40	Normal	—	○
Signal Beam	Bug	Special	75	100	15	Normal	—	—
Uproar	Normal	Special	90	100	10	1 Random	—	—
Magnet Rise	Electric	Status	—	—	10	Self	—	—
Iron Tail	Steel	Physical	100	75	15	Normal	—	○
Snore	Normal	Special	40	100	15	Normal	—	—
Helping Hand	Normal	Status	—	—	20	1 Ally	—	—
Sleep Talk	Normal	Status	—	—	10	Self	—	—

EGG MOVES

Name	Type	Kind	Pow.	Acc.	PP	Range	Long	DA
Reversal	Fighting	Physical	—	100	15	Normal	—	○
Bide	Normal	Physical	—	—	10	Self	—	○
Present	Normal	Physical	—	90	15	Normal	—	○
Encore	Normal	Status	—	100	5	Normal	—	—
DoubleSlap	Normal	Physical	15	85	10	Normal	—	—
Wish	Normal	Status	—	—	10	Self	—	—
Charge	Electric	Status	—	—	20	Self	—	—
Fake Out	Normal	Physical	40	100	10	Normal	—	○
ThunderPunch	Electric	Physical	75	100	15	Normal	—	○
Tickle	Normal	Status	—	100	20	Normal	—	—
Flail	Normal	Physical	—	100	15	Normal	—	○
Endure	Normal	Status	—	—	10	Self	—	○
Lucky Chant	Normal	Status	—	—	30	Your Side	—	—
Bestow	Normal	Status	—	—	15	Normal	—	—

Pokémon AR Marker

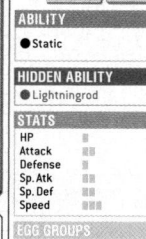

173 Cleffa
Star Shape Pokémon

TYPE Normal

ABILITIES
- Cute Charm
- Magic Guard

HIDDEN ABILITY
- Friend Guard

- **HEIGHT:** 1'00"
- **WEIGHT:** 6.6 lbs.
- **GENDER:** ♂ / ♀

According to local rumors, Cleffa are often seen in places where shooting stars have fallen.

STATS
HP	▪
Attack	▪▪
Defense	▪▪
Sp. Atk	▪▪
Sp. Def	▪▪
Speed	▪

EGG GROUPS
No Egg has ever been discovered

ITEMS SOMETIMES HELD
- None

Same form for ♂ / ♀

Pokémon AR Marker

EVOLUTION

Cleffa → (Level up with high friendship) → Clefairy → (Use Moon Stone) → Clefable

→ p. 31 → p. 31

HOW TO OBTAIN
Pokémon Black Version 2	Catch a Clefairy or Clefable, leave it at the Pokémon Day Care, and hatch the Egg that is found
Pokémon White Version 2	Catch a Clefairy or Clefable, leave it at the Pokémon Day Care, and hatch the Egg that is found

HOW TO OBTAIN FROM OTHER GAMES
Pokémon Platinum Version	Mt. Coronet (morning and night only)

LEVEL-UP AND LEARNED MOVES
Lv.	Name	Type	Kind	Pow.	Acc.	PP	Range	Long	DA
1	Pound	Normal	Physical	40	100	35	Normal	—	○
1	Charm	Normal	Status	—	100	20	Normal	—	—
4	Encore	Normal	Status	—	100	5	Normal	—	—
7	Sing	Normal	Status	—	55	15	Normal	—	—
10	Sweet Kiss	Normal	Status	—	75	10	Normal	—	—
13	Copycat	Normal	Status	—	—	20	Self	—	—
16	Magical Leaf	Grass	Special	60	—	20	Normal	—	—

TM & HM MOVES
Lv.	Name	Type	Kind	Pow.	Acc.	PP	Range	Long	DA
TM03	Psyshock	Psychic	Special	80	100	10	Normal	—	—
TM06	Toxic	Poison	Status	—	90	10	Normal	—	—
TM10	Hidden Power	Normal	Special	—	100	15	Normal	—	—
TM11	Sunny Day	Fire	Status	—	—	5	Both Sides	—	—
TM16	Light Screen	Psychic	Status	—	—	30	Your Side	—	—
TM17	Protect	Normal	Status	—	—	10	Self	—	—
TM18	Rain Dance	Water	Status	—	—	5	Both Sides	—	—
TM19	Telekinesis	Psychic	Status	—	—	15	Normal	—	—
TM20	Safeguard	Normal	Status	—	—	25	Your Side	—	—
TM21	Frustration	Normal	Physical	—	100	20	Normal	—	○
TM22	SolarBeam	Grass	Special	120	100	10	Normal	—	—
TM27	Return	Normal	Physical	—	100	20	Normal	—	○
TM28	Dig	Ground	Physical	80	100	10	Normal	—	○
TM29	Psychic	Psychic	Special	90	100	10	Normal	—	—
TM30	Shadow Ball	Ghost	Special	80	100	15	Normal	—	—
TM32	Double Team	Normal	Status	—	—	15	Self	—	—
TM33	Reflect	Psychic	Status	—	—	20	Your Side	—	—
TM35	Flamethrower	Fire	Special	95	100	15	Normal	—	—
TM38	Fire Blast	Fire	Special	120	85	5	Normal	—	—
TM42	Facade	Normal	Physical	70	100	20	Normal	—	○
TM44	Rest	Psychic	Status	—	—	10	Self	—	—
TM45	Attract	Normal	Status	—	100	15	Normal	—	—
TM48	Round	Normal	Special	60	100	15	Normal	—	—
TM49	Echoed Voice	Normal	Special	40	100	15	Normal	—	—
TM56	Fling	Dark	Physical	—	100	10	Normal	—	○
TM59	Incinerate	Fire	Special	30	100	15	Many Others	—	—
TM70	Flash	Normal	Status	—	100	20	Normal	—	—
TM73	Thunder Wave	Electric	Status	—	100	20	Normal	—	—
TM77	Psych Up	Normal	Status	—	—	10	Self	—	—
TM83	Work Up	Normal	Status	—	—	30	Self	—	—
TM85	Dream Eater	Psychic	Special	100	100	15	Normal	—	—
TM86	Grass Knot	Grass	Special	—	100	20	Normal	—	○
TM87	Swagger	Normal	Status	—	90	15	Normal	—	—
TM90	Substitute	Normal	Status	—	—	10	Self	—	—

MOVES TAUGHT BY PEOPLE
Name	Type	Kind	Pow.	Acc.	PP	Range	Long	DA

MOVES TAUGHT BY MOVE TUTORS FOR SHARDS
Name	Type	Kind	Pow.	Acc.	PP	Range	Long	DA
Covet	Normal	Physical	60	100	40	Normal	—	○
Signal Beam	Bug	Special	75	100	15	Normal	—	—
Uproar	Normal	Special	90	100	10	1 Random	—	—
Last Resort	Normal	Physical	140	100	5	Normal	—	○
Magic Coat	Psychic	Status	—	—	15	Self	—	—
Hyper Voice	Normal	Special	90	100	10	Many Others	—	—
Icy Wind	Ice	Special	55	95	15	Many Others	—	—
Iron Tail	Steel	Physical	100	75	15	Normal	—	○
Zen Headbutt	Psychic	Physical	80	90	15	Normal	—	○
Gravity	Psychic	Status	—	—	5	Both Sides	—	—
Snore	Normal	Special	40	100	15	Normal	—	—
Role Play	Psychic	Status	—	—	10	Normal	—	—
Helping Hand	Normal	Status	—	—	20	1 Ally	—	—
After You	Normal	Status	—	—	15	Normal	—	—
Wonder Room	Psychic	Status	—	—	10	Both Sides	—	—
Recycle	Normal	Status	—	—	10	Self	—	—
Trick	Psychic	Status	—	100	10	Normal	—	—
Endeavor	Normal	Physical	—	100	5	Normal	—	○
Sleep Talk	Normal	Status	—	—	10	Self	—	—

EGG MOVES
Name	Type	Kind	Pow.	Acc.	PP	Range	Long	DA
Present	Normal	Physical	—	90	15	Normal	—	—
Metronome	Normal	Status	—	—	10	Self	—	—
Amnesia	Psychic	Status	—	—	20	Self	—	—
Belly Drum	Normal	Status	—	—	10	Self	—	—
Splash	Normal	Status	—	—	40	Self	—	—
Mimic	Normal	Status	—	—	10	Normal	—	—
Wish	Normal	Status	—	—	10	Self	—	—
Fake Tears	Dark	Status	—	100	20	Normal	—	—
Covet	Normal	Physical	60	100	40	Normal	—	○
Aromatherapy	Grass	Status	—	—	5	Your Party	—	—
Stored Power	Psychic	Special	20	100	10	Normal	—	—
Tickle	Normal	Status	—	100	20	Normal	—	—

174 Igglybuff
Balloon Pokémon

TYPE Normal

ABILITY
- Cute Charm

HIDDEN ABILITY
- Friend Guard

- **HEIGHT:** 1'00"
- **WEIGHT:** 2.2 lbs.
- **GENDER:** ♂ / ♀

Its body has a faintly sweet scent and is bouncy and soft. If it bounces even once, it cannot stop.

STATS
HP	▪▪▪▪
Attack	▪▪
Defense	▪
Sp. Atk	▪▪
Sp. Def	▪
Speed	▪

EGG GROUPS
No Egg has ever been discovered

ITEMS SOMETIMES HELD
- None

Same form for ♂ / ♀

Pokémon AR Marker

EVOLUTION
Igglybuff → (Level up with high friendship) → Jigglypuff → (Use Moon Stone) → Wigglytuff

→ p. 33 → p. 33

HOW TO OBTAIN
Pokémon Black Version 2	Catch a Jigglypuff or Wigglytuff, leave it at the Pokémon Day Care, and hatch the Egg that is found
Pokémon White Version 2	Catch a Jigglypuff or Wigglytuff, leave it at the Pokémon Day Care, and hatch the Egg that is found

HOW TO OBTAIN FROM OTHER GAMES
Pokémon Platinum Version	Pokémon Mansion on Route 212 (after obtaining the National Pokédex, talk to Mr. Backlot)

LEVEL-UP AND LEARNED MOVES
Lv.	Name	Type	Kind	Pow.	Acc.	PP	Range	Long	DA
1	Sing	Normal	Status	—	55	15	Normal	—	—
1	Charm	Normal	Status	—	100	20	Normal	—	—
5	Defense Curl	Normal	Status	—	—	40	Self	—	—
9	Pound	Normal	Physical	40	100	35	Normal	—	○
13	Sweet Kiss	Normal	Status	—	75	10	Normal	—	—
17	Copycat	Normal	Status	—	—	20	Self	—	—

TM & HM MOVES
Lv.	Name	Type	Kind	Pow.	Acc.	PP	Range	Long	DA
TM06	Toxic	Poison	Status	—	90	10	Normal	—	—
TM10	Hidden Power	Normal	Special	—	100	15	Normal	—	—
TM11	Sunny Day	Fire	Status	—	—	5	Both Sides	—	—
TM16	Light Screen	Psychic	Status	—	—	30	Your Side	—	—
TM17	Protect	Normal	Status	—	—	10	Self	—	—
TM18	Rain Dance	Water	Status	—	—	5	Both Sides	—	—
TM20	Safeguard	Normal	Status	—	—	25	Your Side	—	—
TM21	Frustration	Normal	Physical	—	100	20	Normal	—	○
TM22	SolarBeam	Grass	Special	120	100	10	Normal	—	—
TM27	Return	Normal	Physical	—	100	20	Normal	—	○
TM28	Dig	Ground	Physical	80	100	10	Normal	—	○
TM29	Psychic	Psychic	Special	90	100	10	Normal	—	—
TM30	Shadow Ball	Ghost	Special	80	100	15	Normal	—	—
TM32	Double Team	Normal	Status	—	—	15	Self	—	—
TM33	Reflect	Psychic	Status	—	—	20	Your Side	—	—
TM35	Flamethrower	Fire	Special	95	100	15	Normal	—	—
TM38	Fire Blast	Fire	Special	120	85	5	Normal	—	—
TM42	Facade	Normal	Physical	70	100	20	Normal	—	○
TM44	Rest	Psychic	Status	—	—	10	Self	—	—
TM45	Attract	Normal	Status	—	100	15	Normal	—	—
TM48	Round	Normal	Special	60	100	15	Normal	—	—
TM49	Echoed Voice	Normal	Special	40	100	15	Normal	—	—
TM56	Fling	Dark	Physical	—	100	10	Normal	—	○
TM59	Incinerate	Fire	Special	30	100	15	Many Others	—	—
TM70	Flash	Normal	Status	—	100	20	Normal	—	—
TM73	Thunder Wave	Electric	Status	—	100	20	Normal	—	—
TM77	Psych Up	Normal	Status	—	—	10	Self	—	—
TM83	Work Up	Normal	Status	—	—	30	Self	—	—
TM85	Dream Eater	Psychic	Special	100	100	15	Normal	—	—
TM86	Grass Knot	Grass	Special	—	100	20	Normal	—	○
TM87	Swagger	Normal	Status	—	90	15	Normal	—	—
TM90	Substitute	Normal	Status	—	—	10	Self	—	—
TM93	Wild Charge	Electric	Physical	90	100	15	Normal	—	○

MOVES TAUGHT BY PEOPLE
Name	Type	Kind	Pow.	Acc.	PP	Range	Long	DA

MOVES TAUGHT BY MOVE TUTORS FOR SHARDS
Name	Type	Kind	Pow.	Acc.	PP	Range	Long	DA
Covet	Normal	Physical	60	100	40	Normal	—	○
Bounce	Flying	Physical	85	85	5	Normal	○	○
Uproar	Normal	Special	90	100	10	1 Random	—	—
Last Resort	Normal	Physical	140	100	5	Normal	—	○
Magic Coat	Psychic	Status	—	—	15	Self	—	—
Hyper Voice	Normal	Special	90	100	10	Many Others	—	—
Icy Wind	Ice	Special	55	95	15	Many Others	—	—
Gravity	Psychic	Status	—	—	5	Both Sides	—	—
Snore	Normal	Special	40	100	15	Normal	—	—
Heal Bell	Normal	Status	—	—	5	Your Party	—	—
Role Play	Psychic	Status	—	—	10	Normal	—	—
Pain Split	Normal	Status	—	—	20	Normal	—	—
Helping Hand	Normal	Status	—	—	20	1 Ally	—	—
Recycle	Normal	Status	—	—	10	Self	—	—
Endeavor	Normal	Physical	—	100	5	Normal	—	○
Sleep Talk	Normal	Status	—	—	10	Self	—	—

EGG MOVES
Name	Type	Kind	Pow.	Acc.	PP	Range	Long	DA
Perish Song	Normal	Status	—	—	5	Adjacent	○	—
Present	Normal	Physical	—	90	15	Normal	—	—
Faint Attack	Dark	Physical	60	—	20	Normal	—	—
Wish	Normal	Status	—	—	10	Self	—	—
Fake Tears	Dark	Status	—	100	20	Normal	—	—
Last Resort	Normal	Physical	140	100	5	Normal	—	○
Covet	Normal	Physical	60	100	40	Normal	—	○
Gravity	Psychic	Status	—	—	5	Both Sides	—	—
Sleep Talk	Normal	Status	—	—	10	Self	—	—
Captivate	Normal	Status	—	100	20	Many Others	—	—
Punishment	Dark	Physical	—	100	5	Normal	—	○

175 Togepi

Spike Ball Pokémon

- HEIGHT: 1'00"
- WEIGHT: 3.3 lbs.
- GENDER: ♂ / ♀

It transforms the kindness and joy of others into happiness, which it stores in its shell.

TYPE: Normal

ABILITIES
- Hustle
- Serene Grace

HIDDEN ABILITY
- Super Luck

STATS
HP
Attack
Defense
Sp. Atk
Sp. Def
Speed

EGG GROUPS
No Egg has ever been discovered

Same form for ♂ / ♀

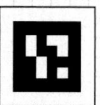

ITEMS SOMETIMES HELD
- None

Pokémon AR Marker

EVOLUTION

Togepi
Level up with high friendship
Togetic
Use Shiny Stone
Togekiss

➡ p. 250

HOW TO OBTAIN

Pokémon Black Version 2	Trade Pokémon during a date with Yancy or Curtis (12th time)
Pokémon White Version 2	Trade Pokémon during a date with Yancy or Curtis (12th time)

HOW TO OBTAIN FROM OTHER GAMES

Pokémon HeartGold Version	Hatch the Mystery Egg received from Mr. Pokémon on Route 30
Pokémon SoulSilver Version	Hatch the Mystery Egg received from Mr. Pokémon on Route 30

LEVEL-UP AND LEARNED MOVES

Lv.	Name	Type	Kind	Pow.	Acc.	PP	Range	Long	DA
1	Growl	Normal	Status	—	100	40	Many Others	—	—
1	Charm	Normal	Status	—	100	20	Normal	—	—
5	Metronome	Normal	Status	—	—	10	Self	—	—
9	Sweet Kiss	Normal	Status	—	75	10	Normal	—	—
13	Yawn	Normal	Status	—	—	10	Normal	—	—
17	Encore	Normal	Status	—	100	5	Normal	—	—
21	Follow Me	Normal	Status	—	—	20	Self	—	—
25	Bestow	Normal	Status	—	—	15	Normal	—	—
29	Wish	Normal	Status	—	—	10	Self	—	—
33	AncientPower	Rock	Special	60	100	5	Normal	—	—
37	Safeguard	Normal	Status	—	—	25	Your Side	—	—
41	Baton Pass	Normal	Status	—	—	40	Self	—	—
45	Double-Edge	Normal	Physical	120	100	15	Normal	—	○
49	Last Resort	Normal	Physical	140	100	5	Normal	—	○
53	After You	Normal	Status	—	—	15	Normal	—	—

TM & HM MOVES

Lv.	Name	Type	Kind	Pow.	Acc.	PP	Range	Long	DA
TM03	Psyshock	Psychic	Special	80	100	10	Normal	—	—
TM06	Toxic	Poison	Status	—	90	10	Normal	—	—
TM10	Hidden Power	Normal	Special	—	100	15	Normal	—	—
TM11	Sunny Day	Fire	Status	—	—	5	Both Sides	—	—
TM16	Light Screen	Psychic	Status	—	—	30	Your Side	—	—
TM17	Protect	Normal	Status	—	—	10	Self	—	—
TM18	Rain Dance	Water	Status	—	—	5	Both Sides	—	—
TM19	Telekinesis	Psychic	Status	—	—	15	Normal	—	—
TM20	Safeguard	Normal	Status	—	—	25	Your Side	—	—
TM21	Frustration	Normal	Physical	—	100	20	Normal	—	○
TM22	SolarBeam	Grass	Special	120	100	10	Normal	—	—
TM27	Return	Normal	Physical	—	100	20	Normal	—	○
TM29	Psychic	Psychic	Special	90	100	10	Normal	—	—
TM30	Shadow Ball	Ghost	Special	80	100	15	Normal	—	—
TM32	Double Team	Normal	Status	—	—	15	Self	—	—
TM33	Reflect	Psychic	Status	—	—	20	Your Side	—	—
TM35	Flamethrower	Fire	Special	95	100	15	Normal	—	—
TM38	Fire Blast	Fire	Special	120	85	5	Normal	—	—
TM42	Facade	Normal	Physical	70	100	20	Normal	—	○
TM44	Rest	Psychic	Status	—	—	10	Self	—	—
TM45	Attract	Normal	Status	—	100	15	Normal	—	—
TM48	Round	Normal	Special	60	100	15	Normal	—	—
TM49	Echoed Voice	Normal	Special	40	100	15	Normal	—	—
TM56	Fling	Dark	Physical	—	100	10	Normal	—	—
TM59	Incinerate	Fire	Special	30	100	15	Many Others	—	—
TM70	Flash	Normal	Status	—	100	20	Normal	—	—
TM73	Thunder Wave	Electric	Status	—	100	20	Normal	—	—
TM77	Psych Up	Normal	Status	—	—	10	Normal	—	—
TM83	Work Up	Normal	Status	—	—	30	Self	—	—
TM85	Dream Eater	Psychic	Special	100	100	15	Normal	—	—
TM86	Grass Knot	Grass	Special	—	100	20	Normal	—	○
TM87	Swagger	Normal	Status	—	90	15	Normal	—	—
TM90	Substitute	Normal	Status	—	—	10	Self	—	—
TM94	Rock Smash	Fighting	Physical	40	100	15	Normal	—	○

MOVES TAUGHT BY PEOPLE

Name	Type	Kind	Pow.	Acc.	PP	Range	Long	DA

MOVES TAUGHT BY MOVE TUTORS FOR SHARDS

Name	Type	Kind	Pow.	Acc.	PP	Range	Long	DA
Covet	Normal	Physical	60	100	40	Normal	—	○
Signal Beam	Bug	Special	75	100	15	Normal	—	—
Uproar	Normal	Special	90	100	10	1 Random	—	—
Last Resort	Normal	Physical	140	100	5	Normal	—	○
Magic Coat	Psychic	Status	—	—	15	Self	—	—
Hyper Voice	Normal	Special	90	100	10	Many Others	—	—
Zen Headbutt	Psychic	Physical	80	90	15	Normal	—	○
Snore	Normal	Special	40	100	15	Normal	—	—
Heal Bell	Normal	Status	—	—	5	Your Party	—	—
After You	Normal	Status	—	—	15	Normal	—	—
Trick	Psychic	Status	—	100	10	Normal	—	—
Endeavor	Normal	Physical	—	100	5	Normal	—	○
Sleep Talk	Normal	Status	—	—	10	Self	—	—

EGG MOVES

Name	Type	Kind	Pow.	Acc.	PP	Range	Long	DA
Present	Normal	Physical	—	90	15	Normal	—	—
Mirror Move	Flying	Status	—	—	20	Normal	—	—
Peck	Flying	Physical	35	100	35	Normal	○	○
Foresight	Normal	Status	—	—	40	Normal	—	—
Future Sight	Psychic	Special	100	100	10	Normal	—	—
Nasty Plot	Dark	Status	—	—	20	Self	—	—
Psycho Shift	Psychic	Status	—	90	10	Normal	—	—
Lucky Chant	Normal	Status	—	—	30	Your Side	—	—
Extrasensory	Psychic	Special	80	100	30	Normal	—	—
Secret Power	Normal	Physical	70	100	20	Normal	—	—
Stored Power	Psychic	Special	20	100	10	Normal	—	—
Morning Sun	Normal	Status	—	—	5	Self	—	—

176 Togetic

Happiness Pokémon

- HEIGHT: 2'00"
- WEIGHT: 7.1 lbs.
- GENDER: ♂ / ♀

To share its happiness, it flies around the world seeking kind-hearted people.

TYPE: Normal / Flying

ABILITIES
- Hustle
- Serene Grace

HIDDEN ABILITY
- Super Luck

STATS
HP
Attack
Defense
Sp. Atk
Sp. Def
Speed

EGG GROUPS
Flying/Fairy

Same form for ♂ / ♀

ITEMS SOMETIMES HELD
- None

Pokémon AR Marker

EVOLUTION

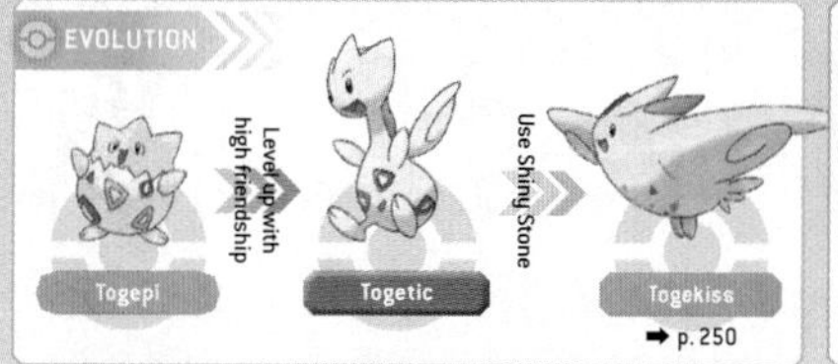
Togepi
Level up with high friendship
Togetic
Use Shiny Stone
Togekiss

➡ p. 250

HOW TO OBTAIN

Pokémon Black Version 2	Level up the Togepi you receive from Yancy or Curtis with high friendship
Pokémon White Version 2	Level up the Togepi you receive from Yancy or Curtis with high friendship

HOW TO OBTAIN FROM OTHER GAMES

—

—

LEVEL-UP AND LEARNED MOVES

Lv.	Name	Type	Kind	Pow.	Acc.	PP	Range	Long	DA
1	Magical Leaf	Grass	Special	60	—	20	Normal	—	—
1	Growl	Normal	Status	—	100	40	Many Others	—	—
1	Charm	Normal	Status	—	100	20	Normal	—	—
1	Metronome	Normal	Status	—	—	10	Self	—	—
1	Sweet Kiss	Normal	Status	—	75	10	Normal	—	—
5	Metronome	Normal	Status	—	—	10	Self	—	—
9	Sweet Kiss	Normal	Status	—	75	10	Normal	—	—
13	Yawn	Normal	Status	—	—	10	Normal	—	—
17	Encore	Normal	Status	—	100	5	Normal	—	—
21	Follow Me	Normal	Status	—	—	20	Self	—	—
25	Bestow	Normal	Status	—	—	15	Normal	—	—
29	Wish	Normal	Status	—	—	10	Self	—	—
33	AncientPower	Rock	Special	60	100	5	Normal	—	—
37	Safeguard	Normal	Status	—	—	25	Your Side	—	—
41	Baton Pass	Normal	Status	—	—	40	Self	—	—
45	Double-Edge	Normal	Physical	120	100	15	Normal	—	○
49	Last Resort	Normal	Physical	140	100	5	Normal	—	○
53	After You	Normal	Status	—	—	15	Normal	—	—

TM & HM MOVES

Lv.	Name	Type	Kind	Pow.	Acc.	PP	Range	Long	DA
TM03	Psyshock	Psychic	Special	80	100	10	Normal	—	—
TM06	Toxic	Poison	Status	—	90	10	Normal	—	—
TM10	Hidden Power	Normal	Special	—	100	15	Normal	—	—
TM11	Sunny Day	Fire	Status	—	—	5	Both Sides	—	—
TM15	Hyper Beam	Normal	Special	150	90	5	Normal	—	—
TM16	Light Screen	Psychic	Status	—	—	30	Your Side	—	—
TM17	Protect	Normal	Status	—	—	10	Self	—	—
TM18	Rain Dance	Water	Status	—	—	5	Both Sides	—	—
TM19	Telekinesis	Psychic	Status	—	—	15	Normal	—	—
TM20	Safeguard	Normal	Status	—	—	25	Your Side	—	—
TM21	Frustration	Normal	Physical	—	100	20	Normal	—	○
TM22	SolarBeam	Grass	Special	120	100	10	Normal	—	—
TM27	Return	Normal	Physical	—	100	20	Normal	—	○
TM29	Psychic	Psychic	Special	90	100	10	Normal	—	—
TM30	Shadow Ball	Ghost	Special	80	100	15	Normal	—	—
TM31	Brick Break	Fighting	Physical	75	100	15	Normal	—	○
TM32	Double Team	Normal	Status	—	—	15	Self	—	—
TM33	Reflect	Psychic	Status	—	—	20	Your Side	—	—
TM35	Flamethrower	Fire	Special	95	100	15	Normal	—	—
TM38	Fire Blast	Fire	Special	120	85	5	Normal	—	—
TM40	Aerial Ace	Flying	Physical	60	—	20	Normal	○	○
TM42	Facade	Normal	Physical	70	100	20	Normal	—	○
TM44	Rest	Psychic	Status	—	—	10	Self	—	—
TM45	Attract	Normal	Status	—	100	15	Normal	—	—
TM48	Round	Normal	Special	60	100	15	Normal	—	—
TM49	Echoed Voice	Normal	Special	40	100	15	Normal	—	—
TM56	Fling	Dark	Physical	—	100	10	Normal	—	—
TM59	Incinerate	Fire	Special	30	100	15	Many Others	—	—
TM67	Retaliate	Normal	Physical	70	100	5	Normal	—	○
TM68	Giga Impact	Normal	Physical	150	90	5	Normal	—	○
TM70	Flash	Normal	Status	—	100	20	Normal	—	—
TM73	Thunder Wave	Electric	Status	—	100	20	Normal	—	—
TM77	Psych Up	Normal	Status	—	—	10	Normal	—	—
TM83	Work Up	Normal	Status	—	—	30	Self	—	—
TM85	Dream Eater	Psychic	Special	100	100	15	Normal	—	—
TM86	Grass Knot	Grass	Special	—	100	20	Normal	—	○
TM87	Swagger	Normal	Status	—	90	15	Normal	—	—
TM90	Substitute	Normal	Status	—	—	10	Self	—	—
TM94	Rock Smash	Fighting	Physical	40	100	15	Normal	—	○
HM02	Fly	Flying	Physical	90	95	15	Normal	○	○

MOVES TAUGHT BY PEOPLE

Name	Type	Kind	Pow.	Acc.	PP	Range	Long	DA

MOVES TAUGHT BY MOVE TUTORS FOR SHARDS

Name	Type	Kind	Pow.	Acc.	PP	Range	Long	DA
Covet	Normal	Physical	60	100	40	Normal	—	○
Signal Beam	Bug	Special	75	100	15	Normal	—	—
Last Resort	Normal	Physical	140	100	5	Normal	—	○
Magic Coat	Psychic	Status	—	—	15	Self	—	—
Hyper Voice	Normal	Special	90	100	10	Many Others	—	—
Zen Headbutt	Psychic	Physical	80	90	15	Normal	—	○
Snore	Normal	Special	40	100	15	Normal	—	—
Heal Bell	Normal	Status	—	—	5	Your Party	—	—
Roost	Flying	Status	—	—	10	Self	—	—
Heat Wave	Fire	Special	100	90	10	Many Others	—	—
Drain Punch	Fighting	Physical	75	100	10	Normal	—	○
Tailwind	Flying	Status	—	—	30	Your Side	—	—
After You	Normal	Status	—	—	15	Normal	—	—
Trick	Psychic	Status	—	100	10	Normal	—	—
Endeavor	Normal	Physical	—	100	5	Normal	—	○
Sleep Talk	Normal	Status	—	—	10	Self	—	—

Tiny Bird Pokémon
177 Natu

TYPE Psychic / Flying

ABILITIES
- Synchronize
- Early Bird

HIDDEN ABILITY
- Magic Bounce

- HEIGHT: 0'08"
- WEIGHT: 4.4 lbs.
- GENDER: ♂ / ♀

It picks food from cactus plants, deftly avoiding buds and spines. It seems to skip about to move.

STATS
- HP
- Attack
- Defense
- Sp. Atk
- Sp. Def
- Speed

EGG GROUPS
Flying

ITEMS SOMETIMES HELD
- None

Same form for ♂ / ♀

Pokémon AR Marker

EVOLUTION

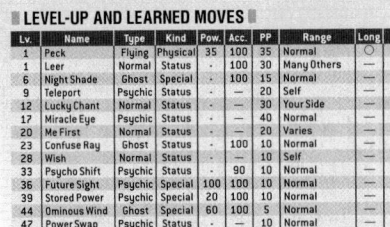

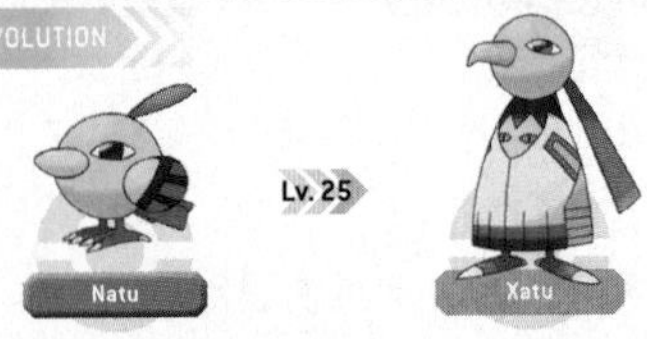

Natu — Lv. 25 → Xatu

HOW TO OBTAIN

| Pokémon Black Version 2 | Route 5 (mass outbreak) |
| Pokémon White Version 2 | Route 5 (mass outbreak) |

HOW TO OBTAIN FROM OTHER GAMES

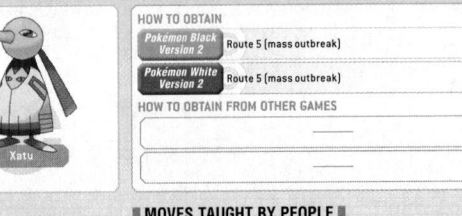

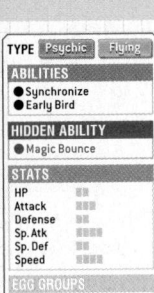

LEVEL-UP AND LEARNED MOVES

Lv.	Name	Type	Kind	Pow.	Acc.	PP	Range	Long	DA
1	Peck	Flying	Physical	35	100	35	Normal	○	—
1	Leer	Normal	Status	-	100	30	Many Others	—	—
6	Night Shade	Ghost	Special	-	100	15	Normal	—	—
9	Teleport	Psychic	Status	-	-	20	Self	—	—
12	Lucky Chant	Normal	Status	-	-	30	Your Side	—	—
17	Miracle Eye	Psychic	Status	-	-	40	Normal	—	—
20	Me First	Normal	Status	-	-	20	Varies	—	—
23	Confuse Ray	Ghost	Status	-	100	10	Normal	—	—
28	Wish	Normal	Status	-	-	10	Self	—	—
33	Psycho Shift	Psychic	Status	-	90	10	Normal	—	—
36	Future Sight	Psychic	Special	100	100	10	Normal	—	—
39	Stored Power	Psychic	Special	20	100	10	Normal	—	—
44	Ominous Wind	Ghost	Special	60	100	5	Normal	—	—
47	Power Swap	Psychic	Status	-	-	10	Normal	—	—
47	Guard Swap	Psychic	Status	-	-	10	Normal	—	—
50	Psychic	Psychic	Special	90	100	10	Normal	—	—

TM & HM MOVES

Lv.	Name	Type	Kind	Pow.	Acc.	PP	Range	Long	DA
TM03	Psyshock	Psychic	Special	80	100	10	Normal	—	—
TM04	Calm Mind	Psychic	Status	—	—	20	Self	—	—
TM06	Toxic	Poison	Status	—	90	10	Normal	—	—
TM10	Hidden Power	Normal	Special	—	100	15	Normal	—	—
TM11	Sunny Day	Fire	Status	—	—	5	Both Sides	—	—
TM16	Light Screen	Psychic	Status	—	—	30	Your Side	—	—
TM17	Protect	Normal	Status	—	—	10	Self	—	—
TM18	Rain Dance	Water	Status	—	—	5	Both Sides	—	—
TM19	Telekinesis	Psychic	Status	—	—	15	Normal	—	—
TM21	Frustration	Normal	Physical	—	100	20	Normal	—	○
TM22	SolarBeam	Grass	Special	120	100	10	Normal	—	—
TM27	Return	Normal	Physical	—	100	20	Normal	—	○
TM29	Psychic	Psychic	Special	90	100	10	Normal	—	—
TM30	Shadow Ball	Ghost	Special	80	100	15	Normal	—	—
TM32	Double Team	Normal	Status	—	—	15	Self	—	—
TM33	Reflect	Psychic	Status	—	—	20	Your Side	—	—
TM40	Aerial Ace	Flying	Physical	60	—	20	Normal	○	—
TM42	Facade	Normal	Physical	70	100	20	Normal	—	○
TM44	Rest	Psychic	Status	—	—	10	Self	—	—
TM45	Attract	Normal	Status	—	100	15	Normal	—	—
TM46	Thief	Dark	Physical	40	100	10	Normal	—	—
TM48	Round	Normal	Special	60	100	15	Normal	—	—
TM51	Ally Switch	Psychic	Status	—	—	15	Self	—	—
TM70	Flash	Normal	Status	—	100	20	Normal	—	—
TM73	Thunder Wave	Electric	Status	—	100	20	Normal	—	—
TM77	Psych Up	Normal	Status	—	—	10	Normal	—	—
TM85	Dream Eater	Psychic	Special	100	100	15	Normal	—	○
TM86	Grass Knot	Grass	Special	—	100	20	Normal	—	○
TM87	Swagger	Normal	Status	—	90	15	Normal	—	—
TM88	Pluck	Flying	Physical	60	100	20	Normal	○	○
TM89	U-turn	Bug	Physical	70	100	20	Normal	—	○
TM90	Substitute	Normal	Status	—	—	10	Self	—	—
TM92	Trick Room	Psychic	Status	—	—	5	Both Sides	—	—

MOVES TAUGHT BY PEOPLE

Name	Type	Kind	Pow.	Acc.	PP	Range	Long	DA

MOVES TAUGHT BY MOVE TUTORS FOR SHARDS

Name	Type	Kind	Pow.	Acc.	PP	Range	Long	DA
Signal Beam	Bug	Special	75	100	15	Normal	—	—
Magic Coat	Psychic	Status	—	—	15	Self	—	—
Zen Headbutt	Psychic	Physical	80	90	15	Normal	—	○
Snore	Normal	Special	40	100	15	Normal	—	—
Roost	Flying	Status	—	—	10	Self	—	—
Heat Wave	Fire	Special	100	90	10	Many Others	—	—
Giga Drain	Grass	Special	75	100	10	Normal	—	—
Pain Split	Normal	Status	—	—	20	Normal	—	—
Tailwind	Flying	Status	—	—	30	Your Side	—	—
Magic Room	Psychic	Status	—	—	10	Both Sides	—	—
Trick	Psychic	Status	—	100	10	Normal	—	—
Sleep Talk	Normal	Status	—	—	10	Self	—	—
Skill Swap	Psychic	Status	—	—	10	Normal	—	—

EGG MOVES

Name	Type	Kind	Pow.	Acc.	PP	Range	Long	DA
Haze	Ice	Status	—	—	30	Both Sides	—	—
Drill Peck	Flying	Physical	80	100	20	Normal	○	—
Quick Attack	Normal	Physical	40	100	30	Normal	—	○
Faint Attack	Dark	Physical	60	—	20	Normal	—	○
Steel Wing	Steel	Physical	70	90	25	Normal	—	○
FeatherDance	Flying	Status	—	100	15	Normal	—	—
Refresh	Normal	Status	—	—	20	Self	—	—
Zen Headbutt	Psychic	Physical	80	90	15	Normal	—	○
Sucker Punch	Dark	Physical	80	100	5	Normal	—	○
Synchronoise	Psychic	Special	70	100	15	Adjacent	—	—
Roost	Flying	Status	—	—	10	Self	—	—
Skill Swap	Psychic	Status	—	—	10	Normal	—	—

Mystic Pokémon
178 Xatu

TYPE Psychic / Flying

ABILITIES
- Synchronize
- Early Bird

HIDDEN ABILITY
- Magic Bounce

- HEIGHT: 4'11"
- WEIGHT: 33.1 lbs.
- GENDER: ♂ / ♀

This odd Pokémon can see both the past and the future. It eyes the sun's movement all day.

STATS
- HP
- Attack
- Defense
- Sp. Atk
- Sp. Def
- Speed

EGG GROUPS
Flying

ITEMS SOMETIMES HELD
- None

♂   ♀

Pokémon AR Marker

EVOLUTION

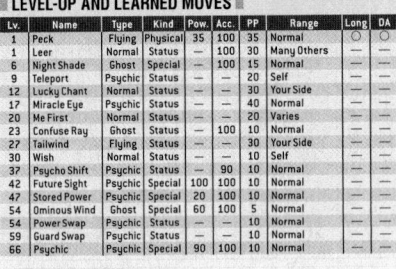

Natu — Lv. 25 → Xatu

HOW TO OBTAIN

| Pokémon Black Version 2 | Level up Natu to Lv. 25 |
| Pokémon White Version 2 | Level up Natu to Lv. 25 |

HOW TO OBTAIN FROM OTHER GAMES

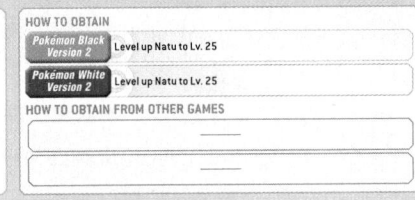

LEVEL-UP AND LEARNED MOVES

Lv.	Name	Type	Kind	Pow.	Acc.	PP	Range	Long	DA
1	Peck	Flying	Physical	35	100	35	Normal	○	—
1	Leer	Normal	Status	—	100	30	Many Others	—	—
6	Night Shade	Ghost	Special	—	100	15	Normal	—	—
9	Teleport	Psychic	Status	—	—	20	Self	—	—
12	Lucky Chant	Normal	Status	—	—	30	Your Side	—	—
17	Miracle Eye	Psychic	Status	—	—	40	Normal	—	—
20	Me First	Normal	Status	—	—	20	Varies	—	—
23	Confuse Ray	Ghost	Status	—	100	10	Normal	—	—
27	Tailwind	Flying	Status	—	—	30	Your Side	—	—
30	Wish	Normal	Status	—	—	10	Self	—	—
37	Psycho Shift	Psychic	Status	—	90	10	Normal	—	—
42	Future Sight	Psychic	Special	100	100	10	Normal	—	—
47	Stored Power	Psychic	Special	20	100	10	Normal	—	—
54	Ominous Wind	Ghost	Special	60	100	5	Normal	—	—
54	Power Swap	Psychic	Status	—	—	10	Normal	—	—
59	Guard Swap	Psychic	Status	—	—	10	Normal	—	—
66	Psychic	Psychic	Special	90	100	10	Normal	—	—

TM & HM MOVES

Lv.	Name	Type	Kind	Pow.	Acc.	PP	Range	Long	DA
TM03	Psyshock	Psychic	Special	80	100	10	Normal	—	—
TM04	Calm Mind	Psychic	Status	—	—	20	Self	—	—
TM06	Toxic	Poison	Status	—	90	10	Normal	—	—
TM10	Hidden Power	Normal	Special	—	100	15	Normal	—	—
TM11	Sunny Day	Fire	Status	—	—	5	Both Sides	—	—
TM15	Hyper Beam	Normal	Special	150	90	5	Normal	—	—
TM16	Light Screen	Psychic	Status	—	—	30	Your Side	—	—
TM17	Protect	Normal	Status	—	—	10	Self	—	—
TM18	Rain Dance	Water	Status	—	—	5	Both Sides	—	—
TM19	Telekinesis	Psychic	Status	—	—	15	Normal	—	—
TM21	Frustration	Normal	Physical	—	100	20	Normal	—	○
TM22	SolarBeam	Grass	Special	120	100	10	Normal	—	—
TM27	Return	Normal	Physical	—	100	20	Normal	—	○
TM29	Psychic	Psychic	Special	90	100	10	Normal	—	—
TM30	Shadow Ball	Ghost	Special	80	100	15	Normal	—	—
TM32	Double Team	Normal	Status	—	—	15	Self	—	—
TM33	Reflect	Psychic	Status	—	—	20	Your Side	—	—
TM40	Aerial Ace	Flying	Physical	60	—	20	Normal	○	—
TM42	Facade	Normal	Physical	70	100	20	Normal	—	○
TM44	Rest	Psychic	Status	—	—	10	Self	—	—
TM45	Attract	Normal	Status	—	100	15	Normal	—	—
TM46	Thief	Dark	Physical	40	100	10	Normal	—	—
TM48	Round	Normal	Special	60	100	15	Normal	—	—
TM51	Ally Switch	Psychic	Status	—	—	15	Self	—	—
TM68	Giga Impact	Normal	Physical	150	90	5	Normal	—	—
TM70	Flash	Normal	Status	—	100	20	Normal	—	—
TM73	Thunder Wave	Electric	Status	—	100	20	Normal	—	—
TM77	Psych Up	Normal	Status	—	—	10	Normal	—	—
TM85	Dream Eater	Psychic	Special	100	100	15	Normal	—	○
TM86	Grass Knot	Grass	Special	—	100	20	Normal	—	○
TM87	Swagger	Normal	Status	—	90	15	Normal	—	—
TM88	Pluck	Flying	Physical	60	100	20	Normal	○	○
TM89	U-turn	Bug	Physical	70	100	20	Normal	—	○
TM90	Substitute	Normal	Status	—	—	10	Self	—	—
TM92	Trick Room	Psychic	Status	—	—	5	Both Sides	—	—
HM02	Fly	Flying	Physical	90	95	15	Normal	○	—

MOVES TAUGHT BY PEOPLE

Name	Type	Kind	Pow.	Acc.	PP	Range	Long	DA

MOVES TAUGHT BY MOVE TUTORS FOR SHARDS

Name	Type	Kind	Pow.	Acc.	PP	Range	Long	DA
Signal Beam	Bug	Special	75	100	15	Normal	—	—
Magic Coat	Psychic	Status	—	—	15	Self	—	—
Zen Headbutt	Psychic	Physical	80	90	15	Normal	—	○
Foul Play	Dark	Physical	95	100	15	Normal	—	○
Snore	Normal	Special	40	100	15	Normal	—	—
Roost	Flying	Status	—	—	10	Self	—	—
Sky Attack	Flying	Physical	140	90	5	Normal	○	—
Heat Wave	Fire	Special	100	90	10	Many Others	—	—
Giga Drain	Grass	Special	75	100	10	Normal	—	—
Pain Split	Normal	Status	—	—	20	Normal	—	—
Tailwind	Flying	Status	—	—	30	Your Side	—	—
Magic Room	Psychic	Status	—	—	10	Both Sides	—	—
Trick	Psychic	Status	—	100	10	Normal	—	—
Sleep Talk	Normal	Status	—	—	10	Self	—	—
Skill Swap	Psychic	Status	—	—	10	Normal	—	—

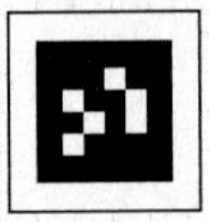

179 Mareep — Wool Pokémon

TYPE Electric

ABILITY
- Static

HIDDEN ABILITY
- Plus

- HEIGHT: 2'00"
- WEIGHT: 17.2 lbs.
- GENDER: ♂ / ♀

When cold weather increases static electricity, its wool doubles in size and the tip of its tail glows slightly.

STATS
- HP
- Attack
- Defense
- Sp. Atk
- Sp. Def
- Speed

EGG GROUPS
Monster/Field

ITEMS SOMETIMES HELD
- None

Same form for ♂ / ♀

EVOLUTION

Mareep — Lv. 15 — Flaaffy — Lv. 30 — Ampharos

HOW TO OBTAIN

Pokémon Black Version 2	Floccesy Ranch
Pokémon White Version 2	Floccesy Ranch

HOW TO OBTAIN FROM OTHER GAMES

—
—

LEVEL-UP AND LEARNED MOVES

Lv.	Name	Type	Kind	Pow.	Acc.	PP	Range	Long	DA
1	Tackle	Normal	Physical	50	100	35	Normal	—	○
1	Growl	Normal	Status	—	100	40	Many Others	—	—
4	Thunder Wave	Electric	Status	—	100	20	Normal	—	—
8	ThunderShock	Electric	Special	40	100	30	Normal	—	—
11	Cotton Spore	Grass	Status	—	100	40	Normal	—	—
15	Charge	Electric	Status	—	—	20	Self	—	—
18	Take Down	Normal	Physical	90	85	20	Normal	—	○
22	Electro Ball	Electric	Special	—	100	10	Normal	—	—
25	Confuse Ray	Ghost	Status	—	100	10	Normal	—	—
29	Power Gem	Rock	Special	70	100	20	Normal	—	—
32	Discharge	Electric	Special	80	100	15	Adjacent	—	—
36	Cotton Guard	Grass	Status	—	—	10	Self	—	—
39	Signal Beam	Bug	Special	75	100	15	Normal	—	—
43	Light Screen	Psychic	Status	—	—	30	Your Side	—	—
46	Thunder	Electric	Special	120	70	10	Normal	—	—

TM & HM MOVES

Lv.	Name	Type	Kind	Pow.	Acc.	PP	Range	Long	DA
TM06	Toxic	Poison	Status	—	90	10	Normal	—	—
TM10	Hidden Power	Normal	Special	—	100	15	Normal	—	—
TM16	Light Screen	Psychic	Status	—	—	30	Your Side	—	—
TM17	Protect	Normal	Status	—	—	10	Self	—	—
TM18	Rain Dance	Water	Status	—	—	5	Both Sides	—	—
TM20	Safeguard	Normal	Status	—	—	25	Your Side	—	—
TM21	Frustration	Normal	Physical	—	100	20	Normal	—	○
TM24	Thunderbolt	Electric	Special	95	100	15	Normal	—	—
TM25	Thunder	Electric	Special	120	70	10	Normal	—	—
TM27	Return	Normal	Physical	—	100	20	Normal	—	○
TM32	Double Team	Normal	Status	—	—	15	Self	—	—
TM42	Facade	Normal	Physical	70	100	20	Normal	—	○
TM44	Rest	Psychic	Status	—	—	10	Self	—	—
TM45	Attract	Normal	Status	—	100	15	Normal	—	—
TM48	Round	Normal	Special	60	100	15	Normal	—	—
TM49	Echoed Voice	Normal	Special	40	100	15	Normal	—	—
TM57	Charge Beam	Electric	Special	50	90	10	Normal	—	—
TM70	Flash	Normal	Status	—	100	20	Normal	—	—
TM73	Thunder Wave	Electric	Status	—	100	20	Normal	—	—
TM87	Swagger	Normal	Status	—	90	15	Normal	—	—
TM90	Substitute	Normal	Status	—	—	10	Self	—	—
TM93	Wild Charge	Electric	Physical	90	100	15	Normal	—	—

MOVES TAUGHT BY PEOPLE

Name	Type	Kind	Pow.	Acc.	PP	Range	Long	DA

MOVES TAUGHT BY MOVE TUTORS FOR SHARDS

Name	Type	Kind	Pow.	Acc.	PP	Range	Long	DA
Signal Beam	Bug	Special	75	100	15	Normal	—	—
Magnet Rise	Electric	Status	—	—	10	Self	—	—
Iron Tail	Steel	Physical	100	75	15	Normal	—	○
Snore	Normal	Special	40	100	15	Normal	—	—
Heal Bell	Normal	Status	—	—	5	Your Party	—	—
After You	Normal	Status	—	—	15	Normal	—	—
Sleep Talk	Normal	Status	—	—	10	Self	—	—

EGG MOVES

Name	Type	Kind	Pow.	Acc.	PP	Range	Long	DA
Take Down	Normal	Physical	90	85	20	Normal	—	○
Body Slam	Normal	Physical	85	100	15	Normal	—	○
Screech	Normal	Status	—	85	40	Normal	—	—
Odor Sleuth	Normal	Status	—	—	40	Normal	—	—
Charge	Electric	Status	—	—	20	Self	—	—
Flatter	Dark	Status	—	100	15	Normal	—	—
Sand-Attack	Ground	Status	—	100	15	Normal	—	—
Iron Tail	Steel	Physical	100	75	15	Normal	—	—
After You	Normal	Status	—	—	15	Normal	—	—
Agility	Psychic	Status	—	—	30	Self	—	—

Pokémon AR Marker

---

180 Flaaffy — Wool Pokémon

TYPE Electric

ABILITY
- Static

HIDDEN ABILITY
- Plus

- HEIGHT: 2'07"
- WEIGHT: 29.3 lbs.
- GENDER: ♂ / ♀

Not even downy wool will grow on its rubbery, nonconductive patches of skin that prevent electrical shock.

STATS
- HP
- Attack
- Defense
- Sp. Atk
- Sp. Def
- Speed

EGG GROUPS
Monster/Field

ITEMS SOMETIMES HELD
- None

Same form for ♂ / ♀

EVOLUTION

Mareep — Lv. 15 — Flaaffy — Lv. 30 — Ampharos

HOW TO OBTAIN

Pokémon Black Version 2	Level up Mareep to Lv. 15
Pokémon White Version 2	Level up Mareep to Lv. 15

HOW TO OBTAIN FROM OTHER GAMES

—
—

LEVEL-UP AND LEARNED MOVES

Lv.	Name	Type	Kind	Pow.	Acc.	PP	Range	Long	DA
1	Tackle	Normal	Physical	50	100	35	Normal	—	○
1	Growl	Normal	Status	—	100	40	Many Others	—	—
1	Thunder Wave	Electric	Status	—	100	20	Normal	—	—
1	ThunderShock	Electric	Special	40	100	30	Normal	—	—
4	Thunder Wave	Electric	Status	—	100	20	Normal	—	—
8	ThunderShock	Electric	Special	40	100	30	Normal	—	—
11	Cotton Spore	Grass	Status	—	100	40	Normal	—	—
16	Charge	Electric	Status	—	—	20	Self	—	—
20	Take Down	Normal	Physical	90	85	20	Normal	—	○
25	Electro Ball	Electric	Special	—	100	10	Normal	—	—
29	Confuse Ray	Ghost	Status	—	100	10	Normal	—	—
34	Power Gem	Rock	Special	70	100	20	Normal	—	—
38	Discharge	Electric	Special	80	100	15	Adjacent	—	—
43	Cotton Guard	Grass	Status	—	—	10	Self	—	—
47	Signal Beam	Bug	Special	75	100	15	Normal	—	—
52	Light Screen	Psychic	Status	—	—	30	Your Side	—	—
56	Thunder	Electric	Special	120	70	10	Normal	—	—

TM & HM MOVES

Lv.	Name	Type	Kind	Pow.	Acc.	PP	Range	Long	DA
TM06	Toxic	Poison	Status	—	90	10	Normal	—	—
TM10	Hidden Power	Normal	Special	—	100	15	Normal	—	—
TM16	Light Screen	Psychic	Status	—	—	30	Your Side	—	—
TM17	Protect	Normal	Status	—	—	10	Self	—	—
TM18	Rain Dance	Water	Status	—	—	5	Both Sides	—	—
TM20	Safeguard	Normal	Status	—	—	25	Your Side	—	—
TM21	Frustration	Normal	Physical	—	100	20	Normal	—	○
TM24	Thunderbolt	Electric	Special	95	100	15	Normal	—	—
TM25	Thunder	Electric	Special	120	70	10	Normal	—	—
TM27	Return	Normal	Physical	—	100	20	Normal	—	○
TM31	Brick Break	Fighting	Physical	75	100	15	Normal	—	○
TM32	Double Team	Normal	Status	—	—	15	Self	—	—
TM42	Facade	Normal	Physical	70	100	20	Normal	—	○
TM44	Rest	Psychic	Status	—	—	10	Self	—	—
TM45	Attract	Normal	Status	—	100	15	Normal	—	—
TM48	Round	Normal	Special	60	100	15	Normal	—	—
TM49	Echoed Voice	Normal	Special	40	100	15	Normal	—	—
TM56	Fling	Dark	Physical	—	100	10	Normal	—	○
TM57	Charge Beam	Electric	Special	50	90	10	Normal	—	—
TM70	Flash	Normal	Status	—	100	20	Normal	—	—
TM72	Volt Switch	Electric	Special	70	100	20	Normal	—	—
TM73	Thunder Wave	Electric	Status	—	100	20	Normal	—	—
TM87	Swagger	Normal	Status	—	90	15	Normal	—	—
TM90	Substitute	Normal	Status	—	—	10	Self	—	—
TM93	Wild Charge	Electric	Physical	90	100	15	Normal	—	—
TM94	Rock Smash	Fighting	Physical	40	100	15	Normal	—	○
HM04	Strength	Normal	Physical	80	100	15	Normal	—	○

MOVES TAUGHT BY PEOPLE

Name	Type	Kind	Pow.	Acc.	PP	Range	Long	DA

MOVES TAUGHT BY MOVE TUTORS FOR SHARDS

Name	Type	Kind	Pow.	Acc.	PP	Range	Long	DA
Signal Beam	Bug	Special	75	100	15	Normal	—	—
Fire Punch	Fire	Physical	75	100	15	Normal	—	○
ThunderPunch	Electric	Physical	75	100	15	Normal	—	○
Magnet Rise	Electric	Status	—	—	10	Self	—	—
Iron Tail	Steel	Physical	100	75	15	Normal	—	○
Snore	Normal	Special	40	100	15	Normal	—	—
Heal Bell	Normal	Status	—	—	5	Your Party	—	—
After You	Normal	Status	—	—	15	Normal	—	—
Sleep Talk	Normal	Status	—	—	10	Self	—	—

Pokémon AR Marker

181 Ampharos
Light Pokémon

TYPE Electric

ABILITY
● Static

HIDDEN ABILITY
● Plus

● HEIGHT: 4'07"
● WEIGHT: 135.6 lbs.
● GENDER: ♂ / ♀

The tip of its tail shines so brightly it can be used to send sea-navigation beacons to distant foreign shores.

STATS
HP	
Attack	
Defense	
Sp. Atk	
Sp. Def	
Speed	

EGG GROUPS
Monster/Field

ITEMS SOMETIMES HELD
● None

Same form for ♂ / ♀

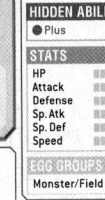

EVOLUTION

Mareep — Lv. 15 → Flaaffy — Lv. 30 → Ampharos

HOW TO OBTAIN
Pokémon Black Version 2	Level up Flaaffy to Lv. 30
Pokémon White Version 2	Level up Flaaffy to Lv. 30

HOW TO OBTAIN FROM OTHER GAMES
—

LEVEL-UP AND LEARNED MOVES
Lv.	Name	Type	Kind	Pow.	Acc.	PP	Range	Long	DA
1	Fire Punch	Fire	Physical	75	100	15	Normal	—	○
1	Tackle	Normal	Physical	50	100	35	Normal	—	—
1	Growl	Normal	Status	—	100	40	Many Others	—	—
1	Thunder Wave	Electric	Status	—	100	20	Normal	—	—
1	ThunderShock	Electric	Special	40	100	30	Normal	—	—
4	Thunder Wave	Electric	Status	—	100	20	Normal	—	—
8	ThunderShock	Electric	Special	40	100	30	Normal	—	—
11	Cotton Spore	Grass	Status	—	100	40	Many Others	—	—
15	Charge	Electric	Status	—	—	20	Self	—	—
20	Take Down	Normal	Physical	90	85	20	Normal	—	—
25	Electro Ball	Electric	Special	—	100	10	Normal	—	—
29	Confuse Ray	Ghost	Status	—	100	10	Normal	—	—
30	ThunderPunch	Electric	Physical	75	100	15	Normal	—	○
35	Power Gem	Rock	Special	70	100	20	Normal	—	—
40	Discharge	Electric	Special	80	100	15	Adjacent	—	—
46	Cotton Guard	Grass	Status	—	—	10	Self	—	—
51	Signal Beam	Bug	Special	75	100	15	Normal	—	—
57	Light Screen	Psychic	Status	—	—	30	Your Side	—	—
62	Thunder	Electric	Special	120	70	10	Normal	—	—

TM & HM MOVES
Lv.	Name	Type	Kind	Pow.	Acc.	PP	Range	Long	DA
TM06	Toxic	Poison	Status	—	90	10	Normal	—	—
TM10	Hidden Power	Normal	Special	—	100	15	Normal	—	—
TM15	Hyper Beam	Normal	Special	150	90	5	Normal	—	—
TM16	Light Screen	Psychic	Status	—	—	30	Your Side	—	—
TM17	Protect	Normal	Status	—	—	10	Self	—	—
TM18	Rain Dance	Water	Status	—	—	5	Both Sides	—	—
TM20	Safeguard	Normal	Status	—	—	25	Your Side	—	—
TM21	Frustration	Normal	Physical	—	100	20	Normal	—	○
TM24	Thunderbolt	Electric	Special	95	100	15	Normal	—	—
TM25	Thunder	Electric	Special	120	70	10	Normal	—	—
TM27	Return	Normal	Physical	—	100	20	Normal	—	○
TM31	Brick Break	Fighting	Physical	75	100	15	Normal	—	○
TM32	Double Team	Normal	Status	—	—	15	Self	—	—
TM42	Facade	Normal	Physical	70	100	20	Normal	—	○
TM44	Rest	Psychic	Status	—	—	10	Self	—	—
TM45	Attract	Normal	Status	—	100	15	Normal	—	—
TM48	Round	Normal	Special	60	100	15	Normal	—	—
TM49	Echoed Voice	Normal	Special	40	100	15	Normal	—	—
TM52	Focus Blast	Fighting	Special	120	70	5	Normal	—	—
TM56	Fling	Dark	Physical	—	100	10	Normal	—	—
TM57	Charge Beam	Electric	Special	50	90	10	Normal	—	—
TM68	Giga Impact	Normal	Physical	150	90	5	Normal	—	○
TM70	Flash	Normal	Status	—	100	20	Normal	—	—
TM72	Volt Switch	Electric	Special	70	100	20	Normal	—	—
TM73	Thunder Wave	Electric	Status	—	100	20	Normal	—	—
TM78	Bulldoze	Ground	Physical	60	100	20	Adjacent	—	—
TM87	Swagger	Normal	Status	—	90	15	Normal	—	—
TM90	Substitute	Normal	Status	—	—	10	Self	—	—
TM93	Wild Charge	Electric	Physical	90	100	15	Normal	—	○
TM94	Rock Smash	Fighting	Physical	40	100	15	Normal	—	○
HM04	Strength	Normal	Physical	80	100	15	Normal	—	○

MOVES TAUGHT BY PEOPLE
Name	Type	Kind	Pow.	Acc.	PP	Range	Long	DA

MOVES TAUGHT BY MOVE TUTORS FOR SHARDS
Name	Type	Kind	Pow.	Acc.	PP	Range	Long	DA
Signal Beam	Bug	Special	75	100	15	Normal	—	—
Fire Punch	Fire	Physical	75	100	15	Normal	—	○
ThunderPunch	Electric	Physical	75	100	15	Normal	—	○
Magnet Rise	Electric	Status	—	—	10	Self	—	—
Iron Tail	Steel	Physical	100	75	15	Normal	—	○
Snore	Normal	Special	40	100	15	Normal	—	—
Heal Bell	Normal	Status	—	—	5	Your Party	—	—
After You	Normal	Status	—	—	15	Normal	—	—
Outrage	Dragon	Physical	120	100	10	1 Random	—	○
Sleep Talk	Normal	Status	—	—	10	Self	—	—

Pokémon AR Marker

---

182 Bellossom
Flower Pokémon

TYPE Grass

ABILITY
● Chlorophyll

HIDDEN ABILITY
● Healer

● HEIGHT: 1'04"
● WEIGHT: 12.8 lbs.
● GENDER: ♂ / ♀

When the heavy rainfall season ends, it is drawn out by warm sunlight to dance in the open.

STATS
HP	
Attack	
Defense	
Sp. Atk	
Sp. Def	
Speed	

EGG GROUPS
Grass

ITEMS SOMETIMES HELD
● None

Same form for ♂ / ♀

EVOLUTION
Oddish → p. 35 — Lv. 21 → Gloom → p. 35

Use Leaf Stone → Vileplume → p. 36

Use Sun Stone → Bellossom

HOW TO OBTAIN
Pokémon Black Version 2	Use Sun Stone on a Gloom you obtain via Link Trade or Poké Transfer
Pokémon White Version 2	Use Sun Stone on a Gloom you obtain via Link Trade or Poké Transfer

HOW TO OBTAIN FROM OTHER GAMES
—

LEVEL-UP AND LEARNED MOVES
Lv.	Name	Type	Kind	Pow.	Acc.	PP	Range	Long	DA
1	Leaf Blade	Grass	Physical	90	100	15	Normal	—	○
1	Mega Drain	Grass	Special	40	100	15	Normal	—	—
1	Sweet Scent	Normal	Status	—	100	20	Many Others	—	—
1	Stun Spore	Grass	Status	—	75	30	Normal	—	—
1	Sunny Day	Fire	Status	—	—	5	Both Sides	—	—
23	Magical Leaf	Grass	Special	60	—	20	Normal	—	—
53	Leaf Storm	Grass	Special	140	90	5	Normal	—	—

TM & HM MOVES
Lv.	Name	Type	Kind	Pow.	Acc.	PP	Range	Long	DA
TM06	Toxic	Poison	Status	—	90	10	Normal	—	—
TM09	Venoshock	Poison	Special	65	100	10	Normal	—	—
TM10	Hidden Power	Normal	Special	—	100	15	Normal	—	—
TM11	Sunny Day	Fire	Status	—	—	5	Both Sides	—	—
TM15	Hyper Beam	Normal	Special	150	90	5	Normal	—	—
TM17	Protect	Normal	Status	—	—	10	Self	—	—
TM20	Safeguard	Normal	Status	—	—	25	Your Side	—	—
TM21	Frustration	Normal	Physical	—	100	20	Normal	—	○
TM22	SolarBeam	Grass	Special	120	100	10	Normal	—	—
TM27	Return	Normal	Physical	—	100	20	Normal	—	○
TM32	Double Team	Normal	Status	—	—	15	Self	—	—
TM36	Sludge Bomb	Poison	Special	90	100	10	Normal	—	—
TM42	Facade	Normal	Physical	70	100	20	Normal	—	○
TM44	Rest	Psychic	Status	—	—	10	Self	—	—
TM45	Attract	Normal	Status	—	100	15	Normal	—	—
TM48	Round	Normal	Special	60	100	15	Normal	—	—
TM53	Energy Ball	Grass	Special	80	100	10	Normal	—	—
TM56	Fling	Dark	Physical	—	100	10	Normal	—	—
TM68	Giga Impact	Normal	Physical	150	90	5	Normal	—	○
TM70	Flash	Normal	Status	—	100	20	Normal	—	—
TM75	Swords Dance	Normal	Status	—	—	30	Self	—	—
TM86	Grass Knot	Grass	Special	—	100	20	Normal	—	—
TM87	Swagger	Normal	Status	—	90	15	Normal	—	—
TM90	Substitute	Normal	Status	—	—	10	Self	—	—
HM01	Cut	Normal	Physical	50	95	30	Normal	—	—

MOVES TAUGHT BY PEOPLE
Name	Type	Kind	Pow.	Acc.	PP	Range	Long	DA

MOVES TAUGHT BY MOVE TUTORS FOR SHARDS
Name	Type	Kind	Pow.	Acc.	PP	Range	Long	DA
Uproar	Normal	Special	90	100	10	1 Random	—	—
Seed Bomb	Grass	Physical	80	100	15	Normal	—	—
Snore	Normal	Special	40	100	15	Normal	—	—
Synthesis	Grass	Status	—	—	5	Self	—	—
Giga Drain	Grass	Special	75	100	10	Normal	—	—
Drain Punch	Fighting	Physical	75	100	10	Normal	—	○
Worry Seed	Grass	Status	—	100	10	Normal	—	—
Gastro Acid	Poison	Status	—	100	10	Normal	—	—
After You	Normal	Status	—	—	15	Normal	—	—
Sleep Talk	Normal	Status	—	—	10	Self	—	—

Pokémon AR Marker

183 Marill

Aqua Mouse Pokémon

- HEIGHT: 1'04"
- WEIGHT: 18.7 lbs.
- GENDER: ♂ / ♀

The oil-filled tail functions as a buoy, so it's fine even in rivers with strong currents.

Same form for ♂ / ♀

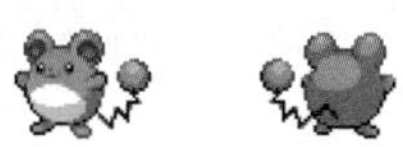

TYPE Water

ABILITIES
- Thick Fat
- Huge Power

HIDDEN ABILITY
- Sap Sipper

STATS
HP
Attack
Defense
Sp. Atk
Sp. Def
Speed

EGG GROUPS
Water ❶ / Fairy

ITEMS SOMETIMES HELD
- None

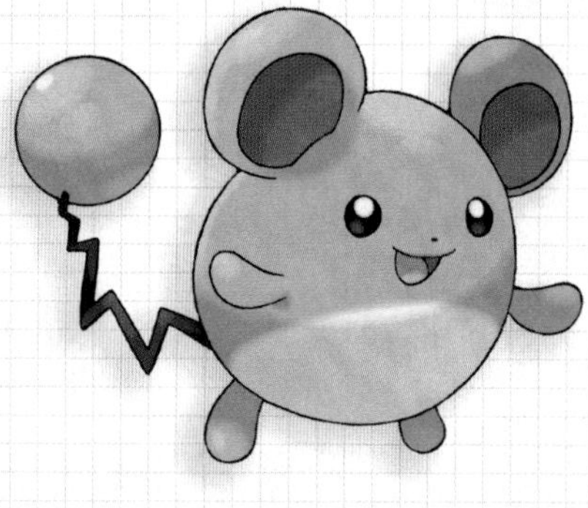

Pokémon AR Marker

EVOLUTION

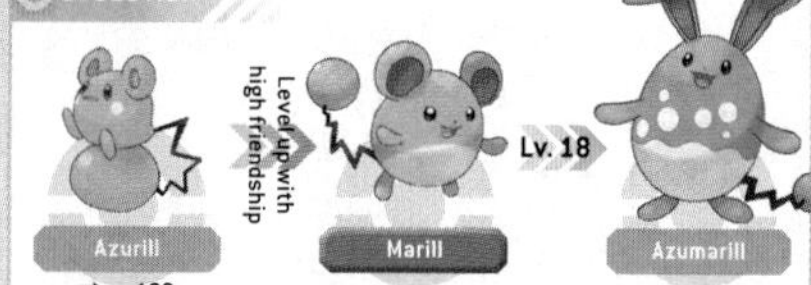

Level up with high friendship
Lv. 18
Azurill
Marill
Azumarill

➡ p. 162

HOW TO OBTAIN

Pokémon Black Version 2	❶ Route 6 ❷ Village Bridge
Pokémon White Version 2	❶ Route 6 ❷ Village Bridge

HOW TO OBTAIN FROM OTHER GAMES

—

—

LEVEL-UP AND LEARNED MOVES

Lv.	Name	Type	Kind	Pow.	Acc.	PP	Range	Long	DA
1	Tackle	Normal	Physical	50	100	35	Normal	—	○
1	Bubble	Water	Special	20	100	30	Many Others	—	—
2	Tail Whip	Normal	Status	—	100	30	Many Others	—	—
5	Water Sport	Water	Status	—	—	15	Both Sides	—	—
7	Water Gun	Water	Special	40	100	25	Normal	—	—
10	Defense Curl	Normal	Status	—	—	40	Self	—	—
10	Rollout	Rock	Physical	30	90	20	Normal	—	○
13	BubbleBeam	Water	Special	65	100	20	Normal	—	—
16	Helping Hand	Normal	Status	—	—	20	1 Ally	—	—
20	Aqua Tail	Water	Physical	90	90	10	Normal	—	○
23	Double-Edge	Normal	Physical	120	100	15	Normal	—	○
28	Aqua Ring	Water	Status	—	—	20	Self	—	—
31	Rain Dance	Water	Status	—	—	5	Both Sides	—	—
37	Superpower	Fighting	Physical	120	100	5	Normal	—	○
40	Hydro Pump	Water	Special	120	80	5	Normal	—	—

TM & HM MOVES

Lv.	Name	Type	Kind	Pow.	Acc.	PP	Range	Long	DA
TM06	Toxic	Poison	Status	—	90	10	Normal	—	—
TM07	Hail	Ice	Status	—	—	10	Both Sides	—	—
TM10	Hidden Power	Normal	Special	—	100	15	Normal	—	—
TM13	Ice Beam	Ice	Special	95	100	10	Normal	—	—
TM14	Blizzard	Ice	Special	120	70	5	Many Others	—	—
TM16	Light Screen	Psychic	Status	—	—	30	Your Side	—	—
TM17	Protect	Normal	Status	—	—	10	Self	—	—
TM18	Rain Dance	Water	Status	—	—	5	Both Sides	—	—
TM21	Frustration	Normal	Physical	—	100	20	Normal	—	○
TM27	Return	Normal	Physical	—	100	20	Normal	—	○
TM28	Dig	Ground	Physical	80	100	10	Normal	—	○
TM31	Brick Break	Fighting	Physical	75	100	15	Normal	—	○
TM32	Double Team	Normal	Status	—	—	15	Self	—	—
TM42	Facade	Normal	Physical	70	100	20	Normal	—	○
TM44	Rest	Psychic	Status	—	—	10	Self	—	—
TM45	Attract	Normal	Status	—	100	15	Normal	—	—
TM48	Round	Normal	Special	60	100	15	Normal	—	—
TM55	Scald	Water	Special	80	100	15	Normal	—	—
TM56	Fling	Dark	Physical	—	100	10	Normal	—	—
TM83	Work Up	Normal	Status	—	—	30	Self	—	—
TM86	Grass Knot	Grass	Special	—	100	20	Normal	—	○
TM87	Swagger	Normal	Status	—	90	15	Normal	—	—
TM90	Substitute	Normal	Status	—	—	10	Self	—	—
TM94	Rock Smash	Fighting	Physical	40	100	15	Normal	—	○
HM03	Surf	Water	Special	95	100	15	Adjacent	—	—
HM04	Strength	Normal	Physical	80	100	15	Normal	—	○
HM05	Waterfall	Water	Physical	80	100	15	Normal	—	○
HM06	Dive	Water	Physical	80	100	10	Normal	—	○

MOVES TAUGHT BY PEOPLE

Name	Type	Kind	Pow.	Acc.	PP	Range	Long	DA

MOVES TAUGHT BY MOVE TUTORS FOR SHARDS

Name	Type	Kind	Pow.	Acc.	PP	Range	Long	DA
Covet	Normal	Physical	60	100	40	Normal	—	○
Bounce	Flying	Physical	85	85	5	Normal	○	○
Ice Punch	Ice	Physical	75	100	15	Normal	—	○
Hyper Voice	Normal	Special	90	100	10	Many Others	—	—
Icy Wind	Ice	Special	55	95	15	Many Others	—	—
Iron Tail	Steel	Physical	100	75	15	Normal	—	○
Aqua Tail	Water	Physical	90	90	10	Normal	—	○
Superpower	Fighting	Physical	120	100	5	Normal	—	○
Snore	Normal	Special	40	100	15	Normal	—	—
Knock Off	Dark	Physical	20	100	20	Normal	—	○
Helping Hand	Normal	Status	—	—	20	1 Ally	—	—
Sleep Talk	Normal	Status	—	—	10	Self	—	—

EGG MOVES

Name	Type	Kind	Pow.	Acc.	PP	Range	Long	DA
Present	Normal	Physical	—	90	15	Normal	—	—
Amnesia	Psychic	Status	—	—	20	Self	—	—
Future Sight	Psychic	Special	100	100	10	Normal	—	—
Belly Drum	Normal	Status	—	—	10	Self	—	—
Perish Song	Normal	Status	—	—	5	Adjacent	○	—
Supersonic	Normal	Status	—	55	20	Normal	—	—
Aqua Jet	Water	Physical	40	100	20	Normal	—	○
Superpower	Fighting	Physical	120	100	5	Normal	—	○
Refresh	Normal	Status	—	—	20	Self	—	—
Body Slam	Normal	Physical	85	100	15	Normal	—	○
Water Sport	Water	Status	—	—	15	Both Sides	—	—
Muddy Water	Water	Special	95	85	10	Many Others	—	—

184 Azumarill

Aqua Rabbit Pokémon

- HEIGHT: 2'07"
- WEIGHT: 62.8 lbs.
- GENDER: ♂ / ♀

Its long ears are superb sensors. It can distinguish the movements of things in water and tell what they are.

Same form for ♂ / ♀

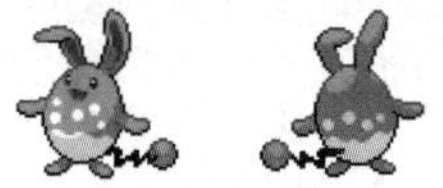

TYPE Water

ABILITIES
- Thick Fat
- Huge Power

HIDDEN ABILITY
- Sap Sipper

STATS
HP
Attack
Defense
Sp. Atk
Sp. Def
Speed

EGG GROUPS
Water ❶ / Fairy

ITEMS SOMETIMES HELD
- None

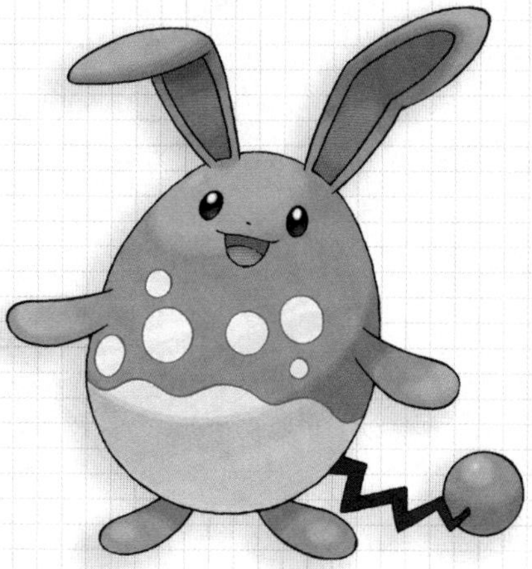

Pokémon AR Marker

EVOLUTION

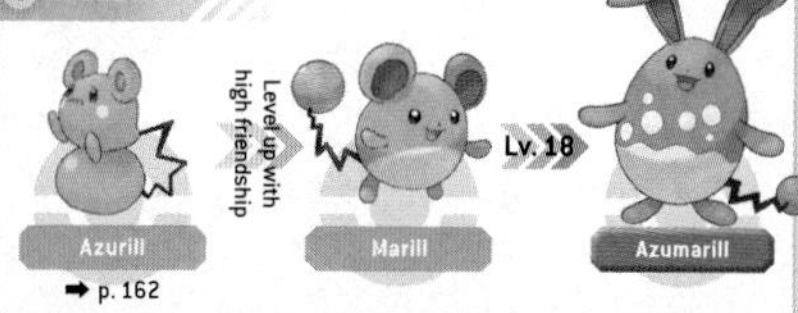

Level up with high friendship
Lv. 18
Azurill
Marill
Azumarill

➡ p. 162

HOW TO OBTAIN

Pokémon Black Version 2	❶ Route 6 (rustling grass) ❷ Village Bridge (rustling grass)
Pokémon White Version 2	Route 6 (rustling grass) Village Bridge (rustling grass)

HOW TO OBTAIN FROM OTHER GAMES

—

—

LEVEL-UP AND LEARNED MOVES

Lv.	Name	Type	Kind	Pow.	Acc.	PP	Range	Long	DA
1	Tackle	Normal	Physical	50	100	35	Normal	—	○
1	Bubble	Water	Special	20	100	30	Many Others	—	—
1	Tail Whip	Normal	Status	—	100	30	Many Others	—	—
1	Water Sport	Water	Status	—	—	15	Both Sides	—	—
2	Tail Whip	Normal	Status	—	100	30	Many Others	—	—
5	Water Sport	Water	Status	—	—	15	Both Sides	—	—
7	Water Gun	Water	Special	40	100	25	Normal	—	—
10	Defense Curl	Normal	Status	—	—	40	Self	—	—
10	Rollout	Rock	Physical	30	90	20	Normal	—	○
13	BubbleBeam	Water	Special	65	100	20	Normal	—	—
16	Helping Hand	Normal	Status	—	—	20	1 Ally	—	—
21	Aqua Tail	Water	Physical	90	90	10	Normal	—	○
25	Double-Edge	Normal	Physical	120	100	15	Normal	—	○
31	Aqua Ring	Water	Status	—	—	20	Self	—	—
35	Rain Dance	Water	Status	—	—	5	Both Sides	—	—
42	Superpower	Fighting	Physical	120	100	5	Normal	—	○
46	Hydro Pump	Water	Special	120	80	5	Normal	—	—

TM & HM MOVES

Lv.	Name	Type	Kind	Pow.	Acc.	PP	Range	Long	DA
TM06	Toxic	Poison	Status	—	90	10	Normal	—	—
TM07	Hail	Ice	Status	—	—	10	Both Sides	—	—
TM10	Hidden Power	Normal	Special	—	100	15	Normal	—	—
TM13	Ice Beam	Ice	Special	95	100	10	Normal	—	—
TM14	Blizzard	Ice	Special	120	70	5	Many Others	—	—
TM15	Hyper Beam	Normal	Special	150	90	5	Normal	—	—
TM16	Light Screen	Psychic	Status	—	—	30	Your Side	—	—
TM17	Protect	Normal	Status	—	—	10	Self	—	—
TM18	Rain Dance	Water	Status	—	—	5	Both Sides	—	—
TM21	Frustration	Normal	Physical	—	100	20	Normal	—	○
TM27	Return	Normal	Physical	—	100	20	Normal	—	○
TM28	Dig	Ground	Physical	80	100	10	Normal	—	○
TM31	Brick Break	Fighting	Physical	75	100	15	Normal	—	○
TM32	Double Team	Normal	Status	—	—	15	Self	—	—
TM42	Facade	Normal	Physical	70	100	20	Normal	—	○
TM44	Rest	Psychic	Status	—	—	10	Self	—	—
TM45	Attract	Normal	Status	—	100	15	Normal	—	—
TM48	Round	Normal	Special	60	100	15	Normal	—	—
TM52	Focus Blast	Fighting	Special	120	70	5	Normal	—	—
TM55	Scald	Water	Special	80	100	15	Normal	—	—
TM56	Fling	Dark	Physical	—	100	10	Normal	—	—
TM68	Giga Impact	Normal	Physical	150	90	5	Normal	—	○
TM78	Bulldoze	Ground	Physical	60	100	20	Adjacent	—	—
TM83	Work Up	Normal	Status	—	—	30	Self	—	—
TM86	Grass Knot	Grass	Special	—	100	20	Normal	—	○
TM87	Swagger	Normal	Status	—	90	15	Normal	—	—
TM90	Substitute	Normal	Status	—	—	10	Self	—	—
TM94	Rock Smash	Fighting	Physical	40	100	15	Normal	—	○
HM03	Surf	Water	Special	95	100	15	Adjacent	—	—
HM04	Strength	Normal	Physical	80	100	15	Normal	—	○
HM05	Waterfall	Water	Physical	80	100	15	Normal	—	○
HM06	Dive	Water	Physical	80	100	10	Normal	—	○

MOVES TAUGHT BY PEOPLE

Name	Type	Kind	Pow.	Acc.	PP	Range	Long	DA

MOVES TAUGHT BY MOVE TUTORS FOR SHARDS

Name	Type	Kind	Pow.	Acc.	PP	Range	Long	DA
Covet	Normal	Physical	60	100	40	Normal	—	○
Bounce	Flying	Physical	85	85	5	Normal	○	○
Ice Punch	Ice	Physical	75	100	15	Normal	—	○
Hyper Voice	Normal	Special	90	100	10	Many Others	—	—
Icy Wind	Ice	Special	55	95	15	Many Others	—	—
Iron Tail	Steel	Physical	100	75	15	Normal	—	○
Aqua Tail	Water	Physical	90	90	10	Normal	—	○
Superpower	Fighting	Physical	120	100	5	Normal	—	○
Snore	Normal	Special	40	100	15	Normal	—	—
Knock Off	Dark	Physical	20	100	20	Normal	—	○
Helping Hand	Normal	Status	—	—	20	1 Ally	—	—
Sleep Talk	Normal	Status	—	—	10	Self	—	—

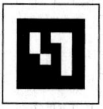

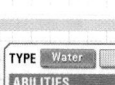

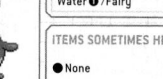

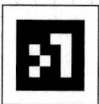

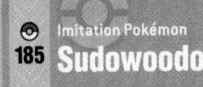

Imitation Pokémon
185 Sudowoodo

- HEIGHT: 3'11"
- WEIGHT: 83.8 lbs.
- GENDER: ♂ / ♀

To avoid being attacked, it does nothing but mimic a tree. It hates water and flees from rain.

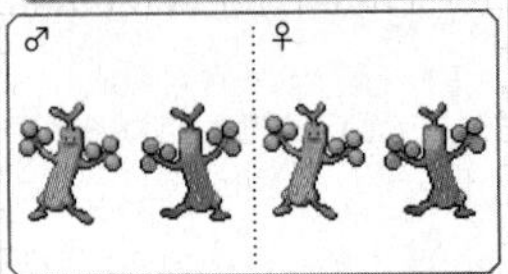

TYPE Rock

ABILITIES
- Sturdy
- Rock Head

HIDDEN ABILITY
- Rattled

STATS
HP
Attack
Defense
Sp. Atk
Sp. Def
Speed

EGG GROUPS
Mineral

ITEMS SOMETIMES HELD
- None

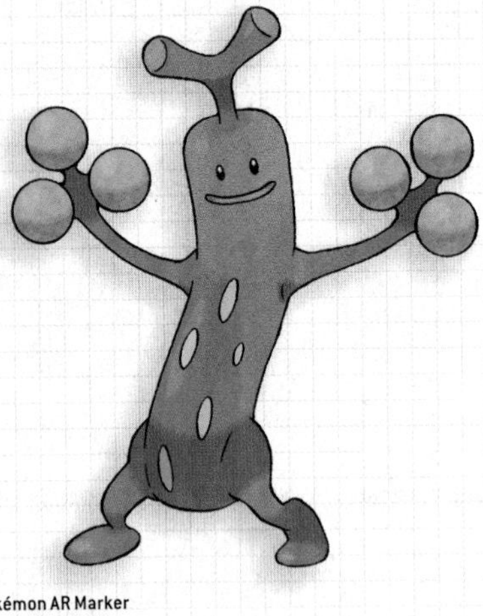

Pokémon AR Marker

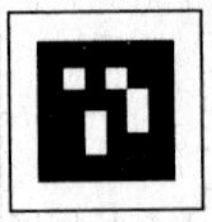

EVOLUTION

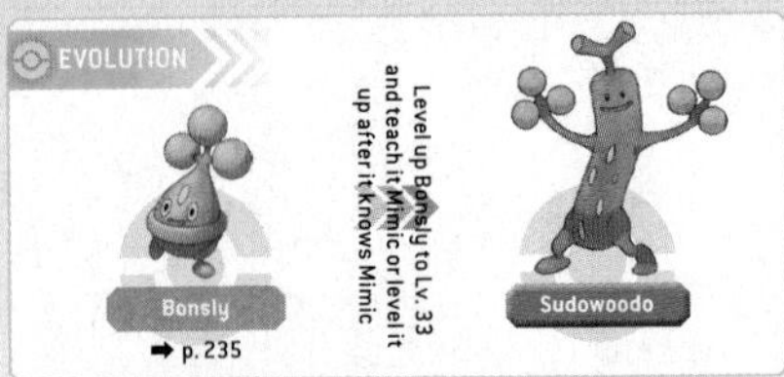
Bonsly
Level up Bonsly to Lv. 33 and teach it Mimic or level it up after it knows Mimic
Sudowoodo

➡ p. 235

HOW TO OBTAIN

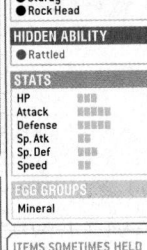

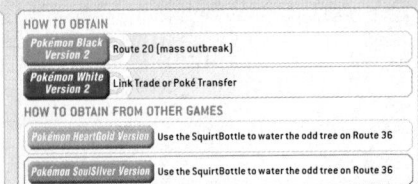

Pokémon Black Version 2	Route 20 (mass outbreak)
Pokémon White Version 2	Link Trade or Poké Transfer

HOW TO OBTAIN FROM OTHER GAMES

Pokémon HeartGold Version	Use the SquirtBottle to water the odd tree on Route 36
Pokémon SoulSilver Version	Use the SquirtBottle to water the odd tree on Route 36

LEVEL-UP AND LEARNED MOVES

Lv.	Name	Type	Kind	Pow.	Acc.	PP	Range	Long	DA
1	Wood Hammer	Grass	Physical	120	100	15	Normal	—	○
1	Copycat	Normal	Status	—	—	20	Self	—	—
1	Flail	Normal	Physical	—	100	15	Normal	—	○
1	Low Kick	Fighting	Physical	—	100	20	Normal	—	○
1	Rock Throw	Rock	Physical	50	90	15	Normal	—	—
5	Flail	Normal	Physical	—	100	15	Normal	—	○
8	Low Kick	Fighting	Physical	—	100	20	Normal	—	○
12	Rock Throw	Rock	Physical	50	90	15	Normal	—	—
15	Mimic	Normal	Status	—	—	10	Normal	—	—
15	Slam	Normal	Physical	80	75	20	Normal	—	○
19	Faint Attack	Dark	Physical	60	—	20	Normal	—	○
22	Rock Tomb	Rock	Physical	50	80	10	Normal	—	—
26	Block	Normal	Status	—	—	5	Normal	—	—
29	Rock Slide	Rock	Physical	75	90	10	Many Others	—	—
33	Counter	Fighting	Physical	—	100	20	Varies	—	○
36	Sucker Punch	Dark	Physical	80	100	5	Normal	—	○
40	Double-Edge	Normal	Physical	120	100	15	Normal	—	○
43	Stone Edge	Rock	Physical	100	80	5	Normal	—	—
47	Hammer Arm	Fighting	Physical	100	90	10	Normal	—	○

TM & HM MOVES

Lv.	Name	Type	Kind	Pow.	Acc.	PP	Range	Long	DA
TM04	Calm Mind	Psychic	Status	—	—	20	Self	—	—
TM06	Toxic	Poison	Status	—	90	10	Normal	—	—
TM10	Hidden Power	Normal	Special	—	100	15	Normal	—	—
TM11	Sunny Day	Fire	Status	—	—	5	Both Sides	—	—
TM12	Taunt	Dark	Status	—	100	20	Normal	—	—
TM17	Protect	Normal	Status	—	—	10	Self	—	—
TM21	Frustration	Normal	Physical	—	100	20	Normal	—	○
TM23	Smack Down	Rock	Physical	50	100	15	Normal	—	—
TM26	Earthquake	Ground	Physical	100	100	10	Adjacent	—	—
TM27	Return	Normal	Physical	—	100	20	Normal	—	○
TM28	Dig	Ground	Physical	80	100	10	Normal	—	○
TM31	Brick Break	Fighting	Physical	75	100	15	Normal	—	○
TM32	Double Team	Normal	Status	—	—	15	Self	—	—
TM37	Sandstorm	Rock	Status	—	—	10	Both Sides	—	—
TM39	Rock Tomb	Rock	Physical	50	80	10	Normal	—	—
TM41	Torment	Dark	Status	—	100	15	Normal	—	—
TM42	Facade	Normal	Physical	70	100	20	Normal	—	○
TM44	Rest	Psychic	Status	—	—	10	Self	—	—
TM45	Attract	Normal	Status	—	100	15	Normal	—	—
TM46	Thief	Dark	Physical	40	100	10	Normal	—	○
TM48	Round	Normal	Special	60	100	15	Normal	—	—
TM56	Fling	Dark	Physical	—	100	10	Normal	—	—
TM64	Explosion	Normal	Physical	250	100	5	Adjacent	—	—
TM69	Rock Polish	Rock	Status	—	—	20	Self	—	—
TM71	Stone Edge	Rock	Physical	100	80	5	Normal	—	—
TM77	Psych Up	Normal	Status	—	—	10	Normal	—	—
TM78	Bulldoze	Ground	Physical	60	100	20	Adjacent	—	—
TM80	Rock Slide	Rock	Physical	75	90	10	Many Others	—	—
TM87	Swagger	Normal	Status	—	90	15	Normal	—	—
TM90	Substitute	Normal	Status	—	—	10	Self	—	—
TM94	Rock Smash	Fighting	Physical	40	100	15	Normal	—	○
HM04	Strength	Normal	Physical	80	100	15	Normal	—	○

MOVES TAUGHT BY PEOPLE

Name	Type	Kind	Pow.	Acc.	PP	Range	Long	DA

MOVES TAUGHT BY MOVE TUTORS FOR SHARDS

Name	Type	Kind	Pow.	Acc.	PP	Range	Long	DA
Covet	Normal	Physical	60	100	40	Normal	—	○
Low Kick	Fighting	Physical	—	100	20	Normal	—	○
Fire Punch	Fire	Physical	75	100	15	Normal	—	○
ThunderPunch	Electric	Physical	75	100	15	Normal	—	○
Ice Punch	Ice	Physical	75	100	15	Normal	—	○
Block	Normal	Status	—	—	5	Normal	—	—
Earth Power	Ground	Special	90	100	10	Normal	—	—
Foul Play	Dark	Physical	95	100	15	Normal	—	○
Snore	Normal	Special	40	100	15	Normal	—	—
Role Play	Psychic	Status	—	—	10	Normal	—	—
Helping Hand	Normal	Status	—	—	20	1 Ally	—	—
After You	Normal	Status	—	—	15	Normal	—	—
Stealth Rock	Rock	Status	—	—	20	Other Side	—	—
Sleep Talk	Normal	Status	—	—	10	Self	—	—

EGG MOVES

Name	Type	Kind	Pow.	Acc.	PP	Range	Long	DA
Selfdestruct	Normal	Physical	200	100	5	Adjacent	—	—
Headbutt	Normal	Physical	70	100	15	Normal	—	○
Harden	Normal	Status	—	—	30	Self	—	—
Defense Curl	Normal	Status	—	—	40	Self	—	—
Rollout	Rock	Physical	30	90	20	Normal	—	○
Sand Tomb	Ground	Physical	35	85	15	Normal	—	—
Stealth Rock	Rock	Status	—	—	20	Other Side	—	—
Curse	Ghost	Status	—	—	10	Varies	—	—
Endure	Normal	Status	—	—	10	Self	—	—

Frog Pokémon
186 Politoed

- HEIGHT: 3'07"
- WEIGHT: 74.7 lbs.
- GENDER: ♂ / ♀

It gathers groups of others as their leader. Its cries make Poliwag obey.

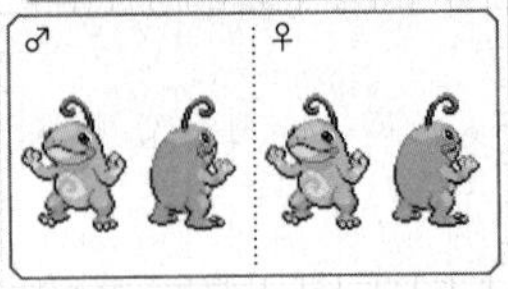

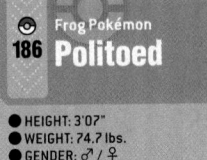

TYPE Water

ABILITIES
- Water Absorb
- Damp

HIDDEN ABILITY
- Drizzle

STATS
HP
Attack
Defense
Sp. Atk
Sp. Def
Speed

EGG GROUPS
Water ❶

ITEMS SOMETIMES HELD
- King's Rock

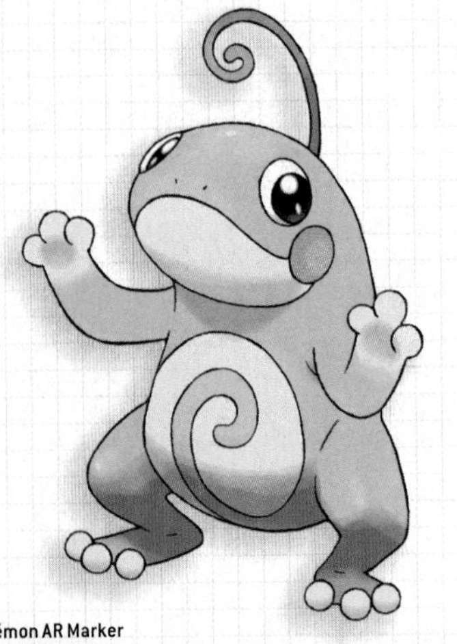

Pokémon AR Marker

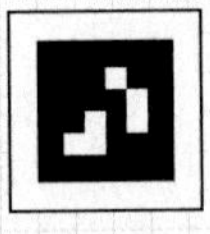

EVOLUTION

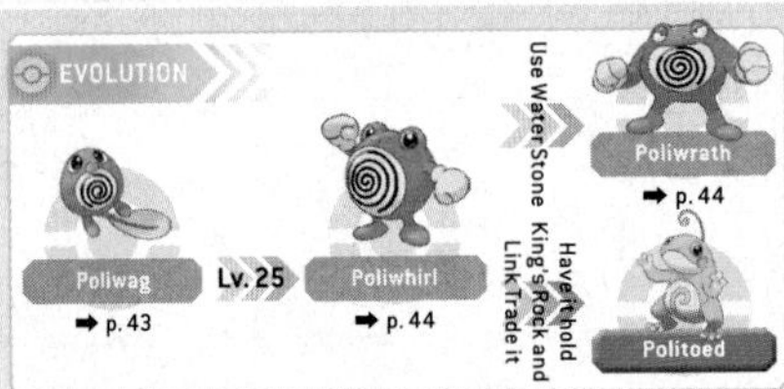
Poliwag
Lv. 25
Poliwhirl
Use Water Stone
Poliwrath
Have it hold King's Rock and Link Trade it
Politoed

➡ p. 43
➡ p. 44
➡ p. 44

HOW TO OBTAIN

Pokémon Black Version 2	❶ Route 19 (Super Rod/ripples in water) ❷ Route 20 (Super Rod/ripples in water)
Pokémon White Version 2	❶ Route 19 (Super Rod/ripples in water) ❷ Route 20 (Super Rod/ripples in water)

HOW TO OBTAIN FROM OTHER GAMES

——
——

LEVEL-UP AND LEARNED MOVES

Lv.	Name	Type	Kind	Pow.	Acc.	PP	Range	Long	DA
1	BubbleBeam	Water	Special	65	100	20	Normal	—	—
1	Hypnosis	Psychic	Status	—	60	20	Normal	—	—
1	DoubleSlap	Normal	Physical	15	85	10	Normal	—	○
1	Perish Song	Normal	Status	—	—	5	Adjacent	○	—
27	Swagger	Normal	Status	—	90	15	Normal	—	—
37	Bounce	Flying	Physical	85	85	5	Normal	○	○
48	Hyper Voice	Normal	Special	90	100	10	Many Others	—	—

TM & HM MOVES

Lv.	Name	Type	Kind	Pow.	Acc.	PP	Range	Long	DA
TM06	Toxic	Poison	Status	—	90	10	Normal	—	—
TM07	Hail	Ice	Status	—	—	10	Both Sides	—	—
TM10	Hidden Power	Normal	Special	—	100	15	Normal	—	—
TM13	Ice Beam	Ice	Special	95	100	10	Normal	—	—
TM14	Blizzard	Ice	Special	120	70	5	Many Others	—	—
TM15	Hyper Beam	Normal	Special	150	90	5	Normal	—	—
TM17	Protect	Normal	Status	—	—	10	Self	—	—
TM18	Rain Dance	Water	Status	—	—	5	Both Sides	—	—
TM21	Frustration	Normal	Physical	—	100	20	Normal	—	○
TM26	Earthquake	Ground	Physical	100	100	10	Adjacent	—	—
TM27	Return	Normal	Physical	—	100	20	Normal	—	○
TM28	Dig	Ground	Physical	80	100	10	Normal	—	○
TM29	Psychic	Psychic	Special	90	100	10	Normal	—	—
TM31	Brick Break	Fighting	Physical	75	100	15	Normal	—	○
TM32	Double Team	Normal	Status	—	—	15	Self	—	—
TM42	Facade	Normal	Physical	70	100	20	Normal	—	○
TM44	Rest	Psychic	Status	—	—	10	Self	—	—
TM45	Attract	Normal	Status	—	100	15	Normal	—	—
TM46	Thief	Dark	Physical	40	100	10	Normal	—	○
TM48	Round	Normal	Special	60	100	15	Normal	—	—
TM49	Echoed Voice	Normal	Special	40	100	15	Normal	—	—
TM52	Focus Blast	Fighting	Special	120	70	5	Normal	—	—
TM55	Scald	Water	Special	80	100	15	Normal	—	—
TM56	Fling	Dark	Physical	—	100	10	Normal	—	—
TM66	Payback	Dark	Physical	50	100	10	Normal	—	○
TM68	Giga Impact	Normal	Physical	150	90	5	Normal	—	○
TM78	Bulldoze	Ground	Physical	60	100	20	Adjacent	—	—
TM87	Swagger	Normal	Status	—	90	15	Normal	—	—
TM90	Substitute	Normal	Status	—	—	10	Self	—	—
TM94	Rock Smash	Fighting	Physical	40	100	15	Normal	—	○
HM03	Surf	Water	Special	95	100	15	Adjacent	—	—
HM04	Strength	Normal	Physical	80	100	15	Normal	—	○
HM05	Waterfall	Water	Physical	80	100	15	Normal	—	○
HM06	Dive	Water	Physical	80	100	10	Normal	—	○

MOVES TAUGHT BY PEOPLE

Name	Type	Kind	Pow.	Acc.	PP	Range	Long	DA

MOVES TAUGHT BY MOVE TUTORS FOR SHARDS

Name	Type	Kind	Pow.	Acc.	PP	Range	Long	DA
Bounce	Flying	Physical	85	85	5	Normal	○	○
Ice Punch	Ice	Physical	75	100	15	Normal	—	○
Hyper Voice	Normal	Special	90	100	10	Many Others	—	—
Icy Wind	Ice	Special	55	95	15	Many Others	—	—
Snore	Normal	Special	40	100	15	Normal	—	—
Helping Hand	Normal	Status	—	—	20	1 Ally	—	—
Endeavor	Normal	Physical	—	100	5	Normal	—	○
Sleep Talk	Normal	Status	—	—	10	Self	—	—

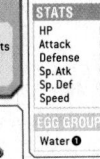

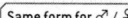

Cottonweed Pokémon

187 Hoppip

- HEIGHT: 1'04"
- WEIGHT: 1.1 lbs.
- GENDER: ♂ / ♀

It drifts on winds. It is said that when Hoppip gather in fields and mountains, spring is on the way.

Same form for ♂ / ♀

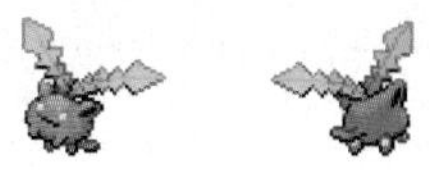

TYPE Grass Flying

ABILITIES
- Chlorophyll
- Leaf Guard

HIDDEN ABILITY
- Infiltrator

STATS
HP
Attack
Defense
Sp. Atk
Sp. Def
Speed

EGG GROUPS
Fairy/Grass

ITEMS SOMETIMES HELD
- None

Pokémon AR Marker

EVOLUTION

Hoppip
Lv. 18
Skiploom
Lv. 27
Jumpluff

HOW TO OBTAIN

Pokémon Black Version 2	Route 18 (mass outbreak)
Pokémon White Version 2	Route 18 (mass outbreak)

HOW TO OBTAIN FROM OTHER GAMES

	—
	—

LEVEL-UP AND LEARNED MOVES

Lv.	Name	Type	Kind	Pow.	Acc.	PP	Range	Long	DA
1	Splash	Normal	Status	—	—	40	Self	—	—
4	Synthesis	Grass	Status	—	—	5	Self	—	—
7	Tail Whip	Normal	Status	—	100	30	Many Others	—	—
10	Tackle	Normal	Physical	50	100	35	Normal	—	○
12	PoisonPowder	Poison	Status	—	75	35	Normal	—	—
14	Stun Spore	Grass	Status	—	75	30	Normal	—	—
16	Sleep Powder	Grass	Status	—	75	15	Normal	—	—
19	Bullet Seed	Grass	Physical	25	100	30	Normal	—	—
22	Leech Seed	Grass	Status	—	90	10	Normal	—	—
25	Mega Drain	Grass	Special	40	100	15	Normal	—	—
28	Acrobatics	Flying	Physical	55	100	15	Normal	○	○
31	Rage Powder	Bug	Status	—	—	20	Self	—	—
34	Cotton Spore	Grass	Status	—	100	40	Normal	—	—
37	U-turn	Bug	Physical	70	100	20	Normal	—	○
40	Worry Seed	Grass	Status	—	100	10	Normal	—	—
43	Giga Drain	Grass	Special	75	100	10	Normal	—	—
46	Bounce	Flying	Physical	85	85	5	Normal	○	○
49	Memento	Dark	Status	—	100	10	Normal	—	—

TM & HM MOVES

Lv.	Name	Type	Kind	Pow.	Acc.	PP	Range	Long	DA
TM06	Toxic	Poison	Status	—	90	10	Normal	—	—
TM10	Hidden Power	Normal	Special	—	100	15	Normal	—	—
TM11	Sunny Day	Fire	Status	—	—	5	Both Sides	—	—
TM17	Protect	Normal	Status	—	—	10	Self	—	—
TM21	Frustration	Normal	Physical	—	100	20	Normal	—	○
TM22	SolarBeam	Grass	Special	120	100	10	Normal	—	—
TM27	Return	Normal	Physical	—	100	20	Normal	—	○
TM32	Double Team	Normal	Status	—	—	15	Self	—	—
TM33	Reflect	Psychic	Status	—	—	20	Your Side	—	—
TM40	Aerial Ace	Flying	Physical	60	—	20	Normal	○	○
TM42	Facade	Normal	Physical	70	100	20	Normal	—	○
TM44	Rest	Psychic	Status	—	—	10	Self	—	—
TM45	Attract	Normal	Status	—	100	15	Normal	—	—
TM48	Round	Normal	Special	60	100	15	Normal	—	—
TM53	Energy Ball	Grass	Special	80	100	10	Normal	—	—
TM62	Acrobatics	Flying	Physical	55	100	15	Normal	○	○
TM70	Flash	Normal	Status	—	100	20	Normal	—	—
TM75	Swords Dance	Normal	Status	—	—	30	Self	—	—
TM77	Psych Up	Normal	Status	—	—	10	Normal	—	—
TM86	Grass Knot	Grass	Special	—	100	20	Normal	—	○
TM87	Swagger	Normal	Status	—	90	15	Normal	—	—
TM89	U-turn	Bug	Physical	70	100	20	Normal	—	○
TM90	Substitute	Normal	Status	—	—	10	Self	—	—

MOVES TAUGHT BY PEOPLE

Name	Type	Kind	Pow.	Acc.	PP	Range	Long	DA

MOVES TAUGHT BY MOVE TUTORS FOR SHARDS

Name	Type	Kind	Pow.	Acc.	PP	Range	Long	DA
Bounce	Flying	Physical	85	85	5	Normal	○	○
Seed Bomb	Grass	Physical	80	100	15	Normal	—	—
Snore	Normal	Special	40	100	15	Normal	—	—
Synthesis	Grass	Status	—	—	5	Self	—	—
Giga Drain	Grass	Special	75	100	10	Normal	—	—
Worry Seed	Grass	Status	—	100	10	Normal	—	—
Helping Hand	Normal	Status	—	—	20	1 Ally	—	—
Sleep Talk	Normal	Status	—	—	10	Self	—	—

EGG MOVES

Name	Type	Kind	Pow.	Acc.	PP	Range	Long	DA
Confusion	Psychic	Special	50	100	25	Normal	—	—
Encore	Normal	Status	—	100	5	Normal	—	—
Double-Edge	Normal	Physical	120	100	15	Normal	—	○
Amnesia	Psychic	Status	—	—	20	Self	—	—
Helping Hand	Normal	Status	—	—	20	1 Ally	—	—
Aromatherapy	Grass	Status	—	—	5	Your Party	—	—
Worry Seed	Grass	Status	—	100	10	Normal	—	—
Cotton Guard	Grass	Status	—	—	10	Self	—	—
Seed Bomb	Grass	Physical	80	100	15	Normal	—	—
Endure	Normal	Status	—	—	10	Self	—	—

Cottonweed Pokémon

188 Skiploom

- HEIGHT: 2'00"
- WEIGHT: 2.2 lbs.
- GENDER: ♂ / ♀

It blooms when the weather warms. It floats in the sky to soak up as much sunlight as possible.

Same form for ♂ / ♀

TYPE Grass Flying

ABILITIES
- Chlorophyll
- Leaf Guard

HIDDEN ABILITY
- Infiltrator

STATS
HP
Attack
Defense
Sp. Atk
Sp. Def
Speed

EGG GROUPS
Fairy/Grass

ITEMS SOMETIMES HELD
- None

Pokémon AR Marker

EVOLUTION

Hoppip
Lv. 18
Skiploom
Lv. 27
Jumpluff

HOW TO OBTAIN

Pokémon Black Version 2	Level up Hoppip to Lv. 18
Pokémon White Version 2	Level up Hoppip to Lv. 18

HOW TO OBTAIN FROM OTHER GAMES

Pokémon HeartGold Version	Route 14 (morning and afternoon only)
Pokémon SoulSilver Version	Route 14 (morning and afternoon only)

LEVEL-UP AND LEARNED MOVES

Lv.	Name	Type	Kind	Pow.	Acc.	PP	Range	Long	DA
1	Splash	Normal	Status	—	—	40	Self	—	—
1	Synthesis	Grass	Status	—	—	5	Self	—	—
1	Tail Whip	Normal	Status	—	100	30	Many Others	—	—
1	Tackle	Normal	Physical	50	100	35	Normal	—	○
4	Synthesis	Grass	Status	—	—	5	Self	—	—
7	Tail Whip	Normal	Status	—	100	30	Many Others	—	—
10	Tackle	Normal	Physical	50	100	35	Normal	—	○
12	PoisonPowder	Poison	Status	—	75	35	Normal	—	—
14	Stun Spore	Grass	Status	—	75	30	Normal	—	—
16	Sleep Powder	Grass	Status	—	75	15	Normal	—	—
20	Bullet Seed	Grass	Physical	25	100	30	Normal	—	—
24	Leech Seed	Grass	Status	—	90	10	Normal	—	—
28	Mega Drain	Grass	Special	40	100	15	Normal	—	—
32	Acrobatics	Flying	Physical	55	100	15	Normal	○	○
36	Rage Powder	Bug	Status	—	—	20	Self	—	—
40	Cotton Spore	Grass	Status	—	100	40	Normal	—	—
44	U-turn	Bug	Physical	70	100	20	Normal	—	○
48	Worry Seed	Grass	Status	—	100	10	Normal	—	—
52	Giga Drain	Grass	Special	75	100	10	Normal	—	—
56	Bounce	Flying	Physical	85	85	5	Normal	○	○
60	Memento	Dark	Status	—	100	10	Normal	—	—

TM & HM MOVES

Lv.	Name	Type	Kind	Pow.	Acc.	PP	Range	Long	DA
TM06	Toxic	Poison	Status	—	90	10	Normal	—	—
TM10	Hidden Power	Normal	Special	—	100	15	Normal	—	—
TM11	Sunny Day	Fire	Status	—	—	5	Both Sides	—	—
TM17	Protect	Normal	Status	—	—	10	Self	—	—
TM21	Frustration	Normal	Physical	—	100	20	Normal	—	○
TM22	SolarBeam	Grass	Special	120	100	10	Normal	—	—
TM27	Return	Normal	Physical	—	100	20	Normal	—	○
TM32	Double Team	Normal	Status	—	—	15	Self	—	—
TM33	Reflect	Psychic	Status	—	—	20	Your Side	—	—
TM40	Aerial Ace	Flying	Physical	60	—	20	Normal	○	○
TM42	Facade	Normal	Physical	70	100	20	Normal	—	○
TM44	Rest	Psychic	Status	—	—	10	Self	—	—
TM45	Attract	Normal	Status	—	100	15	Normal	—	—
TM48	Round	Normal	Special	60	100	15	Normal	—	—
TM53	Energy Ball	Grass	Special	80	100	10	Normal	—	—
TM62	Acrobatics	Flying	Physical	55	100	15	Normal	○	○
TM70	Flash	Normal	Status	—	100	20	Normal	—	—
TM75	Swords Dance	Normal	Status	—	—	30	Self	—	—
TM77	Psych Up	Normal	Status	—	—	10	Normal	—	—
TM86	Grass Knot	Grass	Special	—	100	20	Normal	—	○
TM87	Swagger	Normal	Status	—	90	15	Normal	—	—
TM89	U-turn	Bug	Physical	70	100	20	Normal	—	○
TM90	Substitute	Normal	Status	—	—	10	Self	—	—

MOVES TAUGHT BY PEOPLE

Name	Type	Kind	Pow.	Acc.	PP	Range	Long	DA

MOVES TAUGHT BY MOVE TUTORS FOR SHARDS

Name	Type	Kind	Pow.	Acc.	PP	Range	Long	DA
Bounce	Flying	Physical	85	85	5	Normal	○	○
Seed Bomb	Grass	Physical	80	100	15	Normal	—	—
Snore	Normal	Special	40	100	15	Normal	—	—
Synthesis	Grass	Status	—	—	5	Self	—	—
Giga Drain	Grass	Special	75	100	10	Normal	—	—
Worry Seed	Grass	Status	—	100	10	Normal	—	—
Helping Hand	Normal	Status	—	—	20	1 Ally	—	—
Sleep Talk	Normal	Status	—	—	10	Self	—	—

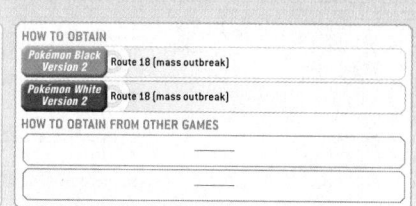

Cottonweed Pokémon

189 Jumpluff

- HEIGHT: 2'07"
- WEIGHT: 6.6 lbs.
- GENDER: ♂ / ♀

Blown by seasonal winds, it circles the globe, scattering cotton spores as it goes.

Same form for ♂ / ♀

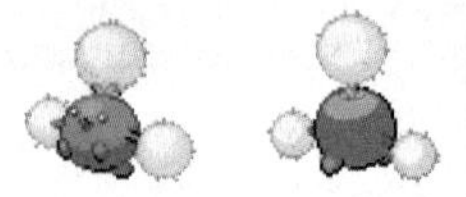

TYPE Grass Flying

ABILITIES
- Chlorophyll
- Leaf Guard

HIDDEN ABILITY
- Infiltrator

STATS
HP
Attack
Defense
Sp. Atk
Sp. Def
Speed

EGG GROUPS
Fairy/Grass

ITEMS SOMETIMES HELD
- None

EVOLUTION

Hoppip
Lv. 18
Skiploom
Lv. 27
Jumpluff

HOW TO OBTAIN

Pokémon Black Version 2	Level up Skiploom to Lv. 27
Pokémon White Version 2	Level up Skiploom to Lv. 27

HOW TO OBTAIN FROM OTHER GAMES

—

—

Pokémon AR Marker

LEVEL-UP AND LEARNED MOVES

Lv.	Name	Type	Kind	Pow.	Acc.	PP	Range	Long	DA
1	Splash	Normal	Status	—	—	40	Self	—	—
1	Synthesis	Grass	Status	—	—	5	Self	—	—
1	Tail Whip	Normal	Status	—	100	30	Many Others	—	—
1	Tackle	Normal	Physical	50	100	35	Normal	—	○
4	Synthesis	Grass	Status	—	—	5	Self	—	—
7	Tail Whip	Normal	Status	—	100	30	Many Others	—	—
10	Tackle	Normal	Physical	50	100	35	Normal	—	○
12	PoisonPowder	Poison	Status	—	75	35	Normal	—	—
14	Stun Spore	Grass	Status	—	75	30	Normal	—	—
16	Sleep Powder	Grass	Status	—	75	15	Normal	—	—
20	Bullet Seed	Grass	Physical	25	100	30	Normal	—	—
24	Leech Seed	Grass	Status	—	90	10	Normal	—	—
29	Mega Drain	Grass	Special	40	100	15	Normal	—	—
34	Acrobatics	Flying	Physical	55	100	15	Normal	○	○
39	Rage Powder	Bug	Status	—	—	20	Self	—	—
44	Cotton Spore	Grass	Status	—	100	40	Normal	—	—
49	U-turn	Bug	Physical	70	100	20	Normal	—	○
54	Worry Seed	Grass	Status	—	100	10	Normal	—	—
59	Giga Drain	Grass	Special	75	100	10	Normal	—	—
64	Bounce	Flying	Physical	85	85	5	Normal	○	○
69	Memento	Dark	Status	—	100	10	Normal	—	—

TM & HM MOVES

Lv.	Name	Type	Kind	Pow.	Acc.	PP	Range	Long	DA
TM06	Toxic	Poison	Status	—	90	10	Normal	—	—
TM10	Hidden Power	Normal	Special	—	100	15	Normal	—	—
TM11	Sunny Day	Fire	Status	—	—	5	Both Sides	—	—
TM15	Hyper Beam	Normal	Special	150	90	5	Normal	—	—
TM17	Protect	Normal	Status	—	—	10	Self	—	—
TM21	Frustration	Normal	Physical	—	100	20	Normal	—	○
TM22	SolarBeam	Grass	Special	120	100	10	Normal	—	—
TM27	Return	Normal	Physical	—	100	20	Normal	—	○
TM32	Double Team	Normal	Status	—	—	15	Self	—	—
TM33	Reflect	Psychic	Status	—	—	20	Your Side	—	—
TM40	Aerial Ace	Flying	Physical	60	—	20	Normal	○	○
TM42	Facade	Normal	Physical	70	100	20	Normal	—	○
TM44	Rest	Psychic	Status	—	—	10	Self	—	—
TM45	Attract	Normal	Status	—	100	15	Normal	—	—
TM48	Round	Normal	Special	60	100	15	Normal	—	—
TM53	Energy Ball	Grass	Special	80	100	10	Normal	—	—
TM62	Acrobatics	Flying	Physical	55	100	15	Normal	○	○
TM68	Giga Impact	Normal	Physical	150	90	5	Normal	—	○
TM70	Flash	Normal	Status	—	100	20	Normal	—	—
TM75	Swords Dance	Normal	Status	—	—	30	Self	—	—
TM77	Psych Up	Normal	Status	—	—	10	Normal	—	—
TM86	Grass Knot	Grass	Special	—	100	20	Normal	—	○
TM87	Swagger	Normal	Status	—	90	15	Normal	—	—
TM89	U-turn	Bug	Physical	70	100	20	Normal	—	○
TM90	Substitute	Normal	Status	—	—	10	Self	—	—

MOVES TAUGHT BY PEOPLE

Name	Type	Kind	Pow.	Acc.	PP	Range	Long	DA

MOVES TAUGHT BY MOVE TUTORS FOR SHARDS

Name	Type	Kind	Pow.	Acc.	PP	Range	Long	DA
Bounce	Flying	Physical	85	85	5	Normal	○	○
Seed Bomb	Grass	Physical	80	100	15	Normal	—	—
Snore	Normal	Special	40	100	15	Normal	—	—
Synthesis	Grass	Status	—	—	5	Self	—	—
Giga Drain	Grass	Special	75	100	10	Normal	—	—
Worry Seed	Grass	Status	—	100	10	Normal	—	—
Helping Hand	Normal	Status	—	—	20	1 Ally	—	—
Sleep Talk	Normal	Status	—	—	10	Self	—	—

Long Tail Pokémon

190 Aipom

- HEIGHT: 2'07"
- WEIGHT: 25.4 lbs.
- GENDER: ♂ / ♀

It lives high among the treetops. It can use its tail as freely and cleverly as its hands.

♂ ♀

TYPE Normal

ABILITIES
- Run Away
- Pickup

HIDDEN ABILITY
—

STATS
HP
Attack
Defense
Sp. Atk
Sp. Def
Speed

EGG GROUPS
Field

ITEMS SOMETIMES HELD
- None

EVOLUTION

Aipom
Level up Aipom to Lv. 32 and teach it Double Hit or level it up after it knows Double Hit
Ambipom

➡ p. 228

HOW TO OBTAIN

Pokémon Black Version 2	Catch an Ambipom, leave it at the Pokémon Day Care, and hatch the Egg that is found
Pokémon White Version 2	Catch an Ambipom, leave it at the Pokémon Day Care, and hatch the Egg that is found

HOW TO OBTAIN FROM OTHER GAMES

Pokémon HeartGold Version	Azalea Town (use Headbutt on tree)
Pokémon SoulSilver Version	Azalea Town (use Headbutt on tree)

Pokémon AR Marker

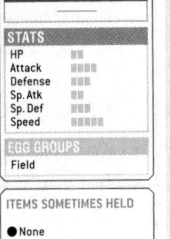

LEVEL-UP AND LEARNED MOVES

Lv.	Name	Type	Kind	Pow.	Acc.	PP	Range	Long	DA
1	Scratch	Normal	Physical	40	100	35	Normal	—	○
1	Tail Whip	Normal	Status	—	100	30	Many Others	—	—
4	Sand-Attack	Ground	Status	—	100	15	Normal	—	—
8	Astonish	Ghost	Physical	30	100	15	Normal	—	○
11	Baton Pass	Normal	Status	—	—	40	Self	—	—
15	Tickle	Normal	Status	—	100	20	Normal	—	—
18	Fury Swipes	Normal	Physical	18	80	15	Normal	—	○
22	Swift	Normal	Special	60	—	20	Many Others	—	—
25	Screech	Normal	Status	—	85	40	Normal	—	—
29	Agility	Psychic	Status	—	—	30	Self	—	—
32	Double Hit	Normal	Physical	35	90	10	Normal	—	○
36	Fling	Dark	Physical	—	100	10	Normal	—	—
39	Nasty Plot	Dark	Status	—	—	20	Self	—	—
43	Last Resort	Normal	Physical	140	100	5	Normal	—	○

TM & HM MOVES

Lv.	Name	Type	Kind	Pow.	Acc.	PP	Range	Long	DA
TM01	Hone Claws	Dark	Status	—	—	15	Self	—	—
TM06	Toxic	Poison	Status	—	90	10	Normal	—	—
TM10	Hidden Power	Normal	Special	—	100	15	Normal	—	—
TM11	Sunny Day	Fire	Status	—	—	5	Both Sides	—	—
TM12	Taunt	Dark	Status	—	100	20	Normal	—	—
TM17	Protect	Normal	Status	—	—	10	Self	—	—
TM18	Rain Dance	Water	Status	—	—	5	Both Sides	—	—
TM21	Frustration	Normal	Physical	—	100	20	Normal	—	○
TM22	SolarBeam	Grass	Special	120	100	10	Normal	—	—
TM24	Thunderbolt	Electric	Special	95	100	15	Normal	—	—
TM25	Thunder	Electric	Special	120	70	10	Normal	—	—
TM27	Return	Normal	Physical	—	100	20	Normal	—	○
TM28	Dig	Ground	Physical	80	100	10	Normal	—	○
TM30	Shadow Ball	Ghost	Special	80	100	15	Normal	—	—
TM31	Brick Break	Fighting	Physical	75	100	15	Normal	—	○
TM32	Double Team	Normal	Status	—	—	15	Self	—	—
TM40	Aerial Ace	Flying	Physical	60	—	20	Normal	○	○
TM42	Facade	Normal	Physical	70	100	20	Normal	—	○
TM44	Rest	Psychic	Status	—	—	10	Self	—	—
TM45	Attract	Normal	Status	—	100	15	Normal	—	—
TM46	Thief	Dark	Physical	40	100	10	Normal	—	○
TM47	Low Sweep	Fighting	Physical	60	100	20	Normal	—	○
TM48	Round	Normal	Special	60	100	15	Normal	—	—
TM56	Fling	Dark	Physical	—	100	10	Normal	—	—
TM62	Acrobatics	Flying	Physical	55	100	15	Normal	○	○
TM65	Shadow Claw	Ghost	Physical	70	100	15	Normal	—	○
TM66	Payback	Dark	Physical	50	100	10	Normal	—	○
TM67	Retaliate	Normal	Physical	70	100	5	Normal	—	○
TM73	Thunder Wave	Electric	Status	—	100	20	Normal	—	—
TM83	Work Up	Normal	Status	—	—	30	Self	—	—
TM85	Dream Eater	Psychic	Special	100	100	15	Normal	—	—
TM86	Grass Knot	Grass	Special	—	100	20	Normal	—	○
TM87	Swagger	Normal	Status	—	90	15	Normal	—	—
TM89	U-turn	Bug	Physical	70	100	20	Normal	—	○
TM90	Substitute	Normal	Status	—	—	10	Self	—	—
TM94	Rock Smash	Fighting	Physical	40	100	15	Normal	—	○
HM01	Cut	Normal	Physical	50	95	30	Normal	—	○
HM04	Strength	Normal	Physical	80	100	15	Normal	—	○

MOVES TAUGHT BY PEOPLE

Name	Type	Kind	Pow.	Acc.	PP	Range	Long	DA

MOVES TAUGHT BY MOVE TUTORS FOR SHARDS

Name	Type	Kind	Pow.	Acc.	PP	Range	Long	DA
Covet	Normal	Physical	60	100	40	Normal	—	○
Bounce	Flying	Physical	85	85	5	Normal	○	○
Uproar	Normal	Special	90	100	10	1 Random	—	—
Seed Bomb	Grass	Physical	80	100	15	Normal	—	—
Low Kick	Fighting	Physical	—	100	20	Normal	—	○
Gunk Shot	Poison	Physical	120	70	5	Normal	—	—
Fire Punch	Fire	Physical	75	100	15	Normal	—	○
ThunderPunch	Electric	Physical	75	100	15	Normal	—	○
Ice Punch	Ice	Physical	75	100	15	Normal	—	○
Last Resort	Normal	Physical	140	100	5	Normal	—	○
Iron Tail	Steel	Physical	100	75	15	Normal	—	○
Foul Play	Dark	Physical	95	100	15	Normal	—	○
Snore	Normal	Special	40	100	15	Normal	—	—
Knock Off	Dark	Physical	20	100	20	Normal	—	○
Role Play	Psychic	Status	—	—	10	Normal	—	—
Spite	Ghost	Status	—	100	10	Normal	—	—
Sleep Talk	Normal	Status	—	—	10	Self	—	—
Snatch	Dark	Status	—	—	10	Self	—	—

EGG MOVES

Name	Type	Kind	Pow.	Acc.	PP	Range	Long	DA
Counter	Fighting	Physical	—	100	20	Varies	—	○
Screech	Normal	Status	—	85	40	Normal	—	—
Pursuit	Dark	Physical	40	100	20	Normal	—	○
Agility	Psychic	Status	—	—	30	Self	—	—
Spite	Ghost	Status	—	100	10	Normal	—	—
Slam	Normal	Physical	80	75	20	Normal	—	○
DoubleSlap	Normal	Physical	15	85	10	Normal	—	○
Beat Up	Dark	Physical	—	100	10	Normal	—	—
Fake Out	Normal	Physical	40	100	10	Normal	—	○
Covet	Normal	Physical	60	100	40	Normal	—	○
Bounce	Flying	Physical	85	85	5	Normal	○	○
Revenge	Fighting	Physical	60	100	10	Normal	—	○
Switcheroo	Dark	Status	—	100	10	Normal	—	—

191 Sunkern

 Seed Pokémon

- HEIGHT: 1'00"
- WEIGHT: 4.0 lbs.
- GENDER: ♂ / ♀

It suddenly falls out of the sky in the morning. Knowing it's weak, it simply feeds until it evolves.

Same form for ♂ / ♀

Pokémon AR Marker

TYPE Grass

ABILITIES
- Chlorophyll
- Solar Power

HIDDEN ABILITY
- Early Bird

STATS
- HP
- Attack
- Defense
- Sp. Atk
- Sp. Def
- Speed

EGG GROUPS
Grass

ITEMS SOMETIMES HELD
- None

EVOLUTION

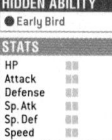

Sunkern — Use Sun Stone → Sunflora

LEVEL-UP AND LEARNED MOVES

Lv.	Name	Type	Kind	Pow.	Acc.	PP	Range	Long	DA
1	Absorb	Grass	Special	20	100	25	Normal	—	—
1	Growth	Normal	Status	—	—	40	Self	—	—
4	Ingrain	Grass	Status	—	—	20	Self	—	—
7	GrassWhistle	Grass	Status	—	55	15	Normal	—	—
10	Mega Drain	Grass	Special	40	100	15	Normal	—	—
13	Leech Seed	Grass	Status	—	90	10	Normal	—	—
16	Razor Leaf	Grass	Physical	55	95	25	Many Others	—	—
19	Worry Seed	Grass	Status	—	100	10	Normal	—	—
22	Giga Drain	Grass	Special	75	100	10	Normal	—	—
25	Endeavor	Normal	Physical	—	100	5	Normal	—	○
28	Synthesis	Grass	Status	—	—	5	Self	—	—
31	Natural Gift	Normal	Physical	—	100	15	Normal	—	—
34	SolarBeam	Grass	Special	120	100	10	Normal	—	—
37	Double-Edge	Normal	Physical	120	100	15	Normal	—	○
40	Sunny Day	Fire	Status	—	—	5	Both Sides	—	—
43	Seed Bomb	Grass	Physical	80	100	15	Normal	—	—

TM & HM MOVES

Lv.	Name	Type	Kind	Pow.	Acc.	PP	Range	Long	DA
TM06	Toxic	Poison	Status	—	90	10	Normal	—	—
TM10	Hidden Power	Normal	Special	—	100	15	Normal	—	—
TM11	Sunny Day	Fire	Status	—	—	5	Both Sides	—	—
TM16	Light Screen	Psychic	Status	—	—	30	Your Side	—	—
TM17	Protect	Normal	Status	—	—	10	Self	—	—
TM20	Safeguard	Normal	Status	—	—	25	Your Side	—	—
TM21	Frustration	Normal	Physical	—	100	20	Normal	—	○
TM22	SolarBeam	Grass	Special	120	100	10	Normal	—	—
TM27	Return	Normal	Physical	—	100	20	Normal	—	○
TM32	Double Team	Normal	Status	—	—	15	Self	—	—
TM36	Sludge Bomb	Poison	Special	90	100	10	Normal	—	—
TM42	Facade	Normal	Physical	70	100	20	Normal	—	—
TM44	Rest	Psychic	Status	—	—	10	Self	—	—
TM45	Attract	Normal	Status	—	100	15	Normal	—	—
TM48	Round	Normal	Special	60	100	15	Normal	—	—
TM53	Energy Ball	Grass	Special	80	100	10	Normal	—	—
TM70	Flash	Normal	Status	—	100	20	Normal	—	—
TM75	Swords Dance	Normal	Status	—	—	30	Self	—	—
TM86	Grass Knot	Grass	Special	—	100	20	Normal	—	○
TM87	Swagger	Normal	Status	—	90	15	Normal	—	—
TM90	Substitute	Normal	Status	—	—	10	Self	—	—
HM01	Cut	Normal	Physical	50	95	30	Normal	—	—

MOVES TAUGHT BY PEOPLE

Name	Type	Kind	Pow.	Acc.	PP	Range	Long	DA

MOVES TAUGHT BY MOVE TUTORS FOR SHARDS

Name	Type	Kind	Pow.	Acc.	PP	Range	Long	DA
Uproar	Normal	Special	90	100	10	1 Random	—	—
Seed Bomb	Grass	Physical	80	100	15	Normal	—	—
Earth Power	Ground	Special	90	100	10	Normal	—	—
Snore	Normal	Special	40	100	15	Normal	—	—
Synthesis	Grass	Status	—	—	5	Self	—	—
Giga Drain	Grass	Special	75	100	10	Normal	—	—
Worry Seed	Grass	Status	—	100	10	Normal	—	—
Helping Hand	Normal	Status	—	—	20	1 Ally	—	—
After You	Normal	Status	—	—	15	Normal	—	—
Endeavor	Normal	Physical	—	100	5	Normal	—	○
Sleep Talk	Normal	Status	—	—	10	Self	—	—

EGG MOVES

Name	Type	Kind	Pow.	Acc.	PP	Range	Long	DA
GrassWhistle	Grass	Status	—	55	15	Normal	—	—
Encore	Normal	Status	—	100	5	Normal	—	—
Leech Seed	Grass	Status	—	90	10	Normal	—	—
Nature Power	Normal	Status	—	—	20	Varies	—	—
Curse	Ghost	Status	—	—	10	Varies	—	—
Helping Hand	Normal	Status	—	—	20	1 Ally	—	—
Ingrain	Grass	Status	—	—	20	Self	—	—
Sweet Scent	Normal	Status	—	100	20	Many Others	—	—
Endure	Normal	Status	—	—	10	Self	—	—
Bide	Normal	Physical	—	—	10	Self	—	○
Natural Gift	Normal	Physical	—	100	15	Normal	—	—
Morning Sun	Normal	Status	—	—	5	Self	—	—

---

192 Sunflora

 Sun Pokémon

- HEIGHT: 2'07"
- WEIGHT: 18.7 lbs.
- GENDER: ♂ / ♀

Since it converts sunlight into energy, it is always looking in the direction of the sun.

Same form for ♂ / ♀

Pokémon AR Marker

TYPE Grass

ABILITIES
- Chlorophyll
- Solar Power

HIDDEN ABILITY
- Early Bird

STATS
- HP
- Attack
- Defense
- Sp. Atk
- Sp. Def
- Speed

EGG GROUPS
Grass

ITEMS SOMETIMES HELD
- None

EVOLUTION

Sunkern — Use Sun Stone → Sunflora

LEVEL-UP AND LEARNED MOVES

Lv.	Name	Type	Kind	Pow.	Acc.	PP	Range	Long	DA
1	Absorb	Grass	Special	20	100	25	Normal	—	—
1	Pound	Normal	Physical	40	100	35	Normal	—	○
1	Growth	Normal	Status	—	—	40	Self	—	—
4	Ingrain	Grass	Status	—	—	20	Self	—	—
7	GrassWhistle	Grass	Status	—	55	15	Normal	—	—
10	Mega Drain	Grass	Special	40	100	15	Normal	—	—
13	Leech Seed	Grass	Status	—	90	10	Normal	—	—
16	Razor Leaf	Grass	Physical	55	95	25	Many Others	—	—
19	Worry Seed	Grass	Status	—	100	10	Normal	—	—
22	Giga Drain	Grass	Special	75	100	10	Normal	—	—
25	Bullet Seed	Grass	Physical	25	100	30	Normal	—	—
28	Petal Dance	Grass	Special	120	100	10	1 Random	—	○
31	Natural Gift	Normal	Physical	—	100	15	Normal	—	—
34	SolarBeam	Grass	Special	120	100	10	Normal	—	—
37	Double-Edge	Normal	Physical	120	100	15	Normal	—	○
40	Sunny Day	Fire	Status	—	—	5	Both Sides	—	—
43	Leaf Storm	Grass	Special	140	90	5	Normal	—	—

TM & HM MOVES

Lv.	Name	Type	Kind	Pow.	Acc.	PP	Range	Long	DA
TM06	Toxic	Poison	Status	—	90	10	Normal	—	—
TM10	Hidden Power	Normal	Special	—	100	15	Normal	—	—
TM11	Sunny Day	Fire	Status	—	—	5	Both Sides	—	—
TM15	Hyper Beam	Normal	Special	150	90	5	Normal	—	—
TM16	Light Screen	Psychic	Status	—	—	30	Your Side	—	—
TM17	Protect	Normal	Status	—	—	10	Self	—	—
TM20	Safeguard	Normal	Status	—	—	25	Your Side	—	—
TM21	Frustration	Normal	Physical	—	100	20	Normal	—	○
TM22	SolarBeam	Grass	Special	120	100	10	Normal	—	—
TM27	Return	Normal	Physical	—	100	20	Normal	—	○
TM32	Double Team	Normal	Status	—	—	15	Self	—	—
TM36	Sludge Bomb	Poison	Special	90	100	10	Normal	—	—
TM42	Facade	Normal	Physical	70	100	20	Normal	—	—
TM44	Rest	Psychic	Status	—	—	10	Self	—	—
TM45	Attract	Normal	Status	—	100	15	Normal	—	—
TM48	Round	Normal	Special	60	100	15	Normal	—	—
TM53	Energy Ball	Grass	Special	80	100	10	Normal	—	—
TM68	Giga Impact	Normal	Physical	150	90	5	Normal	—	—
TM70	Flash	Normal	Status	—	100	20	Normal	—	—
TM75	Swords Dance	Normal	Status	—	—	30	Self	—	—
TM86	Grass Knot	Grass	Special	—	100	20	Normal	—	○
TM87	Swagger	Normal	Status	—	90	15	Normal	—	—
TM90	Substitute	Normal	Status	—	—	10	Self	—	—
HM01	Cut	Normal	Physical	50	95	30	Normal	—	—

MOVES TAUGHT BY PEOPLE

Name	Type	Kind	Pow.	Acc.	PP	Range	Long	DA

MOVES TAUGHT BY MOVE TUTORS FOR SHARDS

Name	Type	Kind	Pow.	Acc.	PP	Range	Long	DA
Uproar	Normal	Special	90	100	10	1 Random	—	—
Seed Bomb	Grass	Physical	80	100	15	Normal	—	—
Earth Power	Ground	Special	90	100	10	Normal	—	—
Snore	Normal	Special	40	100	15	Normal	—	—
Synthesis	Grass	Status	—	—	5	Self	—	—
Giga Drain	Grass	Special	75	100	10	Normal	—	—
Worry Seed	Grass	Status	—	100	10	Normal	—	—
Helping Hand	Normal	Status	—	—	20	1 Ally	—	—
After You	Normal	Status	—	—	15	Normal	—	—
Endeavor	Normal	Physical	—	100	5	Normal	—	○
Sleep Talk	Normal	Status	—	—	10	Self	—	—

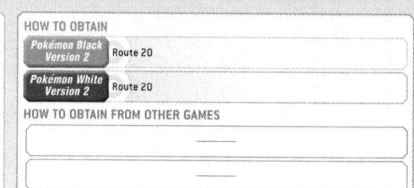

193 Yanma

Clear Wing Pokémon

- HEIGHT: 3'11"
- WEIGHT: 83.8 lbs.
- GENDER: ♂ / ♀

By flapping its wings at high speed, it can fly freely through the air. Even sudden stops are no problem.

Same form for ♂ / ♀

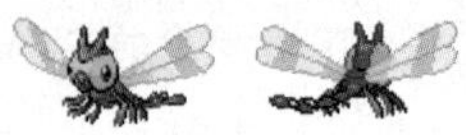

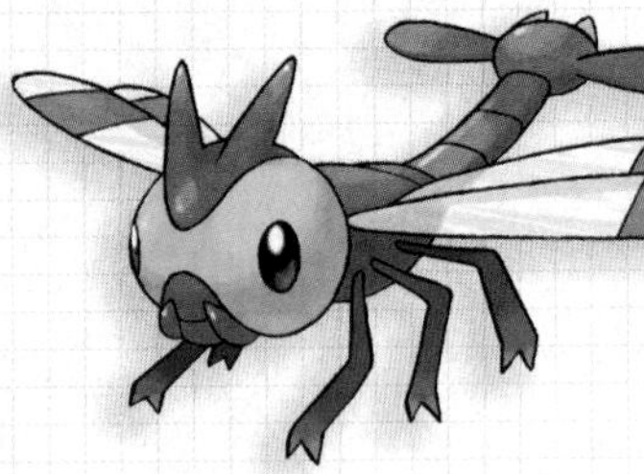

Pokémon AR Marker

TYPE Bug / Flying

ABILITIES
- Speed Boost
- Compoundeyes

HIDDEN ABILITY
- Frisk

STATS
HP
Attack
Defense
Sp. Atk
Sp. Def
Speed

EGG GROUPS
Bug

ITEMS SOMETIMES HELD
- Wide Lens

EVOLUTION

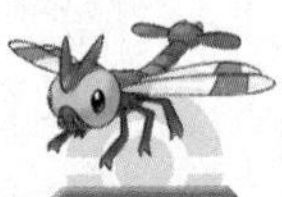

Yanma

Level up Yanma to Lv. 33 and teach it AncientPower or level it up after it knows AncientPower

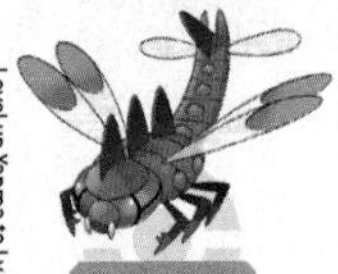

Yanmega

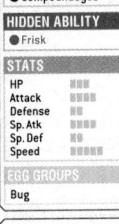

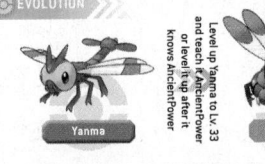

➡ p. 250

HOW TO OBTAIN

Pokémon Black Version 2	❶ Pinwheel Forest entrance ❷ Route 3
Pokémon White Version 2	❶ Pinwheel Forest entrance ❷ Route 3

HOW TO OBTAIN FROM OTHER GAMES

—

—

LEVEL-UP AND LEARNED MOVES

Lv.	Name	Type	Kind	Pow.	Acc.	PP	Range	Long	DA
1	Tackle	Normal	Physical	50	100	35	Normal	—	○
1	Foresight	Normal	Status	—	—	40	Normal	—	—
6	Quick Attack	Normal	Physical	40	100	30	Normal	—	○
11	Double Team	Normal	Status	—	—	15	Self	—	—
14	SonicBoom	Normal	Special	—	90	20	Normal	—	—
17	Detect	Fighting	Status	—	—	5	Self	—	—
22	Supersonic	Normal	Status	—	55	20	Normal	—	—
27	Uproar	Normal	Special	90	100	10	1 Random	—	—
30	Pursuit	Dark	Physical	40	100	20	Normal	—	○
33	AncientPower	Rock	Special	60	100	5	Normal	—	—
38	Hypnosis	Psychic	Status	—	60	20	Normal	—	—
43	Wing Attack	Flying	Physical	60	100	35	Normal	○	○
46	Screech	Normal	Status	—	85	40	Normal	—	—
49	U-turn	Bug	Physical	70	100	20	Normal	—	○
54	Air Slash	Flying	Special	75	95	20	Normal	○	—
57	Bug Buzz	Bug	Special	90	100	10	Normal	—	—

TM & HM MOVES

Lv.	Name	Type	Kind	Pow.	Acc.	PP	Range	Long	DA
TM06	Toxic	Poison	Status	—	90	10	Normal	—	—
TM10	Hidden Power	Normal	Special	—	100	15	Normal	—	—
TM11	Sunny Day	Fire	Status	—	—	5	Both Sides	—	—
TM17	Protect	Normal	Status	—	—	10	Self	—	—
TM21	Frustration	Normal	Physical	—	100	20	Normal	—	○
TM22	SolarBeam	Grass	Special	120	100	10	Normal	—	—
TM27	Return	Normal	Physical	—	100	20	Normal	—	○
TM29	Psychic	Psychic	Special	90	100	10	Normal	—	—
TM30	Shadow Ball	Ghost	Special	80	100	15	Normal	—	—
TM32	Double Team	Normal	Status	—	—	15	Self	—	—
TM40	Aerial Ace	Flying	Physical	60	—	20	Normal	○	○
TM42	Facade	Normal	Physical	70	100	20	Normal	—	○
TM44	Rest	Psychic	Status	—	—	10	Self	—	—
TM45	Attract	Normal	Status	—	100	15	Normal	—	—
TM46	Thief	Dark	Physical	40	100	10	Normal	—	○
TM48	Round	Normal	Special	60	100	15	Normal	—	—
TM70	Flash	Normal	Status	—	100	20	Normal	—	—
TM85	Dream Eater	Psychic	Special	100	100	15	Normal	—	—
TM87	Swagger	Normal	Status	—	90	15	Normal	—	—
TM89	U-turn	Bug	Physical	70	100	20	Normal	—	○
TM90	Substitute	Normal	Status	—	—	10	Self	—	—

MOVES TAUGHT BY PEOPLE

Name	Type	Kind	Pow.	Acc.	PP	Range	Long	DA

MOVES TAUGHT BY MOVE TUTORS FOR SHARDS

Name	Type	Kind	Pow.	Acc.	PP	Range	Long	DA
Bug Bite	Bug	Physical	60	100	20	Normal	—	○
Signal Beam	Bug	Special	75	100	15	Normal	—	—
Uproar	Normal	Special	90	100	10	1 Random	—	—
Snore	Normal	Special	40	100	15	Normal	—	—
Roost	Flying	Status	—	—	10	Self	—	—
Giga Drain	Grass	Special	75	100	10	Normal	—	—
Tailwind	Flying	Status	—	—	30	Your Side	—	—
Sleep Talk	Normal	Status	—	—	10	Self	—	—

EGG MOVES

Name	Type	Kind	Pow.	Acc.	PP	Range	Long	DA
Whirlwind	Normal	Status	—	100	20	Normal	—	—
Reversal	Fighting	Physical	—	100	15	Normal	—	○
Leech Life	Bug	Physical	20	100	15	Normal	—	○
Signal Beam	Bug	Special	75	100	15	Normal	—	—
Silver Wind	Bug	Special	60	100	5	Normal	—	—
Feint	Normal	Physical	30	100	10	Normal	—	—
Faint Attack	Dark	Physical	60	—	20	Normal	—	○
Pursuit	Dark	Physical	40	100	20	Normal	—	○
Double-Edge	Normal	Physical	120	100	15	Normal	—	○
Secret Power	Normal	Physical	70	100	20	Normal	—	—

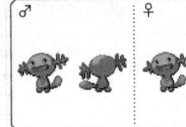

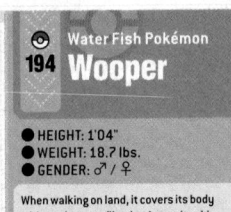

194 Wooper

Water Fish Pokémon

- HEIGHT: 1'04"
- WEIGHT: 18.7 lbs.
- GENDER: ♂ / ♀

When walking on land, it covers its body with a poisonous film that keeps its skin from dehydrating.

♂ ♀

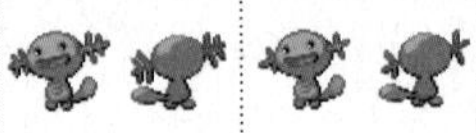

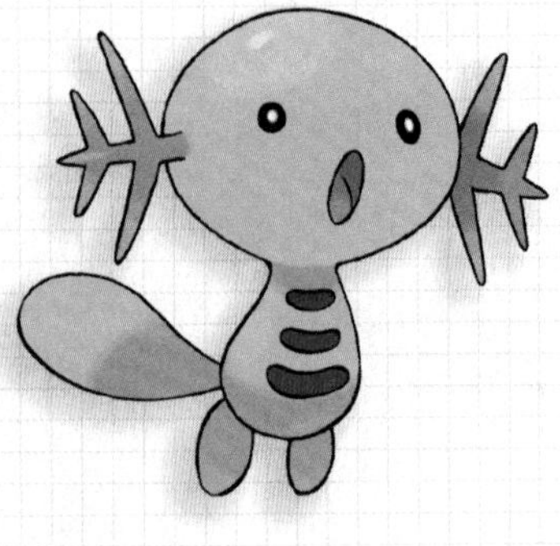

Pokémon AR Marker

TYPE Water / Ground

ABILITIES
- Damp
- Water Absorb

HIDDEN ABILITY
- Unaware

STATS
HP
Attack
Defense
Sp. Atk
Sp. Def
Speed

EGG GROUPS
Water ❶ / Field

ITEMS SOMETIMES HELD
- None

EVOLUTION

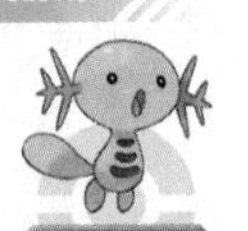

Wooper

Lv. 20

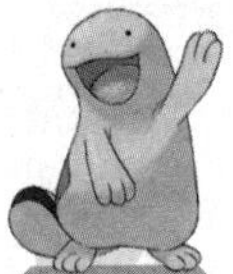

Quagsire

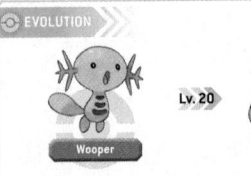

HOW TO OBTAIN

Pokémon Black Version 2	Catch a Quagsire, leave it at the Pokémon Day Care, and hatch the Egg that is found
Pokémon White Version 2	Catch a Quagsire, leave it at the Pokémon Day Care, and hatch the Egg that is found

HOW TO OBTAIN FROM OTHER GAMES

Pokémon HeartGold Version	Route 32 (night only)
Pokémon SoulSilver Version	Route 32 (night only)

LEVEL-UP AND LEARNED MOVES

Lv.	Name	Type	Kind	Pow.	Acc.	PP	Range	Long	DA
1	Water Gun	Water	Special	40	100	25	Normal	—	—
1	Tail Whip	Normal	Status	—	100	30	Many Others	—	—
5	Mud Sport	Ground	Status	—	—	15	Both Sides	—	—
9	Mud Shot	Ground	Special	55	95	15	Normal	—	—
15	Slam	Normal	Physical	80	75	20	Normal	—	○
19	Mud Bomb	Ground	Special	65	85	10	Normal	—	—
23	Amnesia	Psychic	Status	—	—	20	Self	—	—
29	Yawn	Normal	Status	—	—	10	Normal	—	—
33	Earthquake	Ground	Physical	100	100	10	Adjacent	—	—
37	Rain Dance	Water	Status	—	—	5	Both Sides	—	—
43	Mist	Ice	Status	—	—	30	Your Side	—	—
43	Haze	Ice	Status	—	—	30	Both Sides	—	—
47	Muddy Water	Water	Special	95	85	10	Many Others	—	—

TM & HM MOVES

Lv.	Name	Type	Kind	Pow.	Acc.	PP	Range	Long	DA
TM06	Toxic	Poison	Status	—	90	10	Normal	—	—
TM07	Hail	Ice	Status	—	—	10	Both Sides	—	—
TM10	Hidden Power	Normal	Special	—	100	15	Normal	—	—
TM13	Ice Beam	Ice	Special	95	100	10	Normal	—	—
TM14	Blizzard	Ice	Special	120	70	5	Many Others	—	—
TM17	Protect	Normal	Status	—	—	10	Self	—	—
TM18	Rain Dance	Water	Status	—	—	5	Both Sides	—	—
TM20	Safeguard	Normal	Status	—	—	25	Your Side	—	—
TM21	Frustration	Normal	Physical	—	100	20	Normal	—	○
TM26	Earthquake	Ground	Physical	100	100	10	Adjacent	—	—
TM27	Return	Normal	Physical	—	100	20	Normal	—	○
TM28	Dig	Ground	Physical	80	100	10	Normal	—	○
TM32	Double Team	Normal	Status	—	—	15	Self	—	—
TM34	Sludge Wave	Poison	Special	95	100	10	Adjacent	—	—
TM36	Sludge Bomb	Poison	Special	90	100	10	Normal	—	—
TM37	Sandstorm	Rock	Status	—	—	10	Both Sides	—	—
TM42	Facade	Normal	Physical	70	100	20	Normal	—	○
TM44	Rest	Psychic	Status	—	—	10	Self	—	—
TM45	Attract	Normal	Status	—	100	15	Normal	—	—
TM48	Round	Normal	Special	60	100	15	Normal	—	—
TM55	Scald	Water	Special	80	100	15	Normal	—	—
TM70	Flash	Normal	Status	—	100	20	Normal	—	—
TM78	Bulldoze	Ground	Physical	60	100	20	Adjacent	—	—
TM87	Swagger	Normal	Status	—	90	15	Normal	—	—
TM90	Substitute	Normal	Status	—	—	10	Self	—	—
TM94	Rock Smash	Fighting	Physical	40	100	15	Normal	—	○
HM03	Surf	Water	Special	95	100	15	Adjacent	—	—
HM05	Waterfall	Water	Physical	80	100	15	Normal	—	○
HM06	Dive	Water	Physical	80	100	10	Normal	—	○

MOVES TAUGHT BY PEOPLE

Name	Type	Kind	Pow.	Acc.	PP	Range	Long	DA

MOVES TAUGHT BY MOVE TUTORS FOR SHARDS

Name	Type	Kind	Pow.	Acc.	PP	Range	Long	DA
Ice Punch	Ice	Physical	75	100	15	Normal	—	○
Icy Wind	Ice	Special	55	95	15	Many Others	—	—
Iron Tail	Steel	Physical	100	75	15	Normal	—	○
Aqua Tail	Water	Physical	90	90	10	Normal	—	○
Earth Power	Ground	Special	90	100	10	Normal	—	—
Snore	Normal	Special	40	100	15	Normal	—	—
After You	Normal	Status	—	—	15	Normal	—	—
Sleep Talk	Normal	Status	—	—	10	Self	—	—

EGG MOVES

Name	Type	Kind	Pow.	Acc.	PP	Range	Long	DA
Body Slam	Normal	Physical	85	100	15	Normal	—	○
AncientPower	Rock	Special	60	100	5	Normal	—	—
Curse	Ghost	Status	—	—	10	Varies	—	—
Mud Sport	Ground	Status	—	—	15	Both Sides	—	—
Stockpile	Normal	Status	—	—	20	Self	—	—
Swallow	Normal	Status	—	—	10	Self	—	—
Spit Up	Normal	Special	—	100	10	Normal	—	—
Counter	Fighting	Physical	—	100	20	Varies	—	○
Encore	Normal	Status	—	100	5	Normal	—	—
Double Kick	Fighting	Physical	30	100	30	Normal	—	○
Recover	Normal	Status	—	—	10	Self	—	—
After You	Normal	Status	—	—	15	Normal	—	—
Sleep Talk	Normal	Status	—	—	10	Self	—	—
Acid Spray	Poison	Special	40	100	20	Normal	—	—

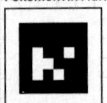

195 Quagsire

Water Fish Pokémon

- HEIGHT: 4'07"
- WEIGHT: 165.3 lbs.
- GENDER: ♂ / ♀

It has an easygoing nature. It doesn't care if it bumps its head on boats and boulders while swimming.

♂ ♀

TYPE Water Ground

ABILITIES
- Damp
- Water Absorb

HIDDEN ABILITY
- Unaware

STATS
HP
Attack
Defense
Sp. Atk
Sp. Def
Speed

EGG GROUPS
Water ❶ / Field

ITEMS SOMETIMES HELD
- None

EVOLUTION

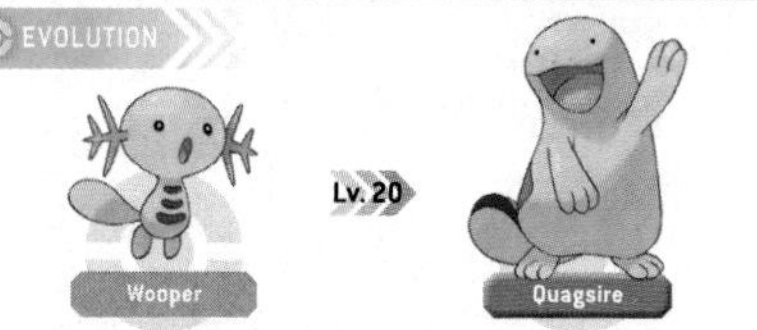

HOW TO OBTAIN

Pokémon Black Version 2	Route 8 (mass outbreak)
Pokémon White Version 2	Route 8 (mass outbreak)

HOW TO OBTAIN FROM OTHER GAMES

———

———

Pokémon AR Marker

LEVEL-UP AND LEARNED MOVES

Lv.	Name	Type	Kind	Pow.	Acc.	PP	Range	Long	DA
1	Water Gun	Water	Special	40	100	25	Normal	—	—
1	Tail Whip	Normal	Status	—	100	30	Many Others	—	—
1	Mud Sport	Ground	Status	—	—	15	Both Sides	—	—
5	Mud Sport	Ground	Status	—	—	15	Both Sides	—	—
9	Mud Shot	Ground	Special	55	95	15	Normal	—	—
15	Slam	Normal	Physical	80	75	20	Normal	—	○
19	Mud Bomb	Ground	Special	65	85	10	Normal	—	—
24	Amnesia	Psychic	Status	—	—	20	Self	—	—
31	Yawn	Normal	Status	—	—	10	Normal	—	—
36	Earthquake	Ground	Physical	100	100	10	Adjacent	—	—
41	Rain Dance	Water	Status	—	—	5	Both Sides	—	—
48	Mist	Ice	Status	—	—	30	Your Side	—	—
48	Haze	Ice	Status	—	—	30	Both Sides	—	—
53	Muddy Water	Water	Special	95	85	10	Many Others	—	—

TM & HM MOVES

Lv.	Name	Type	Kind	Pow.	Acc.	PP	Range	Long	DA
TM06	Toxic	Poison	Status	—	90	10	Normal	—	—
TM07	Hail	Ice	Status	—	—	10	Both Sides	—	—
TM10	Hidden Power	Normal	Special	—	100	15	Normal	—	—
TM13	Ice Beam	Ice	Special	95	100	10	Normal	—	—
TM14	Blizzard	Ice	Special	120	70	5	Many Others	—	—
TM15	Hyper Beam	Normal	Special	150	90	5	Normal	—	—
TM17	Protect	Normal	Status	—	—	10	Self	—	—
TM18	Rain Dance	Water	Status	—	—	5	Both Sides	—	—
TM20	Safeguard	Normal	Status	—	—	25	Your Side	—	—
TM21	Frustration	Normal	Physical	—	100	20	Normal	—	○
TM26	Earthquake	Ground	Physical	100	100	10	Adjacent	—	—
TM27	Return	Normal	Physical	—	100	20	Normal	—	○
TM28	Dig	Ground	Physical	80	100	10	Normal	—	○
TM31	Brick Break	Fighting	Physical	75	100	15	Normal	—	○
TM32	Double Team	Normal	Status	—	—	15	Self	—	—
TM34	Sludge Wave	Poison	Special	95	100	10	Adjacent	—	—
TM36	Sludge Bomb	Poison	Special	90	100	10	Normal	—	—
TM37	Sandstorm	Rock	Status	—	—	10	Both Sides	—	—
TM39	Rock Tomb	Rock	Physical	50	80	10	Normal	—	—
TM42	Facade	Normal	Physical	70	100	20	Normal	—	○
TM44	Rest	Psychic	Status	—	—	10	Self	—	—
TM45	Attract	Normal	Status	—	100	15	Normal	—	—
TM46	Thief	Dark	Physical	40	100	10	Normal	—	○
TM48	Round	Normal	Special	60	100	15	Normal	—	—
TM52	Focus Blast	Fighting	Special	120	70	5	Normal	—	—
TM55	Scald	Water	Special	80	100	15	Normal	—	—
TM56	Fling	Dark	Physical	—	100	10	Normal	—	—
TM68	Giga Impact	Normal	Physical	150	90	5	Normal	—	○
TM70	Flash	Normal	Status	—	100	20	Normal	—	—
TM71	Stone Edge	Rock	Physical	100	80	5	Normal	—	—
TM78	Bulldoze	Ground	Physical	60	100	20	Adjacent	—	—
TM80	Rock Slide	Rock	Physical	75	90	10	Many Others	—	—
TM87	Swagger	Normal	Status	—	90	15	Normal	—	—
TM90	Substitute	Normal	Status	—	—	10	Self	—	—
TM94	Rock Smash	Fighting	Physical	40	100	15	Normal	—	○
HM03	Surf	Water	Special	95	100	15	Adjacent	—	—
HM04	Strength	Normal	Physical	80	100	15	Normal	—	○
HM05	Waterfall	Water	Physical	80	100	15	Normal	—	○
HM06	Dive	Water	Physical	80	100	10	Normal	—	○

MOVES TAUGHT BY PEOPLE

Name	Type	Kind	Pow.	Acc.	PP	Range	Long	DA

MOVES TAUGHT BY MOVE TUTORS FOR SHARDS

Name	Type	Kind	Pow.	Acc.	PP	Range	Long	DA
Ice Punch	Ice	Physical	75	100	15	Normal	—	○
Icy Wind	Ice	Special	55	95	15	Many Others	—	—
Iron Tail	Steel	Physical	100	75	15	Normal	—	○
Aqua Tail	Water	Physical	90	90	10	Normal	—	○
Earth Power	Ground	Special	90	100	10	Normal	—	—
Snore	Normal	Special	40	100	15	Normal	—	—
After You	Normal	Status	—	—	15	Normal	—	—
Sleep Talk	Normal	Status	—	—	10	Self	—	—

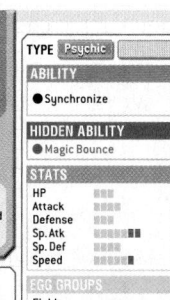

196 Espeon

Sun Pokémon

- HEIGHT: 2'11"
- WEIGHT: 58.4 lbs.
- GENDER: ♂ / ♀

Its fur is so sensitive, it can feel minute shifts in the air and predict the weather...and its foes' thoughts.

Same form for ♂ / ♀

TYPE Psychic

ABILITY
- Synchronize

HIDDEN ABILITY
- Magic Bounce

STATS
HP
Attack
Defense
Sp. Atk
Sp. Def
Speed

EGG GROUPS
Field

ITEMS SOMETIMES HELD
- None

EVOLUTION

Eevee ➡ p. 80

Vaporeon ➡ p. 80
Use Water Stone on Eevee

Jolteon ➡ p. 81
Use Thunderstone on Eevee

Flareon ➡ p. 81
Use Fire Stone on Eevee

Espeon
Level up Eevee with high friendship in the morning, afternoon, or evening

Umbreon
Level up Eevee with high friendship at night or late night

Leafeon ➡ p. 251
Level up Eevee around the moss-covered rock in Pinwheel Forest

Glaceon ➡ p. 251
Level up Eevee around the ice-covered rock in Twist Mountain

HOW TO OBTAIN

Pokémon Black Version 2	Level up Eevee with high friendship in the morning, afternoon, or evening
Pokémon White Version 2	Level up Eevee with high friendship in the morning, afternoon, or evening

HOW TO OBTAIN FROM OTHER GAMES

———

———

Pokémon AR Marker

LEVEL-UP AND LEARNED MOVES

Lv.	Name	Type	Kind	Pow.	Acc.	PP	Range	Long	DA
1	Helping Hand	Normal	Status	—	—	20	1 Ally	—	—
1	Tackle	Normal	Physical	50	100	35	Normal	—	○
1	Tail Whip	Normal	Status	—	100	30	Many Others	—	—
5	Sand-Attack	Ground	Status	—	100	15	Normal	—	—
9	Confusion	Psychic	Special	50	100	25	Normal	—	—
13	Quick Attack	Normal	Physical	40	100	30	Normal	—	○
17	Swift	Normal	Special	60	—	20	Many Others	—	—
21	Psybeam	Psychic	Special	65	100	20	Normal	—	—
25	Future Sight	Psychic	Special	100	100	10	Normal	—	—
29	Psych Up	Normal	Status	—	—	10	Normal	—	—
33	Morning Sun	Normal	Status	—	—	5	Self	—	—
37	Psychic	Psychic	Special	90	100	10	Normal	—	—
41	Last Resort	Normal	Physical	140	100	5	Normal	—	○
45	Power Swap	Psychic	Status	—	—	10	Normal	—	—

TM & HM MOVES

Lv.	Name	Type	Kind	Pow.	Acc.	PP	Range	Long	DA
TM03	Psyshock	Psychic	Special	80	100	10	Normal	—	—
TM04	Calm Mind	Psychic	Status	—	—	20	Self	—	—
TM06	Toxic	Poison	Status	—	90	10	Normal	—	—
TM10	Hidden Power	Normal	Special	—	100	15	Normal	—	—
TM11	Sunny Day	Fire	Status	—	—	5	Both Sides	—	—
TM15	Hyper Beam	Normal	Special	150	90	5	Normal	—	—
TM16	Light Screen	Psychic	Status	—	—	30	Your Side	—	—
TM17	Protect	Normal	Status	—	—	10	Self	—	—
TM18	Rain Dance	Water	Status	—	—	5	Both Sides	—	—
TM19	Telekinesis	Psychic	Status	—	—	15	Normal	—	—
TM21	Frustration	Normal	Physical	—	100	20	Normal	—	○
TM27	Return	Normal	Physical	—	100	20	Normal	—	○
TM28	Dig	Ground	Physical	80	100	10	Normal	—	○
TM29	Psychic	Psychic	Special	90	100	10	Normal	—	—
TM30	Shadow Ball	Ghost	Special	80	100	15	Normal	—	—
TM32	Double Team	Normal	Status	—	—	15	Self	—	—
TM33	Reflect	Psychic	Status	—	—	20	Your Side	—	—
TM42	Facade	Normal	Physical	70	100	20	Normal	—	○
TM44	Rest	Psychic	Status	—	—	10	Self	—	—
TM45	Attract	Normal	Status	—	100	15	Normal	—	—
TM48	Round	Normal	Special	60	100	15	Normal	—	—
TM49	Echoed Voice	Normal	Special	40	100	15	Normal	—	—
TM67	Retaliate	Normal	Physical	70	100	5	Normal	—	○
TM68	Giga Impact	Normal	Physical	150	90	5	Normal	—	○
TM70	Flash	Normal	Status	—	100	20	Normal	—	—
TM77	Psych Up	Normal	Status	—	—	10	Normal	—	—
TM83	Work Up	Normal	Status	—	—	30	Self	—	—
TM85	Dream Eater	Psychic	Special	100	100	15	Normal	—	—
TM86	Grass Knot	Grass	Special	—	100	20	Normal	—	○
TM87	Swagger	Normal	Status	—	90	15	Normal	—	—
TM90	Substitute	Normal	Status	—	—	10	Self	—	—
TM92	Trick Room	Psychic	Status	—	—	5	Both Sides	—	—
HM01	Cut	Normal	Physical	50	95	30	Normal	—	○

MOVES TAUGHT BY PEOPLE

Name	Type	Kind	Pow.	Acc.	PP	Range	Long	DA

MOVES TAUGHT BY MOVE TUTORS FOR SHARDS

Name	Type	Kind	Pow.	Acc.	PP	Range	Long	DA
Covet	Normal	Physical	60	100	40	Normal	—	○
Signal Beam	Bug	Special	75	100	15	Normal	—	—
Last Resort	Normal	Physical	140	100	5	Normal	—	○
Magic Coat	Psychic	Status	—	—	15	Self	—	—
Hyper Voice	Normal	Special	90	100	10	Many Others	—	—
Iron Tail	Steel	Physical	100	75	15	Normal	—	○
Zen Headbutt	Psychic	Physical	80	90	15	Normal	—	○
Snore	Normal	Special	40	100	15	Normal	—	—
Heal Bell	Normal	Status	—	—	5	Your Party	—	—
Helping Hand	Normal	Status	—	—	20	1 Ally	—	—
Magic Room	Psychic	Status	—	—	10	Both Sides	—	—
Trick	Psychic	Status	—	100	10	Normal	—	—
Sleep Talk	Normal	Status	—	—	10	Self	—	—
Skill Swap	Psychic	Status	—	—	10	Normal	—	—

197 Umbreon

Moonlight Pokémon

● HEIGHT: 3'03"
● WEIGHT: 59.5 lbs.
● GENDER: ♂ / ♀

When exposed to the moon's aura, the rings on its body glow faintly and it's filled with a mysterious power.

Same form for ♂ / ♀

TYPE Dark

ABILITY
● Synchronize

HIDDEN ABILITY
● Inner Focus

STATS

Stat	
HP	■■■■
Attack	■■■■
Defense	■■■■■
Sp. Atk	■■■
Sp. Def	■■■■■■
Speed	■■■■

EGG GROUPS
Field

ITEMS SOMETIMES HELD
● None

Pokémon AR Marker

EVOLUTION

- Eevee ➡ p. 80
- Vaporeon ➡ p. 80 — Use Water Stone on Eevee
- Jolteon ➡ p. 81 — Use Thunderstone on Eevee
- Flareon ➡ p. 81 — Use Fire Stone on Eevee
- Espeon — Level up Eevee with high friendship in the morning, afternoon, or evening
- Umbreon — Level up Eevee with high friendship at night or late night
- Leafeon ➡ p. 251 — Level up Eevee around the moss-covered rock in Pinwheel Forest
- Glaceon ➡ p. 251 — Level up Eevee around the ice-covered rock in Twist Mountain

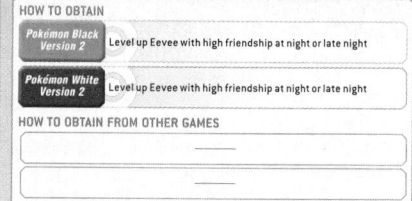

HOW TO OBTAIN

Pokémon Black Version 2	Level up Eevee with high friendship at night or late night
Pokémon White Version 2	Level up Eevee with high friendship at night or late night

HOW TO OBTAIN FROM OTHER GAMES

—
—

LEVEL-UP AND LEARNED MOVES

Lv.	Name	Type	Kind	Pow.	Acc.	PP	Range	Long	DA
1	Helping Hand	Normal	Status	—	—	20	1 Ally	—	—
1	Tackle	Normal	Physical	50	100	35	Normal	—	○
1	Tail Whip	Normal	Status	—	100	30	Many Others	—	—
5	Sand-Attack	Ground	Status	—	100	15	Normal	—	—
9	Pursuit	Dark	Physical	40	100	20	Normal	—	○
13	Quick Attack	Normal	Physical	40	100	30	Normal	—	○
17	Confuse Ray	Ghost	Status	—	100	10	Normal	—	—
21	Faint Attack	Dark	Physical	60	—	20	Normal	—	○
25	Assurance	Dark	Physical	50	100	10	Normal	—	○
29	Screech	Normal	Status	—	85	40	Normal	—	—
33	Moonlight	Normal	Status	—	—	5	Self	—	—
37	Mean Look	Normal	Status	—	—	5	Normal	—	—
41	Last Resort	Normal	Physical	140	100	5	Normal	—	○
45	Guard Swap	Psychic	Status	—	—	10	Normal	—	—

TM & HM MOVES

Lv.	Name	Type	Kind	Pow.	Acc.	PP	Range	Long	DA
TM06	Toxic	Poison	Status	—	90	10	Normal	—	—
TM10	Hidden Power	Normal	Special	—	100	15	Normal	—	—
TM11	Sunny Day	Fire	Status	—	—	5	Both Sides	—	—
TM12	Taunt	Dark	Status	—	100	20	Normal	—	—
TM15	Hyper Beam	Normal	Special	150	90	5	Normal	—	—
TM17	Protect	Normal	Status	—	—	10	Self	—	—
TM18	Rain Dance	Water	Status	—	—	5	Both Sides	—	—
TM21	Frustration	Normal	Physical	—	100	20	Normal	—	○
TM27	Return	Normal	Physical	—	100	20	Normal	—	○
TM28	Dig	Ground	Physical	80	100	10	Normal	—	○
TM29	Psychic	Psychic	Special	90	100	10	Normal	—	—
TM30	Shadow Ball	Ghost	Special	80	100	15	Normal	—	—
TM32	Double Team	Normal	Status	—	—	15	Self	—	—
TM41	Torment	Dark	Status	—	100	15	Normal	—	—
TM42	Facade	Normal	Physical	70	100	20	Normal	—	○
TM44	Rest	Psychic	Status	—	—	10	Self	—	—
TM45	Attract	Normal	Status	—	100	15	Normal	—	—
TM48	Round	Normal	Special	60	100	15	Normal	—	—
TM49	Echoed Voice	Normal	Special	40	100	15	Normal	—	—
TM66	Payback	Dark	Physical	50	100	10	Normal	—	○
TM67	Retaliate	Normal	Physical	70	100	5	Normal	—	○
TM68	Giga Impact	Normal	Physical	150	90	5	Normal	—	○
TM70	Flash	Normal	Status	—	100	20	Normal	—	—
TM77	Psych Up	Normal	Status	—	—	10	Normal	—	—
TM83	Work Up	Normal	Status	—	—	30	Self	—	—
TM85	Dream Eater	Psychic	Special	100	100	15	Normal	—	—
TM87	Swagger	Normal	Status	—	90	15	Normal	—	—
TM90	Substitute	Normal	Status	—	—	10	Self	—	—
TM95	Snarl	Dark	Special	55	95	15	Many Others	—	—
HM01	Cut	Normal	Physical	50	95	30	Normal	—	○

MOVES TAUGHT BY PEOPLE

Name	Type	Kind	Pow.	Acc.	PP	Range	Long	DA

MOVES TAUGHT BY MOVE TUTORS FOR SHARDS

Name	Type	Kind	Pow.	Acc.	PP	Range	Long	DA
Covet	Normal	Physical	60	100	40	Normal	—	○
Last Resort	Normal	Physical	140	100	5	Normal	—	○
Hyper Voice	Normal	Special	90	100	10	Many Others	—	—
Iron Tail	Steel	Physical	100	75	15	Normal	—	○
Foul Play	Dark	Physical	95	100	15	Normal	—	○
Dark Pulse	Dark	Special	80	100	15	Normal	○	—
Snore	Normal	Special	40	100	15	Normal	—	—
Heal Bell	Normal	Status	—	—	5	Your Party	—	—
Helping Hand	Normal	Status	—	—	20	1 Ally	—	—
Wonder Room	Psychic	Status	—	—	10	Both Sides	—	—
Spite	Ghost	Status	—	100	10	Normal	—	—
Sleep Talk	Normal	Status	—	—	10	Self	—	—
Snatch	Dark	Status	—	—	10	Self	—	—

198 Murkrow

Darkness Pokémon

● HEIGHT: 1'08"
● WEIGHT: 4.6 lbs.
● GENDER: ♂ / ♀

If spotted, it will lure an unwary person into chasing it then lose the pursuer on mountain trails.

♂
♀

TYPE Dark Flying

ABILITIES
● Insomnia
● Super Luck

HIDDEN ABILITY
● Prankster

STATS

Stat	
HP	■■■
Attack	■■■■■
Defense	■■
Sp. Atk	■■■■
Sp. Def	■■
Speed	■■■■■

EGG GROUPS
Flying

ITEMS SOMETIMES HELD
● None

Pokémon AR Marker

EVOLUTION

Murkrow
Use Dusk Stone
Honchkrow

➡ p. 231

HOW TO OBTAIN

Pokémon Black Version 2	Pinwheel Forest interior (Hidden Grotto)
Pokémon White Version 2	Pinwheel Forest interior (Hidden Grotto)

HOW TO OBTAIN FROM OTHER GAMES

—
—

LEVEL-UP AND LEARNED MOVES

Lv.	Name	Type	Kind	Pow.	Acc.	PP	Range	Long	DA
1	Peck	Flying	Physical	35	100	35	Normal	○	○
1	Astonish	Ghost	Physical	30	100	15	Normal	—	○
5	Pursuit	Dark	Physical	40	100	20	Normal	—	○
11	Haze	Ice	Status	—	—	30	Both Sides	—	—
15	Wing Attack	Flying	Physical	60	100	35	Normal	○	○
21	Night Shade	Ghost	Special	—	100	15	Normal	—	—
25	Assurance	Dark	Physical	50	100	10	Normal	—	○
31	Taunt	Dark	Status	—	100	20	Normal	—	—
35	Faint Attack	Dark	Physical	60	—	20	Normal	—	○
41	Mean Look	Normal	Status	—	—	5	Normal	—	—
45	Foul Play	Dark	Physical	95	100	15	Normal	—	○
51	Tailwind	Flying	Status	—	—	30	Your Side	—	—
55	Sucker Punch	Dark	Physical	80	100	5	Normal	—	○
61	Torment	Dark	Status	—	100	15	Normal	—	—
65	Quash	Dark	Status	—	100	15	Normal	—	—

TM & HM MOVES

Lv.	Name	Type	Kind	Pow.	Acc.	PP	Range	Long	DA
TM04	Calm Mind	Psychic	Status	—	—	20	Self	—	—
TM06	Toxic	Poison	Status	—	90	10	Normal	—	—
TM10	Hidden Power	Normal	Special	—	100	15	Normal	—	—
TM11	Sunny Day	Fire	Status	—	—	5	Both Sides	—	—
TM12	Taunt	Dark	Status	—	100	20	Normal	—	—
TM17	Protect	Normal	Status	—	—	10	Self	—	—
TM18	Rain Dance	Water	Status	—	—	5	Both Sides	—	—
TM21	Frustration	Normal	Physical	—	100	20	Normal	—	○
TM27	Return	Normal	Physical	—	100	20	Normal	—	○
TM29	Psychic	Psychic	Special	90	100	10	Normal	—	—
TM30	Shadow Ball	Ghost	Special	80	100	15	Normal	—	—
TM32	Double Team	Normal	Status	—	—	15	Self	—	—
TM40	Aerial Ace	Flying	Physical	60	—	20	Normal	○	○
TM41	Torment	Dark	Status	—	100	15	Normal	—	—
TM42	Facade	Normal	Physical	70	100	20	Normal	—	○
TM44	Rest	Psychic	Status	—	—	10	Self	—	—
TM45	Attract	Normal	Status	—	100	15	Normal	—	—
TM46	Thief	Dark	Physical	40	100	10	Normal	—	○
TM48	Round	Normal	Special	60	100	15	Normal	—	—
TM60	Quash	Dark	Status	—	100	15	Normal	—	—
TM63	Embargo	Dark	Status	—	100	15	Normal	—	—
TM66	Payback	Dark	Physical	50	100	10	Normal	—	○
TM67	Retaliate	Normal	Physical	70	100	5	Normal	—	○
TM73	Thunder Wave	Electric	Status	—	100	20	Normal	—	—
TM77	Psych Up	Normal	Status	—	—	10	Normal	—	—
TM85	Dream Eater	Psychic	Special	100	100	15	Normal	—	—
TM87	Swagger	Normal	Status	—	90	15	Normal	—	—
TM88	Pluck	Flying	Physical	60	100	20	Normal	○	○
TM90	Substitute	Normal	Status	—	—	10	Self	—	—
TM95	Snarl	Dark	Special	55	95	15	Many Others	—	—
HM02	Fly	Flying	Physical	90	95	15	Normal	○	○

MOVES TAUGHT BY PEOPLE

Name	Type	Kind	Pow.	Acc.	PP	Range	Long	DA

MOVES TAUGHT BY MOVE TUTORS FOR SHARDS

Name	Type	Kind	Pow.	Acc.	PP	Range	Long	DA
Uproar	Normal	Special	90	100	10	1 Random	—	—
Icy Wind	Ice	Special	55	95	15	Many Others	—	—
Foul Play	Dark	Physical	95	100	15	Normal	—	○
Dark Pulse	Dark	Special	80	100	15	Normal	○	—
Roost	Flying	Status	—	—	10	Self	—	—
Sky Attack	Flying	Physical	140	90	5	Normal	○	—
Heat Wave	Fire	Special	100	90	10	Many Others	—	—
Tailwind	Flying	Status	—	—	30	Your Side	—	—
Spite	Ghost	Status	—	100	10	Normal	—	—
Sleep Talk	Normal	Status	—	—	10	Self	—	—
Snatch	Dark	Status	—	—	10	Self	—	—

EGG MOVES

Name	Type	Kind	Pow.	Acc.	PP	Range	Long	DA
Whirlwind	Normal	Status	—	100	20	Normal	—	—
Drill Peck	Flying	Physical	80	100	20	Normal	○	○
Mirror Move	Flying	Status	—	—	20	Normal	—	—
Wing Attack	Flying	Physical	60	100	35	Normal	○	○
Sky Attack	Flying	Physical	140	90	5	Normal	○	—
Confuse Ray	Ghost	Status	—	100	10	Normal	—	—
FeatherDance	Flying	Status	—	100	15	Normal	—	—
Perish Song	Normal	Status	—	—	5	Adjacent	○	—
Psycho Shift	Psychic	Status	—	90	10	Normal	—	—
Screech	Normal	Status	—	85	40	Normal	—	—
Faint Attack	Dark	Physical	60	—	20	Normal	—	○
Brave Bird	Flying	Physical	120	100	15	Normal	○	○
Roost	Flying	Status	—	—	10	Self	—	—
Assurance	Dark	Physical	50	100	10	Normal	—	○

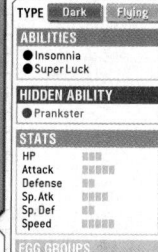

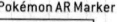

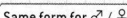

199 Slowking

Royal Pokémon

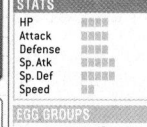

TYPE: Water / Psychic

ABILITIES
- Oblivious
- Own Tempo

HIDDEN ABILITY
- Regenerator

STATS
- HP
- Attack
- Defense
- Sp. Atk
- Sp. Def
- Speed

EGG GROUPS
Monster/Water ❶

- HEIGHT: 6'07"
- WEIGHT: 175.3 lbs.
- GENDER: ♂ / ♀

Being bitten by Shellder gave it intelligence comparable to that of award-winning scientists.

Same form for ♂ / ♀

ITEMS SOMETIMES HELD
- None

Pokémon AR Marker

EVOLUTION

Slowpoke
→ p. 53
Lv. 37
Slowbro
→ p. 53
Have it hold King's Rock and Link Trade it
Slowking

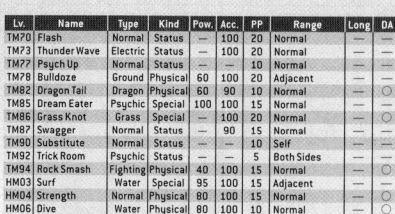

HOW TO OBTAIN

Pokémon Black Version 2	Have Slowpoke sent to you via Link Trade while holding King's Rock to receive Slowking
Pokémon White Version 2	Have Slowpoke sent to you via Link Trade while holding King's Rock to receive Slowking

HOW TO OBTAIN FROM OTHER GAMES

—

—

LEVEL-UP AND LEARNED MOVES

Lv.	Name	Type	Kind	Pow.	Acc.	PP	Range	Long	DA
1	Power Gem	Rock	Special	70	100	20	Normal	—	—
1	Hidden Power	Normal	Special	—	100	15	Normal	—	—
1	Curse	Ghost	Status	—	—	10	Varies	—	—
1	Yawn	Normal	Status	—	—	10	Normal	—	—
1	Tackle	Normal	Physical	50	100	35	Normal	—	○
5	Growl	Normal	Status	—	100	40	Many Others	—	—
9	Water Gun	Water	Special	40	100	25	Normal	—	—
14	Confusion	Psychic	Special	50	100	25	Normal	—	—
19	Disable	Normal	Status	—	100	20	Normal	—	—
23	Headbutt	Normal	Physical	70	100	15	Normal	—	○
28	Water Pulse	Water	Special	60	100	20	Normal	○	—
32	Zen Headbutt	Psychic	Physical	80	90	15	Normal	—	○
36	Nasty Plot	Dark	Status	—	—	20	Self	—	—
41	Swagger	Normal	Status	—	90	15	Normal	—	—
45	Psychic	Psychic	Special	90	100	10	Normal	—	—
49	Trump Card	Normal	Special	—	—	5	Normal	—	○
54	Psych Up	Normal	Status	—	—	10	Normal	—	—
58	Heal Pulse	Psychic	Status	—	—	10	Normal	○	—

TM & HM MOVES

Lv.	Name	Type	Kind	Pow.	Acc.	PP	Range	Long	DA
TM03	Psyshock	Psychic	Special	80	100	10	Normal	—	—
TM04	Calm Mind	Psychic	Status	—	—	20	Self	—	—
TM06	Toxic	Poison	Status	—	90	10	Normal	—	—
TM07	Hail	Ice	Status	—	—	10	Both Sides	—	—
TM10	Hidden Power	Normal	Special	—	100	15	Normal	—	—
TM11	Sunny Day	Fire	Status	—	—	5	Both Sides	—	—
TM13	Ice Beam	Ice	Special	95	100	10	Normal	—	—
TM14	Blizzard	Ice	Special	120	70	5	Many Others	—	—
TM15	Hyper Beam	Normal	Special	150	90	5	Normal	—	—
TM16	Light Screen	Psychic	Status	—	—	30	Your Side	—	—
TM17	Protect	Normal	Status	—	—	10	Self	—	—
TM18	Rain Dance	Water	Status	—	—	5	Both Sides	—	—
TM19	Telekinesis	Psychic	Status	—	—	15	Normal	—	—
TM20	Safeguard	Normal	Status	—	—	25	Your Side	—	—
TM21	Frustration	Normal	Physical	—	100	20	Normal	—	○
TM26	Earthquake	Ground	Physical	100	100	10	Adjacent	—	—
TM27	Return	Normal	Physical	—	100	20	Normal	—	○
TM28	Dig	Ground	Physical	80	100	10	Normal	—	○
TM29	Psychic	Psychic	Special	90	100	10	Normal	—	—
TM30	Shadow Ball	Ghost	Special	80	100	15	Normal	—	—
TM31	Brick Break	Fighting	Physical	75	100	15	Normal	—	○
TM32	Double Team	Normal	Status	—	—	15	Self	—	—
TM35	Flamethrower	Fire	Special	95	100	15	Normal	—	—
TM38	Fire Blast	Fire	Special	120	85	5	Normal	—	—
TM42	Facade	Normal	Physical	70	100	20	Normal	—	○
TM44	Rest	Psychic	Status	—	—	10	Self	—	—
TM45	Attract	Normal	Status	—	100	15	Normal	—	—
TM48	Round	Normal	Special	60	100	15	Normal	—	—
TM49	Echoed Voice	Normal	Special	40	100	15	Normal	—	—
TM52	Focus Blast	Fighting	Special	120	70	5	Normal	—	—
TM55	Scald	Water	Special	80	100	15	Normal	—	—
TM56	Fling	Dark	Physical	—	100	10	Normal	—	—
TM59	Incinerate	Fire	Special	30	100	15	Many Others	—	—
TM60	Quash	Dark	Status	—	100	15	Normal	—	—
TM68	Giga Impact	Normal	Physical	150	90	5	Normal	—	○
TM70	Flash	Normal	Status	—	100	20	Normal	—	—
TM73	Thunder Wave	Electric	Status	—	100	20	Normal	—	—
TM77	Psych Up	Normal	Status	—	—	10	Normal	—	—
TM78	Bulldoze	Ground	Physical	60	100	20	Adjacent	—	—
TM82	Dragon Tail	Dragon	Physical	60	90	10	Normal	—	○
TM85	Dream Eater	Psychic	Special	100	100	15	Normal	—	—
TM86	Grass Knot	Grass	Special	—	100	20	Normal	—	○
TM87	Swagger	Normal	Status	—	90	15	Normal	—	—
TM90	Substitute	Normal	Status	—	—	10	Self	—	—
TM92	Trick Room	Psychic	Status	—	—	5	Both Sides	—	—
TM94	Rock Smash	Fighting	Physical	40	100	15	Normal	—	○
HM03	Surf	Water	Special	95	100	15	Adjacent	—	—
HM04	Strength	Normal	Physical	80	100	15	Normal	—	○
HM06	Dive	Water	Physical	80	100	10	Normal	—	○

MOVES TAUGHT BY PEOPLE

Name	Type	Kind	Pow.	Acc.	PP	Range	Long	DA

MOVES TAUGHT BY MOVE TUTORS FOR SHARDS

Name	Type	Kind	Pow.	Acc.	PP	Range	Long	DA
Signal Beam	Bug	Special	75	100	15	Normal	—	—
Ice Punch	Ice	Physical	75	100	15	Normal	—	○
Iron Defense	Steel	Status	—	—	15	Self	—	—
Magic Coat	Psychic	Status	—	—	15	Self	—	—
Block	Normal	Status	—	—	5	Normal	—	—
Icy Wind	Ice	Special	55	95	15	Many Others	—	—
Iron Tail	Steel	Physical	100	75	15	Normal	—	○
Aqua Tail	Water	Physical	90	90	10	Normal	—	○
Zen Headbutt	Psychic	Physical	80	90	15	Normal	—	○
Foul Play	Dark	Physical	95	100	15	Normal	—	○
Snore	Normal	Special	40	100	15	Normal	—	—
Drain Punch	Fighting	Physical	75	100	10	Normal	—	○
After You	Normal	Status	—	—	15	Normal	—	—
Wonder Room	Psychic	Status	—	—	10	Both Sides	—	—
Recycle	Normal	Status	—	—	10	Self	—	—
Trick	Psychic	Status	—	100	10	Normal	—	—
Sleep Talk	Normal	Status	—	—	10	Self	—	—
Skill Swap	Psychic	Status	—	—	10	Normal	—	—

199 Slowking

200 Misdreavus

Screech Pokémon

TYPE: Ghost

ABILITY
- Levitate

HIDDEN ABILITY
—

STATS
- HP
- Attack
- Defense
- Sp. Atk
- Sp. Def
- Speed

EGG GROUPS
Amorphous

- HEIGHT: 2'04"
- WEIGHT: 2.2 lbs.
- GENDER: ♂ / ♀

A Pokémon that startles people in the middle of the night. It gathers fear as its energy.

Same form for ♂ / ♀

ITEMS SOMETIMES HELD
- None

Pokémon AR Marker

EVOLUTION

Misdreavus
Use Dusk Stone
Mismagius
→ p. 230

HOW TO OBTAIN

Pokémon Black Version 2	Link Trade or Poké Transfer
Pokémon White Version 2	Link Trade or Poké Transfer

HOW TO OBTAIN FROM OTHER GAMES

Pokémon White Version	Abundant Shrine

—

LEVEL-UP AND LEARNED MOVES

Lv.	Name	Type	Kind	Pow.	Acc.	PP	Range	Long	DA
1	Growl	Normal	Status	—	100	40	Many Others	—	—
1	Psywave	Psychic	Special	—	80	15	Normal	—	—
5	Spite	Ghost	Status	—	100	10	Normal	—	—
10	Astonish	Ghost	Physical	30	100	15	Normal	—	○
14	Confuse Ray	Ghost	Status	—	100	10	Normal	—	—
19	Mean Look	Normal	Status	—	—	5	Normal	—	—
23	Hex	Ghost	Special	50	100	10	Normal	—	—
28	Psybeam	Psychic	Special	65	100	20	Normal	—	—
32	Pain Split	Normal	Status	—	—	20	Normal	—	—
37	Payback	Dark	Physical	50	100	10	Normal	—	○
41	Shadow Ball	Ghost	Special	80	100	15	Normal	—	—
46	Perish Song	Normal	Status	—	—	5	Adjacent	○	—
50	Grudge	Ghost	Status	—	—	5	Self	—	—
55	Power Gem	Rock	Special	70	100	20	Normal	—	—

TM & HM MOVES

Lv.	Name	Type	Kind	Pow.	Acc.	PP	Range	Long	DA
TM04	Calm Mind	Psychic	Status	—	—	20	Self	—	—
TM06	Toxic	Poison	Status	—	90	10	Normal	—	—
TM10	Hidden Power	Normal	Special	—	100	15	Normal	—	—
TM11	Sunny Day	Fire	Status	—	—	5	Both Sides	—	—
TM12	Taunt	Dark	Status	—	100	20	Normal	—	—
TM17	Protect	Normal	Status	—	—	10	Self	—	—
TM18	Rain Dance	Water	Status	—	—	5	Both Sides	—	—
TM19	Telekinesis	Psychic	Status	—	—	15	Normal	—	—
TM21	Frustration	Normal	Physical	—	100	20	Normal	—	○
TM24	Thunderbolt	Electric	Special	95	100	15	Normal	—	—
TM25	Thunder	Electric	Special	120	70	10	Normal	—	—
TM27	Return	Normal	Physical	—	100	20	Normal	—	○
TM29	Psychic	Psychic	Special	90	100	10	Normal	—	—
TM30	Shadow Ball	Ghost	Special	80	100	15	Normal	—	—
TM32	Double Team	Normal	Status	—	—	15	Self	—	—
TM40	Aerial Ace	Flying	Physical	60	—	20	Normal	○	○
TM41	Torment	Dark	Status	—	100	15	Normal	—	—
TM42	Facade	Normal	Physical	70	100	20	Normal	—	○
TM44	Rest	Psychic	Status	—	—	10	Self	—	—
TM45	Attract	Normal	Status	—	100	15	Normal	—	—
TM46	Thief	Dark	Physical	40	100	10	Normal	—	○
TM48	Round	Normal	Special	60	100	15	Normal	—	—
TM49	Echoed Voice	Normal	Special	40	100	15	Normal	—	—
TM57	Charge Beam	Electric	Special	50	90	10	Normal	—	—
TM61	Will-O-Wisp	Fire	Status	—	75	15	Normal	—	—
TM63	Embargo	Dark	Status	—	100	15	Normal	—	—
TM66	Payback	Dark	Physical	50	100	10	Normal	—	○
TM70	Flash	Normal	Status	—	100	20	Normal	—	—
TM73	Thunder Wave	Electric	Status	—	100	20	Normal	—	—
TM77	Psych Up	Normal	Status	—	—	10	Normal	—	—
TM85	Dream Eater	Psychic	Special	100	100	15	Normal	—	—
TM87	Swagger	Normal	Status	—	90	15	Normal	—	—
TM90	Substitute	Normal	Status	—	—	10	Self	—	—
TM92	Trick Room	Psychic	Status	—	—	5	Both Sides	—	—

MOVES TAUGHT BY PEOPLE

Name	Type	Kind	Pow.	Acc.	PP	Range	Long	DA

MOVES TAUGHT BY MOVE TUTORS FOR SHARDS

Name	Type	Kind	Pow.	Acc.	PP	Range	Long	DA
Uproar	Normal	Special	90	100	10	1 Random	—	—
Magic Coat	Psychic	Status	—	—	15	Self	—	—
Hyper Voice	Normal	Special	90	100	10	Many Others	—	—
Icy Wind	Ice	Special	55	95	15	Many Others	—	—
Foul Play	Dark	Physical	95	100	15	Normal	—	○
Dark Pulse	Dark	Special	80	100	15	Normal	○	—
Snore	Normal	Special	40	100	15	Normal	—	—
Heal Bell	Normal	Status	—	—	5	Your Party	—	—
Pain Split	Normal	Status	—	—	20	Normal	—	—
Magic Room	Psychic	Status	—	—	10	Both Sides	—	—
Wonder Room	Psychic	Status	—	—	10	Both Sides	—	—
Spite	Ghost	Status	—	100	10	Normal	—	—
Trick	Psychic	Status	—	100	10	Normal	—	—
Sleep Talk	Normal	Status	—	—	10	Self	—	—
Skill Swap	Psychic	Status	—	—	10	Normal	—	—
Snatch	Dark	Status	—	—	10	Self	—	—

EGG MOVES

Name	Type	Kind	Pow.	Acc.	PP	Range	Long	DA
Screech	Normal	Status	—	85	40	Normal	—	—
Destiny Bond	Ghost	Status	—	—	5	Self	—	—
Imprison	Psychic	Status	—	—	10	Self	—	—
Memento	Dark	Status	—	100	10	Normal	—	—
Sucker Punch	Dark	Physical	80	100	5	Normal	—	○
Shadow Sneak	Ghost	Physical	40	100	30	Normal	—	○
Curse	Ghost	Status	—	—	10	Varies	—	—
Spite	Ghost	Status	—	100	10	Normal	—	—
Ominous Wind	Ghost	Special	60	100	5	Normal	—	—
Nasty Plot	Dark	Status	—	—	20	Self	—	—
Skill Swap	Psychic	Status	—	—	10	Normal	—	—
Wonder Room	Psychic	Status	—	—	10	Both Sides	—	—

200 Misdreavus

201 Unown

Symbol Pokémon

TYPE Psychic

ABILITY
● Levitate

HIDDEN ABILITY

STATS
HP
Attack
Defense
Sp. Atk
Sp. Def
Speed

EGG GROUPS
No Egg has ever been discovered

ITEMS SOMETIMES HELD
● None

● HEIGHT: 1'08"
● WEIGHT: 11.0 lbs.
● GENDER: Unknown

When alone, nothing happens. However, if there are two or more, an odd power is said to emerge.

Gender unknown

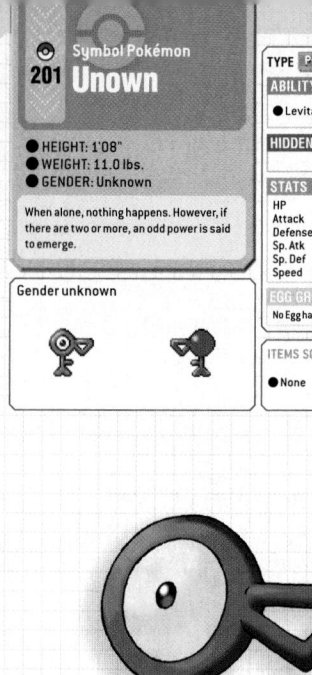

EVOLUTION

Does not evolve

HOW TO OBTAIN
Pokémon Black Version 2	Link Trade or Poké Transfer
Pokémon White Version 2	Link Trade or Poké Transfer

HOW TO OBTAIN FROM OTHER GAMES
Pokémon HeartGold Version	Ruins of Alph
Pokémon SoulSilver Version	Ruins of Alph

LEVEL-UP AND LEARNED MOVES
Lv.	Name	Type	Kind	Pow.	Acc.	PP	Range	Long	DA
1	Hidden Power	Normal	Special	—	100	15	Normal	—	—

TM & HM MOVES
Lv.	Name	Type	Kind	Pow.	Acc.	PP	Range	Long	DA

● Unown Guide and Pokémon AR Markers

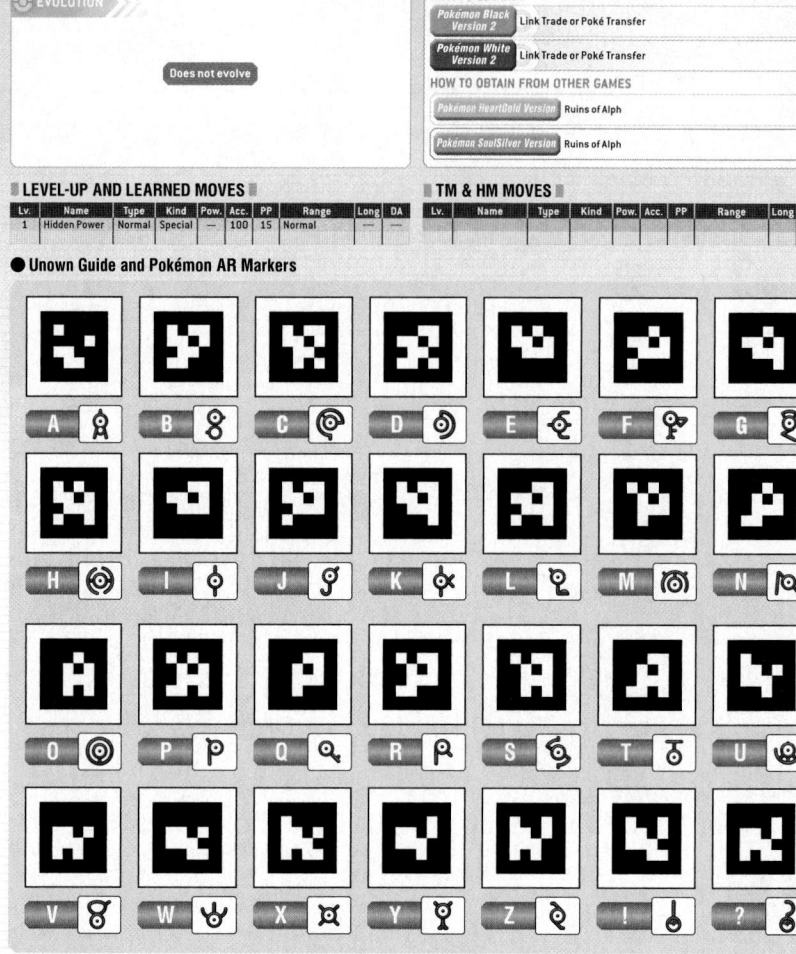

A B C D E F G
H I J K L M N
O P Q R S T U
V W X Y Z ! ?

202 Wobbuffet

Patient Pokémon

TYPE Psychic

ABILITY
● Shadow Tag

HIDDEN ABILITY
● Telepathy

STATS
HP
Attack
Defense
Sp. Atk
Sp. Def
Speed

EGG GROUPS
Amorphous

ITEMS SOMETIMES HELD
● None

● HEIGHT: 4'03"
● WEIGHT: 62.8 lbs.
● GENDER: ♂ / ♀

It desperately tries to keep its black tail hidden. It is said to be proof the tail hides a secret.

♂   ♀

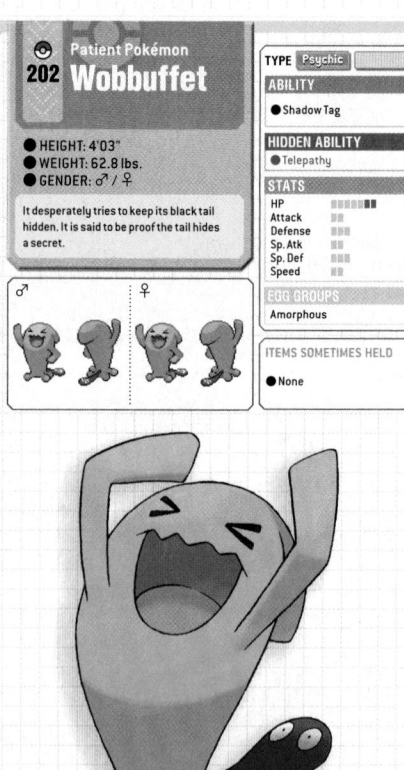

EVOLUTION

Wynaut → Lv. 15 → Wobbuffet
→ p. 193

HOW TO OBTAIN
Pokémon Black Version 2	Trade Pokémon during a date with Yancy or Curtis (second time)
Pokémon White Version 2	Trade Pokémon during a date with Yancy or Curtis (second time)

HOW TO OBTAIN FROM OTHER GAMES
Pokémon HeartGold Version	Dark Cave, Blackthorn City side
Pokémon SoulSilver Version	Dark Cave, Blackthorn City side

LEVEL-UP AND LEARNED MOVES
Lv.	Name	Type	Kind	Pow.	Acc.	PP	Range	Long	DA
1	Counter	Fighting	Physical	—	100	20	Varies	—	○
1	Mirror Coat	Psychic	Special	—	100	20	Varies	—	—
1	Safeguard	Normal	Status	—	—	25	Your Side	—	—
1	Destiny Bond	Ghost	Status	—	—	5	Self	—	—

MOVES TAUGHT BY PEOPLE
Name	Type	Kind	Pow.	Acc.	PP	Range	Long	DA

MOVES TAUGHT BY MOVE TUTORS FOR SHARDS
Name	Type	Kind	Pow.	Acc.	PP	Range	Long	DA

TM & HM MOVES
Lv.	Name	Type	Kind	Pow.	Acc.	PP	Range	Long	DA

EGG MOVES
Name	Type	Kind	Pow.	Acc.	PP	Range	Long	DA

Pokémon AR Marker

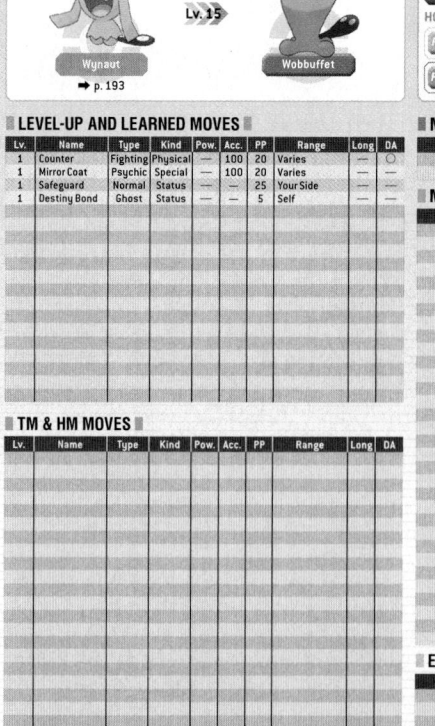
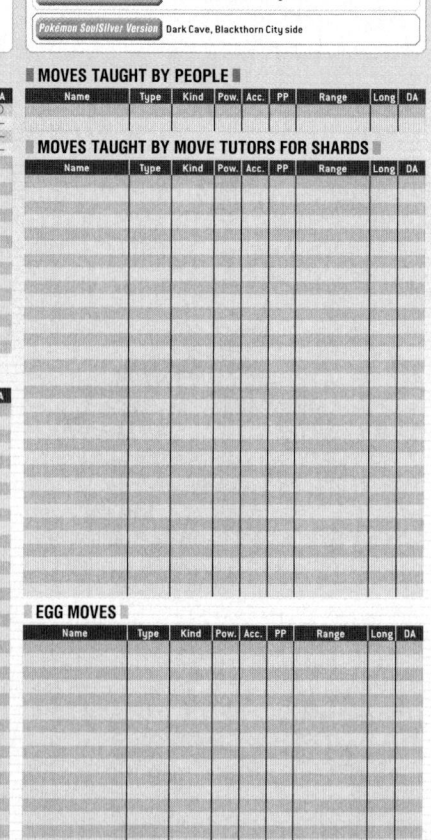

203 **Girafarig**

Long Neck Pokémon

- HEIGHT: 4'11"
- WEIGHT: 91.5 lbs.
- GENDER: ♂ / ♀

The head on its tail contains a small brain. It can instinctively fight even while facing backward.

♂ ♀

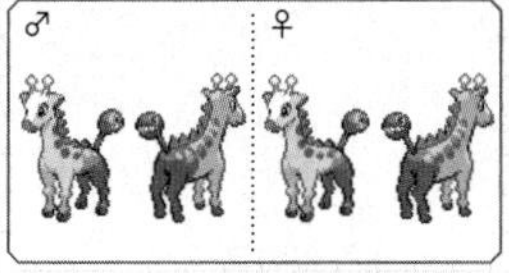

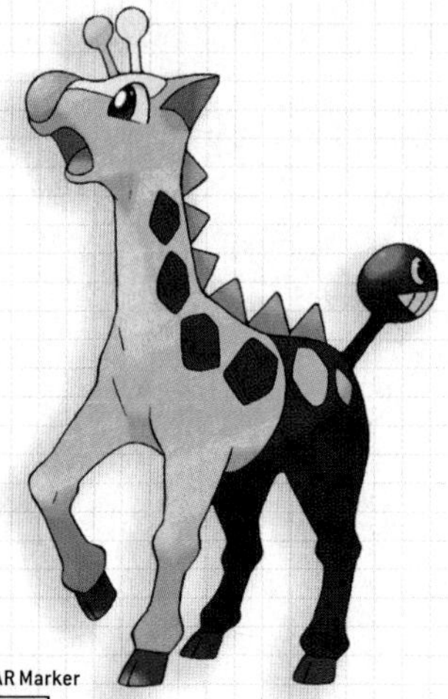

Pokémon AR Marker

TYPE: Normal / Psychic

ABILITIES

- Inner Focus
- Early Bird

HIDDEN ABILITY

- Sap Sipper

STATS

HP
Attack
Defense
Sp. Atk
Sp. Def
Speed

EGG GROUPS

Field

ITEMS SOMETIMES HELD

- Persim Berry

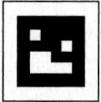

EVOLUTION

Does not evolve

HOW TO OBTAIN

Pokémon Black Version 2	Nature Preserve
Pokémon White Version 2	Nature Preserve

HOW TO OBTAIN FROM OTHER GAMES

—

—

LEVEL-UP AND LEARNED MOVES

Lv.	Name	Type	Kind	Pow.	Acc.	PP	Range	Long	DA
1	Power Swap	Psychic	Status	—	—	10	Normal	—	—
1	Guard Swap	Psychic	Status	—	—	10	Normal	—	—
1	Astonish	Ghost	Physical	30	100	15	Normal	—	○
1	Tackle	Normal	Physical	50	100	35	Normal	—	○
1	Growl	Normal	Status	—	100	40	Many Others	—	—
1	Confusion	Psychic	Special	50	100	25	Normal	—	—
5	Odor Sleuth	Normal	Status	—	—	40	Normal	—	—
10	Stomp	Normal	Physical	65	100	20	Normal	—	○
14	Agility	Psychic	Status	—	—	30	Self	—	—
19	Psybeam	Psychic	Special	65	100	20	Normal	—	—
23	Baton Pass	Normal	Status	—	—	40	Self	—	—
28	Assurance	Dark	Physical	50	100	10	Normal	—	○
32	Double Hit	Normal	Physical	35	90	10	Normal	—	○
37	Psychic	Psychic	Special	90	100	10	Normal	—	—
41	Zen Headbutt	Psychic	Physical	80	90	15	Normal	—	○
46	Crunch	Dark	Physical	80	100	15	Normal	—	○

TM & HM MOVES

Lv.	Name	Type	Kind	Pow.	Acc.	PP	Range	Long	DA
TM03	Psyshock	Psychic	Special	80	100	10	Normal	—	—
TM04	Calm Mind	Psychic	Status	—	—	20	Self	—	—
TM06	Toxic	Poison	Status	—	90	10	Normal	—	—
TM10	Hidden Power	Normal	Special	—	100	15	Normal	—	—
TM11	Sunny Day	Fire	Status	—	—	5	Both Sides	—	—
TM16	Light Screen	Psychic	Status	—	—	30	Your Side	—	—
TM17	Protect	Normal	Status	—	—	10	Self	—	—
TM18	Rain Dance	Water	Status	—	—	5	Both Sides	—	—
TM19	Telekinesis	Psychic	Status	—	—	15	Normal	—	—
TM21	Frustration	Normal	Physical	—	100	20	Normal	—	○
TM24	Thunderbolt	Electric	Special	95	100	15	Normal	—	—
TM25	Thunder	Electric	Special	120	70	10	Normal	—	—
TM26	Earthquake	Ground	Physical	100	100	10	Adjacent	—	—
TM27	Return	Normal	Physical	—	100	20	Normal	—	○
TM29	Psychic	Psychic	Special	90	100	10	Normal	—	—
TM30	Shadow Ball	Ghost	Special	80	100	15	Normal	—	—
TM32	Double Team	Normal	Status	—	—	15	Self	—	—
TM33	Reflect	Psychic	Status	—	—	20	Your Side	—	—
TM42	Facade	Normal	Physical	70	100	20	Normal	—	○
TM44	Rest	Psychic	Status	—	—	10	Self	—	—
TM45	Attract	Normal	Status	—	100	15	Normal	—	—
TM46	Thief	Dark	Physical	40	100	10	Normal	—	○
TM48	Round	Normal	Special	60	100	15	Normal	—	—
TM49	Echoed Voice	Normal	Special	40	100	15	Normal	—	—
TM53	Energy Ball	Grass	Special	80	100	10	Normal	—	—
TM57	Charge Beam	Electric	Special	50	90	10	Normal	—	—
TM67	Retaliate	Normal	Physical	70	100	5	Normal	—	○
TM70	Flash	Normal	Status	—	100	20	Normal	—	—
TM73	Thunder Wave	Electric	Status	—	100	20	Normal	—	—
TM77	Psych Up	Normal	Status	—	—	10	Normal	—	—
TM78	Bulldoze	Ground	Physical	60	100	20	Adjacent	—	—
TM83	Work Up	Normal	Status	—	—	30	Self	—	—
TM85	Dream Eater	Psychic	Special	100	100	15	Normal	—	—
TM86	Grass Knot	Grass	Special	—	100	20	Normal	—	○
TM87	Swagger	Normal	Status	—	90	15	Normal	—	—
TM90	Substitute	Normal	Status	—	—	10	Self	—	—
TM92	Trick Room	Psychic	Status	—	—	5	Both Sides	—	—
TM94	Rock Smash	Fighting	Physical	40	100	15	Normal	—	○
HM04	Strength	Normal	Physical	80	100	15	Normal	—	○

MOVES TAUGHT BY PEOPLE

Name	Type	Kind	Pow.	Acc.	PP	Range	Long	DA

MOVES TAUGHT BY MOVE TUTORS FOR SHARDS

Name	Type	Kind	Pow.	Acc.	PP	Range	Long	DA
Signal Beam	Bug	Special	75	100	15	Normal	—	—
Uproar	Normal	Special	90	100	10	1 Random	—	—
Magic Coat	Psychic	Status	—	—	15	Self	—	—
Hyper Voice	Normal	Special	90	100	10	Many Others	—	—
Iron Tail	Steel	Physical	100	75	15	Normal	—	○
Zen Headbutt	Psychic	Physical	80	90	15	Normal	—	○
Foul Play	Dark	Physical	95	100	15	Normal	—	○
Gravity	Psychic	Status	—	—	5	Both Sides	—	—
Snore	Normal	Special	40	100	15	Normal	—	—
Recycle	Normal	Status	—	—	10	Self	—	—
Trick	Psychic	Status	—	100	10	Normal	—	—
Sleep Talk	Normal	Status	—	—	10	Self	—	—
Skill Swap	Psychic	Status	—	—	10	Normal	—	—

EGG MOVES

Name	Type	Kind	Pow.	Acc.	PP	Range	Long	DA
Take Down	Normal	Physical	90	85	20	Normal	—	○
Amnesia	Psychic	Status	—	—	20	Self	—	—
Foresight	Normal	Status	—	—	40	Normal	—	—
Future Sight	Psychic	Special	100	100	10	Normal	—	—
Beat Up	Dark	Physical	—	100	10	Normal	—	—
Wish	Normal	Status	—	—	10	Self	—	—
Magic Coat	Psychic	Status	—	—	15	Self	—	—
Double Kick	Fighting	Physical	30	100	30	Normal	—	○
Mirror Coat	Psychic	Special	—	100	20	Varies	—	—
Razor Wind	Normal	Special	80	100	10	Many Others	—	—
Skill Swap	Psychic	Status	—	—	10	Normal	—	—
Secret Power	Normal	Physical	70	100	20	Normal	—	—
Mean Look	Normal	Status	—	—	5	Normal	—	—

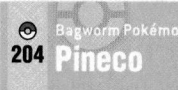

204 **Pineco**

Bagworm Pokémon

- HEIGHT: 2'00"
- WEIGHT: 15.9 lbs.
- GENDER: ♂ / ♀

It looks just like a pinecone. Its shell protects it from bird Pokémon that peck it by mistake.

Same form for ♂ / ♀

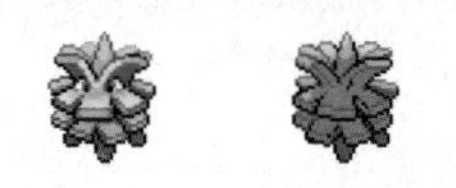

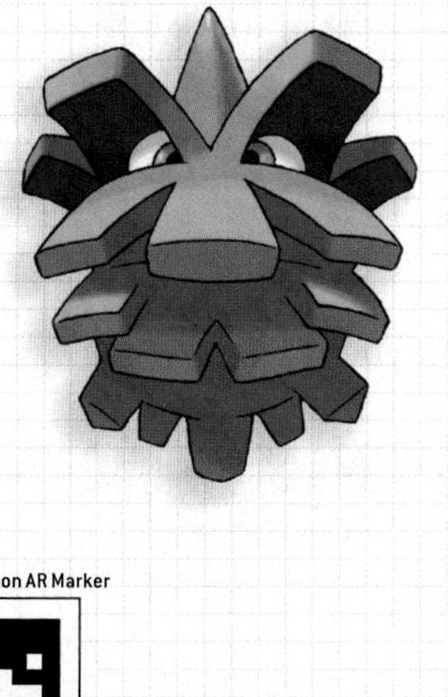

Pokémon AR Marker

TYPE: Bug

ABILITY

- Sturdy

HIDDEN ABILITY

—

STATS

HP
Attack
Defense
Sp. Atk
Sp. Def
Speed

EGG GROUPS

Bug

ITEMS SOMETIMES HELD

- None

EVOLUTION

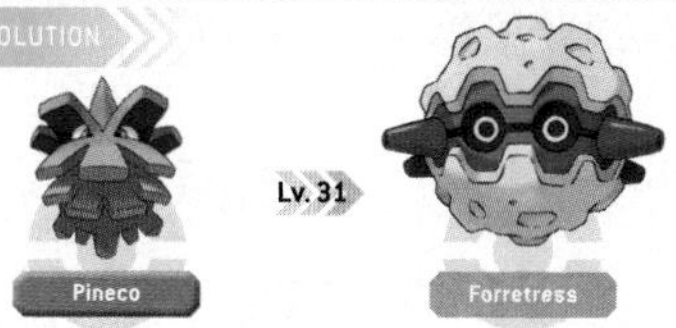

HOW TO OBTAIN

Pokémon Black Version 2	Route 16 (mass outbreak)
Pokémon White Version 2	Route 16 (mass outbreak)

HOW TO OBTAIN FROM OTHER GAMES

—

—

LEVEL-UP AND LEARNED MOVES

Lv.	Name	Type	Kind	Pow.	Acc.	PP	Range	Long	DA
1	Tackle	Normal	Physical	50	100	35	Normal	—	○
1	Protect	Normal	Status	—	—	10	Self	—	—
6	Selfdestruct	Normal	Physical	200	100	5	Adjacent	—	—
9	Bug Bite	Bug	Physical	60	100	20	Normal	—	○
12	Take Down	Normal	Physical	90	85	20	Normal	—	○
17	Rapid Spin	Normal	Physical	20	100	40	Normal	—	○
20	Bide	Normal	Physical	—	—	10	Self	—	○
23	Natural Gift	Normal	Physical	—	100	15	Normal	—	—
28	Spikes	Ground	Status	—	—	20	Other Side	—	—
31	Payback	Dark	Physical	50	100	10	Normal	—	○
34	Explosion	Normal	Physical	250	100	5	Adjacent	—	—
39	Iron Defense	Steel	Status	—	—	15	Self	—	—
42	Gyro Ball	Steel	Physical	—	100	5	Normal	—	○
45	Double-Edge	Normal	Physical	120	100	15	Normal	—	○

TM & HM MOVES

Lv.	Name	Type	Kind	Pow.	Acc.	PP	Range	Long	DA
TM06	Toxic	Poison	Status	—	90	10	Normal	—	—
TM09	Venoshock	Poison	Special	65	100	10	Normal	—	—
TM10	Hidden Power	Normal	Special	—	100	15	Normal	—	—
TM11	Sunny Day	Fire	Status	—	—	5	Both Sides	—	—
TM16	Light Screen	Psychic	Status	—	—	30	Your Side	—	—
TM17	Protect	Normal	Status	—	—	10	Self	—	—
TM21	Frustration	Normal	Physical	—	100	20	Normal	—	○
TM22	SolarBeam	Grass	Special	120	100	10	Normal	—	—
TM26	Earthquake	Ground	Physical	100	100	10	Adjacent	—	—
TM27	Return	Normal	Physical	—	100	20	Normal	—	○
TM28	Dig	Ground	Physical	80	100	10	Normal	—	○
TM32	Double Team	Normal	Status	—	—	15	Self	—	—
TM33	Reflect	Psychic	Status	—	—	20	Your Side	—	—
TM37	Sandstorm	Rock	Status	—	—	10	Both Sides	—	—
TM39	Rock Tomb	Rock	Physical	50	80	10	Normal	—	—
TM42	Facade	Normal	Physical	70	100	20	Normal	—	○
TM44	Rest	Psychic	Status	—	—	10	Self	—	—
TM45	Attract	Normal	Status	—	100	15	Normal	—	—
TM48	Round	Normal	Special	60	100	15	Normal	—	—
TM64	Explosion	Normal	Physical	250	100	5	Adjacent	—	—
TM66	Payback	Dark	Physical	50	100	10	Normal	—	○
TM74	Gyro Ball	Steel	Physical	—	100	5	Normal	—	○
TM76	Struggle Bug	Bug	Special	30	100	20	Many Others	—	—
TM78	Bulldoze	Ground	Physical	60	100	20	Adjacent	—	—
TM80	Rock Slide	Rock	Physical	75	90	10	Many Others	—	—
TM87	Swagger	Normal	Status	—	90	15	Normal	—	—
TM90	Substitute	Normal	Status	—	—	10	Self	—	—
TM94	Rock Smash	Fighting	Physical	40	100	15	Normal	—	○
HM04	Strength	Normal	Physical	80	100	15	Normal	—	○

MOVES TAUGHT BY PEOPLE

Name	Type	Kind	Pow.	Acc.	PP	Range	Long	DA

MOVES TAUGHT BY MOVE TUTORS FOR SHARDS

Name	Type	Kind	Pow.	Acc.	PP	Range	Long	DA
Bug Bite	Bug	Physical	60	100	20	Normal	—	○
Drill Run	Ground	Physical	80	95	10	Normal	—	○
Iron Defense	Steel	Status	—	—	15	Self	—	—
Gravity	Psychic	Status	—	—	5	Both Sides	—	—
Snore	Normal	Special	40	100	15	Normal	—	—
Giga Drain	Grass	Special	75	100	10	Normal	—	—
Pain Split	Normal	Status	—	—	20	Normal	—	—
Stealth Rock	Rock	Status	—	—	20	Other Side	—	—
Sleep Talk	Normal	Status	—	—	10	Self	—	—

EGG MOVES

Name	Type	Kind	Pow.	Acc.	PP	Range	Long	DA
Pin Missile	Bug	Physical	14	85	20	Normal	—	—
Flail	Normal	Physical	—	100	15	Normal	—	○
Swift	Normal	Special	60	—	20	Many Others	—	—
Counter	Fighting	Physical	—	100	20	Varies	—	○
Sand Tomb	Ground	Physical	35	85	15	Normal	—	—
Revenge	Fighting	Physical	60	100	10	Normal	—	○
Double-Edge	Normal	Physical	120	100	15	Normal	—	○
Toxic Spikes	Poison	Status	—	—	20	Other Side	—	—
Power Trick	Psychic	Status	—	—	10	Self	—	—
Endure	Normal	Status	—	—	10	Self	—	—
Stealth Rock	Rock	Status	—	—	20	Other Side	—	—

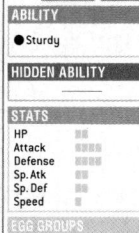

205 Forretress

205 Forretress

Bagworm Pokémon

- HEIGHT: 3'11"
- WEIGHT: 277.3 lbs.
- GENDER: ♂ / ♀

It is encased in a steel shell. Its peering eyes are all that can be seen of its mysterious innards.

Same form for ♂ / ♀

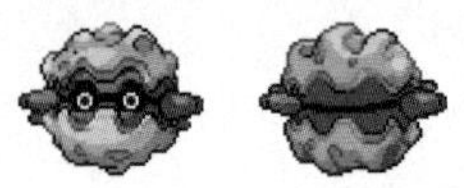

TYPE: Bug / Steel

ABILITY
- Sturdy

HIDDEN ABILITY
—

STATS
HP
Attack
Defense
Sp. Atk
Sp. Def
Speed

EGG GROUPS
Bug

ITEMS SOMETIMES HELD
- None

EVOLUTION

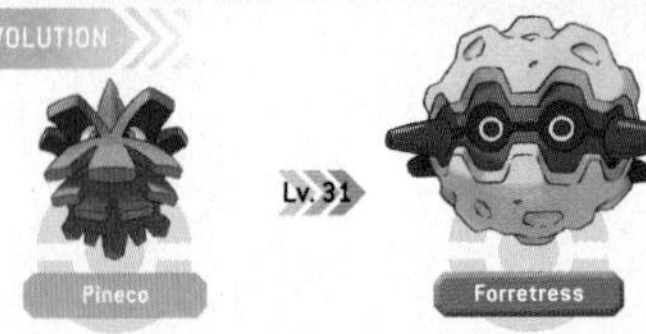

HOW TO OBTAIN

Pokémon Black Version 2	Level up Pineco to Lv. 31
Pokémon White Version 2	Level up Pineco to Lv. 31

HOW TO OBTAIN FROM OTHER GAMES

—

—

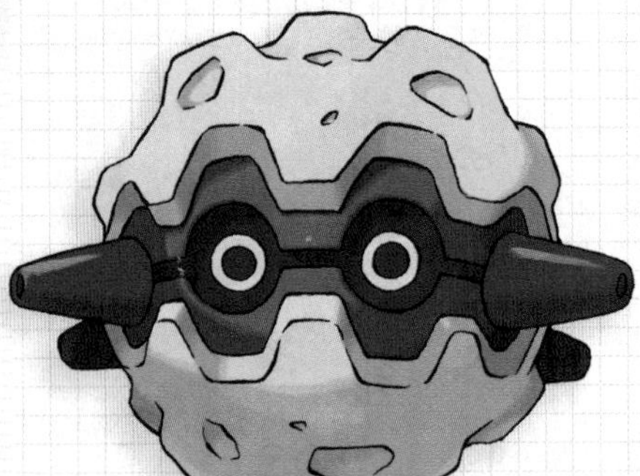

Pokémon AR Marker

LEVEL-UP AND LEARNED MOVES

Lv.	Name	Type	Kind	Pow.	Acc.	PP	Range	Long	DA
1	Toxic Spikes	Poison	Status	—	—	20	Other Side	—	—
1	Tackle	Normal	Physical	50	100	35	Normal	—	○
1	Protect	Normal	Status	—	—	10	Self	—	—
1	Selfdestruct	Normal	Physical	200	100	5	Adjacent	—	—
1	Bug Bite	Bug	Physical	60	100	20	Normal	—	○
6	Selfdestruct	Normal	Physical	200	100	5	Adjacent	—	—
9	Bug Bite	Bug	Physical	60	100	20	Normal	—	○
12	Take Down	Normal	Physical	90	85	20	Normal	—	○
17	Rapid Spin	Normal	Physical	20	100	40	Normal	—	○
20	Bide	Normal	Physical	—	—	10	Self	—	○
23	Natural Gift	Normal	Physical	—	100	15	Normal	—	—
28	Spikes	Ground	Status	—	—	20	Other Side	—	—
31	Mirror Shot	Steel	Special	65	85	10	Normal	—	—
32	Autotomize	Steel	Status	—	—	15	Self	—	—
36	Payback	Dark	Physical	50	100	10	Normal	—	○
42	Explosion	Normal	Physical	250	100	5	Adjacent	—	—
46	Iron Defense	Steel	Status	—	—	15	Self	—	—
50	Gyro Ball	Steel	Physical	—	100	5	Normal	—	○
56	Double-Edge	Normal	Physical	120	100	15	Normal	—	○
60	Magnet Rise	Electric	Status	—	—	10	Self	—	—
64	Zap Cannon	Electric	Special	120	50	5	Normal	—	—
70	Heavy Slam	Steel	Physical	—	100	10	Normal	—	○

TM & HM MOVES

Lv.	Name	Type	Kind	Pow.	Acc.	PP	Range	Long	DA
TM06	Toxic	Poison	Status	—	90	10	Normal	—	—
TM09	Venoshock	Poison	Special	65	100	10	Normal	—	—
TM10	Hidden Power	Normal	Special	—	100	15	Normal	—	—
TM11	Sunny Day	Fire	Status	—	—	5	Both Sides	—	—
TM15	Hyper Beam	Normal	Special	150	90	5	Normal	—	—
TM16	Light Screen	Psychic	Status	—	—	30	Your Side	—	—
TM17	Protect	Normal	Status	—	—	10	Self	—	—
TM21	Frustration	Normal	Physical	—	100	20	Normal	—	○
TM22	SolarBeam	Grass	Special	120	100	10	Normal	—	—
TM26	Earthquake	Ground	Physical	100	100	10	Adjacent	—	—
TM27	Return	Normal	Physical	—	100	20	Normal	—	○
TM28	Dig	Ground	Physical	80	100	10	Normal	—	○
TM32	Double Team	Normal	Status	—	—	15	Self	—	—
TM33	Reflect	Psychic	Status	—	—	20	Your Side	—	—
TM37	Sandstorm	Rock	Status	—	—	10	Both Sides	—	—
TM39	Rock Tomb	Rock	Physical	50	80	10	Normal	—	—
TM42	Facade	Normal	Physical	70	100	20	Normal	—	○
TM44	Rest	Psychic	Status	—	—	10	Self	—	—
TM45	Attract	Normal	Status	—	100	15	Normal	—	—
TM48	Round	Normal	Special	60	100	15	Normal	—	—
TM64	Explosion	Normal	Physical	250	100	5	Adjacent	—	—
TM66	Payback	Dark	Physical	50	100	10	Normal	—	○
TM68	Giga Impact	Normal	Physical	150	90	5	Normal	—	○
TM69	Rock Polish	Rock	Status	—	—	20	Self	—	—
TM72	Volt Switch	Electric	Special	70	100	20	Normal	—	—
TM74	Gyro Ball	Steel	Physical	—	100	5	Normal	—	○
TM76	Struggle Bug	Bug	Special	30	100	20	Many Others	—	—
TM78	Bulldoze	Ground	Physical	60	100	20	Adjacent	—	—
TM80	Rock Slide	Rock	Physical	75	90	10	Many Others	—	—
TM87	Swagger	Normal	Status	—	90	15	Normal	—	—
TM90	Substitute	Normal	Status	—	—	10	Self	—	—
TM91	Flash Cannon	Steel	Special	80	100	10	Normal	—	—
TM94	Rock Smash	Fighting	Physical	40	100	15	Normal	—	○
HM04	Strength	Normal	Physical	80	100	15	Normal	—	○

MOVES TAUGHT BY PEOPLE

Name	Type	Kind	Pow.	Acc.	PP	Range	Long	DA

MOVES TAUGHT BY MOVE TUTORS FOR SHARDS

Name	Type	Kind	Pow.	Acc.	PP	Range	Long	DA
Bug Bite	Bug	Physical	60	100	20	Normal	—	○
Drill Run	Ground	Physical	80	95	10	Normal	—	○
Signal Beam	Bug	Special	75	100	15	Normal	—	—
Iron Defense	Steel	Status	—	—	15	Self	—	—
Magnet Rise	Electric	Status	—	—	10	Self	—	—
Block	Normal	Status	—	—	5	Normal	—	—
Gravity	Psychic	Status	—	—	5	Both Sides	—	—
Snore	Normal	Special	40	100	15	Normal	—	—
Giga Drain	Grass	Special	75	100	10	Normal	—	—
Pain Split	Normal	Status	—	—	20	Normal	—	—
Stealth Rock	Rock	Status	—	—	20	Other Side	—	—
Sleep Talk	Normal	Status	—	—	10	Self	—	—

206 Dunsparce

206 Dunsparce

Land Snake Pokémon

- HEIGHT: 4'11"
- WEIGHT: 30.9 lbs.
- GENDER: ♂ / ♀

It creates mazes in dark locations. When spotted, it flees into the ground by digging with its tail.

Same form for ♂ / ♀

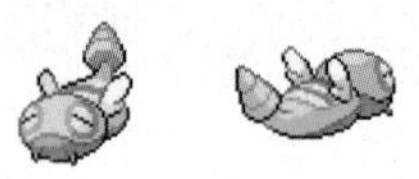

TYPE: Normal

ABILITIES
- Serene Grace
- Run Away

HIDDEN ABILITY
- Rattled

STATS
HP
Attack
Defense
Sp. Atk
Sp. Def
Speed

EGG GROUPS
Field

ITEMS SOMETIMES HELD
- None

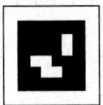

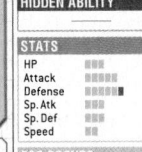

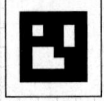

EVOLUTION

Does not evolve

HOW TO OBTAIN

Pokémon Black Version 2	❶ Route 20 (rustling grass) ❷ Floccesy Ranch (rustling grass)
Pokémon White Version 2	❶ Route 20 (rustling grass) ❷ Floccesy Ranch (rustling grass)

HOW TO OBTAIN FROM OTHER GAMES

—

—

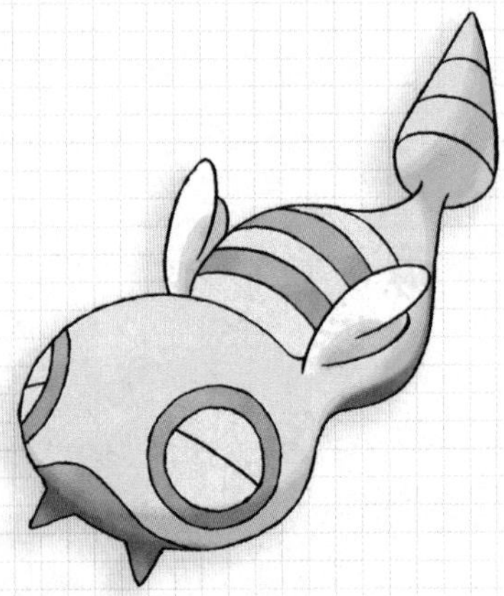

Pokémon AR Marker

LEVEL-UP AND LEARNED MOVES

Lv.	Name	Type	Kind	Pow.	Acc.	PP	Range	Long	DA
1	Rage	Normal	Physical	20	100	20	Normal	—	○
1	Defense Curl	Normal	Status	—	—	40	Self	—	—
4	Rollout	Rock	Physical	30	90	20	Normal	—	○
7	Spite	Ghost	Status	—	100	10	Normal	—	—
10	Pursuit	Dark	Physical	40	100	20	Normal	—	○
13	Screech	Normal	Status	—	85	40	Normal	—	—
16	Yawn	Normal	Status	—	—	10	Normal	—	—
19	AncientPower	Rock	Special	60	100	5	Normal	—	—
22	Take Down	Normal	Physical	90	85	20	Normal	—	○
25	Roost	Flying	Status	—	—	10	Self	—	—
28	Glare	Normal	Status	—	90	30	Normal	—	—
31	Dig	Ground	Physical	80	100	10	Normal	—	○
34	Double-Edge	Normal	Physical	120	100	15	Normal	—	○
37	Coil	Poison	Status	—	—	20	Self	—	—
40	Endure	Normal	Status	—	—	10	Self	—	—
43	Drill Run	Ground	Physical	80	95	10	Normal	—	○
46	Endeavor	Normal	Physical	—	100	5	Normal	—	○
49	Flail	Normal	Physical	—	100	15	Normal	—	○

TM & HM MOVES

Lv.	Name	Type	Kind	Pow.	Acc.	PP	Range	Long	DA
TM04	Calm Mind	Psychic	Status	—	—	20	Self	—	—
TM06	Toxic	Poison	Status	—	90	10	Normal	—	—
TM10	Hidden Power	Normal	Special	—	100	15	Normal	—	—
TM11	Sunny Day	Fire	Status	—	—	5	Both Sides	—	—
TM13	Ice Beam	Ice	Special	95	100	10	Normal	—	—
TM14	Blizzard	Ice	Special	120	70	5	Many Others	—	—
TM17	Protect	Normal	Status	—	—	10	Self	—	—
TM18	Rain Dance	Water	Status	—	—	5	Both Sides	—	—
TM21	Frustration	Normal	Physical	—	100	20	Normal	—	○
TM22	SolarBeam	Grass	Special	120	100	10	Normal	—	—
TM24	Thunderbolt	Electric	Special	95	100	15	Normal	—	—
TM25	Thunder	Electric	Special	120	70	10	Normal	—	—
TM26	Earthquake	Ground	Physical	100	100	10	Adjacent	—	—
TM27	Return	Normal	Physical	—	100	20	Normal	—	○
TM28	Dig	Ground	Physical	80	100	10	Normal	—	○
TM30	Shadow Ball	Ghost	Special	80	100	15	Normal	—	—
TM32	Double Team	Normal	Status	—	—	15	Self	—	—
TM35	Flamethrower	Fire	Special	95	100	15	Normal	—	—
TM38	Fire Blast	Fire	Special	120	85	5	Normal	—	—
TM39	Rock Tomb	Rock	Physical	50	80	10	Normal	—	—
TM42	Facade	Normal	Physical	70	100	20	Normal	—	○
TM44	Rest	Psychic	Status	—	—	10	Self	—	—
TM45	Attract	Normal	Status	—	100	15	Normal	—	—
TM46	Thief	Dark	Physical	40	100	10	Normal	—	○
TM48	Round	Normal	Special	60	100	15	Normal	—	—
TM57	Charge Beam	Electric	Special	50	90	10	Normal	—	—
TM59	Incinerate	Fire	Special	30	100	15	Many Others	—	—
TM67	Retaliate	Normal	Physical	70	100	5	Normal	—	○
TM73	Thunder Wave	Electric	Status	—	100	20	Normal	—	—
TM74	Gyro Ball	Steel	Physical	—	100	5	Normal	—	○
TM77	Psych Up	Normal	Status	—	—	10	Normal	—	—
TM78	Bulldoze	Ground	Physical	60	100	20	Adjacent	—	—
TM80	Rock Slide	Rock	Physical	75	90	10	Many Others	—	—
TM84	Poison Jab	Poison	Physical	80	100	20	Normal	—	○
TM85	Dream Eater	Psychic	Special	100	100	15	Normal	—	—
TM87	Swagger	Normal	Status	—	90	15	Normal	—	—
TM90	Substitute	Normal	Status	—	—	10	Self	—	—
TM93	Wild Charge	Electric	Physical	90	100	15	Normal	—	○
TM94	Rock Smash	Fighting	Physical	40	100	15	Normal	—	○
HM04	Strength	Normal	Physical	80	100	15	Normal	—	○

MOVES TAUGHT BY PEOPLE

Name	Type	Kind	Pow.	Acc.	PP	Range	Long	DA

MOVES TAUGHT BY MOVE TUTORS FOR SHARDS

Name	Type	Kind	Pow.	Acc.	PP	Range	Long	DA
Drill Run	Ground	Physical	80	95	10	Normal	—	○
Last Resort	Normal	Physical	140	100	5	Normal	—	○
Magic Coat	Psychic	Status	—	—	15	Self	—	—
Iron Tail	Steel	Physical	100	75	15	Normal	—	○
Aqua Tail	Water	Physical	90	90	10	Normal	—	○
Zen Headbutt	Psychic	Physical	80	90	15	Normal	—	○
Bind	Normal	Physical	15	85	20	Normal	—	○
Snore	Normal	Special	40	100	15	Normal	—	—
Roost	Flying	Status	—	—	10	Self	—	—
Pain Split	Normal	Status	—	—	20	Normal	—	—
Spite	Ghost	Status	—	100	10	Normal	—	—
Stealth Rock	Rock	Status	—	—	20	Other Side	—	—
Endeavor	Normal	Physical	—	100	5	Normal	—	○
Sleep Talk	Normal	Status	—	—	10	Self	—	—

EGG MOVES

Name	Type	Kind	Pow.	Acc.	PP	Range	Long	DA
Bide	Normal	Physical	—	—	10	Self	—	○
AncientPower	Rock	Special	60	100	5	Normal	—	—
Bite	Dark	Physical	60	100	25	Normal	—	○
Headbutt	Normal	Physical	70	100	15	Normal	—	○
Astonish	Ghost	Physical	30	100	15	Normal	—	○
Curse	Ghost	Status	—	—	10	Varies	—	—
Trump Card	Normal	Special	—	—	5	Normal	—	○
Magic Coat	Psychic	Status	—	—	15	Self	—	—
Snore	Normal	Special	40	100	15	Normal	—	—
Agility	Psychic	Status	—	—	30	Self	—	—
Secret Power	Normal	Physical	70	100	20	Normal	—	—
Sleep Talk	Normal	Status	—	—	10	Self	—	—
Hex	Ghost	Special	50	100	10	Normal	—	—

207 **Gligar**

FlyScorpion Pokémon

- HEIGHT: 3'07"
- WEIGHT: 142.9 lbs.
- GENDER: ♂ / ♀

It clamps on to its chosen prey then jabs the stinger on its tail into the prey while it's stunned with surprise.

♂ ♀

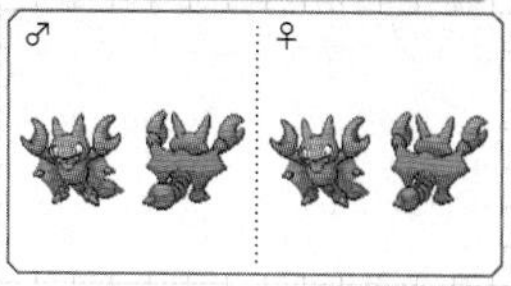

TYPE Ground Flying

ABILITIES
- Hyper Cutter
- Sand Veil

HIDDEN ABILITY
- Immunity

STATS
HP
Attack
Defense
Sp. Atk
Sp. Def
Speed

EGG GROUPS
Bug

ITEMS SOMETIMES HELD
- None

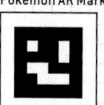

EVOLUTION

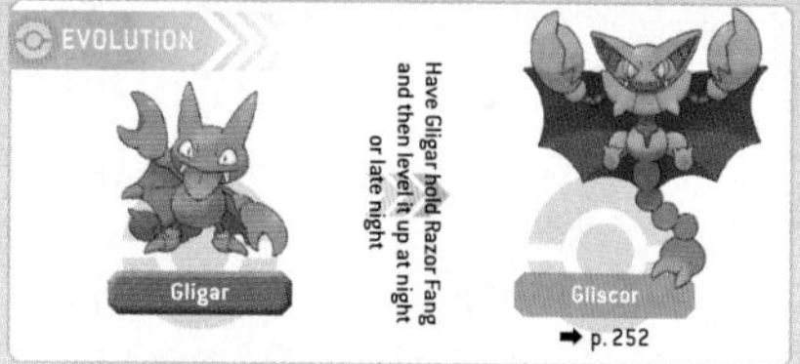

Gligar
Have Gligar hold Razor Fang and then level it up at night or late night
Gliscor

➡ p. 252

HOW TO OBTAIN

Pokémon Black Version 2	❶ Route 11 ❷ Route 23
Pokémon White Version 2	❶ Route 11 ❷ Route 23

HOW TO OBTAIN FROM OTHER GAMES

—

—

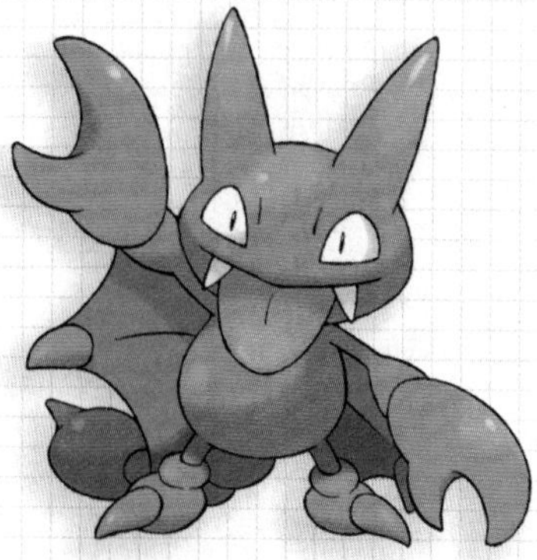

Pokémon AR Marker

LEVEL-UP AND LEARNED MOVES

Lv.	Name	Type	Kind	Pow.	Acc.	PP	Range	Long	DA
1	Poison Sting	Poison	Physical	15	100	35	Normal	—	—
4	Sand-Attack	Ground	Status	—	100	15	Normal	—	—
7	Harden	Normal	Status	—	—	30	Self	—	—
10	Knock Off	Dark	Physical	20	100	20	Normal	—	○
13	Quick Attack	Normal	Physical	40	100	30	Normal	—	○
16	Fury Cutter	Bug	Physical	20	95	20	Normal	—	○
19	Faint Attack	Dark	Physical	60	—	20	Normal	—	○
22	Acrobatics	Flying	Physical	55	100	15	Normal	○	○
27	Slash	Normal	Physical	70	100	20	Normal	—	○
30	U-turn	Bug	Physical	70	100	20	Normal	—	○
35	Screech	Normal	Status	—	85	40	Normal	—	—
40	X-Scissor	Bug	Physical	80	100	15	Normal	—	○
45	Sky Uppercut	Fighting	Physical	85	90	15	Normal	—	○
50	Swords Dance	Normal	Status	—	—	30	Self	—	—
55	Guillotine	Normal	Physical	—	30	5	Normal	—	○

TM & HM MOVES

Lv.	Name	Type	Kind	Pow.	Acc.	PP	Range	Long	DA
TM01	Hone Claws	Dark	Status	—	—	15	Self	—	—
TM06	Toxic	Poison	Status	—	90	10	Normal	—	—
TM09	Venoshock	Poison	Special	65	100	10	Normal	—	—
TM10	Hidden Power	Normal	Special	—	100	15	Normal	—	—
TM11	Sunny Day	Fire	Status	—	—	5	Both Sides	—	—
TM12	Taunt	Dark	Status	—	100	20	Normal	—	—
TM17	Protect	Normal	Status	—	—	10	Self	—	—
TM18	Rain Dance	Water	Status	—	—	5	Both Sides	—	—
TM21	Frustration	Normal	Physical	—	100	20	Normal	—	○
TM26	Earthquake	Ground	Physical	100	100	10	Adjacent	—	—
TM27	Return	Normal	Physical	—	100	20	Normal	—	○
TM28	Dig	Ground	Physical	80	100	10	Normal	—	○
TM31	Brick Break	Fighting	Physical	75	100	15	Normal	—	○
TM32	Double Team	Normal	Status	—	—	15	Self	—	—
TM36	Sludge Bomb	Poison	Special	90	100	10	Normal	—	—
TM37	Sandstorm	Rock	Status	—	—	10	Both Sides	—	—
TM39	Rock Tomb	Rock	Physical	50	80	10	Normal	—	—
TM40	Aerial Ace	Flying	Physical	60	—	20	Normal	○	○
TM41	Torment	Dark	Status	—	100	15	Normal	—	—
TM42	Facade	Normal	Physical	70	100	20	Normal	—	○
TM44	Rest	Psychic	Status	—	—	10	Self	—	—
TM45	Attract	Normal	Status	—	100	15	Normal	—	—
TM46	Thief	Dark	Physical	40	100	10	Normal	—	○
TM48	Round	Normal	Special	60	100	15	Normal	—	—
TM54	False Swipe	Normal	Physical	40	100	40	Normal	—	○
TM56	Fling	Dark	Physical	—	100	10	Normal	—	—
TM62	Acrobatics	Flying	Physical	55	100	15	Normal	○	○
TM66	Payback	Dark	Physical	50	100	10	Normal	—	○
TM69	Rock Polish	Rock	Status	—	—	20	Self	—	—
TM71	Stone Edge	Rock	Physical	100	80	5	Normal	—	—
TM75	Swords Dance	Normal	Status	—	—	30	Self	—	—
TM76	Struggle Bug	Bug	Special	30	100	20	Many Others	—	—
TM78	Bulldoze	Ground	Physical	60	100	20	Adjacent	—	—
TM80	Rock Slide	Rock	Physical	75	90	10	Many Others	—	—
TM81	X-Scissor	Bug	Physical	80	100	15	Normal	—	○
TM84	Poison Jab	Poison	Physical	80	100	20	Normal	—	○
TM87	Swagger	Normal	Status	—	90	15	Normal	—	—
TM89	U-turn	Bug	Physical	70	100	20	Normal	—	○
TM90	Substitute	Normal	Status	—	—	10	Self	—	—
TM94	Rock Smash	Fighting	Physical	40	100	15	Normal	—	○
HM01	Cut	Normal	Physical	50	95	30	Normal	—	○
HM04	Strength	Normal	Physical	80	100	15	Normal	—	○

MOVES TAUGHT BY PEOPLE

Name	Type	Kind	Pow.	Acc.	PP	Range	Long	DA

MOVES TAUGHT BY MOVE TUTORS FOR SHARDS

Name	Type	Kind	Pow.	Acc.	PP	Range	Long	DA
Bug Bite	Bug	Physical	60	100	20	Normal	—	○
Iron Tail	Steel	Physical	100	75	15	Normal	—	○
Aqua Tail	Water	Physical	90	90	10	Normal	—	○
Earth Power	Ground	Special	90	100	10	Normal	—	—
Dark Pulse	Dark	Special	80	100	15	Normal	○	—
Snore	Normal	Special	40	100	15	Normal	—	—
Knock Off	Dark	Physical	20	100	20	Normal	—	○
Roost	Flying	Status	—	—	10	Self	—	—
Tailwind	Flying	Status	—	—	30	Your Side	—	—
Stealth Rock	Rock	Status	—	—	20	Other Side	—	—
Sleep Talk	Normal	Status	—	—	10	Self	—	—

EGG MOVES

Name	Type	Kind	Pow.	Acc.	PP	Range	Long	DA
Metal Claw	Steel	Physical	50	95	35	Normal	—	○
Wing Attack	Flying	Physical	60	100	35	Normal	○	○
Razor Wind	Normal	Special	80	100	10	Many Others	—	—
Counter	Fighting	Physical	—	100	20	Varies	—	○
Sand Tomb	Ground	Physical	35	85	15	Normal	—	—
Agility	Psychic	Status	—	—	30	Self	—	—
Baton Pass	Normal	Status	—	—	40	Self	—	—
Double-Edge	Normal	Physical	120	100	15	Normal	—	○
Feint	Normal	Physical	30	100	10	Normal	—	—
Night Slash	Dark	Physical	70	100	15	Normal	—	○
Cross Poison	Poison	Physical	70	100	20	Normal	—	○
Power Trick	Psychic	Status	—	—	10	Self	—	—
Rock Climb	Normal	Physical	90	85	20	Normal	—	○
Poison Tail	Poison	Physical	50	100	25	Normal	—	○

208 **Steelix**

Iron Snake Pokémon

- HEIGHT: 30'02"
- WEIGHT: 881.8 lbs.
- GENDER: ♂ / ♀

The iron it ingested with the soil it swallowed transformed its body and made it harder than diamonds.

♂ ♀

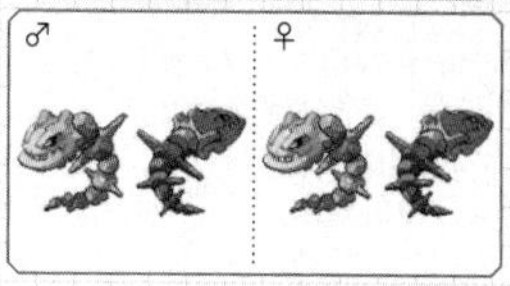

TYPE Steel Ground

ABILITIES
- Rock Head
- Sturdy

HIDDEN ABILITY
- Sheer Force

STATS
HP
Attack
Defense
Sp. Atk
Sp. Def
Speed

EGG GROUPS
Mineral

ITEMS SOMETIMES HELD
- Metal Coat

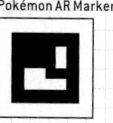

EVOLUTION

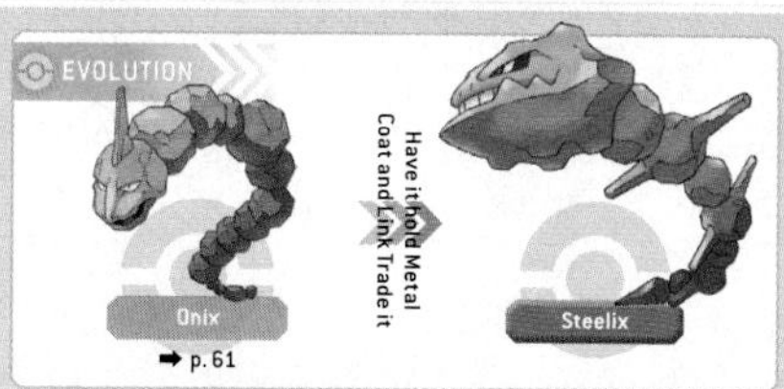

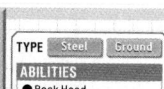

Onix
Have it hold Metal Coat and Link Trade it
Steelix

➡ p. 61

HOW TO OBTAIN

Pokémon Black Version 2	❶ Clay Tunnel (dust cloud) ❷ Twist Mountain (dust cloud)
Pokémon White Version 2	❶ Clay Tunnel (dust cloud) ❷ Twist Mountain (dust cloud)

HOW TO OBTAIN FROM OTHER GAMES

—

—

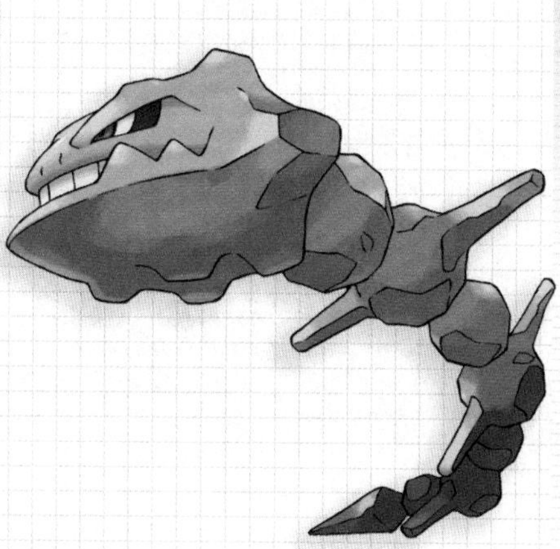

Pokémon AR Marker

LEVEL-UP AND LEARNED MOVES

Lv.	Name	Type	Kind	Pow.	Acc.	PP	Range	Long	DA
1	Thunder Fang	Electric	Physical	65	95	15	Normal	—	○
1	Ice Fang	Ice	Physical	65	95	15	Normal	—	○
1	Fire Fang	Fire	Physical	65	95	15	Normal	—	○
1	Mud Sport	Ground	Status	—	—	15	Both Sides	—	—
1	Tackle	Normal	Physical	50	100	35	Normal	—	○
1	Harden	Normal	Status	—	—	30	Self	—	—
1	Bind	Normal	Physical	15	85	20	Normal	—	○
4	Curse	Ghost	Status	—	—	10	Varies	—	—
7	Rock Throw	Rock	Physical	50	90	15	Normal	—	—
10	Rage	Normal	Physical	20	100	20	Normal	—	○
13	Rock Tomb	Rock	Physical	50	80	10	Normal	—	—
16	Stealth Rock	Rock	Status	—	—	20	Other Side	—	—
19	Autotomize	Steel	Status	—	—	15	Self	—	—
22	Smack Down	Rock	Physical	50	100	15	Normal	—	—
25	DragonBreath	Dragon	Special	60	100	20	Normal	—	—
28	Slam	Normal	Physical	80	75	20	Normal	—	○
31	Screech	Normal	Status	—	85	40	Normal	—	—
34	Rock Slide	Rock	Physical	75	90	10	Many Others	—	—
37	Crunch	Dark	Physical	80	100	15	Normal	—	○
40	Iron Tail	Steel	Physical	100	75	15	Normal	—	○
43	Dig	Ground	Physical	80	100	10	Normal	—	○
46	Stone Edge	Rock	Physical	100	80	5	Normal	—	—
49	Double-Edge	Normal	Physical	120	100	15	Normal	—	○
52	Sandstorm	Rock	Status	—	—	10	Both Sides	—	—

TM & HM MOVES

Lv.	Name	Type	Kind	Pow.	Acc.	PP	Range	Long	DA
TM05	Roar	Normal	Status	—	100	20	Normal	—	—
TM06	Toxic	Poison	Status	—	90	10	Normal	—	—
TM10	Hidden Power	Normal	Special	—	100	15	Normal	—	—
TM11	Sunny Day	Fire	Status	—	—	5	Both Sides	—	—
TM12	Taunt	Dark	Status	—	100	20	Normal	—	—
TM15	Hyper Beam	Normal	Special	150	90	5	Normal	—	—
TM17	Protect	Normal	Status	—	—	10	Self	—	—
TM21	Frustration	Normal	Physical	—	100	20	Normal	—	○
TM23	Smack Down	Rock	Physical	50	100	15	Normal	—	—
TM26	Earthquake	Ground	Physical	100	100	10	Adjacent	—	—
TM27	Return	Normal	Physical	—	100	20	Normal	—	○
TM28	Dig	Ground	Physical	80	100	10	Normal	—	○
TM32	Double Team	Normal	Status	—	—	15	Self	—	—
TM37	Sandstorm	Rock	Status	—	—	10	Both Sides	—	—
TM39	Rock Tomb	Rock	Physical	50	80	10	Normal	—	—
TM41	Torment	Dark	Status	—	100	15	Normal	—	—
TM42	Facade	Normal	Physical	70	100	20	Normal	—	○
TM44	Rest	Psychic	Status	—	—	10	Self	—	—
TM45	Attract	Normal	Status	—	100	15	Normal	—	—
TM48	Round	Normal	Special	60	100	15	Normal	—	—
TM64	Explosion	Normal	Physical	250	100	5	Adjacent	—	—
TM66	Payback	Dark	Physical	50	100	10	Normal	—	○
TM68	Giga Impact	Normal	Physical	150	90	5	Normal	—	○
TM69	Rock Polish	Rock	Status	—	—	20	Self	—	—
TM71	Stone Edge	Rock	Physical	100	80	5	Normal	—	—
TM74	Gyro Ball	Steel	Physical	—	100	5	Normal	—	○
TM77	Psych Up	Normal	Status	—	—	10	Normal	—	—
TM78	Bulldoze	Ground	Physical	60	100	20	Adjacent	—	—
TM80	Rock Slide	Rock	Physical	75	90	10	Many Others	—	—
TM82	Dragon Tail	Dragon	Physical	60	90	10	Normal	—	○
TM87	Swagger	Normal	Status	—	90	15	Normal	—	—
TM90	Substitute	Normal	Status	—	—	10	Self	—	—
TM91	Flash Cannon	Steel	Special	80	100	10	Normal	—	—
TM94	Rock Smash	Fighting	Physical	40	100	15	Normal	—	○
HM01	Cut	Normal	Physical	50	95	30	Normal	—	○
HM04	Strength	Normal	Physical	80	100	15	Normal	—	○

MOVES TAUGHT BY PEOPLE

Name	Type	Kind	Pow.	Acc.	PP	Range	Long	DA

MOVES TAUGHT BY MOVE TUTORS FOR SHARDS

Name	Type	Kind	Pow.	Acc.	PP	Range	Long	DA
Iron Head	Steel	Physical	80	100	15	Normal	—	○
Magnet Rise	Electric	Status	—	—	10	Self	—	—
Block	Normal	Status	—	—	5	Normal	—	—
Iron Tail	Steel	Physical	100	75	15	Normal	—	○
Aqua Tail	Water	Physical	90	90	10	Normal	—	○
Earth Power	Ground	Special	90	100	10	Normal	—	—
Dragon Pulse	Dragon	Special	90	100	10	Normal	○	—
Dark Pulse	Dark	Special	80	100	15	Normal	○	—
Bind	Normal	Physical	15	85	20	Normal	—	○
Snore	Normal	Special	40	100	15	Normal	—	—
Stealth Rock	Rock	Status	—	—	20	Other Side	—	—
Sleep Talk	Normal	Status	—	—	10	Self	—	—

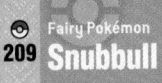

209 Snubbull

Fairy Pokémon

- HEIGHT: 2'00"
- WEIGHT: 17.2 lbs.
- GENDER: ♂ / ♀

Small Pokémon flee from its scary face. It is, however, considered by women to be cute.

Same form for ♂ / ♀

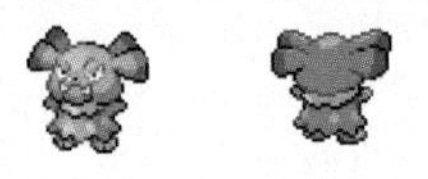

TYPE: Normal

ABILITIES
- Intimidate
- Run Away

HIDDEN ABILITY
- Rattled

STATS
HP
Attack
Defense
Sp. Atk
Sp. Def
Speed

EGG GROUPS
Field/Fairy

ITEMS SOMETIMES HELD
- None

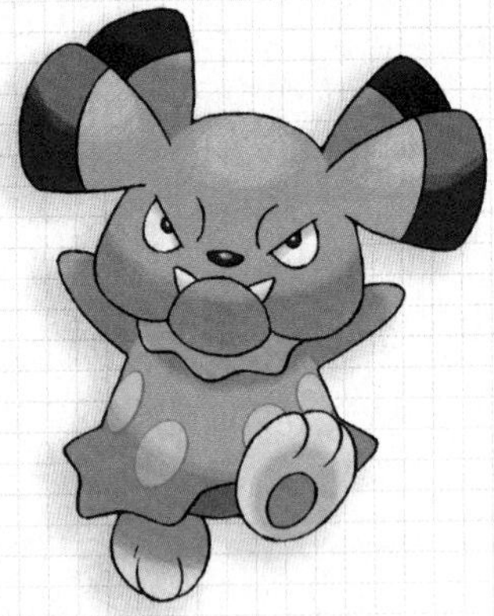

Pokémon AR Marker

EVOLUTION

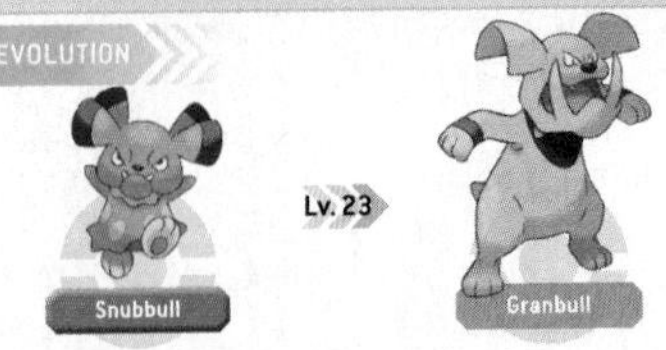

HOW TO OBTAIN

Pokémon Black Version 2	Catch a Granbull, leave it at the Pokémon Day Care, and hatch the Egg that is found
Pokémon White Version 2	Catch a Granbull, leave it at the Pokémon Day Care, and hatch the Egg that is found

HOW TO OBTAIN FROM OTHER GAMES

Pokémon HeartGold Version	Route 38
Pokémon SoulSilver Version	Route 38

LEVEL-UP AND LEARNED MOVES

Lv.	Name	Type	Kind	Pow.	Acc.	PP	Range	Long	DA
1	Ice Fang	Ice	Physical	65	95	15	Normal	—	○
1	Fire Fang	Fire	Physical	65	95	15	Normal	—	○
1	Thunder Fang	Electric	Physical	65	95	15	Normal	—	○
1	Tackle	Normal	Physical	50	100	35	Normal	—	○
1	Scary Face	Normal	Status	—	100	10	Normal	—	—
1	Tail Whip	Normal	Status	—	100	30	Many Others	—	—
1	Charm	Normal	Status	—	100	20	Normal	—	—
7	Bite	Dark	Physical	60	100	25	Normal	—	○
13	Lick	Ghost	Physical	20	100	30	Normal	—	○
19	Headbutt	Normal	Physical	70	100	15	Normal	—	○
25	Roar	Normal	Status	—	100	20	Normal	—	—
31	Rage	Normal	Physical	20	100	20	Normal	—	○
37	Take Down	Normal	Physical	90	85	20	Normal	—	○
43	Payback	Dark	Physical	50	100	10	Normal	—	○
49	Crunch	Dark	Physical	80	100	15	Normal	—	○

TM & HM MOVES

Lv.	Name	Type	Kind	Pow.	Acc.	PP	Range	Long	DA
TM05	Roar	Normal	Status	—	100	20	Normal	—	—
TM06	Toxic	Poison	Status	—	90	10	Normal	—	—
TM08	Bulk Up	Fighting	Status	—	—	20	Self	—	—
TM10	Hidden Power	Normal	Special	—	100	15	Normal	—	—
TM11	Sunny Day	Fire	Status	—	—	5	Both Sides	—	—
TM12	Taunt	Dark	Status	—	100	20	Normal	—	—
TM17	Protect	Normal	Status	—	—	10	Self	—	—
TM18	Rain Dance	Water	Status	—	—	5	Both Sides	—	—
TM21	Frustration	Normal	Physical	—	100	20	Normal	—	○
TM22	SolarBeam	Grass	Special	120	100	10	Normal	—	—
TM24	Thunderbolt	Electric	Special	95	100	15	Normal	—	—
TM25	Thunder	Electric	Special	120	70	10	Normal	—	—
TM26	Earthquake	Ground	Physical	100	100	10	Adjacent	—	—
TM27	Return	Normal	Physical	—	100	20	Normal	—	○
TM28	Dig	Ground	Physical	80	100	10	Normal	—	○
TM30	Shadow Ball	Ghost	Special	80	100	15	Normal	—	—
TM31	Brick Break	Fighting	Physical	75	100	15	Normal	—	○
TM32	Double Team	Normal	Status	—	—	15	Self	—	—
TM33	Reflect	Psychic	Status	—	—	20	Your Side	—	—
TM35	Flamethrower	Fire	Special	95	100	15	Normal	—	—
TM36	Sludge Bomb	Poison	Special	90	100	10	Normal	—	—
TM38	Fire Blast	Fire	Special	120	85	5	Normal	—	—
TM41	Torment	Dark	Status	—	100	15	Normal	—	—
TM42	Facade	Normal	Physical	70	100	20	Normal	—	○
TM44	Rest	Psychic	Status	—	—	10	Self	—	—
TM45	Attract	Normal	Status	—	100	15	Normal	—	—
TM46	Thief	Dark	Physical	40	100	10	Normal	—	○
TM48	Round	Normal	Special	60	100	15	Normal	—	—
TM50	Overheat	Fire	Special	140	90	5	Normal	—	—
TM56	Fling	Dark	Physical	—	100	10	Normal	—	—
TM59	Incinerate	Fire	Special	30	100	15	Many Others	—	—
TM66	Payback	Dark	Physical	50	100	10	Normal	—	○
TM67	Retaliate	Normal	Physical	70	100	5	Normal	—	○
TM73	Thunder Wave	Electric	Status	—	100	20	Normal	—	—
TM78	Bulldoze	Ground	Physical	60	100	20	Adjacent	—	—
TM83	Work Up	Normal	Status	—	—	30	Self	—	—
TM87	Swagger	Normal	Status	—	90	15	Normal	—	—
TM90	Substitute	Normal	Status	—	—	10	Self	—	—
TM93	Wild Charge	Electric	Physical	90	100	15	Normal	—	○
TM94	Rock Smash	Fighting	Physical	40	100	15	Normal	—	○
TM95	Snarl	Dark	Special	55	95	15	Many Others	—	—
HM04	Strength	Normal	Physical	80	100	15	Normal	—	○

MOVES TAUGHT BY PEOPLE

Name	Type	Kind	Pow.	Acc.	PP	Range	Long	DA

MOVES TAUGHT BY MOVE TUTORS FOR SHARDS

Name	Type	Kind	Pow.	Acc.	PP	Range	Long	DA
Covet	Normal	Physical	60	100	40	Normal	—	○
Super Fang	Normal	Physical	—	90	10	Normal	—	○
Low Kick	Fighting	Physical	—	100	20	Normal	—	○
Fire Punch	Fire	Physical	75	100	15	Normal	—	○
ThunderPunch	Electric	Physical	75	100	15	Normal	—	○
Ice Punch	Ice	Physical	75	100	15	Normal	—	○
Last Resort	Normal	Physical	140	100	5	Normal	—	○
Hyper Voice	Normal	Special	90	100	10	Many Others	—	—
Superpower	Fighting	Physical	120	100	5	Normal	—	○
Snore	Normal	Special	40	100	15	Normal	—	—
Heal Bell	Normal	Status	—	—	5	Your Party	—	—
Sleep Talk	Normal	Status	—	—	10	Self	—	—

EGG MOVES

Name	Type	Kind	Pow.	Acc.	PP	Range	Long	DA
Metronome	Normal	Status	—	—	10	Self	—	—
Faint Attack	Dark	Physical	60	—	20	Normal	—	○
Present	Normal	Physical	—	90	15	Normal	—	—
Crunch	Dark	Physical	80	100	15	Normal	—	○
Heal Bell	Normal	Status	—	—	5	Your Party	—	—
Snore	Normal	Special	40	100	15	Normal	—	—
SmellingSalt	Normal	Physical	60	100	10	Normal	—	○
Close Combat	Fighting	Physical	120	100	5	Normal	—	○
Ice Fang	Ice	Physical	65	95	15	Normal	—	○
Fire Fang	Fire	Physical	65	95	15	Normal	—	○
Thunder Fang	Electric	Physical	65	95	15	Normal	—	○
Focus Punch	Fighting	Physical	150	100	20	Normal	—	○
Double-Edge	Normal	Physical	120	100	15	Normal	—	○
Mimic	Normal	Status	—	—	10	Normal	—	—

210 Granbull

Fairy Pokémon

- HEIGHT: 4'07"
- WEIGHT: 107.4 lbs.
- GENDER: ♂ / ♀

It is timid in spite of its looks. If it becomes enraged, however, it will strike with its huge fangs.

Same form for ♂ / ♀

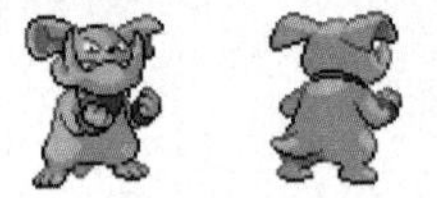

TYPE: Normal

ABILITIES
- Intimidate
- Quick Feet

HIDDEN ABILITY
- Rattled

STATS
HP
Attack
Defense
Sp. Atk
Sp. Def
Speed

EGG GROUPS
Field/Fairy

ITEMS SOMETIMES HELD
- None

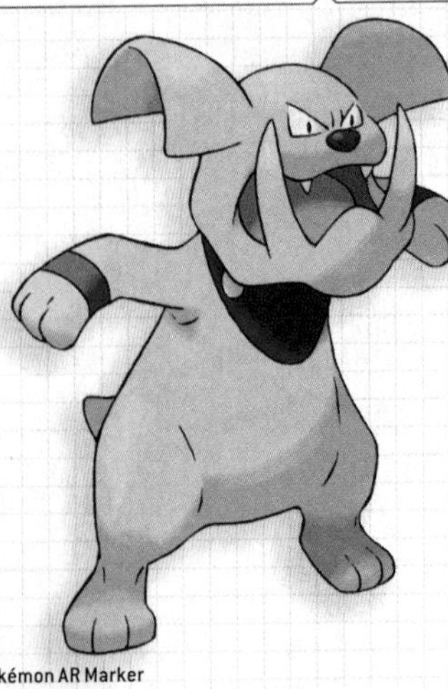

Pokémon AR Marker

EVOLUTION

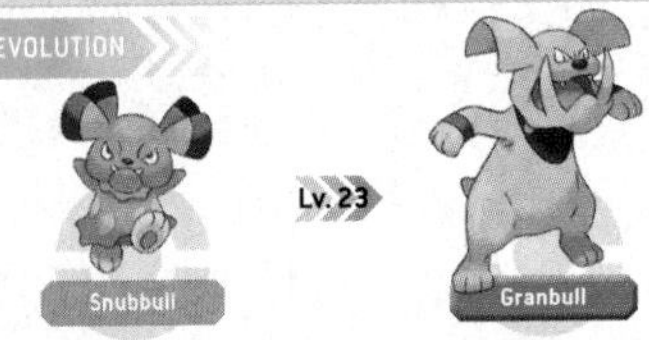

HOW TO OBTAIN

Pokémon Black Version 2	Route 2 (Hidden Grotto)
Pokémon White Version 2	Route 2 (Hidden Grotto)

HOW TO OBTAIN FROM OTHER GAMES

—
—

LEVEL-UP AND LEARNED MOVES

Lv.	Name	Type	Kind	Pow.	Acc.	PP	Range	Long	DA
1	Ice Fang	Ice	Physical	65	95	15	Normal	—	○
1	Fire Fang	Fire	Physical	65	95	15	Normal	—	○
1	Thunder Fang	Electric	Physical	65	95	15	Normal	—	○
1	Tackle	Normal	Physical	50	100	35	Normal	—	○
1	Scary Face	Normal	Status	—	100	10	Normal	—	—
1	Tail Whip	Normal	Status	—	100	30	Many Others	—	—
1	Charm	Normal	Status	—	100	20	Normal	—	—
7	Bite	Dark	Physical	60	100	25	Normal	—	○
13	Lick	Ghost	Physical	20	100	30	Normal	—	○
19	Headbutt	Normal	Physical	70	100	15	Normal	—	○
27	Roar	Normal	Status	—	100	20	Normal	—	—
35	Rage	Normal	Physical	20	100	20	Normal	—	○
43	Take Down	Normal	Physical	90	85	20	Normal	—	○
51	Payback	Dark	Physical	50	100	10	Normal	—	○
59	Crunch	Dark	Physical	80	100	15	Normal	—	○
67	Outrage	Dragon	Physical	120	100	10	1 Random	—	○

TM & HM MOVES

Lv.	Name	Type	Kind	Pow.	Acc.	PP	Range	Long	DA
TM05	Roar	Normal	Status	—	100	20	Normal	—	—
TM06	Toxic	Poison	Status	—	90	10	Normal	—	—
TM08	Bulk Up	Fighting	Status	—	—	20	Self	—	—
TM10	Hidden Power	Normal	Special	—	100	15	Normal	—	—
TM11	Sunny Day	Fire	Status	—	—	5	Both Sides	—	—
TM12	Taunt	Dark	Status	—	100	20	Normal	—	—
TM15	Hyper Beam	Normal	Special	150	90	5	Normal	—	—
TM17	Protect	Normal	Status	—	—	10	Self	—	—
TM18	Rain Dance	Water	Status	—	—	5	Both Sides	—	—
TM21	Frustration	Normal	Physical	—	100	20	Normal	—	○
TM22	SolarBeam	Grass	Special	120	100	10	Normal	—	—
TM24	Thunderbolt	Electric	Special	95	100	15	Normal	—	—
TM25	Thunder	Electric	Special	120	70	10	Normal	—	—
TM26	Earthquake	Ground	Physical	100	100	10	Adjacent	—	—
TM27	Return	Normal	Physical	—	100	20	Normal	—	○
TM28	Dig	Ground	Physical	80	100	10	Normal	—	○
TM30	Shadow Ball	Ghost	Special	80	100	15	Normal	—	—
TM31	Brick Break	Fighting	Physical	75	100	15	Normal	—	○
TM32	Double Team	Normal	Status	—	—	15	Self	—	—
TM33	Reflect	Psychic	Status	—	—	20	Your Side	—	—
TM35	Flamethrower	Fire	Special	95	100	15	Normal	—	—
TM36	Sludge Bomb	Poison	Special	90	100	10	Normal	—	—
TM38	Fire Blast	Fire	Special	120	85	5	Normal	—	—
TM39	Rock Tomb	Rock	Physical	50	80	10	Normal	—	—
TM41	Torment	Dark	Status	—	100	15	Normal	—	—
TM42	Facade	Normal	Physical	70	100	20	Normal	—	○
TM44	Rest	Psychic	Status	—	—	10	Self	—	—
TM45	Attract	Normal	Status	—	100	15	Normal	—	—
TM46	Thief	Dark	Physical	40	100	10	Normal	—	○
TM48	Round	Normal	Special	60	100	15	Normal	—	—
TM50	Overheat	Fire	Special	140	90	5	Normal	—	—
TM52	Focus Blast	Fighting	Special	120	70	5	Normal	—	—
TM56	Fling	Dark	Physical	—	100	10	Normal	—	—
TM59	Incinerate	Fire	Special	30	100	15	Many Others	—	—
TM66	Payback	Dark	Physical	50	100	10	Normal	—	○
TM67	Retaliate	Normal	Physical	70	100	5	Normal	—	○
TM68	Giga Impact	Normal	Physical	150	90	5	Normal	—	○
TM71	Stone Edge	Rock	Physical	100	80	5	Normal	—	—
TM73	Thunder Wave	Electric	Status	—	100	20	Normal	—	—
TM78	Bulldoze	Ground	Physical	60	100	20	Adjacent	—	—
TM80	Rock Slide	Rock	Physical	75	90	10	Many Others	—	—
TM83	Work Up	Normal	Status	—	—	30	Self	—	—
TM87	Swagger	Normal	Status	—	90	15	Normal	—	—
TM90	Substitute	Normal	Status	—	—	10	Self	—	—
TM93	Wild Charge	Electric	Physical	90	100	15	Normal	—	○
TM94	Rock Smash	Fighting	Physical	40	100	15	Normal	—	○
TM95	Snarl	Dark	Special	55	95	15	Many Others	—	—
HM04	Strength	Normal	Physical	80	100	15	Normal	—	○

MOVES TAUGHT BY PEOPLE

Name	Type	Kind	Pow.	Acc.	PP	Range	Long	DA

MOVES TAUGHT BY MOVE TUTORS FOR SHARDS

Name	Type	Kind	Pow.	Acc.	PP	Range	Long	DA
Covet	Normal	Physical	60	100	40	Normal	—	○
Super Fang	Normal	Physical	—	90	10	Normal	—	○
Low Kick	Fighting	Physical	—	100	20	Normal	—	○
Fire Punch	Fire	Physical	75	100	15	Normal	—	○
ThunderPunch	Electric	Physical	75	100	15	Normal	—	○
Ice Punch	Ice	Physical	75	100	15	Normal	—	○
Last Resort	Normal	Physical	140	100	5	Normal	—	○
Hyper Voice	Normal	Special	90	100	10	Many Others	—	—
Iron Tail	Steel	Physical	100	75	15	Normal	—	○
Superpower	Fighting	Physical	120	100	5	Normal	—	○
Snore	Normal	Special	40	100	15	Normal	—	—
Heal Bell	Normal	Status	—	—	5	Your Party	—	—
Outrage	Dragon	Physical	120	100	10	1 Random	—	○
Sleep Talk	Normal	Status	—	—	10	Self	—	—

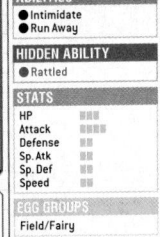

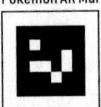

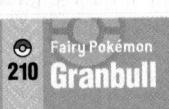

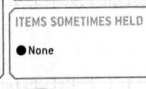

211 Qwilfish
Balloon Pokémon

TYPE: Water | Poison

ABILITIES
- Poison Point
- Swift Swim

HIDDEN ABILITY
- Intimidate

- HEIGHT: 1'08"
- WEIGHT: 8.6 lbs.
- GENDER: ♂ / ♀

It shoots the poison spines on its body in all directions. Its round form makes it a poor swimmer.

STATS
- HP
- Attack
- Defense
- Sp. Atk
- Sp. Def
- Speed

EGG GROUPS
Water ❷

Same form for ♂ / ♀

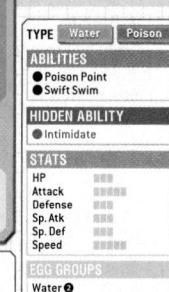
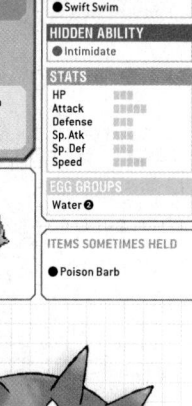

ITEMS SOMETIMES HELD
- Poison Barb

EVOLUTION
Does not evolve

HOW TO OBTAIN

Pokémon Black Version 2	❶ Virbank City (Super Rod) ❷ Virbank Complex (Super Rod)
Pokémon White Version 2	❶ Virbank City (Super Rod) ❷ Virbank Complex (Super Rod)

HOW TO OBTAIN FROM OTHER GAMES
———

LEVEL-UP AND LEARNED MOVES

Lv.	Name	Type	Kind	Pow.	Acc.	PP	Range	Long	DA
1	Spikes	Ground	Status	—	—	20	Other Side	—	—
1	Tackle	Normal	Physical	50	100	35	Normal	—	○
1	Poison Sting	Poison	Physical	15	100	35	Normal	—	○
9	Harden	Normal	Status	—	—	30	Self	—	—
9	Minimize	Normal	Status	—	—	10	Self	—	—
13	Water Gun	Water	Special	40	100	25	Normal	—	—
17	Rollout	Rock	Physical	30	90	20	Normal	—	○
21	Toxic Spikes	Poison	Status	—	—	20	Other Side	—	—
25	Stockpile	Normal	Status	—	—	20	Self	—	—
25	Spit Up	Normal	Special	—	100	10	Normal	—	—
29	Revenge	Fighting	Physical	60	100	10	Normal	—	○
33	Brine	Water	Special	65	100	10	Normal	—	—
37	Pin Missile	Bug	Physical	14	85	20	Normal	—	○
41	Take Down	Normal	Physical	90	85	20	Normal	—	○
45	Aqua Tail	Water	Physical	90	90	10	Normal	—	○
49	Poison Jab	Poison	Physical	80	100	20	Normal	—	○
53	Destiny Bond	Ghost	Status	—	—	5	Self	—	—
57	Hydro Pump	Water	Special	120	80	5	Normal	—	—

TM & HM MOVES

Lv.	Name	Type	Kind	Pow.	Acc.	PP	Range	Long	DA
TM06	Toxic	Poison	Status	—	90	10	Normal	—	—
TM07	Hail	Ice	Status	—	—	10	Both Sides	—	—
TM09	Venoshock	Poison	Special	65	100	10	Normal	—	—
TM10	Hidden Power	Normal	Special	—	100	15	Normal	—	—
TM12	Taunt	Dark	Status	—	100	20	Normal	—	—
TM13	Ice Beam	Ice	Special	95	100	10	Normal	—	—
TM14	Blizzard	Ice	Special	120	70	5	Many Others	—	—
TM17	Protect	Normal	Status	—	—	10	Self	—	—
TM18	Rain Dance	Water	Status	—	—	5	Both Sides	—	—
TM21	Frustration	Normal	Physical	—	100	20	Normal	—	○
TM27	Return	Normal	Physical	—	100	20	Normal	—	○
TM30	Shadow Ball	Ghost	Special	80	100	15	Normal	—	—
TM32	Double Team	Normal	Status	—	—	15	Self	—	—
TM34	Sludge Wave	Poison	Special	95	100	10	Adjacent	—	—
TM36	Sludge Bomb	Poison	Special	90	100	10	Normal	—	—
TM42	Facade	Normal	Physical	70	100	20	Normal	—	○
TM44	Rest	Psychic	Status	—	—	10	Self	—	—
TM45	Attract	Normal	Status	—	100	15	Normal	—	—
TM48	Round	Normal	Special	60	100	15	Normal	—	—
TM55	Scald	Water	Special	80	100	15	Normal	—	—
TM64	Explosion	Normal	Physical	250	100	5	Adjacent	—	—
TM66	Payback	Dark	Physical	50	100	10	Normal	—	○
TM73	Thunder Wave	Electric	Status	—	100	20	Normal	—	—
TM74	Gyro Ball	Steel	Physical	—	100	5	Normal	—	○
TM84	Poison Jab	Poison	Physical	80	100	20	Normal	—	○
TM87	Swagger	Normal	Status	—	90	15	Normal	—	—
TM90	Substitute	Normal	Status	—	—	10	Self	—	—
HM03	Surf	Water	Special	95	100	15	Adjacent	—	—
HM05	Waterfall	Water	Physical	80	100	15	Normal	—	○
HM06	Dive	Water	Physical	80	100	10	Normal	—	○

MOVES TAUGHT BY PEOPLE

Name	Type	Kind	Pow.	Acc.	PP	Range	Long	DA

MOVES TAUGHT BY MOVE TUTORS FOR SHARDS

Name	Type	Kind	Pow.	Acc.	PP	Range	Long	DA
Bounce	Flying	Physical	85	85	5	Normal	○	○
Signal Beam	Bug	Special	75	100	15	Normal	—	—
Icy Wind	Ice	Special	55	95	15	Many Others	—	—
Aqua Tail	Water	Physical	90	90	10	Normal	—	○
Snore	Normal	Special	40	100	15	Normal	—	—
Pain Split	Normal	Status	—	—	20	Normal	—	—
Sleep Talk	Normal	Status	—	—	10	Self	—	—

EGG MOVES

Name	Type	Kind	Pow.	Acc.	PP	Range	Long	DA
Flail	Normal	Physical	—	100	15	Normal	—	○
Haze	Ice	Status	—	—	30	Both Sides	—	—
BubbleBeam	Water	Special	65	100	20	Normal	—	—
Supersonic	Normal	Status	—	55	20	Normal	—	—
Astonish	Ghost	Physical	30	100	15	Normal	—	○
Signal Beam	Bug	Special	75	100	15	Normal	—	—
Aqua Jet	Water	Physical	40	100	20	Normal	—	○
Water Pulse	Water	Special	60	100	20	Normal	○	—
Brine	Water	Special	65	100	10	Normal	—	—
Acid Spray	Poison	Special	40	100	20	Normal	—	—

Pokémon AR Marker

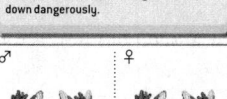

212 Scizor
Pincer Pokémon

TYPE: Bug | Steel

ABILITIES
- Swarm
- Technician

HIDDEN ABILITY
- Light Metal

- HEIGHT: 5'11"
- WEIGHT: 260.1 lbs.
- GENDER: ♂ / ♀

It raises its pincers with eyelike markings for intimidation. It also swings them down dangerously.

STATS
- HP
- Attack
- Defense
- Sp. Atk
- Sp. Def
- Speed

EGG GROUPS
Bug

♂   ♀

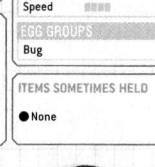

ITEMS SOMETIMES HELD
- None

EVOLUTION

Scyther → Scizor
Have it hold Metal Coat and Link Trade it
→ p. 75

HOW TO OBTAIN

Pokémon Black Version 2	Have Scyther sent to you via Link Trade while holding Metal Coat to receive Scizor
Pokémon White Version 2	Have Scyther sent to you via Link Trade while holding Metal Coat to receive Scizor

HOW TO OBTAIN FROM OTHER GAMES
———

LEVEL-UP AND LEARNED MOVES

Lv.	Name	Type	Kind	Pow.	Acc.	PP	Range	Long	DA
1	Bullet Punch	Steel	Physical	40	100	30	Normal	—	○
1	Quick Attack	Normal	Physical	40	100	30	Normal	—	○
1	Leer	Normal	Status	—	100	30	Many Others	—	—
1	Focus Energy	Normal	Status	—	—	30	Self	—	—
9	Pursuit	Dark	Physical	40	100	20	Normal	—	○
13	False Swipe	Normal	Physical	40	100	40	Normal	—	○
17	Agility	Psychic	Status	—	—	30	Self	—	—
21	Metal Claw	Steel	Physical	50	95	35	Normal	—	○
25	Fury Cutter	Bug	Physical	20	95	20	Normal	—	○
29	Slash	Normal	Physical	70	100	20	Normal	—	○
33	Razor Wind	Normal	Special	80	100	10	Many Others	—	—
37	Iron Defense	Steel	Status	—	—	15	Self	—	—
41	X-Scissor	Bug	Physical	80	100	15	Normal	—	○
45	Night Slash	Dark	Physical	70	100	15	Normal	—	○
49	Double Hit	Normal	Physical	35	90	10	Normal	—	○
53	Iron Head	Steel	Physical	80	100	15	Normal	—	○
57	Swords Dance	Normal	Status	—	—	30	Self	—	—
61	Feint	Normal	Physical	30	100	10	Normal	—	—

TM & HM MOVES

Lv.	Name	Type	Kind	Pow.	Acc.	PP	Range	Long	DA
TM06	Toxic	Poison	Status	—	90	10	Normal	—	—
TM09	Venoshock	Poison	Special	65	100	10	Normal	—	—
TM10	Hidden Power	Normal	Special	—	100	15	Normal	—	—
TM11	Sunny Day	Fire	Status	—	—	5	Both Sides	—	—
TM15	Hyper Beam	Normal	Special	150	90	5	Normal	—	—
TM16	Light Screen	Psychic	Status	—	—	30	Your Side	—	—
TM17	Protect	Normal	Status	—	—	10	Self	—	—
TM18	Rain Dance	Water	Status	—	—	5	Both Sides	—	—
TM20	Safeguard	Normal	Status	—	—	25	Your Side	—	—
TM21	Frustration	Normal	Physical	—	100	20	Normal	—	○
TM27	Return	Normal	Physical	—	100	20	Normal	—	○
TM31	Brick Break	Fighting	Physical	75	100	15	Normal	—	○
TM32	Double Team	Normal	Status	—	—	15	Self	—	—
TM37	Sandstorm	Rock	Status	—	—	10	Both Sides	—	—
TM40	Aerial Ace	Flying	Physical	60	—	20	Normal	○	○
TM42	Facade	Normal	Physical	70	100	20	Normal	—	○
TM44	Rest	Psychic	Status	—	—	10	Self	—	—
TM45	Attract	Normal	Status	—	100	15	Normal	—	—
TM46	Thief	Dark	Physical	40	100	10	Normal	—	○
TM48	Round	Normal	Special	60	100	15	Normal	—	—
TM54	False Swipe	Normal	Physical	40	100	40	Normal	—	○
TM56	Fling	Dark	Physical	—	100	10	Normal	—	—
TM62	Acrobatics	Flying	Physical	55	100	15	Normal	○	○
TM68	Giga Impact	Normal	Physical	150	90	5	Normal	—	○
TM75	Swords Dance	Normal	Status	—	—	30	Self	—	—
TM76	Struggle Bug	Bug	Special	30	100	20	Many Others	—	—
TM81	X-Scissor	Bug	Physical	80	100	15	Normal	—	○
TM87	Swagger	Normal	Status	—	90	15	Normal	—	—
TM89	U-turn	Bug	Physical	70	100	20	Normal	—	○
TM90	Substitute	Normal	Status	—	—	10	Self	—	—
TM91	Flash Cannon	Steel	Special	80	100	10	Normal	—	—
TM94	Rock Smash	Fighting	Physical	40	100	15	Normal	—	○
HM01	Cut	Normal	Physical	50	95	30	Normal	—	○
HM04	Strength	Normal	Physical	80	100	15	Normal	—	○

MOVES TAUGHT BY PEOPLE

Name	Type	Kind	Pow.	Acc.	PP	Range	Long	DA

MOVES TAUGHT BY MOVE TUTORS FOR SHARDS

Name	Type	Kind	Pow.	Acc.	PP	Range	Long	DA
Bug Bite	Bug	Physical	60	100	20	Normal	—	○
Iron Head	Steel	Physical	80	100	15	Normal	—	○
Iron Defense	Steel	Status	—	—	15	Self	—	—
Superpower	Fighting	Physical	120	100	5	Normal	—	○
Snore	Normal	Special	40	100	15	Normal	—	—
Knock Off	Dark	Physical	20	100	20	Normal	—	○
Roost	Flying	Status	—	—	10	Self	—	—
Tailwind	Flying	Status	—	—	30	Your Side	—	—
Sleep Talk	Normal	Status	—	—	10	Self	—	—

Pokémon AR Marker

Mold Pokémon

213 Shuckle

TYPE Bug Rock

ABILITIES
- Sturdy
- Gluttony

HIDDEN ABILITY
- Contrary

STATS
HP
Attack
Defense
Sp. Atk
Sp. Def
Speed

EGG GROUPS
Bug

- HEIGHT: 2'00"
- WEIGHT: 45.2 lbs.
- GENDER: ♂ / ♀

The berries stored in its vaselike shell eventually become a thick, pulpy juice.

Same form for ♂ / ♀

ITEMS SOMETIMES HELD
- Berry Juice

Pokémon AR Marker

EVOLUTION

Does not evolve

HOW TO OBTAIN

Pokémon Black Version 2	Seaside Cave B1F
Pokémon White Version 2	Seaside Cave B1F

HOW TO OBTAIN FROM OTHER GAMES

—

—

LEVEL-UP AND LEARNED MOVES

Lv.	Name	Type	Kind	Pow.	Acc.	PP	Range	Long	DA
1	Withdraw	Water	Status	—	—	40	Self	—	—
1	Constrict	Normal	Physical	10	100	35	Normal	—	○
1	Bide	Normal	Physical	—	—	10	Self	—	○
1	Rollout	Rock	Physical	30	90	20	Normal	—	○
5	Encore	Normal	Status	—	100	5	Normal	—	—
9	Wrap	Normal	Physical	15	90	20	Normal	—	○
12	Struggle Bug	Bug	Special	30	100	20	Many Others	—	—
16	Safeguard	Normal	Status	—	—	25	Your Side	—	—
20	Rest	Psychic	Status	—	—	10	Self	—	—
23	Rock Throw	Rock	Physical	50	90	15	Normal	—	—
27	Gastro Acid	Poison	Status	—	100	10	Normal	—	—
31	Power Trick	Psychic	Status	—	—	10	Self	—	—
34	Shell Smash	Normal	Status	—	—	15	Self	—	—
38	Rock Slide	Rock	Physical	75	90	10	Many Others	—	—
42	Bug Bite	Bug	Physical	60	100	20	Normal	—	○
45	Power Split	Psychic	Status	—	—	10	Normal	—	—
45	Guard Split	Psychic	Status	—	—	10	Normal	—	—
49	Stone Edge	Rock	Physical	100	80	5	Normal	—	—

TM & HM MOVES

Lv.	Name	Type	Kind	Pow.	Acc.	PP	Range	Long	DA
TM06	Toxic	Poison	Status	—	90	10	Normal	—	—
TM09	Venoshock	Poison	Special	65	100	10	Normal	—	—
TM10	Hidden Power	Normal	Special	—	100	15	Normal	—	—
TM11	Sunny Day	Fire	Status	—	—	5	Both Sides	—	—
TM17	Protect	Normal	Status	—	—	10	Self	—	—
TM20	Safeguard	Normal	Status	—	—	25	Your Side	—	—
TM21	Frustration	Normal	Physical	—	100	20	Normal	—	○
TM23	Smack Down	Rock	Physical	50	100	15	Normal	—	—
TM26	Earthquake	Ground	Physical	100	100	10	Adjacent	—	—
TM27	Return	Normal	Physical	—	100	20	Normal	—	○
TM28	Dig	Ground	Physical	80	100	10	Normal	—	○
TM32	Double Team	Normal	Status	—	—	15	Self	—	—
TM34	Sludge Wave	Poison	Special	95	100	10	Adjacent	—	—
TM36	Sludge Bomb	Poison	Special	90	100	10	Normal	—	—
TM37	Sandstorm	Rock	Status	—	—	10	Both Sides	—	—
TM39	Rock Tomb	Rock	Physical	50	80	10	Normal	—	—
TM42	Facade	Normal	Physical	70	100	20	Normal	—	○
TM44	Rest	Psychic	Status	—	—	10	Self	—	—
TM45	Attract	Normal	Status	—	100	15	Normal	—	—
TM48	Round	Normal	Special	60	100	15	Normal	—	—
TM69	Rock Polish	Rock	Status	—	—	20	Self	—	—
TM70	Flash	Normal	Status	—	100	20	Normal	—	—
TM71	Stone Edge	Rock	Physical	100	80	5	Normal	—	—
TM74	Gyro Ball	Steel	Physical	—	100	5	Normal	—	○
TM76	Struggle Bug	Bug	Special	30	100	20	Many Others	—	—
TM78	Bulldoze	Ground	Physical	60	100	20	Adjacent	—	—
TM80	Rock Slide	Rock	Physical	75	90	10	Many Others	—	—
TM87	Swagger	Normal	Status	—	90	15	Normal	—	—
TM90	Substitute	Normal	Status	—	—	10	Self	—	—
TM94	Rock Smash	Fighting	Physical	40	100	15	Normal	—	○
HM04	Strength	Normal	Physical	80	100	15	Normal	—	○

MOVES TAUGHT BY PEOPLE

Name	Type	Kind	Pow.	Acc.	PP	Range	Long	DA

MOVES TAUGHT BY MOVE TUTORS FOR SHARDS

Name	Type	Kind	Pow.	Acc.	PP	Range	Long	DA
Bug Bite	Bug	Physical	60	100	20	Normal	—	○
Earth Power	Ground	Special	90	100	10	Normal	—	—
Bind	Normal	Physical	15	85	20	Normal	—	○
Snore	Normal	Special	40	100	15	Normal	—	—
Knock Off	Dark	Physical	20	100	20	Normal	—	○
Gastro Acid	Poison	Status	—	100	10	Normal	—	—
Helping Hand	Normal	Status	—	—	20	1 Ally	—	—
After You	Normal	Status	—	—	15	Normal	—	—
Stealth Rock	Rock	Status	—	—	20	Other Side	—	—
Sleep Talk	Normal	Status	—	—	10	Self	—	—

EGG MOVES

Name	Type	Kind	Pow.	Acc.	PP	Range	Long	DA
Sweet Scent	Normal	Status	—	100	20	Many Others	—	—
Knock Off	Dark	Physical	20	100	20	Normal	—	○
Helping Hand	Normal	Status	—	—	20	1 Ally	—	—
Acupressure	Normal	Status	—	—	30	Self/Ally	—	—
Sand Tomb	Ground	Physical	35	85	15	Normal	—	—
Mud-Slap	Ground	Special	20	100	10	Normal	—	—
Acid	Poison	Special	40	100	30	Many Others	—	—
Rock Blast	Rock	Physical	25	90	10	Normal	—	—
Final Gambit	Fighting	Special	—	100	5	Normal	—	○

Single Horn Pokémon

214 Heracross

TYPE Bug Fighting

ABILITIES
- Swarm
- Guts

HIDDEN ABILITY
- Moxie

STATS
HP
Attack
Defense
Sp. Atk
Sp. Def
Speed

EGG GROUPS
Bug

- HEIGHT: 4'11"
- WEIGHT: 119.0 lbs.
- GENDER: ♂ / ♀

No matter how heavy its opponents, it flings them far away with its prized horn.

♂ ♀

ITEMS SOMETIMES HELD
- None

Pokémon AR Marker

EVOLUTION

Does not evolve

HOW TO OBTAIN

Pokémon Black Version 2	❶ Lostlorn Forest ❷ Route 12
Pokémon White Version 2	Lostlorn Forest (Hidden Grotto)

HOW TO OBTAIN FROM OTHER GAMES

—

—

LEVEL-UP AND LEARNED MOVES

Lv.	Name	Type	Kind	Pow.	Acc.	PP	Range	Long	DA
1	Night Slash	Dark	Physical	70	100	15	Normal	—	○
1	Tackle	Normal	Physical	50	100	35	Normal	—	○
1	Leer	Normal	Status	—	100	30	Many Others	—	—
1	Horn Attack	Normal	Physical	65	100	25	Normal	—	○
1	Endure	Normal	Status	—	—	10	Self	—	—
7	Fury Attack	Normal	Physical	15	85	20	Normal	—	○
10	Aerial Ace	Flying	Physical	60	—	20	Normal	○	○
16	Chip Away	Normal	Physical	70	100	20	Normal	—	○
19	Counter	Fighting	Physical	—	100	20	Varies	—	○
25	Brick Break	Fighting	Physical	75	100	15	Normal	—	○
28	Take Down	Normal	Physical	90	85	20	Normal	—	○
34	Close Combat	Fighting	Physical	120	100	5	Normal	—	○
37	Feint	Normal	Physical	30	100	10	Normal	—	—
43	Reversal	Fighting	Physical	—	100	15	Normal	—	○
46	Megahorn	Bug	Physical	120	85	10	Normal	—	○

TM & HM MOVES

Lv.	Name	Type	Kind	Pow.	Acc.	PP	Range	Long	DA
TM06	Toxic	Poison	Status	—	90	10	Normal	—	—
TM08	Bulk Up	Fighting	Status	—	—	20	Self	—	—
TM09	Venoshock	Poison	Special	65	100	10	Normal	—	—
TM10	Hidden Power	Normal	Special	—	100	15	Normal	—	—
TM11	Sunny Day	Fire	Status	—	—	5	Both Sides	—	—
TM15	Hyper Beam	Normal	Special	150	90	5	Normal	—	—
TM17	Protect	Normal	Status	—	—	10	Self	—	—
TM18	Rain Dance	Water	Status	—	—	5	Both Sides	—	—
TM21	Frustration	Normal	Physical	—	100	20	Normal	—	○
TM23	Smack Down	Rock	Physical	50	100	15	Normal	—	—
TM26	Earthquake	Ground	Physical	100	100	10	Adjacent	—	—
TM27	Return	Normal	Physical	—	100	20	Normal	—	○
TM28	Dig	Ground	Physical	80	100	10	Normal	—	○
TM31	Brick Break	Fighting	Physical	75	100	15	Normal	—	○
TM32	Double Team	Normal	Status	—	—	15	Self	—	—
TM39	Rock Tomb	Rock	Physical	50	80	10	Normal	—	—
TM40	Aerial Ace	Flying	Physical	60	—	20	Normal	○	○
TM42	Facade	Normal	Physical	70	100	20	Normal	—	○
TM44	Rest	Psychic	Status	—	—	10	Self	—	—
TM45	Attract	Normal	Status	—	100	15	Normal	—	—
TM46	Thief	Dark	Physical	40	100	10	Normal	—	○
TM48	Round	Normal	Special	60	100	15	Normal	—	—
TM52	Focus Blast	Fighting	Special	120	70	5	Normal	—	—
TM54	False Swipe	Normal	Physical	40	100	40	Normal	—	○
TM56	Fling	Dark	Physical	—	100	10	Normal	—	—
TM65	Shadow Claw	Ghost	Physical	70	100	15	Normal	—	○
TM67	Retaliate	Normal	Physical	70	100	5	Normal	—	○
TM68	Giga Impact	Normal	Physical	150	90	5	Normal	—	○
TM71	Stone Edge	Rock	Physical	100	80	5	Normal	—	—
TM75	Swords Dance	Normal	Status	—	—	30	Self	—	—
TM76	Struggle Bug	Bug	Special	30	100	20	Many Others	—	—
TM78	Bulldoze	Ground	Physical	60	100	20	Adjacent	—	—
TM80	Rock Slide	Rock	Physical	75	90	10	Many Others	—	—
TM83	Work Up	Normal	Status	—	—	30	Self	—	—
TM87	Swagger	Normal	Status	—	90	15	Normal	—	—
TM90	Substitute	Normal	Status	—	—	10	Self	—	—
TM94	Rock Smash	Fighting	Physical	40	100	15	Normal	—	○
HM01	Cut	Normal	Physical	50	95	30	Normal	—	○
HM04	Strength	Normal	Physical	80	100	15	Normal	—	○

MOVES TAUGHT BY PEOPLE

Name	Type	Kind	Pow.	Acc.	PP	Range	Long	DA

MOVES TAUGHT BY MOVE TUTORS FOR SHARDS

Name	Type	Kind	Pow.	Acc.	PP	Range	Long	DA
Bug Bite	Bug	Physical	60	100	20	Normal	—	○
Low Kick	Fighting	Physical	—	100	20	Normal	—	○
Iron Defense	Steel	Status	—	—	15	Self	—	—
Snore	Normal	Special	40	100	15	Normal	—	—
Knock Off	Dark	Physical	20	100	20	Normal	—	○
Helping Hand	Normal	Status	—	—	20	1 Ally	—	—
Sleep Talk	Normal	Status	—	—	10	Self	—	—

EGG MOVES

Name	Type	Kind	Pow.	Acc.	PP	Range	Long	DA
Harden	Normal	Status	—	—	30	Self	—	—
Bide	Normal	Physical	—	—	10	Self	—	○
Flail	Normal	Physical	—	100	15	Normal	—	○
Revenge	Fighting	Physical	60	100	10	Normal	—	○
Pursuit	Dark	Physical	40	100	20	Normal	—	○
Double-Edge	Normal	Physical	120	100	15	Normal	—	○
Seismic Toss	Fighting	Physical	—	100	20	Normal	—	○
Focus Punch	Fighting	Physical	150	100	20	Normal	—	○
Megahorn	Bug	Physical	120	85	10	Normal	—	○

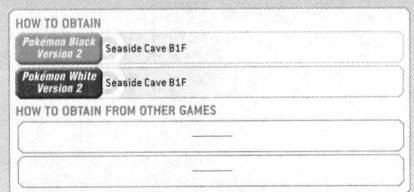

Sharp Claw Pokémon
215 Sneasel

TYPE Dark Ice

ABILITIES
- Inner Focus
- Keen Eye

HIDDEN ABILITY
- Pickpocket

STATS
HP
Attack
Defense
Sp. Atk
Sp. Def
Speed

EGG GROUPS
Field

ITEMS SOMETIMES HELD
- Grip Claw
- Quick Claw

- HEIGHT: 2'11"
- WEIGHT: 61.7 lbs.
- GENDER: ♂ / ♀

A smart and sneaky Pokémon, it makes its opponents flinch by suddenly showing the claws hidden in its paws.

♂ ♀

Pokémon AR Marker

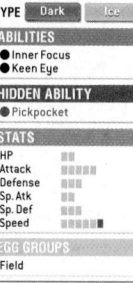

EVOLUTION

Sneasel

Have Sneasel hold Razor Claw and level it up at night or late night

Weavile

➡ p. 246

HOW TO OBTAIN

Pokémon Black Version 2	❶ Giant Chasm caves ❷ Giant Chasm caves (deepest part)
Pokémon White Version 2	❶ Giant Chasm caves ❷ Giant Chasm caves (deepest part)

HOW TO OBTAIN FROM OTHER GAMES

—

—

LEVEL-UP AND LEARNED MOVES

Lv.	Name	Type	Kind	Pow.	Acc.	PP	Range	Long	DA
1	Scratch	Normal	Physical	40	100	35	Normal	—	○
1	Leer	Normal	Status	—	100	30	Many Others	—	—
1	Taunt	Dark	Status	—	100	20	Normal	—	—
8	Quick Attack	Normal	Physical	40	100	30	Normal	—	○
10	Faint Attack	Dark	Physical	60	—	20	Normal	—	○
14	Icy Wind	Ice	Special	55	95	15	Many Others	—	—
16	Fury Swipes	Normal	Physical	18	80	15	Normal	—	○
20	Agility	Psychic	Status	—	—	30	Self	—	—
22	Metal Claw	Steel	Physical	50	95	35	Normal	—	○
25	Hone Claws	Dark	Status	—	—	15	Self	—	—
28	Beat Up	Dark	Physical	—	100	10	Normal	—	—
32	Screech	Normal	Status	—	85	40	Normal	—	—
35	Slash	Normal	Physical	70	100	20	Normal	—	○
40	Snatch	Dark	Status	—	—	10	Self	—	—
44	Punishment	Dark	Physical	—	100	5	Normal	—	○
47	Ice Shard	Ice	Physical	40	100	30	Normal	—	—

TM & HM MOVES

Lv.	Name	Type	Kind	Pow.	Acc.	PP	Range	Long	DA
TM01	Hone Claws	Dark	Status	—	—	15	Self	—	—
TM04	Calm Mind	Psychic	Status	—	—	20	Self	—	—
TM06	Toxic	Poison	Status	—	90	10	Normal	—	—
TM07	Hail	Ice	Status	—	—	10	Both Sides	—	—
TM10	Hidden Power	Normal	Special	—	100	15	Normal	—	—
TM11	Sunny Day	Fire	Status	—	—	5	Both Sides	—	—
TM12	Taunt	Dark	Status	—	100	20	Normal	—	—
TM13	Ice Beam	Ice	Special	95	100	10	Normal	—	—
TM14	Blizzard	Ice	Special	120	70	5	Many Others	—	—
TM17	Protect	Normal	Status	—	—	10	Self	—	—
TM18	Rain Dance	Water	Status	—	—	5	Both Sides	—	—
TM21	Frustration	Normal	Physical	—	100	20	Normal	—	○
TM27	Return	Normal	Physical	—	100	20	Normal	—	○
TM28	Dig	Ground	Physical	80	100	10	Normal	—	○
TM30	Shadow Ball	Ghost	Special	80	100	15	Normal	—	—
TM31	Brick Break	Fighting	Physical	75	100	15	Normal	—	○
TM32	Double Team	Normal	Status	—	—	15	Self	—	—
TM33	Reflect	Psychic	Status	—	—	20	Your Side	—	—
TM40	Aerial Ace	Flying	Physical	60	—	20	Normal	○	○
TM41	Torment	Dark	Status	—	100	15	Normal	—	—
TM42	Facade	Normal	Physical	70	100	20	Normal	—	○
TM44	Rest	Psychic	Status	—	—	10	Self	—	—
TM45	Attract	Normal	Status	—	100	15	Normal	—	—
TM46	Thief	Dark	Physical	40	100	10	Normal	—	○
TM47	Low Sweep	Fighting	Physical	60	100	20	Normal	—	○
TM48	Round	Normal	Special	60	100	15	Normal	—	—
TM54	False Swipe	Normal	Physical	40	100	40	Normal	—	○
TM56	Fling	Dark	Physical	—	100	10	Normal	—	—
TM63	Embargo	Dark	Status	—	100	15	Normal	—	—
TM65	Shadow Claw	Ghost	Physical	70	100	15	Normal	—	○
TM66	Payback	Dark	Physical	50	100	10	Normal	—	○
TM67	Retaliate	Normal	Physical	70	100	5	Normal	—	○
TM75	Swords Dance	Normal	Status	—	—	30	Self	—	—
TM77	Psych Up	Normal	Status	—	—	10	Normal	—	—
TM81	X-Scissor	Bug	Physical	80	100	15	Normal	—	○
TM84	Poison Jab	Poison	Physical	80	100	20	Normal	—	○
TM85	Dream Eater	Psychic	Special	100	100	15	Normal	—	—
TM87	Swagger	Normal	Status	—	90	15	Normal	—	—
TM90	Substitute	Normal	Status	—	—	10	Self	—	—
TM94	Rock Smash	Fighting	Physical	40	100	15	Normal	—	○
TM95	Snarl	Dark	Special	55	95	15	Many Others	—	—
HM01	Cut	Normal	Physical	50	95	30	Normal	—	○
HM03	Surf	Water	Special	95	100	15	Adjacent	—	—
HM04	Strength	Normal	Physical	80	100	15	Normal	—	○

MOVES TAUGHT BY PEOPLE

Name	Type	Kind	Pow.	Acc.	PP	Range	Long	DA

MOVES TAUGHT BY MOVE TUTORS FOR SHARDS

Name	Type	Kind	Pow.	Acc.	PP	Range	Long	DA
Low Kick	Fighting	Physical	—	100	20	Normal	—	○
Ice Punch	Ice	Physical	75	100	15	Normal	—	○
Icy Wind	Ice	Special	55	95	15	Many Others	—	—
Iron Tail	Steel	Physical	100	75	15	Normal	—	○
Foul Play	Dark	Physical	95	100	15	Normal	—	○
Dark Pulse	Dark	Special	80	100	15	Normal	○	—
Snore	Normal	Special	40	100	15	Normal	—	—
Knock Off	Dark	Physical	20	100	20	Normal	—	○
Spite	Ghost	Status	—	100	10	Normal	—	—
Sleep Talk	Normal	Status	—	—	10	Self	—	—
Snatch	Dark	Status	—	—	10	Self	—	—

EGG MOVES

Name	Type	Kind	Pow.	Acc.	PP	Range	Long	DA
Counter	Fighting	Physical	—	100	20	Varies	—	○
Spite	Ghost	Status	—	100	10	Normal	—	—
Foresight	Normal	Status	—	—	40	Normal	—	—
Bite	Dark	Physical	60	100	25	Normal	—	○
Crush Claw	Normal	Physical	75	95	10	Normal	—	○
Fake Out	Normal	Physical	40	100	10	Normal	—	○
Double Hit	Normal	Physical	35	90	10	Normal	—	○
Punishment	Dark	Physical	—	100	5	Normal	—	○
Pursuit	Dark	Physical	40	100	20	Normal	—	○
Ice Shard	Ice	Physical	40	100	30	Normal	—	—
Ice Punch	Ice	Physical	75	100	15	Normal	—	○
Assist	Normal	Status	—	—	20	Self	—	—
Avalanche	Ice	Physical	60	100	10	Normal	—	○
Feint	Normal	Physical	30	100	10	Normal	—	—

215 Sneasel

Little Bear Pokémon
216 Teddiursa

TYPE Normal

ABILITIES
- Pickup
- Quick Feet

HIDDEN ABILITY
- Honey Gather

STATS
HP
Attack
Defense
Sp. Atk
Sp. Def
Speed

EGG GROUPS
Field

ITEMS SOMETIMES HELD
- None

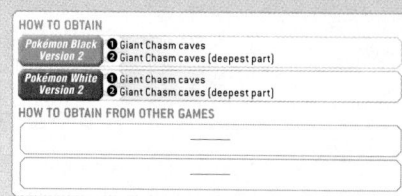

- HEIGHT: 2'00"
- WEIGHT: 19.4 lbs.
- GENDER: ♂ / ♀

It lets honey soak into its paws so it can lick them all the time. Every set of paws tastes unique.

Same form for ♂ / ♀

Pokémon AR Marker

EVOLUTION

Teddiursa

Lv. 30

Ursaring

HOW TO OBTAIN

Pokémon Black Version 2	If your character is a boy, trade Pokémon during a date with Yancy (10th time)
Pokémon White Version 2	If your character is a boy, trade Pokémon during a date with Yancy (10th time)

HOW TO OBTAIN FROM OTHER GAMES

Pokémon SoulSilver Version	Route 45

—

LEVEL-UP AND LEARNED MOVES

Lv.	Name	Type	Kind	Pow.	Acc.	PP	Range	Long	DA
1	Covet	Normal	Physical	60	100	40	Normal	—	○
1	Scratch	Normal	Physical	40	100	35	Normal	—	○
1	Leer	Normal	Status	—	100	30	Many Others	—	—
1	Lick	Ghost	Physical	20	100	30	Normal	—	○
1	Fake Tears	Dark	Status	—	100	20	Normal	—	—
8	Fury Swipes	Normal	Physical	18	80	15	Normal	—	○
15	Faint Attack	Dark	Physical	60	—	20	Normal	—	○
22	Sweet Scent	Normal	Status	—	100	20	Many Others	—	—
29	Slash	Normal	Physical	70	100	20	Normal	—	○
36	Charm	Normal	Status	—	100	20	Normal	—	—
43	Rest	Psychic	Status	—	—	10	Self	—	—
43	Snore	Normal	Special	40	100	15	Normal	—	—
50	Thrash	Normal	Physical	120	100	10	1 Random	—	○
57	Fling	Dark	Physical	—	100	10	Normal	—	—

TM & HM MOVES

Lv.	Name	Type	Kind	Pow.	Acc.	PP	Range	Long	DA
TM01	Hone Claws	Dark	Status	—	—	15	Self	—	—
TM05	Roar	Normal	Status	—	100	20	Normal	—	—
TM06	Toxic	Poison	Status	—	90	10	Normal	—	—
TM08	Bulk Up	Fighting	Status	—	—	20	Self	—	—
TM10	Hidden Power	Normal	Special	—	100	15	Normal	—	—
TM11	Sunny Day	Fire	Status	—	—	5	Both Sides	—	—
TM12	Taunt	Dark	Status	—	100	20	Normal	—	—
TM17	Protect	Normal	Status	—	—	10	Self	—	—
TM18	Rain Dance	Water	Status	—	—	5	Both Sides	—	—
TM21	Frustration	Normal	Physical	—	100	20	Normal	—	○
TM26	Earthquake	Ground	Physical	100	100	10	Adjacent	—	—
TM27	Return	Normal	Physical	—	100	20	Normal	—	○
TM28	Dig	Ground	Physical	80	100	10	Normal	—	○
TM31	Brick Break	Fighting	Physical	75	100	15	Normal	—	○
TM32	Double Team	Normal	Status	—	—	15	Self	—	—
TM39	Rock Tomb	Rock	Physical	50	80	10	Normal	—	—
TM40	Aerial Ace	Flying	Physical	60	—	20	Normal	○	○
TM41	Torment	Dark	Status	—	100	15	Normal	—	—
TM42	Facade	Normal	Physical	70	100	20	Normal	—	○
TM44	Rest	Psychic	Status	—	—	10	Self	—	—
TM45	Attract	Normal	Status	—	100	15	Normal	—	—
TM46	Thief	Dark	Physical	40	100	10	Normal	—	○
TM48	Round	Normal	Special	60	100	15	Normal	—	—
TM56	Fling	Dark	Physical	—	100	10	Normal	—	—
TM65	Shadow Claw	Ghost	Physical	70	100	15	Normal	—	○
TM66	Payback	Dark	Physical	50	100	10	Normal	—	○
TM67	Retaliate	Normal	Physical	70	100	5	Normal	—	○
TM75	Swords Dance	Normal	Status	—	—	30	Self	—	—
TM78	Bulldoze	Ground	Physical	60	100	20	Adjacent	—	—
TM80	Rock Slide	Rock	Physical	75	90	10	Many Others	—	—
TM83	Work Up	Normal	Status	—	—	30	Self	—	—
TM87	Swagger	Normal	Status	—	90	15	Normal	—	—
TM90	Substitute	Normal	Status	—	—	10	Self	—	—
TM94	Rock Smash	Fighting	Physical	40	100	15	Normal	—	○
HM01	Cut	Normal	Physical	50	95	30	Normal	—	○
HM04	Strength	Normal	Physical	80	100	15	Normal	—	○

MOVES TAUGHT BY PEOPLE

Name	Type	Kind	Pow.	Acc.	PP	Range	Long	DA

MOVES TAUGHT BY MOVE TUTORS FOR SHARDS

Name	Type	Kind	Pow.	Acc.	PP	Range	Long	DA
Covet	Normal	Physical	60	100	40	Normal	—	○
Seed Bomb	Grass	Physical	80	100	15	Normal	—	—
Gunk Shot	Poison	Physical	120	70	5	Normal	—	—
Fire Punch	Fire	Physical	75	100	15	Normal	—	○
ThunderPunch	Electric	Physical	75	100	15	Normal	—	○
Ice Punch	Ice	Physical	75	100	15	Normal	—	○
Last Resort	Normal	Physical	140	100	5	Normal	—	○
Hyper Voice	Normal	Special	90	100	10	Many Others	—	—
Superpower	Fighting	Physical	120	100	5	Normal	—	○
Snore	Normal	Special	40	100	15	Normal	—	—
Sleep Talk	Normal	Status	—	—	10	Self	—	—

EGG MOVES

Name	Type	Kind	Pow.	Acc.	PP	Range	Long	DA
Crunch	Dark	Physical	80	100	15	Normal	—	○
Take Down	Normal	Physical	90	85	20	Normal	—	○
Seismic Toss	Fighting	Physical	—	100	20	Normal	—	○
Counter	Fighting	Physical	—	100	20	Varies	—	○
Metal Claw	Steel	Physical	50	95	35	Normal	—	○
Fake Tears	Dark	Status	—	100	20	Normal	—	—
Yawn	Normal	Status	—	—	10	Normal	—	—
Sleep Talk	Normal	Status	—	—	10	Self	—	—
Cross Chop	Fighting	Physical	100	80	5	Normal	—	○
Double-Edge	Normal	Physical	120	100	15	Normal	—	○
Close Combat	Fighting	Physical	120	100	5	Normal	—	○
Night Slash	Dark	Physical	70	100	15	Normal	—	○
Belly Drum	Normal	Status	—	—	10	Self	—	—
Chip Away	Normal	Physical	70	100	20	Normal	—	○

216 Teddiursa

217 Ursaring

Hibernator Pokémon

- HEIGHT: 5'11"
- WEIGHT: 277.3 lbs.
- GENDER: ♂ / ♀

In its territory, it leaves scratches on trees that bear delicious berries or fruits.

♂ ♀

TYPE Normal

ABILITIES
- Guts
- Quick Feet

HIDDEN ABILITY
- Unnerve

STATS
- HP
- Attack
- Defense
- Sp. Atk
- Sp. Def
- Speed

EGG GROUPS
Field

ITEMS SOMETIMES HELD
- None

Pokémon AR Marker

EVOLUTION

HOW TO OBTAIN

Pokémon Black Version 2	If your character is a boy, level up the Teddiursa you receive from Yancy to Lv. 30
Pokémon White Version 2	If your character is a boy, level up the Teddiursa you receive from Yancy to Lv. 30

HOW TO OBTAIN FROM OTHER GAMES

Pokémon SoulSilver Version	Victory Road
—	

LEVEL-UP AND LEARNED MOVES

Lv.	Name	Type	Kind	Pow.	Acc.	PP	Range	Long	DA
1	Covet	Normal	Physical	60	100	40	Normal	—	○
1	Scratch	Normal	Physical	40	100	35	Normal	—	○
1	Leer	Normal	Status	—	100	30	Many Others	—	—
1	Lick	Ghost	Physical	20	100	30	Normal	—	○
1	Fake Tears	Dark	Status	—	100	20	Normal	—	—
8	Fury Swipes	Normal	Physical	18	80	15	Normal	—	○
15	Faint Attack	Dark	Physical	60	—	20	Normal	—	○
22	Sweet Scent	Normal	Status	—	100	20	Many Others	—	—
29	Slash	Normal	Physical	70	100	20	Normal	—	○
38	Scary Face	Normal	Status	—	100	10	Normal	—	—
47	Rest	Psychic	Status	—	—	10	Self	—	—
49	Snore	Normal	Special	40	100	15	Normal	—	—
58	Thrash	Normal	Physical	120	100	10	1 Random	—	○
67	Hammer Arm	Fighting	Physical	100	90	10	Normal	—	○

TM & HM MOVES

Lv.	Name	Type	Kind	Pow.	Acc.	PP	Range	Long	DA
TM01	Hone Claws	Dark	Status	—	—	15	Self	—	—
TM05	Roar	Normal	Status	—	100	20	Normal	—	—
TM06	Toxic	Poison	Status	—	90	10	Normal	—	—
TM08	Bulk Up	Fighting	Status	—	—	20	Self	—	—
TM10	Hidden Power	Normal	Special	—	100	15	Normal	—	—
TM11	Sunny Day	Fire	Status	—	—	5	Both Sides	—	—
TM12	Taunt	Dark	Status	—	100	20	Normal	—	—
TM15	Hyper Beam	Normal	Special	150	90	5	Normal	—	—
TM17	Protect	Normal	Status	—	—	10	Self	—	—
TM18	Rain Dance	Water	Status	—	—	5	Both Sides	—	—
TM21	Frustration	Normal	Physical	—	100	20	Normal	—	○
TM23	Smack Down	Rock	Physical	50	100	15	Normal	—	—
TM26	Earthquake	Ground	Physical	100	100	10	Adjacent	—	—
TM27	Return	Normal	Physical	—	100	20	Normal	—	○
TM28	Dig	Ground	Physical	80	100	10	Normal	—	○
TM31	Brick Break	Fighting	Physical	75	100	15	Normal	—	○
TM32	Double Team	Normal	Status	—	—	15	Self	—	—
TM39	Rock Tomb	Rock	Physical	50	80	10	Normal	—	—
TM40	Aerial Ace	Flying	Physical	60	—	20	Normal	○	○
TM41	Torment	Dark	Status	—	100	15	Normal	—	—
TM42	Facade	Normal	Physical	70	100	20	Normal	—	○
TM44	Rest	Psychic	Status	—	—	10	Self	—	—
TM45	Attract	Normal	Status	—	100	15	Normal	—	—
TM46	Thief	Dark	Physical	40	100	10	Normal	—	○
TM48	Round	Normal	Special	60	100	15	Normal	—	—
TM52	Focus Blast	Fighting	Special	120	70	5	Normal	—	—
TM56	Fling	Dark	Physical	—	100	10	Normal	—	—
TM65	Shadow Claw	Ghost	Physical	70	100	15	Normal	—	○
TM66	Payback	Dark	Physical	50	100	10	Normal	—	○
TM67	Retaliate	Normal	Physical	70	100	5	Normal	—	○
TM68	Giga Impact	Normal	Physical	150	90	5	Normal	—	○
TM71	Stone Edge	Rock	Physical	100	80	5	Normal	—	—
TM75	Swords Dance	Normal	Status	—	—	30	Self	—	—
TM78	Bulldoze	Ground	Physical	60	100	20	Adjacent	—	—
TM80	Rock Slide	Rock	Physical	75	90	10	Many Others	—	—
TM83	Work Up	Normal	Status	—	—	30	Self	—	—
TM87	Swagger	Normal	Status	—	90	15	Normal	—	—
TM90	Substitute	Normal	Status	—	—	10	Self	—	—
TM94	Rock Smash	Fighting	Physical	40	100	15	Normal	—	○
HM01	Cut	Normal	Physical	50	95	30	Normal	—	○
HM04	Strength	Normal	Physical	80	100	15	Normal	—	○

MOVES TAUGHT BY PEOPLE

Name	Type	Kind	Pow.	Acc.	PP	Range	Long	DA

MOVES TAUGHT BY MOVE TUTORS FOR SHARDS

Name	Type	Kind	Pow.	Acc.	PP	Range	Long	DA
Covet	Normal	Physical	60	100	40	Normal	—	○
Uproar	Normal	Special	90	100	10	1 Random	—	—
Seed Bomb	Grass	Physical	80	100	15	Normal	—	—
Low Kick	Fighting	Physical	—	100	20	Normal	—	○
Gunk Shot	Poison	Physical	120	70	5	Normal	—	—
Fire Punch	Fire	Physical	75	100	15	Normal	—	○
ThunderPunch	Electric	Physical	75	100	15	Normal	—	○
Ice Punch	Ice	Physical	75	100	15	Normal	—	○
Last Resort	Normal	Physical	140	100	5	Normal	—	○
Hyper Voice	Normal	Special	90	100	10	Many Others	—	—
Superpower	Fighting	Physical	120	100	5	Normal	—	○
Snore	Normal	Special	40	100	15	Normal	—	—
Sleep Talk	Normal	Status	—	—	10	Self	—	—

218 Slugma

Lava Pokémon

- HEIGHT: 2'04"
- WEIGHT: 77.2 lbs.
- GENDER: ♂ / ♀

Its body is made of magma. If it doesn't keep moving, its body will cool and harden.

Same form for ♂ / ♀

TYPE Fire

ABILITIES
- Magma Armor
- Flame Body

HIDDEN ABILITY
- Weak Armor

STATS
- HP
- Attack
- Defense
- Sp. Atk
- Sp. Def
- Speed

EGG GROUPS
Amorphous

ITEMS SOMETIMES HELD
- None

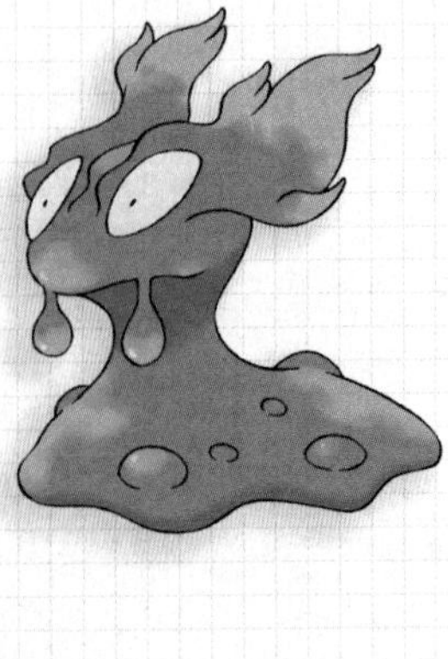

Pokémon AR Marker

EVOLUTION

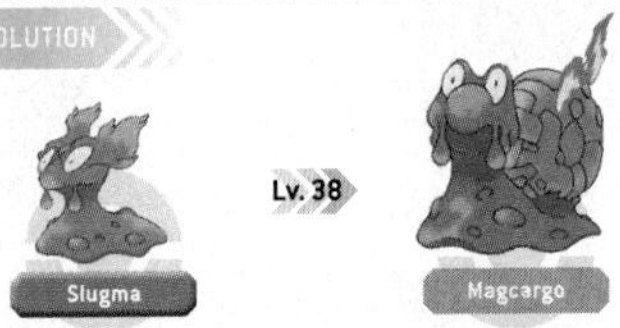

HOW TO OBTAIN

Pokémon Black Version 2	Link Trade or Poké Transfer
Pokémon White Version 2	Link Trade or Poké Transfer

HOW TO OBTAIN FROM OTHER GAMES

Pokémon Platinum Version	Stark Mountain interior
—	

LEVEL-UP AND LEARNED MOVES

Lv.	Name	Type	Kind	Pow.	Acc.	PP	Range	Long	DA
1	Yawn	Normal	Status	—	—	10	Normal	—	—
1	Smog	Poison	Special	20	70	20	Normal	—	—
5	Ember	Fire	Special	40	100	25	Normal	—	—
10	Rock Throw	Rock	Physical	50	90	15	Normal	—	—
14	Harden	Normal	Status	—	—	30	Self	—	—
19	Recover	Normal	Status	—	—	10	Self	—	—
23	Flame Burst	Fire	Special	70	100	15	Normal	—	—
28	AncientPower	Rock	Special	60	100	5	Normal	—	—
32	Amnesia	Psychic	Status	—	—	20	Self	—	—
37	Lava Plume	Fire	Special	80	100	15	Adjacent	—	—
41	Rock Slide	Rock	Physical	75	90	10	Many Others	—	—
46	Body Slam	Normal	Physical	85	100	15	Normal	—	○
50	Flamethrower	Fire	Special	95	100	15	Normal	—	—
55	Earth Power	Ground	Special	90	100	10	Normal	—	—

TM & HM MOVES

Lv.	Name	Type	Kind	Pow.	Acc.	PP	Range	Long	DA
TM06	Toxic	Poison	Status	—	90	10	Normal	—	—
TM10	Hidden Power	Normal	Special	—	100	15	Normal	—	—
TM11	Sunny Day	Fire	Status	—	—	5	Both Sides	—	—
TM16	Light Screen	Psychic	Status	—	—	30	Your Side	—	—
TM17	Protect	Normal	Status	—	—	10	Self	—	—
TM21	Frustration	Normal	Physical	—	100	20	Normal	—	○
TM27	Return	Normal	Physical	—	100	20	Normal	—	○
TM32	Double Team	Normal	Status	—	—	15	Self	—	—
TM33	Reflect	Psychic	Status	—	—	20	Your Side	—	—
TM35	Flamethrower	Fire	Special	95	100	15	Normal	—	—
TM38	Fire Blast	Fire	Special	120	85	5	Normal	—	—
TM39	Rock Tomb	Rock	Physical	50	80	10	Normal	—	—
TM42	Facade	Normal	Physical	70	100	20	Normal	—	○
TM43	Flame Charge	Fire	Physical	50	100	20	Normal	—	○
TM44	Rest	Psychic	Status	—	—	10	Self	—	—
TM45	Attract	Normal	Status	—	100	15	Normal	—	—
TM48	Round	Normal	Special	60	100	15	Normal	—	—
TM50	Overheat	Fire	Special	140	90	5	Normal	—	—
TM59	Incinerate	Fire	Special	30	100	15	Many Others	—	—
TM61	Will-O-Wisp	Fire	Status	—	75	15	Normal	—	—
TM80	Rock Slide	Rock	Physical	75	90	10	Many Others	—	—
TM87	Swagger	Normal	Status	—	90	15	Normal	—	—
TM90	Substitute	Normal	Status	—	—	10	Self	—	—
TM94	Rock Smash	Fighting	Physical	40	100	15	Normal	—	○

MOVES TAUGHT BY PEOPLE

Name	Type	Kind	Pow.	Acc.	PP	Range	Long	DA

MOVES TAUGHT BY MOVE TUTORS FOR SHARDS

Name	Type	Kind	Pow.	Acc.	PP	Range	Long	DA
Iron Defense	Steel	Status	—	—	15	Self	—	—
Earth Power	Ground	Special	90	100	10	Normal	—	—
Snore	Normal	Special	40	100	15	Normal	—	—
Heat Wave	Fire	Special	100	90	10	Many Others	—	—
Pain Split	Normal	Status	—	—	20	Normal	—	—
After You	Normal	Status	—	—	15	Normal	—	—
Sleep Talk	Normal	Status	—	—	10	Self	—	—

EGG MOVES

Name	Type	Kind	Pow.	Acc.	PP	Range	Long	DA
Acid Armor	Poison	Status	—	—	40	Self	—	—
Heat Wave	Fire	Special	100	90	10	Many Others	—	—
Curse	Ghost	Status	—	—	10	Varies	—	—
SmokeScreen	Normal	Status	—	100	20	Normal	—	—
Memento	Dark	Status	—	100	10	Normal	—	—
Stockpile	Normal	Status	—	—	20	Self	—	—
Spit Up	Normal	Special	—	100	10	Normal	—	—
Swallow	Normal	Status	—	—	10	Self	—	—
Rollout	Rock	Physical	30	90	20	Normal	—	○
Inferno	Fire	Special	100	50	5	Normal	—	—
Earth Power	Ground	Special	90	100	10	Normal	—	—

217 Ursaring
218 Slugma

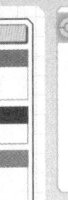

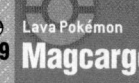

219 Magcargo

Lava Pokémon

TYPE	Fire	Rock

ABILITIES
- Magma Armor
- Flame Body

HIDDEN ABILITY
- Weak Armor

- HEIGHT: 2'07"
- WEIGHT: 121.3 lbs.
- GENDER: ♂ / ♀

It body temperature is roughly 18,000 degrees F. Flames spout from gaps in its hardened shell.

STATS

HP
Attack
Defense
Sp. Atk
Sp. Def
Speed

EGG GROUPS

Amorphous

ITEMS SOMETIMES HELD

- None

Same form for ♂ / ♀

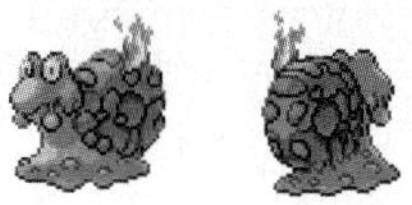

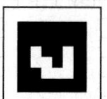

EVOLUTION

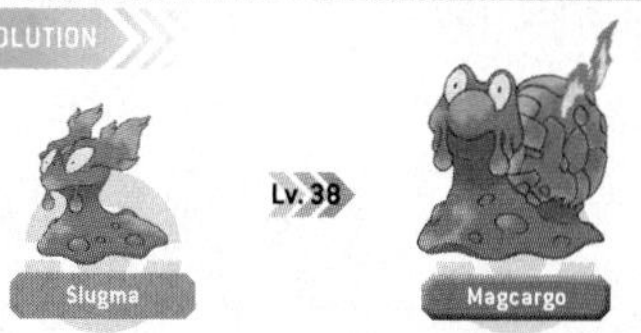

Slugma
Lv. 38
Magcargo

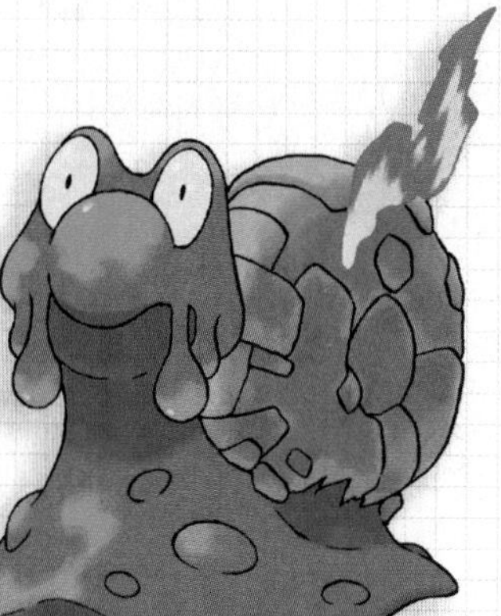

Pokémon AR Marker

HOW TO OBTAIN

Pokémon Black Version 2	Link Trade or Poké Transfer
Pokémon White Version 2	Link Trade or Poké Transfer

HOW TO OBTAIN FROM OTHER GAMES

Pokémon Platinum Version	Stark Mountain interior
	—

LEVEL-UP AND LEARNED MOVES

Lv.	Name	Type	Kind	Pow.	Acc.	PP	Range	Long	DA
1	Yawn	Normal	Status	—	—	10	Normal	—	—
1	Smog	Poison	Special	20	70	20	Normal	—	—
1	Ember	Fire	Special	40	100	25	Normal	—	—
1	Rock Throw	Rock	Physical	50	90	15	Normal	—	—
5	Ember	Fire	Special	40	100	25	Normal	—	—
10	Rock Throw	Rock	Physical	50	90	15	Normal	—	—
14	Harden	Normal	Status	—	—	30	Self	—	—
19	Recover	Normal	Status	—	—	10	Self	—	—
23	Flame Burst	Fire	Special	70	100	15	Normal	—	—
28	AncientPower	Rock	Special	60	100	5	Normal	—	—
32	Amnesia	Psychic	Status	—	—	20	Self	—	—
37	Lava Plume	Fire	Special	80	100	15	Adjacent	—	—
38	Shell Smash	Normal	Status	—	—	15	Self	—	—
44	Rock Slide	Rock	Physical	75	90	10	Many Others	—	—
52	Body Slam	Normal	Physical	85	100	15	Normal	—	○
59	Flamethrower	Fire	Special	95	100	15	Normal	—	—
67	Earth Power	Ground	Special	90	100	10	Normal	—	—

TM & HM MOVES

Lv.	Name	Type	Kind	Pow.	Acc.	PP	Range	Long	DA
TM06	Toxic	Poison	Status	—	90	10	Normal	—	—
TM10	Hidden Power	Normal	Special	—	100	15	Normal	—	—
TM11	Sunny Day	Fire	Status	—	—	5	Both Sides	—	—
TM15	Hyper Beam	Normal	Special	150	90	5	Normal	—	—
TM16	Light Screen	Psychic	Status	—	—	30	Your Side	—	—
TM17	Protect	Normal	Status	—	—	10	Self	—	—
TM21	Frustration	Normal	Physical	—	100	20	Normal	—	○
TM22	SolarBeam	Grass	Special	120	100	10	Normal	—	—
TM23	Smack Down	Rock	Physical	50	100	15	Normal	—	—
TM26	Earthquake	Ground	Physical	100	100	10	Adjacent	—	—
TM27	Return	Normal	Physical	—	100	20	Normal	—	○
TM32	Double Team	Normal	Status	—	—	15	Self	—	—
TM33	Reflect	Psychic	Status	—	—	20	Your Side	—	—
TM35	Flamethrower	Fire	Special	95	100	15	Normal	—	—
TM37	Sandstorm	Rock	Status	—	—	10	Both Sides	—	—
TM38	Fire Blast	Fire	Special	120	85	5	Normal	—	—
TM39	Rock Tomb	Rock	Physical	50	80	10	Normal	—	—
TM42	Facade	Normal	Physical	70	100	20	Normal	—	○
TM43	Flame Charge	Fire	Physical	50	100	20	Normal	—	○
TM44	Rest	Psychic	Status	—	—	10	Self	—	—
TM45	Attract	Normal	Status	—	100	15	Normal	—	—
TM48	Round	Normal	Special	60	100	15	Normal	—	—
TM50	Overheat	Fire	Special	140	90	5	Normal	—	—
TM59	Incinerate	Fire	Special	30	100	15	Many Others	—	—
TM61	Will-O-Wisp	Fire	Status	—	75	15	Normal	—	—
TM64	Explosion	Normal	Physical	250	100	5	Adjacent	—	—
TM68	Giga Impact	Normal	Physical	150	90	5	Normal	—	○
TM69	Rock Polish	Rock	Status	—	—	20	Self	—	—
TM71	Stone Edge	Rock	Physical	100	80	5	Normal	—	—
TM74	Gyro Ball	Steel	Physical	—	100	5	Normal	—	○
TM78	Bulldoze	Ground	Physical	60	100	20	Adjacent	—	—
TM80	Rock Slide	Rock	Physical	75	90	10	Many Others	—	—
TM87	Swagger	Normal	Status	—	90	15	Normal	—	—
TM90	Substitute	Normal	Status	—	—	10	Self	—	—
TM94	Rock Smash	Fighting	Physical	40	100	15	Normal	—	○
HM04	Strength	Normal	Physical	80	100	15	Normal	—	○

MOVES TAUGHT BY PEOPLE

Name	Type	Kind	Pow.	Acc.	PP	Range	Long	DA

MOVES TAUGHT BY MOVE TUTORS FOR SHARDS

Name	Type	Kind	Pow.	Acc.	PP	Range	Long	DA
Iron Defense	Steel	Status	—	—	15	Self	—	—
Earth Power	Ground	Special	90	100	10	Normal	—	—
Snore	Normal	Special	40	100	15	Normal	—	—
Heat Wave	Fire	Special	100	90	10	Many Others	—	—
Pain Split	Normal	Status	—	—	20	Normal	—	—
After You	Normal	Status	—	—	15	Normal	—	—
Stealth Rock	Rock	Status	—	—	20	Other Side	—	—
Sleep Talk	Normal	Status	—	—	10	Self	—	—

220 Swinub

Pig Pokémon

TYPE	Ice	Ground

ABILITIES
- Oblivious
- Snow Cloak

HIDDEN ABILITY
- Thick Fat

- HEIGHT: 1'04"
- WEIGHT: 14.3 lbs.
- GENDER: ♂ / ♀

Rooting the tip of its snout into the ground, it searches for food. Sometimes it even digs up a hot spring.

STATS

HP
Attack
Defense
Sp. Atk
Sp. Def
Speed

EGG GROUPS

Field

ITEMS SOMETIMES HELD

- None

Same form for ♂ / ♀

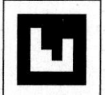

EVOLUTION

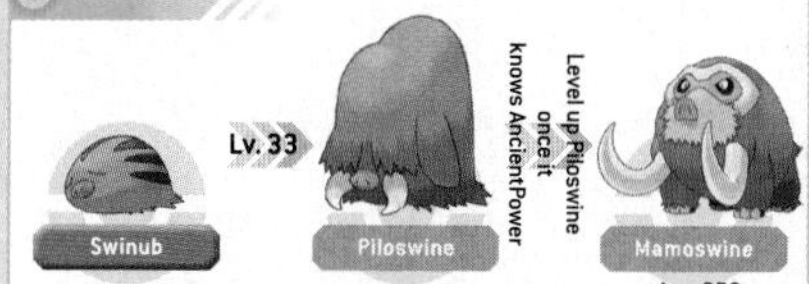

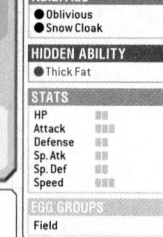

Swinub
Lv. 33
Piloswine
Level up Piloswine once it knows AncientPower
Mamoswine

➡ p. 252

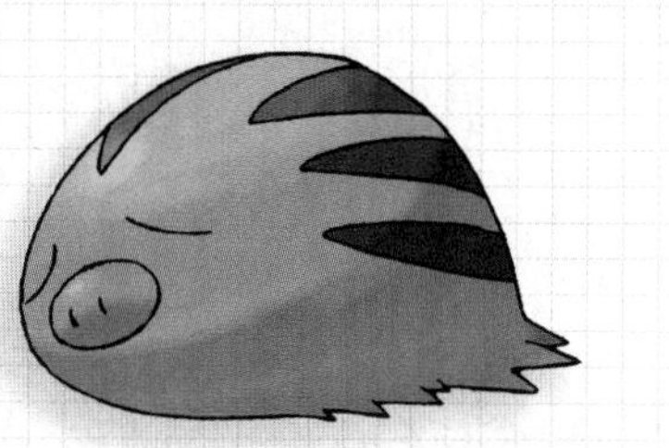

Pokémon AR Marker

HOW TO OBTAIN

Pokémon Black Version 2	Catch a Piloswine or Mamoswine, leave it at the Pokémon Day Care, and hatch the Egg
Pokémon White Version 2	Catch a Piloswine or Mamoswine, leave it at the Pokémon Day Care, and hatch the Egg

HOW TO OBTAIN FROM OTHER GAMES

Pokémon HeartGold Version	Ice Path
Pokémon SoulSilver Version	Ice Path

LEVEL-UP AND LEARNED MOVES

Lv.	Name	Type	Kind	Pow.	Acc.	PP	Range	Long	DA
1	Tackle	Normal	Physical	50	100	35	Normal	-	○
1	Odor Sleuth	Normal	Status	-	-	40	Normal	-	-
5	Mud Sport	Ground	Status	-	-	15	Both Sides	-	-
8	Powder Snow	Ice	Special	40	100	25	Many Others	-	-
11	Mud-Slap	Ground	Special	20	100	10	Normal	-	-
14	Endure	Normal	Status	-	-	10	Self	-	-
18	Mud Bomb	Ground	Special	65	85	10	Normal	-	-
21	Icy Wind	Ice	Special	55	95	15	Many Others	-	-
24	Ice Shard	Ice	Physical	40	100	30	Normal	-	-
28	Take Down	Normal	Physical	90	85	20	Normal	-	○
35	Mist	Ice	Status	-	-	30	Your Side	-	-
37	Earthquake	Ground	Physical	100	100	10	Adjacent	-	-
40	Flail	Normal	Physical	-	100	15	Normal	-	○
44	Blizzard	Ice	Special	120	70	5	Many Others	-	-
48	Amnesia	Psychic	Status	-	-	20	Self	-	-

TM & HM MOVES

Lv.	Name	Type	Kind	Pow.	Acc.	PP	Range	Long	DA
TM05	Roar	Normal	Status	—	100	20	Normal	—	—
TM06	Toxic	Poison	Status	—	90	10	Normal	—	—
TM07	Hail	Ice	Status	—	—	10	Both Sides	—	—
TM10	Hidden Power	Normal	Special	—	100	15	Normal	—	—
TM13	Ice Beam	Ice	Special	95	100	10	Normal	—	—
TM14	Blizzard	Ice	Special	120	70	5	Many Others	—	—
TM16	Light Screen	Psychic	Status	—	—	30	Your Side	—	—
TM17	Protect	Normal	Status	—	—	10	Self	—	—
TM18	Rain Dance	Water	Status	—	—	5	Both Sides	—	—
TM21	Frustration	Normal	Physical	—	100	20	Normal	—	○
TM26	Earthquake	Ground	Physical	100	100	10	Adjacent	—	—
TM27	Return	Normal	Physical	—	100	20	Normal	—	○
TM28	Dig	Ground	Physical	80	100	10	Normal	—	○
TM32	Double Team	Normal	Status	—	—	15	Self	—	—
TM33	Reflect	Psychic	Status	—	—	20	Your Side	—	—
TM37	Sandstorm	Rock	Status	—	—	10	Both Sides	—	—
TM39	Rock Tomb	Rock	Physical	50	80	10	Normal	—	—
TM42	Facade	Normal	Physical	70	100	20	Normal	—	○
TM44	Rest	Psychic	Status	—	—	10	Self	—	—
TM45	Attract	Normal	Status	—	100	15	Normal	—	—
TM48	Round	Normal	Special	60	100	15	Normal	—	—
TM78	Bulldoze	Ground	Physical	60	100	20	Adjacent	—	—
TM80	Rock Slide	Rock	Physical	75	90	10	Many Others	—	—
TM87	Swagger	Normal	Status	—	90	15	Normal	—	—
TM90	Substitute	Normal	Status	—	—	10	Self	—	—
TM94	Rock Smash	Fighting	Physical	40	100	15	Normal	—	○
HM04	Strength	Normal	Physical	80	100	15	Normal	—	○

◆ Give the reminder girl at the PWT a Heart Scale to make Piloswine remember AncientPower

MOVES TAUGHT BY PEOPLE

Name	Type	Kind	Pow.	Acc.	PP	Range	Long	DA

MOVES TAUGHT BY MOVE TUTORS FOR SHARDS

Name	Type	Kind	Pow.	Acc.	PP	Range	Long	DA
Icy Wind	Ice	Special	55	95	15	Many Others	—	—
Earth Power	Ground	Special	90	100	10	Normal	—	—
Superpower	Fighting	Physical	120	100	5	Normal	—	○
Snore	Normal	Special	40	100	15	Normal	—	—
Stealth Rock	Rock	Status	—	—	20	Other Side	—	—
Endeavor	Normal	Physical	—	100	5	Normal	—	○
Sleep Talk	Normal	Status	—	—	10	Self	—	—

EGG MOVES

Name	Type	Kind	Pow.	Acc.	PP	Range	Long	DA
Take Down	Normal	Physical	90	85	20	Normal	—	○
Bite	Dark	Physical	60	100	25	Normal	—	○
Body Slam	Normal	Physical	85	100	15	Normal	—	○
AncientPower	Rock	Special	60	100	5	Normal	—	—
Mud Shot	Ground	Special	55	95	15	Normal	—	—
Icicle Spear	Ice	Physical	25	100	30	Normal	—	—
Double-Edge	Normal	Physical	120	100	15	Normal	—	○
Fissure	Ground	Physical	—	30	5	Normal	—	—
Curse	Ghost	Status	—	—	10	Varies	—	—
Avalanche	Ice	Physical	60	100	10	Normal	—	○
Stealth Rock	Rock	Status	—	—	20	Other Side	—	—
Icicle Crash	Ice	Physical	85	90	10	Normal	—	—

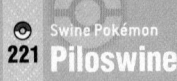

Swine Pokémon

221 Piloswine

TYPE Ice Ground

ABILITIES
- Oblivious
- Snow Cloak

HIDDEN ABILITY
- Thick Fat

- HEIGHT: 3'07"
- WEIGHT: 123.0 lbs.
- GENDER: ♂ / ♀

With its excellent sense of smell, it's even able to find mushrooms that are buried under frozen ground.

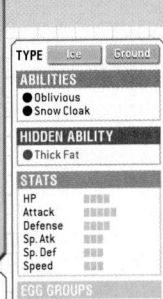

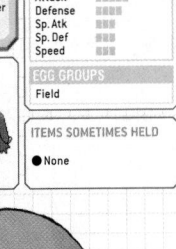

STATS
HP
Attack
Defense
Sp. Atk
Sp. Def
Speed

EGG GROUPS
Field

ITEMS SOMETIMES HELD
- None

♂ ♀

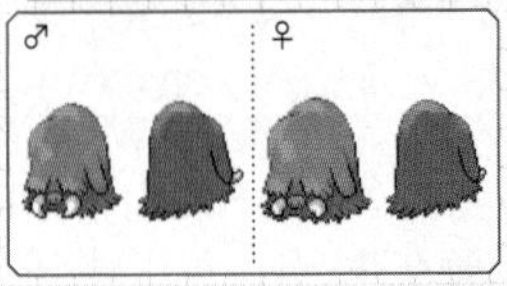

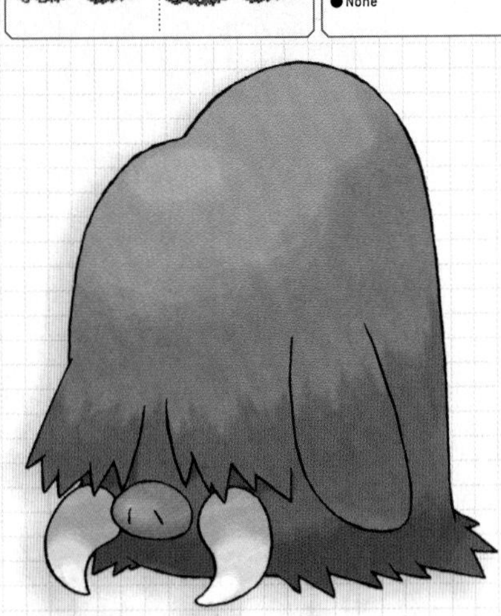

Pokémon AR Marker

EVOLUTION

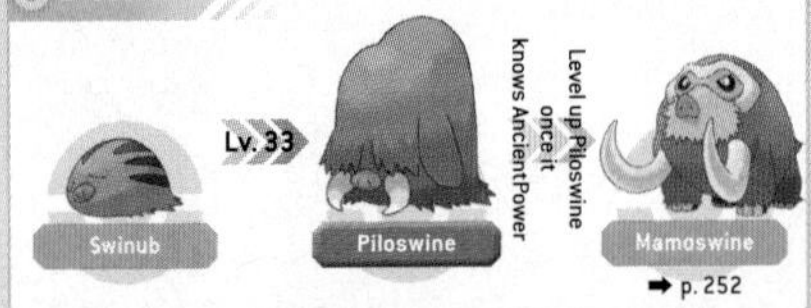

Swinub
Lv. 33
Piloswine
Level up Piloswine once it knows AncientPower
Mamoswine

➡ p. 252

LEVEL-UP AND LEARNED MOVES

Lv.	Name	Type	Kind	Pow.	Acc.	PP	Range	Long	DA
1	AncientPower	Rock	Special	60	100	5	Normal	—	—
1	Peck	Flying	Physical	35	100	35	Normal	○	○
1	Odor Sleuth	Normal	Status	—	—	40	Normal	—	—
1	Mud Sport	Ground	Status	—	—	15	Both Sides	—	—
1	Powder Snow	Ice	Special	40	100	25	Many Others	—	—
5	Mud Sport	Ground	Status	—	—	15	Both Sides	—	—
8	Powder Snow	Ice	Special	40	100	25	Many Others	—	—
11	Mud-Slap	Ground	Special	20	100	10	Normal	—	—
14	Endure	Normal	Status	—	—	10	Self	—	—
18	Mud Bomb	Ground	Special	65	85	10	Normal	—	—
21	Icy Wind	Ice	Special	55	95	15	Many Others	—	—
24	Ice Fang	Ice	Physical	65	95	15	Normal	—	○
28	Take Down	Normal	Physical	90	85	20	Normal	—	○
33	Fury Attack	Normal	Physical	15	85	20	Normal	—	○
37	Mist	Ice	Status	—	—	30	Your Side	—	—
41	Thrash	Normal	Physical	120	100	10	1 Random	—	○
46	Earthquake	Ground	Physical	100	100	10	Adjacent	—	—
52	Blizzard	Ice	Special	120	70	5	Many Others	—	—
58	Amnesia	Psychic	Status	—	—	20	Self	—	—

TM & HM MOVES

Lv.	Name	Type	Kind	Pow.	Acc.	PP	Range	Long	DA
TM05	Roar	Normal	Status	—	100	20	Normal	—	—
TM06	Toxic	Poison	Status	—	90	10	Normal	—	—
TM07	Hail	Ice	Status	—	—	10	Both Sides	—	—
TM10	Hidden Power	Normal	Special	—	100	15	Normal	—	—
TM13	Ice Beam	Ice	Special	95	100	10	Normal	—	—
TM14	Blizzard	Ice	Special	120	70	5	Many Others	—	—
TM15	Hyper Beam	Normal	Special	150	90	5	Normal	—	—
TM16	Light Screen	Psychic	Status	—	—	30	Your Side	—	—
TM17	Protect	Normal	Status	—	—	10	Self	—	—
TM18	Rain Dance	Water	Status	—	—	5	Both Sides	—	—
TM21	Frustration	Normal	Physical	—	100	20	Normal	—	○
TM26	Earthquake	Ground	Physical	100	100	10	Adjacent	—	—
TM27	Return	Normal	Physical	—	100	20	Normal	—	○
TM28	Dig	Ground	Physical	80	100	10	Normal	—	○
TM32	Double Team	Normal	Status	—	—	15	Self	—	—
TM33	Reflect	Psychic	Status	—	—	20	Your Side	—	—
TM37	Sandstorm	Rock	Status	—	—	10	Both Sides	—	—
TM39	Rock Tomb	Rock	Physical	50	80	10	Normal	—	—
TM42	Facade	Normal	Physical	70	100	20	Normal	—	○
TM44	Rest	Psychic	Status	—	—	10	Self	—	—
TM45	Attract	Normal	Status	—	100	15	Normal	—	—
TM48	Round	Normal	Special	60	100	15	Normal	—	—
TM68	Giga Impact	Normal	Physical	150	90	5	Normal	—	○
TM71	Stone Edge	Rock	Physical	100	80	5	Normal	—	—
TM78	Bulldoze	Ground	Physical	60	100	20	Adjacent	—	—
TM80	Rock Slide	Rock	Physical	75	90	10	Many Others	—	—
TM87	Swagger	Normal	Status	—	90	15	Normal	—	—
TM90	Substitute	Normal	Status	—	—	10	Self	—	—
TM94	Rock Smash	Fighting	Physical	40	100	15	Normal	—	○
HM04	Strength	Normal	Physical	80	100	15	Normal	—	○

◆ Give the reminder girl at the PWT a Heart Scale to make Piloswine remember AncientPower

HOW TO OBTAIN

Pokémon Black Version 2	❶ Giant Chasm caves ❷ Giant Chasm crater forest
Pokémon White Version 2	❶ Giant Chasm caves ❷ Giant Chasm crater forest

HOW TO OBTAIN FROM OTHER GAMES

—

—

MOVES TAUGHT BY PEOPLE

Name	Type	Kind	Pow.	Acc.	PP	Range	Long	DA

MOVES TAUGHT BY MOVE TUTORS FOR SHARDS

Name	Type	Kind	Pow.	Acc.	PP	Range	Long	DA
Icy Wind	Ice	Special	55	95	15	Many Others	—	—
Earth Power	Ground	Special	90	100	10	Normal	—	—
Superpower	Fighting	Physical	120	100	5	Normal	—	○
Snore	Normal	Special	40	100	15	Normal	—	—
Stealth Rock	Rock	Status	—	—	20	Other Side	—	—
Endeavor	Normal	Physical	—	100	5	Normal	—	○
Sleep Talk	Normal	Status	—	—	10	Self	—	—

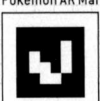

Coral Pokémon

222 Corsola

TYPE Water Rock

ABILITIES
- Hustle
- Natural Cure

HIDDEN ABILITY
- Regenerator

- HEIGHT: 2'00"
- WEIGHT: 11.0 lbs.
- GENDER: ♂ / ♀

They prefer unpolluted southern seas. Their coral branches lose their color and deteriorate in dirty water.

STATS
HP
Attack
Defense
Sp. Atk
Sp. Def
Speed

EGG GROUPS
Water ❶ / Water ❸

ITEMS SOMETIMES HELD
- Hard Stone

Same form for ♂ / ♀

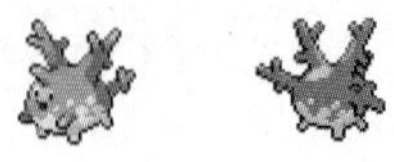

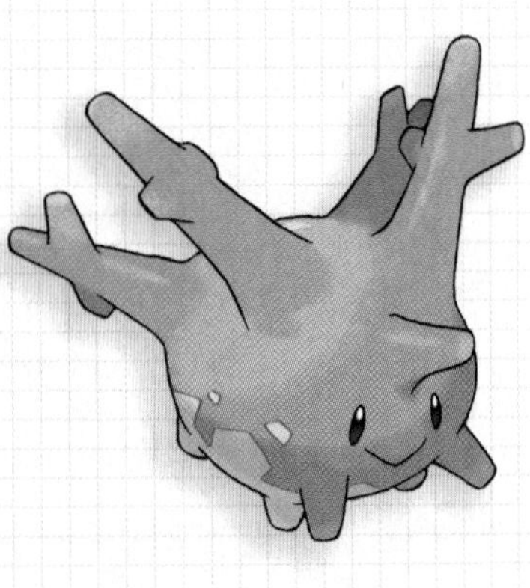

Pokémon AR Marker

EVOLUTION

Does not evolve

LEVEL-UP AND LEARNED MOVES

Lv.	Name	Type	Kind	Pow.	Acc.	PP	Range	Long	DA
1	Tackle	Normal	Physical	50	100	35	Normal	-	○
4	Harden	Normal	Status	-	-	30	Self	-	-
8	Bubble	Water	Special	20	100	30	Many Others	-	-
10	Recover	Normal	Status	-	-	10	Self	-	-
13	Refresh	Normal	Status	-	-	20	Self	-	-
17	BubbleBeam	Water	Special	65	100	20	Normal	-	-
20	AncientPower	Rock	Special	60	100	5	Normal	-	-
23	Lucky Chant	Normal	Status	-	-	30	Your Side	-	-
27	Spike Cannon	Normal	Physical	20	100	15	Normal	-	-
29	Iron Defense	Steel	Status	-	-	15	Self	-	-
31	Rock Blast	Rock	Physical	25	90	10	Normal	-	-
35	Endure	Normal	Status	-	-	10	Self	-	-
38	Aqua Ring	Water	Status	-	-	20	Self	-	-
41	Power Gem	Rock	Special	70	100	20	Normal	-	-
45	Mirror Coat	Psychic	Special	-	100	20	Varies	-	-
47	Earth Power	Ground	Special	90	100	10	Normal	-	-
52	Flail	Normal	Physical	-	100	15	Normal	-	○

TM & HM MOVES

Lv.	Name	Type	Kind	Pow.	Acc.	PP	Range	Long	DA
TM04	Calm Mind	Psychic	Status	—	—	20	Self	—	—
TM06	Toxic	Poison	Status	—	90	10	Normal	—	—
TM07	Hail	Ice	Status	—	—	10	Both Sides	—	—
TM10	Hidden Power	Normal	Special	—	100	15	Normal	—	—
TM11	Sunny Day	Fire	Status	—	—	5	Both Sides	—	—
TM13	Ice Beam	Ice	Special	95	100	10	Normal	—	—
TM14	Blizzard	Ice	Special	120	70	5	Many Others	—	—
TM16	Light Screen	Psychic	Status	—	—	30	Your Side	—	—
TM17	Protect	Normal	Status	—	—	10	Self	—	—
TM18	Rain Dance	Water	Status	—	—	5	Both Sides	—	—
TM20	Safeguard	Normal	Status	—	—	25	Your Side	—	—
TM21	Frustration	Normal	Physical	—	100	20	Normal	—	○
TM26	Earthquake	Ground	Physical	100	100	10	Adjacent	—	—
TM27	Return	Normal	Physical	—	100	20	Normal	—	○
TM28	Dig	Ground	Physical	80	100	10	Normal	—	○
TM29	Psychic	Psychic	Special	90	100	10	Normal	—	—
TM30	Shadow Ball	Ghost	Special	80	100	15	Normal	—	—
TM32	Double Team	Normal	Status	—	—	15	Self	—	—
TM33	Reflect	Psychic	Status	—	—	20	Your Side	—	—
TM37	Sandstorm	Rock	Status	—	—	10	Both Sides	—	—
TM39	Rock Tomb	Rock	Physical	50	80	10	Normal	—	—
TM42	Facade	Normal	Physical	70	100	20	Normal	—	○
TM44	Rest	Psychic	Status	—	—	10	Self	—	—
TM45	Attract	Normal	Status	—	100	15	Normal	—	—
TM48	Round	Normal	Special	60	100	15	Normal	—	—
TM55	Scald	Water	Special	80	100	15	Normal	—	—
TM64	Explosion	Normal	Physical	250	100	5	Adjacent	—	—
TM69	Rock Polish	Rock	Status	—	—	20	Self	—	—
TM71	Stone Edge	Rock	Physical	100	80	5	Normal	—	—
TM78	Bulldoze	Ground	Physical	60	100	20	Adjacent	—	—
TM80	Rock Slide	Rock	Physical	75	90	10	Many Others	—	—
TM87	Swagger	Normal	Status	—	90	15	Normal	—	—
TM90	Substitute	Normal	Status	—	—	10	Self	—	—
TM94	Rock Smash	Fighting	Physical	40	100	15	Normal	—	○
HM03	Surf	Water	Special	95	100	15	Adjacent	—	—
HM04	Strength	Normal	Physical	80	100	15	Normal	—	○

HOW TO OBTAIN

Pokémon Black Version 2	❶ Humilau City (ripples in water) ❷ Route 18 (Super Rod)
Pokémon White Version 2	❶ Humilau City (ripples in water) ❷ Route 18 (Super Rod)

HOW TO OBTAIN FROM OTHER GAMES

—

—

MOVES TAUGHT BY PEOPLE

Name	Type	Kind	Pow.	Acc.	PP	Range	Long	DA

MOVES TAUGHT BY MOVE TUTORS FOR SHARDS

Name	Type	Kind	Pow.	Acc.	PP	Range	Long	DA
Iron Defense	Steel	Status	—	—	15	Self	—	—
Magic Coat	Psychic	Status	—	—	15	Self	—	—
Icy Wind	Ice	Special	55	95	15	Many Others	—	—
Earth Power	Ground	Special	90	100	10	Normal	—	—
Snore	Normal	Special	40	100	15	Normal	—	—
Stealth Rock	Rock	Status	—	—	20	Other Side	—	—
Endeavor	Normal	Physical	—	100	5	Normal	—	○
Sleep Talk	Normal	Status	—	—	10	Self	—	—

EGG MOVES

Name	Type	Kind	Pow.	Acc.	PP	Range	Long	DA
Screech	Normal	Status	—	85	40	Normal	—	—
Mist	Ice	Status	—	—	30	Your Side	—	—
Amnesia	Psychic	Status	—	—	20	Self	—	—
Barrier	Psychic	Status	—	—	30	Self	—	—
Ingrain	Grass	Status	—	—	20	Self	—	—
Confuse Ray	Ghost	Status	—	100	10	Normal	—	—
Icicle Spear	Ice	Physical	25	100	30	Normal	—	—
Nature Power	Normal	Status	—	—	20	Varies	—	—
Aqua Ring	Water	Status	—	—	20	Self	—	—
Curse	Ghost	Status	—	—	10	Varies	—	—
Bide	Normal	Physical	—	—	10	Self	—	○
Water Pulse	Water	Special	60	100	20	Normal	○	—
Head Smash	Rock	Physical	150	80	5	Normal	—	○

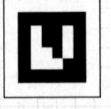

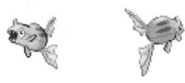

Jet Pokémon

223 Remoraid

- HEIGHT: 2'00"
- WEIGHT: 26.5 lbs.
- GENDER: ♂ / ♀

The water they shoot from their mouths can hit moving prey from more than 300 feet away.

TYPE: Water

ABILITIES
- Hustle
- Sniper

HIDDEN ABILITY
- Moody

STATS
- HP
- Attack
- Defense
- Sp. Atk
- Sp. Def
- Speed

EGG GROUPS
Water ❶ / Water ❷

ITEMS SOMETIMES HELD
- None

Same form for ♂ / ♀

EVOLUTION
Remoraid → Lv. 25 → Octillery

HOW TO OBTAIN

Pokémon Black Version 2	❶ Undella Bay (water surface) ❷ Route 21 (water surface)
Pokémon White Version 2	❶ Undella Bay (water surface) ❷ Route 21 (water surface)

HOW TO OBTAIN FROM OTHER GAMES
—
—

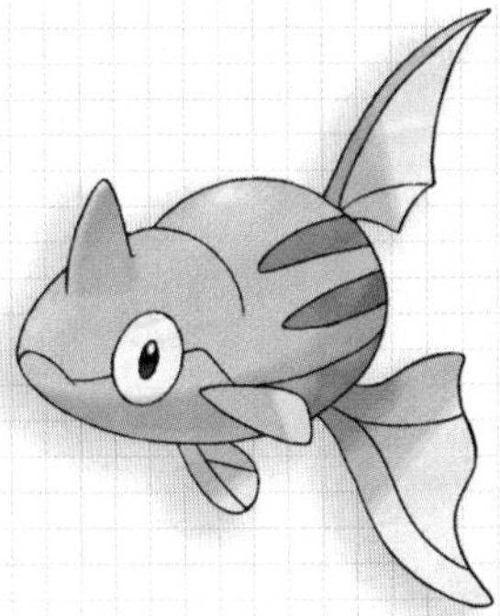

Pokémon AR Marker

LEVEL-UP AND LEARNED MOVES

Lv.	Name	Type	Kind	Pow.	Acc.	PP	Range	Long	DA
1	Water Gun	Water	Special	40	100	25	Normal	—	—
6	Lock-On	Normal	Status	—	—	5	Normal	—	—
10	Psybeam	Psychic	Special	65	100	20	Normal	—	—
14	Aurora Beam	Ice	Special	65	100	20	Normal	—	—
18	BubbleBeam	Water	Special	65	100	20	Normal	—	—
22	Focus Energy	Normal	Status	—	—	30	Self	—	—
26	Water Pulse	Water	Special	60	100	20	Normal	○	—
30	Signal Beam	Bug	Special	75	100	15	Normal	—	—
34	Ice Beam	Ice	Special	95	100	10	Normal	—	—
38	Bullet Seed	Grass	Physical	25	100	30	Normal	—	—
42	Hydro Pump	Water	Special	120	80	5	Normal	—	—
46	Hyper Beam	Normal	Special	150	90	5	Normal	—	—
50	Soak	Water	Status	—	100	20	Normal	—	—

TM & HM MOVES

Lv.	Name	Type	Kind	Pow.	Acc.	PP	Range	Long	DA
TM06	Toxic	Poison	Status	—	90	10	Normal	—	—
TM10	Hidden Power	Normal	Special	—	100	15	Normal	—	—
TM11	Sunny Day	Fire	Status	—	—	5	Both Sides	—	—
TM13	Ice Beam	Ice	Special	95	100	10	Normal	—	—
TM14	Blizzard	Ice	Special	120	70	5	Many Others	—	—
TM15	Hyper Beam	Normal	Special	150	90	5	Normal	—	—
TM17	Protect	Normal	Status	—	—	10	Self	—	—
TM18	Rain Dance	Water	Status	—	—	5	Both Sides	—	—
TM21	Frustration	Normal	Physical	—	100	20	Normal	—	○
TM23	Smack Down	Rock	Physical	50	100	15	Normal	—	—
TM27	Return	Normal	Physical	—	100	20	Normal	—	○
TM29	Psychic	Psychic	Special	90	100	10	Normal	—	—
TM32	Double Team	Normal	Status	—	—	15	Self	—	—
TM35	Flamethrower	Fire	Special	95	100	15	Normal	—	—
TM38	Fire Blast	Fire	Special	120	85	5	Normal	—	—
TM42	Facade	Normal	Physical	70	100	20	Normal	—	○
TM44	Rest	Psychic	Status	—	—	10	Self	—	—
TM45	Attract	Normal	Status	—	100	15	Normal	—	—
TM46	Thief	Dark	Physical	40	100	10	Normal	—	○
TM48	Round	Normal	Special	60	100	15	Normal	—	—
TM55	Scald	Water	Special	80	100	15	Normal	—	—
TM57	Charge Beam	Electric	Special	50	90	10	Normal	—	—
TM59	Incinerate	Fire	Special	30	100	15	Many Others	—	—
TM73	Thunder Wave	Electric	Status	—	100	20	Normal	—	—
TM87	Swagger	Normal	Status	—	90	15	Normal	—	—
TM90	Substitute	Normal	Status	—	—	10	Self	—	—
HM03	Surf	Water	Special	95	100	15	Adjacent	—	—
HM05	Waterfall	Water	Physical	80	100	15	Normal	—	○
HM06	Dive	Water	Physical	80	100	10	Normal	—	○

MOVES TAUGHT BY PEOPLE

Name	Type	Kind	Pow.	Acc.	PP	Range	Long	DA

MOVES TAUGHT BY MOVE TUTORS FOR SHARDS

Name	Type	Kind	Pow.	Acc.	PP	Range	Long	DA
Bounce	Flying	Physical	85	85	5	Normal	○	○
Signal Beam	Bug	Special	75	100	15	Normal	—	—
Seed Bomb	Grass	Physical	80	100	15	Normal	—	—
Gunk Shot	Poison	Physical	120	70	5	Normal	—	—
Icy Wind	Ice	Special	55	95	15	Many Others	—	—
Snore	Normal	Special	40	100	15	Normal	—	—
Sleep Talk	Normal	Status	—	—	10	Self	—	—

EGG MOVES

Name	Type	Kind	Pow.	Acc.	PP	Range	Long	DA
Aurora Beam	Ice	Special	65	100	20	Normal	—	—
Octazooka	Water	Special	65	85	10	Normal	—	—
Supersonic	Normal	Status	—	55	20	Normal	—	—
Haze	Ice	Status	—	—	30	Both Sides	—	—
Screech	Normal	Status	—	85	40	Normal	—	—
Rock Blast	Rock	Physical	25	90	10	Normal	—	—
Snore	Normal	Special	40	100	15	Normal	—	—
Flail	Normal	Physical	—	100	15	Normal	—	○
Water Spout	Water	Special	150	100	5	Many Others	—	—
Mud Shot	Ground	Special	55	95	15	Normal	—	—
Swift	Normal	Special	60	—	20	Many Others	—	—
Acid Spray	Poison	Special	40	100	20	Normal	—	—
Water Pulse	Water	Special	60	100	20	Normal	○	—

Jet Pokémon

224 Octillery

- HEIGHT: 2'11"
- WEIGHT: 62.8 lbs.
- GENDER: ♂ / ♀

It has a tendency to want to be in holes. It prefers rock crags or pots and sprays ink from them before attacking.

TYPE: Water

ABILITIES
- Suction Cups
- Sniper

HIDDEN ABILITY
- Moody

STATS
- HP
- Attack
- Defense
- Sp. Atk
- Sp. Def
- Speed

EGG GROUPS
Water ❶ / Water ❷

ITEMS SOMETIMES HELD
- None

♂ | ♀

EVOLUTION
Remoraid → Lv. 25 → Octillery

HOW TO OBTAIN

Pokémon Black Version 2	❶ Undella Bay (Super Rod—ripples in water) ❷ Route 21 (Super Rod—ripples in water)
Pokémon White Version 2	❶ Undella Bay (Super Rod—ripples in water) ❷ Route 21 (Super Rod—ripples in water)

HOW TO OBTAIN FROM OTHER GAMES
—
—

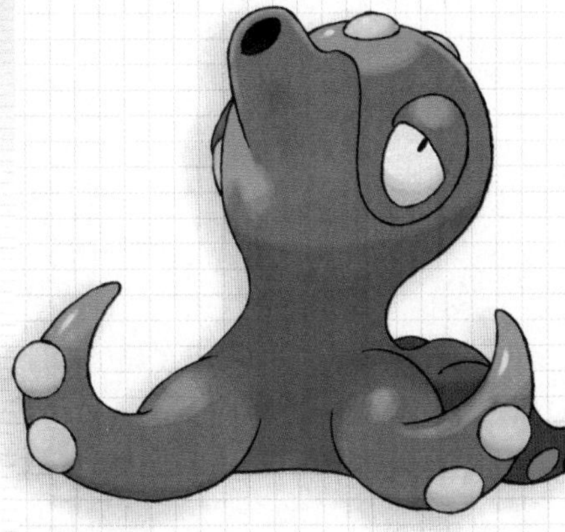

Pokémon AR Marker

LEVEL-UP AND LEARNED MOVES

Lv.	Name	Type	Kind	Pow.	Acc.	PP	Range	Long	DA
1	Gunk Shot	Poison	Physical	120	70	5	Normal	—	—
1	Rock Blast	Rock	Physical	25	90	10	Normal	—	—
1	Water Gun	Water	Special	40	100	25	Normal	—	—
1	Constrict	Normal	Physical	10	100	35	Normal	—	○
1	Psybeam	Psychic	Special	65	100	20	Normal	—	—
1	Aurora Beam	Ice	Special	65	100	20	Normal	—	—
6	Constrict	Normal	Physical	10	100	35	Normal	—	○
10	Psybeam	Psychic	Special	65	100	20	Normal	—	—
14	Aurora Beam	Ice	Special	65	100	20	Normal	—	—
18	BubbleBeam	Water	Special	65	100	20	Normal	—	—
22	Focus Energy	Normal	Status	—	—	30	Self	—	—
25	Octazooka	Water	Special	65	85	10	Normal	—	—
28	Wring Out	Normal	Special	—	100	5	Normal	—	○
34	Signal Beam	Bug	Special	75	100	15	Normal	—	—
40	Ice Beam	Ice	Special	95	100	10	Normal	—	—
46	Bullet Seed	Grass	Physical	25	100	30	Normal	—	—
52	Hydro Pump	Water	Special	120	80	5	Normal	—	—
58	Hyper Beam	Normal	Special	150	90	5	Normal	—	—
64	Soak	Water	Status	—	100	20	Normal	—	—

TM & HM MOVES

Lv.	Name	Type	Kind	Pow.	Acc.	PP	Range	Long	DA
TM06	Toxic	Poison	Status	—	90	10	Normal	—	—
TM10	Hidden Power	Normal	Special	—	100	15	Normal	—	—
TM11	Sunny Day	Fire	Status	—	—	5	Both Sides	—	—
TM13	Ice Beam	Ice	Special	95	100	10	Normal	—	—
TM14	Blizzard	Ice	Special	120	70	5	Many Others	—	—
TM15	Hyper Beam	Normal	Special	150	90	5	Normal	—	—
TM17	Protect	Normal	Status	—	—	10	Self	—	—
TM18	Rain Dance	Water	Status	—	—	5	Both Sides	—	—
TM21	Frustration	Normal	Physical	—	100	20	Normal	—	○
TM23	Smack Down	Rock	Physical	50	100	15	Normal	—	—
TM27	Return	Normal	Physical	—	100	20	Normal	—	○
TM29	Psychic	Psychic	Special	90	100	10	Normal	—	—
TM32	Double Team	Normal	Status	—	—	15	Self	—	—
TM34	Sludge Wave	Poison	Special	95	100	10	Adjacent	—	—
TM35	Flamethrower	Fire	Special	95	100	15	Normal	—	—
TM36	Sludge Bomb	Poison	Special	90	100	10	Normal	—	—
TM38	Fire Blast	Fire	Special	120	85	5	Normal	—	—
TM42	Facade	Normal	Physical	70	100	20	Normal	—	○
TM44	Rest	Psychic	Status	—	—	10	Self	—	—
TM45	Attract	Normal	Status	—	100	15	Normal	—	—
TM46	Thief	Dark	Physical	40	100	10	Normal	—	○
TM48	Round	Normal	Special	60	100	15	Normal	—	—
TM53	Energy Ball	Grass	Special	80	100	10	Normal	—	—
TM55	Scald	Water	Special	80	100	15	Normal	—	—
TM57	Charge Beam	Electric	Special	50	90	10	Normal	—	—
TM59	Incinerate	Fire	Special	30	100	15	Many Others	—	—
TM66	Payback	Dark	Physical	50	100	10	Normal	—	○
TM68	Giga Impact	Normal	Physical	150	90	5	Normal	—	○
TM73	Thunder Wave	Electric	Status	—	100	20	Normal	—	—
TM87	Swagger	Normal	Status	—	90	15	Normal	—	—
TM90	Substitute	Normal	Status	—	—	10	Self	—	—
TM91	Flash Cannon	Steel	Special	80	100	10	Normal	—	—
HM03	Surf	Water	Special	95	100	15	Adjacent	—	—
HM05	Waterfall	Water	Physical	80	100	15	Normal	—	○
HM06	Dive	Water	Physical	80	100	10	Normal	—	○

MOVES TAUGHT BY PEOPLE

Name	Type	Kind	Pow.	Acc.	PP	Range	Long	DA

MOVES TAUGHT BY MOVE TUTORS FOR SHARDS

Name	Type	Kind	Pow.	Acc.	PP	Range	Long	DA
Bounce	Flying	Physical	85	85	5	Normal	○	○
Signal Beam	Bug	Special	75	100	15	Normal	—	—
Seed Bomb	Grass	Physical	80	100	15	Normal	—	—
Gunk Shot	Poison	Physical	120	70	5	Normal	—	—
Icy Wind	Ice	Special	55	95	15	Many Others	—	—
Bind	Normal	Physical	15	85	20	Normal	—	○
Snore	Normal	Special	40	100	15	Normal	—	—
Sleep Talk	Normal	Status	—	—	10	Self	—	—

223 | Remoraid
224 | Octillery

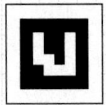

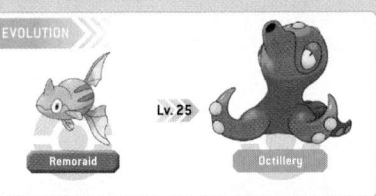

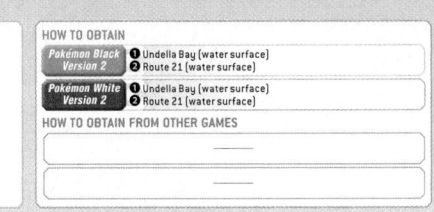

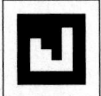

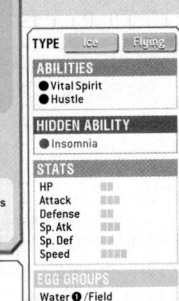

225 Delibird
Delivery Pokémon

TYPE Ice / Flying

ABILITIES
● Vital Spirit
● Hustle

HIDDEN ABILITY
● Insomnia

● HEIGHT: 2'11"
● WEIGHT: 35.3 lbs.
● GENDER: ♂ / ♀

It carries food all day long. When someone is lost in the mountains, it shares that food.

STATS
HP
Attack
Defense
Sp. Atk
Sp. Def
Speed

EGG GROUPS
Water ● / Field

ITEMS SOMETIMES HELD
● None

Same form for ♂ / ♀

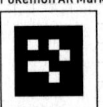

Pokémon AR Marker

EVOLUTION
Does not evolve

HOW TO OBTAIN
Pokémon Black Version 2	❶ Route 22 ❷ Giant Chasm caves
Pokémon White Version 2	❶ Route 22 ❷ Giant Chasm caves

HOW TO OBTAIN FROM OTHER GAMES

LEVEL-UP AND LEARNED MOVES
Lv.	Name	Type	Kind	Pow.	Acc.	PP	Range	Long	DA
1	Present	Normal	Physical	—	90	15	Normal	—	—

MOVES TAUGHT BY PEOPLE
Name	Type	Kind	Pow.	Acc.	PP	Range	Long	DA

MOVES TAUGHT BY MOVE TUTORS FOR SHARDS
Name	Type	Kind	Pow.	Acc.	PP	Range	Long	DA
Bounce	Flying	Physical	85	85	5	Normal	○	—
Signal Beam	Bug	Special	75	100	15	Normal	—	—
Seed Bomb	Grass	Physical	80	100	15	Normal	—	—
Gunk Shot	Poison	Physical	120	70	5	Normal	—	—
Ice Punch	Ice	Physical	75	100	15	Normal	—	—
Icy Wind	Ice	Special	55	95	15	Many Others	—	—
Sky Attack	Flying	Physical	140	90	5	Normal	○	—
Recycle	Normal	Status	—	—	10	Self	—	—
Sleep Talk	Normal	Status	—	—	10	Self	—	—

TM & HM MOVES
Lv.	Name	Type	Kind	Pow.	Acc.	PP	Range	Long	DA
TM06	Toxic	Poison	Status	—	90	10	Normal	—	—
TM07	Hail	Ice	Status	—	—	10	Both Sides	—	—
TM10	Hidden Power	Normal	Special	—	100	15	Normal	—	—
TM13	Ice Beam	Ice	Special	95	100	10	Normal	—	—
TM14	Blizzard	Ice	Special	120	70	5	Many Others	—	—
TM17	Protect	Normal	Status	—	—	10	Self	—	—
TM18	Rain Dance	Water	Status	—	—	5	Both Sides	—	—
TM21	Frustration	Normal	Physical	—	100	20	Normal	—	○
TM27	Return	Normal	Physical	—	100	20	Normal	—	○
TM31	Brick Break	Fighting	Physical	75	100	15	Normal	—	○
TM32	Double Team	Normal	Status	—	—	15	Self	—	—
TM40	Aerial Ace	Flying	Physical	60	—	20	Normal	○	—
TM42	Facade	Normal	Physical	70	100	20	Normal	—	—
TM44	Rest	Psychic	Status	—	—	10	Self	—	—
TM45	Attract	Normal	Status	—	100	15	Normal	—	—
TM46	Thief	Dark	Physical	40	100	10	Normal	—	○
TM48	Round	Normal	Special	60	100	15	Normal	—	—
TM56	Fling	Dark	Physical	—	100	10	Normal	—	—
TM79	Frost Breath	Ice	Special	40	90	10	Normal	—	—
TM87	Swagger	Normal	Status	—	90	15	Normal	—	—
TM88	Pluck	Flying	Physical	60	100	20	Normal	—	—
TM90	Substitute	Normal	Status	—	—	10	Self	—	—
HM02	Fly	Flying	Physical	90	95	15	Normal	○	—

EGG MOVES
Name	Type	Kind	Pow.	Acc.	PP	Range	Long	DA
Aurora Beam	Ice	Special	65	100	20	Normal	—	—
Quick Attack	Normal	Physical	40	100	30	Normal	—	○
Future Sight	Psychic	Special	100	100	10	Normal	—	—
Splash	Normal	Status	—	—	40	Self	—	○
Rapid Spin	Normal	Physical	20	100	40	Normal	—	○
Ice Ball	Ice	Physical	30	90	20	Normal	—	○
Ice Shard	Ice	Physical	40	100	30	Normal	—	○
Ice Punch	Ice	Physical	75	100	15	Normal	—	○
Fake Out	Normal	Physical	40	100	10	Normal	—	○
Bestow	Normal	Status	—	—	15	Normal	—	—
Icy Wind	Ice	Special	55	95	15	Many Others	—	—

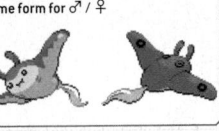

226 Mantine
Kite Pokémon

TYPE Water / Flying

ABILITIES
● Swift Swim
● Water Absorb

HIDDEN ABILITY
● Water Veil

● HEIGHT: 6'11"
● WEIGHT: 485.0 lbs.
● GENDER: ♂ / ♀

If it builds up enough speed swimming, it can fly over 300 feet out of the water from the surface of the ocean.

STATS
HP
Attack
Defense
Sp. Atk
Sp. Def
Speed

EGG GROUPS
Water ●

ITEMS SOMETIMES HELD
● None

Same form for ♂ / ♀

Pokémon AR Marker

EVOLUTION
Mantyke → Mantine

Level up Mantyke while Remoraid is in your party

→ p. 245

HOW TO OBTAIN
Pokémon Black Version 2	❶ Route 21 (ripples in water) ❷ Undella Bay (ripples in water—spring, summer, and autumn only)
Pokémon White Version 2	❶ Route 21 (ripples in water) ❷ Undella Bay (ripples in water—spring, summer, and autumn only)

HOW TO OBTAIN FROM OTHER GAMES

LEVEL-UP AND LEARNED MOVES
Lv.	Name	Type	Kind	Pow.	Acc.	PP	Range	Long	DA
1	Psybeam	Psychic	Special	65	100	20	Normal	-	-
1	Bullet Seed	Grass	Physical	25	100	30	Normal	-	○
1	Signal Beam	Bug	Special	75	100	15	Normal	-	-
1	Tackle	Normal	Physical	50	100	35	Normal	-	-
1	Bubble	Water	Special	20	100	30	Many Others	-	-
1	Supersonic	Normal	Status	-	55	20	Normal	-	-
1	BubbleBeam	Water	Special	65	100	20	Normal	-	-
5	Supersonic	Normal	Status	-	55	20	Normal	-	-
7	BubbleBeam	Water	Special	65	100	20	Normal	-	-
11	Confuse Ray	Ghost	Status	-	100	10	Normal	-	-
14	Wing Attack	Flying	Physical	60	100	35	Normal	○	○
16	Headbutt	Normal	Physical	70	100	15	Normal	-	○
19	Water Pulse	Water	Special	60	100	20	Normal	-	○
23	Wide Guard	Rock	Status	-	-	10	Your Side	-	-
27	Take Down	Normal	Physical	90	85	20	Normal	-	○
32	Agility	Psychic	Status	-	-	30	Self	-	-
36	Air Slash	Flying	Special	75	95	20	Normal	○	-
39	Aqua Ring	Water	Status	-	-	20	Self	-	-
46	Bounce	Flying	Physical	85	85	5	Normal	○	○
49	Hydro Pump	Water	Special	120	80	5	Normal	-	-

MOVES TAUGHT BY PEOPLE
Name	Type	Kind	Pow.	Acc.	PP	Range	Long	DA

MOVES TAUGHT BY MOVE TUTORS FOR SHARDS
Name	Type	Kind	Pow.	Acc.	PP	Range	Long	DA
Bounce	Flying	Physical	85	85	5	Normal	○	—
Signal Beam	Bug	Special	75	100	15	Normal	—	—
Iron Head	Steel	Physical	80	100	15	Normal	—	—
Seed Bomb	Grass	Physical	80	100	15	Normal	—	—
Gunk Shot	Poison	Physical	120	70	5	Normal	—	—
Icy Wind	Ice	Special	55	95	15	Many Others	—	—
Aqua Tail	Water	Physical	90	90	10	Normal	—	—
Snore	Normal	Special	40	100	15	Normal	—	—
Tailwind	Flying	Status	—	—	30	Your Side	—	—
Helping Hand	Normal	Status	—	—	20	1 Ally	—	—
Sleep Talk	Normal	Status	—	—	10	Self	—	—

TM & HM MOVES
Lv.	Name	Type	Kind	Pow.	Acc.	PP	Range	Long	DA
TM06	Toxic	Poison	Status	—	90	10	Normal	—	—
TM07	Hail	Ice	Status	—	—	10	Both Sides	—	—
TM10	Hidden Power	Normal	Special	—	100	15	Normal	—	—
TM13	Ice Beam	Ice	Special	95	100	10	Normal	—	—
TM14	Blizzard	Ice	Special	120	70	5	Many Others	—	—
TM15	Hyper Beam	Normal	Special	150	90	5	Normal	—	—
TM17	Protect	Normal	Status	—	—	10	Self	—	—
TM18	Rain Dance	Water	Status	—	—	5	Both Sides	—	—
TM21	Frustration	Normal	Physical	—	100	20	Normal	—	○
TM26	Earthquake	Ground	Physical	100	100	10	Adjacent	—	—
TM27	Return	Normal	Physical	—	100	20	Normal	—	○
TM32	Double Team	Normal	Status	—	—	15	Self	—	—
TM39	Rock Tomb	Rock	Physical	50	80	10	Normal	—	—
TM40	Aerial Ace	Flying	Physical	60	—	20	Normal	○	—
TM42	Facade	Normal	Physical	70	100	20	Normal	—	—
TM44	Rest	Psychic	Status	—	—	10	Self	—	—
TM45	Attract	Normal	Status	—	100	15	Normal	—	—
TM48	Round	Normal	Special	60	100	15	Normal	—	—
TM55	Scald	Water	Special	80	100	15	Normal	—	—
TM62	Acrobatics	Flying	Physical	55	100	15	Normal	○	—
TM68	Giga Impact	Normal	Physical	150	90	5	Normal	—	—
TM78	Bulldoze	Ground	Physical	60	100	20	Adjacent	—	—
TM80	Rock Slide	Rock	Physical	75	90	10	Many Others	—	—
TM87	Swagger	Normal	Status	—	90	15	Normal	—	—
TM90	Substitute	Normal	Status	—	—	10	Self	—	—
HM03	Surf	Water	Special	95	100	15	Adjacent	—	—
HM05	Waterfall	Water	Physical	80	100	15	Normal	—	○
HM06	Dive	Water	Physical	80	100	10	Normal	—	—

EGG MOVES
Name	Type	Kind	Pow.	Acc.	PP	Range	Long	DA
Twister	Dragon	Special	40	100	20	Many Others	—	—
Hydro Pump	Water	Special	120	80	5	Normal	—	—
Haze	Ice	Status	—	—	30	Both Sides	—	—
Slam	Normal	Physical	80	75	20	Normal	—	—
Mud Sport	Ground	Status	—	—	15	Varies	—	—
Mirror Coat	Psychic	Special	—	100	20	Both Sides	—	—
Water Sport	Water	Status	—	—	15	Both Sides	—	—
Splash	Normal	Status	—	—	40	Self	—	○
Wide Guard	Rock	Status	—	—	10	Your Side	—	—
Amnesia	Psychic	Status	—	—	20	Self	—	—

Armor Bird Pokémon

227 Skarmory

- HEIGHT: 5'07"
- WEIGHT: 111.3 lbs.
- GENDER: ♂ / ♀

Its heavy-looking iron body is actually thin and light, so it can fly at speeds over 180 mph.

Same form for ♂ / ♀

TYPE: Steel / Flying

ABILITIES
- Keen Eye
- Sturdy

HIDDEN ABILITY
- Weak Armor

STATS
HP
Attack
Defense
Sp. Atk
Sp. Def
Speed

EGG GROUPS
Flying

ITEMS SOMETIMES HELD
- None

EVOLUTION
Does not evolve

HOW TO OBTAIN

Pokémon Black Version 2	Reversal Mountain outside
Pokémon White Version 2	Reversal Mountain outside

HOW TO OBTAIN FROM OTHER GAMES
—
—

Pokémon AR Marker

LEVEL-UP AND LEARNED MOVES

Lv.	Name	Type	Kind	Pow.	Acc.	PP	Range	Long	DA
1	Leer	Normal	Status	—	100	30	Many Others	—	—
1	Peck	Flying	Physical	35	100	35	Normal	○	○
6	Sand-Attack	Ground	Status	—	100	15	Normal	—	—
9	Swift	Normal	Special	60	—	20	Many Others	—	—
12	Agility	Psychic	Status	—	—	30	Self	—	—
17	Fury Attack	Normal	Physical	15	85	20	Normal	—	○
20	Feint	Normal	Physical	30	100	10	Normal	—	—
23	Air Cutter	Flying	Special	55	95	25	Many Others	—	—
28	Spikes	Ground	Status	—	—	20	Other Side	—	—
31	Metal Sound	Steel	Status	—	85	40	Normal	—	—
34	Steel Wing	Steel	Physical	70	90	25	Normal	—	○
39	Autotomize	Steel	Status	—	—	15	Self	—	—
42	Air Slash	Flying	Special	75	95	20	Normal	○	—
45	Slash	Normal	Physical	70	100	20	Normal	—	○
50	Night Slash	Dark	Physical	70	100	15	Normal	—	○

TM & HM MOVES

Lv.	Name	Type	Kind	Pow.	Acc.	PP	Range	Long	DA
TM05	Roar	Normal	Status	—	100	20	Normal	—	—
TM06	Toxic	Poison	Status	—	90	10	Normal	—	—
TM10	Hidden Power	Normal	Special	—	100	15	Normal	—	—
TM11	Sunny Day	Fire	Status	—	—	5	Both Sides	—	—
TM12	Taunt	Dark	Status	—	100	20	Normal	—	—
TM17	Protect	Normal	Status	—	—	10	Self	—	—
TM21	Frustration	Normal	Physical	—	100	20	Normal	—	○
TM27	Return	Normal	Physical	—	100	20	Normal	—	○
TM32	Double Team	Normal	Status	—	—	15	Self	—	—
TM37	Sandstorm	Rock	Status	—	—	10	Both Sides	—	—
TM39	Rock Tomb	Rock	Physical	50	80	10	Normal	—	—
TM40	Aerial Ace	Flying	Physical	60	—	20	Normal	○	○
TM41	Torment	Dark	Status	—	100	15	Normal	—	—
TM42	Facade	Normal	Physical	70	100	20	Normal	—	○
TM44	Rest	Psychic	Status	—	—	10	Self	—	—
TM45	Attract	Normal	Status	—	100	15	Normal	—	—
TM46	Thief	Dark	Physical	40	100	10	Normal	—	○
TM48	Round	Normal	Special	60	100	15	Normal	—	—
TM58	Sky Drop	Flying	Physical	60	100	10	Normal	○	○
TM66	Payback	Dark	Physical	50	100	10	Normal	—	○
TM70	Flash	Normal	Status	—	100	20	Normal	—	—
TM75	Swords Dance	Normal	Status	—	—	30	Self	—	—
TM80	Rock Slide	Rock	Physical	75	90	10	Many Others	—	—
TM81	X-Scissor	Bug	Physical	80	100	15	Normal	—	○
TM87	Swagger	Normal	Status	—	90	15	Normal	—	—
TM88	Pluck	Flying	Physical	60	100	20	Normal	○	○
TM90	Substitute	Normal	Status	—	—	10	Self	—	—
TM91	Flash Cannon	Steel	Special	80	100	10	Normal	—	—
TM94	Rock Smash	Fighting	Physical	40	100	15	Normal	—	○
HM01	Cut	Normal	Physical	50	95	30	Normal	—	○
HM02	Fly	Flying	Physical	90	95	15	Normal	○	○

MOVES TAUGHT BY PEOPLE

Name	Type	Kind	Pow.	Acc.	PP	Range	Long	DA

MOVES TAUGHT BY MOVE TUTORS FOR SHARDS

Name	Type	Kind	Pow.	Acc.	PP	Range	Long	DA
Iron Head	Steel	Physical	80	100	15	Normal	—	○
Iron Defense	Steel	Status	—	—	15	Self	—	—
Icy Wind	Ice	Special	55	95	15	Many Others	—	—
Dark Pulse	Dark	Special	80	100	15	Normal	○	—
Snore	Normal	Special	40	100	15	Normal	—	—
Roost	Flying	Status	—	—	10	Self	—	—
Sky Attack	Flying	Physical	140	90	5	Normal	○	—
Tailwind	Flying	Status	—	—	30	Your Side	—	—
Stealth Rock	Rock	Status	—	—	20	Other Side	—	—
Sleep Talk	Normal	Status	—	—	10	Self	—	—

EGG MOVES

Name	Type	Kind	Pow.	Acc.	PP	Range	Long	DA
Drill Peck	Flying	Physical	80	100	20	Normal	○	○
Pursuit	Dark	Physical	40	100	20	Normal	—	○
Whirlwind	Normal	Status	—	100	20	Normal	—	—
Sky Attack	Flying	Physical	140	90	5	Normal	○	—
Curse	Ghost	Status	—	—	10	Varies	—	—
Brave Bird	Flying	Physical	120	100	15	Normal	○	○
Assurance	Dark	Physical	50	100	10	Normal	—	○
Guard Swap	Psychic	Status	—	—	10	Normal	—	—
Stealth Rock	Rock	Status	—	—	20	Other Side	—	—
Endure	Normal	Status	—	—	10	Self	—	—

Dark Pokémon

228 Houndour

- HEIGHT: 2'00"
- WEIGHT: 23.8 lbs.
- GENDER: ♂ / ♀

It is smart enough to hunt in packs. It uses a variety of cries for communicating with others.

Same form for ♂ / ♀

TYPE: Dark / Fire

ABILITIES
- Early Bird
- Flash Fire

HIDDEN ABILITY
- Unnerve

STATS
HP
Attack
Defense
Sp. Atk
Sp. Def
Speed

EGG GROUPS
Field

ITEMS SOMETIMES HELD
- None

EVOLUTION

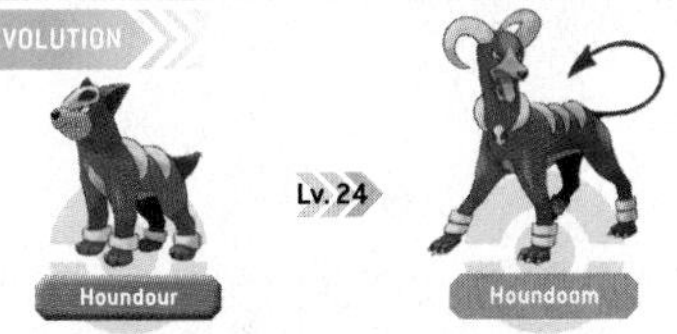

HOW TO OBTAIN

Pokémon Black Version 2	Link Trade or Poké Transfer
Pokémon White Version 2	Link Trade or Poké Transfer

HOW TO OBTAIN FROM OTHER GAMES

Pokémon Black Version	Route 9 (mass outbreak)
—	

Pokémon AR Marker

LEVEL-UP AND LEARNED MOVES

Lv.	Name	Type	Kind	Pow.	Acc.	PP	Range	Long	DA
1	Leer	Normal	Status	—	100	30	Many Others	—	—
1	Ember	Fire	Special	40	100	25	Normal	—	—
4	Howl	Normal	Status	—	—	40	Self	—	—
8	Smog	Poison	Special	20	70	20	Normal	—	—
13	Roar	Normal	Status	—	100	20	Normal	—	—
16	Bite	Dark	Physical	60	100	25	Normal	—	○
20	Odor Sleuth	Normal	Status	—	—	40	Normal	—	—
25	Beat Up	Dark	Physical	—	100	10	Normal	—	—
28	Fire Fang	Fire	Physical	65	95	15	Normal	—	○
32	Faint Attack	Dark	Physical	60	—	20	Normal	—	○
37	Embargo	Dark	Status	—	100	15	Normal	—	—
40	Foul Play	Dark	Physical	95	100	15	Normal	—	○
44	Flamethrower	Fire	Special	95	100	15	Normal	—	—
49	Crunch	Dark	Physical	80	100	15	Normal	—	○
52	Nasty Plot	Dark	Status	—	—	20	Self	—	—
56	Inferno	Fire	Special	100	50	5	Normal	—	—

TM & HM MOVES

Lv.	Name	Type	Kind	Pow.	Acc.	PP	Range	Long	DA
TM05	Roar	Normal	Status	—	100	20	Normal	—	—
TM06	Toxic	Poison	Status	—	90	10	Normal	—	—
TM10	Hidden Power	Normal	Special	—	100	15	Normal	—	—
TM11	Sunny Day	Fire	Status	—	—	5	Both Sides	—	—
TM12	Taunt	Dark	Status	—	100	20	Normal	—	—
TM17	Protect	Normal	Status	—	—	10	Self	—	—
TM21	Frustration	Normal	Physical	—	100	20	Normal	—	○
TM22	SolarBeam	Grass	Special	120	100	10	Normal	—	—
TM27	Return	Normal	Physical	—	100	20	Normal	—	○
TM30	Shadow Ball	Ghost	Special	80	100	15	Normal	—	—
TM32	Double Team	Normal	Status	—	—	15	Self	—	—
TM35	Flamethrower	Fire	Special	95	100	15	Normal	—	—
TM36	Sludge Bomb	Poison	Special	90	100	10	Normal	—	—
TM38	Fire Blast	Fire	Special	120	85	5	Normal	—	—
TM41	Torment	Dark	Status	—	100	15	Normal	—	—
TM42	Facade	Normal	Physical	70	100	20	Normal	—	○
TM43	Flame Charge	Fire	Physical	50	100	20	Normal	—	○
TM44	Rest	Psychic	Status	—	—	10	Self	—	—
TM45	Attract	Normal	Status	—	100	15	Normal	—	—
TM46	Thief	Dark	Physical	40	100	10	Normal	—	○
TM48	Round	Normal	Special	60	100	15	Normal	—	—
TM50	Overheat	Fire	Special	140	90	5	Normal	—	—
TM59	Incinerate	Fire	Special	30	100	15	Many Others	—	—
TM61	Will-O-Wisp	Fire	Status	—	75	15	Normal	—	—
TM63	Embargo	Dark	Status	—	100	15	Normal	—	—
TM66	Payback	Dark	Physical	50	100	10	Normal	—	○
TM67	Retaliate	Normal	Physical	70	100	5	Normal	—	○
TM85	Dream Eater	Psychic	Special	100	100	15	Normal	—	—
TM87	Swagger	Normal	Status	—	90	15	Normal	—	—
TM90	Substitute	Normal	Status	—	—	10	Self	—	—
TM94	Rock Smash	Fighting	Physical	40	100	15	Normal	—	○
TM95	Snarl	Dark	Special	55	95	15	Many Others	—	—

MOVES TAUGHT BY PEOPLE

Name	Type	Kind	Pow.	Acc.	PP	Range	Long	DA

MOVES TAUGHT BY MOVE TUTORS FOR SHARDS

Name	Type	Kind	Pow.	Acc.	PP	Range	Long	DA
Super Fang	Normal	Physical	—	90	10	Normal	—	○
Uproar	Normal	Special	90	100	10	1 Random	—	—
Hyper Voice	Normal	Special	90	100	10	Many Others	—	—
Iron Tail	Steel	Physical	100	75	15	Normal	—	○
Foul Play	Dark	Physical	95	100	15	Normal	—	○
Dark Pulse	Dark	Special	80	100	15	Normal	○	—
Snore	Normal	Special	40	100	15	Normal	—	—
Role Play	Psychic	Status	—	—	10	Normal	—	—
Heat Wave	Fire	Special	100	90	10	Many Others	—	—
Spite	Ghost	Status	—	100	10	Normal	—	—
Sleep Talk	Normal	Status	—	—	10	Self	—	—
Snatch	Dark	Status	—	—	10	Self	—	—

EGG MOVES

Name	Type	Kind	Pow.	Acc.	PP	Range	Long	DA
Fire Spin	Fire	Special	35	85	15	Normal	—	—
Rage	Normal	Physical	20	100	20	Normal	—	○
Pursuit	Dark	Physical	40	100	20	Normal	—	○
Counter	Fighting	Physical	—	100	20	Varies	—	○
Spite	Ghost	Status	—	100	10	Normal	—	—
Reversal	Fighting	Physical	—	100	15	Normal	—	○
Beat Up	Dark	Physical	—	100	10	Normal	—	—
Fire Fang	Fire	Physical	65	95	15	Normal	—	○
Thunder Fang	Electric	Physical	65	95	15	Normal	—	○
Nasty Plot	Dark	Status	—	—	20	Self	—	—
Punishment	Dark	Physical	—	100	5	Normal	—	○
Feint	Normal	Physical	30	100	10	Normal	—	—
Sucker Punch	Dark	Physical	80	100	5	Normal	—	○

229 Houndoom
Dark Pokémon

TYPE Dark / Fire

ABILITIES
- Early Bird
- Flash Fire

HIDDEN ABILITY
- Unnerve

- HEIGHT: 4'07"
- WEIGHT: 77.2 lbs.
- GENDER: ♂ / ♀

The flames it breathes when angry contain toxins. If they cause a burn, it will hurt forever.

STATS
- HP
- Attack
- Defense
- Sp. Atk
- Sp. Def
- Speed

EGG GROUPS
Field

ITEMS SOMETIMES HELD
- None

♂   ♀

Pokémon AR Marker

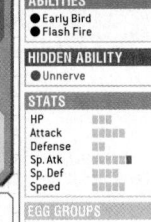 

EVOLUTION

Houndour → Lv. 24 → Houndoom

HOW TO OBTAIN
Pokémon Black Version 2	Link Trade or Poké Transfer
Pokémon White Version 2	Link Trade or Poké Transfer

HOW TO OBTAIN FROM OTHER GAMES
Pokémon Pearl Version	Occasionally appears on Route 214 (use Poké Radar for a better chance)

LEVEL-UP AND LEARNED MOVES
Lv.	Name	Type	Kind	Pow.	Acc.	PP	Range	Long	DA
1	Thunder Fang	Electric	Physical	65	95	15	Normal	—	○
1	Leer	Normal	Status	—	100	30	Many Others	—	—
1	Ember	Fire	Special	40	100	25	Normal	—	—
1	Howl	Normal	Status	—	—	40	Self	—	—
1	Smog	Poison	Special	20	70	20	Normal	—	—
4	Howl	Normal	Status	—	—	40	Self	—	—
8	Smog	Poison	Special	20	70	20	Normal	—	—
13	Roar	Normal	Status	—	100	20	Normal	—	—
16	Bite	Dark	Physical	60	100	25	Normal	—	○
20	Odor Sleuth	Normal	Status	—	—	40	Normal	—	—
26	Beat Up	Dark	Physical	—	100	10	Normal	—	—
30	Fire Fang	Fire	Physical	65	95	15	Normal	—	○
35	Faint Attack	Dark	Physical	60	—	20	Normal	—	—
41	Embargo	Dark	Status	—	100	15	Normal	—	—
45	Foul Play	Dark	Physical	95	100	15	Normal	—	○
50	Flamethrower	Fire	Special	95	100	15	Normal	—	—
56	Crunch	Dark	Physical	80	100	15	Normal	—	○
60	Nasty Plot	Dark	Status	—	—	20	Self	—	—
65	Inferno	Fire	Special	100	50	5	Normal	—	—

TM & HM MOVES
Lv.	Name	Type	Kind	Pow.	Acc.	PP	Range	Long	DA
TM05	Roar	Normal	Status	—	100	20	Normal	—	—
TM06	Toxic	Poison	Status	—	90	10	Normal	—	—
TM10	Hidden Power	Normal	Special	—	100	15	Normal	—	—
TM11	Sunny Day	Fire	Status	—	—	5	Both Sides	—	—
TM12	Taunt	Dark	Status	—	100	20	Normal	—	—
TM15	Hyper Beam	Normal	Special	150	90	5	Normal	—	—
TM17	Protect	Normal	Status	—	—	10	Self	—	—
TM21	Frustration	Normal	Physical	—	100	20	Normal	—	○
TM22	SolarBeam	Grass	Special	120	100	10	Normal	—	—
TM27	Return	Normal	Physical	—	100	20	Normal	—	○
TM30	Shadow Ball	Ghost	Special	80	100	15	Normal	—	—
TM32	Double Team	Normal	Status	—	—	15	Self	—	—
TM35	Flamethrower	Fire	Special	95	100	15	Normal	—	—
TM36	Sludge Bomb	Poison	Special	90	100	10	Normal	—	—
TM38	Fire Blast	Fire	Special	120	85	5	Normal	—	—
TM41	Torment	Dark	Status	—	100	15	Normal	—	—
TM42	Facade	Normal	Physical	70	100	20	Normal	—	○
TM43	Flame Charge	Fire	Physical	50	100	20	Normal	—	○
TM44	Rest	Psychic	Status	—	—	10	Self	—	—
TM45	Attract	Normal	Status	—	100	15	Normal	—	—
TM46	Thief	Dark	Physical	40	100	10	Normal	—	○
TM48	Round	Normal	Special	60	100	15	Normal	—	—
TM50	Overheat	Fire	Special	140	90	5	Normal	—	—
TM59	Incinerate	Fire	Special	30	100	15	Many Others	—	—
TM61	Will-O-Wisp	Fire	Status	—	75	15	Normal	—	—
TM63	Embargo	Dark	Status	—	100	15	Normal	—	—
TM66	Payback	Dark	Physical	50	100	10	Normal	—	○
TM67	Retaliate	Normal	Physical	70	100	5	Normal	—	○
TM68	Giga Impact	Normal	Physical	150	90	5	Normal	—	○
TM85	Dream Eater	Psychic	Special	100	100	15	Normal	—	—
TM87	Swagger	Normal	Status	—	90	15	Normal	—	—
TM90	Substitute	Normal	Status	—	—	10	Self	—	—
TM94	Rock Smash	Fighting	Physical	40	100	15	Normal	—	○
TM95	Snarl	Dark	Special	55	95	15	Many Others	—	—

Lv.	Name	Type	Kind	Pow.	Acc.	PP	Range	Long	DA
HM04	Strength	Normal	Physical	80	100	15	Normal	—	—

MOVES TAUGHT BY PEOPLE
Name	Type	Kind	Pow.	Acc.	PP	Range	Long	DA

MOVES TAUGHT BY MOVE TUTORS FOR SHARDS
Name	Type	Kind	Pow.	Acc.	PP	Range	Long	DA
Super Fang	Normal	Physical	—	90	10	Normal	—	○
Uproar	Normal	Special	90	100	10	1 Random	—	—
Hyper Voice	Normal	Special	90	100	10	Many Others	—	—
Iron Tail	Steel	Physical	100	75	15	Normal	—	○
Foul Play	Dark	Physical	95	100	15	Normal	—	○
Dark Pulse	Dark	Special	80	100	15	Normal	○	—
Snore	Normal	Special	40	100	15	Normal	—	—
Role Play	Psychic	Status	—	—	10	Normal	—	—
Heat Wave	Fire	Special	100	90	10	Many Others	—	—
Spite	Ghost	Status	—	100	10	Normal	—	—
Sleep Talk	Normal	Status	—	—	10	Self	—	—
Snatch	Dark	Status	—	—	10	Self	—	—

---

230 Kingdra
Dragon Pokémon

TYPE Water / Dragon

ABILITIES
- Swift Swim
- Sniper

HIDDEN ABILITY
- Damp

- HEIGHT: 5'11"
- WEIGHT: 335.1 lbs.
- GENDER: ♂ / ♀

It lives in caves on the seafloor and creates giant whirlpools every time it moves.

Same form for ♂ / ♀

STATS
- HP
- Attack
- Defense
- Sp. Atk
- Sp. Def
- Speed

EGG GROUPS
Water ❶ / Dragon

ITEMS SOMETIMES HELD
- Dragon Scale

Pokémon AR Marker

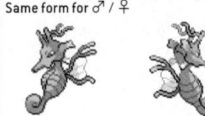

EVOLUTION

Horsea → p.71 → Lv. 32 → Seadra → p.72 → Have it hold the Dragon Scale and Link Trade it → Kingdra

HOW TO OBTAIN
Pokémon Black Version 2	❶ Route 17 (Super Rod—ripples in water) ❷ Route 18 (Super Rod—ripples in water)
Pokémon White Version 2	❶ Route 17 (Super Rod—ripples in water) ❷ Route 18 (Super Rod—ripples in water)

HOW TO OBTAIN FROM OTHER GAMES

LEVEL-UP AND LEARNED MOVES
Lv.	Name	Type	Kind	Pow.	Acc.	PP	Range	Long	DA
1	Yawn	Normal	Status	—	—	10	Normal	—	—
1	Bubble	Water	Special	20	100	30	Many Others	—	—
1	SmokeScreen	Normal	Status	—	100	20	Normal	—	—
1	Leer	Normal	Status	—	100	30	Many Others	—	—
4	Water Gun	Water	Special	40	100	25	Normal	—	—
4	SmokeScreen	Normal	Status	—	100	20	Normal	—	—
8	Leer	Normal	Status	—	100	30	Many Others	—	—
11	Water Gun	Water	Special	40	100	25	Normal	—	—
14	Focus Energy	Normal	Status	—	—	30	Self	—	—
18	BubbleBeam	Water	Special	65	100	20	Normal	—	—
23	Agility	Psychic	Status	—	—	30	Self	—	—
26	Twister	Dragon	Special	40	100	20	Many Others	—	—
30	Brine	Water	Special	65	100	10	Normal	—	—
40	Hydro Pump	Water	Special	120	80	5	Normal	—	—
48	Dragon Dance	Dragon	Status	—	—	20	Self	—	—
57	Dragon Pulse	Dragon	Special	90	100	10	Normal	○	—

TM & HM MOVES
Lv.	Name	Type	Kind	Pow.	Acc.	PP	Range	Long	DA
TM06	Toxic	Poison	Status	—	90	10	Normal	—	—
TM07	Hail	Ice	Status	—	—	10	Both Sides	—	—
TM10	Hidden Power	Normal	Special	—	100	15	Normal	—	—
TM13	Ice Beam	Ice	Special	95	100	10	Normal	—	—
TM14	Blizzard	Ice	Special	120	70	5	Many Others	—	—
TM15	Hyper Beam	Normal	Special	150	90	5	Normal	—	—
TM17	Protect	Normal	Status	—	—	10	Self	—	—
TM18	Rain Dance	Water	Status	—	—	5	Both Sides	—	—
TM21	Frustration	Normal	Physical	—	100	20	Normal	—	○
TM27	Return	Normal	Physical	—	100	20	Normal	—	○
TM32	Double Team	Normal	Status	—	—	15	Self	—	○
TM42	Facade	Normal	Physical	70	100	20	Normal	—	○
TM44	Rest	Psychic	Status	—	—	10	Self	—	—
TM45	Attract	Normal	Status	—	100	15	Normal	—	—
TM48	Round	Normal	Special	60	100	15	Normal	—	—
TM55	Scald	Water	Special	80	100	15	Normal	—	—
TM68	Giga Impact	Normal	Physical	150	90	5	Normal	—	○
TM87	Swagger	Normal	Status	—	90	15	Normal	—	—
TM90	Substitute	Normal	Status	—	—	10	Self	—	—
TM91	Flash Cannon	Steel	Special	80	100	10	Normal	—	—
HM03	Surf	Water	Special	95	100	15	Adjacent	—	—
HM05	Waterfall	Water	Physical	80	100	15	Normal	—	○
HM06	Dive	Water	Physical	80	100	10	Normal	—	○

MOVES TAUGHT BY PEOPLE
Name	Type	Kind	Pow.	Acc.	PP	Range	Long	DA
Draco Meteor	Dragon	Special	140	90	5	Normal	—	—

MOVES TAUGHT BY MOVE TUTORS FOR SHARDS
Name	Type	Kind	Pow.	Acc.	PP	Range	Long	DA
Bounce	Flying	Physical	85	85	5	Normal	○	○
Signal Beam	Bug	Special	75	100	15	Normal	—	—
Iron Head	Steel	Physical	80	100	15	Normal	—	○
Icy Wind	Ice	Special	55	95	15	Many Others	—	—
Dragon Pulse	Dragon	Special	90	100	10	Normal	○	—
Snore	Normal	Special	40	100	15	Normal	—	—
Outrage	Dragon	Physical	120	100	10	1 Random	—	○
Sleep Talk	Normal	Status	—	—	10	Self	—	—

Houndoom | 229
Kingdra | 230

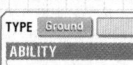

231 Phanpy

Long Nose Pokémon

- HEIGHT: 1'08"
- WEIGHT: 73.9 lbs.
- GENDER: ♂ / ♀

It is strong despite its compact size. It can easily pick up and carry an adult human on its back.

Same form for ♂ / ♀

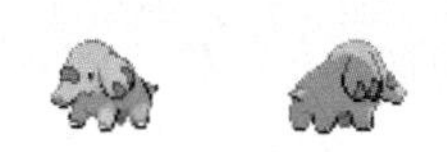

TYPE Ground

ABILITY
- Pickup

HIDDEN ABILITY
- Sand Veil

STATS
HP
Attack
Defense
Sp. Atk
Sp. Def
Speed

EGG GROUPS
Field

ITEMS SOMETIMES HELD
- None

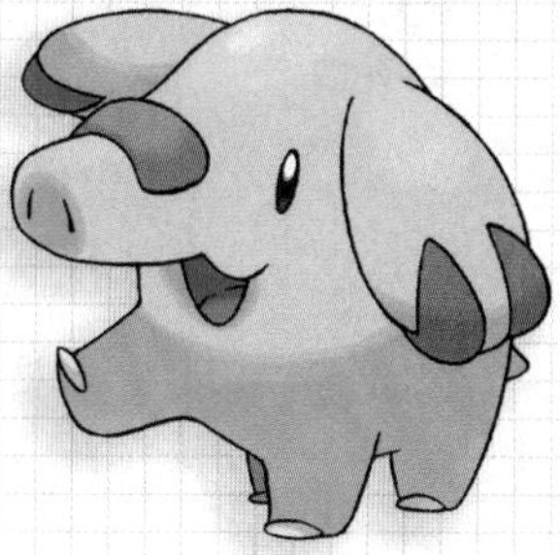

Pokémon AR Marker

EVOLUTION

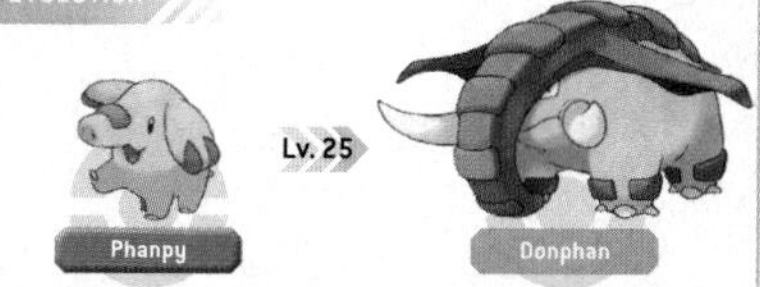

HOW TO OBTAIN

Pokémon Black Version 2	If your character is a girl, trade Pokémon during a date with Curtis (10th time)
Pokémon White Version 2	If your character is a girl, trade Pokémon during a date with Curtis (10th time)

HOW TO OBTAIN FROM OTHER GAMES

Pokémon HeartGold Version	Route 45
Pokémon Platinum Version	Route 207 (mass outbreak)

LEVEL-UP AND LEARNED MOVES

Lv.	Name	Type	Kind	Pow.	Acc.	PP	Range	Long	DA
1	Odor Sleuth	Normal	Status	—	—	40	Normal	—	—
1	Tackle	Normal	Physical	50	100	35	Normal	—	○
1	Growl	Normal	Status	—	100	40	Many Others	—	—
1	Defense Curl	Normal	Status	—	—	40	Self	—	—
6	Flail	Normal	Physical	—	100	15	Normal	—	○
10	Take Down	Normal	Physical	90	85	20	Normal	—	○
15	Rollout	Rock	Physical	30	90	20	Normal	—	○
19	Natural Gift	Normal	Physical	—	100	15	Normal	—	—
24	Slam	Normal	Physical	80	75	20	Normal	—	○
28	Endure	Normal	Status	—	—	10	Self	—	—
33	Charm	Normal	Status	—	100	20	Normal	—	—
37	Last Resort	Normal	Physical	140	100	5	Normal	—	○
42	Double-Edge	Normal	Physical	120	100	15	Normal	—	○

TM & HM MOVES

Lv.	Name	Type	Kind	Pow.	Acc.	PP	Range	Long	DA
TM05	Roar	Normal	Status	—	100	20	Normal	—	—
TM06	Toxic	Poison	Status	—	90	10	Normal	—	—
TM10	Hidden Power	Normal	Special	—	100	15	Normal	—	—
TM11	Sunny Day	Fire	Status	—	—	5	Both Sides	—	—
TM17	Protect	Normal	Status	—	—	10	Self	—	—
TM21	Frustration	Normal	Physical	—	100	20	Normal	—	○
TM26	Earthquake	Ground	Physical	100	100	10	Adjacent	—	—
TM27	Return	Normal	Physical	—	100	20	Normal	—	○
TM32	Double Team	Normal	Status	—	—	15	Self	—	—
TM37	Sandstorm	Rock	Status	—	—	10	Both Sides	—	—
TM39	Rock Tomb	Rock	Physical	50	80	10	Normal	—	—
TM42	Facade	Normal	Physical	70	100	20	Normal	—	○
TM44	Rest	Psychic	Status	—	—	10	Self	—	—
TM45	Attract	Normal	Status	—	100	15	Normal	—	—
TM48	Round	Normal	Special	60	100	15	Normal	—	—
TM49	Echoed Voice	Normal	Special	40	100	15	Normal	—	—
TM78	Bulldoze	Ground	Physical	60	100	20	Adjacent	—	—
TM80	Rock Slide	Rock	Physical	75	90	10	Many Others	—	—
TM87	Swagger	Normal	Status	—	90	15	Normal	—	—
TM90	Substitute	Normal	Status	—	—	10	Self	—	—
TM94	Rock Smash	Fighting	Physical	40	100	15	Normal	—	○
HM04	Strength	Normal	Physical	80	100	15	Normal	—	○

MOVES TAUGHT BY PEOPLE

Name	Type	Kind	Pow.	Acc.	PP	Range	Long	DA

MOVES TAUGHT BY MOVE TUTORS FOR SHARDS

Name	Type	Kind	Pow.	Acc.	PP	Range	Long	DA
Seed Bomb	Grass	Physical	80	100	15	Normal	—	—
Gunk Shot	Poison	Physical	120	70	5	Normal	—	—
Last Resort	Normal	Physical	140	100	5	Normal	—	○
Hyper Voice	Normal	Special	90	100	10	Many Others	—	—
Iron Tail	Steel	Physical	100	75	15	Normal	—	○
Earth Power	Ground	Special	90	100	10	Normal	—	—
Superpower	Fighting	Physical	120	100	5	Normal	—	○
Snore	Normal	Special	40	100	15	Normal	—	—
Knock Off	Dark	Physical	20	100	20	Normal	—	○
Stealth Rock	Rock	Status	—	—	20	Other Side	—	—
Endeavor	Normal	Physical	—	100	5	Normal	—	○
Sleep Talk	Normal	Status	—	—	10	Self	—	—

EGG MOVES

Name	Type	Kind	Pow.	Acc.	PP	Range	Long	DA
Focus Energy	Normal	Status	—	—	30	Self	—	—
Body Slam	Normal	Physical	85	100	15	Normal	—	○
AncientPower	Rock	Special	60	100	5	Normal	—	—
Snore	Normal	Special	40	100	15	Normal	—	—
Counter	Fighting	Physical	—	100	20	Varies	—	○
Fissure	Ground	Physical	—	30	5	Normal	—	—
Endeavor	Normal	Physical	—	100	5	Normal	—	○
Ice Shard	Ice	Physical	40	100	30	Normal	—	—
Head Smash	Rock	Physical	150	80	5	Normal	—	○
Mud-Slap	Ground	Special	20	100	10	Normal	—	—
Heavy Slam	Steel	Physical	—	100	10	Normal	—	○

232 Donphan

Armor Pokémon

- HEIGHT: 3'07"
- WEIGHT: 264.6 lbs.
- GENDER: ♂ / ♀

It attacks by curling up then rolling into its foe. It can blow apart a house in one hit.

♂ ♀

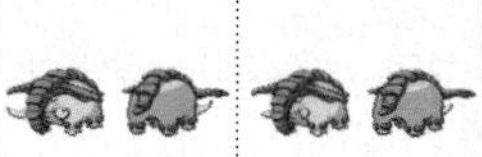

TYPE Ground

ABILITY
- Sturdy

HIDDEN ABILITY
- Sand Veil

STATS
HP
Attack
Defense
Sp. Atk
Sp. Def
Speed

EGG GROUPS
Field

ITEMS SOMETIMES HELD
- None

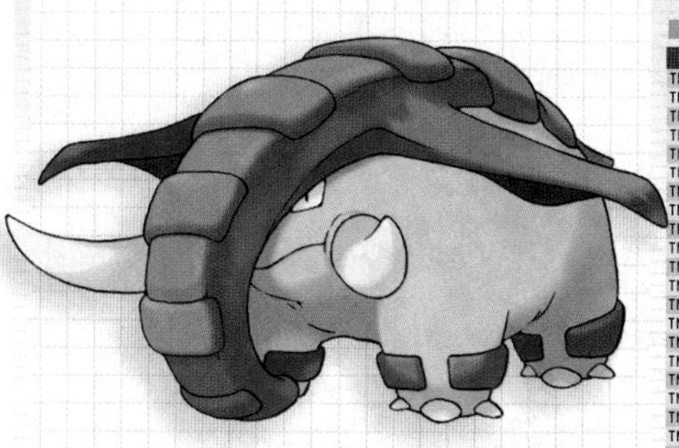

Pokémon AR Marker

EVOLUTION

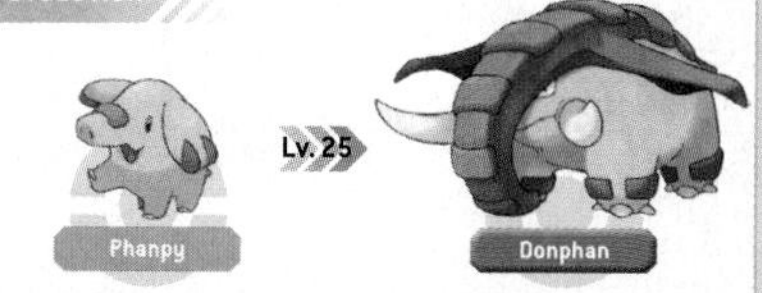

HOW TO OBTAIN

Pokémon Black Version 2	If your character is a girl, level up the Phanpy you receive from Curtis to Lv. 25
Pokémon White Version 2	If your character is a girl, level up the Phanpy you receive from Curtis to Lv. 25

HOW TO OBTAIN FROM OTHER GAMES

Pokémon HeartGold Version	Victory Road
	—

LEVEL-UP AND LEARNED MOVES

Lv.	Name	Type	Kind	Pow.	Acc.	PP	Range	Long	DA
1	Fire Fang	Fire	Physical	65	95	15	Normal	—	○
1	Thunder Fang	Electric	Physical	65	95	15	Normal	—	○
1	Horn Attack	Normal	Physical	65	100	25	Normal	—	○
1	Growl	Normal	Status	—	100	40	Many Others	—	—
1	Defense Curl	Normal	Status	—	—	40	Self	—	—
1	Bulldoze	Ground	Physical	60	100	20	Adjacent	—	—
6	Rapid Spin	Normal	Physical	20	100	40	Normal	—	○
10	Knock Off	Dark	Physical	20	100	20	Normal	—	○
15	Rollout	Rock	Physical	30	90	20	Normal	—	○
19	Magnitude	Ground	Physical	—	100	30	Adjacent	—	—
24	Slam	Normal	Physical	80	75	20	Normal	—	○
25	Fury Attack	Normal	Physical	15	85	20	Normal	—	○
31	Assurance	Dark	Physical	50	100	10	Normal	—	○
39	Scary Face	Normal	Status	—	100	10	Normal	—	—
46	Earthquake	Ground	Physical	100	100	10	Adjacent	—	—
54	Giga Impact	Normal	Physical	150	90	5	Normal	—	○

TM & HM MOVES

Lv.	Name	Type	Kind	Pow.	Acc.	PP	Range	Long	DA
TM05	Roar	Normal	Status	—	100	20	Normal	—	—
TM06	Toxic	Poison	Status	—	90	10	Normal	—	—
TM10	Hidden Power	Normal	Special	—	100	15	Normal	—	—
TM11	Sunny Day	Fire	Status	—	—	5	Both Sides	—	—
TM15	Hyper Beam	Normal	Special	150	90	5	Normal	—	—
TM17	Protect	Normal	Status	—	—	10	Self	—	—
TM21	Frustration	Normal	Physical	—	100	20	Normal	—	○
TM26	Earthquake	Ground	Physical	100	100	10	Adjacent	—	—
TM27	Return	Normal	Physical	—	100	20	Normal	—	○
TM32	Double Team	Normal	Status	—	—	15	Self	—	—
TM37	Sandstorm	Rock	Status	—	—	10	Both Sides	—	—
TM39	Rock Tomb	Rock	Physical	50	80	10	Normal	—	—
TM42	Facade	Normal	Physical	70	100	20	Normal	—	○
TM44	Rest	Psychic	Status	—	—	10	Self	—	—
TM45	Attract	Normal	Status	—	100	15	Normal	—	—
TM48	Round	Normal	Special	60	100	15	Normal	—	—
TM49	Echoed Voice	Normal	Special	40	100	15	Normal	—	—
TM68	Giga Impact	Normal	Physical	150	90	5	Normal	—	○
TM69	Rock Polish	Rock	Status	—	—	20	Self	—	—
TM71	Stone Edge	Rock	Physical	100	80	5	Normal	—	—
TM74	Gyro Ball	Steel	Physical	—	100	5	Normal	—	○
TM78	Bulldoze	Ground	Physical	60	100	20	Adjacent	—	—
TM80	Rock Slide	Rock	Physical	75	90	10	Many Others	—	—
TM84	Poison Jab	Poison	Physical	80	100	20	Normal	—	○
TM87	Swagger	Normal	Status	—	90	15	Normal	—	—
TM90	Substitute	Normal	Status	—	—	10	Self	—	—
TM94	Rock Smash	Fighting	Physical	40	100	15	Normal	—	○
HM04	Strength	Normal	Physical	80	100	15	Normal	—	○

MOVES TAUGHT BY PEOPLE

Name	Type	Kind	Pow.	Acc.	PP	Range	Long	DA

MOVES TAUGHT BY MOVE TUTORS FOR SHARDS

Name	Type	Kind	Pow.	Acc.	PP	Range	Long	DA
Bounce	Flying	Physical	85	85	5	Normal	○	○
Seed Bomb	Grass	Physical	80	100	15	Normal	—	—
Gunk Shot	Poison	Physical	120	70	5	Normal	—	—
Last Resort	Normal	Physical	140	100	5	Normal	—	○
Iron Defense	Steel	Status	—	—	15	Self	—	—
Block	Normal	Status	—	—	5	Normal	—	—
Hyper Voice	Normal	Special	90	100	10	Many Others	—	—
Iron Tail	Steel	Physical	100	75	15	Normal	—	○
Earth Power	Ground	Special	90	100	10	Normal	—	—
Superpower	Fighting	Physical	120	100	5	Normal	—	○
Snore	Normal	Special	40	100	15	Normal	—	—
Knock Off	Dark	Physical	20	100	20	Normal	—	○
Stealth Rock	Rock	Status	—	—	20	Other Side	—	—
Endeavor	Normal	Physical	—	100	5	Normal	—	○
Sleep Talk	Normal	Status	—	—	10	Self	—	—

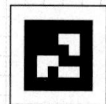

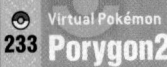

Virtual Pokémon

233 Porygon2

- HEIGHT: 2'00"
- WEIGHT: 71.6 lbs.
- GENDER: Unknown

It was upgraded to enable the exploration of other planets. However, it failed to measure up.

Gender unknown

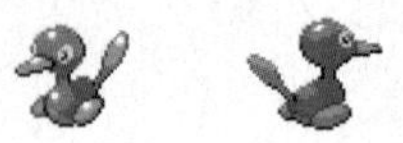

TYPE Normal

ABILITIES
- Trace
- Download

HIDDEN ABILITY
- Analytic

STATS
HP
Attack
Defense
Sp. Atk
Sp. Def
Speed

EGG GROUPS
Mineral

ITEMS SOMETIMES HELD
- None

EVOLUTION

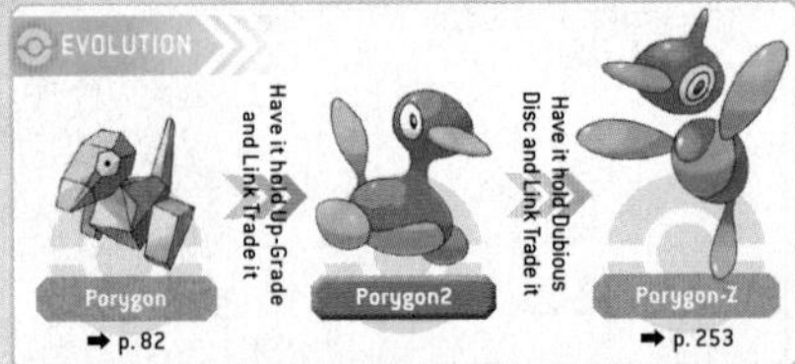
Porygon
Have it hold Up-Grade and Link Trade it
Porygon2
Have it hold Dubious Disc and Link Trade it
Porygon-Z

➡ p. 82
➡ p. 253

HOW TO OBTAIN

Pokémon Black Version 2	Have Porygon sent to you via Link Trade while holding Up-Grade to receive Porygon2
Pokémon White Version 2	Have Porygon sent to you via Link Trade while holding Up-Grade to receive Porygon2

HOW TO OBTAIN FROM OTHER GAMES

——
——

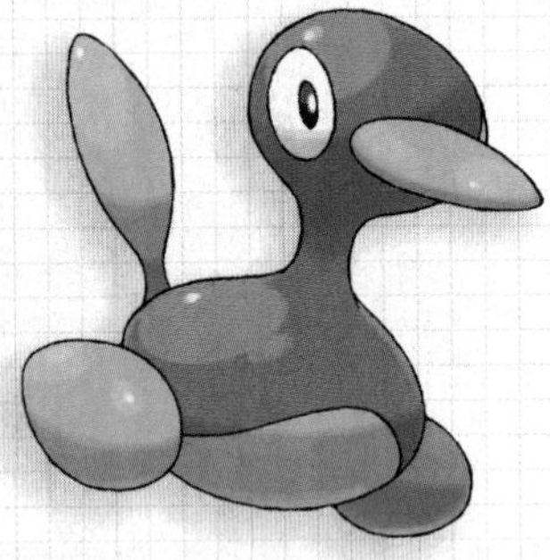

LEVEL-UP AND LEARNED MOVES

Lv.	Name	Type	Kind	Pow.	Acc.	PP	Range	Long	DA
1	Conversion 2	Normal	Status	—	—	30	Normal	—	—
1	Tackle	Normal	Physical	50	100	35	Normal	—	○
1	Conversion	Normal	Status	—	—	30	Self	—	—
1	Defense Curl	Normal	Status	—	—	40	Self	—	—
7	Psybeam	Psychic	Special	65	100	20	Normal	—	—
12	Agility	Psychic	Status	—	—	30	Self	—	—
18	Recover	Normal	Status	—	—	10	Self	—	—
23	Magnet Rise	Electric	Status	—	—	10	Self	—	—
29	Signal Beam	Bug	Special	75	100	15	Normal	—	—
34	Recycle	Normal	Status	—	—	10	Self	—	—
40	Discharge	Electric	Special	80	100	15	Adjacent	—	—
45	Lock—On	Normal	Status	—	—	5	Normal	—	—
51	Tri Attack	Normal	Special	80	100	10	Normal	—	—
56	Magic Coat	Psychic	Status	—	—	15	Self	—	—
62	Zap Cannon	Electric	Special	120	50	5	Normal	—	—
67	Hyper Beam	Normal	Special	150	90	5	Normal	—	—

TM & HM MOVES

Lv.	Name	Type	Kind	Pow.	Acc.	PP	Range	Long	DA
TM03	Psyshock	Psychic	Special	80	100	10	Normal	—	—
TM06	Toxic	Poison	Status	—	90	10	Normal	—	—
TM10	Hidden Power	Normal	Special	—	100	15	Normal	—	—
TM11	Sunny Day	Fire	Status	—	—	5	Both Sides	—	—
TM13	Ice Beam	Ice	Special	95	100	10	Normal	—	—
TM14	Blizzard	Ice	Special	120	70	5	Many Others	—	—
TM15	Hyper Beam	Normal	Special	150	90	5	Normal	—	—
TM17	Protect	Normal	Status	—	—	10	Self	—	—
TM18	Rain Dance	Water	Status	—	—	5	Both Sides	—	—
TM21	Frustration	Normal	Physical	—	100	20	Normal	—	○
TM22	SolarBeam	Grass	Special	120	100	10	Normal	—	—
TM24	Thunderbolt	Electric	Special	95	100	15	Normal	—	—
TM25	Thunder	Electric	Special	120	70	10	Normal	—	—
TM27	Return	Normal	Physical	—	100	20	Normal	—	○
TM29	Psychic	Psychic	Special	90	100	10	Normal	—	—
TM30	Shadow Ball	Ghost	Special	80	100	15	Normal	—	—
TM32	Double Team	Normal	Status	—	—	15	Self	—	—
TM40	Aerial Ace	Flying	Physical	60	—	20	Normal	○	○
TM42	Facade	Normal	Physical	70	100	20	Normal	—	○
TM44	Rest	Psychic	Status	—	—	10	Self	—	—
TM46	Thief	Dark	Physical	40	100	10	Normal	—	○
TM48	Round	Normal	Special	60	100	15	Normal	—	—
TM57	Charge Beam	Electric	Special	50	90	10	Normal	—	—
TM68	Giga Impact	Normal	Physical	150	90	5	Normal	—	○
TM70	Flash	Normal	Status	—	100	20	Normal	—	—
TM73	Thunder Wave	Electric	Status	—	100	20	Normal	—	—
TM77	Psych Up	Normal	Status	—	—	10	Normal	—	—
TM85	Dream Eater	Psychic	Special	100	100	15	Normal	—	—
TM87	Swagger	Normal	Status	—	90	15	Normal	—	—
TM90	Substitute	Normal	Status	—	—	10	Self	—	—
TM92	Trick Room	Psychic	Status	—	—	5	Both Sides	—	—

MOVES TAUGHT BY PEOPLE

Name	Type	Kind	Pow.	Acc.	PP	Range	Long	DA

MOVES TAUGHT BY MOVE TUTORS FOR SHARDS

Name	Type	Kind	Pow.	Acc.	PP	Range	Long	DA
Signal Beam	Bug	Special	75	100	15	Normal	—	—
Last Resort	Normal	Physical	140	100	5	Normal	—	○
Magnet Rise	Electric	Status	—	—	10	Self	—	—
Magic Coat	Psychic	Status	—	—	15	Self	—	—
Electroweb	Electric	Special	55	95	15	Many Others	—	—
Icy Wind	Ice	Special	55	95	15	Many Others	—	—
Iron Tail	Steel	Physical	100	75	15	Normal	—	○
Zen Headbutt	Psychic	Physical	80	90	15	Normal	—	○
Foul Play	Dark	Physical	95	100	15	Normal	—	○
Gravity	Psychic	Status	—	—	5	Both Sides	—	—
Snore	Normal	Special	40	100	15	Normal	—	—
Pain Split	Normal	Status	—	—	20	Normal	—	—
Wonder Room	Psychic	Status	—	—	10	Both Sides	—	—
Recycle	Normal	Status	—	—	10	Self	—	—
Trick	Psychic	Status	—	100	10	Normal	—	—
Sleep Talk	Normal	Status	—	—	10	Self	—	—

Pokémon AR Marker

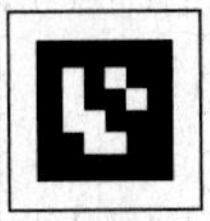

Big Horn Pokémon

234 Stantler

- HEIGHT: 4'07"
- WEIGHT: 157.0 lbs.
- GENDER: ♂ / ♀

Staring at its antlers creates an odd sensation as if one were being drawn into their centers.

Same form for ♂ / ♀

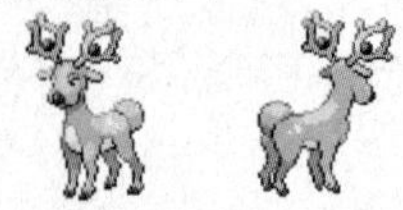

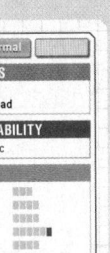

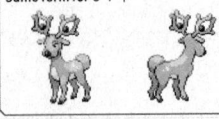

TYPE Normal

ABILITIES
- Intimidate
- Frisk

HIDDEN ABILITY
- Sap Sipper

STATS
HP
Attack
Defense
Sp. Atk
Sp. Def
Speed

EGG GROUPS
Field

ITEMS SOMETIMES HELD
- None

EVOLUTION

Does not evolve

HOW TO OBTAIN

Pokémon Black Version 2	Link Trade or Poké Transfer
Pokémon White Version 2	Link Trade or Poké Transfer

HOW TO OBTAIN FROM OTHER GAMES

Pokémon Black Version	Abundant Shrine
Pokémon White Version	Abundant Shrine

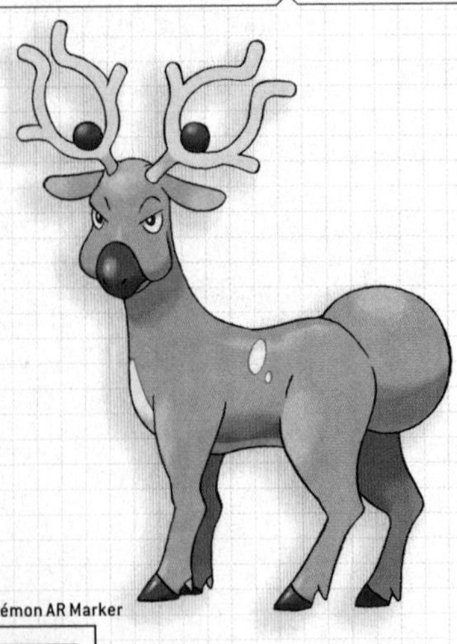

LEVEL-UP AND LEARNED MOVES

Lv.	Name	Type	Kind	Pow.	Acc.	PP	Range	Long	DA
1	Tackle	Normal	Physical	50	100	35	Normal	—	○
3	Leer	Normal	Status	—	100	30	Many Others	—	—
7	Astonish	Ghost	Physical	30	100	15	Normal	—	○
10	Hypnosis	Psychic	Status	—	60	20	Normal	—	—
13	Stomp	Normal	Physical	65	100	20	Normal	—	○
16	Sand-Attack	Ground	Status	—	100	15	Normal	—	—
21	Take Down	Normal	Physical	90	85	20	Normal	—	○
23	Confuse Ray	Ghost	Status	—	100	10	Normal	—	—
27	Calm Mind	Psychic	Status	—	—	20	Self	—	—
33	Role Play	Psychic	Status	—	—	10	Normal	—	—
38	Zen Headbutt	Psychic	Physical	80	90	15	Normal	—	○
43	Jump Kick	Fighting	Physical	100	95	10	Normal	—	○
49	Imprison	Psychic	Status	—	—	10	Self	—	—
53	Captivate	Normal	Status	—	100	20	Many Others	—	—
55	Me First	Normal	Status	—	—	20	Varies	—	—

TM & HM MOVES

Lv.	Name	Type	Kind	Pow.	Acc.	PP	Range	Long	DA
TM03	Psyshock	Psychic	Special	80	100	10	Normal	—	—
TM04	Calm Mind	Psychic	Status	—	—	20	Self	—	—
TM05	Roar	Normal	Status	—	100	20	Normal	—	—
TM06	Toxic	Poison	Status	—	90	10	Normal	—	—
TM10	Hidden Power	Normal	Special	—	100	15	Normal	—	—
TM11	Sunny Day	Fire	Status	—	—	5	Both Sides	—	—
TM16	Light Screen	Psychic	Status	—	—	30	Your Side	—	—
TM17	Protect	Normal	Status	—	—	10	Self	—	—
TM18	Rain Dance	Water	Status	—	—	5	Both Sides	—	—
TM21	Frustration	Normal	Physical	—	100	20	Normal	—	○
TM22	SolarBeam	Grass	Special	120	100	10	Normal	—	—
TM24	Thunderbolt	Electric	Special	95	100	15	Normal	—	—
TM25	Thunder	Electric	Special	120	70	10	Normal	—	—
TM26	Earthquake	Ground	Physical	100	100	10	Adjacent	—	—
TM27	Return	Normal	Physical	—	100	20	Normal	—	○
TM29	Psychic	Psychic	Special	90	100	10	Normal	—	—
TM30	Shadow Ball	Ghost	Special	80	100	15	Normal	—	—
TM32	Double Team	Normal	Status	—	—	15	Self	—	—
TM33	Reflect	Psychic	Status	—	—	20	Your Side	—	—
TM42	Facade	Normal	Physical	70	100	20	Normal	—	○
TM44	Rest	Psychic	Status	—	—	10	Self	—	—
TM45	Attract	Normal	Status	—	100	15	Normal	—	—
TM46	Thief	Dark	Physical	40	100	10	Normal	—	○
TM48	Round	Normal	Special	60	100	15	Normal	—	—
TM53	Energy Ball	Grass	Special	80	100	10	Normal	—	—
TM57	Charge Beam	Electric	Special	50	90	10	Normal	—	—
TM67	Retaliate	Normal	Physical	70	100	5	Normal	—	○
TM68	Giga Impact	Normal	Physical	150	90	5	Normal	—	○
TM70	Flash	Normal	Status	—	100	20	Normal	—	—
TM73	Thunder Wave	Electric	Status	—	100	20	Normal	—	—
TM77	Psych Up	Normal	Status	—	—	10	Normal	—	—
TM78	Bulldoze	Ground	Physical	60	100	20	Adjacent	—	—
TM83	Work Up	Normal	Status	—	—	30	Self	—	—
TM85	Dream Eater	Psychic	Special	100	100	15	Normal	—	—
TM87	Swagger	Normal	Status	—	90	15	Normal	—	—
TM90	Substitute	Normal	Status	—	—	10	Self	—	—
TM92	Trick Room	Psychic	Status	—	—	5	Both Sides	—	—
TM93	Wild Charge	Electric	Physical	90	100	15	Normal	—	○

MOVES TAUGHT BY PEOPLE

Name	Type	Kind	Pow.	Acc.	PP	Range	Long	DA

MOVES TAUGHT BY MOVE TUTORS FOR SHARDS

Name	Type	Kind	Pow.	Acc.	PP	Range	Long	DA
Bounce	Flying	Physical	85	85	5	Normal	○	○
Signal Beam	Bug	Special	75	100	15	Normal	—	—
Uproar	Normal	Special	90	100	10	1 Random	—	—
Last Resort	Normal	Physical	140	100	5	Normal	—	○
Iron Tail	Steel	Physical	100	75	15	Normal	—	○
Zen Headbutt	Psychic	Physical	80	90	15	Normal	—	○
Gravity	Psychic	Status	—	—	5	Both Sides	—	—
Snore	Normal	Special	40	100	15	Normal	—	—
Role Play	Psychic	Status	—	—	10	Normal	—	—
Magic Room	Psychic	Status	—	—	10	Both Sides	—	—
Spite	Ghost	Status	—	100	10	Normal	—	—
Sleep Talk	Normal	Status	—	—	10	Self	—	—
Skill Swap	Psychic	Status	—	—	10	Normal	—	—

EGG MOVES

Name	Type	Kind	Pow.	Acc.	PP	Range	Long	DA
Spite	Ghost	Status	—	100	10	Normal	—	—
Disable	Normal	Status	—	100	20	Normal	—	—
Bite	Dark	Physical	60	100	25	Normal	—	○
Extrasensory	Psychic	Special	80	100	30	Normal	—	—
Thrash	Normal	Physical	120	100	10	1 Random	—	○
Double Kick	Fighting	Physical	30	100	30	Normal	—	○
Zen Headbutt	Psychic	Physical	80	90	15	Normal	—	○
Megahorn	Bug	Physical	120	85	10	Normal	—	○
Mud Sport	Ground	Status	—	—	15	Both Sides	—	—
Rage	Normal	Physical	20	100	20	Normal	—	○
Me First	Normal	Status	—	—	20	Varies	—	—

Pokémon AR Marker

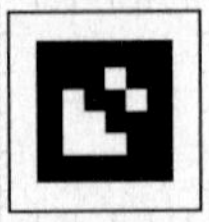

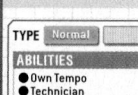

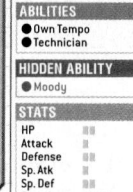

235 Smeargle
Painter Pokémon

TYPE Normal

ABILITIES
- Own Tempo
- Technician

HIDDEN ABILITY
- Moody

- HEIGHT: 3'11"
- WEIGHT: 127.9 lbs.
- GENDER: ♂ / ♀

It marks its territory by using its tail like a paintbrush. There are more than 5,000 different marks.

STATS
- HP
- Attack
- Defense
- Sp. Atk
- Sp. Def
- Speed

Same form for ♂ / ♀

EGG GROUPS
Field

ITEMS SOMETIMES HELD
- None

Pokémon AR Marker

EVOLUTION

Does not evolve

HOW TO OBTAIN
Pokémon Black Version 2	Link Trade or Poké Transfer
Pokémon White Version 2	Link Trade or Poké Transfer

HOW TO OBTAIN FROM OTHER GAMES
Pokémon Black Version	Route 5 (mass outbreak)
Pokémon White Version	Route 5 (mass outbreak)

LEVEL-UP AND LEARNED MOVES
Lv.	Name	Type	Kind	Pow.	Acc.	PP	Range	Long	DA
1	Sketch	Normal	Status	—	—	1	Normal	—	—
11	Sketch	Normal	Status	—	—	1	Normal	—	—
21	Sketch	Normal	Status	—	—	1	Normal	—	—
31	Sketch	Normal	Status	—	—	1	Normal	—	—
41	Sketch	Normal	Status	—	—	1	Normal	—	—
51	Sketch	Normal	Status	—	—	1	Normal	—	—
61	Sketch	Normal	Status	—	—	1	Normal	—	—
71	Sketch	Normal	Status	—	—	1	Normal	—	—
81	Sketch	Normal	Status	—	—	1	Normal	—	—
91	Sketch	Normal	Status	—	—	1	Normal	—	—

TM & HM MOVES
Lv.	Name	Type	Kind	Pow.	Acc.	PP	Range	Long	DA

MOVES TAUGHT BY PEOPLE
Name	Type	Kind	Pow.	Acc.	PP	Range	Long	DA

MOVES TAUGHT BY MOVE TUTORS FOR SHARDS
Name	Type	Kind	Pow.	Acc.	PP	Range	Long	DA

EGG MOVES
Name	Type	Kind	Pow.	Acc.	PP	Range	Long	DA

---

236 Tyrogue
Scuffle Pokémon

TYPE Fighting

ABILITIES
- Guts
- Steadfast

HIDDEN ABILITY
- Vital Spirit

- HEIGHT: 2'04"
- WEIGHT: 46.3 lbs.
- GENDER: ♂

It is famous for its eagerness to fight and always nurses injuries from challenging larger foes.

STATS
- HP
- Attack
- Defense
- Sp. Atk
- Sp. Def
- Speed

♂

EGG GROUPS
No Egg has ever been discovered

ITEMS SOMETIMES HELD
- None

Pokémon AR Marker

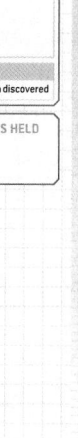

EVOLUTION

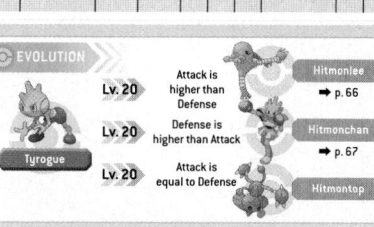

Tyrogue	Lv. 20 — Attack is higher than Defense	Hitmonlee ➡ p.66
	Lv. 20 — Defense is higher than Attack	Hitmonchan ➡ p.67
	Lv. 20 — Attack is equal to Defense	Hitmontop

HOW TO OBTAIN
Pokémon Black Version 2	Link Trade or Poké Transfer
Pokémon White Version 2	Link Trade or Poké Transfer

HOW TO OBTAIN FROM OTHER GAMES
Pokémon Black Version	Route 10 (mass outbreak)
Pokémon White Version	Route 10 (mass outbreak)

LEVEL-UP AND LEARNED MOVES
Lv.	Name	Type	Kind	Pow.	Acc.	PP	Range	Long	DA
1	Tackle	Normal	Physical	50	100	35	Normal	—	○
1	Helping Hand	Normal	Status	—	—	20	1 Ally	—	○
1	Fake Out	Normal	Physical	40	100	10	Normal	—	○
1	Foresight	Normal	Status	—	—	40	Normal	—	○

TM & HM MOVES
Lv.	Name	Type	Kind	Pow.	Acc.	PP	Range	Long	DA
TM06	Toxic	Poison	Status	—	90	10	Normal	—	—
TM08	Bulk Up	Fighting	Status	—	—	20	Self	—	—
TM10	Hidden Power	Normal	Special	—	100	15	Normal	—	—
TM11	Sunny Day	Fire	Status	—	—	5	Both Sides	—	—
TM17	Protect	Normal	Status	—	—	10	Self	—	—
TM18	Rain Dance	Water	Status	—	—	5	Both Sides	—	—
TM21	Frustration	Normal	Physical	—	100	20	Normal	—	○
TM26	Earthquake	Ground	Physical	100	100	10	Adjacent	—	○
TM27	Return	Normal	Physical	—	100	20	Normal	—	○
TM31	Brick Break	Fighting	Physical	75	100	15	Normal	—	○
TM32	Double Team	Normal	Status	—	—	15	Self	—	—
TM42	Facade	Normal	Physical	70	100	20	Normal	—	○
TM44	Rest	Psychic	Status	—	—	10	Self	—	—
TM45	Attract	Normal	Status	—	100	15	Normal	—	—
TM46	Thief	Dark	Physical	40	100	10	Normal	—	○
TM47	Low Sweep	Fighting	Physical	60	100	20	Normal	—	○
TM48	Round	Normal	Special	60	100	15	Normal	—	○
TM67	Retaliate	Normal	Physical	70	100	5	Normal	—	○
TM78	Bulldoze	Ground	Physical	60	100	20	Adjacent	—	○
TM80	Rock Slide	Rock	Physical	75	90	10	Many Others	—	○
TM83	Work Up	Normal	Status	—	—	30	Self	—	—
TM87	Swagger	Normal	Status	—	90	15	Normal	—	—
TM90	Substitute	Normal	Status	—	—	10	Self	—	—
TM94	Rock Smash	Fighting	Physical	40	100	15	Normal	—	○
HM04	Strength	Normal	Physical	80	100	15	Normal	—	○

MOVES TAUGHT BY PEOPLE
Name	Type	Kind	Pow.	Acc.	PP	Range	Long	DA

MOVES TAUGHT BY MOVE TUTORS FOR SHARDS
Name	Type	Kind	Pow.	Acc.	PP	Range	Long	DA
Covet	Normal	Physical	60	100	40	Normal	—	○
Uproar	Normal	Special	90	100	10	1 Random	—	○
Low Kick	Fighting	Physical	—	100	20	Normal	—	○
Snore	Normal	Special	40	100	15	Normal	—	○
Role Play	Psychic	Status	—	—	10	Normal	—	—
Helping Hand	Normal	Status	—	—	20	1 Ally	—	—
Sleep Talk	Normal	Status	—	—	10	Self	—	—

EGG MOVES
Name	Type	Kind	Pow.	Acc.	PP	Range	Long	DA
Rapid Spin	Normal	Physical	20	100	40	Normal	—	○
Hi Jump Kick	Fighting	Physical	130	90	10	Normal	—	○
Mach Punch	Fighting	Physical	40	100	30	Normal	—	○
Mind Reader	Normal	Status	—	—	5	Normal	—	—
Helping Hand	Normal	Status	—	—	20	1 Ally	—	—
Counter	Fighting	Physical	—	100	20	Varies	—	○
Vacuum Wave	Fighting	Special	40	100	30	Normal	—	○
Bullet Punch	Steel	Physical	40	100	30	Normal	—	○
Endure	Normal	Status	—	—	10	Self	—	—
Pursuit	Dark	Physical	40	100	20	Normal	—	○
Feint	Normal	Physical	30	100	10	Normal	—	○

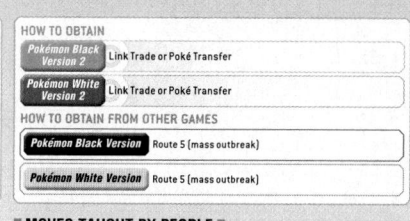

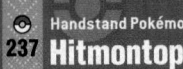

Hitmontop 237

Handstand Pokémon

237 Hitmontop

- HEIGHT: 4'07"
- WEIGHT: 105.8 lbs.
- GENDER: ♂

It fights while spinning like a top. The centrifugal force boosts its destructive power by 10.

TYPE: Fighting

ABILITIES
- Intimidate
- Technician

HIDDEN ABILITY
- Steadfast

STATS
HP
Attack
Defense
Sp. Atk
Sp. Def
Speed

EGG GROUPS
Human-Like

ITEMS SOMETIMES HELD
- None

♂

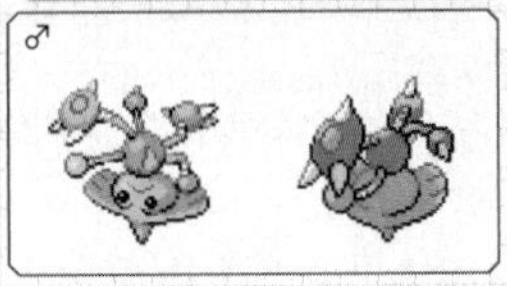

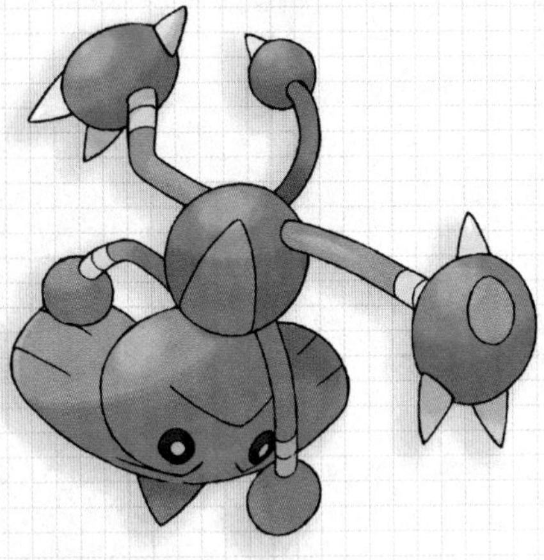

Pokémon AR Marker

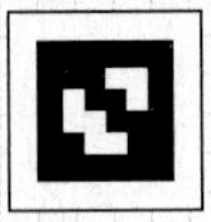

EVOLUTION

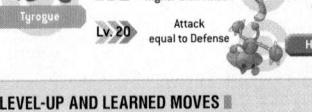

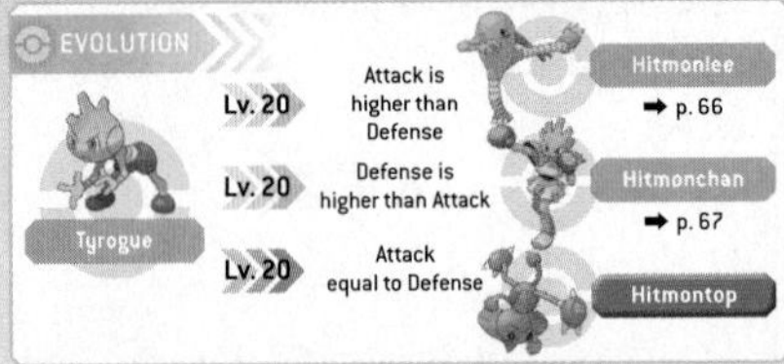
Tyrogue
Lv. 20
Attack is higher than Defense
Hitmonlee
➡ p. 66
Lv. 20
Defense is higher than Attack
Hitmonchan
➡ p. 67
Lv. 20
Attack equal to Defense
Hitmontop

HOW TO OBTAIN

Pokémon Black Version 2	Level up Tyrogue to Lv. 20 when its Attack and Defense are equal
Pokémon White Version 2	Level up Tyrogue to Lv. 20 when its Attack and Defense are equal

HOW TO OBTAIN FROM OTHER GAMES

—

—

LEVEL-UP AND LEARNED MOVES

Lv.	Name	Type	Kind	Pow.	Acc.	PP	Range	Long	DA
1	Revenge	Fighting	Physical	60	100	10	Normal	—	○
1	Rolling Kick	Fighting	Physical	60	85	15	Normal	—	○
6	Focus Energy	Normal	Status	—	—	30	Self	—	—
10	Pursuit	Dark	Physical	40	100	20	Normal	—	○
15	Quick Attack	Normal	Physical	40	100	30	Normal	—	○
19	Triple Kick	Fighting	Physical	10	90	10	Normal	—	○
24	Rapid Spin	Normal	Physical	20	100	40	Normal	—	○
28	Counter	Fighting	Physical	—	100	20	Varies	—	○
33	Feint	Normal	Physical	30	100	10	Normal	—	—
37	Agility	Psychic	Status	—	—	30	Self	—	—
42	Gyro Ball	Steel	Physical	—	100	5	Normal	—	○
46	Wide Guard	Rock	Status	—	—	10	Your Side	—	—
46	Quick Guard	Fighting	Status	—	—	15	Your Side	—	—
51	Detect	Fighting	Status	—	—	5	Self	—	—
55	Close Combat	Fighting	Physical	120	100	5	Normal	—	○
60	Endeavor	Normal	Physical	—	100	5	Normal	—	○

TM & HM MOVES

Lv.	Name	Type	Kind	Pow.	Acc.	PP	Range	Long	DA
TM06	Toxic	Poison	Status	—	90	10	Normal	—	—
TM08	Bulk Up	Fighting	Status	—	—	20	Self	—	—
TM10	Hidden Power	Normal	Special	—	100	15	Normal	—	—
TM11	Sunny Day	Fire	Status	—	—	5	Both Sides	—	—
TM17	Protect	Normal	Status	—	—	10	Self	—	—
TM18	Rain Dance	Water	Status	—	—	5	Both Sides	—	—
TM21	Frustration	Normal	Physical	—	100	20	Normal	—	○
TM26	Earthquake	Ground	Physical	100	100	10	Adjacent	—	—
TM27	Return	Normal	Physical	—	100	20	Normal	—	○
TM28	Dig	Ground	Physical	80	100	10	Normal	—	○
TM31	Brick Break	Fighting	Physical	75	100	15	Normal	—	○
TM32	Double Team	Normal	Status	—	—	15	Self	—	—
TM37	Sandstorm	Rock	Status	—	—	10	Both Sides	—	—
TM40	Aerial Ace	Flying	Physical	60	—	20	Normal	○	○
TM42	Facade	Normal	Physical	70	100	20	Normal	—	○
TM44	Rest	Psychic	Status	—	—	10	Self	—	—
TM45	Attract	Normal	Status	—	100	15	Normal	—	—
TM46	Thief	Dark	Physical	40	100	10	Normal	—	○
TM47	Low Sweep	Fighting	Physical	60	100	20	Normal	—	○
TM48	Round	Normal	Special	60	100	15	Normal	—	—
TM67	Retaliate	Normal	Physical	70	100	5	Normal	—	○
TM71	Stone Edge	Rock	Physical	100	80	5	Normal	—	—
TM74	Gyro Ball	Steel	Physical	—	100	5	Normal	—	○
TM78	Bulldoze	Ground	Physical	60	100	20	Adjacent	—	—
TM80	Rock Slide	Rock	Physical	75	90	10	Many Others	—	—
TM83	Work Up	Normal	Status	—	—	30	Self	—	—
TM87	Swagger	Normal	Status	—	90	15	Normal	—	—
TM90	Substitute	Normal	Status	—	—	10	Self	—	—
TM94	Rock Smash	Fighting	Physical	40	100	15	Normal	—	○
HM04	Strength	Normal	Physical	80	100	15	Normal	—	○

MOVES TAUGHT BY PEOPLE

Name	Type	Kind	Pow.	Acc.	PP	Range	Long	DA

MOVES TAUGHT BY MOVE TUTORS FOR SHARDS

Name	Type	Kind	Pow.	Acc.	PP	Range	Long	DA
Covet	Normal	Physical	60	100	40	Normal	—	○
Drill Run	Ground	Physical	80	95	10	Normal	—	○
Low Kick	Fighting	Physical	—	100	20	Normal	—	○
Snore	Normal	Special	40	100	15	Normal	—	—
Role Play	Psychic	Status	—	—	10	Normal	—	—
Helping Hand	Normal	Status	—	—	20	1 Ally	—	—
Endeavor	Normal	Physical	—	100	5	Normal	—	○
Sleep Talk	Normal	Status	—	—	10	Self	—	—

Smoochum 238

Kiss Pokémon

238 Smoochum

- HEIGHT: 1'04"
- WEIGHT: 13.2 lbs.
- GENDER: ♀

It tests everything by touching with its lips, which remember what it likes and dislikes.

TYPE: Ice Psychic

ABILITIES
- Oblivious
- Forewarn

HIDDEN ABILITY
- Hydration

STATS
HP
Attack
Defense
Sp. Atk
Sp. Def
Speed

EGG GROUPS
No Egg has ever been discovered

ITEMS SOMETIMES HELD
- None

♀

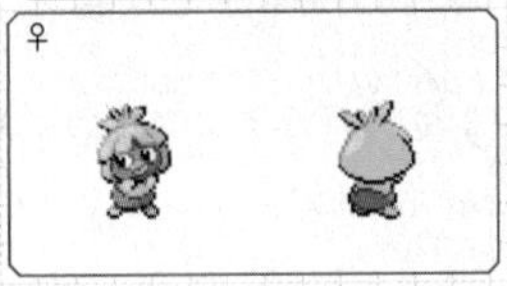

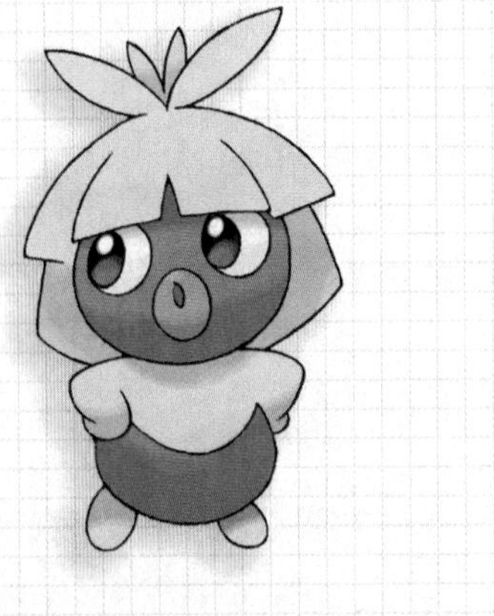

Pokémon AR Marker

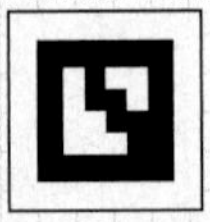

EVOLUTION

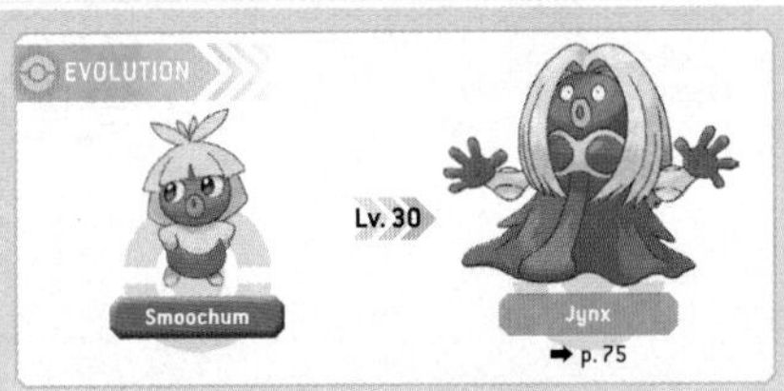
Smoochum
Lv. 30
Jynx
➡ p. 75

HOW TO OBTAIN

Pokémon Black Version 2	Link Trade or Poké Transfer
Pokémon White Version 2	Link Trade or Poké Transfer

HOW TO OBTAIN FROM OTHER GAMES

Pokémon Platinum Version	Snowpoint Temple 1F

—

LEVEL-UP AND LEARNED MOVES

Lv.	Name	Type	Kind	Pow.	Acc.	PP	Range	Long	DA
1	Pound	Normal	Physical	40	100	35	Normal	—	○
5	Lick	Ghost	Physical	20	100	30	Normal	—	○
8	Sweet Kiss	Normal	Status	—	75	10	Normal	—	—
11	Powder Snow	Ice	Special	40	100	25	Many Others	—	—
15	Confusion	Psychic	Special	50	100	25	Normal	—	—
18	Sing	Normal	Status	—	55	15	Normal	—	—
21	Heart Stamp	Psychic	Physical	60	100	25	Normal	—	○
25	Mean Look	Normal	Status	—	—	5	Normal	—	—
28	Fake Tears	Dark	Status	—	100	20	Normal	—	—
31	Lucky Chant	Normal	Status	—	—	30	Your Side	—	—
35	Avalanche	Ice	Physical	60	100	10	Normal	—	○
38	Psychic	Psychic	Special	90	100	10	Normal	—	—
41	Copycat	Normal	Status	—	—	20	Self	—	—
45	Perish Song	Normal	Status	—	—	5	Adjacent	○	—
48	Blizzard	Ice	Special	120	70	5	Many Others	—	—

TM & HM MOVES

Lv.	Name	Type	Kind	Pow.	Acc.	PP	Range	Long	DA
TM03	Psyshock	Psychic	Special	80	100	10	Normal	—	—
TM04	Calm Mind	Psychic	Status	—	—	20	Self	—	—
TM06	Toxic	Poison	Status	—	90	10	Normal	—	—
TM07	Hail	Ice	Status	—	—	10	Both Sides	—	—
TM10	Hidden Power	Normal	Special	—	100	15	Normal	—	—
TM13	Ice Beam	Ice	Special	95	100	10	Normal	—	—
TM14	Blizzard	Ice	Special	120	70	5	Many Others	—	—
TM16	Light Screen	Psychic	Status	—	—	30	Your Side	—	—
TM17	Protect	Normal	Status	—	—	10	Self	—	—
TM18	Rain Dance	Water	Status	—	—	5	Both Sides	—	—
TM21	Frustration	Normal	Physical	—	100	20	Normal	—	○
TM27	Return	Normal	Physical	—	100	20	Normal	—	○
TM29	Psychic	Psychic	Special	90	100	10	Normal	—	—
TM30	Shadow Ball	Ghost	Special	80	100	15	Normal	—	—
TM32	Double Team	Normal	Status	—	—	15	Self	—	—
TM33	Reflect	Psychic	Status	—	—	20	Your Side	—	—
TM42	Facade	Normal	Physical	70	100	20	Normal	—	○
TM44	Rest	Psychic	Status	—	—	10	Self	—	—
TM45	Attract	Normal	Status	—	100	15	Normal	—	—
TM46	Thief	Dark	Physical	40	100	10	Normal	—	○
TM48	Round	Normal	Special	60	100	15	Normal	—	—
TM49	Echoed Voice	Normal	Special	40	100	15	Normal	—	—
TM56	Fling	Dark	Physical	—	100	10	Normal	—	—
TM66	Payback	Dark	Physical	50	100	10	Normal	—	○
TM70	Flash	Normal	Status	—	100	20	Normal	—	—
TM77	Psych Up	Normal	Status	—	—	10	Normal	—	—
TM79	Frost Breath	Ice	Special	40	90	10	Normal	—	—
TM85	Dream Eater	Psychic	Special	100	100	15	Normal	—	—
TM86	Grass Knot	Grass	Special	—	100	20	Normal	—	○
TM87	Swagger	Normal	Status	—	90	15	Normal	—	—
TM90	Substitute	Normal	Status	—	—	10	Self	—	—
TM92	Trick Room	Psychic	Status	—	—	5	Both Sides	—	—

MOVES TAUGHT BY PEOPLE

Name	Type	Kind	Pow.	Acc.	PP	Range	Long	DA

MOVES TAUGHT BY MOVE TUTORS FOR SHARDS

Name	Type	Kind	Pow.	Acc.	PP	Range	Long	DA
Covet	Normal	Physical	60	100	40	Normal	—	○
Signal Beam	Bug	Special	75	100	15	Normal	—	—
Uproar	Normal	Special	90	100	10	1 Random	—	—
Ice Punch	Ice	Physical	75	100	15	Normal	—	○
Magic Coat	Psychic	Status	—	—	15	Self	—	—
Icy Wind	Ice	Special	55	95	15	Many Others	—	—
Zen Headbutt	Psychic	Physical	80	90	15	Normal	—	○
Snore	Normal	Special	40	100	15	Normal	—	—
Heal Bell	Normal	Status	—	—	5	Your Party	—	—
Role Play	Psychic	Status	—	—	10	Normal	—	—
Helping Hand	Normal	Status	—	—	20	1 Ally	—	—
Magic Room	Psychic	Status	—	—	10	Both Sides	—	—
Recycle	Normal	Status	—	—	10	Self	—	—
Trick	Psychic	Status	—	100	10	Normal	—	—
Sleep Talk	Normal	Status	—	—	10	Self	—	—
Skill Swap	Psychic	Status	—	—	10	Normal	—	—

EGG MOVES

Name	Type	Kind	Pow.	Acc.	PP	Range	Long	DA
Meditate	Psychic	Status	—	—	40	Self	—	—
Fake Out	Normal	Physical	40	100	10	Normal	—	○
Wish	Normal	Status	—	—	10	Self	—	—
Ice Punch	Ice	Physical	75	100	15	Normal	—	○
Miracle Eye	Psychic	Status	—	—	40	Normal	—	—
Nasty Plot	Dark	Status	—	—	20	Self	—	—
Wake-Up Slap	Fighting	Physical	60	100	10	Normal	—	○
Captivate	Normal	Status	—	100	20	Many Others	—	—

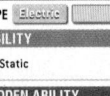

Electric Pokémon

239 Elekid

- HEIGHT: 2'00"
- WEIGHT: 51.8 lbs.
- GENDER: ♂ / ♀

Spinning its arms around to generate electricity makes the area between its horns shine light blue.

Same form for ♂ / ♀

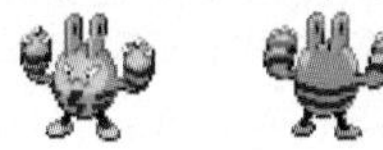

TYPE Electric

ABILITY
- Static

HIDDEN ABILITY
- Vital Spirit

STATS
HP
Attack
Defense
Sp. Atk
Sp. Def
Speed

EGG GROUPS
No Egg has ever been discovered

ITEMS SOMETIMES HELD
- None

EVOLUTION

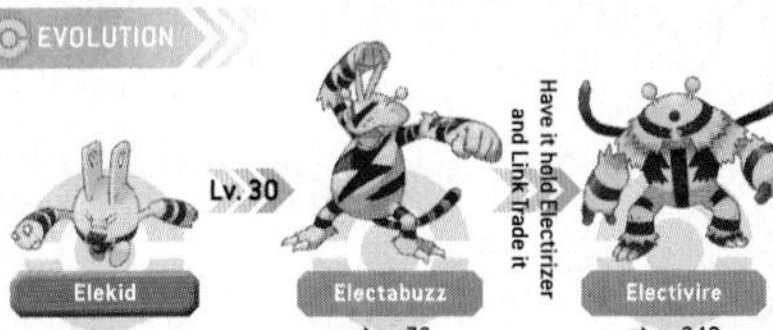
Lv. 30
Have it hold Electirizer and Link Trade it
Elekid
Electabuzz
Electivire

➡ p. 76
➡ p. 249

HOW TO OBTAIN

Pokémon Black Version 2	Link Trade or Poké Transfer
Pokémon White Version 2	❶ Virbank Complex entrance ❷ Virbank Complex interior

HOW TO OBTAIN FROM OTHER GAMES

Pokémon White Version	When Robbie is in White Forest
	———

LEVEL-UP AND LEARNED MOVES

Lv.	Name	Type	Kind	Pow.	Acc.	PP	Range	Long	DA
1	Quick Attack	Normal	Physical	40	100	30	Normal	—	○
1	Leer	Normal	Status	—	100	30	Many Others	—	—
5	ThunderShock	Electric	Special	40	100	30	Normal	—	—
8	Low Kick	Fighting	Physical	—	100	20	Normal	—	○
12	Swift	Normal	Special	60	—	20	Many Others	—	—
15	Shock Wave	Electric	Special	60	—	20	Normal	—	—
19	Thunder Wave	Electric	Status	—	100	20	Normal	—	—
22	Electro Ball	Electric	Special	—	100	10	Normal	—	—
26	Light Screen	Psychic	Status	—	—	30	Your Side	—	—
29	ThunderPunch	Electric	Physical	75	100	15	Normal	—	○
33	Discharge	Electric	Special	80	100	15	Adjacent	—	—
36	Screech	Normal	Status	—	85	40	Normal	—	—
40	Thunderbolt	Electric	Special	95	100	15	Normal	—	—
43	Thunder	Electric	Special	120	70	10	Normal	—	—

TM & HM MOVES

Lv.	Name	Type	Kind	Pow.	Acc.	PP	Range	Long	DA
TM06	Toxic	Poison	Status	—	90	10	Normal	—	—
TM10	Hidden Power	Normal	Special	—	100	15	Normal	—	—
TM16	Light Screen	Psychic	Status	—	—	30	Your Side	—	—
TM17	Protect	Normal	Status	—	—	10	Self	—	—
TM18	Rain Dance	Water	Status	—	—	5	Both Sides	—	—
TM21	Frustration	Normal	Physical	—	100	20	Normal	—	○
TM24	Thunderbolt	Electric	Special	95	100	15	Normal	—	—
TM25	Thunder	Electric	Special	120	70	10	Normal	—	—
TM27	Return	Normal	Physical	—	100	20	Normal	—	○
TM29	Psychic	Psychic	Special	90	100	10	Normal	—	—
TM31	Brick Break	Fighting	Physical	75	100	15	Normal	—	○
TM32	Double Team	Normal	Status	—	—	15	Self	—	—
TM42	Facade	Normal	Physical	70	100	20	Normal	—	○
TM44	Rest	Psychic	Status	—	—	10	Self	—	—
TM45	Attract	Normal	Status	—	100	15	Normal	—	—
TM46	Thief	Dark	Physical	40	100	10	Normal	—	○
TM48	Round	Normal	Special	60	100	15	Normal	—	—
TM56	Fling	Dark	Physical	—	100	10	Normal	—	—
TM57	Charge Beam	Electric	Special	50	90	10	Normal	—	—
TM70	Flash	Normal	Status	—	100	20	Normal	—	—
TM72	Volt Switch	Electric	Special	70	100	20	Normal	—	—
TM73	Thunder Wave	Electric	Status	—	100	20	Normal	—	—
TM87	Swagger	Normal	Status	—	90	15	Normal	—	—
TM90	Substitute	Normal	Status	—	—	10	Self	—	—
TM93	Wild Charge	Electric	Physical	90	100	15	Normal	—	○
TM94	Rock Smash	Fighting	Physical	40	100	15	Normal	—	○

MOVES TAUGHT BY PEOPLE

Name	Type	Kind	Pow.	Acc.	PP	Range	Long	DA

MOVES TAUGHT BY MOVE TUTORS FOR SHARDS

Name	Type	Kind	Pow.	Acc.	PP	Range	Long	DA
Covet	Normal	Physical	60	100	40	Normal	—	○
Signal Beam	Bug	Special	75	100	15	Normal	—	—
Uproar	Normal	Special	90	100	10	1 Random	—	—
Dual Chop	Dragon	Physical	40	90	15	Normal	—	○
Low Kick	Fighting	Physical	—	100	20	Normal	—	○
Fire Punch	Fire	Physical	75	100	15	Normal	—	○
ThunderPunch	Electric	Physical	75	100	15	Normal	—	○
Ice Punch	Ice	Physical	75	100	15	Normal	—	○
Magnet Rise	Electric	Status	—	—	10	Self	—	—
Electroweb	Electric	Special	55	95	15	Many Others	—	—
Snore	Normal	Special	40	100	15	Normal	—	—
Helping Hand	Normal	Status	—	—	20	1 Ally	—	—
Sleep Talk	Normal	Status	—	—	10	Self	—	—

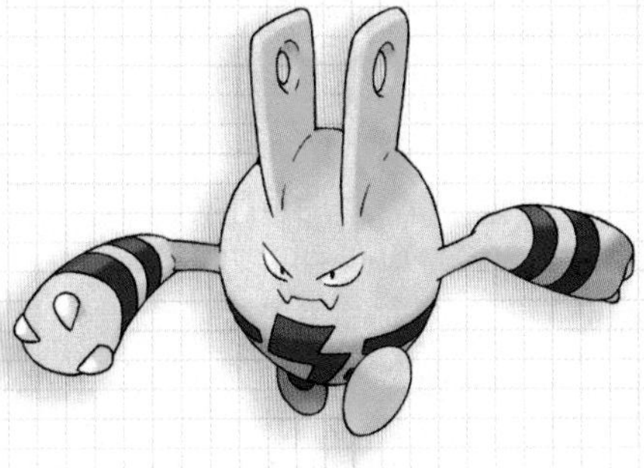

EGG MOVES

Name	Type	Kind	Pow.	Acc.	PP	Range	Long	DA
Karate Chop	Fighting	Physical	50	100	25	Normal	—	○
Barrier	Psychic	Status	—	—	30	Self	—	—
Rolling Kick	Fighting	Physical	60	85	15	Normal	—	○
Meditate	Psychic	Status	—	—	40	Self	—	—
Cross Chop	Fighting	Physical	100	80	5	Normal	—	○
Fire Punch	Fire	Physical	75	100	15	Normal	—	○
Ice Punch	Ice	Physical	75	100	15	Normal	—	○
DynamicPunch	Fighting	Physical	100	50	5	Normal	—	○
Feint	Normal	Physical	30	100	10	Normal	—	—
Hammer Arm	Fighting	Physical	100	90	10	Normal	—	○
Focus Punch	Fighting	Physical	150	100	20	Normal	—	○

Pokémon AR Marker

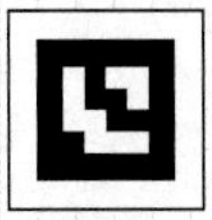

Live Coal Pokémon

240 Magby

- HEIGHT: 2'04"
- WEIGHT: 47.2 lbs.
- GENDER: ♂ / ♀

It's small, but its body temperature is over 1,100 degrees F. Embers escape its mouth and nose when it breathes.

Same form for ♂ / ♀

TYPE Fire

ABILITY
- Flame Body

HIDDEN ABILITY
- Vital Spirit

STATS
HP
Attack
Defense
Sp. Atk
Sp. Def
Speed

EGG GROUPS
No Egg has ever been discovered

ITEMS SOMETIMES HELD
- None

EVOLUTION

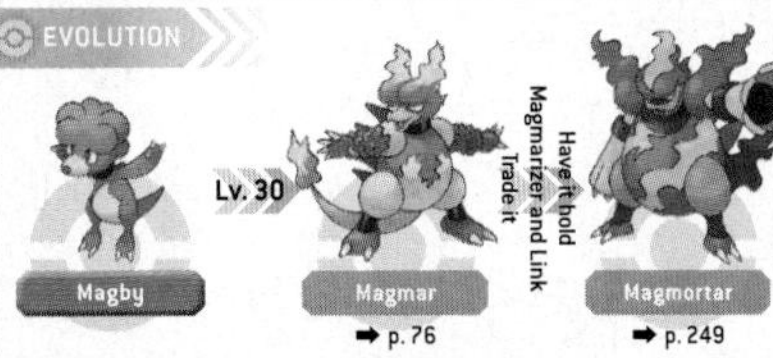
Lv. 30
Have it hold Magmarizer and Link Trade it
Magby
Magmar
Magmortar

➡ p. 76
➡ p. 249

HOW TO OBTAIN

Pokémon Black Version 2	❶ Virbank Complex entrance ❷ Virbank Complex interior
Pokémon White Version 2	Link Trade or Poké Transfer

HOW TO OBTAIN FROM OTHER GAMES

Pokémon White Version	When Vincent is in White Forest
	———

LEVEL-UP AND LEARNED MOVES

Lv.	Name	Type	Kind	Pow.	Acc.	PP	Range	Long	DA
1	Smog	Poison	Special	20	70	20	Normal	—	—
1	Leer	Normal	Status	—	100	30	Many Others	—	—
5	Ember	Fire	Special	40	100	25	Normal	—	—
8	SmokeScreen	Normal	Status	—	100	20	Normal	—	—
12	Faint Attack	Dark	Physical	60	—	20	Normal	—	○
15	Fire Spin	Fire	Special	35	85	15	Normal	—	—
19	Clear Smog	Poison	Special	50	—	15	Normal	—	—
22	Flame Burst	Fire	Special	70	100	15	Normal	—	—
26	Confuse Ray	Ghost	Status	—	100	10	Normal	—	—
29	Fire Punch	Fire	Physical	75	100	15	Normal	—	○
33	Lava Plume	Fire	Special	80	100	15	Adjacent	—	—
36	Sunny Day	Fire	Status	—	—	5	Both Sides	—	—
40	Flamethrower	Fire	Special	95	100	15	Normal	—	—
43	Fire Blast	Fire	Special	120	85	5	Normal	—	—

TM & HM MOVES

Lv.	Name	Type	Kind	Pow.	Acc.	PP	Range	Long	DA
TM06	Toxic	Poison	Status	—	90	10	Normal	—	—
TM10	Hidden Power	Normal	Special	—	100	15	Normal	—	—
TM11	Sunny Day	Fire	Status	—	—	5	Both Sides	—	—
TM17	Protect	Normal	Status	—	—	10	Self	—	—
TM21	Frustration	Normal	Physical	—	100	20	Normal	—	○
TM27	Return	Normal	Physical	—	100	20	Normal	—	○
TM29	Psychic	Psychic	Special	90	100	10	Normal	—	—
TM31	Brick Break	Fighting	Physical	75	100	15	Normal	—	○
TM32	Double Team	Normal	Status	—	—	15	Self	—	—
TM35	Flamethrower	Fire	Special	95	100	15	Normal	—	—
TM38	Fire Blast	Fire	Special	120	85	5	Normal	—	—
TM42	Facade	Normal	Physical	70	100	20	Normal	—	○
TM43	Flame Charge	Fire	Physical	50	100	20	Normal	—	○
TM44	Rest	Psychic	Status	—	—	10	Self	—	—
TM45	Attract	Normal	Status	—	100	15	Normal	—	—
TM46	Thief	Dark	Physical	40	100	10	Normal	—	○
TM48	Round	Normal	Special	60	100	15	Normal	—	—
TM50	Overheat	Fire	Special	140	90	5	Normal	—	—
TM56	Fling	Dark	Physical	—	100	10	Normal	—	—
TM59	Incinerate	Fire	Special	30	100	15	Many Others	—	—
TM61	Will-O-Wisp	Fire	Status	—	75	15	Normal	—	—
TM87	Swagger	Normal	Status	—	90	15	Normal	—	—
TM90	Substitute	Normal	Status	—	—	10	Self	—	—
TM94	Rock Smash	Fighting	Physical	40	100	15	Normal	—	○

MOVES TAUGHT BY PEOPLE

Name	Type	Kind	Pow.	Acc.	PP	Range	Long	DA

MOVES TAUGHT BY MOVE TUTORS FOR SHARDS

Name	Type	Kind	Pow.	Acc.	PP	Range	Long	DA
Covet	Normal	Physical	60	100	40	Normal	—	○
Uproar	Normal	Special	90	100	10	1 Random	—	—
Dual Chop	Dragon	Physical	40	90	15	Normal	—	○
Fire Punch	Fire	Physical	75	100	15	Normal	—	○
ThunderPunch	Electric	Physical	75	100	15	Normal	—	○
Iron Tail	Steel	Physical	100	75	15	Normal	—	○
Snore	Normal	Special	40	100	15	Normal	—	—
Heat Wave	Fire	Special	100	90	10	Many Others	—	—
Helping Hand	Normal	Status	—	—	20	1 Ally	—	—
Sleep Talk	Normal	Status	—	—	10	Self	—	—

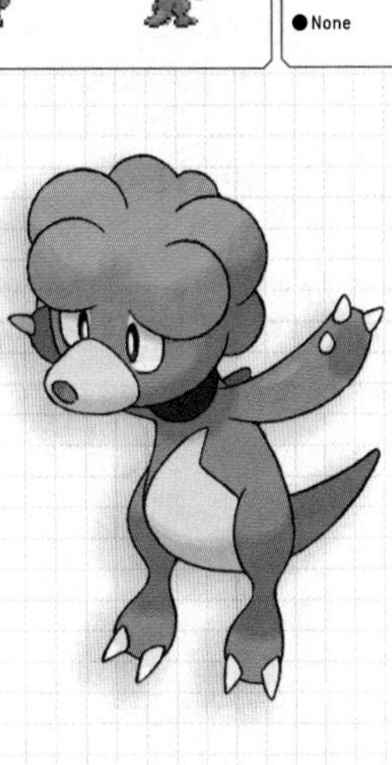

EGG MOVES

Name	Type	Kind	Pow.	Acc.	PP	Range	Long	DA
Karate Chop	Fighting	Physical	50	100	25	Normal	—	○
Mega Punch	Normal	Physical	80	85	20	Normal	—	○
Barrier	Psychic	Status	—	—	30	Self	—	—
Screech	Normal	Status	—	85	40	Normal	—	—
Cross Chop	Fighting	Physical	100	80	5	Normal	—	○
ThunderPunch	Electric	Physical	75	100	15	Normal	—	○
Mach Punch	Fighting	Physical	40	100	30	Normal	—	○
DynamicPunch	Fighting	Physical	100	50	5	Normal	—	○
Flare Blitz	Fire	Physical	120	100	15	Normal	—	○
Belly Drum	Normal	Status	—	—	10	Self	—	—
Iron Tail	Steel	Physical	100	75	15	Normal	—	○
Focus Energy	Normal	Status	—	—	30	Self	—	—

Pokémon AR Marker

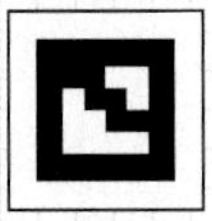

Milk Cow Pokémon

241 Miltank

- HEIGHT: 3'11"
- WEIGHT: 166.4 lbs.
- GENDER: ♀

It is said that kids who drink Miltank's milk grow up to become hearty, healthy adults.

♀

Pokémon AR Marker

TYPE Normal

ABILITIES
- Thick Fat
- Scrappy

HIDDEN ABILITY
- Sap Sipper

STATS
HP
Attack
Defense
Sp. Atk
Sp. Def
Speed

EGG GROUPS
Field

ITEMS SOMETIMES HELD
- None

EVOLUTION

Does not evolve

HOW TO OBTAIN

Pokémon Black Version 2	Link Trade or Poké Transfer
Pokémon White Version 2	Link Trade or Poké Transfer

HOW TO OBTAIN FROM OTHER GAMES

Pokémon HeartGold Version	Route 38
Pokémon SoulSilver Version	Route 38

LEVEL-UP AND LEARNED MOVES

Lv.	Name	Type	Kind	Pow.	Acc.	PP	Range	Long	DA
1	Tackle	Normal	Physical	50	100	35	Normal	—	○
3	Growl	Normal	Status	—	100	40	Many Others	—	—
5	Defense Curl	Normal	Status	—	—	40	Self	—	—
8	Stomp	Normal	Physical	65	100	20	Normal	—	○
11	Milk Drink	Normal	Status	—	—	10	Self	—	—
15	Bide	Normal	Physical	—	—	10	Self	—	○
19	Rollout	Rock	Physical	30	90	20	Normal	—	○
24	Body Slam	Normal	Physical	85	100	15	Normal	—	○
29	Zen Headbutt	Psychic	Physical	80	90	15	Normal	—	○
35	Captivate	Normal	Status	—	100	20	Many Others	—	—
41	Gyro Ball	Steel	Physical	—	100	5	Normal	—	○
48	Heal Bell	Normal	Status	—	—	5	Your Party	—	—
55	Wake-Up Slap	Fighting	Physical	60	100	10	Normal	—	○

TM & HM MOVES

Lv.	Name	Type	Kind	Pow.	Acc.	PP	Range	Long	DA
TM06	Toxic	Poison	Status	—	90	10	Normal	—	—
TM10	Hidden Power	Normal	Special	—	100	15	Normal	—	—
TM11	Sunny Day	Fire	Status	—	—	5	Both Sides	—	—
TM13	Ice Beam	Ice	Special	95	100	10	Normal	—	—
TM14	Blizzard	Ice	Special	120	70	5	Many Others	—	—
TM15	Hyper Beam	Normal	Special	150	90	5	Normal	—	—
TM17	Protect	Normal	Status	—	—	10	Self	—	—
TM18	Rain Dance	Water	Status	—	—	5	Both Sides	—	—
TM21	Frustration	Normal	Physical	—	100	20	Normal	—	○
TM22	SolarBeam	Grass	Special	120	100	10	Normal	—	—
TM24	Thunderbolt	Electric	Special	95	100	15	Normal	—	—
TM25	Thunder	Electric	Special	120	70	10	Normal	—	—
TM26	Earthquake	Ground	Physical	100	100	10	Adjacent	—	—
TM27	Return	Normal	Physical	—	100	20	Normal	—	○
TM30	Shadow Ball	Ghost	Special	80	100	15	Normal	—	—
TM31	Brick Break	Fighting	Physical	75	100	15	Normal	—	○
TM32	Double Team	Normal	Status	—	—	15	Self	—	—
TM37	Sandstorm	Rock	Status	—	—	10	Both Sides	—	—
TM39	Rock Tomb	Rock	Physical	50	80	10	Normal	—	—
TM42	Facade	Normal	Physical	70	100	20	Normal	—	○
TM44	Rest	Psychic	Status	—	—	10	Self	—	—
TM45	Attract	Normal	Status	—	100	15	Normal	—	—
TM48	Round	Normal	Special	60	100	15	Normal	—	—
TM49	Echoed Voice	Normal	Special	40	100	15	Normal	—	—
TM52	Focus Blast	Fighting	Special	120	70	5	Normal	—	—
TM56	Fling	Dark	Physical	—	100	10	Normal	—	—
TM67	Retaliate	Normal	Physical	70	100	5	Normal	—	○
TM68	Giga Impact	Normal	Physical	150	90	5	Normal	—	○
TM73	Thunder Wave	Electric	Status	—	100	20	Normal	—	—
TM74	Gyro Ball	Steel	Physical	—	100	5	Normal	—	○
TM77	Psych Up	Normal	Status	—	—	10	Normal	—	—
TM78	Bulldoze	Ground	Physical	60	100	20	Adjacent	—	—
TM80	Rock Slide	Rock	Physical	75	90	10	Many Others	—	—
TM83	Work Up	Normal	Status	—	—	30	Self	—	—
TM87	Swagger	Normal	Status	—	90	15	Normal	—	—
TM90	Substitute	Normal	Status	—	—	10	Self	—	—
TM94	Rock Smash	Fighting	Physical	40	100	15	Normal	—	○
HM03	Surf	Water	Special	95	100	15	Adjacent	—	—
HM04	Strength	Normal	Physical	80	100	15	Normal	—	○

MOVES TAUGHT BY PEOPLE

Name	Type	Kind	Pow.	Acc.	PP	Range	Long	DA

MOVES TAUGHT BY MOVE TUTORS FOR SHARDS

Name	Type	Kind	Pow.	Acc.	PP	Range	Long	DA
Iron Head	Steel	Physical	80	100	15	Normal	—	○
Fire Punch	Fire	Physical	75	100	15	Normal	—	○
ThunderPunch	Electric	Physical	75	100	15	Normal	—	○
Ice Punch	Ice	Physical	75	100	15	Normal	—	○
Block	Normal	Status	—	—	5	Normal	—	—
Icy Wind	Ice	Special	55	95	15	Many Others	—	—
Iron Tail	Steel	Physical	100	75	15	Normal	—	○
Zen Headbutt	Psychic	Physical	80	90	15	Normal	—	○
Snore	Normal	Special	40	100	15	Normal	—	—
Heal Bell	Normal	Status	—	—	5	Your Party	—	—
Helping Hand	Normal	Status	—	—	20	1 Ally	—	—
After You	Normal	Status	—	—	15	Normal	—	—
Stealth Rock	Rock	Status	—	—	20	Other Side	—	—
Sleep Talk	Normal	Status	—	—	10	Self	—	—

EGG MOVES

Name	Type	Kind	Pow.	Acc.	PP	Range	Long	DA
Present	Normal	Physical	—	90	15	Normal	—	—
Reversal	Fighting	Physical	—	100	15	Normal	—	○
Seismic Toss	Fighting	Physical	—	100	20	Normal	—	○
Endure	Normal	Status	—	—	10	Self	—	—
Curse	Ghost	Status	—	—	10	Varies	—	—
Helping Hand	Normal	Status	—	—	20	1 Ally	—	—
Sleep Talk	Normal	Status	—	—	10	Self	—	—
Dizzy Punch	Normal	Physical	70	100	10	Normal	—	○
Hammer Arm	Fighting	Physical	100	90	10	Normal	—	○
Double-Edge	Normal	Physical	120	100	15	Normal	—	○
Punishment	Dark	Physical	—	100	5	Normal	—	○
Natural Gift	Normal	Physical	—	100	15	Normal	—	—
Heart Stamp	Psychic	Physical	60	100	25	Normal	—	○

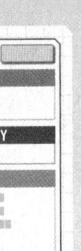

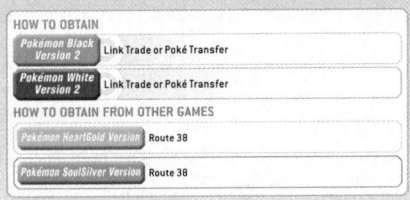

Happiness Pokémon

242 Blissey

- HEIGHT: 4'11"
- WEIGHT: 103.2 lbs.
- GENDER: ♀

The eggs it lays are filled with happiness. Eating even one bite will bring a smile to anyone.

♀

Pokémon AR Marker

TYPE Normal

ABILITIES
- Natural Cure
- Serene Grace

HIDDEN ABILITY
- Healer

STATS
HP
Attack
Defense
Sp. Atk
Sp. Def
Speed

EGG GROUPS
Fairy

ITEMS SOMETIMES HELD
- None

EVOLUTION

Have it hold Oval Stone and level it up in the morning, afternoon, or evening
Level up with high friendship
Happiny
Chansey
Blissey

➡ p. 236 ➡ p. 70

HOW TO OBTAIN

Pokémon Black Version 2	Level up Chansey with high friendship
Pokémon White Version 2	Level up Chansey with high friendship

HOW TO OBTAIN FROM OTHER GAMES

—
—

LEVEL-UP AND LEARNED MOVES

Lv.	Name	Type	Kind	Pow.	Acc.	PP	Range	Long	DA
1	Defense Curl	Normal	Status	—	—	40	Self	—	—
1	Pound	Normal	Physical	40	100	35	Normal	—	○
1	Growl	Normal	Status	—	100	40	Many Others	—	—
5	Tail Whip	Normal	Status	—	100	30	Many Others	—	—
9	Refresh	Normal	Status	—	—	20	Self	—	—
12	DoubleSlap	Normal	Physical	15	85	10	Normal	—	○
16	Softboiled	Normal	Status	—	—	10	Self	—	—
20	Bestow	Normal	Status	—	—	15	Normal	—	—
23	Minimize	Normal	Status	—	—	20	Self	—	—
27	Take Down	Normal	Physical	90	85	20	Normal	—	○
31	Sing	Normal	Status	—	55	15	Normal	—	—
34	Fling	Dark	Physical	—	100	10	Normal	—	—
38	Heal Pulse	Psychic	Status	—	—	10	Normal	○	—
42	Egg Bomb	Normal	Physical	100	75	10	Normal	—	—
46	Light Screen	Psychic	Status	—	—	30	Your Side	—	—
50	Healing Wish	Psychic	Status	—	—	10	Self	—	—
54	Double-Edge	Normal	Physical	120	100	15	Normal	—	○

TM & HM MOVES

Lv.	Name	Type	Kind	Pow.	Acc.	PP	Range	Long	DA
TM04	Calm Mind	Psychic	Status	—	—	20	Self	—	—
TM06	Toxic	Poison	Status	—	90	10	Normal	—	—
TM07	Hail	Ice	Status	—	—	10	Both Sides	—	—
TM10	Hidden Power	Normal	Special	—	100	15	Normal	—	—
TM11	Sunny Day	Fire	Status	—	—	5	Both Sides	—	—
TM13	Ice Beam	Ice	Special	95	100	10	Normal	—	—
TM14	Blizzard	Ice	Special	120	70	5	Many Others	—	—
TM15	Hyper Beam	Normal	Special	150	90	5	Normal	—	—
TM16	Light Screen	Psychic	Status	—	—	30	Your Side	—	—
TM17	Protect	Normal	Status	—	—	10	Self	—	—
TM18	Rain Dance	Water	Status	—	—	5	Both Sides	—	—
TM20	Safeguard	Normal	Status	—	—	25	Your Side	—	—
TM21	Frustration	Normal	Physical	—	100	20	Normal	—	○
TM22	SolarBeam	Grass	Special	120	100	10	Normal	—	—
TM24	Thunderbolt	Electric	Special	95	100	15	Normal	—	—
TM25	Thunder	Electric	Special	120	70	10	Normal	—	—
TM26	Earthquake	Ground	Physical	100	100	10	Adjacent	—	—
TM27	Return	Normal	Physical	—	100	20	Normal	—	○
TM29	Psychic	Psychic	Special	90	100	10	Normal	—	—
TM30	Shadow Ball	Ghost	Special	80	100	15	Normal	—	—
TM31	Brick Break	Fighting	Physical	75	100	15	Normal	—	○
TM32	Double Team	Normal	Status	—	—	15	Self	—	—
TM35	Flamethrower	Fire	Special	95	100	15	Normal	—	—
TM37	Sandstorm	Rock	Status	—	—	10	Both Sides	—	—
TM38	Fire Blast	Fire	Special	120	85	5	Normal	—	—
TM39	Rock Tomb	Rock	Physical	50	80	10	Normal	—	—
TM42	Facade	Normal	Physical	70	100	20	Normal	—	○
TM44	Rest	Psychic	Status	—	—	10	Self	—	—
TM45	Attract	Normal	Status	—	100	15	Normal	—	—
TM48	Round	Normal	Special	60	100	15	Normal	—	—
TM49	Echoed Voice	Normal	Special	40	100	15	Normal	—	—
TM52	Focus Blast	Fighting	Special	120	70	5	Normal	—	—
TM56	Fling	Dark	Physical	—	100	10	Normal	—	—
TM57	Charge Beam	Electric	Special	50	90	10	Normal	—	—
TM59	Incinerate	Fire	Special	30	100	15	Many Others	—	—
TM67	Retaliate	Normal	Physical	70	100	5	Normal	—	○
TM68	Giga Impact	Normal	Physical	150	90	5	Normal	—	○
TM70	Flash	Normal	Status	—	100	20	Normal	—	—
TM73	Thunder Wave	Electric	Status	—	100	20	Normal	—	—
TM77	Psych Up	Normal	Status	—	—	10	Normal	—	—
TM78	Bulldoze	Ground	Physical	60	100	20	Adjacent	—	—
TM80	Rock Slide	Rock	Physical	75	90	10	Many Others	—	—
TM83	Work Up	Normal	Status	—	—	30	Self	—	—
TM85	Dream Eater	Psychic	Special	100	100	15	Normal	—	—
TM86	Grass Knot	Grass	Special	—	100	20	Normal	—	○
TM87	Swagger	Normal	Status	—	90	15	Normal	—	—
TM90	Substitute	Normal	Status	—	—	10	Self	—	—
TM93	Wild Charge	Electric	Physical	90	100	15	Normal	—	○
TM94	Rock Smash	Fighting	Physical	40	100	15	Normal	—	○
HM04	Strength	Normal	Physical	80	100	15	Normal	—	○

MOVES TAUGHT BY PEOPLE

Name	Type	Kind	Pow.	Acc.	PP	Range	Long	DA

MOVES TAUGHT BY MOVE TUTORS FOR SHARDS

Name	Type	Kind	Pow.	Acc.	PP	Range	Long	DA
Covet	Normal	Physical	60	100	40	Normal	—	○
Fire Punch	Fire	Physical	75	100	15	Normal	—	○
ThunderPunch	Electric	Physical	75	100	15	Normal	—	○
Ice Punch	Ice	Physical	75	100	15	Normal	—	○
Last Resort	Normal	Physical	140	100	5	Normal	—	○
Block	Normal	Status	—	—	5	Normal	—	—
Hyper Voice	Normal	Special	90	100	10	Many Others	—	—
Icy Wind	Ice	Special	55	95	15	Many Others	—	—
Iron Tail	Steel	Physical	100	75	15	Normal	—	○
Zen Headbutt	Psychic	Physical	80	90	15	Normal	—	○
Gravity	Psychic	Status	—	—	5	Both Sides	—	—
Snore	Normal	Special	40	100	15	Normal	—	—
Heal Bell	Normal	Status	—	—	5	Your Party	—	—
Drain Punch	Fighting	Physical	75	100	10	Normal	—	○
Helping Hand	Normal	Status	—	—	20	1 Ally	—	—
Recycle	Normal	Status	—	—	10	Self	—	—
Stealth Rock	Rock	Status	—	—	20	Other Side	—	—
Endeavor	Normal	Physical	—	100	5	Normal	—	○
Sleep Talk	Normal	Status	—	—	10	Self	—	—
Skill Swap	Psychic	Status	—	—	10	Normal	—	—
Snatch	Dark	Status	—	—	10	Self	—	—

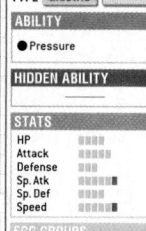

Thunder Pokémon

243 Raikou

TYPE Electric

ABILITY

● Pressure

HIDDEN ABILITY

—

● HEIGHT: 6'03"
● WEIGHT: 392.4 lbs.
● GENDER: Unknown

It is said to have fallen with lightning. It can fire thunderbolts from the rain clouds on its back.

STATS

HP
Attack
Defense
Sp. Atk
Sp. Def
Speed

EGG GROUPS

No Egg has ever been discovered

Gender unknown

ITEMS SOMETIMES HELD

● None

Pokémon AR Marker

EVOLUTION

Does not evolve

HOW TO OBTAIN

Pokémon Black Version 2	Link Trade or Poké Transfer
Pokémon White Version 2	Link Trade or Poké Transfer

HOW TO OBTAIN FROM OTHER GAMES

Pokémon HeartGold Version	After the encounter at the Burned Tower, it starts roaming the Johto region
Pokémon SoulSilver Version	After the encounter at the Burned Tower, it starts roaming the Johto region

LEVEL-UP AND LEARNED MOVES

Lv.	Name	Type	Kind	Pow.	Acc.	PP	Range	Long	DA
1	Bite	Dark	Physical	60	100	25	Normal	—	○
1	Leer	Normal	Status	—	100	30	Many Others	—	—
8	ThunderShock	Electric	Special	40	100	30	Normal	—	—
15	Roar	Normal	Status	—	100	20	Normal	—	—
22	Quick Attack	Normal	Physical	40	100	30	Normal	—	○
29	Spark	Electric	Physical	65	100	20	Normal	—	○
36	Reflect	Psychic	Status	—	—	20	Your Side	—	—
43	Crunch	Dark	Physical	80	100	15	Normal	—	○
50	Thunder Fang	Electric	Physical	65	95	15	Normal	—	○
57	Discharge	Electric	Special	80	100	15	Adjacent	—	—
64	Extrasensory	Psychic	Special	80	100	30	Normal	—	—
71	Rain Dance	Water	Status	—	—	5	Both Sides	—	—
78	Calm Mind	Psychic	Status	—	—	20	Self	—	—
85	Thunder	Electric	Special	120	70	10	Normal	—	—

TM & HM MOVES

Lv.	Name	Type	Kind	Pow.	Acc.	PP	Range	Long	DA
TM04	Calm Mind	Psychic	Status	—	—	20	Self	—	—
TM05	Roar	Normal	Status	—	100	20	Normal	—	—
TM06	Toxic	Poison	Status	—	90	10	Normal	—	—
TM10	Hidden Power	Normal	Special	—	100	15	Normal	—	—
TM11	Sunny Day	Fire	Status	—	—	5	Both Sides	—	—
TM15	Hyper Beam	Normal	Special	150	90	5	Normal	—	—
TM16	Light Screen	Psychic	Status	—	—	30	Your Side	—	—
TM17	Protect	Normal	Status	—	—	10	Self	—	—
TM18	Rain Dance	Water	Status	—	—	5	Both Sides	—	—
TM21	Frustration	Normal	Physical	—	100	20	Normal	—	○
TM24	Thunderbolt	Electric	Special	95	100	15	Normal	—	—
TM25	Thunder	Electric	Special	120	70	10	Normal	—	—
TM27	Return	Normal	Physical	—	100	20	Normal	—	○
TM28	Dig	Ground	Physical	80	100	10	Normal	—	○
TM30	Shadow Ball	Ghost	Special	80	100	15	Normal	—	—
TM32	Double Team	Normal	Status	—	—	15	Self	—	—
TM33	Reflect	Psychic	Status	—	—	20	Your Side	—	—
TM37	Sandstorm	Rock	Status	—	—	10	Both Sides	—	—
TM42	Facade	Normal	Physical	70	100	20	Normal	—	○
TM44	Rest	Psychic	Status	—	—	10	Self	—	—
TM48	Round	Normal	Special	60	100	15	Normal	—	—
TM57	Charge Beam	Electric	Special	50	90	10	Normal	—	—
TM60	Quash	Dark	Status	—	100	15	Normal	—	—
TM68	Giga Impact	Normal	Physical	150	90	5	Normal	—	○
TM70	Flash	Normal	Status	—	100	20	Normal	—	—
TM72	Volt Switch	Electric	Special	70	100	20	Normal	—	—
TM73	Thunder Wave	Electric	Status	—	100	20	Normal	—	—
TM77	Psych Up	Normal	Status	—	—	10	Normal	—	—
TM78	Bulldoze	Ground	Physical	60	100	20	Adjacent	—	—
TM87	Swagger	Normal	Status	—	90	15	Normal	—	—
TM90	Substitute	Normal	Status	—	—	10	Self	—	—
TM93	Wild Charge	Electric	Physical	90	100	15	Normal	—	○
TM94	Rock Smash	Fighting	Physical	40	100	15	Normal	—	○
TM95	Snarl	Dark	Special	55	95	15	Many Others	—	—
HM01	Cut	Normal	Physical	50	95	30	Normal	—	○
HM04	Strength	Normal	Physical	80	100	15	Normal	—	○

MOVES TAUGHT BY PEOPLE

Name	Type	Kind	Pow.	Acc.	PP	Range	Long	DA

MOVES TAUGHT BY MOVE TUTORS FOR SHARDS

Name	Type	Kind	Pow.	Acc.	PP	Range	Long	DA
Signal Beam	Bug	Special	75	100	15	Normal	—	—
Iron Head	Steel	Physical	80	100	15	Normal	—	○
Magnet Rise	Electric	Status	—	—	10	Self	—	—
Iron Tail	Steel	Physical	100	75	15	Normal	—	○
Snore	Normal	Special	40	100	15	Normal	—	—
Sleep Talk	Normal	Status	—	—	10	Self	—	—

243 Raikou

Volcano Pokémon

244 Entei

TYPE Fire

ABILITY

● Pressure

HIDDEN ABILITY

—

● HEIGHT: 6'11"
● WEIGHT: 436.5 lbs.
● GENDER: Unknown

It is said that when it roars, a volcano erupts somewhere around the globe.

STATS

HP
Attack
Defense
Sp. Atk
Sp. Def
Speed

EGG GROUPS

No Egg has ever been discovered

Gender unknown

ITEMS SOMETIMES HELD

● None

Pokémon AR Marker

EVOLUTION

Does not evolve

HOW TO OBTAIN

Pokémon Black Version 2	Link Trade or Poké Transfer
Pokémon White Version 2	Link Trade or Poké Transfer

HOW TO OBTAIN FROM OTHER GAMES

Pokémon HeartGold Version	After the encounter at the Burned Tower, it starts roaming the Johto region
Pokémon SoulSilver Version	After the encounter at the Burned Tower, it starts roaming the Johto region

LEVEL-UP AND LEARNED MOVES

Lv.	Name	Type	Kind	Pow.	Acc.	PP	Range	Long	DA
1	Bite	Dark	Physical	60	100	25	Normal	—	○
1	Leer	Normal	Status	—	100	30	Many Others	—	—
8	Ember	Fire	Special	40	100	25	Normal	—	—
15	Roar	Normal	Status	—	100	20	Normal	—	—
22	Fire Spin	Fire	Special	35	85	15	Normal	—	—
29	Stomp	Normal	Physical	65	100	20	Normal	—	○
36	Flamethrower	Fire	Special	95	100	15	Normal	—	—
43	Swagger	Normal	Status	—	90	15	Normal	—	—
50	Fire Fang	Fire	Physical	65	95	15	Normal	—	○
57	Lava Plume	Fire	Special	80	100	15	Adjacent	—	—
64	Extrasensory	Psychic	Special	80	100	30	Normal	—	—
71	Fire Blast	Fire	Special	120	85	5	Normal	—	—
78	Calm Mind	Psychic	Status	—	—	20	Self	—	—
85	Eruption	Fire	Special	150	100	5	Many Others	—	—

TM & HM MOVES

Lv.	Name	Type	Kind	Pow.	Acc.	PP	Range	Long	DA
TM04	Calm Mind	Psychic	Status	—	—	20	Self	—	—
TM05	Roar	Normal	Status	—	100	20	Normal	—	—
TM06	Toxic	Poison	Status	—	90	10	Normal	—	—
TM10	Hidden Power	Normal	Special	—	100	15	Normal	—	—
TM11	Sunny Day	Fire	Status	—	—	5	Both Sides	—	—
TM15	Hyper Beam	Normal	Special	150	90	5	Normal	—	—
TM17	Protect	Normal	Status	—	—	10	Self	—	—
TM18	Rain Dance	Water	Status	—	—	5	Both Sides	—	—
TM21	Frustration	Normal	Physical	—	100	20	Normal	—	○
TM22	SolarBeam	Grass	Special	120	100	10	Normal	—	—
TM27	Return	Normal	Physical	—	100	20	Normal	—	○
TM28	Dig	Ground	Physical	80	100	10	Normal	—	○
TM30	Shadow Ball	Ghost	Special	80	100	15	Normal	—	—
TM32	Double Team	Normal	Status	—	—	15	Self	—	—
TM33	Reflect	Psychic	Status	—	—	20	Your Side	—	—
TM35	Flamethrower	Fire	Special	95	100	15	Normal	—	—
TM37	Sandstorm	Rock	Status	—	—	10	Both Sides	—	—
TM38	Fire Blast	Fire	Special	120	85	5	Normal	—	—
TM42	Facade	Normal	Physical	70	100	20	Normal	—	○
TM43	Flame Charge	Fire	Physical	50	100	20	Normal	—	○
TM44	Rest	Psychic	Status	—	—	10	Self	—	—
TM48	Round	Normal	Special	60	100	15	Normal	—	—
TM50	Overheat	Fire	Special	140	90	5	Normal	—	—
TM59	Incinerate	Fire	Special	30	100	15	Many Others	—	—
TM60	Quash	Dark	Status	—	100	15	Normal	—	—
TM61	Will—O—Wisp	Fire	Status	—	75	15	Normal	—	—
TM68	Giga Impact	Normal	Physical	150	90	5	Normal	—	○
TM70	Flash	Normal	Status	—	100	20	Normal	—	—
TM71	Stone Edge	Rock	Physical	100	80	5	Normal	—	—
TM77	Psych Up	Normal	Status	—	—	10	Normal	—	—
TM78	Bulldoze	Ground	Physical	60	100	20	Adjacent	—	—
TM87	Swagger	Normal	Status	—	90	15	Normal	—	—
TM90	Substitute	Normal	Status	—	—	10	Self	—	—
TM94	Rock Smash	Fighting	Physical	40	100	15	Normal	—	○
TM95	Snarl	Dark	Special	55	95	15	Many Others	—	—
HM01	Cut	Normal	Physical	50	95	30	Normal	—	○
HM04	Strength	Normal	Physical	80	100	15	Normal	—	○

MOVES TAUGHT BY PEOPLE

Name	Type	Kind	Pow.	Acc.	PP	Range	Long	DA

MOVES TAUGHT BY MOVE TUTORS FOR SHARDS

Name	Type	Kind	Pow.	Acc.	PP	Range	Long	DA
Iron Head	Steel	Physical	80	100	15	Normal	—	○
Iron Tail	Steel	Physical	100	75	15	Normal	—	○
Snore	Normal	Special	40	100	15	Normal	—	—
Heat Wave	Fire	Special	100	90	10	Many Others	—	—
Sleep Talk	Normal	Status	—	—	10	Self	—	—

244 Entei

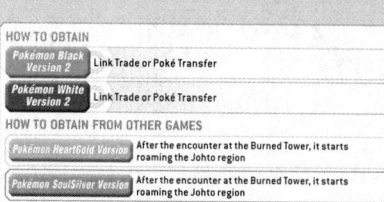

245 Suicune
Aurora Pokémon

- HEIGHT: 6'07"
- WEIGHT: 412.3 lbs.
- GENDER: Unknown

It races around the world to purify fouled water. It dashes away with the north wind.

Gender unknown

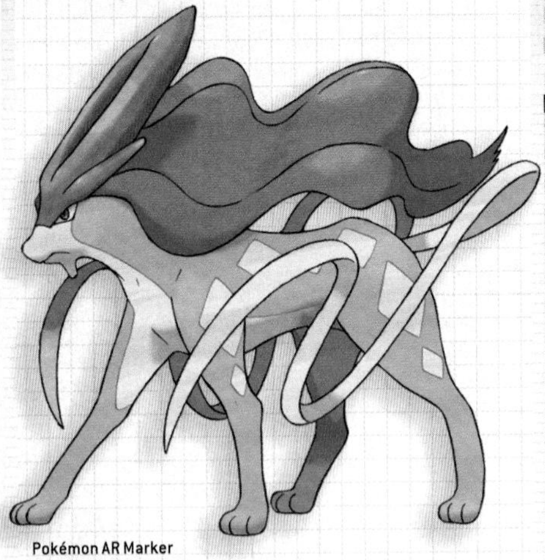

Pokémon AR Marker

TYPE Water

ABILITY
- Pressure

HIDDEN ABILITY
—

STATS
HP
Attack
Defense
Sp. Atk
Sp. Def
Speed

EGG GROUPS
No Egg has ever been discovered

ITEMS SOMETIMES HELD
- None

EVOLUTION

Does not evolve

HOW TO OBTAIN

Pokémon Black Version 2	Link Trade or Poké Transfer
Pokémon White Version 2	Link Trade or Poké Transfer

HOW TO OBTAIN FROM OTHER GAMES

Pokémon HeartGold Version	Hill on Route 25 (after seeing Suicune at all the places it appears)
Pokémon SoulSilver Version	Hill on Route 25 (after seeing Suicune at all the places it appears)

LEVEL-UP AND LEARNED MOVES

Lv.	Name	Type	Kind	Pow.	Acc.	PP	Range	Long	DA
1	Bite	Dark	Physical	60	100	25	Normal	—	○
1	Leer	Normal	Status	—	100	30	Many Others	—	—
8	BubbleBeam	Water	Special	65	100	20	Normal	—	—
15	Rain Dance	Water	Status	—	—	5	Both Sides	—	—
22	Gust	Flying	Special	40	100	35	Normal	○	—
29	Aurora Beam	Ice	Special	65	100	20	Normal	—	—
36	Mist	Ice	Status	—	—	30	Your Side	—	—
43	Mirror Coat	Psychic	Special	—	100	20	Varies	—	—
50	Ice Fang	Ice	Physical	65	95	15	Normal	—	○
57	Tailwind	Flying	Status	—	—	30	Your Side	—	—
64	Extrasensory	Psychic	Special	80	100	30	Normal	—	—
71	Hydro Pump	Water	Special	120	80	5	Normal	—	—
78	Calm Mind	Psychic	Status	—	—	20	Self	—	—
85	Blizzard	Ice	Special	120	70	5	Many Others	—	—

TM & HM MOVES

Lv.	Name	Type	Kind	Pow.	Acc.	PP	Range	Long	DA
TM04	Calm Mind	Psychic	Status	—	—	20	Self	—	—
TM05	Roar	Normal	Status	—	100	20	Normal	—	—
TM06	Toxic	Poison	Status	—	90	10	Normal	—	—
TM07	Hail	Ice	Status	—	—	10	Both Sides	—	—
TM10	Hidden Power	Normal	Special	—	100	15	Normal	—	—
TM11	Sunny Day	Fire	Status	—	—	5	Both Sides	—	—
TM13	Ice Beam	Ice	Special	95	100	10	Normal	—	—
TM14	Blizzard	Ice	Special	120	70	5	Many Others	—	—
TM15	Hyper Beam	Normal	Special	150	90	5	Normal	—	—
TM17	Protect	Normal	Status	—	—	10	Self	—	—
TM18	Rain Dance	Water	Status	—	—	5	Both Sides	—	—
TM21	Frustration	Normal	Physical	—	100	20	Normal	—	○
TM27	Return	Normal	Physical	—	100	20	Normal	—	○
TM28	Dig	Ground	Physical	80	100	10	Normal	—	○
TM30	Shadow Ball	Ghost	Special	80	100	15	Normal	—	—
TM32	Double Team	Normal	Status	—	—	15	Self	—	—
TM33	Reflect	Psychic	Status	—	—	20	Your Side	—	—
TM37	Sandstorm	Rock	Status	—	—	10	Both Sides	—	—
TM42	Facade	Normal	Physical	70	100	20	Normal	—	○
TM44	Rest	Psychic	Status	—	—	10	Self	—	—
TM48	Round	Normal	Special	60	100	15	Normal	—	—
TM55	Scald	Water	Special	80	100	15	Normal	—	—
TM60	Quash	Dark	Status	—	100	15	Normal	—	—
TM68	Giga Impact	Normal	Physical	150	90	5	Normal	—	○
TM77	Psych Up	Normal	Status	—	—	10	Normal	—	—
TM78	Bulldoze	Ground	Physical	60	100	20	Adjacent	—	—
TM87	Swagger	Normal	Status	—	90	15	Normal	—	—
TM90	Substitute	Normal	Status	—	—	10	Self	—	—
TM94	Rock Smash	Fighting	Physical	40	100	15	Normal	—	○
TM95	Snarl	Dark	Special	55	95	15	Many Others	—	—
HM01	Cut	Normal	Physical	50	95	30	Normal	—	○
HM03	Surf	Water	Special	95	100	15	Adjacent	—	—
HM05	Waterfall	Water	Physical	80	100	15	Normal	—	○
HM06	Dive	Water	Physical	80	100	10	Normal	—	○

MOVES TAUGHT BY PEOPLE

Name	Type	Kind	Pow.	Acc.	PP	Range	Long	DA

MOVES TAUGHT BY MOVE TUTORS FOR SHARDS

Name	Type	Kind	Pow.	Acc.	PP	Range	Long	DA
Signal Beam	Bug	Special	75	100	15	Normal	—	—
Iron Head	Steel	Physical	80	100	15	Normal	—	○
Icy Wind	Ice	Special	55	95	15	Many Others	—	—
Iron Tail	Steel	Physical	100	75	15	Normal	—	○
Snore	Normal	Special	40	100	15	Normal	—	—
Tailwind	Flying	Status	—	—	30	Your Side	—	—
Sleep Talk	Normal	Status	—	—	10	Self	—	—

246 Larvitar
Rock Skin Pokémon

- HEIGHT: 2'00"
- WEIGHT: 158.7 lbs.
- GENDER: ♂ / ♀

Born deep underground, it comes aboveground and becomes a pupa once it has finished eating the surrounding soil.

Same form for ♂ / ♀

Pokémon AR Marker

TYPE Rock Ground

ABILITY
- Guts

HIDDEN ABILITY
- Sand Veil

STATS
HP
Attack
Defense
Sp. Atk
Sp. Def
Speed

EGG GROUPS
Monster

ITEMS SOMETIMES HELD
- None

EVOLUTION

HOW TO OBTAIN

Pokémon Black Version 2	Catch a Pupitar or Tyranitar, leave it at the Pokémon Day Care, and hatch the Egg that is found
Pokémon White Version 2	Catch a Pupitar or Tyranitar, leave it at the Pokémon Day Care, and hatch the Egg that is found

HOW TO OBTAIN FROM OTHER GAMES

Pokémon HeartGold Version	Mt. Silver cave interior
Pokémon SoulSilver Version	Mt. Silver cave interior

LEVEL-UP AND LEARNED MOVES

Lv.	Name	Type	Kind	Pow.	Acc.	PP	Range	Long	DA
1	Bite	Dark	Physical	60	100	25	Normal	-	○
1	Leer	Normal	Status	-	100	30	Many Others	-	-
5	Sandstorm	Rock	Status	-	-	10	Both Sides	-	-
10	Screech	Normal	Status	-	85	40	Normal	-	-
14	Chip Away	Normal	Physical	70	100	20	Normal	-	○
19	Rock Slide	Rock	Physical	75	90	10	Many Others	-	-
23	Scary Face	Normal	Status	-	100	10	Normal	-	-
28	Thrash	Normal	Physical	120	100	10	1 Random	-	○
32	Dark Pulse	Dark	Special	80	100	15	Normal	○	-
37	Payback	Dark	Physical	50	100	10	Normal	-	○
41	Crunch	Dark	Physical	80	100	15	Normal	-	○
46	Earthquake	Ground	Physical	100	100	10	Adjacent	-	-
50	Stone Edge	Rock	Physical	100	80	5	Normal	-	-
55	Hyper Beam	Normal	Special	150	90	5	Normal	-	-

TM & HM MOVES

Lv.	Name	Type	Kind	Pow.	Acc.	PP	Range	Long	DA
TM06	Toxic	Poison	Status	—	90	10	Normal	—	—
TM10	Hidden Power	Normal	Special	—	100	15	Normal	—	—
TM11	Sunny Day	Fire	Status	—	—	5	Both Sides	—	—
TM12	Taunt	Dark	Status	—	100	20	Normal	—	—
TM15	Hyper Beam	Normal	Special	150	90	5	Normal	—	—
TM17	Protect	Normal	Status	—	—	10	Self	—	—
TM18	Rain Dance	Water	Status	—	—	5	Both Sides	—	—
TM21	Frustration	Normal	Physical	—	100	20	Normal	—	○
TM23	Smack Down	Rock	Physical	50	100	15	Normal	—	—
TM26	Earthquake	Ground	Physical	100	100	10	Adjacent	—	—
TM27	Return	Normal	Physical	—	100	20	Normal	—	○
TM28	Dig	Ground	Physical	80	100	10	Normal	—	○
TM31	Brick Break	Fighting	Physical	75	100	15	Normal	—	○
TM32	Double Team	Normal	Status	—	—	15	Self	—	—
TM37	Sandstorm	Rock	Status	—	—	10	Both Sides	—	—
TM39	Rock Tomb	Rock	Physical	50	80	10	Normal	—	—
TM41	Torment	Dark	Status	—	100	15	Normal	—	—
TM42	Facade	Normal	Physical	70	100	20	Normal	—	○
TM44	Rest	Psychic	Status	—	—	10	Self	—	—
TM45	Attract	Normal	Status	—	100	15	Normal	—	—
TM48	Round	Normal	Special	60	100	15	Normal	—	—
TM66	Payback	Dark	Physical	50	100	10	Normal	—	○
TM67	Retaliate	Normal	Physical	70	100	5	Normal	—	○
TM69	Rock Polish	Rock	Status	—	—	20	Self	—	—
TM71	Stone Edge	Rock	Physical	100	80	5	Normal	—	—
TM78	Bulldoze	Ground	Physical	60	100	20	Adjacent	—	—
TM80	Rock Slide	Rock	Physical	75	90	10	Many Others	—	—
TM87	Swagger	Normal	Status	—	90	15	Normal	—	—
TM90	Substitute	Normal	Status	—	—	10	Self	—	—
TM94	Rock Smash	Fighting	Physical	40	100	15	Normal	—	○
TM95	Snarl	Dark	Special	55	95	15	Many Others	—	—

MOVES TAUGHT BY PEOPLE

Name	Type	Kind	Pow.	Acc.	PP	Range	Long	DA

MOVES TAUGHT BY MOVE TUTORS FOR SHARDS

Name	Type	Kind	Pow.	Acc.	PP	Range	Long	DA
Iron Head	Steel	Physical	80	100	15	Normal	—	○
Uproar	Normal	Special	90	100	10	1 Random	—	—
Iron Defense	Steel	Status	—	—	15	Self	—	—
Iron Tail	Steel	Physical	100	75	15	Normal	—	○
Earth Power	Ground	Special	90	100	10	Normal	—	—
Superpower	Fighting	Physical	120	100	5	Normal	—	○
Dark Pulse	Dark	Special	80	100	15	Normal	○	—
Snore	Normal	Special	40	100	15	Normal	—	—
Spite	Ghost	Status	—	100	10	Normal	—	—
Stealth Rock	Rock	Status	—	—	20	Other Side	—	—
Outrage	Dragon	Physical	120	100	10	1 Random	—	○
Sleep Talk	Normal	Status	—	—	10	Self	—	—

EGG MOVES

Name	Type	Kind	Pow.	Acc.	PP	Range	Long	DA
Pursuit	Dark	Physical	40	100	20	Normal	—	○
Stomp	Normal	Physical	65	100	20	Normal	—	○
Outrage	Dragon	Physical	120	100	10	1 Random	—	○
Focus Energy	Normal	Status	—	—	30	Self	—	—
AncientPower	Rock	Special	60	100	5	Normal	—	—
Dragon Dance	Dragon	Status	—	—	20	Self	—	—
Curse	Ghost	Status	—	—	10	Varies	—	—
Iron Defense	Steel	Status	—	—	15	Self	—	—
Assurance	Dark	Physical	50	100	10	Normal	—	○
Iron Head	Steel	Physical	80	100	15	Normal	—	○
Stealth Rock	Rock	Status	—	—	20	Other Side	—	—
Iron Tail	Steel	Physical	100	75	15	Normal	—	○

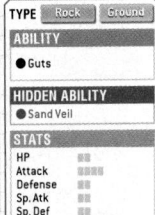

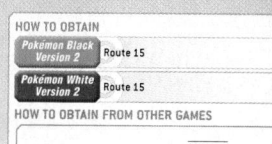

247 Pupitar

Hard Shell Pokémon

- HEIGHT: 3'11"
- WEIGHT: 335.1 lbs.
- GENDER: ♂ / ♀

This pupa flies around wildly by venting with great force the gas pressurized inside its body.

Same form for ♂ / ♀

TYPE Rock Ground

ABILITY
- Shed Skin

HIDDEN ABILITY
—

STATS
HP
Attack
Defense
Sp. Atk
Sp. Def
Speed

EGG GROUPS
Monster

ITEMS SOMETIMES HELD
- None

EVOLUTION

HOW TO OBTAIN

Pokémon Black Version 2	Route 15
Pokémon White Version 2	Route 15

HOW TO OBTAIN FROM OTHER GAMES

—

—

Pokémon AR Marker

LEVEL-UP AND LEARNED MOVES

Lv.	Name	Type	Kind	Pow.	Acc.	PP	Range	Long	DA
1	Bite	Dark	Physical	60	100	25	Normal	—	○
1	Leer	Normal	Status	—	100	30	Many Others	—	—
1	Sandstorm	Rock	Status	—	—	10	Both Sides	—	—
1	Screech	Normal	Status	—	85	40	Normal	—	—
5	Sandstorm	Rock	Status	—	—	10	Both Sides	—	—
10	Screech	Normal	Status	—	85	40	Normal	—	—
14	Chip Away	Normal	Physical	70	100	20	Normal	—	○
19	Rock Slide	Rock	Physical	75	90	10	Many Others	—	—
23	Scary Face	Normal	Status	—	100	10	Normal	—	—
28	Thrash	Normal	Physical	120	100	10	1 Random	—	○
34	Dark Pulse	Dark	Special	80	100	15	Normal	○	—
41	Payback	Dark	Physical	50	100	10	Normal	—	○
47	Crunch	Dark	Physical	80	100	15	Normal	—	○
54	Earthquake	Ground	Physical	100	100	10	Adjacent	—	—
60	Stone Edge	Rock	Physical	100	80	5	Normal	—	—
67	Hyper Beam	Normal	Special	150	90	5	Normal	—	—

TM & HM MOVES

Lv.	Name	Type	Kind	Pow.	Acc.	PP	Range	Long	DA
TM06	Toxic	Poison	Status	—	90	10	Normal	—	—
TM10	Hidden Power	Normal	Special	—	100	15	Normal	—	—
TM11	Sunny Day	Fire	Status	—	—	5	Both Sides	—	—
TM12	Taunt	Dark	Status	—	100	20	Normal	—	—
TM15	Hyper Beam	Normal	Special	150	90	5	Normal	—	—
TM17	Protect	Normal	Status	—	—	10	Self	—	—
TM18	Rain Dance	Water	Status	—	—	5	Both Sides	—	—
TM21	Frustration	Normal	Physical	—	100	20	Normal	—	○
TM23	Smack Down	Rock	Physical	50	100	15	Normal	—	—
TM26	Earthquake	Ground	Physical	100	100	10	Adjacent	—	—
TM27	Return	Normal	Physical	—	100	20	Normal	—	○
TM28	Dig	Ground	Physical	80	100	10	Normal	—	○
TM31	Brick Break	Fighting	Physical	75	100	15	Normal	—	○
TM32	Double Team	Normal	Status	—	—	15	Self	—	—
TM37	Sandstorm	Rock	Status	—	—	10	Both Sides	—	—
TM39	Rock Tomb	Rock	Physical	50	80	10	Normal	—	—
TM41	Torment	Dark	Status	—	100	15	Normal	—	—
TM42	Facade	Normal	Physical	70	100	20	Normal	—	○
TM44	Rest	Psychic	Status	—	—	10	Self	—	—
TM45	Attract	Normal	Status	—	100	15	Normal	—	—
TM48	Round	Normal	Special	60	100	15	Normal	—	—
TM66	Payback	Dark	Physical	50	100	10	Normal	—	○
TM67	Retaliate	Normal	Physical	70	100	5	Normal	—	○
TM69	Rock Polish	Rock	Status	—	—	20	Self	—	—
TM71	Stone Edge	Rock	Physical	100	80	5	Normal	—	—
TM78	Bulldoze	Ground	Physical	60	100	20	Adjacent	—	—
TM80	Rock Slide	Rock	Physical	75	90	10	Many Others	—	—
TM87	Swagger	Normal	Status	—	90	15	Normal	—	—
TM90	Substitute	Normal	Status	—	—	10	Self	—	—
TM94	Rock Smash	Fighting	Physical	40	100	15	Normal	—	○
TM95	Snarl	Dark	Special	55	95	15	Many Others	—	—

MOVES TAUGHT BY PEOPLE

Name	Type	Kind	Pow.	Acc.	PP	Range	Long	DA

MOVES TAUGHT BY MOVE TUTORS FOR SHARDS

Name	Type	Kind	Pow.	Acc.	PP	Range	Long	DA
Iron Head	Steel	Physical	80	100	15	Normal	—	○
Uproar	Normal	Special	90	100	10	1 Random	—	—
Iron Defense	Steel	Status	—	—	15	Self	—	—
Iron Tail	Steel	Physical	100	75	15	Normal	—	○
Earth Power	Ground	Special	90	100	10	Normal	—	—
Superpower	Fighting	Physical	120	100	5	Normal	—	○
Dark Pulse	Dark	Special	80	100	15	Normal	○	—
Snore	Normal	Special	40	100	15	Normal	—	—
Spite	Ghost	Status	—	100	10	Normal	—	—
Stealth Rock	Rock	Status	—	—	20	Other Side	—	—
Outrage	Dragon	Physical	120	100	10	1 Random	—	○
Sleep Talk	Normal	Status	—	—	10	Self	—	—

248 Tyranitar

Armor Pokémon

- HEIGHT: 6'07"
- WEIGHT: 445.3 lbs.
- GENDER: ♂ / ♀

The quakes caused when it walks make even great mountains crumble and change the surrounding terrain.

Same form for ♂ / ♀

TYPE Rock Dark

ABILITY
- Sand Stream

HIDDEN ABILITY
- Unnerve

STATS
HP
Attack
Defense
Sp. Atk
Sp. Def
Speed

EGG GROUPS
Monster

ITEMS SOMETIMES HELD
- None

EVOLUTION

HOW TO OBTAIN

Pokémon Black Version 2	Route 15 (rustling grass)
Pokémon White Version 2	Route 15 (rustling grass)

HOW TO OBTAIN FROM OTHER GAMES

—

—

Pokémon AR Marker

LEVEL-UP AND LEARNED MOVES

Lv.	Name	Type	Kind	Pow.	Acc.	PP	Range	Long	DA
1	Thunder Fang	Electric	Physical	65	95	15	Normal	—	○
1	Ice Fang	Ice	Physical	65	95	15	Normal	—	○
1	Fire Fang	Fire	Physical	65	95	15	Normal	—	○
1	Bite	Dark	Physical	60	100	25	Normal	—	○
1	Leer	Normal	Status	—	100	30	Many Others	—	—
1	Sandstorm	Rock	Status	—	—	10	Both Sides	—	—
1	Screech	Normal	Status	—	85	40	Normal	—	—
5	Sandstorm	Rock	Status	—	—	10	Both Sides	—	—
10	Screech	Normal	Status	—	85	40	Normal	—	—
14	Chip Away	Normal	Physical	70	100	20	Normal	—	○
19	Rock Slide	Rock	Physical	75	90	10	Many Others	—	—
23	Scary Face	Normal	Status	—	100	10	Normal	—	—
28	Thrash	Normal	Physical	120	100	10	1 Random	—	○
34	Dark Pulse	Dark	Special	80	100	15	Normal	○	—
41	Payback	Dark	Physical	50	100	10	Normal	—	○
47	Crunch	Dark	Physical	80	100	15	Normal	—	○
54	Earthquake	Ground	Physical	100	100	10	Adjacent	—	—
63	Stone Edge	Rock	Physical	100	80	5	Normal	—	—
73	Hyper Beam	Normal	Special	150	90	5	Normal	—	—
82	Giga Impact	Normal	Physical	150	90	5	Normal	—	○

TM & HM MOVES

Lv.	Name	Type	Kind	Pow.	Acc.	PP	Range	Long	DA
TM01	Hone Claws	Dark	Status	—	—	15	Self	—	—
TM02	Dragon Claw	Dragon	Physical	80	100	15	Normal	—	○
TM05	Roar	Normal	Status	—	100	20	Normal	—	—
TM06	Toxic	Poison	Status	—	90	10	Normal	—	—
TM10	Hidden Power	Normal	Special	—	100	15	Normal	—	—
TM11	Sunny Day	Fire	Status	—	—	5	Both Sides	—	—
TM12	Taunt	Dark	Status	—	100	20	Normal	—	—
TM13	Ice Beam	Ice	Special	95	100	10	Normal	—	—
TM14	Blizzard	Ice	Special	120	70	5	Many Others	—	—
TM15	Hyper Beam	Normal	Special	150	90	5	Normal	—	—
TM17	Protect	Normal	Status	—	—	10	Self	—	—
TM18	Rain Dance	Water	Status	—	—	5	Both Sides	—	—
TM21	Frustration	Normal	Physical	—	100	20	Normal	—	○
TM23	Smack Down	Rock	Physical	50	100	15	Normal	—	—
TM24	Thunderbolt	Electric	Special	95	100	15	Normal	—	—
TM25	Thunder	Electric	Special	120	70	10	Normal	—	—
TM26	Earthquake	Ground	Physical	100	100	10	Adjacent	—	—
TM27	Return	Normal	Physical	—	100	20	Normal	—	○
TM28	Dig	Ground	Physical	80	100	10	Normal	—	○
TM31	Brick Break	Fighting	Physical	75	100	15	Normal	—	○
TM32	Double Team	Normal	Status	—	—	15	Self	—	—
TM35	Flamethrower	Fire	Special	95	100	15	Normal	—	—
TM37	Sandstorm	Rock	Status	—	—	10	Both Sides	—	—
TM38	Fire Blast	Fire	Special	120	85	5	Normal	—	—
TM39	Rock Tomb	Rock	Physical	50	80	10	Normal	—	—
TM40	Aerial Ace	Flying	Physical	60	—	20	Normal	○	○
TM41	Torment	Dark	Status	—	100	15	Normal	—	—
TM42	Facade	Normal	Physical	70	100	20	Normal	—	○
TM44	Rest	Psychic	Status	—	—	10	Self	—	—
TM45	Attract	Normal	Status	—	100	15	Normal	—	—
TM48	Round	Normal	Special	60	100	15	Normal	—	—
TM52	Focus Blast	Fighting	Special	120	70	5	Normal	—	—
TM56	Fling	Dark	Physical	—	100	10	Normal	—	—
TM59	Incinerate	Fire	Special	30	100	15	Many Others	—	—
TM65	Shadow Claw	Ghost	Physical	70	100	15	Normal	—	○
TM66	Payback	Dark	Physical	50	100	10	Normal	—	○
TM67	Retaliate	Normal	Physical	70	100	5	Normal	—	○
TM68	Giga Impact	Normal	Physical	150	90	5	Normal	—	○
TM69	Rock Polish	Rock	Status	—	—	20	Self	—	—
TM71	Stone Edge	Rock	Physical	100	80	5	Normal	—	—
TM73	Thunder Wave	Electric	Status	—	100	20	Normal	—	—
TM78	Bulldoze	Ground	Physical	60	100	20	Adjacent	—	—
TM80	Rock Slide	Rock	Physical	75	90	10	Many Others	—	—
TM82	Dragon Tail	Dragon	Physical	60	90	10	Normal	—	○
TM87	Swagger	Normal	Status	—	90	15	Normal	—	—
TM90	Substitute	Normal	Status	—	—	10	Self	—	—
TM94	Rock Smash	Fighting	Physical	40	100	15	Normal	—	○
TM95	Snarl	Dark	Special	55	95	15	Many Others	—	—
HM01	Cut	Normal	Physical	50	95	30	Normal	—	○
HM03	Surf	Water	Special	95	100	15	Adjacent	—	—
HM04	Strength	Normal	Physical	80	100	15	Normal	—	○

MOVES TAUGHT BY PEOPLE

Name	Type	Kind	Pow.	Acc.	PP	Range	Long	DA

MOVES TAUGHT BY MOVE TUTORS FOR SHARDS

Name	Type	Kind	Pow.	Acc.	PP	Range	Long	DA
Iron Head	Steel	Physical	80	100	15	Normal	—	○
Uproar	Normal	Special	90	100	10	1 Random	—	—
Low Kick	Fighting	Physical	—	100	20	Normal	—	○
Fire Punch	Fire	Physical	75	100	15	Normal	—	○
ThunderPunch	Electric	Physical	75	100	15	Normal	—	○
Ice Punch	Ice	Physical	75	100	15	Normal	—	○
Iron Defense	Steel	Status	—	—	15	Self	—	—
Block	Normal	Status	—	—	5	Normal	—	—
Iron Tail	Steel	Physical	100	75	15	Normal	—	○
Aqua Tail	Water	Physical	90	90	10	Normal	—	○
Earth Power	Ground	Special	90	100	10	Normal	—	—
Foul Play	Dark	Physical	95	100	15	Normal	—	○
Superpower	Fighting	Physical	120	100	5	Normal	—	○
Dragon Pulse	Dragon	Special	90	100	10	Normal	○	—
Dark Pulse	Dark	Special	80	100	15	Normal	○	—
Snore	Normal	Special	40	100	15	Normal	—	—
Spite	Ghost	Status	—	100	10	Normal	—	—
Stealth Rock	Rock	Status	—	—	20	Other Side	—	—
Outrage	Dragon	Physical	120	100	10	1 Random	—	○
Sleep Talk	Normal	Status	—	—	10	Self	—	—

Diving Pokémon

249 Lugia

- HEIGHT: 17'01"
- WEIGHT: 476.2 lbs.
- GENDER: Unknown

It sleeps in a deep-sea trench. If it flaps its wings, it is said to cause a 40-day storm.

Gender unknown

TYPE Psychic Flying

ABILITY
- Pressure

HIDDEN ABILITY
- Multiscale

STATS
HP
Attack
Defense
Sp. Atk
Sp. Def
Speed

EGG GROUPS
No Egg has ever been discovered

ITEMS SOMETIMES HELD
- None

Pokémon AR Marker

EVOLUTION

Does not evolve

HOW TO OBTAIN

Pokémon Black Version 2	Link Trade or Poké Transfer
Pokémon White Version 2	Link Trade or Poké Transfer

HOW TO OBTAIN FROM OTHER GAMES

Pokémon HeartGold Version	Whirl Islands (after entering the Hall of Fame)
Pokémon SoulSilver Version	Whirl Islands

LEVEL-UP AND LEARNED MOVES

Lv.	Name	Type	Kind	Pow.	Acc.	PP	Range	Long	DA
1	Whirlwind	Normal	Status	—	100	20	Normal	—	—
1	Weather Ball	Normal	Special	50	100	10	Normal	—	—
9	Gust	Flying	Special	40	100	35	Normal	○	—
15	Dragon Rush	Dragon	Physical	100	75	10	Normal	—	○
23	Extrasensory	Psychic	Special	80	100	30	Normal	—	—
29	Rain Dance	Water	Status	—	—	5	Both Sides	—	—
37	Hydro Pump	Water	Special	120	80	5	Normal	—	—
43	Aeroblast	Flying	Special	100	95	5	Normal	○	—
50	Punishment	Dark	Physical	—	100	5	Normal	—	○
57	AncientPower	Rock	Special	60	100	5	Normal	—	—
65	Safeguard	Normal	Status	—	—	25	Your Side	—	—
71	Recover	Normal	Status	—	—	10	Self	—	—
79	Future Sight	Psychic	Special	100	100	10	Normal	—	—
85	Natural Gift	Normal	Physical	—	100	15	Normal	—	—
93	Calm Mind	Psychic	Status	—	—	20	Self	—	—
99	Sky Attack	Flying	Physical	140	90	5	Normal	○	—

TM & HM MOVES

Lv.	Name	Type	Kind	Pow.	Acc.	PP	Range	Long	DA
TM03	Psyshock	Psychic	Special	80	100	10	Normal	—	—
TM04	Calm Mind	Psychic	Status	—	—	20	Self	—	—
TM05	Roar	Normal	Status	—	100	20	Normal	—	—
TM06	Toxic	Poison	Status	—	90	10	Normal	—	—
TM07	Hail	Ice	Status	—	—	10	Both Sides	—	—
TM10	Hidden Power	Normal	Special	—	100	15	Normal	—	—
TM11	Sunny Day	Fire	Status	—	—	5	Both Sides	—	—
TM13	Ice Beam	Ice	Special	95	100	10	Normal	—	—
TM14	Blizzard	Ice	Special	120	70	5	Many Others	—	—
TM15	Hyper Beam	Normal	Special	150	90	5	Normal	—	—
TM16	Light Screen	Psychic	Status	—	—	30	Your Side	—	—
TM17	Protect	Normal	Status	—	—	10	Self	—	—
TM18	Rain Dance	Water	Status	—	—	5	Both Sides	—	—
TM19	Telekinesis	Psychic	Status	—	—	15	Normal	—	—
TM20	Safeguard	Normal	Status	—	—	25	Your Side	—	—
TM21	Frustration	Normal	Physical	—	100	20	Normal	—	○
TM24	Thunderbolt	Electric	Special	95	100	15	Normal	—	—
TM25	Thunder	Electric	Special	120	70	10	Normal	—	—
TM26	Earthquake	Ground	Physical	100	100	10	Adjacent	—	—
TM27	Return	Normal	Physical	—	100	20	Normal	—	○
TM29	Psychic	Psychic	Special	90	100	10	Normal	—	—
TM30	Shadow Ball	Ghost	Special	80	100	15	Normal	—	—
TM32	Double Team	Normal	Status	—	—	15	Self	—	—
TM33	Reflect	Psychic	Status	—	—	20	Your Side	—	—
TM37	Sandstorm	Rock	Status	—	—	10	Both Sides	—	—
TM40	Aerial Ace	Flying	Physical	60	—	20	Normal	○	○
TM42	Facade	Normal	Physical	70	100	20	Normal	—	○
TM44	Rest	Psychic	Status	—	—	10	Self	—	—
TM48	Round	Normal	Special	60	100	15	Normal	—	—
TM49	Echoed Voice	Normal	Special	40	100	15	Normal	—	—
TM57	Charge Beam	Electric	Special	50	90	10	Normal	—	—
TM58	Sky Drop	Flying	Physical	60	100	10	Normal	○	○
TM68	Giga Impact	Normal	Physical	150	90	5	Normal	—	○
TM70	Flash	Normal	Status	—	100	20	Normal	—	—
TM73	Thunder Wave	Electric	Status	—	100	20	Normal	—	—
TM77	Psych Up	Normal	Status	—	—	10	Normal	—	—
TM78	Bulldoze	Ground	Physical	60	100	20	Adjacent	—	—
TM82	Dragon Tail	Dragon	Physical	60	90	10	Normal	—	○
TM85	Dream Eater	Psychic	Special	100	100	15	Normal	—	—
TM87	Swagger	Normal	Status	—	90	15	Normal	—	—
TM90	Substitute	Normal	Status	—	—	10	Self	—	—
TM94	Rock Smash	Fighting	Physical	40	100	15	Normal	—	○
HM02	Fly	Flying	Physical	90	95	15	Normal	○	○
HM03	Surf	Water	Special	95	100	15	Adjacent	—	—
HM04	Strength	Normal	Physical	80	100	15	Normal	—	○
HM05	Waterfall	Water	Physical	80	100	15	Normal	—	○
HM06	Dive	Water	Physical	80	100	10	Normal	—	○

MOVES TAUGHT BY PEOPLE

Name	Type	Kind	Pow.	Acc.	PP	Range	Long	DA

MOVES TAUGHT BY MOVE TUTORS FOR SHARDS

Name	Type	Kind	Pow.	Acc.	PP	Range	Long	DA
Signal Beam	Bug	Special	75	100	15	Normal	—	—
Iron Head	Steel	Physical	80	100	15	Normal	—	○
Hyper Voice	Normal	Special	90	100	10	Many Others	—	—
Icy Wind	Ice	Special	55	95	15	Many Others	—	—
Iron Tail	Steel	Physical	100	75	15	Normal	—	○
Aqua Tail	Water	Physical	90	90	10	Normal	—	○
Earth Power	Ground	Special	90	100	10	Normal	—	—
Zen Headbutt	Psychic	Physical	80	90	15	Normal	—	○
Dragon Pulse	Dragon	Special	90	100	10	Normal	○	—
Snore	Normal	Special	40	100	15	Normal	—	—
Roost	Flying	Status	—	—	10	Self	—	—
Sky Attack	Flying	Physical	140	90	5	Normal	○	—
Giga Drain	Grass	Special	75	100	10	Normal	—	—
Tailwind	Flying	Status	—	—	30	Your Side	—	—
Wonder Room	Psychic	Status	—	—	10	Both Sides	—	—
Trick	Psychic	Status	—	100	10	Normal	—	—
Sleep Talk	Normal	Status	—	—	10	Self	—	—
Skill Swap	Psychic	Status	—	—	10	Normal	—	—

Rainbow Pokémon

250 Ho-Oh

- HEIGHT: 12'06"
- WEIGHT: 438.7 lbs.
- GENDER: Unknown

Its feathers are in seven colors. It is said that anyone seeing it is promised eternal happiness.

Gender unknown

TYPE Fire Flying

ABILITY
- Pressure

HIDDEN ABILITY
- Regenerator

STATS
HP
Attack
Defense
Sp. Atk
Sp. Def
Speed

EGG GROUPS
No Egg has ever been discovered

ITEMS SOMETIMES HELD
- None

Pokémon AR Marker

EVOLUTION

Does not evolve

HOW TO OBTAIN

Pokémon Black Version 2	Link Trade or Poké Transfer
Pokémon White Version 2	Link Trade or Poké Transfer

HOW TO OBTAIN FROM OTHER GAMES

Pokémon HeartGold Version	Bell Tower
Pokémon SoulSilver Version	Bell Tower (after entering the Hall of Fame)

LEVEL-UP AND LEARNED MOVES

Lv.	Name	Type	Kind	Pow.	Acc.	PP	Range	Long	DA
1	Whirlwind	Normal	Status	—	100	20	Normal	—	—
1	Weather Ball	Normal	Special	50	100	10	Normal	—	—
9	Gust	Flying	Special	40	100	35	Normal	○	—
15	Brave Bird	Flying	Physical	120	100	15	Normal	○	○
23	Extrasensory	Psychic	Special	80	100	30	Normal	—	—
29	Sunny Day	Fire	Status	—	—	5	Both Sides	—	—
37	Fire Blast	Fire	Special	120	85	5	Normal	—	—
43	Sacred Fire	Fire	Physical	100	95	5	Normal	—	—
50	Punishment	Dark	Physical	—	100	5	Normal	—	○
57	AncientPower	Rock	Special	60	100	5	Normal	—	—
65	Safeguard	Normal	Status	—	—	25	Your Side	—	—
71	Recover	Normal	Status	—	—	10	Self	—	—
79	Future Sight	Psychic	Special	100	100	10	Normal	—	—
85	Natural Gift	Normal	Physical	—	100	15	Normal	—	—
93	Calm Mind	Psychic	Status	—	—	20	Self	—	—
99	Sky Attack	Flying	Physical	140	90	5	Normal	○	—

TM & HM MOVES

Lv.	Name	Type	Kind	Pow.	Acc.	PP	Range	Long	DA
TM04	Calm Mind	Psychic	Status	—	—	20	Self	—	—
TM05	Roar	Normal	Status	—	100	20	Normal	—	—
TM06	Toxic	Poison	Status	—	90	10	Normal	—	—
TM10	Hidden Power	Normal	Special	—	100	15	Normal	—	—
TM11	Sunny Day	Fire	Status	—	—	5	Both Sides	—	—
TM15	Hyper Beam	Normal	Special	150	90	5	Normal	—	—
TM16	Light Screen	Psychic	Status	—	—	30	Your Side	—	—
TM17	Protect	Normal	Status	—	—	10	Self	—	—
TM18	Rain Dance	Water	Status	—	—	5	Both Sides	—	—
TM20	Safeguard	Normal	Status	—	—	25	Your Side	—	—
TM21	Frustration	Normal	Physical	—	100	20	Normal	—	○
TM22	SolarBeam	Grass	Special	120	100	10	Normal	—	—
TM24	Thunderbolt	Electric	Special	95	100	15	Normal	—	—
TM25	Thunder	Electric	Special	120	70	10	Normal	—	—
TM26	Earthquake	Ground	Physical	100	100	10	Adjacent	—	—
TM27	Return	Normal	Physical	—	100	20	Normal	—	○
TM29	Psychic	Psychic	Special	90	100	10	Normal	—	—
TM30	Shadow Ball	Ghost	Special	80	100	15	Normal	—	—
TM32	Double Team	Normal	Status	—	—	15	Self	—	—
TM33	Reflect	Psychic	Status	—	—	20	Your Side	—	—
TM35	Flamethrower	Fire	Special	95	100	15	Normal	—	—
TM37	Sandstorm	Rock	Status	—	—	10	Both Sides	—	—
TM38	Fire Blast	Fire	Special	120	85	5	Normal	—	—
TM40	Aerial Ace	Flying	Physical	60	—	20	Normal	○	○
TM42	Facade	Normal	Physical	70	100	20	Normal	—	○
TM43	Flame Charge	Fire	Physical	50	100	20	Normal	—	○
TM44	Rest	Psychic	Status	—	—	10	Self	—	—
TM48	Round	Normal	Special	60	100	15	Normal	—	—
TM49	Echoed Voice	Normal	Special	40	100	15	Normal	—	—
TM50	Overheat	Fire	Special	140	90	5	Normal	—	—
TM57	Charge Beam	Electric	Special	50	90	10	Normal	—	—
TM58	Sky Drop	Flying	Physical	60	100	10	Normal	○	○
TM59	Incinerate	Fire	Special	30	100	15	Many Others	—	—
TM61	Will-O-Wisp	Fire	Status	—	75	15	Normal	—	—
TM68	Giga Impact	Normal	Physical	150	90	5	Normal	—	○
TM70	Flash	Normal	Status	—	100	20	Normal	—	—
TM73	Thunder Wave	Electric	Status	—	100	20	Normal	—	—
TM77	Psych Up	Normal	Status	—	—	10	Normal	—	—
TM78	Bulldoze	Ground	Physical	60	100	20	Adjacent	—	—
TM85	Dream Eater	Psychic	Special	100	100	15	Normal	—	—
TM87	Swagger	Normal	Status	—	90	15	Normal	—	—
TM88	Pluck	Flying	Physical	60	100	20	Normal	○	○
TM90	Substitute	Normal	Status	—	—	10	Self	—	—
TM94	Rock Smash	Fighting	Physical	40	100	15	Normal	—	○
HM02	Fly	Flying	Physical	90	95	15	Normal	○	○
HM04	Strength	Normal	Physical	80	100	15	Normal	—	○

MOVES TAUGHT BY PEOPLE

Name	Type	Kind	Pow.	Acc.	PP	Range	Long	DA

MOVES TAUGHT BY MOVE TUTORS FOR SHARDS

Name	Type	Kind	Pow.	Acc.	PP	Range	Long	DA
Signal Beam	Bug	Special	75	100	15	Normal	—	—
Iron Head	Steel	Physical	80	100	15	Normal	—	○
Hyper Voice	Normal	Special	90	100	10	Many Others	—	—
Earth Power	Ground	Special	90	100	10	Normal	—	—
Zen Headbutt	Psychic	Physical	80	90	15	Normal	—	○
Snore	Normal	Special	40	100	15	Normal	—	—
Roost	Flying	Status	—	—	10	Self	—	—
Sky Attack	Flying	Physical	140	90	5	Normal	○	—
Heat Wave	Fire	Special	100	90	10	Many Others	—	—
Giga Drain	Grass	Special	75	100	10	Normal	—	—
Tailwind	Flying	Status	—	—	30	Your Side	—	—
Sleep Talk	Normal	Status	—	—	10	Self	—	—

251 Celebi

Time Travel Pokémon

TYPE: Psychic / Grass

ABILITY
- Natural Cure

HIDDEN ABILITY
—

- HEIGHT: 2'00"
- WEIGHT: 11.0 lbs.
- GENDER: Unknown

It has the power to travel across time, but it is said to appear only in peaceful times.

STATS
HP
Attack
Defense
Sp. Atk
Sp. Def
Speed

EGG GROUPS
No Egg has ever been discovered

Gender unknown

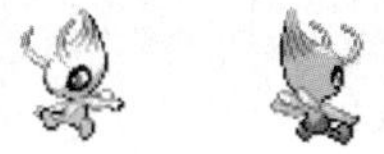

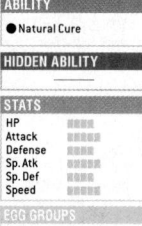

EVOLUTION

Does not evolve

HOW TO OBTAIN

Only available through special distribution events. Check www.pokemon.com for the latest information on how to catch this Pokémon.

Pokémon AR Marker

LEVEL-UP AND LEARNED MOVES

Lv.	Name	Type	Kind	Pow.	Acc.	PP	Range	Long	DA
1	Leech Seed	Grass	Status	—	90	10	Normal	—	—
1	Confusion	Psychic	Special	50	100	25	Normal	—	—
1	Recover	Normal	Status	—	—	10	Self	—	—
1	Heal Bell	Normal	Status	—	—	5	Your Party	—	—
10	Safeguard	Normal	Status	—	—	25	Your Side	—	—
19	Magical Leaf	Grass	Special	60	—	20	Normal	—	—
28	AncientPower	Rock	Special	60	100	5	Normal	—	—
37	Baton Pass	Normal	Status	—	—	40	Self	—	—
46	Natural Gift	Normal	Physical	—	100	15	Normal	—	—
55	Heal Block	Psychic	Status	—	100	15	Many Others	—	—
64	Future Sight	Psychic	Special	100	100	10	Normal	—	—
73	Healing Wish	Psychic	Status	—	—	10	Self	—	—
82	Leaf Storm	Grass	Special	140	90	5	Normal	—	—
91	Perish Song	Normal	Status	—	—	5	Adjacent	○	—

TM & HM MOVES

Lv.	Name	Type	Kind	Pow.	Acc.	PP	Range	Long	DA
TM04	Calm Mind	Psychic	Status	—	—	20	Self	—	—
TM06	Toxic	Poison	Status	—	90	10	Normal	—	—
TM10	Hidden Power	Normal	Special	—	100	15	Normal	—	—
TM11	Sunny Day	Fire	Status	—	—	5	Both Sides	—	—
TM15	Hyper Beam	Normal	Special	150	90	5	Normal	—	—
TM16	Light Screen	Psychic	Status	—	—	30	Your Side	—	—
TM17	Protect	Normal	Status	—	—	10	Self	—	—
TM18	Rain Dance	Water	Status	—	—	5	Both Sides	—	—
TM20	Safeguard	Normal	Status	—	—	25	Your Side	—	—
TM21	Frustration	Normal	Physical	—	100	20	Normal	—	○
TM22	SolarBeam	Grass	Special	120	100	10	Normal	—	—
TM27	Return	Normal	Physical	—	100	20	Normal	—	○
TM29	Psychic	Psychic	Special	90	100	10	Normal	—	—
TM30	Shadow Ball	Ghost	Special	80	100	15	Normal	—	—
TM32	Double Team	Normal	Status	—	—	15	Self	—	—
TM33	Reflect	Psychic	Status	—	—	20	Your Side	—	—
TM37	Sandstorm	Rock	Status	—	—	10	Both Sides	—	—
TM40	Aerial Ace	Flying	Physical	60	—	20	Normal	○	○
TM42	Facade	Normal	Physical	70	100	20	Normal	—	○
TM44	Rest	Psychic	Status	—	—	10	Self	—	—
TM48	Round	Normal	Special	60	100	15	Normal	—	—
TM49	Echoed Voice	Normal	Special	40	100	15	Normal	—	—
TM53	Energy Ball	Grass	Special	80	100	10	Normal	—	—
TM56	Fling	Dark	Physical	—	100	10	Normal	—	—
TM57	Charge Beam	Electric	Special	50	90	10	Normal	—	—
TM68	Giga Impact	Normal	Physical	150	90	5	Normal	—	○
TM70	Flash	Normal	Status	—	100	20	Normal	—	—
TM73	Thunder Wave	Electric	Status	—	100	20	Normal	—	—
TM75	Swords Dance	Normal	Status	—	—	30	Self	—	—
TM77	Psych Up	Normal	Status	—	—	10	Normal	—	—
TM85	Dream Eater	Psychic	Special	100	100	15	Normal	—	—
TM86	Grass Knot	Grass	Special	—	100	20	Normal	—	○
TM87	Swagger	Normal	Status	—	90	15	Normal	—	—
TM89	U-turn	Bug	Physical	70	100	20	Normal	—	○
TM90	Substitute	Normal	Status	—	—	10	Self	—	—
TM92	Trick Room	Psychic	Status	—	—	5	Both Sides	—	—
HM01	Cut	Normal	Physical	50	95	30	Normal	—	○

MOVES TAUGHT BY PEOPLE

Name	Type	Kind	Pow.	Acc.	PP	Range	Long	DA

MOVES TAUGHT BY MOVE TUTORS FOR SHARDS

Name	Type	Kind	Pow.	Acc.	PP	Range	Long	DA
Signal Beam	Bug	Special	75	100	15	Normal	—	—
Uproar	Normal	Special	90	100	10	1 Random	—	—
Seed Bomb	Grass	Physical	80	100	15	Normal	—	—
Last Resort	Normal	Physical	140	100	5	Normal	—	○
Magic Coat	Psychic	Status	—	—	15	Self	—	—
Earth Power	Ground	Special	90	100	10	Normal	—	—
Zen Headbutt	Psychic	Physical	80	90	15	Normal	—	○
Snore	Normal	Special	40	100	15	Normal	—	—
Heal Bell	Normal	Status	—	—	5	Your Party	—	—
Synthesis	Grass	Status	—	—	5	Self	—	—
Giga Drain	Grass	Special	75	100	10	Normal	—	—
Worry Seed	Grass	Status	—	100	10	Normal	—	—
Helping Hand	Normal	Status	—	—	20	1 Ally	—	—
Magic Room	Psychic	Status	—	—	10	Both Sides	—	—
Wonder Room	Psychic	Status	—	—	10	Both Sides	—	—
Trick	Psychic	Status	—	100	10	Normal	—	—
Stealth Rock	Rock	Status	—	—	20	Other Side	—	—
Sleep Talk	Normal	Status	—	—	10	Self	—	—
Skill Swap	Psychic	Status	—	—	10	Normal	—	—

252 Treecko

Wood Gecko Pokémon

TYPE: Grass

ABILITY
- Overgrow

HIDDEN ABILITY
- Unburden

- HEIGHT: 1'08"
- WEIGHT: 11.0 lbs.
- GENDER: ♂ / ♀

The soles of its feet are covered by countless tiny spikes, enabling it to walk on walls and ceilings.

STATS
HP
Attack
Defense
Sp. Atk
Sp. Def
Speed

EGG GROUPS
Monster/Dragon

ITEMS SOMETIMES HELD
- None

Same form for ♂ / ♀

EVOLUTION

Lv. 16
Lv. 36
Treecko
Grovyle
Sceptile

HOW TO OBTAIN

Pokémon Black Version 2	Link Trade or Poké Transfer
Pokémon White Version 2	Link Trade or Poké Transfer

HOW TO OBTAIN FROM OTHER GAMES

Pokémon HeartGold Version	Receive from Steven at Silph Co. in Saffron City (after defeating Red)
Pokémon SoulSilver Version	Receive from Steven at Silph Co. in Saffron City (after defeating Red)

Pokémon AR Marker

LEVEL-UP AND LEARNED MOVES

Lv.	Name	Type	Kind	Pow.	Acc.	PP	Range	Long	DA
1	Pound	Normal	Physical	40	100	35	Normal	—	○
1	Leer	Normal	Status	—	100	30	Many Others	—	—
6	Absorb	Grass	Special	20	100	25	Normal	—	—
11	Quick Attack	Normal	Physical	40	100	30	Normal	—	○
16	Pursuit	Dark	Physical	40	100	20	Normal	—	○
21	Screech	Normal	Status	—	85	40	Normal	—	—
26	Mega Drain	Grass	Special	40	100	15	Normal	—	—
31	Agility	Psychic	Status	—	—	30	Self	—	—
36	Slam	Normal	Physical	80	75	20	Normal	—	○
41	Detect	Fighting	Status	—	—	5	Self	—	—
46	Giga Drain	Grass	Special	75	100	10	Normal	—	—
51	Energy Ball	Grass	Special	80	100	10	Normal	—	—

TM & HM MOVES

Lv.	Name	Type	Kind	Pow.	Acc.	PP	Range	Long	DA
TM06	Toxic	Poison	Status	—	90	10	Normal	—	—
TM10	Hidden Power	Normal	Special	—	100	15	Normal	—	—
TM11	Sunny Day	Fire	Status	—	—	5	Both Sides	—	—
TM17	Protect	Normal	Status	—	—	10	Self	—	—
TM20	Safeguard	Normal	Status	—	—	25	Your Side	—	—
TM21	Frustration	Normal	Physical	—	100	20	Normal	—	○
TM22	SolarBeam	Grass	Special	120	100	10	Normal	—	—
TM27	Return	Normal	Physical	—	100	20	Normal	—	○
TM28	Dig	Ground	Physical	80	100	10	Normal	—	○
TM31	Brick Break	Fighting	Physical	75	100	15	Normal	—	○
TM32	Double Team	Normal	Status	—	—	15	Self	—	—
TM39	Rock Tomb	Rock	Physical	50	80	10	Normal	—	—
TM40	Aerial Ace	Flying	Physical	60	—	20	Normal	○	○
TM42	Facade	Normal	Physical	70	100	20	Normal	—	○
TM44	Rest	Psychic	Status	—	—	10	Self	—	—
TM45	Attract	Normal	Status	—	100	15	Normal	—	—
TM48	Round	Normal	Special	60	100	15	Normal	—	—
TM53	Energy Ball	Grass	Special	80	100	10	Normal	—	—
TM56	Fling	Dark	Physical	—	100	10	Normal	—	—
TM62	Acrobatics	Flying	Physical	55	100	15	Normal	○	○
TM70	Flash	Normal	Status	—	100	20	Normal	—	—
TM75	Swords Dance	Normal	Status	—	—	30	Self	—	—
TM80	Rock Slide	Rock	Physical	75	90	10	Many Others	—	—
TM86	Grass Knot	Grass	Special	—	100	20	Normal	—	○
TM87	Swagger	Normal	Status	—	90	15	Normal	—	—
TM90	Substitute	Normal	Status	—	—	10	Self	—	—
TM94	Rock Smash	Fighting	Physical	40	100	15	Normal	—	○
HM01	Cut	Normal	Physical	50	95	30	Normal	—	○
HM04	Strength	Normal	Physical	80	100	15	Normal	—	○

MOVES TAUGHT BY PEOPLE

Name	Type	Kind	Pow.	Acc.	PP	Range	Long	DA
Grass Pledge	Grass	Special	50	100	10	Normal	—	—

MOVES TAUGHT BY MOVE TUTORS FOR SHARDS

Name	Type	Kind	Pow.	Acc.	PP	Range	Long	DA
Seed Bomb	Grass	Physical	80	100	15	Normal	—	—
Low Kick	Fighting	Physical	—	100	20	Normal	—	○
ThunderPunch	Electric	Physical	75	100	15	Normal	—	○
Iron Tail	Steel	Physical	100	75	15	Normal	—	○
Snore	Normal	Special	40	100	15	Normal	—	—
Synthesis	Grass	Status	—	—	5	Self	—	—
Giga Drain	Grass	Special	75	100	10	Normal	—	—
Drain Punch	Fighting	Physical	75	100	10	Normal	—	○
Worry Seed	Grass	Status	—	100	10	Normal	—	—
Endeavor	Normal	Physical	—	100	5	Normal	—	○
Sleep Talk	Normal	Status	—	—	10	Self	—	—

EGG MOVES

Name	Type	Kind	Pow.	Acc.	PP	Range	Long	DA
Crunch	Dark	Physical	80	100	15	Normal	—	○
Mud Sport	Ground	Status	—	—	15	Both Sides	—	—
Endeavor	Normal	Physical	—	100	5	Normal	—	○
Leech Seed	Grass	Status	—	90	10	Normal	—	—
DragonBreath	Dragon	Special	60	100	20	Normal	—	—
Crush Claw	Normal	Physical	75	95	10	Normal	—	○
Worry Seed	Grass	Status	—	100	10	Normal	—	—
Double Kick	Fighting	Physical	30	100	30	Normal	—	○
GrassWhistle	Grass	Status	—	55	15	Normal	—	—
Synthesis	Grass	Status	—	—	5	Self	—	—
Magical Leaf	Grass	Special	60	—	20	Normal	—	—
Leaf Storm	Grass	Special	140	90	5	Normal	—	—
Razor Wind	Normal	Special	80	100	10	Many Others	—	—
Bullet Seed	Grass	Physical	25	100	30	Normal	—	—
Natural Gift	Normal	Physical	—	100	15	Normal	—	—

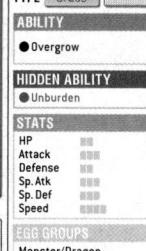

253 Grovyle

Wood Gecko Pokémon

● HEIGHT: 2'11"
● WEIGHT: 47.6 lbs.
● GENDER: ♂ / ♀

It lives in dense jungles. While closing in on its prey, it leaps from branch to branch.

Same form for ♂ / ♀

TYPE Grass

ABILITY
● Overgrow

HIDDEN ABILITY
● Unburden

STATS
HP
Attack
Defense
Sp. Atk
Sp. Def
Speed

EGG GROUPS
Monster/Dragon

ITEMS SOMETIMES HELD
● None

EVOLUTION

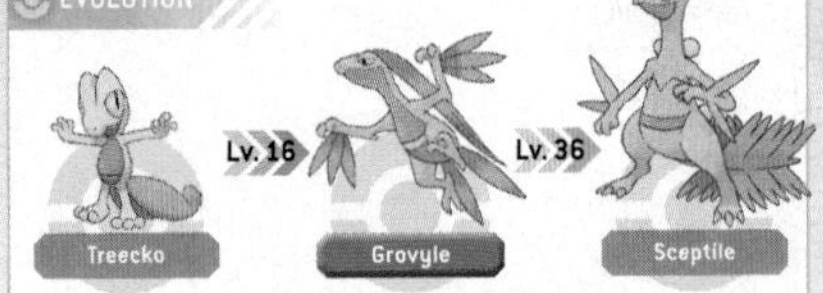

HOW TO OBTAIN

Pokémon Black Version 2	Level up a Treecko you obtain via Link Trade or Poké Transfer to Lv. 16
Pokémon White Version 2	Level up a Treecko you obtain via Link Trade or Poké Transfer to Lv. 16

HOW TO OBTAIN FROM OTHER GAMES

—

—

LEVEL-UP AND LEARNED MOVES

Lv.	Name	Type	Kind	Pow.	Acc.	PP	Range	Long	DA
1	Pound	Normal	Physical	40	100	35	Normal	—	○
1	Leer	Normal	Status	—	100	30	Many Others	—	—
1	Absorb	Grass	Special	20	100	25	Normal	—	—
1	Quick Attack	Normal	Physical	40	100	30	Normal	—	○
6	Absorb	Grass	Special	20	100	25	Normal	—	—
11	Quick Attack	Normal	Physical	40	100	30	Normal	—	○
16	Fury Cutter	Bug	Physical	20	95	20	Normal	—	○
17	Pursuit	Dark	Physical	40	100	20	Normal	—	○
23	Screech	Normal	Status	—	85	40	Normal	—	—
29	Leaf Blade	Grass	Physical	90	100	15	Normal	—	○
35	Agility	Psychic	Status	—	—	30	Self	—	—
41	Slam	Normal	Physical	80	75	20	Normal	—	○
47	Detect	Fighting	Status	—	—	5	Self	—	—
53	False Swipe	Normal	Physical	40	100	40	Normal	—	○
59	Leaf Storm	Grass	Special	140	90	5	Normal	—	—

TM & HM MOVES

Lv.	Name	Type	Kind	Pow.	Acc.	PP	Range	Long	DA
TM06	Toxic	Poison	Status	—	90	10	Normal	—	—
TM10	Hidden Power	Normal	Special	—	100	15	Normal	—	—
TM11	Sunny Day	Fire	Status	—	—	5	Both Sides	—	—
TM17	Protect	Normal	Status	—	—	10	Self	—	—
TM20	Safeguard	Normal	Status	—	—	25	Your Side	—	—
TM21	Frustration	Normal	Physical	—	100	20	Normal	—	○
TM22	SolarBeam	Grass	Special	120	100	10	Normal	—	—
TM27	Return	Normal	Physical	—	100	20	Normal	—	○
TM28	Dig	Ground	Physical	80	100	10	Normal	—	○
TM31	Brick Break	Fighting	Physical	75	100	15	Normal	—	○
TM32	Double Team	Normal	Status	—	—	15	Self	—	—
TM39	Rock Tomb	Rock	Physical	50	80	10	Normal	—	—
TM40	Aerial Ace	Flying	Physical	60	—	20	Normal	○	○
TM42	Facade	Normal	Physical	70	100	20	Normal	—	○
TM44	Rest	Psychic	Status	—	—	10	Self	—	—
TM45	Attract	Normal	Status	—	100	15	Normal	—	—
TM47	Low Sweep	Fighting	Physical	60	100	20	Normal	—	○
TM48	Round	Normal	Special	60	100	15	Normal	—	—
TM53	Energy Ball	Grass	Special	80	100	10	Normal	—	—
TM54	False Swipe	Normal	Physical	40	100	40	Normal	—	○
TM56	Fling	Dark	Physical	—	100	10	Normal	—	—
TM62	Acrobatics	Flying	Physical	55	100	15	Normal	○	○
TM70	Flash	Normal	Status	—	100	20	Normal	—	—
TM75	Swords Dance	Normal	Status	—	—	30	Self	—	—
TM80	Rock Slide	Rock	Physical	75	90	10	Many Others	—	—
TM81	X-Scissor	Bug	Physical	80	100	15	Normal	—	○
TM86	Grass Knot	Grass	Special	—	100	20	Normal	—	○
TM87	Swagger	Normal	Status	—	90	15	Normal	—	—
TM90	Substitute	Normal	Status	—	—	10	Self	—	—
TM94	Rock Smash	Fighting	Physical	40	100	15	Normal	—	○
HM01	Cut	Normal	Physical	50	95	30	Normal	—	○
HM04	Strength	Normal	Physical	80	100	15	Normal	—	○

MOVES TAUGHT BY PEOPLE

Name	Type	Kind	Pow.	Acc.	PP	Range	Long	DA
Grass Pledge	Grass	Special	50	100	10	Normal	—	—

MOVES TAUGHT BY MOVE TUTORS FOR SHARDS

Name	Type	Kind	Pow.	Acc.	PP	Range	Long	DA
Seed Bomb	Grass	Physical	80	100	15	Normal	—	—
Low Kick	Fighting	Physical	—	100	20	Normal	—	○
ThunderPunch	Electric	Physical	75	100	15	Normal	—	○
Iron Tail	Steel	Physical	100	75	15	Normal	—	○
Snore	Normal	Special	40	100	15	Normal	—	—
Synthesis	Grass	Status	—	—	5	Self	—	—
Giga Drain	Grass	Special	75	100	10	Normal	—	—
Drain Punch	Fighting	Physical	75	100	10	Normal	—	○
Worry Seed	Grass	Status	—	100	10	Normal	—	—
Endeavor	Normal	Physical	—	100	5	Normal	—	○
Sleep Talk	Normal	Status	—	—	10	Self	—	—

Pokémon AR Marker

254 Sceptile

Forest Pokémon

● HEIGHT: 5'07"
● WEIGHT: 115.1 lbs.
● GENDER: ♂ / ♀

The leaves that grow on its arms can slice down thick trees. It is without peer in jungle combat.

Same form for ♂ / ♀

TYPE Grass

ABILITY
● Overgrow

HIDDEN ABILITY
● Unburden

STATS
HP
Attack
Defense
Sp. Atk
Sp. Def
Speed

EGG GROUPS
Monster/Dragon

ITEMS SOMETIMES HELD
● None

EVOLUTION

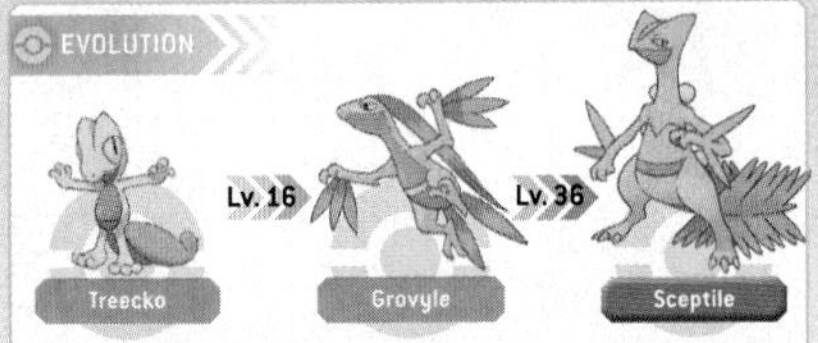

HOW TO OBTAIN

Pokémon Black Version 2	Level up a Grovyle you obtain via Link Trade or Poké Transfer to Lv. 36
Pokémon White Version 2	Level up a Grovyle you obtain via Link Trade or Poké Transfer to Lv. 36

HOW TO OBTAIN FROM OTHER GAMES

—

—

LEVEL-UP AND LEARNED MOVES

Lv.	Name	Type	Kind	Pow.	Acc.	PP	Range	Long	DA
1	Night Slash	Dark	Physical	70	100	15	Normal	—	○
1	Pound	Normal	Physical	40	100	35	Normal	—	○
1	Leer	Normal	Status	—	100	30	Many Others	—	—
1	Absorb	Grass	Special	20	100	25	Normal	—	—
1	Quick Attack	Normal	Physical	40	100	30	Normal	—	○
6	Absorb	Grass	Special	20	100	25	Normal	—	—
11	Quick Attack	Normal	Physical	40	100	30	Normal	—	○
16	X-Scissor	Bug	Physical	80	100	15	Normal	—	○
17	Pursuit	Dark	Physical	40	100	20	Normal	—	○
23	Screech	Normal	Status	—	85	40	Normal	—	—
29	Leaf Blade	Grass	Physical	90	100	15	Normal	—	○
35	Agility	Psychic	Status	—	—	30	Self	—	—
43	Slam	Normal	Physical	80	75	20	Normal	—	○
51	Detect	Fighting	Status	—	—	5	Self	—	—
59	False Swipe	Normal	Physical	40	100	40	Normal	—	○
67	Leaf Storm	Grass	Special	140	90	5	Normal	—	—

TM & HM MOVES

Lv.	Name	Type	Kind	Pow.	Acc.	PP	Range	Long	DA
TM01	Hone Claws	Dark	Status	—	—	15	Self	—	—
TM02	Dragon Claw	Dragon	Physical	80	100	15	Normal	—	○
TM05	Roar	Normal	Status	—	100	20	Normal	—	—
TM06	Toxic	Poison	Status	—	90	10	Normal	—	—
TM10	Hidden Power	Normal	Special	—	100	15	Normal	—	—
TM11	Sunny Day	Fire	Status	—	—	5	Both Sides	—	—
TM15	Hyper Beam	Normal	Special	150	90	5	Normal	—	—
TM17	Protect	Normal	Status	—	—	10	Self	—	—
TM20	Safeguard	Normal	Status	—	—	25	Your Side	—	—
TM21	Frustration	Normal	Physical	—	100	20	Normal	—	○
TM22	SolarBeam	Grass	Special	120	100	10	Normal	—	—
TM26	Earthquake	Ground	Physical	100	100	10	Adjacent	—	—
TM27	Return	Normal	Physical	—	100	20	Normal	—	○
TM28	Dig	Ground	Physical	80	100	10	Normal	—	○
TM31	Brick Break	Fighting	Physical	75	100	15	Normal	—	○
TM32	Double Team	Normal	Status	—	—	15	Self	—	—
TM39	Rock Tomb	Rock	Physical	50	80	10	Normal	—	—
TM40	Aerial Ace	Flying	Physical	60	—	20	Normal	○	○
TM42	Facade	Normal	Physical	70	100	20	Normal	—	○
TM44	Rest	Psychic	Status	—	—	10	Self	—	—
TM45	Attract	Normal	Status	—	100	15	Normal	—	—
TM47	Low Sweep	Fighting	Physical	60	100	20	Normal	—	○
TM48	Round	Normal	Special	60	100	15	Normal	—	—
TM52	Focus Blast	Fighting	Special	120	70	5	Normal	—	—
TM53	Energy Ball	Grass	Special	80	100	10	Normal	—	—
TM54	False Swipe	Normal	Physical	40	100	40	Normal	—	○
TM56	Fling	Dark	Physical	—	100	10	Normal	—	—
TM62	Acrobatics	Flying	Physical	55	100	15	Normal	○	○
TM68	Giga Impact	Normal	Physical	150	90	5	Normal	—	○
TM70	Flash	Normal	Status	—	100	20	Normal	—	—
TM75	Swords Dance	Normal	Status	—	—	30	Self	—	—
TM78	Bulldoze	Ground	Physical	60	100	20	Adjacent	—	—
TM80	Rock Slide	Rock	Physical	75	90	10	Many Others	—	—
TM81	X-Scissor	Bug	Physical	80	100	15	Normal	—	○
TM86	Grass Knot	Grass	Special	—	100	20	Normal	—	○
TM87	Swagger	Normal	Status	—	90	15	Normal	—	—
TM90	Substitute	Normal	Status	—	—	10	Self	—	—
TM94	Rock Smash	Fighting	Physical	40	100	15	Normal	—	○
HM01	Cut	Normal	Physical	50	95	30	Normal	—	○
HM04	Strength	Normal	Physical	80	100	15	Normal	—	○

MOVES TAUGHT BY PEOPLE

Name	Type	Kind	Pow.	Acc.	PP	Range	Long	DA
Grass Pledge	Grass	Special	50	100	10	Normal	—	—
Frenzy Plant	Grass	Special	150	90	5	Normal	—	—

MOVES TAUGHT BY MOVE TUTORS FOR SHARDS

Name	Type	Kind	Pow.	Acc.	PP	Range	Long	DA
Seed Bomb	Grass	Physical	80	100	15	Normal	—	—
Low Kick	Fighting	Physical	—	100	20	Normal	—	○
ThunderPunch	Electric	Physical	75	100	15	Normal	—	○
Iron Tail	Steel	Physical	100	75	15	Normal	—	○
Dragon Pulse	Dragon	Special	90	100	10	Normal	○	—
Snore	Normal	Special	40	100	15	Normal	—	—
Synthesis	Grass	Status	—	—	5	Self	—	—
Giga Drain	Grass	Special	75	100	10	Normal	—	—
Drain Punch	Fighting	Physical	75	100	10	Normal	—	○
Worry Seed	Grass	Status	—	100	10	Normal	—	—
Outrage	Dragon	Physical	120	100	10	1 Random	—	○
Endeavor	Normal	Physical	—	100	5	Normal	—	○
Sleep Talk	Normal	Status	—	—	10	Self	—	—

Pokémon AR Marker

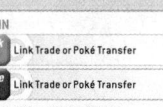

255 Torchic

Chick Pokémon

- HEIGHT: 1'04"
- WEIGHT: 5.5 lbs.
- GENDER: ♂ / ♀

A fire burns inside, so it feels very warm to hug. It launches fireballs of 1,800 degrees F.

♂ ♀

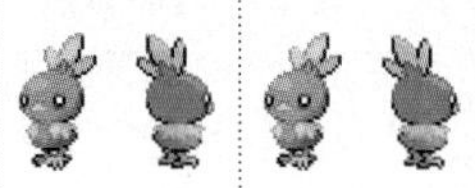

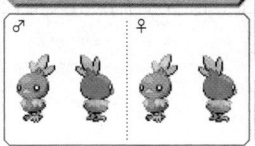

TYPE: Fire

ABILITY
- Blaze

HIDDEN ABILITY
- Speed Boost

STATS
HP
Attack
Defense
Sp. Atk
Sp. Def
Speed

EGG GROUPS
Field

ITEMS SOMETIMES HELD
- None

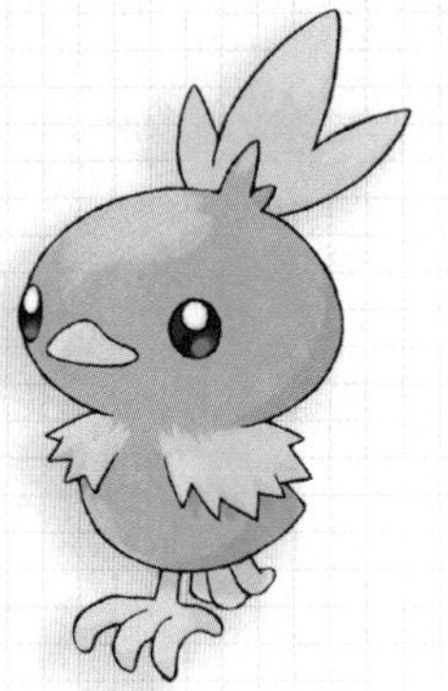

Pokémon AR Marker

EVOLUTION

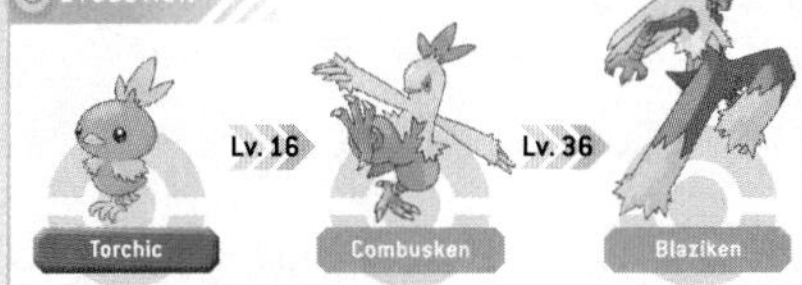

HOW TO OBTAIN

Pokémon Black Version 2	Link Trade or Poké Transfer
Pokémon White Version 2	Link Trade or Poké Transfer

HOW TO OBTAIN FROM OTHER GAMES

Pokémon HeartGold Version	Receive from Steven at Silph Co. in Saffron City (after defeating Red)
Pokémon SoulSilver Version	Receive from Steven at Silph Co. in Saffron City (after defeating Red)

LEVEL-UP AND LEARNED MOVES

Lv.	Name	Type	Kind	Pow.	Acc.	PP	Range	Long	DA
1	Scratch	Normal	Physical	40	100	35	Normal	—	○
1	Growl	Normal	Status	—	100	40	Many Others	—	—
7	Focus Energy	Normal	Status	—	—	30	Self	—	—
10	Ember	Fire	Special	40	100	25	Normal	—	—
16	Peck	Flying	Physical	35	100	35	Normal	○	○
19	Sand-Attack	Ground	Status	—	100	15	Normal	—	—
25	Fire Spin	Fire	Special	35	85	15	Normal	—	—
28	Quick Attack	Normal	Physical	40	100	30	Normal	—	○
34	Slash	Normal	Physical	70	100	20	Normal	—	○
37	Mirror Move	Flying	Status	—	—	20	Normal	—	—
43	Flamethrower	Fire	Special	95	100	15	Normal	—	—

TM & HM MOVES

Lv.	Name	Type	Kind	Pow.	Acc.	PP	Range	Long	DA
TM01	Hone Claws	Dark	Status	—	—	15	Self	—	—
TM06	Toxic	Poison	Status	—	90	10	Normal	—	—
TM10	Hidden Power	Normal	Special	—	100	15	Normal	—	—
TM11	Sunny Day	Fire	Status	—	—	5	Both Sides	—	—
TM17	Protect	Normal	Status	—	—	10	Self	—	—
TM21	Frustration	Normal	Physical	—	100	20	Normal	—	○
TM27	Return	Normal	Physical	—	100	20	Normal	—	○
TM28	Dig	Ground	Physical	80	100	10	Normal	—	○
TM32	Double Team	Normal	Status	—	—	15	Self	—	—
TM35	Flamethrower	Fire	Special	95	100	15	Normal	—	—
TM38	Fire Blast	Fire	Special	120	85	5	Normal	—	—
TM39	Rock Tomb	Rock	Physical	50	80	10	Normal	—	—
TM40	Aerial Ace	Flying	Physical	60	—	20	Normal	○	○
TM42	Facade	Normal	Physical	70	100	20	Normal	—	○
TM43	Flame Charge	Fire	Physical	50	100	20	Normal	—	○
TM44	Rest	Psychic	Status	—	—	10	Self	—	—
TM45	Attract	Normal	Status	—	100	15	Normal	—	—
TM48	Round	Normal	Special	60	100	15	Normal	—	—
TM49	Echoed Voice	Normal	Special	40	100	15	Normal	—	—
TM50	Overheat	Fire	Special	140	90	5	Normal	—	—
TM59	Incinerate	Fire	Special	30	100	15	Many Others	—	—
TM61	Will-O-Wisp	Fire	Status	—	75	15	Normal	—	—
TM65	Shadow Claw	Ghost	Physical	70	100	15	Normal	—	○
TM75	Swords Dance	Normal	Status	—	—	30	Self	—	—
TM80	Rock Slide	Rock	Physical	75	90	10	Many Others	—	—
TM87	Swagger	Normal	Status	—	90	15	Normal	—	—
TM90	Substitute	Normal	Status	—	—	10	Self	—	—
TM94	Rock Smash	Fighting	Physical	40	100	15	Normal	—	○
HM01	Cut	Normal	Physical	50	95	30	Normal	—	○
HM04	Strength	Normal	Physical	80	100	15	Normal	—	○

MOVES TAUGHT BY PEOPLE

Name	Type	Kind	Pow.	Acc.	PP	Range	Long	DA
Fire Pledge	Fire	Special	50	100	10	Normal	—	—

MOVES TAUGHT BY MOVE TUTORS FOR SHARDS

Name	Type	Kind	Pow.	Acc.	PP	Range	Long	DA
Bounce	Flying	Physical	85	85	5	Normal	○	○
Low Kick	Fighting	Physical	—	100	20	Normal	—	○
Last Resort	Normal	Physical	140	100	5	Normal	—	○
Snore	Normal	Special	40	100	15	Normal	—	—
Heat Wave	Fire	Special	100	90	10	Many Others	—	—
Helping Hand	Normal	Status	—	—	20	1 Ally	—	—
Sleep Talk	Normal	Status	—	—	10	Self	—	—

EGG MOVES

Name	Type	Kind	Pow.	Acc.	PP	Range	Long	DA
Counter	Fighting	Physical	—	100	20	Varies	—	○
Reversal	Fighting	Physical	—	100	15	Normal	—	○
Endure	Normal	Status	—	—	10	Self	—	—
SmellingSalt	Normal	Physical	60	100	10	Normal	—	○
Crush Claw	Normal	Physical	75	95	10	Normal	—	○
Baton Pass	Normal	Status	—	—	40	Self	—	—
Agility	Psychic	Status	—	—	30	Self	—	—
Night Slash	Dark	Physical	70	100	15	Normal	—	○
Last Resort	Normal	Physical	140	100	5	Normal	—	○
Feint	Normal	Physical	30	100	10	Normal	—	—
FeatherDance	Flying	Status	—	100	15	Normal	—	—
Curse	Ghost	Status	—	—	10	Varies	—	—
Flame Burst	Fire	Special	70	100	15	Normal	—	—
Low Kick	Fighting	Physical	—	100	20	Normal	—	○

256 Combusken

Young Fowl Pokémon

- HEIGHT: 2'11"
- WEIGHT: 43.0 lbs.
- GENDER: ♂ / ♀

Its kicking mastery lets it loose 10 kicks per second. It emits sharp cries to intimidate foes.

♂ ♀

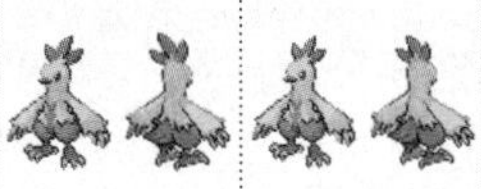

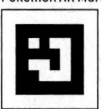

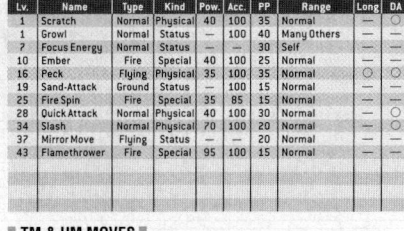

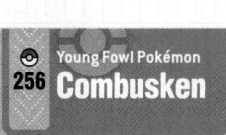

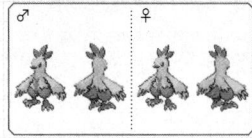

TYPE: Fire / Fighting

ABILITY
- Blaze

HIDDEN ABILITY
- Speed Boost

STATS
HP
Attack
Defense
Sp. Atk
Sp. Def
Speed

EGG GROUPS
Field

ITEMS SOMETIMES HELD
- None

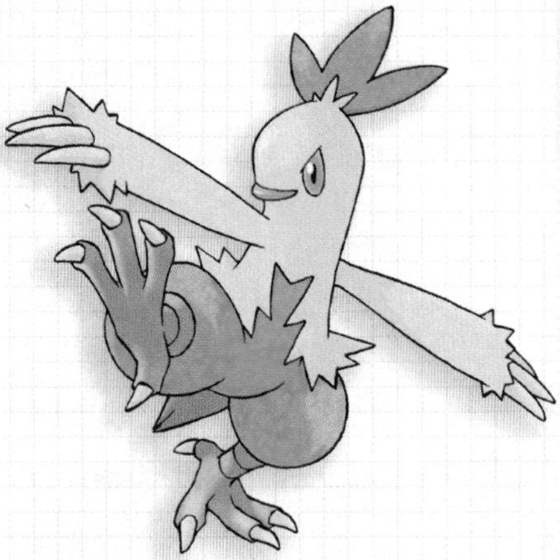

Pokémon AR Marker

EVOLUTION

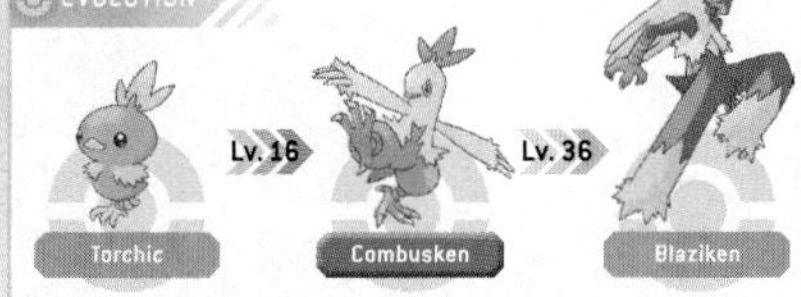

HOW TO OBTAIN

Pokémon Black Version 2	Level up a Torchic you obtain via Link Trade or Poké Transfer to Lv. 16
Pokémon White Version 2	Level up a Torchic you obtain via Link Trade or Poké Transfer to Lv. 16

HOW TO OBTAIN FROM OTHER GAMES

—

—

LEVEL-UP AND LEARNED MOVES

Lv.	Name	Type	Kind	Pow.	Acc.	PP	Range	Long	DA
1	Scratch	Normal	Physical	40	100	35	Normal	—	○
1	Growl	Normal	Status	—	100	40	Many Others	—	—
1	Focus Energy	Normal	Status	—	—	30	Self	—	—
1	Ember	Fire	Special	40	100	25	Normal	—	—
7	Focus Energy	Normal	Status	—	—	30	Self	—	—
13	Ember	Fire	Special	40	100	25	Normal	—	—
16	Double Kick	Fighting	Physical	30	100	30	Normal	—	○
17	Peck	Flying	Physical	35	100	35	Normal	○	○
21	Sand-Attack	Ground	Status	—	100	15	Normal	—	—
28	Bulk Up	Fighting	Status	—	—	20	Self	—	—
32	Quick Attack	Normal	Physical	40	100	30	Normal	—	○
39	Slash	Normal	Physical	70	100	20	Normal	—	○
43	Mirror Move	Flying	Status	—	—	20	Normal	—	—
50	Sky Uppercut	Fighting	Physical	85	90	15	Normal	—	○
54	Flare Blitz	Fire	Physical	120	100	15	Normal	—	○

TM & HM MOVES

Lv.	Name	Type	Kind	Pow.	Acc.	PP	Range	Long	DA
TM01	Hone Claws	Dark	Status	—	—	15	Self	—	—
TM06	Toxic	Poison	Status	—	90	10	Normal	—	—
TM08	Bulk Up	Fighting	Status	—	—	20	Self	—	—
TM10	Hidden Power	Normal	Special	—	100	15	Normal	—	—
TM11	Sunny Day	Fire	Status	—	—	5	Both Sides	—	—
TM17	Protect	Normal	Status	—	—	10	Self	—	—
TM21	Frustration	Normal	Physical	—	100	20	Normal	—	○
TM27	Return	Normal	Physical	—	100	20	Normal	—	○
TM28	Dig	Ground	Physical	80	100	10	Normal	—	○
TM31	Brick Break	Fighting	Physical	75	100	15	Normal	—	○
TM32	Double Team	Normal	Status	—	—	15	Self	—	—
TM35	Flamethrower	Fire	Special	95	100	15	Normal	—	—
TM38	Fire Blast	Fire	Special	120	85	5	Normal	—	—
TM39	Rock Tomb	Rock	Physical	50	80	10	Normal	—	—
TM40	Aerial Ace	Flying	Physical	60	—	20	Normal	○	○
TM42	Facade	Normal	Physical	70	100	20	Normal	—	○
TM43	Flame Charge	Fire	Physical	50	100	20	Normal	—	○
TM44	Rest	Psychic	Status	—	—	10	Self	—	—
TM45	Attract	Normal	Status	—	100	15	Normal	—	—
TM47	Low Sweep	Fighting	Physical	60	100	20	Normal	—	○
TM48	Round	Normal	Special	60	100	15	Normal	—	—
TM49	Echoed Voice	Normal	Special	40	100	15	Normal	—	—
TM50	Overheat	Fire	Special	140	90	5	Normal	—	—
TM52	Focus Blast	Fighting	Special	120	70	5	Normal	—	—
TM56	Fling	Dark	Physical	—	100	10	Normal	—	—
TM59	Incinerate	Fire	Special	30	100	15	Many Others	—	—
TM61	Will-O-Wisp	Fire	Status	—	75	15	Normal	—	—
TM65	Shadow Claw	Ghost	Physical	70	100	15	Normal	—	○
TM75	Swords Dance	Normal	Status	—	—	30	Self	—	—
TM80	Rock Slide	Rock	Physical	75	90	10	Many Others	—	—
TM83	Work Up	Normal	Status	—	—	30	Self	—	—
TM84	Poison Jab	Poison	Physical	80	100	20	Normal	—	○
TM87	Swagger	Normal	Status	—	90	15	Normal	—	—
TM90	Substitute	Normal	Status	—	—	10	Self	—	—
TM94	Rock Smash	Fighting	Physical	40	100	15	Normal	—	○
HM01	Cut	Normal	Physical	50	95	30	Normal	—	○
HM04	Strength	Normal	Physical	80	100	15	Normal	—	○

MOVES TAUGHT BY PEOPLE

Name	Type	Kind	Pow.	Acc.	PP	Range	Long	DA
Fire Pledge	Fire	Special	50	100	10	Normal	—	—

MOVES TAUGHT BY MOVE TUTORS FOR SHARDS

Name	Type	Kind	Pow.	Acc.	PP	Range	Long	DA
Bounce	Flying	Physical	85	85	5	Normal	○	○
Dual Chop	Dragon	Physical	40	90	15	Normal	—	○
Low Kick	Fighting	Physical	—	100	20	Normal	—	○
Fire Punch	Fire	Physical	75	100	15	Normal	—	○
ThunderPunch	Electric	Physical	75	100	15	Normal	—	○
Last Resort	Normal	Physical	140	100	5	Normal	—	○
Snore	Normal	Special	40	100	15	Normal	—	—
Heat Wave	Fire	Special	100	90	10	Many Others	—	—
Helping Hand	Normal	Status	—	—	20	1 Ally	—	—
Sleep Talk	Normal	Status	—	—	10	Self	—	—

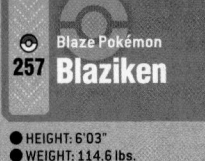

Blaze Pokémon

257 Blaziken

- HEIGHT: 6'03"
- WEIGHT: 114.6 lbs.
- GENDER: ♂ / ♀

Flames spout from its wrists, enveloping its knuckles. Its punches scorch its foes.

TYPE Fire Fighting

ABILITY
- Blaze

HIDDEN ABILITY
- Speed Boost

STATS
HP
Attack
Defense
Sp. Atk
Sp. Def
Speed

EGG GROUPS
Field

ITEMS SOMETIMES HELD
- None

♂ ♀

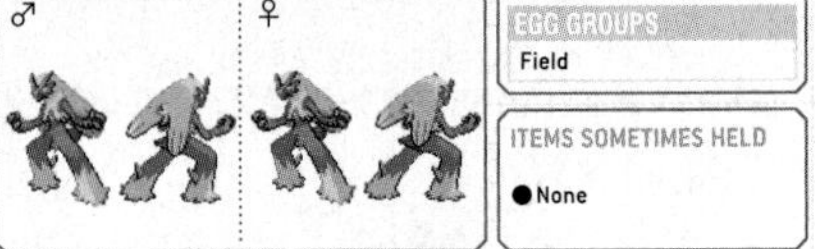

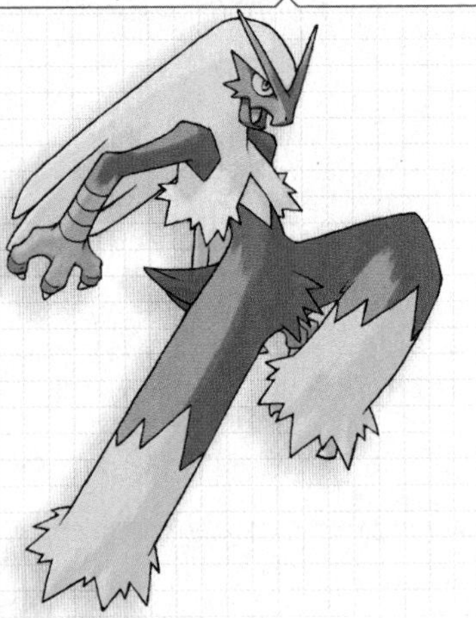

Pokémon AR Marker

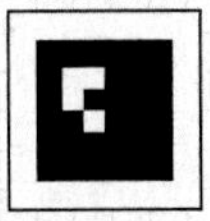

EVOLUTION

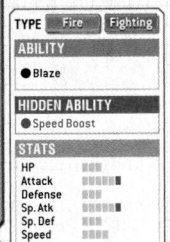

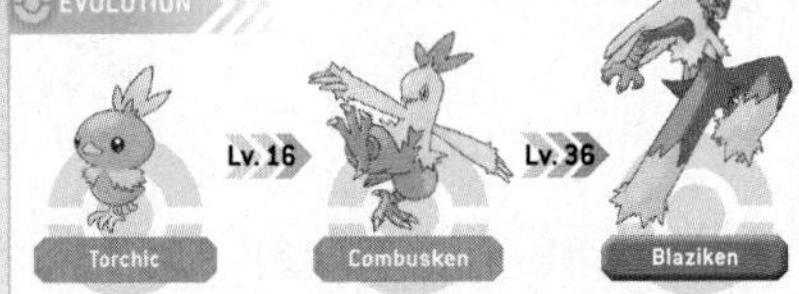
Torchic
Lv. 16
Combusken
Lv. 36
Blaziken

HOW TO OBTAIN

Pokémon Black Version 2	Level up a Combusken you obtain via Link Trade or Poké Transfer to Lv. 36
Pokémon White Version 2	Level up a Combusken you obtain via Link Trade or Poké Transfer to Lv. 36

HOW TO OBTAIN FROM OTHER GAMES

—

—

LEVEL-UP AND LEARNED MOVES

Lv.	Name	Type	Kind	Pow.	Acc.	PP	Range	Long	DA
1	Fire Punch	Fire	Physical	75	100	15	Normal	—	○
1	Hi Jump Kick	Fighting	Physical	130	90	10	Normal	—	○
1	Scratch	Normal	Physical	40	100	35	Normal	—	○
1	Growl	Normal	Status	—	100	40	Many Others	—	—
1	Focus Energy	Normal	Status	—	—	30	Self	—	—
1	Ember	Fire	Special	40	100	25	Normal	—	—
7	Focus Energy	Normal	Status	—	—	30	Self	—	—
13	Ember	Fire	Special	40	100	25	Normal	—	—
16	Double Kick	Fighting	Physical	30	100	30	Normal	—	○
17	Peck	Flying	Physical	35	100	35	Normal	○	○
21	Sand-Attack	Ground	Status	—	100	15	Normal	—	—
28	Bulk Up	Fighting	Status	—	—	20	Self	—	—
32	Quick Attack	Normal	Physical	40	100	30	Normal	—	○
36	Blaze Kick	Fire	Physical	85	90	10	Normal	—	○
42	Slash	Normal	Physical	70	100	20	Normal	—	○
49	Brave Bird	Flying	Physical	120	100	15	Normal	○	○
59	Sky Uppercut	Fighting	Physical	85	90	15	Normal	—	○
66	Flare Blitz	Fire	Physical	120	100	15	Normal	—	○

TM & HM MOVES

Lv.	Name	Type	Kind	Pow.	Acc.	PP	Range	Long	DA
TM01	Hone Claws	Dark	Status	—	—	15	Self	—	—
TM05	Roar	Normal	Status	—	100	20	Normal	—	—
TM06	Toxic	Poison	Status	—	90	10	Normal	—	—
TM08	Bulk Up	Fighting	Status	—	—	20	Self	—	—
TM10	Hidden Power	Normal	Special	—	100	15	Normal	—	—
TM11	Sunny Day	Fire	Status	—	—	5	Both Sides	—	—
TM15	Hyper Beam	Normal	Special	150	90	5	Normal	—	—
TM17	Protect	Normal	Status	—	—	10	Self	—	—
TM21	Frustration	Normal	Physical	—	100	20	Normal	—	○
TM22	SolarBeam	Grass	Special	120	100	10	Normal	—	—
TM26	Earthquake	Ground	Physical	100	100	10	Adjacent	—	—
TM27	Return	Normal	Physical	—	100	20	Normal	—	○
TM28	Dig	Ground	Physical	80	100	10	Normal	—	○
TM31	Brick Break	Fighting	Physical	75	100	15	Normal	—	○
TM32	Double Team	Normal	Status	—	—	15	Self	—	—
TM35	Flamethrower	Fire	Special	95	100	15	Normal	—	—
TM38	Fire Blast	Fire	Special	120	85	5	Normal	—	—
TM39	Rock Tomb	Rock	Physical	50	80	10	Normal	—	—
TM40	Aerial Ace	Flying	Physical	60	—	20	Normal	○	○
TM42	Facade	Normal	Physical	70	100	20	Normal	—	○
TM43	Flame Charge	Fire	Physical	50	100	20	Normal	—	○
TM44	Rest	Psychic	Status	—	—	10	Self	—	—
TM45	Attract	Normal	Status	—	100	15	Normal	—	—
TM47	Low Sweep	Fighting	Physical	60	100	20	Normal	—	○
TM48	Round	Normal	Special	60	100	15	Normal	—	—
TM49	Echoed Voice	Normal	Special	40	100	15	Normal	—	—
TM50	Overheat	Fire	Special	140	90	5	Normal	—	—
TM52	Focus Blast	Fighting	Special	120	70	5	Normal	—	—
TM56	Fling	Dark	Physical	—	100	10	Normal	—	—
TM59	Incinerate	Fire	Special	30	100	15	Many Others	—	—
TM61	Will-O-Wisp	Fire	Status	—	75	15	Normal	—	—
TM62	Acrobatics	Flying	Physical	55	100	15	Normal	○	○
TM65	Shadow Claw	Ghost	Physical	70	100	15	Normal	—	○
TM68	Giga Impact	Normal	Physical	150	90	5	Normal	—	○
TM71	Stone Edge	Rock	Physical	100	80	5	Normal	—	—
TM75	Swords Dance	Normal	Status	—	—	30	Self	—	—
TM78	Bulldoze	Ground	Physical	60	100	20	Adjacent	—	—
TM80	Rock Slide	Rock	Physical	75	90	10	Many Others	—	—
TM83	Work Up	Normal	Status	—	—	30	Self	—	—
TM84	Poison Jab	Poison	Physical	80	100	20	Normal	—	○
TM87	Swagger	Normal	Status	—	90	15	Normal	—	—
TM90	Substitute	Normal	Status	—	—	10	Self	—	—
TM94	Rock Smash	Fighting	Physical	40	100	15	Normal	—	○
HM01	Cut	Normal	Physical	50	95	30	Normal	—	○
HM04	Strength	Normal	Physical	80	100	15	Normal	—	○

MOVES TAUGHT BY PEOPLE

Name	Type	Kind	Pow.	Acc.	PP	Range	Long	DA
Fire Pledge	Fire	Special	50	100	10	Normal	—	—
Blast Burn	Fire	Special	150	90	5	Normal	—	—

MOVES TAUGHT BY MOVE TUTORS FOR SHARDS

Name	Type	Kind	Pow.	Acc.	PP	Range	Long	DA
Bounce	Flying	Physical	85	85	5	Normal	○	○
Dual Chop	Dragon	Physical	40	90	15	Normal	—	○
Low Kick	Fighting	Physical	—	100	20	Normal	—	○
Fire Punch	Fire	Physical	75	100	15	Normal	—	○
ThunderPunch	Electric	Physical	75	100	15	Normal	—	○
Last Resort	Normal	Physical	140	100	5	Normal	—	○
Superpower	Fighting	Physical	120	100	5	Normal	—	○
Snore	Normal	Special	40	100	15	Normal	—	—
Knock Off	Dark	Physical	20	100	20	Normal	—	○
Role Play	Psychic	Status	—	—	10	Normal	—	—
Heat Wave	Fire	Special	100	90	10	Many Others	—	—
Helping Hand	Normal	Status	—	—	20	1 Ally	—	—
Sleep Talk	Normal	Status	—	—	10	Self	—	—

Mud Fish Pokémon

258 Mudkip

- HEIGHT: 1'04"
- WEIGHT: 16.8 lbs.
- GENDER: ♂ / ♀

To alert it, the fin on its head senses the flow of water. It has the strength to heft boulders.

TYPE Water

ABILITY
- Torrent

HIDDEN ABILITY
- Damp

STATS
HP
Attack
Defense
Sp. Atk
Sp. Def
Speed

EGG GROUPS
Monster/Water 1

ITEMS SOMETIMES HELD
- None

Same form for ♂ / ♀

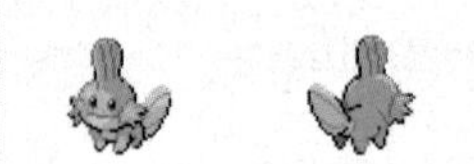

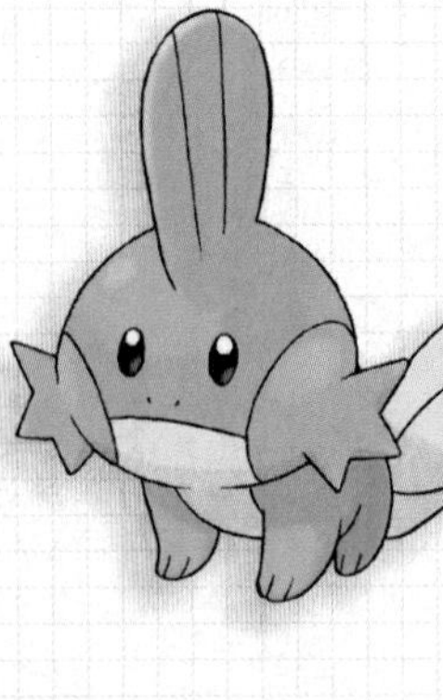

Pokémon AR Marker

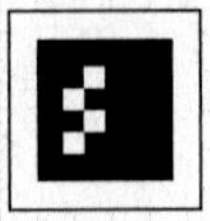

EVOLUTION

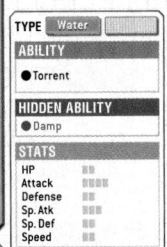

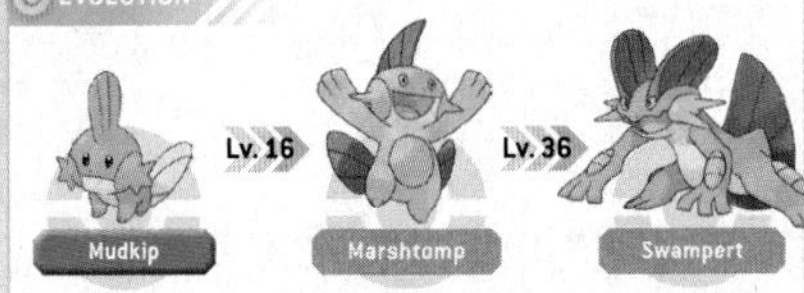
Mudkip
Lv. 16
Marshtomp
Lv. 36
Swampert

HOW TO OBTAIN

Pokémon Black Version 2	Link Trade or Poké Transfer
Pokémon White Version 2	Link Trade or Poké Transfer

HOW TO OBTAIN FROM OTHER GAMES

Pokémon HeartGold Version	Receive from Steven at Silph Co. in Saffron City (after defeating Red)
Pokémon SoulSilver Version	Receive from Steven at Silph Co. in Saffron City (after defeating Red)

LEVEL-UP AND LEARNED MOVES

Lv.	Name	Type	Kind	Pow.	Acc.	PP	Range	Long	DA
1	Tackle	Normal	Physical	50	100	35	Normal	—	○
1	Growl	Normal	Status	—	100	40	Many Others	—	—
6	Mud-Slap	Ground	Special	20	100	10	Normal	—	—
10	Water Gun	Water	Special	40	100	25	Normal	—	—
15	Bide	Normal	Physical	—	—	10	Self	—	○
19	Foresight	Normal	Status	—	—	40	Normal	—	—
24	Mud Sport	Ground	Status	—	—	15	Both Sides	—	—
28	Take Down	Normal	Physical	90	85	20	Normal	—	○
33	Whirlpool	Water	Special	35	85	15	Normal	—	—
37	Protect	Normal	Status	—	—	10	Self	—	—
42	Hydro Pump	Water	Special	120	80	5	Normal	—	—
46	Endeavor	Normal	Physical	—	100	5	Normal	—	○

TM & HM MOVES

Lv.	Name	Type	Kind	Pow.	Acc.	PP	Range	Long	DA
TM06	Toxic	Poison	Status	—	90	10	Normal	—	—
TM07	Hail	Ice	Status	—	—	10	Both Sides	—	—
TM10	Hidden Power	Normal	Special	—	100	15	Normal	—	—
TM13	Ice Beam	Ice	Special	95	100	10	Normal	—	—
TM14	Blizzard	Ice	Special	120	70	5	Many Others	—	—
TM17	Protect	Normal	Status	—	—	10	Self	—	—
TM18	Rain Dance	Water	Status	—	—	5	Both Sides	—	—
TM21	Frustration	Normal	Physical	—	100	20	Normal	—	○
TM27	Return	Normal	Physical	—	100	20	Normal	—	○
TM28	Dig	Ground	Physical	80	100	10	Normal	—	○
TM32	Double Team	Normal	Status	—	—	15	Self	—	—
TM34	Sludge Wave	Poison	Special	95	100	10	Adjacent	—	—
TM39	Rock Tomb	Rock	Physical	50	80	10	Normal	—	—
TM42	Facade	Normal	Physical	70	100	20	Normal	—	○
TM44	Rest	Psychic	Status	—	—	10	Self	—	—
TM45	Attract	Normal	Status	—	100	15	Normal	—	—
TM48	Round	Normal	Special	60	100	15	Normal	—	—
TM49	Echoed Voice	Normal	Special	40	100	15	Normal	—	—
TM55	Scald	Water	Special	80	100	15	Normal	—	—
TM80	Rock Slide	Rock	Physical	75	90	10	Many Others	—	—
TM87	Swagger	Normal	Status	—	90	15	Normal	—	—
TM90	Substitute	Normal	Status	—	—	10	Self	—	—
TM94	Rock Smash	Fighting	Physical	40	100	15	Normal	—	○
HM03	Surf	Water	Special	95	100	15	Adjacent	—	—
HM04	Strength	Normal	Physical	80	100	15	Normal	—	○
HM05	Waterfall	Water	Physical	80	100	15	Normal	—	○
HM06	Dive	Water	Physical	80	100	10	Normal	—	○

MOVES TAUGHT BY PEOPLE

Name	Type	Kind	Pow.	Acc.	PP	Range	Long	DA
Water Pledge	Water	Special	50	100	10	Normal	—	—

MOVES TAUGHT BY MOVE TUTORS FOR SHARDS

Name	Type	Kind	Pow.	Acc.	PP	Range	Long	DA
Low Kick	Fighting	Physical	—	100	20	Normal	—	○
Icy Wind	Ice	Special	55	95	15	Many Others	—	—
Iron Tail	Steel	Physical	100	75	15	Normal	—	○
Aqua Tail	Water	Physical	90	90	10	Normal	—	○
Earth Power	Ground	Special	90	100	10	Normal	—	—
Superpower	Fighting	Physical	120	100	5	Normal	—	○
Snore	Normal	Special	40	100	15	Normal	—	—
Endeavor	Normal	Physical	—	100	5	Normal	—	○
Sleep Talk	Normal	Status	—	—	10	Self	—	—

EGG MOVES

Name	Type	Kind	Pow.	Acc.	PP	Range	Long	DA
Refresh	Normal	Status	—	—	20	Self	—	—
Uproar	Normal	Special	90	100	10	1 Random	—	—
Curse	Ghost	Status	—	—	10	Varies	—	—
Stomp	Normal	Physical	65	100	20	Normal	—	○
Ice Ball	Ice	Physical	30	90	20	Normal	—	○
Mirror Coat	Psychic	Special	—	100	20	Varies	—	—
Counter	Fighting	Physical	—	100	20	Varies	—	○
AncientPower	Rock	Special	60	100	5	Normal	—	—
Whirlpool	Water	Special	35	85	15	Normal	—	—
Bite	Dark	Physical	60	100	25	Normal	—	○
Double-Edge	Normal	Physical	120	100	15	Normal	—	○
Mud Bomb	Ground	Special	65	85	10	Normal	—	—
Yawn	Normal	Status	—	—	10	Normal	—	—
Sludge	Poison	Special	65	100	20	Normal	—	—
Avalanche	Ice	Physical	60	100	10	Normal	—	○
Wide Guard	Rock	Status	—	—	10	Your Side	—	—

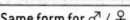

Mud Fish Pokémon

259 Marshtomp

TYPE: Water / Ground

ABILITY
● Torrent

HIDDEN ABILITY
● Damp

● HEIGHT: 2'04"
● WEIGHT: 61.7 lbs.
● GENDER: ♂ / ♀

Its sturdy legs give it sure footing, even in mud. It burrows into dirt to sleep.

STATS
HP
Attack
Defense
Sp. Atk
Sp. Def
Speed

Same form for ♂ / ♀

EGG GROUPS
Monster/Water ❶

ITEMS SOMETIMES HELD
● None

Pokémon AR Marker

EVOLUTION

HOW TO OBTAIN

Pokémon Black Version 2	Level up a Mudkip you obtain via Link Trade or Poké Transfer to Lv. 16
Pokémon White Version 2	Level up a Mudkip you obtain via Link Trade or Poké Transfer to Lv. 16

HOW TO OBTAIN FROM OTHER GAMES

—

—

LEVEL-UP AND LEARNED MOVES

Lv.	Name	Type	Kind	Pow.	Acc.	PP	Range	Long	DA
1	Tackle	Normal	Physical	50	100	35	Normal	—	○
1	Growl	Normal	Status	—	100	40	Many Others	—	—
1	Mud-Slap	Ground	Special	20	100	10	Normal	—	—
1	Water Gun	Water	Special	40	100	25	Normal	—	—
6	Mud-Slap	Ground	Special	20	100	10	Normal	—	—
10	Water Gun	Water	Special	40	100	25	Normal	—	—
15	Bide	Normal	Physical	—	—	10	Self	—	○
16	Mud Shot	Ground	Special	55	95	15	Normal	—	—
20	Foresight	Normal	Status	—	—	40	Normal	—	—
25	Mud Bomb	Ground	Special	65	85	10	Normal	—	—
31	Take Down	Normal	Physical	90	85	20	Normal	—	○
37	Muddy Water	Water	Special	95	85	10	Many Others	—	—
42	Protect	Normal	Status	—	—	10	Self	—	—
46	Earthquake	Ground	Physical	100	100	10	Adjacent	—	—
53	Endeavor	Normal	Physical	—	100	5	Normal	—	○

TM & HM MOVES

Lv.	Name	Type	Kind	Pow.	Acc.	PP	Range	Long	DA
TM06	Toxic	Poison	Status	—	90	10	Normal	—	—
TM07	Hail	Ice	Status	—	—	10	Both Sides	—	—
TM10	Hidden Power	Normal	Special	—	100	15	Normal	—	—
TM13	Ice Beam	Ice	Special	95	100	10	Normal	—	—
TM14	Blizzard	Ice	Special	120	70	5	Many Others	—	—
TM17	Protect	Normal	Status	—	—	10	Self	—	—
TM18	Rain Dance	Water	Status	—	—	5	Both Sides	—	—
TM21	Frustration	Normal	Physical	—	100	20	Normal	—	○
TM26	Earthquake	Ground	Physical	100	100	10	Adjacent	—	—
TM27	Return	Normal	Physical	—	100	20	Normal	—	○
TM28	Dig	Ground	Physical	80	100	10	Normal	—	○
TM31	Brick Break	Fighting	Physical	75	100	15	Normal	—	○
TM32	Double Team	Normal	Status	—	—	15	Self	—	—
TM34	Sludge Wave	Poison	Special	95	100	10	Adjacent	—	—
TM39	Rock Tomb	Rock	Physical	50	80	10	Normal	—	—
TM42	Facade	Normal	Physical	70	100	20	Normal	—	○
TM44	Rest	Psychic	Status	—	—	10	Self	—	—
TM45	Attract	Normal	Status	—	100	15	Normal	—	—
TM48	Round	Normal	Special	60	100	15	Normal	—	—
TM49	Echoed Voice	Normal	Special	40	100	15	Normal	—	—
TM55	Scald	Water	Special	80	100	15	Normal	—	—
TM56	Fling	Dark	Physical	—	100	10	Normal	—	—
TM78	Bulldoze	Ground	Physical	60	100	20	Adjacent	—	—
TM80	Rock Slide	Rock	Physical	75	90	10	Many Others	—	—
TM87	Swagger	Normal	Status	—	90	15	Normal	—	—
TM90	Substitute	Normal	Status	—	—	10	Self	—	—
TM94	Rock Smash	Fighting	Physical	40	100	15	Normal	—	○
HM03	Surf	Water	Special	95	100	15	Adjacent	—	—
HM04	Strength	Normal	Physical	80	100	15	Normal	—	○
HM05	Waterfall	Water	Physical	80	100	15	Normal	—	○
HM06	Dive	Water	Physical	80	100	10	Normal	—	○

MOVES TAUGHT BY PEOPLE

Name	Type	Kind	Pow.	Acc.	PP	Range	Long	DA
Water Pledge	Water	Special	50	100	10	Normal	—	—

MOVES TAUGHT BY MOVE TUTORS FOR SHARDS

Name	Type	Kind	Pow.	Acc.	PP	Range	Long	DA
Low Kick	Fighting	Physical	—	100	20	Normal	—	○
Ice Punch	Ice	Physical	75	100	15	Normal	—	○
Icy Wind	Ice	Special	55	95	15	Many Others	—	—
Iron Tail	Steel	Physical	100	75	15	Normal	—	○
Aqua Tail	Water	Physical	90	90	10	Normal	—	○
Earth Power	Ground	Special	90	100	10	Normal	—	—
Superpower	Fighting	Physical	120	100	5	Normal	—	○
Snore	Normal	Special	40	100	15	Normal	—	—
Stealth Rock	Rock	Status	—	—	20	Other Side	—	—
Endeavor	Normal	Physical	—	100	5	Normal	—	○
Sleep Talk	Normal	Status	—	—	10	Self	—	—

Mud Fish Pokémon

260 Swampert

TYPE: Water / Ground

ABILITY
● Torrent

HIDDEN ABILITY
● Damp

● HEIGHT: 4'11"
● WEIGHT: 180.6 lbs.
● GENDER: ♂ / ♀

It can swim while towing a large ship. It bashes down foes with a swing of its thick arms.

STATS
HP
Attack
Defense
Sp. Atk
Sp. Def
Speed

Same form for ♂ / ♀

EGG GROUPS
Monster/Water ❶

ITEMS SOMETIMES HELD
● None

Pokémon AR Marker

EVOLUTION

HOW TO OBTAIN

Pokémon Black Version 2	Get Marshtomp with Link Trade or Poké Transfer, then level it up to Lv. 36
Pokémon White Version 2	Get Marshtomp with Link Trade or Poké Transfer, then level it up to Lv. 36

HOW TO OBTAIN FROM OTHER GAMES

—

—

LEVEL-UP AND LEARNED MOVES

Lv.	Name	Type	Kind	Pow.	Acc.	PP	Range	Long	DA
1	Tackle	Normal	Physical	50	100	35	Normal	—	○
1	Growl	Normal	Status	—	100	40	Many Others	—	—
1	Mud-Slap	Ground	Special	20	100	10	Normal	—	—
1	Water Gun	Water	Special	40	100	25	Normal	—	—
6	Mud-Slap	Ground	Special	20	100	10	Normal	—	—
10	Water Gun	Water	Special	40	100	25	Normal	—	—
15	Bide	Normal	Physical	—	—	10	Self	—	○
16	Mud Shot	Ground	Special	55	95	15	Normal	—	—
20	Foresight	Normal	Status	—	—	40	Normal	—	—
25	Mud Bomb	Ground	Special	65	85	10	Normal	—	—
31	Take Down	Normal	Physical	90	85	20	Normal	—	○
39	Muddy Water	Water	Special	95	85	10	Many Others	—	—
46	Protect	Normal	Status	—	—	10	Self	—	—
52	Earthquake	Ground	Physical	100	100	10	Adjacent	—	—
61	Endeavor	Normal	Physical	—	100	5	Normal	—	○
69	Hammer Arm	Fighting	Physical	100	90	10	Normal	—	○

TM & HM MOVES

Lv.	Name	Type	Kind	Pow.	Acc.	PP	Range	Long	DA
TM05	Roar	Normal	Status	—	100	20	Normal	—	—
TM06	Toxic	Poison	Status	—	90	10	Normal	—	—
TM07	Hail	Ice	Status	—	—	10	Both Sides	—	—
TM10	Hidden Power	Normal	Special	—	100	15	Normal	—	—
TM13	Ice Beam	Ice	Special	95	100	10	Normal	—	—
TM14	Blizzard	Ice	Special	120	70	5	Many Others	—	—
TM15	Hyper Beam	Normal	Special	150	90	5	Normal	—	—
TM17	Protect	Normal	Status	—	—	10	Self	—	—
TM18	Rain Dance	Water	Status	—	—	5	Both Sides	—	—
TM21	Frustration	Normal	Physical	—	100	20	Normal	—	○
TM26	Earthquake	Ground	Physical	100	100	10	Adjacent	—	—
TM27	Return	Normal	Physical	—	100	20	Normal	—	○
TM28	Dig	Ground	Physical	80	100	10	Normal	—	○
TM31	Brick Break	Fighting	Physical	75	100	15	Normal	—	○
TM32	Double Team	Normal	Status	—	—	15	Self	—	—
TM34	Sludge Wave	Poison	Special	95	100	10	Adjacent	—	—
TM39	Rock Tomb	Rock	Physical	50	80	10	Normal	—	—
TM42	Facade	Normal	Physical	70	100	20	Normal	—	○
TM44	Rest	Psychic	Status	—	—	10	Self	—	—
TM45	Attract	Normal	Status	—	100	15	Normal	—	—
TM48	Round	Normal	Special	60	100	15	Normal	—	—
TM49	Echoed Voice	Normal	Special	40	100	15	Normal	—	—
TM52	Focus Blast	Fighting	Special	120	70	5	Normal	—	—
TM55	Scald	Water	Special	80	100	15	Normal	—	—
TM56	Fling	Dark	Physical	—	100	10	Normal	—	—
TM68	Giga Impact	Normal	Physical	150	90	5	Normal	—	○
TM71	Stone Edge	Rock	Physical	100	80	5	Normal	—	—
TM78	Bulldoze	Ground	Physical	60	100	20	Adjacent	—	—
TM80	Rock Slide	Rock	Physical	75	90	10	Many Others	—	—
TM87	Swagger	Normal	Status	—	90	15	Normal	—	—
TM90	Substitute	Normal	Status	—	—	10	Self	—	—
TM94	Rock Smash	Fighting	Physical	40	100	15	Normal	—	○
HM03	Surf	Water	Special	95	100	15	Adjacent	—	—
HM04	Strength	Normal	Physical	80	100	15	Normal	—	○
HM05	Waterfall	Water	Physical	80	100	15	Normal	—	○
HM06	Dive	Water	Physical	80	100	10	Normal	—	○

MOVES TAUGHT BY PEOPLE

Name	Type	Kind	Pow.	Acc.	PP	Range	Long	DA
Water Pledge	Water	Special	50	100	10	Normal	—	—
Hydro Cannon	Water	Special	150	90	5	Normal	—	—

MOVES TAUGHT BY MOVE TUTORS FOR SHARDS

Name	Type	Kind	Pow.	Acc.	PP	Range	Long	DA
Low Kick	Fighting	Physical	—	100	20	Normal	—	○
Ice Punch	Ice	Physical	75	100	15	Normal	—	○
Icy Wind	Ice	Special	55	95	15	Many Others	—	—
Iron Tail	Steel	Physical	100	75	15	Normal	—	○
Aqua Tail	Water	Physical	90	90	10	Normal	—	○
Earth Power	Ground	Special	90	100	10	Normal	—	—
Superpower	Fighting	Physical	120	100	5	Normal	—	○
Snore	Normal	Special	40	100	15	Normal	—	—
Stealth Rock	Rock	Status	—	—	20	Other Side	—	—
Outrage	Dragon	Physical	120	100	10	1 Random	—	○
Endeavor	Normal	Physical	—	100	5	Normal	—	○
Sleep Talk	Normal	Status	—	—	10	Self	—	—

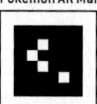

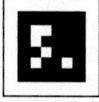

Bite Pokémon

261 Poochyena

- HEIGHT: 1'08"
- WEIGHT: 30.0 lbs.
- GENDER: ♂ / ♀

A Pokémon with a persistent nature, it chases its chosen prey until the prey becomes exhausted.

Same form for ♂ / ♀

Pokémon AR Marker

TYPE Dark

ABILITIES
- Run Away
- Quick Feet

HIDDEN ABILITY
- Rattled

STATS
HP
Attack
Defense
Sp. Atk
Sp. Def
Speed

EGG GROUPS
Field

ITEMS SOMETIMES HELD
- None

EVOLUTION

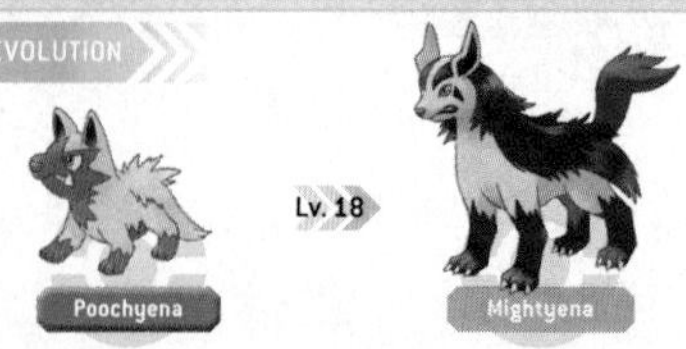

HOW TO OBTAIN

Pokémon Black Version 2	Link Trade or Poké Transfer
Pokémon White Version 2	Link Trade or Poké Transfer

HOW TO OBTAIN FROM OTHER GAMES

Pokémon White Version	Route 9 (mass outbreak)
—	

LEVEL-UP AND LEARNED MOVES

Lv.	Name	Type	Kind	Pow.	Acc.	PP	Range	Long	DA
1	Tackle	Normal	Physical	50	100	35	Normal	—	○
5	Howl	Normal	Status	—	—	40	Self	—	—
9	Sand-Attack	Ground	Status	—	100	15	Normal	—	—
13	Bite	Dark	Physical	60	100	25	Normal	—	○
17	Odor Sleuth	Normal	Status	—	—	40	Normal	—	—
21	Roar	Normal	Status	—	100	20	Normal	—	—
25	Swagger	Normal	Status	—	90	15	Normal	—	—
29	Assurance	Dark	Physical	50	100	10	Normal	—	○
33	Scary Face	Normal	Status	—	100	10	Normal	—	—
37	Taunt	Dark	Status	—	100	20	Normal	—	—
41	Embargo	Dark	Status	—	100	15	Normal	—	—
45	Take Down	Normal	Physical	90	85	20	Normal	—	○
49	Sucker Punch	Dark	Physical	80	100	5	Normal	—	○
53	Crunch	Dark	Physical	80	100	15	Normal	—	○

TM & HM MOVES

Lv.	Name	Type	Kind	Pow.	Acc.	PP	Range	Long	DA
TM05	Roar	Normal	Status	—	100	20	Normal	—	—
TM06	Toxic	Poison	Status	—	90	10	Normal	—	—
TM10	Hidden Power	Normal	Special	—	100	15	Normal	—	—
TM11	Sunny Day	Fire	Status	—	—	5	Both Sides	—	—
TM12	Taunt	Dark	Status	—	100	20	Normal	—	—
TM17	Protect	Normal	Status	—	—	10	Self	—	—
TM18	Rain Dance	Water	Status	—	—	5	Both Sides	—	—
TM21	Frustration	Normal	Physical	—	100	20	Normal	—	○
TM27	Return	Normal	Physical	—	100	20	Normal	—	○
TM28	Dig	Ground	Physical	80	100	10	Normal	—	○
TM30	Shadow Ball	Ghost	Special	80	100	15	Normal	—	—
TM32	Double Team	Normal	Status	—	—	15	Self	—	—
TM41	Torment	Dark	Status	—	100	15	Normal	—	—
TM42	Facade	Normal	Physical	70	100	20	Normal	—	○
TM44	Rest	Psychic	Status	—	—	10	Self	—	—
TM45	Attract	Normal	Status	—	100	15	Normal	—	—
TM46	Thief	Dark	Physical	40	100	10	Normal	—	○
TM48	Round	Normal	Special	60	100	15	Normal	—	—
TM59	Incinerate	Fire	Special	30	100	15	Many Others	—	—
TM63	Embargo	Dark	Status	—	100	15	Normal	—	—
TM66	Payback	Dark	Physical	50	100	10	Normal	—	○
TM67	Retaliate	Normal	Physical	70	100	5	Normal	—	○
TM87	Swagger	Normal	Status	—	90	15	Normal	—	—
TM90	Substitute	Normal	Status	—	—	10	Self	—	—
TM94	Rock Smash	Fighting	Physical	40	100	15	Normal	—	○
TM95	Snarl	Dark	Special	55	95	15	Many Others	—	—

MOVES TAUGHT BY PEOPLE

Name	Type	Kind	Pow.	Acc.	PP	Range	Long	DA

MOVES TAUGHT BY MOVE TUTORS FOR SHARDS

Name	Type	Kind	Pow.	Acc.	PP	Range	Long	DA
Covet	Normal	Physical	60	100	40	Normal	—	○
Super Fang	Normal	Physical	—	90	10	Normal	—	○
Uproar	Normal	Special	90	100	10	1 Random	—	—
Hyper Voice	Normal	Special	90	100	10	Many Others	—	—
Iron Tail	Steel	Physical	100	75	15	Normal	—	○
Foul Play	Dark	Physical	95	100	15	Normal	—	○
Dark Pulse	Dark	Special	80	100	15	Normal	○	—
Snore	Normal	Special	40	100	15	Normal	—	—
Spite	Ghost	Status	—	100	10	Normal	—	—
Sleep Talk	Normal	Status	—	—	10	Self	—	—
Snatch	Dark	Status	—	—	10	Self	—	—

EGG MOVES

Name	Type	Kind	Pow.	Acc.	PP	Range	Long	DA
Astonish	Ghost	Physical	30	100	15	Normal	—	○
Poison Fang	Poison	Physical	50	100	15	Normal	—	○
Covet	Normal	Physical	60	100	40	Normal	—	○
Leer	Normal	Status	—	100	30	Many Others	—	—
Yawn	Normal	Status	—	—	10	Normal	—	—
Sucker Punch	Dark	Physical	80	100	5	Normal	—	○
Ice Fang	Ice	Physical	65	95	15	Normal	—	○
Fire Fang	Fire	Physical	65	95	15	Normal	—	○
Thunder Fang	Electric	Physical	65	95	15	Normal	—	○
Me First	Normal	Status	—	—	20	Varies	—	—
Snatch	Dark	Status	—	—	10	Self	—	—
Sleep Talk	Normal	Status	—	—	10	Self	—	—

Bite Pokémon

262 Mightyena

- HEIGHT: 3'03"
- WEIGHT: 81.6 lbs.
- GENDER: ♂ / ♀

It chases down prey in a pack. It will never disobey the commands of a skilled Trainer.

Same form for ♂ / ♀

Pokémon AR Marker

TYPE Dark

ABILITIES
- Intimidate
- Quick Feet

HIDDEN ABILITY
- Moxie

STATS
HP
Attack
Defense
Sp. Atk
Sp. Def
Speed

EGG GROUPS
Field

ITEMS SOMETIMES HELD
- None

EVOLUTION

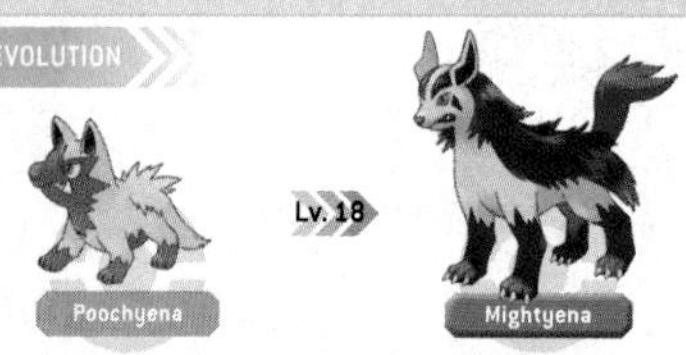

HOW TO OBTAIN

Pokémon Black Version 2	Link Trade or Poké Transfer
Pokémon White Version 2	Link Trade or Poké Transfer

HOW TO OBTAIN FROM OTHER GAMES

Pokémon Diamond Version	Occasionally appears on Route 214 (use Poké Radar for a better chance)
—	

LEVEL-UP AND LEARNED MOVES

Lv.	Name	Type	Kind	Pow.	Acc.	PP	Range	Long	DA
1	Tackle	Normal	Physical	50	100	35	Normal	—	○
1	Howl	Normal	Status	—	—	40	Self	—	—
1	Sand-Attack	Ground	Status	—	100	15	Normal	—	—
1	Bite	Dark	Physical	60	100	25	Normal	—	○
5	Howl	Normal	Status	—	—	40	Self	—	—
9	Sand-Attack	Ground	Status	—	100	15	Normal	—	—
13	Bite	Dark	Physical	60	100	25	Normal	—	○
17	Odor Sleuth	Normal	Status	—	—	40	Normal	—	—
22	Roar	Normal	Status	—	100	20	Normal	—	—
27	Swagger	Normal	Status	—	90	15	Normal	—	—
32	Assurance	Dark	Physical	50	100	10	Normal	—	○
37	Scary Face	Normal	Status	—	100	10	Normal	—	—
42	Taunt	Dark	Status	—	100	20	Normal	—	—
47	Embargo	Dark	Status	—	100	15	Normal	—	—
52	Take Down	Normal	Physical	90	85	20	Normal	—	○
57	Thief	Dark	Physical	40	100	10	Normal	—	○
62	Sucker Punch	Dark	Physical	80	100	5	Normal	—	○

TM & HM MOVES

Lv.	Name	Type	Kind	Pow.	Acc.	PP	Range	Long	DA
TM05	Roar	Normal	Status	—	100	20	Normal	—	—
TM06	Toxic	Poison	Status	—	90	10	Normal	—	—
TM10	Hidden Power	Normal	Special	—	100	15	Normal	—	—
TM11	Sunny Day	Fire	Status	—	—	5	Both Sides	—	—
TM12	Taunt	Dark	Status	—	100	20	Normal	—	—
TM15	Hyper Beam	Normal	Special	150	90	5	Normal	—	—
TM17	Protect	Normal	Status	—	—	10	Self	—	—
TM18	Rain Dance	Water	Status	—	—	5	Both Sides	—	—
TM21	Frustration	Normal	Physical	—	100	20	Normal	—	○
TM27	Return	Normal	Physical	—	100	20	Normal	—	○
TM28	Dig	Ground	Physical	80	100	10	Normal	—	○
TM30	Shadow Ball	Ghost	Special	80	100	15	Normal	—	—
TM32	Double Team	Normal	Status	—	—	15	Self	—	—
TM41	Torment	Dark	Status	—	100	15	Normal	—	—
TM42	Facade	Normal	Physical	70	100	20	Normal	—	○
TM44	Rest	Psychic	Status	—	—	10	Self	—	—
TM45	Attract	Normal	Status	—	100	15	Normal	—	—
TM46	Thief	Dark	Physical	40	100	10	Normal	—	○
TM48	Round	Normal	Special	60	100	15	Normal	—	—
TM59	Incinerate	Fire	Special	30	100	15	Many Others	—	—
TM63	Embargo	Dark	Status	—	100	15	Normal	—	—
TM66	Payback	Dark	Physical	50	100	10	Normal	—	○
TM67	Retaliate	Normal	Physical	70	100	5	Normal	—	○
TM68	Giga Impact	Normal	Physical	150	90	5	Normal	—	○
TM87	Swagger	Normal	Status	—	90	15	Normal	—	—
TM90	Substitute	Normal	Status	—	—	10	Self	—	—
TM94	Rock Smash	Fighting	Physical	40	100	15	Normal	—	○
TM95	Snarl	Dark	Special	55	95	15	Many Others	—	—
HM04	Strength	Normal	Physical	80	100	15	Normal	—	○

MOVES TAUGHT BY PEOPLE

Name	Type	Kind	Pow.	Acc.	PP	Range	Long	DA

MOVES TAUGHT BY MOVE TUTORS FOR SHARDS

Name	Type	Kind	Pow.	Acc.	PP	Range	Long	DA
Covet	Normal	Physical	60	100	40	Normal	—	○
Super Fang	Normal	Physical	—	90	10	Normal	—	○
Uproar	Normal	Special	90	100	10	1 Random	—	—
Hyper Voice	Normal	Special	90	100	10	Many Others	—	—
Iron Tail	Steel	Physical	100	75	15	Normal	—	○
Foul Play	Dark	Physical	95	100	15	Normal	—	○
Dark Pulse	Dark	Special	80	100	15	Normal	○	—
Snore	Normal	Special	40	100	15	Normal	—	—
Spite	Ghost	Status	—	100	10	Normal	—	—
Sleep Talk	Normal	Status	—	—	10	Self	—	—
Snatch	Dark	Status	—	—	10	Self	—	—

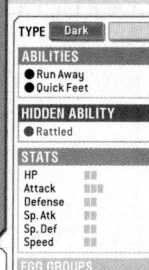

TinyRaccoon Pokémon

263 Zigzagoon

- HEIGHT: 1'04"
- WEIGHT: 38.6 lbs.
- GENDER: ♂ / ♀

It walks in zigzag fashion. It is good at finding items in the grass and even in the ground.

Same form for ♂ / ♀

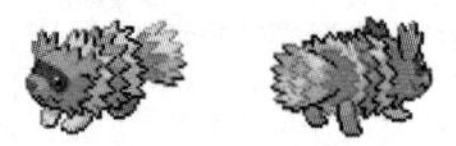

TYPE Normal

ABILITIES
- Pickup
- Gluttony

HIDDEN ABILITY
- Quick Feet

STATS
HP
Attack
Defense
Sp. Atk
Sp. Def
Speed

EGG GROUPS
Field

ITEMS SOMETIMES HELD
- None

Pokémon AR Marker

EVOLUTION

HOW TO OBTAIN

Pokémon Black Version 2	Link Trade or Poké Transfer
Pokémon White Version 2	Link Trade or Poké Transfer

HOW TO OBTAIN FROM OTHER GAMES

Pokémon HeartGold Version	Burned Tower (Hoenn Sound)
Pokémon SoulSilver Version	Burned Tower (Hoenn Sound)

LEVEL-UP AND LEARNED MOVES

Lv.	Name	Type	Kind	Pow.	Acc.	PP	Range	Long	DA
1	Tackle	Normal	Physical	50	100	35	Normal	—	○
1	Growl	Normal	Status	—	100	40	Many Others	—	—
5	Tail Whip	Normal	Status	—	100	30	Many Others	—	—
9	Headbutt	Normal	Physical	70	100	15	Normal	—	○
13	Sand-Attack	Ground	Status	—	100	15	Normal	—	—
17	Odor Sleuth	Normal	Status	—	—	40	Normal	—	—
21	Mud Sport	Ground	Status	—	—	15	Both Sides	—	—
25	Pin Missile	Bug	Physical	14	85	20	Normal	—	—
29	Covet	Normal	Physical	60	100	40	Normal	—	○
33	Bestow	Normal	Status	—	—	15	Normal	—	—
37	Flail	Normal	Physical	—	100	15	Normal	—	○
41	Rest	Psychic	Status	—	—	10	Self	—	—
45	Belly Drum	Normal	Status	—	—	10	Self	—	—
49	Fling	Dark	Physical	—	100	10	Normal	—	—

TM & HM MOVES

Lv.	Name	Type	Kind	Pow.	Acc.	PP	Range	Long	DA
TM01	Hone Claws	Dark	Status	—	—	15	Self	—	—
TM06	Toxic	Poison	Status	—	90	10	Normal	—	—
TM10	Hidden Power	Normal	Special	—	100	15	Normal	—	—
TM11	Sunny Day	Fire	Status	—	—	5	Both Sides	—	—
TM13	Ice Beam	Ice	Special	95	100	10	Normal	—	—
TM14	Blizzard	Ice	Special	120	70	5	Many Others	—	—
TM17	Protect	Normal	Status	—	—	10	Self	—	—
TM18	Rain Dance	Water	Status	—	—	5	Both Sides	—	—
TM21	Frustration	Normal	Physical	—	100	20	Normal	—	○
TM24	Thunderbolt	Electric	Special	95	100	15	Normal	—	—
TM25	Thunder	Electric	Special	120	70	10	Normal	—	—
TM27	Return	Normal	Physical	—	100	20	Normal	—	○
TM28	Dig	Ground	Physical	80	100	10	Normal	—	○
TM30	Shadow Ball	Ghost	Special	80	100	15	Normal	—	—
TM32	Double Team	Normal	Status	—	—	15	Self	—	—
TM42	Facade	Normal	Physical	70	100	20	Normal	—	○
TM44	Rest	Psychic	Status	—	—	10	Self	—	—
TM45	Attract	Normal	Status	—	100	15	Normal	—	—
TM46	Thief	Dark	Physical	40	100	10	Normal	—	○
TM48	Round	Normal	Special	60	100	15	Normal	—	—
TM49	Echoed Voice	Normal	Special	40	100	15	Normal	—	—
TM56	Fling	Dark	Physical	—	100	10	Normal	—	—
TM57	Charge Beam	Electric	Special	50	90	10	Normal	—	—
TM67	Retaliate	Normal	Physical	70	100	5	Normal	—	○
TM73	Thunder Wave	Electric	Status	—	100	20	Normal	—	—
TM83	Work Up	Normal	Status	—	—	30	Self	—	—
TM86	Grass Knot	Grass	Special	—	100	20	Normal	—	○
TM87	Swagger	Normal	Status	—	90	15	Normal	—	—
TM90	Substitute	Normal	Status	—	—	10	Self	—	—
TM94	Rock Smash	Fighting	Physical	40	100	15	Normal	—	○
HM01	Cut	Normal	Physical	50	95	30	Normal	—	○
HM03	Surf	Water	Special	95	100	15	Adjacent	—	—

MOVES TAUGHT BY PEOPLE

Name	Type	Kind	Pow.	Acc.	PP	Range	Long	DA

MOVES TAUGHT BY MOVE TUTORS FOR SHARDS

Name	Type	Kind	Pow.	Acc.	PP	Range	Long	DA
Covet	Normal	Physical	60	100	40	Normal	—	○
Super Fang	Normal	Physical	—	90	10	Normal	—	○
Seed Bomb	Grass	Physical	80	100	15	Normal	—	—
Gunk Shot	Poison	Physical	120	70	5	Normal	—	—
Last Resort	Normal	Physical	140	100	5	Normal	—	○
Hyper Voice	Normal	Special	90	100	10	Many Others	—	—
Icy Wind	Ice	Special	55	95	15	Many Others	—	—
Iron Tail	Steel	Physical	100	75	15	Normal	—	○
Snore	Normal	Special	40	100	15	Normal	—	—
Helping Hand	Normal	Status	—	—	20	1 Ally	—	—
Trick	Psychic	Status	—	100	10	Normal	—	—
Sleep Talk	Normal	Status	—	—	10	Self	—	—

EGG MOVES

Name	Type	Kind	Pow.	Acc.	PP	Range	Long	DA
Charm	Normal	Status	—	100	20	Normal	—	—
Pursuit	Dark	Physical	40	100	20	Normal	—	○
Tickle	Normal	Status	—	100	20	Normal	—	—
Trick	Psychic	Status	—	100	10	Normal	—	—
Helping Hand	Normal	Status	—	—	20	1 Ally	—	—
Mud-Slap	Ground	Special	20	100	10	Normal	—	—
Sleep Talk	Normal	Status	—	—	10	Self	—	—
Rock Climb	Normal	Physical	90	85	20	Normal	—	○
Simple Beam	Normal	Status	—	100	15	Normal	—	—

Rushing Pokémon

264 Linoone

- HEIGHT: 1'08"
- WEIGHT: 71.6 lbs.
- GENDER: ♂ / ♀

It charges prey at speeds over 60 mph. However, because it can only run straight, it often fails.

Same form for ♂ / ♀

TYPE Normal

ABILITIES
- Pickup
- Gluttony

HIDDEN ABILITY
- Quick Feet

STATS
HP
Attack
Defense
Sp. Atk
Sp. Def
Speed

EGG GROUPS
Field

ITEMS SOMETIMES HELD
- None

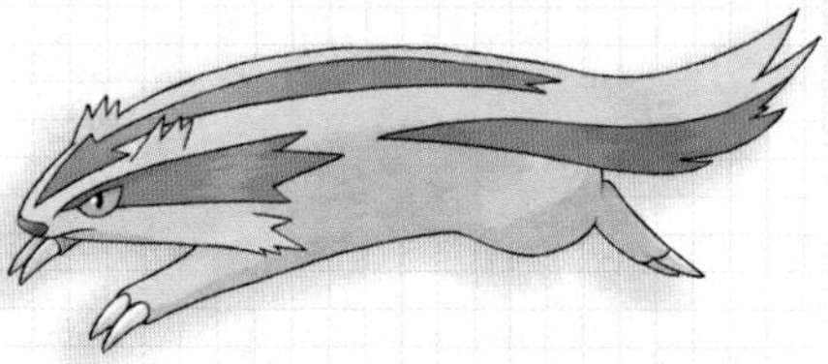

Pokémon AR Marker

EVOLUTION

HOW TO OBTAIN

Pokémon Black Version 2	Link Trade or Poké Transfer
Pokémon White Version 2	Link Trade or Poké Transfer

HOW TO OBTAIN FROM OTHER GAMES

Pokémon HeartGold Version	Route 42 (Hoenn Sound)
Pokémon SoulSilver Version	Route 42 (Hoenn Sound)

LEVEL-UP AND LEARNED MOVES

Lv.	Name	Type	Kind	Pow.	Acc.	PP	Range	Long	DA
1	Switcheroo	Dark	Status	—	100	10	Normal	—	—
1	Tackle	Normal	Physical	50	100	35	Normal	—	○
1	Growl	Normal	Status	—	100	40	Many Others	—	—
1	Tail Whip	Normal	Status	—	100	30	Many Others	—	—
1	Headbutt	Normal	Physical	70	100	15	Normal	—	○
5	Tail Whip	Normal	Status	—	100	30	Many Others	—	—
9	Headbutt	Normal	Physical	70	100	15	Normal	—	○
13	Sand-Attack	Ground	Status	—	100	15	Normal	—	—
17	Odor Sleuth	Normal	Status	—	—	40	Normal	—	—
23	Mud Sport	Ground	Status	—	—	15	Both Sides	—	—
29	Fury Swipes	Normal	Physical	18	80	15	Normal	—	○
35	Covet	Normal	Physical	60	100	40	Normal	—	○
41	Bestow	Normal	Status	—	—	15	Normal	—	—
47	Slash	Normal	Physical	70	100	20	Normal	—	○
53	Rest	Psychic	Status	—	—	10	Self	—	—
59	Belly Drum	Normal	Status	—	—	10	Self	—	—
65	Fling	Dark	Physical	—	100	10	Normal	—	—

Lv.	Name	Type	Kind	Pow.	Acc.	PP	Range	Long	DA
HM04	Strength	Normal	Physical	80	100	15	Normal	—	○

TM & HM MOVES

Lv.	Name	Type	Kind	Pow.	Acc.	PP	Range	Long	DA
TM01	Hone Claws	Dark	Status	—	—	15	Self	—	—
TM05	Roar	Normal	Status	—	100	20	Normal	—	—
TM06	Toxic	Poison	Status	—	90	10	Normal	—	—
TM10	Hidden Power	Normal	Special	—	100	15	Normal	—	—
TM11	Sunny Day	Fire	Status	—	—	5	Both Sides	—	—
TM13	Ice Beam	Ice	Special	95	100	10	Normal	—	—
TM14	Blizzard	Ice	Special	120	70	5	Many Others	—	—
TM15	Hyper Beam	Normal	Special	150	90	5	Normal	—	—
TM17	Protect	Normal	Status	—	—	10	Self	—	—
TM18	Rain Dance	Water	Status	—	—	5	Both Sides	—	—
TM21	Frustration	Normal	Physical	—	100	20	Normal	—	○
TM24	Thunderbolt	Electric	Special	95	100	15	Normal	—	—
TM25	Thunder	Electric	Special	120	70	10	Normal	—	—
TM27	Return	Normal	Physical	—	100	20	Normal	—	○
TM28	Dig	Ground	Physical	80	100	10	Normal	—	○
TM30	Shadow Ball	Ghost	Special	80	100	15	Normal	—	—
TM32	Double Team	Normal	Status	—	—	15	Self	—	—
TM42	Facade	Normal	Physical	70	100	20	Normal	—	○
TM44	Rest	Psychic	Status	—	—	10	Self	—	—
TM45	Attract	Normal	Status	—	100	15	Normal	—	—
TM46	Thief	Dark	Physical	40	100	10	Normal	—	○
TM48	Round	Normal	Special	60	100	15	Normal	—	—
TM49	Echoed Voice	Normal	Special	40	100	15	Normal	—	—
TM56	Fling	Dark	Physical	—	100	10	Normal	—	—
TM57	Charge Beam	Electric	Special	50	90	10	Normal	—	—
TM65	Shadow Claw	Ghost	Physical	70	100	15	Normal	—	○
TM67	Retaliate	Normal	Physical	70	100	5	Normal	—	○
TM68	Giga Impact	Normal	Physical	150	90	5	Normal	—	○
TM73	Thunder Wave	Electric	Status	—	100	20	Normal	—	—
TM83	Work Up	Normal	Status	—	—	30	Self	—	—
TM86	Grass Knot	Grass	Special	—	100	20	Normal	—	○
TM87	Swagger	Normal	Status	—	90	15	Normal	—	—
TM90	Substitute	Normal	Status	—	—	10	Self	—	—
TM94	Rock Smash	Fighting	Physical	40	100	15	Normal	—	○
HM01	Cut	Normal	Physical	50	95	30	Normal	—	○
HM03	Surf	Water	Special	95	100	15	Adjacent	—	—

MOVES TAUGHT BY PEOPLE

Name	Type	Kind	Pow.	Acc.	PP	Range	Long	DA

MOVES TAUGHT BY MOVE TUTORS FOR SHARDS

Name	Type	Kind	Pow.	Acc.	PP	Range	Long	DA
Covet	Normal	Physical	60	100	40	Normal	—	○
Super Fang	Normal	Physical	—	90	10	Normal	—	○
Seed Bomb	Grass	Physical	80	100	15	Normal	—	—
Gunk Shot	Poison	Physical	120	70	5	Normal	—	—
Last Resort	Normal	Physical	140	100	5	Normal	—	○
Hyper Voice	Normal	Special	90	100	10	Many Others	—	—
Icy Wind	Ice	Special	55	95	15	Many Others	—	—
Iron Tail	Steel	Physical	100	75	15	Normal	—	○
Snore	Normal	Special	40	100	15	Normal	—	—
Helping Hand	Normal	Status	—	—	20	1 Ally	—	—
Trick	Psychic	Status	—	100	10	Normal	—	—
Sleep Talk	Normal	Status	—	—	10	Self	—	—

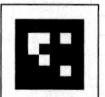

265
Wurmple
● Worm Pokémon

TYPE Bug

ABILITY
● Shield Dust

HIDDEN ABILITY

● HEIGHT: 1'00"
● WEIGHT: 7.9 lbs.
● GENDER: ♂ / ♀

Often targeted by bird Pokémon, it desperately resists by releasing poison from its tail spikes.

STATS
HP
Attack
Defense
Sp. Atk
Sp. Def
Speed

EGG GROUPS
Bug

ITEMS SOMETIMES HELD
● None

Same form for ♂ / ♀

Pokémon AR Marker

● Wurmple evolves into either Silcoon or Cascoon when it reaches Lv. 7.

EVOLUTION

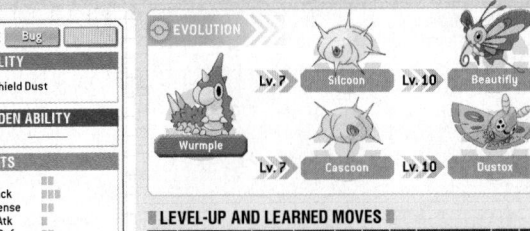

Wurmple — Lv. 7 → Silcoon — Lv. 10 → Beautifly
Wurmple — Lv. 7 → Cascoon — Lv. 10 → Dustox

LEVEL-UP AND LEARNED MOVES

Lv.	Name	Type	Kind	Pow.	Acc.	PP	Range	Long	DA
1	Tackle	Normal	Physical	50	100	35	Normal	—	○
1	String Shot	Bug	Status	—	95	40	Many Others	—	—
5	Poison Sting	Poison	Physical	15	100	35	Normal	—	○
15	Bug Bite	Bug	Physical	60	100	20	Normal	—	○

TM & HM MOVES

Lv.	Name	Type	Kind	Pow.	Acc.	PP	Range	Long	DA

MOVES TAUGHT BY PEOPLE

Name	Type	Kind	Pow.	Acc.	PP	Range	Long	DA

MOVES TAUGHT BY MOVE TUTORS FOR SHARDS

Name	Type	Kind	Pow.	Acc.	PP	Range	Long	DA
Bug Bite	Bug	Physical	60	100	20	Normal	—	○
Electroweb	Electric	Special	55	95	15	Many Others	—	—
Snore	Normal	Special	40	100	15	Normal	—	—

EGG MOVES

Name	Type	Kind	Pow.	Acc.	PP	Range	Long	DA

HOW TO OBTAIN

Pokémon Black Version 2	Link Trade or Poké Transfer
Pokémon White Version 2	Link Trade or Poké Transfer

HOW TO OBTAIN FROM OTHER GAMES

Pokémon Platinum Version	Route 204 (morning and afternoon only)

266
Silcoon
● Cocoon Pokémon

TYPE Bug

ABILITY
● Shed Skin

HIDDEN ABILITY

● HEIGHT: 2'00"
● WEIGHT: 22.0 lbs.
● GENDER: ♂ / ♀

It wraps silk around the branches of a tree. It drinks rainwater on its silk while awaiting evolution.

STATS
HP
Attack
Defense
Sp. Atk
Sp. Def
Speed

EGG GROUPS
Bug

ITEMS SOMETIMES HELD
● None

Same form for ♂ / ♀

Pokémon AR Marker

146

● Wurmple evolves into either Silcoon or Cascoon when it reaches Lv. 7.

EVOLUTION

Wurmple — Lv. 7 → Silcoon — Lv. 10 → Beautifly
Wurmple — Lv. 7 → Cascoon — Lv. 10 → Dustox

LEVEL-UP AND LEARNED MOVES

Lv.	Name	Type	Kind	Pow.	Acc.	PP	Range	Long	DA
1	Harden	Normal	Status	—	—	30	Self	—	—
7	Harden	Normal	Status	—	—	30	Self	—	—

TM & HM MOVES

Lv.	Name	Type	Kind	Pow.	Acc.	PP	Range	Long	DA

MOVES TAUGHT BY PEOPLE

Name	Type	Kind	Pow.	Acc.	PP	Range	Long	DA

MOVES TAUGHT BY MOVE TUTORS FOR SHARDS

Name	Type	Kind	Pow.	Acc.	PP	Range	Long	DA
Bug Bite	Bug	Physical	60	100	20	Normal	—	○
Iron Defense	Steel	Status	—	—	15	Self	—	—
Electroweb	Electric	Special	55	95	15	Many Others	—	—

HOW TO OBTAIN

Pokémon Black Version 2	Link Trade or Poké Transfer
Pokémon White Version 2	Link Trade or Poké Transfer

HOW TO OBTAIN FROM OTHER GAMES

Pokémon Diamond Version	Eterna Forest
Pokémon Platinum Version	Route 205, Eterna City side

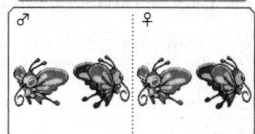

267 Beautifly
Butterfly Pokémon

- HEIGHT: 3'03"
- WEIGHT: 62.6 lbs.
- GENDER: ♂/♀

Despite its looks, it is aggressive. It jabs with its long, thin mouth if disturbed while collecting pollen.

Pokémon AR Marker

TYPE	Bug	Flying

ABILITY
- Swarm

HIDDEN ABILITY

STATS
HP	▪▪▪
Attack	▪▪
Defense	▪▪
Sp. Atk	▪▪▪▪
Sp. Def	▪▪
Speed	▪▪▪

EGG GROUPS
Bug

ITEMS SOMETIMES HELD
- None

EVOLUTION

Wurmple → Lv. 7 → Silcoon → Lv. 10 → Beautifly
Wurmple → Lv. 7 → Cascoon → Lv. 10 → Dustox

HOW TO OBTAIN

Pokémon Black Version 2	Link Trade or Poké Transfer
Pokémon White Version 2	Link Trade or Poké Transfer

HOW TO OBTAIN FROM OTHER GAMES

Pokémon Platinum Version	Route 224

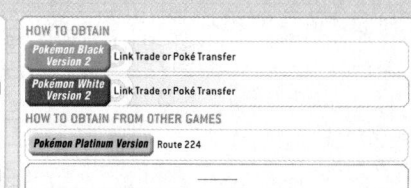

LEVEL-UP AND LEARNED MOVES

Lv.	Name	Type	Kind	Pow.	Acc.	PP	Range	Long	DA
1	Absorb	Grass	Special	20	100	25	Normal	—	—
10	Absorb	Grass	Special	20	100	25	Normal	—	—
13	Gust	Flying	Special	40	100	35	Normal	○	—
17	Stun Spore	Grass	Status	—	75	30	Normal	—	—
20	Morning Sun	Normal	Status	—	—	5	Self	—	—
24	Mega Drain	Grass	Special	40	100	15	Normal	—	—
27	Whirlwind	Normal	Status	—	100	20	Normal	—	—
31	Attract	Normal	Status	—	100	15	Normal	—	—
34	Silver Wind	Bug	Special	60	100	5	Normal	—	—
38	Giga Drain	Grass	Special	75	100	10	Normal	—	—
41	Bug Buzz	Bug	Special	90	100	10	Normal	—	—
45	Quiver Dance	Bug	Status	—	—	20	Self	—	—

TM & HM MOVES

Lv.	Name	Type	Kind	Pow.	Acc.	PP	Range	Long	DA
TM06	Toxic	Poison	Status	—	90	10	Normal	—	—
TM09	Venoshock	Poison	Special	65	100	10	Normal	—	—
TM10	Hidden Power	Normal	Special	—	100	15	Normal	—	—
TM11	Sunny Day	Fire	Status	—	—	5	Both Sides	—	—
TM15	Hyper Beam	Normal	Special	150	90	5	Normal	—	—
TM17	Protect	Normal	Status	—	—	10	Self	—	—
TM20	Safeguard	Normal	Status	—	—	25	Your Side	—	—
TM21	Frustration	Normal	Physical	—	100	20	Normal	—	○
TM22	SolarBeam	Grass	Special	120	100	10	Normal	—	—
TM27	Return	Normal	Physical	—	100	20	Normal	—	○
TM29	Psychic	Psychic	Special	90	100	10	Normal	—	—
TM30	Shadow Ball	Ghost	Special	80	100	15	Normal	—	—
TM32	Double Team	Normal	Status	—	—	15	Self	—	—
TM40	Aerial Ace	Flying	Physical	60	—	20	Normal	○	○
TM42	Facade	Normal	Physical	70	100	20	Normal	—	○
TM44	Rest	Psychic	Status	—	—	10	Self	—	—
TM45	Attract	Normal	Status	—	100	15	Normal	—	—
TM46	Thief	Dark	Physical	40	100	10	Normal	—	○
TM48	Round	Normal	Special	60	100	15	Normal	—	—
TM53	Energy Ball	Grass	Special	80	100	10	Normal	—	—
TM62	Acrobatics	Flying	Physical	55	100	15	Normal	○	○
TM68	Giga Impact	Normal	Physical	150	90	5	Normal	—	○
TM70	Flash	Normal	Status	—	100	20	Normal	—	—
TM76	Struggle Bug	Bug	Special	30	100	20	Many Others	—	—
TM87	Swagger	Normal	Status	—	90	15	Normal	—	—
TM89	U-turn	Bug	Physical	70	100	20	Normal	—	○
TM90	Substitute	Normal	Status	—	—	10	Self	—	—

MOVES TAUGHT BY PEOPLE

Name	Type	Kind	Pow.	Acc.	PP	Range	Long	DA

MOVES TAUGHT BY MOVE TUTORS FOR SHARDS

Name	Type	Kind	Pow.	Acc.	PP	Range	Long	DA
Bug Bite	Bug	Physical	60	100	20	Normal	—	○
Signal Beam	Bug	Special	75	100	15	Normal	—	—
Electroweb	Electric	Special	55	95	15	Many Others	—	—
Snore	Normal	Special	40	100	15	Normal	—	—
Roost	Flying	Status	—	—	10	Self	—	—
Giga Drain	Grass	Special	75	100	10	Normal	—	—
Tailwind	Flying	Status	—	—	30	Your Side	—	—
Sleep Talk	Normal	Status	—	—	10	Self	—	—

- Wurmple evolves into either Silcoon or Cascoon when it reaches Lv. 7.

268 Cascoon
Cocoon Pokémon

- HEIGHT: 2'04"
- WEIGHT: 25.4 lbs.
- GENDER: ♂/♀

It never forgets any attack it endured while in the cocoon. After evolution, it seeks payback.

Same form for ♂/♀

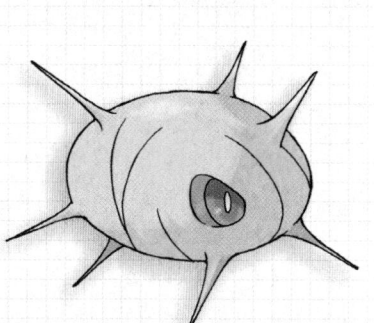

Pokémon AR Marker

TYPE	Bug	

ABILITY
- Shed Skin

HIDDEN ABILITY

STATS
HP	▪▪
Attack	▪▪
Defense	▪
Sp. Atk	▪
Sp. Def	▪
Speed	▪

EGG GROUPS
Bug

ITEMS SOMETIMES HELD
- None

EVOLUTION

Wurmple → Lv. 7 → Silcoon → Lv. 10 → Beautifly
Wurmple → Lv. 7 → Cascoon → Lv. 10 → Dustox

HOW TO OBTAIN

Pokémon Black Version 2	Link Trade or Poké Transfer
Pokémon White Version 2	Link Trade or Poké Transfer

HOW TO OBTAIN FROM OTHER GAMES

Pokémon Pearl Version	Eterna Forest
Pokémon Platinum Version	Route 205, Eterna City side

LEVEL-UP AND LEARNED MOVES

Lv.	Name	Type	Kind	Pow.	Acc.	PP	Range	Long	DA
1	Harden	Normal	Status	—	—	30	Self	—	—
7	Harden	Normal	Status	—	—	30	Self	—	—

MOVES TAUGHT BY PEOPLE

Name	Type	Kind	Pow.	Acc.	PP	Range	Long	DA

MOVES TAUGHT BY MOVE TUTORS FOR SHARDS

Name	Type	Kind	Pow.	Acc.	PP	Range	Long	DA
Bug Bite	Bug	Physical	60	100	20	Normal	—	○
Iron Defense	Steel	Status	—	—	15	Self	—	—
Electroweb	Electric	Special	55	95	15	Many Others	—	—

TM & HM MOVES

Lv.	Name	Type	Kind	Pow.	Acc.	PP	Range	Long	DA

- Wurmple evolves into either Silcoon or Cascoon when it reaches Lv. 7.

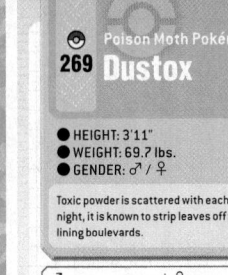

269 Dustox
Poison Moth Pokémon

TYPE Bug | Poison

ABILITY
● Shield Dust

HIDDEN ABILITY
—

● HEIGHT: 3'11"
● WEIGHT: 69.7 lbs.
● GENDER: ♂ / ♀

Toxic powder is scattered with each flap. At night, it is known to strip leaves off trees lining boulevards.

STATS
HP	■■■
Attack	■■■
Defense	■■■
Sp. Atk	■■■
Sp. Def	■■■■
Speed	■■■■

EGG GROUPS
Bug

ITEMS SOMETIMES HELD
● None

269 Dustox

EVOLUTION

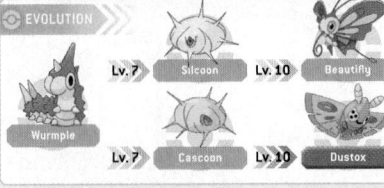

Wurmple → Lv. 7 → Silcoon → Lv. 10 → Beautifly
Wurmple → Lv. 7 → Cascoon → Lv. 10 → Dustox

HOW TO OBTAIN

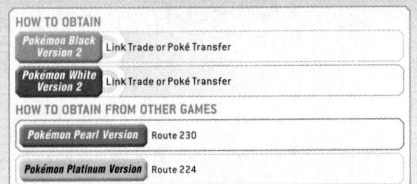

Pokémon Black Version 2	Link Trade or Poké Transfer
Pokémon White Version 2	Link Trade or Poké Transfer

HOW TO OBTAIN FROM OTHER GAMES
Pokémon Pearl Version	Route 230
Pokémon Platinum Version	Route 224

LEVEL-UP AND LEARNED MOVES
Lv.	Name	Type	Kind	Pow.	Acc.	PP	Range	Long	DA
1	Confusion	Psychic	Special	50	100	25	Normal	—	—
10	Confusion	Psychic	Special	50	100	25	Normal	—	—
13	Gust	Flying	Special	40	100	35	Normal	○	—
17	Protect	Normal	Status	—	—	10	Self	—	—
20	Moonlight	Normal	Status	—	—	5	Self	—	—
24	Psybeam	Psychic	Special	65	100	20	Normal	—	—
27	Whirlwind	Normal	Status	—	100	20	Normal	—	—
31	Light Screen	Psychic	Status	—	—	30	Your Side	—	—
34	Silver Wind	Bug	Special	60	100	5	Normal	—	—
38	Toxic	Poison	Status	—	90	10	Normal	—	—
41	Bug Buzz	Bug	Special	90	100	10	Normal	—	—
45	Quiver Dance	Bug	Status	—	—	20	Self	—	—

TM & HM MOVES
Lv.	Name	Type	Kind	Pow.	Acc.	PP	Range	Long	DA
TM06	Toxic	Poison	Status	—	90	10	Normal	—	—
TM09	Venoshock	Poison	Special	65	100	10	Normal	—	—
TM10	Hidden Power	Normal	Special	—	100	15	Normal	—	—
TM11	Sunny Day	Fire	Status	—	—	5	Both Sides	—	—
TM15	Hyper Beam	Normal	Special	150	90	5	Normal	—	—
TM16	Light Screen	Psychic	Status	—	—	30	Your Side	—	—
TM17	Protect	Normal	Status	—	—	10	Self	—	—
TM21	Frustration	Normal	Physical	—	100	20	Normal	—	○
TM22	SolarBeam	Grass	Special	120	100	10	Normal	—	—
TM27	Return	Normal	Physical	—	100	20	Normal	—	○
TM29	Psychic	Psychic	Special	90	100	10	Normal	—	—
TM30	Shadow Ball	Ghost	Special	80	100	15	Normal	—	—
TM32	Double Team	Normal	Status	—	—	15	Self	—	—
TM36	Sludge Bomb	Poison	Special	90	100	10	Normal	—	—
TM40	Aerial Ace	Flying	Physical	60	—	20	Normal	○	○
TM42	Facade	Normal	Physical	70	100	20	Normal	—	—
TM44	Rest	Psychic	Status	—	—	10	Self	—	—
TM45	Attract	Normal	Status	—	100	15	Normal	—	—
TM46	Thief	Dark	Physical	40	100	10	Normal	—	—
TM48	Round	Normal	Special	60	100	15	Normal	—	—
TM53	Energy Ball	Grass	Special	80	100	10	Normal	—	—
TM62	Acrobatics	Flying	Physical	55	100	15	Normal	○	○
TM68	Giga Impact	Normal	Physical	150	90	5	Normal	—	—
TM70	Flash	Normal	Status	—	100	20	Normal	—	—
TM76	Struggle Bug	Bug	Special	30	100	20	Many Others	—	—
TM87	Swagger	Normal	Status	—	90	15	Normal	—	—
TM89	U-turn	Bug	Physical	70	100	20	Normal	—	—
TM90	Substitute	Normal	Status	—	—	10	Self	—	—

MOVES TAUGHT BY PEOPLE
Name	Type	Kind	Pow.	Acc.	PP	Range	Long	DA

MOVES TAUGHT BY MOVE TUTORS FOR SHARDS
Name	Type	Kind	Pow.	Acc.	PP	Range	Long	DA
Bug Bite	Bug	Physical	60	100	20	Normal	—	○
Signal Beam	Bug	Special	75	100	15	Normal	—	—
Electroweb	Electric	Special	55	95	15	Many Others	—	—
Snore	Normal	Special	40	100	15	Normal	—	—
Roost	Flying	Status	—	—	10	Self	—	—
Giga Drain	Grass	Special	75	100	10	Normal	—	—
Tailwind	Flying	Status	—	—	30	Your Side	—	—
Sleep Talk	Normal	Status	—	—	10	Self	—	—

Pokémon AR Marker

● Wurmple evolves into either Silcoon or Cascoon when it reaches Lv. 7.

---

270 Lotad
Water Weed Pokémon

TYPE Water | Grass

ABILITIES
● Swift Swim
● Rain Dish

HIDDEN ABILITY
● Own Tempo

● HEIGHT: 1'08"
● WEIGHT: 5.7 lbs.
● GENDER: ♂ / ♀

It looks like an aquatic plant and serves as a ferry to Pokémon that can't swim.

Same form for ♂ / ♀

STATS
HP	■■
Attack	■■
Defense	■■
Sp. Atk	■■
Sp. Def	■■
Speed	■■

EGG GROUPS
Water ❶ / Grass

ITEMS SOMETIMES HELD
● None

270 Lotad

EVOLUTION

Lotad → Lv. 14 → Lombre → Use Water Stone → Ludicolo

HOW TO OBTAIN
Pokémon Black Version 2	Catch a Lombre, leave it at the Pokémon Day Care, and hatch the Egg that is found
Pokémon White Version 2	Catch a Lombre, leave it at the Pokémon Day Care, and hatch the Egg that is found

HOW TO OBTAIN FROM OTHER GAMES
Pokémon White Version	When Ralph is in White Forest

LEVEL-UP AND LEARNED MOVES
Lv.	Name	Type	Kind	Pow.	Acc.	PP	Range	Long	DA
1	Astonish	Ghost	Physical	30	100	15	Normal	—	—
3	Growl	Normal	Status	—	100	40	Many Others	—	—
5	Absorb	Grass	Special	20	100	25	Normal	—	—
7	Nature Power	Normal	Status	—	—	20	Varies	—	—
11	Mist	Ice	Status	—	—	30	Your Side	—	—
15	Natural Gift	Normal	Physical	—	100	15	Normal	—	—
19	Mega Drain	Grass	Special	40	100	15	Normal	—	—
25	BubbleBeam	Water	Special	65	100	20	Normal	—	—
31	Zen Headbutt	Psychic	Physical	80	90	15	Normal	—	○
37	Rain Dance	Water	Status	—	—	5	Both Sides	—	—
45	Energy Ball	Grass	Special	80	100	10	Normal	—	—

TM & HM MOVES
Lv.	Name	Type	Kind	Pow.	Acc.	PP	Range	Long	DA
TM06	Toxic	Poison	Status	—	90	10	Normal	—	—
TM07	Hail	Ice	Status	—	—	10	Both Sides	—	—
TM10	Hidden Power	Normal	Special	—	100	15	Normal	—	—
TM11	Sunny Day	Fire	Status	—	—	5	Both Sides	—	—
TM13	Ice Beam	Ice	Special	95	100	10	Normal	—	—
TM14	Blizzard	Ice	Special	120	70	5	Many Others	—	—
TM17	Protect	Normal	Status	—	—	10	Self	—	—
TM18	Rain Dance	Water	Status	—	—	5	Both Sides	—	—
TM21	Frustration	Normal	Physical	—	100	20	Normal	—	○
TM22	SolarBeam	Grass	Special	120	100	10	Normal	—	—
TM27	Return	Normal	Physical	—	100	20	Normal	—	○
TM32	Double Team	Normal	Status	—	—	15	Self	—	—
TM42	Facade	Normal	Physical	70	100	20	Normal	—	—
TM44	Rest	Psychic	Status	—	—	10	Self	—	—
TM45	Attract	Normal	Status	—	100	15	Normal	—	—
TM46	Thief	Dark	Physical	40	100	10	Normal	—	—
TM48	Round	Normal	Special	60	100	15	Normal	—	—
TM49	Echoed Voice	Normal	Special	40	100	15	Normal	—	—
TM53	Energy Ball	Grass	Special	80	100	10	Normal	—	—
TM55	Scald	Water	Special	80	100	15	Normal	—	—
TM70	Flash	Normal	Status	—	100	20	Normal	—	—
TM75	Swords Dance	Normal	Status	—	—	30	Self	—	—
TM86	Grass Knot	Grass	Special	—	100	20	Normal	—	○
TM87	Swagger	Normal	Status	—	90	15	Normal	—	—
TM90	Substitute	Normal	Status	—	—	10	Self	—	—
HM03	Surf	Water	Special	95	100	15	Adjacent	—	—

MOVES TAUGHT BY PEOPLE
Name	Type	Kind	Pow.	Acc.	PP	Range	Long	DA

MOVES TAUGHT BY MOVE TUTORS FOR SHARDS
Name	Type	Kind	Pow.	Acc.	PP	Range	Long	DA
Uproar	Normal	Special	90	100	10	1 Random	—	—
Seed Bomb	Grass	Physical	80	100	15	Normal	—	—
Icy Wind	Ice	Special	55	95	15	Many Others	—	—
Zen Headbutt	Psychic	Physical	80	90	15	Normal	—	—
Snore	Normal	Special	40	100	15	Normal	—	—
Synthesis	Grass	Status	—	—	5	Self	—	—
Giga Drain	Grass	Special	75	100	10	Normal	—	—
Sleep Talk	Normal	Status	—	—	10	Self	—	—

EGG MOVES
Name	Type	Kind	Pow.	Acc.	PP	Range	Long	DA
Synthesis	Grass	Status	—	—	5	Self	—	—
Razor Leaf	Grass	Physical	55	95	25	Many Others	—	—
Sweet Scent	Normal	Status	—	100	20	Many Others	—	—
Leech Seed	Grass	Status	—	90	10	Normal	—	—
Flail	Normal	Physical	—	100	15	Normal	—	○
Water Gun	Water	Special	40	100	25	Normal	—	—
Tickle	Normal	Status	—	100	20	Normal	—	—
Counter	Fighting	Physical	—	100	20	Varies	—	○
Giga Drain	Grass	Special	75	100	10	Normal	—	—
Teeter Dance	Normal	Status	—	100	20	Adjacent	—	—

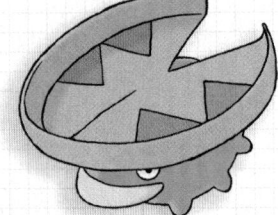

Pokémon AR Marker

271 Lombre

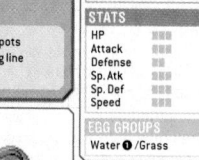

Jolly Pokémon

TYPE Water Grass

ABILITIES
- Swift Swim
- Rain Dish

HIDDEN ABILITY
- Own Tempo

- HEIGHT: 3'11"
- WEIGHT: 71.6 lbs.
- GENDER: ♂ / ♀

It has a mischievous spirit. If it spots an angler, it will tug on the fishing line to interfere.

STATS
HP
Attack
Defense
Sp. Atk
Sp. Def
Speed

EGG GROUPS
Water 1 /Grass

Same form for ♂ / ♀

ITEMS SOMETIMES HELD
- None

EVOLUTION

HOW TO OBTAIN

Pokémon Black Version 2	Route 3 (Hidden Grotto)
Pokémon White Version 2	Route 3 (Hidden Grotto)

HOW TO OBTAIN FROM OTHER GAMES

—

—

Pokémon AR Marker

LEVEL-UP AND LEARNED MOVES

Lv.	Name	Type	Kind	Pow.	Acc.	PP	Range	Long	DA
1	Astonish	Ghost	Physical	30	100	15	Normal	—	○
3	Growl	Normal	Status	—	100	40	Many Others	—	—
5	Absorb	Grass	Special	20	100	25	Normal	—	—
7	Nature Power	Normal	Status	—	—	20	Varies	—	—
11	Fake Out	Normal	Physical	40	100	10	Normal	—	○
15	Fury Swipes	Normal	Physical	18	80	15	Normal	—	○
19	Water Sport	Water	Status	—	—	15	Both Sides	—	—
25	BubbleBeam	Water	Special	65	100	20	Normal	—	—
31	Zen Headbutt	Psychic	Physical	80	90	15	Normal	—	○
37	Uproar	Normal	Special	90	100	10	1 Random	—	—
45	Hydro Pump	Water	Special	120	80	5	Normal	—	—

TM & HM MOVES

Lv.	Name	Type	Kind	Pow.	Acc.	PP	Range	Long	DA
TM01	Hone Claws	Dark	Status	—	—	15	Self	—	—
TM06	Toxic	Poison	Status	—	90	10	Normal	—	—
TM07	Hail	Ice	Status	—	—	10	Both Sides	—	—
TM10	Hidden Power	Normal	Special	—	100	15	Normal	—	—
TM11	Sunny Day	Fire	Status	—	—	5	Both Sides	—	—
TM13	Ice Beam	Ice	Special	95	100	10	Normal	—	—
TM14	Blizzard	Ice	Special	120	70	5	Many Others	—	—
TM17	Protect	Normal	Status	—	—	10	Self	—	—
TM18	Rain Dance	Water	Status	—	—	5	Both Sides	—	—
TM21	Frustration	Normal	Physical	—	100	20	Normal	—	○
TM22	SolarBeam	Grass	Special	120	100	10	Normal	—	—
TM27	Return	Normal	Physical	—	100	20	Normal	—	○
TM31	Brick Break	Fighting	Physical	75	100	15	Normal	—	○
TM32	Double Team	Normal	Status	—	—	15	Self	—	—
TM42	Facade	Normal	Physical	70	100	20	Normal	—	○
TM44	Rest	Psychic	Status	—	—	10	Self	—	—
TM45	Attract	Normal	Status	—	100	15	Normal	—	—
TM46	Thief	Dark	Physical	40	100	10	Normal	—	○
TM48	Round	Normal	Special	60	100	15	Normal	—	—
TM49	Echoed Voice	Normal	Special	40	100	15	Normal	—	—
TM53	Energy Ball	Grass	Special	80	100	10	Normal	—	—
TM55	Scald	Water	Special	80	100	15	Normal	—	—
TM56	Fling	Dark	Physical	—	100	10	Normal	—	—
TM70	Flash	Normal	Status	—	100	20	Normal	—	—
TM75	Swords Dance	Normal	Status	—	—	30	Self	—	—
TM86	Grass Knot	Grass	Special	—	100	20	Normal	—	○
TM87	Swagger	Normal	Status	—	90	15	Normal	—	—
TM90	Substitute	Normal	Status	—	—	10	Self	—	—
TM94	Rock Smash	Fighting	Physical	40	100	15	Normal	—	○
HM03	Surf	Water	Special	95	100	15	Adjacent	—	—
HM04	Strength	Normal	Physical	80	100	15	Normal	—	○
HM05	Waterfall	Water	Physical	80	100	15	Normal	—	○
HM06	Dive	Water	Physical	80	100	10	Normal	—	○

MOVES TAUGHT BY PEOPLE

Name	Type	Kind	Pow.	Acc.	PP	Range	Long	DA

MOVES TAUGHT BY MOVE TUTORS FOR SHARDS

Name	Type	Kind	Pow.	Acc.	PP	Range	Long	DA
Uproar	Normal	Special	90	100	10	1 Random	—	—
Seed Bomb	Grass	Physical	80	100	15	Normal	—	—
Fire Punch	Fire	Physical	75	100	15	Normal	—	○
ThunderPunch	Electric	Physical	75	100	15	Normal	—	○
Ice Punch	Ice	Physical	75	100	15	Normal	—	○
Hyper Voice	Normal	Special	90	100	10	Many Others	—	—
Icy Wind	Ice	Special	55	95	15	Many Others	—	—
Zen Headbutt	Psychic	Physical	80	90	15	Normal	—	○
Snore	Normal	Special	40	100	15	Normal	—	—
Synthesis	Grass	Status	—	—	5	Self	—	—
Giga Drain	Grass	Special	75	100	10	Normal	—	—
Drain Punch	Fighting	Physical	75	100	10	Normal	—	○
Sleep Talk	Normal	Status	—	—	10	Self	—	—

272 Ludicolo

Carefree Pokémon

TYPE Water Grass

ABILITIES
- Swift Swim
- Rain Dish

HIDDEN ABILITY
- Own Tempo

- HEIGHT: 4'11"
- WEIGHT: 121.3 lbs.
- GENDER: ♂ / ♀

If it hears festive music, all its muscles fill with energy. It can't help breaking out into a dance.

STATS
HP
Attack
Defense
Sp. Atk
Sp. Def
Speed

EGG GROUPS
Water 1 /Grass

♂ ♀

ITEMS SOMETIMES HELD
- None

EVOLUTION

HOW TO OBTAIN

Pokémon Black Version 2	Use Water Stone on Lombre
Pokémon White Version 2	Use Water Stone on Lombre

HOW TO OBTAIN FROM OTHER GAMES

—

—

Pokémon AR Marker

LEVEL-UP AND LEARNED MOVES

Lv.	Name	Type	Kind	Pow.	Acc.	PP	Range	Long	DA
1	Astonish	Ghost	Physical	30	100	15	Normal	—	○
1	Growl	Normal	Status	—	100	40	Many Others	—	—
1	Mega Drain	Grass	Special	40	100	15	Normal	—	—
1	Nature Power	Normal	Status	—	—	20	Varies	—	—

TM & HM MOVES

Lv.	Name	Type	Kind	Pow.	Acc.	PP	Range	Long	DA
TM01	Hone Claws	Dark	Status	—	—	15	Self	—	—
TM06	Toxic	Poison	Status	—	90	10	Normal	—	—
TM07	Hail	Ice	Status	—	—	10	Both Sides	—	—
TM10	Hidden Power	Normal	Special	—	100	15	Normal	—	—
TM11	Sunny Day	Fire	Status	—	—	5	Both Sides	—	—
TM13	Ice Beam	Ice	Special	95	100	10	Normal	—	—
TM14	Blizzard	Ice	Special	120	70	5	Many Others	—	—
TM15	Hyper Beam	Normal	Special	150	90	5	Normal	—	—
TM17	Protect	Normal	Status	—	—	10	Self	—	—
TM18	Rain Dance	Water	Status	—	—	5	Both Sides	—	—
TM21	Frustration	Normal	Physical	—	100	20	Normal	—	○
TM22	SolarBeam	Grass	Special	120	100	10	Normal	—	—
TM27	Return	Normal	Physical	—	100	20	Normal	—	○
TM31	Brick Break	Fighting	Physical	75	100	15	Normal	—	○
TM32	Double Team	Normal	Status	—	—	15	Self	—	—
TM42	Facade	Normal	Physical	70	100	20	Normal	—	○
TM44	Rest	Psychic	Status	—	—	10	Self	—	—
TM45	Attract	Normal	Status	—	100	15	Normal	—	—
TM46	Thief	Dark	Physical	40	100	10	Normal	—	○
TM48	Round	Normal	Special	60	100	15	Normal	—	—
TM49	Echoed Voice	Normal	Special	40	100	15	Normal	—	—
TM52	Focus Blast	Fighting	Special	120	70	5	Normal	—	—
TM53	Energy Ball	Grass	Special	80	100	10	Normal	—	—
TM55	Scald	Water	Special	80	100	15	Normal	—	—
TM56	Fling	Dark	Physical	—	100	10	Normal	—	—
TM68	Giga Impact	Normal	Physical	150	90	5	Normal	—	○
TM70	Flash	Normal	Status	—	100	20	Normal	—	—
TM75	Swords Dance	Normal	Status	—	—	30	Self	—	—
TM86	Grass Knot	Grass	Special	—	100	20	Normal	—	○
TM87	Swagger	Normal	Status	—	90	15	Normal	—	—
TM90	Substitute	Normal	Status	—	—	10	Self	—	—
TM94	Rock Smash	Fighting	Physical	40	100	15	Normal	—	○
HM03	Surf	Water	Special	95	100	15	Adjacent	—	—
HM04	Strength	Normal	Physical	80	100	15	Normal	—	○
HM05	Waterfall	Water	Physical	80	100	15	Normal	—	○
HM06	Dive	Water	Physical	80	100	10	Normal	—	○

MOVES TAUGHT BY PEOPLE

Name	Type	Kind	Pow.	Acc.	PP	Range	Long	DA

MOVES TAUGHT BY MOVE TUTORS FOR SHARDS

Name	Type	Kind	Pow.	Acc.	PP	Range	Long	DA
Uproar	Normal	Special	90	100	10	1 Random	—	—
Seed Bomb	Grass	Physical	80	100	15	Normal	—	—
Fire Punch	Fire	Physical	75	100	15	Normal	—	○
ThunderPunch	Electric	Physical	75	100	15	Normal	—	○
Ice Punch	Ice	Physical	75	100	15	Normal	—	○
Hyper Voice	Normal	Special	90	100	10	Many Others	—	—
Icy Wind	Ice	Special	55	95	15	Many Others	—	—
Zen Headbutt	Psychic	Physical	80	90	15	Normal	—	○
Snore	Normal	Special	40	100	15	Normal	—	—
Synthesis	Grass	Status	—	—	5	Self	—	—
Giga Drain	Grass	Special	75	100	10	Normal	—	—
Drain Punch	Fighting	Physical	75	100	10	Normal	—	○
Sleep Talk	Normal	Status	—	—	10	Self	—	—

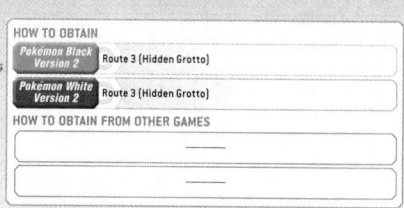

Acorn Pokémon
273 Seedot

TYPE Grass

ABILITIES
- Chlorophyll
- Early Bird

HIDDEN ABILITY

- HEIGHT: 1'08"
- WEIGHT: 8.8 lbs.
- GENDER: ♂ / ♀

When it dangles from a tree branch, it looks just like an acorn. It enjoys scaring other Pokémon.

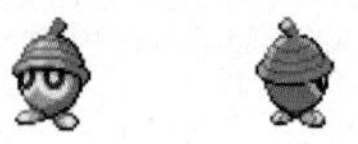

STATS
HP	
Attack	
Defense	
Sp. Atk	
Sp. Def	
Speed	

EGG GROUPS
Field/Grass

ITEMS SOMETIMES HELD
- None

Same form for ♂ / ♀

EVOLUTION

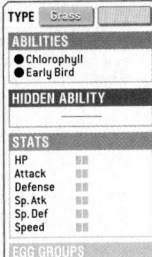

Seedot — Lv. 14 → Nuzleaf — Use Leaf Stone → Shiftry

HOW TO OBTAIN

Pokémon Black Version 2	Catch a Nuzleaf or Shiftry, leave it at the Pokémon Day Care, and hatch the Egg that is found
Pokémon White Version 2	Catch a Nuzleaf or Shiftry, leave it at the Pokémon Day Care, and hatch the Egg that is found

HOW TO OBTAIN FROM OTHER GAMES

Pokémon HeartGold Version	Viridian Forest (use Headbutt on tree)
Pokémon SoulSilver Version	Viridian Forest (use Headbutt on tree)

LEVEL-UP AND LEARNED MOVES

Lv.	Name	Type	Kind	Pow.	Acc.	PP	Range	Long	DA
1	Bide	Normal	Physical	—	—	10	Self	—	—
3	Harden	Normal	Status	—	—	30	Self	—	—
7	Growth	Normal	Status	—	—	40	Self	—	—
13	Nature Power	Normal	Status	—	—	20	Varies	—	—
21	Synthesis	Grass	Status	—	—	5	Self	—	—
31	Sunny Day	Fire	Status	—	—	5	Both Sides	—	—
43	Explosion	Normal	Physical	250	100	5	Adjacent	—	—

TM & HM MOVES

Lv.	Name	Type	Kind	Pow.	Acc.	PP	Range	Long	DA
TM06	Toxic	Poison	Status	—	90	10	Normal	—	—
TM10	Hidden Power	Normal	Special	—	100	15	Normal	—	—
TM11	Sunny Day	Fire	Status	—	—	5	Both Sides	—	—
TM17	Protect	Normal	Status	—	—	10	Self	—	—
TM21	Frustration	Normal	Physical	—	100	20	Normal	—	○
TM22	SolarBeam	Grass	Special	120	100	10	Normal	—	—
TM27	Return	Normal	Physical	—	100	20	Normal	—	○
TM28	Dig	Ground	Physical	80	100	10	Normal	—	○
TM30	Shadow Ball	Ghost	Special	80	100	15	Normal	—	—
TM32	Double Team	Normal	Status	—	—	15	Self	—	—
TM42	Facade	Normal	Physical	70	100	20	Normal	—	○
TM44	Rest	Psychic	Status	—	—	10	Self	—	—
TM45	Attract	Normal	Status	—	100	15	Normal	—	—
TM48	Round	Normal	Special	60	100	15	Normal	—	—
TM53	Energy Ball	Grass	Special	80	100	10	Normal	—	—
TM54	False Swipe	Normal	Physical	40	100	40	Normal	—	○
TM64	Explosion	Normal	Physical	250	100	5	Adjacent	—	—
TM67	Retaliate	Normal	Physical	70	100	5	Normal	—	○
TM70	Flash	Normal	Status	—	100	20	Normal	—	—
TM75	Swords Dance	Normal	Status	—	—	30	Self	—	—
TM86	Grass Knot	Grass	Special	—	100	20	Normal	—	○
TM87	Swagger	Normal	Status	—	90	15	Normal	—	—
TM90	Substitute	Normal	Status	—	—	10	Self	—	—
TM94	Rock Smash	Fighting	Physical	40	100	15	Normal	—	○

MOVES TAUGHT BY PEOPLE

Name	Type	Kind	Pow.	Acc.	PP	Range	Long	DA

MOVES TAUGHT BY MOVE TUTORS FOR SHARDS

Name	Type	Kind	Pow.	Acc.	PP	Range	Long	DA
Seed Bomb	Grass	Physical	80	100	15	Normal	—	—
Foul Play	Dark	Physical	95	100	15	Normal	—	○
Snore	Normal	Special	40	100	15	Normal	—	—
Synthesis	Grass	Status	—	—	5	Self	—	—
Giga Drain	Grass	Special	75	100	10	Normal	—	—
Worry Seed	Grass	Status	—	100	10	Normal	—	—
Spite	Ghost	Status	—	100	10	Normal	—	—
Sleep Talk	Normal	Status	—	—	10	Self	—	—

EGG MOVES

Name	Type	Kind	Pow.	Acc.	PP	Range	Long	DA
Leech Seed	Grass	Status	—	90	10	Normal	—	—
Amnesia	Psychic	Status	—	—	20	Self	—	—
Quick Attack	Normal	Physical	40	100	30	Normal	—	○
Razor Wind	Normal	Special	80	100	10	Many Others	—	—
Take Down	Normal	Physical	90	85	20	Normal	—	○
Worry Seed	Grass	Status	—	100	10	Normal	—	—
Nasty Plot	Dark	Status	—	—	20	Self	—	—
Power Swap	Psychic	Status	—	—	10	Normal	—	—
Defog	Flying	Status	—	—	15	Normal	—	—
Foul Play	Dark	Physical	95	100	15	Normal	—	○
Beat Up	Dark	Physical	—	100	10	Normal	—	—
Bullet Seed	Grass	Physical	25	100	30	Normal	—	—

Seedot | 273

Pokémon AR Marker

Wily Pokémon
274 Nuzleaf

TYPE Grass Dark

ABILITIES
- Chlorophyll
- Early Bird

HIDDEN ABILITY

- HEIGHT: 3'03"
- WEIGHT: 61.7 lbs.
- GENDER: ♂ / ♀

The sound of its grass flute makes its listeners uneasy. It lives deep in forests.

STATS
HP	
Attack	
Defense	
Sp. Atk	
Sp. Def	
Speed	

EGG GROUPS
Field/Grass

ITEMS SOMETIMES HELD
- None

♂   ♀

EVOLUTION

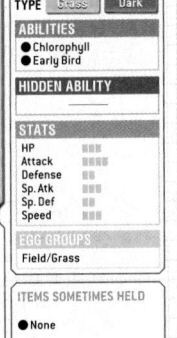

Seedot — Lv. 14 → Nuzleaf — Use Leaf Stone → Shiftry

HOW TO OBTAIN

Pokémon Black Version 2	Nature Preserve
Pokémon White Version 2	Nature Preserve

HOW TO OBTAIN FROM OTHER GAMES

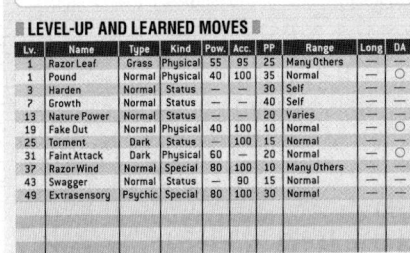

LEVEL-UP AND LEARNED MOVES

Lv.	Name	Type	Kind	Pow.	Acc.	PP	Range	Long	DA
1	Razor Leaf	Grass	Physical	55	95	25	Many Others	—	—
1	Pound	Normal	Physical	40	100	35	Normal	—	○
3	Harden	Normal	Status	—	—	30	Self	—	—
7	Growth	Normal	Status	—	—	40	Self	—	—
13	Nature Power	Normal	Status	—	—	20	Varies	—	—
19	Fake Out	Normal	Physical	40	100	10	Normal	—	○
25	Torment	Dark	Status	—	100	15	Normal	—	—
31	Faint Attack	Dark	Physical	60	—	20	Normal	—	○
37	Razor Wind	Normal	Special	80	100	10	Many Others	—	—
43	Swagger	Normal	Status	—	90	15	Normal	—	—
49	Extrasensory	Psychic	Special	80	100	30	Normal	—	—

TM & HM MOVES

Lv.	Name	Type	Kind	Pow.	Acc.	PP	Range	Long	DA
TM06	Toxic	Poison	Status	—	90	10	Normal	—	—
TM10	Hidden Power	Normal	Special	—	100	15	Normal	—	—
TM11	Sunny Day	Fire	Status	—	—	5	Both Sides	—	—
TM15	Hyper Beam	Normal	Special	150	90	5	Normal	—	—
TM17	Protect	Normal	Status	—	—	10	Self	—	—
TM21	Frustration	Normal	Physical	—	100	20	Normal	—	○
TM22	SolarBeam	Grass	Special	120	100	10	Normal	—	—
TM27	Return	Normal	Physical	—	100	20	Normal	—	○
TM28	Dig	Ground	Physical	80	100	10	Normal	—	○
TM30	Shadow Ball	Ghost	Special	80	100	15	Normal	—	—
TM31	Brick Break	Fighting	Physical	75	100	15	Normal	—	○
TM32	Double Team	Normal	Status	—	—	15	Self	—	—
TM39	Rock Tomb	Rock	Physical	50	80	10	Normal	—	—
TM41	Torment	Dark	Status	—	100	15	Normal	—	—
TM42	Facade	Normal	Physical	70	100	20	Normal	—	○
TM44	Rest	Psychic	Status	—	—	10	Self	—	—
TM45	Attract	Normal	Status	—	100	15	Normal	—	—
TM46	Thief	Dark	Physical	40	100	10	Normal	—	—
TM47	Low Sweep	Fighting	Physical	60	100	20	Normal	—	○
TM48	Round	Normal	Special	60	100	15	Normal	—	—
TM53	Energy Ball	Grass	Special	80	100	10	Normal	—	—
TM54	False Swipe	Normal	Physical	40	100	40	Normal	—	○
TM56	Fling	Dark	Physical	—	100	10	Normal	—	○
TM63	Embargo	Dark	Status	—	100	15	Normal	—	—
TM64	Explosion	Normal	Physical	250	100	5	Adjacent	—	—
TM66	Payback	Dark	Physical	50	100	10	Normal	—	○
TM67	Retaliate	Normal	Physical	70	100	5	Normal	—	○
TM70	Flash	Normal	Status	—	100	20	Normal	—	—
TM75	Swords Dance	Normal	Status	—	—	30	Self	—	—
TM77	Psych Up	Normal	Status	—	—	10	Self	—	—
TM80	Rock Slide	Rock	Physical	75	90	10	Many Others	—	—
TM86	Grass Knot	Grass	Special	—	100	20	Normal	—	○
TM87	Swagger	Normal	Status	—	90	15	Normal	—	—
TM90	Substitute	Normal	Status	—	—	10	Self	—	—
TM94	Rock Smash	Fighting	Physical	40	100	15	Normal	—	○
TM95	Snarl	Dark	Special	55	95	15	Many Others	—	—
HM01	Cut	Normal	Physical	50	95	30	Normal	—	—
HM04	Strength	Normal	Physical	80	100	15	Normal	—	—

MOVES TAUGHT BY PEOPLE

Name	Type	Kind	Pow.	Acc.	PP	Range	Long	DA

MOVES TAUGHT BY MOVE TUTORS FOR SHARDS

Name	Type	Kind	Pow.	Acc.	PP	Range	Long	DA
Seed Bomb	Grass	Physical	80	100	15	Normal	—	—
Low Kick	Fighting	Physical	—	100	20	Normal	—	○
Foul Play	Dark	Physical	95	100	15	Normal	—	○
Dark Pulse	Dark	Special	80	100	15	Normal	○	—
Snore	Normal	Special	40	100	15	Normal	—	—
Synthesis	Grass	Status	—	—	5	Self	—	—
Giga Drain	Grass	Special	75	100	10	Normal	—	—
Worry Seed	Grass	Status	—	100	10	Normal	—	—
Spite	Ghost	Status	—	100	10	Normal	—	—
Sleep Talk	Normal	Status	—	—	10	Self	—	—

Nuzleaf | 274

Pokémon AR Marker

Wicked Pokémon
275 Shiftry

TYPE Grass | Dark

ABILITIES
● Chlorophyll
● Early Bird

HIDDEN ABILITY

● HEIGHT: 4'03"
● WEIGHT: 131.4 lbs.
● GENDER: ♂ / ♀

By flapping its leafy fan, it can whip up gusts of 100 ft/second that can level houses.

♂   ♀

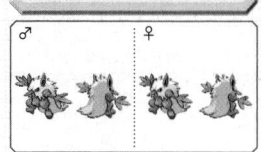

STATS
HP
Attack
Defense
Sp. Atk
Sp. Def
Speed

EGG GROUPS
Field/Grass

ITEMS SOMETIMES HELD
● None

EVOLUTION

Seedot → Lv. 14 → Nuzleaf → Use Leaf Stone → Shiftry

HOW TO OBTAIN

Pokémon Black Version 2	Nature Preserve (rustling grass)
Pokémon White Version 2	Nature Preserve (rustling grass)

HOW TO OBTAIN FROM OTHER GAMES

LEVEL-UP AND LEARNED MOVES

Lv.	Name	Type	Kind	Pow.	Acc.	PP	Range	Long	DA
1	Faint Attack	Dark	Physical	60	—	20	Normal	—	○
1	Whirlwind	Normal	Status	—	100	20	Normal	—	—
1	Nasty Plot	Dark	Status	—	—	20	Self	—	—
1	Razor Leaf	Grass	Physical	55	95	25	Many Others	—	—
19	Leaf Tornado	Grass	Special	65	90	10	Normal	—	—
49	Leaf Storm	Grass	Special	140	90	5	Normal	—	—

TM & HM MOVES

	Name	Type	Kind	Pow.	Acc.	PP	Range	Long	DA
TM06	Toxic	Poison	Status	—	90	10	Normal	—	—
TM10	Hidden Power	Normal	Special	—	100	15	Normal	—	○
TM11	Sunny Day	Fire	Status	—	—	5	Both Sides	—	—
TM15	Hyper Beam	Normal	Special	150	90	5	Normal	—	—
TM17	Protect	Normal	Status	—	—	10	Self	—	—
TM21	Frustration	Normal	Physical	—	100	20	Normal	—	○
TM22	SolarBeam	Grass	Special	120	100	10	Normal	—	—
TM27	Return	Normal	Physical	—	100	20	Normal	—	○
TM28	Dig	Ground	Physical	80	100	10	Normal	—	—
TM30	Shadow Ball	Ghost	Special	80	100	15	Normal	—	○
TM31	Brick Break	Fighting	Physical	75	100	15	Normal	—	—
TM32	Double Team	Normal	Status	—	—	15	Self	—	—
TM39	Rock Tomb	Rock	Physical	50	80	10	Normal	—	—
TM40	Aerial Ace	Flying	Physical	60	—	20	Normal	○	○
TM41	Torment	Dark	Status	—	100	15	Normal	—	○
TM42	Facade	Normal	Physical	70	100	20	Normal	—	○
TM44	Rest	Psychic	Status	—	—	10	Self	—	—
TM45	Attract	Normal	Status	—	100	15	Normal	—	—
TM46	Thief	Dark	Physical	40	100	10	Normal	—	○
TM47	Low Sweep	Fighting	Physical	60	100	20	Normal	—	○
TM48	Round	Normal	Special	60	100	15	Normal	—	—
TM52	Focus Blast	Fighting	Special	120	70	5	Normal	—	○
TM53	Energy Ball	Grass	Special	80	100	10	Normal	—	○
TM54	False Swipe	Normal	Physical	40	100	40	Normal	—	○
TM56	Fling	Dark	Physical	—	100	10	Normal	—	—
TM63	Embargo	Dark	Status	—	100	15	Normal	—	—
TM64	Explosion	Normal	Physical	250	100	5	Adjacent	—	—
TM66	Payback	Dark	Physical	50	100	10	Normal	—	○
TM67	Retaliate	Normal	Physical	70	100	5	Normal	—	○
TM68	Giga Impact	Normal	Physical	150	90	5	Normal	—	—
TM70	Flash	Normal	Status	—	100	20	Normal	—	—
TM75	Swords Dance	Normal	Status	—	—	30	Self	—	—
TM77	Psych Up	Normal	Status	—	—	10	Normal	—	—
TM80	Rock Slide	Rock	Physical	75	90	10	Many Others	—	—
TM81	X-Scissor	Bug	Physical	80	100	15	Normal	—	○
TM86	Grass Knot	Grass	Special	—	100	20	Normal	—	○
TM87	Swagger	Normal	Status	—	90	15	Normal	—	—
TM90	Substitute	Normal	Status	—	—	10	Self	—	—
TM94	Rock Smash	Fighting	Physical	40	100	15	Normal	—	—
TM95	Snarl	Dark	Special	55	95	15	Many Others	—	—
HM01	Cut	Normal	Physical	50	95	30	Normal	—	—
HM04	Strength	Normal	Physical	80	100	15	Normal	—	—

MOVES TAUGHT BY PEOPLE

Name	Type	Kind	Pow.	Acc.	PP	Range	Long	DA

MOVES TAUGHT BY MOVE TUTORS FOR SHARDS

Name	Type	Kind	Pow.	Acc.	PP	Range	Long	DA
Bounce	Flying	Physical	85	85	5	Normal	○	○
Seed Bomb	Grass	Physical	80	100	15	Normal	—	○
Low Kick	Fighting	Physical	—	100	20	Normal	—	○
Icy Wind	Ice	Special	55	95	15	Many Others	—	—
Foul Play	Dark	Physical	95	100	15	Normal	—	○
Dark Pulse	Dark	Special	80	100	15	Normal	○	○
Snore	Normal	Special	40	100	15	Normal	—	○
Knock Off	Dark	Physical	20	100	20	Normal	—	○
Synthesis	Grass	Status	—	—	5	Self	—	—
Giga Drain	Grass	Special	75	100	10	Normal	—	○
Tailwind	Flying	Status	—	—	30	Your Side	—	—
Worry Seed	Grass	Status	—	100	10	Normal	—	—
Spite	Ghost	Status	—	100	10	Normal	—	—
Sleep Talk	Normal	Status	—	—	10	Self	—	—

Pokémon AR Marker

TinySwallow Pokémon
276 Taillow

TYPE Normal | Flying

ABILITY
● Guts

HIDDEN ABILITY
● Scrappy

● HEIGHT: 1'00"
● WEIGHT: 5.1 lbs.
● GENDER: ♂ / ♀

It has a gutsy spirit that makes it bravely take on tough foes. It flies in search of warm climates.

Same form for ♂ / ♀

STATS
HP
Attack
Defense
Sp. Atk
Sp. Def
Speed

EGG GROUPS
Flying

ITEMS SOMETIMES HELD
● None

EVOLUTION

Taillow → Lv. 22 → Swellow

HOW TO OBTAIN

Pokémon Black Version 2	Catch a Swellow, leave it at the Pokémon Day Care, and hatch the Egg that is found
Pokémon White Version 2	Catch a Swellow, leave it at the Pokémon Day Care, and hatch the Egg that is found

HOW TO OBTAIN FROM OTHER GAMES

Pokémon HeartGold Version	Cherrygrove City (use Headbutt on tree)
Pokémon SoulSilver Version	Cherrygrove City (use Headbutt on tree)

LEVEL-UP AND LEARNED MOVES

Lv.	Name	Type	Kind	Pow.	Acc.	PP	Range	Long	DA
1	Peck	Flying	Physical	35	100	35	Normal	○	—
1	Growl	Normal	Status	—	100	40	Many Others	—	—
4	Focus Energy	Normal	Status	—	—	30	Self	—	—
8	Quick Attack	Normal	Physical	40	100	30	Normal	—	○
13	Wing Attack	Flying	Physical	60	100	35	Normal	○	—
19	Double Team	Normal	Status	—	—	15	Self	—	—
26	Endeavor	Normal	Physical	—	100	5	Normal	—	○
34	Aerial Ace	Flying	Physical	60	—	20	Normal	○	○
43	Agility	Psychic	Status	—	—	30	Self	—	—
53	Air Slash	Flying	Special	75	95	20	Normal	—	—

TM & HM MOVES

	Name	Type	Kind	Pow.	Acc.	PP	Range	Long	DA
TM06	Toxic	Poison	Status	—	90	10	Normal	—	—
TM10	Hidden Power	Normal	Special	—	100	15	Normal	—	—
TM11	Sunny Day	Fire	Status	—	—	5	Both Sides	—	—
TM17	Protect	Normal	Status	—	—	10	Self	—	—
TM18	Rain Dance	Water	Status	—	—	5	Both Sides	—	—
TM21	Frustration	Normal	Physical	—	100	20	Normal	—	○
TM27	Return	Normal	Physical	—	100	20	Normal	—	○
TM32	Double Team	Normal	Status	—	—	15	Self	—	—
TM40	Aerial Ace	Flying	Physical	60	—	20	Normal	○	○
TM42	Facade	Normal	Physical	70	100	20	Normal	—	○
TM44	Rest	Psychic	Status	—	—	10	Self	—	—
TM45	Attract	Normal	Status	—	100	15	Normal	—	—
TM46	Thief	Dark	Physical	40	100	10	Normal	—	○
TM48	Round	Normal	Special	60	100	15	Normal	—	—
TM49	Echoed Voice	Normal	Special	40	100	15	Normal	—	—
TM83	Work Up	Normal	Status	—	—	30	Self	—	—
TM87	Swagger	Normal	Status	—	90	15	Normal	—	—
TM88	Pluck	Flying	Physical	60	100	20	Normal	○	○
TM89	U-turn	Bug	Physical	70	100	20	Normal	—	○
TM90	Substitute	Normal	Status	—	—	10	Self	—	—
HM02	Fly	Flying	Physical	90	95	15	Normal	○	○

MOVES TAUGHT BY PEOPLE

Name	Type	Kind	Pow.	Acc.	PP	Range	Long	DA

MOVES TAUGHT BY MOVE TUTORS FOR SHARDS

Name	Type	Kind	Pow.	Acc.	PP	Range	Long	DA
Snore	Normal	Special	40	100	15	Normal	—	—
Roost	Flying	Status	—	—	10	Self	—	—
Heat Wave	Fire	Special	100	90	10	Many Others	—	—
Tailwind	Flying	Status	—	—	30	Your Side	—	—
Endeavor	Normal	Physical	—	100	5	Normal	—	○
Sleep Talk	Normal	Status	—	—	10	Self	—	—

EGG MOVES

Name	Type	Kind	Pow.	Acc.	PP	Range	Long	DA
Pursuit	Dark	Physical	40	100	20	Normal	—	○
Supersonic	Normal	Status	—	55	20	Normal	—	—
Refresh	Normal	Status	—	—	20	Self	—	—
Mirror Move	Flying	Status	—	—	20	Normal	—	—
Rage	Normal	Physical	20	100	20	Normal	—	—
Sky Attack	Flying	Physical	140	90	5	Normal	○	—
Whirlwind	Normal	Status	—	100	20	Normal	—	—
Brave Bird	Flying	Physical	120	100	15	Normal	—	○
Roost	Flying	Status	—	—	10	Self	—	—
Steel Wing	Steel	Physical	70	90	25	Normal	—	○
Defog	Flying	Status	—	—	15	Normal	—	—

Pokémon AR Marker

Swallow Pokémon
277 Swellow

| TYPE | Normal | Flying |

ABILITY
- Guts

HIDDEN ABILITY
- Scrappy

- HEIGHT: 2'04"
- WEIGHT: 43.7 lbs.
- GENDER: ♂ / ♀

It circles the sky in search of prey. When it spots one, it dives steeply to catch the prey.

STATS

HP	
Attack	
Defense	
Sp. Atk	
Sp. Def	
Speed	

Same form for ♂ / ♀

EGG GROUPS
Flying

ITEMS SOMETIMES HELD
- Charti Berry

EVOLUTION

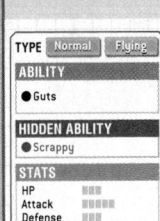

Taillow → Lv. 22 → Swellow

HOW TO OBTAIN

| Pokémon Black Version 2 | Route 13 (mass outbreak) |
| Pokémon White Version 2 | Route 13 (mass outbreak) |

HOW TO OBTAIN FROM OTHER GAMES
| ——— |
| ——— |

LEVEL-UP AND LEARNED MOVES

Lv.	Name	Type	Kind	Pow.	Acc.	PP	Range	Long	DA
1	Pluck	Flying	Physical	60	100	20	Normal	○	
1	Peck	Flying	Physical	35	100	35	Normal	○	
1	Growl	Normal	Status	—	100	40	Many Others		
1	Focus Energy	Normal	Status	—	—	30	Self		
1	Quick Attack	Normal	Physical	40	100	30	Normal		
4	Focus Energy	Normal	Status	—	—	30	Self		
8	Quick Attack	Normal	Physical	40	100	30	Normal		
13	Wing Attack	Flying	Physical	60	100	35	Normal		
19	Double Team	Normal	Status	—	—	15	Self		
28	Endeavor	Normal	Physical	—	100	5	Normal		○
38	Aerial Ace	Flying	Physical	60	—	20	Normal		
49	Agility	Psychic	Status	—	—	30	Self		
61	Air Slash	Flying	Special	75	95	20	Normal	○	

MOVES TAUGHT BY PEOPLE

Name	Type	Kind	Pow.	Acc.	PP	Range	Long	DA

MOVES TAUGHT BY MOVE TUTORS FOR SHARDS

Name	Type	Kind	Pow.	Acc.	PP	Range	Long	DA
Snore	Normal	Special	40	100	15	Normal	—	—
Roost	Flying	Status	—	—	10	Self	○	—
Sky Attack	Flying	Physical	140	90	5	Normal	○	—
Heat Wave	Fire	Special	100	90	10	Many Others	—	—
Tailwind	Flying	Status	—	—	30	Your Side	—	—
Endeavor	Normal	Physical	—	100	5	Normal	—	○
Sleep Talk	Normal	Status	—	—	10	Self	—	—

TM & HM MOVES

Lv.	Name	Type	Kind	Pow.	Acc.	PP	Range	Long	DA
TM06	Toxic	Poison	Status	—	90	10	Normal	—	—
TM10	Hidden Power	Normal	Special	—	100	15	Normal	—	—
TM11	Sunny Day	Fire	Status	—	—	5	Both Sides	—	—
TM15	Hyper Beam	Normal	Special	150	90	5	Normal	—	—
TM17	Protect	Normal	Status	—	—	10	Self	—	—
TM18	Rain Dance	Water	Status	—	—	5	Both Sides	—	—
TM21	Frustration	Normal	Physical	—	100	20	Normal	—	○
TM27	Return	Normal	Physical	—	100	20	Normal	—	○
TM32	Double Team	Normal	Status	—	—	15	Self	—	—
TM40	Aerial Ace	Flying	Physical	60	—	20	Normal	○	—
TM42	Facade	Normal	Physical	70	100	20	Normal	—	○
TM44	Rest	Psychic	Status	—	—	10	Self	—	—
TM45	Attract	Normal	Status	—	100	15	Normal	—	—
TM46	Thief	Dark	Physical	40	100	10	Normal	—	—
TM48	Round	Normal	Special	60	100	15	Normal	—	—
TM49	Echoed Voice	Normal	Special	40	100	15	Normal	—	—
TM68	Giga Impact	Normal	Physical	150	90	5	Normal	—	—
TM83	Work Up	Normal	Status	—	—	30	Self	—	—
TM87	Swagger	Normal	Status	—	90	15	Normal	—	—
TM88	Pluck	Flying	Physical	60	100	20	Normal	○	—
TM89	U-turn	Bug	Physical	70	100	20	Normal	—	—
TM90	Substitute	Normal	Status	—	—	10	Self	—	—
HM02	Fly	Flying	Physical	90	95	15	Normal	○	—

Pokémon AR Marker

Seagull Pokémon
278 Wingull

| TYPE | Water | Flying |

ABILITY
- Keen Eye

HIDDEN ABILITY
- Rain Dish

- HEIGHT: 2'00"
- WEIGHT: 20.9 lbs.
- GENDER: ♂ / ♀

It makes its nest on sheer cliffs. Riding the sea breeze, it glides up into the expansive skies.

STATS

HP	
Attack	
Defense	
Sp. Atk	
Sp. Def	
Speed	

Same form for ♂ / ♀

EGG GROUPS
Water ❶ / Flying

ITEMS SOMETIMES HELD
- None

EVOLUTION

Wingull → Lv. 25 → Pelipper

HOW TO OBTAIN

| Pokémon Black Version 2 | Catch a Pelipper, leave it at the Pokémon Day Care, and hatch the Egg that is found |
| Pokémon White Version 2 | Catch a Pelipper, leave it at the Pokémon Day Care, and hatch the Egg that is found |

HOW TO OBTAIN FROM OTHER GAMES

| Pokémon Black Version | Route 13 (Water Surface) |
| Pokémon White Version | Route 13 (Water Surface) |

LEVEL-UP AND LEARNED MOVES

Lv.	Name	Type	Kind	Pow.	Acc.	PP	Range	Long	DA
1	Growl	Normal	Status	—	100	40	Many Others	—	—
1	Water Gun	Water	Special	40	100	25	Normal	—	—
6	Supersonic	Normal	Status	—	55	20	Normal	—	—
9	Wing Attack	Flying	Physical	60	100	35	Normal	—	—
14	Mist	Ice	Status	—	—	30	Your Side	—	—
17	Water Pulse	Water	Special	60	100	20	Normal	—	—
22	Quick Attack	Normal	Physical	40	100	30	Normal	—	—
26	Roost	Flying	Status	—	—	10	Self	—	—
30	Pursuit	Dark	Physical	40	100	20	Normal	—	—
33	Air Cutter	Flying	Special	55	95	25	Many Others	—	—
38	Agility	Psychic	Status	—	—	30	Self	—	—
42	Aerial Ace	Flying	Physical	60	—	20	Normal	—	—
46	Air Slash	Flying	Special	75	95	20	Normal	—	—
49	Hurricane	Flying	Special	120	70	10	Normal	—	—

MOVES TAUGHT BY PEOPLE

Name	Type	Kind	Pow.	Acc.	PP	Range	Long	DA

MOVES TAUGHT BY MOVE TUTORS FOR SHARDS

Name	Type	Kind	Pow.	Acc.	PP	Range	Long	DA
Uproar	Normal	Special	90	100	10	1 Random	—	—
Icy Wind	Ice	Special	55	95	15	Many Others	—	—
Snore	Normal	Special	40	100	15	Normal	—	—
Knock Off	Dark	Physical	20	100	20	Normal	—	○
Roost	Flying	Status	—	—	10	Self	—	—
Tailwind	Flying	Status	—	—	30	Your Side	—	—
Sleep Talk	Normal	Status	—	—	10	Self	—	—

TM & HM MOVES

Lv.	Name	Type	Kind	Pow.	Acc.	PP	Range	Long	DA
TM06	Toxic	Poison	Status	—	90	10	Normal	—	—
TM07	Hail	Ice	Status	—	—	10	Both Sides	—	—
TM10	Hidden Power	Normal	Special	—	100	15	Normal	—	—
TM13	Ice Beam	Ice	Special	95	100	10	Normal	—	—
TM14	Blizzard	Ice	Special	120	70	5	Many Others	—	—
TM17	Protect	Normal	Status	—	—	10	Self	—	—
TM18	Rain Dance	Water	Status	—	—	5	Both Sides	—	—
TM21	Frustration	Normal	Physical	—	100	20	Normal	—	○
TM27	Return	Normal	Physical	—	100	20	Normal	—	○
TM32	Double Team	Normal	Status	—	—	15	Self	—	—
TM40	Aerial Ace	Flying	Physical	60	—	20	Normal	○	—
TM42	Facade	Normal	Physical	70	100	20	Normal	—	○
TM44	Rest	Psychic	Status	—	—	10	Self	—	—
TM45	Attract	Normal	Status	—	100	15	Normal	—	—
TM46	Thief	Dark	Physical	40	100	10	Normal	—	—
TM48	Round	Normal	Special	60	100	15	Normal	—	—
TM49	Echoed Voice	Normal	Special	40	100	15	Normal	—	—
TM55	Scald	Water	Special	80	100	15	Normal	—	—
TM87	Swagger	Normal	Status	—	90	15	Normal	—	—
TM88	Pluck	Flying	Physical	60	100	20	Normal	○	—
TM89	U-turn	Bug	Physical	70	100	20	Normal	—	—
TM90	Substitute	Normal	Status	—	—	10	Self	—	—
HM02	Fly	Flying	Physical	90	95	15	Normal	○	—

EGG MOVES

Name	Type	Kind	Pow.	Acc.	PP	Range	Long	DA
Mist	Ice	Status	—	—	30	Your Side	—	—
Twister	Dragon	Special	40	100	20	Many Others	—	—
Agility	Psychic	Status	—	—	30	Self	—	—
Gust	Flying	Special	40	100	35	Normal	○	—
Water Sport	Water	Status	—	—	15	Both Sides	—	—
Aqua Ring	Water	Status	—	—	20	Self	—	—
Knock Off	Dark	Physical	20	100	20	Normal	—	○
Brine	Water	Special	65	100	10	Normal	—	—
Roost	Flying	Status	—	—	10	Self	—	—

Pokémon AR Marker

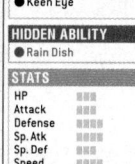

Water Bird Pokémon

279 Pelipper

- HEIGHT: 3'11"
- WEIGHT: 61.7 lbs.
- GENDER: ♂ / ♀

Skimming the water's surface, it dips its large bill in the sea, scoops up food and water, and carries it.

Same form for ♂ / ♀

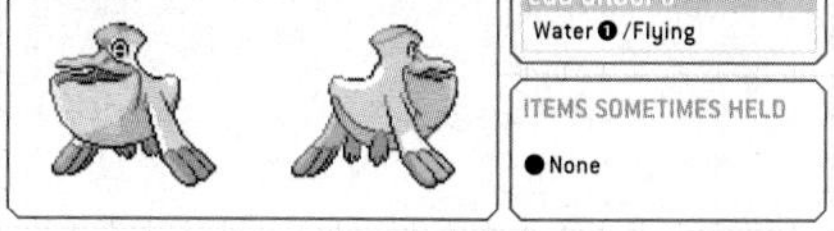

TYPE Water Flying

ABILITY

- Keen Eye

HIDDEN ABILITY

- Rain Dish

STATS

HP
Attack
Defense
Sp. Atk
Sp. Def
Speed

EGG GROUPS

Water 1 / Flying

ITEMS SOMETIMES HELD

- None

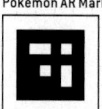

EVOLUTION

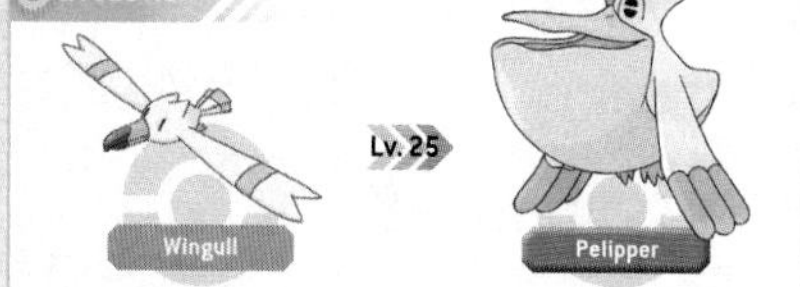
Wingull
Lv. 25
Pelipper

HOW TO OBTAIN

Pokémon Black Version 2	1 Route 13 2 Route 22
Pokémon White Version 2	1 Route 13 2 Route 22

HOW TO OBTAIN FROM OTHER GAMES

—

—

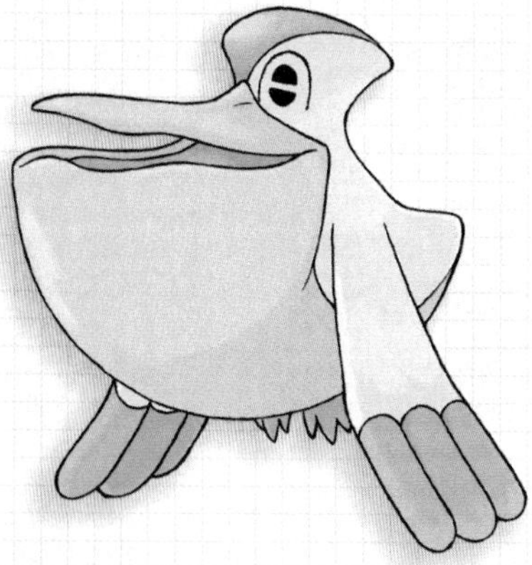

Pokémon AR Marker

LEVEL-UP AND LEARNED MOVES

Lv.	Name	Type	Kind	Pow.	Acc.	PP	Range	Long	DA
1	Soak	Water	Status	—	100	20	Normal	—	—
1	Growl	Normal	Status	—	100	40	Many Others	—	—
1	Water Gun	Water	Special	40	100	25	Normal	—	—
1	Water Sport	Water	Status	—	—	15	Both Sides	—	—
1	Wing Attack	Flying	Physical	60	100	35	Normal	○	○
6	Supersonic	Normal	Status	—	55	20	Normal	—	—
9	Wing Attack	Flying	Physical	60	100	35	Normal	○	○
14	Mist	Ice	Status	—	—	30	Your Side	—	—
17	Water Pulse	Water	Special	60	100	20	Normal	○	—
22	Payback	Dark	Physical	50	100	10	Normal	—	○
25	Protect	Normal	Status	—	—	10	Self	—	—
28	Roost	Flying	Status	—	—	10	Self	—	—
34	Brine	Water	Special	65	100	10	Normal	—	—
39	Stockpile	Normal	Status	—	—	20	Self	—	—
39	Swallow	Normal	Status	—	—	10	Self	—	—
39	Spit Up	Normal	Special	—	100	10	Normal	—	—
46	Fling	Dark	Physical	—	100	10	Normal	—	—
52	Tailwind	Flying	Status	—	—	30	Your Side	—	—
58	Hydro Pump	Water	Special	120	80	5	Normal	—	—
63	Hurricane	Flying	Special	120	70	10	Normal	○	—

TM & HM MOVES

Lv.	Name	Type	Kind	Pow.	Acc.	PP	Range	Long	DA
TM06	Toxic	Poison	Status	—	90	10	Normal	—	—
TM07	Hail	Ice	Status	—	—	10	Both Sides	—	—
TM10	Hidden Power	Normal	Special	—	100	15	Normal	—	—
TM13	Ice Beam	Ice	Special	95	100	10	Normal	—	—
TM14	Blizzard	Ice	Special	120	70	5	Many Others	—	—
TM15	Hyper Beam	Normal	Special	150	90	5	Normal	—	—
TM17	Protect	Normal	Status	—	—	10	Self	—	—
TM18	Rain Dance	Water	Status	—	—	5	Both Sides	—	—
TM21	Frustration	Normal	Physical	—	100	20	Normal	—	○
TM27	Return	Normal	Physical	—	100	20	Normal	—	○
TM32	Double Team	Normal	Status	—	—	15	Self	—	—
TM40	Aerial Ace	Flying	Physical	60	—	20	Normal	○	○
TM42	Facade	Normal	Physical	70	100	20	Normal	—	○
TM44	Rest	Psychic	Status	—	—	10	Self	—	—
TM45	Attract	Normal	Status	—	100	15	Normal	—	—
TM46	Thief	Dark	Physical	40	100	10	Normal	—	○
TM48	Round	Normal	Special	60	100	15	Normal	—	—
TM49	Echoed Voice	Normal	Special	40	100	15	Normal	—	—
TM55	Scald	Water	Special	80	100	15	Normal	—	—
TM56	Fling	Dark	Physical	—	100	10	Normal	—	—
TM58	Sky Drop	Flying	Physical	60	100	10	Normal	○	○
TM66	Payback	Dark	Physical	50	100	10	Normal	—	○
TM68	Giga Impact	Normal	Physical	150	90	5	Normal	—	○
TM87	Swagger	Normal	Status	—	90	15	Normal	—	—
TM88	Pluck	Flying	Physical	60	100	20	Normal	○	○
TM89	U-turn	Bug	Physical	70	100	20	Normal	—	○
TM90	Substitute	Normal	Status	—	—	10	Self	—	—
HM02	Fly	Flying	Physical	90	95	15	Normal	○	○
HM03	Surf	Water	Special	95	100	15	Adjacent	—	—

MOVES TAUGHT BY PEOPLE

Name	Type	Kind	Pow.	Acc.	PP	Range	Long	DA

MOVES TAUGHT BY MOVE TUTORS FOR SHARDS

Name	Type	Kind	Pow.	Acc.	PP	Range	Long	DA
Uproar	Normal	Special	90	100	10	1 Random	—	—
Seed Bomb	Grass	Physical	80	100	15	Normal	—	—
Gunk Shot	Poison	Physical	120	70	5	Normal	—	—
Icy Wind	Ice	Special	55	95	15	Many Others	—	—
Snore	Normal	Special	40	100	15	Normal	—	—
Knock Off	Dark	Physical	20	100	20	Normal	—	○
Roost	Flying	Status	—	—	10	Self	—	—
Sky Attack	Flying	Physical	140	90	5	Normal	○	—
Tailwind	Flying	Status	—	—	30	Your Side	—	—
Sleep Talk	Normal	Status	—	—	10	Self	—	—

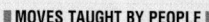

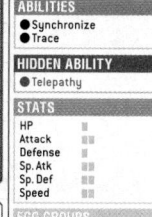

Feeling Pokémon

280 Ralts

- HEIGHT: 1'04"
- WEIGHT: 14.6 lbs.
- GENDER: ♂ / ♀

If its horns capture the warm feelings of people or Pokémon, its body warms up slightly.

Same form for ♂ / ♀

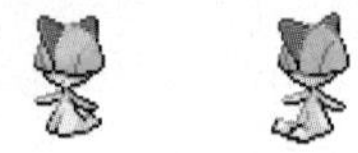

TYPE Psychic

ABILITIES

- Synchronize
- Trace

HIDDEN ABILITY

- Telepathy

STATS

HP
Attack
Defense
Sp. Atk
Sp. Def
Speed

EGG GROUPS

Amorphous

ITEMS SOMETIMES HELD

- None

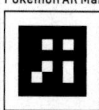

EVOLUTION

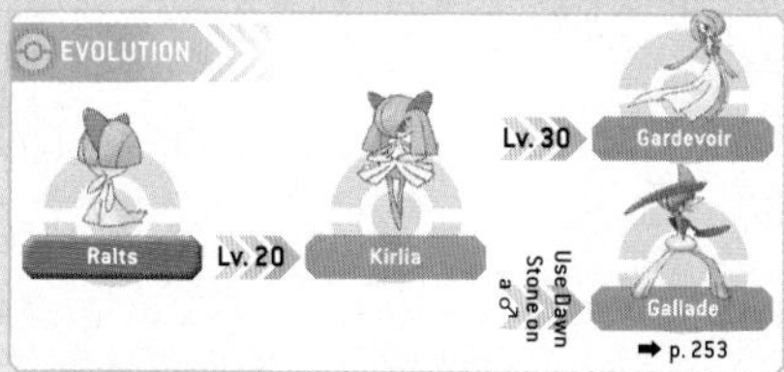
Ralts
Lv. 20
Kirlia
Lv. 30
Gardevoir
Use Dawn Stone on a ♂
Gallade

➡ p. 253

HOW TO OBTAIN

Pokémon Black Version 2	Trade Pokémon during a date with Yancy or Curtis (third time)
Pokémon White Version 2	Trade Pokémon during a date with Yancy or Curtis (third time)

HOW TO OBTAIN FROM OTHER GAMES

Pokémon Platinum Version	Route 208

—

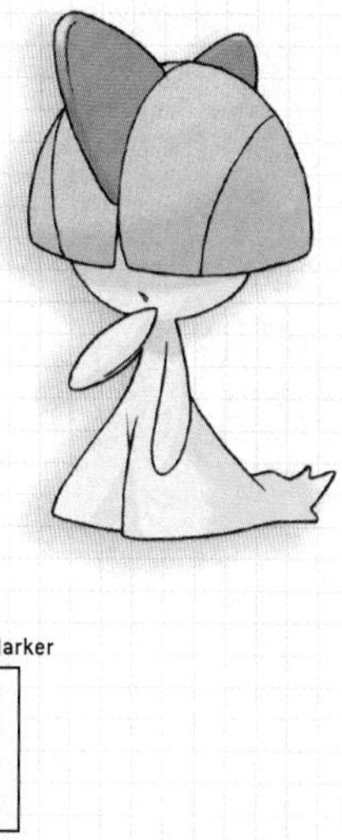

Pokémon AR Marker

LEVEL-UP AND LEARNED MOVES

Lv.	Name	Type	Kind	Pow.	Acc.	PP	Range	Long	DA
1	Growl	Normal	Status	—	100	40	Many Others	—	—
6	Confusion	Psychic	Special	50	100	25	Normal	—	—
10	Double Team	Normal	Status	—	—	15	Self	—	—
12	Teleport	Psychic	Status	—	—	20	Self	—	—
17	Lucky Chant	Normal	Status	—	—	30	Your Side	—	—
21	Magical Leaf	Grass	Special	60	—	20	Normal	—	—
23	Heal Pulse	Psychic	Status	—	—	10	Normal	○	—
28	Calm Mind	Psychic	Status	—	—	20	Self	—	—
32	Psychic	Psychic	Special	90	100	10	Normal	—	—
34	Imprison	Psychic	Status	—	—	10	Self	—	—
39	Future Sight	Psychic	Special	100	100	10	Normal	—	—
43	Charm	Normal	Status	—	100	20	Normal	—	—
45	Hypnosis	Psychic	Status	—	60	20	Normal	—	—
50	Dream Eater	Psychic	Special	100	100	15	Normal	—	—
54	Stored Power	Psychic	Special	20	100	10	Normal	—	—

TM & HM MOVES

Lv.	Name	Type	Kind	Pow.	Acc.	PP	Range	Long	DA
TM03	Psyshock	Psychic	Special	80	100	10	Normal	—	—
TM04	Calm Mind	Psychic	Status	—	—	20	Self	—	—
TM06	Toxic	Poison	Status	—	90	10	Normal	—	—
TM10	Hidden Power	Normal	Special	—	100	15	Normal	—	—
TM11	Sunny Day	Fire	Status	—	—	5	Both Sides	—	—
TM12	Taunt	Dark	Status	—	100	20	Normal	—	—
TM16	Light Screen	Psychic	Status	—	—	30	Your Side	—	—
TM17	Protect	Normal	Status	—	—	10	Self	—	—
TM18	Rain Dance	Water	Status	—	—	5	Both Sides	—	—
TM19	Telekinesis	Psychic	Status	—	—	15	Normal	—	—
TM20	Safeguard	Normal	Status	—	—	25	Your Side	—	—
TM21	Frustration	Normal	Physical	—	100	20	Normal	—	○
TM24	Thunderbolt	Electric	Special	95	100	15	Normal	—	—
TM27	Return	Normal	Physical	—	100	20	Normal	—	○
TM29	Psychic	Psychic	Special	90	100	10	Normal	—	—
TM30	Shadow Ball	Ghost	Special	80	100	15	Normal	—	—
TM32	Double Team	Normal	Status	—	—	15	Self	—	—
TM33	Reflect	Psychic	Status	—	—	20	Your Side	—	—
TM41	Torment	Dark	Status	—	100	15	Normal	—	—
TM42	Facade	Normal	Physical	70	100	20	Normal	—	○
TM44	Rest	Psychic	Status	—	—	10	Self	—	—
TM45	Attract	Normal	Status	—	100	15	Normal	—	—
TM46	Thief	Dark	Physical	40	100	10	Normal	—	○
TM48	Round	Normal	Special	60	100	15	Normal	—	—
TM49	Echoed Voice	Normal	Special	40	100	15	Normal	—	—
TM51	Ally Switch	Psychic	Status	—	—	15	Self	—	—
TM56	Fling	Dark	Physical	—	100	10	Normal	—	—
TM57	Charge Beam	Electric	Special	50	90	10	Normal	—	—
TM61	Will-O-Wisp	Fire	Status	—	75	15	Normal	—	—
TM70	Flash	Normal	Status	—	100	20	Normal	—	—
TM73	Thunder Wave	Electric	Status	—	100	20	Normal	—	—
TM77	Psych Up	Normal	Status	—	—	10	Normal	—	—
TM85	Dream Eater	Psychic	Special	100	100	15	Normal	—	—
TM86	Grass Knot	Grass	Special	—	100	20	Normal	—	○
TM87	Swagger	Normal	Status	—	90	15	Normal	—	—
TM90	Substitute	Normal	Status	—	—	10	Self	—	—
TM92	Trick Room	Psychic	Status	—	—	5	Both Sides	—	—

MOVES TAUGHT BY PEOPLE

Name	Type	Kind	Pow.	Acc.	PP	Range	Long	DA

MOVES TAUGHT BY MOVE TUTORS FOR SHARDS

Name	Type	Kind	Pow.	Acc.	PP	Range	Long	DA
Signal Beam	Bug	Special	75	100	15	Normal	—	—
Fire Punch	Fire	Physical	75	100	15	Normal	—	○
ThunderPunch	Electric	Physical	75	100	15	Normal	—	○
Ice Punch	Ice	Physical	75	100	15	Normal	—	○
Magic Coat	Psychic	Status	—	—	15	Self	—	—
Hyper Voice	Normal	Special	90	100	10	Many Others	—	—
Icy Wind	Ice	Special	55	95	15	Many Others	—	—
Zen Headbutt	Psychic	Physical	80	90	15	Normal	—	○
Snore	Normal	Special	40	100	15	Normal	—	—
Pain Split	Normal	Status	—	—	20	Normal	—	—
Helping Hand	Normal	Status	—	—	20	1 Ally	—	—
Magic Room	Psychic	Status	—	—	10	Both Sides	—	—
Wonder Room	Psychic	Status	—	—	10	Both Sides	—	—
Recycle	Normal	Status	—	—	10	Self	—	—
Trick	Psychic	Status	—	100	10	Normal	—	—
Sleep Talk	Normal	Status	—	—	10	Self	—	—
Skill Swap	Psychic	Status	—	—	10	Normal	—	—
Snatch	Dark	Status	—	—	10	Self	—	—

EGG MOVES

Name	Type	Kind	Pow.	Acc.	PP	Range	Long	DA
Disable	Normal	Status	—	100	20	Normal	—	—
Mean Look	Normal	Status	—	—	5	Normal	—	—
Memento	Dark	Status	—	100	10	Normal	—	—
Destiny Bond	Ghost	Status	—	—	5	Self	—	—
Grudge	Ghost	Status	—	—	5	Self	—	—
Shadow Sneak	Ghost	Physical	40	100	30	Normal	—	○
Confuse Ray	Ghost	Status	—	100	10	Normal	—	—
Encore	Normal	Status	—	100	5	Normal	—	—
Synchronoise	Psychic	Special	70	100	15	Adjacent	—	—
Skill Swap	Psychic	Status	—	—	10	Normal	—	—

281 Kirlia

281 Kirlia

Emotion Pokémon

● HEIGHT: 2'07"
● WEIGHT: 44.5 lbs.
● GENDER: ♂ / ♀

If its Trainer becomes happy, it overflows with energy, dancing joyously while spinning about.

Same form for ♂ / ♀

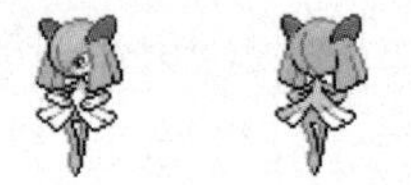

TYPE Psychic

ABILITIES
● Synchronize
● Trace

HIDDEN ABILITY
● Telepathy

STATS
HP
Attack
Defense
Sp. Atk
Sp. Def
Speed

EGG GROUPS
Amorphous

ITEMS SOMETIMES HELD
● None

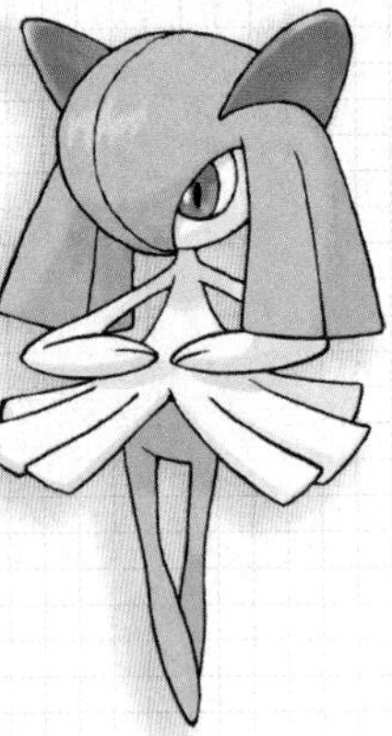

Pokémon AR Marker

EVOLUTION

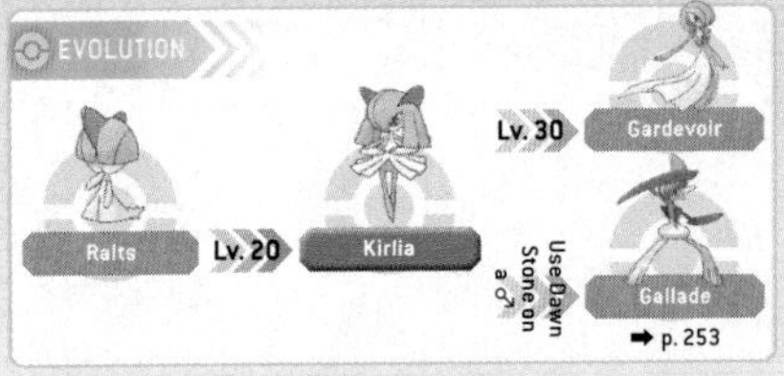

Ralts
Lv. 20
Kirlia
Lv. 30
Gardevoir
Use Dawn Stone on a ♂
Gallade

➡ p. 253

HOW TO OBTAIN

Pokémon Black Version 2	Level up the Ralts you receive from Yancy or Curtis to Lv. 20
Pokémon White Version 2	Level up the Ralts you receive from Yancy or Curtis to Lv. 20

HOW TO OBTAIN FROM OTHER GAMES

Pokémon Platinum Version	Route 212, Hearthome City side
—	

LEVEL-UP AND LEARNED MOVES

Lv.	Name	Type	Kind	Pow.	Acc.	PP	Range	Long	DA
1	Growl	Normal	Status	—	100	40	Many Others	—	—
1	Confusion	Psychic	Special	50	100	25	Normal	—	—
1	Double Team	Normal	Status	—	—	15	Self	—	—
1	Teleport	Psychic	Status	—	—	20	Self	—	—
6	Confusion	Psychic	Special	50	100	25	Normal	—	—
10	Double Team	Normal	Status	—	—	15	Self	—	—
12	Teleport	Psychic	Status	—	—	20	Self	—	—
17	Lucky Chant	Normal	Status	—	—	30	Your Side	—	—
22	Magical Leaf	Grass	Special	60	—	20	Normal	—	—
25	Heal Pulse	Psychic	Status	—	—	10	Normal	○	—
31	Calm Mind	Psychic	Status	—	—	20	Self	—	—
36	Psychic	Psychic	Special	90	100	10	Normal	—	—
39	Imprison	Psychic	Status	—	—	10	Self	—	—
45	Future Sight	Psychic	Special	100	100	10	Normal	—	—
50	Charm	Normal	Status	—	100	20	Normal	—	—
53	Hypnosis	Psychic	Status	—	60	20	Normal	—	—
59	Dream Eater	Psychic	Special	100	100	15	Normal	—	—
64	Stored Power	Psychic	Special	20	100	10	Normal	—	—

TM & HM MOVES

Lv.	Name	Type	Kind	Pow.	Acc.	PP	Range	Long	DA
TM03	Psyshock	Psychic	Special	80	100	10	Normal	—	—
TM04	Calm Mind	Psychic	Status	—	—	20	Self	—	—
TM06	Toxic	Poison	Status	—	90	10	Normal	—	—
TM10	Hidden Power	Normal	Special	—	100	15	Normal	—	—
TM11	Sunny Day	Fire	Status	—	—	5	Both Sides	—	—
TM12	Taunt	Dark	Status	—	100	20	Normal	—	—
TM16	Light Screen	Psychic	Status	—	—	30	Your Side	—	—
TM17	Protect	Normal	Status	—	—	10	Self	—	—
TM18	Rain Dance	Water	Status	—	—	5	Both Sides	—	—
TM19	Telekinesis	Psychic	Status	—	—	15	Normal	—	—
TM20	Safeguard	Normal	Status	—	—	25	Your Side	—	—
TM21	Frustration	Normal	Physical	—	100	20	Normal	—	○
TM24	Thunderbolt	Electric	Special	95	100	15	Normal	—	—
TM27	Return	Normal	Physical	—	100	20	Normal	—	○
TM29	Psychic	Psychic	Special	90	100	10	Normal	—	—
TM30	Shadow Ball	Ghost	Special	80	100	15	Normal	—	—
TM32	Double Team	Normal	Status	—	—	15	Self	—	—
TM33	Reflect	Psychic	Status	—	—	20	Your Side	—	—
TM41	Torment	Dark	Status	—	100	15	Normal	—	—
TM42	Facade	Normal	Physical	70	100	20	Normal	—	○
TM44	Rest	Psychic	Status	—	—	10	Self	—	—
TM45	Attract	Normal	Status	—	100	15	Normal	—	—
TM46	Thief	Dark	Physical	40	100	10	Normal	—	○
TM48	Round	Normal	Special	60	100	15	Normal	—	—
TM49	Echoed Voice	Normal	Special	40	100	15	Normal	—	—
TM51	Ally Switch	Psychic	Status	—	—	15	Self	—	—
TM56	Fling	Dark	Physical	—	100	10	Normal	—	—
TM57	Charge Beam	Electric	Special	50	90	10	Normal	—	—
TM61	Will-O-Wisp	Fire	Status	—	75	15	Normal	—	—
TM70	Flash	Normal	Status	—	100	20	Normal	—	—
TM73	Thunder Wave	Electric	Status	—	100	20	Normal	—	—
TM77	Psych Up	Normal	Status	—	—	10	Normal	—	—
TM85	Dream Eater	Psychic	Special	100	100	15	Normal	—	—
TM86	Grass Knot	Grass	Special	—	100	20	Normal	—	○
TM87	Swagger	Normal	Status	—	90	15	Normal	—	—
TM90	Substitute	Normal	Status	—	—	10	Self	—	—
TM92	Trick Room	Psychic	Status	—	—	5	Both Sides	—	—

MOVES TAUGHT BY PEOPLE

Name	Type	Kind	Pow.	Acc.	PP	Range	Long	DA

MOVES TAUGHT BY MOVE TUTORS FOR SHARDS

Name	Type	Kind	Pow.	Acc.	PP	Range	Long	DA
Signal Beam	Bug	Special	75	100	15	Normal	—	—
Fire Punch	Fire	Physical	75	100	15	Normal	—	○
ThunderPunch	Electric	Physical	75	100	15	Normal	—	○
Ice Punch	Ice	Physical	75	100	15	Normal	—	○
Magic Coat	Psychic	Status	—	—	15	Self	—	—
Hyper Voice	Normal	Special	90	100	10	Many Others	—	—
Icy Wind	Ice	Special	55	95	15	Many Others	—	—
Zen Headbutt	Psychic	Physical	80	90	15	Normal	—	○
Snore	Normal	Special	40	100	15	Normal	—	—
Pain Split	Normal	Status	—	—	20	Normal	—	—
Helping Hand	Normal	Status	—	—	20	1 Ally	—	—
Magic Room	Psychic	Status	—	—	10	Both Sides	—	—
Wonder Room	Psychic	Status	—	—	10	Both Sides	—	—
Recycle	Normal	Status	—	—	10	Self	—	—
Trick	Psychic	Status	—	100	10	Normal	—	—
Sleep Talk	Normal	Status	—	—	10	Self	—	—
Skill Swap	Psychic	Status	—	—	10	Normal	—	—
Snatch	Dark	Status	—	—	10	Self	—	—

282 Gardevoir

282 Gardevoir

Embrace Pokémon

● HEIGHT: 5'03"
● WEIGHT: 106.7 lbs.
● GENDER: ♂ / ♀

To protect its Trainer, it will expend all its psychic power to create a small black hole.

Same form for ♂ / ♀

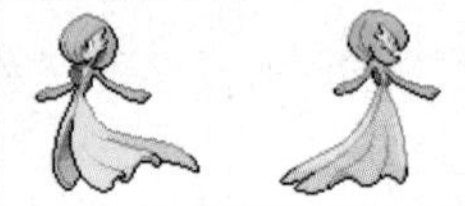

TYPE Psychic

ABILITIES
● Synchronize
● Trace

HIDDEN ABILITY
● Telepathy

STATS
HP
Attack
Defense
Sp. Atk
Sp. Def
Speed

EGG GROUPS
Amorphous

ITEMS SOMETIMES HELD
● None

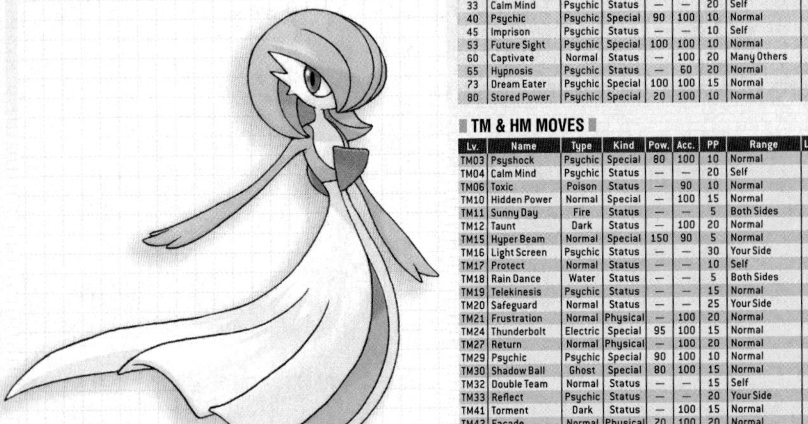

Pokémon AR Marker

EVOLUTION

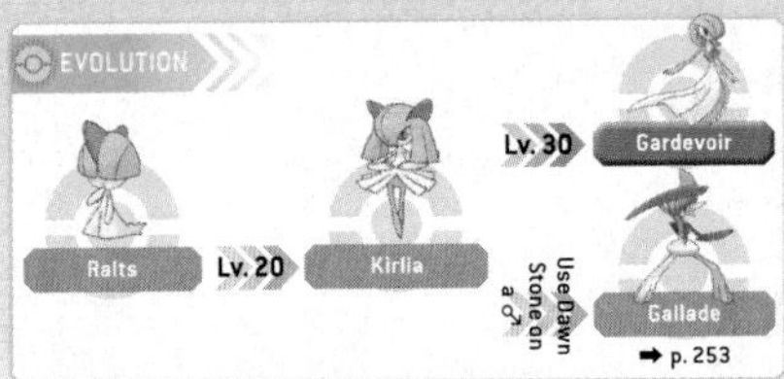

Ralts
Lv. 20
Kirlia
Lv. 30
Gardevoir
Use Dawn Stone on a ♂
Gallade

➡ p. 253

HOW TO OBTAIN

Pokémon Black Version 2	Evolve the Ralts you received from Yancy or Curtis into Kirlia, then level up Kirlia to Lv. 30
Pokémon White Version 2	Evolve the Ralts you received from Yancy or Curtis into Kirlia, then level up Kirlia to Lv. 30

HOW TO OBTAIN FROM OTHER GAMES

—

—

LEVEL-UP AND LEARNED MOVES

Lv.	Name	Type	Kind	Pow.	Acc.	PP	Range	Long	DA
1	Healing Wish	Psychic	Status	—	—	10	Self	—	—
1	Growl	Normal	Status	—	100	40	Many Others	—	—
1	Confusion	Psychic	Special	50	100	25	Normal	—	—
1	Double Team	Normal	Status	—	—	15	Self	—	—
1	Teleport	Psychic	Status	—	—	20	Self	—	—
6	Confusion	Psychic	Special	50	100	25	Normal	—	—
10	Double Team	Normal	Status	—	—	15	Self	—	—
12	Teleport	Psychic	Status	—	—	20	Self	—	—
17	Wish	Normal	Status	—	—	10	Self	—	—
22	Magical Leaf	Grass	Special	60	—	20	Normal	—	—
25	Heal Pulse	Psychic	Status	—	—	10	Normal	○	—
33	Calm Mind	Psychic	Status	—	—	20	Self	—	—
40	Psychic	Psychic	Special	90	100	10	Normal	—	—
45	Imprison	Psychic	Status	—	—	10	Self	—	—
53	Future Sight	Psychic	Special	100	100	10	Normal	—	—
60	Captivate	Normal	Status	—	100	20	Many Others	—	—
65	Hypnosis	Psychic	Status	—	60	20	Normal	—	—
73	Dream Eater	Psychic	Special	100	100	15	Normal	—	—
80	Stored Power	Psychic	Special	20	100	10	Normal	—	—

TM & HM MOVES

Lv.	Name	Type	Kind	Pow.	Acc.	PP	Range	Long	DA
TM03	Psyshock	Psychic	Special	80	100	10	Normal	—	—
TM04	Calm Mind	Psychic	Status	—	—	20	Self	—	—
TM06	Toxic	Poison	Status	—	90	10	Normal	—	—
TM10	Hidden Power	Normal	Special	—	100	15	Normal	—	—
TM11	Sunny Day	Fire	Status	—	—	5	Both Sides	—	—
TM12	Taunt	Dark	Status	—	100	20	Normal	—	—
TM15	Hyper Beam	Normal	Special	150	90	5	Normal	—	—
TM16	Light Screen	Psychic	Status	—	—	30	Your Side	—	—
TM17	Protect	Normal	Status	—	—	10	Self	—	—
TM18	Rain Dance	Water	Status	—	—	5	Both Sides	—	—
TM19	Telekinesis	Psychic	Status	—	—	15	Normal	—	—
TM20	Safeguard	Normal	Status	—	—	25	Your Side	—	—
TM21	Frustration	Normal	Physical	—	100	20	Normal	—	○
TM24	Thunderbolt	Electric	Special	95	100	15	Normal	—	—
TM27	Return	Normal	Physical	—	100	20	Normal	—	○
TM29	Psychic	Psychic	Special	90	100	10	Normal	—	—
TM30	Shadow Ball	Ghost	Special	80	100	15	Normal	—	—
TM32	Double Team	Normal	Status	—	—	15	Self	—	—
TM33	Reflect	Psychic	Status	—	—	20	Your Side	—	—
TM41	Torment	Dark	Status	—	100	15	Normal	—	—
TM42	Facade	Normal	Physical	70	100	20	Normal	—	○
TM44	Rest	Psychic	Status	—	—	10	Self	—	—
TM45	Attract	Normal	Status	—	100	15	Normal	—	—
TM46	Thief	Dark	Physical	40	100	10	Normal	—	○
TM48	Round	Normal	Special	60	100	15	Normal	—	—
TM49	Echoed Voice	Normal	Special	40	100	15	Normal	—	—
TM51	Ally Switch	Psychic	Status	—	—	15	Self	—	—
TM52	Focus Blast	Fighting	Special	120	70	5	Normal	—	—
TM53	Energy Ball	Grass	Special	80	100	10	Normal	—	—
TM56	Fling	Dark	Physical	—	100	10	Normal	—	—
TM57	Charge Beam	Electric	Special	50	90	10	Normal	—	—
TM61	Will-O-Wisp	Fire	Status	—	75	15	Normal	—	—
TM68	Giga Impact	Normal	Physical	150	90	5	Normal	—	○
TM70	Flash	Normal	Status	—	100	20	Normal	—	—
TM73	Thunder Wave	Electric	Status	—	100	20	Normal	—	—
TM77	Psych Up	Normal	Status	—	—	10	Normal	—	—
TM85	Dream Eater	Psychic	Special	100	100	15	Normal	—	—
TM86	Grass Knot	Grass	Special	—	100	20	Normal	—	○
TM87	Swagger	Normal	Status	—	90	15	Normal	—	—
TM90	Substitute	Normal	Status	—	—	10	Self	—	—
TM92	Trick Room	Psychic	Status	—	—	5	Both Sides	—	—

MOVES TAUGHT BY PEOPLE

Name	Type	Kind	Pow.	Acc.	PP	Range	Long	DA

MOVES TAUGHT BY MOVE TUTORS FOR SHARDS

Name	Type	Kind	Pow.	Acc.	PP	Range	Long	DA
Signal Beam	Bug	Special	75	100	15	Normal	—	—
Fire Punch	Fire	Physical	75	100	15	Normal	—	○
ThunderPunch	Electric	Physical	75	100	15	Normal	—	○
Ice Punch	Ice	Physical	75	100	15	Normal	—	○
Magic Coat	Psychic	Status	—	—	15	Self	—	—
Hyper Voice	Normal	Special	90	100	10	Many Others	—	—
Icy Wind	Ice	Special	55	95	15	Many Others	—	—
Zen Headbutt	Psychic	Physical	80	90	15	Normal	—	○
Snore	Normal	Special	40	100	15	Normal	—	—
Heal Bell	Normal	Status	—	—	5	Your Party	—	—
Pain Split	Normal	Status	—	—	20	Normal	—	—
Helping Hand	Normal	Status	—	—	20	1 Ally	—	—
Magic Room	Psychic	Status	—	—	10	Both Sides	—	—
Wonder Room	Psychic	Status	—	—	10	Both Sides	—	—
Recycle	Normal	Status	—	—	10	Self	—	—
Trick	Psychic	Status	—	100	10	Normal	—	—
Sleep Talk	Normal	Status	—	—	10	Self	—	—
Skill Swap	Psychic	Status	—	—	10	Normal	—	—
Snatch	Dark	Status	—	—	10	Self	—	—

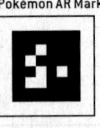

283 Surskit

Pond Skater Pokémon

TYPE: Bug / Water

ABILITY: Swift Swim

HIDDEN ABILITY: Rain Dish

- HEIGHT: 1'08"
- WEIGHT: 3.7 lbs.
- GENDER: ♂/♀

It appears as if it is skating on water. It draws prey with a sweet scent from the tip of its head.

Same form for ♂/♀

STATS
HP / Attack / Defense / Sp. Atk / Sp. Def / Speed

EGG GROUPS: Water ❶ /Bug

ITEMS SOMETIMES HELD: None

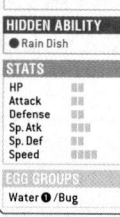

Pokémon AR Marker

EVOLUTION

Surskit → Lv. 22 → Masquerain

HOW TO OBTAIN

Pokémon Black Version 2	Catch a Masquerain, leave it at the Pokémon Day Care, and hatch the Egg that is found
Pokémon White Version 2	Catch a Masquerain, leave it at the Pokémon Day Care, and hatch the Egg that is found

HOW TO OBTAIN FROM OTHER GAMES

Pokémon Platinum Version	Route 229 (water surface)

LEVEL-UP AND LEARNED MOVES

Lv.	Name	Type	Kind	Pow.	Acc.	PP	Range	Long	DA
1	Bubble	Water	Special	20	100	30	Many Others	—	—
7	Quick Attack	Normal	Physical	40	100	30	Normal	—	○
13	Sweet Scent	Normal	Status	—	100	20	Many Others	—	—
19	Water Sport	Water	Status	—	—	15	Both Sides	—	—
25	BubbleBeam	Water	Special	65	100	20	Normal	—	—
31	Agility	Psychic	Status	—	—	30	Self	—	—
37	Mist	Ice	Status	—	—	30	Your Side	—	—
37	Haze	Ice	Status	—	—	30	Both Sides	—	—
43	Baton Pass	Normal	Status	—	—	40	Self	—	—

TM & HM MOVES

Lv.	Name	Type	Kind	Pow.	Acc.	PP	Range	Long	DA
TM06	Toxic	Poison	Status	—	90	10	Normal	—	—
TM10	Hidden Power	Normal	Special	—	100	15	Normal	—	—
TM11	Sunny Day	Fire	Status	—	—	5	Both Sides	—	—
TM13	Ice Beam	Ice	Special	95	100	10	Normal	—	—
TM14	Blizzard	Ice	Special	120	70	5	Many Others	—	—
TM17	Protect	Normal	Status	—	—	10	Self	—	—
TM18	Rain Dance	Water	Status	—	—	5	Both Sides	—	—
TM21	Frustration	Normal	Physical	—	100	20	Normal	—	○
TM22	SolarBeam	Grass	Special	120	100	10	Normal	—	—
TM27	Return	Normal	Physical	—	100	20	Normal	—	○
TM30	Shadow Ball	Ghost	Special	80	100	15	Normal	—	—
TM32	Double Team	Normal	Status	—	—	15	Self	—	—
TM42	Facade	Normal	Physical	70	100	20	Normal	—	○
TM44	Rest	Psychic	Status	—	—	10	Self	—	—
TM45	Attract	Normal	Status	—	100	15	Normal	—	—
TM46	Thief	Dark	Physical	40	100	10	Normal	—	○
TM48	Round	Normal	Special	60	100	15	Normal	—	—
TM55	Scald	Water	Special	80	100	15	Normal	—	—
TM70	Flash	Normal	Status	—	100	20	Normal	—	—
TM76	Struggle Bug	Bug	Special	30	100	20	Many Others	—	—
TM77	Psych Up	Normal	Status	—	—	10	Normal	—	—
TM87	Swagger	Normal	Status	—	90	15	Normal	—	—
TM90	Substitute	Normal	Status	—	—	10	Self	—	—

MOVES TAUGHT BY PEOPLE

Name	Type	Kind	Pow.	Acc.	PP	Range	Long	DA

MOVES TAUGHT BY MOVE TUTORS FOR SHARDS

Name	Type	Kind	Pow.	Acc.	PP	Range	Long	DA
Bug Bite	Bug	Physical	60	100	20	Normal	—	○
Signal Beam	Bug	Special	75	100	15	Normal	—	—
Icy Wind	Ice	Special	55	95	15	Many Others	—	—
Snore	Normal	Special	40	100	15	Normal	—	—
Giga Drain	Grass	Special	75	100	10	Normal	—	—
Sleep Talk	Normal	Status	—	—	10	Self	—	—

EGG MOVES

Name	Type	Kind	Pow.	Acc.	PP	Range	Long	DA
Foresight	Normal	Status	—	—	40	Normal	—	—
Mud Shot	Ground	Special	55	95	15	Normal	—	—
Psybeam	Psychic	Special	65	100	20	Normal	—	—
Hydro Pump	Water	Special	120	80	5	Normal	—	—
Mind Reader	Normal	Status	—	—	5	Normal	—	—
Signal Beam	Bug	Special	75	100	15	Normal	—	—
Bug Bite	Bug	Physical	60	100	20	Normal	—	○
Aqua Jet	Water	Physical	40	100	20	Normal	—	○
Endure	Normal	Status	—	—	10	Self	—	—

---

284 Masquerain

Eyeball Pokémon

TYPE: Bug / Flying

ABILITY: Intimidate

HIDDEN ABILITY: Unnerve

- HEIGHT: 2'07"
- WEIGHT: 7.9 lbs.
- GENDER: ♂/♀

Its antennae have eye patterns on them. Its four wings enable it to hover and fly in any direction.

Same form for ♂/♀

STATS
HP / Attack / Defense / Sp. Atk / Sp. Def / Speed

EGG GROUPS: Water ❶ /Bug

ITEMS SOMETIMES HELD: SilverPowder

Pokémon AR Marker

EVOLUTION

Surskit → Lv. 22 → Masquerain

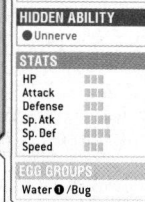

HOW TO OBTAIN

Pokémon Black Version 2	Route 11 (mass outbreak)
Pokémon White Version 2	Route 11 (mass outbreak)

HOW TO OBTAIN FROM OTHER GAMES

—	
—	

LEVEL-UP AND LEARNED MOVES

Lv.	Name	Type	Kind	Pow.	Acc.	PP	Range	Long	DA
1	Ominous Wind	Ghost	Special	60	100	5	Normal	—	—
1	Bubble	Water	Special	20	100	30	Many Others	—	—
1	Quick Attack	Normal	Physical	40	100	30	Normal	—	○
1	Sweet Scent	Normal	Status	—	100	20	Many Others	—	—
1	Water Sport	Water	Status	—	—	15	Both Sides	—	—
7	Quick Attack	Normal	Physical	40	100	30	Normal	—	○
13	Sweet Scent	Normal	Status	—	100	20	Many Others	—	—
19	Water Sport	Water	Status	—	—	15	Both Sides	—	—
22	Gust	Flying	Special	40	100	35	Normal	○	—
26	Scary Face	Normal	Status	—	100	10	Normal	—	—
33	Stun Spore	Grass	Status	—	75	30	Normal	—	—
40	Silver Wind	Bug	Special	60	100	5	Normal	—	—
47	Air Slash	Flying	Special	75	95	20	Normal	○	—
54	Whirlwind	Normal	Status	—	100	20	Normal	—	—
61	Bug Buzz	Bug	Special	90	100	10	Normal	—	—
68	Quiver Dance	Bug	Status	—	—	20	Self	—	—

TM & HM MOVES

Lv.	Name	Type	Kind	Pow.	Acc.	PP	Range	Long	DA
TM06	Toxic	Poison	Status	—	90	10	Normal	—	—
TM10	Hidden Power	Normal	Special	—	100	15	Normal	—	—
TM11	Sunny Day	Fire	Status	—	—	5	Both Sides	—	—
TM13	Ice Beam	Ice	Special	95	100	10	Normal	—	—
TM14	Blizzard	Ice	Special	120	70	5	Many Others	—	—
TM15	Hyper Beam	Normal	Special	150	90	5	Normal	—	—
TM17	Protect	Normal	Status	—	—	10	Self	—	—
TM18	Rain Dance	Water	Status	—	—	5	Both Sides	—	—
TM21	Frustration	Normal	Physical	—	100	20	Normal	—	○
TM22	SolarBeam	Grass	Special	120	100	10	Normal	—	—
TM27	Return	Normal	Physical	—	100	20	Normal	—	○
TM30	Shadow Ball	Ghost	Special	80	100	15	Normal	—	—
TM32	Double Team	Normal	Status	—	—	15	Self	—	—
TM40	Aerial Ace	Flying	Physical	60	—	20	Normal	○	○
TM42	Facade	Normal	Physical	70	100	20	Normal	—	○
TM44	Rest	Psychic	Status	—	—	10	Self	—	—
TM45	Attract	Normal	Status	—	100	15	Normal	—	—
TM46	Thief	Dark	Physical	40	100	10	Normal	—	○
TM48	Round	Normal	Special	60	100	15	Normal	—	—
TM53	Energy Ball	Grass	Special	80	100	10	Normal	—	—
TM55	Scald	Water	Special	80	100	15	Normal	—	—
TM68	Giga Impact	Normal	Physical	150	90	5	Normal	—	○
TM70	Flash	Normal	Status	—	100	20	Normal	—	—
TM76	Struggle Bug	Bug	Special	30	100	20	Many Others	—	—
TM77	Psych Up	Normal	Status	—	—	10	Normal	—	—
TM87	Swagger	Normal	Status	—	90	15	Normal	—	—
TM89	U-turn	Bug	Physical	70	100	20	Normal	—	○
TM90	Substitute	Normal	Status	—	—	10	Self	—	—

MOVES TAUGHT BY PEOPLE

Name	Type	Kind	Pow.	Acc.	PP	Range	Long	DA

MOVES TAUGHT BY MOVE TUTORS FOR SHARDS

Name	Type	Kind	Pow.	Acc.	PP	Range	Long	DA
Bug Bite	Bug	Physical	60	100	20	Normal	—	○
Signal Beam	Bug	Special	75	100	15	Normal	—	—
Icy Wind	Ice	Special	55	95	15	Many Others	—	—
Snore	Normal	Special	40	100	15	Normal	—	—
Roost	Flying	Status	—	—	10	Self	—	—
Giga Drain	Grass	Special	75	100	10	Normal	—	—
Tailwind	Flying	Status	—	—	30	Your Side	—	—
Sleep Talk	Normal	Status	—	—	10	Self	—	—

...oom Pokémon

...oomish

...bs.

♀

...ores from the top of its head. These spores cause pain all over if inhaled.

Same form for ♂ / ♀

TYPE Grass

ABILITIES
- Effect Spore
- Poison Heal

HIDDEN ABILITY
- Quick Feet

STATS

HP
Attack
Defense
Sp. Atk
Sp. Def
Speed

EGG GROUPS

Fairy/Grass

ITEMS SOMETIMES HELD
- None

EVOLUTION

Shroomish → Lv. 23 → Breloom

HOW TO OBTAIN

Pokémon Black Version 2	Catch a Breloom, leave it at the Pokémon Day Care, and hatch the Egg that is found
Pokémon White Version 2	Catch a Breloom, leave it at the Pokémon Day Care, and hatch the Egg that is found

HOW TO OBTAIN FROM OTHER GAMES

Pokémon Black Version	Route 11 (mass outbreak)
	—

Pokémon AR Marker

LEVEL-UP AND LEARNED MOVES

Lv.	Name	Type	Kind	Pow.	Acc.	PP	Range	Long	DA
1	Absorb	Grass	Special	20	100	25	Normal	—	—
5	Tackle	Normal	Physical	50	100	35	Normal	—	○
9	Stun Spore	Grass	Status	—	75	30	Normal	—	—
13	Leech Seed	Grass	Status	—	90	10	Normal	—	—
17	Mega Drain	Grass	Special	40	100	15	Normal	—	—
21	Headbutt	Normal	Physical	70	100	15	Normal	—	○
25	PoisonPowder	Poison	Status	—	75	35	Normal	—	—
29	Worry Seed	Grass	Status	—	100	10	Normal	—	—
33	Growth	Normal	Status	—	—	40	Self	—	—
37	Giga Drain	Grass	Special	75	100	10	Normal	—	—
41	Seed Bomb	Grass	Physical	80	100	15	Normal	—	—
45	Spore	Grass	Status	—	100	15	Normal	—	—

TM & HM MOVES

Lv.	Name	Type	Kind	Pow.	Acc.	PP	Range	Long	DA
TM06	Toxic	Poison	Status	—	90	10	Normal	—	—
TM09	Venoshock	Poison	Special	65	100	10	Normal	—	—
TM10	Hidden Power	Normal	Special	—	100	15	Normal	—	—
TM11	Sunny Day	Fire	Status	—	—	5	Both Sides	—	—
TM17	Protect	Normal	Status	—	—	10	Self	—	—
TM20	Safeguard	Normal	Status	—	—	25	Your Side	—	—
TM21	Frustration	Normal	Physical	—	100	20	Normal	—	○
TM22	SolarBeam	Grass	Special	120	100	10	Normal	—	—
TM27	Return	Normal	Physical	—	100	20	Normal	—	○
TM32	Double Team	Normal	Status	—	—	15	Self	—	—
TM36	Sludge Bomb	Poison	Special	90	100	10	Normal	—	—
TM42	Facade	Normal	Physical	70	100	20	Normal	—	○
TM44	Rest	Psychic	Status	—	—	10	Self	—	—
TM45	Attract	Normal	Status	—	100	15	Normal	—	—
TM48	Round	Normal	Special	60	100	15	Normal	—	—
TM53	Energy Ball	Grass	Special	80	100	10	Normal	—	—
TM54	False Swipe	Normal	Physical	40	100	40	Normal	—	○
TM70	Flash	Normal	Status	—	100	20	Normal	—	—
TM75	Swords Dance	Normal	Status	—	—	30	Self	—	—
TM86	Grass Knot	Grass	Special	—	100	20	Normal	—	○
TM87	Swagger	Normal	Status	—	90	15	Normal	—	—
TM90	Substitute	Normal	Status	—	—	10	Self	—	—

MOVES TAUGHT BY PEOPLE

Name	Type	Kind	Pow.	Acc.	PP	Range	Long	DA

MOVES TAUGHT BY MOVE TUTORS FOR SHARDS

Name	Type	Kind	Pow.	Acc.	PP	Range	Long	DA
Seed Bomb	Grass	Physical	80	100	15	Normal	—	—
Snore	Normal	Special	40	100	15	Normal	—	—
Synthesis	Grass	Status	—	—	5	Self	—	—
Giga Drain	Grass	Special	75	100	10	Normal	—	—
Drain Punch	Fighting	Physical	75	100	10	Normal	—	○
Worry Seed	Grass	Status	—	100	10	Normal	—	—
Helping Hand	Normal	Status	—	—	20	1 Ally	—	—
Sleep Talk	Normal	Status	—	—	10	Self	—	—
Snatch	Dark	Status	—	—	10	Self	—	—

EGG MOVES

Name	Type	Kind	Pow.	Acc.	PP	Range	Long	DA
Fake Tears	Dark	Status	—	100	20	Normal	—	—
Charm	Normal	Status	—	100	20	Normal	—	—
Helping Hand	Normal	Status	—	—	20	1 Ally	—	—
Worry Seed	Grass	Status	—	100	10	Normal	—	—
Wake-Up Slap	Fighting	Physical	60	100	10	Normal	—	○
Seed Bomb	Grass	Physical	80	100	15	Normal	—	—
Bullet Seed	Grass	Physical	25	100	30	Normal	—	—
Focus Punch	Fighting	Physical	150	100	20	Normal	—	○
Natural Gift	Normal	Physical	—	100	15	Normal	—	—
Drain Punch	Fighting	Physical	75	100	10	Normal	—	○

Mushroom Pokémon

286 Breloom

- HEIGHT: 3'11"
- WEIGHT: 86.4 lbs.
- GENDER: ♂ / ♀

Its short arms stretch when it throws punches. Its technique is equal to that of pro boxers.

Same form for ♂ / ♀

TYPE Grass Fighting

ABILITIES
- Effect Spore
- Poison Heal

HIDDEN ABILITY
- Technician

STATS

HP
Attack
Defense
Sp. Atk
Sp. Def
Speed

EGG GROUPS

Fairy/Grass

ITEMS SOMETIMES HELD
- Kebia Berry

EVOLUTION

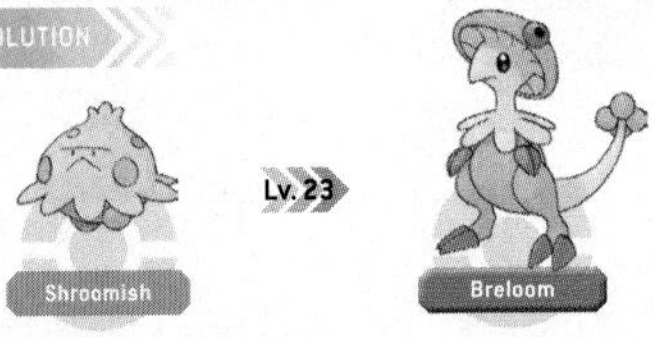

Shroomish → Lv. 23 → Breloom

HOW TO OBTAIN

Pokémon Black Version 2	Pinwheel Forest interior (Hidden Grotto)
Pokémon White Version 2	Pinwheel Forest interior (Hidden Grotto)

HOW TO OBTAIN FROM OTHER GAMES

—
—

Pokémon AR Marker

LEVEL-UP AND LEARNED MOVES

Lv.	Name	Type	Kind	Pow.	Acc.	PP	Range	Long	DA
1	Absorb	Grass	Special	20	100	25	Normal	—	—
1	Tackle	Normal	Physical	50	100	35	Normal	—	○
1	Stun Spore	Grass	Status	—	75	30	Normal	—	—
1	Leech Seed	Grass	Status	—	90	10	Normal	—	—
5	Tackle	Normal	Physical	50	100	35	Normal	—	○
9	Stun Spore	Grass	Status	—	75	30	Normal	—	—
13	Leech Seed	Grass	Status	—	90	10	Normal	—	—
17	Mega Drain	Grass	Special	40	100	15	Normal	—	—
21	Headbutt	Normal	Physical	70	100	15	Normal	—	○
23	Mach Punch	Fighting	Physical	40	100	30	Normal	—	○
25	Counter	Fighting	Physical	—	100	20	Varies	—	○
29	Force Palm	Fighting	Physical	60	100	10	Normal	—	○
33	Sky Uppercut	Fighting	Physical	85	90	15	Normal	—	○
37	Mind Reader	Normal	Status	—	—	5	Normal	—	—
41	Seed Bomb	Grass	Physical	80	100	15	Normal	—	—
45	DynamicPunch	Fighting	Physical	100	50	5	Normal	—	○

TM & HM MOVES

Lv.	Name	Type	Kind	Pow.	Acc.	PP	Range	Long	DA
TM06	Toxic	Poison	Status	—	90	10	Normal	—	—
TM08	Bulk Up	Fighting	Status	—	—	20	Self	—	—
TM09	Venoshock	Poison	Special	65	100	10	Normal	—	—
TM10	Hidden Power	Normal	Special	—	100	15	Normal	—	—
TM11	Sunny Day	Fire	Status	—	—	5	Both Sides	—	—
TM15	Hyper Beam	Normal	Special	150	90	5	Normal	—	—
TM17	Protect	Normal	Status	—	—	10	Self	—	—
TM20	Safeguard	Normal	Status	—	—	25	Your Side	—	—
TM21	Frustration	Normal	Physical	—	100	20	Normal	—	○
TM22	SolarBeam	Grass	Special	120	100	10	Normal	—	—
TM27	Return	Normal	Physical	—	100	20	Normal	—	○
TM31	Brick Break	Fighting	Physical	75	100	15	Normal	—	○
TM32	Double Team	Normal	Status	—	—	15	Self	—	—
TM36	Sludge Bomb	Poison	Special	90	100	10	Normal	—	—
TM39	Rock Tomb	Rock	Physical	50	80	10	Normal	—	—
TM42	Facade	Normal	Physical	70	100	20	Normal	—	○
TM44	Rest	Psychic	Status	—	—	10	Self	—	—
TM45	Attract	Normal	Status	—	100	15	Normal	—	—
TM47	Low Sweep	Fighting	Physical	60	100	20	Normal	—	○
TM48	Round	Normal	Special	60	100	15	Normal	—	—
TM52	Focus Blast	Fighting	Special	120	70	5	Normal	—	—
TM53	Energy Ball	Grass	Special	80	100	10	Normal	—	—
TM54	False Swipe	Normal	Physical	40	100	40	Normal	—	○
TM56	Fling	Dark	Physical	—	100	10	Normal	—	—
TM67	Retaliate	Normal	Physical	70	100	5	Normal	—	○
TM68	Giga Impact	Normal	Physical	150	90	5	Normal	—	○
TM70	Flash	Normal	Status	—	100	20	Normal	—	—
TM71	Stone Edge	Rock	Physical	100	80	5	Normal	—	—
TM75	Swords Dance	Normal	Status	—	—	30	Self	—	—
TM80	Rock Slide	Rock	Physical	75	90	10	Many Others	—	—
TM83	Work Up	Normal	Status	—	—	30	Self	—	—
TM86	Grass Knot	Grass	Special	—	100	20	Normal	—	○
TM87	Swagger	Normal	Status	—	90	15	Normal	—	—
TM90	Substitute	Normal	Status	—	—	10	Self	—	—
TM94	Rock Smash	Fighting	Physical	40	100	15	Normal	—	○
HM01	Cut	Normal	Physical	50	95	30	Normal	—	○
HM04	Strength	Normal	Physical	80	100	15	Normal	—	○

MOVES TAUGHT BY PEOPLE

Name	Type	Kind	Pow.	Acc.	PP	Range	Long	DA

MOVES TAUGHT BY MOVE TUTORS FOR SHARDS

Name	Type	Kind	Pow.	Acc.	PP	Range	Long	DA
Seed Bomb	Grass	Physical	80	100	15	Normal	—	—
ThunderPunch	Electric	Physical	75	100	15	Normal	—	○
Iron Tail	Steel	Physical	100	75	15	Normal	—	○
Superpower	Fighting	Physical	120	100	5	Normal	—	○
Snore	Normal	Special	40	100	15	Normal	—	—
Synthesis	Grass	Status	—	—	5	Self	—	—
Giga Drain	Grass	Special	75	100	10	Normal	—	—
Drain Punch	Fighting	Physical	75	100	10	Normal	—	○
Worry Seed	Grass	Status	—	100	10	Normal	—	—
Helping Hand	Normal	Status	—	—	20	1 Ally	—	—
Sleep Talk	Normal	Status	—	—	10	Self	—	—
Snatch	Dark	Status	—	—	10	Self	—	—

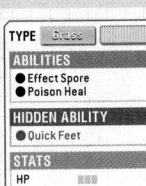

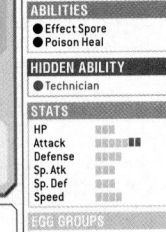

287 Slakoth

Slacker Pokémon

- HEIGHT: 2'07"
- WEIGHT: 52.9 lbs.
- GENDER: ♂ / ♀

If it eats just three leaves in a day, it is satisfied. Other than that, it sleeps for 20 hours a day.

Same form for ♂ / ♀

TYPE Normal

ABILITY
- Truant

HIDDEN ABILITY
—

STATS
HP
Attack
Defense
Sp. Atk
Sp. Def
Speed

EGG GROUPS
Field

ITEMS SOMETIMES HELD
- None

EVOLUTION

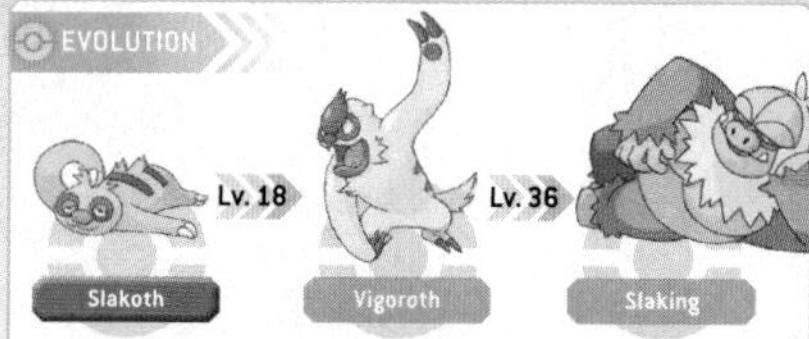

HOW TO OBTAIN

Pokémon Black Version 2	Catch a Vigoroth, leave it at the Pokémon Day Care, and the Egg that is found
Pokémon White Version 2	Catch a Vigoroth, leave it at the Pokémon Day Care, and hatch the Egg that is found

HOW TO OBTAIN FROM OTHER GAMES

Pokémon HeartGold Version	Route 25 (use Headbutt on tree)
Pokémon SoulSilver Version	Route 25 (use Headbutt on tree)

Pokémon AR Marker

LEVEL-UP AND LEARNED MOVES

Lv.	Name	Type	Kind	Pow.	Acc.	PP	Range	Long	DA
1	Scratch	Normal	Physical	40	100	35	Normal	—	○
1	Yawn	Normal	Status	—	—	10	Normal	—	—
7	Encore	Normal	Status	—	100	5	Normal	—	—
13	Slack Off	Normal	Status	—	—	10	Self	—	—
19	Faint Attack	Dark	Physical	60	—	20	Normal	—	○
25	Amnesia	Psychic	Status	—	—	20	Self	—	—
31	Covet	Normal	Physical	60	100	40	Normal	—	○
37	Chip Away	Normal	Physical	70	100	20	Normal	—	○
43	Counter	Fighting	Physical	—	100	20	Varies	—	○
49	Flail	Normal	Physical	—	100	15	Normal	—	○

TM & HM MOVES

Lv.	Name	Type	Kind	Pow.	Acc.	PP	Range	Long	DA
TM01	Hone Claws	Dark	Status	—	—	15	Self	—	—
TM06	Toxic	Poison	Status	—	90	10	Normal	—	—
TM08	Bulk Up	Fighting	Status	—	—	20	Self	—	—
TM10	Hidden Power	Normal	Special	—	100	15	Normal	—	—
TM11	Sunny Day	Fire	Status	—	—	5	Both Sides	—	—
TM13	Ice Beam	Ice	Special	95	100	10	Normal	—	—
TM14	Blizzard	Ice	Special	120	70	5	Many Others	—	—
TM17	Protect	Normal	Status	—	—	10	Self	—	—
TM18	Rain Dance	Water	Status	—	—	5	Both Sides	—	—
TM21	Frustration	Normal	Physical	—	100	20	Normal	—	○
TM22	SolarBeam	Grass	Special	120	100	10	Normal	—	—
TM24	Thunderbolt	Electric	Special	95	100	15	Normal	—	—
TM25	Thunder	Electric	Special	120	70	10	Normal	—	—
TM27	Return	Normal	Physical	—	100	20	Normal	—	○
TM30	Shadow Ball	Ghost	Special	80	100	15	Normal	—	—
TM31	Brick Break	Fighting	Physical	75	100	15	Normal	—	○
TM32	Double Team	Normal	Status	—	—	15	Self	—	—
TM35	Flamethrower	Fire	Special	95	100	15	Normal	—	—
TM38	Fire Blast	Fire	Special	120	85	5	Normal	—	—
TM39	Rock Tomb	Rock	Physical	50	80	10	Normal	—	—
TM40	Aerial Ace	Flying	Physical	60	—	20	Normal	○	○
TM42	Facade	Normal	Physical	70	100	20	Normal	—	○
TM44	Rest	Psychic	Status	—	—	10	Self	—	—
TM45	Attract	Normal	Status	—	100	15	Normal	—	—
TM48	Round	Normal	Special	60	100	15	Normal	—	—
TM56	Fling	Dark	Physical	—	100	10	Normal	—	—
TM59	Incinerate	Fire	Special	30	100	15	Many Others	—	—
TM65	Shadow Claw	Ghost	Physical	70	100	15	Normal	—	○
TM67	Retaliate	Normal	Physical	70	100	5	Normal	—	○
TM80	Rock Slide	Rock	Physical	75	90	10	Many Others	—	—
TM83	Work Up	Normal	Status	—	—	30	Self	—	—
TM87	Swagger	Normal	Status	—	90	15	Normal	—	—
TM90	Substitute	Normal	Status	—	—	10	Self	—	—
TM94	Rock Smash	Fighting	Physical	40	100	15	Normal	—	○
HM01	Cut	Normal	Physical	50	95	30	Normal	—	○
HM04	Strength	Normal	Physical	80	100	15	Normal	—	○

MOVES TAUGHT BY PEOPLE

Name	Type	Kind	Pow.	Acc.	PP	Range	Long	DA

MOVES TAUGHT BY MOVE TUTORS FOR SHARDS

Name	Type	Kind	Pow.	Acc.	PP	Range	Long	DA
Covet	Normal	Physical	60	100	40	Normal	—	○
Gunk Shot	Poison	Physical	120	70	5	Normal	—	—
Fire Punch	Fire	Physical	75	100	15	Normal	—	○
ThunderPunch	Electric	Physical	75	100	15	Normal	—	○
Ice Punch	Ice	Physical	75	100	15	Normal	—	○
Icy Wind	Ice	Special	55	95	15	Many Others	—	—
Snore	Normal	Special	40	100	15	Normal	—	—
After You	Normal	Status	—	—	15	Normal	—	—
Sleep Talk	Normal	Status	—	—	10	Self	—	—

EGG MOVES

Name	Type	Kind	Pow.	Acc.	PP	Range	Long	DA
Pursuit	Dark	Physical	40	100	20	Normal	—	○
Slash	Normal	Physical	70	100	20	Normal	—	○
Body Slam	Normal	Physical	85	100	15	Normal	—	○
Snore	Normal	Special	40	100	15	Normal	—	—
Crush Claw	Normal	Physical	75	95	10	Normal	—	○
Curse	Ghost	Status	—	—	10	Varies	—	—
Sleep Talk	Normal	Status	—	—	10	Self	—	—
Hammer Arm	Fighting	Physical	100	90	10	Normal	—	○
Night Slash	Dark	Physical	70	100	15	Normal	—	○
After You	Normal	Status	—	—	15	Normal	—	—
Tickle	Normal	Status	—	100	20	Normal	—	—

288 Vigoroth

Wild Monkey Pokémon

- HEIGHT: 4'07"
- WEIGHT: 102.5 lbs.
- GENDER: ♂ / ♀

Its heartbeat is fast and its blood so agitated that it can't sit still for one second.

Same form for ♂ / ♀

TYPE Normal

ABILITY
- Vital Spirit

HIDDEN ABILITY
—

STATS
HP
Attack
Defense
Sp. Atk
Sp. Def
Speed

EGG GROUPS
Field

ITEMS SOMETIMES HELD
- None

EVOLUTION

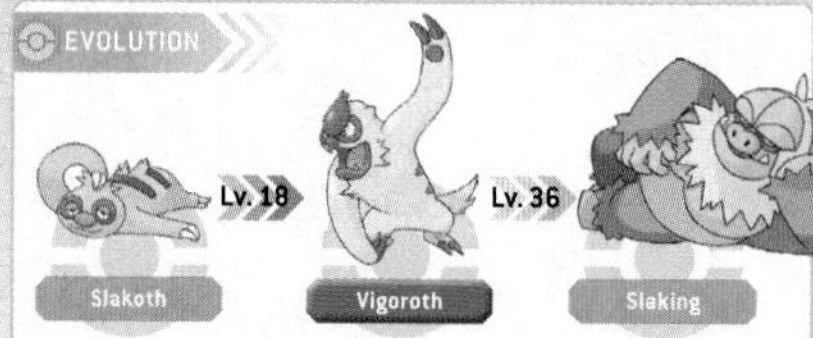

HOW TO OBTAIN

Pokémon Black Version 2	Pinwheel Forest interior
Pokémon White Version 2	Pinwheel Forest interior

HOW TO OBTAIN FROM OTHER GAMES

—

—

Pokémon AR Marker

LEVEL-UP AND LEARNED MOVES

Lv.	Name	Type	Kind	Pow.	Acc.	PP	Range	Long	DA
1	Scratch	Normal	Physical	40	100	35	Normal	—	○
1	Focus Energy	Normal	Status	—	—	30	Self	—	—
1	Encore	Normal	Status	—	100	5	Normal	—	—
1	Uproar	Normal	Special	90	100	10	1 Random	—	—
7	Encore	Normal	Status	—	100	5	Normal	—	—
13	Uproar	Normal	Special	90	100	10	1 Random	—	—
19	Fury Swipes	Normal	Physical	18	80	15	Normal	—	○
25	Endure	Normal	Status	—	—	10	Self	—	—
31	Slash	Normal	Physical	70	100	20	Normal	—	○
37	Counter	Fighting	Physical	—	100	20	Varies	—	○
43	Chip Away	Normal	Physical	70	100	20	Normal	—	○
49	Focus Punch	Fighting	Physical	150	100	20	Normal	—	○
55	Reversal	Fighting	Physical	—	100	15	Normal	—	○

TM & HM MOVES

Lv.	Name	Type	Kind	Pow.	Acc.	PP	Range	Long	DA
TM01	Hone Claws	Dark	Status	—	—	15	Self	—	—
TM05	Roar	Normal	Status	—	100	20	Normal	—	—
TM06	Toxic	Poison	Status	—	90	10	Normal	—	—
TM08	Bulk Up	Fighting	Status	—	—	20	Self	—	—
TM10	Hidden Power	Normal	Special	—	100	15	Normal	—	—
TM11	Sunny Day	Fire	Status	—	—	5	Both Sides	—	—
TM12	Taunt	Dark	Status	—	100	20	Normal	—	—
TM13	Ice Beam	Ice	Special	95	100	10	Normal	—	—
TM14	Blizzard	Ice	Special	120	70	5	Many Others	—	—
TM17	Protect	Normal	Status	—	—	10	Self	—	—
TM18	Rain Dance	Water	Status	—	—	5	Both Sides	—	—
TM21	Frustration	Normal	Physical	—	100	20	Normal	—	○
TM22	SolarBeam	Grass	Special	120	100	10	Normal	—	—
TM24	Thunderbolt	Electric	Special	95	100	15	Normal	—	—
TM25	Thunder	Electric	Special	120	70	10	Normal	—	—
TM26	Earthquake	Ground	Physical	100	100	10	Adjacent	—	—
TM27	Return	Normal	Physical	—	100	20	Normal	—	○
TM30	Shadow Ball	Ghost	Special	80	100	15	Normal	—	—
TM31	Brick Break	Fighting	Physical	75	100	15	Normal	—	○
TM32	Double Team	Normal	Status	—	—	15	Self	—	—
TM35	Flamethrower	Fire	Special	95	100	15	Normal	—	—
TM38	Fire Blast	Fire	Special	120	85	5	Normal	—	—
TM39	Rock Tomb	Rock	Physical	50	80	10	Normal	—	—
TM40	Aerial Ace	Flying	Physical	60	—	20	Normal	○	○
TM42	Facade	Normal	Physical	70	100	20	Normal	—	○
TM44	Rest	Psychic	Status	—	—	10	Self	—	—
TM45	Attract	Normal	Status	—	100	15	Normal	—	—
TM47	Low Sweep	Fighting	Physical	60	100	20	Normal	—	○
TM48	Round	Normal	Special	60	100	15	Normal	—	—
TM52	Focus Blast	Fighting	Special	120	70	5	Normal	—	—
TM56	Fling	Dark	Physical	—	100	10	Normal	—	—
TM59	Incinerate	Fire	Special	30	100	15	Many Others	—	—
TM65	Shadow Claw	Ghost	Physical	70	100	15	Normal	—	○
TM67	Retaliate	Normal	Physical	70	100	5	Normal	—	○
TM78	Bulldoze	Ground	Physical	60	100	20	Adjacent	—	—
TM80	Rock Slide	Rock	Physical	75	90	10	Many Others	—	—
TM83	Work Up	Normal	Status	—	—	30	Self	—	—
TM87	Swagger	Normal	Status	—	90	15	Normal	—	—
TM90	Substitute	Normal	Status	—	—	10	Self	—	—
TM94	Rock Smash	Fighting	Physical	40	100	15	Normal	—	○

Lv.	Name	Type	Kind	Pow.	Acc.	PP	Range	Long	DA
HM01	Cut	Normal	Physical	50	95	30	Normal	-	○
HM04	Strength	Normal	Physical	80	100	15	Normal	-	○

MOVES TAUGHT BY PEOPLE

Name	Type	Kind	Pow.	Acc.	PP	Range	Long	DA

MOVES TAUGHT BY MOVE TUTORS FOR SHARDS

Name	Type	Kind	Pow.	Acc.	PP	Range	Long	DA
Covet	Normal	Physical	60	100	40	Normal	—	○
Uproar	Normal	Special	90	100	10	1 Random	—	—
Low Kick	Fighting	Physical	—	100	20	Normal	—	○
Gunk Shot	Poison	Physical	120	70	5	Normal	—	—
Fire Punch	Fire	Physical	75	100	15	Normal	—	○
ThunderPunch	Electric	Physical	75	100	15	Normal	—	○
Ice Punch	Ice	Physical	75	100	15	Normal	—	○
Icy Wind	Ice	Special	55	95	15	Many Others	—	—
After You	Normal	Status	—	—	15	Normal	—	—
Sleep Talk	Normal	Status	—	—	10	Self	—	—

kémon

king

7 lbs.
♀

lying on its side. It only
es when there is no more grass to eat.

Same form for ♂ / ♀

TYPE Normal

ABILITY
● Truant

HIDDEN ABILITY
—

STATS
HP
Attack
Defense
Sp. Atk
Sp. Def
Speed

EGG GROUPS
Field

ITEMS SOMETIMES HELD
● None

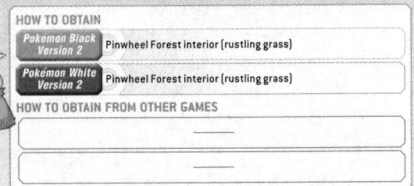

EVOLUTION

Slakoth
Lv. 18
Vigoroth
Lv. 36
Slaking

HOW TO OBTAIN

Pokémon Black Version 2	Pinwheel Forest interior (rustling grass)
Pokémon White Version 2	Pinwheel Forest interior (rustling grass)

HOW TO OBTAIN FROM OTHER GAMES

—

—

LEVEL-UP AND LEARNED MOVES

Lv.	Name	Type	Kind	Pow.	Acc.	PP	Range	Long	DA
1	Scratch	Normal	Physical	40	100	35	Normal	—	○
1	Yawn	Normal	Status	—	—	10	Normal	—	—
1	Encore	Normal	Status	—	100	5	Normal	—	—
1	Slack Off	Normal	Status	—	—	10	Self	—	—
7	Encore	Normal	Status	—	100	5	Normal	—	—
13	Slack Off	Normal	Status	—	—	10	Self	—	—
19	Faint Attack	Dark	Physical	60	—	20	Normal	—	○
25	Amnesia	Psychic	Status	—	—	20	Self	—	—
31	Covet	Normal	Physical	60	100	40	Normal	—	○
36	Swagger	Normal	Status	—	90	15	Normal	—	—
37	Chip Away	Normal	Physical	70	100	20	Normal	—	○
43	Counter	Fighting	Physical	—	100	20	Varies	—	○
49	Flail	Normal	Physical	—	100	15	Normal	—	○
55	Fling	Dark	Physical	—	100	10	Normal	—	—
61	Punishment	Dark	Physical	—	100	5	Normal	—	○
67	Hammer Arm	Fighting	Physical	100	90	10	Normal	—	○

TM & HM MOVES

Lv.	Name	Type	Kind	Pow.	Acc.	PP	Range	Long	DA
TM01	Hone Claws	Dark	Status	—	—	15	Self	—	—
TM05	Roar	Normal	Status	—	100	20	Normal	—	—
TM06	Toxic	Poison	Status	—	90	10	Normal	—	—
TM08	Bulk Up	Fighting	Status	—	—	20	Self	—	—
TM10	Hidden Power	Normal	Special	—	100	15	Normal	—	—
TM11	Sunny Day	Fire	Status	—	—	5	Both Sides	—	—
TM12	Taunt	Dark	Status	—	100	20	Normal	—	—
TM13	Ice Beam	Ice	Special	95	100	10	Normal	—	—
TM14	Blizzard	Ice	Special	120	70	5	Many Others	—	—
TM15	Hyper Beam	Normal	Special	150	90	5	Normal	—	—
TM17	Protect	Normal	Status	—	—	10	Self	—	—
TM18	Rain Dance	Water	Status	—	—	5	Both Sides	—	—
TM21	Frustration	Normal	Physical	—	100	20	Normal	—	○
TM22	SolarBeam	Grass	Special	120	100	10	Normal	—	—
TM23	Smack Down	Rock	Physical	50	100	15	Normal	—	—
TM24	Thunderbolt	Electric	Special	95	100	15	Normal	—	—
TM25	Thunder	Electric	Special	120	70	10	Normal	—	—
TM26	Earthquake	Ground	Physical	100	100	10	Adjacent	—	—
TM27	Return	Normal	Physical	—	100	20	Normal	—	○
TM30	Shadow Ball	Ghost	Special	80	100	15	Normal	—	—
TM31	Brick Break	Fighting	Physical	75	100	15	Normal	—	○
TM32	Double Team	Normal	Status	—	—	15	Self	—	—
TM35	Flamethrower	Fire	Special	95	100	15	Normal	—	—
TM38	Fire Blast	Fire	Special	120	85	5	Normal	—	—
TM39	Rock Tomb	Rock	Physical	50	80	10	Normal	—	—
TM40	Aerial Ace	Flying	Physical	60	—	20	Normal	○	○
TM42	Facade	Normal	Physical	70	100	20	Normal	—	○
TM44	Rest	Psychic	Status	—	—	10	Self	—	—
TM45	Attract	Normal	Status	—	100	15	Normal	—	—
TM47	Low Sweep	Fighting	Physical	60	100	20	Normal	—	○
TM48	Round	Normal	Special	60	100	15	Normal	—	—
TM52	Focus Blast	Fighting	Special	120	70	5	Normal	—	—
TM56	Fling	Dark	Physical	—	100	10	Normal	—	—
TM59	Incinerate	Fire	Special	30	100	15	Many Others	—	—
TM60	Quash	Dark	Status	—	100	15	Normal	—	—
TM65	Shadow Claw	Ghost	Physical	70	100	15	Normal	—	○
TM67	Retaliate	Normal	Physical	70	100	5	Normal	—	○
TM68	Giga Impact	Normal	Physical	150	90	5	Normal	—	○
TM78	Bulldoze	Ground	Physical	60	100	20	Adjacent	—	—
TM80	Rock Slide	Rock	Physical	75	90	10	Many Others	—	—
TM83	Work Up	Normal	Status	—	—	30	Self	—	—
TM87	Swagger	Normal	Status	—	90	15	Normal	—	—
TM90	Substitute	Normal	Status	—	—	10	Self	—	—
TM94	Rock Smash	Fighting	Physical	40	100	15	Normal	—	○
HM01	Cut	Normal	Physical	50	95	30	Normal	—	○
HM04	Strength	Normal	Physical	80	100	15	Normal	—	○

MOVES TAUGHT BY PEOPLE

Name	Type	Kind	Pow.	Acc.	PP	Range	Long	DA

MOVES TAUGHT BY MOVE TUTORS FOR SHARDS

Name	Type	Kind	Pow.	Acc.	PP	Range	Long	DA
Covet	Normal	Physical	60	100	40	Normal	—	○
Low Kick	Fighting	Physical	—	100	20	Normal	—	○
Gunk Shot	Poison	Physical	120	70	5	Normal	—	—
Fire Punch	Fire	Physical	75	100	15	Normal	—	○
ThunderPunch	Electric	Physical	75	100	15	Normal	—	○
Ice Punch	Ice	Physical	75	100	15	Normal	—	○
Block	Normal	Status	—	—	5	Normal	—	—
Icy Wind	Ice	Special	55	95	15	Many Others	—	—
Snore	Normal	Special	40	100	15	Normal	—	—
After You	Normal	Status	—	—	15	Normal	—	—
Sleep Talk	Normal	Status	—	—	10	Self	—	—

Pokémon AR Marker

Trainee Pokémon

290 Nincada

● HEIGHT: 1'08"
● WEIGHT: 12.1 lbs.
● GENDER: ♂ / ♀

It grows underground, sensing its surroundings using antennae instead of its virtually blind eyes.

Same form for ♂ / ♀

TYPE Bug Ground

ABILITY
● Compoundeyes

HIDDEN ABILITY
—

STATS
HP
Attack
Defense
Sp. Atk
Sp. Def
Speed

EGG GROUPS
Bug

ITEMS SOMETIMES HELD
● None

EVOLUTION

Nincada
Lv. 20
Ninjask
Lv. 20
Have at least one free space in your party and a Poké Ball
Shedinja

HOW TO OBTAIN

Pokémon Black Version 2	Link Trade or Poké Transfer
Pokémon White Version 2	Link Trade or Poké Transfer

HOW TO OBTAIN FROM OTHER GAMES

Pokémon Platinum Version	Occasionally appears in Eterna Forest (use Poké Radar for a better chance)

—

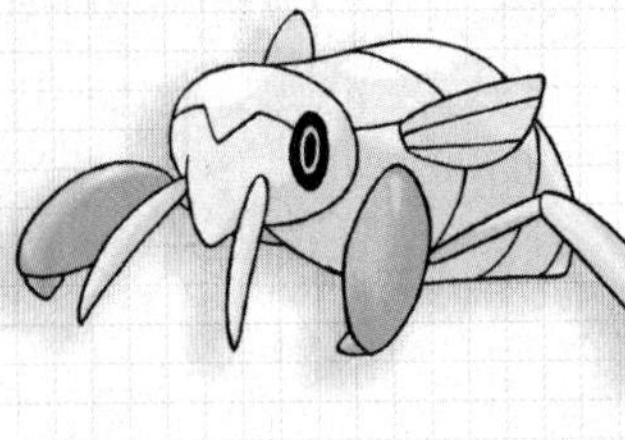

LEVEL-UP AND LEARNED MOVES

Lv.	Name	Type	Kind	Pow.	Acc.	PP	Range	Long	DA
1	Scratch	Normal	Physical	40	100	35	Normal	—	○
1	Harden	Normal	Status	—	—	30	Self	—	—
5	Leech Life	Bug	Physical	20	100	15	Normal	—	○
9	Sand-Attack	Ground	Status	—	100	15	Normal	—	—
14	Fury Swipes	Normal	Physical	18	80	15	Normal	—	○
19	Mind Reader	Normal	Status	—	—	5	Normal	—	—
25	False Swipe	Normal	Physical	40	100	40	Normal	—	○
31	Mud-Slap	Ground	Special	20	100	10	Normal	—	—
38	Metal Claw	Steel	Physical	50	95	35	Normal	—	○
45	Dig	Ground	Physical	80	100	10	Normal	—	○

TM & HM MOVES

Lv.	Name	Type	Kind	Pow.	Acc.	PP	Range	Long	DA
TM01	Hone Claws	Dark	Status	—	—	15	Self	—	—
TM06	Toxic	Poison	Status	—	90	10	Normal	—	—
TM10	Hidden Power	Normal	Special	—	100	15	Normal	—	—
TM11	Sunny Day	Fire	Status	—	—	5	Both Sides	—	—
TM17	Protect	Normal	Status	—	—	10	Self	—	—
TM21	Frustration	Normal	Physical	—	100	20	Normal	—	○
TM22	SolarBeam	Grass	Special	120	100	10	Normal	—	—
TM27	Return	Normal	Physical	—	100	20	Normal	—	○
TM28	Dig	Ground	Physical	80	100	10	Normal	—	○
TM30	Shadow Ball	Ghost	Special	80	100	15	Normal	—	—
TM32	Double Team	Normal	Status	—	—	15	Self	—	—
TM37	Sandstorm	Rock	Status	—	—	10	Both Sides	—	—
TM40	Aerial Ace	Flying	Physical	60	—	20	Normal	○	○
TM42	Facade	Normal	Physical	70	100	20	Normal	—	○
TM44	Rest	Psychic	Status	—	—	10	Self	—	—
TM48	Round	Normal	Special	60	100	15	Normal	—	—
TM54	False Swipe	Normal	Physical	40	100	40	Normal	—	○
TM70	Flash	Normal	Status	—	100	20	Normal	—	—
TM76	Struggle Bug	Bug	Special	30	100	20	Many Others	—	—
TM81	X-Scissor	Bug	Physical	80	100	15	Normal	—	○
TM87	Swagger	Normal	Status	—	90	15	Normal	—	—
TM90	Substitute	Normal	Status	—	—	10	Self	—	—
HM01	Cut	Normal	Physical	50	95	30	Normal	—	○

MOVES TAUGHT BY PEOPLE

Name	Type	Kind	Pow.	Acc.	PP	Range	Long	DA

MOVES TAUGHT BY MOVE TUTORS FOR SHARDS

Name	Type	Kind	Pow.	Acc.	PP	Range	Long	DA
Bug Bite	Bug	Physical	60	100	20	Normal	—	○
Snore	Normal	Special	40	100	15	Normal	—	—
Giga Drain	Grass	Special	75	100	10	Normal	—	—
Spite	Ghost	Status	—	100	10	Normal	—	—
Sleep Talk	Normal	Status	—	—	10	Self	—	—

EGG MOVES

Name	Type	Kind	Pow.	Acc.	PP	Range	Long	DA
Endure	Normal	Status	—	—	10	Self	—	—
Faint Attack	Dark	Physical	60	—	20	Normal	—	○
Gust	Flying	Special	40	100	35	Normal	○	—
Silver Wind	Bug	Special	60	100	5	Normal	—	—
Bug Buzz	Bug	Special	90	100	10	Normal	—	—
Night Slash	Dark	Physical	70	100	15	Normal	—	○
Bug Bite	Bug	Physical	60	100	20	Normal	—	○
Final Gambit	Fighting	Special	—	100	5	Normal	—	○

Pokémon AR Marker

291 Ninjask
Ninja Pokémon

TYPE: Bug / Flying

ABILITY
● Speed Boost

HIDDEN ABILITY
—

STATS
HP
Attack
Defense
Sp. Atk
Sp. Def
Speed

EGG GROUPS
Bug

ITEMS SOMETIMES HELD
● None

● HEIGHT: 2'07"
● WEIGHT: 26.5 lbs.
● GENDER: ♂ / ♀

Because it moves so quickly, it sometimes becomes unseeable. It congregates around tree sap.

Same form for ♂ / ♀

EVOLUTION

Nincada — Lv. 20 → Ninjask
Nincada — Lv. 20 → Shedinja (Have at least one free space in your party and a Poké Ball)

HOW TO OBTAIN
| Pokémon Black Version 2 | Level up a Nincada you obtain via Link Trade or Poké Transfer to Lv. 20 |
| Pokémon White Version 2 | Level up a Nincada you obtain via Link Trade or Poké Transfer to Lv. 20 |

HOW TO OBTAIN FROM OTHER GAMES
——
——

LEVEL-UP AND LEARNED MOVES

Lv.	Name	Type	Kind	Pow.	Acc.	PP	Range	Long	DA
1	Bug Bite	Bug	Physical	60	100	20	Normal	—	○
1	Scratch	Normal	Physical	40	100	35	Normal	—	○
1	Harden	Normal	Status	—	—	30	Self	—	—
1	Leech Life	Bug	Physical	20	100	15	Normal	—	○
5	Sand-Attack	Ground	Status	—	100	15	Normal	—	—
5	Leech Life	Bug	Physical	20	100	15	Normal	—	○
9	Sand-Attack	Ground	Status	—	100	15	Normal	—	—
14	Fury Swipes	Normal	Physical	18	80	15	Normal	—	○
19	Mind Reader	Normal	Status	—	—	5	Normal	—	—
20	Double Team	Normal	Status	—	—	15	Self	—	—
20	Fury Cutter	Bug	Physical	20	95	20	Normal	—	○
20	Screech	Normal	Status	—	85	40	Normal	—	—
25	Swords Dance	Normal	Status	—	—	30	Self	—	—
31	Slash	Normal	Physical	70	100	20	Normal	—	○
38	Agility	Psychic	Status	—	—	30	Self	—	—
45	Baton Pass	Normal	Status	—	—	40	Self	—	—
52	X-Scissor	Bug	Physical	80	100	15	Normal	—	○

TM & HM MOVES

Lv.	Name	Type	Kind	Pow.	Acc.	PP	Range	Long	DA
TM01	Hone Claws	Dark	Status	—	—	15	Self	—	—
TM06	Toxic	Poison	Status	—	90	10	Normal	—	—
TM10	Hidden Power	Normal	Special	—	100	15	Normal	—	—
TM11	Sunny Day	Fire	Status	—	—	5	Both Sides	—	—
TM15	Hyper Beam	Normal	Special	150	90	5	Normal	—	—
TM17	Protect	Normal	Status	—	—	10	Self	—	—
TM21	Frustration	Normal	Physical	—	100	20	Normal	—	○
TM22	SolarBeam	Grass	Special	120	100	10	Normal	—	—
TM27	Return	Normal	Physical	—	100	20	Normal	—	○
TM28	Dig	Ground	Physical	80	100	10	Normal	—	○
TM30	Shadow Ball	Ghost	Special	80	100	15	Normal	—	—
TM32	Double Team	Normal	Status	—	—	15	Self	—	—
TM37	Sandstorm	Rock	Status	—	—	10	Both Sides	—	—
TM40	Aerial Ace	Flying	Physical	60	—	20	Normal	○	○
TM42	Facade	Normal	Physical	70	100	20	Normal	—	○
TM44	Rest	Psychic	Status	—	—	10	Self	—	—
TM45	Attract	Normal	Status	—	100	15	Normal	—	—
TM46	Thief	Dark	Physical	40	100	10	Normal	—	○
TM48	Round	Normal	Special	60	100	15	Normal	—	—
TM54	False Swipe	Normal	Physical	40	100	40	Normal	—	○
TM68	Giga Impact	Normal	Physical	150	90	5	Normal	—	○
TM70	Flash	Normal	Status	—	100	20	Normal	—	—
TM75	Swords Dance	Normal	Status	—	—	30	Self	—	—
TM76	Struggle Bug	Bug	Special	30	100	20	Many Others	—	—
TM81	X-Scissor	Bug	Physical	80	100	15	Normal	—	○
TM87	Swagger	Normal	Status	—	90	15	Normal	—	—
TM89	U-turn	Bug	Physical	70	100	20	Normal	—	○
TM90	Substitute	Normal	Status	—	—	10	Self	—	—
HM01	Cut	Normal	Physical	50	95	30	Normal	—	○

MOVES TAUGHT BY PEOPLE

Name	Type	Kind	Pow.	Acc.	PP	Range	Long	DA

MOVES TAUGHT BY MOVE TUTORS FOR SHARDS

Name	Type	Kind	Pow.	Acc.	PP	Range	Long	DA
Bug Bite	Bug	Physical	60	100	20	Normal	—	○
Uproar	Normal	Special	90	100	10	1 Random	—	—
Snore	Normal	Special	40	100	15	Normal	—	—
Roost	Flying	Status	—	—	10	Self	—	—
Giga Drain	Grass	Special	75	100	10	Normal	—	—
Spite	Ghost	Status	—	100	10	Normal	—	—
Sleep Talk	Normal	Status	—	—	10	Self	—	—

Pokémon AR Marker

292 Shedinja
Shed Pokémon

TYPE: Bug / Ghost

ABILITY
● Wonder Guard

HIDDEN ABILITY
—

STATS
HP
Attack
Defense
Sp. Atk
Sp. Def
Speed

EGG GROUPS
Mineral

ITEMS SOMETIMES HELD
● None

● HEIGHT: 2'07"
● WEIGHT: 2.6 lbs.
● GENDER: ♂ / ♀

A discarded bug shell that came to life. Peering into the crack on its back is said to steal one's spirit.

Same form for ♂ / ♀

EVOLUTION

Nincada — Lv. 20 → Ninjask
Nincada — Lv. 20 → Shedinja (Have at least one free space in your party and a Poké Ball)

HOW TO OBTAIN
| Pokémon Black Version 2 | Have at least one free space in your party and a Poké Ball and level up Nincada to Lv. 20 |
| Pokémon White Version 2 | Have at least one free space in your party and a Poké Ball and level up Nincada to Lv. 20 |

HOW TO OBTAIN FROM OTHER GAMES
——
——

LEVEL-UP AND LEARNED MOVES

Lv.	Name	Type	Kind	Pow.	Acc.	PP	Range	Long	DA
1	Scratch	Normal	Physical	40	100	35	Normal	—	○
1	Harden	Normal	Status	—	—	30	Self	—	—
5	Leech Life	Bug	Physical	20	100	15	Normal	—	○
9	Sand-Attack	Ground	Status	—	100	15	Normal	—	—
14	Fury Swipes	Normal	Physical	18	80	15	Normal	—	○
19	Mind Reader	Normal	Status	—	—	5	Normal	—	—
25	Spite	Ghost	Status	—	100	10	Normal	—	—
31	Confuse Ray	Ghost	Status	—	100	10	Normal	—	—
38	Shadow Sneak	Ghost	Physical	40	100	30	Normal	—	○
45	Grudge	Ghost	Status	—	—	5	Self	—	—
52	Heal Block	Psychic	Status	—	100	15	Many Others	—	—
59	Shadow Ball	Ghost	Special	80	100	15	Normal	—	—

TM & HM MOVES

Lv.	Name	Type	Kind	Pow.	Acc.	PP	Range	Long	DA
TM01	Hone Claws	Dark	Status	—	—	15	Self	—	—
TM06	Toxic	Poison	Status	—	90	10	Normal	—	—
TM10	Hidden Power	Normal	Special	—	100	15	Normal	—	—
TM11	Sunny Day	Fire	Status	—	—	5	Both Sides	—	—
TM15	Hyper Beam	Normal	Special	150	90	5	Normal	—	—
TM17	Protect	Normal	Status	—	—	10	Self	—	—
TM19	Telekinesis	Psychic	Status	—	—	15	Normal	—	—
TM21	Frustration	Normal	Physical	—	100	20	Normal	—	○
TM22	SolarBeam	Grass	Special	120	100	10	Normal	—	○
TM27	Return	Normal	Physical	—	100	20	Normal	—	○
TM28	Dig	Ground	Physical	80	100	10	Normal	—	○
TM30	Shadow Ball	Ghost	Special	80	100	15	Normal	—	—
TM32	Double Team	Normal	Status	—	—	15	Self	—	—
TM37	Sandstorm	Rock	Status	—	—	10	Both Sides	—	—
TM40	Aerial Ace	Flying	Physical	60	—	20	Normal	○	○
TM42	Facade	Normal	Physical	70	100	20	Normal	—	○
TM44	Rest	Psychic	Status	—	—	10	Self	—	—
TM46	Thief	Dark	Physical	40	100	10	Normal	—	○
TM48	Round	Normal	Special	60	100	15	Normal	—	—
TM54	False Swipe	Normal	Physical	40	100	40	Normal	—	○
TM61	Will-O-Wisp	Fire	Status	—	75	15	Normal	—	—
TM65	Shadow Claw	Ghost	Physical	70	100	15	Normal	—	○
TM68	Giga Impact	Normal	Physical	150	90	5	Normal	—	○
TM70	Flash	Normal	Status	—	100	20	Normal	—	—
TM76	Struggle Bug	Bug	Special	30	100	20	Many Others	—	—
TM81	X-Scissor	Bug	Physical	80	100	15	Normal	—	○
TM85	Dream Eater	Psychic	Special	100	100	15	Normal	—	—
TM87	Swagger	Normal	Status	—	90	15	Normal	—	—
TM90	Substitute	Normal	Status	—	—	10	Self	—	—
HM01	Cut	Normal	Physical	50	95	30	Normal	—	○

MOVES TAUGHT BY PEOPLE

Name	Type	Kind	Pow.	Acc.	PP	Range	Long	DA

MOVES TAUGHT BY MOVE TUTORS FOR SHARDS

Name	Type	Kind	Pow.	Acc.	PP	Range	Long	DA
Bug Bite	Bug	Physical	60	100	20	Normal	—	○
Snore	Normal	Special	40	100	15	Normal	—	—
Giga Drain	Grass	Special	75	100	10	Normal	—	—
Spite	Ghost	Status	—	100	10	Normal	—	—
Trick	Psychic	Status	—	100	10	Normal	—	—
Sleep Talk	Normal	Status	—	—	10	Self	—	—

Pokémon AR Marker

Whisper Pokémon

293 Whismur

TYPE: Normal

ABILITY
- Soundproof

HIDDEN ABILITY
- Rattled

- HEIGHT: 2'00"
- WEIGHT: 35.9 lbs.
- GENDER: ♂ / ♀

STATS
HP
Attack
Defense
Sp. Atk
Sp. Def
Speed

EGG GROUPS
Monster/Field

Usually, its cries are like quiet murmurs. If frightened, it shrieks at the same volume as a jet plane.

ITEMS SOMETIMES HELD
- None

Same form for ♂ / ♀

EVOLUTION

Lv. 20
Lv. 40
Whismur
Loudred
Exploud

HOW TO OBTAIN

Pokémon Black Version 2	Link Trade or Poké Transfer
Pokémon White Version 2	Link Trade or Poké Transfer

HOW TO OBTAIN FROM OTHER GAMES

Pokémon HeartGold Version	Route 30 (Hoenn Sound)
Pokémon SoulSilver Version	Route 30 (Hoenn Sound)

LEVEL-UP AND LEARNED MOVES

Lv.	Name	Type	Kind	Pow.	Acc.	PP	Range	Long	DA
1	Pound	Normal	Physical	40	100	35	Normal	—	○
5	Uproar	Normal	Special	90	100	10	1 Random	—	—
11	Astonish	Ghost	Physical	30	100	15	Normal	—	○
15	Howl	Normal	Status	—	—	40	Self	—	—
21	Supersonic	Normal	Status	—	55	20	Normal	—	—
25	Stomp	Normal	Physical	65	100	20	Normal	—	○
31	Screech	Normal	Status	—	85	40	Normal	—	—
35	Roar	Normal	Status	—	100	20	Normal	—	—
41	Synchronoise	Psychic	Special	70	100	15	Adjacent	—	—
45	Rest	Psychic	Status	—	—	10	Self	—	—
45	Sleep Talk	Normal	Status	—	—	10	Self	—	—
51	Hyper Voice	Normal	Special	90	100	10	Many Others	—	—

MOVES TAUGHT BY PEOPLE

Name	Type	Kind	Pow.	Acc.	PP	Range	Long	DA

MOVES TAUGHT BY MOVE TUTORS FOR SHARDS

Name	Type	Kind	Pow.	Acc.	PP	Range	Long	DA
Uproar	Normal	Special	90	100	10	1 Random	—	—
Fire Punch	Fire	Physical	75	100	15	Normal	—	○
ThunderPunch	Electric	Physical	75	100	15	Normal	—	○
Ice Punch	Ice	Physical	75	100	15	Normal	—	○
Hyper Voice	Normal	Special	90	100	10	Many Others	—	—
Icy Wind	Ice	Special	55	95	15	Many Others	—	—
Zen Headbutt	Psychic	Physical	80	90	15	Normal	—	○
Snore	Normal	Special	40	100	15	Normal	—	—
Endeavor	Normal	Physical	—	100	5	Normal	—	○
Sleep Talk	Normal	Status	—	—	10	Self	—	—

TM & HM MOVES

Lv.	Name	Type	Kind	Pow.	Acc.	PP	Range	Long	DA
TM05	Roar	Normal	Status	—	100	20	Normal	—	—
TM06	Toxic	Poison	Status	—	90	10	Normal	—	—
TM10	Hidden Power	Normal	Special	—	100	15	Normal	—	—
TM11	Sunny Day	Fire	Status	—	—	5	Both Sides	—	—
TM13	Ice Beam	Ice	Special	95	100	10	Normal	—	—
TM14	Blizzard	Ice	Special	120	70	5	Many Others	—	—
TM17	Protect	Normal	Status	—	—	10	Self	—	—
TM18	Rain Dance	Water	Status	—	—	5	Both Sides	—	—
TM21	Frustration	Normal	Physical	—	100	20	Normal	—	○
TM22	SolarBeam	Grass	Special	120	100	10	Normal	—	—
TM27	Return	Normal	Physical	—	100	20	Normal	—	○
TM30	Shadow Ball	Ghost	Special	80	100	15	Normal	—	—
TM32	Double Team	Normal	Status	—	—	15	Self	—	—
TM35	Flamethrower	Fire	Special	95	100	15	Normal	—	—
TM38	Fire Blast	Fire	Special	120	85	5	Normal	—	—
TM42	Facade	Normal	Physical	70	100	20	Normal	—	○
TM44	Rest	Psychic	Status	—	—	10	Self	—	—
TM45	Attract	Normal	Status	—	100	15	Normal	—	—
TM48	Round	Normal	Special	60	100	15	Normal	—	—
TM49	Echoed Voice	Normal	Special	40	100	15	Normal	—	—
TM56	Fling	Dark	Physical	—	100	10	Normal	—	—
TM59	Incinerate	Fire	Special	30	100	15	Many Others	—	—
TM67	Retaliate	Normal	Physical	70	100	5	Normal	—	○
TM83	Work Up	Normal	Status	—	—	30	Self	—	—
TM87	Swagger	Normal	Status	—	90	15	Normal	—	—
TM90	Substitute	Normal	Status	—	—	10	Self	—	—

EGG MOVES

Name	Type	Kind	Pow.	Acc.	PP	Range	Long	DA
Take Down	Normal	Physical	90	85	20	Normal	—	○
Snore	Normal	Special	40	100	15	Normal	—	—
Extrasensory	Psychic	Special	80	100	30	Normal	—	—
SmellingSalt	Normal	Physical	60	100	10	Normal	—	○
SmokeScreen	Normal	Status	—	100	20	Normal	—	—
Endeavor	Normal	Physical	—	100	5	Normal	—	○
Hammer Arm	Fighting	Physical	100	90	10	Normal	—	○
Fake Tears	Dark	Status	—	100	20	Normal	—	—
Circle Throw	Fighting	Physical	60	90	10	Normal	—	○

Pokémon AR Marker

Big Voice Pokémon

294 Loudred

TYPE: Normal

ABILITY
- Soundproof

HIDDEN ABILITY
- Scrappy

- HEIGHT: 3'03"
- WEIGHT: 89.3 lbs.
- GENDER: ♂ / ♀

STATS
HP
Attack
Defense
Sp. Atk
Sp. Def
Speed

EGG GROUPS
Monster/Field

The shock waves from its cries can tip over trucks. It stamps its feet to power up.

ITEMS SOMETIMES HELD
- None

Same form for ♂ / ♀

EVOLUTION

Lv. 20
Lv. 40
Whismur
Loudred
Exploud

HOW TO OBTAIN

Pokémon Black Version 2	Link Trade or Poké Transfer
Pokémon White Version 2	Link Trade or Poké Transfer

HOW TO OBTAIN FROM OTHER GAMES

Pokémon Platinum Version	Occasionally appears at Mt. Coronet exterior (use Poké Radar for a better chance)
	———

LEVEL-UP AND LEARNED MOVES

Lv.	Name	Type	Kind	Pow.	Acc.	PP	Range	Long	DA
1	Pound	Normal	Physical	40	100	35	Normal	—	○
1	Uproar	Normal	Special	90	100	10	1 Random	—	—
1	Astonish	Ghost	Physical	30	100	15	Normal	—	○
1	Howl	Normal	Status	—	—	40	Self	—	—
5	Uproar	Normal	Special	90	100	10	1 Random	—	—
11	Astonish	Ghost	Physical	30	100	15	Normal	—	○
15	Howl	Normal	Status	—	—	40	Self	—	—
20	Bite	Dark	Physical	60	100	25	Normal	—	○
23	Supersonic	Normal	Status	—	55	20	Normal	—	—
29	Stomp	Normal	Physical	65	100	20	Normal	—	○
37	Screech	Normal	Status	—	85	40	Normal	—	—
43	Roar	Normal	Status	—	100	20	Normal	—	—
51	Synchronoise	Psychic	Special	70	100	15	Adjacent	—	—
57	Rest	Psychic	Status	—	—	10	Self	—	—
57	Sleep Talk	Normal	Status	—	—	10	Self	—	—
65	Hyper Voice	Normal	Special	90	100	10	Many Others	—	—

MOVES TAUGHT BY PEOPLE

Name	Type	Kind	Pow.	Acc.	PP	Range	Long	DA

MOVES TAUGHT BY MOVE TUTORS FOR SHARDS

Name	Type	Kind	Pow.	Acc.	PP	Range	Long	DA
Uproar	Normal	Special	90	100	10	1 Random	—	—
Low Kick	Fighting	Physical	—	100	20	Normal	—	○
Fire Punch	Fire	Physical	75	100	15	Normal	—	○
ThunderPunch	Electric	Physical	75	100	15	Normal	—	○
Ice Punch	Ice	Physical	75	100	15	Normal	—	○
Hyper Voice	Normal	Special	90	100	10	Many Others	—	—
Icy Wind	Ice	Special	55	95	15	Many Others	—	—
Zen Headbutt	Psychic	Physical	80	90	15	Normal	—	○
Snore	Normal	Special	40	100	15	Normal	—	—
Endeavor	Normal	Physical	—	100	5	Normal	—	○
Sleep Talk	Normal	Status	—	—	10	Self	—	—

TM & HM MOVES

Lv.	Name	Type	Kind	Pow.	Acc.	PP	Range	Long	DA
TM05	Roar	Normal	Status	—	100	20	Normal	—	—
TM06	Toxic	Poison	Status	—	90	10	Normal	—	—
TM10	Hidden Power	Normal	Special	—	100	15	Normal	—	—
TM11	Sunny Day	Fire	Status	—	—	5	Both Sides	—	—
TM12	Taunt	Dark	Status	—	100	20	Normal	—	—
TM13	Ice Beam	Ice	Special	95	100	10	Normal	—	—
TM14	Blizzard	Ice	Special	120	70	5	Many Others	—	—
TM17	Protect	Normal	Status	—	—	10	Self	—	—
TM18	Rain Dance	Water	Status	—	—	5	Both Sides	—	—
TM21	Frustration	Normal	Physical	—	100	20	Normal	—	○
TM22	SolarBeam	Grass	Special	120	100	10	Normal	—	—
TM23	Smack Down	Rock	Physical	50	100	15	Normal	—	—
TM26	Earthquake	Ground	Physical	100	100	10	Adjacent	—	—
TM27	Return	Normal	Physical	—	100	20	Normal	—	○
TM30	Shadow Ball	Ghost	Special	80	100	15	Normal	—	—
TM31	Brick Break	Fighting	Physical	75	100	15	Normal	—	○
TM32	Double Team	Normal	Status	—	—	15	Self	—	—
TM35	Flamethrower	Fire	Special	95	100	15	Normal	—	—
TM38	Fire Blast	Fire	Special	120	85	5	Normal	—	—
TM39	Rock Tomb	Rock	Physical	50	80	10	Normal	—	—
TM41	Torment	Dark	Status	—	100	15	Normal	—	—
TM42	Facade	Normal	Physical	70	100	20	Normal	—	○
TM44	Rest	Psychic	Status	—	—	10	Self	—	—
TM45	Attract	Normal	Status	—	100	15	Normal	—	—
TM48	Round	Normal	Special	60	100	15	Normal	—	—
TM49	Echoed Voice	Normal	Special	40	100	15	Normal	—	—
TM50	Overheat	Fire	Special	140	90	5	Normal	—	—
TM56	Fling	Dark	Physical	—	100	10	Normal	—	—
TM59	Incinerate	Fire	Special	30	100	15	Many Others	—	—
TM67	Retaliate	Normal	Physical	70	100	5	Normal	—	○
TM78	Bulldoze	Ground	Physical	60	100	20	Adjacent	—	—
TM80	Rock Slide	Rock	Physical	75	90	10	Many Others	—	—
TM83	Work Up	Normal	Status	—	—	30	Self	—	—
TM87	Swagger	Normal	Status	—	90	15	Normal	—	—
TM90	Substitute	Normal	Status	—	—	10	Self	—	—
TM94	Rock Smash	Fighting	Physical	40	100	15	Normal	—	○
HM04	Strength	Normal	Physical	80	100	15	Normal	—	○

Pokémon AR Marker

293 Whismur
294 Loudred

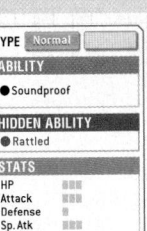

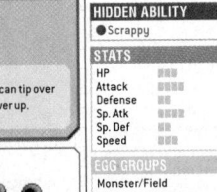

Loud Noise Pokémon

295 Exploud

● HEIGHT: 4'11"
● WEIGHT: 185.2 lbs.
● GENDER: ♂ / ♀

Its howls can be heard over six miles away. It emits all sorts of noises from the ports on its body.

Same form for ♂ / ♀

TYPE: Normal

ABILITY
● Soundproof

HIDDEN ABILITY
● Scrappy

STATS
HP
Attack
Defense
Sp. Atk
Sp. Def
Speed

EGG GROUPS
Monster/Field

ITEMS SOMETIMES HELD
● None

EVOLUTION

HOW TO OBTAIN

Pokémon Black Version 2	Level up a Loudred you obtain via Link Trade or Poké Transfer to Lv. 40
Pokémon White Version 2	Level up a Loudred you obtain via Link Trade or Poké Transfer to Lv. 40

HOW TO OBTAIN FROM OTHER GAMES

—

—

Pokémon AR Marker

LEVEL-UP AND LEARNED MOVES

Lv.	Name	Type	Kind	Pow.	Acc.	PP	Range	Long	DA
1	Ice Fang	Ice	Physical	65	95	15	Normal	—	○
1	Fire Fang	Fire	Physical	65	95	15	Normal	—	○
1	Thunder Fang	Electric	Physical	65	95	15	Normal	—	○
1	Pound	Normal	Physical	40	100	35	Normal	—	○
1	Uproar	Normal	Special	90	100	10	1 Random	—	—
1	Astonish	Ghost	Physical	30	100	15	Normal	—	○
1	Howl	Normal	Status	—	—	40	Self	—	—
5	Uproar	Normal	Special	90	100	10	1 Random	—	—
11	Astonish	Ghost	Physical	30	100	15	Normal	—	○
15	Howl	Normal	Status	—	—	40	Self	—	—
20	Bite	Dark	Physical	60	100	25	Normal	—	○
23	Supersonic	Normal	Status	—	55	20	Normal	—	—
29	Stomp	Normal	Physical	65	100	20	Normal	—	○
37	Screech	Normal	Status	—	85	40	Normal	—	—
40	Crunch	Dark	Physical	80	100	15	Normal	—	○
45	Roar	Normal	Status	—	100	20	Normal	—	—
55	Synchronoise	Psychic	Special	70	100	15	Adjacent	—	—
55	Rest	Psychic	Status	—	—	10	Self	—	—
63	Sleep Talk	Normal	Status	—	—	10	Self	—	—
71	Hyper Voice	Normal	Special	90	100	10	Many Others	—	—
79	Hyper Beam	Normal	Special	150	90	5	Normal	—	—

TM & HM MOVES

Lv.	Name	Type	Kind	Pow.	Acc.	PP	Range	Long	DA
TM05	Roar	Normal	Status	—	100	20	Normal	—	—
TM06	Toxic	Poison	Status	—	90	10	Normal	—	—
TM10	Hidden Power	Normal	Special	—	100	15	Normal	—	—
TM11	Sunny Day	Fire	Status	—	—	5	Both Sides	—	—
TM12	Taunt	Dark	Status	—	100	20	Normal	—	—
TM13	Ice Beam	Ice	Special	95	100	10	Normal	—	—
TM14	Blizzard	Ice	Special	120	70	5	Many Others	—	—
TM15	Hyper Beam	Normal	Special	150	90	5	Normal	—	—
TM17	Protect	Normal	Status	—	—	10	Self	—	—
TM18	Rain Dance	Water	Status	—	—	5	Both Sides	—	—
TM21	Frustration	Normal	Physical	—	100	20	Normal	—	○
TM22	SolarBeam	Grass	Special	120	100	10	Normal	—	—
TM23	Smack Down	Rock	Physical	50	100	15	Normal	—	—
TM26	Earthquake	Ground	Physical	100	100	10	Adjacent	—	—
TM27	Return	Normal	Physical	—	100	20	Normal	—	○
TM30	Shadow Ball	Ghost	Special	80	100	15	Normal	—	—
TM31	Brick Break	Fighting	Physical	75	100	15	Normal	—	○
TM32	Double Team	Normal	Status	—	—	15	Self	—	—
TM35	Flamethrower	Fire	Special	95	100	15	Normal	—	—
TM38	Fire Blast	Fire	Special	120	85	5	Normal	—	—
TM39	Rock Tomb	Rock	Physical	50	80	10	Normal	—	—
TM41	Torment	Dark	Status	—	100	15	Normal	—	—
TM42	Facade	Normal	Physical	70	100	20	Normal	—	○
TM44	Rest	Psychic	Status	—	—	10	Self	—	—
TM45	Attract	Normal	Status	—	100	15	Normal	—	—
TM48	Round	Normal	Special	60	100	15	Normal	—	—
TM49	Echoed Voice	Normal	Special	40	100	15	Normal	—	—
TM50	Overheat	Fire	Special	140	90	5	Normal	—	—
TM52	Focus Blast	Fighting	Special	120	70	5	Normal	—	—
TM56	Fling	Dark	Physical	—	100	10	Normal	—	—
TM59	Incinerate	Fire	Special	30	100	15	Many Others	—	—
TM67	Retaliate	Normal	Physical	70	100	5	Normal	—	○
TM68	Giga Impact	Normal	Physical	150	90	5	Normal	—	○
TM78	Bulldoze	Ground	Physical	60	100	20	Adjacent	—	—
TM80	Rock Slide	Rock	Physical	75	90	10	Many Others	—	—
TM83	Work Up	Normal	Status	—	—	30	Self	—	—
TM87	Swagger	Normal	Status	—	90	15	Normal	—	—
TM90	Substitute	Normal	Status	—	—	10	Self	—	—
TM94	Rock Smash	Fighting	Physical	40	100	15	Normal	—	○
HM03	Surf	Water	Special	95	100	15	Adjacent	—	—
HM04	Strength	Normal	Physical	80	100	15	Normal	—	○

MOVES TAUGHT BY PEOPLE

Name	Type	Kind	Pow.	Acc.	PP	Range	Long	DA

MOVES TAUGHT BY MOVE TUTORS FOR SHARDS

Name	Type	Kind	Pow.	Acc.	PP	Range	Long	DA
Uproar	Normal	Special	90	100	10	1 Random	—	—
Low Kick	Fighting	Physical	—	100	20	Normal	—	○
Fire Punch	Fire	Physical	75	100	15	Normal	—	○
ThunderPunch	Electric	Physical	75	100	15	Normal	—	○
Ice Punch	Ice	Physical	75	100	15	Normal	—	○
Hyper Voice	Normal	Special	90	100	10	Many Others	—	—
Icy Wind	Ice	Special	55	95	15	Many Others	—	—
Zen Headbutt	Psychic	Physical	80	90	15	Normal	—	○
Snore	Normal	Special	40	100	15	Normal	—	—
Outrage	Dragon	Physical	120	100	10	1 Random	—	○
Endeavor	Normal	Physical	—	100	5	Normal	—	○
Sleep Talk	Normal	Status	—	—	10	Self	—	—

Guts Pokémon

296 Makuhita

● HEIGHT: 3'03"
● WEIGHT: 190.5 lbs.
● GENDER: ♂ / ♀

It toughens its body by slamming into thick trees. Many snapped trees can be found near its nest.

Same form for ♂ / ♀

TYPE: Fighting

ABILITIES
● Thick Fat
● Guts

HIDDEN ABILITY
● Sheer Force

STATS
HP
Attack
Defense
Sp. Atk
Sp. Def
Speed

EGG GROUPS
Human-Like

ITEMS SOMETIMES HELD
● None

EVOLUTION

HOW TO OBTAIN

Pokémon Black Version 2	Catch a Hariyama, leave it at the Pokémon Day Care, and hatch the Egg that is found
Pokémon White Version 2	Catch a Hariyama, leave it at the Pokémon Day Care, and hatch the Egg that is found

HOW TO OBTAIN FROM OTHER GAMES

Pokémon HeartGold Version	Union Cave (Hoenn Sound)
Pokémon SoulSilver Version	Union Cave (Hoenn Sound)

Pokémon AR Marker

LEVEL-UP AND LEARNED MOVES

Lv.	Name	Type	Kind	Pow.	Acc.	PP	Range	Long	DA
1	Tackle	Normal	Physical	50	100	35	Normal	—	○
1	Focus Energy	Normal	Status	—	—	30	Self	—	—
4	Sand-Attack	Ground	Status	—	100	15	Normal	—	—
7	Arm Thrust	Fighting	Physical	15	100	20	Normal	—	○
10	Vital Throw	Fighting	Physical	70	—	10	Normal	—	○
13	Fake Out	Normal	Physical	40	100	10	Normal	—	○
16	Whirlwind	Normal	Status	—	100	20	Normal	—	—
19	Knock Off	Dark	Physical	20	100	20	Normal	—	○
22	SmellingSalt	Normal	Physical	60	100	10	Normal	—	○
25	Belly Drum	Normal	Status	—	—	10	Self	—	—
28	Force Palm	Fighting	Physical	60	100	10	Normal	—	○
31	Seismic Toss	Fighting	Physical	—	100	20	Normal	—	○
34	Wake-Up Slap	Fighting	Physical	60	100	10	Normal	—	○
37	Endure	Normal	Status	—	—	10	Self	—	—
40	Close Combat	Fighting	Physical	120	100	5	Normal	—	○
43	Reversal	Fighting	Physical	—	100	15	Normal	—	○
46	Heavy Slam	Steel	Physical	—	100	10	Normal	—	○

TM & HM MOVES

Lv.	Name	Type	Kind	Pow.	Acc.	PP	Range	Long	DA
TM06	Toxic	Poison	Status	—	90	10	Normal	—	—
TM08	Bulk Up	Fighting	Status	—	—	20	Self	—	—
TM10	Hidden Power	Normal	Special	—	100	15	Normal	—	—
TM11	Sunny Day	Fire	Status	—	—	5	Both Sides	—	—
TM17	Protect	Normal	Status	—	—	10	Self	—	—
TM18	Rain Dance	Water	Status	—	—	5	Both Sides	—	—
TM21	Frustration	Normal	Physical	—	100	20	Normal	—	○
TM23	Smack Down	Rock	Physical	50	100	15	Normal	—	—
TM26	Earthquake	Ground	Physical	100	100	10	Adjacent	—	—
TM27	Return	Normal	Physical	—	100	20	Normal	—	○
TM28	Dig	Ground	Physical	80	100	10	Normal	—	○
TM31	Brick Break	Fighting	Physical	75	100	15	Normal	—	○
TM32	Double Team	Normal	Status	—	—	15	Self	—	—
TM39	Rock Tomb	Rock	Physical	50	80	10	Normal	—	—
TM42	Facade	Normal	Physical	70	100	20	Normal	—	○
TM44	Rest	Psychic	Status	—	—	10	Self	—	—
TM45	Attract	Normal	Status	—	100	15	Normal	—	—
TM47	Low Sweep	Fighting	Physical	60	100	20	Normal	—	○
TM48	Round	Normal	Special	60	100	15	Normal	—	—
TM52	Focus Blast	Fighting	Special	120	70	5	Normal	—	—
TM56	Fling	Dark	Physical	—	100	10	Normal	—	—
TM67	Retaliate	Normal	Physical	70	100	5	Normal	—	○
TM78	Bulldoze	Ground	Physical	60	100	20	Adjacent	—	—
TM80	Rock Slide	Rock	Physical	75	90	10	Many Others	—	—
TM83	Work Up	Normal	Status	—	—	30	Self	—	—
TM84	Poison Jab	Poison	Physical	80	100	20	Normal	—	○
TM87	Swagger	Normal	Status	—	90	15	Normal	—	—
TM90	Substitute	Normal	Status	—	—	10	Self	—	—
TM94	Rock Smash	Fighting	Physical	40	100	15	Normal	—	○
HM03	Surf	Water	Special	95	100	15	Adjacent	—	—
HM04	Strength	Normal	Physical	80	100	15	Normal	—	○

MOVES TAUGHT BY PEOPLE

Name	Type	Kind	Pow.	Acc.	PP	Range	Long	DA

MOVES TAUGHT BY MOVE TUTORS FOR SHARDS

Name	Type	Kind	Pow.	Acc.	PP	Range	Long	DA
Low Kick	Fighting	Physical	—	100	20	Normal	—	○
Fire Punch	Fire	Physical	75	100	15	Normal	—	○
ThunderPunch	Electric	Physical	75	100	15	Normal	—	○
Ice Punch	Ice	Physical	75	100	15	Normal	—	○
Superpower	Fighting	Physical	120	100	5	Normal	—	○
Snore	Normal	Special	40	100	15	Normal	—	—
Knock Off	Dark	Physical	20	100	20	Normal	—	○
Role Play	Psychic	Status	—	—	10	Normal	—	—
Helping Hand	Normal	Status	—	—	20	1 Ally	—	—
Sleep Talk	Normal	Status	—	—	10	Self	—	—

EGG MOVES

Name	Type	Kind	Pow.	Acc.	PP	Range	Long	DA
Faint Attack	Dark	Physical	60	—	20	Normal	—	○
Detect	Fighting	Status	—	—	5	Self	—	—
Foresight	Normal	Status	—	—	40	Normal	—	—
Helping Hand	Normal	Status	—	—	20	1 Ally	—	—
Cross Chop	Fighting	Physical	100	80	5	Normal	—	○
Revenge	Fighting	Physical	60	100	10	Normal	—	○
DynamicPunch	Fighting	Physical	100	50	5	Normal	—	○
Counter	Fighting	Physical	—	100	20	Varies	—	○
Wake-Up Slap	Fighting	Physical	60	100	10	Normal	—	○
Bullet Punch	Steel	Physical	40	100	30	Normal	—	○
Feint	Normal	Physical	30	100	10	Normal	—	—
Wide Guard	Rock	Status	—	—	10	Your Side	—	—
Focus Punch	Fighting	Physical	150	100	20	Normal	—	○
Chip Away	Normal	Physical	70	100	20	Normal	—	○

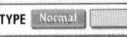

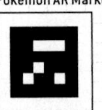

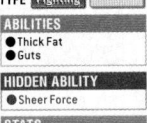

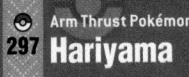

297 Hariyama

Arm Thrust Pokémon

TYPE Fighting

ABILITIES
- Thick Fat
- Guts

HIDDEN ABILITY
- Sheer Force

- HEIGHT: 7'07"
- WEIGHT: 559.5 lbs.
- GENDER: ♂ / ♀

It loves to match power with big-bodied Pokémon. It can knock a truck flying with its arm thrusts.

Same form for ♂ / ♀

STATS
HP	▪▪▪▪▪
Attack	▪▪▪▪
Defense	▪▪▪
Sp. Atk	▪▪
Sp. Def	▪▪▪
Speed	▪

EGG GROUPS
Human-Like

ITEMS SOMETIMES HELD
- King's Rock

Pokémon AR Marker

EVOLUTION

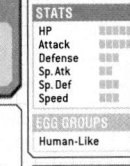

Makuhita → Lv. 24 → Hariyama

HOW TO OBTAIN

Pokémon Black Version 2	Pinwheel Forest (Hidden Grotto)
Pokémon White Version 2	Pinwheel Forest (Hidden Grotto)

HOW TO OBTAIN FROM OTHER GAMES

LEVEL-UP AND LEARNED MOVES

Lv.	Name	Type	Kind	Pow.	Acc.	PP	Range	Long	DA
1	Brine	Water	Special	65	100	10	Normal	—	—
1	Tackle	Normal	Physical	50	100	35	Normal	—	○
1	Focus Energy	Normal	Status	—	—	30	Self	—	—
1	Sand-Attack	Ground	Status	—	100	15	Normal	—	—
1	Arm Thrust	Fighting	Physical	15	100	20	Normal	—	○
4	Sand-Attack	Ground	Status	—	100	15	Normal	—	—
7	Arm Thrust	Fighting	Physical	15	100	20	Normal	—	○
10	Vital Throw	Fighting	Physical	70	—	10	Normal	—	○
13	Fake Out	Normal	Physical	40	100	10	Normal	—	○
16	Whirlwind	Normal	Status	—	100	20	Normal	—	—
19	Knock Off	Dark	Physical	20	100	20	Normal	—	○
22	SmellingSalt	Normal	Physical	60	100	10	Normal	—	○
27	Belly Drum	Normal	Status	—	—	10	Self	—	—
32	Force Palm	Fighting	Physical	60	100	10	Normal	—	○
37	Seismic Toss	Fighting	Physical	—	100	20	Normal	—	—
42	Wake-Up Slap	Fighting	Physical	60	100	10	Normal	—	○
47	Endure	Normal	Status	—	—	10	Self	—	—
52	Close Combat	Fighting	Physical	120	100	5	Normal	—	○
57	Reversal	Fighting	Physical	—	100	15	Normal	—	○
62	Heavy Slam	Steel	Physical	—	100	10	Normal	—	○

TM & HM MOVES

Lv.	Name	Type	Kind	Pow.	Acc.	PP	Range	Long	DA
TM06	Toxic	Poison	Status	—	90	10	Normal	—	—
TM08	Bulk Up	Fighting	Status	—	—	20	Self	—	—
TM10	Hidden Power	Normal	Special	—	100	15	Normal	—	—
TM11	Sunny Day	Fire	Status	—	—	5	Both Sides	—	—
TM15	Hyper Beam	Normal	Special	150	90	5	Normal	—	—
TM17	Protect	Normal	Status	—	—	10	Self	—	—
TM18	Rain Dance	Water	Status	—	—	5	Both Sides	—	—
TM21	Frustration	Normal	Physical	—	100	20	Normal	—	○
TM23	Smack Down	Rock	Physical	50	100	15	Normal	—	—
TM26	Earthquake	Ground	Physical	100	100	10	Adjacent	—	—
TM27	Return	Normal	Physical	—	100	20	Normal	—	○
TM28	Dig	Ground	Physical	80	100	10	Normal	—	○
TM31	Brick Break	Fighting	Physical	75	100	15	Normal	—	○
TM32	Double Team	Normal	Status	—	—	15	Self	—	—
TM39	Rock Tomb	Rock	Physical	50	80	10	Normal	—	○
TM42	Facade	Normal	Physical	70	100	20	Normal	—	○
TM44	Rest	Psychic	Status	—	—	10	Self	—	—
TM45	Attract	Normal	Status	—	100	15	Normal	—	—
TM47	Low Sweep	Fighting	Physical	60	100	20	Normal	—	○
TM48	Round	Normal	Special	60	100	15	Normal	—	—
TM52	Focus Blast	Fighting	Special	120	70	5	Normal	—	—
TM56	Fling	Dark	Physical	—	100	10	Normal	—	—
TM66	Payback	Dark	Physical	50	100	10	Normal	—	—
TM67	Retaliate	Normal	Physical	70	100	5	Normal	—	○
TM68	Giga Impact	Normal	Physical	150	90	5	Normal	—	—
TM71	Stone Edge	Rock	Physical	100	80	5	Normal	—	—
TM78	Bulldoze	Ground	Physical	60	100	20	Adjacent	—	—
TM80	Rock Slide	Rock	Physical	75	90	10	Many Others	—	—
TM83	Work Up	Normal	Status	—	—	30	Self	—	—
TM84	Poison Jab	Poison	Physical	80	100	20	Normal	—	○
TM87	Swagger	Normal	Status	—	90	15	Normal	—	—
TM90	Substitute	Normal	Status	—	—	10	Self	—	—
TM94	Rock Smash	Fighting	Physical	40	100	15	Normal	—	—

Lv.	Name	Type	Kind	Pow.	Acc.	PP	Range	Long	DA
HM03	Surf	Water	Special	95	100	15	Adjacent	—	—
HM04	Strength	Normal	Physical	80	100	15	Normal	—	○

MOVES TAUGHT BY PEOPLE

Name	Type	Kind	Pow.	Acc.	PP	Range	Long	DA

MOVES TAUGHT BY MOVE TUTORS FOR SHARDS

Name	Type	Kind	Pow.	Acc.	PP	Range	Long	DA
Iron Head	Steel	Physical	80	100	15	Normal	—	○
Low Kick	Fighting	Physical	—	100	20	Normal	—	○
Fire Punch	Fire	Physical	75	100	15	Normal	—	○
ThunderPunch	Electric	Physical	75	100	15	Normal	—	○
Ice Punch	Ice	Physical	75	100	15	Normal	—	○
Superpower	Fighting	Physical	120	100	5	Normal	—	○
Snore	Normal	Special	40	100	15	Normal	—	—
Knock Off	Dark	Physical	20	100	20	Normal	—	○
Role Play	Psychic	Status	—	—	10	Normal	—	—
Helping Hand	Normal	Status	—	—	20	1 Ally	—	—
Sleep Talk	Normal	Status	—	—	10	Self	—	—

---

298 Azurill

Polka Dot Pokémon

TYPE Normal

ABILITIES
- Thick Fat
- Huge Power

HIDDEN ABILITY
- Sap Sipper

- HEIGHT: 0'08"
- WEIGHT: 4.4 lbs.
- GENDER: ♂ / ♀

It swings its large, nutrient-filled tail around to fight opponents bigger than itself.

Same form for ♂ / ♀

STATS
HP	▪▪
Attack	▪
Defense	▪▪
Sp. Atk	▪
Sp. Def	▪▪
Speed	▪

EGG GROUPS
No Egg has ever been discovered

ITEMS SOMETIMES HELD
- None

Pokémon AR Marker

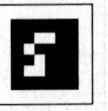

EVOLUTION

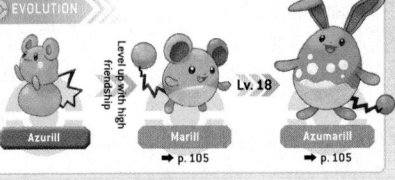

Azurill → Level up with high friendship → Marill → Lv. 18 → Azumarill

→ p. 105   → p. 105

HOW TO OBTAIN

Pokémon Black Version 2	① Floccesy Ranch ② Route 20 (water surface)
Pokémon White Version 2	① Floccesy Ranch ② Route 20 (water surface)

HOW TO OBTAIN FROM OTHER GAMES

LEVEL-UP AND LEARNED MOVES

Lv.	Name	Type	Kind	Pow.	Acc.	PP	Range	Long	DA
1	Splash	Normal	Status	—	—	40	Self	—	—
1	Bubble	Water	Special	20	100	30	Many Others	—	—
3	Tail Whip	Normal	Status	—	100	30	Many Others	—	—
5	Water Sport	Water	Status	—	—	15	Both Sides	—	—
7	Water Gun	Water	Special	40	100	25	Normal	—	—
10	Charm	Normal	Status	—	100	20	Normal	—	—
13	BubbleBeam	Water	Special	65	100	20	Normal	—	—
16	Helping Hand	Normal	Status	—	—	20	1 Ally	—	—
20	Slam	Normal	Physical	80	75	20	Normal	—	○
23	Bounce	Flying	Physical	85	85	5	Normal	○	○

TM & HM MOVES

Lv.	Name	Type	Kind	Pow.	Acc.	PP	Range	Long	DA
TM06	Toxic	Poison	Status	—	90	10	Normal	—	—
TM07	Hail	Ice	Status	—	—	10	Both Sides	—	—
TM10	Hidden Power	Normal	Special	—	100	15	Normal	—	—
TM13	Ice Beam	Ice	Special	95	100	10	Normal	—	—
TM14	Blizzard	Ice	Special	120	70	5	Many Others	—	—
TM16	Light Screen	Psychic	Status	—	—	30	Your Side	—	—
TM17	Protect	Normal	Status	—	—	10	Self	—	—
TM18	Rain Dance	Water	Status	—	—	5	Both Sides	—	—
TM21	Frustration	Normal	Physical	—	100	20	Normal	—	○
TM27	Return	Normal	Physical	—	100	20	Normal	—	○
TM32	Double Team	Normal	Status	—	—	15	Self	—	—
TM42	Facade	Normal	Physical	70	100	20	Normal	—	○
TM44	Rest	Psychic	Status	—	—	10	Self	—	—
TM45	Attract	Normal	Status	—	100	15	Normal	—	—
TM48	Round	Normal	Special	60	100	15	Normal	—	—
TM55	Scald	Water	Special	80	100	15	Normal	—	—
TM83	Work Up	Normal	Status	—	—	30	Self	—	—
TM87	Swagger	Normal	Status	—	90	15	Normal	—	—
TM90	Substitute	Normal	Status	—	—	10	Self	—	—
HM03	Surf	Water	Special	95	100	15	Adjacent	—	—
HM05	Waterfall	Water	Physical	80	100	15	Normal	—	—

MOVES TAUGHT BY PEOPLE

Name	Type	Kind	Pow.	Acc.	PP	Range	Long	DA

MOVES TAUGHT BY MOVE TUTORS FOR SHARDS

Name	Type	Kind	Pow.	Acc.	PP	Range	Long	DA
Covet	Normal	Physical	60	100	40	Normal	—	—
Bounce	Flying	Physical	85	85	5	Normal	○	○
Uproar	Normal	Special	90	100	10	1 Random	—	—
Hyper Voice	Normal	Special	90	100	10	Many Others	—	—
Icy Wind	Ice	Special	55	95	15	Many Others	—	—
Iron Tail	Steel	Physical	100	75	15	Normal	—	○
Snore	Normal	Special	40	100	15	Normal	—	—
Knock Off	Dark	Physical	20	100	20	Normal	—	○
Helping Hand	Normal	Status	—	—	20	1 Ally	—	—
Sleep Talk	Normal	Status	—	—	10	Self	—	—

EGG MOVES

Name	Type	Kind	Pow.	Acc.	PP	Range	Long	DA
Encore	Normal	Status	—	100	5	Normal	—	—
Sing	Normal	Status	—	55	15	Normal	—	—
Refresh	Normal	Status	—	—	20	Self	—	—
Slam	Normal	Physical	80	75	20	Normal	—	○
Tickle	Normal	Status	—	100	20	Normal	—	—
Fake Tears	Dark	Status	—	100	20	Normal	—	—
Body Slam	Normal	Physical	85	100	15	Normal	—	○
Water Sport	Water	Status	—	—	15	Both Sides	—	—
Soak	Water	Status	—	100	20	Normal	—	—
Muddy Water	Water	Special	95	85	10	Many Others	—	—

299 Nosepass

Compass Pokémon

TYPE: Rock

ABILITIES
- Sturdy
- Magnet Pull

HIDDEN ABILITY
- Sand Force

STATS
HP
Attack
Defense
Sp. Atk
Sp. Def
Speed

EGG GROUPS
Mineral

ITEMS SOMETIMES HELD
- Hard Stone

- HEIGHT: 3'03"
- WEIGHT: 213.8 lbs.
- GENDER: ♂ / ♀

Its magnetic nose always faces north and draws iron objects to its body to protect itself better.

Same form for ♂ / ♀

Pokémon AR Marker

EVOLUTION

Nosepass

Level up Nosepass in Chargestone Cave

Probopass

➡ p. 254

HOW TO OBTAIN

Pokémon Black Version 2	❶ Chargestone Cave 1F ❷ Clay Tunnel
Pokémon White Version 2	❶ Chargestone Cave 1F ❷ Clay Tunnel

HOW TO OBTAIN FROM OTHER GAMES

—

—

LEVEL-UP AND LEARNED MOVES

Lv.	Name	Type	Kind	Pow.	Acc.	PP	Range	Long	DA
1	Tackle	Normal	Physical	50	100	35	Normal	—	○
4	Harden	Normal	Status	—	—	30	Self	—	—
8	Block	Normal	Status	—	—	5	Normal	—	—
11	Rock Throw	Rock	Physical	50	90	15	Normal	—	—
15	Thunder Wave	Electric	Status	—	100	20	Normal	—	—
18	Rock Blast	Rock	Physical	25	90	10	Normal	—	—
22	Rest	Psychic	Status	—	—	10	Self	—	—
25	Spark	Electric	Physical	65	100	20	Normal	—	○
29	Rock Slide	Rock	Physical	75	90	10	Many Others	—	—
32	Power Gem	Rock	Special	70	100	20	Normal	—	—
36	Sandstorm	Rock	Status	—	—	10	Both Sides	—	—
39	Discharge	Electric	Special	80	100	15	Adjacent	—	—
43	Earth Power	Ground	Special	90	100	10	Normal	—	—
46	Stone Edge	Rock	Physical	100	80	5	Normal	—	—
50	Lock-On	Normal	Status	—	—	5	Normal	—	—
50	Zap Cannon	Electric	Special	120	50	5	Normal	—	—

TM & HM MOVES

Lv.	Name	Type	Kind	Pow.	Acc.	PP	Range	Long	DA
TM06	Toxic	Poison	Status	—	90	10	Normal	—	—
TM10	Hidden Power	Normal	Special	—	100	15	Normal	—	—
TM11	Sunny Day	Fire	Status	—	—	5	Both Sides	—	—
TM12	Taunt	Dark	Status	—	100	20	Normal	—	—
TM17	Protect	Normal	Status	—	—	10	Self	—	—
TM21	Frustration	Normal	Physical	—	100	20	Normal	—	○
TM23	Smack Down	Rock	Physical	50	100	15	Normal	—	—
TM24	Thunderbolt	Electric	Special	95	100	15	Normal	—	—
TM25	Thunder	Electric	Special	120	70	10	Normal	—	—
TM26	Earthquake	Ground	Physical	100	100	10	Adjacent	—	—
TM27	Return	Normal	Physical	—	100	20	Normal	—	○
TM32	Double Team	Normal	Status	—	—	15	Self	—	—
TM37	Sandstorm	Rock	Status	—	—	10	Both Sides	—	—
TM39	Rock Tomb	Rock	Physical	50	80	10	Normal	—	—
TM41	Torment	Dark	Status	—	100	15	Normal	—	—
TM42	Facade	Normal	Physical	70	100	20	Normal	—	○
TM44	Rest	Psychic	Status	—	—	10	Self	—	—
TM45	Attract	Normal	Status	—	100	15	Normal	—	—
TM48	Round	Normal	Special	60	100	15	Normal	—	—
TM64	Explosion	Normal	Physical	250	100	5	Adjacent	—	—
TM69	Rock Polish	Rock	Status	—	—	20	Self	—	—
TM71	Stone Edge	Rock	Physical	100	80	5	Normal	—	—
TM72	Volt Switch	Electric	Special	70	100	20	Normal	—	—
TM73	Thunder Wave	Electric	Status	—	100	20	Normal	—	—
TM78	Bulldoze	Ground	Physical	60	100	20	Adjacent	—	—
TM80	Rock Slide	Rock	Physical	75	90	10	Many Others	—	—
TM87	Swagger	Normal	Status	—	90	15	Normal	—	—
TM90	Substitute	Normal	Status	—	—	10	Self	—	—
TM94	Rock Smash	Fighting	Physical	40	100	15	Normal	—	○
HM04	Strength	Normal	Physical	80	100	15	Normal	—	○

MOVES TAUGHT BY PEOPLE

Name	Type	Kind	Pow.	Acc.	PP	Range	Long	DA

MOVES TAUGHT BY MOVE TUTORS FOR SHARDS

Name	Type	Kind	Pow.	Acc.	PP	Range	Long	DA
Fire Punch	Fire	Physical	75	100	15	Normal	—	○
ThunderPunch	Electric	Physical	75	100	15	Normal	—	○
Ice Punch	Ice	Physical	75	100	15	Normal	—	○
Iron Defense	Steel	Status	—	—	15	Self	—	—
Magnet Rise	Electric	Status	—	—	10	Self	—	—
Magic Coat	Psychic	Status	—	—	15	Self	—	—
Block	Normal	Status	—	—	5	Normal	—	—
Earth Power	Ground	Special	90	100	10	Normal	—	—
Gravity	Psychic	Status	—	—	5	Both Sides	—	—
Snore	Normal	Special	40	100	15	Normal	—	—
Pain Split	Normal	Status	—	—	20	Normal	—	—
Stealth Rock	Rock	Status	—	—	20	Other Side	—	—
Sleep Talk	Normal	Status	—	—	10	Self	—	—

EGG MOVES

Name	Type	Kind	Pow.	Acc.	PP	Range	Long	DA
Magnitude	Ground	Physical	—	100	30	Adjacent	—	—
Rollout	Rock	Physical	30	90	20	Normal	—	○
Double-Edge	Normal	Physical	120	100	15	Normal	—	○
Block	Normal	Status	—	—	5	Normal	—	—
Stealth Rock	Rock	Status	—	—	20	Other Side	—	—
Endure	Normal	Status	—	—	10	Self	—	—

300 Skitty

Kitten Pokémon

TYPE: Normal

ABILITIES
- Cute Charm
- Normalize

HIDDEN ABILITY
- Wonder Skin

STATS
HP
Attack
Defense
Sp. Atk
Sp. Def
Speed

EGG GROUPS
Field/Fairy

ITEMS SOMETIMES HELD
- Pecha Berry

- HEIGHT: 2'00"
- WEIGHT: 24.3 lbs.
- GENDER: ♂ / ♀

It shows its cute side by chasing its own tail until it gets dizzy.

Same form for ♂ / ♀

Pokémon AR Marker

EVOLUTION

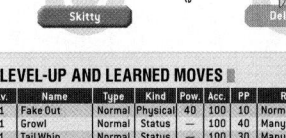

Skitty

Use Moon Stone

Delcatty

HOW TO OBTAIN

Pokémon Black Version 2	Link Trade or Poké Transfer
Pokémon White Version 2	Castelia City empty lot

HOW TO OBTAIN FROM OTHER GAMES

Pokémon Platinum Version	Route 222 (mass outbreak)

—

LEVEL-UP AND LEARNED MOVES

Lv.	Name	Type	Kind	Pow.	Acc.	PP	Range	Long	DA
1	Fake Out	Normal	Physical	40	100	10	Normal	—	○
1	Growl	Normal	Status	—	100	40	Many Others	—	—
1	Tail Whip	Normal	Status	—	100	30	Many Others	—	—
1	Tackle	Normal	Physical	50	100	35	Normal	—	○
4	Foresight	Normal	Status	—	—	40	Normal	—	—
8	Attract	Normal	Status	—	100	15	Normal	—	—
11	Sing	Normal	Status	—	55	15	Normal	—	—
15	DoubleSlap	Normal	Physical	15	85	10	Normal	—	○
18	Copycat	Normal	Status	—	—	20	Self	—	—
22	Assist	Normal	Status	—	—	20	Self	—	—
25	Charm	Normal	Status	—	100	20	Normal	—	—
29	Faint Attack	Dark	Physical	60	—	20	Normal	—	○
32	Wake-Up Slap	Fighting	Physical	60	100	10	Normal	—	○
36	Covet	Normal	Physical	60	100	40	Normal	—	○
39	Heal Bell	Normal	Status	—	—	5	Your Party	—	—
42	Double-Edge	Normal	Physical	120	100	15	Normal	—	○
46	Captivate	Normal	Status	—	100	20	Many Others	—	—

TM & HM MOVES

Lv.	Name	Type	Kind	Pow.	Acc.	PP	Range	Long	DA
TM04	Calm Mind	Psychic	Status	—	—	20	Self	—	—
TM06	Toxic	Poison	Status	—	90	10	Normal	—	—
TM10	Hidden Power	Normal	Special	—	100	15	Normal	—	—
TM11	Sunny Day	Fire	Status	—	—	5	Both Sides	—	—
TM13	Ice Beam	Ice	Special	95	100	10	Normal	—	—
TM14	Blizzard	Ice	Special	120	70	5	Many Others	—	—
TM17	Protect	Normal	Status	—	—	10	Self	—	—
TM18	Rain Dance	Water	Status	—	—	5	Both Sides	—	—
TM20	Safeguard	Normal	Status	—	—	25	Your Side	—	—
TM21	Frustration	Normal	Physical	—	100	20	Normal	—	○
TM22	SolarBeam	Grass	Special	120	100	10	Normal	—	—
TM24	Thunderbolt	Electric	Special	95	100	15	Normal	—	—
TM25	Thunder	Electric	Special	120	70	10	Normal	—	—
TM27	Return	Normal	Physical	—	100	20	Normal	—	○
TM28	Dig	Ground	Physical	80	100	10	Normal	—	○
TM30	Shadow Ball	Ghost	Special	80	100	15	Normal	—	—
TM32	Double Team	Normal	Status	—	—	15	Self	—	—
TM42	Facade	Normal	Physical	70	100	20	Normal	—	○
TM44	Rest	Psychic	Status	—	—	10	Self	—	—
TM45	Attract	Normal	Status	—	100	15	Normal	—	—
TM48	Round	Normal	Special	60	100	15	Normal	—	—
TM49	Echoed Voice	Normal	Special	40	100	15	Normal	—	—
TM57	Charge Beam	Electric	Special	50	90	10	Normal	—	—
TM66	Payback	Dark	Physical	50	100	10	Normal	—	○
TM67	Retaliate	Normal	Physical	70	100	5	Normal	—	○
TM70	Flash	Normal	Status	—	100	20	Normal	—	—
TM73	Thunder Wave	Electric	Status	—	100	20	Normal	—	—
TM77	Psych Up	Normal	Status	—	—	10	Normal	—	—
TM83	Work Up	Normal	Status	—	—	30	Self	—	—
TM85	Dream Eater	Psychic	Special	100	100	15	Normal	—	—
TM86	Grass Knot	Grass	Special	—	100	20	Normal	—	○
TM87	Swagger	Normal	Status	—	90	15	Normal	—	—
TM90	Substitute	Normal	Status	—	—	10	Self	—	—
TM93	Wild Charge	Electric	Physical	90	100	15	Normal	—	○

MOVES TAUGHT BY PEOPLE

Name	Type	Kind	Pow.	Acc.	PP	Range	Long	DA

MOVES TAUGHT BY MOVE TUTORS FOR SHARDS

Name	Type	Kind	Pow.	Acc.	PP	Range	Long	DA
Covet	Normal	Physical	60	100	40	Normal	—	○
Uproar	Normal	Special	90	100	10	1 Random	—	—
Last Resort	Normal	Physical	140	100	5	Normal	—	○
Hyper Voice	Normal	Special	90	100	10	Many Others	—	—
Icy Wind	Ice	Special	55	95	15	Many Others	—	—
Iron Tail	Steel	Physical	100	75	15	Normal	—	○
Zen Headbutt	Psychic	Physical	80	90	15	Normal	—	○
Snore	Normal	Special	40	100	15	Normal	—	—
Heal Bell	Normal	Status	—	—	5	Your Party	—	—
Helping Hand	Normal	Status	—	—	20	1 Ally	—	—
Sleep Talk	Normal	Status	—	—	10	Self	—	—

EGG MOVES

Name	Type	Kind	Pow.	Acc.	PP	Range	Long	DA
Helping Hand	Normal	Status	—	—	20	1 Ally	—	—
Uproar	Normal	Special	90	100	10	1 Random	—	—
Fake Tears	Dark	Status	—	100	20	Normal	—	—
Wish	Normal	Status	—	—	10	Self	—	—
Baton Pass	Normal	Status	—	—	40	Self	—	—
Tickle	Normal	Status	—	100	20	Normal	—	—
Last Resort	Normal	Physical	140	100	5	Normal	—	○
Fake Out	Normal	Physical	40	100	10	Normal	—	○
Zen Headbutt	Psychic	Physical	80	90	15	Normal	—	○
Sucker Punch	Dark	Physical	80	100	5	Normal	—	○
Mud Bomb	Ground	Special	65	85	10	Normal	—	—
Simple Beam	Normal	Status	—	100	15	Normal	—	—
Captivate	Normal	Status	—	100	20	Many Others	—	—

Prim Pokémon

301 Delcatty

- HEIGHT: 3'07"
- WEIGHT: 71.9 lbs.
- GENDER: ♂ / ♀

The reason it does not have a nest is that it simply searches for a clean, comfortable place then sleeps there.

Same form for ♂ / ♀

Pokémon AR Marker

TYPE Normal

ABILITIES
- Cute Charm
- Normalize

HIDDEN ABILITY
- Wonder Skin

STATS
HP
Attack
Defense
Sp. Atk
Sp. Def
Speed

EGG GROUPS
Field/Fairy

ITEMS SOMETIMES HELD
- Pecha Berry

EVOLUTION

HOW TO OBTAIN

Pokémon Black Version 2	Use Moon Stone on a Skitty you obtain via Link Trade or Poké Transfer
Pokémon White Version 2	Castelia City empty lot (rustling grass)

HOW TO OBTAIN FROM OTHER GAMES

—
—

LEVEL-UP AND LEARNED MOVES

Lv.	Name	Type	Kind	Pow.	Acc.	PP	Range	Long	DA
1	Fake Out	Normal	Physical	40	100	10	Normal	—	○
1	Attract	Normal	Status	—	100	15	Normal	—	—
1	Sing	Normal	Status	—	55	15	Normal	—	—
1	DoubleSlap	Normal	Physical	15	85	10	Normal	—	○

TM & HM MOVES

Lv.	Name	Type	Kind	Pow.	Acc.	PP	Range	Long	DA
TM04	Calm Mind	Psychic	Status	—	—	20	Self	—	—
TM06	Toxic	Poison	Status	—	90	10	Normal	—	—
TM10	Hidden Power	Normal	Special	—	100	15	Normal	—	—
TM11	Sunny Day	Fire	Status	—	—	5	Both Sides	—	—
TM13	Ice Beam	Ice	Special	95	100	10	Normal	—	—
TM14	Blizzard	Ice	Special	120	70	5	Many Others	—	—
TM15	Hyper Beam	Normal	Special	150	90	5	Normal	—	—
TM17	Protect	Normal	Status	—	—	10	Self	—	—
TM18	Rain Dance	Water	Status	—	—	5	Both Sides	—	—
TM20	Safeguard	Normal	Status	—	—	25	Your Side	—	—
TM21	Frustration	Normal	Physical	—	100	20	Normal	—	○
TM22	SolarBeam	Grass	Special	120	100	10	Normal	—	—
TM24	Thunderbolt	Electric	Special	95	100	15	Normal	—	—
TM25	Thunder	Electric	Special	120	70	10	Normal	—	—
TM27	Return	Normal	Physical	—	100	20	Normal	—	○
TM28	Dig	Ground	Physical	80	100	10	Normal	—	○
TM30	Shadow Ball	Ghost	Special	80	100	15	Normal	—	—
TM32	Double Team	Normal	Status	—	—	15	Self	—	—
TM42	Facade	Normal	Physical	70	100	20	Normal	—	○
TM44	Rest	Psychic	Status	—	—	10	Self	—	—
TM45	Attract	Normal	Status	—	100	15	Normal	—	—
TM48	Round	Normal	Special	60	100	15	Normal	—	—
TM49	Echoed Voice	Normal	Special	40	100	15	Normal	—	—
TM57	Charge Beam	Electric	Special	50	90	10	Normal	—	—
TM66	Payback	Dark	Physical	50	100	10	Normal	—	○
TM67	Retaliate	Normal	Physical	70	100	5	Normal	—	○
TM68	Giga Impact	Normal	Physical	150	90	5	Normal	—	○
TM70	Flash	Normal	Status	—	100	20	Normal	—	—
TM73	Thunder Wave	Electric	Status	—	100	20	Normal	—	—
TM77	Psych Up	Normal	Status	—	—	10	Normal	—	—
TM83	Work Up	Normal	Status	—	—	30	Self	—	—
TM85	Dream Eater	Psychic	Special	100	100	15	Normal	—	—
TM86	Grass Knot	Grass	Special	—	100	20	Normal	—	○
TM87	Swagger	Normal	Status	—	90	15	Normal	—	—
TM90	Substitute	Normal	Status	—	—	10	Self	—	—
TM93	Wild Charge	Electric	Physical	90	100	15	Normal	—	○
TM94	Rock Smash	Fighting	Physical	40	100	15	Normal	—	○
HM04	Strength	Normal	Physical	80	100	15	Normal	—	○

MOVES TAUGHT BY PEOPLE

Name	Type	Kind	Pow.	Acc.	PP	Range	Long	DA

MOVES TAUGHT BY MOVE TUTORS FOR SHARDS

Name	Type	Kind	Pow.	Acc.	PP	Range	Long	DA
Covet	Normal	Physical	60	100	40	Normal	—	○
Uproar	Normal	Special	90	100	10	1 Random	—	—
Last Resort	Normal	Physical	140	100	5	Normal	—	○
Hyper Voice	Normal	Special	90	100	10	Many Others	—	—
Icy Wind	Ice	Special	55	95	15	Many Others	—	—
Iron Tail	Steel	Physical	100	75	15	Normal	—	○
Zen Headbutt	Psychic	Physical	80	90	15	Normal	—	○
Snore	Normal	Special	40	100	15	Normal	—	—
Heal Bell	Normal	Status	—	—	5	Your Party	—	—
Helping Hand	Normal	Status	—	—	20	1 Ally	—	—
Sleep Talk	Normal	Status	—	—	10	Self	—	—

Darkness Pokémon

302 Sableye

- HEIGHT: 1'08"
- WEIGHT: 24.3 lbs.
- GENDER: ♂ / ♀

It hides in the darkness of caves. Its diet of gems has transformed its eyes into gemstones.

Same form for ♂ / ♀

Pokémon AR Marker

TYPE Dark Ghost

ABILITIES
- Keen Eye
- Stall

HIDDEN ABILITY
- Prankster

STATS
HP
Attack
Defense
Sp. Atk
Sp. Def
Speed

EGG GROUPS
Human-Like

ITEMS SOMETIMES HELD
- None

EVOLUTION

Does not evolve

HOW TO OBTAIN

Pokémon Black Version 2	If your character is a girl, trade Pokémon during a date with Curtis (seventh time)
Pokémon White Version 2	If your character is a girl, trade Pokémon during a date with Curtis (seventh time)

HOW TO OBTAIN FROM OTHER GAMES

Pokémon Black Version	Challenger's Cave 1F
Pokémon White Version	Challenger's Cave 1F

LEVEL-UP AND LEARNED MOVES

Lv.	Name	Type	Kind	Pow.	Acc.	PP	Range	Long	DA
1	Leer	Normal	Status	—	100	30	Many Others	—	—
1	Scratch	Normal	Physical	40	100	35	Normal	—	○
4	Foresight	Normal	Status	—	—	40	Normal	—	—
8	Night Shade	Ghost	Special	—	100	15	Normal	—	—
11	Astonish	Ghost	Physical	30	100	15	Normal	—	○
15	Fury Swipes	Normal	Physical	18	80	15	Normal	—	○
18	Fake Out	Normal	Physical	40	100	10	Normal	—	○
22	Detect	Fighting	Status	—	—	5	Self	—	—
25	Shadow Sneak	Ghost	Physical	40	100	30	Normal	—	○
29	Knock Off	Dark	Physical	20	100	20	Normal	—	○
32	Faint Attack	Dark	Physical	60	—	20	Normal	—	○
36	Punishment	Dark	Physical	—	100	5	Normal	—	○
39	Shadow Claw	Ghost	Physical	70	100	15	Normal	—	○
43	Power Gem	Rock	Special	70	100	20	Normal	—	—
46	Confuse Ray	Ghost	Status	—	100	10	Normal	—	—
50	Foul Play	Dark	Physical	95	100	15	Normal	—	○
53	Zen Headbutt	Psychic	Physical	80	90	15	Normal	—	○
57	Shadow Ball	Ghost	Special	80	100	15	Normal	—	—
60	Mean Look	Normal	Status	—	—	5	Normal	—	—

TM & HM MOVES

Lv.	Name	Type	Kind	Pow.	Acc.	PP	Range	Long	DA
TM01	Hone Claws	Dark	Status	—	—	15	Self	—	—
TM04	Calm Mind	Psychic	Status	—	—	20	Self	—	—
TM06	Toxic	Poison	Status	—	90	10	Normal	—	—
TM10	Hidden Power	Normal	Special	—	100	15	Normal	—	—
TM11	Sunny Day	Fire	Status	—	—	5	Both Sides	—	—
TM12	Taunt	Dark	Status	—	100	20	Normal	—	—
TM17	Protect	Normal	Status	—	—	10	Self	—	—
TM18	Rain Dance	Water	Status	—	—	5	Both Sides	—	—
TM19	Telekinesis	Psychic	Status	—	—	15	Normal	—	—
TM21	Frustration	Normal	Physical	—	100	20	Normal	—	○
TM27	Return	Normal	Physical	—	100	20	Normal	—	○
TM28	Dig	Ground	Physical	80	100	10	Normal	—	○
TM29	Psychic	Psychic	Special	90	100	10	Normal	—	—
TM30	Shadow Ball	Ghost	Special	80	100	15	Normal	—	—
TM31	Brick Break	Fighting	Physical	75	100	15	Normal	—	○
TM32	Double Team	Normal	Status	—	—	15	Self	—	—
TM39	Rock Tomb	Rock	Physical	50	80	10	Normal	—	—
TM40	Aerial Ace	Flying	Physical	60	—	20	Normal	○	○
TM41	Torment	Dark	Status	—	100	15	Normal	—	—
TM42	Facade	Normal	Physical	70	100	20	Normal	—	○
TM44	Rest	Psychic	Status	—	—	10	Self	—	—
TM45	Attract	Normal	Status	—	100	15	Normal	—	—
TM46	Thief	Dark	Physical	40	100	10	Normal	—	○
TM47	Low Sweep	Fighting	Physical	60	100	20	Normal	—	○
TM48	Round	Normal	Special	60	100	15	Normal	—	—
TM56	Fling	Dark	Physical	—	100	10	Normal	—	—
TM59	Incinerate	Fire	Special	30	100	15	Many Others	—	—
TM61	Will-O-Wisp	Fire	Status	—	75	15	Normal	—	—
TM63	Embargo	Dark	Status	—	100	15	Normal	—	—
TM65	Shadow Claw	Ghost	Physical	70	100	15	Normal	—	○
TM66	Payback	Dark	Physical	50	100	10	Normal	—	○
TM67	Retaliate	Normal	Physical	70	100	5	Normal	—	○
TM70	Flash	Normal	Status	—	100	20	Normal	—	—
TM77	Psych Up	Normal	Status	—	—	10	Normal	—	—
TM84	Poison Jab	Poison	Physical	80	100	20	Normal	—	○
TM85	Dream Eater	Psychic	Special	100	100	15	Normal	—	—
TM87	Swagger	Normal	Status	—	90	15	Normal	—	—
TM90	Substitute	Normal	Status	—	—	10	Self	—	—
TM94	Rock Smash	Fighting	Physical	40	100	15	Normal	—	○
TM95	Snarl	Dark	Special	55	95	15	Many Others	—	—
HM01	Cut	Normal	Physical	50	95	30	Normal	—	○

MOVES TAUGHT BY PEOPLE

Name	Type	Kind	Pow.	Acc.	PP	Range	Long	DA

MOVES TAUGHT BY MOVE TUTORS FOR SHARDS

Name	Type	Kind	Pow.	Acc.	PP	Range	Long	DA
Signal Beam	Bug	Special	75	100	15	Normal	—	—
Low Kick	Fighting	Physical	—	100	20	Normal	—	○
Fire Punch	Fire	Physical	75	100	15	Normal	—	○
ThunderPunch	Electric	Physical	75	100	15	Normal	—	○
Ice Punch	Ice	Physical	75	100	15	Normal	—	○
Magic Coat	Psychic	Status	—	—	15	Self	—	—
Icy Wind	Ice	Special	55	95	15	Many Others	—	—
Zen Headbutt	Psychic	Physical	80	90	15	Normal	—	○
Foul Play	Dark	Physical	95	100	15	Normal	—	○
Gravity	Psychic	Status	—	—	5	Both Sides	—	—
Dark Pulse	Dark	Special	80	100	15	Normal	○	—
Snore	Normal	Special	40	100	15	Normal	—	—
Knock Off	Dark	Physical	20	100	20	Normal	—	○
Role Play	Psychic	Status	—	—	10	Normal	—	—
Wonder Room	Psychic	Status	—	—	10	Both Sides	—	—
Spite	Ghost	Status	—	100	10	Normal	—	—
Trick	Psychic	Status	—	100	10	Normal	—	—
Sleep Talk	Normal	Status	—	—	10	Self	—	—
Snatch	Dark	Status	—	—	10	Self	—	—

EGG MOVES

Name	Type	Kind	Pow.	Acc.	PP	Range	Long	DA
Recover	Normal	Status	—	—	10	Self	—	—
Moonlight	Normal	Status	—	—	5	Self	—	—
Nasty Plot	Dark	Status	—	—	20	Self	—	—
Flatter	Dark	Status	—	100	15	Normal	—	—
Feint	Normal	Physical	30	100	10	Normal	—	—
Sucker Punch	Dark	Physical	80	100	5	Normal	—	○
Trick	Psychic	Status	—	100	10	Normal	—	—
Captivate	Normal	Status	—	100	20	Many Others	—	—
Mean Look	Normal	Status	—	—	5	Normal	—	—
Metal Burst	Steel	Physical	—	100	10	Varies	—	—

303 Mawile

Deceiver Pokémon

TYPE Steel

ABILITIES
- Hyper Cutter
- Intimidate

HIDDEN ABILITY
- Sheer Force

STATS
HP
Attack
Defense
Sp. Atk
Sp. Def
Speed

EGG GROUPS
Field/Fairy

ITEMS SOMETIMES HELD
- None

- HEIGHT: 2'00"
- WEIGHT: 25.4 lbs.
- GENDER: ♂ / ♀

Attached to its head is a huge set of jaws formed by horns. It can chew through iron beams.

Same form for ♂ / ♀

Pokémon AR Marker

EVOLUTION

Does not evolve

HOW TO OBTAIN

Pokémon Black Version 2	If your character is a girl, trade Pokémon during a date with Curtis (seventh time)
Pokémon White Version 2	If your character is a girl, trade Pokémon during a date with Curtis (seventh time)

HOW TO OBTAIN FROM OTHER GAMES

Pokémon Black Version	Challenger's Cave 1F
Pokémon White Version	Challenger's Cave 1F

LEVEL-UP AND LEARNED MOVES

Lv.	Name	Type	Kind	Pow.	Acc.	PP	Range	Long	DA
1	Astonish	Ghost	Physical	30	100	15	Normal	—	○
6	Fake Tears	Dark	Status	—	100	20	Normal	—	—
11	Bite	Dark	Physical	60	100	25	Normal	—	○
16	Sweet Scent	Normal	Status	—	100	20	Many Others	—	—
21	ViceGrip	Normal	Physical	55	100	30	Normal	—	○
26	Faint Attack	Dark	Physical	60	—	20	Normal	—	○
31	Baton Pass	Normal	Status	—	—	40	Self	—	—
36	Crunch	Dark	Physical	80	100	15	Normal	—	○
41	Iron Defense	Steel	Status	—	—	15	Self	—	—
46	Sucker Punch	Dark	Physical	80	100	5	Normal	—	○
51	Stockpile	Normal	Status	—	—	20	Self	—	—
51	Swallow	Normal	Status	—	—	10	Self	—	—
51	Spit Up	Normal	Special	—	100	10	Normal	—	—
56	Iron Head	Steel	Physical	80	100	15	Normal	—	○

TM & HM MOVES

Lv.	Name	Type	Kind	Pow.	Acc.	PP	Range	Long	DA
TM06	Toxic	Poison	Status	—	90	10	Normal	—	—
TM10	Hidden Power	Normal	Special	—	100	15	Normal	—	—
TM11	Sunny Day	Fire	Status	—	—	5	Both Sides	—	—
TM12	Taunt	Dark	Status	—	100	20	Normal	—	—
TM13	Ice Beam	Ice	Special	95	100	10	Normal	—	—
TM15	Hyper Beam	Normal	Special	150	90	5	Normal	—	—
TM17	Protect	Normal	Status	—	—	10	Self	—	—
TM18	Rain Dance	Water	Status	—	—	5	Both Sides	—	—
TM21	Frustration	Normal	Physical	—	100	20	Normal	—	○
TM22	SolarBeam	Grass	Special	120	100	10	Normal	—	—
TM27	Return	Normal	Physical	—	100	20	Normal	—	○
TM30	Shadow Ball	Ghost	Special	80	100	15	Normal	—	—
TM31	Brick Break	Fighting	Physical	75	100	15	Normal	—	○
TM32	Double Team	Normal	Status	—	—	15	Self	—	—
TM35	Flamethrower	Fire	Special	95	100	15	Normal	—	—
TM36	Sludge Bomb	Poison	Special	90	100	10	Normal	—	—
TM37	Sandstorm	Rock	Status	—	—	10	Both Sides	—	—
TM38	Fire Blast	Fire	Special	120	85	5	Normal	—	—
TM39	Rock Tomb	Rock	Physical	50	80	10	Normal	—	—
TM41	Torment	Dark	Status	—	100	15	Normal	—	—
TM42	Facade	Normal	Physical	70	100	20	Normal	—	○
TM44	Rest	Psychic	Status	—	—	10	Self	—	—
TM45	Attract	Normal	Status	—	100	15	Normal	—	—
TM48	Round	Normal	Special	60	100	15	Normal	—	—
TM52	Focus Blast	Fighting	Special	120	70	5	Normal	—	—
TM54	False Swipe	Normal	Physical	40	100	40	Normal	—	○
TM56	Fling	Dark	Physical	—	100	10	Normal	—	—
TM57	Charge Beam	Electric	Special	50	90	10	Normal	—	—
TM59	Incinerate	Fire	Special	30	100	15	Many Others	—	—
TM63	Embargo	Dark	Status	—	100	15	Normal	—	—
TM66	Payback	Dark	Physical	50	100	10	Normal	—	○
TM68	Giga Impact	Normal	Physical	150	90	5	Normal	—	○
TM71	Stone Edge	Rock	Physical	100	80	5	Normal	—	—
TM75	Swords Dance	Normal	Status	—	—	30	Self	—	—
TM77	Psych Up	Normal	Status	—	—	10	Normal	—	—
TM80	Rock Slide	Rock	Physical	75	90	10	Many Others	—	—
TM86	Grass Knot	Grass	Special	—	100	20	Normal	—	○
TM87	Swagger	Normal	Status	—	90	15	Normal	—	—
TM90	Substitute	Normal	Status	—	—	10	Self	—	—
TM91	Flash Cannon	Steel	Special	80	100	10	Normal	—	—
TM94	Rock Smash	Fighting	Physical	40	100	15	Normal	—	○
HM04	Strength	Normal	Physical	80	100	15	Normal	—	○

MOVES TAUGHT BY PEOPLE

Name	Type	Kind	Pow.	Acc.	PP	Range	Long	DA

MOVES TAUGHT BY MOVE TUTORS FOR SHARDS

Name	Type	Kind	Pow.	Acc.	PP	Range	Long	DA
Iron Head	Steel	Physical	80	100	15	Normal	—	○
Super Fang	Normal	Physical	—	90	10	Normal	—	○
ThunderPunch	Electric	Physical	75	100	15	Normal	—	○
Ice Punch	Ice	Physical	75	100	15	Normal	—	○
Last Resort	Normal	Physical	140	100	5	Normal	—	○
Iron Defense	Steel	Status	—	—	15	Self	—	—
Magnet Rise	Electric	Status	—	—	10	Self	—	—
Icy Wind	Ice	Special	55	95	15	Many Others	—	—
Foul Play	Dark	Physical	95	100	15	Normal	—	○
Dark Pulse	Dark	Special	80	100	15	Normal	○	—
Snore	Normal	Special	40	100	15	Normal	—	—
Knock Off	Dark	Physical	20	100	20	Normal	—	○
Pain Split	Normal	Status	—	—	20	Normal	—	—
Stealth Rock	Rock	Status	—	—	20	Other Side	—	—
Sleep Talk	Normal	Status	—	—	10	Self	—	—
Snatch	Dark	Status	—	—	10	Self	—	—

EGG MOVES

Name	Type	Kind	Pow.	Acc.	PP	Range	Long	DA
Poison Fang	Poison	Physical	50	100	15	Normal	—	○
AncientPower	Rock	Special	60	100	5	Normal	—	—
Tickle	Normal	Status	—	100	20	Normal	—	—
Sucker Punch	Dark	Physical	80	100	5	Normal	—	○
Ice Fang	Ice	Physical	65	95	15	Normal	—	○
Fire Fang	Fire	Physical	65	95	15	Normal	—	○
Thunder Fang	Electric	Physical	65	95	15	Normal	—	○
Punishment	Dark	Physical	—	100	5	Normal	—	○
Guard Swap	Psychic	Status	—	—	10	Normal	—	—
Captivate	Normal	Status	—	100	20	Many Others	—	—
Slam	Normal	Physical	80	75	20	Normal	—	○
Metal Burst	Steel	Physical	—	100	10	Varies	—	—

304 Aron

Iron Armor Pokémon

TYPE Steel Rock

ABILITIES
- Sturdy
- Rock Head

HIDDEN ABILITY
- Heavy Metal

STATS
HP
Attack
Defense
Sp. Atk
Sp. Def
Speed

EGG GROUPS
Monster

ITEMS SOMETIMES HELD
- Hard Stone

- HEIGHT: 1'04"
- WEIGHT: 132.3 lbs.
- GENDER: ♂ / ♀

In order to build up its steel body, it eats iron ore. This pesky Pokémon is known to eat railroad tracks.

Same form for ♂ / ♀

Pokémon AR Marker

EVOLUTION

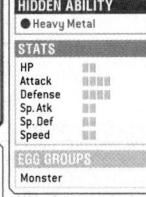

Aron
Lv. 32
Lairon
Lv. 42
Aggron

HOW TO OBTAIN

Pokémon Black Version 2	❶ Mistralton Cave 1F ❷ Mistralton Cave 2F
Pokémon White Version 2	❶ Mistralton Cave 1F ❷ Mistralton Cave 2F

HOW TO OBTAIN FROM OTHER GAMES

—
—

LEVEL-UP AND LEARNED MOVES

Lv.	Name	Type	Kind	Pow.	Acc.	PP	Range	Long	DA
1	Tackle	Normal	Physical	50	100	35	Normal	—	○
1	Harden	Normal	Status	—	—	30	Self	—	—
4	Mud-Slap	Ground	Special	20	100	10	Normal	—	—
8	Headbutt	Normal	Physical	70	100	15	Normal	—	○
11	Metal Claw	Steel	Physical	50	95	35	Normal	—	○
15	Iron Defense	Steel	Status	—	—	15	Self	—	—
18	Roar	Normal	Status	—	100	20	Normal	—	—
22	Take Down	Normal	Physical	90	85	20	Normal	—	○
25	Iron Head	Steel	Physical	80	100	15	Normal	—	○
29	Protect	Normal	Status	—	—	10	Self	—	—
32	Metal Sound	Steel	Status	—	85	40	Normal	—	—
36	Iron Tail	Steel	Physical	100	75	15	Normal	—	○
39	Autotomize	Steel	Status	—	—	15	Self	—	—
43	Heavy Slam	Steel	Physical	—	100	10	Normal	—	○
46	Double-Edge	Normal	Physical	120	100	15	Normal	—	○
50	Metal Burst	Steel	Physical	—	100	10	Varies	—	—

TM & HM MOVES

Lv.	Name	Type	Kind	Pow.	Acc.	PP	Range	Long	DA
TM01	Hone Claws	Dark	Status	—	—	15	Self	—	—
TM05	Roar	Normal	Status	—	100	20	Normal	—	—
TM06	Toxic	Poison	Status	—	90	10	Normal	—	—
TM10	Hidden Power	Normal	Special	—	100	15	Normal	—	—
TM11	Sunny Day	Fire	Status	—	—	5	Both Sides	—	—
TM17	Protect	Normal	Status	—	—	10	Self	—	—
TM18	Rain Dance	Water	Status	—	—	5	Both Sides	—	—
TM21	Frustration	Normal	Physical	—	100	20	Normal	—	○
TM26	Earthquake	Ground	Physical	100	100	10	Adjacent	—	—
TM27	Return	Normal	Physical	—	100	20	Normal	—	○
TM28	Dig	Ground	Physical	80	100	10	Normal	—	○
TM32	Double Team	Normal	Status	—	—	15	Self	—	—
TM37	Sandstorm	Rock	Status	—	—	10	Both Sides	—	—
TM39	Rock Tomb	Rock	Physical	50	80	10	Normal	—	—
TM40	Aerial Ace	Flying	Physical	60	—	20	Normal	○	○
TM42	Facade	Normal	Physical	70	100	20	Normal	—	○
TM44	Rest	Psychic	Status	—	—	10	Self	—	—
TM45	Attract	Normal	Status	—	100	15	Normal	—	—
TM48	Round	Normal	Special	60	100	15	Normal	—	—
TM65	Shadow Claw	Ghost	Physical	70	100	15	Normal	—	○
TM69	Rock Polish	Rock	Status	—	—	20	Self	—	—
TM78	Bulldoze	Ground	Physical	60	100	20	Adjacent	—	—
TM80	Rock Slide	Rock	Physical	75	90	10	Many Others	—	—
TM87	Swagger	Normal	Status	—	90	15	Normal	—	—
TM90	Substitute	Normal	Status	—	—	10	Self	—	—
TM94	Rock Smash	Fighting	Physical	40	100	15	Normal	—	○
HM01	Cut	Normal	Physical	50	95	30	Normal	—	○
HM04	Strength	Normal	Physical	80	100	15	Normal	—	○

MOVES TAUGHT BY PEOPLE

Name	Type	Kind	Pow.	Acc.	PP	Range	Long	DA

MOVES TAUGHT BY MOVE TUTORS FOR SHARDS

Name	Type	Kind	Pow.	Acc.	PP	Range	Long	DA
Iron Head	Steel	Physical	80	100	15	Normal	—	○
Uproar	Normal	Special	90	100	10	1 Random	—	—
Iron Defense	Steel	Status	—	—	15	Self	—	—
Magnet Rise	Electric	Status	—	—	10	Self	—	—
Iron Tail	Steel	Physical	100	75	15	Normal	—	○
Earth Power	Ground	Special	90	100	10	Normal	—	—
Superpower	Fighting	Physical	120	100	5	Normal	—	○
Snore	Normal	Special	40	100	15	Normal	—	—
Spite	Ghost	Status	—	100	10	Normal	—	—
Stealth Rock	Rock	Status	—	—	20	Other Side	—	—
Endeavor	Normal	Physical	—	100	5	Normal	—	○
Sleep Talk	Normal	Status	—	—	10	Self	—	—

EGG MOVES

Name	Type	Kind	Pow.	Acc.	PP	Range	Long	DA
Endeavor	Normal	Physical	—	100	5	Normal	—	○
Body Slam	Normal	Physical	85	100	15	Normal	—	○
Stomp	Normal	Physical	65	100	20	Normal	—	○
SmellingSalt	Normal	Physical	60	100	10	Normal	—	○
Curse	Ghost	Status	—	—	10	Varies	—	—
Screech	Normal	Status	—	85	40	Normal	—	—
Iron Head	Steel	Physical	80	100	15	Normal	—	○
Dragon Rush	Dragon	Physical	100	75	10	Normal	—	○
Head Smash	Rock	Physical	150	80	5	Normal	—	○
Superpower	Fighting	Physical	120	100	5	Normal	—	○
Stealth Rock	Rock	Status	—	—	20	Other Side	—	—

303 Mawile
304 Aron

Iron Armor Pokémon

305 Lairon

- HEIGHT: 2'11"
- WEIGHT: 264.6 lbs.
- GENDER: ♂ / ♀

Lairon fight over territory, and when their steel bodies collide, sparks fly.

TYPE: Steel / Rock

ABILITIES
- Sturdy
- Rock Head

HIDDEN ABILITY
- Heavy Metal

STATS
HP
Attack
Defense
Sp. Atk
Sp. Def
Speed

EGG GROUPS
Monster

Same form for ♂ / ♀

ITEMS SOMETIMES HELD
- Hard Stone

EVOLUTION

Lv. 32
Lv. 42
Aron
Lairon
Aggron

HOW TO OBTAIN

Pokémon Black Version 2	Clay Tunnel
Pokémon White Version 2	Clay Tunnel

HOW TO OBTAIN FROM OTHER GAMES

—

—

Pokémon AR Marker

LEVEL-UP AND LEARNED MOVES

Lv.	Name	Type	Kind	Pow.	Acc.	PP	Range	Long	DA
1	Tackle	Normal	Physical	50	100	35	Normal	—	○
1	Harden	Normal	Status	—	—	30	Self	—	—
1	Mud-Slap	Ground	Special	20	100	10	Normal	—	—
1	Headbutt	Normal	Physical	70	100	15	Normal	—	○
4	Mud-Slap	Ground	Special	20	100	10	Normal	—	—
8	Headbutt	Normal	Physical	70	100	15	Normal	—	○
11	Metal Claw	Steel	Physical	50	95	35	Normal	—	○
15	Iron Defense	Steel	Status	—	—	15	Self	—	—
18	Roar	Normal	Status	—	100	20	Normal	—	—
22	Take Down	Normal	Physical	90	85	20	Normal	—	○
25	Iron Head	Steel	Physical	80	100	15	Normal	—	○
29	Protect	Normal	Status	—	—	10	Self	—	—
34	Metal Sound	Steel	Status	—	85	40	Normal	—	—
40	Iron Tail	Steel	Physical	100	75	15	Normal	—	○
45	Autotomize	Steel	Status	—	—	15	Self	—	—
51	Heavy Slam	Steel	Physical	—	100	10	Normal	—	○
56	Double-Edge	Normal	Physical	120	100	15	Normal	—	○
62	Metal Burst	Steel	Physical	—	100	10	Varies	—	—

TM & HM MOVES

Lv.	Name	Type	Kind	Pow.	Acc.	PP	Range	Long	DA
TM01	Hone Claws	Dark	Status	—	—	15	Self	—	—
TM05	Roar	Normal	Status	—	100	20	Normal	—	—
TM06	Toxic	Poison	Status	—	90	10	Normal	—	—
TM10	Hidden Power	Normal	Special	—	100	15	Normal	—	—
TM11	Sunny Day	Fire	Status	—	—	5	Both Sides	—	—
TM17	Protect	Normal	Status	—	—	10	Self	—	—
TM18	Rain Dance	Water	Status	—	—	5	Both Sides	—	—
TM21	Frustration	Normal	Physical	—	100	20	Normal	—	○
TM26	Earthquake	Ground	Physical	100	100	10	Adjacent	—	—
TM27	Return	Normal	Physical	—	100	20	Normal	—	○
TM28	Dig	Ground	Physical	80	100	10	Normal	—	○
TM32	Double Team	Normal	Status	—	—	15	Self	—	—
TM37	Sandstorm	Rock	Status	—	—	10	Both Sides	—	—
TM39	Rock Tomb	Rock	Physical	50	80	10	Normal	—	—
TM40	Aerial Ace	Flying	Physical	60	—	20	Normal	○	○
TM42	Facade	Normal	Physical	70	100	20	Normal	—	○
TM44	Rest	Psychic	Status	—	—	10	Self	—	—
TM45	Attract	Normal	Status	—	100	15	Normal	—	—
TM48	Round	Normal	Special	60	100	15	Normal	—	—
TM65	Shadow Claw	Ghost	Physical	70	100	15	Normal	—	○
TM69	Rock Polish	Rock	Status	—	—	20	Self	—	—
TM71	Stone Edge	Rock	Physical	100	80	5	Normal	—	—
TM78	Bulldoze	Ground	Physical	60	100	20	Adjacent	—	—
TM80	Rock Slide	Rock	Physical	75	90	10	Many Others	—	—
TM87	Swagger	Normal	Status	—	90	15	Normal	—	—
TM90	Substitute	Normal	Status	—	—	10	Self	—	—
TM94	Rock Smash	Fighting	Physical	40	100	15	Normal	—	○
HM01	Cut	Normal	Physical	50	95	30	Normal	—	○
HM04	Strength	Normal	Physical	80	100	15	Normal	—	○

MOVES TAUGHT BY PEOPLE

Name	Type	Kind	Pow.	Acc.	PP	Range	Long	DA

MOVES TAUGHT BY MOVE TUTORS FOR SHARDS

Name	Type	Kind	Pow.	Acc.	PP	Range	Long	DA
Iron Head	Steel	Physical	80	100	15	Normal	—	○
Uproar	Normal	Special	90	100	10	1 Random	—	—
Iron Defense	Steel	Status	—	—	15	Self	—	—
Magnet Rise	Electric	Status	—	—	10	Self	—	—
Iron Tail	Steel	Physical	100	75	15	Normal	—	○
Earth Power	Ground	Special	90	100	10	Normal	—	—
Superpower	Fighting	Physical	120	100	5	Normal	—	○
Snore	Normal	Special	40	100	15	Normal	—	—
Spite	Ghost	Status	—	100	10	Normal	—	—
Stealth Rock	Rock	Status	—	—	20	Other Side	—	—
Endeavor	Normal	Physical	—	100	5	Normal	—	○
Sleep Talk	Normal	Status	—	—	10	Self	—	—

Iron Armor Pokémon

306 Aggron

- HEIGHT: 6'11"
- WEIGHT: 793.7 lbs.
- GENDER: ♂ / ♀

It claims an entire mountain as its own. The more wounds it has, the more it has battled, so don't take it lightly.

TYPE: Steel / Rock

ABILITIES
- Sturdy
- Rock Head

HIDDEN ABILITY
- Heavy Metal

STATS
HP
Attack
Defense
Sp. Atk
Sp. Def
Speed

EGG GROUPS
Monster

Same form for ♂ / ♀

ITEMS SOMETIMES HELD
- None

EVOLUTION

Lv. 32
Lv. 42
Aron
Lairon
Aggron

HOW TO OBTAIN

Pokémon Black Version 2	Level up Lairon to Lv. 42
Pokémon White Version 2	Level up Lairon to Lv. 42

HOW TO OBTAIN FROM OTHER GAMES

—

—

Pokémon AR Marker

LEVEL-UP AND LEARNED MOVES

Lv.	Name	Type	Kind	Pow.	Acc.	PP	Range	Long	DA
1	Tackle	Normal	Physical	50	100	35	Normal	—	○
1	Harden	Normal	Status	—	—	30	Self	—	—
1	Mud-Slap	Ground	Special	20	100	10	Normal	—	—
1	Headbutt	Normal	Physical	70	100	15	Normal	—	○
4	Mud-Slap	Ground	Special	20	100	10	Normal	—	—
8	Headbutt	Normal	Physical	70	100	15	Normal	—	○
11	Metal Claw	Steel	Physical	50	95	35	Normal	—	○
15	Iron Defense	Steel	Status	—	—	15	Self	—	—
18	Roar	Normal	Status	—	100	20	Normal	—	—
22	Take Down	Normal	Physical	90	85	20	Normal	—	○
25	Iron Head	Steel	Physical	80	100	15	Normal	—	○
29	Protect	Normal	Status	—	—	10	Self	—	—
34	Metal Sound	Steel	Status	—	85	40	Normal	—	—
40	Iron Tail	Steel	Physical	100	75	15	Normal	—	○
48	Autotomize	Steel	Status	—	—	15	Self	—	—
57	Heavy Slam	Steel	Physical	—	100	10	Normal	—	○
65	Double-Edge	Normal	Physical	120	100	15	Normal	—	○
74	Metal Burst	Steel	Physical	—	100	10	Varies	—	—

TM & HM MOVES

Lv.	Name	Type	Kind	Pow.	Acc.	PP	Range	Long	DA
TM01	Hone Claws	Dark	Status	—	—	15	Self	—	—
TM02	Dragon Claw	Dragon	Physical	80	100	15	Normal	—	○
TM05	Roar	Normal	Status	—	100	20	Normal	—	—
TM06	Toxic	Poison	Status	—	90	10	Normal	—	—
TM10	Hidden Power	Normal	Special	—	100	15	Normal	—	—
TM11	Sunny Day	Fire	Status	—	—	5	Both Sides	—	—
TM12	Taunt	Dark	Status	—	100	20	Normal	—	—
TM13	Ice Beam	Ice	Special	95	100	10	Normal	—	—
TM14	Blizzard	Ice	Special	120	70	5	Many Others	—	—
TM15	Hyper Beam	Normal	Special	150	90	5	Normal	—	—
TM17	Protect	Normal	Status	—	—	10	Self	—	—
TM18	Rain Dance	Water	Status	—	—	5	Both Sides	—	—
TM21	Frustration	Normal	Physical	—	100	20	Normal	—	○
TM22	SolarBeam	Grass	Special	120	100	10	Normal	—	—
TM23	Smack Down	Rock	Physical	50	100	15	Normal	—	—
TM24	Thunderbolt	Electric	Special	95	100	15	Normal	—	—
TM25	Thunder	Electric	Special	120	70	10	Normal	—	—
TM26	Earthquake	Ground	Physical	100	100	10	Adjacent	—	—
TM27	Return	Normal	Physical	—	100	20	Normal	—	○
TM28	Dig	Ground	Physical	80	100	10	Normal	—	○
TM31	Brick Break	Fighting	Physical	75	100	15	Normal	—	○
TM32	Double Team	Normal	Status	—	—	15	Self	—	—
TM35	Flamethrower	Fire	Special	95	100	15	Normal	—	—
TM37	Sandstorm	Rock	Status	—	—	10	Both Sides	—	—
TM38	Fire Blast	Fire	Special	120	85	5	Normal	—	—
TM39	Rock Tomb	Rock	Physical	50	80	10	Normal	—	—
TM40	Aerial Ace	Flying	Physical	60	—	20	Normal	○	○
TM42	Facade	Normal	Physical	70	100	20	Normal	—	○
TM44	Rest	Psychic	Status	—	—	10	Self	—	—
TM45	Attract	Normal	Status	—	100	15	Normal	—	—
TM48	Round	Normal	Special	60	100	15	Normal	—	—
TM52	Focus Blast	Fighting	Special	120	70	5	Normal	—	—
TM56	Fling	Dark	Physical	—	100	10	Normal	—	—
TM59	Incinerate	Fire	Special	30	100	15	Many Others	—	—
TM65	Shadow Claw	Ghost	Physical	70	100	15	Normal	—	○
TM66	Payback	Dark	Physical	50	100	10	Normal	—	○
TM68	Giga Impact	Normal	Physical	150	90	5	Normal	—	○
TM69	Rock Polish	Rock	Status	—	—	20	Self	—	—
TM71	Stone Edge	Rock	Physical	100	80	5	Normal	—	—
TM73	Thunder Wave	Electric	Status	—	100	20	Normal	—	—
TM78	Bulldoze	Ground	Physical	60	100	20	Adjacent	—	—
TM80	Rock Slide	Rock	Physical	75	90	10	Many Others	—	—
TM82	Dragon Tail	Dragon	Physical	60	90	10	Normal	—	○
TM87	Swagger	Normal	Status	—	90	15	Normal	—	—
TM90	Substitute	Normal	Status	—	—	10	Self	—	—
TM91	Flash Cannon	Steel	Special	80	100	10	Normal	—	—
TM94	Rock Smash	Fighting	Physical	40	100	15	Normal	—	○
HM01	Cut	Normal	Physical	50	95	30	Normal	—	○
HM03	Surf	Water	Special	95	100	15	Adjacent	—	—
HM04	Strength	Normal	Physical	80	100	15	Normal	—	○

MOVES TAUGHT BY PEOPLE

Name	Type	Kind	Pow.	Acc.	PP	Range	Long	DA

MOVES TAUGHT BY MOVE TUTORS FOR SHARDS

Name	Type	Kind	Pow.	Acc.	PP	Range	Long	DA
Iron Head	Steel	Physical	80	100	15	Normal	—	○
Uproar	Normal	Special	90	100	10	1 Random	—	—
Low Kick	Fighting	Physical	—	100	20	Normal	—	○
Fire Punch	Fire	Physical	75	100	15	Normal	—	○
ThunderPunch	Electric	Physical	75	100	15	Normal	—	○
Ice Punch	Ice	Physical	75	100	15	Normal	—	○
Iron Defense	Steel	Status	—	—	15	Self	—	—
Magnet Rise	Electric	Status	—	—	10	Self	—	—
Block	Normal	Status	—	—	5	Normal	—	—
Icy Wind	Ice	Special	55	95	15	Many Others	—	—
Iron Tail	Steel	Physical	100	75	15	Normal	—	○
Aqua Tail	Water	Physical	90	90	10	Normal	—	○
Earth Power	Ground	Special	90	100	10	Normal	—	—
Superpower	Fighting	Physical	120	100	5	Normal	—	○
Dragon Pulse	Dragon	Special	90	100	10	Normal	○	—
Dark Pulse	Dark	Special	80	100	15	Normal	○	—
Snore	Normal	Special	40	100	15	Normal	—	—
Spite	Ghost	Status	—	100	10	Normal	—	—
Stealth Rock	Rock	Status	—	—	20	Other Side	—	—
Outrage	Dragon	Physical	120	100	10	1 Random	—	○
Endeavor	Normal	Physical	—	100	5	Normal	—	○
Sleep Talk	Normal	Status	—	—	10	Self	—	—

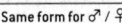

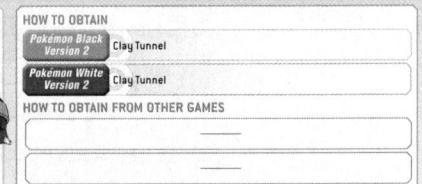

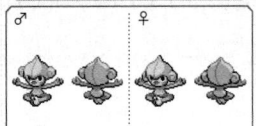

307 Meditite

Meditate Pokémon

- HEIGHT: 2'00"
- WEIGHT: 24.7 lbs.
- GENDER: ♂ / ♀

It always trains deep in mountains. It levitates when it heightens its spiritual power through meditation.

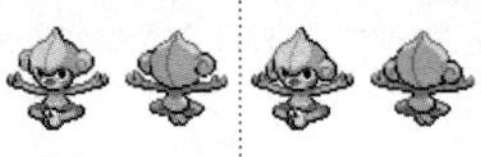

TYPE Fighting Psychic

ABILITY
- Pure Power

HIDDEN ABILITY
- Telepathy

STATS
HP
Attack
Defense
Sp. Atk
Sp. Def
Speed

EGG GROUPS
Human-Like

ITEMS SOMETIMES HELD
- None

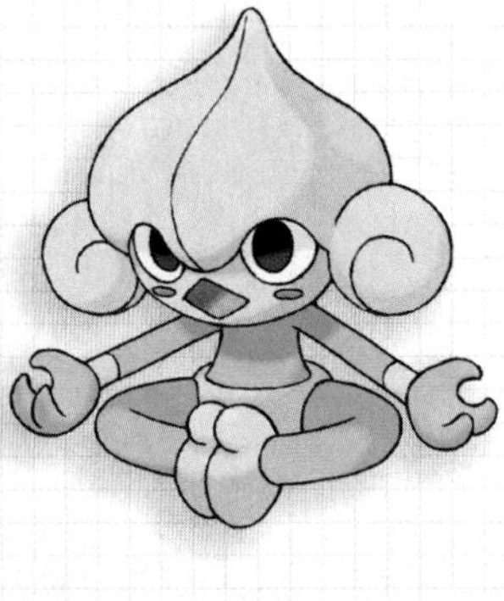

Pokémon AR Marker

EVOLUTION

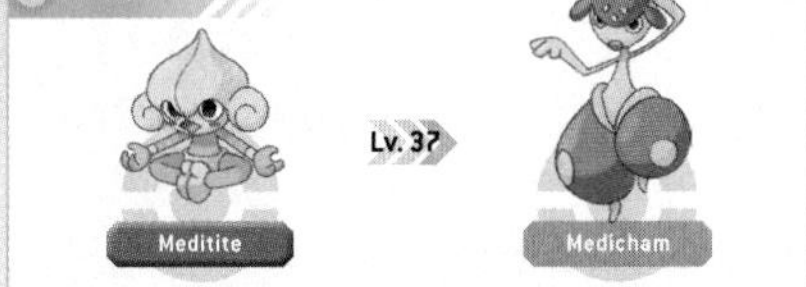

HOW TO OBTAIN

Pokémon Black Version 2	Catch a Medicham, leave it at the Pokémon Day Care, and hatch the Egg that is found
Pokémon White Version 2	Catch a Medicham, leave it at the Pokémon Day Care, and hatch the Egg that is found

HOW TO OBTAIN FROM OTHER GAMES

Pokémon Platinum Version	Route 211
—	

LEVEL-UP AND LEARNED MOVES

Lv.	Name	Type	Kind	Pow.	Acc.	PP	Range	Long	DA
1	Bide	Normal	Physical	—	—	10	Self	—	○
4	Meditate	Psychic	Status	—	—	40	Self	—	—
8	Confusion	Psychic	Special	50	100	25	Normal	—	—
11	Detect	Fighting	Status	—	—	5	Self	—	—
15	Hidden Power	Normal	Special	—	100	15	Normal	—	—
18	Mind Reader	Normal	Status	—	—	5	Normal	—	—
22	Feint	Normal	Physical	30	100	10	Normal	—	—
25	Calm Mind	Psychic	Status	—	—	20	Self	—	—
29	Force Palm	Fighting	Physical	60	100	10	Normal	—	○
32	Hi Jump Kick	Fighting	Physical	130	90	10	Normal	—	○
36	Psych Up	Normal	Status	—	—	10	Normal	—	—
39	Acupressure	Normal	Status	—	—	30	Self/Ally	—	—
43	Power Trick	Psychic	Status	—	—	10	Self	—	—
46	Reversal	Fighting	Physical	—	100	15	Normal	—	○
50	Recover	Normal	Status	—	—	10	Self	—	—

TM & HM MOVES

Lv.	Name	Type	Kind	Pow.	Acc.	PP	Range	Long	DA
TM03	Psyshock	Psychic	Special	80	100	10	Normal	—	—
TM04	Calm Mind	Psychic	Status	—	—	20	Self	—	—
TM06	Toxic	Poison	Status	—	90	10	Normal	—	—
TM08	Bulk Up	Fighting	Status	—	—	20	Self	—	—
TM10	Hidden Power	Normal	Special	—	100	15	Normal	—	—
TM11	Sunny Day	Fire	Status	—	—	5	Both Sides	—	—
TM16	Light Screen	Psychic	Status	—	—	30	Your Side	—	—
TM17	Protect	Normal	Status	—	—	10	Self	—	—
TM18	Rain Dance	Water	Status	—	—	5	Both Sides	—	—
TM19	Telekinesis	Psychic	Status	—	—	15	Normal	—	—
TM21	Frustration	Normal	Physical	—	100	20	Normal	—	○
TM27	Return	Normal	Physical	—	100	20	Normal	—	○
TM29	Psychic	Psychic	Special	90	100	10	Normal	—	—
TM30	Shadow Ball	Ghost	Special	80	100	15	Normal	—	—
TM31	Brick Break	Fighting	Physical	75	100	15	Normal	—	○
TM32	Double Team	Normal	Status	—	—	15	Self	—	—
TM33	Reflect	Psychic	Status	—	—	20	Your Side	—	—
TM39	Rock Tomb	Rock	Physical	50	80	10	Normal	—	—
TM42	Facade	Normal	Physical	70	100	20	Normal	—	○
TM44	Rest	Psychic	Status	—	—	10	Self	—	—
TM45	Attract	Normal	Status	—	100	15	Normal	—	—
TM47	Low Sweep	Fighting	Physical	60	100	20	Normal	—	○
TM48	Round	Normal	Special	60	100	15	Normal	—	—
TM52	Focus Blast	Fighting	Special	120	70	5	Normal	—	—
TM56	Fling	Dark	Physical	—	100	10	Normal	—	—
TM67	Retaliate	Normal	Physical	70	100	5	Normal	—	○
TM70	Flash	Normal	Status	—	100	20	Normal	—	—
TM77	Psych Up	Normal	Status	—	—	10	Normal	—	—
TM80	Rock Slide	Rock	Physical	75	90	10	Many Others	—	—
TM83	Work Up	Normal	Status	—	—	30	Self	—	—
TM84	Poison Jab	Poison	Physical	80	100	20	Normal	—	○
TM85	Dream Eater	Psychic	Special	100	100	15	Normal	—	—
TM86	Grass Knot	Grass	Special	—	100	20	Normal	—	○
TM87	Swagger	Normal	Status	—	90	15	Normal	—	—
TM90	Substitute	Normal	Status	—	—	10	Self	—	—
TM94	Rock Smash	Fighting	Physical	40	100	15	Normal	—	○
HM04	Strength	Normal	Physical	80	100	15	Normal	—	○

MOVES TAUGHT BY PEOPLE

Name	Type	Kind	Pow.	Acc.	PP	Range	Long	DA

MOVES TAUGHT BY MOVE TUTORS FOR SHARDS

Name	Type	Kind	Pow.	Acc.	PP	Range	Long	DA
Signal Beam	Bug	Special	75	100	15	Normal	—	—
Low Kick	Fighting	Physical	—	100	20	Normal	—	○
Fire Punch	Fire	Physical	75	100	15	Normal	—	○
ThunderPunch	Electric	Physical	75	100	15	Normal	—	○
Ice Punch	Ice	Physical	75	100	15	Normal	—	○
Magic Coat	Psychic	Status	—	—	15	Self	—	—
Zen Headbutt	Psychic	Physical	80	90	15	Normal	—	○
Gravity	Psychic	Status	—	—	5	Both Sides	—	—
Snore	Normal	Special	40	100	15	Normal	—	—
Role Play	Psychic	Status	—	—	10	Normal	—	—
Drain Punch	Fighting	Physical	75	100	10	Normal	—	○
Pain Split	Normal	Status	—	—	20	Normal	—	—
Helping Hand	Normal	Status	—	—	20	1 Ally	—	—
Recycle	Normal	Status	—	—	10	Self	—	—
Trick	Psychic	Status	—	100	10	Normal	—	—
Sleep Talk	Normal	Status	—	—	10	Self	—	—

EGG MOVES

Name	Type	Kind	Pow.	Acc.	PP	Range	Long	DA
Fire Punch	Fire	Physical	75	100	15	Normal	—	○
ThunderPunch	Electric	Physical	75	100	15	Normal	—	○
Ice Punch	Ice	Physical	75	100	15	Normal	—	○
Foresight	Normal	Status	—	—	40	Normal	—	—
Fake Out	Normal	Physical	40	100	10	Normal	—	○
Baton Pass	Normal	Status	—	—	40	Self	—	—
DynamicPunch	Fighting	Physical	100	50	5	Normal	—	○
Power Swap	Psychic	Status	—	—	10	Normal	—	—
Guard Swap	Psychic	Status	—	—	10	Normal	—	—
Psycho Cut	Psychic	Physical	70	100	20	Normal	—	—
Bullet Punch	Steel	Physical	40	100	30	Normal	—	○
Drain Punch	Fighting	Physical	75	100	10	Normal	—	○
Secret Power	Normal	Physical	70	100	20	Normal	—	—

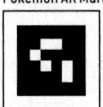

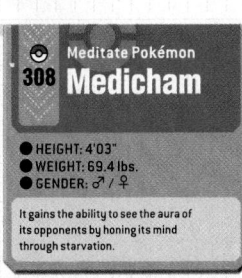

308 Medicham

Meditate Pokémon

- HEIGHT: 4'03"
- WEIGHT: 69.4 lbs.
- GENDER: ♂ / ♀

It gains the ability to see the aura of its opponents by honing its mind through starvation.

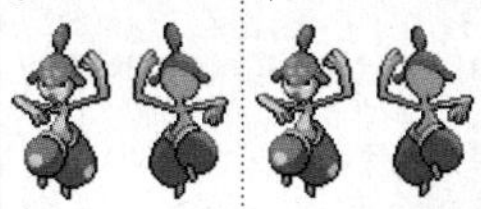

TYPE Fighting Psychic

ABILITY
- Pure Power

HIDDEN ABILITY
- Telepathy

STATS
HP
Attack
Defense
Sp. Atk
Sp. Def
Speed

EGG GROUPS
Human-Like

ITEMS SOMETIMES HELD
- None

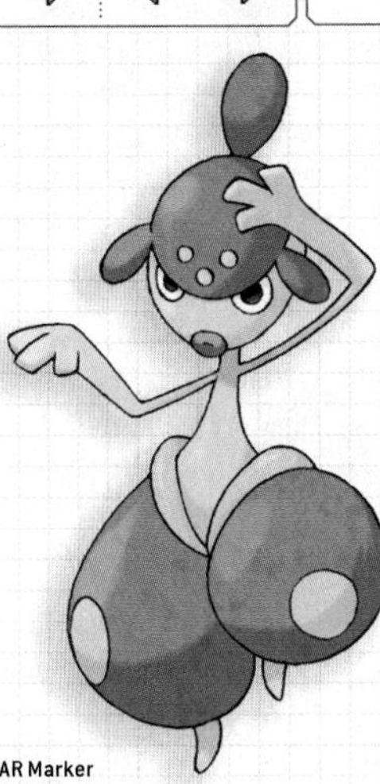

Pokémon AR Marker

EVOLUTION

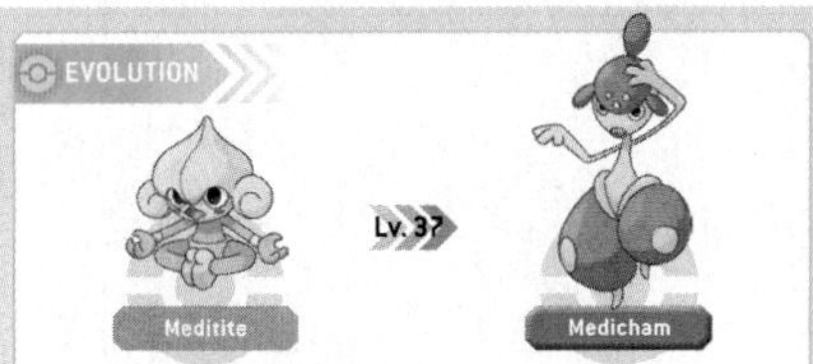

HOW TO OBTAIN

Pokémon Black Version 2	Pinwheel Forest entrance (Hidden Grotto)
Pokémon White Version 2	Pinwheel Forest entrance (Hidden Grotto)

HOW TO OBTAIN FROM OTHER GAMES

—
—

LEVEL-UP AND LEARNED MOVES

Lv.	Name	Type	Kind	Pow.	Acc.	PP	Range	Long	DA
1	Fire Punch	Fire	Physical	75	100	15	Normal	—	○
1	ThunderPunch	Electric	Physical	75	100	15	Normal	—	○
1	Ice Punch	Ice	Physical	75	100	15	Normal	—	○
1	Bide	Normal	Physical	—	—	10	Self	—	○
1	Meditate	Psychic	Status	—	—	40	Self	—	—
1	Confusion	Psychic	Special	50	100	25	Normal	—	—
1	Detect	Fighting	Status	—	—	5	Self	—	—
4	Meditate	Psychic	Status	—	—	40	Self	—	—
8	Confusion	Psychic	Special	50	100	25	Normal	—	—
11	Detect	Fighting	Status	—	—	5	Self	—	—
15	Hidden Power	Normal	Special	—	100	15	Normal	—	—
18	Mind Reader	Normal	Status	—	—	5	Normal	—	—
22	Feint	Normal	Physical	30	100	10	Normal	—	—
25	Calm Mind	Psychic	Status	—	—	20	Self	—	—
29	Force Palm	Fighting	Physical	60	100	10	Normal	—	○
32	Hi Jump Kick	Fighting	Physical	130	90	10	Normal	—	○
36	Psych Up	Normal	Status	—	—	10	Normal	—	—
42	Acupressure	Normal	Status	—	—	30	Self/Ally	—	—
49	Power Trick	Psychic	Status	—	—	10	Self	—	—
55	Reversal	Fighting	Physical	—	100	15	Normal	—	○
62	Recover	Normal	Status	—	—	10	Self	—	—

TM & HM MOVES

Lv.	Name	Type	Kind	Pow.	Acc.	PP	Range	Long	DA
TM03	Psyshock	Psychic	Special	80	100	10	Normal	—	—
TM04	Calm Mind	Psychic	Status	—	—	20	Self	—	—
TM06	Toxic	Poison	Status	—	90	10	Normal	—	—
TM08	Bulk Up	Fighting	Status	—	—	20	Self	—	—
TM10	Hidden Power	Normal	Special	—	100	15	Normal	—	—
TM11	Sunny Day	Fire	Status	—	—	5	Both Sides	—	—
TM15	Hyper Beam	Normal	Special	150	90	5	Normal	—	—
TM16	Light Screen	Psychic	Status	—	—	30	Your Side	—	—
TM17	Protect	Normal	Status	—	—	10	Self	—	—
TM18	Rain Dance	Water	Status	—	—	5	Both Sides	—	—
TM19	Telekinesis	Psychic	Status	—	—	15	Normal	—	—
TM21	Frustration	Normal	Physical	—	100	20	Normal	—	○
TM27	Return	Normal	Physical	—	100	20	Normal	—	○
TM29	Psychic	Psychic	Special	90	100	10	Normal	—	—
TM30	Shadow Ball	Ghost	Special	80	100	15	Normal	—	—
TM31	Brick Break	Fighting	Physical	75	100	15	Normal	—	○
TM32	Double Team	Normal	Status	—	—	15	Self	—	—
TM33	Reflect	Psychic	Status	—	—	20	Your Side	—	—
TM39	Rock Tomb	Rock	Physical	50	80	10	Normal	—	—
TM42	Facade	Normal	Physical	70	100	20	Normal	—	○
TM44	Rest	Psychic	Status	—	—	10	Self	—	—
TM45	Attract	Normal	Status	—	100	15	Normal	—	—
TM47	Low Sweep	Fighting	Physical	60	100	20	Normal	—	○
TM48	Round	Normal	Special	60	100	15	Normal	—	—
TM52	Focus Blast	Fighting	Special	120	70	5	Normal	—	—
TM53	Energy Ball	Grass	Special	80	100	10	Normal	—	—
TM56	Fling	Dark	Physical	—	100	10	Normal	—	—
TM67	Retaliate	Normal	Physical	70	100	5	Normal	—	○
TM68	Giga Impact	Normal	Physical	150	90	5	Normal	—	○
TM70	Flash	Normal	Status	—	100	20	Normal	—	—
TM77	Psych Up	Normal	Status	—	—	10	Normal	—	—
TM80	Rock Slide	Rock	Physical	75	90	10	Many Others	—	—
TM83	Work Up	Normal	Status	—	—	30	Self	—	—
TM84	Poison Jab	Poison	Physical	80	100	20	Normal	—	○
TM85	Dream Eater	Psychic	Special	100	100	15	Normal	—	—
TM86	Grass Knot	Grass	Special	—	100	20	Normal	—	○
TM87	Swagger	Normal	Status	—	90	15	Normal	—	—
TM90	Substitute	Normal	Status	—	—	10	Self	—	—
TM94	Rock Smash	Fighting	Physical	40	100	15	Normal	—	○
HM04	Strength	Normal	Physical	80	100	15	Normal	—	○

MOVES TAUGHT BY PEOPLE

Name	Type	Kind	Pow.	Acc.	PP	Range	Long	DA

MOVES TAUGHT BY MOVE TUTORS FOR SHARDS

Name	Type	Kind	Pow.	Acc.	PP	Range	Long	DA
Signal Beam	Bug	Special	75	100	15	Normal	—	—
Low Kick	Fighting	Physical	—	100	20	Normal	—	○
Fire Punch	Fire	Physical	75	100	15	Normal	—	○
ThunderPunch	Electric	Physical	75	100	15	Normal	—	○
Ice Punch	Ice	Physical	75	100	15	Normal	—	○
Magic Coat	Psychic	Status	—	—	15	Self	—	—
Zen Headbutt	Psychic	Physical	80	90	15	Normal	—	○
Gravity	Psychic	Status	—	—	5	Both Sides	—	—
Snore	Normal	Special	40	100	15	Normal	—	—
Role Play	Psychic	Status	—	—	10	Normal	—	—
Drain Punch	Fighting	Physical	75	100	10	Normal	—	○
Pain Split	Normal	Status	—	—	20	Normal	—	—
Helping Hand	Normal	Status	—	—	20	1 Ally	—	—
Recycle	Normal	Status	—	—	10	Self	—	—
Trick	Psychic	Status	—	100	10	Normal	—	—
Sleep Talk	Normal	Status	—	—	10	Self	—	—

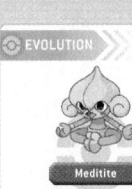

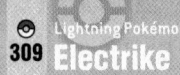

Lightning Pokémon

309 Electrike

● HEIGHT: 2'00"
● WEIGHT: 33.5 lbs.
● GENDER: ♂ / ♀

Using electricity stored in its fur, it stimulates its muscles to heighten its reaction speed.

Same form for ♂ / ♀

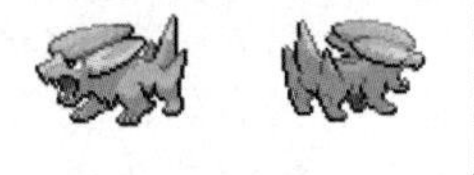

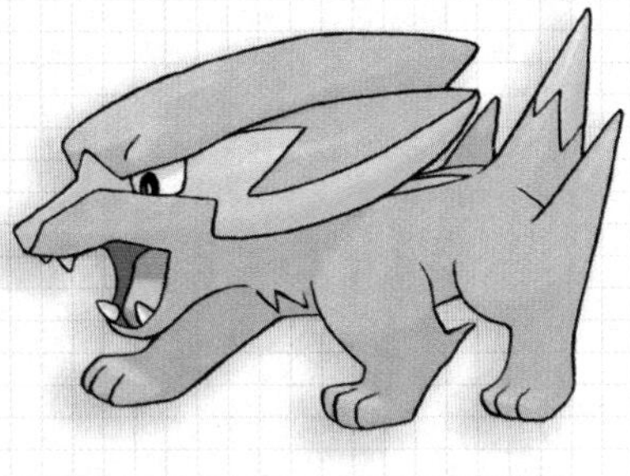

TYPE Electric

ABILITIES
● Static
● Lightningrod

HIDDEN ABILITY
● Minus

STATS
HP
Attack
Defense
Sp. Atk
Sp. Def
Speed

EGG GROUPS
Field

ITEMS SOMETIMES HELD
● None

Pokémon AR Marker

EVOLUTION

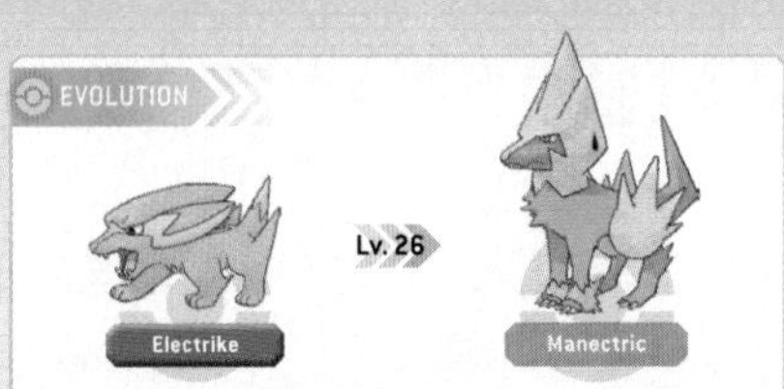

HOW TO OBTAIN

Pokémon Black Version 2	Catch a Manectric, leave it at the Pokémon Day Care, and hatch the Egg that is found
Pokémon White Version 2	Catch a Manectric, leave it at the Pokémon Day Care, and hatch the Egg that is found

HOW TO OBTAIN FROM OTHER GAMES

Pokémon Platinum Version	Valley Windworks (mass outbreak)
—	

LEVEL-UP AND LEARNED MOVES

Lv.	Name	Type	Kind	Pow.	Acc.	PP	Range	Long	DA
1	Tackle	Normal	Physical	50	100	35	Normal	—	○
4	Thunder Wave	Electric	Status	—	100	20	Normal	—	—
9	Leer	Normal	Status	—	100	30	Many Others	—	—
12	Howl	Normal	Status	—	—	40	Self	—	—
17	Quick Attack	Normal	Physical	40	100	30	Normal	—	○
20	Spark	Electric	Physical	65	100	20	Normal	—	○
25	Odor Sleuth	Normal	Status	—	—	40	Normal	—	—
28	Bite	Dark	Physical	60	100	25	Normal	—	○
33	Thunder Fang	Electric	Physical	65	95	15	Normal	—	○
36	Roar	Normal	Status	—	100	20	Normal	—	—
41	Discharge	Electric	Special	80	100	15	Adjacent	—	—
44	Charge	Electric	Status	—	—	20	Self	—	—
49	Wild Charge	Electric	Physical	90	100	15	Normal	—	○
52	Thunder	Electric	Special	120	70	10	Normal	—	—

TM & HM MOVES

Lv.	Name	Type	Kind	Pow.	Acc.	PP	Range	Long	DA
TM05	Roar	Normal	Status	—	100	20	Normal	—	—
TM06	Toxic	Poison	Status	—	90	10	Normal	—	—
TM10	Hidden Power	Normal	Special	—	100	15	Normal	—	—
TM16	Light Screen	Psychic	Status	—	—	30	Your Side	—	—
TM17	Protect	Normal	Status	—	—	10	Self	—	—
TM18	Rain Dance	Water	Status	—	—	5	Both Sides	—	—
TM21	Frustration	Normal	Physical	—	100	20	Normal	—	○
TM24	Thunderbolt	Electric	Special	95	100	15	Normal	—	—
TM25	Thunder	Electric	Special	120	70	10	Normal	—	—
TM27	Return	Normal	Physical	—	100	20	Normal	—	○
TM32	Double Team	Normal	Status	—	—	15	Self	—	—
TM35	Flamethrower	Fire	Special	95	100	15	Normal	—	—
TM42	Facade	Normal	Physical	70	100	20	Normal	—	○
TM44	Rest	Psychic	Status	—	—	10	Self	—	—
TM45	Attract	Normal	Status	—	100	15	Normal	—	—
TM46	Thief	Dark	Physical	40	100	10	Normal	—	○
TM48	Round	Normal	Special	60	100	15	Normal	—	—
TM57	Charge Beam	Electric	Special	50	90	10	Normal	—	—
TM70	Flash	Normal	Status	—	100	20	Normal	—	—
TM72	Volt Switch	Electric	Special	70	100	20	Normal	—	—
TM73	Thunder Wave	Electric	Status	—	100	20	Normal	—	—
TM87	Swagger	Normal	Status	—	90	15	Normal	—	—
TM90	Substitute	Normal	Status	—	—	10	Self	—	—
TM93	Wild Charge	Electric	Physical	90	100	15	Normal	—	○
TM95	Snarl	Dark	Special	55	95	15	Many Others	—	—
HM04	Strength	Normal	Physical	80	100	15	Normal	—	○

MOVES TAUGHT BY PEOPLE

Name	Type	Kind	Pow.	Acc.	PP	Range	Long	DA

MOVES TAUGHT BY MOVE TUTORS FOR SHARDS

Name	Type	Kind	Pow.	Acc.	PP	Range	Long	DA
Signal Beam	Bug	Special	75	100	15	Normal	—	—
Uproar	Normal	Special	90	100	10	1 Random	—	—
Magnet Rise	Electric	Status	—	—	10	Self	—	—
Iron Tail	Steel	Physical	100	75	15	Normal	—	○
Snore	Normal	Special	40	100	15	Normal	—	—
Sleep Talk	Normal	Status	—	—	10	Self	—	—

EGG MOVES

Name	Type	Kind	Pow.	Acc.	PP	Range	Long	DA
Crunch	Dark	Physical	80	100	15	Normal	—	○
Headbutt	Normal	Physical	70	100	15	Normal	—	○
Uproar	Normal	Special	90	100	10	1 Random	—	—
Curse	Ghost	Status	—	—	10	Varies	—	—
Swift	Normal	Special	60	—	20	Many Others	—	—
Discharge	Electric	Special	80	100	15	Adjacent	—	—
Ice Fang	Ice	Physical	65	95	15	Normal	—	○
Fire Fang	Fire	Physical	65	95	15	Normal	—	○
Thunder Fang	Electric	Physical	65	95	15	Normal	—	○
Switcheroo	Dark	Status	—	100	10	Normal	—	—
Electro Ball	Electric	Special	—	100	10	Normal	—	—
Shock Wave	Electric	Special	60	—	20	Normal	—	—
Flame Burst	Fire	Special	70	100	15	Normal	—	—

Discharge Pokémon

310 Manectric

● HEIGHT: 4'11"
● WEIGHT: 88.6 lbs.
● GENDER: ♂ / ♀

It discharges electricity from its mane. It creates a thundercloud overhead to drop lightning bolts.

Same form for ♂ / ♀

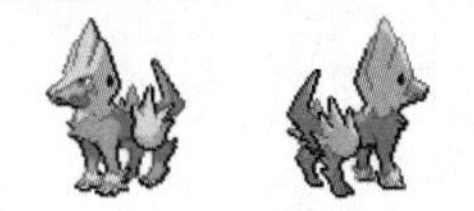

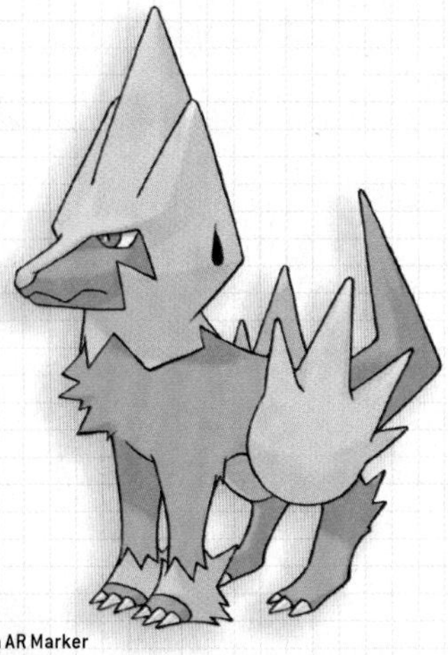

TYPE Electric

ABILITIES
● Static
● Lightningrod

HIDDEN ABILITY
● Minus

STATS
HP
Attack
Defense
Sp. Atk
Sp. Def
Speed

EGG GROUPS
Field

ITEMS SOMETIMES HELD
● None

Pokémon AR Marker

EVOLUTION

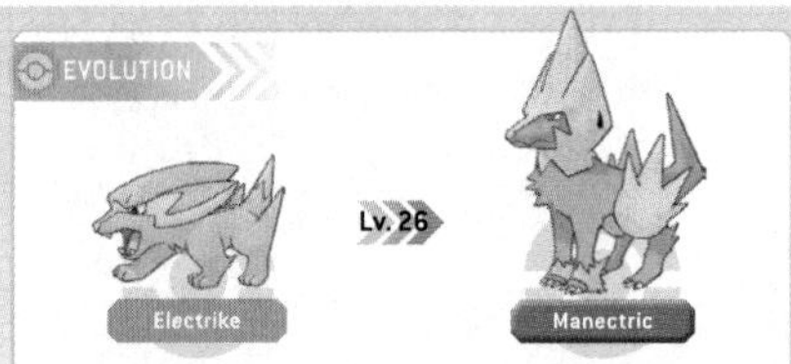

HOW TO OBTAIN

Pokémon Black Version 2	Route 3 (Hidden Grotto)
Pokémon White Version 2	Route 3 (Hidden Grotto)

HOW TO OBTAIN FROM OTHER GAMES

—	
—	

LEVEL-UP AND LEARNED MOVES

Lv.	Name	Type	Kind	Pow.	Acc.	PP	Range	Long	DA
1	Fire Fang	Fire	Physical	65	95	15	Normal	—	○
1	Tackle	Normal	Physical	50	100	35	Normal	—	○
1	Thunder Wave	Electric	Status	—	100	20	Normal	—	—
1	Leer	Normal	Status	—	100	30	Many Others	—	—
1	Howl	Normal	Status	—	—	40	Self	—	—
4	Thunder Wave	Electric	Status	—	100	20	Normal	—	—
9	Leer	Normal	Status	—	100	30	Many Others	—	—
12	Howl	Normal	Status	—	—	40	Self	—	—
17	Quick Attack	Normal	Physical	40	100	30	Normal	—	○
20	Spark	Electric	Physical	65	100	20	Normal	—	○
25	Odor Sleuth	Normal	Status	—	—	40	Normal	—	—
30	Bite	Dark	Physical	60	100	25	Normal	—	○
37	Thunder Fang	Electric	Physical	65	95	15	Normal	—	○
42	Roar	Normal	Status	—	100	20	Normal	—	—
49	Discharge	Electric	Special	80	100	15	Adjacent	—	—
54	Charge	Electric	Status	—	—	20	Self	—	—
61	Wild Charge	Electric	Physical	90	100	15	Normal	—	○
66	Thunder	Electric	Special	120	70	10	Normal	—	—

TM & HM MOVES

Lv.	Name	Type	Kind	Pow.	Acc.	PP	Range	Long	DA
TM05	Roar	Normal	Status	—	100	20	Normal	—	—
TM06	Toxic	Poison	Status	—	90	10	Normal	—	—
TM10	Hidden Power	Normal	Special	—	100	15	Normal	—	—
TM15	Hyper Beam	Normal	Special	150	90	5	Normal	—	—
TM16	Light Screen	Psychic	Status	—	—	30	Your Side	—	—
TM17	Protect	Normal	Status	—	—	10	Self	—	—
TM18	Rain Dance	Water	Status	—	—	5	Both Sides	—	—
TM21	Frustration	Normal	Physical	—	100	20	Normal	—	○
TM24	Thunderbolt	Electric	Special	95	100	15	Normal	—	—
TM25	Thunder	Electric	Special	120	70	10	Normal	—	—
TM27	Return	Normal	Physical	—	100	20	Normal	—	○
TM32	Double Team	Normal	Status	—	—	15	Self	—	—
TM35	Flamethrower	Fire	Special	95	100	15	Normal	—	—
TM42	Facade	Normal	Physical	70	100	20	Normal	—	○
TM44	Rest	Psychic	Status	—	—	10	Self	—	—
TM45	Attract	Normal	Status	—	100	15	Normal	—	—
TM46	Thief	Dark	Physical	40	100	10	Normal	—	○
TM48	Round	Normal	Special	60	100	15	Normal	—	—
TM50	Overheat	Fire	Special	140	90	5	Normal	—	—
TM57	Charge Beam	Electric	Special	50	90	10	Normal	—	—
TM68	Giga Impact	Normal	Physical	150	90	5	Normal	—	○
TM70	Flash	Normal	Status	—	100	20	Normal	—	—
TM72	Volt Switch	Electric	Special	70	100	20	Normal	—	—
TM73	Thunder Wave	Electric	Status	—	100	20	Normal	—	—
TM87	Swagger	Normal	Status	—	90	15	Normal	—	—
TM90	Substitute	Normal	Status	—	—	10	Self	—	—
TM93	Wild Charge	Electric	Physical	90	100	15	Normal	—	○
TM95	Snarl	Dark	Special	55	95	15	Many Others	—	—
HM04	Strength	Normal	Physical	80	100	15	Normal	—	○

MOVES TAUGHT BY PEOPLE

Name	Type	Kind	Pow.	Acc.	PP	Range	Long	DA

MOVES TAUGHT BY MOVE TUTORS FOR SHARDS

Name	Type	Kind	Pow.	Acc.	PP	Range	Long	DA
Signal Beam	Bug	Special	75	100	15	Normal	—	—
Uproar	Normal	Special	90	100	10	1 Random	—	—
Magnet Rise	Electric	Status	—	—	10	Self	—	—
Iron Tail	Steel	Physical	100	75	15	Normal	—	○
Snore	Normal	Special	40	100	15	Normal	—	—
Sleep Talk	Normal	Status	—	—	10	Self	—	—

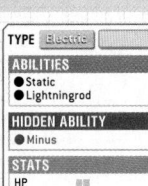

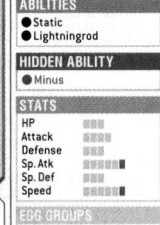

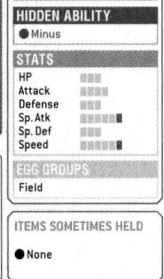

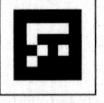

311 Plusle

Cheering Pokémon

- HEIGHT: 1'04"
- WEIGHT: 9.3 lbs.
- GENDER: ♂ / ♀

It cheers on friends with pom-poms made of sparks. It drains power from telephone poles.

Same form for ♂ / ♀

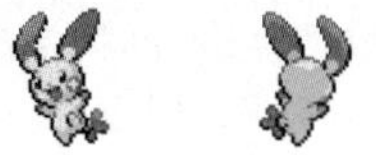

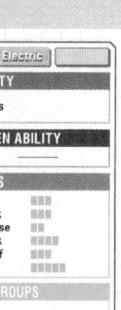

TYPE Electric

ABILITY
- Plus

HIDDEN ABILITY
—

STATS
HP
Attack
Defense
Sp. Atk
Sp. Def
Speed

EGG GROUPS
Fairy

ITEMS SOMETIMES HELD
- None

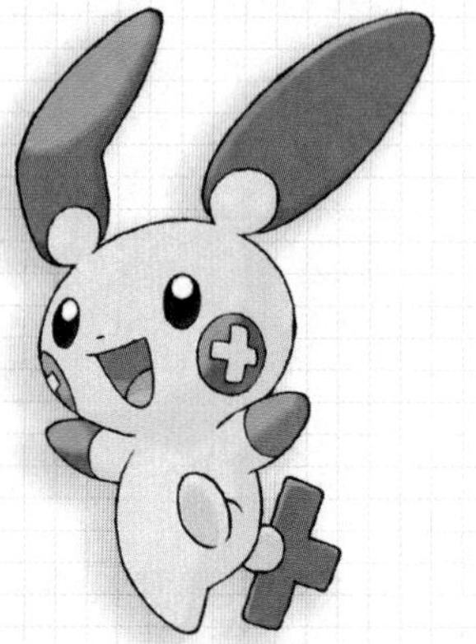

Pokémon AR Marker

EVOLUTION

Does not evolve

HOW TO OBTAIN

Pokémon Black Version 2	Route 6 (mass outbreak)
Pokémon White Version 2	Link Trade or Poké Transfer

HOW TO OBTAIN FROM OTHER GAMES

Pokémon HeartGold Version	Route 29 (Hoenn Sound)
Pokémon SoulSilver Version	Route 29 (Hoenn Sound)

LEVEL-UP AND LEARNED MOVES

Lv.	Name	Type	Kind	Pow.	Acc.	PP	Range	Long	DA
1	Growl	Normal	Status	—	100	40	Many Others	—	—
3	Thunder Wave	Electric	Status	—	100	20	Normal	—	—
7	Quick Attack	Normal	Physical	40	100	30	Normal	—	○
10	Helping Hand	Normal	Status	—	—	20	1 Ally	—	—
15	Spark	Electric	Physical	65	100	20	Normal	—	○
17	Encore	Normal	Status	—	100	5	Normal	—	—
21	Fake Tears	Dark	Status	—	100	20	Normal	—	—
24	Copycat	Normal	Status	—	—	20	Self	—	—
29	Electro Ball	Electric	Special	—	100	10	Normal	—	—
31	Swift	Normal	Special	60	—	20	Many Others	—	—
35	Fake Tears	Dark	Status	—	100	20	Normal	—	—
38	Charge	Electric	Status	—	—	20	Self	—	—
42	Thunder	Electric	Special	120	70	10	Normal	—	—
44	Baton Pass	Normal	Status	—	—	40	Self	—	—
48	Agility	Psychic	Status	—	—	30	Self	—	—
51	Last Resort	Normal	Physical	140	100	5	Normal	—	○
56	Nasty Plot	Dark	Status	—	—	20	Self	—	—
63	Entrainment	Normal	Status	—	100	15	Normal	—	—

TM & HM MOVES

Lv.	Name	Type	Kind	Pow.	Acc.	PP	Range	Long	DA
TM06	Toxic	Poison	Status	—	90	10	Normal	—	—
TM10	Hidden Power	Normal	Special	—	100	15	Normal	—	—
TM16	Light Screen	Psychic	Status	—	—	30	Your Side	—	—
TM17	Protect	Normal	Status	—	—	10	Self	—	—
TM18	Rain Dance	Water	Status	—	—	5	Both Sides	—	—
TM21	Frustration	Normal	Physical	—	100	20	Normal	—	○
TM24	Thunderbolt	Electric	Special	95	100	15	Normal	—	—
TM25	Thunder	Electric	Special	120	70	10	Normal	—	—
TM27	Return	Normal	Physical	—	100	20	Normal	—	○
TM32	Double Team	Normal	Status	—	—	15	Self	—	—
TM42	Facade	Normal	Physical	70	100	20	Normal	—	○
TM44	Rest	Psychic	Status	—	—	10	Self	—	—
TM45	Attract	Normal	Status	—	100	15	Normal	—	—
TM48	Round	Normal	Special	60	100	15	Normal	—	—
TM49	Echoed Voice	Normal	Special	40	100	15	Normal	—	—
TM56	Fling	Dark	Physical	—	100	10	Normal	—	—
TM57	Charge Beam	Electric	Special	50	90	10	Normal	—	—
TM70	Flash	Normal	Status	—	100	20	Normal	—	—
TM72	Volt Switch	Electric	Special	70	100	20	Normal	—	—
TM73	Thunder Wave	Electric	Status	—	100	20	Normal	—	—
TM86	Grass Knot	Grass	Special	—	100	20	Normal	—	○
TM87	Swagger	Normal	Status	—	90	15	Normal	—	—
TM90	Substitute	Normal	Status	—	—	10	Self	—	—
TM93	Wild Charge	Electric	Physical	90	100	15	Normal	—	○

MOVES TAUGHT BY PEOPLE

Name	Type	Kind	Pow.	Acc.	PP	Range	Long	DA

MOVES TAUGHT BY MOVE TUTORS FOR SHARDS

Name	Type	Kind	Pow.	Acc.	PP	Range	Long	DA
Signal Beam	Bug	Special	75	100	15	Normal	—	—
Uproar	Normal	Special	90	100	10	1 Random	—	—
ThunderPunch	Electric	Physical	75	100	15	Normal	—	○
Last Resort	Normal	Physical	140	100	5	Normal	—	○
Magnet Rise	Electric	Status	—	—	10	Self	—	—
Iron Tail	Steel	Physical	100	75	15	Normal	—	○
Snore	Normal	Special	40	100	15	Normal	—	—
Helping Hand	Normal	Status	—	—	20	1 Ally	—	—
Sleep Talk	Normal	Status	—	—	10	Self	—	—

EGG MOVES

Name	Type	Kind	Pow.	Acc.	PP	Range	Long	DA
Wish	Normal	Status	—	—	10	Self	—	—
Sing	Normal	Status	—	55	15	Normal	—	—
Sweet Kiss	Normal	Status	—	75	10	Normal	—	—
Discharge	Electric	Special	80	100	15	Adjacent	—	—
Lucky Chant	Normal	Status	—	—	30	Your Side	—	—

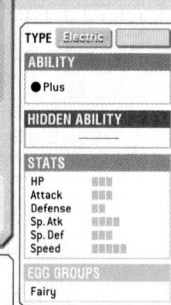

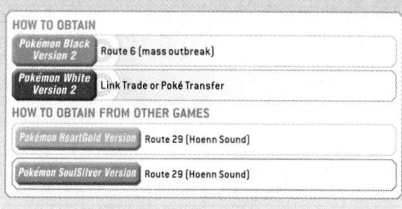

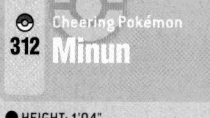

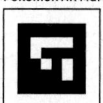

312 Minun

Cheering Pokémon

- HEIGHT: 1'04"
- WEIGHT: 9.3 lbs.
- GENDER: ♂ / ♀

It cheers on friends. If its friends are losing, its body lets off more and more sparks.

Same form for ♂ / ♀

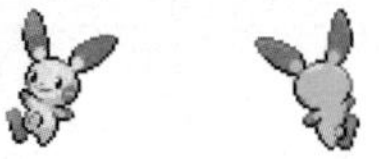

TYPE Electric

ABILITY
- Minus

HIDDEN ABILITY
—

STATS
HP
Attack
Defense
Sp. Atk
Sp. Def
Speed

EGG GROUPS
Fairy

ITEMS SOMETIMES HELD
- None

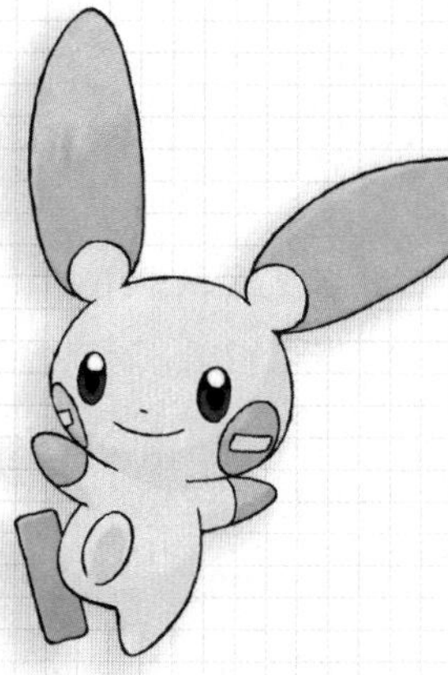

Pokémon AR Marker

EVOLUTION

Does not evolve

HOW TO OBTAIN

Pokémon Black Version 2	Link Trade or Poké Transfer
Pokémon White Version 2	Route 6 (mass outbreak)

HOW TO OBTAIN FROM OTHER GAMES

Pokémon HeartGold Version	Route 29 (Hoenn Sound)
Pokémon SoulSilver Version	Route 29 (Hoenn Sound)

LEVEL-UP AND LEARNED MOVES

Lv.	Name	Type	Kind	Pow.	Acc.	PP	Range	Long	DA
1	Growl	Normal	Status	—	100	40	Many Others	—	—
3	Thunder Wave	Electric	Status	—	100	20	Normal	—	—
7	Quick Attack	Normal	Physical	40	100	30	Normal	—	○
10	Helping Hand	Normal	Status	—	—	20	1 Ally	—	—
15	Spark	Electric	Physical	65	100	20	Normal	—	○
17	Encore	Normal	Status	—	100	5	Normal	—	—
21	Charm	Normal	Status	—	100	20	Normal	—	—
24	Copycat	Normal	Status	—	—	20	Self	—	—
29	Electro Ball	Electric	Special	—	100	10	Normal	—	—
31	Swift	Normal	Special	60	—	20	Many Others	—	—
35	Fake Tears	Dark	Status	—	100	20	Normal	—	—
38	Charge	Electric	Status	—	—	20	Self	—	—
42	Thunder	Electric	Special	120	70	10	Normal	—	—
44	Baton Pass	Normal	Status	—	—	40	Self	—	—
48	Agility	Psychic	Status	—	—	30	Self	—	—
51	Trump Card	Normal	Special	—	—	5	Normal	—	○
56	Nasty Plot	Dark	Status	—	—	20	Self	—	—
63	Entrainment	Normal	Status	—	100	15	Normal	—	—

TM & HM MOVES

Lv.	Name	Type	Kind	Pow.	Acc.	PP	Range	Long	DA
TM06	Toxic	Poison	Status	—	90	10	Normal	—	—
TM10	Hidden Power	Normal	Special	—	100	15	Normal	—	—
TM16	Light Screen	Psychic	Status	—	—	30	Your Side	—	—
TM17	Protect	Normal	Status	—	—	10	Self	—	—
TM18	Rain Dance	Water	Status	—	—	5	Both Sides	—	—
TM21	Frustration	Normal	Physical	—	100	20	Normal	—	○
TM24	Thunderbolt	Electric	Special	95	100	15	Normal	—	—
TM25	Thunder	Electric	Special	120	70	10	Normal	—	—
TM27	Return	Normal	Physical	—	100	20	Normal	—	○
TM32	Double Team	Normal	Status	—	—	15	Self	—	—
TM42	Facade	Normal	Physical	70	100	20	Normal	—	○
TM44	Rest	Psychic	Status	—	—	10	Self	—	—
TM45	Attract	Normal	Status	—	100	15	Normal	—	—
TM48	Round	Normal	Special	60	100	15	Normal	—	—
TM49	Echoed Voice	Normal	Special	40	100	15	Normal	—	—
TM56	Fling	Dark	Physical	—	100	10	Normal	—	—
TM57	Charge Beam	Electric	Special	50	90	10	Normal	—	—
TM70	Flash	Normal	Status	—	100	20	Normal	—	—
TM72	Volt Switch	Electric	Special	70	100	20	Normal	—	—
TM73	Thunder Wave	Electric	Status	—	100	20	Normal	—	—
TM86	Grass Knot	Grass	Special	—	100	20	Normal	—	○
TM87	Swagger	Normal	Status	—	90	15	Normal	—	—
TM90	Substitute	Normal	Status	—	—	10	Self	—	—
TM93	Wild Charge	Electric	Physical	90	100	15	Normal	—	○

MOVES TAUGHT BY PEOPLE

Name	Type	Kind	Pow.	Acc.	PP	Range	Long	DA

MOVES TAUGHT BY MOVE TUTORS FOR SHARDS

Name	Type	Kind	Pow.	Acc.	PP	Range	Long	DA
Signal Beam	Bug	Special	75	100	15	Normal	—	—
Uproar	Normal	Special	90	100	10	1 Random	—	—
ThunderPunch	Electric	Physical	75	100	15	Normal	—	○
Last Resort	Normal	Physical	140	100	5	Normal	—	○
Magnet Rise	Electric	Status	—	—	10	Self	—	—
Iron Tail	Steel	Physical	100	75	15	Normal	—	○
Snore	Normal	Special	40	100	15	Normal	—	—
Helping Hand	Normal	Status	—	—	20	1 Ally	—	—
Sleep Talk	Normal	Status	—	—	10	Self	—	—

EGG MOVES

Name	Type	Kind	Pow.	Acc.	PP	Range	Long	DA
Wish	Normal	Status	—	—	10	Self	—	—
Sing	Normal	Status	—	55	15	Normal	—	—
Sweet Kiss	Normal	Status	—	75	10	Normal	—	—
Discharge	Electric	Special	80	100	15	Adjacent	—	—
Lucky Chant	Normal	Status	—	—	30	Your Side	—	—

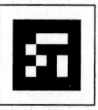

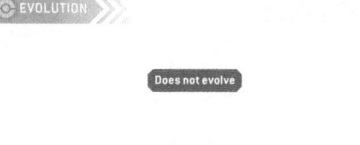

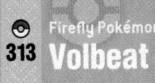

Firefly Pokémon

313 Volbeat

- HEIGHT: 2'04"
- WEIGHT: 39.0 lbs.
- GENDER: ♂

It communicates with others by lighting up its rear at night. It loves Illumise's sweet aroma.

♂

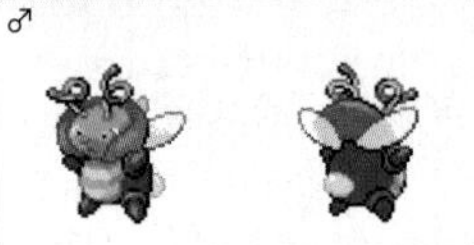

TYPE: Bug

ABILITIES
- Illuminate
- Swarm

HIDDEN ABILITY
- Prankster

STATS
- HP
- Attack
- Defense
- Sp. Atk
- Sp. Def
- Speed

EGG GROUPS
Bug/Human-Like

ITEMS SOMETIMES HELD
- None

EVOLUTION

Does not evolve

HOW TO OBTAIN

Pokémon Black Version 2	Route 3 (mass outbreak)
Pokémon White Version 2	Link Trade or Poké Transfer

HOW TO OBTAIN FROM OTHER GAMES

Pokémon Platinum Version	Route 229
	—

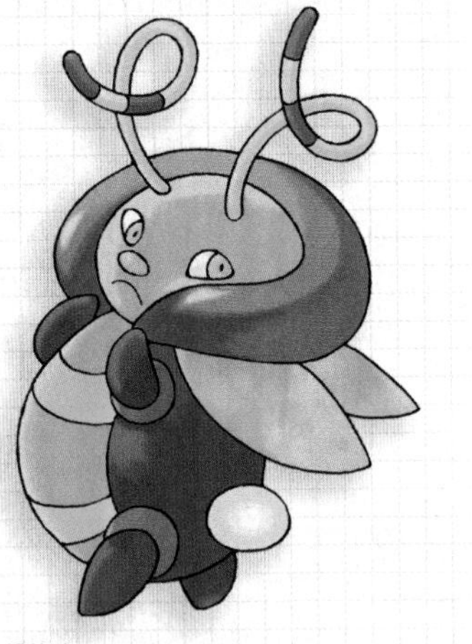

Pokémon AR Marker

LEVEL-UP AND LEARNED MOVES

Lv.	Name	Type	Kind	Pow.	Acc.	PP	Range	Long	DA
1	Flash	Normal	Status	—	100	20	Normal	—	—
1	Tackle	Normal	Physical	50	100	35	Normal	—	○
5	Double Team	Normal	Status	—	—	15	Self	—	—
9	Confuse Ray	Ghost	Status	—	100	10	Normal	—	—
13	Moonlight	Normal	Status	—	—	5	Self	—	—
17	Quick Attack	Normal	Physical	40	100	30	Normal	—	○
21	Tail Glow	Bug	Status	—	—	20	Self	—	—
25	Signal Beam	Bug	Special	75	100	15	Normal	—	—
29	Protect	Normal	Status	—	—	10	Self	—	—
33	Helping Hand	Normal	Status	—	—	20	1 Ally	—	—
37	Zen Headbutt	Psychic	Physical	80	90	15	Normal	—	○
41	Bug Buzz	Bug	Special	90	100	10	Normal	—	—
45	Double-Edge	Normal	Physical	120	100	15	Normal	—	○

TM & HM MOVES

Lv.	Name	Type	Kind	Pow.	Acc.	PP	Range	Long	DA
TM06	Toxic	Poison	Status	—	90	10	Normal	—	—
TM10	Hidden Power	Normal	Special	—	100	15	Normal	—	—
TM11	Sunny Day	Fire	Status	—	—	5	Both Sides	—	—
TM16	Light Screen	Psychic	Status	—	—	30	Your Side	—	—
TM17	Protect	Normal	Status	—	—	10	Self	—	—
TM18	Rain Dance	Water	Status	—	—	5	Both Sides	—	—
TM21	Frustration	Normal	Physical	—	100	20	Normal	—	○
TM22	SolarBeam	Grass	Special	120	100	10	Normal	—	—
TM24	Thunderbolt	Electric	Special	95	100	15	Normal	—	—
TM25	Thunder	Electric	Special	120	70	10	Normal	—	—
TM27	Return	Normal	Physical	—	100	20	Normal	—	○
TM30	Shadow Ball	Ghost	Special	80	100	15	Normal	—	—
TM31	Brick Break	Fighting	Physical	75	100	15	Normal	—	○
TM32	Double Team	Normal	Status	—	—	15	Self	—	—
TM40	Aerial Ace	Flying	Physical	60	—	20	Normal	○	○
TM42	Facade	Normal	Physical	70	100	20	Normal	—	○
TM44	Rest	Psychic	Status	—	—	10	Self	—	—
TM45	Attract	Normal	Status	—	100	15	Normal	—	—
TM46	Thief	Dark	Physical	40	100	10	Normal	—	○
TM48	Round	Normal	Special	60	100	15	Normal	—	—
TM56	Fling	Dark	Physical	—	100	10	Normal	—	—
TM57	Charge Beam	Electric	Special	50	90	10	Normal	—	—
TM62	Acrobatics	Flying	Physical	55	100	15	Normal	○	○
TM70	Flash	Normal	Status	—	100	20	Normal	—	—
TM73	Thunder Wave	Electric	Status	—	100	20	Normal	—	—
TM76	Struggle Bug	Bug	Special	30	100	20	Many Others	—	—
TM77	Psych Up	Normal	Status	—	—	10	Normal	—	—
TM87	Swagger	Normal	Status	—	90	15	Normal	—	—
TM89	U-turn	Bug	Physical	70	100	20	Normal	—	○
TM90	Substitute	Normal	Status	—	—	10	Self	—	—

MOVES TAUGHT BY PEOPLE

Name	Type	Kind	Pow.	Acc.	PP	Range	Long	DA

MOVES TAUGHT BY MOVE TUTORS FOR SHARDS

Name	Type	Kind	Pow.	Acc.	PP	Range	Long	DA
Bug Bite	Bug	Physical	60	100	20	Normal	—	○
Signal Beam	Bug	Special	75	100	15	Normal	—	—
ThunderPunch	Electric	Physical	75	100	15	Normal	—	○
Ice Punch	Ice	Physical	75	100	15	Normal	—	○
Zen Headbutt	Psychic	Physical	80	90	15	Normal	—	○
Snore	Normal	Special	40	100	15	Normal	—	—
Roost	Flying	Status	—	—	10	Self	—	—
Giga Drain	Grass	Special	75	100	10	Normal	—	—
Tailwind	Flying	Status	—	—	30	Your Side	—	—
Helping Hand	Normal	Status	—	—	20	1 Ally	—	—
Trick	Psychic	Status	—	100	10	Normal	—	—
Sleep Talk	Normal	Status	—	—	10	Self	—	—

EGG MOVES

Name	Type	Kind	Pow.	Acc.	PP	Range	Long	DA
Baton Pass	Normal	Status	—	—	40	Self	—	—
Silver Wind	Bug	Special	60	100	5	Normal	—	—
Trick	Psychic	Status	—	100	10	Normal	—	—
Encore	Normal	Status	—	100	5	Normal	—	—
Bug Buzz	Bug	Special	90	100	10	Normal	—	—
Dizzy Punch	Normal	Physical	70	100	10	Normal	—	○
Seismic Toss	Fighting	Physical	—	100	20	Normal	—	○

Firefly Pokémon

314 Illumise

- HEIGHT: 2'00"
- WEIGHT: 39.0 lbs.
- GENDER: ♀

With its sweet aroma, it guides Volbeat to draw signs with light in the night sky.

♀

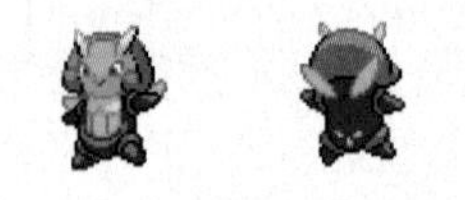

TYPE: Bug

ABILITIES
- Oblivious
- Tinted Lens

HIDDEN ABILITY
- Prankster

STATS
- HP
- Attack
- Defense
- Sp. Atk
- Sp. Def
- Speed

EGG GROUPS
Bug/Human-Like

ITEMS SOMETIMES HELD
- None

EVOLUTION

Does not evolve

HOW TO OBTAIN

Pokémon Black Version 2	Link Trade or Poké Transfer
Pokémon White Version 2	Route 3 (mass outbreak)

HOW TO OBTAIN FROM OTHER GAMES

Pokémon Platinum Version	Route 229
	—

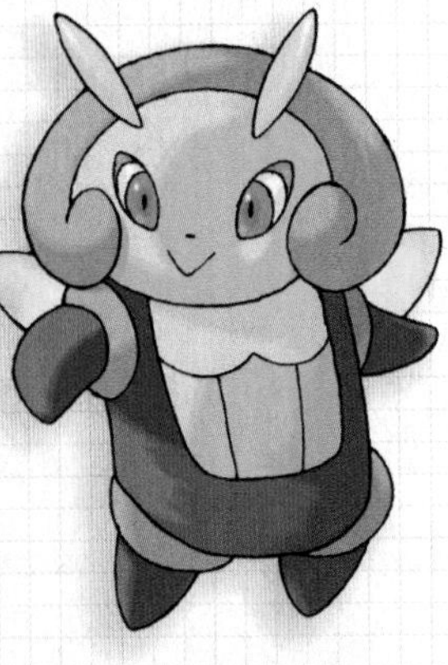

Pokémon AR Marker

LEVEL-UP AND LEARNED MOVES

Lv.	Name	Type	Kind	Pow.	Acc.	PP	Range	Long	DA
1	Tackle	Normal	Physical	50	100	35	Normal	—	○
5	Sweet Scent	Normal	Status	—	100	20	Many Others	—	—
9	Charm	Normal	Status	—	100	20	Normal	—	—
13	Moonlight	Normal	Status	—	—	5	Self	—	—
17	Quick Attack	Normal	Physical	40	100	30	Normal	—	○
21	Wish	Normal	Status	—	—	10	Self	—	—
25	Encore	Normal	Status	—	100	5	Normal	—	—
29	Flatter	Dark	Status	—	100	15	Normal	—	—
33	Helping Hand	Normal	Status	—	—	20	1 Ally	—	—
37	Zen Headbutt	Psychic	Physical	80	90	15	Normal	—	○
41	Bug Buzz	Bug	Special	90	100	10	Normal	—	—
45	Covet	Normal	Physical	60	100	40	Normal	—	○

TM & HM MOVES

Lv.	Name	Type	Kind	Pow.	Acc.	PP	Range	Long	DA
TM06	Toxic	Poison	Status	—	90	10	Normal	—	—
TM10	Hidden Power	Normal	Special	—	100	15	Normal	—	—
TM11	Sunny Day	Fire	Status	—	—	5	Both Sides	—	—
TM16	Light Screen	Psychic	Status	—	—	30	Your Side	—	—
TM17	Protect	Normal	Status	—	—	10	Self	—	—
TM18	Rain Dance	Water	Status	—	—	5	Both Sides	—	—
TM21	Frustration	Normal	Physical	—	100	20	Normal	—	○
TM22	SolarBeam	Grass	Special	120	100	10	Normal	—	—
TM24	Thunderbolt	Electric	Special	95	100	15	Normal	—	—
TM25	Thunder	Electric	Special	120	70	10	Normal	—	—
TM27	Return	Normal	Physical	—	100	20	Normal	—	○
TM30	Shadow Ball	Ghost	Special	80	100	15	Normal	—	—
TM31	Brick Break	Fighting	Physical	75	100	15	Normal	—	○
TM32	Double Team	Normal	Status	—	—	15	Self	—	—
TM40	Aerial Ace	Flying	Physical	60	—	20	Normal	○	○
TM42	Facade	Normal	Physical	70	100	20	Normal	—	○
TM44	Rest	Psychic	Status	—	—	10	Self	—	—
TM45	Attract	Normal	Status	—	100	15	Normal	—	—
TM46	Thief	Dark	Physical	40	100	10	Normal	—	○
TM48	Round	Normal	Special	60	100	15	Normal	—	—
TM56	Fling	Dark	Physical	—	100	10	Normal	—	—
TM57	Charge Beam	Electric	Special	50	90	10	Normal	—	—
TM62	Acrobatics	Flying	Physical	55	100	15	Normal	○	○
TM70	Flash	Normal	Status	—	100	20	Normal	—	—
TM73	Thunder Wave	Electric	Status	—	100	20	Normal	—	—
TM76	Struggle Bug	Bug	Special	30	100	20	Many Others	—	—
TM77	Psych Up	Normal	Status	—	—	10	Normal	—	—
TM87	Swagger	Normal	Status	—	90	15	Normal	—	—
TM89	U-turn	Bug	Physical	70	100	20	Normal	—	○
TM90	Substitute	Normal	Status	—	—	10	Self	—	—

MOVES TAUGHT BY PEOPLE

Name	Type	Kind	Pow.	Acc.	PP	Range	Long	DA

MOVES TAUGHT BY MOVE TUTORS FOR SHARDS

Name	Type	Kind	Pow.	Acc.	PP	Range	Long	DA
Covet	Normal	Physical	60	100	40	Normal	—	○
Bug Bite	Bug	Physical	60	100	20	Normal	—	○
ThunderPunch	Electric	Physical	75	100	15	Normal	—	○
Ice Punch	Ice	Physical	75	100	15	Normal	—	○
Zen Headbutt	Psychic	Physical	80	90	15	Normal	—	○
Snore	Normal	Special	40	100	15	Normal	—	—
Roost	Flying	Status	—	—	10	Self	—	—
Giga Drain	Grass	Special	75	100	10	Normal	—	—
Tailwind	Flying	Status	—	—	30	Your Side	—	—
Helping Hand	Normal	Status	—	—	20	1 Ally	—	—
Sleep Talk	Normal	Status	—	—	10	Self	—	—

EGG MOVES

Name	Type	Kind	Pow.	Acc.	PP	Range	Long	DA
Baton Pass	Normal	Status	—	—	40	Self	—	—
Silver Wind	Bug	Special	60	100	5	Normal	—	—
Growth	Normal	Status	—	—	40	Self	—	—
Encore	Normal	Status	—	100	5	Normal	—	—
Bug Buzz	Bug	Special	90	100	10	Normal	—	—
Captivate	Normal	Status	—	100	20	Many Others	—	—
Fake Tears	Dark	Status	—	100	20	Normal	—	—
Confuse Ray	Ghost	Status	—	100	10	Normal	—	—

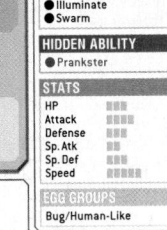

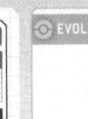

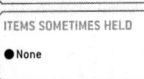

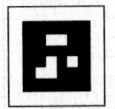

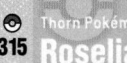

315 **Roselia**

Thorn Pokémon

- HEIGHT: 1'00"
- WEIGHT: 4.4 lbs.
- GENDER: ♂ / ♀

It uses the different poisons in each hand separately when it attacks. The stronger its aroma, the healthier it is.

♂ ♀

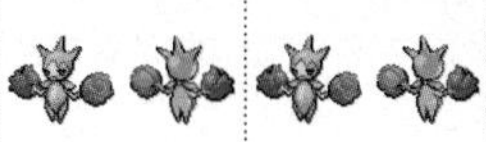

TYPE: Grass / Poison

ABILITIES
- Natural Cure
- Poison Point

HIDDEN ABILITY
—

STATS
HP
Attack
Defense
Sp. Atk
Sp. Def
Speed

EGG GROUPS
Fairy/Grass

ITEMS SOMETIMES HELD
- Poison Barb
- Absorb Bulb

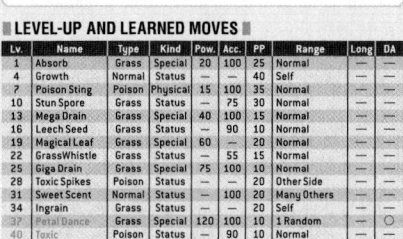

EVOLUTION

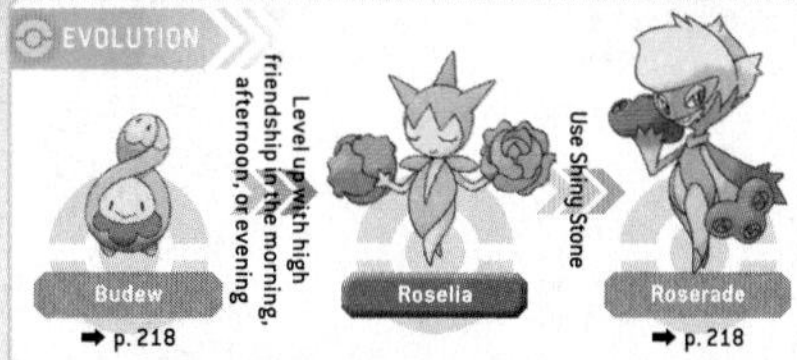

Budew
Level up with high friendship in the morning, afternoon, or evening
Roselia
Use Shiny Stone
Roserade

➡ p. 218 ➡ p. 218

HOW TO OBTAIN

Pokémon Black Version 2	❶ Lostlorn Forest ❷ Route 12
Pokémon White Version 2	❶ Lostlorn Forest ❷ Route 12

HOW TO OBTAIN FROM OTHER GAMES

—

—

LEVEL-UP AND LEARNED MOVES

Lv.	Name	Type	Kind	Pow.	Acc.	PP	Range	Long	DA
1	Absorb	Grass	Special	20	100	25	Normal	—	—
4	Growth	Normal	Status	—	—	40	Self	—	—
7	Poison Sting	Poison	Physical	15	100	35	Normal	—	—
10	Stun Spore	Grass	Status	—	75	30	Normal	—	—
13	Mega Drain	Grass	Special	40	100	15	Normal	—	—
16	Leech Seed	Grass	Status	—	90	10	Normal	—	—
19	Magical Leaf	Grass	Special	60	—	20	Normal	—	—
22	GrassWhistle	Grass	Status	—	55	15	Normal	—	—
25	Giga Drain	Grass	Special	75	100	10	Normal	—	—
28	Toxic Spikes	Poison	Status	—	—	20	Other Side	—	—
31	Sweet Scent	Normal	Status	—	100	20	Many Others	—	—
34	Ingrain	Grass	Status	—	—	20	Self	—	—
37	Petal Dance	Grass	Special	120	100	10	1 Random	—	○
40	Toxic	Poison	Status	—	90	10	Normal	—	—
43	Aromatherapy	Grass	Status	—	—	5	Your Party	—	—
46	Synthesis	Grass	Status	—	—	5	Self	—	—

TM & HM MOVES

Lv.	Name	Type	Kind	Pow.	Acc.	PP	Range	Long	DA
TM06	Toxic	Poison	Status	—	90	10	Normal	—	—
TM09	Venoshock	Poison	Special	65	100	10	Normal	—	—
TM10	Hidden Power	Normal	Special	—	100	15	Normal	—	—
TM11	Sunny Day	Fire	Status	—	—	5	Both Sides	—	—
TM17	Protect	Normal	Status	—	—	10	Self	—	—
TM18	Rain Dance	Water	Status	—	—	5	Both Sides	—	—
TM21	Frustration	Normal	Physical	—	100	20	Normal	—	○
TM22	SolarBeam	Grass	Special	120	100	10	Normal	—	—
TM27	Return	Normal	Physical	—	100	20	Normal	—	○
TM30	Shadow Ball	Ghost	Special	80	100	15	Normal	—	—
TM32	Double Team	Normal	Status	—	—	15	Self	—	—
TM36	Sludge Bomb	Poison	Special	90	100	10	Normal	—	—
TM42	Facade	Normal	Physical	70	100	20	Normal	—	○
TM44	Rest	Psychic	Status	—	—	10	Self	—	—
TM45	Attract	Normal	Status	—	100	15	Normal	—	—
TM48	Round	Normal	Special	60	100	15	Normal	—	—
TM53	Energy Ball	Grass	Special	80	100	10	Normal	—	—
TM70	Flash	Normal	Status	—	100	20	Normal	—	—
TM75	Swords Dance	Normal	Status	—	—	30	Self	—	—
TM77	Psych Up	Normal	Status	—	—	10	Normal	—	—
TM84	Poison Jab	Poison	Physical	80	100	20	Normal	—	○
TM86	Grass Knot	Grass	Special	—	100	20	Normal	—	○
TM87	Swagger	Normal	Status	—	90	15	Normal	—	—
TM90	Substitute	Normal	Status	—	—	10	Self	—	—
HM01	Cut	Normal	Physical	50	95	30	Normal	—	○

MOVES TAUGHT BY PEOPLE

Name	Type	Kind	Pow.	Acc.	PP	Range	Long	DA

MOVES TAUGHT BY MOVE TUTORS FOR SHARDS

Name	Type	Kind	Pow.	Acc.	PP	Range	Long	DA
Covet	Normal	Physical	60	100	40	Normal	—	○
Seed Bomb	Grass	Physical	80	100	15	Normal	—	—
Snore	Normal	Special	40	100	15	Normal	—	—
Synthesis	Grass	Status	—	—	5	Self	—	—
Giga Drain	Grass	Special	75	100	10	Normal	—	—
Worry Seed	Grass	Status	—	100	10	Normal	—	—
Sleep Talk	Normal	Status	—	—	10	Self	—	—

EGG MOVES

Name	Type	Kind	Pow.	Acc.	PP	Range	Long	DA
Spikes	Ground	Status	—	—	20	Other Side	—	—
Synthesis	Grass	Status	—	—	5	Self	—	—
Pin Missile	Bug	Physical	14	85	20	Normal	—	—
Cotton Spore	Grass	Status	—	100	40	Normal	—	—
Sleep Powder	Grass	Status	—	75	15	Normal	—	—
Razor Leaf	Grass	Physical	55	95	25	Many Others	—	—
Mind Reader	Normal	Status	—	—	5	Normal	—	—
Leaf Storm	Grass	Special	140	90	5	Normal	—	—
Seed Bomb	Grass	Physical	80	100	15	Normal	—	—
Giga Drain	Grass	Special	75	100	10	Normal	—	—
Natural Gift	Normal	Physical	—	100	15	Normal	—	—
GrassWhistle	Grass	Status	—	55	15	Normal	—	—

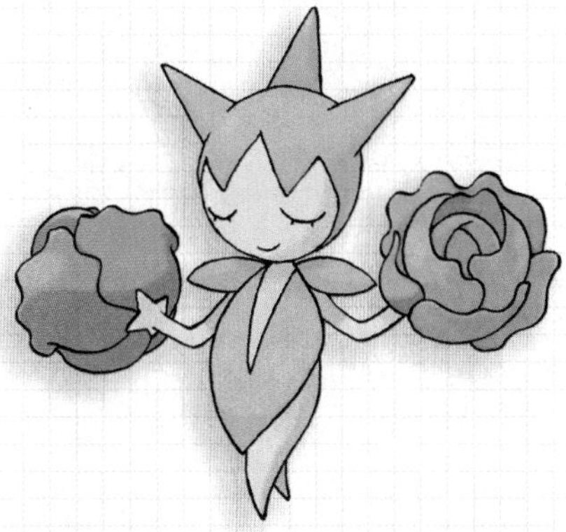

Pokémon AR Marker

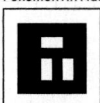

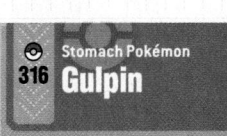

316 **Gulpin**

Stomach Pokémon

- HEIGHT: 1'04"
- WEIGHT: 22.7 lbs.
- GENDER: ♂ / ♀

Almost all its body is its stomach. Its harsh digestive juices quickly dissolve anything it swallows.

♂ ♀

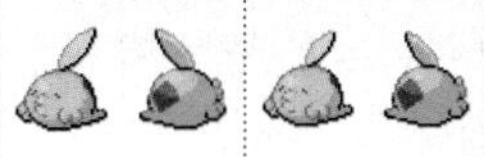

TYPE: Poison

ABILITIES
- Liquid Ooze
- Sticky Hold

HIDDEN ABILITY
—

STATS
HP
Attack
Defense
Sp. Atk
Sp. Def
Speed

EGG GROUPS
Amorphous

ITEMS SOMETIMES HELD
- None

EVOLUTION

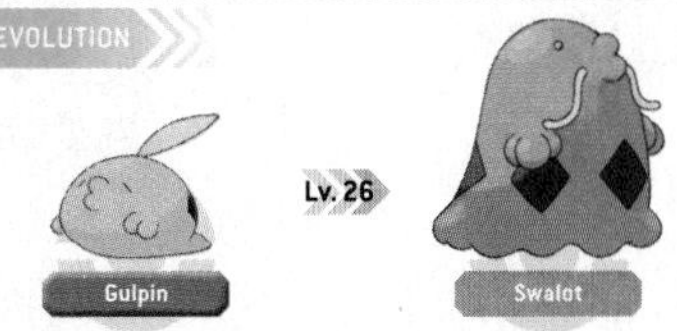

Gulpin
Lv. 26
Swalot

HOW TO OBTAIN

Pokémon Black Version 2	Catch a Swalot, leave it at the Pokémon Day Care, and hatch the Egg that is found
Pokémon White Version 2	Catch a Swalot, leave it at the Pokémon Day Care, and hatch the Egg that is found

HOW TO OBTAIN FROM OTHER GAMES

Pokémon SoulSilver Version	Route 3 (mass outbreak)
Pokémon Platinum Version	Pastoria Great Marsh (after obtaining the National Pokédex/changes daily)

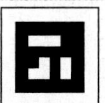

LEVEL-UP AND LEARNED MOVES

Lv.	Name	Type	Kind	Pow.	Acc.	PP	Range	Long	DA
1	Pound	Normal	Physical	40	100	35	Normal	—	○
6	Yawn	Normal	Status	—	—	10	Normal	—	—
9	Poison Gas	Poison	Status	—	80	40	Many Others	—	—
14	Sludge	Poison	Special	65	100	20	Normal	—	—
17	Amnesia	Psychic	Status	—	—	20	Self	—	—
23	Encore	Normal	Status	—	100	5	Normal	—	—
28	Toxic	Poison	Status	—	90	10	Normal	—	—
34	Acid Spray	Poison	Special	40	100	20	Normal	—	—
39	Stockpile	Normal	Status	—	—	20	Self	—	—
39	Spit Up	Normal	Special	—	100	10	Normal	—	—
39	Swallow	Normal	Status	—	—	10	Self	—	—
44	Sludge Bomb	Poison	Special	90	100	10	Normal	—	—
49	Gastro Acid	Poison	Status	—	100	10	Normal	—	—
54	Wring Out	Normal	Special	—	100	5	Normal	—	○
59	Gunk Shot	Poison	Physical	120	70	5	Normal	—	—

TM & HM MOVES

Lv.	Name	Type	Kind	Pow.	Acc.	PP	Range	Long	DA
TM06	Toxic	Poison	Status	—	90	10	Normal	—	—
TM09	Venoshock	Poison	Special	65	100	10	Normal	—	—
TM10	Hidden Power	Normal	Special	—	100	15	Normal	—	—
TM11	Sunny Day	Fire	Status	—	—	5	Both Sides	—	—
TM13	Ice Beam	Ice	Special	95	100	10	Normal	—	—
TM17	Protect	Normal	Status	—	—	10	Self	—	—
TM18	Rain Dance	Water	Status	—	—	5	Both Sides	—	—
TM21	Frustration	Normal	Physical	—	100	20	Normal	—	○
TM22	SolarBeam	Grass	Special	120	100	10	Normal	—	—
TM27	Return	Normal	Physical	—	100	20	Normal	—	○
TM30	Shadow Ball	Ghost	Special	80	100	15	Normal	—	—
TM32	Double Team	Normal	Status	—	—	15	Self	—	—
TM34	Sludge Wave	Poison	Special	95	100	10	Adjacent	—	—
TM36	Sludge Bomb	Poison	Special	90	100	10	Normal	—	—
TM42	Facade	Normal	Physical	70	100	20	Normal	—	○
TM44	Rest	Psychic	Status	—	—	10	Self	—	—
TM45	Attract	Normal	Status	—	100	15	Normal	—	—
TM48	Round	Normal	Special	60	100	15	Normal	—	—
TM64	Explosion	Normal	Physical	250	100	5	Adjacent	—	—
TM85	Dream Eater	Psychic	Special	100	100	15	Normal	—	—
TM87	Swagger	Normal	Status	—	90	15	Normal	—	—
TM90	Substitute	Normal	Status	—	—	10	Self	—	—
TM94	Rock Smash	Fighting	Physical	40	100	15	Normal	—	○
HM04	Strength	Normal	Physical	80	100	15	Normal	—	○

MOVES TAUGHT BY PEOPLE

Name	Type	Kind	Pow.	Acc.	PP	Range	Long	DA

MOVES TAUGHT BY MOVE TUTORS FOR SHARDS

Name	Type	Kind	Pow.	Acc.	PP	Range	Long	DA
Seed Bomb	Grass	Physical	80	100	15	Normal	—	—
Gunk Shot	Poison	Physical	120	70	5	Normal	—	—
Fire Punch	Fire	Physical	75	100	15	Normal	—	○
ThunderPunch	Electric	Physical	75	100	15	Normal	—	○
Ice Punch	Ice	Physical	75	100	15	Normal	—	○
Snore	Normal	Special	40	100	15	Normal	—	—
Giga Drain	Grass	Special	75	100	10	Normal	—	—
Pain Split	Normal	Status	—	—	20	Normal	—	—
Gastro Acid	Poison	Status	—	100	10	Normal	—	—
Sleep Talk	Normal	Status	—	—	10	Self	—	—
Snatch	Dark	Status	—	—	10	Self	—	—

EGG MOVES

Name	Type	Kind	Pow.	Acc.	PP	Range	Long	DA
Acid Armor	Poison	Status	—	—	40	Self	—	—
Smog	Poison	Special	20	70	20	Normal	—	—
Pain Split	Normal	Status	—	—	20	Normal	—	—
Curse	Ghost	Status	—	—	10	Varies	—	—
Destiny Bond	Ghost	Status	—	—	5	Self	—	—
Mud-Slap	Ground	Special	20	100	10	Normal	—	—
Gunk Shot	Poison	Physical	120	70	5	Normal	—	—

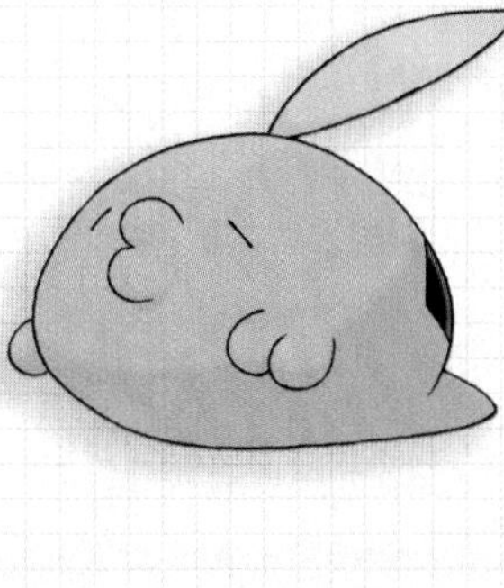

Pokémon AR Marker

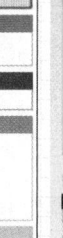

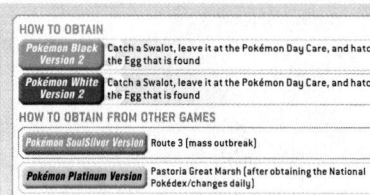

NATIONAL POKÉDEX

317 Swalot

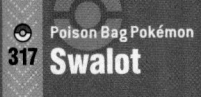

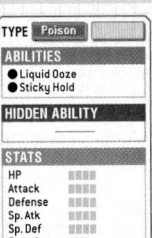

317 Swalot

Poison Bag Pokémon

- HEIGHT: 5'07"
- WEIGHT: 176.4 lbs.
- GENDER: ♂ / ♀

It swallows anything whole. It sweats toxic fluids from its follicles to douse foes.

♂ ♀

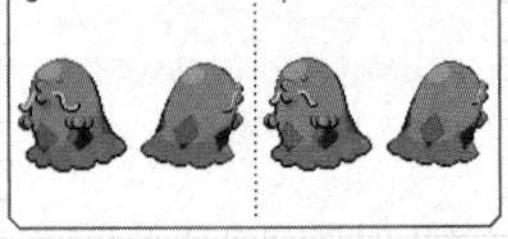

TYPE Poison

ABILITIES
- Liquid Ooze
- Sticky Hold

HIDDEN ABILITY
—

STATS
HP
Attack
Defense
Sp. Atk
Sp. Def
Speed

EGG GROUPS
Amorphous

ITEMS SOMETIMES HELD
- Big Pearl

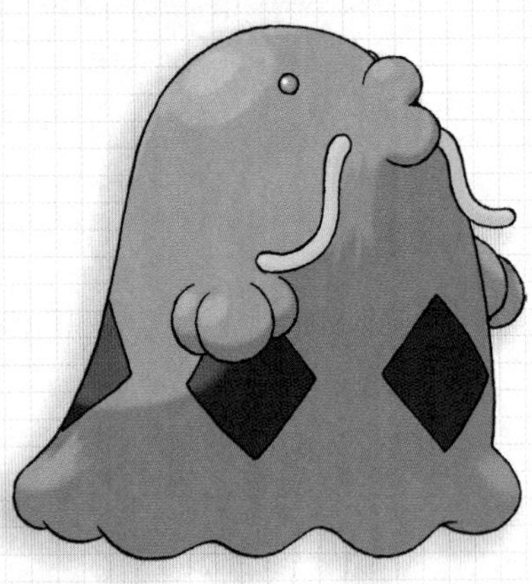

Pokémon AR Marker

EVOLUTION

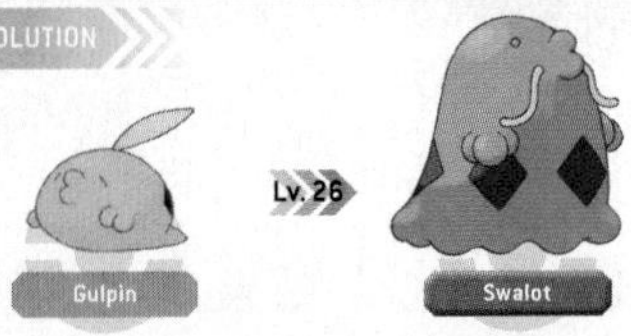

HOW TO OBTAIN

Pokémon Black Version 2	Route 9 (mass outbreak)
Pokémon White Version 2	Route 9 (mass outbreak)

HOW TO OBTAIN FROM OTHER GAMES

—

—

LEVEL-UP AND LEARNED MOVES

Lv.	Name	Type	Kind	Pow.	Acc.	PP	Range	Long	DA
1	Pound	Normal	Physical	40	100	35	Normal	—	○
1	Yawn	Normal	Status	—	—	10	Normal	—	—
1	Poison Gas	Poison	Status	—	80	40	Many Others	—	—
1	Sludge	Poison	Special	65	100	20	Normal	—	—
6	Yawn	Normal	Status	—	—	10	Normal	—	—
9	Poison Gas	Poison	Status	—	80	40	Many Others	—	—
14	Sludge	Poison	Special	65	100	20	Normal	—	—
17	Amnesia	Psychic	Status	—	—	20	Self	—	—
23	Encore	Normal	Status	—	100	5	Normal	—	—
26	Body Slam	Normal	Physical	85	100	15	Normal	—	○
30	Toxic	Poison	Status	—	90	10	Normal	—	—
38	Acid Spray	Poison	Special	40	100	20	Normal	—	—
45	Stockpile	Normal	Status	—	—	20	Self	—	—
45	Spit Up	Normal	Special	—	100	10	Normal	—	—
45	Swallow	Normal	Status	—	—	10	Self	—	—
52	Sludge Bomb	Poison	Special	90	100	10	Normal	—	—
59	Gastro Acid	Poison	Status	—	100	10	Normal	—	—
66	Wring Out	Normal	Special	—	100	5	Normal	—	○
73	Gunk Shot	Poison	Physical	120	70	5	Normal	—	—

TM & HM MOVES

Lv.	Name	Type	Kind	Pow.	Acc.	PP	Range	Long	DA
TM06	Toxic	Poison	Status	—	90	10	Normal	—	—
TM09	Venoshock	Poison	Special	65	100	10	Normal	—	—
TM10	Hidden Power	Normal	Special	—	100	15	Normal	—	—
TM11	Sunny Day	Fire	Status	—	—	5	Both Sides	—	—
TM13	Ice Beam	Ice	Special	95	100	10	Normal	—	—
TM15	Hyper Beam	Normal	Special	150	90	5	Normal	—	—
TM17	Protect	Normal	Status	—	—	10	Self	—	—
TM18	Rain Dance	Water	Status	—	—	5	Both Sides	—	—
TM21	Frustration	Normal	Physical	—	100	20	Normal	—	○
TM22	SolarBeam	Grass	Special	120	100	10	Normal	—	—
TM26	Earthquake	Ground	Physical	100	100	10	Adjacent	—	—
TM27	Return	Normal	Physical	—	100	20	Normal	—	○
TM30	Shadow Ball	Ghost	Special	80	100	15	Normal	—	—
TM32	Double Team	Normal	Status	—	—	15	Self	—	—
TM34	Sludge Wave	Poison	Special	95	100	10	Adjacent	—	—
TM36	Sludge Bomb	Poison	Special	90	100	10	Normal	—	—
TM42	Facade	Normal	Physical	70	100	20	Normal	—	○
TM44	Rest	Psychic	Status	—	—	10	Self	—	—
TM45	Attract	Normal	Status	—	100	15	Normal	—	—
TM48	Round	Normal	Special	60	100	15	Normal	—	—
TM64	Explosion	Normal	Physical	250	100	5	Adjacent	—	—
TM68	Giga Impact	Normal	Physical	150	90	5	Normal	—	○
TM78	Bulldoze	Ground	Physical	60	100	20	Adjacent	—	—
TM85	Dream Eater	Psychic	Special	100	100	15	Normal	—	—
TM87	Swagger	Normal	Status	—	90	15	Normal	—	—
TM90	Substitute	Normal	Status	—	—	10	Self	—	—
TM94	Rock Smash	Fighting	Physical	40	100	15	Normal	—	○
HM04	Strength	Normal	Physical	80	100	15	Normal	—	○

MOVES TAUGHT BY PEOPLE

Name	Type	Kind	Pow.	Acc.	PP	Range	Long	DA

MOVES TAUGHT BY MOVE TUTORS FOR SHARDS

Name	Type	Kind	Pow.	Acc.	PP	Range	Long	DA
Seed Bomb	Grass	Physical	80	100	15	Normal	—	—
Gunk Shot	Poison	Physical	120	70	5	Normal	—	—
Fire Punch	Fire	Physical	75	100	15	Normal	—	○
ThunderPunch	Electric	Physical	75	100	15	Normal	—	○
Ice Punch	Ice	Physical	75	100	15	Normal	—	○
Block	Normal	Status	—	—	5	Normal	—	—
Snore	Normal	Special	40	100	15	Normal	—	—
Giga Drain	Grass	Special	75	100	10	Normal	—	—
Pain Split	Normal	Status	—	—	20	Normal	—	—
Gastro Acid	Poison	Status	—	100	10	Normal	—	—
Sleep Talk	Normal	Status	—	—	10	Self	—	—
Snatch	Dark	Status	—	—	10	Self	—	—

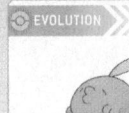

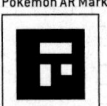

318 Carvanha

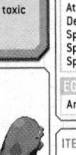

318 Carvanha

Savage Pokémon

- HEIGHT: 2'07"
- WEIGHT: 45.9 lbs.
- GENDER: ♂ / ♀

They swarm any foe that invades their territory. Their sharp fangs can tear out boat hulls.

Same form for ♂ / ♀

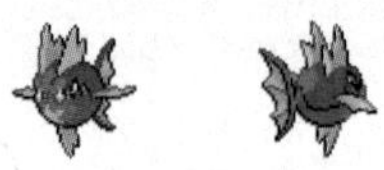

TYPE Water Dark

ABILITY
- Rough Skin

HIDDEN ABILITY
- Speed Boost

STATS
HP
Attack
Defense
Sp. Atk
Sp. Def
Speed

EGG GROUPS
Water 2

ITEMS SOMETIMES HELD
- DeepSeaTooth

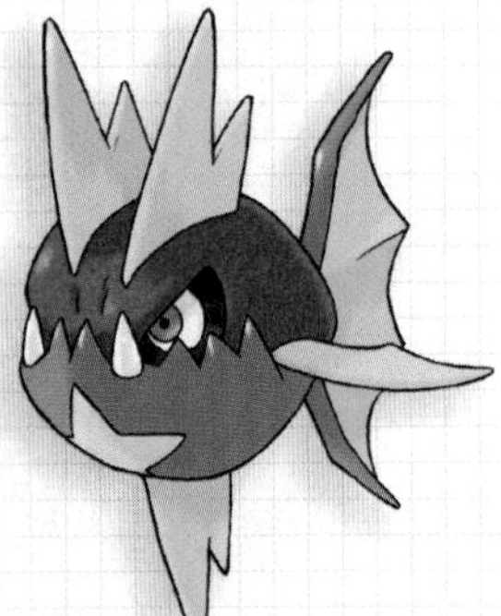

Pokémon AR Marker

EVOLUTION

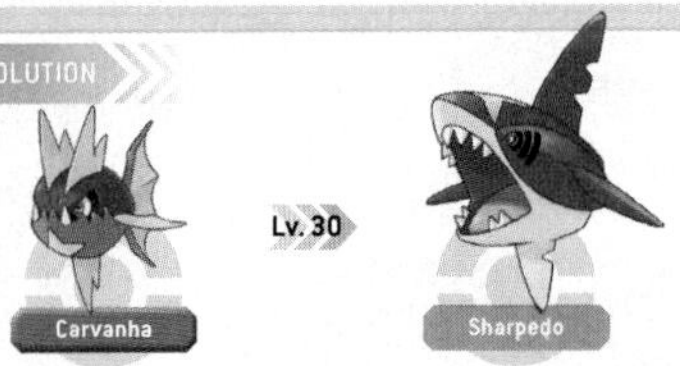

HOW TO OBTAIN

Pokémon Black Version 2	Village Bridge (Super Rod)
Pokémon White Version 2	Village Bridge (Super Rod)

HOW TO OBTAIN FROM OTHER GAMES

—

—

LEVEL-UP AND LEARNED MOVES

Lv.	Name	Type	Kind	Pow.	Acc.	PP	Range	Long	DA
1	Leer	Normal	Status	—	100	30	Many Others	—	—
1	Bite	Dark	Physical	60	100	25	Normal	—	○
6	Rage	Normal	Physical	20	100	20	Normal	—	○
8	Focus Energy	Normal	Status	—	—	30	Self	—	—
11	Scary Face	Normal	Status	—	100	10	Normal	—	—
16	Ice Fang	Ice	Physical	65	95	15	Normal	—	○
18	Screech	Normal	Status	—	85	40	Normal	—	—
21	Swagger	Normal	Status	—	90	15	Normal	—	—
26	Assurance	Dark	Physical	50	100	10	Normal	—	○
28	Crunch	Dark	Physical	80	100	15	Normal	—	○
31	Aqua Jet	Water	Physical	40	100	20	Normal	—	○
36	Agility	Psychic	Status	—	—	30	Self	—	—
38	Take Down	Normal	Physical	90	85	20	Normal	—	○

TM & HM MOVES

Lv.	Name	Type	Kind	Pow.	Acc.	PP	Range	Long	DA
TM06	Toxic	Poison	Status	—	90	10	Normal	—	—
TM07	Hail	Ice	Status	—	—	10	Both Sides	—	—
TM10	Hidden Power	Normal	Special	—	100	15	Normal	—	—
TM12	Taunt	Dark	Status	—	100	20	Normal	—	—
TM13	Ice Beam	Ice	Special	95	100	10	Normal	—	—
TM14	Blizzard	Ice	Special	120	70	5	Many Others	—	—
TM17	Protect	Normal	Status	—	—	10	Self	—	—
TM18	Rain Dance	Water	Status	—	—	5	Both Sides	—	—
TM21	Frustration	Normal	Physical	—	100	20	Normal	—	○
TM27	Return	Normal	Physical	—	100	20	Normal	—	○
TM32	Double Team	Normal	Status	—	—	15	Self	—	—
TM41	Torment	Dark	Status	—	100	15	Normal	—	—
TM42	Facade	Normal	Physical	70	100	20	Normal	—	○
TM44	Rest	Psychic	Status	—	—	10	Self	—	—
TM45	Attract	Normal	Status	—	100	15	Normal	—	—
TM46	Thief	Dark	Physical	40	100	10	Normal	—	○
TM48	Round	Normal	Special	60	100	15	Normal	—	—
TM55	Scald	Water	Special	80	100	15	Normal	—	—
TM66	Payback	Dark	Physical	50	100	10	Normal	—	○
TM67	Retaliate	Normal	Physical	70	100	5	Normal	—	○
TM87	Swagger	Normal	Status	—	90	15	Normal	—	—
TM90	Substitute	Normal	Status	—	—	10	Self	—	—
TM95	Snarl	Dark	Special	55	95	15	Many Others	—	—
HM03	Surf	Water	Special	95	100	15	Adjacent	—	—
HM05	Waterfall	Water	Physical	80	100	15	Normal	—	○
HM06	Dive	Water	Physical	80	100	10	Normal	—	○

MOVES TAUGHT BY PEOPLE

Name	Type	Kind	Pow.	Acc.	PP	Range	Long	DA

MOVES TAUGHT BY MOVE TUTORS FOR SHARDS

Name	Type	Kind	Pow.	Acc.	PP	Range	Long	DA
Bounce	Flying	Physical	85	85	5	Normal	○	○
Super Fang	Normal	Physical	—	90	10	Normal	—	○
Uproar	Normal	Special	90	100	10	1 Random	—	—
Icy Wind	Ice	Special	55	95	15	Many Others	—	—
Zen Headbutt	Psychic	Physical	80	90	15	Normal	—	○
Dark Pulse	Dark	Special	80	100	15	Normal	○	—
Snore	Normal	Special	40	100	15	Normal	—	—
Spite	Ghost	Status	—	100	10	Normal	—	—
Sleep Talk	Normal	Status	—	—	10	Self	—	—

EGG MOVES

Name	Type	Kind	Pow.	Acc.	PP	Range	Long	DA
Hydro Pump	Water	Special	120	80	5	Normal	—	—
Double-Edge	Normal	Physical	120	100	15	Normal	—	○
Thrash	Normal	Physical	120	100	10	1 Random	—	○
AncientPower	Rock	Special	60	100	5	Normal	—	—
Swift	Normal	Special	60	—	20	Many Others	—	—
Brine	Water	Special	65	100	10	Normal	—	—

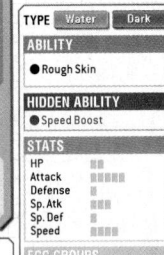

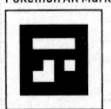

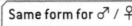

Brutal Pokémon
319 Sharpedo

- HEIGHT: 5'11"
- WEIGHT: 195.8 lbs.
- GENDER: ♂ / ♀

Its fangs rip through sheet iron. It swims at 75 mph and is known as "The Bully of the Sea."

Same form for ♂ / ♀

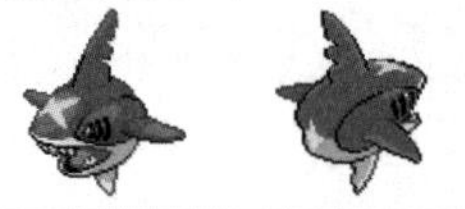

TYPE Water Dark

ABILITY
- Rough Skin

HIDDEN ABILITY
- Speed Boost

STATS
HP
Attack
Defense
Sp. Atk
Sp. Def
Speed

EGG GROUPS
Water ❷

ITEMS SOMETIMES HELD
- DeepSeaTooth

EVOLUTION

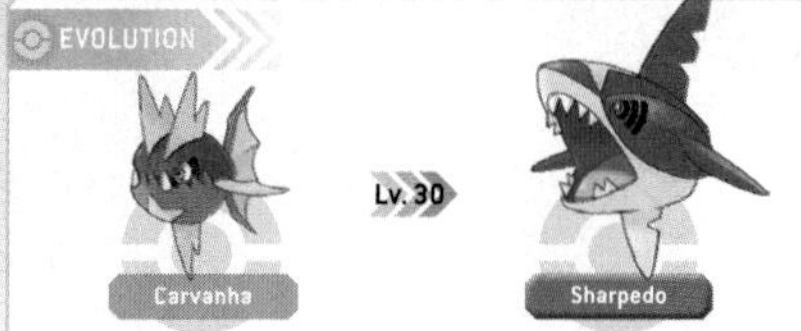

HOW TO OBTAIN

Pokémon Black Version 2	Village Bridge (Super Rod—ripples in water)
Pokémon White Version 2	Village Bridge (Super Rod—ripples in water)

HOW TO OBTAIN FROM OTHER GAMES

—

—

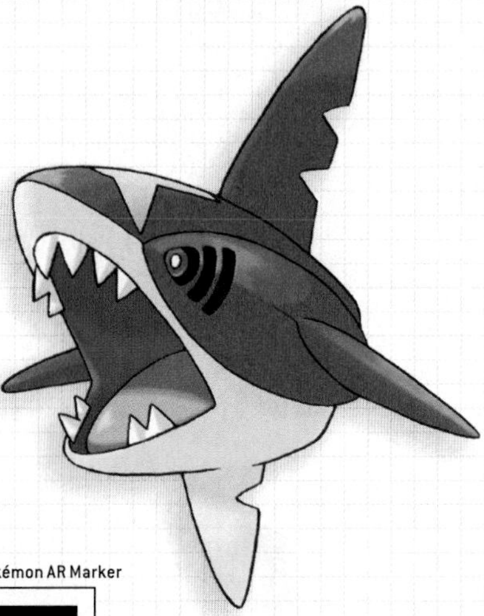

Pokémon AR Marker

LEVEL-UP AND LEARNED MOVES

Lv.	Name	Type	Kind	Pow.	Acc.	PP	Range	Long	DA
1	Feint	Normal	Physical	30	100	10	Normal	—	—
1	Leer	Normal	Status	—	100	30	Many Others	—	—
1	Bite	Dark	Physical	60	100	25	Normal	—	○
1	Rage	Normal	Physical	20	100	20	Normal	—	○
1	Focus Energy	Normal	Status	—	—	30	Self	—	—
6	Rage	Normal	Physical	20	100	20	Normal	—	○
8	Focus Energy	Normal	Status	—	—	30	Self	—	—
11	Scary Face	Normal	Status	—	100	10	Normal	—	—
16	Ice Fang	Ice	Physical	65	95	15	Normal	—	○
18	Screech	Normal	Status	—	85	40	Normal	—	—
21	Swagger	Normal	Status	—	90	15	Normal	—	—
26	Assurance	Dark	Physical	50	100	10	Normal	—	○
28	Crunch	Dark	Physical	80	100	15	Normal	—	○
30	Slash	Normal	Physical	70	100	20	Normal	—	○
34	Aqua Jet	Water	Physical	40	100	20	Normal	—	○
40	Taunt	Dark	Status	—	100	20	Normal	—	—
45	Agility	Psychic	Status	—	—	30	Self	—	—
50	Skull Bash	Normal	Physical	100	100	15	Normal	—	○
56	Night Slash	Dark	Physical	70	100	15	Normal	—	○

TM & HM MOVES

Lv.	Name	Type	Kind	Pow.	Acc.	PP	Range	Long	DA
TM05	Roar	Normal	Status	—	100	20	Normal	—	—
TM06	Toxic	Poison	Status	—	90	10	Normal	—	—
TM07	Hail	Ice	Status	—	—	10	Both Sides	—	—
TM10	Hidden Power	Normal	Special	—	100	15	Normal	—	—
TM12	Taunt	Dark	Status	—	100	20	Normal	—	—
TM13	Ice Beam	Ice	Special	95	100	10	Normal	—	—
TM14	Blizzard	Ice	Special	120	70	5	Many Others	—	—
TM15	Hyper Beam	Normal	Special	150	90	5	Normal	—	—
TM17	Protect	Normal	Status	—	—	10	Self	—	—
TM18	Rain Dance	Water	Status	—	—	5	Both Sides	—	—
TM21	Frustration	Normal	Physical	—	100	20	Normal	—	○
TM26	Earthquake	Ground	Physical	100	100	10	Adjacent	—	—
TM27	Return	Normal	Physical	—	100	20	Normal	—	○
TM32	Double Team	Normal	Status	—	—	15	Self	—	—
TM39	Rock Tomb	Rock	Physical	50	80	10	Normal	—	—
TM41	Torment	Dark	Status	—	100	15	Normal	—	—
TM42	Facade	Normal	Physical	70	100	20	Normal	—	○
TM44	Rest	Psychic	Status	—	—	10	Self	—	—
TM45	Attract	Normal	Status	—	100	15	Normal	—	—
TM46	Thief	Dark	Physical	40	100	10	Normal	—	○
TM48	Round	Normal	Special	60	100	15	Normal	—	—
TM55	Scald	Water	Special	80	100	15	Normal	—	—
TM66	Payback	Dark	Physical	50	100	10	Normal	—	○
TM67	Retaliate	Normal	Physical	70	100	5	Normal	—	○
TM68	Giga Impact	Normal	Physical	150	90	5	Normal	—	○
TM78	Bulldoze	Ground	Physical	60	100	20	Adjacent	—	—
TM84	Poison Jab	Poison	Physical	80	100	20	Normal	—	○
TM87	Swagger	Normal	Status	—	90	15	Normal	—	—
TM90	Substitute	Normal	Status	—	—	10	Self	—	—
TM94	Rock Smash	Fighting	Physical	40	100	15	Normal	—	○
TM95	Snarl	Dark	Special	55	95	15	Many Others	—	—
HM03	Surf	Water	Special	95	100	15	Adjacent	—	—
HM04	Strength	Normal	Physical	80	100	15	Normal	—	○
HM05	Waterfall	Water	Physical	80	100	15	Normal	—	○
HM06	Dive	Water	Physical	80	100	10	Normal	—	○

MOVES TAUGHT BY PEOPLE

Name	Type	Kind	Pow.	Acc.	PP	Range	Long	DA

MOVES TAUGHT BY MOVE TUTORS FOR SHARDS

Name	Type	Kind	Pow.	Acc.	PP	Range	Long	DA
Bounce	Flying	Physical	85	85	5	Normal	○	○
Super Fang	Normal	Physical	—	90	10	Normal	—	○
Uproar	Normal	Special	90	100	10	1 Random	—	—
Icy Wind	Ice	Special	55	95	15	Many Others	—	—
Zen Headbutt	Psychic	Physical	80	90	15	Normal	—	○
Dark Pulse	Dark	Special	80	100	15	Normal	○	—
Snore	Normal	Special	40	100	15	Normal	—	—
Spite	Ghost	Status	—	100	10	Normal	—	—
Sleep Talk	Normal	Status	—	—	10	Self	—	—

NATIONAL POKÉDEX

319 Sharpedo

Ball Whale Pokémon
320 Wailmer

- HEIGHT: 6'07"
- WEIGHT: 286.6 lbs.
- GENDER: ♂ / ♀

It eats one ton of food every day. It plays by shooting stored seawater out its blowholes with great force.

Same form for ♂ / ♀

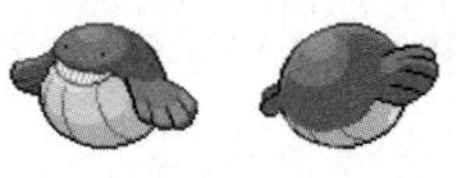

TYPE Water

ABILITIES
- Water Veil
- Oblivious

HIDDEN ABILITY
- Pressure

STATS
HP
Attack
Defense
Sp. Atk
Sp. Def
Speed

EGG GROUPS
Field/Water ❷

ITEMS SOMETIMES HELD
- None

EVOLUTION

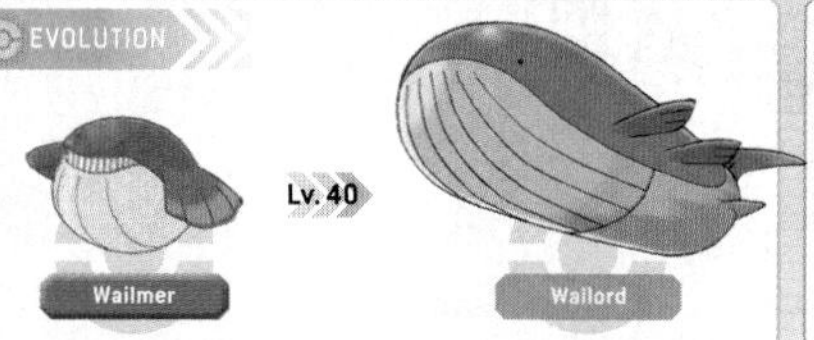

HOW TO OBTAIN

Pokémon Black Version 2	Undella Bay (ripples in water)
Pokémon White Version 2	Undella Bay (ripples in water)

HOW TO OBTAIN FROM OTHER GAMES

—

—

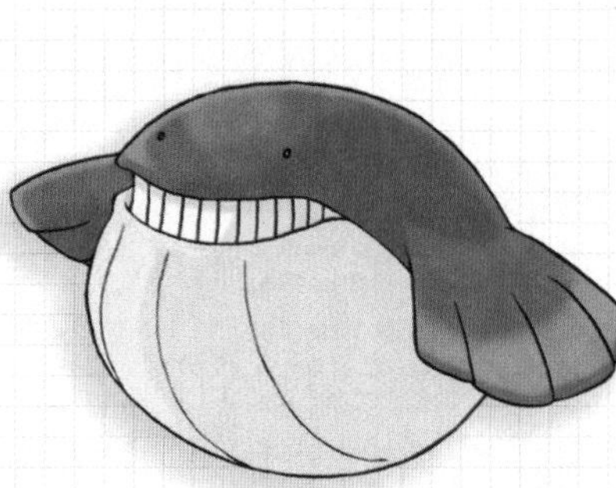

Pokémon AR Marker

LEVEL-UP AND LEARNED MOVES

Lv.	Name	Type	Kind	Pow.	Acc.	PP	Range	Long	DA
1	Splash	Normal	Status	—	—	40	Self	—	—
4	Growl	Normal	Status	—	100	40	Many Others	—	—
7	Water Gun	Water	Special	40	100	25	Normal	—	—
11	Rollout	Rock	Physical	30	90	20	Normal	—	○
14	Whirlpool	Water	Special	35	85	15	Normal	—	—
17	Astonish	Ghost	Physical	30	100	15	Normal	—	○
21	Water Pulse	Water	Special	60	100	20	Normal	○	—
24	Mist	Ice	Status	—	—	30	Your Side	—	—
27	Rest	Psychic	Status	—	—	10	Self	—	—
31	Brine	Water	Special	65	100	10	Normal	—	—
34	Water Spout	Water	Special	150	100	5	Many Others	—	—
37	Amnesia	Psychic	Status	—	—	20	Self	—	—
41	Dive	Water	Physical	80	100	10	Normal	—	○
44	Bounce	Flying	Physical	85	85	5	Normal	○	○
47	Hydro Pump	Water	Special	120	80	5	Normal	—	—
50	Heavy Slam	Steel	Physical	—	100	10	Normal	—	○

TM & HM MOVES

Lv.	Name	Type	Kind	Pow.	Acc.	PP	Range	Long	DA
TM05	Roar	Normal	Status	—	100	20	Normal	—	—
TM06	Toxic	Poison	Status	—	90	10	Normal	—	—
TM07	Hail	Ice	Status	—	—	10	Both Sides	—	—
TM10	Hidden Power	Normal	Special	—	100	15	Normal	—	—
TM13	Ice Beam	Ice	Special	95	100	10	Normal	—	—
TM14	Blizzard	Ice	Special	120	70	5	Many Others	—	—
TM17	Protect	Normal	Status	—	—	10	Self	—	—
TM18	Rain Dance	Water	Status	—	—	5	Both Sides	—	—
TM21	Frustration	Normal	Physical	—	100	20	Normal	—	○
TM26	Earthquake	Ground	Physical	100	100	10	Adjacent	—	—
TM27	Return	Normal	Physical	—	100	20	Normal	—	○
TM32	Double Team	Normal	Status	—	—	15	Self	—	—
TM39	Rock Tomb	Rock	Physical	50	80	10	Normal	—	—
TM42	Facade	Normal	Physical	70	100	20	Normal	—	○
TM44	Rest	Psychic	Status	—	—	10	Self	—	—
TM45	Attract	Normal	Status	—	100	15	Normal	—	—
TM48	Round	Normal	Special	60	100	15	Normal	—	—
TM49	Echoed Voice	Normal	Special	40	100	15	Normal	—	—
TM55	Scald	Water	Special	80	100	15	Normal	—	—
TM78	Bulldoze	Ground	Physical	60	100	20	Adjacent	—	—
TM87	Swagger	Normal	Status	—	90	15	Normal	—	—
TM90	Substitute	Normal	Status	—	—	10	Self	—	—
TM94	Rock Smash	Fighting	Physical	40	100	15	Normal	—	○
HM03	Surf	Water	Special	95	100	15	Adjacent	—	—
HM04	Strength	Normal	Physical	80	100	15	Normal	—	○
HM05	Waterfall	Water	Physical	80	100	15	Normal	—	○
HM06	Dive	Water	Physical	80	100	10	Normal	—	○

MOVES TAUGHT BY PEOPLE

Name	Type	Kind	Pow.	Acc.	PP	Range	Long	DA

MOVES TAUGHT BY MOVE TUTORS FOR SHARDS

Name	Type	Kind	Pow.	Acc.	PP	Range	Long	DA
Bounce	Flying	Physical	85	85	5	Normal	○	○
Hyper Voice	Normal	Special	90	100	10	Many Others	—	—
Icy Wind	Ice	Special	55	95	15	Many Others	—	—
Zen Headbutt	Psychic	Physical	80	90	15	Normal	—	○
Snore	Normal	Special	40	100	15	Normal	—	—
Sleep Talk	Normal	Status	—	—	10	Self	—	—

EGG MOVES

Name	Type	Kind	Pow.	Acc.	PP	Range	Long	DA
Double-Edge	Normal	Physical	120	100	15	Normal	—	○
Thrash	Normal	Physical	120	100	10	1 Random	—	○
Snore	Normal	Special	40	100	15	Normal	—	—
Sleep Talk	Normal	Status	—	—	10	Self	—	—
Curse	Ghost	Status	—	—	10	Varies	—	—
Fissure	Ground	Physical	—	30	5	Normal	—	—
Tickle	Normal	Status	—	100	20	Normal	—	—
Defense Curl	Normal	Status	—	—	40	Self	—	—
Body Slam	Normal	Physical	85	100	15	Normal	—	○
Aqua Ring	Water	Status	—	—	20	Self	—	—
Soak	Water	Status	—	100	20	Normal	—	—
Zen Headbutt	Psychic	Physical	80	90	15	Normal	—	○

320 Wailmer

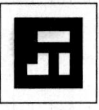

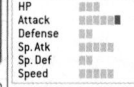

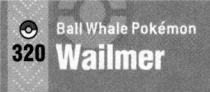

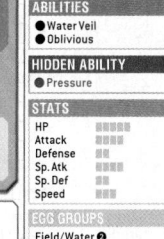

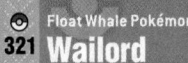

321 Wailord

Float Whale Pokémon

- HEIGHT: 47'07"
- WEIGHT: 877.4 lbs.
- GENDER: ♂ / ♀

It can sometimes knock out opponents with the shock created by breaching and crashing its big body onto the water.

Same form for ♂ / ♀

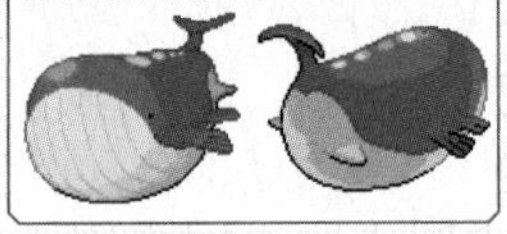

TYPE Water

ABILITIES
- Water Veil
- Oblivious

HIDDEN ABILITY
- Pressure

STATS

HP
Attack
Defense
Sp. Atk
Sp. Def
Speed

EGG GROUPS

Field/Water ❷

ITEMS SOMETIMES HELD
- None

EVOLUTION

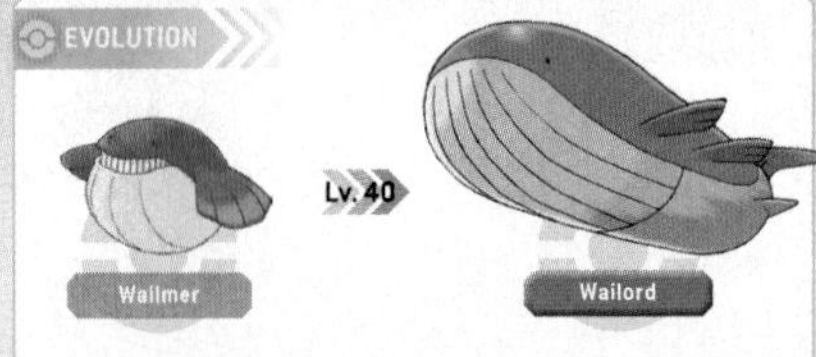
Wailmer
Lv. 40
Wailord

HOW TO OBTAIN

Pokémon Black Version 2	Undella Bay (ripples in water)
Pokémon White Version 2	Undella Bay (ripples in water)

HOW TO OBTAIN FROM OTHER GAMES

—

—

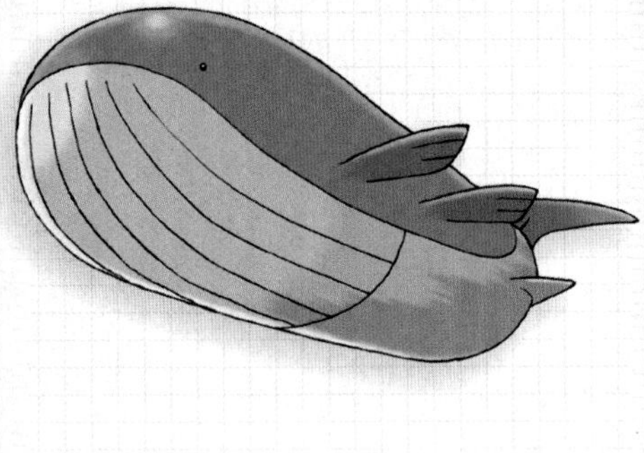

LEVEL-UP AND LEARNED MOVES

Lv.	Name	Type	Kind	Pow.	Acc.	PP	Range	Long	DA
1	Splash	Normal	Status	—	—	40	Self	—	—
1	Growl	Normal	Status	—	100	40	Many Others	—	—
1	Water Gun	Water	Special	40	100	25	Normal	—	—
1	Rollout	Rock	Physical	30	90	20	Normal	—	○
4	Growl	Normal	Status	—	100	40	Many Others	—	—
7	Water Gun	Water	Special	40	100	25	Normal	—	—
11	Rollout	Rock	Physical	30	90	20	Normal	—	○
14	Whirlpool	Water	Special	35	85	15	Normal	—	—
17	Astonish	Ghost	Physical	30	100	15	Normal	—	○
21	Water Pulse	Water	Special	60	100	20	Normal	○	—
24	Mist	Ice	Status	—	—	30	Your Side	—	—
27	Rest	Psychic	Status	—	—	10	Self	—	—
31	Brine	Water	Special	65	100	10	Normal	—	—
34	Water Spout	Water	Special	150	100	5	Many Others	—	—
37	Amnesia	Psychic	Status	—	—	20	Self	—	—
46	Dive	Water	Physical	80	100	10	Normal	—	○
54	Bounce	Flying	Physical	85	85	5	Normal	○	○
62	Hydro Pump	Water	Special	120	80	5	Normal	—	—
70	Heavy Slam	Steel	Physical	—	100	10	Normal	—	○

TM & HM MOVES

Lv.	Name	Type	Kind	Pow.	Acc.	PP	Range	Long	DA
TM05	Roar	Normal	Status	—	100	20	Normal	—	—
TM06	Toxic	Poison	Status	—	90	10	Normal	—	—
TM07	Hail	Ice	Status	—	—	10	Both Sides	—	—
TM10	Hidden Power	Normal	Special	—	100	15	Normal	—	—
TM13	Ice Beam	Ice	Special	95	100	10	Normal	—	—
TM14	Blizzard	Ice	Special	120	70	5	Many Others	—	—
TM15	Hyper Beam	Normal	Special	150	90	5	Normal	—	—
TM17	Protect	Normal	Status	—	—	10	Self	—	—
TM18	Rain Dance	Water	Status	—	—	5	Both Sides	—	—
TM21	Frustration	Normal	Physical	—	100	20	Normal	—	○
TM26	Earthquake	Ground	Physical	100	100	10	Adjacent	—	—
TM27	Return	Normal	Physical	—	100	20	Normal	—	○
TM32	Double Team	Normal	Status	—	—	15	Self	—	—
TM39	Rock Tomb	Rock	Physical	50	80	10	Normal	—	—
TM42	Facade	Normal	Physical	70	100	20	Normal	—	○
TM44	Rest	Psychic	Status	—	—	10	Self	—	—
TM45	Attract	Normal	Status	—	100	15	Normal	—	—
TM48	Round	Normal	Special	60	100	15	Normal	—	—
TM49	Echoed Voice	Normal	Special	40	100	15	Normal	—	—
TM55	Scald	Water	Special	80	100	15	Normal	—	—
TM68	Giga Impact	Normal	Physical	150	90	5	Normal	—	○
TM78	Bulldoze	Ground	Physical	60	100	20	Adjacent	—	—
TM87	Swagger	Normal	Status	—	90	15	Normal	—	—
TM90	Substitute	Normal	Status	—	—	10	Self	—	—
TM94	Rock Smash	Fighting	Physical	40	100	15	Normal	—	○
HM03	Surf	Water	Special	95	100	15	Adjacent	—	—
HM04	Strength	Normal	Physical	80	100	15	Normal	—	○
HM05	Waterfall	Water	Physical	80	100	15	Normal	—	○
HM06	Dive	Water	Physical	80	100	10	Normal	—	○

MOVES TAUGHT BY PEOPLE

Name	Type	Kind	Pow.	Acc.	PP	Range	Long	DA

MOVES TAUGHT BY MOVE TUTORS FOR SHARDS

Name	Type	Kind	Pow.	Acc.	PP	Range	Long	DA
Bounce	Flying	Physical	85	85	5	Normal	○	○
Iron Head	Steel	Physical	80	100	15	Normal	—	○
Block	Normal	Status	—	—	5	Normal	—	—
Hyper Voice	Normal	Special	90	100	10	Many Others	—	—
Icy Wind	Ice	Special	55	95	15	Many Others	—	—
Zen Headbutt	Psychic	Physical	80	90	15	Normal	—	○
Snore	Normal	Special	40	100	15	Normal	—	—
Sleep Talk	Normal	Status	—	—	10	Self	—	—

Pokémon AR Marker

322 Numel

Numb Pokémon

- HEIGHT: 2'04"
- WEIGHT: 52.9 lbs.
- GENDER: ♂ / ♀

The magma in its body reaches 2,200 degrees F. Its hump gets smaller when it uses Fire-type moves.

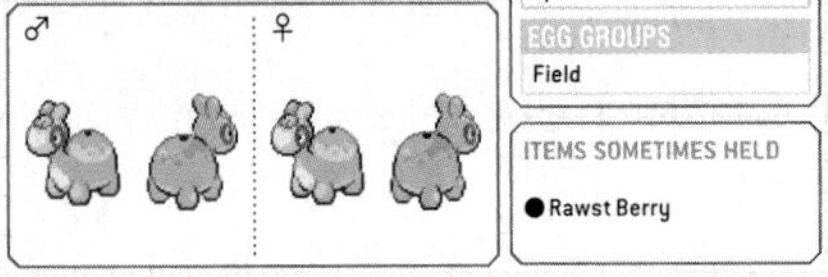
♂
♀

TYPE Fire Ground

ABILITIES
- Oblivious
- Simple

HIDDEN ABILITY
- Own Tempo

STATS

HP
Attack
Defense
Sp. Atk
Sp. Def
Speed

EGG GROUPS

Field

ITEMS SOMETIMES HELD
- Rawst Berry

EVOLUTION

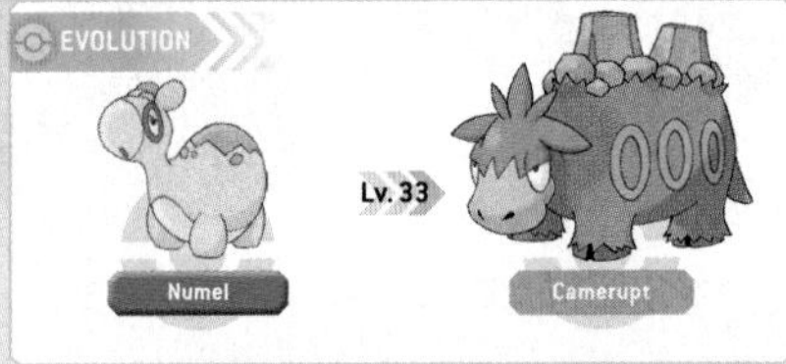
Numel
Lv. 33
Camerupt

HOW TO OBTAIN

Pokémon Black Version 2	Link Trade or Poké Transfer
Pokémon White Version 2	❶ Reversal Mountain outside ❷ Reversal Mountain entrance

HOW TO OBTAIN FROM OTHER GAMES

Pokémon Platinum Version	Route 227

—

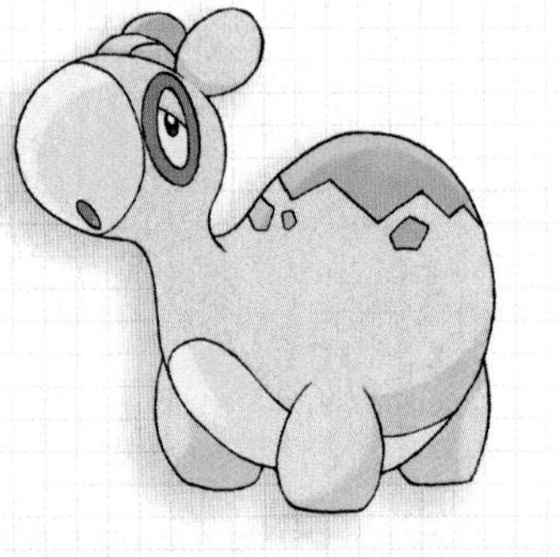

LEVEL-UP AND LEARNED MOVES

Lv.	Name	Type	Kind	Pow.	Acc.	PP	Range	Long	DA
1	Growl	Normal	Status	—	100	40	Many Others	—	—
1	Tackle	Normal	Physical	50	100	35	Normal	—	○
5	Ember	Fire	Special	40	100	25	Normal	—	—
8	Magnitude	Ground	Physical	—	100	30	Adjacent	—	—
12	Focus Energy	Normal	Status	—	—	30	Self	—	—
15	Flame Burst	Fire	Special	70	100	15	Normal	—	—
19	Amnesia	Psychic	Status	—	—	20	Self	—	—
22	Lava Plume	Fire	Special	80	100	15	Adjacent	—	—
26	Earth Power	Ground	Special	90	100	10	Normal	—	—
29	Curse	Ghost	Status	—	—	10	Varies	—	—
31	Take Down	Normal	Physical	90	85	20	Normal	—	○
36	Yawn	Normal	Status	—	—	10	Normal	—	—
40	Earthquake	Ground	Physical	100	100	10	Adjacent	—	—
43	Flamethrower	Fire	Special	95	100	15	Normal	—	—
47	Double-Edge	Normal	Physical	120	100	15	Normal	—	○

TM & HM MOVES

Lv.	Name	Type	Kind	Pow.	Acc.	PP	Range	Long	DA
TM06	Toxic	Poison	Status	—	90	10	Normal	—	—
TM10	Hidden Power	Normal	Special	—	100	15	Normal	—	—
TM11	Sunny Day	Fire	Status	—	—	5	Both Sides	—	—
TM17	Protect	Normal	Status	—	—	10	Self	—	—
TM21	Frustration	Normal	Physical	—	100	20	Normal	—	○
TM26	Earthquake	Ground	Physical	100	100	10	Adjacent	—	—
TM27	Return	Normal	Physical	—	100	20	Normal	—	○
TM28	Dig	Ground	Physical	80	100	10	Normal	—	○
TM32	Double Team	Normal	Status	—	—	15	Self	—	—
TM35	Flamethrower	Fire	Special	95	100	15	Normal	—	—
TM37	Sandstorm	Rock	Status	—	—	10	Both Sides	—	—
TM38	Fire Blast	Fire	Special	120	85	5	Normal	—	—
TM39	Rock Tomb	Rock	Physical	50	80	10	Normal	—	—
TM42	Facade	Normal	Physical	70	100	20	Normal	—	○
TM43	Flame Charge	Fire	Physical	50	100	20	Normal	—	○
TM44	Rest	Psychic	Status	—	—	10	Self	—	—
TM45	Attract	Normal	Status	—	100	15	Normal	—	—
TM48	Round	Normal	Special	60	100	15	Normal	—	—
TM49	Echoed Voice	Normal	Special	40	100	15	Normal	—	—
TM50	Overheat	Fire	Special	140	90	5	Normal	—	—
TM59	Incinerate	Fire	Special	30	100	15	Many Others	—	—
TM61	Will-O-Wisp	Fire	Status	—	75	15	Normal	—	—
TM78	Bulldoze	Ground	Physical	60	100	20	Adjacent	—	—
TM80	Rock Slide	Rock	Physical	75	90	10	Many Others	—	—
TM87	Swagger	Normal	Status	—	90	15	Normal	—	—
TM90	Substitute	Normal	Status	—	—	10	Self	—	—
TM94	Rock Smash	Fighting	Physical	40	100	15	Normal	—	○
HM04	Strength	Normal	Physical	80	100	15	Normal	—	○

MOVES TAUGHT BY PEOPLE

Name	Type	Kind	Pow.	Acc.	PP	Range	Long	DA

MOVES TAUGHT BY MOVE TUTORS FOR SHARDS

Name	Type	Kind	Pow.	Acc.	PP	Range	Long	DA
Iron Head	Steel	Physical	80	100	15	Normal	—	○
Earth Power	Ground	Special	90	100	10	Normal	—	—
Snore	Normal	Special	40	100	15	Normal	—	—
Heat Wave	Fire	Special	100	90	10	Many Others	—	—
After You	Normal	Status	—	—	15	Normal	—	—
Stealth Rock	Rock	Status	—	—	20	Other Side	—	—
Sleep Talk	Normal	Status	—	—	10	Self	—	—

EGG MOVES

Name	Type	Kind	Pow.	Acc.	PP	Range	Long	DA
Howl	Normal	Status	—	—	40	Self	—	—
Scary Face	Normal	Status	—	100	10	Normal	—	—
Body Slam	Normal	Physical	85	100	15	Normal	—	○
Rollout	Rock	Physical	30	90	20	Normal	—	○
Defense Curl	Normal	Status	—	—	40	Self	—	—
Stomp	Normal	Physical	65	100	20	Normal	—	○
Yawn	Normal	Status	—	—	10	Normal	—	—
AncientPower	Rock	Special	60	100	5	Normal	—	—
Mud Bomb	Ground	Special	65	85	10	Normal	—	—
Heat Wave	Fire	Special	100	90	10	Many Others	—	—
Stockpile	Normal	Status	—	—	20	Self	—	—
Swallow	Normal	Status	—	—	10	Self	—	—
Spit Up	Normal	Special	—	100	10	Normal	—	—
Endure	Normal	Status	—	—	10	Self	—	—
Iron Head	Steel	Physical	80	100	15	Normal	—	○

Pokémon AR Marker

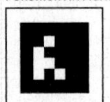

323 Camerupt

Eruption Pokémon

TYPE: Fire / Ground

ABILITIES
- Magma Armor
- Solid Rock

HIDDEN ABILITY
- Anger Point

- HEIGHT: 6'03"
- WEIGHT: 485.0 lbs.
- GENDER: ♂ / ♀

STATS
HP
Attack
Defense
Sp. Atk
Sp. Def
Speed

The volcanoes on its back have a major eruption every 10 years--or whenever it becomes really angry.

EGG GROUPS
Field

♂ ♀

ITEMS SOMETIMES HELD
- Rawst Berry

EVOLUTION

HOW TO OBTAIN

Pokémon Black Version 2	Link Trade or Poké Transfer
Pokémon White Version 2	❶ Reversal Mountain outside ❷ Reversal Mountain entrance

HOW TO OBTAIN FROM OTHER GAMES

Pokémon Platinum Version	Route 227
	—

LEVEL-UP AND LEARNED MOVES

Lv.	Name	Type	Kind	Pow.	Acc.	PP	Range	Long	DA
1	Growl	Normal	Status	—	100	40	Many Others	—	—
1	Tackle	Normal	Physical	50	100	35	Normal	—	○
1	Ember	Fire	Special	40	100	25	Normal	—	—
1	Magnitude	Ground	Physical	—	100	30	Adjacent	—	—
5	Ember	Fire	Special	40	100	25	Normal	—	—
8	Magnitude	Ground	Physical	—	100	30	Adjacent	—	—
12	Focus Energy	Normal	Status	—	—	30	Self	—	—
15	Flame Burst	Fire	Special	70	100	15	Normal	—	—
19	Amnesia	Psychic	Status	—	—	20	Self	—	—
22	Lava Plume	Fire	Special	80	100	15	Adjacent	—	—
26	Earth Power	Ground	Special	90	100	10	Normal	—	—
29	Curse	Ghost	Status	—	—	10	Varies	—	—
31	Take Down	Normal	Physical	90	85	20	Normal	—	○
33	Rock Slide	Rock	Physical	75	90	10	Many Others	—	—
39	Yawn	Normal	Status	—	—	10	Normal	—	—
46	Earthquake	Ground	Physical	100	100	10	Adjacent	—	—
52	Eruption	Fire	Special	150	100	5	Many Others	—	—
59	Fissure	Ground	Physical	—	30	5	Normal	—	—

TM & HM MOVES

Lv.	Name	Type	Kind	Pow.	Acc.	PP	Range	Long	DA
TM05	Roar	Normal	Status	—	100	20	Normal	—	—
TM06	Toxic	Poison	Status	—	90	10	Normal	—	—
TM10	Hidden Power	Normal	Special	—	100	15	Normal	—	—
TM11	Sunny Day	Fire	Status	—	—	5	Both Sides	—	—
TM15	Hyper Beam	Normal	Special	150	90	5	Normal	—	—
TM17	Protect	Normal	Status	—	—	10	Self	—	—
TM21	Frustration	Normal	Physical	—	100	20	Normal	—	○
TM22	SolarBeam	Grass	Special	120	100	10	Normal	—	—
TM26	Earthquake	Ground	Physical	100	100	10	Adjacent	—	—
TM27	Return	Normal	Physical	—	100	20	Normal	—	○
TM28	Dig	Ground	Physical	80	100	10	Normal	—	○
TM32	Double Team	Normal	Status	—	—	15	Self	—	—
TM35	Flamethrower	Fire	Special	95	100	15	Normal	—	—
TM37	Sandstorm	Rock	Status	—	—	10	Both Sides	—	—
TM38	Fire Blast	Fire	Special	120	85	5	Normal	—	—
TM39	Rock Tomb	Rock	Physical	50	80	10	Normal	—	—
TM42	Facade	Normal	Physical	70	100	20	Normal	—	○
TM43	Flame Charge	Fire	Physical	50	100	20	Normal	—	○
TM44	Rest	Psychic	Status	—	—	10	Self	—	—
TM45	Attract	Normal	Status	—	100	15	Normal	—	—
TM48	Round	Normal	Special	60	100	15	Normal	—	—
TM49	Echoed Voice	Normal	Special	40	100	15	Normal	—	—
TM50	Overheat	Fire	Special	140	90	5	Normal	—	—
TM59	Incinerate	Fire	Special	30	100	15	Many Others	—	—
TM61	Will—O—Wisp	Fire	Status	—	75	15	Normal	—	—
TM64	Explosion	Normal	Physical	250	100	5	Adjacent	—	—
TM68	Giga Impact	Normal	Physical	150	90	5	Normal	—	○
TM69	Rock Polish	Rock	Status	—	—	20	Self	—	—
TM71	Stone Edge	Rock	Physical	100	80	5	Normal	—	—
TM78	Bulldoze	Ground	Physical	60	100	20	Adjacent	—	—
TM80	Rock Slide	Rock	Physical	75	90	10	Many Others	—	—
TM87	Swagger	Normal	Status	—	90	15	Normal	—	—
TM90	Substitute	Normal	Status	—	—	10	Self	—	—
TM91	Flash Cannon	Steel	Special	80	100	10	Normal	—	—
TM94	Rock Smash	Fighting	Physical	40	100	15	Normal	—	○

Lv.	Name	Type	Kind	Pow.	Acc.	PP	Range	Long	DA
HM04	Strength	Normal	Physical	80	100	15	Normal	—	○

MOVES TAUGHT BY PEOPLE

Name	Type	Kind	Pow.	Acc.	PP	Range	Long	DA

MOVES TAUGHT BY MOVE TUTORS FOR SHARDS

Name	Type	Kind	Pow.	Acc.	PP	Range	Long	DA
Iron Head	Steel	Physical	80	100	15	Normal	—	○
Earth Power	Ground	Special	90	100	10	Normal	—	—
Snore	Normal	Special	40	100	15	Normal	—	—
Heat Wave	Fire	Special	100	90	10	Many Others	—	—
After You	Normal	Status	—	—	15	Normal	—	—
Stealth Rock	Rock	Status	—	—	20	Other Side	—	—
Sleep Talk	Normal	Status	—	—	10	Self	—	—

Pokémon AR Marker

324 Torkoal

Coal Pokémon

TYPE: Fire

ABILITY
- White Smoke

HIDDEN ABILITY
- Shell Armor

- HEIGHT: 1'08"
- WEIGHT: 177.2 lbs.
- GENDER: ♂ / ♀

STATS
HP
Attack
Defense
Sp. Atk
Sp. Def
Speed

It burns coal inside its shell for energy. It blows out black soot if it is endangered.

EGG GROUPS
Field

Same form for ♂ / ♀

ITEMS SOMETIMES HELD
- None

EVOLUTION

Does not evolve

HOW TO OBTAIN

Pokémon Black Version 2	Link Trade or Poké Transfer
Pokémon White Version 2	Link Trade or Poké Transfer

HOW TO OBTAIN FROM OTHER GAMES

Pokémon Platinum Version	Occasionally appears on Route 227 (use Poké Radar for a better chance)
	—

LEVEL-UP AND LEARNED MOVES

Lv.	Name	Type	Kind	Pow.	Acc.	PP	Range	Long	DA
1	Ember	Fire	Special	40	100	25	Normal	—	—
4	Smog	Poison	Special	20	70	20	Normal	—	—
7	Withdraw	Water	Status	—	—	40	Self	—	—
12	Curse	Ghost	Status	—	—	10	Varies	—	—
17	Fire Spin	Fire	Special	35	85	15	Normal	—	—
20	SmokeScreen	Normal	Status	—	100	20	Normal	—	—
23	Rapid Spin	Normal	Physical	20	100	40	Normal	—	○
28	Flamethrower	Fire	Special	95	100	15	Normal	—	—
33	Body Slam	Normal	Physical	85	100	15	Normal	—	○
36	Protect	Normal	Status	—	—	10	Self	—	—
39	Lava Plume	Fire	Special	80	100	15	Adjacent	—	—
44	Iron Defense	Steel	Status	—	—	15	Self	—	—
49	Amnesia	Psychic	Status	—	—	20	Self	—	—
52	Flail	Normal	Physical	—	100	15	Normal	—	○
55	Heat Wave	Fire	Special	100	90	10	Many Others	—	—
60	Inferno	Fire	Special	100	50	5	Normal	—	—
65	Shell Smash	Normal	Status	—	—	15	Self	—	—

TM & HM MOVES

Lv.	Name	Type	Kind	Pow.	Acc.	PP	Range	Long	DA
TM06	Toxic	Poison	Status	—	90	10	Normal	—	—
TM10	Hidden Power	Normal	Special	—	100	15	Normal	—	—
TM11	Sunny Day	Fire	Status	—	—	5	Both Sides	—	—
TM15	Hyper Beam	Normal	Special	150	90	5	Normal	—	—
TM17	Protect	Normal	Status	—	—	10	Self	—	—
TM21	Frustration	Normal	Physical	—	100	20	Normal	—	○
TM22	SolarBeam	Grass	Special	120	100	10	Normal	—	—
TM26	Earthquake	Ground	Physical	100	100	10	Adjacent	—	—
TM27	Return	Normal	Physical	—	100	20	Normal	—	○
TM32	Double Team	Normal	Status	—	—	15	Self	—	—
TM35	Flamethrower	Fire	Special	95	100	15	Normal	—	—
TM36	Sludge Bomb	Poison	Special	90	100	10	Normal	—	—
TM38	Fire Blast	Fire	Special	120	85	5	Normal	—	—
TM39	Rock Tomb	Rock	Physical	50	80	10	Normal	—	—
TM42	Facade	Normal	Physical	70	100	20	Normal	—	○
TM43	Flame Charge	Fire	Physical	50	100	20	Normal	—	○
TM44	Rest	Psychic	Status	—	—	10	Self	—	—
TM45	Attract	Normal	Status	—	100	15	Normal	—	—
TM48	Round	Normal	Special	60	100	15	Normal	—	—
TM50	Overheat	Fire	Special	140	90	5	Normal	—	—
TM59	Incinerate	Fire	Special	30	100	15	Many Others	—	—
TM61	Will-O-Wisp	Fire	Status	—	75	15	Normal	—	—
TM64	Explosion	Normal	Physical	250	100	5	Adjacent	—	—
TM68	Giga Impact	Normal	Physical	150	90	5	Normal	—	○
TM71	Stone Edge	Rock	Physical	100	80	5	Normal	—	—
TM74	Gyro Ball	Steel	Physical	—	100	5	Normal	—	○
TM78	Bulldoze	Ground	Physical	60	100	20	Adjacent	—	—
TM80	Rock Slide	Rock	Physical	75	90	10	Many Others	—	—
TM87	Swagger	Normal	Status	—	90	15	Normal	—	—
TM90	Substitute	Normal	Status	—	—	10	Self	—	—
TM94	Rock Smash	Fighting	Physical	40	100	15	Normal	—	○
HM04	Strength	Normal	Physical	80	100	15	Normal	—	○

MOVES TAUGHT BY PEOPLE

Name	Type	Kind	Pow.	Acc.	PP	Range	Long	DA

MOVES TAUGHT BY MOVE TUTORS FOR SHARDS

Name	Type	Kind	Pow.	Acc.	PP	Range	Long	DA
Iron Defense	Steel	Status	—	—	15	Self	—	—
Iron Tail	Steel	Physical	100	75	15	Normal	—	○
Earth Power	Ground	Special	90	100	10	Normal	—	—
Snore	Normal	Special	40	100	15	Normal	—	—
Heat Wave	Fire	Special	100	90	10	Many Others	—	—
After You	Normal	Status	—	—	15	Normal	—	—
Stealth Rock	Rock	Status	—	—	20	Other Side	—	—
Sleep Talk	Normal	Status	—	—	10	Self	—	—

EGG MOVES

Name	Type	Kind	Pow.	Acc.	PP	Range	Long	DA
Eruption	Fire	Special	150	100	5	Many Others	—	—
Endure	Normal	Status	—	—	10	Self	—	—
Sleep Talk	Normal	Status	—	—	10	Self	—	—
Yawn	Normal	Status	—	—	10	Normal	—	—
Fissure	Ground	Physical	—	30	5	Normal	—	—
Skull Bash	Normal	Physical	100	100	15	Normal	—	○
Flame Burst	Fire	Special	70	100	15	Normal	—	—
Clear Smog	Poison	Special	50	—	15	Normal	—	—

Pokémon AR Marker

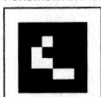

Bounce Pokémon

325 Spoink

- HEIGHT: 2'04"
- WEIGHT: 67.5 lbs.
- GENDER: ♂ / ♀

Using its tail like a spring, it keeps its heart beating by bouncing constantly. If it stops, it dies.

Same form for ♂ / ♀

TYPE Psychic

ABILITIES
- Thick Fat
- Own Tempo

HIDDEN ABILITY
- Gluttony

STATS
HP
Attack
Defense
Sp. Atk
Sp. Def
Speed

EGG GROUPS
Field

ITEMS SOMETIMES HELD
- Persim Berry

Pokémon AR Marker

EVOLUTION

HOW TO OBTAIN

Pokémon Black Version 2	❶ Reversal Mountain outside ❷ Reversal Mountain entrance
Pokémon White Version 2	Link Trade or Poké Transfer

HOW TO OBTAIN FROM OTHER GAMES

Pokémon HeartGold Version	Ilex Forest (Hoenn Sound)
Pokémon SoulSilver Version	Ilex Forest (Hoenn Sound)

LEVEL-UP AND LEARNED MOVES

Lv.	Name	Type	Kind	Pow.	Acc.	PP	Range	Long	DA
1	Splash	Normal	Status	—	—	40	Self	—	—
7	Psywave	Psychic	Special	—	80	15	Normal	—	—
10	Odor Sleuth	Normal	Status	—	—	40	Normal	—	—
14	Psybeam	Psychic	Special	65	100	20	Normal	—	—
15	Psych Up	Normal	Status	—	—	10	Normal	—	—
18	Confuse Ray	Ghost	Status	—	100	10	Normal	—	—
21	Magic Coat	Psychic	Status	—	—	15	Self	—	—
26	Zen Headbutt	Psychic	Physical	80	90	15	Normal	—	○
29	Rest	Psychic	Status	—	—	10	Self	—	—
29	Snore	Normal	Special	40	100	15	Normal	—	—
33	Power Gem	Rock	Special	70	100	20	Normal	—	—
38	Psyshock	Psychic	Special	80	100	10	Normal	—	—
40	Payback	Dark	Physical	50	100	10	Normal	—	○
44	Psychic	Psychic	Special	90	100	10	Normal	—	—
50	Bounce	Flying	Physical	85	85	5	Normal	○	○

TM & HM MOVES

Lv.	Name	Type	Kind	Pow.	Acc.	PP	Range	Long	DA
TM03	Psyshock	Psychic	Special	80	100	10	Normal	—	—
TM04	Calm Mind	Psychic	Status	—	—	20	Self	—	—
TM06	Toxic	Poison	Status	—	90	10	Normal	—	—
TM10	Hidden Power	Normal	Special	—	100	15	Normal	—	—
TM11	Sunny Day	Fire	Status	—	—	5	Both Sides	—	—
TM12	Taunt	Dark	Status	—	100	20	Normal	—	—
TM16	Light Screen	Psychic	Status	—	—	30	Your Side	—	—
TM17	Protect	Normal	Status	—	—	10	Self	—	—
TM18	Rain Dance	Water	Status	—	—	5	Both Sides	—	—
TM19	Telekinesis	Psychic	Status	—	—	15	Normal	—	—
TM21	Frustration	Normal	Physical	—	100	20	Normal	—	○
TM27	Return	Normal	Physical	—	100	20	Normal	—	○
TM29	Psychic	Psychic	Special	90	100	10	Normal	—	—
TM30	Shadow Ball	Ghost	Special	80	100	15	Normal	—	—
TM32	Double Team	Normal	Status	—	—	15	Self	—	—
TM33	Reflect	Psychic	Status	—	—	20	Your Side	—	—
TM41	Torment	Dark	Status	—	100	15	Normal	—	—
TM42	Facade	Normal	Physical	70	100	20	Normal	—	○
TM44	Rest	Psychic	Status	—	—	10	Self	—	—
TM45	Attract	Normal	Status	—	100	15	Normal	—	—
TM46	Thief	Dark	Physical	40	100	10	Normal	—	○
TM48	Round	Normal	Special	60	100	15	Normal	—	—
TM57	Charge Beam	Electric	Special	50	90	10	Normal	—	—
TM66	Payback	Dark	Physical	50	100	10	Normal	—	○
TM70	Flash	Normal	Status	—	100	20	Normal	—	—
TM73	Thunder Wave	Electric	Status	—	100	20	Normal	—	—
TM77	Psych Up	Normal	Status	—	—	10	Normal	—	—
TM85	Dream Eater	Psychic	Special	100	100	15	Normal	—	—
TM86	Grass Knot	Grass	Special	—	100	20	Normal	—	○
TM87	Swagger	Normal	Status	—	90	15	Normal	—	—
TM90	Substitute	Normal	Status	—	—	10	Self	—	—
TM92	Trick Room	Psychic	Status	—	—	5	Both Sides	—	—

MOVES TAUGHT BY PEOPLE

Name	Type	Kind	Pow.	Acc.	PP	Range	Long	DA

MOVES TAUGHT BY MOVE TUTORS FOR SHARDS

Name	Type	Kind	Pow.	Acc.	PP	Range	Long	DA
Covet	Normal	Physical	60	100	40	Normal	—	○
Bounce	Flying	Physical	85	85	5	Normal	○	○
Signal Beam	Bug	Special	75	100	15	Normal	—	—
Magic Coat	Psychic	Status	—	—	15	Self	—	—
Icy Wind	Ice	Special	55	95	15	Many Others	—	—
Iron Tail	Steel	Physical	100	75	15	Normal	—	○
Zen Headbutt	Psychic	Physical	80	90	15	Normal	—	○
Snore	Normal	Special	40	100	15	Normal	—	—
Heal Bell	Normal	Status	—	—	5	Your Party	—	—
Role Play	Psychic	Status	—	—	10	Normal	—	—
Recycle	Normal	Status	—	—	10	Self	—	—
Trick	Psychic	Status	—	100	10	Normal	—	—
Sleep Talk	Normal	Status	—	—	10	Self	—	—
Skill Swap	Psychic	Status	—	—	10	Normal	—	—
Snatch	Dark	Status	—	—	10	Self	—	—

EGG MOVES

Name	Type	Kind	Pow.	Acc.	PP	Range	Long	DA
Future Sight	Psychic	Special	100	100	10	Normal	—	—
Extrasensory	Psychic	Special	80	100	30	Normal	—	—
Trick	Psychic	Status	—	100	10	Normal	—	—
Zen Headbutt	Psychic	Physical	80	90	15	Normal	—	○
Amnesia	Psychic	Status	—	—	20	Self	—	—
Mirror Coat	Psychic	Special	—	100	20	Varies	—	—
Skill Swap	Psychic	Status	—	—	10	Normal	—	—
Whirlwind	Normal	Status	—	100	20	Normal	—	—
Lucky Chant	Normal	Status	—	—	30	Your Side	—	—
Endure	Normal	Status	—	—	10	Self	—	—

Manipulate Pokémon

326 Grumpig

- HEIGHT: 2'11"
- WEIGHT: 157.6 lbs.
- GENDER: ♂ / ♀

It uses black pearls to amplify its psychic power. It does a strange dance to control foes' minds.

Same form for ♂ / ♀

TYPE Psychic

ABILITIES
- Thick Fat
- Own Tempo

HIDDEN ABILITY
- Gluttony

STATS
HP
Attack
Defense
Sp. Atk
Sp. Def
Speed

EGG GROUPS
Field

ITEMS SOMETIMES HELD
- Persim Berry

Pokémon AR Marker

EVOLUTION

HOW TO OBTAIN

Pokémon Black Version 2	❶ Reversal Mountain outside ❷ Reversal Mountain entrance
Pokémon White Version 2	Level up a Spoink you obtain via Link Trade or Poké Transfer to Lv. 32

HOW TO OBTAIN FROM OTHER GAMES

	—
	—

LEVEL-UP AND LEARNED MOVES

Lv.	Name	Type	Kind	Pow.	Acc.	PP	Range	Long	DA
1	Splash	Normal	Status	—	—	40	Self	—	—
1	Psywave	Psychic	Special	—	80	15	Normal	—	—
1	Odor Sleuth	Normal	Status	—	—	40	Normal	—	—
1	Psybeam	Psychic	Special	65	100	20	Normal	—	—
7	Psywave	Psychic	Special	—	80	15	Normal	—	—
10	Odor Sleuth	Normal	Status	—	—	40	Normal	—	—
14	Psybeam	Psychic	Special	65	100	20	Normal	—	—
15	Psych Up	Normal	Status	—	—	10	Normal	—	—
18	Confuse Ray	Ghost	Status	—	100	10	Normal	—	—
21	Magic Coat	Psychic	Status	—	—	15	Self	—	—
26	Zen Headbutt	Psychic	Physical	80	90	15	Normal	—	○
29	Rest	Psychic	Status	—	—	10	Self	—	—
29	Snore	Normal	Special	40	100	15	Normal	—	—
35	Power Gem	Rock	Special	70	100	20	Normal	—	—
42	Psyshock	Psychic	Special	80	100	10	Normal	—	—
46	Payback	Dark	Physical	50	100	10	Normal	—	○
52	Psychic	Psychic	Special	90	100	10	Normal	—	—
60	Bounce	Flying	Physical	85	85	5	Normal	○	○

TM & HM MOVES

Lv.	Name	Type	Kind	Pow.	Acc.	PP	Range	Long	DA
TM03	Psyshock	Psychic	Special	80	100	10	Normal	—	—
TM04	Calm Mind	Psychic	Status	—	—	20	Self	—	—
TM06	Toxic	Poison	Status	—	90	10	Normal	—	—
TM10	Hidden Power	Normal	Special	—	100	15	Normal	—	—
TM11	Sunny Day	Fire	Status	—	—	5	Both Sides	—	—
TM12	Taunt	Dark	Status	—	100	20	Normal	—	—
TM15	Hyper Beam	Normal	Special	150	90	5	Normal	—	—
TM16	Light Screen	Psychic	Status	—	—	30	Your Side	—	—
TM17	Protect	Normal	Status	—	—	10	Self	—	—
TM18	Rain Dance	Water	Status	—	—	5	Both Sides	—	—
TM19	Telekinesis	Psychic	Status	—	—	15	Normal	—	—
TM21	Frustration	Normal	Physical	—	100	20	Normal	—	○
TM27	Return	Normal	Physical	—	100	20	Normal	—	○
TM29	Psychic	Psychic	Special	90	100	10	Normal	—	—
TM30	Shadow Ball	Ghost	Special	80	100	15	Normal	—	—
TM31	Brick Break	Fighting	Physical	75	100	15	Normal	—	○
TM32	Double Team	Normal	Status	—	—	15	Self	—	—
TM33	Reflect	Psychic	Status	—	—	20	Your Side	—	—
TM41	Torment	Dark	Status	—	100	15	Normal	—	—
TM42	Facade	Normal	Physical	70	100	20	Normal	—	○
TM44	Rest	Psychic	Status	—	—	10	Self	—	—
TM45	Attract	Normal	Status	—	100	15	Normal	—	—
TM46	Thief	Dark	Physical	40	100	10	Normal	—	○
TM48	Round	Normal	Special	60	100	15	Normal	—	—
TM52	Focus Blast	Fighting	Special	120	70	5	Normal	—	—
TM53	Energy Ball	Grass	Special	80	100	10	Normal	—	—
TM56	Fling	Dark	Physical	—	100	10	Normal	—	—
TM57	Charge Beam	Electric	Special	50	90	10	Normal	—	—
TM66	Payback	Dark	Physical	50	100	10	Normal	—	○
TM68	Giga Impact	Normal	Physical	150	90	5	Normal	—	○
TM70	Flash	Normal	Status	—	100	20	Normal	—	—
TM73	Thunder Wave	Electric	Status	—	100	20	Normal	—	—
TM77	Psych Up	Normal	Status	—	—	10	Normal	—	—
TM78	Bulldoze	Ground	Physical	60	100	20	Adjacent	—	—
TM85	Dream Eater	Psychic	Special	100	100	15	Normal	—	—
TM86	Grass Knot	Grass	Special	—	100	20	Normal	—	○
TM87	Swagger	Normal	Status	—	90	15	Normal	—	—
TM90	Substitute	Normal	Status	—	—	10	Self	—	—
TM92	Trick Room	Psychic	Status	—	—	5	Both Sides	—	—

MOVES TAUGHT BY PEOPLE

Name	Type	Kind	Pow.	Acc.	PP	Range	Long	DA

MOVES TAUGHT BY MOVE TUTORS FOR SHARDS

Name	Type	Kind	Pow.	Acc.	PP	Range	Long	DA
Covet	Normal	Physical	60	100	40	Normal	—	○
Bounce	Flying	Physical	85	85	5	Normal	○	○
Signal Beam	Bug	Special	75	100	15	Normal	—	—
Fire Punch	Fire	Physical	75	100	15	Normal	—	○
ThunderPunch	Electric	Physical	75	100	15	Normal	—	○
Ice Punch	Ice	Physical	75	100	15	Normal	—	○
Magic Coat	Psychic	Status	—	—	15	Self	—	—
Icy Wind	Ice	Special	55	95	15	Many Others	—	—
Iron Tail	Steel	Physical	100	75	15	Normal	—	○
Zen Headbutt	Psychic	Physical	80	90	15	Normal	—	○
Snore	Normal	Special	40	100	15	Normal	—	—
Heal Bell	Normal	Status	—	—	5	Your Party	—	—
Role Play	Psychic	Status	—	—	10	Normal	—	—
Drain Punch	Fighting	Physical	75	100	10	Normal	—	○
Recycle	Normal	Status	—	—	10	Self	—	—
Trick	Psychic	Status	—	100	10	Normal	—	—
Sleep Talk	Normal	Status	—	—	10	Self	—	—
Skill Swap	Psychic	Status	—	—	10	Normal	—	—
Snatch	Dark	Status	—	—	10	Self	—	—

327 Spinda

Spot Panda Pokémon

- HEIGHT: 3'07"
- WEIGHT: 11.0 lbs.
- GENDER: ♂ / ♀

No two Spinda have the same pattern of spots. Its tottering step fouls the aim of foes.

TYPE Normal

ABILITIES
- Own Tempo
- Tangled Feet

HIDDEN ABILITY
- Contrary

STATS
HP, Attack, Defense, Sp. Atk, Sp. Def, Speed

EGG GROUPS
Field/Human-Like

ITEMS SOMETIMES HELD
- None

Same form for ♂ / ♀

Pokémon AR Marker

EVOLUTION

Does not evolve

HOW TO OBTAIN

Pokémon Black Version 2	Trade Pokémon during a date with Yancy or Curtis (11th time)
Pokémon White Version 2	Trade Pokémon during a date with Yancy or Curtis (11th time)

HOW TO OBTAIN FROM OTHER GAMES

Pokémon HeartGold Version	Sprout Tower (Hoenn Sound)
Pokémon SoulSilver Version	Sprout Tower (Hoenn Sound)

LEVEL-UP AND LEARNED MOVES

Lv.	Name	Type	Kind	Pow.	Acc.	PP	Range	Long	DA
1	Tackle	Normal	Physical	50	100	35	Normal	—	○
5	Uproar	Normal	Special	90	100	10	1 Random	—	—
10	Copycat	Normal	Status	—	—	20	Self	—	—
14	Faint Attack	Dark	Physical	60	—	20	Normal	—	○
19	Psybeam	Psychic	Special	65	100	20	Normal	—	—
23	Hypnosis	Psychic	Status	—	60	20	Normal	—	—
28	Dizzy Punch	Normal	Physical	70	100	10	Normal	—	○
32	Sucker Punch	Dark	Physical	80	100	5	Normal	—	○
37	Teeter Dance	Normal	Status	—	100	20	Adjacent	—	—
41	Psych Up	Normal	Status	—	—	10	Normal	—	—
46	Double-Edge	Normal	Physical	120	100	15	Normal	—	○
50	Flail	Normal	Physical	—	100	15	Normal	—	○
55	Thrash	Normal	Physical	120	100	10	1 Random	—	○

TM & HM MOVES

Lv.	Name	Type	Kind	Pow.	Acc.	PP	Range	Long	DA
TM04	Calm Mind	Psychic	Status	—	—	20	Self	—	—
TM06	Toxic	Poison	Status	—	90	10	Normal	—	—
TM10	Hidden Power	Normal	Special	—	100	15	Normal	—	—
TM11	Sunny Day	Fire	Status	—	—	5	Both Sides	—	—
TM17	Protect	Normal	Status	—	—	10	Self	—	—
TM18	Rain Dance	Water	Status	—	—	5	Both Sides	—	—
TM20	Safeguard	Normal	Status	—	—	25	Your Side	—	—
TM21	Frustration	Normal	Physical	—	100	20	Normal	—	○
TM27	Return	Normal	Physical	—	100	20	Normal	—	○
TM28	Dig	Ground	Physical	80	100	10	Normal	—	○
TM29	Psychic	Psychic	Special	90	100	10	Normal	—	—
TM30	Shadow Ball	Ghost	Special	80	100	15	Normal	—	—
TM31	Brick Break	Fighting	Physical	75	100	15	Normal	—	○
TM32	Double Team	Normal	Status	—	—	15	Self	—	—
TM39	Rock Tomb	Rock	Physical	50	80	10	Normal	—	—
TM42	Facade	Normal	Physical	70	100	20	Normal	—	○
TM44	Rest	Psychic	Status	—	—	10	Self	—	—
TM45	Attract	Normal	Status	—	100	15	Normal	—	—
TM46	Thief	Dark	Physical	40	100	10	Normal	—	○
TM48	Round	Normal	Special	60	100	15	Normal	—	—
TM56	Fling	Dark	Physical	—	100	10	Normal	—	—
TM67	Retaliate	Normal	Physical	70	100	5	Normal	—	○
TM70	Flash	Normal	Status	—	100	20	Normal	—	—
TM77	Psych Up	Normal	Status	—	—	10	Normal	—	—
TM80	Rock Slide	Rock	Physical	75	90	10	Many Others	—	—
TM83	Work Up	Normal	Status	—	—	30	Self	—	—
TM85	Dream Eater	Psychic	Special	100	100	15	Normal	—	—
TM87	Swagger	Normal	Status	—	90	15	Normal	—	—
TM90	Substitute	Normal	Status	—	—	10	Self	—	—
TM92	Trick Room	Psychic	Status	—	—	5	Both Sides	—	—
TM93	Wild Charge	Electric	Physical	90	100	15	Normal	—	○
TM94	Rock Smash	Fighting	Physical	40	100	15	Normal	—	○
HM04	Strength	Normal	Physical	80	100	15	Normal	—	○

MOVES TAUGHT BY PEOPLE

Name	Type	Kind	Pow.	Acc.	PP	Range	Long	DA

MOVES TAUGHT BY MOVE TUTORS FOR SHARDS

Name	Type	Kind	Pow.	Acc.	PP	Range	Long	DA
Covet	Normal	Physical	60	100	40	Normal	—	○
Uproar	Normal	Special	90	100	10	1 Random	—	—
Low Kick	Fighting	Physical	—	100	20	Normal	—	○
Fire Punch	Fire	Physical	75	100	15	Normal	—	○
ThunderPunch	Electric	Physical	75	100	15	Normal	—	○
Ice Punch	Ice	Physical	75	100	15	Normal	—	○
Last Resort	Normal	Physical	140	100	5	Normal	—	○
Hyper Voice	Normal	Special	90	100	10	Many Others	—	—
Icy Wind	Ice	Special	55	95	15	Many Others	—	—
Zen Headbutt	Psychic	Physical	80	90	15	Normal	—	○
Snore	Normal	Special	40	100	15	Normal	—	—
Role Play	Psychic	Status	—	—	10	Normal	—	—
Drain Punch	Fighting	Physical	75	100	10	Normal	—	○
Helping Hand	Normal	Status	—	—	20	1 Ally	—	—
Recycle	Normal	Status	—	—	10	Self	—	—
Trick	Psychic	Status	—	100	10	Normal	—	—
Sleep Talk	Normal	Status	—	—	10	Self	—	—
Skill Swap	Psychic	Status	—	—	10	Normal	—	—
Snatch	Dark	Status	—	—	10	Self	—	—

EGG MOVES

Name	Type	Kind	Pow.	Acc.	PP	Range	Long	DA
Encore	Normal	Status	—	100	5	Normal	—	—
Assist	Normal	Status	—	—	20	Self	—	—
Disable	Normal	Status	—	100	20	Normal	—	—
Baton Pass	Normal	Status	—	—	40	Self	—	—
Wish	Normal	Status	—	—	10	Self	—	—
Trick	Psychic	Status	—	100	10	Normal	—	—
SmellingSalt	Normal	Physical	60	100	10	Normal	—	○
Fake Out	Normal	Physical	40	100	10	Normal	—	○
Role Play	Psychic	Status	—	—	10	Normal	—	—
Psycho Cut	Psychic	Physical	70	100	20	Normal	—	—
Fake Tears	Dark	Status	—	100	20	Normal	—	—
Rapid Spin	Normal	Physical	20	100	40	Normal	—	○
Icy Wind	Ice	Special	55	95	15	Many Others	—	—
Water Pulse	Water	Special	60	100	20	Normal	○	—

328 Trapinch

Ant Pit Pokémon

- HEIGHT: 2'04"
- WEIGHT: 33.1 lbs.
- GENDER: ♂ / ♀

It makes an inescapable conical pit and lies in wait at the bottom for prey to come tumbling down.

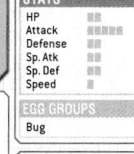

TYPE Ground

ABILITIES
- Hyper Cutter
- Arena Trap

HIDDEN ABILITY
- Sheer Force

STATS
HP, Attack, Defense, Sp. Atk, Sp. Def, Speed

EGG GROUPS
Bug

ITEMS SOMETIMES HELD
- Soft Sand

Same form for ♂ / ♀

Pokémon AR Marker

EVOLUTION

Lv. 35
Lv. 45
Trapinch
Vibrava
Flygon

HOW TO OBTAIN

Pokémon Black Version 2	❶ Desert Resort interior ❷ Reversal Mountain outside
Pokémon White Version 2	❶ Desert Resort interior ❷ Reversal Mountain outside

HOW TO OBTAIN FROM OTHER GAMES

—
—

LEVEL-UP AND LEARNED MOVES

Lv.	Name	Type	Kind	Pow.	Acc.	PP	Range	Long	DA
1	Bite	Dark	Physical	60	100	25	Normal	—	○
4	Sand-Attack	Ground	Status	—	100	15	Normal	—	—
7	Faint Attack	Dark	Physical	60	—	20	Normal	—	○
10	Sand Tomb	Ground	Physical	35	85	15	Normal	—	—
13	Mud-Slap	Ground	Special	20	100	10	Normal	—	—
17	Bide	Normal	Physical	—	—	10	Self	—	○
21	Bulldoze	Ground	Physical	60	100	20	Adjacent	—	—
25	Rock Slide	Rock	Physical	75	90	10	Many Others	—	—
29	Dig	Ground	Physical	80	100	10	Normal	—	○
34	Crunch	Dark	Physical	80	100	15	Normal	—	○
39	Earth Power	Ground	Special	90	100	10	Normal	—	—
44	Sandstorm	Rock	Status	—	—	10	Both Sides	—	—
49	Hyper Beam	Normal	Special	150	90	5	Normal	—	—
55	Earthquake	Ground	Physical	100	100	10	Adjacent	—	—
61	Feint	Normal	Physical	30	100	10	Normal	—	—
67	Superpower	Fighting	Physical	120	100	5	Normal	—	○
73	Fissure	Ground	Physical	—	30	5	Normal	—	—

TM & HM MOVES

Lv.	Name	Type	Kind	Pow.	Acc.	PP	Range	Long	DA
TM06	Toxic	Poison	Status	—	90	10	Normal	—	—
TM10	Hidden Power	Normal	Special	—	100	15	Normal	—	—
TM11	Sunny Day	Fire	Status	—	—	5	Both Sides	—	—
TM15	Hyper Beam	Normal	Special	150	90	5	Normal	—	—
TM17	Protect	Normal	Status	—	—	10	Self	—	—
TM21	Frustration	Normal	Physical	—	100	20	Normal	—	○
TM22	SolarBeam	Grass	Special	120	100	10	Normal	—	—
TM26	Earthquake	Ground	Physical	100	100	10	Adjacent	—	—
TM27	Return	Normal	Physical	—	100	20	Normal	—	○
TM28	Dig	Ground	Physical	80	100	10	Normal	—	○
TM32	Double Team	Normal	Status	—	—	15	Self	—	—
TM37	Sandstorm	Rock	Status	—	—	10	Both Sides	—	—
TM39	Rock Tomb	Rock	Physical	50	80	10	Normal	—	—
TM42	Facade	Normal	Physical	70	100	20	Normal	—	○
TM44	Rest	Psychic	Status	—	—	10	Self	—	—
TM45	Attract	Normal	Status	—	100	15	Normal	—	—
TM48	Round	Normal	Special	60	100	15	Normal	—	—
TM76	Struggle Bug	Bug	Special	30	100	20	Many Others	—	—
TM78	Bulldoze	Ground	Physical	60	100	20	Adjacent	—	—
TM80	Rock Slide	Rock	Physical	75	90	10	Many Others	—	—
TM87	Swagger	Normal	Status	—	90	15	Normal	—	—
TM90	Substitute	Normal	Status	—	—	10	Self	—	—
TM94	Rock Smash	Fighting	Physical	40	100	15	Normal	—	○
HM04	Strength	Normal	Physical	80	100	15	Normal	—	○

MOVES TAUGHT BY PEOPLE

Name	Type	Kind	Pow.	Acc.	PP	Range	Long	DA

MOVES TAUGHT BY MOVE TUTORS FOR SHARDS

Name	Type	Kind	Pow.	Acc.	PP	Range	Long	DA
Bug Bite	Bug	Physical	60	100	20	Normal	—	○
Signal Beam	Bug	Special	75	100	15	Normal	—	—
Earth Power	Ground	Special	90	100	10	Normal	—	—
Superpower	Fighting	Physical	120	100	5	Normal	—	○
Snore	Normal	Special	40	100	15	Normal	—	—
Giga Drain	Grass	Special	75	100	10	Normal	—	—
Sleep Talk	Normal	Status	—	—	10	Self	—	—

EGG MOVES

Name	Type	Kind	Pow.	Acc.	PP	Range	Long	DA
Focus Energy	Normal	Status	—	—	30	Self	—	—
Quick Attack	Normal	Physical	40	100	30	Normal	—	○
Gust	Flying	Special	40	100	35	Normal	○	—
Flail	Normal	Physical	—	100	15	Normal	—	○
Fury Cutter	Bug	Physical	20	95	20	Normal	—	○
Mud Shot	Ground	Special	55	95	15	Normal	—	—
Endure	Normal	Status	—	—	10	Self	—	—
Earth Power	Ground	Special	90	100	10	Normal	—	—
Bug Bite	Bug	Physical	60	100	20	Normal	—	○
Signal Beam	Bug	Special	75	100	15	Normal	—	—

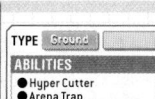

Vibration Pokémon
329 Vibrava

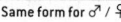

- HEIGHT: 3'07"
- WEIGHT: 33.7 lbs.
- GENDER: ♂ / ♀

The ultrasonic waves it generates by rubbing its two wings together cause severe headaches.

Same form for ♂ / ♀

TYPE Ground Dragon

ABILITY
- Levitate

HIDDEN ABILITY
—

STATS
HP
Attack
Defense
Sp. Atk
Sp. Def
Speed

EGG GROUPS
Bug

ITEMS SOMETIMES HELD
- None

EVOLUTION

HOW TO OBTAIN

Pokémon Black Version 2	Reversal Mountain outside (dark grass)
Pokémon White Version 2	Reversal Mountain outside (dark grass)

HOW TO OBTAIN FROM OTHER GAMES
—
—

Pokémon AR Marker

LEVEL-UP AND LEARNED MOVES

Lv.	Name	Type	Kind	Pow.	Acc.	PP	Range	Long	DA
1	SonicBoom	Normal	Special	—	90	20	Normal	—	—
1	Sand-Attack	Ground	Status	—	100	15	Normal	—	—
1	Faint Attack	Dark	Physical	60	—	20	Normal	—	○
1	Sand Tomb	Ground	Physical	35	85	15	Normal	—	—
4	Sand-Attack	Ground	Status	—	100	15	Normal	—	—
7	Faint Attack	Dark	Physical	60	—	20	Normal	—	○
10	Sand Tomb	Ground	Physical	35	85	15	Normal	—	—
13	Mud-Slap	Ground	Special	20	100	10	Normal	—	—
17	Bide	Normal	Physical	—	—	10	Self	—	○
21	Bulldoze	Ground	Physical	60	100	20	Adjacent	—	—
25	Rock Slide	Rock	Physical	75	90	10	Many Others	—	—
29	Supersonic	Normal	Status	—	55	20	Normal	—	—
34	Screech	Normal	Status	—	85	40	Normal	—	—
35	DragonBreath	Dragon	Special	60	100	20	Normal	—	—
39	Earth Power	Ground	Special	90	100	10	Normal	—	—
44	Sandstorm	Rock	Status	—	—	10	Both Sides	—	—
49	Hyper Beam	Normal	Special	150	90	5	Normal	—	—

TM & HM MOVES

Lv.	Name	Type	Kind	Pow.	Acc.	PP	Range	Long	DA
TM06	Toxic	Poison	Status	—	90	10	Normal	—	—
TM10	Hidden Power	Normal	Special	—	100	15	Normal	—	—
TM11	Sunny Day	Fire	Status	—	—	5	Both Sides	—	—
TM15	Hyper Beam	Normal	Special	150	90	5	Normal	—	—
TM17	Protect	Normal	Status	—	—	10	Self	—	—
TM21	Frustration	Normal	Physical	—	100	20	Normal	—	○
TM22	SolarBeam	Grass	Special	120	100	10	Normal	—	—
TM26	Earthquake	Ground	Physical	100	100	10	Adjacent	—	—
TM27	Return	Normal	Physical	—	100	20	Normal	—	○
TM28	Dig	Ground	Physical	80	100	10	Normal	—	○
TM32	Double Team	Normal	Status	—	—	15	Self	—	—
TM37	Sandstorm	Rock	Status	—	—	10	Both Sides	—	—
TM39	Rock Tomb	Rock	Physical	50	80	10	Normal	—	—
TM42	Facade	Normal	Physical	70	100	20	Normal	—	○
TM44	Rest	Psychic	Status	—	—	10	Self	—	—
TM45	Attract	Normal	Status	—	100	15	Normal	—	—
TM48	Round	Normal	Special	60	100	15	Normal	—	—
TM76	Struggle Bug	Bug	Special	30	100	20	Many Others	—	—
TM78	Bulldoze	Ground	Physical	60	100	20	Adjacent	—	—
TM80	Rock Slide	Rock	Physical	75	90	10	Many Others	—	—
TM87	Swagger	Normal	Status	—	90	15	Normal	—	—
TM89	U-turn	Bug	Physical	70	100	20	Normal	—	○
TM90	Substitute	Normal	Status	—	—	10	Self	—	—
TM94	Rock Smash	Fighting	Physical	40	100	15	Normal	—	○
HM02	Fly	Flying	Physical	90	95	15	Normal	○	○
HM04	Strength	Normal	Physical	80	100	15	Normal	—	○

MOVES TAUGHT BY PEOPLE

Name	Type	Kind	Pow.	Acc.	PP	Range	Long	DA
Draco Meteor	Dragon	Special	140	90	5	Normal	—	—

MOVES TAUGHT BY MOVE TUTORS FOR SHARDS

Name	Type	Kind	Pow.	Acc.	PP	Range	Long	DA
Bug Bite	Bug	Physical	60	100	20	Normal	—	○
Signal Beam	Bug	Special	75	100	15	Normal	—	—
Earth Power	Ground	Special	90	100	10	Normal	—	—
Superpower	Fighting	Physical	120	100	5	Normal	—	○
Dragon Pulse	Dragon	Special	90	100	10	Normal	○	—
Snore	Normal	Special	40	100	15	Normal	—	—
Roost	Flying	Status	—	—	10	Self	—	—
Heat Wave	Fire	Special	100	90	10	Many Others	—	—
Giga Drain	Grass	Special	75	100	10	Normal	—	—
Tailwind	Flying	Status	—	—	30	Your Side	—	—
Outrage	Dragon	Physical	120	100	10	1 Random	—	○
Sleep Talk	Normal	Status	—	—	10	Self	—	—

Mystic Pokémon
330 Flygon

- HEIGHT: 6'07"
- WEIGHT: 180.8 lbs.
- GENDER: ♂ / ♀

Known as "The Desert Spirit," this Pokémon hides in the sandstorms it causes by beating its wings.

Same form for ♂ / ♀

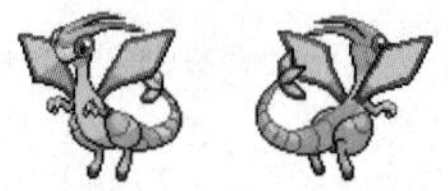

TYPE Ground Dragon

ABILITY
- Levitate

HIDDEN ABILITY
—

STATS
HP
Attack
Defense
Sp. Atk
Sp. Def
Speed

EGG GROUPS
Bug

ITEMS SOMETIMES HELD
- None

EVOLUTION

HOW TO OBTAIN

Pokémon Black Version 2	Level up Vibrava to Lv. 45
Pokémon White Version 2	Level up Vibrava to Lv. 45

HOW TO OBTAIN FROM OTHER GAMES
—
—

Pokémon AR Marker

LEVEL-UP AND LEARNED MOVES

Lv.	Name	Type	Kind	Pow.	Acc.	PP	Range	Long	DA
1	SonicBoom	Normal	Special	—	90	20	Normal	—	—
1	Sand-Attack	Ground	Status	—	100	15	Normal	—	—
1	Faint Attack	Dark	Physical	60	—	20	Normal	—	○
1	Sand Tomb	Ground	Physical	35	85	15	Normal	—	—
4	Sand-Attack	Ground	Status	—	100	15	Normal	—	—
7	Faint Attack	Dark	Physical	60	—	20	Normal	—	○
10	Sand Tomb	Ground	Physical	35	85	15	Normal	—	—
13	Mud-Slap	Ground	Special	20	100	10	Normal	—	—
17	Bide	Normal	Physical	—	—	10	Self	—	○
21	Bulldoze	Ground	Physical	60	100	20	Adjacent	—	—
25	Rock Slide	Rock	Physical	75	90	10	Many Others	—	—
29	Supersonic	Normal	Status	—	55	20	Normal	—	—
34	Screech	Normal	Status	—	85	40	Normal	—	—
35	DragonBreath	Dragon	Special	60	100	20	Normal	—	—
39	Earth Power	Ground	Special	90	100	10	Normal	—	—
44	Sandstorm	Rock	Status	—	—	10	Both Sides	—	—
45	Dragon Tail	Dragon	Physical	60	90	10	Normal	—	○
49	Hyper Beam	Normal	Special	150	90	5	Normal	—	—
55	Dragon Claw	Dragon	Physical	80	100	15	Normal	—	○

TM & HM MOVES

Lv.	Name	Type	Kind	Pow.	Acc.	PP	Range	Long	DA
TM01	Hone Claws	Dark	Status	—	—	15	Self	—	—
TM02	Dragon Claw	Dragon	Physical	80	100	15	Normal	—	○
TM06	Toxic	Poison	Status	—	90	10	Normal	—	—
TM10	Hidden Power	Normal	Special	—	100	15	Normal	—	—
TM11	Sunny Day	Fire	Status	—	—	5	Both Sides	—	—
TM15	Hyper Beam	Normal	Special	150	90	5	Normal	—	—
TM17	Protect	Normal	Status	—	—	10	Self	—	—
TM21	Frustration	Normal	Physical	—	100	20	Normal	—	○
TM22	SolarBeam	Grass	Special	120	100	10	Normal	—	—
TM26	Earthquake	Ground	Physical	100	100	10	Adjacent	—	—
TM27	Return	Normal	Physical	—	100	20	Normal	—	○
TM28	Dig	Ground	Physical	80	100	10	Normal	—	○
TM32	Double Team	Normal	Status	—	—	15	Self	—	—
TM35	Flamethrower	Fire	Special	95	100	15	Normal	—	—
TM37	Sandstorm	Rock	Status	—	—	10	Both Sides	—	—
TM38	Fire Blast	Fire	Special	120	85	5	Normal	—	—
TM39	Rock Tomb	Rock	Physical	50	80	10	Normal	—	—
TM40	Aerial Ace	Flying	Physical	60	—	20	Normal	○	○
TM42	Facade	Normal	Physical	70	100	20	Normal	—	○
TM44	Rest	Psychic	Status	—	—	10	Self	—	—
TM45	Attract	Normal	Status	—	100	15	Normal	—	—
TM48	Round	Normal	Special	60	100	15	Normal	—	—
TM59	Incinerate	Fire	Special	30	100	15	Many Others	—	—
TM68	Giga Impact	Normal	Physical	150	90	5	Normal	—	○
TM71	Stone Edge	Rock	Physical	100	80	5	Normal	—	—
TM76	Struggle Bug	Bug	Special	30	100	20	Many Others	—	—
TM78	Bulldoze	Ground	Physical	60	100	20	Adjacent	—	—
TM80	Rock Slide	Rock	Physical	75	90	10	Many Others	—	—
TM82	Dragon Tail	Dragon	Physical	60	90	10	Normal	—	○
TM87	Swagger	Normal	Status	—	90	15	Normal	—	—
TM89	U-turn	Bug	Physical	70	100	20	Normal	—	○
TM90	Substitute	Normal	Status	—	—	10	Self	—	—
TM94	Rock Smash	Fighting	Physical	40	100	15	Normal	—	○
HM02	Fly	Flying	Physical	90	95	15	Normal	○	○
HM04	Strength	Normal	Physical	80	100	15	Normal	—	○

MOVES TAUGHT BY PEOPLE

Name	Type	Kind	Pow.	Acc.	PP	Range	Long	DA
Draco Meteor	Dragon	Special	140	90	5	Normal	—	—

MOVES TAUGHT BY MOVE TUTORS FOR SHARDS

Name	Type	Kind	Pow.	Acc.	PP	Range	Long	DA
Bug Bite	Bug	Physical	60	100	20	Normal	—	○
Signal Beam	Bug	Special	75	100	15	Normal	—	—
Fire Punch	Fire	Physical	75	100	15	Normal	—	○
ThunderPunch	Electric	Physical	75	100	15	Normal	—	○
Iron Tail	Steel	Physical	100	75	15	Normal	—	○
Earth Power	Ground	Special	90	100	10	Normal	—	—
Superpower	Fighting	Physical	120	100	5	Normal	—	○
Dragon Pulse	Dragon	Special	90	100	10	Normal	○	—
Snore	Normal	Special	40	100	15	Normal	—	—
Roost	Flying	Status	—	—	10	Self	—	—
Heat Wave	Fire	Special	100	90	10	Many Others	—	—
Giga Drain	Grass	Special	75	100	10	Normal	—	—
Tailwind	Flying	Status	—	—	30	Your Side	—	—
Outrage	Dragon	Physical	120	100	10	1 Random	—	○
Sleep Talk	Normal	Status	—	—	10	Self	—	—

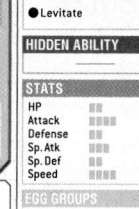

Cactus Pokémon

331 Cacnea

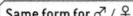

TYPE: Grass

ABILITY
- Sand Veil

HIDDEN ABILITY
- Water Absorb

- HEIGHT: 1'04"
- WEIGHT: 113.1 lbs.
- GENDER: ♂ / ♀

By storing water in its body, this desert dweller can survive for 30 days without water.

STATS
HP
Attack
Defense
Sp. Atk
Sp. Def
Speed

EGG GROUPS
Grass/Human-Like

Same form for ♂ / ♀

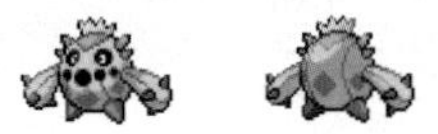

ITEMS SOMETIMES HELD
- None

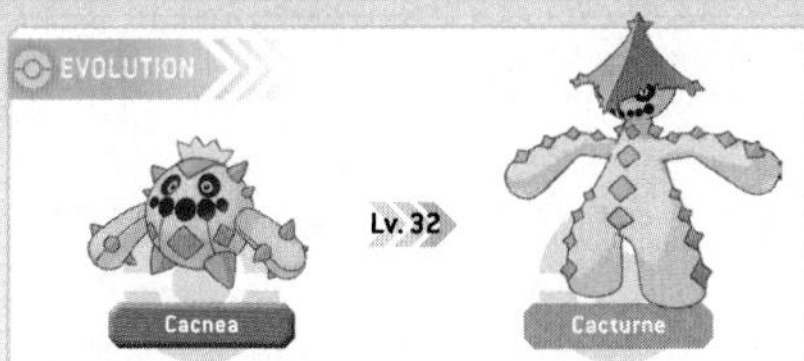
EVOLUTION
Cacnea
Lv. 32
Cacturne

HOW TO OBTAIN

Pokémon Black Version 2	Catch a Cacturne, leave it at the Pokémon Day Care, and hatch the Egg that is found
Pokémon White Version 2	Catch a Cacturne, leave it at the Pokémon Day Care, and hatch the Egg that is found

HOW TO OBTAIN FROM OTHER GAMES

Pokémon Platinum Version	Route 228
—	

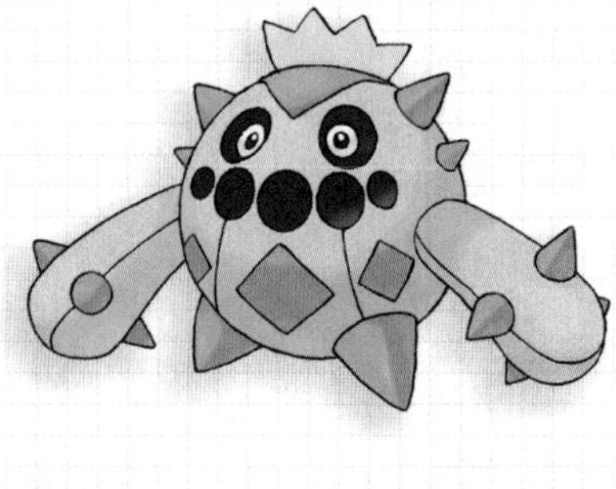

LEVEL-UP AND LEARNED MOVES

Lv.	Name	Type	Kind	Pow.	Acc.	PP	Range	Long	DA
1	Poison Sting	Poison	Physical	15	100	35	Normal	—	—
1	Leer	Normal	Status	—	100	30	Many Others	—	—
5	Absorb	Grass	Special	20	100	25	Normal	—	—
9	Growth	Normal	Status	—	—	40	Self	—	—
13	Leech Seed	Grass	Status	—	90	10	Normal	—	—
17	Sand-Attack	Ground	Status	—	100	15	Normal	—	—
21	Pin Missile	Bug	Physical	14	85	20	Normal	—	—
25	Ingrain	Grass	Status	—	—	20	Self	—	—
29	Faint Attack	Dark	Physical	60	—	20	Normal	—	○
33	Spikes	Ground	Status	—	—	20	Other Side	—	—
37	Sucker Punch	Dark	Physical	80	100	5	Normal	—	○
41	Payback	Dark	Physical	50	100	10	Normal	—	○
45	Needle Arm	Grass	Physical	60	100	15	Normal	—	○
49	Cotton Spore	Grass	Status	—	100	40	Normal	—	—
53	Sandstorm	Rock	Status	—	—	10	Both Sides	—	—
57	Destiny Bond	Ghost	Status	—	—	5	Self	—	—

TM & HM MOVES

Lv.	Name	Type	Kind	Pow.	Acc.	PP	Range	Long	DA
TM06	Toxic	Poison	Status	—	90	10	Normal	—	—
TM09	Venoshock	Poison	Special	65	100	10	Normal	—	—
TM10	Hidden Power	Normal	Special	—	100	15	Normal	—	—
TM11	Sunny Day	Fire	Status	—	—	5	Both Sides	—	—
TM17	Protect	Normal	Status	—	—	10	Self	—	—
TM21	Frustration	Normal	Physical	—	100	20	Normal	—	○
TM22	SolarBeam	Grass	Special	120	100	10	Normal	—	—
TM27	Return	Normal	Physical	—	100	20	Normal	—	○
TM31	Brick Break	Fighting	Physical	75	100	15	Normal	—	○
TM32	Double Team	Normal	Status	—	—	15	Self	—	—
TM37	Sandstorm	Rock	Status	—	—	10	Both Sides	—	—
TM42	Facade	Normal	Physical	70	100	20	Normal	—	○
TM44	Rest	Psychic	Status	—	—	10	Self	—	—
TM45	Attract	Normal	Status	—	100	15	Normal	—	—
TM48	Round	Normal	Special	60	100	15	Normal	—	—
TM53	Energy Ball	Grass	Special	80	100	10	Normal	—	—
TM56	Fling	Dark	Physical	—	100	10	Normal	—	—
TM66	Payback	Dark	Physical	50	100	10	Normal	—	○
TM70	Flash	Normal	Status	—	100	20	Normal	—	—
TM75	Swords Dance	Normal	Status	—	—	30	Self	—	—
TM84	Poison Jab	Poison	Physical	80	100	20	Normal	—	○
TM86	Grass Knot	Grass	Special	—	100	20	Normal	—	○
TM87	Swagger	Normal	Status	—	90	15	Normal	—	—
TM90	Substitute	Normal	Status	—	—	10	Self	—	—
HM01	Cut	Normal	Physical	50	95	30	Normal	—	○

MOVES TAUGHT BY PEOPLE

Name	Type	Kind	Pow.	Acc.	PP	Range	Long	DA

MOVES TAUGHT BY MOVE TUTORS FOR SHARDS

Name	Type	Kind	Pow.	Acc.	PP	Range	Long	DA
Seed Bomb	Grass	Physical	80	100	15	Normal	—	—
Low Kick	Fighting	Physical	—	100	20	Normal	—	○
ThunderPunch	Electric	Physical	75	100	15	Normal	—	○
Block	Normal	Status	—	—	5	Normal	—	—
Dark Pulse	Dark	Special	80	100	15	Normal	○	—
Snore	Normal	Special	40	100	15	Normal	—	—
Synthesis	Grass	Status	—	—	5	Self	—	—
Role Play	Psychic	Status	—	—	10	Normal	—	—
Giga Drain	Grass	Special	75	100	10	Normal	—	—
Drain Punch	Fighting	Physical	75	100	10	Normal	—	○
Worry Seed	Grass	Status	—	100	10	Normal	—	—
Spite	Ghost	Status	—	100	10	Normal	—	—
Sleep Talk	Normal	Status	—	—	10	Self	—	—

EGG MOVES

Name	Type	Kind	Pow.	Acc.	PP	Range	Long	DA
GrassWhistle	Grass	Status	—	55	15	Normal	—	—
Acid	Poison	Special	40	100	30	Many Others	—	—
Teeter Dance	Normal	Status	—	100	20	Adjacent	—	—
DynamicPunch	Fighting	Physical	100	50	5	Normal	—	○
Counter	Fighting	Physical	—	100	20	Varies	—	○
Low Kick	Fighting	Physical	—	100	20	Normal	—	○
SmellingSalt	Normal	Physical	60	100	10	Normal	—	○
Magical Leaf	Grass	Special	60	—	20	Normal	—	—
Seed Bomb	Grass	Physical	80	100	15	Normal	—	—
Nasty Plot	Dark	Status	—	—	20	Self	—	—
Disable	Normal	Status	—	100	20	Normal	—	—
Block	Normal	Status	—	—	5	Normal	—	—
Worry Seed	Grass	Status	—	100	10	Normal	—	—
Switcheroo	Dark	Status	—	100	10	Normal	—	—

Pokémon AR Marker

331 Cacnea

Scarecrow Pokémon

332 Cacturne

TYPE: Grass / Dark

ABILITY
- Sand Veil

HIDDEN ABILITY
- Water Absorb

- HEIGHT: 4'03"
- WEIGHT: 170.6 lbs.
- GENDER: ♂ / ♀

It becomes active at night, seeking prey that is exhausted from the day's desert heat.

STATS
HP
Attack
Defense
Sp. Atk
Sp. Def
Speed

EGG GROUPS
Grass/Human-Like

♂ ♀

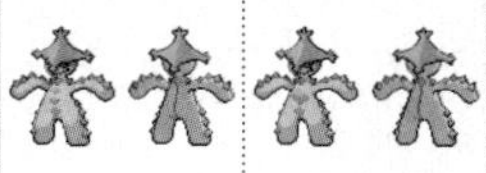

ITEMS SOMETIMES HELD
- Sticky Barb

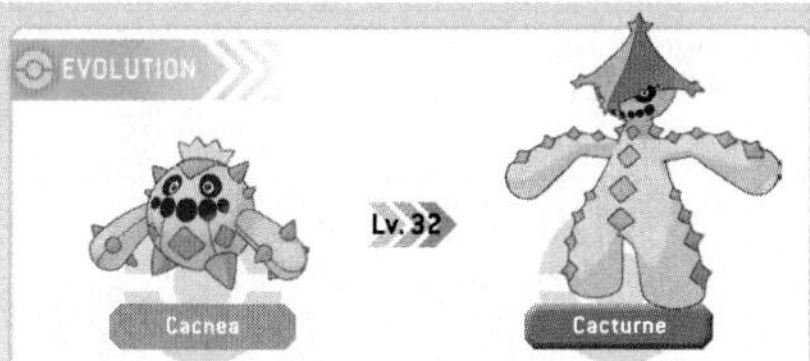
EVOLUTION
Cacnea
Lv. 32
Cacturne

HOW TO OBTAIN

Pokémon Black Version 2	Reversal Mountain entrance (mass outbreak)
Pokémon White Version 2	Reversal Mountain entrance (mass outbreak)

HOW TO OBTAIN FROM OTHER GAMES

—
—

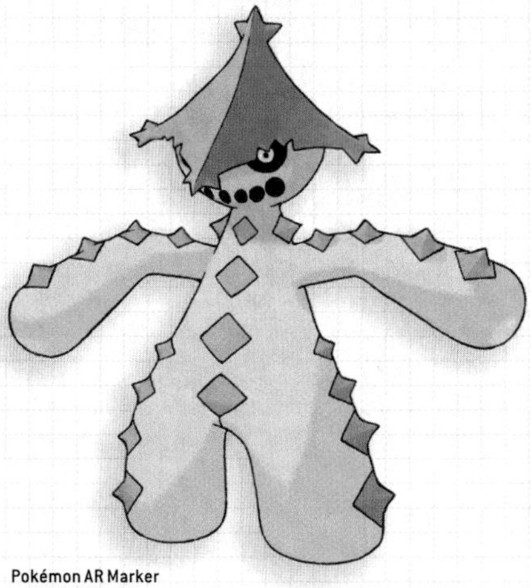

LEVEL-UP AND LEARNED MOVES

Lv.	Name	Type	Kind	Pow.	Acc.	PP	Range	Long	DA
1	Revenge	Fighting	Physical	60	100	10	Normal	—	○
1	Poison Sting	Poison	Physical	15	100	35	Normal	—	—
1	Leer	Normal	Status	—	100	30	Many Others	—	—
1	Absorb	Grass	Special	20	100	25	Normal	—	—
1	Growth	Normal	Status	—	—	40	Self	—	—
5	Absorb	Grass	Special	20	100	25	Normal	—	—
9	Growth	Normal	Status	—	—	40	Self	—	—
13	Leech Seed	Grass	Status	—	90	10	Normal	—	—
17	Sand-Attack	Ground	Status	—	100	15	Normal	—	—
21	Pin Missile	Bug	Physical	14	85	20	Normal	—	—
25	Ingrain	Grass	Status	—	—	20	Self	—	—
29	Faint Attack	Dark	Physical	60	—	20	Normal	—	○
35	Spikes	Ground	Status	—	—	20	Other Side	—	—
41	Sucker Punch	Dark	Physical	80	100	5	Normal	—	○
47	Payback	Dark	Physical	50	100	10	Normal	—	○
53	Needle Arm	Grass	Physical	60	100	15	Normal	—	○
59	Cotton Spore	Grass	Status	—	100	40	Normal	—	—
65	Sandstorm	Rock	Status	—	—	10	Both Sides	—	—
71	Destiny Bond	Ghost	Status	—	—	5	Self	—	—

TM & HM MOVES

Lv.	Name	Type	Kind	Pow.	Acc.	PP	Range	Long	DA
TM06	Toxic	Poison	Status	—	90	10	Normal	—	—
TM09	Venoshock	Poison	Special	65	100	10	Normal	—	—
TM10	Hidden Power	Normal	Special	—	100	15	Normal	—	—
TM11	Sunny Day	Fire	Status	—	—	5	Both Sides	—	—
TM15	Hyper Beam	Normal	Special	150	90	5	Normal	—	—
TM17	Protect	Normal	Status	—	—	10	Self	—	—
TM21	Frustration	Normal	Physical	—	100	20	Normal	—	○
TM22	SolarBeam	Grass	Special	120	100	10	Normal	—	—
TM27	Return	Normal	Physical	—	100	20	Normal	—	○
TM31	Brick Break	Fighting	Physical	75	100	15	Normal	—	○
TM32	Double Team	Normal	Status	—	—	15	Self	—	—
TM37	Sandstorm	Rock	Status	—	—	10	Both Sides	—	—
TM42	Facade	Normal	Physical	70	100	20	Normal	—	○
TM44	Rest	Psychic	Status	—	—	10	Self	—	—
TM45	Attract	Normal	Status	—	100	15	Normal	—	—
TM48	Round	Normal	Special	60	100	15	Normal	—	—
TM52	Focus Blast	Fighting	Special	120	70	5	Normal	—	—
TM53	Energy Ball	Grass	Special	80	100	10	Normal	—	—
TM56	Fling	Dark	Physical	—	100	10	Normal	—	—
TM63	Embargo	Dark	Status	—	100	15	Normal	—	—
TM66	Payback	Dark	Physical	50	100	10	Normal	—	○
TM67	Retaliate	Normal	Physical	70	100	5	Normal	—	○
TM68	Giga Impact	Normal	Physical	150	90	5	Normal	—	○
TM70	Flash	Normal	Status	—	100	20	Normal	—	—
TM75	Swords Dance	Normal	Status	—	—	30	Self	—	—
TM84	Poison Jab	Poison	Physical	80	100	20	Normal	—	○
TM86	Grass Knot	Grass	Special	—	100	20	Normal	—	○
TM87	Swagger	Normal	Status	—	90	15	Normal	—	—
TM90	Substitute	Normal	Status	—	—	10	Self	—	—
HM01	Cut	Normal	Physical	50	95	30	Normal	—	○
HM04	Strength	Normal	Physical	80	100	15	Normal	—	○

MOVES TAUGHT BY PEOPLE

Name	Type	Kind	Pow.	Acc.	PP	Range	Long	DA

MOVES TAUGHT BY MOVE TUTORS FOR SHARDS

Name	Type	Kind	Pow.	Acc.	PP	Range	Long	DA
Seed Bomb	Grass	Physical	80	100	15	Normal	—	—
Low Kick	Fighting	Physical	—	100	20	Normal	—	○
ThunderPunch	Electric	Physical	75	100	15	Normal	—	○
Block	Normal	Status	—	—	5	Normal	—	—
Foul Play	Dark	Physical	95	100	15	Normal	—	○
Superpower	Fighting	Physical	120	100	5	Normal	—	○
Dark Pulse	Dark	Special	80	100	15	Normal	○	—
Snore	Normal	Special	40	100	15	Normal	—	—
Synthesis	Grass	Status	—	—	5	Self	—	—
Role Play	Psychic	Status	—	—	10	Normal	—	—
Giga Drain	Grass	Special	75	100	10	Normal	—	—
Drain Punch	Fighting	Physical	75	100	10	Normal	—	○
Worry Seed	Grass	Status	—	100	10	Normal	—	—
Spite	Ghost	Status	—	100	10	Normal	—	—
Sleep Talk	Normal	Status	—	—	10	Self	—	—

Pokémon AR Marker

332 Cacturne

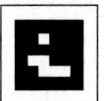

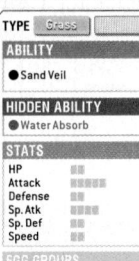

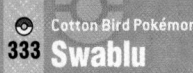

NATIONAL POKÉDEX

333 Swablu

Cotton Bird Pokémon

- HEIGHT: 1'04"
- WEIGHT: 2.6 lbs.
- GENDER: ♂ / ♀

For some reason, it likes to land on people's heads softly and act like it's a hat.

Same form for ♂ / ♀

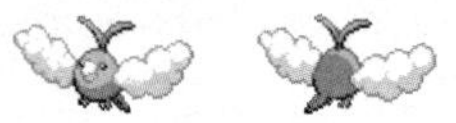

TYPE: Normal / Flying

ABILITY
- Natural Cure

HIDDEN ABILITY
- Cloud Nine

STATS
HP
Attack
Defense
Sp. Atk
Sp. Def
Speed

EGG GROUPS
Flying/Dragon

ITEMS SOMETIMES HELD
- None

EVOLUTION

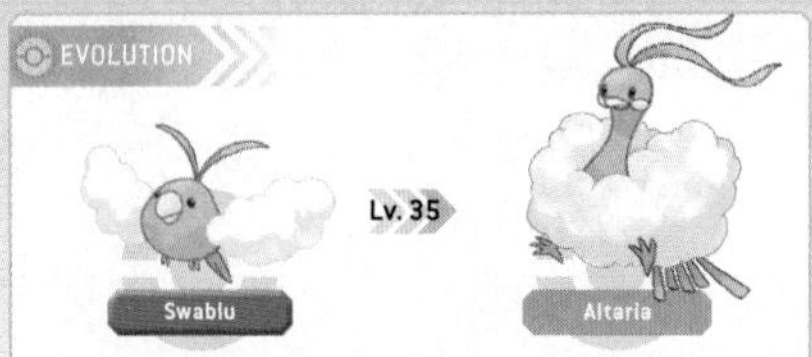

HOW TO OBTAIN

Pokémon Black Version 2	❶ Route 14 ❷ Abundant Shrine
Pokémon White Version 2	❶ Route 14 ❷ Abundant Shrine

HOW TO OBTAIN FROM OTHER GAMES

—

—

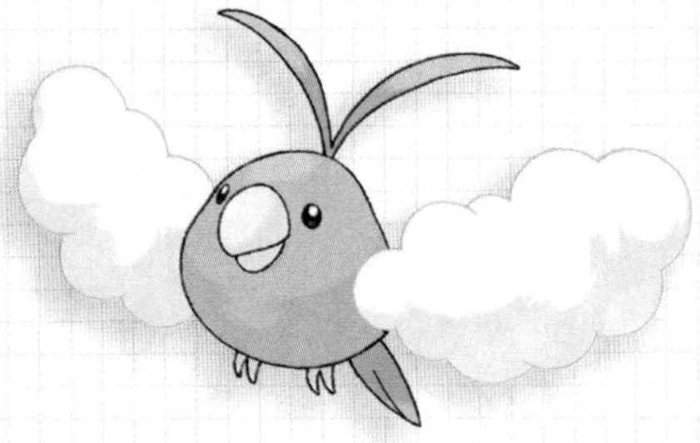

Pokémon AR Marker

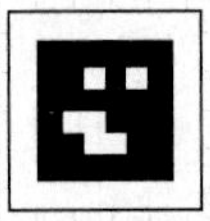

LEVEL-UP AND LEARNED MOVES

Lv.	Name	Type	Kind	Pow.	Acc.	PP	Range	Long	DA
1	Peck	Flying	Physical	35	100	35	Normal	○	○
1	Growl	Normal	Status	—	100	40	Many Others	—	—
4	Astonish	Ghost	Physical	30	100	15	Normal	—	○
8	Sing	Normal	Status	—	55	15	Normal	—	—
10	Fury Attack	Normal	Physical	15	85	20	Normal	—	○
13	Safeguard	Normal	Status	—	—	25	Your Side	—	—
15	Mist	Ice	Status	—	—	30	Your Side	—	—
18	Round	Normal	Special	60	100	15	Normal	—	—
21	Natural Gift	Normal	Physical	—	100	15	Normal	—	—
25	Take Down	Normal	Physical	90	85	20	Normal	—	○
29	Refresh	Normal	Status	—	—	20	Self	—	—
34	Mirror Move	Flying	Status	—	—	20	Normal	—	—
39	Cotton Guard	Grass	Status	—	—	10	Self	—	—
42	Dragon Pulse	Dragon	Special	90	100	10	Normal	○	—
48	Perish Song	Normal	Status	—	—	5	Adjacent	○	—

TM & HM MOVES

Lv.	Name	Type	Kind	Pow.	Acc.	PP	Range	Long	DA
TM06	Toxic	Poison	Status	—	90	10	Normal	—	—
TM10	Hidden Power	Normal	Special	—	100	15	Normal	—	—
TM11	Sunny Day	Fire	Status	—	—	5	Both Sides	—	—
TM13	Ice Beam	Ice	Special	95	100	10	Normal	—	—
TM17	Protect	Normal	Status	—	—	10	Self	—	—
TM18	Rain Dance	Water	Status	—	—	5	Both Sides	—	—
TM20	Safeguard	Normal	Status	—	—	25	Your Side	—	—
TM21	Frustration	Normal	Physical	—	100	20	Normal	—	○
TM22	SolarBeam	Grass	Special	120	100	10	Normal	—	—
TM27	Return	Normal	Physical	—	100	20	Normal	—	○
TM32	Double Team	Normal	Status	—	—	15	Self	—	—
TM40	Aerial Ace	Flying	Physical	60	—	20	Normal	○	○
TM42	Facade	Normal	Physical	70	100	20	Normal	—	○
TM44	Rest	Psychic	Status	—	—	10	Self	—	—
TM45	Attract	Normal	Status	—	100	15	Normal	—	—
TM46	Thief	Dark	Physical	40	100	10	Normal	—	○
TM48	Round	Normal	Special	60	100	15	Normal	—	—
TM49	Echoed Voice	Normal	Special	40	100	15	Normal	—	—
TM77	Psych Up	Normal	Status	—	—	10	Normal	—	—
TM85	Dream Eater	Psychic	Special	100	100	15	Normal	—	—
TM87	Swagger	Normal	Status	—	90	15	Normal	—	—
TM88	Pluck	Flying	Physical	60	100	20	Normal	○	○
TM90	Substitute	Normal	Status	—	—	10	Self	—	—
HM02	Fly	Flying	Physical	90	95	15	Normal	○	○

MOVES TAUGHT BY PEOPLE

Name	Type	Kind	Pow.	Acc.	PP	Range	Long	DA

MOVES TAUGHT BY MOVE TUTORS FOR SHARDS

Name	Type	Kind	Pow.	Acc.	PP	Range	Long	DA
Uproar	Normal	Special	90	100	10	1 Random	—	—
Hyper Voice	Normal	Special	90	100	10	Many Others	—	—
Dragon Pulse	Dragon	Special	90	100	10	Normal	○	—
Snore	Normal	Special	40	100	15	Normal	—	—
Heal Bell	Normal	Status	—	—	5	Your Party	—	—
Roost	Flying	Status	—	—	10	Self	—	—
Heat Wave	Fire	Special	100	90	10	Many Others	—	—
Tailwind	Flying	Status	—	—	30	Your Side	—	—
Outrage	Dragon	Physical	120	100	10	1 Random	—	○
Sleep Talk	Normal	Status	—	—	10	Self	—	—

EGG MOVES

Name	Type	Kind	Pow.	Acc.	PP	Range	Long	DA
Agility	Psychic	Status	—	—	30	Self	—	—
Haze	Ice	Status	—	—	30	Both Sides	—	—
Pursuit	Dark	Physical	40	100	20	Normal	—	○
Rage	Normal	Physical	20	100	20	Normal	—	○
FeatherDance	Flying	Status	—	100	15	Normal	—	—
Dragon Rush	Dragon	Physical	100	75	10	Normal	—	○
Power Swap	Psychic	Status	—	—	10	Normal	—	—
Roost	Flying	Status	—	—	10	Self	—	—
Hyper Voice	Normal	Special	90	100	10	Many Others	—	—
Steel Wing	Steel	Physical	70	90	25	Normal	—	○

334 Altaria

Humming Pokémon

- HEIGHT: 3'07"
- WEIGHT: 45.4 lbs.
- GENDER: ♂ / ♀

On sunny days, it flies freely through the sky and blends into the clouds. It sings in a beautiful soprano.

Same form for ♂ / ♀

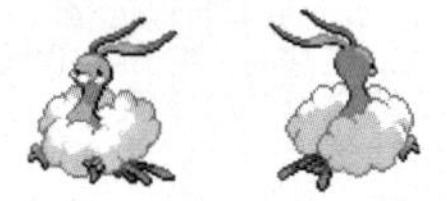

TYPE: Dragon / Flying

ABILITY
- Natural Cure

HIDDEN ABILITY
- Cloud Nine

STATS
HP
Attack
Defense
Sp. Atk
Sp. Def
Speed

EGG GROUPS
Flying/Dragon

ITEMS SOMETIMES HELD
- None

EVOLUTION

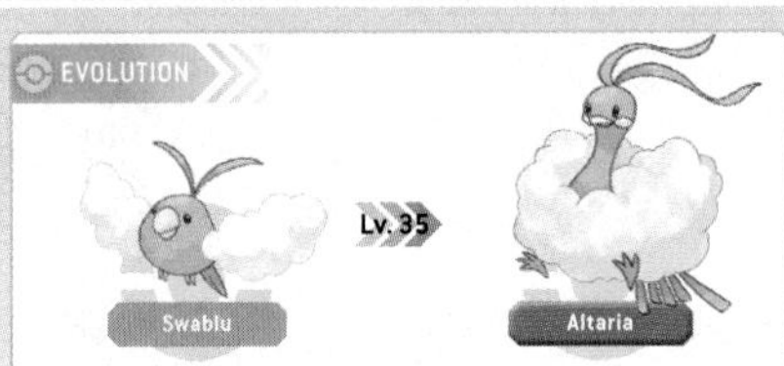

HOW TO OBTAIN

Pokémon Black Version 2	❶ Route 14 ❷ Abundant Shrine
Pokémon White Version 2	❶ Route 14 ❷ Abundant Shrine

HOW TO OBTAIN FROM OTHER GAMES

—

—

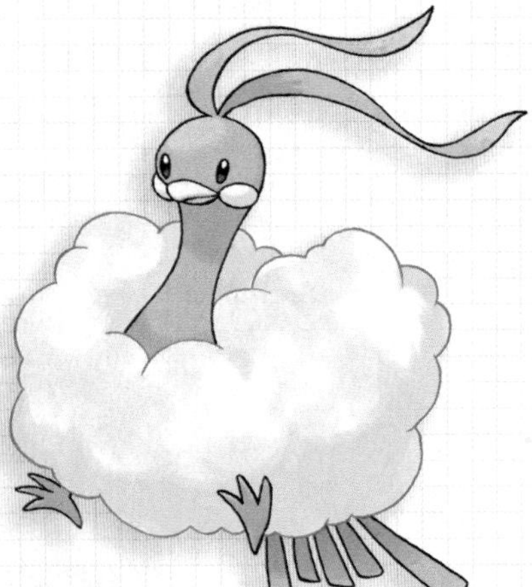

Pokémon AR Marker

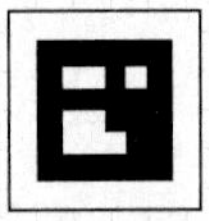

LEVEL-UP AND LEARNED MOVES

Lv.	Name	Type	Kind	Pow.	Acc.	PP	Range	Long	DA
1	Pluck	Flying	Physical	60	100	20	Normal	○	○
1	Peck	Flying	Physical	35	100	35	Normal	○	○
1	Growl	Normal	Status	—	100	40	Many Others	—	—
1	Astonish	Ghost	Physical	30	100	15	Normal	—	○
1	Sing	Normal	Status	—	55	15	Normal	—	—
4	Astonish	Ghost	Physical	30	100	15	Normal	—	○
8	Sing	Normal	Status	—	55	15	Normal	—	—
10	Fury Attack	Normal	Physical	15	85	20	Normal	—	○
13	Safeguard	Normal	Status	—	—	25	Your Side	—	—
15	Mist	Ice	Status	—	—	30	Your Side	—	—
18	Round	Normal	Special	60	100	15	Normal	—	—
21	Natural Gift	Normal	Physical	—	100	15	Normal	—	—
25	Take Down	Normal	Physical	90	85	20	Normal	—	○
29	Refresh	Normal	Status	—	—	20	Self	—	—
34	Dragon Dance	Dragon	Status	—	—	20	Self	—	—
35	DragonBreath	Dragon	Special	60	100	20	Normal	—	—
42	Cotton Guard	Grass	Status	—	—	10	Self	—	—
48	Dragon Pulse	Dragon	Special	90	100	10	Normal	○	—
57	Perish Song	Normal	Status	—	—	5	Adjacent	○	—
64	Sky Attack	Flying	Physical	140	90	5	Normal	○	—

TM & HM MOVES

Lv.	Name	Type	Kind	Pow.	Acc.	PP	Range	Long	DA
TM01	Hone Claws	Dark	Status	—	—	15	Self	—	—
TM02	Dragon Claw	Dragon	Physical	80	100	15	Normal	—	○
TM05	Roar	Normal	Status	—	100	20	Normal	—	—
TM06	Toxic	Poison	Status	—	90	10	Normal	—	—
TM10	Hidden Power	Normal	Special	—	100	15	Normal	—	—
TM11	Sunny Day	Fire	Status	—	—	5	Both Sides	—	—
TM13	Ice Beam	Ice	Special	95	100	10	Normal	—	—
TM15	Hyper Beam	Normal	Special	150	90	5	Normal	—	—
TM17	Protect	Normal	Status	—	—	10	Self	—	—
TM18	Rain Dance	Water	Status	—	—	5	Both Sides	—	—
TM20	Safeguard	Normal	Status	—	—	25	Your Side	—	—
TM21	Frustration	Normal	Physical	—	100	20	Normal	—	○
TM22	SolarBeam	Grass	Special	120	100	10	Normal	—	—
TM26	Earthquake	Ground	Physical	100	100	10	Adjacent	—	—
TM27	Return	Normal	Physical	—	100	20	Normal	—	○
TM32	Double Team	Normal	Status	—	—	15	Self	—	—
TM35	Flamethrower	Fire	Special	95	100	15	Normal	—	—
TM38	Fire Blast	Fire	Special	120	85	5	Normal	—	—
TM40	Aerial Ace	Flying	Physical	60	—	20	Normal	○	○
TM42	Facade	Normal	Physical	70	100	20	Normal	—	○
TM44	Rest	Psychic	Status	—	—	10	Self	—	—
TM45	Attract	Normal	Status	—	100	15	Normal	—	—
TM46	Thief	Dark	Physical	40	100	10	Normal	—	○
TM48	Round	Normal	Special	60	100	15	Normal	—	—
TM49	Echoed Voice	Normal	Special	40	100	15	Normal	—	—
TM59	Incinerate	Fire	Special	30	100	15	Many Others	—	—
TM68	Giga Impact	Normal	Physical	150	90	5	Normal	—	○
TM77	Psych Up	Normal	Status	—	—	10	Normal	—	—
TM78	Bulldoze	Ground	Physical	60	100	20	Adjacent	—	—
TM85	Dream Eater	Psychic	Special	100	100	15	Normal	—	—
TM87	Swagger	Normal	Status	—	90	15	Normal	—	—
TM88	Pluck	Flying	Physical	60	100	20	Normal	○	○
TM90	Substitute	Normal	Status	—	—	10	Self	—	—
TM94	Rock Smash	Fighting	Physical	40	100	15	Normal	—	○
HM02	Fly	Flying	Physical	90	95	15	Normal	○	○

MOVES TAUGHT BY PEOPLE

Name	Type	Kind	Pow.	Acc.	PP	Range	Long	DA
Draco Meteor	Dragon	Special	140	90	5	Normal	—	—

MOVES TAUGHT BY MOVE TUTORS FOR SHARDS

Name	Type	Kind	Pow.	Acc.	PP	Range	Long	DA
Uproar	Normal	Special	90	100	10	1 Random	—	—
Hyper Voice	Normal	Special	90	100	10	Many Others	—	—
Iron Tail	Steel	Physical	100	75	15	Normal	—	○
Dragon Pulse	Dragon	Special	90	100	10	Normal	○	—
Snore	Normal	Special	40	100	15	Normal	—	—
Heal Bell	Normal	Status	—	—	5	Your Party	—	—
Roost	Flying	Status	—	—	10	Self	—	—
Sky Attack	Flying	Physical	140	90	5	Normal	○	—
Heat Wave	Fire	Special	100	90	10	Many Others	—	—
Tailwind	Flying	Status	—	—	30	Your Side	—	—
Wonder Room	Psychic	Status	—	—	10	Both Sides	—	—
Outrage	Dragon	Physical	120	100	10	1 Random	—	○
Sleep Talk	Normal	Status	—	—	10	Self	—	—

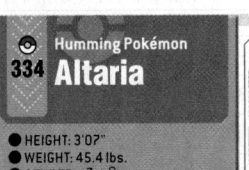

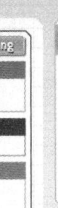

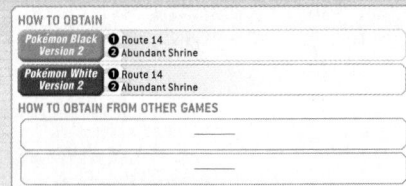

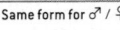

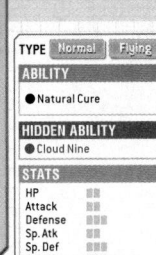

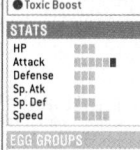

335 **Zangoose**

Cat Ferret Pokémon

- HEIGHT: 4'03"
- WEIGHT: 88.8 lbs.
- GENDER: ♂ / ♀

It's Seviper's archrival. To threaten those it encounters, it fans out the claws on its front paws.

Same form for ♂ / ♀

TYPE: Normal

ABILITY
- Immunity

HIDDEN ABILITY
- Toxic Boost

STATS
HP
Attack
Defense
Sp. Atk
Sp. Def
Speed

EGG GROUPS
Field

ITEMS SOMETIMES HELD
- Quick Claw

Pokémon AR Marker

EVOLUTION

Does not evolve

HOW TO OBTAIN

Pokémon Black Version 2: ❶ Route 7 ❷ Village Bridge

Pokémon White Version 2: ❶ Route 7 ❷ Village Bridge

HOW TO OBTAIN FROM OTHER GAMES

—

—

LEVEL-UP AND LEARNED MOVES

Lv.	Name	Type	Kind	Pow.	Acc.	PP	Range	Long	DA
1	Scratch	Normal	Physical	40	100	35	Normal	—	○
1	Leer	Normal	Status	—	100	30	Many Others	—	—
5	Quick Attack	Normal	Physical	40	100	30	Normal	—	○
8	Fury Cutter	Bug	Physical	20	95	20	Normal	—	○
12	Pursuit	Dark	Physical	40	100	20	Normal	—	○
15	Slash	Normal	Physical	70	100	20	Normal	—	○
19	Embargo	Dark	Status	—	100	15	Normal	—	—
22	Crush Claw	Normal	Physical	75	95	10	Normal	—	○
26	Revenge	Fighting	Physical	60	100	10	Normal	—	○
29	False Swipe	Normal	Physical	40	100	40	Normal	—	○
33	Detect	Fighting	Status	—	—	5	Self	—	—
36	X-Scissor	Bug	Physical	80	100	15	Normal	—	○
40	Taunt	Dark	Status	—	100	20	Normal	—	—
43	Swords Dance	Normal	Status	—	—	30	Self	—	—
47	Close Combat	Fighting	Physical	120	100	5	Normal	—	○

TM & HM MOVES

Lv.	Name	Type	Kind	Pow.	Acc.	PP	Range	Long	DA
TM01	Hone Claws	Dark	Status	—	—	15	Self	—	—
TM05	Roar	Normal	Status	—	100	20	Normal	—	—
TM06	Toxic	Poison	Status	—	90	10	Normal	—	—
TM10	Hidden Power	Normal	Special	—	100	15	Normal	—	—
TM11	Sunny Day	Fire	Status	—	—	5	Both Sides	—	—
TM12	Taunt	Dark	Status	—	100	20	Normal	—	—
TM13	Ice Beam	Ice	Special	95	100	10	Normal	—	—
TM14	Blizzard	Ice	Special	120	70	5	Many Others	—	—
TM17	Protect	Normal	Status	—	—	10	Self	—	—
TM18	Rain Dance	Water	Status	—	—	5	Both Sides	—	—
TM21	Frustration	Normal	Physical	—	100	20	Normal	—	○
TM22	SolarBeam	Grass	Special	120	100	10	Normal	—	—
TM24	Thunderbolt	Electric	Special	95	100	15	Normal	—	—
TM25	Thunder	Electric	Special	120	70	10	Normal	—	—
TM27	Return	Normal	Physical	—	100	20	Normal	—	○
TM28	Dig	Ground	Physical	80	100	10	Normal	—	○
TM30	Shadow Ball	Ghost	Special	80	100	15	Normal	—	—
TM31	Brick Break	Fighting	Physical	75	100	15	Normal	—	○
TM32	Double Team	Normal	Status	—	—	15	Self	—	—
TM35	Flamethrower	Fire	Special	95	100	15	Normal	—	—
TM38	Fire Blast	Fire	Special	120	85	5	Normal	—	—
TM39	Rock Tomb	Rock	Physical	50	80	10	Normal	—	—
TM40	Aerial Ace	Flying	Physical	60	—	20	Normal	○	○
TM42	Facade	Normal	Physical	70	100	20	Normal	—	○
TM44	Rest	Psychic	Status	—	—	10	Self	—	—
TM45	Attract	Normal	Status	—	100	15	Normal	—	—
TM46	Thief	Dark	Physical	40	100	10	Normal	—	○
TM48	Round	Normal	Special	60	100	15	Normal	—	—
TM52	Focus Blast	Fighting	Special	120	70	5	Normal	—	—
TM54	False Swipe	Normal	Physical	40	100	40	Normal	—	○
TM56	Fling	Dark	Physical	—	100	10	Normal	—	—
TM59	Incinerate	Fire	Special	30	100	15	Many Others	—	—
TM63	Embargo	Dark	Status	—	100	15	Normal	—	—
TM65	Shadow Claw	Ghost	Physical	70	100	15	Normal	—	○
TM66	Payback	Dark	Physical	50	100	10	Normal	—	○
TM67	Retaliate	Normal	Physical	70	100	5	Normal	—	○
TM75	Swords Dance	Normal	Status	—	—	30	Self	—	—
TM80	Rock Slide	Rock	Physical	75	90	10	Many Others	—	—
TM81	X-Scissor	Bug	Physical	80	100	15	Normal	—	○
TM83	Work Up	Normal	Status	—	—	30	Self	—	—
TM84	Poison Jab	Poison	Physical	80	100	20	Normal	—	○
TM87	Swagger	Normal	Status	—	90	15	Normal	—	—
TM90	Substitute	Normal	Status	—	—	10	Self	—	—
TM94	Rock Smash	Fighting	Physical	40	100	15	Normal	—	○
HM04	Strength	Normal	Physical	80	100	15	Normal	—	○

MOVES TAUGHT BY PEOPLE

Name	Type	Kind	Pow.	Acc.	PP	Range	Long	DA

MOVES TAUGHT BY MOVE TUTORS FOR SHARDS

Name	Type	Kind	Pow.	Acc.	PP	Range	Long	DA
Low Kick	Fighting	Physical	—	100	20	Normal	—	○
Fire Punch	Fire	Physical	75	100	15	Normal	—	○
ThunderPunch	Electric	Physical	75	100	15	Normal	—	○
Ice Punch	Ice	Physical	75	100	15	Normal	—	○
Last Resort	Normal	Physical	140	100	5	Normal	—	○
Icy Wind	Ice	Special	55	95	15	Many Others	—	—
Iron Tail	Steel	Physical	100	75	15	Normal	—	○
Snore	Normal	Special	40	100	15	Normal	—	—
Knock Off	Dark	Physical	20	100	20	Normal	—	○
Giga Drain	Grass	Special	75	100	10	Normal	—	—
Endeavor	Normal	Physical	—	100	5	Normal	—	○
Sleep Talk	Normal	Status	—	—	10	Self	—	—

EGG MOVES

Name	Type	Kind	Pow.	Acc.	PP	Range	Long	DA
Flail	Normal	Physical	—	100	15	Normal	—	○
Double Kick	Fighting	Physical	30	100	30	Normal	—	○
Razor Wind	Normal	Special	80	100	10	Many Others	—	—
Counter	Fighting	Physical	—	100	20	Varies	—	○
Curse	Ghost	Status	—	—	10	Varies	—	—
Fury Swipes	Normal	Physical	18	80	15	Normal	—	○
Night Slash	Dark	Physical	70	100	15	Normal	—	○
Metal Claw	Steel	Physical	50	95	35	Normal	—	○
Double Hit	Normal	Physical	35	90	10	Normal	—	○
Disable	Normal	Status	—	100	20	Normal	—	—
Iron Tail	Steel	Physical	100	75	15	Normal	—	○
Final Gambit	Fighting	Special	—	100	5	Normal	—	○
Feint	Normal	Physical	30	100	10	Normal	—	—

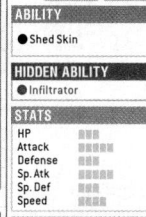

336 **Seviper**

Fang Snake Pokémon

- HEIGHT: 8'10"
- WEIGHT: 115.7 lbs.
- GENDER: ♂ / ♀

Constant polishing makes the edge of the blade on its tail extremely sharp. It's Zangoose's archrival.

Same form for ♂ / ♀

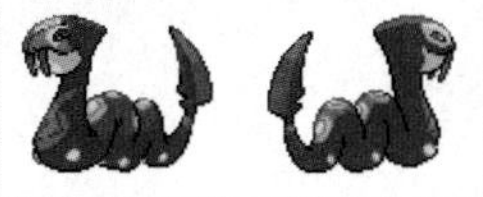

TYPE: Poison

ABILITY
- Shed Skin

HIDDEN ABILITY
- Infiltrator

STATS
HP
Attack
Defense
Sp. Atk
Sp. Def
Speed

EGG GROUPS
Field/Dragon

ITEMS SOMETIMES HELD
- None

Pokémon AR Marker

EVOLUTION

Does not evolve

HOW TO OBTAIN

Pokémon Black Version 2: ❶ Route 7 ❷ Village Bridge

Pokémon White Version 2: ❶ Route 7 ❷ Village Bridge

HOW TO OBTAIN FROM OTHER GAMES

—

—

LEVEL-UP AND LEARNED MOVES

Lv.	Name	Type	Kind	Pow.	Acc.	PP	Range	Long	DA
1	Wrap	Normal	Physical	15	90	20	Normal	—	○
1	Lick	Ghost	Physical	20	100	30	Normal	—	○
5	Bite	Dark	Physical	60	100	25	Normal	—	○
9	Swagger	Normal	Status	—	90	15	Normal	—	—
12	Poison Tail	Poison	Physical	50	100	25	Normal	—	○
16	Screech	Normal	Status	—	85	40	Normal	—	—
20	Venoshock	Poison	Special	65	100	10	Normal	—	—
23	Glare	Normal	Status	—	90	30	Normal	—	—
27	Poison Fang	Poison	Physical	50	100	15	Normal	—	○
31	Night Slash	Dark	Physical	70	100	15	Normal	—	○
34	Gastro Acid	Poison	Status	—	100	10	Normal	—	—
38	Haze	Ice	Status	—	—	30	Both Sides	—	—
42	Poison Jab	Poison	Physical	80	100	20	Normal	—	○
45	Crunch	Dark	Physical	80	100	15	Normal	—	○
49	Coil	Poison	Status	—	—	20	Self	—	—
53	Wring Out	Normal	Special	—	100	5	Normal	—	○

TM & HM MOVES

Lv.	Name	Type	Kind	Pow.	Acc.	PP	Range	Long	DA
TM06	Toxic	Poison	Status	—	90	10	Normal	—	—
TM09	Venoshock	Poison	Special	65	100	10	Normal	—	—
TM10	Hidden Power	Normal	Special	—	100	15	Normal	—	—
TM11	Sunny Day	Fire	Status	—	—	5	Both Sides	—	—
TM12	Taunt	Dark	Status	—	100	20	Normal	—	—
TM17	Protect	Normal	Status	—	—	10	Self	—	—
TM18	Rain Dance	Water	Status	—	—	5	Both Sides	—	—
TM21	Frustration	Normal	Physical	—	100	20	Normal	—	○
TM26	Earthquake	Ground	Physical	100	100	10	Adjacent	—	—
TM27	Return	Normal	Physical	—	100	20	Normal	—	○
TM28	Dig	Ground	Physical	80	100	10	Normal	—	○
TM32	Double Team	Normal	Status	—	—	15	Self	—	—
TM34	Sludge Wave	Poison	Special	95	100	10	Adjacent	—	—
TM35	Flamethrower	Fire	Special	95	100	15	Normal	—	—
TM36	Sludge Bomb	Poison	Special	90	100	10	Normal	—	—
TM42	Facade	Normal	Physical	70	100	20	Normal	—	○
TM44	Rest	Psychic	Status	—	—	10	Self	—	—
TM45	Attract	Normal	Status	—	100	15	Normal	—	—
TM46	Thief	Dark	Physical	40	100	10	Normal	—	○
TM48	Round	Normal	Special	60	100	15	Normal	—	—
TM66	Payback	Dark	Physical	50	100	10	Normal	—	○
TM67	Retaliate	Normal	Physical	70	100	5	Normal	—	○
TM78	Bulldoze	Ground	Physical	60	100	20	Adjacent	—	—
TM81	X-Scissor	Bug	Physical	80	100	15	Normal	—	○
TM82	Dragon Tail	Dragon	Physical	60	90	10	Normal	—	○
TM84	Poison Jab	Poison	Physical	80	100	20	Normal	—	○
TM87	Swagger	Normal	Status	—	90	15	Normal	—	—
TM90	Substitute	Normal	Status	—	—	10	Self	—	—
TM94	Rock Smash	Fighting	Physical	40	100	15	Normal	—	○
HM04	Strength	Normal	Physical	80	100	15	Normal	—	○

MOVES TAUGHT BY PEOPLE

Name	Type	Kind	Pow.	Acc.	PP	Range	Long	DA

MOVES TAUGHT BY MOVE TUTORS FOR SHARDS

Name	Type	Kind	Pow.	Acc.	PP	Range	Long	DA
Iron Tail	Steel	Physical	100	75	15	Normal	—	○
Aqua Tail	Water	Physical	90	90	10	Normal	—	○
Dark Pulse	Dark	Special	80	100	15	Normal	○	—
Bind	Normal	Physical	15	85	20	Normal	—	○
Snore	Normal	Special	40	100	15	Normal	—	—
Knock Off	Dark	Physical	20	100	20	Normal	—	○
Giga Drain	Grass	Special	75	100	10	Normal	—	—
Gastro Acid	Poison	Status	—	100	10	Normal	—	—
Sleep Talk	Normal	Status	—	—	10	Self	—	—
Snatch	Dark	Status	—	—	10	Self	—	—

EGG MOVES

Name	Type	Kind	Pow.	Acc.	PP	Range	Long	DA
Stockpile	Normal	Status	—	—	20	Self	—	—
Swallow	Normal	Status	—	—	10	Self	—	—
Spit Up	Normal	Special	—	100	10	Normal	—	—
Body Slam	Normal	Physical	85	100	15	Normal	—	○
Scary Face	Normal	Status	—	100	10	Normal	—	—
Assurance	Dark	Physical	50	100	10	Normal	—	○
Night Slash	Dark	Physical	70	100	15	Normal	—	○
Switcheroo	Dark	Status	—	100	10	Normal	—	—
Iron Tail	Steel	Physical	100	75	15	Normal	—	○
Wring Out	Normal	Special	—	100	5	Normal	—	○
Punishment	Dark	Physical	—	100	5	Normal	—	○
Final Gambit	Fighting	Special	—	100	5	Normal	—	○

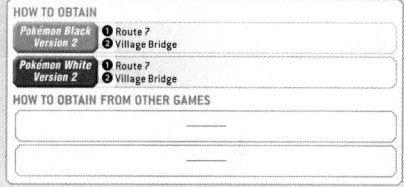

337 Lunatone
Meteorite Pokémon

TYPE: Rock / Psychic

ABILITY: ● Levitate

HIDDEN ABILITY: —

● HEIGHT: 3'03"
● WEIGHT: 370.4 lbs.
● GENDER: Unknown

The phase of the moon apparently has some effect on its power. It's active on the night of a full moon.

Gender unknown

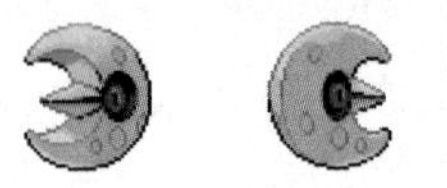

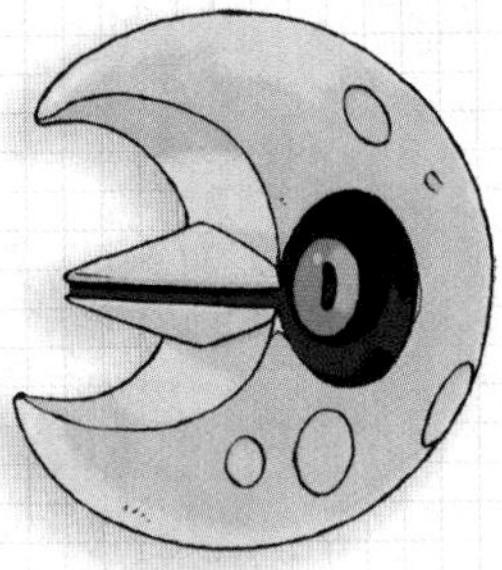

STATS
HP / Attack / Defense / Sp. Atk / Sp. Def / Speed

EGG GROUPS
Mineral

ITEMS SOMETIMES HELD
● Moon Stone
● Comet Shard

337 · Lunatone

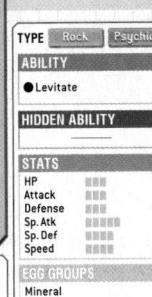

EVOLUTION
Does not evolve

HOW TO OBTAIN
Pokémon Black Version 2	❶ Route 13	❷ Route 22
Pokémon White Version 2	❶ Route 13	❷ Route 22

HOW TO OBTAIN FROM OTHER GAMES
—

LEVEL-UP AND LEARNED MOVES

Lv.	Name	Type	Kind	Pow.	Acc.	PP	Range	Long	DA
1	Tackle	Normal	Physical	50	100	35	Normal	—	—
1	Harden	Normal	Status	—	—	30	Self	—	—
1	Confusion	Psychic	Special	50	100	25	Normal	—	—
5	Rock Throw	Rock	Physical	50	90	15	Normal	—	—
9	Hypnosis	Psychic	Status	—	60	20	Normal	—	—
13	Rock Polish	Rock	Status	—	—	20	Self	—	—
17	Psywave	Psychic	Special	—	80	15	Normal	—	—
21	Embargo	Dark	Status	—	100	15	Normal	—	—
25	Rock Slide	Rock	Physical	75	90	10	Many Others	—	—
29	Cosmic Power	Psychic	Status	—	—	20	Self	—	—
33	Psychic	Psychic	Special	90	100	10	Normal	—	—
37	Heal Block	Psychic	Status	—	100	15	Many Others	—	—
41	Stone Edge	Rock	Physical	100	80	5	Normal	—	—
45	Future Sight	Psychic	Special	100	100	10	Normal	—	—
49	Explosion	Normal	Physical	250	100	5	Adjacent	—	—
53	Magic Room	Psychic	Status	—	—	10	Both Sides	—	—

TM & HM MOVES

Lv.	Name	Type	Kind	Pow.	Acc.	PP	Range	Long	DA
TM03	Psyshock	Psychic	Special	80	100	10	Normal	—	—
TM04	Calm Mind	Psychic	Status	—	—	20	Self	—	—
TM06	Toxic	Poison	Status	—	90	10	Normal	—	—
TM10	Hidden Power	Normal	Special	—	100	15	Normal	—	—
TM13	Ice Beam	Ice	Special	95	100	10	Normal	—	—
TM14	Blizzard	Ice	Special	120	70	5	Many Others	—	—
TM15	Hyper Beam	Normal	Special	150	90	5	Normal	—	—
TM16	Light Screen	Psychic	Status	—	—	30	Your Side	—	—
TM17	Protect	Normal	Status	—	—	10	Self	—	—
TM18	Rain Dance	Water	Status	—	—	5	Both Sides	—	—
TM19	Telekinesis	Psychic	Status	—	—	15	Normal	—	—
TM20	Safeguard	Normal	Status	—	—	25	Your Side	—	—
TM21	Frustration	Normal	Physical	—	100	20	Normal	—	○
TM23	Smack Down	Rock	Physical	50	100	15	Normal	—	—
TM26	Earthquake	Ground	Physical	100	100	10	Adjacent	—	—
TM27	Return	Normal	Physical	—	100	20	Normal	—	○
TM29	Psychic	Psychic	Special	90	100	10	Normal	—	—
TM30	Shadow Ball	Ghost	Special	80	100	15	Normal	—	—
TM32	Double Team	Normal	Status	—	—	15	Self	—	—
TM33	Reflect	Psychic	Status	—	—	20	Your Side	—	—
TM37	Sandstorm	Rock	Status	—	—	10	Both Sides	—	—
TM39	Rock Tomb	Rock	Physical	50	80	10	Normal	—	—
TM42	Facade	Normal	Physical	70	100	20	Normal	—	—
TM44	Rest	Psychic	Status	—	—	10	Self	—	—
TM48	Round	Normal	Special	60	100	15	Normal	—	—
TM57	Charge Beam	Electric	Special	50	90	10	Normal	—	—
TM62	Acrobatics	Flying	Physical	55	100	15	Normal	○	—
TM63	Embargo	Dark	Status	—	100	15	Normal	—	—
TM64	Explosion	Normal	Physical	250	100	5	Adjacent	—	—
TM68	Giga Impact	Normal	Physical	150	90	5	Normal	—	○
TM69	Rock Polish	Rock	Status	—	—	20	Self	—	—
TM70	Flash	Normal	Status	—	100	20	Normal	—	—
TM71	Stone Edge	Rock	Physical	100	80	5	Normal	—	—
TM74	Gyro Ball	Steel	Physical	—	100	5	Normal	—	○
TM77	Psych Up	Normal	Status	—	—	10	Self	—	—
TM78	Bulldoze	Ground	Physical	60	100	20	Adjacent	—	—
TM80	Rock Slide	Rock	Physical	75	90	10	Many Others	—	—
TM85	Dream Eater	Psychic	Special	100	100	15	Normal	—	—
TM86	Grass Knot	Grass	Special	—	100	20	Normal	—	○
TM87	Swagger	Normal	Status	—	90	15	Normal	—	—
TM90	Substitute	Normal	Status	—	—	10	Self	—	—
TM92	Trick Room	Psychic	Status	—	—	5	Both Sides	—	—

MOVES TAUGHT BY PEOPLE

Name	Type	Kind	Pow.	Acc.	PP	Range	Long	DA

MOVES TAUGHT BY MOVE TUTORS FOR SHARDS

Name	Type	Kind	Pow.	Acc.	PP	Range	Long	DA
Signal Beam	Bug	Special	75	100	15	Normal	—	—
Iron Head	Steel	Physical	80	100	15	Normal	—	○
Magic Coat	Psychic	Status	—	—	15	Self	—	—
Icy Wind	Ice	Special	55	95	15	Many Others	—	—
Earth Power	Ground	Special	90	100	10	Normal	—	—
Zen Headbutt	Psychic	Physical	80	90	15	Normal	—	○
Gravity	Psychic	Status	—	—	5	Both Sides	—	—
Snore	Normal	Special	40	100	15	Normal	—	—
Pain Split	Normal	Status	—	—	20	Normal	—	—
Helping Hand	Normal	Status	—	—	20	1 Ally	—	—
Magic Room	Psychic	Status	—	—	10	Both Sides	—	—
Recycle	Normal	Status	—	—	10	Self	—	—
Stealth Rock	Rock	Status	—	—	20	Other Side	—	—
Sleep Talk	Normal	Status	—	—	10	Self	—	—
Skill Swap	Psychic	Status	—	—	10	Normal	—	—

EGG MOVES

Name	Type	Kind	Pow.	Acc.	PP	Range	Long	DA

Pokémon AR Marker

---

338 Solrock
Meteorite Pokémon

TYPE: Rock / Psychic

ABILITY: ● Levitate

HIDDEN ABILITY: —

● HEIGHT: 3'11"
● WEIGHT: 339.5 lbs.
● GENDER: Unknown

Solar energy is the source of its power, so it is strong during the daytime. When it spins, its body shines.

Gender unknown

STATS
HP / Attack / Defense / Sp. Atk / Sp. Def / Speed

EGG GROUPS
Mineral

ITEMS SOMETIMES HELD
● Sun Stone
● Comet Shard

338 · Solrock

EVOLUTION
Does not evolve

HOW TO OBTAIN
Pokémon Black Version 2	❶ Route 13	❷ Route 22
Pokémon White Version 2	❶ Route 13	❷ Route 22

HOW TO OBTAIN FROM OTHER GAMES
—

LEVEL-UP AND LEARNED MOVES

Lv.	Name	Type	Kind	Pow.	Acc.	PP	Range	Long	DA
1	Tackle	Normal	Physical	50	100	35	Normal	—	○
1	Harden	Normal	Status	—	—	30	Self	—	—
1	Confusion	Psychic	Special	50	100	25	Normal	—	—
5	Rock Throw	Rock	Physical	50	90	15	Normal	—	—
9	Fire Spin	Fire	Special	35	85	15	Normal	—	—
13	Rock Polish	Rock	Status	—	—	20	Self	—	—
17	Psywave	Psychic	Special	—	80	15	Normal	—	—
21	Embargo	Dark	Status	—	100	15	Normal	—	—
25	Rock Slide	Rock	Physical	75	90	10	Many Others	—	—
29	Cosmic Power	Psychic	Status	—	—	20	Self	—	—
33	Psychic	Psychic	Special	90	100	10	Normal	—	—
37	Heal Block	Psychic	Status	—	100	15	Many Others	—	—
41	Stone Edge	Rock	Physical	100	80	5	Normal	—	—
45	SolarBeam	Grass	Special	120	100	10	Normal	—	—
49	Explosion	Normal	Physical	250	100	5	Adjacent	—	—
53	Wonder Room	Psychic	Status	—	—	10	Both Sides	—	—

TM & HM MOVES

Lv.	Name	Type	Kind	Pow.	Acc.	PP	Range	Long	DA
TM03	Psyshock	Psychic	Special	80	100	10	Normal	—	—
TM04	Calm Mind	Psychic	Status	—	—	20	Self	—	—
TM06	Toxic	Poison	Status	—	90	10	Normal	—	—
TM10	Hidden Power	Normal	Special	—	100	15	Normal	—	—
TM11	Sunny Day	Fire	Status	—	—	5	Both Sides	—	—
TM15	Hyper Beam	Normal	Special	150	90	5	Normal	—	—
TM16	Light Screen	Psychic	Status	—	—	30	Your Side	—	—
TM17	Protect	Normal	Status	—	—	10	Self	—	—
TM19	Telekinesis	Psychic	Status	—	—	15	Normal	—	—
TM20	Safeguard	Normal	Status	—	—	25	Your Side	—	—
TM21	Frustration	Normal	Physical	—	100	20	Normal	—	○
TM22	SolarBeam	Grass	Special	120	100	10	Normal	—	—
TM23	Smack Down	Rock	Physical	50	100	15	Normal	—	—
TM26	Earthquake	Ground	Physical	100	100	10	Adjacent	—	—
TM27	Return	Normal	Physical	—	100	20	Normal	—	○
TM29	Psychic	Psychic	Special	90	100	10	Normal	—	—
TM30	Shadow Ball	Ghost	Special	80	100	15	Normal	—	—
TM32	Double Team	Normal	Status	—	—	15	Self	—	—
TM33	Reflect	Psychic	Status	—	—	20	Your Side	—	—
TM35	Flamethrower	Fire	Special	95	100	15	Normal	—	—
TM37	Sandstorm	Rock	Status	—	—	10	Both Sides	—	—
TM38	Fire Blast	Fire	Special	120	85	5	Normal	—	—
TM39	Rock Tomb	Rock	Physical	50	80	10	Normal	—	—
TM42	Facade	Normal	Physical	70	100	20	Normal	—	—
TM44	Rest	Psychic	Status	—	—	10	Self	—	—
TM48	Round	Normal	Special	60	100	15	Normal	—	—
TM50	Overheat	Fire	Special	140	90	5	Normal	—	—
TM57	Charge Beam	Electric	Special	50	90	10	Normal	—	—
TM59	Incinerate	Fire	Special	30	100	15	Many Others	—	—
TM61	Will-O-Wisp	Fire	Status	—	75	15	Normal	—	—
TM62	Acrobatics	Flying	Physical	55	100	15	Normal	○	—
TM63	Embargo	Dark	Status	—	100	15	Normal	—	—
TM64	Explosion	Normal	Physical	250	100	5	Adjacent	—	—
TM68	Giga Impact	Normal	Physical	150	90	5	Normal	—	○
TM69	Rock Polish	Rock	Status	—	—	20	Self	—	—
TM70	Flash	Normal	Status	—	100	20	Normal	—	—
TM71	Stone Edge	Rock	Physical	100	80	5	Normal	—	—
TM74	Gyro Ball	Steel	Physical	—	100	5	Normal	—	○
TM77	Psych Up	Normal	Status	—	—	10	Self	—	—
TM78	Bulldoze	Ground	Physical	60	100	20	Adjacent	—	—
TM80	Rock Slide	Rock	Physical	75	90	10	Many Others	—	—
TM85	Dream Eater	Psychic	Special	100	100	15	Normal	—	—
TM86	Grass Knot	Grass	Special	—	100	20	Normal	—	○
TM87	Swagger	Normal	Status	—	90	15	Normal	—	—
TM90	Substitute	Normal	Status	—	—	10	Self	—	—
TM92	Trick Room	Psychic	Status	—	—	5	Both Sides	—	—

MOVES TAUGHT BY PEOPLE

Name	Type	Kind	Pow.	Acc.	PP	Range	Long	DA

MOVES TAUGHT BY MOVE TUTORS FOR SHARDS

Name	Type	Kind	Pow.	Acc.	PP	Range	Long	DA
Signal Beam	Bug	Special	75	100	15	Normal	—	—
Iron Head	Steel	Physical	80	100	15	Normal	—	○
Iron Defense	Steel	Status	—	—	15	Self	—	—
Magic Coat	Psychic	Status	—	—	15	Self	—	—
Earth Power	Ground	Special	90	100	10	Normal	—	—
Zen Headbutt	Psychic	Physical	80	90	15	Normal	—	○
Gravity	Psychic	Status	—	—	5	Both Sides	—	—
Snore	Normal	Special	40	100	15	Normal	—	—
Heat Wave	Fire	Special	100	90	10	Many Others	—	—
Pain Split	Normal	Status	—	—	20	Normal	—	—
Helping Hand	Normal	Status	—	—	20	1 Ally	—	—
Wonder Room	Psychic	Status	—	—	10	Both Sides	—	—
Recycle	Normal	Status	—	—	10	Self	—	—
Stealth Rock	Rock	Status	—	—	20	Other Side	—	—
Sleep Talk	Normal	Status	—	—	10	Self	—	—
Skill Swap	Psychic	Status	—	—	10	Normal	—	—

EGG MOVES

Name	Type	Kind	Pow.	Acc.	PP	Range	Long	DA

Pokémon AR Marker

339 Barboach
Whiskers Pokémon

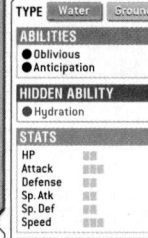

- HEIGHT: 1'04"
- WEIGHT: 4.2 lbs.
- GENDER: ♂ / ♀

Its slimy body is hard to grasp. In one region, it is said to have been born from hardened mud.

Same form for ♂ / ♀

TYPE Water Ground

ABILITIES
- Oblivious
- Anticipation

HIDDEN ABILITY
- Hydration

STATS
- HP
- Attack
- Defense
- Sp. Atk
- Sp. Def
- Speed

EGG GROUPS
Water ❷

ITEMS SOMETIMES HELD
- None

Pokémon AR Marker

EVOLUTION

Barboach → (Lv. 30) → Whiscash

HOW TO OBTAIN

Pokémon Black Version 2	❶ Route 8 (Super Rod) ❷ Icirrus City (Super Rod)
Pokémon White Version 2	❶ Route 8 (Super Rod) ❷ Icirrus City (Super Rod)

HOW TO OBTAIN FROM OTHER GAMES

———

———

LEVEL-UP AND LEARNED MOVES

Lv.	Name	Type	Kind	Pow.	Acc.	PP	Range	Long	DA
1	Mud-Slap	Ground	Special	20	100	10	Normal	—	—
6	Mud Sport	Ground	Status	—	—	15	Both Sides	—	—
6	Water Sport	Water	Status	—	—	15	Both Sides	—	—
10	Water Gun	Water	Special	40	100	25	Normal	—	—
14	Mud Bomb	Ground	Special	65	85	10	Normal	—	—
18	Amnesia	Psychic	Status	—	—	20	Self	—	—
22	Water Pulse	Water	Special	60	100	20	Normal	○	—
26	Magnitude	Ground	Physical	—	100	30	Adjacent	—	—
31	Rest	Psychic	Status	—	—	10	Self	—	—
31	Snore	Normal	Special	40	100	15	Normal	—	—
35	Aqua Tail	Water	Physical	90	90	10	Normal	—	○
39	Earthquake	Ground	Physical	100	100	10	Adjacent	—	—
43	Future Sight	Psychic	Special	100	100	10	Normal	—	—
47	Fissure	Ground	Physical	—	30	5	Normal	—	—

TM & HM MOVES

Lv.	Name	Type	Kind	Pow.	Acc.	PP	Range	Long	DA
TM06	Toxic	Poison	Status	—	90	10	Normal	—	—
TM07	Hail	Ice	Status	—	—	10	Both Sides	—	—
TM10	Hidden Power	Normal	Special	—	100	15	Normal	—	—
TM13	Ice Beam	Ice	Special	95	100	10	Normal	—	—
TM14	Blizzard	Ice	Special	120	70	5	Many Others	—	—
TM17	Protect	Normal	Status	—	—	10	Self	—	—
TM18	Rain Dance	Water	Status	—	—	5	Both Sides	—	—
TM21	Frustration	Normal	Physical	—	100	20	Normal	—	○
TM26	Earthquake	Ground	Physical	100	100	10	Adjacent	—	—
TM27	Return	Normal	Physical	—	100	20	Normal	—	○
TM32	Double Team	Normal	Status	—	—	15	Self	—	—
TM37	Sandstorm	Rock	Status	—	—	10	Both Sides	—	—
TM39	Rock Tomb	Rock	Physical	50	80	10	Normal	—	—
TM42	Facade	Normal	Physical	70	100	20	Normal	—	○
TM44	Rest	Psychic	Status	—	—	10	Self	—	—
TM45	Attract	Normal	Status	—	100	15	Normal	—	—
TM48	Round	Normal	Special	60	100	15	Normal	—	—
TM55	Scald	Water	Special	80	100	15	Normal	—	—
TM78	Bulldoze	Ground	Physical	60	100	20	Adjacent	—	—
TM87	Swagger	Normal	Status	—	90	15	Normal	—	—
TM90	Substitute	Normal	Status	—	—	10	Self	—	—
HM03	Surf	Water	Special	95	100	15	Adjacent	—	—
HM05	Waterfall	Water	Physical	80	100	15	Normal	—	○
HM06	Dive	Water	Physical	80	100	10	Normal	—	○

MOVES TAUGHT BY PEOPLE

Name	Type	Kind	Pow.	Acc.	PP	Range	Long	DA

MOVES TAUGHT BY MOVE TUTORS FOR SHARDS

Name	Type	Kind	Pow.	Acc.	PP	Range	Long	DA
Bounce	Flying	Physical	85	85	5	Normal	○	○
Icy Wind	Ice	Special	55	95	15	Many Others	—	—
Aqua Tail	Water	Physical	90	90	10	Normal	—	○
Earth Power	Ground	Special	90	100	10	Normal	—	—
Snore	Normal	Special	40	100	15	Normal	—	—
Sleep Talk	Normal	Status	—	—	10	Self	—	—

EGG MOVES

Name	Type	Kind	Pow.	Acc.	PP	Range	Long	DA
Thrash	Normal	Physical	120	100	10	1 Random	—	○
Whirlpool	Water	Special	35	85	15	Normal	—	—
Spark	Electric	Physical	65	100	20	Normal	—	○
Hydro Pump	Water	Special	120	80	5	Normal	—	—
Flail	Normal	Physical	—	100	15	Normal	—	○
Take Down	Normal	Physical	90	85	20	Normal	—	○
Dragon Dance	Dragon	Status	—	—	20	Self	—	—
Earth Power	Ground	Special	90	100	10	Normal	—	—
Mud Shot	Ground	Special	55	95	15	Normal	—	—
Muddy Water	Water	Special	95	85	10	Many Others	—	—

---

340 Whiscash
Whiskers Pokémon

- HEIGHT: 2'11"
- WEIGHT: 52.0 lbs.
- GENDER: ♂ / ♀

It is extremely protective of its territory. If any foe approaches, it attacks using vicious tremors.

Same form for ♂ / ♀

TYPE Water Ground

ABILITIES
- Oblivious
- Anticipation

HIDDEN ABILITY
- Hydration

STATS
- HP
- Attack
- Defense
- Sp. Atk
- Sp. Def
- Speed

EGG GROUPS
Water ❷

ITEMS SOMETIMES HELD
- None

Pokémon AR Marker

EVOLUTION

Barboach → (Lv. 30) → Whiscash

HOW TO OBTAIN

Pokémon Black Version 2	❶ Route 8 (Super Rod—ripples in water) ❷ Icirrus City (Super Rod—ripples in water)
Pokémon White Version 2	❶ Route 8 (Super Rod—ripples in water) ❷ Icirrus City (Super Rod—ripples in water)

HOW TO OBTAIN FROM OTHER GAMES

———

———

LEVEL-UP AND LEARNED MOVES

Lv.	Name	Type	Kind	Pow.	Acc.	PP	Range	Long	DA
1	Zen Headbutt	Psychic	Physical	80	90	15	Normal	—	○
1	Tickle	Normal	Status	—	100	20	Normal	—	—
1	Mud-Slap	Ground	Special	20	100	10	Normal	—	—
1	Mud Sport	Ground	Status	—	—	15	Both Sides	—	—
1	Water Sport	Water	Status	—	—	15	Both Sides	—	—
6	Mud Sport	Ground	Status	—	—	15	Both Sides	—	—
6	Water Sport	Water	Status	—	—	15	Both Sides	—	—
10	Water Gun	Water	Special	40	100	25	Normal	—	—
14	Mud Bomb	Ground	Special	65	85	10	Normal	—	—
18	Amnesia	Psychic	Status	—	—	20	Self	—	—
22	Water Pulse	Water	Special	60	100	20	Normal	○	—
26	Magnitude	Ground	Physical	—	100	30	Adjacent	—	—
33	Rest	Psychic	Status	—	—	10	Self	—	—
33	Snore	Normal	Special	40	100	15	Normal	—	—
39	Aqua Tail	Water	Physical	90	90	10	Normal	—	○
45	Earthquake	Ground	Physical	100	100	10	Adjacent	—	—
51	Future Sight	Psychic	Special	100	100	10	Normal	—	—
57	Fissure	Ground	Physical	—	30	5	Normal	—	—

TM & HM MOVES

Lv.	Name	Type	Kind	Pow.	Acc.	PP	Range	Long	DA
TM06	Toxic	Poison	Status	—	90	10	Normal	—	—
TM07	Hail	Ice	Status	—	—	10	Both Sides	—	—
TM10	Hidden Power	Normal	Special	—	100	15	Normal	—	—
TM13	Ice Beam	Ice	Special	95	100	10	Normal	—	—
TM14	Blizzard	Ice	Special	120	70	5	Many Others	—	—
TM15	Hyper Beam	Normal	Special	150	90	5	Normal	—	—
TM17	Protect	Normal	Status	—	—	10	Self	—	—
TM18	Rain Dance	Water	Status	—	—	5	Both Sides	—	—
TM21	Frustration	Normal	Physical	—	100	20	Normal	—	○
TM26	Earthquake	Ground	Physical	100	100	10	Adjacent	—	—
TM27	Return	Normal	Physical	—	100	20	Normal	—	○
TM32	Double Team	Normal	Status	—	—	15	Self	—	—
TM37	Sandstorm	Rock	Status	—	—	10	Both Sides	—	—
TM39	Rock Tomb	Rock	Physical	50	80	10	Normal	—	—
TM42	Facade	Normal	Physical	70	100	20	Normal	—	○
TM44	Rest	Psychic	Status	—	—	10	Self	—	—
TM45	Attract	Normal	Status	—	100	15	Normal	—	—
TM48	Round	Normal	Special	60	100	15	Normal	—	—
TM55	Scald	Water	Special	80	100	15	Normal	—	—
TM68	Giga Impact	Normal	Physical	150	90	5	Normal	—	—
TM71	Stone Edge	Rock	Physical	100	80	5	Normal	—	—
TM78	Bulldoze	Ground	Physical	60	100	20	Adjacent	—	—
TM80	Rock Slide	Rock	Physical	75	90	10	Many Others	—	—
TM87	Swagger	Normal	Status	—	90	15	Normal	—	—
TM90	Substitute	Normal	Status	—	—	10	Self	—	—
TM94	Rock Smash	Fighting	Physical	40	100	15	Normal	—	—
HM03	Surf	Water	Special	95	100	15	Adjacent	—	—
HM04	Strength	Normal	Physical	80	100	15	Normal	—	○
HM05	Waterfall	Water	Physical	80	100	15	Normal	—	○
HM06	Dive	Water	Physical	80	100	10	Normal	—	○

MOVES TAUGHT BY PEOPLE

Name	Type	Kind	Pow.	Acc.	PP	Range	Long	DA

MOVES TAUGHT BY MOVE TUTORS FOR SHARDS

Name	Type	Kind	Pow.	Acc.	PP	Range	Long	DA
Bounce	Flying	Physical	85	85	5	Normal	○	○
Icy Wind	Ice	Special	55	95	15	Many Others	—	—
Aqua Tail	Water	Physical	90	90	10	Normal	—	○
Earth Power	Ground	Special	90	100	10	Normal	—	—
Zen Headbutt	Psychic	Physical	80	90	15	Normal	—	○
Snore	Normal	Special	40	100	15	Normal	—	—
Sleep Talk	Normal	Status	—	—	10	Self	—	—

341 Corphish
Ruffian Pokémon

TYPE Water

ABILITIES
- Hyper Cutter
- Shell Armor

HIDDEN ABILITY
- Adaptability

- HEIGHT: 2'00"
- WEIGHT: 25.4 lbs.
- GENDER: ♂ / ♀

No matter how dirty the water in the river, it will adapt and thrive. It has a strong will to survive.

STATS
HP	■■
Attack	■■■
Defense	■■■
Sp. Atk	■■
Sp. Def	■■
Speed	■■

EGG GROUPS
Water ❶/Water ❸

ITEMS SOMETIMES HELD
- None

Same form for ♂ / ♀

Pokémon AR Marker

◉ EVOLUTION

Corphish — Lv. 30 → Crawdaunt

HOW TO OBTAIN
Pokémon Black Version 2	❶ Route 3 (water surface) ❷ Striaton City (water surface)
Pokémon White Version 2	❶ Route 3 (water surface) ❷ Striaton City (water surface)

HOW TO OBTAIN FROM OTHER GAMES
—
—

▌LEVEL-UP AND LEARNED MOVES▐
Lv.	Name	Type	Kind	Pow.	Acc.	PP	Range	Long	DA
1	Bubble	Water	Special	20	100	30	Many Others	—	—
7	Harden	Normal	Status	—	—	30	Self	—	—
10	ViceGrip	Normal	Physical	55	100	30	Many Others	—	○
13	Leer	Normal	Status	—	100	30	Many Others	—	—
20	BubbleBeam	Water	Special	65	100	20	Normal	—	—
23	Protect	Normal	Status	—	—	10	Self	—	—
26	Knock Off	Dark	Physical	20	100	20	Normal	—	○
32	Taunt	Dark	Status	—	100	20	Normal	—	—
35	Night Slash	Dark	Physical	70	100	15	Normal	—	○
38	Crabhammer	Water	Physical	90	90	10	Normal	—	○
44	Swords Dance	Normal	Status	—	—	30	Self	—	—
47	Crunch	Dark	Physical	80	100	15	Normal	—	○
53	Guillotine	Normal	Physical	—	30	5	Normal	—	○

▌TM & HM MOVES▐
Lv.	Name	Type	Kind	Pow.	Acc.	PP	Range	Long	DA
TM01	Hone Claws	Dark	Status	—	—	15	Self	—	—
TM06	Toxic	Poison	Status	—	90	10	Normal	—	—
TM07	Hail	Ice	Status	—	—	10	Both Sides	—	—
TM10	Hidden Power	Normal	Special	—	100	15	Normal	—	—
TM12	Taunt	Dark	Status	—	100	20	Normal	—	—
TM13	Ice Beam	Ice	Special	95	100	10	Normal	—	—
TM14	Blizzard	Ice	Special	120	70	5	Many Others	—	—
TM17	Protect	Normal	Status	—	—	10	Self	—	—
TM18	Rain Dance	Water	Status	—	—	5	Both Sides	—	—
TM21	Frustration	Normal	Physical	—	100	20	Normal	—	○
TM27	Return	Normal	Physical	—	100	20	Normal	—	○
TM28	Dig	Ground	Physical	80	100	10	Normal	—	○
TM31	Brick Break	Fighting	Physical	75	100	15	Normal	—	○
TM32	Double Team	Normal	Status	—	—	15	Self	—	—
TM36	Sludge Bomb	Poison	Special	90	100	10	Normal	—	—
TM39	Rock Tomb	Rock	Physical	50	80	10	Normal	—	○
TM40	Aerial Ace	Flying	Physical	60	—	20	Normal	○	○
TM42	Facade	Normal	Physical	70	100	20	Normal	—	○
TM44	Rest	Psychic	Status	—	—	10	Self	—	—
TM45	Attract	Normal	Status	—	100	15	Normal	—	—
TM48	Round	Normal	Special	60	100	15	Normal	—	—
TM54	False Swipe	Normal	Physical	40	100	40	Normal	—	○
TM55	Scald	Water	Special	80	100	15	Normal	—	—
TM56	Fling	Dark	Physical	—	100	10	Normal	—	○
TM66	Payback	Dark	Physical	50	100	10	Normal	—	○
TM75	Swords Dance	Normal	Status	—	—	30	Self	—	—
TM80	Rock Slide	Rock	Physical	75	90	10	Many Others	—	○
TM81	X-Scissor	Bug	Physical	80	100	15	Normal	—	○
TM87	Swagger	Normal	Status	—	90	15	Normal	—	—
TM90	Substitute	Normal	Status	—	—	10	Self	—	—
TM94	Rock Smash	Fighting	Physical	40	100	15	Normal	—	○
HM01	Cut	Normal	Physical	50	95	30	Normal	—	○
HM03	Surf	Water	Special	95	100	15	Adjacent	—	—
HM04	Strength	Normal	Physical	80	100	15	Normal	—	○
HM05	Waterfall	Water	Physical	80	100	15	Normal	—	○

▌MOVES TAUGHT BY PEOPLE▐
Name	Type	Kind	Pow.	Acc.	PP	Range	Long	DA

▌MOVES TAUGHT BY MOVE TUTORS FOR SHARDS▐
Name	Type	Kind	Pow.	Acc.	PP	Range	Long	DA
Iron Defense	Steel	Status	—	—	15	Self	—	—
Icy Wind	Ice	Special	55	95	15	Many Others	—	—
Superpower	Fighting	Physical	120	100	5	Normal	—	○
Snore	Normal	Special	40	100	15	Normal	—	—
Knock Off	Dark	Physical	20	100	20	Normal	—	○
Spite	Ghost	Status	—	100	10	Normal	—	—
Endeavor	Normal	Physical	—	100	5	Normal	—	○
Sleep Talk	Normal	Status	—	—	10	Self	—	—

▌EGG MOVES▐
Name	Type	Kind	Pow.	Acc.	PP	Range	Long	DA
Mud Sport	Ground	Status	—	—	15	Both Sides	—	○
Endeavor	Normal	Physical	—	100	5	Normal	—	○
Body Slam	Normal	Physical	85	100	15	Normal	—	○
AncientPower	Rock	Special	60	100	5	Normal	—	—
Knock Off	Dark	Physical	20	100	20	Normal	—	○
Superpower	Fighting	Physical	120	100	5	Normal	—	○
Metal Claw	Steel	Physical	50	95	35	Normal	—	○
Dragon Dance	Dragon	Status	—	—	20	Self	—	—
Trump Card	Normal	Special	—	—	5	Normal	—	—
Chip Away	Normal	Physical	70	100	20	Normal	—	○
Double-Edge	Normal	Physical	120	100	15	Normal	—	○

---

342 Crawdaunt
Rogue Pokémon

TYPE Water Dark

ABILITIES
- Hyper Cutter
- Shell Armor

HIDDEN ABILITY
- Adaptability

- HEIGHT: 3'07"
- WEIGHT: 72.3 lbs.
- GENDER: ♂ / ♀

Loving to battle, this Pokémon pinches all Pokémon that enter its territory with its pincers and throws them out.

STATS
HP	■■
Attack	■■■■■
Defense	■■■■
Sp. Atk	■■■
Sp. Def	■■
Speed	■■■

EGG GROUPS
Water ❶/Water ❸

ITEMS SOMETIMES HELD
- None

Same form for ♂ / ♀

Pokémon AR Marker

◉ EVOLUTION

Corphish — Lv. 30 → Crawdaunt

HOW TO OBTAIN
Pokémon Black Version 2	❶ Route 3 (ripples in water) ❷ Striaton City (ripples in water)
Pokémon White Version 2	❶ Route 3 (ripples in water) ❷ Striaton City (ripples in water)

HOW TO OBTAIN FROM OTHER GAMES
—
—

▌LEVEL-UP AND LEARNED MOVES▐
Lv.	Name	Type	Kind	Pow.	Acc.	PP	Range	Long	DA
1	Bubble	Water	Special	20	100	30	Many Others	—	—
1	Harden	Normal	Status	—	—	30	Self	—	—
1	ViceGrip	Normal	Physical	55	100	30	Normal	—	○
1	Leer	Normal	Status	—	100	30	Many Others	—	—
7	Harden	Normal	Status	—	—	30	Self	—	—
10	ViceGrip	Normal	Physical	55	100	30	Normal	—	○
13	Leer	Normal	Status	—	100	30	Many Others	—	—
20	BubbleBeam	Water	Special	65	100	20	Normal	—	—
23	Protect	Normal	Status	—	—	10	Self	—	—
26	Knock Off	Dark	Physical	20	100	20	Normal	—	○
30	Swift	Normal	Special	60	—	20	Many Others	—	—
34	Taunt	Dark	Status	—	100	20	Normal	—	—
39	Night Slash	Dark	Physical	70	100	15	Normal	—	○
44	Crabhammer	Water	Physical	90	90	10	Normal	—	○
52	Swords Dance	Normal	Status	—	—	30	Self	—	—
57	Crunch	Dark	Physical	80	100	15	Normal	—	○
65	Guillotine	Normal	Physical	—	30	5	Normal	—	○

▌TM & HM MOVES▐
Lv.	Name	Type	Kind	Pow.	Acc.	PP	Range	Long	DA
TM01	Hone Claws	Dark	Status	—	—	15	Self	—	—
TM06	Toxic	Poison	Status	—	90	10	Normal	—	—
TM07	Hail	Ice	Status	—	—	10	Both Sides	—	—
TM10	Hidden Power	Normal	Special	—	100	15	Normal	—	—
TM12	Taunt	Dark	Status	—	100	20	Normal	—	—
TM13	Ice Beam	Ice	Special	95	100	10	Normal	—	—
TM14	Blizzard	Ice	Special	120	70	5	Many Others	—	—
TM15	Hyper Beam	Normal	Special	150	90	5	Normal	—	—
TM17	Protect	Normal	Status	—	—	10	Self	—	—
TM18	Rain Dance	Water	Status	—	—	5	Both Sides	—	—
TM21	Frustration	Normal	Physical	—	100	20	Normal	—	○
TM27	Return	Normal	Physical	—	100	20	Normal	—	○
TM28	Dig	Ground	Physical	80	100	10	Normal	—	○
TM31	Brick Break	Fighting	Physical	75	100	15	Normal	—	○
TM32	Double Team	Normal	Status	—	—	15	Self	—	—
TM34	Sludge Wave	Poison	Special	95	100	10	Adjacent	—	—
TM36	Sludge Bomb	Poison	Special	90	100	10	Normal	—	—
TM39	Rock Tomb	Rock	Physical	50	80	10	Normal	—	○
TM40	Aerial Ace	Flying	Physical	60	—	20	Normal	○	○
TM42	Facade	Normal	Physical	70	100	20	Normal	—	○
TM44	Rest	Psychic	Status	—	—	10	Self	—	—
TM45	Attract	Normal	Status	—	100	15	Normal	—	—
TM48	Round	Normal	Special	60	100	15	Normal	—	—
TM54	False Swipe	Normal	Physical	40	100	40	Normal	—	○
TM55	Scald	Water	Special	80	100	15	Normal	—	—
TM56	Fling	Dark	Physical	—	100	10	Normal	—	○
TM66	Payback	Dark	Physical	50	100	10	Normal	—	○
TM67	Retaliate	Normal	Physical	70	100	5	Normal	—	○
TM68	Giga Impact	Normal	Physical	150	90	5	Normal	—	○
TM75	Swords Dance	Normal	Status	—	—	30	Self	—	—
TM80	Rock Slide	Rock	Physical	75	90	10	Many Others	—	○
TM81	X-Scissor	Bug	Physical	80	100	15	Normal	—	○
TM87	Swagger	Normal	Status	—	90	15	Normal	—	—
TM90	Substitute	Normal	Status	—	—	10	Self	—	—
TM94	Rock Smash	Fighting	Physical	40	100	15	Normal	—	○
TM95	Snarl	Dark	Special	55	95	15	Many Others	—	—

Lv.	Name	Type	Kind	Pow.	Acc.	PP	Range	Long	DA
HM01	Cut	Normal	Physical	50	95	30	Normal	—	○
HM03	Surf	Water	Special	95	100	15	Adjacent	—	—
HM04	Strength	Normal	Physical	80	100	15	Normal	—	○
HM05	Waterfall	Water	Physical	80	100	15	Normal	—	○
HM06	Dive	Water	Physical	80	100	10	Normal	—	—

▌MOVES TAUGHT BY PEOPLE▐
Name	Type	Kind	Pow.	Acc.	PP	Range	Long	DA

▌MOVES TAUGHT BY MOVE TUTORS FOR SHARDS▐
Name	Type	Kind	Pow.	Acc.	PP	Range	Long	DA
Iron Defense	Steel	Status	—	—	15	Self	—	—
Icy Wind	Ice	Special	55	95	15	Many Others	—	—
Superpower	Fighting	Physical	120	100	5	Normal	—	○
Dark Pulse	Dark	Special	80	100	15	Normal	○	—
Snore	Normal	Special	40	100	15	Normal	—	—
Knock Off	Dark	Physical	20	100	20	Normal	—	○
Spite	Ghost	Status	—	100	10	Normal	—	—
Endeavor	Normal	Physical	—	100	5	Normal	—	○
Sleep Talk	Normal	Status	—	—	10	Self	—	—

Clay Doll Pokémon
343 Baltoy

● HEIGHT: 1'08"
● WEIGHT: 47.4 lbs.
● GENDER: Unknown

Discovered in ancient ruins, it moves by spinning around and forms a group when it finds others.

Gender unknown

TYPE Ground Psychic

ABILITY
● Levitate

HIDDEN ABILITY
———

STATS
HP	■■
Attack	■■
Defense	■■■
Sp. Atk	■■
Sp. Def	■■■
Speed	■■■

EGG GROUPS
Mineral

ITEMS SOMETIMES HELD
● None

EVOLUTION

HOW TO OBTAIN

Pokémon Black Version 2	Relic Castle lowest floor passageway ③
Pokémon White Version 2	Relic Castle lowest floor passageway ③

HOW TO OBTAIN FROM OTHER GAMES

———
———

LEVEL-UP AND LEARNED MOVES

Lv.	Name	Type	Kind	Pow.	Acc.	PP	Range	Long	DA
1	Harden	Normal	Status	—	—	30	Self	—	—
1	Confusion	Psychic	Special	50	100	25	Normal	—	—
4	Rapid Spin	Normal	Physical	20	100	40	Normal	—	○
7	Mud-Slap	Ground	Special	20	100	10	Normal	—	—
10	Rock Tomb	Rock	Physical	50	80	10	Normal	—	—
13	Psybeam	Psychic	Special	65	100	20	Normal	—	—
17	Power Trick	Psychic	Status	—	—	10	Self	—	—
21	AncientPower	Rock	Special	60	100	5	Normal	—	—
25	Selfdestruct	Normal	Physical	200	100	5	Adjacent	—	—
28	Extrasensory	Psychic	Special	80	100	30	Normal	—	—
31	Cosmic Power	Psychic	Status	—	—	20	Self	—	—
34	Guard Split	Psychic	Status	—	—	10	Normal	—	—
34	Power Split	Psychic	Status	—	—	10	Normal	—	—
37	Earth Power	Ground	Special	90	100	10	Normal	—	—
41	Sandstorm	Rock	Status	—	—	10	Both Sides	—	—
45	Heal Block	Psychic	Status	—	100	15	Many Others	—	—
49	Explosion	Normal	Physical	250	100	5	Adjacent	—	—

TM & HM MOVES

Lv.	Name	Type	Kind	Pow.	Acc.	PP	Range	Long	DA
TM03	Psyshock	Psychic	Special	80	100	10	Normal	—	—
TM04	Calm Mind	Psychic	Status	—	—	20	Self	—	—
TM06	Toxic	Poison	Status	—	90	10	Normal	—	—
TM10	Hidden Power	Normal	Special	—	100	15	Normal	—	—
TM11	Sunny Day	Fire	Status	—	—	5	Both Sides	—	—
TM13	Ice Beam	Ice	Special	95	100	10	Normal	—	—
TM16	Light Screen	Psychic	Status	—	—	30	Your Side	—	—
TM17	Protect	Normal	Status	—	—	10	Self	—	—
TM18	Rain Dance	Water	Status	—	—	5	Both Sides	—	—
TM19	Telekinesis	Psychic	Status	—	—	15	Normal	—	—
TM20	Safeguard	Normal	Status	—	—	25	Your Side	—	—
TM21	Frustration	Normal	Physical	—	100	20	Normal	—	○
TM22	SolarBeam	Grass	Special	120	100	10	Normal	—	—
TM23	Smack Down	Rock	Physical	50	100	15	Normal	—	—
TM26	Earthquake	Ground	Physical	100	100	10	Adjacent	—	—
TM27	Return	Normal	Physical	—	100	20	Normal	—	○
TM28	Dig	Ground	Physical	80	100	10	Normal	—	○
TM29	Psychic	Psychic	Special	90	100	10	Normal	—	—
TM30	Shadow Ball	Ghost	Special	80	100	15	Normal	—	—
TM32	Double Team	Normal	Status	—	—	15	Self	—	—
TM33	Reflect	Psychic	Status	—	—	20	Your Side	—	—
TM37	Sandstorm	Rock	Status	—	—	10	Both Sides	—	—
TM39	Rock Tomb	Rock	Physical	50	80	10	Normal	—	—
TM42	Facade	Normal	Physical	70	100	20	Normal	—	○
TM44	Rest	Psychic	Status	—	—	10	Self	—	—
TM48	Round	Normal	Special	60	100	15	Normal	—	—
TM51	Ally Switch	Psychic	Status	—	—	15	Self	—	—
TM57	Charge Beam	Electric	Special	50	90	10	Normal	—	—
TM64	Explosion	Normal	Physical	250	100	5	Adjacent	—	—
TM69	Rock Polish	Rock	Status	—	—	20	Self	—	—
TM70	Flash	Normal	Status	—	100	20	Normal	—	—
TM74	Gyro Ball	Steel	Physical	—	100	5	Normal	—	○
TM77	Psych Up	Normal	Status	—	—	10	Normal	—	—
TM78	Bulldoze	Ground	Physical	60	100	20	Adjacent	—	—
TM80	Rock Slide	Rock	Physical	75	90	10	Many Others	—	—
TM85	Dream Eater	Psychic	Special	100	100	15	Normal	—	—
TM86	Grass Knot	Grass	Special	—	100	20	Normal	—	○
TM87	Swagger	Normal	Status	—	90	15	Normal	—	—
TM90	Substitute	Normal	Status	—	—	10	Self	—	—
TM92	Trick Room	Psychic	Status	—	—	5	Both Sides	—	—

MOVES TAUGHT BY PEOPLE

Name	Type	Kind	Pow.	Acc.	PP	Range	Long	DA

MOVES TAUGHT BY MOVE TUTORS FOR SHARDS

Name	Type	Kind	Pow.	Acc.	PP	Range	Long	DA
Drill Run	Ground	Physical	80	95	10	Normal	—	○
Signal Beam	Bug	Special	75	100	15	Normal	—	—
Magic Coat	Psychic	Status	—	—	15	Self	—	—
Earth Power	Ground	Special	90	100	10	Normal	—	—
Zen Headbutt	Psychic	Physical	80	90	15	Normal	—	○
Gravity	Psychic	Status	—	—	5	Both Sides	—	—
Snore	Normal	Special	40	100	15	Normal	—	—
Wonder Room	Psychic	Status	—	—	10	Both Sides	—	—
Recycle	Normal	Status	—	—	10	Self	—	—
Trick	Psychic	Status	—	100	10	Normal	—	—
Stealth Rock	Rock	Status	—	—	20	Other Side	—	—
Sleep Talk	Normal	Status	—	—	10	Self	—	—
Skill Swap	Psychic	Status	—	—	10	Normal	—	—

EGG MOVES

Name	Type	Kind	Pow.	Acc.	PP	Range	Long	DA

Pokémon AR Marker

Clay Doll Pokémon
344 Claydol

● HEIGHT: 4'11"
● WEIGHT: 238.1 lbs.
● GENDER: Unknown

This mysterious Pokémon started life as an ancient clay figurine made over 20,000 years ago.

Gender unknown

TYPE Ground Psychic

ABILITY
● Levitate

HIDDEN ABILITY
———

STATS
HP	■■■
Attack	■■■■
Defense	■■■■■
Sp. Atk	■■■■
Sp. Def	■■■■■
Speed	■■■■

EGG GROUPS
Mineral

ITEMS SOMETIMES HELD
● None

EVOLUTION

HOW TO OBTAIN

Pokémon Black Version 2	Level up Baltoy to Lv. 36
Pokémon White Version 2	Level up Baltoy to Lv. 36

HOW TO OBTAIN FROM OTHER GAMES

———
———

LEVEL-UP AND LEARNED MOVES

Lv.	Name	Type	Kind	Pow.	Acc.	PP	Range	Long	DA
1	Teleport	Psychic	Status	—	—	20	Self	—	—
1	Harden	Normal	Status	—	—	30	Self	—	—
1	Confusion	Psychic	Special	50	100	25	Normal	—	—
1	Rapid Spin	Normal	Physical	20	100	40	Normal	—	○
4	Rapid Spin	Normal	Physical	20	100	40	Normal	—	○
7	Mud-Slap	Ground	Special	20	100	10	Normal	—	—
10	Rock Tomb	Rock	Physical	50	80	10	Normal	—	—
13	Psybeam	Psychic	Special	65	100	20	Normal	—	—
17	Power Trick	Psychic	Status	—	—	10	Self	—	—
21	AncientPower	Rock	Special	60	100	5	Normal	—	—
25	Selfdestruct	Normal	Physical	200	100	5	Adjacent	—	—
28	Extrasensory	Psychic	Special	80	100	30	Normal	—	—
31	Cosmic Power	Psychic	Status	—	—	20	Self	—	—
34	Guard Split	Psychic	Status	—	—	10	Normal	—	—
34	Power Split	Psychic	Status	—	—	10	Normal	—	—
36	Hyper Beam	Normal	Special	150	90	5	Normal	—	—
40	Earth Power	Ground	Special	90	100	10	Normal	—	—
47	Sandstorm	Rock	Status	—	—	10	Both Sides	—	—
54	Heal Block	Psychic	Status	—	100	15	Many Others	—	—
61	Explosion	Normal	Physical	250	100	5	Adjacent	—	—

TM & HM MOVES

Lv.	Name	Type	Kind	Pow.	Acc.	PP	Range	Long	DA
TM03	Psyshock	Psychic	Special	80	100	10	Normal	—	—
TM04	Calm Mind	Psychic	Status	—	—	20	Self	—	—
TM06	Toxic	Poison	Status	—	90	10	Normal	—	—
TM10	Hidden Power	Normal	Special	—	100	15	Normal	—	—
TM11	Sunny Day	Fire	Status	—	—	5	Both Sides	—	—
TM13	Ice Beam	Ice	Special	95	100	10	Normal	—	—
TM15	Hyper Beam	Normal	Special	150	90	5	Normal	—	—
TM16	Light Screen	Psychic	Status	—	—	30	Your Side	—	—
TM17	Protect	Normal	Status	—	—	10	Self	—	—
TM18	Rain Dance	Water	Status	—	—	5	Both Sides	—	—
TM19	Telekinesis	Psychic	Status	—	—	15	Normal	—	—
TM20	Safeguard	Normal	Status	—	—	25	Your Side	—	—
TM21	Frustration	Normal	Physical	—	100	20	Normal	—	○
TM22	SolarBeam	Grass	Special	120	100	10	Normal	—	—
TM23	Smack Down	Rock	Physical	50	100	15	Normal	—	—
TM26	Earthquake	Ground	Physical	100	100	10	Adjacent	—	—
TM27	Return	Normal	Physical	—	100	20	Normal	—	○
TM28	Dig	Ground	Physical	80	100	10	Normal	—	○
TM29	Psychic	Psychic	Special	90	100	10	Normal	—	—
TM30	Shadow Ball	Ghost	Special	80	100	15	Normal	—	—
TM32	Double Team	Normal	Status	—	—	15	Self	—	—
TM33	Reflect	Psychic	Status	—	—	20	Your Side	—	—
TM37	Sandstorm	Rock	Status	—	—	10	Both Sides	—	—
TM39	Rock Tomb	Rock	Physical	50	80	10	Normal	—	—
TM42	Facade	Normal	Physical	70	100	20	Normal	—	○
TM44	Rest	Psychic	Status	—	—	10	Self	—	—
TM48	Round	Normal	Special	60	100	15	Normal	—	—
TM51	Ally Switch	Psychic	Status	—	—	15	Self	—	—
TM57	Charge Beam	Electric	Special	50	90	10	Normal	—	—
TM64	Explosion	Normal	Physical	250	100	5	Adjacent	—	—
TM68	Giga Impact	Normal	Physical	150	90	5	Normal	—	○
TM69	Rock Polish	Rock	Status	—	—	20	Self	—	—
TM70	Flash	Normal	Status	—	100	20	Normal	—	—
TM71	Stone Edge	Rock	Physical	100	80	5	Normal	—	—
TM74	Gyro Ball	Steel	Physical	—	100	5	Normal	—	○
TM77	Psych Up	Normal	Status	—	—	10	Normal	—	—
TM78	Bulldoze	Ground	Physical	60	100	20	Adjacent	—	—
TM80	Rock Slide	Rock	Physical	75	90	10	Many Others	—	—
TM85	Dream Eater	Psychic	Special	100	100	15	Normal	—	—
TM86	Grass Knot	Grass	Special	—	100	20	Normal	—	○
TM87	Swagger	Normal	Status	—	90	15	Normal	—	—
TM90	Substitute	Normal	Status	—	—	10	Self	—	—
TM92	Trick Room	Psychic	Status	—	—	5	Both Sides	—	—
TM94	Rock Smash	Fighting	Physical	40	100	15	Normal	—	○
HM04	Strength	Normal	Physical	80	100	15	Normal	—	○

MOVES TAUGHT BY PEOPLE

Name	Type	Kind	Pow.	Acc.	PP	Range	Long	DA

MOVES TAUGHT BY MOVE TUTORS FOR SHARDS

Name	Type	Kind	Pow.	Acc.	PP	Range	Long	DA
Drill Run	Ground	Physical	80	95	10	Normal	—	○
Signal Beam	Bug	Special	75	100	15	Normal	—	—
Magic Coat	Psychic	Status	—	—	15	Self	—	—
Earth Power	Ground	Special	90	100	10	Normal	—	—
Zen Headbutt	Psychic	Physical	80	90	15	Normal	—	○
Gravity	Psychic	Status	—	—	5	Both Sides	—	—
Snore	Normal	Special	40	100	15	Normal	—	—
Wonder Room	Psychic	Status	—	—	10	Both Sides	—	—
Recycle	Normal	Status	—	—	10	Self	—	—
Trick	Psychic	Status	—	100	10	Normal	—	—
Stealth Rock	Rock	Status	—	—	20	Other Side	—	—
Sleep Talk	Normal	Status	—	—	10	Self	—	—
Skill Swap	Psychic	Status	—	—	10	Normal	—	—

Pokémon AR Marker

Sea Lily Pokémon

345 Lileep

● HEIGHT: 3'03"
● WEIGHT: 52.5 lbs.
● GENDER: ♂ / ♀

It lived on the seafloor 100 million years ago and was reanimated scientifically.

Same form for ♂ / ♀

TYPE Rock Grass

ABILITY
● Suction Cups

HIDDEN ABILITY
● Storm Drain

STATS
HP
Attack
Defense
Sp. Atk
Sp. Def
Speed

EGG GROUPS
Water ❸

ITEMS SOMETIMES HELD
● None

EVOLUTION

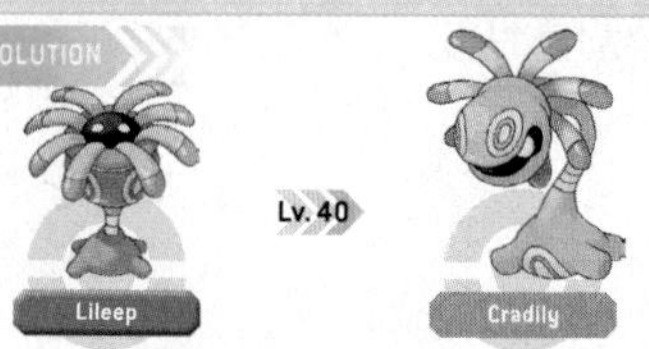

HOW TO OBTAIN

Pokémon Black Version 2	Get the Root Fossil in Twist Mountain and have it restored at the Nacrene Museum
Pokémon White Version 2	Get the Root Fossil in Twist Mountain and have it restored at the Nacrene Museum

HOW TO OBTAIN FROM OTHER GAMES

—

—

Pokémon AR Marker

LEVEL-UP AND LEARNED MOVES

Lv.	Name	Type	Kind	Pow.	Acc.	PP	Range	Long	DA
1	Astonish	Ghost	Physical	30	100	15	Normal	—	○
1	Constrict	Normal	Physical	10	100	35	Normal	—	○
8	Acid	Poison	Special	40	100	30	Many Others	—	—
15	Ingrain	Grass	Status	—	—	20	Self	—	—
22	Confuse Ray	Ghost	Status	—	100	10	Normal	—	—
29	Amnesia	Psychic	Status	—	—	20	Self	—	—
36	Gastro Acid	Poison	Status	—	100	10	Normal	—	—
43	AncientPower	Rock	Special	60	100	5	Normal	—	—
50	Energy Ball	Grass	Special	80	100	10	Normal	—	—
57	Stockpile	Normal	Status	—	—	20	Self	—	—
57	Spit Up	Normal	Special	—	100	10	Normal	—	—
57	Swallow	Normal	Status	—	—	10	Self	—	—
64	Wring Out	Normal	Special	—	100	5	Normal	—	○

TM & HM MOVES

Lv.	Name	Type	Kind	Pow.	Acc.	PP	Range	Long	DA
TM06	Toxic	Poison	Status	—	90	10	Normal	—	—
TM10	Hidden Power	Normal	Special	—	100	15	Normal	—	—
TM11	Sunny Day	Fire	Status	—	—	5	Both Sides	—	—
TM17	Protect	Normal	Status	—	—	10	Self	—	—
TM21	Frustration	Normal	Physical	—	100	20	Normal	—	○
TM22	SolarBeam	Grass	Special	120	100	10	Normal	—	—
TM23	Smack Down	Rock	Physical	50	100	15	Normal	—	—
TM27	Return	Normal	Physical	—	100	20	Normal	—	○
TM32	Double Team	Normal	Status	—	—	15	Self	—	—
TM36	Sludge Bomb	Poison	Special	90	100	10	Normal	—	—
TM37	Sandstorm	Rock	Status	—	—	10	Both Sides	—	—
TM39	Rock Tomb	Rock	Physical	50	80	10	Normal	—	—
TM42	Facade	Normal	Physical	70	100	20	Normal	—	○
TM44	Rest	Psychic	Status	—	—	10	Self	—	—
TM45	Attract	Normal	Status	—	100	15	Normal	—	—
TM48	Round	Normal	Special	60	100	15	Normal	—	—
TM53	Energy Ball	Grass	Special	80	100	10	Normal	—	—
TM69	Rock Polish	Rock	Status	—	—	20	Self	—	—
TM70	Flash	Normal	Status	—	100	20	Normal	—	—
TM75	Swords Dance	Normal	Status	—	—	30	Self	—	—
TM80	Rock Slide	Rock	Physical	75	90	10	Many Others	—	—
TM86	Grass Knot	Grass	Special	—	100	20	Normal	—	○
TM87	Swagger	Normal	Status	—	90	15	Normal	—	—
TM90	Substitute	Normal	Status	—	—	10	Self	—	—

MOVES TAUGHT BY PEOPLE

Name	Type	Kind	Pow.	Acc.	PP	Range	Long	DA

MOVES TAUGHT BY MOVE TUTORS FOR SHARDS

Name	Type	Kind	Pow.	Acc.	PP	Range	Long	DA
Seed Bomb	Grass	Physical	80	100	15	Normal	—	—
Earth Power	Ground	Special	90	100	10	Normal	—	—
Bind	Normal	Physical	15	85	20	Normal	—	○
Snore	Normal	Special	40	100	15	Normal	—	—
Synthesis	Grass	Status	—	—	5	Self	—	—
Giga Drain	Grass	Special	75	100	10	Normal	—	—
Pain Split	Normal	Status	—	—	20	Normal	—	—
Worry Seed	Grass	Status	—	100	10	Normal	—	—
Gastro Acid	Poison	Status	—	100	10	Normal	—	—
Stealth Rock	Rock	Status	—	—	20	Other Side	—	—
Sleep Talk	Normal	Status	—	—	10	Self	—	—

EGG MOVES

Name	Type	Kind	Pow.	Acc.	PP	Range	Long	DA
Barrier	Psychic	Status	—	—	30	Self	—	—
Recover	Normal	Status	—	—	10	Self	—	—
Mirror Coat	Psychic	Special	—	100	20	Varies	—	—
Wring Out	Normal	Special	—	100	5	Normal	—	○
Tickle	Normal	Status	—	100	20	Normal	—	—
Curse	Ghost	Status	—	—	10	Varies	—	—
Mega Drain	Grass	Special	40	100	15	Normal	—	—
Endure	Normal	Status	—	—	10	Self	—	—
Stealth Rock	Rock	Status	—	—	20	Other Side	—	—

Barnacle Pokémon

346 Cradily

● HEIGHT: 4'11"
● WEIGHT: 133.2 lbs.
● GENDER: ♂ / ♀

It lives in the shallows of warm seas. When the tide goes out, it digs up prey from beaches.

Same form for ♂ / ♀

TYPE Rock Grass

ABILITY
● Suction Cups

HIDDEN ABILITY
● Storm Drain

STATS
HP
Attack
Defense
Sp. Atk
Sp. Def
Speed

EGG GROUPS
Water ❸

ITEMS SOMETIMES HELD
● None

EVOLUTION

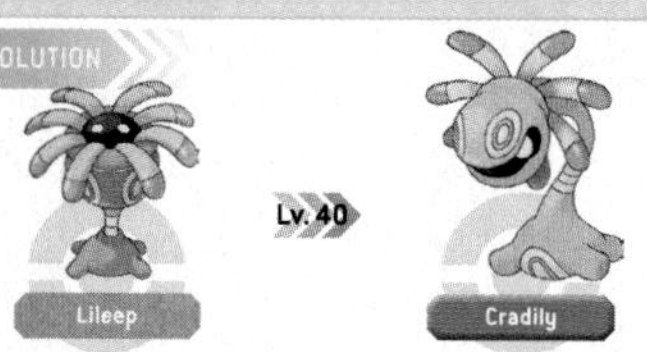

HOW TO OBTAIN

Pokémon Black Version 2	Level up Lileep to Lv. 40
Pokémon White Version 2	Level up Lileep to Lv. 40

HOW TO OBTAIN FROM OTHER GAMES

—

—

Pokémon AR Marker

LEVEL-UP AND LEARNED MOVES

Lv.	Name	Type	Kind	Pow.	Acc.	PP	Range	Long	DA
1	Astonish	Ghost	Physical	30	100	15	Normal	—	○
1	Constrict	Normal	Physical	10	100	35	Normal	—	○
1	Acid	Poison	Special	40	100	30	Many Others	—	—
1	Ingrain	Grass	Status	—	—	20	Self	—	—
8	Acid	Poison	Special	40	100	30	Many Others	—	—
15	Ingrain	Grass	Status	—	—	20	Self	—	—
22	Confuse Ray	Ghost	Status	—	100	10	Normal	—	—
29	Amnesia	Psychic	Status	—	—	20	Self	—	—
36	AncientPower	Rock	Special	60	100	5	Normal	—	—
46	Gastro Acid	Poison	Status	—	100	10	Normal	—	—
56	Energy Ball	Grass	Special	80	100	10	Normal	—	—
66	Stockpile	Normal	Status	—	—	20	Self	—	—
66	Spit Up	Normal	Special	—	100	10	Normal	—	—
66	Swallow	Normal	Status	—	—	10	Self	—	—
76	Wring Out	Normal	Special	—	100	5	Normal	—	○

TM & HM MOVES

Lv.	Name	Type	Kind	Pow.	Acc.	PP	Range	Long	DA
TM06	Toxic	Poison	Status	—	90	10	Normal	—	—
TM10	Hidden Power	Normal	Special	—	100	15	Normal	—	—
TM11	Sunny Day	Fire	Status	—	—	5	Both Sides	—	—
TM15	Hyper Beam	Normal	Special	150	90	5	Normal	—	—
TM17	Protect	Normal	Status	—	—	10	Self	—	—
TM21	Frustration	Normal	Physical	—	100	20	Normal	—	○
TM22	SolarBeam	Grass	Special	120	100	10	Normal	—	—
TM23	Smack Down	Rock	Physical	50	100	15	Normal	—	—
TM26	Earthquake	Ground	Physical	100	100	10	Adjacent	—	—
TM27	Return	Normal	Physical	—	100	20	Normal	—	○
TM32	Double Team	Normal	Status	—	—	15	Self	—	—
TM34	Sludge Wave	Poison	Special	95	100	10	Adjacent	—	—
TM36	Sludge Bomb	Poison	Special	90	100	10	Normal	—	—
TM37	Sandstorm	Rock	Status	—	—	10	Both Sides	—	—
TM39	Rock Tomb	Rock	Physical	50	80	10	Normal	—	—
TM42	Facade	Normal	Physical	70	100	20	Normal	—	○
TM44	Rest	Psychic	Status	—	—	10	Self	—	—
TM45	Attract	Normal	Status	—	100	15	Normal	—	—
TM48	Round	Normal	Special	60	100	15	Normal	—	—
TM53	Energy Ball	Grass	Special	80	100	10	Normal	—	—
TM68	Giga Impact	Normal	Physical	150	90	5	Normal	—	○
TM69	Rock Polish	Rock	Status	—	—	20	Self	—	—
TM70	Flash	Normal	Status	—	100	20	Normal	—	—
TM71	Stone Edge	Rock	Physical	100	80	5	Normal	—	—
TM75	Swords Dance	Normal	Status	—	—	30	Self	—	—
TM78	Bulldoze	Ground	Physical	60	100	20	Adjacent	—	—
TM80	Rock Slide	Rock	Physical	75	90	10	Many Others	—	—
TM86	Grass Knot	Grass	Special	—	100	20	Normal	—	○
TM87	Swagger	Normal	Status	—	90	15	Normal	—	—
TM90	Substitute	Normal	Status	—	—	10	Self	—	—
TM94	Rock Smash	Fighting	Physical	40	100	15	Normal	—	○
HM04	Strength	Normal	Physical	80	100	15	Normal	—	○

MOVES TAUGHT BY PEOPLE

Name	Type	Kind	Pow.	Acc.	PP	Range	Long	DA

MOVES TAUGHT BY MOVE TUTORS FOR SHARDS

Name	Type	Kind	Pow.	Acc.	PP	Range	Long	DA
Seed Bomb	Grass	Physical	80	100	15	Normal	—	—
Block	Normal	Status	—	—	5	Normal	—	—
Earth Power	Ground	Special	90	100	10	Normal	—	—
Bind	Normal	Physical	15	85	20	Normal	—	○
Snore	Normal	Special	40	100	15	Normal	—	—
Synthesis	Grass	Status	—	—	5	Self	—	—
Giga Drain	Grass	Special	75	100	10	Normal	—	—
Pain Split	Normal	Status	—	—	20	Normal	—	—
Worry Seed	Grass	Status	—	100	10	Normal	—	—
Gastro Acid	Poison	Status	—	100	10	Normal	—	—
Stealth Rock	Rock	Status	—	—	20	Other Side	—	—
Sleep Talk	Normal	Status	—	—	10	Self	—	—

Anorith

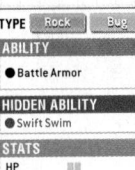

Old Shrimp Pokémon

347 Anorith

- HEIGHT: 2'04"
- WEIGHT: 27.6 lbs.
- GENDER: ♂ / ♀

A Pokémon ancestor that was reanimated from a fossil. It lived in the sea and hunted with claws.

Same form for ♂ / ♀

Pokémon AR Marker

TYPE Rock Bug

ABILITY
- Battle Armor

HIDDEN ABILITY
- Swift Swim

STATS
- HP
- Attack
- Defense
- Sp. Atk
- Sp. Def
- Speed

EGG GROUPS
Water ❸

ITEMS SOMETIMES HELD
- None

EVOLUTION

Anorith — Lv. 40 → Armaldo

HOW TO OBTAIN

Pokémon Black Version 2	Get the Claw Fossil in Twist Mountain and have it restored at the Nacrene Museum
Pokémon White Version 2	Get the Claw Fossil in Twist Mountain and have it restored at the Nacrene Museum

HOW TO OBTAIN FROM OTHER GAMES

LEVEL-UP AND LEARNED MOVES

Lv.	Name	Type	Kind	Pow.	Acc.	PP	Range	Long	DA
1	Scratch	Normal	Physical	40	100	35	Normal	—	○
1	Harden	Normal	Status	—	—	30	Self	—	—
7	Mud Sport	Ground	Status	—	—	15	Both Sides	—	—
13	Water Gun	Water	Special	40	100	25	Normal	—	—
19	Metal Claw	Steel	Physical	50	95	35	Normal	—	○
25	Protect	Normal	Status	—	—	10	Self	—	—
31	AncientPower	Rock	Special	60	100	5	Normal	—	—
37	Fury Cutter	Bug	Physical	20	95	20	Normal	—	○
43	Slash	Normal	Physical	70	100	20	Normal	—	○
49	Rock Blast	Rock	Physical	25	90	10	Normal	—	○
55	Crush Claw	Normal	Physical	75	95	10	Normal	—	○
61	X-Scissor	Bug	Physical	80	100	15	Normal	—	○

TM & HM MOVES

Lv.	Name	Type	Kind	Pow.	Acc.	PP	Range	Long	DA
TM01	Hone Claws	Dark	Status	—	—	15	Self	—	—
TM06	Toxic	Poison	Status	—	90	10	Normal	—	—
TM10	Hidden Power	Normal	Special	—	100	15	Normal	—	—
TM11	Sunny Day	Fire	Status	—	—	5	Both Sides	—	—
TM17	Protect	Normal	Status	—	—	10	Self	—	—
TM21	Frustration	Normal	Physical	—	100	20	Normal	—	○
TM23	Smack Down	Rock	Physical	50	100	15	Normal	—	—
TM27	Return	Normal	Physical	—	100	20	Normal	—	○
TM28	Dig	Ground	Physical	80	100	10	Normal	—	—
TM31	Brick Break	Fighting	Physical	75	100	15	Normal	—	○
TM32	Double Team	Normal	Status	—	—	15	Self	—	—
TM37	Sandstorm	Normal	Status	—	—	10	Both Sides	—	—
TM39	Rock Tomb	Rock	Physical	50	80	10	Normal	—	—
TM40	Aerial Ace	Flying	Physical	60	—	20	Normal	○	○
TM42	Facade	Normal	Physical	70	100	20	Normal	—	○
TM44	Rest	Psychic	Status	—	—	10	Self	—	—
TM45	Attract	Normal	Status	—	100	15	Normal	—	—
TM48	Round	Normal	Special	60	100	15	Normal	—	—
TM54	False Swipe	Normal	Physical	40	100	40	Normal	—	○
TM69	Rock Polish	Rock	Status	—	—	20	Self	—	—
TM75	Swords Dance	Normal	Status	—	—	30	Self	—	—
TM76	Struggle Bug	Bug	Special	30	100	20	Many Others	—	—
TM80	Rock Slide	Rock	Physical	75	90	10	Many Others	—	—
TM81	X-Scissor	Bug	Physical	80	100	15	Normal	—	○
TM87	Swagger	Normal	Status	—	90	15	Normal	—	—
TM90	Substitute	Normal	Status	—	—	10	Self	—	—
TM94	Rock Smash	Fighting	Physical	40	100	15	Normal	—	○
HM01	Cut	Normal	Physical	50	95	30	Normal	—	○

MOVES TAUGHT BY PEOPLE

Name	Type	Kind	Pow.	Acc.	PP	Range	Long	DA

MOVES TAUGHT BY MOVE TUTORS FOR SHARDS

Name	Type	Kind	Pow.	Acc.	PP	Range	Long	DA
Bug Bite	Bug	Physical	60	100	20	Normal	—	○
Iron Defense	Steel	Status	—	—	15	Self	—	—
Earth Power	Ground	Special	90	100	10	Normal	—	—
Snore	Normal	Special	40	100	15	Normal	—	—
Knock Off	Dark	Physical	20	100	20	Normal	—	○
Stealth Rock	Rock	Status	—	—	20	Other Side	—	—
Sleep Talk	Normal	Status	—	—	10	Self	—	—

EGG MOVES

Name	Type	Kind	Pow.	Acc.	PP	Range	Long	DA
Rapid Spin	Normal	Physical	20	100	40	Normal	—	○
Knock Off	Dark	Physical	20	100	20	Normal	—	○
Screech	Normal	Status	—	85	40	Normal	—	—
Sand-Attack	Ground	Status	—	100	15	Normal	—	—
Cross Poison	Poison	Physical	70	100	20	Normal	—	○
Curse	Ghost	Status	—	—	10	Varies	—	—
Iron Defense	Steel	Status	—	—	15	Self	—	—
Water Pulse	Water	Special	60	100	20	Normal	—	○

Armaldo

Plate Pokémon

348 Armaldo

- HEIGHT: 4'11"
- WEIGHT: 150.4 lbs.
- GENDER: ♂ / ♀

It went ashore after evolving. Its entire body is clad in a sturdy armor.

Same form for ♂ / ♀

Pokémon AR Marker

TYPE Rock Bug

ABILITY
- Battle Armor

HIDDEN ABILITY
- Swift Swim

STATS
- HP
- Attack
- Defense
- Sp. Atk
- Sp. Def
- Speed

EGG GROUPS
Water ❸

ITEMS SOMETIMES HELD
- None

EVOLUTION

Anorith — Lv. 40 → Armaldo

HOW TO OBTAIN

Pokémon Black Version 2	Level up Anorith to Lv. 40
Pokémon White Version 2	Level up Anorith to Lv. 40

HOW TO OBTAIN FROM OTHER GAMES

LEVEL-UP AND LEARNED MOVES

Lv.	Name	Type	Kind	Pow.	Acc.	PP	Range	Long	DA
1	Scratch	Normal	Physical	40	100	35	Normal	—	○
1	Harden	Normal	Status	—	—	30	Self	—	—
1	Mud Sport	Ground	Status	—	—	15	Both Sides	—	—
1	Water Gun	Water	Special	40	100	25	Normal	—	—
7	Mud Sport	Ground	Status	—	—	15	Both Sides	—	—
13	Water Gun	Water	Special	40	100	25	Normal	—	—
19	Metal Claw	Steel	Physical	50	95	35	Normal	—	○
25	Protect	Normal	Status	—	—	10	Self	—	—
31	AncientPower	Rock	Special	60	100	5	Normal	—	—
37	Fury Cutter	Bug	Physical	20	95	20	Normal	—	○
46	Slash	Normal	Physical	70	100	20	Normal	—	○
55	Rock Blast	Rock	Physical	25	90	10	Normal	—	○
67	Crush Claw	Normal	Physical	75	95	10	Normal	—	○
73	X-Scissor	Bug	Physical	80	100	15	Normal	—	○

TM & HM MOVES

Lv.	Name	Type	Kind	Pow.	Acc.	PP	Range	Long	DA
TM01	Hone Claws	Dark	Status	—	—	15	Self	—	—
TM06	Toxic	Poison	Status	—	90	10	Normal	—	—
TM10	Hidden Power	Normal	Special	—	100	15	Normal	—	—
TM11	Sunny Day	Fire	Status	—	—	5	Both Sides	—	—
TM15	Hyper Beam	Normal	Special	150	90	5	Normal	—	—
TM17	Protect	Normal	Status	—	—	10	Self	—	—
TM21	Frustration	Normal	Physical	—	100	20	Normal	—	○
TM23	Smack Down	Rock	Physical	50	100	15	Normal	—	—
TM26	Earthquake	Ground	Physical	100	100	10	Adjacent	—	—
TM27	Return	Normal	Physical	—	100	20	Normal	—	○
TM28	Dig	Ground	Physical	80	100	10	Normal	—	—
TM31	Brick Break	Fighting	Physical	75	100	15	Normal	—	○
TM32	Double Team	Normal	Status	—	—	15	Self	—	—
TM37	Sandstorm	Normal	Status	—	—	10	Both Sides	—	—
TM39	Rock Tomb	Rock	Physical	50	80	10	Normal	—	—
TM40	Aerial Ace	Flying	Physical	60	—	20	Normal	○	○
TM42	Facade	Normal	Physical	70	100	20	Normal	—	○
TM44	Rest	Psychic	Status	—	—	10	Self	—	—
TM45	Attract	Normal	Status	—	100	15	Normal	—	—
TM48	Round	Normal	Special	60	100	15	Normal	—	—
TM54	False Swipe	Normal	Physical	40	100	40	Normal	—	○
TM68	Giga Impact	Normal	Physical	150	90	5	Normal	—	—
TM69	Rock Polish	Rock	Status	—	—	20	Self	—	—
TM71	Stone Edge	Rock	Physical	100	80	5	Normal	—	—
TM75	Swords Dance	Normal	Status	—	—	30	Self	—	—
TM76	Struggle Bug	Bug	Special	30	100	20	Many Others	—	—
TM78	Bulldoze	Ground	Physical	60	100	20	Adjacent	—	—
TM80	Rock Slide	Rock	Physical	75	90	10	Many Others	—	—
TM81	X-Scissor	Bug	Physical	80	100	15	Normal	—	○
TM87	Swagger	Normal	Status	—	90	15	Normal	—	—
TM90	Substitute	Normal	Status	—	—	10	Self	—	—
TM91	Flash Cannon	Steel	Special	80	100	10	Normal	—	—
TM94	Rock Smash	Fighting	Physical	40	100	15	Normal	—	○
HM01	Cut	Normal	Physical	50	95	30	Normal	—	○
HM04	Strength	Normal	Physical	80	100	15	Normal	—	—

MOVES TAUGHT BY PEOPLE

Name	Type	Kind	Pow.	Acc.	PP	Range	Long	DA

MOVES TAUGHT BY MOVE TUTORS FOR SHARDS

Name	Type	Kind	Pow.	Acc.	PP	Range	Long	DA
Bug Bite	Bug	Physical	60	100	20	Normal	—	○
Low Kick	Fighting	Physical	—	100	20	Normal	—	○
Iron Defense	Steel	Status	—	—	15	Self	—	—
Block	Normal	Status	—	100	5	Normal	—	—
Iron Tail	Steel	Physical	100	75	15	Normal	—	—
Aqua Tail	Water	Physical	90	90	10	Normal	—	—
Earth Power	Ground	Special	90	100	10	Normal	—	—
Superpower	Fighting	Physical	120	100	5	Normal	—	—
Snore	Normal	Special	40	100	15	Normal	—	—
Knock Off	Dark	Physical	20	100	20	Normal	—	○
Stealth Rock	Rock	Status	—	—	20	Other Side	—	—
Sleep Talk	Normal	Status	—	—	10	Self	—	—

349 Feebas
Fish Pokémon

- HEIGHT: 2'00"
- WEIGHT: 16.3 lbs.
- GENDER: ♂ / ♀

It is a shabby and ugly Pokémon. However, it is very hardy and can survive on little water.

Same form for ♂ / ♀

Pokémon AR Marker

TYPE Water

ABILITY
- Swift Swim

HIDDEN ABILITY
- Adaptability

STATS
HP
Attack
Defense
Sp. Atk
Sp. Def
Speed

EGG GROUPS
Water ❶ / Dragon

ITEMS SOMETIMES HELD
- None

EVOLUTION
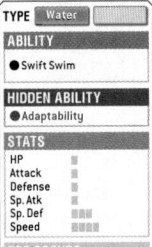 Feebas → (Have it hold Prism Scale and Link Trade it) →  Milotic

HOW TO OBTAIN
Pokémon Black Version 2	Route 1 (Super Rod)
Pokémon White Version 2	Route 1 (Super Rod)

HOW TO OBTAIN FROM OTHER GAMES

LEVEL-UP AND LEARNED MOVES
Lv.	Name	Type	Kind	Pow.	Acc.	PP	Range	Long	DA
1	Splash	Normal	Status	—	—	40	Self	—	—
15	Tackle	Normal	Physical	50	100	35	Normal	—	○
30	Flail	Normal	Physical	—	100	15	Normal	—	○

TM & HM MOVES
Lv.	Name	Type	Kind	Pow.	Acc.	PP	Range	Long	DA
TM06	Toxic	Poison	Status	—	90	10	Normal	—	—
TM07	Hail	Ice	Status	—	—	10	Both Sides	—	—
TM10	Hidden Power	Normal	Special	—	100	15	Normal	—	—
TM13	Ice Beam	Ice	Special	95	100	10	Normal	—	—
TM14	Blizzard	Ice	Special	120	70	5	Many Others	—	—
TM16	Light Screen	Psychic	Status	—	—	30	Your Side	—	—
TM17	Protect	Normal	Status	—	—	10	Self	—	—
TM18	Rain Dance	Water	Status	—	—	5	Both Sides	—	—
TM21	Frustration	Normal	Physical	—	100	20	Normal	—	○
TM27	Return	Normal	Physical	—	100	20	Normal	—	○
TM32	Double Team	Normal	Status	—	—	15	Self	—	—
TM42	Facade	Normal	Physical	70	100	20	Normal	—	○
TM44	Rest	Psychic	Status	—	—	10	Self	—	—
TM45	Attract	Normal	Status	—	100	15	Normal	—	—
TM48	Round	Normal	Special	60	100	15	Normal	—	—
TM55	Scald	Water	Special	80	100	15	Normal	—	—
TM87	Swagger	Normal	Status	—	90	15	Normal	—	—
TM90	Substitute	Normal	Status	—	—	10	Self	—	—
HM03	Surf	Water	Special	95	100	15	Adjacent	—	—
HM05	Waterfall	Water	Physical	80	100	15	Normal	—	○
HM06	Dive	Water	Physical	80	100	10	Normal	—	—

MOVES TAUGHT BY PEOPLE
Name	Type	Kind	Pow.	Acc.	PP	Range	Long	DA

MOVES TAUGHT BY MOVE TUTORS FOR SHARDS
Name	Type	Kind	Pow.	Acc.	PP	Range	Long	DA
Icy Wind	Ice	Special	55	95	15	Many Others	—	—
Iron Tail	Steel	Physical	100	75	15	Normal	—	○
Dragon Pulse	Dragon	Special	90	100	10	Normal	—	—
Snore	Normal	Special	40	100	15	Normal	—	—
Sleep Talk	Normal	Status	—	—	10	Self	—	—

EGG MOVES
Name	Type	Kind	Pow.	Acc.	PP	Range	Long	DA
Mirror Coat	Psychic	Special	—	100	20	Varies	—	—
DragonBreath	Dragon	Special	60	100	20	Normal	—	—
Mud Sport	Ground	Status	—	—	15	Both Sides	—	—
Hypnosis	Psychic	Status	—	60	20	Normal	—	—
Confuse Ray	Ghost	Status	—	100	10	Normal	—	—
Mist	Ice	Status	—	—	30	Your Side	—	—
Haze	Ice	Status	—	—	30	Both Sides	—	—
Tickle	Normal	Status	—	100	20	Normal	—	—
Brine	Water	Special	65	100	10	Normal	—	—
Iron Tail	Steel	Physical	100	75	15	Normal	—	○
Dragon Pulse	Dragon	Special	90	100	10	Normal	○	—
Captivate	Normal	Status	—	100	20	Many Others	—	—

350 Milotic
Tender Pokémon

- HEIGHT: 20'04"
- WEIGHT: 357.1 lbs.
- GENDER: ♂ / ♀

Its lovely scales are described as rainbow colored. They change color depending on the viewing angle.

♂　　♀

Pokémon AR Marker

TYPE Water

ABILITY
- Marvel Scale

HIDDEN ABILITY
- Cute Charm

STATS
HP
Attack
Defense
Sp. Atk
Sp. Def
Speed

EGG GROUPS
Water ❶ / Dragon

ITEMS SOMETIMES HELD
- None

EVOLUTION
Feebas → (Have it hold Prism Scale and Link Trade it) → Milotic

HOW TO OBTAIN
Pokémon Black Version 2	Route 1 (Super Rod—ripples in water)
Pokémon White Version 2	Route 1 (Super Rod—ripples in water)

HOW TO OBTAIN FROM OTHER GAMES

LEVEL-UP AND LEARNED MOVES
Lv.	Name	Type	Kind	Pow.	Acc.	PP	Range	Long	DA
1	Water Gun	Water	Special	40	100	25	Normal	—	—
1	Wrap	Normal	Physical	15	90	20	Normal	—	○
5	Water Sport	Water	Status	—	—	15	Both Sides	—	—
9	Refresh	Normal	Status	—	—	20	Self	—	—
13	Water Pulse	Water	Special	60	100	20	Normal	○	—
17	Twister	Dragon	Special	40	100	20	Many Others	—	—
21	Recover	Normal	Status	—	—	10	Self	—	—
25	Captivate	Normal	Status	—	100	20	Many Others	—	—
29	Aqua Tail	Water	Physical	90	90	10	Normal	—	○
33	Rain Dance	Water	Status	—	—	5	Both Sides	—	—
37	Hydro Pump	Water	Special	120	80	5	Normal	—	—
41	Attract	Normal	Status	—	100	15	Normal	—	—
45	Safeguard	Normal	Status	—	—	25	Your Side	—	—
49	Aqua Ring	Water	Status	—	—	20	Self	—	—

TM & HM MOVES
Lv.	Name	Type	Kind	Pow.	Acc.	PP	Range	Long	DA
TM06	Toxic	Poison	Status	—	90	10	Normal	—	—
TM07	Hail	Ice	Status	—	—	10	Both Sides	—	—
TM10	Hidden Power	Normal	Special	—	100	15	Normal	—	—
TM13	Ice Beam	Ice	Special	95	100	10	Normal	—	—
TM14	Blizzard	Ice	Special	120	70	5	Many Others	—	—
TM15	Hyper Beam	Normal	Special	150	90	5	Normal	—	—
TM16	Light Screen	Psychic	Status	—	—	30	Your Side	—	—
TM17	Protect	Normal	Status	—	—	10	Self	—	—
TM18	Rain Dance	Water	Status	—	—	5	Both Sides	—	—
TM20	Safeguard	Normal	Status	—	—	25	Your Side	—	—
TM21	Frustration	Normal	Physical	—	100	20	Normal	—	○
TM27	Return	Normal	Physical	—	100	20	Normal	—	○
TM32	Double Team	Normal	Status	—	—	15	Self	—	—
TM42	Facade	Normal	Physical	70	100	20	Normal	—	○
TM44	Rest	Psychic	Status	—	—	10	Self	—	—
TM45	Attract	Normal	Status	—	100	15	Normal	—	—
TM48	Round	Normal	Special	60	100	15	Normal	—	—
TM55	Scald	Water	Special	80	100	15	Normal	—	—
TM68	Giga Impact	Normal	Physical	150	90	5	Normal	—	—
TM77	Psych Up	Normal	Status	—	—	10	Self	—	—
TM78	Bulldoze	Ground	Physical	60	100	20	Adjacent	—	—
TM82	Dragon Tail	Dragon	Physical	60	90	10	Normal	—	—
TM87	Swagger	Normal	Status	—	90	15	Normal	—	—
TM90	Substitute	Normal	Status	—	—	10	Self	—	—
HM03	Surf	Water	Special	95	100	15	Adjacent	—	—
HM05	Waterfall	Water	Physical	80	100	15	Normal	—	○
HM06	Dive	Water	Physical	80	100	10	Normal	—	—

MOVES TAUGHT BY PEOPLE
Name	Type	Kind	Pow.	Acc.	PP	Range	Long	DA

MOVES TAUGHT BY MOVE TUTORS FOR SHARDS
Name	Type	Kind	Pow.	Acc.	PP	Range	Long	DA
Iron Head	Steel	Physical	80	100	15	Normal	—	○
Magic Coat	Psychic	Status	—	—	15	Self	—	—
Icy Wind	Ice	Special	55	95	15	Many Others	—	—
Iron Tail	Steel	Physical	100	75	15	Normal	—	○
Aqua Tail	Water	Physical	90	90	10	Normal	—	○
Dragon Pulse	Dragon	Special	90	100	10	Normal	○	—
Bind	Normal	Physical	15	85	20	Normal	—	○
Snore	Normal	Special	40	100	15	Normal	—	—
Sleep Talk	Normal	Status	—	—	10	Self	—	—

Weather Pokémon

351 Castform

TYPE Normal

ABILITY

● Forecast

HIDDEN ABILITY

—

STATS

HP
Attack
Defense
Sp. Atk
Sp. Def
Speed

EGG GROUPS

Fairy/Amorphous

ITEMS SOMETIMES HELD

● Mystic Water

● HEIGHT: 1'00"
● WEIGHT: 1.8 lbs.
● GENDER: ♂ / ♀

Temperature and weather affect its cellular structure, so this Pokémon changes form according to the weather.

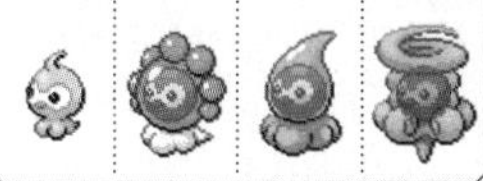

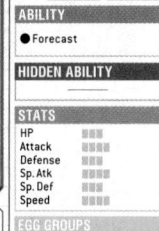

◆ Castform changes to its Sunny Form when the weather condition is Sunny, to its Rainy Form when the weather condition is Rain, and to its Snowy Form when the weather condition is Hail.

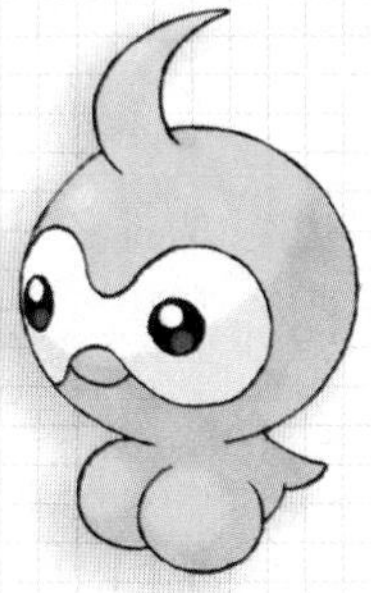

Pokémon AR Marker

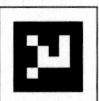

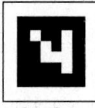

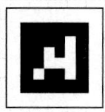

Normal Form Sunny Form Rainy Form Snowy Form

EVOLUTION

Does not evolve

HOW TO OBTAIN

Pokémon Black Version 2	Route 6 (rustling grass)
Pokémon White Version 2	Route 6 (rustling grass)

HOW TO OBTAIN FROM OTHER GAMES

—

—

LEVEL-UP AND LEARNED MOVES

Lv.	Name	Type	Kind	Pow.	Acc.	PP	Range	Long	DA
1	Tackle	Normal	Physical	50	100	35	Normal	—	○
10	Water Gun	Water	Special	40	100	25	Normal	—	—
10	Ember	Fire	Special	40	100	25	Normal	—	—
10	Powder Snow	Ice	Special	40	100	25	Many Others	—	—
15	Headbutt	Normal	Physical	70	100	15	Normal	—	○
20	Rain Dance	Water	Status	—	—	5	Both Sides	—	—
20	Sunny Day	Fire	Status	—	—	5	Both Sides	—	—
20	Hail	Ice	Status	—	—	10	Both Sides	—	—
30	Weather Ball	Normal	Special	50	100	10	Normal	—	—
40	Hydro Pump	Water	Special	120	80	5	Normal	—	—
40	Fire Blast	Fire	Special	120	85	5	Normal	—	—
40	Blizzard	Ice	Special	120	70	5	Many Others	—	—

TM & HM MOVES

Lv.	Name	Type	Kind	Pow.	Acc.	PP	Range	Long	DA
TM06	Toxic	Poison	Status	—	90	10	Normal	—	—
TM07	Hail	Ice	Status	—	—	10	Both Sides	—	—
TM10	Hidden Power	Normal	Special	—	100	15	Normal	—	—
TM11	Sunny Day	Fire	Status	—	—	5	Both Sides	—	—
TM13	Ice Beam	Ice	Special	95	100	10	Normal	—	—
TM14	Blizzard	Ice	Special	120	70	5	Many Others	—	—
TM17	Protect	Normal	Status	—	—	10	Self	—	—
TM18	Rain Dance	Water	Status	—	—	5	Both Sides	—	—
TM21	Frustration	Normal	Physical	—	100	20	Normal	—	○
TM22	SolarBeam	Grass	Special	120	100	10	Normal	—	—
TM24	Thunderbolt	Electric	Special	95	100	15	Normal	—	—
TM25	Thunder	Electric	Special	120	70	10	Normal	—	—
TM27	Return	Normal	Physical	—	100	20	Normal	—	○
TM30	Shadow Ball	Ghost	Special	80	100	15	Normal	—	—
TM32	Double Team	Normal	Status	—	—	15	Self	—	—
TM35	Flamethrower	Fire	Special	95	100	15	Normal	—	—
TM37	Sandstorm	Rock	Status	—	—	10	Both Sides	—	—
TM38	Fire Blast	Fire	Special	120	85	5	Normal	—	—
TM42	Facade	Normal	Physical	70	100	20	Normal	—	○
TM44	Rest	Psychic	Status	—	—	10	Self	—	—
TM45	Attract	Normal	Status	—	100	15	Normal	—	—
TM46	Thief	Dark	Physical	40	100	10	Normal	—	○
TM48	Round	Normal	Special	60	100	15	Normal	—	—
TM53	Energy Ball	Grass	Special	80	100	10	Normal	—	—
TM55	Scald	Water	Special	80	100	15	Normal	—	—
TM59	Incinerate	Fire	Special	30	100	15	Many Others	—	—
TM67	Retaliate	Normal	Physical	70	100	5	Normal	—	○
TM70	Flash	Normal	Status	—	100	20	Normal	—	—
TM73	Thunder Wave	Electric	Status	—	100	20	Normal	—	—
TM77	Psych Up	Normal	Status	—	—	10	Normal	—	—
TM83	Work Up	Normal	Status	—	—	30	Self	—	—
TM87	Swagger	Normal	Status	—	90	15	Normal	—	—
TM90	Substitute	Normal	Status	—	—	10	Self	—	—

MOVES TAUGHT BY PEOPLE

Name	Type	Kind	Pow.	Acc.	PP	Range	Long	DA

MOVES TAUGHT BY MOVE TUTORS FOR SHARDS

Name	Type	Kind	Pow.	Acc.	PP	Range	Long	DA
Last Resort	Normal	Physical	140	100	5	Normal	—	○
Icy Wind	Ice	Special	55	95	15	Many Others	—	—
Snore	Normal	Special	40	100	15	Normal	—	—
Tailwind	Flying	Status	—	—	30	Your Side	—	—
Sleep Talk	Normal	Status	—	—	10	Self	—	—

EGG MOVES

Name	Type	Kind	Pow.	Acc.	PP	Range	Long	DA
Future Sight	Psychic	Special	100	100	10	Normal	—	—
Lucky Chant	Normal	Status	—	—	30	Your Side	—	—
Disable	Normal	Status	—	100	20	Normal	—	—
Amnesia	Psychic	Status	—	—	20	Self	—	—
Ominous Wind	Ghost	Special	60	100	5	Normal	—	—
Hex	Ghost	Special	50	100	10	Normal	—	—
Clear Smog	Poison	Special	50	—	15	Normal	—	—

Color Swap Pokémon

352 Kecleon

TYPE Normal

ABILITY

● Color Change

HIDDEN ABILITY

—

STATS

HP
Attack
Defense
Sp. Atk
Sp. Def
Speed

EGG GROUPS

Field

ITEMS SOMETIMES HELD

● Persim Berry

● HEIGHT: 3'03"
● WEIGHT: 48.5 lbs.
● GENDER: ♂ / ♀

It can freely change its body's color. The zigzag pattern on its belly doesn't change, however.

Same form for ♂ / ♀

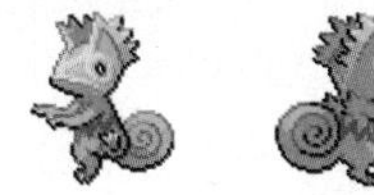

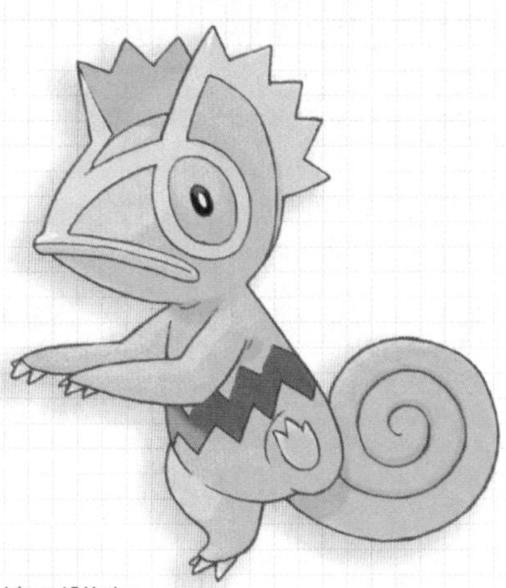

Pokémon AR Marker

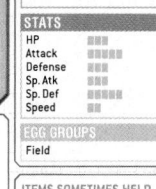

EVOLUTION

Does not evolve

HOW TO OBTAIN

Pokémon Black Version 2	Nature Preserve
Pokémon White Version 2	Nature Preserve

HOW TO OBTAIN FROM OTHER GAMES

—

—

LEVEL-UP AND LEARNED MOVES

Lv.	Name	Type	Kind	Pow.	Acc.	PP	Range	Long	DA
1	Thief	Dark	Physical	40	100	10	Normal	—	○
1	Tail Whip	Normal	Status	—	100	30	Many Others	—	—
1	Astonish	Ghost	Physical	30	100	15	Normal	—	○
1	Lick	Ghost	Physical	20	100	30	Normal	—	○
1	Scratch	Normal	Physical	40	100	35	Normal	—	○
4	Bind	Normal	Physical	15	85	20	Normal	—	○
7	Faint Attack	Dark	Physical	60	—	20	Normal	—	○
10	Fury Swipes	Normal	Physical	18	80	15	Normal	—	○
14	Feint	Normal	Physical	30	100	10	Normal	—	—
18	Psybeam	Psychic	Special	65	100	20	Normal	—	—
22	Shadow Sneak	Ghost	Physical	40	100	30	Normal	—	○
27	Slash	Normal	Physical	70	100	20	Normal	—	○
32	Screech	Normal	Status	—	85	40	Normal	—	—
37	Substitute	Normal	Status	—	—	10	Self	—	—
43	Sucker Punch	Dark	Physical	80	100	5	Normal	—	○
49	Shadow Claw	Ghost	Physical	70	100	15	Normal	—	○
55	AncientPower	Rock	Special	60	100	5	Normal	—	—
58	Synchronoise	Psychic	Special	70	100	15	Adjacent	—	—

TM & HM MOVES

Lv.	Name	Type	Kind	Pow.	Acc.	PP	Range	Long	DA
TM01	Hone Claws	Dark	Status	—	—	15	Self	—	—
TM06	Toxic	Poison	Status	—	90	10	Normal	—	—
TM10	Hidden Power	Normal	Special	—	100	15	Normal	—	—
TM11	Sunny Day	Fire	Status	—	—	5	Both Sides	—	—
TM13	Ice Beam	Ice	Special	95	100	10	Normal	—	—
TM14	Blizzard	Ice	Special	120	70	5	Many Others	—	—
TM17	Protect	Normal	Status	—	—	10	Self	—	—
TM18	Rain Dance	Water	Status	—	—	5	Both Sides	—	—
TM21	Frustration	Normal	Physical	—	100	20	Normal	—	○
TM22	SolarBeam	Grass	Special	120	100	10	Normal	—	—
TM24	Thunderbolt	Electric	Special	95	100	15	Normal	—	—
TM25	Thunder	Electric	Special	120	70	10	Normal	—	—
TM27	Return	Normal	Physical	—	100	20	Normal	—	○
TM28	Dig	Ground	Physical	80	100	10	Normal	—	○
TM30	Shadow Ball	Ghost	Special	80	100	15	Normal	—	—
TM31	Brick Break	Fighting	Physical	75	100	15	Normal	—	○
TM32	Double Team	Normal	Status	—	—	15	Self	—	—
TM35	Flamethrower	Fire	Special	95	100	15	Normal	—	—
TM38	Fire Blast	Fire	Special	120	85	5	Normal	—	—
TM39	Rock Tomb	Rock	Physical	50	80	10	Normal	—	—
TM40	Aerial Ace	Flying	Physical	60	—	20	Normal	○	○
TM42	Facade	Normal	Physical	70	100	20	Normal	—	○
TM44	Rest	Psychic	Status	—	—	10	Self	—	—
TM45	Attract	Normal	Status	—	100	15	Normal	—	—
TM46	Thief	Dark	Physical	40	100	10	Normal	—	○
TM48	Round	Normal	Special	60	100	15	Normal	—	—
TM56	Fling	Dark	Physical	—	100	10	Normal	—	—
TM57	Charge Beam	Electric	Special	50	90	10	Normal	—	—
TM59	Incinerate	Fire	Special	30	100	15	Many Others	—	—
TM65	Shadow Claw	Ghost	Physical	70	100	15	Normal	—	○
TM67	Retaliate	Normal	Physical	70	100	5	Normal	—	○
TM70	Flash	Normal	Status	—	100	20	Normal	—	—
TM73	Thunder Wave	Electric	Status	—	100	20	Normal	—	—
TM77	Psych Up	Normal	Status	—	—	10	Normal	—	—
TM80	Rock Slide	Rock	Physical	75	90	10	Many Others	—	—
TM83	Work Up	Normal	Status	—	—	30	Self	—	—
TM86	Grass Knot	Grass	Special	—	100	20	Normal	—	○
TM87	Swagger	Normal	Status	—	90	15	Normal	—	—
TM90	Substitute	Normal	Status	—	—	10	Self	—	—
TM92	Trick Room	Psychic	Status	—	—	5	Both Sides	—	—
TM94	Rock Smash	Fighting	Physical	40	100	15	Normal	—	○
HM01	Cut	Normal	Physical	50	95	30	Normal	—	○
HM04	Strength	Normal	Physical	80	100	15	Normal	—	○

MOVES TAUGHT BY PEOPLE

Name	Type	Kind	Pow.	Acc.	PP	Range	Long	DA

MOVES TAUGHT BY MOVE TUTORS FOR SHARDS

Name	Type	Kind	Pow.	Acc.	PP	Range	Long	DA
Low Kick	Fighting	Physical	—	100	20	Normal	—	○
Fire Punch	Fire	Physical	75	100	15	Normal	—	○
ThunderPunch	Electric	Physical	75	100	15	Normal	—	○
Ice Punch	Ice	Physical	75	100	15	Normal	—	○
Last Resort	Normal	Physical	140	100	5	Normal	—	○
Magic Coat	Psychic	Status	—	—	15	Self	—	—
Icy Wind	Ice	Special	55	95	15	Many Others	—	—
Iron Tail	Steel	Physical	100	75	15	Normal	—	○
Aqua Tail	Water	Physical	90	90	10	Normal	—	○
Foul Play	Dark	Physical	95	100	15	Normal	—	○
Bind	Normal	Physical	15	85	20	Normal	—	○
Snore	Normal	Special	40	100	15	Normal	—	—
Knock Off	Dark	Physical	20	100	20	Normal	—	○
Role Play	Psychic	Status	—	—	10	Normal	—	—
Drain Punch	Fighting	Physical	75	100	10	Normal	—	○
After You	Normal	Status	—	—	15	Normal	—	—
Wonder Room	Psychic	Status	—	—	10	Both Sides	—	—
Recycle	Normal	Status	—	—	10	Self	—	—
Trick	Psychic	Status	—	100	10	Normal	—	—
Stealth Rock	Rock	Status	—	—	20	Other Side	—	—
Sleep Talk	Normal	Status	—	—	10	Self	—	—
Skill Swap	Psychic	Status	—	—	10	Normal	—	—
Snatch	Dark	Status	—	—	10	Self	—	—

EGG MOVES

Name	Type	Kind	Pow.	Acc.	PP	Range	Long	DA
Disable	Normal	Status	—	100	20	Normal	—	—
Magic Coat	Psychic	Status	—	—	15	Self	—	—
Trick	Psychic	Status	—	100	10	Normal	—	—
Fake Out	Normal	Physical	40	100	10	Normal	—	○
Nasty Plot	Dark	Status	—	—	20	Self	—	—
Dizzy Punch	Normal	Physical	70	100	10	Normal	—	○
Recover	Normal	Status	—	—	10	Self	—	—
Skill Swap	Psychic	Status	—	—	10	Normal	—	—
Snatch	Dark	Status	—	—	10	Self	—	—
Foul Play	Dark	Physical	95	100	15	Normal	—	○

Puppet Pokémon

353 Shuppet

- HEIGHT: 2'00"
- WEIGHT: 5.1 lbs.
- GENDER: ♂ / ♀

It feeds on the dark emotions of sadness and hatred, which make it grow steadily stronger.

Same form for ♂ / ♀

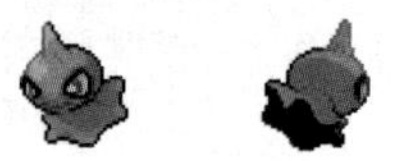

TYPE Ghost

ABILITIES
- Insomnia
- Frisk

HIDDEN ABILITY
- Cursed Body

STATS
HP
Attack
Defense
Sp. Atk
Sp. Def
Speed

EGG GROUPS
Amorphous

ITEMS SOMETIMES HELD
- None

EVOLUTION

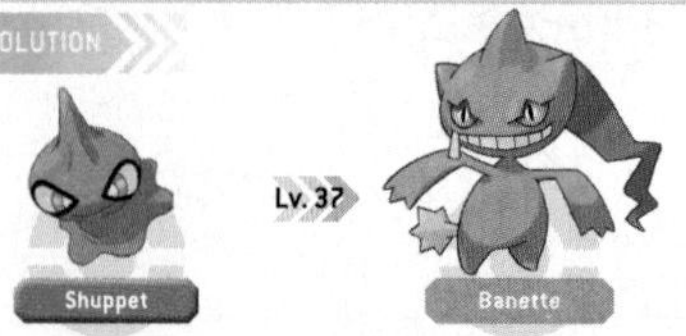

HOW TO OBTAIN

Pokémon Black Version 2	Catch a Banette, leave it at the Pokémon Day Care, and hatch the Egg that is found
Pokémon White Version 2	Catch a Banette, leave it at the Pokémon Day Care, and hatch the Egg that is found

HOW TO OBTAIN FROM OTHER GAMES

—

—

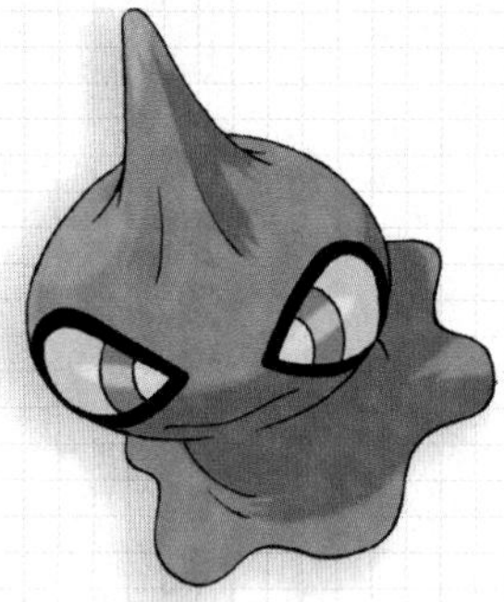

Pokémon AR Marker

LEVEL-UP AND LEARNED MOVES

Lv.	Name	Type	Kind	Pow.	Acc.	PP	Range	Long	DA
1	Knock Off	Dark	Physical	20	100	20	Normal	—	○
4	Screech	Normal	Status	—	85	40	Normal	—	—
7	Night Shade	Ghost	Special	—	100	15	Normal	—	—
10	Spite	Ghost	Status	—	100	10	Normal	—	—
13	Will-O-Wisp	Fire	Status	—	75	15	Normal	—	—
16	Shadow Sneak	Ghost	Physical	40	100	30	Normal	—	○
19	Curse	Ghost	Status	—	—	10	Varies	—	—
22	Faint Attack	Dark	Physical	60	—	20	Normal	—	○
26	Hex	Ghost	Special	50	100	10	Normal	—	—
30	Shadow Ball	Ghost	Special	80	100	15	Normal	—	—
34	Sucker Punch	Dark	Physical	80	100	5	Normal	—	○
38	Embargo	Dark	Status	—	100	15	Normal	—	—
42	Snatch	Dark	Status	—	—	10	Self	—	—
46	Grudge	Ghost	Status	—	—	5	Self	—	—
50	Trick	Psychic	Status	—	100	10	Normal	—	—

TM & HM MOVES

Lv.	Name	Type	Kind	Pow.	Acc.	PP	Range	Long	DA
TM04	Calm Mind	Psychic	Status	—	—	20	Self	—	—
TM06	Toxic	Poison	Status	—	90	10	Normal	—	—
TM10	Hidden Power	Normal	Special	—	100	15	Normal	—	—
TM11	Sunny Day	Fire	Status	—	—	5	Both Sides	—	—
TM12	Taunt	Dark	Status	—	100	20	Normal	—	—
TM17	Protect	Normal	Status	—	—	10	Self	—	—
TM18	Rain Dance	Water	Status	—	—	5	Both Sides	—	—
TM19	Telekinesis	Psychic	Status	—	—	15	Normal	—	—
TM21	Frustration	Normal	Physical	—	100	20	Normal	—	○
TM24	Thunderbolt	Electric	Special	95	100	15	Normal	—	—
TM25	Thunder	Electric	Special	120	70	10	Normal	—	—
TM27	Return	Normal	Physical	—	100	20	Normal	—	○
TM29	Psychic	Psychic	Special	90	100	10	Normal	—	—
TM30	Shadow Ball	Ghost	Special	80	100	15	Normal	—	—
TM32	Double Team	Normal	Status	—	—	15	Self	—	—
TM41	Torment	Dark	Status	—	100	15	Normal	—	—
TM42	Facade	Normal	Physical	70	100	20	Normal	—	○
TM44	Rest	Psychic	Status	—	—	10	Self	—	—
TM45	Attract	Normal	Status	—	100	15	Normal	—	—
TM46	Thief	Dark	Physical	40	100	10	Normal	—	○
TM48	Round	Normal	Special	60	100	15	Normal	—	—
TM57	Charge Beam	Electric	Special	50	90	10	Normal	—	—
TM61	Will-O-Wisp	Fire	Status	—	75	15	Normal	—	—
TM63	Embargo	Dark	Status	—	100	15	Normal	—	—
TM66	Payback	Dark	Physical	50	100	10	Normal	—	○
TM70	Flash	Normal	Status	—	100	20	Normal	—	—
TM73	Thunder Wave	Electric	Status	—	100	20	Normal	—	—
TM77	Psych Up	Normal	Status	—	—	10	Normal	—	—
TM85	Dream Eater	Psychic	Special	100	100	15	Normal	—	—
TM87	Swagger	Normal	Status	—	90	15	Normal	—	—
TM90	Substitute	Normal	Status	—	—	10	Self	—	—
TM92	Trick Room	Psychic	Status	—	—	5	Both Sides	—	—

MOVES TAUGHT BY PEOPLE

Name	Type	Kind	Pow.	Acc.	PP	Range	Long	DA

MOVES TAUGHT BY MOVE TUTORS FOR SHARDS

Name	Type	Kind	Pow.	Acc.	PP	Range	Long	DA
Magic Coat	Psychic	Status	—	—	15	Self	—	—
Icy Wind	Ice	Special	55	95	15	Many Others	—	—
Foul Play	Dark	Physical	95	100	15	Normal	—	○
Dark Pulse	Dark	Special	80	100	15	Normal	○	—
Knock Off	Dark	Physical	20	100	20	Normal	—	○
Role Play	Psychic	Status	—	—	10	Normal	—	—
Pain Split	Normal	Status	—	—	20	Normal	—	—
Magic Room	Psychic	Status	—	—	10	Both Sides	—	—
Spite	Ghost	Status	—	100	10	Normal	—	—
Trick	Psychic	Status	—	100	10	Normal	—	—
Sleep Talk	Normal	Status	—	—	10	Self	—	—
Skill Swap	Psychic	Status	—	—	10	Normal	—	—
Snatch	Dark	Status	—	—	10	Self	—	—

EGG MOVES

Name	Type	Kind	Pow.	Acc.	PP	Range	Long	DA
Disable	Normal	Status	—	100	20	Normal	—	—
Destiny Bond	Ghost	Status	—	—	5	Self	—	—
Foresight	Normal	Status	—	—	40	Normal	—	—
Astonish	Ghost	Physical	30	100	15	Normal	—	○
Imprison	Psychic	Status	—	—	10	Self	—	—
Pursuit	Dark	Physical	40	100	20	Normal	—	○
Shadow Sneak	Ghost	Physical	40	100	30	Normal	—	○
Confuse Ray	Ghost	Status	—	100	10	Normal	—	—
Ominous Wind	Ghost	Special	60	100	5	Normal	—	—
Gunk Shot	Poison	Physical	120	70	5	Normal	—	—

Shuppet | 353

Marionette Pokémon

354 Banette

- HEIGHT: 3'07"
- WEIGHT: 27.6 lbs.
- GENDER: ♂ / ♀

A doll that became a Pokémon over its grudge from being thrown away. It seeks the child who disowned it.

Same form for ♂ / ♀

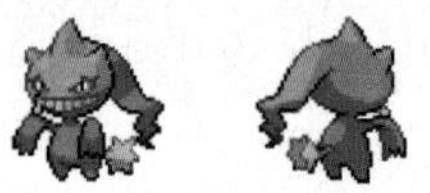

TYPE Ghost

ABILITIES
- Insomnia
- Frisk

HIDDEN ABILITY
- Cursed Body

STATS
HP
Attack
Defense
Sp. Atk
Sp. Def
Speed

EGG GROUPS
Amorphous

ITEMS SOMETIMES HELD
- Spell Tag

EVOLUTION

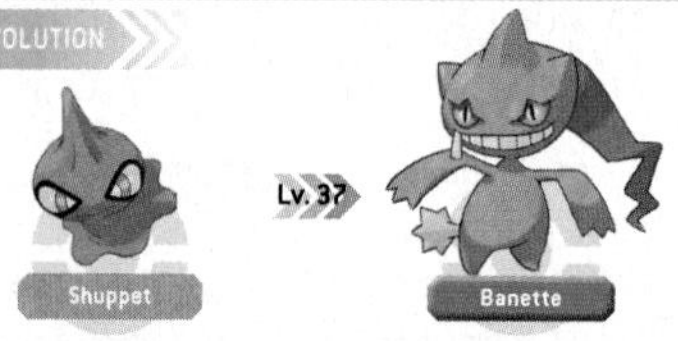

HOW TO OBTAIN

Pokémon Black Version 2	❶ Strange House entrance ❷ Victory Road caves 1F
Pokémon White Version 2	❶ Strange House entrance ❷ Victory Road caves 1F

HOW TO OBTAIN FROM OTHER GAMES

—

—

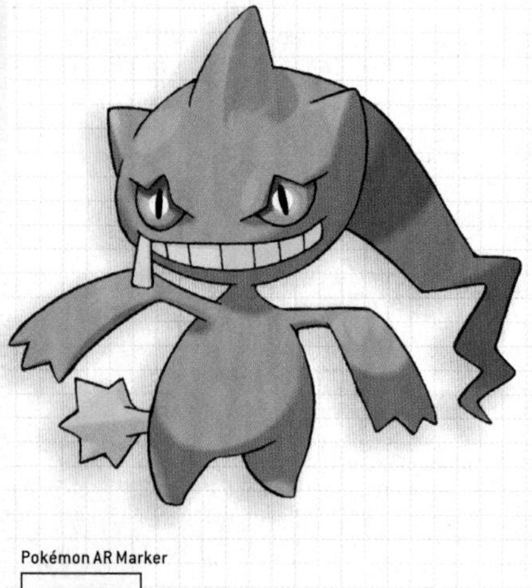

Pokémon AR Marker

LEVEL-UP AND LEARNED MOVES

Lv.	Name	Type	Kind	Pow.	Acc.	PP	Range	Long	DA
1	Knock Off	Dark	Physical	20	100	20	Normal	—	○
1	Screech	Normal	Status	—	85	40	Normal	—	—
1	Night Shade	Ghost	Special	—	100	15	Normal	—	—
1	Curse	Ghost	Status	—	—	10	Varies	—	—
4	Screech	Normal	Status	—	85	40	Normal	—	—
7	Night Shade	Ghost	Special	—	100	15	Normal	—	—
10	Spite	Ghost	Status	—	100	10	Normal	—	—
13	Will-O-Wisp	Fire	Status	—	75	15	Normal	—	—
16	Shadow Sneak	Ghost	Physical	40	100	30	Normal	—	○
19	Curse	Ghost	Status	—	—	10	Varies	—	—
22	Faint Attack	Dark	Physical	60	—	20	Normal	—	○
26	Hex	Ghost	Special	50	100	10	Normal	—	—
30	Shadow Ball	Ghost	Special	80	100	15	Normal	—	—
34	Sucker Punch	Dark	Physical	80	100	5	Normal	—	○
40	Embargo	Dark	Status	—	100	15	Normal	—	—
46	Snatch	Dark	Status	—	—	10	Self	—	—
52	Grudge	Ghost	Status	—	—	5	Self	—	—
58	Trick	Psychic	Status	—	100	10	Normal	—	—

TM & HM MOVES

Lv.	Name	Type	Kind	Pow.	Acc.	PP	Range	Long	DA
TM04	Calm Mind	Psychic	Status	—	—	20	Self	—	—
TM06	Toxic	Poison	Status	—	90	10	Normal	—	—
TM10	Hidden Power	Normal	Special	—	100	15	Normal	—	—
TM11	Sunny Day	Fire	Status	—	—	5	Both Sides	—	—
TM12	Taunt	Dark	Status	—	100	20	Normal	—	—
TM15	Hyper Beam	Normal	Special	150	90	5	Normal	—	—
TM17	Protect	Normal	Status	—	—	10	Self	—	—
TM18	Rain Dance	Water	Status	—	—	5	Both Sides	—	—
TM19	Telekinesis	Psychic	Status	—	—	15	Normal	—	—
TM21	Frustration	Normal	Physical	—	100	20	Normal	—	○
TM24	Thunderbolt	Electric	Special	95	100	15	Normal	—	—
TM25	Thunder	Electric	Special	120	70	10	Normal	—	—
TM27	Return	Normal	Physical	—	100	20	Normal	—	○
TM29	Psychic	Psychic	Special	90	100	10	Normal	—	—
TM30	Shadow Ball	Ghost	Special	80	100	15	Normal	—	—
TM32	Double Team	Normal	Status	—	—	15	Self	—	—
TM41	Torment	Dark	Status	—	100	15	Normal	—	—
TM42	Facade	Normal	Physical	70	100	20	Normal	—	○
TM44	Rest	Psychic	Status	—	—	10	Self	—	—
TM45	Attract	Normal	Status	—	100	15	Normal	—	—
TM46	Thief	Dark	Physical	40	100	10	Normal	—	○
TM48	Round	Normal	Special	60	100	15	Normal	—	—
TM56	Fling	Dark	Physical	—	100	10	Normal	—	—
TM57	Charge Beam	Electric	Special	50	90	10	Normal	—	—
TM61	Will-O-Wisp	Fire	Status	—	75	15	Normal	—	—
TM63	Embargo	Dark	Status	—	100	15	Normal	—	—
TM65	Shadow Claw	Ghost	Physical	70	100	15	Normal	—	○
TM66	Payback	Dark	Physical	50	100	10	Normal	—	○
TM68	Giga Impact	Normal	Physical	150	90	5	Normal	—	○
TM70	Flash	Normal	Status	—	100	20	Normal	—	—
TM73	Thunder Wave	Electric	Status	—	100	20	Normal	—	—
TM77	Psych Up	Normal	Status	—	—	10	Normal	—	—
TM85	Dream Eater	Psychic	Special	100	100	15	Normal	—	—
TM87	Swagger	Normal	Status	—	90	15	Normal	—	—
TM90	Substitute	Normal	Status	—	—	10	Self	—	—

Lv.	Name	Type	Kind	Pow.	Acc.	PP	Range	Long	DA
TM92	Trick Room	Psychic	Status	—	—	5	Both Sides	—	—

MOVES TAUGHT BY PEOPLE

Name	Type	Kind	Pow.	Acc.	PP	Range	Long	DA

MOVES TAUGHT BY MOVE TUTORS FOR SHARDS

Name	Type	Kind	Pow.	Acc.	PP	Range	Long	DA
Magic Coat	Psychic	Status	—	—	15	Self	—	—
Icy Wind	Ice	Special	55	95	15	Many Others	—	—
Foul Play	Dark	Physical	95	100	15	Normal	—	○
Dark Pulse	Dark	Special	80	100	15	Normal	○	—
Knock Off	Dark	Physical	20	100	20	Normal	—	○
Role Play	Psychic	Status	—	—	10	Normal	—	—
Pain Split	Normal	Status	—	—	20	Normal	—	—
Magic Room	Psychic	Status	—	—	10	Both Sides	—	—
Spite	Ghost	Status	—	100	10	Normal	—	—
Trick	Psychic	Status	—	100	10	Normal	—	—
Sleep Talk	Normal	Status	—	—	10	Self	—	—
Skill Swap	Psychic	Status	—	—	10	Normal	—	—
Snatch	Dark	Status	—	—	10	Self	—	—

Banette | 354

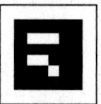

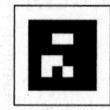

355 Duskull

Requiem Pokémon

TYPE Ghost

ABILITY
● Levitate

HIDDEN ABILITY

● HEIGHT: 2'07"
● WEIGHT: 33.1 lbs.
● GENDER: ♂ / ♀

It loves the crying of children. It startles bad kids by passing through walls and making them cry.

STATS
HP
Attack
Defense
Sp. Atk
Sp. Def
Speed

EGG GROUPS
Amorphous

ITEMS SOMETIMES HELD
● None

Same form for ♂ / ♀

Pokémon AR Marker

EVOLUTION

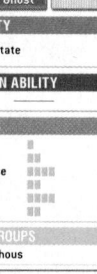 Duskull — Lv. 37 →  Dusclops — Have it hold Reaper Cloth and Link Trade it → 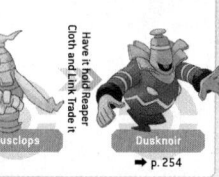 Dusknoir
➡ p. 254

HOW TO OBTAIN
| Pokémon Black Version 2 | Link Trade or Poké Transfer |
| Pokémon White Version 2 | Link Trade or Poké Transfer |

HOW TO OBTAIN FROM OTHER GAMES
| Pokémon Platinum Version | Route 209 (night only) |

LEVEL-UP AND LEARNED MOVES
Lv.	Name	Type	Kind	Pow.	Acc.	PP	Range	Long	DA
1	Leer	Normal	Status	—	100	30	Many Others	—	—
1	Night Shade	Ghost	Special	—	100	15	Normal	—	—
6	Disable	Normal	Status	—	100	20	Normal	—	—
9	Foresight	Normal	Status	—	—	40	Normal	—	—
14	Astonish	Ghost	Physical	30	100	15	Normal	—	○
17	Confuse Ray	Ghost	Status	—	100	10	Normal	—	—
22	Shadow Sneak	Ghost	Physical	40	100	30	Normal	—	○
25	Pursuit	Dark	Physical	40	100	20	Normal	—	—
30	Curse	Ghost	Status	—	—	10	Varies	—	—
33	Will-O-Wisp	Fire	Status	—	75	15	Normal	—	—
38	Hex	Ghost	Special	50	100	10	Normal	—	—
41	Mean Look	Normal	Status	—	—	5	Normal	—	—
46	Payback	Dark	Physical	50	100	10	Normal	—	○
49	Future Sight	Psychic	Special	100	100	10	Normal	—	—

TM & HM MOVES
Lv.	Name	Type	Kind	Pow.	Acc.	PP	Range	Long	DA
TM04	Calm Mind	Psychic	Status	—	—	20	Self	—	—
TM06	Toxic	Poison	Status	—	90	10	Normal	—	—
TM10	Hidden Power	Normal	Special	—	100	15	Normal	—	—
TM11	Sunny Day	Fire	Status	—	—	5	Both Sides	—	—
TM12	Taunt	Dark	Status	—	100	20	Normal	—	—
TM13	Ice Beam	Ice	Special	95	100	10	Normal	—	—
TM14	Blizzard	Ice	Special	120	70	5	Many Others	—	—
TM17	Protect	Normal	Status	—	—	10	Self	—	—
TM18	Rain Dance	Water	Status	—	—	5	Both Sides	—	—
TM19	Telekinesis	Psychic	Status	—	—	15	Normal	—	—
TM21	Frustration	Normal	Physical	—	100	20	Normal	—	○
TM27	Return	Normal	Physical	—	100	20	Normal	—	○
TM29	Psychic	Psychic	Special	90	100	10	Normal	—	—
TM30	Shadow Ball	Ghost	Special	80	100	15	Normal	—	—
TM32	Double Team	Normal	Status	—	—	15	Self	—	—
TM41	Torment	Dark	Status	—	100	15	Normal	—	—
TM42	Facade	Normal	Physical	70	100	20	Normal	—	—
TM44	Rest	Psychic	Status	—	—	10	Self	—	—
TM45	Attract	Normal	Status	—	100	15	Normal	—	—
TM46	Thief	Dark	Physical	40	100	10	Normal	—	○
TM48	Round	Normal	Special	60	100	15	Normal	—	—
TM56	Fling	Dark	Physical	—	100	10	Normal	—	○
TM57	Charge Beam	Electric	Special	50	90	10	Normal	—	—
TM61	Will-O-Wisp	Fire	Status	—	75	15	Normal	—	—
TM63	Embargo	Dark	Status	—	100	15	Normal	—	—
TM66	Payback	Dark	Physical	50	100	10	Normal	—	○
TM70	Flash	Normal	Status	—	100	20	Normal	—	—
TM77	Psych Up	Normal	Status	—	—	10	Normal	—	—
TM85	Dream Eater	Psychic	Special	100	100	15	Normal	—	—
TM87	Swagger	Normal	Status	—	90	15	Normal	—	—
TM90	Substitute	Normal	Status	—	—	10	Self	—	—
TM92	Trick Room	Psychic	Status	—	—	5	Both Sides	—	—

MOVES TAUGHT BY PEOPLE
Name	Type	Kind	Pow.	Acc.	PP	Range	Long	DA

MOVES TAUGHT BY MOVE TUTORS FOR SHARDS
Name	Type	Kind	Pow.	Acc.	PP	Range	Long	DA
Icy Wind	Ice	Special	55	95	15	Many Others	—	—
Gravity	Psychic	Status	—	—	5	Both Sides	—	—
Dark Pulse	Dark	Special	80	100	15	Normal	○	—
Snore	Normal	Special	40	100	15	Normal	—	—
Pain Split	Normal	Status	—	—	20	Normal	—	—
Wonder Room	Psychic	Status	—	—	10	Both Sides	—	—
Spite	Ghost	Status	—	100	10	Normal	—	—
Trick	Psychic	Status	—	100	10	Normal	—	—
Sleep Talk	Normal	Status	—	—	10	Self	—	—
Skill Swap	Psychic	Status	—	—	10	Normal	—	—
Snatch	Dark	Status	—	—	10	Self	—	—

EGG MOVES
Name	Type	Kind	Pow.	Acc.	PP	Range	Long	DA
Imprison	Psychic	Status	—	—	10	Self	—	—
Destiny Bond	Ghost	Status	—	—	5	Self	—	—
Pain Split	Normal	Status	—	—	20	Normal	—	—
Grudge	Ghost	Status	—	—	5	Self	—	—
Memento	Dark	Status	—	100	10	Normal	—	—
Faint Attack	Dark	Physical	60	—	20	Normal	—	○
Ominous Wind	Ghost	Special	60	100	5	Normal	—	—
Dark Pulse	Dark	Special	80	100	15	Normal	—	—
Skill Swap	Psychic	Status	—	—	10	Normal	—	—

356 Dusclops

Beckon Pokémon

TYPE Ghost

ABILITY
● Pressure

HIDDEN ABILITY

● HEIGHT: 5'03"
● WEIGHT: 67.5 lbs.
● GENDER: ♂ / ♀

It seeks drifting will-o'-the-wisps and sucks them into its empty body. What happens inside is a mystery.

STATS
HP
Attack
Defense
Sp. Atk
Sp. Def
Speed

EGG GROUPS
Amorphous

ITEMS SOMETIMES HELD
● None

Same form for ♂ / ♀

Pokémon AR Marker

EVOLUTION

 Duskull — Lv. 37 → Dusclops — Have it hold Reaper Cloth and Link Trade it → Dusknoir
➡ p. 254

HOW TO OBTAIN
| Pokémon Black Version 2 | Link Trade or Poké Transfer |
| Pokémon White Version 2 | Link Trade or Poké Transfer |

HOW TO OBTAIN FROM OTHER GAMES
| Pokémon Platinum Version | Sendoff Spring |

LEVEL-UP AND LEARNED MOVES
Lv.	Name	Type	Kind	Pow.	Acc.	PP	Range	Long	DA
1	Fire Punch	Fire	Physical	75	100	15	Normal	—	○
1	Ice Punch	Ice	Physical	75	100	15	Normal	—	○
1	ThunderPunch	Electric	Physical	75	100	15	Normal	—	○
1	Gravity	Psychic	Status	—	—	5	Both Sides	—	—
1	Bind	Normal	Physical	15	85	20	Normal	—	—
1	Leer	Normal	Status	—	100	30	Many Others	—	—
1	Night Shade	Ghost	Special	—	100	15	Normal	—	—
1	Disable	Normal	Status	—	100	20	Normal	—	—
6	Disable	Normal	Status	—	100	20	Normal	—	—
9	Foresight	Normal	Status	—	—	40	Normal	—	—
14	Astonish	Ghost	Physical	30	100	15	Normal	—	○
17	Confuse Ray	Ghost	Status	—	100	10	Normal	—	—
22	Shadow Sneak	Ghost	Physical	40	100	30	Normal	—	○
25	Pursuit	Dark	Physical	40	100	20	Normal	—	—
30	Curse	Ghost	Status	—	—	10	Varies	—	—
33	Will-O-Wisp	Fire	Status	—	75	15	Normal	—	—
37	Shadow Punch	Ghost	Physical	60	—	20	Normal	—	○
42	Hex	Ghost	Special	50	100	10	Normal	—	—
49	Mean Look	Normal	Status	—	—	5	Normal	—	—
58	Payback	Dark	Physical	50	100	10	Normal	—	○
61	Future Sight	Psychic	Special	100	100	10	Normal	—	—

TM & HM MOVES
Lv.	Name	Type	Kind	Pow.	Acc.	PP	Range	Long	DA
TM04	Calm Mind	Psychic	Status	—	—	20	Self	—	—
TM06	Toxic	Poison	Status	—	90	10	Normal	—	—
TM10	Hidden Power	Normal	Special	—	100	15	Normal	—	—
TM11	Sunny Day	Fire	Status	—	—	5	Both Sides	—	—
TM12	Taunt	Dark	Status	—	100	20	Normal	—	—
TM13	Ice Beam	Ice	Special	95	100	10	Normal	—	—
TM14	Blizzard	Ice	Special	120	70	5	Many Others	—	—
TM15	Hyper Beam	Normal	Special	150	90	5	Normal	—	—
TM17	Protect	Normal	Status	—	—	10	Self	—	—
TM18	Rain Dance	Water	Status	—	—	5	Both Sides	—	—
TM19	Telekinesis	Psychic	Status	—	—	15	Normal	—	—
TM21	Frustration	Normal	Physical	—	100	20	Normal	—	○
TM26	Earthquake	Ground	Physical	100	100	10	Adjacent	—	—
TM27	Return	Normal	Physical	—	100	20	Normal	—	○
TM29	Psychic	Psychic	Special	90	100	10	Normal	—	—
TM30	Shadow Ball	Ghost	Special	80	100	15	Normal	—	—
TM31	Brick Break	Fighting	Physical	75	100	15	Normal	—	—
TM32	Double Team	Normal	Status	—	—	15	Self	—	—
TM39	Rock Tomb	Rock	Physical	50	80	10	Normal	—	—
TM41	Torment	Dark	Status	—	100	15	Normal	—	—
TM42	Facade	Normal	Physical	70	100	20	Normal	—	—
TM44	Rest	Psychic	Status	—	—	10	Self	—	—
TM45	Attract	Normal	Status	—	100	15	Normal	—	—
TM46	Thief	Dark	Physical	40	100	10	Normal	—	○
TM48	Round	Normal	Special	60	100	15	Normal	—	—
TM56	Fling	Dark	Physical	—	100	10	Normal	—	○
TM57	Charge Beam	Electric	Special	50	90	10	Normal	—	—
TM61	Will-O-Wisp	Fire	Status	—	75	15	Normal	—	—
TM63	Embargo	Dark	Status	—	100	15	Normal	—	—
TM66	Payback	Dark	Physical	50	100	10	Normal	—	○
TM68	Giga Impact	Normal	Physical	150	90	5	Normal	—	—
TM70	Flash	Normal	Status	—	100	20	Normal	—	—
TM77	Psych Up	Normal	Status	—	—	10	Normal	—	—
TM78	Bulldoze	Ground	Physical	60	100	20	Adjacent	—	—
TM80	Rock Slide	Rock	Physical	75	90	10	Many Others	—	—
TM85	Dream Eater	Psychic	Special	100	100	15	Normal	—	—
TM87	Swagger	Normal	Status	—	90	15	Normal	—	—
TM90	Substitute	Normal	Status	—	—	10	Self	—	—
TM92	Trick Room	Psychic	Status	—	—	5	Both Sides	—	—
TM94	Rock Smash	Fighting	Physical	40	100	15	Normal	—	○
HM04	Strength	Normal	Physical	80	100	15	Normal	—	—

MOVES TAUGHT BY PEOPLE
Name	Type	Kind	Pow.	Acc.	PP	Range	Long	DA

MOVES TAUGHT BY MOVE TUTORS FOR SHARDS
Name	Type	Kind	Pow.	Acc.	PP	Range	Long	DA
Fire Punch	Fire	Physical	75	100	15	Normal	—	○
ThunderPunch	Electric	Physical	75	100	15	Normal	—	○
Ice Punch	Ice	Physical	75	100	15	Normal	—	○
Icy Wind	Ice	Special	55	95	15	Many Others	—	—
Gravity	Psychic	Status	—	—	5	Both Sides	—	—
Dark Pulse	Dark	Special	80	100	15	Normal	○	—
Bind	Normal	Physical	15	85	20	Normal	—	—
Snore	Normal	Special	40	100	15	Normal	—	—
Pain Split	Normal	Status	—	—	20	Normal	—	—
Wonder Room	Psychic	Status	—	—	10	Both Sides	—	—
Spite	Ghost	Status	—	100	10	Normal	—	—
Trick	Psychic	Status	—	100	10	Normal	—	—
Sleep Talk	Normal	Status	—	—	10	Self	—	—
Skill Swap	Psychic	Status	—	—	10	Normal	—	—
Snatch	Dark	Status	—	—	10	Self	—	—

191

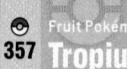

357 Tropius

Fruit Pokémon

- HEIGHT: 6'07"
- WEIGHT: 220.5 lbs.
- GENDER: ♂ / ♀

It flies by flapping its broad leaves and gives the sweet, delicious fruit around its neck to children.

TYPE Grass Flying

ABILITIES
- Chlorophyll
- Solar Power

HIDDEN ABILITY
- Harvest

STATS
HP
Attack
Defense
Sp. Atk
Sp. Def
Speed

EGG GROUPS
Monster/Grass

ITEMS SOMETIMES HELD
- None

Same form for ♂ / ♀

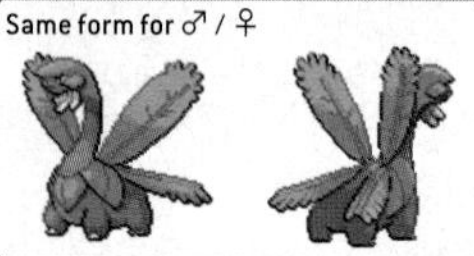

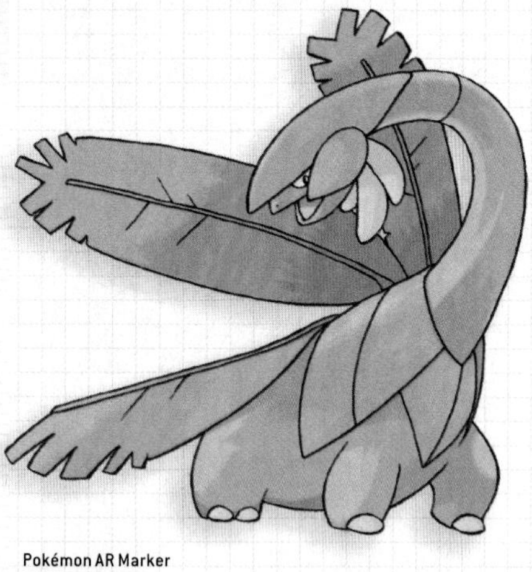

Pokémon AR Marker

EVOLUTION

Does not evolve

HOW TO OBTAIN

Pokémon Black Version 2	Route 18
Pokémon White Version 2	Route 18

HOW TO OBTAIN FROM OTHER GAMES

—
—

LEVEL-UP AND LEARNED MOVES

Lv.	Name	Type	Kind	Pow.	Acc.	PP	Range	Long	DA
1	Leer	Normal	Status	—	100	30	Many Others	—	—
1	Gust	Flying	Special	40	100	35	Normal	○	—
7	Growth	Normal	Status	—	—	40	Self	—	—
11	Razor Leaf	Grass	Physical	55	95	25	Many Others	—	—
17	Stomp	Normal	Physical	65	100	20	Normal	—	○
21	Sweet Scent	Normal	Status	—	100	20	Many Others	—	—
27	Whirlwind	Normal	Status	—	100	20	Normal	—	—
31	Magical Leaf	Grass	Special	60	—	20	Normal	—	—
37	Body Slam	Normal	Physical	85	100	15	Normal	—	○
41	Synthesis	Grass	Status	—	—	5	Self	—	—
47	Leaf Tornado	Grass	Special	65	90	10	Normal	—	—
51	Air Slash	Flying	Special	75	95	20	Normal	○	—
57	Bestow	Normal	Status	—	—	15	Normal	—	—
61	SolarBeam	Grass	Special	120	100	10	Normal	—	—
67	Natural Gift	Normal	Physical	—	100	15	Normal	—	—
71	Leaf Storm	Grass	Special	140	90	5	Normal	—	—

TM & HM MOVES

Lv.	Name	Type	Kind	Pow.	Acc.	PP	Range	Long	DA
TM05	Roar	Normal	Status	—	100	20	Normal	—	—
TM06	Toxic	Poison	Status	—	90	10	Normal	—	—
TM10	Hidden Power	Normal	Special	—	100	15	Normal	—	—
TM11	Sunny Day	Fire	Status	—	—	5	Both Sides	—	—
TM15	Hyper Beam	Normal	Special	150	90	5	Normal	—	—
TM17	Protect	Normal	Status	—	—	10	Self	—	—
TM20	Safeguard	Normal	Status	—	—	25	Your Side	—	—
TM21	Frustration	Normal	Physical	—	100	20	Normal	—	○
TM22	SolarBeam	Grass	Special	120	100	10	Normal	—	—
TM26	Earthquake	Ground	Physical	100	100	10	Adjacent	—	—
TM27	Return	Normal	Physical	—	100	20	Normal	—	○
TM32	Double Team	Normal	Status	—	—	15	Self	—	—
TM40	Aerial Ace	Flying	Physical	60	—	20	Normal	○	○
TM42	Facade	Normal	Physical	70	100	20	Normal	—	○
TM44	Rest	Psychic	Status	—	—	10	Self	—	—
TM45	Attract	Normal	Status	—	100	15	Normal	—	—
TM48	Round	Normal	Special	60	100	15	Normal	—	—
TM53	Energy Ball	Grass	Special	80	100	10	Normal	—	—
TM68	Giga Impact	Normal	Physical	150	90	5	Normal	—	○
TM70	Flash	Normal	Status	—	100	20	Normal	—	—
TM75	Swords Dance	Normal	Status	—	—	30	Self	—	—
TM78	Bulldoze	Ground	Physical	60	100	20	Adjacent	—	—
TM86	Grass Knot	Grass	Special	—	100	20	Normal	—	○
TM87	Swagger	Normal	Status	—	90	15	Normal	—	—
TM90	Substitute	Normal	Status	—	—	10	Self	—	—
TM94	Rock Smash	Fighting	Physical	40	100	15	Normal	—	○
HM01	Cut	Normal	Physical	50	95	30	Normal	—	○
HM02	Fly	Flying	Physical	90	95	15	Normal	○	○
HM04	Strength	Normal	Physical	80	100	15	Normal	—	○

MOVES TAUGHT BY PEOPLE

Name	Type	Kind	Pow.	Acc.	PP	Range	Long	DA

MOVES TAUGHT BY MOVE TUTORS FOR SHARDS

Name	Type	Kind	Pow.	Acc.	PP	Range	Long	DA
Seed Bomb	Grass	Physical	80	100	15	Normal	—	—
Dragon Pulse	Dragon	Special	90	100	10	Normal	○	—
Snore	Normal	Special	40	100	15	Normal	—	—
Synthesis	Grass	Status	—	—	5	Self	—	—
Roost	Flying	Status	—	—	10	Self	—	—
Giga Drain	Grass	Special	75	100	10	Normal	—	—
Tailwind	Flying	Status	—	—	30	Your Side	—	—
Worry Seed	Grass	Status	—	100	10	Normal	—	—
Outrage	Dragon	Physical	120	100	10	1 Random	—	○
Sleep Talk	Normal	Status	—	—	10	Self	—	—

EGG MOVES

Name	Type	Kind	Pow.	Acc.	PP	Range	Long	DA
Headbutt	Normal	Physical	70	100	15	Normal	—	○
Slam	Normal	Physical	80	75	20	Normal	—	○
Razor Wind	Normal	Special	80	100	10	Many Others	—	—
Leech Seed	Grass	Status	—	90	10	Normal	—	—
Nature Power	Normal	Status	—	—	20	Varies	—	—
Leaf Storm	Grass	Special	140	90	5	Normal	—	—
Synthesis	Grass	Status	—	—	5	Self	—	—
Curse	Ghost	Status	—	—	10	Varies	—	—
Leaf Blade	Grass	Physical	90	100	15	Normal	—	○
Dragon Dance	Dragon	Status	—	—	20	Self	—	—
Bullet Seed	Grass	Physical	25	100	30	Normal	—	—
Natural Gift	Normal	Physical	—	100	15	Normal	—	—

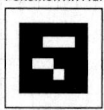

358 Chimecho

Wind Chime Pokémon

- HEIGHT: 2'00"
- WEIGHT: 2.2 lbs.
- GENDER: ♂ / ♀

Its cries echo inside its hollow body to emerge as beautiful notes for startling and repelling foes.

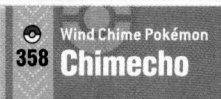

TYPE Psychic

ABILITY
- Levitate

HIDDEN ABILITY
—

STATS
HP
Attack
Defense
Sp. Atk
Sp. Def
Speed

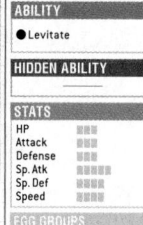

EGG GROUPS
Amorphous

ITEMS SOMETIMES HELD
- None

Same form for ♂ / ♀

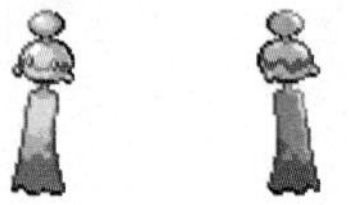

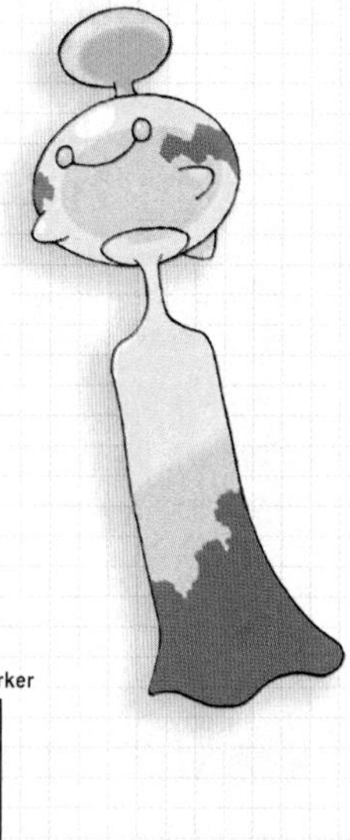

Pokémon AR Marker

EVOLUTION

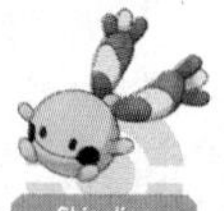

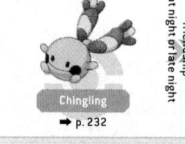

Chingling

➡ p. 232

Level up with high friendship at night or late night

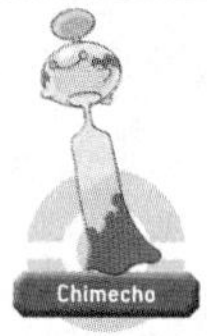

Chimecho

HOW TO OBTAIN

Pokémon Black Version 2	Link Trade or Poké Transfer
Pokémon White Version 2	Link Trade or Poké Transfer

HOW TO OBTAIN FROM OTHER GAMES

Pokémon Black Version	Abundant Shrine
Pokémon White Version	Abundant Shrine

LEVEL-UP AND LEARNED MOVES

Lv.	Name	Type	Kind	Pow.	Acc.	PP	Range	Long	DA
1	Wrap	Normal	Physical	15	90	20	Normal	—	○
6	Growl	Normal	Status	—	100	40	Many Others	—	—
9	Astonish	Ghost	Physical	30	100	15	Normal	—	○
14	Confusion	Psychic	Special	50	100	25	Normal	—	—
17	Uproar	Normal	Special	90	100	10	1 Random	—	—
22	Take Down	Normal	Physical	90	85	20	Normal	—	○
25	Yawn	Normal	Status	—	—	10	Normal	—	—
30	Psywave	Psychic	Special	—	80	15	Normal	—	—
33	Double-Edge	Normal	Physical	120	100	15	Normal	—	○
38	Heal Bell	Normal	Status	—	—	5	Your Party	—	—
41	Safeguard	Normal	Status	—	—	25	Your Side	—	—
46	Extrasensory	Psychic	Special	80	100	30	Normal	—	—
49	Heal Pulse	Psychic	Status	—	—	10	Normal	○	—
54	Synchronoise	Psychic	Special	70	100	15	Adjacent	—	—
57	Healing Wish	Psychic	Status	—	—	10	Self	—	—

TM & HM MOVES

Lv.	Name	Type	Kind	Pow.	Acc.	PP	Range	Long	DA
TM03	Psyshock	Psychic	Special	80	100	10	Normal	—	—
TM04	Calm Mind	Psychic	Status	—	—	20	Self	—	—
TM06	Toxic	Poison	Status	—	90	10	Normal	—	—
TM10	Hidden Power	Normal	Special	—	100	15	Normal	—	—
TM11	Sunny Day	Fire	Status	—	—	5	Both Sides	—	—
TM12	Taunt	Dark	Status	—	100	20	Normal	—	—
TM16	Light Screen	Psychic	Status	—	—	30	Your Side	—	—
TM17	Protect	Normal	Status	—	—	10	Self	—	—
TM18	Rain Dance	Water	Status	—	—	5	Both Sides	—	—
TM19	Telekinesis	Psychic	Status	—	—	15	Normal	—	—
TM20	Safeguard	Normal	Status	—	—	25	Your Side	—	—
TM21	Frustration	Normal	Physical	—	100	20	Normal	—	○
TM27	Return	Normal	Physical	—	100	20	Normal	—	○
TM29	Psychic	Psychic	Special	90	100	10	Normal	—	—
TM30	Shadow Ball	Ghost	Special	80	100	15	Normal	—	—
TM32	Double Team	Normal	Status	—	—	15	Self	—	—
TM33	Reflect	Psychic	Status	—	—	20	Your Side	—	—
TM41	Torment	Dark	Status	—	100	15	Normal	—	—
TM42	Facade	Normal	Physical	70	100	20	Normal	—	○
TM44	Rest	Psychic	Status	—	—	10	Self	—	—
TM45	Attract	Normal	Status	—	100	15	Normal	—	—
TM48	Round	Normal	Special	60	100	15	Normal	—	—
TM49	Echoed Voice	Normal	Special	40	100	15	Normal	—	—
TM53	Energy Ball	Grass	Special	80	100	10	Normal	—	—
TM57	Charge Beam	Electric	Special	50	90	10	Normal	—	—
TM70	Flash	Normal	Status	—	100	20	Normal	—	—
TM73	Thunder Wave	Electric	Status	—	100	20	Normal	—	—
TM77	Psych Up	Normal	Status	—	—	10	Normal	—	—
TM85	Dream Eater	Psychic	Special	100	100	15	Normal	—	—
TM86	Grass Knot	Grass	Special	—	100	20	Normal	—	○
TM87	Swagger	Normal	Status	—	90	15	Normal	—	—
TM90	Substitute	Normal	Status	—	—	10	Self	—	—
TM92	Trick Room	Psychic	Status	—	—	5	Both Sides	—	—

MOVES TAUGHT BY PEOPLE

Name	Type	Kind	Pow.	Acc.	PP	Range	Long	DA

MOVES TAUGHT BY MOVE TUTORS FOR SHARDS

Name	Type	Kind	Pow.	Acc.	PP	Range	Long	DA
Signal Beam	Bug	Special	75	100	15	Normal	—	—
Uproar	Normal	Special	90	100	10	1 Random	—	—
Last Resort	Normal	Physical	140	100	5	Normal	—	○
Magic Coat	Psychic	Status	—	—	15	Self	—	—
Hyper Voice	Normal	Special	90	100	15	Many Others	—	—
Icy Wind	Ice	Special	55	95	15	Many Others	—	—
Zen Headbutt	Psychic	Physical	80	90	15	Normal	—	○
Gravity	Psychic	Status	—	—	5	Both Sides	—	—
Bind	Normal	Physical	15	85	20	Normal	—	○
Snore	Normal	Special	40	100	15	Normal	—	—
Heal Bell	Normal	Status	—	—	5	Your Party	—	—
Knock Off	Dark	Physical	20	100	20	Normal	—	○
Helping Hand	Normal	Status	—	—	20	1 Ally	—	—
Recycle	Normal	Status	—	—	10	Self	—	—
Trick	Psychic	Status	—	100	10	Normal	—	—
Sleep Talk	Normal	Status	—	—	10	Self	—	—
Skill Swap	Psychic	Status	—	—	10	Normal	—	—
Snatch	Dark	Status	—	—	10	Self	—	—

EGG MOVES

Name	Type	Kind	Pow.	Acc.	PP	Range	Long	DA
Disable	Normal	Status	—	100	20	Normal	—	—
Curse	Ghost	Status	—	—	10	Varies	—	—
Hypnosis	Psychic	Status	—	60	20	Normal	—	—
Wish	Normal	Status	—	—	10	Self	—	—
Future Sight	Psychic	Special	100	100	10	Normal	—	—
Stored Power	Psychic	Special	20	100	10	Normal	—	—
Skill Swap	Psychic	Status	—	—	10	Normal	—	—

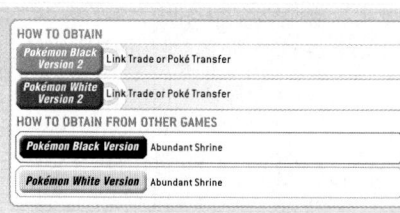

359 Disaster Pokémon
Absol

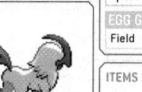

TYPE: Dark

ABILITIES
- Pressure
- Super Luck

HIDDEN ABILITY
- Justified

- HEIGHT: 3'11"
- WEIGHT: 103.6 lbs.
- GENDER: ♂ / ♀

It appears from deep in the mountains to warn people about upcoming disasters it has sensed with its horn.

STATS
HP
Attack
Defense
Sp. Atk
Sp. Def
Speed

EGG GROUPS
Field

Same form for ♂ / ♀

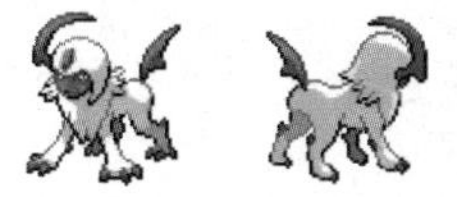

ITEMS SOMETIMES HELD
- None

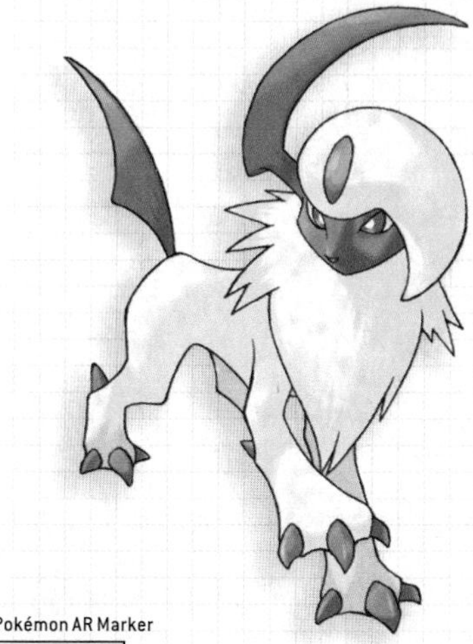

Pokémon AR Marker

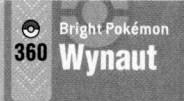

EVOLUTION

Does not evolve

HOW TO OBTAIN

Pokémon Black Version 2	❶ Route 13 ❷ Route 14
Pokémon White Version 2	❶ Route 13 ❷ Route 14

HOW TO OBTAIN FROM OTHER GAMES

	—
	—

LEVEL-UP AND LEARNED MOVES

Lv.	Name	Type	Kind	Pow.	Acc.	PP	Range	Long	DA
1	Scratch	Normal	Physical	40	100	35	Normal	—	○
1	Feint	Normal	Physical	30	100	10	Normal	—	—
4	Leer	Normal	Status	—	100	30	Many Others	—	—
9	Quick Attack	Normal	Physical	40	100	30	Normal	—	○
12	Pursuit	Dark	Physical	40	100	20	Normal	—	○
17	Taunt	Dark	Status	—	100	20	Normal	—	—
20	Bite	Dark	Physical	60	100	25	Normal	—	○
25	Double Team	Normal	Status	—	—	15	Self	—	—
28	Slash	Normal	Physical	70	100	20	Normal	—	○
33	Swords Dance	Normal	Status	—	—	30	Self	—	—
36	Future Sight	Psychic	Special	100	100	10	Normal	—	—
41	Night Slash	Dark	Physical	70	100	15	Normal	—	○
44	Detect	Fighting	Status	—	—	5	Self	—	—
49	Psycho Cut	Psychic	Physical	70	100	20	Normal	—	—
52	Sucker Punch	Dark	Physical	80	100	5	Normal	—	○
57	Razor Wind	Normal	Special	80	100	10	Many Others	—	—
60	Me First	Normal	Status	—	—	20	Varies	—	—
65	Perish Song	Normal	Status	—	—	5	Adjacent	○	—

TM & HM MOVES

Lv.	Name	Type	Kind	Pow.	Acc.	PP	Range	Long	DA
TM01	Hone Claws	Dark	Status	—	—	15	Self	—	—
TM04	Calm Mind	Psychic	Status	—	—	20	Self	—	—
TM06	Toxic	Poison	Status	—	90	10	Normal	—	—
TM07	Hail	Ice	Status	—	—	10	Both Sides	—	—
TM10	Hidden Power	Normal	Special	—	100	15	Normal	—	—
TM11	Sunny Day	Fire	Status	—	—	5	Both Sides	—	—
TM12	Taunt	Dark	Status	—	100	20	Normal	—	—
TM13	Ice Beam	Ice	Special	95	100	10	Normal	—	—
TM14	Blizzard	Ice	Special	120	70	5	Many Others	—	—
TM15	Hyper Beam	Normal	Special	150	90	5	Normal	—	—
TM17	Protect	Normal	Status	—	—	10	Self	—	—
TM18	Rain Dance	Water	Status	—	—	5	Both Sides	—	—
TM21	Frustration	Normal	Physical	—	100	20	Normal	—	○
TM24	Thunderbolt	Electric	Special	95	100	15	Normal	—	—
TM25	Thunder	Electric	Special	120	70	10	Normal	—	—
TM27	Return	Normal	Physical	—	100	20	Normal	—	○
TM30	Shadow Ball	Ghost	Special	80	100	15	Normal	—	—
TM32	Double Team	Normal	Status	—	—	15	Self	—	—
TM35	Flamethrower	Fire	Special	95	100	15	Normal	—	—
TM37	Sandstorm	Rock	Status	—	—	10	Both Sides	—	—
TM38	Fire Blast	Fire	Special	120	85	5	Normal	—	—
TM39	Rock Tomb	Rock	Physical	50	80	10	Normal	—	—
TM40	Aerial Ace	Flying	Physical	60	—	20	Normal	○	○
TM41	Torment	Dark	Status	—	100	15	Normal	—	—
TM42	Facade	Normal	Physical	70	100	20	Normal	—	○
TM44	Rest	Psychic	Status	—	—	10	Self	—	—
TM45	Attract	Normal	Status	—	100	15	Normal	—	—
TM46	Thief	Dark	Physical	40	100	10	Normal	—	○
TM48	Round	Normal	Special	60	100	15	Normal	—	—
TM49	Echoed Voice	Normal	Special	40	100	15	Normal	—	—
TM54	False Swipe	Normal	Physical	40	100	40	Normal	—	○
TM57	Charge Beam	Electric	Special	50	90	10	Normal	—	—
TM59	Incinerate	Fire	Special	30	100	15	Many Others	—	—
TM61	Will-O-Wisp	Fire	Status	—	75	15	Normal	—	—
TM65	Shadow Claw	Ghost	Physical	70	100	15	Normal	—	○
TM66	Payback	Dark	Physical	50	100	10	Normal	—	○
TM67	Retaliate	Normal	Physical	70	100	5	Normal	—	○
TM68	Giga Impact	Normal	Physical	150	90	5	Normal	—	○
TM70	Flash	Normal	Status	—	100	20	Normal	—	—
TM71	Stone Edge	Rock	Physical	100	80	5	Normal	—	—
TM73	Thunder Wave	Electric	Status	—	100	20	Normal	—	—
TM75	Swords Dance	Normal	Status	—	—	30	Self	—	—
TM77	Psych Up	Normal	Status	—	—	10	Normal	—	—
TM80	Rock Slide	Rock	Physical	75	90	10	Many Others	—	—
TM81	X-Scissor	Bug	Physical	80	100	15	Normal	—	○
TM85	Dream Eater	Psychic	Special	100	100	15	Normal	—	—
TM87	Swagger	Normal	Status	—	90	15	Normal	—	—
TM90	Substitute	Normal	Status	—	—	10	Self	—	—
TM94	Rock Smash	Fighting	Physical	40	100	15	Normal	—	○
TM95	Snarl	Dark	Special	55	95	15	Many Others	—	—
HM01	Cut	Normal	Physical	50	95	30	Normal	—	○
HM04	Strength	Normal	Physical	80	100	15	Normal	—	○

MOVES TAUGHT BY PEOPLE

Name	Type	Kind	Pow.	Acc.	PP	Range	Long	DA

MOVES TAUGHT BY MOVE TUTORS FOR SHARDS

Name	Type	Kind	Pow.	Acc.	PP	Range	Long	DA
Bounce	Flying	Physical	85	85	5	Normal	○	○
Magic Coat	Psychic	Status	—	—	15	Self	—	—
Icy Wind	Ice	Special	55	95	15	Many Others	—	—
Iron Tail	Steel	Physical	100	75	15	Normal	—	○
Zen Headbutt	Psychic	Physical	80	90	15	Normal	—	○
Foul Play	Dark	Physical	95	100	15	Normal	—	○
Superpower	Fighting	Physical	120	100	5	Normal	—	○
Dark Pulse	Dark	Special	80	100	15	Normal	○	—
Snore	Normal	Special	40	100	15	Normal	—	—
Knock Off	Dark	Physical	20	100	20	Normal	—	○
Role Play	Psychic	Status	—	—	10	Normal	—	—
Spite	Ghost	Status	—	100	10	Normal	—	—
Sleep Talk	Normal	Status	—	—	10	Self	—	—
Snatch	Dark	Status	—	—	10	Self	—	—

EGG MOVES

Name	Type	Kind	Pow.	Acc.	PP	Range	Long	DA
Baton Pass	Normal	Status	—	—	40	Self	—	—
Faint Attack	Dark	Physical	60	—	20	Normal	—	○
Double-Edge	Normal	Physical	120	100	15	Normal	—	○
Magic Coat	Psychic	Status	—	—	15	Self	—	—
Curse	Ghost	Status	—	—	10	Varies	—	—
Mean Look	Normal	Status	—	—	5	Normal	—	—
Zen Headbutt	Psychic	Physical	80	90	15	Normal	—	○
Punishment	Dark	Physical	—	100	5	Normal	—	○
Sucker Punch	Dark	Physical	80	100	5	Normal	—	○
Assurance	Dark	Physical	50	100	10	Normal	—	○
Me First	Normal	Status	—	—	20	Varies	—	—
Megahorn	Bug	Physical	120	85	10	Normal	—	○
Hex	Ghost	Special	50	100	10	Normal	—	—
Perish Song	Normal	Status	—	—	5	Adjacent	○	—

360 Bright Pokémon
Wynaut

TYPE: Psychic

ABILITY
- Shadow Tag

HIDDEN ABILITY
- Telepathy

- HEIGHT: 2'00"
- WEIGHT: 30.9 lbs.
- GENDER: ♂ / ♀

It grows strong by pushing up against others en masse. It loves eating sweet fruit.

STATS
HP
Attack
Defense
Sp. Atk
Sp. Def
Speed

EGG GROUPS
No Egg has ever been discovered

Same form for ♂ / ♀

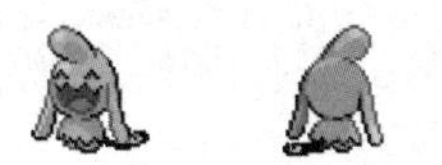

ITEMS SOMETIMES HELD
- None

EVOLUTION

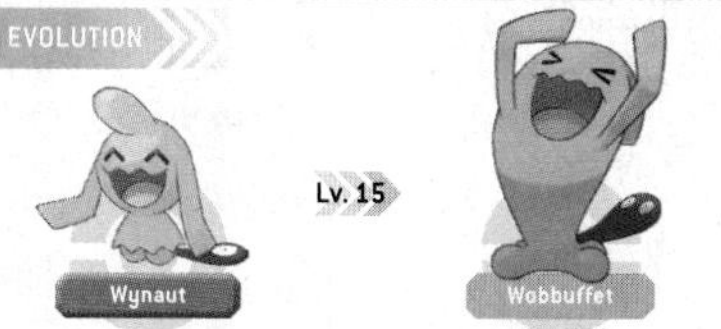

➡ p. 114

HOW TO OBTAIN

Pokémon Black Version 2	Have the Wobbuffet you receive from Yancy or Curtis hold Lax Incense and leave it at the Pokémon Day Care. Hatch the Egg that is found.
Pokémon White Version 2	Have the Wobbuffet you receive from Yancy or Curtis hold Lax Incense and leave it at the Pokémon Day Care. Hatch the Egg that is found.

HOW TO OBTAIN FROM OTHER GAMES

Pokémon Black Version	Route 2 (mass outbreak)
Pokémon White Version	Route 2 (mass outbreak)

LEVEL-UP AND LEARNED MOVES

Lv.	Name	Type	Kind	Pow.	Acc.	PP	Range	Long	DA
1	Splash	Normal	Status	—	—	40	Self	—	—
1	Charm	Normal	Status	—	100	20	Normal	—	—
1	Encore	Normal	Status	—	100	5	Normal	—	—
15	Counter	Fighting	Physical	—	100	20	Varies	—	○
15	Mirror Coat	Psychic	Special	—	100	20	Varies	—	—
15	Safeguard	Normal	Status	—	—	25	Your Side	—	—
15	Destiny Bond	Ghost	Status	—	—	5	Self	—	—

TM & HM MOVES

Lv.	Name	Type	Kind	Pow.	Acc.	PP	Range	Long	DA

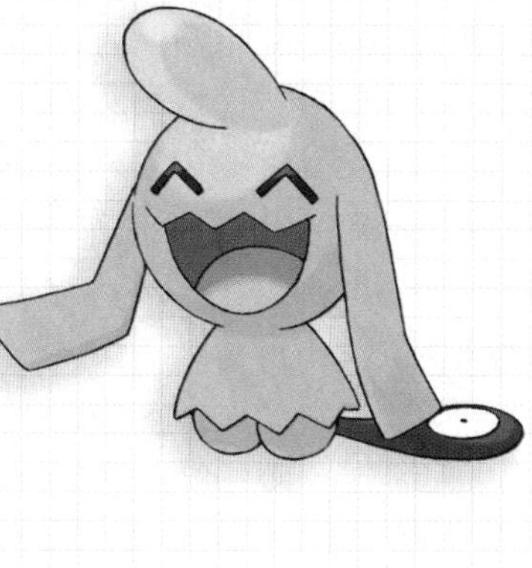

Pokémon AR Marker

MOVES TAUGHT BY PEOPLE

Name	Type	Kind	Pow.	Acc.	PP	Range	Long	DA

MOVES TAUGHT BY MOVE TUTORS FOR SHARDS

Name	Type	Kind	Pow.	Acc.	PP	Range	Long	DA

EGG MOVES

Name	Type	Kind	Pow.	Acc.	PP	Range	Long	DA

POKÉDEX
359 Absol
360 Wynaut

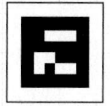

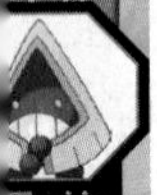

…ow Hat Pokémon
Snorunt

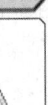

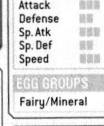

- HEIGHT: 2'04"
- WEIGHT: 37.0 lbs.
- GENDER: ♂ / ♀

It is said that several Snorunt gather under giant leaves and live together in harmony.

Same form for ♂ / ♀

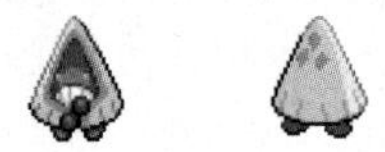

TYPE Ice

ABILITIES
- Inner Focus
- Ice Body

HIDDEN ABILITY
- Moody

STATS
HP
Attack
Defense
Sp. Atk
Sp. Def
Speed

EGG GROUPS
Fairy/Mineral

ITEMS SOMETIMES HELD
- None

EVOLUTION

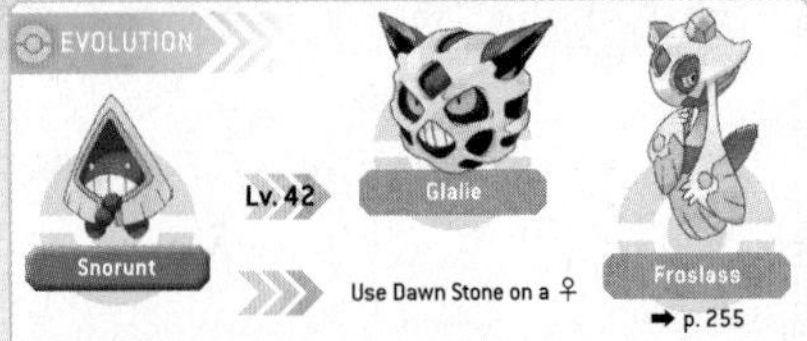

Snorunt
Lv. 42
Glalie
Use Dawn Stone on a ♀
Froslass

➡ p. 255

HOW TO OBTAIN

Pokémon Black Version 2	Link Trade or Poké Transfer
Pokémon White Version 2	Link Trade or Poké Transfer

HOW TO OBTAIN FROM OTHER GAMES

Pokémon Platinum Version	Route 216 (night only)
	——

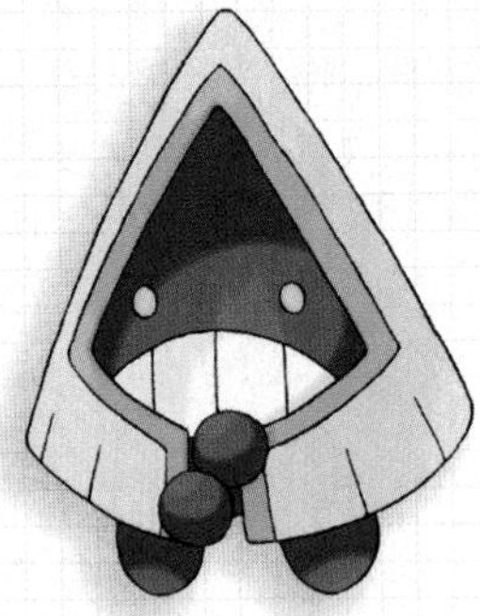

Pokémon AR Marker

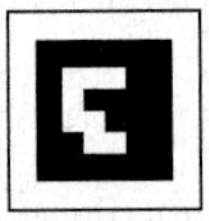

LEVEL-UP AND LEARNED MOVES

Lv.	Name	Type	Kind	Pow.	Acc.	PP	Range	Long	DA
1	Powder Snow	Ice	Special	40	100	25	Many Others	—	—
1	Leer	Normal	Status	—	100	30	Many Others	—	—
4	Double Team	Normal	Status	—	—	15	Self	—	—
10	Bite	Dark	Physical	60	100	25	Normal	—	○
13	Icy Wind	Ice	Special	55	95	15	Many Others	—	—
19	Headbutt	Normal	Physical	70	100	15	Normal	—	○
22	Protect	Normal	Status	—	—	10	Self	—	—
28	Ice Fang	Ice	Physical	65	95	15	Normal	—	○
31	Crunch	Dark	Physical	80	100	15	Normal	—	○
37	Ice Shard	Ice	Physical	40	100	30	Normal	—	—
40	Hail	Ice	Status	—	—	10	Both Sides	—	—
46	Blizzard	Ice	Special	120	70	5	Many Others	—	—

TM & HM MOVES

Lv.	Name	Type	Kind	Pow.	Acc.	PP	Range	Long	DA
TM06	Toxic	Poison	Status	—	90	10	Normal	—	—
TM07	Hail	Ice	Status	—	—	10	Both Sides	—	—
TM10	Hidden Power	Normal	Special	—	100	15	Normal	—	—
TM13	Ice Beam	Ice	Special	95	100	10	Normal	—	—
TM14	Blizzard	Ice	Special	120	70	5	Many Others	—	—
TM16	Light Screen	Psychic	Status	—	—	30	Your Side	—	—
TM17	Protect	Normal	Status	—	—	10	Self	—	—
TM18	Rain Dance	Water	Status	—	—	5	Both Sides	—	—
TM20	Safeguard	Normal	Status	—	—	25	Your Side	—	—
TM21	Frustration	Normal	Physical	—	100	20	Normal	—	○
TM27	Return	Normal	Physical	—	100	20	Normal	—	○
TM30	Shadow Ball	Ghost	Special	80	100	15	Normal	—	—
TM32	Double Team	Normal	Status	—	—	15	Self	—	—
TM42	Facade	Normal	Physical	70	100	20	Normal	—	○
TM44	Rest	Psychic	Status	—	—	10	Self	—	—
TM45	Attract	Normal	Status	—	100	15	Normal	—	—
TM48	Round	Normal	Special	60	100	15	Normal	—	—
TM70	Flash	Normal	Status	—	100	20	Normal	—	—
TM79	Frost Breath	Ice	Special	40	90	10	Normal	—	—
TM87	Swagger	Normal	Status	—	90	15	Normal	—	—
TM90	Substitute	Normal	Status	—	—	10	Self	—	—

MOVES TAUGHT BY PEOPLE

Name	Type	Kind	Pow.	Acc.	PP	Range	Long	DA

MOVES TAUGHT BY MOVE TUTORS FOR SHARDS

Name	Type	Kind	Pow.	Acc.	PP	Range	Long	DA
Block	Normal	Status	—	—	5	Normal	—	—
Icy Wind	Ice	Special	55	95	15	Many Others	—	—
Snore	Normal	Special	40	100	15	Normal	—	—
Spite	Ghost	Status	—	100	10	Normal	—	—
Sleep Talk	Normal	Status	—	—	10	Self	—	—

EGG MOVES

Name	Type	Kind	Pow.	Acc.	PP	Range	Long	DA
Block	Normal	Status	—	—	5	Normal	—	—
Spikes	Ground	Status	—	—	20	3 Foes	—	—
Rollout	Rock	Physical	30	90	20	Normal	—	○
Disable	Normal	Status	—	100	20	Normal	—	—
Bide	Normal	Physical	—	—	10	Self	—	○
Weather Ball	Normal	Special	50	100	10	Normal	—	—
Avalanche	Ice	Physical	60	100	10	Normal	—	○
Hex	Ghost	Special	50	100	10	Normal	—	—
Fake Tears	Dark	Status	—	100	20	Normal	—	—

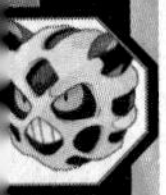

Face Pokémon
362 Glalie

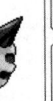

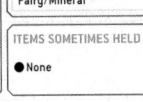

- HEIGHT: 4'11"
- WEIGHT: 565.5 lbs.
- GENDER: ♂ / ♀

It prevents prey from escaping by instantaneously freezing moisture in the air.

Same form for ♂ / ♀

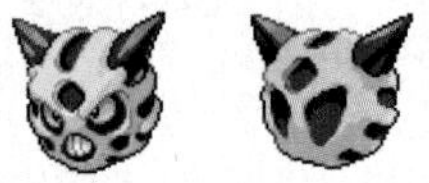

TYPE Ice

ABILITIES
- Inner Focus
- Ice Body

HIDDEN ABILITY
- Moody

STATS
HP
Attack
Defense
Sp. Atk
Sp. Def
Speed

EGG GROUPS
Fairy/Mineral

ITEMS SOMETIMES HELD
- None

EVOLUTION

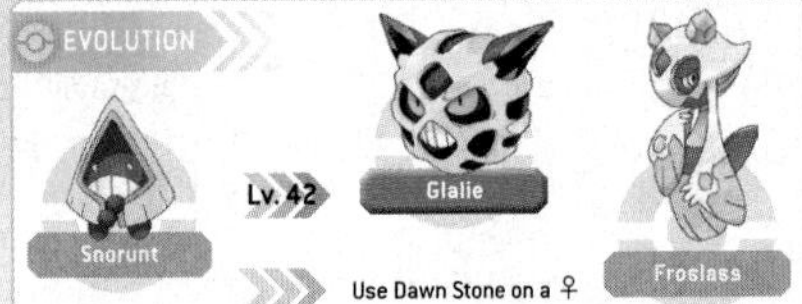

Snorunt
Lv. 42
Glalie
Use Dawn Stone on a ♀
Froslass

➡ p. 255

HOW TO OBTAIN

Pokémon Black Version 2	Get Snorunt with Link Trade or Poké Transfer, then level up to Lv. 42
Pokémon White Version 2	Get Snorunt with Link Trade or Poké Transfer, then level up to Lv. 42

HOW TO OBTAIN FROM OTHER GAMES

——
——

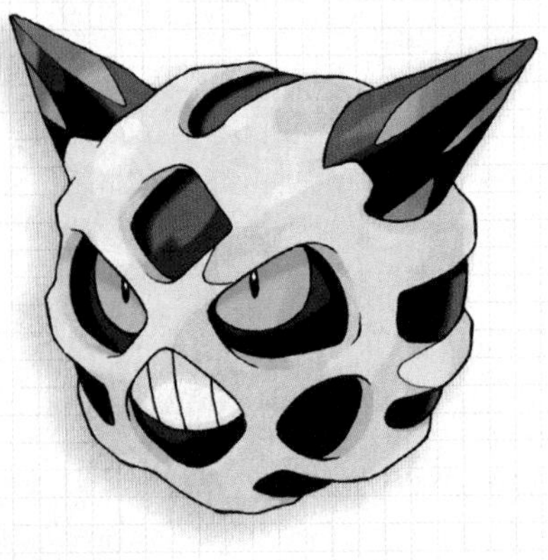

Pokémon AR Marker

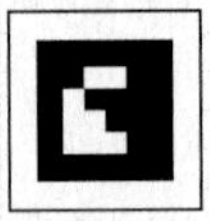

LEVEL-UP AND LEARNED MOVES

Lv.	Name	Type	Kind	Pow.	Acc.	PP	Range	Long	DA
1	Powder Snow	Ice	Special	40	100	25	Many Others	—	—
1	Leer	Normal	Status	—	100	30	Many Others	—	—
1	Double Team	Normal	Status	—	—	15	Self	—	—
1	Bite	Dark	Physical	60	100	25	Normal	—	○
4	Double Team	Normal	Status	—	—	15	Self	—	—
10	Bite	Dark	Physical	60	100	25	Normal	—	○
13	Icy Wind	Ice	Special	55	95	15	Many Others	—	—
19	Headbutt	Normal	Physical	70	100	15	Normal	—	○
22	Protect	Normal	Status	—	—	10	Self	—	—
28	Ice Fang	Ice	Physical	65	95	15	Normal	—	○
31	Crunch	Dark	Physical	80	100	15	Normal	—	○
37	Ice Beam	Ice	Special	95	100	10	Normal	—	—
40	Hail	Ice	Status	—	—	10	Both Sides	—	—
51	Blizzard	Ice	Special	120	70	5	Many Others	—	—
59	Sheer Cold	Ice	Special	—	30	5	Normal	—	—

TM & HM MOVES

Lv.	Name	Type	Kind	Pow.	Acc.	PP	Range	Long	DA
TM06	Toxic	Poison	Status	—	90	10	Normal	—	—
TM07	Hail	Ice	Status	—	—	10	Both Sides	—	—
TM10	Hidden Power	Normal	Special	—	100	15	Normal	—	—
TM12	Taunt	Dark	Status	—	100	20	Normal	—	—
TM13	Ice Beam	Ice	Special	95	100	10	Normal	—	—
TM14	Blizzard	Ice	Special	120	70	5	Multiple Foes	—	—
TM15	Hyper Beam	Normal	Special	150	90	5	Normal	—	—
TM16	Light Screen	Psychic	Status	—	—	30	Your Side	—	—
TM17	Protect	Normal	Status	—	—	10	Self	—	—
TM18	Rain Dance	Water	Status	—	—	5	Both Sides	—	—
TM20	Safeguard	Normal	Status	—	—	25	Your Side	—	—
TM21	Frustration	Normal	Physical	—	100	20	Normal	—	○
TM26	Earthquake	Ground	Physical	100	100	10	Adjacent	—	—
TM27	Return	Normal	Physical	—	100	20	Normal	—	○
TM30	Shadow Ball	Ghost	Special	80	100	15	Normal	—	—
TM32	Double Team	Normal	Status	—	—	15	Self	—	—
TM41	Torment	Dark	Status	—	100	15	Normal	—	—
TM42	Facade	Normal	Physical	70	100	20	Normal	—	○
TM44	Rest	Psychic	Status	—	—	10	Self	—	—
TM45	Attract	Normal	Status	—	100	15	Normal	—	—
TM48	Round	Normal	Special	60	100	15	Normal	—	—
TM64	Explosion	Normal	Physical	250	100	5	Adjacent	—	—
TM66	Payback	Dark	Physical	50	100	10	Normal	—	○
TM68	Giga Impact	Normal	Physical	150	90	5	Normal	—	○
TM70	Flash	Normal	Status	—	100	20	Normal	—	—
TM74	Gyro Ball	Steel	Physical	—	100	5	Normal	—	○
TM78	Bulldoze	Ground	Physical	60	100	20	Adjacent	—	—
TM79	Frost Breath	Ice	Special	40	90	10	Normal	—	—
TM87	Swagger	Normal	Status	—	90	15	Normal	—	—
TM90	Substitute	Normal	Status	—	—	10	Self	—	—

MOVES TAUGHT BY PEOPLE

Name	Type	Kind	Pow.	Acc.	PP	Range	Long	DA

MOVES TAUGHT BY MOVE TUTORS FOR SHARDS

Name	Type	Kind	Pow.	Acc.	PP	Range	Long	DA
Signal Beam	Bug	Special	75	100	15	Normal	—	—
Iron Head	Steel	Physical	80	100	15	Normal	—	○
Super Fang	Normal	Physical	—	90	10	Normal	—	○
Block	Normal	Status	—	—	5	Normal	—	—
Icy Wind	Ice	Special	55	95	15	Many Others	—	—
Dark Pulse	Dark	Special	80	100	15	Normal	○	—
Snore	Normal	Special	40	100	15	Normal	—	—
Spite	Ghost	Status	—	100	10	Normal	—	—
Sleep Talk	Normal	Status	—	—	10	Self	—	—

Spheal

 Clap Pokémon

363 Spheal

- HEIGHT: 2'07"
- WEIGHT: 87.1 lbs.
- GENDER: ♂ / ♀

They can't swim well yet, and they move much faster by rolling. When they're happy, they clap fins.

Same form for ♂ / ♀

TYPE Ice | Water

ABILITIES
- Thick Fat
- Ice Body

HIDDEN ABILITY
- Oblivious

STATS
HP
Attack
Defense
Sp. Atk
Sp. Def
Speed

EGG GROUPS
Water ❶ / Field

ITEMS SOMETIMES HELD
- None

EVOLUTION

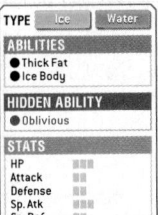 Spheal — Lv. 32 →  Sealeo — Lv. 44 → Walrein

HOW TO OBTAIN
Pokémon Black Version 2	❶ Undella Bay (water surface—winter only) ❷ Route 13 (Hidden Grotto)
Pokémon White Version 2	❶ Undella Bay (water surface—winter only) ❷ Route 13 (Hidden Grotto)

HOW TO OBTAIN FROM OTHER GAMES

Pokémon AR Marker

LEVEL-UP AND LEARNED MOVES

Lv.	Name	Type	Kind	Pow.	Acc.	PP	Range	Long	DA
1	Defense Curl	Normal	Status	—	—	40	Self	—	—
1	Powder Snow	Ice	Special	40	100	25	Many Others	—	—
1	Growl	Normal	Status	—	100	40	Many Others	—	—
1	Water Gun	Water	Special	40	100	25	Normal	—	—
7	Encore	Normal	Status	—	100	5	Normal	—	—
13	Ice Ball	Ice	Physical	30	90	20	Normal	—	○
19	Body Slam	Normal	Physical	85	100	15	Normal	—	—
25	Aurora Beam	Ice	Special	65	100	20	Normal	—	—
31	Hail	Ice	Status	—	—	10	Both Sides	—	—
37	Rest	Psychic	Status	—	—	10	Self	—	—
37	Snore	Normal	Special	40	100	15	Normal	—	○
43	Blizzard	Ice	Special	120	70	5	Many Others	—	—
49	Sheer Cold	Ice	Special	—	30	5	Normal	—	—

TM & HM MOVES

Lv.	Name	Type	Kind	Pow.	Acc.	PP	Range	Long	DA
TM06	Toxic	Poison	Status	—	90	10	Normal	—	—
TM07	Hail	Ice	Status	—	—	10	Both Sides	—	—
TM10	Hidden Power	Normal	Special	—	100	15	Normal	—	—
TM13	Ice Beam	Ice	Special	95	100	10	Normal	—	—
TM14	Blizzard	Ice	Special	120	70	5	Many Others	—	—
TM17	Protect	Normal	Status	—	—	10	Self	—	—
TM18	Rain Dance	Water	Status	—	—	5	Both Sides	—	—
TM21	Frustration	Normal	Physical	—	100	20	Normal	—	○
TM26	Earthquake	Ground	Physical	100	100	10	Adjacent	—	—
TM27	Return	Normal	Physical	—	100	20	Normal	—	—
TM32	Double Team	Normal	Status	—	—	15	Self	—	—
TM39	Rock Tomb	Rock	Physical	50	80	10	Normal	—	—
TM42	Facade	Normal	Physical	70	100	20	Normal	—	—
TM44	Rest	Psychic	Status	—	—	10	Self	—	—
TM45	Attract	Normal	Status	—	100	15	Normal	—	—
TM48	Round	Normal	Special	60	100	15	Normal	—	—
TM49	Echoed Voice	Normal	Special	40	100	15	Normal	—	—
TM78	Bulldoze	Ground	Physical	60	100	20	Adjacent	—	—
TM79	Frost Breath	Ice	Special	40	90	10	Normal	—	—
TM80	Rock Slide	Rock	Physical	75	90	10	Many Others	—	—
TM87	Swagger	Normal	Status	—	90	15	Normal	—	—
TM90	Substitute	Normal	Status	—	—	10	Self	—	—
TM94	Rock Smash	Fighting	Physical	40	100	15	Normal	—	○
HM03	Surf	Water	Special	95	100	15	Adjacent	—	—
HM04	Strength	Normal	Physical	80	100	15	Normal	—	—
HM05	Waterfall	Water	Physical	80	100	15	Normal	—	—
HM06	Dive	Water	Physical	80	100	10	Normal	—	—

MOVES TAUGHT BY PEOPLE

Name	Type	Kind	Pow.	Acc.	PP	Range	Long	DA

MOVES TAUGHT BY MOVE TUTORS FOR SHARDS

Name	Type	Kind	Pow.	Acc.	PP	Range	Long	DA
Signal Beam	Bug	Special	75	100	15	Normal	—	○
Super Fang	Normal	Physical	—	90	10	Normal	—	○
Icy Wind	Ice	Special	55	95	15	Many Others	—	—
Iron Tail	Steel	Physical	100	75	15	Normal	—	○
Aqua Tail	Water	Physical	90	90	10	Normal	—	—
Snore	Normal	Special	40	100	15	Normal	—	○
Sleep Talk	Normal	Status	—	—	10	Self	—	—

EGG MOVES

Name	Type	Kind	Pow.	Acc.	PP	Range	Long	DA
Water Sport	Water	Status	—	—	15	Both Sides	—	—
Stockpile	Normal	Status	—	—	20	Self	—	—
Swallow	Normal	Status	—	—	10	Self	—	—
Spit Up	Normal	Special	—	100	10	Normal	—	—
Yawn	Normal	Status	—	—	10	Normal	—	—
Curse	Ghost	Status	—	—	10	Varies	—	—
Fissure	Ground	Physical	—	30	5	Normal	—	—
Signal Beam	Bug	Special	75	100	15	Normal	—	—
Aqua Ring	Water	Status	—	—	20	Self	—	—
Rollout	Rock	Physical	30	90	20	Normal	—	○
Sleep Talk	Normal	Status	—	—	10	Self	—	—
Water Pulse	Water	Special	60	100	20	Normal	○	—

Sealeo

 Ball Roll Pokémon

364 Sealeo

- HEIGHT: 3'07"
- WEIGHT: 193.1 lbs.
- GENDER: ♂ / ♀

Be it Spheal or Poké Ball, it will spin any round object on its nose with the greatest of ease.

Same form for ♂ / ♀

TYPE Ice | Water

ABILITIES
- Thick Fat
- Ice Body

HIDDEN ABILITY
- Oblivious

STATS
HP
Attack
Defense
Sp. Atk
Sp. Def
Speed

EGG GROUPS
Water ❶ / Field

ITEMS SOMETIMES HELD
- None

EVOLUTION

 Spheal — Lv. 32 → Sealeo — Lv. 44 → Walrein

HOW TO OBTAIN
Pokémon Black Version 2	Undella Bay (ripples in water—winter only)
Pokémon White Version 2	Undella Bay (ripples in water—winter only)

HOW TO OBTAIN FROM OTHER GAMES

Pokémon AR Marker

LEVEL-UP AND LEARNED MOVES

Lv.	Name	Type	Kind	Pow.	Acc.	PP	Range	Long	DA
1	Powder Snow	Ice	Special	40	100	25	Many Others	—	—
1	Growl	Normal	Status	—	100	40	Many Others	—	—
1	Water Gun	Water	Special	40	100	25	Normal	—	—
1	Encore	Normal	Status	—	100	5	Normal	—	—
7	Encore	Normal	Status	—	100	5	Normal	—	—
13	Ice Ball	Ice	Physical	30	90	20	Normal	—	○
19	Body Slam	Normal	Physical	85	100	15	Normal	—	—
25	Aurora Beam	Ice	Special	65	100	20	Normal	—	—
31	Hail	Ice	Status	—	—	10	Both Sides	—	—
32	Swagger	Normal	Status	—	90	15	Normal	—	—
35	Rest	Psychic	Status	—	—	10	Self	—	—
39	Snore	Normal	Special	40	100	15	Normal	—	○
47	Blizzard	Ice	Special	120	70	5	Many Others	—	—
55	Sheer Cold	Ice	Special	—	30	5	Normal	—	—

TM & HM MOVES

Lv.	Name	Type	Kind	Pow.	Acc.	PP	Range	Long	DA
TM05	Roar	Normal	Status	—	100	20	Normal	—	—
TM06	Toxic	Poison	Status	—	90	10	Normal	—	—
TM07	Hail	Ice	Status	—	—	10	Both Sides	—	—
TM10	Hidden Power	Normal	Special	—	100	15	Normal	—	—
TM13	Ice Beam	Ice	Special	95	100	10	Normal	—	—
TM14	Blizzard	Ice	Special	120	70	5	Many Others	—	—
TM17	Protect	Normal	Status	—	—	10	Self	—	—
TM18	Rain Dance	Water	Status	—	—	5	Both Sides	—	—
TM21	Frustration	Normal	Physical	—	100	20	Normal	—	○
TM26	Earthquake	Ground	Physical	100	100	10	Adjacent	—	—
TM27	Return	Normal	Physical	—	100	20	Normal	—	—
TM32	Double Team	Normal	Status	—	—	15	Self	—	—
TM39	Rock Tomb	Rock	Physical	50	80	10	Normal	—	—
TM42	Facade	Normal	Physical	70	100	20	Normal	—	—
TM44	Rest	Psychic	Status	—	—	10	Self	—	—
TM45	Attract	Normal	Status	—	100	15	Normal	—	—
TM48	Round	Normal	Special	60	100	15	Normal	—	—
TM49	Echoed Voice	Normal	Special	40	100	15	Normal	—	—
TM78	Bulldoze	Ground	Physical	60	100	20	Adjacent	—	—
TM79	Frost Breath	Ice	Special	40	90	10	Normal	—	—
TM80	Rock Slide	Rock	Physical	75	90	10	Many Others	—	—
TM87	Swagger	Normal	Status	—	90	15	Normal	—	—
TM90	Substitute	Normal	Status	—	—	10	Self	—	—
TM94	Rock Smash	Fighting	Physical	40	100	15	Normal	—	○
HM03	Surf	Water	Special	95	100	15	Adjacent	—	—
HM04	Strength	Normal	Physical	80	100	15	Normal	—	—
HM05	Waterfall	Water	Physical	80	100	15	Normal	—	—
HM06	Dive	Water	Physical	80	100	10	Normal	—	—

MOVES TAUGHT BY PEOPLE

Name	Type	Kind	Pow.	Acc.	PP	Range	Long	DA

MOVES TAUGHT BY MOVE TUTORS FOR SHARDS

Name	Type	Kind	Pow.	Acc.	PP	Range	Long	DA
Signal Beam	Bug	Special	75	100	15	Normal	—	○
Super Fang	Normal	Physical	—	90	10	Normal	—	○
Icy Wind	Ice	Special	55	95	15	Many Others	—	—
Iron Tail	Steel	Physical	100	75	15	Normal	—	○
Aqua Tail	Water	Physical	90	90	10	Normal	—	—
Snore	Normal	Special	40	100	15	Normal	—	○
Sleep Talk	Normal	Status	—	—	10	Self	—	—

365 Walrein
Ice Break Pokémon

TYPE Ice / Water

ABILITIES
- Thick Fat
- Ice Body

HIDDEN ABILITY
- Oblivious

- HEIGHT: 4'07"
- WEIGHT: 332.0 lbs.
- GENDER: ♂ / ♀

Not only does its thick blubber keep it warm, it also protects it from attacks. It shatters ice with its prized tusks.

STATS
- HP
- Attack
- Defense
- Sp. Atk
- Sp. Def
- Speed

EGG GROUPS
Water ❶ / Field

ITEMS SOMETIMES HELD
- None

Same form for ♂ / ♀

Pokémon AR Marker

EVOLUTION

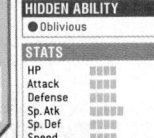

Spheal → (Lv. 32) Sealeo → (Lv. 44) Walrein

HOW TO OBTAIN

| Pokémon Black Version 2 | Undella Bay (ripples in water—winter only) |
| Pokémon White Version 2 | Undella Bay (ripples in water—winter only) |

HOW TO OBTAIN FROM OTHER GAMES

LEVEL-UP AND LEARNED MOVES

Lv.	Name	Type	Kind	Pow.	Acc.	PP	Range	Long	DA
1	Crunch	Dark	Physical	80	100	15	Normal	—	○
1	Powder Snow	Ice	Special	40	100	25	Many Others	—	—
1	Growl	Normal	Status	—	100	40	Many Others	—	—
1	Water Gun	Water	Special	40	100	25	Normal	—	—
1	Encore	Normal	Status	—	100	5	Normal	—	—
7	Encore	Normal	Status	—	100	5	Normal	—	—
13	Ice Ball	Ice	Physical	30	90	20	Normal	—	—
19	Body Slam	Normal	Physical	85	100	15	Normal	—	○
25	Aurora Beam	Ice	Special	65	100	20	Normal	—	—
31	Hail	Ice	Status	—	—	10	Both Sides	—	—
32	Swagger	Normal	Status	—	90	15	Normal	—	—
39	Rest	Psychic	Status	—	—	10	Self	—	—
39	Snore	Normal	Special	40	100	15	Normal	—	—
44	Ice Fang	Ice	Physical	65	95	15	Normal	—	○
52	Blizzard	Ice	Special	120	70	5	Many Others	—	—
65	Sheer Cold	Ice	Special	—	30	5	Normal	—	—

TM & HM MOVES

Lv.	Name	Type	Kind	Pow.	Acc.	PP	Range	Long	DA
TM05	Roar	Normal	Status	—	100	20	Normal	—	—
TM06	Toxic	Poison	Status	—	90	10	Normal	—	—
TM07	Hail	Ice	Status	—	—	10	Both Sides	—	—
TM10	Hidden Power	Normal	Special	—	100	15	Normal	—	—
TM13	Ice Beam	Ice	Special	95	100	10	Normal	—	—
TM14	Blizzard	Ice	Special	120	70	5	Many Others	—	—
TM15	Hyper Beam	Normal	Special	150	90	5	Normal	—	—
TM17	Protect	Normal	Status	—	—	10	Self	—	—
TM18	Rain Dance	Water	Status	—	—	5	Both Sides	—	—
TM21	Frustration	Normal	Physical	—	100	20	Normal	—	○
TM26	Earthquake	Ground	Physical	100	100	10	Adjacent	—	—
TM27	Return	Normal	Physical	—	100	20	Normal	—	○
TM32	Double Team	Normal	Status	—	—	15	Self	—	—
TM39	Rock Tomb	Rock	Physical	50	80	10	Normal	—	—
TM42	Facade	Normal	Physical	70	100	20	Normal	—	—
TM44	Rest	Psychic	Status	—	—	10	Self	—	—
TM45	Attract	Normal	Status	—	100	15	Normal	—	—
TM48	Round	Normal	Special	60	100	15	Normal	—	—
TM49	Echoed Voice	Normal	Special	40	100	15	Normal	—	—
TM68	Giga Impact	Normal	Physical	150	90	5	Normal	—	○
TM78	Bulldoze	Ground	Physical	60	100	20	Adjacent	—	—
TM79	Frost Breath	Ice	Special	40	90	10	Normal	—	—
TM80	Rock Slide	Rock	Physical	75	90	10	Many Others	—	—
TM87	Swagger	Normal	Status	—	90	15	Normal	—	—
TM90	Substitute	Normal	Status	—	—	10	Self	—	—
TM94	Rock Smash	Fighting	Physical	40	100	15	Normal	—	○
HM03	Surf	Water	Special	95	100	15	Adjacent	—	—
HM04	Strength	Normal	Physical	80	100	15	Normal	—	○
HM05	Waterfall	Water	Physical	80	100	15	Normal	—	○
HM06	Dive	Water	Physical	80	100	10	Normal	—	○

MOVES TAUGHT BY PEOPLE

Name	Type	Kind	Pow.	Acc.	PP	Range	Long	DA

MOVES TAUGHT BY MOVE TUTORS FOR SHARDS

Name	Type	Kind	Pow.	Acc.	PP	Range	Long	DA
Signal Beam	Bug	Special	75	100	15	Normal	—	—
Iron Head	Steel	Physical	80	100	15	Normal	—	○
Super Fang	Normal	Physical	—	90	10	Normal	—	—
Block	Normal	Status	—	—	5	Normal	—	—
Icy Wind	Ice	Special	55	95	15	Many Others	—	—
Iron Tail	Steel	Physical	100	75	15	Normal	—	○
Aqua Tail	Water	Physical	90	90	10	Normal	—	—
Snore	Normal	Special	40	100	15	Normal	—	—
Sleep Talk	Normal	Status	—	—	10	Self	—	—

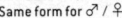

366 Clamperl
Bivalve Pokémon

TYPE Water

ABILITY
- Shell Armor

HIDDEN ABILITY
- Rattled

- HEIGHT: 1'04"
- WEIGHT: 115.7 lbs.
- GENDER: ♂ / ♀

It makes a single pearl during its lifetime. The pearl is said to amplify psychic power.

STATS
- HP
- Attack
- Defense
- Sp. Atk
- Sp. Def
- Speed

EGG GROUPS
Water ❶

ITEMS SOMETIMES HELD
- Big Pearl

Same form for ♂ / ♀

Pokémon AR Marker

EVOLUTION

Clamperl → Have it hold DeepSeaTooth and Link Trade it → Huntail

Clamperl → Have it hold DeepSeaScale and Link Trade it → Gorebyss

HOW TO OBTAIN

| Pokémon Black Version 2 | Route 4 (Super Rod) |
| Pokémon White Version 2 | Route 4 (Super Rod) |

HOW TO OBTAIN FROM OTHER GAMES

LEVEL-UP AND LEARNED MOVES

Lv.	Name	Type	Kind	Pow.	Acc.	PP	Range	Long	DA
1	Clamp	Water	Physical	35	85	15	Normal	—	—
1	Water Gun	Water	Special	40	100	25	Normal	—	—
1	Whirlpool	Water	Special	35	85	15	Normal	—	—
1	Iron Defense	Steel	Status	—	—	15	Self	—	—
51	Shell Smash	Normal	Status	—	—	15	Self	—	—

TM & HM MOVES

Lv.	Name	Type	Kind	Pow.	Acc.	PP	Range	Long	DA
TM06	Toxic	Poison	Status	—	90	10	Normal	—	—
TM07	Hail	Ice	Status	—	—	10	Both Sides	—	—
TM10	Hidden Power	Normal	Special	—	100	15	Normal	—	—
TM13	Ice Beam	Ice	Special	95	100	10	Normal	—	—
TM14	Blizzard	Ice	Special	120	70	5	Many Others	—	—
TM17	Protect	Normal	Status	—	—	10	Self	—	—
TM18	Rain Dance	Water	Status	—	—	5	Both Sides	—	—
TM21	Frustration	Normal	Physical	—	100	20	Normal	—	○
TM27	Return	Normal	Physical	—	100	20	Normal	—	○
TM32	Double Team	Normal	Status	—	—	15	Self	—	—
TM42	Facade	Normal	Physical	70	100	20	Normal	—	—
TM44	Rest	Psychic	Status	—	—	10	Self	—	—
TM45	Attract	Normal	Status	—	100	15	Normal	—	—
TM48	Round	Normal	Special	60	100	15	Normal	—	—
TM55	Scald	Water	Special	80	100	15	Normal	—	—
TM87	Swagger	Normal	Status	—	90	15	Normal	—	—
TM90	Substitute	Normal	Status	—	—	10	Self	—	—
HM03	Surf	Water	Special	95	100	15	Adjacent	—	—
HM05	Waterfall	Water	Physical	80	100	15	Normal	—	○
HM06	Dive	Water	Physical	80	100	10	Normal	—	—

MOVES TAUGHT BY PEOPLE

Name	Type	Kind	Pow.	Acc.	PP	Range	Long	DA

MOVES TAUGHT BY MOVE TUTORS FOR SHARDS

Name	Type	Kind	Pow.	Acc.	PP	Range	Long	DA
Iron Defense	Steel	Status	—	—	15	Self	—	—
Icy Wind	Ice	Special	55	95	15	Many Others	—	—
Snore	Normal	Special	40	100	15	Normal	—	—
Sleep Talk	Normal	Status	—	—	10	Self	—	—

EGG MOVES

Name	Type	Kind	Pow.	Acc.	PP	Range	Long	DA
Refresh	Normal	Status	—	—	20	Self	—	—
Mud Sport	Ground	Status	—	—	15	Both Sides	—	—
Body Slam	Normal	Physical	85	100	15	Normal	—	○
Supersonic	Normal	Status	—	55	20	Normal	—	—
Barrier	Psychic	Status	—	—	30	Self	—	—
Confuse Ray	Ghost	Status	—	100	10	Normal	—	—
Aqua Ring	Water	Status	—	—	20	Self	—	—
Muddy Water	Water	Special	95	85	10	Many Others	—	—
Water Pulse	Water	Special	60	100	20	Normal	○	—
Brine	Water	Special	65	100	10	Normal	—	—
Endure	Normal	Status	—	—	10	Self	—	—

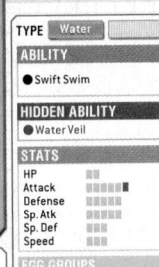

367 Huntail

Deep Sea Pokémon

TYPE Water

ABILITY
● Swift Swim

HIDDEN ABILITY
● Water Veil

● HEIGHT: 5'07"
● WEIGHT: 59.5 lbs.
● GENDER: ♂/♀

It lives deep in the sea. With a tail shaped like a small fish, it attracts unsuspecting prey.

STATS
HP
Attack
Defense
Sp. Atk
Sp. Def
Speed

EGG GROUPS
Water ❶

ITEMS SOMETIMES HELD
● DeepSeaTooth

Same form for ♂ / ♀

EVOLUTION

Clamperl

→→→ Have it hold DeepSeaTooth and Link Trade it → Huntail

→→→ Have it hold DeepSeaScale and Link Trade it → Gorebyss

HOW TO OBTAIN

| Pokémon Black Version 2 | Route 4 (Super Rod—ripples in water) |
| Pokémon White Version 2 | Have Clamperl sent to you via Link Trade while holding DeepSeaTooth to receive Huntail |

HOW TO OBTAIN FROM OTHER GAMES

LEVEL-UP AND LEARNED MOVES

Lv.	Name	Type	Kind	Pow.	Acc.	PP	Range	Long	DA
1	Whirlpool	Water	Special	35	85	15	Normal	—	—
6	Bite	Dark	Physical	60	100	25	Normal	—	○
10	Screech	Normal	Status	—	85	40	Normal	—	—
15	Water Pulse	Water	Special	60	100	20	Normal	○	—
19	Scary Face	Normal	Status	—	100	10	Normal	—	—
24	Ice Fang	Ice	Physical	65	95	15	Normal	—	○
28	Brine	Water	Special	65	100	10	Normal	—	—
33	Baton Pass	Normal	Status	—	—	40	Self	—	—
37	Dive	Water	Physical	80	100	10	Normal	—	○
42	Crunch	Dark	Physical	80	100	15	Normal	—	○
46	Aqua Tail	Water	Physical	90	90	10	Normal	—	○
51	Hydro Pump	Water	Special	120	80	5	Normal	—	—

TM & HM MOVES

Lv.	Name	Type	Kind	Pow.	Acc.	PP	Range	Long	DA
TM06	Toxic	Poison	Status	—	90	10	Normal	—	—
TM07	Hail	Ice	Status	—	—	10	Both Sides	—	—
TM10	Hidden Power	Normal	Special	—	100	15	Normal	—	—
TM13	Ice Beam	Ice	Special	95	100	10	Normal	—	—
TM14	Blizzard	Ice	Special	120	70	5	Many Others	—	—
TM15	Hyper Beam	Normal	Special	150	90	5	Normal	—	—
TM17	Protect	Normal	Status	—	—	10	Self	—	—
TM18	Rain Dance	Water	Status	—	—	5	Both Sides	—	—
TM21	Frustration	Normal	Physical	—	100	20	Normal	—	○
TM27	Return	Normal	Physical	—	100	20	Normal	—	○
TM32	Double Team	Normal	Status	—	—	15	Self	—	—
TM39	Rock Tomb	Rock	Physical	50	80	10	Normal	—	—
TM42	Facade	Normal	Physical	70	100	20	Normal	—	○
TM44	Rest	Psychic	Status	—	—	10	Self	—	—
TM45	Attract	Normal	Status	—	100	15	Normal	—	—
TM48	Round	Normal	Special	60	100	15	Normal	—	—
TM55	Scald	Water	Special	80	100	15	Normal	—	—
TM68	Giga Impact	Normal	Physical	150	90	5	Normal	—	○
TM87	Swagger	Normal	Status	—	90	15	Normal	—	—
TM90	Substitute	Normal	Status	—	—	10	Self	—	—
HM03	Surf	Water	Special	95	100	15	Adjacent	—	—
HM05	Waterfall	Water	Physical	80	100	15	Normal	—	○
HM06	Dive	Water	Physical	80	100	10	Normal	—	○

MOVES TAUGHT BY PEOPLE

Name	Type	Kind	Pow.	Acc.	PP	Range	Long	DA

MOVES TAUGHT BY MOVE TUTORS FOR SHARDS

Name	Type	Kind	Pow.	Acc.	PP	Range	Long	DA
Bounce	Flying	Physical	85	85	5	Normal	○	○
Super Fang	Normal	Physical	—	90	10	Normal	—	—
Icy Wind	Ice	Special	55	95	15	Many Others	—	—
Aqua Tail	Water	Physical	90	90	10	Normal	—	○
Bind	Normal	Physical	15	85	20	Normal	—	—
Snore	Normal	Special	40	100	15	Normal	—	—
Sleep Talk	Normal	Status	—	—	10	Self	—	—
Snatch	Dark	Status	—	—	10	Self	—	—

Pokémon AR Marker

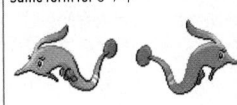

368 Gorebyss

South Sea Pokémon

TYPE Water

ABILITY
● Swift Swim

HIDDEN ABILITY
● Hydration

● HEIGHT: 5'11"
● WEIGHT: 49.8 lbs.
● GENDER: ♂/♀

It lives at the bottom of the sea. In the springtime, its pink body turns more vivid for some reason.

STATS
HP
Attack
Defense
Sp. Atk
Sp. Def
Speed

EGG GROUPS
Water ❶

ITEMS SOMETIMES HELD
● DeepSeaScale

Same form for ♂ / ♀

EVOLUTION

Clamperl

→→→ Have it hold DeepSeaTooth and Link Trade it → Huntail

→→→ Have it hold DeepSeaScale and Link Trade it → Gorebyss

HOW TO OBTAIN

| Pokémon Black Version 2 | Have Clamperl sent to you via Link Trade while holding DeepSeaScale to receive Gorebyss |
| Pokémon White Version 2 | Route 4 (Super Rod—ripples in water) |

HOW TO OBTAIN FROM OTHER GAMES

LEVEL-UP AND LEARNED MOVES

Lv.	Name	Type	Kind	Pow.	Acc.	PP	Range	Long	DA
1	Whirlpool	Water	Special	35	85	15	Normal	—	—
6	Confusion	Psychic	Special	50	100	25	Normal	—	—
10	Agility	Psychic	Status	—	—	30	Self	—	—
15	Water Pulse	Water	Special	60	100	20	Normal	○	—
19	Amnesia	Psychic	Status	—	—	20	Self	—	—
24	Aqua Ring	Water	Status	—	—	20	Self	—	—
28	Captivate	Normal	Status	—	100	20	Many Others	—	—
33	Baton Pass	Normal	Status	—	—	40	Self	—	—
37	Dive	Water	Physical	80	100	10	Normal	—	○
42	Psychic	Psychic	Special	90	100	10	Normal	—	—
46	Aqua Tail	Water	Physical	90	90	10	Normal	—	○
51	Hydro Pump	Water	Special	120	80	5	Normal	—	—

TM & HM MOVES

Lv.	Name	Type	Kind	Pow.	Acc.	PP	Range	Long	DA
TM06	Toxic	Poison	Status	—	90	10	Normal	—	—
TM07	Hail	Ice	Status	—	—	10	Both Sides	—	—
TM10	Hidden Power	Normal	Special	—	100	15	Normal	—	—
TM13	Ice Beam	Ice	Special	95	100	10	Normal	—	—
TM14	Blizzard	Ice	Special	120	70	5	Many Others	—	—
TM15	Hyper Beam	Normal	Special	150	90	5	Normal	—	—
TM17	Protect	Normal	Status	—	—	10	Self	—	—
TM18	Rain Dance	Water	Status	—	—	5	Both Sides	—	—
TM20	Safeguard	Normal	Status	—	—	25	Your Side	—	—
TM21	Frustration	Normal	Physical	—	100	20	Normal	—	○
TM27	Return	Normal	Physical	—	100	20	Normal	—	○
TM29	Psychic	Psychic	Special	90	100	10	Normal	—	—
TM30	Shadow Ball	Ghost	Special	80	100	15	Normal	—	—
TM32	Double Team	Normal	Status	—	—	15	Self	—	—
TM42	Facade	Normal	Physical	70	100	20	Normal	—	○
TM44	Rest	Psychic	Status	—	—	10	Self	—	—
TM45	Attract	Normal	Status	—	100	15	Normal	—	—
TM48	Round	Normal	Special	60	100	15	Normal	—	—
TM55	Scald	Water	Special	80	100	15	Normal	—	—
TM68	Giga Impact	Normal	Physical	150	90	5	Normal	—	○
TM77	Psych Up	Normal	Status	—	—	10	Normal	—	—
TM87	Swagger	Normal	Status	—	90	15	Normal	—	—
TM90	Substitute	Normal	Status	—	—	10	Self	—	—
HM03	Surf	Water	Special	95	100	15	Adjacent	—	—
HM05	Waterfall	Water	Physical	80	100	15	Normal	—	○
HM06	Dive	Water	Physical	80	100	10	Normal	—	○

MOVES TAUGHT BY PEOPLE

Name	Type	Kind	Pow.	Acc.	PP	Range	Long	DA

MOVES TAUGHT BY MOVE TUTORS FOR SHARDS

Name	Type	Kind	Pow.	Acc.	PP	Range	Long	DA
Bounce	Flying	Physical	85	85	5	Normal	○	○
Signal Beam	Bug	Special	75	100	15	Normal	—	—
Icy Wind	Ice	Special	55	95	15	Many Others	—	—
Aqua Tail	Water	Physical	90	90	10	Normal	—	○
Bind	Normal	Physical	15	85	20	Normal	—	—
Snore	Normal	Special	40	100	15	Normal	—	—
Sleep Talk	Normal	Status	—	—	10	Self	—	—

Pokémon AR Marker

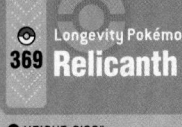

369 Relicanth
Longevity Pokémon

- HEIGHT: 3'03"
- WEIGHT: 51.6 lbs.
- GENDER: ♂ / ♀

A rare Pokémon discovered during a deep-sea exploration. It has not changed in over 100 million years.

♂ ♀

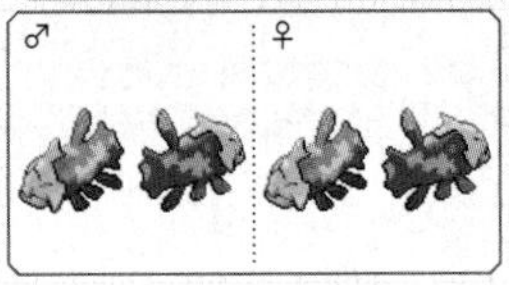

TYPE: Water / Rock

ABILITIES
- Swift Swim
- Rock Head

HIDDEN ABILITY
- Sturdy

STATS
HP
Attack
Defense
Sp. Atk
Sp. Def
Speed

EGG GROUPS
Water ❶ / Water ❷

ITEMS SOMETIMES HELD
- DeepSeaScale

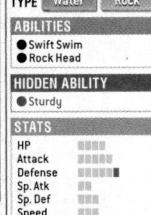

EVOLUTION

Does not evolve

HOW TO OBTAIN

Pokémon Black Version 2	Route 4 (Super Rod/ripples in water)
Pokémon White Version 2	Route 4 (Super Rod/ripples in water)

HOW TO OBTAIN FROM OTHER GAMES

—

—

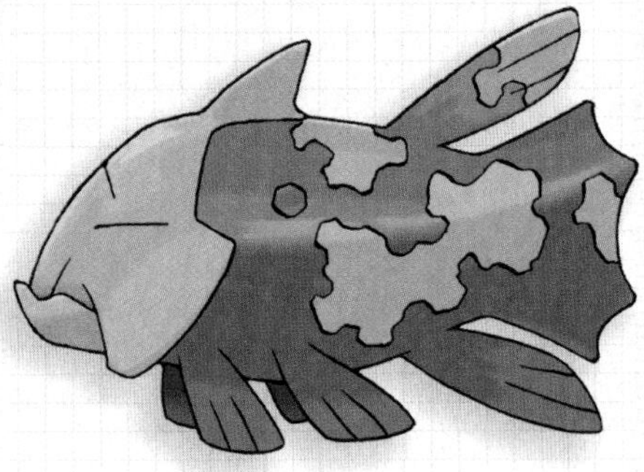

LEVEL-UP AND LEARNED MOVES

Lv.	Name	Type	Kind	Pow.	Acc.	PP	Range	Long	DA
1	Tackle	Normal	Physical	50	100	35	Normal	—	○
1	Harden	Normal	Status	—	—	30	Self	—	—
8	Water Gun	Water	Special	40	100	25	Normal	—	—
15	Rock Tomb	Rock	Physical	50	80	10	Normal	—	—
22	Yawn	Normal	Status	—	—	10	Normal	—	—
29	Take Down	Normal	Physical	90	85	20	Normal	—	○
36	Mud Sport	Ground	Status	—	—	15	Both Sides	—	—
43	AncientPower	Rock	Special	60	100	5	Normal	—	—
50	Double-Edge	Normal	Physical	120	100	15	Normal	—	○
57	Dive	Water	Physical	80	100	10	Normal	—	○
64	Rest	Psychic	Status	—	—	10	Self	—	—
71	Hydro Pump	Water	Special	120	80	5	Normal	—	—
78	Head Smash	Rock	Physical	150	80	5	Normal	—	○

TM & HM MOVES

Lv.	Name	Type	Kind	Pow.	Acc.	PP	Range	Long	DA
TM04	Calm Mind	Psychic	Status	—	—	20	Self	—	—
TM06	Toxic	Poison	Status	—	90	10	Normal	—	—
TM07	Hail	Ice	Status	—	—	10	Both Sides	—	—
TM10	Hidden Power	Normal	Special	—	100	15	Normal	—	—
TM13	Ice Beam	Ice	Special	95	100	10	Normal	—	—
TM14	Blizzard	Ice	Special	120	70	5	Many Others	—	—
TM15	Hyper Beam	Normal	Special	150	90	5	Normal	—	—
TM17	Protect	Normal	Status	—	—	10	Self	—	—
TM18	Rain Dance	Water	Status	—	—	5	Both Sides	—	—
TM20	Safeguard	Normal	Status	—	—	25	Your Side	—	—
TM21	Frustration	Normal	Physical	—	100	20	Normal	—	○
TM23	Smack Down	Rock	Physical	50	100	15	Normal	—	—
TM26	Earthquake	Ground	Physical	100	100	10	Adjacent	—	—
TM27	Return	Normal	Physical	—	100	20	Normal	—	○
TM32	Double Team	Normal	Status	—	—	15	Self	—	—
TM37	Sandstorm	Rock	Status	—	—	10	Both Sides	—	—
TM39	Rock Tomb	Rock	Physical	50	80	10	Normal	—	—
TM42	Facade	Normal	Physical	70	100	20	Normal	—	○
TM44	Rest	Psychic	Status	—	—	10	Self	—	—
TM45	Attract	Normal	Status	—	100	15	Normal	—	—
TM48	Round	Normal	Special	60	100	15	Normal	—	—
TM55	Scald	Water	Special	80	100	15	Normal	—	—
TM68	Giga Impact	Normal	Physical	150	90	5	Normal	—	○
TM69	Rock Polish	Rock	Status	—	—	20	Self	—	—
TM71	Stone Edge	Rock	Physical	100	80	5	Normal	—	—
TM77	Psych Up	Normal	Status	—	—	10	Normal	—	—
TM78	Bulldoze	Ground	Physical	60	100	20	Adjacent	—	—
TM80	Rock Slide	Rock	Physical	75	90	10	Many Others	—	—
TM87	Swagger	Normal	Status	—	90	15	Normal	—	—
TM90	Substitute	Normal	Status	—	—	10	Self	—	—
TM94	Rock Smash	Fighting	Physical	40	100	15	Normal	—	○
HM03	Surf	Water	Special	95	100	15	Adjacent	—	—
HM05	Waterfall	Water	Physical	80	100	15	Normal	—	○
HM06	Dive	Water	Physical	80	100	10	Normal	—	○

MOVES TAUGHT BY PEOPLE

Name	Type	Kind	Pow.	Acc.	PP	Range	Long	DA

MOVES TAUGHT BY MOVE TUTORS FOR SHARDS

Name	Type	Kind	Pow.	Acc.	PP	Range	Long	DA
Bounce	Flying	Physical	85	85	5	Normal	○	○
Icy Wind	Ice	Special	55	95	15	Many Others	—	—
Aqua Tail	Water	Physical	90	90	10	Normal	—	○
Earth Power	Ground	Special	90	100	10	Normal	—	—
Zen Headbutt	Psychic	Physical	80	90	15	Normal	—	○
Snore	Normal	Special	40	100	15	Normal	—	—
Stealth Rock	Rock	Status	—	—	20	3 Foes	—	—
Sleep Talk	Normal	Status	—	—	10	Self	—	—

EGG MOVES

Name	Type	Kind	Pow.	Acc.	PP	Range	Long	DA
Magnitude	Ground	Physical	—	100	30	Adjacent	—	—
Skull Bash	Normal	Physical	100	100	15	Normal	—	○
Water Sport	Water	Status	—	—	15	Both Sides	—	—
Amnesia	Psychic	Status	—	—	20	Self	—	—
Sleep Talk	Normal	Status	—	—	10	Self	—	—
Aqua Tail	Water	Physical	90	90	10	Normal	—	○
Snore	Normal	Special	40	100	15	Normal	—	—
Mud-Slap	Ground	Special	20	100	10	Normal	—	—
Muddy Water	Water	Special	95	85	10	Many Others	—	—
Mud Shot	Ground	Special	55	95	15	Normal	—	—
Brine	Water	Special	65	100	10	Normal	—	—
Zen Headbutt	Psychic	Physical	80	90	15	Normal	—	○

Pokémon AR Marker

370 Luvdisc
Rendezvous Pokémon

- HEIGHT: 2'00"
- WEIGHT: 19.2 lbs.
- GENDER: ♂ / ♀

It lives in warm seas. It is said that a couple finding this Pokémon will be blessed with eternal love.

Same form for ♂ / ♀

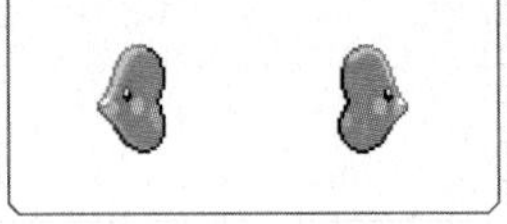

TYPE: Water

ABILITY
- Swift Swim

HIDDEN ABILITY
- Hydration

STATS
HP
Attack
Defense
Sp. Atk
Sp. Def
Speed

EGG GROUPS
Water ❷

ITEMS SOMETIMES HELD
- Heart Scale

EVOLUTION

Does not evolve

HOW TO OBTAIN

Pokémon Black Version 2	❶ Undella Town (Super Rod) ❷ Humilau City (Super Rod)
Pokémon White Version 2	❶ Undella Town (Super Rod) ❷ Humilau City (Super Rod)

HOW TO OBTAIN FROM OTHER GAMES

—

—

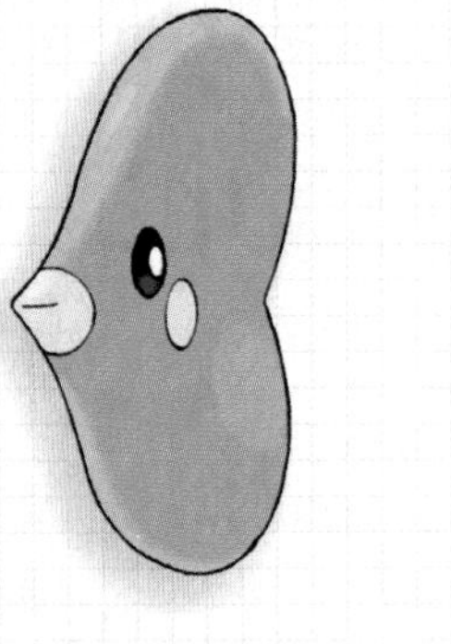

LEVEL-UP AND LEARNED MOVES

Lv.	Name	Type	Kind	Pow.	Acc.	PP	Range	Long	DA
1	Tackle	Normal	Physical	50	100	35	Normal	—	○
4	Charm	Normal	Status	—	100	20	Normal	—	—
7	Water Gun	Water	Special	40	100	25	Normal	—	—
9	Agility	Psychic	Status	—	—	30	Self	—	—
14	Take Down	Normal	Physical	90	85	20	Normal	—	○
17	Lucky Chant	Normal	Status	—	—	30	Your Side	—	—
22	Water Pulse	Water	Special	60	100	20	Normal	○	—
27	Attract	Normal	Status	—	100	15	Normal	—	—
31	Flail	Normal	Physical	—	100	15	Normal	—	○
37	Sweet Kiss	Normal	Status	—	75	10	Normal	—	—
40	Hydro Pump	Water	Special	120	80	5	Normal	—	—
46	Aqua Ring	Water	Status	—	—	20	Self	—	—
51	Captivate	Normal	Status	—	100	20	Many Others	—	—
55	Safeguard	Normal	Status	—	—	25	Your Side	—	—

TM & HM MOVES

Lv.	Name	Type	Kind	Pow.	Acc.	PP	Range	Long	DA
TM06	Toxic	Poison	Status	—	90	10	Normal	—	—
TM07	Hail	Ice	Status	—	—	10	Both Sides	—	—
TM10	Hidden Power	Normal	Special	—	100	15	Normal	—	—
TM13	Ice Beam	Ice	Special	95	100	10	Normal	—	—
TM14	Blizzard	Ice	Special	120	70	5	Many Others	—	—
TM17	Protect	Normal	Status	—	—	10	Self	—	—
TM18	Rain Dance	Water	Status	—	—	5	Both Sides	—	—
TM20	Safeguard	Normal	Status	—	—	25	Your Side	—	—
TM21	Frustration	Normal	Physical	—	100	20	Normal	—	○
TM27	Return	Normal	Physical	—	100	20	Normal	—	○
TM32	Double Team	Normal	Status	—	—	15	Self	—	—
TM42	Facade	Normal	Physical	70	100	20	Normal	—	○
TM44	Rest	Psychic	Status	—	—	10	Self	—	—
TM45	Attract	Normal	Status	—	100	15	Normal	—	—
TM48	Round	Normal	Special	60	100	15	Normal	—	—
TM55	Scald	Water	Special	80	100	15	Normal	—	—
TM77	Psych Up	Normal	Status	—	—	10	Normal	—	—
TM87	Swagger	Normal	Status	—	90	15	Normal	—	—
TM90	Substitute	Normal	Status	—	—	10	Self	—	—
HM03	Surf	Water	Special	95	100	15	Adjacent	—	—
HM05	Waterfall	Water	Physical	80	100	15	Normal	—	○
HM06	Dive	Water	Physical	80	100	10	Normal	—	○

MOVES TAUGHT BY PEOPLE

Name	Type	Kind	Pow.	Acc.	PP	Range	Long	DA

MOVES TAUGHT BY MOVE TUTORS FOR SHARDS

Name	Type	Kind	Pow.	Acc.	PP	Range	Long	DA
Bounce	Flying	Physical	85	85	5	Normal	○	○
Icy Wind	Ice	Special	55	95	15	Many Others	—	—
Snore	Normal	Special	40	100	15	Normal	—	—
Sleep Talk	Normal	Status	—	—	10	Self	—	—

EGG MOVES

Name	Type	Kind	Pow.	Acc.	PP	Range	Long	DA
Splash	Normal	Status	—	—	40	Self	—	—
Supersonic	Normal	Status	—	55	20	Normal	—	—
Water Sport	Water	Status	—	—	15	Both Sides	—	—
Mud Sport	Ground	Status	—	—	15	Both Sides	—	—
Captivate	Normal	Status	—	100	20	Many Others	—	—
Aqua Ring	Water	Status	—	—	20	Self	—	—
Aqua Jet	Water	Physical	40	100	20	Normal	—	○
Heal Pulse	Psychic	Status	—	—	10	Normal	○	—
Brine	Water	Special	65	100	10	Normal	—	—

Pokémon AR Marker

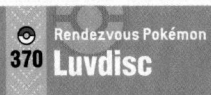

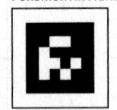

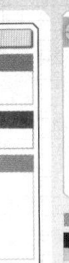

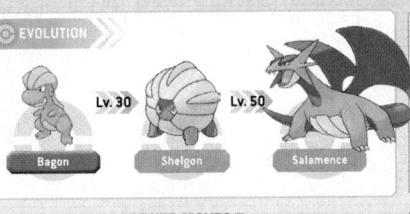

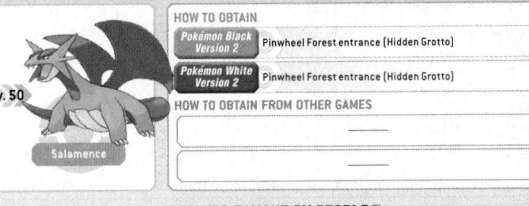

Rock Head Pokémon

371 Bagon

- HEIGHT: 2'00"
- WEIGHT: 92.8 lbs.
- GENDER: ♂ / ♀

Dreaming of one day flying, it practices by leaping off cliffs every day.

Same form for ♂ / ♀

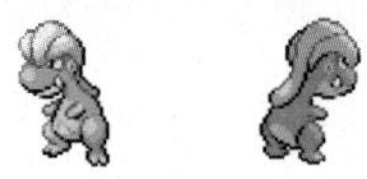

TYPE Dragon

ABILITY
- Rock Head

HIDDEN ABILITY
- Sheer Force

STATS
HP
Attack
Defense
Sp. Atk
Sp. Def
Speed

EGG GROUPS
Dragon

ITEMS SOMETIMES HELD
- Dragon Fang

EVOLUTION

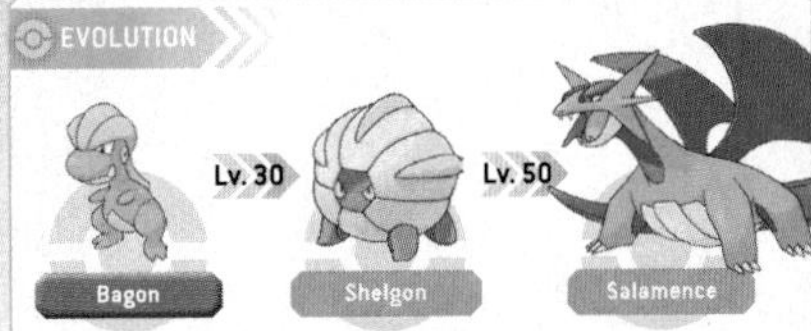

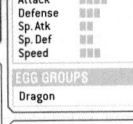

HOW TO OBTAIN

Pokémon Black Version 2	Pinwheel Forest entrance (Hidden Grotto)
Pokémon White Version 2	Pinwheel Forest entrance (Hidden Grotto)

HOW TO OBTAIN FROM OTHER GAMES

—

—

LEVEL-UP AND LEARNED MOVES

Lv.	Name	Type	Kind	Pow.	Acc.	PP	Range	Long	DA
1	Rage	Normal	Physical	20	100	20	Normal	—	○
5	Bite	Dark	Physical	60	100	25	Normal	—	○
10	Leer	Normal	Status	—	100	30	Many Others	—	—
16	Headbutt	Normal	Physical	70	100	15	Normal	—	○
20	Focus Energy	Normal	Status	—	—	30	Self	—	—
25	Ember	Fire	Special	40	100	25	Normal	—	—
31	DragonBreath	Dragon	Special	60	100	20	Normal	—	—
35	Zen Headbutt	Psychic	Physical	80	90	15	Normal	—	○
40	Scary Face	Normal	Status	—	100	10	Normal	—	—
46	Crunch	Dark	Physical	80	100	15	Normal	—	○
50	Dragon Claw	Dragon	Physical	80	100	15	Normal	—	○
55	Double-Edge	Normal	Physical	120	100	15	Normal	—	○

TM & HM MOVES

Lv.	Name	Type	Kind	Pow.	Acc.	PP	Range	Long	DA
TM01	Hone Claws	Dark	Status	—	—	15	Self	—	—
TM02	Dragon Claw	Dragon	Physical	80	100	15	Normal	—	○
TM05	Roar	Normal	Status	—	100	20	Normal	—	—
TM06	Toxic	Poison	Status	—	90	10	Normal	—	—
TM10	Hidden Power	Normal	Special	—	100	15	Normal	—	—
TM11	Sunny Day	Fire	Status	—	—	5	Both Sides	—	—
TM17	Protect	Normal	Status	—	—	10	Self	—	—
TM18	Rain Dance	Water	Status	—	—	5	Both Sides	—	—
TM21	Frustration	Normal	Physical	—	100	20	Normal	—	○
TM27	Return	Normal	Physical	—	100	20	Normal	—	○
TM31	Brick Break	Fighting	Physical	75	100	15	Normal	—	○
TM32	Double Team	Normal	Status	—	—	15	Self	—	—
TM35	Flamethrower	Fire	Special	95	100	15	Normal	—	—
TM38	Fire Blast	Fire	Special	120	85	5	Normal	—	—
TM39	Rock Tomb	Rock	Physical	50	80	10	Normal	—	—
TM40	Aerial Ace	Flying	Physical	60	—	20	Normal	○	○
TM42	Facade	Normal	Physical	70	100	20	Normal	—	○
TM44	Rest	Psychic	Status	—	—	10	Self	—	—
TM45	Attract	Normal	Status	—	100	15	Normal	—	—
TM48	Round	Normal	Special	60	100	15	Normal	—	—
TM59	Incinerate	Fire	Special	30	100	15	Many Others	—	—
TM65	Shadow Claw	Ghost	Physical	70	100	15	Normal	—	○
TM80	Rock Slide	Rock	Physical	75	90	10	Many Others	—	—
TM87	Swagger	Normal	Status	—	90	15	Normal	—	—
TM90	Substitute	Normal	Status	—	—	10	Self	—	—
TM94	Rock Smash	Fighting	Physical	40	100	15	Normal	—	○
HM01	Cut	Normal	Physical	50	95	30	Normal	—	○
HM04	Strength	Normal	Physical	80	100	15	Normal	—	○

MOVES TAUGHT BY PEOPLE

Name	Type	Kind	Pow.	Acc.	PP	Range	Long	DA
Draco Meteor	Dragon	Special	140	90	5	Normal	—	—

MOVES TAUGHT BY MOVE TUTORS FOR SHARDS

Name	Type	Kind	Pow.	Acc.	PP	Range	Long	DA
Hyper Voice	Normal	Special	90	100	10	Many Others	—	—
Zen Headbutt	Psychic	Physical	80	90	15	Normal	—	○
Dragon Pulse	Dragon	Special	90	100	10	Normal	○	—
Snore	Normal	Special	40	100	15	Normal	—	—
Outrage	Dragon	Physical	120	100	10	1 Random	—	○
Sleep Talk	Normal	Status	—	—	10	Self	—	—

EGG MOVES

Name	Type	Kind	Pow.	Acc.	PP	Range	Long	DA
Hydro Pump	Water	Special	120	80	5	Normal	—	—
Thrash	Normal	Physical	120	100	10	1 Random	—	○
Dragon Rage	Dragon	Special	—	100	10	Normal	—	—
Twister	Dragon	Special	40	100	20	Many Others	—	—
Dragon Dance	Dragon	Status	—	—	20	Self	—	—
Fire Fang	Fire	Physical	65	95	15	Normal	—	○
Dragon Rush	Dragon	Physical	100	75	10	Normal	—	○
Dragon Pulse	Dragon	Special	90	100	10	Normal	○	—
Endure	Normal	Status	—	—	10	Self	—	—
Defense Curl	Normal	Status	—	—	40	Self	—	—

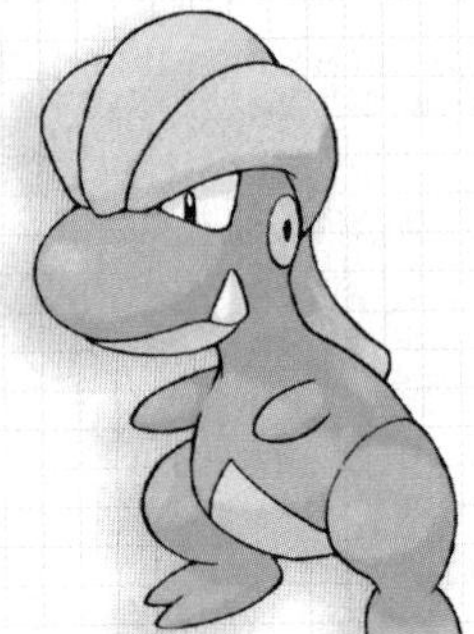

Pokémon AR Marker

Endurance Pokémon

372 Shelgon

- HEIGHT: 3'07"
- WEIGHT: 243.6 lbs.
- GENDER: ♂ / ♀

Within its rugged shell, its cells have begun changing. The shell peels off the instant it evolves.

Same form for ♂ / ♀

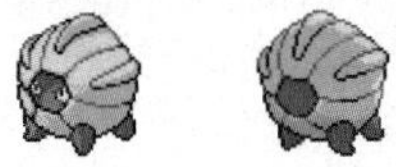

TYPE Dragon

ABILITY
- Rock Head

HIDDEN ABILITY
- Overcoat

STATS
HP
Attack
Defense
Sp. Atk
Sp. Def
Speed

EGG GROUPS
Dragon

ITEMS SOMETIMES HELD
- None

EVOLUTION

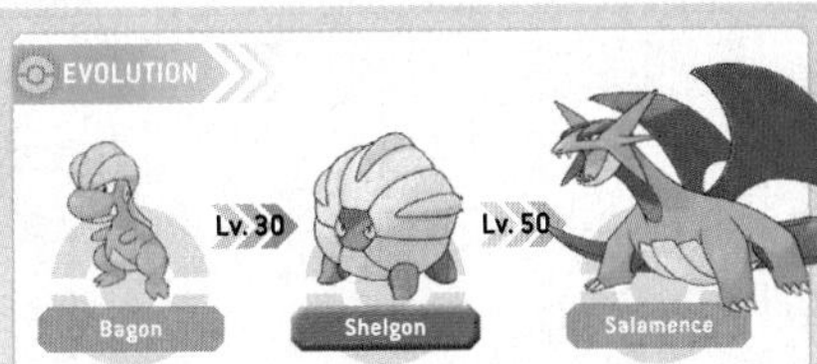

HOW TO OBTAIN

Pokémon Black Version 2	Level up Bagon to Lv. 30
Pokémon White Version 2	Level up Bagon to Lv. 30

HOW TO OBTAIN FROM OTHER GAMES

—

—

LEVEL-UP AND LEARNED MOVES

Lv.	Name	Type	Kind	Pow.	Acc.	PP	Range	Long	DA
1	Rage	Normal	Physical	20	100	20	Normal	—	○
1	Bite	Dark	Physical	60	100	25	Normal	—	○
1	Leer	Normal	Status	—	100	30	Many Others	—	—
1	Headbutt	Normal	Physical	70	100	15	Normal	—	○
5	Bite	Dark	Physical	60	100	25	Normal	—	○
10	Leer	Normal	Status	—	100	30	Many Others	—	—
16	Headbutt	Normal	Physical	70	100	15	Normal	—	○
20	Focus Energy	Normal	Status	—	—	30	Self	—	—
25	Ember	Fire	Special	40	100	25	Normal	—	—
30	Protect	Normal	Status	—	—	10	Self	—	—
32	DragonBreath	Dragon	Special	60	100	20	Normal	—	—
37	Zen Headbutt	Psychic	Physical	80	90	15	Normal	—	○
43	Scary Face	Normal	Status	—	100	10	Normal	—	—
50	Crunch	Dark	Physical	80	100	15	Normal	—	○
55	Dragon Claw	Dragon	Physical	80	100	15	Normal	—	○
61	Double-Edge	Normal	Physical	120	100	15	Normal	—	○

TM & HM MOVES

Lv.	Name	Type	Kind	Pow.	Acc.	PP	Range	Long	DA
TM01	Hone Claws	Dark	Status	—	—	15	Self	—	—
TM02	Dragon Claw	Dragon	Physical	80	100	15	Normal	—	○
TM05	Roar	Normal	Status	—	100	20	Normal	—	—
TM06	Toxic	Poison	Status	—	90	10	Normal	—	—
TM10	Hidden Power	Normal	Special	—	100	15	Normal	—	—
TM11	Sunny Day	Fire	Status	—	—	5	Both Sides	—	—
TM17	Protect	Normal	Status	—	—	10	Self	—	—
TM18	Rain Dance	Water	Status	—	—	5	Both Sides	—	—
TM21	Frustration	Normal	Physical	—	100	20	Normal	—	○
TM27	Return	Normal	Physical	—	100	20	Normal	—	○
TM31	Brick Break	Fighting	Physical	75	100	15	Normal	—	○
TM32	Double Team	Normal	Status	—	—	15	Self	—	—
TM35	Flamethrower	Fire	Special	95	100	15	Normal	—	—
TM38	Fire Blast	Fire	Special	120	85	5	Normal	—	—
TM39	Rock Tomb	Rock	Physical	50	80	10	Normal	—	—
TM40	Aerial Ace	Flying	Physical	60	—	20	Normal	○	○
TM42	Facade	Normal	Physical	70	100	20	Normal	—	○
TM44	Rest	Psychic	Status	—	—	10	Self	—	—
TM45	Attract	Normal	Status	—	100	15	Normal	—	—
TM48	Round	Normal	Special	60	100	15	Normal	—	—
TM59	Incinerate	Fire	Special	30	100	15	Many Others	—	—
TM65	Shadow Claw	Ghost	Physical	70	100	15	Normal	—	○
TM80	Rock Slide	Rock	Physical	75	90	10	Many Others	—	—
TM87	Swagger	Normal	Status	—	90	15	Normal	—	—
TM90	Substitute	Normal	Status	—	—	10	Self	—	—
TM94	Rock Smash	Fighting	Physical	40	100	15	Normal	—	○
HM01	Cut	Normal	Physical	50	95	30	Normal	—	○
HM04	Strength	Normal	Physical	80	100	15	Normal	—	○

MOVES TAUGHT BY PEOPLE

Name	Type	Kind	Pow.	Acc.	PP	Range	Long	DA
Draco Meteor	Dragon	Special	140	90	5	Normal	—	—

MOVES TAUGHT BY MOVE TUTORS FOR SHARDS

Name	Type	Kind	Pow.	Acc.	PP	Range	Long	DA
Iron Defense	Steel	Status	—	—	15	Self	—	—
Hyper Voice	Normal	Special	90	100	10	Many Others	—	—
Zen Headbutt	Psychic	Physical	80	90	15	Normal	—	○
Dragon Pulse	Dragon	Special	90	100	10	Normal	○	—
Snore	Normal	Special	40	100	15	Normal	—	—
Outrage	Dragon	Physical	120	100	10	1 Random	—	○
Sleep Talk	Normal	Status	—	—	10	Self	—	—

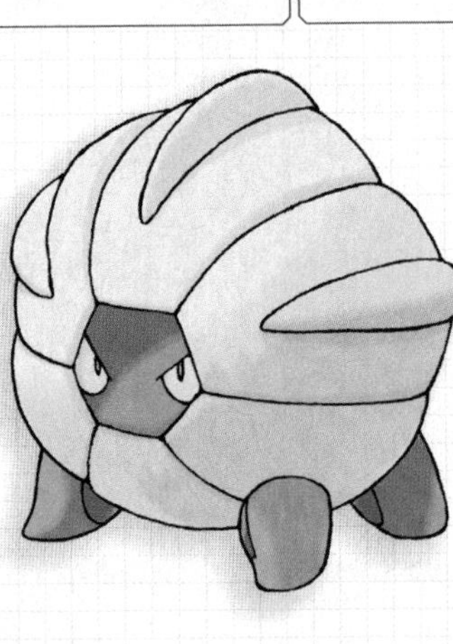

Pokémon AR Marker

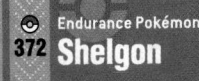

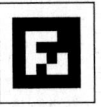

373 Salamence

Dragon Pokémon

TYPE Dragon / Flying

ABILITY
- Intimidate

HIDDEN ABILITY
- Moxie

- HEIGHT: 4'11"
- WEIGHT: 226.2 lbs.
- GENDER: ♂ / ♀

As a result of its long-held dream of flying, its cellular structure changed, and wings grew out.

STATS
- HP
- Attack
- Defense
- Sp. Atk
- Sp. Def
- Speed

EGG GROUPS
Dragon

ITEMS SOMETIMES HELD
- None

Same form for ♂ / ♀

Pokémon AR Marker

EVOLUTION

Bagon — Lv. 30 → Shelgon — Lv. 50 → Salamence

HOW TO OBTAIN

| Pokémon Black Version 2 | Level up Shelgon to Lv. 50 |
| Pokémon White Version 2 | Level up Shelgon to Lv. 50 |

HOW TO OBTAIN FROM OTHER GAMES

| —— |
| —— |

LEVEL-UP AND LEARNED MOVES

Lv.	Name	Type	Kind	Pow.	Acc.	PP	Range	Long	DA
1	Fire Fang	Fire	Physical	65	95	15	Normal	—	○
1	Thunder Fang	Electric	Physical	65	95	15	Normal	—	○
1	Rage	Normal	Physical	20	100	20	Normal	—	○
1	Bite	Dark	Physical	60	100	25	Normal	—	○
1	Leer	Normal	Status	—	100	30	Many Others	—	—
1	Headbutt	Normal	Physical	70	100	15	Normal	—	○
1	Bite	Dark	Physical	60	100	25	Normal	—	○
10	Leer	Normal	Status	—	100	30	Many Others	—	—
16	Headbutt	Normal	Physical	70	100	15	Normal	—	○
20	Focus Energy	Normal	Status	—	—	30	Self	—	—
25	Ember	Fire	Special	40	100	25	Normal	—	—
30	Protect	Normal	Status	—	—	10	Self	—	—
32	DragonBreath	Dragon	Special	60	100	20	Normal	—	—
37	Zen Headbutt	Psychic	Physical	80	90	15	Normal	—	○
43	Scary Face	Normal	Status	—	100	10	Normal	—	—
50	Fly	Flying	Physical	90	95	15	Normal	○	○
53	Crunch	Dark	Physical	80	100	15	Normal	—	○
61	Dragon Claw	Dragon	Physical	80	100	15	Normal	—	○
70	Double-Edge	Normal	Physical	120	100	15	Normal	—	○
80	Dragon Tail	Dragon	Physical	60	90	10	Normal	—	○

TM & HM MOVES

Lv.	Name	Type	Kind	Pow.	Acc.	PP	Range	Long	DA
TM01	Hone Claws	Dark	Status	—	—	15	Self	—	—
TM02	Dragon Claw	Dragon	Physical	80	100	15	Normal	—	○
TM05	Roar	Normal	Status	—	100	20	Normal	—	—
TM06	Toxic	Poison	Status	—	90	10	Normal	—	—
TM10	Hidden Power	Normal	Special	60	100	15	Normal	—	—
TM11	Sunny Day	Fire	Status	—	—	5	Both Sides	—	—
TM15	Hyper Beam	Normal	Special	150	90	5	Normal	—	—
TM17	Protect	Normal	Status	—	—	10	Self	—	—
TM18	Rain Dance	Water	Status	—	—	5	Both Sides	—	—
TM21	Frustration	Normal	Physical	—	100	20	Normal	—	○
TM26	Earthquake	Ground	Physical	100	100	10	Adjacent	—	—
TM27	Return	Normal	Physical	—	100	20	Normal	—	○
TM31	Brick Break	Fighting	Physical	75	100	15	Normal	—	○
TM32	Double Team	Normal	Status	—	—	15	Self	—	—
TM35	Flamethrower	Fire	Special	95	100	15	Normal	—	—
TM38	Fire Blast	Fire	Special	120	85	5	Normal	—	—
TM39	Rock Tomb	Rock	Physical	50	80	10	Normal	—	—
TM40	Aerial Ace	Flying	Physical	60	—	20	Normal	○	○
TM42	Facade	Normal	Physical	70	100	20	Normal	—	○
TM44	Rest	Psychic	Status	—	—	10	Self	—	—
TM45	Attract	Normal	Status	—	100	15	Normal	—	—
TM48	Round	Normal	Special	60	100	15	Normal	—	—
TM59	Incinerate	Fire	Special	30	100	15	Many Others	—	—
TM65	Shadow Claw	Ghost	Physical	70	100	15	Normal	—	○
TM68	Giga Impact	Normal	Physical	150	90	5	Normal	—	○
TM71	Stone Edge	Rock	Physical	100	80	5	Normal	—	—
TM78	Bulldoze	Ground	Physical	60	100	20	Adjacent	—	—
TM80	Rock Slide	Rock	Physical	75	90	10	Many Others	—	—
TM82	Dragon Tail	Dragon	Physical	60	90	10	Normal	—	○
TM87	Swagger	Normal	Status	—	90	15	Normal	—	—
TM90	Substitute	Normal	Status	—	—	10	Self	—	—
TM94	Rock Smash	Fighting	Physical	40	100	15	Normal	—	○
HM01	Cut	Normal	Physical	50	95	30	Normal	—	—
HM02	Fly	Flying	Physical	90	95	15	Normal	○	○
HM04	Strength	Normal	Physical	80	100	15	Normal	—	○

MOVES TAUGHT BY PEOPLE

Name	Type	Kind	Pow.	Acc.	PP	Range	Long	DA
Draco Meteor	Dragon	Special	140	90	5	Normal	—	—

MOVES TAUGHT BY MOVE TUTORS FOR SHARDS

Name	Type	Kind	Pow.	Acc.	PP	Range	Long	DA
Hyper Voice	Normal	Special	90	100	10	Many Others	—	—
Iron Tail	Steel	Physical	100	75	15	Normal	—	○
Aqua Tail	Water	Physical	90	90	10	Normal	—	○
Zen Headbutt	Psychic	Physical	80	90	15	Normal	—	○
Dragon Pulse	Dragon	Special	90	100	10	Normal	○	—
Snore	Normal	Special	40	100	15	Normal	—	—
Roost	Flying	Status	—	—	10	Self	—	—
Heat Wave	Fire	Special	100	90	10	Many Others	—	—
Tailwind	Flying	Status	—	—	30	Your Side	—	—
Outrage	Dragon	Physical	120	100	10	1 Random	—	○
Sleep Talk	Normal	Status	—	—	10	Self	—	—

---

374 Beldum

Iron Ball Pokémon

TYPE Steel / Psychic

ABILITY
- Clear Body

HIDDEN ABILITY
- Light Metal

- HEIGHT: 2'00"
- WEIGHT: 209.9 lbs.
- GENDER: Unknown

Its cells are all magnetic, and it communicates with others by using magnetic pulses.

STATS
- HP
- Attack
- Defense
- Sp. Atk
- Sp. Def
- Speed

EGG GROUPS
Mineral

ITEMS SOMETIMES HELD
- None

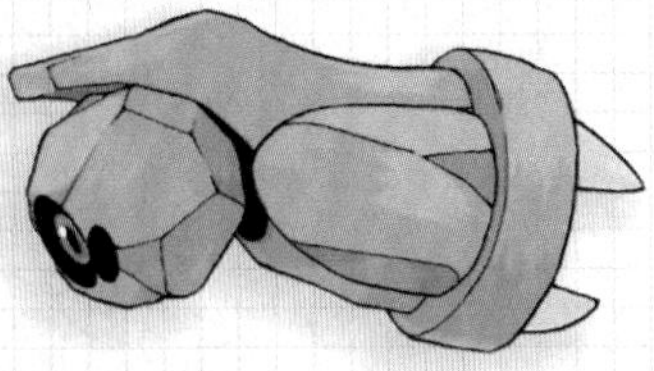

Gender unknown

Pokémon AR Marker

EVOLUTION

Beldum — Lv. 20 → Metang — Lv. 45 → Metagross

HOW TO OBTAIN

| Pokémon Black Version 2 | Catch a Metang or Metagross, leave it at the Pokémon Day Care, and hatch the Egg that is found |
| Pokémon White Version 2 | Catch a Metang or Metagross, leave it at the Pokémon Day Care, and hatch the Egg that is found |

HOW TO OBTAIN FROM OTHER GAMES

| Pokémon HeartGold Version | Trade Forretress to Steven at Silph Co. in Saffron City |
| Pokémon SoulSilver Version | Trade Forretress to Steven at Silph Co. in Saffron City |

LEVEL-UP AND LEARNED MOVES

Lv.	Name	Type	Kind	Pow.	Acc.	PP	Range	Long	DA
1	Take Down	Normal	Physical	90	85	20	Normal	—	○

MOVES TAUGHT BY PEOPLE

Name	Type	Kind	Pow.	Acc.	PP	Range	Long	DA

MOVES TAUGHT BY MOVE TUTORS FOR SHARDS

Name	Type	Kind	Pow.	Acc.	PP	Range	Long	DA
Iron Head	Steel	Physical	80	100	15	Normal	—	○
Iron Defense	Steel	Status	—	—	15	Self	—	—
Zen Headbutt	Psychic	Physical	80	90	15	Normal	—	○

TM & HM MOVES

Lv.	Name	Type	Kind	Pow.	Acc.	PP	Range	Long	DA

EGG MOVES

Name	Type	Kind	Pow.	Acc.	PP	Range	Long	DA

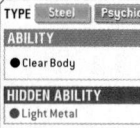

375 Metang

Iron Claw Pokémon

- HEIGHT: 3'11"
- WEIGHT: 446.4 lbs.
- GENDER: Unknown

It is formed by two Beldum joining together. Its two brains are linked, amplifying its psychic power.

Gender unknown

TYPE: Steel / Psychic

ABILITY
- Clear Body

HIDDEN ABILITY
- Light Metal

STATS
HP
Attack
Defense
Sp. Atk
Sp. Def
Speed

EGG GROUPS
Mineral

ITEMS SOMETIMES HELD
- Metal Coat

EVOLUTION

HOW TO OBTAIN

Pokémon Black Version 2	❶ Giant Chasm Crater Forest ❷ Giant Chasm (Hidden Grotto)
Pokémon White Version 2	❶ Giant Chasm Crater Forest ❷ Giant Chasm (Hidden Grotto)

HOW TO OBTAIN FROM OTHER GAMES

—

—

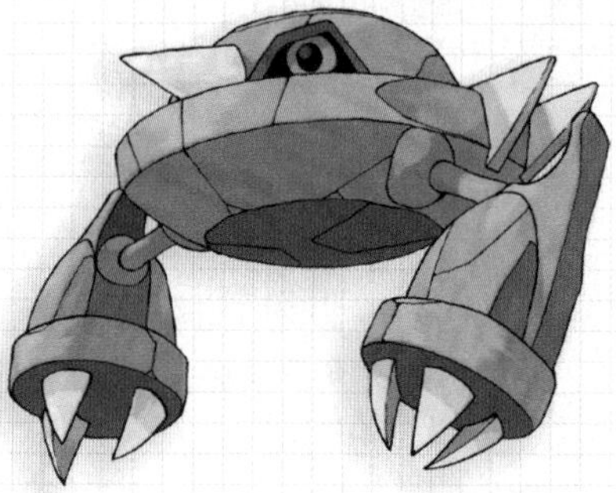

Pokémon AR Marker

LEVEL-UP AND LEARNED MOVES

Lv.	Name	Type	Kind	Pow.	Acc.	PP	Range	Long	DA
1	Magnet Rise	Electric	Status	-	—	10	Self	—	—
1	Take Down	Normal	Physical	90	85	20	Normal	—	○
1	Metal Claw	Steel	Physical	50	95	35	Normal	—	○
1	Confusion	Psychic	Special	50	100	25	Normal	—	—
20	Confusion	Psychic	Special	50	100	25	Normal	—	—
20	Metal Claw	Steel	Physical	50	95	35	Normal	—	○
23	Pursuit	Dark	Physical	40	100	20	Normal	—	○
26	Miracle Eye	Psychic	Status	-	—	40	Normal	—	—
29	Zen Headbutt	Psychic	Physical	80	90	15	Normal	—	○
32	Bullet Punch	Steel	Physical	40	100	30	Normal	—	○
35	Scary Face	Normal	Status	-	100	10	Normal	—	—
38	Agility	Psychic	Status	-	—	30	Self	—	—
41	Psychic	Psychic	Special	90	100	10	Normal	—	—
44	Meteor Mash	Steel	Physical	100	85	10	Normal	—	○
47	Iron Defense	Steel	Status	-	—	15	Self	—	—
50	Hyper Beam	Normal	Special	150	90	5	Normal	—	—

TM & HM MOVES

Lv.	Name	Type	Kind	Pow.	Acc.	PP	Range	Long	DA
TM01	Hone Claws	Dark	Status	—	—	15	Self	—	—
TM03	Psyshock	Psychic	Special	80	100	10	Normal	—	—
TM06	Toxic	Poison	Status	—	90	10	Normal	—	—
TM10	Hidden Power	Normal	Special	—	100	15	Normal	—	—
TM11	Sunny Day	Fire	Status	—	—	5	Both Sides	—	—
TM15	Hyper Beam	Normal	Special	150	90	5	Normal	—	—
TM16	Light Screen	Psychic	Status	—	—	30	Your Side	—	—
TM17	Protect	Normal	Status	—	—	10	Self	—	—
TM18	Rain Dance	Water	Status	—	—	5	Both Sides	—	—
TM19	Telekinesis	Psychic	Status	—	—	15	Normal	—	—
TM21	Frustration	Normal	Physical	—	100	20	Normal	—	○
TM26	Earthquake	Ground	Physical	100	100	10	Adjacent	—	—
TM27	Return	Normal	Physical	—	100	20	Normal	—	○
TM29	Psychic	Psychic	Special	90	100	10	Normal	—	—
TM30	Shadow Ball	Ghost	Special	80	100	15	Normal	—	—
TM31	Brick Break	Fighting	Physical	75	100	15	Normal	—	○
TM32	Double Team	Normal	Status	—	—	15	Self	—	—
TM33	Reflect	Psychic	Status	—	—	20	Your Side	—	—
TM36	Sludge Bomb	Poison	Special	90	100	10	Normal	—	—
TM37	Sandstorm	Rock	Status	—	—	10	Both Sides	—	—
TM39	Rock Tomb	Rock	Physical	50	80	10	Normal	—	—
TM40	Aerial Ace	Flying	Physical	60	—	20	Normal	○	○
TM42	Facade	Normal	Physical	70	100	20	Normal	—	○
TM44	Rest	Psychic	Status	—	—	10	Self	—	—
TM48	Round	Normal	Special	60	100	15	Normal	—	—
TM64	Explosion	Normal	Physical	250	100	5	Adjacent	—	—
TM69	Rock Polish	Rock	Status	—	—	20	Self	—	—
TM70	Flash	Normal	Status	—	100	20	Normal	—	—
TM74	Gyro Ball	Steel	Physical	—	100	5	Normal	—	○
TM77	Psych Up	Normal	Status	—	—	10	Normal	—	—
TM78	Bulldoze	Ground	Physical	60	100	20	Adjacent	—	—
TM80	Rock Slide	Rock	Physical	75	90	10	Many Others	—	—
TM86	Grass Knot	Grass	Special	—	100	20	Normal	—	○
TM87	Swagger	Normal	Status	—	90	15	Normal	—	—
TM90	Substitute	Normal	Status	—	—	10	Self	—	—
TM91	Flash Cannon	Steel	Special	80	100	10	Normal	—	—
TM94	Rock Smash	Fighting	Physical	40	100	15	Normal	—	○
HM01	Cut	Normal	Physical	50	95	30	Normal	—	○
HM04	Strength	Normal	Physical	80	100	15	Normal	—	○

MOVES TAUGHT BY PEOPLE

Name	Type	Kind	Pow.	Acc.	PP	Range	Long	DA

MOVES TAUGHT BY MOVE TUTORS FOR SHARDS

Name	Type	Kind	Pow.	Acc.	PP	Range	Long	DA
Signal Beam	Bug	Special	75	100	15	Normal	—	—
Iron Head	Steel	Physical	80	100	15	Normal	—	○
ThunderPunch	Electric	Physical	75	100	15	Normal	—	○
Ice Punch	Ice	Physical	75	100	15	Normal	—	○
Iron Defense	Steel	Status	—	—	15	Self	—	—
Magnet Rise	Electric	Status	—	—	10	Self	—	—
Icy Wind	Ice	Special	55	95	15	Many Others	—	—
Zen Headbutt	Psychic	Physical	80	90	15	Normal	—	○
Gravity	Psychic	Status	—	—	5	Both Sides	—	—
Snore	Normal	Special	40	100	15	Normal	—	—
Trick	Psychic	Status	—	100	10	Normal	—	—
Stealth Rock	Rock	Status	—	—	20	3 Foes	—	—
Sleep Talk	Normal	Status	—	—	10	Self	—	—

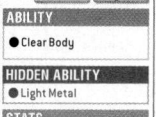

376 Metagross

Iron Leg Pokémon

- HEIGHT: 5'03"
- WEIGHT: 1,212.5 lbs.
- GENDER: Unknown

With four linked brains, it's more intelligent than a supercomputer, and it uses calculations to analyze foes.

Gender unknown

TYPE: Steel / Psychic

ABILITY
- Clear Body

HIDDEN ABILITY
- Light Metal

STATS
HP
Attack
Defense
Sp. Atk
Sp. Def
Speed

EGG GROUPS
Mineral

ITEMS SOMETIMES HELD
- Metal Coat

EVOLUTION

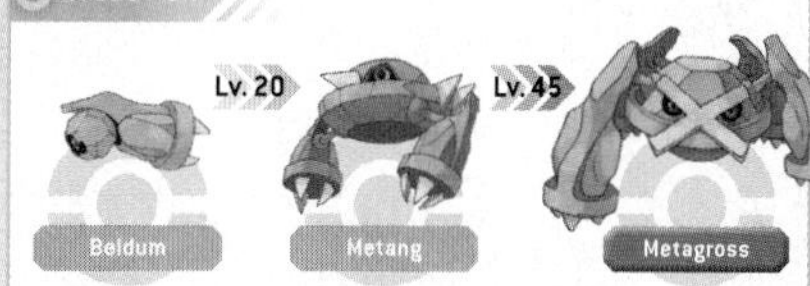

HOW TO OBTAIN

Pokémon Black Version 2	Giant Chasm Crater Forest (rustling grass)
Pokémon White Version 2	Giant Chasm Crater Forest (rustling grass)

HOW TO OBTAIN FROM OTHER GAMES

—

—

Pokémon AR Marker

LEVEL-UP AND LEARNED MOVES

Lv.	Name	Type	Kind	Pow.	Acc.	PP	Range	Long	DA
1	Magnet Rise	Electric	Status	—	—	10	Self	—	—
1	Take Down	Normal	Physical	90	85	20	Normal	—	○
1	Metal Claw	Steel	Physical	50	95	35	Normal	—	○
1	Confusion	Psychic	Special	50	100	25	Normal	—	—
20	Confusion	Psychic	Special	50	100	25	Normal	—	—
20	Metal Claw	Steel	Physical	50	95	35	Normal	—	○
23	Pursuit	Dark	Physical	40	100	20	Normal	—	○
26	Miracle Eye	Psychic	Status	—	—	40	Normal	—	—
29	Zen Headbutt	Psychic	Physical	80	90	15	Normal	—	○
32	Bullet Punch	Steel	Physical	40	100	30	Normal	—	○
35	Scary Face	Normal	Status	—	100	10	Normal	—	—
38	Agility	Psychic	Status	—	—	30	Self	—	—
41	Psychic	Psychic	Special	90	100	10	Normal	—	—
44	Meteor Mash	Steel	Physical	100	85	10	Normal	—	○
45	Hammer Arm	Fighting	Physical	100	90	10	Normal	—	○
53	Iron Defense	Steel	Status	—	—	15	Self	—	—
62	Hyper Beam	Normal	Special	150	90	5	Normal	—	—

TM & HM MOVES

Lv.	Name	Type	Kind	Pow.	Acc.	PP	Range	Long	DA
TM01	Hone Claws	Dark	Status	—	—	15	Self	—	—
TM03	Psyshock	Psychic	Special	80	100	10	Normal	—	—
TM06	Toxic	Poison	Status	—	90	10	Normal	—	—
TM10	Hidden Power	Normal	Special	—	100	15	Normal	—	—
TM11	Sunny Day	Fire	Status	—	—	5	Both Sides	—	—
TM15	Hyper Beam	Normal	Special	150	90	5	Normal	—	—
TM16	Light Screen	Psychic	Status	—	—	30	Your Side	—	—
TM17	Protect	Normal	Status	—	—	10	Self	—	—
TM18	Rain Dance	Water	Status	—	—	5	Both Sides	—	—
TM19	Telekinesis	Psychic	Status	—	—	15	Normal	—	—
TM21	Frustration	Normal	Physical	—	100	20	Normal	—	○
TM26	Earthquake	Ground	Physical	100	100	10	Adjacent	—	—
TM27	Return	Normal	Physical	—	100	20	Normal	—	○
TM29	Psychic	Psychic	Special	90	100	10	Normal	—	—
TM30	Shadow Ball	Ghost	Special	80	100	15	Normal	—	—
TM31	Brick Break	Fighting	Physical	75	100	15	Normal	—	○
TM32	Double Team	Normal	Status	—	—	15	Self	—	—
TM33	Reflect	Psychic	Status	—	—	20	Your Side	—	—
TM36	Sludge Bomb	Poison	Special	90	100	10	Normal	—	—
TM37	Sandstorm	Rock	Status	—	—	10	Both Sides	—	—
TM39	Rock Tomb	Rock	Physical	50	80	10	Normal	—	—
TM40	Aerial Ace	Flying	Physical	60	—	20	Normal	○	○
TM42	Facade	Normal	Physical	70	100	20	Normal	—	○
TM44	Rest	Psychic	Status	—	—	10	Self	—	—
TM48	Round	Normal	Special	60	100	15	Normal	—	—
TM64	Explosion	Normal	Physical	250	100	5	Adjacent	—	—
TM68	Giga Impact	Normal	Physical	150	90	5	Normal	—	○
TM69	Rock Polish	Rock	Status	—	—	20	Self	—	—
TM70	Flash	Normal	Status	—	100	20	Normal	—	—
TM74	Gyro Ball	Steel	Physical	—	100	5	Normal	—	○
TM77	Psych Up	Normal	Status	—	—	10	Normal	—	—
TM78	Bulldoze	Ground	Physical	60	100	20	Adjacent	—	—
TM80	Rock Slide	Rock	Physical	75	90	10	Many Others	—	—
TM86	Grass Knot	Grass	Special	—	100	20	Normal	—	○
TM87	Swagger	Normal	Status	—	90	15	Normal	—	—
TM90	Substitute	Normal	Status	—	—	10	Self	—	—
TM91	Flash Cannon	Steel	Special	80	100	10	Normal	—	—
TM94	Rock Smash	Fighting	Physical	40	100	15	Normal	—	○
HM01	Cut	Normal	Physical	50	95	30	Normal	—	○
HM04	Strength	Normal	Physical	80	100	15	Normal	—	○

MOVES TAUGHT BY PEOPLE

Name	Type	Kind	Pow.	Acc.	PP	Range	Long	DA

MOVES TAUGHT BY MOVE TUTORS FOR SHARDS

Name	Type	Kind	Pow.	Acc.	PP	Range	Long	DA
Signal Beam	Bug	Special	75	100	15	Normal	—	—
Iron Head	Steel	Physical	80	100	15	Normal	—	○
ThunderPunch	Electric	Physical	75	100	15	Normal	—	○
Ice Punch	Ice	Physical	75	100	15	Normal	—	○
Iron Defense	Steel	Status	—	—	15	Self	—	—
Magnet Rise	Electric	Status	—	—	10	Self	—	—
Block	Normal	Status	—	—	5	Normal	—	—
Icy Wind	Ice	Special	55	95	15	Many Others	—	—
Zen Headbutt	Psychic	Physical	80	90	15	Normal	—	○
Gravity	Psychic	Status	—	—	5	Both Sides	—	—
Snore	Normal	Special	40	100	15	Normal	—	—
Trick	Psychic	Status	—	100	10	Normal	—	—
Stealth Rock	Rock	Status	—	—	20	3 Foes	—	—
Sleep Talk	Normal	Status	—	—	10	Self	—	—

377 Regirock
Rock Peak Pokémon

- HEIGHT: 5'07"
- WEIGHT: 507.1 lbs.
- GENDER: Unknown

Its entire body is made of rock. If any part chips off in battle, it attaches rocks to repair itself.

Gender unknown

TYPE Rock

ABILITY
- Clear Body

HIDDEN ABILITY

STATS
- HP ■■■
- Attack ■■■■
- Defense ■■■■■■■
- Sp. Atk ■■■
- Sp. Def ■■■■■
- Speed ■■

EGG GROUPS
No Egg has ever been discovered

ITEMS SOMETIMES HELD
- None

EVOLUTION
Does not evolve

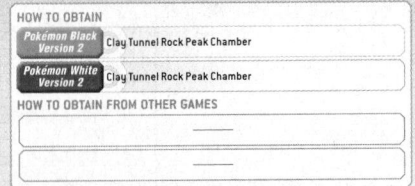

HOW TO OBTAIN
Pokémon Black Version 2	Clay Tunnel Rock Peak Chamber
Pokémon White Version 2	Clay Tunnel Rock Peak Chamber

HOW TO OBTAIN FROM OTHER GAMES

LEVEL-UP AND LEARNED MOVES

Lv.	Name	Type	Kind	Pow.	Acc.	PP	Range	Long	DA
1	Explosion	Normal	Physical	250	100	5	Adjacent	—	
1	Stomp	Normal	Physical	65	100	20	Normal	—	○
9	Rock Throw	Rock	Physical	50	90	15	Normal	—	
17	Curse	Ghost	Status	—	—	10	Varies	—	
25	Superpower	Fighting	Physical	120	100	5	Normal	—	○
33	AncientPower	Rock	Special	60	100	5	Normal	—	
41	Iron Defense	Steel	Status	—	—	15	Self	—	
49	Charge Beam	Electric	Special	50	90	10	Normal	—	
57	Lock-On	Normal	Status	—	—	5	Normal	—	
65	Zap Cannon	Electric	Special	120	50	5	Normal	—	
73	Stone Edge	Rock	Physical	100	80	5	Normal	—	
81	Hammer Arm	Fighting	Physical	100	90	10	Normal	—	
89	Hyper Beam	Normal	Special	150	90	5	Normal	—	

TM & HM MOVES

	Name	Type	Kind	Pow.	Acc.	PP	Range	Long	DA
TM06	Toxic	Poison	Status	—	90	10	Normal	—	
TM10	Hidden Power	Normal	Special	—	100	15	Normal	—	
TM11	Sunny Day	Fire	Status	—	—	5	Both Sides	—	
TM15	Hyper Beam	Normal	Special	150	90	5	Normal	—	
TM17	Protect	Normal	Status	—	—	10	Self	—	
TM20	Safeguard	Normal	Status	—	—	25	Your Side	—	
TM21	Frustration	Normal	Physical	—	100	20	Normal	—	○
TM23	Smack Down	Rock	Physical	50	100	15	Normal	—	
TM24	Thunderbolt	Electric	Special	95	100	15	Normal	—	
TM25	Thunder	Electric	Special	120	70	10	Normal	—	
TM26	Earthquake	Ground	Physical	100	100	10	Adjacent	—	
TM27	Return	Normal	Physical	—	100	20	Normal	—	○
TM28	Dig	Ground	Physical	80	100	10	Normal	—	○
TM31	Brick Break	Fighting	Physical	75	100	15	Normal	—	
TM32	Double Team	Normal	Status	—	—	15	Both Sides	—	
TM37	Sandstorm	Rock	Status	—	—	10	Both Sides	—	
TM39	Rock Tomb	Rock	Physical	50	80	10	Normal	—	
TM42	Facade	Normal	Physical	70	100	20	Normal	—	
TM44	Rest	Psychic	Status	—	—	10	Self	—	
TM48	Round	Normal	Special	60	100	15	Normal	—	
TM52	Focus Blast	Fighting	Special	120	70	5	Normal	—	
TM56	Fling	Dark	Physical	—	100	10	Normal	—	
TM57	Charge Beam	Electric	Special	50	90	10	Normal	—	
TM64	Explosion	Normal	Physical	250	100	5	Adjacent	—	
TM68	Giga Impact	Normal	Physical	150	90	5	Normal	—	
TM69	Rock Polish	Rock	Status	—	—	20	Self	—	
TM71	Stone Edge	Rock	Physical	100	80	5	Normal	—	
TM73	Thunder Wave	Electric	Status	—	100	20	Normal	—	
TM77	Psych Up	Normal	Status	—	—	10	Normal	—	
TM78	Bulldoze	Ground	Physical	60	100	20	Adjacent	—	
TM80	Rock Slide	Rock	Physical	75	90	10	Many Others	—	
TM87	Swagger	Normal	Status	—	90	15	Normal	—	
TM90	Substitute	Normal	Status	—	—	10	Self	—	
TM94	Rock Smash	Fighting	Physical	40	100	15	Normal	—	○
HM04	Strength	Normal	Physical	80	100	15	Normal	—	

MOVES TAUGHT BY PEOPLE

Name	Type	Kind	Pow.	Acc.	PP	Range	Long	DA

MOVES TAUGHT BY MOVE TUTORS FOR SHARDS

Name	Type	Kind	Pow.	Acc.	PP	Range	Long	DA
Iron Head	Steel	Physical	80	100	15	Normal	—	○
Fire Punch	Fire	Physical	75	100	15	Normal	—	○
ThunderPunch	Electric	Physical	75	100	15	Normal	—	○
Ice Punch	Ice	Physical	75	100	15	Normal	—	○
Iron Defense	Steel	Status	—	—	15	Self	—	
Block	Normal	Status	—	—	5	Normal	—	
Earth Power	Ground	Special	90	100	10	Normal	—	
Superpower	Fighting	Physical	120	100	5	Normal	—	○
Gravity	Psychic	Status	—	—	5	Both Sides	—	
Snore	Normal	Special	40	100	15	Normal	—	
Drain Punch	Fighting	Physical	75	100	10	Normal	—	○
Stealth Rock	Rock	Status	—	—	20	3 Foes	—	
Sleep Talk	Normal	Status	—	—	10	Self	—	

Pokémon AR Marker

378 Regice
Iceberg Pokémon

- HEIGHT: 5'11"
- WEIGHT: 385.8 lbs.
- GENDER: Unknown

Its body is made of ice from the ice age. It controls frigid air of −328 degrees Fahrenheit.

Gender unknown

TYPE Ice

ABILITY
- Clear Body

HIDDEN ABILITY

STATS
- HP ■■■
- Attack ■■■
- Defense ■■■
- Sp. Atk ■■■
- Sp. Def ■■■■■■■
- Speed ■■■

EGG GROUPS
No Egg has ever been discovered

ITEMS SOMETIMES HELD
- None

EVOLUTION
Does not evolve

HOW TO OBTAIN
Pokémon Black Version 2	Clay Tunnel Iceberg Chamber
Pokémon White Version 2	Clay Tunnel Iceberg Chamber

HOW TO OBTAIN FROM OTHER GAMES

LEVEL-UP AND LEARNED MOVES

Lv.	Name	Type	Kind	Pow.	Acc.	PP	Range	Long	DA
1	Explosion	Normal	Physical	250	100	5	Adjacent	—	
1	Stomp	Normal	Physical	65	100	20	Normal	—	○
9	Icy Wind	Ice	Special	55	95	15	Many Others	—	
17	Curse	Ghost	Status	—	—	10	Varies	—	
25	Superpower	Fighting	Physical	120	100	5	Normal	—	○
33	AncientPower	Rock	Special	60	100	5	Normal	—	
41	Amnesia	Psychic	Status	—	—	20	Self	—	
49	Charge Beam	Electric	Special	50	90	10	Normal	—	
57	Lock-On	Normal	Status	—	—	5	Normal	—	
65	Zap Cannon	Electric	Special	120	50	5	Normal	—	
73	Ice Beam	Ice	Special	95	100	10	Normal	—	
81	Hammer Arm	Fighting	Physical	100	90	10	Normal	—	
89	Hyper Beam	Normal	Special	150	90	5	Normal	—	

TM & HM MOVES

	Name	Type	Kind	Pow.	Acc.	PP	Range	Long	DA
TM06	Toxic	Poison	Status	—	90	10	Normal	—	
TM07	Hail	Ice	Status	—	—	10	Both Sides	—	
TM10	Hidden Power	Normal	Special	—	100	15	Normal	—	
TM13	Ice Beam	Ice	Special	95	100	10	Normal	—	
TM14	Blizzard	Ice	Special	120	70	5	Many Others	—	
TM15	Hyper Beam	Normal	Special	150	90	5	Normal	—	
TM17	Protect	Normal	Status	—	—	10	Self	—	
TM18	Rain Dance	Water	Status	—	—	5	Both Sides	—	
TM20	Safeguard	Normal	Status	—	—	25	Your Side	—	
TM21	Frustration	Normal	Physical	—	100	20	Normal	—	○
TM24	Thunderbolt	Electric	Special	95	100	15	Normal	—	
TM25	Thunder	Electric	Special	120	70	10	Normal	—	
TM26	Earthquake	Ground	Physical	100	100	10	Adjacent	—	
TM27	Return	Normal	Physical	—	100	20	Normal	—	○
TM31	Brick Break	Fighting	Physical	75	100	15	Normal	—	
TM32	Double Team	Normal	Status	—	—	15	Self	—	
TM39	Rock Tomb	Rock	Physical	50	80	10	Normal	—	
TM42	Facade	Normal	Physical	70	100	20	Normal	—	
TM44	Rest	Psychic	Status	—	—	10	Self	—	
TM48	Round	Normal	Special	60	100	15	Normal	—	
TM52	Focus Blast	Fighting	Special	120	70	5	Normal	—	
TM56	Fling	Dark	Physical	—	100	10	Normal	—	
TM57	Charge Beam	Electric	Special	50	90	10	Normal	—	
TM64	Explosion	Normal	Physical	250	100	5	Adjacent	—	
TM68	Giga Impact	Normal	Physical	150	90	5	Normal	—	
TM69	Rock Polish	Rock	Status	—	—	20	Self	—	
TM73	Thunder Wave	Electric	Status	—	100	20	Normal	—	
TM77	Psych Up	Normal	Status	—	—	10	Normal	—	
TM78	Bulldoze	Ground	Physical	60	100	20	Adjacent	—	
TM79	Frost Breath	Ice	Special	40	90	10	Normal	—	
TM80	Rock Slide	Rock	Physical	75	90	10	Many Others	—	
TM87	Swagger	Normal	Status	—	90	15	Normal	—	
TM90	Substitute	Normal	Status	—	—	10	Self	—	
TM91	Flash Cannon	Steel	Special	80	100	10	Normal	—	
TM94	Rock Smash	Fighting	Physical	40	100	15	Normal	—	○
HM04	Strength	Normal	Physical	80	100	15	Normal	—	

MOVES TAUGHT BY PEOPLE

Name	Type	Kind	Pow.	Acc.	PP	Range	Long	DA

MOVES TAUGHT BY MOVE TUTORS FOR SHARDS

Name	Type	Kind	Pow.	Acc.	PP	Range	Long	DA
Signal Beam	Bug	Special	75	100	15	Normal	—	
Iron Head	Steel	Physical	80	100	15	Normal	—	○
ThunderPunch	Electric	Physical	75	100	15	Normal	—	○
Ice Punch	Ice	Physical	75	100	15	Normal	—	○
Block	Normal	Status	—	—	5	Normal	—	
Icy Wind	Ice	Special	55	95	15	Many Others	—	
Superpower	Fighting	Physical	120	100	5	Normal	—	○
Gravity	Psychic	Status	—	—	5	Both Sides	—	
Snore	Normal	Special	40	100	15	Normal	—	
Sleep Talk	Normal	Status	—	—	10	Self	—	

Pokémon AR Marker

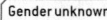

379 Iron Pokémon
Registeel

TYPE: Steel

ABILITY
- Clear Body

HIDDEN ABILITY
—

- HEIGHT: 6'03"
- WEIGHT: 451.9 lbs.
- GENDER: Unknown

Tempered by pressure underground over tens of thousands of years, its body cannot be scratched.

STATS
HP
Attack
Defense
Sp. Atk
Sp. Def
Speed

EGG GROUPS
No Egg has ever been discovered

ITEMS SOMETIMES HELD
- None

Gender unknown

Pokémon AR Marker

EVOLUTION

Does not evolve

HOW TO OBTAIN

Pokémon Black Version 2	Clay Tunnel Iron Chamber
Pokémon White Version 2	Clay Tunnel Iron Chamber

HOW TO OBTAIN FROM OTHER GAMES

—

—

LEVEL-UP AND LEARNED MOVES

Lv.	Name	Type	Kind	Pow.	Acc.	PP	Range	Long	DA
1	Explosion	Normal	Physical	250	100	5	Adjacent	—	—
1	Stomp	Normal	Physical	65	100	20	Normal	—	○
9	Metal Claw	Steel	Physical	50	95	35	Normal	—	○
17	Curse	Ghost	Status	—	—	10	Varies	—	—
25	Superpower	Fighting	Physical	120	100	5	Normal	—	○
33	AncientPower	Rock	Special	60	100	5	Normal	—	—
41	Iron Defense	Steel	Status	—	—	15	Self	—	—
41	Amnesia	Psychic	Status	—	—	20	Self	—	—
49	Charge Beam	Electric	Special	50	90	10	Normal	—	—
57	Lock-On	Normal	Status	—	—	5	Normal	—	—
65	Zap Cannon	Electric	Special	120	50	5	Normal	—	—
73	Iron Head	Steel	Physical	80	100	15	Normal	—	○
73	Flash Cannon	Steel	Special	80	100	10	Normal	—	—
81	Hammer Arm	Fighting	Physical	100	90	10	Normal	—	○
89	Hyper Beam	Normal	Special	150	90	5	Normal	—	—

TM & HM MOVES

Lv.	Name	Type	Kind	Pow.	Acc.	PP	Range	Long	DA
TM01	Hone Claws	Dark	Status	—	—	15	Self	—	—
TM06	Toxic	Poison	Status	—	90	10	Normal	—	—
TM10	Hidden Power	Normal	Special	—	100	15	Normal	—	—
TM11	Sunny Day	Fire	Status	—	—	5	Both Sides	—	—
TM15	Hyper Beam	Normal	Special	150	90	5	Normal	—	—
TM17	Protect	Normal	Status	—	—	10	Self	—	—
TM18	Rain Dance	Water	Status	—	—	5	Both Sides	—	—
TM20	Safeguard	Normal	Status	—	—	25	Your Side	—	—
TM21	Frustration	Normal	Physical	—	100	20	Normal	—	○
TM24	Thunderbolt	Electric	Special	95	100	15	Normal	—	—
TM25	Thunder	Electric	Special	120	70	10	Normal	—	—
TM26	Earthquake	Ground	Physical	100	100	10	Adjacent	—	—
TM27	Return	Normal	Physical	—	100	20	Normal	—	○
TM31	Brick Break	Fighting	Physical	75	100	15	Normal	—	○
TM32	Double Team	Normal	Status	—	—	15	Self	—	—
TM37	Sandstorm	Rock	Status	—	—	10	Both Sides	—	—
TM39	Rock Tomb	Rock	Physical	50	80	10	Normal	—	—
TM40	Aerial Ace	Flying	Physical	60	—	20	Normal	○	○
TM42	Facade	Normal	Physical	70	100	20	Normal	—	○
TM44	Rest	Psychic	Status	—	—	10	Self	—	—
TM48	Round	Normal	Special	60	100	15	Normal	—	—
TM52	Focus Blast	Fighting	Special	120	70	5	Normal	—	—
TM56	Fling	Dark	Physical	—	100	10	Normal	—	—
TM57	Charge Beam	Electric	Special	50	90	10	Normal	—	—
TM64	Explosion	Normal	Physical	250	100	5	Adjacent	—	—
TM65	Shadow Claw	Ghost	Physical	70	100	15	Normal	—	○
TM68	Giga Impact	Normal	Physical	150	90	5	Normal	—	○
TM69	Rock Polish	Rock	Status	—	—	20	Self	—	—
TM73	Thunder Wave	Electric	Status	—	100	20	Normal	—	—
TM77	Psych Up	Normal	Status	—	—	10	Normal	—	—
TM78	Bulldoze	Ground	Physical	60	100	20	Adjacent	—	—
TM80	Rock Slide	Rock	Physical	75	90	10	Many Others	—	—
TM87	Swagger	Normal	Status	—	90	15	Normal	—	—
TM90	Substitute	Normal	Status	—	—	10	Self	—	—
TM91	Flash Cannon	Steel	Special	80	100	10	Normal	—	—
TM94	Rock Smash	Fighting	Physical	40	100	15	Normal	—	○
HM04	Strength	Normal	Physical	80	100	15	Normal	—	○

MOVES TAUGHT BY PEOPLE

Name	Type	Kind	Pow.	Acc.	PP	Range	Long	DA

MOVES TAUGHT BY MOVE TUTORS FOR SHARDS

Name	Type	Kind	Pow.	Acc.	PP	Range	Long	DA
Iron Head	Steel	Physical	80	100	15	Normal	—	○
ThunderPunch	Electric	Physical	75	100	15	Normal	—	○
Ice Punch	Ice	Physical	75	100	15	Normal	—	○
Iron Defense	Steel	Status	—	—	15	Self	—	—
Magnet Rise	Electric	Status	—	—	10	Self	—	—
Block	Normal	Status	—	—	5	Normal	—	—
Superpower	Fighting	Physical	120	100	5	Normal	—	○
Gravity	Psychic	Status	—	—	5	Both Sides	—	—
Snore	Normal	Special	40	100	15	Normal	—	—
Stealth Rock	Rock	Status	—	—	20	3 Foes	—	—
Sleep Talk	Normal	Status	—	—	10	Self	—	—

380 Eon Pokémon
Latias

TYPE: Dragon Psychic

ABILITY
- Levitate

HIDDEN ABILITY
—

- HEIGHT: 4'07"
- WEIGHT: 88.2 lbs.
- GENDER: ♀

Its body is covered with a down that can refract light in such a way that it becomes invisible.

STATS
HP
Attack
Defense
Sp. Atk
Sp. Def
Speed

EGG GROUPS
No Egg has ever been discovered

ITEMS SOMETIMES HELD
- None

♀

Pokémon AR Marker

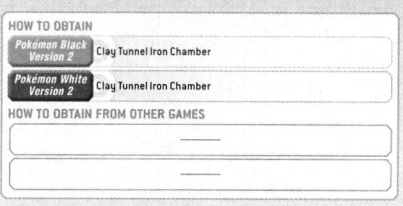

EVOLUTION

Does not evolve

HOW TO OBTAIN

Pokémon Black Version 2	Link Trade or Poké Transfer
Pokémon White Version 2	Dreamyard

HOW TO OBTAIN FROM OTHER GAMES

Pokémon HeartGold Version	Starts roaming the Kanto region after you talk to Steven at the Pokémon Fan Club in Vermilion City

—

LEVEL-UP AND LEARNED MOVES

Lv.	Name	Type	Kind	Pow.	Acc.	PP	Range	Long	DA
1	Psywave	Psychic	Special	—	80	15	Normal	—	—
5	Wish	Normal	Status	—	—	10	Self	—	—
10	Helping Hand	Normal	Status	—	—	20	1 Ally	—	—
15	Safeguard	Normal	Status	—	—	25	Your Side	—	—
20	DragonBreath	Dragon	Special	60	100	20	Normal	—	—
25	Water Sport	Water	Status	—	—	15	Both Sides	—	—
30	Refresh	Normal	Status	—	—	20	Self	—	—
35	Mist Ball	Psychic	Special	70	100	5	Normal	—	—
40	Zen Headbutt	Psychic	Physical	80	90	15	Normal	—	○
45	Recover	Normal	Status	—	—	10	Self	—	—
50	Psycho Shift	Psychic	Status	—	90	10	Normal	—	—
55	Charm	Normal	Status	—	100	20	Normal	—	—
60	Psychic	Psychic	Special	90	100	10	Normal	—	—
65	Heal Pulse	Psychic	Status	—	—	10	Normal	○	—
70	Reflect Type	Normal	Status	—	—	15	Normal	—	—
75	Guard Split	Psychic	Status	—	—	10	Normal	—	—
80	Dragon Pulse	Dragon	Special	90	100	10	Normal	○	—
85	Healing Wish	Psychic	Status	—	—	10	Self	—	—

TM & HM MOVES

Lv.	Name	Type	Kind	Pow.	Acc.	PP	Range	Long	DA
TM01	Hone Claws	Dark	Status	—	—	15	Self	—	—
TM02	Dragon Claw	Dragon	Physical	80	100	15	Normal	—	○
TM03	Psyshock	Psychic	Special	80	100	10	Normal	—	—
TM04	Calm Mind	Psychic	Status	—	—	20	Self	—	—
TM05	Roar	Normal	Status	—	100	20	Normal	—	—
TM06	Toxic	Poison	Status	—	90	10	Normal	—	—
TM10	Hidden Power	Normal	Special	—	100	15	Normal	—	—
TM11	Sunny Day	Fire	Status	—	—	5	Both Sides	—	—
TM13	Ice Beam	Ice	Special	95	100	10	Normal	—	—
TM15	Hyper Beam	Normal	Special	150	90	5	Normal	—	—
TM16	Light Screen	Psychic	Status	—	—	30	Your Side	—	—
TM17	Protect	Normal	Status	—	—	10	Self	—	—
TM18	Rain Dance	Water	Status	—	—	5	Both Sides	—	—
TM19	Telekinesis	Psychic	Status	—	—	15	Normal	—	—
TM20	Safeguard	Normal	Status	—	—	25	Your Side	—	—
TM21	Frustration	Normal	Physical	—	100	20	Normal	—	○
TM22	SolarBeam	Grass	Special	120	100	10	Normal	—	—
TM24	Thunderbolt	Electric	Special	95	100	15	Normal	—	—
TM25	Thunder	Electric	Special	120	70	10	Normal	—	—
TM26	Earthquake	Ground	Physical	100	100	10	Adjacent	—	—
TM27	Return	Normal	Physical	—	100	20	Normal	—	○
TM29	Psychic	Psychic	Special	90	100	10	Normal	—	—
TM30	Shadow Ball	Ghost	Special	80	100	15	Normal	—	—
TM32	Double Team	Normal	Status	—	—	15	Self	—	—
TM33	Reflect	Psychic	Status	—	—	20	Your Side	—	—
TM37	Sandstorm	Rock	Status	—	—	10	Both Sides	—	—
TM40	Aerial Ace	Flying	Physical	60	—	20	Normal	○	○
TM42	Facade	Normal	Physical	70	100	20	Normal	—	○
TM44	Rest	Psychic	Status	—	—	10	Self	—	—
TM45	Attract	Normal	Status	—	100	15	Normal	—	—
TM48	Round	Normal	Special	60	100	15	Normal	—	—
TM53	Energy Ball	Grass	Special	80	100	10	Normal	—	—
TM57	Charge Beam	Electric	Special	50	90	10	Normal	—	—
TM65	Shadow Claw	Ghost	Physical	70	100	15	Normal	—	○
TM67	Retaliate	Normal	Physical	70	100	5	Normal	—	○
TM68	Giga Impact	Normal	Physical	150	90	5	Normal	—	○
TM70	Flash	Normal	Status	—	100	20	Normal	—	—
TM73	Thunder Wave	Electric	Status	—	100	20	Normal	—	—
TM77	Psych Up	Normal	Status	—	—	10	Normal	—	—
TM78	Bulldoze	Ground	Physical	60	100	20	Adjacent	—	—
TM85	Dream Eater	Psychic	Special	100	100	15	Normal	—	—
TM86	Grass Knot	Grass	Special	—	100	20	Normal	—	○
TM87	Swagger	Normal	Status	—	90	15	Normal	—	—
TM90	Substitute	Normal	Status	—	—	10	Self	—	—
HM01	Cut	Normal	Physical	50	95	30	Normal	—	○
HM02	Fly	Flying	Physical	90	95	15	Normal	○	○
HM03	Surf	Water	Special	95	100	15	Adjacent	—	—
HM05	Waterfall	Water	Physical	80	100	15	Normal	—	○
HM06	Dive	Water	Physical	80	100	10	Normal	—	○

MOVES TAUGHT BY PEOPLE

Name	Type	Kind	Pow.	Acc.	PP	Range	Long	DA
Draco Meteor	Dragon	Special	140	90	5	Normal	—	—

MOVES TAUGHT BY MOVE TUTORS FOR SHARDS

Name	Type	Kind	Pow.	Acc.	PP	Range	Long	DA
Covet	Normal	Physical	60	100	40	Normal	—	○
Last Resort	Normal	Physical	140	100	5	Normal	—	○
Magic Coat	Psychic	Status	—	—	15	Self	—	—
Icy Wind	Ice	Special	55	95	15	Many Others	—	—
Zen Headbutt	Psychic	Physical	80	90	15	Normal	—	○
Dragon Pulse	Dragon	Special	90	100	10	Normal	○	—
Snore	Normal	Special	40	100	15	Normal	—	—
Roost	Flying	Status	—	—	10	Self	—	—
Role Play	Psychic	Status	—	—	10	Normal	—	—
Tailwind	Flying	Status	—	—	30	Your Side	—	—
Helping Hand	Normal	Status	—	—	20	1 Ally	—	—
Magic Room	Psychic	Status	—	—	10	Both Sides	—	—
Trick	Psychic	Status	—	100	10	Normal	—	—
Outrage	Dragon	Physical	120	100	10	1 Random	—	○
Sleep Talk	Normal	Status	—	—	10	Self	—	—

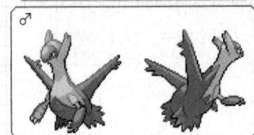

Eon Pokémon
381 Latios

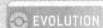

TYPE Dragon | Psychic

ABILITY
● Levitate

HIDDEN ABILITY

- HEIGHT: 6'07"
- WEIGHT: 132.3 lbs.
- GENDER: ♂

A highly intelligent Pokémon. By folding back its wings in flight, it can overtake jet planes.

STATS
HP	
Attack	
Defense	
Sp. Atk	
Sp. Def	
Speed	

EGG GROUPS
No Egg has ever been discovered

ITEMS SOMETIMES HELD
● None

EVOLUTION
Does not evolve

HOW TO OBTAIN
Pokémon Black Version 2	Dreamyard
Pokémon White Version 2	Link Trade or Poké Transfer

HOW TO OBTAIN FROM OTHER GAMES
Pokémon SoulSilver Version	Starts roaming the Kanto region after you talk to Steven at the Pokémon Fan Club in Vermilion City

LEVEL-UP AND LEARNED MOVES
Lv.	Name	Type	Kind	Pow.	Acc.	PP	Range	Long	DA
1	Psywave	Psychic	Special	—	80	15	Normal	—	—
5	Heal Block	Psychic	Status	—	100	15	Many Others	—	—
10	Helping Hand	Normal	Status	—	—	20	1 Ally	—	—
15	Safeguard	Normal	Status	—	—	25	Your Side	—	—
20	DragonBreath	Dragon	Special	60	100	20	Normal	—	—
25	Protect	Normal	Status	—	—	10	Self	—	—
30	Refresh	Normal	Status	—	—	20	Self	—	—
35	Luster Purge	Psychic	Special	70	100	5	Normal	—	—
40	Zen Headbutt	Psychic	Physical	80	90	15	Normal	—	○
45	Recover	Normal	Status	—	—	10	Self	—	—
50	Psycho Shift	Psychic	Status	—	90	10	Normal	—	—
55	Dragon Dance	Dragon	Status	—	—	20	Self	—	—
60	Psychic	Psychic	Special	90	100	10	Normal	—	—
65	Heal Pulse	Psychic	Status	—	—	10	Normal	○	—
70	Telekinesis	Psychic	Status	—	—	15	Normal	—	—
75	Power Split	Psychic	Status	—	—	10	Normal	—	—
80	Dragon Pulse	Dragon	Special	90	100	10	Normal	○	—
85	Memento	Dark	Status	—	100	10	Normal	—	—

TM & HM MOVES
Lv.	Name	Type	Kind	Pow.	Acc.	PP	Range	Long	DA
TM01	Hone Claws	Dark	Status	—	—	15	Self	—	—
TM02	Dragon Claw	Dragon	Physical	80	100	15	Normal	—	○
TM03	Psyshock	Psychic	Special	80	100	10	Normal	—	—
TM04	Calm Mind	Psychic	Status	—	—	20	Self	—	—
TM05	Roar	Normal	Status	—	100	20	Normal	—	—
TM06	Toxic	Poison	Status	—	90	10	Normal	—	—
TM10	Hidden Power	Normal	Special	—	100	15	Normal	—	—
TM11	Sunny Day	Fire	Status	—	—	5	Both Sides	—	—
TM13	Ice Beam	Ice	Special	95	100	10	Normal	—	—
TM15	Hyper Beam	Normal	Special	150	90	5	Normal	—	—
TM16	Light Screen	Psychic	Status	—	—	30	Your Side	—	—
TM17	Protect	Normal	Status	—	—	10	Self	—	—
TM18	Rain Dance	Water	Status	—	—	5	Both Sides	—	—
TM19	Telekinesis	Psychic	Status	—	—	15	Normal	—	—
TM20	Safeguard	Normal	Status	—	—	25	Your Side	—	—
TM21	Frustration	Normal	Physical	—	100	20	Normal	—	○
TM22	SolarBeam	Grass	Special	120	100	10	Normal	—	—
TM24	Thunderbolt	Electric	Special	95	100	15	Normal	—	—
TM25	Thunder	Electric	Special	120	70	10	Normal	—	—
TM26	Earthquake	Ground	Physical	100	100	10	Adjacent	—	○
TM27	Return	Normal	Physical	—	100	20	Normal	—	○
TM29	Psychic	Psychic	Special	90	100	10	Normal	—	—
TM30	Shadow Ball	Ghost	Special	80	100	15	Normal	—	—
TM32	Double Team	Normal	Status	—	—	15	Self	—	—
TM33	Reflect	Psychic	Status	—	—	20	Your Side	—	—
TM37	Sandstorm	Rock	Status	—	—	10	Both Sides	—	—
TM40	Aerial Ace	Flying	Physical	60	—	20	Normal	○	○
TM42	Facade	Normal	Physical	70	100	20	Normal	—	○
TM44	Rest	Psychic	Status	—	—	10	Self	—	—
TM45	Attract	Normal	Status	—	100	15	Normal	—	—
TM48	Round	Normal	Special	60	100	15	Normal	—	—
TM53	Energy Ball	Grass	Special	80	100	10	Normal	—	—
TM57	Charge Beam	Electric	Special	50	90	10	Normal	—	—
TM65	Shadow Claw	Ghost	Physical	70	100	15	Normal	—	○
TM67	Retaliate	Normal	Physical	70	100	5	Normal	—	○

Lv.	Name	Type	Kind	Pow.	Acc.	PP	Range	Long	DA
TM68	Giga Impact	Normal	Physical	150	90	5	Normal	—	○
TM70	Flash	Normal	Status	—	100	20	Normal	—	—
TM73	Thunder Wave	Electric	Status	—	100	20	Normal	—	—
TM77	Psych Up	Normal	Status	—	—	10	Normal	—	—
TM78	Bulldoze	Ground	Physical	60	100	20	Adjacent	—	—
TM85	Dream Eater	Psychic	Special	100	100	15	Normal	—	—
TM86	Grass Knot	Grass	Special	—	100	20	Normal	—	—
TM87	Swagger	Normal	Status	—	90	15	Normal	—	—
TM90	Substitute	Normal	Status	—	—	10	Self	—	—
HM01	Cut	Normal	Physical	50	95	30	Normal	—	○
HM02	Fly	Flying	Physical	90	95	15	Normal	○	○
HM03	Surf	Water	Special	95	100	15	Adjacent	—	—
HM05	Waterfall	Water	Physical	80	100	15	Normal	—	○
HM06	Dive	Water	Physical	80	100	10	Normal	—	○

MOVES TAUGHT BY PEOPLE
Name	Type	Kind	Pow.	Acc.	PP	Range	Long	DA
Draco Meteor	Dragon	Special	140	90	5	Normal	—	—

MOVES TAUGHT BY MOVE TUTORS FOR SHARDS
Name	Type	Kind	Pow.	Acc.	PP	Range	Long	DA
Last Resort	Normal	Physical	140	100	5	Normal	—	○
Magic Coat	Psychic	Status	—	—	15	Self	—	—
Icy Wind	Ice	Special	55	95	15	Many Others	—	—
Zen Headbutt	Psychic	Physical	80	90	15	Normal	—	○
Dragon Pulse	Dragon	Special	90	100	10	Normal	○	—
Snore	Normal	Special	40	100	15	Normal	—	—
Roost	Flying	Status	—	—	10	Self	—	—
Tailwind	Flying	Status	—	—	30	Your Side	—	—
Helping Hand	Normal	Status	—	—	20	1 Ally	—	—
Wonder Room	Psychic	Status	—	—	10	Both Sides	—	—
Trick	Psychic	Status	—	100	10	Normal	—	—
Outrage	Dragon	Physical	120	100	10	1 Random	—	○
Sleep Talk	Normal	Status	—	—	10	Self	—	—

Pokémon AR Marker

Sea Basin Pokémon
382 Kyogre

TYPE Water

ABILITY
● Drizzle

HIDDEN ABILITY

- HEIGHT: 14'09"
- WEIGHT: 776.0 lbs.
- GENDER: Unknown

It is said to have widened the seas by causing downpours. It had been asleep in a marine trench.

Gender unknown

STATS
HP	
Attack	
Defense	
Sp. Atk	
Sp. Def	
Speed	

EGG GROUPS
No Egg has ever been discovered

ITEMS SOMETIMES HELD
● None

EVOLUTION
Does not evolve

HOW TO OBTAIN
Pokémon Black Version 2	Link Trade or Poké Transfer
Pokémon White Version 2	Link Trade or Poké Transfer

HOW TO OBTAIN FROM OTHER GAMES
Pokémon HeartGold Version	Encounter at the Embedded Tower once you have the Blue Orb

LEVEL-UP AND LEARNED MOVES
Lv.	Name	Type	Kind	Pow.	Acc.	PP	Range	Long	DA
1	Water Pulse	Water	Special	60	100	20	Normal	○	—
5	Scary Face	Normal	Status	—	100	10	Normal	—	—
15	Body Slam	Normal	Physical	85	100	15	Normal	—	○
20	Muddy Water	Water	Special	95	85	10	Many Others	—	—
30	Aqua Ring	Water	Status	—	—	20	Self	—	—
35	Ice Beam	Ice	Special	95	100	10	Normal	—	—
45	AncientPower	Rock	Special	60	100	5	Normal	—	—
50	Water Spout	Water	Special	150	100	5	Many Others	—	—
60	Calm Mind	Psychic	Status	—	—	20	Self	—	—
65	Aqua Tail	Water	Physical	90	90	10	Normal	—	○
75	Sheer Cold	Ice	Special	—	30	5	Normal	—	—
80	Double-Edge	Normal	Physical	120	100	15	Normal	—	○
90	Hydro Pump	Water	Special	120	80	5	Normal	—	—

TM & HM MOVES
Lv.	Name	Type	Kind	Pow.	Acc.	PP	Range	Long	DA
TM04	Calm Mind	Psychic	Status	—	—	20	Self	—	—
TM05	Roar	Normal	Status	—	100	20	Normal	—	—
TM06	Toxic	Poison	Status	—	90	10	Normal	—	—
TM07	Hail	Ice	Status	—	—	10	Both Sides	—	—
TM10	Hidden Power	Normal	Special	—	100	15	Normal	—	—
TM13	Ice Beam	Ice	Special	95	100	10	Normal	—	—
TM14	Blizzard	Ice	Special	120	70	5	Many Others	—	—
TM15	Hyper Beam	Normal	Special	150	90	5	Normal	—	—
TM17	Protect	Normal	Status	—	—	10	Self	—	—
TM18	Rain Dance	Water	Status	—	—	5	Both Sides	—	—
TM20	Safeguard	Normal	Status	—	—	25	Your Side	—	—
TM21	Frustration	Normal	Physical	—	100	20	Normal	—	○
TM24	Thunderbolt	Electric	Special	95	100	15	Normal	—	—
TM25	Thunder	Electric	Special	120	70	10	Normal	—	—
TM26	Earthquake	Ground	Physical	100	100	10	Adjacent	—	○
TM27	Return	Normal	Physical	—	100	20	Normal	—	○
TM31	Brick Break	Fighting	Physical	75	100	15	Normal	—	○
TM32	Double Team	Normal	Status	—	—	15	Self	—	—
TM39	Rock Tomb	Rock	Physical	50	80	10	Normal	—	○
TM42	Facade	Normal	Physical	70	100	20	Normal	—	○
TM44	Rest	Psychic	Status	—	—	10	Self	—	—
TM48	Round	Normal	Special	60	100	15	Normal	—	—
TM55	Scald	Water	Special	80	100	15	Normal	—	—
TM68	Giga Impact	Normal	Physical	150	90	5	Normal	—	○
TM73	Thunder Wave	Electric	Status	—	100	20	Normal	—	—
TM77	Psych Up	Normal	Status	—	—	10	Normal	—	—
TM78	Bulldoze	Ground	Physical	60	100	20	Adjacent	—	—
TM80	Rock Slide	Rock	Physical	75	90	10	Many Others	—	—
TM87	Swagger	Normal	Status	—	90	15	Normal	—	—
TM90	Substitute	Normal	Status	—	—	10	Self	—	—
TM94	Rock Smash	Fighting	Physical	40	100	15	Normal	—	○
HM03	Surf	Water	Special	95	100	15	Adjacent	—	—
HM04	Strength	Normal	Physical	80	100	15	Normal	—	○
HM05	Waterfall	Water	Physical	80	100	15	Normal	—	○
HM06	Dive	Water	Physical	80	100	10	Normal	—	○

MOVES TAUGHT BY PEOPLE
Name	Type	Kind	Pow.	Acc.	PP	Range	Long	DA

MOVES TAUGHT BY MOVE TUTORS FOR SHARDS
Name	Type	Kind	Pow.	Acc.	PP	Range	Long	DA
Signal Beam	Bug	Special	75	100	15	Normal	—	—
Iron Head	Steel	Physical	80	100	15	Normal	—	○
Uproar	Normal	Special	90	100	10	1 Random	—	—
Block	Normal	Status	—	—	5	Normal	—	—
Icy Wind	Ice	Special	55	95	15	Many Others	—	—
Aqua Tail	Water	Physical	90	90	10	Normal	—	○
Snore	Normal	Special	40	100	15	Normal	—	—
Sleep Talk	Normal	Status	—	—	10	Self	—	—

Pokémon AR Marker

Continent Pokémon

383 Groudon

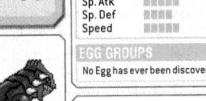

TYPE Ground

ABILITY
- Drought

HIDDEN ABILITY
—

- HEIGHT: 11'06"
- WEIGHT: 2,094.4 lbs.
- GENDER: Unknown

It had been asleep in underground magma ever since it fiercely fought Kyogre long ago.

STATS
HP
Attack
Defense
Sp. Atk
Sp. Def
Speed

EGG GROUPS
No Egg has ever been discovered

Gender unknown

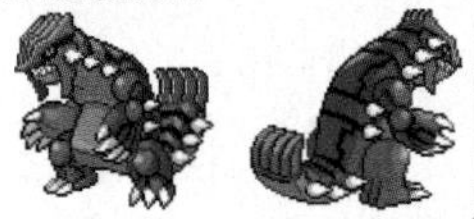

ITEMS SOMETIMES HELD
- None

EVOLUTION
Does not evolve

HOW TO OBTAIN

Pokémon Black Version 2	Link Trade or Poké Transfer
Pokémon White Version 2	Link Trade or Poké Transfer

HOW TO OBTAIN FROM OTHER GAMES

Pokémon SoulSilver Version	Encounter it at the Embedded Tower once you have the Red Orb
	—

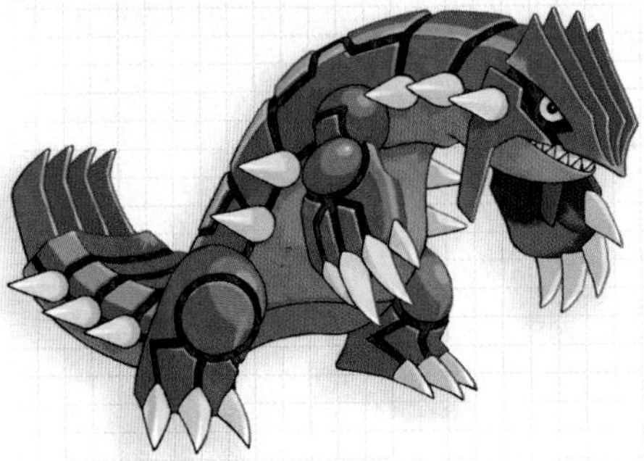

Pokémon AR Marker

LEVEL-UP AND LEARNED MOVES

Lv.	Name	Type	Kind	Pow.	Acc.	PP	Range	Long	DA
1	Mud Shot	Ground	Special	55	95	15	Normal	—	—
5	Scary Face	Normal	Status	—	100	10	Normal	—	—
15	Lava Plume	Fire	Special	80	100	15	Adjacent	—	—
20	Hammer Arm	Fighting	Physical	100	90	10	Normal	—	○
30	Rest	Psychic	Status	—	—	10	Self	—	—
35	Earthquake	Ground	Physical	100	100	10	Adjacent	—	—
45	AncientPower	Rock	Special	60	100	5	Normal	—	—
50	Eruption	Fire	Special	150	100	5	Many Others	—	—
60	Bulk Up	Fighting	Status	—	—	20	Self	—	—
65	Earth Power	Ground	Special	90	100	10	Normal	—	—
75	Fissure	Ground	Physical	—	30	5	Normal	—	—
80	SolarBeam	Grass	Special	120	100	10	Normal	—	—
90	Fire Blast	Fire	Special	120	85	5	Normal	—	—

TM & HM MOVES

Lv.	Name	Type	Kind	Pow.	Acc.	PP	Range	Long	DA
TM01	Hone Claws	Dark	Status	—	—	15	Self	—	—
TM02	Dragon Claw	Dragon	Physical	80	100	15	Normal	—	○
TM05	Roar	Normal	Status	—	100	20	Normal	—	—
TM06	Toxic	Poison	Status	—	90	10	Normal	—	—
TM08	Bulk Up	Fighting	Status	—	—	20	Self	—	—
TM10	Hidden Power	Normal	Special	—	100	15	Normal	—	—
TM11	Sunny Day	Fire	Status	—	—	5	Both Sides	—	—
TM15	Hyper Beam	Normal	Special	150	90	5	Normal	—	—
TM17	Protect	Normal	Status	—	—	10	Self	—	—
TM20	Safeguard	Normal	Status	—	—	25	Your Side	—	—
TM21	Frustration	Normal	Physical	—	100	20	Normal	—	○
TM22	SolarBeam	Grass	Special	120	100	10	Normal	—	—
TM23	Smack Down	Rock	Physical	50	100	15	Normal	—	—
TM24	Thunderbolt	Electric	Special	95	100	15	Normal	—	—
TM25	Thunder	Electric	Special	120	70	10	Normal	—	—
TM26	Earthquake	Ground	Physical	100	100	10	Adjacent	—	—
TM27	Return	Normal	Physical	—	100	20	Normal	—	○
TM28	Dig	Ground	Physical	80	100	10	Normal	—	○
TM31	Brick Break	Fighting	Physical	75	100	15	Normal	—	○
TM32	Double Team	Normal	Status	—	—	15	Self	—	—
TM35	Flamethrower	Fire	Special	95	100	15	Normal	—	—
TM37	Sandstorm	Rock	Status	—	—	10	Both Sides	—	—
TM38	Fire Blast	Fire	Special	120	85	5	Normal	—	—
TM39	Rock Tomb	Rock	Physical	50	80	10	Normal	—	—
TM40	Aerial Ace	Flying	Physical	60	—	20	Normal	○	○
TM42	Facade	Normal	Physical	70	100	20	Normal	—	○
TM44	Rest	Psychic	Status	—	—	10	Self	—	—
TM48	Round	Normal	Special	60	100	15	Normal	—	—
TM50	Overheat	Fire	Special	140	90	5	Normal	—	—
TM52	Focus Blast	Fighting	Special	120	70	5	Normal	—	—
TM56	Fling	Dark	Physical	—	100	10	Normal	—	—
TM59	Incinerate	Fire	Special	30	100	15	Many Others	—	—
TM65	Shadow Claw	Ghost	Physical	70	100	15	Normal	—	○
TM68	Giga Impact	Normal	Physical	150	90	5	Normal	—	○
TM69	Rock Polish	Rock	Status	—	—	20	Self	—	—
TM71	Stone Edge	Rock	Physical	100	80	5	Normal	—	—
TM73	Thunder Wave	Electric	Status	—	100	20	Normal	—	—
TM75	Swords Dance	Normal	Status	—	—	30	Self	—	—
TM77	Psych Up	Normal	Status	—	—	10	Normal	—	—
TM78	Bulldoze	Ground	Physical	60	100	20	Adjacent	—	—
TM80	Rock Slide	Rock	Physical	75	90	10	Many Others	—	—
TM82	Dragon Tail	Dragon	Physical	60	90	10	Normal	—	○
TM87	Swagger	Normal	Status	—	90	15	Normal	—	—
TM90	Substitute	Normal	Status	—	—	10	Self	—	—
TM94	Rock Smash	Fighting	Physical	40	100	15	Normal	—	○
HM01	Cut	Normal	Physical	50	95	30	Normal	—	○
HM04	Strength	Normal	Physical	80	100	15	Normal	—	○

MOVES TAUGHT BY PEOPLE

Name	Type	Kind	Pow.	Acc.	PP	Range	Long	DA

MOVES TAUGHT BY MOVE TUTORS FOR SHARDS

Name	Type	Kind	Pow.	Acc.	PP	Range	Long	DA
Iron Head	Steel	Physical	80	100	15	Normal	—	○
Uproar	Normal	Special	90	100	10	1 Random	—	—
Fire Punch	Fire	Physical	75	100	15	Normal	—	○
ThunderPunch	Electric	Physical	75	100	15	Normal	—	○
Block	Normal	Status	—	—	5	Normal	—	—
Iron Tail	Steel	Physical	100	75	15	Normal	—	○
Earth Power	Ground	Special	90	100	10	Normal	—	—
Dragon Pulse	Dragon	Special	90	100	10	Normal	○	—
Snore	Normal	Special	40	100	15	Normal	—	—
Stealth Rock	Rock	Status	—	—	20	3 Foes	—	—
Sleep Talk	Normal	Status	—	—	10	Self	—	—

383 Groudon

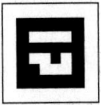

Sky High Pokémon

384 Rayquaza

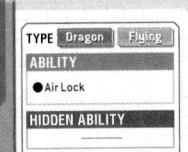

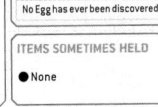

TYPE Dragon Flying

ABILITY
- Air Lock

HIDDEN ABILITY
—

- HEIGHT: 23'00"
- WEIGHT: 455.2 lbs.
- GENDER: Unknown

It lives in the ozone layer far above the clouds and cannot be seen from the ground.

STATS
HP
Attack
Defense
Sp. Atk
Sp. Def
Speed

EGG GROUPS
No Egg has ever been discovered

Gender unknown

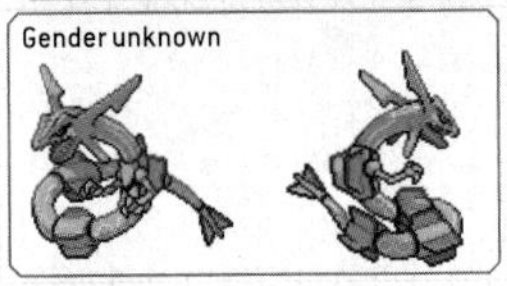

ITEMS SOMETIMES HELD
- None

EVOLUTION
Does not evolve

HOW TO OBTAIN

Pokémon Black Version 2	Link Trade or Poké Transfer
Pokémon White Version 2	Link Trade or Poké Transfer

HOW TO OBTAIN FROM OTHER GAMES

Pokémon HeartGold Version	Encounter at the Embedded Tower once you have the Jade Orb
Pokémon SoulSilver Version	Encounter at the Embedded Tower once you have the Jade Orb

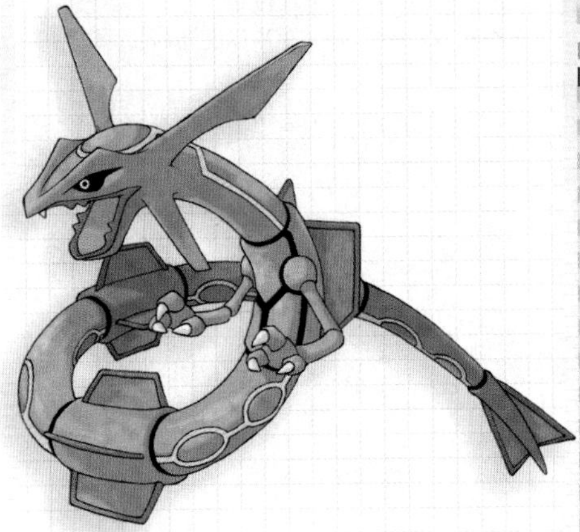

Pokémon AR Marker

LEVEL-UP AND LEARNED MOVES

Lv.	Name	Type	Kind	Pow.	Acc.	PP	Range	Long	DA
1	Twister	Dragon	Special	40	100	20	Many Others	—	—
5	Scary Face	Normal	Status	—	100	10	Normal	—	—
15	Crunch	Dark	Physical	80	100	15	Normal	—	○
20	Hyper Voice	Normal	Special	90	100	10	Many Others	—	—
30	Rest	Psychic	Status	—	—	10	Self	—	—
35	Air Slash	Flying	Special	75	95	20	Normal	○	—
45	AncientPower	Rock	Special	60	100	5	Normal	—	—
50	Outrage	Dragon	Physical	120	100	10	1 Random	—	○
60	Dragon Dance	Dragon	Status	—	—	20	Self	—	—
65	Fly	Flying	Physical	90	95	15	Normal	○	○
75	ExtremeSpeed	Normal	Physical	80	100	5	Normal	—	○
80	Hyper Beam	Normal	Special	150	90	5	Normal	—	—
90	Dragon Pulse	Dragon	Special	90	100	10	Normal	○	—

TM & HM MOVES

Lv.	Name	Type	Kind	Pow.	Acc.	PP	Range	Long	DA
TM01	Hone Claws	Dark	Status	—	—	15	Self	—	—
TM02	Dragon Claw	Dragon	Physical	80	100	15	Normal	—	○
TM05	Roar	Normal	Status	—	100	20	Normal	—	—
TM06	Toxic	Poison	Status	—	90	10	Normal	—	—
TM08	Bulk Up	Fighting	Status	—	—	20	Self	—	—
TM10	Hidden Power	Normal	Special	—	100	15	Normal	—	—
TM11	Sunny Day	Fire	Status	—	—	5	Both Sides	—	—
TM13	Ice Beam	Ice	Special	95	100	10	Normal	—	—
TM14	Blizzard	Ice	Special	120	70	5	Many Others	—	—
TM15	Hyper Beam	Normal	Special	150	90	5	Normal	—	—
TM17	Protect	Normal	Status	—	—	10	Self	—	—
TM18	Rain Dance	Water	Status	—	—	5	Both Sides	—	—
TM21	Frustration	Normal	Physical	—	100	20	Normal	—	○
TM22	SolarBeam	Grass	Special	120	100	10	Normal	—	—
TM24	Thunderbolt	Electric	Special	95	100	15	Normal	—	—
TM25	Thunder	Electric	Special	120	70	10	Normal	—	—
TM26	Earthquake	Ground	Physical	100	100	10	Adjacent	—	—
TM27	Return	Normal	Physical	—	100	20	Normal	—	○
TM31	Brick Break	Fighting	Physical	75	100	15	Normal	—	○
TM32	Double Team	Normal	Status	—	—	15	Self	—	—
TM35	Flamethrower	Fire	Special	95	100	15	Normal	—	—
TM37	Sandstorm	Rock	Status	—	—	10	Both Sides	—	—
TM38	Fire Blast	Fire	Special	120	85	5	Normal	—	—
TM39	Rock Tomb	Rock	Physical	50	80	10	Normal	—	—
TM40	Aerial Ace	Flying	Physical	60	—	20	Normal	○	○
TM42	Facade	Normal	Physical	70	100	20	Normal	—	○
TM44	Rest	Psychic	Status	—	—	10	Self	—	—
TM48	Round	Normal	Special	60	100	15	Normal	—	—
TM49	Echoed Voice	Normal	Special	40	100	15	Normal	—	—
TM50	Overheat	Fire	Special	140	90	5	Normal	—	—
TM52	Focus Blast	Fighting	Special	120	70	5	Normal	—	—
TM53	Energy Ball	Grass	Special	80	100	10	Normal	—	—
TM56	Fling	Dark	Physical	—	100	10	Normal	—	—
TM58	Sky Drop	Flying	Physical	60	100	10	Normal	○	○
TM59	Incinerate	Fire	Special	30	100	15	Many Others	—	—
TM65	Shadow Claw	Ghost	Physical	70	100	15	Normal	—	○
TM68	Giga Impact	Normal	Physical	150	90	5	Normal	—	○
TM71	Stone Edge	Rock	Physical	100	80	5	Normal	—	—
TM73	Thunder Wave	Electric	Status	—	100	20	Normal	—	—
TM74	Gyro Ball	Steel	Physical	—	100	5	Normal	—	○
TM75	Swords Dance	Normal	Status	—	—	30	Self	—	—
TM77	Psych Up	Normal	Status	—	—	10	Normal	—	—
TM78	Bulldoze	Ground	Physical	60	100	20	Adjacent	—	—
TM80	Rock Slide	Rock	Physical	75	90	10	Many Others	—	—
TM82	Dragon Tail	Dragon	Physical	60	90	10	Normal	—	○
TM87	Swagger	Normal	Status	—	90	15	Normal	—	—
TM90	Substitute	Normal	Status	—	—	10	Self	—	—
TM94	Rock Smash	Fighting	Physical	40	100	15	Normal	—	○
HM02	Fly	Flying	Physical	90	95	15	Normal	○	○
HM03	Surf	Water	Special	95	100	15	Adjacent	—	—
HM04	Strength	Normal	Physical	80	100	15	Normal	—	○
HM05	Waterfall	Water	Physical	80	100	15	Normal	—	○
HM06	Dive	Water	Physical	80	100	10	Normal	—	○

MOVES TAUGHT BY PEOPLE

Name	Type	Kind	Pow.	Acc.	PP	Range	Long	DA
Draco Meteor	Dragon	Special	140	90	5	Normal	—	—

MOVES TAUGHT BY MOVE TUTORS FOR SHARDS

Name	Type	Kind	Pow.	Acc.	PP	Range	Long	DA
Iron Head	Steel	Physical	80	100	15	Normal	—	○
Uproar	Normal	Special	90	100	10	1 Random	—	—
Hyper Voice	Normal	Special	90	100	10	Many Others	—	—
Icy Wind	Ice	Special	55	95	15	Many Others	—	—
Iron Tail	Steel	Physical	100	75	15	Normal	—	○
Aqua Tail	Water	Physical	90	90	10	Normal	—	○
Earth Power	Ground	Special	90	100	10	Normal	—	—
Dragon Pulse	Dragon	Special	90	100	10	Normal	○	—
Bind	Normal	Physical	15	85	20	Normal	—	○
Snore	Normal	Special	40	100	15	Normal	—	—
Tailwind	Flying	Status	—	—	30	Your Side	—	—
Outrage	Dragon	Physical	120	100	10	1 Random	—	○
Sleep Talk	Normal	Status	—	—	10	Self	—	—

384 Rayquaza

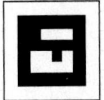

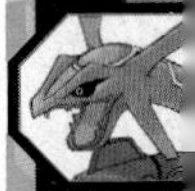

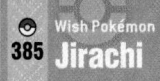

385 Jirachi

Wish Pokémon

- HEIGHT: 1'00"
- WEIGHT: 2.4 lbs.
- GENDER: Unknown

It is said to have the ability to grant any wish for just one week every thousand years.

Gender unknown

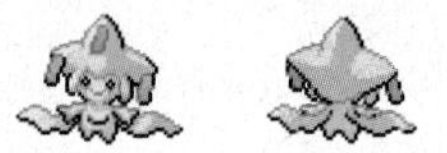

TYPE: Steel / Psychic

ABILITY
- Serene Grace

HIDDEN ABILITY
—

STATS
HP
Attack
Defense
Sp. Atk
Sp. Def
Speed

EGG GROUPS
No Egg has ever been discovered

EVOLUTION
Does not evolve

HOW TO OBTAIN
Only available through special distribution events. Check www.pokemon.com for the latest information on how to catch this Pokémon.

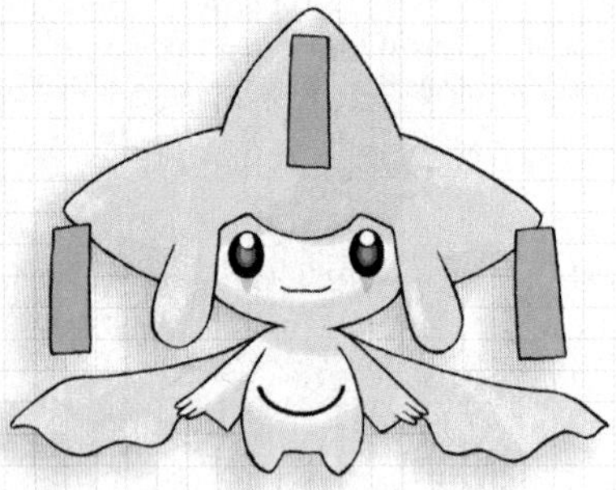

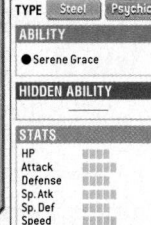

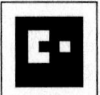

Pokémon AR Marker

LEVEL-UP AND LEARNED MOVES

Lv.	Name	Type	Kind	Pow.	Acc.	PP	Range	Long	DA
1	Wish	Normal	Status	—	—	10	Self	—	—
1	Confusion	Psychic	Special	50	100	25	Normal	—	—
5	Rest	Psychic	Status	—	—	10	Self	—	—
10	Swift	Normal	Special	60	—	20	Many Others	—	—
15	Helping Hand	Normal	Status	—	—	20	1 Ally	—	—
20	Psychic	Psychic	Special	90	100	10	Normal	—	—
25	Refresh	Normal	Status	—	—	20	Self	—	—
30	Rest	Psychic	Status	—	—	10	Self	—	—
35	Zen Headbutt	Psychic	Physical	80	90	15	Normal	—	○
40	Double-Edge	Normal	Physical	120	100	15	Normal	—	○
45	Gravity	Psychic	Status	—	—	5	Both Sides	—	—
50	Healing Wish	Psychic	Status	—	—	10	Self	—	—
55	Future Sight	Psychic	Special	100	100	10	Normal	—	—
60	Cosmic Power	Psychic	Status	—	—	20	Self	—	—
65	Last Resort	Normal	Physical	140	100	5	Normal	—	○
70	Doom Desire	Steel	Special	140	100	5	Normal	—	—

TM & HM MOVES

Lv.	Name	Type	Kind	Pow.	Acc.	PP	Range	Long	DA
TM03	Psyshock	Psychic	Special	80	100	10	Normal	—	—
TM04	Calm Mind	Psychic	Status	—	—	20	Self	—	—
TM06	Toxic	Poison	Status	—	90	10	Normal	—	—
TM10	Hidden Power	Normal	Special	—	100	15	Normal	—	—
TM11	Sunny Day	Fire	Status	—	—	5	Both Sides	—	—
TM15	Hyper Beam	Normal	Special	150	90	5	Normal	—	—
TM16	Light Screen	Psychic	Status	—	—	30	Your Side	—	—
TM17	Protect	Normal	Status	—	—	10	Self	—	—
TM18	Rain Dance	Water	Status	—	—	5	Both Sides	—	—
TM19	Telekinesis	Psychic	Status	—	—	15	Normal	—	—
TM20	Safeguard	Normal	Status	—	—	25	Your Side	—	—
TM21	Frustration	Normal	Physical	—	100	20	Normal	—	○
TM24	Thunderbolt	Electric	Special	95	100	15	Normal	—	—
TM25	Thunder	Electric	Special	120	70	10	Normal	—	—
TM27	Return	Normal	Physical	—	100	20	Normal	—	○
TM29	Psychic	Psychic	Special	90	100	10	Normal	—	—
TM30	Shadow Ball	Ghost	Special	80	100	15	Normal	—	—
TM32	Double Team	Normal	Status	—	—	15	Self	—	—
TM33	Reflect	Psychic	Status	—	—	20	Your Side	—	—
TM37	Sandstorm	Rock	Status	—	—	10	Both Sides	—	—
TM40	Aerial Ace	Flying	Physical	60	—	20	Normal	○	○
TM42	Facade	Normal	Physical	70	100	20	Normal	—	○
TM44	Rest	Psychic	Status	—	—	10	Self	—	—
TM48	Round	Normal	Special	60	100	15	Normal	—	—
TM53	Energy Ball	Grass	Special	80	100	10	Normal	—	—
TM56	Fling	Dark	Physical	—	100	10	Normal	—	—
TM57	Charge Beam	Electric	Special	50	90	10	Normal	—	—
TM68	Giga Impact	Normal	Physical	150	90	5	Normal	—	○
TM70	Flash	Normal	Status	—	100	20	Normal	—	—
TM73	Thunder Wave	Electric	Status	—	100	20	Normal	—	—
TM77	Psych Up	Normal	Status	—	—	10	Normal	—	—
TM85	Dream Eater	Psychic	Special	100	100	15	Normal	—	—
TM86	Grass Knot	Grass	Special	—	100	20	Normal	—	○
TM87	Swagger	Normal	Status	—	90	15	Normal	—	—
TM89	U-turn	Bug	Physical	70	100	20	Normal	—	○
TM90	Substitute	Normal	Status	—	—	10	Self	—	—
TM91	Flash Cannon	Steel	Special	80	100	10	Normal	—	—
TM92	Trick Room	Psychic	Status	—	—	5	Both Sides	—	—

MOVES TAUGHT BY PEOPLE

Name	Type	Kind	Pow.	Acc.	PP	Range	Long	DA

MOVES TAUGHT BY MOVE TUTORS FOR SHARDS

Name	Type	Kind	Pow.	Acc.	PP	Range	Long	DA
Signal Beam	Bug	Special	75	100	15	Normal	—	—
Iron Head	Steel	Physical	80	100	15	Normal	—	○
Uproar	Normal	Special	90	100	10	1 Random	—	—
Fire Punch	Fire	Physical	75	100	15	Normal	—	○
ThunderPunch	Electric	Physical	75	100	15	Normal	—	○
Ice Punch	Ice	Physical	75	100	15	Normal	—	○
Last Resort	Normal	Physical	140	100	5	Normal	—	○
Iron Defense	Steel	Status	—	—	15	Self	—	—
Magic Coat	Psychic	Status	—	—	15	Self	—	—
Icy Wind	Ice	Special	55	95	15	Many Others	—	—
Zen Headbutt	Psychic	Physical	80	90	15	Normal	—	○
Gravity	Psychic	Status	—	—	5	Both Sides	—	—
Snore	Normal	Special	40	100	15	Normal	—	—
Drain Punch	Fighting	Physical	75	100	10	Normal	—	○
Helping Hand	Normal	Status	—	—	20	1 Ally	—	—
Magic Room	Psychic	Status	—	—	10	Both Sides	—	—
Recycle	Normal	Status	—	—	10	Self	—	—
Trick	Psychic	Status	—	100	10	Normal	—	—
Stealth Rock	Rock	Status	—	—	20	3 Foes	—	—
Sleep Talk	Normal	Status	—	—	10	Self	—	—
Skill Swap	Psychic	Status	—	—	10	Normal	—	—

386 Deoxys (Normal Forme)

DNA Pokémon

- HEIGHT: 5'07"
- WEIGHT: 134.0 lbs.
- GENDER: Unknown

An alien virus that fell to earth on a meteor underwent a DNA mutation to become this Pokémon.

Gender unknown

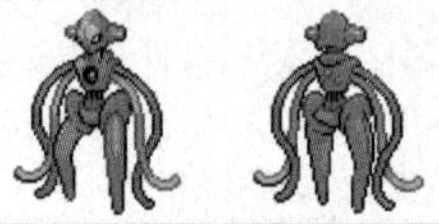

TYPE: Psychic

ABILITY
- Pressure

HIDDEN ABILITY
—

STATS
HP
Attack
Defense
Sp. Atk
Sp. Def
Speed

EGG GROUPS
No Egg has ever been discovered

EVOLUTION
Does not evolve

HOW TO OBTAIN
Only available through special distribution events. Check www.pokemon.com for the latest information on how to obtain this Pokémon.

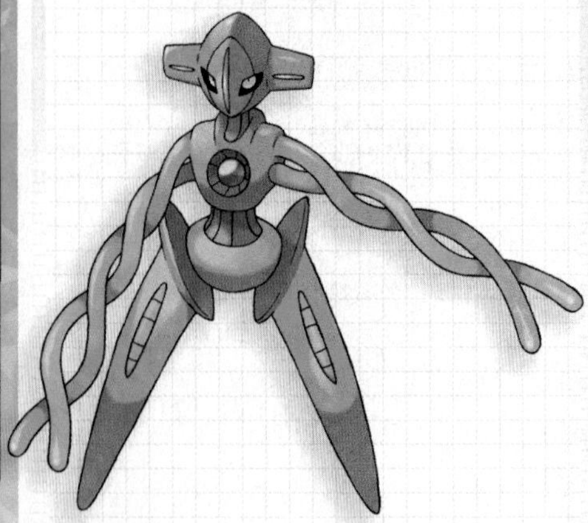

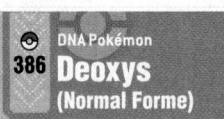

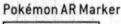

Pokémon AR Marker

LEVEL-UP AND LEARNED MOVES

Lv.	Name	Type	Kind	Pow.	Acc.	PP	Range	Long	DA
1	Leer	Normal	Status	—	100	30	Many Others	—	—
1	Wrap	Normal	Physical	15	90	20	Normal	—	○
9	Night Shade	Ghost	Special	—	100	15	Normal	—	—
17	Teleport	Psychic	Status	—	—	20	Self	—	—
25	Knock Off	Dark	Physical	20	100	20	Normal	—	○
33	Pursuit	Dark	Physical	40	100	20	Normal	—	○
41	Psychic	Psychic	Special	90	100	10	Normal	—	—
49	Snatch	Dark	Status	—	—	10	Self	—	—
57	Psycho Shift	Psychic	Status	—	90	10	Normal	—	—
65	Zen Headbutt	Psychic	Physical	80	90	15	Normal	—	○
73	Cosmic Power	Psychic	Status	—	—	20	Self	—	—
81	Recover	Normal	Status	—	—	10	Self	—	—
89	Psycho Boost	Psychic	Special	140	90	5	Normal	—	—
97	Hyper Beam	Normal	Special	150	90	5	Normal	—	—

TM & HM MOVES

Lv.	Name	Type	Kind	Pow.	Acc.	PP	Range	Long	DA
TM03	Psyshock	Psychic	Special	80	100	10	Normal	—	—
TM04	Calm Mind	Psychic	Status	—	—	20	Self	—	—
TM06	Toxic	Poison	Status	—	90	10	Normal	—	—
TM10	Hidden Power	Normal	Special	—	100	15	Normal	—	—
TM11	Sunny Day	Fire	Status	—	—	5	Both Sides	—	—
TM12	Taunt	Dark	Status	—	100	20	Normal	—	—
TM13	Ice Beam	Ice	Special	95	100	10	Normal	—	—
TM15	Hyper Beam	Normal	Special	150	90	5	Normal	—	—
TM16	Light Screen	Psychic	Status	—	—	30	Your Side	—	—
TM17	Protect	Normal	Status	—	—	10	Self	—	—
TM18	Rain Dance	Water	Status	—	—	5	Both Sides	—	—
TM19	Telekinesis	Psychic	Status	—	—	15	Normal	—	—
TM20	Safeguard	Normal	Status	—	—	25	Your Side	—	—
TM21	Frustration	Normal	Physical	—	100	20	Normal	—	○
TM22	SolarBeam	Grass	Special	120	100	10	Normal	—	—
TM24	Thunderbolt	Electric	Special	95	100	15	Normal	—	—
TM25	Thunder	Electric	Special	120	70	10	Normal	—	—
TM27	Return	Normal	Physical	—	100	20	Normal	—	○
TM29	Psychic	Psychic	Special	90	100	10	Normal	—	—
TM30	Shadow Ball	Ghost	Special	80	100	15	Normal	—	—
TM31	Brick Break	Fighting	Physical	75	100	15	Normal	—	○
TM32	Double Team	Normal	Status	—	—	15	Self	—	—
TM33	Reflect	Psychic	Status	—	—	20	Your Side	—	—
TM39	Rock Tomb	Rock	Physical	50	80	10	Normal	—	—
TM40	Aerial Ace	Flying	Physical	60	—	20	Normal	○	○
TM41	Torment	Dark	Status	—	100	15	Normal	—	—
TM42	Facade	Normal	Physical	70	100	20	Normal	—	○
TM44	Rest	Psychic	Status	—	—	10	Self	—	—
TM47	Low Sweep	Fighting	Physical	60	100	20	Normal	—	○
TM48	Round	Normal	Special	60	100	15	Normal	—	—
TM51	Ally Switch	Psychic	Status	—	—	15	Self	—	—
TM52	Focus Blast	Fighting	Special	120	70	5	Normal	—	—
TM53	Energy Ball	Grass	Special	80	100	10	Normal	—	—
TM56	Fling	Dark	Physical	—	100	10	Normal	—	—
TM57	Charge Beam	Electric	Special	50	90	10	Normal	—	—
TM68	Giga Impact	Normal	Physical	150	90	5	Normal	—	○
TM70	Flash	Normal	Status	—	100	20	Normal	—	—
TM73	Thunder Wave	Electric	Status	—	100	20	Normal	—	—
TM77	Psych Up	Normal	Status	—	—	10	Normal	—	—
TM80	Rock Slide	Rock	Physical	75	90	10	Many Others	—	—
TM84	Poison Jab	Poison	Physical	80	100	20	Normal	—	○
TM85	Dream Eater	Psychic	Special	100	100	15	Normal	—	—
TM86	Grass Knot	Grass	Special	—	100	20	Normal	—	○
TM87	Swagger	Normal	Status	—	90	15	Normal	—	—
TM90	Substitute	Normal	Status	—	—	10	Self	—	—
TM91	Flash Cannon	Steel	Special	80	100	10	Normal	—	—
TM92	Trick Room	Psychic	Status	—	—	5	Both Sides	—	—
TM94	Rock Smash	Fighting	Physical	40	100	15	Normal	—	○
HM01	Cut	Normal	Physical	50	95	30	Normal	—	○
HM04	Strength	Normal	Physical	80	100	15	Normal	—	○

MOVES TAUGHT BY PEOPLE

Name	Type	Kind	Pow.	Acc.	PP	Range	Long	DA

MOVES TAUGHT BY MOVE TUTORS FOR SHARDS

Name	Type	Kind	Pow.	Acc.	PP	Range	Long	DA
Signal Beam	Bug	Special	75	100	15	Normal	—	—
Low Kick	Fighting	Physical	—	100	20	Normal	—	○
Fire Punch	Fire	Physical	75	100	15	Normal	—	○
ThunderPunch	Electric	Physical	75	100	15	Normal	—	○
Ice Punch	Ice	Physical	75	100	15	Normal	—	○
Magic Coat	Psychic	Status	—	—	15	Self	—	—
Icy Wind	Ice	Special	55	95	15	Many Others	—	—
Zen Headbutt	Psychic	Physical	80	90	15	Normal	—	○
Gravity	Psychic	Status	—	—	5	Both Sides	—	—
Bind	Normal	Physical	15	85	20	Normal	—	○
Snore	Normal	Special	40	100	15	Normal	—	—
Knock Off	Dark	Physical	20	100	20	Normal	—	○
Role Play	Psychic	Status	—	—	10	Normal	—	—
Drain Punch	Fighting	Physical	75	100	10	Normal	—	○
Wonder Room	Psychic	Status	—	—	10	Both Sides	—	—
Recycle	Normal	Status	—	—	10	Self	—	—
Trick	Psychic	Status	—	100	10	Normal	—	—
Stealth Rock	Rock	Status	—	—	20	3 Foes	—	—
Sleep Talk	Normal	Status	—	—	10	Self	—	—
Skill Swap	Psychic	Status	—	—	10	Normal	—	—
Snatch	Dark	Status	—	—	10	Self	—	—

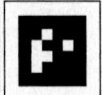

DNA Pokémon

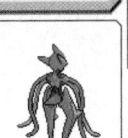

386 Deoxys (Attack Forme)

- HEIGHT: 5'07"
- WEIGHT: 134.0 lbs.
- GENDER: Unknown

An alien virus that fell to earth on a meteor underwent a DNA mutation to become this Pokémon.

Gender unknown

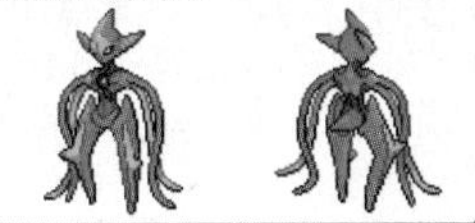

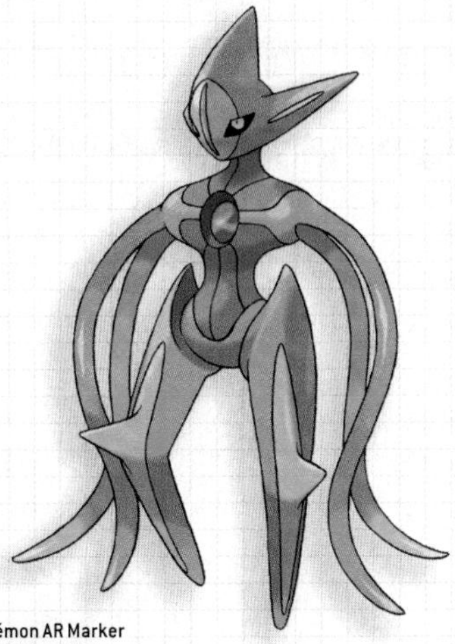

Pokémon AR Marker

TYPE: Psychic

ABILITY
- Pressure

HIDDEN ABILITY
—

STATS
HP
Attack
Defense
Sp. Atk
Sp. Def
Speed

EGG GROUPS
No Egg has ever been discovered

EVOLUTION
Does not evolve

HOW TO OBTAIN

Pokémon Black Version 2	Put Deoxys (Normal Forme) in your party and examine the meteor in the Nacrene Museum
Pokémon White Version 2	Put Deoxys (Normal Forme) in your party and examine the meteor in the Nacrene Museum

HOW TO OBTAIN FROM OTHER GAMES
—
—

LEVEL-UP AND LEARNED MOVES

Lv.	Name	Type	Kind	Pow.	Acc.	PP	Range	Long	DA
1	Leer	Normal	Status	—	100	30	Many Others	—	—
1	Wrap	Normal	Physical	15	90	20	Normal	—	○
9	Night Shade	Ghost	Special	—	100	15	Normal	—	—
17	Teleport	Psychic	Status	—	—	20	Self	—	—
25	Taunt	Dark	Status	—	100	20	Normal	—	—
33	Pursuit	Dark	Physical	40	100	20	Normal	—	○
41	Psychic	Psychic	Special	90	100	10	Normal	—	—
49	Superpower	Fighting	Physical	120	100	5	Normal	—	○
57	Psycho Shift	Psychic	Status	—	90	10	Normal	—	—
65	Zen Headbutt	Psychic	Physical	80	90	15	Normal	—	○
73	Cosmic Power	Psychic	Status	—	—	20	Self	—	—
81	Zap Cannon	Electric	Special	120	50	5	Normal	—	—
89	Psycho Boost	Psychic	Special	140	90	5	Normal	—	—
97	Hyper Beam	Normal	Special	150	90	5	Normal	—	—

TM & HM MOVES

Lv.	Name	Type	Kind	Pow.	Acc.	PP	Range	Long	DA
TM03	Psyshock	Psychic	Special	80	100	10	Normal	—	—
TM04	Calm Mind	Psychic	Status	—	—	20	Self	—	—
TM06	Toxic	Poison	Status	—	90	10	Normal	—	—
TM10	Hidden Power	Normal	Special	—	100	15	Normal	—	—
TM11	Sunny Day	Fire	Status	—	—	5	Both Sides	—	—
TM12	Taunt	Dark	Status	—	100	20	Normal	—	—
TM13	Ice Beam	Ice	Special	95	100	10	Normal	—	—
TM15	Hyper Beam	Normal	Special	150	90	5	Normal	—	—
TM16	Light Screen	Psychic	Status	—	—	30	Your Side	—	—
TM17	Protect	Normal	Status	—	—	10	Self	—	—
TM18	Rain Dance	Water	Status	—	—	5	Both Sides	—	—
TM19	Telekinesis	Psychic	Status	—	—	15	Normal	—	—
TM20	Safeguard	Normal	Status	—	—	25	Your Side	—	—
TM21	Frustration	Normal	Physical	—	100	20	Normal	—	○
TM22	SolarBeam	Grass	Special	120	100	10	Normal	—	—
TM24	Thunderbolt	Electric	Special	95	100	15	Normal	—	—
TM25	Thunder	Electric	Special	120	70	10	Normal	—	—
TM27	Return	Normal	Physical	—	100	20	Normal	—	○
TM29	Psychic	Psychic	Special	90	100	10	Normal	—	—
TM30	Shadow Ball	Ghost	Special	80	100	15	Normal	—	—
TM31	Brick Break	Fighting	Physical	75	100	15	Normal	—	○
TM32	Double Team	Normal	Status	—	—	15	Self	—	—
TM33	Reflect	Psychic	Status	—	—	20	Your Side	—	—
TM39	Rock Tomb	Rock	Physical	50	80	10	Normal	—	—
TM40	Aerial Ace	Flying	Physical	60	—	20	Normal	○	○
TM41	Torment	Dark	Status	—	100	15	Normal	—	—
TM42	Facade	Normal	Physical	70	100	20	Normal	—	○
TM44	Rest	Psychic	Status	—	—	10	Self	—	—
TM47	Low Sweep	Fighting	Physical	60	100	20	Normal	—	○
TM48	Round	Normal	Special	60	100	15	Normal	—	—
TM51	Ally Switch	Psychic	Status	—	—	15	Self	—	—
TM52	Focus Blast	Fighting	Special	120	70	5	Normal	—	—
TM53	Energy Ball	Grass	Special	80	100	10	Normal	—	—
TM56	Fling	Dark	Physical	—	100	10	Normal	—	—
TM57	Charge Beam	Electric	Special	50	90	10	Normal	—	—
TM68	Giga Impact	Normal	Physical	150	90	5	Normal	—	○
TM70	Flash	Normal	Status	—	100	20	Normal	—	—
TM73	Thunder Wave	Electric	Status	—	100	20	Normal	—	—
TM77	Psych Up	Normal	Status	—	—	10	Normal	—	—
TM80	Rock Slide	Rock	Physical	75	90	10	Many Others	—	—
TM84	Poison Jab	Poison	Physical	80	100	20	Normal	—	○
TM85	Dream Eater	Psychic	Special	100	100	15	Normal	—	—
TM86	Grass Knot	Grass	Special	—	100	20	Normal	—	○
TM87	Swagger	Normal	Status	—	90	15	Normal	—	—
TM90	Substitute	Normal	Status	—	—	10	Self	—	—
TM91	Flash Cannon	Steel	Special	80	100	10	Normal	—	—
TM92	Trick Room	Psychic	Status	—	—	5	Both Sides	—	—
TM94	Rock Smash	Fighting	Physical	40	100	15	Normal	—	○
HM01	Cut	Normal	Physical	50	95	30	Normal	—	○
HM04	Strength	Normal	Physical	80	100	15	Normal	—	○

MOVES TAUGHT BY PEOPLE

Name	Type	Kind	Pow.	Acc.	PP	Range	Long	DA

MOVES TAUGHT BY MOVE TUTORS FOR SHARDS

Name	Type	Kind	Pow.	Acc.	PP	Range	Long	DA
Signal Beam	Bug	Special	75	100	15	Normal	—	—
Low Kick	Fighting	Physical	—	100	20	Normal	—	○
Magic Coat	Psychic	Status	—	—	15	Self	—	—
Zen Headbutt	Psychic	Physical	80	90	15	Normal	—	○
Superpower	Fighting	Physical	120	100	5	Normal	—	○
Gravity	Psychic	Status	—	—	5	Both Sides	—	—
Bind	Normal	Physical	15	85	20	Normal	—	○
Snore	Normal	Special	40	100	15	Normal	—	—
Role Play	Psychic	Status	—	—	10	Normal	—	—
Drain Punch	Fighting	Physical	75	100	10	Normal	—	○
Wonder Room	Psychic	Status	—	—	10	Both Sides	—	—
Recycle	Normal	Status	—	—	10	Self	—	—
Trick	Psychic	Status	—	100	10	Normal	—	—
Stealth Rock	Rock	Status	—	—	20	3 Foes	—	—
Sleep Talk	Normal	Status	—	—	10	Self	—	—
Skill Swap	Psychic	Status	—	—	10	Normal	—	—
Snatch	Dark	Status	—	—	10	Self	—	—

DNA Pokémon

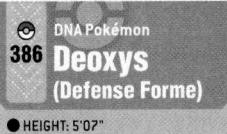

386 Deoxys (Defense Forme)

- HEIGHT: 5'07"
- WEIGHT: 134.0 lbs.
- GENDER: Unknown

An alien virus that fell to earth on a meteor underwent a DNA mutation to become this Pokémon.

Gender unknown

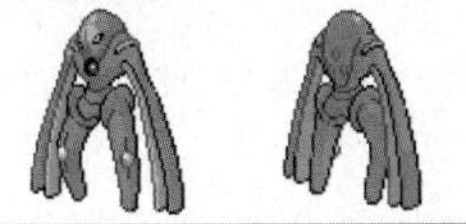

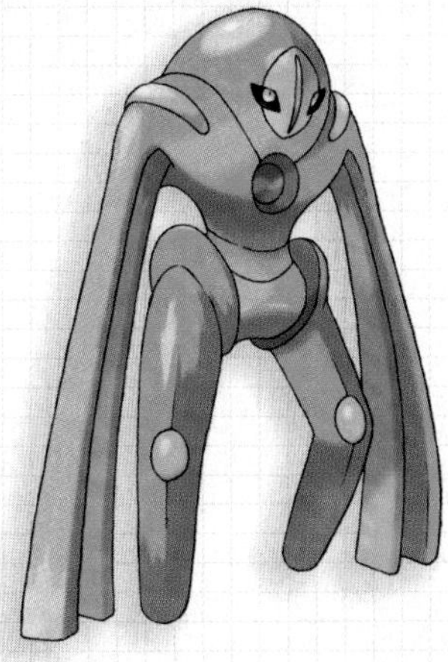

Pokémon AR Marker

TYPE: Psychic

ABILITY
- Pressure

HIDDEN ABILITY
—

STATS
HP
Attack
Defense
Sp. Atk
Sp. Def
Speed

EGG GROUPS
No Egg has ever been discovered

EVOLUTION
Does not evolve

HOW TO OBTAIN

Pokémon Black Version 2	Put Deoxys (Normal Forme) in your party and examine the meteor in the Nacrene Museum
Pokémon White Version 2	Put Deoxys (Normal Forme) in your party and examine the meteor in the Nacrene Museum

HOW TO OBTAIN FROM OTHER GAMES
—
—

LEVEL-UP AND LEARNED MOVES

Lv.	Name	Type	Kind	Pow.	Acc.	PP	Range	Long	DA
1	Leer	Normal	Status	—	100	30	Many Others	—	—
1	Wrap	Normal	Physical	15	90	20	Normal	—	○
9	Night Shade	Ghost	Special	—	100	15	Normal	—	—
17	Teleport	Psychic	Status	—	—	20	Self	—	—
25	Knock Off	Dark	Physical	20	100	20	Normal	—	○
33	Spikes	Ground	Status	—	—	20	3 Foes	—	—
41	Psychic	Psychic	Special	90	100	10	Normal	—	—
49	Snatch	Dark	Status	—	—	10	Self	—	—
57	Psycho Shift	Psychic	Status	—	90	10	Normal	—	—
65	Zen Headbutt	Psychic	Physical	80	90	15	Normal	—	○
73	Iron Defense	Steel	Status	—	—	15	Self	—	—
73	Amnesia	Psychic	Status	—	—	20	Self	—	—
81	Recover	Normal	Status	—	—	10	Self	—	—
89	Psycho Boost	Psychic	Special	140	90	5	Normal	—	—
97	Counter	Fighting	Physical	—	100	20	Varies	—	○
97	Mirror Coat	Psychic	Special	—	100	20	Varies	—	—

TM & HM MOVES

Lv.	Name	Type	Kind	Pow.	Acc.	PP	Range	Long	DA
TM03	Psyshock	Psychic	Special	80	100	10	Normal	—	—
TM04	Calm Mind	Psychic	Status	—	—	20	Self	—	—
TM06	Toxic	Poison	Status	—	90	10	Normal	—	—
TM10	Hidden Power	Normal	Special	—	100	15	Normal	—	—
TM11	Sunny Day	Fire	Status	—	—	5	Both Sides	—	—
TM12	Taunt	Dark	Status	—	100	20	Normal	—	—
TM13	Ice Beam	Ice	Special	95	100	10	Normal	—	—
TM15	Hyper Beam	Normal	Special	150	90	5	Normal	—	—
TM16	Light Screen	Psychic	Status	—	—	30	Your Side	—	—
TM17	Protect	Normal	Status	—	—	10	Self	—	—
TM18	Rain Dance	Water	Status	—	—	5	Both Sides	—	—
TM19	Telekinesis	Psychic	Status	—	—	15	Normal	—	—
TM20	Safeguard	Normal	Status	—	—	25	Your Side	—	—
TM21	Frustration	Normal	Physical	—	100	20	Normal	—	○
TM22	SolarBeam	Grass	Special	120	100	10	Normal	—	—
TM24	Thunderbolt	Electric	Special	95	100	15	Normal	—	—
TM25	Thunder	Electric	Special	120	70	10	Normal	—	—
TM27	Return	Normal	Physical	—	100	20	Normal	—	○
TM29	Psychic	Psychic	Special	90	100	10	Normal	—	—
TM30	Shadow Ball	Ghost	Special	80	100	15	Normal	—	—
TM31	Brick Break	Fighting	Physical	75	100	15	Normal	—	○
TM32	Double Team	Normal	Status	—	—	15	Self	—	—
TM33	Reflect	Psychic	Status	—	—	20	Your Side	—	—
TM39	Rock Tomb	Rock	Physical	50	80	10	Normal	—	—
TM40	Aerial Ace	Flying	Physical	60	—	20	Normal	○	○
TM41	Torment	Dark	Status	—	100	15	Normal	—	—
TM42	Facade	Normal	Physical	70	100	20	Normal	—	○
TM44	Rest	Psychic	Status	—	—	10	Self	—	—
TM47	Low Sweep	Fighting	Physical	60	100	20	Normal	—	○
TM48	Round	Normal	Special	60	100	15	Normal	—	—
TM51	Ally Switch	Psychic	Status	—	—	15	Self	—	—
TM52	Focus Blast	Fighting	Special	120	70	5	Normal	—	—
TM53	Energy Ball	Grass	Special	80	100	10	Normal	—	—
TM56	Fling	Dark	Physical	—	100	10	Normal	—	—
TM57	Charge Beam	Electric	Special	50	90	10	Normal	—	—
TM68	Giga Impact	Normal	Physical	150	90	5	Normal	—	○
TM70	Flash	Normal	Status	—	100	20	Normal	—	—
TM73	Thunder Wave	Electric	Status	—	100	20	Normal	—	—
TM77	Psych Up	Normal	Status	—	—	10	Normal	—	—
TM80	Rock Slide	Rock	Physical	75	90	10	Many Others	—	—
TM84	Poison Jab	Poison	Physical	80	100	20	Normal	—	○
TM85	Dream Eater	Psychic	Special	100	100	15	Normal	—	—
TM86	Grass Knot	Grass	Special	—	100	20	Normal	—	○
TM87	Swagger	Normal	Status	—	90	15	Normal	—	—
TM90	Substitute	Normal	Status	—	—	10	Self	—	—
TM91	Flash Cannon	Steel	Special	80	100	10	Normal	—	—
TM92	Trick Room	Psychic	Status	—	—	5	Both Sides	—	—
TM94	Rock Smash	Fighting	Physical	40	100	15	Normal	—	○
HM01	Cut	Normal	Physical	50	95	30	Normal	—	○
HM04	Strength	Normal	Physical	80	100	15	Normal	—	○

MOVES TAUGHT BY PEOPLE

Name	Type	Kind	Pow.	Acc.	PP	Range	Long	DA

MOVES TAUGHT BY MOVE TUTORS FOR SHARDS

Name	Type	Kind	Pow.	Acc.	PP	Range	Long	DA
Signal Beam	Bug	Special	75	100	15	Normal	—	—
Low Kick	Fighting	Physical	—	100	20	Normal	—	○
Iron Defense	Steel	Status	—	—	15	Self	—	—
Magic Coat	Psychic	Status	—	—	15	Self	—	—
Zen Headbutt	Psychic	Physical	80	90	15	Normal	—	○
Gravity	Psychic	Status	—	—	5	Both Sides	—	—
Bind	Normal	Physical	15	85	20	Normal	—	○
Snore	Normal	Special	40	100	15	Normal	—	—
Knock Off	Dark	Physical	20	100	20	Normal	—	○
Role Play	Psychic	Status	—	—	10	Normal	—	—
Drain Punch	Fighting	Physical	75	100	10	Normal	—	○
Wonder Room	Psychic	Status	—	—	10	Both Sides	—	—
Recycle	Normal	Status	—	—	10	Self	—	—
Trick	Psychic	Status	—	100	10	Normal	—	—
Stealth Rock	Rock	Status	—	—	20	3 Foes	—	—
Sleep Talk	Normal	Status	—	—	10	Self	—	—
Skill Swap	Psychic	Status	—	—	10	Normal	—	—
Snatch	Dark	Status	—	—	10	Self	—	—

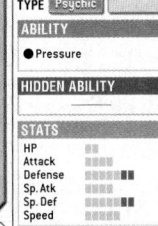

386 Deoxys (Speed Forme)
DNA Pokémon

TYPE Psychic

ABILITY
- Pressure

HIDDEN ABILITY

HEIGHT: 5'07"
WEIGHT: 134.0 lbs.
GENDER: Unknown

An alien virus that fell to earth on a meteor underwent a DNA mutation to become this Pokémon.

STATS
- HP
- Attack
- Defense
- Sp. Atk
- Sp. Def
- Speed

EGG GROUPS
No Egg has ever been discovered

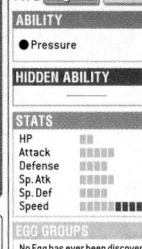

Gender unknown

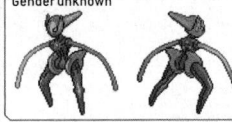

EVOLUTION
Does not evolve

HOW TO OBTAIN
Pokémon Black Version 2	Put Deoxys (Normal Forme) in your party and examine the meteor in the Nacrene Museum
Pokémon White Version 2	Put Deoxys (Normal Forme) in your party and examine the meteor in the Nacrene Museum

HOW TO OBTAIN FROM OTHER GAMES

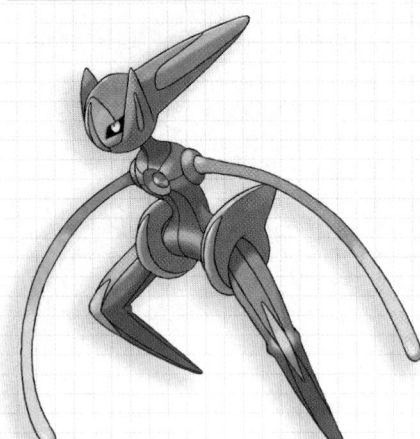

Pokémon AR Marker

LEVEL-UP AND LEARNED MOVES
Lv.	Name	Type	Kind	Pow.	Acc.	PP	Range	Long	DA
1	Leer	Normal	Status	—	100	30	Many Others	—	—
1	Wrap	Normal	Physical	15	90	20	Normal	—	○
9	Night Shade	Ghost	Special	—	100	15	Normal	—	—
17	Double Team	Normal	Status	—	—	15	Self	—	—
25	Knock Off	Dark	Physical	20	100	20	Normal	—	○
33	Pursuit	Dark	Physical	40	100	20	Normal	—	○
41	Psychic	Psychic	Special	90	100	10	Normal	—	—
49	Swift	Normal	Special	60	—	20	Many Others	—	—
57	Psycho Shift	Psychic	Status	—	90	10	Normal	—	—
65	Zen Headbutt	Psychic	Physical	80	90	15	Normal	—	○
73	Agility	Psychic	Status	—	—	30	Self	—	—
81	Recover	Normal	Status	—	—	10	Self	—	—
89	Psycho Boost	Psychic	Special	140	90	5	Normal	—	—
97	ExtremeSpeed	Normal	Physical	80	100	5	Normal	—	○

TM & HM MOVES
Lv.	Name	Type	Kind	Pow.	Acc.	PP	Range	Long	DA
TM03	Psyshock	Psychic	Special	80	100	10	Normal	—	—
TM04	Calm Mind	Psychic	Status	—	—	20	Self	—	—
TM06	Toxic	Poison	Status	—	90	10	Normal	—	—
TM10	Hidden Power	Normal	Special	—	100	15	Normal	—	—
TM11	Sunny Day	Fire	Status	—	—	5	Both Sides	—	—
TM12	Taunt	Dark	Status	—	100	20	Normal	—	—
TM13	Ice Beam	Ice	Special	95	100	10	Normal	—	—
TM15	Hyper Beam	Normal	Special	150	90	5	Normal	—	—
TM16	Light Screen	Psychic	Status	—	—	30	Your Side	—	—
TM17	Protect	Normal	Status	—	—	10	Self	—	—
TM18	Rain Dance	Water	Status	—	—	5	Both Sides	—	—
TM19	Telekinesis	Psychic	Status	—	—	15	Normal	—	—
TM20	Safeguard	Normal	Status	—	—	25	Your Side	—	—
TM21	Frustration	Normal	Physical	—	100	20	Normal	—	○
TM22	SolarBeam	Grass	Special	120	100	10	Normal	—	—
TM24	Thunderbolt	Electric	Special	95	100	15	Normal	—	—
TM25	Thunder	Electric	Special	120	70	10	Normal	—	—
TM27	Return	Normal	Physical	—	100	20	Normal	—	○
TM29	Psychic	Psychic	Special	90	100	10	Normal	—	—
TM30	Shadow Ball	Ghost	Special	80	100	15	Normal	—	—
TM31	Brick Break	Fighting	Physical	75	100	15	Normal	—	—
TM32	Double Team	Normal	Status	—	—	15	Self	—	—
TM33	Reflect	Psychic	Status	—	—	20	Your Side	—	—
TM39	Rock Tomb	Rock	Physical	50	80	10	Normal	—	—
TM40	Aerial Ace	Flying	Physical	60	—	20	Normal	○	○
TM41	Torment	Dark	Status	—	100	15	Normal	—	—
TM42	Facade	Normal	Physical	70	100	20	Normal	—	—
TM44	Rest	Psychic	Status	—	—	10	Self	—	—
TM47	Low Sweep	Fighting	Physical	60	100	20	Normal	—	—
TM48	Round	Normal	Special	60	100	15	Normal	—	—
TM51	Ally Switch	Psychic	Status	—	—	15	Self	—	—
TM52	Focus Blast	Fighting	Special	120	70	5	Normal	—	—
TM53	Energy Ball	Grass	Special	80	100	10	Normal	—	—
TM56	Fling	Dark	Physical	—	100	10	Normal	—	—
TM57	Charge Beam	Electric	Special	50	90	10	Normal	—	—
TM68	Giga Impact	Normal	Physical	150	90	5	Normal	—	○
TM70	Flash	Normal	Status	—	100	20	Normal	—	—
TM73	Thunder Wave	Electric	Status	—	100	20	Normal	—	—
TM77	Psych Up	Normal	Status	—	—	10	Normal	—	—

MOVES TAUGHT BY PEOPLE
Name	Type	Kind	Pow.	Acc.	PP	Range	Long	DA

MOVES TAUGHT BY MOVE TUTORS FOR SHARDS
Name	Type	Kind	Pow.	Acc.	PP	Range	Long	DA
Signal Beam	Bug	Special	75	100	15	Normal	—	—
Low Kick	Fighting	Physical	—	100	20	Normal	—	○
Fire Punch	Fire	Physical	75	100	15	Normal	—	—
ThunderPunch	Electric	Physical	75	100	15	Normal	—	—
Ice Punch	Ice	Physical	75	100	15	Normal	—	—
Magic Coat	Psychic	Status	—	—	15	Self	—	—
Zen Headbutt	Psychic	Physical	80	90	15	Normal	—	○
Gravity	Psychic	Status	—	—	5	Both Sides	—	—
Bind	Normal	Physical	15	85	20	Normal	—	○
Snore	Normal	Special	40	100	15	Normal	—	—
Knock Off	Dark	Physical	20	100	20	Normal	—	○
Role Play	Psychic	Status	—	—	10	Normal	—	—
Drain Punch	Fighting	Physical	75	100	10	Normal	—	—
Wonder Room	Psychic	Status	—	—	10	Both Sides	—	—
Recycle	Normal	Status	—	—	10	Self	—	—
Trick	Psychic	Status	—	100	10	Normal	—	—
Stealth Rock	Rock	Status	—	—	20	3 Foes	—	—
Sleep Talk	Normal	Status	—	—	10	Self	—	—
Skill Swap	Psychic	Status	—	—	10	Normal	—	—
Snatch	Dark	Status	—	—	10	Self	—	—

387 Turtwig
Tiny Leaf Pokémon

TYPE Grass

ABILITY
- Overgrow

HIDDEN ABILITY
- Shell Armor

HEIGHT: 1'04"
WEIGHT: 22.5 lbs.
GENDER: ♂/♀

The shell on its back is made of soil. On a very healthy Turtwig, the shell should feel moist.

Same form for ♂/♀

STATS
- HP
- Attack
- Defense
- Sp. Atk
- Sp. Def
- Speed

EGG GROUPS
Monster/Grass

ITEMS SOMETIMES HELD
- None

Pokémon AR Marker

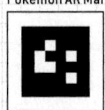

EVOLUTION

Turtwig — Lv. 18 → Grotle — Lv. 32 → Torterra

HOW TO OBTAIN
Pokémon Black Version 2	Link Trade or Poké Transfer
Pokémon White Version 2	Link Trade or Poké Transfer

HOW TO OBTAIN FROM OTHER GAMES
Pokémon Platinum Version	Get from Professor Rowan at the start of the adventure

LEVEL-UP AND LEARNED MOVES
Lv.	Name	Type	Kind	Pow.	Acc.	PP	Range	Long	DA
1	Tackle	Normal	Physical	50	100	35	Normal	—	—
5	Withdraw	Water	Status	—	—	40	Self	—	—
9	Absorb	Grass	Special	20	100	25	Normal	—	—
13	Razor Leaf	Grass	Physical	55	95	25	Many Others	—	—
17	Curse	Ghost	Status	—	—	10	Varies	—	—
21	Bite	Dark	Physical	60	100	25	Normal	—	○
25	Mega Drain	Grass	Special	40	100	15	Normal	—	—
29	Leech Seed	Grass	Status	—	90	10	Normal	—	—
33	Synthesis	Grass	Status	—	—	5	Self	—	—
37	Crunch	Dark	Physical	80	100	15	Normal	—	○
41	Giga Drain	Grass	Special	75	100	10	Normal	—	—
45	Leaf Storm	Grass	Special	140	90	5	Normal	—	—

TM & HM MOVES
Lv.	Name	Type	Kind	Pow.	Acc.	PP	Range	Long	DA
TM06	Toxic	Poison	Status	—	90	10	Normal	—	—
TM10	Hidden Power	Normal	Special	—	100	15	Normal	—	—
TM11	Sunny Day	Fire	Status	—	—	5	Both Sides	—	—
TM16	Light Screen	Psychic	Status	—	—	30	Your Side	—	—
TM17	Protect	Normal	Status	—	—	10	Self	—	—
TM20	Safeguard	Normal	Status	—	—	25	Your Side	—	—
TM21	Frustration	Normal	Physical	—	100	20	Normal	—	○
TM22	SolarBeam	Grass	Special	120	100	10	Normal	—	—
TM27	Return	Normal	Physical	—	100	20	Normal	—	○
TM32	Double Team	Normal	Status	—	—	15	Self	—	—
TM33	Reflect	Psychic	Status	—	—	20	Your Side	—	—
TM42	Facade	Normal	Physical	70	100	20	Normal	—	—
TM44	Rest	Psychic	Status	—	—	10	Self	—	—
TM45	Attract	Normal	Status	—	100	15	Normal	—	—
TM48	Round	Normal	Special	60	100	15	Normal	—	—
TM53	Energy Ball	Grass	Special	80	100	10	Normal	—	—
TM70	Flash	Normal	Status	—	100	20	Normal	—	—
TM75	Swords Dance	Normal	Status	—	—	30	Self	—	—
TM86	Grass Knot	Grass	Special	—	100	20	Normal	—	—
TM87	Swagger	Normal	Status	—	90	15	Normal	—	—
TM90	Substitute	Normal	Status	—	—	10	Self	—	—
TM94	Rock Smash	Fighting	Physical	40	100	15	Normal	—	○
HM01	Cut	Normal	Physical	50	95	30	Normal	—	—
HM04	Strength	Normal	Physical	80	100	15	Normal	—	—

MOVES TAUGHT BY PEOPLE
Name	Type	Kind	Pow.	Acc.	PP	Range	Long	DA
Grass Pledge	Grass	Special	50	100	10	Normal	—	—

MOVES TAUGHT BY MOVE TUTORS FOR SHARDS
Name	Type	Kind	Pow.	Acc.	PP	Range	Long	DA
Seed Bomb	Grass	Physical	80	100	15	Normal	—	○
Iron Tail	Steel	Physical	100	75	15	Normal	—	○
Earth Power	Ground	Special	90	100	10	Normal	—	—
Superpower	Fighting	Physical	120	100	5	Normal	—	—
Snore	Normal	Special	40	100	15	Normal	—	—
Synthesis	Grass	Status	—	—	5	Self	—	—
Giga Drain	Grass	Special	75	100	10	Normal	—	—
Worry Seed	Grass	Status	—	100	10	Normal	—	—
Stealth Rock	Rock	Status	—	—	20	3 Foes	—	—
Sleep Talk	Normal	Status	—	—	10	Self	—	—

EGG MOVES
Name	Type	Kind	Pow.	Acc.	PP	Range	Long	DA
Worry Seed	Grass	Status	—	100	10	Normal	—	—
Growth	Normal	Status	—	—	40	Self	—	—
Tickle	Normal	Status	—	100	20	Normal	—	—
Body Slam	Normal	Physical	85	100	15	Normal	—	○
Double-Edge	Normal	Physical	120	100	15	Normal	—	—
Sand Tomb	Ground	Physical	35	85	15	Normal	—	—
Seed Bomb	Grass	Physical	80	100	15	Normal	—	○
Thrash	Normal	Physical	120	100	10	1 Random	—	—
Amnesia	Psychic	Status	—	—	20	Self	—	—
Superpower	Fighting	Physical	120	100	5	Normal	—	—
Stockpile	Normal	Status	—	—	20	Self	—	—
Swallow	Normal	Status	—	—	10	Self	—	—
Spit Up	Normal	Special	—	100	10	Normal	—	—
Earth Power	Ground	Special	90	100	10	Normal	—	—
Wide Guard	Rock	Status	—	—	10	Your Side	—	—

388 Grotle

Grove Pokémon

TYPE Grass

ABILITY
- Overgrow

HIDDEN ABILITY
- Shell Armor

- HEIGHT: 3'07"
- WEIGHT: 213.8 lbs.
- GENDER: ♂ / ♀

It knows where pure water wells up. It carries fellow Pokémon there on its back.

STATS

HP
Attack
Defense
Sp. Atk
Sp. Def
Speed

EGG GROUPS

Monster/Grass

ITEMS SOMETIMES HELD
- None

Same form for ♂ / ♀

EVOLUTION

HOW TO OBTAIN

Pokémon Black Version 2	Level up a Turtwig obtained via Link Trade or Poké Transfer to Lv. 18
Pokémon White Version 2	Level up a Turtwig obtained via Link Trade or Poké Transfer to Lv. 18

HOW TO OBTAIN FROM OTHER GAMES

—

—

Pokémon AR Marker

LEVEL-UP AND LEARNED MOVES

Lv.	Name	Type	Kind	Pow.	Acc.	PP	Range	Long	DA
1	Tackle	Normal	Physical	50	100	35	Normal	—	○
1	Withdraw	Water	Status	—	—	40	Self	—	—
5	Withdraw	Water	Status	—	—	40	Self	—	—
9	Absorb	Grass	Special	20	100	25	Normal	—	—
13	Razor Leaf	Grass	Physical	55	95	25	Many Others	—	—
17	Curse	Ghost	Status	—	—	10	Varies	—	—
22	Bite	Dark	Physical	60	100	25	Normal	—	○
27	Mega Drain	Grass	Special	40	100	15	Normal	—	—
32	Leech Seed	Grass	Status	—	90	10	Normal	—	—
37	Synthesis	Grass	Status	—	—	5	Self	—	—
42	Crunch	Dark	Physical	80	100	15	Normal	—	○
47	Giga Drain	Grass	Special	75	100	10	Normal	—	—
52	Leaf Storm	Grass	Special	140	90	5	Normal	—	—

TM & HM MOVES

Lv.	Name	Type	Kind	Pow.	Acc.	PP	Range	Long	DA
TM06	Toxic	Poison	Status	—	90	10	Normal	—	—
TM10	Hidden Power	Normal	Special	—	100	15	Normal	—	—
TM11	Sunny Day	Fire	Status	—	—	5	Both Sides	—	—
TM16	Light Screen	Psychic	Status	—	—	30	Your Side	—	—
TM17	Protect	Normal	Status	—	—	10	Self	—	—
TM20	Safeguard	Normal	Status	—	—	25	Your Side	—	—
TM21	Frustration	Normal	Physical	—	100	20	Normal	—	○
TM22	SolarBeam	Grass	Special	120	100	10	Normal	—	—
TM27	Return	Normal	Physical	—	100	20	Normal	—	○
TM32	Double Team	Normal	Status	—	—	15	Self	—	—
TM33	Reflect	Psychic	Status	—	—	20	Your Side	—	—
TM42	Facade	Normal	Physical	70	100	20	Normal	—	○
TM44	Rest	Psychic	Status	—	—	10	Self	—	—
TM45	Attract	Normal	Status	—	100	15	Normal	—	—
TM48	Round	Normal	Special	60	100	15	Normal	—	—
TM53	Energy Ball	Grass	Special	80	100	10	Normal	—	—
TM70	Flash	Normal	Status	—	100	20	Normal	—	—
TM75	Swords Dance	Normal	Status	—	—	30	Self	—	—
TM86	Grass Knot	Grass	Special	—	100	20	Normal	—	○
TM87	Swagger	Normal	Status	—	90	15	Normal	—	—
TM90	Substitute	Normal	Status	—	—	10	Self	—	—
TM94	Rock Smash	Fighting	Physical	40	100	15	Normal	—	○
HM01	Cut	Normal	Physical	50	95	30	Normal	—	○
HM04	Strength	Normal	Physical	80	100	15	Normal	—	○

MOVES TAUGHT BY PEOPLE

Name	Type	Kind	Pow.	Acc.	PP	Range	Long	DA
Grass Pledge	Grass	Special	50	100	10	Normal	—	—

MOVES TAUGHT BY MOVE TUTORS FOR SHARDS

Name	Type	Kind	Pow.	Acc.	PP	Range	Long	DA
Seed Bomb	Grass	Physical	80	100	15	Normal	—	—
Iron Tail	Steel	Physical	100	75	15	Normal	—	○
Earth Power	Ground	Special	90	100	10	Normal	—	—
Superpower	Fighting	Physical	120	100	5	Normal	—	○
Snore	Normal	Special	40	100	15	Normal	—	—
Synthesis	Grass	Status	—	—	5	Self	—	—
Giga Drain	Grass	Special	75	100	10	Normal	—	—
Worry Seed	Grass	Status	—	100	10	Normal	—	—
Stealth Rock	Rock	Status	—	—	20	3 Foes	—	—
Sleep Talk	Normal	Status	—	—	10	Self	—	—

389 Torterra

Continent Pokémon

TYPE Grass Ground

ABILITY
- Overgrow

HIDDEN ABILITY
- Shell Armor

- HEIGHT: 7'03"
- WEIGHT: 683.4 lbs.
- GENDER: ♂ / ♀

Some Pokémon are born on a Torterra's back and spend their entire life there.

STATS

HP
Attack
Defense
Sp. Atk
Sp. Def
Speed

EGG GROUPS

Monster/Grass

ITEMS SOMETIMES HELD
- None

Same form for ♂ / ♀

EVOLUTION

HOW TO OBTAIN

Pokémon Black Version 2	Level up a Grotle obtained via Link Trade or Poké Transfer to Lv. 32
Pokémon White Version 2	Level up a Grotle obtained via Link Trade or Poké Transfer to Lv. 32

HOW TO OBTAIN FROM OTHER GAMES

—

—

Pokémon AR Marker

LEVEL-UP AND LEARNED MOVES

Lv.	Name	Type	Kind	Pow.	Acc.	PP	Range	Long	DA
1	Wood Hammer	Grass	Physical	120	100	15	Normal	—	○
1	Tackle	Normal	Physical	50	100	35	Normal	—	○
1	Withdraw	Water	Status	—	—	40	Self	—	—
1	Absorb	Grass	Special	20	100	25	Normal	—	—
1	Razor Leaf	Grass	Physical	55	95	25	Many Others	—	—
5	Withdraw	Water	Status	—	—	40	Self	—	—
9	Absorb	Grass	Special	20	100	25	Normal	—	—
13	Razor Leaf	Grass	Physical	55	95	25	Many Others	—	—
17	Curse	Ghost	Status	—	—	10	Varies	—	—
22	Bite	Dark	Physical	60	100	25	Normal	—	○
27	Mega Drain	Grass	Special	40	100	15	Normal	—	—
32	Earthquake	Ground	Physical	100	100	10	Adjacent	—	—
33	Leech Seed	Grass	Status	—	90	10	Normal	—	—
39	Synthesis	Grass	Status	—	—	5	Self	—	—
45	Crunch	Dark	Physical	80	100	15	Normal	—	○
51	Giga Drain	Grass	Special	75	100	10	Normal	—	—
57	Leaf Storm	Grass	Special	140	90	5	Normal	—	—

TM & HM MOVES

Lv.	Name	Type	Kind	Pow.	Acc.	PP	Range	Long	DA
TM05	Roar	Normal	Status	—	100	20	Normal	—	—
TM06	Toxic	Poison	Status	—	90	10	Normal	—	—
TM10	Hidden Power	Normal	Special	—	100	15	Normal	—	—
TM11	Sunny Day	Fire	Status	—	—	5	Both Sides	—	—
TM15	Hyper Beam	Normal	Special	150	90	5	Normal	—	—
TM16	Light Screen	Psychic	Status	—	—	30	Your Side	—	—
TM17	Protect	Normal	Status	—	—	10	Self	—	—
TM20	Safeguard	Normal	Status	—	—	25	Your Side	—	—
TM21	Frustration	Normal	Physical	—	100	20	Normal	—	○
TM22	SolarBeam	Grass	Special	120	100	10	Normal	—	—
TM26	Earthquake	Ground	Physical	100	100	10	Adjacent	—	—
TM27	Return	Normal	Physical	—	100	20	Normal	—	○
TM32	Double Team	Normal	Status	—	—	15	Self	—	—
TM33	Reflect	Psychic	Status	—	—	20	Your Side	—	—
TM37	Sandstorm	Rock	Status	—	—	10	Both Sides	—	—
TM39	Rock Tomb	Rock	Physical	50	80	10	Normal	—	—
TM42	Facade	Normal	Physical	70	100	20	Normal	—	○
TM44	Rest	Psychic	Status	—	—	10	Self	—	—
TM45	Attract	Normal	Status	—	100	15	Normal	—	—
TM48	Round	Normal	Special	60	100	15	Normal	—	—
TM53	Energy Ball	Grass	Special	80	100	10	Normal	—	—
TM68	Giga Impact	Normal	Physical	150	90	5	Normal	—	○
TM69	Rock Polish	Rock	Status	—	—	20	Self	—	—
TM70	Flash	Normal	Status	—	100	20	Normal	—	—
TM71	Stone Edge	Rock	Physical	100	80	5	Normal	—	—
TM75	Swords Dance	Normal	Status	—	—	30	Self	—	—
TM78	Bulldoze	Ground	Physical	60	100	20	Adjacent	—	—
TM80	Rock Slide	Rock	Physical	75	90	10	Many Others	—	—
TM86	Grass Knot	Grass	Special	—	100	20	Normal	—	○
TM87	Swagger	Normal	Status	—	90	15	Normal	—	—
TM90	Substitute	Normal	Status	—	—	10	Self	—	—
TM94	Rock Smash	Fighting	Physical	40	100	15	Normal	—	○
HM01	Cut	Normal	Physical	50	95	30	Normal	—	○
HM04	Strength	Normal	Physical	80	100	15	Normal	—	○

MOVES TAUGHT BY PEOPLE

Name	Type	Kind	Pow.	Acc.	PP	Range	Long	DA
Grass Pledge	Grass	Special	50	100	10	Normal	—	—
Frenzy Plant	Grass	Special	150	90	5	Normal	—	—

MOVES TAUGHT BY MOVE TUTORS FOR SHARDS

Name	Type	Kind	Pow.	Acc.	PP	Range	Long	DA
Iron Head	Steel	Physical	80	100	15	Normal	—	○
Seed Bomb	Grass	Physical	80	100	15	Normal	—	—
Block	Normal	Status	—	—	5	Normal	—	—
Iron Tail	Steel	Physical	100	75	15	Normal	—	○
Earth Power	Ground	Special	90	100	10	Normal	—	—
Superpower	Fighting	Physical	120	100	5	Normal	—	○
Snore	Normal	Special	40	100	15	Normal	—	—
Synthesis	Grass	Status	—	—	5	Self	—	—
Giga Drain	Grass	Special	75	100	10	Normal	—	—
Worry Seed	Grass	Status	—	100	10	Normal	—	—
Stealth Rock	Rock	Status	—	—	20	3 Foes	—	—
Outrage	Dragon	Physical	120	100	10	1 Random	—	○
Sleep Talk	Normal	Status	—	—	10	Self	—	—

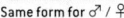

390 Chimchar

Chimp Pokémon

● HEIGHT: 1'08"
● WEIGHT: 13.7 lbs.
● GENDER: ♂ / ♀

It is very agile. Before going to sleep, it extinguishes the flame on its tail to prevent fires.

Same form for ♂ / ♀

TYPE Fire

ABILITY
● Blaze

HIDDEN ABILITY
● Iron Fist

STATS

HP	■■
Attack	■■■
Defense	■■
Sp. Atk	■■■
Sp. Def	■■
Speed	■■■

EGG GROUPS
Field/Human-like

ITEMS SOMETIMES HELD
● None

Pokémon AR Marker

EVOLUTION

Lv. 14
Lv. 36
Chimchar
Monferno
Infernape

HOW TO OBTAIN

Pokémon Black Version 2	Link Trade or Poké Transfer
Pokémon White Version 2	Link Trade or Poké Transfer

HOW TO OBTAIN FROM OTHER GAMES

Pokémon Platinum Version	Get from Professor Rowan at the start of the adventure
	—

LEVEL-UP AND LEARNED MOVES

Lv.	Name	Type	Kind	Pow.	Acc.	PP	Range	Long	DA
1	Scratch	Normal	Physical	40	100	35	Normal	—	○
1	Leer	Normal	Status	—	100	30	Many Others	—	—
7	Ember	Fire	Special	40	100	25	Normal	—	—
9	Taunt	Dark	Status	—	100	20	Normal	—	—
15	Fury Swipes	Normal	Physical	18	80	15	Normal	—	○
17	Flame Wheel	Fire	Physical	60	100	25	Normal	—	○
23	Nasty Plot	Dark	Status	—	—	20	Self	—	—
25	Torment	Dark	Status	—	100	15	Normal	—	—
31	Facade	Normal	Physical	70	100	20	Normal	—	○
33	Fire Spin	Fire	Special	35	85	15	Normal	—	—
39	Acrobatics	Flying	Physical	55	100	15	Normal	○	○
41	Slack Off	Normal	Status	—	—	10	Self	—	—
47	Flamethrower	Fire	Special	95	100	15	Normal	—	—

TM & HM MOVES

Lv.	Name	Type	Kind	Pow.	Acc.	PP	Range	Long	DA
TM01	Hone Claws	Dark	Status	—	—	15	Self	—	—
TM06	Toxic	Poison	Status	—	90	10	Normal	—	—
TM08	Bulk Up	Fighting	Status	—	—	20	Self	—	—
TM10	Hidden Power	Normal	Special	—	100	15	Normal	—	—
TM11	Sunny Day	Fire	Status	—	—	5	Both Sides	—	—
TM12	Taunt	Dark	Status	—	100	20	Normal	—	—
TM17	Protect	Normal	Status	—	—	10	Self	—	—
TM21	Frustration	Normal	Physical	—	100	20	Normal	—	○
TM27	Return	Normal	Physical	—	100	20	Normal	—	○
TM28	Dig	Ground	Physical	80	100	10	Normal	—	○
TM31	Brick Break	Fighting	Physical	75	100	15	Normal	—	○
TM32	Double Team	Normal	Status	—	—	15	Self	—	—
TM35	Flamethrower	Fire	Special	95	100	15	Normal	—	—
TM38	Fire Blast	Fire	Special	120	85	5	Normal	—	—
TM40	Aerial Ace	Flying	Physical	60	—	20	Normal	○	○
TM41	Torment	Dark	Status	—	100	15	Normal	—	—
TM42	Facade	Normal	Physical	70	100	20	Normal	—	○
TM43	Flame Charge	Fire	Physical	50	100	20	Normal	—	○
TM44	Rest	Psychic	Status	—	—	10	Self	—	—
TM45	Attract	Normal	Status	—	100	15	Normal	—	—
TM47	Low Sweep	Fighting	Physical	60	100	20	Normal	—	○
TM48	Round	Normal	Special	60	100	15	Normal	—	—
TM50	Overheat	Fire	Special	140	90	5	Normal	—	—
TM56	Fling	Dark	Physical	—	100	10	Normal	—	—
TM59	Incinerate	Fire	Special	30	100	15	Many Others	—	—
TM61	Will-O-Wisp	Fire	Status	—	75	15	Normal	—	—
TM62	Acrobatics	Flying	Physical	55	100	15	Normal	○	○
TM65	Shadow Claw	Ghost	Physical	70	100	15	Normal	—	○
TM75	Swords Dance	Normal	Status	—	—	30	Self	—	—
TM86	Grass Knot	Grass	Special	—	100	20	Normal	—	○
TM87	Swagger	Normal	Status	—	90	15	Normal	—	—
TM89	U-turn	Bug	Physical	70	100	20	Normal	—	○
TM90	Substitute	Normal	Status	—	—	10	Self	—	—
TM94	Rock Smash	Fighting	Physical	40	100	15	Normal	—	○
HM01	Cut	Normal	Physical	50	95	30	Normal	—	○
HM04	Strength	Normal	Physical	80	100	15	Normal	—	○

MOVES TAUGHT BY PEOPLE

Name	Type	Kind	Pow.	Acc.	PP	Range	Long	DA
Fire Pledge	Fire	Special	50	100	10	Normal	—	—

MOVES TAUGHT BY MOVE TUTORS FOR SHARDS

Name	Type	Kind	Pow.	Acc.	PP	Range	Long	DA
Covet	Normal	Physical	60	100	40	Normal	—	○
Uproar	Normal	Special	90	100	10	1 Random	—	—
Low Kick	Fighting	Physical	—	100	20	Normal	—	○
Gunk Shot	Poison	Physical	120	70	5	Normal	—	—
Fire Punch	Fire	Physical	75	100	15	Normal	—	○
ThunderPunch	Electric	Physical	75	100	15	Normal	—	○
Iron Tail	Steel	Physical	100	75	15	Normal	—	○
Snore	Normal	Special	40	100	15	Normal	—	—
Role Play	Psychic	Status	—	—	10	Normal	—	—
Heat Wave	Fire	Special	100	90	10	Many Others	—	—
Helping Hand	Normal	Status	—	—	20	1 Ally	—	—
Stealth Rock	Rock	Status	—	—	20	3 Foes	—	—
Endeavor	Normal	Physical	—	100	5	Normal	—	○
Sleep Talk	Normal	Status	—	—	10	Self	—	—

EGG MOVES

Name	Type	Kind	Pow.	Acc.	PP	Range	Long	DA
Fire Punch	Fire	Physical	75	100	15	Normal	—	○
ThunderPunch	Electric	Physical	75	100	15	Normal	—	○
Double Kick	Fighting	Physical	30	100	30	Normal	—	○
Encore	Normal	Status	—	100	5	Normal	—	—
Heat Wave	Fire	Special	100	90	10	Many Others	—	—
Focus Energy	Normal	Status	—	—	30	Self	—	—
Helping Hand	Normal	Status	—	—	20	1 Ally	—	—
Fake Out	Normal	Physical	40	100	10	Normal	—	○
Blaze Kick	Fire	Physical	85	90	10	Normal	—	○
Counter	Fighting	Physical	—	100	20	Varies	—	○
Assist	Normal	Status	—	—	20	Self	—	—
Quick Guard	Fighting	Status	—	—	15	Your Side	—	—
Focus Punch	Fighting	Physical	150	100	20	Normal	—	○
Submission	Fighting	Physical	80	80	25	Normal	—	○

391 Monferno

Playful Pokémon

● HEIGHT: 2'11"
● WEIGHT: 48.5 lbs.
● GENDER: ♂ / ♀

It skillfully controls the intensity of the fire on its tail to keep its foes at an ideal distance.

Same form for ♂ / ♀

TYPE Fire Fighting

ABILITY
● Blaze

HIDDEN ABILITY
● Iron Fist

STATS

HP	■■■
Attack	■■■■
Defense	■■
Sp. Atk	■■■■
Sp. Def	■■
Speed	■■■■

EGG GROUPS
Field/Human-like

ITEMS SOMETIMES HELD
● None

Pokémon AR Marker

EVOLUTION

Lv. 14
Lv. 36
Chimchar
Monferno
Infernape

HOW TO OBTAIN

Pokémon Black Version 2	Level up a Chimchar obtained via Link Trade or Poké Transfer to Lv. 14
Pokémon White Version 2	Level up a Chimchar obtained via Link Trade or Poké Transfer to Lv. 14

HOW TO OBTAIN FROM OTHER GAMES

—
—

LEVEL-UP AND LEARNED MOVES

Lv.	Name	Type	Kind	Pow.	Acc.	PP	Range	Long	DA
1	Scratch	Normal	Physical	40	100	35	Normal	—	○
1	Leer	Normal	Status	—	100	30	Many Others	—	—
1	Ember	Fire	Special	40	100	25	Normal	—	—
7	Ember	Fire	Special	40	100	25	Normal	—	—
9	Taunt	Dark	Status	—	100	20	Normal	—	—
14	Mach Punch	Fighting	Physical	40	100	30	Normal	—	○
16	Fury Swipes	Normal	Physical	18	80	15	Normal	—	○
19	Flame Wheel	Fire	Physical	60	100	25	Normal	—	○
26	Feint	Normal	Physical	30	100	10	Normal	—	—
29	Torment	Dark	Status	—	100	15	Normal	—	—
36	Close Combat	Fighting	Physical	120	100	5	Normal	—	○
39	Fire Spin	Fire	Special	35	85	15	Normal	—	—
46	Acrobatics	Flying	Physical	55	100	15	Normal	○	○
49	Slack Off	Normal	Status	—	—	10	Self	—	—
56	Flare Blitz	Fire	Physical	120	100	15	Normal	—	○

TM & HM MOVES

Lv.	Name	Type	Kind	Pow.	Acc.	PP	Range	Long	DA
TM01	Hone Claws	Dark	Status	—	—	15	Self	—	—
TM06	Toxic	Poison	Status	—	90	10	Normal	—	—
TM08	Bulk Up	Fighting	Status	—	—	20	Self	—	—
TM10	Hidden Power	Normal	Special	—	100	15	Normal	—	—
TM11	Sunny Day	Fire	Status	—	—	5	Both Sides	—	—
TM12	Taunt	Dark	Status	—	100	20	Normal	—	—
TM17	Protect	Normal	Status	—	—	10	Self	—	—
TM21	Frustration	Normal	Physical	—	100	20	Normal	—	○
TM27	Return	Normal	Physical	—	100	20	Normal	—	○
TM28	Dig	Ground	Physical	80	100	10	Normal	—	○
TM31	Brick Break	Fighting	Physical	75	100	15	Normal	—	○
TM32	Double Team	Normal	Status	—	—	15	Self	—	—
TM35	Flamethrower	Fire	Special	95	100	15	Normal	—	—
TM38	Fire Blast	Fire	Special	120	85	5	Normal	—	—
TM39	Rock Tomb	Rock	Physical	50	80	10	Normal	—	—
TM40	Aerial Ace	Flying	Physical	60	—	20	Normal	○	○
TM41	Torment	Dark	Status	—	100	15	Normal	—	—
TM42	Facade	Normal	Physical	70	100	20	Normal	—	○
TM43	Flame Charge	Fire	Physical	50	100	20	Normal	—	○
TM44	Rest	Psychic	Status	—	—	10	Self	—	—
TM45	Attract	Normal	Status	—	100	15	Normal	—	—
TM47	Low Sweep	Fighting	Physical	60	100	20	Normal	—	○
TM48	Round	Normal	Special	60	100	15	Normal	—	—
TM50	Overheat	Fire	Special	140	90	5	Normal	—	—
TM52	Focus Blast	Fighting	Special	120	70	5	Normal	—	—
TM56	Fling	Dark	Physical	—	100	10	Normal	—	—
TM59	Incinerate	Fire	Special	30	100	15	Many Others	—	—
TM61	Will-O-Wisp	Fire	Status	—	75	15	Normal	—	—
TM62	Acrobatics	Flying	Physical	55	100	15	Normal	○	○
TM65	Shadow Claw	Ghost	Physical	70	100	15	Normal	—	○
TM67	Retaliate	Normal	Physical	70	100	5	Normal	—	○
TM75	Swords Dance	Normal	Status	—	—	30	Self	—	—
TM80	Rock Slide	Rock	Physical	75	90	10	Many Others	—	—
TM83	Work Up	Normal	Status	—	—	30	Self	—	—
TM84	Poison Jab	Poison	Physical	80	100	20	Normal	—	○
TM86	Grass Knot	Grass	Special	—	100	20	Normal	—	○
TM87	Swagger	Normal	Status	—	90	15	Normal	—	—
TM89	U-turn	Bug	Physical	70	100	20	Normal	—	○
TM90	Substitute	Normal	Status	—	—	10	Self	—	—
TM94	Rock Smash	Fighting	Physical	40	100	15	Normal	—	○
HM01	Cut	Normal	Physical	50	95	30	Normal	—	○
HM04	Strength	Normal	Physical	80	100	15	Normal	—	○

MOVES TAUGHT BY PEOPLE

Name	Type	Kind	Pow.	Acc.	PP	Range	Long	DA
Fire Pledge	Fire	Special	50	100	10	Normal	—	—

MOVES TAUGHT BY MOVE TUTORS FOR SHARDS

Name	Type	Kind	Pow.	Acc.	PP	Range	Long	DA
Covet	Normal	Physical	60	100	40	Normal	—	○
Dual Chop	Dragon	Physical	40	90	15	Normal	—	○
Low Kick	Fighting	Physical	—	100	20	Normal	—	○
Gunk Shot	Poison	Physical	120	70	5	Normal	—	—
Fire Punch	Fire	Physical	75	100	15	Normal	—	○
ThunderPunch	Electric	Physical	75	100	15	Normal	—	○
Iron Tail	Steel	Physical	100	75	15	Normal	—	○
Snore	Normal	Special	40	100	15	Normal	—	—
Role Play	Psychic	Status	—	—	10	Normal	—	—
Heat Wave	Fire	Special	100	90	10	Many Others	—	—
Helping Hand	Normal	Status	—	—	20	1 Ally	—	—
Stealth Rock	Rock	Status	—	—	20	3 Foes	—	—
Endeavor	Normal	Physical	—	100	5	Normal	—	○
Sleep Talk	Normal	Status	—	—	10	Self	—	—

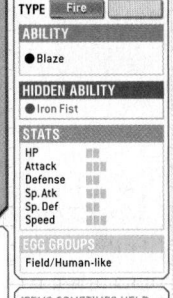

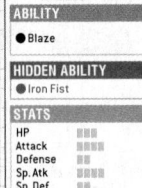

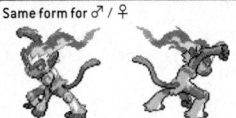

392 Infernape
Flame Pokémon

TYPE	Fire	Fighting

ABILITY
● Blaze

HIDDEN ABILITY
● Iron Fist

STATS
HP
Attack
Defense
Sp. Atk
Sp. Def
Speed

EGG GROUPS
Field/Human-like

ITEMS SOMETIMES HELD
● None

● HEIGHT: 3'11"
● WEIGHT: 121.3 lbs.
● GENDER: ♂/♀

It uses unique fighting moves with fire on its hands and feet. It will take on any opponent.

Same form for ♂/♀

Pokémon AR Marker

EVOLUTION

Chimchar — Lv. 14 → Monferno — Lv. 36 → Infernape

HOW TO OBTAIN
Pokémon Black Version 2	Level up a Monferno obtained via Link Trade or Poké Transfer to Lv. 36
Pokémon White Version 2	Level up a Monferno obtained via Link Trade or Poké Transfer to Lv. 36

HOW TO OBTAIN FROM OTHER GAMES
——
——

LEVEL-UP AND LEARNED MOVES

Lv.	Name	Type	Kind	Pow.	Acc.	PP	Range	Long	DA
1	Scratch	Normal	Physical	40	100	35	Normal	—	○
1	Leer	Normal	Status	—	100	30	Many Others	—	—
1	Ember	Fire	Special	40	100	25	Normal	—	—
1	Taunt	Dark	Status	—	100	20	Normal	—	—
7	Ember	Fire	Special	40	100	25	Normal	—	—
9	Taunt	Dark	Status	—	100	20	Normal	—	—
14	Mach Punch	Fighting	Physical	40	100	30	Normal	—	○
16	Fury Swipes	Normal	Physical	18	80	15	Normal	—	○
19	Flame Wheel	Fire	Physical	60	100	25	Normal	—	○
26	Feint	Normal	Physical	30	100	10	Normal	—	—
29	Punishment	Dark	Physical	—	100	5	Normal	—	○
36	Close Combat	Fighting	Physical	120	100	5	Normal	—	○
42	Fire Spin	Fire	Special	35	85	15	Normal	—	—
52	Acrobatics	Flying	Physical	55	100	15	Normal	○	○
58	Calm Mind	Psychic	Status	—	—	20	Self	—	—
68	Flare Blitz	Fire	Physical	120	100	15	Normal	—	○

TM & HM MOVES

Lv.	Name	Type	Kind	Pow.	Acc.	PP	Range	Long	DA
TM01	Hone Claws	Dark	Status	—	—	15	Self	—	—
TM04	Calm Mind	Psychic	Status	—	—	20	Self	—	—
TM05	Roar	Normal	Status	—	100	20	Normal	—	—
TM06	Toxic	Poison	Status	—	90	10	Normal	—	—
TM08	Bulk Up	Fighting	Status	—	—	20	Self	—	—
TM10	Hidden Power	Normal	Special	—	100	15	Normal	—	○
TM11	Sunny Day	Fire	Status	—	—	5	Both Sides	—	—
TM12	Taunt	Dark	Status	—	100	20	Normal	—	—
TM15	Hyper Beam	Normal	Special	150	90	5	Normal	—	○
TM17	Protect	Normal	Status	—	—	10	Self	—	—
TM21	Frustration	Normal	Physical	—	100	20	Normal	—	○
TM22	SolarBeam	Grass	Special	120	100	10	Normal	—	—
TM26	Earthquake	Ground	Physical	100	100	10	Adjacent	—	—
TM27	Return	Normal	Physical	—	100	20	Normal	—	○
TM28	Dig	Ground	Physical	80	100	10	Normal	—	○
TM31	Brick Break	Fighting	Physical	75	100	15	Normal	—	○
TM32	Double Team	Normal	Status	—	—	15	Self	—	—
TM35	Flamethrower	Fire	Special	95	100	15	Normal	—	—
TM38	Fire Blast	Fire	Special	120	85	5	Normal	—	—
TM39	Rock Tomb	Rock	Physical	50	80	10	Normal	—	—
TM40	Aerial Ace	Flying	Physical	60	—	20	Normal	○	○
TM41	Torment	Dark	Status	—	100	15	Normal	—	—
TM42	Facade	Normal	Physical	70	100	20	Normal	—	○
TM43	Flame Charge	Fire	Physical	50	100	20	Normal	—	○
TM44	Rest	Psychic	Status	—	—	10	Self	—	—
TM45	Attract	Normal	Status	—	100	15	Normal	—	—
TM47	Low Sweep	Fighting	Physical	60	100	20	Normal	—	○
TM48	Round	Normal	Special	60	100	15	Normal	—	—
TM50	Overheat	Fire	Special	140	90	5	Normal	—	—
TM52	Focus Blast	Fighting	Special	120	70	5	Normal	—	—
TM56	Fling	Dark	Physical	—	100	10	Normal	—	—
TM59	Incinerate	Fire	Special	30	100	15	Many Others	—	—
TM61	Will-O-Wisp	Fire	Status	—	75	15	Normal	—	—
TM62	Acrobatics	Flying	Physical	55	100	15	Normal	○	○
TM65	Shadow Claw	Ghost	Physical	70	100	15	Normal	—	○
TM67	Retaliate	Normal	Physical	70	100	5	Normal	—	○
TM68	Giga Impact	Normal	Physical	150	90	5	Normal	—	○

Additional TMs/HMs (right of Level-Up table):

Lv.	Name	Type	Kind	Pow.	Acc.	PP	Range	Long	DA
TM71	Stone Edge	Rock	Physical	100	80	5	Normal	—	—
TM75	Swords Dance	Normal	Status	—	—	30	Self	—	—
TM78	Bulldoze	Ground	Physical	60	100	20	Adjacent	—	—
TM80	Rock Slide	Rock	Physical	75	90	10	Many Others	—	—
TM83	Work Up	Normal	Status	—	—	30	Self	—	—
TM84	Poison Jab	Poison	Physical	80	100	20	Normal	—	○
TM86	Grass Knot	Grass	Special	—	100	20	Normal	—	—
TM87	Swagger	Normal	Status	—	90	15	Normal	—	—
TM89	U-turn	Bug	Physical	70	100	20	Normal	—	○
TM90	Substitute	Normal	Status	—	—	10	Self	—	—
TM94	Rock Smash	Fighting	Physical	40	100	15	Normal	—	○
HM01	Cut	Normal	Physical	50	95	30	Normal	—	○
HM04	Strength	Normal	Physical	80	100	15	Normal	—	○

MOVES TAUGHT BY PEOPLE

Name	Type	Kind	Pow.	Acc.	PP	Range	Long	DA
Fire Pledge	Fire	Special	50	100	10	Normal	—	—
Blast Burn	Fire	Special	150	90	5	Normal	—	—

MOVES TAUGHT BY MOVE TUTORS FOR SHARDS

Name	Type	Kind	Pow.	Acc.	PP	Range	Long	DA
Covet	Normal	Physical	60	100	40	Normal	—	○
Dual Chop	Dragon	Physical	40	90	15	Normal	—	○
Low Kick	Fighting	Physical	—	100	20	Normal	—	○
Gunk Shot	Poison	Physical	120	70	5	Normal	—	—
Fire Punch	Fire	Physical	75	100	15	Normal	—	○
ThunderPunch	Electric	Physical	75	100	15	Normal	—	○
Iron Tail	Steel	Physical	100	75	15	Normal	—	—
Snore	Normal	Special	40	100	15	Normal	—	—
Role Play	Psychic	Status	—	—	10	Normal	—	—
Heat Wave	Fire	Special	100	90	10	Many Others	—	—
Helping Hand	Normal	Status	—	—	20	1 Ally	—	—
Stealth Rock	Rock	Status	—	—	20	3 Foes	—	—
Endeavor	Normal	Physical	—	100	5	Normal	—	○
Sleep Talk	Normal	Status	—	—	10	Self	—	—

---

393 Piplup
Penguin Pokémon

TYPE	Water

ABILITY
● Torrent

HIDDEN ABILITY
● Defiant

STATS
HP
Attack
Defense
Sp. Atk
Sp. Def
Speed

EGG GROUPS
Water ❶ /Field

ITEMS SOMETIMES HELD
● None

● HEIGHT: 1'04"
● WEIGHT: 11.5 lbs.
● GENDER: ♂/♀

A poor walker, it often falls down. However, its strong pride makes it puff up its chest without a care.

Same form for ♂/♀

Pokémon AR Marker

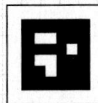

EVOLUTION

Piplup — Lv. 16 → Prinplup — Lv. 36 → Empoleon

HOW TO OBTAIN
Pokémon Black Version 2	Link Trade or Poké Transfer
Pokémon White Version 2	Link Trade or Poké Transfer

HOW TO OBTAIN FROM OTHER GAMES
Pokémon Platinum Version	Get from Professor Rowan at the start of the adventure

LEVEL-UP AND LEARNED MOVES

Lv.	Name	Type	Kind	Pow.	Acc.	PP	Range	Long	DA
1	Pound	Normal	Physical	40	100	35	Normal	—	○
4	Growl	Normal	Status	—	100	40	Many Others	—	—
8	Bubble	Water	Special	20	100	30	Many Others	—	—
11	Water Sport	Water	Status	—	—	15	Both Sides	—	—
15	Peck	Flying	Physical	35	100	35	Normal	○	○
18	BubbleBeam	Water	Special	65	100	20	Normal	—	—
22	Bide	Normal	Physical	—	—	10	Self	—	—
25	Fury Attack	Normal	Physical	15	85	20	Normal	—	○
29	Brine	Water	Special	65	100	10	Normal	—	—
32	Whirlpool	Water	Special	35	85	15	Normal	—	—
36	Mist	Ice	Status	—	—	30	Your Side	—	—
39	Drill Peck	Flying	Physical	80	100	20	Normal	○	○
43	Hydro Pump	Water	Special	120	80	5	Normal	—	—

TM & HM MOVES

Lv.	Name	Type	Kind	Pow.	Acc.	PP	Range	Long	DA
TM06	Toxic	Poison	Status	—	90	10	Normal	—	—
TM07	Hail	Ice	Status	—	—	10	Both Sides	—	—
TM10	Hidden Power	Normal	Special	—	100	15	Normal	—	—
TM13	Ice Beam	Ice	Special	95	100	10	Normal	—	—
TM14	Blizzard	Ice	Special	120	70	5	Many Others	—	—
TM17	Protect	Normal	Status	—	—	10	Self	—	—
TM18	Rain Dance	Water	Status	—	—	5	Both Sides	—	—
TM21	Frustration	Normal	Physical	—	100	20	Normal	—	○
TM27	Return	Normal	Physical	—	100	20	Normal	—	○
TM28	Dig	Ground	Physical	80	100	10	Normal	—	○
TM31	Brick Break	Fighting	Physical	75	100	15	Normal	—	○
TM32	Double Team	Normal	Status	—	—	15	Self	—	—
TM39	Rock Tomb	Rock	Physical	50	80	10	Normal	—	—
TM40	Aerial Ace	Flying	Physical	60	—	20	Normal	○	○
TM42	Facade	Normal	Physical	70	100	20	Normal	—	○
TM44	Rest	Psychic	Status	—	—	10	Self	—	—
TM45	Attract	Normal	Status	—	100	15	Normal	—	—
TM48	Round	Normal	Special	60	100	15	Normal	—	—
TM49	Echoed Voice	Normal	Special	40	100	15	Normal	—	—
TM55	Scald	Water	Special	80	100	15	Normal	—	—
TM56	Fling	Dark	Physical	—	100	10	Normal	—	—
TM60	Quash	Dark	Status	—	100	15	Normal	—	—
TM86	Grass Knot	Grass	Special	—	100	20	Normal	—	—
TM87	Swagger	Normal	Status	—	90	15	Normal	—	—
TM88	Pluck	Flying	Physical	60	100	20	Normal	—	○
TM90	Substitute	Normal	Status	—	—	10	Self	—	—
HM01	Cut	Normal	Physical	50	95	30	Normal	—	○
HM03	Surf	Water	Special	95	100	15	Adjacent	—	—
HM05	Waterfall	Water	Physical	80	100	15	Normal	—	○
HM06	Dive	Water	Physical	80	100	10	Normal	—	○

MOVES TAUGHT BY PEOPLE

Name	Type	Kind	Pow.	Acc.	PP	Range	Long	DA
Water Pledge	Water	Special	50	100	10	Normal	—	—

MOVES TAUGHT BY MOVE TUTORS FOR SHARDS

Name	Type	Kind	Pow.	Acc.	PP	Range	Long	DA
Covet	Normal	Physical	60	100	40	Normal	—	○
Signal Beam	Bug	Special	75	100	15	Normal	—	—
Icy Wind	Ice	Special	55	95	15	Many Others	—	—
Snore	Normal	Special	40	100	15	Normal	—	—
Stealth Rock	Rock	Status	—	—	20	3 Foes	—	—
Sleep Talk	Normal	Status	—	—	10	Self	—	—

EGG MOVES

Name	Type	Kind	Pow.	Acc.	PP	Range	Long	DA
Double Hit	Normal	Physical	35	90	10	Normal	—	○
Supersonic	Normal	Status	—	55	20	Normal	—	—
Yawn	Normal	Status	—	—	10	Normal	—	—
Mud Sport	Ground	Status	—	—	15	Both Sides	—	—
Mud-Slap	Ground	Special	20	100	10	Normal	—	—
Snore	Normal	Special	40	100	15	Normal	—	—
Flail	Normal	Physical	—	100	15	Normal	—	○
Agility	Psychic	Status	—	—	30	Self	—	—
Aqua Ring	Water	Status	—	—	20	Self	—	—
Hydro Pump	Water	Special	120	80	5	Normal	—	—
FeatherDance	Flying	Status	—	100	15	Normal	—	—
Bide	Normal	Physical	—	—	10	Self	—	—
Icy Wind	Ice	Special	55	95	15	Many Others	—	—

394 Prinplup — Penguin Pokémon

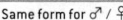

TYPE Water

ABILITY
● Torrent

HIDDEN ABILITY
● Defiant

STATS
HP
Attack
Defense
Sp. Atk
Sp. Def
Speed

● HEIGHT: 2'07"
● WEIGHT: 50.7 lbs.
● GENDER: ♂ / ♀

Because every Prinplup considers itself to be the most important, they can never form a group.

Same form for ♂ / ♀

EGG GROUPS
Water ❶ /Field

ITEMS SOMETIMES HELD
● None

Pokémon AR Marker

EVOLUTION

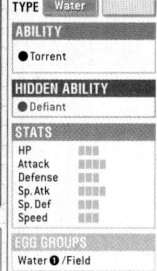

Piplup → (Lv. 16) → Prinplup → (Lv. 36) → Empoleon

HOW TO OBTAIN

Pokémon Black Version 2	Level up a Piplup obtained via Link Trade or Poké Transfer to Lv. 16
Pokémon White Version 2	Level up a Piplup obtained via Link Trade or Poké Transfer to Lv. 16

HOW TO OBTAIN FROM OTHER GAMES

LEVEL-UP AND LEARNED MOVES

Lv.	Name	Type	Kind	Pow.	Acc.	PP	Range	Long	DA
1	Tackle	Normal	Physical	50	100	35	Normal	—	
1	Growl	Normal	Status	—	100	40	Many Others	—	
4	Growl	Normal	Status	—	100	40	Many Others	—	
8	Bubble	Water	Special	20	100	30	Many Others	—	
11	Water Sport	Water	Status	—	—	15	Both Sides	—	
15	Peck	Flying	Physical	35	100	35	Normal	○	○
16	Metal Claw	Steel	Physical	50	95	35	Normal	—	
19	BubbleBeam	Water	Special	65	100	20	Normal	—	
24	Bide	Normal	Physical	—	—	10	Self	—	
28	Fury Attack	Normal	Physical	15	85	20	Normal	—	
33	Brine	Water	Special	65	100	10	Normal	—	
37	Whirlpool	Water	Special	35	85	15	Normal	—	
42	Mist	Ice	Status	—	—	30	Your Side	—	
46	Drill Peck	Flying	Physical	80	100	20	Normal	○	○
51	Hydro Pump	Water	Special	120	80	5	Normal	—	

TM & HM MOVES

Lv.	Name	Type	Kind	Pow.	Acc.	PP	Range	Long	DA
TM01	Hone Claws	Dark	Status	—	—	15	Self	—	
TM06	Toxic	Poison	Status	—	90	10	Normal	—	
TM07	Hail	Ice	Status	—	—	10	Both Sides	—	
TM10	Hidden Power	Normal	Special	—	100	15	Normal	—	
TM13	Ice Beam	Ice	Special	95	100	10	Normal	—	
TM14	Blizzard	Ice	Special	120	70	5	Many Others	—	
TM17	Protect	Normal	Status	—	—	10	Self	—	
TM18	Rain Dance	Water	Status	—	—	5	Both Sides	—	
TM21	Frustration	Normal	Physical	—	100	20	Normal	—	○
TM27	Return	Normal	Physical	—	100	20	Normal	—	○
TM28	Dig	Ground	Physical	80	100	10	Normal	—	○
TM31	Brick Break	Fighting	Physical	75	100	15	Normal	—	○
TM32	Double Team	Normal	Status	—	—	15	Self	—	○
TM39	Rock Tomb	Rock	Physical	50	80	10	Normal	—	
TM40	Aerial Ace	Flying	Physical	60	—	20	Normal	○	○
TM42	Facade	Normal	Physical	70	100	20	Normal	—	○
TM44	Rest	Psychic	Status	—	—	10	Self	—	
TM45	Attract	Normal	Status	—	100	15	Normal	—	○
TM48	Round	Normal	Special	60	100	15	Normal	—	
TM49	Echoed Voice	Normal	Special	40	100	15	Normal	—	
TM55	Scald	Water	Special	80	100	15	Normal	—	
TM56	Fling	Dark	Physical	—	100	10	Normal	—	○
TM60	Quash	Dark	Status	—	100	15	Normal	—	
TM65	Shadow Claw	Ghost	Physical	70	100	15	Normal	—	○
TM86	Grass Knot	Grass	Special	—	100	20	Normal	—	○
TM87	Swagger	Normal	Status	—	90	15	Normal	—	
TM88	Pluck	Flying	Physical	60	100	20	Normal	○	○
TM90	Substitute	Normal	Status	—	—	10	Self	—	
TM94	Rock Smash	Fighting	Physical	40	100	15	Normal	—	○
HM01	Cut	Normal	Physical	50	95	30	Normal	—	
HM03	Surf	Water	Special	95	100	15	Adjacent	—	
HM04	Strength	Normal	Physical	80	100	15	Normal	—	
HM05	Waterfall	Water	Physical	80	100	15	Normal	—	
HM06	Dive	Water	Physical	80	100	10	Normal	—	

MOVES TAUGHT BY PEOPLE

Name	Type	Kind	Pow.	Acc.	PP	Range	Long	DA
Water Pledge	Water	Special	50	100	10	Normal	—	—

MOVES TAUGHT BY MOVE TUTORS FOR SHARDS

Name	Type	Kind	Pow.	Acc.	PP	Range	Long	DA
Covet	Normal	Physical	60	100	40	Normal	—	○
Signal Beam	Bug	Special	75	100	15	Normal	—	
Icy Wind	Ice	Special	55	95	15	Many Others	—	
Snore	Normal	Special	40	100	15	Normal	—	
Stealth Rock	Rock	Status	—	—	20	3 Foes	—	
Sleep Talk	Normal	Status	—	—	10	Self	—	

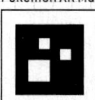

395 Empoleon — Emperor Pokémon

TYPE Water Steel

ABILITY
● Torrent

HIDDEN ABILITY
● Defiant

STATS
HP
Attack
Defense
Sp. Atk
Sp. Def
Speed

● HEIGHT: 5'07"
● WEIGHT: 186.3 lbs.
● GENDER: ♂ / ♀

If anyone were to hurt its pride, it would slash them with wings that can cleave through an ice floe.

Same form for ♂ / ♀

EGG GROUPS
Water ❶ /Field

ITEMS SOMETIMES HELD
● None

Pokémon AR Marker

EVOLUTION

Piplup → (Lv. 16) → Prinplup → (Lv. 36) → Empoleon

HOW TO OBTAIN

Pokémon Black Version 2	Level up a Prinplup obtained via Link Trade or Poké Transfer to Lv. 36
Pokémon White Version 2	Level up a Prinplup obtained via Link Trade or Poké Transfer to Lv. 36

HOW TO OBTAIN FROM OTHER GAMES

LEVEL-UP AND LEARNED MOVES

Lv.	Name	Type	Kind	Pow.	Acc.	PP	Range	Long	DA
1	Tackle	Normal	Physical	50	100	35	Normal	—	
1	Growl	Normal	Status	—	100	40	Many Others	—	
1	Bubble	Water	Special	20	100	30	Many Others	—	
4	Growl	Normal	Status	—	100	40	Many Others	—	
8	Bubble	Water	Special	20	100	30	Many Others	—	
11	Swords Dance	Normal	Status	—	—	30	Self	—	
15	Peck	Flying	Physical	35	100	35	Normal	○	○
16	Metal Claw	Steel	Physical	50	95	35	Normal	—	
19	BubbleBeam	Water	Special	65	100	20	Normal	—	
24	Swagger	Normal	Status	—	90	15	Normal	—	
28	Fury Attack	Normal	Physical	15	85	20	Normal	—	
33	Brine	Water	Special	65	100	10	Normal	—	
36	Aqua Jet	Water	Physical	40	100	20	Normal	—	
39	Whirlpool	Water	Special	35	85	15	Normal	—	
46	Mist	Ice	Status	—	—	30	Your Side	—	
52	Drill Peck	Flying	Physical	80	100	20	Normal	○	○
59	Hydro Pump	Water	Special	120	80	5	Normal	—	

TM & HM MOVES

Lv.	Name	Type	Kind	Pow.	Acc.	PP	Range	Long	DA
TM01	Hone Claws	Dark	Status	—	—	15	Self	—	
TM05	Roar	Normal	Status	—	100	20	Normal	—	
TM06	Toxic	Poison	Status	—	90	10	Normal	—	
TM07	Hail	Ice	Status	—	—	10	Both Sides	—	
TM10	Hidden Power	Normal	Special	—	100	15	Normal	—	
TM13	Ice Beam	Ice	Special	95	100	10	Normal	—	
TM14	Blizzard	Ice	Special	120	70	5	Many Others	—	
TM15	Hyper Beam	Normal	Special	150	90	5	Normal	—	
TM17	Protect	Normal	Status	—	—	10	Self	—	
TM18	Rain Dance	Water	Status	—	—	5	Both Sides	—	
TM21	Frustration	Normal	Physical	—	100	20	Normal	—	○
TM26	Earthquake	Ground	Physical	100	100	10	Adjacent	—	○
TM27	Return	Normal	Physical	—	100	20	Normal	—	○
TM28	Dig	Ground	Physical	80	100	10	Normal	—	○
TM31	Brick Break	Fighting	Physical	75	100	15	Normal	—	○
TM32	Double Team	Normal	Status	—	—	15	Self	—	○
TM39	Rock Tomb	Rock	Physical	50	80	10	Normal	—	
TM40	Aerial Ace	Flying	Physical	60	—	20	Normal	○	○
TM42	Facade	Normal	Physical	70	100	20	Normal	—	○
TM44	Rest	Psychic	Status	—	—	10	Self	—	
TM45	Attract	Normal	Status	—	100	15	Normal	—	○
TM48	Round	Normal	Special	60	100	15	Normal	—	
TM49	Echoed Voice	Normal	Special	40	100	15	Normal	—	
TM55	Scald	Water	Special	80	100	15	Normal	—	
TM56	Fling	Dark	Physical	—	100	10	Normal	—	○
TM60	Quash	Dark	Status	—	100	15	Normal	—	
TM65	Shadow Claw	Ghost	Physical	70	100	15	Normal	—	○
TM68	Giga Impact	Normal	Physical	150	90	5	Normal	—	○
TM75	Swords Dance	Normal	Status	—	—	30	Self	—	
TM78	Bulldoze	Ground	Physical	60	100	20	Adjacent	—	○
TM80	Rock Slide	Rock	Physical	75	90	10	Many Others	—	
TM86	Grass Knot	Grass	Special	—	100	20	Normal	—	○
TM87	Swagger	Normal	Status	—	90	15	Normal	—	
TM88	Pluck	Flying	Physical	60	100	20	Normal	○	○
TM90	Substitute	Normal	Status	—	—	10	Self	—	
TM91	Flash Cannon	Steel	Special	80	100	10	Normal	—	
TM94	Rock Smash	Fighting	Physical	40	100	15	Normal	—	○
HM01	Cut	Normal	Physical	50	95	30	Normal	—	
HM03	Surf	Water	Special	95	100	15	Adjacent	—	
HM04	Strength	Normal	Physical	80	100	15	Normal	—	
HM05	Waterfall	Water	Physical	80	100	15	Normal	—	
HM06	Dive	Water	Physical	80	100	10	Normal	—	

MOVES TAUGHT BY PEOPLE

Name	Type	Kind	Pow.	Acc.	PP	Range	Long	DA
Water Pledge	Water	Special	50	100	10	Normal	—	—
Hydro Cannon	Water	Special	150	90	5	Normal	—	—

MOVES TAUGHT BY MOVE TUTORS FOR SHARDS

Name	Type	Kind	Pow.	Acc.	PP	Range	Long	DA
Covet	Normal	Physical	60	100	40	Normal	—	○
Signal Beam	Bug	Special	75	100	15	Normal	—	
Iron Defense	Steel	Status	—	—	15	Self	—	
Icy Wind	Ice	Special	55	95	15	Many Others	—	
Snore	Normal	Special	40	100	15	Normal	—	
Knock Off	Dark	Physical	20	100	20	Normal	—	○
Stealth Rock	Rock	Status	—	—	20	3 Foes	—	
Sleep Talk	Normal	Status	—	—	10	Self	—	

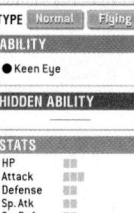

396 Starly

Starling Pokémon

TYPE Normal / Flying

ABILITY
- Keen Eye

HIDDEN ABILITY
- —

- HEIGHT: 1'00"
- WEIGHT: 4.4 lbs.
- GENDER: ♂ / ♀

Because they are weak individually, they form groups. However, they bicker if the group grows too big.

STATS
- HP
- Attack
- Defense
- Sp. Atk
- Sp. Def
- Speed

EGG GROUPS
Flying

ITEMS SOMETIMES HELD
- None

Pokémon AR Marker

EVOLUTION

Starly → Lv. 14 → Staravia → Lv. 34 → Staraptor

HOW TO OBTAIN

Pokémon Black Version 2	Link Trade or Poké Transfer
Pokémon White Version 2	Link Trade or Poké Transfer

HOW TO OBTAIN FROM OTHER GAMES

Pokémon Platinum Version	Route 201

LEVEL-UP AND LEARNED MOVES

Lv.	Name	Type	Kind	Pow.	Acc.	PP	Range	Long	DA
1	Tackle	Normal	Physical	50	100	35	Normal	—	○
1	Growl	Normal	Status	—	100	40	Many Others	—	—
5	Quick Attack	Normal	Physical	40	100	30	Normal	—	○
9	Wing Attack	Flying	Physical	60	100	35	Normal	○	○
13	Double Team	Normal	Status	—	—	15	Self	—	—
17	Endeavor	Normal	Physical	—	100	5	Normal	—	○
21	Whirlwind	Normal	Status	—	100	20	Normal	—	—
25	Aerial Ace	Flying	Physical	60	—	20	Normal	○	○
29	Take Down	Normal	Physical	90	85	20	Normal	—	○
33	Agility	Psychic	Status	—	—	30	Self	—	—
37	Brave Bird	Flying	Physical	120	100	15	Normal	○	○
41	Final Gambit	Fighting	Special	—	100	5	Normal	—	—

TM & HM MOVES

Lv.	Name	Type	Kind	Pow.	Acc.	PP	Range	Long	DA
TM06	Toxic	Poison	Status	—	90	10	Normal	—	—
TM10	Hidden Power	Normal	Special	—	100	15	Normal	—	—
TM11	Sunny Day	Fire	Status	—	—	5	Both Sides	—	—
TM17	Protect	Normal	Status	—	—	10	Self	—	—
TM18	Rain Dance	Water	Status	—	—	5	Both Sides	—	—
TM21	Frustration	Normal	Physical	—	100	20	Normal	—	○
TM27	Return	Normal	Physical	—	100	20	Normal	—	○
TM32	Double Team	Normal	Status	—	—	15	Self	—	—
TM40	Aerial Ace	Flying	Physical	60	—	20	Normal	○	○
TM42	Facade	Normal	Physical	70	100	20	Normal	—	○
TM44	Rest	Psychic	Status	—	—	10	Self	—	—
TM45	Attract	Normal	Status	—	100	15	Normal	—	—
TM46	Thief	Dark	Physical	40	100	10	Normal	—	○
TM48	Round	Normal	Special	60	100	15	Normal	—	—
TM49	Echoed Voice	Normal	Special	40	100	15	Normal	—	—
TM83	Work Up	Normal	Status	—	—	30	Self	—	—
TM87	Swagger	Normal	Status	—	90	15	Normal	—	—
TM88	Pluck	Flying	Physical	60	100	20	Normal	○	○
TM89	U-turn	Bug	Physical	70	100	20	Normal	—	○
TM90	Substitute	Normal	Status	—	—	10	Self	—	—
HM02	Fly	Flying	Physical	90	95	15	Normal	○	○

MOVES TAUGHT BY PEOPLE

Name	Type	Kind	Pow.	Acc.	PP	Range	Long	DA

MOVES TAUGHT BY MOVE TUTORS FOR SHARDS

Name	Type	Kind	Pow.	Acc.	PP	Range	Long	DA
Snore	Normal	Special	40	100	15	Normal	—	—
Roost	Flying	Status	—	—	10	Self	—	—
Heat Wave	Fire	Special	100	90	10	Many Others	—	○
Tailwind	Flying	Status	—	—	30	Your Side	—	—
Endeavor	Normal	Physical	—	100	5	Normal	—	○
Sleep Talk	Normal	Status	—	—	10	Self	—	—

EGG MOVES

Name	Type	Kind	Pow.	Acc.	PP	Range	Long	DA
FeatherDance	Flying	Status	—	100	15	Normal	—	—
Fury Attack	Normal	Physical	15	85	20	Normal	—	○
Pursuit	Dark	Physical	40	100	20	Normal	—	○
Astonish	Ghost	Physical	30	100	15	Normal	—	○
Sand-Attack	Ground	Status	—	100	15	Normal	—	—
Foresight	Normal	Status	—	—	40	Normal	—	—
Double-Edge	Normal	Physical	120	100	15	Normal	—	○
Steel Wing	Steel	Physical	70	90	25	Normal	—	○
Uproar	Normal	Special	90	100	10	1 Random	—	—
Roost	Flying	Status	—	—	10	Self	—	—
Detect	Fighting	Status	—	—	5	Self	—	—
Revenge	Fighting	Physical	60	100	10	Normal	—	○

---

397 Staravia

Starling Pokémon

TYPE Normal / Flying

ABILITY
- Intimidate

HIDDEN ABILITY
- Reckless

- HEIGHT: 2'00"
- WEIGHT: 34.2 lbs.
- GENDER: ♂ / ♀

Recognizing their own weakness, they always live in a group. When alone, a Staravia cries noisily.

STATS
- HP
- Attack
- Defense
- Sp. Atk
- Sp. Def
- Speed

EGG GROUPS
Flying

ITEMS SOMETIMES HELD
- None

Pokémon AR Marker

EVOLUTION

Starly → Lv. 14 → Staravia → Lv. 34 → Staraptor

HOW TO OBTAIN

Pokémon Black Version 2	Link Trade or Poké Transfer
Pokémon White Version 2	Link Trade or Poké Transfer

HOW TO OBTAIN FROM OTHER GAMES

Pokémon Platinum Version	Route 209

LEVEL-UP AND LEARNED MOVES

Lv.	Name	Type	Kind	Pow.	Acc.	PP	Range	Long	DA
1	Tackle	Normal	Physical	50	100	35	Normal	—	○
1	Growl	Normal	Status	—	100	40	Many Others	—	—
1	Quick Attack	Normal	Physical	40	100	30	Normal	—	○
5	Quick Attack	Normal	Physical	40	100	30	Normal	—	○
9	Wing Attack	Flying	Physical	60	100	35	Normal	○	○
13	Double Team	Normal	Status	—	—	15	Self	—	—
18	Endeavor	Normal	Physical	—	100	5	Normal	—	○
23	Whirlwind	Normal	Status	—	100	20	Normal	—	—
28	Aerial Ace	Flying	Physical	60	—	20	Normal	○	○
33	Take Down	Normal	Physical	90	85	20	Normal	—	○
38	Agility	Psychic	Status	—	—	30	Self	—	—
43	Brave Bird	Flying	Physical	120	100	15	Normal	○	○
48	Final Gambit	Fighting	Special	—	100	5	Normal	—	—

TM & HM MOVES

Lv.	Name	Type	Kind	Pow.	Acc.	PP	Range	Long	DA
TM06	Toxic	Poison	Status	—	90	10	Normal	—	—
TM10	Hidden Power	Normal	Special	—	100	15	Normal	—	—
TM11	Sunny Day	Fire	Status	—	—	5	Both Sides	—	—
TM17	Protect	Normal	Status	—	—	10	Self	—	—
TM18	Rain Dance	Water	Status	—	—	5	Both Sides	—	—
TM21	Frustration	Normal	Physical	—	100	20	Normal	—	○
TM27	Return	Normal	Physical	—	100	20	Normal	—	○
TM32	Double Team	Normal	Status	—	—	15	Self	—	—
TM40	Aerial Ace	Flying	Physical	60	—	20	Normal	○	○
TM42	Facade	Normal	Physical	70	100	20	Normal	—	○
TM44	Rest	Psychic	Status	—	—	10	Self	—	—
TM45	Attract	Normal	Status	—	100	15	Normal	—	—
TM46	Thief	Dark	Physical	40	100	10	Normal	—	○
TM48	Round	Normal	Special	60	100	15	Normal	—	—
TM49	Echoed Voice	Normal	Special	40	100	15	Normal	—	—
TM67	Retaliate	Normal	Physical	70	100	5	Normal	—	○
TM83	Work Up	Normal	Status	—	—	30	Self	—	—
TM87	Swagger	Normal	Status	—	90	15	Normal	—	—
TM88	Pluck	Flying	Physical	60	100	20	Normal	○	○
TM89	U-turn	Bug	Physical	70	100	20	Normal	—	○
TM90	Substitute	Normal	Status	—	—	10	Self	—	—
HM02	Fly	Flying	Physical	90	95	15	Normal	○	○

MOVES TAUGHT BY PEOPLE

Name	Type	Kind	Pow.	Acc.	PP	Range	Long	DA

MOVES TAUGHT BY MOVE TUTORS FOR SHARDS

Name	Type	Kind	Pow.	Acc.	PP	Range	Long	DA
Snore	Normal	Special	40	100	15	Normal	—	—
Roost	Flying	Status	—	—	10	Self	—	—
Heat Wave	Fire	Special	100	90	10	Many Others	—	○
Tailwind	Flying	Status	—	—	30	Your Side	—	—
Endeavor	Normal	Physical	—	100	5	Normal	—	○
Sleep Talk	Normal	Status	—	—	10	Self	—	—

Predator Pokémon

398 Staraptor

TYPE Normal / Flying

ABILITY
● Intimidate

HIDDEN ABILITY
● Reckless

● HEIGHT: 3'11"
● WEIGHT: 54.9 lbs.
● GENDER: ♂ / ♀

It never stops attacking even if it is injured. It fusses over the shape of its comb.

♂   ♀

STATS
HP	
Attack	
Defense	
Sp. Atk	
Sp. Def	
Speed	

EGG GROUPS
Flying

ITEMS SOMETIMES HELD
● None

Pokémon AR Marker

EVOLUTION

Starly → Lv. 14 → Staravia → Lv. 34 → Staraptor

HOW TO OBTAIN

Pokémon Black Version 2	Level up a Staravia you obtain via Link Trade or Poké Transfer to Lv. 34
Pokémon White Version 2	Level up a Staravia you obtain via Link Trade or Poké Transfer to Lv. 34

HOW TO OBTAIN FROM OTHER GAMES

LEVEL-UP AND LEARNED MOVES

Lv.	Name	Type	Kind	Pow.	Acc.	PP	Range	Long	DA
1	Tackle	Normal	Physical	50	100	35	Normal	—	○
1	Growl	Normal	Status	—	100	40	Many Others	—	○
1	Quick Attack	Normal	Physical	40	100	30	Normal	—	○
5	Quick Attack	Normal	Physical	40	100	30	Normal	—	○
9	Wing Attack	Flying	Physical	60	100	35	Normal	○	○
9	Quick Attack	Normal	Physical	40	100	30	Normal	—	○
13	Wing Attack	Flying	Physical	60	100	35	Normal	○	○
13	Double Team	Normal	Status	—	—	15	Self	—	—
18	Endeavor	Normal	Physical	—	100	5	Normal	—	○
23	Whirlwind	Normal	Status	—	100	20	Normal	—	—
28	Aerial Ace	Flying	Physical	60	—	20	Normal	—	○
33	Take Down	Normal	Physical	90	85	20	Normal	—	○
34	Close Combat	Fighting	Physical	120	100	5	Normal	—	○
41	Agility	Psychic	Status	—	—	30	Self	—	—
49	Brave Bird	Flying	Physical	120	100	15	Normal	○	○
57	Final Gambit	Fighting	Status	—	100	5	Normal	—	○

TM & HM MOVES

Lv.	Name	Type	Kind	Pow.	Acc.	PP	Range	Long	DA
TM06	Toxic	Poison	Status	—	90	10	Normal	—	—
TM10	Hidden Power	Normal	Special	—	100	15	Normal	—	○
TM11	Sunny Day	Fire	Status	—	—	5	Both Sides	—	—
TM15	Hyper Beam	Normal	Special	150	90	5	Normal	—	○
TM17	Protect	Normal	Status	—	—	10	Self	—	—
TM18	Rain Dance	Water	Status	—	—	5	Both Sides	—	—
TM21	Frustration	Normal	Physical	—	100	20	Normal	—	○
TM27	Return	Normal	Physical	—	100	20	Normal	—	○
TM32	Double Team	Normal	Status	—	—	15	Self	—	—
TM40	Aerial Ace	Flying	Physical	60	—	20	Normal	—	○
TM42	Facade	Normal	Physical	70	100	20	Normal	—	○
TM44	Rest	Psychic	Status	—	—	10	Self	—	—
TM45	Attract	Normal	Status	—	100	15	Normal	—	—
TM46	Thief	Dark	Physical	40	100	10	Normal	—	○
TM48	Round	Normal	Special	60	100	15	Normal	—	—
TM49	Echoed Voice	Normal	Special	40	100	15	Normal	—	—
TM67	Retaliate	Normal	Physical	70	100	5	Normal	—	○
TM68	Giga Impact	Normal	Physical	150	90	5	Normal	—	○
TM83	Work Up	Normal	Status	—	—	30	Self	—	—
TM87	Swagger	Normal	Status	—	90	15	Normal	—	—
TM88	Pluck	Flying	Physical	60	100	20	Normal	—	○
TM89	U-turn	Bug	Physical	70	100	20	Normal	—	○
TM90	Substitute	Normal	Status	—	—	10	Self	—	—
HM02	Fly	Flying	Physical	90	95	15	Normal	○	○

MOVES TAUGHT BY PEOPLE

Name	Type	Kind	Pow.	Acc.	PP	Range	Long	DA

MOVES TAUGHT BY MOVE TUTORS FOR SHARDS

Name	Type	Kind	Pow.	Acc.	PP	Range	Long	DA
Snore	Normal	Special	40	100	15	Normal	—	—
Roost	Flying	Status	—	—	10	Self	○	—
Sky Attack	Flying	Physical	140	90	5	Normal	—	○
Heat Wave	Fire	Special	100	90	10	Many Others	—	—
Tailwind	Flying	Status	—	—	30	Your Side	—	—
Endeavor	Normal	Physical	—	100	5	Normal	—	○
Sleep Talk	Normal	Status	—	—	10	Self	—	—

Plump Mouse Pokémon

399 Bidoof

TYPE Normal

ABILITIES
● Simple
● Unaware

HIDDEN ABILITY
● Moody

● HEIGHT: 1'08"
● WEIGHT: 44.1 lbs.
● GENDER: ♂ / ♀

A comparison revealed that Bidoof's front teeth grow at the same rate as Rattata's.

 ♂   ♀

STATS
HP	
Attack	
Defense	
Sp. Atk	
Sp. Def	
Speed	

EGG GROUPS
Water ❶ /Field

ITEMS SOMETIMES HELD
● None

Pokémon AR Marker

EVOLUTION

Bidoof → Lv. 15 → Bibarel

HOW TO OBTAIN

Pokémon Black Version 2	Catch a Bibarel, leave it at the Pokémon Day Care, and hatch the Egg that is found
Pokémon White Version 2	Catch a Bibarel, leave it at the Pokémon Day Care, and hatch the Egg that is found

HOW TO OBTAIN FROM OTHER GAMES

Pokémon Platinum Version	Route 201

LEVEL-UP AND LEARNED MOVES

Lv.	Name	Type	Kind	Pow.	Acc.	PP	Range	Long	DA
1	Tackle	Normal	Physical	50	100	35	Normal	—	○
5	Growl	Normal	Status	—	100	40	Many Others	—	○
9	Defense Curl	Normal	Status	—	—	40	Self	—	—
13	Rollout	Rock	Physical	30	90	20	Normal	—	○
17	Headbutt	Normal	Physical	70	100	15	Normal	—	○
21	Hyper Fang	Normal	Physical	80	90	15	Normal	—	○
25	Yawn	Normal	Status	—	—	10	Normal	—	—
29	Amnesia	Psychic	Status	—	—	20	Self	—	—
33	Take Down	Normal	Physical	90	85	20	Normal	—	○
37	Super Fang	Normal	Physical	—	90	10	Normal	—	○
41	Superpower	Fighting	Physical	120	100	5	Normal	—	○
45	Curse	Ghost	Status	—	—	10	Varies	—	—

TM & HM MOVES

Lv.	Name	Type	Kind	Pow.	Acc.	PP	Range	Long	DA
TM06	Toxic	Poison	Status	—	90	10	Normal	—	—
TM10	Hidden Power	Normal	Special	—	100	15	Normal	—	○
TM11	Sunny Day	Fire	Status	—	—	5	Both Sides	—	—
TM12	Taunt	Dark	Status	—	100	20	Normal	—	—
TM13	Ice Beam	Ice	Special	95	100	10	Normal	—	—
TM14	Blizzard	Ice	Special	120	70	5	Many Others	—	—
TM17	Protect	Normal	Status	—	—	10	Self	—	—
TM18	Rain Dance	Water	Status	—	—	5	Both Sides	—	—
TM21	Frustration	Normal	Physical	—	100	20	Normal	—	○
TM24	Thunderbolt	Electric	Special	95	100	15	Normal	—	—
TM25	Thunder	Electric	Special	120	70	10	Normal	—	—
TM27	Return	Normal	Physical	—	100	20	Normal	—	○
TM28	Dig	Ground	Physical	80	100	10	Normal	—	○
TM30	Shadow Ball	Ghost	Special	80	100	15	Normal	—	—
TM32	Double Team	Normal	Status	—	—	15	Self	—	—
TM42	Facade	Normal	Physical	70	100	20	Normal	—	○
TM44	Rest	Psychic	Status	—	—	10	Self	—	—
TM45	Attract	Normal	Status	—	100	15	Normal	—	—
TM46	Thief	Dark	Physical	40	100	10	Normal	—	○
TM48	Round	Normal	Special	60	100	15	Normal	—	—
TM49	Echoed Voice	Normal	Special	40	100	15	Normal	—	—
TM57	Charge Beam	Electric	Special	50	90	10	Normal	—	—
TM67	Retaliate	Normal	Physical	70	100	5	Normal	—	○
TM73	Thunder Wave	Electric	Status	—	100	20	Normal	—	—
TM83	Work Up	Normal	Status	—	—	30	Self	—	—
TM86	Grass Knot	Grass	Special	—	100	20	Normal	—	○
TM87	Swagger	Normal	Status	—	90	15	Normal	—	—
TM88	Pluck	Flying	Physical	60	100	20	Normal	—	○
TM90	Substitute	Normal	Status	—	—	10	Self	—	—
TM94	Rock Smash	Fighting	Physical	40	100	15	Normal	—	○
HM01	Cut	Normal	Physical	50	95	30	Normal	—	○

MOVES TAUGHT BY PEOPLE

Name	Type	Kind	Pow.	Acc.	PP	Range	Long	DA

MOVES TAUGHT BY MOVE TUTORS FOR SHARDS

Name	Type	Kind	Pow.	Acc.	PP	Range	Long	DA
Covet	Normal	Physical	60	100	40	Normal	—	○
Super Fang	Normal	Physical	—	90	10	Normal	—	○
Last Resort	Normal	Physical	140	100	5	Normal	—	○
Icy Wind	Ice	Special	55	95	15	Many Others	—	—
Iron Tail	Steel	Physical	100	75	15	Normal	—	○
Aqua Tail	Water	Physical	90	90	10	Normal	—	○
Superpower	Fighting	Physical	120	100	5	Normal	—	○
Snore	Normal	Special	40	100	15	Normal	—	—
Stealth Rock	Rock	Status	—	—	20	3 Foes	—	—
Sleep Talk	Normal	Status	—	—	10	Self	—	—

EGG MOVES

Name	Type	Kind	Pow.	Acc.	PP	Range	Long	DA
Quick Attack	Normal	Physical	40	100	30	Normal	—	○
Water Sport	Water	Status	—	—	15	Both Sides	—	—
Double-Edge	Normal	Physical	120	100	15	Normal	—	○
Fury Swipes	Normal	Physical	18	80	15	Normal	—	○
Defense Curl	Normal	Status	—	—	40	Self	—	—
Rollout	Rock	Physical	30	90	20	Normal	—	○
Odor Sleuth	Normal	Status	—	—	40	Normal	—	—
Aqua Tail	Water	Physical	90	90	10	Normal	—	○
Rock Climb	Normal	Physical	90	85	20	Normal	—	○
Sleep Talk	Normal	Status	—	—	10	Self	—	—
Endure	Normal	Status	—	—	10	Self	—	—
Skull Bash	Normal	Physical	100	100	15	Normal	—	○

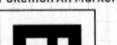

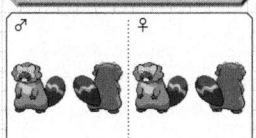

400 Bibarel
Beaver Pokémon

TYPE Normal | Water

ABILITIES
● Simple
● Unaware

HIDDEN ABILITY
● Moody

● HEIGHT: 3'03"
● WEIGHT: 69.4 lbs.
● GENDER: ♂ / ♀

A river dammed by Bibarel will never overflow its banks, which is appreciated by people nearby.

STATS
HP
Attack
Defense
Sp. Atk
Sp. Def
Speed

EGG GROUPS
Water ❶ /Field

ITEMS SOMETIMES HELD
● Oran Berry
● Sitrus Berry

EVOLUTION

Bidoof — Lv. 15 → Bibarel

HOW TO OBTAIN

| Pokémon Black Version 2 | Route 3 (Hidden Grotto) |
| Pokémon White Version 2 | Route 3 (Hidden Grotto) |

HOW TO OBTAIN FROM OTHER GAMES

| ——— |
| |

LEVEL-UP AND LEARNED MOVES

Lv.	Name	Type	Kind	Pow.	Acc.	PP	Range	Long	DA
1	Tackle	Normal	Physical	50	100	35	Normal	—	○
1	Growl	Normal	Status	—	100	40	Many Others	—	—
5	Growl	Normal	Status	—	100	40	Many Others	—	—
9	Defense Curl	Normal	Status	—	—	40	Self	—	—
13	Rollout	Rock	Physical	30	90	20	Normal	—	○
15	Water Gun	Water	Special	40	100	25	Normal	—	—
18	Headbutt	Normal	Physical	70	100	15	Normal	—	○
23	Hyper Fang	Normal	Physical	80	90	15	Normal	—	○
28	Yawn	Normal	Status	—	—	10	Normal	—	—
33	Amnesia	Psychic	Status	—	—	20	Self	—	—
38	Take Down	Normal	Physical	90	85	20	Normal	—	○
43	Super Fang	Normal	Physical	—	90	10	Normal	—	○
48	Superpower	Fighting	Physical	120	100	5	Normal	—	○
53	Curse	Ghost	Status	—	—	10	Varies	—	—

TM & HM MOVES

Lv.	Name	Type	Kind	Pow.	Acc.	PP	Range	Long	DA
TM06	Toxic	Poison	Status	—	90	10	Normal	—	—
TM10	Hidden Power	Normal	Special	—	100	15	Normal	—	—
TM11	Sunny Day	Fire	Status	—	—	5	Both Sides	—	—
TM12	Taunt	Dark	Status	—	100	20	Normal	—	—
TM13	Ice Beam	Ice	Special	95	100	10	Normal	—	—
TM14	Blizzard	Ice	Special	120	70	5	Many Others	—	—
TM15	Hyper Beam	Normal	Special	150	90	5	Normal	—	—
TM17	Protect	Normal	Status	—	—	10	Self	—	—
TM18	Rain Dance	Water	Status	—	—	5	Both Sides	—	—
TM21	Frustration	Normal	Physical	—	100	20	Normal	—	○
TM24	Thunderbolt	Electric	Special	95	100	15	Normal	—	—
TM25	Thunder	Electric	Special	120	70	10	Normal	—	—
TM27	Return	Normal	Physical	—	100	20	Normal	—	○
TM28	Dig	Ground	Physical	80	100	10	Normal	—	○
TM30	Shadow Ball	Ghost	Special	80	100	15	Normal	—	—
TM32	Double Team	Normal	Status	—	—	15	Self	—	—
TM42	Facade	Normal	Physical	70	100	20	Normal	—	○
TM44	Rest	Psychic	Status	—	—	10	Self	—	—
TM45	Attract	Normal	Status	—	100	15	Normal	—	—
TM46	Thief	Dark	Physical	40	100	10	Normal	—	○
TM48	Round	Normal	Special	60	100	15	Normal	—	—
TM49	Echoed Voice	Normal	Special	40	100	15	Normal	—	—
TM55	Scald	Water	Special	80	100	15	Normal	—	—
TM56	Fling	Dark	Physical	—	100	10	Normal	—	○
TM57	Charge Beam	Electric	Special	50	90	10	Normal	—	—
TM67	Retaliate	Normal	Physical	70	100	5	Normal	—	○
TM68	Giga Impact	Normal	Physical	150	90	5	Normal	—	○
TM73	Thunder Wave	Electric	Status	—	100	20	Normal	—	—
TM78	Bulldoze	Ground	Physical	60	100	20	Adjacent	—	○
TM83	Work Up	Normal	Status	—	—	30	Self	—	—
TM86	Grass Knot	Grass	Special	—	100	20	Normal	—	—
TM87	Swagger	Normal	Status	—	90	15	Normal	—	—
TM88	Pluck	Flying	Physical	60	100	20	Normal	○	○
TM90	Substitute	Normal	Status	—	—	10	Self	—	—
TM94	Rock Smash	Fighting	Physical	40	100	15	Normal	—	○
HM01	Cut	Normal	Physical	50	95	30	Adjacent	—	○
HM03	Surf	Water	Special	95	100	15	Normal	—	—
HM04	Strength	Normal	Physical	80	100	15	Normal	—	○
HM05	Waterfall	Water	Physical	80	100	15	Normal	—	○

Lv.	Name	Type	Kind	Pow.	Acc.	PP	Range	Long	DA
HM06	Dive	Water	Physical	80	100	10	Normal	—	○

MOVES TAUGHT BY PEOPLE

Name	Type	Kind	Pow.	Acc.	PP	Range	Long	DA

MOVES TAUGHT BY MOVE TUTORS FOR SHARDS

Name	Type	Kind	Pow.	Acc.	PP	Range	Long	DA
Covet	Normal	Physical	60	100	40	Normal	—	○
Super Fang	Normal	Physical	—	90	10	Normal	—	○
Last Resort	Normal	Physical	140	100	5	Normal	—	○
Icy Wind	Ice	Special	55	95	15	Many Others	—	—
Iron Tail	Steel	Physical	100	75	15	Normal	—	○
Aqua Tail	Water	Physical	90	90	10	Normal	—	○
Superpower	Fighting	Physical	120	100	5	Normal	—	○
Snore	Normal	Special	40	100	15	Normal	—	—
Stealth Rock	Rock	Status	—	—	20	3 Foes	—	—
Sleep Talk	Normal	Status	—	—	10	Self	—	—

Pokémon AR Marker

401 Kricketot
Cricket Pokémon

TYPE Bug

ABILITY
● Shed Skin

HIDDEN ABILITY

● HEIGHT: 1'00"
● WEIGHT: 4.9 lbs.
● GENDER: ♂ / ♀

Its legs are short. Whenever it stumbles, its stiff antennae clack with a xylophone-like sound.

STATS
HP
Attack
Defense
Sp. Atk
Sp. Def
Speed

EGG GROUPS
Bug

ITEMS SOMETIMES HELD
● None

EVOLUTION

Kricketot — Lv. 10 → Kricketune

HOW TO OBTAIN

| Pokémon Black Version 2 | Link Trade or Poké Transfer |
| Pokémon White Version 2 | Link Trade or Poké Transfer |

HOW TO OBTAIN FROM OTHER GAMES

| Pokémon Platinum Version | Route 202 (morning, night only) |
| | |

LEVEL-UP AND LEARNED MOVES

Lv.	Name	Type	Kind	Pow.	Acc.	PP	Range	Long	DA
1	Growl	Normal	Status	—	100	40	Many Others	—	—
1	Bide	Normal	Physical	—	—	10	Self	—	○
6	Struggle Bug	Bug	Special	30	100	20	Many Others	—	—
16	Bug Bite	Bug	Physical	60	100	20	Normal	—	○

TM & HM MOVES

Lv.	Name	Type	Kind	Pow.	Acc.	PP	Range	Long	DA

MOVES TAUGHT BY PEOPLE

Name	Type	Kind	Pow.	Acc.	PP	Range	Long	DA

MOVES TAUGHT BY MOVE TUTORS FOR SHARDS

Name	Type	Kind	Pow.	Acc.	PP	Range	Long	DA
Bug Bite	Bug	Physical	60	100	20	Normal	—	○
Uproar	Normal	Special	90	100	10	1 Random	—	—
Snore	Normal	Special	40	100	15	Normal	—	—
Endeavor	Normal	Physical	—	100	5	Normal	—	○

EGG MOVES

Name	Type	Kind	Pow.	Acc.	PP	Range	Long	DA

Pokémon AR Marker

Cricket Pokémon
402 Kricketune

- HEIGHT: 3'03"
- WEIGHT: 56.2 lbs.
- GENDER: ♂ / ♀

There is a village that hosts a contest based on the amazingly variable cries of this Pokémon.

Pokémon AR Marker

TYPE: Bug

ABILITY
- Swarm

HIDDEN ABILITY
—

STATS
- HP
- Attack
- Defense
- Sp. Atk
- Sp. Def
- Speed

EGG GROUPS
- Bug

ITEMS SOMETIMES HELD
- None

EVOLUTION

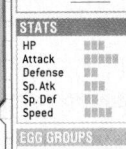

Kricketot — Lv. 10 → Kricketune

HOW TO OBTAIN

| Pokémon Black Version 2 | Link Trade or Poké Transfer |
| Pokémon White Version 2 | Link Trade or Poké Transfer |

HOW TO OBTAIN FROM OTHER GAMES

| Pokémon Black Version | Dreamyard basement (after finishing the main story—dark grass) |
| Pokémon White Version | Dreamyard basement (after finishing the main story—dark grass) |

LEVEL-UP AND LEARNED MOVES

Lv.	Name	Type	Kind	Pow.	Acc.	PP	Range	Long	DA
1	Growl	Normal	Status	—	100	40	Many Others	—	—
1	Bide	Normal	Physical	—	—	10	Self	—	○
10	Fury Cutter	Bug	Physical	20	95	20	Normal	—	○
14	Leech Life	Bug	Physical	20	100	15	Normal	—	—
18	Sing	Normal	Status	—	55	15	Normal	—	—
22	Focus Energy	Normal	Status	—	—	30	Self	—	—
26	Slash	Normal	Physical	70	100	20	Normal	—	○
30	X-Scissor	Bug	Physical	80	100	15	Normal	—	○
34	Screech	Normal	Status	—	85	40	Normal	—	—
38	Taunt	Dark	Status	—	100	20	Normal	—	—
42	Night Slash	Dark	Physical	70	100	15	Normal	—	○
46	Bug Buzz	Bug	Special	90	100	10	Normal	—	—
50	Perish Song	Normal	Status	—	—	5	Adjacent	○	—

TM & HM MOVES

Lv.	Name	Type	Kind	Pow.	Acc.	PP	Range	Long	DA
TM01	Hone Claws	Dark	Status	—	—	15	Self	—	—
TM06	Toxic	Poison	Status	—	90	10	Normal	—	—
TM10	Hidden Power	Normal	Special	—	100	15	Normal	—	—
TM11	Sunny Day	Fire	Status	—	—	5	Both Sides	—	—
TM12	Taunt	Dark	Status	—	100	20	Normal	—	—
TM15	Hyper Beam	Normal	Special	150	90	5	Normal	—	—
TM17	Protect	Normal	Status	—	—	10	Self	—	—
TM18	Rain Dance	Water	Status	—	—	5	Both Sides	—	—
TM21	Frustration	Normal	Physical	—	100	20	Normal	—	○
TM27	Return	Normal	Physical	—	100	20	Normal	—	○
TM31	Brick Break	Fighting	Physical	75	100	15	Normal	—	—
TM32	Double Team	Normal	Status	—	—	15	Self	—	—
TM40	Aerial Ace	Flying	Physical	60	—	20	Normal	○	○
TM42	Facade	Normal	Physical	70	100	20	Normal	—	○
TM44	Rest	Psychic	Status	—	—	10	Self	—	—
TM45	Attract	Normal	Status	—	100	15	Normal	—	—
TM48	Round	Normal	Special	60	100	15	Normal	—	—
TM49	Echoed Voice	Normal	Special	40	100	15	Normal	—	—
TM54	False Swipe	Normal	Physical	40	100	40	Normal	—	○
TM68	Giga Impact	Normal	Physical	150	90	5	Normal	—	—
TM70	Flash	Normal	Status	—	100	20	Normal	—	—
TM75	Swords Dance	Normal	Status	—	—	30	Self	—	—
TM76	Struggle Bug	Bug	Special	30	100	20	Many Others	—	—
TM81	X-Scissor	Bug	Physical	80	100	15	Normal	—	○
TM87	Swagger	Normal	Status	—	90	15	Normal	—	—
TM90	Substitute	Normal	Status	—	—	10	Self	—	—
TM94	Rock Smash	Fighting	Physical	40	100	15	Normal	—	○
HM01	Cut	Normal	Physical	50	95	30	Normal	—	—
HM04	Strength	Normal	Physical	80	100	15	Normal	—	—

MOVES TAUGHT BY PEOPLE

Name	Type	Kind	Pow.	Acc.	PP	Range	Long	DA

MOVES TAUGHT BY MOVE TUTORS FOR SHARDS

Name	Type	Kind	Pow.	Acc.	PP	Range	Long	DA
Bug Bite	Bug	Physical	60	100	20	Normal	—	—
Uproar	Normal	Special	90	100	10	1 Random	—	—
Hyper Voice	Normal	Special	90	100	10	Many Others	—	—
Snore	Normal	Special	40	100	15	Normal	—	—
Heal Bell	Normal	Status	—	—	5	Your Party	—	—
Knock Off	Dark	Physical	20	100	20	Normal	—	○
Endeavor	Normal	Physical	—	100	5	Normal	—	○
Sleep Talk	Normal	Status	—	—	10	Self	—	—

Flash Pokémon
403 Shinx

- HEIGHT: 1'08"
- WEIGHT: 20.9 lbs.
- GENDER: ♂ / ♀

The extension and contraction of its muscles generates electricity. It glows when in trouble.

Pokémon AR Marker

TYPE: Electric

ABILITIES
- Rivalry
- Intimidate

HIDDEN ABILITY
- Guts

STATS
- HP
- Attack
- Defense
- Sp. Atk
- Sp. Def
- Speed

EGG GROUPS
- Field

ITEMS SOMETIMES HELD
- None

EVOLUTION

Shinx — Lv. 15 → Luxio — Lv. 30 → Luxray

HOW TO OBTAIN

| Pokémon Black Version 2 | Link Trade or Poké Transfer |
| Pokémon White Version 2 | Link Trade or Poké Transfer |

HOW TO OBTAIN FROM OTHER GAMES

| Pokémon Platinum Version | Route 202 |

LEVEL-UP AND LEARNED MOVES

Lv.	Name	Type	Kind	Pow.	Acc.	PP	Range	Long	DA
1	Tackle	Normal	Physical	50	100	35	Normal	—	—
5	Leer	Normal	Status	—	100	30	Many Others	—	—
9	Charge	Electric	Status	—	—	20	Self	—	—
13	Spark	Electric	Physical	65	100	20	Normal	—	○
17	Bite	Dark	Physical	60	100	25	Normal	—	○
21	Roar	Normal	Status	—	100	20	Normal	—	—
25	Swagger	Normal	Status	—	90	15	Normal	—	—
29	Thunder Fang	Electric	Physical	65	95	15	Normal	—	○
33	Crunch	Dark	Physical	80	100	15	Normal	—	○
37	Scary Face	Normal	Status	—	100	10	Normal	—	—
41	Discharge	Electric	Special	80	100	15	Adjacent	—	—
45	Wild Charge	Electric	Physical	90	100	15	Normal	—	○

TM & HM MOVES

Lv.	Name	Type	Kind	Pow.	Acc.	PP	Range	Long	DA
TM05	Roar	Normal	Status	—	100	20	Normal	—	—
TM06	Toxic	Poison	Status	—	90	10	Normal	—	—
TM10	Hidden Power	Normal	Special	—	100	15	Normal	—	—
TM16	Light Screen	Psychic	Status	—	—	30	Your Side	—	—
TM17	Protect	Normal	Status	—	—	10	Self	—	—
TM18	Rain Dance	Water	Status	—	—	5	Both Sides	—	—
TM21	Frustration	Normal	Physical	—	100	20	Normal	—	○
TM24	Thunderbolt	Electric	Special	95	100	15	Normal	—	—
TM25	Thunder	Electric	Special	120	70	10	Normal	—	—
TM27	Return	Normal	Physical	—	100	20	Normal	—	○
TM32	Double Team	Normal	Status	—	—	15	Self	—	—
TM42	Facade	Normal	Physical	70	100	20	Normal	—	○
TM44	Rest	Psychic	Status	—	—	10	Self	—	—
TM45	Attract	Normal	Status	—	100	15	Normal	—	—
TM46	Thief	Dark	Physical	40	100	10	Normal	—	—
TM48	Round	Normal	Special	60	100	15	Normal	—	—
TM57	Charge Beam	Electric	Special	50	90	10	Normal	—	—
TM70	Flash	Normal	Status	—	100	20	Normal	—	—
TM72	Volt Switch	Electric	Special	70	100	20	Normal	—	—
TM73	Thunder Wave	Electric	Status	—	100	20	Normal	—	—
TM87	Swagger	Normal	Status	—	90	15	Normal	—	—
TM90	Substitute	Normal	Status	—	—	10	Self	—	—
TM93	Wild Charge	Electric	Physical	90	100	15	Normal	—	○
TM95	Snarl	Dark	Special	55	95	15	Many Others	—	—
HM04	Strength	Normal	Physical	80	100	15	Normal	—	—

MOVES TAUGHT BY PEOPLE

Name	Type	Kind	Pow.	Acc.	PP	Range	Long	DA

MOVES TAUGHT BY MOVE TUTORS FOR SHARDS

Name	Type	Kind	Pow.	Acc.	PP	Range	Long	DA
Signal Beam	Bug	Special	75	100	15	Normal	—	—
Magnet Rise	Electric	Status	—	—	10	Self	—	—
Iron Tail	Steel	Physical	100	75	15	Normal	—	○
Snore	Normal	Special	40	100	15	Normal	—	—
Sleep Talk	Normal	Status	—	—	10	Self	—	—

EGG MOVES

Name	Type	Kind	Pow.	Acc.	PP	Range	Long	DA
Ice Fang	Ice	Physical	65	95	15	Normal	—	○
Fire Fang	Fire	Physical	65	95	15	Normal	—	○
Thunder Fang	Electric	Physical	65	95	15	Normal	—	○
Quick Attack	Normal	Physical	40	100	30	Normal	—	○
Howl	Normal	Status	—	—	40	Self	—	—
Take Down	Normal	Physical	90	85	20	Normal	—	○
Night Slash	Dark	Physical	70	100	15	Normal	—	○
Shock Wave	Electric	Special	60	—	20	Normal	—	—
Swift	Normal	Special	60	—	20	Many Others	—	—
Double Kick	Fighting	Physical	30	100	30	Normal	—	—
Signal Beam	Bug	Special	75	100	15	Normal	—	—
Helping Hand	Normal	Status	—	—	20	1 Ally	—	—

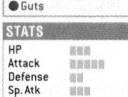

404 Luxio

Spark Pokémon

- HEIGHT: 2'11"
- WEIGHT: 67.2 lbs.
- GENDER: ♂ / ♀

Strong electricity courses through the tips of its sharp claws. A light scratch causes fainting in foes.

TYPE Electric

ABILITIES
- Rivalry
- Intimidate

HIDDEN ABILITY
- Guts

STATS
HP / Attack / Defense / Sp. Atk / Sp. Def / Speed

EGG GROUPS
Field

ITEMS SOMETIMES HELD
- None

Pokémon AR Marker

EVOLUTION

Shinx — Lv. 15 → Luxio — Lv. 30 → Luxray

HOW TO OBTAIN

Pokémon Black Version 2	Link Trade or Poké Transfer
Pokémon White Version 2	Link Trade or Poké Transfer

HOW TO OBTAIN FROM OTHER GAMES

Pokémon Platinum Version	Route 222

LEVEL-UP AND LEARNED MOVES

Lv.	Name	Type	Kind	Pow.	Acc.	PP	Range	Long	DA
1	Tackle	Normal	Physical	50	100	35	Normal	—	—
1	Leer	Normal	Status	—	100	30	Many Others	—	—
5	Leer	Normal	Status	—	100	30	Many Others	—	—
9	Charge	Electric	Status	—	—	20	Self	—	—
13	Spark	Electric	Physical	65	100	20	Normal	—	○
18	Bite	Dark	Physical	60	100	25	Normal	—	○
23	Roar	Normal	Status	—	100	20	Normal	—	—
28	Swagger	Normal	Status	—	90	15	Normal	—	—
33	Thunder Fang	Electric	Physical	65	95	15	Normal	—	○
38	Crunch	Dark	Physical	80	100	15	Normal	—	○
43	Scary Face	Normal	Status	—	100	10	Normal	—	—
48	Discharge	Electric	Special	80	100	15	Adjacent	—	—
53	Wild Charge	Electric	Physical	90	100	15	Normal	—	○

TM & HM MOVES

Lv.	Name	Type	Kind	Pow.	Acc.	PP	Range	Long	DA
TM05	Roar	Normal	Status	—	100	20	Normal	—	—
TM06	Toxic	Poison	Status	—	90	10	Normal	—	—
TM10	Hidden Power	Normal	Special	—	100	15	Normal	—	—
TM16	Light Screen	Psychic	Status	—	—	30	Your Side	—	—
TM17	Protect	Normal	Status	—	—	10	Self	—	—
TM18	Rain Dance	Water	Status	—	—	5	Both Sides	—	—
TM21	Frustration	Normal	Physical	—	100	20	Normal	—	○
TM24	Thunderbolt	Electric	Special	95	100	15	Normal	—	—
TM25	Thunder	Electric	Special	120	70	10	Normal	—	—
TM27	Return	Normal	Physical	—	100	20	Normal	—	○
TM32	Double Team	Normal	Status	—	—	15	Self	—	—
TM42	Facade	Normal	Physical	70	100	20	Normal	—	○
TM44	Rest	Psychic	Status	—	—	10	Self	—	—
TM45	Attract	Normal	Status	—	100	15	Normal	—	—
TM46	Thief	Dark	Physical	40	100	10	Normal	—	—
TM48	Round	Normal	Special	60	100	15	Normal	—	—
TM57	Charge Beam	Electric	Special	50	90	10	Normal	—	—
TM70	Flash	Normal	Status	—	100	20	Normal	—	—
TM72	Volt Switch	Electric	Special	70	100	20	Normal	—	—
TM73	Thunder Wave	Electric	Status	—	100	20	Normal	—	—
TM87	Swagger	Normal	Status	—	90	15	Normal	—	—
TM90	Substitute	Normal	Status	—	—	10	Self	—	—
TM93	Wild Charge	Electric	Physical	90	100	15	Normal	—	○
TM95	Snarl	Dark	Special	55	95	15	Many Others	—	—
HM04	Strength	Normal	Physical	80	100	15	Normal	—	—

MOVES TAUGHT BY PEOPLE

Name	Type	Kind	Pow.	Acc.	PP	Range	Long	DA

MOVES TAUGHT BY MOVE TUTORS FOR SHARDS

Name	Type	Kind	Pow.	Acc.	PP	Range	Long	DA
Signal Beam	Bug	Special	75	100	15	Normal	—	—
Magnet Rise	Electric	Status	—	—	10	Self	—	—
Iron Tail	Steel	Physical	100	75	15	Normal	—	○
Snore	Normal	Special	40	100	15	Normal	—	—
Sleep Talk	Normal	Status	—	—	10	Self	—	—

---

405 Luxray

Gleam Eyes Pokémon

- HEIGHT: 4'07"
- WEIGHT: 92.6 lbs.
- GENDER: ♂ / ♀

It can see clearly through walls to track down its prey and seek its lost young.

TYPE Electric

ABILITIES
- Rivalry
- Intimidate

HIDDEN ABILITY
- Guts

STATS
HP / Attack / Defense / Sp. Atk / Sp. Def / Speed

EGG GROUPS
Field

ITEMS SOMETIMES HELD
- None

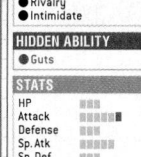

Pokémon AR Marker

EVOLUTION

Shinx — Lv. 15 → Luxio — Lv. 30 → Luxray

HOW TO OBTAIN

Pokémon Black Version 2	Level up a Luxio you obtain via Link Trade or Poké Transfer to Lv. 30
Pokémon White Version 2	Level up a Luxio you obtain via Link Trade or Poké Transfer to Lv. 30

HOW TO OBTAIN FROM OTHER GAMES

LEVEL-UP AND LEARNED MOVES

Lv.	Name	Type	Kind	Pow.	Acc.	PP	Range	Long	DA
1	Tackle	Normal	Physical	50	100	35	Normal	—	○
1	Leer	Normal	Status	—	100	30	Many Others	—	—
1	Charge	Electric	Status	—	—	20	Self	—	—
5	Leer	Normal	Status	—	100	30	Many Others	—	—
9	Charge	Electric	Status	—	—	20	Self	—	—
13	Spark	Electric	Physical	65	100	20	Normal	—	○
18	Bite	Dark	Physical	60	100	25	Normal	—	○
23	Roar	Normal	Status	—	100	20	Normal	—	—
28	Swagger	Normal	Status	—	90	15	Normal	—	—
35	Thunder Fang	Electric	Physical	65	95	15	Normal	—	○
42	Crunch	Dark	Physical	80	100	15	Normal	—	○
49	Scary Face	Normal	Status	—	100	10	Normal	—	—
56	Discharge	Electric	Special	80	100	15	Adjacent	—	—
63	Wild Charge	Electric	Physical	90	100	15	Normal	—	○

TM & HM MOVES

Lv.	Name	Type	Kind	Pow.	Acc.	PP	Range	Long	DA
TM05	Roar	Normal	Status	—	100	20	Normal	—	—
TM06	Toxic	Poison	Status	—	90	10	Normal	—	—
TM10	Hidden Power	Normal	Special	—	100	15	Normal	—	—
TM15	Hyper Beam	Normal	Special	150	90	5	Normal	—	—
TM16	Light Screen	Psychic	Status	—	—	30	Your Side	—	—
TM17	Protect	Normal	Status	—	—	10	Self	—	—
TM18	Rain Dance	Water	Status	—	—	5	Both Sides	—	—
TM21	Frustration	Normal	Physical	—	100	20	Normal	—	○
TM24	Thunderbolt	Electric	Special	95	100	15	Normal	—	—
TM25	Thunder	Electric	Special	120	70	10	Normal	—	—
TM27	Return	Normal	Physical	—	100	20	Normal	—	○
TM32	Double Team	Normal	Status	—	—	15	Self	—	—
TM42	Facade	Normal	Physical	70	100	20	Normal	—	○
TM44	Rest	Psychic	Status	—	—	10	Self	—	—
TM45	Attract	Normal	Status	—	100	15	Normal	—	—
TM46	Thief	Dark	Physical	40	100	10	Normal	—	—
TM48	Round	Normal	Special	60	100	15	Normal	—	—
TM57	Charge Beam	Electric	Special	50	90	10	Normal	—	—
TM68	Giga Impact	Normal	Physical	150	90	5	Normal	—	—
TM70	Flash	Normal	Status	—	100	20	Normal	—	—
TM72	Volt Switch	Electric	Special	70	100	20	Normal	—	—
TM73	Thunder Wave	Electric	Status	—	100	20	Normal	—	—
TM87	Swagger	Normal	Status	—	90	15	Normal	—	—
TM90	Substitute	Normal	Status	—	—	10	Self	—	—
TM93	Wild Charge	Electric	Physical	90	100	15	Normal	—	○
TM95	Snarl	Dark	Special	55	95	15	Many Others	—	—
HM04	Strength	Normal	Physical	80	100	15	Normal	—	—

MOVES TAUGHT BY PEOPLE

Name	Type	Kind	Pow.	Acc.	PP	Range	Long	DA

MOVES TAUGHT BY MOVE TUTORS FOR SHARDS

Name	Type	Kind	Pow.	Acc.	PP	Range	Long	DA
Signal Beam	Bug	Special	75	100	15	Normal	—	—
Magnet Rise	Electric	Status	—	—	10	Self	—	—
Iron Tail	Steel	Physical	100	75	15	Normal	—	○
Superpower	Fighting	Physical	120	100	5	Normal	—	—
Snore	Normal	Special	40	100	15	Normal	—	—
Sleep Talk	Normal	Status	—	—	10	Self	—	—

Budew
Bud Pokémon
406

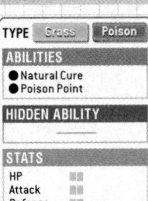

TYPE Grass | Poison

ABILITIES
● Natural Cure
● Poison Point

HIDDEN ABILITY
—

● HEIGHT: 0'08"
● WEIGHT: 2.6 lbs.
● GENDER: ♂ / ♀

Sensitive to changing temperatures, the bud blooms when it's warm, releasing toxic pollen.

STATS
HP
Attack
Defense
Sp. Atk
Sp. Def
Speed

EGG GROUPS
No Egg has ever been discovered

ITEMS SOMETIMES HELD
● None

Same form for ♂ / ♀

Budew | 406

Pokémon AR Marker

◉ EVOLUTION
Budew → (Level up with high friendship in the morning, afternoon, or evening) Roselia → (Use Shiny Stone) Roserade
→ p. 171

HOW TO OBTAIN
Pokémon Black Version 2	Catch a Roselia or Roserade, leave it at the Pokémon Day Care, and hatch the Egg that is found
Pokémon White Version 2	Catch a Roselia or Roserade, leave it at the Pokémon Day Care, and hatch the Egg that is found

HOW TO OBTAIN FROM OTHER GAMES
Pokémon Platinum Version	Route 204

LEVEL-UP AND LEARNED MOVES
Lv.	Name	Type	Kind	Pow.	Acc.	PP	Range	Long	DA
1	Absorb	Grass	Special	20	100	25	Normal	—	—
4	Growth	Normal	Status	—	—	40	Self	—	—
7	Water Sport	Water	Status	—	—	15	Both Sides	—	—
10	Stun Spore	Grass	Status	—	75	30	Normal	—	—
13	Mega Drain	Grass	Special	40	100	15	Normal	—	—
16	Worry Seed	Grass	Status	—	100	10	Normal	—	—

TM & HM MOVES
Lv.	Name	Type	Kind	Pow.	Acc.	PP	Range	Long	DA
TM06	Toxic	Poison	Status	—	90	10	Normal	—	—
TM09	Venoshock	Poison	Special	65	100	10	Normal	—	—
TM10	Hidden Power	Normal	Special	—	100	15	Normal	—	—
TM11	Sunny Day	Fire	Status	—	—	5	Both Sides	—	—
TM17	Protect	Normal	Status	—	—	10	Self	—	—
TM18	Rain Dance	Water	Status	—	—	5	Both Sides	—	—
TM21	Frustration	Normal	Physical	—	100	20	Normal	—	○
TM22	SolarBeam	Grass	Special	120	100	10	Normal	—	—
TM27	Return	Normal	Physical	—	100	20	Normal	—	○
TM30	Shadow Ball	Ghost	Special	80	100	15	Normal	—	—
TM32	Double Team	Normal	Status	—	—	15	Self	—	—
TM36	Sludge Bomb	Poison	Special	90	100	10	Normal	—	—
TM42	Facade	Normal	Physical	70	100	20	Normal	—	—
TM44	Rest	Psychic	Status	—	—	10	Self	—	—
TM45	Attract	Normal	Status	—	100	15	Normal	—	—
TM48	Round	Normal	Special	60	100	15	Normal	—	—
TM53	Energy Ball	Grass	Special	80	100	10	Normal	—	—
TM70	Flash	Normal	Status	—	100	20	Normal	—	—
TM75	Swords Dance	Normal	Status	—	—	30	Self	—	—
TM77	Psych Up	Normal	Status	—	—	10	Normal	—	—
TM86	Grass Knot	Grass	Special	—	100	20	Normal	—	—
TM87	Swagger	Normal	Status	—	90	15	Normal	—	—
TM90	Substitute	Normal	Status	—	—	10	Self	—	—
HM01	Cut	Normal	Physical	50	95	30	Normal	—	○

MOVES TAUGHT BY PEOPLE
Name	Type	Kind	Pow.	Acc.	PP	Range	Long	DA

MOVES TAUGHT BY MOVE TUTORS FOR SHARDS
Name	Type	Kind	Pow.	Acc.	PP	Range	Long	DA
Covet	Normal	Physical	60	100	40	Normal	—	○
Uproar	Normal	Special	90	100	10	1 Random	—	—
Seed Bomb	Grass	Physical	80	100	15	Normal	—	—
Snore	Normal	Special	40	100	15	Normal	—	—
Synthesis	Grass	Status	—	—	5	Self	—	—
Giga Drain	Grass	Special	75	100	10	Normal	—	—
Worry Seed	Grass	Status	—	100	10	Normal	—	—
Sleep Talk	Normal	Status	—	—	10	Self	—	—

EGG MOVES
Name	Type	Kind	Pow.	Acc.	PP	Range	Long	DA
Spikes	Ground	Status	—	—	20	3 Foes	—	—
Synthesis	Grass	Status	—	—	5	Self	—	—
Pin Missile	Bug	Physical	14	85	20	Normal	—	—
Cotton Spore	Grass	Status	—	100	40	Normal	—	—
Sleep Powder	Grass	Status	—	75	15	Normal	—	—
Razor Leaf	Grass	Physical	55	95	25	Many Others	—	—
Mind Reader	Normal	Status	—	—	5	Normal	—	—
Leaf Storm	Grass	Special	140	90	5	Normal	—	—
Extrasensory	Psychic	Special	80	100	30	Normal	—	—
Seed Bomb	Grass	Physical	80	100	15	Normal	—	—
Giga Drain	Grass	Special	75	100	10	Normal	—	—
Natural Gift	Normal	Physical	—	100	15	Normal	—	—
GrassWhistle	Grass	Status	—	55	15	Normal	—	—

Roserade
Bouquet Pokémon
407

TYPE Grass | Poison

ABILITIES
● Natural Cure
● Poison Point

HIDDEN ABILITY
—

● HEIGHT: 2'11"
● WEIGHT: 32.0 lbs.
● GENDER: ♂ / ♀

Luring prey with a sweet scent, it uses poison whips on its arms to poison, bind, and finish off the prey.

STATS
HP
Attack
Defense
Sp. Atk
Sp. Def
Speed

EGG GROUPS
Fairy/Grass

ITEMS SOMETIMES HELD
● Poison Barb

♂   ♀

Roserade | 407

◉ EVOLUTION
Budew → (Level up with high friendship in the morning, afternoon, or evening) Roselia → (Use Shiny Stone) Roserade
→ p. 171

HOW TO OBTAIN
Pokémon Black Version 2	❶ Lostlorn Forest (rustling grass) ❷ Route 12 (rustling grass)
Pokémon White Version 2	❶ Lostlorn Forest (rustling grass) ❷ Route 12 (rustling grass)

HOW TO OBTAIN FROM OTHER GAMES
—	
—	

LEVEL-UP AND LEARNED MOVES
Lv.	Name	Type	Kind	Pow.	Acc.	PP	Range	Long	DA
1	Weather Ball	Normal	Special	50	100	10	Normal	—	—
1	Poison Sting	Poison	Physical	15	100	35	Normal	—	—
1	Mega Drain	Grass	Special	40	100	15	Normal	—	—
1	Magical Leaf	Grass	Special	60	—	20	Normal	—	—
1	Sweet Scent	Normal	Status	—	100	20	Many Others	—	—

TM & HM MOVES
Lv.	Name	Type	Kind	Pow.	Acc.	PP	Range	Long	DA
TM06	Toxic	Poison	Status	—	90	10	Normal	—	—
TM09	Venoshock	Poison	Special	65	100	10	Normal	—	—
TM10	Hidden Power	Normal	Special	—	100	15	Normal	—	—
TM11	Sunny Day	Fire	Status	—	—	5	Both Sides	—	—
TM15	Hyper Beam	Normal	Special	150	90	5	Normal	—	—
TM17	Protect	Normal	Status	—	—	10	Self	—	—
TM18	Rain Dance	Water	Status	—	—	5	Both Sides	—	—
TM21	Frustration	Normal	Physical	—	100	20	Normal	—	○
TM22	SolarBeam	Grass	Special	120	100	10	Normal	—	—
TM27	Return	Normal	Physical	—	100	20	Normal	—	○
TM30	Shadow Ball	Ghost	Special	80	100	15	Normal	—	—
TM32	Double Team	Normal	Status	—	—	15	Self	—	—
TM36	Sludge Bomb	Poison	Special	90	100	10	Normal	—	—
TM42	Facade	Normal	Physical	70	100	20	Normal	—	—
TM44	Rest	Psychic	Status	—	—	10	Self	—	—
TM45	Attract	Normal	Status	—	100	15	Normal	—	—
TM48	Round	Normal	Special	60	100	15	Normal	—	—
TM53	Energy Ball	Grass	Special	80	100	10	Normal	—	—
TM68	Giga Impact	Normal	Physical	150	90	5	Normal	—	○
TM70	Flash	Normal	Status	—	100	20	Normal	—	—
TM75	Swords Dance	Normal	Status	—	—	30	Self	—	—
TM77	Psych Up	Normal	Status	—	—	10	Normal	—	—
TM84	Poison Jab	Poison	Physical	80	100	20	Normal	—	○
TM86	Grass Knot	Grass	Special	—	100	20	Normal	—	—
TM87	Swagger	Normal	Status	—	90	15	Normal	—	—
TM90	Substitute	Normal	Status	—	—	10	Self	—	—
HM01	Cut	Normal	Physical	50	95	30	Normal	—	○

MOVES TAUGHT BY PEOPLE
Name	Type	Kind	Pow.	Acc.	PP	Range	Long	DA

MOVES TAUGHT BY MOVE TUTORS FOR SHARDS
Name	Type	Kind	Pow.	Acc.	PP	Range	Long	DA
Covet	Normal	Physical	60	100	40	Normal	—	○
Seed Bomb	Grass	Physical	80	100	15	Normal	—	—
Snore	Normal	Special	40	100	15	Normal	—	—
Synthesis	Grass	Status	—	—	5	Self	—	—
Giga Drain	Grass	Special	75	100	10	Normal	—	—
Worry Seed	Grass	Status	—	100	10	Normal	—	—
Sleep Talk	Normal	Status	—	—	10	Self	—	—

Pokémon AR Marker

(res bars on pg. 218 and 219) = I.D. #

Head Butt Pokémon

408 Cranidos

● HEIGHT: 2'11"
● WEIGHT: 69.4 lbs.
● GENDER: ♂ / ♀

A lifelong jungle dweller from 100 million years ago, it would snap obstructing trees with head butts.

Same form for ♂ / ♀

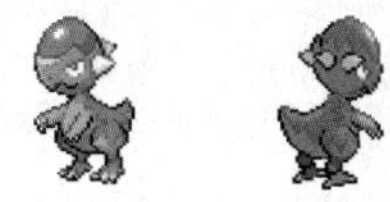

TYPE: Rock

ABILITY
● Mold Breaker

HIDDEN ABILITY
● Sheer Force

STATS

HP	■■■
Attack	■■■■■■■■
Defense	■■
Sp. Atk	■■
Sp. Def	■■
Speed	■■■

EGG GROUPS
Monster

ITEMS SOMETIMES HELD
● None

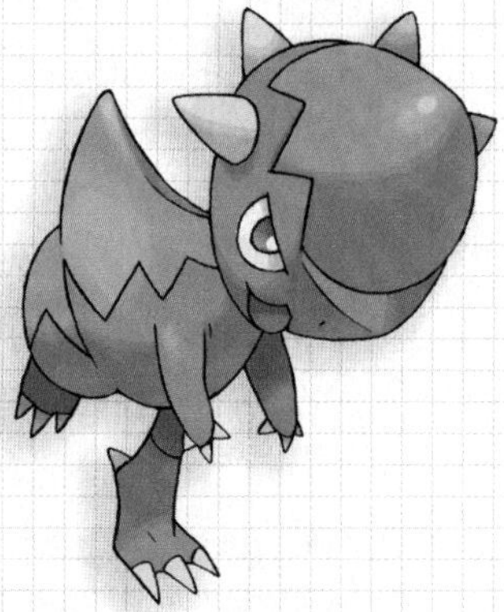

Pokémon AR Marker

EVOLUTION

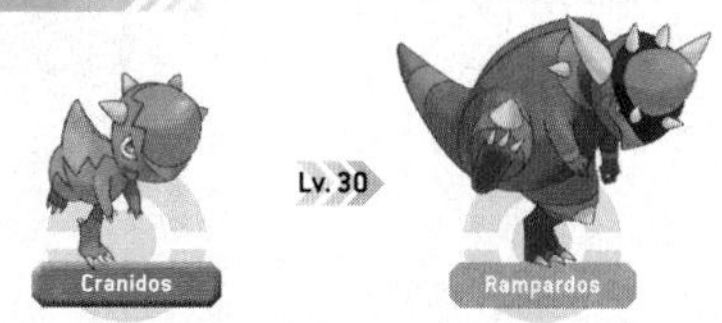

HOW TO OBTAIN

Pokémon Black Version 2	❶ Get the Skull Fossil in Twist Mountain and have it restored at the Nacrene Museum ❷ If your character is a girl, trade Pokémon during a date with Curtis (fourth time)
Pokémon White Version 2	❶ Get the Skull Fossil in Twist Mountain and have it restored at the Nacrene Museum ❷ If your character is a girl, trade Pokémon during a date with Curtis (fourth time)

HOW TO OBTAIN FROM OTHER GAMES

—

—

LEVEL-UP AND LEARNED MOVES

Lv.	Name	Type	Kind	Pow.	Acc.	PP	Range	Long	DA
1	Headbutt	Normal	Physical	70	100	15	Normal	—	○
1	Leer	Normal	Status	—	100	30	Many Others	—	—
6	Focus Energy	Normal	Status	—	—	30	Self	—	—
10	Pursuit	Dark	Physical	40	100	20	Normal	—	○
15	Take Down	Normal	Physical	90	85	20	Normal	—	○
19	Scary Face	Normal	Status	—	100	10	Normal	—	—
24	Assurance	Dark	Physical	50	100	10	Normal	—	○
28	Chip Away	Normal	Physical	70	100	20	Normal	—	○
33	AncientPower	Rock	Special	60	100	5	Normal	—	—
37	Zen Headbutt	Psychic	Physical	80	90	15	Normal	—	○
42	Screech	Normal	Status	—	85	40	Normal	—	—
46	Head Smash	Rock	Physical	150	80	5	Normal	—	○

TM & HM MOVES

Lv.	Name	Type	Kind	Pow.	Acc.	PP	Range	Long	DA
TM05	Roar	Normal	Status	—	100	20	Normal	—	—
TM06	Toxic	Poison	Status	—	90	10	Normal	—	—
TM10	Hidden Power	Normal	Special	—	100	15	Normal	—	—
TM11	Sunny Day	Fire	Status	—	—	5	Both Sides	—	—
TM13	Ice Beam	Ice	Special	95	100	10	Normal	—	—
TM14	Blizzard	Ice	Special	120	70	5	Many Others	—	—
TM17	Protect	Normal	Status	—	—	10	Self	—	—
TM18	Rain Dance	Water	Status	—	—	5	Both Sides	—	—
TM21	Frustration	Normal	Physical	—	100	20	Normal	—	○
TM23	Smack Down	Rock	Physical	50	100	15	Normal	—	—
TM24	Thunderbolt	Electric	Special	95	100	15	Normal	—	—
TM25	Thunder	Electric	Special	120	70	10	Normal	—	—
TM26	Earthquake	Ground	Physical	100	100	10	Adjacent	—	—
TM27	Return	Normal	Physical	—	100	20	Normal	—	○
TM28	Dig	Ground	Physical	80	100	10	Normal	—	○
TM32	Double Team	Normal	Status	—	—	15	Self	—	—
TM35	Flamethrower	Fire	Special	95	100	15	Normal	—	—
TM37	Sandstorm	Rock	Status	—	—	10	Both Sides	—	—
TM38	Fire Blast	Fire	Special	120	85	5	Normal	—	—
TM39	Rock Tomb	Rock	Physical	50	80	10	Normal	—	—
TM42	Facade	Normal	Physical	70	100	20	Normal	—	○
TM44	Rest	Psychic	Status	—	—	10	Self	—	—
TM45	Attract	Normal	Status	—	100	15	Normal	—	—
TM46	Thief	Dark	Physical	40	100	10	Normal	—	○
TM48	Round	Normal	Special	60	100	15	Normal	—	—
TM56	Fling	Dark	Physical	—	100	10	Normal	—	—
TM59	Incinerate	Fire	Special	30	100	15	Many Others	—	—
TM66	Payback	Dark	Physical	50	100	10	Normal	—	○
TM69	Rock Polish	Rock	Status	—	—	20	Self	—	—
TM71	Stone Edge	Rock	Physical	100	80	5	Normal	—	—
TM75	Swords Dance	Normal	Status	—	—	30	Self	—	—
TM78	Bulldoze	Ground	Physical	60	100	20	Adjacent	—	—
TM80	Rock Slide	Rock	Physical	75	90	10	Many Others	—	—
TM87	Swagger	Normal	Status	—	90	15	Normal	—	—
TM90	Substitute	Normal	Status	—	—	10	Self	—	—
TM94	Rock Smash	Fighting	Physical	40	100	15	Normal	—	○
HM04	Strength	Normal	Physical	80	100	15	Normal	—	○

MOVES TAUGHT BY PEOPLE

Name	Type	Kind	Pow.	Acc.	PP	Range	Long	DA

MOVES TAUGHT BY MOVE TUTORS FOR SHARDS

Name	Type	Kind	Pow.	Acc.	PP	Range	Long	DA
Iron Head	Steel	Physical	80	100	15	Normal	—	○
Uproar	Normal	Special	90	100	10	1 Random	—	—
Fire Punch	Fire	Physical	75	100	15	Normal	—	○
ThunderPunch	Electric	Physical	75	100	15	Normal	—	○
Iron Tail	Steel	Physical	100	75	15	Normal	—	○
Earth Power	Ground	Special	90	100	10	Normal	—	—
Zen Headbutt	Psychic	Physical	80	90	15	Normal	—	○
Superpower	Fighting	Physical	120	100	5	Normal	—	○
Dragon Pulse	Dragon	Special	90	100	10	Normal	○	—
Snore	Normal	Special	40	100	15	Normal	—	—
Spite	Ghost	Status	—	100	10	Normal	—	—
Stealth Rock	Rock	Status	—	—	20	3 Foes	—	—
Endeavor	Normal	Physical	—	100	5	Normal	—	○
Sleep Talk	Normal	Status	—	—	10	Self	—	—

EGG MOVES

Name	Type	Kind	Pow.	Acc.	PP	Range	Long	DA
Crunch	Dark	Physical	80	100	15	Normal	—	○
Thrash	Normal	Physical	120	100	10	1 Random	—	○
Double-Edge	Normal	Physical	120	100	15	Normal	—	○
Leer	Normal	Status	—	100	30	Many Others	—	—
Slam	Normal	Physical	80	75	20	Normal	—	○
Stomp	Normal	Physical	65	100	20	Normal	—	○
Whirlwind	Normal	Status	—	100	20	Normal	—	—
Hammer Arm	Fighting	Physical	100	90	10	Normal	—	○
Curse	Ghost	Status	—	—	10	Varies	—	—
Iron Tail	Steel	Physical	100	75	15	Normal	—	○
Iron Head	Steel	Physical	80	100	15	Normal	—	○

Head Butt Pokémon

409 Rampardos

● HEIGHT: 5'03"
● WEIGHT: 226.0 lbs.
● GENDER: ♂ / ♀

If two were to smash their heads together, their foot-thick skulls would keep them from fainting.

Same form for ♂ / ♀

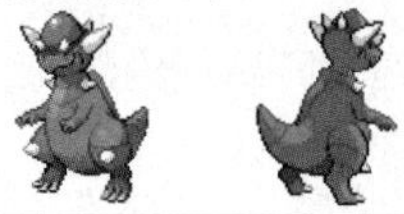

TYPE: Rock

ABILITY
● Mold Breaker

HIDDEN ABILITY
● Sheer Force

STATS

HP	■■■■
Attack	■■■■■■■■■
Defense	■■■
Sp. Atk	■■■
Sp. Def	■■
Speed	■■■

EGG GROUPS
Monster

ITEMS SOMETIMES HELD
● None

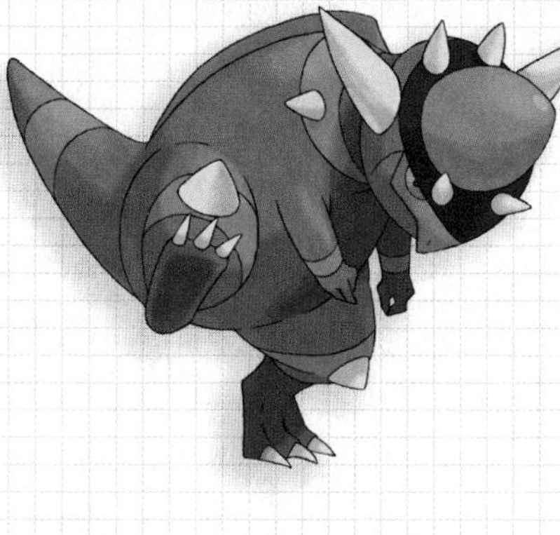

Pokémon AR Marker

EVOLUTION

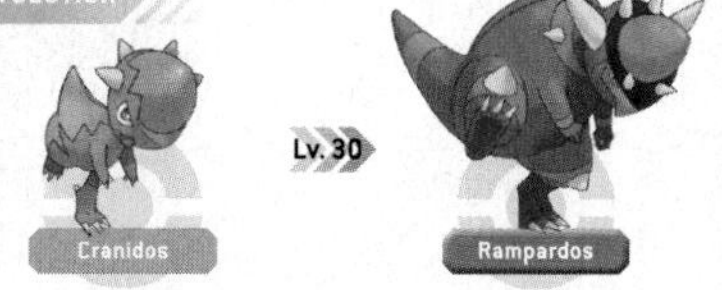

HOW TO OBTAIN

Pokémon Black Version 2	Level up Cranidos to Lv. 30
Pokémon White Version 2	Level up Cranidos to Lv. 30

HOW TO OBTAIN FROM OTHER GAMES

—

—

LEVEL-UP AND LEARNED MOVES

Lv.	Name	Type	Kind	Pow.	Acc.	PP	Range	Long	DA
1	Headbutt	Normal	Physical	70	100	15	Normal	—	○
1	Leer	Normal	Status	—	100	30	Many Others	—	—
6	Focus Energy	Normal	Status	—	—	30	Self	—	—
10	Pursuit	Dark	Physical	40	100	20	Normal	—	○
15	Take Down	Normal	Physical	90	85	20	Normal	—	○
19	Scary Face	Normal	Status	—	100	10	Normal	—	—
24	Assurance	Dark	Physical	50	100	10	Normal	—	○
28	Chip Away	Normal	Physical	70	100	20	Normal	—	○
30	Endeavor	Normal	Physical	—	100	5	Normal	—	○
36	AncientPower	Rock	Special	60	100	5	Normal	—	—
43	Zen Headbutt	Psychic	Physical	80	90	15	Normal	—	○
51	Screech	Normal	Status	—	85	40	Normal	—	—
58	Head Smash	Rock	Physical	150	80	5	Normal	—	○

TM & HM MOVES

Lv.	Name	Type	Kind	Pow.	Acc.	PP	Range	Long	DA
TM05	Roar	Normal	Status	—	100	20	Normal	—	—
TM06	Toxic	Poison	Status	—	90	10	Normal	—	—
TM10	Hidden Power	Normal	Special	—	100	15	Normal	—	—
TM11	Sunny Day	Fire	Status	—	—	5	Both Sides	—	—
TM13	Ice Beam	Ice	Special	95	100	10	Normal	—	—
TM14	Blizzard	Ice	Special	120	70	5	Many Others	—	—
TM15	Hyper Beam	Normal	Special	150	90	5	Normal	—	—
TM17	Protect	Normal	Status	—	—	10	Self	—	—
TM18	Rain Dance	Water	Status	—	—	5	Both Sides	—	—
TM21	Frustration	Normal	Physical	—	100	20	Normal	—	○
TM23	Smack Down	Rock	Physical	50	100	15	Normal	—	—
TM24	Thunderbolt	Electric	Special	95	100	15	Normal	—	—
TM25	Thunder	Electric	Special	120	70	10	Normal	—	—
TM26	Earthquake	Ground	Physical	100	100	10	Adjacent	—	—
TM27	Return	Normal	Physical	—	100	20	Normal	—	○
TM28	Dig	Ground	Physical	80	100	10	Normal	—	○
TM31	Brick Break	Fighting	Physical	75	100	15	Normal	—	○
TM32	Double Team	Normal	Status	—	—	15	Self	—	—
TM35	Flamethrower	Fire	Special	95	100	15	Normal	—	—
TM37	Sandstorm	Rock	Status	—	—	10	Both Sides	—	—
TM38	Fire Blast	Fire	Special	120	85	5	Normal	—	—
TM39	Rock Tomb	Rock	Physical	50	80	10	Normal	—	—
TM42	Facade	Normal	Physical	70	100	20	Normal	—	○
TM44	Rest	Psychic	Status	—	—	10	Self	—	—
TM45	Attract	Normal	Status	—	100	15	Normal	—	—
TM46	Thief	Dark	Physical	40	100	10	Normal	—	○
TM48	Round	Normal	Special	60	100	15	Normal	—	—
TM52	Focus Blast	Fighting	Special	120	70	5	Normal	—	—
TM56	Fling	Dark	Physical	—	100	10	Normal	—	—
TM59	Incinerate	Fire	Special	30	100	15	Many Others	—	—
TM66	Payback	Dark	Physical	50	100	10	Normal	—	○
TM68	Giga Impact	Normal	Physical	150	90	5	Normal	—	○
TM69	Rock Polish	Rock	Status	—	—	20	Self	—	—
TM71	Stone Edge	Rock	Physical	100	80	5	Normal	—	—
TM75	Swords Dance	Normal	Status	—	—	30	Self	—	—
TM78	Bulldoze	Ground	Physical	60	100	20	Adjacent	—	—
TM80	Rock Slide	Rock	Physical	75	90	10	Many Others	—	—
TM82	Dragon Tail	Dragon	Physical	60	90	10	Normal	—	○
TM87	Swagger	Normal	Status	—	90	15	Normal	—	—
TM90	Substitute	Normal	Status	—	—	10	Self	—	—
TM94	Rock Smash	Fighting	Physical	40	100	15	Normal	—	○
HM01	Cut	Normal	Physical	50	95	30	Normal	—	○
HM03	Surf	Water	Special	95	100	15	Adjacent	—	—
HM04	Strength	Normal	Physical	80	100	15	Normal	—	○

MOVES TAUGHT BY PEOPLE

Name	Type	Kind	Pow.	Acc.	PP	Range	Long	DA

MOVES TAUGHT BY MOVE TUTORS FOR SHARDS

Name	Type	Kind	Pow.	Acc.	PP	Range	Long	DA
Iron Head	Steel	Physical	80	100	15	Normal	—	○
Uproar	Normal	Special	90	100	10	1 Random	—	—
Fire Punch	Fire	Physical	75	100	15	Normal	—	○
ThunderPunch	Electric	Physical	75	100	15	Normal	—	○
Iron Tail	Steel	Physical	100	75	15	Normal	—	○
Earth Power	Ground	Special	90	100	10	Normal	—	—
Zen Headbutt	Psychic	Physical	80	90	15	Normal	—	○
Superpower	Fighting	Physical	120	100	5	Normal	—	○
Dragon Pulse	Dragon	Special	90	100	10	Normal	○	—
Snore	Normal	Special	40	100	15	Normal	—	—
Pain Split	Normal	Status	—	—	20	Normal	—	—
Spite	Ghost	Status	—	100	10	Normal	—	—
Stealth Rock	Rock	Status	—	—	20	3 Foes	—	—
Outrage	Dragon	Physical	120	100	10	1 Random	—	○
Endeavor	Normal	Physical	—	100	5	Normal	—	○
Sleep Talk	Normal	Status	—	—	10	Self	—	—

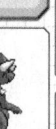

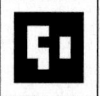

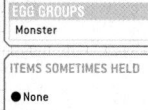

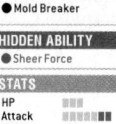

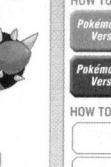

Shield Pokémon
410 Shieldon

TYPE	Rock	Steel

ABILITY
- Sturdy

HIDDEN ABILITY
- Soundproof

- HEIGHT: 1'08"
- WEIGHT: 125.7 lbs.
- GENDER: ♂ / ♀

It is outstandingly armored. As a result, it can eat grass and berries without having to fight.

STATS
HP
Attack
Defense
Sp. Atk
Sp. Def
Speed

EGG GROUPS
Monster

Same form for ♂ / ♀

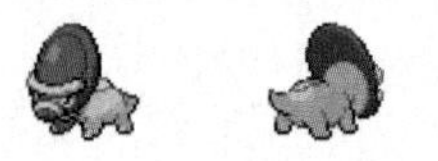

ITEMS SOMETIMES HELD
- None

EVOLUTION

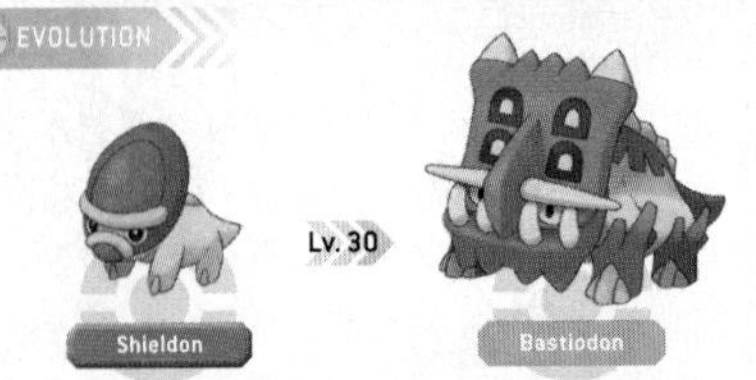

HOW TO OBTAIN

Pokémon Black Version 2	❶ Get the Armor Fossil in Twist Mountain and have it restored at the Nacrene Museum ❷ If your character is a boy, trade Pokémon during a date with Yancy (fourth time)
Pokémon White Version 2	❶ Get the Armor Fossil in Twist Mountain and have it restored at the Nacrene Museum ❷ If your character is a boy, trade Pokémon during a date with Yancy (fourth time)

HOW TO OBTAIN FROM OTHER GAMES

—

—

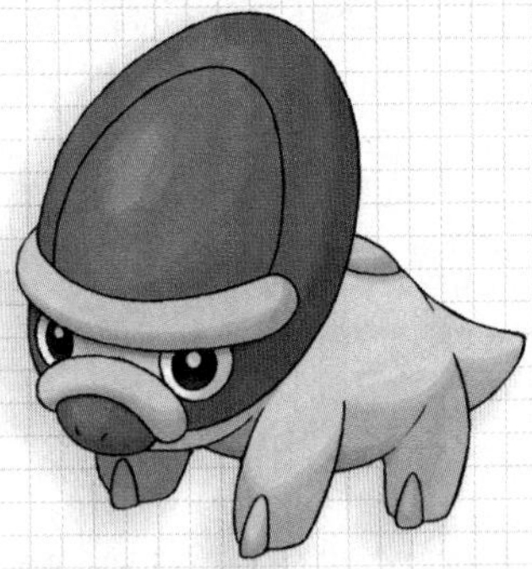

LEVEL-UP AND LEARNED MOVES

Lv.	Name	Type	Kind	Pow.	Acc.	PP	Range	Long	DA
1	Tackle	Normal	Physical	50	100	35	Normal	—	○
1	Protect	Normal	Status	—	—	10	Self	—	—
6	Taunt	Dark	Status	—	100	20	Normal	—	—
10	Metal Sound	Steel	Status	—	85	40	Normal	—	—
15	Take Down	Normal	Physical	90	85	20	Normal	—	○
19	Iron Defense	Steel	Status	—	—	15	Self	—	—
24	Swagger	Normal	Status	—	90	15	Normal	—	—
28	AncientPower	Rock	Special	60	100	5	Normal	—	—
33	Endure	Normal	Status	—	—	10	Self	—	—
37	Metal Burst	Steel	Physical	—	100	10	Varies	—	—
42	Iron Head	Steel	Physical	80	100	15	Normal	—	○
46	Heavy Slam	Steel	Physical	—	100	10	Normal	—	○

TM & HM MOVES

Lv.	Name	Type	Kind	Pow.	Acc.	PP	Range	Long	DA
TM05	Roar	Normal	Status	—	100	20	Normal	—	—
TM06	Toxic	Poison	Status	—	90	10	Normal	—	—
TM10	Hidden Power	Normal	Special	—	100	15	Normal	—	—
TM11	Sunny Day	Fire	Status	—	—	5	Both Sides	—	—
TM12	Taunt	Dark	Status	—	100	20	Normal	—	—
TM13	Ice Beam	Ice	Special	95	100	10	Normal	—	—
TM14	Blizzard	Ice	Special	120	70	5	Many Others	—	—
TM17	Protect	Normal	Status	—	—	10	Self	—	—
TM18	Rain Dance	Water	Status	—	—	5	Both Sides	—	—
TM21	Frustration	Normal	Physical	—	100	20	Normal	—	○
TM23	Smack Down	Rock	Physical	50	100	15	Normal	—	—
TM24	Thunderbolt	Electric	Special	95	100	15	Normal	—	—
TM25	Thunder	Electric	Special	120	70	10	Normal	—	—
TM26	Earthquake	Ground	Physical	100	100	10	Adjacent	—	—
TM27	Return	Normal	Physical	—	100	20	Normal	—	○
TM28	Dig	Ground	Physical	80	100	10	Normal	—	○
TM32	Double Team	Normal	Status	—	—	15	Self	—	—
TM35	Flamethrower	Fire	Special	95	100	15	Normal	—	—
TM37	Sandstorm	Rock	Status	—	—	10	Both Sides	—	—
TM38	Fire Blast	Fire	Special	120	85	5	Normal	—	—
TM39	Rock Tomb	Rock	Physical	50	80	10	Normal	—	—
TM41	Torment	Dark	Status	—	100	15	Normal	—	—
TM42	Facade	Normal	Physical	70	100	20	Normal	—	○
TM44	Rest	Psychic	Status	—	—	10	Self	—	—
TM45	Attract	Normal	Status	—	100	15	Normal	—	—
TM48	Round	Normal	Special	60	100	15	Normal	—	—
TM59	Incinerate	Fire	Special	30	100	15	Many Others	—	—
TM69	Rock Polish	Rock	Status	—	—	20	Self	—	—
TM71	Stone Edge	Rock	Physical	100	80	5	Normal	—	—
TM78	Bulldoze	Ground	Physical	60	100	20	Adjacent	—	—
TM80	Rock Slide	Rock	Physical	75	90	10	Many Others	—	—
TM87	Swagger	Normal	Status	—	90	15	Normal	—	—
TM90	Substitute	Normal	Status	—	—	10	Self	—	—
TM91	Flash Cannon	Steel	Special	80	100	10	Normal	—	—
TM94	Rock Smash	Fighting	Physical	40	100	15	Normal	—	○
HM04	Strength	Normal	Physical	80	100	15	Normal	—	○

MOVES TAUGHT BY PEOPLE

Name	Type	Kind	Pow.	Acc.	PP	Range	Long	DA

MOVES TAUGHT BY MOVE TUTORS FOR SHARDS

Name	Type	Kind	Pow.	Acc.	PP	Range	Long	DA
Iron Head	Steel	Physical	80	100	15	Normal	—	○
Iron Defense	Steel	Status	—	—	15	Self	—	—
Magnet Rise	Electric	Status	—	—	10	Self	—	—
Iron Tail	Steel	Physical	100	75	15	Normal	—	○
Earth Power	Ground	Special	90	100	10	Normal	—	—
Snore	Normal	Special	40	100	15	Normal	—	—
Stealth Rock	Rock	Status	—	—	20	3 Foes	—	—
Sleep Talk	Normal	Status	—	—	10	Self	—	—

EGG MOVES

Name	Type	Kind	Pow.	Acc.	PP	Range	Long	DA
Headbutt	Normal	Physical	70	100	15	Normal	—	○
Scary Face	Normal	Status	—	100	10	Normal	—	—
Focus Energy	Normal	Status	—	—	30	Self	—	—
Double-Edge	Normal	Physical	120	100	15	Normal	—	○
Rock Blast	Rock	Physical	25	90	10	Normal	—	—
Body Slam	Normal	Physical	85	100	15	Normal	—	○
Screech	Normal	Status	—	85	40	Normal	—	—
Curse	Ghost	Status	—	—	10	Varies	—	—
Fissure	Ground	Physical	—	30	5	Normal	—	—
Counter	Fighting	Physical	—	100	20	Varies	—	○
Stealth Rock	Rock	Status	—	—	20	3 Foes	—	—
Wide Guard	Rock	Status	—	—	10	Your Side	—	—

Pokémon AR Marker

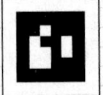

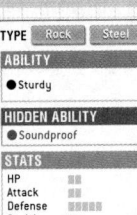

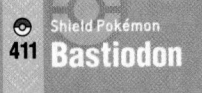

Shield Pokémon
411 Bastiodon

TYPE	Rock	Steel

ABILITY
- Sturdy

HIDDEN ABILITY
- Soundproof

- HEIGHT: 4'03"
- WEIGHT: 329.6 lbs.
- GENDER: ♂ / ♀

When they lined up side by side, no foe could break through. They shielded their young in that way.

STATS
HP
Attack
Defense
Sp. Atk
Sp. Def
Speed

EGG GROUPS
Monster

Same form for ♂ / ♀

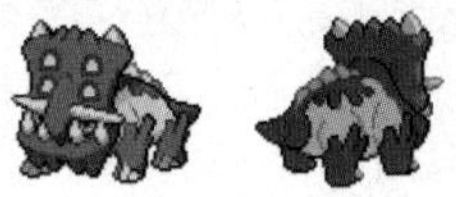

ITEMS SOMETIMES HELD
- None

EVOLUTION

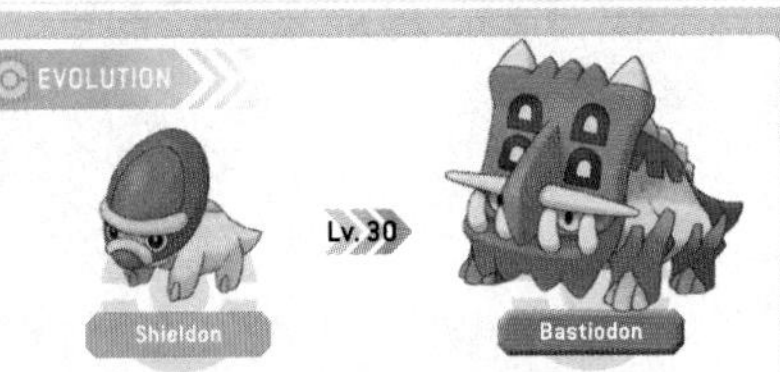

HOW TO OBTAIN

Pokémon Black Version 2	Level up Shieldon to Lv. 30
Pokémon White Version 2	Level up Shieldon to Lv. 30

HOW TO OBTAIN FROM OTHER GAMES

—

—

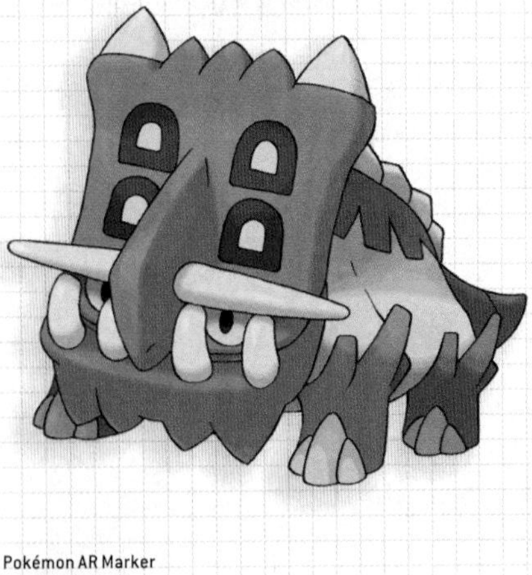

LEVEL-UP AND LEARNED MOVES

Lv.	Name	Type	Kind	Pow.	Acc.	PP	Range	Long	DA
1	Tackle	Normal	Physical	50	100	35	Normal	—	○
1	Protect	Normal	Status	—	—	10	Self	—	—
1	Taunt	Dark	Status	—	100	20	Normal	—	—
1	Metal Sound	Steel	Status	—	85	40	Normal	—	—
6	Taunt	Dark	Status	—	100	20	Normal	—	—
10	Metal Sound	Steel	Status	—	85	40	Normal	—	—
15	Take Down	Normal	Physical	90	85	20	Normal	—	○
19	Iron Defense	Steel	Status	—	—	15	Self	—	—
24	Swagger	Normal	Status	—	90	15	Normal	—	—
28	AncientPower	Rock	Special	60	100	5	Normal	—	—
30	Block	Normal	Status	—	—	5	Normal	—	—
36	Endure	Normal	Status	—	—	10	Self	—	—
43	Metal Burst	Steel	Physical	—	100	10	Varies	—	—
51	Iron Head	Steel	Physical	80	100	15	Normal	—	○
58	Heavy Slam	Steel	Physical	—	100	10	Normal	—	○

TM & HM MOVES

Lv.	Name	Type	Kind	Pow.	Acc.	PP	Range	Long	DA
TM05	Roar	Normal	Status	—	100	20	Normal	—	—
TM06	Toxic	Poison	Status	—	90	10	Normal	—	—
TM10	Hidden Power	Normal	Special	—	100	15	Normal	—	—
TM11	Sunny Day	Fire	Status	—	—	5	Both Sides	—	—
TM12	Taunt	Dark	Status	—	100	20	Normal	—	—
TM13	Ice Beam	Ice	Special	95	100	10	Normal	—	—
TM14	Blizzard	Ice	Special	120	70	5	Many Others	—	—
TM15	Hyper Beam	Normal	Special	150	90	5	Normal	—	—
TM17	Protect	Normal	Status	—	—	10	Self	—	—
TM18	Rain Dance	Water	Status	—	—	5	Both Sides	—	—
TM21	Frustration	Normal	Physical	—	100	20	Normal	—	○
TM23	Smack Down	Rock	Physical	50	100	15	Normal	—	—
TM24	Thunderbolt	Electric	Special	95	100	15	Normal	—	—
TM25	Thunder	Electric	Special	120	70	10	Normal	—	—
TM26	Earthquake	Ground	Physical	100	100	10	Adjacent	—	—
TM27	Return	Normal	Physical	—	100	20	Normal	—	○
TM28	Dig	Ground	Physical	80	100	10	Normal	—	○
TM32	Double Team	Normal	Status	—	—	15	Self	—	—
TM35	Flamethrower	Fire	Special	95	100	15	Normal	—	—
TM37	Sandstorm	Rock	Status	—	—	10	Both Sides	—	—
TM38	Fire Blast	Fire	Special	120	85	5	Normal	—	—
TM39	Rock Tomb	Rock	Physical	50	80	10	Normal	—	—
TM41	Torment	Dark	Status	—	100	15	Normal	—	—
TM42	Facade	Normal	Physical	70	100	20	Normal	—	○
TM44	Rest	Psychic	Status	—	—	10	Self	—	—
TM45	Attract	Normal	Status	—	100	15	Normal	—	—
TM48	Round	Normal	Special	60	100	15	Normal	—	—
TM59	Incinerate	Fire	Special	30	100	15	Many Others	—	—
TM68	Giga Impact	Normal	Physical	150	90	5	Normal	—	○
TM69	Rock Polish	Rock	Status	—	—	20	Self	—	—
TM71	Stone Edge	Rock	Physical	100	80	5	Normal	—	—
TM78	Bulldoze	Ground	Physical	60	100	20	Adjacent	—	—
TM80	Rock Slide	Rock	Physical	75	90	10	Many Others	—	—
TM87	Swagger	Normal	Status	—	90	15	Normal	—	—
TM90	Substitute	Normal	Status	—	—	10	Self	—	—
TM91	Flash Cannon	Steel	Special	80	100	10	Normal	—	—
TM94	Rock Smash	Fighting	Physical	40	100	15	Normal	—	○
HM04	Strength	Normal	Physical	80	100	15	Normal	—	○

MOVES TAUGHT BY PEOPLE

Name	Type	Kind	Pow.	Acc.	PP	Range	Long	DA

MOVES TAUGHT BY MOVE TUTORS FOR SHARDS

Name	Type	Kind	Pow.	Acc.	PP	Range	Long	DA
Iron Head	Steel	Physical	80	100	15	Normal	—	○
Iron Defense	Steel	Status	—	—	15	Self	—	—
Magnet Rise	Electric	Status	—	—	10	Self	—	—
Magic Coat	Psychic	Status	—	—	15	Self	—	—
Block	Normal	Status	—	—	5	Normal	—	—
Iron Tail	Steel	Physical	100	75	15	Normal	—	○
Earth Power	Ground	Special	90	100	10	Normal	—	—
Snore	Normal	Special	40	100	15	Normal	—	—
Stealth Rock	Rock	Status	—	—	20	3 Foes	—	—
Outrage	Dragon	Physical	120	100	10	1 Random	—	○
Sleep Talk	Normal	Status	—	—	10	Self	—	—

Pokémon AR Marker

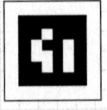

412 Burmy
● Bagworm Pokémon

TYPE Bug

ABILITY
● Shed Skin

HIDDEN ABILITY
● Overcoat

STATS
HP
Attack
Defense
Sp. Atk
Sp. Def
Speed

EGG GROUPS
Bug

ITEMS SOMETIMES HELD
● None

● HEIGHT: 0'08"
● WEIGHT: 7.5 lbs.
● GENDER: ♂ / ♀

Even if it is born where there are no cocooning materials, it somehow always ends up with a cloak.

Plant Cloak	Sandy Cloak	Trash Cloak

Plant Cloak

Trash Cloak

Sandy Cloak

Pokémon AR Marker

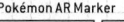   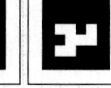

Plant Cloak Sandy Cloak Trash Cloak

EVOLUTION
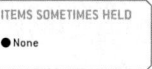

	Lv.	
Burmy ♀ Plant Cloak	Lv. 20	Wormadam Plant Cloak
Burmy ♀ Sandy Cloak	Lv. 20	Wormadam Sandy Cloak
Burmy ♀ Trash Cloak	Lv. 20	Wormadam Trash Cloak
Burmy ♂	Lv. 20	Mothim

HOW TO OBTAIN
Pokémon Black Version 2	Link Trade or Poké Transfer
Pokémon White Version 2	Link Trade or Poké Transfer

HOW TO OBTAIN FROM OTHER GAMES
Pokémon HeartGold Version	Route 38 (use Headbutt)
Pokémon SoulSilver Version	Route 38 (use Headbutt)

LEVEL-UP AND LEARNED MOVES
Lv.	Name	Type	Kind	Pow.	Acc.	PP	Range	Long	DA
1	Protect	Normal	Status	—	—	10	Self	—	—
10	Tackle	Normal	Physical	50	100	35	Normal	—	○
15	Bug Bite	Bug	Physical	60	100	20	Normal	—	○
20	Hidden Power	Normal	Special	—	100	15	Normal	—	—

TM & HM MOVES

MOVES TAUGHT BY PEOPLE
Name	Type	Kind	Pow.	Acc.	PP	Range	Long	DA

MOVES TAUGHT BY MOVE TUTORS FOR SHARDS
Name	Type	Kind	Pow.	Acc.	PP	Range	Long	DA
Bug Bite	Bug	Physical	60	100	20	Normal	—	○
Electroweb	Electric	Special	55	95	15	Many Others	—	—
Snore	Normal	Special	40	100	15	Normal	—	—

EGG MOVES
Name	Type	Kind	Pow.	Acc.	PP	Range	Long	DA

---

413 Wormadam (Plant Cloak)
● Bagworm Pokémon

TYPE Bug Grass

ABILITY
● Anticipation

HIDDEN ABILITY
● Overcoat

STATS
HP
Attack
Defense
Sp. Atk
Sp. Def
Speed

EGG GROUPS
Bug

ITEMS SOMETIMES HELD
● None

● HEIGHT: 1'08"
● WEIGHT: 14.3 lbs.
● GENDER: ♀

When evolving, its body takes in surrounding materials. As a result, there are many body variations.

Pokémon AR Marker

EVOLUTION
	Lv.	
Burmy ♀ Plant Cloak	Lv. 20	Wormadam Plant Cloak
Burmy ♀ Sandy Cloak	Lv. 20	Wormadam Sandy Cloak
Burmy ♀ Trash Cloak	Lv. 20	Wormadam Trash Cloak
Burmy ♂	Lv. 20	Mothim

HOW TO OBTAIN
Pokémon Black Version 2	Get Burmy ♀ (Plant Cloak) with Link Trade or Poké Transfer, then level it up to Lv. 20
Pokémon White Version 2	Get Burmy ♀ (Plant Cloak) with Link Trade or Poké Transfer, then level it up to Lv. 20

HOW TO OBTAIN FROM OTHER GAMES

LEVEL-UP AND LEARNED MOVES
Lv.	Name	Type	Kind	Pow.	Acc.	PP	Range	Long	DA
1	Tackle	Normal	Physical	50	100	35	Normal	—	○
10	Protect	Normal	Status	—	—	10	Self	—	—
15	Bug Bite	Bug	Physical	60	100	20	Normal	—	○
20	Hidden Power	Normal	Special	—	100	15	Normal	—	—
23	Confusion	Psychic	Special	50	100	25	Normal	—	—
26	Razor Leaf	Grass	Physical	55	95	25	Many Others	—	—
29	Growth	Normal	Status	—	—	40	Self	—	—
32	Psybeam	Psychic	Special	65	100	20	Normal	—	—
35	Captivate	Normal	Status	—	100	20	Many Others	—	—
38	Flail	Normal	Physical	—	100	15	Normal	—	○
41	Attract	Normal	Status	—	100	15	Normal	—	—
44	Psychic	Psychic	Special	90	100	10	Normal	—	—
47	Leaf Storm	Grass	Special	140	90	5	Normal	—	—

TM & HM MOVES
Lv.	Name	Type	Kind	Pow.	Acc.	PP	Range	Long	DA
TM06	Toxic	Poison	Status	—	90	10	Normal	—	—
TM09	Venoshock	Poison	Special	65	100	10	Normal	—	—
TM10	Hidden Power	Normal	Special	—	100	15	Normal	—	—
TM11	Sunny Day	Fire	Status	—	—	5	Both Sides	—	—
TM15	Hyper Beam	Normal	Special	150	90	5	Normal	—	—
TM17	Protect	Normal	Status	—	—	10	Self	—	—
TM18	Rain Dance	Water	Status	—	—	5	Both Sides	—	—
TM20	Safeguard	Normal	Status	—	—	25	Your Side	—	—
TM21	Frustration	Normal	Physical	—	100	20	Normal	—	○
TM22	SolarBeam	Grass	Special	120	100	10	Normal	—	—
TM27	Return	Normal	Physical	—	100	20	Normal	—	○
TM29	Psychic	Psychic	Special	90	100	10	Normal	—	—
TM30	Shadow Ball	Ghost	Special	80	100	15	Normal	—	—
TM32	Double Team	Normal	Status	—	—	15	Self	—	—
TM42	Facade	Normal	Physical	70	100	20	Normal	—	○
TM44	Rest	Psychic	Status	—	—	10	Self	—	—
TM45	Attract	Normal	Status	—	100	15	Normal	—	—
TM46	Thief	Dark	Physical	40	100	10	Normal	—	○
TM48	Round	Normal	Special	60	100	15	Normal	—	—
TM53	Energy Ball	Grass	Special	80	100	10	Normal	—	—
TM68	Giga Impact	Normal	Physical	150	90	5	Normal	—	○
TM70	Flash	Normal	Status	—	100	20	Normal	—	—
TM76	Struggle Bug	Bug	Special	30	100	20	Many Others	—	—
TM77	Psych Up	Normal	Status	—	—	10	Normal	—	—
TM85	Dream Eater	Psychic	Special	100	100	15	Normal	—	—
TM86	Grass Knot	Grass	Special	—	100	20	Normal	—	—
TM87	Swagger	Normal	Status	—	90	15	Normal	—	—
TM90	Substitute	Normal	Status	—	—	10	Self	—	—

MOVES TAUGHT BY PEOPLE
Name	Type	Kind	Pow.	Acc.	PP	Range	Long	DA

MOVES TAUGHT BY MOVE TUTORS FOR SHARDS
Name	Type	Kind	Pow.	Acc.	PP	Range	Long	DA
Bug Bite	Bug	Physical	60	100	20	Normal	—	○
Signal Beam	Bug	Special	75	100	15	Normal	—	—
Uproar	Normal	Special	90	100	10	1 Random	—	—
Seed Bomb	Grass	Physical	80	100	15	Normal	—	—
Electroweb	Electric	Special	55	95	15	Many Others	—	—
Snore	Normal	Special	40	100	15	Normal	—	—
Synthesis	Grass	Status	—	—	5	Self	—	—
Giga Drain	Grass	Special	75	100	10	Normal	—	—
Worry Seed	Grass	Status	—	100	10	Normal	—	—
Endeavor	Normal	Physical	—	100	5	Normal	—	○
Sleep Talk	Normal	Status	—	—	10	Self	—	—
Skill Swap	Psychic	Status	—	—	10	Normal	—	—

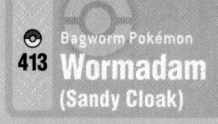

Bagworm Pokémon
413 Wormadam (Sandy Cloak)

- HEIGHT: 1'08"
- WEIGHT: 14.3 lbs.
- GENDER: ♀

When evolving, its body takes in surrounding materials. As a result, there are many body variations.

TYPE: Bug / Ground

ABILITY
- Anticipation

HIDDEN ABILITY
- Overcoat

STATS
HP
Attack
Defense
Sp. Atk
Sp. Def
Speed

EGG GROUPS
Bug

ITEMS SOMETIMES HELD
- None

♀
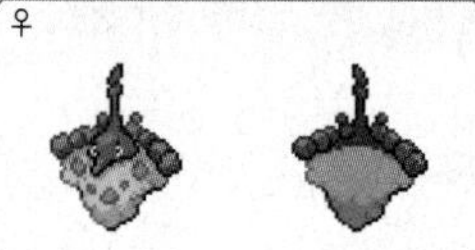

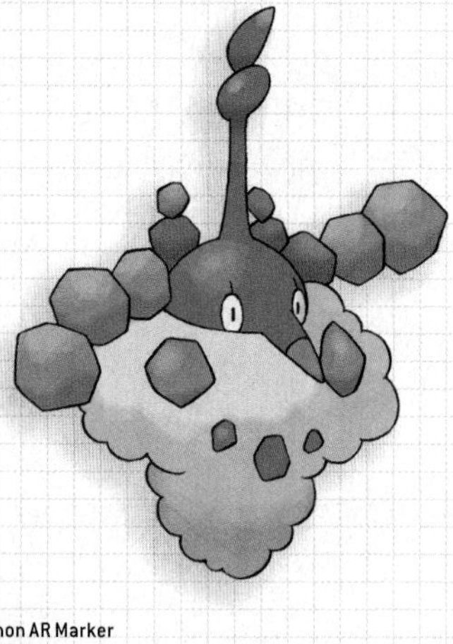

Pokémon AR Marker

EVOLUTION

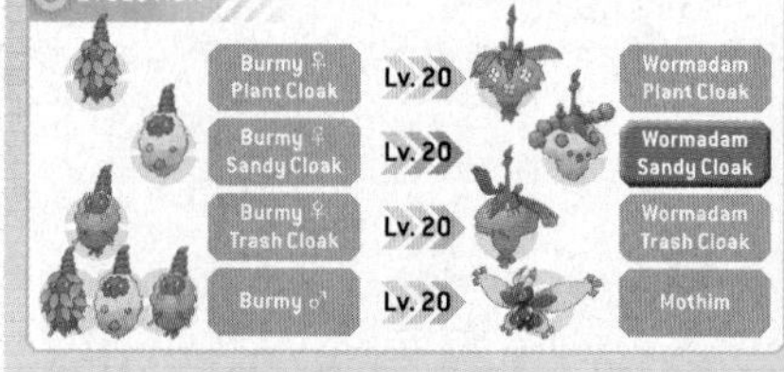
Burmy ♀ Plant Cloak
Lv. 20
Wormadam Plant Cloak
Burmy ♀ Sandy Cloak
Lv. 20
Wormadam Sandy Cloak
Burmy ♀ Trash Cloak
Lv. 20
Wormadam Trash Cloak
Burmy ♂
Lv. 20
Mothim

HOW TO OBTAIN

Pokémon Black Version 2	Get Burmy ♀ (Sandy Cloak) with Link Trade or Poké Transfer, then level it up to Lv. 20
Pokémon White Version 2	Get Burmy ♀ (Sandy Cloak) with Link Trade or Poké Transfer, then level it up to Lv. 20

HOW TO OBTAIN FROM OTHER GAMES

———

———

LEVEL-UP AND LEARNED MOVES

Lv.	Name	Type	Kind	Pow.	Acc.	PP	Range	Long	DA
1	Tackle	Normal	Physical	50	100	35	Normal	—	○
10	Protect	Normal	Status	—	—	10	Self	—	—
15	Bug Bite	Bug	Physical	60	100	20	Normal	—	○
20	Hidden Power	Normal	Special	—	100	15	Normal	—	—
23	Confusion	Psychic	Special	50	100	25	Normal	—	—
26	Rock Blast	Rock	Physical	25	90	10	Normal	—	—
29	Harden	Normal	Status	—	—	30	Self	—	—
32	Psybeam	Psychic	Special	65	100	20	Normal	—	—
35	Captivate	Normal	Status	—	100	20	Many Others	—	—
38	Flail	Normal	Physical	—	100	15	Normal	—	○
41	Attract	Normal	Status	—	100	15	Normal	—	—
44	Psychic	Psychic	Special	90	100	10	Normal	—	—
47	Fissure	Ground	Physical	—	30	5	Normal	—	—

TM & HM MOVES

Lv.	Name	Type	Kind	Pow.	Acc.	PP	Range	Long	DA
TM06	Toxic	Poison	Status	—	90	10	Normal	—	—
TM09	Venoshock	Poison	Special	65	100	10	Normal	—	—
TM10	Hidden Power	Normal	Special	—	100	15	Normal	—	—
TM11	Sunny Day	Fire	Status	—	—	5	Both Sides	—	—
TM15	Hyper Beam	Normal	Special	150	90	5	Normal	—	—
TM17	Protect	Normal	Status	—	—	10	Self	—	—
TM18	Rain Dance	Water	Status	—	—	5	Both Sides	—	—
TM20	Safeguard	Normal	Status	—	—	25	Your Side	—	—
TM21	Frustration	Normal	Physical	—	100	20	Normal	—	○
TM26	Earthquake	Ground	Physical	100	100	10	Adjacent	—	—
TM27	Return	Normal	Physical	—	100	20	Normal	—	○
TM28	Dig	Ground	Physical	80	100	10	Normal	—	○
TM29	Psychic	Psychic	Special	90	100	10	Normal	—	—
TM30	Shadow Ball	Ghost	Special	80	100	15	Normal	—	—
TM32	Double Team	Normal	Status	—	—	15	Self	—	—
TM37	Sandstorm	Rock	Status	—	—	10	Both Sides	—	—
TM39	Rock Tomb	Rock	Physical	50	80	10	Normal	—	—
TM42	Facade	Normal	Physical	70	100	20	Normal	—	○
TM44	Rest	Psychic	Status	—	—	10	Self	—	—
TM45	Attract	Normal	Status	—	100	15	Normal	—	—
TM46	Thief	Dark	Physical	40	100	10	Normal	—	○
TM48	Round	Normal	Special	60	100	15	Normal	—	—
TM68	Giga Impact	Normal	Physical	150	90	5	Normal	—	○
TM70	Flash	Normal	Status	—	100	20	Normal	—	—
TM76	Struggle Bug	Bug	Special	30	100	20	Many Others	—	—
TM77	Psych Up	Normal	Status	—	—	10	Normal	—	—
TM78	Bulldoze	Ground	Physical	60	100	20	Adjacent	—	—
TM85	Dream Eater	Psychic	Special	100	100	15	Normal	—	—
TM87	Swagger	Normal	Status	—	90	15	Normal	—	—
TM90	Substitute	Normal	Status	—	—	10	Self	—	—

MOVES TAUGHT BY PEOPLE

Name	Type	Kind	Pow.	Acc.	PP	Range	Long	DA

MOVES TAUGHT BY MOVE TUTORS FOR SHARDS

Name	Type	Kind	Pow.	Acc.	PP	Range	Long	DA
Bug Bite	Bug	Physical	60	100	20	Normal	—	○
Signal Beam	Bug	Special	75	100	15	Normal	—	—
Uproar	Normal	Special	90	100	10	1 Random	—	—
Electroweb	Electric	Special	55	95	15	Many Others	—	—
Earth Power	Ground	Special	90	100	10	Normal	—	—
Snore	Normal	Special	40	100	15	Normal	—	—
Stealth Rock	Rock	Status	—	—	20	3 Foes	—	—
Endeavor	Normal	Physical	—	100	5	Normal	—	○
Sleep Talk	Normal	Status	—	—	10	Self	—	—
Skill Swap	Psychic	Status	—	—	10	Normal	—	—

Bagworm Pokémon
413 Wormadam (Trash Cloak)

- HEIGHT: 1'08"
- WEIGHT: 14.3 lbs.
- GENDER: ♀

When evolving, its body takes in surrounding materials. As a result, there are many body variations.

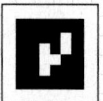

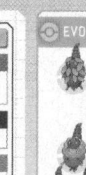

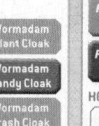

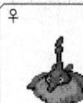

TYPE: Bug / Steel

ABILITY
- Anticipation

HIDDEN ABILITY
- Overcoat

STATS
HP
Attack
Defense
Sp. Atk
Sp. Def
Speed

EGG GROUPS
Bug

ITEMS SOMETIMES HELD
- None

♀
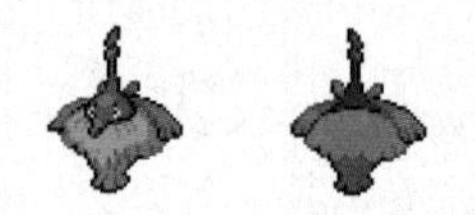

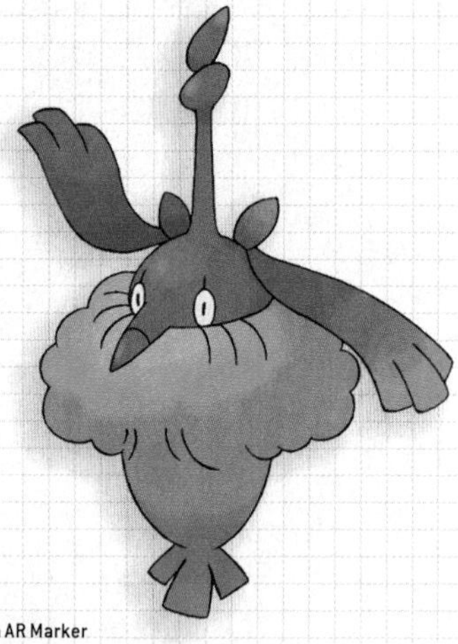

Pokémon AR Marker

EVOLUTION

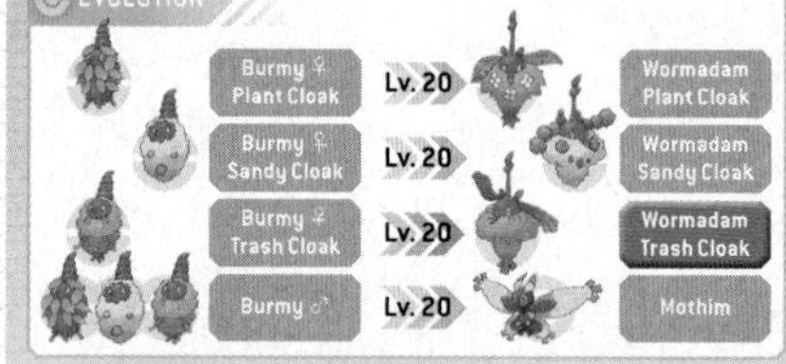
Burmy ♀ Plant Cloak
Lv. 20
Wormadam Plant Cloak
Burmy ♀ Sandy Cloak
Lv. 20
Wormadam Sandy Cloak
Burmy ♀ Trash Cloak
Lv. 20
Wormadam Trash Cloak
Burmy ♂
Lv. 20
Mothim

HOW TO OBTAIN

Pokémon Black Version 2	Get Burmy ♀ (Trash Cloak) with Link Trade or Poké Transfer, then level it up to Lv. 20
Pokémon White Version 2	Get Burmy ♀ (Trash Cloak) with Link Trade or Poké Transfer, then level it up to Lv. 20

HOW TO OBTAIN FROM OTHER GAMES

———

———

LEVEL-UP AND LEARNED MOVES

Lv.	Name	Type	Kind	Pow.	Acc.	PP	Range	Long	DA
1	Tackle	Normal	Physical	50	100	35	Normal	—	○
10	Protect	Normal	Status	—	—	10	Self	—	—
15	Bug Bite	Bug	Physical	60	100	20	Normal	—	○
20	Hidden Power	Normal	Special	—	100	15	Normal	—	—
23	Confusion	Psychic	Special	50	100	25	Normal	—	—
26	Mirror Shot	Steel	Special	65	85	10	Normal	—	—
29	Metal Sound	Steel	Status	—	85	40	Normal	—	—
32	Psybeam	Psychic	Special	65	100	20	Normal	—	—
35	Captivate	Normal	Status	—	100	20	Many Others	—	—
38	Flail	Normal	Physical	—	100	15	Normal	—	○
41	Attract	Normal	Status	—	100	15	Normal	—	—
44	Psychic	Psychic	Special	90	100	10	Normal	—	—
47	Iron Head	Steel	Physical	80	100	15	Normal	—	○

TM & HM MOVES

Lv.	Name	Type	Kind	Pow.	Acc.	PP	Range	Long	DA
TM06	Toxic	Poison	Status	—	90	10	Normal	—	—
TM09	Venoshock	Poison	Special	65	100	10	Normal	—	—
TM10	Hidden Power	Normal	Special	—	100	15	Normal	—	—
TM11	Sunny Day	Fire	Status	—	—	5	Both Sides	—	—
TM15	Hyper Beam	Normal	Special	150	90	5	Normal	—	—
TM17	Protect	Normal	Status	—	—	10	Self	—	—
TM18	Rain Dance	Water	Status	—	—	5	Both Sides	—	—
TM20	Safeguard	Normal	Status	—	—	25	Your Side	—	—
TM21	Frustration	Normal	Physical	—	100	20	Normal	—	○
TM27	Return	Normal	Physical	—	100	20	Normal	—	○
TM29	Psychic	Psychic	Special	90	100	10	Normal	—	—
TM30	Shadow Ball	Ghost	Special	80	100	15	Normal	—	—
TM32	Double Team	Normal	Status	—	—	15	Self	—	—
TM42	Facade	Normal	Physical	70	100	20	Normal	—	○
TM44	Rest	Psychic	Status	—	—	10	Self	—	—
TM45	Attract	Normal	Status	—	100	15	Normal	—	—
TM46	Thief	Dark	Physical	40	100	10	Normal	—	○
TM48	Round	Normal	Special	60	100	15	Normal	—	—
TM68	Giga Impact	Normal	Physical	150	90	5	Normal	—	○
TM70	Flash	Normal	Status	—	100	20	Normal	—	—
TM74	Gyro Ball	Steel	Physical	—	100	5	Normal	—	○
TM76	Struggle Bug	Bug	Special	30	100	20	Many Others	—	—
TM77	Psych Up	Normal	Status	—	—	10	Normal	—	—
TM85	Dream Eater	Psychic	Special	100	100	15	Normal	—	—
TM87	Swagger	Normal	Status	—	90	15	Normal	—	—
TM90	Substitute	Normal	Status	—	—	10	Self	—	—
TM91	Flash Cannon	Steel	Special	80	100	10	Normal	—	—

MOVES TAUGHT BY PEOPLE

Name	Type	Kind	Pow.	Acc.	PP	Range	Long	DA

MOVES TAUGHT BY MOVE TUTORS FOR SHARDS

Name	Type	Kind	Pow.	Acc.	PP	Range	Long	DA
Bug Bite	Bug	Physical	60	100	20	Normal	—	○
Signal Beam	Bug	Special	75	100	15	Normal	—	—
Iron Head	Steel	Physical	80	100	15	Normal	—	○
Uproar	Normal	Special	90	100	10	1 Random	—	—
Gunk Shot	Poison	Physical	120	70	5	Normal	—	—
Iron Defense	Steel	Status	—	—	15	Self	—	—
Magnet Rise	Electric	Status	—	—	10	Self	—	—
Electroweb	Electric	Special	55	95	15	Many Others	—	—
Snore	Normal	Special	40	100	15	Normal	—	—
Stealth Rock	Rock	Status	—	—	20	3 Foes	—	—
Endeavor	Normal	Physical	—	100	5	Normal	—	○
Sleep Talk	Normal	Status	—	—	10	Self	—	—
Skill Swap	Psychic	Status	—	—	10	Normal	—	—

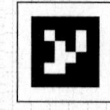

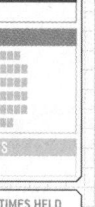

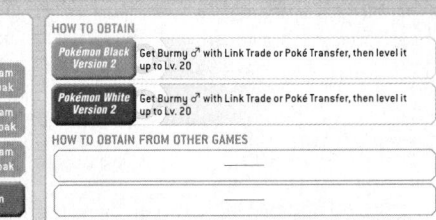

414 Mothim
Moth Pokémon

- HEIGHT: 2'11"
- WEIGHT: 51.4 lbs.
- GENDER: ♂

While it loves floral honey, it won't gather any itself. Instead, it plots to steal some from Combee.

TYPE
Bug / Flying

ABILITY
- Swarm

HIDDEN ABILITY
- Tinted Lens

STATS
HP	
Attack	
Defense	
Sp. Atk	
Sp. Def	
Speed	

EGG GROUPS
Bug

ITEMS SOMETIMES HELD
- None

Pokémon AR Marker

EVOLUTION
Burmy ♀ Plant Cloak	Lv. 20	Wormadam Plant Cloak
Burmy ♀ Sandy Cloak	Lv. 20	Wormadam Sandy Cloak
Burmy ♀ Trash Cloak	Lv. 20	Wormadam Trash Cloak
Burmy ♂	Lv. 20	Mothim

HOW TO OBTAIN
Pokémon Black Version 2	Get Burmy ♂ with Link Trade or Poké Transfer, then level it up to Lv. 20
Pokémon White Version 2	Get Burmy ♂ with Link Trade or Poké Transfer, then level it up to Lv. 20

HOW TO OBTAIN FROM OTHER GAMES
| — |
| — |

LEVEL-UP AND LEARNED MOVES
Lv.	Name	Type	Kind	Pow.	Acc.	PP	Range	Long	DA
1	Tackle	Normal	Physical	50	100	35	Normal	—	○
10	Protect	Normal	Status	—	—	10	Self	—	—
15	Bug Bite	Bug	Physical	60	100	20	Normal	—	○
20	Hidden Power	Normal	Special	—	100	15	Normal	—	—
23	Confusion	Psychic	Special	50	100	25	Normal	—	—
26	Gust	Flying	Special	40	100	35	Normal	○	—
29	PoisonPowder	Poison	Status	—	75	35	Normal	—	—
32	Psybeam	Psychic	Special	65	100	20	Normal	—	—
35	Camouflage	Normal	Status	—	—	20	Self	—	—
38	Silver Wind	Bug	Special	60	100	5	Normal	—	—
41	Air Slash	Flying	Special	75	95	20	Normal	○	—
44	Psychic	Psychic	Special	90	100	10	Normal	—	—
47	Bug Buzz	Bug	Special	90	100	10	Normal	—	—
50	Quiver Dance	Bug	Status	—	—	20	Self	—	—

TM & HM MOVES
Lv.	Name	Type	Kind	Pow.	Acc.	PP	Range	Long	DA
TM06	Toxic	Poison	Status	—	90	10	Normal	—	—
TM09	Venoshock	Poison	Special	65	100	10	Normal	—	—
TM10	Hidden Power	Normal	Special	—	100	15	Normal	—	—
TM11	Sunny Day	Fire	Status	—	—	5	Both Sides	—	—
TM15	Hyper Beam	Normal	Special	150	90	5	Normal	—	—
TM17	Protect	Normal	Status	—	—	10	Self	—	—
TM18	Rain Dance	Water	Status	—	—	5	Both Sides	—	—
TM20	Safeguard	Normal	Status	—	—	25	Your Side	—	—
TM21	Frustration	Normal	Physical	—	100	20	Normal	—	○
TM22	SolarBeam	Grass	Special	120	100	10	Normal	—	—
TM27	Return	Normal	Physical	—	100	20	Normal	—	○
TM29	Psychic	Psychic	Special	90	100	10	Normal	—	—
TM30	Shadow Ball	Ghost	Special	80	100	15	Normal	—	—
TM32	Double Team	Normal	Status	—	—	15	Self	—	—
TM40	Aerial Ace	Flying	Physical	60	—	20	Normal	○	○
TM42	Facade	Normal	Physical	70	100	20	Normal	—	○
TM44	Rest	Psychic	Status	—	—	10	Self	—	—
TM45	Attract	Normal	Status	—	100	15	Normal	—	—
TM46	Thief	Dark	Physical	40	100	10	Normal	—	○
TM48	Round	Normal	Special	60	100	15	Normal	—	—
TM53	Energy Ball	Grass	Special	80	100	10	Normal	—	—
TM62	Acrobatics	Flying	Physical	55	100	15	Normal	○	○
TM68	Giga Impact	Normal	Physical	150	90	5	Normal	—	○
TM70	Flash	Normal	Status	—	100	20	Normal	—	—
TM76	Struggle Bug	Bug	Special	30	100	20	Many Others	—	—
TM77	Psych Up	Normal	Status	—	—	10	Normal	—	—
TM85	Dream Eater	Psychic	Special	100	100	15	Normal	—	—
TM87	Swagger	Normal	Status	—	90	15	Normal	—	—
TM89	U-turn	Bug	Physical	70	100	20	Normal	—	○
TM90	Substitute	Normal	Status	—	—	10	Self	—	—

MOVES TAUGHT BY PEOPLE
Name	Type	Kind	Pow.	Acc.	PP	Range	Long	DA

MOVES TAUGHT BY MOVE TUTORS FOR SHARDS
Name	Type	Kind	Pow.	Acc.	PP	Range	Long	DA
Bug Bite	Bug	Physical	60	100	20	Normal	—	○
Signal Beam	Bug	Special	75	100	15	Normal	—	—
Electroweb	Electric	Special	55	95	15	Many Others	—	—
Snore	Normal	Special	40	100	15	Normal	—	—
Roost	Flying	Status	—	—	10	Self	—	—
Giga Drain	Grass	Special	75	100	10	Normal	—	—
Tailwind	Flying	Status	—	—	30	Your Side	—	—
Sleep Talk	Normal	Status	—	—	10	Self	—	—
Skill Swap	Psychic	Status	—	—	10	Normal	—	—

---

415 Combee
Tiny Bee Pokémon

- HEIGHT: 1'00"
- WEIGHT: 12.1 lbs.
- GENDER: ♂ / ♀

This Pokémon is a set of three. When they sleep, they gather up and form a giant hive of 100 Combee.

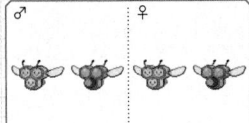

TYPE
Bug / Flying

ABILITY
- Honey Gather

HIDDEN ABILITY
- Hustle

STATS
HP	
Attack	
Defense	
Sp. Atk	
Sp. Def	
Speed	

EGG GROUPS
Bug

ITEMS SOMETIMES HELD
- Honey

Pokémon AR Marker

EVOLUTION
Combee	Lv. 21	Vespiquen

HOW TO OBTAIN
Pokémon Black Version 2	❶ Lostlorn Forest ❷ Route 12
Pokémon White Version 2	❶ Lostlorn Forest ❷ Route 12

HOW TO OBTAIN FROM OTHER GAMES
| |
| |

LEVEL-UP AND LEARNED MOVES
Lv.	Name	Type	Kind	Pow.	Acc.	PP	Range	Long	DA
1	Sweet Scent	Normal	Status	—	100	20	Many Others	—	—
1	Gust	Flying	Special	40	100	35	Normal	○	—
13	Bug Bite	Bug	Physical	60	100	20	Normal	—	○
29	Bug Buzz	Bug	Special	90	100	10	Normal	—	—

TM & HM MOVES
Lv.	Name	Type	Kind	Pow.	Acc.	PP	Range	Long	DA

MOVES TAUGHT BY PEOPLE
Name	Type	Kind	Pow.	Acc.	PP	Range	Long	DA

MOVES TAUGHT BY MOVE TUTORS FOR SHARDS
Name	Type	Kind	Pow.	Acc.	PP	Range	Long	DA
Bug Bite	Bug	Physical	60	100	20	Normal	—	—
Snore	Normal	Special	40	100	15	Normal	—	—
Tailwind	Flying	Status	—	—	30	Your Side	—	—
Endeavor	Normal	Physical	—	100	5	Normal	—	○

EGG MOVES
Name	Type	Kind	Pow.	Acc.	PP	Range	Long	DA

◆ Male Combee do not evolve.

416 Vespiquen
Beehive Pokémon

TYPE Bug / Flying

ABILITY
● Pressure

HIDDEN ABILITY
● Unnerve

● HEIGHT: 3'11"
● WEIGHT: 84.9 lbs.
● GENDER: ♀

It houses its colony in cells in its body and releases various pheromones to make those grubs do its bidding.

♀

STATS
HP
Attack
Defense
Sp. Atk
Sp. Def
Speed

EGG GROUPS
Bug

ITEMS SOMETIMES HELD
● Poison Barb

EVOLUTION

Combee ♀ → Lv. 21 → Vespiquen
→ p. 223

HOW TO OBTAIN
Pokémon Black Version 2	❶ Lostlorn Forest (rustling grass) ❷ Route 12 (rustling grass)
Pokémon White Version 2	❶ Lostlorn Forest (rustling grass) ❷ Route 12 (rustling grass)

HOW TO OBTAIN FROM OTHER GAMES

LEVEL-UP AND LEARNED MOVES
Lv.	Name	Type	Kind	Pow.	Acc.	PP	Range	Long	DA
1	Sweet Scent	Normal	Status	—	100	20	Many Others	—	—
1	Gust	Flying	Special	40	100	35	Normal	○	—
1	Poison Sting	Poison	Physical	15	100	35	Normal	—	—
1	Confuse Ray	Ghost	Status	—	100	10	Normal	—	—
5	Fury Cutter	Bug	Physical	20	95	20	Normal	—	○
9	Pursuit	Dark	Physical	40	100	20	Normal	—	○
13	Fury Swipes	Normal	Physical	18	80	15	Normal	—	○
17	Defend Order	Bug	Status	—	—	10	Self	—	—
21	Slash	Normal	Physical	70	100	20	Normal	—	○
25	Power Gem	Rock	Special	70	100	20	Normal	—	—
29	Heal Order	Bug	Status	—	—	10	Self	—	—
33	Toxic	Poison	Status	—	90	10	Normal	—	—
37	Air Slash	Flying	Special	75	95	20	Normal	○	—
41	Captivate	Normal	Status	—	100	20	Many Others	—	—
45	Attack Order	Bug	Physical	90	100	15	Normal	—	—
49	Swagger	Normal	Status	—	90	15	Normal	—	—
53	Destiny Bond	Ghost	Status	—	—	5	Self	—	—

TM & HM MOVES
Lv.	Name	Type	Kind	Pow.	Acc.	PP	Range	Long	DA
TM01	Hone Claws	Dark	Status	—	—	15	Self	—	—
TM06	Toxic	Poison	Status	—	90	10	Normal	—	—
TM09	Venoshock	Poison	Special	65	100	10	Normal	—	—
TM10	Hidden Power	Normal	Special	—	100	15	Normal	—	—
TM11	Sunny Day	Fire	Status	—	—	5	Both Sides	—	—
TM15	Hyper Beam	Normal	Special	150	90	5	Normal	—	—
TM17	Protect	Normal	Status	—	—	10	Self	—	—
TM18	Rain Dance	Water	Status	—	—	5	Both Sides	—	—
TM21	Frustration	Normal	Physical	—	100	20	Normal	—	○
TM27	Return	Normal	Physical	—	100	20	Normal	—	○
TM32	Double Team	Normal	Status	—	—	15	Self	—	—
TM36	Sludge Bomb	Poison	Special	90	100	10	Normal	—	—
TM40	Aerial Ace	Flying	Physical	60	—	20	Normal	○	—
TM42	Facade	Normal	Physical	70	100	20	Normal	—	○
TM44	Rest	Psychic	Status	—	—	10	Self	—	—
TM45	Attract	Normal	Status	—	100	15	Normal	—	—
TM46	Thief	Dark	Physical	40	100	10	Normal	—	—
TM48	Round	Normal	Special	60	100	15	Normal	—	—
TM56	Fling	Dark	Physical	—	100	10	Normal	—	—
TM60	Quash	Dark	Status	—	100	15	Normal	—	—
TM62	Acrobatics	Flying	Physical	55	100	15	Normal	○	—
TM68	Giga Impact	Normal	Physical	150	90	5	Normal	—	—
TM70	Flash	Normal	Status	—	100	20	Normal	—	—
TM76	Struggle Bug	Bug	Special	30	100	20	Many Others	—	—
TM81	X-Scissor	Bug	Physical	80	100	15	Normal	—	—
TM87	Swagger	Normal	Status	—	90	15	Normal	—	—
TM89	U-turn	Bug	Physical	70	100	20	Normal	—	○
TM90	Substitute	Normal	Status	—	—	10	Self	—	—
HM01	Cut	Normal	Physical	50	95	30	Normal	—	—

MOVES TAUGHT BY PEOPLE
Name	Type	Kind	Pow.	Acc.	PP	Range	Long	DA

MOVES TAUGHT BY MOVE TUTORS FOR SHARDS
Name	Type	Kind	Pow.	Acc.	PP	Range	Long	DA
Bug Bite	Bug	Physical	60	100	20	Normal	—	—
Signal Beam	Bug	Special	75	100	15	Normal	—	—
Snore	Normal	Special	40	100	15	Normal	—	—
Roost	Flying	Status	—	—	10	Self	—	—
Tailwind	Flying	Status	—	—	30	Your Side	—	—
Endeavor	Normal	Physical	—	100	5	Normal	—	○
Sleep Talk	Normal	Status	—	—	10	Self	—	—

Pokémon AR Marker

417 Pachirisu
EleSquirrel Pokémon

TYPE Electric

ABILITIES
● Run Away
● Pickup

HIDDEN ABILITY
● Volt Absorb

● HEIGHT: 1'04"
● WEIGHT: 8.6 lbs.
● GENDER: ♂ / ♀

A pair may be seen rubbing their cheek pouches together in an effort to share stored electricity.

♂   ♀

STATS
HP
Attack
Defense
Sp. Atk
Sp. Def
Speed

EGG GROUPS
Field/Fairy

ITEMS SOMETIMES HELD
● None

EVOLUTION
Does not evolve

HOW TO OBTAIN
Pokémon Black Version 2	Route 3 (Hidden Grotto)
Pokémon White Version 2	Route 3 (Hidden Grotto)

HOW TO OBTAIN FROM OTHER GAMES

LEVEL-UP AND LEARNED MOVES
Lv.	Name	Type	Kind	Pow.	Acc.	PP	Range	Long	DA
1	Growl	Normal	Status	—	100	40	Many Others	—	—
1	Bide	Normal	Physical	—	—	10	Self	—	○
5	Quick Attack	Normal	Physical	40	100	30	Normal	—	○
9	Charm	Normal	Status	—	100	20	Normal	—	—
13	Spark	Electric	Physical	65	100	20	Normal	—	○
17	Endure	Normal	Status	—	—	10	Self	—	—
21	Swift	Normal	Special	60	—	20	Many Others	—	—
25	Electro Ball	Electric	Special	—	100	10	Normal	—	—
29	Sweet Kiss	Normal	Status	—	75	10	Normal	—	—
33	Thunder Wave	Electric	Status	—	100	20	Normal	—	—
37	Super Fang	Normal	Physical	—	90	10	Normal	—	○
41	Discharge	Electric	Special	80	100	15	Adjacent	—	—
45	Last Resort	Normal	Physical	140	100	5	Normal	—	○
49	Hyper Fang	Normal	Physical	80	90	15	Normal	—	○

TM & HM MOVES
Lv.	Name	Type	Kind	Pow.	Acc.	PP	Range	Long	DA
TM06	Toxic	Poison	Status	—	90	10	Normal	—	—
TM10	Hidden Power	Normal	Special	—	100	15	Normal	—	—
TM16	Light Screen	Psychic	Status	—	—	30	Your Side	—	—
TM17	Protect	Normal	Status	—	—	10	Self	—	—
TM18	Rain Dance	Water	Status	—	—	5	Both Sides	—	—
TM21	Frustration	Normal	Physical	—	100	20	Normal	—	○
TM24	Thunderbolt	Electric	Special	95	100	15	Normal	—	—
TM25	Thunder	Electric	Special	120	70	10	Normal	—	—
TM27	Return	Normal	Physical	—	100	20	Normal	—	○
TM28	Dig	Ground	Physical	80	100	10	Normal	—	—
TM32	Double Team	Normal	Status	—	—	15	Self	—	—
TM42	Facade	Normal	Physical	70	100	20	Normal	—	○
TM44	Rest	Psychic	Status	—	—	10	Self	—	—
TM45	Attract	Normal	Status	—	100	15	Normal	—	—
TM48	Round	Normal	Special	60	100	15	Normal	—	—
TM49	Echoed Voice	Normal	Special	40	100	15	Normal	—	—
TM56	Fling	Dark	Physical	—	100	10	Normal	—	—
TM57	Charge Beam	Electric	Special	50	90	10	Normal	—	—
TM70	Flash	Normal	Status	—	100	20	Normal	—	—
TM72	Volt Switch	Electric	Special	70	100	20	Normal	—	○
TM73	Thunder Wave	Electric	Status	—	100	20	Normal	—	—
TM86	Grass Knot	Grass	Special	—	100	20	Normal	—	—
TM87	Swagger	Normal	Status	—	90	15	Normal	—	—
TM89	U-turn	Bug	Physical	70	100	20	Normal	—	○
TM90	Substitute	Normal	Status	—	—	10	Self	—	—
HM01	Cut	Normal	Physical	50	95	30	Normal	—	—

MOVES TAUGHT BY PEOPLE
Name	Type	Kind	Pow.	Acc.	PP	Range	Long	DA

MOVES TAUGHT BY MOVE TUTORS FOR SHARDS
Name	Type	Kind	Pow.	Acc.	PP	Range	Long	DA
Covet	Normal	Physical	60	100	40	Normal	—	○
Super Fang	Normal	Physical	—	90	10	Normal	—	○
Uproar	Normal	Special	90	100	10	1 Random	—	—
Seed Bomb	Grass	Physical	80	100	15	Normal	—	—
Gunk Shot	Poison	Physical	120	70	5	Normal	—	—
ThunderPunch	Electric	Physical	75	100	15	Normal	—	○
Last Resort	Normal	Physical	140	100	5	Normal	—	○
Magnet Rise	Electric	Status	—	—	10	Self	—	—
Iron Tail	Steel	Physical	100	75	15	Normal	—	○
Snore	Normal	Special	40	100	15	Normal	—	—
Helping Hand	Normal	Status	—	—	20	1 Ally	—	—
Sleep Talk	Normal	Status	—	—	10	Self	—	—

EGG MOVES
Name	Type	Kind	Pow.	Acc.	PP	Range	Long	DA
Covet	Normal	Physical	60	100	40	Normal	—	○
Bite	Dark	Physical	60	100	25	Normal	—	○
Fake Tears	Dark	Status	—	100	20	Normal	—	—
Defense Curl	Normal	Status	—	—	40	Self	—	—
Rollout	Rock	Physical	30	90	20	Normal	—	○
Flatter	Dark	Status	—	100	15	Normal	—	—
Flail	Normal	Physical	—	100	15	Normal	—	○
Iron Tail	Steel	Physical	100	75	15	Normal	—	○
Tail Whip	Normal	Status	—	100	30	Many Others	—	—
Follow Me	Normal	Status	—	—	20	Self	—	—
Charge	Electric	Status	—	—	20	Self	—	—
Bestow	Normal	Status	—	—	15	Normal	—	—

Pokémon AR Marker

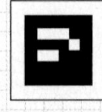

418 Buizel

Sea Weasel Pokémon

- HEIGHT: 2'04"
- WEIGHT: 65.0 lbs.
- GENDER: ♂ / ♀

It inflates the flotation sac around its neck and pokes its head out of the water to see what is going on.

♂ ♀

TYPE Water

ABILITY
- Swift Swim

HIDDEN ABILITY
- Water Veil

STATS
HP
Attack
Defense
Sp. Atk
Sp. Def
Speed

EGG GROUPS
Water ❶ / Field

ITEMS SOMETIMES HELD
- None

EVOLUTION

HOW TO OBTAIN

Pokémon Black Version 2	❶ Lostlorn Forest (water surface) ❷ Route 14 (water surface)
Pokémon White Version 2	❶ Lostlorn Forest (water surface) ❷ Route 14 (water surface)

HOW TO OBTAIN FROM OTHER GAMES

—

—

LEVEL-UP AND LEARNED MOVES

Lv.	Name	Type	Kind	Pow.	Acc.	PP	Range	Long	DA
1	SonicBoom	Normal	Special	—	90	20	Normal	—	—
4	Growl	Normal	Status	—	100	40	Many Others	—	—
7	Water Sport	Water	Status	—	—	15	Both Sides	—	—
11	Quick Attack	Normal	Physical	40	100	30	Normal	—	○
15	Water Gun	Water	Special	40	100	25	Normal	—	—
18	Pursuit	Dark	Physical	40	100	20	Normal	—	○
21	Swift	Normal	Special	60	—	20	Many Others	—	—
24	Aqua Jet	Water	Physical	40	100	20	Normal	—	○
27	Double Hit	Normal	Physical	35	90	10	Normal	—	○
31	Whirlpool	Water	Special	35	85	15	Normal	—	—
35	Razor Wind	Normal	Special	80	100	10	Many Others	—	—
38	Aqua Tail	Water	Physical	90	90	10	Normal	—	○
41	Agility	Psychic	Status	—	—	30	Self	—	—
45	Hydro Pump	Water	Special	120	80	5	Normal	—	—

TM & HM MOVES

Lv.	Name	Type	Kind	Pow.	Acc.	PP	Range	Long	DA
TM06	Toxic	Poison	Status	—	90	10	Normal	—	—
TM07	Hail	Ice	Status	—	—	10	Both Sides	—	—
TM08	Bulk Up	Fighting	Status	—	—	20	Self	—	—
TM10	Hidden Power	Normal	Special	—	100	15	Normal	—	—
TM13	Ice Beam	Ice	Special	95	100	10	Normal	—	—
TM14	Blizzard	Ice	Special	120	70	5	Many Others	—	—
TM17	Protect	Normal	Status	—	—	10	Self	—	—
TM18	Rain Dance	Water	Status	—	—	5	Both Sides	—	—
TM21	Frustration	Normal	Physical	—	100	20	Normal	—	○
TM27	Return	Normal	Physical	—	100	20	Normal	—	○
TM28	Dig	Ground	Physical	80	100	10	Normal	—	○
TM31	Brick Break	Fighting	Physical	75	100	15	Normal	—	○
TM32	Double Team	Normal	Status	—	—	15	Self	—	—
TM39	Rock Tomb	Rock	Physical	50	80	10	Normal	—	—
TM42	Facade	Normal	Physical	70	100	20	Normal	—	○
TM44	Rest	Psychic	Status	—	—	10	Self	—	—
TM45	Attract	Normal	Status	—	100	15	Normal	—	—
TM48	Round	Normal	Special	60	100	15	Normal	—	—
TM49	Echoed Voice	Normal	Special	40	100	15	Normal	—	—
TM55	Scald	Water	Special	80	100	15	Normal	—	—
TM87	Swagger	Normal	Status	—	90	15	Normal	—	—
TM90	Substitute	Normal	Status	—	—	10	Self	—	—
TM94	Rock Smash	Fighting	Physical	40	100	15	Normal	—	○
HM03	Surf	Water	Special	95	100	15	Adjacent	—	—
HM04	Strength	Normal	Physical	80	100	15	Normal	—	○
HM05	Waterfall	Water	Physical	80	100	15	Normal	—	○
HM06	Dive	Water	Physical	80	100	10	Normal	—	○

MOVES TAUGHT BY PEOPLE

Name	Type	Kind	Pow.	Acc.	PP	Range	Long	DA

MOVES TAUGHT BY MOVE TUTORS FOR SHARDS

Name	Type	Kind	Pow.	Acc.	PP	Range	Long	DA
Ice Punch	Ice	Physical	75	100	15	Normal	—	○
Icy Wind	Ice	Special	55	95	15	Many Others	—	—
Iron Tail	Steel	Physical	100	75	15	Normal	—	○
Aqua Tail	Water	Physical	90	90	10	Normal	—	○
Snore	Normal	Special	40	100	15	Normal	—	—
Sleep Talk	Normal	Status	—	—	10	Self	—	—

EGG MOVES

Name	Type	Kind	Pow.	Acc.	PP	Range	Long	DA
Mud-Slap	Ground	Special	20	100	10	Normal	—	—
Headbutt	Normal	Physical	70	100	15	Normal	—	○
Fury Swipes	Normal	Physical	18	80	15	Normal	—	○
Slash	Normal	Physical	70	100	20	Normal	—	○
Odor Sleuth	Normal	Status	—	—	40	Normal	—	—
DoubleSlap	Normal	Physical	15	85	10	Normal	—	○
Fury Cutter	Bug	Physical	20	95	20	Normal	—	○
Baton Pass	Normal	Status	—	—	40	Self	—	—
Aqua Tail	Water	Physical	90	90	10	Normal	—	○
Aqua Ring	Water	Status	—	—	20	Self	—	—
Me First	Normal	Status	—	—	20	Varies	—	—
Switcheroo	Dark	Status	—	100	10	Normal	—	—
Tail Slap	Normal	Physical	25	85	10	Normal	—	○

Pokémon AR Marker

419 Floatzel

Sea Weasel Pokémon

- HEIGHT: 3'07"
- WEIGHT: 73.9 lbs.
- GENDER: ♂ / ♀

It is a common sight around fishing ports. It is known to rescue people and carry off prey.

♂ ♀

TYPE Water

ABILITY
- Swift Swim

HIDDEN ABILITY
- Water Veil

STATS
HP
Attack
Defense
Sp. Atk
Sp. Def
Speed

EGG GROUPS
Water ❶ / Field

ITEMS SOMETIMES HELD
- None

EVOLUTION

HOW TO OBTAIN

Pokémon Black Version 2	❶ Lostlorn Forest (ripples in water) ❷ Route 14 (ripples in water)
Pokémon White Version 2	❶ Lostlorn Forest (ripples in water) ❷ Route 14 (ripples in water)

HOW TO OBTAIN FROM OTHER GAMES

—

—

LEVEL-UP AND LEARNED MOVES

Lv.	Name	Type	Kind	Pow.	Acc.	PP	Range	Long	DA
1	Ice Fang	Ice	Physical	65	95	15	Normal	—	○
1	Crunch	Dark	Physical	80	100	15	Normal	—	○
1	SonicBoom	Normal	Special	—	90	20	Normal	—	—
1	Growl	Normal	Status	—	100	40	Many Others	—	—
1	Water Sport	Water	Status	—	—	15	Both Sides	—	—
1	Quick Attack	Normal	Physical	40	100	30	Normal	—	○
4	Growl	Normal	Status	—	100	40	Many Others	—	—
7	Water Sport	Water	Status	—	—	15	Both Sides	—	—
11	Quick Attack	Normal	Physical	40	100	30	Normal	—	○
15	Water Gun	Water	Special	40	100	25	Normal	—	—
18	Pursuit	Dark	Physical	40	100	20	Normal	—	○
21	Swift	Normal	Special	60	—	20	Many Others	—	—
24	Aqua Jet	Water	Physical	40	100	20	Normal	—	○
29	Double Hit	Normal	Physical	35	90	10	Normal	—	○
35	Whirlpool	Water	Special	35	85	15	Normal	—	—
41	Razor Wind	Normal	Special	80	100	10	Many Others	—	—
46	Aqua Tail	Water	Physical	90	90	10	Normal	—	○
51	Agility	Psychic	Status	—	—	30	Self	—	—
57	Hydro Pump	Water	Special	120	80	5	Normal	—	—

TM & HM MOVES

Lv.	Name	Type	Kind	Pow.	Acc.	PP	Range	Long	DA
TM05	Roar	Normal	Status	—	100	20	Normal	—	—
TM06	Toxic	Poison	Status	—	90	10	Normal	—	—
TM07	Hail	Ice	Status	—	—	10	Both Sides	—	—
TM08	Bulk Up	Fighting	Status	—	—	20	Self	—	—
TM10	Hidden Power	Normal	Special	—	100	15	Normal	—	—
TM12	Taunt	Dark	Status	—	100	20	Normal	—	—
TM13	Ice Beam	Ice	Special	95	100	10	Normal	—	—
TM14	Blizzard	Ice	Special	120	70	5	Many Others	—	—
TM15	Hyper Beam	Normal	Special	150	90	5	Normal	—	—
TM17	Protect	Normal	Status	—	—	10	Self	—	—
TM18	Rain Dance	Water	Status	—	—	5	Both Sides	—	—
TM21	Frustration	Normal	Physical	—	100	20	Normal	—	○
TM27	Return	Normal	Physical	—	100	20	Normal	—	○
TM28	Dig	Ground	Physical	80	100	10	Normal	—	○
TM31	Brick Break	Fighting	Physical	75	100	15	Normal	—	○
TM32	Double Team	Normal	Status	—	—	15	Self	—	—
TM39	Rock Tomb	Rock	Physical	50	80	10	Normal	—	—
TM41	Torment	Dark	Status	—	100	15	Normal	—	—
TM42	Facade	Normal	Physical	70	100	20	Normal	—	○
TM44	Rest	Psychic	Status	—	—	10	Self	—	—
TM45	Attract	Normal	Status	—	100	15	Normal	—	—
TM48	Round	Normal	Special	60	100	15	Normal	—	—
TM49	Echoed Voice	Normal	Special	40	100	15	Normal	—	—
TM52	Focus Blast	Fighting	Special	120	70	5	Normal	—	—
TM55	Scald	Water	Special	80	100	15	Normal	—	—
TM66	Payback	Dark	Physical	50	100	10	Normal	—	○
TM68	Giga Impact	Normal	Physical	150	90	5	Normal	—	○
TM87	Swagger	Normal	Status	—	90	15	Normal	—	—
TM90	Substitute	Normal	Status	—	—	10	Self	—	—
TM94	Rock Smash	Fighting	Physical	40	100	15	Normal	—	○
HM03	Surf	Water	Special	95	100	15	Adjacent	—	—
HM04	Strength	Normal	Physical	80	100	15	Normal	—	○
HM05	Waterfall	Water	Physical	80	100	15	Normal	—	○
HM06	Dive	Water	Physical	80	100	10	Normal	—	○

MOVES TAUGHT BY PEOPLE

Name	Type	Kind	Pow.	Acc.	PP	Range	Long	DA

MOVES TAUGHT BY MOVE TUTORS FOR SHARDS

Name	Type	Kind	Pow.	Acc.	PP	Range	Long	DA
Low Kick	Fighting	Physical	—	100	20	Normal	—	○
Ice Punch	Ice	Physical	75	100	15	Normal	—	○
Icy Wind	Ice	Special	55	95	15	Many Others	—	—
Iron Tail	Steel	Physical	100	75	15	Normal	—	○
Aqua Tail	Water	Physical	90	90	10	Normal	—	○
Snore	Normal	Special	40	100	15	Normal	—	—
Sleep Talk	Normal	Status	—	—	10	Self	—	—

Pokémon AR Marker

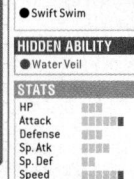

420
Cherubi

Cherry Pokémon
420 Cherubi

TYPE Grass

ABILITY
● Chlorophyll

HIDDEN ABILITY
___

● HEIGHT: 1'04"
● WEIGHT: 7.3 lbs.
● GENDER: ♂ / ♀

The small ball is not only filled with nutrients, it is also tasty. Starly try to peck it off.

STATS
HP
Attack
Defense
Sp. Atk
Sp. Def
Speed

EGG GROUPS
Fairy/Grass

ITEMS SOMETIMES HELD
● None

Same form for ♂/♀

Pokémon AR Marker

EVOLUTION

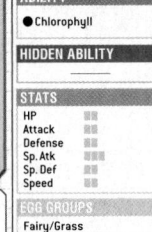

Cherubi → Lv. 25 → Cherrim

HOW TO OBTAIN

Pokémon Black Version 2	Link Trade or Poké Transfer
Pokémon White Version 2	Link Trade or Poké Transfer

HOW TO OBTAIN FROM OTHER GAMES

Pokémon HeartGold Version	National Park (use Headbutt)
Pokémon SoulSilver Version	National Park (use Headbutt)

LEVEL-UP AND LEARNED MOVES

Lv.	Name	Type	Kind	Pow.	Acc.	PP	Range	Long	DA
1	Morning Sun	Normal	Status	—	—	5	Self	—	—
1	Tackle	Normal	Physical	50	100	35	Normal	—	○
7	Growth	Normal	Status	—	—	40	Self	—	—
10	Leech Seed	Grass	Status	—	90	10	Normal	—	—
13	Magical Leaf	Grass	Special	60	—	20	Normal	—	—
19	Helping Hand	Normal	Status	—	—	20	1 Ally	—	—
22	Sunny Day	Fire	Status	—	—	5	Both Sides	—	—
28	Worry Seed	Grass	Status	—	100	10	Normal	—	—
31	Take Down	Normal	Physical	90	85	20	Normal	—	○
37	SolarBeam	Grass	Special	120	100	10	Normal	—	—
40	Lucky Chant	Normal	Status	—	—	30	Your Side	—	—

TM & HM MOVES

Lv.	Name	Type	Kind	Pow.	Acc.	PP	Range	Long	DA
TM06	Toxic	Poison	Status	—	90	10	Normal	—	—
TM10	Hidden Power	Normal	Special	—	100	15	Normal	—	—
TM11	Sunny Day	Fire	Status	—	—	5	Both Sides	—	—
TM17	Protect	Normal	Status	—	—	10	Self	—	—
TM20	Safeguard	Normal	Status	—	—	25	Your Side	—	—
TM21	Frustration	Normal	Physical	—	100	20	Normal	—	○
TM22	SolarBeam	Grass	Special	120	100	10	Normal	—	—
TM27	Return	Normal	Physical	—	100	20	Normal	—	○
TM32	Double Team	Normal	Status	—	—	15	Self	—	—
TM42	Facade	Normal	Physical	70	100	20	Normal	—	○
TM44	Rest	Psychic	Status	—	—	10	Self	—	—
TM45	Attract	Normal	Status	—	100	15	Normal	—	—
TM48	Round	Normal	Special	60	100	15	Normal	—	—
TM53	Energy Ball	Grass	Special	80	100	10	Normal	—	—
TM70	Flash	Normal	Status	—	100	20	Normal	—	—
TM75	Swords Dance	Normal	Status	—	—	30	Self	—	—
TM86	Grass Knot	Grass	Special	—	100	20	Normal	—	○
TM87	Swagger	Normal	Status	—	90	15	Normal	—	—
TM90	Substitute	Normal	Status	—	—	10	Self	—	—

MOVES TAUGHT BY PEOPLE

Name	Type	Kind	Pow.	Acc.	PP	Range	Long	DA

MOVES TAUGHT BY MOVE TUTORS FOR SHARDS

Name	Type	Kind	Pow.	Acc.	PP	Range	Long	DA
Seed Bomb	Grass	Physical	80	100	15	Normal	—	—
Snore	Normal	Special	40	100	15	Normal	—	—
Synthesis	Grass	Status	—	—	5	Self	—	—
Giga Drain	Grass	Special	75	100	10	Normal	—	—
Worry Seed	Grass	Status	—	100	10	Normal	—	—
Helping Hand	Normal	Status	—	—	20	1 Ally	—	—
Sleep Talk	Normal	Status	—	—	10	Self	—	—

EGG MOVES

Name	Type	Kind	Pow.	Acc.	PP	Range	Long	DA
Razor Leaf	Grass	Physical	55	95	25	Many Others	—	—
Sweet Scent	Normal	Status	—	100	20	Many Others	—	—
Tickle	Normal	Status	—	100	20	Normal	—	—
Nature Power	Normal	Status	—	—	20	Varies	—	—
GrassWhistle	Grass	Status	—	55	15	Normal	—	—
Aromatherapy	Grass	Status	—	—	5	Your Party	—	—
Weather Ball	Normal	Special	50	100	10	Normal	—	—
Heal Pulse	Psychic	Status	—	—	10	Normal	○	—
Healing Wish	Psychic	Status	—	—	10	Self	—	—
Seed Bomb	Grass	Physical	80	100	15	Normal	—	—
Natural Gift	Normal	Physical	—	100	15	Normal	—	—
Defense Curl	Normal	Status	—	—	40	Self	—	—
Rollout	Rock	Physical	30	90	20	Normal	—	○

421
Cherrim

Blossom Pokémon
421 Cherrim

TYPE Grass

ABILITY
● Flower Gift

HIDDEN ABILITY
___

● HEIGHT: 1'08"
● WEIGHT: 20.5 lbs.
● GENDER: ♂ / ♀

If it senses strong sunlight, it opens its folded petals to absorb the sun's rays with its whole body.

STATS
HP
Attack
Defense
Sp. Atk
Sp. Def
Speed

EGG GROUPS
Fairy/Grass

ITEMS SOMETIMES HELD
● None

Overcast **Sunshine**

Overcast Form

Sunshine Form

Pokémon AR Marker

 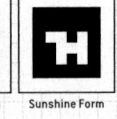

Overcast Form   Sunshine Form

EVOLUTION

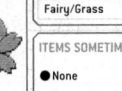

Cherubi → Lv. 25 → Cherrim

HOW TO OBTAIN

Pokémon Black Version 2	Link Trade or Poké Transfer
Pokémon White Version 2	Link Trade or Poké Transfer

HOW TO OBTAIN FROM OTHER GAMES

Pokémon Black Version	Route 12
Pokémon White Version	Route 12

LEVEL-UP AND LEARNED MOVES

Lv.	Name	Type	Kind	Pow.	Acc.	PP	Range	Long	DA
1	Morning Sun	Normal	Status	—	—	5	Self	—	—
1	Tackle	Normal	Physical	50	100	35	Normal	—	○
1	Growth	Normal	Status	—	—	40	Self	—	—
7	Growth	Normal	Status	—	—	40	Self	—	—
10	Leech Seed	Grass	Status	—	90	10	Normal	—	—
13	Helping Hand	Normal	Status	—	—	20	1 Ally	—	—
19	Magical Leaf	Grass	Special	60	—	20	Normal	—	—
22	Sunny Day	Fire	Status	—	—	5	Both Sides	—	—
25	Petal Dance	Grass	Special	120	100	10	1 Random	—	○
30	Worry Seed	Grass	Status	—	100	10	Normal	—	—
35	Take Down	Normal	Physical	90	85	20	Normal	—	○
43	SolarBeam	Grass	Special	120	100	10	Normal	—	—
48	Lucky Chant	Normal	Status	—	—	30	Your Side	—	—

TM & HM MOVES

Lv.	Name	Type	Kind	Pow.	Acc.	PP	Range	Long	DA
TM06	Toxic	Poison	Status	—	90	10	Normal	—	—
TM10	Hidden Power	Normal	Special	—	100	15	Normal	—	—
TM11	Sunny Day	Fire	Status	—	—	5	Both Sides	—	—
TM15	Hyper Beam	Normal	Special	150	90	5	Normal	—	—
TM17	Protect	Normal	Status	—	—	10	Self	—	—
TM20	Safeguard	Normal	Status	—	—	25	Your Side	—	—
TM21	Frustration	Normal	Physical	—	100	20	Normal	—	○
TM22	SolarBeam	Grass	Special	120	100	10	Normal	—	—
TM27	Return	Normal	Physical	—	100	20	Normal	—	○
TM32	Double Team	Normal	Status	—	—	15	Self	—	—
TM42	Facade	Normal	Physical	70	100	20	Normal	—	○
TM44	Rest	Psychic	Status	—	—	10	Self	—	—
TM45	Attract	Normal	Status	—	100	15	Normal	—	—
TM48	Round	Normal	Special	60	100	15	Normal	—	—
TM53	Energy Ball	Grass	Special	80	100	10	Normal	—	—
TM68	Giga Impact	Normal	Physical	150	90	5	Normal	—	○
TM70	Flash	Normal	Status	—	100	20	Normal	—	—
TM75	Swords Dance	Normal	Status	—	—	30	Self	—	—
TM86	Grass Knot	Grass	Special	—	100	20	Normal	—	○
TM87	Swagger	Normal	Status	—	90	15	Normal	—	—
TM90	Substitute	Normal	Status	—	—	10	Self	—	—

MOVES TAUGHT BY PEOPLE

Name	Type	Kind	Pow.	Acc.	PP	Range	Long	DA

MOVES TAUGHT BY MOVE TUTORS FOR SHARDS

Name	Type	Kind	Pow.	Acc.	PP	Range	Long	DA
Seed Bomb	Grass	Physical	80	100	15	Normal	—	—
Snore	Normal	Special	40	100	15	Normal	—	—
Synthesis	Grass	Status	—	—	5	Self	—	—
Giga Drain	Grass	Special	75	100	10	Normal	—	—
Worry Seed	Grass	Status	—	100	10	Normal	—	—
Helping Hand	Normal	Status	—	—	20	1 Ally	—	—
Sleep Talk	Normal	Status	—	—	10	Self	—	—

Sunshine Form

Overcast Form

◆ When the weather condition becomes Sunny from either Cherrim's move Sunny Day or the Drought Ability, it will change forms from Overcast Form to Sunshine Form.

422 Shellos

Sea Slug Pokémon

TYPE Water

ABILITIES
- Sticky Hold
- Storm Drain

HIDDEN ABILITY
- Sand Force

- HEIGHT: 1'00"
- WEIGHT: 13.9 lbs.
- GENDER: ♂ / ♀

Beware of pushing strongly on its squishy body, as it makes a mysterious purple fluid ooze out.

STATS
HP	■■■
Attack	■■
Defense	■■
Sp. Atk	■■
Sp. Def	■■■
Speed	■■

EGG GROUPS
Water ❶ /Amorphous

ITEMS SOMETIMES HELD
- None

West Sea **East Sea**

Pokémon AR Marker

West Sea | East Sea

West Sea
East Sea

⟳ EVOLUTION
Lv. 30
Lv. 30
Shellos | Gastrodon

HOW TO OBTAIN
Pokémon Black Version 2 — Trade Pokémon during a date with Yancy or Curtis (sixth time). If your character is a boy, you can receive Shellos (West Sea). If your character is a girl, you can receive Shellos (East Sea).

Pokémon White Version 2 — Trade Pokémon during a date with Yancy or Curtis (sixth time). If your character is a boy, you can receive Shellos (West Sea). If your character is a girl, you can receive Shellos (East Sea).

HOW TO OBTAIN FROM OTHER GAMES
Pokémon Platinum Version — Valley Windworks (West Sea)/Route 213 (East Sea)

LEVEL-UP AND LEARNED MOVES
Lv.	Name	Type	Kind	Pow.	Acc.	PP	Range	Long	DA
1	Mud-Slap	Ground	Special	20	100	10	Normal	—	—
2	Mud Sport	Ground	Status	—	—	15	Both Sides	—	—
4	Harden	Normal	Status	—	—	30	Self	—	—
7	Water Pulse	Water	Special	60	100	20	Normal	○	—
11	Mud Bomb	Ground	Special	65	85	10	Normal	—	—
16	Hidden Power	Normal	Special	—	100	15	Normal	—	—
22	Rain Dance	Water	Status	—	—	5	Both Sides	—	—
29	Body Slam	Normal	Physical	85	100	15	Normal	—	—
37	Muddy Water	Water	Special	95	85	10	Many Others	—	—
46	Recover	Normal	Status	—	—	10	Self	—	—

TM & HM MOVES
Lv.	Name	Type	Kind	Pow.	Acc.	PP	Range	Long	DA
TM06	Toxic	Poison	Status	—	90	10	Normal	—	—
TM07	Hail	Ice	Status	—	—	10	Both Sides	—	—
TM10	Hidden Power	Normal	Special	—	100	15	Normal	—	—
TM13	Ice Beam	Ice	Special	95	100	10	Normal	—	—
TM14	Blizzard	Ice	Special	120	70	5	Many Others	—	—
TM17	Protect	Normal	Status	—	—	10	Self	—	—
TM18	Rain Dance	Water	Status	—	—	5	Both Sides	—	—
TM21	Frustration	Normal	Physical	—	100	20	Normal	—	○
TM27	Return	Normal	Physical	—	100	20	Normal	—	○
TM32	Double Team	Normal	Status	—	—	15	Self	—	—
TM42	Facade	Normal	Physical	70	100	20	Normal	—	—
TM44	Rest	Psychic	Status	—	—	10	Self	—	—
TM45	Attract	Normal	Status	—	100	15	Normal	—	—
TM48	Round	Normal	Special	60	100	15	Normal	—	—
TM55	Scald	Water	Special	80	100	15	Normal	—	—
TM87	Swagger	Normal	Status	—	90	15	Normal	—	—
TM90	Substitute	Normal	Status	—	—	10	Self	—	—
HM03	Surf	Water	Special	95	100	15	Adjacent	—	—
HM06	Dive	Water	Physical	80	100	10	Normal	—	—

MOVES TAUGHT BY PEOPLE
Name	Type	Kind	Pow.	Acc.	PP	Range	Long	DA

MOVES TAUGHT BY MOVE TUTORS FOR SHARDS
Name	Type	Kind	Pow.	Acc.	PP	Range	Long	DA
Icy Wind	Ice	Special	55	95	15	Many Others	—	—
Earth Power	Ground	Special	90	100	10	Normal	—	—
Snore	Normal	Special	40	100	15	Normal	—	—
Pain Split	Normal	Status	—	—	20	Normal	—	—
Sleep Talk	Normal	Status	—	—	10	Self	—	—

EGG MOVES
Name	Type	Kind	Pow.	Acc.	PP	Range	Long	DA
Counter	Fighting	Physical	—	100	20	Varies	—	—
Mirror Coat	Psychic	Special	—	100	20	Varies	—	—
Stockpile	Normal	Status	—	—	20	Self	—	—
Swallow	Normal	Status	—	—	10	Self	—	—
Spit Up	Normal	Special	—	100	10	Normal	—	—
Yawn	Normal	Status	—	—	10	Normal	—	—
Memento	Dark	Status	—	100	10	Normal	—	—
Curse	Ghost	Status	—	—	10	Varies	—	—
Amnesia	Psychic	Status	—	—	20	Self	—	—
Fissure	Ground	Physical	—	30	5	Normal	—	—
Trump Card	Normal	Special	—	—	5	Normal	—	○
Sludge	Poison	Special	65	100	20	Normal	—	—
Clear Smog	Poison	Special	50	—	15	Normal	—	—
Brine	Water	Special	65	100	10	Normal	—	—
Mist	Ice	Status	—	—	30	Your Side	—	—

---

423 Gastrodon

Sea Slug Pokémon

TYPE Water Ground

ABILITIES
- Sticky Hold
- Storm Drain

HIDDEN ABILITY
- Sand Force

- HEIGHT: 2'11"
- WEIGHT: 65.9 lbs.
- GENDER: ♂ / ♀

Long ago, its entire back was shielded with a sturdy shell. There are traces of it left in its cells.

STATS
HP	■■■■
Attack	■■■
Defense	■■■
Sp. Atk	■■■
Sp. Def	■■■
Speed	■■

EGG GROUPS
Water ❶ /Amorphous

ITEMS SOMETIMES HELD
- None

West Sea **East Sea**

Pokémon AR Marker

West Sea | East Sea

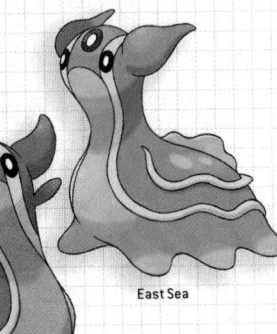

West Sea
East Sea

⟳ EVOLUTION
Lv. 30
Lv. 30
Shellos | Gastrodon

HOW TO OBTAIN
Pokémon Black Version 2 — Level up the Shellos you receive from Yancy or Curtis to Lv. 30

Pokémon White Version 2 — Level up the Shellos you receive from Yancy or Curtis to Lv. 30

HOW TO OBTAIN FROM OTHER GAMES
Pokémon Platinum Version — Route 218 (West Sea)/Route 224 (East Sea)

LEVEL-UP AND LEARNED MOVES
Lv.	Name	Type	Kind	Pow.	Acc.	PP	Range	Long	DA
1	Mud-Slap	Ground	Special	20	100	10	Normal	—	—
1	Mud Sport	Ground	Status	—	—	15	Both Sides	—	—
1	Harden	Normal	Status	—	—	30	Self	—	—
1	Water Pulse	Water	Special	60	100	20	Normal	○	—
2	Mud Sport	Ground	Status	—	—	15	Both Sides	—	—
4	Harden	Normal	Status	—	—	30	Self	—	—
7	Water Pulse	Water	Special	60	100	20	Normal	○	—
11	Mud Bomb	Ground	Special	65	85	10	Normal	—	—
16	Hidden Power	Normal	Special	—	100	15	Normal	—	—
22	Rain Dance	Water	Status	—	—	5	Both Sides	—	—
29	Body Slam	Normal	Physical	85	100	15	Normal	—	—
41	Muddy Water	Water	Special	95	85	10	Many Others	—	—
54	Recover	Normal	Status	—	—	10	Self	—	—

TM & HM MOVES
Lv.	Name	Type	Kind	Pow.	Acc.	PP	Range	Long	DA
TM06	Toxic	Poison	Status	—	90	10	Normal	—	—
TM07	Hail	Ice	Status	—	—	10	Both Sides	—	—
TM10	Hidden Power	Normal	Special	—	100	15	Normal	—	—
TM13	Ice Beam	Ice	Special	95	100	10	Normal	—	—
TM14	Blizzard	Ice	Special	120	70	5	Many Others	—	—
TM15	Hyper Beam	Normal	Special	150	90	5	Normal	—	—
TM17	Protect	Normal	Status	—	—	10	Self	—	—
TM18	Rain Dance	Water	Status	—	—	5	Both Sides	—	—
TM21	Frustration	Normal	Physical	—	100	20	Normal	—	○
TM26	Earthquake	Ground	Physical	100	100	10	Adjacent	—	—
TM27	Return	Normal	Physical	—	100	20	Normal	—	○
TM28	Dig	Ground	Physical	80	100	10	Normal	—	—
TM32	Double Team	Normal	Status	—	—	15	Self	—	—
TM34	Sludge Wave	Poison	Special	95	100	10	Adjacent	—	—
TM36	Sludge Bomb	Poison	Special	90	100	10	Normal	—	—
TM37	Sandstorm	Rock	Status	—	—	10	Both Sides	—	—
TM39	Rock Tomb	Rock	Physical	50	80	10	Normal	—	—
TM42	Facade	Normal	Physical	70	100	20	Normal	—	—
TM44	Rest	Psychic	Status	—	—	10	Self	—	—
TM45	Attract	Normal	Status	—	100	15	Normal	—	—
TM48	Round	Normal	Special	60	100	15	Normal	—	—
TM55	Scald	Water	Special	80	100	15	Normal	—	—
TM68	Giga Impact	Normal	Physical	150	90	5	Normal	—	—
TM70	Flash	Normal	Status	—	100	20	Normal	—	—
TM71	Stone Edge	Rock	Physical	100	80	5	Normal	—	—
TM78	Bulldoze	Ground	Physical	60	100	20	Adjacent	—	—
TM80	Rock Slide	Rock	Physical	75	90	10	Many Others	—	—
TM87	Swagger	Normal	Status	—	90	15	Normal	—	—
TM90	Substitute	Normal	Status	—	—	10	Self	—	—
TM94	Rock Smash	Fighting	Physical	40	100	15	Normal	—	—
HM03	Surf	Water	Special	95	100	15	Adjacent	—	—
HM04	Strength	Normal	Physical	80	100	15	Normal	—	—
HM05	Waterfall	Water	Physical	80	100	15	Normal	—	—
HM06	Dive	Water	Physical	80	100	10	Normal	—	—

MOVES TAUGHT BY PEOPLE
Name	Type	Kind	Pow.	Acc.	PP	Range	Long	DA

MOVES TAUGHT BY MOVE TUTORS FOR SHARDS
Name	Type	Kind	Pow.	Acc.	PP	Range	Long	DA
Block	Normal	Status	—	—	5	Normal	—	—
Icy Wind	Ice	Special	55	95	15	Many Others	—	—
Earth Power	Ground	Special	90	100	10	Normal	—	—
Snore	Normal	Special	40	100	15	Normal	—	—
Pain Split	Normal	Status	—	—	20	Normal	—	—
Sleep Talk	Normal	Status	—	—	10	Self	—	—

Long Tail Pokémon

424 Ambipom

- HEIGHT: 3'11"
- WEIGHT: 44.8 lbs.
- GENDER: ♂ / ♀

Split into two, the tails are so adept at handling and doing things, Ambipom rarely uses its hands.

♂ ♀

TYPE Normal

ABILITIES
- Technician
- Pickup

HIDDEN ABILITY
—

STATS
HP
Attack
Defense
Sp. Atk
Sp. Def
Speed

EGG GROUPS
Field

ITEMS SOMETIMES HELD
- None

Pokémon AR Marker

EVOLUTION

Aipom

➡ p. 108

Level up Aipom to Lv. 32 and teach it Double Hit, or level it up once it knows Double Hit

Ambipom

HOW TO OBTAIN

Pokémon Black Version 2	Trade an Excadrill to a woman in Accumula Town
Pokémon White Version 2	Trade an Excadrill to a woman in Accumula Town

HOW TO OBTAIN FROM OTHER GAMES

—

—

LEVEL-UP AND LEARNED MOVES

Lv.	Name	Type	Kind	Pow.	Acc.	PP	Range	Long	DA
1	Scratch	Normal	Physical	40	100	35	Normal	—	○
1	Tail Whip	Normal	Status	—	100	30	Many Others	—	—
1	Sand-Attack	Ground	Status	—	100	15	Normal	—	—
1	Astonish	Ghost	Physical	30	100	15	Normal	—	○
4	Sand-Attack	Ground	Status	—	100	15	Normal	—	—
8	Astonish	Ghost	Physical	30	100	15	Normal	—	○
11	Baton Pass	Normal	Status	—	—	40	Self	—	—
15	Tickle	Normal	Status	—	100	20	Normal	—	—
18	Fury Swipes	Normal	Physical	18	80	15	Normal	—	○
22	Swift	Normal	Special	60	—	20	Many Others	—	—
25	Screech	Normal	Status	—	85	40	Normal	—	—
29	Agility	Psychic	Status	—	—	30	Self	—	—
32	Double Hit	Normal	Physical	35	90	10	Normal	—	○
36	Fling	Dark	Physical	—	100	10	Normal	—	—
39	Nasty Plot	Dark	Status	—	—	20	Self	—	—
43	Last Resort	Normal	Physical	140	100	5	Normal	—	○

TM & HM MOVES

Lv.	Name	Type	Kind	Pow.	Acc.	PP	Range	Long	DA
TM01	Hone Claws	Dark	Status	—	—	15	Self	—	—
TM06	Toxic	Poison	Status	—	90	10	Normal	—	—
TM10	Hidden Power	Normal	Special	—	100	15	Normal	—	—
TM11	Sunny Day	Fire	Status	—	—	5	Both Sides	—	—
TM12	Taunt	Dark	Status	—	100	20	Normal	—	—
TM15	Hyper Beam	Normal	Special	150	90	5	Normal	—	—
TM17	Protect	Normal	Status	—	—	10	Self	—	—
TM18	Rain Dance	Water	Status	—	—	5	Both Sides	—	—
TM21	Frustration	Normal	Physical	—	100	20	Normal	—	○
TM22	SolarBeam	Grass	Special	120	100	10	Normal	—	—
TM24	Thunderbolt	Electric	Special	95	100	15	Normal	—	—
TM25	Thunder	Electric	Special	120	70	10	Normal	—	—
TM27	Return	Normal	Physical	—	100	20	Normal	—	○
TM28	Dig	Ground	Physical	80	100	10	Normal	—	○
TM30	Shadow Ball	Ghost	Special	80	100	15	Normal	—	—
TM31	Brick Break	Fighting	Physical	75	100	15	Normal	—	○
TM32	Double Team	Normal	Status	—	—	15	Self	—	—
TM40	Aerial Ace	Flying	Physical	60	—	20	Normal	○	○
TM42	Facade	Normal	Physical	70	100	20	Normal	—	○
TM44	Rest	Psychic	Status	—	—	10	Self	—	—
TM45	Attract	Normal	Status	—	100	15	Normal	—	—
TM46	Thief	Dark	Physical	40	100	10	Normal	—	○
TM47	Low Sweep	Fighting	Physical	60	100	20	Normal	—	○
TM48	Round	Normal	Special	60	100	15	Normal	—	—
TM56	Fling	Dark	Physical	—	100	10	Normal	—	—
TM62	Acrobatics	Flying	Physical	55	100	15	Normal	○	○
TM65	Shadow Claw	Ghost	Physical	70	100	15	Normal	—	○
TM66	Payback	Dark	Physical	50	100	10	Normal	—	○
TM67	Retaliate	Normal	Physical	70	100	5	Normal	—	○
TM68	Giga Impact	Normal	Physical	150	90	5	Normal	—	○
TM73	Thunder Wave	Electric	Status	—	100	20	Normal	—	—
TM83	Work Up	Normal	Status	—	—	30	Self	—	—
TM85	Dream Eater	Psychic	Special	100	100	15	Normal	—	—
TM86	Grass Knot	Grass	Special	—	100	20	Normal	—	○
TM87	Swagger	Normal	Status	—	90	15	Normal	—	—
TM89	U-turn	Bug	Physical	70	100	20	Normal	—	○
TM90	Substitute	Normal	Status	—	—	10	Self	—	—
TM94	Rock Smash	Fighting	Physical	40	100	15	Normal	—	○
HM01	Cut	Normal	Physical	50	95	30	Normal	—	○
HM04	Strength	Normal	Physical	80	100	15	Normal	—	○

MOVES TAUGHT BY PEOPLE

Name	Type	Kind	Pow.	Acc.	PP	Range	Long	DA

MOVES TAUGHT BY MOVE TUTORS FOR SHARDS

Name	Type	Kind	Pow.	Acc.	PP	Range	Long	DA
Covet	Normal	Physical	60	100	40	Normal	—	○
Bounce	Flying	Physical	85	85	5	Normal	○	○
Uproar	Normal	Special	90	100	10	1 Random	—	—
Seed Bomb	Grass	Physical	80	100	15	Normal	—	—
Low Kick	Fighting	Physical	—	100	20	Normal	—	○
Gunk Shot	Poison	Physical	120	70	5	Normal	—	—
Fire Punch	Fire	Physical	75	100	15	Normal	—	○
ThunderPunch	Electric	Physical	75	100	15	Normal	—	○
Ice Punch	Ice	Physical	75	100	15	Normal	—	○
Last Resort	Normal	Physical	140	100	5	Normal	—	○
Iron Tail	Steel	Physical	100	75	15	Normal	—	○
Foul Play	Dark	Physical	95	100	15	Normal	—	○
Snore	Normal	Special	40	100	15	Normal	—	—
Knock Off	Dark	Physical	20	100	20	Normal	—	○
Role Play	Psychic	Status	—	—	10	Normal	—	—
Spite	Ghost	Status	—	100	10	Normal	—	—
Sleep Talk	Normal	Status	—	—	10	Self	—	—
Snatch	Dark	Status	—	—	10	Self	—	—

Balloon Pokémon

425 Drifloon

- HEIGHT: 1'04"
- WEIGHT: 2.6 lbs.
- GENDER: ♂ / ♀

These Pokémon are called the "Signpost for Wandering Spirits." Children holding them sometimes vanish.

Same form for ♂ / ♀

TYPE Ghost Flying

ABILITIES
- Aftermath
- Unburden

HIDDEN ABILITY
- Flare Boost

STATS
HP
Attack
Defense
Sp. Atk
Sp. Def
Speed

EGG GROUPS
Amorphous

ITEMS SOMETIMES HELD
- None

Pokémon AR Marker

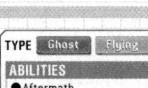

EVOLUTION

Drifloon

Lv. 28

Drifblim

HOW TO OBTAIN

Pokémon Black Version 2	Route 13 (Hidden Grotto)
Pokémon White Version 2	Route 13 (Hidden Grotto)

HOW TO OBTAIN FROM OTHER GAMES

—

—

LEVEL-UP AND LEARNED MOVES

Lv.	Name	Type	Kind	Pow.	Acc.	PP	Range	Long	DA
1	Constrict	Normal	Physical	10	100	35	Normal	—	○
1	Minimize	Normal	Status	—	—	20	Self	—	—
4	Astonish	Ghost	Physical	30	100	15	Normal	—	○
8	Gust	Flying	Special	40	100	35	Normal	○	—
13	Focus Energy	Normal	Status	—	—	30	Self	—	—
16	Payback	Dark	Physical	50	100	10	Normal	—	○
20	Ominous Wind	Ghost	Special	60	100	5	Normal	—	—
25	Stockpile	Normal	Status	—	—	20	Self	—	—
27	Hex	Ghost	Special	50	100	10	Normal	—	—
32	Swallow	Normal	Status	—	—	10	Self	—	—
32	Spit Up	Normal	Special	—	100	10	Normal	—	—
36	Shadow Ball	Ghost	Special	80	100	15	Normal	—	—
40	Amnesia	Psychic	Status	—	—	20	Self	—	—
44	Baton Pass	Normal	Status	—	—	40	Self	—	—
50	Explosion	Normal	Physical	250	100	5	Adjacent	—	—

TM & HM MOVES

Lv.	Name	Type	Kind	Pow.	Acc.	PP	Range	Long	DA
TM04	Calm Mind	Psychic	Status	—	—	20	Self	—	—
TM06	Toxic	Poison	Status	—	90	10	Normal	—	—
TM10	Hidden Power	Normal	Special	—	100	15	Normal	—	—
TM11	Sunny Day	Fire	Status	—	—	5	Both Sides	—	—
TM17	Protect	Normal	Status	—	—	10	Self	—	—
TM18	Rain Dance	Water	Status	—	—	5	Both Sides	—	—
TM19	Telekinesis	Psychic	Status	—	—	15	Normal	—	—
TM21	Frustration	Normal	Physical	—	100	20	Normal	—	○
TM24	Thunderbolt	Electric	Special	95	100	15	Normal	—	—
TM25	Thunder	Electric	Special	120	70	10	Normal	—	—
TM27	Return	Normal	Physical	—	100	20	Normal	—	○
TM29	Psychic	Psychic	Special	90	100	10	Normal	—	—
TM30	Shadow Ball	Ghost	Special	80	100	15	Normal	—	—
TM32	Double Team	Normal	Status	—	—	15	Self	—	—
TM42	Facade	Normal	Physical	70	100	20	Normal	—	○
TM44	Rest	Psychic	Status	—	—	10	Self	—	—
TM45	Attract	Normal	Status	—	100	15	Normal	—	—
TM46	Thief	Dark	Physical	40	100	10	Normal	—	○
TM48	Round	Normal	Special	60	100	15	Normal	—	—
TM57	Charge Beam	Electric	Special	50	90	10	Normal	—	—
TM61	Will-O-Wisp	Fire	Status	—	75	15	Normal	—	—
TM62	Acrobatics	Flying	Physical	55	100	15	Normal	○	○
TM63	Embargo	Dark	Status	—	100	15	Normal	—	—
TM64	Explosion	Normal	Physical	250	100	5	Adjacent	—	—
TM66	Payback	Dark	Physical	50	100	10	Normal	—	○
TM70	Flash	Normal	Status	—	100	20	Normal	—	—
TM73	Thunder Wave	Electric	Status	—	100	20	Normal	—	—
TM74	Gyro Ball	Steel	Physical	—	100	5	Normal	—	○
TM77	Psych Up	Normal	Status	—	—	10	Normal	—	—
TM85	Dream Eater	Psychic	Special	100	100	15	Normal	—	—
TM87	Swagger	Normal	Status	—	90	15	Normal	—	—
TM90	Substitute	Normal	Status	—	—	10	Self	—	—
HM01	Cut	Normal	Physical	50	95	30	Normal	—	○

MOVES TAUGHT BY PEOPLE

Name	Type	Kind	Pow.	Acc.	PP	Range	Long	DA

MOVES TAUGHT BY MOVE TUTORS FOR SHARDS

Name	Type	Kind	Pow.	Acc.	PP	Range	Long	DA
Magic Coat	Psychic	Status	—	—	15	Self	—	—
Icy Wind	Ice	Special	55	95	15	Many Others	—	—
Bind	Normal	Physical	15	85	20	Normal	—	○
Snore	Normal	Special	40	100	15	Normal	—	—
Knock Off	Dark	Physical	20	100	20	Normal	—	○
Pain Split	Normal	Status	—	—	20	Normal	—	—
Tailwind	Flying	Status	—	—	30	Your Side	—	—
Spite	Ghost	Status	—	100	10	Normal	—	—
Recycle	Normal	Status	—	—	10	Self	—	—
Trick	Psychic	Status	—	100	10	Normal	—	—
Sleep Talk	Normal	Status	—	—	10	Self	—	—
Skill Swap	Psychic	Status	—	—	10	Normal	—	—

EGG MOVES

Name	Type	Kind	Pow.	Acc.	PP	Range	Long	DA
Memento	Dark	Status	—	100	10	Normal	—	—
Body Slam	Normal	Physical	85	100	15	Normal	—	○
Destiny Bond	Ghost	Status	—	—	5	Self	—	—
Disable	Normal	Status	—	100	20	Normal	—	—
Haze	Ice	Status	—	—	30	Both Sides	—	—
Hypnosis	Psychic	Status	—	60	20	Normal	—	—
Weather Ball	Normal	Special	50	100	10	Normal	—	—
Clear Smog	Poison	Special	50	—	15	Normal	—	—
Defog	Flying	Status	—	—	15	Normal	—	—

426 Drifblim

Blimp Pokémon

- HEIGHT: 3'11"
- WEIGHT: 33.1 lbs.
- GENDER: ♂ / ♀

They carry people and Pokémon, but the wind can catch them, so there can't be a fixed destination.

Same form for ♂ / ♀

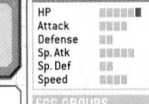

TYPE: Ghost / Flying

ABILITIES
- Aftermath
- Unburden

HIDDEN ABILITY
- Flare Boost

STATS
HP
Attack
Defense
Sp. Atk
Sp. Def
Speed

EGG GROUPS
Amorphous

ITEMS SOMETIMES HELD
- Air Balloon

Pokémon AR Marker

EVOLUTION

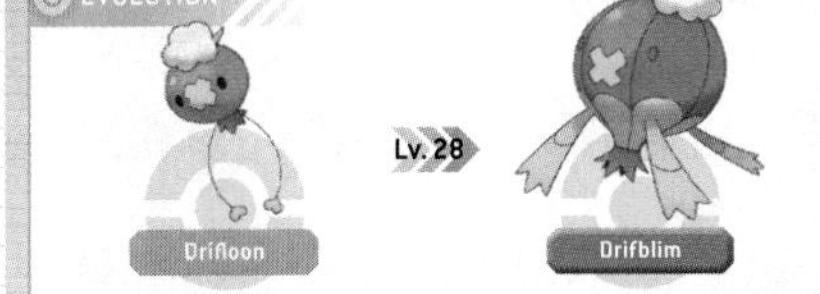
Drifloon
Lv. 28
Drifblim

HOW TO OBTAIN

Pokémon Black Version 2	❶ Reversal Mountain outside ❷ Route 14
Pokémon White Version 2	❶ Reversal Mountain outside ❷ Route 14

HOW TO OBTAIN FROM OTHER GAMES

—

—

LEVEL-UP AND LEARNED MOVES

Lv.	Name	Type	Kind	Pow.	Acc.	PP	Range	Long	DA
1	Constrict	Normal	Physical	10	100	35	Normal	—	○
1	Minimize	Normal	Status	—	—	20	Self	—	—
1	Astonish	Ghost	Physical	30	100	15	Normal	—	○
1	Gust	Flying	Special	40	100	35	Normal	○	—
4	Astonish	Ghost	Physical	30	100	15	Normal	—	○
8	Gust	Flying	Special	40	100	35	Normal	○	—
13	Focus Energy	Normal	Status	—	—	30	Self	—	—
16	Payback	Dark	Physical	50	100	10	Normal	—	○
20	Ominous Wind	Ghost	Special	60	100	5	Normal	—	—
25	Stockpile	Normal	Status	—	—	20	Self	—	—
27	Hex	Ghost	Special	50	100	10	Normal	—	—
34	Swallow	Normal	Status	—	—	10	Self	—	—
34	Spit Up	Normal	Special	—	100	10	Normal	—	—
40	Shadow Ball	Ghost	Special	80	100	15	Normal	—	—
46	Amnesia	Psychic	Status	—	—	20	Self	—	—
52	Baton Pass	Normal	Status	—	—	40	Self	—	—
60	Explosion	Normal	Physical	250	100	5	Adjacent	—	—

TM & HM MOVES

Lv.	Name	Type	Kind	Pow.	Acc.	PP	Range	Long	DA
TM04	Calm Mind	Psychic	Status	—	—	20	Self	—	—
TM06	Toxic	Poison	Status	—	90	10	Normal	—	—
TM10	Hidden Power	Normal	Special	—	100	15	Normal	—	—
TM11	Sunny Day	Fire	Status	—	—	5	Both Sides	—	—
TM15	Hyper Beam	Normal	Special	150	90	5	Normal	—	—
TM17	Protect	Normal	Status	—	—	10	Self	—	—
TM18	Rain Dance	Water	Status	—	—	5	Both Sides	—	—
TM19	Telekinesis	Psychic	Status	—	—	15	Normal	—	—
TM21	Frustration	Normal	Physical	—	100	20	Normal	—	○
TM24	Thunderbolt	Electric	Special	95	100	15	Normal	—	—
TM25	Thunder	Electric	Special	120	70	10	Normal	—	—
TM27	Return	Normal	Physical	—	100	20	Normal	—	○
TM29	Psychic	Psychic	Special	90	100	10	Normal	—	—
TM30	Shadow Ball	Ghost	Special	80	100	15	Normal	—	—
TM32	Double Team	Normal	Status	—	—	15	Self	—	—
TM42	Facade	Normal	Physical	70	100	20	Normal	—	○
TM44	Rest	Psychic	Status	—	—	10	Self	—	—
TM45	Attract	Normal	Status	—	100	15	Normal	—	—
TM46	Thief	Dark	Physical	40	100	10	Normal	—	○
TM48	Round	Normal	Special	60	100	15	Normal	—	—
TM57	Charge Beam	Electric	Special	50	90	10	Normal	—	—
TM61	Will-O-Wisp	Fire	Status	—	75	15	Normal	—	—
TM62	Acrobatics	Flying	Physical	55	100	15	Normal	○	○
TM63	Embargo	Dark	Status	—	100	15	Normal	—	—
TM64	Explosion	Normal	Physical	250	100	5	Adjacent	—	—
TM66	Payback	Dark	Physical	50	100	10	Normal	—	○
TM68	Giga Impact	Normal	Physical	150	90	5	Normal	—	○
TM70	Flash	Normal	Status	—	100	20	Normal	—	—
TM73	Thunder Wave	Electric	Status	—	100	20	Normal	—	—
TM74	Gyro Ball	Steel	Physical	—	100	5	Normal	—	○
TM77	Psych Up	Normal	Status	—	—	10	Normal	—	—
TM85	Dream Eater	Psychic	Special	100	100	15	Normal	—	—
TM87	Swagger	Normal	Status	—	90	15	Normal	—	—
TM90	Substitute	Normal	Status	—	—	10	Self	—	—
HM01	Cut	Normal	Physical	50	95	30	Normal	—	○
HM02	Fly	Flying	Physical	90	95	15	Normal	○	○

MOVES TAUGHT BY PEOPLE

Name	Type	Kind	Pow.	Acc.	PP	Range	Long	DA

MOVES TAUGHT BY MOVE TUTORS FOR SHARDS

Name	Type	Kind	Pow.	Acc.	PP	Range	Long	DA
Magic Coat	Psychic	Status	—	—	15	Self	—	—
Icy Wind	Ice	Special	55	95	15	Many Others	—	—
Bind	Normal	Physical	15	85	20	Normal	—	○
Snore	Normal	Special	40	100	15	Normal	—	—
Knock Off	Dark	Physical	20	100	20	Normal	—	○
Pain Split	Normal	Status	—	—	20	Normal	—	—
Tailwind	Flying	Status	—	—	30	Your Side	—	—
Spite	Ghost	Status	—	100	10	Normal	—	—
Recycle	Normal	Status	—	—	10	Self	—	—
Trick	Psychic	Status	—	100	10	Normal	—	—
Sleep Talk	Normal	Status	—	—	10	Self	—	—
Skill Swap	Psychic	Status	—	—	10	Normal	—	—

427 Buneary

Rabbit Pokémon

- HEIGHT: 1'04"
- WEIGHT: 12.1 lbs.
- GENDER: ♂ / ♀

By extending its rolled-up ears and striking the ground, it can bound so high it surprises itself.

Same form for ♂ / ♀

TYPE: Normal

ABILITIES
- Run Away
- Klutz

HIDDEN ABILITY
- Limber

STATS
HP
Attack
Defense
Sp. Atk
Sp. Def
Speed

EGG GROUPS
Field/Human-Like

ITEMS SOMETIMES HELD
- Pecha Berry

Pokémon AR Marker

EVOLUTION

Buneary
Level up with high friendship
Lopunny

HOW TO OBTAIN

Pokémon Black Version 2	Castelia City empty lot
Pokémon White Version 2	Link Trade or Poké Transfer

HOW TO OBTAIN FROM OTHER GAMES

Pokémon Platinum Version	Eterna Forest

—

LEVEL-UP AND LEARNED MOVES

Lv.	Name	Type	Kind	Pow.	Acc.	PP	Range	Long	DA
1	Splash	Normal	Status	—	—	40	Self	—	—
1	Pound	Normal	Physical	40	100	35	Normal	—	○
1	Defense Curl	Normal	Status	—	—	40	Self	—	—
1	Foresight	Normal	Status	—	—	40	Normal	—	—
6	Endure	Normal	Status	—	—	10	Self	—	—
13	Frustration	Normal	Physical	—	100	20	Normal	—	○
16	Quick Attack	Normal	Physical	40	100	30	Normal	—	○
23	Jump Kick	Fighting	Physical	100	95	10	Normal	—	○
26	Baton Pass	Normal	Status	—	—	40	Self	—	—
33	Agility	Psychic	Status	—	—	30	Self	—	—
36	Dizzy Punch	Normal	Physical	70	100	10	Normal	—	○
43	After You	Normal	Status	—	—	15	Normal	—	—
46	Charm	Normal	Status	—	100	20	Normal	—	—
53	Entrainment	Normal	Status	—	100	15	Normal	—	—
56	Bounce	Flying	Physical	85	85	5	Normal	○	○
63	Healing Wish	Psychic	Status	—	—	10	Self	—	—

TM & HM MOVES

Lv.	Name	Type	Kind	Pow.	Acc.	PP	Range	Long	DA
TM06	Toxic	Poison	Status	—	90	10	Normal	—	—
TM10	Hidden Power	Normal	Special	—	100	15	Normal	—	—
TM11	Sunny Day	Fire	Status	—	—	5	Both Sides	—	—
TM13	Ice Beam	Ice	Special	95	100	10	Normal	—	—
TM17	Protect	Normal	Status	—	—	10	Self	—	—
TM18	Rain Dance	Water	Status	—	—	5	Both Sides	—	—
TM21	Frustration	Normal	Physical	—	100	20	Normal	—	○
TM22	SolarBeam	Grass	Special	120	100	10	Normal	—	—
TM24	Thunderbolt	Electric	Special	95	100	15	Normal	—	—
TM27	Return	Normal	Physical	—	100	20	Normal	—	○
TM28	Dig	Ground	Physical	80	100	10	Normal	—	○
TM30	Shadow Ball	Ghost	Special	80	100	15	Normal	—	—
TM32	Double Team	Normal	Status	—	—	15	Self	—	—
TM42	Facade	Normal	Physical	70	100	20	Normal	—	○
TM44	Rest	Psychic	Status	—	—	10	Self	—	—
TM45	Attract	Normal	Status	—	100	15	Normal	—	—
TM48	Round	Normal	Special	60	100	15	Normal	—	—
TM56	Fling	Dark	Physical	—	100	10	Normal	—	—
TM57	Charge Beam	Electric	Special	50	90	10	Normal	—	—
TM67	Retaliate	Normal	Physical	70	100	5	Normal	—	○
TM73	Thunder Wave	Electric	Status	—	100	20	Normal	—	—
TM83	Work Up	Normal	Status	—	—	30	Self	—	—
TM86	Grass Knot	Grass	Special	—	100	20	Normal	—	○
TM87	Swagger	Normal	Status	—	90	15	Normal	—	—
TM90	Substitute	Normal	Status	—	—	10	Self	—	—
TM94	Rock Smash	Fighting	Physical	40	100	15	Normal	—	○
HM01	Cut	Normal	Physical	50	95	30	Normal	—	○

MOVES TAUGHT BY PEOPLE

Name	Type	Kind	Pow.	Acc.	PP	Range	Long	DA

MOVES TAUGHT BY MOVE TUTORS FOR SHARDS

Name	Type	Kind	Pow.	Acc.	PP	Range	Long	DA
Covet	Normal	Physical	60	100	40	Normal	—	○
Bounce	Flying	Physical	85	85	5	Normal	○	○
Uproar	Normal	Special	90	100	10	1 Random	—	—
Low Kick	Fighting	Physical	—	100	20	Normal	—	○
Fire Punch	Fire	Physical	75	100	15	Normal	—	○
ThunderPunch	Electric	Physical	75	100	15	Normal	—	○
Ice Punch	Ice	Physical	75	100	15	Normal	—	○
Last Resort	Normal	Physical	140	100	5	Normal	—	○
Magic Coat	Psychic	Status	—	—	15	Self	—	—
Hyper Voice	Normal	Special	90	100	10	Many Others	—	—
Iron Tail	Steel	Physical	100	75	15	Normal	—	○
Snore	Normal	Special	40	100	15	Normal	—	—
Heal Bell	Normal	Status	—	—	5	Your Party	—	—
Drain Punch	Fighting	Physical	75	100	10	Normal	—	○
Helping Hand	Normal	Status	—	—	20	1 Ally	—	—
After You	Normal	Status	—	—	15	Normal	—	—
Endeavor	Normal	Physical	—	100	5	Normal	—	○
Sleep Talk	Normal	Status	—	—	10	Self	—	—

EGG MOVES

Name	Type	Kind	Pow.	Acc.	PP	Range	Long	DA
Fake Tears	Dark	Status	—	100	20	Normal	—	—
Fake Out	Normal	Physical	40	100	10	Normal	—	○
Encore	Normal	Status	—	100	5	Normal	—	—
Sweet Kiss	Normal	Status	—	75	10	Normal	—	—
Double Hit	Normal	Physical	35	90	10	Normal	—	○
Low Kick	Fighting	Physical	—	100	20	Normal	—	○
Sky Uppercut	Fighting	Physical	85	90	15	Normal	—	○
Switcheroo	Dark	Status	—	100	10	Normal	—	—
ThunderPunch	Electric	Physical	75	100	15	Normal	—	○
Ice Punch	Ice	Physical	75	100	15	Normal	—	○
Fire Punch	Fire	Physical	75	100	15	Normal	—	○
Flail	Normal	Physical	—	100	15	Normal	—	○
Focus Punch	Fighting	Physical	150	100	20	Normal	—	○
Circle Throw	Fighting	Physical	60	90	10	Normal	—	○
Copycat	Normal	Status	—	—	20	Self	—	—

Rabbit Pokémon

428 Lopunny

- HEIGHT: 3'11"
- WEIGHT: 73.4 lbs.
- GENDER: ♂ / ♀

Extremely cautious, it quickly bounds off when it senses danger.

TYPE Normal

ABILITIES
- Cute Charm
- Klutz

HIDDEN ABILITY
- Limber

STATS
HP
Attack
Defense
Sp. Atk
Sp. Def
Speed

EGG GROUPS
Field/Human-Like

ITEMS SOMETIMES HELD
- Pecha Berry

Same form for ♂ / ♀

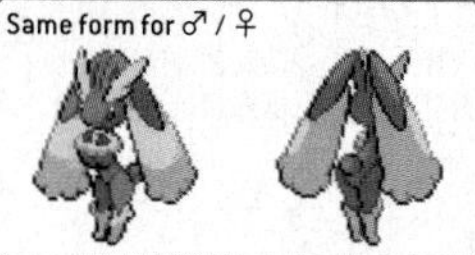

Pokémon AR Marker

EVOLUTION

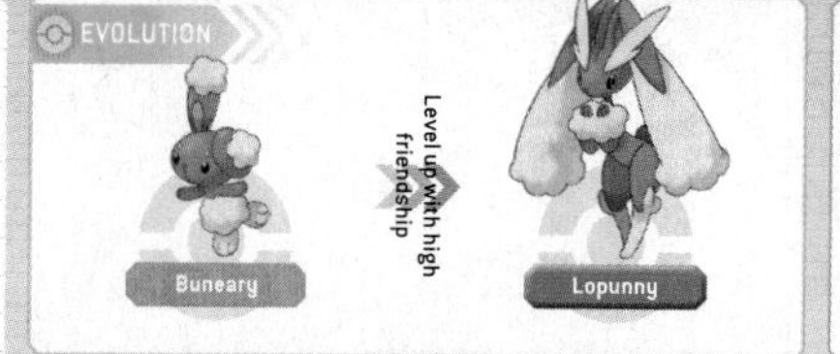

HOW TO OBTAIN

Pokémon Black Version 2	Castelia City empty lot (rustling grass)
Pokémon White Version 2	Level up a Buneary you obtain via Link Trade or Poké Transfer with high friendship

HOW TO OBTAIN FROM OTHER GAMES

—

—

LEVEL-UP AND LEARNED MOVES

Lv.	Name	Type	Kind	Pow.	Acc.	PP	Range	Long	DA
1	Mirror Coat	Psychic	Special	—	100	20	Varies	—	—
1	Magic Coat	Psychic	Status	—	—	15	Self	—	—
1	Splash	Normal	Status	—	—	40	Self	—	—
1	Pound	Normal	Physical	40	100	35	Normal	—	○
1	Defense Curl	Normal	Status	—	—	40	Self	—	—
1	Foresight	Normal	Status	—	—	40	Normal	—	—
6	Endure	Normal	Status	—	—	10	Self	—	—
13	Return	Normal	Physical	—	100	20	Normal	—	○
16	Quick Attack	Normal	Physical	40	100	30	Normal	—	○
23	Jump Kick	Fighting	Physical	100	95	10	Normal	—	○
26	Baton Pass	Normal	Status	—	—	40	Self	—	—
33	Agility	Psychic	Status	—	—	30	Self	—	—
36	Dizzy Punch	Normal	Physical	70	100	10	Normal	—	○
43	After You	Normal	Status	—	—	15	Normal	—	—
46	Charm	Normal	Status	—	100	20	Normal	—	—
53	Entrainment	Normal	Status	—	100	15	Normal	—	—
56	Bounce	Flying	Physical	85	85	5	Normal	○	○
63	Healing Wish	Psychic	Status	—	—	10	Self	—	—

TM & HM MOVES

Lv.	Name	Type	Kind	Pow.	Acc.	PP	Range	Long	DA
TM06	Toxic	Poison	Status	—	90	10	Normal	—	—
TM10	Hidden Power	Normal	Special	—	100	15	Normal	—	—
TM11	Sunny Day	Fire	Status	—	—	5	Both Sides	—	—
TM13	Ice Beam	Ice	Special	95	100	10	Normal	—	—
TM14	Blizzard	Ice	Special	120	70	5	Many Others	—	—
TM15	Hyper Beam	Normal	Special	150	90	5	Normal	—	—
TM17	Protect	Normal	Status	—	—	10	Self	—	—
TM18	Rain Dance	Water	Status	—	—	5	Both Sides	—	—
TM21	Frustration	Normal	Physical	—	100	20	Normal	—	○
TM22	SolarBeam	Grass	Special	120	100	10	Normal	—	—
TM24	Thunderbolt	Electric	Special	95	100	15	Normal	—	—
TM25	Thunder	Electric	Special	120	70	10	Normal	—	—
TM27	Return	Normal	Physical	—	100	20	Normal	—	○
TM28	Dig	Ground	Physical	80	100	10	Normal	—	○
TM30	Shadow Ball	Ghost	Special	80	100	15	Normal	—	—
TM32	Double Team	Normal	Status	—	—	15	Self	—	—
TM42	Facade	Normal	Physical	70	100	20	Normal	—	○
TM44	Rest	Psychic	Status	—	—	10	Self	—	—
TM45	Attract	Normal	Status	—	100	15	Normal	—	—
TM47	Low Sweep	Fighting	Physical	60	100	20	Normal	—	○
TM48	Round	Normal	Special	60	100	15	Normal	—	—
TM52	Focus Blast	Fighting	Special	120	70	5	Normal	—	—
TM56	Fling	Dark	Physical	—	100	10	Normal	—	—
TM57	Charge Beam	Electric	Special	50	90	10	Normal	—	—
TM67	Retaliate	Normal	Physical	70	100	5	Normal	—	○
TM68	Giga Impact	Normal	Physical	150	90	5	Normal	—	○
TM73	Thunder Wave	Electric	Status	—	100	20	Normal	—	—
TM83	Work Up	Normal	Status	—	—	30	Self	—	—
TM86	Grass Knot	Grass	Special	—	100	20	Normal	—	○
TM87	Swagger	Normal	Status	—	90	15	Normal	—	—
TM90	Substitute	Normal	Status	—	—	10	Self	—	—
TM94	Rock Smash	Fighting	Physical	40	100	15	Normal	—	○
HM01	Cut	Normal	Physical	50	95	30	Normal	—	○
HM04	Strength	Normal	Physical	80	100	15	Normal	—	○

MOVES TAUGHT BY PEOPLE

Name	Type	Kind	Pow.	Acc.	PP	Range	Long	DA

MOVES TAUGHT BY MOVE TUTORS FOR SHARDS

Name	Type	Kind	Pow.	Acc.	PP	Range	Long	DA
Covet	Normal	Physical	60	100	40	Normal	—	○
Bounce	Flying	Physical	85	85	5	Normal	○	○
Uproar	Normal	Special	90	100	10	1 Random	—	—
Low Kick	Fighting	Physical	—	100	20	Normal	—	○
Fire Punch	Fire	Physical	75	100	15	Normal	—	○
ThunderPunch	Electric	Physical	75	100	15	Normal	—	○
Ice Punch	Ice	Physical	75	100	15	Normal	—	○
Last Resort	Normal	Physical	140	100	5	Normal	—	○
Magic Coat	Psychic	Status	—	—	15	Self	—	—
Hyper Voice	Normal	Special	90	100	10	Many Others	—	—
Iron Tail	Steel	Physical	100	75	15	Normal	—	○
Snore	Normal	Special	40	100	15	Normal	—	—
Heal Bell	Normal	Status	—	—	5	Your Party	—	—
Drain Punch	Fighting	Physical	75	100	10	Normal	—	○
Helping Hand	Normal	Status	—	—	20	1 Ally	—	—
After You	Normal	Status	—	—	15	Normal	—	—
Endeavor	Normal	Physical	—	100	5	Normal	—	○
Sleep Talk	Normal	Status	—	—	10	Self	—	—

Magical Pokémon

429 Mismagius

- HEIGHT: 2'11"
- WEIGHT: 9.7 lbs.
- GENDER: ♂ / ♀

Its cry sounds like an incantation. It is said the cry may rarely be imbued with happiness-giving power.

TYPE Ghost

ABILITY
- Levitate

HIDDEN ABILITY
—

STATS
HP
Attack
Defense
Sp. Atk
Sp. Def
Speed

EGG GROUPS
Amorphous

ITEMS SOMETIMES HELD
- None

Same form for ♂ / ♀

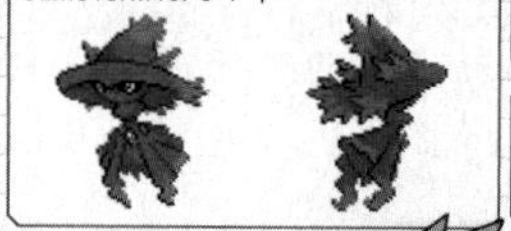

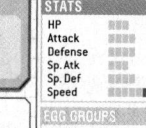

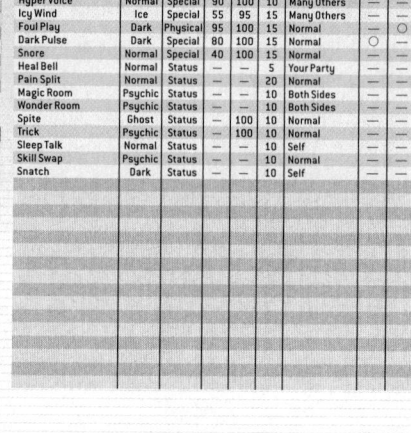

Pokémon AR Marker

EVOLUTION

➡ p. 113

HOW TO OBTAIN

Pokémon Black Version 2	Use Dusk Stone on a Misdreavus you obtain via Link Trade or Poké Transfer
Pokémon White Version 2	Use Dusk Stone on a Misdreavus you obtain via Link Trade or Poké Transfer

HOW TO OBTAIN FROM OTHER GAMES

Pokémon White Version	Abundant Shrine (rustling grass)

—

LEVEL-UP AND LEARNED MOVES

Lv.	Name	Type	Kind	Pow.	Acc.	PP	Range	Long	DA
1	Lucky Chant	Normal	Status	—	—	30	Your Side	—	—
1	Magical Leaf	Grass	Special	60	—	20	Normal	—	—
1	Growl	Normal	Status	—	100	40	Many Others	—	—
1	Psywave	Psychic	Special	—	80	15	Normal	—	—
1	Spite	Ghost	Status	—	100	10	Normal	—	—
1	Astonish	Ghost	Physical	30	100	15	Normal	—	○

TM & HM MOVES

Lv.	Name	Type	Kind	Pow.	Acc.	PP	Range	Long	DA
TM04	Calm Mind	Psychic	Status	—	—	20	Self	—	—
TM06	Toxic	Poison	Status	—	90	10	Normal	—	—
TM10	Hidden Power	Normal	Special	—	100	15	Normal	—	—
TM11	Sunny Day	Fire	Status	—	—	5	Both Sides	—	—
TM12	Taunt	Dark	Status	—	100	20	Normal	—	—
TM15	Hyper Beam	Normal	Special	150	90	5	Normal	—	—
TM17	Protect	Normal	Status	—	—	10	Self	—	—
TM18	Rain Dance	Water	Status	—	—	5	Both Sides	—	—
TM19	Telekinesis	Psychic	Status	—	—	15	Normal	—	—
TM21	Frustration	Normal	Physical	—	100	20	Normal	—	○
TM24	Thunderbolt	Electric	Special	95	100	15	Normal	—	—
TM25	Thunder	Electric	Special	120	70	10	Normal	—	—
TM27	Return	Normal	Physical	—	100	20	Normal	—	○
TM29	Psychic	Psychic	Special	90	100	10	Normal	—	—
TM30	Shadow Ball	Ghost	Special	80	100	15	Normal	—	—
TM32	Double Team	Normal	Status	—	—	15	Self	—	—
TM40	Aerial Ace	Flying	Physical	60	—	20	Normal	○	○
TM41	Torment	Dark	Status	—	100	15	Normal	—	—
TM42	Facade	Normal	Physical	70	100	20	Normal	—	○
TM44	Rest	Psychic	Status	—	—	10	Self	—	—
TM45	Attract	Normal	Status	—	100	15	Normal	—	—
TM46	Thief	Dark	Physical	40	100	10	Normal	—	○
TM48	Round	Normal	Special	60	100	15	Normal	—	—
TM49	Echoed Voice	Normal	Special	40	100	15	Normal	—	—
TM53	Energy Ball	Grass	Special	80	100	10	Normal	—	—
TM57	Charge Beam	Electric	Special	50	90	10	Normal	—	—
TM61	Will-O-Wisp	Fire	Status	—	75	15	Normal	—	—
TM63	Embargo	Dark	Status	—	100	15	Normal	—	—
TM66	Payback	Dark	Physical	50	100	10	Normal	—	○
TM68	Giga Impact	Normal	Physical	150	90	5	Normal	—	○
TM70	Flash	Normal	Status	—	100	20	Normal	—	—
TM73	Thunder Wave	Electric	Status	—	100	20	Normal	—	—
TM77	Psych Up	Normal	Status	—	—	10	Normal	—	—
TM85	Dream Eater	Psychic	Special	100	100	15	Normal	—	—
TM87	Swagger	Normal	Status	—	90	15	Normal	—	—
TM90	Substitute	Normal	Status	—	—	10	Self	—	—
TM92	Trick Room	Psychic	Status	—	—	5	Both Sides	—	—

MOVES TAUGHT BY PEOPLE

Name	Type	Kind	Pow.	Acc.	PP	Range	Long	DA

MOVES TAUGHT BY MOVE TUTORS FOR SHARDS

Name	Type	Kind	Pow.	Acc.	PP	Range	Long	DA
Uproar	Normal	Special	90	100	10	1 Random	—	—
Magic Coat	Psychic	Status	—	—	15	Self	—	—
Hyper Voice	Normal	Special	90	100	10	Many Others	—	—
Icy Wind	Ice	Special	55	95	15	Many Others	—	—
Foul Play	Dark	Physical	95	100	15	Normal	—	○
Dark Pulse	Dark	Special	80	100	15	Normal	○	—
Snore	Normal	Special	40	100	15	Normal	—	—
Heal Bell	Normal	Status	—	—	5	Your Party	—	—
Pain Split	Normal	Status	—	—	20	Normal	—	—
Magic Room	Psychic	Status	—	—	10	Both Sides	—	—
Wonder Room	Psychic	Status	—	—	10	Both Sides	—	—
Spite	Ghost	Status	—	100	10	Normal	—	—
Trick	Psychic	Status	—	100	10	Normal	—	—
Sleep Talk	Normal	Status	—	—	10	Self	—	—
Skill Swap	Psychic	Status	—	—	10	Normal	—	—
Snatch	Dark	Status	—	—	10	Self	—	—

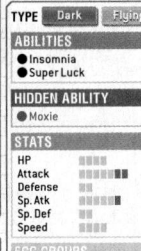

Big Boss Pokémon

430 Honchkrow

- HEIGHT: 2'11"
- WEIGHT: 60.2 lbs.
- GENDER: ♂ / ♀

If one utters a deep cry, many Murkrow gather quickly. For this, it is called "Summoner of Night."

Same form for ♂ / ♀

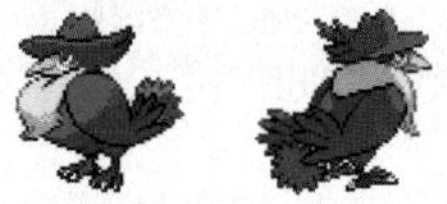

TYPE: Dark / Flying

ABILITIES
- Insomnia
- Super Luck

HIDDEN ABILITY
- Moxie

STATS
HP
Attack
Defense
Sp. Atk
Sp. Def
Speed

EGG GROUPS
Flying

ITEMS SOMETIMES HELD
- None

EVOLUTION

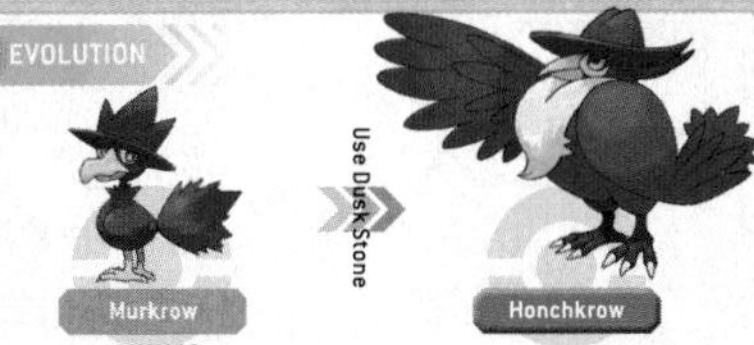

➡ p. 112

HOW TO OBTAIN

Pokémon Black Version 2	Use Dusk Stone on Murkrow
Pokémon White Version 2	Use Dusk Stone on Murkrow

HOW TO OBTAIN FROM OTHER GAMES

—
—

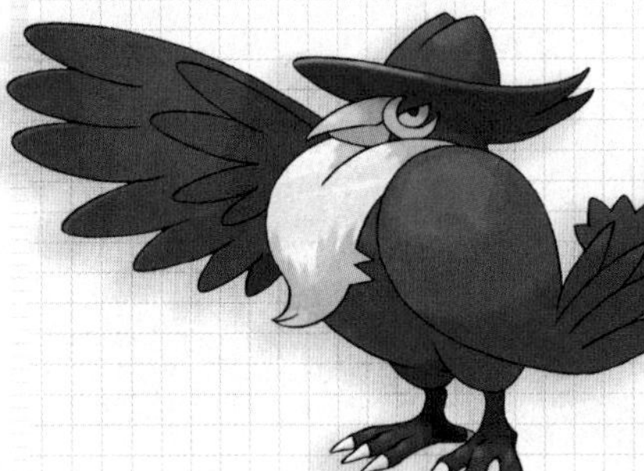

Pokémon AR Marker

LEVEL-UP AND LEARNED MOVES

Lv.	Name	Type	Kind	Pow.	Acc.	PP	Range	Long	DA
1	Astonish	Ghost	Physical	30	100	15	Normal	—	○
1	Pursuit	Dark	Physical	40	100	20	Normal	—	○
1	Haze	Ice	Status	—	—	30	Both Sides	—	—
1	Wing Attack	Flying	Physical	60	100	35	Normal	○	○
25	Swagger	Normal	Status	—	90	15	Normal	—	—
35	Nasty Plot	Dark	Status	—	—	20	Self	—	—
45	Foul Play	Dark	Physical	95	100	15	Normal	—	○
55	Night Slash	Dark	Physical	70	100	15	Normal	—	○
65	Quash	Dark	Status	—	100	15	Normal	—	—
75	Dark Pulse	Dark	Special	80	100	15	Normal	○	—

TM & HM MOVES

Lv.	Name	Type	Kind	Pow.	Acc.	PP	Range	Long	DA
TM04	Calm Mind	Psychic	Status	—	—	20	Self	—	—
TM06	Toxic	Poison	Status	—	90	10	Normal	—	—
TM10	Hidden Power	Normal	Special	—	100	15	Normal	—	—
TM11	Sunny Day	Fire	Status	—	—	5	Both Sides	—	—
TM12	Taunt	Dark	Status	—	100	20	Normal	—	—
TM15	Hyper Beam	Normal	Special	150	90	5	Normal	—	—
TM17	Protect	Normal	Status	—	—	10	Self	—	—
TM18	Rain Dance	Water	Status	—	—	5	Both Sides	—	—
TM21	Frustration	Normal	Physical	—	100	20	Normal	—	○
TM27	Return	Normal	Physical	—	100	20	Normal	—	○
TM29	Psychic	Psychic	Special	90	100	10	Normal	—	—
TM30	Shadow Ball	Ghost	Special	80	100	15	Normal	—	—
TM32	Double Team	Normal	Status	—	—	15	Self	—	—
TM40	Aerial Ace	Flying	Physical	60	—	20	Normal	○	○
TM41	Torment	Dark	Status	—	100	15	Normal	—	—
TM42	Facade	Normal	Physical	70	100	20	Normal	—	○
TM44	Rest	Psychic	Status	—	—	10	Self	—	—
TM45	Attract	Normal	Status	—	100	15	Normal	—	—
TM46	Thief	Dark	Physical	40	100	10	Normal	—	○
TM48	Round	Normal	Special	60	100	15	Normal	—	—
TM59	Incinerate	Fire	Special	30	100	15	Many Others	—	—
TM60	Quash	Dark	Status	—	100	15	Normal	—	—
TM63	Embargo	Dark	Status	—	100	15	Normal	—	—
TM66	Payback	Dark	Physical	50	100	10	Normal	—	○
TM67	Retaliate	Normal	Physical	70	100	5	Normal	—	○
TM68	Giga Impact	Normal	Physical	150	90	5	Normal	—	○
TM73	Thunder Wave	Electric	Status	—	100	20	Normal	—	—
TM77	Psych Up	Normal	Status	—	—	10	Normal	—	—
TM85	Dream Eater	Psychic	Special	100	100	15	Normal	—	—
TM87	Swagger	Normal	Status	—	90	15	Normal	—	—
TM88	Pluck	Flying	Physical	60	100	20	Normal	○	○
TM90	Substitute	Normal	Status	—	—	10	Self	—	—
TM95	Snarl	Dark	Special	55	95	15	Many Others	—	—
HM02	Fly	Flying	Physical	90	95	15	Normal	○	○

MOVES TAUGHT BY PEOPLE

Name	Type	Kind	Pow.	Acc.	PP	Range	Long	DA

MOVES TAUGHT BY MOVE TUTORS FOR SHARDS

Name	Type	Kind	Pow.	Acc.	PP	Range	Long	DA
Uproar	Normal	Special	90	100	10	1 Random	—	—
Icy Wind	Ice	Special	55	95	15	Many Others	—	—
Foul Play	Dark	Physical	95	100	15	Normal	—	○
Superpower	Fighting	Physical	120	100	5	Normal	—	○
Dark Pulse	Dark	Special	80	100	15	Normal	○	—
Roost	Flying	Status	—	—	10	Self	—	—
Sky Attack	Flying	Physical	140	90	5	Normal	○	—
Heat Wave	Fire	Special	100	90	10	Many Others	—	—
Tailwind	Flying	Status	—	—	30	Your Side	—	—
Spite	Ghost	Status	—	100	10	Normal	—	—
Sleep Talk	Normal	Status	—	—	10	Self	—	—
Snatch	Dark	Status	—	—	10	Self	—	—

Catty Pokémon

431 Glameow

- HEIGHT: 1'08"
- WEIGHT: 8.6 lbs.
- GENDER: ♂ / ♀

It hides its spiteful tendency of hooking its claws into the nose of its Trainer if it isn't fed.

Same form for ♂ / ♀

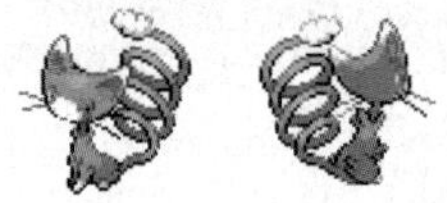

TYPE: Normal

ABILITIES
- Limber
- Own Tempo

HIDDEN ABILITY
- Keen Eye

STATS
HP
Attack
Defense
Sp. Atk
Sp. Def
Speed

EGG GROUPS
Field

ITEMS SOMETIMES HELD
- None

EVOLUTION

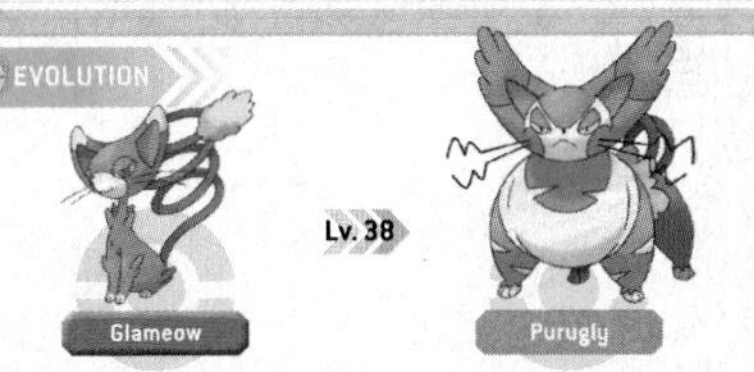

HOW TO OBTAIN

Pokémon Black Version 2	Link Trade or Poké Transfer
Pokémon White Version 2	Link Trade or Poké Transfer

HOW TO OBTAIN FROM OTHER GAMES

Pokémon Pearl Version	Route 218
—	

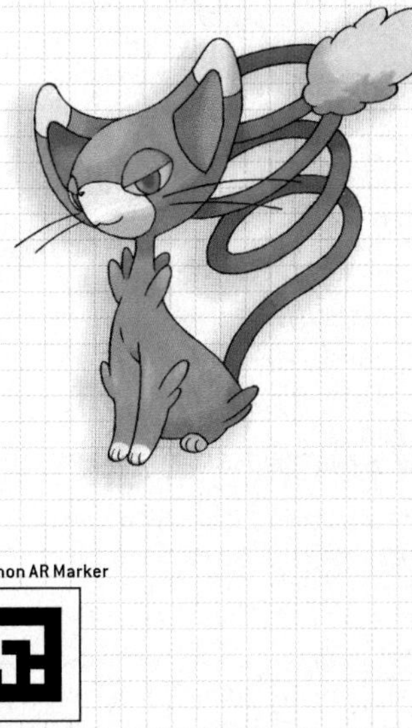

Pokémon AR Marker

LEVEL-UP AND LEARNED MOVES

Lv.	Name	Type	Kind	Pow.	Acc.	PP	Range	Long	DA
1	Fake Out	Normal	Physical	40	100	10	Normal	—	○
5	Scratch	Normal	Physical	40	100	35	Normal	—	○
8	Growl	Normal	Status	—	100	40	Many Others	—	—
13	Hypnosis	Psychic	Status	—	60	20	Normal	—	—
17	Faint Attack	Dark	Physical	60	—	20	Normal	—	○
20	Fury Swipes	Normal	Physical	18	80	15	Normal	—	○
25	Charm	Normal	Status	—	100	20	Normal	—	—
29	Assist	Normal	Status	—	—	20	Self	—	—
32	Captivate	Normal	Status	—	100	20	Many Others	—	—
37	Slash	Normal	Physical	70	100	20	Normal	—	○
41	Sucker Punch	Dark	Physical	80	100	5	Normal	—	○
44	Attract	Normal	Status	—	100	15	Normal	—	—
48	Hone Claws	Dark	Status	—	—	15	Self	—	—

TM & HM MOVES

Lv.	Name	Type	Kind	Pow.	Acc.	PP	Range	Long	DA
TM01	Hone Claws	Dark	Status	—	—	15	Self	—	—
TM06	Toxic	Poison	Status	—	90	10	Normal	—	—
TM10	Hidden Power	Normal	Special	—	100	15	Normal	—	—
TM11	Sunny Day	Fire	Status	—	—	5	Both Sides	—	—
TM12	Taunt	Dark	Status	—	100	20	Normal	—	—
TM17	Protect	Normal	Status	—	—	10	Self	—	—
TM18	Rain Dance	Water	Status	—	—	5	Both Sides	—	—
TM21	Frustration	Normal	Physical	—	100	20	Normal	—	○
TM24	Thunderbolt	Electric	Special	95	100	15	Normal	—	—
TM25	Thunder	Electric	Special	120	70	10	Normal	—	—
TM27	Return	Normal	Physical	—	100	20	Normal	—	○
TM28	Dig	Ground	Physical	80	100	10	Normal	—	○
TM30	Shadow Ball	Ghost	Special	80	100	15	Normal	—	—
TM32	Double Team	Normal	Status	—	—	15	Self	—	—
TM40	Aerial Ace	Flying	Physical	60	—	20	Normal	○	○
TM41	Torment	Dark	Status	—	100	15	Normal	—	—
TM42	Facade	Normal	Physical	70	100	20	Normal	—	○
TM44	Rest	Psychic	Status	—	—	10	Self	—	—
TM45	Attract	Normal	Status	—	100	15	Normal	—	—
TM46	Thief	Dark	Physical	40	100	10	Normal	—	○
TM48	Round	Normal	Special	60	100	15	Normal	—	—
TM49	Echoed Voice	Normal	Special	40	100	15	Normal	—	—
TM65	Shadow Claw	Ghost	Physical	70	100	15	Normal	—	○
TM66	Payback	Dark	Physical	50	100	10	Normal	—	○
TM67	Retaliate	Normal	Physical	70	100	5	Normal	—	○
TM70	Flash	Normal	Status	—	100	20	Normal	—	—
TM77	Psych Up	Normal	Status	—	—	10	Normal	—	—
TM83	Work Up	Normal	Status	—	—	30	Self	—	—
TM85	Dream Eater	Psychic	Special	100	100	15	Normal	—	—
TM87	Swagger	Normal	Status	—	90	15	Normal	—	—
TM89	U-turn	Bug	Physical	70	100	20	Normal	—	○
TM90	Substitute	Normal	Status	—	—	10	Self	—	—
HM01	Cut	Normal	Physical	50	95	30	Normal	—	○

MOVES TAUGHT BY PEOPLE

Name	Type	Kind	Pow.	Acc.	PP	Range	Long	DA

MOVES TAUGHT BY MOVE TUTORS FOR SHARDS

Name	Type	Kind	Pow.	Acc.	PP	Range	Long	DA
Covet	Normal	Physical	60	100	40	Normal	—	○
Super Fang	Normal	Physical	—	90	10	Normal	—	○
Last Resort	Normal	Physical	140	100	5	Normal	—	○
Hyper Voice	Normal	Special	90	100	10	Many Others	—	—
Iron Tail	Steel	Physical	100	75	15	Normal	—	○
Foul Play	Dark	Physical	95	100	15	Normal	—	○
Snore	Normal	Special	40	100	15	Normal	—	—
Knock Off	Dark	Physical	20	100	20	Normal	—	○
Sleep Talk	Normal	Status	—	—	10	Self	—	—
Snatch	Dark	Status	—	—	10	Self	—	—

EGG MOVES

Name	Type	Kind	Pow.	Acc.	PP	Range	Long	DA
Bite	Dark	Physical	60	100	25	Normal	—	○
Tail Whip	Normal	Status	—	100	30	Many Others	—	—
Quick Attack	Normal	Physical	40	100	30	Normal	—	○
Sand-Attack	Ground	Status	—	100	15	Normal	—	—
Fake Tears	Dark	Status	—	100	20	Normal	—	—
Assurance	Dark	Physical	50	100	10	Normal	—	○
Flail	Normal	Physical	—	100	15	Normal	—	○
Snatch	Dark	Status	—	—	10	Self	—	—
Wake-Up Slap	Fighting	Physical	60	100	10	Normal	—	○
Last Resort	Normal	Physical	140	100	5	Normal	—	○

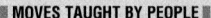

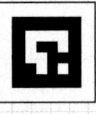

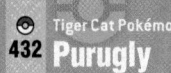

Tiger Cat Pokémon
432 Purugly

- HEIGHT: 3'03"
- WEIGHT: 96.6 lbs.
- GENDER: ♂ / ♀

It binds its body with its tails to make itself look bigger. If it locks eyes, it will glare ceaselessly.

Same form for ♂ / ♀

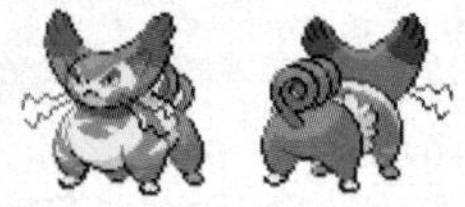

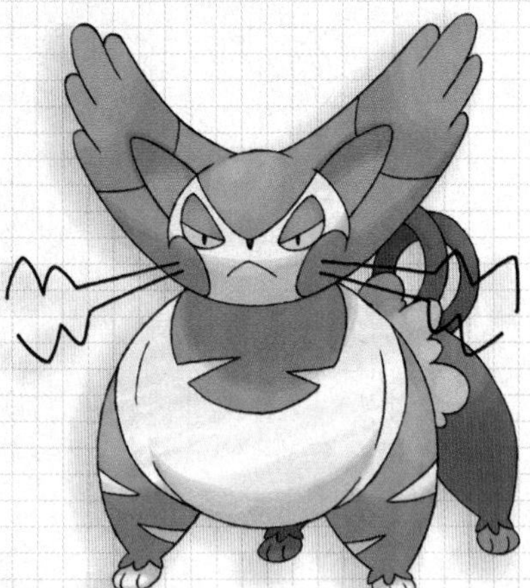

Pokémon AR Marker

TYPE Normal

ABILITIES
- Thick Fat
- Own Tempo

HIDDEN ABILITY
- Defiant

STATS
HP
Attack
Defense
Sp. Atk
Sp. Def
Speed

EGG GROUPS
Field

ITEMS SOMETIMES HELD
- None

EVOLUTION

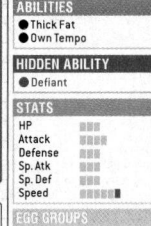

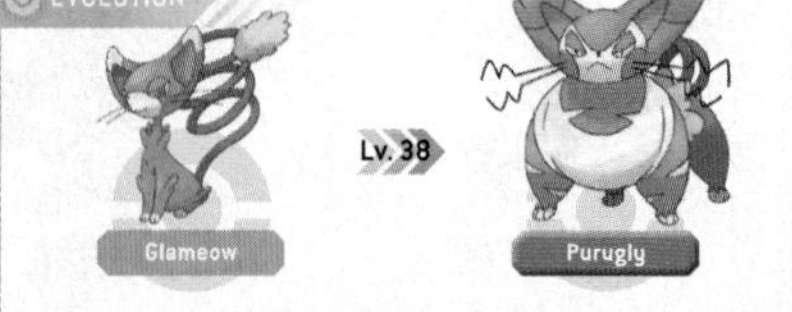
Glameow
Lv. 38
Purugly

HOW TO OBTAIN

Pokémon Black Version 2	Link Trade or Poké Transfer
Pokémon White Version 2	Link Trade or Poké Transfer

HOW TO OBTAIN FROM OTHER GAMES

Pokémon Pearl Version	Route 222

LEVEL-UP AND LEARNED MOVES

Lv.	Name	Type	Kind	Pow.	Acc.	PP	Range	Long	DA
1	Fake Out	Normal	Physical	40	100	10	Normal	—	○
1	Scratch	Normal	Physical	40	100	35	Normal	—	○
1	Growl	Normal	Status	—	100	40	Many Others	—	—
5	Scratch	Normal	Physical	40	100	35	Normal	—	○
8	Growl	Normal	Status	—	100	40	Many Others	—	—
13	Hypnosis	Psychic	Status	—	60	20	Normal	—	—
17	Faint Attack	Dark	Physical	60	—	20	Normal	—	○
20	Fury Swipes	Normal	Physical	18	80	15	Normal	—	○
25	Charm	Normal	Status	—	100	20	Normal	—	—
29	Assist	Normal	Status	—	—	20	Self	—	—
32	Captivate	Normal	Status	—	100	20	Many Others	—	—
37	Slash	Normal	Physical	70	100	20	Normal	—	○
38	Swagger	Normal	Status	—	90	15	Normal	—	—
45	Body Slam	Normal	Physical	85	100	15	Normal	—	○
52	Attract	Normal	Status	—	100	15	Normal	—	—
60	Hone Claws	Dark	Status	—	—	15	Self	—	—

TM & HM MOVES

Lv.	Name	Type	Kind	Pow.	Acc.	PP	Range	Long	DA
TM01	Hone Claws	Dark	Status	—	—	15	Self	—	—
TM05	Roar	Normal	Status	—	100	20	Normal	—	—
TM06	Toxic	Poison	Status	—	90	10	Normal	—	—
TM10	Hidden Power	Normal	Special	—	100	15	Normal	—	—
TM11	Sunny Day	Fire	Status	—	—	5	Both Sides	—	—
TM12	Taunt	Dark	Status	—	100	20	Normal	—	—
TM15	Hyper Beam	Normal	Special	150	90	5	Normal	—	—
TM17	Protect	Normal	Status	—	—	10	Self	—	—
TM18	Rain Dance	Water	Status	—	—	5	Both Sides	—	—
TM21	Frustration	Normal	Physical	—	100	20	Normal	—	○
TM24	Thunderbolt	Electric	Special	95	100	15	Normal	—	—
TM25	Thunder	Electric	Special	120	70	10	Normal	—	—
TM27	Return	Normal	Physical	—	100	20	Normal	—	○
TM28	Dig	Ground	Physical	80	100	10	Normal	—	○
TM30	Shadow Ball	Ghost	Special	80	100	15	Normal	—	—
TM32	Double Team	Normal	Status	—	—	15	Self	—	—
TM40	Aerial Ace	Flying	Physical	60	—	20	Normal	○	○
TM41	Torment	Dark	Status	—	100	15	Normal	—	—
TM42	Facade	Normal	Physical	70	100	20	Normal	—	○
TM44	Rest	Psychic	Status	—	—	10	Self	—	—
TM45	Attract	Normal	Status	—	100	15	Normal	—	—
TM46	Thief	Dark	Physical	40	100	10	Normal	—	○
TM48	Round	Normal	Special	60	100	15	Normal	—	—
TM49	Echoed Voice	Normal	Special	40	100	15	Normal	—	—
TM65	Shadow Claw	Ghost	Physical	70	100	15	Normal	—	○
TM66	Payback	Dark	Physical	50	100	10	Normal	—	○
TM67	Retaliate	Normal	Physical	70	100	5	Normal	—	○
TM68	Giga Impact	Normal	Physical	150	90	5	Normal	—	○
TM70	Flash	Normal	Status	—	100	20	Normal	—	—
TM77	Psych Up	Normal	Status	—	—	10	Normal	—	—
TM78	Bulldoze	Ground	Physical	60	100	20	Adjacent	—	—
TM83	Work Up	Normal	Status	—	—	30	Self	—	—
TM85	Dream Eater	Psychic	Special	100	100	15	Normal	—	—
TM87	Swagger	Normal	Status	—	90	15	Normal	—	—
TM89	U-turn	Bug	Physical	70	100	20	Normal	—	○
TM90	Substitute	Normal	Status	—	—	10	Self	—	—
HM01	Cut	Normal	Physical	50	95	30	Normal	—	○

MOVES TAUGHT BY PEOPLE

Name	Type	Kind	Pow.	Acc.	PP	Range	Long	DA

MOVES TAUGHT BY MOVE TUTORS FOR SHARDS

Name	Type	Kind	Pow.	Acc.	PP	Range	Long	DA
Covet	Normal	Physical	60	100	40	Normal	—	○
Super Fang	Normal	Physical	—	90	10	Normal	—	○
Last Resort	Normal	Physical	140	100	5	Normal	—	○
Hyper Voice	Normal	Special	90	100	10	Many Others	—	—
Iron Tail	Steel	Physical	100	75	15	Normal	—	○
Foul Play	Dark	Physical	95	100	15	Normal	—	○
Snore	Normal	Special	40	100	15	Normal	—	—
Knock Off	Dark	Physical	20	100	20	Normal	—	○
Sleep Talk	Normal	Status	—	—	10	Self	—	—
Snatch	Dark	Status	—	—	10	Self	—	—

Bell Pokémon
433 Chingling

- HEIGHT: 0'08"
- WEIGHT: 1.3 lbs.
- GENDER: ♂ / ♀

There is an orb inside its mouth. When it hops, the orb bounces all over and makes a ringing sound.

Same form for ♂ / ♀

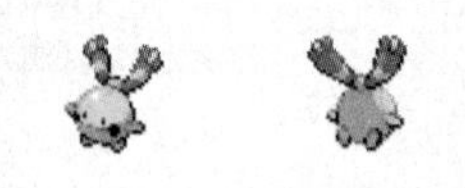

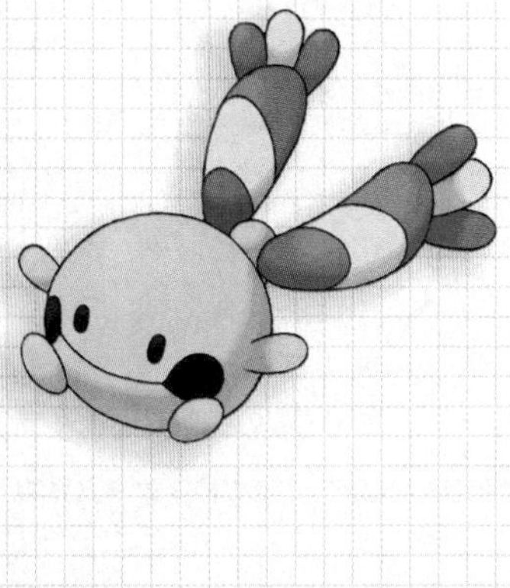

Pokémon AR Marker

TYPE Psychic

ABILITY
- Levitate

HIDDEN ABILITY
—

STATS
HP
Attack
Defense
Sp. Atk
Sp. Def
Speed

EGG GROUPS
No Egg has ever been discovered

ITEMS SOMETIMES HELD
- None

EVOLUTION

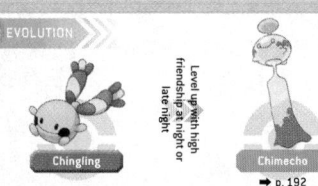

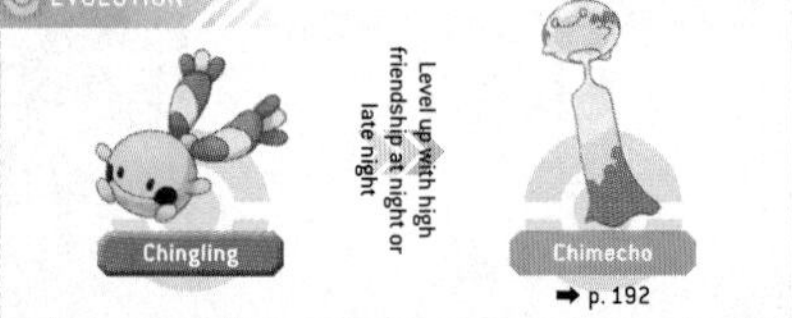
Chingling
Level up with high friendship at night or late night
Chimecho

➡ p. 192

HOW TO OBTAIN

Pokémon Black Version 2	Link Trade or Poké Transfer
Pokémon White Version 2	Link Trade or Poké Transfer

HOW TO OBTAIN FROM OTHER GAMES

Pokémon Platinum Version	Route 211

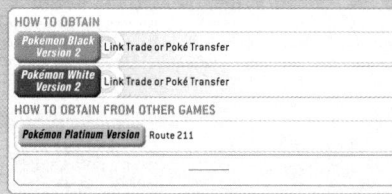

LEVEL-UP AND LEARNED MOVES

Lv.	Name	Type	Kind	Pow.	Acc.	PP	Range	Long	DA
1	Wrap	Normal	Physical	15	90	20	Normal	—	○
6	Growl	Normal	Status	—	100	40	Many Others	—	—
9	Astonish	Ghost	Physical	30	100	15	Normal	—	○
14	Confusion	Psychic	Special	50	100	25	Normal	—	—
17	Uproar	Normal	Special	90	100	10	1 Random	—	—
22	Last Resort	Normal	Physical	140	100	5	Normal	—	○
25	Entrainment	Normal	Status	—	100	15	Normal	—	—

TM & HM MOVES

Lv.	Name	Type	Kind	Pow.	Acc.	PP	Range	Long	DA
TM03	Psyshock	Psychic	Special	80	100	10	Normal	—	—
TM04	Calm Mind	Psychic	Status	—	—	20	Self	—	—
TM06	Toxic	Poison	Status	—	90	10	Normal	—	—
TM10	Hidden Power	Normal	Special	—	100	15	Normal	—	—
TM11	Sunny Day	Fire	Status	—	—	5	Both Sides	—	—
TM12	Taunt	Dark	Status	—	100	20	Normal	—	—
TM16	Light Screen	Psychic	Status	—	—	30	Your Side	—	—
TM17	Protect	Normal	Status	—	—	10	Self	—	—
TM18	Rain Dance	Water	Status	—	—	5	Both Sides	—	—
TM19	Telekinesis	Psychic	Status	—	—	15	Normal	—	—
TM20	Safeguard	Normal	Status	—	—	25	Your Side	—	—
TM21	Frustration	Normal	Physical	—	100	20	Normal	—	○
TM27	Return	Normal	Physical	—	100	20	Normal	—	○
TM29	Psychic	Psychic	Special	90	100	10	Normal	—	—
TM30	Shadow Ball	Ghost	Special	80	100	15	Normal	—	—
TM32	Double Team	Normal	Status	—	—	15	Self	—	—
TM33	Reflect	Psychic	Status	—	—	20	Your Side	—	—
TM41	Torment	Dark	Status	—	100	15	Normal	—	—
TM42	Facade	Normal	Physical	70	100	20	Normal	—	○
TM44	Rest	Psychic	Status	—	—	10	Self	—	—
TM45	Attract	Normal	Status	—	100	15	Normal	—	—
TM48	Round	Normal	Special	60	100	15	Normal	—	—
TM49	Echoed Voice	Normal	Special	40	100	15	Normal	—	—
TM57	Charge Beam	Electric	Special	50	90	10	Normal	—	—
TM70	Flash	Normal	Status	—	100	20	Normal	—	—
TM73	Thunder Wave	Electric	Status	—	100	20	Normal	—	—
TM77	Psych Up	Normal	Status	—	—	10	Normal	—	—
TM85	Dream Eater	Psychic	Special	100	100	15	Normal	—	—
TM86	Grass Knot	Grass	Special	—	100	20	Normal	—	○
TM87	Swagger	Normal	Status	—	90	15	Normal	—	—
TM90	Substitute	Normal	Status	—	—	10	Self	—	—
TM92	Trick Room	Psychic	Status	—	—	5	Both Sides	—	—

MOVES TAUGHT BY PEOPLE

Name	Type	Kind	Pow.	Acc.	PP	Range	Long	DA

MOVES TAUGHT BY MOVE TUTORS FOR SHARDS

Name	Type	Kind	Pow.	Acc.	PP	Range	Long	DA
Signal Beam	Bug	Special	75	100	15	Normal	—	—
Uproar	Normal	Special	90	100	10	1 Random	—	—
Last Resort	Normal	Physical	140	100	5	Normal	—	○
Magic Coat	Psychic	Status	—	—	15	Self	—	—
Hyper Voice	Normal	Special	90	100	10	Many Others	—	—
Icy Wind	Ice	Special	55	95	15	Many Others	—	—
Zen Headbutt	Psychic	Physical	80	90	15	Normal	—	○
Gravity	Psychic	Status	—	—	5	Both Sides	—	—
Bind	Normal	Physical	15	85	20	Normal	—	○
Snore	Normal	Special	40	100	15	Normal	—	—
Heal Bell	Normal	Status	—	—	5	Your Party	—	—
Knock Off	Dark	Physical	20	100	20	Normal	—	○
Helping Hand	Normal	Status	—	—	20	1 Ally	—	—
Recycle	Normal	Status	—	—	10	Self	—	—
Trick	Psychic	Status	—	100	10	Normal	—	—
Sleep Talk	Normal	Status	—	—	10	Self	—	—
Skill Swap	Psychic	Status	—	—	10	Normal	—	—
Snatch	Dark	Status	—	—	10	Self	—	—

EGG MOVES

Name	Type	Kind	Pow.	Acc.	PP	Range	Long	DA
Disable	Normal	Status	—	100	20	Normal	—	—
Curse	Ghost	Status	—	—	10	Varies	—	—
Hypnosis	Psychic	Status	—	60	20	Normal	—	—
Wish	Normal	Status	—	—	10	Self	—	—
Future Sight	Psychic	Special	100	100	10	Normal	—	—
Recover	Normal	Status	—	—	10	Self	—	—
Stored Power	Psychic	Special	20	100	10	Normal	—	—
Skill Swap	Psychic	Status	—	—	10	Normal	—	—

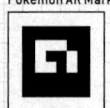

434 Stunky

Skunk Pokémon

TYPE Poison | Dark

ABILITIES
● Stench
● Aftermath

HIDDEN ABILITY
● Keen Eye

STATS
HP
Attack
Defense
Sp. Atk
Sp. Def
Speed

EGG GROUPS
Field

ITEMS SOMETIMES HELD
● None

● HEIGHT: 1'04"
● WEIGHT: 42.3 lbs.
● GENDER: ♂ / ♀

It sprays a foul fluid from its rear. Its stench spreads over a mile radius, driving Pokémon away.

Same form for ♂ / ♀

Pokémon AR Marker

EVOLUTION

Stunky — Lv. 34 → Skuntank

HOW TO OBTAIN

Pokémon Black Version 2	Link Trade or Poké Transfer
Pokémon White Version 2	Link Trade or Poké Transfer

HOW TO OBTAIN FROM OTHER GAMES

Pokémon Diamond Version	Route 206

LEVEL-UP AND LEARNED MOVES

Lv.	Name	Type	Kind	Pow.	Acc.	PP	Range	Long	DA
1	Scratch	Normal	Physical	40	100	35	Normal	—	○
1	Focus Energy	Normal	Status	—	—	30	Self	—	—
4	Poison Gas	Poison	Status	—	80	40	Many Others	—	—
7	Screech	Normal	Status	—	85	40	Normal	—	—
10	Fury Swipes	Normal	Physical	18	80	15	Normal	—	○
14	SmokeScreen	Normal	Status	—	100	20	Normal	—	—
18	Feint	Normal	Physical	30	100	10	Normal	—	○
22	Slash	Normal	Physical	70	100	20	Normal	—	○
27	Toxic	Poison	Status	—	90	10	Normal	—	—
32	Acid Spray	Poison	Special	40	100	20	Normal	—	—
37	Night Slash	Dark	Physical	70	100	15	Normal	—	○
43	Memento	Dark	Status	—	100	10	Normal	—	—
49	Explosion	Normal	Physical	250	100	5	Adjacent	—	—

TM & HM MOVES

Lv.	Name	Type	Kind	Pow.	Acc.	PP	Range	Long	DA
TM01	Hone Claws	Dark	Status	—	—	15	Self	—	—
TM05	Roar	Normal	Status	—	100	20	Normal	—	—
TM06	Toxic	Poison	Status	—	90	10	Normal	—	—
TM09	Venoshock	Poison	Special	65	100	10	Normal	—	—
TM10	Hidden Power	Normal	Special	—	100	15	Normal	—	—
TM11	Sunny Day	Fire	Status	—	—	5	Both Sides	—	—
TM12	Taunt	Dark	Status	—	100	20	Normal	—	—
TM17	Protect	Normal	Status	—	—	10	Self	—	—
TM18	Rain Dance	Water	Status	—	—	5	Both Sides	—	—
TM21	Frustration	Normal	Physical	—	100	20	Normal	—	○
TM27	Return	Normal	Physical	—	100	20	Normal	—	○
TM28	Dig	Ground	Physical	80	100	10	Normal	—	○
TM30	Shadow Ball	Ghost	Special	80	100	15	Normal	—	—
TM32	Double Team	Normal	Status	—	—	15	Self	—	—
TM35	Flamethrower	Fire	Special	95	100	15	Normal	—	—
TM36	Sludge Bomb	Poison	Special	90	100	10	Normal	—	—
TM38	Fire Blast	Fire	Special	120	85	5	Normal	—	—
TM41	Torment	Dark	Status	—	100	15	Normal	—	—
TM42	Facade	Normal	Physical	70	100	20	Normal	—	○
TM44	Rest	Psychic	Status	—	—	10	Self	—	—
TM45	Attract	Normal	Status	—	100	15	Normal	—	—
TM46	Thief	Dark	Physical	40	100	10	Normal	—	○
TM48	Round	Normal	Special	60	100	15	Normal	—	—
TM59	Incinerate	Fire	Special	30	100	15	Many Others	—	—
TM64	Explosion	Normal	Physical	250	100	5	Adjacent	—	—
TM65	Shadow Claw	Ghost	Physical	70	100	15	Normal	—	○
TM66	Payback	Dark	Physical	50	100	10	Normal	—	○
TM87	Swagger	Normal	Status	—	90	15	Normal	—	—
TM90	Substitute	Normal	Status	—	—	10	Self	—	—
TM94	Rock Smash	Fighting	Physical	40	100	15	Normal	—	○
TM95	Snarl	Dark	Special	55	95	15	Many Others	—	—
HM01	Cut	Normal	Physical	50	95	30	Normal	—	○

MOVES TAUGHT BY PEOPLE

Name	Type	Kind	Pow.	Acc.	PP	Range	Long	DA

MOVES TAUGHT BY MOVE TUTORS FOR SHARDS

Name	Type	Kind	Pow.	Acc.	PP	Range	Long	DA
Iron Tail	Steel	Physical	100	75	15	Normal	—	○
Foul Play	Dark	Physical	95	100	15	Normal	—	○
Dark Pulse	Dark	Special	80	100	15	Normal	○	—
Snore	Normal	Special	40	100	15	Normal	—	—
Sleep Talk	Normal	Status	—	—	10	Self	—	—
Snatch	Dark	Status	—	—	10	Self	—	—

EGG MOVES

Name	Type	Kind	Pow.	Acc.	PP	Range	Long	DA
Pursuit	Dark	Physical	40	100	20	Normal	—	○
Leer	Normal	Status	—	100	30	Many Others	—	—
Smog	Poison	Special	20	70	20	Normal	—	—
Double-Edge	Normal	Physical	120	100	15	Normal	—	○
Crunch	Dark	Physical	80	100	15	Normal	—	○
Scary Face	Normal	Status	—	100	10	Normal	—	—
Astonish	Ghost	Physical	30	100	15	Normal	—	○
Punishment	Dark	Physical	—	100	5	Normal	—	○
Haze	Ice	Status	—	—	30	Both Sides	—	—
Iron Tail	Steel	Physical	100	75	15	Normal	—	○
Foul Play	Dark	Physical	95	100	15	Normal	—	○
Flame Burst	Fire	Special	70	100	15	Normal	—	—

---

435 Skuntank

Skunk Pokémon

TYPE Poison | Dark

ABILITIES
● Stench
● Aftermath

HIDDEN ABILITY
● Keen Eye

STATS
HP
Attack
Defense
Sp. Atk
Sp. Def
Speed

EGG GROUPS
Field

ITEMS SOMETIMES HELD
● None

● HEIGHT: 3'03"
● WEIGHT: 83.8 lbs.
● GENDER: ♂ / ♀

It attacks by spraying a horribly smelly fluid from the tip of its tail. Attacks from above confound it.

Same form for ♂ / ♀

Pokémon AR Marker

EVOLUTION

Stunky — Lv. 34 → Skuntank

HOW TO OBTAIN

Pokémon Black Version 2	Link Trade or Poké Transfer
Pokémon White Version 2	Link Trade or Poké Transfer

HOW TO OBTAIN FROM OTHER GAMES

Pokémon Diamond Version	Route 221

LEVEL-UP AND LEARNED MOVES

Lv.	Name	Type	Kind	Pow.	Acc.	PP	Range	Long	DA
1	Scratch	Normal	Physical	40	100	35	Normal	—	○
1	Focus Energy	Normal	Status	—	—	30	Self	—	—
1	Poison Gas	Poison	Status	—	80	40	Many Others	—	—
4	Poison Gas	Poison	Status	—	80	40	Many Others	—	—
7	Screech	Normal	Status	—	85	40	Normal	—	—
10	Fury Swipes	Normal	Physical	18	80	15	Normal	—	○
14	SmokeScreen	Normal	Status	—	100	20	Normal	—	—
18	Feint	Normal	Physical	30	100	10	Normal	—	○
22	Slash	Normal	Physical	70	100	20	Normal	—	○
27	Toxic	Poison	Status	—	90	10	Normal	—	—
32	Acid Spray	Poison	Special	40	100	20	Normal	—	—
34	Flamethrower	Fire	Special	95	100	15	Normal	—	—
41	Night Slash	Dark	Physical	70	100	15	Normal	—	○
51	Memento	Dark	Status	—	100	10	Normal	—	—
61	Explosion	Normal	Physical	250	100	5	Adjacent	—	—

TM & HM MOVES

Lv.	Name	Type	Kind	Pow.	Acc.	PP	Range	Long	DA
TM01	Hone Claws	Dark	Status	—	—	15	Self	—	—
TM05	Roar	Normal	Status	—	100	20	Normal	—	—
TM06	Toxic	Poison	Status	—	90	10	Normal	—	—
TM09	Venoshock	Poison	Special	65	100	10	Normal	—	—
TM10	Hidden Power	Normal	Special	—	100	15	Normal	—	—
TM11	Sunny Day	Fire	Status	—	—	5	Both Sides	—	—
TM12	Taunt	Dark	Status	—	100	20	Normal	—	—
TM15	Hyper Beam	Normal	Special	150	90	5	Normal	—	—
TM17	Protect	Normal	Status	—	—	10	Self	—	—
TM18	Rain Dance	Water	Status	—	—	5	Both Sides	—	—
TM21	Frustration	Normal	Physical	—	100	20	Normal	—	○
TM27	Return	Normal	Physical	—	100	20	Normal	—	○
TM28	Dig	Ground	Physical	80	100	10	Normal	—	○
TM30	Shadow Ball	Ghost	Special	80	100	15	Normal	—	—
TM32	Double Team	Normal	Status	—	—	15	Self	—	—
TM35	Flamethrower	Fire	Special	95	100	15	Normal	—	—
TM36	Sludge Bomb	Poison	Special	90	100	10	Normal	—	—
TM38	Fire Blast	Fire	Special	120	85	5	Normal	—	—
TM41	Torment	Dark	Status	—	100	15	Normal	—	—
TM42	Facade	Normal	Physical	70	100	20	Normal	—	○
TM44	Rest	Psychic	Status	—	—	10	Self	—	—
TM45	Attract	Normal	Status	—	100	15	Normal	—	—
TM46	Thief	Dark	Physical	40	100	10	Normal	—	○
TM48	Round	Normal	Special	60	100	15	Normal	—	—
TM59	Incinerate	Fire	Special	30	100	15	Many Others	—	—
TM64	Explosion	Normal	Physical	250	100	5	Adjacent	—	—
TM65	Shadow Claw	Ghost	Physical	70	100	15	Normal	—	○
TM66	Payback	Dark	Physical	50	100	10	Normal	—	○
TM68	Giga Impact	Normal	Physical	150	90	5	Normal	—	○
TM84	Poison Jab	Poison	Physical	80	100	20	Normal	—	○
TM87	Swagger	Normal	Status	—	90	15	Normal	—	—
TM90	Substitute	Normal	Status	—	—	10	Self	—	—
TM94	Rock Smash	Fighting	Physical	40	100	15	Normal	—	○
TM95	Snarl	Dark	Special	55	95	15	Many Others	—	—
HM01	Cut	Normal	Physical	50	95	30	Normal	—	○
HM04	Strength	Normal	Physical	80	100	15	Normal	—	○

MOVES TAUGHT BY PEOPLE

Name	Type	Kind	Pow.	Acc.	PP	Range	Long	DA

MOVES TAUGHT BY MOVE TUTORS FOR SHARDS

Name	Type	Kind	Pow.	Acc.	PP	Range	Long	DA
Iron Tail	Steel	Physical	100	75	15	Normal	—	○
Foul Play	Dark	Physical	95	100	15	Normal	—	○
Dark Pulse	Dark	Special	80	100	15	Normal	○	—
Snore	Normal	Special	40	100	15	Normal	—	—
Sleep Talk	Normal	Status	—	—	10	Self	—	—
Snatch	Dark	Status	—	—	10	Self	—	—

436 Bronzor
Bronze Pokémon

TYPE Steel Psychic

ABILITIES
- Levitate
- Heatproof

HIDDEN ABILITY
- Heavy Metal

- HEIGHT: 1'08"
- WEIGHT: 133.4 lbs.
- GENDER: Unknown

They are found in ancient tombs. The patterns on their backs are said to be imbued with mysterious power.

STATS
HP / Attack / Defense / Sp. Atk / Sp. Def / Speed

EGG GROUPS
Mineral

ITEMS SOMETIMES HELD
- Metal Coat

Gender unknown

EVOLUTION
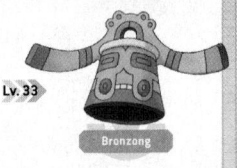
Bronzor → Lv. 33 → Bronzong

HOW TO OBTAIN
Pokémon Black Version 2	❶ Abundant Shrine ❷ Abundant Shrine (Hidden Grotto)
Pokémon White Version 2	❶ Abundant Shrine ❷ Abundant Shrine (Hidden Grotto)

HOW TO OBTAIN FROM OTHER GAMES

LEVEL-UP AND LEARNED MOVES

Lv.	Name	Type	Kind	Pow.	Acc.	PP	Range	Long	DA
1	Tackle	Normal	Physical	50	100	35	Normal	—	○
1	Confusion	Psychic	Special	50	100	25	Normal	—	—
5	Hypnosis	Psychic	Status	—	60	20	Normal	—	—
9	Imprison	Psychic	Status	—	—	10	Self	—	—
11	Confuse Ray	Ghost	Status	—	100	10	Normal	—	—
15	Psywave	Psychic	Special	—	80	15	Normal	—	—
19	Iron Defense	Steel	Status	—	—	15	Self	—	—
21	Faint Attack	Dark	Physical	60	—	20	Normal	—	—
25	Safeguard	Normal	Status	—	—	25	Your Side	—	—
29	Future Sight	Psychic	Special	100	100	10	Normal	—	—
31	Metal Sound	Steel	Status	—	85	40	Normal	—	—
35	Gyro Ball	Steel	Physical	—	100	5	Normal	—	—
39	Extrasensory	Psychic	Special	80	100	30	Normal	—	—
41	Payback	Dark	Physical	50	100	10	Normal	—	—
45	Heal Block	Psychic	Status	—	100	15	Many Others	—	—
49	Heavy Slam	Steel	Physical	—	100	10	Normal	—	—

TM & HM MOVES

Lv.	Name	Type	Kind	Pow.	Acc.	PP	Range	Long	DA
TM03	Psyshock	Psychic	Special	80	100	10	Normal	—	○
TM04	Calm Mind	Psychic	Status	—	—	20	Self	—	—
TM06	Toxic	Poison	Status	—	90	10	Normal	—	—
TM10	Hidden Power	Normal	Special	—	100	15	Normal	—	—
TM11	Sunny Day	Fire	Status	—	—	5	Both Sides	—	—
TM16	Light Screen	Psychic	Status	—	—	30	Your Side	—	—
TM17	Protect	Normal	Status	—	—	10	Self	—	—
TM18	Rain Dance	Water	Status	—	—	5	Both Sides	—	—
TM19	Telekinesis	Psychic	Status	—	—	15	Normal	—	—
TM20	Safeguard	Normal	Status	—	—	25	Your Side	—	—
TM21	Frustration	Normal	Physical	—	100	20	Normal	—	○
TM22	SolarBeam	Grass	Special	120	100	10	Normal	—	—
TM26	Earthquake	Ground	Physical	100	100	10	Adjacent	—	○
TM27	Return	Normal	Physical	—	100	20	Normal	—	○
TM29	Psychic	Psychic	Special	90	100	10	Normal	—	—
TM30	Shadow Ball	Ghost	Special	80	100	15	Normal	—	—
TM32	Double Team	Normal	Status	—	—	15	Self	—	—
TM33	Reflect	Psychic	Status	—	—	20	Your Side	—	—
TM37	Sandstorm	Rock	Status	—	—	10	Both Sides	—	—
TM39	Rock Tomb	Rock	Physical	50	80	10	Normal	—	—
TM42	Facade	Normal	Physical	70	100	20	Normal	—	—
TM44	Rest	Psychic	Status	—	—	10	Self	—	—
TM48	Round	Normal	Special	60	100	15	Normal	—	—
TM57	Charge Beam	Electric	Special	50	90	10	Normal	—	—
TM66	Payback	Dark	Physical	50	100	10	Normal	—	—
TM69	Rock Polish	Rock	Status	—	—	20	Self	—	—
TM70	Flash	Normal	Status	—	100	20	Normal	—	—
TM74	Gyro Ball	Steel	Physical	—	100	5	Normal	—	—
TM77	Psych Up	Normal	Status	—	—	10	Normal	—	—
TM78	Bulldoze	Ground	Physical	60	100	20	Adjacent	—	—
TM80	Rock Slide	Rock	Physical	75	90	10	Many Others	—	—
TM85	Dream Eater	Psychic	Special	100	100	15	Normal	—	—
TM86	Grass Knot	Grass	Special	—	100	20	Normal	—	—
TM87	Swagger	Normal	Status	—	90	15	Normal	—	—
TM90	Substitute	Normal	Status	—	—	10	Self	—	—
TM91	Flash Cannon	Steel	Special	80	100	10	Normal	—	—
TM92	Trick Room	Psychic	Status	—	—	5	Both Sides	—	—

MOVES TAUGHT BY PEOPLE

Name	Type	Kind	Pow.	Acc.	PP	Range	Long	DA

MOVES TAUGHT BY MOVE TUTORS FOR SHARDS

Name	Type	Kind	Pow.	Acc.	PP	Range	Long	DA
Signal Beam	Bug	Special	75	100	15	Normal	—	—
Iron Defense	Steel	Status	—	—	15	Self	—	—
Gravity	Psychic	Status	—	—	5	Both Sides	—	—
Snore	Normal	Special	40	100	15	Normal	—	—
Wonder Room	Psychic	Status	—	—	10	Both Sides	—	—
Recycle	Normal	Status	—	—	10	Self	—	—
Trick	Psychic	Status	—	100	10	Normal	—	—
Stealth Rock	Rock	Status	—	—	20	3 Foes	—	—
Sleep Talk	Normal	Status	—	—	10	Self	—	—
Skill Swap	Psychic	Status	—	—	10	Normal	—	—

EGG MOVES

Name	Type	Kind	Pow.	Acc.	PP	Range	Long	DA

Pokémon AR Marker

437 Bronzong
Bronze Bell Pokémon

TYPE Steel Psychic

ABILITIES
- Levitate
- Heatproof

HIDDEN ABILITY
- Heavy Metal

- HEIGHT: 4'03"
- WEIGHT: 412.3 lbs.
- GENDER: Unknown

In ages past, this Pokémon was revered as a bringer of rain. It was found buried in the ground.

STATS
HP / Attack / Defense / Sp. Atk / Sp. Def / Speed

EGG GROUPS
Mineral

ITEMS SOMETIMES HELD
- None

Gender unknown

EVOLUTION

Bronzor → Lv. 33 → Bronzong

HOW TO OBTAIN
Pokémon Black Version 2	Abundant Shrine (dark grass)
Pokémon White Version 2	Abundant Shrine (dark grass)

HOW TO OBTAIN FROM OTHER GAMES

LEVEL-UP AND LEARNED MOVES

Lv.	Name	Type	Kind	Pow.	Acc.	PP	Range	Long	DA
1	Sunny Day	Fire	Status	—	—	5	Both Sides	—	—
1	Rain Dance	Water	Status	—	—	5	Both Sides	—	—
1	Tackle	Normal	Physical	50	100	35	Normal	—	○
1	Confusion	Psychic	Special	50	100	25	Normal	—	—
1	Hypnosis	Psychic	Status	—	60	20	Normal	—	—
1	Imprison	Psychic	Status	—	—	10	Self	—	—
5	Hypnosis	Psychic	Status	—	60	20	Normal	—	—
9	Imprison	Psychic	Status	—	—	10	Self	—	—
11	Confuse Ray	Ghost	Status	—	100	10	Normal	—	—
15	Psywave	Psychic	Special	—	80	15	Normal	—	—
19	Iron Defense	Steel	Status	—	—	15	Self	—	—
21	Faint Attack	Dark	Physical	60	—	20	Normal	—	—
25	Safeguard	Normal	Status	—	—	25	Your Side	—	—
29	Future Sight	Psychic	Special	100	100	10	Normal	—	—
31	Metal Sound	Steel	Status	—	85	40	Normal	—	—
33	Block	Normal	Status	—	—	5	Normal	—	—
36	Gyro Ball	Steel	Physical	—	100	5	Normal	—	—
42	Extrasensory	Psychic	Special	80	100	30	Normal	—	—
46	Payback	Dark	Physical	50	100	10	Normal	—	—
52	Heal Block	Psychic	Status	—	100	15	Many Others	—	—
58	Heavy Slam	Steel	Physical	—	100	10	Normal	—	—

TM & HM MOVES

Lv.	Name	Type	Kind	Pow.	Acc.	PP	Range	Long	DA
TM03	Psyshock	Psychic	Special	80	100	10	Normal	—	○
TM04	Calm Mind	Psychic	Status	—	—	20	Self	—	—
TM06	Toxic	Poison	Status	—	90	10	Normal	—	—
TM10	Hidden Power	Normal	Special	—	100	15	Normal	—	—
TM11	Sunny Day	Fire	Status	—	—	5	Both Sides	—	—
TM15	Hyper Beam	Normal	Special	150	90	5	Normal	—	—
TM16	Light Screen	Psychic	Status	—	—	30	Your Side	—	—
TM17	Protect	Normal	Status	—	—	10	Self	—	—
TM18	Rain Dance	Water	Status	—	—	5	Both Sides	—	—
TM19	Telekinesis	Psychic	Status	—	—	15	Normal	—	—
TM20	Safeguard	Normal	Status	—	—	25	Your Side	—	—
TM21	Frustration	Normal	Physical	—	100	20	Normal	—	○
TM22	SolarBeam	Grass	Special	120	100	10	Normal	—	—
TM26	Earthquake	Ground	Physical	100	100	10	Adjacent	—	○
TM27	Return	Normal	Physical	—	100	20	Normal	—	○
TM29	Psychic	Psychic	Special	90	100	10	Normal	—	—
TM30	Shadow Ball	Ghost	Special	80	100	15	Normal	—	—
TM32	Double Team	Normal	Status	—	—	15	Self	—	—
TM33	Reflect	Psychic	Status	—	—	20	Your Side	—	—
TM37	Sandstorm	Rock	Status	—	—	10	Both Sides	—	—
TM39	Rock Tomb	Rock	Physical	50	80	10	Normal	—	—
TM42	Facade	Normal	Physical	70	100	20	Normal	—	—
TM44	Rest	Psychic	Status	—	—	10	Self	—	—
TM48	Round	Normal	Special	60	100	15	Normal	—	—
TM57	Charge Beam	Electric	Special	50	90	10	Normal	—	—
TM64	Explosion	Normal	Physical	250	100	5	Adjacent	—	—
TM66	Payback	Dark	Physical	50	100	10	Normal	—	—
TM68	Giga Impact	Normal	Physical	150	90	5	Normal	—	—
TM69	Rock Polish	Rock	Status	—	—	20	Self	—	—
TM70	Flash	Normal	Status	—	100	20	Normal	—	—
TM74	Gyro Ball	Steel	Physical	—	100	5	Normal	—	—
TM77	Psych Up	Normal	Status	—	—	10	Normal	—	—
TM78	Bulldoze	Ground	Physical	60	100	20	Adjacent	—	—
TM80	Rock Slide	Rock	Physical	75	90	10	Many Others	—	—
TM85	Dream Eater	Psychic	Special	100	100	15	Normal	—	—
TM86	Grass Knot	Grass	Special	—	100	20	Normal	—	○
TM87	Swagger	Normal	Status	—	90	15	Normal	—	—
TM90	Substitute	Normal	Status	—	—	10	Self	—	—
TM91	Flash Cannon	Steel	Special	80	100	10	Normal	—	—
TM92	Trick Room	Psychic	Status	—	—	5	Both Sides	—	—
TM94	Rock Smash	Fighting	Physical	40	100	15	Normal	—	○
HM04	Strength	Normal	Physical	80	100	15	Normal	—	—

MOVES TAUGHT BY PEOPLE

Name	Type	Kind	Pow.	Acc.	PP	Range	Long	DA

MOVES TAUGHT BY MOVE TUTORS FOR SHARDS

Name	Type	Kind	Pow.	Acc.	PP	Range	Long	DA
Signal Beam	Bug	Special	75	100	15	Normal	—	—
Iron Head	Steel	Physical	80	100	15	Normal	—	○
Iron Defense	Steel	Status	—	—	15	Self	—	—
Block	Normal	Status	—	—	5	Normal	—	—
Zen Headbutt	Psychic	Physical	80	90	15	Normal	—	—
Gravity	Psychic	Status	—	—	5	Both Sides	—	—
Snore	Normal	Special	40	100	15	Normal	—	—
Wonder Room	Psychic	Status	—	—	10	Both Sides	—	—
Recycle	Normal	Status	—	—	10	Self	—	—
Trick	Psychic	Status	—	100	10	Normal	—	—
Stealth Rock	Rock	Status	—	—	20	3 Foes	—	—
Sleep Talk	Normal	Status	—	—	10	Self	—	—
Skill Swap	Psychic	Status	—	—	10	Normal	—	—

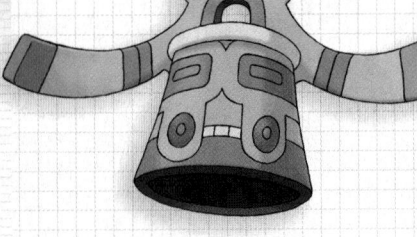

Pokémon AR Marker

438 **Bonsly**

Bonsai Pokémon

- HEIGHT: 1'08"
- WEIGHT: 33.1 lbs.
- GENDER: ♂ / ♀

It prefers an arid atmosphere. It leaks water that looks like tears when adjusting its moisture level.

Same form for ♂ / ♀

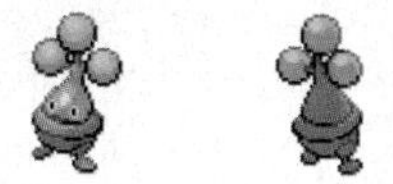

Pokémon AR Marker

TYPE Rock

ABILITIES
- Sturdy
- Rock Head

HIDDEN ABILITY
- Rattled

STATS
HP
Attack
Defense
Sp. Atk
Sp. Def
Speed

EGG GROUPS
No Egg has ever been discovered

ITEMS SOMETIMES HELD
- None

EVOLUTION

Bonsly

Level up Bonsly to Lv. 33 and teach it Mimic, or level it up after it knows Mimic

Sudowoodo

➡ p. 106

HOW TO OBTAIN

Pokémon Black Version 2	Catch a Sudowoodo, leave it at the Pokémon Day Care, and hatch the Egg that is found
Pokémon White Version 2	Link Trade or use the Poké Transfer

HOW TO OBTAIN FROM OTHER GAMES

Pokémon Pearl Version	Route 209
	—

LEVEL-UP AND LEARNED MOVES

Lv.	Name	Type	Kind	Pow.	Acc.	PP	Range	Long	DA
1	Fake Tears	Dark	Status	—	100	20	Normal	—	—
1	Copycat	Normal	Status	—	—	20	Self	—	—
5	Flail	Normal	Physical	—	100	15	Normal	—	○
8	Low Kick	Fighting	Physical	—	100	20	Normal	—	○
12	Rock Throw	Rock	Physical	50	90	15	Normal	—	—
15	Slam	Normal	Physical	80	75	20	Normal	—	○
19	Faint Attack	Dark	Physical	60	—	20	Normal	—	○
22	Rock Tomb	Rock	Physical	50	80	10	Normal	—	—
26	Block	Normal	Status	—	—	5	Normal	—	—
29	Rock Slide	Rock	Physical	75	90	10	Many Others	—	—
33	Mimic	Normal	Status	—	—	10	Normal	—	—
36	Sucker Punch	Dark	Physical	80	100	5	Normal	—	○
40	Double-Edge	Normal	Physical	120	100	15	Normal	—	○

TM & HM MOVES

Lv.	Name	Type	Kind	Pow.	Acc.	PP	Range	Long	DA
TM04	Calm Mind	Psychic	Status	—	—	20	Self	—	—
TM06	Toxic	Poison	Status	—	90	10	Normal	—	—
TM10	Hidden Power	Normal	Special	—	100	15	Normal	—	—
TM11	Sunny Day	Fire	Status	—	—	5	Both Sides	—	—
TM17	Protect	Normal	Status	—	—	10	Self	—	—
TM21	Frustration	Normal	Physical	—	100	20	Normal	—	○
TM23	Smack Down	Rock	Physical	50	100	15	Normal	—	—
TM27	Return	Normal	Physical	—	100	20	Normal	—	○
TM28	Dig	Ground	Physical	80	100	10	Normal	—	○
TM31	Brick Break	Fighting	Physical	75	100	15	Normal	—	○
TM32	Double Team	Normal	Status	—	—	15	Self	—	—
TM37	Sandstorm	Rock	Status	—	—	10	Both Sides	—	—
TM39	Rock Tomb	Rock	Physical	50	80	10	Normal	—	—
TM42	Facade	Normal	Physical	70	100	20	Normal	—	○
TM44	Rest	Psychic	Status	—	—	10	Self	—	—
TM45	Attract	Normal	Status	—	100	15	Normal	—	—
TM46	Thief	Dark	Physical	40	100	10	Normal	—	○
TM48	Round	Normal	Special	60	100	15	Normal	—	—
TM64	Explosion	Normal	Physical	250	100	5	Adjacent	—	—
TM69	Rock Polish	Rock	Status	—	—	20	Self	—	—
TM77	Psych Up	Normal	Status	—	—	10	Normal	—	—
TM80	Rock Slide	Rock	Physical	75	90	10	Many Others	—	—
TM87	Swagger	Normal	Status	—	90	15	Normal	—	—
TM90	Substitute	Normal	Status	—	—	10	Self	—	—

MOVES TAUGHT BY PEOPLE

Name	Type	Kind	Pow.	Acc.	PP	Range	Long	DA

MOVES TAUGHT BY MOVE TUTORS FOR SHARDS

Name	Type	Kind	Pow.	Acc.	PP	Range	Long	DA
Covet	Normal	Physical	60	100	40	Normal	—	○
Uproar	Normal	Special	90	100	10	1 Random	—	—
Low Kick	Fighting	Physical	—	100	20	Normal	—	○
Block	Normal	Status	—	—	5	Normal	—	—
Earth Power	Ground	Special	90	100	10	Normal	—	—
Foul Play	Dark	Physical	95	100	15	Normal	—	○
Snore	Normal	Special	40	100	15	Normal	—	—
Role Play	Psychic	Status	—	—	10	Normal	—	—
Helping Hand	Normal	Status	—	—	20	1 Ally	—	—
After You	Normal	Status	—	—	15	Normal	—	—
Stealth Rock	Rock	Status	—	—	20	3 Foes	—	—
Sleep Talk	Normal	Status	—	—	10	Self	—	—

EGG MOVES

Name	Type	Kind	Pow.	Acc.	PP	Range	Long	DA
Selfdestruct	Normal	Physical	200	100	5	Adjacent	—	—
Headbutt	Normal	Physical	70	100	15	Normal	—	○
Harden	Normal	Status	—	—	30	Self	—	—
Defense Curl	Normal	Status	—	—	40	Self	—	—
Rollout	Rock	Physical	30	90	20	Normal	—	○
Sand Tomb	Ground	Physical	35	85	15	Normal	—	—
Stealth Rock	Rock	Status	—	—	20	3 Foes	—	—
Curse	Ghost	Status	—	—	10	Varies	—	—
Endure	Normal	Status	—	—	10	Self	—	—

439 **Mime Jr.**

Mime Pokémon

- HEIGHT: 2'00"
- WEIGHT: 28.7 lbs.
- GENDER: ♂ / ♀

It mimics the expressions and motions of those it sees to understand the feelings of others.

Same form for ♂ / ♀

Pokémon AR Marker

TYPE Psychic

ABILITIES
- Soundproof
- Filter

HIDDEN ABILITY
- Technician

STATS
HP
Attack
Defense
Sp. Atk
Sp. Def
Speed

EGG GROUPS
No Egg has ever been discovered

ITEMS SOMETIMES HELD
- None

EVOLUTION

Mime Jr.

Level up Mime Jr. to Lv. 15, then teach it Mimic, or level it up after it knows Mimic

Mr. Mime

➡ p. 74

HOW TO OBTAIN

Pokémon Black Version 2	Link Trade or Poké Transfer
Pokémon White Version 2	Catch a Mr. Mime, leave it at the Pokémon Day Care, and hatch the Egg that is found

HOW TO OBTAIN FROM OTHER GAMES

Pokémon Diamond Version	Route 209
	—

LEVEL-UP AND LEARNED MOVES

Lv.	Name	Type	Kind	Pow.	Acc.	PP	Range	Long	DA
1	Tickle	Normal	Status	—	100	20	Normal	—	—
1	Barrier	Psychic	Status	—	—	30	Self	—	—
1	Confusion	Psychic	Special	50	100	25	Normal	—	—
4	Copycat	Normal	Status	—	—	20	Self	—	—
8	Meditate	Psychic	Status	—	—	40	Self	—	—
11	DoubleSlap	Normal	Physical	15	85	10	Normal	—	○
15	Mimic	Normal	Status	—	—	10	Normal	—	—
18	Encore	Normal	Status	—	100	5	Normal	—	—
22	Light Screen	Psychic	Status	—	—	30	Your Side	—	—
22	Reflect	Psychic	Status	—	—	20	Your Side	—	—
25	Psybeam	Psychic	Special	65	100	20	Normal	—	—
29	Substitute	Normal	Status	—	—	10	Self	—	—
32	Recycle	Normal	Status	—	—	10	Self	—	—
36	Trick	Psychic	Status	—	100	10	Normal	—	—
39	Psychic	Psychic	Special	90	100	10	Normal	—	—
43	Role Play	Psychic	Status	—	—	10	Normal	—	—
46	Baton Pass	Normal	Status	—	—	40	Self	—	—
50	Safeguard	Normal	Status	—	—	25	Your Side	—	—

TM & HM MOVES

Lv.	Name	Type	Kind	Pow.	Acc.	PP	Range	Long	DA
TM03	Psyshock	Psychic	Special	80	100	10	Normal	—	—
TM04	Calm Mind	Psychic	Status	—	—	20	Self	—	—
TM06	Toxic	Poison	Status	—	90	10	Normal	—	—
TM10	Hidden Power	Normal	Special	—	100	15	Normal	—	—
TM11	Sunny Day	Fire	Status	—	—	5	Both Sides	—	—
TM12	Taunt	Dark	Status	—	100	20	Normal	—	—
TM16	Light Screen	Psychic	Status	—	—	30	Your Side	—	—
TM17	Protect	Normal	Status	—	—	10	Self	—	—
TM18	Rain Dance	Water	Status	—	—	5	Both Sides	—	—
TM19	Telekinesis	Psychic	Status	—	—	15	Normal	—	—
TM20	Safeguard	Normal	Status	—	—	25	Your Side	—	—
TM21	Frustration	Normal	Physical	—	100	20	Normal	—	○
TM22	SolarBeam	Grass	Special	120	100	10	Normal	—	—
TM24	Thunderbolt	Electric	Special	95	100	15	Normal	—	—
TM25	Thunder	Electric	Special	120	70	10	Normal	—	—
TM27	Return	Normal	Physical	—	100	20	Normal	—	○
TM29	Psychic	Psychic	Special	90	100	10	Normal	—	—
TM30	Shadow Ball	Ghost	Special	80	100	15	Normal	—	—
TM31	Brick Break	Fighting	Physical	75	100	15	Normal	—	○
TM32	Double Team	Normal	Status	—	—	15	Self	—	—
TM33	Reflect	Psychic	Status	—	—	20	Your Side	—	—
TM41	Torment	Dark	Status	—	100	15	Normal	—	—
TM42	Facade	Normal	Physical	70	100	20	Normal	—	○
TM44	Rest	Psychic	Status	—	—	10	Self	—	—
TM45	Attract	Normal	Status	—	100	15	Normal	—	—
TM46	Thief	Dark	Physical	40	100	10	Normal	—	○
TM48	Round	Normal	Special	60	100	15	Normal	—	—
TM56	Fling	Dark	Physical	—	100	10	Normal	—	—
TM57	Charge Beam	Electric	Special	50	90	10	Normal	—	—
TM70	Flash	Normal	Status	—	100	20	Normal	—	—
TM73	Thunder Wave	Electric	Status	—	100	20	Normal	—	—
TM77	Psych Up	Normal	Status	—	—	10	Normal	—	—
TM85	Dream Eater	Psychic	Special	100	100	15	Normal	—	—
TM86	Grass Knot	Grass	Special	—	100	20	Normal	—	○
TM87	Swagger	Normal	Status	—	90	15	Normal	—	—
TM90	Substitute	Normal	Status	—	—	10	Self	—	—
TM92	Trick Room	Psychic	Status	—	—	5	Both Sides	—	—

MOVES TAUGHT BY PEOPLE

Name	Type	Kind	Pow.	Acc.	PP	Range	Long	DA

MOVES TAUGHT BY MOVE TUTORS FOR SHARDS

Name	Type	Kind	Pow.	Acc.	PP	Range	Long	DA
Covet	Normal	Physical	60	100	40	Normal	—	○
Signal Beam	Bug	Special	75	100	15	Normal	—	—
Uproar	Normal	Special	90	100	10	1 Random	—	—
Magic Coat	Psychic	Status	—	—	15	Self	—	—
Icy Wind	Ice	Special	55	95	15	Many Others	—	—
Snore	Normal	Special	40	100	15	Normal	—	—
Role Play	Psychic	Status	—	—	10	Normal	—	—
Drain Punch	Fighting	Physical	75	100	10	Normal	—	○
Helping Hand	Normal	Status	—	—	20	1 Ally	—	—
Magic Room	Psychic	Status	—	—	10	Both Sides	—	—
Wonder Room	Psychic	Status	—	—	10	Both Sides	—	—
Recycle	Normal	Status	—	—	10	Self	—	—
Trick	Psychic	Status	—	100	10	Normal	—	—
Sleep Talk	Normal	Status	—	—	10	Self	—	—
Skill Swap	Psychic	Status	—	—	10	Normal	—	—
Snatch	Dark	Status	—	—	10	Self	—	—

EGG MOVES

Name	Type	Kind	Pow.	Acc.	PP	Range	Long	DA
Future Sight	Psychic	Special	100	100	10	Normal	—	—
Hypnosis	Psychic	Status	—	60	20	Normal	—	—
Mimic	Normal	Status	—	—	10	Normal	—	—
Fake Out	Normal	Physical	40	100	10	Normal	—	○
Trick	Psychic	Status	—	100	10	Normal	—	—
Confuse Ray	Ghost	Status	—	100	10	Normal	—	—
Wake-Up Slap	Fighting	Physical	60	100	10	Normal	—	○
Teeter Dance	Normal	Status	—	100	20	Adjacent	—	—
Healing Wish	Psychic	Status	—	—	10	Self	—	—
Charm	Normal	Status	—	100	20	Normal	—	—
Nasty Plot	Dark	Status	—	—	20	Self	—	—
Power Split	Psychic	Status	—	—	10	Normal	—	—
Magic Room	Psychic	Status	—	—	10	Both Sides	—	—
Icy Wind	Ice	Special	55	95	15	Many Others	—	—

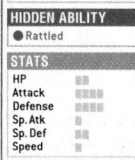

440 Happiny
Playhouse Pokémon

- HEIGHT: 2'00"
- WEIGHT: 53.8 lbs.
- GENDER: ♀

It likes to carry around a small rock. It may wander around others' feet and cause them to stumble.

TYPE Normal

ABILITIES
- Natural Cure
- Serene Grace

HIDDEN ABILITY
- Friend Guard

STATS
HP	▪▪▪▪
Attack	▪
Defense	▪
Sp. Atk	▪
Sp. Def	▪▪▪
Speed	▪▪

EGG GROUPS
No Egg has ever been discovered

ITEMS SOMETIMES HELD
- None

♀

Pokémon AR Marker

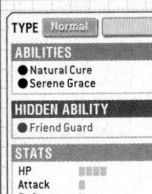

EVOLUTION

Happiny	Chansey → p.70	Blissey → p.134

Have it hold Oval Stone, and level it up in the morning, afternoon, or evening.

Level up with high friendship.

HOW TO OBTAIN
Pokémon Black Version 2	Hatch the Egg the woman in Nacrene City gives you
Pokémon White Version 2	Hatch the Egg the woman in Nacrene City gives you

HOW TO OBTAIN FROM OTHER GAMES

LEVEL-UP AND LEARNED MOVES
Lv.	Name	Type	Kind	Pow.	Acc.	PP	Range	Long	DA
1	Pound	Normal	Physical	40	100	35	Normal	—	—
1	Charm	Normal	Status	—	100	20	Normal	—	—
3	Copycat	Normal	Status	—	—	20	Self	—	—
9	Refresh	Normal	Status	—	—	20	Self	—	—
12	Sweet Kiss	Normal	Status	—	75	10	Normal	—	—

TM & HM MOVES
Lv.	Name	Type	Kind	Pow.	Acc.	PP	Range	Long	DA
TM06	Toxic	Poison	Status	—	90	10	Normal	—	—
TM07	Hail	Ice	Status	—	—	10	Both Sides	—	—
TM10	Hidden Power	Normal	Special	—	100	15	Normal	—	—
TM11	Sunny Day	Fire	Status	—	—	5	Both Sides	—	—
TM16	Light Screen	Psychic	Status	—	—	30	Your Side	—	—
TM17	Protect	Normal	Status	—	—	10	Self	—	—
TM18	Rain Dance	Water	Status	—	—	5	Both Sides	—	—
TM20	Safeguard	Normal	Status	—	—	25	Your Side	—	—
TM21	Frustration	Normal	Physical	—	100	20	Normal	—	○
TM22	SolarBeam	Grass	Special	120	100	10	Normal	—	—
TM27	Return	Normal	Physical	—	100	20	Normal	—	○
TM29	Psychic	Psychic	Special	90	100	10	Normal	—	—
TM30	Shadow Ball	Ghost	Special	80	100	15	Normal	—	—
TM32	Double Team	Normal	Status	—	—	15	Self	—	—
TM35	Flamethrower	Fire	Special	95	100	15	Normal	—	—
TM38	Fire Blast	Fire	Special	120	85	5	Normal	—	—
TM42	Facade	Normal	Physical	70	100	20	Normal	—	—
TM44	Rest	Psychic	Status	—	—	10	Self	—	—
TM45	Attract	Normal	Status	—	100	15	Normal	—	—
TM48	Round	Normal	Special	60	100	15	Normal	—	—
TM49	Echoed Voice	Normal	Special	40	100	15	Normal	—	—
TM56	Fling	Dark	Physical	—	100	10	Normal	—	—
TM59	Incinerate	Fire	Special	30	100	15	Many Others	—	—
TM70	Flash	Normal	Status	—	100	20	Normal	—	—
TM73	Thunder Wave	Electric	Status	—	100	20	Normal	—	—
TM77	Psych Up	Normal	Status	—	—	10	Normal	—	—
TM83	Work Up	Normal	Status	—	—	30	Self	—	—
TM85	Dream Eater	Psychic	Special	100	100	15	Normal	—	—
TM86	Grass Knot	Grass	Special	—	100	20	Normal	—	○
TM87	Swagger	Normal	Status	—	90	15	Normal	—	—
TM90	Substitute	Normal	Status	—	—	10	Self	—	—

MOVES TAUGHT BY PEOPLE
Name	Type	Kind	Pow.	Acc.	PP	Range	Long	DA

MOVES TAUGHT BY MOVE TUTORS FOR SHARDS
Name	Type	Kind	Pow.	Acc.	PP	Range	Long	DA
Covet	Normal	Physical	60	100	40	Normal	—	—
Uproar	Normal	Special	90	100	10	1 Random	—	—
Last Resort	Normal	Physical	140	100	5	Normal	—	○
Hyper Voice	Normal	Special	90	100	10	Many Others	—	—
Icy Wind	Ice	Special	55	95	15	Many Others	—	—
Zen Headbutt	Psychic	Physical	80	90	15	Normal	—	—
Gravity	Psychic	Status	—	—	5	Both Sides	—	○
Snore	Normal	Special	40	100	15	Normal	—	—
Heal Bell	Normal	Status	—	—	5	Your Party	—	—
Drain Punch	Fighting	Physical	75	100	10	Normal	—	○
Helping Hand	Normal	Status	—	—	20	1 Ally	—	—
Recycle	Normal	Status	—	—	10	Self	—	—
Endeavor	Normal	Physical	—	100	5	Normal	—	—
Sleep Talk	Normal	Status	—	—	10	Self	—	—

EGG MOVES
Name	Type	Kind	Pow.	Acc.	PP	Range	Long	DA
Present	Normal	Physical	—	90	15	Normal	—	—
Metronome	Normal	Status	—	—	10	Self	—	—
Heal Bell	Normal	Status	—	—	5	Your Party	—	—
Aromatherapy	Grass	Status	—	—	5	Your Party	—	—
Counter	Fighting	Physical	—	100	20	Varies	—	○
Helping Hand	Normal	Status	—	—	20	1 Ally	—	—
Gravity	Psychic	Status	—	—	5	Both Sides	—	○
Last Resort	Normal	Physical	140	100	5	Normal	—	○
Mud Bomb	Ground	Special	65	85	10	Normal	—	—
Natural Gift	Normal	Physical	—	100	15	Normal	—	—
Endure	Normal	Status	—	—	10	Self	—	—

---

441 Chatot
Music Note Pokémon

- HEIGHT: 1'08"
- WEIGHT: 4.2 lbs.
- GENDER: ♂ / ♀

Its tongue is just like a human's. As a result, it can cleverly mimic human speech.

TYPE Normal Flying

ABILITIES
- Keen Eye
- Tangled Feet

HIDDEN ABILITY
- Big Pecks

STATS
HP	▪▪▪
Attack	▪▪▪
Defense	▪▪
Sp. Atk	▪▪▪▪
Sp. Def	▪▪
Speed	▪▪▪▪

EGG GROUPS
Flying

ITEMS SOMETIMES HELD
- Metronome

Same form for ♂ / ♀

Pokémon AR Marker

EVOLUTION
Does not evolve

HOW TO OBTAIN
Pokémon Black Version 2	Route 18 (Hidden Grotto)
Pokémon White Version 2	Route 18 (Hidden Grotto)

HOW TO OBTAIN FROM OTHER GAMES

LEVEL-UP AND LEARNED MOVES
Lv.	Name	Type	Kind	Pow.	Acc.	PP	Range	Long	DA
1	Peck	Flying	Physical	35	100	35	Normal	○	—
5	Growl	Normal	Status	—	100	40	Many Others	—	—
9	Mirror Move	Flying	Status	—	—	20	Normal	—	—
13	Sing	Normal	Status	—	55	15	Normal	—	—
17	Fury Attack	Normal	Physical	15	85	20	Normal	—	—
21	Chatter	Flying	Special	60	100	20	Normal	○	—
25	Taunt	Dark	Status	—	100	20	Normal	—	—
29	Round	Normal	Special	60	100	15	Normal	—	—
33	Mimic	Normal	Status	—	—	10	Normal	—	—
37	Echoed Voice	Normal	Special	40	100	15	Normal	—	—
41	Roost	Flying	Status	—	—	10	Self	—	—
45	Uproar	Normal	Special	90	100	10	1 Random	—	—
49	Synchronoise	Psychic	Special	70	100	15	Adjacent	—	—
53	FeatherDance	Flying	Status	—	100	15	Normal	—	—
57	Hyper Voice	Normal	Special	90	100	10	Many Others	—	—

TM & HM MOVES
Lv.	Name	Type	Kind	Pow.	Acc.	PP	Range	Long	DA
TM06	Toxic	Poison	Status	—	90	10	Normal	—	—
TM10	Hidden Power	Normal	Special	—	100	15	Normal	—	—
TM11	Sunny Day	Fire	Status	—	—	5	Both Sides	—	—
TM12	Taunt	Dark	Status	—	100	20	Normal	—	—
TM17	Protect	Normal	Status	—	—	10	Self	—	—
TM18	Rain Dance	Water	Status	—	—	5	Both Sides	—	—
TM21	Frustration	Normal	Physical	—	100	20	Normal	—	○
TM27	Return	Normal	Physical	—	100	20	Normal	—	○
TM32	Double Team	Normal	Status	—	—	15	Self	—	—
TM40	Aerial Ace	Flying	Physical	60	—	20	Normal	—	—
TM41	Torment	Dark	Status	—	100	15	Normal	—	—
TM42	Facade	Normal	Physical	70	100	20	Normal	—	—
TM44	Rest	Psychic	Status	—	—	10	Self	—	—
TM45	Attract	Normal	Status	—	100	15	Normal	—	—
TM46	Thief	Dark	Physical	40	100	10	Normal	—	—
TM48	Round	Normal	Special	60	100	15	Normal	—	—
TM49	Echoed Voice	Normal	Special	40	100	15	Normal	—	—
TM83	Work Up	Normal	Status	—	—	30	Self	—	—
TM87	Swagger	Normal	Status	—	90	15	Normal	—	—
TM88	Pluck	Flying	Physical	60	100	20	Normal	○	—
TM89	U-turn	Bug	Physical	70	100	20	Normal	—	—
TM90	Substitute	Normal	Status	—	—	10	Self	—	—
HM02	Fly	Flying	Physical	90	95	15	Normal	—	—

MOVES TAUGHT BY PEOPLE
Name	Type	Kind	Pow.	Acc.	PP	Range	Long	DA

MOVES TAUGHT BY MOVE TUTORS FOR SHARDS
Name	Type	Kind	Pow.	Acc.	PP	Range	Long	DA
Uproar	Normal	Special	90	100	10	1 Random	—	—
Hyper Voice	Normal	Special	90	100	10	Many Others	—	—
Snore	Normal	Special	40	100	15	Normal	—	—
Roost	Flying	Status	—	—	10	Self	—	—
Sky Attack	Flying	Physical	140	90	5	Normal	○	—
Role Play	Psychic	Status	—	—	10	Normal	—	—
Heat Wave	Fire	Special	100	90	10	Many Others	—	—
Tailwind	Flying	Status	—	—	30	Your Side	—	—
Sleep Talk	Normal	Status	—	—	10	Self	—	—

EGG MOVES
Name	Type	Kind	Pow.	Acc.	PP	Range	Long	DA
Encore	Normal	Status	—	100	5	Normal	—	—
Night Shade	Ghost	Special	—	100	15	Normal	—	—
Agility	Psychic	Status	—	—	30	Self	—	—
Nasty Plot	Dark	Status	—	—	20	Self	—	—
Supersonic	Normal	Status	—	55	20	Normal	—	—
Steel Wing	Steel	Physical	70	90	25	Normal	—	—
Sleep Talk	Normal	Status	—	—	10	Self	—	—
Defog	Flying	Status	—	—	15	Normal	—	—
Air Cutter	Flying	Special	55	95	25	Many Others	—	—

Forbidden Pokémon

442 Spiritomb

- HEIGHT: 3'03"
- WEIGHT: 238.1 lbs.
- GENDER: ♂ / ♀

Its constant mischief and misdeeds resulted in it being bound to an Odd Keystone by a mysterious spell.

Same form for ♂ / ♀

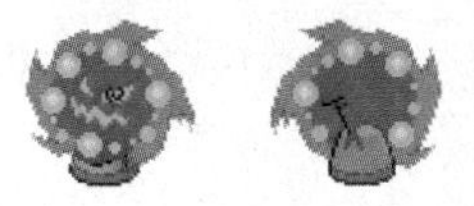

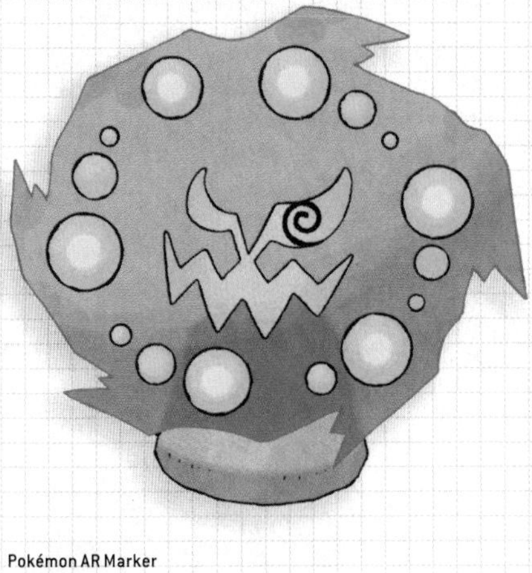

Pokémon AR Marker

TYPE Ghost Dark

ABILITY

- Pressure

HIDDEN ABILITY

- Infiltrator

STATS

HP
Attack
Defense
Sp. Atk
Sp. Def
Speed

EGG GROUPS

Amorphous

ITEMS SOMETIMES HELD

- None

EVOLUTION

Does not evolve

HOW TO OBTAIN

Pokémon Black Version 2	You can receive one if you trade Pokémon during a date with Yancy or Curtis (eighth time)
Pokémon White Version 2	You can receive one if you trade Pokémon during a date with Yancy or Curtis (eighth time)

HOW TO OBTAIN FROM OTHER GAMES

Pokémon Platinum Version	Broken stone tower on Route 209
—	

LEVEL-UP AND LEARNED MOVES

Lv.	Name	Type	Kind	Pow.	Acc.	PP	Range	Long	DA
1	Curse	Ghost	Status	—	—	10	Varies	—	—
1	Pursuit	Dark	Physical	40	100	20	Normal	—	○
1	Confuse Ray	Ghost	Status	—	100	10	Normal	—	—
1	Spite	Ghost	Status	—	100	10	Normal	—	—
1	Shadow Sneak	Ghost	Physical	40	100	30	Normal	—	○
7	Faint Attack	Dark	Physical	60	—	20	Normal	—	○
13	Hypnosis	Psychic	Status	—	60	20	Normal	—	—
19	Dream Eater	Psychic	Special	100	100	15	Normal	—	—
25	Ominous Wind	Ghost	Special	60	100	5	Normal	—	—
31	Sucker Punch	Dark	Physical	80	100	5	Normal	—	○
37	Nasty Plot	Dark	Status	—	—	20	Self	—	—
43	Memento	Dark	Status	—	100	10	Normal	—	—
49	Dark Pulse	Dark	Special	80	100	15	Normal	○	—

TM & HM MOVES

Lv.	Name	Type	Kind	Pow.	Acc.	PP	Range	Long	DA
TM04	Calm Mind	Psychic	Status	—	—	20	Self	—	—
TM06	Toxic	Poison	Status	—	90	10	Normal	—	—
TM10	Hidden Power	Normal	Special	—	100	15	Normal	—	—
TM11	Sunny Day	Fire	Status	—	—	5	Both Sides	—	—
TM12	Taunt	Dark	Status	—	100	20	Normal	—	—
TM15	Hyper Beam	Normal	Special	150	90	5	Normal	—	—
TM17	Protect	Normal	Status	—	—	10	Self	—	—
TM18	Rain Dance	Water	Status	—	—	5	Both Sides	—	—
TM19	Telekinesis	Psychic	Status	—	—	15	Normal	—	—
TM21	Frustration	Normal	Physical	—	100	20	Normal	—	○
TM27	Return	Normal	Physical	—	100	20	Normal	—	○
TM29	Psychic	Psychic	Special	90	100	10	Normal	—	—
TM30	Shadow Ball	Ghost	Special	80	100	15	Normal	—	—
TM32	Double Team	Normal	Status	—	—	15	Self	—	—
TM39	Rock Tomb	Rock	Physical	50	80	10	Normal	—	—
TM41	Torment	Dark	Status	—	100	15	Normal	—	—
TM42	Facade	Normal	Physical	70	100	20	Normal	—	○
TM44	Rest	Psychic	Status	—	—	10	Self	—	—
TM45	Attract	Normal	Status	—	100	15	Normal	—	—
TM46	Thief	Dark	Physical	40	100	10	Normal	—	○
TM48	Round	Normal	Special	60	100	15	Normal	—	—
TM60	Quash	Dark	Status	—	100	15	Normal	—	—
TM61	Will-O-Wisp	Fire	Status	—	75	15	Normal	—	—
TM63	Embargo	Dark	Status	—	100	15	Normal	—	—
TM67	Retaliate	Normal	Physical	70	100	5	Normal	—	○
TM68	Giga Impact	Normal	Physical	150	90	5	Normal	—	○
TM70	Flash	Normal	Status	—	100	20	Normal	—	—
TM77	Psych Up	Normal	Status	—	—	10	Normal	—	—
TM85	Dream Eater	Psychic	Special	100	100	15	Normal	—	—
TM87	Swagger	Normal	Status	—	90	15	Normal	—	—
TM90	Substitute	Normal	Status	—	—	10	Self	—	—
TM95	Snarl	Dark	Special	55	95	15	Many Others	—	—

MOVES TAUGHT BY PEOPLE

Name	Type	Kind	Pow.	Acc.	PP	Range	Long	DA

MOVES TAUGHT BY MOVE TUTORS FOR SHARDS

Name	Type	Kind	Pow.	Acc.	PP	Range	Long	DA
Uproar	Normal	Special	90	100	10	1 Random	—	—
Icy Wind	Ice	Special	55	95	15	Many Others	—	—
Foul Play	Dark	Physical	95	100	15	Normal	—	○
Dark Pulse	Dark	Special	80	100	15	Normal	○	—
Snore	Normal	Special	40	100	15	Normal	—	—
Pain Split	Normal	Status	—	—	20	Normal	—	—
Wonder Room	Psychic	Status	—	—	10	Both Sides	—	—
Spite	Ghost	Status	—	100	10	Normal	—	—
Trick	Psychic	Status	—	100	10	Normal	—	—
Sleep Talk	Normal	Status	—	—	10	Self	—	—
Snatch	Dark	Status	—	—	10	Self	—	—

EGG MOVES

Name	Type	Kind	Pow.	Acc.	PP	Range	Long	DA
Destiny Bond	Ghost	Status	—	—	5	Self	—	—
Pain Split	Normal	Status	—	—	20	Normal	—	—
SmokeScreen	Normal	Status	—	100	20	Normal	—	—
Imprison	Psychic	Status	—	—	10	Self	—	—
Grudge	Ghost	Status	—	—	5	Self	—	—
Shadow Sneak	Ghost	Physical	40	100	30	Normal	—	○
Captivate	Normal	Status	—	100	20	Many Others	—	—
Nightmare	Ghost	Status	—	100	15	Normal	—	—

Land Shark Pokémon

443 Gible

- HEIGHT: 2'04"
- WEIGHT: 45.2 lbs.
- GENDER: ♂ / ♀

It attacks using its huge mouth. While its attacks are powerful, it hurts itself out of clumsiness, too.

♂ ♀

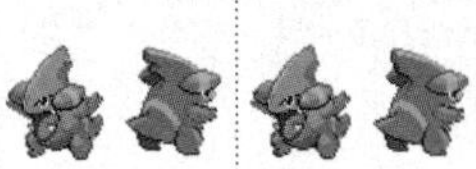

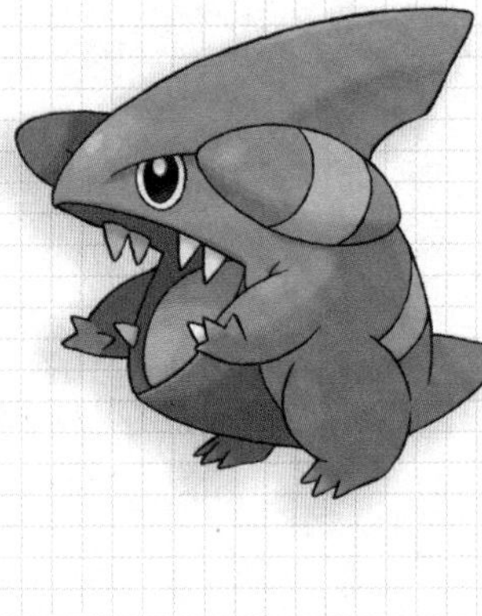

Pokémon AR Marker

TYPE Dragon Ground

ABILITY

- Sand Veil

HIDDEN ABILITY

- Rough Skin

STATS

HP
Attack
Defense
Sp. Atk
Sp. Def
Speed

EGG GROUPS

Monster/Dragon

ITEMS SOMETIMES HELD

- None

EVOLUTION

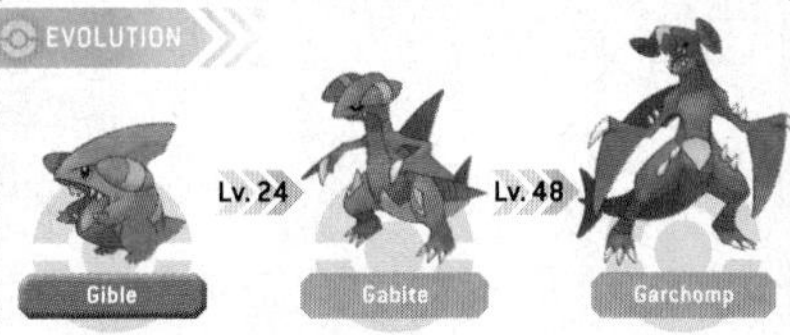

Lv. 24
Lv. 48
Gible
Gabite
Garchomp

HOW TO OBTAIN

Pokémon Black Version 2	Link Trade or Poké Transfer
Pokémon White Version 2	Link Trade or Poké Transfer

HOW TO OBTAIN FROM OTHER GAMES

Pokémon Platinum Version	Wayward Cave (beneath Cycling Road)
—	

LEVEL-UP AND LEARNED MOVES

Lv.	Name	Type	Kind	Pow.	Acc.	PP	Range	Long	DA
1	Tackle	Normal	Physical	50	100	35	Normal	—	○
3	Sand-Attack	Ground	Status	—	100	15	Normal	—	—
7	Dragon Rage	Dragon	Special	—	100	10	Normal	—	—
13	Sandstorm	Rock	Status	—	—	10	Both Sides	—	—
15	Take Down	Normal	Physical	90	85	20	Normal	—	○
19	Sand Tomb	Ground	Physical	35	85	15	Normal	—	—
25	Slash	Normal	Physical	70	100	20	Normal	—	○
27	Dragon Claw	Dragon	Physical	80	100	15	Normal	—	○
31	Dig	Ground	Physical	80	100	10	Normal	—	○
37	Dragon Rush	Dragon	Physical	100	75	10	Normal	—	○

TM & HM MOVES

Lv.	Name	Type	Kind	Pow.	Acc.	PP	Range	Long	DA
TM01	Hone Claws	Dark	Status	—	—	15	Self	—	—
TM02	Dragon Claw	Dragon	Physical	80	100	15	Normal	—	○
TM05	Roar	Normal	Status	—	100	20	Normal	—	—
TM06	Toxic	Poison	Status	—	90	10	Normal	—	—
TM10	Hidden Power	Normal	Special	—	100	15	Normal	—	—
TM11	Sunny Day	Fire	Status	—	—	5	Both Sides	—	—
TM17	Protect	Normal	Status	—	—	10	Self	—	—
TM18	Rain Dance	Water	Status	—	—	5	Both Sides	—	—
TM21	Frustration	Normal	Physical	—	100	20	Normal	—	○
TM26	Earthquake	Ground	Physical	100	100	10	Adjacent	—	—
TM27	Return	Normal	Physical	—	100	20	Normal	—	○
TM28	Dig	Ground	Physical	80	100	10	Normal	—	○
TM32	Double Team	Normal	Status	—	—	15	Self	—	—
TM35	Flamethrower	Fire	Special	95	100	15	Normal	—	—
TM37	Sandstorm	Rock	Status	—	—	10	Both Sides	—	—
TM38	Fire Blast	Fire	Special	120	85	5	Normal	—	—
TM39	Rock Tomb	Rock	Physical	50	80	10	Normal	—	—
TM40	Aerial Ace	Flying	Physical	60	—	20	Normal	○	○
TM42	Facade	Normal	Physical	70	100	20	Normal	—	○
TM44	Rest	Psychic	Status	—	—	10	Self	—	—
TM45	Attract	Normal	Status	—	100	15	Normal	—	—
TM48	Round	Normal	Special	60	100	15	Normal	—	—
TM59	Incinerate	Fire	Special	30	100	15	Many Others	—	—
TM65	Shadow Claw	Ghost	Physical	70	100	15	Normal	—	○
TM71	Stone Edge	Rock	Physical	100	80	5	Normal	—	—
TM78	Bulldoze	Ground	Physical	60	100	20	Adjacent	—	—
TM80	Rock Slide	Rock	Physical	75	90	10	Many Others	—	—
TM87	Swagger	Normal	Status	—	90	15	Normal	—	—
TM90	Substitute	Normal	Status	—	—	10	Self	—	—
TM94	Rock Smash	Fighting	Physical	40	100	15	Normal	—	○
HM01	Cut	Normal	Physical	50	95	30	Normal	—	○
HM04	Strength	Normal	Physical	80	100	15	Normal	—	○

MOVES TAUGHT BY PEOPLE

Name	Type	Kind	Pow.	Acc.	PP	Range	Long	DA
Draco Meteor	Dragon	Special	140	90	5	Normal	—	—

MOVES TAUGHT BY MOVE TUTORS FOR SHARDS

Name	Type	Kind	Pow.	Acc.	PP	Range	Long	DA
Iron Head	Steel	Physical	80	100	15	Normal	—	○
Iron Tail	Steel	Physical	100	75	15	Normal	—	○
Earth Power	Ground	Special	90	100	10	Normal	—	—
Dragon Pulse	Dragon	Special	90	100	10	Normal	○	—
Snore	Normal	Special	40	100	15	Normal	—	—
Stealth Rock	Rock	Status	—	—	20	3 Foes	—	—
Outrage	Dragon	Physical	120	100	10	1 Random	—	○
Sleep Talk	Normal	Status	—	—	10	Self	—	—

EGG MOVES

Name	Type	Kind	Pow.	Acc.	PP	Range	Long	DA
DragonBreath	Dragon	Special	60	100	20	Normal	—	—
Outrage	Dragon	Physical	120	100	10	1 Random	—	○
Twister	Dragon	Special	40	100	20	Many Others	—	—
Scary Face	Normal	Status	—	100	10	Normal	—	—
Double-Edge	Normal	Physical	120	100	15	Normal	—	○
Thrash	Normal	Physical	120	100	10	1 Random	—	○
Metal Claw	Steel	Physical	50	95	35	Normal	—	○
Sand Tomb	Ground	Physical	35	85	15	Normal	—	—
Body Slam	Normal	Physical	85	100	15	Normal	—	○
Iron Head	Steel	Physical	80	100	15	Normal	—	○
Mud Shot	Ground	Special	55	95	15	Normal	—	—
Rock Climb	Normal	Physical	90	85	20	Normal	—	○
Iron Tail	Steel	Physical	100	75	15	Normal	—	○

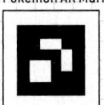

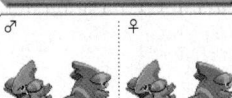

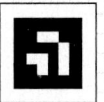

NATIONAL POKÉDEX

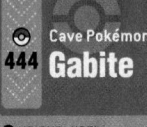

444 Gabite

Cave Pokémon

444 Gabite

- HEIGHT: 4'07"
- WEIGHT: 123.5 lbs.
- GENDER: ♂ / ♀

It loves sparkly things. It seeks treasures in caves and hoards the loot in its nest.

♂ ♀

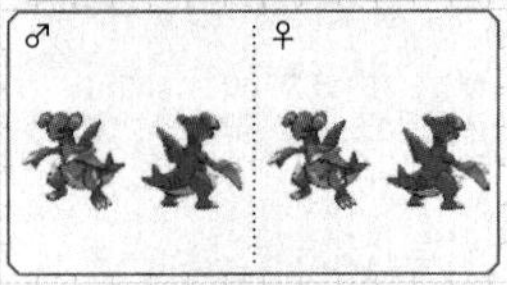

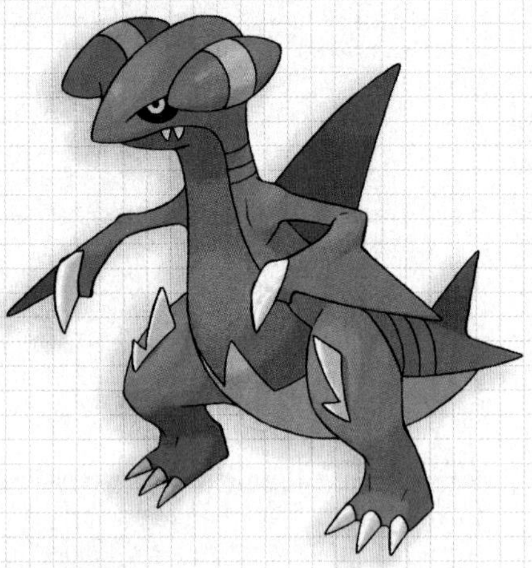

Pokémon AR Marker

TYPE Dragon Ground

ABILITY
- Sand Veil

HIDDEN ABILITY
- Rough Skin

STATS
- HP
- Attack
- Defense
- Sp. Atk
- Sp. Def
- Speed

EGG GROUPS
Monster/Dragon

ITEMS SOMETIMES HELD
- None

EVOLUTION

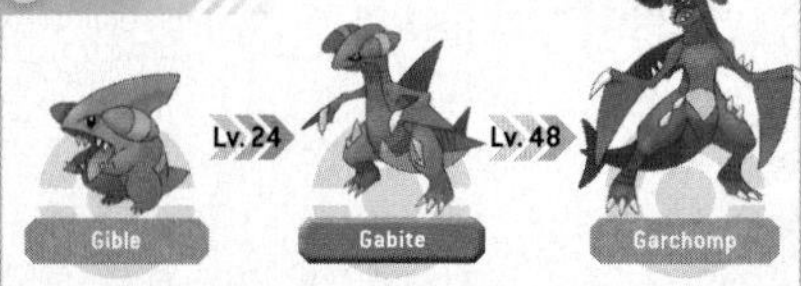

HOW TO OBTAIN

Pokémon Black Version 2	Link Trade or Poké Transfer
Pokémon White Version 2	Link Trade or Poké Transfer

HOW TO OBTAIN FROM OTHER GAMES

Pokémon Platinum Version	Victory Road 1F
	—

LEVEL-UP AND LEARNED MOVES

Lv.	Name	Type	Kind	Pow.	Acc.	PP	Range	Long	DA
1	Tackle	Normal	Physical	50	100	35	Normal	—	○
1	Sand-Attack	Ground	Status	—	100	15	Normal	—	—
3	Sand-Attack	Ground	Status	—	100	15	Normal	—	—
7	Dragon Rage	Dragon	Special	—	100	10	Normal	—	—
13	Sandstorm	Rock	Status	—	—	10	Both Sides	—	—
15	Take Down	Normal	Physical	90	85	20	Normal	—	○
19	Sand Tomb	Ground	Physical	35	85	15	Normal	—	—
24	Dual Chop	Dragon	Physical	40	90	15	Normal	—	○
28	Slash	Normal	Physical	70	100	20	Normal	—	○
33	Dragon Claw	Dragon	Physical	80	100	15	Normal	—	○
40	Dig	Ground	Physical	80	100	10	Normal	—	○
49	Dragon Rush	Dragon	Physical	100	75	10	Normal	—	○

MOVES TAUGHT BY PEOPLE

Name	Type	Kind	Pow.	Acc.	PP	Range	Long	DA
Draco Meteor	Dragon	Special	140	90	5	Normal	—	—

MOVES TAUGHT BY MOVE TUTORS FOR SHARDS

Name	Type	Kind	Pow.	Acc.	PP	Range	Long	DA
Iron Head	Steel	Physical	80	100	15	Normal	—	○
Dual Chop	Dragon	Physical	40	90	15	Normal	—	○
Iron Tail	Steel	Physical	100	75	15	Normal	—	○
Earth Power	Ground	Special	90	100	10	Normal	—	—
Dragon Pulse	Dragon	Special	90	100	10	Normal	○	—
Snore	Normal	Special	40	100	15	Normal	—	—
Stealth Rock	Rock	Status	—	—	20	3 Foes	—	—
Outrage	Dragon	Physical	120	100	10	1 Random	—	○
Sleep Talk	Normal	Status	—	—	10	Self	—	—

TM & HM MOVES

Lv.	Name	Type	Kind	Pow.	Acc.	PP	Range	Long	DA
TM01	Hone Claws	Dark	Status	—	—	15	Self	—	—
TM02	Dragon Claw	Dragon	Physical	80	100	15	Normal	—	○
TM05	Roar	Normal	Status	—	100	20	Normal	—	—
TM06	Toxic	Poison	Status	—	90	10	Normal	—	—
TM10	Hidden Power	Normal	Special	—	100	15	Normal	—	—
TM11	Sunny Day	Fire	Status	—	—	5	Both Sides	—	—
TM17	Protect	Normal	Status	—	—	10	Self	—	—
TM18	Rain Dance	Water	Status	—	—	5	Both Sides	—	—
TM21	Frustration	Normal	Physical	—	100	20	Normal	—	○
TM26	Earthquake	Ground	Physical	100	100	10	Adjacent	—	—
TM27	Return	Normal	Physical	—	100	20	Normal	—	○
TM28	Dig	Ground	Physical	80	100	10	Normal	—	○
TM32	Double Team	Normal	Status	—	—	15	Self	—	—
TM35	Flamethrower	Fire	Special	95	100	15	Normal	—	—
TM37	Sandstorm	Rock	Status	—	—	10	Both Sides	—	—
TM38	Fire Blast	Fire	Special	120	85	5	Normal	—	—
TM39	Rock Tomb	Rock	Physical	50	80	10	Normal	—	—
TM40	Aerial Ace	Flying	Physical	60	—	20	Normal	○	○
TM42	Facade	Normal	Physical	70	100	20	Normal	—	○
TM44	Rest	Psychic	Status	—	—	10	Self	—	—
TM45	Attract	Normal	Status	—	100	15	Normal	—	—
TM48	Round	Normal	Special	60	100	15	Normal	—	—
TM59	Incinerate	Fire	Special	30	100	15	Many Others	—	—
TM65	Shadow Claw	Ghost	Physical	70	100	15	Normal	—	○
TM71	Stone Edge	Rock	Physical	100	80	5	Normal	—	—
TM78	Bulldoze	Ground	Physical	60	100	20	Adjacent	—	—
TM80	Rock Slide	Rock	Physical	75	90	10	Many Others	—	—
TM87	Swagger	Normal	Status	—	90	15	Normal	—	—
TM90	Substitute	Normal	Status	—	—	10	Self	—	—
TM94	Rock Smash	Fighting	Physical	40	100	15	Normal	—	○
HM01	Cut	Normal	Physical	50	95	30	Normal	—	○
HM04	Strength	Normal	Physical	80	100	15	Normal	—	○

445 Garchomp

Mach Pokémon

445 Garchomp

- HEIGHT: 6'03"
- WEIGHT: 209.4 lbs.
- GENDER: ♂ / ♀

It is said that when one runs at high speed, its wings create blades of wind that can fell nearby trees.

♂ ♀

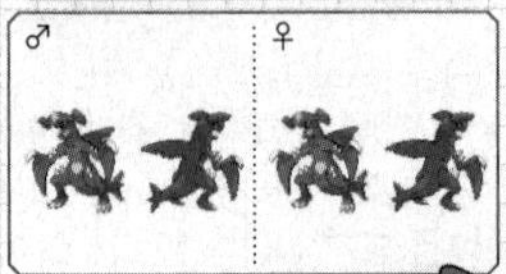

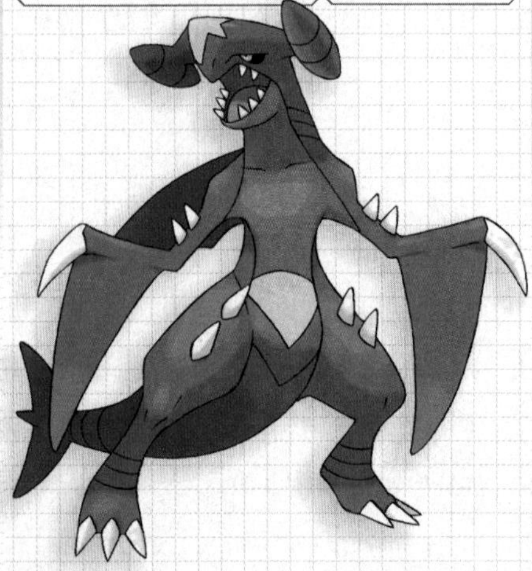

Pokémon AR Marker

TYPE Dragon Ground

ABILITY
- Sand Veil

HIDDEN ABILITY
- Rough Skin

STATS
- HP
- Attack
- Defense
- Sp. Atk
- Sp. Def
- Speed

EGG GROUPS
Monster/Dragon

ITEMS SOMETIMES HELD
- None

EVOLUTION

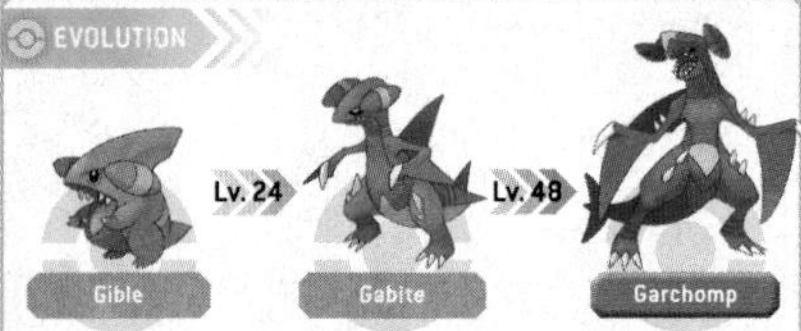

HOW TO OBTAIN

Pokémon Black Version 2	Level up a Gabite you obtain via Link Trade or Poké Transfer to Lv. 48
Pokémon White Version 2	Level up a Gabite you obtain via Link Trade or Poké Transfer to Lv. 48

HOW TO OBTAIN FROM OTHER GAMES

—
—

LEVEL-UP AND LEARNED MOVES

Lv.	Name	Type	Kind	Pow.	Acc.	PP	Range	Long	DA
1	Fire Fang	Fire	Physical	65	95	15	Normal	—	○
1	Tackle	Normal	Physical	50	100	35	Normal	—	○
1	Sand-Attack	Ground	Status	—	100	15	Normal	—	—
1	Dragon Rage	Dragon	Special	—	100	10	Normal	—	—
1	Sandstorm	Rock	Status	—	—	10	Both Sides	—	—
3	Sand-Attack	Ground	Status	—	100	15	Normal	—	—
7	Dragon Rage	Dragon	Special	—	100	10	Normal	—	—
13	Sandstorm	Rock	Status	—	—	10	Both Sides	—	—
15	Take Down	Normal	Physical	90	85	20	Normal	—	○
19	Sand Tomb	Ground	Physical	35	85	15	Normal	—	—
24	Dual Chop	Dragon	Physical	40	90	15	Normal	—	○
28	Slash	Normal	Physical	70	100	20	Normal	—	○
33	Dragon Claw	Dragon	Physical	80	100	15	Normal	—	○
40	Dig	Ground	Physical	80	100	10	Normal	—	○
48	Crunch	Dark	Physical	80	100	15	Normal	—	○
55	Dragon Rush	Dragon	Physical	100	75	10	Normal	—	○

TM & HM MOVES

Lv.	Name	Type	Kind	Pow.	Acc.	PP	Range	Long	DA
TM01	Hone Claws	Dark	Status	—	—	15	Self	—	—
TM02	Dragon Claw	Dragon	Physical	80	100	15	Normal	—	○
TM05	Roar	Normal	Status	—	100	20	Normal	—	—
TM06	Toxic	Poison	Status	—	90	10	Normal	—	—
TM10	Hidden Power	Normal	Special	—	100	15	Normal	—	—
TM11	Sunny Day	Fire	Status	—	—	5	Both Sides	—	—
TM15	Hyper Beam	Normal	Special	150	90	5	Normal	—	—
TM17	Protect	Normal	Status	—	—	10	Self	—	—
TM18	Rain Dance	Water	Status	—	—	5	Both Sides	—	—
TM21	Frustration	Normal	Physical	—	100	20	Normal	—	○
TM26	Earthquake	Ground	Physical	100	100	10	Adjacent	—	—
TM27	Return	Normal	Physical	—	100	20	Normal	—	○
TM28	Dig	Ground	Physical	80	100	10	Normal	—	○
TM31	Brick Break	Fighting	Physical	75	100	15	Normal	—	○
TM32	Double Team	Normal	Status	—	—	15	Self	—	—
TM35	Flamethrower	Fire	Special	95	100	15	Normal	—	—
TM37	Sandstorm	Rock	Status	—	—	10	Both Sides	—	—
TM38	Fire Blast	Fire	Special	120	85	5	Normal	—	—
TM39	Rock Tomb	Rock	Physical	50	80	10	Normal	—	—
TM40	Aerial Ace	Flying	Physical	60	—	20	Normal	○	○
TM42	Facade	Normal	Physical	70	100	20	Normal	—	○
TM44	Rest	Psychic	Status	—	—	10	Self	—	—
TM45	Attract	Normal	Status	—	100	15	Normal	—	—
TM48	Round	Normal	Special	60	100	15	Normal	—	—
TM54	False Swipe	Normal	Physical	40	100	40	Normal	—	○
TM56	Fling	Dark	Physical	—	100	10	Normal	—	—
TM59	Incinerate	Fire	Special	30	100	15	Many Others	—	—
TM65	Shadow Claw	Ghost	Physical	70	100	15	Normal	—	○
TM68	Giga Impact	Normal	Physical	150	90	5	Normal	—	○
TM71	Stone Edge	Rock	Physical	100	80	5	Normal	—	—
TM75	Swords Dance	Normal	Status	—	—	30	Self	—	—
TM78	Bulldoze	Ground	Physical	60	100	20	Adjacent	—	—
TM80	Rock Slide	Rock	Physical	75	90	10	Many Others	—	—
TM82	Dragon Tail	Dragon	Physical	60	90	10	Normal	—	○
TM84	Poison Jab	Poison	Physical	80	100	20	Normal	—	○
TM87	Swagger	Normal	Status	—	90	15	Normal	—	—
TM90	Substitute	Normal	Status	—	—	10	Self	—	—

Lv.	Name	Type	Kind	Pow.	Acc.	PP	Range	Long	DA
TM94	Rock Smash	Fighting	Physical	40	100	15	Normal	—	○
HM01	Cut	Normal	Physical	50	95	30	Normal	—	○
HM03	Surf	Water	Special	95	100	15	Adjacent	—	—
HM04	Strength	Normal	Physical	80	100	15	Normal	—	○

MOVES TAUGHT BY PEOPLE

Name	Type	Kind	Pow.	Acc.	PP	Range	Long	DA
Draco Meteor	Dragon	Special	140	90	5	Normal	—	—

MOVES TAUGHT BY MOVE TUTORS FOR SHARDS

Name	Type	Kind	Pow.	Acc.	PP	Range	Long	DA
Iron Head	Steel	Physical	80	100	15	Normal	—	○
Dual Chop	Dragon	Physical	40	90	15	Normal	—	○
Iron Tail	Steel	Physical	100	75	15	Normal	—	○
Aqua Tail	Water	Physical	90	90	10	Normal	—	○
Earth Power	Ground	Special	90	100	10	Normal	—	—
Dragon Pulse	Dragon	Special	90	100	10	Normal	○	—
Snore	Normal	Special	40	100	15	Normal	—	—
Stealth Rock	Rock	Status	—	—	20	3 Foes	—	—
Outrage	Dragon	Physical	120	100	10	1 Random	—	○
Sleep Talk	Normal	Status	—	—	10	Self	—	—

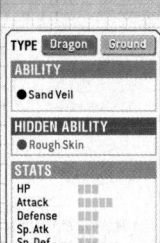

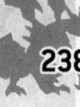

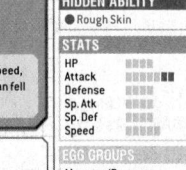

446 Munchlax

Big Eater Pokémon

- HEIGHT: 2'00"
- WEIGHT: 231.5 lbs.
- GENDER: ♂ / ♀

In its desperation to gulp down food, it forgets about the food it has hidden under its fur.

Same form for ♂ / ♀

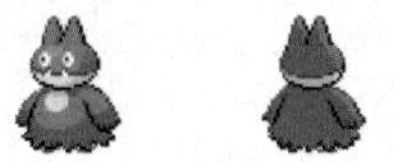

TYPE: Normal

ABILITIES
- Pickup
- Thick Fat

HIDDEN ABILITY
- Gluttony

STATS
HP, Attack, Defense, Sp. Atk, Sp. Def, Speed

EGG GROUPS
No Egg has ever been discovered

ITEMS SOMETIMES HELD
- None

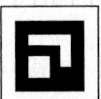

EVOLUTION

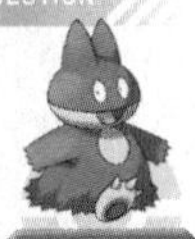

Munchlax → Level up with high friendship → Snorlax

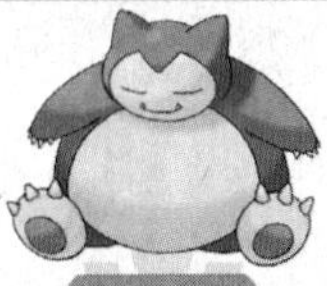

➡ p. 85

HOW TO OBTAIN

Pokémon Black Version 2	Have the Snorlax you receive from Yancy or Curtis hold the Full Incense and leave it at the Pokémon Day Care. Hatch the Egg that is found.
Pokémon White Version 2	Have the Snorlax you receive from Yancy or Curtis hold the Full Incense and leave it at the Pokémon Day Care. Hatch the Egg that is found.

HOW TO OBTAIN FROM OTHER GAMES

Pokémon Black Version	Trade the man in Undella Town a Cinccino for it (summer)
Pokémon White Version	Trade the man in Undella Town a Cinccino for it (summer)

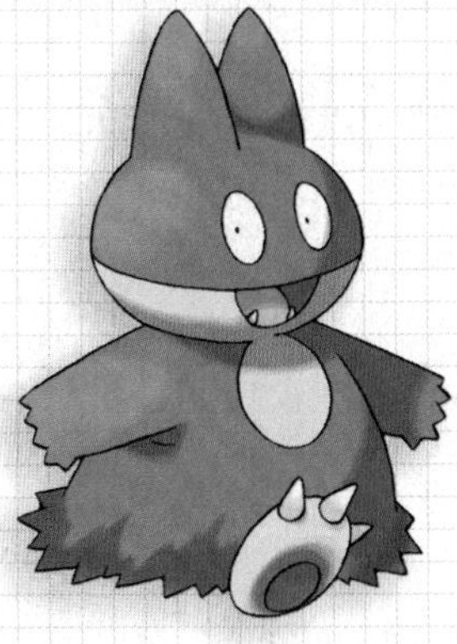

Pokémon AR Marker

LEVEL-UP AND LEARNED MOVES

Lv.	Name	Type	Kind	Pow.	Acc.	PP	Range	Long	DA
1	Metronome	Normal	Status	—	—	10	Self	—	—
1	Odor Sleuth	Normal	Status	—	—	40	Normal	—	—
1	Tackle	Normal	Physical	50	100	35	Normal	—	○
4	Defense Curl	Normal	Status	—	—	40	Self	—	—
9	Amnesia	Psychic	Status	—	—	20	Self	—	—
12	Lick	Ghost	Physical	20	100	30	Normal	—	○
17	Recycle	Normal	Status	—	—	10	Self	—	—
20	Screech	Normal	Status	—	85	40	Normal	—	—
25	Chip Away	Normal	Physical	70	100	20	Normal	—	○
28	Stockpile	Normal	Status	—	—	20	Self	—	—
33	Swallow	Normal	Status	—	—	10	Self	—	—
36	Body Slam	Normal	Physical	85	100	15	Normal	—	○
41	Fling	Dark	Physical	—	100	10	Normal	—	—
44	Rollout	Rock	Physical	30	90	20	Normal	—	○
49	Natural Gift	Normal	Physical	—	100	15	Normal	—	—
52	Snatch	Dark	Status	—	—	10	Self	—	—
57	Last Resort	Normal	Physical	140	100	5	Normal	—	○

TM & HM MOVES

Lv.	Name	Type	Kind	Pow.	Acc.	PP	Range	Long	DA
TM06	Toxic	Poison	Status	—	90	10	Normal	—	—
TM10	Hidden Power	Normal	Special	—	100	15	Normal	—	—
TM11	Sunny Day	Fire	Status	—	—	5	Both Sides	—	—
TM13	Ice Beam	Ice	Special	95	100	10	Normal	—	—
TM14	Blizzard	Ice	Special	120	70	5	Many Others	—	—
TM17	Protect	Normal	Status	—	—	10	Self	—	—
TM18	Rain Dance	Water	Status	—	—	5	Both Sides	—	—
TM21	Frustration	Normal	Physical	—	100	20	Normal	—	○
TM22	SolarBeam	Grass	Special	120	100	10	Normal	—	—
TM24	Thunderbolt	Electric	Special	95	100	15	Normal	—	—
TM25	Thunder	Electric	Special	120	70	10	Normal	—	—
TM26	Earthquake	Ground	Physical	100	100	10	Adjacent	—	—
TM27	Return	Normal	Physical	—	100	20	Normal	—	○
TM29	Psychic	Psychic	Special	90	100	10	Normal	—	—
TM30	Shadow Ball	Ghost	Special	80	100	15	Normal	—	—
TM31	Brick Break	Fighting	Physical	75	100	15	Normal	—	○
TM32	Double Team	Normal	Status	—	—	15	Self	—	—
TM35	Flamethrower	Fire	Special	95	100	15	Normal	—	—
TM37	Sandstorm	Rock	Status	—	—	10	Both Sides	—	—
TM38	Fire Blast	Fire	Special	120	85	5	Normal	—	—
TM39	Rock Tomb	Rock	Physical	50	80	10	Normal	—	—
TM42	Facade	Normal	Physical	70	100	20	Normal	—	○
TM44	Rest	Psychic	Status	—	—	10	Self	—	—
TM45	Attract	Normal	Status	—	100	15	Normal	—	—
TM48	Round	Normal	Special	60	100	15	Normal	—	—
TM56	Fling	Dark	Physical	—	100	10	Normal	—	—
TM59	Incinerate	Fire	Special	30	100	15	Many Others	—	—
TM67	Retaliate	Normal	Physical	70	100	5	Normal	—	○
TM78	Bulldoze	Ground	Physical	60	100	20	Adjacent	—	—
TM80	Rock Slide	Rock	Physical	75	90	10	Many Others	—	—
TM83	Work Up	Normal	Status	—	—	30	Self	—	—
TM87	Swagger	Normal	Status	—	90	15	Normal	—	—
TM90	Substitute	Normal	Status	—	—	10	Self	—	—
TM94	Rock Smash	Fighting	Physical	40	100	15	Normal	—	○
HM03	Surf	Water	Special	95	100	15	Adjacent	—	—
HM04	Strength	Normal	Physical	80	100	15	Normal	—	○

MOVES TAUGHT BY PEOPLE

Name	Type	Kind	Pow.	Acc.	PP	Range	Long	DA

MOVES TAUGHT BY MOVE TUTORS FOR SHARDS

Name	Type	Kind	Pow.	Acc.	PP	Range	Long	DA
Covet	Normal	Physical	60	100	40	Normal	—	○
Uproar	Normal	Special	90	100	10	1 Random	—	—
Seed Bomb	Grass	Physical	80	100	15	Normal	—	—
Gunk Shot	Poison	Physical	120	70	5	Normal	—	—
Fire Punch	Fire	Physical	75	100	15	Normal	—	○
ThunderPunch	Electric	Physical	75	100	15	Normal	—	○
Ice Punch	Ice	Physical	75	100	15	Normal	—	○
Last Resort	Normal	Physical	140	100	5	Normal	—	○
Hyper Voice	Normal	Special	90	100	10	Many Others	—	—
Icy Wind	Ice	Special	55	95	15	Many Others	—	—
Zen Headbutt	Psychic	Physical	80	90	15	Normal	—	○
Superpower	Fighting	Physical	120	100	5	Normal	—	○
Snore	Normal	Special	40	100	15	Normal	—	—
After You	Normal	Status	—	—	15	Normal	—	—
Recycle	Normal	Status	—	—	10	Self	—	—
Sleep Talk	Normal	Status	—	—	10	Self	—	—
Snatch	Dark	Status	—	—	10	Self	—	—

EGG MOVES

Name	Type	Kind	Pow.	Acc.	PP	Range	Long	DA
Lick	Ghost	Physical	20	100	30	Normal	—	○
Charm	Normal	Status	—	100	20	Normal	—	—
Double-Edge	Normal	Physical	120	100	15	Normal	—	○
Curse	Ghost	Status	—	—	10	Varies	—	—
Whirlwind	Normal	Status	—	100	20	Normal	—	—
Pursuit	Dark	Physical	40	100	20	Normal	—	○
Zen Headbutt	Psychic	Physical	80	90	15	Normal	—	○
Counter	Fighting	Physical	—	100	20	Varies	—	○
Natural Gift	Normal	Physical	—	100	15	Normal	—	—
After You	Normal	Status	—	—	15	Normal	—	—
Selfdestruct	Normal	Physical	200	100	5	Adjacent	—	—

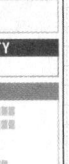

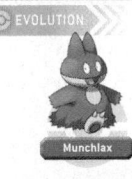

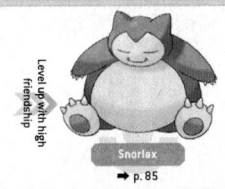

447 Riolu

Emanation Pokémon

- HEIGHT: 2'04"
- WEIGHT: 44.5 lbs.
- GENDER: ♂ / ♀

It uses the shapes of auras, which change according to emotion, to communicate with others.

Same form for ♂ / ♀

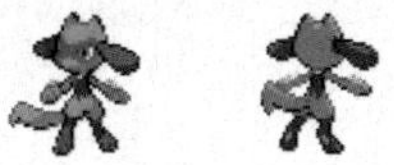

TYPE: Fighting

ABILITIES
- Steadfast
- Inner Focus

HIDDEN ABILITY
- Prankster

STATS
HP, Attack, Defense, Sp. Atk, Sp. Def, Speed

EGG GROUPS
No Egg has ever been discovered

ITEMS SOMETIMES HELD
- None

EVOLUTION

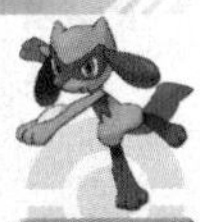

Riolu → Level up with high friendship in the morning, afternoon, or evening → Lucario

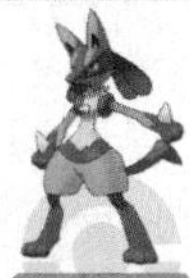

HOW TO OBTAIN

Pokémon Black Version 2	Floccesy Ranch
Pokémon White Version 2	Floccesy Ranch

HOW TO OBTAIN FROM OTHER GAMES

——
——

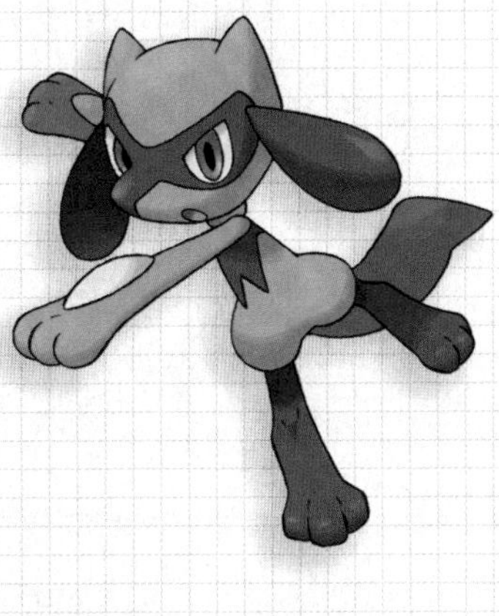

Pokémon AR Marker

LEVEL-UP AND LEARNED MOVES

Lv.	Name	Type	Kind	Pow.	Acc.	PP	Range	Long	DA
1	Foresight	Normal	Status	—	—	40	Normal	—	—
1	Quick Attack	Normal	Physical	40	100	30	Normal	—	○
1	Endure	Normal	Status	—	—	10	Self	—	—
6	Counter	Fighting	Physical	—	100	20	Varies	—	○
11	Feint	Normal	Physical	30	100	10	Normal	—	—
15	Force Palm	Fighting	Physical	60	100	10	Normal	—	○
19	Copycat	Normal	Status	—	—	20	Self	—	—
24	Screech	Normal	Status	—	85	40	Normal	—	—
29	Reversal	Fighting	Physical	—	100	15	Normal	—	○
47	Nasty Plot	Dark	Status	—	—	20	Self	—	—
55	Final Gambit	Fighting	Special	—	100	5	Normal	—	○

TM & HM MOVES

Lv.	Name	Type	Kind	Pow.	Acc.	PP	Range	Long	DA
TM05	Roar	Normal	Status	—	100	20	Normal	—	—
TM06	Toxic	Poison	Status	—	90	10	Normal	—	—
TM08	Bulk Up	Fighting	Status	—	—	20	Self	—	—
TM10	Hidden Power	Normal	Special	—	100	15	Normal	—	—
TM11	Sunny Day	Fire	Status	—	—	5	Both Sides	—	—
TM17	Protect	Normal	Status	—	—	10	Self	—	—
TM18	Rain Dance	Water	Status	—	—	5	Both Sides	—	—
TM21	Frustration	Normal	Physical	—	100	20	Normal	—	○
TM26	Earthquake	Ground	Physical	100	100	10	Adjacent	—	—
TM27	Return	Normal	Physical	—	100	20	Normal	—	○
TM28	Dig	Ground	Physical	80	100	10	Normal	—	○
TM31	Brick Break	Fighting	Physical	75	100	15	Normal	—	○
TM32	Double Team	Normal	Status	—	—	15	Self	—	—
TM39	Rock Tomb	Rock	Physical	50	80	10	Normal	—	—
TM42	Facade	Normal	Physical	70	100	20	Normal	—	○
TM44	Rest	Psychic	Status	—	—	10	Self	—	—
TM45	Attract	Normal	Status	—	100	15	Normal	—	—
TM47	Low Sweep	Fighting	Physical	60	100	20	Normal	—	○
TM48	Round	Normal	Special	60	100	15	Normal	—	—
TM52	Focus Blast	Fighting	Special	120	70	5	Normal	—	—
TM56	Fling	Dark	Physical	—	100	10	Normal	—	—
TM65	Shadow Claw	Ghost	Physical	70	100	15	Normal	—	○
TM66	Payback	Dark	Physical	50	100	10	Normal	—	○
TM67	Retaliate	Normal	Physical	70	100	5	Normal	—	○
TM75	Swords Dance	Normal	Status	—	—	30	Self	—	—
TM78	Bulldoze	Ground	Physical	60	100	20	Adjacent	—	—
TM80	Rock Slide	Rock	Physical	75	90	10	Many Others	—	—
TM83	Work Up	Normal	Status	—	—	30	Self	—	—
TM84	Poison Jab	Poison	Physical	80	100	20	Normal	—	○
TM87	Swagger	Normal	Status	—	90	15	Normal	—	—
TM90	Substitute	Normal	Status	—	—	10	Self	—	—
TM94	Rock Smash	Fighting	Physical	40	100	15	Normal	—	○
HM04	Strength	Normal	Physical	80	100	15	Normal	—	○

MOVES TAUGHT BY PEOPLE

Name	Type	Kind	Pow.	Acc.	PP	Range	Long	DA

MOVES TAUGHT BY MOVE TUTORS FOR SHARDS

Name	Type	Kind	Pow.	Acc.	PP	Range	Long	DA
Dual Chop	Dragon	Physical	40	90	15	Normal	—	○
Low Kick	Fighting	Physical	—	100	20	Normal	—	○
ThunderPunch	Electric	Physical	75	100	15	Normal	—	○
Ice Punch	Ice	Physical	75	100	15	Normal	—	○
Iron Defense	Steel	Status	—	—	15	Self	—	—
Magnet Rise	Electric	Status	—	—	10	Self	—	—
Iron Tail	Steel	Physical	100	75	15	Normal	—	○
Zen Headbutt	Psychic	Physical	80	90	15	Normal	—	○
Snore	Normal	Special	40	100	15	Normal	—	—
Role Play	Psychic	Status	—	—	10	Normal	—	—
Drain Punch	Fighting	Physical	75	100	10	Normal	—	○
Helping Hand	Normal	Status	—	—	20	1 Ally	—	—
Sleep Talk	Normal	Status	—	—	10	Self	—	—

EGG MOVES

Name	Type	Kind	Pow.	Acc.	PP	Range	Long	DA
Cross Chop	Fighting	Physical	100	80	5	Normal	—	○
Detect	Fighting	Status	—	—	5	Self	—	—
Bite	Dark	Physical	60	100	25	Normal	—	○
Mind Reader	Normal	Status	—	—	5	Normal	—	—
Sky Uppercut	Fighting	Physical	85	90	15	Normal	—	○
Hi Jump Kick	Fighting	Physical	130	90	10	Normal	—	○
Agility	Psychic	Status	—	—	30	Self	—	—
Vacuum Wave	Fighting	Special	40	100	30	Normal	—	—
Crunch	Dark	Physical	80	100	15	Normal	—	○
Low Kick	Fighting	Physical	—	100	20	Normal	—	○
Iron Defense	Steel	Status	—	—	15	Self	—	—
Blaze Kick	Fire	Physical	85	90	10	Normal	—	○
Bullet Punch	Steel	Physical	40	100	30	Normal	—	○
Follow Me	Normal	Status	—	—	20	Self	—	—
Circle Throw	Fighting	Physical	60	90	10	Normal	—	○

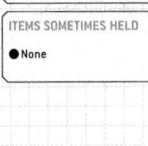

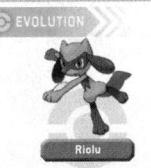

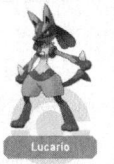

448 Lucario
Aura Pokémon

TYPE Fighting | Steel

ABILITIES
● Steadfast
● Inner Focus

HIDDEN ABILITY
● Justified

● HEIGHT: 3'11"
● WEIGHT: 119.0 lbs.
● GENDER: ♂ / ♀

By reading the auras of all things, it can tell how others are feeling from over half a mile away.

Same form for ♂ / ♀

STATS
HP	▮▮▮
Attack	▮▮▮▮▮
Defense	▮▮▮
Sp. Atk	▮▮▮▮▮
Sp. Def	▮▮▮
Speed	▮▮▮▮

EGG GROUPS
Field/Human-like

ITEMS SOMETIMES HELD
● None

EVOLUTION
 Riolu → Level up with high friendship in the morning, afternoon, or evening →  Lucario

HOW TO OBTAIN
Pokémon Black Version 2	Level up Riolu with high friendship in the morning, afternoon, or evening
Pokémon White Version 2	Level up Riolu with high friendship in the morning, afternoon, or evening

HOW TO OBTAIN FROM OTHER GAMES

Pokémon AR Marker

LEVEL-UP AND LEARNED MOVES
Lv.	Name	Type	Kind	Pow.	Acc.	PP	Range	Long	DA
1	Dark Pulse	Dark	Special	80	100	15	Normal	○	
1	Foresight	Normal	Status	—	—	40	Normal	—	
1	Quick Attack	Normal	Physical	40	100	30	Normal	—	○
1	Detect	Fighting	Status	—	—	5	Self	—	
1	Metal Claw	Steel	Physical	50	95	35	Normal	—	○
6	Counter	Fighting	Physical	—	100	20	Varies	—	
11	Feint	Normal	Physical	30	100	10	Normal	—	○
15	Force Palm	Fighting	Physical	60	100	10	Normal	—	○
19	Me First	Normal	Status	—	—	20	Varies	—	
24	Metal Sound	Steel	Status	—	85	40	Normal	—	
28	Bone Rush	Ground	Physical	25	90	10	Normal	—	
33	Quick Guard	Fighting	Status	—	—	15	Your Side	—	
37	Swords Dance	Normal	Status	—	—	30	Self	—	
42	Heal Pulse	Psychic	Status	—	—	10	Normal	○	
47	Calm Mind	Psychic	Status	—	—	20	Self	—	
51	Aura Sphere	Fighting	Special	90	—	20	Normal	○	
55	Close Combat	Fighting	Physical	120	100	5	Normal	—	
60	Dragon Pulse	Dragon	Special	90	100	10	Normal	○	
65	ExtremeSpeed	Normal	Physical	80	100	5	Normal	—	

TM & HM MOVES
Lv.	Name	Type	Kind	Pow.	Acc.	PP	Range	Long	DA
TM01	Hone Claws	Dark	Status	—	—	15	Self	—	
TM04	Calm Mind	Psychic	Status	—	—	20	Self	—	
TM05	Roar	Normal	Status	—	100	20	Normal	—	
TM06	Toxic	Poison	Status	—	90	10	Normal	—	
TM08	Bulk Up	Fighting	Status	—	—	20	Self	—	
TM10	Hidden Power	Normal	Special	—	100	15	Normal	○	
TM11	Sunny Day	Fire	Status	—	—	5	Both Sides	—	
TM15	Hyper Beam	Normal	Special	150	90	5	Normal	—	
TM17	Protect	Normal	Status	—	—	10	Self	—	
TM18	Rain Dance	Water	Status	—	—	5	Both Sides	—	
TM21	Frustration	Normal	Physical	—	100	20	Normal	—	○
TM26	Earthquake	Ground	Physical	100	100	10	Adjacent	—	
TM27	Return	Normal	Physical	—	100	20	Normal	—	○
TM28	Dig	Ground	Physical	80	100	10	Normal	—	○
TM29	Psychic	Psychic	Special	90	100	10	Normal	—	
TM30	Shadow Ball	Ghost	Special	80	100	15	Normal	—	○
TM31	Brick Break	Fighting	Physical	75	100	15	Normal	—	○
TM32	Double Team	Normal	Status	—	—	15	Self	—	
TM39	Rock Tomb	Rock	Physical	50	80	10	Normal	—	○
TM42	Facade	Normal	Physical	70	100	20	Normal	—	○
TM44	Rest	Psychic	Status	—	—	10	Self	—	
TM45	Attract	Normal	Status	—	100	15	Normal	—	
TM47	Low Sweep	Fighting	Physical	60	100	20	Normal	—	○
TM48	Round	Normal	Special	60	100	15	Normal	—	
TM52	Focus Blast	Fighting	Special	120	70	5	Normal	○	
TM56	Fling	Dark	Physical	—	100	10	Normal	—	○
TM65	Shadow Claw	Ghost	Physical	70	100	15	Normal	—	○
TM66	Payback	Dark	Physical	50	100	10	Normal	—	○
TM67	Retaliate	Normal	Physical	70	100	5	Normal	—	○
TM68	Giga Impact	Normal	Physical	150	90	5	Normal	—	
TM71	Stone Edge	Rock	Physical	100	80	5	Normal	—	
TM75	Swords Dance	Normal	Status	—	—	30	Self	—	
TM78	Bulldoze	Ground	Physical	60	100	20	Adjacent	—	○
TM80	Rock Slide	Rock	Physical	75	90	10	Many Others	—	○
TM83	Work Up	Normal	Status	—	—	30	Self	—	
TM84	Poison Jab	Poison	Physical	80	100	20	Normal	—	
TM87	Swagger	Normal	Status	—	90	15	Normal	—	
TM90	Substitute	Normal	Status	—	—	10	Self	—	
TM91	Flash Cannon	Steel	Special	80	100	10	Normal	○	
TM94	Rock Smash	Fighting	Physical	40	100	15	Normal	—	○
HM04	Strength	Normal	Physical	80	100	15	Normal	—	

MOVES TAUGHT BY PEOPLE
Name	Type	Kind	Pow.	Acc.	PP	Range	Long	DA

MOVES TAUGHT BY MOVE TUTORS FOR SHARDS
Name	Type	Kind	Pow.	Acc.	PP	Range	Long	DA
Dual Chop	Dragon	Physical	40	90	15	Normal	—	○
Low Kick	Fighting	Physical	—	100	20	Normal	—	○
ThunderPunch	Electric	Physical	75	100	15	Normal	—	○
Ice Punch	Ice	Physical	75	100	15	Normal	—	○
Iron Defense	Steel	Status	—	—	15	Self	—	
Magnet Rise	Electric	Status	—	—	10	Self	—	
Iron Tail	Steel	Physical	100	75	15	Normal	—	○
Zen Headbutt	Psychic	Physical	80	90	15	Normal	—	○
Dragon Pulse	Dragon	Special	90	100	10	Normal	○	
Dark Pulse	Dark	Special	80	100	15	Normal	○	
Snore	Normal	Special	40	100	15	Normal	—	
Role Play	Psychic	Status	—	—	10	Normal	—	
Drain Punch	Fighting	Physical	75	100	10	Normal	—	○
Helping Hand	Normal	Status	—	—	20	1 Ally	—	
Sleep Talk	Normal	Status	—	—	10	Self	—	

449 Hippopotas
Hippo Pokémon

TYPE Ground

ABILITY
● Sand Stream

HIDDEN ABILITY
● Sand Force

● HEIGHT: 2'07"
● WEIGHT: 109.1 lbs.
● GENDER: ♂ / ♀

It shuts its nostrils tight then travels through sand as if walking. They form colonies of around 10.

♂   ♀

STATS
HP	▮▮▮
Attack	▮▮▮
Defense	▮▮▮
Sp. Atk	▮▮
Sp. Def	▮▮
Speed	▮▮

EGG GROUPS
Field

ITEMS SOMETIMES HELD
● None

EVOLUTION
 Hippopotas → Lv. 34 → Hippowdon

HOW TO OBTAIN
Pokémon Black Version 2	Catch a Hippowdon, leave it at the Pokémon Day Care, and hatch the Egg that is found
Pokémon White Version 2	Catch a Hippowdon, leave it at the Pokémon Day Care, and hatch the Egg that is found

HOW TO OBTAIN FROM OTHER GAMES
Pokémon Black Version	Route 4 (mass outbreak)
Pokémon White Version	Route 4 (mass outbreak)

LEVEL-UP AND LEARNED MOVES
Lv.	Name	Type	Kind	Pow.	Acc.	PP	Range	Long	DA
1	Tackle	Normal	Physical	50	100	35	Normal	—	
1	Sand-Attack	Ground	Status	—	100	15	Normal	—	
7	Bite	Dark	Physical	60	100	25	Normal	—	○
13	Yawn	Normal	Status	—	—	10	Normal	—	
19	Take Down	Normal	Physical	90	85	20	Normal	—	
19	Dig	Ground	Physical	80	100	10	Normal	—	○
25	Sand Tomb	Ground	Physical	35	85	15	Normal	—	
31	Crunch	Dark	Physical	80	100	15	Normal	—	○
37	Earthquake	Ground	Physical	100	100	10	Adjacent	—	
44	Double-Edge	Normal	Physical	120	100	15	Normal	—	
50	Fissure	Ground	Physical	—	30	5	Normal	—	

TM & HM MOVES
Lv.	Name	Type	Kind	Pow.	Acc.	PP	Range	Long	DA
TM05	Roar	Normal	Status	—	100	20	Normal	—	
TM06	Toxic	Poison	Status	—	90	10	Normal	—	
TM10	Hidden Power	Normal	Special	—	100	15	Normal	○	
TM11	Sunny Day	Fire	Status	—	—	5	Both Sides	—	
TM17	Protect	Normal	Status	—	—	10	Self	—	
TM21	Frustration	Normal	Physical	—	100	20	Normal	—	○
TM26	Earthquake	Ground	Physical	100	100	10	Adjacent	—	
TM27	Return	Normal	Physical	—	100	20	Normal	—	○
TM28	Dig	Ground	Physical	80	100	10	Normal	—	○
TM32	Double Team	Normal	Status	—	—	15	Self	—	
TM37	Sandstorm	Rock	Status	—	—	10	Both Sides	—	
TM39	Rock Tomb	Rock	Physical	50	80	10	Normal	—	○
TM42	Facade	Normal	Physical	70	100	20	Normal	—	○
TM44	Rest	Psychic	Status	—	—	10	Self	—	
TM45	Attract	Normal	Status	—	100	15	Normal	—	
TM48	Round	Normal	Special	60	100	15	Normal	—	
TM78	Bulldoze	Ground	Physical	60	100	20	Adjacent	—	○
TM80	Rock Slide	Rock	Physical	75	90	10	Many Others	—	○
TM87	Swagger	Normal	Status	—	90	15	Normal	—	
TM90	Substitute	Normal	Status	—	—	10	Self	—	
TM94	Rock Smash	Fighting	Physical	40	100	15	Normal	—	○
HM04	Strength	Normal	Physical	80	100	15	Normal	—	

MOVES TAUGHT BY PEOPLE
Name	Type	Kind	Pow.	Acc.	PP	Range	Long	DA

MOVES TAUGHT BY MOVE TUTORS FOR SHARDS
Name	Type	Kind	Pow.	Acc.	PP	Range	Long	DA
Iron Tail	Steel	Physical	100	75	15	Normal	—	○
Earth Power	Ground	Special	90	100	10	Normal	—	
Superpower	Fighting	Physical	120	100	5	Normal	—	○
Snore	Normal	Special	40	100	15	Normal	—	
Stealth Rock	Rock	Status	—	—	20	3 Foes	—	
Sleep Talk	Normal	Status	—	—	10	Self	—	

EGG MOVES
Name	Type	Kind	Pow.	Acc.	PP	Range	Long	DA
Stockpile	Normal	Status	—	—	20	Self	—	
Swallow	Normal	Status	—	—	10	Self	—	
Spit Up	Normal	Special	—	100	10	Self	—	
Curse	Ghost	Status	—	—	10	Varies	—	
Slack Off	Normal	Status	—	—	10	Self	—	
Body Slam	Normal	Physical	85	100	15	Normal	—	
Sand Tomb	Ground	Physical	35	85	15	Normal	—	
Revenge	Fighting	Physical	60	100	10	Normal	—	○
Sleep Talk	Normal	Status	—	—	10	Self	—	
Whirlwind	Normal	Status	—	100	20	Normal	—	

Pokémon AR Marker

450 Hippowdon
Heavyweight Pokémon

TYPE Ground

ABILITY
● Sand Stream

HIDDEN ABILITY
● Sand Force

● HEIGHT: 6'07"
● WEIGHT: 661.4 lbs.
● GENDER: ♂ / ♀

It is surprisingly quick to anger. It holds its mouth agape as a display of its strength.

STATS
HP
Attack
Defense
Sp. Atk
Sp. Def
Speed

EGG GROUPS
Field

ITEMS SOMETIMES HELD
● None

♂　　　　　♀

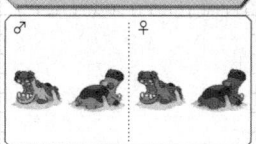

Pokémon AR Marker

EVOLUTION

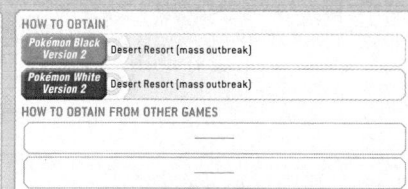

Hippopotas → Lv. 34 → Hippowdon

HOW TO OBTAIN
Pokémon Black Version 2	Desert Resort (mass outbreak)
Pokémon White Version 2	Desert Resort (mass outbreak)

HOW TO OBTAIN FROM OTHER GAMES

LEVEL-UP AND LEARNED MOVES
Lv.	Name	Type	Kind	Pow.	Acc.	PP	Range	Long	DA
1	Ice Fang	Ice	Physical	65	95	15	Normal	—	○
1	Fire Fang	Fire	Physical	65	95	15	Normal	—	○
1	Thunder Fang	Electric	Physical	65	95	15	Normal	—	○
1	Tackle	Normal	Physical	50	100	35	Normal	—	—
1	Sand-Attack	Ground	Status	—	100	15	Normal	—	—
1	Bite	Dark	Physical	60	100	25	Normal	—	○
1	Yawn	Normal	Status	—	—	10	Normal	—	—
7	Bite	Dark	Physical	60	100	25	Normal	—	○
13	Yawn	Normal	Status	—	—	10	Normal	—	—
19	Take Down	Normal	Physical	90	85	20	Normal	—	○
19	Dig	Ground	Physical	80	100	10	Normal	—	—
25	Sand Tomb	Ground	Physical	35	85	15	Normal	—	—
31	Crunch	Dark	Physical	80	100	15	Normal	—	○
40	Earthquake	Ground	Physical	100	100	10	Adjacent	—	—
50	Double-Edge	Normal	Physical	120	100	15	Normal	—	○
60	Fissure	Ground	Physical	—	30	5	Normal	—	—

TM & HM MOVES
Lv.	Name	Type	Kind	Pow.	Acc.	PP	Range	Long	DA
TM05	Roar	Normal	Status	—	100	20	Normal	—	—
TM06	Toxic	Poison	Status	—	90	10	Normal	—	—
TM10	Hidden Power	Normal	Special	—	100	15	Normal	—	—
TM11	Sunny Day	Fire	Status	—	—	5	Both Sides	—	—
TM15	Hyper Beam	Normal	Special	150	90	5	Normal	—	—
TM17	Protect	Normal	Status	—	—	10	Self	—	—
TM21	Frustration	Normal	Physical	—	100	20	Normal	—	○
TM26	Earthquake	Ground	Physical	100	100	10	Adjacent	—	—
TM27	Return	Normal	Physical	—	100	20	Normal	—	○
TM28	Dig	Ground	Physical	80	100	10	Normal	—	—
TM32	Double Team	Normal	Status	—	—	15	Self	—	—
TM37	Sandstorm	Rock	Status	—	—	10	Both Sides	—	—
TM39	Rock Tomb	Rock	Physical	50	80	10	Normal	—	—
TM42	Facade	Normal	Physical	70	100	20	Normal	—	○
TM44	Rest	Psychic	Status	—	—	10	Self	—	—
TM45	Attract	Normal	Status	—	100	15	Normal	—	—
TM48	Round	Normal	Special	60	100	15	Normal	—	—
TM68	Giga Impact	Normal	Physical	150	90	5	Normal	—	○
TM71	Stone Edge	Rock	Physical	100	80	5	Normal	—	—
TM78	Bulldoze	Ground	Physical	60	100	20	Adjacent	—	—
TM80	Rock Slide	Rock	Physical	75	90	10	Many Others	—	—
TM87	Swagger	Normal	Status	—	90	15	Normal	—	—
TM90	Substitute	Normal	Status	—	—	10	Self	—	—
TM94	Rock Smash	Fighting	Physical	40	100	15	Normal	—	○
HM04	Strength	Normal	Physical	80	100	15	Normal	—	—

MOVES TAUGHT BY PEOPLE
Name	Type	Kind	Pow.	Acc.	PP	Range	Long	DA

MOVES TAUGHT BY MOVE TUTORS FOR SHARDS
Name	Type	Kind	Pow.	Acc.	PP	Range	Long	DA
Iron Head	Steel	Physical	80	100	15	Normal	—	○
Iron Tail	Steel	Physical	100	75	15	Normal	—	—
Earth Power	Ground	Special	90	100	10	Normal	—	—
Superpower	Fighting	Physical	120	100	5	Normal	—	○
Snore	Normal	Special	40	100	15	Normal	—	—
Stealth Rock	Rock	Status	—	—	20	3 Foes	—	—
Sleep Talk	Normal	Status	—	—	10	Self	—	—

---

451 Skorupi
Scorpion Pokémon

TYPE Poison　Bug

ABILITIES
● Battle Armor
● Sniper

HIDDEN ABILITY
● Keen Eye

● HEIGHT: 2'07"
● WEIGHT: 26.5 lbs.
● GENDER: ♂ / ♀

It lives in arid regions and can go without food for a year while waiting for prey.

STATS
HP
Attack
Defense
Sp. Atk
Sp. Def
Speed

EGG GROUPS
Bug/Water ❺

ITEMS SOMETIMES HELD
● Poison Barb

Same form for ♂ / ♀

Pokémon AR Marker

EVOLUTION

Skorupi → Lv. 40 → Drapion

HOW TO OBTAIN
Pokémon Black Version 2	❶ Reversal Mountain outside ❷ Reversal Mountain entrance
Pokémon White Version 2	❶ Reversal Mountain outside ❷ Reversal Mountain entrance

HOW TO OBTAIN FROM OTHER GAMES

LEVEL-UP AND LEARNED MOVES
Lv.	Name	Type	Kind	Pow.	Acc.	PP	Range	Long	DA
1	Bite	Dark	Physical	60	100	25	Normal	—	○
1	Poison Sting	Poison	Physical	15	100	35	Normal	—	—
1	Leer	Normal	Status	—	100	30	Many Others	—	—
5	Knock Off	Dark	Physical	20	100	20	Normal	—	○
9	Pin Missile	Bug	Physical	14	85	20	Normal	—	—
13	Acupressure	Normal	Status	—	—	30	Self/Ally	—	—
16	Pursuit	Dark	Physical	40	100	20	Normal	—	○
20	Bug Bite	Bug	Physical	60	100	20	Normal	—	○
23	Poison Fang	Poison	Physical	50	100	15	Normal	—	—
27	Venoshock	Poison	Special	65	100	10	Normal	—	—
30	Hone Claws	Dark	Status	—	—	15	Self	—	—
34	Toxic Spikes	Poison	Status	—	—	20	3 Foes	—	—
38	Night Slash	Dark	Physical	70	100	15	Normal	—	○
41	Scary Face	Normal	Status	—	100	10	Normal	—	—
45	Crunch	Dark	Physical	80	100	15	Normal	—	○
49	Cross Poison	Poison	Physical	70	100	20	Normal	—	—

TM & HM MOVES
Lv.	Name	Type	Kind	Pow.	Acc.	PP	Range	Long	DA
TM01	Hone Claws	Dark	Status	—	—	15	Self	—	—
TM06	Toxic	Poison	Status	—	90	10	Normal	—	—
TM09	Venoshock	Poison	Special	65	100	10	Normal	—	—
TM10	Hidden Power	Normal	Special	—	100	15	Normal	—	—
TM11	Sunny Day	Fire	Status	—	—	5	Both Sides	—	—
TM12	Taunt	Dark	Status	—	100	20	Normal	—	—
TM17	Protect	Normal	Status	—	—	10	Self	—	—
TM18	Rain Dance	Water	Status	—	—	5	Both Sides	—	—
TM21	Frustration	Normal	Physical	—	100	20	Normal	—	○
TM27	Return	Normal	Physical	—	100	20	Normal	—	○
TM28	Dig	Ground	Physical	80	100	10	Normal	—	—
TM30	Shadow Ball	Ghost	Special	80	100	15	Normal	—	—
TM31	Brick Break	Fighting	Physical	75	100	15	Normal	—	—
TM32	Double Team	Normal	Status	—	—	15	Self	—	—
TM36	Sludge Bomb	Poison	Special	90	100	10	Normal	—	—
TM39	Rock Tomb	Rock	Physical	50	80	10	Normal	—	—
TM40	Aerial Ace	Flying	Physical	60	—	20	Normal	○	○
TM41	Torment	Dark	Status	—	100	15	Normal	—	—
TM42	Facade	Normal	Physical	70	100	20	Normal	—	○
TM44	Rest	Psychic	Status	—	—	10	Self	—	—
TM45	Attract	Normal	Status	—	100	15	Normal	—	—
TM46	Thief	Dark	Physical	40	100	10	Normal	—	○
TM48	Round	Normal	Special	60	100	15	Normal	—	—
TM54	False Swipe	Normal	Physical	40	100	40	Normal	—	○
TM56	Fling	Dark	Physical	—	100	10	Normal	—	—
TM66	Payback	Dark	Physical	50	100	10	Normal	—	○
TM70	Flash	Normal	Status	—	100	20	Normal	—	—
TM75	Swords Dance	Normal	Status	—	—	30	Self	—	—
TM76	Struggle Bug	Bug	Special	30	100	20	Many Others	—	—
TM81	X-Scissor	Bug	Physical	80	100	15	Normal	—	○
TM84	Poison Jab	Poison	Physical	80	100	20	Normal	—	—
TM87	Swagger	Normal	Status	—	90	15	Normal	—	—
TM90	Substitute	Normal	Status	—	—	10	Self	—	—
TM94	Rock Smash	Fighting	Physical	40	100	15	Normal	—	○
HM01	Cut	Normal	Physical	50	95	30	Normal	—	—
HM04	Strength	Normal	Physical	80	100	15	Normal	—	—

MOVES TAUGHT BY PEOPLE
Name	Type	Kind	Pow.	Acc.	PP	Range	Long	DA

MOVES TAUGHT BY MOVE TUTORS FOR SHARDS
Name	Type	Kind	Pow.	Acc.	PP	Range	Long	DA
Bug Bite	Bug	Physical	60	100	20	Normal	—	○
Iron Tail	Steel	Physical	100	75	15	Normal	—	—
Aqua Tail	Water	Physical	90	90	10	Normal	—	—
Dark Pulse	Dark	Special	80	100	15	Normal	—	○
Snore	Normal	Special	40	100	15	Normal	—	—
Knock Off	Dark	Physical	20	100	20	Normal	—	○
Sleep Talk	Normal	Status	—	—	10	Self	—	—

EGG MOVES
Name	Type	Kind	Pow.	Acc.	PP	Range	Long	DA
Faint Attack	Dark	Physical	60	—	20	Normal	—	○
Screech	Normal	Status	—	85	40	Normal	—	—
Sand-Attack	Ground	Status	—	100	15	Normal	—	—
Slash	Normal	Physical	70	100	20	Normal	—	○
Confuse Ray	Ghost	Status	—	100	10	Normal	—	—
Whirlwind	Normal	Status	—	100	20	Normal	—	—
Agility	Psychic	Status	—	—	30	Self	—	—
Pursuit	Dark	Physical	40	100	20	Normal	—	○
Night Slash	Dark	Physical	70	100	15	Normal	—	○
Iron Tail	Steel	Physical	100	75	15	Normal	—	—
Twineedle	Bug	Physical	25	100	20	Normal	—	—
Poison Tail	Poison	Physical	50	100	25	Normal	—	—

452 Drapion

452 Drapion

Ogre Scorp Pokémon

- HEIGHT: 4'03"
- WEIGHT: 135.6 lbs.
- GENDER: ♂ / ♀

It takes pride in its strength. Even though it can tear foes apart, it finishes them off with powerful poison.

Same form for ♂ / ♀

TYPE: Poison / Dark

ABILITIES
- Battle Armor
- Sniper

HIDDEN ABILITY
- Keen Eye

STATS
- HP
- Attack
- Defense
- Sp. Atk
- Sp. Def
- Speed

EGG GROUPS
Bug/Water 3

ITEMS SOMETIMES HELD
- None

EVOLUTION

HOW TO OBTAIN

Pokémon Black Version 2	Level up Skorupi to Lv. 40
Pokémon White Version 2	Level up Skorupi to Lv. 40

HOW TO OBTAIN FROM OTHER GAMES

—

—

Pokémon AR Marker

LEVEL-UP AND LEARNED MOVES

Lv.	Name	Type	Kind	Pow.	Acc.	PP	Range	Long	DA
1	Thunder Fang	Electric	Physical	65	95	15	Normal	—	○
1	Ice Fang	Ice	Physical	65	95	15	Normal	—	○
1	Fire Fang	Fire	Physical	65	95	15	Normal	—	○
1	Bite	Dark	Physical	60	100	25	Normal	—	○
1	Poison Sting	Poison	Physical	15	100	35	Normal	—	—
1	Leer	Normal	Status	—	100	30	Many Others	—	—
1	Knock Off	Dark	Physical	20	100	20	Normal	—	○
5	Knock Off	Dark	Physical	20	100	20	Normal	—	○
9	Pin Missile	Bug	Physical	14	85	20	Normal	—	—
13	Acupressure	Normal	Status	—	—	30	Self/Ally	—	—
16	Pursuit	Dark	Physical	40	100	20	Normal	—	○
20	Bug Bite	Bug	Physical	60	100	20	Normal	—	○
23	Poison Fang	Poison	Physical	50	100	15	Normal	—	○
27	Venoshock	Poison	Special	65	100	10	Normal	—	—
30	Hone Claws	Dark	Status	—	—	15	Self	—	—
34	Toxic Spikes	Poison	Status	—	—	20	3 Foes	—	—
38	Night Slash	Dark	Physical	70	100	15	Normal	—	○
43	Scary Face	Normal	Status	—	100	10	Normal	—	—
49	Crunch	Dark	Physical	80	100	15	Normal	—	○
57	Cross Poison	Poison	Physical	70	100	20	Normal	—	○

TM & HM MOVES

Lv.	Name	Type	Kind	Pow.	Acc.	PP	Range	Long	DA
TM01	Hone Claws	Dark	Status	—	—	15	Self	—	—
TM05	Roar	Normal	Status	—	100	20	Normal	—	—
TM06	Toxic	Poison	Status	—	90	10	Normal	—	—
TM09	Venoshock	Poison	Special	65	100	10	Normal	—	—
TM10	Hidden Power	Normal	Special	—	100	15	Normal	—	—
TM11	Sunny Day	Fire	Status	—	—	5	Both Sides	—	—
TM12	Taunt	Dark	Status	—	100	20	Normal	—	—
TM15	Hyper Beam	Normal	Special	150	90	5	Normal	—	—
TM17	Protect	Normal	Status	—	—	10	Self	—	—
TM18	Rain Dance	Water	Status	—	—	5	Both Sides	—	—
TM21	Frustration	Normal	Physical	—	100	20	Normal	—	○
TM26	Earthquake	Ground	Physical	100	100	10	Adjacent	—	—
TM27	Return	Normal	Physical	—	100	20	Normal	—	○
TM28	Dig	Ground	Physical	80	100	10	Normal	—	○
TM30	Shadow Ball	Ghost	Special	80	100	15	Normal	—	—
TM31	Brick Break	Fighting	Physical	75	100	15	Normal	—	○
TM32	Double Team	Normal	Status	—	—	15	Self	—	—
TM36	Sludge Bomb	Poison	Special	90	100	10	Normal	—	—
TM39	Rock Tomb	Rock	Physical	50	80	10	Normal	—	—
TM40	Aerial Ace	Flying	Physical	60	—	20	Normal	○	○
TM41	Torment	Dark	Status	—	100	15	Normal	—	—
TM42	Facade	Normal	Physical	70	100	20	Normal	—	○
TM44	Rest	Psychic	Status	—	—	10	Self	—	—
TM45	Attract	Normal	Status	—	100	15	Normal	—	—
TM46	Thief	Dark	Physical	40	100	10	Normal	—	○
TM48	Round	Normal	Special	60	100	15	Normal	—	—
TM54	False Swipe	Normal	Physical	40	100	40	Normal	—	○
TM56	Fling	Dark	Physical	—	100	10	Normal	—	—
TM66	Payback	Dark	Physical	50	100	10	Normal	—	○
TM67	Retaliate	Normal	Physical	70	100	5	Normal	—	○
TM68	Giga Impact	Normal	Physical	150	90	5	Normal	—	○
TM70	Flash	Normal	Status	—	100	20	Normal	—	—
TM75	Swords Dance	Normal	Status	—	—	30	Self	—	—
TM76	Struggle Bug	Bug	Special	30	100	20	Many Others	—	—
TM78	Bulldoze	Ground	Physical	60	100	20	Adjacent	—	—
TM80	Rock Slide	Rock	Physical	75	90	10	Many Others	—	—
TM81	X-Scissor	Bug	Physical	80	100	15	Normal	—	○
TM84	Poison Jab	Poison	Physical	80	100	20	Normal	—	○
TM87	Swagger	Normal	Status	—	90	15	Normal	—	—
TM90	Substitute	Normal	Status	—	—	10	Self	—	—
TM94	Rock Smash	Fighting	Physical	40	100	15	Normal	—	○
TM95	Snarl	Dark	Special	55	95	15	Many Others	—	—
HM01	Cut	Normal	Physical	50	95	30	Normal	—	○
HM04	Strength	Normal	Physical	80	100	15	Normal	—	○

MOVES TAUGHT BY PEOPLE

Name	Type	Kind	Pow.	Acc.	PP	Range	Long	DA

MOVES TAUGHT BY MOVE TUTORS FOR SHARDS

Name	Type	Kind	Pow.	Acc.	PP	Range	Long	DA
Bug Bite	Bug	Physical	60	100	20	Normal	—	○
Iron Tail	Steel	Physical	100	75	15	Normal	—	○
Aqua Tail	Water	Physical	90	90	10	Normal	—	○
Dark Pulse	Dark	Special	80	100	15	Normal	○	—
Snore	Normal	Special	40	100	15	Normal	—	—
Knock Off	Dark	Physical	20	100	20	Normal	—	○
Sleep Talk	Normal	Status	—	—	10	Self	—	—

453 Croagunk

453 Croagunk

Toxic Mouth Pokémon

- HEIGHT: 2'04"
- WEIGHT: 50.7 lbs.
- GENDER: ♂ / ♀

Inflating its poison sacs, it fills the area with an odd sound and hits flinching opponents with a poison jab.

TYPE: Poison / Fighting

ABILITIES
- Anticipation
- Dry Skin

HIDDEN ABILITY
- Poison Touch

STATS
- HP
- Attack
- Defense
- Sp. Atk
- Sp. Def
- Speed

EGG GROUPS
Human-like

ITEMS SOMETIMES HELD
- Black Sludge

EVOLUTION

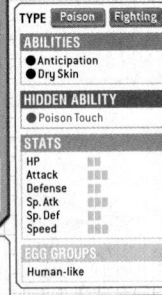

HOW TO OBTAIN

Pokémon Black Version 2	1 Route 8 (spring, summer, and autumn only) 2 Icirrus City (spring, summer, and autumn only)
Pokémon White Version 2	1 Route 8 (spring, summer, and autumn only) 2 Icirrus City (spring, summer, and autumn only)

HOW TO OBTAIN FROM OTHER GAMES

—

—

Pokémon AR Marker

LEVEL-UP AND LEARNED MOVES

Lv.	Name	Type	Kind	Pow.	Acc.	PP	Range	Long	DA
1	Astonish	Ghost	Physical	30	100	15	Normal	—	○
3	Mud-Slap	Ground	Special	20	100	10	Normal	—	—
8	Poison Sting	Poison	Physical	15	100	35	Normal	—	—
10	Taunt	Dark	Status	—	100	20	Normal	—	—
15	Pursuit	Dark	Physical	40	100	20	Normal	—	○
17	Faint Attack	Dark	Physical	60	—	20	Normal	—	○
22	Revenge	Fighting	Physical	60	100	10	Normal	—	○
24	Swagger	Normal	Status	—	90	15	Normal	—	—
29	Mud Bomb	Ground	Special	65	85	10	Normal	—	—
31	Sucker Punch	Dark	Physical	80	100	5	Normal	—	○
36	Venoshock	Poison	Special	65	100	10	Normal	—	—
38	Nasty Plot	Dark	Status	—	—	20	Self	—	—
43	Poison Jab	Poison	Physical	80	100	20	Normal	—	○
45	Sludge Bomb	Poison	Special	90	100	10	Normal	—	—
50	Flatter	Dark	Status	—	100	15	Normal	—	—

TM & HM MOVES

Lv.	Name	Type	Kind	Pow.	Acc.	PP	Range	Long	DA
TM06	Toxic	Poison	Status	—	90	10	Normal	—	—
TM08	Bulk Up	Fighting	Status	—	—	20	Self	—	—
TM09	Venoshock	Poison	Special	65	100	10	Normal	—	—
TM10	Hidden Power	Normal	Special	—	100	15	Normal	—	—
TM11	Sunny Day	Fire	Status	—	—	5	Both Sides	—	—
TM12	Taunt	Dark	Status	—	100	20	Normal	—	—
TM17	Protect	Normal	Status	—	—	10	Self	—	—
TM18	Rain Dance	Water	Status	—	—	5	Both Sides	—	—
TM21	Frustration	Normal	Physical	—	100	20	Normal	—	○
TM26	Earthquake	Ground	Physical	100	100	10	Adjacent	—	—
TM27	Return	Normal	Physical	—	100	20	Normal	—	○
TM28	Dig	Ground	Physical	80	100	10	Normal	—	○
TM30	Shadow Ball	Ghost	Special	80	100	15	Normal	—	—
TM31	Brick Break	Fighting	Physical	75	100	15	Normal	—	○
TM32	Double Team	Normal	Status	—	—	15	Self	—	—
TM34	Sludge Wave	Poison	Special	95	100	10	Adjacent	—	—
TM36	Sludge Bomb	Poison	Special	90	100	10	Normal	—	—
TM39	Rock Tomb	Rock	Physical	50	80	10	Normal	—	—
TM41	Torment	Dark	Status	—	100	15	Normal	—	—
TM42	Facade	Normal	Physical	70	100	20	Normal	—	○
TM44	Rest	Psychic	Status	—	—	10	Self	—	—
TM45	Attract	Normal	Status	—	100	15	Normal	—	—
TM46	Thief	Dark	Physical	40	100	10	Normal	—	○
TM47	Low Sweep	Fighting	Physical	60	100	20	Normal	—	○
TM48	Round	Normal	Special	60	100	15	Normal	—	—
TM52	Focus Blast	Fighting	Special	120	70	5	Normal	—	—
TM56	Fling	Dark	Physical	—	100	10	Normal	—	—
TM63	Embargo	Dark	Status	—	100	15	Normal	—	—
TM66	Payback	Dark	Physical	50	100	10	Normal	—	○
TM67	Retaliate	Normal	Physical	70	100	5	Normal	—	○
TM78	Bulldoze	Ground	Physical	60	100	20	Adjacent	—	—
TM80	Rock Slide	Rock	Physical	75	90	10	Many Others	—	—
TM81	X-Scissor	Bug	Physical	80	100	15	Normal	—	○
TM83	Work Up	Normal	Status	—	—	30	Self	—	—
TM84	Poison Jab	Poison	Physical	80	100	20	Normal	—	○
TM87	Swagger	Normal	Status	—	90	15	Normal	—	—
TM90	Substitute	Normal	Status	—	—	10	Self	—	—
TM94	Rock Smash	Fighting	Physical	40	100	15	Normal	—	○
HM04	Strength	Normal	Physical	80	100	15	Normal	—	○

MOVES TAUGHT BY PEOPLE

Name	Type	Kind	Pow.	Acc.	PP	Range	Long	DA

MOVES TAUGHT BY MOVE TUTORS FOR SHARDS

Name	Type	Kind	Pow.	Acc.	PP	Range	Long	DA
Bounce	Flying	Physical	85	85	5	Normal	○	○
Super Fang	Normal	Physical	—	90	10	Normal	—	○
Dual Chop	Dragon	Physical	40	90	15	Normal	—	○
Low Kick	Fighting	Physical	—	100	20	Normal	—	○
Gunk Shot	Poison	Physical	120	70	5	Normal	—	—
ThunderPunch	Electric	Physical	75	100	15	Normal	—	○
Ice Punch	Ice	Physical	75	100	15	Normal	—	○
Icy Wind	Ice	Special	55	95	15	Many Others	—	—
Foul Play	Dark	Physical	95	100	15	Normal	—	○
Dark Pulse	Dark	Special	80	100	15	Normal	○	—
Snore	Normal	Special	40	100	15	Normal	—	—
Knock Off	Dark	Physical	20	100	20	Normal	—	○
Role Play	Psychic	Status	—	—	10	Normal	—	—
Drain Punch	Fighting	Physical	75	100	10	Normal	—	○
Helping Hand	Normal	Status	—	—	20	1 Ally	—	—
Spite	Ghost	Status	—	100	10	Normal	—	—
Sleep Talk	Normal	Status	—	—	10	Self	—	—
Snatch	Dark	Status	—	—	10	Self	—	—

EGG MOVES

Name	Type	Kind	Pow.	Acc.	PP	Range	Long	DA
Me First	Normal	Status	—	—	20	Varies	—	—
Feint	Normal	Physical	30	100	10	Normal	—	—
DynamicPunch	Fighting	Physical	100	50	5	Normal	—	○
Headbutt	Normal	Physical	70	100	15	Normal	—	○
Vacuum Wave	Fighting	Special	40	100	30	Normal	—	—
Meditate	Psychic	Status	—	—	40	Self	—	—
Fake Out	Normal	Physical	40	100	10	Normal	—	○
Wake-Up Slap	Fighting	Physical	60	100	10	Normal	—	○
SmellingSalt	Normal	Physical	60	100	10	Normal	—	○
Cross Chop	Fighting	Physical	100	80	5	Normal	—	○
Bullet Punch	Steel	Physical	40	100	30	Normal	—	○
Counter	Fighting	Physical	—	100	20	Varies	—	○
Drain Punch	Fighting	Physical	75	100	10	Normal	—	○
Acupressure	Normal	Status	—	—	30	Self/Ally	—	—

Toxic Mouth Pokémon

454 Toxicroak

- HEIGHT: 4'03"
- WEIGHT: 97.9 lbs.
- GENDER: ♂ / ♀

The croaking that Toxicroak produces before a battle is for churning the poison it has stored in its poison sac.

♂ ♀

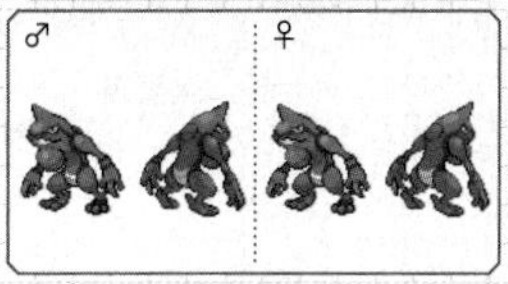

TYPE: Poison, Fighting

ABILITIES
- Anticipation
- Dry Skin

HIDDEN ABILITY
- Poison Touch

STATS
HP
Attack
Defense
Sp. Atk
Sp. Def
Speed

EGG GROUPS
Human-like

ITEMS SOMETIMES HELD
- Black Sludge

EVOLUTION

Croagunk
Lv. 37
Toxicroak

HOW TO OBTAIN

Pokémon Black Version 2	Pinwheel Forest entrance
Pokémon White Version 2	Pinwheel Forest entrance

HOW TO OBTAIN FROM OTHER GAMES

—

—

LEVEL-UP AND LEARNED MOVES

Lv.	Name	Type	Kind	Pow.	Acc.	PP	Range	Long	DA
1	Astonish	Ghost	Physical	30	100	15	Normal	—	○
1	Mud-Slap	Ground	Special	20	100	10	Normal	—	—
1	Poison Sting	Poison	Physical	15	100	35	Normal	—	—
3	Mud-Slap	Ground	Special	20	100	10	Normal	—	—
8	Poison Sting	Poison	Physical	15	100	35	Normal	—	—
10	Taunt	Dark	Status	—	100	20	Normal	—	—
15	Pursuit	Dark	Physical	40	100	20	Normal	—	○
17	Faint Attack	Dark	Physical	60	—	20	Normal	—	○
22	Revenge	Fighting	Physical	60	100	10	Normal	—	○
24	Swagger	Normal	Status	—	90	15	Normal	—	—
29	Mud Bomb	Ground	Special	65	85	10	Normal	—	—
31	Sucker Punch	Dark	Physical	80	100	5	Normal	—	○
36	Venoshock	Poison	Special	65	100	10	Normal	—	—
41	Nasty Plot	Dark	Status	—	—	20	Self	—	—
49	Poison Jab	Poison	Physical	80	100	20	Normal	—	○
54	Sludge Bomb	Poison	Special	90	100	10	Normal	—	—
62	Flatter	Dark	Status	—	100	15	Normal	—	—

TM & HM MOVES

Lv.	Name	Type	Kind	Pow.	Acc.	PP	Range	Long	DA
TM06	Toxic	Poison	Status	—	90	10	Normal	—	—
TM08	Bulk Up	Fighting	Status	—	—	20	Self	—	—
TM09	Venoshock	Poison	Special	65	100	10	Normal	—	—
TM10	Hidden Power	Normal	Special	—	100	15	Normal	—	—
TM11	Sunny Day	Fire	Status	—	—	5	Both Sides	—	—
TM12	Taunt	Dark	Status	—	100	20	Normal	—	—
TM15	Hyper Beam	Normal	Special	150	90	5	Normal	—	—
TM17	Protect	Normal	Status	—	—	10	Self	—	—
TM18	Rain Dance	Water	Status	—	—	5	Both Sides	—	—
TM21	Frustration	Normal	Physical	—	100	20	Normal	—	○
TM26	Earthquake	Ground	Physical	100	100	10	Adjacent	—	—
TM27	Return	Normal	Physical	—	100	20	Normal	—	○
TM28	Dig	Ground	Physical	80	100	10	Normal	—	○
TM30	Shadow Ball	Ghost	Special	80	100	15	Normal	—	—
TM31	Brick Break	Fighting	Physical	75	100	15	Normal	—	○
TM32	Double Team	Normal	Status	—	—	15	Self	—	—
TM34	Sludge Wave	Poison	Special	95	100	10	Adjacent	—	—
TM36	Sludge Bomb	Poison	Special	90	100	10	Normal	—	—
TM39	Rock Tomb	Rock	Physical	50	80	10	Normal	—	—
TM41	Torment	Dark	Status	—	100	15	Normal	—	—
TM42	Facade	Normal	Physical	70	100	20	Normal	—	○
TM44	Rest	Psychic	Status	—	—	10	Self	—	—
TM45	Attract	Normal	Status	—	100	15	Normal	—	—
TM46	Thief	Dark	Physical	40	100	10	Normal	—	○
TM47	Low Sweep	Fighting	Physical	60	100	20	Normal	—	○
TM48	Round	Normal	Special	60	100	15	Normal	—	—
TM52	Focus Blast	Fighting	Special	120	70	5	Normal	—	—
TM56	Fling	Dark	Physical	—	100	10	Normal	—	—
TM63	Embargo	Dark	Status	—	100	15	Normal	—	—
TM66	Payback	Dark	Physical	50	100	10	Normal	—	○
TM67	Retaliate	Normal	Physical	70	100	5	Normal	—	○
TM68	Giga Impact	Normal	Physical	150	90	5	Normal	—	○
TM71	Stone Edge	Rock	Physical	100	80	5	Normal	—	—
TM75	Swords Dance	Normal	Status	—	—	30	Self	—	—
TM78	Bulldoze	Ground	Physical	60	100	20	Adjacent	—	—
TM80	Rock Slide	Rock	Physical	75	90	10	Many Others	—	—
TM81	X-Scissor	Bug	Physical	80	100	15	Normal	—	○
TM83	Work Up	Normal	Status	—	—	30	Self	—	—
TM84	Poison Jab	Poison	Physical	80	100	20	Normal	—	○
TM87	Swagger	Normal	Status	—	90	15	Normal	—	—
TM90	Substitute	Normal	Status	—	—	10	Self	—	—
TM94	Rock Smash	Fighting	Physical	40	100	15	Normal	—	○
HM01	Cut	Normal	Physical	50	95	30	Normal	—	○
HM04	Strength	Normal	Physical	80	100	15	Normal	—	○

MOVES TAUGHT BY PEOPLE

Name	Type	Kind	Pow.	Acc.	PP	Range	Long	DA

MOVES TAUGHT BY MOVE TUTORS FOR SHARDS

Name	Type	Kind	Pow.	Acc.	PP	Range	Long	DA
Bounce	Flying	Physical	85	85	5	Normal	○	○
Super Fang	Normal	Physical	—	90	10	Normal	—	○
Dual Chop	Dragon	Physical	40	90	15	Normal	—	○
Low Kick	Fighting	Physical	—	100	20	Normal	—	○
Gunk Shot	Poison	Physical	120	70	5	Normal	—	—
ThunderPunch	Electric	Physical	75	100	15	Normal	—	○
Ice Punch	Ice	Physical	75	100	15	Normal	—	○
Icy Wind	Ice	Special	55	95	15	Many Others	—	—
Foul Play	Dark	Physical	95	100	15	Normal	—	○
Dark Pulse	Dark	Special	80	100	15	Normal	○	—
Snore	Normal	Special	40	100	15	Normal	—	—
Knock Off	Dark	Physical	20	100	20	Normal	—	○
Role Play	Psychic	Status	—	—	10	Normal	—	—
Drain Punch	Fighting	Physical	75	100	10	Normal	—	○
Helping Hand	Normal	Status	—	—	20	1 Ally	—	—
Spite	Ghost	Status	—	100	10	Normal	—	—
Sleep Talk	Normal	Status	—	—	10	Self	—	—
Snatch	Dark	Status	—	—	10	Self	—	—

Pokémon AR Marker

454 Toxicroak

Bug Catcher Pokémon

455 Carnivine

- HEIGHT: 4'07"
- WEIGHT: 59.5 lbs.
- GENDER: ♂ / ♀

Using its tentacles to lash itself to trees, it lies in wait for prey, luring it close with sweet-smelling drool.

Same form for ♂ / ♀

TYPE: Grass

ABILITY
- Levitate

HIDDEN ABILITY
—

STATS
HP
Attack
Defense
Sp. Atk
Sp. Def
Speed

EGG GROUPS
Grass

ITEMS SOMETIMES HELD
- None

EVOLUTION

Does not evolve

HOW TO OBTAIN

Pokémon Black Version 2	Route 18
Pokémon White Version 2	Route 18

HOW TO OBTAIN FROM OTHER GAMES

—

—

LEVEL-UP AND LEARNED MOVES

Lv.	Name	Type	Kind	Pow.	Acc.	PP	Range	Long	DA
1	Bind	Normal	Physical	15	85	20	Normal	—	○
1	Growth	Normal	Status	—	—	40	Self	—	—
7	Bite	Dark	Physical	60	100	25	Normal	—	○
11	Vine Whip	Grass	Physical	35	100	15	Normal	—	○
17	Sweet Scent	Normal	Status	—	100	20	Many Others	—	—
21	Ingrain	Grass	Status	—	—	20	Self	—	—
27	Faint Attack	Dark	Physical	60	—	20	Normal	—	○
31	Leaf Tornado	Grass	Special	65	90	10	Normal	—	—
37	Stockpile	Normal	Status	—	—	20	Self	—	—
37	Spit Up	Normal	Special	—	100	10	Normal	—	—
37	Swallow	Normal	Status	—	—	10	Self	—	—
41	Crunch	Dark	Physical	80	100	15	Normal	—	○
47	Wring Out	Normal	Special	—	100	5	Normal	—	○
51	Power Whip	Grass	Physical	120	85	10	Normal	—	○

TM & HM MOVES

Lv.	Name	Type	Kind	Pow.	Acc.	PP	Range	Long	DA
TM06	Toxic	Poison	Status	—	90	10	Normal	—	—
TM10	Hidden Power	Normal	Special	—	100	15	Normal	—	—
TM11	Sunny Day	Fire	Status	—	—	5	Both Sides	—	—
TM15	Hyper Beam	Normal	Special	150	90	5	Normal	—	—
TM17	Protect	Normal	Status	—	—	10	Self	—	—
TM21	Frustration	Normal	Physical	—	100	20	Normal	—	○
TM22	SolarBeam	Grass	Special	120	100	10	Normal	—	—
TM27	Return	Normal	Physical	—	100	20	Normal	—	○
TM32	Double Team	Normal	Status	—	—	15	Self	—	—
TM36	Sludge Bomb	Poison	Special	90	100	10	Normal	—	—
TM42	Facade	Normal	Physical	70	100	20	Normal	—	○
TM44	Rest	Psychic	Status	—	—	10	Self	—	—
TM45	Attract	Normal	Status	—	100	15	Normal	—	—
TM46	Thief	Dark	Physical	40	100	10	Normal	—	○
TM48	Round	Normal	Special	60	100	15	Normal	—	—
TM53	Energy Ball	Grass	Special	80	100	10	Normal	—	—
TM56	Fling	Dark	Physical	—	100	10	Normal	—	—
TM66	Payback	Dark	Physical	50	100	10	Normal	—	○
TM68	Giga Impact	Normal	Physical	150	90	5	Normal	—	○
TM70	Flash	Normal	Status	—	100	20	Normal	—	—
TM75	Swords Dance	Normal	Status	—	—	30	Self	—	—
TM86	Grass Knot	Grass	Special	—	100	20	Normal	—	○
TM87	Swagger	Normal	Status	—	90	15	Normal	—	—
TM90	Substitute	Normal	Status	—	—	10	Self	—	—
HM01	Cut	Normal	Physical	50	95	30	Normal	—	○

MOVES TAUGHT BY PEOPLE

Name	Type	Kind	Pow.	Acc.	PP	Range	Long	DA

MOVES TAUGHT BY MOVE TUTORS FOR SHARDS

Name	Type	Kind	Pow.	Acc.	PP	Range	Long	DA
Bug Bite	Bug	Physical	60	100	20	Normal	—	○
Seed Bomb	Grass	Physical	80	100	15	Normal	—	—
Bind	Normal	Physical	15	85	20	Normal	—	○
Snore	Normal	Special	40	100	15	Normal	—	—
Knock Off	Dark	Physical	20	100	20	Normal	—	○
Synthesis	Grass	Status	—	—	5	Self	—	—
Giga Drain	Grass	Special	75	100	10	Normal	—	—
Worry Seed	Grass	Status	—	100	10	Normal	—	—
Gastro Acid	Poison	Status	—	100	10	Normal	—	—
Sleep Talk	Normal	Status	—	—	10	Self	—	—

Pokémon AR Marker

455 Carnivine

456 Finneon
Wing Fish Pokémon

TYPE Water

ABILITIES
- Swift Swim
- Storm Drain

HIDDEN ABILITY
- Water Veil

- HEIGHT: 1'04"
- WEIGHT: 15.4 lbs.
- GENDER: ♂ / ♀

STATS
- HP
- Attack
- Defense
- Sp. Atk
- Sp. Def
- Speed

The line running down its side can store sunlight. It shines vividly at night.

EGG GROUPS
Water ❷

ITEMS SOMETIMES HELD
- Rindo Berry

Pokémon AR Marker

EVOLUTION

Finneon — Lv. 31 → Lumineon

HOW TO OBTAIN
Pokémon Black Version 2	❶ Route 17 (Super Rod) ❷ Route 18 (Super Rod)
Pokémon White Version 2	❶ Route 17 (Super Rod) ❷ Route 18 (Super Rod)

HOW TO OBTAIN FROM OTHER GAMES
———
———

LEVEL-UP AND LEARNED MOVES
Lv.	Name	Type	Kind	Pow.	Acc.	PP	Range	Long	DA
1	Pound	Normal	Physical	40	100	35	Normal	—	—
6	Water Gun	Water	Special	40	100	25	Normal	—	—
10	Attract	Normal	Status	—	100	15	Normal	—	—
13	Rain Dance	Water	Status	—	—	5	Both Sides	—	—
17	Gust	Flying	Special	40	100	35	Normal	○	—
22	Water Pulse	Water	Special	60	100	20	Normal	○	—
26	Captivate	Normal	Status	—	100	20	Many Others	—	—
29	Safeguard	Normal	Status	—	—	25	Your Side	—	—
33	Aqua Ring	Water	Status	—	—	20	Self	—	—
38	Whirlpool	Water	Special	35	85	15	Normal	—	—
42	U-turn	Bug	Physical	70	100	20	Normal	—	—
45	Bounce	Flying	Physical	85	85	5	Normal	○	—
49	Silver Wind	Bug	Special	60	100	5	Normal	—	—
54	Soak	Water	Status	—	100	20	Normal	—	—

TM & HM MOVES
Lv.	Name	Type	Kind	Pow.	Acc.	PP	Range	Long	DA
TM06	Toxic	Poison	Status	—	90	10	Normal	—	—
TM07	Hail	Ice	Status	—	—	10	Both Sides	—	—
TM10	Hidden Power	Normal	Special	—	100	15	Normal	—	—
TM13	Ice Beam	Ice	Special	95	100	10	Normal	—	—
TM14	Blizzard	Ice	Special	120	70	5	Many Others	—	—
TM17	Protect	Normal	Status	—	—	10	Self	—	—
TM18	Rain Dance	Water	Status	—	—	5	Both Sides	—	—
TM20	Safeguard	Normal	Status	—	—	25	Your Side	—	—
TM21	Frustration	Normal	Physical	—	100	20	Normal	—	○
TM27	Return	Normal	Physical	—	100	20	Normal	—	○
TM32	Double Team	Normal	Status	—	—	15	Self	—	—
TM42	Facade	Normal	Physical	70	100	20	Normal	—	—
TM44	Rest	Psychic	Status	—	—	10	Self	—	—
TM45	Attract	Normal	Status	—	100	15	Normal	—	—
TM48	Round	Normal	Special	60	100	15	Normal	—	—
TM55	Scald	Water	Special	80	100	15	Normal	—	—
TM66	Payback	Dark	Physical	50	100	10	Normal	—	—
TM70	Flash	Normal	Status	—	100	20	Normal	—	—
TM77	Psych Up	Normal	Status	—	—	10	Normal	—	—
TM87	Swagger	Normal	Status	—	90	15	Normal	—	—
TM89	U-turn	Bug	Physical	70	100	20	Normal	—	—
TM90	Substitute	Normal	Status	—	—	10	Self	—	—
HM03	Surf	Water	Special	95	100	15	Adjacent	—	—
HM05	Waterfall	Water	Physical	80	100	15	Normal	—	—
HM06	Dive	Water	Physical	80	100	10	Normal	—	—

MOVES TAUGHT BY PEOPLE
Name	Type	Kind	Pow.	Acc.	PP	Range	Long	DA

MOVES TAUGHT BY MOVE TUTORS FOR SHARDS
Name	Type	Kind	Pow.	Acc.	PP	Range	Long	DA
Bounce	Flying	Physical	85	85	5	Normal	○	—
Signal Beam	Bug	Special	75	100	15	Normal	—	—
Icy Wind	Ice	Special	55	95	15	Many Others	—	—
Aqua Tail	Water	Physical	90	90	10	Normal	—	○
Snore	Normal	Special	40	100	15	Normal	—	—
Tailwind	Flying	Status	—	—	30	Your Side	—	—
Sleep Talk	Normal	Status	—	—	10	Self	—	—

EGG MOVES
Name	Type	Kind	Pow.	Acc.	PP	Range	Long	DA
Sweet Kiss	Normal	Status	—	75	10	Normal	—	—
Charm	Normal	Status	—	100	20	Normal	—	—
Flail	Normal	Physical	—	100	15	Normal	—	○
Aqua Tail	Water	Physical	90	90	10	Normal	—	—
Splash	Normal	Status	—	—	40	Self	—	—
Psybeam	Psychic	Special	65	100	20	Normal	—	—
Tickle	Normal	Status	—	100	20	Normal	—	—
Agility	Psychic	Status	—	—	30	Self	—	—
Brine	Water	Special	65	100	10	Normal	—	—
Aurora Beam	Ice	Special	65	100	20	Normal	—	—
Signal Beam	Bug	Special	75	100	15	Normal	—	—

457 Lumineon
Neon Pokémon

TYPE Water

ABILITIES
- Swift Swim
- Storm Drain

HIDDEN ABILITY
- Water Veil

- HEIGHT: 3'11"
- WEIGHT: 52.9 lbs.
- GENDER: ♂ / ♀

STATS
- HP
- Attack
- Defense
- Sp. Atk
- Sp. Def
- Speed

It crawls along the seafloor using its long front fins like legs. It competes for food with Lanturn.

EGG GROUPS
Water ❷

ITEMS SOMETIMES HELD
- Rindo Berry

Pokémon AR Marker

EVOLUTION
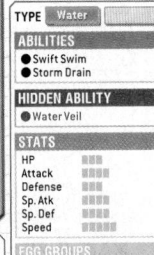
Finneon — Lv. 31 → Lumineon

HOW TO OBTAIN
Pokémon Black Version 2	❶ Route 17 (Super Rod/ripples in water) ❷ Route 18 (Super Rod/ripples in water)
Pokémon White Version 2	❶ Route 17 (Super Rod/ripples in water) ❷ Route 18 (Super Rod/ripples in water)

HOW TO OBTAIN FROM OTHER GAMES
———
———

LEVEL-UP AND LEARNED MOVES
Lv.	Name	Type	Kind	Pow.	Acc.	PP	Range	Long	DA
1	Pound	Normal	Physical	40	100	35	Normal	—	—
1	Water Gun	Water	Special	40	100	25	Normal	—	—
1	Attract	Normal	Status	—	100	15	Normal	—	—
6	Water Gun	Water	Special	40	100	25	Normal	—	—
10	Attract	Normal	Status	—	100	15	Normal	—	—
13	Rain Dance	Water	Status	—	—	5	Both Sides	—	—
17	Gust	Flying	Special	40	100	35	Normal	○	—
22	Water Pulse	Water	Special	60	100	20	Normal	○	—
26	Captivate	Normal	Status	—	100	20	Many Others	—	—
29	Safeguard	Normal	Status	—	—	25	Your Side	—	—
35	Aqua Ring	Water	Status	—	—	20	Self	—	—
42	Whirlpool	Water	Special	35	85	15	Normal	—	—
48	U-turn	Bug	Physical	70	100	20	Normal	—	—
53	Bounce	Flying	Physical	85	85	5	Normal	○	—
59	Silver Wind	Bug	Special	60	100	5	Normal	—	—
66	Soak	Water	Status	—	100	20	Normal	—	—

TM & HM MOVES
Lv.	Name	Type	Kind	Pow.	Acc.	PP	Range	Long	DA
TM06	Toxic	Poison	Status	—	90	10	Normal	—	—
TM07	Hail	Ice	Status	—	—	10	Both Sides	—	—
TM10	Hidden Power	Normal	Special	—	100	15	Normal	—	—
TM13	Ice Beam	Ice	Special	95	100	10	Normal	—	—
TM14	Blizzard	Ice	Special	120	70	5	Many Others	—	—
TM15	Hyper Beam	Normal	Special	150	90	5	Normal	—	—
TM17	Protect	Normal	Status	—	—	10	Self	—	—
TM18	Rain Dance	Water	Status	—	—	5	Both Sides	—	—
TM20	Safeguard	Normal	Status	—	—	25	Your Side	—	—
TM21	Frustration	Normal	Physical	—	100	20	Normal	—	○
TM27	Return	Normal	Physical	—	100	20	Normal	—	○
TM32	Double Team	Normal	Status	—	—	15	Self	—	—
TM42	Facade	Normal	Physical	70	100	20	Normal	—	—
TM44	Rest	Psychic	Status	—	—	10	Self	—	—
TM45	Attract	Normal	Status	—	100	15	Normal	—	—
TM48	Round	Normal	Special	60	100	15	Normal	—	—
TM55	Scald	Water	Special	80	100	15	Normal	—	—
TM66	Payback	Dark	Physical	50	100	10	Normal	—	—
TM68	Giga Impact	Normal	Physical	150	90	5	Normal	—	—
TM70	Flash	Normal	Status	—	100	20	Normal	—	—
TM77	Psych Up	Normal	Status	—	—	10	Normal	—	—
TM87	Swagger	Normal	Status	—	90	15	Normal	—	—
TM89	U-turn	Bug	Physical	70	100	20	Normal	—	—
TM90	Substitute	Normal	Status	—	—	10	Self	—	—
HM03	Surf	Water	Special	95	100	15	Adjacent	—	—
HM05	Waterfall	Water	Physical	80	100	15	Normal	—	—
HM06	Dive	Water	Physical	80	100	10	Normal	—	—

MOVES TAUGHT BY PEOPLE
Name	Type	Kind	Pow.	Acc.	PP	Range	Long	DA

MOVES TAUGHT BY MOVE TUTORS FOR SHARDS
Name	Type	Kind	Pow.	Acc.	PP	Range	Long	DA
Bounce	Flying	Physical	85	85	5	Normal	○	—
Signal Beam	Bug	Special	75	100	15	Normal	—	—
Icy Wind	Ice	Special	55	95	15	Many Others	—	—
Aqua Tail	Water	Physical	90	90	10	Normal	—	○
Snore	Normal	Special	40	100	15	Normal	—	—
Tailwind	Flying	Status	—	—	30	Your Side	—	—
Sleep Talk	Normal	Status	—	—	10	Self	—	—

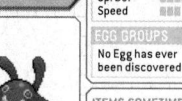

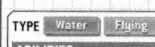

Kite Pokémon

458 Mantyke

● HEIGHT: 3'03"
● WEIGHT: 143.3 lbs.
● GENDER: ♂ / ♀

The pattern on its back varies by region. It often swims in a school of Remoraid.

Same form for ♂ / ♀

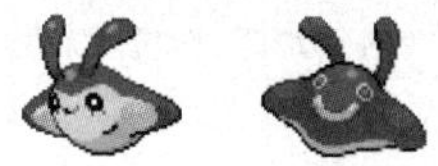

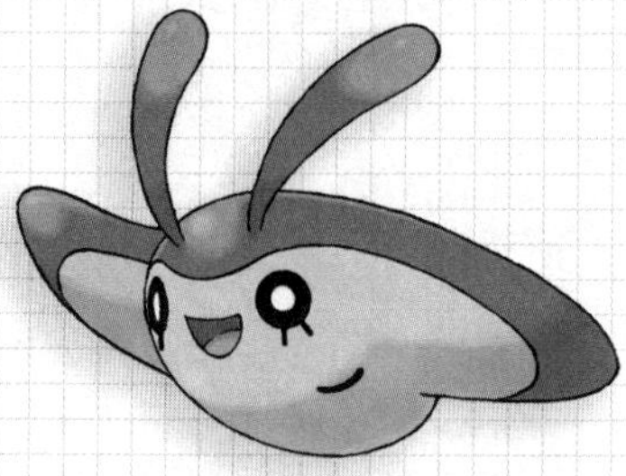

Pokémon AR Marker

TYPE: Water / Flying

ABILITIES
● Swift Swim
● Water Absorb

HIDDEN ABILITY
● Water Veil

STATS
HP
Attack
Defense
Sp. Atk
Sp. Def
Speed

EGG GROUPS
No Egg has ever been discovered

ITEMS SOMETIMES HELD
● None

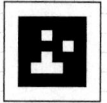

EVOLUTION

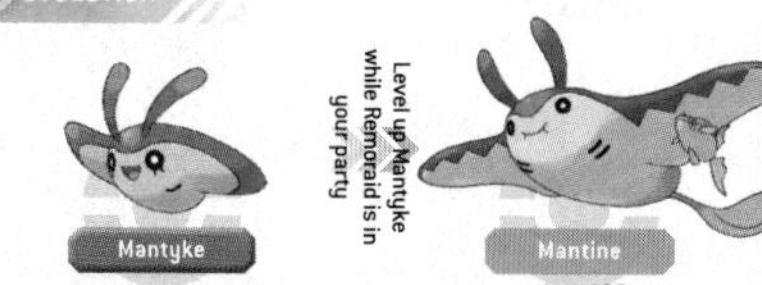
Mantyke
Level up Mantyke while Remoraid is in your party
Mantine

➡ p. 126

HOW TO OBTAIN

Pokémon Black Version 2: ❶ Route 21 (water surface) ❷ Undella Bay (water surface/spring, summer, autumn only)

Pokémon White Version 2: ❶ Route 21 (water surface) ❷ Undella Bay (water surface/spring, summer, autumn only)

HOW TO OBTAIN FROM OTHER GAMES

—

—

LEVEL-UP AND LEARNED MOVES

Lv.	Name	Type	Kind	Pow.	Acc.	PP	Range	Long	DA
1	Tackle	Normal	Physical	50	100	35	Normal	—	○
1	Bubble	Water	Special	20	100	30	Many Others	—	—
3	Supersonic	Normal	Status	—	55	20	Normal	—	—
7	BubbleBeam	Water	Special	65	100	20	Normal	—	—
11	Confuse Ray	Ghost	Status	—	100	10	Normal	—	—
14	Wing Attack	Flying	Physical	60	100	35	Normal	○	○
16	Headbutt	Normal	Physical	70	100	15	Normal	—	○
19	Water Pulse	Water	Special	60	100	20	Normal	○	—
23	Wide Guard	Rock	Status	—	—	10	Your Side	—	—
27	Take Down	Normal	Physical	90	85	20	Normal	—	○
32	Agility	Psychic	Status	—	—	30	Self	—	—
36	Air Slash	Flying	Special	75	95	20	Normal	○	—
39	Aqua Ring	Water	Status	—	—	20	Self	—	—
46	Bounce	Flying	Physical	85	85	5	Normal	○	○
49	Hydro Pump	Water	Special	120	80	5	Normal	—	—

TM & HM MOVES

Lv.	Name	Type	Kind	Pow.	Acc.	PP	Range	Long	DA
TM06	Toxic	Poison	Status	—	90	10	Normal	—	—
TM07	Hail	Ice	Status	—	—	10	Both Sides	—	—
TM10	Hidden Power	Normal	Special	—	100	15	Normal	—	—
TM13	Ice Beam	Ice	Special	95	100	10	Normal	—	—
TM14	Blizzard	Ice	Special	120	70	5	Many Others	—	—
TM17	Protect	Normal	Status	—	—	10	Self	—	—
TM18	Rain Dance	Water	Status	—	—	5	Both Sides	—	—
TM21	Frustration	Normal	Physical	—	100	20	Normal	—	○
TM26	Earthquake	Ground	Physical	100	100	10	Adjacent	—	—
TM27	Return	Normal	Physical	—	100	20	Normal	—	○
TM32	Double Team	Normal	Status	—	—	15	Self	—	—
TM40	Aerial Ace	Flying	Physical	60	—	20	Normal	○	○
TM42	Facade	Normal	Physical	70	100	20	Normal	—	○
TM44	Rest	Psychic	Status	—	—	10	Self	—	—
TM45	Attract	Normal	Status	—	100	15	Normal	—	—
TM48	Round	Normal	Special	60	100	15	Normal	—	—
TM55	Scald	Water	Special	80	100	15	Normal	—	—
TM62	Acrobatics	Flying	Physical	55	100	15	Normal	○	○
TM78	Bulldoze	Ground	Physical	60	100	20	Adjacent	—	—
TM80	Rock Slide	Rock	Physical	75	90	10	Many Others	—	—
TM87	Swagger	Normal	Status	—	90	15	Normal	—	—
TM90	Substitute	Normal	Status	—	—	10	Self	—	—
HM03	Surf	Water	Special	95	100	15	Adjacent	—	—
HM05	Waterfall	Water	Physical	80	100	15	Normal	—	○
HM06	Dive	Water	Physical	80	100	10	Normal	—	○

MOVES TAUGHT BY PEOPLE

Name	Type	Kind	Pow.	Acc.	PP	Range	Long	DA

MOVES TAUGHT BY MOVE TUTORS FOR SHARDS

Name	Type	Kind	Pow.	Acc.	PP	Range	Long	DA
Bounce	Flying	Physical	85	85	5	Normal	○	○
Signal Beam	Bug	Special	75	100	15	Normal	—	—
Icy Wind	Ice	Special	55	95	15	Many Others	—	—
Snore	Normal	Special	40	100	15	Normal	—	—
Helping Hand	Normal	Status	—	—	20	1 Ally	—	—
Sleep Talk	Normal	Status	—	—	10	Self	—	—

EGG MOVES

Name	Type	Kind	Pow.	Acc.	PP	Range	Long	DA
Twister	Dragon	Special	40	100	20	Many Others	—	—
Hydro Pump	Water	Special	120	80	5	Normal	—	—
Haze	Ice	Status	—	—	30	Both Sides	—	—
Slam	Normal	Physical	80	75	20	Normal	—	○
Mud Sport	Ground	Status	—	—	15	Both Sides	—	—
Mirror Coat	Psychic	Special	—	100	20	Varies	—	—
Water Sport	Water	Status	—	—	15	Both Sides	—	—
Splash	Normal	Status	—	—	40	Self	—	—
Signal Beam	Bug	Special	75	100	15	Normal	—	—
Wide Guard	Rock	Status	—	—	10	Your Side	—	—
Amnesia	Psychic	Status	—	—	20	Self	—	—

Frost Tree Pokémon

459 Snover

● HEIGHT: 3'03"
● WEIGHT: 111.3 lbs.
● GENDER: ♂ / ♀

Seemingly curious about people, they gather around footsteps they find on snowy mountains.

♂ ♀

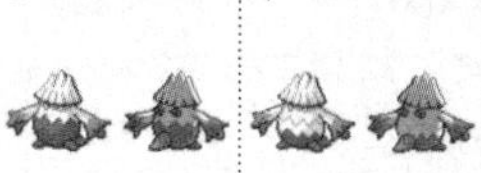

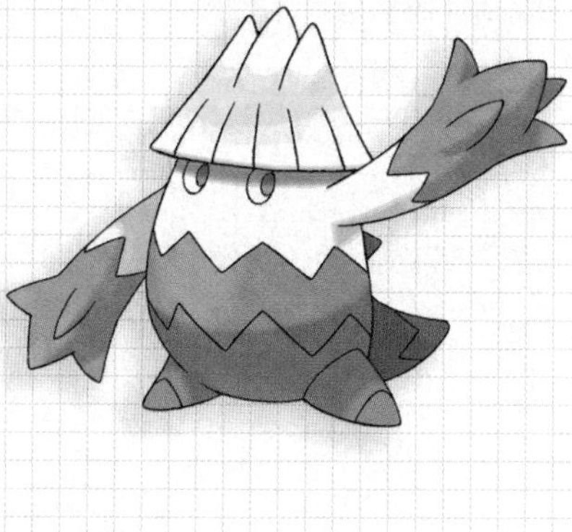

Pokémon AR Marker

TYPE: Grass / Ice

ABILITY
● Snow Warning

HIDDEN ABILITY
● Soundproof

STATS
HP
Attack
Defense
Sp. Atk
Sp. Def
Speed

EGG GROUPS
Monster/Grass

ITEMS SOMETIMES HELD
● None

EVOLUTION

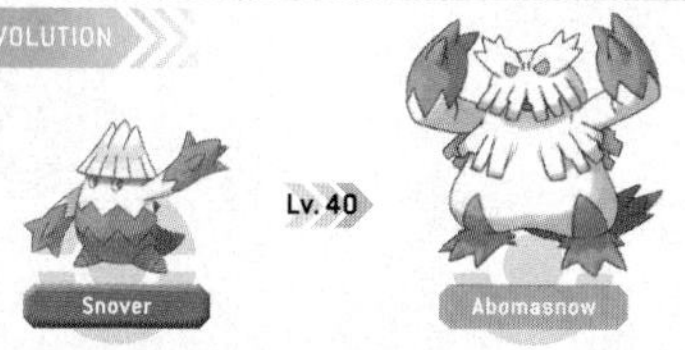
Snover
Lv. 40
Abomasnow

HOW TO OBTAIN

Pokémon Black Version 2: Link Trade or Poké Transfer

Pokémon White Version 2: Link Trade or Poké Transfer

HOW TO OBTAIN FROM OTHER GAMES

Pokémon Platinum Version: Route 216

—

LEVEL-UP AND LEARNED MOVES

Lv.	Name	Type	Kind	Pow.	Acc.	PP	Range	Long	DA
1	Powder Snow	Ice	Special	40	100	25	Many Others	—	—
1	Leer	Normal	Status	—	100	30	Many Others	—	—
5	Razor Leaf	Grass	Physical	55	95	25	Many Others	—	—
9	Icy Wind	Ice	Special	55	95	15	Many Others	—	—
13	GrassWhistle	Grass	Status	—	55	15	Normal	—	—
17	Swagger	Normal	Status	—	90	15	Normal	—	—
21	Mist	Ice	Status	—	—	30	Your Side	—	—
26	Ice Shard	Ice	Physical	40	100	30	Normal	—	—
31	Ingrain	Grass	Status	—	—	20	Self	—	—
36	Wood Hammer	Grass	Physical	120	100	15	Normal	—	○
41	Blizzard	Ice	Special	120	70	5	Many Others	—	—
46	Sheer Cold	Ice	Special	—	30	5	Normal	—	—

TM & HM MOVES

Lv.	Name	Type	Kind	Pow.	Acc.	PP	Range	Long	DA
TM06	Toxic	Poison	Status	—	90	10	Normal	—	—
TM07	Hail	Ice	Status	—	—	10	Both Sides	—	—
TM10	Hidden Power	Normal	Special	—	100	15	Normal	—	—
TM13	Ice Beam	Ice	Special	95	100	10	Normal	—	—
TM14	Blizzard	Ice	Special	120	70	5	Many Others	—	—
TM16	Light Screen	Psychic	Status	—	—	30	Your Side	—	—
TM17	Protect	Normal	Status	—	—	10	Self	—	—
TM18	Rain Dance	Water	Status	—	—	5	Both Sides	—	—
TM20	Safeguard	Normal	Status	—	—	25	Your Side	—	—
TM21	Frustration	Normal	Physical	—	100	20	Normal	—	○
TM22	SolarBeam	Grass	Special	120	100	10	Normal	—	—
TM27	Return	Normal	Physical	—	100	20	Normal	—	○
TM30	Shadow Ball	Ghost	Special	80	100	15	Normal	—	—
TM32	Double Team	Normal	Status	—	—	15	Self	—	—
TM42	Facade	Normal	Physical	70	100	20	Normal	—	○
TM44	Rest	Psychic	Status	—	—	10	Self	—	—
TM45	Attract	Normal	Status	—	100	15	Normal	—	—
TM48	Round	Normal	Special	60	100	15	Normal	—	—
TM53	Energy Ball	Grass	Special	80	100	10	Normal	—	—
TM70	Flash	Normal	Status	—	100	20	Normal	—	—
TM75	Swords Dance	Normal	Status	—	—	30	Self	—	—
TM79	Frost Breath	Ice	Special	40	90	10	Normal	—	—
TM86	Grass Knot	Grass	Special	—	100	20	Normal	—	○
TM87	Swagger	Normal	Status	—	90	15	Normal	—	—
TM90	Substitute	Normal	Status	—	—	10	Self	—	—

MOVES TAUGHT BY PEOPLE

Name	Type	Kind	Pow.	Acc.	PP	Range	Long	DA

MOVES TAUGHT BY MOVE TUTORS FOR SHARDS

Name	Type	Kind	Pow.	Acc.	PP	Range	Long	DA
Seed Bomb	Grass	Physical	80	100	15	Normal	—	—
Ice Punch	Ice	Physical	75	100	15	Normal	—	○
Icy Wind	Ice	Special	55	95	15	Many Others	—	—
Iron Tail	Steel	Physical	100	75	15	Normal	—	○
Snore	Normal	Special	40	100	15	Normal	—	—
Synthesis	Grass	Status	—	—	5	Self	—	—
Role Play	Psychic	Status	—	—	10	Normal	—	—
Giga Drain	Grass	Special	75	100	10	Normal	—	—
Worry Seed	Grass	Status	—	100	10	Normal	—	—
Sleep Talk	Normal	Status	—	—	10	Self	—	—

EGG MOVES

Name	Type	Kind	Pow.	Acc.	PP	Range	Long	DA
Leech Seed	Grass	Status	—	90	10	Normal	—	—
Magical Leaf	Grass	Special	60	—	20	Normal	—	—
Seed Bomb	Grass	Physical	80	100	15	Normal	—	—
Growth	Normal	Status	—	—	40	Self	—	—
Double-Edge	Normal	Physical	120	100	15	Normal	—	○
Mist	Ice	Status	—	—	30	Your Side	—	—
Stomp	Normal	Physical	65	100	20	Normal	—	○
Skull Bash	Normal	Physical	100	100	15	Normal	—	○
Avalanche	Ice	Physical	60	100	10	Normal	—	○
Natural Gift	Normal	Physical	—	100	15	Normal	—	—
Bullet Seed	Grass	Physical	25	100	30	Normal	—	—

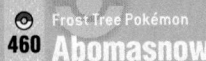

Frost Tree Pokémon

460 Abomasnow

● HEIGHT: 7'03"
● WEIGHT: 298.7 lbs.
● GENDER: ♂ / ♀

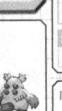

They appear when the snow flowers bloom. When the petals fall, they retreat to places unknown again.

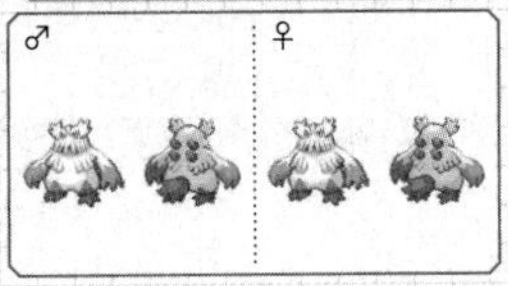

TYPE Grass / Ice

ABILITY
● Snow Warning

HIDDEN ABILITY
● Soundproof

STATS
HP
Attack
Defense
Sp. Atk
Sp. Def
Speed

EGG GROUPS
Monster/Grass

ITEMS SOMETIMES HELD
● None

EVOLUTION

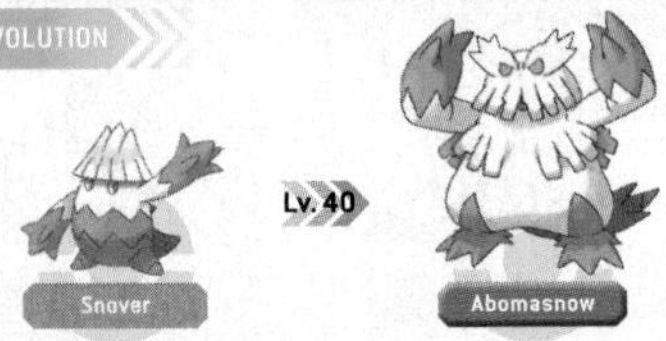

HOW TO OBTAIN

Pokémon Black Version 2	Link Trade or Poké Transfer
Pokémon White Version 2	Link Trade or Poké Transfer

HOW TO OBTAIN FROM OTHER GAMES

Pokémon Platinum Version	Mt. Coronet outside
	—

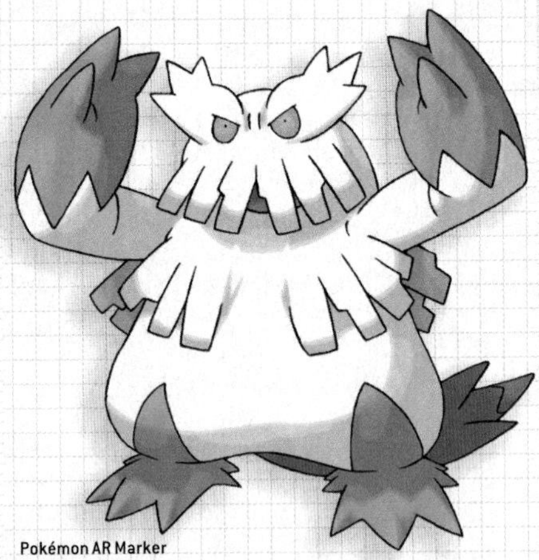

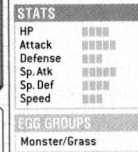

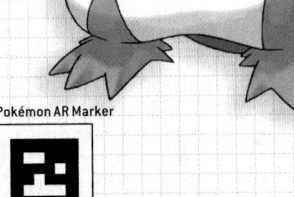

Pokémon AR Marker

LEVEL-UP AND LEARNED MOVES

Lv.	Name	Type	Kind	Pow.	Acc.	PP	Range	Long	DA
1	Ice Punch	Ice	Physical	75	100	15	Normal	—	○
1	Powder Snow	Ice	Special	40	100	25	Many Others	—	—
1	Leer	Normal	Status	—	100	30	Many Others	—	—
1	Razor Leaf	Grass	Physical	55	95	25	Many Others	—	—
1	Icy Wind	Ice	Special	55	95	15	Many Others	—	—
5	Razor Leaf	Grass	Physical	55	95	25	Many Others	—	—
9	Icy Wind	Ice	Special	55	95	15	Many Others	—	—
13	GrassWhistle	Grass	Status	—	55	15	Normal	—	—
17	Swagger	Normal	Status	—	90	15	Normal	—	—
21	Mist	Ice	Status	—	—	30	Your Side	—	—
26	Ice Shard	Ice	Physical	40	100	30	Normal	—	—
31	Ingrain	Grass	Status	—	—	20	Self	—	—
36	Wood Hammer	Grass	Physical	120	100	15	Normal	—	○
47	Blizzard	Ice	Special	120	70	5	Many Others	—	—
58	Sheer Cold	Ice	Special	—	30	5	Normal	—	—

TM & HM MOVES

Lv.	Name	Type	Kind	Pow.	Acc.	PP	Range	Long	DA
TM06	Toxic	Poison	Status	—	90	10	Normal	—	—
TM07	Hail	Ice	Status	—	—	10	Both Sides	—	—
TM10	Hidden Power	Normal	Special	—	100	15	Normal	—	—
TM13	Ice Beam	Ice	Special	95	100	10	Normal	—	—
TM14	Blizzard	Ice	Special	120	70	5	Many Others	—	—
TM15	Hyper Beam	Normal	Special	150	90	5	Normal	—	—
TM16	Light Screen	Psychic	Status	—	—	30	Your Side	—	—
TM17	Protect	Normal	Status	—	—	10	Self	—	—
TM18	Rain Dance	Water	Status	—	—	5	Both Sides	—	—
TM20	Safeguard	Normal	Status	—	—	25	Your Side	—	—
TM21	Frustration	Normal	Physical	—	100	20	Normal	—	○
TM22	SolarBeam	Grass	Special	120	100	10	Normal	—	—
TM26	Earthquake	Ground	Physical	100	100	10	Adjacent	—	—
TM27	Return	Normal	Physical	—	100	20	Normal	—	○
TM30	Shadow Ball	Ghost	Special	80	100	15	Normal	—	—
TM31	Brick Break	Fighting	Physical	75	100	15	Normal	—	○
TM32	Double Team	Normal	Status	—	—	15	Self	—	—
TM39	Rock Tomb	Rock	Physical	50	80	10	Normal	—	—
TM42	Facade	Normal	Physical	70	100	20	Normal	—	○
TM44	Rest	Psychic	Status	—	—	10	Self	—	—
TM45	Attract	Normal	Status	—	100	15	Normal	—	—
TM48	Round	Normal	Special	60	100	15	Normal	—	—
TM52	Focus Blast	Fighting	Special	120	70	5	Normal	—	—
TM53	Energy Ball	Grass	Special	80	100	10	Normal	—	—
TM56	Fling	Dark	Physical	—	100	10	Normal	—	—
TM68	Giga Impact	Normal	Physical	150	90	5	Normal	—	○
TM70	Flash	Normal	Status	—	100	20	Normal	—	—
TM75	Swords Dance	Normal	Status	—	—	30	Self	—	—
TM78	Bulldoze	Ground	Physical	60	100	20	Adjacent	—	—
TM79	Frost Breath	Ice	Special	40	90	10	Normal	—	—
TM80	Rock Slide	Rock	Physical	75	90	10	Many Others	—	—
TM86	Grass Knot	Grass	Special	—	100	20	Normal	—	○
TM87	Swagger	Normal	Status	—	90	15	Normal	—	—
TM90	Substitute	Normal	Status	—	—	10	Self	—	—
TM94	Rock Smash	Fighting	Physical	40	100	15	Normal	—	○
HM04	Strength	Normal	Physical	80	100	15	Normal	—	○

MOVES TAUGHT BY PEOPLE

Name	Type	Kind	Pow.	Acc.	PP	Range	Long	DA

MOVES TAUGHT BY MOVE TUTORS FOR SHARDS

Name	Type	Kind	Pow.	Acc.	PP	Range	Long	DA
Seed Bomb	Grass	Physical	80	100	15	Normal	—	—
Ice Punch	Ice	Physical	75	100	15	Normal	—	○
Block	Normal	Status	—	—	5	Normal	—	—
Icy Wind	Ice	Special	55	95	15	Many Others	—	—
Iron Tail	Steel	Physical	100	75	15	Normal	—	○
Snore	Normal	Special	40	100	15	Normal	—	—
Synthesis	Grass	Status	—	—	5	Self	—	—
Role Play	Psychic	Status	—	—	10	Normal	—	—
Giga Drain	Grass	Special	75	100	10	Normal	—	—
Worry Seed	Grass	Status	—	100	10	Normal	—	—
Outrage	Dragon	Physical	120	100	10	1 Random	—	○
Sleep Talk	Normal	Status	—	—	10	Self	—	—

Sharp Claw Pokémon

461 Weavile

● HEIGHT: 3'07"
● WEIGHT: 75.0 lbs.
● GENDER: ♂ / ♀

They communicate by clawing signs in boulders and work together to surround enemies.

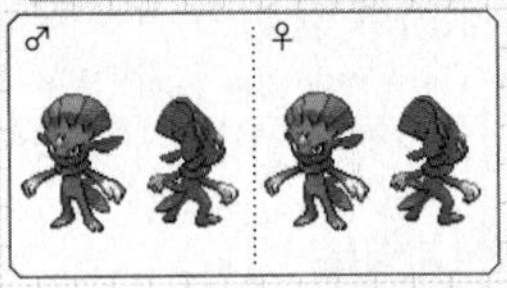

TYPE Dark / Ice

ABILITY
● Pressure

HIDDEN ABILITY
● Pickpocket

STATS
HP
Attack
Defense
Sp. Atk
Sp. Def
Speed

EGG GROUPS
Field

ITEMS SOMETIMES HELD
● None

EVOLUTION

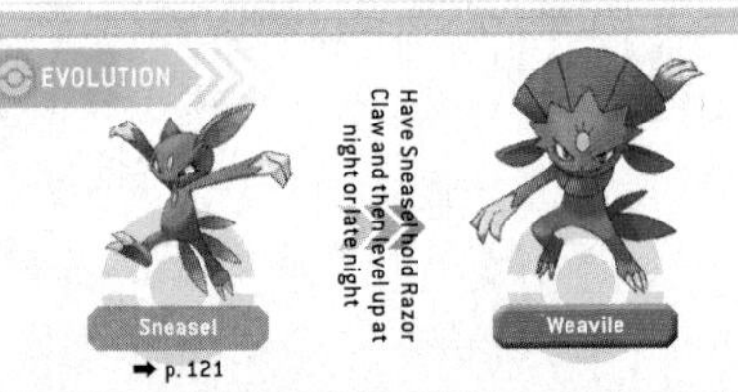

➡ p. 121

HOW TO OBTAIN

Pokémon Black Version 2	Have Sneasel hold Razor Claw and then level up at night or late night
Pokémon White Version 2	Have Sneasel hold Razor Claw and then level up at night or late night

HOW TO OBTAIN FROM OTHER GAMES

—
—

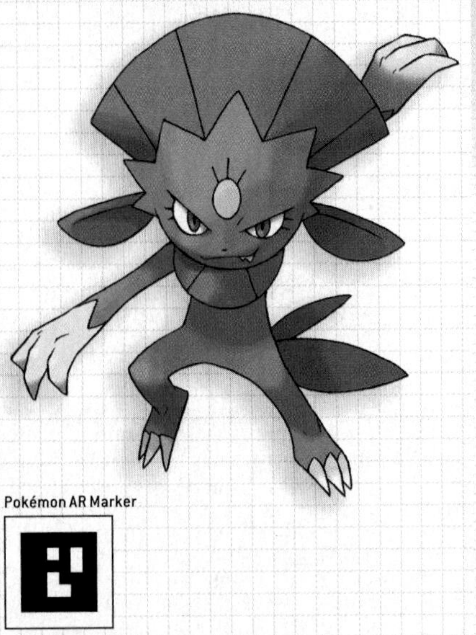

Pokémon AR Marker

LEVEL-UP AND LEARNED MOVES

Lv.	Name	Type	Kind	Pow.	Acc.	PP	Range	Long	DA
1	Embargo	Dark	Status	—	100	15	Normal	—	—
1	Revenge	Fighting	Physical	60	100	10	Normal	—	○
1	Assurance	Dark	Physical	50	100	10	Normal	—	○
1	Scratch	Normal	Physical	40	100	35	Normal	—	○
1	Leer	Normal	Status	—	100	30	Many Others	—	—
1	Taunt	Dark	Status	—	100	20	Normal	—	—
1	Quick Attack	Normal	Physical	40	100	30	Normal	—	○
8	Quick Attack	Normal	Physical	40	100	30	Normal	—	○
10	Faint Attack	Dark	Physical	60	—	20	Normal	—	○
14	Icy Wind	Ice	Special	55	95	15	Many Others	—	—
16	Fury Swipes	Normal	Physical	18	80	15	Normal	—	○
20	Nasty Plot	Dark	Status	—	—	20	Self	—	—
22	Metal Claw	Steel	Physical	50	95	35	Normal	—	○
25	Hone Claws	Dark	Status	—	—	15	Self	—	—
28	Fling	Dark	Physical	—	100	10	Normal	—	—
32	Screech	Normal	Status	—	85	40	Normal	—	—
35	Night Slash	Dark	Physical	70	100	15	Normal	—	○
40	Snatch	Dark	Status	—	—	10	Self	—	—
44	Punishment	Dark	Physical	—	100	5	Normal	—	○
47	Dark Pulse	Dark	Special	80	100	15	Normal	○	—

TM & HM MOVES

Lv.	Name	Type	Kind	Pow.	Acc.	PP	Range	Long	DA
TM01	Hone Claws	Dark	Status	—	—	15	Self	—	—
TM04	Calm Mind	Psychic	Status	—	—	20	Self	—	—
TM06	Toxic	Poison	Status	—	90	10	Normal	—	—
TM07	Hail	Ice	Status	—	—	10	Both Sides	—	—
TM10	Hidden Power	Normal	Special	—	100	15	Normal	—	—
TM11	Sunny Day	Fire	Status	—	—	5	Both Sides	—	—
TM12	Taunt	Dark	Status	—	100	20	Normal	—	—
TM13	Ice Beam	Ice	Special	95	100	10	Normal	—	—
TM14	Blizzard	Ice	Special	120	70	5	Many Others	—	—
TM15	Hyper Beam	Normal	Special	150	90	5	Normal	—	—
TM17	Protect	Normal	Status	—	—	10	Self	—	—
TM18	Rain Dance	Water	Status	—	—	5	Both Sides	—	—
TM21	Frustration	Normal	Physical	—	100	20	Normal	—	○
TM27	Return	Normal	Physical	—	100	20	Normal	—	○
TM28	Dig	Ground	Physical	80	100	10	Normal	—	○
TM30	Shadow Ball	Ghost	Special	80	100	15	Normal	—	—
TM31	Brick Break	Fighting	Physical	75	100	15	Normal	—	○
TM32	Double Team	Normal	Status	—	—	15	Self	—	—
TM33	Reflect	Psychic	Status	—	—	20	Your Side	—	—
TM40	Aerial Ace	Flying	Physical	60	—	20	Normal	○	○
TM41	Torment	Dark	Status	—	100	15	Normal	—	—
TM42	Facade	Normal	Physical	70	100	20	Normal	—	○
TM44	Rest	Psychic	Status	—	—	10	Self	—	—
TM45	Attract	Normal	Status	—	100	15	Normal	—	—
TM46	Thief	Dark	Physical	40	100	10	Normal	—	○
TM47	Low Sweep	Fighting	Physical	60	100	20	Normal	—	○
TM48	Round	Normal	Special	60	100	15	Normal	—	—
TM52	Focus Blast	Fighting	Special	120	70	5	Normal	—	—
TM54	False Swipe	Normal	Physical	40	100	40	Normal	—	○
TM56	Fling	Dark	Physical	—	100	10	Normal	—	—
TM63	Embargo	Dark	Status	—	100	15	Normal	—	—
TM65	Shadow Claw	Ghost	Physical	70	100	15	Normal	—	○
TM66	Payback	Dark	Physical	50	100	10	Normal	—	○
TM67	Retaliate	Normal	Physical	70	100	5	Normal	—	○
TM68	Giga Impact	Normal	Physical	150	90	5	Normal	—	○
TM75	Swords Dance	Normal	Status	—	—	30	Self	—	—
TM77	Psych Up	Normal	Status	—	—	10	Normal	—	—
TM81	X-Scissor	Bug	Physical	80	100	15	Normal	—	○
TM84	Poison Jab	Poison	Physical	80	100	20	Normal	—	○
TM85	Dream Eater	Psychic	Special	100	100	15	Normal	—	—
TM87	Swagger	Normal	Status	—	90	15	Normal	—	—
TM90	Substitute	Normal	Status	—	—	10	Self	—	—
TM94	Rock Smash	Fighting	Physical	40	100	15	Normal	—	○
TM95	Snarl	Dark	Special	55	95	15	Many Others	—	—
HM01	Cut	Normal	Physical	50	95	30	Normal	—	○
HM03	Surf	Water	Special	95	100	15	Adjacent	—	—
HM04	Strength	Normal	Physical	80	100	15	Normal	—	○

MOVES TAUGHT BY PEOPLE

Name	Type	Kind	Pow.	Acc.	PP	Range	Long	DA

MOVES TAUGHT BY MOVE TUTORS FOR SHARDS

Name	Type	Kind	Pow.	Acc.	PP	Range	Long	DA
Low Kick	Fighting	Physical	—	100	20	Normal	—	○
Ice Punch	Ice	Physical	75	100	15	Normal	—	○
Icy Wind	Ice	Special	55	95	15	Many Others	—	—
Iron Tail	Steel	Physical	100	75	15	Normal	—	○
Foul Play	Dark	Physical	95	100	15	Normal	—	○
Dark Pulse	Dark	Special	80	100	15	Normal	○	—
Snore	Normal	Special	40	100	15	Normal	—	—
Knock Off	Dark	Physical	20	100	20	Normal	—	○
Spite	Ghost	Status	—	100	10	Normal	—	—
Sleep Talk	Normal	Status	—	—	10	Self	—	—
Snatch	Dark	Status	—	—	10	Self	—	—

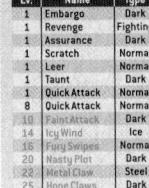

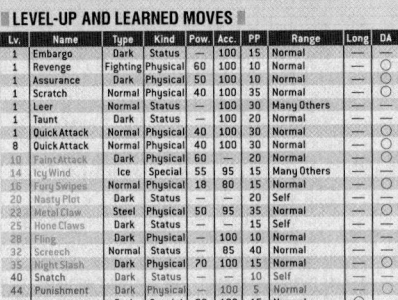

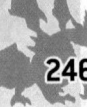

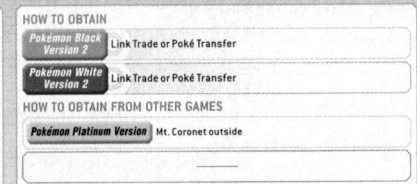

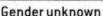

462 Magnezone

Magnet Area Pokémon

- HEIGHT: 3'11"
- WEIGHT: 396.8 lbs.
- GENDER: ♂ / ♀

Sometimes the magnetism emitted by Magnezone is too strong, making them attract each other so they cannot move.

Gender unknown

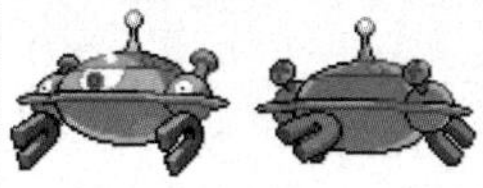

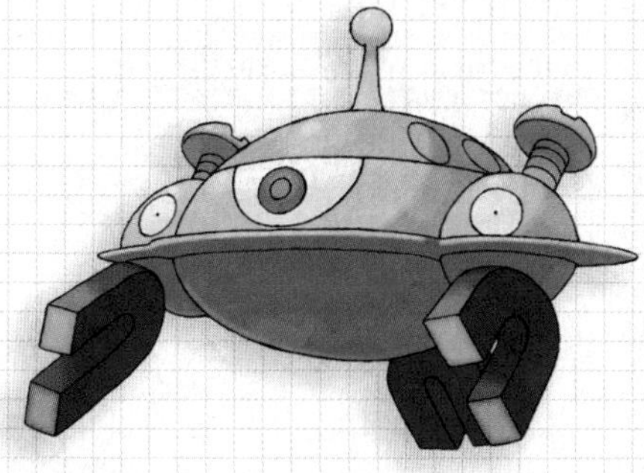

Pokémon AR Marker

TYPE Electric / Steel

ABILITIES
- Magnet Pull
- Sturdy

HIDDEN ABILITY
- Analytic

STATS
HP
Attack
Defense
Sp. Atk
Sp. Def
Speed

EGG GROUPS
Mineral

ITEMS SOMETIMES HELD
- Metal Coat

EVOLUTION

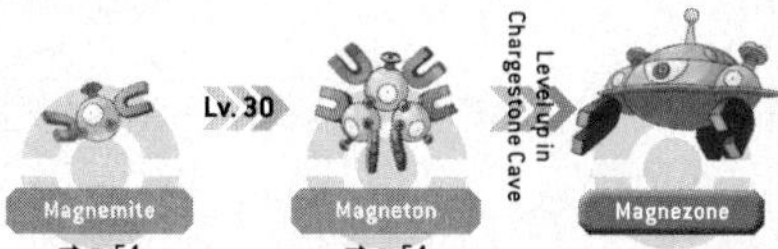

Magnemite ➡ p. 54 → Lv. 30 → Magneton ➡ p. 54 → Level up in Chargestone Cave → Magnezone

HOW TO OBTAIN

Pokémon Black Version 2	P2 Laboratory (rustling grass)
Pokémon White Version 2	P2 Laboratory (rustling grass)

HOW TO OBTAIN FROM OTHER GAMES

—

—

LEVEL-UP AND LEARNED MOVES

Lv.	Name	Type	Kind	Pow.	Acc.	PP	Range	Long	DA
1	Mirror Coat	Psychic	Special	—	100	20	Varies	—	—
1	Barrier	Psychic	Status	—	—	30	Self	—	—
1	Tackle	Normal	Physical	50	100	35	Normal	—	○
1	Supersonic	Normal	Status	—	55	20	Normal	—	—
1	ThunderShock	Electric	Special	40	100	30	Normal	—	—
1	SonicBoom	Normal	Special	—	90	20	Normal	—	—
4	Supersonic	Normal	Status	—	55	20	Normal	—	—
7	ThunderShock	Electric	Special	40	100	30	Normal	—	—
11	SonicBoom	Normal	Special	—	90	20	Normal	—	—
15	Thunder Wave	Electric	Status	—	100	20	Normal	—	—
18	Magnet Bomb	Steel	Physical	60	—	20	Normal	—	—
21	Spark	Electric	Physical	65	100	20	Normal	—	○
25	Mirror Shot	Steel	Special	65	85	10	Normal	—	—
29	Metal Sound	Steel	Status	—	85	40	Normal	—	—
34	Electro Ball	Electric	Special	—	100	10	Normal	—	—
39	Flash Cannon	Steel	Special	80	100	10	Normal	—	—
45	Screech	Normal	Status	—	85	40	Normal	—	—
51	Discharge	Electric	Special	80	100	15	Adjacent	—	—
56	Lock-On	Normal	Status	—	—	5	Normal	—	—
62	Magnet Rise	Electric	Status	—	—	10	Self	—	—
67	Gyro Ball	Steel	Physical	—	100	5	Normal	—	○
73	Zap Cannon	Electric	Special	120	50	5	Normal	—	—

TM & HM MOVES

Lv.	Name	Type	Kind	Pow.	Acc.	PP	Range	Long	DA
TM06	Toxic	Poison	Status	—	90	10	Normal	—	—
TM10	Hidden Power	Normal	Special	—	100	15	Normal	—	—
TM11	Sunny Day	Fire	Status	—	—	5	Both Sides	—	—
TM15	Hyper Beam	Normal	Special	150	90	5	Normal	—	—
TM16	Light Screen	Psychic	Status	—	—	30	Your Side	—	—
TM17	Protect	Normal	Status	—	—	10	Self	—	—
TM18	Rain Dance	Water	Status	—	—	5	Both Sides	—	—
TM21	Frustration	Normal	Physical	—	100	20	Normal	—	○
TM24	Thunderbolt	Electric	Special	95	100	15	Normal	—	—
TM25	Thunder	Electric	Special	120	70	10	Normal	—	—
TM27	Return	Normal	Physical	—	100	20	Normal	—	○
TM32	Double Team	Normal	Status	—	—	15	Self	—	—
TM33	Reflect	Psychic	Status	—	—	20	Your Side	—	—
TM42	Facade	Normal	Physical	70	100	20	Normal	—	○
TM44	Rest	Psychic	Status	—	—	10	Self	—	—
TM48	Round	Normal	Special	60	100	15	Normal	—	—
TM57	Charge Beam	Electric	Special	50	90	10	Normal	—	—
TM64	Explosion	Normal	Physical	250	100	5	Adjacent	—	—
TM68	Giga Impact	Normal	Physical	150	90	5	Normal	—	○
TM70	Flash	Normal	Status	—	100	20	Normal	—	—
TM72	Volt Switch	Electric	Special	70	100	20	Normal	—	—
TM73	Thunder Wave	Electric	Status	—	100	20	Normal	—	—
TM74	Gyro Ball	Steel	Physical	—	100	5	Normal	—	○
TM77	Psych Up	Normal	Status	—	—	10	Normal	—	—
TM87	Swagger	Normal	Status	—	90	15	Normal	—	—
TM90	Substitute	Normal	Status	—	—	10	Self	—	—
TM91	Flash Cannon	Steel	Special	80	100	10	Normal	—	—
TM93	Wild Charge	Electric	Physical	90	100	15	Normal	—	○

MOVES TAUGHT BY PEOPLE

Name	Type	Kind	Pow.	Acc.	PP	Range	Long	DA

MOVES TAUGHT BY MOVE TUTORS FOR SHARDS

Name	Type	Kind	Pow.	Acc.	PP	Range	Long	DA
Signal Beam	Bug	Special	75	100	15	Normal	—	—
Iron Head	Steel	Physical	80	100	15	Normal	—	○
Iron Defense	Steel	Status	—	—	15	Self	—	—
Magnet Rise	Electric	Status	—	—	10	Self	—	—
Magic Coat	Psychic	Status	—	—	15	Self	—	—
Electroweb	Electric	Special	55	95	15	Many Others	—	—
Gravity	Psychic	Status	—	—	5	Both Sides	—	—
Snore	Normal	Special	40	100	15	Normal	—	—
Recycle	Normal	Status	—	—	10	Self	—	—
Sleep Talk	Normal	Status	—	—	10	Self	—	—

463 Lickilicky

Licking Pokémon

- HEIGHT: 5'07"
- WEIGHT: 308.6 lbs.
- GENDER: ♂ / ♀

Their saliva contains lots of components that can dissolve anything. The numbness caused by their lick does not dissipate.

Same form for ♂ / ♀

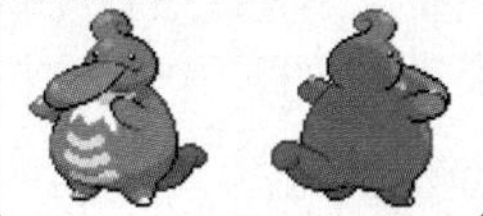

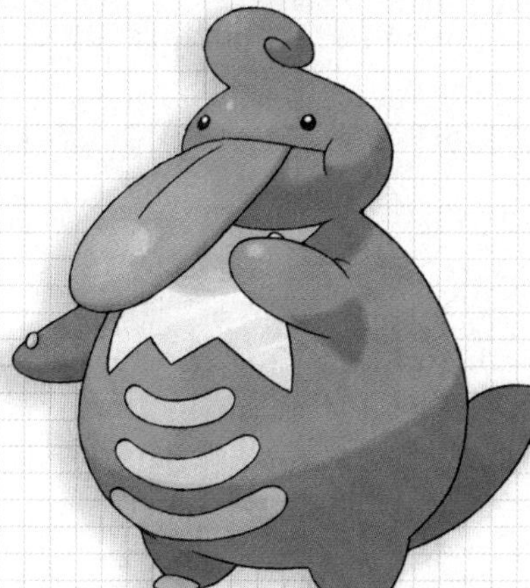

Pokémon AR Marker

TYPE Normal

ABILITIES
- Own Tempo
- Oblivious

HIDDEN ABILITY
- Cloud Nine

STATS
HP
Attack
Defense
Sp. Atk
Sp. Def
Speed

EGG GROUPS
Monster

ITEMS SOMETIMES HELD
- Lagging Tail

EVOLUTION

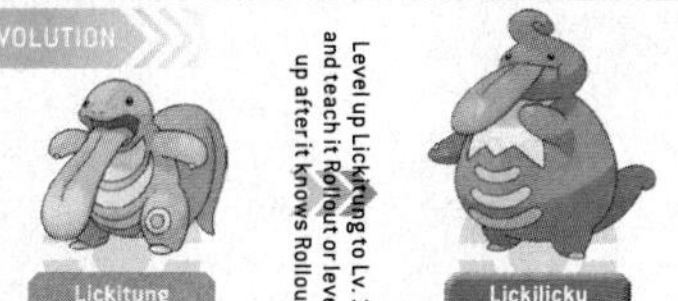

Lickitung ➡ p. 67 → Level up Lickitung to Lv. 33 and teach it Rollout or level it up after it knows Rollout → Lickilicky

HOW TO OBTAIN

Pokémon Black Version 2	Route 2 (rustling grass)
Pokémon White Version 2	Route 2 (rustling grass)

HOW TO OBTAIN FROM OTHER GAMES

—

—

LEVEL-UP AND LEARNED MOVES

Lv.	Name	Type	Kind	Pow.	Acc.	PP	Range	Long	DA
1	Lick	Ghost	Physical	20	100	30	Normal	—	○
5	Supersonic	Normal	Status	—	55	20	Normal	—	—
9	Defense Curl	Normal	Status	—	—	40	Self	—	—
13	Knock Off	Dark	Physical	20	100	20	Normal	—	○
17	Wrap	Normal	Physical	15	90	20	Normal	—	○
21	Stomp	Normal	Physical	65	100	20	Normal	—	○
25	Disable	Normal	Status	—	100	20	Normal	—	—
29	Slam	Normal	Physical	80	75	20	Normal	—	○
33	Rollout	Rock	Physical	30	90	20	Normal	—	○
37	Chip Away	Normal	Physical	70	100	20	Normal	—	○
41	Me First	Normal	Status	—	—	20	Varies	—	—
45	Refresh	Normal	Status	—	—	20	Self	—	—
49	Screech	Normal	Status	—	85	40	Normal	—	—
53	Power Whip	Grass	Physical	120	85	10	Normal	—	○
57	Wring Out	Normal	Special	—	100	5	Normal	—	○
61	Gyro Ball	Steel	Physical	—	100	5	Normal	—	○

TM & HM MOVES

Lv.	Name	Type	Kind	Pow.	Acc.	PP	Range	Long	DA
TM06	Toxic	Poison	Status	—	90	10	Normal	—	—
TM10	Hidden Power	Normal	Special	—	100	15	Normal	—	—
TM11	Sunny Day	Fire	Status	—	—	5	Both Sides	—	—
TM13	Ice Beam	Ice	Special	95	100	10	Normal	—	—
TM14	Blizzard	Ice	Special	120	70	5	Many Others	—	—
TM15	Hyper Beam	Normal	Special	150	90	5	Normal	—	—
TM17	Protect	Normal	Status	—	—	10	Self	—	—
TM18	Rain Dance	Water	Status	—	—	5	Both Sides	—	—
TM21	Frustration	Normal	Physical	—	100	20	Normal	—	○
TM22	SolarBeam	Grass	Special	120	100	10	Normal	—	—
TM24	Thunderbolt	Electric	Special	95	100	15	Normal	—	—
TM25	Thunder	Electric	Special	120	70	10	Normal	—	—
TM26	Earthquake	Ground	Physical	100	100	10	Adjacent	—	—
TM27	Return	Normal	Physical	—	100	20	Normal	—	○
TM28	Dig	Ground	Physical	80	100	10	Normal	—	○
TM30	Shadow Ball	Ghost	Special	80	100	15	Normal	—	—
TM31	Brick Break	Fighting	Physical	75	100	15	Normal	—	○
TM32	Double Team	Normal	Status	—	—	15	Self	—	—
TM35	Flamethrower	Fire	Special	95	100	15	Normal	—	—
TM37	Sandstorm	Rock	Status	—	—	10	Both Sides	—	—
TM38	Fire Blast	Fire	Special	120	85	5	Normal	—	—
TM39	Rock Tomb	Rock	Physical	50	80	10	Normal	—	—
TM42	Facade	Normal	Physical	70	100	20	Normal	—	○
TM44	Rest	Psychic	Status	—	—	10	Self	—	—
TM45	Attract	Normal	Status	—	100	15	Normal	—	—
TM46	Thief	Dark	Physical	40	100	10	Normal	—	○
TM48	Round	Normal	Special	60	100	15	Normal	—	—
TM52	Focus Blast	Fighting	Special	120	70	5	Normal	—	—
TM56	Fling	Dark	Physical	—	100	10	Normal	—	—
TM59	Incinerate	Fire	Special	30	100	15	Many Others	—	—
TM64	Explosion	Normal	Physical	250	100	5	Adjacent	—	—
TM67	Retaliate	Normal	Physical	70	100	5	Normal	—	○
TM68	Giga Impact	Normal	Physical	150	90	5	Normal	—	○
TM74	Gyro Ball	Steel	Physical	—	100	5	Normal	—	○
TM75	Swords Dance	Normal	Status	—	—	30	Self	—	—
TM77	Psych Up	Normal	Status	—	—	10	Normal	—	—
TM78	Bulldoze	Ground	Physical	60	100	20	Adjacent	—	—
TM80	Rock Slide	Rock	Physical	75	90	10	Many Others	—	—
TM82	Dragon Tail	Dragon	Physical	60	90	10	Normal	—	○
TM83	Work Up	Normal	Status	—	—	30	Self	—	—
TM85	Dream Eater	Psychic	Special	100	100	15	Normal	—	—
TM87	Swagger	Normal	Status	—	90	15	Normal	—	—
TM90	Substitute	Normal	Status	—	—	10	Self	—	—
TM94	Rock Smash	Fighting	Physical	40	100	15	Normal	—	○
HM01	Cut	Normal	Physical	50	95	30	Normal	—	○
HM03	Surf	Water	Special	95	100	15	Adjacent	—	—
HM04	Strength	Normal	Physical	80	100	15	Normal	—	○

MOVES TAUGHT BY PEOPLE

Name	Type	Kind	Pow.	Acc.	PP	Range	Long	DA

MOVES TAUGHT BY MOVE TUTORS FOR SHARDS

Name	Type	Kind	Pow.	Acc.	PP	Range	Long	DA
Fire Punch	Fire	Physical	75	100	15	Normal	—	○
ThunderPunch	Electric	Physical	75	100	15	Normal	—	○
Ice Punch	Ice	Physical	75	100	15	Normal	—	○
Block	Normal	Status	—	—	5	Normal	—	—
Icy Wind	Ice	Special	55	95	15	Many Others	—	—
Iron Tail	Steel	Physical	100	75	15	Normal	—	○
Aqua Tail	Water	Physical	90	90	10	Normal	—	○
Zen Headbutt	Psychic	Physical	80	90	15	Normal	—	○
Bind	Normal	Physical	15	85	20	Normal	—	○
Snore	Normal	Special	40	100	15	Normal	—	—
Knock Off	Dark	Physical	20	100	20	Normal	—	○
Sleep Talk	Normal	Status	—	—	10	Self	—	—

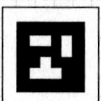

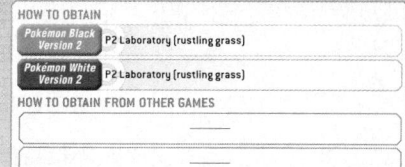

Drill Pokémon

464 Rhyperior

● HEIGHT: 7'10"
● WEIGHT: 623.5 lbs.
● GENDER: ♂ / ♀

It can launch a rock held in its hand like a missile by tightening then expanding muscles instantly.

♂ ♀

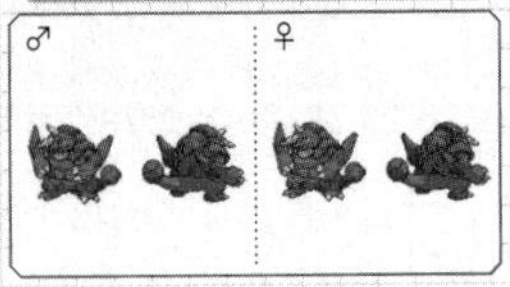

TYPE: Ground, Rock

ABILITIES
● Lightningrod
● Solid Rock

HIDDEN ABILITY
● Reckless

STATS
HP
Attack
Defense
Sp. Atk
Sp. Def
Speed

EGG GROUPS
Monster/Field

ITEMS SOMETIMES HELD
● None

EVOLUTION

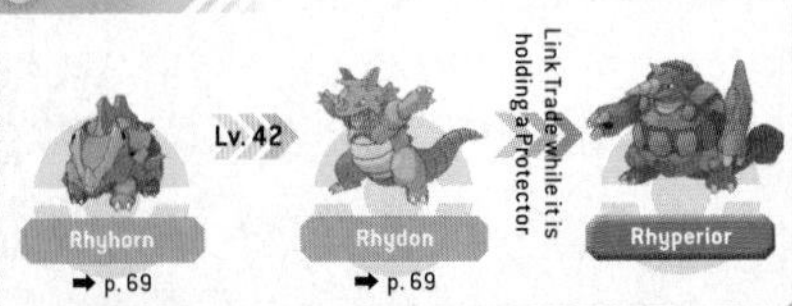

Rhyhorn ➡ p. 69 → Lv. 42 → Rhydon ➡ p. 69 → Link Trade while it is holding a Protector → Rhyperior

HOW TO OBTAIN

Pokémon Black Version 2	Have Rhydon sent to you by Link Trade while it's holding Protector to receive Rhyperior
Pokémon White Version 2	Have Rhydon sent to you by Link Trade while it's holding Protector to receive Rhyperior

HOW TO OBTAIN FROM OTHER GAMES

—

—

Pokémon AR Marker

LEVEL-UP AND LEARNED MOVES

Lv.	Name	Type	Kind	Pow.	Acc.	PP	Range	Long	DA
1	Poison Jab	Poison	Physical	80	100	20	Normal	—	○
1	Horn Attack	Normal	Physical	65	100	25	Normal	—	○
1	Tail Whip	Normal	Status	—	100	30	Many Others	—	—
1	Stomp	Normal	Physical	65	100	20	Normal	—	○
1	Fury Attack	Normal	Physical	15	85	20	Normal	—	○
9	Stomp	Normal	Physical	65	100	20	Normal	—	○
19	Fury Attack	Normal	Physical	15	85	20	Normal	—	○
19	Scary Face	Normal	Status	—	100	10	Normal	—	—
23	Rock Blast	Rock	Physical	25	90	10	Normal	—	—
30	Chip Away	Normal	Physical	70	100	20	Normal	—	○
41	Take Down	Normal	Physical	90	85	20	Normal	—	○
42	Hammer Arm	Fighting	Physical	100	90	10	Normal	—	○
47	Drill Run	Ground	Physical	80	95	10	Normal	—	○
56	Stone Edge	Rock	Physical	100	80	5	Normal	—	—
62	Earthquake	Ground	Physical	100	100	10	Adjacent	—	—
71	Horn Drill	Normal	Physical	—	30	5	Normal	—	○
77	Megahorn	Bug	Physical	120	85	10	Normal	—	○
86	Rock Wrecker	Rock	Physical	150	90	5	Normal	—	—

TM & HM MOVES

Lv.	Name	Type	Kind	Pow.	Acc.	PP	Range	Long	DA
TM05	Roar	Normal	Status	—	100	20	Normal	—	—
TM06	Toxic	Poison	Status	—	90	10	Normal	—	—
TM10	Hidden Power	Normal	Special	—	100	15	Normal	—	—
TM11	Sunny Day	Fire	Status	—	—	5	Both Sides	—	—
TM13	Ice Beam	Ice	Special	95	100	10	Normal	—	—
TM14	Blizzard	Ice	Special	120	70	5	Many Others	—	—
TM15	Hyper Beam	Normal	Special	150	90	5	Normal	—	—
TM17	Protect	Normal	Status	—	—	10	Self	—	—
TM18	Rain Dance	Water	Status	—	—	5	Both Sides	—	—
TM21	Frustration	Normal	Physical	—	100	20	Normal	—	○
TM23	Smack Down	Rock	Physical	50	100	15	Normal	—	—
TM24	Thunderbolt	Electric	Special	95	100	15	Normal	—	—
TM25	Thunder	Electric	Special	120	70	10	Normal	—	—
TM26	Earthquake	Ground	Physical	100	100	10	Adjacent	—	—
TM27	Return	Normal	Physical	—	100	20	Normal	—	○
TM28	Dig	Ground	Physical	80	100	10	Normal	—	○
TM31	Brick Break	Fighting	Physical	75	100	15	Normal	—	○
TM32	Double Team	Normal	Status	—	—	15	Self	—	—
TM35	Flamethrower	Fire	Special	95	100	15	Normal	—	—
TM37	Sandstorm	Rock	Status	—	—	10	Both Sides	—	—
TM38	Fire Blast	Fire	Special	120	85	5	Normal	—	—
TM39	Rock Tomb	Rock	Physical	50	80	10	Normal	—	—
TM42	Facade	Normal	Physical	70	100	20	Normal	—	○
TM44	Rest	Psychic	Status	—	—	10	Self	—	—
TM45	Attract	Normal	Status	—	100	15	Normal	—	—
TM46	Thief	Dark	Physical	40	100	10	Normal	—	○
TM48	Round	Normal	Special	60	100	15	Normal	—	—
TM52	Focus Blast	Fighting	Special	120	70	5	Normal	—	—
TM56	Fling	Dark	Physical	—	100	10	Normal	—	—
TM59	Incinerate	Fire	Special	30	100	15	Many Others	—	—
TM65	Shadow Claw	Ghost	Physical	70	100	15	Normal	—	○
TM66	Payback	Dark	Physical	50	100	10	Normal	—	○
TM68	Giga Impact	Normal	Physical	150	90	5	Normal	—	○
TM69	Rock Polish	Rock	Status	—	—	20	Self	—	—
TM71	Stone Edge	Rock	Physical	100	80	5	Normal	—	—
TM75	Swords Dance	Normal	Status	—	—	30	Self	—	—
TM78	Bulldoze	Ground	Physical	60	100	20	Adjacent	—	—
TM80	Rock Slide	Rock	Physical	75	90	10	Many Others	—	—
TM82	Dragon Tail	Dragon	Physical	60	90	10	Normal	—	○
TM84	Poison Jab	Poison	Physical	80	100	20	Normal	—	○
TM87	Swagger	Normal	Status	—	90	15	Normal	—	—
TM90	Substitute	Normal	Status	—	—	10	Self	—	—
TM91	Flash Cannon	Steel	Special	80	100	10	Normal	—	—
TM94	Rock Smash	Fighting	Physical	40	100	15	Normal	—	○
HM01	Cut	Normal	Physical	50	95	30	Normal	—	○
HM03	Surf	Water	Special	95	100	15	Adjacent	—	—
HM04	Strength	Normal	Physical	80	100	15	Normal	—	○

MOVES TAUGHT BY PEOPLE

Name	Type	Kind	Pow.	Acc.	PP	Range	Long	DA

MOVES TAUGHT BY MOVE TUTORS FOR SHARDS

Name	Type	Kind	Pow.	Acc.	PP	Range	Long	DA
Drill Run	Ground	Physical	80	95	10	Normal	—	○
Iron Head	Steel	Physical	80	100	15	Normal	—	○
Uproar	Normal	Special	90	100	10	1 Random	—	—
Fire Punch	Fire	Physical	75	100	15	Normal	—	○
ThunderPunch	Electric	Physical	75	100	15	Normal	—	○
Ice Punch	Ice	Physical	75	100	15	Normal	—	○
Block	Normal	Status	—	—	5	Normal	—	—
Icy Wind	Ice	Special	55	95	15	Many Others	—	—
Iron Tail	Steel	Physical	100	75	15	Normal	—	○
Aqua Tail	Water	Physical	90	90	10	Normal	—	○
Earth Power	Ground	Special	90	100	10	Normal	—	—
Superpower	Fighting	Physical	120	100	5	Normal	—	○
Dragon Pulse	Dragon	Special	90	100	10	Normal	○	—
Snore	Normal	Special	40	100	15	Normal	—	—
Spite	Ghost	Status	—	100	10	Normal	—	—
Stealth Rock	Rock	Status	—	—	20	3 Foes	—	—
Outrage	Dragon	Physical	120	100	10	1 Random	—	○
Endeavor	Normal	Physical	—	100	5	Normal	—	○
Sleep Talk	Normal	Status	—	—	10	Self	—	—

Rhyperior | 464

Vine Pokémon

465 Tangrowth

● HEIGHT: 6'07"
● WEIGHT: 283.5 lbs.
● GENDER: ♂ / ♀

Even if one of its arms is eaten, it's fine. The Pokémon regrows quickly and will go right back to normal.

♂ ♀

TYPE: Grass

ABILITIES
● Chlorophyll
● Leaf Guard

HIDDEN ABILITY
● Regenerator

STATS
HP
Attack
Defense
Sp. Atk
Sp. Def
Speed

EGG GROUPS
Grass

ITEMS SOMETIMES HELD
● None

EVOLUTION

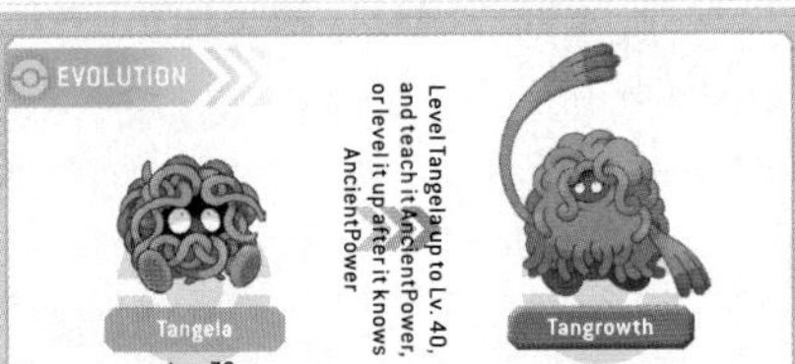

Tangela ➡ p. 70 → Level Tangela up to Lv. 40, and teach it AncientPower, or level it up after it knows AncientPower → Tangrowth

HOW TO OBTAIN

Pokémon Black Version 2	❶ Route 13 (rustling grass) ❷ Giant Chasm entrance (rustling grass)
Pokémon White Version 2	❶ Route 13 (rustling grass) ❷ Giant Chasm entrance (rustling grass)

HOW TO OBTAIN FROM OTHER GAMES

—

—

Pokémon AR Marker

LEVEL-UP AND LEARNED MOVES

Lv.	Name	Type	Kind	Pow.	Acc.	PP	Range	Long	DA
1	Ingrain	Grass	Status	—	—	20	Self	—	—
1	Constrict	Normal	Physical	10	100	35	Normal	—	○
4	Sleep Powder	Grass	Status	—	75	15	Normal	—	—
7	Vine Whip	Grass	Physical	35	100	15	Normal	—	○
10	Absorb	Grass	Special	20	100	25	Normal	—	—
14	PoisonPowder	Poison	Status	—	75	35	Normal	—	—
17	Bind	Normal	Physical	15	85	20	Normal	—	○
20	Growth	Normal	Status	—	—	40	Self	—	—
23	Mega Drain	Grass	Special	40	100	15	Normal	—	—
27	Knock Off	Dark	Physical	20	100	20	Normal	—	○
30	Stun Spore	Grass	Status	—	75	30	Normal	—	—
33	Natural Gift	Normal	Physical	—	100	15	Normal	—	—
36	Giga Drain	Grass	Special	75	100	10	Normal	—	—
40	AncientPower	Rock	Special	60	100	5	Normal	—	—
43	Slam	Normal	Physical	80	75	20	Normal	—	○
46	Tickle	Normal	Status	—	100	20	Normal	—	—
49	Wring Out	Normal	Special	—	100	5	Normal	—	○
53	Power Whip	Grass	Physical	120	85	10	Normal	—	○
56	Block	Normal	Status	—	—	5	Normal	—	—

TM & HM MOVES

Lv.	Name	Type	Kind	Pow.	Acc.	PP	Range	Long	DA
TM06	Toxic	Poison	Status	—	90	10	Normal	—	—
TM10	Hidden Power	Normal	Special	—	100	15	Normal	—	—
TM11	Sunny Day	Fire	Status	—	—	5	Both Sides	—	—
TM15	Hyper Beam	Normal	Special	150	90	5	Normal	—	—
TM17	Protect	Normal	Status	—	—	10	Self	—	—
TM21	Frustration	Normal	Physical	—	100	20	Normal	—	○
TM22	SolarBeam	Grass	Special	120	100	10	Normal	—	—
TM26	Earthquake	Ground	Physical	100	100	10	Adjacent	—	—
TM27	Return	Normal	Physical	—	100	20	Normal	—	○
TM31	Brick Break	Fighting	Physical	75	100	15	Normal	—	○
TM32	Double Team	Normal	Status	—	—	15	Self	—	—
TM33	Reflect	Psychic	Status	—	—	20	Your Side	—	—
TM36	Sludge Bomb	Poison	Special	90	100	10	Normal	—	—
TM39	Rock Tomb	Rock	Physical	50	80	10	Normal	—	—
TM40	Aerial Ace	Flying	Physical	60	—	20	Normal	○	○
TM42	Facade	Normal	Physical	70	100	20	Normal	—	○
TM44	Rest	Psychic	Status	—	—	10	Self	—	—
TM45	Attract	Normal	Status	—	100	15	Normal	—	—
TM46	Thief	Dark	Physical	40	100	10	Normal	—	○
TM48	Round	Normal	Special	60	100	15	Normal	—	—
TM52	Focus Blast	Fighting	Special	120	70	5	Normal	—	—
TM53	Energy Ball	Grass	Special	80	100	10	Normal	—	—
TM56	Fling	Dark	Physical	—	100	10	Normal	—	—
TM66	Payback	Dark	Physical	50	100	10	Normal	—	○
TM68	Giga Impact	Normal	Physical	150	90	5	Normal	—	○
TM70	Flash	Normal	Status	—	100	20	Normal	—	—
TM75	Swords Dance	Normal	Status	—	—	30	Self	—	—
TM77	Psych Up	Normal	Status	—	—	10	Normal	—	—
TM78	Bulldoze	Ground	Physical	60	100	20	Adjacent	—	—
TM80	Rock Slide	Rock	Physical	75	90	10	Many Others	—	—
TM84	Poison Jab	Poison	Physical	80	100	20	Normal	—	○
TM86	Grass Knot	Grass	Special	—	100	20	Normal	—	○
TM87	Swagger	Normal	Status	—	90	15	Normal	—	—
TM90	Substitute	Normal	Status	—	—	10	Self	—	—
TM94	Rock Smash	Fighting	Physical	40	100	15	Normal	—	○
HM01	Cut	Normal	Physical	50	95	30	Normal	—	○
HM04	Strength	Normal	Physical	80	100	15	Normal	—	○

MOVES TAUGHT BY PEOPLE

Name	Type	Kind	Pow.	Acc.	PP	Range	Long	DA

MOVES TAUGHT BY MOVE TUTORS FOR SHARDS

Name	Type	Kind	Pow.	Acc.	PP	Range	Long	DA
Seed Bomb	Grass	Physical	80	100	15	Normal	—	—
Block	Normal	Status	—	—	5	Normal	—	—
Bind	Normal	Physical	15	85	20	Normal	—	○
Snore	Normal	Special	40	100	15	Normal	—	—
Knock Off	Dark	Physical	20	100	20	Normal	—	○
Synthesis	Grass	Status	—	—	5	Self	—	—
Giga Drain	Grass	Special	75	100	10	Normal	—	—
Pain Split	Normal	Status	—	—	20	Normal	—	—
Worry Seed	Grass	Status	—	100	10	Normal	—	—
Endeavor	Normal	Physical	—	100	5	Normal	—	○
Sleep Talk	Normal	Status	—	—	10	Self	—	—

Tangrowth | 465

Thunderbolt Pokémon

466 Electivire

- HEIGHT: 5'11"
- WEIGHT: 305.6 lbs.
- GENDER: ♂ / ♀

The instant it presses the tips of its tails onto an opponent, it sends over 20,000 volts of electricity into the foe.

Same form for ♂ / ♀

Pokémon AR Marker

TYPE Electric

ABILITY

- Motor Drive

HIDDEN ABILITY

- Vital Spirit

STATS

HP
Attack
Defense
Sp. Atk
Sp. Def
Speed

EGG GROUPS

Human-like

ITEMS SOMETIMES HELD

- None

EVOLUTION

Lv. 30
Link Trade while it is holding an Electirizer
Elekid
Electabuzz
Electivire

➡ p. 133
➡ p. 76

HOW TO OBTAIN

Pokémon Black Version 2	Have Electabuzz sent to you by Link Trade while it's holding Electirizer to receive Electivire
Pokémon White Version 2	Have Electabuzz sent to you by Link Trade while it's holding Electirizer to receive Electivire

HOW TO OBTAIN FROM OTHER GAMES

—

—

LEVEL-UP AND LEARNED MOVES

Lv.	Name	Type	Kind	Pow.	Acc.	PP	Range	Long	DA
1	Fire Punch	Fire	Physical	75	100	15	Normal	—	○
1	Quick Attack	Normal	Physical	40	100	30	Normal	—	○
1	Leer	Normal	Status	—	100	30	Many Others	—	—
1	ThunderShock	Electric	Special	40	100	30	Normal	—	—
1	Low Kick	Fighting	Physical	—	100	20	Normal	—	○
5	ThunderShock	Electric	Special	40	100	30	Normal	—	—
8	Low Kick	Fighting	Physical	—	100	20	Normal	—	○
12	Swift	Normal	Special	60	—	20	Many Others	—	—
15	Shock Wave	Electric	Special	60	—	20	Normal	—	—
19	Thunder Wave	Electric	Status	—	100	20	Normal	—	—
22	Electro Ball	Electric	Special	—	100	10	Normal	—	—
26	Light Screen	Psychic	Status	—	—	30	Your Side	—	—
29	ThunderPunch	Electric	Physical	75	100	15	Normal	—	○
36	Discharge	Electric	Special	80	100	15	Adjacent	—	—
42	Screech	Normal	Status	—	85	40	Normal	—	—
49	Thunderbolt	Electric	Special	95	100	15	Normal	—	—
55	Thunder	Electric	Special	120	70	10	Normal	—	—
62	Giga Impact	Normal	Physical	150	90	5	Normal	—	○

TM & HM MOVES

Lv.	Name	Type	Kind	Pow.	Acc.	PP	Range	Long	DA
TM06	Toxic	Poison	Status	—	90	10	Normal	—	—
TM10	Hidden Power	Normal	Special	—	100	15	Normal	—	—
TM12	Taunt	Dark	Status	—	100	20	Normal	—	—
TM15	Hyper Beam	Normal	Special	150	90	5	Normal	—	—
TM16	Light Screen	Psychic	Status	—	—	30	Your Side	—	—
TM17	Protect	Normal	Status	—	—	10	Self	—	—
TM18	Rain Dance	Water	Status	—	—	5	Both Sides	—	—
TM21	Frustration	Normal	Physical	—	100	20	Normal	—	○
TM24	Thunderbolt	Electric	Special	95	100	15	Normal	—	—
TM25	Thunder	Electric	Special	120	70	10	Normal	—	—
TM26	Earthquake	Ground	Physical	100	100	10	Adjacent	—	—
TM27	Return	Normal	Physical	—	100	20	Normal	—	○
TM28	Dig	Ground	Physical	80	100	10	Normal	—	○
TM29	Psychic	Psychic	Special	90	100	10	Normal	—	—
TM31	Brick Break	Fighting	Physical	75	100	15	Normal	—	○
TM32	Double Team	Normal	Status	—	—	15	Self	—	—
TM35	Flamethrower	Fire	Special	95	100	15	Normal	—	—
TM39	Rock Tomb	Rock	Physical	50	80	10	Normal	—	—
TM41	Torment	Dark	Status	—	100	15	Normal	—	—
TM42	Facade	Normal	Physical	70	100	20	Normal	—	○
TM44	Rest	Psychic	Status	—	—	10	Self	—	—
TM45	Attract	Normal	Status	—	100	15	Normal	—	—
TM46	Thief	Dark	Physical	40	100	10	Normal	—	○
TM47	Low Sweep	Fighting	Physical	60	100	20	Normal	—	○
TM48	Round	Normal	Special	60	100	15	Normal	—	—
TM52	Focus Blast	Fighting	Special	120	70	5	Normal	—	—
TM56	Fling	Dark	Physical	—	100	10	Normal	—	—
TM57	Charge Beam	Electric	Special	50	90	10	Normal	—	—
TM68	Giga Impact	Normal	Physical	150	90	5	Normal	—	○
TM70	Flash	Normal	Status	—	100	20	Normal	—	—
TM72	Volt Switch	Electric	Special	70	100	20	Normal	—	—
TM73	Thunder Wave	Electric	Status	—	100	20	Normal	—	—
TM78	Bulldoze	Ground	Physical	60	100	20	Adjacent	—	—
TM80	Rock Slide	Rock	Physical	75	90	10	Many Others	—	—
TM87	Swagger	Normal	Status	—	90	15	Normal	—	—
TM90	Substitute	Normal	Status	—	—	10	Self	—	—
TM93	Wild Charge	Electric	Physical	90	100	15	Normal	—	○
TM94	Rock Smash	Fighting	Physical	40	100	15	Normal	—	○
HM04	Strength	Normal	Physical	80	100	15	Normal	—	○

MOVES TAUGHT BY PEOPLE

Name	Type	Kind	Pow.	Acc.	PP	Range	Long	DA

MOVES TAUGHT BY MOVE TUTORS FOR SHARDS

Name	Type	Kind	Pow.	Acc.	PP	Range	Long	DA
Covet	Normal	Physical	60	100	40	Normal	—	○
Signal Beam	Bug	Special	75	100	15	Normal	—	—
Dual Chop	Dragon	Physical	40	90	15	Normal	—	○
Low Kick	Fighting	Physical	—	100	20	Normal	—	○
Fire Punch	Fire	Physical	75	100	15	Normal	—	○
ThunderPunch	Electric	Physical	75	100	15	Normal	—	○
Ice Punch	Ice	Physical	75	100	15	Normal	—	○
Magnet Rise	Electric	Status	—	—	10	Self	—	—
Electroweb	Electric	Special	55	95	15	Many Others	—	—
Iron Tail	Steel	Physical	100	75	15	Normal	—	○
Snore	Normal	Special	40	100	15	Normal	—	—
Helping Hand	Normal	Status	—	—	20	1 Ally	—	—
Sleep Talk	Normal	Status	—	—	10	Self	—	—

Blast Pokémon

467 Magmortar

- HEIGHT: 5'03"
- WEIGHT: 149.9 lbs.
- GENDER: ♂ / ♀

When shooting 3,600 degree F fireballs from its arms, its body takes on a whitish hue from the intense heat.

Same form for ♂ / ♀

Pokémon AR Marker

TYPE Fire

ABILITY

- Flame Body

HIDDEN ABILITY

- Vital Spirit

STATS

HP
Attack
Defense
Sp. Atk
Sp. Def
Speed

EGG GROUPS

Human-like

ITEMS SOMETIMES HELD

- None

EVOLUTION

Lv. 30
Have Magmar hold the Magmarizer and Link Trade it
Magby
Magmar
Magmortar

➡ p. 133
➡ p. 76

HOW TO OBTAIN

Pokémon Black Version 2	Have Magmar sent to you by Link Trade while it's holding Magmarizer to receive Magmortar
Pokémon White Version 2	Have Magmar sent to you by Link Trade while it's holding Magmarizer to receive Magmortar

HOW TO OBTAIN FROM OTHER GAMES

—

—

LEVEL-UP AND LEARNED MOVES

Lv.	Name	Type	Kind	Pow.	Acc.	PP	Range	Long	DA
1	ThunderPunch	Electric	Physical	75	100	15	Normal	—	○
1	Smog	Poison	Special	20	70	20	Normal	—	—
1	Leer	Normal	Status	—	100	30	Many Others	—	—
1	Ember	Fire	Special	40	100	25	Normal	—	—
1	SmokeScreen	Normal	Status	—	100	20	Normal	—	—
5	Ember	Fire	Special	40	100	25	Normal	—	—
8	SmokeScreen	Normal	Status	—	100	20	Normal	—	—
12	Faint Attack	Dark	Physical	60	—	20	Normal	—	○
15	Fire Spin	Fire	Special	35	85	15	Normal	—	—
19	Clear Smog	Poison	Special	50	—	15	Normal	—	—
22	Flame Burst	Fire	Special	70	100	15	Normal	—	—
26	Confuse Ray	Ghost	Status	—	100	10	Normal	—	—
29	Fire Punch	Fire	Physical	75	100	15	Normal	—	○
36	Lava Plume	Fire	Special	80	100	15	Adjacent	—	—
42	Sunny Day	Fire	Status	—	—	5	Both Sides	—	—
49	Flamethrower	Fire	Special	95	100	15	Normal	—	—
55	Fire Blast	Fire	Special	120	85	5	Normal	—	—
62	Hyper Beam	Normal	Special	150	90	5	Normal	—	—

TM & HM MOVES

Lv.	Name	Type	Kind	Pow.	Acc.	PP	Range	Long	DA
TM06	Toxic	Poison	Status	—	90	10	Normal	—	—
TM10	Hidden Power	Normal	Special	—	100	15	Normal	—	—
TM11	Sunny Day	Fire	Status	—	—	5	Both Sides	—	—
TM12	Taunt	Dark	Status	—	100	20	Normal	—	—
TM15	Hyper Beam	Normal	Special	150	90	5	Normal	—	—
TM17	Protect	Normal	Status	—	—	10	Self	—	—
TM21	Frustration	Normal	Physical	—	100	20	Normal	—	○
TM22	SolarBeam	Grass	Special	120	100	10	Normal	—	—
TM24	Thunderbolt	Electric	Special	95	100	15	Normal	—	—
TM26	Earthquake	Ground	Physical	100	100	10	Adjacent	—	—
TM27	Return	Normal	Physical	—	100	20	Normal	—	○
TM29	Psychic	Psychic	Special	90	100	10	Normal	—	—
TM31	Brick Break	Fighting	Physical	75	100	15	Normal	—	○
TM32	Double Team	Normal	Status	—	—	15	Self	—	—
TM35	Flamethrower	Fire	Special	95	100	15	Normal	—	—
TM38	Fire Blast	Fire	Special	120	85	5	Normal	—	—
TM39	Rock Tomb	Rock	Physical	50	80	10	Normal	—	—
TM41	Torment	Dark	Status	—	100	15	Normal	—	—
TM42	Facade	Normal	Physical	70	100	20	Normal	—	○
TM43	Flame Charge	Fire	Physical	50	100	20	Normal	—	○
TM44	Rest	Psychic	Status	—	—	10	Self	—	—
TM45	Attract	Normal	Status	—	100	15	Normal	—	—
TM46	Thief	Dark	Physical	40	100	10	Normal	—	○
TM47	Low Sweep	Fighting	Physical	60	100	20	Normal	—	○
TM48	Round	Normal	Special	60	100	15	Normal	—	—
TM50	Overheat	Fire	Special	140	90	5	Normal	—	—
TM52	Focus Blast	Fighting	Special	120	70	5	Normal	—	—
TM56	Fling	Dark	Physical	—	100	10	Normal	—	—
TM59	Incinerate	Fire	Special	30	100	15	Many Others	—	—
TM61	Will-O-Wisp	Fire	Status	—	75	15	Normal	—	—
TM68	Giga Impact	Normal	Physical	150	90	5	Normal	—	○
TM78	Bulldoze	Ground	Physical	60	100	20	Adjacent	—	—
TM80	Rock Slide	Rock	Physical	75	90	10	Many Others	—	—
TM87	Swagger	Normal	Status	—	90	15	Normal	—	—
TM90	Substitute	Normal	Status	—	—	10	Self	—	—
TM94	Rock Smash	Fighting	Physical	40	100	15	Normal	—	○
HM04	Strength	Normal	Physical	80	100	15	Normal	—	○

MOVES TAUGHT BY PEOPLE

Name	Type	Kind	Pow.	Acc.	PP	Range	Long	DA

MOVES TAUGHT BY MOVE TUTORS FOR SHARDS

Name	Type	Kind	Pow.	Acc.	PP	Range	Long	DA
Covet	Normal	Physical	60	100	40	Normal	—	○
Dual Chop	Dragon	Physical	40	90	15	Normal	—	○
Low Kick	Fighting	Physical	—	100	20	Normal	—	○
Fire Punch	Fire	Physical	75	100	15	Normal	—	○
ThunderPunch	Electric	Physical	75	100	15	Normal	—	○
Iron Tail	Steel	Physical	100	75	15	Normal	—	○
Snore	Normal	Special	40	100	15	Normal	—	—
Heat Wave	Fire	Special	100	90	10	Many Others	—	—
Helping Hand	Normal	Status	—	—	20	1 Ally	—	—
Sleep Talk	Normal	Status	—	—	10	Self	—	—

468 Togekiss

Jubilee Pokémon

TYPE Normal / Flying

ABILITIES
- Hustle
- Serene Grace

HIDDEN ABILITY
- Super Luck

- HEIGHT: 4'11"
- WEIGHT: 83.8 lbs.
- GENDER: ♂ / ♀

It shares many blessings with people who respect one another's rights and avoid needless strife.

STATS
- HP
- Attack
- Defense
- Sp. Atk
- Sp. Def
- Speed

Same form for ♂ / ♀

EGG GROUPS
Flying/Fairy

ITEMS SOMETIMES HELD
- None

EVOLUTION

Togepi → p. 101 | Level up with high friendship | Togetic → p. 101 | Use Shiny Stone | Togekiss

HOW TO OBTAIN

Pokémon Black Version 2	Level up the Togepi you receive from Yancy or Curtis and use the Shiny Stone on Togetic
Pokémon White Version 2	Level up the Togepi you receive from Yancy or Curtis and use the Shiny Stone on Togetic

HOW TO OBTAIN FROM OTHER GAMES

LEVEL-UP AND LEARNED MOVES

Lv.	Name	Type	Kind	Pow.	Acc.	PP	Range	Long	DA
1	Sky Attack	Flying	Physical	140	90	5	Normal	○	
1	ExtremeSpeed	Normal	Physical	80	100	5	Normal		○
1	Aura Sphere	Fighting	Special	90	—	20	Normal		○
1	Air Slash	Flying	Special	75	95	20	Normal		

TM & HM MOVES

Lv.	Name	Type	Kind	Pow.	Acc.	PP	Range	Long	DA
TM03	Psyshock	Psychic	Special	80	100	10	Normal	—	
TM06	Toxic	Poison	Status	—	90	10	Normal	—	
TM10	Hidden Power	Normal	Special	—	100	15	Normal	—	
TM11	Sunny Day	Fire	Status	—	—	5	Both Sides	—	
TM15	Hyper Beam	Normal	Special	150	90	5	Normal	—	
TM16	Light Screen	Psychic	Status	—	—	30	Your Side	—	
TM17	Protect	Normal	Status	—	—	10	Self	—	
TM18	Rain Dance	Water	Status	—	—	5	Both Sides	—	
TM19	Telekinesis	Psychic	Status	—	—	15	Normal	—	
TM20	Safeguard	Normal	Status	—	—	25	Your Side	—	
TM21	Frustration	Normal	Physical	—	100	20	Normal	—	○
TM22	SolarBeam	Grass	Special	120	100	10	Normal	—	
TM27	Return	Normal	Physical	—	100	20	Normal	—	○
TM29	Psychic	Psychic	Special	90	100	10	Normal	—	
TM30	Shadow Ball	Ghost	Special	80	100	15	Normal	—	
TM31	Brick Break	Fighting	Physical	75	100	15	Normal	—	
TM32	Double Team	Normal	Status	—	—	15	Self	—	
TM33	Reflect	Psychic	Status	—	—	20	Your Side	—	
TM35	Flamethrower	Fire	Special	95	100	15	Normal	—	
TM38	Fire Blast	Fire	Special	120	85	5	Normal	—	
TM40	Aerial Ace	Flying	Physical	60	—	20	Normal	○	○
TM42	Facade	Normal	Physical	70	100	20	Normal	—	○
TM44	Rest	Psychic	Status	—	—	10	Self	—	
TM45	Attract	Normal	Status	—	100	15	Normal	—	
TM48	Round	Normal	Special	60	100	15	Normal	—	
TM49	Echoed Voice	Normal	Special	40	100	15	Normal	—	
TM56	Fling	Dark	Physical	—	100	10	Normal	—	
TM59	Incinerate	Fire	Special	30	100	15	Many Others	—	
TM67	Retaliate	Normal	Physical	70	100	5	Normal	—	
TM68	Giga Impact	Normal	Physical	150	90	5	Normal	—	
TM70	Flash	Normal	Status	—	100	20	Normal	—	
TM73	Thunder Wave	Electric	Status	—	100	20	Normal	—	
TM77	Psych Up	Normal	Status	—	—	10	Self	—	
TM83	Work Up	Normal	Status	—	—	30	Self	—	
TM85	Dream Eater	Psychic	Special	100	100	15	Normal	—	
TM86	Grass Knot	Grass	Special	—	100	20	Normal	—	
TM87	Swagger	Normal	Status	—	90	15	Normal	—	
TM88	Pluck	Flying	Physical	60	100	20	Normal	○	○
TM90	Substitute	Normal	Status	—	—	10	Self	—	
TM94	Rock Smash	Fighting	Physical	40	100	15	Normal	—	○
HM02	Fly	Flying	Physical	90	95	15	Normal	○	○

MOVES TAUGHT BY PEOPLE

Name	Type	Kind	Pow.	Acc.	PP	Range	Long	DA

MOVES TAUGHT BY MOVE TUTORS FOR SHARDS

Name	Type	Kind	Pow.	Acc.	PP	Range	Long	DA
Covet	Normal	Physical	60	100	40	Normal	—	○
Signal Beam	Bug	Special	75	100	15	Normal	—	
Last Resort	Normal	Physical	140	100	5	Normal	—	○
Magic Coat	Psychic	Status	—	—	15	Self	—	
Hyper Voice	Normal	Special	90	100	10	Many Others	—	
Zen Headbutt	Psychic	Physical	80	90	15	Normal	—	○
Snore	Normal	Special	40	100	15	Normal	—	
Heal Bell	Normal	Status	—	—	5	Your Party	—	
Roost	Flying	Status	—	—	10	Self	—	
Sky Attack	Flying	Physical	140	90	5	Normal	○	
Heat Wave	Fire	Special	100	90	10	Many Others	—	○
Drain Punch	Fighting	Physical	75	100	10	Normal	—	○
Tailwind	Flying	Status	—	—	30	Your Side	—	
Trick	Psychic	Status	—	100	10	Normal	—	
Endeavor	Normal	Physical	—	100	5	Normal	—	○
Sleep Talk	Normal	Status	—	—	10	Self	—	

Pokémon AR Marker

469 Yanmega

Ogre Darner Pokémon

TYPE Bug / Flying

ABILITIES
- Speed Boost
- Tinted Lens

HIDDEN ABILITY
- Frisk

- HEIGHT: 6'03"
- WEIGHT: 113.5 lbs.
- GENDER: ♂ / ♀

It prefers to battle by biting apart foes' heads instantly while flying by at high speed.

STATS
- HP
- Attack
- Defense
- Sp. Atk
- Sp. Def
- Speed

Same form for ♂ / ♀

EGG GROUPS
Bug

ITEMS SOMETIMES HELD
- Wide Lens

EVOLUTION

Yanma → p. 110 | Level up Yanma to Lv. 33 and teach it AncientPower, or level it up after it knows AncientPower. | Yanmega

HOW TO OBTAIN

Pokémon Black Version 2	① Pinwheel Forest entrance (rustling grass) ② Route 3 (rustling grass)
Pokémon White Version 2	① Pinwheel Forest entrance (rustling grass) ② Route 3 (rustling grass)

HOW TO OBTAIN FROM OTHER GAMES

LEVEL-UP AND LEARNED MOVES

Lv.	Name	Type	Kind	Pow.	Acc.	PP	Range	Long	DA
1	Night Slash	Dark	Physical	70	100	15	Normal	—	○
1	Bug Bite	Bug	Physical	60	100	20	Normal	—	○
1	Tackle	Normal	Physical	50	100	35	Normal	—	
1	Foresight	Normal	Status	—	—	40	Normal	—	
1	Quick Attack	Normal	Physical	40	100	30	Normal	—	
6	Quick Attack	Normal	Physical	40	100	30	Normal	—	
11	Double Team	Normal	Status	—	—	15	Self	—	
14	SonicBoom	Normal	Special	—	90	20	Normal	—	
17	Detect	Fighting	Status	—	—	5	Self	—	
22	Supersonic	Normal	Status	—	55	20	Normal	—	
27	Uproar	Normal	Special	90	100	10	1 Random	—	
30	Pursuit	Normal	Physical	40	100	20	Normal	—	
33	AncientPower	Rock	Special	60	100	5	Normal	—	
38	Feint	Normal	Physical	30	100	10	Normal	—	
43	Slash	Normal	Physical	70	100	20	Normal	—	
46	Screech	Normal	Status	—	85	40	Normal	—	
49	U-turn	Bug	Physical	70	100	20	Normal	—	
54	Air Slash	Flying	Special	75	95	20	Normal	—	○
57	Bug Buzz	Bug	Special	90	100	10	Normal	—	

TM & HM MOVES

Lv.	Name	Type	Kind	Pow.	Acc.	PP	Range	Long	DA
TM06	Toxic	Poison	Status	—	90	10	Normal	—	
TM10	Hidden Power	Normal	Special	—	100	15	Normal	—	
TM11	Sunny Day	Fire	Status	—	—	5	Both Sides	—	
TM15	Hyper Beam	Normal	Special	150	90	5	Normal	—	
TM17	Protect	Normal	Status	—	—	10	Self	—	
TM21	Frustration	Normal	Physical	—	100	20	Normal	—	○
TM22	SolarBeam	Grass	Special	120	100	10	Normal	—	
TM27	Return	Normal	Physical	—	100	20	Normal	—	○
TM29	Psychic	Psychic	Special	90	100	10	Normal	—	
TM30	Shadow Ball	Ghost	Special	80	100	15	Normal	—	
TM32	Double Team	Normal	Status	—	—	15	Self	—	
TM40	Aerial Ace	Flying	Physical	60	—	20	Normal	○	○
TM42	Facade	Normal	Physical	70	100	20	Normal	—	○
TM44	Rest	Psychic	Status	—	—	10	Self	—	
TM45	Attract	Normal	Status	—	100	15	Normal	—	
TM46	Thief	Dark	Physical	40	100	10	Normal	—	
TM48	Round	Normal	Special	60	100	15	Normal	—	
TM68	Giga Impact	Normal	Physical	150	90	5	Normal	—	
TM70	Flash	Normal	Status	—	100	20	Normal	—	
TM76	Struggle Bug	Bug	Special	30	100	20	Many Others	—	
TM77	Psych Up	Normal	Status	—	—	10	Self	—	
TM85	Dream Eater	Psychic	Special	100	100	15	Normal	—	
TM87	Swagger	Normal	Status	—	90	15	Normal	—	
TM89	U-turn	Bug	Physical	70	100	20	Normal	—	
TM90	Substitute	Normal	Status	—	—	10	Self	—	

MOVES TAUGHT BY PEOPLE

Name	Type	Kind	Pow.	Acc.	PP	Range	Long	DA

MOVES TAUGHT BY MOVE TUTORS FOR SHARDS

Name	Type	Kind	Pow.	Acc.	PP	Range	Long	DA
Bug Bite	Bug	Physical	60	100	20	Normal	—	○
Signal Beam	Bug	Special	75	100	15	Normal	—	
Uproar	Normal	Special	90	100	10	1 Random	—	
Snore	Normal	Special	40	100	15	Normal	—	
Roost	Flying	Status	—	—	10	Self	—	
Giga Drain	Grass	Special	75	100	10	Normal	—	
Tailwind	Flying	Status	—	—	30	Your Side	—	
Sleep Talk	Normal	Status	—	—	10	Self	—	

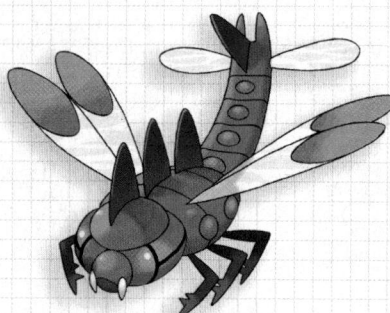

Pokémon AR Marker

470 Leafeon

Verdant Pokémon

● HEIGHT: 3'03"
● WEIGHT: 56.2 lbs.
● GENDER: ♂ / ♀

With cells similar to those of plants, it performs photosynthesis inside its body and creates pure air.

Same form for ♂ / ♀

Pokémon AR Marker

TYPE Grass

ABILITY
● Leaf Guard

HIDDEN ABILITY
● Chlorophyll

STATS

HP	■■■
Attack	■■■■■■
Defense	■■■■■■
Sp. Atk	■■■
Sp. Def	■■■
Speed	■■■■■

EGG GROUPS
Field

ITEMS SOMETIMES HELD
● None

EVOLUTION

- Eevee ➡ p. 80
- Vaporeon ➡ p. 80 — Use Water Stone on Eevee
- Jolteon ➡ p. 81 — Use Thunderstone on Eevee
- Flareon ➡ p. 81 — Use Fire Stone on Eevee
- Espeon ➡ p. 111 — Level up with high friendship in the morning, afternoon, or evening
- Umbreon ➡ p. 112 — Level up with high friendship at night
- Leafeon — Level up Eevee around the moss-covered rock in the Pinwheel Forest
- Glaceon — Level up Eevee around the ice-covered rock in Twist Mountain

HOW TO OBTAIN

Pokémon Black Version 2	Level up Eevee around the moss-covered rock in the Pinwheel Forest
Pokémon White Version 2	Level up Eevee around the moss-covered rock in the Pinwheel Forest

HOW TO OBTAIN FROM OTHER GAMES

—

—

LEVEL-UP AND LEARNED MOVES

Lv.	Name	Type	Kind	Pow.	Acc.	PP	Range	Long	DA
1	Tail Whip	Normal	Status	—	100	30	Many Others	—	—
1	Tackle	Normal	Physical	50	100	35	Normal	—	○
1	Helping Hand	Normal	Status	—	—	20	1 Ally	—	—
5	Sand-Attack	Ground	Status	—	100	15	Normal	—	—
9	Razor Leaf	Grass	Physical	55	95	25	Many Others	—	—
13	Quick Attack	Normal	Physical	40	100	30	Normal	—	○
17	GrassWhistle	Grass	Status	—	55	15	Normal	—	—
21	Magical Leaf	Grass	Special	60	—	20	Normal	—	—
25	Giga Drain	Grass	Special	75	100	10	Normal	—	—
29	Swords Dance	Normal	Status	—	—	30	Self	—	—
33	Synthesis	Grass	Status	—	—	5	Self	—	—
37	Sunny Day	Fire	Status	—	—	5	Both Sides	—	—
41	Last Resort	Normal	Physical	140	100	5	Normal	—	○
45	Leaf Blade	Grass	Physical	90	100	15	Normal	—	○

TM & HM MOVES

Lv.	Name	Type	Kind	Pow.	Acc.	PP	Range	Long	DA
TM05	Roar	Normal	Status	—	100	20	Normal	—	—
TM06	Toxic	Poison	Status	—	90	10	Normal	—	—
TM10	Hidden Power	Normal	Special	—	100	15	Normal	—	—
TM11	Sunny Day	Fire	Status	—	—	5	Both Sides	—	—
TM15	Hyper Beam	Normal	Special	150	90	5	Normal	—	—
TM17	Protect	Normal	Status	—	—	10	Self	—	—
TM18	Rain Dance	Water	Status	—	—	5	Both Sides	—	—
TM21	Frustration	Normal	Physical	—	100	20	Normal	—	○
TM22	SolarBeam	Grass	Special	120	100	10	Normal	—	—
TM27	Return	Normal	Physical	—	100	20	Normal	—	○
TM28	Dig	Ground	Physical	80	100	10	Normal	—	○
TM30	Shadow Ball	Ghost	Special	80	100	15	Normal	—	—
TM32	Double Team	Normal	Status	—	—	15	Self	—	—
TM40	Aerial Ace	Flying	Physical	60	—	20	Normal	○	○
TM42	Facade	Normal	Physical	70	100	20	Normal	—	○
TM44	Rest	Psychic	Status	—	—	10	Self	—	—
TM45	Attract	Normal	Status	—	100	15	Normal	—	—
TM48	Round	Normal	Special	60	100	15	Normal	—	—
TM49	Echoed Voice	Normal	Special	40	100	15	Normal	—	—
TM53	Energy Ball	Grass	Special	80	100	10	Normal	—	—
TM67	Retaliate	Normal	Physical	70	100	5	Normal	—	○
TM68	Giga Impact	Normal	Physical	150	90	5	Normal	—	○
TM70	Flash	Normal	Status	—	100	20	Normal	—	—
TM75	Swords Dance	Normal	Status	—	—	30	Self	—	—
TM81	X-Scissor	Bug	Physical	80	100	15	Normal	—	○
TM83	Work Up	Normal	Status	—	—	30	Self	—	—
TM86	Grass Knot	Grass	Special	—	100	20	Normal	—	○
TM87	Swagger	Normal	Status	—	90	15	Normal	—	—
TM90	Substitute	Normal	Status	—	—	10	Self	—	—
TM94	Rock Smash	Fighting	Physical	40	100	15	Normal	—	○
HM04	Strength	Normal	Physical	80	100	15	Normal	—	○

MOVES TAUGHT BY PEOPLE

Name	Type	Kind	Pow.	Acc.	PP	Range	Long	DA

MOVES TAUGHT BY MOVE TUTORS FOR SHARDS

Name	Type	Kind	Pow.	Acc.	PP	Range	Long	DA
Covet	Normal	Physical	60	100	40	Normal	—	○
Seed Bomb	Grass	Physical	80	100	15	Normal	—	—
Last Resort	Normal	Physical	140	100	5	Normal	—	○
Hyper Voice	Normal	Special	90	100	10	Many Others	—	—
Iron Tail	Steel	Physical	100	75	15	Normal	—	○
Snore	Normal	Special	40	100	15	Normal	—	—
Heal Bell	Normal	Status	—	—	5	Your Party	—	—
Knock Off	Dark	Physical	20	100	20	Normal	—	○
Synthesis	Grass	Status	—	—	5	Self	—	—
Giga Drain	Grass	Special	75	100	10	Normal	—	—
Worry Seed	Grass	Status	—	100	10	Normal	—	—
Helping Hand	Normal	Status	—	—	20	1 Ally	—	—
Sleep Talk	Normal	Status	—	—	10	Self	—	—

471 Glaceon

Fresh Snow Pokémon

● HEIGHT: 2'07"
● WEIGHT: 57.1 lbs.
● GENDER: ♂ / ♀

It lowers its body heat to freeze its fur. The hairs then become like needles it can fire.

Same form for ♂ / ♀

Pokémon AR Marker

TYPE Ice

ABILITY
● Snow Cloak

HIDDEN ABILITY
● Ice Body

STATS

HP	■■■
Attack	■■■
Defense	■■■■■
Sp. Atk	■■■■■■■
Sp. Def	■■■■
Speed	■■■■

EGG GROUPS
Field

ITEMS SOMETIMES HELD
● None

EVOLUTION

- Eevee ➡ p. 80
- Vaporeon ➡ p. 80 — Use Water Stone on Eevee
- Jolteon ➡ p. 81 — Use Thunderstone on Eevee
- Flareon ➡ p. 81 — Use Fire Stone on Eevee
- Espeon ➡ p. 111 — Level up with high friendship in the morning, afternoon, or evening
- Umbreon ➡ p. 112 — Level up with high friendship at night
- Leafeon — Level up Eevee around the moss-covered rock in the Pinwheel Forest
- Glaceon — Level up Eevee around the ice-covered rock in Twist Mountain

HOW TO OBTAIN

Pokémon Black Version 2	Level up Eevee around the ice-covered rock in Twist Mountain
Pokémon White Version 2	Level up Eevee around the ice-covered rock in Twist Mountain

HOW TO OBTAIN FROM OTHER GAMES

—

—

LEVEL-UP AND LEARNED MOVES

Lv.	Name	Type	Kind	Pow.	Acc.	PP	Range	Long	DA
1	Helping Hand	Normal	Status	—	—	20	1 Ally	—	—
1	Tackle	Normal	Physical	50	100	35	Normal	—	○
1	Tail Whip	Normal	Status	—	100	30	Many Others	—	—
5	Sand-Attack	Ground	Status	—	100	15	Normal	—	—
9	Icy Wind	Ice	Special	55	95	15	Many Others	—	—
13	Quick Attack	Normal	Physical	40	100	30	Normal	—	○
17	Bite	Dark	Physical	60	100	25	Normal	—	○
21	Ice Fang	Ice	Physical	65	95	15	Normal	—	○
25	Ice Shard	Ice	Physical	40	100	30	Normal	—	—
29	Barrier	Psychic	Status	—	—	30	Self	—	—
33	Mirror Coat	Psychic	Special	—	100	20	Varies	—	—
37	Hail	Ice	Status	—	—	10	Both Sides	—	—
41	Last Resort	Normal	Physical	140	100	5	Normal	—	○
45	Blizzard	Ice	Special	120	70	5	Many Others	—	—

TM & HM MOVES

Lv.	Name	Type	Kind	Pow.	Acc.	PP	Range	Long	DA
TM05	Roar	Normal	Status	—	100	20	Normal	—	—
TM06	Toxic	Poison	Status	—	90	10	Normal	—	—
TM07	Hail	Ice	Status	—	—	10	Both Sides	—	—
TM10	Hidden Power	Normal	Special	—	100	15	Normal	—	—
TM11	Sunny Day	Fire	Status	—	—	5	Both Sides	—	—
TM13	Ice Beam	Ice	Special	95	100	10	Normal	—	—
TM14	Blizzard	Ice	Special	120	70	5	Many Others	—	—
TM15	Hyper Beam	Normal	Special	150	90	5	Normal	—	—
TM17	Protect	Normal	Status	—	—	10	Self	—	—
TM18	Rain Dance	Water	Status	—	—	5	Both Sides	—	—
TM21	Frustration	Normal	Physical	—	100	20	Normal	—	○
TM27	Return	Normal	Physical	—	100	20	Normal	—	○
TM28	Dig	Ground	Physical	80	100	10	Normal	—	○
TM30	Shadow Ball	Ghost	Special	80	100	15	Normal	—	—
TM32	Double Team	Normal	Status	—	—	15	Self	—	—
TM42	Facade	Normal	Physical	70	100	20	Normal	—	○
TM44	Rest	Psychic	Status	—	—	10	Self	—	—
TM45	Attract	Normal	Status	—	100	15	Normal	—	—
TM48	Round	Normal	Special	60	100	15	Normal	—	—
TM49	Echoed Voice	Normal	Special	40	100	15	Normal	—	—
TM67	Retaliate	Normal	Physical	70	100	5	Normal	—	○
TM68	Giga Impact	Normal	Physical	150	90	5	Normal	—	○
TM79	Frost Breath	Ice	Special	40	90	10	Normal	—	—
TM83	Work Up	Normal	Status	—	—	30	Self	—	—
TM87	Swagger	Normal	Status	—	90	15	Normal	—	—
TM90	Substitute	Normal	Status	—	—	10	Self	—	—
TM94	Rock Smash	Fighting	Physical	40	100	15	Normal	—	○
HM04	Strength	Normal	Physical	80	100	15	Normal	—	○

MOVES TAUGHT BY PEOPLE

Name	Type	Kind	Pow.	Acc.	PP	Range	Long	DA

MOVES TAUGHT BY MOVE TUTORS FOR SHARDS

Name	Type	Kind	Pow.	Acc.	PP	Range	Long	DA
Covet	Normal	Physical	60	100	40	Normal	—	○
Signal Beam	Bug	Special	75	100	15	Normal	—	—
Last Resort	Normal	Physical	140	100	5	Normal	—	○
Hyper Voice	Normal	Special	90	100	10	Many Others	—	—
Icy Wind	Ice	Special	55	95	15	Many Others	—	—
Iron Tail	Steel	Physical	100	75	15	Normal	—	○
Aqua Tail	Water	Physical	90	90	10	Normal	—	○
Snore	Normal	Special	40	100	15	Normal	—	—
Heal Bell	Normal	Status	—	—	5	Your Party	—	—
Helping Hand	Normal	Status	—	—	20	1 Ally	—	—
Sleep Talk	Normal	Status	—	—	10	Self	—	—

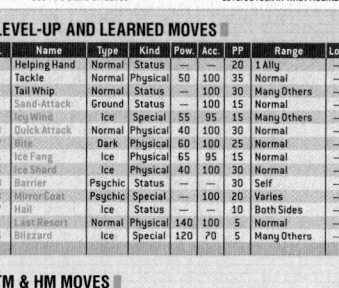

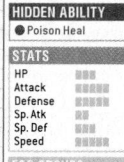

Fang Scorp Pokémon

472 Gliscor

- HEIGHT: 6'07"
- WEIGHT: 93.7 lbs.
- GENDER: ♂ / ♀

It dances silently through the sky. When it approaches prey, it can land a critical hit in an instant.

Gender unknown

TYPE Ground Flying

ABILITIES
- Hyper Cutter
- Sand Veil

HIDDEN ABILITY
- Poison Heal

STATS
HP
Attack
Defense
Sp. Atk
Sp. Def
Speed

EGG GROUPS
Bug

ITEMS SOMETIMES HELD
- None

EVOLUTION

Gligar

➡ p. 117

Have Gligar hold Razor Fang and level it up at night

Gliscor

HOW TO OBTAIN

Pokémon Black Version 2	❶ Route 11 (rustling grass) ❷ Route 23 (rustling grass)
Pokémon White Version 2	❶ Route 11 (rustling grass) ❷ Route 23 (rustling grass)

HOW TO OBTAIN FROM OTHER GAMES

—

—

Pokémon AR Marker

LEVEL-UP AND LEARNED MOVES

Lv.	Name	Type	Kind	Pow.	Acc.	PP	Range	Long	DA
1	Thunder Fang	Electric	Physical	65	95	15	Normal	—	○
1	Ice Fang	Ice	Physical	65	95	15	Normal	—	○
1	Fire Fang	Fire	Physical	65	95	15	Normal	—	○
1	Poison Jab	Poison	Physical	80	100	20	Normal	—	○
1	Sand-Attack	Ground	Status	—	100	15	Normal	—	—
1	Harden	Normal	Status	—	—	30	Self	—	—
1	Knock Off	Dark	Physical	20	100	20	Normal	—	○
4	Sand-Attack	Ground	Status	—	100	15	Normal	—	—
7	Harden	Normal	Status	—	—	30	Self	—	—
10	Knock Off	Dark	Physical	20	100	20	Normal	—	○
13	Quick Attack	Normal	Physical	40	100	30	Normal	—	○
16	Fury Cutter	Bug	Physical	20	95	20	Normal	—	○
19	Faint Attack	Dark	Physical	60	—	20	Normal	—	○
22	Acrobatics	Flying	Physical	55	100	15	Normal	○	○
27	Night Slash	Dark	Physical	70	100	15	Normal	—	○
30	U-turn	Bug	Physical	70	100	20	Normal	—	○
35	Screech	Normal	Status	—	85	40	Normal	—	—
40	X-Scissor	Bug	Physical	80	100	15	Normal	—	○
45	Sky Uppercut	Fighting	Physical	85	90	15	Normal	—	○
50	Swords Dance	Normal	Status	—	—	30	Self	—	—
55	Guillotine	Normal	Physical	—	30	5	Normal	—	○

TM & HM MOVES

Lv.	Name	Type	Kind	Pow.	Acc.	PP	Range	Long	DA
TM01	Hone Claws	Dark	Status	—	—	15	Self	—	—
TM06	Toxic	Poison	Status	—	90	10	Normal	—	—
TM09	Venoshock	Poison	Special	65	100	10	Normal	—	—
TM10	Hidden Power	Normal	Special	—	100	15	Normal	—	—
TM11	Sunny Day	Fire	Status	—	—	5	Both Sides	—	—
TM12	Taunt	Dark	Status	—	100	20	Normal	—	—
TM15	Hyper Beam	Normal	Special	150	90	5	Normal	—	—
TM17	Protect	Normal	Status	—	—	10	Self	—	—
TM18	Rain Dance	Water	Status	—	—	5	Both Sides	—	—
TM21	Frustration	Normal	Physical	—	100	20	Normal	—	○
TM26	Earthquake	Ground	Physical	100	100	10	Adjacent	—	—
TM27	Return	Normal	Physical	—	100	20	Normal	—	○
TM28	Dig	Ground	Physical	80	100	10	Normal	—	○
TM31	Brick Break	Fighting	Physical	75	100	15	Normal	—	○
TM32	Double Team	Normal	Status	—	—	15	Self	—	—
TM36	Sludge Bomb	Poison	Special	90	100	10	Normal	—	—
TM37	Sandstorm	Rock	Status	—	—	10	Both Sides	—	—
TM39	Rock Tomb	Rock	Physical	50	80	10	Normal	—	—
TM40	Aerial Ace	Flying	Physical	60	—	20	Normal	○	○
TM41	Torment	Dark	Status	—	100	15	Normal	—	—
TM42	Facade	Normal	Physical	70	100	20	Normal	—	○
TM44	Rest	Psychic	Status	—	—	10	Self	—	—
TM45	Attract	Normal	Status	—	100	15	Normal	—	—
TM46	Thief	Dark	Physical	40	100	10	Normal	—	○
TM48	Round	Normal	Special	60	100	15	Normal	—	—
TM54	False Swipe	Normal	Physical	40	100	40	Normal	—	○
TM56	Fling	Dark	Physical	—	100	10	Normal	—	—
TM62	Acrobatics	Flying	Physical	55	100	15	Normal	○	○
TM66	Payback	Dark	Physical	50	100	10	Normal	—	○
TM68	Giga Impact	Normal	Physical	150	90	5	Normal	—	○
TM69	Rock Polish	Rock	Status	—	—	20	Self	—	—
TM71	Stone Edge	Rock	Physical	100	80	5	Normal	—	—
TM75	Swords Dance	Normal	Status	—	—	30	Self	—	—
TM76	Struggle Bug	Bug	Special	30	100	20	Many Others	—	—
TM78	Bulldoze	Ground	Physical	60	100	20	Adjacent	—	—
TM80	Rock Slide	Rock	Physical	75	90	10	Many Others	—	—
TM81	X-Scissor	Bug	Physical	80	100	15	Normal	—	○
TM84	Poison Jab	Poison	Physical	80	100	20	Normal	—	○
TM87	Swagger	Normal	Status	—	90	15	Normal	—	—
TM89	U-turn	Bug	Physical	70	100	20	Normal	—	○
TM90	Substitute	Normal	Status	—	—	10	Self	—	—
TM94	Rock Smash	Fighting	Physical	40	100	15	Normal	—	○
HM01	Cut	Normal	Physical	50	95	30	Normal	—	○
HM04	Strength	Normal	Physical	80	100	15	Normal	—	○

MOVES TAUGHT BY PEOPLE

Name	Type	Kind	Pow.	Acc.	PP	Range	Long	DA

MOVES TAUGHT BY MOVE TUTORS FOR SHARDS

Name	Type	Kind	Pow.	Acc.	PP	Range	Long	DA
Bug Bite	Bug	Physical	60	100	20	Normal	—	○
Iron Tail	Steel	Physical	100	75	15	Normal	—	○
Aqua Tail	Water	Physical	90	90	10	Normal	—	○
Earth Power	Ground	Special	90	100	10	Normal	—	—
Dark Pulse	Dark	Special	80	100	15	Normal	○	—
Snore	Normal	Special	40	100	15	Normal	—	—
Knock Off	Dark	Physical	20	100	20	Normal	—	○
Roost	Flying	Status	—	—	10	Self	—	—
Sky Attack	Flying	Physical	140	90	5	Normal	○	—
Tailwind	Flying	Status	—	—	30	Your Side	—	—
Stealth Rock	Rock	Status	—	—	20	3 Foes	—	—
Sleep Talk	Normal	Status	—	—	10	Self	—	—

Twin Tusk Pokémon

473 Mamoswine

- HEIGHT: 8'02"
- WEIGHT: 641.5 lbs.
- GENDER: ♂ / ♀

When the temperature rose at the end of the ice age, most Mamoswine disappeared.

♂ ♀

TYPE Ice Ground

ABILITIES
- Oblivious
- Snow Cloak

HIDDEN ABILITY
- Thick Fat

STATS
HP
Attack
Defense
Sp. Atk
Sp. Def
Speed

EGG GROUPS
Field

ITEMS SOMETIMES HELD
- None

EVOLUTION

Swinub

➡ p. 123

Lv. 33

Piloswine

➡ p. 124

Level up Piloswine once it knows AncientPower

Mamoswine

HOW TO OBTAIN

Pokémon Black Version 2	Giant Chasm Crater Forest (rustling grass)
Pokémon White Version 2	Giant Chasm Crater Forest (rustling grass)

HOW TO OBTAIN FROM OTHER GAMES

—

—

Pokémon AR Marker

LEVEL-UP AND LEARNED MOVES

Lv.	Name	Type	Kind	Pow.	Acc.	PP	Range	Long	DA
1	AncientPower	Rock	Special	60	100	5	Normal	—	—
1	Peck	Flying	Physical	35	100	35	Normal	○	○
1	Odor Sleuth	Normal	Status	—	—	40	Normal	—	—
1	Mud Sport	Ground	Status	—	—	15	Both Sides	—	—
1	Powder Snow	Ice	Special	40	100	25	Many Others	—	—
5	Mud Sport	Ground	Status	—	—	15	Both Sides	—	—
8	Powder Snow	Ice	Special	40	100	25	Many Others	—	—
11	Mud-Slap	Ground	Special	20	100	10	Normal	—	—
14	Endure	Normal	Status	—	—	10	Self	—	—
18	Mud Bomb	Ground	Special	65	85	10	Normal	—	—
21	Hail	Ice	Status	—	—	10	Both Sides	—	—
24	Ice Fang	Ice	Physical	65	95	15	Normal	—	○
28	Take Down	Normal	Physical	90	85	20	Normal	—	○
33	Double Hit	Normal	Physical	35	90	10	Normal	—	○
37	Mist	Ice	Status	—	—	30	Your Side	—	—
41	Thrash	Normal	Physical	120	100	10	1 Random	—	○
46	Earthquake	Ground	Physical	100	100	10	Adjacent	—	—
52	Blizzard	Ice	Special	120	70	5	Many Others	—	—
58	Scary Face	Normal	Status	—	100	10	Normal	—	—

TM & HM MOVES

Lv.	Name	Type	Kind	Pow.	Acc.	PP	Range	Long	DA
TM05	Roar	Normal	Status	—	100	20	Normal	—	—
TM06	Toxic	Poison	Status	—	90	10	Normal	—	—
TM07	Hail	Ice	Status	—	—	10	Both Sides	—	—
TM10	Hidden Power	Normal	Special	—	100	15	Normal	—	—
TM13	Ice Beam	Ice	Special	95	100	10	Normal	—	—
TM14	Blizzard	Ice	Special	120	70	5	Many Others	—	—
TM15	Hyper Beam	Normal	Special	150	90	5	Normal	—	—
TM16	Light Screen	Psychic	Status	—	—	30	Your Side	—	—
TM17	Protect	Normal	Status	—	—	10	Self	—	—
TM18	Rain Dance	Water	Status	—	—	5	Both Sides	—	—
TM21	Frustration	Normal	Physical	—	100	20	Normal	—	○
TM26	Earthquake	Ground	Physical	100	100	10	Adjacent	—	—
TM27	Return	Normal	Physical	—	100	20	Normal	—	○
TM28	Dig	Ground	Physical	80	100	10	Normal	—	○
TM32	Double Team	Normal	Status	—	—	15	Self	—	—
TM33	Reflect	Psychic	Status	—	—	20	Your Side	—	—
TM37	Sandstorm	Rock	Status	—	—	10	Both Sides	—	—
TM39	Rock Tomb	Rock	Physical	50	80	10	Normal	—	—
TM42	Facade	Normal	Physical	70	100	20	Normal	—	○
TM44	Rest	Psychic	Status	—	—	10	Self	—	—
TM45	Attract	Normal	Status	—	100	15	Normal	—	—
TM48	Round	Normal	Special	60	100	15	Normal	—	—
TM68	Giga Impact	Normal	Physical	150	90	5	Normal	—	○
TM71	Stone Edge	Rock	Physical	100	80	5	Normal	—	—
TM78	Bulldoze	Ground	Physical	60	100	20	Adjacent	—	—
TM80	Rock Slide	Rock	Physical	75	90	10	Many Others	—	—
TM87	Swagger	Normal	Status	—	90	15	Normal	—	—
TM90	Substitute	Normal	Status	—	—	10	Self	—	—
TM94	Rock Smash	Fighting	Physical	40	100	15	Normal	—	○
HM04	Strength	Normal	Physical	80	100	15	Normal	—	○

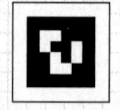

◆ Give the reminder girl at the PWT a Heart Scale to make Piloswine remember AncientPower.

MOVES TAUGHT BY PEOPLE

Name	Type	Kind	Pow.	Acc.	PP	Range	Long	DA

MOVES TAUGHT BY MOVE TUTORS FOR SHARDS

Name	Type	Kind	Pow.	Acc.	PP	Range	Long	DA
Iron Head	Steel	Physical	80	100	15	Normal	—	○
Block	Normal	Status	—	—	5	Normal	—	—
Icy Wind	Ice	Special	55	95	15	Many Others	—	—
Earth Power	Ground	Special	90	100	10	Normal	—	—
Superpower	Fighting	Physical	120	100	5	Normal	—	○
Snore	Normal	Special	40	100	15	Normal	—	—
Knock Off	Dark	Physical	20	100	20	Normal	—	○
Stealth Rock	Rock	Status	—	—	20	3 Foes	—	—
Endeavor	Normal	Physical	—	100	5	Normal	—	○
Sleep Talk	Normal	Status	—	—	10	Self	—	—

474 Porygon-Z
Virtual Pokémon

- HEIGHT: 2'11"
- WEIGHT: 75.0 lbs.
- GENDER: Unknown

Its programming was modified to enable work in alien dimensions. It did not work as planned.

TYPE Normal

ABILITIES
- Adaptability
- Download

HIDDEN ABILITY
- Analytic

STATS
HP
Attack
Defense
Sp. Atk
Sp. Def
Speed

EGG GROUPS
Mineral

ITEMS SOMETIMES HELD
- None

Gender unknown

EVOLUTION
Porygon
Link Trade it while it is holding an Up-Grade
Porygon2
Link Trade it while it is holding a Dubious Disc
Porygon-Z

➡ p. 82
➡ p. 130

HOW TO OBTAIN

Pokémon Black Version 2	Have Porygon sent to you by Link Trade while it's holding Dubious Disc to receive Porygon-Z
Pokémon White Version 2	Have Porygon sent to you by Link Trade while it's holding Dubious Disc to receive Porygon-Z

HOW TO OBTAIN FROM OTHER GAMES

—

—

Pokémon AR Marker

LEVEL-UP AND LEARNED MOVES

Lv.	Name	Type	Kind	Pow.	Acc.	PP	Range	Long	DA
1	Trick Room	Psychic	Status	—	—	5	Both Sides	—	—
1	Conversion 2	Normal	Status	—	—	30	Normal	—	—
1	Tackle	Normal	Physical	50	100	35	Normal	—	○
1	Conversion	Normal	Status	—	—	30	Self	—	—
1	Nasty Plot	Dark	Status	—	—	20	Self	—	—
7	Psybeam	Psychic	Special	65	100	20	Normal	—	—
12	Agility	Psychic	Status	—	—	30	Self	—	—
18	Recover	Normal	Status	—	—	10	Self	—	—
23	Magnet Rise	Electric	Status	—	—	10	Self	—	—
29	Signal Beam	Bug	Special	75	100	15	Normal	—	—
34	Embargo	Dark	Status	—	100	15	Normal	—	—
40	Discharge	Electric	Special	80	100	15	Adjacent	—	—
45	Lock-On	Normal	Status	—	—	5	Normal	—	—
51	Tri Attack	Normal	Special	80	100	10	Normal	—	—
56	Magic Coat	Psychic	Status	—	—	15	Self	—	—
62	Zap Cannon	Electric	Special	120	50	5	Normal	—	—
67	Hyper Beam	Normal	Special	150	90	5	Normal	—	—

TM & HM MOVES

Lv.	Name	Type	Kind	Pow.	Acc.	PP	Range	Long	DA
TM03	Psyshock	Psychic	Special	80	100	10	Normal	—	—
TM06	Toxic	Poison	Status	—	90	10	Normal	—	—
TM10	Hidden Power	Normal	Special	—	100	15	Normal	—	—
TM11	Sunny Day	Fire	Status	—	—	5	Both Sides	—	—
TM13	Ice Beam	Ice	Special	95	100	10	Normal	—	—
TM14	Blizzard	Ice	Special	120	70	5	Many Others	—	—
TM15	Hyper Beam	Normal	Special	150	90	5	Normal	—	—
TM17	Protect	Normal	Status	—	—	10	Self	—	—
TM18	Rain Dance	Water	Status	—	—	5	Both Sides	—	—
TM21	Frustration	Normal	Physical	—	100	20	Normal	—	○
TM22	SolarBeam	Grass	Special	120	100	10	Normal	—	—
TM24	Thunderbolt	Electric	Special	95	100	15	Normal	—	—
TM25	Thunder	Electric	Special	120	70	10	Normal	—	—
TM27	Return	Normal	Physical	—	100	20	Normal	—	○
TM29	Psychic	Psychic	Special	90	100	10	Normal	—	—
TM30	Shadow Ball	Ghost	Special	80	100	15	Normal	—	—
TM32	Double Team	Normal	Status	—	—	15	Self	—	—
TM40	Aerial Ace	Flying	Physical	60	—	20	Normal	○	○
TM42	Facade	Normal	Physical	70	100	20	Normal	—	○
TM44	Rest	Psychic	Status	—	—	10	Self	—	—
TM46	Thief	Dark	Physical	40	100	10	Normal	—	○
TM48	Round	Normal	Special	60	100	15	Normal	—	—
TM57	Charge Beam	Electric	Special	50	90	10	Normal	—	—
TM63	Embargo	Dark	Status	—	100	15	Normal	—	—
TM68	Giga Impact	Normal	Physical	150	90	5	Normal	—	○
TM70	Flash	Normal	Status	—	100	20	Normal	—	—
TM73	Thunder Wave	Electric	Status	—	100	20	Normal	—	—
TM77	Psych Up	Normal	Status	—	—	10	Normal	—	—
TM85	Dream Eater	Psychic	Special	100	100	15	Normal	—	—
TM87	Swagger	Normal	Status	—	90	15	Normal	—	—
TM90	Substitute	Normal	Status	—	—	10	Self	—	—
TM92	Trick Room	Psychic	Status	—	—	5	Both Sides	—	—

MOVES TAUGHT BY PEOPLE

Name	Type	Kind	Pow.	Acc.	PP	Range	Long	DA

MOVES TAUGHT BY MOVE TUTORS FOR SHARDS

Name	Type	Kind	Pow.	Acc.	PP	Range	Long	DA
Signal Beam	Bug	Special	75	100	15	Normal	—	—
Uproar	Normal	Special	90	100	10	1 Random	—	—
Last Resort	Normal	Physical	140	100	5	Normal	—	○
Magnet Rise	Electric	Status	—	—	10	Self	—	—
Magic Coat	Psychic	Status	—	—	15	Self	—	—
Electroweb	Electric	Special	55	95	15	Many Others	—	—
Icy Wind	Ice	Special	55	95	15	Many Others	—	—
Iron Tail	Steel	Physical	100	75	15	Normal	—	○
Zen Headbutt	Psychic	Physical	80	90	15	Normal	—	○
Foul Play	Dark	Physical	95	100	15	Normal	—	○
Gravity	Psychic	Status	—	—	5	Both Sides	—	—
Dark Pulse	Dark	Special	80	100	15	Normal	○	—
Snore	Normal	Special	40	100	15	Normal	—	—
Pain Split	Normal	Status	—	—	20	Normal	—	—
Wonder Room	Psychic	Status	—	—	10	Both Sides	—	—
Recycle	Normal	Status	—	—	10	Self	—	—
Trick	Psychic	Status	—	100	10	Normal	—	—
Sleep Talk	Normal	Status	—	—	10	Self	—	—

475 Gallade
Blade Pokémon

- HEIGHT: 5'03"
- WEIGHT: 114.6 lbs.
- GENDER: ♂

When trying to protect someone, it extends its elbows as if they were swords and fights savagely.

TYPE Psychic Fighting

ABILITY
- Steadfast

HIDDEN ABILITY
- Justified

STATS
HP
Attack
Defense
Sp. Atk
Sp. Def
Speed

EGG GROUPS
Amorphous

ITEMS SOMETIMES HELD
- None

♂

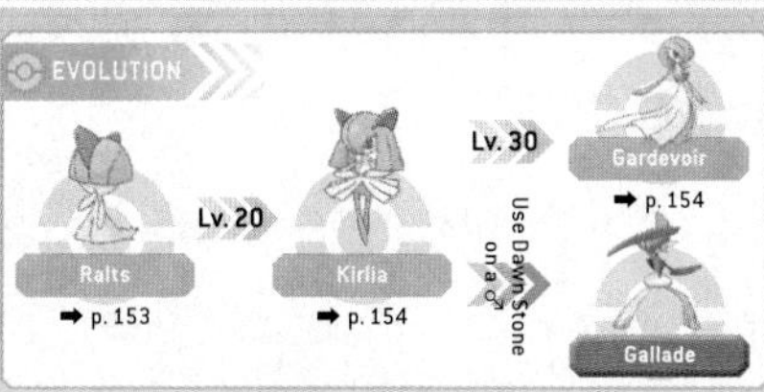
EVOLUTION
Ralts
Lv. 20
Kirlia
Lv. 30
Gardevoir
Use Dawn Stone on a ♂
Gallade

➡ p. 153
➡ p. 154
➡ p. 154

HOW TO OBTAIN

Pokémon Black Version 2	If the Ralts you receive from Yancy or Curtis is male, level it up to evolve it to Kirlia and then use the Dawn Stone on Kirlia
Pokémon White Version 2	If the Ralts you receive from Yancy or Curtis is male, level it up to evolve it to Kirlia and then use the Dawn Stone on Kirlia

HOW TO OBTAIN FROM OTHER GAMES

—

—

Pokémon AR Marker

LEVEL-UP AND LEARNED MOVES

Lv.	Name	Type	Kind	Pow.	Acc.	PP	Range	Long	DA
1	Leaf Blade	Grass	Physical	90	100	15	Normal	—	○
1	Night Slash	Dark	Physical	70	100	15	Normal	—	○
1	Leer	Normal	Status	—	100	30	Many Others	—	—
1	Confusion	Psychic	Special	50	100	25	Normal	—	—
1	Double Team	Normal	Status	—	—	15	Self	—	—
1	Teleport	Psychic	Status	—	—	20	Self	—	—
6	Confusion	Psychic	Special	50	100	25	Normal	—	—
10	Double Team	Normal	Status	—	—	15	Self	—	—
12	Teleport	Psychic	Status	—	—	20	Self	—	—
17	Fury Cutter	Bug	Physical	20	95	20	Normal	—	○
22	Slash	Normal	Physical	70	100	20	Normal	—	○
25	Heal Pulse	Psychic	Status	—	—	10	Normal	○	—
31	Swords Dance	Normal	Status	—	—	30	Self	—	—
36	Psycho Cut	Psychic	Physical	70	100	20	Normal	—	—
39	Helping Hand	Normal	Status	—	—	20	1 Ally	—	—
45	Feint	Normal	Physical	30	100	10	Normal	—	—
50	False Swipe	Normal	Physical	40	100	40	Normal	—	○
53	Protect	Normal	Status	—	—	10	Self	—	—
59	Close Combat	Fighting	Physical	120	100	5	Normal	—	○
64	Stored Power	Psychic	Special	20	100	10	Normal	—	—

TM & HM MOVES

Lv.	Name	Type	Kind	Pow.	Acc.	PP	Range	Long	DA
TM03	Psyshock	Psychic	Special	80	100	10	Normal	—	—
TM04	Calm Mind	Psychic	Status	—	—	20	Self	—	—
TM06	Toxic	Poison	Status	—	90	10	Normal	—	—
TM08	Bulk Up	Fighting	Status	—	—	20	Self	—	—
TM10	Hidden Power	Normal	Special	—	100	15	Normal	—	—
TM11	Sunny Day	Fire	Status	—	—	5	Both Sides	—	—
TM12	Taunt	Dark	Status	—	100	20	Normal	—	—
TM15	Hyper Beam	Normal	Special	150	90	5	Normal	—	—
TM16	Light Screen	Psychic	Status	—	—	30	Your Side	—	—
TM17	Protect	Normal	Status	—	—	10	Self	—	—
TM18	Rain Dance	Water	Status	—	—	5	Both Sides	—	—
TM19	Telekinesis	Psychic	Status	—	—	15	Normal	—	—
TM20	Safeguard	Normal	Status	—	—	25	Your Side	—	—
TM21	Frustration	Normal	Physical	—	100	20	Normal	—	○
TM24	Thunderbolt	Electric	Special	95	100	15	Normal	—	—
TM26	Earthquake	Ground	Physical	100	100	10	Adjacent	—	—
TM27	Return	Normal	Physical	—	100	20	Normal	—	○
TM29	Psychic	Psychic	Special	90	100	10	Normal	—	—
TM30	Shadow Ball	Ghost	Special	80	100	15	Normal	—	—
TM31	Brick Break	Fighting	Physical	75	100	15	Normal	—	○
TM32	Double Team	Normal	Status	—	—	15	Self	—	—
TM33	Reflect	Psychic	Status	—	—	20	Your Side	—	—
TM39	Rock Tomb	Rock	Physical	50	80	10	Normal	—	—
TM40	Aerial Ace	Flying	Physical	60	—	20	Normal	○	○
TM41	Torment	Dark	Status	—	100	15	Normal	—	—
TM42	Facade	Normal	Physical	70	100	20	Normal	—	○
TM44	Rest	Psychic	Status	—	—	10	Self	—	—
TM45	Attract	Normal	Status	—	100	15	Normal	—	—
TM46	Thief	Dark	Physical	40	100	10	Normal	—	○
TM47	Low Sweep	Fighting	Physical	60	100	20	Normal	—	○
TM48	Round	Normal	Special	60	100	15	Normal	—	—
TM49	Echoed Voice	Normal	Special	40	100	15	Normal	—	—
TM51	Ally Switch	Psychic	Status	—	—	15	Self	—	—
TM52	Focus Blast	Fighting	Special	120	70	5	Normal	—	—
TM54	False Swipe	Normal	Physical	40	100	40	Normal	—	○
TM56	Fling	Dark	Physical	—	100	10	Normal	—	—
TM57	Charge Beam	Electric	Special	50	90	10	Normal	—	—
TM61	Will-O-Wisp	Fire	Status	—	75	15	Normal	—	—
TM67	Retaliate	Normal	Physical	70	100	5	Normal	—	○
TM68	Giga Impact	Normal	Physical	150	90	5	Normal	—	○
TM70	Flash	Normal	Status	—	100	20	Normal	—	—
TM71	Stone Edge	Rock	Physical	100	80	5	Normal	—	—
TM73	Thunder Wave	Electric	Status	—	100	20	Normal	—	—
TM75	Swords Dance	Normal	Status	—	—	30	Self	—	—
TM77	Psych Up	Normal	Status	—	—	10	Normal	—	—
TM78	Bulldoze	Ground	Physical	60	100	20	Adjacent	—	—
TM80	Rock Slide	Rock	Physical	75	90	10	Many Others	—	—
TM81	X-Scissor	Bug	Physical	80	100	15	Normal	—	○
TM83	Work Up	Normal	Status	—	—	30	Self	—	—
TM84	Poison Jab	Poison	Physical	80	100	20	Normal	—	○
TM85	Dream Eater	Psychic	Special	100	100	15	Normal	—	—
TM86	Grass Knot	Grass	Special	—	100	20	Normal	—	○
TM87	Swagger	Normal	Status	—	90	15	Normal	—	—
TM90	Substitute	Normal	Status	—	—	10	Self	—	—
TM92	Trick Room	Psychic	Status	—	—	5	Both Sides	—	—
TM94	Rock Smash	Fighting	Physical	40	100	15	Normal	—	○
HM01	Cut	Normal	Physical	50	95	30	Normal	—	○
HM04	Strength	Normal	Physical	80	100	15	Normal	—	○

MOVES TAUGHT BY PEOPLE

Name	Type	Kind	Pow.	Acc.	PP	Range	Long	DA

MOVES TAUGHT BY MOVE TUTORS FOR SHARDS

Name	Type	Kind	Pow.	Acc.	PP	Range	Long	DA
Signal Beam	Bug	Special	75	100	15	Normal	—	—
Dual Chop	Dragon	Physical	40	90	15	Normal	—	○
Low Kick	Fighting	Physical	—	100	20	Normal	—	○
Fire Punch	Fire	Physical	75	100	15	Normal	—	○
ThunderPunch	Electric	Physical	75	100	15	Normal	—	○
Ice Punch	Ice	Physical	75	100	15	Normal	—	○
Magic Coat	Psychic	Status	—	—	15	Self	—	—
Hyper Voice	Normal	Special	90	100	10	Many Others	—	—
Zen Headbutt	Psychic	Physical	80	90	15	Normal	—	○
Snore	Normal	Special	40	100	15	Normal	—	—
Knock Off	Dark	Physical	20	100	20	Normal	—	○
Drain Punch	Fighting	Physical	75	100	10	Normal	—	○
Pain Split	Normal	Status	—	—	20	Normal	—	—
Helping Hand	Normal	Status	—	—	20	1 Ally	—	—
Magic Room	Psychic	Status	—	—	10	Both Sides	—	—
Wonder Room	Psychic	Status	—	—	10	Both Sides	—	—
Recycle	Normal	Status	—	—	10	Self	—	—
Trick	Psychic	Status	—	100	10	Normal	—	—
Sleep Talk	Normal	Status	—	—	10	Self	—	—
Skill Swap	Psychic	Status	—	—	10	Normal	—	—
Snatch	Dark	Status	—	—	10	Self	—	—

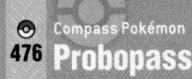

Compass Pokémon
476 Probopass

- HEIGHT: 4'07"
- WEIGHT: 749.6 lbs.
- GENDER: ♂/♀

It freely controls three units called Mini-Noses using magnetic force.

TYPE Rock | Steel

ABILITIES
- Sturdy
- Magnet Pull

HIDDEN ABILITY
- Sand Force

STATS
- HP
- Attack
- Defense
- Sp. Atk
- Sp. Def
- Speed

EGG GROUPS
Mineral

ITEMS SOMETIMES HELD
- None

Same form for ♂/♀

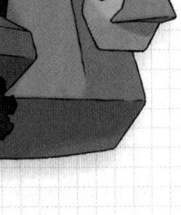

EVOLUTION

Nosepass → Probopass

Level up in Chargestone Cave

→ p. 163

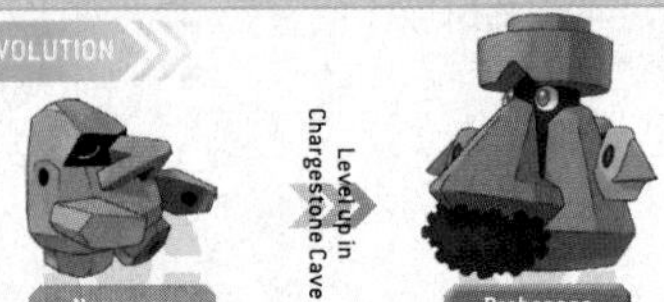

→ p. 163

HOW TO OBTAIN

| Pokémon Black Version 2 | Level up Nosepass in Chargestone Cave |
| Pokémon White Version 2 | Level up Nosepass in Chargestone Cave |

HOW TO OBTAIN FROM OTHER GAMES

LEVEL-UP AND LEARNED MOVES

Lv.	Name	Type	Kind	Pow.	Acc.	PP	Range	Long	DA
1	Magnet Rise	Electric	Status	—	—	10	Self	—	—
1	Gravity	Psychic	Status	—	—	5	Both Sides	—	—
1	Tackle	Normal	Physical	50	100	35	Normal	—	○
1	Iron Defense	Steel	Status	—	—	15	Self	—	—
1	Block	Normal	Status	—	—	5	Normal	—	—
1	Magnet Bomb	Steel	Physical	60	—	20	Normal	—	—
4	Iron Defense	Steel	Status	—	—	15	Self	—	—
8	Block	Normal	Status	—	—	5	Normal	—	—
11	Magnet Bomb	Steel	Physical	60	—	20	Normal	—	—
15	Thunder Wave	Electric	Status	—	100	20	Normal	—	—
18	Rock Blast	Rock	Physical	25	90	10	Normal	—	—
22	Rest	Psychic	Status	—	—	10	Self	—	—
25	Spark	Electric	Physical	65	100	20	Normal	—	○
29	Rock Slide	Rock	Physical	75	90	10	Many Others	—	—
32	Power Gem	Rock	Special	70	100	20	Normal	—	—
36	Sandstorm	Rock	Status	—	—	10	Both Sides	—	—
39	Discharge	Electric	Special	80	100	15	Adjacent	—	—
43	Earth Power	Ground	Special	90	100	10	Normal	—	—
46	Stone Edge	Rock	Physical	100	80	5	Normal	—	—
50	Lock-On	Normal	Status	—	—	5	Normal	—	—
50	Zap Cannon	Electric	Special	120	50	5	Normal	—	—

TM & HM MOVES

Lv.	Name	Type	Kind	Pow.	Acc.	PP	Range	Long	DA
TM06	Toxic	Poison	Status	—	90	10	Normal	—	—
TM10	Hidden Power	Normal	Special	—	100	15	Normal	—	—
TM11	Sunny Day	Fire	Status	—	—	5	Both Sides	—	—
TM12	Taunt	Dark	Status	—	100	20	Normal	—	—
TM15	Hyper Beam	Normal	Special	150	90	5	Normal	—	—
TM17	Protect	Normal	Status	—	—	10	Self	—	—
TM21	Frustration	Normal	Physical	—	100	20	Normal	—	○
TM23	Smack Down	Rock	Physical	50	100	15	Normal	—	—
TM24	Thunderbolt	Electric	Special	95	100	15	Normal	—	—
TM25	Thunder	Electric	Special	120	70	10	Normal	—	—
TM26	Earthquake	Ground	Physical	100	100	10	Adjacent	—	—
TM27	Return	Normal	Physical	—	100	20	Normal	—	○
TM32	Double Team	Normal	Status	—	—	15	Self	—	—
TM37	Sandstorm	Rock	Status	—	—	10	Both Sides	—	—
TM39	Rock Tomb	Rock	Physical	50	80	10	Normal	—	—
TM41	Torment	Dark	Status	—	100	15	Normal	—	—
TM42	Facade	Normal	Physical	70	100	20	Normal	—	—
TM44	Rest	Psychic	Status	—	—	10	Self	—	—
TM45	Attract	Normal	Status	—	100	15	Normal	—	—
TM48	Round	Normal	Special	60	100	15	Normal	—	—
TM64	Explosion	Normal	Physical	250	100	5	Adjacent	—	—
TM68	Giga Impact	Normal	Physical	150	90	5	Normal	—	○
TM69	Rock Polish	Rock	Status	—	—	20	Self	—	—
TM71	Stone Edge	Rock	Physical	100	80	5	Normal	—	—
TM72	Volt Switch	Electric	Special	70	100	20	Normal	—	—
TM73	Thunder Wave	Electric	Status	—	100	20	Normal	—	—
TM78	Bulldoze	Ground	Physical	60	100	20	Adjacent	—	—
TM80	Rock Slide	Rock	Physical	75	90	10	Many Others	—	—
TM87	Swagger	Normal	Status	—	90	15	Normal	—	—
TM90	Substitute	Normal	Status	—	—	10	Self	—	—
TM91	Flash Cannon	Steel	Special	80	100	10	Normal	—	—
TM94	Rock Smash	Fighting	Physical	40	100	15	Normal	—	○

Lv.	Name	Type	Kind	Pow.	Acc.	PP	Range	Long	DA
HM04	Strength	Normal	Physical	80	100	15	Normal	—	—

MOVES TAUGHT BY PEOPLE

Name	Type	Kind	Pow.	Acc.	PP	Range	Long	DA

MOVES TAUGHT BY MOVE TUTORS FOR SHARDS

Name	Type	Kind	Pow.	Acc.	PP	Range	Long	DA
Iron Head	Steel	Physical	80	100	15	Normal	—	○
Fire Punch	Fire	Physical	75	100	15	Normal	—	○
ThunderPunch	Electric	Physical	75	100	15	Normal	—	○
Ice Punch	Ice	Physical	75	100	15	Normal	—	○
Iron Defense	Steel	Status	—	—	15	Self	—	—
Magnet Rise	Electric	Status	—	—	10	Self	—	—
Magic Coat	Psychic	Status	—	—	15	Self	—	—
Block	Normal	Status	—	—	5	Normal	—	—
Earth Power	Ground	Special	90	100	10	Normal	—	—
Gravity	Psychic	Status	—	—	5	Both Sides	—	—
Snore	Normal	Special	40	100	15	Normal	—	—
Pain Split	Normal	Status	—	—	20	Normal	—	—
Stealth Rock	Rock	Status	—	—	20	3 Foes	—	—
Sleep Talk	Normal	Status	—	—	10	Self	—	—

Pokémon AR Marker

Gripper Pokémon
477 Dusknoir

- HEIGHT: 7'03"
- WEIGHT: 235.0 lbs.
- GENDER: ♂/♀

It is said to take lost spirits into its pliant body and guide them home.

TYPE Ghost

ABILITY
- Pressure

HIDDEN ABILITY

STATS
- HP
- Attack
- Defense
- Sp. Atk
- Sp. Def
- Speed

EGG GROUPS
Amorphous

ITEMS SOMETIMES HELD
- None

Same form for ♂/♀

EVOLUTION

Duskull → Dusclops → Dusknoir

Lv. 37

Have it hold a Reaper Cloth and Link Trade it

→ p. 191 → p. 191

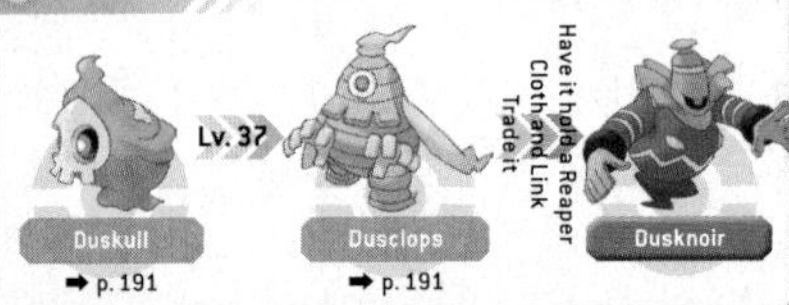

→ p. 191 → p. 191

HOW TO OBTAIN

| Pokémon Black Version 2 | Have Dusclops sent to you while it's holding a Reaper Cloth to receive Dusknoir |
| Pokémon White Version 2 | Have Dusclops sent to you while it's holding a Reaper Cloth to receive Dusknoir |

HOW TO OBTAIN FROM OTHER GAMES

LEVEL-UP AND LEARNED MOVES

Lv.	Name	Type	Kind	Pow.	Acc.	PP	Range	Long	DA
1	Fire Punch	Fire	Physical	75	100	15	Normal	—	○
1	Ice Punch	Ice	Physical	75	100	15	Normal	—	○
1	ThunderPunch	Electric	Physical	75	100	15	Normal	—	○
1	Gravity	Psychic	Status	—	—	5	Both Sides	—	—
1	Bind	Normal	Physical	15	85	20	Normal	—	—
1	Leer	Normal	Status	—	100	30	Many Others	—	—
1	Night Shade	Ghost	Special	—	100	15	Normal	—	—
1	Disable	Normal	Status	—	100	20	Normal	—	—
6	Disable	Normal	Status	—	100	20	Normal	—	—
9	Foresight	Normal	Status	—	—	40	Normal	—	—
14	Astonish	Ghost	Physical	30	100	15	Normal	—	○
17	Confuse Ray	Ghost	Status	—	100	10	Normal	—	—
22	Shadow Sneak	Ghost	Physical	40	100	30	Normal	—	—
25	Pursuit	Dark	Physical	40	100	20	Normal	—	—
30	Curse	Ghost	Status	—	—	10	Varies	—	—
33	Will-O-Wisp	Fire	Status	—	75	15	Normal	—	—
37	Shadow Punch	Ghost	Physical	60	—	20	Normal	—	—
42	Hex	Ghost	Special	50	100	10	Normal	—	—
49	Mean Look	Normal	Status	—	—	5	Normal	—	—
58	Payback	Dark	Physical	50	100	10	Normal	—	—
61	Future Sight	Psychic	Special	100	100	10	Normal	—	—

TM & HM MOVES

Lv.	Name	Type	Kind	Pow.	Acc.	PP	Range	Long	DA
TM04	Calm Mind	Psychic	Status	—	—	20	Self	—	—
TM06	Toxic	Poison	Status	—	90	10	Normal	—	—
TM10	Hidden Power	Normal	Special	—	100	15	Normal	—	—
TM11	Sunny Day	Fire	Status	—	—	5	Both Sides	—	—
TM12	Taunt	Dark	Status	—	100	20	Normal	—	—
TM13	Ice Beam	Ice	Special	95	100	10	Normal	—	—
TM14	Blizzard	Ice	Special	120	70	5	Many Others	—	—
TM15	Hyper Beam	Normal	Special	150	90	5	Normal	—	—
TM17	Protect	Normal	Status	—	—	10	Self	—	—
TM18	Rain Dance	Water	Status	—	—	5	Both Sides	—	—
TM19	Telekinesis	Psychic	Status	—	—	15	Normal	—	—
TM21	Frustration	Normal	Physical	—	100	20	Normal	—	○
TM26	Earthquake	Ground	Physical	100	100	10	Adjacent	—	—
TM27	Return	Normal	Physical	—	100	20	Normal	—	○
TM29	Psychic	Psychic	Special	90	100	10	Normal	—	—
TM30	Shadow Ball	Ghost	Special	80	100	15	Normal	—	—
TM31	Brick Break	Fighting	Physical	75	100	15	Normal	—	—
TM32	Double Team	Normal	Status	—	—	15	Self	—	—
TM39	Rock Tomb	Rock	Physical	50	80	10	Normal	—	—
TM41	Torment	Dark	Status	—	100	15	Normal	—	—
TM42	Facade	Normal	Physical	70	100	20	Normal	—	—
TM44	Rest	Psychic	Status	—	—	10	Self	—	—
TM45	Attract	Normal	Status	—	100	15	Normal	—	—
TM46	Thief	Dark	Physical	40	100	10	Normal	—	—
TM48	Round	Normal	Special	60	100	15	Normal	—	—
TM52	Focus Blast	Fighting	Special	120	70	5	Normal	—	—
TM56	Fling	Dark	Physical	—	100	10	Normal	—	—
TM57	Charge Beam	Electric	Special	50	90	10	Normal	—	—
TM61	Will-O-Wisp	Fire	Status	—	75	15	Normal	—	—
TM63	Embargo	Dark	Status	—	100	15	Normal	—	—
TM66	Payback	Dark	Physical	50	100	10	Normal	—	—
TM68	Giga Impact	Normal	Physical	150	90	5	Normal	—	○

Lv.	Name	Type	Kind	Pow.	Acc.	PP	Range	Long	DA
TM70	Flash	Normal	Status	—	100	20	Normal	—	—
TM77	Psych Up	Normal	Status	—	—	10	Normal	—	—
TM78	Bulldoze	Ground	Physical	60	100	20	Adjacent	—	—
TM80	Rock Slide	Rock	Physical	75	90	10	Many Others	—	—
TM85	Dream Eater	Psychic	Special	100	100	15	Normal	—	—
TM87	Swagger	Normal	Status	—	90	15	Normal	—	—
TM90	Substitute	Normal	Status	—	—	10	Self	—	—
TM92	Trick Room	Psychic	Status	—	—	5	Both Sides	—	—
TM94	Rock Smash	Fighting	Physical	40	100	15	Normal	—	○
HM04	Strength	Normal	Physical	80	100	15	Normal	—	—

MOVES TAUGHT BY PEOPLE

Name	Type	Kind	Pow.	Acc.	PP	Range	Long	DA

MOVES TAUGHT BY MOVE TUTORS FOR SHARDS

Name	Type	Kind	Pow.	Acc.	PP	Range	Long	DA
Fire Punch	Fire	Physical	75	100	15	Normal	—	○
ThunderPunch	Electric	Physical	75	100	15	Normal	—	○
Ice Punch	Ice	Physical	75	100	15	Normal	—	○
Icy Wind	Ice	Special	55	95	15	Many Others	—	—
Gravity	Psychic	Status	—	—	5	Both Sides	—	—
Dark Pulse	Dark	Special	60	100	15	Normal	○	—
Bind	Normal	Physical	15	85	20	Normal	—	—
Snore	Normal	Special	40	100	15	Normal	—	—
Pain Split	Normal	Status	—	—	20	Normal	—	—
Spite	Ghost	Status	—	100	10	Normal	—	—
Trick	Psychic	Status	—	100	10	Normal	—	—
Sleep Talk	Normal	Status	—	—	10	Self	—	—
Skill Swap	Psychic	Status	—	—	10	Normal	—	—
Snatch	Dark	Status	—	—	10	Self	—	—

Pokémon AR Marker

478 Froslass
Snow Land Pokémon

| TYPE | Ice | Ghost |

ABILITY
- Snow Cloak

HIDDEN ABILITY
- Cursed Body

- HEIGHT: 4'03"
- WEIGHT: 58.6 lbs.
- GENDER: ♀

It freezes prey by blowing its -58 degrees F breath. It is said to then secretly display its prey.

♀

STATS
HP
Attack
Defense
Sp. Atk
Sp. Def
Speed

EGG GROUPS
Fairy/Mineral

ITEMS SOMETIMES HELD
- None

Pokémon AR Marker

EVOLUTION

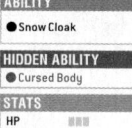

Snorunt → p.194

Lv. 42 → Glalie → p.194

Use Dawn Stone on a ♀

Froslass

HOW TO OBTAIN

| Pokémon Black Version 2 | Use Dawn Stone on a female Snorunt you obtain via Link Trade or Poké Transfer |
| Pokémon White Version 2 | Use Dawn Stone on a female Snorunt you obtain via Link Trade or Poké Transfer |

HOW TO OBTAIN FROM OTHER GAMES
——
——

LEVEL-UP AND LEARNED MOVES

Lv.	Name	Type	Kind	Pow.	Acc.	PP	Range	Long	DA
1	Powder Snow	Ice	Special	40	100	25	Many Others	—	—
1	Leer	Normal	Status	—	100	30	Many Others	—	—
1	Double Team	Normal	Status	—	—	15	Self	—	—
1	Astonish	Ghost	Physical	30	100	15	Normal	—	○
4	Double Team	Normal	Status	—	—	15	Self	—	—
10	Astonish	Ghost	Physical	30	100	15	Normal	—	○
13	Icy Wind	Ice	Special	55	95	15	Many Others	—	—
19	Confuse Ray	Ghost	Status	—	100	10	Normal	—	—
22	Ominous Wind	Ghost	Special	60	100	5	Normal	—	—
28	Wake-Up Slap	Fighting	Physical	60	100	10	Normal	—	○
31	Captivate	Normal	Status	—	100	20	Many Others	—	—
37	Ice Shard	Ice	Physical	40	100	30	Normal	—	—
40	Hail	Ice	Status	—	—	10	Both Sides	—	—
51	Blizzard	Ice	Special	120	70	5	Many Others	—	—
59	Destiny Bond	Ghost	Status	—	—	5	Self	—	—

TM & HM MOVES

Lv.	Name	Type	Kind	Pow.	Acc.	PP	Range	Long	DA
TM06	Toxic	Poison	Status	—	90	10	Normal	—	—
TM07	Hail	Ice	Status	—	—	10	Both Sides	—	—
TM10	Hidden Power	Normal	Special	—	100	15	Normal	—	—
TM12	Taunt	Dark	Status	—	100	20	Normal	—	—
TM13	Ice Beam	Ice	Special	95	100	10	Normal	—	—
TM14	Blizzard	Ice	Special	120	70	5	Many Others	—	—
TM15	Hyper Beam	Normal	Special	150	90	5	Normal	—	—
TM16	Light Screen	Psychic	Status	—	—	30	Your Side	—	—
TM17	Protect	Normal	Status	—	—	10	Self	—	—
TM18	Rain Dance	Water	Status	—	—	5	Both Sides	—	—
TM19	Telekinesis	Psychic	Status	—	—	15	Normal	—	—
TM20	Safeguard	Normal	Status	—	—	25	Your Side	—	—
TM21	Frustration	Normal	Physical	—	100	20	Normal	—	○
TM24	Thunderbolt	Electric	Special	95	100	15	Normal	—	—
TM25	Thunder	Electric	Special	120	70	10	Normal	—	—
TM27	Return	Normal	Physical	—	100	20	Normal	—	○
TM29	Psychic	Psychic	Special	90	100	10	Normal	—	—
TM30	Shadow Ball	Ghost	Special	80	100	15	Normal	—	—
TM32	Double Team	Normal	Status	—	—	15	Self	—	—
TM41	Torment	Dark	Status	—	100	15	Normal	—	—
TM42	Facade	Normal	Physical	70	100	20	Normal	—	○
TM44	Rest	Psychic	Status	—	—	10	Self	—	—
TM45	Attract	Normal	Status	—	100	15	Normal	—	—
TM48	Round	Normal	Special	60	100	15	Normal	—	—
TM56	Fling	Dark	Physical	—	100	10	Normal	—	—
TM63	Embargo	Dark	Status	—	100	15	Normal	—	—
TM66	Payback	Dark	Physical	50	100	10	Normal	—	○
TM68	Giga Impact	Normal	Physical	150	90	5	Normal	—	○
TM70	Flash	Normal	Status	—	100	20	Normal	—	—
TM73	Thunder Wave	Electric	Status	—	100	20	Normal	—	—
TM77	Psych Up	Normal	Status	—	—	10	Normal	—	—
TM79	Frost Breath	Ice	Special	40	90	10	Normal	—	—
TM85	Dream Eater	Psychic	Special	100	100	15	Normal	—	—
TM87	Swagger	Normal	Status	—	90	15	Normal	—	—
TM90	Substitute	Normal	Status	—	—	10	Self	—	—

MOVES TAUGHT BY PEOPLE

Name	Type	Kind	Pow.	Acc.	PP	Range	Long	DA

MOVES TAUGHT BY MOVE TUTORS FOR SHARDS

Name	Type	Kind	Pow.	Acc.	PP	Range	Long	DA
Signal Beam	Bug	Special	75	100	15	Normal	—	○
Ice Punch	Ice	Physical	75	100	15	Normal	—	○
Block	Normal	Status	—	—	5	Normal	—	—
Icy Wind	Ice	Special	55	95	15	Many Others	—	—
Snore	Normal	Special	40	100	15	Normal	—	—
Pain Split	Normal	Status	—	—	20	Normal	—	—
Spite	Ghost	Status	—	100	10	Normal	—	—
Trick	Psychic	Status	—	100	10	Normal	—	—
Sleep Talk	Normal	Status	—	—	10	Self	—	—
Snatch	Dark	Status	—	—	10	Self	—	—

479 Rotom
Plasma Pokémon

| TYPE | Electric | Ghost |

ABILITY
- Levitate

HIDDEN ABILITY

- HEIGHT: 1'00"
- WEIGHT: 0.7 lbs.
- GENDER: Unknown

Its electric-like body can enter some kinds of machines and take control in order to make mischief.

Gender unknown

STATS
HP
Attack
Defense
Sp. Atk
Sp. Def
Speed

EGG GROUPS
Amorphous

ITEMS SOMETIMES HELD
- None

Pokémon AR Marker

EVOLUTION

Does not evolve

HOW TO OBTAIN

| Pokémon Black Version 2 | Trade a Ditto to the woman in the trailer on Route 15 |
| Pokémon White Version 2 | Trade a Ditto to the woman in the trailer on Route 15 |

HOW TO OBTAIN FROM OTHER GAMES
——
——

LEVEL-UP AND LEARNED MOVES

Lv.	Name	Type	Kind	Pow.	Acc.	PP	Range	Long	DA
1	Trick	Psychic	Status	—	100	10	Normal	—	—
1	Astonish	Ghost	Physical	30	100	15	Normal	—	○
1	Thunder Wave	Electric	Status	—	100	20	Normal	—	—
1	ThunderShock	Electric	Special	40	100	30	Normal	—	—
1	Confuse Ray	Ghost	Status	—	100	10	Normal	—	—
8	Uproar	Normal	Special	90	100	10	1 Random	—	—
15	Double Team	Normal	Status	—	—	15	Self	—	—
22	Shock Wave	Electric	Special	60	—	20	Normal	—	—
29	Ominous Wind	Ghost	Special	60	100	5	Normal	—	—
36	Substitute	Normal	Status	—	—	10	Self	—	—
43	Electro Ball	Electric	Special	—	100	10	Normal	—	—
50	Hex	Ghost	Special	50	100	10	Normal	—	—
57	Charge	Electric	Status	—	—	20	Self	—	—
64	Discharge	Electric	Special	80	100	15	Adjacent	—	—

TM & HM MOVES

Lv.	Name	Type	Kind	Pow.	Acc.	PP	Range	Long	DA
TM06	Toxic	Poison	Status	—	90	10	Normal	—	—
TM10	Hidden Power	Normal	Special	—	100	15	Normal	—	—
TM11	Sunny Day	Fire	Status	—	—	5	Both Sides	—	—
TM16	Light Screen	Psychic	Status	—	—	30	Your Side	—	—
TM17	Protect	Normal	Status	—	—	10	Self	—	—
TM18	Rain Dance	Water	Status	—	—	5	Both Sides	—	—
TM19	Telekinesis	Psychic	Status	—	—	15	Normal	—	—
TM21	Frustration	Normal	Physical	—	100	20	Normal	—	○
TM24	Thunderbolt	Electric	Special	95	100	15	Normal	—	—
TM25	Thunder	Electric	Special	120	70	10	Normal	—	—
TM27	Return	Normal	Physical	—	100	20	Normal	—	○
TM30	Shadow Ball	Ghost	Special	80	100	15	Normal	—	—
TM32	Double Team	Normal	Status	—	—	15	Self	—	—
TM33	Reflect	Psychic	Status	—	—	20	Your Side	—	—
TM42	Facade	Normal	Physical	70	100	20	Normal	—	○
TM44	Rest	Psychic	Status	—	—	10	Self	—	—
TM46	Thief	Dark	Physical	40	100	10	Normal	—	○
TM48	Round	Normal	Special	60	100	15	Normal	—	—
TM57	Charge Beam	Electric	Special	50	90	10	Normal	—	—
TM61	Will-O-Wisp	Fire	Status	—	75	15	Normal	—	—
TM70	Flash	Normal	Status	—	100	20	Normal	—	—
TM72	Volt Switch	Electric	Special	70	100	20	Normal	—	—
TM73	Thunder Wave	Electric	Status	—	100	20	Normal	—	—
TM77	Psych Up	Normal	Status	—	—	10	Normal	—	—
TM85	Dream Eater	Psychic	Special	100	100	15	Normal	—	—
TM87	Swagger	Normal	Status	—	90	15	Normal	—	—
TM90	Substitute	Normal	Status	—	—	10	Self	—	—

MOVES TAUGHT BY PEOPLE

Name	Type	Kind	Pow.	Acc.	PP	Range	Long	DA

MOVES TAUGHT BY MOVE TUTORS FOR SHARDS

Name	Type	Kind	Pow.	Acc.	PP	Range	Long	DA
Signal Beam	Bug	Special	75	100	15	Normal	—	—
Uproar	Normal	Special	90	100	10	1 Random	—	—
Electroweb	Electric	Special	55	95	15	Many Others	—	—
Dark Pulse	Dark	Special	80	100	15	Normal	○	—
Snore	Normal	Special	40	100	15	Normal	—	—
Pain Split	Normal	Status	—	—	20	Normal	—	—
Spite	Ghost	Status	—	100	10	Normal	—	—
Trick	Psychic	Status	—	100	10	Normal	—	—
Sleep Talk	Normal	Status	—	—	10	Self	—	—
Snatch	Dark	Status	—	—	10	Self	—	—

EGG MOVES

Name	Type	Kind	Pow.	Acc.	PP	Range	Long	DA

479 Rotom (Heat Rotom)

Plasma Pokémon

TYPE: Electric / Fire

ABILITY: Levitate

HIDDEN ABILITY:

- HEIGHT: 1'00"
- WEIGHT: 0.7 lbs.
- GENDER: Unknown

Its electric-like body can enter some kinds of machines and take control in order to make mischief.

Gender unknown

STATS
HP, Attack, Defense, Sp. Atk, Sp. Def, Speed

EGG GROUPS: Amorphous

ITEMS SOMETIMES HELD: None

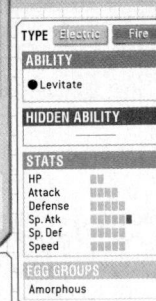

Pokémon AR Marker

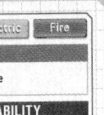
EVOLUTION — Does not evolve

HOW TO OBTAIN

| Pokémon Black Version 2 | Go to the back room on the first floor of Shopping Mall Nine and check the cardboard boxes while Rotom is in your party |
| Pokémon White Version 2 | Go to the back room on the first floor of Shopping Mall Nine and check the cardboard boxes while Rotom is in your party |

HOW TO OBTAIN FROM OTHER GAMES

LEVEL-UP AND LEARNED MOVES

Lv.	Name	Type	Kind	Pow.	Acc.	PP	Range	Long	DA
1	Trick	Psychic	Status	—	100	10	Normal	—	—
1	Astonish	Ghost	Physical	30	100	15	Normal	—	○
1	Thunder Wave	Electric	Status	—	100	20	Normal	—	—
1	ThunderShock	Electric	Special	40	100	30	Normal	—	—
1	Confuse Ray	Ghost	Status	—	100	10	Normal	—	—
8	Uproar	Normal	Special	90	100	10	1 Random	—	—
15	Double Team	Normal	Status	—	—	15	Self	—	—
22	Shock Wave	Electric	Special	60	—	20	Normal	—	—
29	Ominous Wind	Ghost	Special	60	100	5	Normal	—	—
36	Substitute	Normal	Status	—	—	10	Self	—	—
43	Electro Ball	Electric	Special	—	100	10	Normal	—	—
50	Hex	Ghost	Special	50	100	10	Normal	—	—
57	Charge	Electric	Status	—	—	20	Self	—	—
64	Discharge	Electric	Special	80	100	15	Adjacent	—	—
◆	Overheat	Fire	Special	140	90	5	Normal	—	—

TM & HM MOVES

Lv.	Name	Type	Kind	Pow.	Acc.	PP	Range	Long	DA
TM06	Toxic	Poison	Status	—	90	10	Normal	—	—
TM10	Hidden Power	Normal	Special	—	100	15	Normal	—	—
TM11	Sunny Day	Fire	Status	—	—	5	Both Sides	—	—
TM16	Light Screen	Psychic	Status	—	—	30	Your Side	—	—
TM17	Protect	Normal	Status	—	—	10	Self	—	—
TM18	Rain Dance	Water	Status	—	—	5	Both Sides	—	—
TM19	Telekinesis	Psychic	Status	—	—	15	Normal	—	—
TM21	Frustration	Normal	Physical	—	100	20	Normal	—	○
TM24	Thunderbolt	Electric	Special	95	100	15	Normal	—	—
TM25	Thunder	Electric	Special	120	70	10	Normal	—	—
TM27	Return	Normal	Physical	—	100	20	Normal	—	○
TM30	Shadow Ball	Ghost	Special	80	100	15	Normal	—	—
TM32	Double Team	Normal	Status	—	—	15	Self	—	—
TM33	Reflect	Psychic	Status	—	—	20	Your Side	—	—
TM42	Facade	Normal	Physical	70	100	20	Normal	—	○
TM44	Rest	Psychic	Status	—	—	10	Self	—	—
TM46	Thief	Dark	Physical	40	100	10	Normal	—	○
TM48	Round	Normal	Special	60	100	15	Normal	—	—
TM57	Charge Beam	Electric	Special	50	90	10	Normal	—	—
TM61	Will-O-Wisp	Fire	Status	—	75	15	Normal	—	—
TM70	Flash	Normal	Status	—	100	20	Normal	—	—
TM72	Volt Switch	Electric	Special	70	100	20	Normal	—	—
TM73	Thunder Wave	Electric	Status	—	100	20	Normal	—	—
TM77	Psych Up	Normal	Status	—	—	10	Normal	—	—
TM85	Dream Eater	Psychic	Special	100	100	15	Normal	—	—
TM87	Swagger	Normal	Status	—	90	15	Normal	—	—
TM90	Substitute	Normal	Status	—	—	10	Self	—	—

MOVES TAUGHT BY PEOPLE

Name	Type	Kind	Pow.	Acc.	PP	Range	Long	DA

MOVES TAUGHT BY MOVE TUTORS FOR SHARDS

Name	Type	Kind	Pow.	Acc.	PP	Range	Long	DA
Signal Beam	Bug	Special	75	100	15	Normal	—	—
Uproar	Normal	Special	90	100	10	1 Random	—	—
Electroweb	Electric	Special	55	95	15	Many Others	—	—
Dark Pulse	Dark	Special	80	100	15	Normal	○	—
Snore	Normal	Special	40	100	15	Normal	—	—
Pain Split	Normal	Status	—	—	20	Normal	—	—
Spite	Ghost	Status	—	100	10	Normal	—	—
Trick	Psychic	Status	—	100	10	Normal	—	—
Sleep Talk	Normal	Status	—	—	10	Self	—	—
Snatch	Dark	Status	—	—	10	Self	—	—

◆ It learns one move when it changes its form. When it goes back to Rotom, it forgets that move.

---

479 Rotom (Wash Rotom)

Plasma Pokémon

TYPE: Electric / Water

ABILITY: Levitate

HIDDEN ABILITY:

- HEIGHT: 1'00"
- WEIGHT: 0.7 lbs.
- GENDER: Unknown

Its electric-like body can enter some kinds of machines and take control in order to make mischief.

Gender unknown

STATS
HP, Attack, Defense, Sp. Atk, Sp. Def, Speed

EGG GROUPS: Amorphous

ITEMS SOMETIMES HELD: None

Pokémon AR Marker

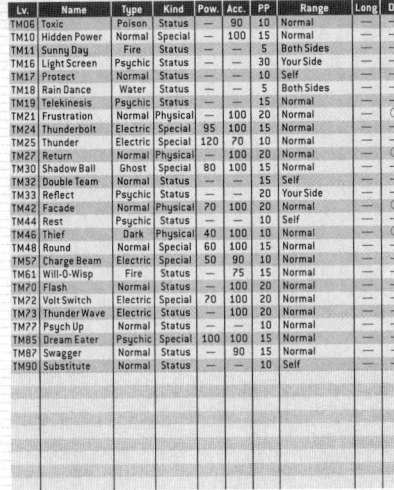

EVOLUTION — Does not evolve

HOW TO OBTAIN

| Pokémon Black Version 2 | Go to the back room on the first floor of Shopping Mall Nine and check the cardboard boxes while Rotom is in your party |
| Pokémon White Version 2 | Go to the back room on the first floor of Shopping Mall Nine and check the cardboard boxes while Rotom is in your party |

HOW TO OBTAIN FROM OTHER GAMES

LEVEL-UP AND LEARNED MOVES

Lv.	Name	Type	Kind	Pow.	Acc.	PP	Range	Long	DA
1	Trick	Psychic	Status	—	100	10	Normal	—	—
1	Astonish	Ghost	Physical	30	100	15	Normal	—	○
1	Thunder Wave	Electric	Status	—	100	20	Normal	—	—
1	ThunderShock	Electric	Special	40	100	30	Normal	—	—
1	Confuse Ray	Ghost	Status	—	100	10	Normal	—	—
8	Uproar	Normal	Special	90	100	10	1 Random	—	—
15	Double Team	Normal	Status	—	—	15	Self	—	—
22	Shock Wave	Electric	Special	60	—	20	Normal	—	—
29	Ominous Wind	Ghost	Special	60	100	5	Normal	—	—
36	Substitute	Normal	Status	—	—	10	Self	—	—
43	Electro Ball	Electric	Special	—	100	10	Normal	—	—
50	Hex	Ghost	Special	50	100	10	Normal	—	—
57	Charge	Electric	Status	—	—	20	Self	—	—
64	Discharge	Electric	Special	80	100	15	Adjacent	—	—
◆	Hydro Pump	Water	Special	120	80	5	Normal	—	—

TM & HM MOVES

Lv.	Name	Type	Kind	Pow.	Acc.	PP	Range	Long	DA
TM06	Toxic	Poison	Status	—	90	10	Normal	—	—
TM10	Hidden Power	Normal	Special	—	100	15	Normal	—	—
TM11	Sunny Day	Fire	Status	—	—	5	Both Sides	—	—
TM16	Light Screen	Psychic	Status	—	—	30	Your Side	—	—
TM17	Protect	Normal	Status	—	—	10	Self	—	—
TM18	Rain Dance	Water	Status	—	—	5	Both Sides	—	—
TM19	Telekinesis	Psychic	Status	—	—	15	Normal	—	—
TM21	Frustration	Normal	Physical	—	100	20	Normal	—	○
TM24	Thunderbolt	Electric	Special	95	100	15	Normal	—	—
TM25	Thunder	Electric	Special	120	70	10	Normal	—	—
TM27	Return	Normal	Physical	—	100	20	Normal	—	○
TM30	Shadow Ball	Ghost	Special	80	100	15	Normal	—	—
TM32	Double Team	Normal	Status	—	—	15	Self	—	—
TM33	Reflect	Psychic	Status	—	—	20	Your Side	—	—
TM42	Facade	Normal	Physical	70	100	20	Normal	—	○
TM44	Rest	Psychic	Status	—	—	10	Self	—	—
TM46	Thief	Dark	Physical	40	100	10	Normal	—	○
TM48	Round	Normal	Special	60	100	15	Normal	—	—
TM57	Charge Beam	Electric	Special	50	90	10	Normal	—	—
TM61	Will-O-Wisp	Fire	Status	—	75	15	Normal	—	—
TM70	Flash	Normal	Status	—	100	20	Normal	—	—
TM72	Volt Switch	Electric	Special	70	100	20	Normal	—	—
TM73	Thunder Wave	Electric	Status	—	100	20	Normal	—	—
TM77	Psych Up	Normal	Status	—	—	10	Normal	—	—
TM85	Dream Eater	Psychic	Special	100	100	15	Normal	—	—
TM87	Swagger	Normal	Status	—	90	15	Normal	—	—
TM90	Substitute	Normal	Status	—	—	10	Self	—	—

MOVES TAUGHT BY PEOPLE

Name	Type	Kind	Pow.	Acc.	PP	Range	Long	DA

MOVES TAUGHT BY MOVE TUTORS FOR SHARDS

Name	Type	Kind	Pow.	Acc.	PP	Range	Long	DA
Signal Beam	Bug	Special	75	100	15	Normal	—	—
Uproar	Normal	Special	90	100	10	1 Random	—	—
Electroweb	Electric	Special	55	95	15	Many Others	—	—
Dark Pulse	Dark	Special	80	100	15	Normal	○	—
Snore	Normal	Special	40	100	15	Normal	—	—
Pain Split	Normal	Status	—	—	20	Normal	—	—
Spite	Ghost	Status	—	100	10	Normal	—	—
Trick	Psychic	Status	—	100	10	Normal	—	—
Sleep Talk	Normal	Status	—	—	10	Self	—	—
Snatch	Dark	Status	—	—	10	Self	—	—

◆ It learns one move when it changes its form. When it goes back to Rotom, it forgets that move.

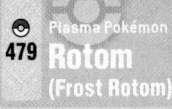

479 Rotom (Frost Rotom)
Plasma Pokémon

● HEIGHT: 1'00"
● WEIGHT: 0.7 lbs.
● GENDER: Unknown

Its electric-like body can enter some kinds of machines and take control in order to make mischief.

Gender unknown

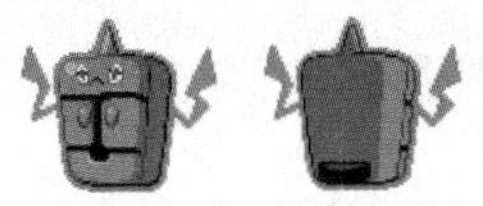

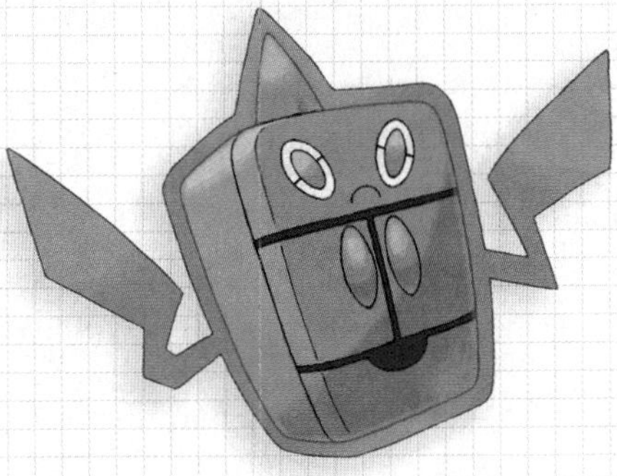

Pokémon AR Marker

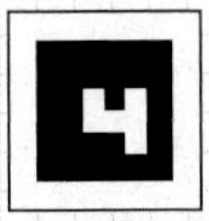

TYPE Electric Ice

ABILITY
● Levitate

HIDDEN ABILITY
—

STATS
HP
Attack
Defense
Sp. Atk
Sp. Def
Speed

EGG GROUPS
Amorphous

ITEMS SOMETIMES HELD
● None

EVOLUTION
Does not evolve

HOW TO OBTAIN

Pokémon Black Version 2	Go to the back room on the first floor of Shopping Mall Nine and check the cardboard boxes while Rotom is in your party
Pokémon White Version 2	Go to the back room on the first floor of Shopping Mall Nine and check the cardboard boxes while Rotom is in your party

HOW TO OBTAIN FROM OTHER GAMES
—
—

LEVEL-UP AND LEARNED MOVES

Lv.	Name	Type	Kind	Pow.	Acc.	PP	Range	Long	DA
1	Trick	Psychic	Status	-	100	10	Normal	-	-
1	Astonish	Ghost	Physical	30	100	15	Normal	-	○
1	Thunder Wave	Electric	Status	-	100	20	Normal	-	-
1	ThunderShock	Electric	Special	40	100	30	Normal	-	-
1	Confuse Ray	Ghost	Status	-	100	10	Normal	-	-
8	Uproar	Normal	Special	90	100	10	1 Random	-	-
15	Double Team	Normal	Status	-	-	15	Self	-	-
22	Shock Wave	Electric	Special	60	-	20	Normal	-	-
29	Ominous Wind	Ghost	Special	60	100	5	Normal	-	-
36	Substitute	Normal	Status	-	-	10	Self	-	-
43	Electro Ball	Electric	Special	-	100	10	Normal	-	-
50	Hex	Ghost	Special	50	100	10	Normal	-	-
57	Charge	Electric	Status	-	-	20	Self	-	-
64	Discharge	Electric	Special	80	100	15	Adjacent	-	-
◆	Blizzard	Ice	Special	120	70	5	Many Others	-	-

TM & HM MOVES

Lv.	Name	Type	Kind	Pow.	Acc.	PP	Range	Long	DA
TM06	Toxic	Poison	Status	—	90	10	Normal	—	—
TM10	Hidden Power	Normal	Special	—	100	15	Normal	—	—
TM11	Sunny Day	Fire	Status	—	—	5	Both Sides	—	—
TM16	Light Screen	Psychic	Status	—	—	30	Your Side	—	—
TM17	Protect	Normal	Status	—	—	10	Self	—	—
TM18	Rain Dance	Water	Status	—	—	5	Both Sides	—	—
TM19	Telekinesis	Psychic	Status	—	—	15	Normal	—	—
TM21	Frustration	Normal	Physical	—	100	20	Normal	—	○
TM24	Thunderbolt	Electric	Special	95	100	15	Normal	—	—
TM25	Thunder	Electric	Special	120	70	10	Normal	—	—
TM27	Return	Normal	Physical	—	100	20	Normal	—	○
TM30	Shadow Ball	Ghost	Special	80	100	15	Normal	—	—
TM32	Double Team	Normal	Status	—	—	15	Self	—	—
TM33	Reflect	Psychic	Status	—	—	20	Your Side	—	—
TM42	Facade	Normal	Physical	70	100	20	Normal	—	○
TM44	Rest	Psychic	Status	—	—	10	Self	—	—
TM46	Thief	Dark	Physical	40	100	10	Normal	—	○
TM48	Round	Normal	Special	60	100	15	Normal	—	—
TM57	Charge Beam	Electric	Special	50	90	10	Normal	—	—
TM61	Will-O-Wisp	Fire	Status	—	75	15	Normal	—	—
TM70	Flash	Normal	Status	—	100	20	Normal	—	—
TM72	Volt Switch	Electric	Special	70	100	20	Normal	—	—
TM73	Thunder Wave	Electric	Status	—	100	20	Normal	—	—
TM77	Psych Up	Normal	Status	—	—	10	Normal	—	—
TM85	Dream Eater	Psychic	Special	100	100	15	Normal	—	—
TM87	Swagger	Normal	Status	—	90	15	Normal	—	—
TM90	Substitute	Normal	Status	—	—	10	Self	—	—

◆ It learns one move when it changes its form. When it goes back to Rotom, it forgets that move.

MOVES TAUGHT BY PEOPLE

Name	Type	Kind	Pow.	Acc.	PP	Range	Long	DA

MOVES TAUGHT BY MOVE TUTORS FOR SHARDS

Name	Type	Kind	Pow.	Acc.	PP	Range	Long	DA
Signal Beam	Bug	Special	75	100	15	Normal	—	—
Uproar	Normal	Special	90	100	10	1 Random	—	—
Electroweb	Electric	Special	55	95	15	Many Others	—	—
Dark Pulse	Dark	Special	80	100	15	Normal	○	—
Snore	Normal	Special	40	100	15	Normal	—	—
Pain Split	Normal	Status	—	—	20	Normal	—	—
Spite	Ghost	Status	—	100	10	Normal	—	—
Trick	Psychic	Status	—	100	10	Normal	—	—
Sleep Talk	Normal	Status	—	—	10	Self	—	—
Snatch	Dark	Status	—	—	10	Self	—	—

479 Rotom (Fan Rotom)
Plasma Pokémon

● HEIGHT: 1'00"
● WEIGHT: 0.7 lbs.
● GENDER: Unknown

Its electric-like body can enter some kinds of machines and take control in order to make mischief.

Gender unknown

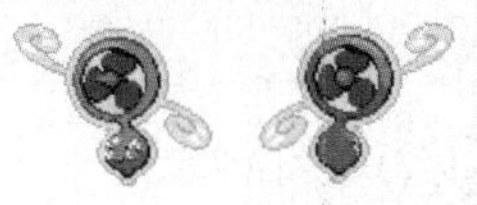

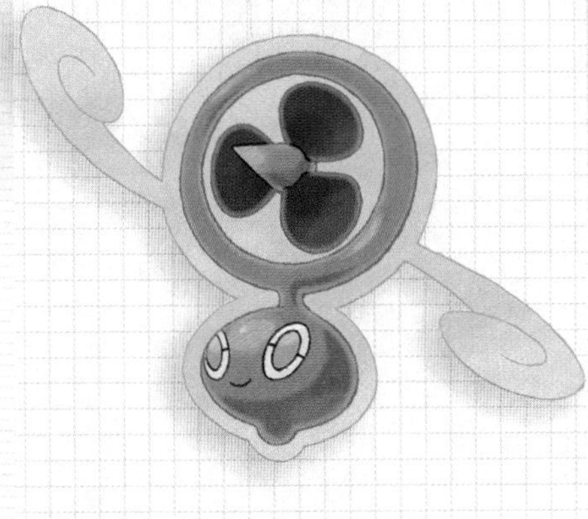

Pokémon AR Marker

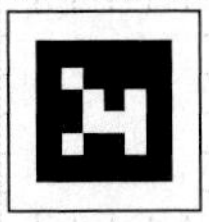

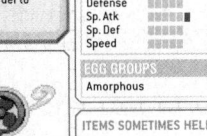

TYPE Electric Flying

ABILITY
● Levitate

HIDDEN ABILITY
—

STATS
HP
Attack
Defense
Sp. Atk
Sp. Def
Speed

EGG GROUPS
Amorphous

ITEMS SOMETIMES HELD
● None

EVOLUTION
Does not evolve

HOW TO OBTAIN

Pokémon Black Version 2	Go to the back room on the first floor of Shopping Mall Nine and check the cardboard boxes while Rotom is in your party
Pokémon White Version 2	Go to the back room on the first floor of Shopping Mall Nine and check the cardboard boxes while Rotom is in your party

HOW TO OBTAIN FROM OTHER GAMES
—
—

LEVEL-UP AND LEARNED MOVES

Lv.	Name	Type	Kind	Pow.	Acc.	PP	Range	Long	DA
1	Trick	Psychic	Status	-	100	10	Normal	-	-
1	Astonish	Ghost	Physical	30	100	15	Normal	-	○
1	Thunder Wave	Electric	Status	-	100	20	Normal	-	-
1	ThunderShock	Electric	Special	40	100	30	Normal	-	-
1	Confuse Ray	Ghost	Status	-	100	10	Normal	-	-
8	Uproar	Normal	Special	90	100	10	1 Random	-	-
15	Double Team	Normal	Status	-	-	15	Self	-	-
22	Shock Wave	Electric	Special	60	-	20	Normal	-	-
29	Ominous Wind	Ghost	Special	60	100	5	Normal	-	-
36	Substitute	Normal	Status	-	-	10	Self	-	-
43	Electro Ball	Electric	Special	-	100	10	Normal	-	-
50	Hex	Ghost	Special	50	100	10	Normal	-	-
57	Charge	Electric	Status	-	-	20	Self	-	-
64	Discharge	Electric	Special	80	100	15	Adjacent	-	-
◆	Air Slash	Flying	Special	75	95	20	Normal	○	-

TM & HM MOVES

Lv.	Name	Type	Kind	Pow.	Acc.	PP	Range	Long	DA
TM06	Toxic	Poison	Status	—	90	10	Normal	—	—
TM10	Hidden Power	Normal	Special	—	100	15	Normal	—	—
TM11	Sunny Day	Fire	Status	—	—	5	Both Sides	—	—
TM16	Light Screen	Psychic	Status	—	—	30	Your Side	—	—
TM17	Protect	Normal	Status	—	—	10	Self	—	—
TM18	Rain Dance	Water	Status	—	—	5	Both Sides	—	—
TM19	Telekinesis	Psychic	Status	—	—	15	Normal	—	—
TM21	Frustration	Normal	Physical	—	100	20	Normal	—	○
TM24	Thunderbolt	Electric	Special	95	100	15	Normal	—	—
TM25	Thunder	Electric	Special	120	70	10	Normal	—	—
TM27	Return	Normal	Physical	—	100	20	Normal	—	○
TM30	Shadow Ball	Ghost	Special	80	100	15	Normal	—	—
TM32	Double Team	Normal	Status	—	—	15	Self	—	—
TM33	Reflect	Psychic	Status	—	—	20	Your Side	—	—
TM42	Facade	Normal	Physical	70	100	20	Normal	—	○
TM44	Rest	Psychic	Status	—	—	10	Self	—	—
TM46	Thief	Dark	Physical	40	100	10	Normal	—	○
TM48	Round	Normal	Special	60	100	15	Normal	—	—
TM57	Charge Beam	Electric	Special	50	90	10	Normal	—	—
TM61	Will-O-Wisp	Fire	Status	—	75	15	Normal	—	—
TM70	Flash	Normal	Status	—	100	20	Normal	—	—
TM72	Volt Switch	Electric	Special	70	100	20	Normal	—	—
TM73	Thunder Wave	Electric	Status	—	100	20	Normal	—	—
TM77	Psych Up	Normal	Status	—	—	10	Normal	—	—
TM85	Dream Eater	Psychic	Special	100	100	15	Normal	—	—
TM87	Swagger	Normal	Status	—	90	15	Normal	—	—
TM90	Substitute	Normal	Status	—	—	10	Self	—	—

◆ It learns one move when it changes its form. When it goes back to Rotom, it forgets that move.

MOVES TAUGHT BY PEOPLE

Name	Type	Kind	Pow.	Acc.	PP	Range	Long	DA

MOVES TAUGHT BY MOVE TUTORS FOR SHARDS

Name	Type	Kind	Pow.	Acc.	PP	Range	Long	DA
Signal Beam	Bug	Special	75	100	15	Normal	—	—
Uproar	Normal	Special	90	100	10	1 Random	—	—
Electroweb	Electric	Special	55	95	15	Many Others	—	—
Dark Pulse	Dark	Special	80	100	15	Normal	○	—
Snore	Normal	Special	40	100	15	Normal	—	—
Pain Split	Normal	Status	—	—	20	Normal	—	—
Spite	Ghost	Status	—	100	10	Normal	—	—
Trick	Psychic	Status	—	100	10	Normal	—	—
Sleep Talk	Normal	Status	—	—	10	Self	—	—
Snatch	Dark	Status	—	—	10	Self	—	—

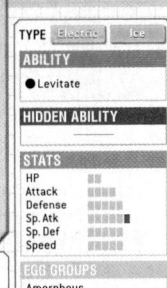

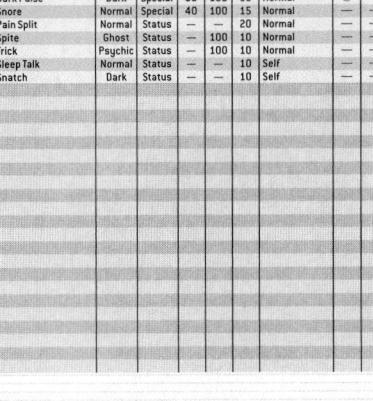

Plasma Pokémon

479 Rotom (Mow Rotom)

- HEIGHT: 1'00"
- WEIGHT: 0.7 lbs.
- GENDER: Unknown

Its electric-like body can enter some kinds of machines and take control in order to make mischief.

Gender unknown

TYPE Electric Grass

ABILITY

- Levitate

HIDDEN ABILITY

—

STATS

HP
Attack
Defense
Sp. Atk
Sp. Def
Speed

EGG GROUPS

Amorphous

ITEMS SOMETIMES HELD

- None

Pokémon AR Marker

EVOLUTION

Does not evolve

HOW TO OBTAIN

Pokémon Black Version 2	Go to the back room on the first floor of Shopping Mall Nine and check the cardboard boxes while Rotom is in your party
Pokémon White Version 2	Go to the back room on the first floor of Shopping Mall Nine and check the cardboard boxes while Rotom is in your party

HOW TO OBTAIN FROM OTHER GAMES

—

—

LEVEL-UP AND LEARNED MOVES

Lv.	Name	Type	Kind	Pow.	Acc.	PP	Range	Long	DA
1	Trick	Psychic	Status	-	100	10	Normal	-	-
1	Astonish	Ghost	Physical	30	100	15	Normal	-	○
1	Thunder Wave	Electric	Status	-	100	20	Normal	-	-
1	ThunderShock	Electric	Special	40	100	30	Normal	-	-
1	Confuse Ray	Ghost	Status	-	100	10	Normal	-	-
8	Uproar	Normal	Special	90	100	10	1 Random	-	-
15	Double Team	Normal	Status	-	-	15	Self	-	-
22	Shock Wave	Electric	Special	60	-	20	Normal	-	-
29	Ominous Wind	Ghost	Special	60	100	5	Normal	-	-
36	Substitute	Normal	Status	-	-	10	Self	-	-
43	Electro Ball	Electric	Special	-	100	10	Normal	-	-
50	Hex	Ghost	Special	50	100	10	Normal	-	-
57	Charge	Electric	Status	-	-	20	Self	-	-
64	Discharge	Electric	Special	80	100	15	Adjacent	-	-
◆	Leaf Storm	Grass	Special	140	90	5	Normal	-	-

TM & HM MOVES

Lv.	Name	Type	Kind	Pow.	Acc.	PP	Range	Long	DA
TM06	Toxic	Poison	Status	—	90	10	Normal	—	—
TM10	Hidden Power	Normal	Special	—	100	15	Normal	—	—
TM11	Sunny Day	Fire	Status	—	—	5	Both Sides	—	—
TM16	Light Screen	Psychic	Status	—	—	30	Your Side	—	—
TM17	Protect	Normal	Status	—	—	10	Self	—	—
TM18	Rain Dance	Water	Status	—	—	5	Both Sides	—	—
TM19	Telekinesis	Psychic	Status	—	—	15	Normal	—	—
TM21	Frustration	Normal	Physical	—	100	20	Normal	—	○
TM24	Thunderbolt	Electric	Special	95	100	15	Normal	—	—
TM25	Thunder	Electric	Special	120	70	10	Normal	—	—
TM27	Return	Normal	Physical	—	100	20	Normal	—	○
TM30	Shadow Ball	Ghost	Special	80	100	15	Normal	—	—
TM32	Double Team	Normal	Status	—	—	15	Self	—	—
TM33	Reflect	Psychic	Status	—	—	20	Your Side	—	—
TM42	Facade	Normal	Physical	70	100	20	Normal	—	○
TM44	Rest	Psychic	Status	—	—	10	Self	—	—
TM46	Thief	Dark	Physical	40	100	10	Normal	—	○
TM48	Round	Normal	Special	60	100	15	Normal	—	—
TM57	Charge Beam	Electric	Special	50	90	10	Normal	—	—
TM61	Will-O-Wisp	Fire	Status	—	75	15	Normal	—	—
TM70	Flash	Normal	Status	—	100	20	Normal	—	—
TM72	Volt Switch	Electric	Special	70	100	20	Normal	—	—
TM73	Thunder Wave	Electric	Status	—	100	20	Normal	—	—
TM77	Psych Up	Normal	Status	—	—	10	Normal	—	—
TM85	Dream Eater	Psychic	Special	100	100	15	Normal	—	—
TM87	Swagger	Normal	Status	—	90	15	Normal	—	—
TM90	Substitute	Normal	Status	—	—	10	Self	—	—

◆ It learns one move when it changes its form. When it goes back to Rotom, it forgets that move.

MOVES TAUGHT BY PEOPLE

Name	Type	Kind	Pow.	Acc.	PP	Range	Long	DA

MOVES TAUGHT BY MOVE TUTORS FOR SHARDS

Name	Type	Kind	Pow.	Acc.	PP	Range	Long	DA
Signal Beam	Bug	Special	75	100	15	Normal	—	—
Uproar	Normal	Special	90	100	10	1 Random	—	—
Electroweb	Electric	Special	55	95	15	Many Others	—	—
Dark Pulse	Dark	Special	80	100	15	Normal	○	—
Snore	Normal	Special	40	100	15	Normal	—	—
Pain Split	Normal	Status	—	—	20	Normal	—	—
Spite	Ghost	Status	—	100	10	Normal	—	—
Trick	Psychic	Status	—	100	10	Normal	—	—
Sleep Talk	Normal	Status	—	—	10	Self	—	—
Snatch	Dark	Status	—	—	10	Self	—	—

Knowledge Pokémon

480 Uxie

- HEIGHT: 1'00"
- WEIGHT: 0.7 lbs.
- GENDER: Unknown

When Uxie flew, people gained the ability to solve problems. It was the birth of knowledge.

Gender unknown

TYPE Psychic

ABILITY

- Levitate

HIDDEN ABILITY

—

STATS

HP
Attack
Defense
Sp. Atk
Sp. Def
Speed

EGG GROUPS

No Egg has ever been discovered

ITEMS SOMETIMES HELD

- None

Pokémon AR Marker

EVOLUTION

Does not evolve

HOW TO OBTAIN

Pokémon Black Version 2	In front of the Nacrene Museum (after visiting the Cave of Being)
Pokémon White Version 2	In front of the Nacrene Museum (after visiting the Cave of Being)

HOW TO OBTAIN FROM OTHER GAMES

—

—

LEVEL-UP AND LEARNED MOVES

Lv.	Name	Type	Kind	Pow.	Acc.	PP	Range	Long	DA
1	Rest	Psychic	Status	—	—	10	Self	—	—
1	Confusion	Psychic	Special	50	100	25	Normal	—	—
6	Imprison	Psychic	Status	—	—	10	Self	—	—
16	Endure	Normal	Status	—	—	10	Self	—	—
21	Swift	Normal	Special	60	—	20	Many Others	—	—
31	Yawn	Normal	Status	—	—	10	Normal	—	—
36	Future Sight	Psychic	Special	100	100	10	Normal	—	—
46	Amnesia	Psychic	Status	—	—	20	Self	—	—
51	Extrasensory	Psychic	Special	80	100	30	Normal	—	—
61	Flail	Normal	Physical	—	100	15	Normal	—	○
66	Natural Gift	Normal	Physical	—	100	15	Normal	—	—
76	Memento	Dark	Status	—	100	10	Normal	—	—

TM & HM MOVES

Lv.	Name	Type	Kind	Pow.	Acc.	PP	Range	Long	DA
TM03	Psyshock	Psychic	Special	80	100	10	Normal	—	—
TM04	Calm Mind	Psychic	Status	—	—	20	Self	—	—
TM06	Toxic	Poison	Status	—	90	10	Normal	—	—
TM10	Hidden Power	Normal	Special	—	100	15	Normal	—	—
TM11	Sunny Day	Fire	Status	—	—	5	Both Sides	—	—
TM15	Hyper Beam	Normal	Special	150	90	5	Normal	—	—
TM16	Light Screen	Psychic	Status	—	—	30	Your Side	—	—
TM17	Protect	Normal	Status	—	—	10	Self	—	—
TM18	Rain Dance	Water	Status	—	—	5	Both Sides	—	—
TM19	Telekinesis	Psychic	Status	—	—	15	Normal	—	—
TM20	Safeguard	Normal	Status	—	—	25	Your Side	—	—
TM21	Frustration	Normal	Physical	—	100	20	Normal	—	○
TM22	SolarBeam	Grass	Special	120	100	10	Normal	—	—
TM24	Thunderbolt	Electric	Special	95	100	15	Normal	—	—
TM25	Thunder	Electric	Special	120	70	10	Normal	—	—
TM27	Return	Normal	Physical	—	100	20	Normal	—	○
TM29	Psychic	Psychic	Special	90	100	10	Normal	—	—
TM30	Shadow Ball	Ghost	Special	80	100	15	Normal	—	—
TM32	Double Team	Normal	Status	—	—	15	Self	—	—
TM33	Reflect	Psychic	Status	—	—	20	Your Side	—	—
TM37	Sandstorm	Rock	Status	—	—	10	Both Sides	—	—
TM42	Facade	Normal	Physical	70	100	20	Normal	—	○
TM44	Rest	Psychic	Status	—	—	10	Self	—	—
TM48	Round	Normal	Special	60	100	15	Normal	—	—
TM53	Energy Ball	Grass	Special	80	100	10	Normal	—	—
TM56	Fling	Dark	Physical	—	100	10	Normal	—	—
TM57	Charge Beam	Electric	Special	50	90	10	Normal	—	—
TM62	Acrobatics	Flying	Physical	55	100	15	Normal	○	○
TM68	Giga Impact	Normal	Physical	150	90	5	Normal	—	○
TM70	Flash	Normal	Status	—	100	20	Normal	—	—
TM73	Thunder Wave	Electric	Status	—	100	20	Normal	—	—
TM77	Psych Up	Normal	Status	—	—	10	Normal	—	—
TM85	Dream Eater	Psychic	Special	100	100	15	Normal	—	—
TM86	Grass Knot	Grass	Special	—	100	20	Normal	—	○
TM87	Swagger	Normal	Status	—	90	15	Normal	—	—
TM89	U-turn	Bug	Physical	70	100	20	Normal	—	○
TM90	Substitute	Normal	Status	—	—	10	Self	—	—
TM92	Trick Room	Psychic	Status	—	—	5	Both Sides	—	—

MOVES TAUGHT BY PEOPLE

Name	Type	Kind	Pow.	Acc.	PP	Range	Long	DA

MOVES TAUGHT BY MOVE TUTORS FOR SHARDS

Name	Type	Kind	Pow.	Acc.	PP	Range	Long	DA
Signal Beam	Bug	Special	75	100	15	Normal	—	—
Fire Punch	Fire	Physical	75	100	15	Normal	—	○
ThunderPunch	Electric	Physical	75	100	15	Normal	—	○
Ice Punch	Ice	Physical	75	100	15	Normal	—	○
Magic Coat	Psychic	Status	—	—	15	Self	—	—
Iron Tail	Steel	Physical	100	75	15	Normal	—	○
Zen Headbutt	Psychic	Physical	80	90	15	Normal	—	○
Foul Play	Dark	Physical	95	100	15	Normal	—	○
Snore	Normal	Special	40	100	15	Normal	—	—
Heal Bell	Normal	Status	—	—	5	Your Party	—	—
Knock Off	Dark	Physical	20	100	20	Normal	—	○
Role Play	Psychic	Status	—	—	10	Normal	—	—
Giga Drain	Grass	Special	75	100	10	Normal	—	—
Helping Hand	Normal	Status	—	—	20	1 Ally	—	—
Magic Room	Psychic	Status	—	—	10	Both Sides	—	—
Wonder Room	Psychic	Status	—	—	10	Both Sides	—	—
Recycle	Normal	Status	—	—	10	Self	—	—
Trick	Psychic	Status	—	100	10	Normal	—	—
Stealth Rock	Rock	Status	—	—	20	Other Side	—	—
Sleep Talk	Normal	Status	—	—	10	Self	—	—
Skill Swap	Psychic	Status	—	—	10	Normal	—	—

Mesprit

 Emotion Pokémon
481 Mesprit

- **TYPE:** Psychic
- **ABILITY:** Levitate
- **HIDDEN ABILITY:**

- **HEIGHT:** 1'00"
- **WEIGHT:** 0.7 lbs.
- **GENDER:** Unknown

When Mesprit flew, people learned the joy and sadness of living. It was the birth of emotions.

STATS: HP, Attack, Defense, Sp. Atk, Sp. Def, Speed

EGG GROUPS: No Egg has ever been discovered

ITEMS SOMETIMES HELD: None

Gender unknown

EVOLUTION
Does not evolve

HOW TO OBTAIN
Pokémon Black Version 2	Celestial Tower top floor (after visiting the Cave of Being)
Pokémon White Version 2	Celestial Tower top floor (after visiting the Cave of Being)

HOW TO OBTAIN FROM OTHER GAMES
———
———

LEVEL-UP AND LEARNED MOVES
Lv.	Name	Type	Kind	Pow.	Acc.	PP	Range	Long	DA
1	Rest	Psychic	Status	—	—	10	Self	—	—
1	Confusion	Psychic	Special	50	100	25	Normal	—	—
6	Imprison	Psychic	Status	—	—	10	Self	—	—
16	Protect	Normal	Status	—	—	10	Self	—	—
21	Swift	Normal	Special	60	—	20	Many Others	—	—
31	Lucky Chant	Normal	Status	—	—	30	Your Side	—	—
36	Future Sight	Psychic	Special	100	100	10	Normal	—	—
46	Charm	Normal	Status	—	100	20	Normal	—	—
51	Extrasensory	Psychic	Special	80	100	10	Normal	—	—
61	Copycat	Normal	Status	—	—	20	Self	—	—
66	Natural Gift	Normal	Physical	—	100	15	Normal	—	—
76	Healing Wish	Psychic	Status	—	—	10	Self	—	—

TM & HM MOVES
Lv.	Name	Type	Kind	Pow.	Acc.	PP	Range	Long	DA
TM03	Psyshock	Psychic	Special	80	100	10	Normal	—	—
TM04	Calm Mind	Psychic	Status	—	—	20	Self	—	—
TM06	Toxic	Poison	Status	—	90	10	Normal	—	—
TM10	Hidden Power	Normal	Special	—	100	15	Normal	—	—
TM11	Sunny Day	Fire	Status	—	—	5	Both Sides	—	—
TM13	Ice Beam	Ice	Special	95	100	10	Normal	—	—
TM14	Blizzard	Ice	Special	120	70	5	Many Others	—	—
TM15	Hyper Beam	Normal	Special	150	90	5	Normal	—	—
TM16	Light Screen	Psychic	Status	—	—	30	Your Side	—	—
TM17	Protect	Normal	Status	—	—	10	Self	—	—
TM18	Rain Dance	Water	Status	—	—	5	Both Sides	—	—
TM19	Telekinesis	Psychic	Status	—	—	15	Normal	—	—
TM20	Safeguard	Normal	Status	—	—	25	Your Side	—	—
TM21	Frustration	Normal	Physical	—	100	20	Normal	—	○
TM24	Thunderbolt	Electric	Special	95	100	15	Normal	—	—
TM25	Thunder	Electric	Special	120	70	10	Normal	—	—
TM27	Return	Normal	Physical	—	100	20	Normal	—	○
TM29	Psychic	Psychic	Special	90	100	10	Normal	—	—
TM30	Shadow Ball	Ghost	Special	80	100	15	Normal	—	—
TM32	Double Team	Normal	Status	—	—	15	Self	—	—
TM33	Reflect	Psychic	Status	—	—	20	Your Side	—	—
TM37	Sandstorm	Rock	Status	—	—	10	Both Sides	—	—
TM42	Facade	Normal	Physical	70	100	20	Normal	—	○
TM44	Rest	Psychic	Status	—	—	10	Self	—	—
TM48	Round	Normal	Special	60	100	15	Normal	—	—
TM53	Energy Ball	Grass	Special	80	100	10	Normal	—	—
TM56	Fling	Dark	Physical	—	100	10	Normal	—	○
TM57	Charge Beam	Electric	Special	50	90	10	Normal	—	—
TM62	Acrobatics	Flying	Physical	55	100	15	Normal	○	○
TM68	Giga Impact	Normal	Physical	150	90	5	Normal	—	○
TM70	Flash	Normal	Status	—	100	20	Normal	—	—
TM73	Thunder Wave	Electric	Status	—	100	20	Normal	—	—
TM77	Psych Up	Normal	Status	—	—	10	Self	—	—
TM85	Dream Eater	Psychic	Special	100	100	15	Normal	—	—
TM86	Grass Knot	Grass	Special	—	100	20	Normal	—	○
TM87	Swagger	Normal	Status	—	90	15	Normal	—	—
TM89	U-turn	Bug	Physical	70	100	20	Normal	—	○
TM90	Substitute	Normal	Status	—	—	10	Self	—	—
TM92	Trick Room	Psychic	Status	—	—	5	Both Sides	—	—

MOVES TAUGHT BY PEOPLE
Name	Type	Kind	Pow.	Acc.	PP	Range	Long	DA

MOVES TAUGHT BY MOVE TUTORS FOR SHARDS
Name	Type	Kind	Pow.	Acc.	PP	Range	Long	DA
Signal Beam	Bug	Special	75	100	15	Normal	—	—
Fire Punch	Fire	Physical	75	100	15	Normal	—	○
ThunderPunch	Electric	Physical	75	100	15	Normal	—	○
Ice Punch	Ice	Physical	75	100	15	Normal	—	○
Magic Coat	Psychic	Status	—	—	15	Self	—	—
Iron Tail	Steel	Physical	100	75	15	Normal	—	○
Zen Headbutt	Psychic	Physical	80	90	15	Normal	—	○
Snore	Normal	Special	40	100	15	Normal	—	—
Knock Off	Dark	Physical	20	100	20	Normal	—	○
Role Play	Psychic	Status	—	—	10	Normal	—	—
Helping Hand	Normal	Status	—	—	20	1 Ally	—	—
Magic Room	Psychic	Status	—	—	10	Both Sides	—	—
Wonder Room	Psychic	Status	—	—	10	Both Sides	—	—
Recycle	Normal	Status	—	—	10	Self	—	—
Trick	Psychic	Status	—	100	10	Normal	—	—
Stealth Rock	Rock	Status	—	—	20	Other Side	—	—
Sleep Talk	Normal	Status	—	—	10	Self	—	—
Skill Swap	Psychic	Status	—	—	10	Normal	—	—

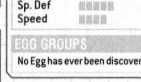

Pokémon AR Marker

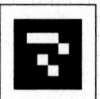

481 | Mesprit

Azelf

 Willpower Pokémon
482 Azelf

- **TYPE:** Psychic
- **ABILITY:** Levitate
- **HIDDEN ABILITY:**

- **HEIGHT:** 1'00"
- **WEIGHT:** 0.7 lbs.
- **GENDER:** Unknown

When Azelf flew, people gained the determination to do things. It was the birth of willpower.

STATS: HP, Attack, Defense, Sp. Atk, Sp. Def, Speed

EGG GROUPS: No Egg has ever been discovered

ITEMS SOMETIMES HELD: None

Gender unknown

EVOLUTION
Does not evolve

HOW TO OBTAIN
Pokémon Black Version 2	Route 23 (after visiting the Cave of Being)
Pokémon White Version 2	Route 23 (after visiting the Cave of Being)

HOW TO OBTAIN FROM OTHER GAMES
———
———

LEVEL-UP AND LEARNED MOVES
Lv.	Name	Type	Kind	Pow.	Acc.	PP	Range	Long	DA
1	Rest	Psychic	Status	—	—	10	Self	—	—
1	Confusion	Psychic	Special	50	100	25	Normal	—	—
6	Imprison	Psychic	Status	—	—	10	Self	—	—
16	Detect	Fighting	Status	—	—	5	Self	—	—
21	Swift	Normal	Special	60	—	20	Many Others	—	—
31	Uproar	Normal	Special	90	100	10	1 Random	—	—
36	Future Sight	Psychic	Special	100	100	10	Normal	—	—
46	Nasty Plot	Dark	Status	—	—	20	Self	—	—
51	Extrasensory	Psychic	Special	80	100	30	Normal	—	—
61	Last Resort	Normal	Physical	140	100	5	Normal	—	○
66	Natural Gift	Normal	Physical	—	100	15	Normal	—	—
76	Explosion	Normal	Physical	250	100	5	Adjacent	—	—

TM & HM MOVES
Lv.	Name	Type	Kind	Pow.	Acc.	PP	Range	Long	DA
TM03	Psyshock	Psychic	Special	80	100	10	Normal	—	—
TM04	Calm Mind	Psychic	Status	—	—	20	Self	—	—
TM06	Toxic	Poison	Status	—	90	10	Normal	—	—
TM10	Hidden Power	Normal	Special	—	100	15	Normal	—	—
TM11	Sunny Day	Fire	Status	—	—	5	Both Sides	—	—
TM12	Taunt	Dark	Status	—	100	20	Normal	—	—
TM15	Hyper Beam	Normal	Special	150	90	5	Normal	—	—
TM16	Light Screen	Psychic	Status	—	—	30	Your Side	—	—
TM17	Protect	Normal	Status	—	—	10	Self	—	—
TM18	Rain Dance	Water	Status	—	—	5	Both Sides	—	—
TM19	Telekinesis	Psychic	Status	—	—	15	Normal	—	—
TM20	Safeguard	Normal	Status	—	—	25	Your Side	—	—
TM21	Frustration	Normal	Physical	—	100	20	Normal	—	○
TM24	Thunderbolt	Electric	Special	95	100	15	Normal	—	—
TM25	Thunder	Electric	Special	120	70	10	Normal	—	—
TM27	Return	Normal	Physical	—	100	20	Normal	—	○
TM29	Psychic	Psychic	Special	90	100	10	Normal	—	—
TM30	Shadow Ball	Ghost	Special	80	100	15	Normal	—	—
TM32	Double Team	Normal	Status	—	—	15	Self	—	—
TM33	Reflect	Psychic	Status	—	—	20	Your Side	—	—
TM35	Flamethrower	Fire	Special	95	100	15	Normal	—	—
TM37	Sandstorm	Rock	Status	—	—	10	Both Sides	—	—
TM38	Fire Blast	Fire	Special	120	85	5	Normal	—	—
TM41	Torment	Dark	Status	—	100	15	Normal	—	—
TM42	Facade	Normal	Physical	70	100	20	Normal	—	○
TM44	Rest	Psychic	Status	—	—	10	Self	—	—
TM48	Round	Normal	Special	60	100	15	Normal	—	—
TM53	Energy Ball	Grass	Special	80	100	10	Normal	—	—
TM56	Fling	Dark	Physical	—	100	10	Normal	—	○
TM57	Charge Beam	Electric	Special	50	90	10	Normal	—	—
TM59	Incinerate	Fire	Special	30	100	15	Many Others	—	—
TM62	Acrobatics	Flying	Physical	55	100	15	Normal	○	○
TM64	Explosion	Normal	Physical	250	100	5	Adjacent	—	—
TM66	Payback	Dark	Physical	50	100	10	Normal	—	○
TM68	Giga Impact	Normal	Physical	150	90	5	Normal	—	○
TM70	Flash	Normal	Status	—	100	20	Normal	—	—
TM73	Thunder Wave	Electric	Status	—	100	20	Normal	—	—
TM77	Psych Up	Normal	Status	—	—	10	Self	—	—
TM85	Dream Eater	Psychic	Special	100	100	15	Normal	—	—
TM86	Grass Knot	Grass	Special	—	100	20	Normal	—	○
TM87	Swagger	Normal	Status	—	90	15	Normal	—	—
TM89	U-turn	Bug	Physical	70	100	20	Normal	-	○
TM90	Substitute	Normal	Status	—	—	10	Self	-	-
TM92	Trick Room	Psychic	Status	-	-	5	Both Sides	-	-

MOVES TAUGHT BY PEOPLE
Name	Type	Kind	Pow.	Acc.	PP	Range	Long	DA

MOVES TAUGHT BY MOVE TUTORS FOR SHARDS
Name	Type	Kind	Pow.	Acc.	PP	Range	Long	DA
Signal Beam	Bug	Special	75	100	15	Normal	—	—
Uproar	Normal	Special	90	100	10	1 Random	—	—
Fire Punch	Fire	Physical	75	100	15	Normal	—	○
ThunderPunch	Electric	Physical	75	100	15	Normal	—	○
Ice Punch	Ice	Physical	75	100	15	Normal	—	○
Last Resort	Normal	Physical	140	100	5	Normal	—	○
Magic Coat	Psychic	Status	—	—	15	Self	—	—
Iron Tail	Steel	Physical	100	75	15	Normal	—	○
Zen Headbutt	Psychic	Physical	80	90	15	Normal	—	○
Snore	Normal	Special	40	100	15	Normal	—	—
Knock Off	Dark	Physical	20	100	20	Normal	—	○
Role Play	Psychic	Status	—	—	10	Normal	—	—
Helping Hand	Normal	Status	—	—	20	1 Ally	—	—
Magic Room	Psychic	Status	—	—	10	Both Sides	—	—
Wonder Room	Psychic	Status	—	—	10	Both Sides	—	—
Recycle	Normal	Status	—	—	10	Self	—	—
Trick	Psychic	Status	—	100	10	Normal	—	—
Stealth Rock	Rock	Status	—	—	20	Other Side	—	—
Sleep Talk	Normal	Status	—	—	10	Self	—	—
Skill Swap	Psychic	Status	—	—	10	Normal	—	—

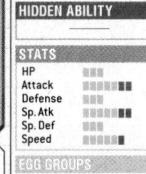

Pokémon AR Marker

482 | Azelf

Temporal Pokémon

483 Dialga

- HEIGHT: 17'09"
- WEIGHT: 1,505.8 lbs.
- GENDER: Unknown

A legendary Pokémon of Sinnoh. It is said that time flows when Dialga's heart beats.

Gender unknown

Pokémon AR Marker

TYPE Steel Dragon

ABILITY
- Pressure

HIDDEN ABILITY
- Telepathy

STATS
HP
Attack
Defense
Sp. Atk
Sp. Def
Speed

EGG GROUPS
No Egg has ever been discovered

ITEMS SOMETIMES HELD
- None

EVOLUTION
Does not evolve

HOW TO OBTAIN

Pokémon Black Version 2	Link Trade or Poké Transfer
Pokémon White Version 2	Link Trade or Poké Transfer

HOW TO OBTAIN FROM OTHER GAMES

Pokémon Diamond Version	Spear Pillar on Mt. Coronet
Pokémon Platinum Version	Spear Pillar on Mt. Coronet (after entering the Hall of Fame)

LEVEL-UP AND LEARNED MOVES

Lv.	Name	Type	Kind	Pow.	Acc.	PP	Range	Long	DA
1	DragonBreath	Dragon	Special	60	100	20	Normal	—	—
1	Scary Face	Normal	Status	—	100	10	Normal	—	—
6	Metal Claw	Steel	Physical	50	95	35	Normal	—	○
10	AncientPower	Rock	Special	60	100	5	Normal	—	—
15	Slash	Normal	Physical	70	100	20	Normal	—	○
19	Power Gem	Rock	Special	70	100	20	Normal	—	—
24	Metal Burst	Steel	Physical	—	100	10	Varies	—	—
28	Dragon Claw	Dragon	Physical	80	100	15	Normal	—	○
33	Earth Power	Ground	Special	90	100	10	Normal	—	—
37	Aura Sphere	Fighting	Special	90	—	20	Normal	○	—
42	Iron Tail	Steel	Physical	100	75	15	Normal	—	○
46	Roar of Time	Dragon	Special	150	90	5	Normal	—	—
50	Flash Cannon	Steel	Special	80	100	10	Normal	—	—

TM & HM MOVES

Lv.	Name	Type	Kind	Pow.	Acc.	PP	Range	Long	DA
TM01	Hone Claws	Dark	Status	—	—	15	Self	—	—
TM02	Dragon Claw	Dragon	Physical	80	100	15	Normal	—	○
TM05	Roar	Normal	Status	—	100	20	Normal	—	—
TM06	Toxic	Poison	Status	—	90	10	Normal	—	—
TM08	Bulk Up	Fighting	Status	—	—	20	Self	—	—
TM10	Hidden Power	Normal	Special	—	100	15	Normal	—	—
TM11	Sunny Day	Fire	Status	—	—	5	Both Sides	—	—
TM13	Ice Beam	Ice	Special	95	100	10	Normal	—	—
TM14	Blizzard	Ice	Special	120	70	5	Many Others	—	—
TM15	Hyper Beam	Normal	Special	150	90	5	Normal	—	—
TM17	Protect	Normal	Status	—	—	10	Self	—	—
TM18	Rain Dance	Water	Status	—	—	5	Both Sides	—	—
TM20	Safeguard	Normal	Status	—	—	25	Your Side	—	—
TM21	Frustration	Normal	Physical	—	100	20	Normal	—	○
TM24	Thunderbolt	Electric	Special	95	100	15	Normal	—	—
TM25	Thunder	Electric	Special	120	70	10	Normal	—	—
TM26	Earthquake	Ground	Physical	100	100	10	Adjacent	—	—
TM27	Return	Normal	Physical	—	100	20	Normal	—	○
TM31	Brick Break	Fighting	Physical	75	100	15	Normal	—	○
TM32	Double Team	Normal	Status	—	—	15	Self	—	—
TM35	Flamethrower	Fire	Special	95	100	15	Normal	—	—
TM37	Sandstorm	Rock	Status	—	—	10	Both Sides	—	—
TM38	Fire Blast	Fire	Special	120	85	5	Normal	—	—
TM39	Rock Tomb	Rock	Physical	50	80	10	Normal	—	—
TM40	Aerial Ace	Flying	Physical	60	—	20	Normal	○	○
TM42	Facade	Normal	Physical	70	100	20	Normal	—	○
TM44	Rest	Psychic	Status	—	—	10	Self	—	—
TM48	Round	Normal	Special	60	100	15	Normal	—	—
TM49	Echoed Voice	Normal	Special	40	100	15	Normal	—	—
TM50	Overheat	Fire	Special	140	90	5	Normal	—	—
TM59	Incinerate	Fire	Special	30	100	15	Many Others	—	—
TM65	Shadow Claw	Ghost	Physical	70	100	15	Normal	—	○
TM68	Giga Impact	Normal	Physical	150	90	5	Normal	—	○
TM70	Flash	Normal	Status	—	100	20	Normal	—	—
TM71	Stone Edge	Rock	Physical	100	80	5	Normal	—	—
TM73	Thunder Wave	Electric	Status	—	100	20	Normal	—	—
TM77	Psych Up	Normal	Status	—	—	10	Normal	—	—
TM78	Bulldoze	Ground	Physical	60	100	20	Adjacent	—	—
TM80	Rock Slide	Rock	Physical	75	90	10	Many Others	—	—
TM82	Dragon Tail	Dragon	Physical	60	90	10	Normal	—	○
TM87	Swagger	Normal	Status	—	90	15	Normal	—	—
TM90	Substitute	Normal	Status	—	—	10	Self	—	—
TM91	Flash Cannon	Steel	Special	80	100	10	Normal	—	—
TM92	Trick Room	Psychic	Status	—	—	5	Both Sides	—	—
TM94	Rock Smash	Fighting	Physical	40	100	15	Normal	—	○
HM01	Cut	Normal	Physical	50	95	30	Normal	—	○
HM04	Strength	Normal	Physical	80	100	15	Normal	—	○

MOVES TAUGHT BY PEOPLE

Name	Type	Kind	Pow.	Acc.	PP	Range	Long	DA
Draco Meteor	Dragon	Special	140	90	5	Normal	—	—

MOVES TAUGHT BY MOVE TUTORS FOR SHARDS

Name	Type	Kind	Pow.	Acc.	PP	Range	Long	DA
Iron Head	Steel	Physical	80	100	15	Normal	—	○
Iron Defense	Steel	Status	—	—	15	Self	—	—
Magnet Rise	Electric	Status	—	—	10	Self	—	—
Hyper Voice	Normal	Special	90	100	10	Many Others	—	—
Iron Tail	Steel	Physical	100	75	15	Normal	—	○
Earth Power	Ground	Special	90	100	10	Normal	—	—
Gravity	Psychic	Status	—	—	5	Both Sides	—	—
Dragon Pulse	Dragon	Special	90	100	10	Normal	○	—
Snore	Normal	Special	40	100	15	Normal	—	—
Stealth Rock	Rock	Status	—	—	20	Other Side	—	—
Outrage	Dragon	Physical	120	100	10	1 Random	—	○
Sleep Talk	Normal	Status	—	—	10	Self	—	—

Spatial Pokémon

484 Palkia

- HEIGHT: 13'09"
- WEIGHT: 740.8 lbs.
- GENDER: Unknown

A legendary Pokémon of Sinnoh. It is said that space becomes more stable with Palkia's every breath.

Gender unknown

Pokémon AR Marker

TYPE Water Dragon

ABILITY
- Pressure

HIDDEN ABILITY
- Telepathy

STATS
HP
Attack
Defense
Sp. Atk
Sp. Def
Speed

EGG GROUPS
No Egg has ever been discovered

ITEMS SOMETIMES HELD
- None

EVOLUTION
Does not evolve

HOW TO OBTAIN

Pokémon Black Version 2	Link Trade or Poké Transfer
Pokémon White Version 2	Link Trade or Poké Transfer

HOW TO OBTAIN FROM OTHER GAMES

Pokémon Pearl Version	Spear Pillar on Mt. Coronet
Pokémon Platinum Version	Spear Pillar on Mt. Coronet (after entering the Hall of Fame)

LEVEL-UP AND LEARNED MOVES

Lv.	Name	Type	Kind	Pow.	Acc.	PP	Range	Long	DA
1	DragonBreath	Dragon	Special	60	100	20	Normal	—	—
1	Scary Face	Normal	Status	—	100	10	Normal	—	—
6	Water Pulse	Water	Special	60	100	20	Normal	○	—
10	AncientPower	Rock	Special	60	100	5	Normal	—	—
15	Slash	Normal	Physical	70	100	20	Normal	—	○
19	Power Gem	Rock	Special	70	100	20	Normal	—	—
24	Aqua Tail	Water	Physical	90	90	10	Normal	—	○
28	Dragon Claw	Dragon	Physical	80	100	15	Normal	—	○
33	Earth Power	Ground	Special	90	100	10	Normal	—	—
37	Aura Sphere	Fighting	Special	90	—	20	Normal	○	—
42	Aqua Tail	Water	Physical	90	90	10	Normal	—	○
46	Spacial Rend	Dragon	Special	100	95	5	Normal	—	—
50	Hydro Pump	Water	Special	120	80	5	Normal	—	—

TM & HM MOVES

Lv.	Name	Type	Kind	Pow.	Acc.	PP	Range	Long	DA
TM01	Hone Claws	Dark	Status	—	—	15	Self	—	—
TM02	Dragon Claw	Dragon	Physical	80	100	15	Normal	—	○
TM05	Roar	Normal	Status	—	100	20	Normal	—	—
TM06	Toxic	Poison	Status	—	90	10	Normal	—	—
TM07	Hail	Ice	Status	—	—	10	Both Sides	—	—
TM08	Bulk Up	Fighting	Status	—	—	20	Self	—	—
TM10	Hidden Power	Normal	Special	—	100	15	Normal	—	—
TM11	Sunny Day	Fire	Status	—	—	5	Both Sides	—	—
TM13	Ice Beam	Ice	Special	95	100	10	Normal	—	—
TM14	Blizzard	Ice	Special	120	70	5	Many Others	—	—
TM15	Hyper Beam	Normal	Special	150	90	5	Normal	—	—
TM17	Protect	Normal	Status	—	—	10	Self	—	—
TM18	Rain Dance	Water	Status	—	—	5	Both Sides	—	—
TM20	Safeguard	Normal	Status	—	—	25	Your Side	—	—
TM21	Frustration	Normal	Physical	—	100	20	Normal	—	○
TM24	Thunderbolt	Electric	Special	95	100	15	Normal	—	—
TM25	Thunder	Electric	Special	120	70	10	Normal	—	—
TM26	Earthquake	Ground	Physical	100	100	10	Adjacent	—	—
TM27	Return	Normal	Physical	—	100	20	Normal	—	○
TM31	Brick Break	Fighting	Physical	75	100	15	Normal	—	○
TM32	Double Team	Normal	Status	—	—	15	Self	—	—
TM35	Flamethrower	Fire	Special	95	100	15	Normal	—	—
TM37	Sandstorm	Rock	Status	—	—	10	Both Sides	—	—
TM38	Fire Blast	Fire	Special	120	85	5	Normal	—	—
TM39	Rock Tomb	Rock	Physical	50	80	10	Normal	—	—
TM40	Aerial Ace	Flying	Physical	60	—	20	Normal	○	○
TM42	Facade	Normal	Physical	70	100	20	Normal	—	○
TM44	Rest	Psychic	Status	—	—	10	Self	—	—
TM48	Round	Normal	Special	60	100	15	Normal	—	—
TM49	Echoed Voice	Normal	Special	40	100	15	Normal	—	—
TM52	Focus Blast	Fighting	Special	120	70	5	Normal	—	—
TM56	Fling	Dark	Physical	—	100	10	Normal	—	—
TM59	Incinerate	Fire	Special	30	100	15	Many Others	—	—
TM65	Shadow Claw	Ghost	Physical	70	100	15	Normal	—	○
TM68	Giga Impact	Normal	Physical	150	90	5	Normal	—	○
TM71	Stone Edge	Rock	Physical	100	80	5	Normal	—	—
TM73	Thunder Wave	Electric	Status	—	100	20	Normal	—	—
TM77	Psych Up	Normal	Status	—	—	10	Normal	—	—
TM78	Bulldoze	Ground	Physical	60	100	20	Adjacent	—	—
TM80	Rock Slide	Rock	Physical	75	90	10	Many Others	—	—
TM82	Dragon Tail	Dragon	Physical	60	90	10	Normal	—	○
TM87	Swagger	Normal	Status	—	90	15	Normal	—	—
TM90	Substitute	Normal	Status	—	—	10	Self	—	—
TM92	Trick Room	Psychic	Status	—	—	5	Both Sides	—	—
TM94	Rock Smash	Fighting	Physical	40	100	15	Normal	—	○
HM01	Cut	Normal	Physical	50	95	30	Normal	—	○
HM03	Surf	Water	Special	95	100	15	Adjacent	—	—
HM04	Strength	Normal	Physical	80	100	15	Normal	—	○
HM06	Dive	Water	Physical	80	100	10	Normal	—	○

MOVES TAUGHT BY PEOPLE

Name	Type	Kind	Pow.	Acc.	PP	Range	Long	DA
Draco Meteor	Dragon	Special	140	90	5	Normal	—	—

MOVES TAUGHT BY MOVE TUTORS FOR SHARDS

Name	Type	Kind	Pow.	Acc.	PP	Range	Long	DA
Hyper Voice	Normal	Special	90	100	10	Many Others	—	—
Aqua Tail	Water	Physical	90	90	10	Normal	—	○
Earth Power	Ground	Special	90	100	10	Normal	—	—
Gravity	Psychic	Status	—	—	5	Both Sides	—	—
Dragon Pulse	Dragon	Special	90	100	10	Normal	○	—
Snore	Normal	Special	40	100	15	Normal	—	—
Outrage	Dragon	Physical	120	100	10	1 Random	—	○
Sleep Talk	Normal	Status	—	—	10	Self	—	—

485 Heatran
Lava Dome Pokémon

TYPE: Fire / Steel

ABILITY
- Flash Fire

HIDDEN ABILITY
—

STATS
HP
Attack
Defense
Sp. Atk
Sp. Def
Speed

EGG GROUPS
No Egg has ever been discovered

ITEMS SOMETIMES HELD
- None

- HEIGHT: 5'07"
- WEIGHT: 948.0 lbs.
- GENDER: ♂ / ♀

Its body is made of rugged steel. However, it is partially melted in spots because of its own heat.

Same form for ♂ / ♀

Pokémon AR Marker

EVOLUTION

Does not evolve

HOW TO OBTAIN

Pokémon Black Version 2	Reversal Mountain (after obtaining the Magma Stone)
Pokémon White Version 2	Reversal Mountain (after obtaining the Magma Stone)

HOW TO OBTAIN FROM OTHER GAMES

—

—

LEVEL-UP AND LEARNED MOVES

Lv.	Name	Type	Kind	Pow.	Acc.	PP	Range	Long	DA
1	AncientPower	Rock	Special	60	100	5	Normal	—	—
9	Leer	Normal	Status	—	100	30	Many Others	—	—
17	Fire Fang	Fire	Physical	65	95	15	Normal	—	○
25	Metal Sound	Steel	Status	—	85	40	Normal	—	—
33	Crunch	Dark	Physical	80	100	15	Normal	—	○
41	Scary Face	Normal	Status	—	100	10	Normal	—	—
49	Lava Plume	Fire	Special	80	100	15	Adjacent	—	—
57	Fire Spin	Fire	Special	35	85	15	Normal	—	—
65	Iron Head	Steel	Physical	80	100	15	Normal	—	○
73	Earth Power	Ground	Special	90	100	10	Normal	—	—
81	Heat Wave	Fire	Special	100	90	10	Many Others	—	—
88	Stone Edge	Rock	Physical	100	80	5	Normal	—	—
96	Magma Storm	Fire	Special	120	75	5	Normal	—	—

TM & HM MOVES

Lv.	Name	Type	Kind	Pow.	Acc.	PP	Range	Long	DA
TM05	Roar	Normal	Status	—	100	20	Normal	—	—
TM06	Toxic	Poison	Status	—	90	10	Normal	—	—
TM10	Hidden Power	Normal	Special	—	100	15	Normal	—	—
TM11	Sunny Day	Fire	Status	—	—	5	Both Sides	—	—
TM12	Taunt	Dark	Status	—	100	20	Normal	—	—
TM15	Hyper Beam	Normal	Special	150	90	5	Normal	—	—
TM17	Protect	Normal	Status	—	—	10	Self	—	—
TM21	Frustration	Normal	Physical	—	100	20	Normal	—	○
TM22	SolarBeam	Grass	Special	120	100	10	Normal	—	—
TM26	Earthquake	Ground	Physical	100	100	10	Adjacent	—	—
TM27	Return	Normal	Physical	—	100	20	Normal	—	○
TM28	Dig	Ground	Physical	80	100	10	Normal	—	○
TM32	Double Team	Normal	Status	—	—	15	Self	—	—
TM35	Flamethrower	Fire	Special	95	100	15	Normal	—	—
TM38	Fire Blast	Fire	Special	120	85	5	Normal	—	—
TM39	Rock Tomb	Rock	Physical	50	80	10	Normal	—	—
TM41	Torment	Dark	Status	—	100	15	Normal	—	—
TM42	Facade	Normal	Physical	70	100	20	Normal	—	○
TM43	Flame Charge	Fire	Physical	50	100	20	Normal	—	○
TM44	Rest	Psychic	Status	—	—	10	Self	—	—
TM45	Attract	Normal	Status	—	100	15	Normal	—	—
TM48	Round	Normal	Special	60	100	15	Normal	—	—
TM50	Overheat	Fire	Special	140	90	5	Normal	—	—
TM59	Incinerate	Fire	Special	30	100	15	Many Others	—	—
TM61	Will-O-Wisp	Fire	Status	—	75	15	Normal	—	—
TM64	Explosion	Normal	Physical	250	100	5	Adjacent	—	—
TM66	Payback	Dark	Physical	50	100	10	Normal	—	○
TM68	Giga Impact	Normal	Physical	150	90	5	Normal	—	○
TM71	Stone Edge	Rock	Physical	100	80	5	Normal	—	—
TM78	Bulldoze	Ground	Physical	60	100	20	Adjacent	—	—
TM80	Rock Slide	Rock	Physical	75	90	10	Many Others	—	—
TM87	Swagger	Normal	Status	—	90	15	Normal	—	—
TM90	Substitute	Normal	Status	—	—	10	Self	—	—
TM91	Flash Cannon	Steel	Special	80	100	10	Normal	—	—
TM94	Rock Smash	Fighting	Physical	40	100	15	Normal	—	○
HM04	Strength	Normal	Physical	80	100	15	Normal	—	○

MOVES TAUGHT BY PEOPLE

Name	Type	Kind	Pow.	Acc.	PP	Range	Long	DA

MOVES TAUGHT BY MOVE TUTORS FOR SHARDS

Name	Type	Kind	Pow.	Acc.	PP	Range	Long	DA
Bug Bite	Bug	Physical	60	100	20	Normal	—	○
Iron Head	Steel	Physical	80	100	15	Normal	—	○
Uproar	Normal	Special	90	100	10	1 Random	—	—
Iron Defense	Steel	Status	—	—	15	Self	—	—
Earth Power	Ground	Special	90	100	10	Normal	—	—
Dragon Pulse	Dragon	Special	90	100	10	Normal	○	—
Dark Pulse	Dark	Special	80	100	15	Normal	○	—
Snore	Normal	Special	40	100	15	Normal	—	—
Heat Wave	Fire	Special	100	90	10	Many Others	—	—
Stealth Rock	Rock	Status	—	—	20	Other Side	—	—
Sleep Talk	Normal	Status	—	—	10	Self	—	—

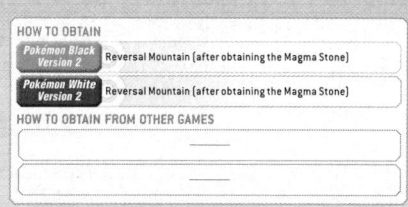

486 Regigigas
Colossal Pokémon

TYPE: Normal

ABILITY
- Slow Start

HIDDEN ABILITY
—

STATS
HP
Attack
Defense
Sp. Atk
Sp. Def
Speed

EGG GROUPS
No Egg has ever been discovered

ITEMS SOMETIMES HELD
- None

- HEIGHT: 12'02"
- WEIGHT: 925.9 lbs.
- GENDER: Unknown

It is said to have made Pokémon that look like itself from a special ice mountain, rocks, and magma.

Gender unknown

Pokémon AR Marker

EVOLUTION

Does not evolve

HOW TO OBTAIN

Pokémon Black Version 2	Go to the lowest level of Twist Mountain with Regirock, Regice, and Registeel in your party
Pokémon White Version 2	Go to the lowest level of Twist Mountain with Regirock, Regice, and Registeel in your party

HOW TO OBTAIN FROM OTHER GAMES

—

—

LEVEL-UP AND LEARNED MOVES

Lv.	Name	Type	Kind	Pow.	Acc.	PP	Range	Long	DA
1	Fire Punch	Fire	Physical	75	100	15	Normal	—	○
1	Ice Punch	Ice	Physical	75	100	15	Normal	—	○
1	ThunderPunch	Electric	Physical	75	100	15	Normal	—	○
1	Dizzy Punch	Normal	Physical	70	100	10	Normal	—	○
1	Knock Off	Dark	Physical	20	100	20	Normal	—	○
1	Confuse Ray	Ghost	Status	—	100	10	Normal	—	—
1	Foresight	Normal	Status	—	—	40	Normal	—	—
25	Revenge	Fighting	Physical	60	100	10	Normal	—	○
40	Wide Guard	Rock	Status	—	—	10	Your Side	—	—
50	Zen Headbutt	Psychic	Physical	80	90	15	Normal	—	○
65	Payback	Dark	Physical	50	100	10	Normal	—	○
75	Crush Grip	Normal	Physical	—	100	5	Normal	—	○
90	Heavy Slam	Steel	Physical	—	100	10	Normal	—	○
100	Giga Impact	Normal	Physical	150	90	5	Normal	—	○

TM & HM MOVES

Lv.	Name	Type	Kind	Pow.	Acc.	PP	Range	Long	DA
TM06	Toxic	Poison	Status	—	90	10	Normal	—	—
TM10	Hidden Power	Normal	Special	—	100	15	Normal	—	—
TM11	Sunny Day	Fire	Status	—	—	5	Both Sides	—	—
TM15	Hyper Beam	Normal	Special	150	90	5	Normal	—	—
TM18	Rain Dance	Water	Status	—	—	5	Both Sides	—	—
TM20	Safeguard	Normal	Status	—	—	25	Your Side	—	—
TM21	Frustration	Normal	Physical	—	100	20	Normal	—	○
TM23	Smack Down	Rock	Physical	50	100	15	Normal	—	—
TM24	Thunderbolt	Electric	Special	95	100	15	Normal	—	—
TM25	Thunder	Electric	Special	120	70	10	Normal	—	—
TM26	Earthquake	Ground	Physical	100	100	10	Adjacent	—	—
TM27	Return	Normal	Physical	—	100	20	Normal	—	○
TM31	Brick Break	Fighting	Physical	75	100	15	Normal	—	○
TM32	Double Team	Normal	Status	—	—	15	Self	—	—
TM39	Rock Tomb	Rock	Physical	50	80	10	Normal	—	—
TM40	Aerial Ace	Flying	Physical	60	—	20	Normal	○	○
TM42	Facade	Normal	Physical	70	100	20	Normal	—	○
TM48	Round	Normal	Special	60	100	15	Normal	—	—
TM52	Focus Blast	Fighting	Special	120	70	5	Normal	—	—
TM56	Fling	Dark	Physical	—	100	10	Normal	—	—
TM66	Payback	Dark	Physical	50	100	10	Normal	—	○
TM67	Retaliate	Normal	Physical	70	100	5	Normal	—	○
TM68	Giga Impact	Normal	Physical	150	90	5	Normal	—	○
TM69	Rock Polish	Rock	Status	—	—	20	Self	—	—
TM71	Stone Edge	Rock	Physical	100	80	5	Normal	—	—
TM73	Thunder Wave	Electric	Status	—	100	20	Normal	—	—
TM77	Psych Up	Normal	Status	—	—	10	Normal	—	—
TM78	Bulldoze	Ground	Physical	60	100	20	Adjacent	—	—
TM80	Rock Slide	Rock	Physical	75	90	10	Many Others	—	—
TM87	Swagger	Normal	Status	—	90	15	Normal	—	—
TM90	Substitute	Normal	Status	—	—	10	Self	—	—
TM94	Rock Smash	Fighting	Physical	40	100	15	Normal	—	○
HM04	Strength	Normal	Physical	80	100	15	Normal	—	○

MOVES TAUGHT BY PEOPLE

Name	Type	Kind	Pow.	Acc.	PP	Range	Long	DA

MOVES TAUGHT BY MOVE TUTORS FOR SHARDS

Name	Type	Kind	Pow.	Acc.	PP	Range	Long	DA
Iron Head	Steel	Physical	80	100	15	Normal	—	○
Fire Punch	Fire	Physical	75	100	15	Normal	—	○
ThunderPunch	Electric	Physical	75	100	15	Normal	—	○
Ice Punch	Ice	Physical	75	100	15	Normal	—	○
Block	Normal	Status	—	—	5	Normal	—	—
Icy Wind	Ice	Special	55	95	15	Many Others	—	—
Earth Power	Ground	Special	90	100	10	Normal	—	—
Zen Headbutt	Psychic	Physical	80	90	15	Normal	—	○
Superpower	Fighting	Physical	120	100	5	Normal	—	○
Gravity	Psychic	Status	—	—	5	Both Sides	—	—
Snore	Normal	Special	40	100	15	Normal	—	—
Knock Off	Dark	Physical	20	100	20	Normal	—	○
Drain Punch	Fighting	Physical	75	100	10	Normal	—	○
Sleep Talk	Normal	Status	—	—	10	Self	—	—

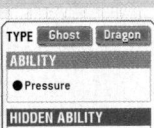

487 Giratina (Altered Forme)
Renegade Pokémon

TYPE Ghost　Dragon

ABILITY
● Pressure

HIDDEN ABILITY
● Telepathy

● HEIGHT: 14'09"
● WEIGHT: 1,653.5 lbs.
● GENDER: Unknown

It was banished for its violence. It silently gazed upon the old world from the Distortion World.

Gender unknown

STATS
HP
Attack
Defense
Sp. Atk
Sp. Def
Speed

EGG GROUPS
No Egg has ever been discovered

ITEMS SOMETIMES HELD
● None

EVOLUTION
Does not evolve

HOW TO OBTAIN
| Pokémon Black Version 2 | Link Trade or Poké Transfer |
| Pokémon White Version 2 | Link Trade or Poké Transfer |

HOW TO OBTAIN FROM OTHER GAMES
| Pokémon Diamond Version | Turnback Cave |
| Pokémon Pearl Version | Turnback Cave |

LEVEL-UP AND LEARNED MOVES

Lv.	Name	Type	Kind	Pow.	Acc.	PP	Range	Long	DA
1	DragonBreath	Dragon	Special	60	100	20	Normal	—	—
1	Scary Face	Normal	Status	—	100	10	Normal	—	—
6	Ominous Wind	Ghost	Special	60	100	5	Normal	—	—
10	AncientPower	Rock	Special	60	100	5	Normal	—	—
15	Slash	Normal	Physical	70	100	20	Normal	—	○
19	Shadow Sneak	Ghost	Physical	40	100	30	Normal	—	○
24	Destiny Bond	Ghost	Status	—	—	5	Self	—	—
28	Dragon Claw	Dragon	Physical	80	100	15	Normal	—	○
33	Earth Power	Ground	Special	90	100	10	Normal	—	—
37	Aura Sphere	Fighting	Special	90	—	20	Normal	○	—
42	Shadow Claw	Ghost	Physical	70	100	15	Normal	—	○
46	Shadow Force	Ghost	Physical	120	100	5	Normal	—	○
50	Hex	Ghost	Special	50	100	10	Normal	—	—

TM & HM MOVES

Lv.	Name	Type	Kind	Pow.	Acc.	PP	Range	Long	DA
TM01	Hone Claws	Dark	Status	—	—	15	Self	—	—
TM02	Dragon Claw	Dragon	Physical	80	100	15	Normal	—	○
TM04	Calm Mind	Psychic	Status	—	—	20	Self	—	—
TM05	Roar	Normal	Status	—	100	20	Normal	—	—
TM06	Toxic	Poison	Status	—	90	10	Normal	—	—
TM10	Hidden Power	Normal	Special	—	100	15	Normal	—	—
TM11	Sunny Day	Fire	Status	—	—	5	Both Sides	—	—
TM15	Hyper Beam	Normal	Special	150	90	5	Normal	—	—
TM17	Protect	Normal	Status	—	—	10	Self	—	—
TM18	Rain Dance	Water	Status	—	—	5	Both Sides	—	—
TM19	Telekinesis	Psychic	Status	—	—	15	Normal	—	—
TM20	Safeguard	Normal	Status	—	—	25	Your Side	—	—
TM21	Frustration	Normal	Physical	—	100	20	Normal	—	○
TM24	Thunderbolt	Electric	Special	95	100	15	Normal	—	—
TM25	Thunder	Electric	Special	120	70	10	Normal	—	—
TM26	Earthquake	Ground	Physical	100	100	10	Adjacent	—	—
TM27	Return	Normal	Physical	—	100	20	Normal	—	○
TM29	Psychic	Psychic	Special	90	100	10	Normal	—	—
TM30	Shadow Ball	Ghost	Special	80	100	15	Normal	—	—
TM32	Double Team	Normal	Status	—	—	15	Self	—	—
TM40	Aerial Ace	Flying	Physical	60	—	20	Normal	○	○
TM42	Facade	Normal	Physical	70	100	20	Normal	—	—
TM44	Rest	Psychic	Status	—	—	10	Self	—	—
TM48	Round	Normal	Special	60	100	15	Normal	—	—
TM49	Echoed Voice	Normal	Special	40	100	15	Normal	—	—
TM53	Energy Ball	Grass	Special	80	100	10	Normal	—	—
TM57	Charge Beam	Electric	Special	50	90	10	Normal	—	—
TM61	Will-O-Wisp	Fire	Status	—	75	15	Normal	—	—
TM65	Shadow Claw	Ghost	Physical	70	100	15	Normal	—	○
TM66	Payback	Dark	Physical	50	100	10	Normal	—	—
TM68	Giga Impact	Normal	Physical	150	90	5	Normal	—	—
TM71	Stone Edge	Rock	Physical	100	80	5	Normal	—	—
TM73	Thunder Wave	Electric	Status	—	100	20	Normal	—	—
TM77	Psych Up	Normal	Status	—	—	10	Normal	—	—
TM78	Bulldoze	Ground	Physical	60	100	20	Adjacent	—	—
TM82	Dragon Tail	Dragon	Physical	60	90	10	Normal	—	—
TM85	Dream Eater	Psychic	Special	100	100	15	Normal	—	—
TM87	Swagger	Normal	Status	—	90	15	Normal	—	—
TM90	Substitute	Normal	Status	—	—	10	Self	—	—
TM94	Rock Smash	Fighting	Physical	40	100	15	Normal	—	○

Lv.	Name	Type	Kind	Pow.	Acc.	PP	Range	Long	DA
HM01	Cut	Normal	Physical	50	95	30	Normal	—	○
HM02	Fly	Flying	Physical	90	95	15	Normal	○	○
HM04	Strength	Normal	Physical	80	100	15	Normal	—	○

MOVES TAUGHT BY PEOPLE

Name	Type	Kind	Pow.	Acc.	PP	Range	Long	DA
Draco Meteor	Dragon	Special	140	90	5	Normal	—	—

MOVES TAUGHT BY MOVE TUTORS FOR SHARDS

Name	Type	Kind	Pow.	Acc.	PP	Range	Long	DA
Iron Head	Steel	Physical	80	100	15	Normal	—	○
Hyper Voice	Normal	Special	90	100	10	Many Others	—	—
Icy Wind	Ice	Special	55	95	15	Many Others	—	—
Iron Tail	Steel	Physical	100	75	15	Normal	—	○
Aqua Tail	Water	Physical	90	90	10	Normal	—	—
Earth Power	Ground	Special	90	100	10	Normal	—	—
Gravity	Psychic	Status	—	—	5	Both Sides	—	—
Dragon Pulse	Dragon	Special	90	100	10	Normal	○	—
Dark Pulse	Dark	Special	80	100	15	Normal	—	—
Snore	Normal	Special	40	100	15	Normal	—	—
Pain Split	Normal	Status	—	—	20	Normal	—	—
Spite	Ghost	Status	—	100	10	Normal	—	—
Outrage	Dragon	Physical	120	100	10	1 Random	—	○
Sleep Talk	Normal	Status	—	—	10	Self	—	—

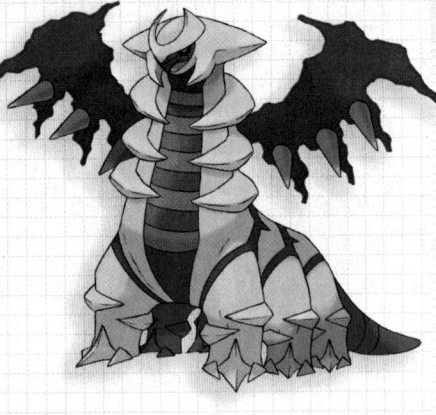

Pokémon AR Marker

---

487 Giratina (Origin Forme)
Renegade Pokémon

TYPE Ghost　Dragon

ABILITY
● Levitate

HIDDEN ABILITY
● Telepathy

● HEIGHT: 22'08"
● WEIGHT: 1,433.0 lbs.
● GENDER: Unknown

It was banished for its violence. It silently gazed upon the old world from the Distortion World.

Gender unknown

STATS
HP
Attack
Defense
Sp. Atk
Sp. Def
Speed

EGG GROUPS
No Egg has ever been discovered

ITEMS SOMETIMES HELD
● None

EVOLUTION
Does not evolve

HOW TO OBTAIN
| Pokémon Black Version 2 | Have Giratina (Altered Forme) hold the Griseous Orb |
| Pokémon White Version 2 | Have Giratina (Altered Forme) hold the Griseous Orb |

HOW TO OBTAIN FROM OTHER GAMES
| —— |
| —— |

LEVEL-UP AND LEARNED MOVES

Lv.	Name	Type	Kind	Pow.	Acc.	PP	Range	Long	DA
1	DragonBreath	Dragon	Special	60	100	20	Normal	—	—
1	Scary Face	Normal	Status	—	100	10	Normal	—	—
6	Ominous Wind	Ghost	Special	60	100	5	Normal	—	—
10	AncientPower	Rock	Special	60	100	5	Normal	—	—
15	Slash	Normal	Physical	70	100	20	Normal	—	○
19	Shadow Sneak	Ghost	Physical	40	100	30	Normal	—	○
24	Destiny Bond	Ghost	Status	—	—	5	Self	—	—
28	Dragon Claw	Dragon	Physical	80	100	15	Normal	—	○
33	Earth Power	Ground	Special	90	100	10	Normal	—	—
37	Aura Sphere	Fighting	Special	90	—	20	Normal	○	—
42	Shadow Claw	Ghost	Physical	70	100	15	Normal	—	○
46	Shadow Force	Ghost	Physical	120	100	5	Normal	—	○
50	Hex	Ghost	Special	50	100	10	Normal	—	—

TM & HM MOVES

Lv.	Name	Type	Kind	Pow.	Acc.	PP	Range	Long	DA
TM01	Hone Claws	Dark	Status	—	—	15	Self	—	—
TM02	Dragon Claw	Dragon	Physical	80	100	15	Normal	—	○
TM04	Calm Mind	Psychic	Status	—	—	20	Self	—	—
TM05	Roar	Normal	Status	—	100	20	Normal	—	—
TM06	Toxic	Poison	Status	—	90	10	Normal	—	—
TM10	Hidden Power	Normal	Special	—	100	15	Normal	—	—
TM11	Sunny Day	Fire	Status	—	—	5	Both Sides	—	—
TM15	Hyper Beam	Normal	Special	150	90	5	Normal	—	—
TM17	Protect	Normal	Status	—	—	10	Self	—	—
TM18	Rain Dance	Water	Status	—	—	5	Both Sides	—	—
TM19	Telekinesis	Psychic	Status	—	—	15	Normal	—	—
TM20	Safeguard	Normal	Status	—	—	25	Your Side	—	—
TM21	Frustration	Normal	Physical	—	100	20	Normal	—	—
TM24	Thunderbolt	Electric	Special	95	100	15	Normal	—	—
TM25	Thunder	Electric	Special	120	70	10	Normal	—	—
TM26	Earthquake	Ground	Physical	100	100	10	Adjacent	—	—
TM27	Return	Normal	Physical	—	100	20	Normal	—	○
TM29	Psychic	Psychic	Special	90	100	10	Normal	—	—
TM30	Shadow Ball	Ghost	Special	80	100	15	Normal	—	—
TM32	Double Team	Normal	Status	—	—	15	Self	—	—
TM40	Aerial Ace	Flying	Physical	60	—	20	Normal	○	○
TM42	Facade	Normal	Physical	70	100	20	Normal	—	—
TM44	Rest	Psychic	Status	—	—	10	Self	—	—
TM48	Round	Normal	Special	60	100	15	Normal	—	—
TM49	Echoed Voice	Normal	Special	40	100	15	Normal	—	—
TM53	Energy Ball	Grass	Special	80	100	10	Normal	—	—
TM57	Charge Beam	Electric	Special	50	90	10	Normal	—	—
TM61	Will-O-Wisp	Fire	Status	—	75	15	Normal	—	—
TM65	Shadow Claw	Ghost	Physical	70	100	15	Normal	—	○
TM66	Payback	Dark	Physical	50	100	10	Normal	—	—
TM68	Giga Impact	Normal	Physical	150	90	5	Normal	—	—
TM71	Stone Edge	Rock	Physical	100	80	5	Normal	—	—
TM73	Thunder Wave	Electric	Status	—	100	20	Normal	—	—
TM77	Psych Up	Normal	Status	—	—	10	Normal	—	—
TM78	Bulldoze	Ground	Physical	60	100	20	Adjacent	—	—
TM82	Dragon Tail	Dragon	Physical	60	90	10	Normal	—	—
TM85	Dream Eater	Psychic	Special	100	100	15	Normal	—	—
TM87	Swagger	Normal	Status	—	90	15	Normal	—	—
TM90	Substitute	Normal	Status	—	—	10	Self	—	—
TM94	Rock Smash	Fighting	Physical	40	100	15	Normal	—	○

Lv.	Name	Type	Kind	Pow.	Acc.	PP	Range	Long	DA
HM01	Cut	Normal	Physical	50	95	30	Normal	—	○
HM02	Fly	Flying	Physical	90	95	15	Normal	○	○
HM04	Strength	Normal	Physical	80	100	15	Normal	—	○

MOVES TAUGHT BY PEOPLE

Name	Type	Kind	Pow.	Acc.	PP	Range	Long	DA
Draco Meteor	Dragon	Special	140	90	5	Normal	—	—

MOVES TAUGHT BY MOVE TUTORS FOR SHARDS

Name	Type	Kind	Pow.	Acc.	PP	Range	Long	DA
Iron Head	Steel	Physical	80	100	15	Normal	—	○
Magic Coat	Psychic	Status	—	—	15	Self	—	—
Hyper Voice	Normal	Special	90	100	10	Many Others	—	—
Icy Wind	Ice	Special	55	95	15	Many Others	—	—
Iron Tail	Steel	Physical	100	75	15	Normal	—	○
Aqua Tail	Water	Physical	90	90	10	Normal	—	—
Earth Power	Ground	Special	90	100	10	Normal	—	—
Gravity	Psychic	Status	—	—	5	Both Sides	—	—
Dragon Pulse	Dragon	Special	90	100	10	Normal	○	—
Dark Pulse	Dark	Special	80	100	15	Normal	—	—
Snore	Normal	Special	40	100	15	Normal	—	—
Tailwind	Flying	Status	—	—	30	Your Side	—	—
Spite	Ghost	Status	—	100	10	Normal	—	—
Outrage	Dragon	Physical	120	100	10	1 Random	—	○
Sleep Talk	Normal	Status	—	—	10	Self	—	—

Pokémon AR Marker

488 Cresselia
Lunar Pokémon

TYPE Psychic

ABILITY
● Levitate

HIDDEN ABILITY

- HEIGHT: 4'11"
- WEIGHT: 188.7 lbs.
- GENDER: ♀

On nights around the quarter moon, the aurora from its tail extends and undulates beautifully.

STATS
HP	
Attack	
Defense	
Sp. Atk	
Sp. Def	
Speed	

EGG GROUPS
No Egg has ever been discovered

ITEMS SOMETIMES HELD
● None

♀

EVOLUTION
Does not evolve

HOW TO OBTAIN
Pokémon Black Version 2	Marvelous Bridge (after obtaining the Lunar Wing)
Pokémon White Version 2	Marvelous Bridge (after obtaining the Lunar Wing)

HOW TO OBTAIN FROM OTHER GAMES
—
—

LEVEL-UP AND LEARNED MOVES
Lv.	Name	Type	Kind	Pow.	Acc.	PP	Range	Long	DA
1	Confusion	Psychic	Special	50	100	25	Normal	—	—
1	Double Team	Normal	Status	—	—	15	Self	—	—
11	Safeguard	Normal	Status	—	—	25	Your Side	—	—
20	Mist	Ice	Status	—	—	30	Your Side	—	—
29	Aurora Beam	Ice	Special	65	100	20	Normal	—	—
38	Future Sight	Psychic	Special	100	100	10	Normal	—	—
47	Slash	Normal	Physical	70	100	20	Normal	—	○
57	Moonlight	Normal	Status	—	—	5	Self	—	—
66	Psycho Cut	Psychic	Physical	70	100	20	Normal	—	—
75	Psycho Shift	Psychic	Status	—	90	10	Normal	—	—
84	Lunar Dance	Psychic	Status	—	—	10	Self	—	—
93	Psychic	Psychic	Special	90	100	10	Normal	—	—

TM & HM MOVES
Lv.	Name	Type	Kind	Pow.	Acc.	PP	Range	Long	DA
TM03	Psyshock	Psychic	Special	80	100	10	Normal	—	—
TM04	Calm Mind	Psychic	Status	—	—	20	Self	—	—
TM06	Toxic	Poison	Status	—	90	10	Normal	—	—
TM10	Hidden Power	Normal	Special	—	100	15	Normal	—	—
TM11	Sunny Day	Fire	Status	—	—	5	Both Sides	—	—
TM13	Ice Beam	Ice	Special	95	100	10	Normal	—	—
TM15	Hyper Beam	Normal	Special	150	90	5	Normal	—	—
TM16	Light Screen	Psychic	Status	—	—	30	Your Side	—	—
TM17	Protect	Normal	Status	—	—	10	Self	—	—
TM18	Rain Dance	Water	Status	—	—	5	Both Sides	—	—
TM19	Telekinesis	Psychic	Status	—	—	15	Normal	—	—
TM20	Safeguard	Normal	Status	—	—	25	Your Side	—	—
TM21	Frustration	Normal	Physical	—	100	20	Normal	—	○
TM22	SolarBeam	Grass	Special	120	100	10	Normal	—	—
TM27	Return	Normal	Physical	—	100	20	Normal	—	○
TM29	Psychic	Psychic	Special	90	100	10	Normal	—	—
TM30	Shadow Ball	Ghost	Special	80	100	15	Normal	—	—
TM32	Double Team	Normal	Status	—	—	15	Self	—	—
TM33	Reflect	Psychic	Status	—	—	20	Your Side	—	—
TM42	Facade	Normal	Physical	70	100	20	Normal	—	○
TM44	Rest	Psychic	Status	—	—	10	Self	—	—
TM45	Attract	Normal	Status	—	100	15	Normal	—	—
TM48	Round	Normal	Special	60	100	15	Normal	—	—
TM53	Energy Ball	Grass	Special	80	100	10	Normal	—	—
TM57	Charge Beam	Electric	Special	50	90	10	Normal	—	—
TM68	Giga Impact	Normal	Physical	150	90	5	Normal	—	○
TM70	Flash	Normal	Status	—	100	20	Normal	—	—
TM73	Thunder Wave	Electric	Status	—	100	20	Normal	—	—
TM77	Psych Up	Normal	Status	—	—	10	Self	—	—
TM85	Dream Eater	Psychic	Special	100	100	15	Normal	—	—
TM86	Grass Knot	Grass	Special	—	100	20	Normal	—	○
TM87	Swagger	Normal	Status	—	90	15	Normal	—	—
TM90	Substitute	Normal	Status	—	—	10	Self	—	—
TM92	Trick Room	Psychic	Status	—	—	5	Both Sides	—	—

MOVES TAUGHT BY PEOPLE
Name	Type	Kind	Pow.	Acc.	PP	Range	Long	DA

MOVES TAUGHT BY MOVE TUTORS FOR SHARDS
Name	Type	Kind	Pow.	Acc.	PP	Range	Long	DA
Signal Beam	Bug	Special	75	100	15	Normal	—	—
Magic Coat	Psychic	Status	—	—	15	Self	—	—
Icy Wind	Ice	Special	55	95	15	Many Others	—	—
Zen Headbutt	Psychic	Physical	80	90	15	Normal	—	○
Gravity	Psychic	Status	—	—	5	Both Sides	—	—
Snore	Normal	Special	40	100	15	Normal	—	—
Helping Hand	Normal	Status	—	—	20	1 Ally	—	—
Magic Room	Psychic	Status	—	—	10	Both Sides	—	—
Recycle	Normal	Status	—	—	10	Self	—	—
Trick	Psychic	Status	—	100	10	Normal	—	—
Sleep Talk	Normal	Status	—	—	10	Self	—	—
Skill Swap	Psychic	Status	—	—	10	Normal	—	—

Pokémon AR Marker

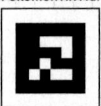

---

489 Phione
Sea Drifter Pokémon

TYPE Water

ABILITY
● Hydration

HIDDEN ABILITY

- HEIGHT: 1'04"
- WEIGHT: 6.8 lbs.
- GENDER: Unknown

It drifts in warm seas. It always returns to where it was born, no matter how far it may have drifted.

STATS
HP	
Attack	
Defense	
Sp. Atk	
Sp. Def	
Speed	

EGG GROUPS
Water ❶/Fairy

Gender unknown

EVOLUTION
Does not evolve

HOW TO OBTAIN
Pokémon Black Version 2	Link Trade or Poké Transfer
Pokémon White Version 2	Link Trade or Poké Transfer

HOW TO OBTAIN FROM OTHER GAMES
Leave a Manaphy ◆ at the Pokémon Day Care and hatch the Egg that is found
Leave a Manaphy ◆ at the Pokémon Day Care and hatch the Egg that is found

LEVEL-UP AND LEARNED MOVES
Lv.	Name	Type	Kind	Pow.	Acc.	PP	Range	Long	DA
1	Bubble	Water	Special	20	100	30	Many Others	—	—
1	Water Sport	Water	Status	—	—	15	Both Sides	—	—
9	Charm	Normal	Status	—	100	20	Normal	—	—
16	Supersonic	Normal	Status	—	55	20	Normal	—	—
24	BubbleBeam	Water	Special	65	100	20	Normal	—	—
31	Acid Armor	Poison	Status	—	—	40	Self	—	—
39	Whirlpool	Water	Special	35	85	15	Normal	—	—
46	Water Pulse	Water	Special	60	100	20	Normal	○	—
54	Aqua Ring	Water	Status	—	—	20	Self	—	—
61	Dive	Water	Physical	80	100	10	Normal	—	○
69	Rain Dance	Water	Status	—	—	5	Both Sides	—	—

TM & HM MOVES
Lv.	Name	Type	Kind	Pow.	Acc.	PP	Range	Long	DA
TM06	Toxic	Poison	Status	—	90	10	Normal	—	—
TM07	Hail	Ice	Status	—	—	10	Both Sides	—	—
TM10	Hidden Power	Normal	Special	—	100	15	Normal	—	—
TM13	Ice Beam	Ice	Special	95	100	10	Normal	—	—
TM14	Blizzard	Ice	Special	120	70	5	Many Others	—	—
TM17	Protect	Normal	Status	—	—	10	Self	—	—
TM18	Rain Dance	Water	Status	—	—	5	Both Sides	—	—
TM20	Safeguard	Normal	Status	—	—	25	Your Side	—	—
TM21	Frustration	Normal	Physical	—	100	20	Normal	—	○
TM27	Return	Normal	Physical	—	100	20	Normal	—	○
TM32	Double Team	Normal	Status	—	—	15	Self	—	—
TM42	Facade	Normal	Physical	70	100	20	Normal	—	○
TM44	Rest	Psychic	Status	—	—	10	Self	—	—
TM48	Round	Normal	Special	60	100	15	Normal	—	—
TM55	Scald	Water	Special	80	100	15	Normal	—	—
TM56	Fling	Dark	Physical	—	100	10	Normal	—	—
TM77	Psych Up	Normal	Status	—	—	10	Self	—	—
TM86	Grass Knot	Grass	Special	—	100	20	Normal	—	○
TM87	Swagger	Normal	Status	—	90	15	Normal	—	—
TM89	U-turn	Bug	Physical	70	100	20	Normal	—	○
TM90	Substitute	Normal	Status	—	—	10	Self	—	—
HM03	Surf	Water	Special	95	100	15	Adjacent	—	—
HM05	Waterfall	Water	Physical	80	100	15	Normal	—	○
HM06	Dive	Water	Physical	80	100	10	Normal	—	○

MOVES TAUGHT BY PEOPLE
Name	Type	Kind	Pow.	Acc.	PP	Range	Long	DA

MOVES TAUGHT BY MOVE TUTORS FOR SHARDS
Name	Type	Kind	Pow.	Acc.	PP	Range	Long	DA
Covet	Normal	Physical	60	100	40	Normal	—	—
Bounce	Flying	Physical	85	85	5	Normal	○	○
Signal Beam	Bug	Special	75	100	15	Normal	—	—
Uproar	Normal	Special	90	100	10	1 Random	—	—
Last Resort	Normal	Physical	140	100	5	Normal	—	○
Icy Wind	Ice	Special	55	95	15	Many Others	—	—
Snore	Normal	Special	40	100	15	Normal	—	—
Heal Bell	Normal	Status	—	—	5	Your Party	—	—
Knock Off	Dark	Physical	20	100	20	Normal	—	○
Helping Hand	Normal	Status	—	—	20	1 Ally	—	—
Sleep Talk	Normal	Status	—	—	10	Self	—	—

EGG MOVES
Name	Type	Kind	Pow.	Acc.	PP	Range	Long	DA

Pokémon AR Marker

◆ Manaphy is only available through special distribution events. Check www.pokemon.com for the latest information on how to catch this Pokémon.

490 Manaphy

Seafaring Pokémon

TYPE Water

ABILITY
● Hydration

HIDDEN ABILITY
—

STATS
HP
Attack
Defense
Sp. Atk
Sp. Def
Speed

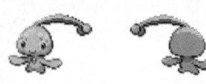

EGG GROUPS
Water ❶ /Fairy

● HEIGHT: 1'00"
● WEIGHT: 3.1 lbs.
● GENDER: Unknown

It is born with a wondrous power that lets it bond with any kind of Pokémon.

Gender unknown

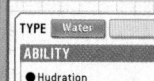

EVOLUTION

Does not evolve

HOW TO OBTAIN

Only available through special distribution events. Check www.pokemon.com for the latest information on how to catch this Pokémon.

Pokémon AR Marker

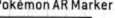

LEVEL-UP AND LEARNED MOVES

Lv.	Name	Type	Kind	Pow.	Acc.	PP	Range	Long	DA
1	Tail Glow	Bug	Status	—	—	20	Self	—	—
1	Bubble	Water	Special	20	100	30	Many Others	—	—
1	Water Sport	Water	Status	—	—	15	Both Sides	—	—
9	Charm	Normal	Status	—	100	20	Normal	—	—
16	Supersonic	Normal	Status	—	55	20	Normal	—	—
24	BubbleBeam	Water	Special	65	100	20	Normal	—	—
31	Acid Armor	Poison	Status	—	—	40	Self	—	—
39	Whirlpool	Water	Special	35	85	15	Normal	—	—
46	Water Pulse	Water	Special	60	100	20	Normal	○	—
54	Aqua Ring	Water	Status	—	—	20	Self	—	—
61	Dive	Water	Physical	80	100	10	Normal	—	○
69	Rain Dance	Water	Status	—	—	5	Both Sides	—	—
76	Heart Swap	Psychic	Status	—	—	10	Normal	—	—

TM & HM MOVES

Lv.	Name	Type	Kind	Pow.	Acc.	PP	Range	Long	DA
TM04	Calm Mind	Psychic	Status	—	—	20	Self	—	—
TM06	Toxic	Poison	Status	—	90	10	Normal	—	—
TM07	Hail	Ice	Status	—	—	10	Both Sides	—	—
TM10	Hidden Power	Normal	Special	—	100	15	Normal	—	—
TM13	Ice Beam	Ice	Special	95	100	10	Normal	—	—
TM14	Blizzard	Ice	Special	120	70	5	Many Others	—	—
TM15	Hyper Beam	Normal	Special	150	90	5	Normal	—	—
TM16	Light Screen	Psychic	Status	—	—	30	Your Side	—	—
TM17	Protect	Normal	Status	—	—	10	Self	—	—
TM18	Rain Dance	Water	Status	—	—	5	Both Sides	—	—
TM20	Safeguard	Normal	Status	—	—	25	Your Side	—	—
TM21	Frustration	Normal	Physical	—	100	20	Normal	—	○
TM27	Return	Normal	Physical	—	100	20	Normal	—	○
TM29	Psychic	Psychic	Special	90	100	10	Normal	—	—
TM30	Shadow Ball	Ghost	Special	80	100	15	Normal	—	—
TM32	Double Team	Normal	Status	—	—	15	Self	—	—
TM33	Reflect	Psychic	Status	—	—	20	Your Side	—	—
TM42	Facade	Normal	Physical	70	100	20	Normal	—	—
TM44	Rest	Psychic	Status	—	—	10	Self	—	—
TM48	Round	Normal	Special	60	100	15	Normal	—	—
TM53	Energy Ball	Grass	Special	80	100	10	Normal	—	—
TM55	Scald	Water	Special	80	100	15	Normal	—	—
TM56	Fling	Dark	Physical	—	100	10	Normal	—	○
TM68	Giga Impact	Normal	Physical	150	90	5	Normal	—	—
TM70	Flash	Normal	Status	—	100	20	Normal	—	—
TM77	Psych Up	Normal	Status	—	—	10	Normal	—	—
TM86	Grass Knot	Grass	Special	—	100	20	Normal	—	—
TM87	Swagger	Normal	Status	—	90	15	Normal	—	—
TM89	U-turn	Bug	Physical	70	100	20	Normal	—	—
TM90	Substitute	Normal	Status	—	—	10	Self	—	—
HM03	Surf	Water	Special	95	100	15	Adjacent	—	—
HM05	Waterfall	Water	Physical	80	100	15	Normal	—	○
HM06	Dive	Water	Physical	80	100	10	Normal	—	○

MOVES TAUGHT BY PEOPLE

Name	Type	Kind	Pow.	Acc.	PP	Range	Long	DA

MOVES TAUGHT BY MOVE TUTORS FOR SHARDS

Name	Type	Kind	Pow.	Acc.	PP	Range	Long	DA
Covet	Normal	Physical	60	100	40	Normal	—	—
Bounce	Flying	Physical	85	85	5	Normal	○	○
Signal Beam	Bug	Special	75	100	15	Normal	—	—
Uproar	Normal	Special	90	100	10	1 Random	—	—
Last Resort	Normal	Physical	140	100	5	Normal	—	—
Icy Wind	Ice	Special	55	95	15	Many Others	—	—
Snore	Normal	Special	40	100	15	Normal	—	—
Heal Bell	Normal	Status	—	—	5	Your Party	—	—
Knock Off	Dark	Physical	20	100	20	Normal	—	—
Helping Hand	Normal	Status	—	—	20	1 Ally	—	—
Sleep Talk	Normal	Status	—	—	10	Self	—	—
Skill Swap	Psychic	Status	—	—	10	Normal	—	—

---

491 Darkrai

Pitch-Black Pokémon

TYPE Dark

ABILITIES
● Bad Dreams

HIDDEN ABILITY
—

STATS
HP
Attack
Defense
Sp. Atk
Sp. Def
Speed

EGG GROUPS
No Egg has ever been discovered

● HEIGHT: 4'11"
● WEIGHT: 111.3 lbs.
● GENDER: Unknown

To protect itself, it afflicts those around it with nightmares. However, it means no harm.

Gender unknown

EVOLUTION

Does not evolve

HOW TO OBTAIN

Only available through special distribution events. Check www.pokemon.com for the latest information on how to catch this Pokémon.

Pokémon AR Marker

LEVEL-UP AND LEARNED MOVES

Lv.	Name	Type	Kind	Pow.	Acc.	PP	Range	Long	DA		Lv.	Name	Type	Kind	Pow.	Acc.	PP	Range	Long	DA
1	Ominous Wind	Ghost	Special	60	100	5	Normal	—	—		TM81	X-Scissor	Bug	Physical	80	100	15	Normal	—	—
1	Disable	Normal	Status	—	100	20	Normal	—	—		TM84	Poison Jab	Poison	Physical	80	100	20	Normal	—	○
11	Quick Attack	Normal	Physical	40	100	30	Normal	—	—		TM85	Dream Eater	Psychic	Special	100	100	15	Normal	—	—
20	Hypnosis	Psychic	Status	—	60	20	Normal	—	—		TM87	Swagger	Normal	Status	—	90	15	Normal	—	—
29	Faint Attack	Dark	Physical	60	—	20	Normal	—	○		TM90	Substitute	Normal	Status	—	—	10	Self	—	—
38	Nightmare	Ghost	Status	—	100	15	Normal	—	—		TM94	Rock Smash	Fighting	Physical	40	100	15	Normal	—	○
47	Double Team	Normal	Status	—	—	15	Self	—	—		TM95	Snarl	Dark	Special	55	95	15	Many Others	—	—
57	Haze	Ice	Status	—	—	30	Both Sides	—	—		HM01	Cut	Normal	Physical	50	95	30	Normal	—	—
66	Dark Void	Dark	Status	—	80	10	Many Others	—	—		HM04	Strength	Normal	Physical	80	100	15	Normal	—	—
75	Nasty Plot	Dark	Status	—	—	20	Self	—	—											
84	Dream Eater	Psychic	Special	100	100	15	Normal	—	—											
93	Dark Pulse	Dark	Special	80	100	15	Normal	○	—											

TM & HM MOVES

Lv.	Name	Type	Kind	Pow.	Acc.	PP	Range	Long	DA
TM04	Calm Mind	Psychic	Status	—	—	20	Self	—	—
TM06	Toxic	Poison	Status	—	90	10	Normal	—	—
TM10	Hidden Power	Normal	Special	—	100	15	Normal	—	—
TM11	Sunny Day	Fire	Status	—	—	5	Both Sides	—	—
TM12	Taunt	Dark	Status	—	100	20	Normal	—	—
TM13	Ice Beam	Ice	Special	95	100	10	Normal	—	—
TM14	Blizzard	Ice	Special	120	70	5	Many Others	—	—
TM15	Hyper Beam	Normal	Special	150	90	5	Normal	—	—
TM17	Protect	Normal	Status	—	—	10	Self	—	—
TM18	Rain Dance	Water	Status	—	—	5	Both Sides	—	—
TM21	Frustration	Normal	Physical	—	100	20	Normal	—	○
TM24	Thunderbolt	Electric	Special	95	100	15	Normal	—	—
TM25	Thunder	Electric	Special	120	70	10	Normal	—	—
TM27	Return	Normal	Physical	—	100	20	Normal	—	○
TM29	Psychic	Psychic	Special	90	100	10	Normal	—	—
TM30	Shadow Ball	Ghost	Special	80	100	15	Normal	—	—
TM31	Brick Break	Fighting	Physical	75	100	15	Normal	—	—
TM32	Double Team	Normal	Status	—	—	15	Self	—	—
TM36	Sludge Bomb	Poison	Special	90	100	10	Normal	—	—
TM39	Rock Tomb	Rock	Physical	50	80	10	Normal	—	—
TM40	Aerial Ace	Flying	Physical	60	—	20	Normal	—	—
TM41	Torment	Dark	Status	—	100	15	Normal	—	○
TM42	Facade	Normal	Physical	70	100	20	Normal	—	—
TM44	Rest	Psychic	Status	—	—	10	Self	—	—
TM46	Thief	Dark	Physical	40	100	10	Normal	—	○
TM48	Round	Normal	Special	60	100	15	Normal	—	—
TM52	Focus Blast	Fighting	Special	120	70	5	Normal	—	—
TM56	Fling	Dark	Physical	—	100	10	Normal	—	○
TM57	Charge Beam	Electric	Special	50	90	10	Normal	—	—
TM59	Incinerate	Fire	Special	30	100	15	Many Others	—	—
TM61	Will-O-Wisp	Fire	Status	—	75	15	Normal	—	—
TM63	Embargo	Dark	Status	—	100	15	Normal	—	—
TM65	Shadow Claw	Ghost	Physical	70	100	15	Normal	—	○
TM66	Payback	Dark	Physical	50	100	10	Normal	—	○
TM67	Retaliate	Normal	Physical	70	100	5	Normal	—	○
TM68	Giga Impact	Normal	Physical	150	90	5	Normal	—	—
TM70	Flash	Normal	Status	—	100	20	Normal	—	—
TM73	Thunder Wave	Electric	Status	—	100	20	Normal	—	—
TM75	Swords Dance	Normal	Status	—	—	30	Self	—	—
TM77	Psych Up	Normal	Status	—	—	10	Normal	—	—
TM80	Rock Slide	Rock	Physical	75	90	10	Many Others	—	—

MOVES TAUGHT BY PEOPLE

Name	Type	Kind	Pow.	Acc.	PP	Range	Long	DA

MOVES TAUGHT BY MOVE TUTORS FOR SHARDS

Name	Type	Kind	Pow.	Acc.	PP	Range	Long	DA
Last Resort	Normal	Physical	140	100	5	Normal	—	—
Icy Wind	Ice	Special	55	95	15	Many Others	—	—
Foul Play	Dark	Physical	95	100	15	Normal	—	—
Dark Pulse	Dark	Special	80	100	15	Normal	○	—
Snore	Normal	Special	40	100	15	Normal	—	—
Knock Off	Dark	Physical	20	100	20	Normal	—	—
Drain Punch	Fighting	Physical	75	100	10	Normal	—	—
Wonder Room	Psychic	Status	—	—	10	Both Sides	—	—
Spite	Ghost	Status	—	100	10	Normal	—	—
Trick	Psychic	Status	—	100	10	Normal	—	—
Sleep Talk	Normal	Status	—	—	10	Self	—	—
Snatch	Dark	Status	—	—	10	Self	—	—

Gratitude Pokémon

492 Shaymin (Land Forme)

- HEIGHT: 0'08"
- WEIGHT: 4.6 lbs.
- GENDER: Unknown

The flowers all over its body burst into bloom if it is lovingly hugged and senses gratitude.

Gender unknown

TYPE	Grass	

ABILITY
- Natural Cure

HIDDEN ABILITY

STATS
HP	
Attack	
Defense	
Sp. Atk	
Sp. Def	
Speed	

EGG GROUPS
No Egg has ever been discovered

EVOLUTION

Does not evolve

HOW TO OBTAIN

Only available through special distribution events. Check www.pokemon.com for the latest information on how to catch this Pokémon.

LEVEL-UP AND LEARNED MOVES

Lv.	Name	Type	Kind	Pow.	Acc.	PP	Range	Long	DA
1	Growth	Normal	Status	—	—	40	Self	—	—
10	Magical Leaf	Grass	Special	60	—	20	Normal	—	—
19	Leech Seed	Grass	Status	—	90	10	Normal	—	—
28	Synthesis	Grass	Status	—	—	5	Self	—	—
37	Sweet Scent	Normal	Status	—	100	20	Many Others	—	—
46	Natural Gift	Normal	Physical	—	100	15	Normal	—	—
55	Worry Seed	Grass	Status	—	100	10	Normal	—	—
64	Aromatherapy	Grass	Status	—	—	5	Your Party	—	—
73	Energy Ball	Grass	Special	80	100	10	Normal	—	—
82	Sweet Kiss	Normal	Status	—	75	10	Normal	—	—
91	Healing Wish	Psychic	Status	—	—	10	Self	—	—
100	Seed Flare	Grass	Special	120	85	5	Normal	—	—

TM & HM MOVES

Lv.	Name	Type	Kind	Pow.	Acc.	PP	Range	Long	DA
TM06	Toxic	Poison	Status	—	90	10	Normal	—	—
TM10	Hidden Power	Normal	Special	—	100	15	Normal	—	—
TM11	Sunny Day	Fire	Status	—	—	5	Both Sides	—	—
TM15	Hyper Beam	Normal	Special	150	90	5	Normal	—	—
TM17	Protect	Normal	Status	—	—	10	Self	—	—
TM20	Safeguard	Normal	Status	—	—	25	Your Side	—	—
TM21	Frustration	Normal	Physical	—	100	20	Normal	—	○
TM22	SolarBeam	Grass	Special	120	100	10	Normal	—	—
TM27	Return	Normal	Physical	—	100	20	Normal	—	○
TM29	Psychic	Psychic	Special	90	100	10	Normal	—	—
TM32	Double Team	Normal	Status	—	—	15	Self	—	—
TM42	Facade	Normal	Physical	70	100	20	Normal	—	○
TM44	Rest	Psychic	Status	—	—	10	Self	—	—
TM48	Round	Normal	Special	60	100	15	Normal	—	—
TM53	Energy Ball	Grass	Special	80	100	10	Normal	—	—
TM68	Giga Impact	Normal	Physical	150	90	5	Normal	—	○
TM70	Flash	Normal	Status	—	100	20	Normal	—	—
TM75	Swords Dance	Normal	Status	—	—	30	Self	—	—
TM77	Psych Up	Normal	Status	—	—	10	Self	—	—
TM86	Grass Knot	Grass	Special	—	100	20	Normal	—	○
TM87	Swagger	Normal	Status	—	90	15	Normal	—	—
TM90	Substitute	Normal	Status	—	—	10	Self	—	—

MOVES TAUGHT BY PEOPLE

Name	Type	Kind	Pow.	Acc.	PP	Range	Long	DA

MOVES TAUGHT BY MOVE TUTORS FOR SHARDS

Name	Type	Kind	Pow.	Acc.	PP	Range	Long	DA
Covet	Normal	Physical	60	100	40	Normal	—	○
Seed Bomb	Grass	Physical	80	100	15	Normal	—	○
Last Resort	Normal	Physical	140	100	5	Normal	—	○
Earth Power	Ground	Special	90	100	10	Normal	—	○
Zen Headbutt	Psychic	Physical	80	90	15	Normal	—	○
Snore	Normal	Special	40	100	15	Normal	—	—
Synthesis	Grass	Status	—	—	5	Self	—	—
Giga Drain	Grass	Special	75	100	10	Normal	—	—
Worry Seed	Grass	Status	—	100	10	Normal	—	—
Endeavor	Normal	Physical	—	100	5	Normal	—	—
Sleep Talk	Normal	Status	—	—	10	Self	—	—

Pokémon AR Marker

 Gratitude Pokémon

492 Shaymin (Sky Forme)

- HEIGHT: 1'04"
- WEIGHT: 11.5 lbs.
- GENDER: Unknown

The flowers all over its body burst into bloom if it is lovingly hugged and senses gratitude.

Gender unknown

TYPE	Grass	Flying

ABILITY
- Serene Grace

HIDDEN ABILITY

STATS
HP	
Attack	
Defense	
Sp. Atk	
Sp. Def	
Speed	

EGG GROUPS
No Egg has ever been discovered

EVOLUTION

Does not evolve

HOW TO OBTAIN

Pokémon Black Version 2	Use the Gracidea on Shaymin (Land Forme)
Pokémon White Version 2	Use the Gracidea on Shaymin (Land Forme)

HOW TO OBTAIN FROM OTHER GAMES

—
—

LEVEL-UP AND LEARNED MOVES

Lv.	Name	Type	Kind	Pow.	Acc.	PP	Range	Long	DA
1	Growth	Normal	Status	—	—	40	Self	—	—
10	Magical Leaf	Grass	Special	60	—	20	Normal	—	—
19	Leech Seed	Grass	Status	—	90	10	Normal	—	—
28	Quick Attack	Normal	Physical	40	100	30	Normal	—	○
37	Sweet Scent	Normal	Status	—	100	20	Many Others	—	—
46	Natural Gift	Normal	Physical	—	100	15	Normal	—	—
55	Worry Seed	Grass	Status	—	100	10	Normal	—	—
64	Air Slash	Flying	Special	75	95	20	Normal	—	—
73	Energy Ball	Grass	Special	80	100	10	Normal	—	—
82	Sweet Kiss	Normal	Status	—	75	10	Normal	—	—
91	Leaf Storm	Grass	Special	140	90	5	Normal	—	—
100	Seed Flare	Grass	Special	120	85	5	Normal	—	—

TM & HM MOVES

Lv.	Name	Type	Kind	Pow.	Acc.	PP	Range	Long	DA
TM06	Toxic	Poison	Status	—	90	10	Normal	—	—
TM10	Hidden Power	Normal	Special	—	100	15	Normal	—	—
TM11	Sunny Day	Fire	Status	—	—	5	Both Sides	—	—
TM15	Hyper Beam	Normal	Special	150	90	5	Normal	—	—
TM17	Protect	Normal	Status	—	—	10	Self	—	—
TM20	Safeguard	Normal	Status	—	—	25	Your Side	—	—
TM21	Frustration	Normal	Physical	—	100	20	Normal	—	○
TM22	SolarBeam	Grass	Special	120	100	10	Normal	—	—
TM27	Return	Normal	Physical	—	100	20	Normal	—	○
TM29	Psychic	Psychic	Special	90	100	10	Normal	—	—
TM32	Double Team	Normal	Status	—	—	15	Self	—	—
TM42	Facade	Normal	Physical	70	100	20	Normal	—	○
TM44	Rest	Psychic	Status	—	—	10	Self	—	—
TM48	Round	Normal	Special	60	100	15	Normal	—	—
TM53	Energy Ball	Grass	Special	80	100	10	Normal	—	—
TM68	Giga Impact	Normal	Physical	150	90	5	Normal	—	○
TM70	Flash	Normal	Status	—	100	20	Normal	—	—
TM75	Swords Dance	Normal	Status	—	—	30	Self	—	—
TM77	Psych Up	Normal	Status	—	—	10	Self	—	—
TM86	Grass Knot	Grass	Special	—	100	20	Normal	—	○
TM87	Swagger	Normal	Status	—	90	15	Normal	—	—
TM90	Substitute	Normal	Status	—	—	10	Self	—	—

MOVES TAUGHT BY PEOPLE

Name	Type	Kind	Pow.	Acc.	PP	Range	Long	DA

MOVES TAUGHT BY MOVE TUTORS FOR SHARDS

Name	Type	Kind	Pow.	Acc.	PP	Range	Long	DA
Covet	Normal	Physical	60	100	40	Normal	—	○
Seed Bomb	Grass	Physical	80	100	15	Normal	—	○
Last Resort	Normal	Physical	140	100	5	Normal	—	○
Zen Headbutt	Psychic	Physical	80	90	15	Normal	—	○
Snore	Normal	Special	40	100	15	Normal	—	—
Synthesis	Grass	Status	—	—	5	Self	—	—
Giga Drain	Grass	Special	75	100	10	Normal	—	—
Tailwind	Flying	Status	—	—	30	Your Side	—	—
Worry Seed	Grass	Status	—	100	10	Normal	—	—
Sleep Talk	Normal	Status	—	—	10	Self	—	—

Pokémon AR Marker

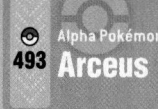

493 Arceus

Alpha Pokémon

- HEIGHT: 10'06"
- WEIGHT: 705.5 lbs.
- GENDER: Unknown

It is said to have emerged from an egg in a place where there was nothing then shaped the world.

TYPE Normal

ABILITY
- Multitype

HIDDEN ABILITY
—

STATS
HP
Attack
Defense
Sp. Atk
Sp. Def
Speed

EGG GROUPS
No Egg has ever been discovered

EVOLUTION
Does not evolve

HOW TO OBTAIN
Only available through special distribution events. Check www.pokemon.com for the latest information on how to catch this Pokémon.

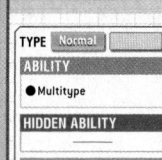

Normal Type

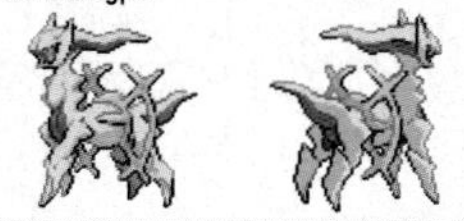

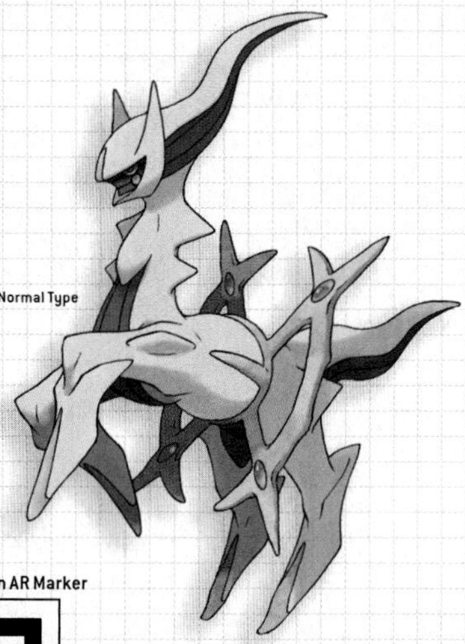

Normal Type

Pokémon AR Marker

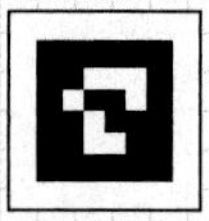

Normal Type

LEVEL-UP AND LEARNED MOVES

Lv.	Name	Type	Kind	Pow.	Acc.	PP	Range	Long	DA
1	Seismic Toss	Fighting	Physical	—	100	20	Normal	—	○
1	Cosmic Power	Psychic	Status	—	—	20	Self	—	—
1	Natural Gift	Normal	Physical	—	100	15	Normal	—	—
1	Punishment	Dark	Physical	—	100	5	Normal	—	○
10	Gravity	Psychic	Status	—	—	5	Both Sides	—	—
20	Earth Power	Ground	Special	90	100	10	Normal	—	—
30	Hyper Voice	Normal	Special	90	100	10	Many Others	—	—
40	ExtremeSpeed	Normal	Physical	80	100	5	Normal	—	○
50	Refresh	Normal	Status	—	—	20	Self	—	—
60	Future Sight	Psychic	Special	100	100	10	Normal	—	—
70	Recover	Normal	Status	—	—	10	Self	—	—
80	Hyper Beam	Normal	Special	150	90	5	Normal	—	—
90	Perish Song	Normal	Status	—	—	5	Adjacent	○	—
100	Judgment	Normal	Special	100	100	10	Normal	—	—

TM & HM MOVES

Lv.	Name	Type	Kind	Pow.	Acc.	PP	Range	Long	DA
TM01	Hone Claws	Dark	Status	—	—	15	Self	—	—
TM02	Dragon Claw	Dragon	Physical	80	100	15	Normal	—	○
TM03	Psyshock	Psychic	Special	80	100	10	Normal	—	—
TM04	Calm Mind	Psychic	Status	—	—	20	Self	—	—
TM05	Roar	Normal	Status	—	100	20	Normal	—	—
TM06	Toxic	Poison	Status	—	90	10	Normal	—	—
TM07	Hail	Ice	Status	—	—	10	Both Sides	—	—
TM10	Hidden Power	Normal	Special	—	100	15	Normal	—	—
TM11	Sunny Day	Fire	Status	—	—	5	Both Sides	—	—
TM13	Ice Beam	Ice	Special	95	100	10	Normal	—	—
TM14	Blizzard	Ice	Special	120	70	5	Many Others	—	—
TM15	Hyper Beam	Normal	Special	150	90	5	Normal	—	—
TM16	Light Screen	Psychic	Status	—	—	30	Your Side	—	—
TM17	Protect	Normal	Status	—	—	10	Self	—	—
TM18	Rain Dance	Water	Status	—	—	5	Both Sides	—	—
TM19	Telekinesis	Psychic	Status	—	—	15	Normal	—	—
TM20	Safeguard	Normal	Status	—	—	25	Your Side	—	—
TM21	Frustration	Normal	Physical	—	100	20	Normal	—	○
TM22	SolarBeam	Grass	Special	120	100	10	Normal	—	—
TM24	Thunderbolt	Electric	Special	95	100	15	Normal	—	—
TM25	Thunder	Electric	Special	120	70	10	Normal	—	—
TM26	Earthquake	Ground	Physical	100	100	10	Adjacent	—	—
TM27	Return	Normal	Physical	—	100	20	Normal	—	○
TM29	Psychic	Psychic	Special	90	100	10	Normal	—	—
TM30	Shadow Ball	Ghost	Special	80	100	15	Normal	—	—
TM31	Brick Break	Fighting	Physical	75	100	15	Normal	—	○
TM32	Double Team	Normal	Status	—	—	15	Self	—	—
TM33	Reflect	Psychic	Status	—	—	20	Your Side	—	—
TM35	Flamethrower	Fire	Special	95	100	15	Normal	—	—
TM36	Sludge Bomb	Poison	Special	90	100	10	Normal	—	—
TM37	Sandstorm	Rock	Status	—	—	10	Both Sides	—	—
TM38	Fire Blast	Fire	Special	120	85	5	Normal	—	—
TM39	Rock Tomb	Rock	Physical	50	80	10	Normal	—	—
TM40	Aerial Ace	Flying	Physical	60	—	20	Normal	○	○
TM42	Facade	Normal	Physical	70	100	20	Normal	—	○
TM44	Rest	Psychic	Status	—	—	10	Self	—	—
TM48	Round	Normal	Special	60	100	15	Normal	—	—
TM49	Echoed Voice	Normal	Special	40	100	15	Normal	—	—
TM50	Overheat	Fire	Special	140	90	5	Normal	—	—
TM52	Focus Blast	Fighting	Special	120	70	5	Normal	—	—
TM53	Energy Ball	Grass	Special	80	100	10	Normal	—	—
TM57	Charge Beam	Electric	Special	50	90	10	Normal	—	—
TM59	Incinerate	Fire	Special	30	100	15	Many Others	—	—
TM60	Quash	Dark	Status	—	100	15	Normal	—	—
TM61	Will—O—Wisp	Fire	Status	—	75	15	Normal	—	—
TM65	Shadow Claw	Ghost	Physical	70	100	15	Normal	—	○
TM66	Payback	Dark	Physical	50	100	10	Normal	—	○
TM67	Retaliate	Normal	Physical	70	100	5	Normal	—	○
TM68	Giga Impact	Normal	Physical	150	90	5	Normal	—	○
TM70	Flash	Normal	Status	—	100	20	Normal	—	—
TM71	Stone Edge	Rock	Physical	100	80	5	Normal	—	—
TM73	Thunder Wave	Electric	Status	—	100	20	Normal	—	—
TM75	Swords Dance	Normal	Status	—	—	30	Self	—	—
TM77	Psych Up	Normal	Status	—	—	10	Normal	—	—
TM78	Bulldoze	Ground	Physical	60	100	20	Adjacent	—	—
TM80	Rock Slide	Rock	Physical	75	90	10	Many Others	—	—
TM81	X—Scissor	Bug	Physical	80	100	15	Normal	—	○
TM83	Work Up	Normal	Status	—	—	30	Self	—	—
TM84	Poison Jab	Poison	Physical	80	100	20	Normal	—	○
TM85	Dream Eater	Psychic	Special	100	100	15	Normal	—	—
TM86	Grass Knot	Grass	Special	—	100	20	Normal	—	○
TM87	Swagger	Normal	Status	—	90	15	Normal	—	—
TM90	Substitute	Normal	Status	—	—	10	Self	—	—
TM91	Flash Cannon	Steel	Special	80	100	10	Normal	—	—
TM92	Trick Room	Psychic	Status	—	—	5	Both Sides	—	—
TM94	Rock Smash	Fighting	Physical	40	100	15	Normal	—	○
TM95	Snarl	Dark	Special	55	95	15	Many Others	—	—
HM01	Cut	Normal	Physical	50	95	30	Normal	—	○
HM02	Fly	Flying	Physical	90	95	15	Normal	○	○
HM03	Surf	Water	Special	95	100	15	Adjacent	—	—
HM04	Strength	Normal	Physical	80	100	15	Normal	—	○
HM05	Waterfall	Water	Physical	80	100	15	Normal	—	○

MOVES TAUGHT BY PEOPLE

Name	Type	Kind	Pow.	Acc.	PP	Range	Long	DA
Draco Meteor◆	Dragon	Special	140	90	5	Normal	—	—

MOVES TAUGHT BY MOVE TUTORS FOR SHARDS

Name	Type	Kind	Pow.	Acc.	PP	Range	Long	DA
Signal Beam	Bug	Special	75	100	15	Normal	—	—
Iron Head	Steel	Physical	80	100	15	Normal	—	○
Last Resort	Normal	Physical	140	100	5	Normal	—	○
Iron Defense	Steel	Status	—	—	15	Self	—	—
Magic Coat	Psychic	Status	—	—	15	Self	—	—
Hyper Voice	Normal	Special	90	100	10	Many Others	—	—
Icy Wind	Ice	Special	55	95	15	Many Others	—	—
Iron Tail	Steel	Physical	100	75	15	Normal	—	○
Aqua Tail	Water	Physical	90	90	10	Normal	—	○
Earth Power	Ground	Special	90	100	10	Normal	—	—
Zen Headbutt	Psychic	Physical	80	90	15	Normal	—	○
Gravity	Psychic	Status	—	—	5	Both Sides	—	—
Dragon Pulse	Dragon	Special	90	100	10	Normal	○	—
Dark Pulse	Dark	Special	80	100	15	Normal	○	—
Snore	Normal	Special	40	100	15	Normal	—	—
Heat Wave	Fire	Special	100	90	10	Many Others	—	—
Giga Drain	Grass	Special	75	100	10	Normal	—	—
Tailwind	Flying	Status	—	—	30	Your Side	—	—
Recycle	Normal	Status	—	—	10	Self	—	—
Trick	Psychic	Status	—	100	10	Normal	—	—
Stealth Rock	Rock	Status	—	—	20	Other Side	—	—
Outrage	Dragon	Physical	120	100	10	1 Random	—	○
Sleep Talk	Normal	Status	—	—	10	Self	—	—

Fire Type

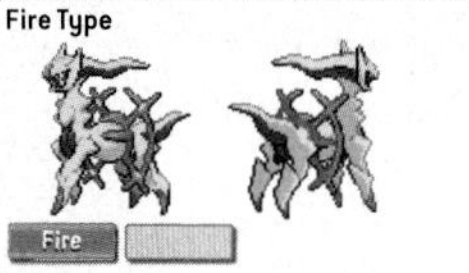

Pokémon AR Marker

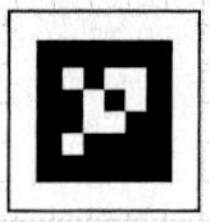

Fire Type

Water Type

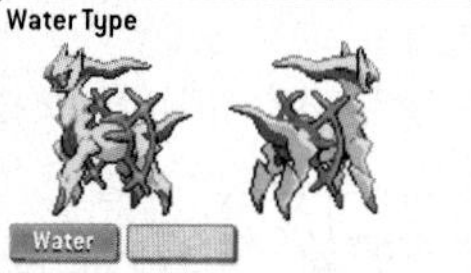

Pokémon AR Marker

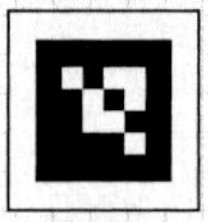

Water Type

Grass Type

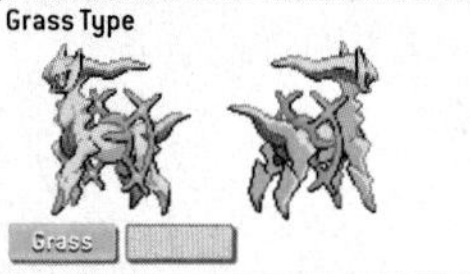

Pokémon AR Marker

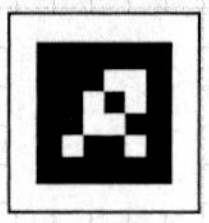

Grass Type

Electric Type

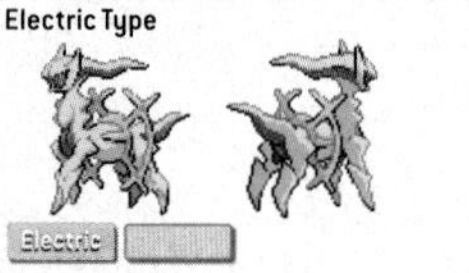

Pokémon AR Marker

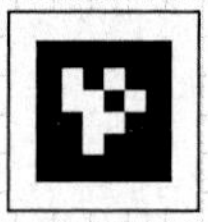

Electric Type

Ice Type

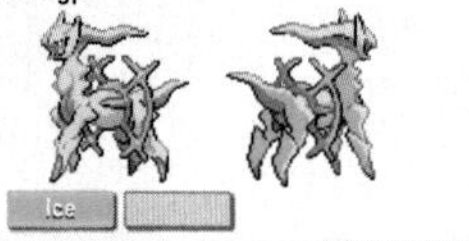

Pokémon AR Marker

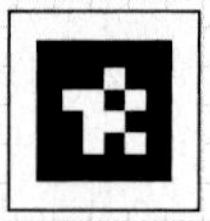

Ice Type

Fighting Type

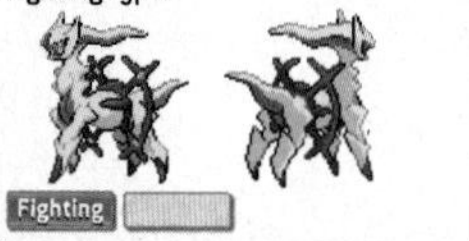

Pokémon AR Marker

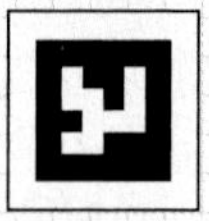

Fighting Type

Poison Type

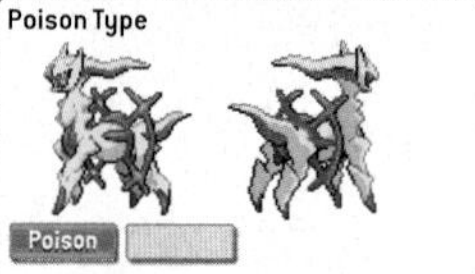

Pokémon AR Marker

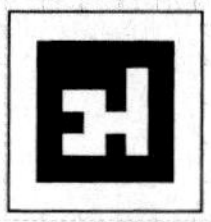

Poison Type

Ground Type

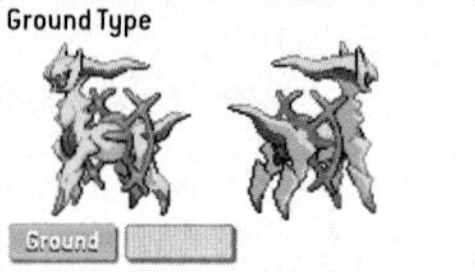

Pokémon AR Marker

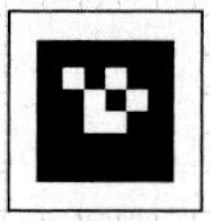

Ground Type

Flying Type

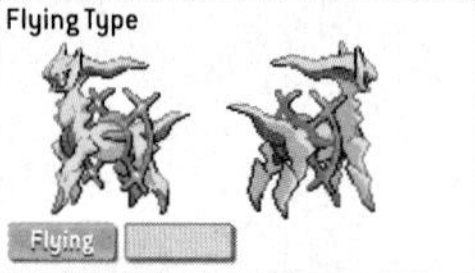

Pokémon AR Marker

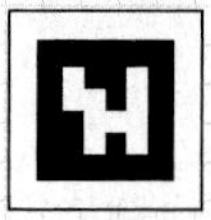

Flying Type

Psychic Type

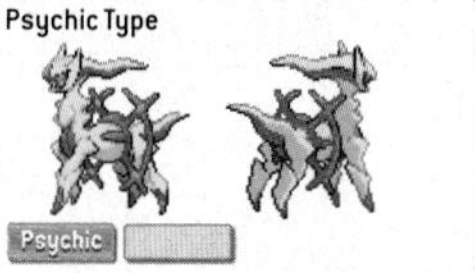

Pokémon AR Marker

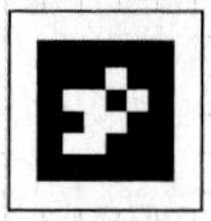

Psychic Type

Bug Type

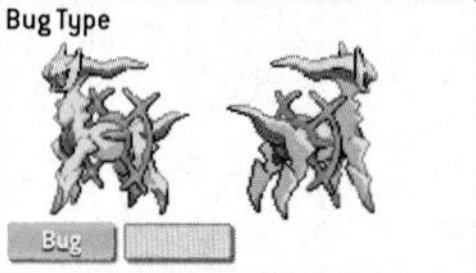

Pokémon AR Marker

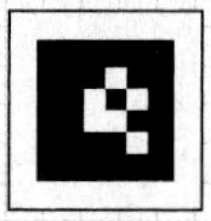

Bug Type

Rock Type

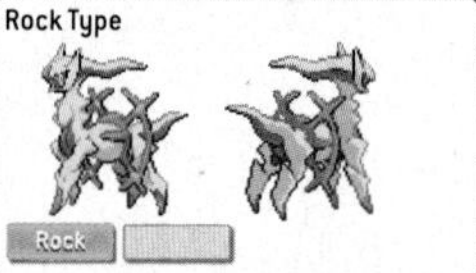

Pokémon AR Marker

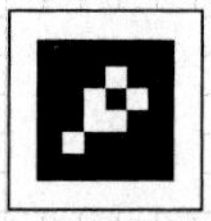

Rock Type

Ghost Type

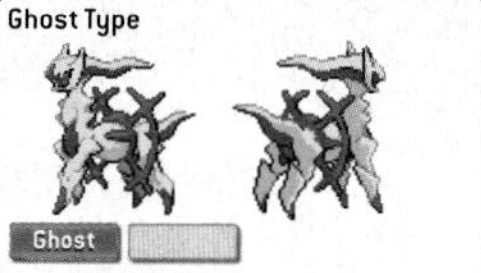

Pokémon AR Marker

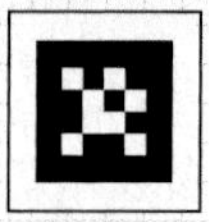

Ghost Type

Dragon Type

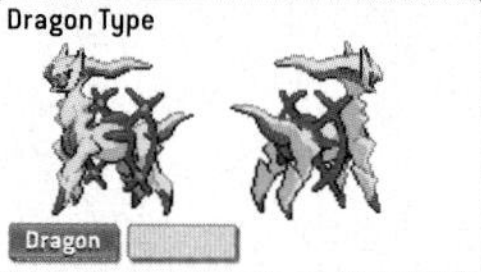

Pokémon AR Marker

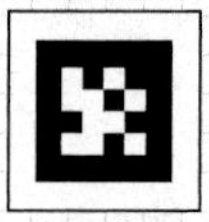

Dragon Type

Dark Type

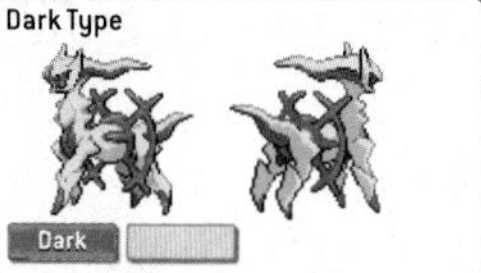

Pokémon AR Marker

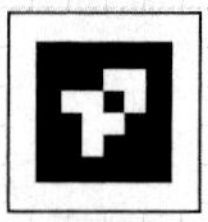

Dark Type

Steel Type

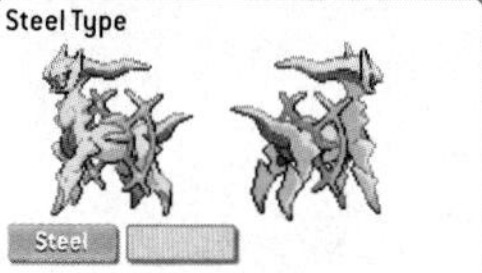

Pokémon AR Marker

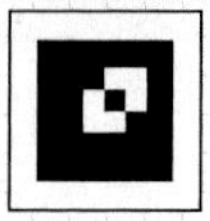

Steel Type

◆ You can have this move taught to Arceus if it is holding the Draco Plate and its friendship is high enough.

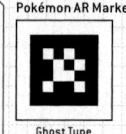

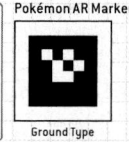

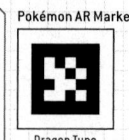

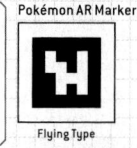

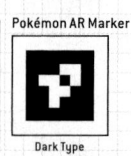

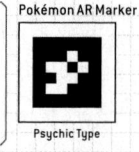

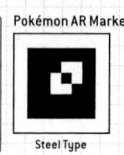

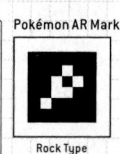

NATIONAL POKÉDEX

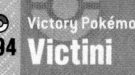

494 Victini

Victory Pokémon

● HEIGHT: 1'04"
● WEIGHT: 8.8 lbs.
● GENDER: Unknown

When it shares the infinite energy it creates, that being's entire body will be overflowing with power.

TYPE: Psychic / Fire

ABILITY
● Victory Star

HIDDEN ABILITY
—

STATS
HP
Attack
Defense
Sp. Atk
Sp. Def
Speed

EGG GROUPS
No Egg has ever been discovered

Gender unknown

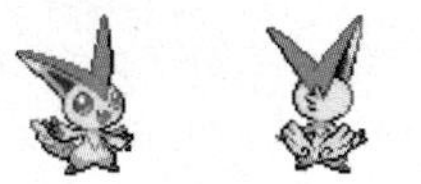

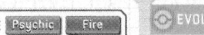

EVOLUTION

Does not evolve

HOW TO OBTAIN

Only available through special distribution events. Check www.pokemon.com for the latest information on how to catch this Pokémon.

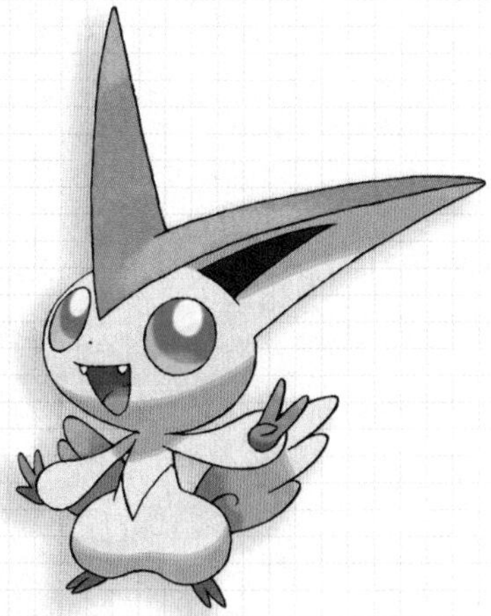

Pokémon AR Marker

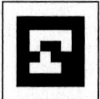

LEVEL-UP AND LEARNED MOVES

Lv.	Name	Type	Kind	Pow.	Acc.	PP	Range	Long	DA
1	Searing Shot	Fire	Special	100	100	5	Adjacent	—	—
1	Focus Energy	Normal	Status	—	—	30	Self	—	—
1	Confusion	Psychic	Special	50	100	25	Normal	—	—
1	Incinerate	Fire	Special	30	100	15	Many Others	—	—
1	Quick Attack	Normal	Physical	40	100	30	Normal	—	○
9	Endure	Normal	Status	—	—	10	Self	—	—
17	Headbutt	Normal	Physical	70	100	15	Normal	—	○
25	Flame Charge	Fire	Physical	50	100	20	Normal	—	○
33	Reversal	Fighting	Physical	—	100	15	Normal	—	○
41	Flame Burst	Fire	Special	70	100	15	Normal	—	—
49	Zen Headbutt	Psychic	Physical	80	90	15	Normal	—	○
57	Inferno	Fire	Special	100	50	5	Normal	—	—
65	Double-Edge	Normal	Physical	120	100	15	Normal	—	○
73	Flare Blitz	Fire	Physical	120	100	15	Normal	—	○
81	Final Gambit	Fighting	Special	—	100	5	Normal	—	○
89	Stored Power	Psychic	Special	20	100	10	Normal	—	—
97	Overheat	Fire	Special	140	90	5	Normal	—	—

TM & HM MOVES

Lv.	Name	Type	Kind	Pow.	Acc.	PP	Range	Long	DA
TM03	Psyshock	Psychic	Special	80	100	10	Normal	—	—
TM06	Toxic	Poison	Status	—	90	10	Normal	—	—
TM10	Hidden Power	Normal	Special	—	100	15	Normal	—	—
TM11	Sunny Day	Fire	Status	—	—	5	Both Sides	—	—
TM12	Taunt	Dark	Status	—	100	20	Normal	—	—
TM15	Hyper Beam	Normal	Special	150	90	5	Normal	—	—
TM16	Light Screen	Psychic	Status	—	—	30	Your Side	—	—
TM17	Protect	Normal	Status	—	—	10	Self	—	—
TM19	Telekinesis	Psychic	Status	—	—	15	Normal	—	—
TM20	Safeguard	Normal	Status	—	—	25	Your Side	—	—
TM21	Frustration	Normal	Physical	—	100	20	Normal	—	○
TM22	SolarBeam	Grass	Special	120	100	10	Normal	—	—
TM24	Thunderbolt	Electric	Special	95	100	15	Normal	—	—
TM25	Thunder	Electric	Special	120	70	10	Normal	—	—
TM27	Return	Normal	Physical	—	100	20	Normal	—	○
TM29	Psychic	Psychic	Special	90	100	10	Normal	—	—
TM30	Shadow Ball	Ghost	Special	80	100	15	Normal	—	—
TM31	Brick Break	Fighting	Physical	75	100	15	Normal	—	○
TM32	Double Team	Normal	Status	—	—	15	Self	—	—
TM35	Flamethrower	Fire	Special	95	100	15	Normal	—	—
TM38	Fire Blast	Fire	Special	120	85	5	Normal	—	—
TM42	Facade	Normal	Physical	70	100	20	Normal	—	○
TM43	Flame Charge	Fire	Physical	50	100	20	Normal	—	○
TM44	Rest	Psychic	Status	—	—	10	Self	—	—
TM48	Round	Normal	Special	60	100	15	Normal	—	—
TM50	Overheat	Fire	Special	140	90	5	Normal	—	—
TM52	Focus Blast	Fighting	Special	120	70	5	Normal	—	—
TM53	Energy Ball	Grass	Special	80	100	10	Normal	—	—
TM56	Fling	Dark	Physical	—	100	10	Normal	—	—
TM57	Charge Beam	Electric	Special	50	90	10	Normal	—	—
TM59	Incinerate	Fire	Special	30	100	15	Many Others	—	—
TM61	Will-O-Wisp	Fire	Status	—	75	15	Normal	—	—
TM63	Embargo	Dark	Status	—	100	15	Normal	—	—
TM68	Giga Impact	Normal	Physical	150	90	5	Normal	—	○
TM70	Flash	Normal	Status	—	100	20	Normal	—	—
TM73	Thunder Wave	Electric	Status	—	100	20	Normal	—	—
TM77	Psych Up	Normal	Status	—	—	10	Normal	—	—
TM83	Work Up	Normal	Status	—	—	30	Self	—	—
TM86	Grass Knot	Grass	Special	—	100	20	Normal	—	○
TM87	Swagger	Normal	Status	—	90	15	Normal	—	—
TM89	U-turn	Bug	Physical	70	100	20	Normal	—	○
TM90	Substitute	Normal	Status	—	—	10	Self	—	—
TM92	Trick Room	Psychic	Status	—	—	5	Both Sides	—	—
TM93	Wild Charge	Electric	Physical	90	100	15	Normal	—	○
TM94	Rock Smash	Fighting	Physical	40	100	15	Normal	—	○

MOVES TAUGHT BY PEOPLE

Name	Type	Kind	Pow.	Acc.	PP	Range	Long	DA

MOVES TAUGHT BY MOVE TUTORS FOR SHARDS

Name	Type	Kind	Pow.	Acc.	PP	Range	Long	DA
Bounce	Flying	Physical	85	85	5	Normal	○	○
Signal Beam	Bug	Special	75	100	15	Normal	—	—
Uproar	Normal	Special	90	100	10	1 Random	—	—
Fire Punch	Fire	Physical	75	100	15	Normal	—	○
ThunderPunch	Electric	Physical	75	100	15	Normal	—	○
Last Resort	Normal	Physical	140	100	5	Normal	—	○
Magic Coat	Psychic	Status	—	—	15	Self	—	—
Zen Headbutt	Psychic	Physical	80	90	15	Normal	—	○
Snore	Normal	Special	40	100	15	Normal	—	—
Role Play	Psychic	Status	—	—	10	Normal	—	—
Heat Wave	Fire	Special	100	90	10	Many Others	—	—
Helping Hand	Normal	Status	—	—	20	1 Ally	—	—
Trick	Psychic	Status	—	100	10	Normal	—	—
Sleep Talk	Normal	Status	—	—	10	Self	—	—
Skill Swap	Psychic	Status	—	—	10	Normal	—	—

495 Snivy

Grass Snake Pokémon

● HEIGHT: 2'00"
● WEIGHT: 17.9 lbs.
● GENDER: ♂ / ♀

Being exposed to sunlight makes its movements swifter. It uses vines more adeptly than its hands.

TYPE: Grass

ABILITY
● Overgrow

HIDDEN ABILITY
—

STATS
HP
Attack
Defense
Sp. Atk
Sp. Def
Speed

EGG GROUPS
Field/Grass

ITEMS SOMETIMES HELD
● None

Same form for ♂ / ♀

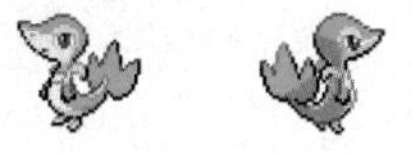

EVOLUTION

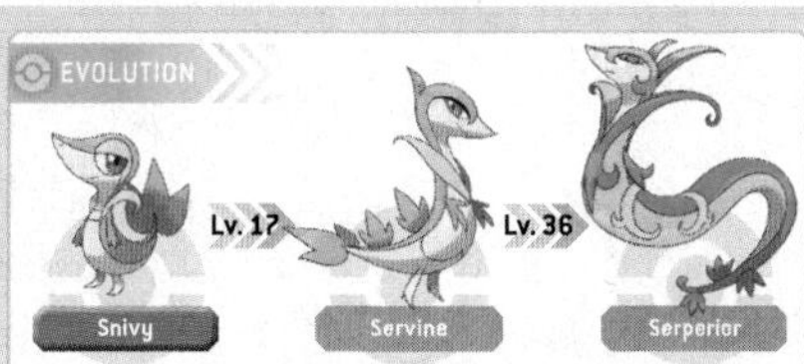

Lv. 17
Lv. 36
Snivy
Servine
Serperior

HOW TO OBTAIN

Pokémon Black Version 2	Get from Bianca at the start of the adventure
Pokémon White Version 2	Get from Bianca at the start of the adventure

HOW TO OBTAIN FROM OTHER GAMES

—

—

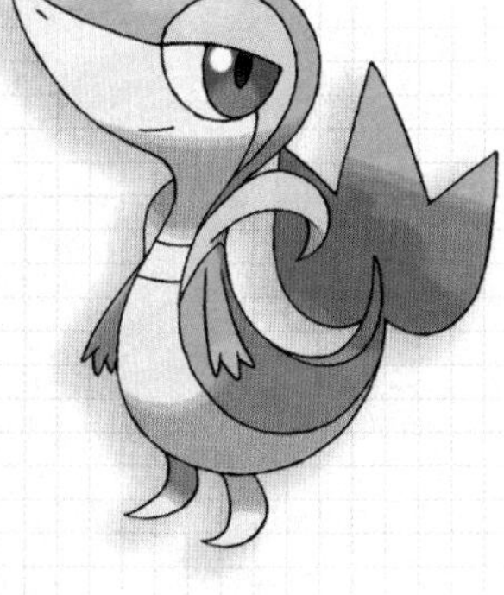

Pokémon AR Marker

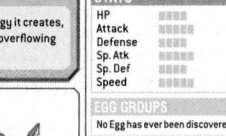

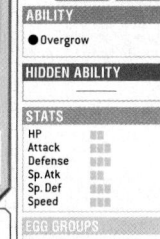

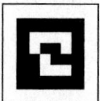

LEVEL-UP AND LEARNED MOVES

Lv.	Name	Type	Kind	Pow.	Acc.	PP	Range	Long	DA
1	Tackle	Normal	Physical	50	100	35	Normal	—	○
4	Leer	Normal	Status	—	100	30	Many Others	—	—
7	Vine Whip	Grass	Physical	35	100	15	Normal	—	○
10	Wrap	Normal	Physical	15	90	20	Normal	—	○
13	Growth	Normal	Status	—	—	40	Self	—	—
16	Leaf Tornado	Grass	Special	65	90	10	Normal	—	—
19	Leech Seed	Grass	Status	—	90	10	Normal	—	—
22	Mega Drain	Grass	Special	40	100	15	Normal	—	—
25	Slam	Normal	Physical	80	75	20	Normal	—	○
28	Leaf Blade	Grass	Physical	90	100	15	Normal	—	○
31	Coil	Poison	Status	—	—	20	Self	—	—
34	Giga Drain	Grass	Special	75	100	10	Normal	—	—
37	Wring Out	Normal	Special	—	100	5	Normal	—	○
40	Gastro Acid	Poison	Status	—	100	10	Normal	—	—
43	Leaf Storm	Grass	Special	140	90	5	Normal	—	—

TM & HM MOVES

Lv.	Name	Type	Kind	Pow.	Acc.	PP	Range	Long	DA
TM04	Calm Mind	Psychic	Status	—	—	20	Self	—	—
TM06	Toxic	Poison	Status	—	90	10	Normal	—	—
TM10	Hidden Power	Normal	Special	—	100	15	Normal	—	—
TM11	Sunny Day	Fire	Status	—	—	5	Both Sides	—	—
TM12	Taunt	Dark	Status	—	100	20	Normal	—	—
TM16	Light Screen	Psychic	Status	—	—	30	Your Side	—	—
TM17	Protect	Normal	Status	—	—	10	Self	—	—
TM20	Safeguard	Normal	Status	—	—	25	Your Side	—	—
TM21	Frustration	Normal	Physical	—	100	20	Normal	—	○
TM22	SolarBeam	Grass	Special	120	100	10	Normal	—	—
TM27	Return	Normal	Physical	—	100	20	Normal	—	○
TM32	Double Team	Normal	Status	—	—	15	Self	—	—
TM33	Reflect	Psychic	Status	—	—	20	Your Side	—	—
TM40	Aerial Ace	Flying	Physical	60	—	20	Normal	○	○
TM41	Torment	Dark	Status	—	100	15	Normal	—	—
TM42	Facade	Normal	Physical	70	100	20	Normal	—	○
TM44	Rest	Psychic	Status	—	—	10	Self	—	—
TM45	Attract	Normal	Status	—	100	15	Normal	—	—
TM48	Round	Normal	Special	60	100	15	Normal	—	—
TM53	Energy Ball	Grass	Special	80	100	10	Normal	—	—
TM70	Flash	Normal	Status	—	100	20	Normal	—	—
TM75	Swords Dance	Normal	Status	—	—	30	Self	—	—
TM86	Grass Knot	Grass	Special	—	100	20	Normal	—	○
TM87	Swagger	Normal	Status	—	90	15	Normal	—	—
TM90	Substitute	Normal	Status	—	—	10	Self	—	—
HM01	Cut	Normal	Physical	50	95	30	Normal	—	○

MOVES TAUGHT BY PEOPLE

Name	Type	Kind	Pow.	Acc.	PP	Range	Long	DA
Grass Pledge	Grass	Special	50	100	10	Normal	—	—

MOVES TAUGHT BY MOVE TUTORS FOR SHARDS

Name	Type	Kind	Pow.	Acc.	PP	Range	Long	DA
Seed Bomb	Grass	Physical	80	100	15	Normal	—	—
Iron Tail	Steel	Physical	100	75	15	Normal	—	○
Aqua Tail	Water	Physical	90	90	10	Normal	—	○
Bind	Normal	Physical	15	85	20	Normal	—	○
Snore	Normal	Special	40	100	15	Normal	—	—
Knock Off	Dark	Physical	20	100	20	Normal	—	○
Synthesis	Grass	Status	—	—	5	Self	—	—
Giga Drain	Grass	Special	75	100	10	Normal	—	—
Worry Seed	Grass	Status	—	100	10	Normal	—	—
Gastro Acid	Poison	Status	—	100	10	Normal	—	—
Sleep Talk	Normal	Status	—	—	10	Self	—	—
Snatch	Dark	Status	—	—	10	Self	—	—

EGG MOVES

Name	Type	Kind	Pow.	Acc.	PP	Range	Long	DA
Captivate	Normal	Status	—	100	20	Many Others	—	—
Natural Gift	Normal	Physical	—	100	15	Normal	—	—
Glare	Normal	Status	—	90	30	Normal	—	—
Iron Tail	Steel	Physical	100	75	15	Normal	—	○
Magical Leaf	Grass	Special	60	—	20	Normal	—	—
Sweet Scent	Normal	Status	—	100	20	Many Others	—	—
Mirror Coat	Psychic	Special	—	100	20	Varies	—	—
Pursuit	Dark	Physical	40	100	20	Normal	—	○
Mean Look	Normal	Status	—	—	5	Normal	—	—
Twister	Dragon	Special	40	100	20	Many Others	—	—

494 Victini
495 Snivy

496 Servine

Grass Snake Pokémon

- HEIGHT: 2'07"
- WEIGHT: 35.3 lbs.
- GENDER: ♂ / ♀

When it gets dirty, its leaves can't be used in photosynthesis, so it always keeps itself clean.

TYPE: Grass

ABILITY
- Overgrow

HIDDEN ABILITY
—

STATS
HP
Attack
Defense
Sp. Atk
Sp. Def
Speed

EGG GROUPS
Field/Grass

ITEMS SOMETIMES HELD
- None

Same form for ♂ / ♀

Pokémon AR Marker

EVOLUTION

HOW TO OBTAIN

Pokémon Black Version 2	Level up Snivy to Lv. 17
Pokémon White Version 2	Level up Snivy to Lv. 17

HOW TO OBTAIN FROM OTHER GAMES

—

—

LEVEL-UP AND LEARNED MOVES

Lv.	Name	Type	Kind	Pow.	Acc.	PP	Range	Long	DA
1	Tackle	Normal	Physical	50	100	35	Normal	—	○
1	Leer	Normal	Status	—	100	30	Many Others	—	—
1	Vine Whip	Grass	Physical	35	100	15	Normal	—	○
1	Wrap	Normal	Physical	15	90	20	Normal	—	○
4	Leer	Normal	Status	—	100	30	Many Others	—	—
7	Vine Whip	Grass	Physical	35	100	15	Normal	—	○
10	Wrap	Normal	Physical	15	90	20	Normal	—	○
13	Growth	Normal	Status	—	—	40	Self	—	—
16	Leaf Tornado	Grass	Special	65	90	10	Normal	—	—
20	Leech Seed	Grass	Status	—	90	10	Normal	—	—
24	Mega Drain	Grass	Special	40	100	15	Normal	—	—
28	Slam	Normal	Physical	80	75	20	Normal	—	○
32	Leaf Blade	Grass	Physical	90	100	15	Normal	—	○
36	Coil	Poison	Status	—	—	20	Self	—	—
40	Giga Drain	Grass	Special	75	100	10	Normal	—	—
44	Wring Out	Normal	Special	—	100	5	Normal	—	○
48	Gastro Acid	Poison	Status	—	100	10	Normal	—	—
52	Leaf Storm	Grass	Special	140	90	5	Normal	—	—

TM & HM MOVES

Lv.	Name	Type	Kind	Pow.	Acc.	PP	Range	Long	DA
TM04	Calm Mind	Psychic	Status	—	—	20	Self	—	—
TM06	Toxic	Poison	Status	—	90	10	Normal	—	—
TM10	Hidden Power	Normal	Special	—	100	15	Normal	—	—
TM11	Sunny Day	Fire	Status	—	—	5	Both Sides	—	—
TM12	Taunt	Dark	Status	—	100	20	Normal	—	—
TM16	Light Screen	Psychic	Status	—	—	30	Your Side	—	—
TM17	Protect	Normal	Status	—	—	10	Self	—	—
TM20	Safeguard	Normal	Status	—	—	25	Your Side	—	—
TM21	Frustration	Normal	Physical	—	100	20	Normal	—	○
TM22	SolarBeam	Grass	Special	120	100	10	Normal	—	—
TM27	Return	Normal	Physical	—	100	20	Normal	—	○
TM32	Double Team	Normal	Status	—	—	15	Self	—	—
TM33	Reflect	Psychic	Status	—	—	20	Your Side	—	—
TM40	Aerial Ace	Flying	Physical	60	—	20	Normal	○	○
TM41	Torment	Dark	Status	—	100	15	Normal	—	—
TM42	Facade	Normal	Physical	70	100	20	Normal	—	○
TM44	Rest	Psychic	Status	—	—	10	Self	—	—
TM45	Attract	Normal	Status	—	100	15	Normal	—	—
TM48	Round	Normal	Special	60	100	15	Normal	—	—
TM53	Energy Ball	Grass	Special	80	100	10	Normal	—	—
TM70	Flash	Normal	Status	—	100	20	Normal	—	—
TM75	Swords Dance	Normal	Status	—	—	30	Self	—	—
TM86	Grass Knot	Grass	Special	—	100	20	Normal	—	○
TM87	Swagger	Normal	Status	—	90	15	Normal	—	—
TM90	Substitute	Normal	Status	—	—	10	Self	—	—
HM01	Cut	Normal	Physical	50	95	30	Normal	—	○

MOVES TAUGHT BY PEOPLE

Name	Type	Kind	Pow.	Acc.	PP	Range	Long	DA
Grass Pledge	Grass	Special	50	100	10	Normal	—	—

MOVES TAUGHT BY MOVE TUTORS FOR SHARDS

Name	Type	Kind	Pow.	Acc.	PP	Range	Long	DA
Seed Bomb	Grass	Physical	80	100	15	Normal	—	—
Iron Tail	Steel	Physical	100	75	15	Normal	—	○
Aqua Tail	Water	Physical	90	90	10	Normal	—	○
Bind	Normal	Physical	15	85	20	Normal	—	○
Snore	Normal	Special	40	100	15	Normal	—	—
Knock Off	Dark	Physical	20	100	20	Normal	—	○
Synthesis	Grass	Status	—	—	5	Self	—	—
Giga Drain	Grass	Special	75	100	10	Normal	—	—
Worry Seed	Grass	Status	—	100	10	Normal	—	—
Gastro Acid	Poison	Status	—	100	10	Normal	—	—
Sleep Talk	Normal	Status	—	—	10	Self	—	—
Snatch	Dark	Status	—	—	10	Self	—	—

497 Serperior

Regal Pokémon

- HEIGHT: 10'10"
- WEIGHT: 138.9 lbs.
- GENDER: ♂ / ♀

It only gives its all against strong opponents who are not fazed by the glare from Serperior's noble eyes.

TYPE: Grass

ABILITY
- Overgrow

HIDDEN ABILITY
—

STATS
HP
Attack
Defense
Sp. Atk
Sp. Def
Speed

EGG GROUPS
Field/Grass

ITEMS SOMETIMES HELD
- None

Same form for ♂ / ♀

Pokémon AR Marker

EVOLUTION

HOW TO OBTAIN

Pokémon Black Version 2	Level up Servine to Lv. 36
Pokémon White Version 2	Level up Servine to Lv. 36

HOW TO OBTAIN FROM OTHER GAMES

—

—

LEVEL-UP AND LEARNED MOVES

Lv.	Name	Type	Kind	Pow.	Acc.	PP	Range	Long	DA
1	Tackle	Normal	Physical	50	100	35	Normal	—	○
1	Leer	Normal	Status	—	100	30	Many Others	—	—
1	Vine Whip	Grass	Physical	35	100	15	Normal	—	○
1	Wrap	Normal	Physical	15	90	20	Normal	—	○
4	Leer	Normal	Status	—	100	30	Many Others	—	—
7	Vine Whip	Grass	Physical	35	100	15	Normal	—	○
10	Wrap	Normal	Physical	15	90	20	Normal	—	○
13	Growth	Normal	Status	—	—	40	Self	—	—
16	Leaf Tornado	Grass	Special	65	90	10	Normal	—	—
20	Leech Seed	Grass	Status	—	90	10	Normal	—	—
24	Mega Drain	Grass	Special	40	100	15	Normal	—	—
28	Slam	Normal	Physical	80	75	20	Normal	—	○
32	Leaf Blade	Grass	Physical	90	100	15	Normal	—	○
38	Coil	Poison	Status	—	—	20	Self	—	—
44	Giga Drain	Grass	Special	75	100	10	Normal	—	—
50	Wring Out	Normal	Special	—	100	5	Normal	—	○
56	Gastro Acid	Poison	Status	—	100	10	Normal	—	—
62	Leaf Storm	Grass	Special	140	90	5	Normal	—	—

TM & HM MOVES

Lv.	Name	Type	Kind	Pow.	Acc.	PP	Range	Long	DA
TM04	Calm Mind	Psychic	Status	—	—	20	Self	—	—
TM06	Toxic	Poison	Status	—	90	10	Normal	—	—
TM10	Hidden Power	Normal	Special	—	100	15	Normal	—	—
TM11	Sunny Day	Fire	Status	—	—	5	Both Sides	—	—
TM12	Taunt	Dark	Status	—	100	20	Normal	—	—
TM15	Hyper Beam	Normal	Special	150	90	5	Normal	—	—
TM16	Light Screen	Psychic	Status	—	—	30	Your Side	—	—
TM17	Protect	Normal	Status	—	—	10	Self	—	—
TM20	Safeguard	Normal	Status	—	—	25	Your Side	—	—
TM21	Frustration	Normal	Physical	—	100	20	Normal	—	○
TM22	SolarBeam	Grass	Special	120	100	10	Normal	—	—
TM27	Return	Normal	Physical	—	100	20	Normal	—	○
TM32	Double Team	Normal	Status	—	—	15	Self	—	—
TM33	Reflect	Psychic	Status	—	—	20	Your Side	—	—
TM40	Aerial Ace	Flying	Physical	60	—	20	Normal	○	○
TM41	Torment	Dark	Status	—	100	15	Normal	—	—
TM42	Facade	Normal	Physical	70	100	20	Normal	—	○
TM44	Rest	Psychic	Status	—	—	10	Self	—	—
TM45	Attract	Normal	Status	—	100	15	Normal	—	—
TM48	Round	Normal	Special	60	100	15	Normal	—	—
TM53	Energy Ball	Grass	Special	80	100	10	Normal	—	—
TM68	Giga Impact	Normal	Physical	150	90	5	Normal	—	○
TM70	Flash	Normal	Status	—	100	20	Normal	—	—
TM75	Swords Dance	Normal	Status	—	—	30	Self	—	—
TM82	Dragon Tail	Dragon	Physical	60	90	10	Normal	—	○
TM86	Grass Knot	Grass	Special	—	100	20	Normal	—	○
TM87	Swagger	Normal	Status	—	90	15	Normal	—	—
TM90	Substitute	Normal	Status	—	—	10	Self	—	—
TM94	Rock Smash	Fighting	Physical	40	100	15	Normal	—	○
HM01	Cut	Normal	Physical	50	95	30	Normal	—	○
HM04	Strength	Normal	Physical	80	100	15	Normal	—	○

MOVES TAUGHT BY PEOPLE

Name	Type	Kind	Pow.	Acc.	PP	Range	Long	DA
Grass Pledge	Grass	Special	50	100	10	Normal	—	—
Frenzy Plant	Grass	Special	150	90	5	Normal	—	—

MOVES TAUGHT BY MOVE TUTORS FOR SHARDS

Name	Type	Kind	Pow.	Acc.	PP	Range	Long	DA
Seed Bomb	Grass	Physical	80	100	15	Normal	—	—
Iron Tail	Steel	Physical	100	75	15	Normal	—	○
Aqua Tail	Water	Physical	90	90	10	Normal	—	○
Dragon Pulse	Dragon	Special	90	100	10	Normal	○	—
Bind	Normal	Physical	15	85	20	Normal	—	○
Snore	Normal	Special	40	100	15	Normal	—	—
Knock Off	Dark	Physical	20	100	20	Normal	—	○
Synthesis	Grass	Status	—	—	5	Self	—	—
Giga Drain	Grass	Special	75	100	10	Normal	—	—
Worry Seed	Grass	Status	—	100	10	Normal	—	—
Gastro Acid	Poison	Status	—	100	10	Normal	—	—
Outrage	Dragon	Physical	120	100	10	1 Random	—	○
Sleep Talk	Normal	Status	—	—	10	Self	—	—
Snatch	Dark	Status	—	—	10	Self	—	—

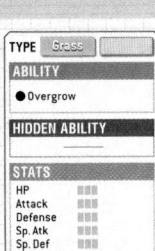

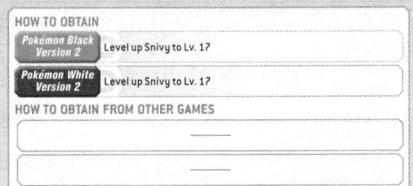

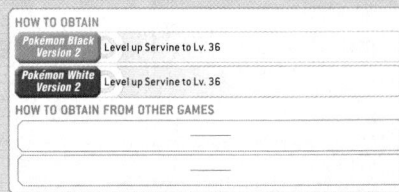

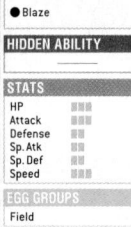

Fire Pig Pokémon

498 Tepig

- HEIGHT: 1'08"
- WEIGHT: 21.8 lbs.
- GENDER: ♂ / ♀

It loves to eat roasted berries, but sometimes it gets too excited and burns them to a crisp.

Same form for ♂ / ♀

Pokémon AR Marker

TYPE Fire

ABILITY
- Blaze

HIDDEN ABILITY
—

STATS
HP
Attack
Defense
Sp. Atk
Sp. Def
Speed

EGG GROUPS
Field

ITEMS SOMETIMES HELD
- None

EVOLUTION

HOW TO OBTAIN

Pokémon Black Version 2	Get from Bianca at the start of the adventure
Pokémon White Version 2	Get from Bianca at the start of the adventure

HOW TO OBTAIN FROM OTHER GAMES

—

—

LEVEL-UP AND LEARNED MOVES

Lv.	Name	Type	Kind	Pow.	Acc.	PP	Range	Long	DA
1	Tackle	Normal	Physical	50	100	35	Normal	—	○
3	Tail Whip	Normal	Status	—	100	30	Many Others	—	—
7	Ember	Fire	Special	40	100	25	Normal	—	—
9	Odor Sleuth	Normal	Status	—	—	40	Normal	—	—
13	Defense Curl	Normal	Status	—	—	40	Self	—	—
15	Flame Charge	Fire	Physical	50	100	20	Normal	—	○
19	Smog	Poison	Special	20	70	20	Normal	—	—
21	Rollout	Rock	Physical	30	90	20	Normal	—	○
25	Take Down	Normal	Physical	90	85	20	Normal	—	○
27	Heat Crash	Fire	Physical	—	100	10	Normal	—	○
31	Assurance	Dark	Physical	50	100	10	Normal	—	○
33	Flamethrower	Fire	Special	95	100	15	Normal	—	—
37	Head Smash	Rock	Physical	150	80	5	Normal	—	○
39	Roar	Normal	Status	—	100	20	Normal	—	—
43	Flare Blitz	Fire	Physical	120	100	15	Normal	—	○

TM & HM MOVES

Lv.	Name	Type	Kind	Pow.	Acc.	PP	Range	Long	DA
TM05	Roar	Normal	Status	—	100	20	Normal	—	—
TM06	Toxic	Poison	Status	—	90	10	Normal	—	—
TM10	Hidden Power	Normal	Special	—	100	15	Normal	—	—
TM11	Sunny Day	Fire	Status	—	—	5	Both Sides	—	—
TM12	Taunt	Dark	Status	—	100	20	Normal	—	—
TM17	Protect	Normal	Status	—	—	10	Self	—	—
TM21	Frustration	Normal	Physical	—	100	20	Normal	—	○
TM22	SolarBeam	Grass	Special	120	100	10	Normal	—	—
TM27	Return	Normal	Physical	—	100	20	Normal	—	○
TM32	Double Team	Normal	Status	—	—	15	Self	—	—
TM35	Flamethrower	Fire	Special	95	100	15	Normal	—	—
TM38	Fire Blast	Fire	Special	120	85	5	Normal	—	—
TM39	Rock Tomb	Rock	Physical	50	80	10	Normal	—	—
TM42	Facade	Normal	Physical	70	100	20	Normal	—	○
TM43	Flame Charge	Fire	Physical	50	100	20	Normal	—	○
TM44	Rest	Psychic	Status	—	—	10	Self	—	—
TM45	Attract	Normal	Status	—	100	15	Normal	—	—
TM48	Round	Normal	Special	60	100	15	Normal	—	—
TM49	Echoed Voice	Normal	Special	40	100	15	Normal	—	—
TM50	Overheat	Fire	Special	140	90	5	Normal	—	—
TM59	Incinerate	Fire	Special	30	100	15	Many Others	—	—
TM61	Will-O-Wisp	Fire	Status	—	75	15	Normal	—	—
TM74	Gyro Ball	Steel	Physical	—	100	5	Normal	—	○
TM86	Grass Knot	Grass	Special	—	100	20	Normal	—	○
TM87	Swagger	Normal	Status	—	90	15	Normal	—	—
TM90	Substitute	Normal	Status	—	—	10	Self	—	—
TM93	Wild Charge	Electric	Physical	90	100	15	Normal	—	○
TM94	Rock Smash	Fighting	Physical	40	100	15	Normal	—	○
HM04	Strength	Normal	Physical	80	100	15	Normal	—	○

MOVES TAUGHT BY PEOPLE

Name	Type	Kind	Pow.	Acc.	PP	Range	Long	DA
Fire Pledge	Fire	Special	50	100	10	Normal	—	—

MOVES TAUGHT BY MOVE TUTORS FOR SHARDS

Name	Type	Kind	Pow.	Acc.	PP	Range	Long	DA
Covet	Normal	Physical	60	100	40	Normal	—	○
Iron Tail	Steel	Physical	100	75	15	Normal	—	○
Superpower	Fighting	Physical	120	100	5	Normal	—	○
Snore	Normal	Special	40	100	15	Normal	—	—
Heat Wave	Fire	Special	100	90	10	Many Others	—	—
Helping Hand	Normal	Status	—	—	20	1 Ally	—	—
Endeavor	Normal	Physical	—	100	5	Normal	—	○
Sleep Talk	Normal	Status	—	—	10	Self	—	—

EGG MOVES

Name	Type	Kind	Pow.	Acc.	PP	Range	Long	DA
Covet	Normal	Physical	60	100	40	Normal	—	○
Body Slam	Normal	Physical	85	100	15	Normal	—	○
Thrash	Normal	Physical	120	100	10	1 Random	—	○
Magnitude	Ground	Physical	—	100	30	Adjacent	—	—
Superpower	Fighting	Physical	120	100	5	Normal	—	○
Curse	Ghost	Status	—	—	10	Varies	—	—
Endeavor	Normal	Physical	—	100	5	Normal	—	○
Yawn	Normal	Status	—	—	10	Normal	—	—
Sleep Talk	Normal	Status	—	—	10	Self	—	—
Heavy Slam	Steel	Physical	—	100	10	Normal	—	○

Fire Pig Pokémon

499 Pignite

- HEIGHT: 3'03"
- WEIGHT: 122.4 lbs.
- GENDER: ♂ / ♀

The more it eats, the more fuel it has to make the fire in its stomach stronger. This fills it with even more power.

Same form for ♂ / ♀

Pokémon AR Marker

TYPE Fire Fighting

ABILITY
- Blaze

HIDDEN ABILITY
—

STATS
HP
Attack
Defense
Sp. Atk
Sp. Def
Speed

EGG GROUPS
Field

ITEMS SOMETIMES HELD
- None

EVOLUTION

HOW TO OBTAIN

Pokémon Black Version 2	Level up Tepig to Lv. 17
Pokémon White Version 2	Level up Tepig to Lv. 17

HOW TO OBTAIN FROM OTHER GAMES

—

—

LEVEL-UP AND LEARNED MOVES

Lv.	Name	Type	Kind	Pow.	Acc.	PP	Range	Long	DA
1	Tackle	Normal	Physical	50	100	35	Normal	—	○
1	Tail Whip	Normal	Status	—	100	30	Many Others	—	—
1	Ember	Fire	Special	40	100	25	Normal	—	—
1	Odor Sleuth	Normal	Status	—	—	40	Normal	—	—
3	Tail Whip	Normal	Status	—	100	30	Many Others	—	—
7	Ember	Fire	Special	40	100	25	Normal	—	—
9	Odor Sleuth	Normal	Status	—	—	40	Normal	—	—
13	Defense Curl	Normal	Status	—	—	40	Self	—	—
15	Flame Charge	Fire	Physical	50	100	20	Normal	—	○
17	Arm Thrust	Fighting	Physical	15	100	20	Normal	—	○
20	Smog	Poison	Special	20	70	20	Normal	—	—
23	Rollout	Rock	Physical	30	90	20	Normal	—	○
28	Take Down	Normal	Physical	90	85	20	Normal	—	○
31	Heat Crash	Fire	Physical	—	100	10	Normal	—	○
36	Assurance	Dark	Physical	50	100	10	Normal	—	○
39	Flamethrower	Fire	Special	95	100	15	Normal	—	—
44	Head Smash	Rock	Physical	150	80	5	Normal	—	○
47	Roar	Normal	Status	—	100	20	Normal	—	—
52	Flare Blitz	Fire	Physical	120	100	15	Normal	—	○

TM & HM MOVES

Lv.	Name	Type	Kind	Pow.	Acc.	PP	Range	Long	DA
TM05	Roar	Normal	Status	—	100	20	Normal	—	—
TM06	Toxic	Poison	Status	—	90	10	Normal	—	—
TM10	Hidden Power	Normal	Special	—	100	15	Normal	—	—
TM11	Sunny Day	Fire	Status	—	—	5	Both Sides	—	—
TM12	Taunt	Dark	Status	—	100	20	Normal	—	—
TM17	Protect	Normal	Status	—	—	10	Self	—	—
TM21	Frustration	Normal	Physical	—	100	20	Normal	—	○
TM22	SolarBeam	Grass	Special	120	100	10	Normal	—	—
TM27	Return	Normal	Physical	—	100	20	Normal	—	○
TM31	Brick Break	Fighting	Physical	75	100	15	Normal	—	○
TM32	Double Team	Normal	Status	—	—	15	Self	—	—
TM35	Flamethrower	Fire	Special	95	100	15	Normal	—	—
TM38	Fire Blast	Fire	Special	120	85	5	Normal	—	—
TM39	Rock Tomb	Rock	Physical	50	80	10	Normal	—	—
TM42	Facade	Normal	Physical	70	100	20	Normal	—	○
TM43	Flame Charge	Fire	Physical	50	100	20	Normal	—	○
TM44	Rest	Psychic	Status	—	—	10	Self	—	—
TM45	Attract	Normal	Status	—	100	15	Normal	—	—
TM47	Low Sweep	Fighting	Physical	60	100	20	Normal	—	○
TM48	Round	Normal	Special	60	100	15	Normal	—	—
TM49	Echoed Voice	Normal	Special	40	100	15	Normal	—	—
TM50	Overheat	Fire	Special	140	90	5	Normal	—	—
TM52	Focus Blast	Fighting	Special	120	70	5	Normal	—	—
TM56	Fling	Dark	Physical	—	100	10	Normal	—	—
TM59	Incinerate	Fire	Special	30	100	15	Many Others	—	—
TM61	Will-O-Wisp	Fire	Status	—	75	15	Normal	—	—
TM71	Stone Edge	Rock	Physical	100	80	5	Normal	—	—
TM74	Gyro Ball	Steel	Physical	—	100	5	Normal	—	○
TM78	Bulldoze	Ground	Physical	60	100	20	Adjacent	—	—
TM80	Rock Slide	Rock	Physical	75	90	10	Many Others	—	—
TM83	Work Up	Normal	Status	—	—	30	Self	—	—
TM84	Poison Jab	Poison	Physical	80	100	20	Normal	—	○
TM86	Grass Knot	Grass	Special	—	100	20	Normal	—	○
TM87	Swagger	Normal	Status	—	90	15	Normal	—	—
TM90	Substitute	Normal	Status	—	—	10	Self	—	—
TM93	Wild Charge	Electric	Physical	90	100	15	Normal	—	○
TM94	Rock Smash	Fighting	Physical	40	100	15	Normal	—	○
HM04	Strength	Normal	Physical	80	100	15	Normal	—	○

MOVES TAUGHT BY PEOPLE

Name	Type	Kind	Pow.	Acc.	PP	Range	Long	DA
Fire Pledge	Fire	Special	50	100	10	Normal	—	—

MOVES TAUGHT BY MOVE TUTORS FOR SHARDS

Name	Type	Kind	Pow.	Acc.	PP	Range	Long	DA
Covet	Normal	Physical	60	100	40	Normal	—	○
Low Kick	Fighting	Physical	—	100	20	Normal	—	○
Fire Punch	Fire	Physical	75	100	15	Normal	—	○
ThunderPunch	Electric	Physical	75	100	15	Normal	—	○
Iron Tail	Steel	Physical	100	75	15	Normal	—	○
Superpower	Fighting	Physical	120	100	5	Normal	—	○
Snore	Normal	Special	40	100	15	Normal	—	—
Heat Wave	Fire	Special	100	90	10	Many Others	—	—
Helping Hand	Normal	Status	—	—	20	1 Ally	—	—
Endeavor	Normal	Physical	—	100	5	Normal	—	○
Sleep Talk	Normal	Status	—	—	10	Self	—	—

Mega Fire Pig Pokémon
500 Emboar

- HEIGHT: 5'03"
- WEIGHT: 330.7 lbs.
- GENDER: ♂ / ♀

A flaring beard of fire is proof that it is fired up. It is adept at using many different moves.

Same form for ♂ / ♀

TYPE | Fire | Fighting

ABILITY
- Blaze

HIDDEN ABILITY
—

STATS
- HP
- Attack
- Defense
- Sp. Atk
- Sp. Def
- Speed

EGG GROUPS
Field

ITEMS SOMETIMES HELD
- None

Pokémon AR Marker

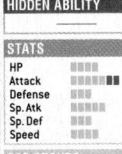

EVOLUTION

Tepig → Lv. 17 → Pignite → Lv. 36 → Emboar

HOW TO OBTAIN
Pokémon Black Version 2	Level up Pignite to Lv. 36
Pokémon White Version 2	Level up Pignite to Lv. 36

HOW TO OBTAIN FROM OTHER GAMES

LEVEL-UP AND LEARNED MOVES

Lv.	Name	Type	Kind	Pow.	Acc.	PP	Range	Long	DA
1	Hammer Arm	Fighting	Physical	100	90	10	Normal	—	○
1	Tackle	Normal	Physical	50	100	35	Normal	—	—
1	Tail Whip	Normal	Status	—	100	30	Many Others	—	—
1	Ember	Fire	Special	40	100	25	Normal	—	—
1	Odor Sleuth	Normal	Status	—	—	40	Normal	—	—
3	Tail Whip	Normal	Status	—	100	30	Many Others	—	—
7	Ember	Fire	Special	40	100	25	Normal	—	—
9	Odor Sleuth	Normal	Status	—	—	40	Normal	—	—
13	Defense Curl	Normal	Status	—	—	40	Self	—	—
15	Flame Charge	Fire	Physical	50	100	20	Normal	—	○
17	Arm Thrust	Fighting	Physical	15	100	20	Normal	—	○
20	Smog	Poison	Special	20	70	20	Normal	—	—
23	Rollout	Rock	Physical	30	90	20	Normal	—	○
28	Take Down	Normal	Physical	90	85	20	Normal	—	○
31	Heat Crash	Fire	Physical	—	100	10	Normal	—	○
38	Assurance	Dark	Physical	50	100	10	Normal	—	○
43	Flamethrower	Fire	Special	95	100	15	Normal	—	—
50	Head Smash	Rock	Physical	150	80	5	Normal	—	○
55	Roar	Normal	Status	—	100	20	Normal	—	—
62	Flare Blitz	Fire	Physical	120	100	15	Normal	—	○

TM & HM MOVES

Lv.	Name	Type	Kind	Pow.	Acc.	PP	Range	Long	DA
TM05	Roar	Normal	Status	—	100	20	Normal	—	—
TM06	Toxic	Poison	Status	—	90	10	Normal	—	—
TM08	Bulk Up	Fighting	Status	—	—	20	Self	—	—
TM10	Hidden Power	Normal	Special	—	100	15	Normal	—	—
TM11	Sunny Day	Fire	Status	—	—	5	Both Sides	—	—
TM12	Taunt	Dark	Status	—	100	20	Normal	—	—
TM15	Hyper Beam	Normal	Special	150	90	5	Normal	—	—
TM17	Protect	Normal	Status	—	—	10	Self	—	—
TM21	Frustration	Normal	Physical	—	100	20	Normal	—	○
TM22	SolarBeam	Grass	Special	120	100	10	Normal	—	—
TM23	Smack Down	Rock	Physical	50	100	15	Normal	—	—
TM26	Earthquake	Ground	Physical	100	100	10	Adjacent	—	○
TM27	Return	Normal	Physical	—	100	20	Normal	—	○
TM31	Brick Break	Fighting	Physical	75	100	15	Normal	—	○
TM32	Double Team	Normal	Status	—	—	15	Self	—	—
TM35	Flamethrower	Fire	Special	95	100	15	Normal	—	—
TM38	Fire Blast	Fire	Special	120	85	5	Normal	—	—
TM39	Rock Tomb	Rock	Physical	50	80	10	Normal	—	—
TM42	Facade	Normal	Physical	70	100	20	Normal	—	—
TM43	Flame Charge	Fire	Physical	50	100	20	Normal	—	○
TM44	Rest	Psychic	Status	—	—	10	Self	—	—
TM45	Attract	Normal	Status	—	100	15	Normal	—	—
TM47	Low Sweep	Fighting	Physical	60	100	20	Normal	—	○
TM48	Round	Normal	Special	60	100	15	Normal	—	—
TM49	Echoed Voice	Normal	Special	40	100	15	Normal	—	—
TM50	Overheat	Fire	Special	140	90	5	Normal	—	—
TM52	Focus Blast	Fighting	Special	120	70	5	Normal	—	—
TM55	Scald	Water	Special	80	100	15	Normal	—	—
TM56	Fling	Dark	Physical	—	100	10	Normal	—	—
TM59	Incinerate	Fire	Special	30	100	15	Many Others	—	—
TM61	Will-O-Wisp	Fire	Status	—	75	15	Normal	—	—
TM68	Giga Impact	Normal	Physical	150	90	5	Normal	—	○
TM71	Stone Edge	Rock	Physical	100	80	5	Normal	—	—

Lv.	Name	Type	Kind	Pow.	Acc.	PP	Range	Long	DA
TM74	Gyro Ball	Steel	Physical	—	100	5	Normal	—	○
TM78	Bulldoze	Ground	Physical	60	100	20	Adjacent	—	—
TM80	Rock Slide	Rock	Physical	75	90	10	Many Others	—	—
TM83	Work Up	Normal	Status	—	—	30	Self	—	—
TM84	Poison Jab	Poison	Physical	80	100	20	Normal	—	○
TM86	Grass Knot	Grass	Special	—	100	20	Normal	—	—
TM87	Swagger	Normal	Status	—	90	15	Normal	—	—
TM90	Substitute	Normal	Status	—	—	10	Self	—	—
TM93	Wild Charge	Electric	Physical	90	100	15	Normal	—	○
TM94	Rock Smash	Fighting	Physical	40	100	15	Normal	—	○
HM04	Strength	Normal	Physical	80	100	15	Normal	—	—

MOVES TAUGHT BY PEOPLE

Name	Type	Kind	Pow.	Acc.	PP	Range	Long	DA
Fire Pledge	Fire	Special	50	100	10	Normal	—	—
Blast Burn	Fire	Special	150	90	5	Normal	—	—

MOVES TAUGHT BY MOVE TUTORS FOR SHARDS

Name	Type	Kind	Pow.	Acc.	PP	Range	Long	DA
Covet	Normal	Physical	60	100	40	Normal	—	○
Iron Head	Steel	Physical	80	100	15	Normal	—	○
Low Kick	Fighting	Physical	—	100	20	Normal	—	—
Fire Punch	Fire	Physical	75	100	15	Normal	—	○
ThunderPunch	Electric	Physical	75	100	15	Normal	—	○
Block	Normal	Status	—	—	5	Normal	—	—
Iron Tail	Steel	Physical	100	75	15	Normal	—	○
Superpower	Fighting	Physical	120	100	5	Normal	—	—
Snore	Normal	Special	40	100	15	Many Others	—	—
Heat Wave	Fire	Special	100	90	10	Many Others	—	—
Helping Hand	Normal	Status	—	—	20	1 Ally	—	—
Endeavor	Normal	Physical	—	100	5	Normal	—	○
Sleep Talk	Normal	Status	—	—	10	Self	—	—

Sea Otter Pokémon
501 Oshawott

- HEIGHT: 1'08"
- WEIGHT: 13.0 lbs.
- GENDER: ♂ / ♀

The scalchop on its stomach isn't just used for battle—it can be used to break open hard berries as well.

Same form for ♂ / ♀

TYPE | Water

ABILITY
- Torrent

HIDDEN ABILITY
—

STATS
- HP
- Attack
- Defense
- Sp. Atk
- Sp. Def
- Speed

EGG GROUPS
Field

ITEMS SOMETIMES HELD
- None

Pokémon AR Marker

EVOLUTION

Oshawott → Lv. 17 → Dewott → Lv. 36 → Samurott

HOW TO OBTAIN
Pokémon Black Version 2	Get from Bianca at the start of the adventure
Pokémon White Version 2	Get from Bianca at the start of the adventure

HOW TO OBTAIN FROM OTHER GAMES

LEVEL-UP AND LEARNED MOVES

Lv.	Name	Type	Kind	Pow.	Acc.	PP	Range	Long	DA
1	Tackle	Normal	Physical	50	100	35	Normal	—	—
5	Tail Whip	Normal	Status	—	100	30	Many Others	—	—
7	Water Gun	Water	Special	40	100	25	Normal	—	—
11	Water Sport	Water	Status	—	—	15	Both Sides	—	—
13	Focus Energy	Normal	Status	—	—	30	Self	—	—
17	Razor Shell	Water	Physical	75	95	10	Normal	—	○
19	Fury Cutter	Bug	Physical	20	95	20	Normal	—	○
23	Water Pulse	Water	Special	60	100	20	Normal	○	—
25	Revenge	Fighting	Physical	60	100	10	Normal	—	○
29	Aqua Jet	Water	Physical	40	100	20	Normal	—	○
31	Encore	Normal	Status	—	100	5	Normal	—	—
35	Aqua Tail	Water	Physical	90	90	10	Normal	—	○
37	Retaliate	Normal	Physical	70	100	5	Normal	—	—
41	Swords Dance	Normal	Status	—	—	30	Self	—	—
43	Hydro Pump	Water	Special	120	80	5	Normal	—	—

TM & HM MOVES

Lv.	Name	Type	Kind	Pow.	Acc.	PP	Range	Long	DA
TM06	Toxic	Poison	Status	—	90	10	Normal	—	—
TM07	Hail	Ice	Status	—	—	10	Both Sides	—	—
TM10	Hidden Power	Normal	Special	—	100	15	Normal	—	—
TM12	Taunt	Dark	Status	—	100	20	Normal	—	—
TM13	Ice Beam	Ice	Special	95	100	10	Normal	—	—
TM14	Blizzard	Ice	Special	120	70	5	Many Others	—	—
TM17	Protect	Normal	Status	—	—	10	Self	—	—
TM18	Rain Dance	Water	Status	—	—	5	Both Sides	—	—
TM21	Frustration	Normal	Physical	—	100	20	Normal	—	○
TM27	Return	Normal	Physical	—	100	20	Normal	—	○
TM28	Dig	Ground	Physical	80	100	10	Normal	—	○
TM32	Double Team	Normal	Status	—	—	15	Self	—	—
TM40	Aerial Ace	Flying	Physical	60	—	20	Normal	○	○
TM42	Facade	Normal	Physical	70	100	20	Normal	—	—
TM44	Rest	Psychic	Status	—	—	10	Self	—	—
TM45	Attract	Normal	Status	—	100	15	Normal	—	—
TM48	Round	Normal	Special	60	100	15	Normal	—	—
TM54	False Swipe	Normal	Physical	40	100	40	Normal	—	○
TM55	Scald	Water	Special	80	100	15	Normal	—	—
TM56	Fling	Dark	Physical	—	100	10	Normal	—	—
TM67	Retaliate	Normal	Physical	70	100	5	Normal	—	—
TM75	Swords Dance	Normal	Status	—	—	30	Self	—	—
TM81	X-Scissor	Bug	Physical	80	100	15	Normal	—	○
TM86	Grass Knot	Grass	Special	—	100	20	Normal	—	—
TM87	Swagger	Normal	Status	—	90	15	Normal	—	—
TM90	Substitute	Normal	Status	—	—	10	Self	—	—
TM94	Rock Smash	Fighting	Physical	40	100	15	Normal	—	○
HM01	Cut	Normal	Physical	50	95	30	Normal	—	—
HM03	Surf	Water	Special	95	100	15	Adjacent	—	—
HM05	Waterfall	Water	Physical	80	100	15	Normal	—	○
HM06	Dive	Water	Physical	80	100	10	Normal	—	—

MOVES TAUGHT BY PEOPLE

Name	Type	Kind	Pow.	Acc.	PP	Range	Long	DA
Water Pledge	Water	Special	50	100	10	Normal	—	—

MOVES TAUGHT BY MOVE TUTORS FOR SHARDS

Name	Type	Kind	Pow.	Acc.	PP	Range	Long	DA
Covet	Normal	Physical	60	100	40	Normal	—	○
Icy Wind	Ice	Special	55	95	15	Many Others	—	—
Iron Tail	Steel	Physical	100	75	15	Normal	—	○
Aqua Tail	Water	Physical	90	90	10	Normal	—	○
Snore	Normal	Special	40	100	15	Many Others	—	—
Helping Hand	Normal	Status	—	—	20	1 Ally	—	—
Sleep Talk	Normal	Status	—	—	10	Self	—	—

EGG MOVES

Name	Type	Kind	Pow.	Acc.	PP	Range	Long	DA
Copycat	Normal	Status	—	—	20	Self	—	—
Detect	Fighting	Status	—	—	5	Self	—	—
Air Slash	Flying	Special	75	95	20	Normal	○	—
Assurance	Dark	Physical	50	100	10	Normal	—	○
Brine	Water	Special	65	100	10	Normal	—	—
Night Slash	Dark	Physical	70	100	15	Normal	—	○
Trump Card	Normal	Special	—	—	5	Normal	—	—
Screech	Normal	Status	—	85	40	Normal	—	—

502 Dewott

Discipline Pokémon

- HEIGHT: 2'07"
- WEIGHT: 54.0 lbs.
- GENDER: ♂ / ♀

As a result of strict training, each Dewott learns different forms for using the scalchops.

Same form for ♂ / ♀

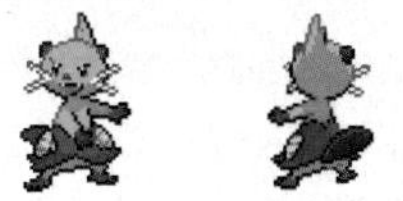

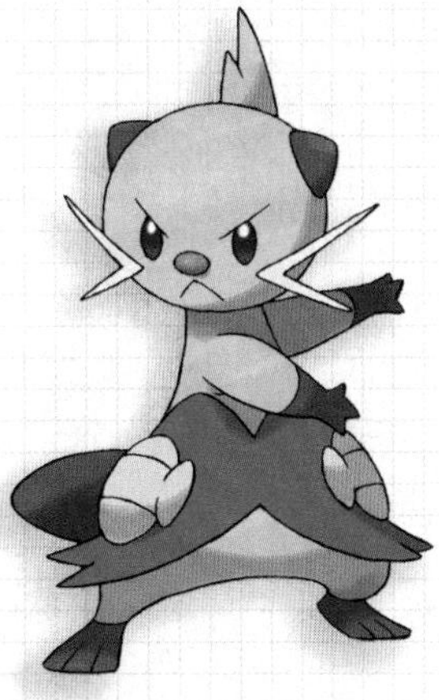

Pokémon AR Marker

TYPE Water

ABILITY

- Torrent

HIDDEN ABILITY

—

STATS

HP
Attack
Defense
Sp. Atk
Sp. Def
Speed

EGG GROUPS

Field

ITEMS SOMETIMES HELD

- None

EVOLUTION

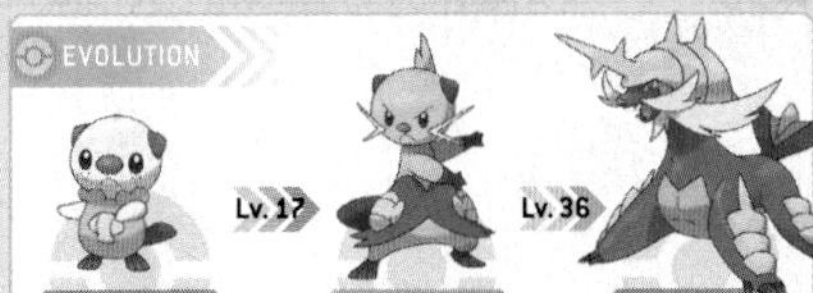

HOW TO OBTAIN

Pokémon Black Version 2	Level up Oshawott to Lv. 17
Pokémon White Version 2	Level up Oshawott to Lv. 17

HOW TO OBTAIN FROM OTHER GAMES

—

—

LEVEL-UP AND LEARNED MOVES

Lv.	Name	Type	Kind	Pow.	Acc.	PP	Range	Long	DA
1	Tackle	Normal	Physical	50	100	35	Normal	—	○
1	Tail Whip	Normal	Status	—	100	30	Many Others	—	—
1	Water Gun	Water	Special	40	100	25	Normal	—	—
1	Water Sport	Water	Status	—	—	15	Both Sides	—	—
5	Tail Whip	Normal	Status	—	100	30	Many Others	—	—
7	Water Gun	Water	Special	40	100	25	Normal	—	—
11	Water Sport	Water	Status	—	—	15	Both Sides	—	—
13	Focus Energy	Normal	Status	—	—	30	Self	—	—
17	Razor Shell	Water	Physical	75	95	10	Normal	—	○
20	Fury Cutter	Bug	Physical	20	95	20	Normal	—	○
25	Water Pulse	Water	Special	60	100	20	Normal	○	—
28	Revenge	Fighting	Physical	60	100	10	Normal	—	○
33	Aqua Jet	Water	Physical	40	100	20	Normal	—	○
36	Encore	Normal	Status	—	100	5	Normal	—	—
41	Aqua Tail	Water	Physical	90	90	10	Normal	—	○
44	Retaliate	Normal	Physical	70	100	5	Normal	—	○
49	Swords Dance	Normal	Status	—	—	30	Self	—	—
52	Hydro Pump	Water	Special	120	80	5	Normal	—	—

TM & HM MOVES

Lv.	Name	Type	Kind	Pow.	Acc.	PP	Range	Long	DA
TM06	Toxic	Poison	Status	—	90	10	Normal	—	—
TM07	Hail	Ice	Status	—	—	10	Both Sides	—	—
TM10	Hidden Power	Normal	Special	—	100	15	Normal	—	—
TM12	Taunt	Dark	Status	—	100	20	Normal	—	—
TM13	Ice Beam	Ice	Special	95	100	10	Normal	—	—
TM14	Blizzard	Ice	Special	120	70	5	Many Others	—	—
TM17	Protect	Normal	Status	—	—	10	Self	—	—
TM18	Rain Dance	Water	Status	—	—	5	Both Sides	—	—
TM21	Frustration	Normal	Physical	—	100	20	Normal	—	○
TM27	Return	Normal	Physical	—	100	20	Normal	—	○
TM28	Dig	Ground	Physical	80	100	10	Normal	—	○
TM32	Double Team	Normal	Status	—	—	15	Self	—	—
TM40	Aerial Ace	Flying	Physical	60	—	20	Normal	○	○
TM42	Facade	Normal	Physical	70	100	20	Normal	—	○
TM44	Rest	Psychic	Status	—	—	10	Self	—	—
TM45	Attract	Normal	Status	—	100	15	Normal	—	—
TM48	Round	Normal	Special	60	100	15	Normal	—	—
TM54	False Swipe	Normal	Physical	40	100	40	Normal	—	○
TM55	Scald	Water	Special	80	100	15	Normal	—	—
TM56	Fling	Dark	Physical	—	100	10	Normal	—	—
TM67	Retaliate	Normal	Physical	70	100	5	Normal	—	○
TM75	Swords Dance	Normal	Status	—	—	30	Self	—	—
TM81	X-Scissor	Bug	Physical	80	100	15	Normal	—	○
TM86	Grass Knot	Grass	Special	—	100	20	Normal	—	○
TM87	Swagger	Normal	Status	—	90	15	Normal	—	—
TM90	Substitute	Normal	Status	—	—	10	Self	—	—
TM94	Rock Smash	Fighting	Physical	40	100	15	Normal	—	○
HM01	Cut	Normal	Physical	50	95	30	Normal	—	○
HM03	Surf	Water	Special	95	100	15	Adjacent	—	—
HM05	Waterfall	Water	Physical	80	100	15	Normal	—	○
HM06	Dive	Water	Physical	80	100	10	Normal	—	○

MOVES TAUGHT BY PEOPLE

Name	Type	Kind	Pow.	Acc.	PP	Range	Long	DA
Water Pledge	Water	Special	50	100	10	Normal	—	—

MOVES TAUGHT BY MOVE TUTORS FOR SHARDS

Name	Type	Kind	Pow.	Acc.	PP	Range	Long	DA
Covet	Normal	Physical	60	100	40	Normal	—	○
Icy Wind	Ice	Special	55	95	15	Many Others	—	—
Iron Tail	Steel	Physical	100	75	15	Normal	—	○
Aqua Tail	Water	Physical	90	90	10	Normal	—	○
Snore	Normal	Special	40	100	15	Normal	—	—
Helping Hand	Normal	Status	—	—	20	1 Ally	—	—
Sleep Talk	Normal	Status	—	—	10	Self	—	—

503 Samurott

Formidable Pokémon

- HEIGHT: 4'11"
- WEIGHT: 208.6 lbs.
- GENDER: ♂ / ♀

In the time it takes a foe to blink, it can draw and sheathe the seamitars attached to its front legs.

Same form for ♂ / ♀

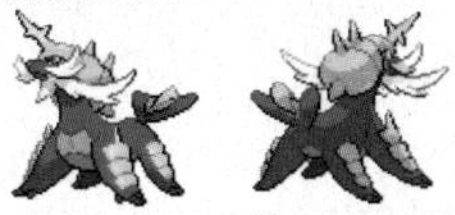

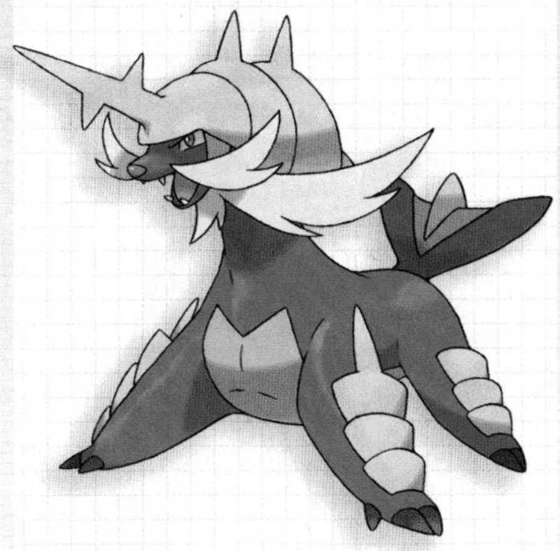

Pokémon AR Marker

TYPE Water

ABILITY

- Torrent

HIDDEN ABILITY

—

STATS

HP
Attack
Defense
Sp. Atk
Sp. Def
Speed

EGG GROUPS

Field

ITEMS SOMETIMES HELD

- None

EVOLUTION

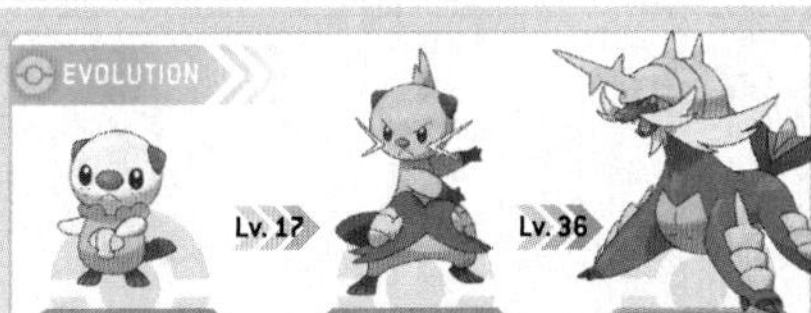

HOW TO OBTAIN

Pokémon Black Version 2	Level up Dewott to Lv. 36
Pokémon White Version 2	Level up Dewott to Lv. 36

HOW TO OBTAIN FROM OTHER GAMES

—

—

LEVEL-UP AND LEARNED MOVES

Lv.	Name	Type	Kind	Pow.	Acc.	PP	Range	Long	DA
1	Megahorn	Bug	Physical	120	85	10	Normal	—	○
1	Tackle	Normal	Physical	50	100	35	Normal	—	○
1	Tail Whip	Normal	Status	—	100	30	Many Others	—	—
1	Water Gun	Water	Special	40	100	25	Normal	—	—
1	Water Sport	Water	Status	—	—	15	Both Sides	—	—
5	Tail Whip	Normal	Status	—	100	30	Many Others	—	—
7	Water Gun	Water	Special	40	100	25	Normal	—	—
11	Water Sport	Water	Status	—	—	15	Both Sides	—	—
13	Focus Energy	Normal	Status	—	—	30	Self	—	—
17	Razor Shell	Water	Physical	75	95	10	Normal	—	○
20	Fury Cutter	Bug	Physical	20	95	20	Normal	—	○
25	Water Pulse	Water	Special	60	100	20	Normal	○	—
28	Revenge	Fighting	Physical	60	100	10	Normal	—	○
33	Aqua Jet	Water	Physical	40	100	20	Normal	—	○
36	Slash	Normal	Physical	70	100	20	Normal	—	○
38	Encore	Normal	Status	—	100	5	Normal	—	—
45	Aqua Tail	Water	Physical	90	90	10	Normal	—	○
50	Retaliate	Normal	Physical	70	100	5	Normal	—	○
57	Swords Dance	Normal	Status	—	—	30	Self	—	—
62	Hydro Pump	Water	Special	120	80	5	Normal	—	—

TM & HM MOVES

Lv.	Name	Type	Kind	Pow.	Acc.	PP	Range	Long	DA
TM06	Toxic	Poison	Status	—	90	10	Normal	—	—
TM07	Hail	Ice	Status	—	—	10	Both Sides	—	—
TM10	Hidden Power	Normal	Special	—	100	15	Normal	—	—
TM12	Taunt	Dark	Status	—	100	20	Normal	—	—
TM13	Ice Beam	Ice	Special	95	100	10	Normal	—	—
TM14	Blizzard	Ice	Special	120	70	5	Many Others	—	—
TM15	Hyper Beam	Normal	Special	150	90	5	Normal	—	—
TM17	Protect	Normal	Status	—	—	10	Self	—	—
TM18	Rain Dance	Water	Status	—	—	5	Both Sides	—	—
TM21	Frustration	Normal	Physical	—	100	20	Normal	—	○
TM27	Return	Normal	Physical	—	100	20	Normal	—	○
TM28	Dig	Ground	Physical	80	100	10	Normal	—	○
TM32	Double Team	Normal	Status	—	—	15	Self	—	—
TM40	Aerial Ace	Flying	Physical	60	—	20	Normal	○	○
TM42	Facade	Normal	Physical	70	100	20	Normal	—	○
TM44	Rest	Psychic	Status	—	—	10	Self	—	—
TM45	Attract	Normal	Status	—	100	15	Normal	—	—
TM48	Round	Normal	Special	60	100	15	Normal	—	—
TM54	False Swipe	Normal	Physical	40	100	40	Normal	—	○
TM55	Scald	Water	Special	80	100	15	Normal	—	—
TM56	Fling	Dark	Physical	—	100	10	Normal	—	—
TM67	Retaliate	Normal	Physical	70	100	5	Normal	—	○
TM68	Giga Impact	Normal	Physical	150	90	5	Normal	—	○
TM75	Swords Dance	Normal	Status	—	—	30	Self	—	—
TM81	X-Scissor	Bug	Physical	80	100	15	Normal	—	○
TM82	Dragon Tail	Dragon	Physical	60	90	10	Normal	—	○
TM86	Grass Knot	Grass	Special	—	100	20	Normal	—	○
TM87	Swagger	Normal	Status	—	90	15	Normal	—	—
TM90	Substitute	Normal	Status	—	—	10	Self	—	—
TM94	Rock Smash	Fighting	Physical	40	100	15	Normal	—	○
HM01	Cut	Normal	Physical	50	95	30	Normal	—	○
HM03	Surf	Water	Special	95	100	15	Adjacent	—	—
HM04	Strength	Normal	Physical	80	100	15	Normal	—	○
HM05	Waterfall	Water	Physical	80	100	15	Normal	—	○
HM06	Dive	Water	Physical	80	100	10	Normal	—	○

MOVES TAUGHT BY PEOPLE

Name	Type	Kind	Pow.	Acc.	PP	Range	Long	DA
Water Pledge	Water	Special	50	100	10	Normal	—	—
Hydro Cannon	Water	Special	150	90	5	Normal	—	—

MOVES TAUGHT BY MOVE TUTORS FOR SHARDS

Name	Type	Kind	Pow.	Acc.	PP	Range	Long	DA
Covet	Normal	Physical	60	100	40	Normal	—	○
Block	Normal	Status	—	—	5	Normal	—	—
Icy Wind	Ice	Special	55	95	15	Many Others	—	—
Iron Tail	Steel	Physical	100	75	15	Normal	—	○
Aqua Tail	Water	Physical	90	90	10	Normal	—	○
Superpower	Fighting	Physical	120	100	5	Normal	—	○
Snore	Normal	Special	40	100	15	Normal	—	—
Knock Off	Dark	Physical	20	100	20	Normal	—	○
Helping Hand	Normal	Status	—	—	20	1 Ally	—	—
Sleep Talk	Normal	Status	—	—	10	Self	—	—

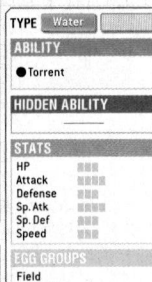

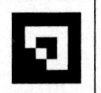

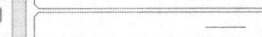

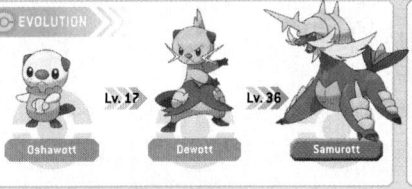

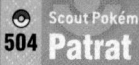

504 Patrat

Scout Pokémon

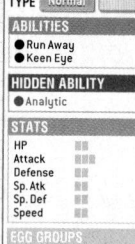

- HEIGHT: 1'08"
- WEIGHT: 25.6 lbs.
- GENDER: ♂ / ♀

Extremely cautious, one of them will always be on the lookout, but it won't notice a foe coming from behind.

Same form for ♂ / ♀

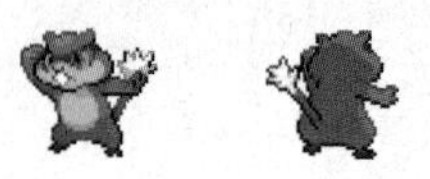

TYPE: Normal

ABILITIES
- Run Away
- Keen Eye

HIDDEN ABILITY
- Analytic

STATS
HP
Attack
Defense
Sp. Atk
Sp. Def
Speed

EGG GROUPS
Field

ITEMS SOMETIMES HELD
- None

EVOLUTION

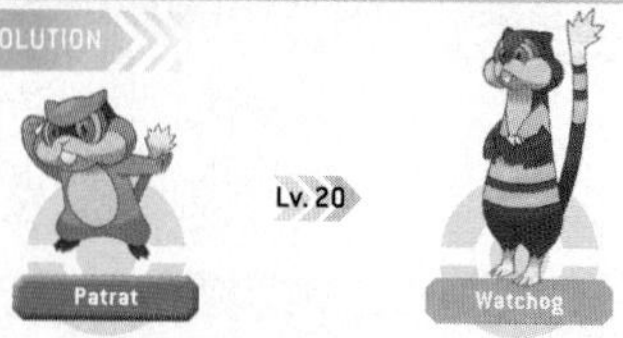

HOW TO OBTAIN

Pokémon Black Version 2	❶ Route 19 ❷ Route 20
Pokémon White Version 2	❶ Route 19 ❷ Route 20

HOW TO OBTAIN FROM OTHER GAMES

—

—

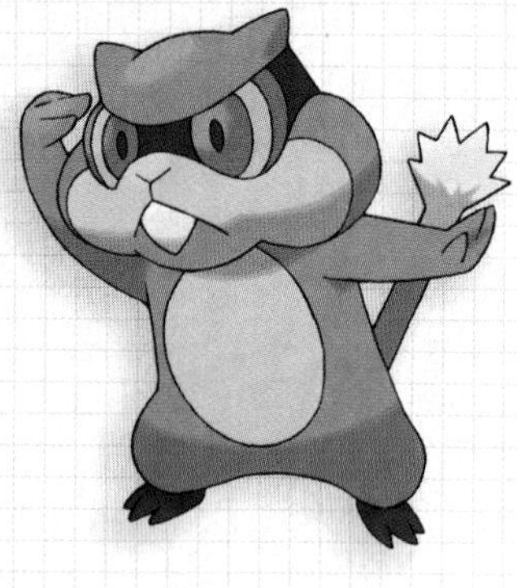

Pokémon AR Marker

LEVEL-UP AND LEARNED MOVES

Lv.	Name	Type	Kind	Pow.	Acc.	PP	Range	Long	DA
1	Tackle	Normal	Physical	50	100	35	Normal	—	○
3	Leer	Normal	Status	—	100	30	Many Others	—	—
6	Bite	Dark	Physical	60	100	25	Normal	—	○
8	Bide	Normal	Physical	—	—	10	Self	—	○
11	Detect	Fighting	Status	—	—	5	Self	—	—
13	Sand-Attack	Ground	Status	—	100	15	Normal	—	—
16	Crunch	Dark	Physical	80	100	15	Normal	—	○
18	Hypnosis	Psychic	Status	—	60	20	Normal	—	—
21	Super Fang	Normal	Physical	—	90	10	Normal	—	○
23	After You	Normal	Status	—	—	15	Normal	—	—
26	Work Up	Normal	Status	—	—	30	Self	—	—
28	Hyper Fang	Normal	Physical	80	90	15	Normal	—	○
31	Mean Look	Normal	Status	—	—	5	Normal	—	—
33	Baton Pass	Normal	Status	—	—	40	Self	—	—
36	Slam	Normal	Physical	80	75	20	Normal	—	○

TM & HM MOVES

Lv.	Name	Type	Kind	Pow.	Acc.	PP	Range	Long	DA
TM06	Toxic	Poison	Status	—	90	10	Normal	—	—
TM10	Hidden Power	Normal	Special	—	100	15	Normal	—	—
TM11	Sunny Day	Fire	Status	—	—	5	Both Sides	—	—
TM17	Protect	Normal	Status	—	—	10	Self	—	—
TM18	Rain Dance	Water	Status	—	—	5	Both Sides	—	—
TM21	Frustration	Normal	Physical	—	100	20	Normal	—	○
TM24	Thunderbolt	Electric	Special	95	100	15	Normal	—	—
TM27	Return	Normal	Physical	—	100	20	Normal	—	○
TM28	Dig	Ground	Physical	80	100	10	Normal	—	○
TM30	Shadow Ball	Ghost	Special	80	100	15	Normal	—	—
TM32	Double Team	Normal	Status	—	—	15	Self	—	—
TM42	Facade	Normal	Physical	70	100	20	Normal	—	○
TM44	Rest	Psychic	Status	—	—	10	Self	—	—
TM45	Attract	Normal	Status	—	100	15	Normal	—	—
TM48	Round	Normal	Special	60	100	15	Normal	—	—
TM56	Fling	Dark	Physical	—	100	10	Normal	—	—
TM67	Retaliate	Normal	Physical	70	100	5	Normal	—	○
TM75	Swords Dance	Normal	Status	—	—	30	Self	—	—
TM83	Work Up	Normal	Status	—	—	30	Self	—	—
TM86	Grass Knot	Grass	Special	—	100	20	Normal	—	○
TM87	Swagger	Normal	Status	—	90	15	Normal	—	—
TM90	Substitute	Normal	Status	—	—	10	Self	—	—
HM01	Cut	Normal	Physical	50	95	30	Normal	—	○

MOVES TAUGHT BY PEOPLE

Name	Type	Kind	Pow.	Acc.	PP	Range	Long	DA

MOVES TAUGHT BY MOVE TUTORS FOR SHARDS

Name	Type	Kind	Pow.	Acc.	PP	Range	Long	DA
Covet	Normal	Physical	60	100	40	Normal	—	○
Super Fang	Normal	Physical	—	90	10	Normal	—	○
Seed Bomb	Grass	Physical	80	100	15	Normal	—	—
Low Kick	Fighting	Physical	—	100	20	Normal	—	○
Gunk Shot	Poison	Physical	120	70	5	Normal	—	—
Last Resort	Normal	Physical	140	100	5	Normal	—	○
Iron Tail	Steel	Physical	100	75	15	Normal	—	○
Aqua Tail	Water	Physical	90	90	10	Normal	—	○
Zen Headbutt	Psychic	Physical	80	90	15	Normal	—	○
Snore	Normal	Special	40	100	15	Normal	—	—
Helping Hand	Normal	Status	—	—	20	1 Ally	—	—
After You	Normal	Status	—	—	15	Normal	—	—
Endeavor	Normal	Physical	—	100	5	Normal	—	○
Sleep Talk	Normal	Status	—	—	10	Self	—	—

EGG MOVES

Name	Type	Kind	Pow.	Acc.	PP	Range	Long	DA
Foresight	Normal	Status	—	—	40	Normal	—	—
Iron Tail	Steel	Physical	100	75	15	Normal	—	○
Screech	Normal	Status	—	85	40	Normal	—	—
Assurance	Dark	Physical	50	100	10	Normal	—	○
Pursuit	Dark	Physical	40	100	20	Normal	—	○
Revenge	Fighting	Physical	60	100	10	Normal	—	○
Flail	Normal	Physical	—	100	15	Normal	—	○

505 Watchog

Lookout Pokémon

- HEIGHT: 3'07"
- WEIGHT: 59.5 lbs.
- GENDER: ♂ / ♀

Using luminescent matter, it makes its eyes and body glow and stuns attacking opponents.

Same form for ♂ / ♀

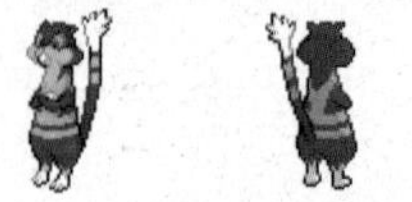

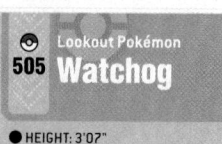

TYPE: Normal

ABILITIES
- Illuminate
- Keen Eye

HIDDEN ABILITY
- Analytic

STATS
HP
Attack
Defense
Sp. Atk
Sp. Def
Speed

EGG GROUPS
Field

ITEMS SOMETIMES HELD
- None

EVOLUTION

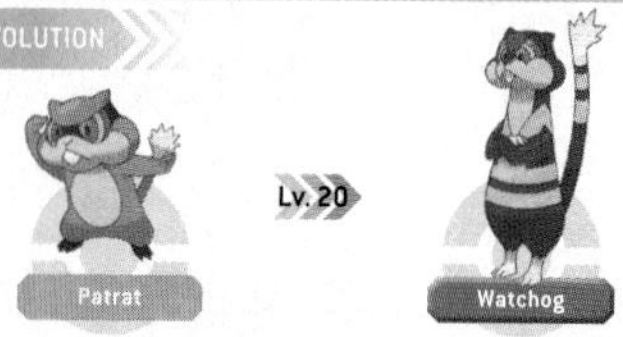

HOW TO OBTAIN

Pokémon Black Version 2	❶ Route 7 ❷ Route 3
Pokémon White Version 2	❶ Route 7 ❷ Route 3

HOW TO OBTAIN FROM OTHER GAMES

—

—

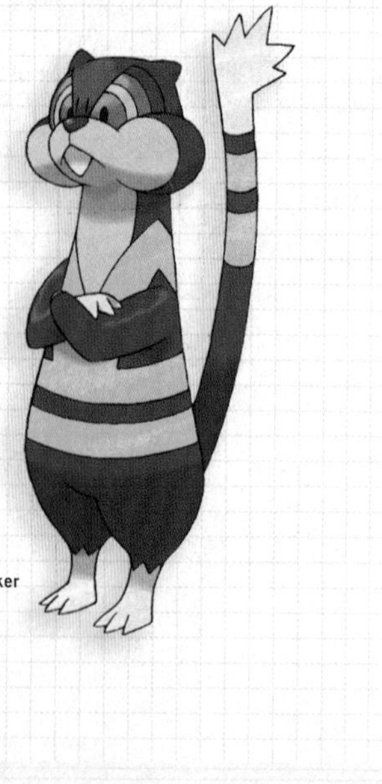

Pokémon AR Marker

LEVEL-UP AND LEARNED MOVES

Lv.	Name	Type	Kind	Pow.	Acc.	PP	Range	Long	DA
1	Tackle	Normal	Physical	50	100	35	Normal	—	○
1	Leer	Normal	Status	—	100	30	Many Others	—	—
1	Bite	Dark	Physical	60	100	25	Normal	—	○
1	Low Kick	Fighting	Physical	—	100	20	Normal	—	○
3	Leer	Normal	Status	—	100	30	Many Others	—	—
6	Bite	Dark	Physical	60	100	25	Normal	—	○
8	Bide	Normal	Physical	—	—	10	Self	—	○
11	Detect	Fighting	Status	—	—	5	Self	—	—
13	Sand-Attack	Ground	Status	—	100	15	Normal	—	—
16	Crunch	Dark	Physical	80	100	15	Normal	—	○
18	Hypnosis	Psychic	Status	—	60	20	Normal	—	—
20	Confuse Ray	Ghost	Status	—	100	10	Normal	—	—
22	Super Fang	Normal	Physical	—	90	10	Normal	—	○
25	After You	Normal	Status	—	—	15	Normal	—	—
29	Psych Up	Normal	Status	—	—	10	Normal	—	—
32	Hyper Fang	Normal	Physical	80	90	15	Normal	—	○
36	Mean Look	Normal	Status	—	—	5	Normal	—	—
39	Baton Pass	Normal	Status	—	—	40	Self	—	—
43	Slam	Normal	Physical	80	75	20	Normal	—	○

TM & HM MOVES

Lv.	Name	Type	Kind	Pow.	Acc.	PP	Range	Long	DA
TM06	Toxic	Poison	Status	—	90	10	Normal	—	—
TM10	Hidden Power	Normal	Special	—	100	15	Normal	—	—
TM11	Sunny Day	Fire	Status	—	—	5	Both Sides	—	—
TM15	Hyper Beam	Normal	Special	150	90	5	Normal	—	—
TM16	Light Screen	Psychic	Status	—	—	30	Your Side	—	—
TM17	Protect	Normal	Status	—	—	10	Self	—	—
TM18	Rain Dance	Water	Status	—	—	5	Both Sides	—	—
TM21	Frustration	Normal	Physical	—	100	20	Normal	—	○
TM24	Thunderbolt	Electric	Special	95	100	15	Normal	—	—
TM25	Thunder	Electric	Special	120	70	10	Normal	—	—
TM27	Return	Normal	Physical	—	100	20	Normal	—	○
TM28	Dig	Ground	Physical	80	100	10	Normal	—	○
TM30	Shadow Ball	Ghost	Special	80	100	15	Normal	—	—
TM32	Double Team	Normal	Status	—	—	15	Self	—	—
TM35	Flamethrower	Fire	Special	95	100	15	Normal	—	—
TM42	Facade	Normal	Physical	70	100	20	Normal	—	○
TM44	Rest	Psychic	Status	—	—	10	Self	—	—
TM45	Attract	Normal	Status	—	100	15	Normal	—	—
TM48	Round	Normal	Special	60	100	15	Normal	—	—
TM52	Focus Blast	Fighting	Special	120	70	5	Normal	—	—
TM56	Fling	Dark	Physical	—	100	10	Normal	—	—
TM67	Retaliate	Normal	Physical	70	100	5	Normal	—	○
TM68	Giga Impact	Normal	Physical	150	90	5	Normal	—	○
TM70	Flash	Normal	Status	—	100	20	Normal	—	—
TM73	Thunder Wave	Electric	Status	—	100	20	Normal	—	—
TM75	Swords Dance	Normal	Status	—	—	30	Self	—	—
TM77	Psych Up	Normal	Status	—	—	10	Normal	—	—
TM83	Work Up	Normal	Status	—	—	30	Self	—	—
TM85	Dream Eater	Psychic	Special	100	100	15	Normal	—	—
TM86	Grass Knot	Grass	Special	—	100	20	Normal	—	○
TM87	Swagger	Normal	Status	—	90	15	Normal	—	—
TM90	Substitute	Normal	Status	—	—	10	Self	—	—
TM94	Rock Smash	Fighting	Physical	40	100	15	Normal	—	○
HM01	Cut	Normal	Physical	50	95	30	Normal	—	○

Lv.	Name	Type	Kind	Pow.	Acc.	PP	Range	Long	DA
HM04	Strength	Normal	Physical	80	100	15	Normal	—	○

MOVES TAUGHT BY PEOPLE

Name	Type	Kind	Pow.	Acc.	PP	Range	Long	DA

MOVES TAUGHT BY MOVE TUTORS FOR SHARDS

Name	Type	Kind	Pow.	Acc.	PP	Range	Long	DA
Covet	Normal	Physical	60	100	40	Normal	—	○
Signal Beam	Bug	Special	75	100	15	Normal	—	—
Super Fang	Normal	Physical	—	90	10	Normal	—	○
Seed Bomb	Grass	Physical	80	100	15	Normal	—	—
Low Kick	Fighting	Physical	—	100	20	Normal	—	○
Gunk Shot	Poison	Physical	120	70	5	Normal	—	—
Fire Punch	Fire	Physical	75	100	15	Normal	—	○
ThunderPunch	Electric	Physical	75	100	15	Normal	—	○
Ice Punch	Ice	Physical	75	100	15	Normal	—	○
Last Resort	Normal	Physical	140	100	5	Normal	—	○
Iron Tail	Steel	Physical	100	75	15	Normal	—	○
Aqua Tail	Water	Physical	90	90	10	Normal	—	○
Zen Headbutt	Psychic	Physical	80	90	15	Normal	—	○
Snore	Normal	Special	40	100	15	Normal	—	—
Knock Off	Dark	Physical	20	100	20	Normal	—	○
Helping Hand	Normal	Status	—	—	20	1 Ally	—	—
After You	Normal	Status	—	—	15	Normal	—	—
Endeavor	Normal	Physical	—	100	5	Normal	—	○
Sleep Talk	Normal	Status	—	—	10	Self	—	—

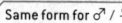

506 Lillipup
Puppy Pokémon

TYPE Normal

ABILITIES
- Vital Spirit
- Pickup

HIDDEN ABILITY
- Run Away

- HEIGHT: 1'04"
- WEIGHT: 9.0 lbs.
- GENDER: ♂ / ♀

Though it is a very brave Pokémon, it's also smart enough to check its foe's strength and avoid battle.

STATS
- HP ▪▪
- Attack ▪▪
- Defense ▪▪
- Sp. Atk ▪
- Sp. Def ▪
- Speed ▪▪▪

EGG GROUPS
Field

ITEMS SOMETIMES HELD
- None

Same form for ♂ / ♀

Pokémon AR Marker

EVOLUTION

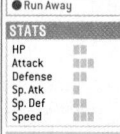

Lillipup → Lv. 16 → Herdier → Lv. 32 → Stoutland

HOW TO OBTAIN
Pokémon Black Version 2	Floccesy Ranch
Pokémon White Version 2	Floccesy Ranch

HOW TO OBTAIN FROM OTHER GAMES

LEVEL-UP AND LEARNED MOVES

Lv.	Name	Type	Kind	Pow.	Acc.	PP	Range	Long	DA
1	Leer	Normal	Status	—	100	30	Many Others	—	—
1	Tackle	Normal	Physical	50	100	35	Normal	—	○
5	Odor Sleuth	Normal	Status	—	—	40	Normal	—	—
8	Bite	Dark	Physical	60	100	25	Normal	—	○
12	Helping Hand	Normal	Status	—	—	20	1 Ally	—	○
15	Take Down	Normal	Physical	90	85	20	Normal	—	○
19	Work Up	Normal	Status	—	—	30	Self	—	—
22	Crunch	Dark	Physical	80	100	15	Normal	—	○
26	Roar	Normal	Status	—	100	20	Normal	—	—
29	Retaliate	Normal	Physical	70	100	5	Normal	—	○
33	Reversal	Fighting	Physical	—	100	15	Normal	—	○
36	Last Resort	Normal	Physical	140	100	5	Normal	—	○
40	Giga Impact	Normal	Physical	150	90	5	Normal	—	○

TM & HM MOVES

Lv.	Name	Type	Kind	Pow.	Acc.	PP	Range	Long	DA
TM05	Roar	Normal	Status	—	100	20	Normal	—	—
TM06	Toxic	Poison	Status	—	90	10	Normal	—	—
TM10	Hidden Power	Normal	Special	—	100	15	Normal	—	—
TM11	Sunny Day	Fire	Status	—	—	5	Both Sides	—	—
TM17	Protect	Normal	Status	—	—	10	Self	—	—
TM18	Rain Dance	Water	Status	—	—	5	Both Sides	—	—
TM21	Frustration	Normal	Physical	—	100	20	Normal	—	○
TM24	Thunderbolt	Electric	Special	95	100	15	Normal	—	—
TM27	Return	Normal	Physical	—	100	15	Normal	—	○
TM28	Dig	Ground	Physical	80	100	10	Normal	—	○
TM30	Shadow Ball	Ghost	Special	80	100	15	Normal	—	—
TM32	Double Team	Normal	Status	—	—	15	Self	—	—
TM39	Rock Tomb	Rock	Physical	50	80	10	Normal	—	○
TM40	Aerial Ace	Flying	Physical	60	—	20	Normal	○	○
TM42	Facade	Normal	Physical	70	100	20	Normal	—	○
TM44	Rest	Psychic	Status	—	—	10	Self	—	—
TM45	Attract	Normal	Status	—	100	15	Normal	—	—
TM48	Round	Normal	Special	60	100	15	Normal	—	—
TM67	Retaliate	Normal	Physical	70	100	5	Normal	—	○
TM68	Giga Impact	Normal	Physical	150	90	5	Normal	—	○
TM73	Thunder Wave	Electric	Status	—	100	20	Normal	—	—
TM83	Work Up	Normal	Status	—	—	30	Self	—	—
TM87	Swagger	Normal	Status	—	90	15	Normal	—	—
TM90	Substitute	Normal	Status	—	—	10	Self	—	—
TM93	Wild Charge	Electric	Physical	90	100	15	Normal	—	○
TM94	Rock Smash	Fighting	Physical	40	100	15	Normal	—	○
TM95	Snarl	Dark	Special	55	95	15	Many Others	—	—

MOVES TAUGHT BY PEOPLE

Name	Type	Kind	Pow.	Acc.	PP	Range	Long	DA

MOVES TAUGHT BY MOVE TUTORS FOR SHARDS

Name	Type	Kind	Pow.	Acc.	PP	Range	Long	DA
Covet	Normal	Physical	60	100	40	Normal	—	○
Uproar	Normal	Special	90	100	10	1 Random	—	—
Last Resort	Normal	Physical	140	100	5	Normal	—	○
Hyper Voice	Normal	Special	90	100	10	Many Others	—	—
Snore	Normal	Special	40	100	15	Normal	—	—
Helping Hand	Normal	Status	—	—	20	1 Ally	—	○
Sleep Talk	Normal	Status	—	—	10	Self	—	—

EGG MOVES

Name	Type	Kind	Pow.	Acc.	PP	Range	Long	DA
Howl	Normal	Status	—	—	40	Self	—	—
Sand-Attack	Ground	Status	—	100	15	Normal	—	—
Mud-Slap	Ground	Special	20	100	10	Normal	—	—
Lick	Ghost	Physical	20	100	30	Normal	—	○
Charm	Normal	Status	—	100	20	Normal	—	—
Endure	Normal	Status	—	—	10	Self	—	—
Yawn	Normal	Status	—	—	10	Normal	—	—
Pursuit	Dark	Physical	40	100	20	Normal	—	○
Fire Fang	Fire	Physical	65	95	15	Normal	—	○
Thunder Fang	Electric	Physical	65	95	15	Normal	—	○
Ice Fang	Ice	Physical	65	95	15	Normal	—	○

---

507 Herdier
Loyal Dog Pokémon

TYPE Normal

ABILITIES
- Intimidate
- Sand Rush

HIDDEN ABILITY
- Scrappy

- HEIGHT: 2'11"
- WEIGHT: 32.4 lbs.
- GENDER: ♂ / ♀

This very loyal Pokémon helps Trainers, and it also takes care of other Pokémon.

STATS
- HP ▪▪▪
- Attack ▪▪▪
- Defense ▪▪▪
- Sp. Atk ▪▪
- Sp. Def ▪▪
- Speed ▪▪▪

EGG GROUPS
Field

ITEMS SOMETIMES HELD
- None

Same form for ♂ / ♀

Pokémon AR Marker

EVOLUTION

 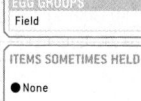

Lillipup → Lv. 16 → Herdier → Lv. 32 → Stoutland

HOW TO OBTAIN
Pokémon Black Version 2	❶ Route 3 ❷ Route 2
Pokémon White Version 2	❶ Route 3 ❷ Route 2

HOW TO OBTAIN FROM OTHER GAMES

LEVEL-UP AND LEARNED MOVES

Lv.	Name	Type	Kind	Pow.	Acc.	PP	Range	Long	DA
1	Leer	Normal	Status	—	100	30	Many Others	—	—
1	Tackle	Normal	Physical	50	100	35	Normal	—	○
1	Odor Sleuth	Normal	Status	—	—	40	Normal	—	—
1	Bite	Dark	Physical	60	100	25	Normal	—	○
5	Odor Sleuth	Normal	Status	—	—	40	Normal	—	—
8	Bite	Dark	Physical	60	100	25	Normal	—	○
12	Helping Hand	Normal	Status	—	—	20	1 Ally	—	○
15	Take Down	Normal	Physical	90	85	20	Normal	—	○
20	Work Up	Normal	Status	—	—	30	Self	—	—
24	Crunch	Dark	Physical	80	100	15	Normal	—	○
29	Roar	Normal	Status	—	100	20	Normal	—	—
33	Retaliate	Normal	Physical	70	100	5	Normal	—	○
38	Reversal	Fighting	Physical	—	100	15	Normal	—	○
42	Last Resort	Normal	Physical	140	100	5	Normal	—	○
47	Giga Impact	Normal	Physical	150	90	5	Normal	—	○

TM & HM MOVES

Lv.	Name	Type	Kind	Pow.	Acc.	PP	Range	Long	DA
TM05	Roar	Normal	Status	—	100	20	Normal	—	—
TM06	Toxic	Poison	Status	—	90	10	Normal	—	—
TM10	Hidden Power	Normal	Special	—	100	15	Normal	—	—
TM11	Sunny Day	Fire	Status	—	—	5	Both Sides	—	—
TM17	Protect	Normal	Status	—	—	10	Self	—	—
TM18	Rain Dance	Water	Status	—	—	5	Both Sides	—	—
TM21	Frustration	Normal	Physical	—	100	20	Normal	—	○
TM24	Thunderbolt	Electric	Special	95	100	15	Normal	—	—
TM27	Return	Normal	Physical	—	100	15	Normal	—	○
TM28	Dig	Ground	Physical	80	100	10	Normal	—	○
TM30	Shadow Ball	Ghost	Special	80	100	15	Normal	—	—
TM32	Double Team	Normal	Status	—	—	15	Self	—	—
TM39	Rock Tomb	Rock	Physical	50	80	10	Normal	—	○
TM40	Aerial Ace	Flying	Physical	60	—	20	Normal	○	○
TM42	Facade	Normal	Physical	70	100	20	Normal	—	○
TM44	Rest	Psychic	Status	—	—	10	Self	—	—
TM45	Attract	Normal	Status	—	100	15	Normal	—	—
TM48	Round	Normal	Special	60	100	15	Normal	—	—
TM66	Payback	Dark	Physical	50	100	10	Normal	—	○
TM67	Retaliate	Normal	Physical	70	100	5	Normal	—	○
TM68	Giga Impact	Normal	Physical	150	90	5	Normal	—	○
TM73	Thunder Wave	Electric	Status	—	100	20	Normal	—	—
TM83	Work Up	Normal	Status	—	—	30	Self	—	—
TM87	Swagger	Normal	Status	—	90	15	Normal	—	—
TM90	Substitute	Normal	Status	—	—	10	Self	—	—
TM93	Wild Charge	Electric	Physical	90	100	15	Normal	—	○
TM94	Rock Smash	Fighting	Physical	40	100	15	Normal	—	○
TM95	Snarl	Dark	Special	55	95	15	Many Others	—	—
HM03	Surf	Water	Special	95	100	15	Adjacent	—	—
HM04	Strength	Normal	Physical	80	100	15	Normal	—	○

MOVES TAUGHT BY PEOPLE

Name	Type	Kind	Pow.	Acc.	PP	Range	Long	DA

MOVES TAUGHT BY MOVE TUTORS FOR SHARDS

Name	Type	Kind	Pow.	Acc.	PP	Range	Long	DA
Covet	Normal	Physical	60	100	40	Normal	—	○
Uproar	Normal	Special	90	100	10	1 Random	—	—
Last Resort	Normal	Physical	140	100	5	Normal	—	○
Hyper Voice	Normal	Special	90	100	10	Many Others	—	—
Snore	Normal	Special	40	100	15	Normal	—	—
Helping Hand	Normal	Status	—	—	20	1 Ally	—	○
Sleep Talk	Normal	Status	—	—	10	Self	—	—

Big-Hearted Pokémon
508 Stoutland

TYPE Normal

ABILITIES
- Intimidate
- Sand Rush

HIDDEN ABILITY
- Scrappy

- HEIGHT: 3'11"
- WEIGHT: 134.5 lbs.
- GENDER: ♂ / ♀

Being wrapped in its long fur is so comfortable that a person would be fine even overnight on a wintry mountain.

Same form for ♂ / ♀

STATS
- HP
- Attack
- Defense
- Sp. Atk
- Sp. Def
- Speed

EGG GROUPS
Field

ITEMS SOMETIMES HELD
- None

EVOLUTION

Lillipup — Lv. 16 → Herdier — Lv. 32 → Stoutland

HOW TO OBTAIN

Pokémon Black Version 2	❶ Route 3 (rustling grass) ❷ Route 2 (rustling grass)
Pokémon White Version 2	❶ Route 3 (rustling grass) ❷ Route 2 (rustling grass)

HOW TO OBTAIN FROM OTHER GAMES

LEVEL-UP AND LEARNED MOVES

Lv.	Name	Type	Kind	Pow.	Acc.	PP	Range	Long	DA
1	Ice Fang	Ice	Physical	65	95	15	Normal	—	O
1	Fire Fang	Fire	Physical	65	95	15	Normal	—	O
1	Thunder Fang	Electric	Physical	65	95	15	Normal	—	O
1	Leer	Normal	Status	—	100	30	Many Others	—	—
1	Tackle	Normal	Physical	50	100	35	Normal	—	O
1	Odor Sleuth	Normal	Status	—	—	40	Normal	—	—
1	Bite	Dark	Physical	60	100	25	Normal	—	O
5	Odor Sleuth	Normal	Status	—	—	40	Normal	—	—
8	Bite	Dark	Physical	60	100	25	Normal	—	O
12	Helping Hand	Normal	Status	—	—	20	1 Ally	—	—
15	Take Down	Normal	Physical	90	85	20	Normal	—	O
20	Work Up	Normal	Status	—	—	30	Self	—	—
24	Crunch	Dark	Physical	80	100	15	Normal	—	O
29	Roar	Normal	Status	—	100	20	Normal	—	—
36	Retaliate	Normal	Physical	70	100	5	Normal	—	O
42	Reversal	Fighting	Physical	—	100	15	Normal	—	O
51	Last Resort	Normal	Physical	140	100	5	Normal	—	O
59	Giga Impact	Normal	Physical	150	90	5	Normal	—	O

TM & HM MOVES

Lv.	Name	Type	Kind	Pow.	Acc.	PP	Range	Long	DA
TM05	Roar	Normal	Status	—	100	20	Normal	—	—
TM06	Toxic	Poison	Status	—	90	10	Normal	—	—
TM10	Hidden Power	Normal	Special	—	100	15	Normal	—	O
TM11	Sunny Day	Fire	Status	—	—	5	Both Sides	—	—
TM15	Hyper Beam	Normal	Special	150	90	5	Normal	—	O
TM17	Protect	Normal	Status	—	—	10	Self	—	—
TM18	Rain Dance	Water	Status	—	—	5	Both Sides	—	—
TM21	Frustration	Normal	Physical	—	100	20	Normal	—	O
TM24	Thunderbolt	Electric	Special	95	100	15	Normal	—	O
TM25	Thunder	Electric	Special	120	70	10	Normal	—	O
TM27	Return	Normal	Physical	—	100	20	Normal	—	O
TM28	Dig	Ground	Physical	80	100	10	Normal	—	O
TM30	Shadow Ball	Ghost	Special	80	100	15	Normal	—	O
TM32	Double Team	Normal	Status	—	—	15	Self	—	—
TM39	Rock Tomb	Rock	Physical	50	80	10	Normal	—	O
TM40	Aerial Ace	Flying	Physical	60	—	20	Normal	O	O
TM42	Facade	Normal	Physical	70	100	20	Normal	—	O
TM44	Rest	Psychic	Status	—	—	10	Self	—	—
TM45	Attract	Normal	Status	—	100	15	Normal	—	—
TM48	Round	Normal	Special	60	100	15	Normal	—	O
TM66	Payback	Dark	Physical	50	100	10	Normal	—	O
TM67	Retaliate	Normal	Physical	70	100	5	Normal	—	O
TM68	Giga Impact	Normal	Physical	150	90	5	Normal	—	O
TM73	Thunder Wave	Electric	Status	—	100	20	Normal	—	—
TM83	Work Up	Normal	Status	—	—	30	Self	—	—
TM87	Swagger	Normal	Status	—	90	15	Normal	—	—
TM90	Substitute	Normal	Status	—	—	10	Self	—	—
TM93	Wild Charge	Electric	Physical	90	100	15	Normal	—	O
TM94	Rock Smash	Fighting	Physical	40	100	15	Normal	—	O
TM95	Snarl	Dark	Special	55	95	15	Many Others	—	—
HM03	Surf	Water	Special	95	100	15	Adjacent	—	O
HM04	Strength	Normal	Physical	80	100	15	Normal	—	O

MOVES TAUGHT BY PEOPLE

Name	Type	Kind	Pow.	Acc.	PP	Range	Long	DA

MOVES TAUGHT BY MOVE TUTORS FOR SHARDS

Name	Type	Kind	Pow.	Acc.	PP	Range	Long	DA
Covet	Normal	Physical	60	100	40	Normal	—	O
Iron Head	Steel	Physical	80	100	15	Normal	—	O
Uproar	Normal	Special	90	100	10	1 Random	—	—
Last Resort	Normal	Physical	140	100	5	Normal	—	O
Hyper Voice	Normal	Special	90	100	10	Many Others	—	—
Superpower	Fighting	Physical	120	100	5	Normal	—	O
Snore	Normal	Special	40	100	15	Normal	—	—
Helping Hand	Normal	Status	—	—	20	1 Ally	—	—
Sleep Talk	Normal	Status	—	—	10	Self	—	—

Pokémon AR Marker

Devious Pokémon
509 Purrloin

TYPE Dark

ABILITIES
- Limber
- Unburden

HIDDEN ABILITY
- Prankster

- HEIGHT: 1'04"
- WEIGHT: 22.3 lbs.
- GENDER: ♂ / ♀

Their cute act is a ruse. They trick people and steal their valuables just to see the looks on their faces.

Same form for ♂ / ♀

STATS
- HP
- Attack
- Defense
- Sp. Atk
- Sp. Def
- Speed

EGG GROUPS
Field

ITEMS SOMETIMES HELD
- None

EVOLUTION

Purrloin — Lv. 20 → Liepard

HOW TO OBTAIN

Pokémon Black Version 2	❶ Route 19 ❷ Route 20
Pokémon White Version 2	❶ Route 19 ❷ Route 20

HOW TO OBTAIN FROM OTHER GAMES

LEVEL-UP AND LEARNED MOVES

Lv.	Name	Type	Kind	Pow.	Acc.	PP	Range	Long	DA
1	Scratch	Normal	Physical	40	100	35	Normal	—	O
3	Growl	Normal	Status	—	100	40	Many Others	—	—
6	Assist	Normal	Status	—	—	20	Self	—	—
10	Sand-Attack	Ground	Status	—	100	15	Normal	—	—
12	Fury Swipes	Normal	Physical	18	80	15	Normal	—	O
15	Pursuit	Dark	Physical	40	100	20	Normal	—	O
19	Torment	Dark	Status	—	100	15	Normal	—	—
21	Fake Out	Normal	Physical	40	100	10	Normal	—	O
24	Hone Claws	Dark	Status	—	—	15	Self	—	—
28	Assurance	Dark	Physical	50	100	10	Normal	—	O
30	Slash	Normal	Physical	70	100	20	Normal	—	O
33	Captivate	Normal	Status	—	100	20	Many Others	—	—
37	Night Slash	Dark	Physical	70	100	15	Normal	—	O
39	Snatch	Dark	Status	—	—	10	Self	—	—
42	Nasty Plot	Dark	Status	—	—	20	Self	—	—
46	Sucker Punch	Dark	Physical	80	100	5	Normal	—	O

TM & HM MOVES

Lv.	Name	Type	Kind	Pow.	Acc.	PP	Range	Long	DA
TM01	Hone Claws	Dark	Status	—	—	15	Self	—	—
TM06	Toxic	Poison	Status	—	90	10	Normal	—	—
TM10	Hidden Power	Normal	Special	—	100	15	Normal	—	O
TM11	Sunny Day	Fire	Status	—	—	5	Both Sides	—	—
TM12	Taunt	Dark	Status	—	100	20	Normal	—	—
TM17	Protect	Normal	Status	—	—	10	Self	—	—
TM18	Rain Dance	Water	Status	—	—	5	Both Sides	—	—
TM21	Frustration	Normal	Physical	—	100	20	Normal	—	O
TM27	Return	Normal	Physical	—	100	20	Normal	—	O
TM30	Shadow Ball	Ghost	Special	80	100	15	Normal	—	O
TM32	Double Team	Normal	Status	—	—	15	Self	—	—
TM40	Aerial Ace	Flying	Physical	60	—	20	Normal	O	O
TM41	Torment	Dark	Status	—	100	15	Normal	—	—
TM42	Facade	Normal	Physical	70	100	20	Normal	—	O
TM44	Rest	Psychic	Status	—	—	10	Self	—	—
TM45	Attract	Normal	Status	—	100	15	Normal	—	—
TM46	Thief	Dark	Physical	40	100	10	Normal	—	O
TM48	Round	Normal	Special	60	100	15	Normal	—	O
TM49	Echoed Voice	Normal	Special	40	100	15	Normal	—	O
TM63	Embargo	Dark	Status	—	100	15	Normal	—	—
TM65	Shadow Claw	Ghost	Physical	70	100	15	Normal	—	O
TM66	Payback	Dark	Physical	50	100	10	Normal	—	O
TM73	Thunder Wave	Electric	Status	—	100	20	Normal	—	—
TM77	Psych Up	Normal	Status	—	—	10	Self	—	—
TM85	Dream Eater	Psychic	Special	100	100	15	Normal	—	O
TM86	Grass Knot	Grass	Special	—	100	20	Normal	—	O
TM87	Swagger	Normal	Status	—	90	15	Normal	—	—
TM89	U-turn	Bug	Physical	70	100	20	Normal	—	O
TM90	Substitute	Normal	Status	—	—	10	Self	—	—
TM95	Snarl	Dark	Special	55	95	15	Many Others	—	—
HM01	Cut	Normal	Physical	50	95	30	Normal	—	—

MOVES TAUGHT BY PEOPLE

Name	Type	Kind	Pow.	Acc.	PP	Range	Long	DA

MOVES TAUGHT BY MOVE TUTORS FOR SHARDS

Name	Type	Kind	Pow.	Acc.	PP	Range	Long	DA
Covet	Normal	Physical	60	100	40	Normal	—	O
Seed Bomb	Grass	Physical	80	100	15	Normal	—	O
Gunk Shot	Poison	Physical	120	70	5	Normal	—	O
Hyper Voice	Normal	Special	90	100	10	Many Others	—	—
Iron Tail	Steel	Physical	100	75	15	Normal	—	O
Foul Play	Dark	Physical	95	100	15	Normal	—	O
Dark Pulse	Dark	Special	80	100	15	Normal	O	O
Snore	Normal	Special	40	100	15	Normal	—	—
Knock Off	Dark	Physical	20	100	20	Normal	—	O
Role Play	Psychic	Status	—	—	10	Normal	—	—
Spite	Ghost	Status	—	100	10	Normal	—	—
Trick	Psychic	Status	—	100	10	Normal	—	—
Sleep Talk	Normal	Status	—	—	10	Self	—	—
Snatch	Dark	Status	—	—	10	Self	—	—

EGG MOVES

Name	Type	Kind	Pow.	Acc.	PP	Range	Long	DA
Pay Day	Normal	Physical	40	100	20	Normal	—	—
Foul Play	Dark	Physical	95	100	15	Normal	—	O
Faint Attack	Dark	Physical	60	—	20	Normal	—	O
Fake Tears	Dark	Status	—	100	20	Normal	—	—
Charm	Normal	Status	—	100	20	Normal	—	—
Encore	Normal	Status	—	100	5	Normal	—	—
Yawn	Normal	Status	—	—	10	Normal	—	—
Covet	Normal	Physical	60	100	40	Normal	—	O

Pokémon AR Marker

510 Liepard

Cruel Pokémon

TYPE: Dark

ABILITIES
- Limber
- Unburden

HIDDEN ABILITY
- Prankster

- HEIGHT: 3'07"
- WEIGHT: 82.7 lbs.
- GENDER: ♂ / ♀

Their beautiful form comes from the muscles they have developed. They run silently in the night.

STATS
HP
Attack
Defense
Sp. Atk
Sp. Def
Speed

EGG GROUPS
Field

Same form for ♂ / ♀

ITEMS SOMETIMES HELD
- None

Pokémon AR Marker

EVOLUTION

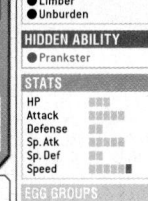

Purrloin

Lv. 20

Liepard

HOW TO OBTAIN

Pokémon Black Version 2	❶ Route 16 ❷ Route 5
Pokémon White Version 2	❶ Route 16 ❷ Route 5

HOW TO OBTAIN FROM OTHER GAMES

—

—

LEVEL-UP AND LEARNED MOVES

Lv.	Name	Type	Kind	Pow.	Acc.	PP	Range	Long	DA
1	Scratch	Normal	Physical	40	100	35	Normal	—	○
1	Growl	Normal	Status	—	100	40	Many Others	—	—
1	Assist	Normal	Status	—	—	20	Self	—	—
1	Sand-Attack	Ground	Status	—	100	15	Normal	—	—
3	Growl	Normal	Status	—	100	40	Many Others	—	—
6	Assist	Normal	Status	—	—	20	Self	—	—
10	Sand-Attack	Ground	Status	—	100	15	Normal	—	—
12	Fury Swipes	Normal	Physical	18	80	15	Normal	—	○
15	Pursuit	Dark	Physical	40	100	20	Normal	—	○
19	Torment	Dark	Status	—	100	15	Normal	—	—
22	Fake Out	Normal	Physical	40	100	10	Normal	—	○
26	Hone Claws	Dark	Status	—	—	15	Self	—	—
31	Assurance	Dark	Physical	50	100	10	Normal	—	○
34	Slash	Normal	Physical	70	100	20	Normal	—	○
38	Taunt	Dark	Status	—	100	20	Normal	—	—
43	Night Slash	Dark	Physical	70	100	15	Normal	—	○
47	Snatch	Dark	Status	—	—	10	Self	—	—
50	Nasty Plot	Dark	Status	—	—	20	Self	—	—
55	Sucker Punch	Dark	Physical	80	100	5	Normal	—	○

TM & HM MOVES

Lv.	Name	Type	Kind	Pow.	Acc.	PP	Range	Long	DA
TM01	Hone Claws	Dark	Status	—	—	15	Self	—	—
TM06	Toxic	Poison	Status	—	90	10	Normal	—	—
TM10	Hidden Power	Normal	Special	—	100	15	Normal	—	—
TM11	Sunny Day	Fire	Status	—	—	5	Both Sides	—	—
TM12	Taunt	Dark	Status	—	100	20	Normal	—	—
TM15	Hyper Beam	Normal	Special	150	90	5	Normal	—	—
TM17	Protect	Normal	Status	—	—	10	Self	—	—
TM18	Rain Dance	Water	Status	—	—	5	Both Sides	—	—
TM21	Frustration	Normal	Physical	—	100	20	Normal	—	○
TM27	Return	Normal	Physical	—	100	20	Normal	—	○
TM30	Shadow Ball	Ghost	Special	80	100	15	Normal	—	—
TM32	Double Team	Normal	Status	—	—	15	Self	—	—
TM40	Aerial Ace	Flying	Physical	60	—	20	Normal	○	○
TM41	Torment	Dark	Status	—	100	15	Normal	—	—
TM42	Facade	Normal	Physical	70	100	20	Normal	—	○
TM44	Rest	Psychic	Status	—	—	10	Self	—	—
TM45	Attract	Normal	Status	—	100	15	Normal	—	—
TM46	Thief	Dark	Physical	40	100	10	Normal	—	○
TM48	Round	Normal	Special	60	100	15	Normal	—	—
TM49	Echoed Voice	Normal	Special	40	100	15	Normal	—	—
TM63	Embargo	Dark	Status	—	100	15	Normal	—	—
TM65	Shadow Claw	Ghost	Physical	70	100	15	Normal	—	○
TM66	Payback	Dark	Physical	50	100	10	Normal	—	○
TM68	Giga Impact	Normal	Physical	150	90	5	Normal	—	○
TM73	Thunder Wave	Electric	Status	—	100	20	Normal	—	—
TM77	Psych Up	Normal	Status	—	—	10	Normal	—	—
TM85	Dream Eater	Psychic	Special	100	100	15	Normal	—	—
TM86	Grass Knot	Grass	Special	—	100	20	Normal	—	○
TM87	Swagger	Normal	Status	—	90	15	Normal	—	—
TM89	U-turn	Bug	Physical	70	100	20	Normal	—	○
TM90	Substitute	Normal	Status	—	—	10	Self	—	—
TM94	Rock Smash	Fighting	Physical	40	100	15	Normal	—	○
TM95	Snarl	Dark	Special	55	95	15	Many Others	—	—
HM01	Cut	Normal	Physical	50	95	30	Normal	—	○

MOVES TAUGHT BY PEOPLE

Name	Type	Kind	Pow.	Acc.	PP	Range	Long	DA

MOVES TAUGHT BY MOVE TUTORS FOR SHARDS

Name	Type	Kind	Pow.	Acc.	PP	Range	Long	DA
Covet	Normal	Physical	60	100	40	Normal	—	○
Seed Bomb	Grass	Physical	80	100	15	Normal	—	—
Gunk Shot	Poison	Physical	120	70	5	Normal	—	—
Hyper Voice	Normal	Special	90	100	10	Many Others	—	—
Iron Tail	Steel	Physical	100	75	15	Normal	—	○
Foul Play	Dark	Physical	95	100	15	Normal	—	○
Dark Pulse	Dark	Special	80	100	15	Normal	○	—
Snore	Normal	Special	40	100	15	Normal	—	—
Knock Off	Dark	Physical	20	100	20	Normal	—	○
Role Play	Psychic	Status	—	—	10	Normal	—	—
Spite	Ghost	Status	—	100	10	Normal	—	—
Trick	Psychic	Status	—	100	10	Normal	—	—
Sleep Talk	Normal	Status	—	—	10	Self	—	—
Snatch	Dark	Status	—	—	10	Self	—	—

511 Pansage

Grass Monkey Pokémon

TYPE: Grass

ABILITY
- Gluttony

HIDDEN ABILITY
—

- HEIGHT: 2'00"
- WEIGHT: 23.1 lbs.
- GENDER: ♂ / ♀

It's good at finding berries and gathers them from all over. It's kind enough to share them with friends.

STATS
HP
Attack
Defense
Sp. Atk
Sp. Def
Speed

EGG GROUPS
Field

Same form for ♂ / ♀

ITEMS SOMETIMES HELD
- Oran Berry
- Occa Berry

Pokémon AR Marker

EVOLUTION

Pansage

Use Leaf Stone

Simisage

HOW TO OBTAIN

Pokémon Black Version 2	❶ Lostlorn Forest (rustling grass) ❷ Pinwheel Forest deep in the forest (rustling grass)
Pokémon White Version 2	❶ Lostlorn Forest (rustling grass) ❷ Pinwheel Forest deep in the forest (rustling grass)

HOW TO OBTAIN FROM OTHER GAMES

—

—

LEVEL-UP AND LEARNED MOVES

Lv.	Name	Type	Kind	Pow.	Acc.	PP	Range	Long	DA
1	Scratch	Normal	Physical	40	100	35	Normal	—	○
4	Leer	Normal	Status	—	100	30	Many Others	—	—
7	Lick	Ghost	Physical	20	100	30	Normal	—	○
10	Vine Whip	Grass	Physical	35	100	15	Normal	—	○
13	Fury Swipes	Normal	Physical	18	80	15	Normal	—	○
16	Leech Seed	Grass	Status	—	90	10	Normal	—	—
19	Bite	Dark	Physical	60	100	25	Normal	—	○
22	Seed Bomb	Grass	Physical	80	100	15	Normal	—	—
25	Torment	Dark	Status	—	100	15	Normal	—	—
28	Fling	Dark	Physical	—	100	10	Normal	—	—
31	Acrobatics	Flying	Physical	55	100	15	Normal	○	○
34	Grass Knot	Grass	Special	—	100	20	Normal	—	○
37	Recycle	Normal	Status	—	—	10	Self	—	—
40	Natural Gift	Normal	Physical	—	100	15	Normal	—	—
43	Crunch	Dark	Physical	80	100	15	Normal	—	○

TM & HM MOVES

Lv.	Name	Type	Kind	Pow.	Acc.	PP	Range	Long	DA
TM01	Hone Claws	Dark	Status	—	—	15	Self	—	—
TM06	Toxic	Poison	Status	—	90	10	Normal	—	—
TM10	Hidden Power	Normal	Special	—	100	15	Normal	—	—
TM11	Sunny Day	Fire	Status	—	—	5	Both Sides	—	—
TM12	Taunt	Dark	Status	—	100	20	Normal	—	—
TM17	Protect	Normal	Status	—	—	10	Self	—	—
TM21	Frustration	Normal	Physical	—	100	20	Normal	—	○
TM22	SolarBeam	Grass	Special	120	100	10	Normal	—	—
TM27	Return	Normal	Physical	—	100	20	Normal	—	○
TM28	Dig	Ground	Physical	80	100	10	Normal	—	○
TM32	Double Team	Normal	Status	—	—	15	Self	—	—
TM39	Rock Tomb	Rock	Physical	50	80	10	Normal	—	—
TM41	Torment	Dark	Status	—	100	15	Normal	—	—
TM42	Facade	Normal	Physical	70	100	20	Normal	—	○
TM44	Rest	Psychic	Status	—	—	10	Self	—	—
TM45	Attract	Normal	Status	—	100	15	Normal	—	—
TM46	Thief	Dark	Physical	40	100	10	Normal	—	○
TM47	Low Sweep	Fighting	Physical	60	100	20	Normal	—	○
TM48	Round	Normal	Special	60	100	15	Normal	—	—
TM53	Energy Ball	Grass	Special	80	100	10	Normal	—	—
TM56	Fling	Dark	Physical	—	100	10	Normal	—	—
TM62	Acrobatics	Flying	Physical	55	100	15	Normal	○	○
TM65	Shadow Claw	Ghost	Physical	70	100	15	Normal	—	○
TM66	Payback	Dark	Physical	50	100	10	Normal	—	○
TM70	Flash	Normal	Status	—	100	20	Normal	—	—
TM83	Work Up	Normal	Status	—	—	30	Self	—	—
TM86	Grass Knot	Grass	Special	—	100	20	Normal	—	○
TM87	Swagger	Normal	Status	—	90	15	Normal	—	—
TM90	Substitute	Normal	Status	—	—	10	Self	—	—
TM94	Rock Smash	Fighting	Physical	40	100	15	Normal	—	○
HM01	Cut	Normal	Physical	50	95	30	Normal	—	○

MOVES TAUGHT BY PEOPLE

Name	Type	Kind	Pow.	Acc.	PP	Range	Long	DA

MOVES TAUGHT BY MOVE TUTORS FOR SHARDS

Name	Type	Kind	Pow.	Acc.	PP	Range	Long	DA
Covet	Normal	Physical	60	100	40	Normal	—	○
Uproar	Normal	Special	90	100	10	1 Random	—	—
Seed Bomb	Grass	Physical	80	100	15	Normal	—	—
Low Kick	Fighting	Physical	—	100	20	Normal	—	○
Gunk Shot	Poison	Physical	120	70	5	Normal	—	—
Iron Tail	Steel	Physical	100	75	15	Normal	—	○
Snore	Normal	Special	40	100	15	Normal	—	—
Knock Off	Dark	Physical	20	100	20	Normal	—	○
Synthesis	Grass	Status	—	—	5	Self	—	—
Role Play	Psychic	Status	—	—	10	Normal	—	—
Giga Drain	Grass	Special	75	100	10	Normal	—	—
Worry Seed	Grass	Status	—	100	10	Normal	—	—
Helping Hand	Normal	Status	—	—	20	1 Ally	—	—
Recycle	Normal	Status	—	—	10	Self	—	—
Endeavor	Normal	Physical	—	100	5	Normal	—	○
Sleep Talk	Normal	Status	—	—	10	Self	—	—

EGG MOVES

Name	Type	Kind	Pow.	Acc.	PP	Range	Long	DA
Covet	Normal	Physical	60	100	40	Normal	—	○
Low Kick	Fighting	Physical	—	100	20	Normal	—	○
Tickle	Normal	Status	—	100	20	Normal	—	—
Nasty Plot	Dark	Status	—	—	20	Self	—	—
Role Play	Psychic	Status	—	—	10	Normal	—	—
Astonish	Ghost	Physical	30	100	15	Normal	—	○
GrassWhistle	Grass	Status	—	55	15	Normal	—	—
Magical Leaf	Grass	Special	60	—	20	Normal	—	—
Bullet Seed	Grass	Physical	25	100	30	Normal	—	—
Leaf Storm	Grass	Special	140	90	5	Normal	—	—

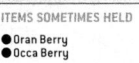

Thorn Monkey Pokémon
512 Simisage

● HEIGHT: 3'07"
● WEIGHT: 67.2 lbs.
● GENDER: ♂ / ♀

It strikes its enemies with a thorn-covered tail. The leaf on its head is bitter.

TYPE Grass

ABILITY
● Gluttony

HIDDEN ABILITY
—

STATS

HP	■■■
Attack	■■■■■
Defense	■■■
Sp. Atk	■■■■■
Sp. Def	■■■
Speed	■■■■■

EGG GROUPS
Field

ITEMS SOMETIMES HELD
● None

Same form for ♂ / ♀

Pokémon AR Marker

EVOLUTION

HOW TO OBTAIN

Pokémon Black Version 2	Use Leaf Stone on Pansage
Pokémon White Version 2	Use Leaf Stone on Pansage

HOW TO OBTAIN FROM OTHER GAMES

—

—

LEVEL-UP AND LEARNED MOVES

Lv.	Name	Type	Kind	Pow.	Acc.	PP	Range	Long	DA
1	Leer	Normal	Status	—	100	30	Many Others	—	—
1	Lick	Ghost	Physical	20	100	30	Normal	—	○
1	Fury Swipes	Normal	Physical	18	80	15	Normal	—	○
1	Seed Bomb	Grass	Physical	80	100	15	Normal	—	—

TM & HM MOVES

Lv.	Name	Type	Kind	Pow.	Acc.	PP	Range	Long	DA
TM01	Hone Claws	Dark	Status	—	—	15	Self	—	—
TM06	Toxic	Poison	Status	—	90	10	Normal	—	—
TM10	Hidden Power	Normal	Special	—	100	15	Normal	—	—
TM11	Sunny Day	Fire	Status	—	—	5	Both Sides	—	—
TM12	Taunt	Dark	Status	—	100	20	Normal	—	—
TM15	Hyper Beam	Normal	Special	150	90	5	Normal	—	—
TM17	Protect	Normal	Status	—	—	10	Self	—	—
TM21	Frustration	Normal	Physical	—	100	20	Normal	—	○
TM22	SolarBeam	Grass	Special	120	100	10	Normal	—	—
TM27	Return	Normal	Physical	—	100	20	Normal	—	○
TM28	Dig	Ground	Physical	80	100	10	Normal	—	○
TM31	Brick Break	Fighting	Physical	75	100	15	Normal	—	○
TM32	Double Team	Normal	Status	—	—	15	Self	—	—
TM39	Rock Tomb	Rock	Physical	50	80	10	Normal	—	—
TM41	Torment	Dark	Status	—	100	15	Normal	—	—
TM42	Facade	Normal	Physical	70	100	20	Normal	—	○
TM44	Rest	Psychic	Status	—	—	10	Self	—	—
TM45	Attract	Normal	Status	—	100	15	Normal	—	—
TM46	Thief	Dark	Physical	40	100	10	Normal	—	○
TM47	Low Sweep	Fighting	Physical	60	100	20	Normal	—	○
TM48	Round	Normal	Special	60	100	15	Normal	—	—
TM52	Focus Blast	Fighting	Special	120	70	5	Normal	—	—
TM53	Energy Ball	Grass	Special	80	100	10	Normal	—	—
TM56	Fling	Dark	Physical	—	100	10	Normal	—	—
TM62	Acrobatics	Flying	Physical	55	100	15	Normal	○	○
TM65	Shadow Claw	Ghost	Physical	70	100	15	Normal	—	○
TM66	Payback	Dark	Physical	50	100	10	Normal	—	○
TM68	Giga Impact	Normal	Physical	150	90	5	Normal	—	○
TM70	Flash	Normal	Status	—	100	20	Normal	—	—
TM80	Rock Slide	Rock	Physical	75	90	10	Many Others	—	—
TM83	Work Up	Normal	Status	—	—	30	Self	—	—
TM86	Grass Knot	Grass	Special	—	100	20	Normal	—	○
TM87	Swagger	Normal	Status	—	90	15	Normal	—	—
TM90	Substitute	Normal	Status	—	—	10	Self	—	—
TM94	Rock Smash	Fighting	Physical	40	100	15	Normal	—	○
HM01	Cut	Normal	Physical	50	95	30	Normal	—	○

MOVES TAUGHT BY PEOPLE

Name	Type	Kind	Pow.	Acc.	PP	Range	Long	DA

MOVES TAUGHT BY MOVE TUTORS FOR SHARDS

Name	Type	Kind	Pow.	Acc.	PP	Range	Long	DA
Covet	Normal	Physical	60	100	40	Normal	—	○
Uproar	Normal	Special	90	100	10	1 Random	—	—
Seed Bomb	Grass	Physical	80	100	15	Normal	—	—
Low Kick	Fighting	Physical	—	100	20	Normal	—	○
Gunk Shot	Poison	Physical	120	70	5	Normal	—	—
Iron Tail	Steel	Physical	100	75	15	Normal	—	○
Superpower	Fighting	Physical	120	100	5	Normal	—	○
Snore	Normal	Special	40	100	15	Normal	—	—
Knock Off	Dark	Physical	20	100	20	Normal	—	○
Synthesis	Grass	Status	—	—	5	Self	—	—
Role Play	Psychic	Status	—	—	10	Normal	—	—
Giga Drain	Grass	Special	75	100	10	Normal	—	—
Worry Seed	Grass	Status	—	100	10	Normal	—	—
Helping Hand	Normal	Status	—	—	20	1 Ally	—	—
Recycle	Normal	Status	—	—	10	Self	—	—
Endeavor	Normal	Physical	—	100	5	Normal	—	○
Sleep Talk	Normal	Status	—	—	10	Self	—	—

High Temp Pokémon
513 Pansear

● HEIGHT: 2'00"
● WEIGHT: 24.3 lbs.
● GENDER: ♂ / ♀

Very intelligent, it roasts berries before eating them. It likes to help people.

TYPE Fire

ABILITY
● Gluttony

HIDDEN ABILITY
—

STATS

HP	■■
Attack	■■■
Defense	■■
Sp. Atk	■■■
Sp. Def	■■
Speed	■■■■

EGG GROUPS
Field

ITEMS SOMETIMES HELD
● Oran Berry
● Passho Berry

Same form for ♂ / ♀

Pokémon AR Marker

EVOLUTION

HOW TO OBTAIN

Pokémon Black Version 2	❶ Lostlorn Forest (rustling grass) ❷ Pinwheel Forest deep in the forest (rustling grass)
Pokémon White Version 2	❶ Lostlorn Forest (rustling grass) ❷ Pinwheel Forest deep in the forest (rustling grass)

HOW TO OBTAIN FROM OTHER GAMES

—

—

LEVEL-UP AND LEARNED MOVES

Lv.	Name	Type	Kind	Pow.	Acc.	PP	Range	Long	DA
1	Scratch	Normal	Physical	40	100	35	Normal	—	○
4	Leer	Normal	Status	—	100	30	Many Others	—	—
7	Lick	Ghost	Physical	20	100	30	Normal	—	○
10	Incinerate	Fire	Special	30	100	15	Many Others	—	—
13	Fury Swipes	Normal	Physical	18	80	15	Normal	—	○
16	Yawn	Normal	Status	—	—	10	Normal	—	—
19	Bite	Dark	Physical	60	100	25	Normal	—	○
22	Flame Burst	Fire	Special	70	100	15	Normal	—	—
25	Amnesia	Psychic	Status	—	—	20	Self	—	—
28	Fling	Dark	Physical	—	100	10	Normal	—	—
31	Acrobatics	Flying	Physical	55	100	15	Normal	○	○
34	Fire Blast	Fire	Special	120	85	5	Normal	—	—
37	Recycle	Normal	Status	—	—	10	Self	—	—
40	Natural Gift	Normal	Physical	—	100	15	Normal	—	—
43	Crunch	Dark	Physical	80	100	15	Normal	—	○

TM & HM MOVES

Lv.	Name	Type	Kind	Pow.	Acc.	PP	Range	Long	DA
TM01	Hone Claws	Dark	Status	—	—	15	Self	—	—
TM06	Toxic	Poison	Status	—	90	10	Normal	—	—
TM10	Hidden Power	Normal	Special	—	100	15	Normal	—	—
TM11	Sunny Day	Fire	Status	—	—	5	Both Sides	—	—
TM12	Taunt	Dark	Status	—	100	20	Normal	—	—
TM17	Protect	Normal	Status	—	—	10	Self	—	—
TM21	Frustration	Normal	Physical	—	100	20	Normal	—	○
TM22	SolarBeam	Grass	Special	120	100	10	Normal	—	—
TM27	Return	Normal	Physical	—	100	20	Normal	—	○
TM28	Dig	Ground	Physical	80	100	10	Normal	—	○
TM32	Double Team	Normal	Status	—	—	15	Self	—	—
TM35	Flamethrower	Fire	Special	95	100	15	Normal	—	—
TM38	Fire Blast	Fire	Special	120	85	5	Normal	—	—
TM39	Rock Tomb	Rock	Physical	50	80	10	Normal	—	—
TM41	Torment	Dark	Status	—	100	15	Normal	—	—
TM42	Facade	Normal	Physical	70	100	20	Normal	—	○
TM43	Flame Charge	Fire	Physical	50	100	20	Normal	—	○
TM44	Rest	Psychic	Status	—	—	10	Self	—	—
TM45	Attract	Normal	Status	—	100	15	Normal	—	—
TM46	Thief	Dark	Physical	40	100	10	Normal	—	○
TM47	Low Sweep	Fighting	Physical	60	100	20	Normal	—	○
TM48	Round	Normal	Special	60	100	15	Normal	—	—
TM50	Overheat	Fire	Special	140	90	5	Normal	—	—
TM56	Fling	Dark	Physical	—	100	10	Normal	—	—
TM59	Incinerate	Fire	Special	30	100	15	Many Others	—	—
TM61	Will-O-Wisp	Fire	Status	—	75	15	Normal	—	—
TM62	Acrobatics	Flying	Physical	55	100	15	Normal	○	○
TM65	Shadow Claw	Ghost	Physical	70	100	15	Normal	—	○
TM66	Payback	Dark	Physical	50	100	10	Normal	—	○
TM83	Work Up	Normal	Status	—	—	30	Self	—	—
TM86	Grass Knot	Grass	Special	—	100	20	Normal	—	○
TM87	Swagger	Normal	Status	—	90	15	Normal	—	—
TM90	Substitute	Normal	Status	—	—	10	Self	—	—
TM94	Rock Smash	Fighting	Physical	40	100	15	Normal	—	○
HM01	Cut	Normal	Physical	50	95	30	Normal	—	○

MOVES TAUGHT BY PEOPLE

Name	Type	Kind	Pow.	Acc.	PP	Range	Long	DA

MOVES TAUGHT BY MOVE TUTORS FOR SHARDS

Name	Type	Kind	Pow.	Acc.	PP	Range	Long	DA
Covet	Normal	Physical	60	100	40	Normal	—	○
Uproar	Normal	Special	90	100	10	1 Random	—	—
Low Kick	Fighting	Physical	—	100	20	Normal	—	○
Gunk Shot	Poison	Physical	120	70	5	Normal	—	—
Fire Punch	Fire	Physical	75	100	15	Normal	—	○
Iron Tail	Steel	Physical	100	75	15	Normal	—	○
Snore	Normal	Special	40	100	15	Normal	—	—
Knock Off	Dark	Physical	20	100	20	Normal	—	○
Role Play	Psychic	Status	—	—	10	Normal	—	—
Heat Wave	Fire	Special	100	90	10	Many Others	—	—
Helping Hand	Normal	Status	—	—	20	1 Ally	—	—
Recycle	Normal	Status	—	—	10	Self	—	—
Endeavor	Normal	Physical	—	100	5	Normal	—	○
Sleep Talk	Normal	Status	—	—	10	Self	—	—

EGG MOVES

Name	Type	Kind	Pow.	Acc.	PP	Range	Long	DA
Covet	Normal	Physical	60	100	40	Normal	—	○
Low Kick	Fighting	Physical	—	100	20	Normal	—	○
Tickle	Normal	Status	—	100	20	Normal	—	—
Nasty Plot	Dark	Status	—	—	20	Self	—	—
Role Play	Psychic	Status	—	—	10	Normal	—	—
Astonish	Ghost	Physical	30	100	15	Normal	—	○
Sleep Talk	Normal	Status	—	—	10	Self	—	—
Fire Spin	Fire	Special	35	85	15	Normal	—	—
Fire Punch	Fire	Physical	75	100	15	Normal	—	○
Heat Wave	Fire	Special	100	90	10	Many Others	—	—

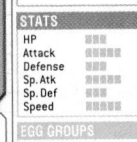

Ember Pokémon

514 Simisear

● HEIGHT: 3'03"
● WEIGHT: 61.7 lbs.
● GENDER: ♂ / ♀

When it gets excited, embers rise from its head and tail and it gets hot. For some reason, it loves sweets.

Same form for ♂ / ♀

TYPE: Fire

ABILITY

● Gluttony

HIDDEN ABILITY

—

STATS

HP	■■■
Attack	■■■■■
Defense	■■■
Sp. Atk	■■■■■
Sp. Def	■■■
Speed	■■■■■

EGG GROUPS

Field

ITEMS SOMETIMES HELD

● None

HOW TO OBTAIN

Pokémon Black Version 2	Use Fire Stone on Pansear
Pokémon White Version 2	Use Fire Stone on Pansear

HOW TO OBTAIN FROM OTHER GAMES

—

—

Pokémon AR Marker

LEVEL-UP AND LEARNED MOVES

Lv.	Name	Type	Kind	Pow.	Acc.	PP	Range	Long	DA
1	Leer	Normal	Status	—	100	30	Many Others	—	—
1	Lick	Ghost	Physical	20	100	30	Normal	—	○
1	Fury Swipes	Normal	Physical	18	80	15	Normal	—	○
1	Flame Burst	Fire	Special	70	100	15	Normal	—	—

TM & HM MOVES

Lv.	Name	Type	Kind	Pow.	Acc.	PP	Range	Long	DA
TM01	Hone Claws	Dark	Status	—	—	15	Self	—	—
TM06	Toxic	Poison	Status	—	90	10	Normal	—	—
TM10	Hidden Power	Normal	Special	—	100	15	Normal	—	—
TM11	Sunny Day	Fire	Status	—	—	5	Both Sides	—	—
TM12	Taunt	Dark	Status	—	100	20	Normal	—	—
TM15	Hyper Beam	Normal	Special	150	90	5	Normal	—	—
TM17	Protect	Normal	Status	—	—	10	Self	—	—
TM21	Frustration	Normal	Physical	—	100	20	Normal	—	○
TM22	SolarBeam	Grass	Special	120	100	10	Normal	—	—
TM27	Return	Normal	Physical	—	100	20	Normal	—	○
TM28	Dig	Ground	Physical	80	100	10	Normal	—	○
TM31	Brick Break	Fighting	Physical	75	100	15	Normal	—	○
TM32	Double Team	Normal	Status	—	—	15	Self	—	—
TM35	Flamethrower	Fire	Special	95	100	15	Normal	—	—
TM38	Fire Blast	Fire	Special	120	85	5	Normal	—	—
TM39	Rock Tomb	Rock	Physical	50	80	10	Normal	—	—
TM41	Torment	Dark	Status	—	100	15	Normal	—	—
TM42	Facade	Normal	Physical	70	100	20	Normal	—	○
TM43	Flame Charge	Fire	Physical	50	100	20	Normal	—	○
TM44	Rest	Psychic	Status	—	—	10	Self	—	—
TM45	Attract	Normal	Status	—	100	15	Normal	—	—
TM46	Thief	Dark	Physical	40	100	10	Normal	—	○
TM47	Low Sweep	Fighting	Physical	60	100	20	Normal	—	○
TM48	Round	Normal	Special	60	100	15	Normal	—	—
TM50	Overheat	Fire	Special	140	90	5	Normal	—	—
TM52	Focus Blast	Fighting	Special	120	70	5	Normal	—	—
TM56	Fling	Dark	Physical	—	100	10	Normal	—	—
TM59	Incinerate	Fire	Special	30	100	15	Many Others	—	—
TM61	Will-O-Wisp	Fire	Status	—	75	15	Normal	—	—
TM62	Acrobatics	Flying	Physical	55	100	15	Normal	○	○
TM65	Shadow Claw	Ghost	Physical	70	100	15	Normal	—	○
TM66	Payback	Dark	Physical	50	100	10	Normal	—	○
TM68	Giga Impact	Normal	Physical	150	90	5	Normal	—	○
TM80	Rock Slide	Rock	Physical	75	90	10	Many Others	—	—
TM83	Work Up	Normal	Status	—	—	30	Self	—	—
TM86	Grass Knot	Grass	Special	—	100	20	Normal	—	○
TM87	Swagger	Normal	Status	—	90	15	Normal	—	—
TM90	Substitute	Normal	Status	—	—	10	Self	—	—
TM94	Rock Smash	Fighting	Physical	40	100	15	Normal	—	○
HM01	Cut	Normal	Physical	50	95	30	Normal	—	○

MOVES TAUGHT BY PEOPLE

Name	Type	Kind	Pow.	Acc.	PP	Range	Long	DA

MOVES TAUGHT BY MOVE TUTORS FOR SHARDS

Name	Type	Kind	Pow.	Acc.	PP	Range	Long	DA
Covet	Normal	Physical	60	100	40	Normal	—	○
Uproar	Normal	Special	90	100	10	1 Random	—	—
Low Kick	Fighting	Physical	—	100	20	Normal	—	○
Gunk Shot	Poison	Physical	120	70	5	Normal	—	—
Fire Punch	Fire	Physical	75	100	15	Normal	—	○
Iron Tail	Steel	Physical	100	75	15	Normal	—	○
Superpower	Fighting	Physical	120	100	5	Normal	—	○
Snore	Normal	Special	40	100	15	Normal	—	—
Knock Off	Dark	Physical	20	100	20	Normal	—	○
Role Play	Psychic	Status	—	—	10	Normal	—	—
Heat Wave	Fire	Special	100	90	10	Many Others	—	—
Helping Hand	Normal	Status	—	—	20	1 Ally	—	—
Recycle	Normal	Status	—	—	10	Self	—	—
Endeavor	Normal	Physical	—	100	5	Normal	—	○
Sleep Talk	Normal	Status	—	—	10	Self	—	—

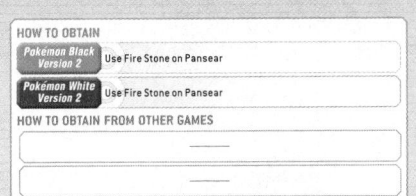

Spray Pokémon

515 Panpour

● HEIGHT: 2'00"
● WEIGHT: 29.8 lbs.
● GENDER: ♂ / ♀

The water stored inside the tuft on its head is full of nutrients. It waters plants with its using its tail.

Same form for ♂ / ♀

TYPE: Water

ABILITY

● Gluttony

HIDDEN ABILITY

—

STATS

HP	■■
Attack	■■■
Defense	■■
Sp. Atk	■■■
Sp. Def	■■
Speed	■■■■

EGG GROUPS

Field

ITEMS SOMETIMES HELD

● Oran Berry
● Rindo Berry

HOW TO OBTAIN

Pokémon Black Version 2	❶ Lostlorn Forest (rustling grass) ❷ Pinwheel Forest deep in the forest (rustling grass)
Pokémon White Version 2	❶ Lostlorn Forest (rustling grass) ❷ Pinwheel Forest deep in the forest (rustling grass)

HOW TO OBTAIN FROM OTHER GAMES

—

—

Pokémon AR Marker

LEVEL-UP AND LEARNED MOVES

Lv.	Name	Type	Kind	Pow.	Acc.	PP	Range	Long	DA
1	Scratch	Normal	Physical	40	100	35	Normal	—	○
4	Leer	Normal	Status	—	100	30	Many Others	—	—
7	Lick	Ghost	Physical	20	100	30	Normal	—	○
10	Water Gun	Water	Special	40	100	25	Normal	—	—
13	Fury Swipes	Normal	Physical	18	80	15	Normal	—	○
16	Water Sport	Water	Status	—	—	15	Both Sides	—	—
19	Bite	Dark	Physical	60	100	25	Normal	—	○
22	Scald	Water	Special	80	100	15	Normal	—	—
25	Taunt	Dark	Status	—	100	20	Normal	—	—
28	Fling	Dark	Physical	—	100	10	Normal	—	—
31	Acrobatics	Flying	Physical	55	100	15	Normal	○	○
34	Brine	Water	Special	65	100	10	Normal	—	—
37	Recycle	Normal	Status	—	—	10	Self	—	—
40	Natural Gift	Normal	Physical	—	100	15	Normal	—	—
43	Crunch	Dark	Physical	80	100	15	Normal	—	○

TM & HM MOVES

Lv.	Name	Type	Kind	Pow.	Acc.	PP	Range	Long	DA
TM01	Hone Claws	Dark	Status	—	—	15	Self	—	—
TM06	Toxic	Poison	Status	—	90	10	Normal	—	—
TM07	Hail	Ice	Status	—	—	10	Both Sides	—	—
TM10	Hidden Power	Normal	Special	—	100	15	Normal	—	—
TM12	Taunt	Dark	Status	—	100	20	Normal	—	—
TM13	Ice Beam	Ice	Special	95	100	10	Normal	—	—
TM14	Blizzard	Ice	Special	120	70	5	Many Others	—	—
TM17	Protect	Normal	Status	—	—	10	Self	—	—
TM18	Rain Dance	Water	Status	—	—	5	Both Sides	—	—
TM21	Frustration	Normal	Physical	—	100	20	Normal	—	○
TM27	Return	Normal	Physical	—	100	20	Normal	—	○
TM28	Dig	Ground	Physical	80	100	10	Normal	—	○
TM32	Double Team	Normal	Status	—	—	15	Self	—	—
TM39	Rock Tomb	Rock	Physical	50	80	10	Normal	—	—
TM41	Torment	Dark	Status	—	100	15	Normal	—	—
TM42	Facade	Normal	Physical	70	100	20	Normal	—	○
TM44	Rest	Psychic	Status	—	—	10	Self	—	—
TM45	Attract	Normal	Status	—	100	15	Normal	—	—
TM46	Thief	Dark	Physical	40	100	10	Normal	—	○
TM47	Low Sweep	Fighting	Physical	60	100	20	Normal	—	○
TM48	Round	Normal	Special	60	100	15	Normal	—	—
TM55	Scald	Water	Special	80	100	15	Normal	—	—
TM56	Fling	Dark	Physical	—	100	10	Normal	—	—
TM62	Acrobatics	Flying	Physical	55	100	15	Normal	○	○
TM65	Shadow Claw	Ghost	Physical	70	100	15	Normal	—	○
TM66	Payback	Dark	Physical	50	100	10	Normal	—	○
TM83	Work Up	Normal	Status	—	—	30	Self	—	—
TM86	Grass Knot	Grass	Special	—	100	20	Normal	—	○
TM87	Swagger	Normal	Status	—	90	15	Normal	—	—
TM90	Substitute	Normal	Status	—	—	10	Self	—	—
TM94	Rock Smash	Fighting	Physical	40	100	15	Normal	—	○
HM01	Cut	Normal	Physical	50	95	30	Normal	—	○
HM03	Surf	Water	Special	95	100	15	Adjacent	—	—
HM05	Waterfall	Water	Physical	80	100	15	Normal	—	○
HM06	Dive	Water	Physical	80	100	10	Normal	—	○

MOVES TAUGHT BY PEOPLE

Name	Type	Kind	Pow.	Acc.	PP	Range	Long	DA

MOVES TAUGHT BY MOVE TUTORS FOR SHARDS

Name	Type	Kind	Pow.	Acc.	PP	Range	Long	DA
Covet	Normal	Physical	60	100	40	Normal	—	○
Uproar	Normal	Special	90	100	10	1 Random	—	—
Low Kick	Fighting	Physical	—	100	20	Normal	—	○
Gunk Shot	Poison	Physical	120	70	5	Normal	—	—
Ice Punch	Ice	Physical	75	100	15	Normal	—	○
Icy Wind	Ice	Special	55	95	15	Many Others	—	—
Iron Tail	Steel	Physical	100	75	15	Normal	—	○
Aqua Tail	Water	Physical	90	90	10	Normal	—	○
Snore	Normal	Special	40	100	15	Normal	—	—
Knock Off	Dark	Physical	20	100	20	Normal	—	○
Role Play	Psychic	Status	—	—	10	Normal	—	—
Helping Hand	Normal	Status	—	—	20	1 Ally	—	—
Recycle	Normal	Status	—	—	10	Self	—	—
Endeavor	Normal	Physical	—	100	5	Normal	—	○
Sleep Talk	Normal	Status	—	—	10	Self	—	

EGG MOVES

Name	Type	Kind	Pow.	Acc.	PP	Range	Long	DA
Covet	Normal	Physical	60	100	40	Normal	—	○
Low Kick	Fighting	Physical	—	100	20	Normal	—	○
Tickle	Normal	Status	—	100	20	Normal	—	—
Nasty Plot	Dark	Status	—	—	20	Self	—	—
Role Play	Psychic	Status	—	—	10	Normal	—	—
Astonish	Ghost	Physical	30	100	15	Normal	—	○
Aqua Ring	Water	Status	—	—	20	Self	—	—
Aqua Tail	Water	Physical	90	90	10	Normal	—	○
Mud Sport	Ground	Status	—	—	15	Both Sides	—	—
Hydro Pump	Water	Special	120	80	5	Normal	—	—

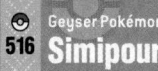

516 Simipour

Geyser Pokémon

- HEIGHT: 3'03"
- WEIGHT: 63.9 lbs.
- GENDER: ♂ / ♀

It prefers places with clean water. When its tuft runs low, it replenishes it by siphoning up water with its tail.

Same form for ♂ / ♀

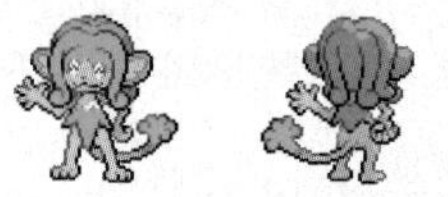

TYPE Water

ABILITY
- Gluttony

HIDDEN ABILITY
—

STATS
HP
Attack
Defense
Sp. Atk
Sp. Def
Speed

EGG GROUPS
Field

ITEMS SOMETIMES HELD
- None

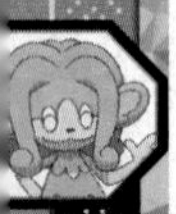

EVOLUTION

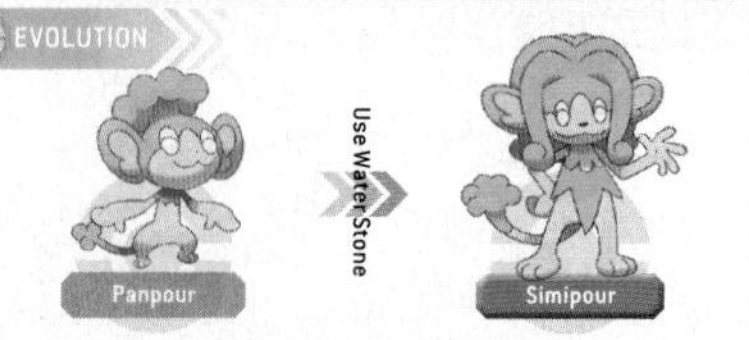

HOW TO OBTAIN

Pokémon Black Version 2	Use Water Stone on Panpour
Pokémon White Version 2	Use Water Stone on Panpour

HOW TO OBTAIN FROM OTHER GAMES

—
—

LEVEL-UP AND LEARNED MOVES

Lv.	Name	Type	Kind	Pow.	Acc.	PP	Range	Long	DA
1	Leer	Normal	Status	—	100	30	Many Others	—	—
1	Lick	Ghost	Physical	20	100	30	Normal	—	○
1	Fury Swipes	Normal	Physical	18	80	15	Normal	—	○
1	Scald	Water	Special	80	100	15	Normal	—	—

TM & HM MOVES

Lv.	Name	Type	Kind	Pow.	Acc.	PP	Range	Long	DA
TM01	Hone Claws	Dark	Status	—	—	15	Self	—	—
TM06	Toxic	Poison	Status	—	90	10	Normal	—	—
TM07	Hail	Ice	Status	—	—	10	Both Sides	—	—
TM10	Hidden Power	Normal	Special	—	100	15	Normal	—	—
TM12	Taunt	Dark	Status	—	100	20	Normal	—	—
TM13	Ice Beam	Ice	Special	95	100	10	Normal	—	—
TM14	Blizzard	Ice	Special	120	70	5	Many Others	—	—
TM15	Hyper Beam	Normal	Special	150	90	5	Normal	—	—
TM17	Protect	Normal	Status	—	—	10	Self	—	—
TM18	Rain Dance	Water	Status	—	—	5	Both Sides	—	—
TM21	Frustration	Normal	Physical	—	100	20	Normal	—	○
TM27	Return	Normal	Physical	—	100	20	Normal	—	○
TM28	Dig	Ground	Physical	80	100	10	Normal	—	○
TM31	Brick Break	Fighting	Physical	75	100	15	Normal	—	○
TM32	Double Team	Normal	Status	—	—	15	Self	—	—
TM39	Rock Tomb	Rock	Physical	50	80	10	Normal	—	—
TM41	Torment	Dark	Status	—	100	15	Normal	—	—
TM42	Facade	Normal	Physical	70	100	20	Normal	—	○
TM44	Rest	Psychic	Status	—	—	10	Self	—	—
TM45	Attract	Normal	Status	—	100	15	Normal	—	—
TM46	Thief	Dark	Physical	40	100	10	Normal	—	○
TM47	Low Sweep	Fighting	Physical	60	100	20	Normal	—	○
TM48	Round	Normal	Special	60	100	15	Normal	—	—
TM52	Focus Blast	Fighting	Special	120	70	5	Normal	—	—
TM55	Scald	Water	Special	80	100	15	Normal	—	—
TM56	Fling	Dark	Physical	—	100	10	Normal	—	—
TM62	Acrobatics	Flying	Physical	55	100	15	Normal	○	○
TM65	Shadow Claw	Ghost	Physical	70	100	15	Normal	—	○
TM66	Payback	Dark	Physical	50	100	10	Normal	—	○
TM68	Giga Impact	Normal	Physical	150	90	5	Normal	—	○
TM80	Rock Slide	Rock	Physical	75	90	10	Many Others	—	—
TM83	Work Up	Normal	Status	—	—	30	Self	—	—
TM86	Grass Knot	Grass	Special	—	100	20	Normal	—	○
TM87	Swagger	Normal	Status	—	90	15	Normal	—	—
TM90	Substitute	Normal	Status	—	—	10	Self	—	—
TM94	Rock Smash	Fighting	Physical	40	100	15	Normal	—	○
HM01	Cut	Normal	Physical	50	95	30	Normal	—	○
HM03	Surf	Water	Special	95	100	15	Adjacent	—	—
HM05	Waterfall	Water	Physical	80	100	15	Normal	—	○
HM06	Dive	Water	Physical	80	100	10	Normal	—	○

MOVES TAUGHT BY PEOPLE

Name	Type	Kind	Pow.	Acc.	PP	Range	Long	DA

MOVES TAUGHT BY MOVE TUTORS FOR SHARDS

Name	Type	Kind	Pow.	Acc.	PP	Range	Long	DA
Covet	Normal	Physical	60	100	40	Normal	—	○
Uproar	Normal	Special	90	100	10	1 Random	—	—
Low Kick	Fighting	Physical	—	100	20	Normal	—	○
Gunk Shot	Poison	Physical	120	70	5	Normal	—	—
Ice Punch	Ice	Physical	75	100	15	Normal	—	○
Icy Wind	Ice	Special	55	95	15	Many Others	—	—
Iron Tail	Steel	Physical	100	75	15	Normal	—	○
Aqua Tail	Water	Physical	90	90	10	Normal	—	○
Superpower	Fighting	Physical	120	100	5	Normal	—	○
Snore	Normal	Special	40	100	15	Normal	—	—
Knock Off	Dark	Physical	20	100	20	Normal	—	○
Role Play	Psychic	Status	—	—	10	Normal	—	—
Helping Hand	Normal	Status	—	—	20	1 Ally	—	—
Recycle	Normal	Status	—	—	10	Self	—	—
Endeavor	Normal	Physical	—	100	5	Normal	—	○
Sleep Talk	Normal	Status	—	—	10	Self	—	—

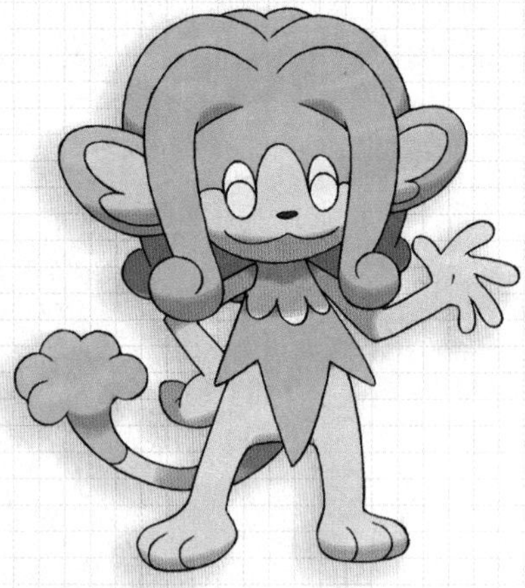

Pokémon AR Marker

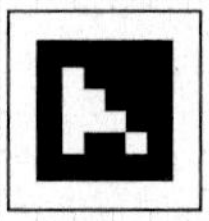

517 Munna

Dream Eater Pokémon

- HEIGHT: 2'00"
- WEIGHT: 51.4 lbs.
- GENDER: ♂ / ♀

This Pokémon appears before people and Pokémon who are having nightmares and eats those dreams.

Same form for ♂ / ♀

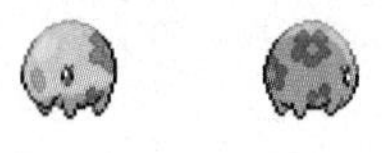

TYPE Psychic

ABILITIES
- Forewarn
- Synchronize

HIDDEN ABILITY
- Telepathy

STATS
HP
Attack
Defense
Sp. Atk
Sp. Def
Speed

EGG GROUPS
Field

ITEMS SOMETIMES HELD
- None

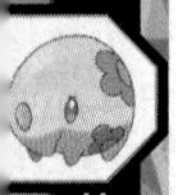

EVOLUTION

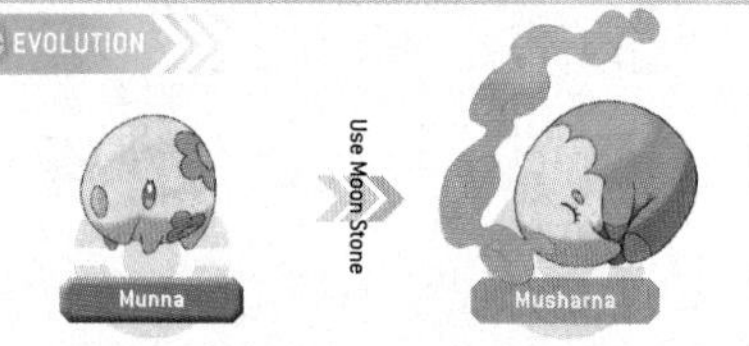

HOW TO OBTAIN

Pokémon Black Version 2	❶ Dreamyard ❷ Dreamyard Basement (dark grass)
Pokémon White Version 2	❶ Dreamyard ❷ Dreamyard Basement (dark grass)

HOW TO OBTAIN FROM OTHER GAMES

—
—

LEVEL-UP AND LEARNED MOVES

Lv.	Name	Type	Kind	Pow.	Acc.	PP	Range	Long	DA
1	Psywave	Psychic	Special	—	80	15	Normal	—	—
1	Defense Curl	Normal	Status	—	—	40	Self	—	—
5	Lucky Chant	Normal	Status	—	—	30	Your Side	—	—
7	Yawn	Normal	Status	—	—	10	Normal	—	—
11	Psybeam	Psychic	Special	65	100	20	Normal	—	—
13	Imprison	Psychic	Status	—	—	10	Self	—	—
17	Moonlight	Normal	Status	—	—	5	Self	—	—
19	Hypnosis	Psychic	Status	—	60	20	Normal	—	—
23	Zen Headbutt	Psychic	Physical	80	90	15	Normal	—	○
25	Synchronoise	Psychic	Special	70	100	15	Adjacent	—	—
29	Nightmare	Ghost	Status	—	100	15	Normal	—	—
31	Future Sight	Psychic	Special	100	100	10	Normal	—	—
35	Calm Mind	Psychic	Status	—	—	20	Self	—	—
37	Psychic	Psychic	Special	90	100	10	Normal	—	—
41	Dream Eater	Psychic	Special	100	100	15	Normal	—	—
43	Telekinesis	Psychic	Status	—	—	15	Normal	—	—
47	Stored Power	Psychic	Special	20	100	10	Normal	—	—

TM & HM MOVES

Lv.	Name	Type	Kind	Pow.	Acc.	PP	Range	Long	DA
TM03	Psyshock	Psychic	Special	80	100	10	Normal	—	—
TM04	Calm Mind	Psychic	Status	—	—	20	Self	—	—
TM06	Toxic	Poison	Status	—	90	10	Normal	—	—
TM10	Hidden Power	Normal	Special	—	100	15	Normal	—	—
TM16	Light Screen	Psychic	Status	—	—	30	Your Side	—	—
TM17	Protect	Normal	Status	—	—	10	Self	—	—
TM18	Rain Dance	Water	Status	—	—	5	Both Sides	—	—
TM19	Telekinesis	Psychic	Status	—	—	15	Normal	—	—
TM20	Safeguard	Normal	Status	—	—	25	Your Side	—	—
TM21	Frustration	Normal	Physical	—	100	20	Normal	—	○
TM27	Return	Normal	Physical	—	100	20	Normal	—	○
TM29	Psychic	Psychic	Special	90	100	10	Normal	—	—
TM30	Shadow Ball	Ghost	Special	80	100	15	Normal	—	—
TM32	Double Team	Normal	Status	—	—	15	Self	—	—
TM33	Reflect	Psychic	Status	—	—	20	Your Side	—	—
TM39	Rock Tomb	Rock	Physical	50	80	10	Normal	—	—
TM41	Torment	Dark	Status	—	100	15	Normal	—	—
TM42	Facade	Normal	Physical	70	100	20	Normal	—	○
TM44	Rest	Psychic	Status	—	—	10	Self	—	—
TM45	Attract	Normal	Status	—	100	15	Normal	—	—
TM48	Round	Normal	Special	60	100	15	Normal	—	—
TM53	Energy Ball	Grass	Special	80	100	10	Normal	—	—
TM57	Charge Beam	Electric	Special	50	90	10	Normal	—	—
TM70	Flash	Normal	Status	—	100	20	Normal	—	—
TM73	Thunder Wave	Electric	Status	—	100	20	Normal	—	—
TM74	Gyro Ball	Steel	Physical	—	100	5	Normal	—	○
TM77	Psych Up	Normal	Status	—	—	10	Normal	—	—
TM80	Rock Slide	Rock	Physical	75	90	10	Many Others	—	—
TM85	Dream Eater	Psychic	Special	100	100	15	Normal	—	—
TM87	Swagger	Normal	Status	—	90	15	Normal	—	—
TM90	Substitute	Normal	Status	—	—	10	Self	—	—
TM92	Trick Room	Psychic	Status	—	—	5	Both Sides	—	—

MOVES TAUGHT BY PEOPLE

Name	Type	Kind	Pow.	Acc.	PP	Range	Long	DA

MOVES TAUGHT BY MOVE TUTORS FOR SHARDS

Name	Type	Kind	Pow.	Acc.	PP	Range	Long	DA
Signal Beam	Bug	Special	75	100	15	Normal	—	—
Magic Coat	Psychic	Status	—	—	15	Self	—	—
Zen Headbutt	Psychic	Physical	80	90	15	Normal	—	○
Gravity	Psychic	Status	—	—	5	Both Sides	—	—
Snore	Normal	Special	40	100	15	Normal	—	—
Heal Bell	Normal	Status	—	—	5	Your Party	—	—
Pain Split	Normal	Status	—	—	20	Normal	—	—
Worry Seed	Grass	Status	—	100	10	Normal	—	—
Helping Hand	Normal	Status	—	—	20	1 Ally	—	—
After You	Normal	Status	—	—	15	Normal	—	—
Wonder Room	Psychic	Status	—	—	10	Both Sides	—	—
Trick	Psychic	Status	—	100	10	Normal	—	—
Sleep Talk	Normal	Status	—	—	10	Self	—	—
Skill Swap	Psychic	Status	—	—	10	Normal	—	—

EGG MOVES

Name	Type	Kind	Pow.	Acc.	PP	Range	Long	DA
Sleep Talk	Normal	Status	—	—	10	Self	—	—
Secret Power	Normal	Physical	70	100	20	Normal	—	—
Barrier	Psychic	Status	—	—	30	Self	—	—
Magic Coat	Psychic	Status	—	—	15	Self	—	—
Helping Hand	Normal	Status	—	—	20	1 Ally	—	—
Baton Pass	Normal	Status	—	—	40	Self	—	—
Swift	Normal	Special	60	—	20	Many Others	—	—
Curse	Ghost	Status	—	—	10	Varies	—	—
SonicBoom	Normal	Special	—	90	20	Normal	—	—

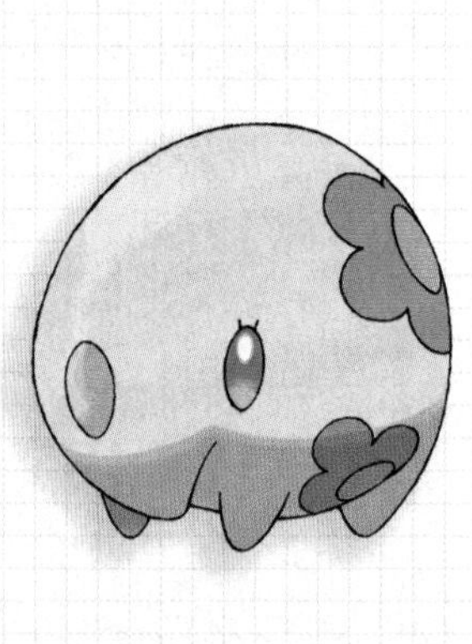

Pokémon AR Marker

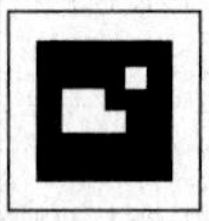

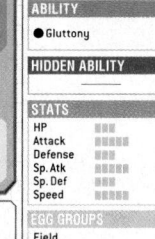

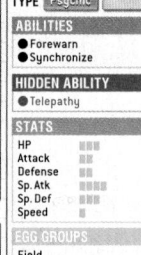

518 Musharna

Drowsing Pokémon

TYPE Psychic

ABILITIES
- Forewarn
- Synchronize

HIDDEN ABILITY
- Telepathy

- **HEIGHT:** 3'07"
- **WEIGHT:** 133.4 lbs.
- **GENDER:** ♂ / ♀

The dream mist coming from its forehead changes into many different colors depending on the dream that was eaten.

STATS
HP
Attack
Defense
Sp. Atk
Sp. Def
Speed

EGG GROUPS
Field

ITEMS SOMETIMES HELD
- None

Same form for ♂ / ♀

Pokémon AR Marker

EVOLUTION

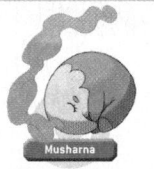

Munna → Use Moon Stone → Musharna

HOW TO OBTAIN

Pokémon Black Version 2	Dreamyard basement (rustling grass)
Pokémon White Version 2	Dreamyard basement (rustling grass)

HOW TO OBTAIN FROM OTHER GAMES

——

518 | Musharna

LEVEL-UP AND LEARNED MOVES

Lv.	Name	Type	Kind	Pow.	Acc.	PP	Range	Long	DA
1	Defense Curl	Normal	Status	—	—	40	Self	—	—
1	Lucky Chant	Normal	Status	—	—	30	Your Side	—	—
1	Psybeam	Psychic	Special	65	100	20	Normal	—	—
1	Hypnosis	Psychic	Status	—	60	20	Normal	—	—

TM & HM MOVES

Lv.	Name	Type	Kind	Pow.	Acc.	PP	Range	Long	DA
TM03	Psyshock	Psychic	Special	80	100	10	Normal	—	—
TM04	Calm Mind	Psychic	Status	—	—	20	Self	—	—
TM06	Toxic	Poison	Status	—	90	10	Normal	—	—
TM10	Hidden Power	Normal	Special	—	100	15	Normal	—	—
TM15	Hyper Beam	Normal	Special	150	90	5	Normal	—	—
TM16	Light Screen	Psychic	Status	—	—	30	Your Side	—	—
TM17	Protect	Normal	Status	—	—	10	Self	—	—
TM18	Rain Dance	Water	Status	—	—	5	Both Sides	—	—
TM19	Telekinesis	Psychic	Status	—	—	15	Normal	—	—
TM20	Safeguard	Normal	Status	—	—	25	Your Side	—	—
TM21	Frustration	Normal	Physical	—	100	20	Normal	—	○
TM27	Return	Normal	Physical	—	100	20	Normal	—	○
TM29	Psychic	Psychic	Special	90	100	10	Normal	—	—
TM30	Shadow Ball	Ghost	Special	80	100	15	Normal	—	—
TM32	Double Team	Normal	Status	—	—	15	Self	—	—
TM33	Reflect	Psychic	Status	—	—	20	Your Side	—	—
TM39	Rock Tomb	Rock	Physical	50	80	10	Normal	—	—
TM41	Torment	Dark	Status	—	100	15	Normal	—	—
TM42	Facade	Normal	Physical	70	100	20	Normal	—	—
TM44	Rest	Psychic	Status	—	—	10	Self	—	—
TM45	Attract	Normal	Status	—	100	15	Normal	—	—
TM48	Round	Normal	Special	60	100	15	Normal	—	—
TM53	Energy Ball	Grass	Special	80	100	10	Normal	—	—
TM57	Charge Beam	Electric	Special	50	90	10	Normal	—	—
TM68	Giga Impact	Normal	Physical	150	90	5	Normal	—	—
TM70	Flash	Normal	Status	—	100	20	Normal	—	—
TM73	Thunder Wave	Electric	Status	—	100	20	Normal	—	—
TM74	Gyro Ball	Steel	Physical	—	100	5	Normal	—	○
TM77	Psych Up	Normal	Status	—	—	10	Self	—	—
TM80	Rock Slide	Rock	Physical	75	90	10	Many Others	—	—
TM85	Dream Eater	Psychic	Special	100	100	15	Normal	—	—
TM87	Swagger	Normal	Status	—	90	15	Normal	—	—
TM90	Substitute	Normal	Status	—	—	10	Self	—	—
TM92	Trick Room	Psychic	Status	—	—	5	Both Sides	—	—

MOVES TAUGHT BY PEOPLE

Name	Type	Kind	Pow.	Acc.	PP	Range	Long	DA

MOVES TAUGHT BY MOVE TUTORS FOR SHARDS

Name	Type	Kind	Pow.	Acc.	PP	Range	Long	DA
Signal Beam	Bug	Special	75	100	15	Normal	—	—
Magic Coat	Psychic	Status	—	—	15	Self	—	—
Zen Headbutt	Psychic	Physical	80	90	15	Normal	—	○
Gravity	Psychic	Status	—	—	5	Both Sides	—	—
Snore	Normal	Special	40	100	15	Normal	—	—
Heal Bell	Normal	Status	—	—	5	Your Party	—	—
Pain Split	Normal	Status	—	—	20	Normal	—	—
Worry Seed	Grass	Status	—	100	10	Normal	—	—
Helping Hand	Normal	Status	—	—	20	1 Ally	—	—
After You	Normal	Status	—	—	15	Normal	—	—
Wonder Room	Psychic	Status	—	—	10	Both Sides	—	—
Trick	Psychic	Status	—	100	10	Normal	—	—
Sleep Talk	Normal	Status	—	—	10	Self	—	—
Skill Swap	Psychic	Status	—	—	10	Normal	—	—

---

519 Pidove

Tiny Pigeon Pokémon

TYPE Normal Flying

ABILITIES
- Big Pecks
- Super Luck

HIDDEN ABILITY
- Rivalry

- **HEIGHT:** 1'00"
- **WEIGHT:** 4.6 lbs.
- **GENDER:** ♂ / ♀

This very forgetful Pokémon will wait for a new order from its Trainer even though it already has one.

STATS
HP
Attack
Defense
Sp. Atk
Sp. Def
Speed

EGG GROUPS
Flying

ITEMS SOMETIMES HELD
- None

Same form for ♂ / ♀

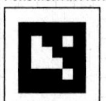

Pokémon AR Marker

EVOLUTION

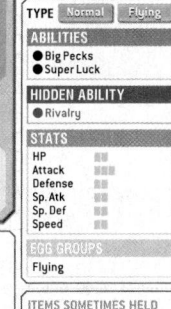

Pidove → Lv. 21 → Tranquill → Lv. 32 → Unfezant

HOW TO OBTAIN

Pokémon Black Version 2	❶ Route 20 ❷ Virbank Complex
Pokémon White Version 2	❶ Route 20 ❷ Virbank Complex

HOW TO OBTAIN FROM OTHER GAMES

519 | Pidove

LEVEL-UP AND LEARNED MOVES

Lv.	Name	Type	Kind	Pow.	Acc.	PP	Range	Long	DA
1	Gust	Flying	Special	40	100	35	Normal	○	—
4	Growl	Normal	Status	—	100	40	Many Others	—	—
8	Leer	Normal	Status	—	100	30	Many Others	—	—
11	Quick Attack	Normal	Physical	40	100	30	Normal	—	○
15	Air Cutter	Flying	Special	55	95	25	Many Others	—	—
18	Roost	Flying	Status	—	—	10	Self	—	—
22	Detect	Fighting	Status	—	—	5	Self	—	—
25	Taunt	Dark	Status	—	100	20	Normal	—	—
29	Air Slash	Flying	Special	75	95	20	Normal	○	—
32	Razor Wind	Normal	Special	80	100	10	Many Others	—	—
36	FeatherDance	Flying	Status	—	100	15	Normal	—	—
39	Swagger	Normal	Status	—	90	15	Normal	—	—
43	Facade	Normal	Physical	70	100	20	Normal	—	—
46	Tailwind	Flying	Status	—	—	30	Your Side	—	—
50	Sky Attack	Flying	Physical	140	90	5	Normal	○	—

TM & HM MOVES

Lv.	Name	Type	Kind	Pow.	Acc.	PP	Range	Long	DA
TM06	Toxic	Poison	Status	—	90	10	Normal	—	—
TM10	Hidden Power	Normal	Special	—	100	15	Normal	—	—
TM11	Sunny Day	Fire	Status	—	—	5	Both Sides	—	—
TM12	Taunt	Dark	Status	—	100	20	Normal	—	—
TM17	Protect	Normal	Status	—	—	10	Self	—	—
TM18	Rain Dance	Water	Status	—	—	5	Both Sides	—	—
TM21	Frustration	Normal	Physical	—	100	20	Normal	—	○
TM27	Return	Normal	Physical	—	100	20	Normal	—	○
TM32	Double Team	Normal	Status	—	—	15	Self	—	—
TM40	Aerial Ace	Flying	Physical	60	—	20	Normal	○	○
TM42	Facade	Normal	Physical	70	100	20	Normal	—	—
TM44	Rest	Psychic	Status	—	—	10	Self	—	—
TM45	Attract	Normal	Status	—	100	15	Normal	—	—
TM48	Round	Normal	Special	60	100	15	Normal	—	—
TM49	Echoed Voice	Normal	Special	40	100	15	Normal	—	—
TM83	Work Up	Normal	Status	—	—	30	Self	—	—
TM87	Swagger	Normal	Status	—	90	15	Normal	—	—
TM88	Pluck	Flying	Physical	60	100	20	Normal	○	○
TM89	U-turn	Bug	Physical	70	100	20	Normal	—	○
TM90	Substitute	Normal	Status	—	—	10	Self	—	—
HM02	Fly	Flying	Physical	90	95	15	Normal	○	—

MOVES TAUGHT BY PEOPLE

Name	Type	Kind	Pow.	Acc.	PP	Range	Long	DA

MOVES TAUGHT BY MOVE TUTORS FOR SHARDS

Name	Type	Kind	Pow.	Acc.	PP	Range	Long	DA
Uproar	Normal	Special	90	100	10	1 Random	—	—
Snore	Normal	Special	40	100	15	Normal	—	—
Roost	Flying	Status	—	—	10	Self	—	—
Sky Attack	Flying	Physical	140	90	5	Normal	○	—
Heat Wave	Fire	Special	100	90	10	Many Others	—	—
Tailwind	Flying	Status	—	—	30	Your Side	—	—
Sleep Talk	Normal	Status	—	—	10	Self	—	—

EGG MOVES

Name	Type	Kind	Pow.	Acc.	PP	Range	Long	DA
Steel Wing	Steel	Physical	70	90	25	Normal	—	○
Hypnosis	Psychic	Status	—	60	20	Normal	—	—
Uproar	Normal	Special	90	100	10	1 Random	—	—
Bestow	Normal	Status	—	—	15	Normal	—	—
Wish	Normal	Status	—	—	10	Self	—	—
Morning Sun	Normal	Status	—	—	5	Self	—	—
Lucky Chant	Normal	Status	—	—	30	Your Side	—	—

520 Tranquill
Wild Pigeon Pokémon

● HEIGHT: 2'00"
● WEIGHT: 33.1 lbs.
● GENDER: ♂ / ♀

No matter where in the world it goes, it knows where its nest is, so it never gets separated from its Trainer.

Same form for ♂ / ♀

Pokémon AR Marker

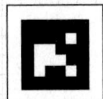

TYPE Normal Flying

ABILITIES
● Big Pecks
● Super Luck

HIDDEN ABILITY
● Rivalry

STATS
HP
Attack
Defense
Sp. Atk
Sp. Def
Speed

EGG GROUPS
Flying

ITEMS SOMETIMES HELD
● None

EVOLUTION

Pidove — Lv. 21 → Tranquill — Lv. 32 → Unfezant

HOW TO OBTAIN

Pokémon Black Version 2	❶ Route 6 ❷ Route 7
Pokémon White Version 2	❶ Route 6 ❷ Route 7

HOW TO OBTAIN FROM OTHER GAMES

LEVEL-UP AND LEARNED MOVES

Lv.	Name	Type	Kind	Pow.	Acc.	PP	Range	Long	DA
1	Gust	Flying	Special	40	100	35	Normal	○	—
1	Growl	Normal	Status	—	100	40	Many Others	—	—
1	Leer	Normal	Status	—	100	30	Many Others	—	—
1	Quick Attack	Normal	Physical	40	100	30	Normal	—	○
4	Growl	Normal	Status	—	100	40	Many Others	—	—
8	Leer	Normal	Status	—	100	30	Many Others	—	—
11	Quick Attack	Normal	Physical	40	100	30	Normal	—	○
15	Air Cutter	Flying	Special	55	95	25	Many Others	—	—
18	Roost	Flying	Status	—	—	10	Self	—	—
23	Detect	Fighting	Status	—	—	5	Self	—	—
27	Taunt	Dark	Status	—	100	20	Normal	—	—
32	Air Slash	Flying	Special	75	95	20	Normal	○	—
36	Razor Wind	Normal	Special	80	100	10	Many Others	—	—
41	FeatherDance	Flying	Status	—	100	15	Normal	—	—
45	Swagger	Normal	Status	—	90	15	Normal	—	—
50	Facade	Normal	Physical	70	100	20	Normal	—	○
54	Tailwind	Flying	Status	—	—	30	Your Side	—	—
59	Sky Attack	Flying	Physical	140	90	5	Normal	○	—

TM & HM MOVES

Lv.	Name	Type	Kind	Pow.	Acc.	PP	Range	Long	DA
TM06	Toxic	Poison	Status	—	90	10	Normal	—	—
TM10	Hidden Power	Normal	Special	—	100	15	Normal	—	—
TM11	Sunny Day	Fire	Status	—	—	5	Both Sides	—	—
TM12	Taunt	Dark	Status	—	100	20	Normal	—	—
TM17	Protect	Normal	Status	—	—	10	Self	—	—
TM18	Rain Dance	Water	Status	—	—	5	Both Sides	—	—
TM21	Frustration	Normal	Physical	—	100	20	Normal	—	○
TM27	Return	Normal	Physical	—	100	20	Normal	—	○
TM32	Double Team	Normal	Status	—	—	15	Self	—	—
TM40	Aerial Ace	Flying	Physical	60	—	20	Normal	○	○
TM42	Facade	Normal	Physical	70	100	20	Normal	—	○
TM44	Rest	Psychic	Status	—	—	10	Self	—	—
TM45	Attract	Normal	Status	—	100	15	Normal	—	—
TM48	Round	Normal	Special	60	100	15	Normal	—	—
TM49	Echoed Voice	Normal	Special	40	100	15	Normal	—	—
TM83	Work Up	Normal	Status	—	—	30	Self	—	—
TM87	Swagger	Normal	Status	—	90	15	Normal	—	—
TM88	Pluck	Flying	Physical	60	100	20	Normal	○	○
TM89	U-turn	Bug	Physical	70	100	20	Normal	—	○
TM90	Substitute	Normal	Status	—	—	10	Self	—	—
HM02	Fly	Flying	Physical	90	95	15	Normal	○	○

MOVES TAUGHT BY PEOPLE

Name	Type	Kind	Pow.	Acc.	PP	Range	Long	DA

MOVES TAUGHT BY MOVE TUTORS FOR SHARDS

Name	Type	Kind	Pow.	Acc.	PP	Range	Long	DA
Uproar	Normal	Special	90	100	10	1 Random	—	—
Snore	Normal	Special	40	100	15	Normal	—	—
Roost	Flying	Status	—	—	10	Self	—	—
Sky Attack	Flying	Physical	140	90	5	Normal	○	—
Heat Wave	Fire	Special	100	90	10	Many Others	—	—
Tailwind	Flying	Status	—	—	30	Your Side	—	—
Sleep Talk	Normal	Status	—	—	10	Self	—	—

521 Unfezant
Proud Pokémon

● HEIGHT: 3'11"
● WEIGHT: 63.9 lbs.
● GENDER: ♂ / ♀

Males swing the plumage on their heads to threaten others, but females are better at flying.

Male Form

Female Form

Pokémon AR Marker

Male Form   Female Form

TYPE Normal Flying

ABILITIES
● Big Pecks
● Super Luck

HIDDEN ABILITY
● Rivalry

STATS
HP
Attack
Defense
Sp. Atk
Sp. Def
Speed

EGG GROUPS
Flying

ITEMS SOMETIMES HELD
● None

EVOLUTION

Pidove — Lv. 21 → Tranquill — Lv. 32 → Unfezant

HOW TO OBTAIN

Pokémon Black Version 2	❶ Route 6 (rustling grass) ❷ Route 7 (rustling grass)
Pokémon White Version 2	❶ Route 6 (rustling grass) ❷ Route 7 (rustling grass)

HOW TO OBTAIN FROM OTHER GAMES

LEVEL-UP AND LEARNED MOVES

Lv.	Name	Type	Kind	Pow.	Acc.	PP	Range	Long	DA
1	Gust	Flying	Special	40	100	35	Normal	○	—
1	Growl	Normal	Status	—	100	40	Many Others	—	—
1	Leer	Normal	Status	—	100	30	Many Others	—	—
1	Quick Attack	Normal	Physical	40	100	30	Normal	—	○
4	Growl	Normal	Status	—	100	40	Many Others	—	—
8	Leer	Normal	Status	—	100	30	Many Others	—	—
11	Quick Attack	Normal	Physical	40	100	30	Normal	—	○
15	Air Cutter	Flying	Special	55	95	25	Many Others	—	—
18	Roost	Flying	Status	—	—	10	Self	—	—
23	Detect	Fighting	Status	—	—	5	Self	—	—
27	Taunt	Dark	Status	—	100	20	Normal	—	—
33	Air Slash	Flying	Special	75	95	20	Normal	○	—
38	Razor Wind	Normal	Special	80	100	10	Many Others	—	—
44	FeatherDance	Flying	Status	—	100	15	Normal	—	—
49	Swagger	Normal	Status	—	90	15	Normal	—	—
55	Facade	Normal	Physical	70	100	20	Normal	—	○
60	Tailwind	Flying	Status	—	—	30	Your Side	—	—
66	Sky Attack	Flying	Physical	140	90	5	Normal	○	—

TM & HM MOVES

Lv.	Name	Type	Kind	Pow.	Acc.	PP	Range	Long	DA
TM06	Toxic	Poison	Status	—	90	10	Normal	—	—
TM10	Hidden Power	Normal	Special	—	100	15	Normal	—	—
TM11	Sunny Day	Fire	Status	—	—	5	Both Sides	—	—
TM12	Taunt	Dark	Status	—	100	20	Normal	—	—
TM15	Hyper Beam	Normal	Special	150	90	5	Normal	—	—
TM17	Protect	Normal	Status	—	—	10	Self	—	—
TM18	Rain Dance	Water	Status	—	—	5	Both Sides	—	—
TM21	Frustration	Normal	Physical	—	100	20	Normal	—	○
TM27	Return	Normal	Physical	—	100	20	Normal	—	○
TM32	Double Team	Normal	Status	—	—	15	Self	—	—
TM40	Aerial Ace	Flying	Physical	60	—	20	Normal	○	○
TM42	Facade	Normal	Physical	70	100	20	Normal	—	○
TM44	Rest	Psychic	Status	—	—	10	Self	—	—
TM45	Attract	Normal	Status	—	100	15	Normal	—	—
TM48	Round	Normal	Special	60	100	15	Normal	—	—
TM49	Echoed Voice	Normal	Special	40	100	15	Normal	—	—
TM68	Giga Impact	Normal	Physical	150	90	5	Normal	—	○
TM77	Psych Up	Normal	Status	—	—	10	Normal	—	—
TM83	Work Up	Normal	Status	—	—	30	Self	—	—
TM87	Swagger	Normal	Status	—	90	15	Normal	—	—
TM88	Pluck	Flying	Physical	60	100	20	Normal	○	○
TM89	U-turn	Bug	Physical	70	100	20	Normal	—	○
TM90	Substitute	Normal	Status	—	—	10	Self	—	—
HM02	Fly	Flying	Physical	90	95	15	Normal	○	○

MOVES TAUGHT BY PEOPLE

Name	Type	Kind	Pow.	Acc.	PP	Range	Long	DA

MOVES TAUGHT BY MOVE TUTORS FOR SHARDS

Name	Type	Kind	Pow.	Acc.	PP	Range	Long	DA
Uproar	Normal	Special	90	100	10	1 Random	—	—
Snore	Normal	Special	40	100	15	Normal	—	—
Roost	Flying	Status	—	—	10	Self	—	—
Sky Attack	Flying	Physical	140	90	5	Normal	○	—
Heat Wave	Fire	Special	100	90	10	Many Others	—	—
Tailwind	Flying	Status	—	—	30	Your Side	—	—
Sleep Talk	Normal	Status	—	—	10	Self	—	—

522 Blitzle

Electrified Pokémon

TYPE Electric

ABILITIES
- Lightningrod
- Motor Drive

HIDDEN ABILITY
- Sap Sipper

STATS
HP	▪▪
Attack	▪▪
Defense	▪▪
Sp. Atk	▪▪
Sp. Def	▪▪
Speed	▪▪▪▪

EGG GROUPS
Field

ITEMS SOMETIMES HELD
- None

- HEIGHT: 2'07"
- WEIGHT: 65.7 lbs.
- GENDER: ♂ / ♀

Its mane shines when it discharges electricity. They use the frequency and rhythm of these flashes to communicate.

Same form for ♂ / ♀

Pokémon AR Marker

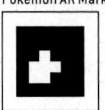

EVOLUTION

 Blitzle → Lv. 27 →  Zebstrika

HOW TO OBTAIN
Pokémon Black Version 2	Catch a Zebstrika, leave it at the Pokémon Day Care, and hatch the Egg that is found
Pokémon White Version 2	Catch a Zebstrika, leave it at the Pokémon Day Care, and hatch the Egg that is found

HOW TO OBTAIN FROM OTHER GAMES
Pokémon Black Version	Route 3
Pokémon White Version	Route 3

LEVEL-UP AND LEARNED MOVES
Lv.	Name	Type	Kind	Pow.	Acc.	PP	Range	Long	DA
1	Quick Attack	Normal	Physical	40	100	30	Normal	—	○
4	Tail Whip	Normal	Status	—	100	30	Many Others	—	—
8	Charge	Electric	Status	—	—	20	Self	—	—
11	Shock Wave	Electric	Special	60	—	20	Normal	—	—
15	Thunder Wave	Electric	Status	—	100	20	Normal	—	—
18	Flame Charge	Fire	Physical	50	100	20	Normal	—	○
22	Pursuit	Dark	Physical	40	100	20	Normal	—	○
25	Spark	Electric	Physical	65	100	20	Normal	—	○
29	Stomp	Normal	Physical	65	100	20	Normal	—	○
32	Discharge	Electric	Special	80	100	15	Adjacent	—	—
36	Agility	Psychic	Status	—	—	30	Self	—	—
39	Wild Charge	Electric	Physical	90	100	15	Normal	—	○
43	Thrash	Normal	Physical	120	100	10	1 Random	—	○

TM & HM MOVES
Lv.	Name	Type	Kind	Pow.	Acc.	PP	Range	Long	DA
TM06	Toxic	Poison	Status	—	90	10	Normal	—	—
TM10	Hidden Power	Normal	Special	—	100	15	Normal	—	—
TM16	Light Screen	Psychic	Status	—	—	30	Your Side	—	—
TM17	Protect	Normal	Status	—	—	10	Self	—	—
TM18	Rain Dance	Water	Status	—	—	5	Both Sides	—	—
TM21	Frustration	Normal	Physical	—	100	20	Normal	—	○
TM24	Thunderbolt	Electric	Special	95	100	15	Normal	—	—
TM25	Thunder	Electric	Special	120	70	10	Normal	—	—
TM27	Return	Normal	Physical	—	100	20	Normal	—	○
TM32	Double Team	Normal	Status	—	—	15	Self	—	—
TM42	Facade	Normal	Physical	70	100	20	Normal	—	○
TM43	Flame Charge	Fire	Physical	50	100	20	Normal	—	○
TM44	Rest	Psychic	Status	—	—	10	Self	—	—
TM45	Attract	Normal	Status	—	100	15	Normal	—	—
TM48	Round	Normal	Special	60	100	15	Normal	—	—
TM57	Charge Beam	Electric	Special	50	90	10	Normal	—	—
TM70	Flash	Normal	Status	—	100	20	Normal	—	—
TM72	Volt Switch	Electric	Special	70	100	20	Normal	—	—
TM73	Thunder Wave	Electric	Status	—	100	20	Normal	—	—
TM87	Swagger	Normal	Status	—	90	15	Normal	—	—
TM90	Substitute	Normal	Status	—	—	10	Self	—	—
TM93	Wild Charge	Electric	Physical	90	100	15	Normal	—	○

MOVES TAUGHT BY PEOPLE
Name	Type	Kind	Pow.	Acc.	PP	Range	Long	DA

MOVES TAUGHT BY MOVE TUTORS FOR SHARDS
Name	Type	Kind	Pow.	Acc.	PP	Range	Long	DA
Bounce	Flying	Physical	85	85	5	Normal	○	○
Signal Beam	Bug	Special	75	100	15	Normal	—	—
Magnet Rise	Electric	Status	—	—	10	Self	—	—
Snore	Normal	Special	40	100	15	Normal	—	—
Sleep Talk	Normal	Status	—	—	10	Self	—	—

EGG MOVES
Name	Type	Kind	Pow.	Acc.	PP	Range	Long	DA
Me First	Normal	Status	—	—	20	Varies	—	—
Take Down	Normal	Physical	90	85	20	Normal	—	○
Sand-Attack	Ground	Status	—	100	15	Normal	—	—
Double Kick	Fighting	Physical	30	100	30	Normal	—	○
Screech	Normal	Status	—	85	40	Normal	—	—
Rage	Normal	Physical	20	100	20	Normal	—	○
Endure	Normal	Status	—	—	10	Self	—	—
Double-Edge	Normal	Physical	120	100	15	Normal	—	○
Shock Wave	Electric	Special	60	—	20	Normal	—	—

522 | Blitzle

---

523 Zebstrika

Thunderbolt Pokémon

TYPE Electric

ABILITIES
- Lightningrod
- Motor Drive

HIDDEN ABILITY
- Sap Sipper

STATS
HP	▪▪▪
Attack	▪▪▪▪
Defense	▪▪▪
Sp. Atk	▪▪▪
Sp. Def	▪▪▪
Speed	▪▪▪▪▪

EGG GROUPS
Field

ITEMS SOMETIMES HELD
- Cheri Berry

- HEIGHT: 5'03"
- WEIGHT: 175.3 lbs.
- GENDER: ♂ / ♀

When this ill-tempered Pokémon runs wild, it shoots lightning from its mane in all directions.

Same form for ♂ / ♀

Pokémon AR Marker

EVOLUTION

 Blitzle → Lv. 27 → Zebstrika

HOW TO OBTAIN
Pokémon Black Version 2	❶ Route 7 ❷ Route 3
Pokémon White Version 2	❶ Route 7 ❷ Route 3

HOW TO OBTAIN FROM OTHER GAMES
	—
	—

LEVEL-UP AND LEARNED MOVES
Lv.	Name	Type	Kind	Pow.	Acc.	PP	Range	Long	DA
1	Quick Attack	Normal	Physical	40	100	30	Normal	—	○
1	Tail Whip	Normal	Status	—	100	30	Many Others	—	—
1	Charge	Electric	Status	—	—	20	Self	—	—
1	Thunder Wave	Electric	Status	—	100	20	Normal	—	—
1	Tail Whip	Normal	Status	—	100	30	Many Others	—	—
8	Charge	Electric	Status	—	—	20	Self	—	—
11	Shock Wave	Electric	Special	60	—	20	Normal	—	—
15	Thunder Wave	Electric	Status	—	100	20	Normal	—	—
18	Flame Charge	Fire	Physical	50	100	20	Normal	—	○
22	Pursuit	Dark	Physical	40	100	20	Normal	—	○
25	Spark	Electric	Physical	65	100	20	Normal	—	○
31	Stomp	Normal	Physical	65	100	20	Normal	—	○
36	Discharge	Electric	Special	80	100	15	Adjacent	—	—
42	Agility	Psychic	Status	—	—	30	Self	—	—
47	Wild Charge	Electric	Physical	90	100	15	Normal	—	○
53	Thrash	Normal	Physical	120	100	10	1 Random	—	○

TM & HM MOVES
Lv.	Name	Type	Kind	Pow.	Acc.	PP	Range	Long	DA
TM06	Toxic	Poison	Status	—	90	10	Normal	—	—
TM10	Hidden Power	Normal	Special	—	100	15	Normal	—	—
TM15	Hyper Beam	Normal	Special	150	90	5	Normal	—	—
TM16	Light Screen	Psychic	Status	—	—	30	Your Side	—	—
TM17	Protect	Normal	Status	—	—	10	Self	—	—
TM18	Rain Dance	Water	Status	—	—	5	Both Sides	—	—
TM21	Frustration	Normal	Physical	—	100	20	Normal	—	○
TM24	Thunderbolt	Electric	Special	95	100	15	Normal	—	—
TM25	Thunder	Electric	Special	120	70	10	Normal	—	—
TM27	Return	Normal	Physical	—	100	20	Normal	—	○
TM32	Double Team	Normal	Status	—	—	15	Self	—	—
TM42	Facade	Normal	Physical	70	100	20	Normal	—	○
TM43	Flame Charge	Fire	Physical	50	100	20	Normal	—	○
TM44	Rest	Psychic	Status	—	—	10	Self	—	—
TM45	Attract	Normal	Status	—	100	15	Normal	—	—
TM48	Round	Normal	Special	60	100	15	Normal	—	—
TM50	Overheat	Fire	Special	140	90	5	Normal	—	—
TM57	Charge Beam	Electric	Special	50	90	10	Normal	—	—
TM68	Giga Impact	Normal	Physical	150	90	5	Normal	—	○
TM70	Flash	Normal	Status	—	100	20	Normal	—	—
TM72	Volt Switch	Electric	Special	70	100	20	Normal	—	—
TM73	Thunder Wave	Electric	Status	—	100	20	Normal	—	—
TM87	Swagger	Normal	Status	—	90	15	Normal	—	—
TM90	Substitute	Normal	Status	—	—	10	Self	—	—
TM93	Wild Charge	Electric	Physical	90	100	15	Normal	—	○
TM94	Rock Smash	Fighting	Physical	40	100	15	Normal	—	○

MOVES TAUGHT BY PEOPLE
Name	Type	Kind	Pow.	Acc.	PP	Range	Long	DA

MOVES TAUGHT BY MOVE TUTORS FOR SHARDS
Name	Type	Kind	Pow.	Acc.	PP	Range	Long	DA
Bounce	Flying	Physical	85	85	5	Normal	○	○
Signal Beam	Bug	Special	75	100	15	Normal	—	—
Magnet Rise	Electric	Status	—	—	10	Self	—	—
Snore	Normal	Special	40	100	15	Normal	—	—
Sleep Talk	Normal	Status	—	—	10	Self	—	—

523 | Zebstrika

Mantle Pokémon
524 Roggenrola

- HEIGHT: 1'04"
- WEIGHT: 39.7 lbs.
- GENDER: ♂ / ♀

The hexagonal-shaped hole is its ear. It has a tendency to walk in the direction the sound is coming from.

Same form for ♂ / ♀

Pokémon AR Marker

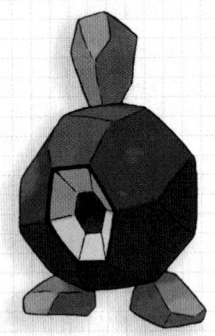

TYPE Rock

ABILITY
- Sturdy

HIDDEN ABILITY
- Sand Force

STATS
- HP
- Attack
- Defense
- Sp. Atk
- Sp. Def
- Speed

EGG GROUPS
Mineral

ITEMS SOMETIMES HELD
- Everstone
- Hard Stone

EVOLUTION

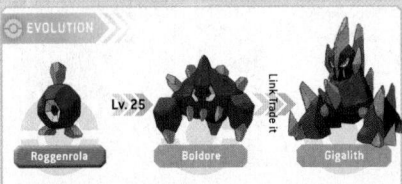

Roggenrola → (Lv. 25) → Boldore → Link Trade it → Gigalith

HOW TO OBTAIN
Pokémon Black Version 2	Relic Passage Castelia City exit
Pokémon White Version 2	Relic Passage Castelia City exit

HOW TO OBTAIN FROM OTHER GAMES
—
—

LEVEL-UP AND LEARNED MOVES

Lv.	Name	Type	Kind	Pow.	Acc.	PP	Range	Long	DA
1	Tackle	Normal	Physical	50	100	35	Normal	—	○
4	Harden	Normal	Status	—	—	30	Self	—	—
7	Sand-Attack	Ground	Status	—	100	15	Normal	—	—
10	Headbutt	Normal	Physical	70	100	15	Normal	—	○
14	Rock Blast	Rock	Physical	25	90	10	Normal	—	—
17	Mud-Slap	Ground	Special	20	100	10	Normal	—	—
20	Iron Defense	Steel	Status	—	—	15	Self	—	—
23	Smack Down	Rock	Physical	50	100	15	Normal	—	—
27	Rock Slide	Rock	Physical	75	90	10	Many Others	—	—
30	Stealth Rock	Rock	Status	—	—	20	Other Side	—	—
33	Sandstorm	Rock	Status	—	—	10	Both Sides	—	—
36	Stone Edge	Rock	Physical	100	80	5	Normal	—	—
40	Explosion	Normal	Physical	250	100	5	Adjacent	—	—

TM & HM MOVES

Lv.	Name	Type	Kind	Pow.	Acc.	PP	Range	Long	DA
TM06	Toxic	Poison	Status	—	90	10	Normal	—	—
TM10	Hidden Power	Normal	Special	—	100	15	Normal	—	—
TM17	Protect	Normal	Status	—	—	10	Self	—	—
TM21	Frustration	Normal	Physical	—	100	20	Normal	—	○
TM23	Smack Down	Rock	Physical	50	100	15	Normal	—	—
TM26	Earthquake	Ground	Physical	100	100	10	Adjacent	—	—
TM27	Return	Normal	Physical	—	100	20	Normal	—	○
TM32	Double Team	Normal	Status	—	—	15	Self	—	—
TM37	Sandstorm	Rock	Status	—	—	10	Both Sides	—	—
TM39	Rock Tomb	Rock	Physical	50	80	10	Normal	—	○
TM42	Facade	Normal	Physical	70	100	20	Normal	—	○
TM44	Rest	Psychic	Status	—	—	10	Self	—	—
TM45	Attract	Normal	Status	—	100	15	Normal	—	—
TM48	Round	Normal	Special	60	100	15	Normal	—	—
TM64	Explosion	Normal	Physical	250	100	5	Adjacent	—	—
TM69	Rock Polish	Rock	Status	—	—	20	Self	—	—
TM71	Stone Edge	Rock	Physical	100	80	5	Normal	—	—
TM78	Bulldoze	Ground	Physical	60	100	20	Adjacent	—	—
TM80	Rock Slide	Rock	Physical	75	90	10	Many Others	—	—
TM87	Swagger	Normal	Status	—	90	15	Normal	—	—
TM90	Substitute	Normal	Status	—	—	10	Self	—	—
TM91	Flash Cannon	Steel	Special	80	100	10	Normal	—	—
TM94	Rock Smash	Fighting	Physical	40	100	15	Normal	—	○
HM04	Strength	Normal	Physical	80	100	15	Normal	—	○

MOVES TAUGHT BY PEOPLE

Name	Type	Kind	Pow.	Acc.	PP	Range	Long	DA

MOVES TAUGHT BY MOVE TUTORS FOR SHARDS

Name	Type	Kind	Pow.	Acc.	PP	Range	Long	DA
Iron Defense	Steel	Status	—	—	15	Self	—	—
Block	Normal	Status	—	—	5	Normal	—	—
Earth Power	Ground	Special	90	100	10	Normal	—	—
Gravity	Psychic	Status	—	—	5	Both Sides	—	—
Snore	Normal	Special	40	100	15	Normal	—	—
Stealth Rock	Rock	Status	—	—	20	Other Side	—	—
Sleep Talk	Normal	Status	—	—	10	Self	—	—

EGG MOVES

Name	Type	Kind	Pow.	Acc.	PP	Range	Long	DA
Magnitude	Ground	Physical	—	100	30	Adjacent	—	—
Curse	Ghost	Status	—	—	10	Varies	—	—
Autotomize	Steel	Status	—	—	15	Self	—	—
Rock Tomb	Rock	Physical	50	80	10	Normal	—	—
Lock-On	Normal	Status	—	—	5	Normal	—	—
Heavy Slam	Steel	Physical	—	100	10	Normal	—	○
Take Down	Normal	Physical	90	85	20	Normal	—	○
Gravity	Psychic	Status	—	—	5	Both Sides	—	—

Ore Pokémon
525 Boldore

- HEIGHT: 2'11"
- WEIGHT: 224.9 lbs.
- GENDER: ♂ / ♀

When it is healthy, its core sticks out. Always facing the same way, it swiftly moves front to back and left to right.

Same form for ♂ / ♀

Pokémon AR Marker

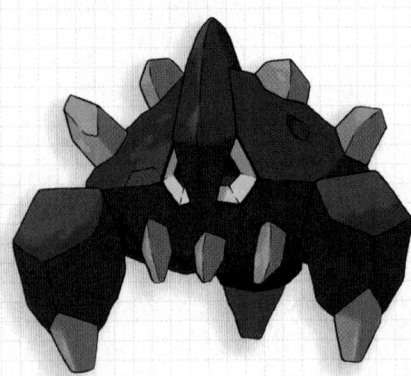

TYPE Rock

ABILITY
- Sturdy

HIDDEN ABILITY
- Sand Force

STATS
- HP
- Attack
- Defense
- Sp. Atk
- Sp. Def
- Speed

EGG GROUPS
Mineral

ITEMS SOMETIMES HELD
- Everstone
- Hard Stone

EVOLUTION

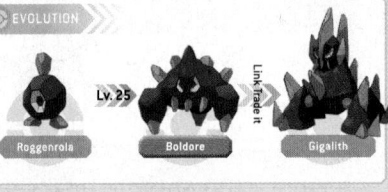

Roggenrola → (Lv. 25) → Boldore → Link Trade it → Gigalith

HOW TO OBTAIN
Pokémon Black Version 2	❶ Relic Passage Driftveil City exit ❷ Mistralton Cave 1F
Pokémon White Version 2	❶ Relic Passage Driftveil City exit ❷ Mistralton Cave 1F

HOW TO OBTAIN FROM OTHER GAMES
—
—

LEVEL-UP AND LEARNED MOVES

Lv.	Name	Type	Kind	Pow.	Acc.	PP	Range	Long	DA
1	Tackle	Normal	Physical	50	100	35	Normal	—	○
1	Harden	Normal	Status	—	—	30	Self	—	—
1	Sand-Attack	Ground	Status	—	100	15	Normal	—	—
1	Headbutt	Normal	Physical	70	100	15	Normal	—	○
4	Harden	Normal	Status	—	—	30	Self	—	—
7	Sand-Attack	Ground	Status	—	100	15	Normal	—	—
10	Headbutt	Normal	Physical	70	100	15	Normal	—	○
14	Rock Blast	Rock	Physical	25	90	10	Normal	—	—
17	Mud-Slap	Ground	Special	20	100	10	Normal	—	—
20	Iron Defense	Steel	Status	—	—	15	Self	—	—
23	Smack Down	Rock	Physical	50	100	15	Normal	—	—
25	Power Gem	Rock	Special	70	100	20	Normal	—	—
30	Rock Slide	Rock	Physical	75	90	10	Many Others	—	—
36	Stealth Rock	Rock	Status	—	—	20	Other Side	—	—
42	Sandstorm	Rock	Status	—	—	10	Both Sides	—	—
48	Stone Edge	Rock	Physical	100	80	5	Normal	—	—
55	Explosion	Normal	Physical	250	100	5	Adjacent	—	—

TM & HM MOVES

Lv.	Name	Type	Kind	Pow.	Acc.	PP	Range	Long	DA
TM06	Toxic	Poison	Status	—	90	10	Normal	—	—
TM10	Hidden Power	Normal	Special	—	100	15	Normal	—	—
TM17	Protect	Normal	Status	—	—	10	Self	—	—
TM21	Frustration	Normal	Physical	—	100	20	Normal	—	○
TM23	Smack Down	Rock	Physical	50	100	15	Normal	—	—
TM26	Earthquake	Ground	Physical	100	100	10	Adjacent	—	—
TM27	Return	Normal	Physical	—	100	20	Normal	—	○
TM32	Double Team	Normal	Status	—	—	15	Self	—	—
TM37	Sandstorm	Rock	Status	—	—	10	Both Sides	—	—
TM39	Rock Tomb	Rock	Physical	50	80	10	Normal	—	○
TM42	Facade	Normal	Physical	70	100	20	Normal	—	○
TM44	Rest	Psychic	Status	—	—	10	Self	—	—
TM45	Attract	Normal	Status	—	100	15	Normal	—	—
TM48	Round	Normal	Special	60	100	15	Normal	—	—
TM64	Explosion	Normal	Physical	250	100	5	Adjacent	—	—
TM69	Rock Polish	Rock	Status	—	—	20	Self	—	—
TM71	Stone Edge	Rock	Physical	100	80	5	Normal	—	—
TM78	Bulldoze	Ground	Physical	60	100	20	Adjacent	—	—
TM80	Rock Slide	Rock	Physical	75	90	10	Many Others	—	—
TM87	Swagger	Normal	Status	—	90	15	Normal	—	—
TM90	Substitute	Normal	Status	—	—	10	Self	—	—
TM91	Flash Cannon	Steel	Special	80	100	10	Normal	—	—
TM94	Rock Smash	Fighting	Physical	40	100	15	Normal	—	○
HM04	Strength	Normal	Physical	80	100	15	Normal	—	○

MOVES TAUGHT BY PEOPLE

Name	Type	Kind	Pow.	Acc.	PP	Range	Long	DA

MOVES TAUGHT BY MOVE TUTORS FOR SHARDS

Name	Type	Kind	Pow.	Acc.	PP	Range	Long	DA
Iron Defense	Steel	Status	—	—	15	Self	—	—
Block	Normal	Status	—	—	5	Normal	—	—
Earth Power	Ground	Special	90	100	10	Normal	—	—
Gravity	Psychic	Status	—	—	5	Both Sides	—	—
Snore	Normal	Special	40	100	15	Normal	—	—
Stealth Rock	Rock	Status	—	—	20	Other Side	—	—
Sleep Talk	Normal	Status	—	—	10	Self	—	—

526 **Gigalith**

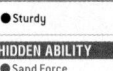

Compressed Pokémon

- HEIGHT: 5'07"
- WEIGHT: 573.2 lbs.
- GENDER: ♂ / ♀

The solar rays it absorbs are processed in its energy core and fired as a ball of light.

Same form for ♂ / ♀

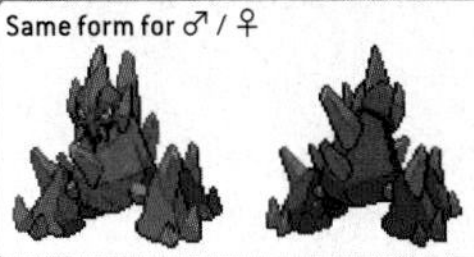

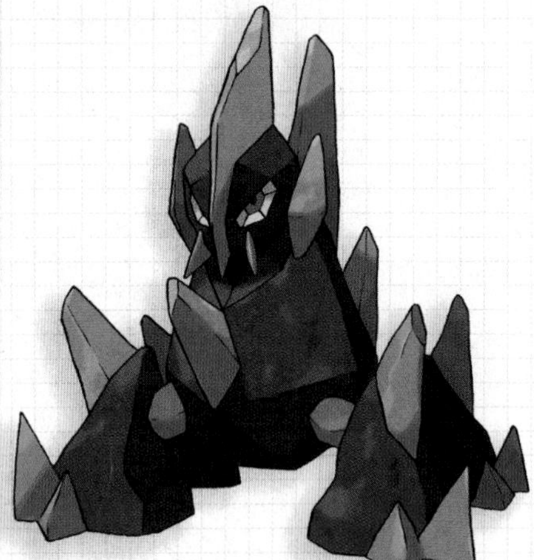

Pokémon AR Marker

TYPE: Rock

ABILITY
- Sturdy

HIDDEN ABILITY
- Sand Force

STATS
HP
Attack
Defense
Sp. Atk
Sp. Def
Speed

EGG GROUPS
Mineral

ITEMS SOMETIMES HELD
- None

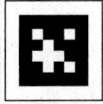

EVOLUTION

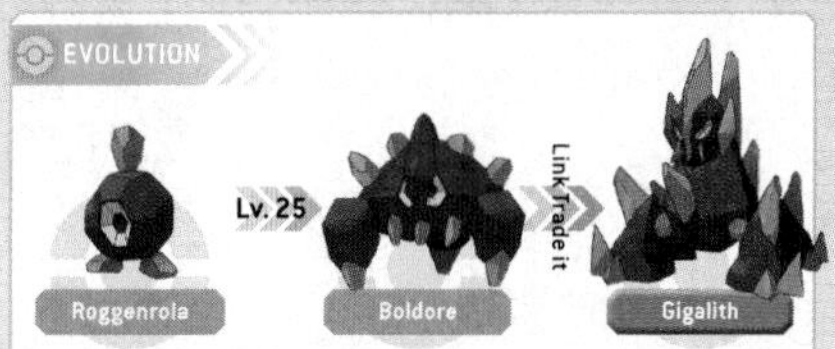

Roggenrola
Lv. 25
Boldore
Link trade it
Gigalith

HOW TO OBTAIN

Pokémon Black Version 2	Trade an Emolga to the Hiker in the house on R
Pokémon White Version 2	Trade an Emolga to the Hiker in the house on

HOW TO OBTAIN FROM OTHER GAMES

—

—

LEVEL-UP AND LEARNED MOVES

Lv.	Name	Type	Kind	Pow.	Acc.	PP	Range	Long	DA
1	Tackle	Normal	Physical	50	100	35	Normal	—	○
1	Harden	Normal	Status	—	—	30	Self	—	—
1	Sand-Attack	Ground	Status	—	100	15	Normal	—	—
1	Headbutt	Normal	Physical	70	100	15	Normal	—	○
4	Harden	Normal	Status	—	—	30	Self	—	—
7	Sand-Attack	Ground	Status	—	100	15	Normal	—	—
10	Headbutt	Normal	Physical	70	100	15	Normal	—	○
14	Rock Blast	Rock	Physical	25	90	10	Normal	—	—
17	Mud-Slap	Ground	Special	20	100	10	Normal	—	—
20	Iron Defense	Steel	Status	—	—	15	Self	—	—
23	Smack Down	Rock	Physical	50	100	15	Normal	—	—
25	Power Gem	Rock	Special	70	100	20	Normal	—	—
30	Rock Slide	Rock	Physical	75	90	10	Many Others	—	—
36	Stealth Rock	Rock	Status	—	—	20	Other Side	—	—
42	Sandstorm	Rock	Status	—	—	10	Both Sides	—	—
48	Stone Edge	Rock	Physical	100	80	5	Normal	—	—
55	Explosion	Normal	Physical	250	100	5	Adjacent	—	—

TM & HM MOVES

Lv.	Name	Type	Kind	Pow.	Acc.	PP	Range	Long	DA
TM06	Toxic	Poison	Status	—	90	10	Normal	—	—
TM10	Hidden Power	Normal	Special	—	100	15	Normal	—	—
TM15	Hyper Beam	Normal	Special	150	90	5	Normal	—	—
TM17	Protect	Normal	Status	—	—	10	Self	—	—
TM21	Frustration	Normal	Physical	—	100	20	Normal	—	○
TM22	SolarBeam	Grass	Special	120	100	10	Normal	—	—
TM23	Smack Down	Rock	Physical	50	100	15	Normal	—	—
TM26	Earthquake	Ground	Physical	100	100	10	Adjacent	—	—
TM27	Return	Normal	Physical	—	100	20	Normal	—	○
TM32	Double Team	Normal	Status	—	—	15	Self	—	—
TM37	Sandstorm	Rock	Status	—	—	10	Both Sides	—	—
TM39	Rock Tomb	Rock	Physical	50	80	10	Normal	—	—
TM42	Facade	Normal	Physical	70	100	20	Normal	—	○
TM44	Rest	Psychic	Status	—	—	10	Self	—	—
TM45	Attract	Normal	Status	—	100	15	Normal	—	—
TM48	Round	Normal	Special	60	100	15	Normal	—	—
TM64	Explosion	Normal	Physical	250	100	5	Adjacent	—	—
TM68	Giga Impact	Normal	Physical	150	90	5	Normal	—	○
TM69	Rock Polish	Rock	Status	—	—	20	Self	—	—
TM71	Stone Edge	Rock	Physical	100	80	5	Normal	—	—
TM78	Bulldoze	Ground	Physical	60	100	20	Adjacent	—	—
TM80	Rock Slide	Rock	Physical	75	90	10	Many Others	—	—
TM87	Swagger	Normal	Status	—	90	15	Normal	—	—
TM90	Substitute	Normal	Status	—	—	10	Self	—	—
TM91	Flash Cannon	Steel	Special	80	100	10	Normal	—	—
TM94	Rock Smash	Fighting	Physical	40	100	15	Normal	—	○
HM04	Strength	Normal	Physical	80	100	15	Normal	—	○

MOVES TAUGHT BY PEOPLE

Name	Type	Kind	Pow.	Acc.	PP	Range	Long	DA

MOVES TAUGHT BY MOVE TUTORS FOR SHARDS

Name	Type	Kind	Pow.	Acc.	PP	Range	Long	DA
Iron Head	Steel	Physical	80	100	15	Normal	—	○
Iron Defense	Steel	Status	—	—	15	Self	—	—
Block	Normal	Status	—	—	5	Normal	—	—
Earth Power	Ground	Special	90	100	10	Normal	—	—
Superpower	Fighting	Physical	120	100	5	Normal	—	○
Gravity	Psychic	Status	—	—	5	Both Sides	—	—
Snore	Normal	Special	40	100	15	Normal	—	—
Stealth Rock	Rock	Status	—	—	20	Other Side	—	—
Sleep Talk	Normal	Status	—	—	10	Self	—	—

527 **Woobat**

Bat Pokémon

- HEIGHT: 1'04"
- WEIGHT: 4.6 lbs.
- GENDER: ♂ / ♀

The heart-shaped mark left on a body after a Woobat has been attached to it is said to bring good fortune.

Same form for ♂ / ♀

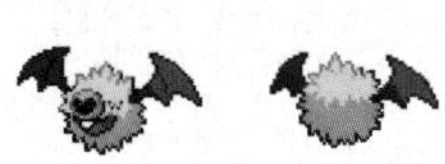

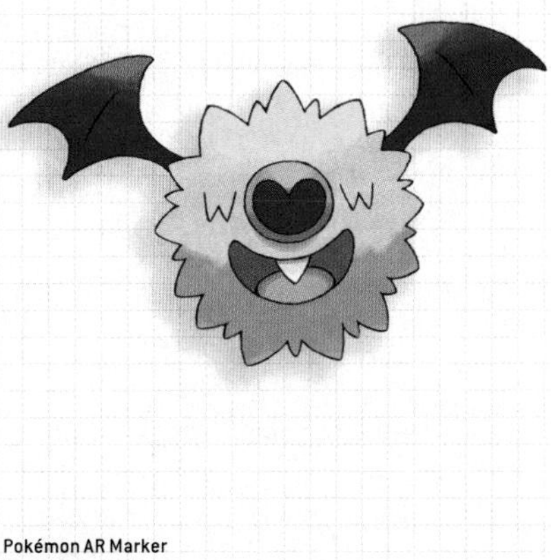

Pokémon AR Marker

TYPE: Psychic / Flying

ABILITIES
- Unaware
- Klutz

HIDDEN ABILITY
- Simple

STATS
HP
Attack
Defense
Sp. Atk
Sp. Def
Speed

EGG GROUPS
Field/Flying

ITEMS SOMETIMES HELD
- None

EVOLUTION

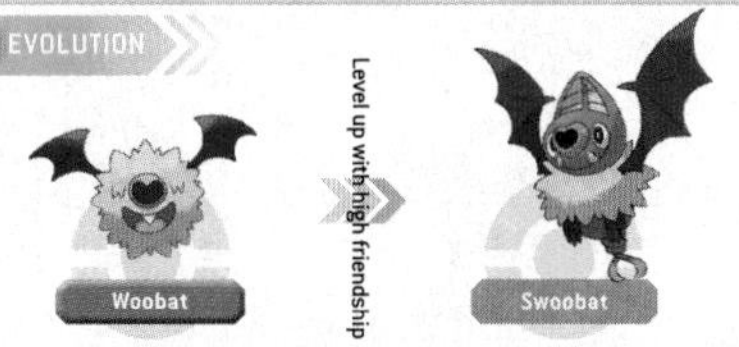

Woobat
Level up with high friendship
Swoobat

HOW TO OBTAIN

Pokémon Black Version 2	❶ Relic Passage Driftveil City exit ❷ Mistralton Cave 1F
Pokémon White Version 2	❶ Relic Passage Driftveil City exit ❷ Mistralton Cave 1F

HOW TO OBTAIN FROM OTHER GAMES

—

—

LEVEL-UP AND LEARNED MOVES

Lv.	Name	Type	Kind	Pow.	Acc.	PP	Range	Long	DA
1	Confusion	Psychic	Special	50	100	25	Normal	—	—
4	Odor Sleuth	Normal	Status	—	—	40	Normal	—	—
8	Gust	Flying	Special	40	100	35	Normal	○	—
12	Assurance	Dark	Physical	50	100	10	Normal	—	○
15	Heart Stamp	Psychic	Physical	60	100	25	Normal	—	○
19	Imprison	Psychic	Status	—	—	10	Self	—	—
21	Air Cutter	Flying	Special	55	95	25	Many Others	—	—
25	Attract	Normal	Status	—	100	15	Normal	—	—
29	Amnesia	Psychic	Status	—	—	20	Self	—	—
29	Calm Mind	Psychic	Status	—	—	20	Self	—	—
32	Air Slash	Flying	Special	75	95	20	Normal	○	—
36	Future Sight	Psychic	Special	100	100	10	Normal	—	—
41	Psychic	Psychic	Special	90	100	10	Normal	—	—
47	Endeavor	Normal	Physical	—	100	5	Normal	—	○

TM & HM MOVES

Lv.	Name	Type	Kind	Pow.	Acc.	PP	Range	Long	DA
TM03	Psyshock	Psychic	Special	80	100	10	Normal	—	—
TM04	Calm Mind	Psychic	Status	—	—	20	Self	—	—
TM06	Toxic	Poison	Status	—	90	10	Normal	—	—
TM10	Hidden Power	Normal	Special	—	100	15	Normal	—	—
TM12	Taunt	Dark	Status	—	100	20	Normal	—	—
TM16	Light Screen	Psychic	Status	—	—	30	Your Side	—	—
TM17	Protect	Normal	Status	—	—	10	Self	—	—
TM18	Rain Dance	Water	Status	—	—	5	Both Sides	—	—
TM19	Telekinesis	Psychic	Status	—	—	15	Normal	—	—
TM20	Safeguard	Normal	Status	—	—	25	Your Side	—	—
TM21	Frustration	Normal	Physical	—	100	20	Normal	—	○
TM27	Return	Normal	Physical	—	100	20	Normal	—	○
TM29	Psychic	Psychic	Special	90	100	10	Normal	—	—
TM30	Shadow Ball	Ghost	Special	80	100	15	Normal	—	—
TM32	Double Team	Normal	Status	—	—	15	Self	—	—
TM33	Reflect	Psychic	Status	—	—	20	Your Side	—	—
TM40	Aerial Ace	Flying	Physical	60	—	20	Normal	○	○
TM41	Torment	Dark	Status	—	100	15	Normal	—	—
TM42	Facade	Normal	Physical	70	100	20	Normal	—	○
TM44	Rest	Psychic	Status	—	—	10	Self	—	—
TM45	Attract	Normal	Status	—	100	15	Normal	—	—
TM46	Thief	Dark	Physical	40	100	10	Normal	—	○
TM48	Round	Normal	Special	60	100	15	Normal	—	—
TM53	Energy Ball	Grass	Special	80	100	10	Normal	—	—
TM57	Charge Beam	Electric	Special	50	90	10	Normal	—	—
TM62	Acrobatics	Flying	Physical	55	100	15	Normal	○	○
TM63	Embargo	Dark	Status	—	100	15	Normal	—	—
TM70	Flash	Normal	Status	—	100	20	Normal	—	—
TM73	Thunder Wave	Electric	Status	—	100	20	Normal	—	—
TM74	Gyro Ball	Steel	Physical	—	100	5	Normal	—	○
TM77	Psych Up	Normal	Status	—	—	10	Normal	—	—
TM85	Dream Eater	Psychic	Special	100	100	15	Normal	—	—
TM87	Swagger	Normal	Status	—	90	15	Normal	—	—
TM88	Pluck	Flying	Physical	60	100	20	Normal	○	○
TM89	U-turn	Bug	Physical	70	100	20	Normal	—	○
TM90	Substitute	Normal	Status	—	—	10	Self	—	—
TM92	Trick Room	Psychic	Status	—	—	5	Both Sides	—	—
HM02	Fly	Flying	Physical	90	95	15	Normal	○	○

MOVES TAUGHT BY PEOPLE

Name	Type	Kind	Pow.	Acc.	PP	Range	Long	DA

MOVES TAUGHT BY MOVE TUTORS FOR SHARDS

Name	Type	Kind	Pow.	Acc.	PP	Range	Long	DA
Signal Beam	Bug	Special	75	100	15	Normal	—	—
Super Fang	Normal	Physical	—	90	10	Normal	—	○
Uproar	Normal	Special	90	100	10	1 Random	—	—
Magic Coat	Psychic	Status	—	—	15	Self	—	—
Zen Headbutt	Psychic	Physical	80	90	15	Normal	—	○
Snore	Normal	Special	40	100	15	Normal	—	—
Knock Off	Dark	Physical	20	100	20	Normal	—	○
Roost	Flying	Status	—	—	10	Self	—	—
Heat Wave	Fire	Special	100	90	10	Many Others	—	—
Giga Drain	Grass	Special	75	100	10	Normal	—	—
Tailwind	Flying	Status	—	—	30	Your Side	—	—
Helping Hand	Normal	Status	—	—	20	1 Ally	—	—
After You	Normal	Status	—	—	15	Normal	—	—
Trick	Psychic	Status	—	100	10	Normal	—	—
Endeavor	Normal	Physical	—	100	5	Normal	—	○
Sleep Talk	Normal	Status	—	—	10	Self	—	—
Skill Swap	Psychic	Status	—	—	10	Normal	—	—

EGG MOVES

Name	Type	Kind	Pow.	Acc.	PP	Range	Long	DA
Charm	Normal	Status	—	100	20	Normal	—	—
Knock Off	Dark	Physical	20	100	20	Normal	—	○
Fake Tears	Dark	Status	—	100	20	Normal	—	—
Supersonic	Normal	Status	—	55	20	Normal	—	—
Synchronoise	Psychic	Special	70	100	15	Adjacent	—	—
Stored Power	Psychic	Special	20	100	10	Normal	—	—
Roost	Flying	Status	—	—	10	Self	—	—
Flatter	Dark	Status	—	100	15	Normal	—	—
Helping Hand	Normal	Status	—	—	20	1 Ally	—	—

528 Swoobat

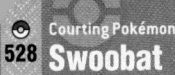

528 Swoobat

Courting Pokémon

- HEIGHT: 2'11"
- WEIGHT: 23.1 lbs.
- GENDER: ♂ / ♀

It shakes its tail vigorously when it emits ultrasonic waves strong enough to reduce concrete to rubble.

TYPE: Psychic / Flying

ABILITIES
- Unaware
- Klutz

HIDDEN ABILITY
- Simple

STATS
HP
Attack
Defense
Sp. Atk
Sp. Def
Speed

EGG GROUPS
Field/Flying

ITEMS SOMETIMES HELD
- None

Same form for ♂ / ♀

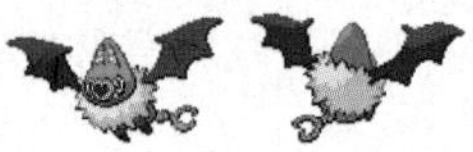

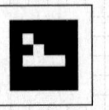

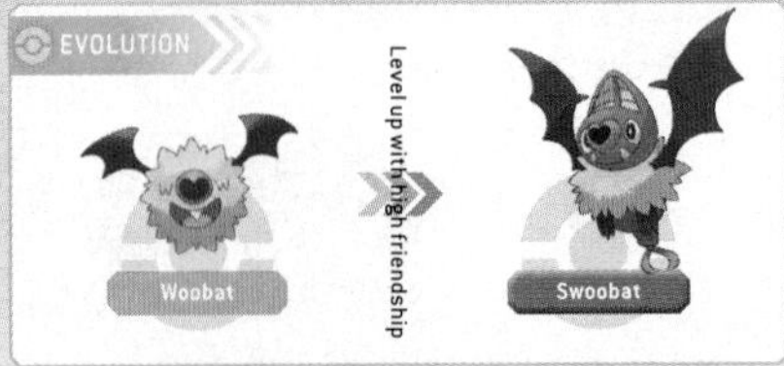
EVOLUTION
Woobat
Level up with high friendship
Swoobat

HOW TO OBTAIN

Pokémon Black Version 2	Level up Woobat with high friendship
Pokémon White Version 2	Level up Woobat with high friendship

HOW TO OBTAIN FROM OTHER GAMES

—

—

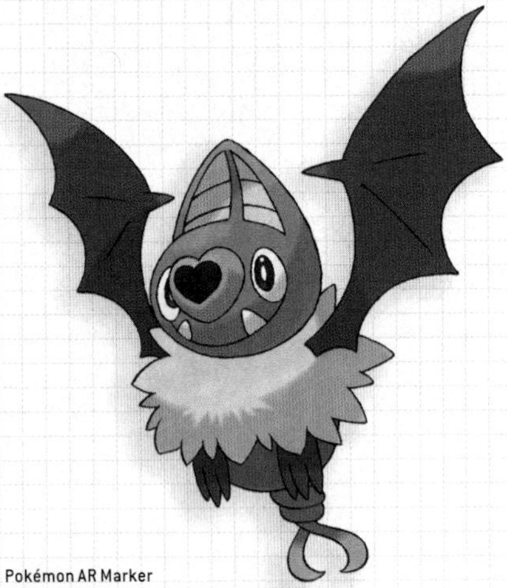

Pokémon AR Marker

LEVEL-UP AND LEARNED MOVES

Lv.	Name	Type	Kind	Pow.	Acc.	PP	Range	Long	DA
1	Confusion	Psychic	Special	50	100	25	Normal	—	—
1	Odor Sleuth	Normal	Status	—	—	40	Normal	—	—
1	Gust	Flying	Special	40	100	35	Normal	○	—
1	Assurance	Dark	Physical	50	100	10	Normal	—	○
4	Odor Sleuth	Normal	Status	—	—	40	Normal	—	—
8	Gust	Flying	Special	40	100	35	Normal	○	—
12	Assurance	Dark	Physical	50	100	10	Normal	—	○
15	Heart Stamp	Psychic	Physical	60	100	25	Normal	—	○
19	Imprison	Psychic	Status	—	—	10	Self	—	—
21	Air Cutter	Flying	Special	55	95	25	Many Others	—	—
25	Attract	Normal	Status	—	100	15	Normal	—	—
29	Amnesia	Psychic	Status	—	—	20	Self	—	—
29	Calm Mind	Psychic	Status	—	—	20	Self	—	—
32	Air Slash	Flying	Special	75	95	20	Normal	○	—
36	Future Sight	Psychic	Special	100	100	10	Normal	—	—
41	Psychic	Psychic	Special	90	100	10	Normal	—	—
47	Endeavor	Normal	Physical	—	100	5	Normal	—	○

TM & HM MOVES

Lv.	Name	Type	Kind	Pow.	Acc.	PP	Range	Long	DA
TM03	Psyshock	Psychic	Special	80	100	10	Normal	—	—
TM04	Calm Mind	Psychic	Status	—	—	20	Self	—	—
TM06	Toxic	Poison	Status	—	90	10	Normal	—	—
TM10	Hidden Power	Normal	Special	—	100	15	Normal	—	—
TM12	Taunt	Dark	Status	—	100	20	Normal	—	—
TM15	Hyper Beam	Normal	Special	150	90	5	Normal	—	—
TM16	Light Screen	Psychic	Status	—	—	30	Your Side	—	—
TM17	Protect	Normal	Status	—	—	10	Self	—	—
TM18	Rain Dance	Water	Status	—	—	5	Both Sides	—	—
TM19	Telekinesis	Psychic	Status	—	—	15	Normal	—	—
TM20	Safeguard	Normal	Status	—	—	25	Your Side	—	—
TM21	Frustration	Normal	Physical	—	100	20	Normal	—	○
TM27	Return	Normal	Physical	—	100	20	Normal	—	○
TM29	Psychic	Psychic	Special	90	100	10	Normal	—	—
TM30	Shadow Ball	Ghost	Special	80	100	15	Normal	—	—
TM32	Double Team	Normal	Status	—	—	15	Self	—	—
TM33	Reflect	Psychic	Status	—	—	20	Your Side	—	—
TM40	Aerial Ace	Flying	Physical	60	—	20	Normal	○	○
TM41	Torment	Dark	Status	—	100	15	Normal	—	—
TM42	Facade	Normal	Physical	70	100	20	Normal	—	○
TM44	Rest	Psychic	Status	—	—	10	Self	—	—
TM45	Attract	Normal	Status	—	100	15	Normal	—	—
TM46	Thief	Dark	Physical	40	100	10	Normal	—	○
TM48	Round	Normal	Special	60	100	15	Normal	—	—
TM53	Energy Ball	Grass	Special	80	100	10	Normal	—	—
TM57	Charge Beam	Electric	Special	50	90	10	Normal	—	—
TM62	Acrobatics	Flying	Physical	55	100	15	Normal	○	○
TM63	Embargo	Dark	Status	—	100	15	Normal	—	—
TM68	Giga Impact	Normal	Physical	150	90	5	Normal	—	○
TM70	Flash	Normal	Status	—	100	20	Normal	—	—
TM73	Thunder Wave	Electric	Status	—	100	20	Normal	—	—
TM74	Gyro Ball	Steel	Physical	—	100	5	Normal	—	○
TM77	Psych Up	Normal	Status	—	—	10	Normal	—	—
TM85	Dream Eater	Psychic	Special	100	100	15	Normal	—	—
TM87	Swagger	Normal	Status	—	90	15	Normal	—	—
TM88	Pluck	Flying	Physical	60	100	20	Normal	○	○
TM89	U-turn	Bug	Physical	70	100	20	Normal	—	○
TM90	Substitute	Normal	Status	—	—	10	Self	—	—
TM92	Trick Room	Psychic	Status	—	—	5	Both Sides	—	—
HM02	Fly	Flying	Physical	90	95	15	Normal	○	○

MOVES TAUGHT BY PEOPLE

Name	Type	Kind	Pow.	Acc.	PP	Range	Long	DA

MOVES TAUGHT BY MOVE TUTORS FOR SHARDS

Name	Type	Kind	Pow.	Acc.	PP	Range	Long	DA
Signal Beam	Bug	Special	75	100	15	Normal	—	—
Super Fang	Normal	Physical	—	90	10	Normal	—	○
Uproar	Normal	Special	90	100	10	1 Random	—	—
Magic Coat	Psychic	Status	—	—	15	Self	—	—
Zen Headbutt	Psychic	Physical	80	90	15	Normal	—	○
Snore	Normal	Special	40	100	15	Normal	—	—
Knock Off	Dark	Physical	20	100	20	Normal	—	○
Roost	Flying	Status	—	—	10	Self	—	—
Sky Attack	Flying	Physical	140	90	5	Normal	○	—
Heat Wave	Fire	Special	100	90	10	Many Others	—	—
Giga Drain	Grass	Special	75	100	10	Normal	—	—
Tailwind	Flying	Status	—	—	30	Your Side	—	—
Helping Hand	Normal	Status	—	—	20	1 Ally	—	—
After You	Normal	Status	—	—	15	Normal	—	—
Trick	Psychic	Status	—	100	10	Normal	—	—
Endeavor	Normal	Physical	—	100	5	Normal	—	○
Sleep Talk	Normal	Status	—	—	10	Self	—	—
Skill Swap	Psychic	Status	—	—	10	Normal	—	—

529 Drilbur

529 Drilbur

Mole Pokémon

- HEIGHT: 1'00"
- WEIGHT: 18.7 lbs.
- GENDER: ♂ / ♀

By spinning its body, it can dig straight through the ground at a speed of 30 mph.

TYPE: Ground

ABILITIES
- Sand Rush
- Sand Force

HIDDEN ABILITY
- Mold Breaker

STATS
HP
Attack
Defense
Sp. Atk
Sp. Def
Speed

EGG GROUPS
Field

ITEMS SOMETIMES HELD
- None

Same form for ♂ / ♀

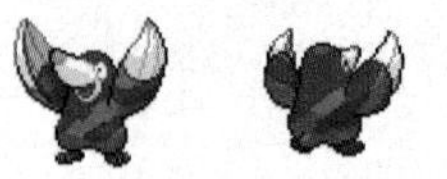

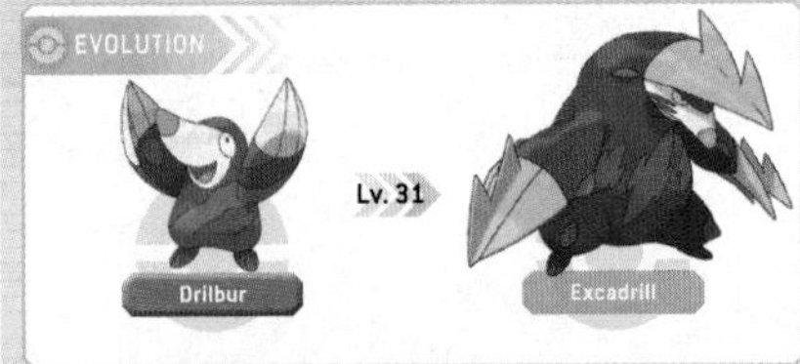
EVOLUTION
Drilbur
Lv. 31
Excadrill

HOW TO OBTAIN

Pokémon Black Version 2	❶ Relic Passage Driftveil City exit (dust clouds) ❷ Mistralton Cave 1F (dust clouds)
Pokémon White Version 2	❶ Relic Passage Driftveil City exit (dust clouds) ❷ Mistralton Cave 1F (dust clouds)

HOW TO OBTAIN FROM OTHER GAMES

—

—

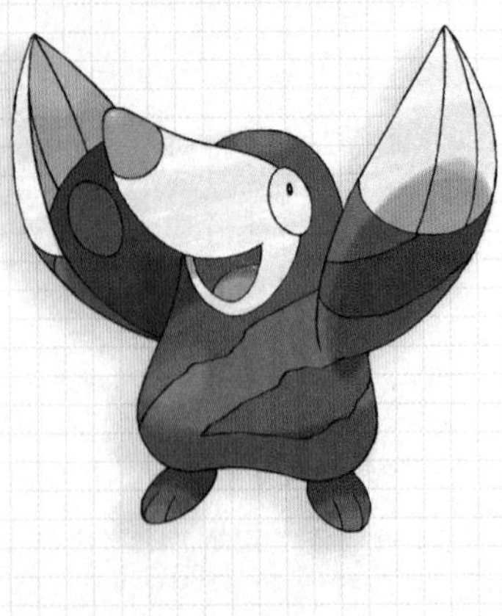

Pokémon AR Marker

LEVEL-UP AND LEARNED MOVES

Lv.	Name	Type	Kind	Pow.	Acc.	PP	Range	Long	DA
1	Scratch	Normal	Physical	40	100	35	Normal	—	○
1	Mud Sport	Ground	Status	—	—	15	Both Sides	—	—
5	Rapid Spin	Normal	Physical	20	100	40	Normal	—	○
8	Mud-Slap	Ground	Special	20	100	10	Normal	—	—
12	Fury Swipes	Normal	Physical	18	80	15	Normal	—	○
15	Metal Claw	Steel	Physical	50	95	35	Normal	—	○
19	Dig	Ground	Physical	80	100	10	Normal	—	○
22	Hone Claws	Dark	Status	—	—	15	Self	—	—
26	Slash	Normal	Physical	70	100	20	Normal	—	○
29	Rock Slide	Rock	Physical	75	90	10	Many Others	—	—
33	Earthquake	Ground	Physical	100	100	10	Adjacent	—	—
36	Swords Dance	Normal	Status	—	—	30	Self	—	—
40	Sandstorm	Rock	Status	—	—	10	Both Sides	—	—
43	Drill Run	Ground	Physical	80	95	10	Normal	—	○
47	Fissure	Ground	Physical	—	30	5	Normal	—	—

TM & HM MOVES

Lv.	Name	Type	Kind	Pow.	Acc.	PP	Range	Long	DA
TM01	Hone Claws	Dark	Status	—	—	15	Self	—	—
TM06	Toxic	Poison	Status	—	90	10	Normal	—	—
TM10	Hidden Power	Normal	Special	—	100	15	Normal	—	—
TM17	Protect	Normal	Status	—	—	10	Self	—	—
TM21	Frustration	Normal	Physical	—	100	20	Normal	—	○
TM26	Earthquake	Ground	Physical	100	100	10	Adjacent	—	—
TM27	Return	Normal	Physical	—	100	20	Normal	—	○
TM28	Dig	Ground	Physical	80	100	10	Normal	—	○
TM31	Brick Break	Fighting	Physical	75	100	15	Normal	—	○
TM32	Double Team	Normal	Status	—	—	15	Self	—	—
TM36	Sludge Bomb	Poison	Special	90	100	10	Normal	—	—
TM37	Sandstorm	Rock	Status	—	—	10	Both Sides	—	—
TM39	Rock Tomb	Rock	Physical	50	80	10	Normal	—	—
TM40	Aerial Ace	Flying	Physical	60	—	20	Normal	○	○
TM42	Facade	Normal	Physical	70	100	20	Normal	—	○
TM44	Rest	Psychic	Status	—	—	10	Self	—	—
TM45	Attract	Normal	Status	—	100	15	Normal	—	—
TM48	Round	Normal	Special	60	100	15	Normal	—	—
TM56	Fling	Dark	Physical	—	100	10	Normal	—	—
TM65	Shadow Claw	Ghost	Physical	70	100	15	Normal	—	○
TM75	Swords Dance	Normal	Status	—	—	30	Self	—	—
TM78	Bulldoze	Ground	Physical	60	100	20	Adjacent	—	—
TM80	Rock Slide	Rock	Physical	75	90	10	Many Others	—	—
TM81	X-Scissor	Bug	Physical	80	100	15	Normal	—	○
TM84	Poison Jab	Poison	Physical	80	100	20	Normal	—	○
TM87	Swagger	Normal	Status	—	90	15	Normal	—	—
TM90	Substitute	Normal	Status	—	—	10	Self	—	—
TM94	Rock Smash	Fighting	Physical	40	100	15	Normal	—	○
HM01	Cut	Normal	Physical	50	95	30	Normal	—	○
HM04	Strength	Normal	Physical	80	100	15	Normal	—	○

MOVES TAUGHT BY PEOPLE

Name	Type	Kind	Pow.	Acc.	PP	Range	Long	DA

MOVES TAUGHT BY MOVE TUTORS FOR SHARDS

Name	Type	Kind	Pow.	Acc.	PP	Range	Long	DA
Drill Run	Ground	Physical	80	95	10	Normal	—	○
Iron Defense	Steel	Status	—	—	15	Self	—	—
Earth Power	Ground	Special	90	100	10	Normal	—	—
Snore	Normal	Special	40	100	15	Normal	—	—
Stealth Rock	Rock	Status	—	—	20	Other Side	—	—
Sleep Talk	Normal	Status	—	—	10	Self	—	—

EGG MOVES

Name	Type	Kind	Pow.	Acc.	PP	Range	Long	DA
Iron Defense	Steel	Status	—	—	15	Self	—	—
Rapid Spin	Normal	Physical	20	100	40	Normal	—	○
Earth Power	Ground	Special	90	100	10	Normal	—	—
Crush Claw	Normal	Physical	75	95	10	Normal	—	○
Metal Sound	Steel	Status	—	85	40	Normal	—	—
Submission	Fighting	Physical	80	80	25	Normal	—	○
Skull Bash	Normal	Physical	100	100	15	Normal	—	○
Rock Climb	Normal	Physical	90	85	20	Normal	—	○

530 Excadrill

Subterrene Pokémon

- HEIGHT: 2'04"
- WEIGHT: 89.1 lbs.
- GENDER: ♂ / ♀

Forming a drill with its steel claws and head, it can bore through a steel plate, no matter how thick it is.

Same form for ♂ / ♀

TYPE Ground Steel

ABILITIES
- Sand Rush
- Sand Force

HIDDEN ABILITY
- Mold Breaker

STATS
HP
Attack
Defense
Sp. Atk
Sp. Def
Speed

EGG GROUPS
Field

ITEMS SOMETIMES HELD
- None

Pokémon AR Marker

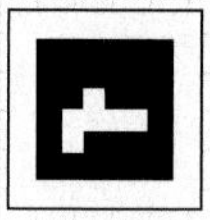

EVOLUTION

HOW TO OBTAIN

Pokémon Black Version 2: ❶ Reversal Mountain Entrance (dust clouds) ❷ Seaside Cave 1F (dust clouds)

Pokémon White Version 2: ❶ Reversal Mountain Entrance (dust clouds) ❷ Seaside Cave 1F (dust clouds)

HOW TO OBTAIN FROM OTHER GAMES

—

—

LEVEL-UP AND LEARNED MOVES

Lv.	Name	Type	Kind	Pow.	Acc.	PP	Range	Long	DA
1	Scratch	Normal	Physical	40	100	35	Normal	—	○
1	Mud Sport	Ground	Status	—	—	15	Both Sides	—	—
1	Rapid Spin	Normal	Physical	20	100	40	Normal	—	○
1	Mud-Slap	Ground	Special	20	100	10	Normal	—	—
5	Rapid Spin	Normal	Physical	20	100	40	Normal	—	○
8	Mud-Slap	Ground	Special	20	100	10	Normal	—	—
12	Fury Swipes	Normal	Physical	18	80	15	Normal	—	○
15	Metal Claw	Steel	Physical	50	95	35	Normal	—	○
19	Dig	Ground	Physical	80	100	10	Normal	—	○
22	Hone Claws	Dark	Status	—	—	15	Self	—	—
26	Slash	Normal	Physical	70	100	20	Normal	—	○
29	Rock Slide	Rock	Physical	75	90	10	Many Others	—	—
31	Horn Drill	Normal	Physical	—	30	5	Normal	—	○
36	Earthquake	Ground	Physical	100	100	10	Adjacent	—	—
42	Swords Dance	Normal	Status	—	—	30	Self	—	—
49	Sandstorm	Rock	Status	—	—	10	Both Sides	—	—
55	Drill Run	Ground	Physical	80	95	10	Normal	—	○
62	Fissure	Ground	Physical	—	30	5	Normal	—	—

TM & HM MOVES

Lv.	Name	Type	Kind	Pow.	Acc.	PP	Range	Long	DA
TM01	Hone Claws	Dark	Status	—	—	15	Self	—	—
TM06	Toxic	Poison	Status	—	90	10	Normal	—	—
TM10	Hidden Power	Normal	Special	—	100	15	Normal	—	—
TM15	Hyper Beam	Normal	Special	150	90	5	Normal	—	—
TM17	Protect	Normal	Status	—	—	10	Self	—	—
TM21	Frustration	Normal	Physical	—	100	20	Normal	—	○
TM26	Earthquake	Ground	Physical	100	100	10	Adjacent	—	—
TM27	Return	Normal	Physical	—	100	20	Normal	—	○
TM28	Dig	Ground	Physical	80	100	10	Normal	—	○
TM31	Brick Break	Fighting	Physical	75	100	15	Normal	—	○
TM32	Double Team	Normal	Status	—	—	15	Self	—	—
TM36	Sludge Bomb	Poison	Special	90	100	10	Normal	—	—
TM37	Sandstorm	Rock	Status	—	—	10	Both Sides	—	—
TM39	Rock Tomb	Rock	Physical	50	80	10	Normal	—	—
TM40	Aerial Ace	Flying	Physical	60	—	20	Normal	○	○
TM42	Facade	Normal	Physical	70	100	20	Normal	—	○
TM44	Rest	Psychic	Status	—	—	10	Self	—	—
TM45	Attract	Normal	Status	—	100	15	Normal	—	—
TM48	Round	Normal	Special	60	100	15	Normal	—	—
TM52	Focus Blast	Fighting	Special	120	70	5	Normal	—	—
TM56	Fling	Dark	Physical	—	100	10	Normal	—	—
TM65	Shadow Claw	Ghost	Physical	70	100	15	Normal	—	○
TM68	Giga Impact	Normal	Physical	150	90	5	Normal	—	○
TM75	Swords Dance	Normal	Status	—	—	30	Self	—	—
TM78	Bulldoze	Ground	Physical	60	100	20	Adjacent	—	—
TM80	Rock Slide	Rock	Physical	75	90	10	Many Others	—	—
TM81	X-Scissor	Bug	Physical	80	100	15	Normal	—	○
TM84	Poison Jab	Poison	Physical	80	100	20	Normal	—	○
TM87	Swagger	Normal	Status	—	90	15	Normal	—	—
TM90	Substitute	Normal	Status	—	—	10	Self	—	—
TM94	Rock Smash	Fighting	Physical	40	100	15	Normal	—	○
HM01	Cut	Normal	Physical	50	95	30	Normal	—	○
HM04	Strength	Normal	Physical	80	100	15	Normal	—	○

MOVES TAUGHT BY PEOPLE

Name	Type	Kind	Pow.	Acc.	PP	Range	Long	DA

MOVES TAUGHT BY MOVE TUTORS FOR SHARDS

Name	Type	Kind	Pow.	Acc.	PP	Range	Long	DA
Drill Run	Ground	Physical	80	95	10	Normal	—	○
Iron Head	Steel	Physical	80	100	15	Normal	—	○
Iron Defense	Steel	Status	—	—	15	Self	—	—
Magnet Rise	Electric	Status	—	—	10	Self	—	—
Earth Power	Ground	Special	90	100	10	Normal	—	—
Snore	Normal	Special	40	100	15	Normal	—	—
Stealth Rock	Rock	Status	—	—	20	Other Side	—	—
Sleep Talk	Normal	Status	—	—	10	Self	—	—

531 Audino

Hearing Pokémon

- HEIGHT: 3'07"
- WEIGHT: 68.3 lbs.
- GENDER: ♂ / ♀

Using the feelers on its ears, it can tell how someone is feeling or when an egg might hatch.

Same form for ♂ / ♀

TYPE Normal

ABILITIES
- Healer
- Regenerator

HIDDEN ABILITY
—

STATS
HP
Attack
Defense
Sp. Atk
Sp. Def
Speed

EGG GROUPS
Fairy

ITEMS SOMETIMES HELD
- Oran Berry
- Sitrus Berry

Pokémon AR Marker

EVOLUTION

Does not evolve

HOW TO OBTAIN

Pokémon Black Version 2: ❶ Route 20 (rustling grass) ❷ Floccesy Ranch (rustling grass)

Pokémon White Version 2: ❶ Route 20 (rustling grass) ❷ Floccesy Ranch (rustling grass)

HOW TO OBTAIN FROM OTHER GAMES

—

—

LEVEL-UP AND LEARNED MOVES

Lv.	Name	Type	Kind	Pow.	Acc.	PP	Range	Long	DA
1	Pound	Normal	Physical	40	100	35	Normal	—	○
1	Growl	Normal	Status	—	100	40	Many Others	—	—
1	Helping Hand	Normal	Status	—	—	20	1 Ally	—	—
5	Refresh	Normal	Status	—	—	20	Self	—	—
10	DoubleSlap	Normal	Physical	15	85	10	Normal	—	○
15	Attract	Normal	Status	—	100	15	Normal	—	—
20	Secret Power	Normal	Physical	70	100	20	Normal	—	—
25	Entrainment	Normal	Status	—	100	15	Normal	—	—
30	Take Down	Normal	Physical	90	85	20	Normal	—	○
35	Heal Pulse	Psychic	Status	—	—	10	Normal	○	—
40	After You	Normal	Status	—	—	15	Normal	—	—
45	Simple Beam	Normal	Status	—	100	15	Normal	—	—
50	Double-Edge	Normal	Physical	120	100	15	Normal	—	○
55	Last Resort	Normal	Physical	140	100	5	Normal	—	○

TM & HM MOVES

Lv.	Name	Type	Kind	Pow.	Acc.	PP	Range	Long	DA
TM03	Psyshock	Psychic	Special	80	100	10	Normal	—	—
TM04	Calm Mind	Psychic	Status	—	—	20	Self	—	—
TM06	Toxic	Poison	Status	—	90	10	Normal	—	—
TM10	Hidden Power	Normal	Special	—	100	15	Normal	—	—
TM11	Sunny Day	Fire	Status	—	—	5	Both Sides	—	—
TM13	Ice Beam	Ice	Special	95	100	10	Normal	—	—
TM14	Blizzard	Ice	Special	120	70	5	Many Others	—	—
TM15	Hyper Beam	Normal	Special	150	90	5	Normal	—	—
TM16	Light Screen	Psychic	Status	—	—	30	Your Side	—	—
TM17	Protect	Normal	Status	—	—	10	Self	—	—
TM18	Rain Dance	Water	Status	—	—	5	Both Sides	—	—
TM19	Telekinesis	Psychic	Status	—	—	15	Normal	—	—
TM20	Safeguard	Normal	Status	—	—	25	Your Side	—	—
TM21	Frustration	Normal	Physical	—	100	20	Normal	—	○
TM22	SolarBeam	Grass	Special	120	100	10	Normal	—	—
TM24	Thunderbolt	Electric	Special	95	100	15	Normal	—	—
TM25	Thunder	Electric	Special	120	70	10	Normal	—	—
TM27	Return	Normal	Physical	—	100	20	Normal	—	○
TM28	Dig	Ground	Physical	80	100	10	Normal	—	○
TM29	Psychic	Psychic	Special	90	100	10	Normal	—	—
TM30	Shadow Ball	Ghost	Special	80	100	15	Normal	—	—
TM32	Double Team	Normal	Status	—	—	15	Self	—	—
TM33	Reflect	Psychic	Status	—	—	20	Your Side	—	—
TM35	Flamethrower	Fire	Special	95	100	15	Normal	—	—
TM38	Fire Blast	Fire	Special	120	85	5	Normal	—	—
TM42	Facade	Normal	Physical	70	100	20	Normal	—	○
TM44	Rest	Psychic	Status	—	—	10	Self	—	—
TM45	Attract	Normal	Status	—	100	15	Normal	—	—
TM48	Round	Normal	Special	60	100	15	Normal	—	—
TM49	Echoed Voice	Normal	Special	40	100	15	Normal	—	—
TM56	Fling	Dark	Physical	—	100	10	Normal	—	—
TM57	Charge Beam	Electric	Special	50	90	10	Normal	—	—
TM59	Incinerate	Fire	Special	30	100	15	Many Others	—	—
TM67	Retaliate	Normal	Physical	70	100	5	Normal	—	○
TM70	Flash	Normal	Status	—	100	20	Normal	—	—
TM73	Thunder Wave	Electric	Status	—	100	20	Normal	—	—
TM77	Psych Up	Normal	Status	—	—	10	Normal	—	—
TM83	Work Up	Normal	Status	—	—	30	Self	—	—
TM85	Dream Eater	Psychic	Special	100	100	15	Normal	—	—
TM86	Grass Knot	Grass	Special	—	100	20	Normal	—	○
TM87	Swagger	Normal	Status	—	90	15	Normal	—	—
TM90	Substitute	Normal	Status	—	—	10	Self	—	—
TM92	Trick Room	Psychic	Status	—	—	5	Both Sides	—	—
TM93	Wild Charge	Electric	Physical	90	100	15	Normal	—	○
HM03	Surf	Water	Special	95	100	15	Adjacent	—	—

MOVES TAUGHT BY PEOPLE

Name	Type	Kind	Pow.	Acc.	PP	Range	Long	DA

MOVES TAUGHT BY MOVE TUTORS FOR SHARDS

Name	Type	Kind	Pow.	Acc.	PP	Range	Long	DA
Covet	Normal	Physical	60	100	40	Normal	—	○
Signal Beam	Bug	Special	75	100	15	Normal	—	—
Uproar	Normal	Special	90	100	10	1 Random	—	—
Low Kick	Fighting	Physical	—	100	20	Normal	—	○
Fire Punch	Fire	Physical	75	100	15	Normal	—	○
ThunderPunch	Electric	Physical	75	100	15	Normal	—	○
Ice Punch	Ice	Physical	75	100	15	Normal	—	○
Last Resort	Normal	Physical	140	100	5	Normal	—	○
Magic Coat	Psychic	Status	—	—	15	Self	—	—
Hyper Voice	Normal	Special	90	100	10	Many Others	—	—
Icy Wind	Ice	Special	55	95	15	Many Others	—	—
Iron Tail	Steel	Physical	100	75	15	Normal	—	○
Zen Headbutt	Psychic	Physical	80	90	15	Normal	—	○
Gravity	Psychic	Status	—	—	5	Both Sides	—	—
Snore	Normal	Special	40	100	15	Normal	—	—
Heal Bell	Normal	Status	—	—	5	Your Party	—	—
Knock Off	Dark	Physical	20	100	20	Normal	—	○
Role Play	Psychic	Status	—	—	10	Normal	—	—
Drain Punch	Fighting	Physical	75	100	10	Normal	—	○
Pain Split	Normal	Status	—	—	20	Normal	—	—
Helping Hand	Normal	Status	—	—	20	1 Ally	—	—
After You	Normal	Status	—	—	15	Normal	—	—
Sleep Talk	Normal	Status	—	—	10	Self	—	—
Skill Swap	Psychic	Status	—	—	10	Normal	—	—
Snatch	Dark	Status	—	—	10	Self	—	—

EGG MOVES

Name	Type	Kind	Pow.	Acc.	PP	Range	Long	DA
Wish	Normal	Status	—	—	10	Self	—	—
Heal Bell	Normal	Status	—	—	5	Your Party	—	—
Lucky Chant	Normal	Status	—	—	30	Your Side	—	—
Encore	Normal	Status	—	100	5	Normal	—	—
Bestow	Normal	Status	—	—	15	Normal	—	—
Sweet Kiss	Normal	Status	—	75	10	Normal	—	—
Yawn	Normal	Status	—	—	10	Normal	—	—
Sleep Talk	Normal	Status	—	—	10	Self	—	—
Healing Wish	Psychic	Status	—	—	10	Self	—	—
Amnesia	Psychic	Status	—	—	20	Self	—	—

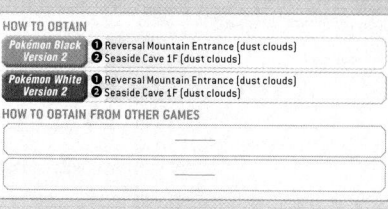

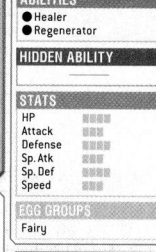

532 Timburr

Muscular Pokémon

TYPE: **Fighting**

ABILITIES
- Guts
- Sheer Force

HIDDEN ABILITY
—

- HEIGHT: 2'00"
- WEIGHT: 27.6 lbs.
- GENDER: ♂ / ♀

Always carrying squared logs, they help out with construction. As they grow, they carry bigger logs.

STATS
HP	■■■
Attack	■■■■
Defense	■■■
Sp. Atk	■
Sp. Def	■
Speed	■■

EGG GROUPS
Human-like

Same form for ♂ / ♀

ITEMS SOMETIMES HELD
- None

Pokémon AR Marker

EVOLUTION

Timburr → Lv. 25 → Gurdurr → Link Trade it → Conkeldurr

HOW TO OBTAIN
Pokémon Black Version 2	Relic Passage Castelia City exit
Pokémon White Version 2	Relic Passage Castelia City exit

HOW TO OBTAIN FROM OTHER GAMES
—

—

LEVEL-UP AND LEARNED MOVES
Lv.	Name	Type	Kind	Pow.	Acc.	PP	Range	Long	DA
1	Pound	Normal	Physical	40	100	35	Normal	—	○
1	Leer	Normal	Status	—	100	30	Many Others	—	—
4	Focus Energy	Normal	Status	—	—	30	Self	—	—
8	Bide	Normal	Physical	—	—	10	Self	—	○
12	Low Kick	Fighting	Physical	—	100	20	Normal	—	○
16	Rock Throw	Rock	Physical	50	90	15	Normal	—	—
20	Wake-Up Slap	Fighting	Physical	60	100	10	Normal	—	○
24	Chip Away	Normal	Physical	70	100	20	Normal	—	○
28	Bulk Up	Fighting	Status	—	—	20	Self	—	—
31	Rock Slide	Rock	Physical	75	90	10	Many Others	—	—
34	DynamicPunch	Fighting	Physical	100	50	5	Normal	—	○
37	Scary Face	Normal	Status	—	100	10	Normal	—	—
40	Hammer Arm	Fighting	Physical	100	90	10	Normal	—	○
43	Stone Edge	Rock	Physical	100	80	5	Normal	—	—
46	Focus Punch	Fighting	Physical	150	100	20	Normal	—	○
49	Superpower	Fighting	Physical	120	100	5	Normal	—	○

TM & HM MOVES
Lv.	Name	Type	Kind	Pow.	Acc.	PP	Range	Long	DA
TM06	Toxic	Poison	Status	—	90	10	Normal	—	—
TM08	Bulk Up	Fighting	Status	—	—	20	Self	—	—
TM10	Hidden Power	Normal	Special	—	100	15	Normal	—	—
TM11	Sunny Day	Fire	Status	—	—	5	Both Sides	—	—
TM12	Taunt	Dark	Status	—	100	20	Normal	—	—
TM17	Protect	Normal	Status	—	—	10	Self	—	—
TM18	Rain Dance	Water	Status	—	—	5	Both Sides	—	—
TM21	Frustration	Normal	Physical	—	100	20	Normal	—	○
TM23	Smack Down	Rock	Physical	50	100	15	Normal	—	○
TM27	Return	Normal	Physical	—	100	20	Normal	—	○
TM28	Dig	Ground	Physical	80	100	10	Normal	—	○
TM31	Brick Break	Fighting	Physical	75	100	15	Normal	—	○
TM32	Double Team	Normal	Status	—	—	15	Self	—	—
TM39	Rock Tomb	Rock	Physical	50	80	10	Normal	—	○
TM42	Facade	Normal	Physical	70	100	20	Normal	—	○
TM44	Rest	Psychic	Status	—	—	10	Self	—	—
TM45	Attract	Normal	Status	—	100	15	Normal	—	—
TM47	Low Sweep	Fighting	Physical	60	100	20	Normal	—	○
TM48	Round	Normal	Special	60	100	15	Normal	—	—
TM52	Focus Blast	Fighting	Special	120	70	5	Normal	—	—
TM56	Fling	Dark	Physical	—	100	10	Normal	—	○
TM66	Payback	Dark	Physical	50	100	10	Normal	—	○
TM67	Retaliate	Normal	Physical	70	100	5	Normal	—	○
TM71	Stone Edge	Rock	Physical	100	80	5	Normal	—	—
TM80	Rock Slide	Rock	Physical	75	90	10	Many Others	—	—
TM83	Work Up	Normal	Status	—	—	30	Self	—	—
TM84	Poison Jab	Poison	Physical	80	100	20	Normal	—	○
TM86	Grass Knot	Grass	Special	—	100	20	Normal	—	○
TM87	Swagger	Normal	Status	—	90	15	Normal	—	—
TM90	Substitute	Normal	Status	—	—	10	Self	—	—
TM94	Rock Smash	Fighting	Physical	40	100	15	Normal	—	○
HM04	Strength	Normal	Physical	80	100	15	Normal	—	○

MOVES TAUGHT BY PEOPLE
Name	Type	Kind	Pow.	Acc.	PP	Range	Long	DA

MOVES TAUGHT BY MOVE TUTORS FOR SHARDS
Name	Type	Kind	Pow.	Acc.	PP	Range	Long	DA
Low Kick	Fighting	Physical	—	100	20	Normal	—	○
Fire Punch	Fire	Physical	75	100	15	Normal	—	○
ThunderPunch	Electric	Physical	75	100	15	Normal	—	○
Ice Punch	Ice	Physical	75	100	15	Normal	—	○
Block	Normal	Status	—	—	5	Normal	—	—
Superpower	Fighting	Physical	120	100	5	Normal	—	○
Snore	Normal	Special	40	100	15	Normal	—	—
Knock Off	Dark	Physical	20	100	20	Normal	—	○
Drain Punch	Fighting	Physical	75	100	10	Normal	—	○
Helping Hand	Normal	Status	—	—	20	1 Ally	—	—
Sleep Talk	Normal	Status	—	—	10	Self	—	—

EGG MOVES
Name	Type	Kind	Pow.	Acc.	PP	Range	Long	DA
Drain Punch	Fighting	Physical	75	100	10	Normal	—	○
Endure	Normal	Status	—	—	10	Self	—	—
Counter	Fighting	Physical	—	100	20	Varies	—	○
Comet Punch	Normal	Physical	18	85	15	Normal	—	○
Foresight	Normal	Status	—	—	40	Normal	—	—
SmellingSalt	Normal	Physical	60	100	10	Normal	—	○
Detect	Fighting	Status	—	—	5	Self	—	—
Wide Guard	Rock	Status	—	—	10	Your Side	—	—
Force Palm	Fighting	Physical	60	100	10	Normal	—	○
Reversal	Fighting	Physical	—	100	15	Normal	—	○
Mach Punch	Fighting	Physical	40	100	30	Normal	—	○

---

533 Gurdurr

Muscular Pokémon

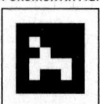

TYPE: **Fighting**

ABILITIES
- Guts
- Sheer Force

HIDDEN ABILITY
—

- HEIGHT: 3'11"
- WEIGHT: 88.2 lbs.
- GENDER: ♂ / ♀

With strengthened bodies, they skillfully wield steel beams to take down buildings.

STATS
HP	■■■
Attack	■■■■■■
Defense	■■■■
Sp. Atk	■
Sp. Def	■■
Speed	■■

EGG GROUPS
Human-like

Same form for ♂ / ♀

ITEMS SOMETIMES HELD
- None

Pokémon AR Marker

EVOLUTION

Timburr → Lv. 25 → Gurdurr → Link Trade it → Conkeldurr

HOW TO OBTAIN
Pokémon Black Version 2	❶ Relic Passage Driftveil City exit ❷ Victory Road outside ②
Pokémon White Version 2	❶ Relic Passage Driftveil City exit ❷ Victory Road outside ②

HOW TO OBTAIN FROM OTHER GAMES
—

—

LEVEL-UP AND LEARNED MOVES
Lv.	Name	Type	Kind	Pow.	Acc.	PP	Range	Long	DA
1	Pound	Normal	Physical	40	100	35	Normal	—	○
1	Leer	Normal	Status	—	100	30	Many Others	—	—
1	Focus Energy	Normal	Status	—	—	30	Self	—	—
1	Bide	Normal	Physical	—	—	10	Self	—	○
4	Focus Energy	Normal	Status	—	—	30	Self	—	—
8	Bide	Normal	Physical	—	—	10	Self	—	○
12	Low Kick	Fighting	Physical	—	100	20	Normal	—	○
16	Rock Throw	Rock	Physical	50	90	15	Normal	—	—
20	Wake-Up Slap	Fighting	Physical	60	100	10	Normal	—	○
24	Chip Away	Normal	Physical	70	100	20	Normal	—	○
29	Bulk Up	Fighting	Status	—	—	20	Self	—	—
33	Rock Slide	Rock	Physical	75	90	10	Many Others	—	—
37	DynamicPunch	Fighting	Physical	100	50	5	Normal	—	○
41	Scary Face	Normal	Status	—	100	10	Normal	—	—
45	Hammer Arm	Fighting	Physical	100	90	10	Normal	—	○
49	Stone Edge	Rock	Physical	100	80	5	Normal	—	—
53	Focus Punch	Fighting	Physical	150	100	20	Normal	—	○
57	Superpower	Fighting	Physical	120	100	5	Normal	—	○

TM & HM MOVES
Lv.	Name	Type	Kind	Pow.	Acc.	PP	Range	Long	DA
TM06	Toxic	Poison	Status	—	90	10	Normal	—	—
TM08	Bulk Up	Fighting	Status	—	—	20	Self	—	—
TM10	Hidden Power	Normal	Special	—	100	15	Normal	—	—
TM11	Sunny Day	Fire	Status	—	—	5	Both Sides	—	—
TM12	Taunt	Dark	Status	—	100	20	Normal	—	—
TM17	Protect	Normal	Status	—	—	10	Self	—	—
TM18	Rain Dance	Water	Status	—	—	5	Both Sides	—	—
TM21	Frustration	Normal	Physical	—	100	20	Normal	—	○
TM23	Smack Down	Rock	Physical	50	100	15	Normal	—	○
TM27	Return	Normal	Physical	—	100	20	Normal	—	○
TM28	Dig	Ground	Physical	80	100	10	Normal	—	○
TM31	Brick Break	Fighting	Physical	75	100	15	Normal	—	○
TM32	Double Team	Normal	Status	—	—	15	Self	—	—
TM39	Rock Tomb	Rock	Physical	50	80	10	Normal	—	○
TM42	Facade	Normal	Physical	70	100	20	Normal	—	○
TM44	Rest	Psychic	Status	—	—	10	Self	—	—
TM45	Attract	Normal	Status	—	100	15	Normal	—	—
TM47	Low Sweep	Fighting	Physical	60	100	20	Normal	—	○
TM48	Round	Normal	Special	60	100	15	Normal	—	—
TM52	Focus Blast	Fighting	Special	120	70	5	Normal	—	—
TM56	Fling	Dark	Physical	—	100	10	Normal	—	○
TM66	Payback	Dark	Physical	50	100	10	Normal	—	○
TM67	Retaliate	Normal	Physical	70	100	5	Normal	—	○
TM71	Stone Edge	Rock	Physical	100	80	5	Normal	—	—
TM80	Rock Slide	Rock	Physical	75	90	10	Many Others	—	—
TM83	Work Up	Normal	Status	—	—	30	Self	—	—
TM84	Poison Jab	Poison	Physical	80	100	20	Normal	—	○
TM86	Grass Knot	Grass	Special	—	100	20	Normal	—	○
TM87	Swagger	Normal	Status	—	90	15	Normal	—	—
TM90	Substitute	Normal	Status	—	—	10	Self	—	—
TM94	Rock Smash	Fighting	Physical	40	100	15	Normal	—	○
HM04	Strength	Normal	Physical	80	100	15	Normal	—	○

MOVES TAUGHT BY PEOPLE
Name	Type	Kind	Pow.	Acc.	PP	Range	Long	DA

MOVES TAUGHT BY MOVE TUTORS FOR SHARDS
Name	Type	Kind	Pow.	Acc.	PP	Range	Long	DA
Low Kick	Fighting	Physical	—	100	20	Normal	—	○
Fire Punch	Fire	Physical	75	100	15	Normal	—	○
ThunderPunch	Electric	Physical	75	100	15	Normal	—	○
Ice Punch	Ice	Physical	75	100	15	Normal	—	○
Block	Normal	Status	—	—	5	Normal	—	—
Superpower	Fighting	Physical	120	100	5	Normal	—	○
Snore	Normal	Special	40	100	15	Normal	—	—
Knock Off	Dark	Physical	20	100	20	Normal	—	○
Drain Punch	Fighting	Physical	75	100	10	Normal	—	○
Helping Hand	Normal	Status	—	—	20	1 Ally	—	—
Sleep Talk	Normal	Status	—	—	10	Self	—	—

534 Conkeldurr

Muscular Pokémon

- HEIGHT: 4'07"
- WEIGHT: 191.8 lbs.
- GENDER: ♂ / ♀

Rather than rely on force, they master moves that utilize the centrifugal force of spinning concrete.

Same form for ♂ / ♀

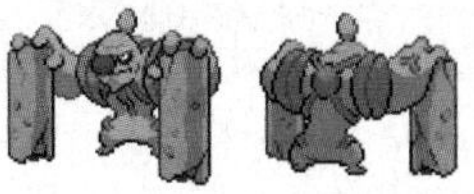

TYPE: Fighting

ABILITIES
- Guts
- Sheer Force

HIDDEN ABILITY

—

STATS

HP / Attack / Defense / Sp. Atk / Sp. Def / Speed

EGG GROUPS

Human-like

ITEMS SOMETIMES HELD
- None

EVOLUTION

HOW TO OBTAIN

Pokémon Black Version 2	Have Gurdurr sent to you by Link Trade to receive Conkeldurr
Pokémon White Version 2	Have Gurdurr sent to you by Link Trade to receive Conkeldurr

HOW TO OBTAIN FROM OTHER GAMES

—

—

Pokémon AR Marker

LEVEL-UP AND LEARNED MOVES

Lv.	Name	Type	Kind	Pow.	Acc.	PP	Range	Long	DA
1	Pound	Normal	Physical	40	100	35	Normal	—	○
1	Leer	Normal	Status	—	100	30	Many Others	—	—
1	Focus Energy	Normal	Status	—	—	30	Self	—	—
1	Bide	Normal	Physical	—	—	10	Self	—	○
4	Focus Energy	Normal	Status	—	—	30	Self	—	—
8	Bide	Normal	Physical	—	—	10	Self	—	○
12	Low Kick	Fighting	Physical	—	100	20	Normal	—	○
16	Rock Throw	Rock	Physical	50	90	15	Normal	—	—
20	Wake-Up Slap	Fighting	Physical	60	100	10	Normal	—	○
24	Chip Away	Normal	Physical	70	100	20	Normal	—	○
29	Bulk Up	Fighting	Status	—	—	20	Self	—	—
33	Rock Slide	Rock	Physical	75	90	10	Many Others	—	—
37	DynamicPunch	Fighting	Physical	100	50	5	Normal	—	○
41	Scary Face	Normal	Status	—	100	10	Normal	—	—
45	Hammer Arm	Fighting	Physical	100	90	10	Normal	—	○
49	Stone Edge	Rock	Physical	100	80	5	Normal	—	—
53	Focus Punch	Fighting	Physical	150	100	20	Normal	—	○
57	Superpower	Fighting	Physical	120	100	5	Normal	—	○

Lv.	Name	Type	Kind	Pow.	Acc.	PP	Range	Long	DA
HM04	Strength	Normal	Physical	80	100	15	Normal	—	○

TM & HM MOVES

Lv.	Name	Type	Kind	Pow.	Acc.	PP	Range	Long	DA
TM06	Toxic	Poison	Status	—	90	10	Normal	—	—
TM08	Bulk Up	Fighting	Status	—	—	20	Self	—	—
TM10	Hidden Power	Normal	Special	—	100	15	Normal	—	—
TM11	Sunny Day	Fire	Status	—	—	5	Both Sides	—	—
TM12	Taunt	Dark	Status	—	100	20	Normal	—	—
TM15	Hyper Beam	Normal	Special	150	90	5	Normal	—	—
TM17	Protect	Normal	Status	—	—	10	Self	—	—
TM18	Rain Dance	Water	Status	—	—	5	Both Sides	—	—
TM21	Frustration	Normal	Physical	—	100	20	Normal	—	○
TM23	Smack Down	Rock	Physical	50	100	15	Normal	—	—
TM26	Earthquake	Ground	Physical	100	100	10	Adjacent	—	—
TM27	Return	Normal	Physical	—	100	20	Normal	—	○
TM28	Dig	Ground	Physical	80	100	10	Normal	—	○
TM31	Brick Break	Fighting	Physical	75	100	15	Normal	—	○
TM32	Double Team	Normal	Status	—	—	15	Self	—	—
TM39	Rock Tomb	Rock	Physical	50	80	10	Normal	—	—
TM42	Facade	Normal	Physical	70	100	20	Normal	—	○
TM44	Rest	Psychic	Status	—	—	10	Self	—	—
TM45	Attract	Normal	Status	—	100	15	Normal	—	—
TM47	Low Sweep	Fighting	Physical	60	100	20	Normal	—	○
TM48	Round	Normal	Special	60	100	15	Normal	—	—
TM52	Focus Blast	Fighting	Special	120	70	5	Normal	—	—
TM56	Fling	Dark	Physical	—	100	10	Normal	—	—
TM66	Payback	Dark	Physical	50	100	10	Normal	—	○
TM67	Retaliate	Normal	Physical	70	100	5	Normal	—	○
TM68	Giga Impact	Normal	Physical	150	90	5	Normal	—	○
TM71	Stone Edge	Rock	Physical	100	80	5	Normal	—	—
TM78	Bulldoze	Ground	Physical	60	100	20	Adjacent	—	—
TM80	Rock Slide	Rock	Physical	75	90	10	Many Others	—	—
TM83	Work Up	Normal	Status	—	—	30	Self	—	—
TM84	Poison Jab	Poison	Physical	80	100	20	Normal	—	○
TM86	Grass Knot	Grass	Special	—	100	20	Normal	—	○
TM87	Swagger	Normal	Status	—	90	15	Normal	—	—
TM90	Substitute	Normal	Status	—	—	10	Self	—	—
TM94	Rock Smash	Fighting	Physical	40	100	15	Normal	—	○

MOVES TAUGHT BY PEOPLE

Name	Type	Kind	Pow.	Acc.	PP	Range	Long	DA

MOVES TAUGHT BY MOVE TUTORS FOR SHARDS

Name	Type	Kind	Pow.	Acc.	PP	Range	Long	DA
Low Kick	Fighting	Physical	—	100	20	Normal	—	○
Fire Punch	Fire	Physical	75	100	15	Normal	—	○
ThunderPunch	Electric	Physical	75	100	15	Normal	—	○
Ice Punch	Ice	Physical	75	100	15	Normal	—	○
Block	Normal	Status	—	—	5	Normal	—	—
Superpower	Fighting	Physical	120	100	5	Normal	—	○
Snore	Normal	Special	40	100	15	Normal	—	—
Knock Off	Dark	Physical	20	100	20	Normal	—	○
Drain Punch	Fighting	Physical	75	100	10	Normal	—	○
Helping Hand	Normal	Status	—	—	20	1 Ally	—	—
Sleep Talk	Normal	Status	—	—	10	Self	—	—

535 Tympole

Tadpole Pokémon

- HEIGHT: 1'08"
- WEIGHT: 9.9 lbs.
- GENDER: ♂ / ♀

By vibrating its cheeks, it emits sound waves imperceptible to humans and warns others of danger.

Same form for ♂ / ♀

TYPE: Water

ABILITIES
- Swift Swim
- Hydration

HIDDEN ABILITY
- Water Absorb

STATS

HP / Attack / Defense / Sp. Atk / Sp. Def / Speed

EGG GROUPS

Water 1

ITEMS SOMETIMES HELD
- None

EVOLUTION

HOW TO OBTAIN

Pokémon Black Version 2	Catch a Palpitoad or Seismitoad, leave it at the Pokémon Day Care, and hatch the Egg that is found
Pokémon White Version 2	Catch a Palpitoad or Seismitoad, leave it at the Pokémon Day Care, and hatch the Egg that is found

HOW TO OBTAIN FROM OTHER GAMES

Pokémon Black Version	Pinwheel Forest Entrance
Pokémon White Version	Pinwheel Forest Entrance

Pokémon AR Marker

LEVEL-UP AND LEARNED MOVES

Lv.	Name	Type	Kind	Pow.	Acc.	PP	Range	Long	DA
1	Bubble	Water	Special	20	100	30	Many Others	—	—
1	Growl	Normal	Status	—	100	40	Many Others	—	—
5	Supersonic	Normal	Status	—	55	20	Normal	—	—
9	Round	Normal	Special	60	100	15	Normal	—	—
12	BubbleBeam	Water	Special	65	100	20	Normal	—	—
16	Mud Shot	Ground	Special	55	95	15	Normal	—	—
20	Aqua Ring	Water	Status	—	—	20	Self	—	—
23	Uproar	Normal	Special	90	100	10	1 Random	—	—
27	Muddy Water	Water	Special	95	85	10	Many Others	—	—
31	Rain Dance	Water	Status	—	—	5	Both Sides	—	—
34	Flail	Normal	Physical	—	100	15	Normal	—	○
38	Echoed Voice	Normal	Special	40	100	15	Normal	—	—
42	Hydro Pump	Water	Special	120	80	5	Normal	—	—
45	Hyper Voice	Normal	Special	90	100	10	Many Others	—	—

TM & HM MOVES

Lv.	Name	Type	Kind	Pow.	Acc.	PP	Range	Long	DA
TM06	Toxic	Poison	Status	—	90	10	Normal	—	—
TM07	Hail	Ice	Status	—	—	10	Both Sides	—	—
TM10	Hidden Power	Normal	Special	—	100	15	Normal	—	—
TM17	Protect	Normal	Status	—	—	10	Self	—	—
TM18	Rain Dance	Water	Status	—	—	5	Both Sides	—	—
TM21	Frustration	Normal	Physical	—	100	20	Normal	—	○
TM27	Return	Normal	Physical	—	100	20	Normal	—	○
TM32	Double Team	Normal	Status	—	—	15	Self	—	—
TM34	Sludge Wave	Poison	Special	95	100	10	Adjacent	—	—
TM36	Sludge Bomb	Poison	Special	90	100	10	Normal	—	—
TM42	Facade	Normal	Physical	70	100	20	Normal	—	○
TM44	Rest	Psychic	Status	—	—	10	Self	—	—
TM45	Attract	Normal	Status	—	100	15	Normal	—	—
TM48	Round	Normal	Special	60	100	15	Normal	—	—
TM49	Echoed Voice	Normal	Special	40	100	15	Normal	—	—
TM55	Scald	Water	Special	80	100	15	Normal	—	—
TM87	Swagger	Normal	Status	—	90	15	Normal	—	—
TM90	Substitute	Normal	Status	—	—	10	Self	—	—
HM03	Surf	Water	Special	95	100	15	Adjacent	—	—

MOVES TAUGHT BY PEOPLE

Name	Type	Kind	Pow.	Acc.	PP	Range	Long	DA

MOVES TAUGHT BY MOVE TUTORS FOR SHARDS

Name	Type	Kind	Pow.	Acc.	PP	Range	Long	DA
Bounce	Flying	Physical	85	85	5	Normal	○	○
Uproar	Normal	Special	90	100	10	1 Random	—	—
Hyper Voice	Normal	Special	90	100	10	Many Others	—	—
Icy Wind	Ice	Special	55	95	15	Many Others	—	—
Earth Power	Ground	Special	90	100	10	Normal	—	—
Snore	Normal	Special	40	100	15	Normal	—	—
Endeavor	Normal	Physical	—	100	5	Normal	—	○
Sleep Talk	Normal	Status	—	—	10	Self	—	—

EGG MOVES

Name	Type	Kind	Pow.	Acc.	PP	Range	Long	DA
Water Pulse	Water	Special	60	100	20	Normal	○	—
Refresh	Normal	Status	—	—	20	Self	—	—
Mud Sport	Ground	Status	—	—	15	Both Sides	—	—
Mud Bomb	Ground	Special	65	85	10	Normal	—	—
Sleep Talk	Normal	Status	—	—	10	Self	—	—
Snore	Normal	Special	40	100	15	Normal	—	—
Mist	Ice	Status	—	—	30	Your Side	—	—
Earth Power	Ground	Special	90	100	10	Normal	—	—

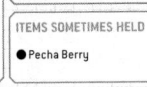

Vibration Pokémon

536 Palpitoad

- HEIGHT: 2'07"
- WEIGHT: 37.5 lbs.
- GENDER: ♂ / ♀

It lives in the water and on land. It uses its long, sticky tongue to immobilize its opponents.

Same form for ♂ / ♀

Pokémon AR Marker

TYPE: Water, Ground

ABILITIES
- Swift Swim
- Hydration

HIDDEN ABILITY
- Water Absorb

STATS
HP
Attack
Defense
Sp. Atk
Sp. Def
Speed

EGG GROUPS
Water ❶

ITEMS SOMETIMES HELD
- Pecha Berry

EVOLUTION

Tympole
Lv. 25
Palpitoad
Lv. 36
Seismitoad

HOW TO OBTAIN

Pokémon Black Version 2	❶ Route 8 (spring, summer, and autumn only) ❷ Icirrus City (spring, summer, and autumn only)
Pokémon White Version 2	❶ Route 8 (spring, summer, and autumn only) ❷ Icirrus City (spring, summer, and autumn only)

HOW TO OBTAIN FROM OTHER GAMES

—

—

LEVEL-UP AND LEARNED MOVES

Lv.	Name	Type	Kind	Pow.	Acc.	PP	Range	Long	DA
1	Bubble	Water	Special	20	100	30	Many Others	—	—
1	Growl	Normal	Status	—	100	40	Many Others	—	—
1	Supersonic	Normal	Status	—	55	20	Normal	—	—
1	Round	Normal	Special	60	100	15	Normal	—	—
5	Supersonic	Normal	Status	—	55	20	Normal	—	—
9	Round	Normal	Special	60	100	15	Normal	—	—
12	BubbleBeam	Water	Special	65	100	20	Normal	—	—
16	Mud Shot	Ground	Special	55	95	15	Normal	—	—
20	Aqua Ring	Water	Status	—	—	20	Self	—	—
23	Uproar	Normal	Special	90	100	10	1 Random	—	—
28	Muddy Water	Water	Special	95	85	10	Many Others	—	—
33	Rain Dance	Water	Status	—	—	5	Both Sides	—	—
37	Flail	Normal	Physical	—	100	15	Normal	—	○
42	Echoed Voice	Normal	Special	40	100	15	Normal	—	—
47	Hydro Pump	Water	Special	120	80	5	Normal	—	—
51	Hyper Voice	Normal	Special	90	100	10	Many Others	—	—

TM & HM MOVES

Lv.	Name	Type	Kind	Pow.	Acc.	PP	Range	Long	DA
TM06	Toxic	Poison	Status	—	90	10	Normal	—	—
TM07	Hail	Ice	Status	—	—	10	Both Sides	—	—
TM10	Hidden Power	Normal	Special	—	100	15	Normal	—	—
TM17	Protect	Normal	Status	—	—	10	Self	—	—
TM18	Rain Dance	Water	Status	—	—	5	Both Sides	—	—
TM21	Frustration	Normal	Physical	—	100	20	Normal	—	○
TM27	Return	Normal	Physical	—	100	20	Normal	—	○
TM32	Double Team	Normal	Status	—	—	15	Self	—	—
TM34	Sludge Wave	Poison	Special	95	100	10	Adjacent	—	—
TM36	Sludge Bomb	Poison	Special	90	100	10	Normal	—	—
TM42	Facade	Normal	Physical	70	100	20	Normal	—	○
TM44	Rest	Psychic	Status	—	—	10	Self	—	—
TM45	Attract	Normal	Status	—	100	15	Normal	—	—
TM48	Round	Normal	Special	60	100	15	Normal	—	—
TM49	Echoed Voice	Normal	Special	40	100	15	Normal	—	—
TM55	Scald	Water	Special	80	100	15	Normal	—	—
TM78	Bulldoze	Ground	Physical	60	100	20	Adjacent	—	—
TM87	Swagger	Normal	Status	—	90	15	Normal	—	—
TM90	Substitute	Normal	Status	—	—	10	Self	—	—
TM94	Rock Smash	Fighting	Physical	40	100	15	Normal	—	○
HM03	Surf	Water	Special	95	100	15	Adjacent	—	—

MOVES TAUGHT BY PEOPLE

Name	Type	Kind	Pow.	Acc.	PP	Range	Long	DA

MOVES TAUGHT BY MOVE TUTORS FOR SHARDS

Name	Type	Kind	Pow.	Acc.	PP	Range	Long	DA
Bounce	Flying	Physical	85	85	5	Normal	○	○
Uproar	Normal	Special	90	100	10	1 Random	—	—
Hyper Voice	Normal	Special	90	100	10	Many Others	—	—
Icy Wind	Ice	Special	55	95	15	Many Others	—	—
Earth Power	Ground	Special	90	100	10	Normal	—	—
Snore	Normal	Special	40	100	15	Normal	—	—
Gastro Acid	Poison	Status	—	100	10	Normal	—	—
Stealth Rock	Rock	Status	—	—	20	Other Side	—	—
Endeavor	Normal	Physical	—	100	5	Normal	—	○
Sleep Talk	Normal	Status	—	—	10	Self	—	—

Vibration Pokémon

537 Seismitoad

- HEIGHT: 4'11"
- WEIGHT: 136.7 lbs.
- GENDER: ♂ / ♀

By putting power into its bumps, it creates vibrations and increases the power of its punches.

Same form for ♂ / ♀

Pokémon AR Marker

TYPE: Water, Ground

ABILITIES
- Swift Swim
- Poison Touch

HIDDEN ABILITY
- Water Absorb

STATS
HP
Attack
Defense
Sp. Atk
Sp. Def
Speed

EGG GROUPS
Water ❶

ITEMS SOMETIMES HELD
- Pecha Berry

EVOLUTION

Tympole
Lv. 25
Palpitoad
Lv. 36
Seismitoad

HOW TO OBTAIN

Pokémon Black Version 2	❶ Route 8 (ripples in water) ❷ Icirrus City (ripples in water)
Pokémon White Version 2	❶ Route 8 (ripples in water) ❷ Icirrus City (ripples in water)

HOW TO OBTAIN FROM OTHER GAMES

—

—

LEVEL-UP AND LEARNED MOVES

Lv.	Name	Type	Kind	Pow.	Acc.	PP	Range	Long	DA
1	Bubble	Water	Special	20	100	30	Many Others	—	—
1	Growl	Normal	Status	—	100	40	Many Others	—	—
1	Supersonic	Normal	Status	—	55	20	Normal	—	—
1	Round	Normal	Special	60	100	15	Normal	—	—
5	Supersonic	Normal	Status	—	55	20	Normal	—	—
9	Round	Normal	Special	60	100	15	Normal	—	—
12	BubbleBeam	Water	Special	65	100	20	Normal	—	—
16	Mud Shot	Ground	Special	55	95	15	Normal	—	—
20	Aqua Ring	Water	Status	—	—	20	Self	—	—
23	Uproar	Normal	Special	90	100	10	1 Random	—	—
28	Muddy Water	Water	Special	95	85	10	Many Others	—	—
33	Rain Dance	Water	Status	—	—	5	Both Sides	—	—
36	Acid	Poison	Special	40	100	30	Many Others	—	—
39	Flail	Normal	Physical	—	100	15	Normal	—	○
44	Drain Punch	Fighting	Physical	75	100	10	Normal	—	○
49	Echoed Voice	Normal	Special	40	100	15	Normal	—	—
53	Hydro Pump	Water	Special	120	80	5	Normal	—	—
59	Hyper Voice	Normal	Special	90	100	10	Many Others	—	—

TM & HM MOVES

Lv.	Name	Type	Kind	Pow.	Acc.	PP	Range	Long	DA
TM06	Toxic	Poison	Status	—	90	10	Normal	—	—
TM07	Hail	Ice	Status	—	—	10	Both Sides	—	—
TM09	Venoshock	Poison	Special	65	100	10	Normal	—	—
TM10	Hidden Power	Normal	Special	—	100	15	Normal	—	—
TM15	Hyper Beam	Normal	Special	150	90	5	Normal	—	—
TM17	Protect	Normal	Status	—	—	10	Self	—	—
TM18	Rain Dance	Water	Status	—	—	5	Both Sides	—	—
TM21	Frustration	Normal	Physical	—	100	20	Normal	—	○
TM26	Earthquake	Ground	Physical	100	100	10	Adjacent	—	—
TM27	Return	Normal	Physical	—	100	20	Normal	—	○
TM28	Dig	Ground	Physical	80	100	10	Normal	—	○
TM31	Brick Break	Fighting	Physical	75	100	15	Normal	—	○
TM32	Double Team	Normal	Status	—	—	15	Self	—	—
TM34	Sludge Wave	Poison	Special	95	100	10	Adjacent	—	—
TM36	Sludge Bomb	Poison	Special	90	100	10	Normal	—	—
TM39	Rock Tomb	Rock	Physical	50	80	10	Normal	—	—
TM42	Facade	Normal	Physical	70	100	20	Normal	—	○
TM44	Rest	Psychic	Status	—	—	10	Self	—	—
TM45	Attract	Normal	Status	—	100	15	Normal	—	—
TM48	Round	Normal	Special	60	100	15	Normal	—	—
TM49	Echoed Voice	Normal	Special	40	100	15	Normal	—	—
TM52	Focus Blast	Fighting	Special	120	70	5	Normal	—	—
TM55	Scald	Water	Special	80	100	15	Normal	—	—
TM56	Fling	Dark	Physical	—	100	10	Normal	—	—
TM66	Payback	Dark	Physical	50	100	10	Normal	—	○
TM68	Giga Impact	Normal	Physical	150	90	5	Normal	—	○
TM78	Bulldoze	Ground	Physical	60	100	20	Adjacent	—	—
TM80	Rock Slide	Rock	Physical	75	90	10	Many Others	—	—
TM84	Poison Jab	Poison	Physical	80	100	20	Normal	—	○
TM86	Grass Knot	Grass	Special	—	100	20	Normal	—	○
TM87	Swagger	Normal	Status	—	90	15	Normal	—	—
TM90	Substitute	Normal	Status	—	—	10	Self	—	—
TM94	Rock Smash	Fighting	Physical	40	100	15	Normal	—	○
HM03	Surf	Water	Special	95	100	15	Adjacent	—	—
HM04	Strength	Normal	Physical	80	100	15	Normal	—	○

MOVES TAUGHT BY PEOPLE

Name	Type	Kind	Pow.	Acc.	PP	Range	Long	DA

MOVES TAUGHT BY MOVE TUTORS FOR SHARDS

Name	Type	Kind	Pow.	Acc.	PP	Range	Long	DA
Bounce	Flying	Physical	85	85	5	Normal	○	○
Uproar	Normal	Special	90	100	10	1 Random	—	—
Low Kick	Fighting	Physical	—	100	20	Normal	—	○
Ice Punch	Ice	Physical	75	100	15	Normal	—	○
Hyper Voice	Normal	Special	90	100	10	Many Others	—	—
Icy Wind	Ice	Special	55	95	15	Many Others	—	—
Earth Power	Ground	Special	90	100	10	Normal	—	—
Snore	Normal	Special	40	100	15	Normal	—	—
Knock Off	Dark	Physical	20	100	20	Normal	—	○
Drain Punch	Fighting	Physical	75	100	10	Normal	—	○
Gastro Acid	Poison	Status	—	100	10	Normal	—	—
Stealth Rock	Rock	Status	—	—	20	Other Side	—	—
Endeavor	Normal	Physical	—	100	5	Normal	—	○
Sleep Talk	Normal	Status	—	—	10	Self	—	—

538 Throh

Judo Pokémon

● HEIGHT: 4'03"
● WEIGHT: 122.4 lbs.
● GENDER: ♂

When it encounters a foe bigger than itself, it wants to throw it. It changes belts as it gets stronger.

♂

TYPE: Fighting

ABILITIES
● Guts
● Inner Focus

HIDDEN ABILITY
—

STATS

HP	■■■■■
Attack	■■■■■
Defense	■■■■
Sp. Atk	■■
Sp. Def	■■■■
Speed	■■■

EGG GROUPS
Human-like

ITEMS SOMETIMES HELD
● Black Belt
● Expert Belt

Pokémon AR Marker

EVOLUTION

Does not evolve

HOW TO OBTAIN

Pokémon Black Version 2	❶ Route 23 (rustling grass) ❷ Victory Road outside ②
Pokémon White Version 2	❶ Route 23 ❷ Victory Road outside ②

HOW TO OBTAIN FROM OTHER GAMES

—

—

LEVEL-UP AND LEARNED MOVES

Lv.	Name	Type	Kind	Pow.	Acc.	PP	Range	Long	DA
1	Bind	Normal	Physical	15	85	20	Normal	—	○
1	Leer	Normal	Status	—	100	30	Many Others	—	—
5	Bide	Normal	Physical	—	—	10	Self	—	○
9	Focus Energy	Normal	Status	—	—	30	Self	—	—
13	Seismic Toss	Fighting	Physical	—	100	20	Normal	—	○
17	Vital Throw	Fighting	Physical	70	—	10	Normal	—	○
21	Revenge	Fighting	Physical	60	100	10	Normal	—	○
25	Storm Throw	Fighting	Physical	40	100	10	Normal	—	○
29	Body Slam	Normal	Physical	85	100	15	Normal	—	○
33	Bulk Up	Fighting	Status	—	—	20	Self	—	—
37	Circle Throw	Fighting	Physical	60	90	10	Normal	—	○
41	Endure	Normal	Status	—	—	10	Self	—	—
45	Wide Guard	Rock	Status	—	—	10	Your Side	—	—
49	Superpower	Fighting	Physical	120	100	5	Normal	—	○
53	Reversal	Fighting	Physical	—	100	15	Normal	—	○

TM & HM MOVES

Lv.	Name	Type	Kind	Pow.	Acc.	PP	Range	Long	DA
TM06	Toxic	Poison	Status	—	90	10	Normal	—	—
TM08	Bulk Up	Fighting	Status	—	—	20	Self	—	—
TM10	Hidden Power	Normal	Special	—	100	15	Normal	—	—
TM11	Sunny Day	Fire	Status	—	—	5	Both Sides	—	—
TM12	Taunt	Dark	Status	—	100	20	Normal	—	—
TM17	Protect	Normal	Status	—	—	10	Self	—	—
TM18	Rain Dance	Water	Status	—	—	5	Both Sides	—	—
TM21	Frustration	Normal	Physical	—	100	20	Normal	—	○
TM26	Earthquake	Ground	Physical	100	100	10	Adjacent	—	—
TM27	Return	Normal	Physical	—	100	20	Normal	—	○
TM28	Dig	Ground	Physical	80	100	10	Normal	—	○
TM31	Brick Break	Fighting	Physical	75	100	15	Normal	—	○
TM32	Double Team	Normal	Status	—	—	15	Self	—	—
TM39	Rock Tomb	Rock	Physical	50	80	10	Normal	—	—
TM42	Facade	Normal	Physical	70	100	20	Normal	—	○
TM44	Rest	Psychic	Status	—	—	10	Self	—	—
TM45	Attract	Normal	Status	—	100	15	Normal	—	—
TM47	Low Sweep	Fighting	Physical	60	100	20	Normal	—	○
TM48	Round	Normal	Special	60	100	15	Normal	—	—
TM52	Focus Blast	Fighting	Special	120	70	5	Normal	—	—
TM56	Fling	Dark	Physical	—	100	10	Normal	—	—
TM66	Payback	Dark	Physical	50	100	10	Normal	—	○
TM67	Retaliate	Normal	Physical	70	100	5	Normal	—	○
TM68	Giga Impact	Normal	Physical	150	90	5	Normal	—	○
TM71	Stone Edge	Rock	Physical	100	80	5	Normal	—	—
TM78	Bulldoze	Ground	Physical	60	100	20	Adjacent	—	—
TM80	Rock Slide	Rock	Physical	75	90	10	Many Others	—	—
TM83	Work Up	Normal	Status	—	—	30	Self	—	—
TM84	Poison Jab	Poison	Physical	80	100	20	Normal	—	○
TM86	Grass Knot	Grass	Special	—	100	20	Normal	—	○
TM87	Swagger	Normal	Status	—	90	15	Normal	—	—
TM90	Substitute	Normal	Status	—	—	10	Self	—	—
TM94	Rock Smash	Fighting	Physical	40	100	15	Normal	—	○
HM04	Strength	Normal	Physical	80	100	15	Normal	—	○

MOVES TAUGHT BY PEOPLE

Name	Type	Kind	Pow.	Acc.	PP	Range	Long	DA

MOVES TAUGHT BY MOVE TUTORS FOR SHARDS

Name	Type	Kind	Pow.	Acc.	PP	Range	Long	DA
Low Kick	Fighting	Physical	—	100	20	Normal	—	○
Fire Punch	Fire	Physical	75	100	15	Normal	—	○
ThunderPunch	Electric	Physical	75	100	15	Normal	—	○
Ice Punch	Ice	Physical	75	100	15	Normal	—	○
Block	Normal	Status	—	—	5	Normal	—	—
Superpower	Fighting	Physical	120	100	5	Normal	—	○
Bind	Normal	Physical	15	85	20	Normal	—	○
Snore	Normal	Special	40	100	15	Normal	—	—
Knock Off	Dark	Physical	20	100	20	Normal	—	○
Pain Split	Normal	Status	—	—	20	Normal	—	—
Helping Hand	Normal	Status	—	—	20	1 Ally	—	—
Sleep Talk	Normal	Status	—	—	10	Self	—	—

EGG MOVES

Name	Type	Kind	Pow.	Acc.	PP	Range	Long	DA

539 Sawk

Karate Pokémon

● HEIGHT: 4'07"
● WEIGHT: 112.4 lbs.
● GENDER: ♂

Desiring the strongest karate chop, they seclude themselves in mountains and train without sleeping.

♂

TYPE: Fighting

ABILITIES
● Sturdy
● Inner Focus

HIDDEN ABILITY
—

STATS

HP	■■■
Attack	■■■■■■■
Defense	■■■
Sp. Atk	■■
Sp. Def	■■■
Speed	■■■■■

EGG GROUPS
Human-like

ITEMS SOMETIMES HELD
● Black Belt
● Expert Belt

Pokémon AR Marker

EVOLUTION

Does not evolve

HOW TO OBTAIN

Pokémon Black Version 2	❶ Route 23 ❷ Victory Road outside ② (rustling grass)
Pokémon White Version 2	❶ Route 23 (rustling grass) ❷ Victory Road outside ② (rustling grass)

HOW TO OBTAIN FROM OTHER GAMES

—

—

LEVEL-UP AND LEARNED MOVES

Lv.	Name	Type	Kind	Pow.	Acc.	PP	Range	Long	DA
1	Rock Smash	Fighting	Physical	40	100	15	Normal	—	○
1	Leer	Normal	Status	—	100	30	Many Others	—	—
5	Bide	Normal	Physical	—	—	10	Self	—	○
9	Focus Energy	Normal	Status	—	—	30	Self	—	—
13	Double Kick	Fighting	Physical	30	100	30	Normal	—	○
17	Low Sweep	Fighting	Physical	60	100	20	Normal	—	○
21	Counter	Fighting	Physical	—	100	20	Varies	—	○
25	Karate Chop	Fighting	Physical	50	100	25	Normal	—	○
29	Brick Break	Fighting	Physical	75	100	15	Normal	—	○
33	Bulk Up	Fighting	Status	—	—	20	Self	—	—
37	Retaliate	Normal	Physical	70	100	5	Normal	—	○
41	Endure	Normal	Status	—	—	10	Self	—	—
45	Quick Guard	Fighting	Status	—	—	15	Your Side	—	—
49	Close Combat	Fighting	Physical	120	100	5	Normal	—	○
53	Reversal	Fighting	Physical	—	100	15	Normal	—	○

TM & HM MOVES

Lv.	Name	Type	Kind	Pow.	Acc.	PP	Range	Long	DA
TM06	Toxic	Poison	Status	—	90	10	Normal	—	—
TM08	Bulk Up	Fighting	Status	—	—	20	Self	—	—
TM10	Hidden Power	Normal	Special	—	100	15	Normal	—	—
TM11	Sunny Day	Fire	Status	—	—	5	Both Sides	—	—
TM12	Taunt	Dark	Status	—	100	20	Normal	—	—
TM17	Protect	Normal	Status	—	—	10	Self	—	—
TM18	Rain Dance	Water	Status	—	—	5	Both Sides	—	—
TM21	Frustration	Normal	Physical	—	100	20	Normal	—	○
TM26	Earthquake	Ground	Physical	100	100	10	Adjacent	—	—
TM27	Return	Normal	Physical	—	100	20	Normal	—	○
TM28	Dig	Ground	Physical	80	100	10	Normal	—	○
TM31	Brick Break	Fighting	Physical	75	100	15	Normal	—	○
TM32	Double Team	Normal	Status	—	—	15	Self	—	—
TM39	Rock Tomb	Rock	Physical	50	80	10	Normal	—	—
TM42	Facade	Normal	Physical	70	100	20	Normal	—	○
TM44	Rest	Psychic	Status	—	—	10	Self	—	—
TM45	Attract	Normal	Status	—	100	15	Normal	—	—
TM47	Low Sweep	Fighting	Physical	60	100	20	Normal	—	○
TM48	Round	Normal	Special	60	100	15	Normal	—	—
TM52	Focus Blast	Fighting	Special	120	70	5	Normal	—	—
TM56	Fling	Dark	Physical	—	100	10	Normal	—	—
TM66	Payback	Dark	Physical	50	100	10	Normal	—	○
TM67	Retaliate	Normal	Physical	70	100	5	Normal	—	○
TM68	Giga Impact	Normal	Physical	150	90	5	Normal	—	○
TM71	Stone Edge	Rock	Physical	100	80	5	Normal	—	—
TM78	Bulldoze	Ground	Physical	60	100	20	Adjacent	—	—
TM80	Rock Slide	Rock	Physical	75	90	10	Many Others	—	—
TM83	Work Up	Normal	Status	—	—	30	Self	—	—
TM84	Poison Jab	Poison	Physical	80	100	20	Normal	—	○
TM86	Grass Knot	Grass	Special	—	100	20	Normal	—	○
TM87	Swagger	Normal	Status	—	90	15	Normal	—	—
TM90	Substitute	Normal	Status	—	—	10	Self	—	—
TM94	Rock Smash	Fighting	Physical	40	100	15	Normal	—	○
HM04	Strength	Normal	Physical	80	100	15	Normal	—	○

MOVES TAUGHT BY PEOPLE

Name	Type	Kind	Pow.	Acc.	PP	Range	Long	DA

MOVES TAUGHT BY MOVE TUTORS FOR SHARDS

Name	Type	Kind	Pow.	Acc.	PP	Range	Long	DA
Dual Chop	Dragon	Physical	40	90	15	Normal	—	○
Low Kick	Fighting	Physical	—	100	20	Normal	—	○
Fire Punch	Fire	Physical	75	100	15	Normal	—	○
ThunderPunch	Electric	Physical	75	100	15	Normal	—	○
Ice Punch	Ice	Physical	75	100	15	Normal	—	○
Block	Normal	Status	—	—	5	Normal	—	—
Superpower	Fighting	Physical	120	100	5	Normal	—	○
Snore	Normal	Special	40	100	15	Normal	—	—
Knock Off	Dark	Physical	20	100	20	Normal	—	○
Pain Split	Normal	Status	—	—	20	Normal	—	—
Helping Hand	Normal	Status	—	—	20	1 Ally	—	—
Sleep Talk	Normal	Status	—	—	10	Self	—	—

EGG MOVES

Name	Type	Kind	Pow.	Acc.	PP	Range	Long	DA

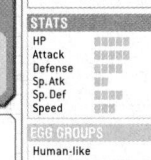

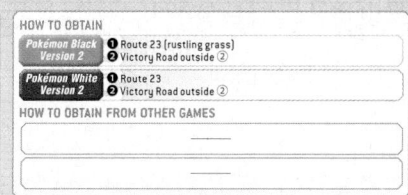

540 Sewaddle

Sewing Pokémon

- HEIGHT: 1'00"
- WEIGHT: 5.5 lbs.
- GENDER: ♂ / ♀

Since this Pokémon makes its own clothes out of leaves, it is a popular mascot for fashion designers.

Same form for ♂ / ♀

TYPE
Bug | Grass

ABILITIES
- Swarm
- Chlorophyll

HIDDEN ABILITY
- Overcoat

STATS
- HP
- Attack
- Defense
- Sp. Atk
- Sp. Def
- Speed

EGG GROUPS
Bug

ITEMS SOMETIMES HELD
- Mental Herb

Pokémon AR Marker

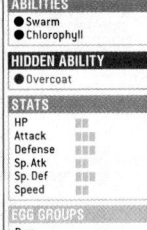 

EVOLUTION

Sewaddle → Lv. 20 → Swadloon → Level up with high friendship → Leavanny

HOW TO OBTAIN

| Pokémon Black Version 2 | ❶ Route 20 ❷ Route 12 |
| Pokémon White Version 2 | ❶ Route 20 ❷ Route 12 |

HOW TO OBTAIN FROM OTHER GAMES

LEVEL-UP AND LEARNED MOVES

Lv.	Name	Type	Kind	Pow.	Acc.	PP	Range	Long	DA
1	Tackle	Normal	Physical	50	100	35	Normal	—	—
1	String Shot	Bug	Status	—	95	40	Many Others	—	—
8	Bug Bite	Bug	Physical	60	100	20	Normal	—	○
15	Razor Leaf	Grass	Physical	55	95	25	Many Others	—	—
22	Struggle Bug	Bug	Special	30	100	20	Many Others	—	—
29	Endure	Normal	Status	—	—	10	Self	—	—
36	Bug Buzz	Bug	Special	90	100	10	Normal	—	—
43	Flail	Normal	Physical	—	100	15	Normal	—	—

TM & HM MOVES

Lv.	Name	Type	Kind	Pow.	Acc.	PP	Range	Long	DA
TM04	Calm Mind	Psychic	Status	—	—	20	Self	—	—
TM06	Toxic	Poison	Status	—	90	10	Normal	—	—
TM10	Hidden Power	Normal	Special	—	100	15	Normal	—	—
TM11	Sunny Day	Fire	Status	—	—	5	Both Sides	—	—
TM16	Light Screen	Psychic	Status	—	—	30	Your Side	—	—
TM17	Protect	Normal	Status	—	—	10	Self	—	—
TM20	Safeguard	Normal	Status	—	—	25	Your Side	—	—
TM21	Frustration	Normal	Physical	—	100	20	Normal	—	○
TM22	SolarBeam	Grass	Special	120	100	10	Normal	—	—
TM27	Return	Normal	Physical	—	100	20	Normal	—	○
TM32	Double Team	Normal	Status	—	—	15	Self	—	—
TM42	Facade	Normal	Physical	70	100	20	Normal	—	○
TM44	Rest	Psychic	Status	—	—	10	Self	—	—
TM45	Attract	Normal	Status	—	100	15	Normal	—	—
TM48	Round	Normal	Special	60	100	15	Normal	—	—
TM53	Energy Ball	Grass	Special	80	100	10	Normal	—	—
TM66	Payback	Dark	Physical	50	100	10	Normal	—	—
TM70	Flash	Normal	Status	—	100	20	Normal	—	—
TM76	Struggle Bug	Bug	Special	30	100	20	Many Others	—	—
TM85	Dream Eater	Psychic	Special	100	100	15	Normal	—	—
TM86	Grass Knot	Grass	Special	—	100	20	Normal	—	—
TM87	Swagger	Normal	Status	—	90	15	Normal	—	—
TM90	Substitute	Normal	Status	—	—	10	Self	—	—
HM01	Cut	Normal	Physical	50	95	30	Normal	—	○

MOVES TAUGHT BY PEOPLE

Name	Type	Kind	Pow.	Acc.	PP	Range	Long	DA

MOVES TAUGHT BY MOVE TUTORS FOR SHARDS

Name	Type	Kind	Pow.	Acc.	PP	Range	Long	DA
Bug Bite	Bug	Physical	60	100	20	Normal	—	○
Signal Beam	Bug	Special	75	100	15	Normal	—	—
Seed Bomb	Grass	Physical	80	100	15	Normal	—	—
Iron Defense	Steel	Status	—	—	15	Self	—	—
Magic Coat	Psychic	Status	—	—	15	Self	—	—
Electroweb	Electric	Special	55	95	15	Many Others	—	—
Snore	Normal	Special	40	100	15	Normal	—	—
Synthesis	Grass	Status	—	—	5	Self	—	—
Giga Drain	Grass	Special	75	100	10	Normal	—	—
Worry Seed	Grass	Status	—	100	10	Normal	—	—
Sleep Talk	Normal	Status	—	—	10	Self	—	—

EGG MOVES

Name	Type	Kind	Pow.	Acc.	PP	Range	Long	DA
Silver Wind	Bug	Special	60	100	5	Normal	—	—
Screech	Normal	Status	—	85	40	Normal	—	—
Razor Wind	Normal	Special	80	100	10	Many Others	—	—
Mind Reader	Normal	Status	—	—	5	Normal	—	—
Agility	Psychic	Status	—	—	30	Self	—	—
Me First	Normal	Status	—	—	20	Varies	—	—
Baton Pass	Normal	Status	—	—	40	Self	—	—
Camouflage	Normal	Status	—	—	20	Self	—	—
Air Slash	Flying	Special	75	95	20	Normal	○	—

---

541 Swadloon

Leaf-Wrapped Pokémon

- HEIGHT: 1'08"
- WEIGHT: 16.1 lbs.
- GENDER: ♂ / ♀

Preferring dark, damp places, it spends the entire day eating fallen leaves that lie around it.

Same form for ♂ / ♀

TYPE
Bug | Grass

ABILITIES
- Leaf Guard
- Chlorophyll

HIDDEN ABILITY
- Overcoat

STATS
- HP
- Attack
- Defense
- Sp. Atk
- Sp. Def
- Speed

EGG GROUPS
Bug

ITEMS SOMETIMES HELD
- Mental Herb

Pokémon AR Marker

EVOLUTION

Sewaddle → Lv. 20 → Swadloon → Level up with high friendship → Leavanny

HOW TO OBTAIN

| Pokémon Black Version 2 | ❶ Lostlorn Forest ❷ Route 6 |
| Pokémon White Version 2 | ❶ Lostlorn Forest ❷ Route 6 |

HOW TO OBTAIN FROM OTHER GAMES

LEVEL-UP AND LEARNED MOVES

Lv.	Name	Type	Kind	Pow.	Acc.	PP	Range	Long	DA
1	GrassWhistle	Grass	Status	—	55	15	Normal	—	—
1	Tackle	Normal	Physical	50	100	35	Normal	—	—
1	String Shot	Bug	Status	—	95	40	Many Others	—	—
1	Bug Bite	Bug	Physical	60	100	20	Normal	—	○
1	Razor Leaf	Grass	Physical	55	95	25	Many Others	—	—
20	Protect	Normal	Status	—	—	10	Self	—	—

TM & HM MOVES

Lv.	Name	Type	Kind	Pow.	Acc.	PP	Range	Long	DA
TM04	Calm Mind	Psychic	Status	—	—	20	Self	—	—
TM06	Toxic	Poison	Status	—	90	10	Normal	—	—
TM10	Hidden Power	Normal	Special	—	100	15	Normal	—	—
TM11	Sunny Day	Fire	Status	—	—	5	Both Sides	—	—
TM16	Light Screen	Psychic	Status	—	—	30	Your Side	—	—
TM17	Protect	Normal	Status	—	—	10	Self	—	—
TM20	Safeguard	Normal	Status	—	—	25	Your Side	—	—
TM21	Frustration	Normal	Physical	—	100	20	Normal	—	○
TM22	SolarBeam	Grass	Special	120	100	10	Normal	—	—
TM27	Return	Normal	Physical	—	100	20	Normal	—	○
TM32	Double Team	Normal	Status	—	—	15	Self	—	—
TM42	Facade	Normal	Physical	70	100	20	Normal	—	○
TM44	Rest	Psychic	Status	—	—	10	Self	—	—
TM45	Attract	Normal	Status	—	100	15	Normal	—	—
TM48	Round	Normal	Special	60	100	15	Normal	—	—
TM53	Energy Ball	Grass	Special	80	100	10	Normal	—	—
TM66	Payback	Dark	Physical	50	100	10	Normal	—	—
TM70	Flash	Normal	Status	—	100	20	Normal	—	—
TM76	Struggle Bug	Bug	Special	30	100	20	Many Others	—	—
TM85	Dream Eater	Psychic	Special	100	100	15	Normal	—	—
TM86	Grass Knot	Grass	Special	—	100	20	Normal	—	—
TM87	Swagger	Normal	Status	—	90	15	Normal	—	—
TM90	Substitute	Normal	Status	—	—	10	Self	—	—
HM01	Cut	Normal	Physical	50	95	30	Normal	—	○

MOVES TAUGHT BY PEOPLE

Name	Type	Kind	Pow.	Acc.	PP	Range	Long	DA

MOVES TAUGHT BY MOVE TUTORS FOR SHARDS

Name	Type	Kind	Pow.	Acc.	PP	Range	Long	DA
Bug Bite	Bug	Physical	60	100	20	Normal	—	○
Signal Beam	Bug	Special	75	100	15	Normal	—	—
Seed Bomb	Grass	Physical	80	100	15	Normal	—	—
Iron Defense	Steel	Status	—	—	15	Self	—	—
Magic Coat	Psychic	Status	—	—	15	Self	—	—
Electroweb	Electric	Special	55	95	15	Many Others	—	—
Snore	Normal	Special	40	100	15	Normal	—	—
Synthesis	Grass	Status	—	—	5	Self	—	—
Giga Drain	Grass	Special	75	100	10	Normal	—	—
Worry Seed	Grass	Status	—	100	10	Normal	—	—
Sleep Talk	Normal	Status	—	—	10	Self	—	—

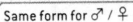

Nurturing Pokémon

542 Leavanny

● HEIGHT: 3'11"
● WEIGHT: 45.2 lbs.
● GENDER: ♂ / ♀

Upon finding a small Pokémon, it weaves clothing for it from leaves by using the sticky silk secreted from its mouth.

Same form for ♂ / ♀

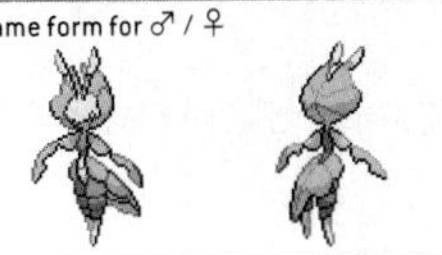

Pokémon AR Marker

TYPE Bug Grass

ABILITIES
● Swarm
● Chlorophyll

HIDDEN ABILITY
● Overcoat

STATS
HP
Attack
Defense
Sp. Atk
Sp. Def
Speed

EGG GROUPS
Bug

ITEMS SOMETIMES HELD
● Mental Herb

EVOLUTION

Sewaddle
Lv. 20
Swadloon
Level up with high friendship
Leavanny

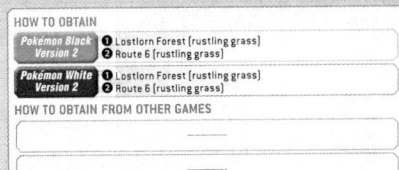

HOW TO OBTAIN

Pokémon Black Version 2	❶ Lostlorn Forest (rustling grass) ❷ Route 6 (rustling grass)
Pokémon White Version 2	❶ Lostlorn Forest (rustling grass) ❷ Route 6 (rustling grass)

HOW TO OBTAIN FROM OTHER GAMES

—

—

LEVEL-UP AND LEARNED MOVES

Lv.	Name	Type	Kind	Pow.	Acc.	PP	Range	Long	DA
1	False Swipe	Normal	Physical	40	100	40	Normal	—	○
1	Tackle	Normal	Physical	50	100	35	Normal	—	○
1	String Shot	Bug	Status	—	95	40	Many Others	—	—
1	Bug Bite	Bug	Physical	60	100	20	Normal	—	○
1	Razor Leaf	Grass	Physical	55	95	25	Many Others	—	—
8	Bug Bite	Bug	Physical	60	100	20	Normal	—	○
15	Razor Leaf	Grass	Physical	55	95	25	Many Others	—	—
22	Struggle Bug	Bug	Special	30	100	20	Many Others	—	—
29	Slash	Normal	Physical	70	100	20	Normal	—	○
32	Helping Hand	Normal	Status	—	—	20	1 Ally	—	—
36	Leaf Blade	Grass	Physical	90	100	15	Normal	—	○
39	X-Scissor	Bug	Physical	80	100	15	Normal	—	○
43	Entrainment	Normal	Status	—	100	15	Normal	—	—
46	Swords Dance	Normal	Status	—	—	30	Self	—	—
50	Leaf Storm	Grass	Special	140	90	5	Normal	—	—

TM & HM MOVES

Lv.	Name	Type	Kind	Pow.	Acc.	PP	Range	Long	DA
TM01	Hone Claws	Dark	Status	—	—	15	Self	—	—
TM04	Calm Mind	Psychic	Status	—	—	20	Self	—	—
TM06	Toxic	Poison	Status	—	90	10	Normal	—	—
TM10	Hidden Power	Normal	Special	—	100	15	Normal	—	—
TM11	Sunny Day	Fire	Status	—	—	5	Both Sides	—	—
TM15	Hyper Beam	Normal	Special	150	90	5	Normal	—	—
TM16	Light Screen	Psychic	Status	—	—	30	Your Side	—	—
TM17	Protect	Normal	Status	—	—	10	Self	—	—
TM20	Safeguard	Normal	Status	—	—	25	Your Side	—	—
TM21	Frustration	Normal	Physical	—	100	20	Normal	—	○
TM22	SolarBeam	Grass	Special	120	100	10	Normal	—	—
TM27	Return	Normal	Physical	—	100	20	Normal	—	○
TM32	Double Team	Normal	Status	—	—	15	Self	—	—
TM33	Reflect	Psychic	Status	—	—	20	Your Side	—	—
TM40	Aerial Ace	Flying	Physical	60	—	20	Normal	○	○
TM42	Facade	Normal	Physical	70	100	20	Normal	—	○
TM44	Rest	Psychic	Status	—	—	10	Self	—	—
TM45	Attract	Normal	Status	—	100	15	Normal	—	—
TM48	Round	Normal	Special	60	100	15	Normal	—	—
TM53	Energy Ball	Grass	Special	80	100	10	Normal	—	—
TM54	False Swipe	Normal	Physical	40	100	40	Normal	—	○
TM65	Shadow Claw	Ghost	Physical	70	100	15	Normal	—	○
TM66	Payback	Dark	Physical	50	100	10	Normal	—	○
TM67	Retaliate	Normal	Physical	70	100	5	Normal	—	○
TM68	Giga Impact	Normal	Physical	150	90	5	Normal	—	○
TM70	Flash	Normal	Status	—	100	20	Normal	—	—
TM75	Swords Dance	Normal	Status	—	—	30	Self	—	—
TM76	Struggle Bug	Bug	Special	30	100	20	Many Others	—	—
TM81	X-Scissor	Bug	Physical	80	100	15	Normal	—	○
TM84	Poison Jab	Poison	Physical	80	100	20	Normal	—	○
TM85	Dream Eater	Psychic	Special	100	100	15	Normal	—	—
TM86	Grass Knot	Grass	Special	—	100	20	Normal	—	○
TM87	Swagger	Normal	Status	—	90	15	Normal	—	—
TM90	Substitute	Normal	Status	—	—	10	Self	—	—
HM01	Cut	Normal	Physical	50	95	30	Normal	—	○

MOVES TAUGHT BY PEOPLE

Name	Type	Kind	Pow.	Acc.	PP	Range	Long	DA

MOVES TAUGHT BY MOVE TUTORS FOR SHARDS

Name	Type	Kind	Pow.	Acc.	PP	Range	Long	DA
Bug Bite	Bug	Physical	60	100	20	Normal	—	○
Signal Beam	Bug	Special	75	100	15	Normal	—	—
Seed Bomb	Grass	Physical	80	100	15	Normal	—	—
Iron Defense	Steel	Status	—	—	15	Self	—	—
Magic Coat	Psychic	Status	—	—	15	Self	—	—
Electroweb	Electric	Special	55	95	15	Many Others	—	—
Snore	Normal	Special	40	100	15	Normal	—	—
Heal Bell	Normal	Status	—	—	5	Your Party	—	—
Knock Off	Dark	Physical	20	100	20	Normal	—	○
Synthesis	Grass	Status	—	—	5	Self	—	—
Giga Drain	Grass	Special	75	100	10	Normal	—	—
Worry Seed	Grass	Status	—	100	10	Normal	—	—
Helping Hand	Normal	Status	—	—	20	1 Ally	—	—
Sleep Talk	Normal	Status	—	—	10	Self	—	—

Centipede Pokémon

543 Venipede

● HEIGHT: 1'04"
● WEIGHT: 11.7 lbs.
● GENDER: ♂ / ♀

Using the feelers on its head and tail, it picks up vibrations in the air to determine its prey's location and state.

Same form for ♂ / ♀

Pokémon AR Marker

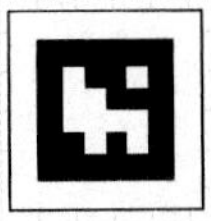

TYPE Bug Poison

ABILITIES
● Poison Point
● Swarm

HIDDEN ABILITY
● Quick Feet

STATS
HP
Attack
Defense
Sp. Atk
Sp. Def
Speed

EGG GROUPS
Bug

ITEMS SOMETIMES HELD
● Poison Barb

EVOLUTION

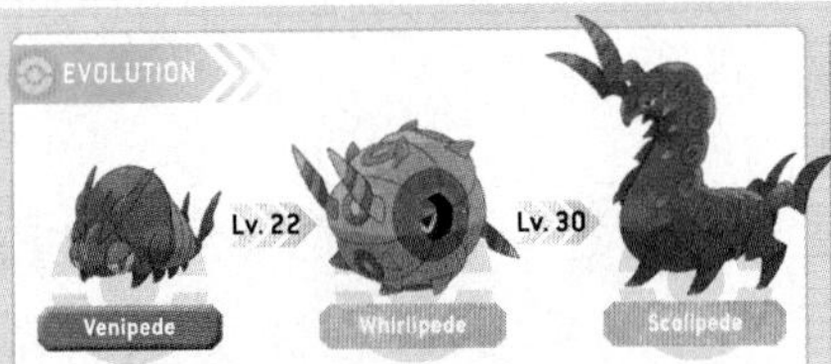
Venipede
Lv. 22
Whirlipede
Lv. 30
Scolipede

HOW TO OBTAIN

Pokémon Black Version 2	❶ Lostlorn Forest ❷ Route 20 (dark grass)
Pokémon White Version 2	❶ Lostlorn Forest ❷ Route 20 (dark grass)

HOW TO OBTAIN FROM OTHER GAMES

—

—

LEVEL-UP AND LEARNED MOVES

Lv.	Name	Type	Kind	Pow.	Acc.	PP	Range	Long	DA
1	Defense Curl	Normal	Status	—	—	40	Self	—	—
1	Rollout	Rock	Physical	30	90	20	Normal	—	○
5	Poison Sting	Poison	Physical	15	100	35	Normal	—	—
8	Screech	Normal	Status	—	85	40	Normal	—	—
12	Pursuit	Dark	Physical	40	100	20	Normal	—	○
15	Protect	Normal	Status	—	—	10	Self	—	—
19	Poison Tail	Poison	Physical	50	100	25	Normal	—	○
22	Bug Bite	Bug	Physical	60	100	20	Normal	—	○
26	Venoshock	Poison	Special	65	100	10	Normal	—	—
29	Agility	Psychic	Status	—	—	30	Self	—	—
33	Steamroller	Bug	Physical	65	100	20	Normal	—	○
36	Toxic	Poison	Status	—	90	10	Normal	—	—
40	Rock Climb	Normal	Physical	90	85	20	Normal	—	○
43	Double-Edge	Normal	Physical	120	100	15	Normal	—	○

TM & HM MOVES

Lv.	Name	Type	Kind	Pow.	Acc.	PP	Range	Long	DA
TM06	Toxic	Poison	Status	—	90	10	Normal	—	—
TM09	Venoshock	Poison	Special	65	100	10	Normal	—	—
TM10	Hidden Power	Normal	Special	—	100	15	Normal	—	—
TM11	Sunny Day	Fire	Status	—	—	5	Both Sides	—	—
TM17	Protect	Normal	Status	—	—	10	Self	—	—
TM21	Frustration	Normal	Physical	—	100	20	Normal	—	○
TM22	SolarBeam	Grass	Special	120	100	10	Normal	—	—
TM27	Return	Normal	Physical	—	100	20	Normal	—	○
TM32	Double Team	Normal	Status	—	—	15	Self	—	—
TM36	Sludge Bomb	Poison	Special	90	100	10	Normal	—	—
TM42	Facade	Normal	Physical	70	100	20	Normal	—	○
TM44	Rest	Psychic	Status	—	—	10	Self	—	—
TM45	Attract	Normal	Status	—	100	15	Normal	—	—
TM48	Round	Normal	Special	60	100	15	Normal	—	—
TM66	Payback	Dark	Physical	50	100	10	Normal	—	○
TM74	Gyro Ball	Steel	Physical	—	100	5	Normal	—	○
TM76	Struggle Bug	Bug	Special	30	100	20	Many Others	—	—
TM84	Poison Jab	Poison	Physical	80	100	20	Normal	—	○
TM87	Swagger	Normal	Status	—	90	15	Normal	—	—
TM90	Substitute	Normal	Status	—	—	10	Self	—	—
TM94	Rock Smash	Fighting	Physical	40	100	15	Normal	—	○

MOVES TAUGHT BY PEOPLE

Name	Type	Kind	Pow.	Acc.	PP	Range	Long	DA

MOVES TAUGHT BY MOVE TUTORS FOR SHARDS

Name	Type	Kind	Pow.	Acc.	PP	Range	Long	DA
Bug Bite	Bug	Physical	60	100	20	Normal	—	○
Iron Defense	Steel	Status	—	—	15	Self	—	—
Snore	Normal	Special	40	100	15	Normal	—	—
Endeavor	Normal	Physical	—	100	5	Normal	—	○
Sleep Talk	Normal	Status	—	—	10	Self	—	—

EGG MOVES

Name	Type	Kind	Pow.	Acc.	PP	Range	Long	DA
Twineedle	Bug	Physical	25	100	20	Normal	—	—
Pin Missile	Bug	Physical	14	85	20	Normal	—	—
Toxic Spikes	Poison	Status	—	—	20	Other Side	—	—
Spikes	Ground	Status	—	—	20	Other Side	—	—
Take Down	Normal	Physical	90	85	20	Normal	—	○
Rock Climb	Normal	Physical	90	85	20	Normal	—	○

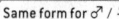

544 Whirlipede
Curlipede Pokémon

- HEIGHT: 3'11"
- WEIGHT: 129.0 lbs.
- GENDER: ♂ / ♀

Storing energy for evolution, it sits. But, when predators approach, it moves to stab them with poison spikes.

Same form for ♂ / ♀

Pokémon AR Marker

TYPE
Bug | Poison

ABILITIES
- Poison Point
- Swarm

HIDDEN ABILITY
- Quick Feet

STATS
- HP
- Attack
- Defense
- Sp. Atk
- Sp. Def
- Speed

EGG GROUPS
Bug

ITEMS SOMETIMES HELD
- Poison Barb

EVOLUTION
Venipede → Lv. 22 → Whirlipede → Lv. 30 → Scolipede

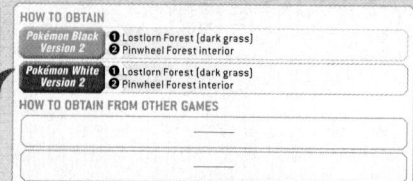

HOW TO OBTAIN
Pokémon Black Version 2	❶ Lostlorn Forest (dark grass) ❷ Pinwheel Forest interior
Pokémon White Version 2	❶ Lostlorn Forest (dark grass) ❷ Pinwheel Forest interior

HOW TO OBTAIN FROM OTHER GAMES

LEVEL-UP AND LEARNED MOVES
Lv.	Name	Type	Kind	Pow.	Acc.	PP	Range	Long	DA
1	Defense Curl	Normal	Status	—	—	40	Self	—	—
1	Rollout	Rock	Physical	30	90	20	Normal	—	○
1	Poison Sting	Poison	Physical	15	100	35	Normal	—	—
1	Screech	Normal	Status	—	85	40	Normal	—	—
5	Poison Sting	Poison	Physical	15	100	35	Normal	—	—
8	Screech	Normal	Status	—	85	40	Normal	—	—
12	Pursuit	Dark	Physical	40	100	20	Normal	—	—
15	Protect	Normal	Status	—	—	10	Self	—	—
19	Poison Tail	Poison	Physical	50	100	25	Normal	—	—
22	Iron Defense	Steel	Status	—	—	15	Self	—	—
23	Bug Bite	Bug	Physical	60	100	20	Normal	—	○
28	Venoshock	Poison	Special	65	100	10	Normal	—	—
32	Agility	Psychic	Status	—	—	30	Self	—	—
37	Steamroller	Bug	Physical	65	100	20	Normal	—	○
41	Toxic	Poison	Status	—	90	10	Normal	—	—
46	Rock Climb	Normal	Physical	90	85	20	Normal	—	○
50	Double-Edge	Normal	Physical	120	100	15	Normal	—	—

TM & HM MOVES
Lv.	Name	Type	Kind	Pow.	Acc.	PP	Range	Long	DA
TM06	Toxic	Poison	Status	—	90	10	Normal	—	—
TM09	Venoshock	Poison	Special	65	100	10	Normal	—	—
TM10	Hidden Power	Normal	Special	—	100	15	Normal	—	—
TM11	Sunny Day	Fire	Status	—	—	5	Both Sides	—	—
TM17	Protect	Normal	Status	—	—	10	Self	—	—
TM21	Frustration	Normal	Physical	—	100	20	Normal	—	○
TM22	SolarBeam	Grass	Special	120	100	10	Normal	—	—
TM27	Return	Normal	Physical	—	100	20	Normal	—	○
TM32	Double Team	Normal	Status	—	—	15	Self	—	—
TM36	Sludge Bomb	Poison	Special	90	100	10	Normal	—	—
TM42	Facade	Normal	Physical	70	100	20	Normal	—	—
TM44	Rest	Psychic	Status	—	—	10	Self	—	—
TM45	Attract	Normal	Status	—	100	15	Normal	—	—
TM48	Round	Normal	Special	60	100	15	Normal	—	—
TM66	Payback	Dark	Physical	50	100	10	Normal	—	—
TM74	Gyro Ball	Steel	Physical	—	100	5	Normal	—	—
TM76	Struggle Bug	Bug	Special	30	100	20	Many Others	—	—
TM84	Poison Jab	Poison	Physical	80	100	20	Normal	—	—
TM87	Swagger	Normal	Status	—	90	15	Normal	—	—
TM90	Substitute	Normal	Status	—	—	10	Self	—	—
TM94	Rock Smash	Fighting	Physical	40	100	15	Normal	—	○

MOVES TAUGHT BY PEOPLE
Name	Type	Kind	Pow.	Acc.	PP	Range	Long	DA

MOVES TAUGHT BY MOVE TUTORS FOR SHARDS
Name	Type	Kind	Pow.	Acc.	PP	Range	Long	DA
Bug Bite	Bug	Physical	60	100	20	Normal	—	○
Iron Defense	Steel	Status	—	—	15	Self	—	—
Snore	Normal	Special	40	100	15	Normal	—	—
Endeavor	Normal	Physical	—	100	5	Normal	—	○
Sleep Talk	Normal	Status	—	—	10	Self	—	—

545 Scolipede
Megapede Pokémon

- HEIGHT: 8'02"
- WEIGHT: 442.0 lbs.
- GENDER: ♂ / ♀

It clasps its prey with the claws on its neck until it stops moving. Then it finishes it off with deadly poison.

Same form for ♂ / ♀

Pokémon AR Marker

TYPE
Bug | Poison

ABILITIES
- Poison Point
- Swarm

HIDDEN ABILITY
- Quick Feet

STATS
- HP
- Attack
- Defense
- Sp. Atk
- Sp. Def
- Speed

EGG GROUPS
Bug

ITEMS SOMETIMES HELD
- Poison Barb

EVOLUTION

Venipede → Lv. 22 → Whirlipede → Lv. 30 → Scolipede

HOW TO OBTAIN
Pokémon Black Version 2	Pinwheel Forest interior (rustling grass)
Pokémon White Version 2	Pinwheel Forest interior (rustling grass)

HOW TO OBTAIN FROM OTHER GAMES

LEVEL-UP AND LEARNED MOVES
Lv.	Name	Type	Kind	Pow.	Acc.	PP	Range	Long	DA
1	Megahorn	Bug	Physical	120	85	10	Normal	—	○
1	Defense Curl	Normal	Status	—	—	40	Self	—	—
1	Rollout	Rock	Physical	30	90	20	Normal	—	○
1	Poison Sting	Poison	Physical	15	100	35	Normal	—	—
1	Screech	Normal	Status	—	85	40	Normal	—	—
5	Poison Sting	Poison	Physical	15	100	35	Normal	—	—
8	Screech	Normal	Status	—	85	40	Normal	—	—
12	Pursuit	Dark	Physical	40	100	20	Normal	—	—
15	Protect	Normal	Status	—	—	10	Self	—	—
19	Poison Tail	Poison	Physical	50	100	25	Normal	—	—
23	Bug Bite	Bug	Physical	60	100	20	Normal	—	○
28	Venoshock	Poison	Special	65	100	10	Normal	—	—
30	Baton Pass	Normal	Status	—	—	40	Self	—	—
33	Agility	Psychic	Status	—	—	30	Self	—	—
39	Steamroller	Bug	Physical	65	100	20	Normal	—	○
44	Toxic	Poison	Status	—	90	10	Normal	—	—
50	Rock Climb	Normal	Physical	90	85	20	Normal	—	○
55	Double-Edge	Normal	Physical	120	100	15	Normal	—	—

TM & HM MOVES
Lv.	Name	Type	Kind	Pow.	Acc.	PP	Range	Long	DA
TM06	Toxic	Poison	Status	—	90	10	Normal	—	—
TM09	Venoshock	Poison	Special	65	100	10	Normal	—	—
TM10	Hidden Power	Normal	Special	—	100	15	Normal	—	—
TM11	Sunny Day	Fire	Status	—	—	5	Both Sides	—	—
TM15	Hyper Beam	Normal	Special	150	90	5	Normal	—	—
TM17	Protect	Normal	Status	—	—	10	Self	—	—
TM21	Frustration	Normal	Physical	—	100	20	Normal	—	○
TM22	SolarBeam	Grass	Special	120	100	10	Normal	—	—
TM26	Earthquake	Ground	Physical	100	100	10	Adjacent	—	—
TM27	Return	Normal	Physical	—	100	20	Normal	—	○
TM28	Dig	Ground	Physical	80	100	10	Normal	—	○
TM32	Double Team	Normal	Status	—	—	15	Self	—	—
TM36	Sludge Bomb	Poison	Special	90	100	10	Normal	—	—
TM39	Rock Tomb	Rock	Physical	50	80	10	Normal	—	—
TM42	Facade	Normal	Physical	70	100	20	Normal	—	—
TM44	Rest	Psychic	Status	—	—	10	Self	—	—
TM45	Attract	Normal	Status	—	100	15	Normal	—	—
TM48	Round	Normal	Special	60	100	15	Normal	—	—
TM66	Payback	Dark	Physical	50	100	10	Normal	—	—
TM68	Giga Impact	Normal	Physical	150	90	5	Normal	—	—
TM74	Gyro Ball	Steel	Physical	—	100	5	Normal	—	—
TM75	Swords Dance	Normal	Status	—	—	30	Self	—	—
TM76	Struggle Bug	Bug	Special	30	100	20	Many Others	—	—
TM78	Bulldoze	Ground	Physical	60	100	20	Adjacent	—	—
TM80	Rock Slide	Rock	Physical	75	90	10	Many Others	—	—
TM81	X-Scissor	Bug	Physical	80	100	15	Normal	—	—
TM84	Poison Jab	Poison	Physical	80	100	20	Normal	—	—
TM87	Swagger	Normal	Status	—	90	15	Normal	—	—
TM90	Substitute	Normal	Status	—	—	10	Self	—	—
TM94	Rock Smash	Fighting	Physical	40	100	15	Normal	—	○
HM01	Cut	Normal	Physical	50	95	30	Normal	—	—
HM04	Strength	Normal	Physical	80	100	15	Normal	—	—

MOVES TAUGHT BY PEOPLE
Name	Type	Kind	Pow.	Acc.	PP	Range	Long	DA

MOVES TAUGHT BY MOVE TUTORS FOR SHARDS
Name	Type	Kind	Pow.	Acc.	PP	Range	Long	DA
Bug Bite	Bug	Physical	60	100	20	Normal	—	○
Iron Defense	Steel	Status	—	—	15	Self	—	—
Iron Tail	Steel	Physical	100	75	15	Normal	—	—
Aqua Tail	Water	Physical	90	90	10	Normal	—	—
Superpower	Fighting	Physical	120	100	5	Normal	—	—
Snore	Normal	Special	40	100	15	Normal	—	—
Endeavor	Normal	Physical	—	100	5	Normal	—	○
Sleep Talk	Normal	Status	—	—	10	Self	—	—
Snatch	Dark	Status	—	—	10	Self	—	—

546 Cottonee
Cotton Puff Pokémon

- HEIGHT: 1'00"
- WEIGHT: 1.3 lbs.
- GENDER: ♂ / ♀

Perhaps because they feel more at ease in a group, they stick to others they find. They end up looking like a cloud.

Same form for ♂ / ♀

Pokémon AR Marker

TYPE
Grass

ABILITIES
- Prankster
- Infiltrator

HIDDEN ABILITY
- Chlorophyll

STATS
HP	
Attack	
Defense	
Sp. Atk	
Sp. Def	
Speed	

EGG GROUPS
Grass/Fairy

ITEMS SOMETIMES HELD
- None

EVOLUTION
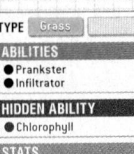

Cottonee → (Use Sun Stone) → Whimsicott

HOW TO OBTAIN

| Pokémon Black Version 2 | ① Castelia City empty lot ② Lostlorn Forest |
| Pokémon White Version 2 | Trade a Petilil to the boy on Route 4 |

HOW TO OBTAIN FROM OTHER GAMES

LEVEL-UP AND LEARNED MOVES
Lv.	Name	Type	Kind	Pow.	Acc.	PP	Range	Long	DA
1	Absorb	Grass	Special	20	100	25	Normal	—	—
4	Growth	Normal	Status	—	—	40	Self	—	—
8	Leech Seed	Grass	Status	—	90	10	Normal	—	—
10	Stun Spore	Grass	Status	—	75	30	Normal	—	—
13	Mega Drain	Grass	Special	40	100	15	Normal	—	—
17	Cotton Spore	Grass	Status	—	100	40	Many Others	—	—
19	Razor Leaf	Grass	Physical	55	95	25	Many Others	—	—
22	PoisonPowder	Poison	Status	—	75	35	Normal	—	—
26	Giga Drain	Grass	Special	75	100	10	Normal	—	—
28	Charm	Normal	Status	—	100	20	Normal	—	—
31	Helping Hand	Normal	Status	—	—	20	1 Ally	—	—
35	Energy Ball	Grass	Special	80	100	10	Normal	—	—
37	Cotton Guard	Grass	Status	—	—	10	Self	—	—
40	Sunny Day	Fire	Status	—	—	5	Both Sides	—	—
44	Endeavor	Normal	Physical	—	100	5	Normal	—	○
46	SolarBeam	Grass	Special	120	100	10	Normal	—	—

TM & HM MOVES
Lv.	Name	Type	Kind	Pow.	Acc.	PP	Range	Long	DA
TM06	Toxic	Poison	Status	—	90	10	Normal	—	—
TM10	Hidden Power	Normal	Special	—	100	15	Normal	—	—
TM11	Sunny Day	Fire	Status	—	—	5	Both Sides	—	—
TM12	Taunt	Dark	Status	—	100	20	Normal	—	—
TM17	Protect	Normal	Status	—	—	10	Self	—	—
TM20	Safeguard	Normal	Status	—	—	25	Your Side	—	—
TM21	Frustration	Normal	Physical	—	100	20	Normal	—	○
TM22	SolarBeam	Grass	Special	120	100	10	Normal	—	—
TM27	Return	Normal	Physical	—	100	20	Normal	—	○
TM32	Double Team	Normal	Status	—	—	15	Self	—	—
TM42	Facade	Normal	Physical	70	100	20	Normal	—	—
TM44	Rest	Psychic	Status	—	—	10	Self	—	—
TM45	Attract	Normal	Status	—	100	15	Normal	—	—
TM48	Round	Normal	Special	60	100	15	Normal	—	—
TM53	Energy Ball	Grass	Special	80	100	10	Normal	—	—
TM70	Flash	Normal	Status	—	100	20	Normal	—	—
TM85	Dream Eater	Psychic	Special	100	100	15	Normal	—	○
TM86	Grass Knot	Grass	Special	—	100	20	Normal	—	—
TM87	Swagger	Normal	Status	—	90	15	Normal	—	—
TM90	Substitute	Normal	Status	—	—	10	Self	—	—

MOVES TAUGHT BY PEOPLE
Name	Type	Kind	Pow.	Acc.	PP	Range	Long	DA

MOVES TAUGHT BY MOVE TUTORS FOR SHARDS
Name	Type	Kind	Pow.	Acc.	PP	Range	Long	DA
Covet	Normal	Physical	60	100	40	Normal	—	○
Seed Bomb	Grass	Physical	80	100	15	Normal	—	—
Snore	Normal	Special	40	100	15	Normal	—	—
Knock Off	Dark	Physical	20	100	20	Normal	—	○
Giga Drain	Grass	Special	75	100	10	Normal	—	—
Tailwind	Flying	Status	—	—	30	Your Side	—	—
Worry Seed	Grass	Status	—	100	10	Normal	—	—
Helping Hand	Normal	Status	—	—	20	1 Ally	—	—
Endeavor	Normal	Physical	—	100	5	Normal	—	—
Sleep Talk	Normal	Status	—	—	10	Self	—	—

EGG MOVES
Name	Type	Kind	Pow.	Acc.	PP	Range	Long	DA
Natural Gift	Normal	Physical	—	100	15	Normal	—	—
Encore	Normal	Status	—	100	5	Normal	—	—
Tickle	Normal	Status	—	100	20	Normal	—	—
Fake Tears	Dark	Status	—	100	20	Normal	—	—
GrassWhistle	Grass	Status	—	55	15	Normal	—	—
Memento	Dark	Status	—	100	10	Normal	—	—
Beat Up	Dark	Physical	—	100	10	Normal	—	—
Switcheroo	Dark	Status	—	100	10	Normal	—	—
Worry Seed	Grass	Status	—	100	10	Normal	—	—

---

547 Whimsicott
Windveiled Pokémon

- HEIGHT: 2'04"
- WEIGHT: 14.6 lbs.
- GENDER: ♂ / ♀

They appear along with whirlwinds. They pull pranks, such as moving furniture and leaving balls of cotton in homes.

Same form for ♂ / ♀

Pokémon AR Marker

TYPE
Grass

ABILITIES
- Prankster
- Infiltrator

HIDDEN ABILITY
- Chlorophyll

STATS
HP	
Attack	
Defense	
Sp. Atk	
Sp. Def	
Speed	

EGG GROUPS
Grass/Fairy

ITEMS SOMETIMES HELD
- None

EVOLUTION
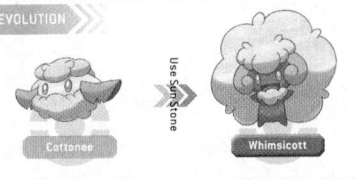

Cottonee → (Use Sun Stone) → Whimsicott

HOW TO OBTAIN
| Pokémon Black Version 2 | ① Castelia City empty lot (rustling grass) ② Lostlorn Forest (rustling grass) |
| Pokémon White Version 2 | Use Sun Stone on Cottonee |

HOW TO OBTAIN FROM OTHER GAMES

LEVEL-UP AND LEARNED MOVES
Lv.	Name	Type	Kind	Pow.	Acc.	PP	Range	Long	DA
1	Growth	Normal	Status	—	—	40	Self	—	—
1	Leech Seed	Grass	Status	—	90	10	Normal	—	—
1	Mega Drain	Grass	Special	40	100	15	Normal	—	—
1	Cotton Spore	Grass	Status	—	100	40	Normal	—	—
10	Gust	Flying	Special	40	100	35	Normal	—	—
28	Tailwind	Flying	Status	—	—	30	Your Side	—	—
46	Hurricane	Flying	Special	120	70	10	Normal	—	—

TM & HM MOVES
Lv.	Name	Type	Kind	Pow.	Acc.	PP	Range	Long	DA
TM06	Toxic	Poison	Status	—	90	10	Normal	—	—
TM10	Hidden Power	Normal	Special	—	100	15	Normal	—	—
TM11	Sunny Day	Fire	Status	—	—	5	Both Sides	—	—
TM12	Taunt	Dark	Status	—	100	20	Normal	—	—
TM15	Hyper Beam	Normal	Special	150	90	5	Normal	—	—
TM16	Light Screen	Psychic	Status	—	—	30	Your Side	—	—
TM17	Protect	Normal	Status	—	—	10	Self	—	—
TM20	Safeguard	Normal	Status	—	—	25	Your Side	—	—
TM21	Frustration	Normal	Physical	—	100	20	Normal	—	○
TM22	SolarBeam	Grass	Special	120	100	10	Normal	—	—
TM27	Return	Normal	Physical	—	100	20	Normal	—	○
TM29	Psychic	Psychic	Special	90	100	10	Normal	—	—
TM30	Shadow Ball	Ghost	Special	80	100	15	Normal	—	—
TM32	Double Team	Normal	Status	—	—	15	Self	—	—
TM42	Facade	Normal	Physical	70	100	20	Normal	—	—
TM44	Rest	Psychic	Status	—	—	10	Self	—	—
TM45	Attract	Normal	Status	—	100	15	Normal	—	—
TM46	Thief	Dark	Physical	40	100	10	Normal	—	○
TM48	Round	Normal	Special	60	100	15	Normal	—	—
TM53	Energy Ball	Grass	Special	80	100	10	Normal	—	—
TM56	Fling	Dark	Physical	—	100	10	Normal	—	○
TM68	Giga Impact	Normal	Physical	150	90	5	Normal	—	○
TM70	Flash	Normal	Status	—	100	20	Normal	—	—
TM85	Dream Eater	Psychic	Special	100	100	15	Normal	—	○
TM86	Grass Knot	Grass	Special	—	100	20	Normal	—	—
TM87	Swagger	Normal	Status	—	90	15	Normal	—	—
TM89	U-turn	Bug	Physical	70	100	20	Normal	—	○
TM90	Substitute	Normal	Status	—	—	10	Self	—	—
TM92	Trick Room	Psychic	Status	—	—	5	Both Sides	—	—

MOVES TAUGHT BY PEOPLE
Name	Type	Kind	Pow.	Acc.	PP	Range	Long	DA

MOVES TAUGHT BY MOVE TUTORS FOR SHARDS
Name	Type	Kind	Pow.	Acc.	PP	Range	Long	DA
Covet	Normal	Physical	60	100	40	Normal	—	○
Seed Bomb	Grass	Physical	80	100	15	Normal	—	—
Snore	Normal	Special	40	100	15	Normal	—	—
Knock Off	Dark	Physical	20	100	20	Normal	—	○
Giga Drain	Grass	Special	75	100	10	Normal	—	—
Tailwind	Flying	Status	—	—	30	Your Side	—	—
Worry Seed	Grass	Status	—	100	10	Normal	—	—
Helping Hand	Normal	Status	—	—	20	1 Ally	—	—
Endeavor	Normal	Physical	—	100	5	Normal	—	—
Sleep Talk	Normal	Status	—	—	10	Self	—	—

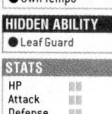 548 Petilil
Bulb Pokémon

TYPE Grass

ABILITIES
- Chlorophyll
- Own Tempo

HIDDEN ABILITY
- Leaf Guard

- HEIGHT: 1'08"
- WEIGHT: 14.6 lbs.
- GENDER: ♀

The leaves on its head grow right back even if they fall out. These bitter leaves refresh those who eat them.

STATS
- HP
- Attack
- Defense
- Sp. Atk
- Sp. Def
- Speed

EGG GROUPS
Grass

ITEMS SOMETIMES HELD
- None

♀

⚙ EVOLUTION

Petilil — Use Sun Stone → Lilligant

HOW TO OBTAIN

Pokémon Black Version 2	Trade a Cottonee to the girl on Route 4
Pokémon White Version 2	❶ Castelia City empty lot ❷ Lostlorn Forest

HOW TO OBTAIN FROM OTHER GAMES

▌ LEVEL-UP AND LEARNED MOVES ▌

Lv.	Name	Type	Kind	Pow.	Acc.	PP	Range	Long	DA
1	Absorb	Grass	Special	20	100	25	Normal	—	—
4	Growth	Normal	Status	—	—	40	Self	—	—
8	Leech Seed	Grass	Status	—	90	10	Normal	—	—
10	Sleep Powder	Grass	Status	—	75	15	Normal	—	—
13	Mega Drain	Grass	Special	40	100	15	Normal	—	—
17	Synthesis	Grass	Status	—	—	5	Self	—	—
19	Magical Leaf	Grass	Special	60	—	20	Normal	—	—
22	Stun Spore	Grass	Status	—	75	30	Normal	—	—
25	Giga Drain	Grass	Special	75	100	10	Normal	—	—
28	Aromatherapy	Grass	Status	—	—	5	Your Party	—	—
31	Helping Hand	Normal	Status	—	—	20	1 Ally	—	—
35	Energy Ball	Grass	Special	80	100	10	Normal	—	—
37	Entrainment	Normal	Status	—	100	15	Normal	—	—
40	Sunny Day	Fire	Status	—	—	5	Both Sides	—	—
44	After You	Normal	Status	—	—	15	Normal	—	—
46	Leaf Storm	Grass	Special	140	90	5	Normal	—	—

▌ TM & HM MOVES ▌

Lv.	Name	Type	Kind	Pow.	Acc.	PP	Range	Long	DA
TM06	Toxic	Poison	Status	—	90	10	Normal	—	—
TM10	Hidden Power	Normal	Special	—	100	15	Normal	—	—
TM11	Sunny Day	Fire	Status	—	—	5	Both Sides	—	—
TM17	Protect	Normal	Status	—	—	10	Self	—	—
TM20	Safeguard	Normal	Status	—	—	25	Your Side	—	—
TM21	Frustration	Normal	Physical	—	100	20	Normal	—	○
TM22	SolarBeam	Grass	Special	120	100	10	Normal	—	—
TM27	Return	Normal	Physical	—	100	20	Normal	—	○
TM32	Double Team	Normal	Status	—	—	15	Self	—	—
TM42	Facade	Normal	Physical	70	100	20	Normal	—	○
TM44	Rest	Psychic	Status	—	—	10	Self	—	—
TM45	Attract	Normal	Status	—	100	15	Normal	—	—
TM48	Round	Normal	Special	60	100	15	Normal	—	—
TM53	Energy Ball	Grass	Special	80	100	10	Normal	—	—
TM70	Flash	Normal	Status	—	100	20	Normal	—	—
TM85	Dream Eater	Psychic	Special	100	100	15	Normal	—	—
TM86	Grass Knot	Grass	Special	—	100	20	Normal	—	○
TM87	Swagger	Normal	Status	—	90	15	Normal	—	—
TM90	Substitute	Normal	Status	—	—	10	Self	—	—
HM01	Cut	Normal	Physical	50	95	30	Normal	—	—

▌ MOVES TAUGHT BY PEOPLE ▌

Name	Type	Kind	Pow.	Acc.	PP	Range	Long	DA

▌ MOVES TAUGHT BY MOVE TUTORS FOR SHARDS ▌

Name	Type	Kind	Pow.	Acc.	PP	Range	Long	DA
Covet	Normal	Physical	60	100	40	Normal	—	○
Seed Bomb	Grass	Physical	80	100	15	Normal	—	—
Snore	Normal	Special	40	100	15	Normal	—	—
Heal Bell	Normal	Status	—	—	5	Your Party	—	—
Synthesis	Grass	Status	—	—	5	Self	—	—
Giga Drain	Grass	Special	75	100	10	Normal	—	—
Worry Seed	Grass	Status	—	100	10	Normal	—	—
Helping Hand	Normal	Status	—	—	20	1 Ally	—	—
After You	Normal	Status	—	—	15	Normal	—	—
Sleep Talk	Normal	Status	—	—	10	Self	—	—

▌ EGG MOVES ▌

Name	Type	Kind	Pow.	Acc.	PP	Range	Long	DA
Natural Gift	Normal	Physical	—	100	15	Normal	—	—
Charm	Normal	Status	—	100	20	Normal	—	—
Endure	Normal	Status	—	—	10	Self	—	—
Ingrain	Grass	Status	—	—	20	Self	—	—
Worry Seed	Grass	Status	—	100	10	Normal	—	—
GrassWhistle	Grass	Status	—	55	15	Normal	—	—
Sweet Scent	Normal	Status	—	100	20	Many Others	—	—
Bide	Normal	Physical	—	—	10	Self	—	○
Healing Wish	Psychic	Status	—	—	10	Self	—	—

Pokémon AR Marker

---

549 Lilligant
Flowering Pokémon

TYPE Grass

ABILITIES
- Chlorophyll
- Own Tempo

HIDDEN ABILITY
- Leaf Guard

- HEIGHT: 3'07"
- WEIGHT: 35.9 lbs.
- GENDER: ♀

The fragrance of the garland on its head has a relaxing effect, but taking care of it is very difficult.

STATS
- HP
- Attack
- Defense
- Sp. Atk
- Sp. Def
- Speed

EGG GROUPS
Grass

ITEMS SOMETIMES HELD
- None

♀

⚙ EVOLUTION

Petilil — Use Sun Stone → Lilligant

HOW TO OBTAIN

Pokémon Black Version 2	Use Sun Stone on Petilil
Pokémon White Version 2	❶ Castelia City empty lot (rustling grass) ❷ Lostlorn Forest (rustling grass)

HOW TO OBTAIN FROM OTHER GAMES

▌ LEVEL-UP AND LEARNED MOVES ▌

Lv.	Name	Type	Kind	Pow.	Acc.	PP	Range	Long	DA
1	Growth	Normal	Status	—	—	40	Self	—	—
1	Leech Seed	Grass	Status	—	90	10	Normal	—	—
1	Mega Drain	Grass	Special	40	100	15	Normal	—	—
1	Synthesis	Grass	Status	—	—	5	Self	—	—
10	Teeter Dance	Normal	Status	—	100	20	Adjacent	—	—
28	Quiver Dance	Bug	Status	—	—	20	Self	—	—
46	Petal Dance	Grass	Special	120	100	10	1 Random	—	○

▌ TM & HM MOVES ▌

Lv.	Name	Type	Kind	Pow.	Acc.	PP	Range	Long	DA
TM06	Toxic	Poison	Status	—	90	10	Normal	—	—
TM10	Hidden Power	Normal	Special	—	100	15	Normal	—	—
TM11	Sunny Day	Fire	Status	—	—	5	Both Sides	—	—
TM15	Hyper Beam	Normal	Special	150	90	5	Normal	—	—
TM16	Light Screen	Psychic	Status	—	—	30	Your Side	—	—
TM17	Protect	Normal	Status	—	—	10	Self	—	—
TM20	Safeguard	Normal	Status	—	—	25	Your Side	—	—
TM21	Frustration	Normal	Physical	—	100	20	Normal	—	○
TM22	SolarBeam	Grass	Special	120	100	10	Normal	—	—
TM27	Return	Normal	Physical	—	100	20	Normal	—	○
TM32	Double Team	Normal	Status	—	—	15	Self	—	—
TM42	Facade	Normal	Physical	70	100	20	Normal	—	○
TM44	Rest	Psychic	Status	—	—	10	Self	—	—
TM45	Attract	Normal	Status	—	100	15	Normal	—	—
TM48	Round	Normal	Special	60	100	15	Normal	—	—
TM53	Energy Ball	Grass	Special	80	100	10	Normal	—	—
TM68	Giga Impact	Normal	Physical	150	90	5	Normal	—	○
TM70	Flash	Normal	Status	—	100	20	Normal	—	—
TM75	Swords Dance	Normal	Status	—	—	30	Self	—	—
TM85	Dream Eater	Psychic	Special	100	100	15	Normal	—	—
TM86	Grass Knot	Grass	Special	—	100	20	Normal	—	○
TM87	Swagger	Normal	Status	—	90	15	Normal	—	—
TM90	Substitute	Normal	Status	—	—	10	Self	—	—
HM01	Cut	Normal	Physical	50	95	30	Normal	—	○

▌ MOVES TAUGHT BY PEOPLE ▌

Name	Type	Kind	Pow.	Acc.	PP	Range	Long	DA

▌ MOVES TAUGHT BY MOVE TUTORS FOR SHARDS ▌

Name	Type	Kind	Pow.	Acc.	PP	Range	Long	DA
Covet	Normal	Physical	60	100	40	Normal	—	○
Seed Bomb	Grass	Physical	80	100	15	Normal	—	—
Snore	Normal	Special	40	100	15	Normal	—	—
Heal Bell	Normal	Status	—	—	5	Your Party	—	—
Synthesis	Grass	Status	—	—	5	Self	—	—
Role Play	Psychic	Status	—	—	10	Normal	—	—
Giga Drain	Grass	Special	75	100	10	Normal	—	—
Worry Seed	Grass	Status	—	100	10	Normal	—	—
Helping Hand	Normal	Status	—	—	20	1 Ally	—	—
After You	Normal	Status	—	—	15	Normal	—	—
Sleep Talk	Normal	Status	—	—	10	Self	—	—

Pokémon AR Marker

Hostile Pokémon

550 Basculin

● HEIGHT: 3'03"
● WEIGHT: 39.7 lbs.
● GENDER: ♂ / ♀

Red- and blue-striped Basculin are very violent and always fighting. They are also remarkably tasty.

Red-Striped Form | Blue-Striped Form

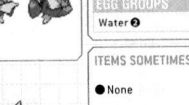

TYPE Water

ABILITIES (Red-Striped Form)
● Reckless
● Adaptability

ABILITIES (Blue-Striped Form)
● Rock Head
● Adaptability

HIDDEN ABILITY (Both)
● Mold Breaker

STATS
HP
Attack
Defense
Sp. Atk
Sp. Def
Speed

EGG GROUPS
Water ❷

ITEMS SOMETIMES HELD
● None

Red-Striped Form

Blue-Striped Form

Pokémon AR Marker

Red-Striped Form | Blue-Striped Form

EVOLUTION

Does not evolve

HOW TO OBTAIN

Red-Striped Form

Pokémon Black Version 2	Aspertia City (water surface)
Pokémon White Version 2	Aspertia City (ripples in water)

Blue-Striped Form

Pokémon Black Version 2	Aspertia City (ripples in water)
Pokémon White Version 2	Aspertia City (water surface)

LEVEL-UP AND LEARNED MOVES

Lv.	Name	Type	Kind	Pow.	Acc.	PP	Range	Long	DA
1	Tackle	Normal	Physical	50	100	35	Normal	—	○
1	Water Gun	Water	Special	40	100	25	Normal	—	—
4	Uproar	Normal	Special	90	100	10	1 Random	—	—
7	Headbutt	Normal	Physical	70	100	15	Normal	—	○
10	Bite	Dark	Physical	60	100	25	Normal	—	○
13	Aqua Jet	Water	Physical	40	100	20	Normal	—	○
16	Chip Away	Normal	Physical	70	100	20	Normal	—	○
20	Take Down	Normal	Physical	90	85	20	Normal	—	○
24	Crunch	Dark	Physical	80	100	15	Normal	—	○
28	Aqua Tail	Water	Physical	90	90	10	Normal	—	○
32	Soak	Water	Status	—	100	20	Normal	—	—
36	Double-Edge	Normal	Physical	120	100	15	Normal	—	○
41	Scary Face	Normal	Status	—	100	10	Normal	—	—
46	Flail	Normal	Physical	—	100	15	Normal	—	○
51	Final Gambit	Fighting	Special	—	100	5	Normal	—	○
56	Thrash	Normal	Physical	120	100	10	1 Random	—	○

TM & HM MOVES

Lv.	Name	Type	Kind	Pow.	Acc.	PP	Range	Long	DA
TM06	Toxic	Poison	Status	—	90	10	Normal	—	—
TM07	Hail	Ice	Status	—	—	10	Both Sides	—	—
TM10	Hidden Power	Normal	Special	—	100	15	Normal	—	—
TM12	Taunt	Dark	Status	—	100	20	Normal	—	—
TM13	Ice Beam	Ice	Special	95	100	10	Normal	—	—
TM17	Protect	Normal	Status	—	—	10	Self	—	—
TM18	Rain Dance	Water	Status	—	—	5	Both Sides	—	—
TM21	Frustration	Normal	Physical	—	100	20	Normal	—	○
TM27	Return	Normal	Physical	—	100	20	Normal	—	○
TM32	Double Team	Normal	Status	—	—	15	Self	—	—
TM42	Facade	Normal	Physical	70	100	20	Normal	—	○
TM44	Rest	Psychic	Status	—	—	10	Self	—	—
TM45	Attract	Normal	Status	—	100	15	Normal	—	—
TM48	Round	Normal	Special	60	100	15	Normal	—	—
TM55	Scald	Water	Special	80	100	15	Normal	—	—
TM87	Swagger	Normal	Status	—	90	15	Normal	—	—
TM90	Substitute	Normal	Status	—	—	10	Self	—	—
HM01	Cut	Normal	Physical	50	95	30	Normal	—	○
HM03	Surf	Water	Special	95	100	15	Adjacent	—	—
HM05	Waterfall	Water	Physical	80	100	15	Normal	—	○
HM06	Dive	Water	Physical	80	100	10	Normal	—	○

MOVES TAUGHT BY PEOPLE

Name	Type	Kind	Pow.	Acc.	PP	Range	Long	DA

MOVES TAUGHT BY MOVE TUTORS FOR SHARDS

Name	Type	Kind	Pow.	Acc.	PP	Range	Long	DA
Bounce	Flying	Physical	85	85	5	Normal	○	○
Uproar	Normal	Special	90	100	10	1 Random	—	—
Icy Wind	Ice	Special	55	95	15	Many Others	—	—
Aqua Tail	Water	Physical	90	90	10	Normal	—	○
Zen Headbutt	Psychic	Physical	80	90	15	Normal	—	○
Superpower	Fighting	Physical	120	100	5	Normal	—	○
Snore	Normal	Special	40	100	15	Normal	—	—
Endeavor	Normal	Physical	—	100	5	Normal	—	○
Sleep Talk	Normal	Status	—	—	10	Self	—	—

EGG MOVES

Name	Type	Kind	Pow.	Acc.	PP	Range	Long	DA
Swift	Normal	Special	60	—	20	Many Others	—	—
BubbleBeam	Water	Special	65	100	20	Normal	—	—
Mud Shot	Ground	Special	55	95	15	Normal	—	—
Muddy Water	Water	Special	95	85	10	Many Others	—	—
Agility	Psychic	Status	—	—	30	Self	—	—
Whirlpool	Water	Special	35	85	15	Normal	—	—
Rage	Normal	Physical	20	100	20	Normal	—	○
Brine	Water	Special	65	100	10	Normal	—	—
Revenge	Fighting	Physical	60	100	10	Normal	—	○

Desert Croc Pokémon

551 Sandile

● HEIGHT: 2'04"
● WEIGHT: 33.5 lbs.
● GENDER: ♂ / ♀

They live hidden under hot desert sands in order to keep their body temperature from dropping.

Same form for ♂ / ♀

TYPE Ground Dark

ABILITIES
● Intimidate
● Moxie

HIDDEN ABILITY
● Anger Point

STATS
HP
Attack
Defense
Sp. Atk
Sp. Def
Speed

EGG GROUPS
Field

ITEMS SOMETIMES HELD
● None

Pokémon AR Marker

EVOLUTION

Lv. 29
Lv. 40
Sandile
Krokorok
Krookodile

HOW TO OBTAIN

Pokémon Black Version 2	❶ Route 4 ❷ Desert Resort entrance
Pokémon White Version 2	❶ Route 4 ❷ Desert Resort entrance

HOW TO OBTAIN FROM OTHER GAMES

———

———

LEVEL-UP AND LEARNED MOVES

Lv.	Name	Type	Kind	Pow.	Acc.	PP	Range	Long	DA
1	Leer	Normal	Status	—	100	30	Many Others	—	—
1	Rage	Normal	Physical	20	100	20	Normal	—	○
4	Bite	Dark	Physical	60	100	25	Normal	—	○
7	Sand-Attack	Ground	Status	—	100	15	Normal	—	—
10	Torment	Dark	Status	—	100	15	Normal	—	—
13	Sand Tomb	Ground	Physical	35	85	15	Normal	—	—
16	Assurance	Dark	Physical	50	100	10	Normal	—	○
19	Mud-Slap	Ground	Special	20	100	10	Normal	—	—
22	Embargo	Dark	Status	—	100	15	Normal	—	—
25	Swagger	Normal	Status	—	90	15	Normal	—	—
28	Crunch	Dark	Physical	80	100	15	Normal	—	○
31	Dig	Ground	Physical	80	100	10	Normal	—	○
34	Scary Face	Normal	Status	—	100	10	Normal	—	—
37	Foul Play	Dark	Physical	95	100	15	Normal	—	○
40	Sandstorm	Rock	Status	—	—	10	Both Sides	—	—
43	Earthquake	Ground	Physical	100	100	10	Adjacent	—	—
46	Thrash	Normal	Physical	120	100	10	1 Random	—	○

TM & HM MOVES

Lv.	Name	Type	Kind	Pow.	Acc.	PP	Range	Long	DA
TM01	Hone Claws	Dark	Status	—	—	15	Self	—	—
TM05	Roar	Normal	Status	—	100	20	Normal	—	—
TM06	Toxic	Poison	Status	—	90	10	Normal	—	—
TM10	Hidden Power	Normal	Special	—	100	15	Normal	—	—
TM12	Taunt	Dark	Status	—	100	20	Normal	—	—
TM17	Protect	Normal	Status	—	—	10	Self	—	—
TM21	Frustration	Normal	Physical	—	100	20	Normal	—	○
TM26	Earthquake	Ground	Physical	100	100	10	Adjacent	—	—
TM27	Return	Normal	Physical	—	100	20	Normal	—	○
TM28	Dig	Ground	Physical	80	100	10	Normal	—	○
TM32	Double Team	Normal	Status	—	—	15	Self	—	—
TM36	Sludge Bomb	Poison	Special	90	100	10	Normal	—	—
TM37	Sandstorm	Rock	Status	—	—	10	Both Sides	—	—
TM39	Rock Tomb	Rock	Physical	50	80	10	Normal	—	—
TM41	Torment	Dark	Status	—	100	15	Normal	—	—
TM42	Facade	Normal	Physical	70	100	20	Normal	—	○
TM44	Rest	Psychic	Status	—	—	10	Self	—	—
TM45	Attract	Normal	Status	—	100	15	Normal	—	—
TM46	Thief	Dark	Physical	40	100	10	Normal	—	○
TM48	Round	Normal	Special	60	100	15	Normal	—	—
TM59	Incinerate	Fire	Special	30	100	15	Many Others	—	—
TM63	Embargo	Dark	Status	—	100	15	Normal	—	—
TM66	Payback	Dark	Physical	50	100	10	Normal	—	○
TM67	Retaliate	Normal	Physical	70	100	5	Normal	—	○
TM71	Stone Edge	Rock	Physical	100	80	5	Normal	—	—
TM78	Bulldoze	Ground	Physical	60	100	20	Adjacent	—	—
TM80	Rock Slide	Rock	Physical	75	90	10	Many Others	—	—
TM87	Swagger	Normal	Status	—	90	15	Normal	—	—
TM90	Substitute	Normal	Status	—	—	10	Self	—	—
TM95	Snarl	Dark	Special	55	95	15	Many Others	—	—
HM01	Cut	Normal	Physical	50	95	30	Normal	—	○

MOVES TAUGHT BY PEOPLE

Name	Type	Kind	Pow.	Acc.	PP	Range	Long	DA

MOVES TAUGHT BY MOVE TUTORS FOR SHARDS

Name	Type	Kind	Pow.	Acc.	PP	Range	Long	DA
Uproar	Normal	Special	90	100	10	1 Random	—	—
Iron Tail	Steel	Physical	100	75	15	Normal	—	○
Aqua Tail	Water	Physical	90	90	10	Normal	—	○
Earth Power	Ground	Special	90	100	10	Normal	—	—
Foul Play	Dark	Physical	95	100	15	Normal	—	○
Dark Pulse	Dark	Special	80	100	15	Normal	○	—
Snore	Normal	Special	40	100	15	Normal	—	—
Spite	Ghost	Status	—	100	10	Normal	—	—
Stealth Rock	Rock	Status	—	—	20	Other Side	—	—
Sleep Talk	Normal	Status	—	—	10	Self	—	—
Snatch	Dark	Status	—	—	10	Self	—	—

EGG MOVES

Name	Type	Kind	Pow.	Acc.	PP	Range	Long	DA
Double-Edge	Normal	Physical	120	100	15	Normal	—	○
Rock Climb	Normal	Physical	90	85	20	Normal	—	○
Pursuit	Dark	Physical	40	100	20	Normal	—	○
Uproar	Normal	Special	90	100	10	1 Random	—	—
Fire Fang	Fire	Physical	65	95	15	Normal	—	○
Thunder Fang	Electric	Physical	65	95	15	Normal	—	○
Beat Up	Dark	Physical	—	100	10	Normal	—	—
Focus Energy	Normal	Status	—	—	30	Self	—	—
Counter	Fighting	Physical	—	100	20	Varies	—	○
Mean Look	Normal	Status	—	—	5	Normal	—	—

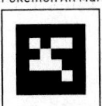

552 Krokorok

Desert Croc Pokémon

- HEIGHT: 3'03"
- WEIGHT: 73.6 lbs.
- GENDER: ♂ / ♀

Protected by thin membranes, their eyes can see even in the dead of night. They live in groups of a few individuals.

Same form for ♂ / ♀

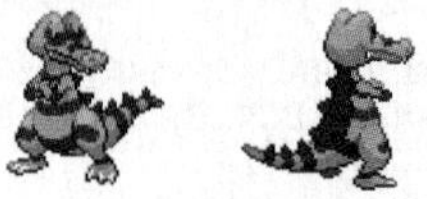

Pokémon AR Marker

TYPE Ground Dark

ABILITIES
- Intimidate
- Moxie

HIDDEN ABILITY
- Anger Point

STATS
HP
Attack
Defense
Sp. Atk
Sp. Def
Speed

EGG GROUPS
Field

ITEMS SOMETIMES HELD
- None

EVOLUTION

HOW TO OBTAIN

Pokémon Black Version 2	Relic Castle lowest floor passageways ①②④⑤
Pokémon White Version 2	Relic Castle lowest floor passageways ①②④⑤

HOW TO OBTAIN FROM OTHER GAMES

—

—

LEVEL-UP AND LEARNED MOVES

Lv.	Name	Type	Kind	Pow.	Acc.	PP	Range	Long	DA
1	Leer	Normal	Status	—	100	30	Many Others	—	—
1	Rage	Normal	Physical	20	100	20	Normal	—	○
1	Bite	Dark	Physical	60	100	25	Normal	—	○
1	Sand-Attack	Ground	Status	—	100	15	Normal	—	—
4	Bite	Dark	Physical	60	100	25	Normal	—	○
7	Sand-Attack	Ground	Status	—	100	15	Normal	—	—
10	Torment	Dark	Status	—	100	15	Normal	—	—
13	Sand Tomb	Ground	Physical	35	85	15	Normal	—	—
16	Assurance	Dark	Physical	50	100	10	Normal	—	○
19	Mud-Slap	Ground	Special	20	100	10	Normal	—	—
22	Embargo	Dark	Status	—	100	15	Normal	—	—
25	Swagger	Normal	Status	—	90	15	Normal	—	—
28	Crunch	Dark	Physical	80	100	15	Normal	—	○
32	Dig	Ground	Physical	80	100	10	Normal	—	○
36	Scary Face	Normal	Status	—	100	10	Normal	—	—
40	Foul Play	Dark	Physical	95	100	15	Normal	—	○
44	Sandstorm	Rock	Status	—	—	10	Both Sides	—	—
48	Earthquake	Ground	Physical	100	100	10	Adjacent	—	—
52	Thrash	Normal	Physical	120	100	10	1 Random	—	○

TM & HM MOVES

Lv.	Name	Type	Kind	Pow.	Acc.	PP	Range	Long	DA
TM01	Hone Claws	Dark	Status	—	—	15	Self	—	—
TM05	Roar	Normal	Status	—	100	20	Normal	—	—
TM06	Toxic	Poison	Status	—	90	10	Normal	—	—
TM10	Hidden Power	Normal	Special	—	100	15	Normal	—	—
TM12	Taunt	Dark	Status	—	100	20	Normal	—	—
TM17	Protect	Normal	Status	—	—	10	Self	—	—
TM21	Frustration	Normal	Physical	—	100	20	Normal	—	○
TM26	Earthquake	Ground	Physical	100	100	10	Adjacent	—	—
TM27	Return	Normal	Physical	—	100	20	Normal	—	○
TM28	Dig	Ground	Physical	80	100	10	Normal	—	○
TM31	Brick Break	Fighting	Physical	75	100	15	Normal	—	○
TM32	Double Team	Normal	Status	—	—	15	Self	—	—
TM36	Sludge Bomb	Poison	Special	90	100	10	Normal	—	—
TM37	Sandstorm	Rock	Status	—	—	10	Both Sides	—	—
TM39	Rock Tomb	Rock	Physical	50	80	10	Normal	—	—
TM41	Torment	Dark	Status	—	100	15	Normal	—	—
TM42	Facade	Normal	Physical	70	100	20	Normal	—	○
TM44	Rest	Psychic	Status	—	—	10	Self	—	—
TM45	Attract	Normal	Status	—	100	15	Normal	—	—
TM46	Thief	Dark	Physical	40	100	10	Normal	—	○
TM47	Low Sweep	Fighting	Physical	60	100	20	Normal	—	○
TM48	Round	Normal	Special	60	100	15	Normal	—	—
TM56	Fling	Dark	Physical	—	100	10	Normal	—	—
TM59	Incinerate	Fire	Special	30	100	15	Many Others	—	—
TM63	Embargo	Dark	Status	—	100	15	Normal	—	—
TM65	Shadow Claw	Ghost	Physical	70	100	15	Normal	—	○
TM66	Payback	Dark	Physical	50	100	10	Normal	—	○
TM67	Retaliate	Normal	Physical	70	100	5	Normal	—	○
TM71	Stone Edge	Rock	Physical	100	80	5	Normal	—	—
TM78	Bulldoze	Ground	Physical	60	100	20	Adjacent	—	—
TM80	Rock Slide	Rock	Physical	75	90	10	Many Others	—	—
TM86	Grass Knot	Grass	Special	—	100	20	Normal	—	○
TM87	Swagger	Normal	Status	—	90	15	Normal	—	—
TM90	Substitute	Normal	Status	—	—	10	Self	—	—
TM94	Rock Smash	Fighting	Physical	40	100	15	Normal	—	○
TM95	Snarl	Dark	Special	55	95	15	Many Others	—	—
HM01	Cut	Normal	Physical	50	95	30	Normal	—	○
HM04	Strength	Normal	Physical	80	100	15	Normal	—	○

MOVES TAUGHT BY PEOPLE

Name	Type	Kind	Pow.	Acc.	PP	Range	Long	DA

MOVES TAUGHT BY MOVE TUTORS FOR SHARDS

Name	Type	Kind	Pow.	Acc.	PP	Range	Long	DA
Uproar	Normal	Special	90	100	10	1 Random	—	—
Low Kick	Fighting	Physical	—	100	20	Normal	—	○
Iron Tail	Steel	Physical	100	75	15	Normal	—	○
Aqua Tail	Water	Physical	90	90	10	Normal	—	○
Earth Power	Ground	Special	90	100	10	Normal	—	—
Foul Play	Dark	Physical	95	100	15	Normal	—	○
Dark Pulse	Dark	Special	80	100	15	Normal	○	—
Snore	Normal	Special	40	100	15	Normal	—	—
Knock Off	Dark	Physical	20	100	20	Normal	—	○
Spite	Ghost	Status	—	100	10	Normal	—	—
Stealth Rock	Rock	Status	—	—	20	Other Side	—	—
Sleep Talk	Normal	Status	—	—	10	Self	—	—
Snatch	Dark	Status	—	—	10	Self	—	—

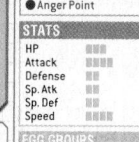

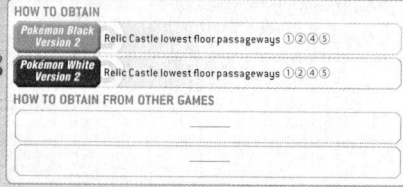

553 Krookodile

Intimidation Pokémon

- HEIGHT: 4'11"
- WEIGHT: 212.3 lbs.
- GENDER: ♂ / ♀

Very violent Pokémon, they try to clamp down on anything that moves in front of their eyes.

Same form for ♂ / ♀

Pokémon AR Marker

TYPE Ground Dark

ABILITIES
- Intimidate
- Moxie

HIDDEN ABILITY
- Anger Point

STATS
HP
Attack
Defense
Sp. Atk
Sp. Def
Speed

EGG GROUPS
Field

ITEMS SOMETIMES HELD
- None

EVOLUTION

HOW TO OBTAIN

Pokémon Black Version 2	Level up Krokorok to Lv. 40
Pokémon White Version 2	Level up Krokorok to Lv. 40

HOW TO OBTAIN FROM OTHER GAMES

—

—

LEVEL-UP AND LEARNED MOVES

Lv.	Name	Type	Kind	Pow.	Acc.	PP	Range	Long	DA
1	Leer	Normal	Status	—	100	30	Many Others	—	—
1	Rage	Normal	Physical	20	100	20	Normal	—	○
1	Bite	Dark	Physical	60	100	25	Normal	—	○
1	Sand-Attack	Ground	Status	—	100	15	Normal	—	—
4	Bite	Dark	Physical	60	100	25	Normal	—	○
7	Sand-Attack	Ground	Status	—	100	15	Normal	—	—
10	Torment	Dark	Status	—	100	15	Normal	—	—
13	Sand Tomb	Ground	Physical	35	85	15	Normal	—	—
16	Assurance	Dark	Physical	50	100	10	Normal	—	○
19	Mud-Slap	Ground	Special	20	100	10	Normal	—	—
22	Embargo	Dark	Status	—	100	15	Normal	—	—
25	Swagger	Normal	Status	—	90	15	Normal	—	—
28	Crunch	Dark	Physical	80	100	15	Normal	—	○
32	Dig	Ground	Physical	80	100	10	Normal	—	○
36	Scary Face	Normal	Status	—	100	10	Normal	—	—
42	Foul Play	Dark	Physical	95	100	15	Normal	—	○
48	Sandstorm	Rock	Status	—	—	10	Both Sides	—	—
54	Earthquake	Ground	Physical	100	100	10	Adjacent	—	—
60	Outrage	Dragon	Physical	120	100	10	1 Random	—	○

TM & HM MOVES

Lv.	Name	Type	Kind	Pow.	Acc.	PP	Range	Long	DA
TM01	Hone Claws	Dark	Status	—	—	15	Self	—	—
TM02	Dragon Claw	Dragon	Physical	80	100	15	Normal	—	○
TM05	Roar	Normal	Status	—	100	20	Normal	—	—
TM06	Toxic	Poison	Status	—	90	10	Normal	—	—
TM08	Bulk Up	Fighting	Status	—	—	20	Self	—	—
TM10	Hidden Power	Normal	Special	—	100	15	Normal	—	—
TM12	Taunt	Dark	Status	—	100	20	Normal	—	—
TM15	Hyper Beam	Normal	Special	150	90	5	Normal	—	—
TM17	Protect	Normal	Status	—	—	10	Self	—	—
TM21	Frustration	Normal	Physical	—	100	20	Normal	—	○
TM23	Smack Down	Rock	Physical	50	100	15	Normal	—	—
TM26	Earthquake	Ground	Physical	100	100	10	Adjacent	—	—
TM27	Return	Normal	Physical	—	100	20	Normal	—	○
TM28	Dig	Ground	Physical	80	100	10	Normal	—	○
TM31	Brick Break	Fighting	Physical	75	100	15	Normal	—	○
TM32	Double Team	Normal	Status	—	—	15	Self	—	—
TM36	Sludge Bomb	Poison	Special	90	100	10	Normal	—	—
TM37	Sandstorm	Rock	Status	—	—	10	Both Sides	—	—
TM39	Rock Tomb	Rock	Physical	50	80	10	Normal	—	—
TM40	Aerial Ace	Flying	Physical	60	—	20	Normal	○	○
TM41	Torment	Dark	Status	—	100	15	Normal	—	—
TM42	Facade	Normal	Physical	70	100	20	Normal	—	○
TM44	Rest	Psychic	Status	—	—	10	Self	—	—
TM45	Attract	Normal	Status	—	100	15	Normal	—	—
TM46	Thief	Dark	Physical	40	100	10	Normal	—	○
TM47	Low Sweep	Fighting	Physical	60	100	20	Normal	—	○
TM48	Round	Normal	Special	60	100	15	Normal	—	—
TM52	Focus Blast	Fighting	Special	120	70	5	Normal	—	—
TM56	Fling	Dark	Physical	—	100	10	Normal	—	—
TM59	Incinerate	Fire	Special	30	100	15	Many Others	—	—
TM63	Embargo	Dark	Status	—	100	15	Normal	—	—
TM65	Shadow Claw	Ghost	Physical	70	100	15	Normal	—	○
TM66	Payback	Dark	Physical	50	100	10	Normal	—	○
TM67	Retaliate	Normal	Physical	70	100	5	Normal	—	○
TM68	Giga Impact	Normal	Physical	150	90	5	Normal	—	○
TM71	Stone Edge	Rock	Physical	100	80	5	Normal	—	—
TM78	Bulldoze	Ground	Physical	60	100	20	Adjacent	—	—
TM80	Rock Slide	Rock	Physical	75	90	10	Many Others	—	—
TM82	Dragon Tail	Dragon	Physical	60	90	10	Normal	—	○
TM86	Grass Knot	Grass	Special	—	100	20	Normal	—	○
TM87	Swagger	Normal	Status	—	90	15	Normal	—	—
TM90	Substitute	Normal	Status	—	—	10	Self	—	—
TM94	Rock Smash	Fighting	Physical	40	100	15	Normal	—	○
TM95	Snarl	Dark	Special	55	95	15	Many Others	—	—
HM01	Cut	Normal	Physical	50	95	30	Normal	—	○
HM04	Strength	Normal	Physical	80	100	15	Normal	—	○

MOVES TAUGHT BY PEOPLE

Name	Type	Kind	Pow.	Acc.	PP	Range	Long	DA

MOVES TAUGHT BY MOVE TUTORS FOR SHARDS

Name	Type	Kind	Pow.	Acc.	PP	Range	Long	DA
Uproar	Normal	Special	90	100	10	1 Random	—	—
Low Kick	Fighting	Physical	—	100	20	Normal	—	○
Block	Normal	Status	—	—	5	Normal	—	—
Iron Tail	Steel	Physical	100	75	15	Normal	—	○
Aqua Tail	Water	Physical	90	90	10	Normal	—	○
Earth Power	Ground	Special	90	100	10	Normal	—	—
Foul Play	Dark	Physical	95	100	15	Normal	—	○
Superpower	Fighting	Physical	120	100	5	Normal	—	○
Dragon Pulse	Dragon	Special	90	100	10	Normal	○	—
Dark Pulse	Dark	Special	80	100	15	Normal	○	—
Snore	Normal	Special	40	100	15	Normal	—	—
Knock Off	Dark	Physical	20	100	20	Normal	—	○
Spite	Ghost	Status	—	100	10	Normal	—	—
Stealth Rock	Rock	Status	—	—	20	Other Side	—	—
Outrage	Dragon	Physical	120	100	10	1 Random	—	○
Sleep Talk	Normal	Status	—	—	10	Self	—	—
Snatch	Dark	Status	—	—	10	Self	—	—

554 Darumaka
Zen Charm Pokémon

- HEIGHT: 2'00"
- WEIGHT: 82.7 lbs.
- GENDER: ♂ / ♀

When it sleeps, it pulls its limbs into its body and its internal fire goes down to 1,100° F.

Same form for ♂ / ♀

Pokémon AR Marker

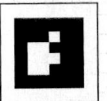

TYPE: Fire

ABILITY
- Hustle

HIDDEN ABILITY
- Inner Focus

STATS
HP
Attack
Defense
Sp. Atk
Sp. Def
Speed

EGG GROUPS
Field

ITEMS SOMETIMES HELD
- Rawst Berry

EVOLUTION

HOW TO OBTAIN

Pokémon Black Version 2	❶ Route 4 ❷ Desert Resort entrance
Pokémon White Version 2	❶ Route 4 ❷ Desert Resort entrance

HOW TO OBTAIN FROM OTHER GAMES

—

—

LEVEL-UP AND LEARNED MOVES

Lv.	Name	Type	Kind	Pow.	Acc.	PP	Range	Long	DA
1	Tackle	Normal	Physical	50	100	35	Normal	—	○
3	Rollout	Rock	Physical	30	90	20	Normal	—	○
6	Incinerate	Fire	Special	30	100	15	Many Others	—	—
9	Rage	Normal	Physical	20	100	20	Normal	—	○
11	Fire Fang	Fire	Physical	65	95	15	Normal	—	○
14	Headbutt	Normal	Physical	70	100	15	Normal	—	○
17	Uproar	Normal	Special	90	100	10	1 Random	—	—
19	Facade	Normal	Physical	70	100	20	Normal	—	○
22	Fire Punch	Fire	Physical	75	100	15	Normal	—	○
25	Work Up	Normal	Status	—	—	30	Self	—	—
27	Thrash	Normal	Physical	120	100	10	1 Random	—	○
30	Belly Drum	Normal	Status	—	—	10	Self	—	—
33	Flare Blitz	Fire	Physical	120	100	15	Normal	—	○
35	Taunt	Dark	Status	—	100	20	Normal	—	—
39	Superpower	Fighting	Physical	120	100	5	Normal	—	○
42	Overheat	Fire	Special	140	90	5	Normal	—	—

TM & HM MOVES

Lv.	Name	Type	Kind	Pow.	Acc.	PP	Range	Long	DA
TM05	Roar	Normal	Status	—	100	20	Normal	—	—
TM06	Toxic	Poison	Status	—	90	10	Normal	—	—
TM10	Hidden Power	Normal	Special	—	100	15	Normal	—	—
TM11	Sunny Day	Fire	Status	—	—	5	Both Sides	—	—
TM12	Taunt	Dark	Status	—	100	20	Normal	—	—
TM17	Protect	Normal	Status	—	—	10	Self	—	—
TM21	Frustration	Normal	Physical	—	100	20	Normal	—	○
TM22	SolarBeam	Grass	Special	120	100	10	Normal	—	—
TM27	Return	Normal	Physical	—	100	20	Normal	—	○
TM28	Dig	Ground	Physical	80	100	10	Normal	—	○
TM31	Brick Break	Fighting	Physical	75	100	15	Normal	—	○
TM32	Double Team	Normal	Status	—	—	15	Self	—	—
TM35	Flamethrower	Fire	Special	95	100	15	Normal	—	—
TM38	Fire Blast	Fire	Special	120	85	5	Normal	—	—
TM39	Rock Tomb	Rock	Physical	50	80	10	Normal	—	—
TM42	Facade	Normal	Physical	70	100	20	Normal	—	○
TM43	Flame Charge	Fire	Physical	50	100	20	Normal	—	○
TM44	Rest	Psychic	Status	—	—	10	Self	—	—
TM45	Attract	Normal	Status	—	100	15	Normal	—	—
TM46	Thief	Dark	Physical	40	100	10	Normal	—	○
TM48	Round	Normal	Special	60	100	15	Normal	—	—
TM50	Overheat	Fire	Special	140	90	5	Normal	—	—
TM56	Fling	Dark	Physical	—	100	10	Normal	—	—
TM59	Incinerate	Fire	Special	30	100	15	Many Others	—	—
TM61	Will-O-Wisp	Fire	Status	—	75	15	Normal	—	—
TM74	Gyro Ball	Steel	Physical	—	100	5	Normal	—	○
TM80	Rock Slide	Rock	Physical	75	90	10	Many Others	—	—
TM83	Work Up	Normal	Status	—	—	30	Self	—	—
TM86	Grass Knot	Grass	Special	—	100	20	Normal	—	○
TM87	Swagger	Normal	Status	—	90	15	Normal	—	—
TM89	U-turn	Bug	Physical	70	100	20	Normal	—	○
TM90	Substitute	Normal	Status	—	—	10	Self	—	—
TM94	Rock Smash	Fighting	Physical	40	100	15	Normal	—	○
HM04	Strength	Normal	Physical	80	100	15	Normal	—	○

MOVES TAUGHT BY PEOPLE

Name	Type	Kind	Pow.	Acc.	PP	Range	Long	DA

MOVES TAUGHT BY MOVE TUTORS FOR SHARDS

Name	Type	Kind	Pow.	Acc.	PP	Range	Long	DA
Uproar	Normal	Special	90	100	10	1 Random	—	—
Fire Punch	Fire	Physical	75	100	15	Normal	—	○
Zen Headbutt	Psychic	Physical	80	90	15	Normal	—	○
Superpower	Fighting	Physical	120	100	5	Normal	—	○
Snore	Normal	Special	40	100	15	Normal	—	—
Heat Wave	Fire	Special	100	90	10	Many Others	—	—
Endeavor	Normal	Physical	—	100	5	Normal	—	○
Sleep Talk	Normal	Status	—	—	10	Self	—	—

EGG MOVES

Name	Type	Kind	Pow.	Acc.	PP	Range	Long	DA
Sleep Talk	Normal	Status	—	—	10	Self	—	—
Focus Punch	Fighting	Physical	150	100	20	Normal	—	○
Focus Energy	Normal	Status	—	—	30	Self	—	—
Endure	Normal	Status	—	—	10	Self	—	—
Hammer Arm	Fighting	Physical	100	90	10	Normal	—	○
Take Down	Normal	Physical	90	85	20	Normal	—	○
Flame Wheel	Fire	Physical	60	100	25	Normal	—	○
Encore	Normal	Status	—	100	5	Normal	—	—
Yawn	Normal	Status	—	—	10	Normal	—	—

555 Darmanitan
Blazing Pokémon

- HEIGHT: 4'03"
- WEIGHT: 204.8 lbs.
- GENDER: ♂ / ♀

When one is injured in a fierce battle, it hardens into a stone-like form. Then it meditates and sharpens its mind.

Standard Mode / Zen Mode

ITEMS SOMETIMES HELD
- None

Pokémon AR Marker

Standard Mode / Zen Mode

TYPE (Standard Mode): Fire

TYPE (Zen Mode): Fire / Psychic

ABILITY
- Sheer Force

HIDDEN ABILITY
- Zen Mode

STATS (Standard Mode)
HP
Attack
Defense
Sp. Atk
Sp. Def
Speed

STATS (Zen Mode)
HP
Attack
Defense
Sp. Atk
Sp. Def
Speed

EGG GROUPS
Field

EVOLUTION

HOW TO OBTAIN

Standard Mode

Pokémon Black Version 2	Level up Darumaka to Lv. 35
Pokémon White Version 2	Level up Darumaka to Lv. 35

Zen Mode

Pokémon Black Version 2	Lower the HP of a Darmanitan with the Hidden Ability Zen Mode to half or less during battle
Pokémon White Version 2	Lower the HP of a Darmanitan with the Hidden Ability Zen Mode to half or less during battle

LEVEL-UP AND LEARNED MOVES

Lv.	Name	Type	Kind	Pow.	Acc.	PP	Range	Long	DA
1	Tackle	Normal	Physical	50	100	35	Normal	—	○
1	Rollout	Rock	Physical	30	90	20	Normal	—	○
1	Incinerate	Fire	Special	30	100	15	Many Others	—	—
1	Rage	Normal	Physical	20	100	20	Normal	—	○
3	Rollout	Rock	Physical	30	90	20	Normal	—	○
6	Incinerate	Fire	Special	30	100	15	Many Others	—	—
9	Rage	Normal	Physical	20	100	20	Normal	—	○
11	Fire Fang	Fire	Physical	65	95	15	Normal	—	○
14	Headbutt	Normal	Physical	70	100	15	Normal	—	○
17	Swagger	Normal	Status	—	90	15	Normal	—	—
19	Facade	Normal	Physical	70	100	20	Normal	—	○
22	Fire Punch	Fire	Physical	75	100	15	Normal	—	○
25	Work Up	Normal	Status	—	—	30	Self	—	—
27	Thrash	Normal	Physical	120	100	10	1 Random	—	○
30	Belly Drum	Normal	Status	—	—	10	Self	—	—
33	Flare Blitz	Fire	Physical	120	100	15	Normal	—	○
35	Hammer Arm	Fighting	Physical	100	90	10	Normal	—	○
39	Taunt	Dark	Status	—	100	20	Normal	—	—
47	Superpower	Fighting	Physical	120	100	5	Normal	—	○
54	Overheat	Fire	Special	140	90	5	Normal	—	—

TM & HM MOVES

Lv.	Name	Type	Kind	Pow.	Acc.	PP	Range	Long	DA
TM05	Roar	Normal	Status	—	100	20	Normal	—	—
TM06	Toxic	Poison	Status	—	90	10	Normal	—	—
TM08	Bulk Up	Fighting	Status	—	—	20	Self	—	—
TM10	Hidden Power	Normal	Special	—	100	15	Normal	—	—
TM11	Sunny Day	Fire	Status	—	—	5	Both Sides	—	—
TM12	Taunt	Dark	Status	—	100	20	Normal	—	—
TM15	Hyper Beam	Normal	Special	150	90	5	Normal	—	—
TM17	Protect	Normal	Status	—	—	10	Self	—	—
TM21	Frustration	Normal	Physical	—	100	20	Normal	—	○
TM22	SolarBeam	Grass	Special	120	100	10	Normal	—	—
TM23	Smack Down	Rock	Physical	50	100	15	Normal	—	—
TM26	Earthquake	Ground	Physical	100	100	10	Adjacent	—	—
TM27	Return	Normal	Physical	—	100	20	Normal	—	○
TM28	Dig	Ground	Physical	80	100	10	Normal	—	○
TM29	Psychic	Psychic	Special	90	100	10	Normal	—	—
TM31	Brick Break	Fighting	Physical	75	100	15	Normal	—	○
TM32	Double Team	Normal	Status	—	—	15	Self	—	—
TM35	Flamethrower	Fire	Special	95	100	15	Normal	—	—
TM38	Fire Blast	Fire	Special	120	85	5	Normal	—	—
TM39	Rock Tomb	Rock	Physical	50	80	10	Normal	—	—
TM41	Torment	Dark	Status	—	100	15	Normal	—	—
TM42	Facade	Normal	Physical	70	100	20	Normal	—	○
TM43	Flame Charge	Fire	Physical	50	100	20	Normal	—	○
TM44	Rest	Psychic	Status	—	—	10	Self	—	—
TM45	Attract	Normal	Status	—	100	15	Normal	—	—
TM46	Thief	Dark	Physical	40	100	10	Normal	—	○
TM48	Round	Normal	Special	60	100	15	Normal	—	—
TM50	Overheat	Fire	Special	140	90	5	Normal	—	—
TM52	Focus Blast	Fighting	Special	120	70	5	Normal	—	—
TM56	Fling	Dark	Physical	—	100	10	Normal	—	—
TM59	Incinerate	Fire	Special	30	100	15	Many Others	—	—
TM61	Will-O-Wisp	Fire	Status	—	75	15	Normal	—	—
TM66	Payback	Dark	Physical	50	100	10	Normal	—	○
TM68	Giga Impact	Normal	Physical	150	90	5	Normal	—	○
TM71	Stone Edge	Rock	Physical	100	80	5	Normal	—	—
TM74	Gyro Ball	Steel	Physical	—	100	5	Normal	—	○
TM78	Bulldoze	Ground	Physical	60	100	20	Adjacent	—	—
TM80	Rock Slide	Rock	Physical	75	90	10	Many Others	—	—
TM83	Work Up	Normal	Status	—	—	30	Self	—	—
TM86	Grass Knot	Grass	Special	—	100	20	Normal	—	○
TM87	Swagger	Normal	Status	—	90	15	Normal	—	—
TM89	U-turn	Bug	Physical	70	100	20	Normal	—	○
TM90	Substitute	Normal	Status	—	—	10	Self	—	—
TM94	Rock Smash	Fighting	Physical	40	100	15	Normal	—	○
HM04	Strength	Normal	Physical	80	100	15	Normal	—	○

MOVES TAUGHT BY PEOPLE

Name	Type	Kind	Pow.	Acc.	PP	Range	Long	DA

MOVES TAUGHT BY MOVE TUTORS FOR SHARDS

Name	Type	Kind	Pow.	Acc.	PP	Range	Long	DA
Uproar	Normal	Special	90	100	10	1 Random	—	—
Fire Punch	Fire	Physical	75	100	15	Normal	—	○
Zen Headbutt	Psychic	Physical	80	90	15	Normal	—	○
Superpower	Fighting	Physical	120	100	5	Normal	—	○
Snore	Normal	Special	40	100	15	Normal	—	—
Heat Wave	Fire	Special	100	90	10	Many Others	—	—
Endeavor	Normal	Physical	-	100	5	Normal	—	○
Sleep Talk	Normal	Status	-	-	10	Self	—	—

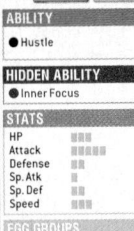

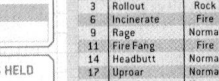

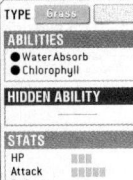

Cactus Pokémon

556 Maractus

- HEIGHT: 3'03"
- WEIGHT: 61.7 lbs.
- GENDER: ♂ / ♀

When it moves rhythmically, it makes a sound similar to maracas, making the surprised Pokémon flee.

Same form for ♂ / ♀

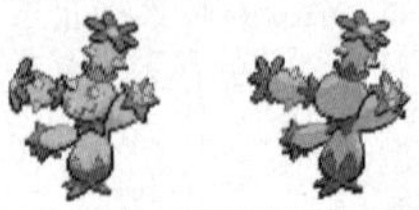

Pokémon AR Marker

TYPE: Grass

ABILITIES
- Water Absorb
- Chlorophyll

HIDDEN ABILITY
—

STATS
HP
Attack
Defense
Sp. Atk
Sp. Def
Speed

EGG GROUPS
Grass

ITEMS SOMETIMES HELD
- Miracle Seed

EVOLUTION

Does not evolve

HOW TO OBTAIN

Pokémon Black Version 2	❶ Desert Resort entrance ❷ Desert Resort interior
Pokémon White Version 2	❶ Desert Resort entrance ❷ Desert Resort interior

HOW TO OBTAIN FROM OTHER GAMES

—

—

LEVEL-UP AND LEARNED MOVES

Lv.	Name	Type	Kind	Pow.	Acc.	PP	Range	Long	DA
1	Peck	Flying	Physical	35	100	35	Normal	○	○
1	Absorb	Grass	Special	20	100	25	Normal	—	—
3	Sweet Scent	Normal	Status	—	100	20	Many Others	—	—
6	Growth	Normal	Status	—	—	40	Self	—	—
10	Pin Missile	Bug	Physical	14	85	20	Normal	—	—
13	Mega Drain	Grass	Special	40	100	15	Normal	—	—
15	Synthesis	Grass	Status	—	—	5	Self	—	—
18	Cotton Spore	Grass	Status	—	100	40	Normal	—	—
22	Needle Arm	Grass	Physical	60	100	15	Normal	—	○
26	Giga Drain	Grass	Special	75	100	10	Normal	—	—
29	Acupressure	Normal	Status	—	—	30	Self/Ally	—	—
33	Ingrain	Grass	Status	—	—	20	Self	—	—
38	Petal Dance	Grass	Special	120	100	10	1 Random	—	○
42	Sucker Punch	Dark	Physical	80	100	5	Normal	—	○
45	Sunny Day	Fire	Status	—	—	5	Both Sides	—	—
50	SolarBeam	Grass	Special	120	100	10	Normal	—	—
55	Cotton Guard	Grass	Status	—	—	10	Self	—	—
57	After You	Normal	Status	—	—	15	Normal	—	—

TM & HM MOVES

Lv.	Name	Type	Kind	Pow.	Acc.	PP	Range	Long	DA
TM06	Toxic	Poison	Status	—	90	10	Normal	—	—
TM10	Hidden Power	Normal	Special	—	100	15	Normal	—	—
TM11	Sunny Day	Fire	Status	—	—	5	Both Sides	—	—
TM17	Protect	Normal	Status	—	—	10	Self	—	—
TM20	Safeguard	Normal	Status	—	—	25	Your Side	—	—
TM21	Frustration	Normal	Physical	—	100	20	Normal	—	○
TM22	SolarBeam	Grass	Special	120	100	10	Normal	—	—
TM27	Return	Normal	Physical	—	100	20	Normal	—	○
TM32	Double Team	Normal	Status	—	—	15	Self	—	—
TM40	Aerial Ace	Flying	Physical	60	—	20	Normal	○	○
TM42	Facade	Normal	Physical	70	100	20	Normal	—	○
TM44	Rest	Psychic	Status	—	—	10	Self	—	—
TM45	Attract	Normal	Status	—	100	15	Normal	—	—
TM48	Round	Normal	Special	60	100	15	Normal	—	—
TM53	Energy Ball	Grass	Special	80	100	10	Normal	—	—
TM84	Poison Jab	Poison	Physical	80	100	20	Normal	—	○
TM86	Grass Knot	Grass	Special	—	100	20	Normal	—	○
TM87	Swagger	Normal	Status	—	90	15	Normal	—	—
TM90	Substitute	Normal	Status	—	—	10	Self	—	—

MOVES TAUGHT BY PEOPLE

Name	Type	Kind	Pow.	Acc.	PP	Range	Long	DA

MOVES TAUGHT BY MOVE TUTORS FOR SHARDS

Name	Type	Kind	Pow.	Acc.	PP	Range	Long	DA
Bounce	Flying	Physical	85	85	5	Normal	○	○
Uproar	Normal	Special	90	100	10	1 Random	—	—
Seed Bomb	Grass	Physical	80	100	15	Normal	—	—
Hyper Voice	Normal	Special	90	100	10	Many Others	—	—
Snore	Normal	Special	40	100	15	Normal	—	—
Knock Off	Dark	Physical	20	100	20	Normal	—	○
Synthesis	Grass	Status	—	—	5	Self	—	—
Giga Drain	Grass	Special	75	100	10	Normal	—	—
Drain Punch	Fighting	Physical	75	100	10	Normal	—	○
Worry Seed	Grass	Status	—	100	10	Normal	—	—
Helping Hand	Normal	Status	—	—	20	1 Ally	—	—
After You	Normal	Status	—	—	15	Normal	—	—
Endeavor	Normal	Physical	—	100	5	Normal	—	○
Sleep Talk	Normal	Status	—	—	10	Self	—	—

EGG MOVES

Name	Type	Kind	Pow.	Acc.	PP	Range	Long	DA
Bullet Seed	Grass	Physical	25	100	30	Normal	—	—
Bounce	Flying	Physical	85	85	5	Normal	○	○
Worry Seed	Grass	Status	—	100	10	Normal	—	—
Leech Seed	Grass	Status	—	90	10	Normal	—	—
Seed Bomb	Grass	Physical	80	100	15	Normal	—	—
Wood Hammer	Grass	Physical	120	100	15	Normal	—	○
Spikes	Ground	Status	—	—	20	Other Side	—	—
GrassWhistle	Grass	Status	—	55	15	Normal	—	—

Rock Inn Pokémon

557 Dwebble

- HEIGHT: 1'00"
- WEIGHT: 32.0 lbs.
- GENDER: ♂ / ♀

When it finds a stone of a suitable size, it secretes a liquid from its mouth to open up a hole to crawl into.

Same form for ♂ / ♀

Pokémon AR Marker

TYPE: Bug / Rock

ABILITIES
- Sturdy
- Shell Armor

HIDDEN ABILITY
- Weak Armor

STATS
HP
Attack
Defense
Sp. Atk
Sp. Def
Speed

EGG GROUPS
Bug/Mineral

ITEMS SOMETIMES HELD
- Hard Stone

EVOLUTION

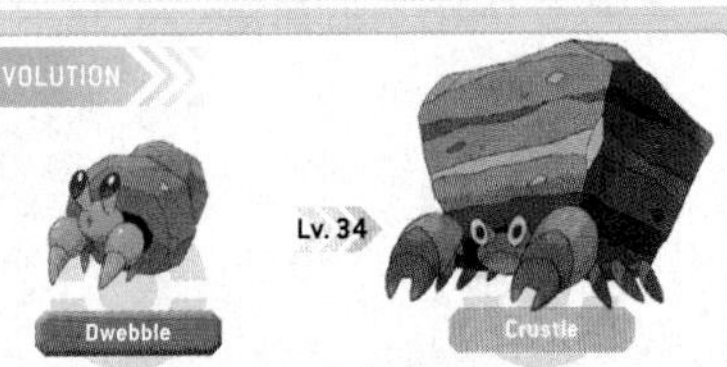

HOW TO OBTAIN

Pokémon Black Version 2	❶ Desert Resort entrance ❷ Desert Resort interior
Pokémon White Version 2	❶ Desert Resort entrance ❷ Desert Resort interior

HOW TO OBTAIN FROM OTHER GAMES

—

—

LEVEL-UP AND LEARNED MOVES

Lv.	Name	Type	Kind	Pow.	Acc.	PP	Range	Long	DA
1	Fury Cutter	Bug	Physical	20	95	20	Normal	—	○
5	Rock Blast	Rock	Physical	25	90	10	Normal	—	—
7	Withdraw	Water	Status	—	—	40	Self	—	—
11	Sand-Attack	Ground	Status	—	100	15	Normal	—	—
13	Faint Attack	Dark	Physical	60	—	20	Normal	—	○
17	Smack Down	Rock	Physical	50	100	15	Normal	—	—
19	Rock Polish	Rock	Status	—	—	20	Self	—	—
23	Bug Bite	Bug	Physical	60	100	20	Normal	—	○
24	Stealth Rock	Rock	Status	—	—	20	Other Side	—	—
29	Rock Slide	Rock	Physical	75	90	10	Many Others	—	—
31	Slash	Normal	Physical	70	100	20	Normal	—	○
35	X-Scissor	Bug	Physical	80	100	15	Normal	—	○
37	Shell Smash	Normal	Status	—	—	15	Self	—	—
41	Flail	Normal	Physical	—	100	15	Normal	—	○
43	Rock Wrecker	Rock	Physical	150	90	5	Normal	—	—

TM & HM MOVES

Lv.	Name	Type	Kind	Pow.	Acc.	PP	Range	Long	DA
TM01	Hone Claws	Dark	Status	—	—	15	Self	—	—
TM06	Toxic	Poison	Status	—	90	10	Normal	—	—
TM10	Hidden Power	Normal	Special	—	100	15	Normal	—	—
TM17	Protect	Normal	Status	—	—	10	Self	—	—
TM21	Frustration	Normal	Physical	—	100	20	Normal	—	○
TM22	SolarBeam	Grass	Special	120	100	10	Normal	—	—
TM23	Smack Down	Rock	Physical	50	100	15	Normal	—	—
TM26	Earthquake	Ground	Physical	100	100	10	Adjacent	—	—
TM27	Return	Normal	Physical	—	100	20	Normal	—	○
TM28	Dig	Ground	Physical	80	100	10	Normal	—	○
TM32	Double Team	Normal	Status	—	—	15	Self	—	—
TM37	Sandstorm	Rock	Status	—	—	10	Both Sides	—	—
TM39	Rock Tomb	Rock	Physical	50	80	10	Normal	—	—
TM40	Aerial Ace	Flying	Physical	60	—	20	Normal	○	○
TM42	Facade	Normal	Physical	70	100	20	Normal	—	○
TM44	Rest	Psychic	Status	—	—	10	Self	—	—
TM45	Attract	Normal	Status	—	100	15	Normal	—	—
TM48	Round	Normal	Special	60	100	15	Normal	—	—
TM65	Shadow Claw	Ghost	Physical	70	100	15	Normal	—	○
TM69	Rock Polish	Rock	Status	—	—	20	Self	—	—
TM71	Stone Edge	Rock	Physical	100	80	5	Normal	—	—
TM75	Swords Dance	Normal	Status	—	—	30	Self	—	—
TM76	Struggle Bug	Bug	Special	30	100	20	Many Others	—	—
TM78	Bulldoze	Ground	Physical	60	100	20	Adjacent	—	—
TM80	Rock Slide	Rock	Physical	75	90	10	Many Others	—	—
TM81	X-Scissor	Bug	Physical	80	100	15	Normal	—	○
TM84	Poison Jab	Poison	Physical	80	100	20	Normal	—	○
TM87	Swagger	Normal	Status	—	90	15	Normal	—	—
TM90	Substitute	Normal	Status	—	—	10	Self	—	—
TM94	Rock Smash	Fighting	Physical	40	100	15	Normal	—	○
HM01	Cut	Normal	Physical	50	95	30	Normal	—	○
HM04	Strength	Normal	Physical	80	100	15	Normal	—	○

MOVES TAUGHT BY PEOPLE

Name	Type	Kind	Pow.	Acc.	PP	Range	Long	DA

MOVES TAUGHT BY MOVE TUTORS FOR SHARDS

Name	Type	Kind	Pow.	Acc.	PP	Range	Long	DA
Bug Bite	Bug	Physical	60	100	20	Normal	—	○
Iron Defense	Steel	Status	—	—	15	Self	—	—
Block	Normal	Status	—	—	5	Normal	—	—
Snore	Normal	Special	40	100	15	Normal	—	—
Knock Off	Dark	Physical	20	100	20	Normal	—	○
Stealth Rock	Rock	Status	—	—	20	Other Side	—	—
Sleep Talk	Normal	Status	—	—	10	Self	—	—

EGG MOVES

Name	Type	Kind	Pow.	Acc.	PP	Range	Long	DA
Endure	Normal	Status	—	—	10	Self	—	—
Iron Defense	Steel	Status	—	—	15	Self	—	—
Night Slash	Dark	Physical	70	100	15	Normal	—	○
Sand Tomb	Ground	Physical	35	85	15	Normal	—	—
Counter	Fighting	Physical	—	100	20	Varies	—	○
Curse	Ghost	Status	—	—	10	Varies	—	—
Spikes	Ground	Status	—	—	20	Other Side	—	—
Block	Normal	Status	—	—	5	Normal	—	—

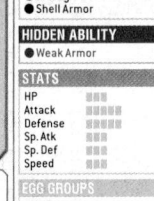

Stone Home Pokémon

558 Crustle

- HEIGHT: 4'07"
- WEIGHT: 440.9 lbs.
- GENDER: ♂ / ♀

When its boulder is broken in battles for territory, it feels unsure and begins to weaken.

Same form for ♂ / ♀

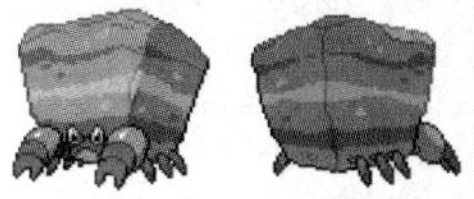

TYPE: Bug / Rock

ABILITIES
- Sturdy
- Shell Armor

HIDDEN ABILITY
- Weak Armor

STATS

HP
Attack
Defense
Sp. Atk
Sp. Def
Speed

EGG GROUPS

Bug/Mineral

ITEMS SOMETIMES HELD
- Hard Stone
- Rare Bone

Pokémon AR Marker

EVOLUTION

Dwebble
Lv. 34
Crustle

HOW TO OBTAIN

Pokémon Black Version 2: ❶ Catch after using the Colress Machine on it in Seaside Cave ❷ Route 18

Pokémon White Version 2: ❶ Catch after using the Colress Machine on it in Seaside Cave ❷ Route 18

HOW TO OBTAIN FROM OTHER GAMES

—

—

LEVEL-UP AND LEARNED MOVES

Lv.	Name	Type	Kind	Pow.	Acc.	PP	Range	Long	DA
1	Shell Smash	Normal	Status	—	—	15	Self	—	—
1	Rock Blast	Rock	Physical	25	90	10	Normal	—	—
1	Withdraw	Water	Status	—	—	40	Self	—	—
1	Sand-Attack	Ground	Status	—	100	15	Normal	—	—
5	Rock Blast	Rock	Physical	25	90	10	Normal	—	—
7	Withdraw	Water	Status	—	—	40	Self	—	—
11	Sand-Attack	Ground	Status	—	100	15	Normal	—	—
13	Faint Attack	Dark	Physical	60	—	20	Normal	—	○
17	Smack Down	Rock	Physical	50	100	15	Normal	—	—
19	Rock Polish	Rock	Status	—	—	20	Self	—	—
23	Bug Bite	Bug	Physical	60	100	20	Normal	—	○
24	Stealth Rock	Rock	Status	—	—	20	Other Side	—	—
29	Rock Slide	Rock	Physical	75	90	10	Many Others	—	—
31	Slash	Normal	Physical	70	100	20	Normal	—	○
38	X-Scissor	Bug	Physical	80	100	15	Normal	—	○
43	Shell Smash	Normal	Status	—	—	15	Self	—	—
50	Flail	Normal	Physical	—	100	15	Normal	—	○
55	Rock Wrecker	Rock	Physical	150	90	5	Normal	—	—

TM & HM MOVES

Lv.	Name	Type	Kind	Pow.	Acc.	PP	Range	Long	DA
TM01	Hone Claws	Dark	Status	—	—	15	Self	—	—
TM06	Toxic	Poison	Status	—	90	10	Normal	—	—
TM10	Hidden Power	Normal	Special	—	100	15	Normal	—	—
TM15	Hyper Beam	Normal	Special	150	90	5	Normal	—	—
TM17	Protect	Normal	Status	—	—	10	Self	—	—
TM21	Frustration	Normal	Physical	—	100	20	Normal	—	○
TM22	SolarBeam	Grass	Special	120	100	10	Normal	—	—
TM23	Smack Down	Rock	Physical	50	100	15	Normal	—	—
TM26	Earthquake	Ground	Physical	100	100	10	Adjacent	—	—
TM27	Return	Normal	Physical	—	100	20	Normal	—	○
TM28	Dig	Ground	Physical	80	100	10	Normal	—	○
TM32	Double Team	Normal	Status	—	—	15	Self	—	—
TM37	Sandstorm	Rock	Status	—	—	10	Both Sides	—	—
TM39	Rock Tomb	Rock	Physical	50	80	10	Normal	—	—
TM40	Aerial Ace	Flying	Physical	60	—	20	Normal	○	○
TM42	Facade	Normal	Physical	70	100	20	Normal	—	○
TM44	Rest	Psychic	Status	—	—	10	Self	—	—
TM45	Attract	Normal	Status	—	100	15	Normal	—	—
TM48	Round	Normal	Special	60	100	15	Normal	—	—
TM65	Shadow Claw	Ghost	Physical	70	100	15	Normal	—	○
TM68	Giga Impact	Normal	Physical	150	90	5	Normal	—	○
TM69	Rock Polish	Rock	Status	—	—	20	Self	—	—
TM71	Stone Edge	Rock	Physical	100	80	5	Normal	—	—
TM75	Swords Dance	Normal	Status	—	—	30	Self	—	—
TM76	Struggle Bug	Bug	Special	30	100	20	Many Others	—	—
TM78	Bulldoze	Ground	Physical	60	100	20	Adjacent	—	—
TM80	Rock Slide	Rock	Physical	75	90	10	Many Others	—	—
TM81	X-Scissor	Bug	Physical	80	100	15	Normal	—	○
TM84	Poison Jab	Poison	Physical	80	100	20	Normal	—	○
TM87	Swagger	Normal	Status	—	90	15	Normal	—	—
TM90	Substitute	Normal	Status	—	—	10	Self	—	—
TM94	Rock Smash	Fighting	Physical	40	100	15	Normal	—	○
HM01	Cut	Normal	Physical	50	95	30	Normal	—	○
HM04	Strength	Normal	Physical	80	100	15	Normal	—	○

MOVES TAUGHT BY PEOPLE

Name	Type	Kind	Pow.	Acc.	PP	Range	Long	DA

MOVES TAUGHT BY MOVE TUTORS FOR SHARDS

Name	Type	Kind	Pow.	Acc.	PP	Range	Long	DA
Bug Bite	Bug	Physical	60	100	20	Normal	—	○
Iron Defense	Steel	Status	—	—	15	Self	—	—
Block	Normal	Status	—	—	5	Normal	—	—
Snore	Normal	Special	40	100	15	Normal	—	—
Knock Off	Dark	Physical	20	100	20	Normal	—	○
Stealth Rock	Rock	Status	—	—	20	Other Side	—	—
Sleep Talk	Normal	Status	—	—	10	Self	—	—

Shedding Pokémon

559 Scraggy

- HEIGHT: 2'00"
- WEIGHT: 26.0 lbs.
- GENDER: ♂ / ♀

Proud of its sturdy skull, it suddenly headbutts everything, but its weight makes it unstable, too.

Same form for ♂ / ♀

TYPE: Dark / Fighting

ABILITIES
- Shed Skin
- Moxie

HIDDEN ABILITY

—

STATS

HP
Attack
Defense
Sp. Atk
Sp. Def
Speed

EGG GROUPS

Field/Dragon

ITEMS SOMETIMES HELD
- Shed Shell

Pokémon AR Marker

EVOLUTION

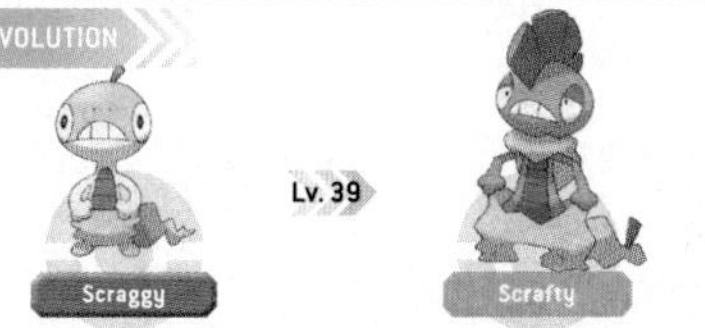
Scraggy
Lv. 39
Scrafty

HOW TO OBTAIN

Pokémon Black Version 2: ❶ Route 4 ❷ Desert Resort entrance

Pokémon White Version 2: ❶ Route 4 ❷ Desert Resort entrance

HOW TO OBTAIN FROM OTHER GAMES

—

—

LEVEL-UP AND LEARNED MOVES

Lv.	Name	Type	Kind	Pow.	Acc.	PP	Range	Long	DA
1	Leer	Normal	Status	—	100	30	Many Others	—	—
1	Low Kick	Fighting	Physical	—	100	20	Normal	—	○
5	Sand-Attack	Ground	Status	—	100	15	Normal	—	—
9	Faint Attack	Dark	Physical	60	—	20	Normal	—	○
12	Headbutt	Normal	Physical	70	100	15	Normal	—	○
16	Swagger	Normal	Status	—	90	15	Normal	—	—
20	Brick Break	Fighting	Physical	75	100	15	Normal	—	○
23	Payback	Dark	Physical	50	100	10	Normal	—	○
27	Chip Away	Normal	Physical	70	100	20	Normal	—	○
31	Hi Jump Kick	Fighting	Physical	130	90	10	Normal	—	○
34	Scary Face	Normal	Status	—	100	10	Normal	—	—
38	Crunch	Dark	Physical	80	100	15	Normal	—	○
42	Facade	Normal	Physical	70	100	20	Normal	—	○
45	Rock Climb	Normal	Physical	90	85	20	Normal	—	○
49	Focus Punch	Fighting	Physical	150	100	20	Normal	—	○
53	Head Smash	Rock	Physical	150	80	5	Normal	—	○

TM & HM MOVES

Lv.	Name	Type	Kind	Pow.	Acc.	PP	Range	Long	DA
TM02	Dragon Claw	Dragon	Physical	80	100	15	Normal	—	○
TM05	Roar	Normal	Status	—	100	20	Normal	—	—
TM06	Toxic	Poison	Status	—	90	10	Normal	—	—
TM08	Bulk Up	Fighting	Status	—	—	20	Self	—	—
TM10	Hidden Power	Normal	Special	—	100	15	Normal	—	—
TM11	Sunny Day	Fire	Status	—	—	5	Both Sides	—	—
TM12	Taunt	Dark	Status	—	100	20	Normal	—	—
TM17	Protect	Normal	Status	—	—	10	Self	—	—
TM18	Rain Dance	Water	Status	—	—	5	Both Sides	—	—
TM21	Frustration	Normal	Physical	—	100	20	Normal	—	○
TM23	Smack Down	Rock	Physical	50	100	15	Normal	—	—
TM27	Return	Normal	Physical	—	100	20	Normal	—	○
TM28	Dig	Ground	Physical	80	100	10	Normal	—	○
TM31	Brick Break	Fighting	Physical	75	100	15	Normal	—	○
TM32	Double Team	Normal	Status	—	—	15	Self	—	—
TM36	Sludge Bomb	Poison	Special	90	100	10	Normal	—	—
TM39	Rock Tomb	Rock	Physical	50	80	10	Normal	—	—
TM41	Torment	Dark	Status	—	100	15	Normal	—	—
TM42	Facade	Normal	Physical	70	100	20	Normal	—	○
TM44	Rest	Psychic	Status	—	—	10	Self	—	—
TM45	Attract	Normal	Status	—	100	15	Normal	—	—
TM47	Low Sweep	Fighting	Physical	60	100	20	Normal	—	○
TM48	Round	Normal	Special	60	100	15	Normal	—	—
TM52	Focus Blast	Fighting	Special	120	70	5	Normal	—	—
TM56	Fling	Dark	Physical	—	100	10	Normal	—	—
TM59	Incinerate	Fire	Special	30	100	15	Many Others	—	—
TM66	Payback	Dark	Physical	50	100	10	Normal	—	○
TM67	Retaliate	Normal	Physical	70	100	5	Normal	—	○
TM71	Stone Edge	Rock	Physical	100	80	5	Normal	—	—
TM80	Rock Slide	Rock	Physical	75	90	10	Many Others	—	—
TM82	Dragon Tail	Dragon	Physical	60	90	10	Normal	—	○
TM83	Work Up	Normal	Status	—	—	30	Self	—	—
TM84	Poison Jab	Poison	Physical	80	100	20	Normal	—	○
TM86	Grass Knot	Grass	Special	—	100	20	Normal	—	○
TM87	Swagger	Normal	Status	—	90	15	Normal	—	—
TM90	Substitute	Normal	Status	—	—	10	Self	—	—
TM94	Rock Smash	Fighting	Physical	40	100	15	Normal	—	○
TM95	Snarl	Dark	Special	55	95	15	Many Others	—	—
HM04	Strength	Normal	Physical	80	100	15	Normal	—	○

MOVES TAUGHT BY PEOPLE

Name	Type	Kind	Pow.	Acc.	PP	Range	Long	DA

MOVES TAUGHT BY MOVE TUTORS FOR SHARDS

Name	Type	Kind	Pow.	Acc.	PP	Range	Long	DA
Iron Head	Steel	Physical	80	100	15	Normal	—	○
Super Fang	Normal	Physical	—	90	10	Normal	—	○
Dual Chop	Dragon	Physical	40	90	15	Normal	—	○
Low Kick	Fighting	Physical	—	100	20	Normal	—	○
Fire Punch	Fire	Physical	75	100	15	Normal	—	○
ThunderPunch	Electric	Physical	75	100	15	Normal	—	○
Ice Punch	Ice	Physical	75	100	15	Normal	—	○
Iron Defense	Steel	Status	—	—	15	Self	—	—
Iron Tail	Steel	Physical	100	75	15	Normal	—	○
Zen Headbutt	Psychic	Physical	80	90	15	Normal	—	○
Foul Play	Dark	Physical	95	100	15	Normal	—	○
Dragon Pulse	Dragon	Special	90	100	10	Normal	○	—
Dark Pulse	Dark	Special	80	100	15	Normal	○	—
Snore	Normal	Special	40	100	15	Normal	—	—
Knock Off	Dark	Physical	20	100	20	Normal	—	○
Drain Punch	Fighting	Physical	75	100	10	Normal	—	○
Spite	Ghost	Status	—	100	10	Normal	—	—
Sleep Talk	Normal	Status	—	—	10	Self	—	—
Snatch	Dark	Status	—	—	10	Self	—	—

EGG MOVES

Name	Type	Kind	Pow.	Acc.	PP	Range	Long	DA
Drain Punch	Fighting	Physical	75	100	10	Normal	—	○
Counter	Fighting	Physical	—	100	20	Varies	—	○
Dragon Dance	Dragon	Status	—	—	20	Self	—	—
Detect	Fighting	Status	—	—	5	Self	—	—
Fake Out	Normal	Physical	40	100	10	Normal	—	○
Fire Punch	Fire	Physical	75	100	15	Normal	—	○
Ice Punch	Ice	Physical	75	100	15	Normal	—	○
ThunderPunch	Electric	Physical	75	100	15	Normal	—	○
Amnesia	Psychic	Status	—	—	20	Self	—	—
Faint Attack	Dark	Physical	60	—	20	Normal	—	○
Zen Headbutt	Psychic	Physical	80	90	15	Normal	—	○

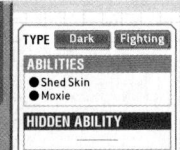

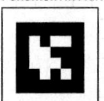

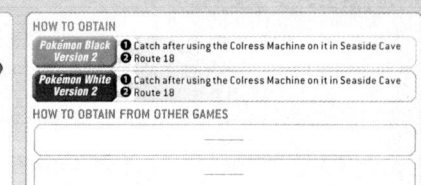

560 Scrafty

Hoodlum Pokémon

- HEIGHT: 3'07"
- WEIGHT: 66.1 lbs.
- GENDER: ♂ / ♀

It pulls up its shed skin to protect itself while it kicks. The bigger the crest, the more respected it is.

TYPE: Dark / Fighting

ABILITIES
- Shed Skin
- Moxie

HIDDEN ABILITY
—

STATS
HP
Attack
Defense
Sp. Atk
Sp. Def
Speed

EGG GROUPS
Field/Dragon

ITEMS SOMETIMES HELD
- Shed Shell

Same form for ♂ / ♀

Pokémon AR Marker

EVOLUTION

HOW TO OBTAIN

Pokémon Black Version 2	❶ Route 15 ❷ Route 18
Pokémon White Version 2	❶ Route 15 ❷ Route 18

HOW TO OBTAIN FROM OTHER GAMES

—

—

LEVEL-UP AND LEARNED MOVES

Lv.	Name	Type	Kind	Pow.	Acc.	PP	Range	Long	DA
1	Leer	Normal	Status	—	100	30	Many Others	—	—
1	Low Kick	Fighting	Physical	—	100	20	Normal	—	○
1	Sand-Attack	Ground	Status	—	100	15	Normal	—	—
1	Faint Attack	Dark	Physical	60	—	20	Normal	—	○
5	Sand-Attack	Ground	Status	—	100	15	Normal	—	—
9	Faint Attack	Dark	Physical	60	—	20	Normal	—	○
12	Headbutt	Normal	Physical	70	100	15	Normal	—	○
16	Swagger	Normal	Status	—	90	15	Normal	—	—
20	Brick Break	Fighting	Physical	75	100	15	Normal	—	○
23	Payback	Dark	Physical	50	100	10	Normal	—	○
27	Chip Away	Normal	Physical	70	100	20	Normal	—	○
31	Hi Jump Kick	Fighting	Physical	130	90	10	Normal	—	○
34	Scary Face	Normal	Status	—	100	10	Normal	—	—
38	Crunch	Dark	Physical	80	100	15	Normal	—	○
45	Facade	Normal	Physical	70	100	20	Normal	—	○
51	Rock Climb	Normal	Physical	90	85	20	Normal	—	○
58	Focus Punch	Fighting	Physical	150	100	20	Normal	—	○
65	Head Smash	Rock	Physical	150	80	5	Normal	—	○

TM & HM MOVES

Lv.	Name	Type	Kind	Pow.	Acc.	PP	Range	Long	DA
TM02	Dragon Claw	Dragon	Physical	80	100	15	Normal	—	○
TM05	Roar	Normal	Status	—	100	20	Normal	—	—
TM06	Toxic	Poison	Status	—	90	10	Normal	—	—
TM08	Bulk Up	Fighting	Status	—	—	20	Self	—	—
TM10	Hidden Power	Normal	Special	—	100	15	Normal	—	—
TM11	Sunny Day	Fire	Status	—	—	5	Both Sides	—	—
TM12	Taunt	Dark	Status	—	100	20	Normal	—	—
TM15	Hyper Beam	Normal	Special	150	90	5	Normal	—	—
TM17	Protect	Normal	Status	—	—	10	Self	—	—
TM18	Rain Dance	Water	Status	—	—	5	Both Sides	—	—
TM21	Frustration	Normal	Physical	—	100	20	Normal	—	○
TM23	Smack Down	Rock	Physical	50	100	15	Normal	—	—
TM27	Return	Normal	Physical	—	100	20	Normal	—	○
TM28	Dig	Ground	Physical	80	100	10	Normal	—	○
TM31	Brick Break	Fighting	Physical	75	100	15	Normal	—	○
TM32	Double Team	Normal	Status	—	—	15	Self	—	—
TM36	Sludge Bomb	Poison	Special	90	100	10	Normal	—	—
TM39	Rock Tomb	Rock	Physical	50	80	10	Normal	—	—
TM41	Torment	Dark	Status	—	100	15	Normal	—	—
TM42	Facade	Normal	Physical	70	100	20	Normal	—	○
TM44	Rest	Psychic	Status	—	—	10	Self	—	—
TM45	Attract	Normal	Status	—	100	15	Normal	—	—
TM46	Thief	Dark	Physical	40	100	10	Normal	—	○
TM47	Low Sweep	Fighting	Physical	60	100	20	Normal	—	○
TM48	Round	Normal	Special	60	100	15	Normal	—	—
TM52	Focus Blast	Fighting	Special	120	70	5	Normal	—	—
TM56	Fling	Dark	Physical	—	100	10	Normal	—	—
TM59	Incinerate	Fire	Special	30	100	15	Many Others	—	—
TM66	Payback	Dark	Physical	50	100	10	Normal	—	○
TM67	Retaliate	Normal	Physical	70	100	5	Normal	—	○
TM68	Giga Impact	Normal	Physical	150	90	5	Normal	—	○
TM71	Stone Edge	Rock	Physical	100	80	5	Normal	—	—
TM80	Rock Slide	Rock	Physical	75	90	10	Many Others	—	—
TM82	Dragon Tail	Dragon	Physical	60	90	10	Normal	—	○
TM83	Work Up	Normal	Status	—	—	30	Self	—	—
TM84	Poison Jab	Poison	Physical	80	100	20	Normal	—	○
TM86	Grass Knot	Grass	Special	—	100	20	Normal	—	○
TM87	Swagger	Normal	Status	—	90	15	Normal	—	—
TM90	Substitute	Normal	Status	—	—	10	Self	—	—
TM94	Rock Smash	Fighting	Physical	40	100	15	Normal	—	○
TM95	Snarl	Dark	Special	55	95	15	Many Others	—	—
HM04	Strength	Normal	Physical	80	100	15	Normal	—	○

MOVES TAUGHT BY PEOPLE

Name	Type	Kind	Pow.	Acc.	PP	Range	Long	DA

MOVES TAUGHT BY MOVE TUTORS FOR SHARDS

Name	Type	Kind	Pow.	Acc.	PP	Range	Long	DA
Iron Head	Steel	Physical	80	100	15	Normal	—	○
Super Fang	Normal	Physical	—	90	10	Normal	—	○
Dual Chop	Dragon	Physical	40	90	15	Normal	—	○
Low Kick	Fighting	Physical	—	100	20	Normal	—	○
Fire Punch	Fire	Physical	75	100	15	Normal	—	○
ThunderPunch	Electric	Physical	75	100	15	Normal	—	○
Ice Punch	Ice	Physical	75	100	15	Normal	—	○
Iron Defense	Steel	Status	—	—	15	Self	—	—
Iron Tail	Steel	Physical	100	75	15	Normal	—	○
Zen Headbutt	Psychic	Physical	80	90	15	Normal	—	○
Foul Play	Dark	Physical	95	100	15	Normal	—	○
Dragon Pulse	Dragon	Special	90	100	10	Normal	○	—
Dark Pulse	Dark	Special	80	100	15	Normal	○	—
Snore	Normal	Special	40	100	15	Normal	—	—
Knock Off	Dark	Physical	20	100	20	Normal	—	○
Drain Punch	Fighting	Physical	75	100	10	Normal	—	○
Spite	Ghost	Status	—	100	10	Normal	—	—
Outrage	Dragon	Physical	120	100	10	1 Random	—	○
Sleep Talk	Normal	Status	—	—	10	Self	—	—
Snatch	Dark	Status	—	—	10	Self	—	—

561 Sigilyph

Avianoid Pokémon

- HEIGHT: 4'07"
- WEIGHT: 30.9 lbs.
- GENDER: ♂ / ♀

The guardians of an ancient city, they always fly the same route while keeping watch for invaders.

TYPE: Psychic / Flying

ABILITIES
- Wonder Skin
- Magic Guard

HIDDEN ABILITY
- Tinted Lens

STATS
HP
Attack
Defense
Sp. Atk
Sp. Def
Speed

EGG GROUPS
Flying

ITEMS SOMETIMES HELD
- None

Same form for ♂ / ♀

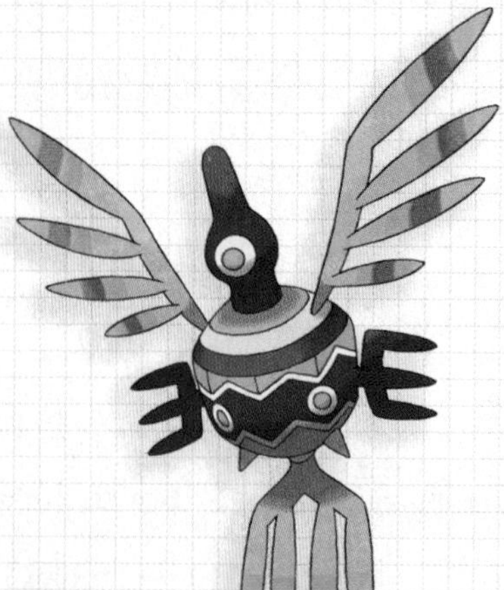

Pokémon AR Marker

EVOLUTION

Does not evolve

HOW TO OBTAIN

Pokémon Black Version 2	Desert Resort deep in the desert
Pokémon White Version 2	Desert Resort deep in the desert

HOW TO OBTAIN FROM OTHER GAMES

—

—

LEVEL-UP AND LEARNED MOVES

Lv.	Name	Type	Kind	Pow.	Acc.	PP	Range	Long	DA
1	Gust	Flying	Special	40	100	35	Normal	○	—
1	Miracle Eye	Psychic	Status	—	—	40	Normal	—	—
4	Hypnosis	Psychic	Status	—	60	20	Normal	—	—
8	Psywave	Psychic	Special	—	80	15	Normal	—	—
11	Tailwind	Flying	Status	—	—	30	Your Side	—	—
14	Whirlwind	Normal	Status	—	100	20	Normal	—	—
18	Psybeam	Psychic	Special	65	100	20	Normal	—	—
21	Air Cutter	Flying	Special	55	95	25	Many Others	—	—
24	Light Screen	Psychic	Status	—	—	30	Your Side	—	—
28	Reflect	Psychic	Status	—	—	20	Your Side	—	—
31	Synchronoise	Psychic	Special	70	100	15	Adjacent	—	—
34	Mirror Move	Flying	Status	—	—	20	Normal	—	—
38	Gravity	Psychic	Status	—	—	5	Both Sides	—	—
41	Air Slash	Flying	Special	75	95	20	Normal	○	—
44	Psychic	Psychic	Special	90	100	10	Normal	—	—
48	Cosmic Power	Psychic	Status	—	—	20	Self	—	—
51	Sky Attack	Flying	Physical	140	90	5	Normal	○	—

TM & HM MOVES

Lv.	Name	Type	Kind	Pow.	Acc.	PP	Range	Long	DA
TM03	Psyshock	Psychic	Special	80	100	10	Normal	—	—
TM04	Calm Mind	Psychic	Status	—	—	20	Self	—	—
TM06	Toxic	Poison	Status	—	90	10	Normal	—	—
TM10	Hidden Power	Normal	Special	—	100	15	Normal	—	—
TM13	Ice Beam	Ice	Special	95	100	10	Normal	—	—
TM15	Hyper Beam	Normal	Special	150	90	5	Normal	—	—
TM16	Light Screen	Psychic	Status	—	—	30	Your Side	—	—
TM17	Protect	Normal	Status	—	—	10	Self	—	—
TM18	Rain Dance	Water	Status	—	—	5	Both Sides	—	—
TM19	Telekinesis	Psychic	Status	—	—	15	Normal	—	—
TM20	Safeguard	Normal	Status	—	—	25	Your Side	—	—
TM21	Frustration	Normal	Physical	—	100	20	Normal	—	○
TM22	SolarBeam	Grass	Special	120	100	10	Normal	—	—
TM23	Smack Down	Rock	Physical	50	100	15	Normal	—	—
TM27	Return	Normal	Physical	—	100	20	Normal	—	○
TM29	Psychic	Psychic	Special	90	100	10	Normal	—	—
TM30	Shadow Ball	Ghost	Special	80	100	15	Normal	—	—
TM32	Double Team	Normal	Status	—	—	15	Self	—	—
TM33	Reflect	Psychic	Status	—	—	20	Your Side	—	—
TM40	Aerial Ace	Flying	Physical	60	—	20	Normal	○	○
TM42	Facade	Normal	Physical	70	100	20	Normal	—	○
TM44	Rest	Psychic	Status	—	—	10	Self	—	—
TM45	Attract	Normal	Status	—	100	15	Normal	—	—
TM46	Thief	Dark	Physical	40	100	10	Normal	—	○
TM48	Round	Normal	Special	60	100	15	Normal	—	—
TM53	Energy Ball	Grass	Special	80	100	10	Normal	—	—
TM57	Charge Beam	Electric	Special	50	90	10	Normal	—	—
TM70	Flash	Normal	Status	—	100	20	Normal	—	—
TM73	Thunder Wave	Electric	Status	—	100	20	Normal	—	—
TM77	Psych Up	Normal	Status	—	—	10	Normal	—	—
TM85	Dream Eater	Psychic	Special	100	100	15	Normal	—	—
TM87	Swagger	Normal	Status	—	90	15	Normal	—	—
TM88	Pluck	Flying	Physical	60	100	20	Normal	○	○
TM90	Substitute	Normal	Status	—	—	10	Self	—	—
TM91	Flash Cannon	Steel	Special	80	100	10	Normal	—	—
TM92	Trick Room	Psychic	Status	—	—	5	Both Sides	—	—
HM02	Fly	Flying	Physical	90	95	15	Normal	○	○

MOVES TAUGHT BY PEOPLE

Name	Type	Kind	Pow.	Acc.	PP	Range	Long	DA

MOVES TAUGHT BY MOVE TUTORS FOR SHARDS

Name	Type	Kind	Pow.	Acc.	PP	Range	Long	DA
Signal Beam	Bug	Special	75	100	15	Normal	—	—
Magic Coat	Psychic	Status	—	—	15	Self	—	—
Icy Wind	Ice	Special	55	95	15	Many Others	—	—
Zen Headbutt	Psychic	Physical	80	90	15	Normal	—	○
Gravity	Psychic	Status	—	—	5	Both Sides	—	—
Dark Pulse	Dark	Special	80	100	15	Normal	○	—
Snore	Normal	Special	40	100	15	Normal	—	—
Roost	Flying	Status	—	—	10	Self	—	—
Sky Attack	Flying	Physical	140	90	5	Normal	○	—
Heat Wave	Fire	Special	100	90	10	Many Others	—	—
Tailwind	Flying	Status	—	—	30	Your Side	—	—
Magic Room	Psychic	Status	—	—	10	Both Sides	—	—
Trick	Psychic	Status	—	100	10	Normal	—	—
Sleep Talk	Normal	Status	—	—	10	Self	—	—
Skill Swap	Psychic	Status	—	—	10	Normal	—	—

EGG MOVES

Name	Type	Kind	Pow.	Acc.	PP	Range	Long	DA
Stored Power	Psychic	Special	20	100	10	Normal	—	—
Psycho Shift	Psychic	Status	—	90	10	Normal	—	—
AncientPower	Rock	Special	60	100	5	Normal	—	—
Steel Wing	Steel	Physical	70	90	25	Normal	—	○
Roost	Flying	Status	—	—	10	Self	—	—
Skill Swap	Psychic	Status	—	—	10	Normal	—	—

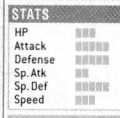

562 Yamask

Spirit Pokémon

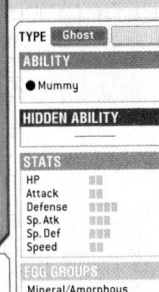

- HEIGHT: 1'08"
- WEIGHT: 3.3 lbs.
- GENDER: ♂ / ♀

These Pokémon arose from the spirits of people interred in graves. Each retains memories of its former life.

TYPE Ghost

ABILITY
- Mummy

HIDDEN ABILITY
—

STATS
HP
Attack
Defense
Sp. Atk
Sp. Def
Speed

EGG GROUPS
Mineral/Amorphous

Same form for ♂ / ♀

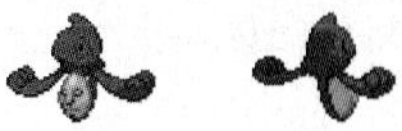

ITEMS SOMETIMES HELD
- Spell Tag

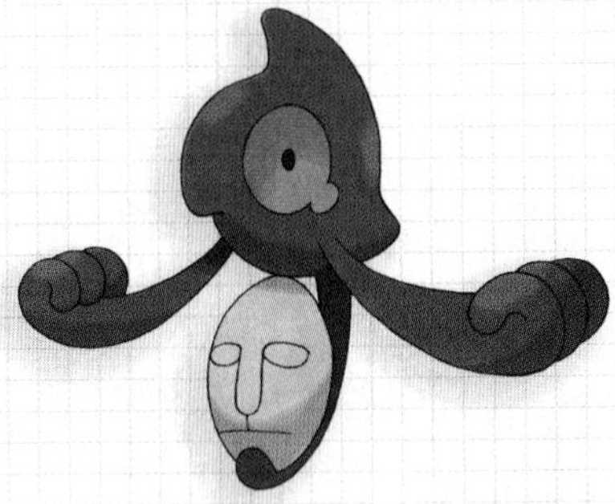

Pokémon AR Marker

EVOLUTION

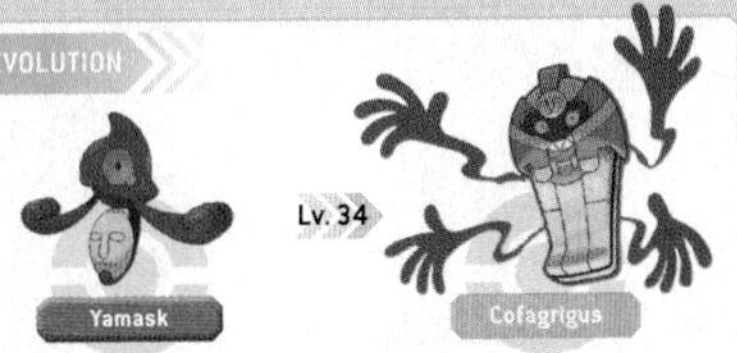

HOW TO OBTAIN

Pokémon Black Version 2	❶ Relic Castle 1F ❷ Relic Castle B1F
Pokémon White Version 2	❶ Relic Castle 1F ❷ Relic Castle B1F

HOW TO OBTAIN FROM OTHER GAMES

—

—

LEVEL-UP AND LEARNED MOVES

Lv.	Name	Type	Kind	Pow.	Acc.	PP	Range	Long	DA
1	Astonish	Ghost	Physical	30	100	15	Normal	—	○
1	Protect	Normal	Status	—	—	10	Self	—	—
5	Disable	Normal	Status	—	100	20	Normal	—	—
9	Haze	Ice	Status	—	—	30	Both Sides	—	—
13	Night Shade	Ghost	Special	—	100	15	Normal	—	—
17	Hex	Ghost	Special	50	100	10	Normal	—	—
21	Will-O-Wisp	Fire	Status	—	75	15	Normal	—	—
25	Ominous Wind	Ghost	Special	60	100	5	Normal	—	—
29	Curse	Ghost	Status	—	—	10	Varies	—	—
33	Power Split	Psychic	Status	—	—	10	Normal	—	—
33	Guard Split	Psychic	Status	—	—	10	Normal	—	—
37	Shadow Ball	Ghost	Special	80	100	15	Normal	—	—
41	Grudge	Ghost	Status	—	—	5	Self	—	—
45	Mean Look	Normal	Status	—	—	5	Normal	—	—
49	Destiny Bond	Ghost	Status	—	—	5	Self	—	—

TM & HM MOVES

Lv.	Name	Type	Kind	Pow.	Acc.	PP	Range	Long	DA
TM04	Calm Mind	Psychic	Status	—	—	20	Self	—	—
TM06	Toxic	Poison	Status	—	90	10	Normal	—	—
TM10	Hidden Power	Normal	Special	—	100	15	Normal	—	—
TM17	Protect	Normal	Status	—	—	10	Self	—	—
TM18	Rain Dance	Water	Status	—	—	5	Both Sides	—	—
TM19	Telekinesis	Psychic	Status	—	—	15	Normal	—	—
TM20	Safeguard	Normal	Status	—	—	25	Your Side	—	—
TM21	Frustration	Normal	Physical	—	100	20	Normal	—	○
TM27	Return	Normal	Physical	—	100	20	Normal	—	○
TM29	Psychic	Psychic	Special	90	100	10	Normal	—	—
TM30	Shadow Ball	Ghost	Special	80	100	15	Normal	—	—
TM32	Double Team	Normal	Status	—	—	15	Self	—	—
TM42	Facade	Normal	Physical	70	100	20	Normal	—	○
TM44	Rest	Psychic	Status	—	—	10	Self	—	—
TM45	Attract	Normal	Status	—	100	15	Normal	—	—
TM46	Thief	Dark	Physical	40	100	10	Normal	—	○
TM48	Round	Normal	Special	60	100	15	Normal	—	—
TM53	Energy Ball	Grass	Special	80	100	10	Normal	—	—
TM61	Will-O-Wisp	Fire	Status	—	75	15	Normal	—	—
TM63	Embargo	Dark	Status	—	100	15	Normal	—	—
TM66	Payback	Dark	Physical	50	100	10	Normal	—	○
TM70	Flash	Normal	Status	—	100	20	Normal	—	—
TM77	Psych Up	Normal	Status	—	—	10	Normal	—	—
TM85	Dream Eater	Psychic	Special	100	100	15	Normal	—	—
TM87	Swagger	Normal	Status	—	90	15	Normal	—	—
TM90	Substitute	Normal	Status	—	—	10	Self	—	—
TM92	Trick Room	Psychic	Status	—	—	5	Both Sides	—	—

MOVES TAUGHT BY PEOPLE

Name	Type	Kind	Pow.	Acc.	PP	Range	Long	DA

MOVES TAUGHT BY MOVE TUTORS FOR SHARDS

Name	Type	Kind	Pow.	Acc.	PP	Range	Long	DA
Iron Defense	Steel	Status	—	—	15	Self	—	—
Magic Coat	Psychic	Status	—	—	15	Self	—	—
Block	Normal	Status	—	—	5	Normal	—	—
Dark Pulse	Dark	Special	80	100	15	Normal	○	—
Snore	Normal	Special	40	100	15	Normal	—	—
Knock Off	Dark	Physical	20	100	20	Normal	—	○
Role Play	Psychic	Status	—	—	10	Normal	—	—
Pain Split	Normal	Status	—	—	20	Normal	—	—
After You	Normal	Status	—	—	15	Normal	—	—
Wonder Room	Psychic	Status	—	—	10	Both Sides	—	—
Spite	Ghost	Status	—	100	10	Normal	—	—
Trick	Psychic	Status	—	100	10	Normal	—	—
Sleep Talk	Normal	Status	—	—	10	Self	—	—
Skill Swap	Psychic	Status	—	—	10	Normal	—	—
Snatch	Dark	Status	—	—	10	Self	—	—

EGG MOVES

Name	Type	Kind	Pow.	Acc.	PP	Range	Long	DA
Memento	Dark	Status	—	100	10	Normal	—	—
Fake Tears	Dark	Status	—	100	20	Normal	—	—
Nasty Plot	Dark	Status	—	—	20	Self	—	—
Endure	Normal	Status	—	—	10	Self	—	—
Heal Block	Psychic	Status	—	100	15	Many Others	—	—
Imprison	Psychic	Status	—	—	10	Self	—	—
Nightmare	Ghost	Status	—	100	15	Normal	—	—
Disable	Normal	Status	—	100	20	Normal	—	—

563 Cofagrigus

Coffin Pokémon

- HEIGHT: 5'07"
- WEIGHT: 168.7 lbs.
- GENDER: ♂ / ♀

Grave robbers who mistake them for real coffins and get too close end up trapped inside their bodies.

TYPE Ghost

ABILITY
- Mummy

HIDDEN ABILITY
—

STATS
HP
Attack
Defense
Sp. Atk
Sp. Def
Speed

EGG GROUPS
Mineral/Amorphous

Same form for ♂ / ♀

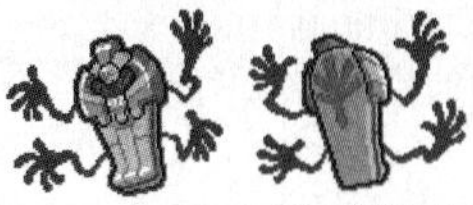

ITEMS SOMETIMES HELD
- None

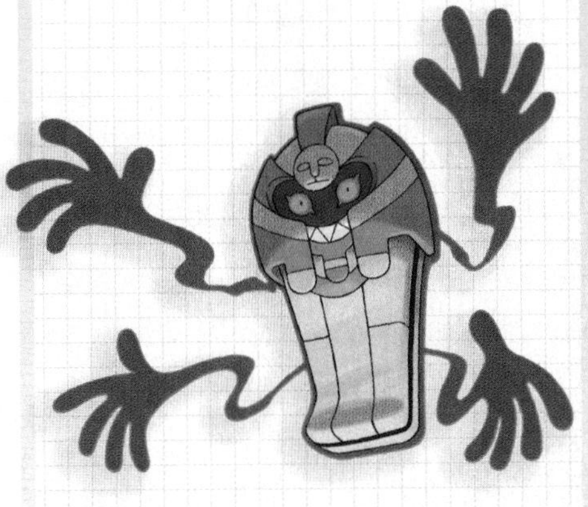

Pokémon AR Marker

EVOLUTION

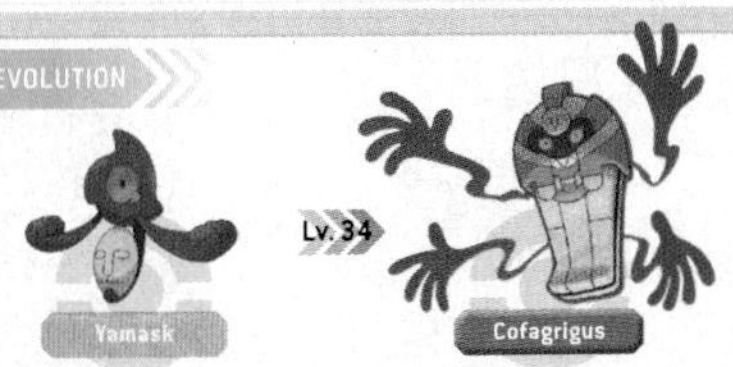

HOW TO OBTAIN

Pokémon Black Version 2	Level up Yamask to Lv. 34
Pokémon White Version 2	Level up Yamask to Lv. 34

HOW TO OBTAIN FROM OTHER GAMES

—

—

LEVEL-UP AND LEARNED MOVES

Lv.	Name	Type	Kind	Pow.	Acc.	PP	Range	Long	DA
1	Astonish	Ghost	Physical	30	100	15	Normal	—	○
1	Protect	Normal	Status	—	—	10	Self	—	—
1	Disable	Normal	Status	—	100	20	Normal	—	—
1	Haze	Ice	Status	—	—	30	Both Sides	—	—
5	Disable	Normal	Status	—	100	20	Normal	—	—
9	Haze	Ice	Status	—	—	30	Both Sides	—	—
13	Night Shade	Ghost	Special	—	100	15	Normal	—	—
17	Hex	Ghost	Special	50	100	10	Normal	—	—
21	Will-O-Wisp	Fire	Status	—	75	15	Normal	—	—
25	Ominous Wind	Ghost	Special	60	100	5	Normal	—	—
29	Curse	Ghost	Status	—	—	10	Varies	—	—
33	Power Split	Psychic	Status	—	—	10	Normal	—	—
33	Guard Split	Psychic	Status	—	—	10	Normal	—	—
34	Scary Face	Normal	Status	—	100	10	Normal	—	—
39	Shadow Ball	Ghost	Special	80	100	15	Normal	—	—
45	Grudge	Ghost	Status	—	—	5	Self	—	—
51	Mean Look	Normal	Status	—	—	5	Normal	—	—
57	Destiny Bond	Ghost	Status	—	—	5	Self	—	—

TM & HM MOVES

Lv.	Name	Type	Kind	Pow.	Acc.	PP	Range	Long	DA
TM04	Calm Mind	Psychic	Status	—	—	20	Self	—	—
TM06	Toxic	Poison	Status	—	90	10	Normal	—	—
TM10	Hidden Power	Normal	Special	—	100	15	Normal	—	—
TM15	Hyper Beam	Normal	Special	150	90	5	Normal	—	—
TM17	Protect	Normal	Status	—	—	10	Self	—	—
TM18	Rain Dance	Water	Status	—	—	5	Both Sides	—	—
TM19	Telekinesis	Psychic	Status	—	—	15	Normal	—	—
TM20	Safeguard	Normal	Status	—	—	25	Your Side	—	—
TM21	Frustration	Normal	Physical	—	100	20	Normal	—	○
TM27	Return	Normal	Physical	—	100	20	Normal	—	○
TM29	Psychic	Psychic	Special	90	100	10	Normal	—	—
TM30	Shadow Ball	Ghost	Special	80	100	15	Normal	—	—
TM32	Double Team	Normal	Status	—	—	15	Self	—	—
TM42	Facade	Normal	Physical	70	100	20	Normal	—	○
TM44	Rest	Psychic	Status	—	—	10	Self	—	—
TM45	Attract	Normal	Status	—	100	15	Normal	—	—
TM46	Thief	Dark	Physical	40	100	10	Normal	—	○
TM48	Round	Normal	Special	60	100	15	Normal	—	—
TM53	Energy Ball	Grass	Special	80	100	10	Normal	—	—
TM61	Will-O-Wisp	Fire	Status	—	75	15	Normal	—	—
TM63	Embargo	Dark	Status	—	100	15	Normal	—	—
TM66	Payback	Dark	Physical	50	100	10	Normal	—	○
TM68	Giga Impact	Normal	Physical	150	90	5	Normal	—	○
TM70	Flash	Normal	Status	—	100	20	Normal	—	—
TM77	Psych Up	Normal	Status	—	—	10	Normal	—	—
TM85	Dream Eater	Psychic	Special	100	100	15	Normal	—	—
TM86	Grass Knot	Grass	Special	—	100	20	Normal	—	○
TM87	Swagger	Normal	Status	—	90	15	Normal	—	—
TM90	Substitute	Normal	Status	—	—	10	Self	—	—
TM92	Trick Room	Psychic	Status	—	—	5	Both Sides	—	—

MOVES TAUGHT BY PEOPLE

Name	Type	Kind	Pow.	Acc.	PP	Range	Long	DA

MOVES TAUGHT BY MOVE TUTORS FOR SHARDS

Name	Type	Kind	Pow.	Acc.	PP	Range	Long	DA
Iron Defense	Steel	Status	—	—	15	Self	—	—
Magic Coat	Psychic	Status	—	—	15	Self	—	—
Block	Normal	Status	—	—	5	Normal	—	—
Dark Pulse	Dark	Special	80	100	15	Normal	○	—
Snore	Normal	Special	40	100	15	Normal	—	—
Knock Off	Dark	Physical	20	100	20	Normal	—	○
Role Play	Psychic	Status	—	—	10	Normal	—	—
Pain Split	Normal	Status	—	—	20	Normal	—	—
After You	Normal	Status	—	—	15	Normal	—	—
Wonder Room	Psychic	Status	—	—	10	Both Sides	—	—
Spite	Ghost	Status	—	100	10	Normal	—	—
Trick	Psychic	Status	—	100	10	Normal	—	—
Sleep Talk	Normal	Status	—	—	10	Self	—	—
Skill Swap	Psychic	Status	—	—	10	Normal	—	—
Snatch	Dark	Status	—	—	10	Self	—	—

564 Tirtouga
Prototurtle Pokémon

TYPE Water / Rock

ABILITIES
- Solid Rock
- Sturdy

HIDDEN ABILITY
- Swift Swim

- HEIGHT: 2'04"
- WEIGHT: 36.4 lbs.
- GENDER: ♂ / ♀

This Pokémon was restored from a fossil. It swam skillfully and dove to depths beyond half a mile.

Same form for ♂ / ♀

STATS
- HP
- Attack
- Defense
- Sp. Atk
- Sp. Def
- Speed

EGG GROUPS
Water ❶ / Water ❸

ITEMS SOMETIMES HELD
- None

Pokémon AR Marker

⬤ EVOLUTION

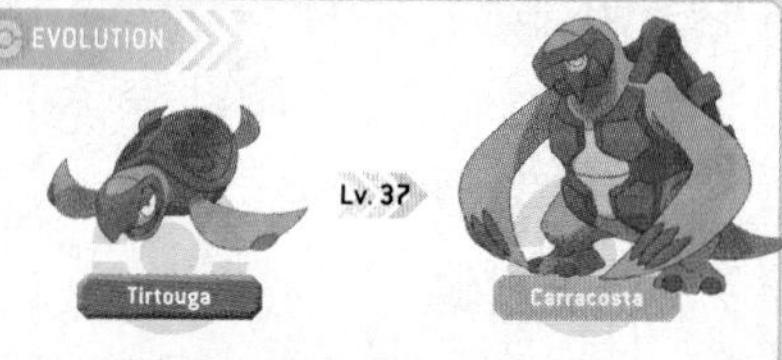

Tirtouga → Lv. 37 → Carracosta

HOW TO OBTAIN

Pokémon Black Version 2	Get the Cover Fossil from Lenora in Nacrene City and have it restored at the Nacrene Museum
Pokémon White Version 2	Get the Cover Fossil from Lenora in Nacrene City and have it restored at the Nacrene Museum

HOW TO OBTAIN FROM OTHER GAMES

—

LEVEL-UP AND LEARNED MOVES

Lv.	Name	Type	Kind	Pow.	Acc.	PP	Range	Long	DA
1	Bide	Normal	Physical	—	—	10	Self	—	
1	Withdraw	Water	Status	—	—	40	Self	—	
1	Water Gun	Water	Special	40	100	25	Normal	—	
5	Rollout	Rock	Physical	30	90	20	Normal	—	○
8	Bite	Dark	Physical	60	100	25	Normal	—	○
11	Protect	Normal	Status	—	—	10	Self	—	
15	Aqua Jet	Water	Physical	40	100	20	Normal	—	○
18	AncientPower	Rock	Special	60	100	5	Normal	—	○
21	Crunch	Dark	Physical	80	100	15	Normal	—	○
25	Wide Guard	Rock	Status	—	—	10	Your Side	—	
28	Brine	Water	Special	65	100	10	Normal	—	○
31	Smack Down	Rock	Physical	50	100	15	Normal	—	○
35	Curse	Ghost	Status	—	—	10	Varies	—	
38	Shell Smash	Normal	Status	—	—	15	Self	—	
41	Aqua Tail	Water	Physical	90	90	10	Normal	—	○
45	Rock Slide	Rock	Physical	75	90	10	Many Others	—	
48	Rain Dance	Water	Status	—	—	5	Both Sides	—	
51	Hydro Pump	Water	Special	120	80	5	Normal	—	○

TM & HM MOVES

Lv.	Name	Type	Kind	Pow.	Acc.	PP	Range	Long	DA
TM06	Toxic	Poison	Status	—	90	10	Normal	—	
TM10	Hidden Power	Normal	Special	—	100	15	Normal	—	
TM13	Ice Beam	Ice	Special	95	100	10	Normal	—	
TM14	Blizzard	Ice	Special	120	70	5	Many Others	—	
TM17	Protect	Normal	Status	—	—	10	Self	—	
TM18	Rain Dance	Water	Status	—	—	5	Both Sides	—	
TM21	Frustration	Normal	Physical	—	100	20	Normal	—	○
TM23	Smack Down	Rock	Physical	50	100	15	Normal	—	○
TM26	Earthquake	Ground	Physical	100	100	10	Adjacent	—	
TM27	Return	Normal	Physical	—	100	20	Normal	—	○
TM28	Dig	Ground	Physical	80	100	10	Normal	—	○
TM32	Double Team	Normal	Status	—	—	15	Self	—	
TM37	Sandstorm	Rock	Status	—	—	10	Both Sides	—	
TM39	Rock Tomb	Rock	Physical	50	80	10	Normal	—	○
TM42	Facade	Normal	Physical	70	100	20	Normal	—	○
TM44	Rest	Psychic	Status	—	—	10	Self	—	
TM45	Attract	Normal	Status	—	100	15	Normal	—	
TM48	Round	Normal	Special	60	100	15	Normal	—	
TM55	Scald	Water	Special	80	100	15	Normal	—	
TM69	Rock Polish	Rock	Status	—	—	20	Self	—	
TM71	Stone Edge	Rock	Physical	100	80	5	Normal	—	○
TM78	Bulldoze	Ground	Physical	60	100	20	Adjacent	—	
TM80	Rock Slide	Rock	Physical	75	90	10	Many Others	—	
TM87	Swagger	Normal	Status	—	90	15	Normal	—	
TM90	Substitute	Normal	Status	—	—	10	Self	—	
TM94	Rock Smash	Fighting	Physical	40	100	15	Normal	—	○
HM03	Surf	Water	Special	95	100	15	Adjacent	—	
HM04	Strength	Normal	Physical	80	100	15	Normal	—	○
HM05	Waterfall	Water	Physical	80	100	15	Normal	—	○
HM06	Dive	Water	Physical	80	100	10	Normal	—	

MOVES TAUGHT BY PEOPLE

Name	Type	Kind	Pow.	Acc.	PP	Range	Long	DA

MOVES TAUGHT BY MOVE TUTORS FOR SHARDS

Name	Type	Kind	Pow.	Acc.	PP	Range	Long	DA
Iron Defense	Steel	Status	—	—	15	Self	—	
Block	Normal	Status	—	—	5	Normal	—	
Icy Wind	Ice	Special	55	95	15	Many Others	—	
Iron Tail	Steel	Physical	100	75	15	Normal	—	○
Aqua Tail	Water	Physical	90	90	10	Normal	—	○
Earth Power	Ground	Special	90	100	10	Normal	—	
Snore	Normal	Special	40	100	15	Normal	—	
Stealth Rock	Rock	Status	—	—	20	Other Side	—	
Sleep Talk	Normal	Status	—	—	10	Self	—	

EGG MOVES

Name	Type	Kind	Pow.	Acc.	PP	Range	Long	DA
Water Pulse	Water	Special	60	100	20	Normal	○	
Knock Off	Dark	Physical	20	100	20	Normal	—	○
Rock Throw	Rock	Physical	50	90	15	Normal	—	
Slam	Normal	Physical	80	75	20	Normal	—	○
Iron Defense	Steel	Status	—	—	15	Self	—	
Flail	Normal	Physical	—	100	15	Normal	—	○
Whirlpool	Water	Special	35	85	15	Normal	—	
Body Slam	Normal	Physical	85	100	15	Normal	—	○
Bide	Normal	Physical	—	—	10	Self	—	

---

565 Carracosta
Prototurtle Pokémon

TYPE Water / Rock

ABILITIES
- Solid Rock
- Sturdy

HIDDEN ABILITY
- Swift Swim

- HEIGHT: 3'11"
- WEIGHT: 178.6 lbs.
- GENDER: ♂ / ♀

It could knock out a foe with a slap from one of its developed front appendages and chew it up, shell or bones and all.

Same form for ♂ / ♀

STATS
- HP
- Attack
- Defense
- Sp. Atk
- Sp. Def
- Speed

EGG GROUPS
Water ❶ / Water ❸

ITEMS SOMETIMES HELD
- None

Pokémon AR Marker

⬤ EVOLUTION

Tirtouga → Lv. 37 → Carracosta

HOW TO OBTAIN

Pokémon Black Version 2	Level up Tirtouga to Lv. 37
Pokémon White Version 2	Level up Tirtouga to Lv. 37

HOW TO OBTAIN FROM OTHER GAMES

LEVEL-UP AND LEARNED MOVES

Lv.	Name	Type	Kind	Pow.	Acc.	PP	Range	Long	DA
1	Bide	Normal	Physical	—	—	10	Self	—	
1	Withdraw	Water	Status	—	—	40	Self	—	
1	Water Gun	Water	Special	40	100	25	Normal	—	
1	Rollout	Rock	Physical	30	90	20	Normal	—	○
5	Rollout	Rock	Physical	30	90	20	Normal	—	○
8	Bite	Dark	Physical	60	100	25	Normal	—	○
11	Protect	Normal	Status	—	—	10	Self	—	
15	Aqua Jet	Water	Physical	40	100	20	Normal	—	○
18	AncientPower	Rock	Special	60	100	5	Normal	—	○
21	Crunch	Dark	Physical	80	100	15	Normal	—	○
25	Wide Guard	Rock	Status	—	—	10	Your Side	—	
28	Brine	Water	Special	65	100	10	Normal	—	○
31	Smack Down	Rock	Physical	50	100	15	Normal	—	○
35	Curse	Ghost	Status	—	—	10	Varies	—	
40	Shell Smash	Normal	Status	—	—	15	Self	—	
45	Aqua Tail	Water	Physical	90	90	10	Normal	—	○
51	Rock Slide	Rock	Physical	75	90	10	Many Others	—	
56	Rain Dance	Water	Status	—	—	5	Both Sides	—	
61	Hydro Pump	Water	Special	120	80	5	Normal	—	○

TM & HM MOVES

Lv.	Name	Type	Kind	Pow.	Acc.	PP	Range	Long	DA
TM06	Toxic	Poison	Status	—	90	10	Normal	—	
TM10	Hidden Power	Normal	Special	—	100	15	Normal	—	
TM13	Ice Beam	Ice	Special	95	100	10	Normal	—	
TM14	Blizzard	Ice	Special	120	70	5	Many Others	—	
TM15	Hyper Beam	Normal	Special	150	90	5	Normal	—	
TM17	Protect	Normal	Status	—	—	10	Self	—	
TM18	Rain Dance	Water	Status	—	—	5	Both Sides	—	
TM21	Frustration	Normal	Physical	—	100	20	Normal	—	○
TM23	Smack Down	Rock	Physical	50	100	15	Normal	—	○
TM26	Earthquake	Ground	Physical	100	100	10	Adjacent	—	
TM27	Return	Normal	Physical	—	100	20	Normal	—	○
TM28	Dig	Ground	Physical	80	100	10	Normal	—	○
TM32	Double Team	Normal	Status	—	—	15	Self	—	
TM37	Sandstorm	Rock	Status	—	—	10	Both Sides	—	
TM39	Rock Tomb	Rock	Physical	50	80	10	Normal	—	○
TM42	Facade	Normal	Physical	70	100	20	Normal	—	○
TM44	Rest	Psychic	Status	—	—	10	Self	—	
TM45	Attract	Normal	Status	—	100	15	Normal	—	
TM48	Round	Normal	Special	60	100	15	Normal	—	
TM52	Focus Blast	Fighting	Special	120	70	5	Normal	—	
TM55	Scald	Water	Special	80	100	15	Normal	—	
TM68	Giga Impact	Normal	Physical	150	90	5	Normal	—	
TM69	Rock Polish	Rock	Status	—	—	20	Self	—	
TM71	Stone Edge	Rock	Physical	100	80	5	Normal	—	○
TM78	Bulldoze	Ground	Physical	60	100	20	Adjacent	—	
TM80	Rock Slide	Rock	Physical	75	90	10	Many Others	—	
TM87	Swagger	Normal	Status	—	90	15	Normal	—	
TM90	Substitute	Normal	Status	—	—	10	Self	—	
TM94	Rock Smash	Fighting	Physical	40	100	15	Normal	—	○
HM03	Surf	Water	Special	95	100	15	Adjacent	—	
HM04	Strength	Normal	Physical	80	100	15	Normal	—	○
HM05	Waterfall	Water	Physical	80	100	15	Normal	—	○
HM06	Dive	Water	Physical	80	100	10	Normal	—	

MOVES TAUGHT BY PEOPLE

Name	Type	Kind	Pow.	Acc.	PP	Range	Long	DA

MOVES TAUGHT BY MOVE TUTORS FOR SHARDS

Name	Type	Kind	Pow.	Acc.	PP	Range	Long	DA
Iron Head	Steel	Physical	80	100	15	Normal	—	○
Low Kick	Fighting	Physical	—	100	20	Normal	—	○
Iron Defense	Steel	Status	—	—	15	Self	—	
Block	Normal	Status	—	—	5	Normal	—	
Icy Wind	Ice	Special	55	95	15	Many Others	—	
Iron Tail	Steel	Physical	100	75	15	Normal	—	○
Aqua Tail	Water	Physical	90	90	10	Normal	—	○
Earth Power	Ground	Special	90	100	10	Normal	—	
Superpower	Fighting	Physical	120	100	5	Normal	—	
Snore	Normal	Special	40	100	15	Normal	—	
Stealth Rock	Rock	Status	—	—	20	Other Side	—	
Sleep Talk	Normal	Status	—	—	10	Self	—	

First Bird Pokémon

566 Archen

TYPE: Rock / Flying

ABILITY
- Defeatist

HIDDEN ABILITY
—

STATS
HP
Attack
Defense
Sp. Atk
Sp. Def
Speed

EGG GROUPS
Flying/Water ❸

- HEIGHT: 1'08"
- WEIGHT: 20.9 lbs.
- GENDER: ♂ / ♀

It was revived from an ancient fossil. Not able to fly, it lived in treetops and hopped from one branch to another.

Same form for ♂ / ♀

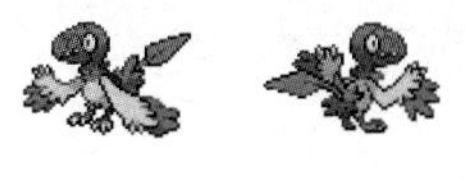

ITEMS SOMETIMES HELD
- None

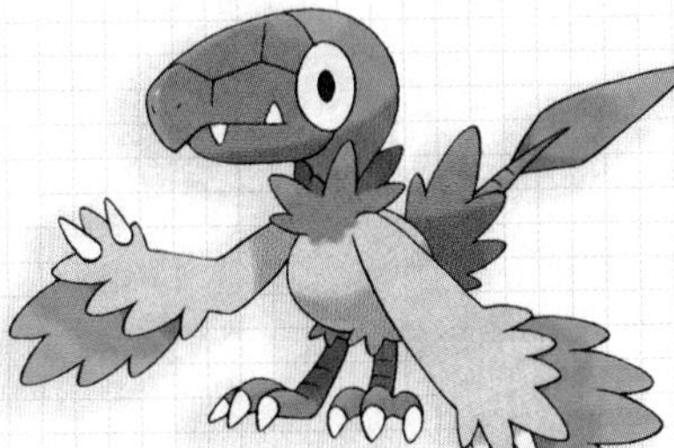

Pokémon AR Marker

EVOLUTION

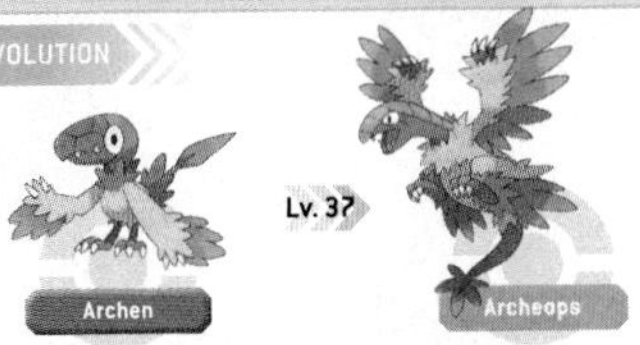

HOW TO OBTAIN

Pokémon Black Version 2	Get the Plume Fossil from Lenora in Nacrene City and have it restored at the Nacrene Museum
Pokémon White Version 2	Get the Plume Fossil from Lenora in Nacrene City and have it restored at the Nacrene Museum

HOW TO OBTAIN FROM OTHER GAMES

—

—

LEVEL-UP AND LEARNED MOVES

Lv.	Name	Type	Kind	Pow.	Acc.	PP	Range	Long	DA
1	Quick Attack	Normal	Physical	40	100	30	Normal	—	○
1	Leer	Normal	Status	—	100	30	Many Others	—	—
1	Wing Attack	Flying	Physical	60	100	35	Normal	○	○
5	Rock Throw	Rock	Physical	50	90	15	Normal	—	—
8	Double Team	Normal	Status	—	—	15	Self	—	—
11	Scary Face	Normal	Status	—	100	10	Normal	—	—
15	Pluck	Flying	Physical	60	100	20	Normal	○	○
18	AncientPower	Rock	Special	60	100	5	Normal	—	—
21	Agility	Psychic	Status	—	—	30	Self	—	—
25	Quick Guard	Fighting	Status	—	—	15	Your Side	—	—
28	Acrobatics	Flying	Physical	55	100	15	Normal	○	○
31	DragonBreath	Dragon	Special	60	100	20	Normal	—	—
35	Crunch	Dark	Physical	80	100	15	Normal	—	○
38	Endeavor	Normal	Physical	—	100	5	Normal	—	○
41	U-turn	Bug	Physical	70	100	20	Normal	—	○
45	Rock Slide	Rock	Physical	75	90	10	Many Others	—	—
48	Dragon Claw	Dragon	Physical	80	100	15	Normal	—	○
51	Thrash	Normal	Physical	120	100	10	1 Random	—	○

TM & HM MOVES

Lv.	Name	Type	Kind	Pow.	Acc.	PP	Range	Long	DA
TM01	Hone Claws	Dark	Status	—	—	15	Self	—	—
TM02	Dragon Claw	Dragon	Physical	80	100	15	Normal	—	○
TM05	Roar	Normal	Status	—	100	20	Normal	—	—
TM06	Toxic	Poison	Status	—	90	10	Normal	—	—
TM10	Hidden Power	Normal	Special	—	100	15	Normal	—	—
TM12	Taunt	Dark	Status	—	100	20	Normal	—	—
TM17	Protect	Normal	Status	—	—	10	Self	—	—
TM21	Frustration	Normal	Physical	—	100	20	Normal	—	○
TM23	Smack Down	Rock	Physical	50	100	15	Normal	—	—
TM26	Earthquake	Ground	Physical	100	100	10	Adjacent	—	—
TM27	Return	Normal	Physical	—	100	20	Normal	—	○
TM28	Dig	Ground	Physical	80	100	10	Normal	—	○
TM32	Double Team	Normal	Status	—	—	15	Self	—	—
TM37	Sandstorm	Rock	Status	—	—	10	Both Sides	—	—
TM39	Rock Tomb	Rock	Physical	50	80	10	Normal	—	—
TM40	Aerial Ace	Flying	Physical	60	—	20	Normal	○	○
TM41	Torment	Dark	Status	—	100	15	Normal	—	—
TM42	Facade	Normal	Physical	70	100	20	Normal	—	○
TM44	Rest	Psychic	Status	—	—	10	Self	—	—
TM45	Attract	Normal	Status	—	100	15	Normal	—	—
TM48	Round	Normal	Special	60	100	15	Normal	—	—
TM62	Acrobatics	Flying	Physical	55	100	15	Normal	○	○
TM65	Shadow Claw	Ghost	Physical	70	100	15	Normal	—	○
TM69	Rock Polish	Rock	Status	—	—	20	Self	—	—
TM71	Stone Edge	Rock	Physical	100	80	5	Normal	—	—
TM78	Bulldoze	Ground	Physical	60	100	20	Adjacent	—	—
TM80	Rock Slide	Rock	Physical	75	90	10	Many Others	—	—
TM87	Swagger	Normal	Status	—	90	15	Normal	—	—
TM88	Pluck	Flying	Physical	60	100	20	Normal	○	○
TM89	U-turn	Bug	Physical	70	100	20	Normal	—	○
TM90	Substitute	Normal	Status	—	—	10	Self	—	—
TM94	Rock Smash	Fighting	Physical	40	100	15	Normal	—	○
HM01	Cut	Normal	Physical	50	95	30	Normal	—	○

MOVES TAUGHT BY PEOPLE

Name	Type	Kind	Pow.	Acc.	PP	Range	Long	DA

MOVES TAUGHT BY MOVE TUTORS FOR SHARDS

Name	Type	Kind	Pow.	Acc.	PP	Range	Long	DA
Bounce	Flying	Physical	85	85	5	Normal	○	○
Uproar	Normal	Special	90	100	10	1 Random	—	—
Iron Defense	Steel	Status	—	—	15	Self	—	—
Iron Tail	Steel	Physical	100	75	15	Normal	—	○
Aqua Tail	Water	Physical	90	90	10	Normal	—	○
Earth Power	Ground	Special	90	100	10	Normal	—	—
Dragon Pulse	Dragon	Special	90	100	10	Normal	○	—
Snore	Normal	Special	40	100	15	Normal	—	—
Roost	Flying	Status	—	—	10	Self	—	—
Heat Wave	Fire	Special	100	90	10	Many Others	—	—
Tailwind	Flying	Status	—	—	30	Your Side	—	—
Stealth Rock	Rock	Status	—	—	20	Other Side	—	—
Endeavor	Normal	Physical	—	100	5	Normal	—	○
Sleep Talk	Normal	Status	—	—	10	Self	—	—

EGG MOVES

Name	Type	Kind	Pow.	Acc.	PP	Range	Long	DA
Steel Wing	Steel	Physical	70	90	25	Normal	—	○
Defog	Flying	Status	—	—	15	Normal	—	—
Dragon Pulse	Dragon	Special	90	100	10	Normal	○	—
Head Smash	Rock	Physical	150	80	5	Normal	—	○
Knock Off	Dark	Physical	20	100	20	Normal	—	○
Earth Power	Ground	Special	90	100	10	Normal	—	—
Bite	Dark	Physical	60	100	25	Normal	—	○

First Bird Pokémon

567 Archeops

TYPE: Rock / Flying

ABILITY
- Defeatist

HIDDEN ABILITY
—

STATS
HP
Attack
Defense
Sp. Atk
Sp. Def
Speed

EGG GROUPS
Flying/Water ❸

- HEIGHT: 4'07"
- WEIGHT: 70.5 lbs.
- GENDER: ♂ / ♀

It runs better than it flies. It takes off into the sky by running at a speed of 25 mph.

Same form for ♂ / ♀

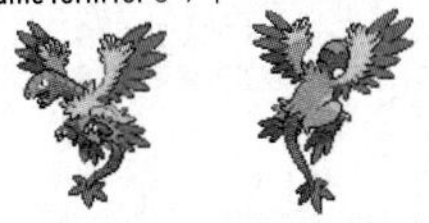

ITEMS SOMETIMES HELD
- None

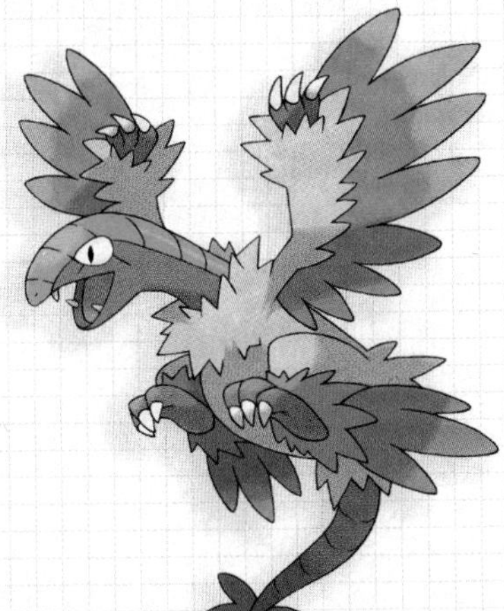

Pokémon AR Marker

EVOLUTION

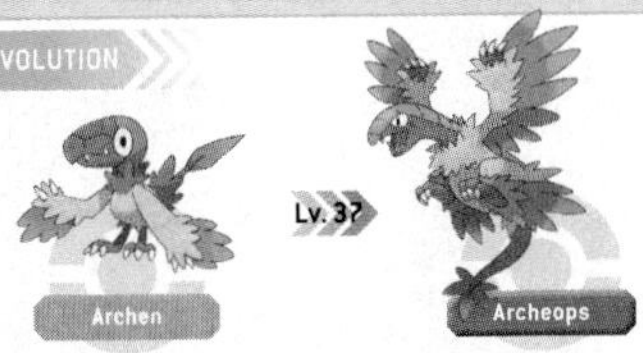

HOW TO OBTAIN

Pokémon Black Version 2	Level up Archen to Lv. 37
Pokémon White Version 2	Level up Archen to Lv. 37

HOW TO OBTAIN FROM OTHER GAMES

—

—

LEVEL-UP AND LEARNED MOVES

Lv.	Name	Type	Kind	Pow.	Acc.	PP	Range	Long	DA
1	Quick Attack	Normal	Physical	40	100	30	Normal	—	○
1	Leer	Normal	Status	—	100	30	Many Others	—	—
1	Wing Attack	Flying	Physical	60	100	35	Normal	○	○
1	Rock Throw	Rock	Physical	50	90	15	Normal	—	—
5	Rock Throw	Rock	Physical	50	90	15	Normal	—	—
8	Double Team	Normal	Status	—	—	15	Self	—	—
11	Scary Face	Normal	Status	—	100	10	Normal	—	—
15	Pluck	Flying	Physical	60	100	20	Normal	○	○
18	AncientPower	Rock	Special	60	100	5	Normal	—	—
21	Agility	Psychic	Status	—	—	30	Self	—	—
25	Quick Guard	Fighting	Status	—	—	15	Your Side	—	—
28	Acrobatics	Flying	Physical	55	100	15	Normal	○	○
31	DragonBreath	Dragon	Special	60	100	20	Normal	—	—
35	Crunch	Dark	Physical	80	100	15	Normal	—	○
40	Endeavor	Normal	Physical	—	100	5	Normal	—	○
45	U-turn	Bug	Physical	70	100	20	Normal	—	○
51	Rock Slide	Rock	Physical	75	90	10	Many Others	—	—
56	Dragon Claw	Dragon	Physical	80	100	15	Normal	—	○
61	Thrash	Normal	Physical	120	100	10	1 Random	—	○

TM & HM MOVES

Lv.	Name	Type	Kind	Pow.	Acc.	PP	Range	Long	DA
TM01	Hone Claws	Dark	Status	—	—	15	Self	—	—
TM02	Dragon Claw	Dragon	Physical	80	100	15	Normal	—	○
TM05	Roar	Normal	Status	—	100	20	Normal	—	—
TM06	Toxic	Poison	Status	—	90	10	Normal	—	—
TM10	Hidden Power	Normal	Special	—	100	15	Normal	—	—
TM12	Taunt	Dark	Status	—	100	20	Normal	—	—
TM15	Hyper Beam	Normal	Special	150	90	5	Normal	—	—
TM17	Protect	Normal	Status	—	—	10	Self	—	—
TM21	Frustration	Normal	Physical	—	100	20	Normal	—	○
TM23	Smack Down	Rock	Physical	50	100	15	Normal	—	—
TM26	Earthquake	Ground	Physical	100	100	10	Adjacent	—	—
TM27	Return	Normal	Physical	—	100	20	Normal	—	○
TM28	Dig	Ground	Physical	80	100	10	Normal	—	○
TM32	Double Team	Normal	Status	—	—	15	Self	—	—
TM37	Sandstorm	Rock	Status	—	—	10	Both Sides	—	—
TM39	Rock Tomb	Rock	Physical	50	80	10	Normal	—	—
TM40	Aerial Ace	Flying	Physical	60	—	20	Normal	○	○
TM41	Torment	Dark	Status	—	100	15	Normal	—	—
TM42	Facade	Normal	Physical	70	100	20	Normal	—	○
TM44	Rest	Psychic	Status	—	—	10	Self	—	—
TM45	Attract	Normal	Status	—	100	15	Normal	—	—
TM48	Round	Normal	Special	60	100	15	Normal	—	—
TM52	Focus Blast	Fighting	Special	120	70	5	Normal	—	—
TM62	Acrobatics	Flying	Physical	55	100	15	Normal	○	○
TM65	Shadow Claw	Ghost	Physical	70	100	15	Normal	—	○
TM68	Giga Impact	Normal	Physical	150	90	5	Normal	—	○
TM69	Rock Polish	Rock	Status	—	—	20	Self	—	—
TM71	Stone Edge	Rock	Physical	100	80	5	Normal	—	—
TM78	Bulldoze	Ground	Physical	60	100	20	Adjacent	—	—
TM80	Rock Slide	Rock	Physical	75	90	10	Many Others	—	—
TM82	Dragon Tail	Dragon	Physical	60	90	10	Normal	—	○
TM87	Swagger	Normal	Status	—	90	15	Normal	—	—
TM88	Pluck	Flying	Physical	60	100	20	Normal	○	○
TM89	U-turn	Bug	Physical	70	100	20	Normal	—	○
TM90	Substitute	Normal	Status	—	—	10	Self	—	—
TM94	Rock Smash	Fighting	Physical	40	100	15	Normal	—	○
HM01	Cut	Normal	Physical	50	95	30	Normal	—	○
HM02	Fly	Flying	Physical	90	95	15	Normal	○	○

MOVES TAUGHT BY PEOPLE

Name	Type	Kind	Pow.	Acc.	PP	Range	Long	DA

MOVES TAUGHT BY MOVE TUTORS FOR SHARDS

Name	Type	Kind	Pow.	Acc.	PP	Range	Long	DA
Bounce	Flying	Physical	85	85	5	Normal	○	○
Uproar	Normal	Special	90	100	10	1 Random	—	—
Iron Defense	Steel	Status	—	—	15	Self	—	—
Iron Tail	Steel	Physical	100	75	15	Normal	—	○
Aqua Tail	Water	Physical	90	90	10	Normal	—	○
Earth Power	Ground	Special	90	100	10	Normal	—	—
Dragon Pulse	Dragon	Special	90	100	10	Normal	○	—
Snore	Normal	Special	40	100	15	Normal	—	—
Roost	Flying	Status	—	—	10	Self	—	—
Sky Attack	Flying	Physical	140	90	5	Normal	○	—
Heat Wave	Fire	Special	100	90	10	Many Others	—	—
Tailwind	Flying	Status	—	—	30	Your Side	—	—
Stealth Rock	Rock	Status	—	—	20	Other Side	—	—
Outrage	Dragon	Physical	120	100	10	1 Random	—	○
Endeavor	Normal	Physical	—	100	5	Normal	—	○
Sleep Talk	Normal	Status	—	—	10	Self	—	—

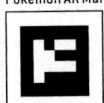

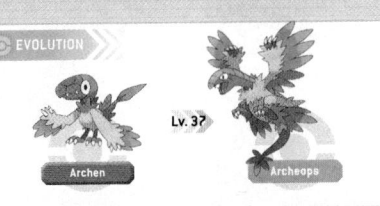

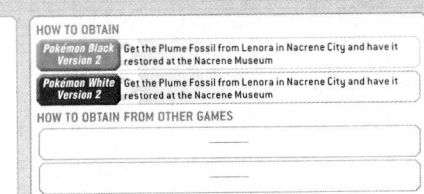

568 Trubbish
Trash Bag Pokémon

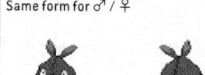

- HEIGHT: 2'00"
- WEIGHT: 68.3 lbs.
- GENDER: ♂ / ♀

Wanting more garbage, they follow people who litter. They always belch poison gas.

Same form for ♂ / ♀

TYPE Poison

ABILITIES
- Stench
- Sticky Hold

HIDDEN ABILITY
- Aftermath

STATS
- HP
- Attack
- Defense
- Sp. Atk
- Sp. Def
- Speed

EGG GROUPS
Mineral

ITEMS SOMETIMES HELD
- Black Sludge
- Nugget

Pokémon AR Marker

EVOLUTION

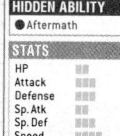

Trubbish → Lv. 36 → Garbodor

HOW TO OBTAIN

Pokémon Black Version 2	❶ Route 4 ❷ Route 16
Pokémon White Version 2	❶ Route 16 ❷ Route 5

HOW TO OBTAIN FROM OTHER GAMES
—
—

LEVEL-UP AND LEARNED MOVES

Lv.	Name	Type	Kind	Pow.	Acc.	PP	Range	Long	DA
1	Pound	Normal	Physical	40	100	35	Normal	—	○
1	Poison Gas	Poison	Status	—	80	40	Many Others	—	—
3	Recycle	Normal	Status	—	—	10	Self	—	—
7	Toxic Spikes	Poison	Status	—	—	20	Other Side	—	—
12	Acid Spray	Poison	Special	40	100	20	Normal	—	—
14	DoubleSlap	Normal	Physical	15	85	10	Normal	—	○
18	Sludge	Poison	Special	65	100	20	Normal	—	—
23	Stockpile	Normal	Status	—	—	20	Self	—	—
23	Swallow	Normal	Status	—	—	10	Self	—	—
25	Take Down	Normal	Physical	90	85	20	Normal	—	○
29	Sludge Bomb	Poison	Special	90	100	10	Normal	—	—
34	Clear Smog	Poison	Special	50	—	15	Normal	—	—
36	Toxic	Poison	Status	—	90	10	Normal	—	—
40	Amnesia	Psychic	Status	—	—	20	Self	—	—
45	Gunk Shot	Poison	Physical	120	70	5	Normal	—	—
47	Explosion	Normal	Physical	250	100	5	Adjacent	—	—

TM & HM MOVES

Lv.	Name	Type	Kind	Pow.	Acc.	PP	Range	Long	DA
TM06	Toxic	Poison	Status	—	90	10	Normal	—	—
TM09	Venoshock	Poison	Special	65	100	10	Normal	—	—
TM10	Hidden Power	Normal	Special	—	100	15	Normal	—	—
TM11	Sunny Day	Fire	Status	—	—	5	Both Sides	—	—
TM17	Protect	Normal	Status	—	—	10	Self	—	—
TM18	Rain Dance	Water	Status	—	—	5	Both Sides	—	—
TM21	Frustration	Normal	Physical	—	100	20	Normal	—	○
TM27	Return	Normal	Physical	—	100	20	Normal	—	○
TM32	Double Team	Normal	Status	—	—	15	Self	—	—
TM34	Sludge Wave	Poison	Special	95	100	10	Adjacent	—	—
TM36	Sludge Bomb	Poison	Special	90	100	10	Normal	—	—
TM42	Facade	Normal	Physical	70	100	20	Normal	—	○
TM44	Rest	Psychic	Status	—	—	10	Self	—	—
TM45	Attract	Normal	Status	—	100	15	Normal	—	—
TM46	Thief	Dark	Physical	40	100	10	Normal	—	—
TM48	Round	Normal	Special	60	100	15	Normal	—	—
TM64	Explosion	Normal	Physical	250	100	5	Adjacent	—	—
TM66	Payback	Dark	Physical	50	100	10	Normal	—	—
TM87	Swagger	Normal	Status	—	90	15	Normal	—	—
TM90	Substitute	Normal	Status	—	—	10	Self	—	—

MOVES TAUGHT BY PEOPLE

Name	Type	Kind	Pow.	Acc.	PP	Range	Long	DA

MOVES TAUGHT BY MOVE TUTORS FOR SHARDS

Name	Type	Kind	Pow.	Acc.	PP	Range	Long	DA
Seed Bomb	Grass	Physical	80	100	15	Normal	—	—
Gunk Shot	Poison	Physical	120	70	5	Normal	—	—
Dark Pulse	Dark	Special	80	100	15	Normal	○	—
Snore	Normal	Special	40	100	15	Normal	—	—
Giga Drain	Grass	Special	75	100	10	Normal	—	—
Drain Punch	Fighting	Physical	75	100	10	Normal	—	○
Pain Split	Normal	Status	—	—	20	Normal	—	—
Spite	Ghost	Status	—	100	10	Normal	—	—
Recycle	Normal	Status	—	—	10	Self	—	—
Sleep Talk	Normal	Status	—	—	10	Self	—	—

EGG MOVES

Name	Type	Kind	Pow.	Acc.	PP	Range	Long	DA
Spikes	Ground	Status	—	—	20	Other Side	—	—
Rollout	Rock	Physical	30	90	20	Normal	—	○
Haze	Ice	Status	—	—	30	Both Sides	—	—
Curse	Ghost	Status	—	—	10	Varies	—	—
Rock Blast	Rock	Physical	25	90	10	Normal	—	—
Sand-Attack	Ground	Status	—	100	15	Normal	—	—
Mud Sport	Ground	Status	—	—	15	Both Sides	—	—
Selfdestruct	Normal	Physical	200	100	5	Adjacent	—	—

---

569 Garbodor
Trash Heap Pokémon

- HEIGHT: 6'03"
- WEIGHT: 236.6 lbs.
- GENDER: ♂ / ♀

Consuming garbage makes new kinds of poison gases and liquids inside their bodies.

Same form for ♂ / ♀

TYPE Poison

ABILITIES
- Stench
- Weak Armor

HIDDEN ABILITY
- Aftermath

STATS
- HP
- Attack
- Defense
- Sp. Atk
- Sp. Def
- Speed

EGG GROUPS
Mineral

ITEMS SOMETIMES HELD
- Black Sludge
- Big Nugget
- Nugget

Pokémon AR Marker

EVOLUTION

Trubbish → Lv. 36 → Garbodor

HOW TO OBTAIN

Pokémon Black Version 2	❶ Route 9 ❷ Route 9 (Hidden Grotto)
Pokémon White Version 2	❶ Route 9 ❷ Route 9 (Hidden Grotto)

HOW TO OBTAIN FROM OTHER GAMES
—
—

LEVEL-UP AND LEARNED MOVES

Lv.	Name	Type	Kind	Pow.	Acc.	PP	Range	Long	DA
1	Pound	Normal	Physical	40	100	35	Normal	—	○
1	Poison Gas	Poison	Status	—	80	40	Many Others	—	—
1	Recycle	Normal	Status	—	—	10	Self	—	—
1	Toxic Spikes	Poison	Status	—	—	20	Other Side	—	—
3	Recycle	Normal	Status	—	—	10	Self	—	—
7	Toxic Spikes	Poison	Status	—	—	20	Other Side	—	—
12	Acid Spray	Poison	Special	40	100	20	Normal	—	—
14	DoubleSlap	Normal	Physical	15	85	10	Normal	—	○
18	Sludge	Poison	Special	65	100	20	Normal	—	—
23	Stockpile	Normal	Status	—	—	20	Self	—	—
23	Swallow	Normal	Status	—	—	10	Self	—	—
25	Body Slam	Normal	Physical	85	100	15	Normal	—	—
29	Sludge Bomb	Poison	Special	90	100	10	Normal	—	—
34	Clear Smog	Poison	Special	50	—	15	Normal	—	—
39	Toxic	Poison	Status	—	90	10	Normal	—	—
46	Amnesia	Psychic	Status	—	—	20	Self	—	—
54	Gunk Shot	Poison	Physical	120	70	5	Normal	—	—
59	Explosion	Normal	Physical	250	100	5	Adjacent	—	—

TM & HM MOVES

Lv.	Name	Type	Kind	Pow.	Acc.	PP	Range	Long	DA
TM06	Toxic	Poison	Status	—	90	10	Normal	—	—
TM09	Venoshock	Poison	Special	65	100	10	Normal	—	—
TM10	Hidden Power	Normal	Special	—	100	15	Normal	—	—
TM11	Sunny Day	Fire	Status	—	—	5	Both Sides	—	—
TM15	Hyper Beam	Normal	Special	150	90	5	Normal	—	—
TM17	Protect	Normal	Status	—	—	10	Self	—	—
TM18	Rain Dance	Water	Status	—	—	5	Both Sides	—	—
TM21	Frustration	Normal	Physical	—	100	20	Normal	—	○
TM22	SolarBeam	Grass	Special	120	100	10	Normal	—	—
TM23	Smack Down	Rock	Physical	50	100	15	Normal	—	—
TM24	Thunderbolt	Electric	Special	95	100	15	Normal	—	—
TM27	Return	Normal	Physical	—	100	20	Normal	—	○
TM29	Psychic	Psychic	Special	90	100	10	Normal	—	—
TM32	Double Team	Normal	Status	—	—	15	Self	—	—
TM34	Sludge Wave	Poison	Special	95	100	10	Adjacent	—	—
TM36	Sludge Bomb	Poison	Special	90	100	10	Normal	—	—
TM42	Facade	Normal	Physical	70	100	20	Normal	—	○
TM44	Rest	Psychic	Status	—	—	10	Self	—	—
TM45	Attract	Normal	Status	—	100	15	Normal	—	—
TM46	Thief	Dark	Physical	40	100	10	Normal	—	—
TM48	Round	Normal	Special	60	100	15	Normal	—	—
TM52	Focus Blast	Fighting	Special	120	70	5	Normal	—	—
TM56	Fling	Dark	Physical	—	100	10	Normal	—	—
TM64	Explosion	Normal	Physical	250	100	5	Adjacent	—	—
TM66	Payback	Dark	Physical	50	100	10	Normal	—	—
TM68	Giga Impact	Normal	Physical	150	90	5	Normal	—	—
TM78	Rock Polish	Rock	Status	—	—	20	Self	—	—
TM87	Swagger	Normal	Status	—	90	15	Normal	—	—
TM90	Substitute	Normal	Status	—	—	10	Self	—	—

MOVES TAUGHT BY PEOPLE

Name	Type	Kind	Pow.	Acc.	PP	Range	Long	DA

MOVES TAUGHT BY MOVE TUTORS FOR SHARDS

Name	Type	Kind	Pow.	Acc.	PP	Range	Long	DA
Seed Bomb	Grass	Physical	80	100	15	Normal	—	—
Gunk Shot	Poison	Physical	120	70	5	Normal	—	—
Dark Pulse	Dark	Special	80	100	15	Normal	○	—
Snore	Normal	Special	40	100	15	Normal	—	—
Giga Drain	Grass	Special	75	100	10	Normal	—	—
Drain Punch	Fighting	Physical	75	100	10	Normal	—	○
Pain Split	Normal	Status	—	—	20	Normal	—	—
Spite	Ghost	Status	—	100	10	Normal	—	—
Recycle	Normal	Status	—	—	10	Self	—	—
Sleep Talk	Normal	Status	—	—	10	Self	—	—

570 Zorua

Tricky Fox Pokémon

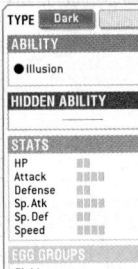

570 Zorua

- HEIGHT: 2'04"
- WEIGHT: 27.6 lbs.
- GENDER: ♂ / ♀

It changes so it looks just like its foe, tricks it, and then uses that opportunity to flee.

Same form for ♂ / ♀

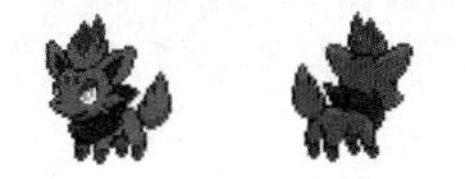

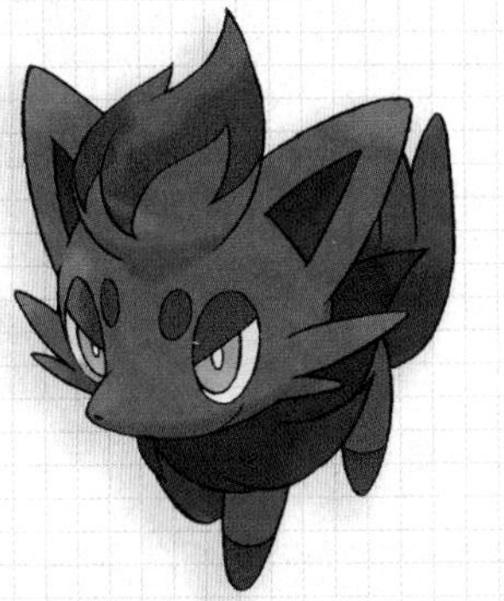

Pokémon AR Marker

TYPE: Dark

ABILITY
- Illusion

HIDDEN ABILITY
—

STATS
- HP
- Attack
- Defense
- Sp. Atk
- Sp. Def
- Speed

EGG GROUPS
Field

ITEMS SOMETIMES HELD
- None

EVOLUTION

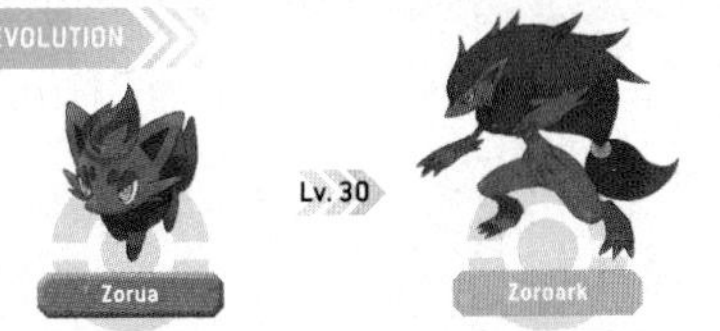

HOW TO OBTAIN

Pokémon Black Version 2	Receive from Rood in Driftveil City
Pokémon White Version 2	Receive from Rood in Driftveil City

HOW TO OBTAIN FROM OTHER GAMES

—

—

LEVEL-UP AND LEARNED MOVES

Lv.	Name	Type	Kind	Pow.	Acc.	PP	Range	Long	DA
1	Scratch	Normal	Physical	40	100	35	Normal	—	○
1	Leer	Normal	Status	—	100	30	Many Others	—	—
5	Pursuit	Dark	Physical	40	100	20	Normal	—	○
9	Fake Tears	Dark	Status	—	100	20	Normal	—	—
13	Fury Swipes	Normal	Physical	18	80	15	Normal	—	○
17	Faint Attack	Dark	Physical	60	—	20	Normal	—	○
21	Scary Face	Normal	Status	—	100	10	Normal	—	—
25	Taunt	Dark	Status	—	100	20	Normal	—	—
29	Foul Play	Dark	Physical	95	100	15	Normal	—	○
33	Torment	Dark	Status	—	100	15	Normal	—	—
37	Agility	Psychic	Status	—	—	30	Self	—	—
41	Embargo	Dark	Status	—	100	15	Normal	—	—
45	Punishment	Dark	Physical	—	100	5	Normal	—	○
49	Nasty Plot	Dark	Status	—	—	20	Self	—	—
53	Imprison	Psychic	Status	—	—	10	Self	—	—
57	Night Daze	Dark	Special	85	95	10	Normal	—	—

TM & HM MOVES

Lv.	Name	Type	Kind	Pow.	Acc.	PP	Range	Long	DA
TM01	Hone Claws	Dark	Status	—	—	15	Self	—	—
TM04	Calm Mind	Psychic	Status	—	—	20	Self	—	—
TM05	Roar	Normal	Status	—	100	20	Normal	—	—
TM06	Toxic	Poison	Status	—	90	10	Normal	—	—
TM10	Hidden Power	Normal	Special	—	100	15	Normal	—	—
TM11	Sunny Day	Fire	Status	—	—	5	Both Sides	—	—
TM12	Taunt	Dark	Status	—	100	20	Normal	—	—
TM17	Protect	Normal	Status	—	—	10	Self	—	—
TM18	Rain Dance	Water	Status	—	—	5	Both Sides	—	—
TM21	Frustration	Normal	Physical	—	100	20	Normal	—	○
TM27	Return	Normal	Physical	—	100	20	Normal	—	○
TM28	Dig	Ground	Physical	80	100	10	Normal	—	○
TM30	Shadow Ball	Ghost	Special	80	100	15	Normal	—	—
TM32	Double Team	Normal	Status	—	—	15	Self	—	—
TM40	Aerial Ace	Flying	Physical	60	—	20	Normal	○	○
TM41	Torment	Dark	Status	—	100	15	Normal	—	—
TM42	Facade	Normal	Physical	70	100	20	Normal	—	○
TM44	Rest	Psychic	Status	—	—	10	Self	—	—
TM45	Attract	Normal	Status	—	100	15	Normal	—	—
TM46	Thief	Dark	Physical	40	100	10	Normal	—	○
TM48	Round	Normal	Special	60	100	15	Normal	—	—
TM56	Fling	Dark	Physical	—	100	10	Normal	—	—
TM59	Incinerate	Fire	Special	30	100	15	Many Others	—	—
TM63	Embargo	Dark	Status	—	100	15	Normal	—	—
TM66	Payback	Dark	Physical	50	100	10	Normal	—	○
TM67	Retaliate	Normal	Physical	70	100	5	Normal	—	○
TM75	Swords Dance	Normal	Status	—	—	30	Self	—	—
TM77	Psych Up	Normal	Status	—	—	10	Normal	—	—
TM86	Grass Knot	Grass	Special	—	100	20	Normal	—	○
TM87	Swagger	Normal	Status	—	90	15	Normal	—	—
TM89	U-turn	Bug	Physical	70	100	20	Normal	—	○
TM90	Substitute	Normal	Status	—	—	10	Self	—	—
TM95	Snarl	Dark	Special	55	95	15	Many Others	—	—
HM01	Cut	Normal	Physical	50	95	30	Normal	—	○

MOVES TAUGHT BY PEOPLE

Name	Type	Kind	Pow.	Acc.	PP	Range	Long	DA

MOVES TAUGHT BY MOVE TUTORS FOR SHARDS

Name	Type	Kind	Pow.	Acc.	PP	Range	Long	DA
Covet	Normal	Physical	60	100	40	Normal	—	○
Bounce	Flying	Physical	85	85	5	Normal	○	○
Uproar	Normal	Special	90	100	10	1 Random	—	—
Hyper Voice	Normal	Special	90	100	10	Many Others	—	—
Foul Play	Dark	Physical	95	100	15	Normal	—	○
Dark Pulse	Dark	Special	80	100	15	Normal	○	—
Snore	Normal	Special	40	100	15	Normal	—	—
Knock Off	Dark	Physical	20	100	20	Normal	—	○
Spite	Ghost	Status	—	100	10	Normal	—	—
Trick	Psychic	Status	—	100	10	Normal	—	—
Sleep Talk	Normal	Status	—	—	10	Self	—	—
Snatch	Dark	Status	—	—	10	Self	—	—

EGG MOVES

Name	Type	Kind	Pow.	Acc.	PP	Range	Long	DA
Detect	Fighting	Status	—	—	5	Self	—	—
Captivate	Normal	Status	—	100	20	Many Others	—	—
Dark Pulse	Dark	Special	80	100	15	Normal	○	—
Snatch	Dark	Status	—	—	10	Self	—	—
Memento	Dark	Status	—	100	10	Normal	—	—
Sucker Punch	Dark	Physical	80	100	5	Normal	—	○
Extrasensory	Psychic	Special	80	100	30	Normal	—	—
Counter	Fighting	Physical	—	100	20	Varies	—	○

571 Zoroark

Illusion Fox Pokémon

571 Zoroark

- HEIGHT: 5'03"
- WEIGHT: 178.8 lbs.
- GENDER: ♂ / ♀

Stories say those who tried to catch Zoroark were trapped in an illusion and punished.

Same form for ♂ / ♀

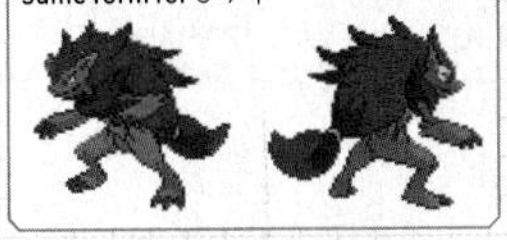

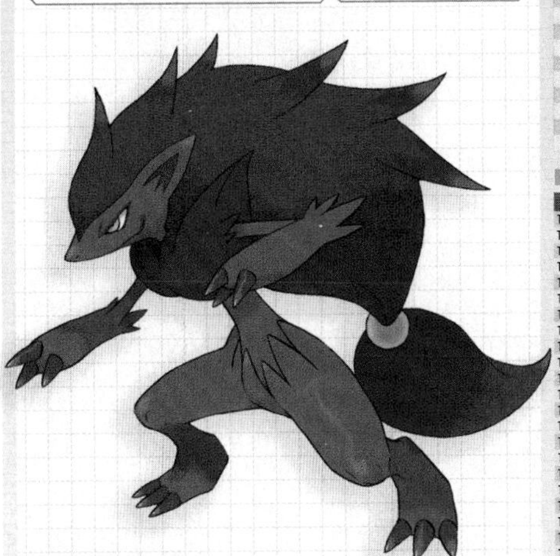

Pokémon AR Marker

TYPE: Dark

ABILITY
- Illusion

HIDDEN ABILITY
—

STATS
- HP
- Attack
- Defense
- Sp. Atk
- Sp. Def
- Speed

EGG GROUPS
Field

ITEMS SOMETIMES HELD
- None

EVOLUTION

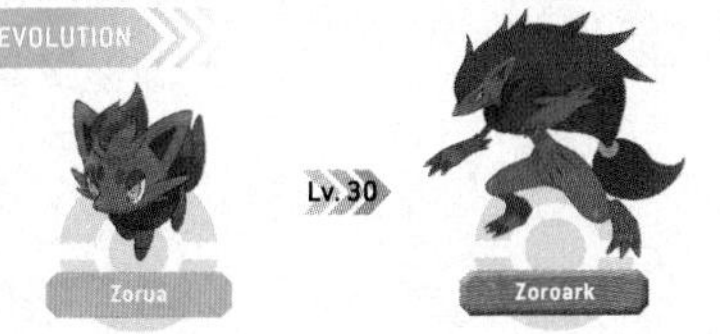

HOW TO OBTAIN

Pokémon Black Version 2	Level up Zorua to Lv. 30
Pokémon White Version 2	Level up Zorua to Lv. 30

HOW TO OBTAIN FROM OTHER GAMES

—

—

LEVEL-UP AND LEARNED MOVES

Lv.	Name	Type	Kind	Pow.	Acc.	PP	Range	Long	DA
1	U-turn	Bug	Physical	70	100	20	Normal	—	○
1	Scratch	Normal	Physical	40	100	35	Normal	—	○
1	Leer	Normal	Status	—	100	30	Many Others	—	—
1	Pursuit	Dark	Physical	40	100	20	Normal	—	○
1	Hone Claws	Dark	Status	—	—	15	Self	—	—
5	Pursuit	Dark	Physical	40	100	20	Normal	—	○
9	Hone Claws	Dark	Status	—	—	15	Self	—	—
13	Fury Swipes	Normal	Physical	18	80	15	Normal	—	○
17	Faint Attack	Dark	Physical	60	—	20	Normal	—	○
21	Scary Face	Normal	Status	—	100	10	Normal	—	—
25	Taunt	Dark	Status	—	100	20	Normal	—	—
29	Foul Play	Dark	Physical	95	100	15	Normal	—	○
30	Night Slash	Dark	Physical	70	100	15	Normal	—	○
34	Torment	Dark	Status	—	100	15	Normal	—	—
39	Agility	Psychic	Status	—	—	30	Self	—	—
44	Embargo	Dark	Status	—	100	15	Normal	—	—
49	Punishment	Dark	Physical	—	100	5	Normal	—	○
54	Nasty Plot	Dark	Status	—	—	20	Self	—	—
59	Imprison	Psychic	Status	—	—	10	Self	—	—
64	Night Daze	Dark	Special	85	95	10	Normal	—	—

TM & HM MOVES

Lv.	Name	Type	Kind	Pow.	Acc.	PP	Range	Long	DA
TM01	Hone Claws	Dark	Status	—	—	15	Self	—	—
TM04	Calm Mind	Psychic	Status	—	—	20	Self	—	—
TM05	Roar	Normal	Status	—	100	20	Normal	—	—
TM06	Toxic	Poison	Status	—	90	10	Normal	—	—
TM10	Hidden Power	Normal	Special	—	100	15	Normal	—	—
TM11	Sunny Day	Fire	Status	—	—	5	Both Sides	—	—
TM12	Taunt	Dark	Status	—	100	20	Normal	—	—
TM15	Hyper Beam	Normal	Special	150	90	5	Normal	—	—
TM17	Protect	Normal	Status	—	—	10	Self	—	—
TM18	Rain Dance	Water	Status	—	—	5	Both Sides	—	—
TM21	Frustration	Normal	Physical	—	100	20	Normal	—	○
TM27	Return	Normal	Physical	—	100	20	Normal	—	○
TM28	Dig	Ground	Physical	80	100	10	Normal	—	○
TM30	Shadow Ball	Ghost	Special	80	100	15	Normal	—	—
TM32	Double Team	Normal	Status	—	—	15	Self	—	—
TM35	Flamethrower	Fire	Special	95	100	15	Normal	—	—
TM40	Aerial Ace	Flying	Physical	60	—	20	Normal	○	○
TM41	Torment	Dark	Status	—	100	15	Normal	—	—
TM42	Facade	Normal	Physical	70	100	20	Normal	—	○
TM44	Rest	Psychic	Status	—	—	10	Self	—	—
TM45	Attract	Normal	Status	—	100	15	Normal	—	—
TM46	Thief	Dark	Physical	40	100	10	Normal	—	○
TM47	Low Sweep	Fighting	Physical	60	100	20	Normal	—	○
TM48	Round	Normal	Special	60	100	15	Normal	—	—
TM52	Focus Blast	Fighting	Special	120	70	5	Normal	—	—
TM56	Fling	Dark	Physical	—	100	10	Normal	—	—
TM59	Incinerate	Fire	Special	30	100	15	Many Others	—	—
TM63	Embargo	Dark	Status	—	100	15	Normal	—	—
TM65	Shadow Claw	Ghost	Physical	70	100	15	Normal	—	○
TM66	Payback	Dark	Physical	50	100	10	Normal	—	○
TM67	Retaliate	Normal	Physical	70	100	5	Normal	—	○
TM68	Giga Impact	Normal	Physical	150	90	5	Normal	—	○
TM75	Swords Dance	Normal	Status	—	—	30	Self	—	—
TM77	Psych Up	Normal	Status	—	—	10	Normal	—	—
TM86	Grass Knot	Grass	Special	—	100	20	Normal	—	○
TM87	Swagger	Normal	Status	—	90	15	Normal	—	—
TM89	U-turn	Bug	Physical	70	100	20	Normal	—	○
TM90	Substitute	Normal	Status	—	—	10	Self	—	—
TM94	Rock Smash	Fighting	Physical	40	100	15	Normal	—	○
TM95	Snarl	Dark	Special	55	95	15	Many Others	—	—
HM01	Cut	Normal	Physical	50	95	30	Normal	—	○

MOVES TAUGHT BY PEOPLE

Name	Type	Kind	Pow.	Acc.	PP	Range	Long	DA

MOVES TAUGHT BY MOVE TUTORS FOR SHARDS

Name	Type	Kind	Pow.	Acc.	PP	Range	Long	DA
Covet	Normal	Physical	60	100	40	Normal	—	○
Bounce	Flying	Physical	85	85	5	Normal	○	○
Uproar	Normal	Special	90	100	10	1 Random	—	—
Low Kick	Fighting	Physical	—	100	20	Normal	—	○
Hyper Voice	Normal	Special	90	100	10	Many Others	—	—
Foul Play	Dark	Physical	95	100	15	Normal	—	○
Dark Pulse	Dark	Special	80	100	15	Normal	○	—
Snore	Normal	Special	40	100	15	Normal	—	—
Knock Off	Dark	Physical	20	100	20	Normal	—	○
Spite	Ghost	Status	—	100	10	Normal	—	—
Trick	Psychic	Status	—	100	10	Normal	—	—
Sleep Talk	Normal	Status	—	—	10	Self	—	—
Snatch	Dark	Status	—	—	10	Self	—	—

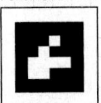

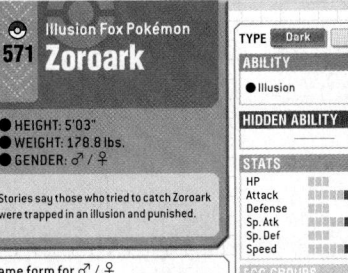

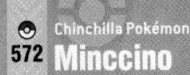

572 Minccino

Chinchilla Pokémon

- HEIGHT: 1'04"
- WEIGHT: 12.8 lbs.
- GENDER: ♂ / ♀

Minccino greet each other by grooming one another thoroughly with their tails.

TYPE Normal

ABILITIES
- Cute Charm
- Technician

HIDDEN ABILITY
- Skill Link

STATS
HP
Attack
Defense
Sp. Atk
Sp. Def
Speed

EGG GROUPS
Field

ITEMS SOMETIMES HELD
- Chesto Berry

Same form for ♂ / ♀

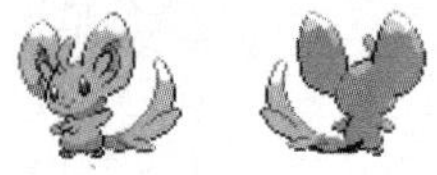

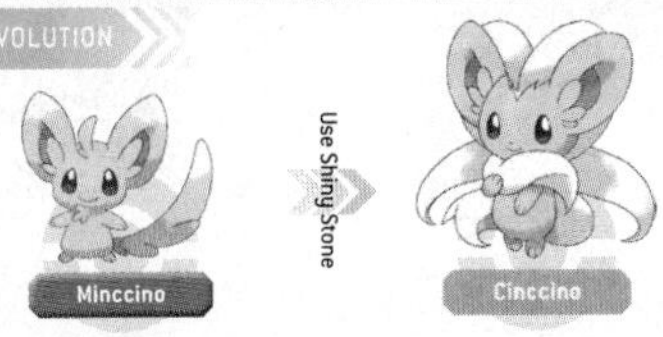
Minccino
Use Shiny Stone
Cinccino

HOW TO OBTAIN

Pokémon Black Version 2	❶ Route 16 ❷ Route 5
Pokémon White Version 2	❶ Route 4 ❷ Route 16

HOW TO OBTAIN FROM OTHER GAMES

—

—

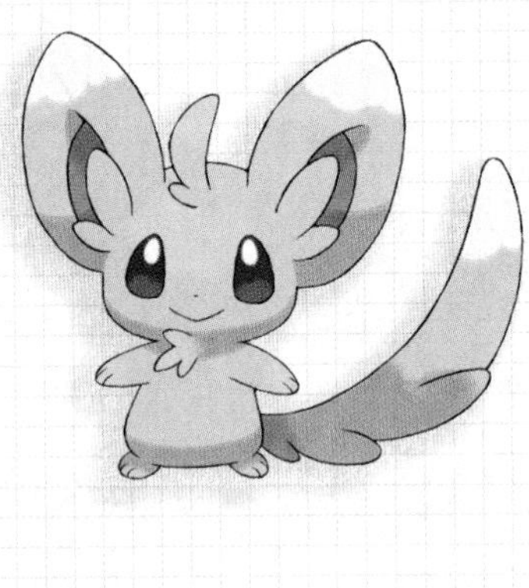

Pokémon AR Marker

LEVEL-UP AND LEARNED MOVES

Lv.	Name	Type	Kind	Pow.	Acc.	PP	Range	Long	DA
1	Pound	Normal	Physical	40	100	35	Normal	—	○
3	Growl	Normal	Status	—	100	40	Many Others	—	—
7	Helping Hand	Normal	Status	—	—	20	1 Ally	—	—
9	Tickle	Normal	Status	—	100	20	Normal	—	—
13	DoubleSlap	Normal	Physical	15	85	10	Normal	—	○
15	Encore	Normal	Status	—	100	5	Normal	—	—
19	Swift	Normal	Special	60	—	20	Many Others	—	—
21	Sing	Normal	Status	—	55	15	Normal	—	—
25	Tail Slap	Normal	Physical	25	85	10	Normal	—	○
27	Charm	Normal	Status	—	100	20	Normal	—	—
31	Wake-Up Slap	Fighting	Physical	60	100	10	Normal	—	○
33	Echoed Voice	Normal	Special	40	100	15	Normal	—	—
37	Slam	Normal	Physical	80	75	20	Normal	—	○
39	Captivate	Normal	Status	—	100	20	Many Others	—	—
43	Hyper Voice	Normal	Special	90	100	10	Many Others	—	—
45	Last Resort	Normal	Physical	140	100	5	Normal	—	○
49	After You	Normal	Status	—	—	15	Normal	—	—

TM & HM MOVES

Lv.	Name	Type	Kind	Pow.	Acc.	PP	Range	Long	DA
TM04	Calm Mind	Psychic	Status	—	—	20	Self	—	—
TM06	Toxic	Poison	Status	—	90	10	Normal	—	—
TM10	Hidden Power	Normal	Special	—	100	15	Normal	—	—
TM11	Sunny Day	Fire	Status	—	—	5	Both Sides	—	—
TM17	Protect	Normal	Status	—	—	10	Self	—	—
TM18	Rain Dance	Water	Status	—	—	5	Both Sides	—	—
TM20	Safeguard	Normal	Status	—	—	25	Your Side	—	—
TM21	Frustration	Normal	Physical	—	100	20	Normal	—	○
TM24	Thunderbolt	Electric	Special	95	100	15	Normal	—	—
TM27	Return	Normal	Physical	—	100	20	Normal	—	○
TM28	Dig	Ground	Physical	80	100	10	Normal	—	○
TM32	Double Team	Normal	Status	—	—	15	Self	—	—
TM42	Facade	Normal	Physical	70	100	20	Normal	—	○
TM44	Rest	Psychic	Status	—	—	10	Self	—	—
TM45	Attract	Normal	Status	—	100	15	Normal	—	—
TM46	Thief	Dark	Physical	40	100	10	Normal	—	○
TM48	Round	Normal	Special	60	100	15	Normal	—	—
TM49	Echoed Voice	Normal	Special	40	100	15	Normal	—	—
TM56	Fling	Dark	Physical	—	100	10	Normal	—	—
TM67	Retaliate	Normal	Physical	70	100	5	Normal	—	○
TM73	Thunder Wave	Electric	Status	—	100	20	Normal	—	—
TM83	Work Up	Normal	Status	—	—	30	Self	—	—
TM86	Grass Knot	Grass	Special	—	100	20	Normal	—	○
TM87	Swagger	Normal	Status	—	90	15	Normal	—	—
TM89	U-turn	Bug	Physical	70	100	20	Normal	—	○
TM90	Substitute	Normal	Status	—	—	10	Self	—	—

MOVES TAUGHT BY PEOPLE

Name	Type	Kind	Pow.	Acc.	PP	Range	Long	DA

MOVES TAUGHT BY MOVE TUTORS FOR SHARDS

Name	Type	Kind	Pow.	Acc.	PP	Range	Long	DA
Covet	Normal	Physical	60	100	40	Normal	—	○
Uproar	Normal	Special	90	100	10	1 Random	—	—
Seed Bomb	Grass	Physical	80	100	15	Normal	—	—
Gunk Shot	Poison	Physical	120	70	5	Normal	—	—
Last Resort	Normal	Physical	140	100	5	Normal	—	○
Hyper Voice	Normal	Special	90	100	10	Many Others	—	—
Iron Tail	Steel	Physical	100	75	15	Normal	—	○
Aqua Tail	Water	Physical	90	90	10	Normal	—	○
Snore	Normal	Special	40	100	15	Normal	—	—
Knock Off	Dark	Physical	20	100	20	Normal	—	○
Helping Hand	Normal	Status	—	—	20	1 Ally	—	—
After You	Normal	Status	—	—	15	Normal	—	—
Sleep Talk	Normal	Status	—	—	10	Self	—	—

EGG MOVES

Name	Type	Kind	Pow.	Acc.	PP	Range	Long	DA
Iron Tail	Steel	Physical	100	75	15	Normal	—	○
Tail Whip	Normal	Status	—	100	30	Many Others	—	—
Aqua Tail	Water	Physical	90	90	10	Normal	—	○
Mud-Slap	Ground	Special	20	100	10	Normal	—	—
Knock Off	Dark	Physical	20	100	20	Normal	—	○
Fake Tears	Dark	Status	—	100	20	Normal	—	—
Sleep Talk	Normal	Status	—	—	10	Self	—	—
Endure	Normal	Status	—	—	10	Self	—	—
Flail	Normal	Physical	—	100	15	Normal	—	○

573 Cinccino

Scarf Pokémon

- HEIGHT: 1'08"
- WEIGHT: 16.5 lbs.
- GENDER: ♂ / ♀

Cinccino's body is coated in a special oil that helps it deflect attacks, such as punches.

TYPE Normal

ABILITIES
- Cute Charm
- Technician

HIDDEN ABILITY
- Skill Link

STATS
HP
Attack
Defense
Sp. Atk
Sp. Def
Speed

EGG GROUPS
Field

ITEMS SOMETIMES HELD
- Chesto Berry

Same form for ♂ / ♀

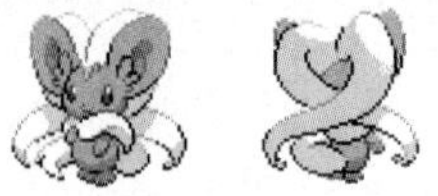

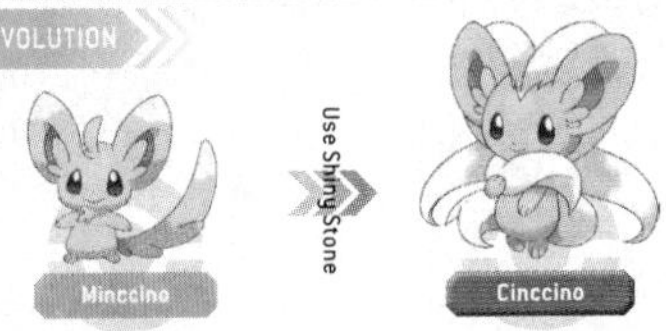
Minccino
Use Shiny Stone
Cinccino

HOW TO OBTAIN

Pokémon Black Version 2	❶ Route 16 (rustling grass) ❷ Route 5 (rustling grass)
Pokémon White Version 2	❶ Route 16 (rustling grass) ❷ Route 5 (rustling grass)

HOW TO OBTAIN FROM OTHER GAMES

—

—

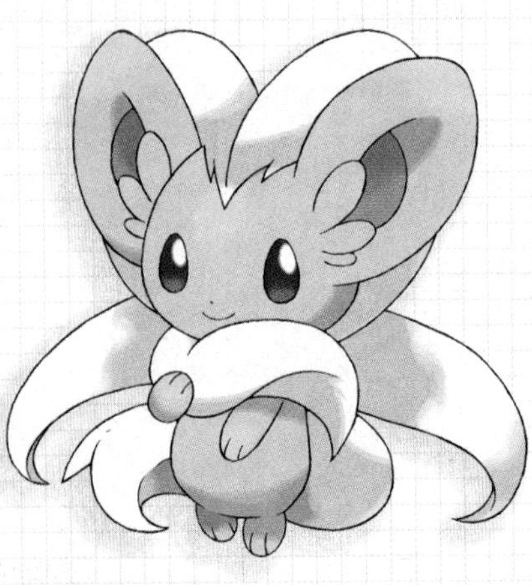

Pokémon AR Marker

LEVEL-UP AND LEARNED MOVES

Lv.	Name	Type	Kind	Pow.	Acc.	PP	Range	Long	DA
1	Bullet Seed	Grass	Physical	25	100	30	Normal	-	-
1	Rock Blast	Rock	Physical	25	90	10	Normal	-	-
1	Helping Hand	Normal	Status	-	-	20	1 Ally	-	-
1	Tickle	Normal	Status	-	100	20	Normal	-	-
1	Sing	Normal	Status	-	55	15	Normal	-	-
1	Tail Slap	Normal	Physical	25	85	10	Normal	-	○

TM & HM MOVES

Lv.	Name	Type	Kind	Pow.	Acc.	PP	Range	Long	DA
TM04	Calm Mind	Psychic	Status	—	—	20	Self	—	—
TM06	Toxic	Poison	Status	—	90	10	Normal	—	—
TM10	Hidden Power	Normal	Special	—	100	15	Normal	—	—
TM11	Sunny Day	Fire	Status	—	—	5	Both Sides	—	—
TM15	Hyper Beam	Normal	Special	150	90	5	Normal	—	—
TM16	Light Screen	Psychic	Status	—	—	30	Your Side	—	—
TM17	Protect	Normal	Status	—	—	10	Self	—	—
TM18	Rain Dance	Water	Status	—	—	5	Both Sides	—	—
TM20	Safeguard	Normal	Status	—	—	25	Your Side	—	—
TM21	Frustration	Normal	Physical	—	100	20	Normal	—	○
TM24	Thunderbolt	Electric	Special	95	100	15	Normal	—	—
TM25	Thunder	Electric	Special	120	70	10	Normal	—	—
TM27	Return	Normal	Physical	—	100	20	Normal	—	○
TM28	Dig	Ground	Physical	80	100	10	Normal	—	○
TM32	Double Team	Normal	Status	—	—	15	Self	—	—
TM42	Facade	Normal	Physical	70	100	20	Normal	—	○
TM44	Rest	Psychic	Status	—	—	10	Self	—	—
TM45	Attract	Normal	Status	—	100	15	Normal	—	—
TM46	Thief	Dark	Physical	40	100	10	Normal	—	○
TM48	Round	Normal	Special	60	100	15	Normal	—	—
TM49	Echoed Voice	Normal	Special	40	100	15	Normal	—	—
TM52	Focus Blast	Fighting	Special	120	70	5	Normal	—	—
TM56	Fling	Dark	Physical	—	100	10	Normal	—	—
TM67	Retaliate	Normal	Physical	70	100	5	Normal	—	○
TM68	Giga Impact	Normal	Physical	150	90	5	Normal	—	○
TM73	Thunder Wave	Electric	Status	—	100	20	Normal	—	—
TM83	Work Up	Normal	Status	—	—	30	Self	—	—
TM86	Grass Knot	Grass	Special	—	100	20	Normal	—	○
TM87	Swagger	Normal	Status	—	90	15	Normal	—	—
TM89	U-turn	Bug	Physical	70	100	20	Normal	—	○
TM90	Substitute	Normal	Status	—	—	10	Self	—	—

MOVES TAUGHT BY PEOPLE

Name	Type	Kind	Pow.	Acc.	PP	Range	Long	DA

MOVES TAUGHT BY MOVE TUTORS FOR SHARDS

Name	Type	Kind	Pow.	Acc.	PP	Range	Long	DA
Covet	Normal	Physical	60	100	40	Normal	—	○
Uproar	Normal	Special	90	100	10	1 Random	—	—
Seed Bomb	Grass	Physical	80	100	15	Normal	—	—
Gunk Shot	Poison	Physical	120	70	5	Normal	—	—
Last Resort	Normal	Physical	140	100	5	Normal	—	○
Hyper Voice	Normal	Special	90	100	10	Many Others	—	—
Iron Tail	Steel	Physical	100	75	15	Normal	—	○
Aqua Tail	Water	Physical	90	90	10	Normal	—	○
Snore	Normal	Special	40	100	15	Normal	—	—
Knock Off	Dark	Physical	20	100	20	Normal	—	○
Helping Hand	Normal	Status	—	—	20	1 Ally	—	—
After You	Normal	Status	—	—	15	Normal	—	—
Sleep Talk	Normal	Status	—	—	10	Self	—	—

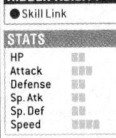

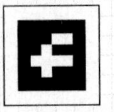

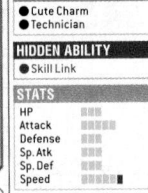

574 Gothita
Fixation Pokémon

TYPE Psychic

ABILITY
- Frisk

HIDDEN ABILITY

STATS
- HP
- Attack
- Defense
- Sp. Atk
- Sp. Def
- Speed

- HEIGHT: 1'04"
- WEIGHT: 12.8 lbs.
- GENDER: ♂ / ♀

It stares intently at everything. It can become so obsessed with watching that it doesn't notice attacks.

EGG GROUPS
Human-like

ITEMS SOMETIMES HELD
- Persim Berry

Same form for ♂ / ♀

Pokémon AR Marker

EVOLUTION

Gothita → Lv. 32 → Gothorita → Lv. 41 → Gothitelle

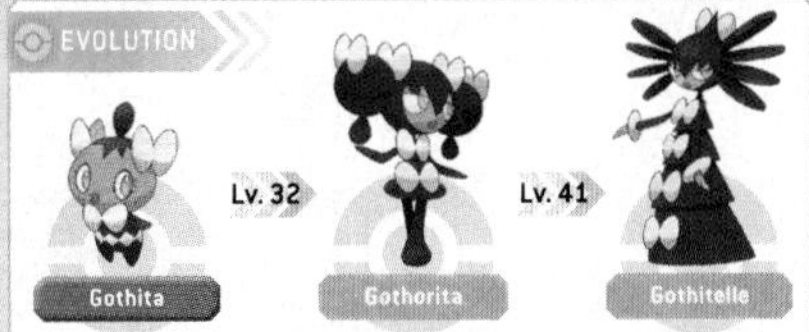

HOW TO OBTAIN
| Pokémon Black Version 2 | ① Route 16 ② Route 5 |
| Pokémon White Version 2 | Link Trade |

HOW TO OBTAIN FROM OTHER GAMES
| Pokémon Black Version | Route 16 |

LEVEL-UP AND LEARNED MOVES
Lv.	Name	Type	Kind	Pow.	Acc.	PP	Range	Long	DA
1	Pound	Normal	Physical	40	100	35	Normal	—	○
3	Confusion	Psychic	Special	50	100	25	Normal	—	—
7	Tickle	Normal	Status	—	100	20	Normal	—	—
10	Fake Tears	Dark	Status	—	100	20	Normal	—	—
14	DoubleSlap	Normal	Physical	15	85	10	Normal	—	—
16	Psybeam	Psychic	Special	65	100	10	Normal	—	—
19	Embargo	Dark	Status	—	100	15	Normal	—	—
24	Faint Attack	Dark	Physical	60	—	20	Normal	—	○
25	Psyshock	Psychic	Special	80	100	10	Normal	—	—
28	Flatter	Dark	Status	—	100	15	Normal	—	—
31	Future Sight	Psychic	Special	100	100	10	Normal	—	—
33	Heal Block	Psychic	Status	—	100	15	Many Others	—	—
37	Psychic	Psychic	Special	90	100	10	Normal	—	—
40	Telekinesis	Psychic	Status	—	—	15	Normal	—	—
46	Charm	Normal	Status	—	100	20	Normal	—	—
48	Magic Room	Psychic	Status	—	—	10	Both Sides	—	—

TM & HM MOVES
Lv.	Name	Type	Kind	Pow.	Acc.	PP	Range	Long	DA
TM03	Psyshock	Psychic	Special	80	100	10	Normal	—	—
TM04	Calm Mind	Psychic	Status	—	—	20	Self	—	—
TM06	Toxic	Poison	Status	—	90	10	Normal	—	—
TM10	Hidden Power	Normal	Special	—	100	15	Normal	—	—
TM12	Taunt	Dark	Status	—	100	20	Normal	—	—
TM16	Light Screen	Psychic	Status	—	—	30	Your Side	—	—
TM17	Protect	Normal	Status	—	—	10	Self	—	—
TM18	Rain Dance	Water	Status	—	—	5	Both Sides	—	—
TM19	Telekinesis	Psychic	Status	—	—	15	Normal	—	—
TM20	Safeguard	Normal	Status	—	—	25	Your Side	—	—
TM21	Frustration	Normal	Physical	—	100	20	Normal	—	○
TM24	Thunderbolt	Electric	Special	95	100	15	Normal	—	—
TM27	Return	Normal	Physical	—	100	20	Normal	—	○
TM29	Psychic	Psychic	Special	90	100	10	Normal	—	—
TM30	Shadow Ball	Ghost	Special	80	100	15	Normal	—	—
TM32	Double Team	Normal	Status	—	—	15	Self	—	—
TM33	Reflect	Psychic	Status	—	—	20	Your Side	—	—
TM39	Rock Tomb	Rock	Physical	50	80	10	Normal	—	—
TM41	Torment	Dark	Status	—	100	15	Normal	—	—
TM42	Facade	Normal	Physical	70	100	20	Normal	—	—
TM44	Rest	Psychic	Status	—	—	10	Self	—	—
TM45	Attract	Normal	Status	—	100	15	Normal	—	—
TM46	Thief	Dark	Physical	40	100	10	Normal	—	—
TM48	Round	Normal	Special	60	100	15	Normal	—	—
TM53	Energy Ball	Grass	Special	80	100	10	Normal	—	—
TM56	Fling	Dark	Physical	—	100	10	Normal	—	—
TM57	Charge Beam	Electric	Special	50	90	10	Normal	—	—
TM63	Embargo	Dark	Status	—	100	15	Normal	—	—
TM66	Payback	Dark	Physical	50	100	10	Normal	—	○
TM70	Flash	Normal	Status	—	100	20	Normal	—	—
TM73	Thunder Wave	Electric	Status	—	100	20	Normal	—	—
TM77	Psych Up	Normal	Status	—	—	10	Normal	—	—
TM80	Rock Slide	Rock	Physical	75	90	10	Many Others	—	—
TM85	Dream Eater	Psychic	Special	100	100	15	Normal	—	—
TM86	Grass Knot	Grass	Special	—	100	20	Normal	—	○
TM87	Swagger	Normal	Status	—	90	15	Normal	—	—
TM90	Substitute	Normal	Status	—	—	10	Self	—	—

Lv.	Name	Type	Kind	Pow.	Acc.	PP	Range	Long	DA
TM92	Trick Room	Psychic	Status	—	—	5	Both Sides	—	—

MOVES TAUGHT BY PEOPLE
Name	Type	Kind	Pow.	Acc.	PP	Range	Long	DA

MOVES TAUGHT BY MOVE TUTORS FOR SHARDS
Name	Type	Kind	Pow.	Acc.	PP	Range	Long	DA
Covet	Normal	Physical	60	100	40	Normal	—	—
Signal Beam	Bug	Special	75	100	15	Normal	—	—
Uproar	Normal	Special	90	100	10	1 Random	—	—
Magic Coat	Psychic	Status	—	—	15	Self	—	—
Zen Headbutt	Psychic	Physical	80	90	15	Normal	—	○
Foul Play	Dark	Physical	95	100	15	Normal	—	○
Gravity	Psychic	Status	—	—	5	Both Sides	—	—
Snore	Normal	Special	40	100	15	Normal	—	—
Heal Bell	Normal	Status	—	—	5	Your Party	—	—
Role Play	Psychic	Status	—	—	10	Normal	—	—
Helping Hand	Normal	Status	—	—	20	1 Ally	—	—
Magic Room	Psychic	Status	—	—	10	Both Sides	—	—
Recycle	Normal	Status	—	—	10	Self	—	—
Trick	Psychic	Status	—	100	10	Normal	—	—
Sleep Talk	Normal	Status	—	—	10	Self	—	—
Skill Swap	Psychic	Status	—	—	10	Normal	—	—
Snatch	Dark	Status	—	—	10	Self	—	—

EGG MOVES
Name	Type	Kind	Pow.	Acc.	PP	Range	Long	DA
Mirror Coat	Psychic	Special	—	100	10	Varies	—	—
Uproar	Normal	Special	90	100	10	1 Random	—	—
Miracle Eye	Psychic	Status	—	—	40	Normal	—	—
Captivate	Normal	Status	—	100	20	Many Others	—	—
Mean Look	Normal	Status	—	—	5	Normal	—	—
Dark Pulse	Dark	Special	80	100	15	Normal	○	—

---

575 Gothorita
Manipulate Pokémon

TYPE Psychic

ABILITY
- Frisk

HIDDEN ABILITY
- Shadow Tag

STATS
- HP
- Attack
- Defense
- Sp. Atk
- Sp. Def
- Speed

- HEIGHT: 2'04"
- WEIGHT: 39.7 lbs.
- GENDER: ♂ / ♀

According to many old tales, it creates friends for itself by controlling sleeping children on starry nights.

EGG GROUPS
Human-like

ITEMS SOMETIMES HELD
- Persim Berry

Same form for ♂ / ♀

Pokémon AR Marker

EVOLUTION
Gothita → Lv. 32 → Gothorita → Lv. 41 → Gothitelle

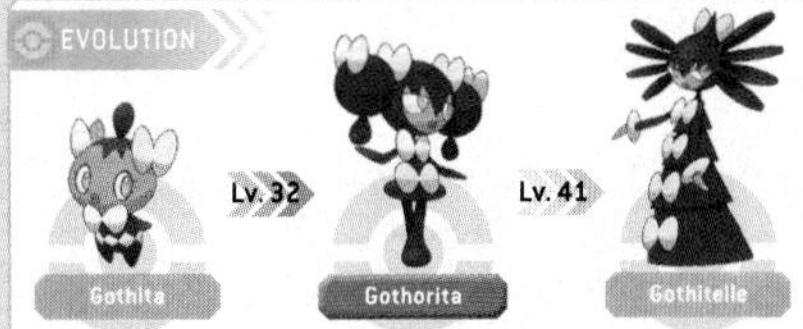

HOW TO OBTAIN
| Pokémon Black Version 2 | ① Strange House room ① ② Route 9 |
| Pokémon White Version 2 | Level up a Gothita you obtain via Link Trade to Lv. 32 |

HOW TO OBTAIN FROM OTHER GAMES
| Pokémon Black Version | Route 9 |

LEVEL-UP AND LEARNED MOVES
Lv.	Name	Type	Kind	Pow.	Acc.	PP	Range	Long	DA
1	Pound	Normal	Physical	40	100	35	Normal	—	○
1	Confusion	Psychic	Special	50	100	25	Normal	—	—
1	Tickle	Normal	Status	—	100	20	Normal	—	—
1	Fake Tears	Dark	Status	—	100	20	Normal	—	—
3	Confusion	Psychic	Special	50	100	25	Normal	—	—
7	Tickle	Normal	Status	—	100	20	Normal	—	—
10	Fake Tears	Dark	Status	—	100	20	Normal	—	—
14	DoubleSlap	Normal	Physical	15	85	10	Normal	—	—
16	Psybeam	Psychic	Special	65	100	10	Normal	—	—
19	Embargo	Dark	Status	—	100	15	Normal	—	—
24	Faint Attack	Dark	Physical	60	—	20	Normal	—	○
25	Psyshock	Psychic	Special	80	100	10	Normal	—	—
28	Flatter	Dark	Status	—	100	15	Normal	—	—
31	Future Sight	Psychic	Special	100	100	10	Normal	—	—
34	Heal Block	Psychic	Status	—	100	15	Many Others	—	—
39	Psychic	Psychic	Special	90	100	10	Normal	—	—
43	Telekinesis	Psychic	Status	—	—	15	Normal	—	—
50	Charm	Normal	Status	—	100	20	Normal	—	—
53	Magic Room	Psychic	Status	—	—	10	Both Sides	—	—

TM & HM MOVES
Lv.	Name	Type	Kind	Pow.	Acc.	PP	Range	Long	DA
TM03	Psyshock	Psychic	Special	80	100	10	Normal	—	—
TM04	Calm Mind	Psychic	Status	—	—	20	Self	—	—
TM06	Toxic	Poison	Status	—	90	10	Normal	—	—
TM10	Hidden Power	Normal	Special	—	100	15	Normal	—	—
TM12	Taunt	Dark	Status	—	100	20	Normal	—	—
TM16	Light Screen	Psychic	Status	—	—	30	Your Side	—	—
TM17	Protect	Normal	Status	—	—	10	Self	—	—
TM18	Rain Dance	Water	Status	—	—	5	Both Sides	—	—
TM19	Telekinesis	Psychic	Status	—	—	15	Normal	—	—
TM20	Safeguard	Normal	Status	—	—	25	Your Side	—	—
TM21	Frustration	Normal	Physical	—	100	20	Normal	—	○
TM24	Thunderbolt	Electric	Special	95	100	15	Normal	—	—
TM27	Return	Normal	Physical	—	100	20	Normal	—	○
TM29	Psychic	Psychic	Special	90	100	10	Normal	—	—
TM30	Shadow Ball	Ghost	Special	80	100	15	Normal	—	—
TM32	Double Team	Normal	Status	—	—	15	Self	—	—
TM33	Reflect	Psychic	Status	—	—	20	Your Side	—	—
TM39	Rock Tomb	Rock	Physical	50	80	10	Normal	—	—
TM41	Torment	Dark	Status	—	100	15	Normal	—	—
TM42	Facade	Normal	Physical	70	100	20	Normal	—	—
TM44	Rest	Psychic	Status	—	—	10	Self	—	—
TM45	Attract	Normal	Status	—	100	15	Normal	—	—
TM46	Thief	Dark	Physical	40	100	10	Normal	—	—
TM48	Round	Normal	Special	60	100	15	Normal	—	—
TM53	Energy Ball	Grass	Special	80	100	10	Normal	—	—
TM56	Fling	Dark	Physical	—	100	10	Normal	—	—
TM57	Charge Beam	Electric	Special	50	90	10	Normal	—	—
TM63	Embargo	Dark	Status	—	100	15	Normal	—	—
TM66	Payback	Dark	Physical	50	100	10	Normal	—	○
TM70	Flash	Normal	Status	—	100	20	Normal	—	—
TM73	Thunder Wave	Electric	Status	—	100	20	Normal	—	—
TM77	Psych Up	Normal	Status	—	—	10	Normal	—	—
TM80	Rock Slide	Rock	Physical	75	90	10	Many Others	—	—
TM85	Dream Eater	Psychic	Special	100	100	15	Normal	—	—

Lv.	Name	Type	Kind	Pow.	Acc.	PP	Range	Long	DA
TM86	Grass Knot	Grass	Special	—	100	20	Normal	—	○
TM87	Swagger	Normal	Status	—	90	15	Normal	—	—
TM90	Substitute	Normal	Status	—	—	10	Self	—	—
TM92	Trick Room	Psychic	Status	—	—	5	Both Sides	—	—

MOVES TAUGHT BY PEOPLE
Name	Type	Kind	Pow.	Acc.	PP	Range	Long	DA

MOVES TAUGHT BY MOVE TUTORS FOR SHARDS
Name	Type	Kind	Pow.	Acc.	PP	Range	Long	DA
Covet	Normal	Physical	60	100	40	Normal	—	—
Signal Beam	Bug	Special	75	100	15	Normal	—	—
Uproar	Normal	Special	90	100	10	1 Random	—	—
Magic Coat	Psychic	Status	—	—	15	Self	—	—
Zen Headbutt	Psychic	Physical	80	90	15	Normal	—	○
Foul Play	Dark	Physical	95	100	15	Normal	—	○
Gravity	Psychic	Status	—	—	5	Both Sides	—	—
Snore	Normal	Special	40	100	15	Normal	—	—
Heal Bell	Normal	Status	—	—	5	Your Party	—	—
Role Play	Psychic	Status	—	—	10	Normal	—	—
Helping Hand	Normal	Status	—	—	20	1 Ally	—	—
Magic Room	Psychic	Status	—	—	10	Both Sides	—	—
Recycle	Normal	Status	—	—	10	Self	—	—
Trick	Psychic	Status	—	100	10	Normal	—	—
Sleep Talk	Normal	Status	—	—	10	Self	—	—
Skill Swap	Psychic	Status	—	—	10	Self	—	—
Snatch	Dark	Status	—	—	10	Self	—	—

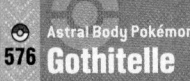

Astral Body Pokémon

576 Gothitelle

- HEIGHT: 4'11"
- WEIGHT: 97.0 lbs.
- GENDER: ♂ / ♀

It can see the future from the movement of the stars. When it learns its Trainer's life span, it cries in sadness.

Same form for ♂ / ♀

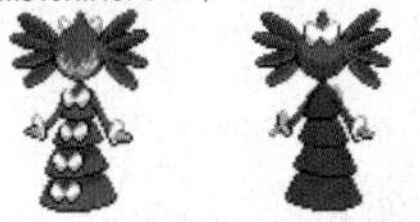

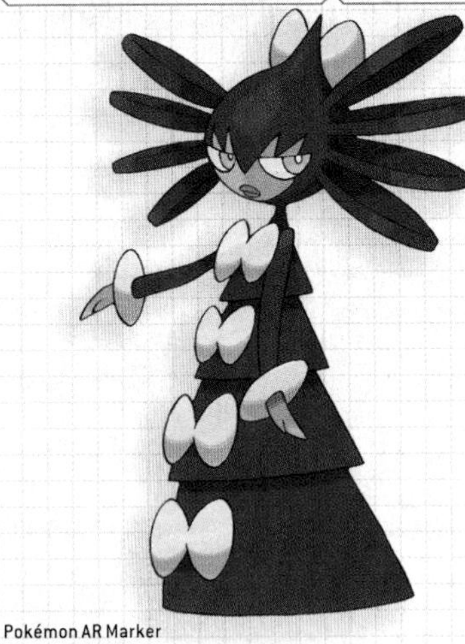

Pokémon AR Marker

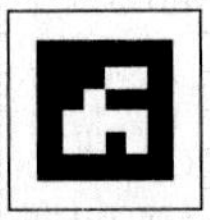

TYPE Psychic

ABILITY
- Frisk

HIDDEN ABILITY
- Shadow Tag

STATS
HP
Attack
Defense
Sp. Atk
Sp. Def
Speed

EGG GROUPS
Human-like

ITEMS SOMETIMES HELD
- Persim Berry

EVOLUTION

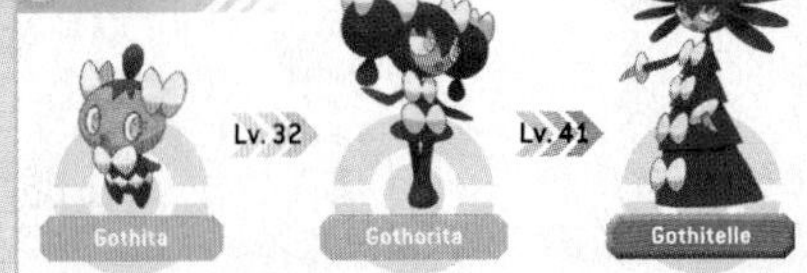

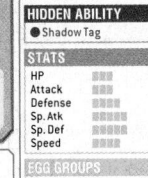

Gothita
Lv. 32
Gothorita
Lv. 41
Gothitelle

HOW TO OBTAIN

Pokémon Black Version 2	Route 9 (rustling grass)
Pokémon White Version 2	Level up a Gothorita you obtain via Link Trade to Lv. 41

HOW TO OBTAIN FROM OTHER GAMES

Pokémon Black Version	Route 9 (rustling grass)
—	

LEVEL-UP AND LEARNED MOVES

Lv.	Name	Type	Kind	Pow.	Acc.	PP	Range	Long	DA
1	Pound	Normal	Physical	40	100	35	Normal	—	○
1	Confusion	Psychic	Special	50	100	25	Normal	—	—
1	Tickle	Normal	Status	—	100	20	Normal	—	—
1	Fake Tears	Dark	Status	—	100	20	Normal	—	—
3	Confusion	Psychic	Special	50	100	25	Normal	—	—
7	Tickle	Normal	Status	—	100	20	Normal	—	—
10	Fake Tears	Dark	Status	—	100	20	Normal	—	—
14	DoubleSlap	Normal	Physical	15	85	10	Normal	—	○
16	Psybeam	Psychic	Special	65	100	20	Normal	—	—
19	Embargo	Dark	Status	—	100	15	Normal	—	—
24	Faint Attack	Dark	Physical	60	—	20	Normal	—	○
25	Psyshock	Psychic	Special	80	100	10	Normal	—	—
28	Flatter	Dark	Status	—	100	15	Normal	—	—
31	Future Sight	Psychic	Special	100	100	10	Normal	—	—
34	Heal Block	Psychic	Status	—	100	15	Many Others	—	—
39	Psychic	Psychic	Special	90	100	10	Normal	—	—
45	Telekinesis	Psychic	Status	—	—	15	Normal	—	—
54	Charm	Normal	Status	—	100	20	Normal	—	—
59	Magic Room	Psychic	Status	—	—	10	Both Sides	—	—

TM & HM MOVES

Lv.	Name	Type	Kind	Pow.	Acc.	PP	Range	Long	DA
TM03	Psyshock	Psychic	Special	80	100	10	Normal	—	—
TM04	Calm Mind	Psychic	Status	—	—	20	Self	—	—
TM06	Toxic	Poison	Status	—	90	10	Normal	—	—
TM10	Hidden Power	Normal	Special	—	100	15	Normal	—	—
TM12	Taunt	Dark	Status	—	100	20	Normal	—	—
TM15	Hyper Beam	Normal	Special	150	90	5	Normal	—	—
TM16	Light Screen	Psychic	Status	—	—	30	Your Side	—	—
TM17	Protect	Normal	Status	—	—	10	Self	—	—
TM18	Rain Dance	Water	Status	—	—	5	Both Sides	—	—
TM19	Telekinesis	Psychic	Status	—	—	15	Normal	—	—
TM20	Safeguard	Normal	Status	—	—	25	Your Side	—	—
TM21	Frustration	Normal	Physical	—	100	20	Normal	—	○
TM24	Thunderbolt	Electric	Special	95	100	15	Normal	—	—
TM27	Return	Normal	Physical	—	100	20	Normal	—	○
TM29	Psychic	Psychic	Special	90	100	10	Normal	—	—
TM30	Shadow Ball	Ghost	Special	80	100	15	Normal	—	—
TM31	Brick Break	Fighting	Physical	75	100	15	Normal	—	○
TM32	Double Team	Normal	Status	—	—	15	Self	—	—
TM33	Reflect	Psychic	Status	—	—	20	Your Side	—	—
TM39	Rock Tomb	Rock	Physical	50	80	10	Normal	—	—
TM41	Torment	Dark	Status	—	100	15	Normal	—	—
TM42	Facade	Normal	Physical	70	100	20	Normal	—	○
TM44	Rest	Psychic	Status	—	—	10	Self	—	—
TM45	Attract	Normal	Status	—	100	15	Normal	—	—
TM46	Thief	Dark	Physical	40	100	10	Normal	—	○
TM47	Low Sweep	Fighting	Physical	60	100	20	Normal	—	○
TM48	Round	Normal	Special	60	100	15	Normal	—	—
TM53	Energy Ball	Grass	Special	80	100	10	Normal	—	—
TM56	Fling	Dark	Physical	—	100	10	Normal	—	—
TM57	Charge Beam	Electric	Special	50	90	10	Normal	—	—
TM63	Embargo	Dark	Status	—	100	15	Normal	—	—
TM66	Payback	Dark	Physical	50	100	10	Normal	—	○
TM68	Giga Impact	Normal	Physical	150	90	5	Normal	—	○
TM70	Flash	Normal	Status	—	100	20	Normal	—	—
TM73	Thunder Wave	Electric	Status	—	100	20	Normal	—	—
TM77	Psych Up	Normal	Status	—	—	10	Normal	—	—
TM80	Rock Slide	Rock	Physical	75	90	10	Many Others	—	—
TM85	Dream Eater	Psychic	Special	100	100	15	Normal	—	—
TM86	Grass Knot	Grass	Special	—	100	20	Normal	—	○
TM87	Swagger	Normal	Status	—	90	15	Normal	—	—
TM90	Substitute	Normal	Status	—	—	10	Self	—	—
TM92	Trick Room	Psychic	Status	—	—	5	Both Sides	—	—

MOVES TAUGHT BY PEOPLE

Name	Type	Kind	Pow.	Acc.	PP	Range	Long	DA

MOVES TAUGHT BY MOVE TUTORS FOR SHARDS

Name	Type	Kind	Pow.	Acc.	PP	Range	Long	DA
Covet	Normal	Physical	60	100	40	Normal	—	○
Signal Beam	Bug	Special	75	100	15	Normal	—	—
Uproar	Normal	Special	90	100	10	1 Random	—	—
Magic Coat	Psychic	Status	—	—	15	Self	—	—
Zen Headbutt	Psychic	Physical	80	90	15	Normal	—	○
Foul Play	Dark	Physical	95	100	15	Normal	—	○
Gravity	Psychic	Status	—	—	5	Both Sides	—	—
Snore	Normal	Special	40	100	15	Normal	—	—
Heal Bell	Normal	Status	—	—	5	Your Party	—	—
Role Play	Psychic	Status	—	—	10	Normal	—	—
Helping Hand	Normal	Status	—	—	20	1 Ally	—	—
Magic Room	Psychic	Status	—	—	10	Both Sides	—	—
Recycle	Normal	Status	—	—	10	Self	—	—
Trick	Psychic	Status	—	100	10	Normal	—	—
Sleep Talk	Normal	Status	—	—	10	Self	—	—
Skill Swap	Psychic	Status	—	—	10	Normal	—	—
Snatch	Dark	Status	—	—	10	Self	—	—

Cell Pokémon

577 Solosis

- HEIGHT: 1'00"
- WEIGHT: 2.2 lbs.
- GENDER: ♂ / ♀

Because their bodies are enveloped in a special liquid, they are fine in any environment, no matter how severe.

Same form for ♂ / ♀

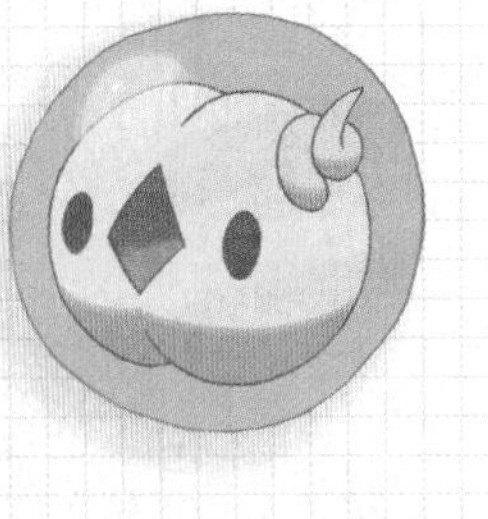

Pokémon AR Marker

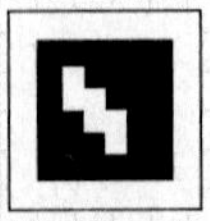

TYPE Psychic

ABILITIES
- Overcoat
- Magic Guard

HIDDEN ABILITY
- Regenerator

STATS
HP
Attack
Defense
Sp. Atk
Sp. Def
Speed

EGG GROUPS
Amorphous

ITEMS SOMETIMES HELD
- Persim Berry

EVOLUTION

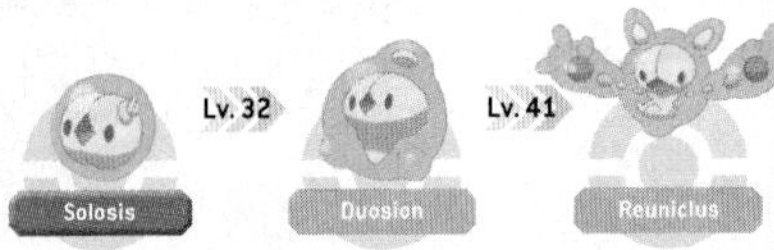

Solosis
Lv. 32
Duosion
Lv. 41
Reuniclus

HOW TO OBTAIN

Pokémon Black Version 2	Link Trade
Pokémon White Version 2	❶ Route 16 ❷ Route 5

HOW TO OBTAIN FROM OTHER GAMES

Pokémon White Version	Route 16
—	

LEVEL-UP AND LEARNED MOVES

Lv.	Name	Type	Kind	Pow.	Acc.	PP	Range	Long	DA
1	Psywave	Psychic	Special	—	80	15	Normal	—	—
3	Reflect	Psychic	Status	—	—	20	Your Side	—	—
7	Rollout	Rock	Physical	30	90	20	Normal	—	○
10	Snatch	Dark	Status	—	—	10	Self	—	—
14	Hidden Power	Normal	Special	—	100	15	Normal	—	—
16	Light Screen	Psychic	Status	—	—	30	Your Side	—	—
19	Charm	Normal	Status	—	100	20	Normal	—	—
24	Recover	Normal	Status	—	—	10	Self	—	—
25	Psyshock	Psychic	Special	80	100	10	Normal	—	—
28	Endeavor	Normal	Physical	—	100	5	Normal	—	○
31	Future Sight	Psychic	Special	100	100	10	Normal	—	—
33	Pain Split	Normal	Status	—	—	20	Normal	—	—
37	Psychic	Psychic	Special	90	100	10	Normal	—	—
40	Skill Swap	Psychic	Status	—	—	10	Normal	—	—
46	Heal Block	Psychic	Status	—	100	15	Many Others	—	—
48	Wonder Room	Psychic	Status	—	—	10	Both Sides	—	—

TM & HM MOVES

Lv.	Name	Type	Kind	Pow.	Acc.	PP	Range	Long	DA
TM03	Psyshock	Psychic	Special	80	100	10	Normal	—	—
TM04	Calm Mind	Psychic	Status	—	—	20	Self	—	—
TM06	Toxic	Poison	Status	—	90	10	Normal	—	—
TM10	Hidden Power	Normal	Special	—	100	15	Normal	—	—
TM16	Light Screen	Psychic	Status	—	—	30	Your Side	—	—
TM17	Protect	Normal	Status	—	—	10	Self	—	—
TM18	Rain Dance	Water	Status	—	—	5	Both Sides	—	—
TM19	Telekinesis	Psychic	Status	—	—	15	Normal	—	—
TM20	Safeguard	Normal	Status	—	—	25	Your Side	—	—
TM21	Frustration	Normal	Physical	—	100	20	Normal	—	○
TM25	Thunder	Electric	Special	120	70	10	Normal	—	—
TM27	Return	Normal	Physical	—	100	20	Normal	—	○
TM29	Psychic	Psychic	Special	90	100	10	Normal	—	—
TM30	Shadow Ball	Ghost	Special	80	100	15	Normal	—	—
TM32	Double Team	Normal	Status	—	—	15	Self	—	—
TM33	Reflect	Psychic	Status	—	—	20	Your Side	—	—
TM39	Rock Tomb	Rock	Physical	50	80	10	Normal	—	—
TM42	Facade	Normal	Physical	70	100	20	Normal	—	○
TM44	Rest	Psychic	Status	—	—	10	Self	—	—
TM45	Attract	Normal	Status	—	100	15	Normal	—	—
TM48	Round	Normal	Special	60	100	15	Normal	—	—
TM53	Energy Ball	Grass	Special	80	100	10	Normal	—	—
TM63	Embargo	Dark	Status	—	100	15	Normal	—	—
TM64	Explosion	Normal	Physical	250	100	5	Adjacent	—	—
TM70	Flash	Normal	Status	—	100	20	Normal	—	—
TM73	Thunder Wave	Electric	Status	—	100	20	Normal	—	—
TM74	Gyro Ball	Steel	Physical	—	100	5	Normal	—	○
TM77	Psych Up	Normal	Status	—	—	10	Normal	—	—
TM80	Rock Slide	Rock	Physical	75	90	10	Many Others	—	—
TM85	Dream Eater	Psychic	Special	100	100	15	Normal	—	—
TM87	Swagger	Normal	Status	—	90	15	Normal	—	—
TM90	Substitute	Normal	Status	—	—	10	Self	—	—
TM91	Flash Cannon	Steel	Special	80	100	10	Normal	—	—
TM92	Trick Room	Psychic	Status	—	—	5	Both Sides	—	—

MOVES TAUGHT BY PEOPLE

Name	Type	Kind	Pow.	Acc.	PP	Range	Long	DA

MOVES TAUGHT BY MOVE TUTORS FOR SHARDS

Name	Type	Kind	Pow.	Acc.	PP	Range	Long	DA
Signal Beam	Bug	Special	75	100	15	Normal	—	—
Magic Coat	Psychic	Status	—	—	15	Self	—	—
Zen Headbutt	Psychic	Physical	80	90	15	Normal	—	○
Gravity	Psychic	Status	—	—	5	Both Sides	—	—
Snore	Normal	Special	40	100	15	Normal	—	—
Role Play	Psychic	Status	—	—	10	Normal	—	—
Pain Split	Normal	Status	—	—	20	Normal	—	—
After You	Normal	Status	—	—	15	Normal	—	—
Wonder Room	Psychic	Status	—	—	10	Both Sides	—	—
Trick	Psychic	Status	—	100	10	Normal	—	—
Endeavor	Normal	Physical	—	100	5	Normal	—	○
Sleep Talk	Normal	Status	—	—	10	Self	—	—
Skill Swap	Psychic	Status	—	—	10	Normal	—	—
Snatch	Dark	Status	—	—	10	Self	—	—

EGG MOVES

Name	Type	Kind	Pow.	Acc.	PP	Range	Long	DA
Night Shade	Ghost	Special	—	100	15	Normal	—	—
Astonish	Ghost	Physical	30	100	15	Normal	—	○
Confuse Ray	Ghost	Status	—	100	10	Normal	—	—
Acid Armor	Poison	Status	—	—	40	Self	—	—
Trick	Psychic	Status	—	100	10	Normal	—	—
Imprison	Psychic	Status	—	—	10	Self	—	—
Secret Power	Normal	Physical	70	100	20	Normal	—	—

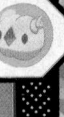

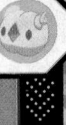

578 Duosion

Mitosis Pokémon

- HEIGHT: 2'00"
- WEIGHT: 17.6 lbs.
- GENDER: ♂ / ♀

When their two divided brains think the same thoughts, their psychic power is maximized.

Same form for ♂ / ♀

Pokémon AR Marker

TYPE Psychic

ABILITIES
- Overcoat
- Magic Guard

HIDDEN ABILITY
- Regenerator

STATS
HP
Attack
Defense
Sp. Atk
Sp. Def
Speed

EGG GROUPS
Amorphous

ITEMS SOMETIMES HELD
- Persim Berry

EVOLUTION

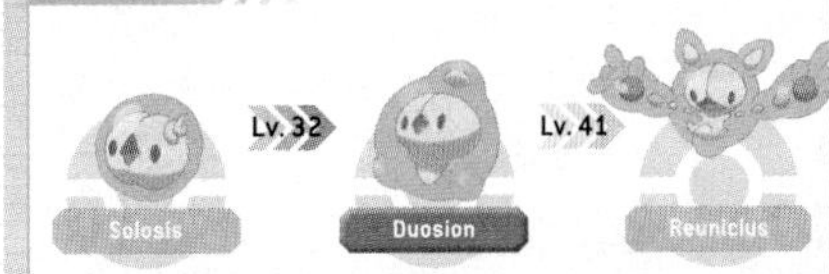

HOW TO OBTAIN

Pokémon Black Version 2	Level up a Solosis you obtain via Link Trade to Lv. 32
Pokémon White Version 2	❶ Strange House room ① ❷ Route 9

HOW TO OBTAIN FROM OTHER GAMES

Pokémon White Version	Route 9
	—

LEVEL-UP AND LEARNED MOVES

Lv.	Name	Type	Kind	Pow.	Acc.	PP	Range	Long	DA
1	Psywave	Psychic	Special	—	80	15	Normal	—	—
1	Reflect	Psychic	Status	—	—	20	Your Side	—	—
1	Rollout	Rock	Physical	30	90	20	Normal	—	○
1	Snatch	Dark	Status	—	—	10	Self	—	—
3	Reflect	Psychic	Status	—	—	20	Your Side	—	—
7	Rollout	Rock	Physical	30	90	20	Normal	—	○
10	Snatch	Dark	Status	—	—	10	Self	—	—
14	Hidden Power	Normal	Special	—	100	15	Normal	—	—
16	Light Screen	Psychic	Status	—	—	30	Your Side	—	—
19	Charm	Normal	Status	—	100	20	Normal	—	—
24	Recover	Normal	Status	—	—	10	Self	—	—
25	Psyshock	Psychic	Special	80	100	10	Normal	—	—
28	Endeavor	Normal	Physical	—	100	5	Normal	—	○
31	Future Sight	Psychic	Special	100	100	10	Normal	—	—
34	Pain Split	Normal	Status	—	—	20	Normal	—	—
39	Psychic	Psychic	Special	90	100	10	Normal	—	—
43	Skill Swap	Psychic	Status	—	—	10	Normal	—	—
50	Heal Block	Psychic	Status	—	100	15	Many Others	—	—
53	Wonder Room	Psychic	Status	—	—	10	Both Sides	—	—

TM & HM MOVES

Lv.	Name	Type	Kind	Pow.	Acc.	PP	Range	Long	DA
TM03	Psyshock	Psychic	Special	80	100	10	Normal	—	—
TM04	Calm Mind	Psychic	Status	—	—	20	Self	—	—
TM06	Toxic	Poison	Status	—	90	10	Normal	—	—
TM10	Hidden Power	Normal	Special	—	100	15	Normal	—	—
TM16	Light Screen	Psychic	Status	—	—	30	Your Side	—	—
TM17	Protect	Normal	Status	—	—	10	Self	—	—
TM18	Rain Dance	Water	Status	—	—	5	Both Sides	—	—
TM19	Telekinesis	Psychic	Status	—	—	15	Normal	—	—
TM20	Safeguard	Normal	Status	—	—	25	Your Side	—	—
TM21	Frustration	Normal	Physical	—	100	20	Normal	—	○
TM25	Thunder	Electric	Special	120	70	10	Normal	—	—
TM27	Return	Normal	Physical	—	100	20	Normal	—	○
TM29	Psychic	Psychic	Special	90	100	10	Normal	—	—
TM30	Shadow Ball	Ghost	Special	80	100	15	Normal	—	—
TM32	Double Team	Normal	Status	—	—	15	Self	—	—
TM33	Reflect	Psychic	Status	—	—	20	Your Side	—	—
TM39	Rock Tomb	Rock	Physical	50	80	10	Normal	—	—
TM42	Facade	Normal	Physical	70	100	20	Normal	—	○
TM44	Rest	Psychic	Status	—	—	10	Self	—	—
TM45	Attract	Normal	Status	—	100	15	Normal	—	—
TM48	Round	Normal	Special	60	100	15	Normal	—	—
TM53	Energy Ball	Grass	Special	80	100	10	Normal	—	—
TM63	Embargo	Dark	Status	—	100	15	Normal	—	—
TM64	Explosion	Normal	Physical	250	100	5	Adjacent	—	—
TM70	Flash	Normal	Status	—	100	20	Normal	—	—
TM73	Thunder Wave	Electric	Status	—	100	20	Normal	—	—
TM74	Gyro Ball	Steel	Physical	—	100	5	Normal	—	○
TM77	Psych Up	Normal	Status	—	—	10	Normal	—	—
TM80	Rock Slide	Rock	Physical	75	90	10	Many Others	—	—
TM85	Dream Eater	Psychic	Special	100	100	15	Normal	—	—
TM87	Swagger	Normal	Status	—	90	15	Normal	—	—
TM90	Substitute	Normal	Status	—	—	10	Self	—	—
TM91	Flash Cannon	Steel	Special	80	100	10	Normal	—	—
TM92	Trick Room	Psychic	Status	—	—	5	Both Sides	—	—

MOVES TAUGHT BY PEOPLE

Name	Type	Kind	Pow.	Acc.	PP	Range	Long	DA

MOVES TAUGHT BY MOVE TUTORS FOR SHARDS

Name	Type	Kind	Pow.	Acc.	PP	Range	Long	DA
Signal Beam	Bug	Special	75	100	15	Normal	—	—
Magic Coat	Psychic	Status	—	—	15	Self	—	—
Zen Headbutt	Psychic	Physical	80	90	15	Normal	—	○
Gravity	Psychic	Status	—	—	5	Both Sides	—	—
Snore	Normal	Special	40	100	15	Normal	—	—
Role Play	Psychic	Status	—	—	10	Normal	—	—
Pain Split	Normal	Status	—	—	20	Normal	—	—
After You	Normal	Status	—	—	15	Normal	—	—
Wonder Room	Psychic	Status	—	—	10	Both Sides	—	—
Trick	Psychic	Status	—	100	10	Normal	—	—
Endeavor	Normal	Physical	—	100	5	Normal	—	○
Sleep Talk	Normal	Status	—	—	10	Self	—	—
Skill Swap	Psychic	Status	—	—	10	Normal	—	—
Snatch	Dark	Status	—	—	10	Self	—	—

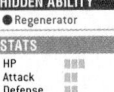

579 Reuniclus

Multiplying Pokémon

- HEIGHT: 3'03"
- WEIGHT: 44.3 lbs.
- GENDER: ♂ / ♀

They use psychic power to control their arms, which are made of a special liquid. They can crush boulders psychically.

Same form for ♂ / ♀

Pokémon AR Marker

TYPE Psychic

ABILITIES
- Overcoat
- Magic Guard

HIDDEN ABILITY
- Regenerator

STATS
HP
Attack
Defense
Sp. Atk
Sp. Def
Speed

EGG GROUPS
Amorphous

ITEMS SOMETIMES HELD
- Persim Berry

EVOLUTION

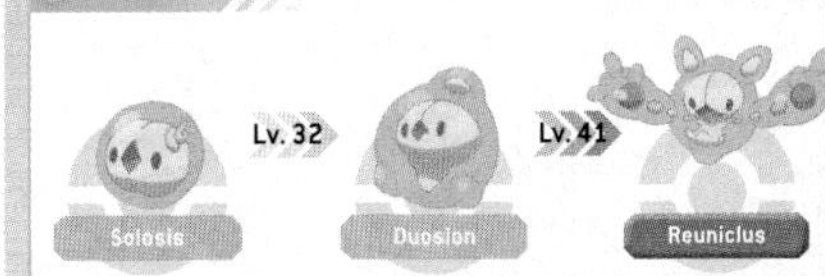

HOW TO OBTAIN

Pokémon Black Version 2	Level up a Duosion you obtain via Link Trade to Lv. 41
Pokémon White Version 2	Route 9 (rustling grass)

HOW TO OBTAIN FROM OTHER GAMES

Pokémon White Version	Route 9 (rustling grass)
	—

LEVEL-UP AND LEARNED MOVES

Lv.	Name	Type	Kind	Pow.	Acc.	PP	Range	Long	DA
1	Psywave	Psychic	Special	—	80	15	Normal	—	—
1	Reflect	Psychic	Status	—	—	20	Your Side	—	—
1	Rollout	Rock	Physical	30	90	20	Normal	—	○
1	Snatch	Dark	Status	—	—	10	Self	—	—
3	Reflect	Psychic	Status	—	—	20	Your Side	—	—
7	Rollout	Rock	Physical	30	90	20	Normal	—	○
10	Snatch	Dark	Status	—	—	10	Self	—	—
14	Hidden Power	Normal	Special	—	100	15	Normal	—	—
16	Light Screen	Psychic	Status	—	—	30	Your Side	—	—
19	Charm	Normal	Status	—	100	20	Normal	—	—
24	Recover	Normal	Status	—	—	10	Self	—	—
25	Psyshock	Psychic	Special	80	100	10	Normal	—	—
28	Endeavor	Normal	Physical	—	100	5	Normal	—	○
31	Future Sight	Psychic	Special	100	100	10	Normal	—	—
34	Pain Split	Normal	Status	—	—	20	Normal	—	—
39	Psychic	Psychic	Special	90	100	10	Normal	—	—
41	Dizzy Punch	Normal	Physical	70	100	10	Normal	—	○
45	Skill Swap	Psychic	Status	—	—	10	Normal	—	—
54	Heal Block	Psychic	Status	—	100	15	Many Others	—	—
59	Wonder Room	Psychic	Status	—	—	10	Both Sides	—	—

TM & HM MOVES

Lv.	Name	Type	Kind	Pow.	Acc.	PP	Range	Long	DA
TM03	Psyshock	Psychic	Special	80	100	10	Normal	—	—
TM04	Calm Mind	Psychic	Status	—	—	20	Self	—	—
TM06	Toxic	Poison	Status	—	90	10	Normal	—	—
TM10	Hidden Power	Normal	Special	—	100	15	Normal	—	—
TM15	Hyper Beam	Normal	Special	150	90	5	Normal	—	—
TM16	Light Screen	Psychic	Status	—	—	30	Your Side	—	—
TM17	Protect	Normal	Status	—	—	10	Self	—	—
TM18	Rain Dance	Water	Status	—	—	5	Both Sides	—	—
TM19	Telekinesis	Psychic	Status	—	—	15	Normal	—	—
TM20	Safeguard	Normal	Status	—	—	25	Your Side	—	—
TM21	Frustration	Normal	Physical	—	100	20	Normal	—	○
TM25	Thunder	Electric	Special	120	70	10	Normal	—	—
TM27	Return	Normal	Physical	—	100	20	Normal	—	○
TM29	Psychic	Psychic	Special	90	100	10	Normal	—	—
TM30	Shadow Ball	Ghost	Special	80	100	15	Normal	—	—
TM32	Double Team	Normal	Status	—	—	15	Self	—	—
TM33	Reflect	Psychic	Status	—	—	20	Your Side	—	—
TM39	Rock Tomb	Rock	Physical	50	80	10	Normal	—	—
TM42	Facade	Normal	Physical	70	100	20	Normal	—	○
TM44	Rest	Psychic	Status	—	—	10	Self	—	—
TM45	Attract	Normal	Status	—	100	15	Normal	—	—
TM48	Round	Normal	Special	60	100	15	Normal	—	—
TM52	Focus Blast	Fighting	Special	120	70	5	Normal	—	—
TM53	Energy Ball	Grass	Special	80	100	10	Normal	—	—
TM56	Fling	Dark	Physical	—	100	10	Normal	—	—
TM63	Embargo	Dark	Status	—	100	15	Normal	—	—
TM64	Explosion	Normal	Physical	250	100	5	Adjacent	—	—
TM68	Giga Impact	Normal	Physical	150	90	5	Normal	—	○
TM70	Flash	Normal	Status	—	100	20	Normal	—	—
TM73	Thunder Wave	Electric	Status	—	100	20	Normal	—	—
TM74	Gyro Ball	Steel	Physical	—	100	5	Normal	—	○
TM77	Psych Up	Normal	Status	—	—	10	Normal	—	—
TM80	Rock Slide	Rock	Physical	75	90	10	Many Others	—	—
TM85	Dream Eater	Psychic	Special	100	100	15	Normal	—	—
TM86	Grass Knot	Grass	Special	—	100	20	Normal	—	○
TM87	Swagger	Normal	Status	—	90	15	Normal	—	—
TM90	Substitute	Normal	Status	—	—	10	Self	—	—
TM91	Flash Cannon	Steel	Special	80	100	10	Normal	—	—
TM92	Trick Room	Psychic	Status	—	—	5	Both Sides	—	—
TM94	Rock Smash	Fighting	Physical	40	100	15	Normal	—	○
HM04	Strength	Normal	Physical	80	100	15	Normal	—	○

MOVES TAUGHT BY PEOPLE

Name	Type	Kind	Pow.	Acc.	PP	Range	Long	DA

MOVES TAUGHT BY MOVE TUTORS FOR SHARDS

Name	Type	Kind	Pow.	Acc.	PP	Range	Long	DA
Signal Beam	Bug	Special	75	100	15	Normal	—	—
Fire Punch	Fire	Physical	75	100	15	Normal	—	○
ThunderPunch	Electric	Physical	75	100	15	Normal	—	○
Ice Punch	Ice	Physical	75	100	15	Normal	—	○
Magic Coat	Psychic	Status	—	—	15	Self	—	—
Zen Headbutt	Psychic	Physical	80	90	15	Normal	—	○
Superpower	Fighting	Physical	120	100	5	Normal	—	○
Gravity	Psychic	Status	—	—	5	Both Sides	—	—
Snore	Normal	Special	40	100	15	Normal	—	—
Knock Off	Dark	Physical	20	100	20	Normal	—	○
Role Play	Psychic	Status	—	—	10	Normal	—	—
Drain Punch	Fighting	Physical	75	100	10	Normal	—	○
Pain Split	Normal	Status	—	—	20	Normal	—	—
Helping Hand	Normal	Status	—	—	20	1 Ally	—	—
After You	Normal	Status	—	—	15	Normal	—	—
Wonder Room	Psychic	Status	—	—	10	Both Sides	—	—
Trick	Psychic	Status	—	100	10	Normal	—	—
Endeavor	Normal	Physical	—	100	5	Normal	—	○
Sleep Talk	Normal	Status	—	—	10	Self	—	—
Skill Swap	Psychic	Status	—	—	10	Normal	—	—
Snatch	Dark	Status	—	—	10	Self	—	—

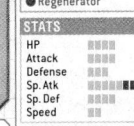

580 Ducklett

Water Bird Pokémon

TYPE Water | Flying

ABILITIES
- Keen Eye
- Big Pecks

HIDDEN ABILITY
- Hydration

- HEIGHT: 1'08"
- WEIGHT: 12.1 lbs.
- GENDER: ♂ / ♀

They are better at swimming than flying, and they happily eat their favorite food, peat moss, as they dive underwater.

Same form for ♂ / ♀

STATS
- HP
- Attack
- Defense
- Sp. Atk
- Sp. Def
- Speed

EGG GROUPS
Water ❶ /Flying

ITEMS SOMETIMES HELD
- None

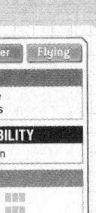

EVOLUTION

 Ducklett — Lv. 35 → Swanna

HOW TO OBTAIN

Pokémon Black Version 2	Driftveil Drawbridge (Pokémon shadows)
Pokémon White Version 2	Driftveil Drawbridge (Pokémon shadows)

HOW TO OBTAIN FROM OTHER GAMES

LEVEL-UP AND LEARNED MOVES

Lv.	Name	Type	Kind	Pow.	Acc.	PP	Range	Long	DA
1	Water Gun	Water	Special	40	100	25	Normal	—	—
3	Water Sport	Water	Status	—	—	15	Both Sides	—	—
6	Defog	Flying	Status	—	—	15	Normal	—	—
9	Wing Attack	Flying	Physical	60	100	35	Normal	○	—
13	Water Pulse	Water	Special	60	100	20	Normal	—	○
15	Aerial Ace	Flying	Physical	60	—	20	Normal	○	—
19	BubbleBeam	Water	Special	65	100	20	Normal	—	○
21	FeatherDance	Flying	Status	—	100	15	Normal	—	—
24	Aqua Ring	Water	Status	—	—	20	Self	—	—
27	Air Slash	Flying	Special	75	95	20	Normal	○	—
30	Roost	Flying	Status	—	—	10	Self	—	—
34	Rain Dance	Water	Status	—	—	5	Both Sides	—	—
37	Tailwind	Flying	Status	—	—	30	Your Side	—	—
41	Brave Bird	Flying	Physical	120	100	15	Normal	○	○
46	Hurricane	Flying	Special	120	70	10	Normal	○	—

TM & HM MOVES

Lv.	Name	Type	Kind	Pow.	Acc.	PP	Range	Long	DA
TM06	Toxic	Poison	Status	—	90	10	Normal	—	—
TM07	Hail	Ice	Status	—	—	10	Both Sides	—	—
TM10	Hidden Power	Normal	Special	—	100	15	Normal	—	—
TM13	Ice Beam	Ice	Special	95	100	10	Normal	—	—
TM17	Protect	Normal	Status	—	—	10	Self	—	—
TM18	Rain Dance	Water	Status	—	—	5	Both Sides	—	—
TM21	Frustration	Normal	Physical	—	100	20	Normal	—	○
TM27	Return	Normal	Physical	—	100	20	Normal	—	○
TM32	Double Team	Normal	Status	—	—	15	Self	—	—
TM40	Aerial Ace	Flying	Physical	60	—	20	Normal	○	—
TM42	Facade	Normal	Physical	70	100	20	Normal	—	—
TM44	Rest	Psychic	Status	—	—	10	Self	—	—
TM45	Attract	Normal	Status	—	100	15	Normal	—	—
TM48	Round	Normal	Special	60	100	15	Normal	—	—
TM55	Scald	Water	Special	80	100	15	Normal	—	○
TM87	Swagger	Normal	Status	—	90	15	Normal	—	—
TM88	Pluck	Flying	Physical	60	100	20	Normal	○	○
TM90	Substitute	Normal	Status	—	—	10	Self	—	—
HM02	Fly	Flying	Physical	90	95	15	Normal	○	—
HM03	Surf	Water	Special	95	100	15	Adjacent	—	—
HM06	Dive	Water	Physical	80	100	10	Normal	—	—

MOVES TAUGHT BY PEOPLE

Name	Type	Kind	Pow.	Acc.	PP	Range	Long	DA

MOVES TAUGHT BY MOVE TUTORS FOR SHARDS

Name	Type	Kind	Pow.	Acc.	PP	Range	Long	DA
Uproar	Normal	Special	90	100	10	1 Random	—	—
Icy Wind	Ice	Special	55	95	15	Many Others	—	—
Snore	Normal	Special	40	100	15	Normal	—	—
Roost	Flying	Status	—	—	10	Self	—	—
Tailwind	Flying	Status	—	—	30	Your Side	—	—
Endeavor	Normal	Physical	—	100	5	Normal	—	○
Sleep Talk	Normal	Status	—	—	10	Self	—	—

EGG MOVES

Name	Type	Kind	Pow.	Acc.	PP	Range	Long	DA
Steel Wing	Steel	Physical	70	90	25	Normal	—	○
Brine	Water	Special	65	100	10	Normal	—	—
Gust	Flying	Special	40	100	35	Normal	○	—
Air Cutter	Flying	Special	55	95	25	Many Others	—	—
Mirror Move	Flying	Status	—	—	20	Normal	—	—
Me First	Normal	Status	—	—	20	Varies	—	—
Lucky Chant	Normal	Status	—	—	30	Your Side	—	—

Pokémon AR Marker

---

581 Swanna

White Bird Pokémon

TYPE Water | Flying

ABILITIES
- Keen Eye
- Big Pecks

HIDDEN ABILITY
- Hydration

- HEIGHT: 4'03"
- WEIGHT: 53.4 lbs.
- GENDER: ♂ / ♀

Despite their elegant appearance, they can flap their wings strongly and fly for thousands of miles.

Same form for ♂ / ♀

STATS
- HP
- Attack
- Defense
- Sp. Atk
- Sp. Def
- Speed

EGG GROUPS
Water ❶ /Flying

ITEMS SOMETIMES HELD
- None

EVOLUTION

 Ducklett — Lv. 35 → Swanna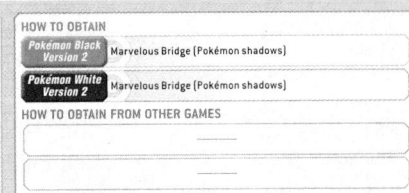

HOW TO OBTAIN

Pokémon Black Version 2	Marvelous Bridge (Pokémon shadows)
Pokémon White Version 2	Marvelous Bridge (Pokémon shadows)

HOW TO OBTAIN FROM OTHER GAMES

LEVEL-UP AND LEARNED MOVES

Lv.	Name	Type	Kind	Pow.	Acc.	PP	Range	Long	DA
1	Water Gun	Water	Special	40	100	25	Normal	—	—
1	Water Sport	Water	Status	—	—	15	Both Sides	—	—
1	Defog	Flying	Status	—	—	15	Normal	—	—
1	Wing Attack	Flying	Physical	60	100	35	Normal	○	—
3	Water Sport	Water	Status	—	—	15	Both Sides	—	—
6	Defog	Flying	Status	—	—	15	Normal	—	—
9	Wing Attack	Flying	Physical	60	100	35	Normal	○	—
13	Water Pulse	Water	Special	60	100	20	Normal	—	○
15	Aerial Ace	Flying	Physical	60	—	20	Normal	○	—
19	BubbleBeam	Water	Special	65	100	20	Normal	—	○
21	FeatherDance	Flying	Status	—	100	15	Normal	—	—
24	Aqua Ring	Water	Status	—	—	20	Self	—	—
27	Air Slash	Flying	Special	75	95	20	Normal	○	—
30	Roost	Flying	Status	—	—	10	Self	—	—
34	Rain Dance	Water	Status	—	—	5	Both Sides	—	—
40	Tailwind	Flying	Status	—	—	30	Your Side	—	—
47	Brave Bird	Flying	Physical	120	100	15	Normal	○	○
55	Hurricane	Flying	Special	120	70	10	Normal	○	—

TM & HM MOVES

Lv.	Name	Type	Kind	Pow.	Acc.	PP	Range	Long	DA
TM06	Toxic	Poison	Status	—	90	10	Normal	—	—
TM07	Hail	Ice	Status	—	—	10	Both Sides	—	—
TM10	Hidden Power	Normal	Special	—	100	15	Normal	—	—
TM13	Ice Beam	Ice	Special	95	100	10	Normal	—	—
TM15	Hyper Beam	Normal	Special	150	90	5	Normal	—	—
TM17	Protect	Normal	Status	—	—	10	Self	—	—
TM18	Rain Dance	Water	Status	—	—	5	Both Sides	—	—
TM21	Frustration	Normal	Physical	—	100	20	Normal	—	○
TM27	Return	Normal	Physical	—	100	20	Normal	—	○
TM32	Double Team	Normal	Status	—	—	15	Self	—	—
TM40	Aerial Ace	Flying	Physical	60	—	20	Normal	○	—
TM42	Facade	Normal	Physical	70	100	20	Normal	—	—
TM44	Rest	Psychic	Status	—	—	10	Self	—	—
TM45	Attract	Normal	Status	—	100	15	Normal	—	—
TM48	Round	Normal	Special	60	100	15	Normal	—	—
TM55	Scald	Water	Special	80	100	15	Normal	—	○
TM68	Giga Impact	Normal	Physical	150	90	5	Normal	—	—
TM87	Swagger	Normal	Status	—	90	15	Normal	—	—
TM88	Pluck	Flying	Physical	60	100	20	Normal	○	○
TM90	Substitute	Normal	Status	—	—	10	Self	—	—
HM02	Fly	Flying	Physical	90	95	15	Normal	○	—
HM03	Surf	Water	Special	95	100	15	Adjacent	—	—
HM06	Dive	Water	Physical	80	100	10	Normal	—	—

MOVES TAUGHT BY PEOPLE

Name	Type	Kind	Pow.	Acc.	PP	Range	Long	DA

MOVES TAUGHT BY MOVE TUTORS FOR SHARDS

Name	Type	Kind	Pow.	Acc.	PP	Range	Long	DA
Uproar	Normal	Special	90	100	10	1 Random	—	—
Icy Wind	Ice	Special	55	95	15	Many Others	—	—
Snore	Normal	Special	40	100	15	Normal	—	—
Roost	Flying	Status	—	—	10	Self	—	—
Sky Attack	Flying	Physical	140	90	5	Normal	○	—
Tailwind	Flying	Status	—	—	30	Your Side	—	—
Endeavor	Normal	Physical	—	100	5	Normal	—	—
Sleep Talk	Normal	Status	—	—	10	Self	—	—

Pokémon AR Marker

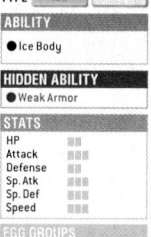

582 Vanillite
Fresh Snow Pokémon

TYPE Ice

ABILITY
- Ice Body

HIDDEN ABILITY
- Weak Armor

- HEIGHT: 1'04"
- WEIGHT: 12.6 lbs.
- GENDER: ♂ / ♀

Theoretically, this Pokémon formed from icicles bathed in energy from the morning sun. Their breath is -58° F.

Same form for ♂ / ♀

STATS
- HP
- Attack
- Defense
- Sp. Atk
- Sp. Def
- Speed

EGG GROUPS
Mineral

ITEMS SOMETIMES HELD
- None

EVOLUTION

Vanillite → Lv. 35 Vanillish → Lv. 47 Vanilluxe

HOW TO OBTAIN

Pokémon Black Version 2 — Catch a Vanillish or Vanilluxe, leave it at the Pokémon Day Care, and hatch the Egg that is found

Pokémon White Version 2 — Catch a Vanillish or Vanilluxe, leave it at the Pokémon Day Care, and hatch the Egg that is found

HOW TO OBTAIN FROM OTHER GAMES

Pokémon Black Version — Cold Storage entrance

Pokémon White Version — Cold Storage entrance

LEVEL-UP AND LEARNED MOVES

Lv.	Name	Type	Kind	Pow.	Acc.	PP	Range	Long	DA
1	Icicle Spear	Ice	Physical	25	100	30	Normal	—	—
4	Harden	Normal	Status	—	—	30	Self	—	—
7	Astonish	Ghost	Physical	30	100	15	Normal	—	○
10	Uproar	Normal	Special	90	100	10	1 Random	—	—
13	Icy Wind	Ice	Special	55	95	15	Many Others	—	—
16	Mist	Ice	Status	—	—	30	Your Side	—	—
19	Avalanche	Ice	Physical	60	100	10	Normal	—	—
22	Taunt	Dark	Status	—	100	20	Normal	—	—
26	Mirror Shot	Steel	Special	65	85	10	Normal	—	—
31	Acid Armor	Poison	Status	—	—	40	Self	—	—
35	Ice Beam	Ice	Special	95	100	10	Normal	—	—
40	Hail	Ice	Status	—	—	10	Both Sides	—	—
44	Mirror Coat	Psychic	Special	—	100	20	Varies	—	—
49	Blizzard	Ice	Special	120	70	5	Many Others	—	—
53	Sheer Cold	Ice	Special	—	30	5	Normal	—	—

TM & HM MOVES

Lv.	Name	Type	Kind	Pow.	Acc.	PP	Range	Long	DA
TM06	Toxic	Poison	Status	—	90	10	Normal	—	—
TM07	Hail	Ice	Status	—	—	10	Both Sides	—	—
TM10	Hidden Power	Normal	Special	—	100	15	Normal	—	—
TM12	Taunt	Dark	Status	—	100	20	Normal	—	—
TM13	Ice Beam	Ice	Special	95	100	10	Normal	—	—
TM14	Blizzard	Ice	Special	120	70	5	Many Others	—	—
TM16	Light Screen	Psychic	Status	—	—	30	Your Side	—	—
TM17	Protect	Normal	Status	—	—	10	Self	—	—
TM18	Rain Dance	Water	Status	—	—	5	Both Sides	—	—
TM21	Frustration	Normal	Physical	—	100	20	Normal	—	○
TM27	Return	Normal	Physical	—	100	20	Normal	—	○
TM32	Double Team	Normal	Status	—	—	15	Self	—	—
TM42	Facade	Normal	Physical	70	100	20	Normal	—	○
TM44	Rest	Psychic	Status	—	—	10	Self	—	—
TM45	Attract	Normal	Status	—	100	15	Normal	—	—
TM48	Round	Normal	Special	60	100	15	Normal	—	—
TM64	Explosion	Normal	Physical	250	100	5	Adjacent	—	—
TM79	Frost Breath	Ice	Special	40	90	10	Normal	—	—
TM87	Swagger	Normal	Status	—	90	15	Normal	—	—
TM90	Substitute	Normal	Status	—	—	10	Self	—	—
TM91	Flash Cannon	Steel	Special	80	100	10	Normal	—	—

MOVES TAUGHT BY PEOPLE

Name	Type	Kind	Pow.	Acc.	PP	Range	Long	DA

MOVES TAUGHT BY MOVE TUTORS FOR SHARDS

Name	Type	Kind	Pow.	Acc.	PP	Range	Long	DA
Signal Beam	Bug	Special	75	100	15	Normal	—	—
Uproar	Normal	Special	90	100	10	1 Random	—	—
Iron Defense	Steel	Status	—	—	15	Self	—	—
Magnet Rise	Electric	Status	—	—	10	Self	—	—
Magic Coat	Psychic	Status	—	—	15	Self	—	—
Icy Wind	Ice	Special	55	95	15	Many Others	—	—
Snore	Normal	Special	40	100	15	Normal	—	—
Sleep Talk	Normal	Status	—	—	10	Self	—	—

EGG MOVES

Name	Type	Kind	Pow.	Acc.	PP	Range	Long	DA
Water Pulse	Water	Special	60	100	20	Normal	○	—
Natural Gift	Normal	Physical	—	100	15	Normal	—	—
Imprison	Psychic	Status	—	—	10	Self	—	—
Autotomize	Steel	Status	—	—	15	Self	—	—
Iron Defense	Steel	Status	—	—	15	Self	—	—
Magnet Rise	Electric	Status	—	—	10	Self	—	—
Ice Shard	Ice	Physical	40	100	30	Normal	—	—
Powder Snow	Ice	Special	40	100	25	Many Others	—	—

Pokémon AR Marker

---

583 Vanillish
Icy Snow Pokémon

TYPE Ice

ABILITY
- Ice Body

HIDDEN ABILITY
- Weak Armor

- HEIGHT: 3'07"
- WEIGHT: 90.4 lbs.
- GENDER: ♂ / ♀

They cool down the surrounding air and create ice particles, which they use to freeze their foes.

Same form for ♂ / ♀

STATS
- HP
- Attack
- Defense
- Sp. Atk
- Sp. Def
- Speed

EGG GROUPS
Mineral

ITEMS SOMETIMES HELD
- None

EVOLUTION

Vanillite → Lv. 35 Vanillish → Lv. 47 Vanilluxe

HOW TO OBTAIN

Pokémon Black Version 2 — ① Giant Chasm caves ② Giant Chasm entrance

Pokémon White Version 2 — ① Giant Chasm caves ② Giant Chasm entrance

HOW TO OBTAIN FROM OTHER GAMES

LEVEL-UP AND LEARNED MOVES

Lv.	Name	Type	Kind	Pow.	Acc.	PP	Range	Long	DA
1	Icicle Spear	Ice	Physical	25	100	30	Normal	—	—
1	Harden	Normal	Status	—	—	30	Self	—	—
1	Astonish	Ghost	Physical	30	100	15	Normal	—	○
1	Uproar	Normal	Special	90	100	10	1 Random	—	—
4	Harden	Normal	Status	—	—	30	Self	—	—
7	Astonish	Ghost	Physical	30	100	15	Normal	—	○
10	Uproar	Normal	Special	90	100	10	1 Random	—	—
13	Icy Wind	Ice	Special	55	95	15	Many Others	—	—
16	Mist	Ice	Status	—	—	30	Your Side	—	—
19	Avalanche	Ice	Physical	60	100	10	Normal	—	—
22	Taunt	Dark	Status	—	100	20	Normal	—	—
26	Mirror Shot	Steel	Special	65	85	10	Normal	—	—
31	Acid Armor	Poison	Status	—	—	40	Self	—	—
36	Ice Beam	Ice	Special	95	100	10	Normal	—	—
42	Hail	Ice	Status	—	—	10	Both Sides	—	—
47	Mirror Coat	Psychic	Special	—	100	20	Varies	—	—
53	Blizzard	Ice	Special	120	70	5	Many Others	—	—
58	Sheer Cold	Ice	Special	—	30	5	Normal	—	—

TM & HM MOVES

Lv.	Name	Type	Kind	Pow.	Acc.	PP	Range	Long	DA
TM06	Toxic	Poison	Status	—	90	10	Normal	—	—
TM07	Hail	Ice	Status	—	—	10	Both Sides	—	—
TM10	Hidden Power	Normal	Special	—	100	15	Normal	—	—
TM12	Taunt	Dark	Status	—	100	20	Normal	—	—
TM13	Ice Beam	Ice	Special	95	100	10	Normal	—	—
TM14	Blizzard	Ice	Special	120	70	5	Many Others	—	—
TM16	Light Screen	Psychic	Status	—	—	30	Your Side	—	—
TM17	Protect	Normal	Status	—	—	10	Self	—	—
TM18	Rain Dance	Water	Status	—	—	5	Both Sides	—	—
TM21	Frustration	Normal	Physical	—	100	20	Normal	—	○
TM27	Return	Normal	Physical	—	100	20	Normal	—	○
TM32	Double Team	Normal	Status	—	—	15	Self	—	—
TM42	Facade	Normal	Physical	70	100	20	Normal	—	○
TM44	Rest	Psychic	Status	—	—	10	Self	—	—
TM45	Attract	Normal	Status	—	100	15	Normal	—	—
TM48	Round	Normal	Special	60	100	15	Normal	—	—
TM64	Explosion	Normal	Physical	250	100	5	Adjacent	—	—
TM79	Frost Breath	Ice	Special	40	90	10	Normal	—	—
TM87	Swagger	Normal	Status	—	90	15	Normal	—	—
TM90	Substitute	Normal	Status	—	—	10	Self	—	—
TM91	Flash Cannon	Steel	Special	80	100	10	Normal	—	—

MOVES TAUGHT BY PEOPLE

Name	Type	Kind	Pow.	Acc.	PP	Range	Long	DA

MOVES TAUGHT BY MOVE TUTORS FOR SHARDS

Name	Type	Kind	Pow.	Acc.	PP	Range	Long	DA
Signal Beam	Bug	Special	75	100	15	Normal	—	—
Uproar	Normal	Special	90	100	10	1 Random	—	—
Iron Defense	Steel	Status	—	—	15	Self	—	—
Magnet Rise	Electric	Status	—	—	10	Self	—	—
Magic Coat	Psychic	Status	—	—	15	Self	—	—
Icy Wind	Ice	Special	55	95	15	Many Others	—	—
Snore	Normal	Special	40	100	15	Normal	—	—
Sleep Talk	Normal	Status	—	—	10	Self	—	—

Pokémon AR Marker

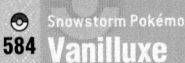

584 Vanilluxe

Snowstorm Pokémon

● HEIGHT: 4'03"
● WEIGHT: 126.8 lbs.
● GENDER: ♂ / ♀

Swallowing large amounts of water, they make snow clouds inside their bodies and, when angry, cause violent blizzards.

TYPE Ice

ABILITY
● Ice Body

HIDDEN ABILITY
● Weak Armor

STATS
HP
Attack
Defense
Sp. Atk
Sp. Def
Speed

EGG GROUPS
Mineral

ITEMS SOMETIMES HELD
● None

Same form for ♂ / ♀

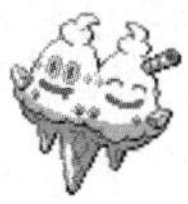

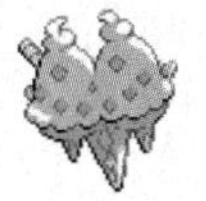

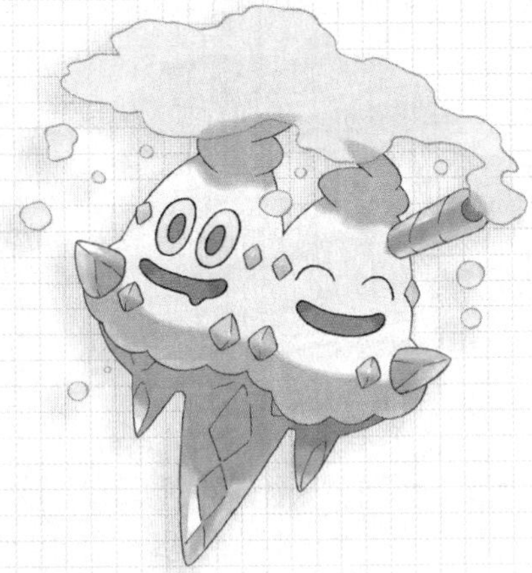

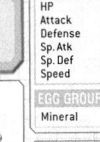

EVOLUTION

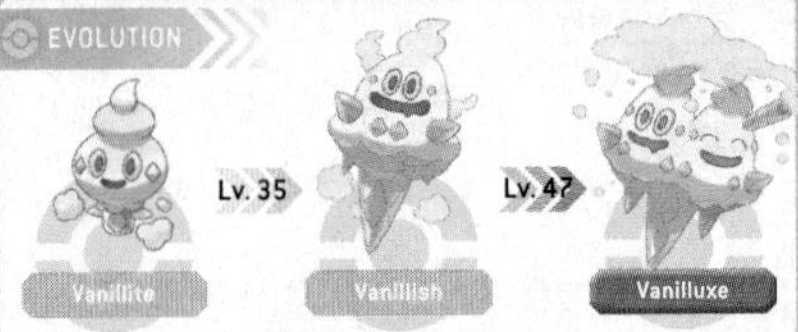
Vanillite
Lv. 35
Vanillish
Lv. 47
Vanilluxe

HOW TO OBTAIN

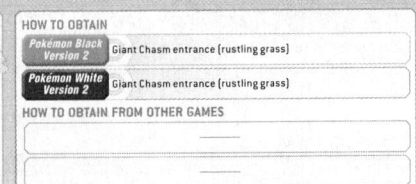

Pokémon Black Version 2	Giant Chasm entrance (rustling grass)
Pokémon White Version 2	Giant Chasm entrance (rustling grass)

HOW TO OBTAIN FROM OTHER GAMES

—
—

LEVEL-UP AND LEARNED MOVES

Lv.	Name	Type	Kind	Pow.	Acc.	PP	Range	Long	DA
1	Weather Ball	Normal	Special	50	100	10	Normal	—	—
1	Icicle Spear	Ice	Physical	25	100	30	Normal	—	—
1	Harden	Normal	Status	—	—	30	Self	—	—
1	Astonish	Ghost	Physical	30	100	15	Normal	—	○
1	Uproar	Normal	Special	90	100	10	1 Random	—	—
4	Harden	Normal	Status	—	—	30	Self	—	—
7	Astonish	Ghost	Physical	30	100	15	Normal	—	○
10	Uproar	Normal	Special	90	100	10	1 Random	—	—
13	Icy Wind	Ice	Special	55	95	15	Many Others	—	—
16	Mist	Ice	Status	—	—	30	Your Side	—	—
19	Avalanche	Ice	Physical	60	100	10	Normal	—	○
22	Taunt	Dark	Status	—	100	20	Normal	—	—
26	Mirror Shot	Steel	Special	65	85	10	Normal	—	—
31	Acid Armor	Poison	Status	—	—	40	Self	—	—
36	Ice Beam	Ice	Special	95	100	10	Normal	—	—
42	Hail	Ice	Status	—	—	10	Both Sides	—	—
50	Mirror Coat	Psychic	Special	—	100	20	Varies	—	—
59	Blizzard	Ice	Special	120	70	5	Many Others	—	—
67	Sheer Cold	Ice	Special	—	30	5	Normal	—	—

TM & HM MOVES

Lv.	Name	Type	Kind	Pow.	Acc.	PP	Range	Long	DA
TM06	Toxic	Poison	Status	—	90	10	Normal	—	—
TM07	Hail	Ice	Status	—	—	10	Both Sides	—	—
TM10	Hidden Power	Normal	Special	—	100	15	Normal	—	—
TM12	Taunt	Dark	Status	—	100	20	Normal	—	—
TM13	Ice Beam	Ice	Special	95	100	10	Normal	—	—
TM14	Blizzard	Ice	Special	120	70	5	Many Others	—	—
TM15	Hyper Beam	Normal	Special	150	90	5	Normal	—	—
TM16	Light Screen	Psychic	Status	—	—	30	Your Side	—	—
TM17	Protect	Normal	Status	—	—	10	Self	—	—
TM18	Rain Dance	Water	Status	—	—	5	Both Sides	—	—
TM21	Frustration	Normal	Physical	—	100	20	Normal	—	○
TM27	Return	Normal	Physical	—	100	20	Normal	—	○
TM32	Double Team	Normal	Status	—	—	15	Self	—	—
TM42	Facade	Normal	Physical	70	100	20	Normal	—	○
TM44	Rest	Psychic	Status	—	—	10	Self	—	—
TM45	Attract	Normal	Status	—	100	15	Normal	—	—
TM48	Round	Normal	Special	60	100	15	Normal	—	—
TM64	Explosion	Normal	Physical	250	100	5	Adjacent	—	—
TM68	Giga Impact	Normal	Physical	150	90	5	Normal	—	○
TM79	Frost Breath	Ice	Special	40	90	10	Normal	—	—
TM87	Swagger	Normal	Status	—	90	15	Normal	—	—
TM90	Substitute	Normal	Status	—	—	10	Self	—	—
TM91	Flash Cannon	Steel	Special	80	100	10	Normal	—	—

MOVES TAUGHT BY PEOPLE

Name	Type	Kind	Pow.	Acc.	PP	Range	Long	DA

MOVES TAUGHT BY MOVE TUTORS FOR SHARDS

Name	Type	Kind	Pow.	Acc.	PP	Range	Long	DA
Signal Beam	Bug	Special	75	100	15	Normal	—	—
Uproar	Normal	Special	90	100	10	1 Random	—	—
Iron Defense	Steel	Status	—	—	15	Self	—	—
Magnet Rise	Electric	Status	—	—	10	Self	—	—
Magic Coat	Psychic	Status	—	—	15	Self	—	—
Icy Wind	Ice	Special	55	95	15	Many Others	—	—
Snore	Normal	Special	40	100	15	Normal	—	—
Sleep Talk	Normal	Status	—	—	10	Self	—	—

Pokémon AR Marker

584 Vanilluxe

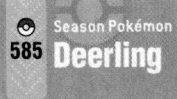

585 Deerling

Season Pokémon

● HEIGHT: 2'00"
● WEIGHT: 43.0 lbs.
● GENDER: ♂ / ♀

Their coloring changes according to the seasons and can be slightly affected by the temperature and humidity as well.

TYPE Normal Grass

ABILITIES
● Chlorophyll
● Sap Sipper

HIDDEN ABILITY
● Serene Grace

STATS
HP
Attack
Defense
Sp. Atk
Sp. Def
Speed

EGG GROUPS
Field

ITEMS SOMETIMES HELD
● None

Spring Form

Summer Form

Autumn Form

Winter Form

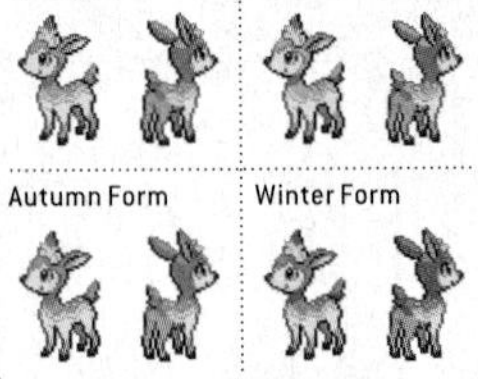

EVOLUTION

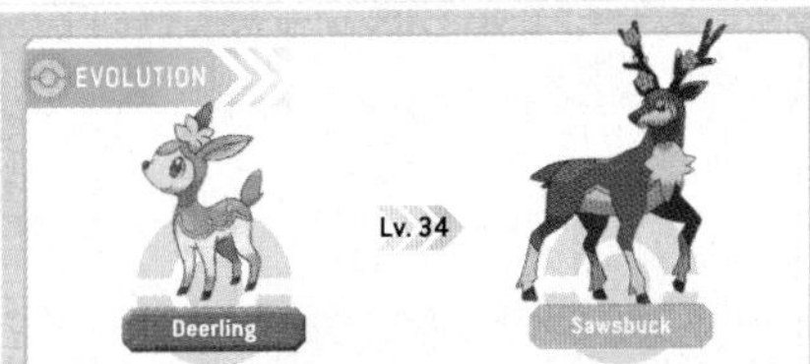
Deerling
Lv. 34
Sawsbuck

HOW TO OBTAIN

Pokémon Black Version 2	❶ Route 6 ❷ Route 7
Pokémon White Version 2	❶ Route 6 ❷ Route 7

HOW TO OBTAIN FROM OTHER GAMES

—
—

LEVEL-UP AND LEARNED MOVES

Lv.	Name	Type	Kind	Pow.	Acc.	PP	Range	Long	DA
1	Tackle	Normal	Physical	50	100	35	Normal	—	○
1	Camouflage	Normal	Status	—	—	20	Self	—	—
4	Growl	Normal	Status	—	100	40	Many Others	—	—
7	Sand-Attack	Ground	Status	—	100	15	Normal	—	—
10	Double Kick	Fighting	Physical	30	100	30	Normal	—	○
13	Leech Seed	Grass	Status	—	90	10	Normal	—	—
16	Faint Attack	Dark	Physical	60	—	20	Normal	—	○
20	Take Down	Normal	Physical	90	85	20	Normal	—	○
24	Jump Kick	Fighting	Physical	100	95	10	Normal	—	○
28	Aromatherapy	Grass	Status	—	—	5	Your Party	—	—
32	Energy Ball	Grass	Special	80	100	10	Normal	—	—
36	Charm	Normal	Status	—	100	20	Normal	—	—
41	Nature Power	Normal	Status	—	—	20	Varies	—	—
46	Double-Edge	Normal	Physical	120	100	15	Normal	—	○
51	SolarBeam	Grass	Special	120	100	10	Normal	—	—

TM & HM MOVES

Lv.	Name	Type	Kind	Pow.	Acc.	PP	Range	Long	DA
TM06	Toxic	Poison	Status	—	90	10	Normal	—	—
TM10	Hidden Power	Normal	Special	—	100	15	Normal	—	—
TM11	Sunny Day	Fire	Status	—	—	5	Both Sides	—	—
TM16	Light Screen	Psychic	Status	—	—	30	Your Side	—	—
TM17	Protect	Normal	Status	—	—	10	Self	—	—
TM18	Rain Dance	Water	Status	—	—	5	Both Sides	—	—
TM20	Safeguard	Normal	Status	—	—	25	Your Side	—	—
TM21	Frustration	Normal	Physical	—	100	20	Normal	—	○
TM22	SolarBeam	Grass	Special	120	100	10	Normal	—	—
TM27	Return	Normal	Physical	—	100	20	Normal	—	○
TM30	Shadow Ball	Ghost	Special	80	100	15	Normal	—	—
TM32	Double Team	Normal	Status	—	—	15	Self	—	—
TM42	Facade	Normal	Physical	70	100	20	Normal	—	○
TM44	Rest	Psychic	Status	—	—	10	Self	—	—
TM45	Attract	Normal	Status	—	100	15	Normal	—	—
TM48	Round	Normal	Special	60	100	15	Normal	—	—
TM49	Echoed Voice	Normal	Special	40	100	15	Normal	—	—
TM53	Energy Ball	Grass	Special	80	100	10	Normal	—	—
TM67	Retaliate	Normal	Physical	70	100	5	Normal	—	○
TM70	Flash	Normal	Status	—	100	20	Normal	—	—
TM73	Thunder Wave	Electric	Status	—	100	20	Normal	—	—
TM83	Work Up	Normal	Status	—	—	30	Self	—	—
TM86	Grass Knot	Grass	Special	—	100	20	Normal	—	○
TM87	Swagger	Normal	Status	—	90	15	Normal	—	—
TM90	Substitute	Normal	Status	—	—	10	Self	—	—
TM93	Wild Charge	Electric	Physical	90	100	15	Normal	—	○

MOVES TAUGHT BY PEOPLE

Name	Type	Kind	Pow.	Acc.	PP	Range	Long	DA

MOVES TAUGHT BY MOVE TUTORS FOR SHARDS

Name	Type	Kind	Pow.	Acc.	PP	Range	Long	DA
Bounce	Flying	Physical	85	85	5	Normal	○	○
Seed Bomb	Grass	Physical	80	100	15	Normal	—	—
Last Resort	Normal	Physical	140	100	5	Normal	—	○
Snore	Normal	Special	40	100	15	Normal	—	—
Synthesis	Grass	Status	—	—	5	Self	—	—
Giga Drain	Grass	Special	75	100	10	Normal	—	—
Worry Seed	Grass	Status	—	100	10	Normal	—	—
Sleep Talk	Normal	Status	—	—	10	Self	—	—

EGG MOVES

Name	Type	Kind	Pow.	Acc.	PP	Range	Long	DA
Fake Tears	Dark	Status	—	100	20	Normal	—	—
Natural Gift	Normal	Physical	—	100	15	Normal	—	—
Synthesis	Grass	Status	—	—	5	Self	—	—
Worry Seed	Grass	Status	—	100	10	Normal	—	—
Odor Sleuth	Normal	Status	—	—	40	Normal	—	—
Agility	Psychic	Status	—	—	30	Self	—	—
Sleep Talk	Normal	Status	—	—	10	Self	—	—
Baton Pass	Normal	Status	—	—	40	Self	—	—
GrassWhistle	Grass	Status	—	55	15	Normal	—	—

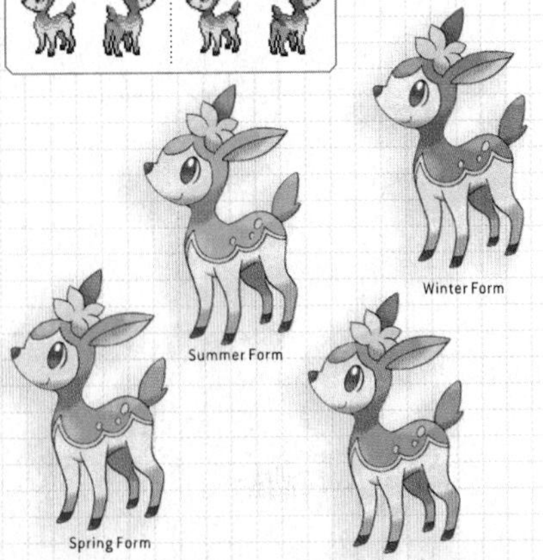
Winter Form
Summer Form
Spring Form
Autumn Form

Pokémon AR Marker

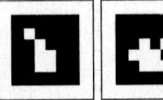

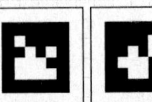

Spring Form | Summer Form | Autumn Form | Winter Form

585 Deerling

Season Pokémon

586 Sawsbuck

TYPE: Normal / Grass

ABILITIES
- Chlorophyll
- Sap Sipper

HIDDEN ABILITY
- Serene Grace

STATS
HP
Attack
Defense
Sp. Atk
Sp. Def
Speed

EGG GROUPS
Field

ITEMS SOMETIMES HELD
- None

- HEIGHT: 6'03"
- WEIGHT: 203.9 lbs.
- GENDER: ♂ / ♀

They migrate according to the seasons, so some people call Sawsbuck the harbingers of spring.

Spring Form / Summer Form / Autumn Form / Winter Form

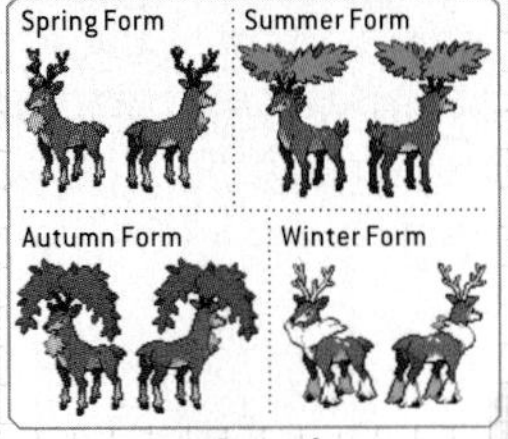

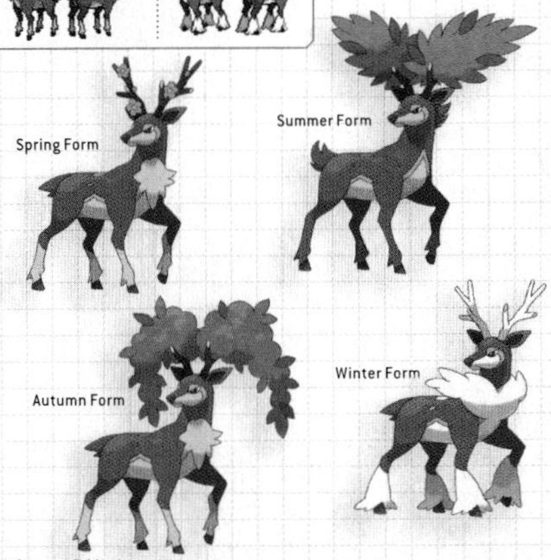

Pokémon AR Marker

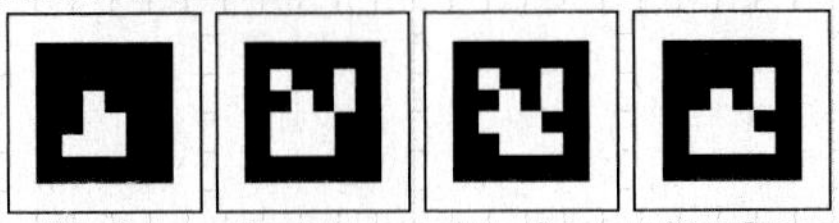

Spring Form / Summer Form / Autumn Form / Winter Form

EVOLUTION

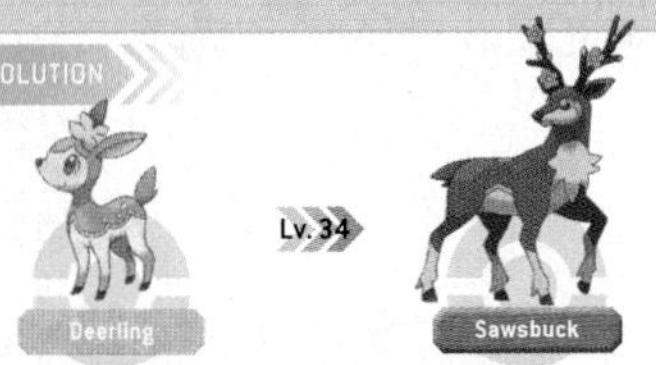

HOW TO OBTAIN

Pokémon Black Version 2	❶ Dragonspiral Tower entrance ❷ Dragonspiral Tower 1F outside
Pokémon White Version 2	❶ Dragonspiral Tower entrance ❷ Dragonspiral Tower 1F outside

HOW TO OBTAIN FROM OTHER GAMES

—

—

LEVEL-UP AND LEARNED MOVES

Lv.	Name	Type	Kind	Pow.	Acc.	PP	Range	Long	DA
1	Megahorn	Bug	Physical	120	85	10	Normal	—	○
1	Tackle	Normal	Physical	50	100	35	Normal	—	○
1	Camouflage	Normal	Status	—	—	20	Self	—	—
1	Growl	Normal	Status	—	100	40	Many Others	—	—
1	Sand-Attack	Ground	Status	—	100	15	Normal	—	—
4	Growl	Normal	Status	—	100	40	Many Others	—	—
7	Sand-Attack	Ground	Status	—	100	15	Normal	—	—
10	Double Kick	Fighting	Physical	30	100	30	Normal	—	○
13	Leech Seed	Grass	Status	—	90	10	Normal	—	—
16	Faint Attack	Dark	Physical	60	—	20	Normal	—	○
20	Take Down	Normal	Physical	90	85	20	Normal	—	○
24	Jump Kick	Fighting	Physical	100	95	10	Normal	—	○
28	Aromatherapy	Grass	Status	—	—	5	Your Party	—	—
32	Energy Ball	Grass	Special	80	100	10	Normal	—	—
36	Charm	Normal	Status	—	100	20	Normal	—	—
37	Horn Leech	Grass	Physical	75	100	10	Normal	—	○
44	Nature Power	Normal	Status	—	—	20	Varies	—	—
52	Double-Edge	Normal	Physical	120	100	15	Normal	—	○
60	SolarBeam	Grass	Special	120	100	10	Normal	—	—

TM & HM MOVES

Lv.	Name	Type	Kind	Pow.	Acc.	PP	Range	Long	DA
TM06	Toxic	Poison	Status	—	90	10	Normal	—	—
TM10	Hidden Power	Normal	Special	—	100	15	Normal	—	—
TM11	Sunny Day	Fire	Status	—	—	5	Both Sides	—	—
TM15	Hyper Beam	Normal	Special	150	90	5	Normal	—	—
TM16	Light Screen	Psychic	Status	—	—	30	Your Side	—	—
TM17	Protect	Normal	Status	—	—	10	Self	—	—
TM18	Rain Dance	Water	Status	—	—	5	Both Sides	—	—
TM20	Safeguard	Normal	Status	—	—	25	Your Side	—	—
TM21	Frustration	Normal	Physical	—	100	20	Normal	—	○
TM22	SolarBeam	Grass	Special	120	100	10	Normal	—	—
TM27	Return	Normal	Physical	—	100	20	Normal	—	○
TM30	Shadow Ball	Ghost	Special	80	100	15	Normal	—	—
TM32	Double Team	Normal	Status	—	—	15	Self	—	—
TM42	Facade	Normal	Physical	70	100	20	Normal	—	○
TM44	Rest	Psychic	Status	—	—	10	Self	—	—
TM45	Attract	Normal	Status	—	100	15	Normal	—	—
TM48	Round	Normal	Special	60	100	15	Normal	—	—
TM49	Echoed Voice	Normal	Special	40	100	15	Normal	—	—
TM53	Energy Ball	Grass	Special	80	100	10	Normal	—	—
TM67	Retaliate	Normal	Physical	70	100	5	Normal	—	○
TM68	Giga Impact	Normal	Physical	150	90	5	Normal	—	○
TM70	Flash	Normal	Status	—	100	20	Normal	—	—
TM73	Thunder Wave	Electric	Status	—	100	20	Normal	—	—
TM75	Swords Dance	Normal	Status	—	—	30	Self	—	—
TM83	Work Up	Normal	Status	—	—	30	Self	—	—
TM86	Grass Knot	Grass	Special	—	100	20	Normal	—	○
TM87	Swagger	Normal	Status	—	90	15	Normal	—	—
TM90	Substitute	Normal	Status	—	—	10	Self	—	—
TM93	Wild Charge	Electric	Physical	90	100	15	Normal	—	○
TM94	Rock Smash	Fighting	Physical	40	100	15	Normal	—	○
HM01	Cut	Normal	Physical	50	95	30	Normal	—	○

MOVES TAUGHT BY PEOPLE

Name	Type	Kind	Pow.	Acc.	PP	Range	Long	DA

MOVES TAUGHT BY MOVE TUTORS FOR SHARDS

Name	Type	Kind	Pow.	Acc.	PP	Range	Long	DA
Bounce	Flying	Physical	85	85	5	Normal	○	○
Seed Bomb	Grass	Physical	80	100	15	Normal	—	—
Last Resort	Normal	Physical	140	100	5	Normal	—	○
Snore	Normal	Special	40	100	15	Normal	—	—
Synthesis	Grass	Status	—	—	5	Self	—	—
Giga Drain	Grass	Special	75	100	10	Normal	—	—
Worry Seed	Grass	Status	—	100	10	Normal	—	—
Sleep Talk	Normal	Status	—	—	10	Self	—	—

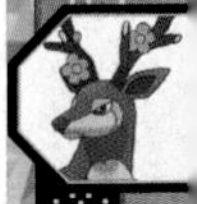

Sky Squirrel Pokémon

587 Emolga

TYPE: Electric / Flying

ABILITY
- Static

HIDDEN ABILITY
- Motor Drive

STATS
HP
Attack
Defense
Sp. Atk
Sp. Def
Speed

EGG GROUPS
Field

ITEMS SOMETIMES HELD
- Cheri Berry

- HEIGHT: 1'04"
- WEIGHT: 11.0 lbs.
- GENDER: ♂ / ♀

It glides on its outstretched membrane while shocking foes with the electricity stored in the pouches on its cheeks.

Same form for ♂ / ♀

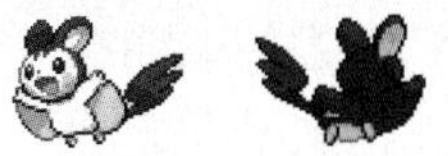

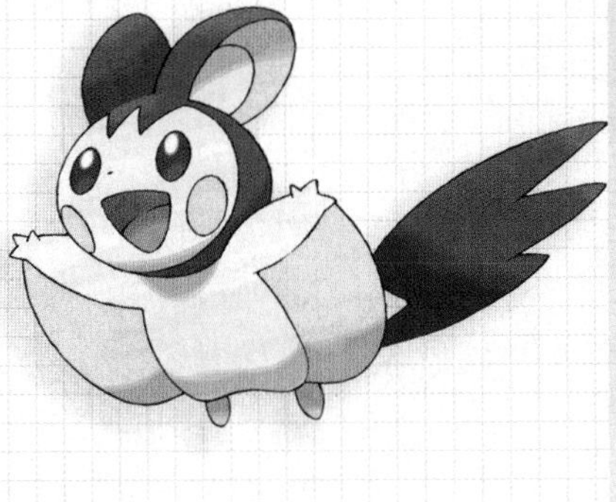

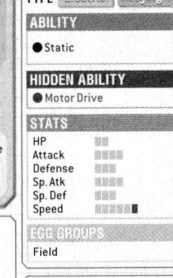

Pokémon AR Marker

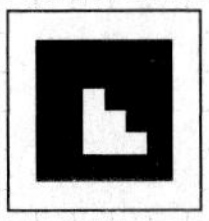

EVOLUTION

Does not evolve

HOW TO OBTAIN

Pokémon Black Version 2	❶ Route 16 (rustling grass) ❷ Route 5 (rustling grass)
Pokémon White Version 2	❶ Route 16 (rustling grass) ❷ Route 5 (rustling grass)

HOW TO OBTAIN FROM OTHER GAMES

—

—

LEVEL-UP AND LEARNED MOVES

Lv.	Name	Type	Kind	Pow.	Acc.	PP	Range	Long	DA
1	ThunderShock	Electric	Special	40	100	30	Normal	—	—
4	Quick Attack	Normal	Physical	40	100	30	Normal	—	○
7	Tail Whip	Normal	Status	—	100	30	Many Others	—	—
10	Charge	Electric	Status	—	—	20	Self	—	—
13	Spark	Electric	Physical	65	100	20	Normal	—	○
16	Pursuit	Dark	Physical	40	100	20	Normal	—	○
19	Double Team	Normal	Status	—	—	15	Self	—	—
22	Shock Wave	Electric	Special	60	—	20	Normal	—	—
26	Electro Ball	Electric	Special	—	100	10	Normal	—	—
30	Acrobatics	Flying	Physical	55	100	15	Normal	○	○
34	Light Screen	Psychic	Status	—	—	30	Your Side	—	—
38	Encore	Normal	Status	—	100	5	Normal	—	—
42	Volt Switch	Electric	Special	70	100	20	Normal	—	—
46	Agility	Psychic	Status	—	—	30	Self	—	—
50	Discharge	Electric	Special	80	100	15	Adjacent	—	—

TM & HM MOVES

Lv.	Name	Type	Kind	Pow.	Acc.	PP	Range	Long	DA
TM06	Toxic	Poison	Status	—	90	10	Normal	—	—
TM10	Hidden Power	Normal	Special	—	100	15	Normal	—	—
TM12	Taunt	Dark	Status	—	100	20	Normal	—	—
TM16	Light Screen	Psychic	Status	—	—	30	Your Side	—	—
TM17	Protect	Normal	Status	—	—	10	Self	—	—
TM18	Rain Dance	Water	Status	—	—	5	Both Sides	—	—
TM21	Frustration	Normal	Physical	—	100	20	Normal	—	○
TM24	Thunderbolt	Electric	Special	95	100	15	Normal	—	—
TM25	Thunder	Electric	Special	120	70	10	Normal	—	—
TM27	Return	Normal	Physical	—	100	20	Normal	—	○
TM32	Double Team	Normal	Status	—	—	15	Self	—	—
TM40	Aerial Ace	Flying	Physical	60	—	20	Normal	○	○
TM42	Facade	Normal	Physical	70	100	20	Normal	—	○
TM44	Rest	Psychic	Status	—	—	10	Self	—	—
TM45	Attract	Normal	Status	—	100	15	Normal	—	—
TM48	Round	Normal	Special	60	100	15	Normal	—	—
TM56	Fling	Dark	Physical	—	100	10	Normal	—	—
TM57	Charge Beam	Electric	Special	50	90	10	Normal	—	—
TM62	Acrobatics	Flying	Physical	55	100	15	Normal	○	○
TM70	Flash	Normal	Status	—	100	20	Normal	—	—
TM72	Volt Switch	Electric	Special	70	100	20	Normal	—	—
TM73	Thunder Wave	Electric	Status	—	100	20	Normal	—	—
TM87	Swagger	Normal	Status	—	90	15	Normal	—	—
TM89	U-turn	Bug	Physical	70	100	20	Normal	—	○
TM90	Substitute	Normal	Status	—	—	10	Self	—	—
TM93	Wild Charge	Electric	Physical	90	100	15	Normal	—	○
HM01	Cut	Normal	Physical	50	95	30	Normal	—	○

MOVES TAUGHT BY PEOPLE

Name	Type	Kind	Pow.	Acc.	PP	Range	Long	DA

MOVES TAUGHT BY MOVE TUTORS FOR SHARDS

Name	Type	Kind	Pow.	Acc.	PP	Range	Long	DA
Covet	Normal	Physical	60	100	40	Normal	—	○
Signal Beam	Bug	Special	75	100	15	Normal	—	—
Last Resort	Normal	Physical	140	100	5	Normal	—	○
Iron Tail	Steel	Physical	100	75	15	Normal	—	○
Snore	Normal	Special	40	100	15	Normal	—	—
Knock Off	Dark	Physical	20	100	20	Normal	—	○
Roost	Flying	Status	—	—	10	Self	—	—
Tailwind	Flying	Status	—	—	30	Your Side	—	—
Helping Hand	Normal	Status	—	—	20	1 Ally	—	—
Sleep Talk	Normal	Status	—	—	10	Self	—	—

EGG MOVES

Name	Type	Kind	Pow.	Acc.	PP	Range	Long	DA
Roost	Flying	Status	—	—	10	Self	—	—
Iron Tail	Steel	Physical	100	75	15	Normal	—	○
Astonish	Ghost	Physical	30	100	15	Normal	—	○
Air Slash	Flying	Special	75	95	20	Normal	○	—
Shock Wave	Electric	Special	60	—	20	Normal	—	—
Charm	Normal	Status	—	100	20	Normal	—	—
Covet	Normal	Physical	60	100	40	Normal	—	○
Tickle	Normal	Status	—	100	20	Normal	—	—
Baton Pass	Normal	Status	—	—	40	Self	—	—

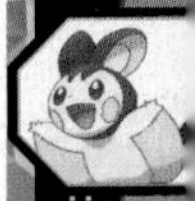

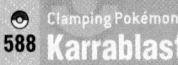

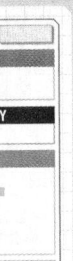

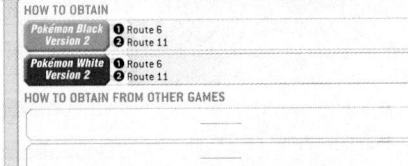

Clamping Pokémon

588 Karrablast

- HEIGHT: 1'08"
- WEIGHT: 13.0 lbs.
- GENDER: ♂ / ♀

For some reason they evolve when they receive electrical energy while they are attacking Shelmet.

Same form for ♂ / ♀

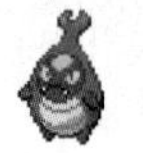

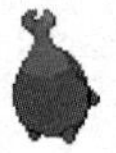

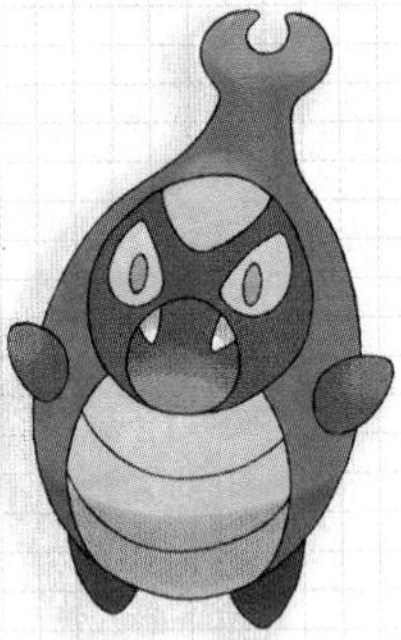

TYPE Bug

ABILITIES
- Swarm
- Shed Skin

HIDDEN ABILITY
- No Guard

STATS
HP
Attack
Defense
Sp. Atk
Sp. Def
Speed

EGG GROUPS
Bug

ITEMS SOMETIMES HELD
- None

EVOLUTION

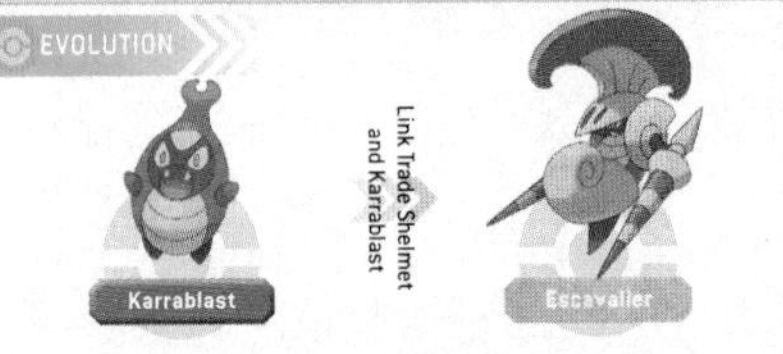

HOW TO OBTAIN

Pokémon Black Version 2	❶ Route 6 ❷ Route 11
Pokémon White Version 2	❶ Route 6 ❷ Route 11

HOW TO OBTAIN FROM OTHER GAMES

—

—

LEVEL-UP AND LEARNED MOVES

Lv.	Name	Type	Kind	Pow.	Acc.	PP	Range	Long	DA
1	Peck	Flying	Physical	35	100	35	Normal	○	○
4	Leer	Normal	Status	—	100	30	Many Others	—	—
8	Endure	Normal	Status	—	—	10	Self	—	—
13	Fury Cutter	Bug	Physical	20	95	20	Normal	—	○
16	Fury Attack	Normal	Physical	15	85	20	Normal	—	○
20	Headbutt	Normal	Physical	70	100	15	Normal	—	○
25	False Swipe	Normal	Physical	40	100	40	Normal	—	○
28	Bug Buzz	Bug	Special	90	100	10	Normal	—	—
32	Slash	Normal	Physical	70	100	20	Normal	—	○
37	Take Down	Normal	Physical	90	85	20	Normal	—	○
40	Scary Face	Normal	Status	—	100	10	Normal	—	—
44	X-Scissor	Bug	Physical	80	100	15	Normal	—	○
49	Flail	Normal	Physical	—	100	15	Normal	—	○
52	Swords Dance	Normal	Status	—	—	30	Self	—	—
56	Double-Edge	Normal	Physical	120	100	15	Normal	—	○

TM & HM MOVES

Lv.	Name	Type	Kind	Pow.	Acc.	PP	Range	Long	DA
TM06	Toxic	Poison	Status	—	90	10	Normal	—	—
TM10	Hidden Power	Normal	Special	—	100	15	Normal	—	—
TM17	Protect	Normal	Status	—	—	10	Self	—	—
TM18	Rain Dance	Water	Status	—	—	5	Both Sides	—	—
TM21	Frustration	Normal	Physical	—	100	20	Normal	—	○
TM27	Return	Normal	Physical	—	100	20	Normal	—	○
TM32	Double Team	Normal	Status	—	—	15	Self	—	—
TM40	Aerial Ace	Flying	Physical	60	—	20	Normal	○	○
TM42	Facade	Normal	Physical	70	100	20	Normal	—	○
TM44	Rest	Psychic	Status	—	—	10	Self	—	—
TM45	Attract	Normal	Status	—	100	15	Normal	—	—
TM48	Round	Normal	Special	60	100	15	Normal	—	—
TM53	Energy Ball	Grass	Special	80	100	10	Normal	—	—
TM54	False Swipe	Normal	Physical	40	100	40	Normal	—	○
TM75	Swords Dance	Normal	Status	—	—	30	Self	—	—
TM76	Struggle Bug	Bug	Special	30	100	20	Many Others	—	—
TM81	X-Scissor	Bug	Physical	80	100	15	Normal	—	○
TM84	Poison Jab	Poison	Physical	80	100	20	Normal	—	○
TM87	Swagger	Normal	Status	—	90	15	Normal	—	—
TM90	Substitute	Normal	Status	—	—	10	Self	—	—
HM01	Cut	Normal	Physical	50	95	30	Normal	—	○

MOVES TAUGHT BY PEOPLE

Name	Type	Kind	Pow.	Acc.	PP	Range	Long	DA

MOVES TAUGHT BY MOVE TUTORS FOR SHARDS

Name	Type	Kind	Pow.	Acc.	PP	Range	Long	DA
Bug Bite	Bug	Physical	60	100	20	Normal	—	○
Iron Defense	Steel	Status	—	—	15	Self	—	—
Snore	Normal	Special	40	100	15	Normal	—	—
Knock Off	Dark	Physical	20	100	20	Normal	—	○
Giga Drain	Grass	Special	75	100	10	Normal	—	—
Sleep Talk	Normal	Status	—	—	10	Self	—	—

EGG MOVES

Name	Type	Kind	Pow.	Acc.	PP	Range	Long	DA
Megahorn	Bug	Physical	120	85	10	Normal	—	○
Pursuit	Dark	Physical	40	100	20	Normal	—	○
Counter	Fighting	Physical	—	100	20	Varies	—	○
Horn Attack	Normal	Physical	65	100	25	Normal	—	○
Faint Attack	Dark	Physical	60	—	20	Normal	—	○
Bug Bite	Bug	Physical	60	100	20	Normal	—	○
Screech	Normal	Status	—	85	40	Normal	—	—
Knock Off	Dark	Physical	20	100	20	Normal	—	○

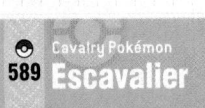

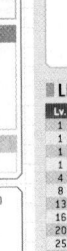

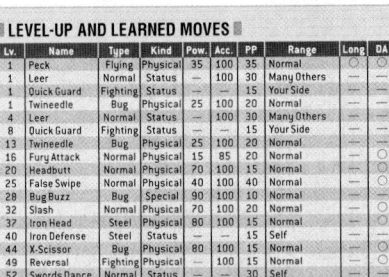

Pokémon AR Marker

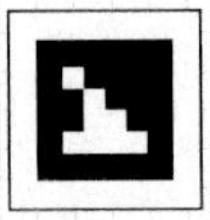

Karrablast | 588

Cavalry Pokémon

589 Escavalier

- HEIGHT: 3'03"
- WEIGHT: 72.8 lbs.
- GENDER: ♂ / ♀

Wearing the shell covering they stole from Shelmet, they defend themselves and attack with two lances.

Same form for ♂ / ♀

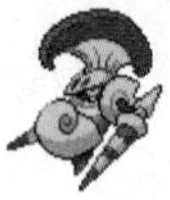

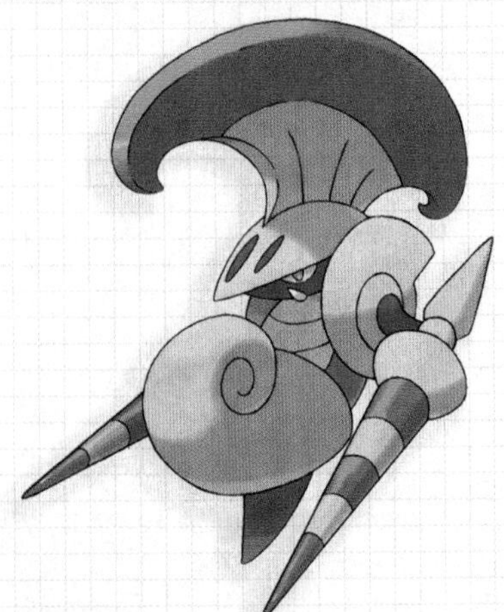

TYPE Bug Steel

ABILITIES
- Swarm
- Shell Armor

HIDDEN ABILITY
- Overcoat

STATS
HP
Attack
Defense
Sp. Atk
Sp. Def
Speed

EGG GROUPS
Bug

ITEMS SOMETIMES HELD
- None

EVOLUTION

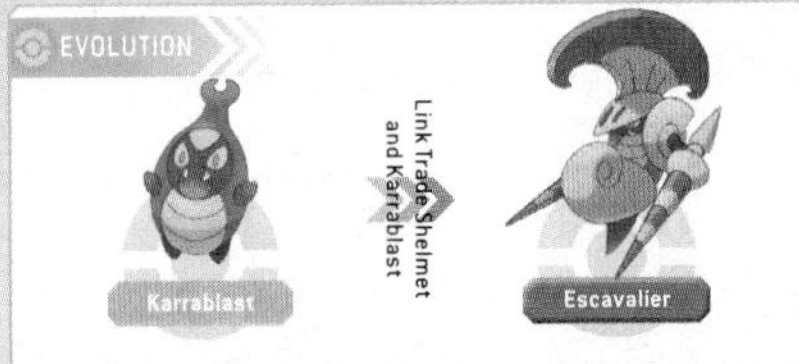

HOW TO OBTAIN

Pokémon Black Version 2	Send Shelmet in exchange for Karrablast in a Link Trade to receive Escavalier
Pokémon White Version 2	Send Shelmet in exchange for Karrablast in a Link Trade to receive Escavalier

HOW TO OBTAIN FROM OTHER GAMES

—

—

LEVEL-UP AND LEARNED MOVES

Lv.	Name	Type	Kind	Pow.	Acc.	PP	Range	Long	DA
1	Peck	Flying	Physical	35	100	35	Normal	○	○
1	Leer	Normal	Status	—	100	30	Many Others	—	—
1	Quick Guard	Fighting	Status	—	—	15	Your Side	—	—
1	Twineedle	Bug	Physical	25	100	20	Normal	—	—
4	Leer	Normal	Status	—	100	30	Many Others	—	—
8	Quick Guard	Fighting	Status	—	—	15	Your Side	—	—
13	Twineedle	Bug	Physical	25	100	20	Normal	—	—
16	Fury Attack	Normal	Physical	15	85	20	Normal	—	○
20	Headbutt	Normal	Physical	70	100	15	Normal	—	○
25	False Swipe	Normal	Physical	40	100	40	Normal	—	○
28	Bug Buzz	Bug	Special	90	100	10	Normal	—	—
32	Slash	Normal	Physical	70	100	20	Normal	—	○
37	Iron Head	Steel	Physical	80	100	15	Normal	—	○
40	Iron Defense	Steel	Status	—	—	15	Self	—	—
44	X-Scissor	Bug	Physical	80	100	15	Normal	—	○
49	Reversal	Fighting	Physical	—	100	15	Normal	—	○
52	Swords Dance	Normal	Status	—	—	30	Self	—	—
56	Giga Impact	Normal	Physical	150	90	5	Normal	—	○

TM & HM MOVES

Lv.	Name	Type	Kind	Pow.	Acc.	PP	Range	Long	DA
TM06	Toxic	Poison	Status	—	90	10	Normal	—	—
TM10	Hidden Power	Normal	Special	—	100	15	Normal	—	—
TM15	Hyper Beam	Normal	Special	150	90	5	Normal	—	—
TM17	Protect	Normal	Status	—	—	10	Self	—	—
TM18	Rain Dance	Water	Status	—	—	5	Both Sides	—	—
TM21	Frustration	Normal	Physical	—	100	20	Normal	—	○
TM27	Return	Normal	Physical	—	100	20	Normal	—	○
TM32	Double Team	Normal	Status	—	—	15	Self	—	—
TM40	Aerial Ace	Flying	Physical	60	—	20	Normal	○	○
TM42	Facade	Normal	Physical	70	100	20	Normal	—	○
TM44	Rest	Psychic	Status	—	—	10	Self	—	—
TM45	Attract	Normal	Status	—	100	15	Normal	—	—
TM48	Round	Normal	Special	60	100	15	Normal	—	—
TM52	Focus Blast	Fighting	Special	120	70	5	Normal	—	—
TM53	Energy Ball	Grass	Special	80	100	10	Normal	—	—
TM54	False Swipe	Normal	Physical	40	100	40	Normal	—	○
TM68	Giga Impact	Normal	Physical	150	90	5	Normal	—	○
TM75	Swords Dance	Normal	Status	—	—	30	Self	—	—
TM76	Struggle Bug	Bug	Special	30	100	20	Many Others	—	—
TM81	X-Scissor	Bug	Physical	80	100	15	Normal	—	○
TM84	Poison Jab	Poison	Physical	80	100	20	Normal	—	○
TM87	Swagger	Normal	Status	—	90	15	Normal	—	—
TM90	Substitute	Normal	Status	—	—	10	Self	—	—
TM94	Rock Smash	Fighting	Physical	40	100	15	Normal	—	○
HM01	Cut	Normal	Physical	50	95	30	Normal	—	○

MOVES TAUGHT BY PEOPLE

Name	Type	Kind	Pow.	Acc.	PP	Range	Long	DA

MOVES TAUGHT BY MOVE TUTORS FOR SHARDS

Name	Type	Kind	Pow.	Acc.	PP	Range	Long	DA
Bug Bite	Bug	Physical	60	100	20	Normal	—	○
Iron Head	Steel	Physical	80	100	15	Normal	—	○
Iron Defense	Steel	Status	—	—	15	Self	—	—
Snore	Normal	Special	40	100	15	Normal	—	—
Knock Off	Dark	Physical	20	100	20	Normal	—	○
Giga Drain	Grass	Special	75	100	10	Normal	—	—
Sleep Talk	Normal	Status	—	—	10	Self	—	—

Pokémon AR Marker

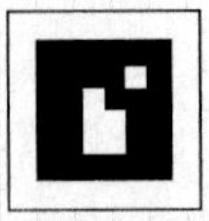

Spring Form

Escavalier | 589

590 Foongus

Mushroom Pokémon

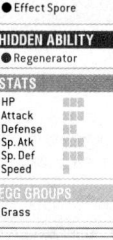

TYPE Grass Poison

ABILITY
● Effect Spore

HIDDEN ABILITY
● Regenerator

● HEIGHT: 0'08"
● WEIGHT: 2.2 lbs.
● GENDER: ♂ / ♀

STATS
HP
Attack
Defense
Sp. Atk
Sp. Def
Speed

It lures Pokémon with its pattern that looks just like a Poké Ball then releases poison spores.

Same form for ♂ / ♀

EGG GROUPS
Grass

ITEMS SOMETIMES HELD
● TinyMushroom
● Big Mushroom
● BalmMushroom

EVOLUTION

Foongus → Lv. 39 → Amoonguss

HOW TO OBTAIN

| Pokémon Black Version 2 | ❶ Route 6 ❷ Route 7 |
| Pokémon White Version 2 | ❶ Route 6 ❷ Route 7 |

HOW TO OBTAIN FROM OTHER GAMES

LEVEL-UP AND LEARNED MOVES

Lv.	Name	Type	Kind	Pow.	Acc.	PP	Range	Long	DA
1	Absorb	Grass	Special	20	100	25	Normal	—	—
6	Growth	Normal	Status	—	—	40	Self	—	—
8	Astonish	Ghost	Physical	30	100	15	Normal	—	○
12	Bide	Normal	Physical	—	—	10	Self	—	—
15	Mega Drain	Grass	Special	40	100	15	Normal	—	—
18	Ingrain	Grass	Status	—	—	20	Self	—	—
20	Faint Attack	Dark	Physical	60	—	20	Normal	—	—
24	Sweet Scent	Normal	Status	—	100	20	Many Others	—	—
28	Giga Drain	Grass	Special	75	100	10	Normal	—	—
32	Toxic	Poison	Status	—	90	10	Normal	—	—
35	Synthesis	Grass	Status	—	—	5	Self	—	—
39	Clear Smog	Poison	Special	50	—	15	Normal	—	—
43	SolarBeam	Grass	Special	120	100	10	Normal	—	—
45	Rage Powder	Bug	Status	—	—	20	Self	—	—
50	Spore	Grass	Status	—	100	15	Normal	—	—

TM & HM MOVES

Lv.	Name	Type	Kind	Pow.	Acc.	PP	Range	Long	DA
TM06	Toxic	Poison	Status	—	90	10	Normal	—	—
TM09	Venoshock	Poison	Special	65	100	10	Normal	—	—
TM10	Hidden Power	Normal	Special	—	100	15	Normal	—	—
TM11	Sunny Day	Fire	Status	—	—	5	Both Sides	—	—
TM17	Protect	Normal	Status	—	—	10	Self	—	—
TM18	Rain Dance	Water	Status	—	—	5	Both Sides	—	—
TM21	Frustration	Normal	Physical	—	100	20	Normal	—	—
TM22	SolarBeam	Grass	Special	120	100	10	Normal	—	—
TM27	Return	Normal	Physical	—	100	20	Normal	—	—
TM32	Double Team	Normal	Status	—	—	15	Self	—	—
TM36	Sludge Bomb	Poison	Special	90	100	10	Normal	—	—
TM42	Facade	Normal	Physical	70	100	20	Normal	—	—
TM44	Rest	Psychic	Status	—	—	10	Self	—	—
TM45	Attract	Normal	Status	—	100	15	Normal	—	—
TM48	Round	Normal	Special	60	100	15	Normal	—	—
TM53	Energy Ball	Grass	Special	80	100	10	Normal	—	—
TM66	Payback	Dark	Physical	50	100	10	Normal	—	—
TM70	Flash	Normal	Status	—	100	20	Normal	—	—
TM86	Grass Knot	Grass	Special	—	100	20	Normal	—	—
TM87	Swagger	Normal	Status	—	90	15	Normal	—	—
TM90	Substitute	Normal	Status	—	—	10	Self	—	—

MOVES TAUGHT BY PEOPLE

Name	Type	Kind	Pow.	Acc.	PP	Range	Long	DA

MOVES TAUGHT BY MOVE TUTORS FOR SHARDS

Name	Type	Kind	Pow.	Acc.	PP	Range	Long	DA
Seed Bomb	Grass	Physical	80	100	15	Normal	—	—
Foul Play	Dark	Physical	95	100	15	Normal	—	○
Snore	Normal	Special	40	100	15	Normal	—	—
Synthesis	Grass	Status	—	—	5	Self	—	—
Giga Drain	Grass	Special	75	100	10	Normal	—	—
Worry Seed	Grass	Status	—	100	10	Normal	—	—
Gastro Acid	Poison	Status	—	100	10	Normal	—	—
After You	Normal	Status	—	—	15	Normal	—	—
Sleep Talk	Normal	Status	—	—	10	Self	—	—

EGG MOVES

Name	Type	Kind	Pow.	Acc.	PP	Range	Long	DA
Gastro Acid	Poison	Status	—	100	10	Normal	—	—
Growth	Normal	Status	—	—	40	Self	—	—
PoisonPowder	Poison	Status	—	75	35	Normal	—	—
Stun Spore	Grass	Status	—	75	30	Normal	—	—
Rollout	Rock	Physical	30	90	20	Normal	—	—
Defense Curl	Normal	Status	—	—	40	Self	—	—
Endure	Normal	Status	—	—	10	Self	—	—
Body Slam	Normal	Physical	85	100	15	Normal	—	○

Pokémon AR Marker

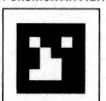

---

591 Amoonguss

Mushroom Pokémon

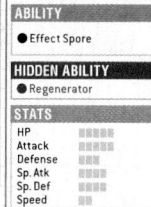

TYPE Grass Poison

ABILITY
● Effect Spore

HIDDEN ABILITY
● Regenerator

● HEIGHT: 2'00"
● WEIGHT: 23.1 lbs.
● GENDER: ♂ / ♀

STATS
HP
Attack
Defense
Sp. Atk
Sp. Def
Speed

It moves the caps on both arms and does a dance to lure prey. It prefers damp places.

Same form for ♂ / ♀

EGG GROUPS
Grass

ITEMS SOMETIMES HELD
● TinyMushroom
● Big Mushroom
● BalmMushroom

EVOLUTION

Foongus → Lv. 39 → Amoonguss

HOW TO OBTAIN

| Pokémon Black Version 2 | ❶ Route 11 ❷ Route 22 |
| Pokémon White Version 2 | ❶ Route 11 ❷ Route 22 |

HOW TO OBTAIN FROM OTHER GAMES

LEVEL-UP AND LEARNED MOVES

Lv.	Name	Type	Kind	Pow.	Acc.	PP	Range	Long	DA
1	Absorb	Grass	Special	20	100	25	Normal	—	—
1	Growth	Normal	Status	—	—	40	Self	—	—
1	Astonish	Ghost	Physical	30	100	15	Normal	—	○
1	Bide	Normal	Physical	—	—	10	Self	—	—
6	Growth	Normal	Status	—	—	40	Self	—	—
8	Astonish	Ghost	Physical	30	100	15	Normal	—	○
12	Bide	Normal	Physical	—	—	10	Self	—	—
15	Mega Drain	Grass	Special	40	100	15	Normal	—	—
18	Ingrain	Grass	Status	—	—	20	Self	—	—
20	Faint Attack	Dark	Physical	60	—	20	Normal	—	—
24	Sweet Scent	Normal	Status	—	100	20	Many Others	—	—
28	Giga Drain	Grass	Special	75	100	10	Normal	—	—
32	Toxic	Poison	Status	—	90	10	Normal	—	—
35	Synthesis	Grass	Status	—	—	5	Self	—	—
43	Clear Smog	Poison	Special	50	—	15	Normal	—	—
49	SolarBeam	Grass	Special	120	100	10	Normal	—	—
54	Rage Powder	Bug	Status	—	—	20	Self	—	—
62	Spore	Grass	Status	—	100	15	Normal	—	—

TM & HM MOVES

Lv.	Name	Type	Kind	Pow.	Acc.	PP	Range	Long	DA
TM06	Toxic	Poison	Status	—	90	10	Normal	—	—
TM09	Venoshock	Poison	Special	65	100	10	Normal	—	—
TM10	Hidden Power	Normal	Special	—	100	15	Normal	—	—
TM11	Sunny Day	Fire	Status	—	—	5	Both Sides	—	—
TM15	Hyper Beam	Normal	Special	150	90	5	Normal	—	—
TM17	Protect	Normal	Status	—	—	10	Self	—	—
TM18	Rain Dance	Water	Status	—	—	5	Both Sides	—	—
TM21	Frustration	Normal	Physical	—	100	20	Normal	—	○
TM22	SolarBeam	Grass	Special	120	100	10	Normal	—	—
TM27	Return	Normal	Physical	—	100	20	Normal	—	○
TM32	Double Team	Normal	Status	—	—	15	Self	—	—
TM36	Sludge Bomb	Poison	Special	90	100	10	Normal	—	—
TM42	Facade	Normal	Physical	70	100	20	Normal	—	○
TM44	Rest	Psychic	Status	—	—	10	Self	—	—
TM45	Attract	Normal	Status	—	100	15	Normal	—	—
TM48	Round	Normal	Special	60	100	15	Normal	—	—
TM53	Energy Ball	Grass	Special	80	100	10	Normal	—	—
TM66	Payback	Dark	Physical	50	100	10	Normal	—	—
TM68	Giga Impact	Normal	Physical	150	90	5	Normal	—	○
TM70	Flash	Normal	Status	—	100	20	Normal	—	—
TM86	Grass Knot	Grass	Special	—	100	20	Normal	—	○
TM87	Swagger	Normal	Status	—	90	15	Normal	—	—
TM90	Substitute	Normal	Status	—	—	10	Self	—	—

MOVES TAUGHT BY PEOPLE

Name	Type	Kind	Pow.	Acc.	PP	Range	Long	DA

MOVES TAUGHT BY MOVE TUTORS FOR SHARDS

Name	Type	Kind	Pow.	Acc.	PP	Range	Long	DA
Seed Bomb	Grass	Physical	80	100	15	Normal	—	—
Foul Play	Dark	Physical	95	100	15	Normal	—	○
Snore	Normal	Special	40	100	15	Normal	—	—
Synthesis	Grass	Status	—	—	5	Self	—	—
Giga Drain	Grass	Special	75	100	10	Normal	—	—
Worry Seed	Grass	Status	—	100	10	Normal	—	—
Gastro Acid	Poison	Status	—	100	10	Normal	—	—
After You	Normal	Status	—	—	15	Normal	—	—
Sleep Talk	Normal	Status	—	—	10	Self	—	—

Pokémon AR Marker

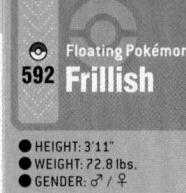

Floating Pokémon

592 Frillish

- HEIGHT: 3'11"
- WEIGHT: 72.8 lbs.
- GENDER: ♂ / ♀

If its veil-like arms stun and wrap a foe, that foe will be dragged miles below the surface, never to return.

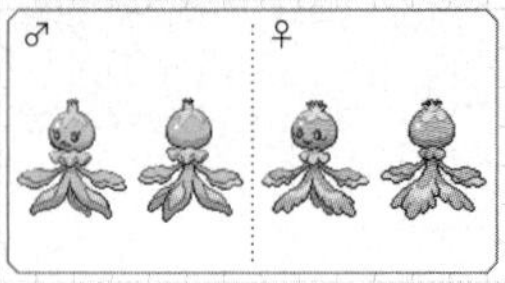

TYPE: Water / Ghost

ABILITIES
- Water Absorb
- Cursed Body

HIDDEN ABILITY
- Damp

STATS
- HP
- Attack
- Defense
- Sp. Atk
- Sp. Def
- Speed

EGG GROUPS
Amorphous

ITEMS SOMETIMES HELD
- None

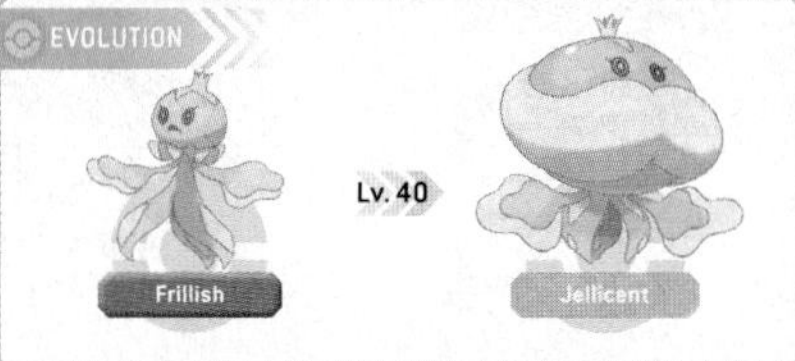

HOW TO OBTAIN

Pokémon Black Version 2	❶ Undella Town (water surface) ❷ Undella Bay (water surface)
Pokémon White Version 2	❶ Undella Town (water surface) ❷ Undella Bay (water surface)

HOW TO OBTAIN FROM OTHER GAMES

—

—

Pokémon AR Marker

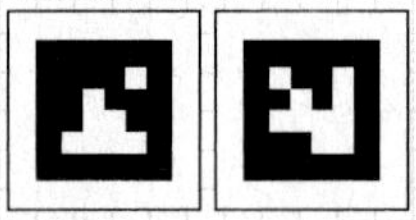

Male Form Female Form

LEVEL-UP AND LEARNED MOVES

Lv.	Name	Type	Kind	Pow.	Acc.	PP	Range	Long	DA
1	Bubble	Water	Special	20	100	30	Many Others	—	—
1	Water Sport	Water	Status	—	—	15	Both Sides	—	—
5	Absorb	Grass	Special	20	100	25	Normal	—	—
9	Night Shade	Ghost	Special	—	100	15	Normal	—	—
13	BubbleBeam	Water	Special	65	100	20	Normal	—	—
17	Recover	Normal	Status	—	—	10	Self	—	—
22	Water Pulse	Water	Special	60	100	20	Normal	○	—
27	Ominous Wind	Ghost	Special	60	100	5	Normal	—	—
32	Brine	Water	Special	65	100	10	Normal	—	—
37	Rain Dance	Water	Status	—	—	5	Both Sides	—	—
43	Hex	Ghost	Special	50	100	10	Normal	—	—
49	Hydro Pump	Water	Special	120	80	5	Normal	—	—
55	Wring Out	Normal	Special	—	100	5	Normal	—	○
61	Water Spout	Water	Special	150	100	5	Many Others	—	—

TM & HM MOVES

Lv.	Name	Type	Kind	Pow.	Acc.	PP	Range	Long	DA
TM06	Toxic	Poison	Status	—	90	10	Normal	—	—
TM07	Hail	Ice	Status	—	—	10	Both Sides	—	—
TM10	Hidden Power	Normal	Special	—	100	15	Normal	—	—
TM12	Taunt	Dark	Status	—	100	20	Normal	—	—
TM13	Ice Beam	Ice	Special	95	100	10	Normal	—	—
TM14	Blizzard	Ice	Special	120	70	5	Many Others	—	—
TM17	Protect	Normal	Status	—	—	10	Self	—	—
TM18	Rain Dance	Water	Status	—	—	5	Both Sides	—	—
TM20	Safeguard	Normal	Status	—	—	25	Your Side	—	—
TM21	Frustration	Normal	Physical	—	100	20	Normal	—	○
TM27	Return	Normal	Physical	—	100	20	Normal	—	○
TM29	Psychic	Psychic	Special	90	100	10	Normal	—	—
TM30	Shadow Ball	Ghost	Special	80	100	15	Normal	—	—
TM32	Double Team	Normal	Status	—	—	15	Self	—	—
TM34	Sludge Wave	Poison	Special	95	100	10	Adjacent	—	—
TM36	Sludge Bomb	Poison	Special	90	100	10	Normal	—	—
TM42	Facade	Normal	Physical	70	100	20	Normal	—	○
TM44	Rest	Psychic	Status	—	—	10	Self	—	—
TM45	Attract	Normal	Status	—	100	15	Normal	—	—
TM48	Round	Normal	Special	60	100	15	Normal	—	—
TM53	Energy Ball	Grass	Special	80	100	10	Normal	—	—
TM55	Scald	Water	Special	80	100	15	Normal	—	—
TM61	Will-O-Wisp	Fire	Status	—	75	15	Normal	—	—
TM70	Flash	Normal	Status	—	100	20	Normal	—	—
TM77	Psych Up	Normal	Status	—	—	10	Normal	—	—
TM85	Dream Eater	Psychic	Special	100	100	15	Normal	—	—
TM87	Swagger	Normal	Status	—	90	15	Normal	—	—
TM90	Substitute	Normal	Status	—	—	10	Self	—	—
TM92	Trick Room	Psychic	Status	—	—	5	Both Sides	—	—
HM03	Surf	Water	Special	95	100	15	Adjacent	—	—
HM05	Waterfall	Water	Physical	80	100	15	Normal	—	○
HM06	Dive	Water	Physical	80	100	10	Normal	—	○

MOVES TAUGHT BY PEOPLE

Name	Type	Kind	Pow.	Acc.	PP	Range	Long	DA

MOVES TAUGHT BY MOVE TUTORS FOR SHARDS

Name	Type	Kind	Pow.	Acc.	PP	Range	Long	DA
Magic Coat	Psychic	Status	—	—	15	Self	—	—
Icy Wind	Ice	Special	55	95	15	Many Others	—	—
Dark Pulse	Dark	Special	80	100	15	Normal	○	—
Bind	Normal	Physical	15	85	20	Normal	—	○
Snore	Normal	Special	40	100	15	Normal	—	—
Giga Drain	Grass	Special	75	100	10	Normal	—	—
Pain Split	Normal	Status	—	—	20	Normal	—	—
Spite	Ghost	Status	—	100	10	Normal	—	—
Trick	Psychic	Status	—	100	10	Normal	—	—
Sleep Talk	Normal	Status	—	—	10	Self	—	—

EGG MOVES

Name	Type	Kind	Pow.	Acc.	PP	Range	Long	DA
Acid Armor	Poison	Status	—	—	40	Self	—	—
Confuse Ray	Ghost	Status	—	100	10	Normal	—	—
Pain Split	Normal	Status	—	—	20	Normal	—	—
Mist	Ice	Status	—	—	30	Your Side	—	—
Recover	Normal	Status	—	—	10	Self	—	—
Constrict	Normal	Physical	10	100	35	Normal	—	○

Floating Pokémon

593 Jellicent

- HEIGHT: 7'03"
- WEIGHT: 297.6 lbs.
- GENDER: ♂ / ♀

Its body is mostly seawater. It's said there's a castle of ships Jellicent have sunk on the seafloor.

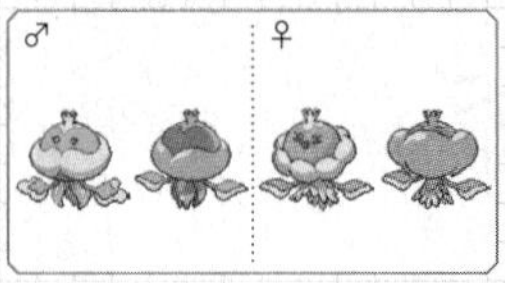

TYPE: Water / Ghost

ABILITIES
- Water Absorb
- Cursed Body

HIDDEN ABILITY
- Damp

STATS
- HP
- Attack
- Defense
- Sp. Atk
- Sp. Def
- Speed

EGG GROUPS
Amorphous

ITEMS SOMETIMES HELD
- None

HOW TO OBTAIN

Pokémon Black Version 2	❶ Undella Town (ripples in water) ❷ Undella Bay (ripples in water/spring, summer, and autumn only)
Pokémon White Version 2	❶ Undella Town (ripples in water) ❷ Undella Bay (ripples in water/spring, summer, and autumn only)

HOW TO OBTAIN FROM OTHER GAMES

—

—

Pokémon AR Marker

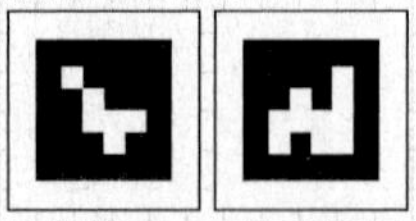

Male Form Female Form

LEVEL-UP AND LEARNED MOVES

Lv.	Name	Type	Kind	Pow.	Acc.	PP	Range	Long	DA
1	Bubble	Water	Special	20	100	30	Many Others	—	—
1	Water Sport	Water	Status	—	—	15	Both Sides	—	—
1	Absorb	Grass	Special	20	100	25	Normal	—	—
1	Night Shade	Ghost	Special	—	100	15	Normal	—	—
5	Absorb	Grass	Special	20	100	25	Normal	—	—
9	Night Shade	Ghost	Special	—	100	15	Normal	—	—
13	BubbleBeam	Water	Special	65	100	20	Normal	—	—
17	Recover	Normal	Status	—	—	10	Self	—	—
22	Water Pulse	Water	Special	60	100	20	Normal	○	—
27	Ominous Wind	Ghost	Special	60	100	5	Normal	—	—
32	Brine	Water	Special	65	100	10	Normal	—	—
37	Rain Dance	Water	Status	—	—	5	Both Sides	—	—
45	Hex	Ghost	Special	50	100	10	Normal	—	—
53	Hydro Pump	Water	Special	120	80	5	Normal	—	—
61	Wring Out	Normal	Special	—	100	5	Normal	—	○
69	Water Spout	Water	Special	150	100	5	Many Others	—	—

TM & HM MOVES

Lv.	Name	Type	Kind	Pow.	Acc.	PP	Range	Long	DA
TM06	Toxic	Poison	Status	—	90	10	Normal	—	—
TM07	Hail	Ice	Status	—	—	10	Both Sides	—	—
TM10	Hidden Power	Normal	Special	—	100	15	Normal	—	—
TM12	Taunt	Dark	Status	—	100	20	Normal	—	—
TM13	Ice Beam	Ice	Special	95	100	10	Normal	—	—
TM14	Blizzard	Ice	Special	120	70	5	Many Others	—	—
TM15	Hyper Beam	Normal	Special	150	90	5	Normal	—	—
TM17	Protect	Normal	Status	—	—	10	Self	—	—
TM18	Rain Dance	Water	Status	—	—	5	Both Sides	—	—
TM20	Safeguard	Normal	Status	—	—	25	Your Side	—	—
TM21	Frustration	Normal	Physical	—	100	20	Normal	—	○
TM27	Return	Normal	Physical	—	100	20	Normal	—	○
TM29	Psychic	Psychic	Special	90	100	10	Normal	—	—
TM30	Shadow Ball	Ghost	Special	80	100	15	Normal	—	—
TM32	Double Team	Normal	Status	—	—	15	Self	—	—
TM34	Sludge Wave	Poison	Special	95	100	10	Adjacent	—	—
TM36	Sludge Bomb	Poison	Special	90	100	10	Normal	—	—
TM42	Facade	Normal	Physical	70	100	20	Normal	—	○
TM44	Rest	Psychic	Status	—	—	10	Self	—	—
TM45	Attract	Normal	Status	—	100	15	Normal	—	—
TM48	Round	Normal	Special	60	100	15	Normal	—	—
TM53	Energy Ball	Grass	Special	80	100	10	Normal	—	—
TM55	Scald	Water	Special	80	100	15	Normal	—	—
TM61	Will-O-Wisp	Fire	Status	—	75	15	Normal	—	—
TM68	Giga Impact	Normal	Physical	150	90	5	Normal	—	○
TM70	Flash	Normal	Status	—	100	20	Normal	—	—
TM77	Psych Up	Normal	Status	—	—	10	Normal	—	—
TM85	Dream Eater	Psychic	Special	100	100	15	Normal	—	—
TM87	Swagger	Normal	Status	—	90	15	Normal	—	—
TM90	Substitute	Normal	Status	—	—	10	Self	—	—
TM92	Trick Room	Psychic	Status	—	—	5	Both Sides	—	—
HM03	Surf	Water	Special	95	100	15	Adjacent	—	—
HM05	Waterfall	Water	Physical	80	100	15	Normal	—	○
HM06	Dive	Water	Physical	80	100	10	Normal	—	○

MOVES TAUGHT BY PEOPLE

Name	Type	Kind	Pow.	Acc.	PP	Range	Long	DA

MOVES TAUGHT BY MOVE TUTORS FOR SHARDS

Name	Type	Kind	Pow.	Acc.	PP	Range	Long	DA
Magic Coat	Psychic	Status	—	—	15	Self	—	—
Icy Wind	Ice	Special	55	95	15	Many Others	—	—
Dark Pulse	Dark	Special	80	100	15	Normal	○	—
Bind	Normal	Physical	15	85	20	Normal	—	○
Snore	Normal	Special	40	100	15	Normal	—	—
Giga Drain	Grass	Special	75	100	10	Normal	—	—
Pain Split	Normal	Status	—	—	20	Normal	—	—
Spite	Ghost	Status	—	100	10	Normal	—	—
Trick	Psychic	Status	—	100	10	Normal	—	—
Sleep Talk	Normal	Status	—	—	10	Self	—	—

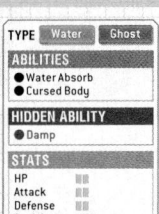

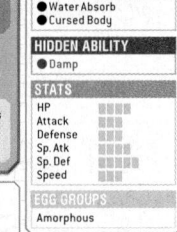

594 Alomomola

Caring Pokémon

TYPE Water

ABILITIES
- Healer
- Hydration

HIDDEN ABILITY
- Regenerator

- HEIGHT: 3'11"
- WEIGHT: 69.7 lbs.
- GENDER: ♂ / ♀

It gently holds injured and weak Pokémon in its fins. Its special membrane heals their wounds.

STATS
- HP
- Attack
- Defense
- Sp. Atk
- Sp. Def
- Speed

EGG GROUPS
Water ❶ / Water ❷

ITEMS SOMETIMES HELD
- None

Same form for ♂ / ♀

Pokémon AR Marker

EVOLUTION

Does not evolve

HOW TO OBTAIN

| Pokémon Black Version 2 | ❶ Virbank City (ripples in water) ❷ Route 4 (ripples in water) |
| Pokémon White Version 2 | ❶ Virbank City (ripples in water) ❷ Route 4 (ripples in water) |

HOW TO OBTAIN FROM OTHER GAMES
———
———

LEVEL-UP AND LEARNED MOVES

Lv.	Name	Type	Kind	Pow.	Acc.	PP	Range	Long	DA
1	Pound	Normal	Physical	40	100	35	Normal	—	○
1	Water Sport	Water	Status	—	—	15	Both Sides	—	—
5	Aqua Ring	Water	Status	—	—	20	Self	—	—
9	Aqua Jet	Water	Physical	40	100	20	Normal	—	○
13	DoubleSlap	Normal	Physical	15	85	10	Normal	—	○
17	Protect	Normal	Status	—	—	10	Self	—	—
21	Heal Pulse	Psychic	Status	—	—	10	Normal	○	—
25	Water Pulse	Water	Special	60	100	20	Normal	○	—
29	Wake-Up Slap	Fighting	Physical	60	100	10	Normal	—	○
33	Soak	Water	Status	—	100	20	Normal	—	—
37	Wish	Normal	Status	—	—	10	Self	—	—
41	Brine	Water	Special	65	100	10	Normal	—	—
45	Safeguard	Normal	Status	—	—	25	Your Side	—	—
49	Helping Hand	Normal	Status	—	—	20	1 Ally	—	—
53	Wide Guard	Rock	Status	—	—	10	Your Side	—	—
57	Healing Wish	Psychic	Status	—	—	10	Self	—	—
61	Hydro Pump	Water	Special	120	80	5	Normal	—	—

TM & HM MOVES

Lv.	Name	Type	Kind	Pow.	Acc.	PP	Range	Long	DA
TM04	Calm Mind	Psychic	Status	—	—	20	Self	—	—
TM06	Toxic	Poison	Status	—	90	10	Normal	—	—
TM07	Hail	Ice	Status	—	—	10	Both Sides	—	—
TM10	Hidden Power	Normal	Special	—	100	15	Normal	—	—
TM13	Ice Beam	Ice	Special	95	100	10	Normal	—	—
TM14	Blizzard	Ice	Special	120	70	5	Many Others	—	—
TM16	Light Screen	Psychic	Status	—	—	30	Your Side	—	—
TM17	Protect	Normal	Status	—	—	10	Self	—	—
TM18	Rain Dance	Water	Status	—	—	5	Both Sides	—	—
TM20	Safeguard	Normal	Status	—	—	25	Your Side	—	—
TM21	Frustration	Normal	Physical	—	100	20	Normal	—	○
TM27	Return	Normal	Physical	—	100	20	Normal	—	○
TM29	Psychic	Psychic	Special	90	100	10	Normal	—	—
TM30	Shadow Ball	Ghost	Special	80	100	15	Normal	—	—
TM32	Double Team	Normal	Status	—	—	15	Self	—	—
TM42	Facade	Normal	Physical	70	100	20	Normal	—	○
TM44	Rest	Psychic	Status	—	—	10	Self	—	—
TM45	Attract	Normal	Status	—	100	15	Normal	—	—
TM48	Round	Normal	Special	60	100	15	Normal	—	—
TM55	Scald	Water	Special	80	100	15	Normal	—	—
TM77	Psych Up	Normal	Status	—	—	10	Normal	—	—
TM87	Swagger	Normal	Status	—	90	15	Normal	—	—
TM90	Substitute	Normal	Status	—	—	10	Self	—	—
HM03	Surf	Water	Special	95	100	15	Adjacent	—	—
HM05	Waterfall	Water	Physical	80	100	15	Normal	—	○
HM06	Dive	Water	Physical	80	100	10	Normal	—	○

MOVES TAUGHT BY PEOPLE

Name	Type	Kind	Pow.	Acc.	PP	Range	Long	DA

MOVES TAUGHT BY MOVE TUTORS FOR SHARDS

Name	Type	Kind	Pow.	Acc.	PP	Range	Long	DA
Bounce	Flying	Physical	85	85	5	Normal	○	○
Magic Coat	Psychic	Status	—	—	15	Self	—	—
Icy Wind	Ice	Special	55	95	15	Many Others	—	—
Snore	Normal	Special	40	100	15	Normal	—	—
Knock Off	Dark	Physical	20	100	20	Normal	—	○
Pain Split	Normal	Status	—	—	20	Normal	—	—
Helping Hand	Normal	Status	—	—	20	1 Ally	—	—
Sleep Talk	Normal	Status	—	—	10	Self	—	—

EGG MOVES

Name	Type	Kind	Pow.	Acc.	PP	Range	Long	DA
Pain Split	Normal	Status	—	—	20	Normal	—	—
Refresh	Normal	Status	—	—	20	Self	—	—
Tickle	Normal	Status	—	100	20	Normal	—	—
Mirror Coat	Psychic	Special	—	100	20	Varies	—	—
Mist	Ice	Status	—	—	30	Your Side	—	—
Endure	Normal	Status	—	—	10	Self	—	—

---

595 Joltik

Attaching Pokémon

TYPE Bug Electric

ABILITIES
- Compoundeyes
- Unnerve

HIDDEN ABILITY
- Swarm

- HEIGHT: 0'04"
- WEIGHT: 1.3 lbs.
- GENDER: ♂ / ♀

Since it can't generate its own electricity, it sticks onto large-bodied Pokémon and absorbs static electricity.

STATS
- HP
- Attack
- Defense
- Sp. Atk
- Sp. Def
- Speed

EGG GROUPS
Bug

ITEMS SOMETIMES HELD
- None

Same form for ♂ / ♀

Pokémon AR Marker

EVOLUTION

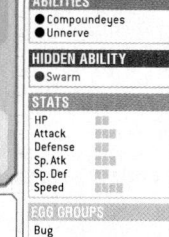

Joltik — Lv. 36 → Galvantula

HOW TO OBTAIN

| Pokémon Black Version 2 | ❶ Chargestone Cave 1F ❷ Chargestone Cave B1F |
| Pokémon White Version 2 | ❶ Chargestone Cave 1F ❷ Chargestone Cave B1F |

HOW TO OBTAIN FROM OTHER GAMES
———
———

LEVEL-UP AND LEARNED MOVES

Lv.	Name	Type	Kind	Pow.	Acc.	PP	Range	Long	DA
1	String Shot	Bug	Status	—	95	40	Many Others	—	—
1	Leech Life	Bug	Physical	20	100	15	Normal	—	○
1	Spider Web	Bug	Status	—	—	10	Normal	—	—
4	Thunder Wave	Electric	Status	—	100	20	Normal	—	—
8	Screech	Normal	Status	—	85	40	Normal	—	—
12	Fury Cutter	Bug	Physical	20	95	20	Normal	—	○
15	Electroweb	Electric	Special	55	95	15	Many Others	—	—
18	Bug Bite	Bug	Physical	60	100	20	Normal	—	○
23	Gastro Acid	Poison	Status	—	100	10	Normal	—	—
26	Slash	Normal	Physical	70	100	20	Normal	—	○
29	Electro Ball	Electric	Special	—	100	10	Normal	—	—
34	Signal Beam	Bug	Special	75	100	15	Normal	—	—
37	Agility	Psychic	Status	—	—	30	Self	—	—
40	Sucker Punch	Dark	Physical	80	100	5	Normal	—	○
45	Discharge	Electric	Special	80	100	15	Adjacent	—	—
48	Bug Buzz	Bug	Special	90	100	10	Normal	—	—

TM & HM MOVES

Lv.	Name	Type	Kind	Pow.	Acc.	PP	Range	Long	DA
TM06	Toxic	Poison	Status	—	90	10	Normal	—	—
TM10	Hidden Power	Normal	Special	—	100	15	Normal	—	—
TM16	Light Screen	Psychic	Status	—	—	30	Your Side	—	—
TM17	Protect	Normal	Status	—	—	10	Self	—	—
TM18	Rain Dance	Water	Status	—	—	5	Both Sides	—	—
TM21	Frustration	Normal	Physical	—	100	20	Normal	—	○
TM24	Thunderbolt	Electric	Special	95	100	15	Normal	—	—
TM27	Return	Normal	Physical	—	100	20	Normal	—	○
TM32	Double Team	Normal	Status	—	—	15	Self	—	—
TM42	Facade	Normal	Physical	70	100	20	Normal	—	○
TM44	Rest	Psychic	Status	—	—	10	Self	—	—
TM45	Attract	Normal	Status	—	100	15	Normal	—	—
TM46	Thief	Dark	Physical	40	100	10	Normal	—	○
TM48	Round	Normal	Special	60	100	15	Normal	—	—
TM53	Energy Ball	Grass	Special	80	100	10	Normal	—	—
TM57	Charge Beam	Electric	Special	50	90	10	Normal	—	—
TM70	Flash	Normal	Status	—	100	20	Normal	—	—
TM72	Volt Switch	Electric	Special	70	100	20	Normal	—	—
TM73	Thunder Wave	Electric	Status	—	100	20	Normal	—	—
TM76	Struggle Bug	Bug	Special	30	100	20	Many Others	—	—
TM81	X-Scissor	Bug	Physical	80	100	15	Normal	—	○
TM84	Poison Jab	Poison	Physical	80	100	20	Normal	—	○
TM87	Swagger	Normal	Status	—	90	15	Normal	—	—
TM90	Substitute	Normal	Status	—	—	10	Self	—	—
TM93	Wild Charge	Electric	Physical	90	100	15	Normal	—	○
HM01	Cut	Normal	Physical	50	95	30	Normal	—	○

MOVES TAUGHT BY PEOPLE

Name	Type	Kind	Pow.	Acc.	PP	Range	Long	DA

MOVES TAUGHT BY MOVE TUTORS FOR SHARDS

Name	Type	Kind	Pow.	Acc.	PP	Range	Long	DA
Bug Bite	Bug	Physical	60	100	20	Normal	—	○
Bounce	Flying	Physical	85	85	5	Normal	○	○
Signal Beam	Bug	Special	75	100	15	Normal	—	—
Magnet Rise	Electric	Status	—	—	10	Self	—	—
Electroweb	Electric	Special	55	95	15	Many Others	—	—
Snore	Normal	Special	40	100	15	Normal	—	—
Giga Drain	Grass	Special	75	100	10	Normal	—	—
Gastro Acid	Poison	Status	—	100	10	Normal	—	—
Sleep Talk	Normal	Status	—	—	10	Self	—	—

EGG MOVES

Name	Type	Kind	Pow.	Acc.	PP	Range	Long	DA
Pin Missile	Bug	Physical	14	85	20	Normal	—	—
Poison Sting	Poison	Physical	15	100	35	Normal	—	—
Cross Poison	Poison	Physical	70	100	20	Normal	—	○
Rock Climb	Normal	Physical	90	85	20	Normal	—	—
Pursuit	Dark	Physical	40	100	20	Normal	—	○
Disable	Normal	Status	—	100	20	Normal	—	—
Faint Attack	Dark	Physical	60	—	20	Normal	—	—

596 Galvantula
EleSpider Pokémon

TYPE Bug | Electric

ABILITIES
- Compoundeyes
- Unnerve

HIDDEN ABILITY
- Swarm

STATS
HP	
Attack	
Defense	
Sp. Atk	
Sp. Def	
Speed	

EGG GROUPS
Bug

ITEMS SOMETIMES HELD
- None

- HEIGHT: 2'07"
- WEIGHT: 31.5 lbs.
- GENDER: ♂ / ♀

It creates barriers from electrified silk that stun foes. This works as a weapon as well as a defense.

Same form for ♂ / ♀

Pokémon AR Marker

EVOLUTION

Joltik → Lv. 36 → Galvantula

HOW TO OBTAIN
Pokémon Black Version 2	Level up Joltik to Lv. 36
Pokémon White Version 2	Level up Joltik to Lv. 36

HOW TO OBTAIN FROM OTHER GAMES
———
———

LEVEL-UP AND LEARNED MOVES
Lv.	Name	Type	Kind	Pow.	Acc.	PP	Range	Long	DA
1	String Shot	Bug	Status	—	95	40	Many Others	—	—
1	Leech Life	Bug	Physical	20	100	15	Normal	—	○
1	Spider Web	Bug	Status	—	—	10	Normal	—	—
4	Thunder Wave	Electric	Status	—	100	20	Normal	—	—
4	Screech	Normal	Status	—	85	40	Normal	—	—
7	Fury Cutter	Bug	Physical	20	95	20	Normal	—	○
12	Electroweb	Electric	Special	55	95	15	Many Others	—	—
15	Bug Bite	Bug	Physical	60	100	20	Normal	—	○
18	Gastro Acid	Poison	Status	—	100	10	Normal	—	—
23	Slash	Normal	Physical	70	100	20	Normal	—	○
26	Electro Ball	Electric	Special	—	100	10	Normal	—	—
29	Signal Beam	Bug	Special	75	100	15	Normal	—	—
34	Agility	Psychic	Status	—	—	30	Self	—	—
40	Sucker Punch	Dark	Physical	80	100	5	Normal	—	○
46	Discharge	Electric	Special	80	100	15	Adjacent	—	—
54	Bug Buzz	Bug	Special	90	100	10	Normal	—	—
60									

TM & HM MOVES
Lv.	Name	Type	Kind	Pow.	Acc.	PP	Range	Long	DA
TM06	Toxic	Poison	Status	—	90	10	Normal	—	—
TM10	Hidden Power	Normal	Special	—	100	15	Normal	—	—
TM15	Hyper Beam	Normal	Special	150	90	5	Normal	—	—
TM16	Light Screen	Psychic	Status	—	—	30	Your Side	—	—
TM17	Protect	Normal	Status	—	—	10	Self	—	—
TM18	Rain Dance	Water	Status	—	—	5	Both Sides	—	—
TM21	Frustration	Normal	Physical	—	100	20	Normal	—	○
TM24	Thunderbolt	Electric	Special	95	100	15	Normal	—	—
TM25	Thunder	Electric	Special	120	70	10	Normal	—	—
TM27	Return	Normal	Physical	—	100	20	Normal	—	○
TM32	Double Team	Normal	Status	—	—	15	Self	—	—
TM42	Facade	Normal	Physical	70	100	20	Normal	—	○
TM44	Rest	Psychic	Status	—	—	10	Self	—	—
TM45	Attract	Normal	Status	—	100	15	Normal	—	—
TM46	Thief	Dark	Physical	40	100	10	Normal	—	○
TM48	Round	Normal	Special	60	100	15	Normal	—	—
TM53	Energy Ball	Grass	Special	80	100	10	Normal	—	—
TM57	Charge Beam	Electric	Special	50	90	10	Normal	—	—
TM68	Giga Impact	Normal	Physical	150	90	5	Normal	—	○
TM70	Flash	Normal	Status	—	100	20	Normal	—	—
TM72	Volt Switch	Electric	Special	70	100	20	Normal	—	—
TM73	Thunder Wave	Electric	Status	—	100	20	Normal	—	—
TM76	Struggle Bug	Bug	Special	30	100	20	Many Others	—	—
TM81	X-Scissor	Bug	Physical	80	100	15	Normal	—	○
TM84	Poison Jab	Poison	Physical	80	100	20	Normal	—	○
TM87	Swagger	Normal	Status	—	90	15	Normal	—	—
TM90	Substitute	Normal	Status	—	—	10	Self	—	—
TM93	Wild Charge	Electric	Physical	90	100	15	Normal	—	○
HM01	Cut	Normal	Physical	50	95	30	Normal	—	—

MOVES TAUGHT BY PEOPLE
Name	Type	Kind	Pow.	Acc.	PP	Range	Long	DA

MOVES TAUGHT BY MOVE TUTORS FOR SHARDS
Name	Type	Kind	Pow.	Acc.	PP	Range	Long	DA
Bug Bite	Bug	Physical	60	100	20	Normal	—	○
Bounce	Flying	Physical	85	85	5	Normal	○	○
Signal Beam	Bug	Special	75	100	15	Normal	—	—
Magnet Rise	Electric	Status	—	—	10	Self	—	—
Electroweb	Electric	Special	55	95	15	Many Others	—	—
Snore	Normal	Special	40	100	15	Normal	—	—
Giga Drain	Grass	Special	75	100	10	Normal	—	—
Gastro Acid	Poison	Status	—	100	10	Normal	—	—
Sleep Talk	Normal	Status	—	—	10	Self	—	—

---

597 Ferroseed
Thorn Seed Pokémon

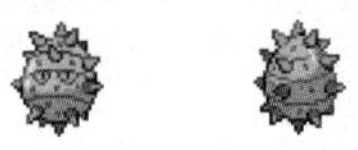

TYPE Grass | Steel

ABILITY
- Iron Barbs

HIDDEN ABILITY
———

STATS
HP	
Attack	
Defense	
Sp. Atk	
Sp. Def	
Speed	

EGG GROUPS
Grass/Mineral

ITEMS SOMETIMES HELD
- Sticky Barb

- HEIGHT: 2'00"
- WEIGHT: 41.4 lbs.
- GENDER: ♂ / ♀

It absorbs the iron it finds in the rock while clinging to the ceiling. It shoots spikes when in danger.

Same form for ♂ / ♀

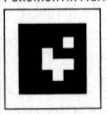
Pokémon AR Marker

EVOLUTION
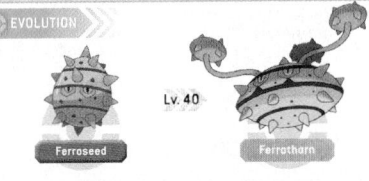

Ferroseed → Lv. 40 → Ferrothorn

HOW TO OBTAIN
Pokémon Black Version 2	❶ Chargestone Cave 1F ❷ Chargestone Cave B1F
Pokémon White Version 2	❶ Chargestone Cave 1F ❷ Chargestone Cave B1F

HOW TO OBTAIN FROM OTHER GAMES

LEVEL-UP AND LEARNED MOVES
Lv.	Name	Type	Kind	Pow.	Acc.	PP	Range	Long	DA
1	Tackle	Normal	Physical	50	100	35	Normal	—	○
1	Harden	Normal	Status	—	—	30	Self	—	—
6	Rollout	Rock	Physical	30	90	20	Normal	—	—
9	Curse	Ghost	Status	—	—	10	Varies	—	—
14	Metal Claw	Steel	Physical	50	95	35	Normal	—	○
18	Pin Missile	Bug	Physical	14	85	20	Normal	—	—
21	Gyro Ball	Steel	Physical	—	100	5	Normal	—	○
26	Iron Defense	Steel	Status	—	—	15	Self	—	—
30	Mirror Shot	Steel	Special	65	85	10	Normal	—	—
35	Ingrain	Grass	Status	—	—	20	Self	—	—
38	Selfdestruct	Normal	Physical	200	100	5	Adjacent	—	—
43	Iron Head	Steel	Physical	80	100	15	Normal	—	○
47	Payback	Dark	Physical	50	100	10	Normal	—	—
52	Flash Cannon	Steel	Special	80	100	10	Normal	—	—
55	Explosion	Normal	Physical	250	100	5	Adjacent	—	—

TM & HM MOVES
Lv.	Name	Type	Kind	Pow.	Acc.	PP	Range	Long	DA
TM01	Hone Claws	Dark	Status	—	—	15	Self	—	—
TM06	Toxic	Poison	Status	—	90	10	Normal	—	—
TM10	Hidden Power	Normal	Special	—	100	15	Normal	—	—
TM11	Sunny Day	Fire	Status	—	—	5	Both Sides	—	—
TM17	Protect	Normal	Status	—	—	10	Self	—	—
TM21	Frustration	Normal	Physical	—	100	20	Normal	—	○
TM22	SolarBeam	Grass	Special	120	100	10	Normal	—	—
TM24	Thunderbolt	Electric	Special	95	100	15	Normal	—	—
TM27	Return	Normal	Physical	—	100	20	Normal	—	○
TM32	Double Team	Normal	Status	—	—	15	Self	—	—
TM42	Facade	Normal	Physical	70	100	20	Normal	—	○
TM44	Rest	Psychic	Status	—	—	10	Self	—	—
TM48	Round	Normal	Special	60	100	15	Normal	—	—
TM53	Energy Ball	Grass	Special	80	100	10	Normal	—	—
TM64	Explosion	Normal	Physical	250	100	5	Adjacent	—	—
TM66	Payback	Dark	Physical	50	100	10	Normal	—	○
TM69	Rock Polish	Rock	Status	—	—	20	Self	—	—
TM70	Flash	Normal	Status	—	100	20	Normal	—	—
TM73	Thunder Wave	Electric	Status	—	100	20	Normal	—	—
TM74	Gyro Ball	Steel	Physical	—	100	5	Normal	—	○
TM84	Poison Jab	Poison	Physical	80	100	20	Normal	—	○
TM87	Swagger	Normal	Status	—	90	15	Normal	—	—
TM90	Substitute	Normal	Status	—	—	10	Self	—	—
TM91	Flash Cannon	Steel	Special	80	100	10	Normal	—	—
TM94	Rock Smash	Fighting	Physical	40	100	15	Normal	—	—

MOVES TAUGHT BY PEOPLE
Name	Type	Kind	Pow.	Acc.	PP	Range	Long	DA

MOVES TAUGHT BY MOVE TUTORS FOR SHARDS
Name	Type	Kind	Pow.	Acc.	PP	Range	Long	DA
Iron Head	Steel	Physical	80	100	15	Normal	—	○
Seed Bomb	Grass	Physical	80	100	15	Normal	—	—
Iron Defense	Steel	Status	—	—	15	Self	—	—
Magnet Rise	Electric	Status	—	—	10	Self	—	—
Gravity	Psychic	Status	—	—	5	Both Sides	—	—
Snore	Normal	Special	40	100	15	Normal	—	—
Giga Drain	Grass	Special	75	100	10	Normal	—	—
Worry Seed	Grass	Status	—	100	10	Normal	—	—
Stealth Rock	Rock	Status	—	—	20	Other Side	—	—
Endeavor	Normal	Physical	—	100	5	Normal	—	○
Sleep Talk	Normal	Status	—	—	10	Self	—	—

EGG MOVES
Name	Type	Kind	Pow.	Acc.	PP	Range	Long	DA
Bullet Seed	Grass	Physical	25	100	30	Normal	—	—
Leech Seed	Grass	Status	—	90	10	Normal	—	—
Spikes	Ground	Status	—	—	20	Other Side	—	—
Worry Seed	Grass	Status	—	100	10	Normal	—	—
Seed Bomb	Grass	Physical	80	100	15	Normal	—	—
Gravity	Psychic	Status	—	—	5	Both Sides	—	—
Rock Climb	Normal	Physical	90	85	20	Normal	—	—
Stealth Rock	Rock	Status	—	—	20	Other Side	—	—

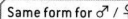
Thorn Pod Pokémon
598 Ferrothorn

- HEIGHT: 3'03"
- WEIGHT: 242.5 lbs.
- GENDER: ♂ / ♀

By swinging around its three spiky feelers and shooting spikes, it can obliterate an opponent.

Same form for ♂ / ♀

TYPE Grass Steel

ABILITY
- Iron Barbs

HIDDEN ABILITY

STATS
- HP
- Attack
- Defense
- Sp. Atk
- Sp. Def
- Speed

EGG GROUPS
Grass/Mineral

ITEMS SOMETIMES HELD
- None

EVOLUTION

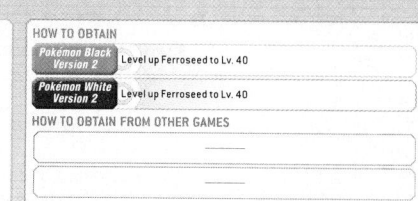

Ferroseed → Lv. 40 → Ferrothorn

HOW TO OBTAIN

Pokémon Black Version 2	Level up Ferroseed to Lv. 40
Pokémon White Version 2	Level up Ferroseed to Lv. 40

HOW TO OBTAIN FROM OTHER GAMES

LEVEL-UP AND LEARNED MOVES

Lv.	Name	Type	Kind	Pow.	Acc.	PP	Range	Long	DA
1	Rock Climb	Normal	Physical	90	85	20	Normal	—	○
1	Tackle	Normal	Physical	50	100	35	Normal	—	—
1	Harden	Normal	Status	—	—	30	Self	—	—
1	Rollout	Rock	Physical	30	90	20	Normal	—	—
1	Curse	Ghost	Status	—	—	10	Varies	—	—
6	Rollout	Rock	Physical	30	90	20	Normal	—	—
9	Curse	Ghost	Status	—	—	10	Varies	—	—
14	Metal Claw	Steel	Physical	50	95	35	Normal	—	—
18	Pin Missile	Bug	Physical	14	85	20	Normal	—	—
21	Gyro Ball	Steel	Physical	—	100	5	Normal	—	—
26	Iron Defense	Steel	Status	—	—	15	Self	—	—
30	Mirror Shot	Steel	Special	65	85	10	Normal	—	—
35	Ingrain	Grass	Status	—	—	20	Self	—	—
38	Selfdestruct	Normal	Physical	200	100	5	Adjacent	—	—
40	Power Whip	Grass	Physical	120	85	10	Normal	—	—
46	Iron Head	Steel	Physical	80	100	15	Normal	—	—
53	Payback	Dark	Physical	50	100	10	Normal	—	—
61	Flash Cannon	Steel	Special	80	100	10	Normal	—	—
67	Explosion	Normal	Physical	250	100	5	Adjacent	—	—

TM & HM MOVES

Lv.	Name	Type	Kind	Pow.	Acc.	PP	Range	Long	DA
TM01	Hone Claws	Dark	Status	—	—	15	Self	—	—
TM06	Toxic	Poison	Status	—	90	10	Normal	—	—
TM10	Hidden Power	Normal	Special	—	100	15	Normal	—	—
TM11	Sunny Day	Fire	Status	—	—	5	Both Sides	—	—
TM15	Hyper Beam	Normal	Special	150	90	5	Normal	—	—
TM17	Protect	Normal	Status	—	—	10	Self	—	—
TM21	Frustration	Normal	Physical	—	100	20	Normal	—	○
TM22	SolarBeam	Grass	Special	120	100	10	Normal	—	—
TM24	Thunderbolt	Electric	Special	95	100	15	Normal	—	—
TM25	Thunder	Electric	Special	120	70	10	Normal	—	—
TM27	Return	Normal	Physical	—	100	20	Normal	—	○
TM32	Double Team	Normal	Status	—	—	15	Self	—	—
TM37	Sandstorm	Rock	Status	—	—	10	Both Sides	—	—
TM40	Aerial Ace	Flying	Physical	60	—	20	Normal	○	—
TM42	Facade	Normal	Physical	70	100	20	Normal	—	—
TM44	Rest	Psychic	Status	—	—	10	Self	—	—
TM48	Round	Normal	Special	60	100	15	Normal	—	—
TM53	Energy Ball	Grass	Special	80	100	10	Normal	—	—
TM64	Explosion	Normal	Physical	250	100	5	Adjacent	—	—
TM65	Shadow Claw	Ghost	Physical	70	100	15	Normal	—	○
TM66	Payback	Dark	Physical	50	100	10	Normal	—	○
TM68	Giga Impact	Normal	Physical	150	90	5	Normal	—	—
TM69	Rock Polish	Rock	Status	—	—	20	Self	—	—
TM70	Flash	Normal	Status	—	100	20	Normal	—	—
TM73	Thunder Wave	Electric	Status	—	100	20	Normal	—	—
TM74	Gyro Ball	Steel	Physical	—	100	5	Normal	—	—
TM75	Swords Dance	Normal	Status	—	—	30	Self	—	—
TM78	Bulldoze	Ground	Physical	60	100	20	Adjacent	—	—
TM84	Poison Jab	Poison	Physical	80	100	20	Normal	—	—
TM86	Grass Knot	Grass	Special	—	100	20	Normal	—	—
TM87	Swagger	Normal	Status	—	90	15	Normal	—	—
TM90	Substitute	Normal	Status	—	—	10	Self	—	—
TM91	Flash Cannon	Steel	Special	80	100	10	Normal	—	—
TM94	Rock Smash	Fighting	Physical	40	100	15	Normal	—	○

Lv.	Name	Type	Kind	Pow.	Acc.	PP	Range	Long	DA
HM01	Cut	Normal	Physical	50	95	30	Normal	—	○
HM04	Strength	Normal	Physical	80	100	15	Normal	—	○

MOVES TAUGHT BY PEOPLE

Name	Type	Kind	Pow.	Acc.	PP	Range	Long	DA

MOVES TAUGHT BY MOVE TUTORS FOR SHARDS

Name	Type	Kind	Pow.	Acc.	PP	Range	Long	DA
Iron Head	Steel	Physical	80	100	15	Normal	—	—
Seed Bomb	Grass	Physical	80	100	15	Normal	—	—
Iron Defense	Steel	Status	—	—	15	Self	—	—
Magnet Rise	Electric	Status	—	—	10	Self	—	—
Gravity	Psychic	Status	—	—	5	Both Sides	—	—
Snore	Normal	Special	40	100	15	Normal	—	—
Knock Off	Dark	Physical	20	100	20	Normal	—	—
Giga Drain	Grass	Special	75	100	10	Normal	—	—
Worry Seed	Grass	Status	—	100	10	Normal	—	—
Stealth Rock	Rock	Status	—	—	20	Other Side	—	—
Endeavor	Normal	Physical	—	100	5	Normal	—	—
Sleep Talk	Normal	Status	—	—	10	Self	—	—

Pokémon AR Marker

Gear Pokémon
599 Klink

- HEIGHT: 1'00"
- WEIGHT: 46.3 lbs.
- GENDER: Unknown

Two bodies comprise a fixed pair. They spin around each other to generate energy.

Gender unknown

TYPE Steel

ABILITIES
- Plus
- Minus

HIDDEN ABILITY

STATS
- HP
- Attack
- Defense
- Sp. Atk
- Sp. Def
- Speed

EGG GROUPS
Mineral

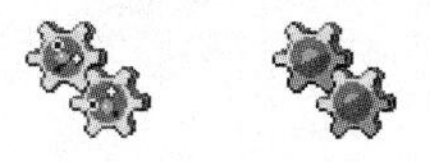

ITEMS SOMETIMES HELD
- None

EVOLUTION

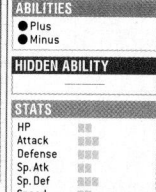

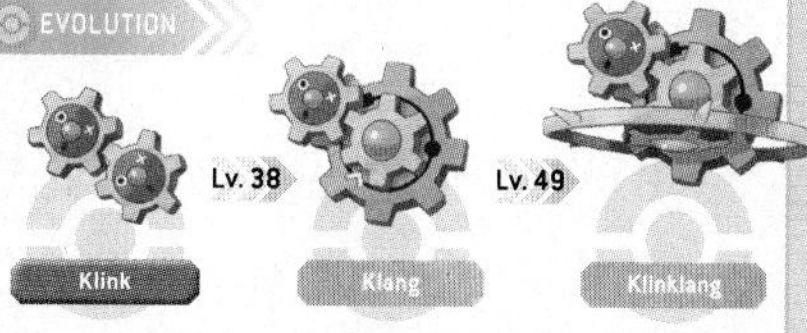

Klink → Lv. 38 → Klang → Lv. 49 → Klinklang

HOW TO OBTAIN

Pokémon Black Version 2	❶	Chargestone Cave 1F
	❷	Chargestone Cave B1F
Pokémon White Version 2	❶	Chargestone Cave 1F
	❷	Chargestone Cave B1F

HOW TO OBTAIN FROM OTHER GAMES

LEVEL-UP AND LEARNED MOVES

Lv.	Name	Type	Kind	Pow.	Acc.	PP	Range	Long	DA
1	ViceGrip	Normal	Physical	55	100	30	Normal	—	○
6	Charge	Electric	Status	—	—	20	Self	—	—
11	ThunderShock	Electric	Special	40	100	30	Normal	—	—
16	Gear Grind	Steel	Physical	50	85	15	Normal	—	○
21	Bind	Normal	Physical	15	85	20	Normal	—	—
26	Charge Beam	Electric	Special	50	90	10	Normal	—	—
31	Autotomize	Steel	Status	—	—	15	Self	—	—
36	Mirror Shot	Steel	Special	65	85	10	Normal	—	—
39	Screech	Normal	Status	—	85	40	Normal	—	—
42	Discharge	Electric	Special	80	100	15	Adjacent	—	—
45	Metal Sound	Steel	Status	—	85	40	Normal	—	—
48	Shift Gear	Steel	Status	—	—	10	Self	—	—
51	Lock-On	Normal	Status	—	—	5	Normal	—	—
54	Zap Cannon	Electric	Special	120	50	5	Normal	—	—
57	Hyper Beam	Normal	Special	150	90	5	Normal	—	—

TM & HM MOVES

Lv.	Name	Type	Kind	Pow.	Acc.	PP	Range	Long	DA
TM06	Toxic	Poison	Status	—	90	10	Normal	—	—
TM10	Hidden Power	Normal	Special	—	100	15	Normal	—	—
TM15	Hyper Beam	Normal	Special	150	90	5	Normal	—	—
TM17	Protect	Normal	Status	—	—	10	Self	—	—
TM21	Frustration	Normal	Physical	—	100	20	Normal	—	○
TM24	Thunderbolt	Electric	Special	95	100	15	Normal	—	—
TM27	Return	Normal	Physical	—	100	20	Normal	—	○
TM32	Double Team	Normal	Status	—	—	15	Self	—	—
TM37	Sandstorm	Rock	Status	—	—	10	Both Sides	—	—
TM42	Facade	Normal	Physical	70	100	20	Normal	—	—
TM44	Rest	Psychic	Status	—	—	10	Self	—	—
TM48	Round	Normal	Special	60	100	15	Normal	—	—
TM57	Charge Beam	Electric	Special	50	90	10	Normal	—	—
TM69	Rock Polish	Rock	Status	—	—	20	Self	—	—
TM72	Volt Switch	Electric	Special	70	100	20	Normal	—	—
TM73	Thunder Wave	Electric	Status	—	100	20	Normal	—	—
TM87	Swagger	Normal	Status	—	90	15	Normal	—	—
TM90	Substitute	Normal	Status	—	—	10	Self	—	—
TM91	Flash Cannon	Steel	Special	80	100	10	Normal	—	—
TM93	Wild Charge	Electric	Physical	90	100	15	Normal	—	○
TM94	Rock Smash	Fighting	Physical	40	100	15	Normal	—	○

MOVES TAUGHT BY PEOPLE

Name	Type	Kind	Pow.	Acc.	PP	Range	Long	DA

MOVES TAUGHT BY MOVE TUTORS FOR SHARDS

Name	Type	Kind	Pow.	Acc.	PP	Range	Long	DA
Signal Beam	Bug	Special	75	100	15	Normal	—	—
Uproar	Normal	Special	90	100	10	1 Random	—	—
Iron Defense	Steel	Status	—	—	15	Self	—	—
Magnet Rise	Electric	Status	—	—	10	Self	—	—
Magic Coat	Psychic	Status	—	—	15	Self	—	—
Gravity	Psychic	Status	—	—	5	Both Sides	—	—
Bind	Normal	Physical	15	85	20	Normal	—	—
Snore	Normal	Special	40	100	15	Normal	—	—
Recycle	Normal	Status	—	—	10	Self	—	—
Sleep Talk	Normal	Status	—	—	10	Self	—	—

EGG MOVES

Name	Type	Kind	Pow.	Acc.	PP	Range	Long	DA

Pokémon AR Marker

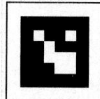

600 Klang
Gear Pokémon

TYPE Steel

ABILITIES
- Plus
- Minus

HIDDEN ABILITY
- Clear Body

- HEIGHT: 2'00"
- WEIGHT: 112.4 lbs.
- GENDER: Unknown

A minigear and big gear comprise its body. If the minigear it launches at a foe doesn't return, it will die.

STATS
- HP
- Attack
- Defense
- Sp. Atk
- Sp. Def
- Speed

EGG GROUPS
Mineral

ITEMS SOMETIMES HELD
- None

Gender unknown

EVOLUTION

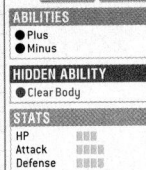

Klink — Lv. 38 → Klang — Lv. 49 → Klinklang

HOW TO OBTAIN
Pokémon Black Version 2	P2 Laboratory
Pokémon White Version 2	P2 Laboratory

HOW TO OBTAIN FROM OTHER GAMES
—

LEVEL-UP AND LEARNED MOVES

Lv.	Name	Type	Kind	Pow.	Acc.	PP	Range	Long	DA
1	ViceGrip	Normal	Physical	55	100	30	Normal	—	
1	Charge	Electric	Status	—	—	20	Self	—	
1	ThunderShock	Electric	Special	40	100	30	Normal	—	
1	Gear Grind	Steel	Physical	50	85	15	Normal	—	○
6	Charge	Electric	Status	—	—	20	Self	—	
11	ThunderShock	Electric	Special	40	100	30	Normal	—	
16	Gear Grind	Steel	Physical	50	85	15	Normal	—	○
21	Bind	Normal	Physical	15	85	20	Normal	—	○
26	Charge Beam	Electric	Special	50	90	10	Normal	—	
31	Autotomize	Steel	Status	—	—	15	Self	—	
36	Mirror Shot	Steel	Special	65	85	10	Normal	—	
40	Screech	Normal	Status	—	85	40	Normal	—	
44	Discharge	Electric	Special	80	100	15	Adjacent	—	
48	Metal Sound	Steel	Status	—	85	40	Normal	—	
52	Shift Gear	Steel	Status	—	—	10	Self	—	
56	Lock-On	Normal	Status	—	—	5	Normal	—	
60	Zap Cannon	Electric	Special	120	50	5	Normal	—	
64	Hyper Beam	Normal	Special	150	90	5	Normal	—	

TM & HM MOVES

Lv.	Name	Type	Kind	Pow.	Acc.	PP	Range	Long	DA
TM06	Toxic	Poison	Status	—	90	10	Normal	—	
TM10	Hidden Power	Normal	Special	—	100	15	Normal	—	
TM15	Hyper Beam	Normal	Special	150	90	5	Normal	—	
TM17	Protect	Normal	Status	—	—	10	Self	—	
TM21	Frustration	Normal	Physical	—	100	20	Normal	—	○
TM24	Thunderbolt	Electric	Special	95	100	15	Normal	—	
TM27	Return	Normal	Physical	—	100	20	Normal	—	○
TM32	Double Team	Normal	Status	—	—	15	Self	—	
TM37	Sandstorm	Rock	Status	—	—	10	Both Sides	—	
TM42	Facade	Normal	Physical	70	100	20	Normal	—	○
TM44	Rest	Psychic	Status	—	—	10	Self	—	
TM48	Round	Normal	Special	60	100	15	Normal	—	
TM57	Charge Beam	Electric	Special	50	90	10	Normal	—	
TM69	Rock Polish	Rock	Status	—	—	20	Self	—	
TM72	Volt Switch	Electric	Special	70	100	20	Normal	—	
TM73	Thunder Wave	Electric	Status	—	100	20	Normal	—	
TM87	Swagger	Normal	Status	—	90	15	Normal	—	
TM90	Substitute	Normal	Status	—	—	10	Self	—	
TM91	Flash Cannon	Steel	Special	80	100	10	Normal	—	
TM93	Wild Charge	Electric	Physical	90	100	15	Normal	—	○
TM94	Rock Smash	Fighting	Physical	40	100	15	Normal	—	○

MOVES TAUGHT BY PEOPLE

Name	Type	Kind	Pow.	Acc.	PP	Range	Long	DA

MOVES TAUGHT BY MOVE TUTORS FOR SHARDS

Name	Type	Kind	Pow.	Acc.	PP	Range	Long	DA
Signal Beam	Bug	Special	75	100	15	Normal	—	
Uproar	Normal	Special	90	100	10	1 Random	—	
Iron Defense	Steel	Status	—	—	15	Self	—	
Magnet Rise	Electric	Status	—	—	10	Self	—	
Magic Coat	Psychic	Status	—	—	15	Self	—	
Gravity	Psychic	Status	—	—	5	Both Sides	—	
Bind	Normal	Physical	15	85	20	Normal	—	○
Snore	Normal	Special	40	100	15	Normal	—	
Recycle	Normal	Status	—	—	10	Self	—	
Sleep Talk	Normal	Status	—	—	10	Self	—	

Pokémon AR Marker

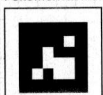

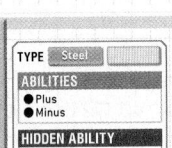

601 Klinklang
Gear Pokémon

TYPE Steel

ABILITIES
- Plus
- Minus

HIDDEN ABILITY
- Clear Body

- HEIGHT: 2'00"
- WEIGHT: 178.6 lbs.
- GENDER: Unknown

The minigear spins at high speed. Then the energy from the red core charges the minigear to make it ready to fire.

STATS
- HP
- Attack
- Defense
- Sp. Atk
- Sp. Def
- Speed

EGG GROUPS
Mineral

ITEMS SOMETIMES HELD
- None

Gender unknown

EVOLUTION

Klink — Lv. 38 → Klang — Lv. 49 → Klinklang

HOW TO OBTAIN
Pokémon Black Version 2	P2 Laboratory (rustling grass)
Pokémon White Version 2	P2 Laboratory (rustling grass)

HOW TO OBTAIN FROM OTHER GAMES
—

LEVEL-UP AND LEARNED MOVES

Lv.	Name	Type	Kind	Pow.	Acc.	PP	Range	Long	DA
1	ViceGrip	Normal	Physical	55	100	30	Normal	—	○
1	Charge	Electric	Status	—	—	20	Self	—	
1	ThunderShock	Electric	Special	40	100	30	Normal	—	
1	Gear Grind	Steel	Physical	50	85	15	Normal	—	○
6	Charge	Electric	Status	—	—	20	Self	—	
11	ThunderShock	Electric	Special	40	100	30	Normal	—	
16	Gear Grind	Steel	Physical	50	85	15	Normal	—	○
21	Bind	Normal	Physical	15	85	20	Normal	—	○
25	Charge Beam	Electric	Special	50	90	10	Normal	—	
31	Autotomize	Steel	Status	—	—	15	Self	—	
36	Mirror Shot	Steel	Special	65	85	10	Normal	—	
40	Screech	Normal	Status	—	85	40	Normal	—	
44	Discharge	Electric	Special	80	100	15	Adjacent	—	
48	Metal Sound	Steel	Status	—	85	40	Normal	—	
54	Shift Gear	Steel	Status	—	—	10	Self	—	
60	Lock-On	Normal	Status	—	—	5	Normal	—	
66	Zap Cannon	Electric	Special	120	50	5	Normal	—	
72	Hyper Beam	Normal	Special	150	90	5	Normal	—	

TM & HM MOVES

Lv.	Name	Type	Kind	Pow.	Acc.	PP	Range	Long	DA
TM06	Toxic	Poison	Status	—	90	10	Normal	—	
TM10	Hidden Power	Normal	Special	—	100	15	Normal	—	
TM15	Hyper Beam	Normal	Special	150	90	5	Normal	—	
TM17	Protect	Normal	Status	—	—	10	Self	—	
TM21	Frustration	Normal	Physical	—	100	20	Normal	—	○
TM24	Thunderbolt	Electric	Special	95	100	15	Normal	—	
TM25	Thunder	Electric	Special	120	70	10	Normal	—	
TM27	Return	Normal	Physical	—	100	20	Normal	—	○
TM32	Double Team	Normal	Status	—	—	15	Self	—	
TM37	Sandstorm	Rock	Status	—	—	10	Both Sides	—	
TM42	Facade	Normal	Physical	70	100	20	Normal	—	○
TM44	Rest	Psychic	Status	—	—	10	Self	—	
TM48	Round	Normal	Special	60	100	15	Normal	—	
TM57	Charge Beam	Electric	Special	50	90	10	Normal	—	
TM68	Giga Impact	Normal	Physical	150	90	5	Normal	—	
TM69	Rock Polish	Rock	Status	—	—	20	Self	—	
TM72	Volt Switch	Electric	Special	70	100	20	Normal	—	
TM73	Thunder Wave	Electric	Status	—	100	20	Normal	—	
TM87	Swagger	Normal	Status	—	90	15	Normal	—	
TM90	Substitute	Normal	Status	—	—	10	Self	—	
TM91	Flash Cannon	Steel	Special	80	100	10	Normal	—	
TM92	Trick Room	Psychic	Status	—	—	5	Both Sides	—	
TM93	Wild Charge	Electric	Physical	90	100	15	Normal	—	○
TM94	Rock Smash	Fighting	Physical	40	100	15	Normal	—	○

MOVES TAUGHT BY PEOPLE

Name	Type	Kind	Pow.	Acc.	PP	Range	Long	DA

MOVES TAUGHT BY MOVE TUTORS FOR SHARDS

Name	Type	Kind	Pow.	Acc.	PP	Range	Long	DA
Signal Beam	Bug	Special	75	100	15	Normal	—	
Uproar	Normal	Special	90	100	10	1 Random	—	
Iron Defense	Steel	Status	—	—	15	Self	—	
Magnet Rise	Electric	Status	—	—	10	Self	—	
Magic Coat	Psychic	Status	—	—	15	Self	—	
Gravity	Psychic	Status	—	—	5	Both Sides	—	
Bind	Normal	Physical	15	85	20	Normal	—	○
Snore	Normal	Special	40	100	15	Normal	—	
Recycle	Normal	Status	—	—	10	Self	—	
Sleep Talk	Normal	Status	—	—	10	Self	—	

Pokémon AR Marker

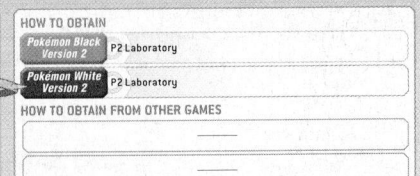

602 Tynamo

EleFish Pokémon

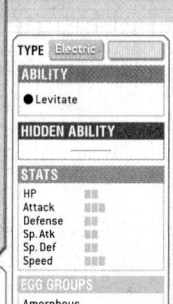

TYPE Electric

ABILITY
● Levitate

HIDDEN ABILITY
—

● HEIGHT: 0'08"
● WEIGHT: 0.7 lbs.
● GENDER: ♂ / ♀

One alone can emit only a trickle of electricity, so a group of them gathers to unleash a powerful electric shock.

STATS
HP
Attack
Defense
Sp. Atk
Sp. Def
Speed

EGG GROUPS
Amorphous

ITEMS SOMETIMES HELD
● None

Same form for ♂ / ♀

EVOLUTION

Tynamo — Lv. 39 → Eelektrik — Use Thunderstone → Eelektross

HOW TO OBTAIN

Pokémon Black Version 2 — ❶ Chargestone Cave 1F ❷ Seaside Cave 1F

Pokémon White Version 2 — ❶ Chargestone Cave 1F ❷ Seaside Cave 1F

HOW TO OBTAIN FROM OTHER GAMES
—

LEVEL-UP AND LEARNED MOVES

Lv.	Name	Type	Kind	Pow.	Acc.	PP	Range	Long	DA
1	Tackle	Normal	Physical	50	100	35	Normal	—	
1	Thunder Wave	Electric	Status	—	100	20	Normal	—	○
1	Spark	Electric	Physical	65	100	20	Normal	—	○
1	Charge Beam	Electric	Special	50	90	10	Normal	—	○

MOVES TAUGHT BY PEOPLE

Name	Type	Kind	Pow.	Acc.	PP	Range	Long	DA

MOVES TAUGHT BY MOVE TUTORS FOR SHARDS

Name	Type	Kind	Pow.	Acc.	PP	Range	Long	DA
Magnet Rise	Electric	Status	—	—	10	Self	—	

TM & HM MOVES

Lv.	Name	Type	Kind	Pow.	Acc.	PP	Range	Long	DA

EGG MOVES

Name	Type	Kind	Pow.	Acc.	PP	Range	Long	DA

Pokémon AR Marker

---

603 Eelektrik

EleFish Pokémon

TYPE Electric

ABILITY
● Levitate

HIDDEN ABILITY
—

● HEIGHT: 3'11"
● WEIGHT: 48.5 lbs.
● GENDER: ♂ / ♀

It wraps itself around its prey and paralyzes it with electricity from the round spots on its sides. Then it chomps.

STATS
HP
Attack
Defense
Sp. Atk
Sp. Def
Speed

EGG GROUPS
Amorphous

ITEMS SOMETIMES HELD
● None

Same form for ♂ / ♀

EVOLUTION

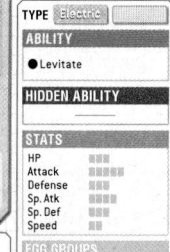

Tynamo — Lv. 39 → Eelektrik — Use Thunderstone → Eelektross

HOW TO OBTAIN

Pokémon Black Version 2 — Seaside Cave B1F

Pokémon White Version 2 — Seaside Cave B1F

HOW TO OBTAIN FROM OTHER GAMES
—

LEVEL-UP AND LEARNED MOVES

Lv.	Name	Type	Kind	Pow.	Acc.	PP	Range	Long	DA
1	Headbutt	Normal	Physical	70	100	15	Normal	—	○
1	Thunder Wave	Electric	Status	—	100	20	Normal	—	○
1	Spark	Electric	Physical	65	100	20	Normal	—	○
1	Charge Beam	Electric	Special	50	90	10	Normal	—	○
9	Bind	Normal	Physical	15	85	20	Normal	—	○
19	Acid	Poison	Special	40	100	30	Many Others	—	
29	Discharge	Electric	Special	80	100	15	Adjacent	—	
39	Crunch	Dark	Physical	80	100	15	Normal	—	○
44	Thunderbolt	Electric	Special	95	100	15	Normal	—	
49	Acid Spray	Poison	Special	40	100	20	Normal	—	
54	Coil	Poison	Status	—	—	20	Self	—	
59	Wild Charge	Electric	Physical	90	100	15	Normal	—	○
64	Gastro Acid	Poison	Status	—	100	10	Normal	—	
69	Zap Cannon	Electric	Special	120	50	5	Normal	—	
74	Thrash	Normal	Physical	120	100	10	1 Random	—	○

MOVES TAUGHT BY PEOPLE

Name	Type	Kind	Pow.	Acc.	PP	Range	Long	DA

MOVES TAUGHT BY MOVE TUTORS FOR SHARDS

Name	Type	Kind	Pow.	Acc.	PP	Range	Long	DA
Bounce	Flying	Physical	85	85	5	Normal	○	○
Signal Beam	Bug	Special	75	100	15	Normal	—	
Super Fang	Normal	Physical	—	90	10	Normal	—	
Magnet Rise	Electric	Status	—	—	10	Self	—	
Iron Tail	Steel	Physical	100	75	15	Normal	—	○
Aqua Tail	Water	Physical	90	90	10	Normal	—	○
Bind	Normal	Physical	15	85	20	Normal	—	○
Snore	Normal	Special	40	100	15	Normal	—	
Knock Off	Dark	Physical	20	100	20	Normal	—	○
Giga Drain	Grass	Special	75	100	10	Normal	—	
Gastro Acid	Poison	Status	—	100	10	Normal	—	
Sleep Talk	Normal	Status	—	—	10	Normal	—	

TM & HM MOVES

Lv.	Name	Type	Kind	Pow.	Acc.	PP	Range	Long	DA
TM06	Toxic	Poison	Status	—	90	10	Normal	—	
TM10	Hidden Power	Normal	Special	—	100	15	Normal	—	
TM16	Light Screen	Psychic	Status	—	—	30	Your Side	—	
TM17	Protect	Normal	Status	—	—	10	Self	—	
TM18	Rain Dance	Water	Status	—	—	5	Both Sides	—	
TM21	Frustration	Normal	Physical	—	100	20	Normal	—	○
TM24	Thunderbolt	Electric	Special	95	100	15	Normal	—	
TM25	Thunder	Electric	Special	120	70	10	Normal	—	
TM27	Return	Normal	Physical	—	100	20	Normal	—	○
TM32	Double Team	Normal	Status	—	—	15	Self	—	
TM42	Facade	Normal	Physical	70	100	20	Normal	—	○
TM44	Rest	Psychic	Status	—	—	10	Self	—	
TM45	Attract	Normal	Status	—	100	15	Normal	—	
TM48	Round	Normal	Special	60	100	15	Normal	—	
TM57	Charge Beam	Electric	Special	50	90	10	Normal	—	○
TM62	Acrobatics	Flying	Physical	55	100	15	Normal	○	○
TM70	Flash	Normal	Status	—	100	20	Normal	—	
TM72	Volt Switch	Electric	Special	70	100	20	Normal	—	
TM73	Thunder Wave	Electric	Status	—	100	20	Normal	—	○
TM87	Swagger	Normal	Status	—	90	15	Normal	—	
TM89	U-turn	Bug	Physical	70	100	20	Normal	—	○
TM90	Substitute	Normal	Status	—	—	10	Self	—	
TM91	Flash Cannon	Steel	Special	80	100	10	Normal	—	
TM93	Wild Charge	Electric	Physical	90	100	15	Normal	—	○

Pokémon AR Marker

604 Eelektross

EleFish Pokémon

● HEIGHT: 6'11"
● WEIGHT: 177.5 lbs.
● GENDER: ♂ / ♀

It latches on to prey with its sucker mouth, sinking in its fangs and shocking the prey with powerful electricity.

Same form for ♂ / ♀

TYPE Electric

ABILITY
● Levitate

HIDDEN ABILITY
—

STATS

Stat	
HP	■■■
Attack	■■■■■■
Defense	■■■■
Sp. Atk	■■■■■■
Sp. Def	■■■■
Speed	■■■

EGG GROUPS
Amorphous

ITEMS SOMETIMES HELD
● None

Pokémon AR Marker

EVOLUTION

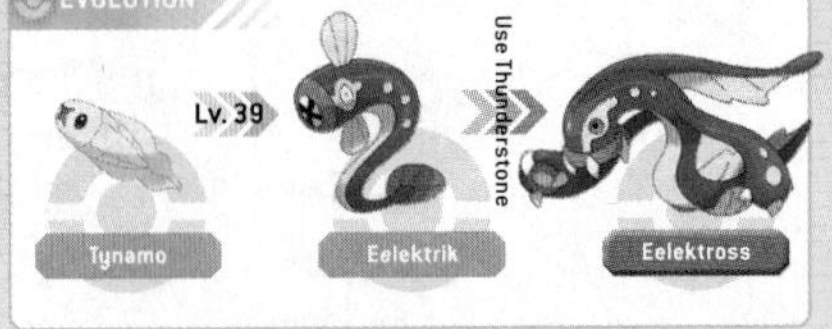

HOW TO OBTAIN

Pokémon Black Version 2	Use Thunderstone on Eelektrik
Pokémon White Version 2	Use Thunderstone on Eelektrik

HOW TO OBTAIN FROM OTHER GAMES

—

—

LEVEL-UP AND LEARNED MOVES

Lv.	Name	Type	Kind	Pow.	Acc.	PP	Range	Long	DA
1	Crush Claw	Normal	Physical	75	95	10	Normal	—	○
1	Headbutt	Normal	Physical	70	100	15	Normal	—	○
1	Acid	Poison	Special	40	100	30	Many Others	—	—
1	Discharge	Electric	Special	80	100	15	Adjacent	—	—
1	Crunch	Dark	Physical	80	100	15	Normal	—	○

TM & HM MOVES

Lv.	Name	Type	Kind	Pow.	Acc.	PP	Range	Long	DA
TM01	Hone Claws	Dark	Status	—	—	15	Self	—	—
TM02	Dragon Claw	Dragon	Physical	80	100	15	Normal	—	○
TM05	Roar	Normal	Status	—	100	20	Normal	—	—
TM06	Toxic	Poison	Status	—	90	10	Normal	—	—
TM10	Hidden Power	Normal	Special	—	100	15	Normal	—	—
TM15	Hyper Beam	Normal	Special	150	90	5	Normal	—	—
TM16	Light Screen	Psychic	Status	—	—	30	Your Side	—	—
TM17	Protect	Normal	Status	—	—	10	Self	—	—
TM18	Rain Dance	Water	Status	—	—	5	Both Sides	—	—
TM21	Frustration	Normal	Physical	—	100	20	Normal	—	○
TM24	Thunderbolt	Electric	Special	95	100	15	Normal	—	—
TM25	Thunder	Electric	Special	120	70	10	Normal	—	—
TM27	Return	Normal	Physical	—	100	20	Normal	—	○
TM31	Brick Break	Fighting	Physical	75	100	15	Normal	—	○
TM32	Double Team	Normal	Status	—	—	15	Self	—	—
TM35	Flamethrower	Fire	Special	95	100	15	Normal	—	—
TM39	Rock Tomb	Rock	Physical	50	80	10	Normal	—	—
TM42	Facade	Normal	Physical	70	100	20	Normal	—	○
TM44	Rest	Psychic	Status	—	—	10	Self	—	—
TM45	Attract	Normal	Status	—	100	15	Normal	—	—
TM48	Round	Normal	Special	60	100	15	Normal	—	—
TM57	Charge Beam	Electric	Special	50	90	10	Normal	—	—
TM62	Acrobatics	Flying	Physical	55	100	15	Normal	○	○
TM68	Giga Impact	Normal	Physical	150	90	5	Normal	—	○
TM70	Flash	Normal	Status	—	100	20	Normal	—	—
TM72	Volt Switch	Electric	Special	70	100	20	Normal	—	—
TM73	Thunder Wave	Electric	Status	—	100	20	Normal	—	—
TM80	Rock Slide	Rock	Physical	75	90	10	Many Others	—	—
TM82	Dragon Tail	Dragon	Physical	60	90	10	Normal	—	○
TM86	Grass Knot	Grass	Special	—	100	20	Normal	—	○
TM87	Swagger	Normal	Status	—	90	15	Normal	—	—
TM89	U-turn	Bug	Physical	70	100	20	Normal	—	○
TM90	Substitute	Normal	Status	—	—	10	Self	—	—
TM91	Flash Cannon	Steel	Special	80	100	10	Normal	—	—
TM93	Wild Charge	Electric	Physical	90	100	15	Normal	—	○
TM94	Rock Smash	Fighting	Physical	40	100	15	Normal	—	○
HM01	Cut	Normal	Physical	50	95	30	Normal	—	○
HM04	Strength	Normal	Physical	80	100	15	Normal	—	○

MOVES TAUGHT BY PEOPLE

Name	Type	Kind	Pow.	Acc.	PP	Range	Long	DA

MOVES TAUGHT BY MOVE TUTORS FOR SHARDS

Name	Type	Kind	Pow.	Acc.	PP	Range	Long	DA
Bounce	Flying	Physical	85	85	5	Normal	○	○
Signal Beam	Bug	Special	75	100	15	Normal	—	—
Super Fang	Normal	Physical	—	90	10	Normal	—	○
Fire Punch	Fire	Physical	75	100	15	Normal	—	○
ThunderPunch	Electric	Physical	75	100	15	Normal	—	○
Magnet Rise	Electric	Status	—	—	10	Self	—	—
Iron Tail	Steel	Physical	100	75	15	Normal	—	○
Aqua Tail	Water	Physical	90	90	10	Normal	—	○
Superpower	Fighting	Physical	120	100	5	Normal	—	○
Bind	Normal	Physical	15	85	20	Normal	—	○
Snore	Normal	Special	40	100	15	Normal	—	—
Knock Off	Dark	Physical	20	100	20	Normal	—	○
Giga Drain	Grass	Special	75	100	10	Normal	—	—
Drain Punch	Fighting	Physical	75	100	10	Normal	—	○
Gastro Acid	Poison	Status	—	100	10	Normal	—	—
Sleep Talk	Normal	Status	—	—	10	Self	—	—

605 Elgyem

Cerebral Pokémon

● HEIGHT: 1'08"
● WEIGHT: 19.8 lbs.
● GENDER: ♂ / ♀

Rumors of its origin are linked to a UFO crash site in the desert 50 years ago.

Same form for ♂ / ♀

TYPE Psychic

ABILITIES
● Telepathy
● Synchronize

HIDDEN ABILITY
● Analytic

STATS

Stat	
HP	■■
Attack	■■■
Defense	■■■
Sp. Atk	■■■■
Sp. Def	■■■
Speed	■■

EGG GROUPS
Human-like

ITEMS SOMETIMES HELD
● None

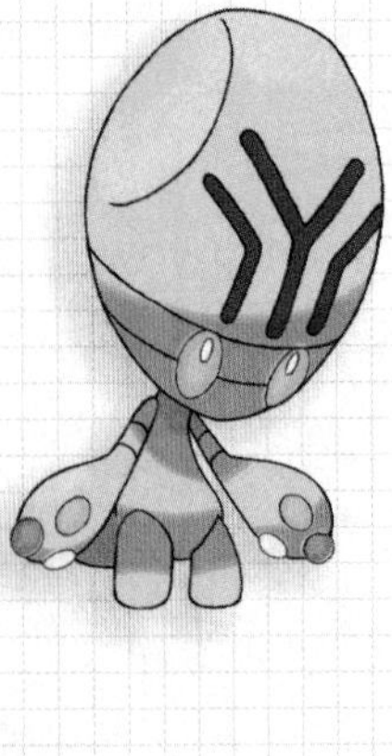

Pokémon AR Marker

EVOLUTION

HOW TO OBTAIN

Pokémon Black Version 2	❶ Celestial Tower 3F ❷ Celestial Tower 4F
Pokémon White Version 2	❶ Celestial Tower 3F ❷ Celestial Tower 4F

HOW TO OBTAIN FROM OTHER GAMES

—

—

LEVEL-UP AND LEARNED MOVES

Lv.	Name	Type	Kind	Pow.	Acc.	PP	Range	Long	DA
1	Confusion	Psychic	Special	50	100	25	Normal	—	—
4	Growl	Normal	Status	—	100	40	Many Others	—	—
8	Heal Block	Psychic	Status	—	100	15	Many Others	—	—
11	Miracle Eye	Psychic	Status	—	—	40	Normal	—	—
15	Psybeam	Psychic	Special	65	100	20	Normal	—	—
18	Headbutt	Normal	Physical	70	100	15	Normal	—	○
22	Hidden Power	Normal	Special	—	100	15	Normal	—	—
25	Imprison	Psychic	Status	—	—	10	Self	—	—
29	Simple Beam	Normal	Status	—	100	15	Normal	—	—
32	Zen Headbutt	Psychic	Physical	80	90	15	Normal	—	○
36	Psych Up	Normal	Status	—	—	10	Normal	—	—
39	Psychic	Psychic	Special	90	100	10	Normal	—	—
43	Calm Mind	Psychic	Status	—	—	20	Self	—	—
46	Recover	Normal	Status	—	—	10	Self	—	—
50	Guard Split	Psychic	Status	—	—	10	Normal	—	—
50	Power Split	Psychic	Status	—	—	10	Normal	—	—
53	Synchronoise	Psychic	Special	70	100	15	Adjacent	—	—
56	Wonder Room	Psychic	Status	—	—	10	Both Sides	—	—

TM & HM MOVES

Lv.	Name	Type	Kind	Pow.	Acc.	PP	Range	Long	DA
TM03	Psyshock	Psychic	Special	80	100	10	Normal	—	—
TM04	Calm Mind	Psychic	Status	—	—	20	Self	—	—
TM06	Toxic	Poison	Status	—	90	10	Normal	—	—
TM10	Hidden Power	Normal	Special	—	100	15	Normal	—	—
TM16	Light Screen	Psychic	Status	—	—	30	Your Side	—	—
TM17	Protect	Normal	Status	—	—	10	Self	—	—
TM18	Rain Dance	Water	Status	—	—	5	Both Sides	—	—
TM19	Telekinesis	Psychic	Status	—	—	15	Normal	—	—
TM20	Safeguard	Normal	Status	—	—	25	Your Side	—	—
TM21	Frustration	Normal	Physical	—	100	20	Normal	—	○
TM24	Thunderbolt	Electric	Special	95	100	15	Normal	—	—
TM27	Return	Normal	Physical	—	100	20	Normal	—	○
TM29	Psychic	Psychic	Special	90	100	10	Normal	—	—
TM30	Shadow Ball	Ghost	Special	80	100	15	Normal	—	—
TM32	Double Team	Normal	Status	—	—	15	Self	—	—
TM33	Reflect	Psychic	Status	—	—	20	Your Side	—	—
TM39	Rock Tomb	Rock	Physical	50	80	10	Normal	—	—
TM42	Facade	Normal	Physical	70	100	20	Normal	—	○
TM44	Rest	Psychic	Status	—	—	10	Self	—	—
TM45	Attract	Normal	Status	—	100	15	Normal	—	—
TM46	Thief	Dark	Physical	40	100	10	Normal	—	○
TM48	Round	Normal	Special	60	100	15	Normal	—	—
TM49	Echoed Voice	Normal	Special	40	100	15	Normal	—	—
TM51	Ally Switch	Psychic	Status	—	—	15	Self	—	—
TM53	Energy Ball	Grass	Special	80	100	10	Normal	—	—
TM57	Charge Beam	Electric	Special	50	90	10	Normal	—	—
TM63	Embargo	Dark	Status	—	100	15	Normal	—	—
TM70	Flash	Normal	Status	—	100	20	Normal	—	—
TM73	Thunder Wave	Electric	Status	—	100	20	Normal	—	—
TM77	Psych Up	Normal	Status	—	—	10	Normal	—	—
TM80	Rock Slide	Rock	Physical	75	90	10	Many Others	—	—
TM85	Dream Eater	Psychic	Special	100	100	15	Normal	—	—
TM87	Swagger	Normal	Status	—	90	15	Normal	—	—
TM90	Substitute	Normal	Status	—	—	10	Self	—	—
TM92	Trick Room	Psychic	Status	—	—	5	Both Sides	—	—

MOVES TAUGHT BY PEOPLE

Name	Type	Kind	Pow.	Acc.	PP	Range	Long	DA

MOVES TAUGHT BY MOVE TUTORS FOR SHARDS

Name	Type	Kind	Pow.	Acc.	PP	Range	Long	DA
Signal Beam	Bug	Special	75	100	15	Normal	—	—
Uproar	Normal	Special	90	100	10	1 Random	—	—
Magic Coat	Psychic	Status	—	—	15	Self	—	—
Zen Headbutt	Psychic	Physical	80	90	15	Normal	—	○
Gravity	Psychic	Status	—	—	5	Both Sides	—	—
Dark Pulse	Dark	Special	80	100	15	Normal	○	—
Snore	Normal	Special	40	100	15	Normal	—	—
Role Play	Psychic	Status	—	—	10	Normal	—	—
Pain Split	Normal	Status	—	—	20	Normal	—	—
After You	Normal	Status	—	—	15	Normal	—	—
Wonder Room	Psychic	Status	—	—	10	Both Sides	—	—
Recycle	Normal	Status	—	—	10	Self	—	—
Trick	Psychic	Status	—	100	10	Normal	—	—
Sleep Talk	Normal	Status	—	—	10	Self	—	—
Skill Swap	Psychic	Status	—	—	10	Normal	—	—
Snatch	Dark	Status	—	—	10	Self	—	—

EGG MOVES

Name	Type	Kind	Pow.	Acc.	PP	Range	Long	DA
Teleport	Psychic	Status	—	—	20	Self	—	—
Disable	Normal	Status	—	100	20	Normal	—	—
Astonish	Ghost	Physical	30	100	15	Normal	—	○
Power Swap	Psychic	Status	—	—	10	Normal	—	—
Guard Swap	Psychic	Status	—	—	10	Normal	—	—
Barrier	Psychic	Status	—	—	30	Self	—	—
Nasty Plot	Dark	Status	—	—	20	Self	—	—
Skill Swap	Psychic	Status	—	—	10	Normal	—	—

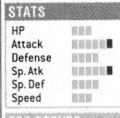

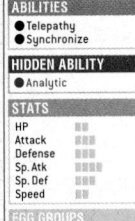

Cerebral Pokémon
606 Beheeyem

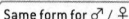

- HEIGHT: 3'03"
- WEIGHT: 76.1 lbs.
- GENDER: ♂ / ♀

Apparently, it communicates by flashing its three fingers, but those patterns haven't been decoded.

Same form for ♂ / ♀

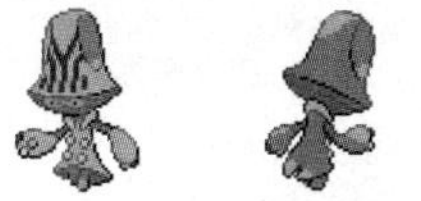

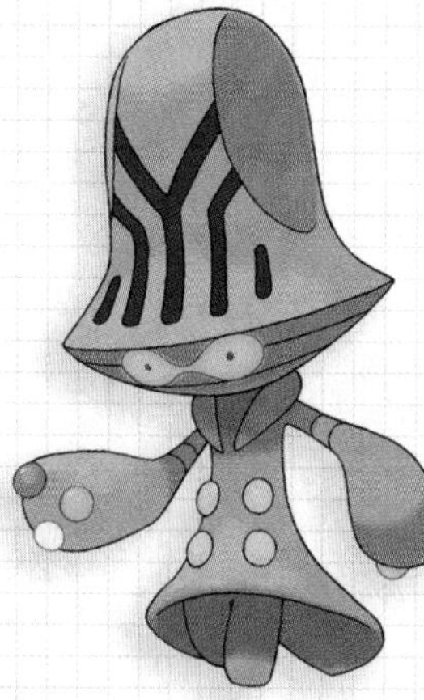

Pokémon AR Marker

TYPE Psychic

ABILITIES
- Telepathy
- Synchronize

HIDDEN ABILITY
- Analytic

STATS
HP
Attack
Defense
Sp. Atk
Sp. Def
Speed

EGG GROUPS
Human-like

ITEMS SOMETIMES HELD
- None

EVOLUTION

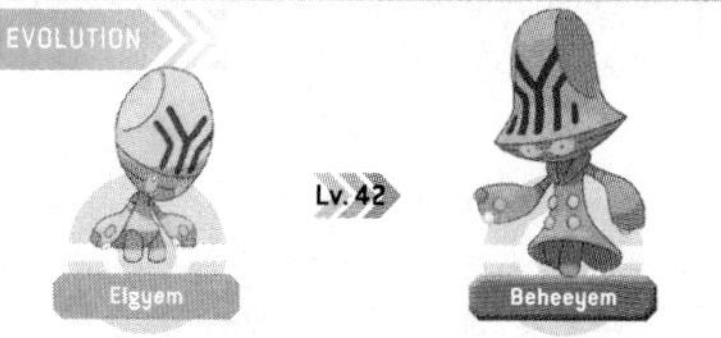

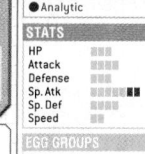

Elgyem
Lv. 42
Beheeyem

HOW TO OBTAIN

Pokémon Black Version 2	Level up Elgyem to Lv. 42
Pokémon White Version 2	Level up Elgyem to Lv. 42

HOW TO OBTAIN FROM OTHER GAMES

—

—

LEVEL-UP AND LEARNED MOVES

Lv.	Name	Type	Kind	Pow.	Acc.	PP	Range	Long	DA
1	Confusion	Psychic	Special	50	100	25	Normal	—	—
1	Growl	Normal	Status	—	100	40	Many Others	—	—
1	Heal Block	Psychic	Status	—	100	15	Many Others	—	—
1	Miracle Eye	Psychic	Status	—	—	40	Normal	—	—
4	Growl	Normal	Status	—	100	40	Many Others	—	—
8	Heal Block	Psychic	Status	—	100	15	Many Others	—	—
11	Miracle Eye	Psychic	Status	—	—	40	Normal	—	—
15	Psybeam	Psychic	Special	65	100	20	Normal	—	—
18	Headbutt	Normal	Physical	70	100	15	Normal	—	○
22	Hidden Power	Normal	Special	—	100	15	Normal	—	—
25	Imprison	Psychic	Status	—	—	10	Self	—	—
29	Simple Beam	Normal	Status	—	100	15	Normal	—	—
32	Zen Headbutt	Psychic	Physical	80	90	15	Normal	—	○
36	Psych Up	Normal	Status	—	—	10	Normal	—	—
39	Psychic	Psychic	Special	90	100	10	Normal	—	—
45	Calm Mind	Psychic	Status	—	—	20	Self	—	—
50	Recover	Normal	Status	—	—	10	Self	—	—
56	Guard Split	Psychic	Status	—	—	10	Normal	—	—
58	Power Split	Psychic	Status	—	—	10	Normal	—	—
63	Synchronoise	Psychic	Special	70	100	15	Adjacent	—	—
68	Wonder Room	Psychic	Status	—	—	10	Both Sides	—	—

TM & HM MOVES

Lv.	Name	Type	Kind	Pow.	Acc.	PP	Range	Long	DA
TM03	Psyshock	Psychic	Special	80	100	10	Normal	—	—
TM04	Calm Mind	Psychic	Status	—	—	20	Self	—	—
TM06	Toxic	Poison	Status	—	90	10	Normal	—	—
TM10	Hidden Power	Normal	Special	—	100	15	Normal	—	—
TM15	Hyper Beam	Normal	Special	150	90	5	Normal	—	—
TM16	Light Screen	Psychic	Status	—	—	30	Your Side	—	—
TM17	Protect	Normal	Status	—	—	10	Self	—	—
TM18	Rain Dance	Water	Status	—	—	5	Both Sides	—	—
TM19	Telekinesis	Psychic	Status	—	—	15	Normal	—	—
TM20	Safeguard	Normal	Status	—	—	25	Your Side	—	—
TM21	Frustration	Normal	Physical	—	100	20	Normal	—	○
TM24	Thunderbolt	Electric	Special	95	100	15	Normal	—	—
TM27	Return	Normal	Physical	—	100	20	Normal	—	○
TM29	Psychic	Psychic	Special	90	100	10	Normal	—	—
TM30	Shadow Ball	Ghost	Special	80	100	15	Normal	—	—
TM32	Double Team	Normal	Status	—	—	15	Self	—	—
TM33	Reflect	Psychic	Status	—	—	20	Your Side	—	—
TM39	Rock Tomb	Rock	Physical	50	80	10	Normal	—	—
TM42	Facade	Normal	Physical	70	100	20	Normal	—	○
TM44	Rest	Psychic	Status	—	—	10	Self	—	—
TM45	Attract	Normal	Status	—	100	15	Normal	—	—
TM46	Thief	Dark	Physical	40	100	10	Normal	—	○
TM48	Round	Normal	Special	60	100	15	Normal	—	—
TM49	Echoed Voice	Normal	Special	40	100	15	Normal	—	—
TM51	Ally Switch	Psychic	Status	—	—	15	Self	—	—
TM53	Energy Ball	Grass	Special	80	100	10	Normal	—	—
TM57	Charge Beam	Electric	Special	50	90	10	Normal	—	—
TM63	Embargo	Dark	Status	—	100	15	Normal	—	—
TM68	Giga Impact	Normal	Physical	150	90	5	Normal	—	○
TM70	Flash	Normal	Status	—	100	20	Normal	—	—
TM73	Thunder Wave	Electric	Status	—	100	20	Normal	—	—
TM77	Psych Up	Normal	Status	—	—	10	Normal	—	—
TM80	Rock Slide	Rock	Physical	75	90	10	Many Others	—	—
TM85	Dream Eater	Psychic	Special	100	100	15	Normal	—	—
TM87	Swagger	Normal	Status	—	90	15	Normal	—	—
TM90	Substitute	Normal	Status	—	—	10	Self	—	—
TM92	Trick Room	Psychic	Status	—	—	5	Both Sides	—	—

MOVES TAUGHT BY PEOPLE

Name	Type	Kind	Pow.	Acc.	PP	Range	Long	DA

MOVES TAUGHT BY MOVE TUTORS FOR SHARDS

Name	Type	Kind	Pow.	Acc.	PP	Range	Long	DA
Signal Beam	Bug	Special	75	100	15	Normal	—	—
Uproar	Normal	Special	90	100	10	1 Random	—	—
Magic Coat	Psychic	Status	—	—	15	Self	—	—
Zen Headbutt	Psychic	Physical	80	90	15	Normal	—	○
Gravity	Psychic	Status	—	—	5	Both Sides	—	—
Dark Pulse	Dark	Special	80	100	15	Normal	○	—
Snore	Normal	Special	40	100	15	Normal	—	—
Role Play	Psychic	Status	—	—	10	Normal	—	—
Pain Split	Normal	Status	—	—	20	Normal	—	—
After You	Normal	Status	—	—	15	Normal	—	—
Wonder Room	Psychic	Status	—	—	10	Both Sides	—	—
Recycle	Normal	Status	—	—	10	Self	—	—
Trick	Psychic	Status	—	100	10	Normal	—	—
Sleep Talk	Normal	Status	—	—	10	Self	—	—
Skill Swap	Psychic	Status	—	—	10	Normal	—	—
Snatch	Dark	Status	—	—	10	Self	—	—

Candle Pokémon
607 Litwick

- HEIGHT: 1'00"
- WEIGHT: 6.8 lbs.
- GENDER: ♂ / ♀

Its flame is usually out, but it starts shining when it absorbs life force from people or Pokémon.

Same form for ♂ / ♀

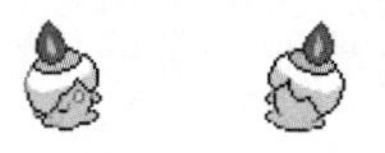

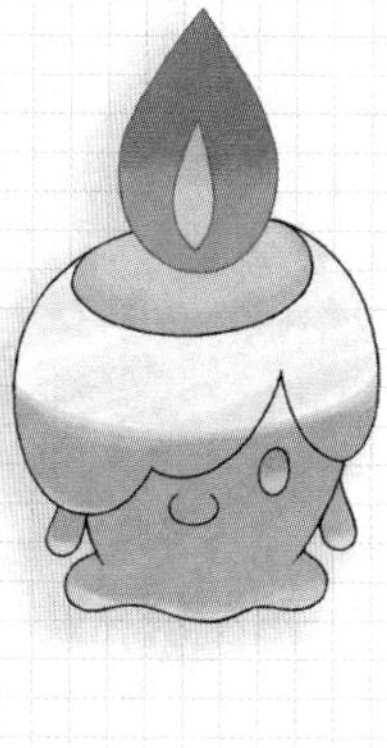

Pokémon AR Marker

TYPE Ghost Fire

ABILITIES
- Flash Fire
- Flame Body

HIDDEN ABILITY
—

STATS
HP
Attack
Defense
Sp. Atk
Sp. Def
Speed

EGG GROUPS
Amorphous

ITEMS SOMETIMES HELD
- None

EVOLUTION

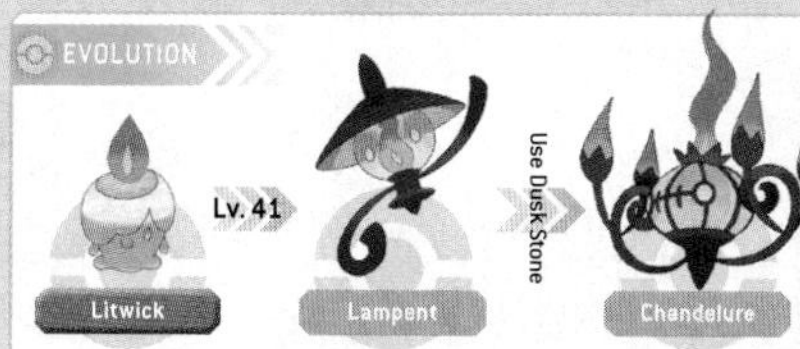

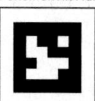

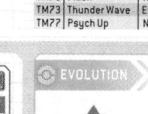

Litwick
Lv. 41
Lampent
Use Dusk Stone
Chandelure

HOW TO OBTAIN

Pokémon Black Version 2	❶ Celestial Tower 2F ❷ Strange House entrance
Pokémon White Version 2	❶ Celestial Tower 2F ❷ Strange House entrance

HOW TO OBTAIN FROM OTHER GAMES

—

—

LEVEL-UP AND LEARNED MOVES

Lv.	Name	Type	Kind	Pow.	Acc.	PP	Range	Long	DA
1	Ember	Fire	Special	40	100	25	Normal	—	—
1	Astonish	Ghost	Physical	30	100	15	Normal	—	○
3	Minimize	Normal	Status	—	—	20	Self	—	—
5	Smog	Poison	Special	20	70	20	Normal	—	—
7	Fire Spin	Fire	Special	35	85	15	Normal	—	—
10	Confuse Ray	Ghost	Status	—	100	10	Normal	—	—
13	Night Shade	Ghost	Special	—	100	15	Normal	—	—
16	Will-O-Wisp	Fire	Status	—	75	15	Normal	—	—
20	Flame Burst	Fire	Special	70	100	15	Normal	—	—
24	Imprison	Psychic	Status	—	—	10	Self	—	—
28	Hex	Ghost	Special	50	100	10	Normal	—	—
33	Memento	Dark	Status	—	100	10	Normal	—	—
38	Inferno	Fire	Special	100	50	5	Normal	—	—
43	Curse	Ghost	Status	—	—	10	Varies	—	—
49	Shadow Ball	Ghost	Special	80	100	15	Normal	—	—
55	Pain Split	Normal	Status	—	—	20	Normal	—	—
61	Overheat	Fire	Special	140	90	5	Normal	—	—

TM & HM MOVES

Lv.	Name	Type	Kind	Pow.	Acc.	PP	Range	Long	DA
TM04	Calm Mind	Psychic	Status	—	—	20	Self	—	—
TM06	Toxic	Poison	Status	—	90	10	Normal	—	—
TM10	Hidden Power	Normal	Special	—	100	15	Normal	—	—
TM11	Sunny Day	Fire	Status	—	—	5	Both Sides	—	—
TM12	Taunt	Dark	Status	—	100	20	Normal	—	—
TM17	Protect	Normal	Status	—	—	10	Self	—	—
TM19	Telekinesis	Psychic	Status	—	—	15	Normal	—	—
TM20	Safeguard	Normal	Status	—	—	25	Your Side	—	—
TM21	Frustration	Normal	Physical	—	100	20	Normal	—	○
TM22	SolarBeam	Grass	Special	120	100	10	Normal	—	—
TM27	Return	Normal	Physical	—	100	20	Normal	—	○
TM29	Psychic	Psychic	Special	90	100	10	Normal	—	—
TM30	Shadow Ball	Ghost	Special	80	100	15	Normal	—	—
TM32	Double Team	Normal	Status	—	—	15	Self	—	—
TM35	Flamethrower	Fire	Special	95	100	15	Normal	—	—
TM38	Fire Blast	Fire	Special	120	85	5	Normal	—	—
TM42	Facade	Normal	Physical	70	100	20	Normal	—	○
TM43	Flame Charge	Fire	Physical	50	100	20	Normal	—	○
TM44	Rest	Psychic	Status	—	—	10	Self	—	—
TM45	Attract	Normal	Status	—	100	15	Normal	—	—
TM46	Thief	Dark	Physical	40	100	10	Normal	—	○
TM48	Round	Normal	Special	60	100	15	Normal	—	—
TM50	Overheat	Fire	Special	140	90	5	Normal	—	—
TM53	Energy Ball	Grass	Special	80	100	10	Normal	—	—
TM59	Incinerate	Fire	Special	30	100	15	Many Others	—	—
TM61	Will-O-Wisp	Fire	Status	—	75	15	Normal	—	—
TM63	Embargo	Dark	Status	—	100	15	Normal	—	—
TM66	Payback	Dark	Physical	50	100	10	Normal	—	○
TM70	Flash	Normal	Status	—	100	20	Normal	—	—
TM77	Psych Up	Normal	Status	—	—	10	Normal	—	—
TM85	Dream Eater	Psychic	Special	100	100	15	Normal	—	—
TM87	Swagger	Normal	Status	—	90	15	Normal	—	—
TM90	Substitute	Normal	Status	—	—	10	Self	—	—
TM92	Trick Room	Psychic	Status	—	—	5	Both Sides	—	—

MOVES TAUGHT BY PEOPLE

Name	Type	Kind	Pow.	Acc.	PP	Range	Long	DA

MOVES TAUGHT BY MOVE TUTORS FOR SHARDS

Name	Type	Kind	Pow.	Acc.	PP	Range	Long	DA
Dark Pulse	Dark	Special	80	100	15	Normal	○	—
Snore	Normal	Special	40	100	15	Normal	—	—
Heat Wave	Fire	Special	100	90	10	Many Others	—	—
Pain Split	Normal	Status	—	—	20	Normal	—	—
Spite	Ghost	Status	—	100	10	Normal	—	—
Trick	Psychic	Status	—	100	10	Normal	—	—
Sleep Talk	Normal	Status	—	—	10	Self	—	—

EGG MOVES

Name	Type	Kind	Pow.	Acc.	PP	Range	Long	DA
Acid Armor	Poison	Status	—	—	40	Self	—	—
Heat Wave	Fire	Special	100	90	10	Many Others	—	—
Haze	Ice	Status	—	—	30	Both Sides	—	—
Endure	Normal	Status	—	—	10	Self	—	—
Captivate	Normal	Status	—	100	20	Many Others	—	—
Acid	Poison	Special	40	100	30	Many Others	—	—
Clear Smog	Poison	Special	50	—	15	Normal	—	—

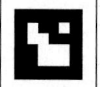

608 Lampent
Lamp Pokémon

TYPE Ghost Fire

ABILITIES
- Flash Fire
- Flame Body

HIDDEN ABILITY

- HEIGHT: 2'00"
- WEIGHT: 28.7 lbs.
- GENDER: ♂ / ♀

The spirits it absorbs fuel its baleful fire. It hangs around hospitals waiting for people to pass on.

STATS
HP
Attack
Defense
Sp. Atk
Sp. Def
Speed

EGG GROUPS
Amorphous

ITEMS SOMETIMES HELD
- None

EVOLUTION
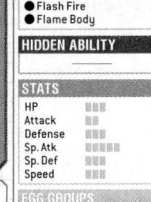

Litwick — Lv. 41 → Lampent — Use Dusk Stone → Chandelure

HOW TO OBTAIN

| Pokémon Black Version 2 | Level up Litwick to Lv. 41 |
| Pokémon White Version 2 | Level up Litwick to Lv. 41 |

HOW TO OBTAIN FROM OTHER GAMES

Same form for ♂ / ♀

Pokémon AR Marker

LEVEL-UP AND LEARNED MOVES

Lv.	Name	Type	Kind	Pow.	Acc.	PP	Range	Long	DA
1	Ember	Fire	Special	40	100	25	Normal	—	
1	Astonish	Ghost	Physical	30	100	15	Normal	—	○
1	Minimize	Normal	Status	—	—	20	Self	—	
1	Smog	Poison	Special	20	70	20	Normal	—	
3	Minimize	Normal	Status	—	—	20	Self	—	
5	Smog	Poison	Special	20	70	20	Normal	—	
7	Fire Spin	Fire	Special	35	85	15	Normal	—	
10	Confuse Ray	Ghost	Status	—	100	10	Normal	—	
13	Night Shade	Ghost	Special	—	100	15	Normal	—	
16	Will-O-Wisp	Fire	Status	—	75	15	Normal	—	
20	Flame Burst	Fire	Special	70	100	15	Normal	—	
24	Imprison	Psychic	Status	—	—	10	Self	—	
28	Hex	Ghost	Special	50	100	10	Normal	—	
33	Memento	Dark	Status	—	100	10	Normal	—	
38	Inferno	Fire	Special	100	50	5	Normal	—	
45	Curse	Ghost	Status	—	—	10	Varies	—	
53	Shadow Ball	Ghost	Special	80	100	15	Normal	—	
61	Pain Split	Normal	Status	—	—	20	Normal	—	
69	Overheat	Fire	Special	140	90	5	Normal	—	

TM & HM MOVES

Lv.	Name	Type	Kind	Pow.	Acc.	PP	Range	Long	DA
TM04	Calm Mind	Psychic	Status	—	—	20	Self	—	
TM06	Toxic	Poison	Status	—	90	10	Normal	—	
TM10	Hidden Power	Normal	Special	—	100	15	Normal	—	
TM11	Sunny Day	Fire	Status	—	—	5	Both Sides	—	
TM12	Taunt	Dark	Status	—	100	20	Normal	—	
TM17	Protect	Normal	Status	—	—	10	Self	—	
TM19	Telekinesis	Psychic	Status	—	—	15	Normal	—	
TM20	Safeguard	Normal	Status	—	—	25	Your Side	—	
TM21	Frustration	Normal	Physical	—	100	20	Normal	—	○
TM22	SolarBeam	Grass	Special	120	100	10	Normal	—	
TM27	Return	Normal	Physical	—	100	20	Normal	—	○
TM29	Psychic	Psychic	Special	90	100	10	Normal	—	
TM30	Shadow Ball	Ghost	Special	80	100	15	Normal	—	
TM32	Double Team	Normal	Status	—	—	15	Self	—	
TM35	Flamethrower	Fire	Special	95	100	15	Normal	—	
TM38	Fire Blast	Fire	Special	120	85	5	Normal	—	
TM42	Facade	Normal	Physical	70	100	20	Normal	—	○
TM43	Flame Charge	Fire	Physical	50	100	20	Normal	—	○
TM44	Rest	Psychic	Status	—	—	10	Self	—	
TM45	Attract	Normal	Status	—	100	15	Normal	—	
TM46	Thief	Dark	Physical	40	100	10	Normal	—	
TM48	Round	Normal	Special	60	100	15	Normal	—	
TM50	Overheat	Fire	Special	140	90	5	Normal	—	
TM53	Energy Ball	Grass	Special	80	100	10	Normal	—	
TM59	Incinerate	Fire	Special	30	100	15	Many Others	—	
TM61	Will-O-Wisp	Fire	Status	—	75	15	Normal	—	
TM63	Embargo	Dark	Status	—	100	15	Normal	—	
TM66	Payback	Dark	Physical	50	100	10	Normal	—	○
TM70	Flash	Normal	Status	—	100	20	Normal	—	
TM77	Psych Up	Normal	Status	—	—	10	Normal	—	
TM85	Dream Eater	Psychic	Special	100	100	15	Normal	—	
TM87	Swagger	Normal	Status	—	90	15	Normal	—	
TM90	Substitute	Normal	Status	—	—	10	Self	—	
TM92	Trick Room	Psychic	Status	—	—	5	Both Sides	—	

MOVES TAUGHT BY PEOPLE

Name	Type	Kind	Pow.	Acc.	PP	Range	Long	DA

MOVES TAUGHT BY MOVE TUTORS FOR SHARDS

Name	Type	Kind	Pow.	Acc.	PP	Range	Long	DA
Dark Pulse	Dark	Special	80	100	15	Normal	○	
Snore	Normal	Special	40	100	15	Normal	—	
Heat Wave	Fire	Special	100	90	10	Many Others	—	
Pain Split	Normal	Status	—	—	20	Normal	—	
Spite	Ghost	Status	—	100	10	Normal	—	
Trick	Psychic	Status	—	100	10	Normal	—	
Sleep Talk	Normal	Status	—	—	10	Self	—	

---

609 Chandelure
Luring Pokémon

TYPE Ghost Fire

ABILITIES
- Flash Fire
- Flame Body

HIDDEN ABILITY

- HEIGHT: 3'03"
- WEIGHT: 75.6 lbs.
- GENDER: ♂ / ♀

The spirits burned up in its ominous flame lose their way and wander this world forever.

STATS
HP
Attack
Defense
Sp. Atk
Sp. Def
Speed

EGG GROUPS
Amorphous

ITEMS SOMETIMES HELD
- None

EVOLUTION

Litwick — Lv. 41 → Lampent — Use Dusk Stone → Chandelure

HOW TO OBTAIN

| Pokémon Black Version 2 | Use Dusk Stone on Lampent |
| Pokémon White Version 2 | Use Dusk Stone on Lampent |

HOW TO OBTAIN FROM OTHER GAMES

Same form for ♂ / ♀

Pokémon AR Marker

LEVEL-UP AND LEARNED MOVES

Lv.	Name	Type	Kind	Pow.	Acc.	PP	Range	Long	DA
1	Smog	Poison	Special	20	70	20	Normal	—	
1	Confuse Ray	Ghost	Status	—	100	10	Normal	—	
1	Flame Burst	Fire	Special	70	100	15	Normal	—	
1	Hex	Ghost	Special	50	100	10	Normal	—	

TM & HM MOVES

Lv.	Name	Type	Kind	Pow.	Acc.	PP	Range	Long	DA
TM04	Calm Mind	Psychic	Status	—	—	20	Self	—	
TM06	Toxic	Poison	Status	—	90	10	Normal	—	
TM10	Hidden Power	Normal	Special	—	100	15	Normal	—	
TM11	Sunny Day	Fire	Status	—	—	5	Both Sides	—	
TM12	Taunt	Dark	Status	—	100	20	Normal	—	
TM15	Hyper Beam	Normal	Special	150	90	5	Normal	—	
TM17	Protect	Normal	Status	—	—	10	Self	—	
TM19	Telekinesis	Psychic	Status	—	—	15	Normal	—	
TM20	Safeguard	Normal	Status	—	—	25	Your Side	—	
TM21	Frustration	Normal	Physical	—	100	20	Normal	—	○
TM22	SolarBeam	Grass	Special	120	100	10	Normal	—	
TM27	Return	Normal	Physical	—	100	20	Normal	—	○
TM29	Psychic	Psychic	Special	90	100	10	Normal	—	
TM30	Shadow Ball	Ghost	Special	80	100	15	Normal	—	
TM32	Double Team	Normal	Status	—	—	15	Self	—	
TM35	Flamethrower	Fire	Special	95	100	15	Normal	—	
TM38	Fire Blast	Fire	Special	120	85	5	Normal	—	
TM42	Facade	Normal	Physical	70	100	20	Normal	—	○
TM43	Flame Charge	Fire	Physical	50	100	20	Normal	—	○
TM44	Rest	Psychic	Status	—	—	10	Self	—	
TM45	Attract	Normal	Status	—	100	15	Normal	—	
TM46	Thief	Dark	Physical	40	100	10	Normal	—	○
TM48	Round	Normal	Special	60	100	15	Normal	—	
TM50	Overheat	Fire	Special	140	90	5	Normal	—	
TM53	Energy Ball	Grass	Special	80	100	10	Normal	—	
TM59	Incinerate	Fire	Special	30	100	15	Many Others	—	
TM61	Will-O-Wisp	Fire	Status	—	75	15	Normal	—	
TM63	Embargo	Dark	Status	—	100	15	Normal	—	
TM66	Payback	Dark	Physical	50	100	10	Normal	—	○
TM68	Giga Impact	Normal	Physical	150	90	5	Normal	—	
TM70	Flash	Normal	Status	—	100	20	Normal	—	
TM77	Psych Up	Normal	Status	—	—	10	Normal	—	
TM85	Dream Eater	Psychic	Special	100	100	15	Normal	—	
TM87	Swagger	Normal	Status	—	90	15	Normal	—	
TM90	Substitute	Normal	Status	—	—	10	Self	—	
TM92	Trick Room	Psychic	Status	—	—	5	Both Sides	—	

MOVES TAUGHT BY PEOPLE

Name	Type	Kind	Pow.	Acc.	PP	Range	Long	DA

MOVES TAUGHT BY MOVE TUTORS FOR SHARDS

Name	Type	Kind	Pow.	Acc.	PP	Range	Long	DA
Dark Pulse	Dark	Special	80	100	15	Normal	○	
Snore	Normal	Special	40	100	15	Normal	—	
Heat Wave	Fire	Special	100	90	10	Many Others	—	
Pain Split	Normal	Status	—	—	20	Normal	—	
Spite	Ghost	Status	—	100	10	Normal	—	
Trick	Psychic	Status	—	100	10	Normal	—	
Sleep Talk	Normal	Status	—	—	10	Self	—	

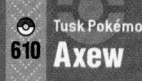

610 Axew
Tusk Pokémon

- HEIGHT: 2'00"
- WEIGHT: 39.7 lbs.
- GENDER: ♂ / ♀

Its large tusks have a tendency to break, but each time they grow back, they grow in harder and sturdier.

Same form for ♂ / ♀

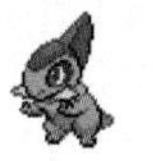

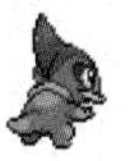

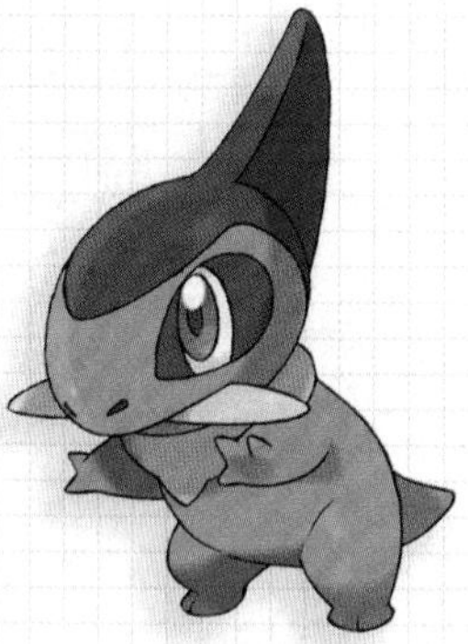

Pokémon AR Marker

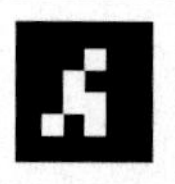

TYPE Dragon

ABILITIES
- Rivalry
- Mold Breaker

HIDDEN ABILITY
- Unnerve

STATS
HP
Attack
Defense
Sp. Atk
Sp. Def
Speed

EGG GROUPS
Monster/Dragon

ITEMS SOMETIMES HELD
- None

EVOLUTION

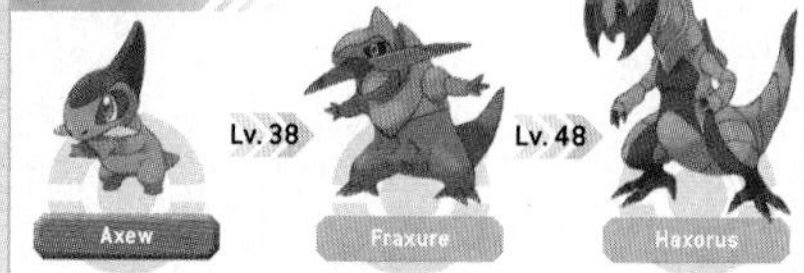

HOW TO OBTAIN

Pokémon Black Version 2: ❶ Mistralton Cave 1F ❷ Mistralton Cave 2F

Pokémon White Version 2: ❶ Mistralton Cave 1F ❷ Mistralton Cave 2F

HOW TO OBTAIN FROM OTHER GAMES

—

—

LEVEL-UP AND LEARNED MOVES

Lv.	Name	Type	Kind	Pow.	Acc.	PP	Range	Long	DA
1	Scratch	Normal	Physical	40	100	35	Normal	—	○
4	Leer	Normal	Status	—	100	30	Many Others	—	—
7	Assurance	Dark	Physical	50	100	10	Normal	—	○
10	Dragon Rage	Dragon	Special	—	100	10	Normal	—	—
13	Dual Chop	Dragon	Physical	40	90	15	Normal	—	○
16	Scary Face	Normal	Status	—	100	10	Normal	—	—
20	Slash	Normal	Physical	70	100	20	Normal	—	○
24	False Swipe	Normal	Physical	40	100	40	Normal	—	○
28	Dragon Claw	Dragon	Physical	80	100	15	Normal	—	○
32	Dragon Dance	Dragon	Status	—	—	20	Self	—	—
36	Taunt	Dark	Status	—	100	20	Normal	—	—
41	Dragon Pulse	Dragon	Special	90	100	10	Normal	○	—
46	Swords Dance	Normal	Status	—	—	30	Self	—	—
51	Guillotine	Normal	Physical	—	30	5	Normal	—	○
56	Outrage	Dragon	Physical	120	100	10	1 Random	—	○
61	Giga Impact	Normal	Physical	150	90	5	Normal	—	○

TM & HM MOVES

Lv.	Name	Type	Kind	Pow.	Acc.	PP	Range	Long	DA
TM01	Hone Claws	Dark	Status	—	—	15	Self	—	—
TM02	Dragon Claw	Dragon	Physical	80	100	15	Normal	—	○
TM05	Roar	Normal	Status	—	100	20	Normal	—	—
TM06	Toxic	Poison	Status	—	90	10	Normal	—	—
TM10	Hidden Power	Normal	Special	—	100	15	Normal	—	—
TM11	Sunny Day	Fire	Status	—	—	5	Both Sides	—	—
TM12	Taunt	Dark	Status	—	100	20	Normal	—	—
TM17	Protect	Normal	Status	—	—	10	Self	—	—
TM18	Rain Dance	Water	Status	—	—	5	Both Sides	—	—
TM21	Frustration	Normal	Physical	—	100	20	Normal	—	○
TM27	Return	Normal	Physical	—	100	20	Normal	—	○
TM28	Dig	Ground	Physical	80	100	10	Normal	—	○
TM32	Double Team	Normal	Status	—	—	15	Self	—	—
TM39	Rock Tomb	Rock	Physical	50	80	10	Normal	—	—
TM40	Aerial Ace	Flying	Physical	60	—	20	Normal	○	○
TM42	Facade	Normal	Physical	70	100	20	Normal	—	○
TM44	Rest	Psychic	Status	—	—	10	Self	—	—
TM45	Attract	Normal	Status	—	100	15	Normal	—	—
TM48	Round	Normal	Special	60	100	15	Normal	—	—
TM54	False Swipe	Normal	Physical	40	100	40	Normal	—	○
TM56	Fling	Dark	Physical	—	100	10	Normal	—	—
TM59	Incinerate	Fire	Special	30	100	15	Many Others	—	—
TM66	Payback	Dark	Physical	50	100	10	Normal	—	○
TM68	Giga Impact	Normal	Physical	150	90	5	Normal	—	○
TM75	Swords Dance	Normal	Status	—	—	30	Self	—	—
TM81	X-Scissor	Bug	Physical	80	100	15	Normal	—	○
TM84	Poison Jab	Poison	Physical	80	100	20	Normal	—	○
TM87	Swagger	Normal	Status	—	90	15	Normal	—	—
TM90	Substitute	Normal	Status	—	—	10	Self	—	—
TM94	Rock Smash	Fighting	Physical	40	100	15	Normal	—	○
HM01	Cut	Normal	Physical	50	95	30	Normal	—	○
HM04	Strength	Normal	Physical	80	100	15	Normal	—	○

MOVES TAUGHT BY PEOPLE

Name	Type	Kind	Pow.	Acc.	PP	Range	Long	DA
Draco Meteor	Dragon	Special	140	90	5	Normal	—	—

MOVES TAUGHT BY MOVE TUTORS FOR SHARDS

Name	Type	Kind	Pow.	Acc.	PP	Range	Long	DA
Dual Chop	Dragon	Physical	40	90	15	Normal	—	○
Iron Tail	Steel	Physical	100	75	15	Normal	—	○
Aqua Tail	Water	Physical	90	90	10	Normal	—	○
Superpower	Fighting	Physical	120	100	5	Normal	—	○
Dragon Pulse	Dragon	Special	90	100	10	Normal	○	—
Snore	Normal	Special	40	100	15	Normal	—	—
Outrage	Dragon	Physical	120	100	10	1 Random	—	○
Endeavor	Normal	Physical	—	100	5	Normal	—	○
Sleep Talk	Normal	Status	—	—	10	Self	—	—

EGG MOVES

Name	Type	Kind	Pow.	Acc.	PP	Range	Long	DA
Counter	Fighting	Physical	—	100	20	Varies	—	○
Focus Energy	Normal	Status	—	—	30	Self	—	—
Reversal	Fighting	Physical	—	100	15	Normal	—	○
Endure	Normal	Status	—	—	10	Self	—	—
Razor Wind	Normal	Special	80	100	10	Many Others	—	—
Night Slash	Dark	Physical	70	100	15	Normal	—	○
Endeavor	Normal	Physical	—	100	5	Normal	—	○
Iron Tail	Steel	Physical	100	75	15	Normal	—	○
Dragon Pulse	Dragon	Special	90	100	10	Normal	○	—
Harden	Normal	Status	—	—	30	Self	—	—

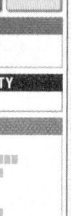

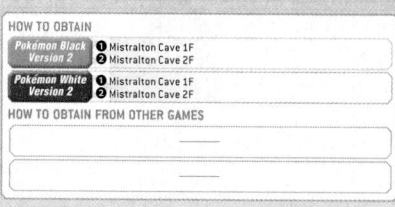

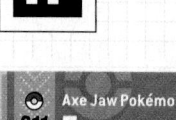

611 Fraxure
Axe Jaw Pokémon

- HEIGHT: 3'03"
- WEIGHT: 79.4 lbs.
- GENDER: ♂ / ♀

A broken tusk will not grow back, so it diligently sharpens its tusks on river rocks after the end of a battle.

Same form for ♂ / ♀

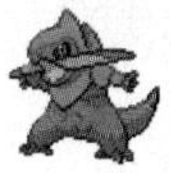

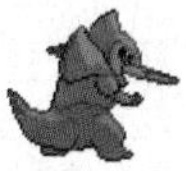

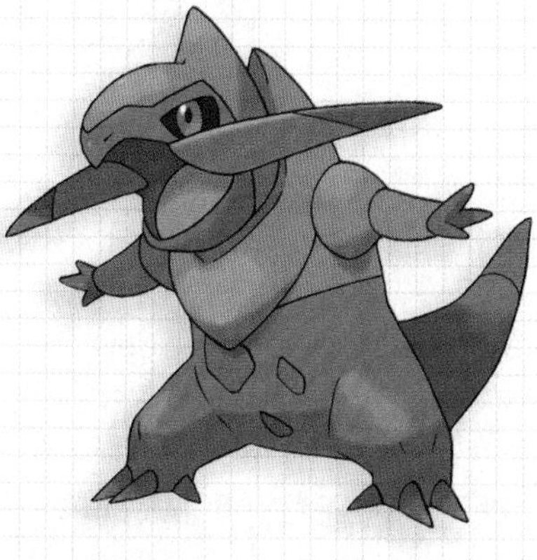

Pokémon AR Marker

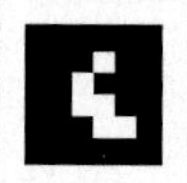

TYPE Dragon

ABILITIES
- Rivalry
- Mold Breaker

HIDDEN ABILITY
- Unnerve

STATS
HP
Attack
Defense
Sp. Atk
Sp. Def
Speed

EGG GROUPS
Monster/Dragon

ITEMS SOMETIMES HELD
- None

EVOLUTION

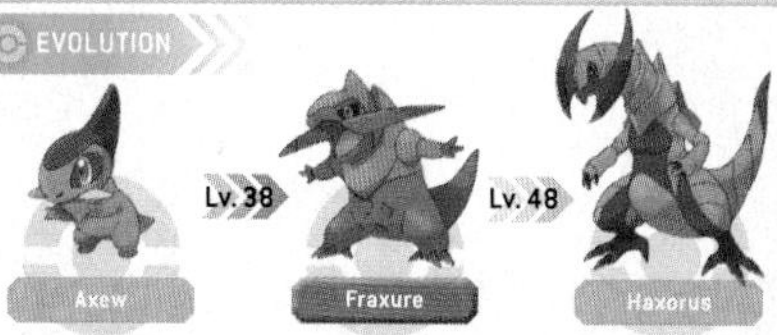

HOW TO OBTAIN

Pokémon Black Version 2: Nature Preserve

Pokémon White Version 2: Nature Preserve

HOW TO OBTAIN FROM OTHER GAMES

—

—

LEVEL-UP AND LEARNED MOVES

Lv.	Name	Type	Kind	Pow.	Acc.	PP	Range	Long	DA
1	Scratch	Normal	Physical	40	100	35	Normal	—	○
1	Leer	Normal	Status	—	100	30	Many Others	—	—
1	Assurance	Dark	Physical	50	100	10	Normal	—	○
1	Dragon Rage	Dragon	Special	—	100	10	Normal	—	—
4	Leer	Normal	Status	—	100	30	Many Others	—	—
7	Assurance	Dark	Physical	50	100	10	Normal	—	○
10	Dragon Rage	Dragon	Special	—	100	10	Normal	—	—
13	Dual Chop	Dragon	Physical	40	90	15	Normal	—	○
16	Scary Face	Normal	Status	—	100	10	Normal	—	—
20	Slash	Normal	Physical	70	100	20	Normal	—	○
24	False Swipe	Normal	Physical	40	100	40	Normal	—	○
28	Dragon Claw	Dragon	Physical	80	100	15	Normal	—	○
32	Dragon Dance	Dragon	Status	—	—	20	Self	—	—
36	Taunt	Dark	Status	—	100	20	Normal	—	—
42	Dragon Pulse	Dragon	Special	90	100	10	Normal	○	—
48	Swords Dance	Normal	Status	—	—	30	Self	—	—
54	Guillotine	Normal	Physical	—	30	5	Normal	—	○
60	Outrage	Dragon	Physical	120	100	10	1 Random	—	○
66	Giga Impact	Normal	Physical	150	90	5	Normal	—	○

TM & HM MOVES

Lv.	Name	Type	Kind	Pow.	Acc.	PP	Range	Long	DA
TM01	Hone Claws	Dark	Status	—	—	15	Self	—	—
TM02	Dragon Claw	Dragon	Physical	80	100	15	Normal	—	○
TM05	Roar	Normal	Status	—	100	20	Normal	—	—
TM06	Toxic	Poison	Status	—	90	10	Normal	—	—
TM10	Hidden Power	Normal	Special	—	100	15	Normal	—	—
TM11	Sunny Day	Fire	Status	—	—	5	Both Sides	—	—
TM12	Taunt	Dark	Status	—	100	20	Normal	—	—
TM17	Protect	Normal	Status	—	—	10	Self	—	—
TM18	Rain Dance	Water	Status	—	—	5	Both Sides	—	—
TM21	Frustration	Normal	Physical	—	100	20	Normal	—	○
TM27	Return	Normal	Physical	—	100	20	Normal	—	○
TM28	Dig	Ground	Physical	80	100	10	Normal	—	○
TM32	Double Team	Normal	Status	—	—	15	Self	—	—
TM39	Rock Tomb	Rock	Physical	50	80	10	Normal	—	—
TM40	Aerial Ace	Flying	Physical	60	—	20	Normal	○	○
TM42	Facade	Normal	Physical	70	100	20	Normal	—	○
TM44	Rest	Psychic	Status	—	—	10	Self	—	—
TM45	Attract	Normal	Status	—	100	15	Normal	—	—
TM48	Round	Normal	Special	60	100	15	Normal	—	—
TM54	False Swipe	Normal	Physical	40	100	40	Normal	—	○
TM56	Fling	Dark	Physical	—	100	10	Normal	—	—
TM59	Incinerate	Fire	Special	30	100	15	Many Others	—	—
TM65	Shadow Claw	Ghost	Physical	70	100	15	Normal	—	○
TM66	Payback	Dark	Physical	50	100	10	Normal	—	○
TM68	Giga Impact	Normal	Physical	150	90	5	Normal	—	○
TM75	Swords Dance	Normal	Status	—	—	30	Self	—	—
TM81	X-Scissor	Bug	Physical	80	100	15	Normal	—	○
TM82	Dragon Tail	Dragon	Physical	60	90	10	Normal	—	○
TM84	Poison Jab	Poison	Physical	80	100	20	Normal	—	○
TM87	Swagger	Normal	Status	—	90	15	Normal	—	—
TM90	Substitute	Normal	Status	—	—	10	Self	—	—
TM94	Rock Smash	Fighting	Physical	40	100	15	Normal	—	○
HM01	Cut	Normal	Physical	50	95	30	Normal	—	○
HM04	Strength	Normal	Physical	80	100	15	Normal	—	○

MOVES TAUGHT BY PEOPLE

Name	Type	Kind	Pow.	Acc.	PP	Range	Long	DA
Draco Meteor	Dragon	Special	140	90	5	Normal	—	—

MOVES TAUGHT BY MOVE TUTORS FOR SHARDS

Name	Type	Kind	Pow.	Acc.	PP	Range	Long	DA
Dual Chop	Dragon	Physical	40	90	15	Normal	—	○
Low Kick	Fighting	Physical	—	100	20	Normal	—	○
Iron Tail	Steel	Physical	100	75	15	Normal	—	○
Aqua Tail	Water	Physical	90	90	10	Normal	—	○
Superpower	Fighting	Physical	120	100	5	Normal	—	○
Dragon Pulse	Dragon	Special	90	100	10	Normal	○	—
Snore	Normal	Special	40	100	15	Normal	—	—
Outrage	Dragon	Physical	120	100	10	1 Random	—	○
Endeavor	Normal	Physical	—	100	5	Normal	—	○
Sleep Talk	Normal	Status	—	—	10	Self	—	—

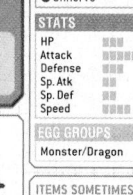

612 Haxorus

Axe Jaw Pokémon

TYPE Dragon

ABILITIES
- Rivalry
- Mold Breaker

HIDDEN ABILITY
- Unnerve

- HEIGHT: 5'11"
- WEIGHT: 232.6 lbs.
- GENDER: ♂ / ♀

Its tusks are incredibly destructive. They can easily slice through a thick, sturdy steel column every time.

Same form for ♂ / ♀

STATS
- HP
- Attack
- Defense
- Sp. Atk
- Sp. Def
- Speed

EGG GROUPS
Monster/Dragon

ITEMS SOMETIMES HELD
- None

EVOLUTION

Axew — Lv. 38 → Fraxure — Lv. 48 → Haxorus

HOW TO OBTAIN

Pokémon Black Version 2	Level up Fraxure to Lv. 48
Pokémon White Version 2	Level up Fraxure to Lv. 48

HOW TO OBTAIN FROM OTHER GAMES

—
—

Pokémon AR Marker

LEVEL-UP AND LEARNED MOVES

Lv.	Name	Type	Kind	Pow.	Acc.	PP	Range	Long	DA
1	Scratch	Normal	Physical	40	100	35	Normal	—	○
1	Leer	Normal	Status	—	100	30	Many Others	—	○
1	Assurance	Dark	Physical	50	100	10	Normal	—	○
1	Dragon Rage	Dragon	Special	—	100	10	Normal	—	—
4	Leer	Normal	Status	—	100	30	Many Others	—	○
10	Dragon Rage	Dragon	Special	—	100	10	Normal	—	—
7	Assurance	Dark	Physical	50	100	10	Normal	—	○
13	Dual Chop	Dragon	Physical	40	90	15	Normal	—	○
16	Scary Face	Normal	Status	—	100	10	Normal	—	○
20	Slash	Normal	Physical	70	100	20	Normal	—	○
24	False Swipe	Normal	Physical	40	100	40	Normal	—	○
28	Dragon Claw	Dragon	Physical	80	100	15	Normal	—	○
32	Dragon Dance	Dragon	Status	—	—	20	Self	—	—
36	Taunt	Dark	Status	—	100	20	Normal	—	—
42	Dragon Pulse	Dragon	Special	90	100	10	Normal	○	—
50	Swords Dance	Normal	Status	—	—	30	Self	—	—
58	Guillotine	Normal	Physical	—	30	5	Normal	—	○
66	Outrage	Dragon	Physical	120	100	10	1 Random	—	○
74	Giga Impact	Normal	Physical	150	90	5	Normal	—	○

TM & HM MOVES

Lv.	Name	Type	Kind	Pow.	Acc.	PP	Range	Long	DA
TM01	Hone Claws	Dark	Status	—	—	15	Self	—	—
TM02	Dragon Claw	Dragon	Physical	80	100	15	Normal	—	○
TM05	Roar	Normal	Status	—	100	20	Normal	—	—
TM06	Toxic	Poison	Status	—	90	10	Normal	—	—
TM10	Hidden Power	Normal	Special	—	100	15	Normal	—	○
TM11	Sunny Day	Fire	Status	—	—	5	Both Sides	—	—
TM12	Taunt	Dark	Status	—	100	20	Normal	—	—
TM15	Hyper Beam	Normal	Special	150	90	5	Normal	—	○
TM17	Protect	Normal	Status	—	—	10	Self	—	—
TM18	Rain Dance	Water	Status	—	—	5	Both Sides	—	—
TM21	Frustration	Normal	Physical	—	100	20	Normal	—	○
TM26	Earthquake	Ground	Physical	100	100	10	Adjacent	—	○
TM27	Return	Normal	Physical	—	100	20	Normal	—	○
TM28	Dig	Ground	Physical	80	100	10	Normal	—	○
TM31	Brick Break	Fighting	Physical	75	100	15	Normal	—	○
TM32	Double Team	Normal	Status	—	—	15	Self	—	—
TM39	Rock Tomb	Rock	Physical	50	80	10	Normal	—	○
TM40	Aerial Ace	Flying	Physical	60	—	20	Normal	○	○
TM42	Facade	Normal	Physical	70	100	20	Normal	—	○
TM44	Rest	Psychic	Status	—	—	10	Self	—	—
TM45	Attract	Normal	Status	—	100	15	Normal	—	—
TM48	Round	Normal	Special	60	100	15	Normal	—	○
TM52	Focus Blast	Fighting	Special	120	70	5	Normal	○	—
TM54	False Swipe	Normal	Physical	40	100	40	Normal	—	○
TM56	Fling	Dark	Physical	—	100	10	Normal	—	○
TM59	Incinerate	Fire	Special	30	100	15	Many Others	—	—
TM65	Shadow Claw	Ghost	Physical	70	100	15	Normal	—	○
TM66	Payback	Dark	Physical	50	100	10	Normal	—	○
TM68	Giga Impact	Normal	Physical	150	90	5	Normal	—	○
TM75	Swords Dance	Normal	Status	—	—	30	Self	—	—
TM78	Bulldoze	Ground	Physical	60	100	20	Adjacent	—	○
TM80	Rock Slide	Rock	Physical	75	90	10	Many Others	—	○
TM81	X-Scissor	Bug	Physical	80	100	15	Normal	—	○
TM82	Dragon Tail	Dragon	Physical	60	90	10	Normal	—	○

Lv.	Name	Type	Kind	Pow.	Acc.	PP	Range	Long	DA
TM84	Poison Jab	Poison	Physical	80	100	20	Normal	—	○
TM86	Grass Knot	Grass	Special	—	100	20	Normal	—	○
TM87	Swagger	Normal	Status	—	90	15	Normal	—	—
TM90	Substitute	Normal	Status	—	—	10	Self	—	—
TM94	Rock Smash	Fighting	Physical	40	100	15	Normal	—	○
HM01	Cut	Normal	Physical	50	95	30	Normal	—	○
HM03	Surf	Water	Special	95	100	15	Adjacent	—	○
HM04	Strength	Normal	Physical	80	100	15	Normal	—	○

MOVES TAUGHT BY PEOPLE

Name	Type	Kind	Pow.	Acc.	PP	Range	Long	DA
Draco Meteor	Dragon	Special	140	90	5	Normal	—	—

MOVES TAUGHT BY MOVE TUTORS FOR SHARDS

Name	Type	Kind	Pow.	Acc.	PP	Range	Long	DA
Dual Chop	Dragon	Physical	40	90	15	Normal	—	○
Low Kick	Fighting	Physical	—	100	20	Normal	—	○
Iron Tail	Steel	Physical	100	75	15	Normal	—	○
Aqua Tail	Water	Physical	90	90	10	Normal	—	○
Superpower	Fighting	Physical	120	100	5	Normal	—	○
Dragon Pulse	Dragon	Special	90	100	10	Normal	○	—
Snore	Normal	Special	40	100	15	Normal	—	—
Outrage	Dragon	Physical	120	100	10	1 Random	—	○
Endeavor	Normal	Physical	—	100	5	Normal	—	○
Sleep Talk	Normal	Status	—	—	10	Self	—	—

---

613 Cubchoo

Chill Pokémon

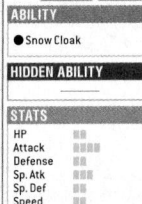

TYPE Ice

ABILITY
- Snow Cloak

HIDDEN ABILITY
- (none listed)

- HEIGHT: 1'08"
- WEIGHT: 18.7 lbs.
- GENDER: ♂ / ♀

Their snot is a barometer of health. When healthy, their snot is sticky and the power of their ice moves increases.

Same form for ♂ / ♀

STATS
- HP
- Attack
- Defense
- Sp. Atk
- Sp. Def
- Speed

EGG GROUPS
Field

ITEMS SOMETIMES HELD
- Aspear Berry

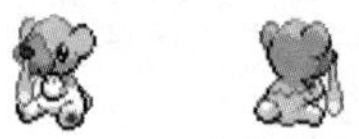

EVOLUTION

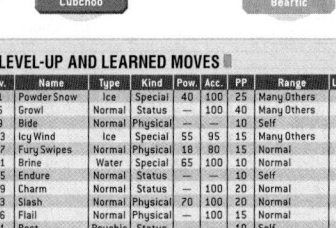

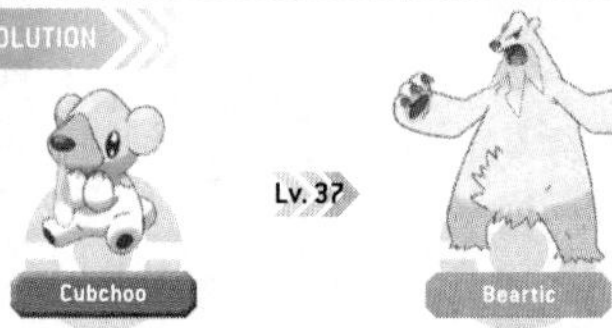

Cubchoo — Lv. 37 → Beartic

HOW TO OBTAIN

Pokémon Black Version 2	❶ Route 7 (winter only) ❷ Route 7 (Hidden Grotto)
Pokémon White Version 2	❶ Route 7 (winter only) ❷ Route 7 (Hidden Grotto)

HOW TO OBTAIN FROM OTHER GAMES

—
—

Pokémon AR Marker

LEVEL-UP AND LEARNED MOVES

Lv.	Name	Type	Kind	Pow.	Acc.	PP	Range	Long	DA
1	Powder Snow	Ice	Special	40	100	25	Many Others	—	—
5	Growl	Normal	Status	—	100	40	Many Others	—	—
9	Bide	Normal	Physical	—	—	10	Self	—	—
13	Icy Wind	Ice	Special	55	95	15	Many Others	—	—
17	Fury Swipes	Normal	Physical	18	80	15	Normal	—	○
21	Brine	Water	Special	65	100	10	Normal	—	—
25	Endure	Normal	Status	—	—	10	Self	—	—
29	Charm	Normal	Status	—	100	20	Normal	—	—
33	Slash	Normal	Physical	70	100	20	Normal	—	○
36	Flail	Normal	Physical	—	100	15	Normal	—	○
41	Rest	Psychic	Status	—	—	10	Self	—	—
45	Blizzard	Ice	Special	120	70	5	Many Others	—	—
49	Hail	Ice	Status	—	—	10	Both Sides	—	—
53	Thrash	Normal	Physical	120	100	10	1 Random	—	○
57	Sheer Cold	Ice	Special	—	30	5	Normal	—	—

TM & HM MOVES

Lv.	Name	Type	Kind	Pow.	Acc.	PP	Range	Long	DA
TM01	Hone Claws	Dark	Status	—	—	15	Self	—	—
TM06	Toxic	Poison	Status	—	90	10	Normal	—	—
TM07	Hail	Ice	Status	—	—	10	Both Sides	—	—
TM10	Hidden Power	Normal	Special	—	100	15	Normal	—	○
TM13	Ice Beam	Ice	Special	95	100	10	Normal	—	—
TM14	Blizzard	Ice	Special	120	70	5	Many Others	—	—
TM17	Protect	Normal	Status	—	—	10	Self	—	—
TM18	Rain Dance	Water	Status	—	—	5	Both Sides	—	—
TM21	Frustration	Normal	Physical	—	100	20	Normal	—	○
TM27	Return	Normal	Physical	—	100	20	Normal	—	○
TM28	Dig	Ground	Physical	80	100	10	Normal	—	○
TM32	Double Team	Normal	Status	—	—	15	Self	—	—
TM39	Rock Tomb	Rock	Physical	50	80	10	Normal	—	○
TM40	Aerial Ace	Flying	Physical	60	—	20	Normal	○	○
TM42	Facade	Normal	Physical	70	100	20	Normal	—	○
TM44	Rest	Psychic	Status	—	—	10	Self	—	—
TM45	Attract	Normal	Status	—	100	15	Normal	—	—
TM48	Round	Normal	Special	60	100	15	Normal	—	○
TM49	Echoed Voice	Normal	Special	40	100	15	Normal	—	—
TM56	Fling	Dark	Physical	—	100	10	Normal	—	○
TM65	Shadow Claw	Ghost	Physical	70	100	15	Normal	—	○
TM79	Frost Breath	Ice	Special	40	90	10	Normal	—	—
TM86	Grass Knot	Grass	Special	—	100	20	Normal	—	○
TM87	Swagger	Normal	Status	—	90	15	Normal	—	—
TM90	Substitute	Normal	Status	—	—	10	Self	—	—
TM94	Rock Smash	Fighting	Physical	40	100	15	Normal	—	○
HM01	Cut	Normal	Physical	50	95	30	Normal	—	○
HM03	Surf	Water	Special	95	100	15	Adjacent	—	○
HM04	Strength	Normal	Physical	80	100	15	Normal	—	○

MOVES TAUGHT BY PEOPLE

Name	Type	Kind	Pow.	Acc.	PP	Range	Long	DA

MOVES TAUGHT BY MOVE TUTORS FOR SHARDS

Name	Type	Kind	Pow.	Acc.	PP	Range	Long	DA
Covet	Normal	Physical	60	100	40	Normal	—	○
Low Kick	Fighting	Physical	—	100	20	Normal	—	○
Ice Punch	Ice	Physical	75	100	15	Normal	—	○
Icy Wind	Ice	Special	55	95	15	Many Others	—	—
Superpower	Fighting	Physical	120	100	5	Normal	—	○
Snore	Normal	Special	40	100	15	Normal	—	—
Sleep Talk	Normal	Status	—	—	10	Self	—	—

EGG MOVES

Name	Type	Kind	Pow.	Acc.	PP	Range	Long	DA
Yawn	Normal	Status	—	—	10	Normal	—	—
Avalanche	Ice	Physical	60	100	10	Normal	—	○
Encore	Normal	Status	—	100	5	Normal	—	—
Ice Punch	Ice	Physical	75	100	15	Normal	—	○
Night Slash	Dark	Physical	70	100	15	Normal	—	○
Assurance	Dark	Physical	50	100	10	Normal	—	○
Sleep Talk	Normal	Status	—	—	10	Self	—	—
Focus Punch	Fighting	Physical	150	100	20	Normal	—	○

614 Freezing Pokémon

Beartic

- HEIGHT: 8'06"
- WEIGHT: 573.2 lbs.
- GENDER: ♂ / ♀

They love the cold seas of the north. They create pathways across the ocean waters by freezing their own breath.

Same form for ♂ / ♀

Pokémon AR Marker

TYPE: Ice

ABILITY
- Snow Cloak

HIDDEN ABILITY
- Swift Swim

STATS
- HP
- Attack
- Defense
- Sp. Atk
- Sp. Def
- Speed

EGG GROUPS
Field

ITEMS SOMETIMES HELD
- Aspear Berry

EVOLUTION

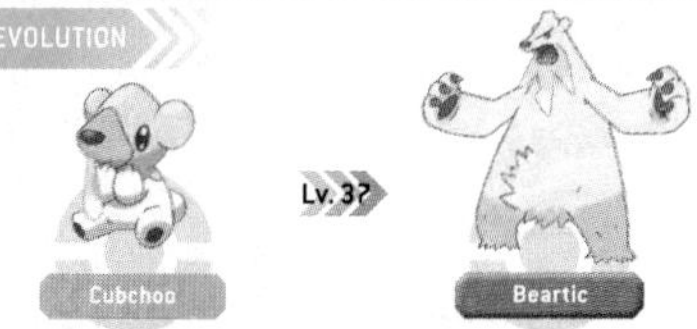

HOW TO OBTAIN
- Pokémon Black Version 2: ❶ Twist Mountain ❷ Dragonspiral Tower entrance (winter only)
- Pokémon White Version 2: ❶ Twist Mountain ❷ Dragonspiral Tower entrance (winter only)

HOW TO OBTAIN FROM OTHER GAMES
- —
- —

LEVEL-UP AND LEARNED MOVES

Lv.	Name	Type	Kind	Pow.	Acc.	PP	Range	Long	DA
1	Superpower	Fighting	Physical	120	100	5	Normal	—	○
1	Aqua Jet	Water	Physical	40	100	20	Normal	—	○
1	Powder Snow	Ice	Special	40	100	25	Many Others	—	—
1	Growl	Normal	Status	—	100	40	Many Others	—	—
1	Bide	Normal	Physical	—	—	10	Self	—	○
1	Icy Wind	Ice	Special	55	95	15	Many Others	—	—
5	Growl	Normal	Status	—	100	40	Many Others	—	—
9	Bide	Normal	Physical	—	—	10	Self	—	○
13	Icy Wind	Ice	Special	55	95	15	Many Others	—	—
17	Fury Swipes	Normal	Physical	18	80	15	Normal	—	○
21	Brine	Water	Special	65	100	10	Normal	—	—
25	Endure	Normal	Status	—	—	10	Self	—	—
29	Swagger	Normal	Status	—	90	15	Normal	—	—
33	Slash	Normal	Physical	70	100	20	Normal	—	○
36	Flail	Normal	Physical	—	100	15	Normal	—	○
37	Icicle Crash	Ice	Physical	85	90	10	Normal	—	—
41	Rest	Psychic	Status	—	—	10	Self	—	—
45	Blizzard	Ice	Special	120	70	5	Many Others	—	—
53	Hail	Ice	Status	—	—	10	Both Sides	—	—
59	Thrash	Normal	Physical	120	100	10	1 Random	—	○
66	Sheer Cold	Ice	Special	—	30	5	Normal	—	—

TM & HM MOVES

Lv.	Name	Type	Kind	Pow.	Acc.	PP	Range	Long	DA
TM01	Hone Claws	Dark	Status	—	—	15	Self	—	—
TM05	Roar	Normal	Status	—	100	20	Normal	—	—
TM06	Toxic	Poison	Status	—	90	10	Normal	—	—
TM07	Hail	Ice	Status	—	—	10	Both Sides	—	—
TM08	Bulk Up	Fighting	Status	—	—	20	Self	—	—
TM10	Hidden Power	Normal	Special	—	100	15	Normal	—	—
TM12	Taunt	Dark	Status	—	100	20	Normal	—	—
TM13	Ice Beam	Ice	Special	95	100	10	Normal	—	—
TM14	Blizzard	Ice	Special	120	70	5	Many Others	—	—
TM15	Hyper Beam	Normal	Special	150	90	5	Normal	—	—
TM17	Protect	Normal	Status	—	—	10	Self	—	—
TM18	Rain Dance	Water	Status	—	—	5	Both Sides	—	—
TM21	Frustration	Normal	Physical	—	100	20	Normal	—	○
TM27	Return	Normal	Physical	—	100	20	Normal	—	○
TM28	Dig	Ground	Physical	80	100	10	Normal	—	○
TM31	Brick Break	Fighting	Physical	75	100	15	Normal	—	○
TM32	Double Team	Normal	Status	—	—	15	Self	—	—
TM39	Rock Tomb	Rock	Physical	50	80	10	Normal	—	—
TM40	Aerial Ace	Flying	Physical	60	—	20	Normal	○	○
TM42	Facade	Normal	Physical	70	100	20	Normal	—	○
TM44	Rest	Psychic	Status	—	—	10	Self	—	—
TM45	Attract	Normal	Status	—	100	15	Normal	—	—
TM48	Round	Normal	Special	60	100	15	Normal	—	—
TM49	Echoed Voice	Normal	Special	40	100	15	Normal	—	—
TM52	Focus Blast	Fighting	Special	120	70	5	Normal	—	—
TM56	Fling	Dark	Physical	—	100	10	Normal	—	—
TM65	Shadow Claw	Ghost	Physical	70	100	15	Normal	—	○
TM68	Giga Impact	Normal	Physical	150	90	5	Normal	—	○
TM71	Stone Edge	Rock	Physical	100	80	5	Normal	—	—
TM75	Swords Dance	Normal	Status	—	—	30	Self	—	—
TM78	Bulldoze	Ground	Physical	60	100	20	Adjacent	—	—
TM79	Frost Breath	Ice	Special	40	90	10	Normal	—	—
TM80	Rock Slide	Rock	Physical	75	90	10	Many Others	—	—
TM86	Grass Knot	Grass	Special	—	100	20	Normal	—	○
TM87	Swagger	Normal	Status	—	90	15	Normal	—	—
TM90	Substitute	Normal	Status	—	—	10	Self	—	—
TM94	Rock Smash	Fighting	Physical	40	100	15	Normal	—	○
HM01	Cut	Normal	Physical	50	95	30	Normal	—	○
HM03	Surf	Water	Special	95	100	15	Adjacent	—	—
HM04	Strength	Normal	Physical	80	100	15	Normal	—	○
HM06	Dive	Water	Physical	80	100	10	Normal	—	○

MOVES TAUGHT BY PEOPLE

Name	Type	Kind	Pow.	Acc.	PP	Range	Long	DA

MOVES TAUGHT BY MOVE TUTORS FOR SHARDS

Name	Type	Kind	Pow.	Acc.	PP	Range	Long	DA
Covet	Normal	Physical	60	100	40	Normal	—	○
Low Kick	Fighting	Physical	—	100	20	Normal	—	○
Ice Punch	Ice	Physical	75	100	15	Normal	—	○
Icy Wind	Ice	Special	55	95	15	Many Others	—	—
Superpower	Fighting	Physical	120	100	5	Normal	—	○
Snore	Normal	Special	40	100	15	Normal	—	—
Sleep Talk	Normal	Status	—	—	10	Self	—	—

615 Crystallizing Pokémon

Cryogonal

- HEIGHT: 3'07"
- WEIGHT: 326.3 lbs.
- GENDER: ♂ / ♀

They are composed of ice crystals. They capture prey with chains of ice, freezing the prey at -148°F.

Same form for ♂ / ♀

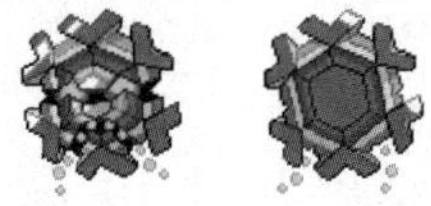

Pokémon AR Marker

TYPE: Ice

ABILITY
- Levitate

HIDDEN ABILITY
—

STATS
- HP
- Attack
- Defense
- Sp. Atk
- Sp. Def
- Speed

EGG GROUPS
Mineral

ITEMS SOMETIMES HELD
- NeverMeltIce

EVOLUTION

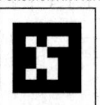

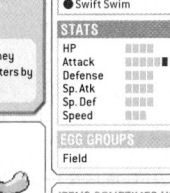

Does not evolve

HOW TO OBTAIN
- Pokémon Black Version 2: Twist Mountain
- Pokémon White Version 2: Twist Mountain

HOW TO OBTAIN FROM OTHER GAMES
- —
- —

LEVEL-UP AND LEARNED MOVES

Lv.	Name	Type	Kind	Pow.	Acc.	PP	Range	Long	DA
1	Bind	Normal	Physical	15	85	20	Normal	—	○
5	Ice Shard	Ice	Physical	40	100	30	Normal	—	—
9	Sharpen	Normal	Status	—	—	30	Self	—	—
13	Rapid Spin	Normal	Physical	20	100	40	Normal	—	○
17	Icy Wind	Ice	Special	55	95	15	Many Others	—	—
21	Mist	Ice	Status	—	—	30	Your Side	—	—
21	Haze	Ice	Status	—	—	30	Both Sides	—	—
25	Aurora Beam	Ice	Special	65	100	20	Normal	—	—
29	Acid Armor	Poison	Status	—	—	40	Self	—	—
33	Ice Beam	Ice	Special	95	100	10	Normal	—	—
37	Light Screen	Psychic	Status	—	—	30	Your Side	—	—
37	Reflect	Psychic	Status	—	—	20	Your Side	—	—
41	Slash	Normal	Physical	70	100	20	Normal	—	○
45	Confuse Ray	Ghost	Status	—	100	10	Normal	—	—
49	Recover	Normal	Status	—	—	10	Self	—	—
53	SolarBeam	Grass	Special	120	100	10	Normal	—	—
57	Night Slash	Dark	Physical	70	100	15	Normal	—	○
61	Sheer Cold	Ice	Special	—	30	5	Normal	—	—

TM & HM MOVES

Lv.	Name	Type	Kind	Pow.	Acc.	PP	Range	Long	DA
TM06	Toxic	Poison	Status	—	90	10	Normal	—	—
TM07	Hail	Ice	Status	—	—	10	Both Sides	—	—
TM10	Hidden Power	Normal	Special	—	100	15	Normal	—	—
TM13	Ice Beam	Ice	Special	95	100	10	Normal	—	—
TM14	Blizzard	Ice	Special	120	70	5	Many Others	—	—
TM15	Hyper Beam	Normal	Special	150	90	5	Normal	—	—
TM16	Light Screen	Psychic	Status	—	—	30	Your Side	—	—
TM17	Protect	Normal	Status	—	—	10	Self	—	—
TM18	Rain Dance	Water	Status	—	—	5	Both Sides	—	—
TM21	Frustration	Normal	Physical	—	100	20	Normal	—	○
TM22	SolarBeam	Grass	Special	120	100	10	Normal	—	—
TM27	Return	Normal	Physical	—	100	20	Normal	—	○
TM32	Double Team	Normal	Status	—	—	15	Self	—	—
TM33	Reflect	Psychic	Status	—	—	20	Your Side	—	—
TM42	Facade	Normal	Physical	70	100	20	Normal	—	○
TM44	Rest	Psychic	Status	—	—	10	Self	—	—
TM45	Attract	Normal	Status	—	100	15	Normal	—	—
TM48	Round	Normal	Special	60	100	15	Normal	—	—
TM62	Acrobatics	Flying	Physical	55	100	15	Normal	○	○
TM64	Explosion	Normal	Physical	250	100	5	Adjacent	—	—
TM79	Frost Breath	Ice	Special	40	90	10	Normal	—	—
TM84	Poison Jab	Poison	Physical	80	100	20	Normal	—	○
TM87	Swagger	Normal	Status	—	90	15	Normal	—	—
TM90	Substitute	Normal	Status	—	—	10	Self	—	—
TM91	Flash Cannon	Steel	Special	80	100	10	Normal	—	—

MOVES TAUGHT BY PEOPLE

Name	Type	Kind	Pow.	Acc.	PP	Range	Long	DA

MOVES TAUGHT BY MOVE TUTORS FOR SHARDS

Name	Type	Kind	Pow.	Acc.	PP	Range	Long	DA
Signal Beam	Bug	Special	75	100	15	Normal	—	—
Iron Defense	Steel	Status	—	—	15	Self	—	—
Magic Coat	Psychic	Status	—	—	15	Self	—	—
Icy Wind	Ice	Special	55	95	15	Many Others	—	—
Bind	Normal	Physical	15	85	20	Normal	—	○
Snore	Normal	Special	40	100	15	Normal	—	—
Knock Off	Dark	Physical	20	100	20	Normal	—	○
Sleep Talk	Normal	Status	—	—	10	Self	—	—

EGG MOVES

Name	Type	Kind	Pow.	Acc.	PP	Range	Long	DA

Snail Pokémon
616 Shelmet

TYPE: Bug

ABILITIES
● Hydration
● Shell Armor

HIDDEN ABILITY
● Overcoat

● HEIGHT: 1'04"
● WEIGHT: 17.0 lbs.
● GENDER: ♂ / ♀

When it and Karrablast are together, and both receive electrical stimulation, they both evolve.

STATS
HP
Attack
Defense
Sp. Atk
Sp. Def
Speed

EGG GROUPS
Bug

ITEMS SOMETIMES HELD
● None

Same form for ♂ / ♀

Pokémon AR Marker

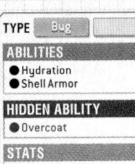

EVOLUTION

Shelmet — Link Trade Karrablast and Shelmet — Accelgor

HOW TO OBTAIN

| Pokémon Black Version 2 | ❶ Route 6 ❷ Route 11 |
| Pokémon White Version 2 | ❶ Route 6 ❷ Route 11 |

HOW TO OBTAIN FROM OTHER GAMES

LEVEL-UP AND LEARNED MOVES

Lv.	Name	Type	Kind	Pow.	Acc.	PP	Range	Long	DA
1	Leech Life	Bug	Physical	20	100	15	Normal	—	○
4	Acid	Poison	Special	40	100	30	Many Others	—	—
8	Bide	Normal	Physical	—	—	10	Self	—	○
13	Curse	Ghost	Status	—	—	10	Varies	—	—
16	Struggle Bug	Bug	Special	30	100	20	Many Others	—	—
20	Mega Drain	Grass	Special	40	100	15	Normal	—	—
25	Yawn	Normal	Status	—	—	10	Normal	—	—
28	Protect	Normal	Status	—	—	10	Self	—	—
32	Acid Armor	Poison	Status	—	—	40	Self	—	—
37	Giga Drain	Grass	Special	75	100	10	Normal	—	—
40	Body Slam	Normal	Physical	85	100	15	Normal	—	○
44	Bug Buzz	Bug	Special	90	100	10	Normal	—	—
49	Recover	Normal	Status	—	—	10	Self	—	—
52	Guard Swap	Psychic	Status	—	—	10	Normal	—	—
56	Final Gambit	Fighting	Special	—	100	5	Normal	—	○

TM & HM MOVES

Lv.	Name	Type	Kind	Pow.	Acc.	PP	Range	Long	DA
TM06	Toxic	Poison	Status	—	90	10	Normal	—	—
TM09	Venoshock	Poison	Special	65	100	10	Normal	—	—
TM10	Hidden Power	Normal	Special	—	100	15	Normal	—	—
TM17	Protect	Normal	Status	—	—	10	Self	—	—
TM18	Rain Dance	Water	Status	—	—	5	Both Sides	—	—
TM21	Frustration	Normal	Physical	—	100	20	Normal	—	○
TM27	Return	Normal	Physical	—	100	20	Normal	—	○
TM32	Double Team	Normal	Status	—	—	15	Self	—	—
TM36	Sludge Bomb	Poison	Special	90	100	10	Normal	—	—
TM42	Facade	Normal	Physical	70	100	20	Normal	—	○
TM44	Rest	Psychic	Status	—	—	10	Self	—	—
TM45	Attract	Normal	Status	—	100	15	Normal	—	—
TM48	Round	Normal	Special	60	100	15	Normal	—	—
TM53	Energy Ball	Grass	Special	80	100	10	Normal	—	—
TM76	Struggle Bug	Bug	Special	30	100	20	Many Others	—	—
TM87	Swagger	Normal	Status	—	90	15	Normal	—	—
TM90	Substitute	Normal	Status	—	—	10	Self	—	—

MOVES TAUGHT BY PEOPLE

Name	Type	Kind	Pow.	Acc.	PP	Range	Long	DA

MOVES TAUGHT BY MOVE TUTORS FOR SHARDS

Name	Type	Kind	Pow.	Acc.	PP	Range	Long	DA
Bug Bite	Bug	Physical	60	100	20	Normal	—	○
Signal Beam	Bug	Special	75	100	15	Normal	—	—
Snore	Normal	Special	40	100	15	Normal	—	—
Giga Drain	Grass	Special	75	100	10	Normal	—	—
Gastro Acid	Poison	Status	—	100	10	Normal	—	—
Sleep Talk	Normal	Status	—	—	10	Self	—	—

EGG MOVES

Name	Type	Kind	Pow.	Acc.	PP	Range	Long	DA
Endure	Normal	Status	—	—	10	Self	—	—
Baton Pass	Normal	Status	—	—	40	Self	—	—
Double-Edge	Normal	Physical	120	100	15	Normal	—	○
Encore	Normal	Status	—	100	5	Normal	—	—
Guard Split	Psychic	Status	—	—	10	Normal	—	—
Mind Reader	Normal	Status	—	—	5	Normal	—	—
Mud-Slap	Ground	Special	20	100	10	Normal	—	—
Spikes	Ground	Status	—	—	20	Other Side	—	—
Feint	Normal	Physical	30	100	10	Normal	—	—
Pursuit	Dark	Physical	40	100	20	Normal	—	○

Shell Out Pokémon
617 Accelgor

TYPE: Bug

ABILITIES
● Hydration
● Sticky Hold

HIDDEN ABILITY
● Unburden

● HEIGHT: 2'07"
● WEIGHT: 55.8 lbs.
● GENDER: ♂ / ♀

When its body dries out, it weakens. So it wraps a membrane around itself for protection while it spits poison.

STATS
HP
Attack
Defense
Sp. Atk
Sp. Def
Speed

EGG GROUPS
Bug

ITEMS SOMETIMES HELD
● None

Same form for ♂ / ♀

Pokémon AR Marker

EVOLUTION

Shelmet — Link Trade Karrablast and Shelmet — Accelgor

HOW TO OBTAIN

| Pokémon Black Version 2 | Send Karrablast in exchange for Shelmet in a Link Trade to receive Accelgor |
| Pokémon White Version 2 | Send Karrablast in exchange for Shelmet in a Link Trade to receive Accelgor |

HOW TO OBTAIN FROM OTHER GAMES

LEVEL-UP AND LEARNED MOVES

Lv.	Name	Type	Kind	Pow.	Acc.	PP	Range	Long	DA
1	Leech Life	Bug	Physical	20	100	15	Normal	—	○
1	Acid Spray	Poison	Special	40	100	20	Normal	—	—
1	Double Team	Normal	Status	—	—	15	Self	—	—
1	Quick Attack	Normal	Physical	40	100	30	Normal	—	—
4	Acid Spray	Poison	Special	40	100	20	Normal	—	—
8	Double Team	Normal	Status	—	—	15	Self	—	—
13	Quick Attack	Normal	Physical	40	100	30	Normal	—	—
16	Struggle Bug	Bug	Special	30	100	20	Many Others	—	—
20	Mega Drain	Grass	Special	40	100	15	Normal	—	—
25	Swift	Normal	Special	60	—	20	Many Others	—	—
28	Me First	Normal	Status	—	—	20	Varies	—	—
32	Agility	Psychic	Status	—	—	30	Self	—	—
37	Giga Drain	Grass	Special	75	100	10	Normal	—	—
40	U-turn	Bug	Physical	70	100	20	Normal	—	○
44	Bug Buzz	Bug	Special	90	100	10	Normal	—	—
49	Recover	Normal	Status	—	—	10	Self	—	—
52	Power Swap	Psychic	Status	—	—	10	Normal	—	—
56	Final Gambit	Fighting	Special	—	100	5	Normal	—	○

TM & HM MOVES

Lv.	Name	Type	Kind	Pow.	Acc.	PP	Range	Long	DA
TM06	Toxic	Poison	Status	—	90	10	Normal	—	—
TM09	Venoshock	Poison	Special	65	100	10	Normal	—	—
TM10	Hidden Power	Normal	Special	—	100	15	Normal	—	—
TM15	Hyper Beam	Normal	Special	150	90	5	Normal	—	—
TM17	Protect	Normal	Status	—	—	10	Self	—	—
TM18	Rain Dance	Water	Status	—	—	5	Both Sides	—	—
TM21	Frustration	Normal	Physical	—	100	20	Normal	—	○
TM27	Return	Normal	Physical	—	100	20	Normal	—	○
TM32	Double Team	Normal	Status	—	—	15	Self	—	—
TM36	Sludge Bomb	Poison	Special	90	100	10	Normal	—	—
TM37	Sandstorm	Rock	Status	—	—	10	Both Sides	—	—
TM42	Facade	Normal	Physical	70	100	20	Normal	—	○
TM44	Rest	Psychic	Status	—	—	10	Self	—	—
TM45	Attract	Normal	Status	—	100	15	Normal	—	—
TM48	Round	Normal	Special	60	100	15	Normal	—	—
TM52	Focus Blast	Fighting	Special	120	70	5	Normal	—	—
TM53	Energy Ball	Grass	Special	80	100	10	Normal	—	—
TM68	Giga Impact	Normal	Physical	150	90	5	Normal	—	○
TM76	Struggle Bug	Bug	Special	30	100	20	Many Others	—	—
TM87	Swagger	Normal	Status	—	90	15	Normal	—	—
TM89	U-turn	Bug	Physical	70	100	20	Normal	—	○
TM90	Substitute	Normal	Status	—	—	10	Self	—	—

MOVES TAUGHT BY PEOPLE

Name	Type	Kind	Pow.	Acc.	PP	Range	Long	DA

MOVES TAUGHT BY MOVE TUTORS FOR SHARDS

Name	Type	Kind	Pow.	Acc.	PP	Range	Long	DA
Bug Bite	Bug	Physical	60	100	20	Normal	—	○
Signal Beam	Bug	Special	75	100	15	Normal	—	—
Snore	Normal	Special	40	100	15	Normal	—	—
Knock Off	Dark	Physical	20	100	20	Normal	—	○
Giga Drain	Grass	Special	75	100	10	Normal	—	—
Gastro Acid	Poison	Status	—	100	10	Normal	—	—
Sleep Talk	Normal	Status	—	—	10	Self	—	—

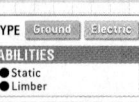

618 Stunfisk
Trap Pokémon

TYPE Ground | Electric

ABILITIES
- Static
- Limber

HIDDEN ABILITY
- Sand Veil

- **HEIGHT:** 2'04"
- **WEIGHT:** 24.3 lbs.
- **GENDER:** ♂ / ♀

When its opponent can't be paralyzed, it contorts itself with unexpected speed and flops away.

STATS
- HP
- Attack
- Defense
- Sp. Atk
- Sp. Def
- Speed

EGG GROUPS
Water ❶/Amorphous

ITEMS SOMETIMES HELD
- Soft Sand

Same form for ♂ / ♀

EVOLUTION

Does not evolve

HOW TO OBTAIN
Pokémon Black Version 2	❶ Route 8 (water surface) ❷ Icirrus City (water surface)
Pokémon White Version 2	❶ Route 8 (water surface) ❷ Icirrus City (water surface)

HOW TO OBTAIN FROM OTHER GAMES

Pokémon AR Marker

LEVEL-UP AND LEARNED MOVES
Lv.	Name	Type	Kind	Pow.	Acc.	PP	Range	Long	DA
1	Mud-Slap	Ground	Special	20	100	10	Normal	—	—
1	Mud Sport	Ground	Status	—	—	15	Both Sides	—	—
5	Bide	Normal	Physical	—	—	10	Self	—	○
9	ThunderShock	Electric	Special	40	100	30	Normal	—	—
13	Mud Shot	Ground	Special	55	95	15	Normal	—	—
17	Camouflage	Normal	Status	—	—	20	Self	—	—
21	Mud Bomb	Ground	Special	65	85	10	Normal	—	—
25	Discharge	Electric	Special	80	100	15	Adjacent	—	—
30	Endure	Normal	Status	—	—	10	Self	—	○
35	Bounce	Flying	Physical	85	85	5	Normal	○	○
40	Muddy Water	Water	Special	95	85	10	Many Others	—	—
45	Thunderbolt	Electric	Special	95	100	15	Normal	—	—
50	Revenge	Fighting	Physical	60	100	10	Normal	—	○
55	Flail	Normal	Physical	—	100	15	Normal	—	○
61	Fissure	Ground	Physical	—	30	5	Normal	—	—

TM & HM MOVES
Lv.	Name	Type	Kind	Pow.	Acc.	PP	Range	Long	DA
TM06	Toxic	Poison	Status	—	90	10	Normal	—	—
TM10	Hidden Power	Normal	Special	—	100	15	Normal	—	—
TM17	Protect	Normal	Status	—	—	10	Self	—	—
TM18	Rain Dance	Water	Status	—	—	5	Both Sides	—	—
TM21	Frustration	Normal	Physical	—	100	20	Normal	—	○
TM24	Thunderbolt	Electric	Special	95	100	15	Normal	—	—
TM25	Thunder	Electric	Special	120	70	10	Normal	—	—
TM26	Earthquake	Ground	Physical	100	100	10	Adjacent	—	—
TM27	Return	Normal	Physical	—	100	20	Normal	—	○
TM28	Dig	Ground	Physical	80	100	10	Normal	—	○
TM32	Double Team	Normal	Status	—	—	15	Self	—	—
TM34	Sludge Wave	Poison	Special	95	100	10	Adjacent	—	—
TM36	Sludge Bomb	Poison	Special	90	100	10	Normal	—	—
TM37	Sandstorm	Rock	Status	—	—	10	Both Sides	—	—
TM39	Rock Tomb	Rock	Physical	50	80	10	Normal	—	—
TM42	Facade	Normal	Physical	70	100	20	Normal	—	○
TM44	Rest	Psychic	Status	—	—	10	Self	—	—
TM45	Attract	Normal	Status	—	100	15	Normal	—	—
TM48	Round	Normal	Special	60	100	15	Normal	—	—
TM55	Scald	Water	Special	80	100	15	Normal	—	—
TM66	Payback	Dark	Physical	50	100	10	Normal	—	—
TM70	Flash	Normal	Status	—	100	20	Normal	—	—
TM71	Stone Edge	Rock	Physical	100	80	5	Normal	—	—
TM73	Thunder Wave	Electric	Status	—	100	20	Normal	—	—
TM78	Bulldoze	Ground	Physical	60	100	20	Adjacent	—	—
TM80	Rock Slide	Rock	Physical	75	90	10	Many Others	—	—
TM87	Swagger	Normal	Status	—	90	15	Normal	—	—
TM90	Substitute	Normal	Status	—	—	10	Self	—	—
HM03	Surf	Water	Special	95	100	15	Adjacent	—	—

MOVES TAUGHT BY PEOPLE
Name	Type	Kind	Pow.	Acc.	PP	Range	Long	DA

MOVES TAUGHT BY MOVE TUTORS FOR SHARDS
Name	Type	Kind	Pow.	Acc.	PP	Range	Long	DA
Bounce	Flying	Physical	85	85	5	Normal	○	○
Uproar	Normal	Special	90	100	10	1 Random	—	—
Magnet Rise	Electric	Status	—	—	10	Self	—	—
Electroweb	Electric	Special	55	95	15	Many Others	—	—
Aqua Tail	Water	Physical	90	90	10	Normal	—	—
Earth Power	Ground	Special	90	100	10	Normal	—	—
Foul Play	Dark	Physical	95	100	15	Normal	—	—
Snore	Normal	Special	40	100	15	Normal	—	—
Pain Split	Normal	Status	—	—	20	Normal	—	—
Spite	Ghost	Status	—	100	10	Normal	—	—
Stealth Rock	Rock	Status	—	—	20	Other Side	—	—
Endeavor	Normal	Physical	—	100	5	Normal	—	—
Sleep Talk	Normal	Status	—	—	10	Self	—	—

EGG MOVES
Name	Type	Kind	Pow.	Acc.	PP	Range	Long	DA
Shock Wave	Electric	Special	60	—	20	Normal	—	—
Earth Power	Ground	Special	90	100	10	Normal	—	—
Yawn	Normal	Status	—	—	10	Normal	—	—
Sleep Talk	Normal	Status	—	—	10	Self	—	—
Astonish	Ghost	Physical	30	100	15	Normal	—	—
Curse	Ghost	Status	—	—	10	Varies	—	—
Spite	Ghost	Status	—	100	10	Normal	—	—
Spark	Electric	Physical	65	100	20	Normal	—	○
Pain Split	Normal	Status	—	—	20	Normal	—	—

---

619 Mienfoo
Martial Arts Pokémon

TYPE Fighting

ABILITIES
- Inner Focus
- Regenerator

HIDDEN ABILITY
- Reckless

- **HEIGHT:** 2'11"
- **WEIGHT:** 44.1 lbs.
- **GENDER:** ♂ / ♀

It takes pride in the speed at which it can use moves. What it loses in power, it makes up for in quantity.

STATS
- HP
- Attack
- Defense
- Sp. Atk
- Sp. Def
- Speed

EGG GROUPS
Field/Human-Like

ITEMS SOMETIMES HELD
- None

Same form for ♂ / ♀

EVOLUTION

 Mienfoo — Lv. 50 →  Mienshao

HOW TO OBTAIN
Pokémon Black Version 2	❶ Route 22 ❷ Route 14
Pokémon White Version 2	❶ Route 22 ❷ Route 14

HOW TO OBTAIN FROM OTHER GAMES

Pokémon AR Marker

LEVEL-UP AND LEARNED MOVES
Lv.	Name	Type	Kind	Pow.	Acc.	PP	Range	Long	DA
1	Pound	Normal	Physical	40	100	35	Normal	—	○
5	Meditate	Psychic	Status	—	—	40	Self	—	—
9	Detect	Fighting	Status	—	—	5	Self	—	—
13	Fake Out	Normal	Physical	40	100	10	Normal	—	○
17	DoubleSlap	Normal	Physical	15	85	10	Normal	—	○
21	Swift	Normal	Special	60	—	20	Many Others	—	—
25	Calm Mind	Psychic	Status	—	—	20	Self	—	—
29	Force Palm	Fighting	Physical	60	100	10	Normal	—	○
33	Drain Punch	Fighting	Physical	75	100	10	Normal	—	○
37	Jump Kick	Fighting	Physical	100	95	10	Normal	—	○
41	U-turn	Bug	Physical	70	100	20	Normal	—	○
45	Quick Guard	Fighting	Status	—	—	15	Your Side	—	—
49	Bounce	Flying	Physical	85	85	5	Normal	○	○
53	Hi Jump Kick	Fighting	Physical	130	90	10	Normal	—	○
57	Reversal	Fighting	Physical	—	100	15	Normal	—	○
61	Aura Sphere	Fighting	Special	90	—	20	Normal	○	—

TM & HM MOVES
Lv.	Name	Type	Kind	Pow.	Acc.	PP	Range	Long	DA
TM04	Calm Mind	Psychic	Status	—	—	20	Self	—	—
TM06	Toxic	Poison	Status	—	90	10	Normal	—	—
TM08	Bulk Up	Fighting	Status	—	—	20	Self	—	—
TM10	Hidden Power	Normal	Special	—	100	15	Normal	—	—
TM11	Sunny Day	Fire	Status	—	—	5	Both Sides	—	—
TM12	Taunt	Dark	Status	—	100	20	Normal	—	—
TM17	Protect	Normal	Status	—	—	10	Self	—	—
TM18	Rain Dance	Water	Status	—	—	5	Both Sides	—	—
TM21	Frustration	Normal	Physical	—	100	20	Normal	—	○
TM27	Return	Normal	Physical	—	100	20	Normal	—	○
TM28	Dig	Ground	Physical	80	100	10	Normal	—	○
TM31	Brick Break	Fighting	Physical	75	100	15	Normal	—	○
TM32	Double Team	Normal	Status	—	—	15	Self	—	—
TM33	Reflect	Psychic	Status	—	—	20	Your Side	—	—
TM39	Rock Tomb	Rock	Physical	50	80	10	Normal	—	—
TM40	Aerial Ace	Flying	Physical	60	—	20	Normal	○	○
TM42	Facade	Normal	Physical	70	100	20	Normal	—	○
TM44	Rest	Psychic	Status	—	—	10	Self	—	—
TM45	Attract	Normal	Status	—	100	15	Normal	—	—
TM47	Low Sweep	Fighting	Physical	60	100	20	Normal	—	○
TM48	Round	Normal	Special	60	100	15	Normal	—	—
TM52	Focus Blast	Fighting	Special	120	70	5	Normal	—	—
TM56	Fling	Dark	Physical	—	100	10	Normal	—	—
TM62	Acrobatics	Flying	Physical	55	100	15	Normal	○	○
TM66	Payback	Dark	Physical	50	100	10	Normal	—	—
TM67	Retaliate	Normal	Physical	70	100	5	Normal	—	—
TM71	Stone Edge	Rock	Physical	100	80	5	Normal	—	—
TM75	Swords Dance	Normal	Status	—	—	30	Self	—	—
TM77	Psych Up	Normal	Status	—	—	10	Self	—	—
TM80	Rock Slide	Rock	Physical	75	90	10	Many Others	—	—
TM83	Work Up	Normal	Status	—	—	30	Self	—	—
TM84	Poison Jab	Poison	Physical	80	100	20	Normal	—	—
TM86	Grass Knot	Grass	Special	—	100	20	Normal	—	—
TM87	Swagger	Normal	Status	—	90	15	Normal	—	—
TM89	U-turn	Bug	Physical	70	100	20	Normal	—	○
TM90	Substitute	Normal	Status	—	—	10	Self	—	—
TM94	Rock Smash	Fighting	Physical	40	100	15	Normal	—	—

LEVEL-UP AND LEARNED MOVES
Lv.	Name	Type	Kind	Pow.	Acc.	PP	Range	Long	DA
HM04	Strength	Normal	Physical	80	100	15	Normal	—	—

MOVES TAUGHT BY PEOPLE
Name	Type	Kind	Pow.	Acc.	PP	Range	Long	DA

MOVES TAUGHT BY MOVE TUTORS FOR SHARDS
Name	Type	Kind	Pow.	Acc.	PP	Range	Long	DA
Bounce	Flying	Physical	85	85	5	Normal	○	○
Dual Chop	Dragon	Physical	40	90	15	Normal	—	○
Low Kick	Fighting	Physical	—	100	20	Normal	—	—
Snore	Normal	Special	40	100	15	Normal	—	—
Knock Off	Dark	Physical	20	100	20	Normal	—	—
Role Play	Psychic	Status	—	—	10	Normal	—	—
Drain Punch	Fighting	Physical	75	100	10	Normal	—	○
Helping Hand	Normal	Status	—	—	20	1 Ally	—	—
Sleep Talk	Normal	Status	—	—	10	Self	—	—

EGG MOVES
Name	Type	Kind	Pow.	Acc.	PP	Range	Long	DA
Endure	Normal	Status	—	—	10	Self	—	○
Vital Throw	Fighting	Physical	70	—	10	Normal	—	○
Baton Pass	Normal	Status	—	—	40	Self	—	—
SmellingSalt	Normal	Physical	60	100	10	Normal	—	—
Low Kick	Fighting	Physical	—	100	20	Normal	—	—
Feint	Normal	Physical	30	100	10	Normal	—	—
Me First	Normal	Status	—	—	20	Varies	—	—
Knock Off	Dark	Physical	20	100	20	Normal	—	—

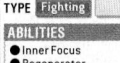

620 Mienshao
Martial Arts Pokémon

TYPE Fighting

ABILITIES
- Inner Focus
- Regenerator

HIDDEN ABILITY
- Reckless

- HEIGHT: 4'07"
- WEIGHT: 78.3 lbs.
- GENDER: ♂ / ♀

STATS
- HP
- Attack
- Defense
- Sp. Atk
- Sp. Def
- Speed

Using the long fur on its arms like whips, it launches into combo attacks that, once started, no one can stop.

Same form for ♂ / ♀

EGG GROUPS
Field/Human-Like

ITEMS SOMETIMES HELD
- None

Pokémon AR Marker

EVOLUTION

 Mienfoo — Lv. 50 →  Mienshao

HOW TO OBTAIN

Pokémon Black Version 2	❶ Route 23 (dark grass)	
	❷ Dragonspiral Tower entrance	
Pokémon White Version 2	❶ Route 23 (dark grass)	
	❷ Dragonspiral Tower entrance	

HOW TO OBTAIN FROM OTHER GAMES

LEVEL-UP AND LEARNED MOVES

Lv.	Name	Type	Kind	Pow.	Acc.	PP	Range	Long	DA
1	Pound	Normal	Physical	40	100	35	Normal	—	○
1	Meditate	Psychic	Status	—	—	40	Self	—	—
1	Detect	Fighting	Status	—	—	5	Self	—	—
1	Fake Out	Normal	Physical	40	100	10	Normal	—	○
5	Meditate	Psychic	Status	—	—	40	Self	—	—
9	Detect	Fighting	Status	—	—	5	Self	—	—
13	Fake Out	Normal	Physical	40	100	10	Normal	—	○
17	DoubleSlap	Normal	Physical	15	85	10	Normal	—	—
21	Swift	Normal	Special	60	—	20	Many Others	—	—
25	Calm Mind	Psychic	Status	—	—	20	Self	—	—
29	Force Palm	Fighting	Physical	60	100	10	Normal	—	○
33	Drain Punch	Fighting	Physical	75	100	10	Normal	—	○
37	Jump Kick	Fighting	Physical	100	95	10	Normal	—	○
41	U-turn	Bug	Physical	70	100	20	Normal	—	○
45	Wide Guard	Rock	Status	—	—	10	Your Side	—	—
49	Bounce	Flying	Physical	85	85	5	Normal	○	○
56	Hi Jump Kick	Fighting	Physical	130	90	10	Normal	—	○
63	Reversal	Fighting	Physical	—	100	15	Normal	—	○
70	Aura Sphere	Fighting	Special	90	—	20	Normal	—	—

TM & HM MOVES

Lv.	Name	Type	Kind	Pow.	Acc.	PP	Range	Long	DA
TM04	Calm Mind	Psychic	Status	—	—	20	Self	—	—
TM06	Toxic	Poison	Status	—	90	10	Normal	—	—
TM08	Bulk Up	Fighting	Status	—	—	20	Self	—	—
TM10	Hidden Power	Normal	Special	—	100	15	Normal	—	—
TM11	Sunny Day	Fire	Status	—	—	5	Both Sides	—	—
TM12	Taunt	Dark	Status	—	100	20	Normal	—	—
TM15	Hyper Beam	Normal	Special	150	90	5	Normal	—	—
TM17	Protect	Normal	Status	—	—	10	Self	—	—
TM18	Rain Dance	Water	Status	—	—	5	Both Sides	—	—
TM21	Frustration	Normal	Physical	—	100	20	Normal	—	○
TM27	Return	Normal	Physical	—	100	20	Normal	—	○
TM28	Dig	Ground	Physical	80	100	10	Normal	—	○
TM31	Brick Break	Fighting	Physical	75	100	15	Normal	—	○
TM32	Double Team	Normal	Status	—	—	15	Self	—	—
TM33	Reflect	Psychic	Status	—	—	20	Your Side	—	—
TM39	Rock Tomb	Rock	Physical	50	80	10	Normal	—	○
TM40	Aerial Ace	Flying	Physical	60	—	20	Normal	—	○
TM42	Facade	Normal	Physical	70	100	20	Normal	—	○
TM44	Rest	Psychic	Status	—	—	10	Self	—	—
TM45	Attract	Normal	Status	—	100	15	Normal	—	—
TM47	Low Sweep	Fighting	Physical	60	100	20	Normal	—	○
TM48	Round	Normal	Special	60	100	15	Normal	—	—
TM52	Focus Blast	Fighting	Special	120	70	5	Normal	—	—
TM56	Fling	Dark	Physical	—	100	10	Normal	—	○
TM62	Acrobatics	Flying	Physical	55	100	15	Normal	—	○
TM66	Payback	Dark	Physical	50	100	10	Normal	—	○
TM67	Retaliate	Normal	Physical	70	100	5	Normal	—	○
TM68	Giga Impact	Normal	Physical	150	90	5	Normal	—	○
TM71	Stone Edge	Rock	Physical	100	80	5	Normal	—	○
TM75	Swords Dance	Normal	Status	—	—	30	Self	—	—
TM77	Psych Up	Normal	Status	—	—	10	Self	—	—
TM80	Rock Slide	Rock	Physical	75	90	10	Many Others	—	○
TM83	Work Up	Normal	Status	—	—	30	Self	—	—
TM84	Poison Jab	Poison	Physical	80	100	20	Normal	—	○

Lv.	Name	Type	Kind	Pow.	Acc.	PP	Range	Long	DA
TM86	Grass Knot	Grass	Special	—	100	20	Normal	—	○
TM87	Swagger	Normal	Status	—	90	15	Normal	—	—
TM89	U-turn	Bug	Physical	70	100	20	Normal	—	○
TM90	Substitute	Normal	Status	—	—	10	Self	—	—
TM94	Rock Smash	Fighting	Physical	40	100	15	Normal	—	○
HM04	Strength	Normal	Physical	80	100	15	Normal	—	○

MOVES TAUGHT BY PEOPLE

Name	Type	Kind	Pow.	Acc.	PP	Range	Long	DA

MOVES TAUGHT BY MOVE TUTORS FOR SHARDS

Name	Type	Kind	Pow.	Acc.	PP	Range	Long	DA
Bounce	Flying	Physical	85	85	5	Normal	○	○
Dual Chop	Dragon	Physical	40	90	15	Normal	—	○
Low Kick	Fighting	Physical	—	100	20	Normal	—	○
Snore	Normal	Special	40	100	15	Normal	—	—
Knock Off	Dark	Physical	20	100	20	Normal	—	○
Role Play	Psychic	Status	—	—	10	Normal	—	—
Drain Punch	Fighting	Physical	75	100	10	Normal	—	○
Helping Hand	Normal	Status	—	—	20	1 Ally	—	—
Sleep Talk	Normal	Status	—	—	10	Self	—	—

621 Druddigon
Cave Pokémon

TYPE Dragon

ABILITIES
- Rough Skin
- Sheer Force

HIDDEN ABILITY
- Mold Breaker

- HEIGHT: 5'03"
- WEIGHT: 306.4 lbs.
- GENDER: ♂ / ♀

STATS
- HP
- Attack
- Defense
- Sp. Atk
- Sp. Def
- Speed

It runs through the narrow tunnels formed by Excadrill and Onix. It uses its sharp claws to catch prey.

Same form for ♂ / ♀

EGG GROUPS
Dragon/Monster

ITEMS SOMETIMES HELD
- Dragon Fang

Pokémon AR Marker

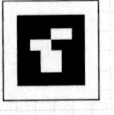

EVOLUTION

Does not evolve

HOW TO OBTAIN

Pokémon Black Version 2	❶ Victory Road 3F in the first part of the cave	
	❷ Dragonspiral Tower 1F	
Pokémon White Version 2	❶ Victory Road 3F in the first part of the cave	
	❷ Dragonspiral Tower 1F	

HOW TO OBTAIN FROM OTHER GAMES

LEVEL-UP AND LEARNED MOVES

Lv.	Name	Type	Kind	Pow.	Acc.	PP	Range	Long	DA
1	Leer	Normal	Status	—	100	30	Many Others	—	—
1	Scratch	Normal	Physical	40	100	35	Normal	—	○
1	Hone Claws	Dark	Status	—	—	15	Self	—	—
9	Bite	Dark	Physical	60	100	25	Normal	—	○
13	Scary Face	Normal	Status	—	100	10	Normal	—	—
18	Dragon Rage	Dragon	Special	—	100	10	Normal	—	—
21	Slash	Normal	Physical	70	100	20	Normal	—	○
25	Crunch	Dark	Physical	80	100	15	Normal	—	○
27	Dragon Claw	Dragon	Physical	80	100	15	Normal	—	○
31	Chip Away	Normal	Physical	70	100	20	Normal	—	○
35	Revenge	Fighting	Physical	60	100	10	Normal	—	○
40	Night Slash	Dark	Physical	70	100	15	Normal	—	○
45	Dragon Tail	Dragon	Physical	60	90	10	Normal	—	○
49	Rock Climb	Normal	Physical	90	85	20	Normal	—	○
55	Superpower	Fighting	Physical	120	100	5	Normal	—	○
62	Outrage	Dragon	Physical	120	100	10	1 Random	—	○

TM & HM MOVES

Lv.	Name	Type	Kind	Pow.	Acc.	PP	Range	Long	DA
TM01	Hone Claws	Dark	Status	—	—	15	Self	—	—
TM02	Dragon Claw	Dragon	Physical	80	100	15	Normal	—	○
TM05	Roar	Normal	Status	—	—	20	Normal	—	—
TM06	Toxic	Poison	Status	—	90	10	Normal	—	—
TM10	Hidden Power	Normal	Special	—	100	15	Normal	—	—
TM11	Sunny Day	Fire	Status	—	—	5	Both Sides	—	—
TM12	Taunt	Dark	Status	—	100	20	Normal	—	—
TM15	Hyper Beam	Normal	Special	150	90	5	Normal	—	—
TM17	Protect	Normal	Status	—	—	10	Self	—	—
TM18	Rain Dance	Water	Status	—	—	5	Both Sides	—	—
TM21	Frustration	Normal	Physical	—	100	20	Normal	—	○
TM23	Smack Down	Rock	Physical	50	100	15	Normal	—	○
TM26	Earthquake	Ground	Physical	100	100	10	Adjacent	—	○
TM27	Return	Normal	Physical	—	100	20	Normal	—	○
TM28	Dig	Ground	Physical	80	100	10	Normal	—	○
TM32	Double Team	Normal	Status	—	—	15	Self	—	—
TM35	Flamethrower	Fire	Special	95	100	15	Normal	—	—
TM36	Sludge Bomb	Poison	Special	90	100	10	Normal	—	—
TM39	Rock Tomb	Rock	Physical	50	80	10	Normal	—	○
TM40	Aerial Ace	Flying	Physical	60	—	20	Normal	—	○
TM41	Torment	Dark	Status	—	100	15	Normal	—	—
TM42	Facade	Normal	Physical	70	100	20	Normal	—	○
TM44	Rest	Psychic	Status	—	—	10	Self	—	—
TM45	Attract	Normal	Status	—	100	15	Normal	—	—
TM48	Round	Normal	Special	60	100	15	Normal	—	—
TM52	Focus Blast	Fighting	Special	120	70	5	Normal	—	—
TM56	Fling	Dark	Physical	—	100	10	Normal	—	○
TM57	Charge Beam	Electric	Special	50	90	10	Normal	—	—
TM59	Incinerate	Fire	Special	30	100	15	Many Others	—	—
TM65	Shadow Claw	Ghost	Physical	70	100	15	Normal	—	○
TM66	Payback	Dark	Physical	50	100	10	Normal	—	○
TM67	Retaliate	Normal	Physical	70	100	5	Normal	—	○
TM68	Giga Impact	Normal	Physical	150	90	5	Normal	—	○
TM78	Bulldoze	Ground	Physical	60	100	20	Adjacent	—	○
TM80	Rock Slide	Rock	Physical	75	90	10	Many Others	—	○
TM82	Dragon Tail	Dragon	Physical	60	90	10	Normal	—	○
TM87	Swagger	Normal	Status	—	90	15	Normal	—	—

Lv.	Name	Type	Kind	Pow.	Acc.	PP	Range	Long	DA
TM90	Substitute	Normal	Status	—	—	10	Self	—	—
TM91	Flash Cannon	Steel	Special	80	100	10	Normal	—	—
TM94	Rock Smash	Fighting	Physical	40	100	15	Normal	—	○
TM95	Snarl	Dark	Special	55	95	15	Many Others	—	—
HM01	Cut	Normal	Physical	50	95	30	Normal	—	○
HM03	Surf	Water	Special	95	100	15	Adjacent	—	—
HM04	Strength	Normal	Physical	80	100	15	Normal	—	○

MOVES TAUGHT BY PEOPLE

Name	Type	Kind	Pow.	Acc.	PP	Range	Long	DA
Draco Meteor	Dragon	Special	140	90	5	Normal	—	—

MOVES TAUGHT BY MOVE TUTORS FOR SHARDS

Name	Type	Kind	Pow.	Acc.	PP	Range	Long	DA
Iron Head	Steel	Physical	80	100	15	Normal	—	○
Gunk Shot	Poison	Physical	120	70	5	Normal	—	○
Fire Punch	Fire	Physical	75	100	15	Normal	—	○
ThunderPunch	Electric	Physical	75	100	15	Normal	—	○
Iron Tail	Steel	Physical	100	75	15	Normal	—	○
Aqua Tail	Water	Physical	90	90	10	Normal	—	○
Superpower	Fighting	Physical	120	100	5	Normal	—	○
Dragon Pulse	Dragon	Special	90	100	10	Normal	—	—
Dark Pulse	Dark	Special	80	100	15	Normal	—	—
Snore	Normal	Special	40	100	15	Normal	—	—
Heat Wave	Fire	Special	100	90	10	Many Others	—	—
Stealth Rock	Rock	Status	—	—	20	Other Side	—	—
Outrage	Dragon	Physical	120	100	10	1 Random	—	○
Sleep Talk	Normal	Status	—	—	10	Self	—	—
Snatch	Dark	Status	—	—	10	Self	—	—

EGG MOVES

Name	Type	Kind	Pow.	Acc.	PP	Range	Long	DA
Fire Fang	Fire	Physical	65	95	15	Normal	—	○
Thunder Fang	Electric	Physical	65	95	15	Normal	—	○
Crush Claw	Normal	Physical	75	95	10	Normal	—	○
Faint Attack	Dark	Physical	60	—	20	Normal	—	○
Pursuit	Dark	Physical	40	100	20	Normal	—	○
Iron Tail	Steel	Physical	100	75	15	Normal	—	○
Poison Tail	Poison	Physical	50	100	25	Normal	—	○
Snatch	Dark	Status	—	—	10	Self	—	—
Metal Claw	Steel	Physical	50	95	35	Normal	—	○
Glare	Normal	Status	—	90	30	Normal	—	—
Sucker Punch	Dark	Physical	80	100	5	Normal	—	○

Automaton Pokémon
622 Golett

- HEIGHT: 3'03"
- WEIGHT: 202.8 lbs.
- GENDER: Unknown

Ancient science fashioned this Pokémon from clay. It's been active for thousands of years.

Gender unknown

Pokémon AR Marker

TYPE Ground Ghost

ABILITIES
- Iron Fist
- Klutz

HIDDEN ABILITY
- No Guard

STATS
- HP
- Attack
- Defense
- Sp. Atk
- Sp. Def
- Speed

EGG GROUPS
Mineral

ITEMS SOMETIMES HELD
- None

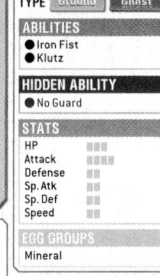

EVOLUTION

Golett — Lv. 43 — Golurk

HOW TO OBTAIN

Pokémon Black Version 2	Catch a Golurk, leave it at the Pokémon Day Care, and hatch the Egg that is found
Pokémon White Version 2	Catch a Golurk, leave it at the Pokémon Day Care, and hatch the Egg that is found

HOW TO OBTAIN FROM OTHER GAMES

Pokémon Black Version	Dragonspiral Tower 1F
Pokémon White Version	Dragonspiral Tower 1F

LEVEL-UP AND LEARNED MOVES

Lv.	Name	Type	Kind	Pow.	Acc.	PP	Range	Long	DA
1	Pound	Normal	Physical	40	100	35	Normal	—	
1	Astonish	Ghost	Physical	30	100	15	Normal	—	○
1	Defense Curl	Normal	Status	—	—	40	Self	—	
5	Mud-Slap	Ground	Special	20	100	10	Normal	—	○
9	Rollout	Rock	Physical	30	90	20	Normal	—	
13	Shadow Punch	Ghost	Physical	60	—	20	Normal	—	○
17	Iron Defense	Steel	Status	—	—	15	Self	—	
21	Mega Punch	Normal	Physical	80	85	20	Normal	—	○
25	Magnitude	Ground	Physical	—	100	30	Adjacent	—	
30	DynamicPunch	Fighting	Physical	100	50	5	Normal	—	○
35	Night Shade	Ghost	Special	—	100	15	Normal	—	
40	Curse	Ghost	Status	—	—	10	Varies	—	
45	Earthquake	Ground	Physical	100	100	10	Adjacent	—	
50	Hammer Arm	Fighting	Physical	100	90	10	Normal	—	○
55	Focus Punch	Fighting	Physical	150	100	20	Normal	—	

TM & HM MOVES

Lv.	Name	Type	Kind	Pow.	Acc.	PP	Range	Long	DA
TM06	Toxic	Poison	Status	—	90	10	Normal	—	
TM10	Hidden Power	Normal	Special	—	100	15	Normal	—	
TM13	Ice Beam	Ice	Special	95	100	10	Normal	—	
TM17	Protect	Normal	Status	—	—	10	Self	—	
TM18	Rain Dance	Water	Status	—	—	5	Both Sides	—	
TM19	Telekinesis	Psychic	Status	—	—	15	Normal	—	
TM20	Safeguard	Normal	Status	—	—	25	Your Side	—	
TM21	Frustration	Normal	Physical	—	100	20	Normal	—	○
TM26	Earthquake	Ground	Physical	100	100	10	Adjacent	—	
TM27	Return	Normal	Physical	—	100	20	Normal	—	○
TM29	Psychic	Psychic	Special	90	100	10	Normal	—	
TM30	Shadow Ball	Ghost	Special	80	100	15	Normal	—	
TM31	Brick Break	Fighting	Physical	75	100	15	Normal	—	
TM32	Double Team	Normal	Status	—	—	15	Self	—	
TM39	Rock Tomb	Rock	Physical	50	80	10	Normal	—	
TM42	Facade	Normal	Physical	70	100	20	Normal	—	○
TM44	Rest	Psychic	Status	—	—	10	Self	—	
TM46	Thief	Dark	Physical	40	100	10	Normal	—	
TM47	Low Sweep	Fighting	Physical	60	100	20	Normal	—	○
TM48	Round	Normal	Special	60	100	15	Normal	—	
TM52	Focus Blast	Fighting	Special	120	70	5	Normal	—	
TM56	Fling	Dark	Physical	—	100	10	Normal	—	○
TM69	Rock Polish	Rock	Status	—	—	20	Self	—	
TM70	Flash	Normal	Status	—	100	20	Normal	—	
TM74	Gyro Ball	Steel	Physical	—	100	5	Normal	—	
TM78	Bulldoze	Ground	Physical	60	100	20	Adjacent	—	
TM80	Rock Slide	Rock	Physical	75	90	10	Many Others	—	
TM86	Grass Knot	Grass	Special	—	100	20	Normal	—	○
TM87	Swagger	Normal	Status	—	90	15	Normal	—	
TM90	Substitute	Normal	Status	—	—	10	Self	—	
TM94	Rock Smash	Fighting	Physical	40	100	15	Normal	—	○
HM04	Strength	Normal	Physical	80	100	15	Normal	—	

MOVES TAUGHT BY PEOPLE

Name	Type	Kind	Pow.	Acc.	PP	Range	Long	DA

MOVES TAUGHT BY MOVE TUTORS FOR SHARDS

Name	Type	Kind	Pow.	Acc.	PP	Range	Long	DA
Signal Beam	Bug	Special	75	100	15	Normal	—	
Low Kick	Fighting	Physical	—	100	20	Normal	—	○
Fire Punch	Fire	Physical	75	100	15	Normal	—	○
ThunderPunch	Electric	Physical	75	100	15	Normal	—	○
Ice Punch	Ice	Physical	75	100	15	Normal	—	○
Iron Defense	Steel	Status	—	—	15	Self	—	
Magic Coat	Psychic	Status	—	—	15	Self	—	
Block	Normal	Status	—	—	5	Normal	—	
Icy Wind	Ice	Special	55	95	15	Many Others	—	
Earth Power	Ground	Special	90	100	10	Normal	—	
Superpower	Fighting	Physical	120	100	5	Normal	—	○
Gravity	Psychic	Status	—	—	5	Both Sides	—	
Snore	Normal	Special	40	100	15	Normal	—	
Drain Punch	Fighting	Physical	75	100	10	Normal	—	○
Stealth Rock	Rock	Status	—	—	20	Other Side	—	
Sleep Talk	Normal	Status	—	—	10	Self	—	

EGG MOVES

Name	Type	Kind	Pow.	Acc.	PP	Range	Long	DA

Automaton Pokémon
623 Golurk

- HEIGHT: 9'02"
- WEIGHT: 727.5 lbs.
- GENDER: Unknown

Golurk were created to protect people and Pokémon. They run on a mysterious energy.

Gender unknown

Pokémon AR Marker

TYPE Ground Ghost

ABILITIES
- Iron Fist
- Klutz

HIDDEN ABILITY
- No Guard

STATS
- HP
- Attack
- Defense
- Sp. Atk
- Sp. Def
- Speed

EGG GROUPS
Mineral

ITEMS SOMETIMES HELD
- Light Clay

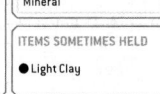

EVOLUTION

Golett — Lv. 43 — Golurk

HOW TO OBTAIN

Pokémon Black Version 2	❶ Victory Road caves 1F ❷ Dragonspiral Tower 1F
Pokémon White Version 2	❶ Victory Road caves 1F ❷ Dragonspiral Tower 1F

HOW TO OBTAIN FROM OTHER GAMES

—
—

LEVEL-UP AND LEARNED MOVES

Lv.	Name	Type	Kind	Pow.	Acc.	PP	Range	Long	DA
1	Pound	Normal	Physical	40	100	35	Normal	—	
1	Astonish	Ghost	Physical	30	100	15	Normal	—	○
1	Defense Curl	Normal	Status	—	—	40	Self	—	
1	Mud-Slap	Ground	Special	20	100	10	Normal	—	○
5	Mud-Slap	Ground	Special	20	100	10	Normal	—	○
9	Rollout	Rock	Physical	30	90	20	Normal	—	
13	Shadow Punch	Ghost	Physical	60	—	20	Normal	—	○
17	Iron Defense	Steel	Status	—	—	15	Self	—	
21	Mega Punch	Normal	Physical	80	85	20	Normal	—	○
25	Magnitude	Ground	Physical	—	100	30	Adjacent	—	
30	DynamicPunch	Fighting	Physical	100	50	5	Normal	—	○
35	Night Shade	Ghost	Special	—	100	15	Normal	—	
40	Curse	Ghost	Status	—	—	10	Varies	—	
43	Heavy Slam	Steel	Physical	—	100	10	Normal	—	
45	Earthquake	Ground	Physical	100	100	10	Adjacent	—	
50	Hammer Arm	Fighting	Physical	100	90	10	Normal	—	○
60	Earthquake	Ground	Physical	100	100	10	Adjacent	—	
70	Focus Punch	Fighting	Physical	150	100	20	Normal	—	

TM & HM MOVES

Lv.	Name	Type	Kind	Pow.	Acc.	PP	Range	Long	DA
TM06	Toxic	Poison	Status	—	90	10	Normal	—	
TM10	Hidden Power	Normal	Special	—	100	15	Normal	—	
TM13	Ice Beam	Ice	Special	95	100	10	Normal	—	
TM15	Hyper Beam	Normal	Special	150	90	5	Normal	—	
TM17	Protect	Normal	Status	—	—	10	Self	—	
TM18	Rain Dance	Water	Status	—	—	5	Both Sides	—	
TM19	Telekinesis	Psychic	Status	—	—	15	Normal	—	
TM20	Safeguard	Normal	Status	—	—	25	Your Side	—	
TM21	Frustration	Normal	Physical	—	100	20	Normal	—	○
TM22	SolarBeam	Grass	Special	120	100	10	Normal	—	
TM24	Thunderbolt	Electric	Special	95	100	15	Normal	—	
TM26	Earthquake	Ground	Physical	100	100	10	Adjacent	—	
TM27	Return	Normal	Physical	—	100	20	Normal	—	○
TM29	Psychic	Psychic	Special	90	100	10	Normal	—	
TM30	Shadow Ball	Ghost	Special	80	100	15	Normal	—	
TM31	Brick Break	Fighting	Physical	75	100	15	Normal	—	
TM32	Double Team	Normal	Status	—	—	15	Self	—	
TM39	Rock Tomb	Rock	Physical	50	80	10	Normal	—	
TM42	Facade	Normal	Physical	70	100	20	Normal	—	○
TM44	Rest	Psychic	Status	—	—	10	Self	—	
TM46	Thief	Dark	Physical	40	100	10	Normal	—	
TM47	Low Sweep	Fighting	Physical	60	100	20	Normal	—	○
TM48	Round	Normal	Special	60	100	15	Normal	—	
TM52	Focus Blast	Fighting	Special	120	70	5	Normal	—	
TM56	Fling	Dark	Physical	—	100	10	Normal	—	○
TM57	Charge Beam	Electric	Special	50	90	10	Normal	—	
TM68	Giga Impact	Normal	Physical	150	90	5	Normal	—	
TM69	Rock Polish	Rock	Status	—	—	20	Self	—	
TM70	Flash	Normal	Status	—	100	20	Normal	—	
TM71	Stone Edge	Rock	Physical	100	80	5	Normal	—	
TM74	Gyro Ball	Steel	Physical	—	100	5	Normal	—	
TM78	Bulldoze	Ground	Physical	60	100	20	Adjacent	—	
TM80	Rock Slide	Rock	Physical	75	90	10	Many Others	—	
TM86	Grass Knot	Grass	Special	—	100	20	Normal	—	○
TM87	Swagger	Normal	Status	—	90	15	Normal	—	
TM90	Substitute	Normal	Status	—	—	10	Self	—	

Lv.	Name	Type	Kind	Pow.	Acc.	PP	Range	Long	DA
TM91	Flash Cannon	Steel	Special	80	100	10	Normal	—	
TM94	Rock Smash	Fighting	Physical	40	100	15	Normal	—	○
HM02	Fly	Flying	Physical	90	95	15	Normal	—	○
HM04	Strength	Normal	Physical	80	100	15	Normal	—	○

MOVES TAUGHT BY PEOPLE

Name	Type	Kind	Pow.	Acc.	PP	Range	Long	DA

MOVES TAUGHT BY MOVE TUTORS FOR SHARDS

Name	Type	Kind	Pow.	Acc.	PP	Range	Long	DA
Signal Beam	Bug	Special	75	100	15	Normal	—	
Low Kick	Fighting	Physical	—	100	20	Normal	—	○
Fire Punch	Fire	Physical	75	100	15	Normal	—	○
ThunderPunch	Electric	Physical	75	100	15	Normal	—	○
Ice Punch	Ice	Physical	75	100	15	Normal	—	○
Iron Defense	Steel	Status	—	—	15	Self	—	
Magic Coat	Psychic	Status	—	—	15	Self	—	
Block	Normal	Status	—	—	5	Normal	—	
Icy Wind	Ice	Special	55	95	15	Many Others	—	
Earth Power	Ground	Special	90	100	10	Normal	—	
Zen Headbutt	Psychic	Physical	80	90	15	Normal	—	○
Superpower	Fighting	Physical	120	100	5	Normal	—	○
Gravity	Psychic	Status	—	—	5	Both Sides	—	
Snore	Normal	Special	40	100	15	Normal	—	
Drain Punch	Fighting	Physical	75	100	10	Normal	—	○
Stealth Rock	Rock	Status	—	—	20	Other Side	—	
Sleep Talk	Normal	Status	—	—	10	Self	—	

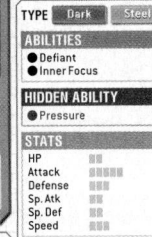

624 Pawniard

Sharp Blade Pokémon

- HEIGHT: 1'08"
- WEIGHT: 22.5 lbs.
- GENDER: ♂ / ♀

Ignoring their injuries, groups attack by sinking the blades that cover their bodies into their prey.

Same form for ♂ / ♀

TYPE: Dark / Steel

ABILITIES
- Defiant
- Inner Focus

HIDDEN ABILITY
- Pressure

STATS
HP
Attack
Defense
Sp. Atk
Sp. Def
Speed

EGG GROUPS
Human-Like

ITEMS SOMETIMES HELD
- None

EVOLUTION

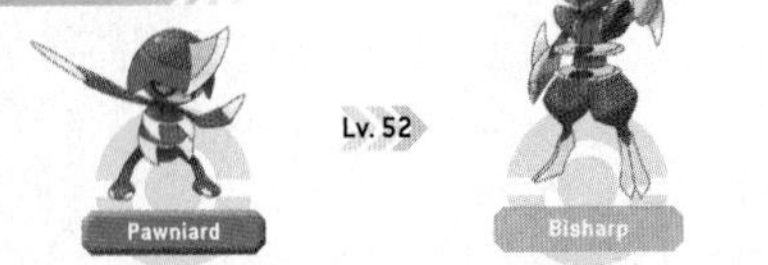

HOW TO OBTAIN

Pokémon Black Version 2	Route 9
Pokémon White Version 2	Route 9

HOW TO OBTAIN FROM OTHER GAMES

	—
	—

Pokémon AR Marker

LEVEL-UP AND LEARNED MOVES

Lv.	Name	Type	Kind	Pow.	Acc.	PP	Range	Long	DA
1	Scratch	Normal	Physical	40	100	35	Normal	—	○
6	Leer	Normal	Status	—	100	30	Many Others	—	—
9	Fury Cutter	Bug	Physical	20	95	20	Normal	—	○
14	Torment	Dark	Status	—	100	15	Normal	—	—
17	Faint Attack	Dark	Physical	60	—	20	Normal	—	○
22	Scary Face	Normal	Status	—	100	10	Normal	—	—
25	Metal Claw	Steel	Physical	50	95	35	Normal	—	○
30	Slash	Normal	Physical	70	100	20	Normal	—	○
33	Assurance	Dark	Physical	50	100	10	Normal	—	○
38	Metal Sound	Steel	Status	—	85	40	Normal	—	—
41	Embargo	Dark	Status	—	100	15	Normal	—	—
46	Iron Defense	Steel	Status	—	—	15	Self	—	—
49	Night Slash	Dark	Physical	70	100	15	Normal	—	○
54	Iron Head	Steel	Physical	80	100	15	Normal	—	○
57	Swords Dance	Normal	Status	—	—	30	Self	—	—
62	Guillotine	Normal	Physical	—	30	5	Normal	—	○

TM & HM MOVES

Lv.	Name	Type	Kind	Pow.	Acc.	PP	Range	Long	DA
TM01	Hone Claws	Dark	Status	—	—	15	Self	—	—
TM06	Toxic	Poison	Status	—	90	10	Normal	—	—
TM10	Hidden Power	Normal	Special	—	100	15	Normal	—	—
TM12	Taunt	Dark	Status	—	100	20	Normal	—	—
TM17	Protect	Normal	Status	—	—	10	Self	—	—
TM18	Rain Dance	Water	Status	—	—	5	Both Sides	—	—
TM21	Frustration	Normal	Physical	—	100	20	Normal	—	○
TM27	Return	Normal	Physical	—	100	20	Normal	—	○
TM28	Dig	Ground	Physical	80	100	10	Normal	—	○
TM31	Brick Break	Fighting	Physical	75	100	15	Normal	—	○
TM32	Double Team	Normal	Status	—	—	15	Self	—	—
TM37	Sandstorm	Rock	Status	—	—	10	Both Sides	—	—
TM39	Rock Tomb	Rock	Physical	50	80	10	Normal	—	—
TM40	Aerial Ace	Flying	Physical	60	—	20	Normal	○	○
TM41	Torment	Dark	Status	—	100	15	Normal	—	—
TM42	Facade	Normal	Physical	70	100	20	Normal	—	○
TM44	Rest	Psychic	Status	—	—	10	Self	—	—
TM45	Attract	Normal	Status	—	100	15	Normal	—	—
TM46	Thief	Dark	Physical	40	100	10	Normal	—	○
TM47	Low Sweep	Fighting	Physical	60	100	20	Normal	—	○
TM48	Round	Normal	Special	60	100	15	Normal	—	—
TM54	False Swipe	Normal	Physical	40	100	40	Normal	—	○
TM56	Fling	Dark	Physical	—	100	10	Normal	—	—
TM63	Embargo	Dark	Status	—	100	15	Normal	—	—
TM65	Shadow Claw	Ghost	Physical	70	100	15	Normal	—	○
TM66	Payback	Dark	Physical	50	100	10	Normal	—	○
TM67	Retaliate	Normal	Physical	70	100	5	Normal	—	○
TM69	Rock Polish	Rock	Status	—	—	20	Self	—	—
TM73	Thunder Wave	Electric	Status	—	100	20	Normal	—	—
TM75	Swords Dance	Normal	Status	—	—	30	Self	—	—
TM81	X-Scissor	Bug	Physical	80	100	15	Normal	—	○
TM84	Poison Jab	Poison	Physical	80	100	20	Normal	—	○
TM86	Grass Knot	Grass	Special	—	100	20	Normal	—	○
TM87	Swagger	Normal	Status	—	90	15	Normal	—	—
TM90	Substitute	Normal	Status	—	—	10	Self	—	—
TM94	Rock Smash	Fighting	Physical	40	100	15	Normal	—	○
TM95	Snarl	Dark	Special	55	95	15	Many Others	—	—
HM01	Cut	Normal	Physical	50	95	30	Normal	—	○

MOVES TAUGHT BY PEOPLE

Name	Type	Kind	Pow.	Acc.	PP	Range	Long	DA

MOVES TAUGHT BY MOVE TUTORS FOR SHARDS

Name	Type	Kind	Pow.	Acc.	PP	Range	Long	DA
Iron Head	Steel	Physical	80	100	15	Normal	—	○
Dual Chop	Dragon	Physical	40	90	15	Normal	—	○
Low Kick	Fighting	Physical	—	100	20	Normal	—	○
Iron Defense	Steel	Status	—	—	15	Self	—	—
Magnet Rise	Electric	Status	—	—	10	Self	—	—
Foul Play	Dark	Physical	95	100	15	Normal	—	○
Dark Pulse	Dark	Special	80	100	15	Normal	○	—
Snore	Normal	Special	40	100	15	Normal	—	—
Knock Off	Dark	Physical	20	100	20	Normal	—	○
Role Play	Psychic	Status	—	—	10	Normal	—	—
Spite	Ghost	Status	—	100	10	Normal	—	—
Stealth Rock	Rock	Status	—	—	20	Other Side	—	—
Sleep Talk	Normal	Status	—	—	10	Self	—	—
Snatch	Dark	Status	—	—	10	Self	—	—

EGG MOVES

Name	Type	Kind	Pow.	Acc.	PP	Range	Long	DA
Revenge	Fighting	Physical	60	100	10	Normal	—	○
Sucker Punch	Dark	Physical	80	100	5	Normal	—	○
Pursuit	Dark	Physical	40	100	20	Normal	—	○
Headbutt	Normal	Physical	70	100	15	Normal	—	○
Stealth Rock	Rock	Status	—	—	20	Other Side	—	—
Psycho Cut	Psychic	Physical	70	100	20	Normal	—	—
Mean Look	Normal	Status	—	—	5	Normal	—	—

625 Bisharp

Sword Blade Pokémon

- HEIGHT: 5'03"
- WEIGHT: 154.3 lbs.
- GENDER: ♂ / ♀

This pitiless Pokémon commands a group of Pawniard to hound prey into immobility. It then moves in to finish the prey off.

Same form for ♂ / ♀

TYPE: Dark / Steel

ABILITIES
- Defiant
- Inner Focus

HIDDEN ABILITY
- Pressure

STATS
HP
Attack
Defense
Sp. Atk
Sp. Def
Speed

EGG GROUPS
Human-Like

ITEMS SOMETIMES HELD
- None

EVOLUTION

HOW TO OBTAIN

Pokémon Black Version 2	Level up Pawniard to Lv. 52
Pokémon White Version 2	Level up Pawniard to Lv. 52

HOW TO OBTAIN FROM OTHER GAMES

Pokémon Black Version	Route 11 (dark grass)
Pokémon White Version	Route 11 (dark grass)

Pokémon AR Marker

LEVEL-UP AND LEARNED MOVES

Lv.	Name	Type	Kind	Pow.	Acc.	PP	Range	Long	DA
1	Metal Burst	Steel	Physical	—	100	10	Varies	—	—
1	Scratch	Normal	Physical	40	100	35	Normal	—	○
1	Leer	Normal	Status	—	100	30	Many Others	—	—
1	Fury Cutter	Bug	Physical	20	95	20	Normal	—	○
1	Torment	Dark	Status	—	100	15	Normal	—	—
6	Leer	Normal	Status	—	100	30	Many Others	—	—
9	Fury Cutter	Bug	Physical	20	95	20	Normal	—	○
14	Torment	Dark	Status	—	100	15	Normal	—	—
17	Faint Attack	Dark	Physical	60	—	20	Normal	—	○
22	Scary Face	Normal	Status	—	100	10	Normal	—	—
25	Metal Claw	Steel	Physical	50	95	35	Normal	—	○
30	Slash	Normal	Physical	70	100	20	Normal	—	○
33	Assurance	Dark	Physical	50	100	10	Normal	—	○
38	Metal Sound	Steel	Status	—	85	40	Normal	—	—
41	Embargo	Dark	Status	—	100	15	Normal	—	—
46	Iron Defense	Steel	Status	—	—	15	Self	—	—
49	Night Slash	Dark	Physical	70	100	15	Normal	—	○
57	Iron Head	Steel	Physical	80	100	15	Normal	—	○
63	Swords Dance	Normal	Status	—	—	30	Self	—	—
71	Guillotine	Normal	Physical	—	30	5	Normal	—	○

TM & HM MOVES

Lv.	Name	Type	Kind	Pow.	Acc.	PP	Range	Long	DA
TM01	Hone Claws	Dark	Status	—	—	15	Self	—	—
TM06	Toxic	Poison	Status	—	90	10	Normal	—	—
TM10	Hidden Power	Normal	Special	—	100	15	Normal	—	—
TM12	Taunt	Dark	Status	—	100	20	Normal	—	—
TM15	Hyper Beam	Normal	Special	150	90	5	Normal	—	—
TM17	Protect	Normal	Status	—	—	10	Self	—	—
TM18	Rain Dance	Water	Status	—	—	5	Both Sides	—	—
TM21	Frustration	Normal	Physical	—	100	20	Normal	—	○
TM27	Return	Normal	Physical	—	100	20	Normal	—	○
TM28	Dig	Ground	Physical	80	100	10	Normal	—	○
TM31	Brick Break	Fighting	Physical	75	100	15	Normal	—	○
TM32	Double Team	Normal	Status	—	—	15	Self	—	—
TM37	Sandstorm	Rock	Status	—	—	10	Both Sides	—	—
TM39	Rock Tomb	Rock	Physical	50	80	10	Normal	—	—
TM40	Aerial Ace	Flying	Physical	60	—	20	Normal	○	○
TM41	Torment	Dark	Status	—	100	15	Normal	—	—
TM42	Facade	Normal	Physical	70	100	20	Normal	—	○
TM44	Rest	Psychic	Status	—	—	10	Self	—	—
TM45	Attract	Normal	Status	—	100	15	Normal	—	—
TM46	Thief	Dark	Physical	40	100	10	Normal	—	○
TM47	Low Sweep	Fighting	Physical	60	100	20	Normal	—	○
TM48	Round	Normal	Special	60	100	15	Normal	—	—
TM52	Focus Blast	Fighting	Special	120	70	5	Normal	—	—
TM54	False Swipe	Normal	Physical	40	100	40	Normal	—	○
TM56	Fling	Dark	Physical	—	100	10	Normal	—	—
TM63	Embargo	Dark	Status	—	100	15	Normal	—	—
TM65	Shadow Claw	Ghost	Physical	70	100	15	Normal	—	○
TM66	Payback	Dark	Physical	50	100	10	Normal	—	○
TM67	Retaliate	Normal	Physical	70	100	5	Normal	—	○
TM68	Giga Impact	Normal	Physical	150	90	5	Normal	—	○
TM69	Rock Polish	Rock	Status	—	—	20	Self	—	—
TM71	Stone Edge	Rock	Physical	100	80	5	Normal	—	—
TM73	Thunder Wave	Electric	Status	—	100	20	Normal	—	—
TM75	Swords Dance	Normal	Status	—	—	30	Self	—	—
TM81	X-Scissor	Bug	Physical	80	100	15	Normal	—	○
TM84	Poison Jab	Poison	Physical	80	100	20	Normal	—	○
TM86	Grass Knot	Grass	Special	—	100	20	Normal	—	○
TM87	Swagger	Normal	Status	—	90	15	Normal	—	—
TM90	Substitute	Normal	Status	—	—	10	Self	—	—
TM94	Rock Smash	Fighting	Physical	40	100	15	Normal	—	○
TM95	Snarl	Dark	Special	55	95	15	Many Others	—	—
HM01	Cut	Normal	Physical	50	95	30	Normal	—	○

MOVES TAUGHT BY PEOPLE

Name	Type	Kind	Pow.	Acc.	PP	Range	Long	DA

MOVES TAUGHT BY MOVE TUTORS FOR SHARDS

Name	Type	Kind	Pow.	Acc.	PP	Range	Long	DA
Iron Head	Steel	Physical	80	100	15	Normal	—	○
Dual Chop	Dragon	Physical	40	90	15	Normal	—	○
Low Kick	Fighting	Physical	—	100	20	Normal	—	○
Iron Defense	Steel	Status	—	—	15	Self	—	—
Magnet Rise	Electric	Status	—	—	10	Self	—	—
Foul Play	Dark	Physical	95	100	15	Normal	—	○
Dark Pulse	Dark	Special	80	100	15	Normal	○	—
Snore	Normal	Special	40	100	15	Normal	—	—
Knock Off	Dark	Physical	20	100	20	Normal	—	○
Role Play	Psychic	Status	—	—	10	Normal	—	—
Spite	Ghost	Status	—	100	10	Normal	—	—
Stealth Rock	Rock	Status	—	—	20	Other Side	—	—
Sleep Talk	Normal	Status	—	—	10	Self	—	—
Snatch	Dark	Status	—	—	10	Self	—	—

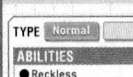

626 Bouffalant
Bash Buffalo Pokémon

TYPE Normal

ABILITIES
- Reckless
- Sap Sipper

HIDDEN ABILITY
- Soundproof

- HEIGHT: 5'03"
- WEIGHT: 208.6 lbs.
- GENDER: ♂ / ♀

They are known to charge so wildly that if a train were to enter their territory, they would send it flying.

STATS
HP / Attack / Defense / Sp. Atk / Sp. Def / Speed

EGG GROUPS
Field

Same form for ♂ / ♀

ITEMS SOMETIMES HELD
- None

Pokémon AR Marker

EVOLUTION
Does not evolve

HOW TO OBTAIN

Pokémon Black Version 2: ❶ Route 23 ❷ Route 9 (Hidden Grotto)
Pokémon White Version 2: ❶ Route 23 ❷ Route 9 (Hidden Grotto)

HOW TO OBTAIN FROM OTHER GAMES

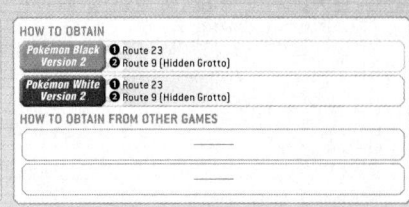

LEVEL-UP AND LEARNED MOVES

Lv.	Name	Type	Kind	Pow.	Acc.	PP	Range	Long	DA
1	Pursuit	Dark	Physical	40	100	20	Normal	—	○
1	Leer	Normal	Status	—	100	30	Many Others	—	○
6	Rage	Normal	Physical	20	100	20	Normal	—	○
11	Fury Attack	Normal	Physical	15	85	20	Normal	—	○
16	Horn Attack	Normal	Physical	65	100	25	Normal	—	○
21	Scary Face	Normal	Status	—	100	10	Normal	—	○
26	Revenge	Fighting	Physical	60	100	10	Normal	—	○
31	Head Charge	Normal	Physical	120	100	15	Normal	—	○
36	Focus Energy	Normal	Status	—	—	30	Self	—	○
41	Megahorn	Bug	Physical	120	85	10	Normal	—	○
46	Reversal	Fighting	Physical	—	100	15	Normal	—	○
51	Thrash	Normal	Physical	120	100	10	1 Random	—	○
56	Swords Dance	Normal	Status	—	—	30	Self	—	○
61	Giga Impact	Normal	Physical	150	90	5	Normal	—	○

TM & HM MOVES

Lv.	Name	Type	Kind	Pow.	Acc.	PP	Range	Long	DA
TM06	Toxic	Poison	Status	—	90	10	Normal	—	—
TM10	Hidden Power	Normal	Special	—	100	15	Normal	—	—
TM11	Sunny Day	Fire	Status	—	—	5	Both Sides	—	—
TM12	Taunt	Dark	Status	—	100	20	Normal	—	—
TM17	Protect	Normal	Status	—	—	10	Self	—	—
TM18	Rain Dance	Water	Status	—	—	5	Both Sides	—	—
TM21	Frustration	Normal	Physical	—	100	20	Normal	—	—
TM26	Earthquake	Ground	Physical	100	100	10	Adjacent	—	—
TM27	Return	Normal	Physical	—	100	20	Normal	—	—
TM32	Double Team	Normal	Status	—	—	15	Self	—	—
TM39	Rock Tomb	Rock	Physical	50	80	10	Normal	○	○
TM40	Aerial Ace	Flying	Physical	60	—	20	Normal	○	○
TM42	Facade	Normal	Physical	70	100	20	Normal	—	○
TM44	Rest	Psychic	Status	—	—	10	Self	—	—
TM45	Attract	Normal	Status	—	100	15	Normal	—	—
TM48	Round	Normal	Special	60	100	15	Normal	—	—
TM66	Payback	Dark	Physical	50	100	10	Normal	—	—
TM67	Retaliate	Normal	Physical	70	100	5	Normal	—	—
TM68	Giga Impact	Normal	Physical	150	90	5	Normal	—	—
TM71	Stone Edge	Rock	Physical	100	80	5	Normal	—	—
TM75	Swords Dance	Normal	Status	—	—	30	Self	—	—
TM78	Bulldoze	Ground	Physical	60	100	20	Adjacent	—	—
TM80	Rock Slide	Rock	Physical	75	90	10	Many Others	—	—
TM83	Work Up	Normal	Status	—	—	30	Self	—	—
TM84	Poison Jab	Poison	Physical	80	100	20	Normal	—	○
TM87	Swagger	Normal	Status	—	90	15	Normal	—	—
TM90	Substitute	Normal	Status	—	—	10	Self	—	—
TM93	Wild Charge	Electric	Physical	90	100	15	Normal	—	○
TM94	Rock Smash	Fighting	Physical	40	100	15	Normal	—	○
HM01	Cut	Normal	Physical	50	95	30	Normal	—	○
HM03	Surf	Water	Special	95	100	15	Adjacent	—	○
HM04	Strength	Normal	Physical	80	100	15	Normal	—	○

MOVES TAUGHT BY PEOPLE

Name	Type	Kind	Pow.	Acc.	PP	Range	Long	DA

MOVES TAUGHT BY MOVE TUTORS FOR SHARDS

Name	Type	Kind	Pow.	Acc.	PP	Range	Long	DA
Iron Head	Steel	Physical	80	100	15	Normal	—	○
Uproar	Normal	Special	90	100	10	1 Random	—	○
Zen Headbutt	Psychic	Physical	80	90	15	Normal	—	○
Superpower	Fighting	Physical	120	100	5	Normal	—	○
Snore	Normal	Special	40	100	15	Normal	—	○
Outrage	Dragon	Physical	120	100	10	1 Random	—	○
Endeavor	Normal	Physical	—	100	5	Normal	—	○
Sleep Talk	Normal	Status	—	—	10	Self	—	—

EGG MOVES

Name	Type	Kind	Pow.	Acc.	PP	Range	Long	DA
Stomp	Normal	Physical	65	100	20	Normal	—	○
Rock Climb	Normal	Physical	90	85	20	Normal	—	○
Headbutt	Normal	Physical	70	100	15	Normal	—	○
Skull Bash	Normal	Physical	100	100	15	Normal	—	○
Mud Shot	Ground	Special	55	95	15	Normal	○	○
Mud-Slap	Ground	Special	20	100	10	Normal	○	○
Iron Head	Steel	Physical	80	100	15	Normal	—	○
Amnesia	Psychic	Status	—	—	20	Self	—	—

---

627 Rufflet
Eaglet Pokémon

TYPE Normal Flying

ABILITIES
- Keen Eye
- Sheer Force

HIDDEN ABILITY

- HEIGHT: 1'08"
- WEIGHT: 23.1 lbs.
- GENDER: ♂

It stands up to massive opponents, not out of courage, but out of recklessness. But that is how it gets stronger.

STATS
HP / Attack / Defense / Sp. Atk / Sp. Def / Speed

EGG GROUPS
Flying

ITEMS SOMETIMES HELD
- None

Pokémon AR Marker

EVOLUTION

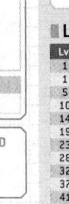

Rufflet → Lv. 54 → Braviary

HOW TO OBTAIN

Pokémon Black Version 2: Link Trade
Pokémon White Version 2: Route 23

HOW TO OBTAIN FROM OTHER GAMES
Pokémon White Version: Route 10

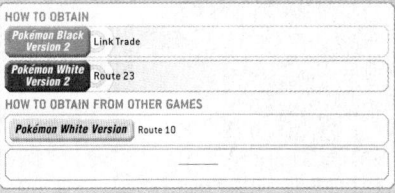

LEVEL-UP AND LEARNED MOVES

Lv.	Name	Type	Kind	Pow.	Acc.	PP	Range	Long	DA
1	Peck	Flying	Physical	35	100	35	Normal	○	○
1	Leer	Normal	Status	—	100	30	Many Others	—	○
5	Fury Attack	Normal	Physical	15	85	20	Normal	—	○
10	Wing Attack	Flying	Physical	60	100	35	Normal	○	○
14	Hone Claws	Dark	Status	—	—	15	Self	—	—
19	Scary Face	Normal	Status	—	100	10	Normal	—	○
23	Aerial Ace	Flying	Physical	60	—	20	Normal	○	○
28	Slash	Normal	Physical	70	100	20	Normal	—	○
32	Defog	Flying	Status	—	—	15	Normal	—	○
37	Tailwind	Flying	Status	—	—	15	Your Side	—	○
41	Air Slash	Flying	Special	75	95	15	Normal	○	○
46	Crush Claw	Normal	Physical	75	95	10	Normal	—	○
50	Sky Drop	Flying	Physical	60	100	10	Normal	○	○
55	Whirlwind	Normal	Status	—	100	20	Normal	—	○
59	Brave Bird	Flying	Physical	120	100	15	Normal	○	○
64	Thrash	Normal	Physical	120	100	10	1 Random	—	○

TM & HM MOVES

Lv.	Name	Type	Kind	Pow.	Acc.	PP	Range	Long	DA
TM01	Hone Claws	Dark	Status	—	—	15	Self	—	—
TM06	Toxic	Poison	Status	—	90	10	Normal	—	—
TM08	Bulk Up	Fighting	Status	—	—	20	Self	—	—
TM10	Hidden Power	Normal	Special	—	100	15	Normal	—	—
TM11	Sunny Day	Fire	Status	—	—	5	Both Sides	—	—
TM17	Protect	Normal	Status	—	—	10	Self	—	—
TM18	Rain Dance	Water	Status	—	—	5	Both Sides	—	—
TM21	Frustration	Normal	Physical	—	100	20	Normal	—	—
TM27	Return	Normal	Physical	—	100	20	Normal	—	—
TM32	Double Team	Normal	Status	—	—	15	Self	—	—
TM39	Rock Tomb	Rock	Physical	50	80	10	Normal	○	○
TM40	Aerial Ace	Flying	Physical	60	—	20	Normal	○	○
TM42	Facade	Normal	Physical	70	100	20	Normal	—	○
TM44	Rest	Psychic	Status	—	—	10	Self	—	—
TM45	Attract	Normal	Status	—	100	15	Normal	—	—
TM48	Round	Normal	Special	60	100	15	Normal	—	—
TM58	Sky Drop	Flying	Physical	60	100	10	Normal	○	○
TM65	Shadow Claw	Ghost	Physical	70	100	15	Normal	—	○
TM67	Retaliate	Normal	Physical	70	100	5	Normal	—	—
TM80	Rock Slide	Rock	Physical	75	90	10	Many Others	—	—
TM83	Work Up	Normal	Status	—	—	30	Self	—	—
TM87	Swagger	Normal	Status	—	90	15	Normal	—	—
TM88	Pluck	Flying	Physical	60	100	20	Normal	—	○
TM89	U-turn	Bug	Physical	70	100	20	Normal	—	○
TM90	Substitute	Normal	Status	—	—	10	Self	—	—
TM94	Rock Smash	Fighting	Physical	40	100	15	Normal	—	○
HM01	Cut	Normal	Physical	50	95	30	Normal	—	○
HM02	Fly	Flying	Physical	90	95	15	Normal	—	○
HM04	Strength	Normal	Physical	80	100	15	Normal	—	○

MOVES TAUGHT BY PEOPLE

Name	Type	Kind	Pow.	Acc.	PP	Range	Long	DA

MOVES TAUGHT BY MOVE TUTORS FOR SHARDS

Name	Type	Kind	Pow.	Acc.	PP	Range	Long	DA
Superpower	Fighting	Physical	120	100	5	Normal	—	○
Snore	Normal	Special	40	100	15	Normal	—	○
Roost	Flying	Status	—	—	10	Self	—	—
Heat Wave	Fire	Special	100	90	10	Many Others	—	○
Tailwind	Flying	Status	—	—	30	Your Side	—	○
Sleep Talk	Normal	Status	—	—	10	Self	—	—

EGG MOVES

Name	Type	Kind	Pow.	Acc.	PP	Range	Long	DA

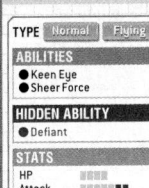

628 Braviary

Valiant Pokémon

- HEIGHT: 4'11"
- WEIGHT: 90.4 lbs.
- GENDER: ♂

For the sake of its friends, this brave warrior of the sky will not stop battling, even if injured.

♂

TYPE Normal Flying

ABILITIES
- Keen Eye
- Sheer Force

HIDDEN ABILITY
- Defiant

STATS
HP
Attack
Defense
Sp. Atk
Sp. Def
Speed

EGG GROUPS
Flying

ITEMS SOMETIMES HELD
- None

EVOLUTION

HOW TO OBTAIN

Pokémon Black Version 2	Level up a Rufflet you obtain via Link Trade to Lv. 54
Pokémon White Version 2	Route 4 (Monday only)

HOW TO OBTAIN FROM OTHER GAMES

Pokémon White Version	Route 11 (dark grass)
—	

Pokémon AR Marker

LEVEL-UP AND LEARNED MOVES

Lv.	Name	Type	Kind	Pow.	Acc.	PP	Range	Long	DA
1	Peck	Flying	Physical	35	100	35	Normal	○	○
1	Leer	Normal	Status	—	100	30	Many Others	—	—
1	Fury Attack	Normal	Physical	15	85	20	Normal	—	○
1	Wing Attack	Flying	Physical	60	100	35	Normal	○	○
5	Fury Attack	Normal	Physical	15	85	20	Normal	—	○
10	Wing Attack	Flying	Physical	60	100	35	Normal	○	○
14	Hone Claws	Dark	Status	—	—	15	Self	—	—
19	Scary Face	Normal	Status	—	100	10	Normal	—	—
23	Aerial Ace	Flying	Physical	60	—	20	Normal	○	○
28	Slash	Normal	Physical	70	100	20	Normal	—	○
32	Defog	Flying	Status	—	—	15	Normal	—	—
37	Tailwind	Flying	Status	—	—	30	Your Side	—	—
41	Air Slash	Flying	Special	75	95	20	Normal	○	—
46	Crush Claw	Normal	Physical	75	95	10	Normal	—	○
50	Sky Drop	Flying	Physical	60	100	10	Normal	○	○
51	Superpower	Fighting	Physical	120	100	5	Normal	—	○
57	Whirlwind	Normal	Status	—	100	20	Normal	—	—
63	Brave Bird	Flying	Physical	120	100	15	Normal	○	○
70	Thrash	Normal	Physical	120	100	10	1 Random	—	○

TM & HM MOVES

Lv.	Name	Type	Kind	Pow.	Acc.	PP	Range	Long	DA
TM01	Hone Claws	Dark	Status	—	—	15	Self	—	—
TM06	Toxic	Poison	Status	—	90	10	Normal	—	—
TM08	Bulk Up	Fighting	Status	—	—	20	Self	—	—
TM10	Hidden Power	Normal	Special	—	100	15	Normal	—	—
TM11	Sunny Day	Fire	Status	—	—	5	Both Sides	—	—
TM15	Hyper Beam	Normal	Special	150	90	5	Normal	—	—
TM17	Protect	Normal	Status	—	—	10	Self	—	—
TM18	Rain Dance	Water	Status	—	—	5	Both Sides	—	—
TM21	Frustration	Normal	Physical	—	100	20	Normal	—	○
TM27	Return	Normal	Physical	—	100	20	Normal	—	○
TM32	Double Team	Normal	Status	—	—	15	Self	—	—
TM39	Rock Tomb	Rock	Physical	50	80	10	Normal	—	—
TM40	Aerial Ace	Flying	Physical	60	—	20	Normal	○	○
TM42	Facade	Normal	Physical	70	100	20	Normal	—	○
TM44	Rest	Psychic	Status	—	—	10	Self	—	—
TM45	Attract	Normal	Status	—	100	15	Normal	—	—
TM48	Round	Normal	Special	60	100	15	Normal	—	—
TM58	Sky Drop	Flying	Physical	60	100	10	Normal	○	○
TM65	Shadow Claw	Ghost	Physical	70	100	15	Normal	—	○
TM67	Retaliate	Normal	Physical	70	100	5	Normal	—	○
TM68	Giga Impact	Normal	Physical	150	90	5	Normal	—	○
TM80	Rock Slide	Rock	Physical	75	90	10	Many Others	—	—
TM83	Work Up	Normal	Status	—	—	30	Self	—	—
TM87	Swagger	Normal	Status	—	90	15	Normal	—	—
TM88	Pluck	Flying	Physical	60	100	20	Normal	○	○
TM89	U-turn	Bug	Physical	70	100	20	Normal	—	○
TM90	Substitute	Normal	Status	—	—	10	Self	—	—
TM94	Rock Smash	Fighting	Physical	40	100	15	Normal	—	○
HM01	Cut	Normal	Physical	50	95	30	Normal	—	○
HM02	Fly	Flying	Physical	90	95	15	Normal	○	○
HM04	Strength	Normal	Physical	80	100	15	Normal	—	○

MOVES TAUGHT BY PEOPLE

Name	Type	Kind	Pow.	Acc.	PP	Range	Long	DA

MOVES TAUGHT BY MOVE TUTORS FOR SHARDS

Name	Type	Kind	Pow.	Acc.	PP	Range	Long	DA
Superpower	Fighting	Physical	120	100	5	Normal	—	○
Snore	Normal	Special	40	100	15	Normal	—	—
Roost	Flying	Status	—	—	10	Self	—	—
Sky Attack	Flying	Physical	140	90	5	Normal	○	—
Heat Wave	Fire	Special	100	90	10	Many Others	—	—
Tailwind	Flying	Status	—	—	30	Your Side	—	—
Sleep Talk	Normal	Status	—	—	10	Self	—	—

629 Vullaby

Diapered Pokémon

- HEIGHT: 1'08"
- WEIGHT: 19.8 lbs.
- GENDER: ♀

Their wings are too tiny to allow them to fly. They guard their posteriors with bones that were gathered by Mandibuzz.

♀

TYPE Dark Flying

ABILITIES
- Big Pecks
- Overcoat

HIDDEN ABILITY
- Weak Armor

STATS
HP
Attack
Defense
Sp. Atk
Sp. Def
Speed

EGG GROUPS
Flying

ITEMS SOMETIMES HELD
- None

EVOLUTION

HOW TO OBTAIN

Pokémon Black Version 2	Route 23
Pokémon White Version 2	Link Trade

HOW TO OBTAIN FROM OTHER GAMES

Pokémon Black Version	Route 10
—	

Pokémon AR Marker

LEVEL-UP AND LEARNED MOVES

Lv.	Name	Type	Kind	Pow.	Acc.	PP	Range	Long	DA
1	Gust	Flying	Special	40	100	35	Normal	○	—
1	Leer	Normal	Status	—	100	30	Many Others	—	—
5	Fury Attack	Normal	Physical	15	85	20	Normal	—	○
10	Pluck	Flying	Physical	60	100	20	Normal	○	○
14	Nasty Plot	Dark	Status	—	—	20	Self	—	—
19	Flatter	Dark	Status	—	100	15	Normal	—	—
23	Faint Attack	Dark	Physical	60	—	20	Normal	—	○
28	Punishment	Dark	Physical	—	100	5	Normal	—	○
32	Defog	Flying	Status	—	—	15	Normal	—	—
37	Tailwind	Flying	Status	—	—	30	Your Side	—	—
41	Air Slash	Flying	Special	75	95	20	Normal	○	—
46	Dark Pulse	Dark	Special	80	100	15	Normal	○	—
50	Embargo	Dark	Status	—	100	15	Normal	—	—
55	Whirlwind	Normal	Status	—	100	20	Normal	—	—
59	Brave Bird	Flying	Physical	120	100	15	Normal	○	○
64	Mirror Move	Flying	Status	—	—	20	Normal	—	—

TM & HM MOVES

Lv.	Name	Type	Kind	Pow.	Acc.	PP	Range	Long	DA
TM06	Toxic	Poison	Status	—	90	10	Normal	—	—
TM10	Hidden Power	Normal	Special	—	100	15	Normal	—	—
TM11	Sunny Day	Fire	Status	—	—	5	Both Sides	—	—
TM12	Taunt	Dark	Status	—	100	20	Normal	—	—
TM17	Protect	Normal	Status	—	—	10	Self	—	—
TM18	Rain Dance	Water	Status	—	—	5	Both Sides	—	—
TM21	Frustration	Normal	Physical	—	100	20	Normal	—	○
TM27	Return	Normal	Physical	—	100	20	Normal	—	○
TM30	Shadow Ball	Ghost	Special	80	100	15	Normal	—	—
TM32	Double Team	Normal	Status	—	—	15	Self	—	—
TM39	Rock Tomb	Rock	Physical	50	80	10	Normal	—	—
TM40	Aerial Ace	Flying	Physical	60	—	20	Normal	○	○
TM41	Torment	Dark	Status	—	100	15	Normal	—	—
TM42	Facade	Normal	Physical	70	100	20	Normal	—	○
TM44	Rest	Psychic	Status	—	—	10	Self	—	—
TM45	Attract	Normal	Status	—	100	15	Normal	—	—
TM46	Thief	Dark	Physical	40	100	10	Normal	—	○
TM48	Round	Normal	Special	60	100	15	Normal	—	—
TM59	Incinerate	Fire	Special	30	100	15	Many Others	—	—
TM63	Embargo	Dark	Status	—	100	15	Normal	—	—
TM66	Payback	Dark	Physical	50	100	10	Normal	—	○
TM67	Retaliate	Normal	Physical	70	100	5	Normal	—	○
TM77	Psych Up	Normal	Status	—	—	10	Normal	—	—
TM87	Swagger	Normal	Status	—	90	15	Normal	—	—
TM88	Pluck	Flying	Physical	60	100	20	Normal	○	○
TM89	U-turn	Bug	Physical	70	100	20	Normal	—	○
TM90	Substitute	Normal	Status	—	—	10	Self	—	—
TM94	Rock Smash	Fighting	Physical	40	100	15	Normal	—	○
TM95	Snarl	Dark	Special	55	95	15	Many Others	—	—
HM01	Cut	Normal	Physical	50	95	30	Normal	—	○
HM02	Fly	Flying	Physical	90	95	15	Normal	○	○

MOVES TAUGHT BY PEOPLE

Name	Type	Kind	Pow.	Acc.	PP	Range	Long	DA

MOVES TAUGHT BY MOVE TUTORS FOR SHARDS

Name	Type	Kind	Pow.	Acc.	PP	Range	Long	DA
Iron Defense	Steel	Status	—	—	15	Self	—	—
Block	Normal	Status	—	—	5	Normal	—	—
Foul Play	Dark	Physical	95	100	15	Normal	—	○
Dark Pulse	Dark	Special	80	100	15	Normal	○	—
Snore	Normal	Special	40	100	15	Normal	—	—
Knock Off	Dark	Physical	20	100	20	Normal	—	○
Roost	Flying	Status	—	—	10	Self	—	—
Heat Wave	Fire	Special	100	90	10	Many Others	—	—
Tailwind	Flying	Status	—	—	30	Your Side	—	—
Sleep Talk	Normal	Status	—	—	10	Self	—	—
Snatch	Dark	Status	—	—	10	Self	—	—

EGG MOVES

Name	Type	Kind	Pow.	Acc.	PP	Range	Long	DA
Steel Wing	Steel	Physical	70	90	25	Normal	—	○
Mean Look	Normal	Status	—	—	5	Normal	—	—
Roost	Flying	Status	—	—	10	Self	—	—
Scary Face	Normal	Status	—	100	10	Normal	—	—
Knock Off	Dark	Physical	20	100	20	Normal	—	○
Fake Tears	Dark	Status	—	100	20	Normal	—	—

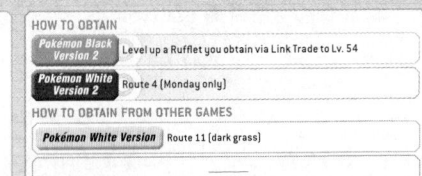

Bone Vulture Pokémon

630 Mandibuzz

- HEIGHT: 3'11"
- WEIGHT: 87.1 lbs.
- GENDER: ♀

They fly in circles around the sky. When they spot prey, they attack and carry it back to their nest with ease.

♀

TYPE Dark Flying

ABILITIES
- Big Pecks
- Overcoat

HIDDEN ABILITY
- Weak Armor

STATS
HP
Attack
Defense
Sp. Atk
Sp. Def
Speed

EGG GROUPS
Flying

ITEMS SOMETIMES HELD
- None

EVOLUTION

HOW TO OBTAIN

Pokémon Black Version 2	Route 4 (Thursday only)
Pokémon White Version 2	Level up a Vullaby you obtain via Link Trade to Lv. 54

HOW TO OBTAIN FROM OTHER GAMES

Pokémon Black Version	Route 11 (dark grass)
	—

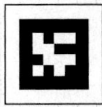

Pokémon AR Marker

LEVEL-UP AND LEARNED MOVES

Lv.	Name	Type	Kind	Pow.	Acc.	PP	Range	Long	DA
1	Gust	Flying	Special	40	100	35	Normal	○	—
1	Leer	Normal	Status	—	100	30	Many Others	—	—
1	Fury Attack	Normal	Physical	15	85	20	Normal	—	○
1	Pluck	Flying	Physical	60	100	20	Normal	○	○
5	Fury Attack	Normal	Physical	15	85	20	Normal	—	○
10	Pluck	Flying	Physical	60	100	20	Normal	○	○
14	Nasty Plot	Dark	Status	—	—	20	Self	—	—
19	Flatter	Dark	Status	—	100	15	Normal	—	—
23	Faint Attack	Dark	Physical	60	—	20	Normal	—	○
28	Punishment	Dark	Physical	—	100	5	Normal	—	○
32	Defog	Flying	Status	—	—	15	Normal	—	—
37	Tailwind	Flying	Status	—	—	30	Your Side	—	—
41	Air Slash	Flying	Special	75	95	20	Normal	○	—
46	Dark Pulse	Dark	Special	80	100	15	Normal	○	—
50	Embargo	Dark	Status	—	100	15	Normal	—	—
51	Bone Rush	Ground	Physical	25	90	10	Normal	—	—
57	Whirlwind	Normal	Status	—	100	20	Normal	—	—
63	Brave Bird	Flying	Physical	120	100	15	Normal	○	○
70	Mirror Move	Flying	Status	—	—	20	Normal	—	—

TM & HM MOVES

Lv.	Name	Type	Kind	Pow.	Acc.	PP	Range	Long	DA
TM06	Toxic	Poison	Status	—	90	10	Normal	—	—
TM10	Hidden Power	Normal	Special	—	100	15	Normal	—	—
TM11	Sunny Day	Fire	Status	—	—	5	Both Sides	—	—
TM12	Taunt	Dark	Status	—	100	20	Normal	—	—
TM15	Hyper Beam	Normal	Special	150	90	5	Normal	—	—
TM17	Protect	Normal	Status	—	—	10	Self	—	—
TM18	Rain Dance	Water	Status	—	—	5	Both Sides	—	—
TM21	Frustration	Normal	Physical	—	100	20	Normal	—	○
TM27	Return	Normal	Physical	—	100	20	Normal	—	○
TM30	Shadow Ball	Ghost	Special	80	100	15	Normal	—	—
TM32	Double Team	Normal	Status	—	—	15	Self	—	—
TM39	Rock Tomb	Rock	Physical	50	80	10	Normal	—	—
TM40	Aerial Ace	Flying	Physical	60	—	20	Normal	○	○
TM41	Torment	Dark	Status	—	100	15	Normal	—	—
TM42	Facade	Normal	Physical	70	100	20	Normal	—	○
TM44	Rest	Psychic	Status	—	—	10	Self	—	—
TM45	Attract	Normal	Status	—	100	15	Normal	—	—
TM46	Thief	Dark	Physical	40	100	10	Normal	—	○
TM48	Round	Normal	Special	60	100	15	Normal	—	—
TM59	Incinerate	Fire	Special	30	100	15	Many Others	—	—
TM63	Embargo	Dark	Status	—	100	15	Normal	—	—
TM66	Payback	Dark	Physical	50	100	10	Normal	—	○
TM67	Retaliate	Normal	Physical	70	100	5	Normal	—	○
TM68	Giga Impact	Normal	Physical	150	90	5	Normal	—	○
TM77	Psych Up	Normal	Status	—	—	10	Normal	—	—
TM87	Swagger	Normal	Status	—	90	15	Normal	—	—
TM88	Pluck	Flying	Physical	60	100	20	Normal	○	○
TM89	U-turn	Bug	Physical	70	100	20	Normal	—	○
TM90	Substitute	Normal	Status	—	—	10	Self	—	—
TM94	Rock Smash	Fighting	Physical	40	100	15	Normal	—	○
TM95	Snarl	Dark	Special	55	95	15	Many Others	—	—
HM01	Cut	Normal	Physical	50	95	30	Normal	—	○
HM02	Fly	Flying	Physical	90	95	15	Normal	○	○

MOVES TAUGHT BY PEOPLE

Name	Type	Kind	Pow.	Acc.	PP	Range	Long	DA

MOVES TAUGHT BY MOVE TUTORS FOR SHARDS

Name	Type	Kind	Pow.	Acc.	PP	Range	Long	DA
Iron Defense	Steel	Status	—	—	15	Self	—	—
Block	Normal	Status	—	—	5	Normal	—	—
Foul Play	Dark	Physical	95	100	15	Normal	—	○
Dark Pulse	Dark	Special	80	100	15	Normal	○	—
Snore	Normal	Special	40	100	15	Normal	—	—
Knock Off	Dark	Physical	20	100	20	Normal	—	○
Roost	Flying	Status	—	—	10	Self	—	—
Sky Attack	Flying	Physical	140	90	5	Normal	○	—
Heat Wave	Fire	Special	100	90	10	Many Others	—	—
Tailwind	Flying	Status	—	—	30	Your Side	—	—
Sleep Talk	Normal	Status	—	—	10	Self	—	—
Snatch	Dark	Status	—	—	10	Self	—	—

Anteater Pokémon

631 Heatmor

- HEIGHT: 4'07"
- WEIGHT: 127.9 lbs.
- GENDER: ♂ / ♀

It draws in air through its tail, transforms it into fire, and uses it like a tongue. It melts Durant and eats them.

Same form for ♂ / ♀

TYPE Fire

ABILITIES
- Gluttony
- Flash Fire

HIDDEN ABILITY
- White Smoke

STATS
HP
Attack
Defense
Sp. Atk
Sp. Def
Speed

EGG GROUPS
Field

ITEMS SOMETIMES HELD
- None

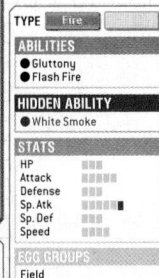

EVOLUTION

Does not evolve

HOW TO OBTAIN

Pokémon Black Version 2	Twist Mountain
Pokémon White Version 2	Twist Mountain

HOW TO OBTAIN FROM OTHER GAMES

—
—

Pokémon AR Marker

LEVEL-UP AND LEARNED MOVES

Lv.	Name	Type	Kind	Pow.	Acc.	PP	Range	Long	DA
1	Incinerate	Fire	Special	30	100	15	Many Others	—	—
1	Lick	Ghost	Physical	20	100	30	Normal	—	○
6	Odor Sleuth	Normal	Status	—	—	40	Normal	—	—
11	Bind	Normal	Physical	15	85	20	Normal	—	○
16	Fire Spin	Fire	Special	35	85	15	Normal	—	—
21	Fury Swipes	Normal	Physical	18	80	15	Normal	—	○
26	Snatch	Dark	Status	—	—	10	Self	—	—
31	Flame Burst	Fire	Special	70	100	15	Normal	—	—
36	Bug Bite	Bug	Physical	60	100	20	Normal	—	○
41	Slash	Normal	Physical	70	100	20	Normal	—	○
46	Amnesia	Psychic	Status	—	—	20	Self	—	—
51	Flamethrower	Fire	Special	95	100	15	Normal	—	—
56	Stockpile	Normal	Status	—	—	20	Self	—	—
56	Spit Up	Normal	Special	—	100	10	Normal	—	—
56	Swallow	Normal	Status	—	—	10	Self	—	—
61	Inferno	Fire	Special	100	50	5	Normal	—	—

TM & HM MOVES

Lv.	Name	Type	Kind	Pow.	Acc.	PP	Range	Long	DA
TM01	Hone Claws	Dark	Status	—	—	15	Self	—	—
TM06	Toxic	Poison	Status	—	90	10	Normal	—	—
TM10	Hidden Power	Normal	Special	—	100	15	Normal	—	—
TM11	Sunny Day	Fire	Status	—	—	5	Both Sides	—	—
TM12	Taunt	Dark	Status	—	100	20	Normal	—	—
TM17	Protect	Normal	Status	—	—	10	Self	—	—
TM18	Rain Dance	Water	Status	—	—	5	Both Sides	—	—
TM21	Frustration	Normal	Physical	—	100	20	Normal	—	○
TM22	SolarBeam	Grass	Special	120	100	10	Normal	—	—
TM27	Return	Normal	Physical	—	100	20	Normal	—	○
TM28	Dig	Ground	Physical	80	100	10	Normal	—	○
TM32	Double Team	Normal	Status	—	—	15	Self	—	—
TM35	Flamethrower	Fire	Special	95	100	15	Normal	—	—
TM38	Fire Blast	Fire	Special	120	85	5	Normal	—	—
TM39	Rock Tomb	Rock	Physical	50	80	10	Normal	—	—
TM40	Aerial Ace	Flying	Physical	60	—	20	Normal	○	○
TM42	Facade	Normal	Physical	70	100	20	Normal	—	○
TM44	Rest	Psychic	Status	—	—	10	Self	—	—
TM45	Attract	Normal	Status	—	100	15	Normal	—	—
TM46	Thief	Dark	Physical	40	100	10	Normal	—	○
TM48	Round	Normal	Special	60	100	15	Normal	—	—
TM52	Focus Blast	Fighting	Special	120	70	5	Normal	—	—
TM56	Fling	Dark	Physical	—	100	10	Normal	—	—
TM59	Incinerate	Fire	Special	30	100	15	Many Others	—	—
TM61	Will-O-Wisp	Fire	Status	—	75	15	Normal	—	—
TM65	Shadow Claw	Ghost	Physical	70	100	15	Normal	—	○
TM68	Giga Impact	Normal	Physical	150	90	5	Normal	—	○
TM87	Swagger	Normal	Status	—	90	15	Normal	—	—
TM90	Substitute	Normal	Status	—	—	10	Self	—	—
TM94	Rock Smash	Fighting	Physical	40	100	15	Normal	—	○
HM01	Cut	Normal	Physical	50	95	30	Normal	—	○

MOVES TAUGHT BY PEOPLE

Name	Type	Kind	Pow.	Acc.	PP	Range	Long	DA

MOVES TAUGHT BY MOVE TUTORS FOR SHARDS

Name	Type	Kind	Pow.	Acc.	PP	Range	Long	DA
Bug Bite	Bug	Physical	60	100	20	Normal	—	○
Low Kick	Fighting	Physical	—	100	20	Normal	—	○
Fire Punch	Fire	Physical	75	100	15	Normal	—	○
ThunderPunch	Electric	Physical	75	100	15	Normal	—	○
Superpower	Fighting	Physical	120	100	5	Normal	—	○
Bind	Normal	Physical	15	85	20	Normal	—	○
Snore	Normal	Special	40	100	15	Normal	—	—
Knock Off	Dark	Physical	20	100	20	Normal	—	○
Heat Wave	Fire	Special	100	90	10	Many Others	—	—
Giga Drain	Grass	Special	75	100	10	Normal	—	—
Gastro Acid	Poison	Status	—	100	10	Normal	—	—
Recycle	Normal	Status	—	—	10	Self	—	—
Sleep Talk	Normal	Status	—	—	10	Self	—	—
Snatch	Dark	Status	—	—	10	Self	—	—

EGG MOVES

Name	Type	Kind	Pow.	Acc.	PP	Range	Long	DA
Pursuit	Dark	Physical	40	100	20	Normal	—	○
Wrap	Normal	Physical	15	90	20	Normal	—	○
Night Slash	Dark	Physical	70	100	15	Normal	—	○
Curse	Ghost	Status	—	—	10	Varies	—	—
Body Slam	Normal	Physical	85	100	15	Normal	—	○
Heat Wave	Fire	Special	100	90	10	Many Others	—	—
Faint Attack	Dark	Physical	60	—	20	Normal	—	○
Sucker Punch	Dark	Physical	80	100	5	Normal	—	○
Tickle	Normal	Status	—	100	20	Normal	—	—
Sleep Talk	Normal	Status	—	—	10	Self	—	—

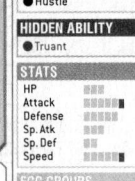

632 Durant

Iron Ant Pokémon

- HEIGHT: 1'00"
- WEIGHT: 72.8 lbs.
- GENDER: ♂ / ♀

Individuals each play different roles in driving Heatmor, their natural predator, away from their colony.

Same form for ♂ / ♀

Pokémon AR Marker

TYPE: Bug / Steel

ABILITIES
- Swarm
- Hustle

HIDDEN ABILITY
- Truant

STATS
HP
Attack
Defense
Sp. Atk
Sp. Def
Speed

EGG GROUPS
Bug

ITEMS SOMETIMES HELD
- None

EVOLUTION

Does not evolve

HOW TO OBTAIN

Pokémon Black Version 2	❶ Clay Tunnel ❷ Twist Mountain
Pokémon White Version 2	❶ Clay Tunnel ❷ Twist Mountain

HOW TO OBTAIN FROM OTHER GAMES

—

—

LEVEL-UP AND LEARNED MOVES

Lv.	Name	Type	Kind	Pow.	Acc.	PP	Range	Long	DA
1	ViceGrip	Normal	Physical	55	100	30	Normal	—	○
1	Sand-Attack	Ground	Status	—	100	15	Normal	—	—
6	Fury Cutter	Bug	Physical	20	95	20	Normal	—	○
11	Bite	Dark	Physical	60	100	25	Normal	—	○
16	Agility	Psychic	Status	—	—	30	Self	—	—
21	Metal Claw	Steel	Physical	50	95	35	Normal	—	○
26	Bug Bite	Bug	Physical	60	100	20	Normal	—	○
31	Crunch	Dark	Physical	80	100	15	Normal	—	○
36	Iron Head	Steel	Physical	80	100	15	Normal	—	○
41	Dig	Ground	Physical	80	100	10	Normal	—	○
46	Entrainment	Normal	Status	—	100	15	Normal	—	—
51	X-Scissor	Bug	Physical	80	100	15	Normal	—	○
56	Iron Defense	Steel	Status	—	—	15	Self	—	—
61	Guillotine	Normal	Physical	—	30	5	Normal	—	○
66	Metal Sound	Steel	Status	—	85	40	Normal	—	—

TM & HM MOVES

Lv.	Name	Type	Kind	Pow.	Acc.	PP	Range	Long	DA
TM01	Hone Claws	Dark	Status	—	—	15	Self	—	—
TM06	Toxic	Poison	Status	—	90	10	Normal	—	—
TM10	Hidden Power	Normal	Special	—	100	15	Normal	—	—
TM17	Protect	Normal	Status	—	—	10	Self	—	—
TM21	Frustration	Normal	Physical	—	100	20	Normal	—	○
TM27	Return	Normal	Physical	—	100	20	Normal	—	○
TM28	Dig	Ground	Physical	80	100	10	Normal	—	○
TM32	Double Team	Normal	Status	—	—	15	Self	—	—
TM37	Sandstorm	Rock	Status	—	—	10	Both Sides	—	—
TM39	Rock Tomb	Rock	Physical	50	80	10	Normal	—	—
TM40	Aerial Ace	Flying	Physical	60	—	20	Normal	○	○
TM42	Facade	Normal	Physical	70	100	20	Normal	—	○
TM44	Rest	Psychic	Status	—	—	10	Self	—	—
TM45	Attract	Normal	Status	—	100	15	Normal	—	—
TM48	Round	Normal	Special	60	100	15	Normal	—	—
TM53	Energy Ball	Grass	Special	80	100	10	Normal	—	—
TM65	Shadow Claw	Ghost	Physical	70	100	15	Normal	—	○
TM67	Retaliate	Normal	Physical	70	100	5	Normal	—	○
TM68	Giga Impact	Normal	Physical	150	90	5	Normal	—	○
TM69	Rock Polish	Rock	Status	—	—	20	Self	—	—
TM71	Stone Edge	Rock	Physical	100	80	5	Normal	—	—
TM73	Thunder Wave	Electric	Status	—	100	20	Normal	—	—
TM76	Struggle Bug	Bug	Special	30	100	20	Many Others	—	—
TM80	Rock Slide	Rock	Physical	75	90	10	Many Others	—	—
TM81	X-Scissor	Bug	Physical	80	100	15	Normal	—	○
TM87	Swagger	Normal	Status	—	90	15	Normal	—	—
TM90	Substitute	Normal	Status	—	—	10	Self	—	—
TM91	Flash Cannon	Steel	Special	80	100	10	Normal	—	—
TM94	Rock Smash	Fighting	Physical	40	100	15	Normal	—	○
HM01	Cut	Normal	Physical	50	95	30	Normal	—	○
HM04	Strength	Normal	Physical	80	100	15	Normal	—	○

MOVES TAUGHT BY PEOPLE

Name	Type	Kind	Pow.	Acc.	PP	Range	Long	DA

MOVES TAUGHT BY MOVE TUTORS FOR SHARDS

Name	Type	Kind	Pow.	Acc.	PP	Range	Long	DA
Bug Bite	Bug	Physical	60	100	20	Normal	—	○
Iron Head	Steel	Physical	80	100	15	Normal	—	○
Iron Defense	Steel	Status	—	—	15	Self	—	—
Superpower	Fighting	Physical	120	100	5	Normal	—	○
Snore	Normal	Special	40	100	15	Normal	—	—
Endeavor	Normal	Physical	—	100	5	Normal	—	○
Sleep Talk	Normal	Status	—	—	10	Self	—	—

EGG MOVES

Name	Type	Kind	Pow.	Acc.	PP	Range	Long	DA
Screech	Normal	Status	—	85	40	Normal	—	—
Endure	Normal	Status	—	—	10	Self	—	—
Rock Climb	Normal	Physical	90	85	20	Normal	—	○
Baton Pass	Normal	Status	—	—	40	Self	—	—
Thunder Fang	Electric	Physical	65	95	15	Normal	—	○
Faint Attack	Dark	Physical	60	—	20	Normal	—	○

633 Deino

Irate Pokémon

- HEIGHT: 2'07"
- WEIGHT: 38.1 lbs.
- GENDER: ♂ / ♀

Lacking sight, it's unaware of its surroundings, so it bumps into things and eats anything that moves.

Same form for ♂ / ♀

Pokémon AR Marker

TYPE: Dark / Dragon

ABILITY
- Hustle

HIDDEN ABILITY
—

STATS
HP
Attack
Defense
Sp. Atk
Sp. Def
Speed

EGG GROUPS
Dragon

ITEMS SOMETIMES HELD
- None

EVOLUTION

HOW TO OBTAIN

Pokémon Black Version 2	Catch a Zweilous, leave it at the Pokémon Day Care, and hatch the Egg that is found
Pokémon White Version 2	Catch a Zweilous, leave it at the Pokémon Day Care, and hatch the Egg that is found

HOW TO OBTAIN FROM OTHER GAMES

Pokémon Black Version	Victory Road 1F
Pokémon White Version	Victory Road 1F

LEVEL-UP AND LEARNED MOVES

Lv.	Name	Type	Kind	Pow.	Acc.	PP	Range	Long	DA
1	Tackle	Normal	Physical	50	100	35	Normal	—	○
1	Dragon Rage	Dragon	Special	—	100	10	Normal	—	—
4	Focus Energy	Normal	Status	—	—	30	Self	—	—
9	Bite	Dark	Physical	60	100	25	Normal	—	○
12	Headbutt	Normal	Physical	70	100	15	Normal	—	○
17	DragonBreath	Dragon	Special	60	100	20	Normal	—	—
20	Roar	Normal	Status	—	100	20	Normal	—	—
25	Crunch	Dark	Physical	80	100	15	Normal	—	○
28	Slam	Normal	Physical	80	75	20	Normal	—	○
32	Dragon Pulse	Dragon	Special	90	100	10	Normal	○	—
38	Work Up	Normal	Status	—	—	30	Self	—	—
42	Dragon Rush	Dragon	Physical	100	75	10	Normal	—	○
48	Body Slam	Normal	Physical	85	100	15	Normal	—	○
52	Scary Face	Normal	Status	—	100	10	Normal	—	—
58	Hyper Voice	Normal	Special	90	100	10	Many Others	—	—
62	Outrage	Dragon	Physical	120	100	10	1 Random	—	○

TM & HM MOVES

Lv.	Name	Type	Kind	Pow.	Acc.	PP	Range	Long	DA
TM05	Roar	Normal	Status	—	100	20	Normal	—	—
TM06	Toxic	Poison	Status	—	90	10	Normal	—	—
TM10	Hidden Power	Normal	Special	—	100	15	Normal	—	—
TM11	Sunny Day	Fire	Status	—	—	5	Both Sides	—	—
TM12	Taunt	Dark	Status	—	100	20	Normal	—	—
TM17	Protect	Normal	Status	—	—	10	Self	—	—
TM18	Rain Dance	Water	Status	—	—	5	Both Sides	—	—
TM21	Frustration	Normal	Physical	—	100	20	Normal	—	○
TM27	Return	Normal	Physical	—	100	20	Normal	—	○
TM32	Double Team	Normal	Status	—	—	15	Self	—	—
TM41	Torment	Dark	Status	—	100	15	Normal	—	—
TM42	Facade	Normal	Physical	70	100	20	Normal	—	○
TM44	Rest	Psychic	Status	—	—	10	Self	—	—
TM45	Attract	Normal	Status	—	100	15	Normal	—	—
TM46	Thief	Dark	Physical	40	100	10	Normal	—	○
TM48	Round	Normal	Special	60	100	15	Normal	—	—
TM59	Incinerate	Fire	Special	30	100	15	Many Others	—	—
TM73	Thunder Wave	Electric	Status	—	100	20	Normal	—	—
TM77	Psych Up	Normal	Status	—	—	10	Normal	—	—
TM82	Dragon Tail	Dragon	Physical	60	90	10	Normal	—	○
TM83	Work Up	Normal	Status	—	—	30	Self	—	—
TM87	Swagger	Normal	Status	—	90	15	Normal	—	—
TM90	Substitute	Normal	Status	—	—	10	Self	—	—
TM94	Rock Smash	Fighting	Physical	40	100	15	Normal	—	○
HM04	Strength	Normal	Physical	80	100	15	Normal	—	○

MOVES TAUGHT BY PEOPLE

Name	Type	Kind	Pow.	Acc.	PP	Range	Long	DA
Draco Meteor	Dragon	Special	140	90	5	Normal	—	—

MOVES TAUGHT BY MOVE TUTORS FOR SHARDS

Name	Type	Kind	Pow.	Acc.	PP	Range	Long	DA
Uproar	Normal	Special	90	100	10	1 Random	—	—
Hyper Voice	Normal	Special	90	100	10	Many Others	—	—
Aqua Tail	Water	Physical	90	90	10	Normal	—	○
Earth Power	Ground	Special	90	100	10	Normal	—	—
Zen Headbutt	Psychic	Physical	80	90	15	Normal	—	○
Superpower	Fighting	Physical	120	100	5	Normal	—	○
Dragon Pulse	Dragon	Special	90	100	10	Normal	○	—
Dark Pulse	Dark	Special	80	100	15	Normal	○	—
Snore	Normal	Special	40	100	15	Normal	—	—
Spite	Ghost	Status	—	100	10	Normal	—	—
Outrage	Dragon	Physical	120	100	10	1 Random	—	○
Sleep Talk	Normal	Status	—	—	10	Self	—	—

EGG MOVES

Name	Type	Kind	Pow.	Acc.	PP	Range	Long	DA
Fire Fang	Fire	Physical	65	95	15	Normal	—	○
Thunder Fang	Electric	Physical	65	95	15	Normal	—	○
Ice Fang	Ice	Physical	65	95	15	Normal	—	○
Double Hit	Normal	Physical	35	90	10	Normal	—	○
Astonish	Ghost	Physical	30	100	15	Normal	—	○
Earth Power	Ground	Special	90	100	10	Normal	—	—
Screech	Normal	Status	—	85	40	Normal	—	—
Head Smash	Rock	Physical	150	80	5	Normal	—	○
Assurance	Dark	Physical	50	100	10	Normal	—	○
Dark Pulse	Dark	Special	80	100	15	Normal	○	—

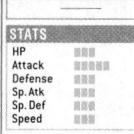

Hostile Pokémon

634 Zweilous

- HEIGHT: 4'07"
- WEIGHT: 110.2 lbs.
- GENDER: ♂ / ♀

The two heads do not get along. Whichever head eats more than the other gets to be the leader.

Same form for ♂ / ♀

TYPE: Dark / Dragon

ABILITY
- Hustle

HIDDEN ABILITY
—

STATS
HP
Attack
Defense
Sp. Atk
Sp. Def
Speed

EGG GROUPS
Dragon

ITEMS SOMETIMES HELD
- None

EVOLUTION

HOW TO OBTAIN

Pokémon Black Version 2	❶ Victory Road 3F in the first part of the cave ❷ Victory Road caves 1F
Pokémon White Version 2	❶ Victory Road 3F in the first part of the cave ❷ Victory Road caves 1F

HOW TO OBTAIN FROM OTHER GAMES

—

—

Pokémon AR Marker

LEVEL-UP AND LEARNED MOVES

Lv.	Name	Type	Kind	Pow.	Acc.	PP	Range	Long	DA
1	Double Hit	Normal	Physical	35	90	10	Normal	—	○
1	Dragon Rage	Dragon	Special	—	100	10	Normal	—	—
1	Focus Energy	Normal	Status	—	—	30	Self	—	—
1	Bite	Dark	Physical	60	100	25	Normal	—	○
4	Focus Energy	Normal	Status	—	—	30	Self	—	—
9	Bite	Dark	Physical	60	100	25	Normal	—	○
12	Headbutt	Normal	Physical	70	100	15	Normal	—	○
17	DragonBreath	Dragon	Special	60	100	20	Normal	—	—
20	Roar	Normal	Status	—	100	20	Normal	—	—
25	Crunch	Dark	Physical	80	100	15	Normal	—	○
28	Slam	Normal	Physical	80	75	20	Normal	—	○
32	Dragon Pulse	Dragon	Special	90	100	10	Normal	○	—
38	Work Up	Normal	Status	—	—	30	Self	—	—
42	Dragon Rush	Dragon	Physical	100	75	10	Normal	—	○
48	Body Slam	Normal	Physical	85	100	15	Normal	—	○
55	Scary Face	Normal	Status	—	100	10	Normal	—	—
64	Hyper Voice	Normal	Special	90	100	10	Many Others	—	—
71	Outrage	Dragon	Physical	120	100	10	1 Random	—	○

TM & HM MOVES

Lv.	Name	Type	Kind	Pow.	Acc.	PP	Range	Long	DA
TM05	Roar	Normal	Status	—	100	20	Normal	—	—
TM06	Toxic	Poison	Status	—	90	10	Normal	—	—
TM10	Hidden Power	Normal	Special	—	100	15	Normal	—	—
TM11	Sunny Day	Fire	Status	—	—	5	Both Sides	—	—
TM12	Taunt	Dark	Status	—	100	20	Normal	—	—
TM17	Protect	Normal	Status	—	—	10	Self	—	—
TM18	Rain Dance	Water	Status	—	—	5	Both Sides	—	—
TM21	Frustration	Normal	Physical	—	100	20	Normal	—	○
TM27	Return	Normal	Physical	—	100	20	Normal	—	○
TM32	Double Team	Normal	Status	—	—	15	Self	—	—
TM41	Torment	Dark	Status	—	100	15	Normal	—	—
TM42	Facade	Normal	Physical	70	100	20	Normal	—	○
TM44	Rest	Psychic	Status	—	—	10	Self	—	—
TM45	Attract	Normal	Status	—	100	15	Normal	—	—
TM46	Thief	Dark	Physical	40	100	10	Normal	—	○
TM48	Round	Normal	Special	60	100	15	Normal	—	—
TM59	Incinerate	Fire	Special	30	100	15	Many Others	—	—
TM73	Thunder Wave	Electric	Status	—	100	20	Normal	—	—
TM77	Psych Up	Normal	Status	—	—	10	Normal	—	—
TM82	Dragon Tail	Dragon	Physical	60	90	10	Normal	—	○
TM83	Work Up	Normal	Status	—	—	30	Self	—	—
TM87	Swagger	Normal	Status	—	90	15	Normal	—	—
TM90	Substitute	Normal	Status	—	—	10	Self	—	—
TM94	Rock Smash	Fighting	Physical	40	100	15	Normal	—	○
HM04	Strength	Normal	Physical	80	100	15	Normal	—	○

MOVES TAUGHT BY PEOPLE

Name	Type	Kind	Pow.	Acc.	PP	Range	Long	DA
Draco Meteor	Dragon	Special	140	90	5	Normal	—	—

MOVES TAUGHT BY MOVE TUTORS FOR SHARDS

Name	Type	Kind	Pow.	Acc.	PP	Range	Long	DA
Uproar	Normal	Special	90	100	10	1 Random	—	—
Hyper Voice	Normal	Special	90	100	10	Many Others	—	—
Aqua Tail	Water	Physical	90	90	10	Normal	—	○
Earth Power	Ground	Special	90	100	10	Normal	—	—
Zen Headbutt	Psychic	Physical	80	90	15	Normal	—	○
Superpower	Fighting	Physical	120	100	5	Normal	—	○
Dragon Pulse	Dragon	Special	90	100	10	Normal	○	—
Dark Pulse	Dark	Special	80	100	15	Normal	○	—
Snore	Normal	Special	40	100	15	Normal	—	—
Spite	Ghost	Status	—	100	10	Normal	—	—
Outrage	Dragon	Physical	120	100	10	1 Random	—	○
Sleep Talk	Normal	Status	—	—	10	Self	—	—

Brutal Pokémon

635 Hydreigon

- HEIGHT: 5'11"
- WEIGHT: 352.7 lbs.
- GENDER: ♂ / ♀

It responds to movement by attacking. This scary, three-headed Pokémon devours everything in its path!

Same form for ♂ / ♀

TYPE: Dark / Dragon

ABILITY
- Levitate

HIDDEN ABILITY
—

STATS
HP
Attack
Defense
Sp. Atk
Sp. Def
Speed

EGG GROUPS
Dragon

ITEMS SOMETIMES HELD
- None

EVOLUTION

HOW TO OBTAIN

Pokémon Black Version 2	Level up Zweilous to Lv. 64
Pokémon White Version 2	Level up Zweilous to Lv. 64

HOW TO OBTAIN FROM OTHER GAMES

—

—

Pokémon AR Marker

LEVEL-UP AND LEARNED MOVES

Lv.	Name	Type	Kind	Pow.	Acc.	PP	Range	Long	DA
1	Tri Attack	Normal	Special	80	100	10	Normal	—	—
1	Dragon Rage	Dragon	Special	—	100	10	Normal	—	—
1	Focus Energy	Normal	Status	—	—	30	Self	—	—
1	Bite	Dark	Physical	60	100	25	Normal	—	○
4	Focus Energy	Normal	Status	—	—	30	Self	—	—
9	Bite	Dark	Physical	60	100	25	Normal	—	○
12	Headbutt	Normal	Physical	70	100	15	Normal	—	○
17	DragonBreath	Dragon	Special	60	100	20	Normal	—	—
20	Roar	Normal	Status	—	100	20	Normal	—	—
25	Crunch	Dark	Physical	80	100	15	Normal	—	○
28	Slam	Normal	Physical	80	75	20	Normal	—	○
32	Dragon Pulse	Dragon	Special	90	100	10	Normal	○	—
38	Work Up	Normal	Status	—	—	30	Self	—	—
42	Dragon Rush	Dragon	Physical	100	75	10	Normal	—	○
48	Body Slam	Normal	Physical	85	100	15	Normal	—	○
55	Scary Face	Normal	Status	—	100	10	Normal	—	—
68	Hyper Voice	Normal	Special	90	100	10	Many Others	—	—
79	Outrage	Dragon	Physical	120	100	10	1 Random	—	○

TM & HM MOVES

Lv.	Name	Type	Kind	Pow.	Acc.	PP	Range	Long	DA
TM05	Roar	Normal	Status	—	100	20	Normal	—	—
TM06	Toxic	Poison	Status	—	90	10	Normal	—	—
TM10	Hidden Power	Normal	Special	—	100	15	Normal	—	—
TM11	Sunny Day	Fire	Status	—	—	5	Both Sides	—	—
TM12	Taunt	Dark	Status	—	100	20	Normal	—	—
TM15	Hyper Beam	Normal	Special	150	90	5	Normal	—	—
TM17	Protect	Normal	Status	—	—	10	Self	—	—
TM18	Rain Dance	Water	Status	—	—	5	Both Sides	—	—
TM21	Frustration	Normal	Physical	—	100	20	Normal	—	○
TM26	Earthquake	Ground	Physical	100	100	10	Adjacent	—	—
TM27	Return	Normal	Physical	—	100	20	Normal	—	○
TM32	Double Team	Normal	Status	—	—	15	Self	—	—
TM33	Reflect	Psychic	Status	—	—	20	Your Side	—	—
TM35	Flamethrower	Fire	Special	95	100	15	Normal	—	—
TM38	Fire Blast	Fire	Special	120	85	5	Normal	—	—
TM39	Rock Tomb	Rock	Physical	50	80	10	Normal	—	—
TM41	Torment	Dark	Status	—	100	15	Normal	—	—
TM42	Facade	Normal	Physical	70	100	20	Normal	—	○
TM44	Rest	Psychic	Status	—	—	10	Self	—	—
TM45	Attract	Normal	Status	—	100	15	Normal	—	—
TM46	Thief	Dark	Physical	40	100	10	Normal	—	○
TM48	Round	Normal	Special	60	100	15	Normal	—	—
TM49	Echoed Voice	Normal	Special	40	100	15	Normal	—	—
TM52	Focus Blast	Fighting	Special	120	70	5	Normal	—	—
TM57	Charge Beam	Electric	Special	50	90	10	Normal	—	—
TM59	Incinerate	Fire	Special	30	100	15	Many Others	—	—
TM62	Acrobatics	Flying	Physical	55	100	15	Normal	○	○
TM66	Payback	Dark	Physical	50	100	10	Normal	—	○
TM68	Giga Impact	Normal	Physical	150	90	5	Normal	—	○
TM71	Stone Edge	Rock	Physical	100	80	5	Normal	—	—
TM73	Thunder Wave	Electric	Status	—	100	20	Normal	—	—
TM77	Psych Up	Normal	Status	—	—	10	Normal	—	—
TM78	Bulldoze	Ground	Physical	60	100	20	Adjacent	—	—
TM80	Rock Slide	Rock	Physical	75	90	10	Many Others	—	—
TM82	Dragon Tail	Dragon	Physical	60	90	10	Normal	—	○
TM83	Work Up	Normal	Status	—	—	30	Self	—	—
TM87	Swagger	Normal	Status	—	90	15	Normal	—	—
TM89	U-turn	Bug	Physical	70	100	20	Normal	—	○
TM90	Substitute	Normal	Status	—	—	10	Self	—	—
TM91	Flash Cannon	Steel	Special	80	100	10	Normal	—	—
TM94	Rock Smash	Fighting	Physical	40	100	15	Normal	—	○
HM02	Fly	Flying	Physical	90	95	15	Normal	○	○
HM03	Surf	Water	Special	95	100	15	Adjacent	—	—
HM04	Strength	Normal	Physical	80	100	15	Normal	—	○

MOVES TAUGHT BY PEOPLE

Name	Type	Kind	Pow.	Acc.	PP	Range	Long	DA
Draco Meteor	Dragon	Special	140	90	5	Normal	—	—

MOVES TAUGHT BY MOVE TUTORS FOR SHARDS

Name	Type	Kind	Pow.	Acc.	PP	Range	Long	DA
Signal Beam	Bug	Special	75	100	15	Normal	—	—
Uproar	Normal	Special	90	100	10	1 Random	—	—
Hyper Voice	Normal	Special	90	100	10	Many Others	—	—
Iron Tail	Steel	Physical	100	75	15	Normal	—	○
Aqua Tail	Water	Physical	90	90	10	Normal	—	○
Earth Power	Ground	Special	90	100	10	Normal	—	—
Zen Headbutt	Psychic	Physical	80	90	15	Normal	—	○
Superpower	Fighting	Physical	120	100	5	Normal	—	○
Dragon Pulse	Dragon	Special	90	100	10	Normal	○	—
Dark Pulse	Dark	Special	80	100	15	Normal	○	—
Snore	Normal	Special	40	100	15	Normal	—	—
Roost	Flying	Status	—	—	10	Self	—	—
Heat Wave	Fire	Special	100	90	10	Many Others	—	—
Tailwind	Flying	Status	—	—	30	Your Side	—	—
Spite	Ghost	Status	—	100	10	Normal	—	—
Outrage	Dragon	Physical	120	100	10	1 Random	—	○
Sleep Talk	Normal	Status	—	—	10	Self	—	—

Torch Pokémon

636 Larvesta

- HEIGHT: 3'07"
- WEIGHT: 63.5 lbs.
- GENDER: ♂ / ♀

Said to have been born from the sun, it spews fire from its horns and encases itself in a cocoon of fire when it evolves.

Same form for ♂ / ♀

TYPE Bug Fire

ABILITY
- Flame Body

HIDDEN ABILITY
—

STATS
HP
Attack
Defense
Sp. Atk
Sp. Def
Speed

EGG GROUPS
Bug

ITEMS SOMETIMES HELD
- None

EVOLUTION

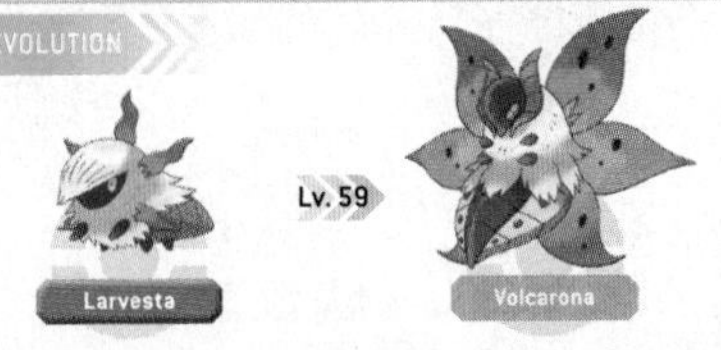

HOW TO OBTAIN

Pokémon Black Version 2	Catch a Volcarona, leave it at the Pokémon Day Care, and hatch the Egg that is found
Pokémon White Version 2	Catch a Volcarona, leave it at the Pokémon Day Care, and hatch the Egg that is found

HOW TO OBTAIN FROM OTHER GAMES

Pokémon Black Version	Hatch the Egg received on Route 18
Pokémon White Version	Hatch the Egg received on Route 18

LEVEL-UP AND LEARNED MOVES

Lv.	Name	Type	Kind	Pow.	Acc.	PP	Range	Long	DA
1	Ember	Fire	Special	40	100	25	Normal	—	—
1	String Shot	Bug	Status	—	95	40	Many Others	—	—
10	Leech Life	Bug	Physical	20	100	15	Normal	—	○
20	Take Down	Normal	Physical	90	85	20	Normal	—	○
30	Flame Charge	Fire	Physical	50	100	20	Normal	—	○
40	Bug Bite	Bug	Physical	60	100	20	Normal	—	○
50	Double-Edge	Normal	Physical	120	100	15	Normal	—	○
60	Flame Wheel	Fire	Physical	60	100	25	Normal	—	○
70	Bug Buzz	Bug	Special	90	100	10	Normal	—	—
80	Amnesia	Psychic	Status	—	—	20	Self	—	—
90	Thrash	Normal	Physical	120	100	10	1 Random	—	○
100	Flare Blitz	Fire	Physical	120	100	15	Normal	—	○

TM & HM MOVES

Lv.	Name	Type	Kind	Pow.	Acc.	PP	Range	Long	DA
TM04	Calm Mind	Psychic	Status	—	—	20	Self	—	—
TM06	Toxic	Poison	Status	—	90	10	Normal	—	—
TM10	Hidden Power	Normal	Special	—	100	15	Normal	—	—
TM11	Sunny Day	Fire	Status	—	—	5	Both Sides	—	—
TM16	Light Screen	Psychic	Status	—	—	30	Your Side	—	—
TM17	Protect	Normal	Status	—	—	10	Self	—	—
TM20	Safeguard	Normal	Status	—	—	25	Your Side	—	—
TM21	Frustration	Normal	Physical	—	100	20	Normal	—	○
TM22	SolarBeam	Grass	Special	120	100	10	Normal	—	—
TM27	Return	Normal	Physical	—	100	20	Normal	—	○
TM29	Psychic	Psychic	Special	90	100	10	Normal	—	—
TM32	Double Team	Normal	Status	—	—	15	Self	—	—
TM35	Flamethrower	Fire	Special	95	100	15	Normal	—	—
TM38	Fire Blast	Fire	Special	120	85	5	Normal	—	—
TM42	Facade	Normal	Physical	70	100	20	Normal	—	○
TM43	Flame Charge	Fire	Physical	50	100	20	Normal	—	○
TM44	Rest	Psychic	Status	—	—	10	Self	—	—
TM48	Round	Normal	Special	60	100	15	Normal	—	—
TM50	Overheat	Fire	Special	140	90	5	Normal	—	—
TM59	Incinerate	Fire	Special	30	100	15	Many Others	—	—
TM61	Will-O-Wisp	Fire	Status	—	75	15	Normal	—	—
TM62	Acrobatics	Flying	Physical	55	100	15	Normal	○	○
TM76	Struggle Bug	Bug	Special	30	100	20	Many Others	—	—
TM87	Swagger	Normal	Status	—	90	15	Normal	—	—
TM89	U-turn	Bug	Physical	70	100	20	Normal	—	○
TM90	Substitute	Normal	Status	—	—	10	Self	—	—
TM93	Wild Charge	Electric	Physical	90	100	15	Normal	—	○

MOVES TAUGHT BY PEOPLE

Name	Type	Kind	Pow.	Acc.	PP	Range	Long	DA

MOVES TAUGHT BY MOVE TUTORS FOR SHARDS

Name	Type	Kind	Pow.	Acc.	PP	Range	Long	DA
Bug Bite	Bug	Physical	60	100	20	Normal	—	○
Signal Beam	Bug	Special	75	100	15	Normal	—	—
Magnet Rise	Electric	Status	—	—	10	Self	—	—
Zen Headbutt	Psychic	Physical	80	90	15	Normal	—	○
Snore	Normal	Special	40	100	15	Normal	—	—
Heat Wave	Fire	Special	100	90	10	Many Others	—	—
Giga Drain	Grass	Special	75	100	10	Normal	—	—
Sleep Talk	Normal	Status	—	—	10	Self	—	—

EGG MOVES

Name	Type	Kind	Pow.	Acc.	PP	Range	Long	DA
String Shot	Bug	Status	—	95	40	Many Others	—	—
Harden	Normal	Status	—	—	30	Self	—	—
Foresight	Normal	Status	—	—	40	Normal	—	—
Endure	Normal	Status	—	—	10	Self	—	—
Zen Headbutt	Psychic	Physical	80	90	15	Normal	—	○
Morning Sun	Normal	Status	—	—	5	Self	—	—
Magnet Rise	Electric	Status	—	—	10	Self	—	—

Pokémon AR Marker

Sun Pokémon

637 Volcarona

- HEIGHT: 5'03"
- WEIGHT: 101.4 lbs.
- GENDER: ♂ / ♀

Thought to be an embodiment of the sun, it appeared during a bitterly cold winter and saved Pokémon from freezing.

Same form for ♂ / ♀

TYPE Bug Fire

ABILITY
- Flame Body

HIDDEN ABILITY
—

STATS
HP
Attack
Defense
Sp. Atk
Sp. Def
Speed

EGG GROUPS
Bug

ITEMS SOMETIMES HELD
- SilverPowder

EVOLUTION

HOW TO OBTAIN

Pokémon Black Version 2	Relic Castle innermost part of the lowest floor
Pokémon White Version 2	Relic Castle innermost part of the lowest floor

HOW TO OBTAIN FROM OTHER GAMES

—

—

LEVEL-UP AND LEARNED MOVES

Lv.	Name	Type	Kind	Pow.	Acc.	PP	Range	Long	DA
1	Ember	Fire	Special	40	100	25	Normal	—	—
1	String Shot	Bug	Status	—	95	40	Many Others	—	—
1	Leech Life	Bug	Physical	20	100	15	Normal	—	○
1	Gust	Flying	Special	40	100	35	Normal	○	—
10	Leech Life	Bug	Physical	20	100	15	Normal	—	○
20	Gust	Flying	Special	40	100	35	Normal	○	—
30	Fire Spin	Fire	Special	35	85	15	Normal	—	—
40	Whirlwind	Normal	Status	—	100	20	Normal	—	—
50	Silver Wind	Bug	Special	60	100	5	Normal	—	—
59	Quiver Dance	Bug	Status	—	—	20	Self	—	—
60	Heat Wave	Fire	Special	100	90	10	Many Others	—	—
70	Bug Buzz	Bug	Special	90	100	10	Normal	—	—
80	Rage Powder	Bug	Status	—	—	20	Self	—	—
90	Hurricane	Flying	Special	120	70	10	Normal	○	—
100	Fiery Dance	Fire	Special	80	100	10	Normal	—	—

TM & HM MOVES

Lv.	Name	Type	Kind	Pow.	Acc.	PP	Range	Long	DA
TM04	Calm Mind	Psychic	Status	—	—	20	Self	—	—
TM06	Toxic	Poison	Status	—	90	10	Normal	—	—
TM10	Hidden Power	Normal	Special	—	100	15	Normal	—	—
TM11	Sunny Day	Fire	Status	—	—	5	Both Sides	—	—
TM15	Hyper Beam	Normal	Special	150	90	5	Normal	—	—
TM16	Light Screen	Psychic	Status	—	—	30	Your Side	—	—
TM17	Protect	Normal	Status	—	—	10	Self	—	—
TM20	Safeguard	Normal	Status	—	—	25	Your Side	—	—
TM21	Frustration	Normal	Physical	—	100	20	Normal	—	○
TM22	SolarBeam	Grass	Special	120	100	10	Normal	—	—
TM27	Return	Normal	Physical	—	100	20	Normal	—	○
TM29	Psychic	Psychic	Special	90	100	10	Normal	—	—
TM32	Double Team	Normal	Status	—	—	15	Self	—	—
TM35	Flamethrower	Fire	Special	95	100	15	Normal	—	—
TM38	Fire Blast	Fire	Special	120	85	5	Normal	—	—
TM40	Aerial Ace	Flying	Physical	60	—	20	Normal	○	○
TM42	Facade	Normal	Physical	70	100	20	Normal	—	○
TM43	Flame Charge	Fire	Physical	50	100	20	Normal	—	○
TM44	Rest	Psychic	Status	—	—	10	Self	—	—
TM48	Round	Normal	Special	60	100	15	Normal	—	—
TM50	Overheat	Fire	Special	140	90	5	Normal	—	—
TM59	Incinerate	Fire	Special	30	100	15	Many Others	—	—
TM61	Will-O-Wisp	Fire	Status	—	75	15	Normal	—	—
TM62	Acrobatics	Flying	Physical	55	100	15	Normal	○	○
TM68	Giga Impact	Normal	Physical	150	90	5	Normal	—	○
TM76	Struggle Bug	Bug	Special	30	100	20	Many Others	—	—
TM84	Poison Jab	Poison	Physical	80	100	20	Normal	—	○
TM87	Swagger	Normal	Status	—	90	15	Normal	—	—
TM89	U-turn	Bug	Physical	70	100	20	Normal	—	○
TM90	Substitute	Normal	Status	—	—	10	Self	—	—
TM93	Wild Charge	Electric	Physical	90	100	15	Normal	—	○
HM02	Fly	Flying	Physical	90	95	15	Normal	○	○

MOVES TAUGHT BY PEOPLE

Name	Type	Kind	Pow.	Acc.	PP	Range	Long	DA

MOVES TAUGHT BY MOVE TUTORS FOR SHARDS

Name	Type	Kind	Pow.	Acc.	PP	Range	Long	DA
Bug Bite	Bug	Physical	60	100	20	Normal	—	○
Signal Beam	Bug	Special	75	100	15	Normal	—	—
Magnet Rise	Electric	Status	—	—	10	Self	—	—
Zen Headbutt	Psychic	Physical	80	90	15	Normal	—	○
Snore	Normal	Special	40	100	15	Normal	—	—
Roost	Flying	Status	—	—	10	Self	—	—
Heat Wave	Fire	Special	100	90	10	Many Others	—	—
Giga Drain	Grass	Special	75	100	10	Normal	—	—
Tailwind	Flying	Status	—	—	30	Your Side	—	—
Sleep Talk	Normal	Status	—	—	10	Self	—	—

Pokémon AR Marker

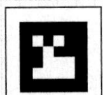

Iron Will Pokémon

638 Cobalion

- HEIGHT: 6'11"
- WEIGHT: 551.2 lbs.
- GENDER: Unknown

It has a body and heart of steel. It worked with its allies to punish people when they hurt Pokémon.

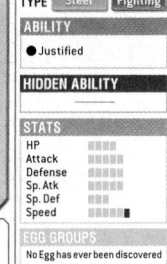

Gender unknown

Pokémon AR Marker

TYPE: Steel / Fighting

ABILITY
- Justified

HIDDEN ABILITY
—

STATS
HP
Attack
Defense
Sp. Atk
Sp. Def
Speed

EGG GROUPS
No Egg has ever been discovered

ITEMS SOMETIMES HELD
- None

EVOLUTION
Does not evolve

HOW TO OBTAIN

Pokémon Black Version 2	Route 13
Pokémon White Version 2	Route 13

HOW TO OBTAIN FROM OTHER GAMES
—
—

LEVEL-UP AND LEARNED MOVES

Lv.	Name	Type	Kind	Pow.	Acc.	PP	Range	Long	DA
1	Quick Attack	Normal	Physical	40	100	30	Normal	—	○
1	Leer	Normal	Status	—	100	30	Many Others	—	—
7	Double Kick	Fighting	Physical	30	100	30	Normal	—	○
13	Metal Claw	Steel	Physical	50	95	35	Normal	—	○
19	Take Down	Normal	Physical	90	85	20	Normal	—	○
25	Helping Hand	Normal	Status	—	—	20	1 Ally	—	—
31	Retaliate	Normal	Physical	70	100	5	Normal	—	○
37	Iron Head	Steel	Physical	80	100	15	Normal	—	○
42	Sacred Sword	Fighting	Physical	90	100	20	Normal	—	○
49	Swords Dance	Normal	Status	—	—	30	Self	—	—
55	Quick Guard	Fighting	Status	—	—	15	Your Side	—	—
61	Work Up	Normal	Status	—	—	30	Self	—	—
67	Metal Burst	Steel	Physical	—	100	10	Varies	—	—
73	Close Combat	Fighting	Physical	120	100	5	Normal	—	○

TM & HM MOVES

Lv.	Name	Type	Kind	Pow.	Acc.	PP	Range	Long	DA
TM01	Hone Claws	Dark	Status	—	—	15	Self	—	—
TM04	Calm Mind	Psychic	Status	—	—	20	Self	—	—
TM05	Roar	Normal	Status	—	100	20	Normal	—	—
TM06	Toxic	Poison	Status	—	90	10	Normal	—	—
TM10	Hidden Power	Normal	Special	—	100	15	Normal	—	—
TM12	Taunt	Dark	Status	—	100	20	Normal	—	—
TM15	Hyper Beam	Normal	Special	150	90	5	Normal	—	—
TM17	Protect	Normal	Status	—	—	10	Self	—	—
TM20	Safeguard	Normal	Status	—	—	25	Your Side	—	—
TM21	Frustration	Normal	Physical	—	100	20	Normal	—	○
TM27	Return	Normal	Physical	—	100	20	Normal	—	○
TM32	Double Team	Normal	Status	—	—	15	Self	—	—
TM33	Reflect	Psychic	Status	—	—	20	Your Side	—	—
TM37	Sandstorm	Rock	Status	—	—	10	Both Sides	—	—
TM40	Aerial Ace	Flying	Physical	60	—	20	Normal	○	○
TM42	Facade	Normal	Physical	70	100	20	Normal	—	○
TM44	Rest	Psychic	Status	—	—	10	Self	—	—
TM48	Round	Normal	Special	60	100	15	Normal	—	—
TM52	Focus Blast	Fighting	Special	120	70	5	Normal	—	—
TM54	False Swipe	Normal	Physical	40	100	40	Normal	—	○
TM67	Retaliate	Normal	Physical	70	100	5	Normal	—	○
TM68	Giga Impact	Normal	Physical	150	90	5	Normal	—	○
TM69	Rock Polish	Rock	Status	—	—	20	Self	—	—
TM71	Stone Edge	Rock	Physical	100	80	5	Normal	—	—
TM72	Volt Switch	Electric	Special	70	100	20	Normal	—	—
TM73	Thunder Wave	Electric	Status	—	100	20	Normal	—	—
TM75	Swords Dance	Normal	Status	—	—	30	Self	—	—
TM77	Psych Up	Normal	Status	—	—	10	Normal	—	—
TM81	X-Scissor	Bug	Physical	80	100	15	Normal	—	○
TM83	Work Up	Normal	Status	—	—	30	Self	—	—
TM84	Poison Jab	Poison	Physical	80	100	20	Normal	—	○
TM87	Swagger	Normal	Status	—	90	15	Normal	—	—
TM90	Substitute	Normal	Status	—	—	10	Self	—	—
TM91	Flash Cannon	Steel	Special	80	100	10	Normal	—	—
TM94	Rock Smash	Fighting	Physical	40	100	15	Normal	—	○
HM01	Cut	Normal	Physical	50	95	30	Normal	—	○
HM04	Strength	Normal	Physical	80	100	15	Normal	—	○

MOVES TAUGHT BY PEOPLE

Name	Type	Kind	Pow.	Acc.	PP	Range	Long	DA

MOVES TAUGHT BY MOVE TUTORS FOR SHARDS

Name	Type	Kind	Pow.	Acc.	PP	Range	Long	DA
Bounce	Flying	Physical	85	85	5	Normal	○	○
Iron Head	Steel	Physical	80	100	15	Normal	—	○
Iron Defense	Steel	Status	—	—	15	Self	—	—
Magnet Rise	Electric	Status	—	—	10	Self	—	—
Block	Normal	Status	—	—	5	Normal	—	—
Zen Headbutt	Psychic	Physical	80	90	15	Normal	—	○
Superpower	Fighting	Physical	120	100	5	Normal	—	○
Snore	Normal	Special	40	100	15	Normal	—	—
Helping Hand	Normal	Status	—	—	20	1 Ally	—	—
Stealth Rock	Rock	Status	—	—	20	Other Side	—	—
Sleep Talk	Normal	Status	—	—	10	Self	—	—

Cavern Pokémon

639 Terrakion

- HEIGHT: 6'03"
- WEIGHT: 573.2 lbs.
- GENDER: Unknown

Spoken of in legend, this Pokémon used its phenomenal power to destroy a castle in its effort to protect Pokémon.

Gender unknown

Pokémon AR Marker

TYPE: Rock / Fighting

ABILITY
- Justified

HIDDEN ABILITY
—

STATS
HP
Attack
Defense
Sp. Atk
Sp. Def
Speed

EGG GROUPS
No Egg has ever been discovered

ITEMS SOMETIMES HELD
- None

EVOLUTION
Does not evolve

HOW TO OBTAIN

Pokémon Black Version 2	Route 22
Pokémon White Version 2	Route 22

HOW TO OBTAIN FROM OTHER GAMES
—
—

LEVEL-UP AND LEARNED MOVES

Lv.	Name	Type	Kind	Pow.	Acc.	PP	Range	Long	DA
1	Quick Attack	Normal	Physical	40	100	30	Normal	—	○
1	Leer	Normal	Status	—	100	30	Many Others	—	—
7	Double Kick	Fighting	Physical	30	100	30	Normal	—	○
13	Smack Down	Rock	Physical	50	100	15	Normal	—	—
19	Take Down	Normal	Physical	90	85	20	Normal	—	○
25	Helping Hand	Normal	Status	—	—	20	1 Ally	—	—
31	Retaliate	Normal	Physical	70	100	5	Normal	—	○
37	Rock Slide	Rock	Physical	75	90	10	Many Others	—	—
42	Sacred Sword	Fighting	Physical	90	100	20	Normal	—	○
49	Swords Dance	Normal	Status	—	—	30	Self	—	—
55	Quick Guard	Fighting	Status	—	—	15	Your Side	—	—
61	Work Up	Normal	Status	—	—	30	Self	—	—
67	Stone Edge	Rock	Physical	100	80	5	Normal	—	—
73	Close Combat	Fighting	Physical	120	100	5	Normal	—	○

TM & HM MOVES

Lv.	Name	Type	Kind	Pow.	Acc.	PP	Range	Long	DA
TM04	Calm Mind	Psychic	Status	—	—	20	Self	—	—
TM05	Roar	Normal	Status	—	100	20	Normal	—	—
TM06	Toxic	Poison	Status	—	90	10	Normal	—	—
TM10	Hidden Power	Normal	Special	—	100	15	Normal	—	—
TM12	Taunt	Dark	Status	—	100	20	Normal	—	—
TM15	Hyper Beam	Normal	Special	150	90	5	Normal	—	—
TM17	Protect	Normal	Status	—	—	10	Self	—	—
TM20	Safeguard	Normal	Status	—	—	25	Your Side	—	—
TM21	Frustration	Normal	Physical	—	100	20	Normal	—	○
TM23	Smack Down	Rock	Physical	50	100	15	Normal	—	—
TM26	Earthquake	Ground	Physical	100	100	10	Adjacent	—	—
TM27	Return	Normal	Physical	—	100	20	Normal	—	○
TM32	Double Team	Normal	Status	—	—	15	Self	—	—
TM33	Reflect	Psychic	Status	—	—	20	Your Side	—	—
TM37	Sandstorm	Rock	Status	—	—	10	Both Sides	—	—
TM39	Rock Tomb	Rock	Physical	50	80	10	Normal	—	—
TM40	Aerial Ace	Flying	Physical	60	—	20	Normal	○	○
TM42	Facade	Normal	Physical	70	100	20	Normal	—	○
TM44	Rest	Psychic	Status	—	—	10	Self	—	—
TM48	Round	Normal	Special	60	100	15	Normal	—	—
TM52	Focus Blast	Fighting	Special	120	70	5	Normal	—	—
TM54	False Swipe	Normal	Physical	40	100	40	Normal	—	○
TM67	Retaliate	Normal	Physical	70	100	5	Normal	—	○
TM68	Giga Impact	Normal	Physical	150	90	5	Normal	—	○
TM69	Rock Polish	Rock	Status	—	—	20	Self	—	—
TM71	Stone Edge	Rock	Physical	100	80	5	Normal	—	—
TM75	Swords Dance	Normal	Status	—	—	30	Self	—	—
TM77	Psych Up	Normal	Status	—	—	10	Normal	—	—
TM78	Bulldoze	Ground	Physical	60	100	20	Adjacent	—	—
TM80	Rock Slide	Rock	Physical	75	90	10	Many Others	—	—
TM81	X-Scissor	Bug	Physical	80	100	15	Normal	—	○
TM83	Work Up	Normal	Status	—	—	30	Self	—	—
TM84	Poison Jab	Poison	Physical	80	100	20	Normal	—	○
TM87	Swagger	Normal	Status	—	90	15	Normal	—	—
TM90	Substitute	Normal	Status	—	—	10	Self	—	—
TM94	Rock Smash	Fighting	Physical	40	100	15	Normal	—	○
HM01	Cut	Normal	Physical	50	95	30	Normal	—	○
HM04	Strength	Normal	Physical	80	100	15	Normal	—	○

MOVES TAUGHT BY PEOPLE

Name	Type	Kind	Pow.	Acc.	PP	Range	Long	DA

MOVES TAUGHT BY MOVE TUTORS FOR SHARDS

Name	Type	Kind	Pow.	Acc.	PP	Range	Long	DA
Iron Head	Steel	Physical	80	100	15	Normal	—	○
Block	Normal	Status	—	—	5	Normal	—	—
Earth Power	Ground	Special	90	100	10	Normal	—	—
Zen Headbutt	Psychic	Physical	80	90	15	Normal	—	○
Superpower	Fighting	Physical	120	100	5	Normal	—	○
Snore	Normal	Special	40	100	15	Normal	—	—
Helping Hand	Normal	Status	—	—	20	1 Ally	—	—
Stealth Rock	Rock	Status	—	—	20	Other Side	—	—
Sleep Talk	Normal	Status	—	—	10	Self	—	—

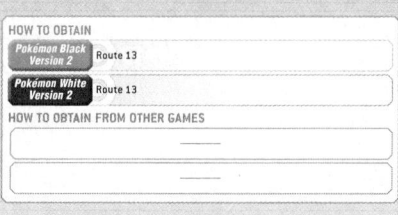

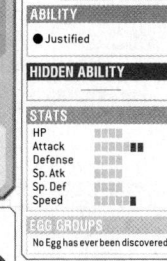

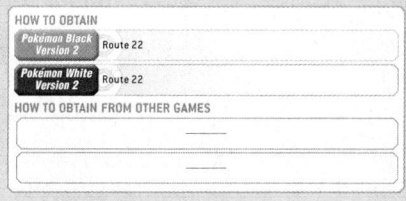

640 Virizion

Grassland Pokémon

- HEIGHT: 6'07"
- WEIGHT: 440.9 lbs.
- GENDER: Unknown

Legends say this Pokémon confounded opponents with its swift movements.

TYPE: Grass / Fighting

ABILITY
- Justified

HIDDEN ABILITY
—

STATS
HP
Attack
Defense
Sp. Atk
Sp. Def
Speed

EGG GROUPS
No Egg has ever been discovered

ITEMS SOMETIMES HELD
- None

Gender unknown

Pokémon AR Marker

EVOLUTION

Does not evolve

HOW TO OBTAIN

Pokémon Black Version 2	Route 11
Pokémon White Version 2	Route 11

HOW TO OBTAIN FROM OTHER GAMES

—

—

LEVEL-UP AND LEARNED MOVES

Lv.	Name	Type	Kind	Pow.	Acc.	PP	Range	Long	DA
1	Quick Attack	Normal	Physical	40	100	30	Normal	—	○
1	Leer	Normal	Status	—	100	30	Many Others	—	—
7	Double Kick	Fighting	Physical	30	100	30	Normal	—	○
13	Magical Leaf	Grass	Special	60	—	20	Normal	—	—
19	Take Down	Normal	Physical	90	85	20	Normal	—	○
25	Helping Hand	Normal	Status	—	—	20	1 Ally	—	—
31	Retaliate	Normal	Physical	70	100	5	Normal	—	○
37	Giga Drain	Grass	Special	75	100	10	Normal	—	—
42	Sacred Sword	Fighting	Physical	90	100	20	Normal	—	○
49	Swords Dance	Normal	Status	—	—	30	Self	—	—
55	Quick Guard	Fighting	Status	—	—	15	Your Side	—	—
61	Work Up	Normal	Status	—	—	30	Self	—	—
67	Leaf Blade	Grass	Physical	90	100	15	Normal	—	○
73	Close Combat	Fighting	Physical	120	100	5	Normal	—	○

TM & HM MOVES

Lv.	Name	Type	Kind	Pow.	Acc.	PP	Range	Long	DA
TM04	Calm Mind	Psychic	Status	—	—	20	Self	—	—
TM05	Roar	Normal	Status	—	100	20	Normal	—	—
TM06	Toxic	Poison	Status	—	90	10	Normal	—	—
TM10	Hidden Power	Normal	Special	—	100	15	Normal	—	—
TM11	Sunny Day	Fire	Status	—	—	5	Both Sides	—	—
TM12	Taunt	Dark	Status	—	100	20	Normal	—	—
TM15	Hyper Beam	Normal	Special	150	90	5	Normal	—	—
TM16	Light Screen	Psychic	Status	—	—	30	Your Side	—	—
TM17	Protect	Normal	Status	—	—	10	Self	—	—
TM20	Safeguard	Normal	Status	—	—	25	Your Side	—	—
TM21	Frustration	Normal	Physical	—	100	20	Normal	—	○
TM22	SolarBeam	Grass	Special	120	100	10	Normal	—	—
TM27	Return	Normal	Physical	—	100	20	Normal	—	○
TM32	Double Team	Normal	Status	—	—	15	Self	—	—
TM33	Reflect	Psychic	Status	—	—	20	Your Side	—	—
TM40	Aerial Ace	Flying	Physical	60	—	20	Normal	○	○
TM42	Facade	Normal	Physical	70	100	20	Normal	—	○
TM44	Rest	Psychic	Status	—	—	10	Self	—	—
TM48	Round	Normal	Special	60	100	15	Normal	—	—
TM52	Focus Blast	Fighting	Special	120	70	5	Normal	—	—
TM53	Energy Ball	Grass	Special	80	100	10	Normal	—	—
TM54	False Swipe	Normal	Physical	40	100	40	Normal	—	○
TM67	Retaliate	Normal	Physical	70	100	5	Normal	—	○
TM68	Giga Impact	Normal	Physical	150	90	5	Normal	—	○
TM70	Flash	Normal	Status	—	100	20	Normal	—	—
TM71	Stone Edge	Rock	Physical	100	80	5	Normal	—	—
TM75	Swords Dance	Normal	Status	—	—	30	Self	—	—
TM77	Psych Up	Normal	Status	—	—	10	Normal	—	—
TM81	X-Scissor	Bug	Physical	80	100	15	Normal	—	○
TM83	Work Up	Normal	Status	—	—	30	Self	—	—
TM86	Grass Knot	Grass	Special	—	100	20	Normal	—	○
TM87	Swagger	Normal	Status	—	90	15	Normal	—	—
TM90	Substitute	Normal	Status	—	—	10	Self	—	—
TM94	Rock Smash	Fighting	Physical	40	100	15	Normal	—	○
HM01	Cut	Normal	Physical	50	95	30	Normal	—	○
HM04	Strength	Normal	Physical	80	100	15	Normal	—	○

MOVES TAUGHT BY PEOPLE

Name	Type	Kind	Pow.	Acc.	PP	Range	Long	DA

MOVES TAUGHT BY MOVE TUTORS FOR SHARDS

Name	Type	Kind	Pow.	Acc.	PP	Range	Long	DA
Bounce	Flying	Physical	85	85	5	Normal	○	○
Seed Bomb	Grass	Physical	80	100	15	Normal	—	—
Block	Normal	Status	—	—	5	Normal	—	—
Zen Headbutt	Psychic	Physical	80	90	15	Normal	—	○
Superpower	Fighting	Physical	120	100	5	Normal	—	○
Snore	Normal	Special	40	100	15	Normal	—	—
Synthesis	Grass	Status	—	—	5	Self	—	—
Giga Drain	Grass	Special	75	100	10	Normal	—	—
Worry Seed	Grass	Status	—	100	10	Normal	—	—
Helping Hand	Normal	Status	—	—	20	1 Ally	—	—
Sleep Talk	Normal	Status	—	—	10	Self	—	—

641 Tornadus (Incarnate Forme)

Cyclone Pokémon

- HEIGHT: 4'11"
- WEIGHT: 138.9 lbs.
- GENDER: ♂

In every direction it flies, creating winds so powerful, they blow everything away.

TYPE: Flying

ABILITY
- Prankster

HIDDEN ABILITY
- Defiant

STATS
HP
Attack
Defense
Sp. Atk
Sp. Def
Speed

EGG GROUPS
No Egg has ever been discovered

ITEMS SOMETIMES HELD
- None

♂

Pokémon AR Marker

EVOLUTION

Does not evolve

HOW TO OBTAIN

Pokémon Black Version 2	Link Trade
Pokémon White Version 2	Link Trade

HOW TO OBTAIN FROM OTHER GAMES

Pokémon Black Version	After you encounter it on Route 7, you can catch it as it roams around the Unova region

—

LEVEL-UP AND LEARNED MOVES

Lv.	Name	Type	Kind	Pow.	Acc.	PP	Range	Long	DA
1	Uproar	Normal	Special	90	100	10	1 Random	—	—
1	Astonish	Ghost	Physical	30	100	15	Normal	—	○
1	Gust	Flying	Special	40	100	35	Normal	○	—
7	Swagger	Normal	Status	—	90	15	Normal	—	—
13	Bite	Dark	Physical	60	100	25	Normal	—	○
19	Revenge	Fighting	Physical	60	100	10	Normal	—	○
25	Air Cutter	Flying	Special	55	95	25	Many Others	—	—
31	Extrasensory	Psychic	Special	80	100	30	Normal	—	—
37	Agility	Psychic	Status	—	—	30	Self	—	—
43	Air Slash	Flying	Special	75	95	20	Normal	○	—
49	Crunch	Dark	Physical	80	100	15	Normal	—	○
55	Tailwind	Flying	Status	—	—	30	Your Side	—	—
61	Rain Dance	Water	Status	—	—	5	Both Sides	—	—
67	Hurricane	Flying	Special	120	70	10	Normal	○	—
73	Dark Pulse	Dark	Special	80	100	15	Normal	○	—
79	Hammer Arm	Fighting	Physical	100	90	10	Normal	—	○
85	Thrash	Normal	Physical	120	100	10	1 Random	—	○

TM & HM MOVES

Lv.	Name	Type	Kind	Pow.	Acc.	PP	Range	Long	DA
TM06	Toxic	Poison	Status	—	90	10	Normal	—	—
TM08	Bulk Up	Fighting	Status	—	—	20	Self	—	—
TM10	Hidden Power	Normal	Special	—	100	15	Normal	—	—
TM12	Taunt	Dark	Status	—	100	20	Normal	—	—
TM15	Hyper Beam	Normal	Special	150	90	5	Normal	—	—
TM17	Protect	Normal	Status	—	—	10	Self	—	—
TM18	Rain Dance	Water	Status	—	—	5	Both Sides	—	—
TM21	Frustration	Normal	Physical	—	100	20	Normal	—	○
TM23	Smack Down	Rock	Physical	50	100	15	Normal	—	—
TM27	Return	Normal	Physical	—	100	20	Normal	—	○
TM29	Psychic	Psychic	Special	90	100	10	Normal	—	—
TM31	Brick Break	Fighting	Physical	75	100	15	Normal	—	○
TM32	Double Team	Normal	Status	—	—	15	Self	—	—
TM34	Sludge Wave	Poison	Special	95	100	10	Adjacent	—	—
TM36	Sludge Bomb	Poison	Special	90	100	10	Normal	—	—
TM40	Aerial Ace	Flying	Physical	60	—	20	Normal	○	○
TM41	Torment	Dark	Status	—	100	15	Normal	—	—
TM42	Facade	Normal	Physical	70	100	20	Normal	—	○
TM44	Rest	Psychic	Status	—	—	10	Self	—	—
TM45	Attract	Normal	Status	—	100	15	Normal	—	—
TM46	Thief	Dark	Physical	40	100	10	Normal	—	○
TM48	Round	Normal	Special	60	100	15	Normal	—	—
TM52	Focus Blast	Fighting	Special	120	70	5	Normal	—	—
TM56	Fling	Dark	Physical	—	100	10	Normal	—	—
TM58	Sky Drop	Flying	Physical	60	100	10	Normal	○	○
TM59	Incinerate	Fire	Special	30	100	15	Many Others	—	—
TM62	Acrobatics	Flying	Physical	55	100	15	Normal	○	○
TM63	Embargo	Dark	Status	—	100	15	Normal	—	—
TM66	Payback	Dark	Physical	50	100	10	Normal	—	○
TM68	Giga Impact	Normal	Physical	150	90	5	Normal	—	○
TM86	Grass Knot	Grass	Special	—	100	20	Normal	—	○
TM87	Swagger	Normal	Status	—	90	15	Normal	—	—
TM89	U-turn	Bug	Physical	70	100	20	Normal	—	○
TM90	Substitute	Normal	Status	—	—	10	Self	—	—
TM94	Rock Smash	Fighting	Physical	40	100	15	Normal	—	○
HM02	Fly	Flying	Physical	90	95	15	Normal	○	○
HM04	Strength	Normal	Physical	80	100	15	Normal	—	○

MOVES TAUGHT BY PEOPLE

Name	Type	Kind	Pow.	Acc.	PP	Range	Long	DA

MOVES TAUGHT BY MOVE TUTORS FOR SHARDS

Name	Type	Kind	Pow.	Acc.	PP	Range	Long	DA
Uproar	Normal	Special	90	100	10	1 Random	—	—
Icy Wind	Ice	Special	55	95	15	Many Others	—	—
Iron Tail	Steel	Physical	100	75	15	Normal	—	○
Foul Play	Dark	Physical	95	100	15	Normal	—	○
Superpower	Fighting	Physical	120	100	5	Normal	—	○
Dark Pulse	Dark	Special	80	100	15	Normal	○	—
Snore	Normal	Special	40	100	15	Normal	—	—
Knock Off	Dark	Physical	20	100	20	Normal	—	○
Role Play	Psychic	Status	—	—	10	Normal	—	—
Heat Wave	Fire	Special	100	90	10	Many Others	—	—
Tailwind	Flying	Status	—	—	30	Your Side	—	—
Sleep Talk	Normal	Status	—	—	10	Self	—	—

Cyclone Pokémon

641 Tornadus (Therian Forme)

- HEIGHT: 4'07"
- WEIGHT: 138.9 lbs.
- GENDER: ♂

In every direction it flies, creating winds so powerful, they blow everything away.

♂

TYPE Flying

ABILITY
- Regenerator

HIDDEN ABILITY
—

STATS
HP
Attack
Defense
Sp. Atk
Sp. Def
Speed

EGG GROUPS
No Egg has ever been discovered

ITEMS SOMETIMES HELD
- None

Pokémon AR Marker

EVOLUTION
Does not evolve

HOW TO OBTAIN

Pokémon Black Version 2	Bring Tornadus Incarnate Forme to your game and use Reveal Glass
Pokémon White Version 2	Bring Tornadus Incarnate Forme to your game and use Reveal Glass

HOW TO OBTAIN FROM OTHER GAMES
—
—

LEVEL-UP AND LEARNED MOVES

Lv.	Name	Type	Kind	Pow.	Acc.	PP	Range	Long	DA
1	Uproar	Normal	Special	90	100	10	1 Random	—	—
1	Astonish	Ghost	Physical	30	100	15	Normal	—	○
1	Gust	Flying	Special	40	100	35	Normal	○	—
7	Swagger	Normal	Status	—	90	15	Normal	—	—
13	Bite	Dark	Physical	60	100	25	Normal	—	○
19	Revenge	Fighting	Physical	60	100	10	Normal	—	○
25	Air Cutter	Flying	Special	55	95	25	Many Others	—	—
31	Extrasensory	Psychic	Special	80	100	30	Normal	—	—
37	Agility	Psychic	Status	—	—	30	Self	—	—
43	Air Slash	Flying	Special	75	95	20	Normal	○	—
49	Crunch	Dark	Physical	80	100	15	Normal	—	○
55	Tailwind	Flying	Status	—	—	30	Your Side	—	—
61	Rain Dance	Water	Status	—	—	5	Both Sides	—	—
67	Hurricane	Flying	Special	120	70	10	Normal	○	—
73	Dark Pulse	Dark	Special	80	100	15	Normal	○	—
79	Hammer Arm	Fighting	Physical	100	90	10	Normal	—	○
85	Thrash	Normal	Physical	120	100	10	1 Random	—	○

TM & HM MOVES

Lv.	Name	Type	Kind	Pow.	Acc.	PP	Range	Long	DA
TM06	Toxic	Poison	Status	—	90	10	Normal	—	—
TM08	Bulk Up	Fighting	Status	—	—	20	Self	—	—
TM10	Hidden Power	Normal	Special	—	100	15	Normal	—	—
TM12	Taunt	Dark	Status	—	100	20	Normal	—	—
TM15	Hyper Beam	Normal	Special	150	90	5	Normal	—	—
TM17	Protect	Normal	Status	—	—	10	Self	—	—
TM18	Rain Dance	Water	Status	—	—	5	Both Sides	—	—
TM21	Frustration	Normal	Physical	—	100	20	Normal	—	○
TM23	Smack Down	Rock	Physical	50	100	15	Normal	—	—
TM27	Return	Normal	Physical	—	100	20	Normal	—	○
TM29	Psychic	Psychic	Special	90	100	10	Normal	—	—
TM31	Brick Break	Fighting	Physical	75	100	15	Normal	—	○
TM32	Double Team	Normal	Status	—	—	15	Self	—	—
TM34	Sludge Wave	Poison	Special	95	100	10	Adjacent	—	—
TM36	Sludge Bomb	Poison	Special	90	100	10	Normal	—	—
TM40	Aerial Ace	Flying	Physical	60	—	20	Normal	○	○
TM41	Torment	Dark	Status	—	100	15	Normal	—	—
TM42	Facade	Normal	Physical	70	100	20	Normal	—	○
TM44	Rest	Psychic	Status	—	—	10	Self	—	—
TM45	Attract	Normal	Status	—	100	15	Normal	—	—
TM46	Thief	Dark	Physical	40	100	10	Normal	—	○
TM48	Round	Normal	Special	60	100	15	Normal	—	—
TM52	Focus Blast	Fighting	Special	120	70	5	Normal	—	—
TM56	Fling	Dark	Physical	—	100	10	Normal	—	—
TM58	Sky Drop	Flying	Physical	60	100	10	Normal	○	○
TM59	Incinerate	Fire	Special	30	100	15	Many Others	—	—
TM62	Acrobatics	Flying	Physical	55	100	15	Normal	○	○
TM63	Embargo	Dark	Status	—	100	15	Normal	—	—
TM66	Payback	Dark	Physical	50	100	10	Normal	—	○
TM68	Giga Impact	Normal	Physical	150	90	5	Normal	—	○
TM86	Grass Knot	Grass	Special	—	100	20	Normal	—	○
TM87	Swagger	Normal	Status	—	90	15	Normal	—	—
TM89	U-turn	Bug	Physical	70	100	20	Normal	—	○
TM90	Substitute	Normal	Status	—	—	10	Self	—	—
TM94	Rock Smash	Fighting	Physical	40	100	15	Normal	—	○
HM02	Fly	Flying	Physical	90	95	15	Normal	○	○
HM04	Strength	Normal	Physical	80	100	15	Normal	-	○

MOVES TAUGHT BY PEOPLE

Name	Type	Kind	Pow.	Acc.	PP	Range	Long	DA

MOVES TAUGHT BY MOVE TUTORS FOR SHARDS

Name	Type	Kind	Pow.	Acc.	PP	Range	Long	DA
Uproar	Normal	Special	90	100	10	1 Random	—	—
Icy Wind	Ice	Special	55	95	15	Many Others	—	—
Iron Tail	Steel	Physical	100	75	15	Normal	—	○
Foul Play	Dark	Physical	95	100	15	Normal	—	○
Superpower	Fighting	Physical	120	100	5	Normal	—	○
Dark Pulse	Dark	Special	80	100	15	Normal	○	—
Snore	Normal	Special	40	100	15	Normal	—	—
Knock Off	Dark	Physical	20	100	20	Normal	—	○
Role Play	Psychic	Status	—	—	10	Normal	—	—
Heat Wave	Fire	Special	100	90	10	Many Others	—	—
Tailwind	Flying	Status	—	—	30	Your Side	—	—
Sleep Talk	Normal	Status	—	—	10	Self	—	—

Bolt Strike Pokémon

642 Thundurus (Incarnate Forme)

- HEIGHT: 4'11"
- WEIGHT: 134.5 lbs.
- GENDER: ♂

As it flies around, it shoots lightning all over the place and causes forest fires. It is therefore disliked.

♂

TYPE Electric Flying

ABILITY
- Prankster

HIDDEN ABILITY
- Defiant

STATS
HP
Attack
Defense
Sp. Atk
Sp. Def
Speed

EGG GROUPS
No Egg has ever been discovered

ITEMS SOMETIMES HELD
- None

Pokémon AR Marker

EVOLUTION
Does not evolve

HOW TO OBTAIN

Pokémon Black Version 2	Link Trade
Pokémon White Version 2	Link Trade

HOW TO OBTAIN FROM OTHER GAMES

Pokémon White Version	After you encounter it on Route 7, you can catch it as it roams around the Unova region
—	

LEVEL-UP AND LEARNED MOVES

Lv.	Name	Type	Kind	Pow.	Acc.	PP	Range	Long	DA
1	Uproar	Normal	Special	90	100	10	1 Random	—	—
1	Astonish	Ghost	Physical	30	100	15	Normal	—	○
1	ThunderShock	Electric	Special	40	100	30	Normal	—	—
7	Swagger	Normal	Status	—	90	15	Normal	—	—
13	Bite	Dark	Physical	60	100	25	Normal	—	○
19	Revenge	Fighting	Physical	60	100	10	Normal	—	○
25	Shock Wave	Electric	Special	60	—	20	Normal	—	—
31	Heal Block	Psychic	Status	—	100	15	Many Others	—	—
37	Agility	Psychic	Status	—	—	30	Self	—	—
43	Discharge	Electric	Special	80	100	15	Adjacent	—	—
49	Crunch	Dark	Physical	80	100	15	Normal	—	○
55	Charge	Electric	Status	—	—	20	Self	—	—
61	Nasty Plot	Dark	Status	—	—	20	Self	—	—
67	Thunder	Electric	Special	120	70	10	Normal	—	—
73	Dark Pulse	Dark	Special	80	100	15	Normal	○	—
79	Hammer Arm	Fighting	Physical	100	90	10	Normal	—	○
85	Thrash	Normal	Physical	120	100	10	1 Random	—	○

TM & HM MOVES

Lv.	Name	Type	Kind	Pow.	Acc.	PP	Range	Long	DA
TM06	Toxic	Poison	Status	—	90	10	Normal	—	—
TM08	Bulk Up	Fighting	Status	—	—	20	Self	—	—
TM10	Hidden Power	Normal	Special	—	100	15	Normal	—	—
TM12	Taunt	Dark	Status	—	100	20	Normal	—	—
TM15	Hyper Beam	Normal	Special	150	90	5	Normal	—	—
TM17	Protect	Normal	Status	—	—	10	Self	—	—
TM18	Rain Dance	Water	Status	—	—	5	Both Sides	—	—
TM21	Frustration	Normal	Physical	—	100	20	Normal	—	○
TM23	Smack Down	Rock	Physical	50	100	15	Normal	—	—
TM24	Thunderbolt	Electric	Special	95	100	15	Normal	—	—
TM25	Thunder	Electric	Special	120	70	10	Normal	—	—
TM27	Return	Normal	Physical	—	100	20	Normal	—	○
TM29	Psychic	Psychic	Special	90	100	10	Normal	—	—
TM31	Brick Break	Fighting	Physical	75	100	15	Normal	—	○
TM32	Double Team	Normal	Status	—	—	15	Self	—	—
TM34	Sludge Wave	Poison	Special	95	100	10	Adjacent	—	—
TM36	Sludge Bomb	Poison	Special	90	100	10	Normal	—	—
TM41	Torment	Dark	Status	—	100	15	Normal	—	—
TM42	Facade	Normal	Physical	70	100	20	Normal	—	○
TM44	Rest	Psychic	Status	—	—	10	Self	—	—
TM45	Attract	Normal	Status	—	100	15	Normal	—	—
TM46	Thief	Dark	Physical	40	100	10	Normal	—	○
TM48	Round	Normal	Special	60	100	15	Normal	—	—
TM52	Focus Blast	Fighting	Special	120	70	5	Normal	—	—
TM56	Fling	Dark	Physical	—	100	10	Normal	—	—
TM57	Charge Beam	Electric	Special	50	90	10	Normal	—	—
TM58	Sky Drop	Flying	Physical	60	100	10	Normal	○	○
TM59	Incinerate	Fire	Special	30	100	15	Many Others	—	—
TM63	Embargo	Dark	Status	—	100	15	Normal	—	—
TM66	Payback	Dark	Physical	50	100	10	Normal	—	○
TM68	Giga Impact	Normal	Physical	150	90	5	Normal	—	○
TM72	Volt Switch	Electric	Special	70	100	20	Normal	—	—
TM73	Thunder Wave	Electric	Status	—	100	20	Normal	—	—
TM86	Grass Knot	Grass	Special	—	100	20	Normal	—	○
TM87	Swagger	Normal	Status	—	90	15	Normal	—	—
TM89	U-turn	Bug	Physical	70	100	20	Normal	—	○
TM90	Substitute	Normal	Status	—	—	10	Self	—	—
TM91	Flash Cannon	Steel	Special	80	100	10	Normal	—	—
TM93	Wild Charge	Electric	Physical	90	100	15	Normal	—	○
TM94	Rock Smash	Fighting	Physical	40	100	15	Normal	—	○
HM02	Fly	Flying	Physical	90	95	15	Normal	○	○
HM04	Strength	Normal	Physical	80	100	15	Normal	—	○

MOVES TAUGHT BY PEOPLE

Name	Type	Kind	Pow.	Acc.	PP	Range	Long	DA

MOVES TAUGHT BY MOVE TUTORS FOR SHARDS

Name	Type	Kind	Pow.	Acc.	PP	Range	Long	DA
Uproar	Normal	Special	90	100	10	1 Random	—	—
ThunderPunch	Electric	Physical	75	100	15	Normal	—	○
Iron Tail	Steel	Physical	100	75	15	Normal	—	○
Foul Play	Dark	Physical	95	100	15	Normal	—	○
Superpower	Fighting	Physical	120	100	5	Normal	—	○
Dark Pulse	Dark	Special	80	100	15	Normal	○	—
Snore	Normal	Special	40	100	15	Normal	—	—
Knock Off	Dark	Physical	20	100	20	Normal	—	○
Role Play	Psychic	Status	—	—	10	Normal	—	—
Sleep Talk	Normal	Status	—	—	10	Self	—	—

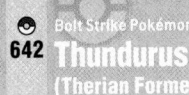

Bolt Strike Pokémon

642 Thundurus (Therian Forme)

- HEIGHT: 9'10"
- WEIGHT: 134.5 lbs.
- GENDER: ♂

As it flies around, it shoots lightning all over the place and causes forest fires. It is therefore disliked.

♂

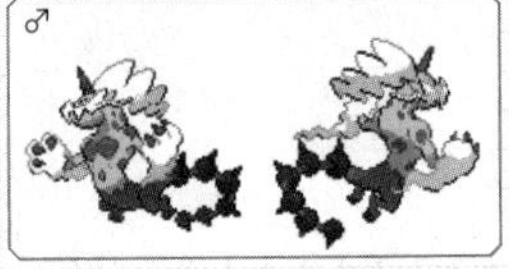

TYPE: Electric / Flying

ABILITY
- Volt Absorb

HIDDEN ABILITY
—

STATS
HP
Attack
Defense
Sp. Atk
Sp. Def
Speed

EGG GROUPS
No Egg has ever been discovered

ITEMS SOMETIMES HELD
- None

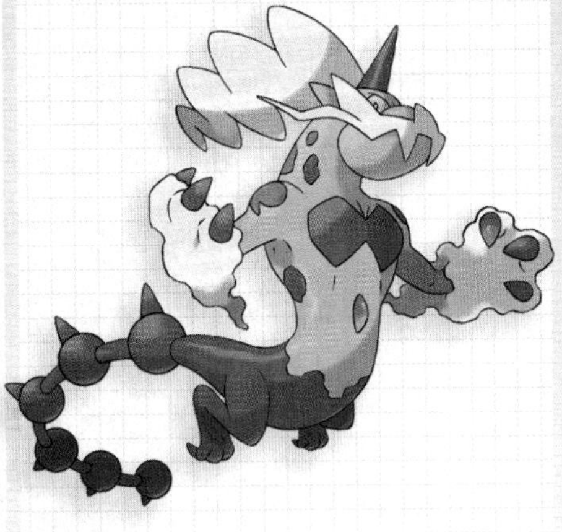

Pokémon AR Marker

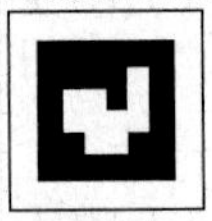

EVOLUTION

Does not evolve

HOW TO OBTAIN

Pokémon Black Version 2	Bring Thundurus Incarnate Forme to your game and use Reveal Glass
Pokémon White Version 2	Bring Thundurus Incarnate Forme to your game and use Reveal Glass

HOW TO OBTAIN FROM OTHER GAMES

—

—

LEVEL-UP AND LEARNED MOVES

Lv.	Name	Type	Kind	Pow.	Acc.	PP	Range	Long	DA
1	Uproar	Normal	Special	90	100	10	1 Random	—	—
1	Astonish	Ghost	Physical	30	100	15	Normal	—	○
1	ThunderShock	Electric	Special	40	100	30	Normal	—	—
7	Swagger	Normal	Status	—	90	15	Normal	—	—
13	Bite	Dark	Physical	60	100	25	Normal	—	○
19	Revenge	Fighting	Physical	60	100	10	Normal	—	○
25	Shock Wave	Electric	Special	60	—	20	Normal	—	—
31	Heal Block	Psychic	Status	—	100	15	Many Others	—	—
37	Agility	Psychic	Status	—	—	30	Self	—	—
43	Discharge	Electric	Special	80	100	15	Adjacent	—	—
49	Crunch	Dark	Physical	80	100	15	Normal	—	○
55	Charge	Electric	Status	—	—	20	Self	—	—
61	Nasty Plot	Dark	Status	—	—	20	Self	—	—
67	Thunder	Electric	Special	120	70	10	Normal	—	—
73	Dark Pulse	Dark	Special	80	100	15	Normal	○	—
79	Hammer Arm	Fighting	Physical	100	90	10	Normal	—	○
85	Thrash	Normal	Physical	120	100	10	1 Random	—	○

TM & HM MOVES

Lv.	Name	Type	Kind	Pow.	Acc.	PP	Range	Long	DA
TM06	Toxic	Poison	Status	—	90	10	Normal	—	—
TM08	Bulk Up	Fighting	Status	—	—	20	Self	—	—
TM10	Hidden Power	Normal	Special	—	100	15	Normal	—	—
TM12	Taunt	Dark	Status	—	100	20	Normal	—	—
TM15	Hyper Beam	Normal	Special	150	90	5	Normal	—	—
TM17	Protect	Normal	Status	—	—	10	Self	—	—
TM18	Rain Dance	Water	Status	—	—	5	Both Sides	—	—
TM21	Frustration	Normal	Physical	—	100	20	Normal	—	○
TM23	Smack Down	Rock	Physical	50	100	15	Normal	—	—
TM24	Thunderbolt	Electric	Special	95	100	15	Normal	—	—
TM25	Thunder	Electric	Special	120	70	10	Normal	—	—
TM27	Return	Normal	Physical	—	100	20	Normal	—	○
TM29	Psychic	Psychic	Special	90	100	10	Normal	—	—
TM31	Brick Break	Fighting	Physical	75	100	15	Normal	—	○
TM32	Double Team	Normal	Status	—	—	15	Self	—	—
TM34	Sludge Wave	Poison	Special	95	100	10	Adjacent	—	—
TM36	Sludge Bomb	Poison	Special	90	100	10	Normal	—	—
TM41	Torment	Dark	Status	—	100	15	Normal	—	—
TM42	Facade	Normal	Physical	70	100	20	Normal	—	○
TM44	Rest	Psychic	Status	—	—	10	Self	—	—
TM45	Attract	Normal	Status	—	100	15	Normal	—	—
TM46	Thief	Dark	Physical	40	100	10	Normal	—	○
TM48	Round	Normal	Special	60	100	15	Normal	—	—
TM52	Focus Blast	Fighting	Special	120	70	5	Normal	—	—
TM56	Fling	Dark	Physical	—	100	10	Normal	—	—
TM57	Charge Beam	Electric	Special	50	90	10	Normal	—	—
TM58	Sky Drop	Flying	Physical	60	100	10	Normal	○	○
TM59	Incinerate	Fire	Special	30	100	15	Many Others	—	—
TM63	Embargo	Dark	Status	—	100	15	Normal	—	—
TM66	Payback	Dark	Physical	50	100	10	Normal	—	○
TM68	Giga Impact	Normal	Physical	150	90	5	Normal	—	○
TM72	Volt Switch	Electric	Special	70	100	20	Normal	—	—
TM73	Thunder Wave	Electric	Status	—	100	20	Normal	—	—
TM86	Grass Knot	Grass	Special	—	100	20	Normal	—	○
TM87	Swagger	Normal	Status	—	90	15	Normal	—	—
TM89	U-turn	Bug	Physical	70	100	20	Normal	—	○
TM90	Substitute	Normal	Status	—	—	10	Self	—	—
TM91	Flash Cannon	Steel	Special	80	100	10	Normal	—	—
TM93	Wild Charge	Electric	Physical	90	100	15	Normal	—	○
TM94	Rock Smash	Fighting	Physical	40	100	15	Normal	—	○
HM02	Fly	Flying	Physical	90	95	15	Normal	○	○
HM04	Strength	Normal	Physical	80	100	15	Normal	—	○

MOVES TAUGHT BY PEOPLE

Name	Type	Kind	Pow.	Acc.	PP	Range	Long	DA

MOVES TAUGHT BY MOVE TUTORS FOR SHARDS

Name	Type	Kind	Pow.	Acc.	PP	Range	Long	DA
Uproar	Normal	Special	90	100	10	1 Random	—	—
ThunderPunch	Electric	Physical	75	100	15	Normal	—	○
Iron Tail	Steel	Physical	100	75	15	Normal	—	○
Foul Play	Dark	Physical	95	100	15	Normal	—	○
Superpower	Fighting	Physical	120	100	5	Normal	—	○
Dark Pulse	Dark	Special	80	100	15	Normal	○	—
Snore	Normal	Special	40	100	15	Normal	—	—
Knock Off	Dark	Physical	20	100	20	Normal	—	○
Role Play	Psychic	Status	—	—	10	Normal	—	—
Sleep Talk	Normal	Status	—	—	10	Self	—	—

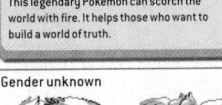

Vast White Pokémon

643 Reshiram

- HEIGHT: 10'06"
- WEIGHT: 727.5 lbs.
- GENDER: Unknown

This legendary Pokémon can scorch the world with fire. It helps those who want to build a world of truth.

Gender unknown

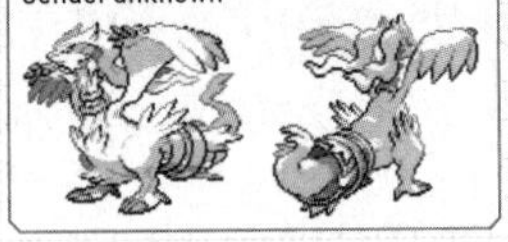

TYPE: Dragon / Fire

ABILITY
- Turboblaze

HIDDEN ABILITY
—

STATS
HP
Attack
Defense
Sp. Atk
Sp. Def
Speed

EGG GROUPS
No Egg has ever been discovered

ITEMS SOMETIMES HELD
- None

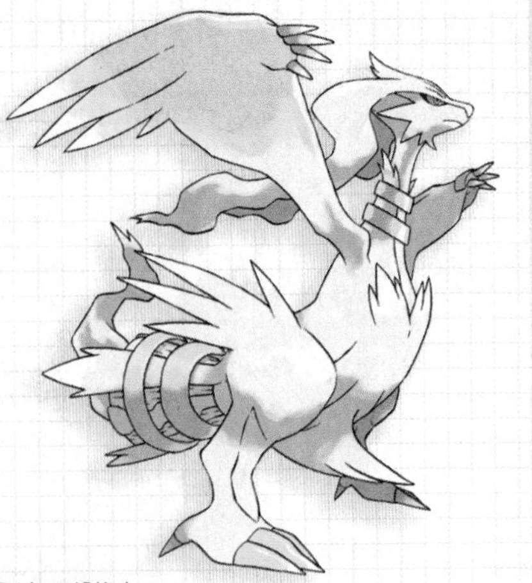

Pokémon AR Marker

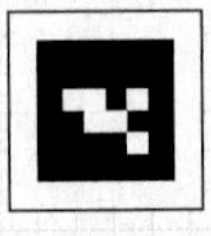

EVOLUTION

Does not evolve

HOW TO OBTAIN

Pokémon Black Version 2	Link Trade
Pokémon White Version 2	Dragonspiral Tower

HOW TO OBTAIN FROM OTHER GAMES

Pokémon Black Version	N's Castle

—

LEVEL-UP AND LEARNED MOVES

Lv.	Name	Type	Kind	Pow.	Acc.	PP	Range	Long	DA
1	Fire Fang	Fire	Physical	65	95	15	Normal	—	○
1	Dragon Rage	Dragon	Special	—	100	10	Normal	—	—
8	Imprison	Psychic	Status	—	—	10	Self	—	—
15	AncientPower	Rock	Special	60	100	5	Normal	—	—
22	Flamethrower	Fire	Special	95	100	15	Normal	—	—
29	DragonBreath	Dragon	Special	60	100	20	Normal	—	—
36	Slash	Normal	Physical	70	100	20	Normal	—	○
43	Extrasensory	Psychic	Special	80	100	30	Normal	—	—
50	Fusion Flare	Fire	Special	100	100	5	Normal	—	—
54	Dragon Pulse	Dragon	Special	90	100	10	Normal	○	—
64	Imprison	Psychic	Status	—	—	10	Self	—	—
71	Crunch	Dark	Physical	80	100	15	Normal	—	○
78	Fire Blast	Fire	Special	120	85	5	Normal	—	—
85	Outrage	Dragon	Physical	120	100	10	1 Random	—	○
92	Hyper Voice	Normal	Special	90	100	10	Many Others	—	—
100	Blue Flare	Fire	Special	130	85	5	Normal	—	—

TM & HM MOVES

Lv.	Name	Type	Kind	Pow.	Acc.	PP	Range	Long	DA
TM01	Hone Claws	Dark	Status	—	—	15	Self	—	—
TM02	Dragon Claw	Dragon	Physical	80	100	15	Normal	—	○
TM06	Toxic	Poison	Status	—	90	10	Normal	—	—
TM10	Hidden Power	Normal	Special	—	100	15	Normal	—	—
TM11	Sunny Day	Fire	Status	—	—	5	Both Sides	—	—
TM15	Hyper Beam	Normal	Special	150	90	5	Normal	—	—
TM16	Light Screen	Psychic	Status	—	—	30	Your Side	—	—
TM17	Protect	Normal	Status	—	—	10	Self	—	—
TM20	Safeguard	Normal	Status	—	—	25	Your Side	—	—
TM21	Frustration	Normal	Physical	—	100	20	Normal	—	○
TM22	SolarBeam	Grass	Special	120	100	10	Normal	—	—
TM27	Return	Normal	Physical	—	100	20	Normal	—	○
TM29	Psychic	Psychic	Special	90	100	10	Normal	—	—
TM30	Shadow Ball	Ghost	Special	80	100	15	Normal	—	—
TM32	Double Team	Normal	Status	—	—	15	Self	—	—
TM33	Reflect	Psychic	Status	—	—	20	Your Side	—	—
TM35	Flamethrower	Fire	Special	95	100	15	Normal	—	—
TM38	Fire Blast	Fire	Special	120	85	5	Normal	—	—
TM39	Rock Tomb	Rock	Physical	50	80	10	Normal	—	—
TM42	Facade	Normal	Physical	70	100	20	Normal	—	○
TM43	Flame Charge	Fire	Physical	50	100	20	Normal	—	○
TM44	Rest	Psychic	Status	—	—	10	Self	—	—
TM48	Round	Normal	Special	60	100	15	Normal	—	—
TM49	Echoed Voice	Normal	Special	40	100	15	Normal	—	—
TM50	Overheat	Fire	Special	140	90	5	Normal	—	—
TM52	Focus Blast	Fighting	Special	120	70	5	Normal	—	—
TM56	Fling	Dark	Physical	—	100	10	Normal	—	—
TM59	Incinerate	Fire	Special	30	100	15	Many Others	—	—
TM61	Will-O-Wisp	Fire	Status	—	75	15	Normal	—	—
TM65	Shadow Claw	Ghost	Physical	70	100	15	Normal	—	○
TM66	Payback	Dark	Physical	50	100	10	Normal	—	○
TM68	Giga Impact	Normal	Physical	150	90	5	Normal	—	○
TM71	Stone Edge	Rock	Physical	100	80	5	Normal	—	—
TM80	Rock Slide	Rock	Physical	75	90	10	Many Others	—	—
TM82	Dragon Tail	Dragon	Physical	60	90	10	Normal	—	○
TM87	Swagger	Normal	Status	—	90	15	Normal	—	—
TM90	Substitute	Normal	Status	—	—	10	Self	—	—
TM94	Rock Smash	Fighting	Physical	40	100	15	Normal	—	○
HM01	Cut	Normal	Physical	50	95	30	Normal	—	○
HM02	Fly	Flying	Physical	90	95	15	Normal	○	○
HM04	Strength	Normal	Physical	80	100	15	Normal	—	○

MOVES TAUGHT BY PEOPLE

Name	Type	Kind	Pow.	Acc.	PP	Range	Long	DA
Draco Meteor	Dragon	Special	140	90	5	Normal	—	—

MOVES TAUGHT BY MOVE TUTORS FOR SHARDS

Name	Type	Kind	Pow.	Acc.	PP	Range	Long	DA
Hyper Voice	Normal	Special	90	100	10	Many Others	—	—
Earth Power	Ground	Special	90	100	10	Normal	—	—
Zen Headbutt	Psychic	Physical	80	90	15	Normal	—	○
Dragon Pulse	Dragon	Special	90	100	10	Normal	○	—
Snore	Normal	Special	40	100	15	Normal	—	—
Roost	Flying	Status	—	—	10	Self	—	—
Heat Wave	Fire	Special	100	90	10	Many Others	—	—
Tailwind	Flying	Status	—	—	30	Your Side	—	—
Outrage	Dragon	Physical	120	100	10	1 Random	—	○
Sleep Talk	Normal	Status	—	—	10	Self	—	—

644 Zekrom

Deep Black Pokémon

- HEIGHT: 9'06"
- WEIGHT: 760.6 lbs.
- GENDER: Unknown

This legendary Pokémon can scorch the world with lightning. It assists those who want to build an ideal world.

Gender unknown

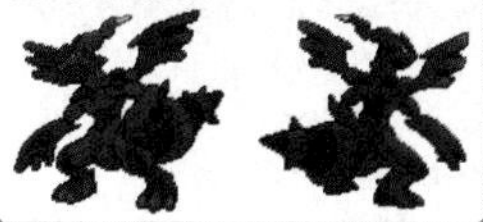

TYPE Dragon Electric

ABILITY
- Teravolt

HIDDEN ABILITY
—

STATS
HP
Attack
Defense
Sp. Atk
Sp. Def
Speed

EGG GROUPS
No Egg has ever been discovered

ITEMS SOMETIMES HELD
- None

EVOLUTION
Does not evolve

HOW TO OBTAIN

Pokémon Black Version 2	Dragonspiral Tower
Pokémon White Version 2	Link Trade

HOW TO OBTAIN FROM OTHER GAMES

Pokémon White Version	N's Castle
—	

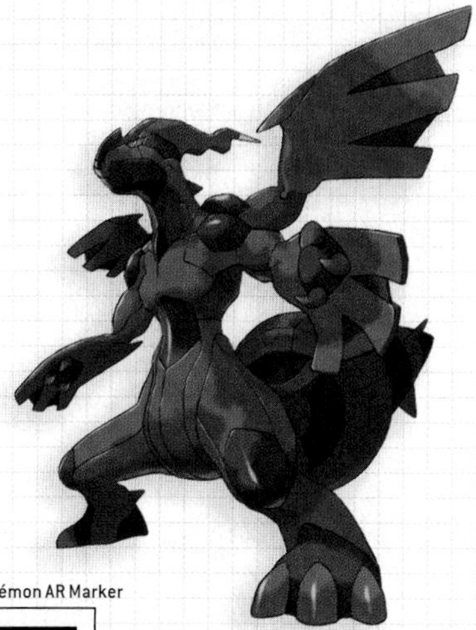

Pokémon AR Marker

LEVEL-UP AND LEARNED MOVES

Lv.	Name	Type	Kind	Pow.	Acc.	PP	Range	Long	DA
1	Thunder Fang	Electric	Physical	65	95	15	Normal	—	○
1	Dragon Rage	Dragon	Special	—	100	10	Normal	—	—
8	Imprison	Psychic	Status	—	—	10	Self	—	—
15	AncientPower	Rock	Special	60	100	5	Normal	—	—
22	Thunderbolt	Electric	Special	95	100	15	Normal	—	—
29	DragonBreath	Dragon	Special	60	100	20	Normal	—	—
36	Slash	Normal	Physical	70	100	20	Normal	—	○
43	Zen Headbutt	Psychic	Physical	80	90	15	Normal	—	○
50	Fusion Bolt	Electric	Physical	100	100	5	Normal	—	—
54	Dragon Claw	Dragon	Physical	80	100	15	Normal	—	○
64	Imprison	Psychic	Status	—	—	10	Self	—	—
71	Crunch	Dark	Physical	80	100	15	Normal	—	○
78	Thunder	Electric	Special	120	70	10	Normal	—	—
85	Outrage	Dragon	Physical	120	100	10	1 Random	—	○
92	Hyper Voice	Normal	Special	90	100	10	Many Others	—	—
100	Bolt Strike	Electric	Physical	130	85	5	Normal	—	○

TM & HM MOVES

Lv.	Name	Type	Kind	Pow.	Acc.	PP	Range	Long	DA
TM01	Hone Claws	Dark	Status	—	—	15	Self	—	—
TM02	Dragon Claw	Dragon	Physical	80	100	15	Normal	—	○
TM06	Toxic	Poison	Status	—	90	10	Normal	—	—
TM10	Hidden Power	Normal	Special	—	100	15	Normal	—	—
TM15	Hyper Beam	Normal	Special	150	90	5	Normal	—	—
TM16	Light Screen	Psychic	Status	—	—	30	Your Side	—	—
TM17	Protect	Normal	Status	—	—	10	Self	—	—
TM18	Rain Dance	Water	Status	—	—	5	Both Sides	—	—
TM20	Safeguard	Normal	Status	—	—	25	Your Side	—	—
TM21	Frustration	Normal	Physical	—	100	20	Normal	—	○
TM24	Thunderbolt	Electric	Special	95	100	15	Normal	—	—
TM25	Thunder	Electric	Special	120	70	10	Normal	—	—
TM27	Return	Normal	Physical	—	100	20	Normal	—	○
TM29	Psychic	Psychic	Special	90	100	10	Normal	—	—
TM30	Shadow Ball	Ghost	Special	80	100	15	Normal	—	—
TM32	Double Team	Normal	Status	—	—	15	Self	—	—
TM33	Reflect	Psychic	Status	—	—	20	Your Side	—	—
TM39	Rock Tomb	Rock	Physical	50	80	10	Normal	—	—
TM42	Facade	Normal	Physical	70	100	20	Normal	—	○
TM44	Rest	Psychic	Status	—	—	10	Self	—	—
TM48	Round	Normal	Special	60	100	15	Normal	—	—
TM49	Echoed Voice	Normal	Special	40	100	15	Normal	—	—
TM52	Focus Blast	Fighting	Special	120	70	5	Normal	—	—
TM56	Fling	Dark	Physical	—	100	10	Normal	—	—
TM57	Charge Beam	Electric	Special	50	90	10	Normal	—	—
TM65	Shadow Claw	Ghost	Physical	70	100	15	Normal	—	○
TM66	Payback	Dark	Physical	50	100	10	Normal	—	○
TM68	Giga Impact	Normal	Physical	150	90	5	Normal	—	○
TM70	Flash	Normal	Status	—	100	20	Normal	—	—
TM71	Stone Edge	Rock	Physical	100	80	5	Normal	—	—
TM72	Volt Switch	Electric	Special	70	100	20	Normal	—	—
TM73	Thunder Wave	Electric	Status	—	100	20	Normal	—	—
TM80	Rock Slide	Rock	Physical	75	90	10	Many Others	—	—
TM82	Dragon Tail	Dragon	Physical	60	90	10	Normal	—	○
TM87	Swagger	Normal	Status	—	90	15	Normal	—	—
TM90	Substitute	Normal	Status	—	—	10	Self	—	—
TM91	Flash Cannon	Steel	Special	80	100	10	Normal	—	—
TM93	Wild Charge	Electric	Physical	90	100	15	Normal	—	○
TM94	Rock Smash	Fighting	Physical	40	100	15	Normal	—	○
HM01	Cut	Normal	Physical	50	95	30	Normal	—	○
HM02	Fly	Flying	Physical	90	95	15	Normal	○	○
HM04	Strength	Normal	Physical	80	100	15	Normal	—	○

MOVES TAUGHT BY PEOPLE

Name	Type	Kind	Pow.	Acc.	PP	Range	Long	DA
Draco Meteor	Dragon	Special	140	90	5	Normal	—	—

MOVES TAUGHT BY MOVE TUTORS FOR SHARDS

Name	Type	Kind	Pow.	Acc.	PP	Range	Long	DA
Signal Beam	Bug	Special	75	100	15	Normal	—	—
ThunderPunch	Electric	Physical	75	100	15	Normal	—	○
Magnet Rise	Electric	Status	—	—	10	Self	—	—
Hyper Voice	Normal	Special	90	100	10	Many Others	—	—
Earth Power	Ground	Special	90	100	10	Normal	—	—
Zen Headbutt	Psychic	Physical	80	90	15	Normal	—	○
Dragon Pulse	Dragon	Special	90	100	10	Normal	○	—
Snore	Normal	Special	40	100	15	Normal	—	—
Roost	Flying	Status	—	—	10	Self	—	—
Tailwind	Flying	Status	—	—	30	Your Side	—	—
Outrage	Dragon	Physical	120	100	10	1 Random	—	○
Sleep Talk	Normal	Status	—	—	10	Self	—	—

645 Landorus (Incarnate Forme)

Abundance Pokémon

- HEIGHT: 4'11"
- WEIGHT: 149.9 lbs.
- GENDER: ♂

From the forces of lightning and wind, it creates energy to give nutrients to the soil and make the land abundant.

♂

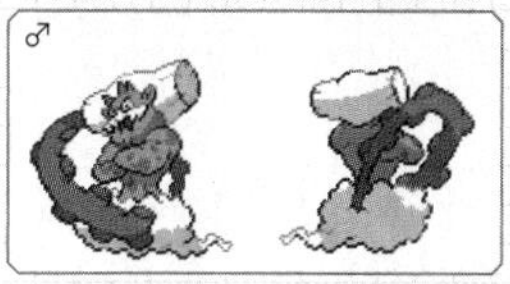

TYPE Ground Flying

ABILITY
- Sand Force

HIDDEN ABILITY
- Sheer Force

STATS
HP
Attack
Defense
Sp. Atk
Sp. Def
Speed

EGG GROUPS
No Egg has ever been discovered

ITEMS SOMETIMES HELD
- None

EVOLUTION
Does not evolve

HOW TO OBTAIN

Pokémon Black Version 2	Link Trade
Pokémon White Version 2	Link Trade

HOW TO OBTAIN FROM OTHER GAMES

Pokémon Black Version	Put both Tornadus and Thundurus in your party, go to the Abundant Shrine, and catch it.
Pokémon White Version	Put both Tornadus and Thundurus in your party, go to the Abundant Shrine, and catch it.

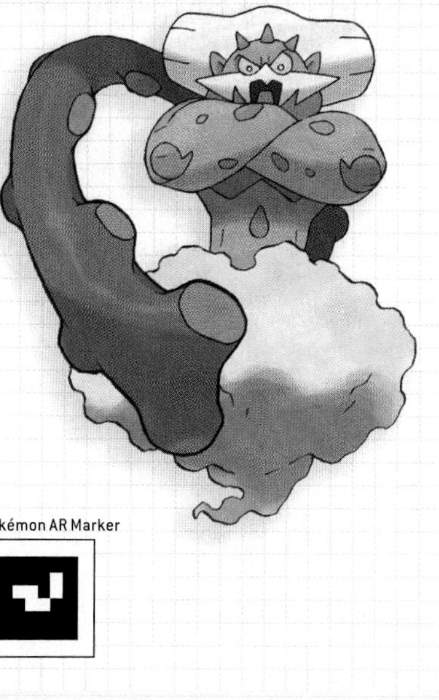

Pokémon AR Marker

LEVEL-UP AND LEARNED MOVES

Lv.	Name	Type	Kind	Pow.	Acc.	PP	Range	Long	DA
1	Block	Normal	Status	—	—	5	Normal	—	—
1	Mud Shot	Ground	Special	55	95	15	Normal	—	—
1	Rock Tomb	Rock	Physical	50	80	10	Normal	—	—
7	Imprison	Psychic	Status	—	—	10	Self	—	—
13	Punishment	Dark	Physical	—	100	5	Normal	—	○
19	Bulldoze	Ground	Physical	60	100	20	Adjacent	—	—
25	Rock Throw	Rock	Physical	50	90	15	Normal	—	—
31	Extrasensory	Psychic	Special	80	100	30	Normal	—	—
37	Swords Dance	Normal	Status	—	—	30	Self	—	—
43	Earth Power	Ground	Special	90	100	10	Normal	—	—
49	Rock Slide	Rock	Physical	75	90	10	Many Others	—	—
55	Earthquake	Ground	Physical	100	100	10	Adjacent	—	—
61	Sandstorm	Rock	Status	—	—	10	Both Sides	—	—
67	Fissure	Ground	Physical	—	30	5	Normal	—	—
73	Stone Edge	Rock	Physical	100	80	5	Normal	—	—
79	Hammer Arm	Fighting	Physical	100	90	10	Normal	—	○
85	Outrage	Dragon	Physical	120	100	10	1 Random	—	○

TM & HM MOVES

Lv.	Name	Type	Kind	Pow.	Acc.	PP	Range	Long	DA
TM04	Calm Mind	Psychic	Status	—	—	20	Self	—	—
TM06	Toxic	Poison	Status	—	90	10	Normal	—	—
TM08	Bulk Up	Fighting	Status	—	—	20	Self	—	—
TM10	Hidden Power	Normal	Special	—	100	15	Normal	—	—
TM15	Hyper Beam	Normal	Special	150	90	5	Normal	—	—
TM17	Protect	Normal	Status	—	—	10	Self	—	—
TM21	Frustration	Normal	Physical	—	100	20	Normal	—	○
TM23	Smack Down	Rock	Physical	50	100	15	Normal	—	—
TM26	Earthquake	Ground	Physical	100	100	10	Adjacent	—	—
TM27	Return	Normal	Physical	—	100	20	Normal	—	○
TM28	Dig	Ground	Physical	80	100	10	Normal	—	○
TM29	Psychic	Psychic	Special	90	100	10	Normal	—	—
TM31	Brick Break	Fighting	Physical	75	100	15	Normal	—	○
TM32	Double Team	Normal	Status	—	—	15	Self	—	—
TM34	Sludge Wave	Poison	Special	95	100	10	Adjacent	—	—
TM36	Sludge Bomb	Poison	Special	90	100	10	Normal	—	—
TM37	Sandstorm	Rock	Status	—	—	10	Both Sides	—	—
TM39	Rock Tomb	Rock	Physical	50	80	10	Normal	—	—
TM42	Facade	Normal	Physical	70	100	20	Normal	—	○
TM44	Rest	Psychic	Status	—	—	10	Self	—	—
TM45	Attract	Normal	Status	—	100	15	Normal	—	—
TM48	Round	Normal	Special	60	100	15	Normal	—	—
TM52	Focus Blast	Fighting	Special	120	70	5	Normal	—	—
TM56	Fling	Dark	Physical	—	100	10	Normal	—	—
TM64	Explosion	Normal	Physical	250	100	5	Adjacent	—	—
TM66	Payback	Dark	Physical	50	100	10	Normal	—	○
TM68	Giga Impact	Normal	Physical	150	90	5	Normal	—	○
TM69	Rock Polish	Rock	Status	—	—	20	Self	—	—
TM71	Stone Edge	Rock	Physical	100	80	5	Normal	—	—
TM75	Swords Dance	Normal	Status	—	—	30	Self	—	—
TM78	Bulldoze	Ground	Physical	60	100	20	Adjacent	—	—
TM80	Rock Slide	Rock	Physical	75	90	10	Many Others	—	—
TM86	Grass Knot	Grass	Special	—	100	20	Normal	—	○
TM87	Swagger	Normal	Status	—	90	15	Normal	—	—
TM89	U-turn	Bug	Physical	70	100	20	Normal	—	○
TM90	Substitute	Normal	Status	—	—	10	Self	—	—
TM94	Rock Smash	Fighting	Physical	40	100	15	Normal	—	○
HM02	Fly	Flying	Physical	90	95	15	Normal	○	○
HM04	Strength	Normal	Physical	80	100	15	Normal	—	○

MOVES TAUGHT BY PEOPLE

Name	Type	Kind	Pow.	Acc.	PP	Range	Long	DA

MOVES TAUGHT BY MOVE TUTORS FOR SHARDS

Name	Type	Kind	Pow.	Acc.	PP	Range	Long	DA
Block	Normal	Status	—	—	5	Normal	—	—
Iron Tail	Steel	Physical	100	75	15	Normal	—	○
Earth Power	Ground	Special	90	100	10	Normal	—	—
Superpower	Fighting	Physical	120	100	5	Normal	—	○
Gravity	Psychic	Status	—	—	5	Both Sides	—	—
Snore	Normal	Special	40	100	15	Normal	—	—
Knock Off	Dark	Physical	20	100	20	Normal	—	○
Role Play	Psychic	Status	—	—	10	Normal	—	—
Stealth Rock	Rock	Status	—	—	20	Other Side	—	—
Outrage	Dragon	Physical	120	100	10	1 Random	—	○
Sleep Talk	Normal	Status	—	—	10	Self	—	—

645 Landorus (Therian Forme)

Abundance Pokémon

TYPE Ground / Flying

ABILITY
● Intimidate

HIDDEN ABILITY

● HEIGHT: 4'03"
● WEIGHT: 149.9 lbs.
● GENDER: ♂

From the forces of lightning and wind, it creates energy to give nutrients to the soil and make the land abundant.

STATS
HP
Attack
Defense
Sp. Atk
Sp. Def
Speed

EGG GROUPS
No Egg has ever been discovered

ITEMS SOMETIMES HELD
● None

Pokémon AR Marker

EVOLUTION

Does not evolve

HOW TO OBTAIN

| Pokémon Black Version 2 | Bring Landorus Incarnate Forme to your game and use Reveal Glass |
| Pokémon White Version 2 | Bring Landorus Incarnate Forme to your game and use Reveal Glass |

HOW TO OBTAIN FROM OTHER GAMES

LEVEL-UP AND LEARNED MOVES

Lv.	Name	Type	Kind	Pow.	Acc.	PP	Range	Long	DA
1	Block	Normal	Status	—	—	5	Normal	—	—
1	Mud Shot	Ground	Special	55	95	15	Normal	—	—
1	Rock Tomb	Rock	Physical	50	80	10	Normal	—	—
7	Imprison	Psychic	Status	—	—	10	Self	—	—
13	Punishment	Dark	Physical	—	100	5	Normal	—	○
19	Bulldoze	Ground	Physical	60	100	20	Adjacent	—	—
25	Rock Throw	Rock	Physical	50	90	15	Normal	—	—
31	Extrasensory	Psychic	Special	80	100	30	Normal	—	—
37	Swords Dance	Normal	Status	—	—	30	Self	—	—
43	Earth Power	Ground	Special	90	100	10	Normal	—	○
49	Rock Slide	Rock	Physical	75	90	10	Many Others	—	—
55	Earthquake	Ground	Physical	100	100	10	Adjacent	—	—
61	Sandstorm	Rock	Status	—	—	10	Both Sides	—	—
67	Fissure	Ground	Physical	—	30	5	Normal	—	—
73	Stone Edge	Rock	Physical	100	80	5	Normal	—	—
79	Hammer Arm	Fighting	Physical	100	90	10	Normal	—	○
85	Outrage	Dragon	Physical	120	100	10	1 Random	—	○

TM & HM MOVES

Lv.	Name	Type	Kind	Pow.	Acc.	PP	Range	Long	DA
TM04	Calm Mind	Psychic	Status	—	—	20	Self	—	—
TM06	Toxic	Poison	Status	—	90	10	Normal	—	—
TM08	Bulk Up	Fighting	Status	—	—	20	Self	—	—
TM10	Hidden Power	Normal	Special	—	100	15	Normal	—	—
TM15	Hyper Beam	Normal	Special	150	90	5	Normal	—	—
TM17	Protect	Normal	Status	—	—	10	Self	—	—
TM21	Frustration	Normal	Physical	—	100	20	Normal	—	○
TM23	Smack Down	Rock	Physical	50	100	15	Normal	—	—
TM26	Earthquake	Ground	Physical	100	100	10	Adjacent	—	—
TM27	Return	Normal	Physical	—	100	20	Normal	—	○
TM28	Dig	Ground	Physical	80	100	10	Normal	—	—
TM29	Psychic	Psychic	Special	90	100	10	Normal	—	○
TM31	Brick Break	Fighting	Physical	75	100	15	Normal	—	○
TM32	Double Team	Normal	Status	—	—	15	Self	—	—
TM34	Sludge Wave	Poison	Special	95	100	10	Adjacent	—	—
TM36	Sludge Bomb	Poison	Special	90	100	10	Normal	—	—
TM37	Sandstorm	Rock	Status	—	—	10	Both Sides	—	—
TM39	Rock Tomb	Rock	Physical	50	80	10	Normal	—	—
TM42	Facade	Normal	Physical	70	100	20	Normal	—	—
TM44	Rest	Psychic	Status	—	—	10	Self	—	—
TM45	Attract	Normal	Status	—	100	15	Normal	—	—
TM48	Round	Normal	Special	60	100	15	Normal	—	—
TM52	Focus Blast	Fighting	Special	120	70	5	Normal	—	—
TM56	Fling	Dark	Physical	—	100	10	Normal	—	○
TM64	Explosion	Normal	Physical	250	100	5	Adjacent	—	—
TM66	Payback	Dark	Physical	50	100	10	Normal	—	○
TM68	Giga Impact	Normal	Physical	150	90	5	Normal	—	—
TM69	Rock Polish	Rock	Status	—	—	20	Self	—	—
TM71	Stone Edge	Rock	Physical	100	80	5	Normal	—	—
TM75	Swords Dance	Normal	Status	—	—	30	Self	—	—
TM78	Bulldoze	Ground	Physical	60	100	20	Adjacent	—	—
TM80	Rock Slide	Rock	Physical	75	90	10	Many Others	—	—
TM86	Grass Knot	Grass	Special	—	100	20	Normal	—	○
TM87	Swagger	Normal	Status	—	90	15	Normal	—	—
TM89	U-turn	Bug	Physical	70	100	20	Normal	—	—
TM90	Substitute	Normal	Status	—	—	10	Self	—	—

Lv.	Name	Type	Kind	Pow.	Acc.	PP	Range	Long	DA
TM94	Rock Smash	Fighting	Physical	40	100	15	Normal	—	○
HM02	Fly	Flying	Physical	90	95	15	Normal	○	○
HM04	Strength	Normal	Physical	80	100	15	Normal	—	—

MOVES TAUGHT BY PEOPLE

Name	Type	Kind	Pow.	Acc.	PP	Range	Long	DA

MOVES TAUGHT BY MOVE TUTORS FOR SHARDS

Name	Type	Kind	Pow.	Acc.	PP	Range	Long	DA
Block	Normal	Status	—	—	5	Normal	—	○
Iron Tail	Steel	Physical	100	75	15	Normal	—	○
Earth Power	Ground	Special	90	100	10	Normal	—	○
Superpower	Fighting	Physical	120	100	5	Normal	—	○
Gravity	Psychic	Status	—	—	5	Both Sides	—	—
Snore	Normal	Special	40	100	15	Normal	—	—
Knock Off	Dark	Physical	20	100	20	Normal	—	○
Role Play	Psychic	Status	—	—	10	Normal	—	—
Stealth Rock	Rock	Status	—	—	20	Other Side	—	—
Outrage	Dragon	Physical	120	100	10	1 Random	—	○
Sleep Talk	Normal	Status	—	—	10	Self	—	—

---

646 Kyurem

Boundary Pokémon

TYPE Dragon / Ice

ABILITY
● Pressure

HIDDEN ABILITY

● HEIGHT: 9'10"
● WEIGHT: 716.5 lbs.
● GENDER: Unknown

This legendary ice Pokémon waits for a hero to fill in the missing parts of its body with truth or ideals.

Gender unknown

STATS
HP
Attack
Defense
Sp. Atk
Sp. Def
Speed

EGG GROUPS
No Egg has ever been discovered

ITEMS SOMETIMES HELD
● None

Pokémon AR Marker

EVOLUTION

Does not evolve

HOW TO OBTAIN

| Pokémon Black Version 2 | Giant Chasm deepest cave (after entering the Hall of Fame) |
| Pokémon White Version 2 | Giant Chasm deepest cave (after entering the Hall of Fame) |

HOW TO OBTAIN FROM OTHER GAMES

LEVEL-UP AND LEARNED MOVES

Lv.	Name	Type	Kind	Pow.	Acc.	PP	Range	Long	DA
1	Icy Wind	Ice	Special	55	95	15	Many Others	—	—
1	Dragon Rage	Dragon	Special	—	100	10	Normal	—	—
8	Imprison	Psychic	Status	—	—	10	Self	—	—
15	AncientPower	Rock	Special	60	100	5	Normal	—	—
22	Ice Beam	Ice	Special	95	100	10	Normal	—	—
29	DragonBreath	Dragon	Special	60	100	20	Normal	—	—
36	Slash	Normal	Physical	70	100	20	Normal	—	—
43	Scary Face	Normal	Status	—	100	10	Normal	—	—
50	Glaciate	Ice	Special	65	95	10	Many Others	○	—
57	Dragon Pulse	Dragon	Special	90	100	10	Normal	○	○
64	Imprison	Psychic	Status	—	—	10	Self	—	—
71	Endeavor	Normal	Physical	—	100	5	Normal	—	—
78	Blizzard	Ice	Special	120	70	5	Many Others	—	—
85	Outrage	Dragon	Physical	120	100	10	1 Random	—	○
92	Hyper Voice	Normal	Special	90	100	10	Many Others	—	—

TM & HM MOVES

Lv.	Name	Type	Kind	Pow.	Acc.	PP	Range	Long	DA
TM01	Hone Claws	Dark	Status	—	—	15	Self	—	—
TM02	Dragon Claw	Dragon	Physical	80	100	15	Normal	—	○
TM06	Toxic	Poison	Status	—	90	10	Normal	—	—
TM07	Hail	Ice	Status	—	—	10	Both Sides	—	—
TM10	Hidden Power	Normal	Special	—	100	15	Normal	—	—
TM11	Sunny Day	Fire	Status	—	—	5	Both Sides	—	—
TM13	Ice Beam	Ice	Special	95	100	10	Normal	—	—
TM14	Blizzard	Ice	Special	120	70	5	Many Others	—	—
TM15	Hyper Beam	Normal	Special	150	90	5	Normal	—	—
TM16	Light Screen	Psychic	Status	—	—	30	Your Side	—	—
TM17	Protect	Normal	Status	—	—	10	Self	—	—
TM18	Rain Dance	Water	Status	—	—	5	Both Sides	—	—
TM20	Safeguard	Normal	Status	—	—	25	Your Side	—	—
TM21	Frustration	Normal	Physical	—	100	20	Normal	—	○
TM27	Return	Normal	Physical	—	100	20	Normal	—	○
TM29	Psychic	Psychic	Special	90	100	10	Normal	—	○
TM30	Shadow Ball	Ghost	Special	80	100	15	Normal	—	○
TM32	Double Team	Normal	Status	—	—	15	Self	—	—
TM33	Reflect	Psychic	Status	—	—	20	Your Side	—	—
TM39	Rock Tomb	Rock	Physical	50	80	10	Normal	—	—
TM42	Facade	Normal	Physical	70	100	20	Normal	—	—
TM44	Rest	Psychic	Status	—	—	10	Self	—	—
TM48	Round	Normal	Special	60	100	15	Normal	—	—
TM49	Echoed Voice	Normal	Special	40	100	15	Normal	—	—
TM52	Focus Blast	Fighting	Special	120	70	5	Normal	—	—
TM56	Fling	Dark	Physical	—	100	10	Normal	—	○
TM65	Shadow Claw	Ghost	Physical	70	100	15	Normal	—	—
TM66	Payback	Dark	Physical	50	100	10	Normal	—	○
TM68	Giga Impact	Normal	Physical	150	90	5	Normal	—	—
TM71	Stone Edge	Rock	Physical	100	80	5	Normal	—	—
TM80	Rock Slide	Rock	Physical	75	90	10	Many Others	—	—
TM82	Dragon Tail	Dragon	Physical	60	90	10	Normal	—	—
TM87	Swagger	Normal	Status	—	90	15	Normal	—	—
TM90	Substitute	Normal	Status	—	—	10	Self	—	—
TM91	Flash Cannon	Steel	Special	80	100	10	Normal	—	—
TM94	Rock Smash	Fighting	Physical	40	100	15	Normal	—	○
HM01	Cut	Normal	Physical	50	95	30	Normal	—	—
HM02	Fly	Flying	Physical	90	95	15	Normal	○	○

Lv.	Name	Type	Kind	Pow.	Acc.	PP	Range	Long	DA
HM04	Strength	Normal	Physical	80	100	15	Normal	—	—

MOVES TAUGHT BY PEOPLE

Name	Type	Kind	Pow.	Acc.	PP	Range	Long	DA
Draco Meteor	Dragon	Special	140	90	5	Normal	—	—

MOVES TAUGHT BY MOVE TUTORS FOR SHARDS

Name	Type	Kind	Pow.	Acc.	PP	Range	Long	DA
Signal Beam	Bug	Special	75	100	15	Normal	—	○
Iron Head	Steel	Physical	80	100	15	Normal	—	○
Hyper Voice	Normal	Special	90	100	10	Many Others	—	—
Icy Wind	Ice	Special	55	95	15	Many Others	—	—
Earth Power	Ground	Special	90	100	10	Normal	—	○
Zen Headbutt	Psychic	Physical	80	90	15	Normal	—	—
Dragon Pulse	Dragon	Special	90	100	10	Normal	○	○
Snore	Normal	Special	40	100	15	Normal	—	—
Roost	Flying	Status	—	—	10	Self	—	—
Outrage	Dragon	Physical	120	100	10	1 Random	—	○
Endeavor	Normal	Physical	—	100	5	Normal	—	○
Sleep Talk	Normal	Status	—	—	10	Self	—	—

646 Kyurem (Black Kyurem)

Boundary Pokémon

TYPE Dragon | Ice

ABILITY
● Teravolt

HIDDEN ABILITY
———

- HEIGHT: 10'10"
- WEIGHT: 716.5 lbs.
- GENDER: Unknown

This legendary ice Pokémon waits for a hero to fill in the missing parts of its body with truth or ideals.

STATS
HP
Attack
Defense
Sp. Atk
Sp. Def
Speed

EGG GROUPS
No Egg has ever been discovered

ITEMS SOMETIMES HELD
● None

Gender unknown

EVOLUTION

Does not evolve

HOW TO OBTAIN

Pokémon Black Version 2	Use the DNA Splicers on Kyurem to create Absofusion with Zekrom
Pokémon White Version 2	Use the DNA Splicers on Kyurem to create Absofusion with Zekrom

HOW TO OBTAIN FROM OTHER GAMES

LEVEL-UP AND LEARNED MOVES

Lv.	Name	Type	Kind	Pow.	Acc.	PP	Range	Long	DA
1	Icy Wind	Ice	Special	55	95	15	Many Others	—	—
1	Dragon Rage	Dragon	Special	—	100	10	Normal	—	—
8	Imprison	Psychic	Status	—	—	10	Self	—	—
15	AncientPower	Rock	Special	60	100	5	Normal	—	—
22	Ice Beam	Ice	Special	95	100	10	Normal	—	—
29	DragonBreath	Dragon	Special	60	100	20	Normal	—	—
36	Slash	Normal	Physical	70	100	20	Normal	—	○
43	Fusion Bolt	Electric	Physical	100	100	5	Normal	—	—
50	Freeze Shock	Ice	Special	140	90	5	Normal	—	—
57	Dragon Pulse	Dragon	Special	90	100	10	Normal	○	—
64	Imprison	Psychic	Status	—	—	10	Self	—	○
71	Endeavor	Normal	Physical	—	100	5	Normal	—	○
78	Blizzard	Ice	Special	120	70	5	Many Others	—	—
85	Outrage	Dragon	Physical	120	100	10	1 Random	—	○
92	Hyper Voice	Normal	Special	90	100	10	Many Others	—	—

Lv.	Name	Type	Kind	Pow.	Acc.	PP	Range	Long	DA
HM04	Strength	Normal	Physical	80	100	15	Normal	—	—

MOVES TAUGHT BY PEOPLE

Name	Type	Kind	Pow.	Acc.	PP	Range	Long	DA
Draco Meteor	Dragon	Special	140	90	5	Normal	—	—

TM & HM MOVES

Lv.	Name	Type	Kind	Pow.	Acc.	PP	Range	Long	DA
TM01	Hone Claws	Dark	Status	—	—	15	Self	—	—
TM02	Dragon Claw	Dragon	Physical	80	100	15	Normal	—	○
TM06	Toxic	Poison	Status	—	90	10	Normal	—	—
TM07	Hail	Ice	Status	—	—	10	Both Sides	—	—
TM10	Hidden Power	Normal	Special	—	100	15	Normal	—	—
TM11	Sunny Day	Fire	Status	—	—	5	Both Sides	—	—
TM13	Ice Beam	Ice	Special	95	100	10	Normal	—	—
TM14	Blizzard	Ice	Special	120	70	5	Many Others	—	—
TM15	Hyper Beam	Normal	Special	150	90	5	Normal	—	—
TM16	Light Screen	Psychic	Status	—	—	30	Your Side	—	—
TM17	Protect	Normal	Status	—	—	10	Self	—	—
TM18	Rain Dance	Water	Status	—	—	5	Both Sides	—	—
TM20	Safeguard	Normal	Status	—	—	25	Your Side	—	—
TM21	Frustration	Normal	Physical	—	100	20	Normal	—	○
TM27	Return	Normal	Physical	—	100	20	Normal	—	○
TM29	Psychic	Psychic	Special	90	100	10	Normal	—	—
TM30	Shadow Ball	Ghost	Special	80	100	15	Normal	—	—
TM32	Double Team	Normal	Status	—	—	15	Self	—	—
TM33	Reflect	Psychic	Status	—	—	20	Your Side	—	—
TM39	Rock Tomb	Rock	Physical	50	80	10	Normal	—	—
TM42	Facade	Normal	Physical	70	100	20	Normal	—	○
TM44	Rest	Psychic	Status	—	—	10	Self	—	—
TM48	Round	Normal	Special	60	100	15	Normal	—	—
TM49	Echoed Voice	Normal	Special	40	100	15	Normal	—	—
TM52	Focus Blast	Fighting	Special	120	70	5	Normal	—	—
TM56	Fling	Dark	Physical	—	100	10	Normal	—	○
TM65	Shadow Claw	Ghost	Physical	70	100	15	Normal	—	○
TM66	Payback	Dark	Physical	50	100	10	Normal	—	○
TM68	Giga Impact	Normal	Physical	150	90	5	Normal	—	○
TM71	Stone Edge	Rock	Physical	100	80	5	Normal	—	—
TM80	Rock Slide	Rock	Physical	75	90	10	Many Others	—	—
TM82	Dragon Tail	Dragon	Physical	60	90	10	Normal	—	○
TM87	Swagger	Normal	Status	—	90	15	Normal	—	—
TM90	Substitute	Normal	Status	—	—	10	Self	—	—
TM91	Flash Cannon	Steel	Special	80	100	10	Normal	—	—
TM94	Rock Smash	Fighting	Physical	40	100	15	Normal	—	○
HM01	Cut	Normal	Physical	50	95	30	Normal	—	○
HM02	Fly	Flying	Physical	90	95	15	Normal	○	○

MOVES TAUGHT BY MOVE TUTORS FOR SHARDS

Name	Type	Kind	Pow.	Acc.	PP	Range	Long	DA
Signal Beam	Bug	Special	75	100	15	Normal	—	—
Iron Head	Steel	Physical	80	100	15	Normal	—	○
Hyper Voice	Normal	Special	90	100	10	Many Others	—	—
Icy Wind	Ice	Special	55	95	15	Many Others	—	—
Earth Power	Ground	Special	90	100	10	Normal	—	—
Zen Headbutt	Psychic	Physical	80	90	15	Normal	—	○
Dragon Pulse	Dragon	Special	90	100	10	Normal	○	—
Snore	Normal	Special	40	100	15	Normal	—	—
Roost	Flying	Status	—	—	10	Self	—	—
Outrage	Dragon	Physical	120	100	10	1 Random	—	○
Endeavor	Normal	Physical	—	100	5	Normal	—	○
Sleep Talk	Normal	Status	—	—	10	Self	—	—

Pokémon AR Marker

---

646 Kyurem (White Kyurem)

Boundary Pokémon

TYPE Dragon | Ice

ABILITY
● Turboblaze

HIDDEN ABILITY
———

- HEIGHT: 11'10"
- WEIGHT: 716.5 lbs.
- GENDER: Unknown

This legendary ice Pokémon waits for a hero to fill in the missing parts of its body with truth or ideals.

STATS
HP
Attack
Defense
Sp. Atk
Sp. Def
Speed

EGG GROUPS
No Egg has ever been discovered

ITEMS SOMETIMES HELD
● None

Gender unknown

EVOLUTION

Does not evolve

HOW TO OBTAIN

Pokémon Black Version 2	Use the DNA Splicers on Kyurem to create Absofusion with Reshiram
Pokémon White Version 2	Use the DNA Splicers on Kyurem to create Absofusion with Reshiram

HOW TO OBTAIN FROM OTHER GAMES

LEVEL-UP AND LEARNED MOVES

Lv.	Name	Type	Kind	Pow.	Acc.	PP	Range	Long	DA
1	Icy Wind	Ice	Special	55	95	15	Many Others	—	—
1	Dragon Rage	Dragon	Special	—	100	10	Normal	—	—
8	Imprison	Psychic	Status	—	—	10	Self	—	—
15	AncientPower	Rock	Special	60	100	5	Normal	—	—
22	Ice Beam	Ice	Special	95	100	10	Normal	—	—
29	DragonBreath	Dragon	Special	60	100	20	Normal	—	—
36	Slash	Normal	Physical	70	100	20	Normal	—	○
43	Fusion Flare	Fire	Special	100	100	5	Normal	—	—
50	Ice Burn	Ice	Special	140	90	5	Normal	—	—
57	Dragon Pulse	Dragon	Special	90	100	10	Normal	○	—
64	Imprison	Psychic	Status	—	—	10	Self	—	○
71	Endeavor	Normal	Physical	—	100	5	Normal	—	○
78	Blizzard	Ice	Special	120	70	5	Many Others	—	—
85	Outrage	Dragon	Physical	120	100	10	1 Random	—	○
92	Hyper Voice	Normal	Special	90	100	10	Many Others	—	—

Lv.	Name	Type	Kind	Pow.	Acc.	PP	Range	Long	DA
HM04	Strength	Normal	Physical	80	100	15	Normal	—	—

MOVES TAUGHT BY PEOPLE

Name	Type	Kind	Pow.	Acc.	PP	Range	Long	DA
Draco Meteor	Dragon	Special	140	90	5	Normal	—	—

TM & HM MOVES

Lv.	Name	Type	Kind	Pow.	Acc.	PP	Range	Long	DA
TM01	Hone Claws	Dark	Status	—	—	15	Self	—	—
TM02	Dragon Claw	Dragon	Physical	80	100	15	Normal	—	○
TM06	Toxic	Poison	Status	—	90	10	Normal	—	—
TM07	Hail	Ice	Status	—	—	10	Both Sides	—	—
TM10	Hidden Power	Normal	Special	—	100	15	Normal	—	—
TM11	Sunny Day	Fire	Status	—	—	5	Both Sides	—	—
TM13	Ice Beam	Ice	Special	95	100	10	Normal	—	—
TM14	Blizzard	Ice	Special	120	70	5	Many Others	—	—
TM15	Hyper Beam	Normal	Special	150	90	5	Normal	—	—
TM16	Light Screen	Psychic	Status	—	—	30	Your Side	—	—
TM17	Protect	Normal	Status	—	—	10	Self	—	—
TM18	Rain Dance	Water	Status	—	—	5	Both Sides	—	—
TM20	Safeguard	Normal	Status	—	—	25	Your Side	—	—
TM21	Frustration	Normal	Physical	—	100	20	Normal	—	○
TM27	Return	Normal	Physical	—	100	20	Normal	—	○
TM29	Psychic	Psychic	Special	90	100	10	Normal	—	—
TM30	Shadow Ball	Ghost	Special	80	100	15	Normal	—	—
TM32	Double Team	Normal	Status	—	—	15	Self	—	—
TM33	Reflect	Psychic	Status	—	—	20	Your Side	—	—
TM39	Rock Tomb	Rock	Physical	50	80	10	Normal	—	—
TM42	Facade	Normal	Physical	70	100	20	Normal	—	○
TM44	Rest	Psychic	Status	—	—	10	Self	—	—
TM48	Round	Normal	Special	60	100	15	Normal	—	—
TM49	Echoed Voice	Normal	Special	40	100	15	Normal	—	—
TM52	Focus Blast	Fighting	Special	120	70	5	Normal	—	—
TM56	Fling	Dark	Physical	—	100	10	Normal	—	○
TM65	Shadow Claw	Ghost	Physical	70	100	15	Normal	—	○
TM66	Payback	Dark	Physical	50	100	10	Normal	—	○
TM68	Giga Impact	Normal	Physical	150	90	5	Normal	—	○
TM71	Stone Edge	Rock	Physical	100	80	5	Normal	—	—
TM80	Rock Slide	Rock	Physical	75	90	10	Many Others	—	—
TM82	Dragon Tail	Dragon	Physical	60	90	10	Normal	—	○
TM87	Swagger	Normal	Status	—	90	15	Normal	—	—
TM90	Substitute	Normal	Status	—	—	10	Self	—	—
TM91	Flash Cannon	Steel	Special	80	100	10	Normal	—	—
TM94	Rock Smash	Fighting	Physical	40	100	15	Normal	—	○
HM01	Cut	Normal	Physical	50	95	30	Normal	—	○
HM02	Fly	Flying	Physical	90	95	15	Normal	○	○

MOVES TAUGHT BY MOVE TUTORS FOR SHARDS

Name	Type	Kind	Pow.	Acc.	PP	Range	Long	DA
Signal Beam	Bug	Special	75	100	15	Normal	—	—
Iron Head	Steel	Physical	80	100	15	Normal	—	○
Hyper Voice	Normal	Special	90	100	10	Many Others	—	—
Icy Wind	Ice	Special	55	95	15	Many Others	—	—
Earth Power	Ground	Special	90	100	10	Normal	—	—
Zen Headbutt	Psychic	Physical	80	90	15	Normal	—	○
Dragon Pulse	Dragon	Special	90	100	10	Normal	○	—
Snore	Normal	Special	40	100	15	Normal	—	—
Roost	Flying	Status	—	—	10	Self	—	—
Outrage	Dragon	Physical	120	100	10	1 Random	—	○
Endeavor	Normal	Physical	—	100	5	Normal	—	○
Sleep Talk	Normal	Status	—	—	10	Self	—	—

Pokémon AR Marker

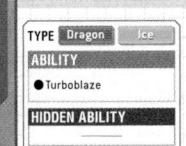

Colt Pokémon

647 Keldeo (Ordinary Form)

- HEIGHT: 4'07"
- WEIGHT: 106.9 lbs.
- GENDER: Unknown

When it is resolute, its body fills with power and it becomes swifter. Its jumps are then too fast to follow.

Gender unknown

TYPE: Water / Fighting

ABILITY
- Justified

HIDDEN ABILITY
—

STATS
HP
Attack
Defense
Sp. Atk
Sp. Def
Speed

EGG GROUPS
No Egg has ever been discovered

EVOLUTION
Does not evolve

HOW TO OBTAIN
Only available through special distribution events.
Check www.pokemon.com for the latest information on how to catch this Pokémon.

Pokémon AR Marker

LEVEL-UP AND LEARNED MOVES

Lv.	Name	Type	Kind	Pow.	Acc.	PP	Range	Long	DA
1	Aqua Jet	Water	Physical	40	100	20	Normal	—	○
1	Leer	Normal	Status	—	100	30	Many Others	—	—
7	Double Kick	Fighting	Physical	30	100	30	Normal	—	○
13	BubbleBeam	Water	Special	65	100	20	Normal	—	—
19	Take Down	Normal	Physical	90	85	20	Normal	—	○
25	Helping Hand	Normal	Status	—	—	20	1 Ally	—	—
31	Retaliate	Normal	Physical	70	100	5	Normal	—	○
37	Aqua Tail	Water	Physical	90	90	10	Normal	—	○
43	Sacred Sword	Fighting	Physical	90	100	20	Normal	—	○
49	Swords Dance	Normal	Status	—	—	30	Self	—	—
55	Quick Guard	Fighting	Status	—	—	15	Your Side	—	—
61	Work Up	Normal	Status	—	—	30	Self	—	—
67	Hydro Pump	Water	Special	120	80	5	Normal	—	—
73	Close Combat	Fighting	Physical	120	100	5	Normal	—	○

TM & HM MOVES

Lv.	Name	Type	Kind	Pow.	Acc.	PP	Range	Long	DA
TM04	Calm Mind	Psychic	Status	—	—	20	Self	—	—
TM05	Roar	Normal	Status	—	100	20	Normal	—	—
TM06	Toxic	Poison	Status	—	90	10	Normal	—	—
TM07	Hail	Ice	Status	—	—	10	Both Sides	—	—
TM10	Hidden Power	Normal	Special	—	100	15	Normal	—	—
TM12	Taunt	Dark	Status	—	100	20	Normal	—	—
TM15	Hyper Beam	Normal	Special	150	90	5	Normal	—	—
TM17	Protect	Normal	Status	—	—	10	Self	—	—
TM18	Rain Dance	Water	Status	—	—	5	Both Sides	—	—
TM20	Safeguard	Normal	Status	—	—	25	Your Side	—	—
TM21	Frustration	Normal	Physical	—	100	20	Normal	—	○
TM27	Return	Normal	Physical	—	100	20	Normal	—	○
TM32	Double Team	Normal	Status	—	—	15	Self	—	—
TM33	Reflect	Psychic	Status	—	—	20	Your Side	—	—
TM40	Aerial Ace	Flying	Physical	60	—	20	Normal	○	○
TM42	Facade	Normal	Physical	70	100	20	Normal	—	○
TM44	Rest	Psychic	Status	—	—	10	Self	—	—
TM48	Round	Normal	Special	60	100	15	Normal	—	—
TM52	Focus Blast	Fighting	Special	120	70	5	Normal	—	—
TM54	False Swipe	Normal	Physical	40	100	40	Normal	—	○
TM55	Scald	Water	Special	80	100	15	Normal	—	—
TM67	Retaliate	Normal	Physical	70	100	5	Normal	—	○
TM68	Giga Impact	Normal	Physical	150	90	5	Normal	—	○
TM71	Stone Edge	Rock	Physical	100	80	5	Normal	—	—
TM75	Swords Dance	Normal	Status	—	—	30	Self	—	—
TM77	Psych Up	Normal	Status	—	—	10	Normal	—	—
TM81	X-Scissor	Bug	Physical	80	100	15	Normal	—	○
TM83	Work Up	Normal	Status	—	—	30	Self	—	—
TM84	Poison Jab	Poison	Physical	80	100	20	Normal	—	○
TM87	Swagger	Normal	Status	—	90	15	Normal	—	—
TM90	Substitute	Normal	Status	—	—	10	Self	—	—
TM94	Rock Smash	Fighting	Physical	40	100	15	Normal	—	○
HM01	Cut	Normal	Physical	50	95	30	Normal	—	○
HM03	Surf	Water	Special	95	100	15	Adjacent	—	—
HM04	Strength	Normal	Physical	80	100	15	Normal	—	○

MOVES TAUGHT BY PEOPLE

Name	Type	Kind	Pow.	Acc.	PP	Range	Long	DA

MOVES TAUGHT BY MOVE TUTORS FOR SHARDS

Name	Type	Kind	Pow.	Acc.	PP	Range	Long	DA
Covet	Normal	Physical	60	100	40	Normal	—	○
Bounce	Flying	Physical	85	85	5	Normal	○	○
Last Resort	Normal	Physical	140	100	5	Normal	—	○
Icy Wind	Ice	Special	55	95	15	Many Others	—	—
Aqua Tail	Water	Physical	90	90	10	Normal	—	○
Superpower	Fighting	Physical	120	100	5	Normal	—	○
Snore	Normal	Special	40	100	15	Normal	—	—
Helping Hand	Normal	Status	—	—	20	1 Ally	—	—
Endeavor	Normal	Physical	—	100	5	Normal	—	○
Sleep Talk	Normal	Status	—	—	10	Self	—	—

Colt Pokémon

647 Keldeo (Resolute Form)

- HEIGHT: 4'07"
- WEIGHT: 106.9 lbs.
- GENDER: Unknown

When it is resolute, its body fills with power and it becomes swifter. Its jumps are then too fast to follow.

Gender unknown

TYPE: Water / Fighting

ABILITY
- Justified

HIDDEN ABILITY
—

STATS
HP
Attack
Defense
Sp. Atk
Sp. Def
Speed

EGG GROUPS
No Egg has ever been discovered

EVOLUTION
Does not evolve

HOW TO OBTAIN
Only available through special distribution events.
Check www.pokemon.com for the latest information on how to catch this Pokémon.

Pokémon AR Marker

LEVEL-UP AND LEARNED MOVES

Lv.	Name	Type	Kind	Pow.	Acc.	PP	Range	Long	DA
1	Aqua Jet	Water	Physical	40	100	20	Normal	—	○
1	Leer	Normal	Status	—	100	30	Many Others	—	—
7	Double Kick	Fighting	Physical	30	100	30	Normal	—	○
13	BubbleBeam	Water	Special	65	100	20	Normal	—	—
19	Take Down	Normal	Physical	90	85	20	Normal	—	○
25	Helping Hand	Normal	Status	—	—	20	1 Ally	—	—
31	Retaliate	Normal	Physical	70	100	5	Normal	—	○
37	Aqua Tail	Water	Physical	90	90	10	Normal	—	○
43	Sacred Sword	Fighting	Physical	90	100	20	Normal	—	○
49	Swords Dance	Normal	Status	—	—	30	Self	—	—
55	Quick Guard	Fighting	Status	—	—	15	Your Side	—	—
61	Work Up	Normal	Status	—	—	30	Self	—	—
67	Hydro Pump	Water	Special	120	80	5	Normal	—	—
73	Close Combat	Fighting	Physical	120	100	5	Normal	—	○
◆	Secret Sword	Fighting	Special	85	100	10	Normal	—	—

TM & HM MOVES

Lv.	Name	Type	Kind	Pow.	Acc.	PP	Range	Long	DA
TM04	Calm Mind	Psychic	Status	—	—	20	Self	—	—
TM05	Roar	Normal	Status	—	100	20	Normal	—	—
TM06	Toxic	Poison	Status	—	90	10	Normal	—	—
TM07	Hail	Ice	Status	—	—	10	Both Sides	—	—
TM10	Hidden Power	Normal	Special	—	100	15	Normal	—	—
TM12	Taunt	Dark	Status	—	100	20	Normal	—	—
TM15	Hyper Beam	Normal	Special	150	90	5	Normal	—	—
TM17	Protect	Normal	Status	—	—	10	Self	—	—
TM18	Rain Dance	Water	Status	—	—	5	Both Sides	—	—
TM20	Safeguard	Normal	Status	—	—	25	Your Side	—	—
TM21	Frustration	Normal	Physical	—	100	20	Normal	—	○
TM27	Return	Normal	Physical	—	100	20	Normal	—	○
TM32	Double Team	Normal	Status	—	—	15	Self	—	—
TM33	Reflect	Psychic	Status	—	—	20	Your Side	—	—
TM40	Aerial Ace	Flying	Physical	60	—	20	Normal	○	○
TM42	Facade	Normal	Physical	70	100	20	Normal	—	○
TM44	Rest	Psychic	Status	—	—	10	Self	—	—
TM48	Round	Normal	Special	60	100	15	Normal	—	—
TM52	Focus Blast	Fighting	Special	120	70	5	Normal	—	—
TM54	False Swipe	Normal	Physical	40	100	40	Normal	—	○
TM55	Scald	Water	Special	80	100	15	Normal	—	—
TM67	Retaliate	Normal	Physical	70	100	5	Normal	—	○
TM68	Giga Impact	Normal	Physical	150	90	5	Normal	—	○
TM71	Stone Edge	Rock	Physical	100	80	5	Normal	—	—
TM75	Swords Dance	Normal	Status	—	—	30	Self	—	—
TM77	Psych Up	Normal	Status	—	—	10	Normal	—	—
TM81	X-Scissor	Bug	Physical	80	100	15	Normal	—	○
TM83	Work Up	Normal	Status	—	—	30	Self	—	—
TM84	Poison Jab	Poison	Physical	80	100	20	Normal	—	○
TM87	Swagger	Normal	Status	—	90	15	Normal	—	—
TM90	Substitute	Normal	Status	—	—	10	Self	—	—
TM94	Rock Smash	Fighting	Physical	40	100	15	Normal	—	○
HM01	Cut	Normal	Physical	50	95	30	Normal	—	○
HM03	Surf	Water	Special	95	100	15	Adjacent	—	—
HM04	Strength	Normal	Physical	80	100	15	Normal	—	○

MOVES TAUGHT BY PEOPLE

Name	Type	Kind	Pow.	Acc.	PP	Range	Long	DA

MOVES TAUGHT BY MOVE TUTORS FOR SHARDS

Name	Type	Kind	Pow.	Acc.	PP	Range	Long	DA
Covet	Normal	Physical	60	100	40	Normal	—	○
Bounce	Flying	Physical	85	85	5	Normal	○	○
Last Resort	Normal	Physical	140	100	5	Normal	—	○
Icy Wind	Ice	Special	55	95	15	Many Others	—	—
Aqua Tail	Water	Physical	90	90	10	Normal	—	○
Superpower	Fighting	Physical	120	100	5	Normal	—	○
Snore	Normal	Special	40	100	15	Normal	—	—
Helping Hand	Normal	Status	—	—	20	1 Ally	—	—
Endeavor	Normal	Physical	—	100	5	Normal	—	○
Sleep Talk	Normal	Status	—	—	10	Self	—	—

◆ Go to the Pledge Grove north of Floccesy Town and check the rock to teach it this move.

Melody Pokémon

648 Meloetta
(Aria Forme)

- HEIGHT: 2'00"
- WEIGHT: 14.3 lbs.
- GENDER: Unknown

The melodies sung by Meloetta have the power to make Pokémon that hear them happy or sad.

Gender unknown

TYPE	Normal	Psychic

ABILITY
- Serene Grace

HIDDEN ABILITY

STATS
HP
Attack
Defense
Sp. Atk
Sp. Def
Speed

EGG GROUPS
No Egg has ever been discovered

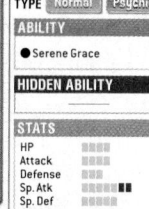

EVOLUTION

Does not evolve

HOW TO OBTAIN

Only available through special distribution events. Check www.pokemon.com for the latest information on how to catch this Pokémon.

LEVEL-UP AND LEARNED MOVES

Lv.	Name	Type	Kind	Pow.	Acc.	PP	Range	Long	DA

This Pokémon has secret moves that are yet to be revealed.

MOVES TAUGHT BY PEOPLE

	Name	Type	Kind	Pow.	Acc.	PP	Range	Long	DA

TM & HM MOVES

Lv.	Name	Type	Kind	Pow.	Acc.	PP	Range	Long	DA

MOVES TAUGHT BY MOVE TUTORS FOR SHARDS

	Name	Type	Kind	Pow.	Acc.	PP	Range	Long	DA

Pokémon AR Marker

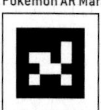

Melody Pokémon

648 Meloetta
(Pirouette Forme)

- HEIGHT: 2'00"
- WEIGHT: 14.3 lbs.
- GENDER: Unknown

The melodies sung by Meloetta have the power to make Pokémon that hear them happy or sad.

Gender unknown

TYPE	Normal	Fighting

ABILITY
- Serene Grace

HIDDEN ABILITY

STATS
HP
Attack
Defense
Sp. Atk
Sp. Def
Speed

EGG GROUPS
No Egg has ever been discovered

EVOLUTION

Does not evolve

HOW TO OBTAIN

Only available through special distribution events. Check www.pokemon.com for the latest information on how to catch this Pokémon.

LEVEL-UP AND LEARNED MOVES

Lv.	Name	Type	Kind	Pow.	Acc.	PP	Range	Long	DA

This Pokémon has secret moves that are yet to be revealed.

MOVES TAUGHT BY PEOPLE

	Name	Type	Kind	Pow.	Acc.	PP	Range	Long	DA

TM & HM MOVES

Lv.	Name	Type	Kind	Pow.	Acc.	PP	Range	Long	DA

MOVES TAUGHT BY MOVE TUTORS FOR SHARDS

	Name	Type	Kind	Pow.	Acc.	PP	Range	Long	DA

Pokémon AR Marker

649 Genesect
Paleozoic Pokémon

TYPE
Bug | Steel

ABILITY
● Download

HIDDEN ABILITY

STATS
HP	▮▮▮
Attack	▮▮▮▮▮
Defense	▮▮▮▮
Sp. Attack	▮▮▮▮▮
Sp. Defense	▮▮▮▮
Speed	▮▮▮▮▮

EGG GROUPS
No Egg has ever been discovered

● HEIGHT: 4'11"
● WEIGHT: 181.9 lbs.
● GENDER: Unknown

This Pokémon existed 300 million years ago. Team Plasma altered it and attached a cannon to its back.

Gender unknown

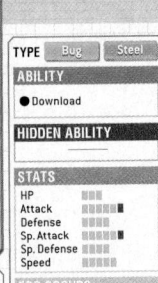

Holding the Douse Drive

Holding the Shock Drive

Holding the Chill Drive

Holding the Burn Drive

Does not evolve

HOW TO OBTAIN

Only available through special distribution events. Check www.pokemon.com for the latest information on how to catch this Pokémon.

LEVEL-UP AND LEARNED MOVES

Lv.	Name	Type	Kind	Pow.	Acc.	PP	Range	Long	DA
1	Techno Blast ◆	Normal	Special	85	100	5	Normal	—	—
1	Quick Attack	Normal	Physical	40	100	30	Normal	—	○
1	Magnet Rise	Electric	Status	—	—	10	Self	—	—
1	Metal Claw	Steel	Physical	50	95	35	Normal	—	○
1	Screech	Normal	Status	—	85	40	Normal	—	—
7	Fury Cutter	Bug	Physical	20	95	20	Normal	—	○
11	Lock-On	Normal	Status	—	—	5	Normal	—	—
18	Flame Charge	Fire	Physical	50	100	20	Normal	—	○
22	Magnet Bomb	Steel	Physical	60	—	20	Normal	—	—
29	Slash	Normal	Physical	70	100	20	Normal	—	○
33	Metal Sound	Steel	Status	—	85	40	Normal	—	—
40	Signal Beam	Bug	Special	75	100	15	Normal	—	—
44	Tri Attack	Normal	Special	80	100	10	Normal	—	—
51	X-Scissor	Bug	Physical	80	100	15	Normal	—	○
55	Bug Buzz	Bug	Special	90	100	10	Normal	—	—
62	Simple Beam	Normal	Status	—	100	15	Normal	—	—
66	Zap Cannon	Electric	Special	120	50	5	Normal	—	—
73	Hyper Beam	Normal	Special	150	90	5	Normal	—	—
77	Selfdestruct	Normal	Physical	200	100	5	Adjacent	—	—

TM & HM MOVES

Lv.	Name	Type	Kind	Pow.	Acc.	PP	Range	Long	DA
TM01	Hone Claws	Dark	Status	—	—	15	Self	—	—
TM06	Toxic	Poison	Status	—	90	10	Normal	—	—
TM10	Hidden Power	Normal	Special	—	100	15	Normal	—	—
TM13	Ice Beam	Ice	Special	95	100	10	Normal	—	—
TM14	Blizzard	Ice	Special	120	70	5	Many Others	—	—
TM15	Hyper Beam	Normal	Special	150	90	5	Normal	—	—
TM16	Light Screen	Psychic	Status	—	—	30	Your Side	—	—
TM17	Protect	Normal	Status	—	—	10	Self	—	—
TM21	Frustration	Normal	Physical	—	100	20	Normal	—	○
TM22	SolarBeam	Grass	Special	120	100	10	Normal	—	—
TM24	Thunderbolt	Electric	Special	95	100	15	Normal	—	—
TM25	Thunder	Electric	Special	120	70	10	Normal	—	—
TM27	Return	Normal	Physical	—	100	20	Normal	—	○
TM29	Psychic	Psychic	Special	90	100	10	Normal	—	—
TM32	Double Team	Normal	Status	—	—	15	Self	—	—
TM33	Reflect	Psychic	Status	—	—	20	Your Side	—	—
TM35	Flamethrower	Fire	Special	95	100	15	Normal	—	—
TM40	Aerial Ace	Flying	Physical	60	—	20	Normal	○	○
TM42	Facade	Normal	Physical	70	100	20	Normal	—	○
TM43	Flame Charge	Fire	Physical	50	100	20	Normal	—	○
TM44	Rest	Psychic	Status	—	—	10	Self	—	—
TM48	Round	Normal	Special	60	100	15	Normal	—	—
TM53	Energy Ball	Grass	Special	80	100	10	Normal	—	—
TM57	Charge Beam	Electric	Special	50	90	10	Normal	—	—
TM64	Explosion	Normal	Physical	250	100	5	Adjacent	—	—
TM65	Shadow Claw	Ghost	Physical	70	100	15	Normal	—	○
TM68	Giga Impact	Normal	Physical	150	90	5	Normal	—	○
TM69	Rock Polish	Rock	Status	—	—	20	Self	—	—
TM70	Flash	Normal	Status	—	100	20	Normal	—	—

Lv.	Name	Type	Kind	Pow.	Acc.	PP	Range	Long	DA
TM73	Thunder Wave	Electric	Status	—	100	20	Normal	—	—
TM76	Struggle Bug	Bug	Special	30	100	20	Many Others	—	—
TM81	X-Scissor	Bug	Physical	80	100	15	Normal	—	○
TM87	Swagger	Normal	Status	—	90	15	Normal	—	—
TM89	U-turn	Bug	Physical	70	100	20	Normal	—	○
TM90	Substitute	Normal	Status	—	—	10	Self	—	—
TM91	Flash Cannon	Steel	Special	80	100	10	Normal	—	—
HM02	Fly	Flying	Physical	90	95	15	Normal	○	○

MOVES TAUGHT BY PEOPLE

Name	Type	Kind	Pow.	Acc.	PP	Range	Long	DA

MOVES TAUGHT BY MOVE TUTORS FOR SHARDS

Name	Type	Kind	Pow.	Acc.	PP	Range	Long	DA
Bug Bite	Bug	Physical	60	100	20	Normal	—	○
Signal Beam	Bug	Special	75	100	15	Normal	—	—
Iron Head	Steel	Physical	80	100	15	Normal	—	○
Gunk Shot	Poison	Physical	120	70	5	Normal	—	—
Last Resort	Normal	Physical	140	100	5	Normal	—	○
Iron Defense	Steel	Status	—	—	15	Self	—	—
Magnet Rise	Electric	Status	—	—	10	Self	—	—
Magic Coat	Psychic	Status	—	—	15	Self	—	—
Electroweb	Electric	Special	55	95	15	Many Others	—	—
Zen Headbutt	Psychic	Physical	80	90	15	Normal	—	○
Gravity	Psychic	Status	—	—	5	Both Sides	—	—
Dark Pulse	Dark	Special	80	100	15	Normal	○	—
Snore	Normal	Special	40	100	15	Normal	—	—
Giga Drain	Grass	Special	75	100	10	Normal	—	—
Recycle	Normal	Status	—	—	10	Self	—	—
Sleep Talk	Normal	Status	—	—	10	Self	—	—

◆ Techno Blast's type changes if Genesect is holding a Drive: it changes to Water type when it holds a Douse Drive, Electric type when it holds a Shock Drive, Ice type when it holds a Chill Drive, and Fire type when it holds a Burn Drive.

Form and Forme Changes in the Unova Region

Certain Pokémon have more than one form or Forme

Some Pokémon, such as Giratina, Shaymin, and Deoxys, are able to change their Formes. Discover how Pokémon may change their forms or Formes after they're sent to Pokémon Black Version 2 or Pokémon White Version 2. This information will help you with completing your Pokédex and in Pokémon battles.

Giratina — Give Giratina the Griseous Orb to change it into its Origin Forme

Giratina is normally in its Altered Forme. When you have it hold the Griseous Orb, it changes into Origin Forme. You'll get the Griseous Orb in Dragonspiral Tower.

Trainer found a Griseous Orb!

Giratina's Forme Changes

Giratina
Altered Forme
Ghost / Dragon

Giratina
Origin Forme
Ghost / Dragon

 Griseous Orb
Dragonspiral Tower 4F

Shaymin — Use the Gracidea flower to change it into its Sky Forme

Use the Gracidea on Shaymin Land Forme, and it will turn Shaymin into Sky Forme. Shaymin Sky Forme is a Grass- and Flying-type Pokémon, and its Ability is Serene Grace.

Trainer obtained the Gracidea!

Conditions that revert Shaymin to Land Forme
- When put in a PC Box
- At night and late night
- When frozen
- When left at the Pokémon Day Care
- When in a Link Trade
- When placed in the GTS

◆ Shaymin can be obtained during special distribution periods. Check www.pokemon.com to find out if any Pokémon are currently being distributed.

Shaymin's Forme Changes

Shaymin
Land Forme
Grass

Shaymin
Sky Forme
Grass / Flying

 Gracidea
Talk to the woman in Striaton City's Pokémon Center while Shaymin is in your party, and she will give you the Gracidea.

Rotom — Check the cardboard boxes in Shopping Mall Nine

To change its form, go through the door on the first floor of Shopping Mall Nine and check the cardboard boxes while Rotom is in your party. Have it enter a microwave oven, a washing machine, a refrigerator, an electric fan, or a lawnmower, and it will become Heat Rotom, Wash Rotom, Frost Rotom, Fan Rotom, or Mow Rotom, respectively.

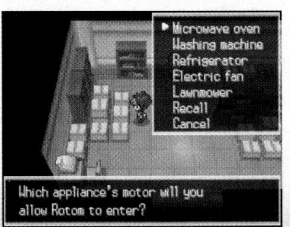

Which appliance's motor will you allow Rotom to enter?

Microwave oven
Washing machine
Refrigerator
Electric fan
Lawnmower
Recall
Cancel

Rotom's Form Changes

Rotom
Electric / Ghost

Rotom
Wash Rotom
Electric / Water

Rotom
Heat Rotom
Electric / Fire

Rotom
Mow Rotom
Electric / Grass

Rotom
Frost Rotom
Electric / Ice

Rotom
Fan Rotom
Electric / Flying

Deoxys ▶ Examine the meteor in the Nacrene Museum

Deoxys can change from its Normal Forme to its Attack Forme, Defense Forme, or Speed Forme. Change its Forme by putting Deoxys in your party and examining the meteor in the Nacrene Museum. Every time you examine the meteor, Deoxys will change into another one of its Formes.

◆ Deoxys can be obtained during special distribution periods. Check www.pokemon.com to find out if any Pokémon are currently being distributed.

Deoxys's Forme Changes

 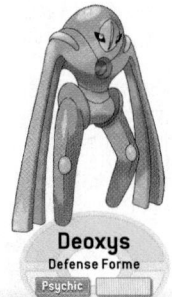 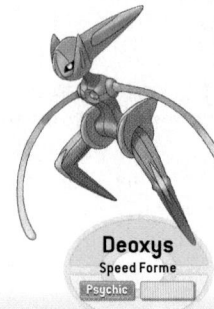

Deoxys	Deoxys	Deoxys	Deoxys
Normal Forme	Attack Forme	Defense Forme	Speed Forme
Psychic	Psychic	Psychic	Psychic

Arceus ▶ Holding a Plate shifts Arceus's type

Arceus is usually a Normal-type Pokémon, but holding a Plate will shift its type and appearance in one of 16 ways. You can obtain various Plates in Undella Bay or at the Abyssal Ruins.

Arceus
Normal

Arceus's Types

Arceus	Arceus	Arceus	Arceus	Arceus	Arceus	Arceus	Arceus	Arceus
Normal	Fire	Water	Grass	Electric	Ice	Fighting	Poison	Ground
	Flame Plate	Splash Plate	Meadow Plate	Zap Plate	Icicle Plate	Fist Plate	Toxic Plate	Earth Plate

Arceus	Arceus	Arceus	Arceus	Arceus	Arceus	Arceus	Arceus
Flying	Psychic	Bug	Rock	Ghost	Dragon	Dark	Steel
Sky Plate	Mind Plate	Insect Plate	Stone Plate	Spooky Plate	Draco Plate	Dread Plate	Iron Plate

◆ Arceus can be obtained during special distribution periods. Check www.pokemon.com to find out if any Pokémon are currently being distributed.

Castform ▶ Castform changes its form and type in battle according to the weather

Castform changes to Sunny Form when the weather condition is Sunny. It changes to Rainy Form when the weather condition is Rain. It changes to Snowy Form when the weather condition is Hail.

Castform
Normal

Castform's Forms

Castform	Castform	Castform	Castform
Normal	Sunny Form	Rainy Form	Snowy Form
Normal	Fire	Water	Ice

Cherrim ▶ Cherrim changes its form when the weather is sunny

During a battle, Cherrim's form changes from Overcast Form to Sunshine Form if the weather condition becomes Sunny. This does not change its stats or type.

The foe's Cherrim transformed!

Cherrim's Form Changes

Cherrim	Cherrim
Overcast Form	Sunshine Form
Grass	Grass

Deerling and Sawsbuck | Changes its form depending on the season

Deerling and Sawsbuck change their forms depending on the season in the Unova region. Deerling's fur becomes pink in spring, green in summer, and so on. Sawsbuck's horns change dramatically, with flowers in spring, green leaves in summer, and so on. The Unova region's season changes with every month of real-world time. For example, August is winter, September is spring, October is summer, and November is autumn. Don't miss your chance to observe Deerling and Sawsbuck as they transform with the season.

A wild Sawsbuck appeared!

Deerling's Seasonal Changes

Deerling
Spring Form
Normal Grass

Deerling
Summer Form
Normal Grass

Deerling
Autumn Form
Normal Grass

Deerling
Winter Form
Normal Grass

Sawsbuck's Seasonal Changes

Sawsbuck
Spring Form
Normal Grass

Sawsbuck
Summer Form
Normal Grass

Sawsbuck
Autumn Form
Normal Grass

Sawsbuck
Winter Form
Normal Grass

Darmanitan | When half its HP is lost, it changes form

A Darmanitan with the Hidden Ability called Zen Mode can change its form during battle. If its HP falls to half or less than half during a battle, it will automatically change into Zen Mode at the end of the turn. This changes its type to Fire- and Psychic-type. Its stats will change, too. This change only happens during battle—once the battle is over, Darmanitan goes back to Standard Mode.

Darmanitan
Fire

Darmanitan's Form Changes

Darmanitan
Standard Mode
Fire

Darmanitan
Zen Mode
Fire Psychic

Tornadus, Thundurus, and Landorus | The Reveal Glass changes its Forme

Tornadus, Thundurus, and Landorus change their Formes when you use the Reveal Glass. They change from Incarnate Forme into Therian Forme with the Reveal Glass, and vice versa.

Reveal Glass

To obtain the Reveal Glass, you first need to get Landorus in Therian Forme. Catch Landorus in *Pokémon Dream Radar* and send it to your game. With Landorus Therian Forme in your party, visit the Abundant Shrine, and you'll be able to obtain the Reveal Glass.

Tornadus's Forme Changes

Tornadus
Incarnate Forme
Flying

Tornadus
Therian Forme
Flying

Thundurus's Forme Changes

Thundurus
Incarnate Forme
Electric Flying

Thundurus
Therian Forme
Electric Flying

Landorus's Forme Changes

Landorus
Incarnate Forme
Ground Flying

Landorus
Therian Forme
Ground Flying

Black Kyurem and White Kyurem >> Absofusion changes its appearance

With Kyurem and Zekrom (Reshiram) in your party, use the DNA Splicers. Choose Kyurem, then Zekrom (Reshiram). Kyurem will merge with Zekrom (Reshiram) in a process called Absofusion to turn into Black Kyurem (White Kyurem). Use the DNA Splicers with Black Kyurem (White Kyurem) in your party to separate Kyurem from Zekrom (Reshiram).

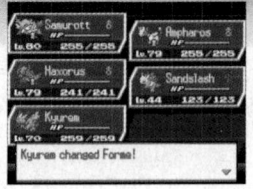
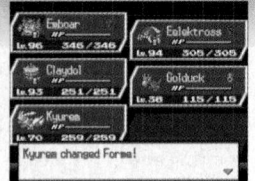

DNA Splicers

Giant Chasm (after catching Kyurem)

Kyurem and Zekrom's Absofusion

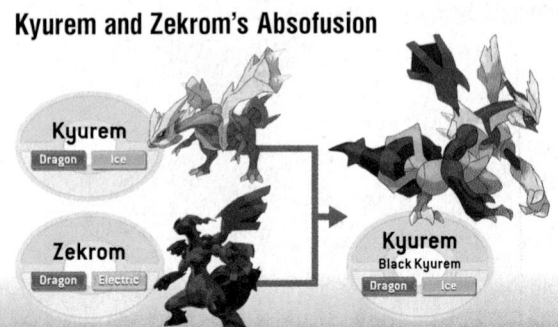

Kyurem and Reshiram's Absofusion

Keldeo >> Check the rock that has deeply cut marks inside Pledge Grove to change Keldeo's Form

With Keldeo in your party, head to Pledge Grove, north of Floccesy Town. Inspect the rock with the deeply cut marks, and Keldeo will learn Secret Sword. Its Form changes to Resolute Form. It goes back to its Ordinary Form when it forgets Secret Sword.

Keldeo's Form Changes

◆ Keldeo Ordinary Form can be obtained during special distribution periods. Check www.pokemon.com to find out if any Pokémon are currently being distributed.

Genesect >> Part of its body changes color when it holds a different Drive

Have Genesect hold one of the four Drives, and it changes its color accordingly. Holding a Drive changes the type of its move Techno Blast to Water, Electric, Ice, or Fire type.

How to obtain the four Drives

Douse Drive

With Genesect in your party, visit the P2 Laboratory and defeat the Scientist in battle (Pokémon White Version 2).

Shock Drive

With Genesect in your party, visit the P2 Laboratory and defeat the Scientist in battle (Pokémon Black Version 2).

Chill Drive

With Genesect in your party, visit the P2 Laboratory and defeat the Scientist in battle (Pokémon White Version 2).

Burn Drive

With Genesect in your party, visit the P2 Laboratory and defeat the Scientist in battle (Pokémon Black Version 2).

Genesect's Appearance Changes

Genesect — Douse Drive | Genesect — Shock Drive | Genesect — Chill Drive | Genesect — Burn Drive

◆ Genesect can be obtained during special distribution periods. Check www.pokemon.com to find out if any Pokémon are currently being distributed.

National Pokédex Challenge

Take the National Pokédex Challenge

Complete the National Pokédex by catching 636 kinds of Pokémon

A Pokémon Trainer's greatest dream is registering every Pokémon in the Pokédex and completing the National Pokédex. Completing the National Pokédex is a lot of effort—you must register more than 600 kinds of Pokémon—so completing it gives you a tremendous sense of joy and accomplishment. Use this book as your guide and do your best!

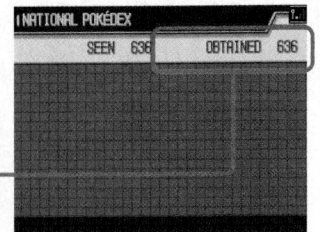

When you're done, this number will have reached 636

Have Cedric Juniper rate your Pokédex completion

Cedric Juniper provides a lot of support as you complete the National Pokédex. You'll find him in Juniper Pokémon Lab in Nuvema Town. Speak to him and he'll rate your Pokédex completion. He provides advice on what kind of Pokémon you might want to go after as he rates your Pokédex.

You're here to show me how your Pokédex is coming along, right?

Pokémon not needed to complete the National Pokédex

Of the 649 known Pokémon, there are 13 that don't need to be registered to complete the National Pokédex. Many of these Pokémon are extremely hard to come by, obtainable only through special distribution events. No need to worry about these—you can complete the National Pokédex without them.

National Pokédex No. 151 **Mew**

National Pokédex No. 251 **Celebi**

National Pokédex No. 385 **Jirachi**

National Pokédex No. 386 **Deoxys**

National Pokédex No. 489 **Phione**

National Pokédex No. 490 **Manaphy**

National Pokédex No. 491 **Darkrai**

National Pokédex No. 492 **Shaymin**

National Pokédex No. 493 **Arceus**

National Pokédex No. 494 **Victini**

National Pokédex No. 647 **Keldeo**

National Pokédex No. 648 **Meloetta**

National Pokédex No. 649 **Genesect**

Bring your Pokémon to *Pokémon Black Version 2* and *Pokémon White Version 2*

To register 636 kinds of Pokémon in your *Pokémon Black Version 2* or *Pokémon White Version 2*, you'll need help not only from both games, but also from *Pokémon Black Version* and *Pokémon White Version*, as well as *Pokémon Diamond, Pearl, Platinum, HeartGold,* and *SoulSilver Versions*. If you don't have these games, trade Pokémon with friends and family.

Games needed to complete the National Pokédex

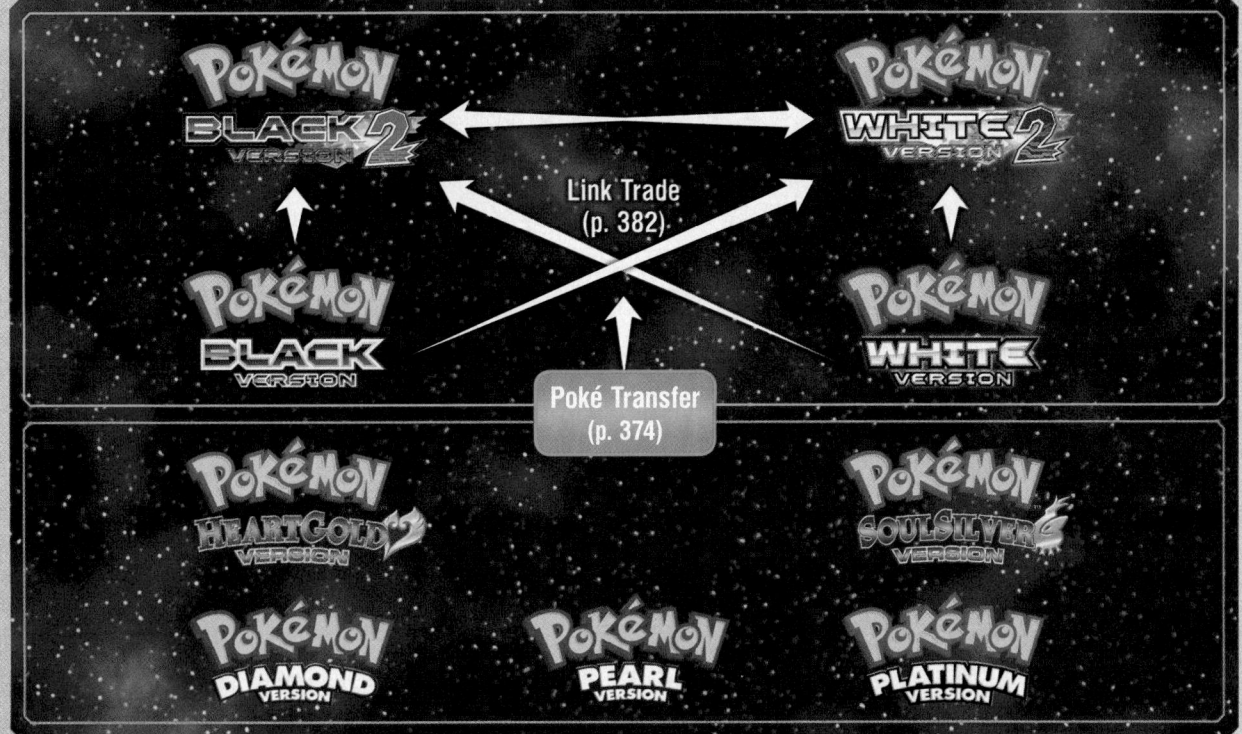

There are several different ways to bring Pokémon into *Pokémon Black Version 2* and *Pokémon White Version 2*, depending on the game. You can use Infrared Connection, DS Wireless Communications, or Nintendo Wi-Fi Connection to trade Pokémon with *Pokémon Black Version* or *Pokémon White Version* (p. 382). You need to use Poké Transfer to bring Pokémon from *Pokémon Diamond, Pearl, Platinum, HeartGold,* or *SoulSilver Versions* (p. 374).

Get a certificate and a Medal for completing it

When you complete the National Pokédex, you can get a stately award certificate from the Game Director in Castelia City's GAME FREAK building. The award certificate will be posted on the wall of your room. You'll also receive a special Medal from Mr. Medal.

Castelia City GAME FREAK

I will send this award certificate to your house, too!

Your room in Aspertia City

It's an award for completing the National Mode Pokédex!

National Catcher

Check p. 531 for the Medal list.

National Pokédex Completion Tip ①

Catch wild Pokémon

Master these techniques to increase your capture rate

The simplest way to fill out your Pokédex is to look for wild Pokémon and catch them with Poké Balls. Mastering the following techniques will help get the Pokémon you're after!

A wild Slakng appeared!

Catching Technique 1 — Push the Pokémon's HP into the red

You could just fling your Poké Ball at a wild Pokémon, but there's a good chance the Pokémon will pop right back out. You probably won't catch it if it's still full of energy, so use attacks to lower its HP. Once it's weakened, you have a much better chance of sealing the deal.

Lower its HP until the bar is red

When the Pokémon has just a few HP left, your odds of a successful catch are higher.

Catching Technique 2 — Inflict status conditions on wild Pokémon

Use Pokémon moves to inflict status conditions. Some status conditions make a Pokémon much easier to catch. That's not all it takes, of course. If you inflict a status condition and lower the Pokémon's HP, you'll maximize your chances of making the catch.

Status conditions that aid in capture

Sleep	Frozen	Paralysis	Poison	Burned
The target cannot attack. Wears off on its own after several turns. **(Easiest to Catch)**	The target cannot attack. Wears off on its own after several turns. **(Easiest to Catch)**	Lowers Speed, and each turn there's a 25% chance that the target can't attack. Does not wear off on its own.	The target's HP decreases each turn. Does not wear off on its own.	Lowers Attack, and HP decreases each turn. Does not wear off on its own.
● Some moves that cause Sleep status	● Some moves that cause Frozen status	● Some moves that cause Paralysis status	● Some moves that cause Poison status	● Some moves that cause Burned status
Sing, Hypnosis	Powder Snow, Ice Beam	Thunder Wave, Lick	PoisonPowder, Poison Gas	Will-O-Wisp, Scald

◆ Some moves can be used when Asleep or Frozen.

Catching Technique 3 — Catching many Pokémon makes it easier to catch other Pokémon

Catching many wild Pokémon increases the likelihood of catching others. Sometimes, when you throw a Poké Ball, it will click shut after rocking only once, and the Pokémon will be caught. This phenomenon is called a "critical capture." The more Pokémon you have caught, the more often this phenomenon occurs, so work on catching many Pokémon from the start of the game.

Critical captures

1. A Pokémon is caught after the Poké Ball rocks only once.

2. The more Pokémon you catch, the more likely this is to happen.

Catching Technique 4 — Use Pokémon moves and Abilities

Certain Pokémon moves and Abilities come in handy for finding and catching wild Pokémon. Use these moves and Abilities to increase your chances of catching the Pokémon you're after.

Examples of useful moves for catching Pokémon

Move Sweet Scent — Normal

Use this in a place where wild Pokémon appear, such as tall grass or a cave, and wild Pokémon will certainly appear.

● Pokémon who can use this move

Roselia, Combee, Tropius, and others

Move False Swipe — Normal

Always leaves at least 1 HP remaining, even if the damage should knock the Pokémon out. Useful for lowering HP as far as it will go without causing the Pokémon to faint.

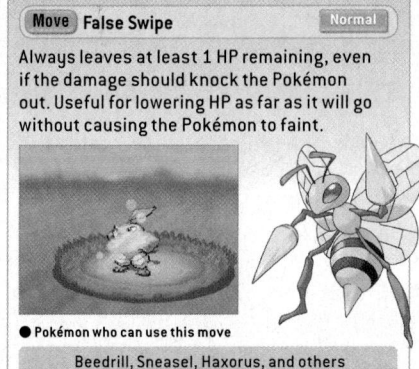

● Pokémon who can use this move

Beedrill, Sneasel, Haxorus, and others

Move Super Fang — Normal

Use this to halve your target's HP. Keep using it over and over until you minimize your target's HP.

● Pokémon who can use this move

Raticate, Pachirisu, Watchog, and others

Examples of useful Abilities for catching wild Pokémon

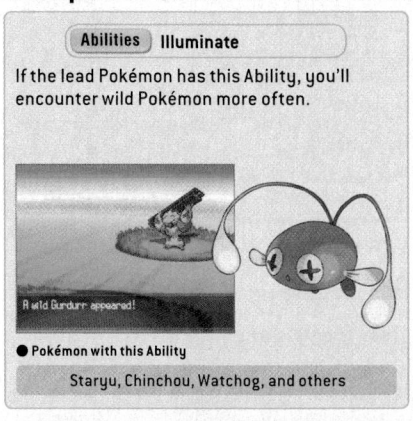

Abilities | **Illuminate**

If the lead Pokémon has this Ability, you'll encounter wild Pokémon more often.

● Pokémon with this Ability

Staryu, Chinchou, Watchog, and others

Abilities | **Sticky Hold**

An Ability that excels at attracting Pokémon to your fishing line.

● Pokémon with this Ability

Grimer, Trubbish, Accelgor, and others

Abilities | **Cute Charm**

An Ability that's good at attracting Pokémon of the opposite gender.

● Pokémon with this Ability

Clefairy, Delcatty, Lopunny, and others

Catching Technique 5 — Add a helpful Pokémon to your party

There are some Pokémon whose move sets are practically custom-made for catching wild Pokémon. Use these Pokémon to increase your chances of catching a wild Pokémon.

Example 1 — Watchog's Moves

Watchog's Illuminate Ability makes it easy to encounter wild Pokémon. It also learns Super Fang at Lv. 22. Give the reminder girl in the PWT area a Heart Scale to have it remember Hypnosis. Teach it Thunder Wave with TM73.

● Mainly Appears at

Route 7

Move | **Super Fang** | Normal

Halves the target's HP.

Move | **Hypnosis** | Psychic

Inflicts Sleep status on the target.

Move | **Thunder Wave** | Electric

Inflicts Paralysis status. Ground-type Pokémon are immune to it.

Example 2 — Leavanny's Moves

Before Swadloon evolves into Leavanny, it knows GrassWhistle from Lv. 1, and after it evolves, you can use TM54 to teach it False Swipe. Use False Swipe to reduce the wild Pokémon's HP to 1, and inflict Sleep status with GrassWhistle. This puts wild Pokémon in the easiest-to-catch state, so throw a Poké Ball.

● How to Obtain

Catch Swadloon in Lostlorn Forest and level it up with high friendship.

Move | **False Swipe** | Normal

Always leaves 1 HP, even if the damage would have made the target faint.

Move | **GrassWhistle** | Grass

Inflicts Sleep status on the target.

National Pokédex Completion Tip 2

Catch wild Pokémon on the water surface

Use the HM Surf to find wild Pokémon

Plenty of Pokémon live in the water, and you'll encounter them while using Surf to move over the water's surface. You should catch these Pokémon just like you catch the ones on land. Dive Balls and Net Balls are especially useful for catching these Pokémon.

National Pokédex Completion Tip ③

Use the Super Rod to catch wild Pokémon

Receive a Super Rod from Cedric Juniper in Nuvema Town

Go to Juniper Pokémon Lab in Nuvema Town after entering the Hall of Fame, and Cedric Juniper will give you a Super Rod. If you walk up to a body of water and use the rod, you can catch wild Pokémon that live underwater. You'll be able to register some Pokémon you won't see while surfing.

A wild Carvanha appeared!

National Pokédex Completion Tip ④

Catch specially appearing wild Pokémon

Pokémon special appearances

Some of the Unova region's Pokémon appear along with a special natural phenomenon. Many of these Pokémon are not usually seen. If you see one of these phenomena, rush right to it and see what Pokémon is there!

A wild Steelix appeared!

Special Pokémon appearances

Rustling Grass

You'll sometimes see rustling in the regular tall grass (not the dark grass). Step into the rustling grass, and a Pokémon will appear.

Dust Cloud

These occur inside caves. Step on a dust cloud and a Pokémon will appear, or you will get an item.

Flying Pokémon Shadows

You may see these shadows on the Driftveil Drawbridge and Marvelous Bridge. Step on a shadow and a Pokémon will appear, or you will get an item.

Ripples in Water

Occurs on the water's surface. Surf over it, or cast your fishing rod into the ripple, and a Pokémon will appear.

National Pokédex Completion Tip ⑤

Obtain Pokémon through Evolution

Give Pokémon Exp. Points in various ways

Many kinds of Pokémon must be registered in the Unova Pokédex by being evolved, and many evolve through leveling up. Here are six tricks for leveling up your Pokémon effectively. If you use these tricks, it will be easier to evolve your Pokémon.

Congratulations! Your Skorupi evolved into Drapion!

Special Pokémon appearances

① Put it into battle, then switch it out immediately

The most basic way to raise the level of a low-level Pokémon is to put it in battle once, then withdraw it immediately. Just by being in battle once, it will receive a share of the Exp. Points you earn.

② Have the first Pokémon in your party hold the Lucky Egg

A Pokémon that holds the Lucky Egg will receive 50% more Exp. Points. Have the first Pokémon in your party hold it. Professor Juniper gives you this item in Celestial Tower.

③ Have one of your party Pokémon hold the Exp. Share

The Exp. Share shares the Exp. Points earned from a battle with the Pokémon that holds it, even if that Pokémon didn't participate in battle. You receive it in the Battle Company in Castelia City.

④ Let the Pokémon Day Care level up your Pokémon

Leaving Pokémon in the Pokémon Day Care is also an effective way to raise levels. When you come to get your Pokémon after you've continued on your adventure, the Pokémon's level may have gone up.

⑤ Use a Rare Candy to raise a Pokémon's level

Rare Candy raises a Pokémon's level by one. Pick a Pokémon, such as one that levels up at a high level, and use Rare Candy on it.

⑥ Defeat many wild Audino

When you encounter an Audino in the rustling grass and defeat it, you'll receive more Exp. Points than you would for defeating other Pokémon. Audino is great for leveling up your Pokémon!

Special Evolution ① **Tyrogue evolves differently depending on its stats**

Tyrogue evolves into Hitmonlee, Hitmonchan, or Hitmontop at Lv. 20. Its stats determine which one it evolves into. Use Protein to raise Attack faster, and use Iron to raise Defense faster.

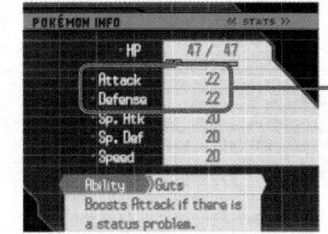

Check Tyrogue's stats closely

How Tyrogue evolves

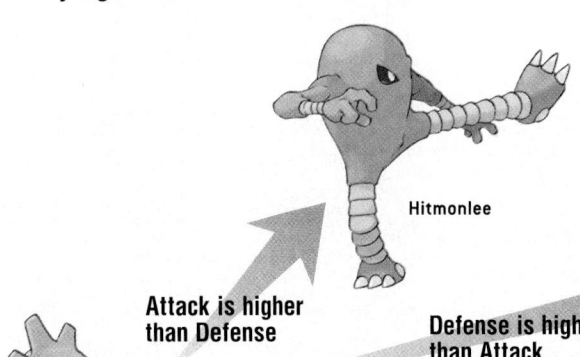

Hitmonlee

Hitmonchan

Attack is higher than Defense

Defense is higher than Attack

Attack and Defense are equal

Hitmontop

Tyrogue

Special Evolution 2 — Wurmple evolves into Silcoon or Cascoon

Wurmple evolves into Silcoon or Cascoon at Lv. 7. You won't know which one it will become until it evolves.

How Wurmple evolves

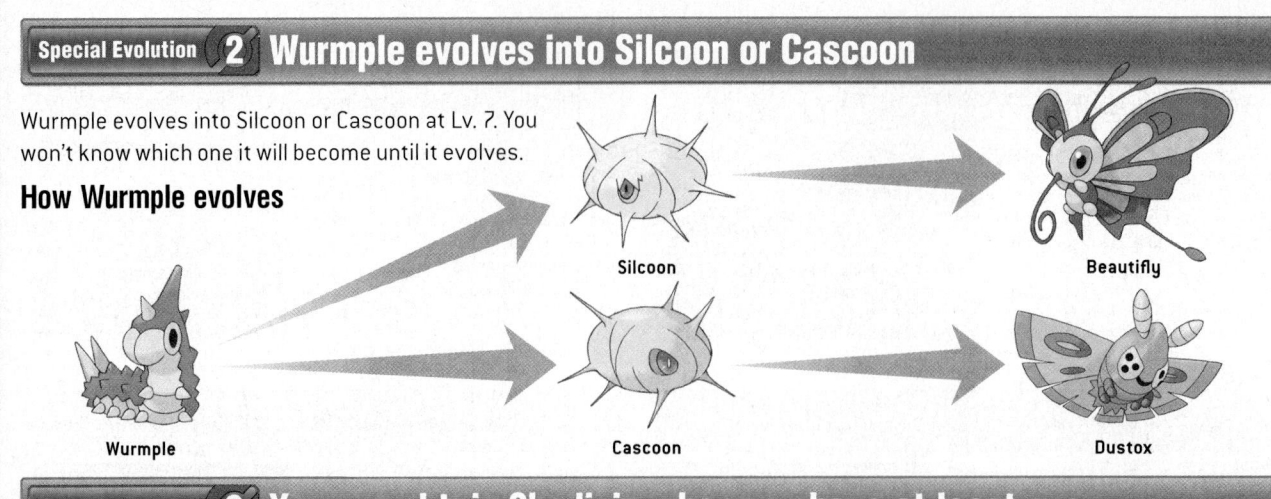

Wurmple

Silcoon

Beautifly

Cascoon

Dustox

Special Evolution 3 — You can obtain Shedinja when you have at least one free space in your party

Level up Nincada to Lv. 20 while you have a free space in your party and a Poké Ball in your Bag, and Shedinja will join your party as Nincada evolves into Ninjask.

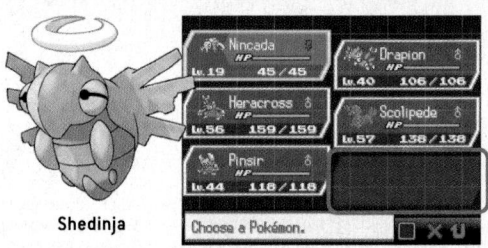

Shedinja

Have an empty slot in your party

Special Evolution 4 — Have Remoraid in your party and Mantyke will evolve

Have Remoraid in your party when Mantyke levels up, and it'll evolve into Mantine.

Mantine

Remoraid

Have Remoraid in your party

National Pokédex Completion Tip 6

Evolve Pokémon with special Stones

Stones trigger an instant Evolution

Some Pokémon evolve from the power hidden in special Stones. Nine types of Stones appear in *Pokémon Black Version 2* and *Pokémon White Version 2*. When you get one of these Stones, use it on a Pokémon you want to evolve.

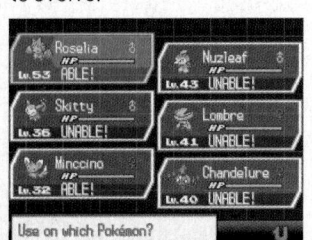

Use on which Pokémon?

Main ways to get Stones

Leaf Stone
Route 7 / Exchange for 3 BP in the PWT or Battle Subway

Fire Stone
Route 19 / Exchange for 3 BP in the PWT or Battle Subway

Water Stone
Route 19 / Exchange for 3 BP in the PWT or Battle Subway

Thunderstone
Chargestone Cave / Exchange for 3 BP in the PWT or Battle Subway

Moon Stone
Route 6 / Giant Chasm's Crater Forest

Sun Stone
Nimbasa City / Giant Chasm

Shiny Stone
Route 6 / Abundant Shrine

Dusk Stone
Strange House / Twist Mountain

Dawn Stone
Dreamyard / Found in dust clouds inside caves

Obtain Pokémon by restoring Fossils

 ## Have Fossils restored to obtain nine different Pokémon

Go to Twist Mountain after entering the Hall of Fame, and you'll receive a Fossil every day. Have it restored at the Nacrene Museum.

The Fossil you gave me turned back into a Pokémon!

Fossils and restored Pokémon

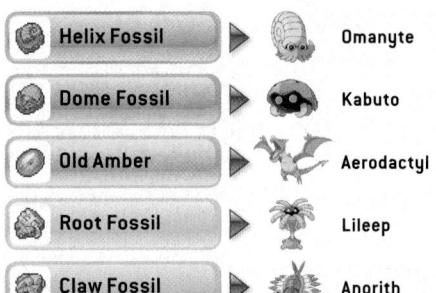

Fossil	Restored Pokémon
Helix Fossil	Omanyte
Dome Fossil	Kabuto
Old Amber	Aerodactyl
Root Fossil	Lileep
Claw Fossil	Anorith

Fossil	Restored Pokémon
Skull Fossil	Cranidos
Armor Fossil	Shieldon
Cover Fossil	Tirtouga
Plume Fossil	Archen

◆ Lenora gives you either the Cover Fossil or the Plume Fossil in Nacrene City.

Evolve Pokémon through Friendship

 ## Make your Pokémon happy

Friendship is the bond of affection and trust that can grow between a Pokémon and its Trainer. Some Pokémon evolve by being leveled up with high friendship. If you do things that make the Pokémon happy, it will grow to like you. Letting it hold the Soothe Bell is especially recommended.

How to improve your friendship with your Pokémon

Quality time while adventuring	Use items	Use a Beauty Salon or a Café
When you go on an adventure with a Pokémon in your party, its friendship will grow.	Use items such as Protein and Zinc to raise base stats. They raise your friendship, too.	Use a Beauty Salon or a Café in Join Avenue, and your friendship goes up (p. 406, 407).

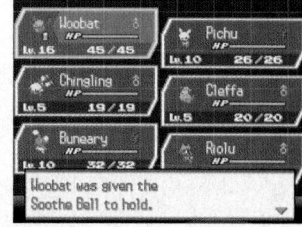

Woobat was given the Soothe Bell to hold.

Trade Pokémon with people in towns

 ## Trade for Pokémon that don't appear in the wild

In towns and houses, there are people waiting to trade Pokémon with you. In *Pokémon Black Version 2* and *Pokémon White Version 2*, some of these Pokémon, such as Ambipom, Alakazam, and Rotom, don't appear as wild Pokémon. They'll help you complete the National Pokédex. Make sure to trade Pokémon when offered.

By any chance, have you caught a Pokémon called Rotom?

Pokémon trades that help you complete the National Pokédex

Pokémon received	Pokémon to trade / How to obtain	Location of trader	The difference between the two versions
Alakazam	Hippowdon (mass outbreaks in the Desert Resort)	Woman in a house in Accumula Town	—
Ambipom	Excadrill (dust clouds outside Reversal Mountain)	Woman in a house in Accumula Town	—
Cottonee	Petilil (Castelia City empty lot)	Boy in building on Route 4	*Pokémon White Version 2*
Gigalith	Emolga (rustling grass on Route 16)	Hiker in building on Route 7	—
Petilil	Cottonee (Castelia City empty lot)	Girl in building on Route 4	*Pokémon Black Version 2*
Rotom	Ditto (Crater Forest in the Giant Chasm)	Woman in a parked camper on Route 15	—
Tangrowth	Mantine (rippling water on Route 21)	Man in a house in Humilau City	—

NATIONAL POKÉDEX CHALLENGE

National Pokédex Completion Tip 10

Catch Pokémon during mass outbreaks

Check the electric bulletin board for mass outbreaks

After you enter the Hall of Fame, a mass outbreak—a large group of Pokémon appearing all at once—will occur in a different location every day. Information about the mass outbreak will be displayed on the electric bulletin boards in every gate. Be sure to check them out!

Pokémon mass outbreaks after entering the Hall of Fame

Pokémon	Location	Version
Cacturne	Reversal Mountain Entrance	
Doduo	Route 12	
Farfetch'd	Route 1	
Fearow	Route 15	
Furret	Route 7	
Hippowdon	Desert Resort	Both *Pokémon Black Version 2* and *Pokémon White Version 2*
Hypno	Dreamyard	
Masquerain	Route 11	
Natu	Route 5	
Pineco	Route 16	
Quagsire	Route 8	
Swellow	Route 13	

Pokémon	Location	Version
Ariados	Route 22	*Pokémon Black Version 2* only
Hoppip	Route 18	Both *Pokémon Black Version 2* and *Pokémon White Version 2*
Illumise	Route 3	*Pokémon White Version 2* only
Ledian	Route 22	*Pokémon White Version 2* only
Minun	Route 6	*Pokémon White Version 2* only
Mr. Mime	Route 20	*Pokémon White Version 2* only
Plusle	Route 6	*Pokémon Black Version 2* only
Slowpoke	Abundant Shrine	Both *Pokémon Black Version 2* and *Pokémon White Version 2*
Sudowoodo	Route 20	*Pokémon Black Version 2* only
Swalot	Route 9	Both *Pokémon Black Version 2* and *Pokémon White Version 2*
Volbeat	Route 3	*Pokémon Black Version 2* only

Tip — Shiny Pokémon, N's Pokémon, and Star Pokémon

There are some special Pokémon that appear in *Pokémon Black Version 2* and *Pokémon White Version 2*. A Pokémon with unusual coloration is called a Shiny Pokémon. When a Shiny Pokémon first appears in battle, you'll see a ring of lights around its body. N's Pokémon start to appear after you use Memory Link to witness the event "MEETING FRIENDS, SAYING GOOD-BYE." Their OT, or original Trainer, is N. A Star Pokémon is one that received a Star Rank from Pokéstar Studios. When a Star Pokémon is sent out to battle, it is surrounded by a sparkling star that breaks into pieces.

Shiny Pokémon

N's Pokémon

Star Pokémon

National Pokédex Completion Tip 11

Get certain Pokémon during story events

Put all of your Pokémon-catching techniques to use

Some Pokémon are encountered only at certain points during the course of the game. Only one each of these Pokémon exists. Zekrom and Latios can be caught only in *Pokémon Black Version 2*, while Reshiram and Latias can be caught only in *Pokémon White Version 2*. Use Link Trade to register them all.

Take the National Pokédex Challenge

Rarely seen Pokémon needed to complete the National Pokédex

National Pokédex No. 380
Latias
When playing Pokémon White Version 2

Appears in the Dreamyard after you enter the Hall of Fame. Follow it and you can battle it.

National Pokédex No. 381
Latios
When playing Pokémon Black Version 2

Appears in the Dreamyard after you enter the Hall of Fame. Follow it and you can battle it.

National Pokédex No. 480
Uxie

After you enter the Hall of Fame, it appears first in the Cave of Being, then in Nacrene City.

National Pokédex No. 481
Mesprit

After you enter the Hall of Fame, it appears first in the Cave of Being, then in Celestial Tower.

National Pokédex No. 482
Azelf

After you enter the Hall of Fame, it appears first in the Cave of Being, then on Route 23.

National Pokédex No. 485
Heatran

Obtain the Magma Stone on Route 18, and it'll appear in Reversal Mountain.

National Pokédex No. 488
Cresselia

Obtain the Lunar Wing in the Strange House, and it'll appear on Marvelous Bridge.

National Pokédex No. 570
Zorua

Get from Rood, formerly of Team Plasma, in Driftveil City. Evolve it to register Zoroark.

National Pokédex No. 637
Volcarona

Relic Castle (Lowest Floor—Deepest Part). If you leave it at the Day Care and find an Egg, you can register Larvesta in the Pokédex, too.

National Pokédex No. 638
Cobalion

It appears first on Route 6, then on Route 13 as you head north.

National Pokédex No. 639
Terrakion

It's on a hill as you head west on Route 22.

National Pokédex No. 640
Virizion

As you head west on Route 11, it will jump down from a ledge.

National Pokédex No. 643
Reshiram
When playing Pokémon White Version 2

Obtain the Light Stone in N's Castle, and it will appear in Dragonspiral Tower.

National Pokédex No. 644
Zekrom
When playing Pokémon Black Version 2

Obtain the Dark Stone in N's Castle, and it will appear in Dragonspiral Tower.

National Pokédex No. 646
Kyurem

Catch Zekrom (Reshiram), and it will appear in the deepest part of the Giant Chasm.

See page 576 if you accidentally defeat one of these Pokémon. ▷

National Pokédex Completion Tip 12

Trade Pokémon with the owner of the Dropped Item

 Trade Pokémon from other regions

The owner of the Dropped Item turns out to be Yancy (if your character is a boy) or Curtis (if your character is a girl). As you talk to this Trainer on the Xtransceiver, you'll be able to trade Pokémon eventually.

Will you trade me one of your Pokémon?

How to trade Pokémon with the owner of the Dropped Item

Pick up the Dropped Item in Nimbasa City

Pick up the Dropped Item in Nimbasa City's amusement park. This is the first step to trading some rare Pokémon.

Have conversations over the Xtransceiver with Yancy (Curtis)

You will receive a call from the owner of the Dropped Item, Yancy (Curtis), and she (he) will ask you to hold on to it for now. Yancy (Curtis) will call you 10 times before moving to the next step.

Give the Dropped Item back to Yancy (Curtis)

You'll make a promise to meet up with Yancy (Curtis) in front of the Nimbasa City Ferris wheel. Return the Dropped Item to its owner.

Have regular chats with Yancy (Curtis)

You'll be able to call Yancy (Curtis) every now and again on the Xtransceiver. Yancy (Curtis) will call you as well. Have 20 of these conversations.

Meet Yancy (Curtis) at the Ferris wheel

Yancy (Curtis) will meet you at Nimbasa City's Ferris wheel for a date.

Trade Pokémon with Yancy (Curtis)

You'll be able to meet up with Yancy (Curtis) at the Ferris wheel daily. After you enter the Hall of Fame, you'll be able to trade Pokémon with her (him).

Yancy (Curtis) will trade to you

Trade	Yancy (if your character is a boy)	Curtis (if your character is a girl)
1st	Meowth	Mankey
2nd	Wobbuffet	Wobbuffet
3rd	Ralts	Ralts
4th	Shieldon	Cranidos
5th	Rhyhorn	Rhyhorn
6th	Shellos (West Sea)	Shellos (East Sea)
7th	Mawile	Sableye
8th	Spiritomb	Spiritomb
9th	Snorlax	Snorlax
10th	Teddiursa	Phanpy
11th	Spinda	Spinda
12th	Togepi	Togepi

The most likely places to receive calls from Yancy (Curtis)

Nimbasa City, Driftveil City, Mistralton City, Lacunosa Town, Undella Town, Lentimas Town, and Routes 5, 6, 7, 9, 11, 12, 13, 14, and 16

◆ The screen shots shown here are boys' versions.

National Pokédex Completion Tip 13

Catch Registeel, Regice, and Regigigas with the Key System

Send each other Keys to catch these three Legendary Pokémon

Use the Key System from Unova Link, and you'll be able to catch Registeel and Regice in Clay Tunnel, and Regigigas in Twist Mountain. Here's how to use the Key System and register these Pokémon.

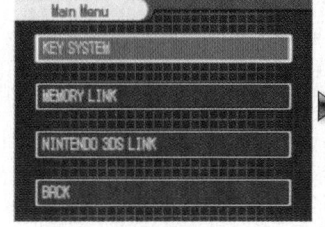

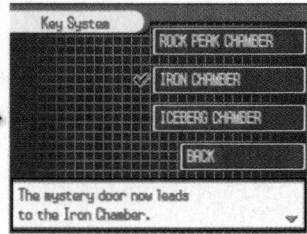

How to catch Regigigas through the Key System

Catch Regirock in the Rock Peak Chamber

Catch Regirock in *Pokémon Black Version 2*, and you'll obtain the Iron Key.
Catch Regirock in *Pokémon White Version 2*, and you'll obtain the Iceberg Key.

 In *Pokémon Black Version 2*, you can obtain the Iron Key.

In *Pokémon White Version 2*, you can obtain the Iceberg Key.

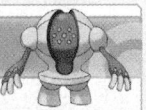

Catch Registeel in the Iron Chamber

With the Iron Key, you'll be able to enter the Iron Chamber using the Key System.

Catch Regice in the Iceberg Chamber

With the Iceberg Key, you'll be able to enter the Iceberg Chamber using the Key System.

Send the Iceberg Key to *Pokémon Black Version 2* or the Iron Key to *Pokémon White Version 2* using the Key System.

Catch Regice in the Iceberg Chamber

Enter the Iceberg Chamber using the Iceberg Key received with the Key System.

Catch Registeel in the Iron Chamber

Enter the Iron Chamber using the Iron Key received with the Key System.

Catch Regigigas in Twist Mountain

Have Regirock, Registeel, and Regice in your party and go to the lowest level of Twist Mountain to catch Regigigas.

National Pokédex Completion Tip 14

Discover Eggs and Get New Pokémon

Obtain earlier evolutionary forms with Pokémon Eggs

If you leave two compatible Pokémon at the Pokémon Day Care on Route 3, you may find a Pokémon Egg when you return. To register certain Pokémon in the National Pokédex, you must hatch them from Eggs. Use these steps to discover Eggs and get the Pokémon you're after.

 **The Pokémon Day Care Man's comments will tell you if an Egg will be found**

When you leave two Pokémon at the Day Care, the old man who stands outside will tell you how well they get along. These messages also tell you how likely it is that an Egg will be discovered.

◆ The Day Care Couple will raise Pokémon left at the Pokémon Day Care, and although these Pokémon's levels will increase, they will not evolve. They will evolve when raised one level after you retrieve them.

The old man's messages

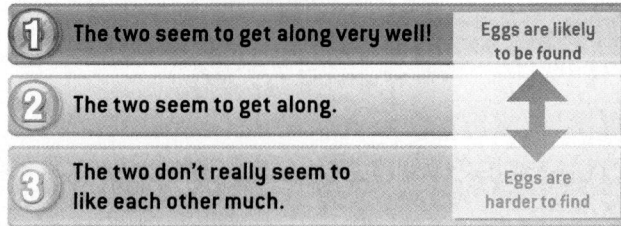

①	The two seem to get along very well!	Eggs are likely to be found
②	The two seem to get along.	
③	The two don't really seem to like each other much.	Eggs are harder to find
④	The two prefer to play with other Pokémon more than with each other.	Eggs will not be found

 **Tip** **The Oval Charm makes it more likely to find Eggs**

Complete the Unova Pokédex and you will receive the Oval Charm from Professor Juniper. This is an item that makes it more likely to find Pokémon Eggs. Finding Eggs is one of the keys to completing the National Pokédex, and the Oval Charm will help!

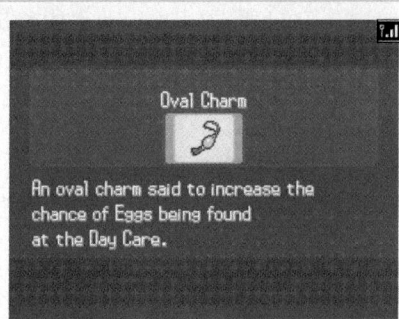

Oval Charm

An oval charm said to increase the chance of Eggs being found at the Day Care.

Oval Charm
Complete the Unova Pokédex

 **Get Medals for hatching Eggs**

As you hatch Pokémon Eggs, Mr. Medal will give you Medals depending on your achievements. You can get four different Medals for hatching Eggs. When you hatch an Egg for the first time, you'll receive the Egg Beginner Medal. When you've hatched 10 Eggs, you'll receive the Egg Breeder Medal. When you've hatched 50 Eggs, you'll receive the Egg Elite Medal. The Hatching Aficionado Medal is given to players who hatch an amazing 100 Eggs!

Egg Beginner | Egg Breeder | Egg Elite | Hatching Aficionado

Check p. 531 for the Medal list.

How to Discover Eggs ① **Learn how to pair up Pokémon and find Eggs**

To find Eggs, you can leave two Pokémon of the same species but opposite genders at the Pokémon Day Care. This is the simplest method, but you can also pair off Pokémon by Egg Group. You can still find an Egg from two different species of Pokémon if they have opposite genders and the same Egg Group. As with Camerupt and Zebstrika to the right, an Egg may be discovered.

♂ ♂ Pokémon   ♀ ♀ Pokémon

Camerupt ♂
Field Group

Zebstrika ♀
Field Group

Egg

Blitzle

For example, if you leave a male Camerupt and a female Zebstrika, both of which are from the Field Egg Group, a Blitzle Egg will be found.

Rules for finding Eggs

① If you leave two Pokémon of opposite genders from the same Egg Group, an Egg will be found.

② The Pokémon that hatches from the Egg is either the same species as the female or an earlier evolutionary form.

③ The hatched Pokémon is almost always in its initial evolutionary stage.

See page 369 for information about Egg Groups.

How to Discover Eggs 2 — With Ditto, you can find almost any kind of Egg

Some Pokémon's genders are unknown. Also, some Pokémon species have only one gender. Under normal circumstances, you can't find Eggs for these Pokémon. But leave one together with a Ditto and you'll find an Egg after all. You can catch Ditto in Crater Forest in the Giant Chasm. Ditto can be a big help when you want more Eggs!

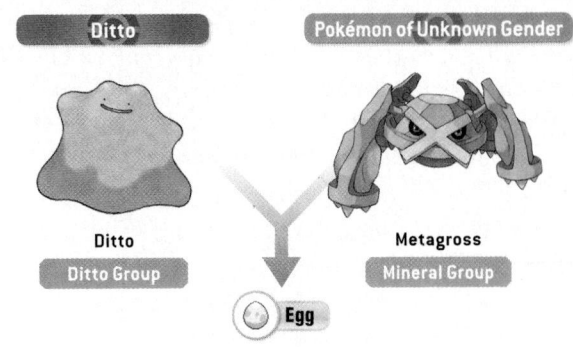

Ditto | Pokémon of Unknown Gender
Ditto — Ditto Group
Metagross — Mineral Group
Egg

Places where wild Ditto appear

Crater Forest in the Giant Chasm

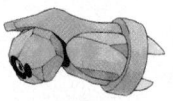

A Beldum Egg will be found when you leave Metagross, whose gender is unknown, with Ditto.

Beldum

Egg Move Rules 1 — Have a Pokémon inherit moves

The two Pokémon you leave at the Pokémon Day Care can pass on a move they have learned to a Pokémon hatched from an Egg. Usually, newly hatched Pokémon only know the moves that the Pokémon would know at Lv. 1. However, if both of the two Pokémon you left at the Pokémon Day Care have learned a move that the hatched Pokémon can learn by leveling up, the hatched Pokémon will know that move. Similarly, moves Pokémon learn with TMs can be passed on, too.

Rules for inheriting moves

1 If both Pokémon at the Pokémon Day Care know the same level-up move, the hatched Pokémon may know that level-up move.

2 A move that the male Pokémon knows and that the hatched Pokémon could learn from a TM can be passed on.

♂ Pokémon | ♀ Pokémon
Rapidash ♂ — Field Group — Move Inferno Fire
Ninetales ♀ — Field Group — Move Inferno Fire
Egg

Hatched with the move Inferno!

Vulpix — Move Inferno Fire

Egg Move Rules 2 — Hatch a Pokémon that knows an Egg Move

Pokémon may hatch from Eggs already knowing moves that they usually can't learn. These moves are called Egg Moves. For example, Riolu can't learn the move Bullet Punch by leveling up. But if the male Pokémon left at the Pokémon Day Care is a Hitmonchan that knows Bullet Punch, the Riolu that hatches from the Egg might know the move Bullet Punch. Because many Egg Moves are so unexpected, you can surprise the opposing Trainer in battle.

♂ Pokémon | ♀ Pokémon
Hitmonchan ♂ — Human-Like Group — Move Bullet Punch Steel
Lucario ♀ — Human-Like Group
Egg

A Riolu with the Egg Move Bullet Punch hatches!

Riolu — Move Bullet Punch Steel

A rule of Egg Moves

1 A move that the male Pokémon knows and that the hatched Pokémon can learn as an Egg Move can be passed on.

Ability Info 1 You can't control the hatched Pokémon's Ability

You don't know which Ability a Pokémon hatched from an Egg will have until it hatches. For example, Axew can have either the Rivalry or Mold Breaker Ability. Sometimes when you leave a female Haxorus with the Mold Breaker Ability at the Pokémon Day Care, the Egg that is found will hatch an Axew with the Rivalry Ability.

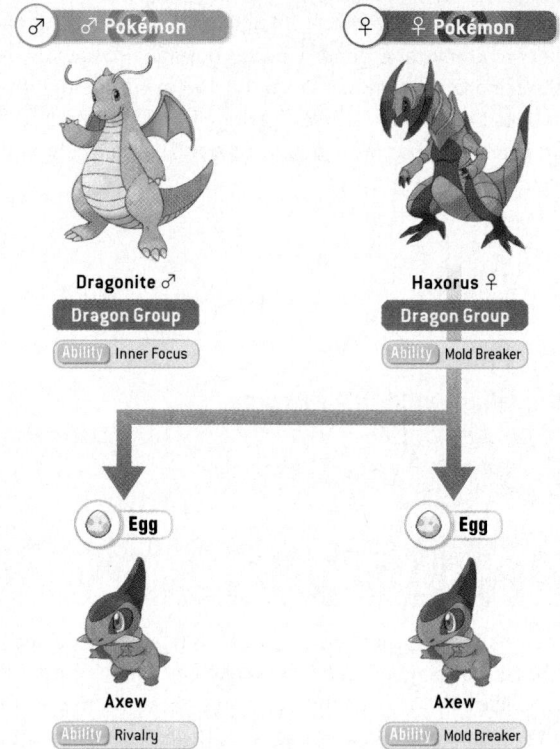

Rules about the Abilities of Hatched Pokémon

1 The Ability of a Pokémon hatched from an Egg can be either of its species' possible Abilities, but it's more likely to be the Ability of the female Pokémon left at the Pokémon Day Care.

◆ If you leave a Pokémon with Ditto, the Ability of the Pokémon that hatches from the Egg will not be influenced.

Ability Info 2 Hidden Abilities can be inherited

If you leave a female Pokémon that has a Hidden Ability at the Pokémon Day Care, you may find an Egg that hatches a Pokémon with the same Ability. For example, Watchog can have the Hidden Ability Analytic. If you leave a female Watchog with Analytic at the Pokémon Day Care, you may find an Egg of a Patrat with one of its usual Abilities—Run Away or Keen Eye—or the same Hidden Ability, Analytic.

Hidden Ability rules

1 When, and only when, the female Pokémon at the Pokémon Day Care has a Hidden Ability, you can sometimes hatch a Pokémon with a Hidden Ability. The Pokémon that hatches this way is more likely to have the Hidden Ability than one of its other possible Abilities.

◆ The Hidden Ability will not be passed on if you leave the female Pokémon with Ditto.

Comprehensive Guide to Pokémon Egg Groups

Some Pokémon belong to more than one Egg Group. Consult the following tables when you want to find an Egg after dropping off a pair of Pokémon at the Pokémon Day Care. This information will be indispensable when you want to pass along Egg Moves!

Grass Group

● Grass Egg Group only

043	Oddish	♂/♀
044	Gloom	♂/♀
045	Vileplume	♂/♀
069	Bellsprout	♂/♀
070	Weepinbell	♂/♀
071	Victreebel	♂/♀
102	Exeggcute	♂/♀
103	Exeggutor	♂/♀
114	Tangela	♂/♀
182	Bellossom	♂/♀
191	Sunkern	♂/♀
192	Sunflora	♂/♀
455	Carnivine	♂/♀
465	Tangrowth	♂/♀
548	Petilil	♀
549	Lilligant	♀
556	Maractus	♂/♀
590	Foongus	♂/♀
591	Amoonguss	♂/♀

● Grass and Bug Egg Groups

046	Paras	♂/♀
047	Parasect	♂/♀

● Grass and Human-Like Egg Groups

331	Cacnea	♂/♀
332	Cacturne	♂/♀

● Grass and Monster Egg Groups

001	Bulbasaur	♂/♀
002	Ivysaur	♂/♀
003	Venusaur	♂/♀
152	Chikorita	♂/♀
153	Bayleef	♂/♀
154	Meganium	♂/♀
357	Tropius	♂/♀
387	Turtwig	♂/♀
388	Grotle	♂/♀
389	Torterra	♂/♀
459	Snover	♂/♀
460	Abomasnow	♂/♀

● Grass and Fairy Egg Groups

187	Hoppip	♂/♀
188	Skiploom	♂/♀
189	Jumpluff	♂/♀
285	Shroomish	♂/♀
286	Breloom	♂/♀
315	Roselia	♂/♀
407	Roserade	♂/♀
420	Cherubi	♂/♀
421	Cherrim	♂/♀
546	Cottonee	♂/♀
547	Whimsicott	♂/♀

● Grass and Mineral Egg Groups

597	Ferroseed	♂/♀
598	Ferrothorn	♂/♀

● Grass and Field Egg Group

273	Seedot	♂/♀
274	Nuzleaf	♂/♀
275	Shiftry	♂/♀
495	Snivy	♂/♀
496	Servine	♂/♀
497	Serperior	♂/♀

● Grass and Water 1 Egg Groups

270	Lotad	♂/♀
271	Lombre	♂/♀
272	Ludicolo	♂/♀

There is no crossover between the Grass Egg Group and the following Egg Groups:
● Flying
● Dragon
● Amorphous
● Water 2
● Water 3
● Ditto
● No Eggs Discovered

Bug Group

● Bug Egg Group only

010	Caterpie	♂/♀
011	Metapod	♂/♀
012	Butterfree	♂/♀
013	Weedle	♂/♀
014	Kakuna	♂/♀
015	Beedrill	♂/♀
048	Venonat	♂/♀
049	Venomoth	♂/♀
123	Scyther	♂/♀
127	Pinsir	♂/♀
165	Ledyba	♂/♀
166	Ledian	♂/♀
167	Spinarak	♂/♀
168	Ariados	♂/♀
193	Yanma	♂/♀
204	Pineco	♂/♀
205	Forretress	♂/♀
207	Gligar	♂/♀
212	Scizor	♂/♀
213	Shuckle	♂/♀
214	Heracross	♂/♀
265	Wurmple	♂/♀
266	Silcoon	♂/♀
267	Beautifly	♂/♀
268	Cascoon	♂/♀
269	Dustox	♂/♀
290	Nincada	♂/♀
291	Ninjask	♂/♀
328	Trapinch	♂/♀
329	Vibrava	♂/♀
330	Flygon	♂/♀
401	Kricketot	♂/♀
402	Kricketune	♂/♀
412	Burmy	♂/♀
413	Wormadam	♀
414	Mothim	♂
415	Combee	♂/♀
416	Vespiquen	♀
469	Yanmega	♂/♀
472	Gliscor	♂/♀
540	Sewaddle	♂/♀
541	Swadloon	♂/♀
542	Leavanny	♂/♀
543	Venipede	♂/♀
544	Whirlipede	♂/♀
545	Scolipede	♂/♀
588	Karrablast	♂/♀
589	Escavalier	♂/♀
595	Joltik	♂/♀
596	Galvantula	♂/♀
616	Shelmet	♂/♀
617	Accelgor	♂/♀
632	Durant	♂/♀
636	Larvesta	♂/♀
637	Volcarona	♂/♀

● Bug and Grass Egg Groups

046	Paras	♂/♀
047	Parasect	♂/♀

● Bug and Human-Like Egg Groups

313	Volbeat	♂
314	Illumise	♀

● Bug and Mineral Egg Groups

557	Dwebble	♂/♀
558	Crustle	♂/♀

● Bug and Water 1 Egg Groups

283	Surskit	♂/♀
284	Masquerain	♂/♀

● Bug and Water 3 Egg Groups

451	Skorupi	♂/♀
452	Drapion	♂/♀

There is no crossover between the Bug Egg Group and the following Egg Groups:
● Flying
● Fairy
● Dragon
● Amorphous
● Water 2
● Ditto
● Monster
● No Eggs Discovered

Flying Group

● Flying Egg Group only

016	Pidgey	♂/♀
017	Pidgeotto	♂/♀
018	Pidgeot	♂/♀
021	Spearow	♂/♀
022	Fearow	♂/♀
041	Zubat	♂/♀
042	Golbat	♂/♀
084	Doduo	♂/♀
085	Dodrio	♂/♀
142	Aerodactyl	♂/♀
163	Hoothoot	♂/♀
164	Noctowl	♂/♀
169	Crobat	♂/♀
177	Natu	♂/♀
178	Xatu	♂/♀
198	Murkrow	♂/♀
227	Skarmory	♂/♀
276	Taillow	♂/♀
277	Swellow	♂/♀
396	Starly	♂/♀
397	Staravia	♂/♀
398	Staraptor	♂/♀
430	Honchkrow	♂/♀
441	Chatot	♂/♀
519	Pidove	♂/♀
520	Tranquill	♂/♀
521	Unfezant	♂/♀
561	Sigilyph	♂/♀
627	Rufflet	♂
628	Braviary	♂
629	Vullaby	♀
630	Mandibuzz	♀

● Flying and Fairy Egg Groups

176	Togetic	♂/♀
468	Togekiss	♂/♀

● Flying and Dragon Egg Groups

333	Swablu	♂/♀
334	Altaria	♂/♀

● Flying and Field Egg Groups

083	Farfetch'd	♂/♀
527	Woobat	♂/♀
528	Swoobat	♂/♀

● Flying and Water 1 Egg Groups

278	Wingull	♂/♀
279	Pelipper	♂/♀
580	Ducklett	♂/♀
581	Swanna	♂/♀

● Flying and Water 3 Egg Group

566	Archen	♂/♀
567	Archeops	♂/♀

There is no crossover between the Flying Egg Group and the following Egg Groups:
● Grass
● Bug
● Human-Like
● Monster
● Mineral
● Amorphous
● Water 2
● Ditto
● No Eggs Discovered

Key to the Tables
● Numbers represent the Pokémon's place in the National Pokédex
● Pokémon listed as ♂ are only male, while those listed as ♀ are only female
● Pokémon listed as ♂/♀ have both male and female
● Pokémon listed as "Unknown" do not have a known gender

🥚 Tip — Special techniques for hatching Eggs

There are a few ways to speed up the hatching of Eggs. If a Pokémon with the Flame Body or Magma Armor Ability is in your party along with the Egg, it will hatch faster. The Pass Power called Hatching Power ↑↑↑ helps a lot (p. 413). You can also use a Nursery on Join Avenue to help your Eggs hatch more quickly (p. 407).

Methods that make it easier to hatch Eggs

1. **Using Abilities wisely**
2. **Using Pass Powers**
3. **Use a Nursery on Join Avenue**

Volcarona

Camerupt

Warn an Egg slowly and carefully. It makes the Egg hatch much faster.

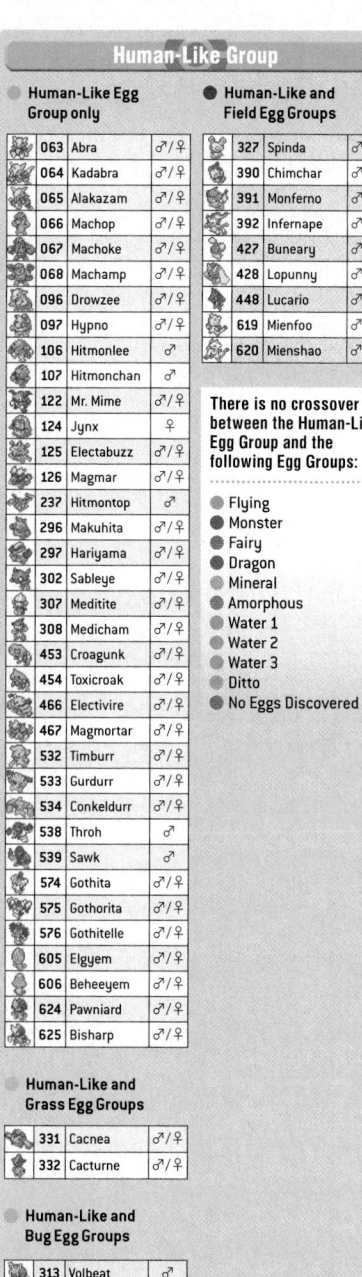

NATIONAL POKÉDEX CHALLENGE

Comprehensive Guide to Pokémon Egg Groups

Human-Like Group

Human-Like Egg Group only

063	Abra	♂/♀
064	Kadabra	♂/♀
065	Alakazam	♂/♀
066	Machop	♂/♀
067	Machoke	♂/♀
068	Machamp	♂/♀
096	Drowzee	♂/♀
097	Hypno	♂/♀
106	Hitmonlee	♂
107	Hitmonchan	♂
122	Mr. Mime	♂/♀
124	Jynx	♀
125	Electabuzz	♂/♀
126	Magmar	♂/♀
237	Hitmontop	♂
296	Makuhita	♂/♀
297	Hariyama	♂/♀
302	Sableye	♂/♀
307	Meditite	♂/♀
308	Medicham	♂/♀
453	Croagunk	♂/♀
454	Toxicroak	♂/♀
466	Electivire	♂/♀
467	Magmortar	♂/♀
532	Timburr	♂/♀
533	Gurdurr	♂/♀
534	Conkeldurr	♂/♀
538	Throh	♂
539	Sawk	♂
574	Gothita	♂/♀
575	Gothorita	♂/♀
576	Gothitelle	♂/♀
605	Elgyem	♂/♀
606	Beheeyem	♂/♀
624	Pawniard	♂/♀
625	Bisharp	♂/♀

Human-Like and Grass Egg Groups

331	Cacnea	♂/♀
332	Cacturne	♂/♀

Human-Like and Bug Egg Groups

313	Volbeat	♂
314	Illumise	♀

Human-Like and Field Egg Groups

327	Spinda	♂/♀
390	Chimchar	♂/♀
391	Monferno	♂/♀
392	Infernape	♂/♀
427	Buneary	♂/♀
428	Lopunny	♂/♀
448	Lucario	♂/♀
619	Mienfoo	♂/♀
620	Mienshao	♂/♀

There is no crossover between the Human-Like Egg Group and the following Egg Groups:
- Flying
- Monster
- Fairy
- Dragon
- Mineral
- Amorphous
- Water 1
- Water 2
- Water 3
- Ditto
- No Eggs Discovered

Monster Group

Monster Egg Group only

104	Cubone	♂/♀
105	Marowak	♂/♀
108	Lickitung	♂/♀
115	Kangaskhan	♀
143	Snorlax	♂/♀
246	Larvitar	♂/♀
247	Pupitar	♂/♀
248	Tyranitar	♂/♀
304	Aron	♂/♀
305	Lairon	♂/♀
306	Aggron	♂/♀
408	Cranidos	♂/♀
409	Rampardos	♂/♀
410	Shieldon	♂/♀
411	Bastiodon	♂/♀
463	Lickilicky	♂/♀

Monster and Grass Egg Groups

001	Bulbasaur	♂/♀
002	Ivysaur	♂/♀
003	Venusaur	♂/♀
152	Chikorita	♂/♀
153	Bayleef	♂/♀
154	Meganium	♂/♀
357	Tropius	♂/♀
387	Turtwig	♂/♀
388	Grotle	♂/♀
389	Torterra	♂/♀
459	Snover	♂/♀
460	Abomasnow	♂/♀

Monster and Dragon Egg Groups

004	Charmander	♂/♀
005	Charmeleon	♂/♀
006	Charizard	♂/♀
252	Treecko	♂/♀
253	Grovyle	♂/♀
254	Sceptile	♂/♀
443	Gible	♂/♀
444	Gabite	♂/♀
445	Garchomp	♂/♀
610	Axew	♂/♀
611	Fraxure	♂/♀
612	Haxorus	♂/♀
621	Druddigon	♂/♀

Monster and Field Egg Groups

029	Nidoran♀	♀
032	Nidoran♂	♂
033	Nidorino	♂
034	Nidoking	♂
111	Rhyhorn	♂/♀
112	Rhydon	♂/♀
179	Mareep	♂/♀
180	Flaaffy	♂/♀
181	Ampharos	♂/♀
293	Whismur	♂/♀
294	Loudred	♂/♀
295	Exploud	♂/♀
464	Rhyperior	♂/♀

Monster and Water 1 Egg Groups

007	Squirtle	♂/♀
008	Wartortle	♂/♀
009	Blastoise	♂/♀
079	Slowpoke	♂/♀
080	Slowbro	♂/♀
131	Lapras	♂/♀
158	Totodile	♂/♀
159	Croconaw	♂/♀
160	Feraligatr	♂/♀
199	Slowking	♂/♀
258	Mudkip	♂/♀
259	Marshtomp	♂/♀
260	Swampert	♂/♀

There is no crossover between the Monster Egg Group and the following Egg Groups:
- Bug
- Flying
- Human-Like
- Fairy
- Mineral
- Amorphous
- Water 2
- Water 3
- Ditto
- No Eggs Discovered

Fairy Group

Fairy Egg Group only

035	Clefairy	♂/♀
036	Clefable	♂/♀
039	Jigglypuff	♂/♀
040	Wigglytuff	♂/♀
113	Chansey	♀
242	Blissey	♀
311	Plusle	♂/♀
312	Minun	♂/♀
531	Audino	♂/♀

Fairy and Grass Egg Groups

187	Hoppip	♂/♀
188	Skiploom	♂/♀
189	Jumpluff	♂/♀
285	Shroomish	♂/♀
286	Breloom	♂/♀
315	Roselia	♂/♀
407	Roserade	♂/♀
420	Cherubi	♂/♀
421	Cherrim	♂/♀
546	Cottonee	♂/♀
547	Whimsicott	♂/♀

Fairy and Flying Egg Groups

176	Togetic	♂/♀
468	Togekiss	♂/♀

Fairy and Mineral Egg Groups

361	Snorunt	♂/♀
362	Glalie	♂/♀
478	Froslass	♀

Fairy and Field Egg Groups

025	Pikachu	♂/♀
026	Raichu	♂/♀
209	Snubbull	♂/♀
210	Granbull	♂/♀
300	Skitty	♂/♀
301	Delcatty	♂/♀
303	Mawile	♂/♀
417	Pachirisu	♂/♀

Fairy and Amorphous Egg Groups

351	Castform	♂/♀

Fairy and Water 1 Egg Groups

183	Marill	♂/♀
184	Azumarill	♂/♀
489	Phione	Unknown
490	Manaphy	Unknown

There is no crossover between the Fairy Egg Group and the following Egg Groups:
- Bug
- Human-Like
- Monster
- Dragon
- Water 2
- Water 3
- Ditto
- No Eggs Discovered

Dragon Group

Dragon Egg Group only

371	Bagon	♂/♀
372	Shelgon	♂/♀
373	Salamence	♂/♀
633	Deino	♂/♀
634	Zweilous	♂/♀
635	Hydreigon	♂/♀

Dragon and Flying Egg Groups

333	Swablu	♂/♀
334	Altaria	♂/♀

Dragon and Monster Egg Groups

004	Charmander	♂/♀
005	Charmeleon	♂/♀
006	Charizard	♂/♀
252	Treecko	♂/♀
253	Grovyle	♂/♀
254	Sceptile	♂/♀
443	Gible	♂/♀
444	Gabite	♂/♀
445	Garchomp	♂/♀
610	Axew	♂/♀
611	Fraxure	♂/♀
612	Haxorus	♂/♀
621	Druddigon	♂/♀

Dragon and Field Egg Groups

023	Ekans	♂/♀
024	Arbok	♂/♀
336	Seviper	♂/♀
559	Scraggy	♂/♀
560	Scrafty	♂/♀

Dragon and Water 1 Egg Groups

116	Horsea	♂/♀
117	Seadra	♂/♀
147	Dratini	♂/♀
148	Dragonair	♂/♀
149	Dragonite	♂/♀
230	Kingdra	♂/♀
349	Feebas	♂/♀
350	Milotic	♂/♀

Dragon and Water 2 Egg Groups

129	Magikarp	♂/♀
130	Gyarados	♂/♀

There is no crossover between the Dragon Egg Group and the following Egg Groups:
- Grass
- Bug
- Human-Like
- Fairy
- Mineral
- Amorphous
- Water 3
- Ditto
- No Eggs Discovered

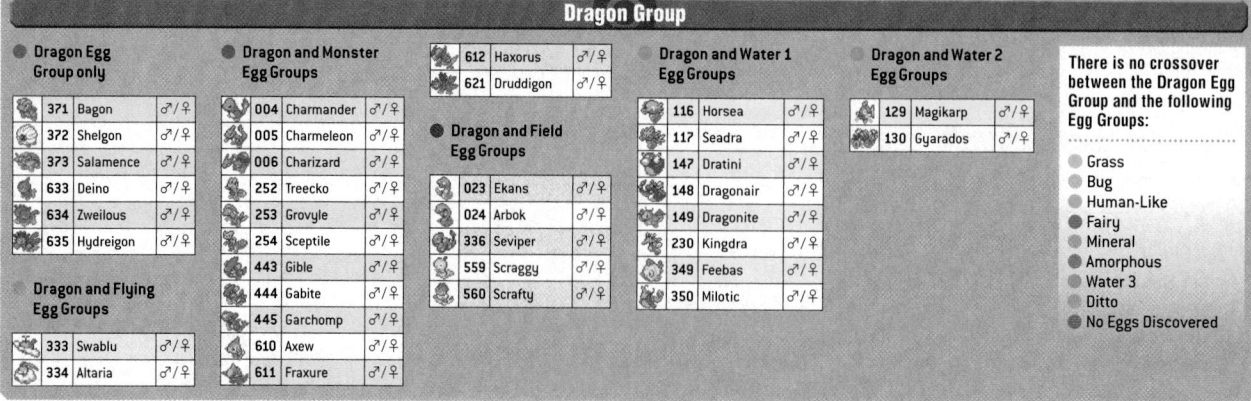

Tip — Drop off a Manaphy to get a Phione Egg

If you have the Mythical Pokémon Manaphy, drop it off at a Pokémon Day Care together with Ditto. Hatch the Egg that is found, and Phione will be yours!

Manaphy

Phione

◆ Manaphy cannot be obtained through normal gameplay.

Mineral Group

Mineral Egg Group only

074	Geodude	♂/♀
075	Graveler	♂/♀
076	Golem	♂/♀
081	Magnemite	Unknown
082	Magneton	Unknown
095	Onix	♂/♀
100	Voltorb	Unknown
101	Electrode	Unknown
137	Porygon	Unknown
185	Sudowoodo	♂/♀
208	Steelix	♂/♀
233	Porygon2	Unknown
292	Shedinja	Unknown
299	Nosepass	♂/♀
337	Lunatone	Unknown
338	Solrock	Unknown
343	Baltoy	Unknown
344	Claydol	Unknown
374	Beldum	Unknown
375	Metang	Unknown
376	Metagross	Unknown
436	Bronzor	Unknown
437	Bronzong	Unknown
462	Magnezone	Unknown
474	Porygon-Z	Unknown
476	Probopass	♂/♀
524	Roggenrola	♂/♀
525	Boldore	♂/♀
526	Gigalith	♂/♀
568	Trubbish	♂/♀
569	Garbodor	♂/♀
582	Vanillite	♂/♀
583	Vanillish	♂/♀
584	Vanilluxe	♂/♀
599	Klink	Unknown
600	Klang	Unknown
601	Klinklang	Unknown
615	Cryogonal	Unknown
622	Golett	Unknown
623	Golurk	Unknown

Mineral and Grass Egg Groups

597	Ferroseed	♂/♀
598	Ferrothorn	♂/♀

Mineral and Bug Egg Groups

557	Dwebble	♂/♀
558	Crustle	♂/♀

Mineral and Fairy Egg Groups

361	Snorunt	♂/♀
362	Glalie	♂/♀
478	Froslass	♀

Mineral and Amorphous Egg Groups

562	Yamask	♂/♀
563	Cofagrigus	♂/♀

There is no crossover between the Mineral Egg Group and the following Egg Groups:

- Flying
- Human-Like
- Monster
- Dragon
- Field
- Water 1
- Water 2
- Water 3
- Ditto
- No Eggs Discovered

Field Group

Field Egg Group only

019	Rattata	♂/♀
020	Raticate	♂/♀
027	Sandshrew	♂/♀
028	Sandslash	♂/♀
037	Vulpix	♂/♀
038	Ninetales	♂/♀
050	Diglett	♂/♀
051	Dugtrio	♂/♀
052	Meowth	♂/♀
053	Persian	♂/♀
056	Mankey	♂/♀
057	Primeape	♂/♀
058	Growlithe	♂/♀
059	Arcanine	♂/♀
077	Ponyta	♂/♀
078	Rapidash	♂/♀
128	Tauros	♂
133	Eevee	♂/♀
134	Vaporeon	♂/♀
135	Jolteon	♂/♀
136	Flareon	♂/♀
155	Cyndaquil	♂/♀
156	Quilava	♂/♀
157	Typhlosion	♂/♀
161	Sentret	♂/♀
162	Furret	♂/♀
190	Aipom	♂/♀
196	Espeon	♂/♀
197	Umbreon	♂/♀
203	Girafarig	♂/♀
206	Dunsparce	♂/♀
215	Sneasel	♂/♀
216	Teddiursa	♂/♀
217	Ursaring	♂/♀
220	Swinub	♂/♀
221	Piloswine	♂/♀
228	Houndour	♂/♀
229	Houndoom	♂/♀
231	Phanpy	♂/♀
232	Donphan	♂/♀
234	Stantler	♂/♀
235	Smeargle	♂/♀
241	Miltank	♀
255	Torchic	♂/♀
256	Combusken	♂/♀
257	Blaziken	♂/♀
261	Poochyena	♂/♀
262	Mightyena	♂/♀
263	Zigzagoon	♂/♀
264	Linoone	♂/♀
287	Slakoth	♂/♀
288	Vigoroth	♂/♀
289	Slaking	♂/♀
309	Electrike	♂/♀
310	Manectric	♂/♀
322	Numel	♂/♀
323	Camerupt	♂/♀
324	Torkoal	♂/♀
325	Spoink	♂/♀
326	Grumpig	♂/♀
335	Zangoose	♂/♀
352	Kecleon	♂/♀
359	Absol	♂/♀
403	Shinx	♂/♀
404	Luxio	♂/♀
405	Luxray	♂/♀
424	Ambipom	♂/♀
431	Glameow	♂/♀
432	Purugly	♂/♀
434	Stunky	♂/♀
435	Skuntank	♂/♀
449	Hippopotas	♂/♀
450	Hippowdon	♂/♀
461	Weavile	♂/♀
470	Leafeon	♂/♀
471	Glaceon	♂/♀
473	Mamoswine	♂/♀
498	Tepig	♂/♀
499	Pignite	♂/♀
500	Emboar	♂/♀
501	Oshawott	♂/♀
502	Dewott	♂/♀
503	Samurott	♂/♀
504	Patrat	♂/♀
505	Watchog	♂/♀
506	Lillipup	♂/♀
507	Herdier	♂/♀
508	Stoutland	♂/♀
509	Purrloin	♂/♀
510	Liepard	♂/♀
511	Pansage	♂/♀
512	Simisage	♂/♀
513	Pansear	♂/♀
514	Simisear	♂/♀
515	Panpour	♂/♀
516	Simipour	♂/♀
517	Munna	♂/♀
518	Musharna	♂/♀
522	Blitzle	♂/♀
523	Zebstrika	♂/♀
529	Drilbur	♂/♀
530	Excadrill	♂/♀
551	Sandile	♂/♀
552	Krokorok	♂/♀
553	Krookodile	♂/♀
554	Darumaka	♂/♀
555	Darmanitan	♂/♀
570	Zorua	♂/♀
571	Zoroark	♂/♀
572	Minccino	♂/♀
573	Cinccino	♂/♀
585	Deerling	♂/♀
586	Sawsbuck	♂/♀
587	Emolga	♂/♀
613	Cubchoo	♂/♀
614	Beartic	♂/♀
626	Bouffalant	♂/♀
631	Heatmor	♂/♀

Field and Grass Egg Groups

273	Seedot	♂/♀
274	Nuzleaf	♂/♀
275	Shiftry	♂/♀
495	Snivy	♂/♀
496	Servine	♂/♀
497	Serperior	♂/♀

Field and Flying Egg Groups

083	Farfetch'd	♂/♀
527	Woobat	♂/♀
528	Swoobat	♂/♀

Field and Human-Like Egg Groups

327	Spinda	♂/♀
390	Chimchar	♂/♀
391	Monferno	♂/♀
392	Infernape	♂/♀
427	Buneary	♂/♀
428	Lopunny	♂/♀
448	Lucario	♂/♀
619	Mienfoo	♂/♀
620	Mienshao	♂/♀

Field and Monster Egg Groups

029	Nidoran ♀	♀
032	Nidoran ♂	♂
033	Nidorino	♂
034	Nidoking	♂
111	Rhyhorn	♂/♀
112	Rhydon	♂/♀
179	Mareep	♂/♀
180	Flaaffy	♂/♀
181	Ampharos	♂/♀
293	Whismur	♂/♀
294	Loudred	♂/♀
295	Exploud	♂/♀
464	Rhyperior	♂/♀

Field and Fairy Egg Groups

025	Pikachu	♂/♀
026	Raichu	♂/♀
209	Snubbull	♂/♀
210	Granbull	♂/♀
300	Skitty	♂/♀
301	Delcatty	♂/♀
303	Mawile	♂/♀
417	Pachirisu	♂/♀

Field and Dragon Egg Groups

023	Ekans	♂/♀
024	Arbok	♂/♀
336	Seviper	♂/♀
559	Scraggy	♂/♀
560	Scrafty	♂/♀

Field and Water 1 Egg Groups

054	Psyduck	♂/♀
055	Golduck	♂/♀
086	Seel	♂/♀
087	Dewgong	♂/♀
194	Wooper	♂/♀
195	Quagsire	♂/♀
225	Delibird	♂/♀
363	Spheal	♂/♀
364	Sealeo	♂/♀
365	Walrein	♂/♀
393	Piplup	♂/♀
394	Prinplup	♂/♀
395	Empoleon	♂/♀
399	Bidoof	♂/♀
400	Bibarel	♂/♀
418	Buizel	♂/♀
419	Floatzel	♂/♀

Field and Water 2 Egg Groups

320	Wailmer	♂/♀
321	Wailord	♂/♀

There is no crossover between the Field Egg Group and the following Egg Groups:

- Bug
- Mineral
- Amorphous
- Water 3
- Ditto
- No Eggs Discovered

 **Tip** — **Hatching Pokémon with certain forms**

Some Pokémon can appear in different Forms, such as Basculin, Shellos, and Gastrodon. If the hatched Pokémon is one of these, it will have the same form as the female Pokémon you left at the Pokémon Day Care.

Shellos
West Sea

Shellos
East Sea

Basculin
Red-Striped Form

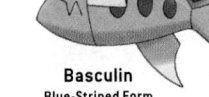

Basculin
Blue-Striped Form

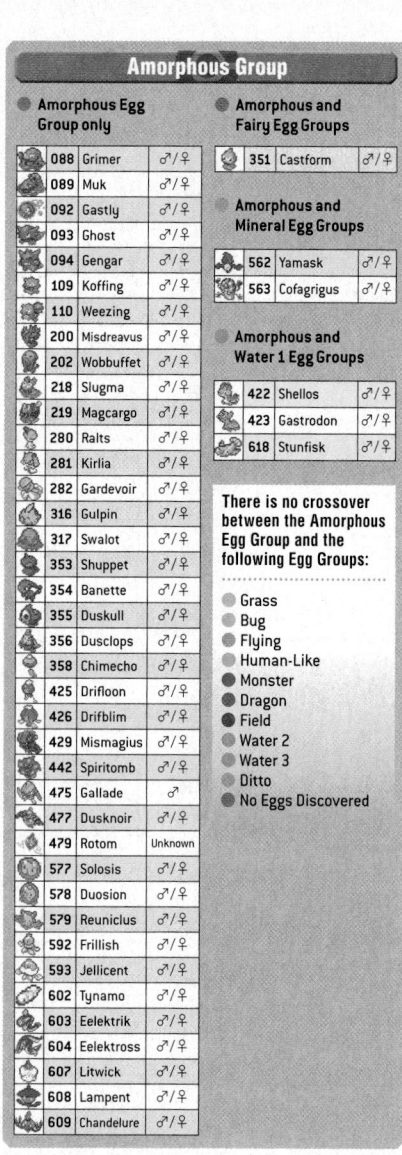

Amorphous Group

Amorphous Egg Group only

088	Grimer	♂/♀
089	Muk	♂/♀
092	Gastly	♂/♀
093	Ghost	♂/♀
094	Gengar	♂/♀
109	Koffing	♂/♀
110	Weezing	♂/♀
200	Misdreavus	♂/♀
202	Wobbuffet	♂/♀
218	Slugma	♂/♀
219	Magcargo	♂/♀
280	Ralts	♂/♀
281	Kirlia	♂/♀
282	Gardevoir	♂/♀
316	Gulpin	♂/♀
317	Swalot	♂/♀
353	Shuppet	♂/♀
354	Banette	♂/♀
355	Duskull	♂/♀
356	Dusclops	♂/♀
358	Chimecho	♂/♀
425	Drifloon	♂/♀
426	Drifblim	♂/♀
429	Mismagius	♂/♀
442	Spiritomb	♂/♀
475	Gallade	♂
477	Dusknoir	♂/♀
479	Rotom	Unknown
577	Solosis	♂/♀
578	Duosion	♂/♀
579	Reuniclus	♂/♀
592	Frillish	♂/♀
593	Jellicent	♂/♀
602	Tynamo	♂/♀
603	Eelektrik	♂/♀
604	Eelektross	♂/♀
607	Litwick	♂/♀
608	Lampent	♂/♀
609	Chandelure	♂/♀

Amorphous and Fairy Egg Groups

351	Castform	♂/♀

Amorphous and Mineral Egg Groups

562	Yamask	♂/♀
563	Cofagrigus	♂/♀

Amorphous and Water 1 Egg Groups

422	Shellos	♂/♀
423	Gastrodon	♂/♀
618	Stunfisk	♂/♀

There is no crossover between the Amorphous Egg Group and the following Egg Groups:
- Grass
- Bug
- Flying
- Human-Like
- Monster
- Dragon
- Field
- Water 2
- Water 3
- Ditto
- No Eggs Discovered

Water Group 1

Water Egg Group 1 only

060	Poliwag	♂/♀
061	Poliwhirl	♂/♀
062	Poliwrath	♂/♀
186	Politoed	♂/♀
226	Mantine	♂/♀
366	Clamperl	♂/♀
367	Huntail	♂/♀
368	Gorebyss	♂/♀
535	Tympole	♂/♀
536	Palpitoad	♂/♀
537	Seismitoad	♂/♀

Water 1 and Grass Egg Groups

270	Lotad	♂/♀
271	Lombre	♂/♀
272	Ludicolo	♂/♀

Water 1 and Bug Egg Groups

283	Surskit	♂/♀
284	Masquerain	♂/♀

Water 1 and Flying Egg Groups

278	Wingull	♂/♀
279	Pelipper	♂/♀
580	Ducklett	♂/♀
581	Swanna	♂/♀

Water 1 and Monster Egg Groups

007	Squirtle	♂/♀
008	Wartortle	♂/♀
009	Blastoise	♂/♀
079	Slowpoke	♂/♀
080	Slowbro	♂/♀
131	Lapras	♂/♀

158	Totodile	♂/♀
159	Croconaw	♂/♀
160	Feraligatr	♂/♀
199	Slowking	♂/♀
258	Mudkip	♂/♀
259	Marshtomp	♂/♀
260	Swampert	♂/♀

Water 1 and Fairy Egg Groups

183	Marill	♂/♀
184	Azumarill	♂/♀
489	Phione	Unknown
490	Manaphy	Unknown

Water 1 and Dragon Egg Groups

116	Horsea	♂/♀
117	Seadra	♂/♀
147	Dratini	♂/♀
148	Dragonair	♂/♀
149	Dragonite	♂/♀
230	Kingdra	♂/♀
349	Feebas	♂/♀
350	Milotic	♂/♀

Water 1 and Field Egg Groups

054	Psyduck	♂/♀
055	Golduck	♂/♀
086	Seel	♂/♀
087	Dewgong	♂/♀
194	Wooper	♂/♀
195	Quagsire	♂/♀
225	Delibird	♂/♀
363	Spheal	♂/♀
364	Sealeo	♂/♀
365	Walrein	♂/♀
393	Piplup	♂/♀
394	Prinplup	♂/♀

395	Empoleon	♂/♀
399	Bidoof	♂/♀
400	Bibarel	♂/♀
418	Buizel	♂/♀
419	Floatzel	♂/♀

Water 1 and Amorphous Egg Groups

422	Shellos	♂/♀
423	Gastrodon	♂/♀
618	Stunfisk	♂/♀

Water 1 and Water 2 Egg Groups

223	Remoraid	♂/♀
224	Octillery	♂/♀
369	Relicanth	♂/♀
594	Alomomola	♂/♀

Water 1 and Water 3 Egg Groups

138	Omanyte	♂/♀
139	Omastar	♂/♀
140	Kabuto	♂/♀
141	Kabutops	♂/♀
222	Corsola	♂/♀
341	Corphish	♂/♀
342	Crawdaunt	♂/♀
564	Tirtouga	♂/♀
565	Carracosta	♂/♀

There is no crossover between Water Egg Group 1 and the following Egg Groups:
- Human-Like
- Mineral
- Ditto
- No Eggs Discovered

 Tip — ## Special pairings can result in two different Eggs

It is usually true that only one kind of Pokémon can be hatched from a given Pokémon pairing, but there are some exceptions. If you drop off a Nidoran ♀ with a male Pokémon from either the Monster Group or the Field Group, the Egg that you find could hatch either a Nidoran ♀ or a Nidoran ♂. If you drop off an Illumise with a compatible Pokémon, the Egg that you find could hatch either an Illumise or a Volbeat. This also works if you leave a Nidoran ♂ or Volbeat at the Pokémon Day Care with a Ditto.

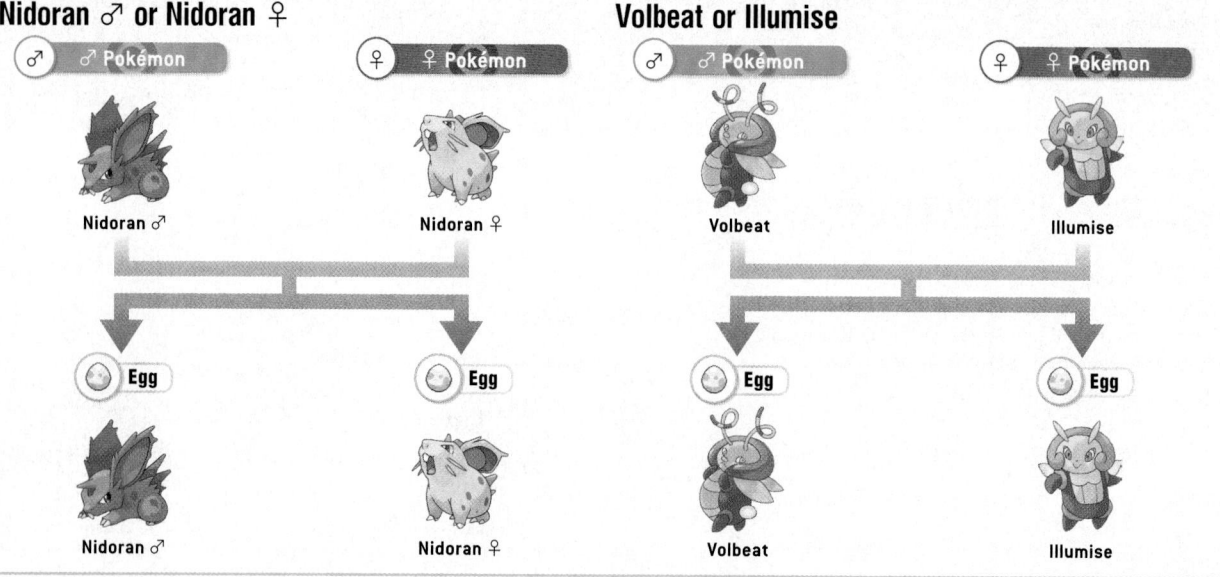

Nidoran ♂ or Nidoran ♀

♂ Pokémon — Nidoran ♂ → Egg → Nidoran ♂

♀ Pokémon — Nidoran ♀ → Egg → Nidoran ♀

Volbeat or Illumise

♂ Pokémon — Volbeat → Egg → Volbeat

♀ Pokémon — Illumise → Egg → Illumise

Water Group 2

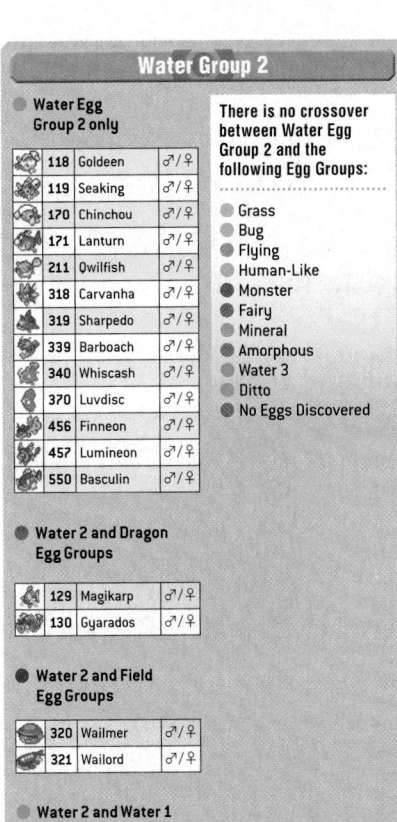

Water Egg Group 2 only

	118	Goldeen	♂/♀
	119	Seaking	♂/♀
	170	Chinchou	♂/♀
	171	Lanturn	♂/♀
	211	Qwilfish	♂/♀
	318	Carvanha	♂/♀
	319	Sharpedo	♂/♀
	339	Barboach	♂/♀
	340	Whiscash	♂/♀
	370	Luvdisc	♂/♀
	456	Finneon	♂/♀
	457	Lumineon	♂/♀
	550	Basculin	♂/♀

There is no crossover between Water Egg Group 2 and the following Egg Groups:

- Grass
- Bug
- Flying
- Human-Like
- Monster
- Fairy
- Mineral
- Amorphous
- Water 3
- Ditto
- No Eggs Discovered

Water 2 and Dragon Egg Groups

	129	Magikarp	♂/♀
	130	Gyarados	♂/♀

Water 2 and Field Egg Groups

	320	Wailmer	♂/♀
	321	Wailord	♂/♀

Water 2 and Water 1 Egg Groups

	223	Remoraid	♂/♀
	224	Octillery	♂/♀
	369	Relicanth	♂/♀
	594	Alomomola	♂/♀

Water Group 3

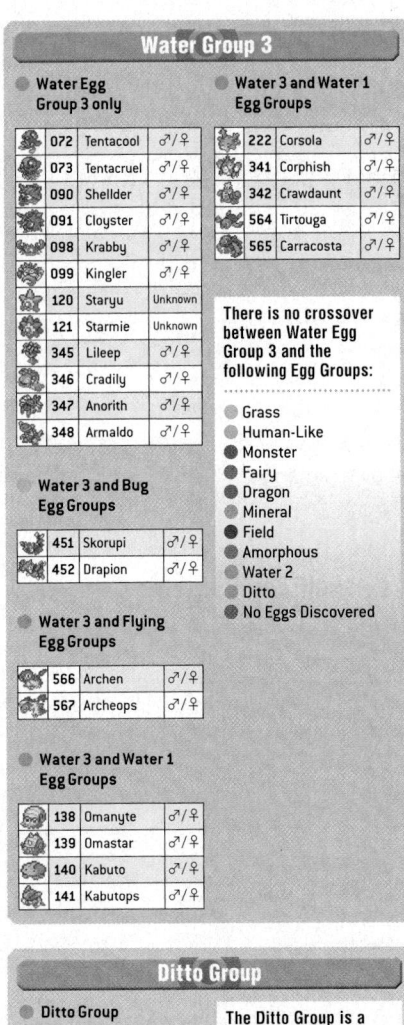

Water Egg Group 3 only

	072	Tentacool	♂/♀
	073	Tentacruel	♂/♀
	090	Shellder	♂/♀
	091	Cloyster	♂/♀
	098	Krabby	♂/♀
	099	Kingler	♂/♀
	120	Staryu	Unknown
	121	Starmie	Unknown
	345	Lileep	♂/♀
	346	Cradily	♂/♀
	347	Anorith	♂/♀
	348	Armaldo	♂/♀

Water 3 and Water 1 Egg Groups

	222	Corsola	♂/♀
	341	Corphish	♂/♀
	342	Crawdaunt	♂/♀
	564	Tirtouga	♂/♀
	565	Carracosta	♂/♀

There is no crossover between Water Egg Group 3 and the following Egg Groups:

- Grass
- Human-Like
- Monster
- Fairy
- Dragon
- Mineral
- Field
- Amorphous
- Water 2
- Ditto
- No Eggs Discovered

Water 3 and Bug Egg Groups

	451	Skorupi	♂/♀
	452	Drapion	♂/♀

Water 3 and Flying Egg Groups

	566	Archen	♂/♀
	567	Archeops	♂/♀

Water 3 and Water 1 Egg Groups

	138	Omanyte	♂/♀
	139	Omastar	♂/♀
	140	Kabuto	♂/♀
	141	Kabutops	♂/♀

Ditto Group

	132	Ditto	Unknown

The Ditto Group is a special Group. Ditto is not a part of any other Egg Group, yet if you drop it off at a Pokémon Day Care with another Pokémon, you will find an Egg for that Pokémon. You cannot find a Ditto Egg.

No Eggs Discovered Group

No Eggs Discovered

	030	Nidorina	♀		458	Mantyke	♂/♀
	031	Nidoqueen	♀		480	Uxie	Unknown
	144	Articuno	Unknown		481	Mesprit	Unknown
	145	Zapdos	Unknown		482	Azelf	Unknown
	146	Moltres	Unknown		483	Dialga	Unknown
	150	Mewtwo	Unknown		484	Palkia	Unknown
	151	Mew	Unknown		485	Heatran	♂/♀
	172	Pichu	♂/♀		486	Regigigas	Unknown
	173	Cleffa	♂/♀		487	Giratina	Unknown
	174	Igglybuff	♂/♀		488	Cresselia	♀
	175	Togepi	♂/♀		491	Darkrai	Unknown
	201	Unown	Unknown		492	Shaymin	Unknown
	236	Tyrogue	♂		493	Arceus	Unknown
	238	Smoochum	♀		494	Victini	Unknown
	239	Elekid	♂/♀		638	Cobalion	Unknown
	240	Magby	♂/♀		639	Terrakion	Unknown
	243	Raikou	Unknown		640	Virizion	Unknown
	244	Entei	Unknown		641	Tornadus	♂
	245	Suicune	Unknown		642	Thundurus	♂
	249	Lugia	Unknown		643	Reshiram	Unknown
	250	Ho-Oh	Unknown		644	Zekrom	Unknown
	251	Celebi	Unknown		645	Landorus	♂
	298	Azurill	♂/♀		646	Kyurem	Unknown
	360	Wynaut	♂/♀		647	Keldeo	Unknown
	377	Regirock	Unknown		648	Meloetta	Unknown
	378	Regice	Unknown		649	Genesect	Unknown
	379	Registeel	Unknown				
	380	Latias	♀				
	381	Latios	♂				
	382	Kyogre	Unknown				
	383	Groudon	Unknown				
	384	Rayquaza	Unknown				
	385	Jirachi	Unknown				
	386	Deoxys	Unknown				
	406	Budew	♂/♀				
	433	Chingling	♂/♀				
	438	Bonsly	♂/♀				
	439	Mime Jr.	♂/♀				
	440	Happiny	♀				
	446	Munchlax	♂/♀				
	447	Riolu	♂/♀				

None of the Pokémon in the No Eggs Discovered Group belongs to any other Egg Group.

 **Tip**

Pokémon Eggs found with the help of items

In general, the Pokémon that hatches from an Egg you find at a Pokémon Day Care will be in its earliest evolutionary stage. However, there are some exceptions. For example, if you drop off a female Wobbuffet and a male Pokémon from the Amorphous Group, you will find a Wobbuffet Egg, not a Wynaut Egg (even though Wobbuffet evolves from Wynaut). If you wish to find a Wynaut Egg, you will need to have one of the Pokémon hold a Lax Incense before you drop it off. The table below lists all nine of these special Eggs.

Eggs that require incense

Egg Discovered	Female Pokémon	Male Pokémon Egg Group	Necessary item
Azurill	Marill or Azumarill	Fairy Group or Water Group 1	Sea Incense
Wynaut	Wobbuffet	Amorphous Group	Lax Incense
Budew	Roselia or Roserade	Fairy Group or Grass Group	Rose Incense
Chingling	Chimecho	Amorphous Group	Pure Incense
Bonsly	Sudowoodo	Mineral Group	Rock Incense
Mime Jr.	Mr. Mime	Human-Like Group	Odd Incense
Happiny	Chansey or Blissey	Fairy Group	Luck Incense
Munchlax	Snorlax	Monster Group	Full Incense
Mantyke	Mantine	Water Group 1	Wave Incense

National Pokédex Completion Tip **15**

Use Poké Transfer to Bring Pokémon Over

Hit the Pokémon popping out of the tall grass with Poké Balls

Poké Transfer is a device that transfers Pokémon from *Pokémon Diamond, Pearl, Platinum, HeartGold,* and *SoulSilver Versions*. When Pokémon pop out of the tall grass, pull the bowstring back and send a Poké Ball flying! When you hit a Pokémon with a Poké Ball, it will be sent to your PC Box. It is also registered in the National Pokédex if it wasn't already.

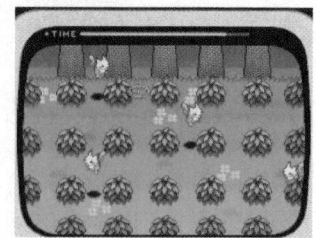

How to use Poké Transfer

1 You need two systems from the Nintendo DS family of systems (Nintendo DS, Nintendo DS Lite, Nintendo DSi, Nintendo DSi XL), two Nintendo 3DS systems, or one of each

2 You can send Pokémon anytime you want

3 Items held by Pokémon can't be taken with them

4 Pokémon that know HMs can't be transferred

5 Once transferred, a Pokémon can't be returned to the game it came from

Games that support Poké Transfer

Pokémon can be brought over from these games via Poké Transfer (Nintendo DS games, also can be played on Nintendo 3DS)

Pokémon can be brought to these games via Poké Transfer (Nintendo DS games, also can be played on Nintendo 3DS)

Move up to six Pokémon at once from Nintendo DS Pokémon series games

With Poké Transfer, you can transfer up to six Pokémon at once from prior Nintendo DS Pokémon series games to *Pokémon Black Version 2* or *Pokémon White Version 2*. You can use it as often as you like. You'll need two systems in the Nintendo DS family of systems to use Poké Transfer. Work together with friends or family members to transfer the Pokémon you need!

How to use Poké Transfer

Game Receiving Pokémon	Game Sending Pokémon	Game Sending Pokémon	Game Receiving Pokémon
Wireless communications begin	Choose the Pokémon to send	Catch the Pokémon within 2 minutes	The Pokémon are put in the Box

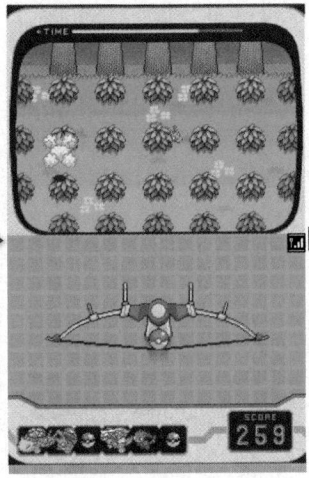

Speak to Professor Park, and wireless communications will begin.

Start the Poké Transfer program from DS Download Play.

Use the stylus to pull the bow and aim the Poké Ball at the Pokémon.

The Pokémon you caught will be sent to the PC Box.

🌸 Tip · Try for a high score

When you hit a Pokémon with a Poké Ball, you score points. If you get enough points, the level goes up and Professor Park's comment changes. Different kinds of Pokémon give you different numbers of points. You get bonus points for catching Pokémon Lv. 50 or higher.

If you hit the Pokémon right in the center of its body with the Poké Ball, you get a lot of stars and more points. If you score 900 points or more, Professor Park says what is shown in the screenshot to the left.

How points work

Number of Stars	Points
8 stars	High
3 stars	Normal
No stars	Low

Level	Points
6	900 points or more
5	800 points or more
4	700 points or more
3	550 points or more
2	400 points or more
1	399 points or lower

Pokémon that give you bonus points

Articuno, Zapdos, Moltres, Mewtwo, Mew, Raikou, Entei, Suicune, Lugia, Ho-Oh, Celebi, Regirock, Regice, Registeel, Latias, Latios, Kyogre, Groudon, Rayquaza, Jirachi, Deoxys, Rotom, Uxie, Mesprit, Azelf, Dialga, Palkia, Heatran, Regigigas, Giratina, Cresselia, Phione, Manaphy, Darkrai, Shaymin, and Arceus

---

Where to find the Poké Transfer Lab

Find the Poké Transfer Lab on Route 15

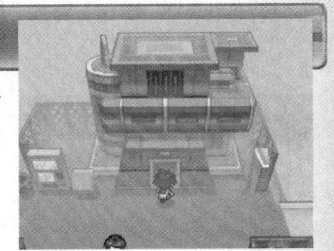

The Poké Transfer Lab is located on Route 15. You can go there after entering the Hall of Fame. If you'd like to use Fly, going to Black City *(Pokémon Black Version 2)* or White Forest *(Pokémon White Version 2)* first is the fastest way there.

 **Tip** Great Ways to Catch Pokémon Using Poké Transfer

Check out the tips below to make catching the Pokémon a breeze

In Poké Transfer, you catch Pokémon by hitting them with Poké Balls shot from a bow. Hit the jumping Pokémon with a Poké Ball. It might seem a little difficult at first, but with the techniques from this page, catching them will become much easier.

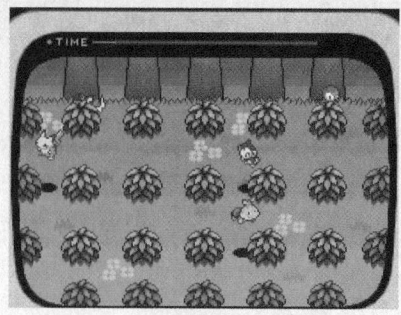

Find the Poké Transfer Lab on Route 15

Pokémon jump between the patches of tall grass. You can't catch Pokémon while they're hiding, so launch a Poké Ball while aiming between the patches of tall grass. Even in the short amount of time it takes the Poké Ball to cross the field after it is launched, the Pokémon will move, so you have to aim for where the Pokémon will be when the ball reaches the field. If no Pokémon is jumping, hit the tall grass with a Poké Ball just as the Pokémon peeks out from the tall grass. The hiding Pokémon will start moving.

Let go the moment the Pokémon jumps

Aim between the patches of tall grass when the Pokémon comes out

Adjust the shot's strength and direction to fire the Poké Ball where you want it to go

When you let go of the bow, the Poké Ball goes flying. If you pull it to the left, the ball goes right, and if you pull it to the right, the ball goes left. When you want to fire the ball a shorter distance, just pull back a little bit. Pull back a long way to fire the Poké Ball farther.

You can aim to the left and right by moving while the bow is drawn

Pull back far to reach faraway places

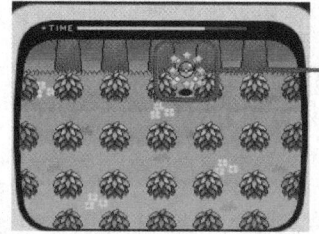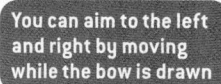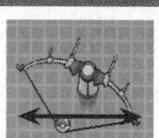

Purple mist makes it easier to catch Pokémon

Sometimes purple mist wafts through the air. If you hit this mist with a Poké Ball, the Pokémon you haven't caught yet will fall asleep for a moment. You can even catch Pokémon hiding in the tall grass when they're sleeping. Sleeping Pokémon don't move, so it's easy to catch them.

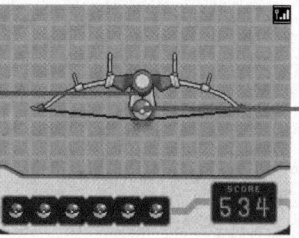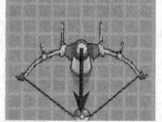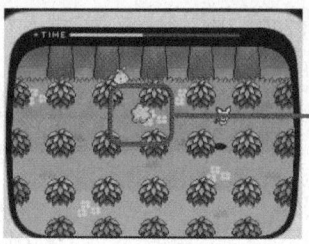

Hit the purple mist and Pokémon fall asleep

Important Pokémon to Transfer from *Pokémon Diamond*, *Pearl*, and *Platinum Versions* with Poké Transfer

Professor Rowan gives you Turtwig, Chimchar, or Piplup

The Turtwig, Chimchar, or Piplup you get from Professor Rowan at the start of your adventure in Sinnoh is a very rare Pokémon. You can only receive one, so register the other two in the National Pokédex by Link Trade or the GTS (p. 382).

National Pokédex No. 387
Turtwig

Pokémon Diamond Version

Pokémon Pearl Version

Pokémon Platinum Version

National Pokédex No. 390
Chimchar

Pokémon Diamond Version

Pokémon Pearl Version

Pokémon Platinum Version

National Pokédex No. 393
Piplup

Pokémon Diamond Version

Pokémon Pearl Version

Pokémon Platinum Version

Screen from Pokémon Platinum Version

Go on! Open the briefcase and choose a Pokémon!

Professor Rowan will ask if you like Pokémon. Answer "YES" and he will give you a Pokémon.

Dialga and Palkia wait on Mt. Coronet's Peak

You can meet Dialga and Palkia at the peak of Mt. Coronet when you bring the Adamant Orb and the Lustrous Orb after entering the Hall of Fame. In *Pokémon Platinum Version*, you can catch both of them.

National Pokédex No. 483
Dialga

Pokémon Diamond Version

Pokémon Platinum Version

National Pokédex No. 484
Palkia

Pokémon Pearl Version

Pokémon Platinum Version

Screen from Pokémon Platinum Version

DIALGA: Gugyugubah!

Screen from Pokémon Platinum Version

PALKIA: Gagyagyaah!

You need the moves Surf, Rock Climb, and Strength to reach it.

Only one or the other appears in *Pokémon Diamond* and *Pokémon Pearl*.

Giratina is found in Turnback Cave or the Distortion World

In *Pokémon Diamond* and *Pearl Versions*, Giratina is found in Turnback Cave. In *Pokémon Platinum Version*, it's found in the Distortion World.

Screen from Pokémon Platinum Version

...Bishaan!

National Pokédex No. 487
Giratina
Origin Forme

Pokémon Platinum Version

National Pokédex No. 487
Giratina
Altered Forme

Pokémon Diamond Version

Pokémon Pearl Version

Screen from Pokémon Diamond or Pearl Version

...Bishaan!

Tip — Use the Poké Radar to find Pokémon

The Poké Radar seeks out uncommon Pokémon deep in the tall grass. Get it from Professor Rowan.

National Pokédex No. 290
Nincada

National Pokédex No. 324
Torkoal

Important Pokémon to Transfer from *Pokémon HeartGold* and *SoulSilver Versions* with Poké Transfer

Professor Elm's gift: Chikorita, Cyndaquil, or Totodile

The Chikorita, Cyndaquil, or Totodile you get from Professor Elm at the start of your adventure in Johto is a very rare Pokémon. You can only receive one, so register the other two in the National Pokédex by Link Trade or the GTS (p. 382).

National Pokédex No. 152
Chikorita

Pokémon HeartGold Version

Pokémon SoulSilver Version

National Pokédex No. 155
Cyndaquil

Pokémon HeartGold Version

Pokémon SoulSilver Version

National Pokédex No. 158
Totodile

Pokémon HeartGold Version

Pokémon SoulSilver Version

Screen from Pokémon HeartGold or SoulSilver Version

You can choose one of the Pokémon over there.

Professor Elm is known far and wide as an authority on Pokémon evolution.

Tip — Headbutt trees to make Pokémon appear

Some Pokémon live in trees in the Johto and Kanto regions. If you use Headbutt on trees, these Pokémon may appear. Also, some Pokémon live only in the trees you can reach by using the move Rock Climb.

National Pokédex No. 420
Cherubi

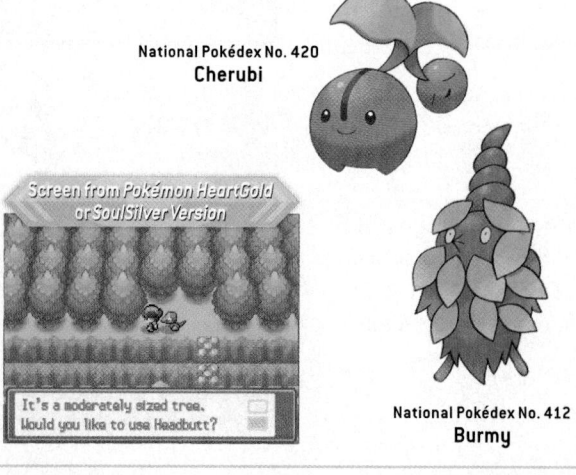

Screen from Pokémon HeartGold or SoulSilver Version

It's a moderately sized tree. Would you like to use Headbutt?

National Pokédex No. 412
Burmy

Legendary Pokémon that roam the Johto region: Raikou, Entei, and Suicune

Raikou and Entei roam around the Johto region. If you encounter them, they run away immediately. Use the moves Spider Web or Mean Look to keep them close enough to catch them. You can catch Suicune only after you have seen it in all the places it appears once you've encountered it in the Burned Tower in Ecruteak City.

Screen from Pokémon HeartGold or SoulSilver Version

Raikou and Entei's positions are displayed on your Pokégear. Always check their locations and approach with caution.

Screen from Pokémon HeartGold or SoulSilver Version

A wild ENTEI appeared!

If you find them, Raikou and Entei flee right away. Use moves and Abilities to keep them from running off.

National Pokédex No. 243
Raikou

Pokémon HeartGold Version

Pokémon SoulSilver Version

National Pokédex No. 244
Entei

Pokémon HeartGold Version

Pokémon SoulSilver Version

National Pokédex No. 245
Suicune

Pokémon HeartGold Version

Pokémon SoulSilver Version

Ho-Oh descends to the Bell Tower

Ho-Oh appears in both *Pokémon HeartGold* and *Pokémon SoulSilver*. It shows up in the Johto region's Bell Tower. In *Pokémon SoulSilver*, you get the Rainbow Wing from an old man in Pewter City in the Kanto region, which you can visit after entering the Hall of Fame.

Screen from *Pokémon HeartGold* or *SoulSilver Version*

HO-OH: Shaoooh!

The Bell Tower is north of Ecruteak City. To reach the top of the tower, you have to solve the mysteries of the warp panels and ladders.

National Pokédex No. 250
Ho-Oh

Pokémon HeartGold Version

Pokémon SoulSilver Version

Lugia sleeps in the Whirl Islands

Lugia appears in both *Pokémon HeartGold* and *Pokémon SoulSilver Versions*. It shows up in the Johto region's Whirl Islands. In *Pokémon HeartGold Version*, you get the Silver Wing from an old man in Pewter City in the Kanto region, which you can visit after entering the Hall of Fame.

Screen from *Pokémon HeartGold* or *SoulSilver Version*

To meet Lugia in the Whirl Islands, you need Pokémon with the moves Surf, Whirlpool, and Flash.

LUGIA: Gyaaas!

National Pokédex No. 249
Lugia

Pokémon HeartGold Version

Pokémon SoulSilver Version

The Kanto region's Legendary Pokémon: Articuno, Zapdos, and Moltres

Articuno is in the Seafoam Islands in the Kanto region. Moltres is in Mt. Silver and Zapdos appears at the entrance of the Power Plant in Kanto after you defeat all of the Gym Leaders in Johto and Kanto and get all 16 Badges.

Screen from *Pokémon HeartGold* or *SoulSilver Version*

To meet Articuno at the Seafoam Islands, use Pokémon with the moves Surf and Strength.

National Pokédex No. 144
Articuno

Pokémon HeartGold Version

Pokémon SoulSilver Version

Screen from *Pokémon HeartGold* or *SoulSilver Version*

National Pokédex No. 145
Zapdos

Pokémon HeartGold Version

Pokémon SoulSilver Version

To reach the Power Plant in Kanto, use Pokémon with the moves Cut and Surf.

Screen from *Pokémon HeartGold* or *SoulSilver Version*

National Pokédex No. 146
Moltres

Pokémon HeartGold Version

Pokémon SoulSilver Version

To meet Moltres, you need the moves Surf, Waterfall, and Rock Climb.

Articuno, Zapdos, and Moltres also appear in *Pokémon Platinum Version*.

Mewtwo hides in Cerulean Cave

Mewtwo is in Cerulean Cave in the Kanto region. You can get to Cerulean Cave by using Surf on Route 25, but someone is blocking the entrance. To get in, you must defeat all of the Gym Leaders in the Kanto region and get all of the Badges.

Screen from *Pokémon HeartGold* or *SoulSilver Version*

To find Mewtwo, you must have Pokémon with the moves Flash, Surf, and Rock Climb.

National Pokédex No. 150
Mewtwo

Pokémon HeartGold Version

Pokémon SoulSilver Version

 **Tip**

Some Pokémon appear when Hoenn Sound or Sinnoh Sound is played on the Pokégear

After you enter the Hall of Fame, the Music Channel on your Pokégear's radio plays Hoenn Sound on Wednesdays and Sinnoh Sound on Thursdays. Play this music, and Pokémon from the Hoenn region or Sinnoh region may appear.

Screen from *Pokémon HeartGold* or *SoulSilver Version*

19:23 WEDNESDAY

Ben
Sound that carries a hint of Hoenn Region taste! The Hoenn music might just lure a

National Pokédex No. 263
Zigzagoon

National Pokédex No. 264
Linoone

National Pokédex No. 293
Whismur

National Pokédex No. 327
Spinda

Professor Oak's gift: Bulbasaur, Charmander, or Squirtle

Visit Pallet Town in the Kanto region after defeating Red on the peak of Mt. Silver. Professor Oak will give you either Bulbasaur, Charmander, or Squirtle.

National Pokédex No. 001 **Bulbasaur**	National Pokédex No. 004 **Charmander**	National Pokédex No. 007 **Squirtle**
Pokémon HeartGold Version	*Pokémon HeartGold Version*	*Pokémon HeartGold Version*
Pokémon SoulSilver Version	*Pokémon SoulSilver Version*	*Pokémon SoulSilver Version*

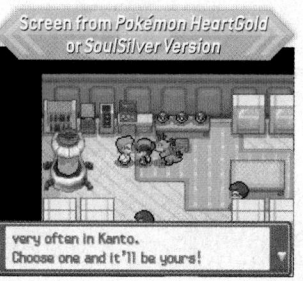

Screen from *Pokémon HeartGold* or *SoulSilver Version*

very often in Kanto.
Choose one and it'll be yours!

Get the other two Pokémon using Link Trade or the GTS to complete your National Pokédex (p. 382).

In Saffron City, Steven gives you Treecko, Torchic, or Mudkip

Talk to Steven in Saffron City after defeating Red. Answer his question with "GREEN STONE," and he gives you Treecko; "RED STONE," and he gives you Torchic; "BLUE STONE," and he gives you Mudkip.

National Pokédex No. 252 **Treecko**	National Pokédex No. 255 **Torchic**	National Pokédex No. 258 **Mudkip**
Pokémon HeartGold Version	*Pokémon HeartGold Version*	*Pokémon HeartGold Version*
Pokémon SoulSilver Version	*Pokémon SoulSilver Version*	*Pokémon SoulSilver Version*

Screen from *Pokémon HeartGold* or *SoulSilver Version*

You can't find the other two. Use Link Trade or the GTS to get them and complete your National Pokédex (p. 382).

front of you.
Which color would you pick?

Kyogre appears in the Embedded Tower

Get the Blue Orb from Mr. Pokémon on Route 30 in the Johto region in *Pokémon HeartGold*. If you go to the Embedded Tower after that, Kyogre will appear.

Screen from *Pokémon HeartGold* or *SoulSilver Version*

KYOGRE: Gyararoooah!

National Pokédex No. 382
Kyogre

Pokémon HeartGold Version

Groudon appears in the Embedded Tower

Get the Red Orb from Mr. Pokémon on Route 30 in the Johto region in *Pokémon SoulSilver*. If you go to the Embedded Tower after that, Groudon will appear.

National Pokédex No. 383
Groudon

Pokémon SoulSilver Version

Screen from *Pokémon HeartGold* or *SoulSilver Version*

Rayquaza appears if you put Kyogre and Groudon in your party

Put the Kyogre and Groudon you caught in the Embedded Tower in your party and talk to Professor Oak in Pallet Town. He gives you the Jade Orb, which you can use to meet Rayquaza in the Embedded Tower. After that, go to the Embedded Tower to catch Rayquaza. Please note that the Kyogre and Groudon that are the keys to finding Rayquaza need to be caught in the Embedded Tower in *Pokémon HeartGold* or *Pokémon SoulSilver*.

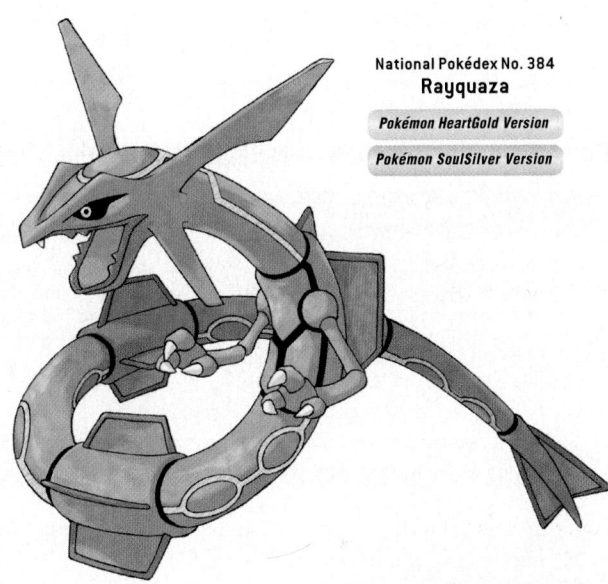

National Pokédex No. 384
Rayquaza

Pokémon HeartGold Version

Pokémon SoulSilver Version

Screen from *Pokémon HeartGold* or *SoulSilver Version*

RAYQURZA: Kiyuryursheeah!

Link Trade to Get Pokémon

📧 Use Link Trade to Complete the National Pokédex

If you use the communication functions in *Pokémon Black Version 2* and *Pokémon White Version 2*, you can trade Pokémon with friends around the corner or all over the world. These communication functions can help you complete the National Pokédex quickly. There are three different ways to Link Trade: IR, Wireless, and Online (Nintendo Wi-Fi Connection).

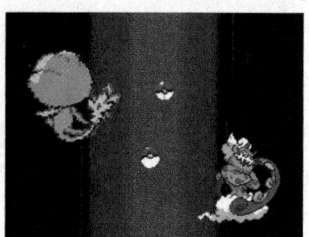

Communication functions available in *Pokémon Black 2* and *Pokémon White 2*

IR (Infrared Connection)	WIRELESS	ONLINE
This is the easiest way to trade Pokémon with nearby people. Each participant offers a Pokémon for the trade.	In this Pokémon trading style, you choose a trading partner from multiple people within about 30 feet from you. In this Negotiation Trade, each person offers three candidate Pokémon.	You can trade Pokémon with far away friends and other Pokémon players using Nintendo Wi-Fi Connection. In this Negotiation Trade, each person offers three candidate Pokémon.

📧 Some Pokémon evolve when they are Link Traded while holding items

Some species of Pokémon evolve when they are Link Traded. Also, some species of Pokémon evolve when they are Link Traded while they are holding items.

Items that evolve Pokémon and how to get them

Metal Coat Chargestone Cave/Clay Tunnel	**Up-Grade** Receive from Cheren in Pinwheel Forest/Striaton City
Reaper Cloth Dreamyard	**DeepSeaScale** Wild Chinchou, Lanturn, and Gorebyss sometimes have one
DeepSeaTooth Wild Carvanha, Sharpedo, and Huntail sometimes have one	**Protector** Wellspring Cave
Magmarizer Plasma Frigate (*Pokémon Black 2* only)	**Electirizer** Plasma Frigate (*Pokémon White 2* only)
Dubious Disc P2 Laboratory	**Prism Scale** Receive from a man in the Pokémon Center in Undella Town/Route 1
King's Rock In Nuvema Town, the home of the hero from *Pokémon Black* or *Pokémon White*	**Dragon Scale** Victory Road

Learn the characteristics of each Link Trade to get Pokémon

Link Trades are an easy way to get the Pokémon you want. Working together with friends to complete the Pokédex makes the process much more fun. Even better, Pokémon received in Link Trades level up more quickly because they get 50% more Experience Points when used in battle. If you want to register a Pokémon by evolving it, getting it in a Link Trade is a good idea.

Pokémon trade using communication functions

IR (Infrared)	WIRELESS	ONLINE
IR Trades are done using the C-Gear displayed on the Touch Screen. Tap IR on the C-Gear, then tap "TRADE." The trade works just like an ordinary Pokémon Link Trade.	Wireless trades are conducted in the Union Room in Pokémon Center 2F. Choose a trading partner from the people in the Union Room. The trading style is a Negotiation Trade.	You can trade Pokémon with your friends using Nintendo Wi-Fi Connection in the Wi-Fi Club in Pokémon Center 2F. Only people you've exchanged Friend Codes with can trade with you. The trading style is a Negotiation Trade.

Tap IR on the C-Gear

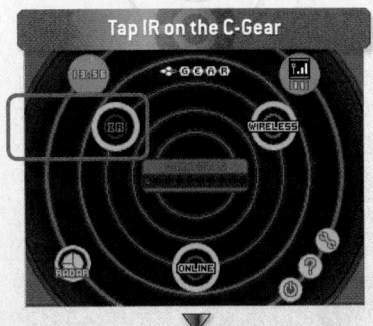

Enter the Union Room

Enter the Wi-Fi Club

Tap "TRADE"

Talk to a friend

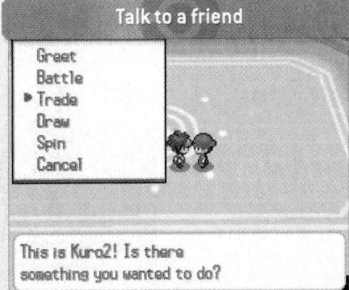

Talk to a friend

Select a Pokémon to trade

Negotiate

Negotiate

The Pokémon will come to you

The Pokémon will come to you

The Pokémon will come to you

Trade Pokémon worldwide using GTS

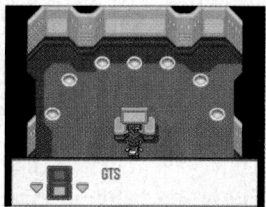

The Global Trade Station (GTS) is a system for trading Pokémon with Pokémon fans worldwide. Use the GTS by going to the Global Terminal in Pokémon Center 2F. There are four ways to trade Pokémon in all. Learn how each one works and choose a method that fits your goals.

Ways to Trade Pokémon through the GTS

① Deposit Pokémon

Deposit a Pokémon and then decide the conditions for the trade. If there is a Pokémon that meets your conditions, the trade will go through.

Select Pokémon to deposit

Choose a Pokémon to trade from your party or PC Box. It will be deposited at the GTS.

Decide what kind of Pokémon you want

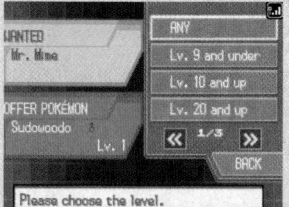

Decide what kind of Pokémon you want to trade the deposited Pokémon for, including gender and level. You can also choose "ANY" or "EITHER" for some conditions.

When you trade, the Pokémon will come to you

After a little time has passed, try accessing the GTS. When the trade is successful, the Pokémon you traded for will come to you.

② Seek Pokémon

Decide the species, level, etc. of the Pokémon you want. People who are offering Pokémon that meet those conditions will be displayed.

Choose the Pokémon you want

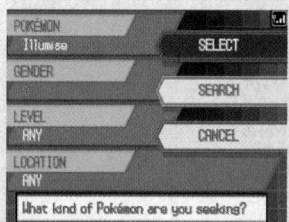

Select "SEEK POKÉMON" after you've decided what kind of Pokémon you want, the gender, etc.

Select a person to trade with

People who have deposited Pokémon that meet your trading conditions are displayed. If you see many people, choose one.

When you trade, the Pokémon will come to you

When you pick a trading partner, choose the Pokémon you want to trade. The trade will begin immediately.

 **Tip** **Check the locations of people you've traded with on Geonet**

Geonet is the high-tech globe in the Pokémon Center 2F. When you register, the place you live and the locations of people you've traded Pokémon with on the GTS are displayed. Of course, players from other countries are displayed as well.

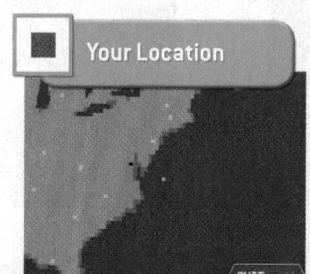
Your Location

Your Trading Partner's Location

GTS Negotiation Pokémon Trade Methods

① Trade with Anyone

You can use Negotiation Trades on the GTS. You select a Pokémon using keywords such as "COOL."

Decide on the trade conditions

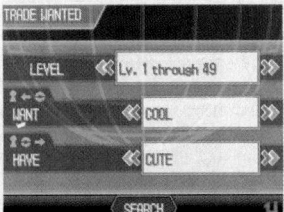

Select the conditions for "WANT" and "HAVE." You can choose keywords such as "COOL" and "CUTE."

Negotiate

A trading partner who meets your requirements is found. When the trading partner appears, the Negotiation Trade begins.

When you trade, the Pokémon will come to you

When the trade is successful, the Pokémon you traded for will come to you. The Pokémon will be added to your party or PC Box.

② Trade Rendezvous

Meet someone you've traded with before and have a Negotiation Trade.

Select a person to trade with

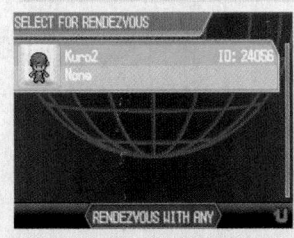

A list of people to trade with will be displayed. Choose the person you want to trade with from the list.

Negotiate

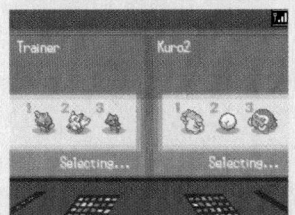

Negotiate with your trading partner. When the trade is successful, the Pokémon you traded for will come to you.

Who's on your Trade Rendezvous list?

- People you've traded with through IR
- People you've traded with at the Wi-Fi Club
- People you've traded with in the Union Room
- People you've traded with through GTS or GTS Negotiations

 **Tip**

Trading with other countries increases the chance to hatch a Shiny Pokémon

If you trade Pokémon with a player from another country through the GTS and leave it in the Pokémon Day Care, the chance to discover an Egg that will hatch a Shiny Pokémon goes up slightly.

Example of Gastly

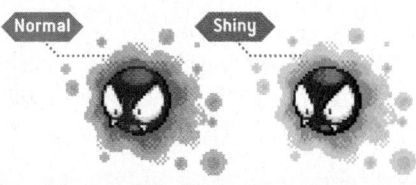

Normal | Shiny

Befriend Pokémon in the Pokémon Dream World

Befriend Pokémon from many different regions

You can meet many Pokémon from other regions in the Pokémon Dream World, part of the Pokémon Global Link website. Some of these Pokémon don't appear in *Pokémon Black 2* and *Pokémon White 2*, so play in the Pokémon Dream World and befriend them all!

Pokémon Global Link home page

Click here to enter the Pokémon Dream World

After you log in, you can check information such as your PGL nickname and tucked-in Pokémon. You can check your profile, too.

Click here to enter the Pokémon Dream World

Click here to enter the Pokémon Dream World. You can play in the Pokémon Dream World for one hour every day. It will be available again 20 hours after the last time you played.

http://www.pokemon-gl.com/

The first time you access the PGL

The first time you access the Pokémon Global Link, you'll need to follow these steps. After you've done that, you can just log in directly.

Steps to follow the first time you access the Pokémon Global Link

1 Get a Game Sync ID

Tap "ONLINE" on the C-Gear and select "GAME SYNC" to get your Game Sync ID.

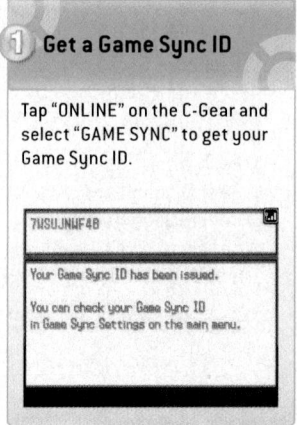

2 Sign up for the Pokémon Trainer Club

Click "SIGN UP!" on the Pokémon Global Link home page to register.

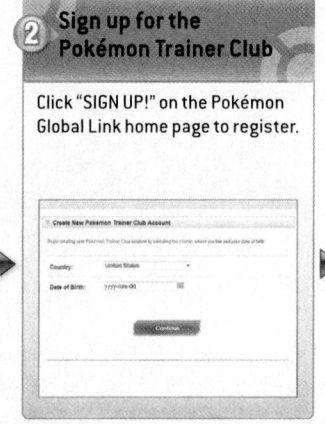

3 Register at the Pokémon Global Link

When you enter a PGL user name and your Game Sync ID after logging in with your Pokémon Trainer Club account, you're done.

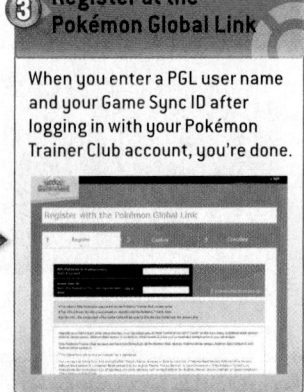

*Membership is free.

Master bringing Pokémon to *Pokémon Black 2* and *Pokémon White 2*

You can befriend many different kinds of Pokémon in the Pokémon Dream World. Follow these steps to bring the Pokémon you befriend in the Pokémon Dream World to your copy of *Pokémon Black 2* or *Pokémon White 2* and register it in the National Pokédex.

Come here, Aron!

Befriending Pokémon in the Pokémon Dream World

Nintendo DS System Steps

Tap "ONLINE" on the C-Gear on the Touch Screen, then tap "GAME SYNC." Choose a Pokémon you want to send to the Pokémon Dream World from your PC Boxes. The selected Pokémon will fall asleep and begin to dream, and you can access its dream in the Pokémon Dream World.

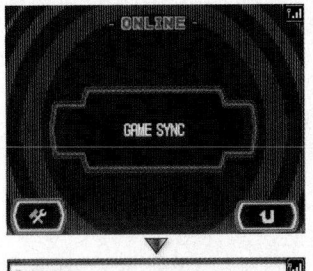

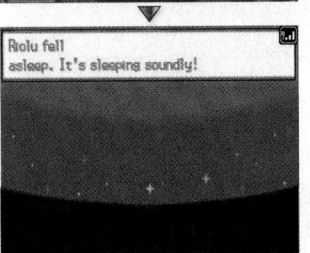

Tap "ONLINE" on the C-Gear
↓
Tap "GAME SYNC"
↓
Choose a Pokémon to tuck in from your PC Boxes
↓
The Pokémon you chose is tucked in

PC Steps

Log in to the Pokémon Global Link on your PC. Select the Pokémon Dream World on the home page and go to the Island of Dreams. Play minigames with the Pokémon you meet on the Island of Dreams to become friends. When you arrive at the Tree of Dreams, select a Pokémon you want to take to *Pokémon Black 2* or *Pokémon White 2*.

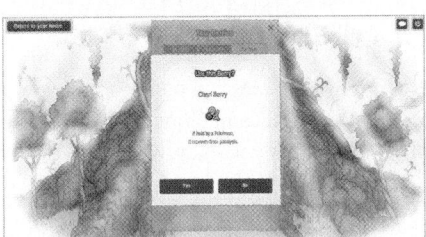

Log in to the Pokémon Global Link
↓
Enter the Pokémon Dream World and go to the Island of Dreams
↓
Play a minigame with the Pokémon you meet to befriend them
↓
Make a wish at the Tree of Dreams to send a Pokémon to your game (only one of the Pokémon you've befriended)
↓
Select "Exit and prepare to wake up" to finish playing in the Pokémon Dream World

Nintendo DS System Steps

Tap "ONLINE" on the C-Gear, then tap "GAME SYNC." The tucked-in Pokémon will wake up. Next, tap "WIRELESS" on the C-Gear, then tap "ENTRALINK." Go to the Entree Forest and you'll meet the Pokémon you befriended in the Pokémon Dream World. Speak to the Pokémon and throw a Dream Ball to catch it.

The Aron your Pokémon saw in the dream appeared!

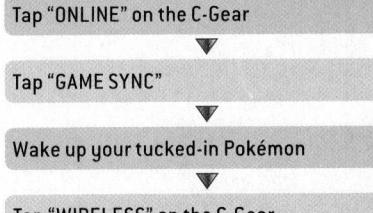

Tap "ONLINE" on the C-Gear
↓
Tap "GAME SYNC"
↓
Wake up your tucked-in Pokémon
↓
Tap "WIRELESS" on the C-Gear
↓
Tap "ENTRALINK"
↓
Go to the Entree Forest
↓
Talk to the Pokémon
↓
Throw a Dream Ball and catch it

Accumulate Dream Points and meet lots of Pokémon

Dream Points make the Pokémon Dream World even more fun as you get more of them. The more you play in the Pokémon Dream World, the more points you'll earn. To meet more kinds of Pokémon in the Pokémon Dream World, collect a lot of Dream Points when you play.

How to accumulate Dream Points

Actions that give you Dream Points	Points received
Watering another player's Berries ◆	★
Befriending a Pokémon on the Island of Dreams	★★
Becoming Dream Pals with another player	★★★
Entering the Pokémon Dream World	★★★★★

◆ This means the points you get for watering Berries per plant. You can water 20 plants per Game Sync.

Areas to visit in the Island of Dreams

Game Cards		How to go to each area					
		Pleasant Forest	Windswept Sky	Sparkling Sea	Spooky Manor	Rugged Mountain	Icy Cave
Pokémon Black 2 and *Pokémon White 2*	Badges you need	8	4 or more	—	4 or more	8	—
	Dream Points you need	3,000	1,500	—	1,500	3,000	—
	Dream Points you need for Level 2	5,000	5,000	5,000	5,000	5,000	5,000
	Dream Points you need for Level 3	10,000	10,000	10,000	10,000	10,000	10,000
Pokémon Black and *Pokémon White*	Badges you need	—	4 or more	8	—	—	—
	Dream Points you need	—	2,500	5,000	—	—	—
	Dream Points you need for Level 2	7,500	7,500	7,500	7,500	7,500	7,500
	Dream Points you need for Level 3	10,000	10,000	10,000	10,000	10,000	10,000

Pokémon types make some areas easier to visit

Tuck in a Pokémon and go to the Pokémon Dream World. You can go to an area such as the Pleasant Forest or the Windswept Sky. The area you explore will be chosen automatically. However, sometimes you'll have a better chance of getting to a certain area, depending on the type of the Pokémon you tucked in with Game Sync. If you want to meet a certain Pokémon, tuck in a Pokémon whose type makes it easier to go to the area where you can find that Pokémon.

How Pokémon types influence your visit

Type	Pleasant Forest	Windswept Sky	Sparkling Sea	Spooky Manor	Rugged Mountain	Icy Cave
Normal	—	—	—	—	—	—
Fire	—	—	—	—	○	—
Water	—	—	◎	—	—	—
Electric	○	—	—	—	—	—
Grass	◎	—	—	—	—	—
Ice	—	—	—	—	—	◎
Fighting	—	—	—	—	○	—
Poison	○	—	—	—	—	—
Ground	—	—	—	—	○	○
Flying	—	◎	—	—	—	—
Psychic	—	—	—	○	—	—
Bug	○	—	—	—	—	—
Rock	—	—	—	—	○	○
Ghost	—	—	◎	—	—	—
Dragon	—	—	—	—	—	—
Dark	—	—	—	○	—	—
Steel	—	—	—	—	○	○

◎ Very easy to go ○ Easier than normal — Normal

Befriend Pokémon by playing minigames

If you successfully complete a minigame with a Pokémon you meet, you will befriend that Pokémon, and you can take it into your game. If you clear the minigame with a high score, the Pokémon you befriend is more likely to know rare moves!

Minigame rules

 The Pokémon you meet chooses the minigame you play.

 Even if it's the same species of Pokémon, the minigame you play may be different depending on its gender.

 If you get a high score, the Pokémon you befriend is more likely to know rare moves.

Nine minigames from the Pokémon Dream World

Ice Cream Scoop

Use one Berry and stack scoops of ice cream. Stack the ice cream higher than 20 inches to win.

High Score 20,000 or more

Wailord's Water Spout

Launch Pokémon from Wailord's spout to open balls that match their colors. If you open 15 or more, you win.

High Score 30,000 or more

Lights Out!

You and your opponent take turns blowing out candles. If your opponent blows out the last candle, you win.

High Score 30,000 or more

Gem Collector

Aim for the goal while collecting gems to get points. Win by reaching the goal before time runs out.

High Score 30,000 or more

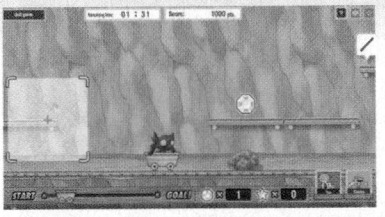

Pokémon Seek

Search for the hiding Pokémon. If you find it before time runs out, you win.

High Score 40,000 or more

Sky Race

Race toward the goal while guiding Pelipper with a flag. Win by reaching the goal before time runs out.

High Score 45,000 or more

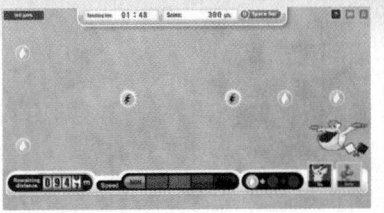

Frozen Treat Sweep

Collect treats while sliding on the ice. If you collect 15,000 points or more before time runs out, you win.

High Score 25,000 or more

Charizard's Treasure Box

Move Charizard and collect 12 Energy symbols before time runs out to open the treasure box to win.

High Score 30,000 or more

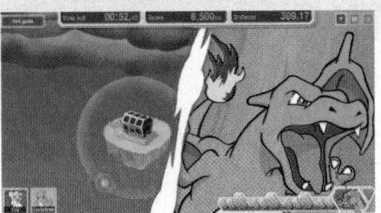

Pokémon Bistro

To win, guide Foongus to serve four correct drinks to your Pokémon customers before time runs out.

High Score 30,000 or more

Pokémon that can be befriended in the
Pokémon Dream World

◎ Pleasant Forest

National Pokédex No. 019
Rattata
Appears at Dream Point Level
● 1

MINIGAME
● Ice Cream Scoop
(both ♂ and ♀ appear)

ABILITIES
● Run Away
● Guts
● Hustle

National Pokédex No. 037
Vulpix
Appears at Dream Point Level
● 3

MINIGAME
● Frozen Treat Sweep
(both ♂ and ♀ appear)

ABILITIES
● Flash Fire
●
● Drought

National Pokédex No. 043
Oddish
Appears at Dream Point Level
● 1

MINIGAME
● Pokémon Bistro
(both ♂ and ♀ appear)

ABILITIES
● Chlorophyll
●
● Run Away

National Pokédex No. 054
Psyduck
Appears at Dream Point Level
● 2

MINIGAME
● Frozen Treat Sweep
(both ♂ and ♀ appear)

ABILITIES
● Damp
● Cloud Nine
● Swift Swim

National Pokédex No. 058
Growlithe
Appears at Dream Point Level
● 2

MINIGAME
● Ice Cream Scoop
(both ♂ and ♀ appear)

ABILITIES
● Intimidate
● Flash Fire
● Justified

National Pokédex No. 060
Poliwag
Appears at Dream Point Level
● 3

MINIGAME
● Pokémon Bistro
(both ♂ and ♀ appear)

ABILITIES
● Water Absorb
● Damp
● Swift Swim

National Pokédex No. 069
Bellsprout
Appears at Dream Point Level
● 1

MINIGAME
● Pokémon Bistro
(both ♂ and ♀ appear)

ABILITIES
● Chlorophyll
●
● Gluttony

National Pokédex No. 077
Ponyta
Appears at Dream Point Level
● 1

MINIGAME
● Pokémon Seek
(both ♂ and ♀ appear)

ABILITIES
● Run Away
● Flash Fire
● Flame Body

National Pokédex No. 083
Farfetch'd
Appears at Dream Point Level
● 1

MINIGAME
● Frozen Treat Sweep
(both ♂ and ♀ appear)

ABILITIES
● Keen Eye
● Inner Focus
● Defiant

National Pokédex No. 084
Doduo
Appears at Dream Point Level
● 1

MINIGAME
● Lights Out!
(both ♂ and ♀ appear)

ABILITIES
● Run Away
● Early Bird
● Tangled Feet

National Pokédex No. 102
Exeggcute
Appears at Dream Point Level
● 1

MINIGAME
● Ice Cream Scoop
(both ♂ and ♀ appear)

ABILITIES
● Chlorophyll
●
● Harvest

National Pokédex No. 108
Lickitung
Appears at Dream Point Level
● 1

MINIGAME
● Pokémon Seek
(both ♂ and ♀ appear)

ABILITIES
● Own Tempo
● Oblivious
● Cloud Nine

National Pokédex No. 114
Tangela
Appears at Dream Point Level
● 1

MINIGAME
● Ice Cream Scoop
(both ♂ and ♀ appear)

ABILITIES
● Chlorophyll
● Leaf Guard
● Regenerator

National Pokédex No. 115
Kangaskhan
Appears at Dream Point Level
● 1

MINIGAME
● Pokémon Seek
(♀ appear)

ABILITIES
● Early Bird
● Scrappy
● Inner Focus

National Pokédex No. 123
Scyther
Appears at Dream Point Level
● 2

MINIGAME
● Pokémon Bistro
(both ♂ and ♀ appear)

ABILITIES
● Swarm
● Technician
● Steadfast

National Pokédex No. 128
Tauros
Appears at Dream Point Level
● 2

MINIGAME
● Frozen Treat Sweep
(♂ appear)

ABILITIES
● Intimidate
● Anger Point
● Sheer Force

National Pokédex No. 161
Sentret
Appears at Dream Point Level
● 1

MINIGAME
● Ice Cream Scoop
(both ♂ and ♀ appear)

ABILITIES
● Run Away
● Keen Eye
● Frisk

National Pokédex No. 177
Natu
Appears at Dream Point Level
● 3

MINIGAME
● Lights Out!
(both ♂ and ♀ appear)

ABILITIES
● Synchronize
● Early Bird
● Magic Bounce

National Pokédex No. 179
Mareep
Appears at Dream Point Level
● 1

MINIGAME
● Pokémon Seek
(both ♂ and ♀ appear)

ABILITIES
● Static
●
● Plus

National Pokédex No. 183
Marill
Appears at Dream Point Level
● 2

MINIGAME
● Frozen Treat
(♂ appear)

ABILITIES
● Thick Fat
● Huge Power
● Sap Sipper

National Pokédex No. 183
Marill
Appears at Dream Point Level
● 3

MINIGAME
● Pokémon Bistro
(both ♂ and ♀ appear)

ABILITIES
● Thick Fat
● Huge Power
● Sap Sipper

National Pokédex No. 185
Sudowoodo
Appears at Dream Point Level
● 2

MINIGAME
● Pokémon Seek
(both ♂ and ♀ appear)

ABILITIES
● Sturdy
● Rock Head
● Rattled

National Pokédex No. 191
Sunkern
Appears at Dream Point Level
● 1

MINIGAME
● Lights Out!
(both ♂ and ♀ appear)

ABILITIES
● Chlorophyll
● Solar Power
● Early Bird

National Pokédex No. 203
Girafarig
Appears at Dream Point Level
● 2

MINIGAME
● Ice Cream Scoop
(both ♂ and ♀ appear)

ABILITIES
● Inner Focus
● Early Bird
● Sap Sipper

National Pokédex No. 234
Stantler
Appears at Dream Point Level
● 2

MINIGAME
● Lights Out!
(both ♂ and ♀ appear)

ABILITIES
● Intimidate
● Frisk
● Sap Sipper

National Pokédex No. 239
Elekid
Appears at Dream Point Level
● 3

MINIGAME
● Frozen Treat Sweep
(both ♂ and ♀ appear)

ABILITIES
● Static
●
● Vital Spirit

National Pokédex No. 241
Miltank
Appears at Dream Point Level
● 2

MINIGAME
● Frozen Treat Sweep
(♀ appear)

ABILITIES
● Thick Fat
● Scrappy
● Sap Sipper

National Pokédex No. 261
Poochyena
Appears at Dream Point Level
● 1

MINIGAME
● Lights Out!
(both ♂ and ♀ appear)

ABILITIES
● Run Away
● Quick Feet
● Rattled

National Pokédex No. 263
Zigzagoon
Appears at Dream Point Level
● 2

MINIGAME
● Frozen Treat Sweep
(both ♂ and ♀ appear)

ABILITIES
● Pickup
● Gluttony
● Quick Feet

National Pokédex No. 283
Surskit
Appears at Dream Point Level
● 1

MINIGAME
● Pokémon Bistro
(both ♂ and ♀ appear)

ABILITIES
● Swift Swim
●
● Rain Dish

National Pokédex No. 300
Skitty
Appears at Dream Point Level
● 3

MINIGAME
● Lights Out!
(both ♂ and ♀ appear)

ABILITIES
● Cute Charm
● Normalize
● Wonder Skin

National Pokédex No. 399
Bidoof
Appears at Dream Point Level
● 1

MINIGAME
● Pokémon Bistro
(both ♂ and ♀ appear)

ABILITIES
● Simple
● Unaware
● Moody

National Pokédex No. 403
Shinx
Appears at Dream Point Level
● 1

MINIGAME
● Frozen Treat Sweep
(both ♂ and ♀ appear)

ABILITIES
● Rivalry
● Intimidate
● Guts

National Pokédex No. 427
Buneary
Appears at Dream Point Level
● 2

MINIGAME
● Pokémon Bistro
(both ♂ and ♀ appear)

ABILITIES
● Run Away
● Klutz
● Limber

National Pokédex No. 431
Glameow
Appears at Dream Point Level
● 2

MINIGAME
● Pokémon Seek
(both ♂ and ♀ appear)

ABILITIES
● Limber
● Own Tempo
● Keen Eye

Pokémon that can be befriended in the Pokémon Dream World

National Pokédex No. 535
Tympole
Appears at Dream Point Level 
● 1

MINIGAME
● Frozen Treat Sweep (both ♂ and ♀ appear)

ABILITIES
● Swift Swim
● Hydration
● Water Absorb

National Pokédex No. 545
Scolipede
Appears at Dream Point Level
● 2

MINIGAME
● Lights Out! (both ♂ and ♀ appear)

ABILITIES
● Poison Point
● Swarm
● Quick Feet

National Pokédex No. 546
Cottonee
Appears at Dream Point Level
● 1

MINIGAME
● Pokémon Bistro (both ♂ and ♀ appear)

ABILITIES
● Prankster
● Infiltrator
● Chlorophyll

National Pokédex No. 548
Petilil
Appears at Dream Point Level
● 1

MINIGAME
● Frozen Treat Sweep (♀ appear)

ABILITIES
● Chlorophyll
● Own Tempo
● Leaf Guard

National Pokédex No. 588
Karrablast
Appears at Dream Point Level
● 1

MINIGAME
● Lights Out! (both ♂ and ♀ appear)

ABILITIES
● Swarm
● Shed Skin
● No Guard

National Pokédex No. 616
Shelmet
Appears at Dream Point Level
● 1

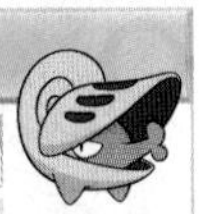

MINIGAME
● Ice Cream Scoop (both ♂ and ♀ appear)

ABILITIES
● Hydration
● Shell Armor
● Overcoat

⊙ Windswept Sky

National Pokédex No. 016
Pidgey
Appears at Dream Point Level 
● 1

MINIGAME
● Pokémon Seek (♂ appear)
● Treasure Box (♀ appear)

ABILITIES
● Keen Eye
● Tangled Feet
● Big Pecks

National Pokédex No. 021
Spearow
Appears at Dream Point Level
● 1

MINIGAME
● Pokémon Seek (both ♂ and ♀ appear)

ABILITIES
● Keen Eye
● —
● Sniper

National Pokédex No. 041
Zubat
Appears at Dream Point Level
● 1

MINIGAME
● Collect Gems with Sableye (both ♂ and ♀ appear)

ABILITIES
● Inner Focus
● —
● Infiltrator

National Pokédex No. 142
Aerodactyl
Appears at Dream Point Level
● 1

MINIGAME
● Sky Race (both ♂ and ♀ appear)

ABILITIES
● Rock Head
● Pressure
● Unnerve

National Pokédex No. 165
Ledyba
Appears at Dream Point Level
● 1

MINIGAME
● Treasure Box (both ♂ and ♀ appear)

ABILITIES
● Swarm
● Early Bird
● Rattled

National Pokédex No. 187
Hoppip
Appears at Dream Point Level
● 1

MINIGAME
● Treasure Box (both ♂ and ♀ appear)

ABILITIES
● Chlorophyll
● Leaf Guard
● Infiltrator

National Pokédex No. 193
Yanma
Appears at Dream Point Level
● 1

MINIGAME
● Collect Gems with Sableye (both ♂ and ♀ appear)

ABILITIES
● Speed Boost
● Compoundeyes
● Frisk

National Pokédex No. 198
Murkrow
Appears at Dream Point Level
● 1

MINIGAME
● Pokémon Seek (both ♂ and ♀ appear)

ABILITIES
● Insomnia
● Super Luck
● Prankster

National Pokédex No. 207
Gligar
Appears at Dream Point Level
● 1

MINIGAME
● Treasure Box (both ♂ and ♀ appear)

ABILITIES
● Hyper Cutter
● Sand Veil
● Immunity

National Pokédex No. 225
Delibird
Appears at Dream Point Level
● 1

MINIGAME
● Sky Race (♂ appear)
● Pokémon Seek (♀ appear)

ABILITIES
● Vital Spirit
● Hustle
● Insomnia

National Pokédex No. 227
Skarmory
Appears at Dream Point Level
● 2

MINIGAME
● Treasure Box (both ♂ and ♀ appear)

ABILITIES
● Keen Eye
● Sturdy
● Weak Armor

National Pokédex No. 276
Taillow
Appears at Dream Point Level
● 1

MINIGAME
● Collect Gems with Sableye (both ♂ and ♀ appear)

ABILITIES
● Guts
● —
● Scrappy

National Pokédex No. 357
Tropius
Appears at Dream Point Level
● 2

MINIGAME
● Treasure Box (both ♂ and ♀ appear)

ABILITIES
● Chlorophyll
● Solar Power
● Harvest

National Pokédex No. 397
Staravia
Appears at Dream Point Level
● 1

MINIGAME
● Collect Gems with Sableye (both ♂ and ♀ appear)

ABILITIES
● Intimidate
● —
● Reckless

National Pokédex No. 519
Pidove
Appears at Dream Point Level
● 1

MINIGAME
● Treasure Box (both ♂ and ♀ appear)

ABILITIES
● Big Pecks
● Super Luck
● Rivalry

National Pokédex No. 561
Sigilyph
Appears at Dream Point Level
● 1

MINIGAME
● Collect Gems with Sableye (both ♂ and ♀ appear)

ABILITIES
● Wonder Skin
● Magic Guard
● Tinted Lens

National Pokédex No. 580
Ducklett
Appears at Dream Point Level
● 1

MINIGAME
● Sky Race (both ♂ and ♀ appear)

ABILITIES
● Keen Eye
● Big Pecks
● Hydration

National Pokédex No. 587
Emolga
Appears at Dream Point Level
● 2

MINIGAME
● Sky Race (both ♂ and ♀ appear)

ABILITIES
● Static
● —
● Motor Drive

⊙ Sparkling Sea

National Pokédex No. 072
Tentacool
Appears at Dream Point Level 
● 2

MINIGAME
● Frozen Treat Sweep (both ♂ and ♀ appear)

ABILITIES
● Clear Body
● Liquid Ooze
● Rain Dish

National Pokédex No. 086
Seel
Appears at Dream Point Level
● 2

MINIGAME
● Sky Race (both ♂ and ♀ appear)

ABILITIES
● Thick Fat
● Hydration
● Ice Body

National Pokédex No. 090
Shellder
Appears at Dream Point Level
● 2

MINIGAME
● Pokémon Bistro (both ♂ and ♀ appear)

ABILITIES
● Shell Armor
● Skill Link
● Overcoat

National Pokédex No. 116
Horsea
Appears at Dream Point Level
● 1

MINIGAME
● Pokémon Bistro (both ♂ and ♀ appear)

ABILITIES
● Swift Swim
● Sniper
● Damp

National Pokédex No. 118
Goldeen
Appears at Dream Point Level
● 1

MINIGAME
● Wailord's Water Spout (both ♂ and ♀ appear)

ABILITIES
● Swift Swim
● Water Veil
● Lightningrod

National Pokédex No. 129
Magikarp
Appears at Dream Point Level
● 1

MINIGAME
● Sky Race (both ♂ and ♀ appear)

ABILITIES
● Swift Swim
● —
● Rattled

National Pokédex No. 131
Lapras
Appears at Dream Point Level
● 3

MINIGAME
● Frozen Treat Sweep (both ♂ and ♀ appear)

ABILITIES
● Water Absorb
● Shell Armor
● Hydration

National Pokédex No. 138
Omanyte
Appears at Dream Point Level
● 1

MINIGAME
● Pokémon Bistro (both ♂ and ♀ appear)

ABILITIES
● Swift Swim
● Shell Armor
● Weak Armor

National Pokédex No. 140
Kabuto
Appears at Dream Point Level
● 1

MINIGAME
● Pokémon Bistro (both ♂ and ♀ appear)

ABILITIES
● Swift Swim
● Battle Armor
● Weak Armor

National Pokédex No. 147
Dratini
Appears at Dream Point Level
● 3

MINIGAME
● Frozen Treat Sweep (both ♂ and ♀ appear)

ABILITIES
● Shed Skin
● —
● Marvel Scale

National Pokédex No. 170
Chinchou
Appears at Dream Point Level
● 2

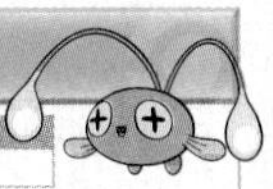

MINIGAME
● Sky Race (♂ appear)
● Pokémon Bistro (♀ appear)

ABILITIES
● Volt Absorb
● Illuminate
● Water Absorb

Pokémon that can be befriended in the Pokémon Dream World

National Pokédex No. 194 — Wooper
Appears at Dream Point Level
- 1

MINIGAME
- Wailord's Water Spout (both ♂ and ♀ appear)

ABILITIES
- Damp
- Water Absorb
- Unaware

National Pokédex No. 211 — Qwilfish
Appears at Dream Point Level
- 1

MINIGAME
- Pokémon Seek (both ♂ and ♀ appear)

ABILITIES
- Poison Point
- Swift Swim
- Intimidate

National Pokédex No. 223 — Remoraid
Appears at Dream Point Level
- 1

MINIGAME
- Frozen Treat Sweep (both ♂ and ♀ appear)

ABILITIES
- Hustle
- Sniper
- Moody

National Pokédex No. 226 — Mantine
Appears at Dream Point Level
- 1

MINIGAME
- Frozen Treat Sweep (both ♂ and ♀ appear)

ABILITIES
- Swift Swim
- Water Absorb
- Water Veil

National Pokédex No. 318 — Carvanha
Appears at Dream Point Level
- 2

MINIGAME
- Wailord's Water Spout (both ♂ and ♀ appear)

ABILITIES
- Rough Skin
- —
- Speed Boost

National Pokédex No. 320 — Wailmer
Appears at Dream Point Level
- 1

MINIGAME
- Frozen Treat Sweep (both ♂ and ♀ appear)

ABILITIES
- Water Veil
- Oblivious
- Pressure

National Pokédex No. 339 — Barboach
Appears at Dream Point Level
- 1

MINIGAME
- Sky Race (both ♂ and ♀ appear)

ABILITIES
- Oblivious
- Anticipation
- Hydration

National Pokédex No. 341 — Corphish
Appears at Dream Point Level
- 2

MINIGAME
- Frozen Treat Sweep (both ♂ and ♀ appear)

ABILITIES
- Hyper Cutter
- Shell Armor
- Adaptability

National Pokédex No. 345 — Lileep
Appears at Dream Point Level
- 2

MINIGAME
- Pokémon Seek (both ♂ and ♀ appear)

ABILITIES
- Suction Cups
- —
- Storm Drain

National Pokédex No. 347 — Anorith
Appears at Dream Point Level
- 2

MINIGAME
- Pokémon Seek (both ♂ and ♀ appear)

ABILITIES
- Battle Armor
- —
- Swift Swim

National Pokédex No. 349 — Feebas
Appears at Dream Point Level
- 2

MINIGAME
- Wailord's Water Spout (both ♂ and ♀ appear)

ABILITIES
- Swift Swim
- —
- Adaptability

National Pokédex No. 366 — Clamperl
Appears at Dream Point Level
- 1

MINIGAME
- Wailord's Water Spout (both ♂ and ♀ appear)

ABILITIES
- Shell Armor
- —
- Rattled

National Pokédex No. 369 — Relicanth
Appears at Dream Point Level
- 1

MINIGAME
- Pokémon Seek (both ♂ and ♀ appear)

ABILITIES
- Swift Swim
- Rock Head
- Sturdy

National Pokédex No. 370 — Luvdisc
Appears at Dream Point Level
- 1

MINIGAME
- Pokémon Bistro (both ♂ and ♀ appear)

ABILITIES
- Swift Swim
- —
- Hydration

National Pokédex No. 418 — Buizel
Appears at Dream Point Level
- 1

MINIGAME
- Frozen Treat Sweep (both ♂ and ♀ appear)

ABILITIES
- Swift Swim
- —
- Water Veil

National Pokédex No. 456 — Finneon
Appears at Dream Point Level
- 1

MINIGAME
- Wailord's Water Spout (both ♂ and ♀ appear)

ABILITIES
- Swift Swim
- Storm Drain
- Water Veil

National Pokédex No. 550 — Basculin (Blue-Striped Form)
Appears at Dream Point Level
- 1

MINIGAME
- Pokémon Seek (both ♂ and ♀ appear)

ABILITIES
- Rock Head
- Adaptability
- Mold Breaker

National Pokédex No. 550 — Basculin (Red-Striped Form)
Appears at Dream Point Level
- 1

MINIGAME
- Pokémon Seek (both ♂ and ♀ appear)

ABILITIES
- Reckless
- Adaptability
- Mold Breaker

National Pokédex No. 564 — Tirtouga
Appears at Dream Point Level
- 2

MINIGAME
- Pokémon Bistro (both ♂ and ♀ appear)

ABILITIES
- Solid Rock
- Sturdy
- Swift Swim

National Pokédex No. 594 — Alomomola
Appears at Dream Point Level
- 1

MINIGAME
- Pokémon Bistro (both ♂ and ♀ appear)

ABILITIES
- Healer
- Hydration
- Regenerator

National Pokédex No. 618 — Stunfisk
Appears at Dream Point Level
- 1

MINIGAME
- Sky Race (both ♂ and ♀ appear)

ABILITIES
- Static
- Limber
- Sand Veil

Spooky Manor
< ∨

National Pokédex No. 063 — Abra
Appears at Dream Point Level
- 3

MINIGAME
- Lights Out! (both ♂ and ♀ appear)

ABILITIES
- Synchronize
- Inner Focus
- Magic Guard

National Pokédex No. 092 — Gastly
Appears at Dream Point Level
- 1

MINIGAME
- Pokémon Seek (both ♂ and ♀ appear)

ABILITIES
- Levitate
- —
- —

National Pokédex No. 096 — Drowzee
Appears at Dream Point Level
- 1

MINIGAME
- Ice Cream Scoop (both ♂ and ♀ appear)

ABILITIES
- Insomnia
- Forewarn
- Inner Focus

National Pokédex No. 122 — Mr. Mime
Appears at Dream Point Level
- 1

MINIGAME
- Pokémon Seek (both ♂ and ♀ appear)

ABILITIES
- Soundproof
- Filter
- Technician

National Pokédex No. 167 — Spinarak
Appears at Dream Point Level
- 1

MINIGAME
- Ice Cream Scoop (both ♂ and ♀ appear)

ABILITIES
- Swarm
- Insomnia
- Sniper

National Pokédex No. 200 — Misdreavus
Appears at Dream Point Level
- 1

MINIGAME
- Wailord's Water Spout (♂ appear)
- Collect Gems with Sableye (♀ appear)

ABILITIES
- Levitate
- —
- —

National Pokédex No. 209 — Snubbull
Appears at Dream Point Level
- 2

MINIGAME
- Lights Out! (both ♂ and ♀ appear)

ABILITIES
- Intimidate
- Run Away
- Rattled

National Pokédex No. 228 — Houndour
Appears at Dream Point Level
- 1

MINIGAME
- Wailord's Water Spout (both ♂ and ♀ appear)

ABILITIES
- Early Bird
- Flash Fire
- Unnerve

National Pokédex No. 235 — Smeargle
Appears at Dream Point Level
- 2

MINIGAME
- Pokémon Seek (both ♂ and ♀ appear)

ABILITIES
- Own Tempo
- Technician
- Moody

National Pokédex No. 313 — Volbeat
Appears at Dream Point Level
- 2

MINIGAME
- Pokémon Seek (♂ appear)

ABILITIES
- Illuminate
- Swarm
- Prankster

National Pokédex No. 314 — Illumise
Appears at Dream Point Level
- 2

MINIGAME
- Lights Out! (♀ appear)

ABILITIES
- Oblivious
- Tinted Lens
- Prankster

National Pokédex No. 325 — Spoink
Appears at Dream Point Level
- 1

MINIGAME
- Collect Gems with Sableye (both ♂ and ♀ appear)

ABILITIES
- Thick Fat
- Own Tempo
- Gluttony

National Pokédex No. 353 — Shuppet
Appears at Dream Point Level
- 1

MINIGAME
- Ice Cream Scoop (both ♂ and ♀ appear)

ABILITIES
- Insomnia
- Frisk
- Cursed Body

National Pokédex No. 355 — Duskull
Appears at Dream Point Level
- 1

MINIGAME
- Collect Gems with Sableye (both ♂ and ♀ appear)

ABILITIES
- Levitate
- —
- —

National Pokédex No. 358 — Chimecho
Appears at Dream Point Level
- 1

MINIGAME
- Ice Cream Scoop (both ♂ and ♀ appear)

ABILITIES
- Levitate
- —
- —

National Pokédex No. 434
Stunky
Appears at Dream Point Level
● 1
MINIGAME
● Collect Gems with Sableye (both ♂ and ♀ appear)
ABILITIES
● Stench
● Aftermath
● Keen Eye

National Pokédex No. 578
Duosion
Appears at Dream Point Level
● 3
MINIGAME
● Wailord's Water Spout (both ♂ and ♀ appear)
ABILITIES
● Overcoat
● Magic Guard
● Regenerator

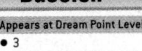

National Pokédex No. 596
Galvantula
Appears at Dream Point Level
● 2
MINIGAME
● Ice Cream Scoop (both ♂ and ♀ appear)
ABILITIES
● Compoundeyes
● Unnerve
● Swarm

National Pokédex No. 605
Elgyem
Appears at Dream Point Level
● 1
MINIGAME
● Lights Out! (both ♂ and ♀ appear)
ABILITIES
● Telepathy
● Synchronize
● Analytic

National Pokédex No. 622
Golett
Appears at Dream Point Level
● 3
MINIGAME
● Collect Gems with Sableye
ABILITIES
● Iron Fist
● Klutz
● No Guard

National Pokédex No. 624
Pawniard
Appears at Dream Point Level
● 1
MINIGAME
● Lights Out! (both ♂ and ♀ appear)
ABILITIES
● Defiant
● Inner Focus
● Pressure

◉ Rugged Mountain

National Pokédex No. 066
Machop
Appears at Dream Point Level
● 1
MINIGAME
● Collect Gems with Sableye (both ♂ and ♀ appear)
ABILITIES
● Guts
● No Guard
● Steadfast

National Pokédex No. 081
Magnemite
Appears at Dream Point Level
● 1
MINIGAME
● Sky Race
ABILITIES
● Magnet Pull
● Sturdy
● Analytic

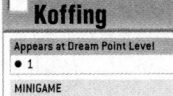

National Pokédex No. 109
Koffing
Appears at Dream Point Level
● 1
MINIGAME
● Treasure Box (both ♂ and ♀ appear)
ABILITIES
● Levitate
● —
● —

National Pokédex No. 218
Slugma
Appears at Dream Point Level
● 1
MINIGAME
● Lights Out! (both ♂ and ♀ appear)
ABILITIES
● Magma Armor
● Flame Body
● Weak Armor

National Pokédex No. 236
Tyrogue
Appears at Dream Point Level
● 3
MINIGAME
● Treasure Box (♂ appear)
ABILITIES
● Guts
● Steadfast
● Vital Spirit

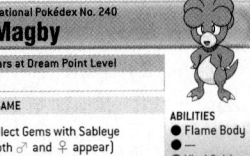

National Pokédex No. 240
Magby
Appears at Dream Point Level
● 2
MINIGAME
● Collect Gems with Sableye (both ♂ and ♀ appear)
ABILITIES
● Flame Body
● —
● Vital Spirit

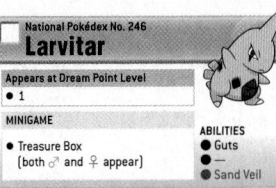

National Pokédex No. 246
Larvitar
Appears at Dream Point Level
● 1
MINIGAME
● Treasure Box (both ♂ and ♀ appear)
ABILITIES
● Guts
● —
● Sand Veil

National Pokédex No. 322
Numel
Appears at Dream Point Level
● 2
MINIGAME
● Collect Gems with Sableye (both ♂ and ♀ appear)
ABILITIES
● Oblivious
● Simple
● Own Tempo

National Pokédex No. 324
Torkoal
Appears at Dream Point Level
● 1
MINIGAME
● Lights Out! (both ♂ and ♀ appear)
ABILITIES
● White Smoke
● —
● Shell Armor

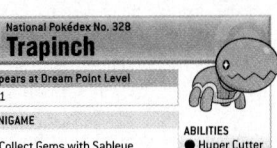

National Pokédex No. 328
Trapinch
Appears at Dream Point Level
● 1
MINIGAME
● Collect Gems with Sableye (both ♂ and ♀ appear)
ABILITIES
● Hyper Cutter
● Arena Trap
● Sheer Force

National Pokédex No. 331
Cacnea
Appears at Dream Point Level
● 1
MINIGAME
● Sky Race (both ♂ and ♀ appear)
ABILITIES
● Sand Veil
● —
● Water Absorb

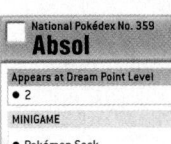

National Pokédex No. 359
Absol
Appears at Dream Point Level
● 2
MINIGAME
● Pokémon Seek (both ♂ and ♀ appear)
ABILITIES
● Pressure
● Super Luck
● Justified

National Pokédex No. 371
Bagon
Appears at Dream Point Level
● 3
MINIGAME
● Treasure Box (both ♂ and ♀ appear)
ABILITIES
● Rock Head
● —
● Sheer Force

National Pokédex No. 412
Burmy (Sandy Cloak)
Appears at Dream Point Level
● 1
MINIGAME
● Collect Gems with Sableye (both ♂ and ♀ appear)
ABILITIES
● Shed Skin
● —
● Overcoat

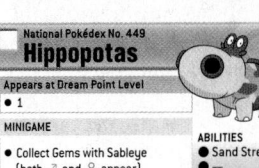

National Pokédex No. 449
Hippopotas
Appears at Dream Point Level
● 1
MINIGAME
● Collect Gems with Sableye (both ♂ and ♀ appear)
ABILITIES
● Sand Stream
● —
● Sand Force

National Pokédex No. 453
Croagunk
Appears at Dream Point Level
● 2
MINIGAME
● Pokémon Seek (both ♂ and ♀ appear)
ABILITIES
● Anticipation
● Dry Skin
● Poison Touch

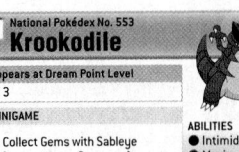

National Pokédex No. 553
Krookodile
Appears at Dream Point Level
● 3
MINIGAME
● Collect Gems with Sableye (both ♂ and ♀ appear)
ABILITIES
● Intimidate
● Moxie
● Anger Point

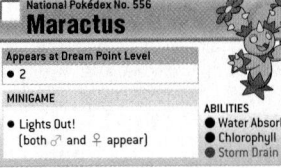

National Pokédex No. 556
Maractus
Appears at Dream Point Level
● 2
MINIGAME
● Lights Out! (both ♂ and ♀ appear)
ABILITIES
● Water Absorb
● Chlorophyll
● Storm Drain

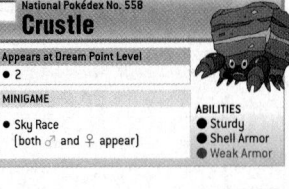

National Pokédex No. 558
Crustle
Appears at Dream Point Level
● 2
MINIGAME
● Sky Race (both ♂ and ♀ appear)
ABILITIES
● Sturdy
● Shell Armor
● Weak Armor

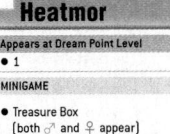

National Pokédex No. 631
Heatmor
Appears at Dream Point Level
● 1
MINIGAME
● Treasure Box (both ♂ and ♀ appear)
ABILITIES
● Gluttony
● Flash Fire
● White Smoke

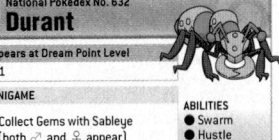

National Pokédex No. 632
Durant
Appears at Dream Point Level
● 1
MINIGAME
● Collect Gems with Sableye (both ♂ and ♀ appear)
ABILITIES
● Swarm
● Hustle
● Truant

◉ Icy Cave

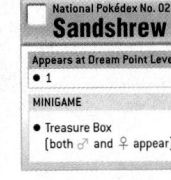

National Pokédex No. 027
Sandshrew
Appears at Dream Point Level
● 1
MINIGAME
● Treasure Box (both ♂ and ♀ appear)
ABILITIES
● Sand Veil
● —
● Sand Rush

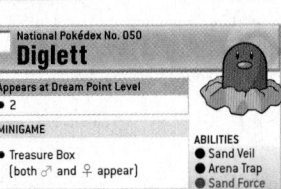

National Pokédex No. 050
Diglett
Appears at Dream Point Level
● 2
MINIGAME
● Treasure Box (both ♂ and ♀ appear)
ABILITIES
● Sand Veil
● Arena Trap
● Sand Force

National Pokédex No. 074
Geodude
Appears at Dream Point Level
● 1
MINIGAME
● Ice Cream Scoop (both ♂ and ♀ appear)
ABILITIES
● Rock Head
● Sturdy
● Sand Veil

National Pokédex No. 095
Onix
Appears at Dream Point Level
● 1
MINIGAME
● Treasure Box (♂ appear)
● Wailord's Water Spout (♀ appear)
ABILITIES
● Rock Head
● Sturdy
● Weak Armor

National Pokédex No. 100
Voltorb
Appears at Dream Point Level
● 1
MINIGAME
● Treasure Box (♀ appear)
ABILITIES
● Soundproof
● Static
● Aftermath

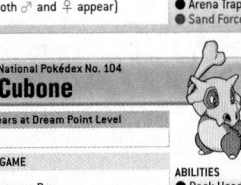

National Pokédex No. 104
Cubone
Appears at Dream Point Level
● 1
MINIGAME
● Treasure Box (both ♂ and ♀ appear)
ABILITIES
● Rock Head
● Lightningrod
● Battle Armor

National Pokédex No. 215
Sneasel
Appears at Dream Point Level
● 2
MINIGAME
● Treasure Box (both ♂ and ♀ appear)
ABILITIES
● Inner Focus
● Keen Eye
● Pickpocket

Swinub

National Pokédex No. 220

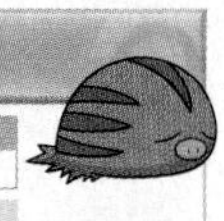

Appears at Dream Point Level
- 3

MINIGAME
- Frozen Treat Sweep (both ♂ and ♀ appear)

ABILITIES
- Oblivious
- Snow Cloak
- Thick Fat

Whismur

National Pokédex No. 293

Appears at Dream Point Level
- 1

MINIGAME
- Ice Cream Scoop (both ♂ and ♀ appear)

ABILITIES
- Soundproof
- —
- Rattled

Aron

National Pokédex No. 304

Appears at Dream Point Level
- 1

MINIGAME
- Pokémon Bistro (both ♂ and ♀ appear)

ABILITIES
- Sturdy
- Rock Head
- Heavy Metal

Lunatone

National Pokédex No. 337

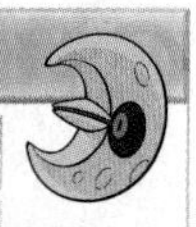

Appears at Dream Point Level
- 1

MINIGAME
- Wailord's Water Spout

ABILITIES
- Levitate
- —
- —

Solrock

National Pokédex No. 338

Appears at Dream Point Level
- 1

MINIGAME
- Wailord's Water Spout

ABILITIES
- Levitate
- —
- —

Baltoy

National Pokédex No. 343

Appears at Dream Point Level
- 1

MINIGAME
- Treasure Box

ABILITIES
- Levitate
- —
- —

Snorunt

National Pokédex No. 361

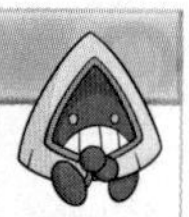

Appears at Dream Point Level
- 3

MINIGAME
- Frozen Treat Sweep (♂ appear)
- Pokémon Bistro (♀ appear)

ABILITIES
- Inner Focus
- Ice Body
- Moody

Gible

National Pokédex No. 443

Appears at Dream Point Level
- 3

MINIGAME
- Pokémon Bistro (both ♂ and ♀ appear)

ABILITIES
- Sand Veil
- —
- Rough Skin

Snover

National Pokédex No. 459

Appears at Dream Point Level
- 1

MINIGAME
- Pokémon Bistro (both ♂ and ♀ appear)

ABILITIES
- Snow Warning
- —
- Soundproof

Boldore

National Pokédex No. 525

Appears at Dream Point Level
- 2

MINIGAME
- Frozen Treat Sweep (both ♂ and ♀ appear)

ABILITIES
- Sturdy
- —
- Sand Force

Drilbur

National Pokédex No. 529

Appears at Dream Point Level
- 1

MINIGAME
- Frozen Treat Sweep (both ♂ and ♀ appear)

ABILITIES
- Sand Rush
- Sand Force
- Mold Breaker

Vanillish

National Pokédex No. 583

Appears at Dream Point Level
- 2

MINIGAME
- Ice Cream Scoop (both ♂ and ♀ appear)

ABILITIES
- Ice Body
- —
- Weak Armor

Klang

National Pokédex No. 600

Appears at Dream Point Level
- 2

MINIGAME
- Wailord's Water Spout

ABILITIES
- Plus
- Minus
- Clear Body

Axew

National Pokédex No. 610

Appears at Dream Point Level
- 3

MINIGAME
- Frozen Treat Sweep (both ♂ and ♀ appear)

ABILITIES
- Rivalry
- Mold Breaker
- Unnerve

Druddigon

National Pokédex No. 621

Appears at Dream Point Level
- 1

MINIGAME
- Frozen Treat Sweep (both ♂ and ♀ appear)

ABILITIES
- Rough Skin
- Sheer Force
- Mold Breaker

Get valuable items in the Pokémon Dream World

Sometimes you will find items when you visit the Island of Dreams. If you see a shining place, be sure to click it! The items you find can be sent back to *Pokémon Black Version 2* and *Pokémon White Version 2* just like you can send Pokémon.

Items you can get in the Pokémon Dream World

🌀 Pleasant Forest

Level	Item
1	Cheri Berry
	Figy Berry
	Heal Ball
	Nest Ball
	Net Ball
	Oran Berry
	Pass Orb
	Pecha Berry
	Poké Ball
	Sitrus Berry
	Super Potion
	Ether
	Great Ball
	Lagging Tail
2	Moomoo Milk
	Mystic Water
	Sharp Beak
	TinyMushroom
	Big Mushroom
3	Stick
	Wide Lens

🌀 Windswept Sky

Level	Item
1	Aguav Berry
	Aspear Berry
	Grepa Berry
	Hondew Berry
	Hyper Potion
	Iapapa Berry
	Kelpsy Berry
	Pass Orb
	Persim Berry
	Pomeg Berry
	Qualot Berry
	Quick Ball
	Tamato Berry
2	Metronome
	SilverPowder
	Stardust
	Ultra Ball
3	Star Piece
	Wide Lens

🌀 Sparkling Sea

Level	Item
1	Chesto Berry
	Dive Ball
	Full Heal
	Mago Berry
	Pass Orb
	Rawst Berry
	Super Potion
	Wiki Berry
2	Big Root
	Hard Stone
	Heart Scale
	Pearl
	Poison Barb
	Revive
3	Big Pearl

🌀 Spooky Manor

Level	Item
1	Bluk Berry
	Calcium
	Carbos
	Elixir
	HP Up
	Iron
	Lum Berry
	Max Ether
	Nanab Berry
	Old Gateau
	Pass Orb
	Protein
	Razz Berry
	Zinc
	Rare Candy
2	Spell Tag
	TwistedSpoon
	Cleanse Tag
3	Reaper Cloth
	Red Card

🌀 Rugged Mountain

Level	Item
1	Black Belt
	Charcoal
	Cornn Berry
	Everstone
	Float Stone
	Magost Berry
	Metal Coat
	Pass Orb
	Pinap Berry
	Repeat Ball
	Soft Sand
	Timer Ball
	Wepear Berry
	Dawn Stone
	Dragon Fang
	Fire Stone
	Leaf Stone
2	Oval Stone
	Rare Candy
	Sticky Barb
	Thunderstone
	Water Stone
	Comet Shard
	Dusk Stone
3	Moon Stone
	Shiny Stone
	Sun Stone

🌀 Icy Cave

Level	Item	Level	Item
1	Belue Berry	2	Blue Shard
	Bug Gem		Green Shard
	Dark Gem		Heart Scale
	Dragon Gem		Rare Bone
	Durin Berry		Red Shard
	Dusk Ball		Yellow Shard
	Electric Gem	3	Damp Rock
	Fighting Gem		Heat Rock
	Fire Gem		Icy Rock
	Flying Gem		Iron Ball
	Ghost Gem		Light Clay
	Grass Gem		NeverMeltIce
	Ground Gem		Rare Candy
	Ice Gem		Smooth Rock
	Leppa Berry		
	Normal Gem		
	Pass Orb		
	Poison Gem		
	Psychic Gem		
	Revive		
	Rock Gem		
	Steel Gem		
	Water Gem		
	Watmel Berry		

National Pokédex Completion Tip 18

Bring Pokémon over from *Pokémon Dream Radar*

Bring Pokémon over from *Pokémon Dream Radar* using Unova Link

Nintendo 3DS Link can be accessed from Unova Link on the main menu. It brings over Pokémon and items from the Nintendo 3DS download software *Pokémon Dream Radar* to *Pokémon Black Version 2* or *Pokémon White Version 2*. Insert *Pokémon Black Version 2* or *Pokémon White Version 2* into your Nintendo 3DS system, and when you receive the research data that was sent, the Pokémon will be transferred.

NINTENDO 3DS LINK

Receiving research data from Pokémon Dream Radar...

Pokémon Dream Radar for the Nintendo 3DS

Catch the Pokémon found in a place called the Interdream Zone in this virtual shooting game. Shoot at the Dream Clouds that float around in this space to find hiding Pokémon or discover items.

How *Pokémon Dream Radar* works

Survey Phase Shoot at Dream Clouds to search for Pokémon

In this Phase, you shoot a Beam at Dream Clouds. You then collect the Pokémon, items, or balls of energy called Dream Orbs that come out of the clouds by shooting the Beam at them. Use Dream Orbs you collected by hitting them with the Beam to power up your equipment in the upgrade phase.

Battle Phase Keep hitting the Pokémon with the Beam to catch it

You catch Pokémon in this phase. Continue to hit the Pokémon with the Beam as it moves around. You can catch the Pokémon by hitting it with the Beam until the gauge in the upper left of the screen is full. If your time runs out, the Pokémon will get away.

Professor Burnet

Strengthening Phase Prepare for your next search by upgrading your device

In this phase, you upgrade your device. Use Dream Orbs to power up your Beam and make it easier to catch Pokémon. If you enhance your Visoscope, you can find more Dream Clouds.

Beam
Lv. 1
Energy Pack
Lv. 1
Support Items
Increases the power of your Beam for catching Pokémon.
Lv. 1

Game Information

Pokémon Dream Radar
- Publisher: The Pokémon Company
- Distributor: Nintendo
- Developer: Creatures Inc. / GAME FREAK inc.
- Platform: Nintendo 3DS
- Genre: Virtual Shooting
- Players: 1
- Connectivity: None
- Release Date: October 7, 2012 (Sunday)
- Rating: E

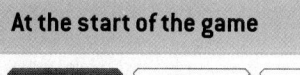 Valuable Pokémon and items await

Catch Therian Forme Tornadus, Thundurus, and Landorus and upgrade your device. After you do, you will come across : many more precious Pokémon and items.

Catching Pokémon and getting items in *Pokémon Dream Radar*

At the start of the game

Pokémon that can be found	 Drifloon	 Swablu	 Munna	 Sigilyph	 Riolu

Items that can be found	
Blue Shard	Red Shard
Green Shard	Revive
Leppa Berry	Yellow Shard
PP Up	

You can catch Therian Forme Tornadus

After you catch Therian Forme Tornadus...

Pokémon that can be found	 Shuckle	 Igglybuff

Items that can be found
Max Revive
Moon Stone
Sun Stone

You can catch Therian Forme Thundurus

After you catch Therian Forme Thundurus...

Pokémon that can be found	 Staryu	 Bronzor	 Porygon	 Ralts

Items that can be found
Fire Stone
Leaf Stone
Thunderstone
Water Stone

You can catch Therian Forme Landorus

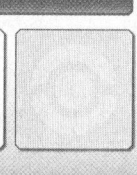

After you catch Therian Forme Landorus...

Pokémon that can be found	 Smoochum	 Spiritomb	 Togepi	 Rotom

Items that can be found
Rare Candy
Sacred Ash

 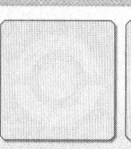   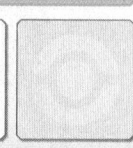

Items you can find with Simulator α

Items you can get when you catch Tornadus
Heart Scale
Life Orb
Max Revive
PP Up
Rare Candy
Star Piece

Items you can find with Simulator β

Items you can get when you catch Thundurus
Dawn Stone
Focus Sash
Heart Scale
King's Rock
Rare Candy
Star Piece

Items you can find with Simulator γ

Items you can get when you catch Landorus
Eviolite
Focus Sash
Heart Scale
Life Orb
Rare Candy
Star Piece

Pokémon Black Version 2 & Pokémon White Version 2: The Official National Pokédex & Guide

Communication Features Guide

Try the Communication Features

Communication features expand your gameplay of *Pokémon Black 2* and *Pokémon White 2*

Use the communication functions in *Pokémon Black 2* and *Pokémon White 2* to enjoy many features as well as battle and trade with your friends. There are three different communication functions: IR, Wireless, and Online (Nintendo Wi-Fi Connection). Each one provides different gameplay features. Try them depending on what you want to play and your communication environment.

The three communication functions available in *Pokémon Black 2* and *Pokémon White 2*

IR (Infrared)

This is the simplest way to link up with your nearby friends and family members. No special equipment is necessary. Just face your systems toward each other to trade, battle, etc.

Main Features

- ◎ Battle
- ◎ Trade
- ◎ Feeling Check

See p. 417 for IR. ▶

Wireless

This communication method allows you to play with people up to 30 feet away. Link up with your friends and family or even new people, and play in the Entralink, Union Room, etc.

Main Features

- ◎ Xtransceiver
- ◎ Entralink
- ◎ Union Room

See p. 418 for wireless communication. ▶

Online (Nintendo Wi-Fi Connection)

Set up your system for Nintendo Wi-Fi Connection (Nintendo WFC) and you can use these features. Exchange Friend Codes with your friends and you can have fun with them no matter where they are!

Main Features

- ◎ Wi-Fi Club
- ◎ Global Terminal
- ◎ Xtransceiver

See p. 419 for Nintendo WFC. ▶

The Pokémon Global Link has been updated

The Pokémon Global Link is a website where you can visit a Pokémon's dream world and check battle records of players all over the world. It was dramatically updated for the release of *Pokémon Black Version 2* and *Pokémon White Version 2*. Access it with a PC and a router connected to the Internet to connect to Nintendo Wi-Fi Connection.

Main Features

- ◎ Pokémon Dream World
- ◎ Global Battle Union
- ◎ Customize

See p. 420 for the Pokémon Global Link. ▶

Enjoy the new features of *Pokémon Black 2* and *Pokémon White 2*

Pokémon Black Version 2 and *Pokémon White Version 2* have new elements that use communication features. Develop an avenue on Join Avenue, and try a lot of Funfest Missions. Also, you can receive different surveys from those in *Pokémon Black Version* and *Pokémon White Version* at Passerby Analytics.

New features of *Pokémon Black 2* and *Pokémon White 2*

Join Avenue

Join Avenue is a large avenue located between Route 4 and Nimbasa City. There's not much to see when you first visit there, but once you become a manager, you can build various shops. Many visitors come to the avenue. Let them be residents to run shops or recommend shops to them to develop Join Avenue.

Main game features on Join Avenue

◎ **Build shops**

Dream ★ Arhippa was built!

◎ **Shop**

A short private training session for a Pokémon. It raises the Pokémon's level by one.

◎ **Guide visitors**

If there is a shop with a male clerk, I want to go there.

◎ **Raise ranks of the avenue and shops**

Join Avenue reached Rank 5!

See p. 400 for Join Avenue. ▶

Entralink Funfest Missions

A Funfest Mission is game in which you try to achieve a target, such as collecting items and defeating Trainers. You can participate in a Funfest Mission hosted by other people and enjoy it with many others. You can also host a mission and play it by yourself if you like.

Features of Funfest Missions

◎ **Funfest Missions**

◎ **Entree**

Checked your Entrees.

See p. 408 for Funfest Missions. ▶

Tag Mode

The game features using Tag Mode have been upgraded in *Pokémon Black 2* and *Pokémon White 2*. You can get new surveys at Passerby Analytics HQ and set three different Pass Powers to give to passersby at a time.

Main game features of Tag Mode

◎ **Tag Log**

Shiro2

Steve

Marci

3 Ppl.
Total: 4

◎ **Passerby Analytics**

▶ Accept a request
Report the result
Nothing

What would you like to do today?

See p. 412 for Tag Mode. ▶

Try the Communication Features

Communications **1**

Develop Join Avenue

Become a manager to develop Join Avenue

Join Avenue is a place where you build shops and invite visitors to develop a vibrant avenue. Once you become the manager, invite visitors to be shop owners. When you recommend shops to visitors, the shops and Join Avenue become more popular and their ranks will go up.

How to develop Join Avenue

1. Invite visitors and build shops.

2. Recommend shops to visitors to raise the shops' popularity.

3. When their popularity goes up, the ranks of the avenue and the shops go up and Join Avenue will develop further.

Use various communication features to invite visitors to the avenue

Even if you don't use the communication features, a few visitors still come to Join Avenue every day. However, if you do use them, people you communicated with will visit Join Avenue. The communication features that attract visitors are listed on the right. Communicate with many people and attract a lot of visitors to the avenue.

People who come as visitors

People you passed by using Tag Mode

People you traded Pokémon with by C-Gear

People you battled by C-Gear

People you exchanged Friend Codes with by C-Gear

People you talked to in the Union Room

People you battled in a Random Matchup in the Global Terminal

People you traded Pokémon with via GTS or GTS Negotiations

People you teamed up with in a Multi Train in the Battle Subway

People you teamed up with in a Super Multi Train in the Battle Subway

People you played with in Entralink Funfest Missions

People whose homes you visited in the Pokémon Dream World

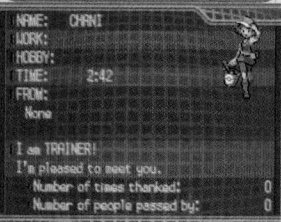

Pass by a person

NAME: CHRNI
WORK:
HOBBY:
TIME: 2:42
FROM:
None

I am TRAINER!
I'm pleased to meet you.
  Number of times thanked: 0
  Number of people passed by: 0

The passerby visits the avenue

Did you know we've passed by each other several times?

💬 Tip   Some visitors give you souvenirs

Some people who visit Join Avenue give you an item as a souvenir when you speak to them. The higher the rank of the avenue is, the better item you can get. Speak to all visitors to get a lot of souvenirs.

Invite visitors to build shops

Speak to a visitor and select "Invite" and the visitor will tell you which shop he or she wants to build out of eight different kinds of shops. Select "Make the person a resident" to build the shop. If the avenue has no more space, you can remove one existing shop and build a new shop.

Eight shops you can build and visitors' lines

Shop		Line	
	Dojo	I would want to train people's Pokémon and make them strong.	
	Market	I would want to collect a lot of things and surprise everyone.	
	Flower Shop	I would want to help everyone relax with beautiful flowers.	
	Raffle Shop	I would want to make everyone excited.	
	Beauty Salon	I would want to make people's Pokémon more beautiful.	
	Antique Shop	I would want to collect unique items and surprise everyone!	
	Café	I would want to make delicious meals for Pokémon and make them happy.	
	Nursery	I would want to spend my days helping Pokémon Eggs hatch.	

The flow to build and develop shops

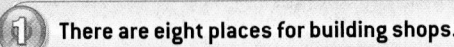
There are eight places for building shops.

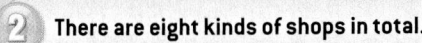
There are eight kinds of shops in total.

Shops will have more products as their ranks go up.

Recommend shops to visitors to raise popularity

Speak to a visitor and select "Recommend" and the visitor will tell you what he or she wants to do. Recommend a shop he or she wants, and the popularity of both the shop and the avenue will go up. When popularity reaches a certain point, the ranks of the shop and the avenue go up.

The flow to recommend a shop to a visitor

1 Speak to a visitor

Speak to a visitor and select "Recommend" and the visitor will tell you what he or she wants to do.

2 Select a desired shop

Choose a shop that the visitor wants among the shops on the avenue to recommend it to the visitor.

3 Popularity goes up if you succeed

If the shop you recommended is what the visitor wants, the popularity of the shop goes up. The popularity of the avenue also goes up.

 **Tip** ## Gym Leaders will visit the avenue when the rank goes up

Gym Leaders of the Unova region will come to Join Avenue if you have entered the Hall of Fame. Recommend shops that the Gym Leaders want, and the popularity goes up more than when you recommend shops to other visitors.

The owner gives you a present when the avenue's rank goes up

Join Avenue's rank goes up when the popularity goes up. When the rank reaches a certain rank, such as Rank 2 and Rank 4, the owner will give you a present. Go to the office to receive the presents.

I have a present for you today.
I've recruited a new assistant for you.

Presents from the owner

Avenue's Rank	Present from the owner
2	An assistant named Gardner comes
4	An assistant named Elethia comes
6	You can change the ceiling color
8	You can recruit a visitor who came from *Pokémon Black 2* or *Pokémon White 2* as your assistant if the visitor's avenue's rank is lower than yours
10	You can change the name of the avenue
15	You can build Nurseries, and products which become available only after the Hall of Fame will be sold
20	You can have a parade with the owner
21 and up	You can receive one of the following: Stardust, Rare Candy, Star Piece, or Comet Shard

Popularity you need to raise the avenue's rank

	Avenue's Rank											
	1	2	3	4	5	6	7	8	9–19	20–40	41–99	100
Popularity You Need	300	350	450	550	650	750	850	950	1,000	1,500	2,000	—

◆ As the avenue's rank goes up, prices at shops get slightly cheaper.

Remember the assistants' jobs

Speak to the assistants in the office, and they will provide various help to run Join Avenue. The owner will assign Gardner and Elethia as your assistants when the avenue's rank goes up.

What the assistants will do when you speak to them

Assistant Jacci

She tells you the avenue's rank and how many more points you need to reach the next rank.

She lets you change your title, favorite phrase, and what you say when impressed.

She lets you change the name of the avenue (Rank 10 and up).

She lets you have a parade (Rank 20 and up).

Assistant Future

He increases the chance that the shop you selected will be the shop visitors want to visit.

Assistant Gardner

He lets you organize your PC Box.

He lets you check your record in ranking.

He can switch roles of the assistants.

He can change the order of shops.

He can change the color of the ceiling (Rank 6 and up).

Assistant Elethia

She fully restores HP and PP of your party Pokémon.

Fully enjoy Join Avenue and collect Medals

You can receive a total of 13 different Medals on Join Avenue. You can receive the Extreme Developer Medal when you build 50 shops or more.

New Guide · Elite Guide · Veteran Guide · Guiding Champ · Shop Starter · Shop Builder · Shop Constructor

Extreme Developer · OK Souvenir Getter · Good Souvenir Getter · Great Souvenir Getter · Tycoon of Souvenirs · Avenue of Fame

Check p. 531 for the Medal list.

Dojo

Shop's Name	● Rank 1 to 3	● Rank 4 to 7	● Rank 8 and up
	(Shop owner name) Fitness	(Shop owner name)'s Ring	(Shop owner name) Colosseum

A Dojo is a place where Pokémon will be trained strong. You can raise Pokémon's levels and base stats. Select a menu item and then a Pokémon you want to train from your party. The menus are different depending on which Game Card the shop owner came from.

► Train a Pokémon
How are you doing lately?
How are you?
See you!

TRAINER Colosseum:
I work hard with your Pokémon!

The effects of the Dojo menu

Menu	Effect
Training	The level of the trained Pokémon goes up by the Lv. number.
HP	The HP base stat of the trained Pokémon goes up. The higher the Lv. is, the higher the stat goes up.
Attack	The Attack stat of the trained Pokémon goes up. The higher the Lv. is, the higher the stat goes up.
Defense	The Defense stat of the trained Pokémon goes up. The higher the Lv. is, the higher the stat goes up.
Sp. Atk	The Sp. Atk stat of the trained Pokémon goes up. The higher the Lv. is, the higher the stat goes up.
Sp. Def	The Sp. Def stat of the trained Pokémon goes up. The higher the Lv. is, the higher the stat goes up.
Speed	The Speed stat of the trained Pokémon goes up. The higher the Lv. is, the higher the stat goes up.

Menu at a Dojo
(When the shop owner came from *Pokémon Black*)

Menu	Rank	Price
Training Lv. 1	Rank 1 and up	15,000
Defense Lv. 4	Rank 1 and up	6,000
Sp. Atk Lv. 4	Rank 1 and up	6,000
Attack Lv. 8	Rank 2 and up	12,000
HP Lv. 8	Rank 3 and up	12,000
Training Lv. 2	Rank 4 and up	30,000
Sp. Def Lv. 16	Rank 4 and up	26,000
Speed Lv. 16	Rank 4 and up	26,000
Sp. Atk Lv. 24	Rank 5 and up	36,000
Defense Lv. 24	Rank 6 and up	36,000
Attack Lv. 32	Rank 7 and up	48,000
Training Lv. 3	Rank 8 and up	45,000
HP Lv. 32	Rank 8 and up	48,000
Speed Lv. 64	Rank 9 and up	96,000
Training Lv. 4	Rank 10	60,000
Sp. Def Lv. 64	Rank 10	96,000

Menu at a Dojo
(When the shop owner came from *Pokémon White*)

Menu	Rank	Price
Training Lv. 1	Rank 1 and up	15,000
Sp. Atk Lv. 4	Rank 1 and up	6,000
Sp. Def Lv. 4	Rank 1 and up	6,000
Defense Lv. 8	Rank 2 and up	12,000
Attack Lv. 8	Rank 3 and up	12,000
Training Lv. 2	Rank 4 and up	30,000
Speed Lv. 16	Rank 4 and up	26,000
HP Lv. 16	Rank 4 and up	26,000
Sp. Def Lv. 24	Rank 5 and up	36,000
Sp. Atk Lv. 24	Rank 6 and up	36,000
Defense Lv. 32	Rank 7 and up	48,000
Training Lv. 3	Rank 8 and up	45,000
Attack Lv. 32	Rank 8 and up	48,000
Speed Lv. 64	Rank 9 and up	96,000
Training Lv. 4	Rank 10	60,000
HP Lv. 64	Rank 10	96,000

Menu at a Dojo
(When the shop owner came from *Pokémon Black 2*)

Menu	Rank	Price
Training Lv. 1	Rank 1 and up	15,000
Sp. Def Lv. 4	Rank 1 and up	6,000
Speed Lv. 4	Rank 1 and up	6,000
Sp. Atk Lv. 8	Rank 2 and up	12,000
Defense Lv. 8	Rank 3 and up	12,000
Training Lv. 2	Rank 4 and up	30,000
HP Lv. 16	Rank 4 and up	26,000
Attack Lv. 16	Rank 4 and up	26,000
Speed Lv. 24	Rank 5 and up	36,000
Sp. Def Lv. 24	Rank 6 and up	36,000
Sp. Atk Lv. 32	Rank 7 and up	48,000
Training Lv. 3	Rank 8 and up	45,000
Defense Lv. 32	Rank 8 and up	48,000
Attack Lv. 64	Rank 9 and up	96,000
Training Lv. 4	Rank 10	60,000
HP Lv. 64	Rank 10	96,000

Menu at a Dojo
(When the shop owner came from *Pokémon White 2*)

Menu	Rank	Price
Training Lv. 1	Rank 1 and up	15,000
HP Lv. 4	Rank 1 and up	6,000
Attack Lv. 4	Rank 1 and up	6,000
Speed Lv. 8	Rank 2 and up	12,000
Sp. Def Lv. 8	Rank 3 and up	12,000
Training Lv. 2	Rank 4 and up	30,000
Defense Lv. 16	Rank 4 and up	26,000
Sp. Atk Lv. 16	Rank 4 and up	26,000
Attack Lv. 24	Rank 5 and up	36,000
HP Lv. 24	Rank 6 and up	36,000
Speed Lv. 32	Rank 7 and up	48,000
Training Lv. 3	Rank 8 and up	45,000
Sp. Def Lv. 32	Rank 8 and up	48,000
Sp. Atk Lv. 64	Rank 9 and up	96,000
Training Lv. 4	Rank 10	60,000
Defense Lv. 64	Rank 10	96,000

 **Tip** ## Shop owners sometimes recommend other shops to customers

When you recommend a shop to a visitor, the shop owner sometimes recommends another shop to the customer. Some customers visit all the shops on the avenue. It's great when this happens because the popularity of the shops go up.

The flow that a shop owner recommends another shop to a customer

The recommended shop's rank goes up

Janus's Flowers's popularity went up by 75 points!

The shop recommends another shop

My favorite shop is right over there. Do you want to have a look?

The customer is guided to the shop

Judith has come to Annetta's Antiques!

The popularity of the shop goes up

Annetta's Antiques's popularity went up by 93 points!

Market

Shop's Name	● Rank 1 to 3	● Rank 4 to 7	● Rank 8 and up
	[Shop owner name] Mart	[Shop owner name]'s Shop	[Shop owner name]'s Emporium

At a Market, you can buy items in bulk at a low price. The selection of items are different depending on which version the shop owner came from.

▶ Buy
How are you doing lately?
How are you?
Give the person a different job
See you!

Marci's Emporium:
You can buy all sorts of things here!

Items at a Market

Items at Rank 1	Price
Fresh Water ×12	2,400
Full Heal ×12◆	5,400
Hyper Potion ×12◆	10,800
Max Repel ×12◆	6,300
Moomoo Milk ×12	6,000
Revive ×12◆	13,500

Items at Rank 2	Price
Fresh Water ×24	4,800
Full Heal ×12◆	5,400
Honey ×12	3,600
Hyper Potion ×12◆	10,800
Max Repel ×12◆	6,300
Moomoo Milk ×12	6,000
Revive ×12◆	13,500

Items at Rank 3	Price
Dire Hit ×12○	5,850
Fresh Water ×36	7,200
Full Heal ×12◆	5,400
Guard Spec. ×12●	6,300
Honey ×12	3,600
Hyper Potion ×12◆	10,800
Max Repel ×12◆	6,300
Moomoo Milk ×24	12,000
Revive ×12◆	13,500
X Attack ×12▲	4,500
X Defend ×12△	4,950

Items at Rank 4	Price
Dire Hit ×12○	5,850
Ether	1,500
Fresh Water ×48	9,600
Full Heal ×24◆	10,800
Guard Spec. ×12●	6,300
Honey ×12	3,600
Hyper Potion ×24◆	21,600
Max Repel ×24◆	12,600
Moomoo Milk ×24	12,000
Revive ×24◆	27,000
X Accuracy ×12○	8,550
X Attack ×12▲	4,500
X Defend ×12△	4,950
X Sp. Def ×12△	3,150
X Special ×12▲	3,150
X Speed ×12●	3,150

Items at Rank 5	Price
Carbos ×12○△	99,960
Dire Hit ×12○	5,850
Ether	1,500
Fresh Water ×48	9,600
Full Heal ×24◆	10,800
Guard Spec. ×12●	6,300
Honey ×12	3,600
HP Up ×12●▲	99,960
Hyper Potion ×24◆	21,600
Max Repel ×24◆	12,600
Moomoo Milk ×36	18,000
Revive ×24◆	27,000
X Accuracy ×12○	8,550
X Attack ×12▲	4,500
X Defend ×12△	4,950
X Sp. Def ×12△	3,150
X Special ×12▲	3,150
X Speed ×12●	3,150

Items at Rank 6	Price
Calcium ×12○△	99,960
Carbos ×12○△	99,960
Dire Hit ×12○	5,850
Ether	1,500
Fresh Water ×48	9,600
Full Heal ×24◆	10,800
Guard Spec. ×12●	6,300
Honey ×12	3,600
HP Up ×12●▲	99,960
Hyper Potion ×24◆	21,600
Max Repel ×24◆	12,600
Moomoo Milk ×36	18,000
Protein ×12●▲	99,960
Revive ×24◆	27,000
X Accuracy ×12○	8,550
X Attack ×12▲	4,500
X Defend ×12△	4,950
X Sp. Def ×12△	3,150
X Special ×12▲	3,150
X Speed ×12●	3,150

Items at Rank 7	Price
Calcium ×12○△	99,960
Carbos ×12○△	99,960
Dire Hit ×12○	5,850
Ether	1,500
Fresh Water ×48	9,600
Full Heal ×24◆	10,800
Guard Spec. ×12●	6,300
Honey ×12	3,600
HP Up ×12●▲	99,960
Hyper Potion ×24◆	21,600
Iron ×12●▲	99,960
Max Repel ×24◆	12,600
Moomoo Milk ×48	24,000
Protein ×12●▲	99,960
Revive ×24◆	27,000
X Accuracy ×12○	8,550
X Attack ×12▲	4,500
X Defend ×12△	4,950
X Sp. Def ×12△	3,150
X Special ×12▲	3,150
X Speed ×12●	3,150
Zinc ×12○△	99,960

Items at Rank 8	Price
Calcium ×12○△	99,960
Carbos ×12○△	99,960
Dire Hit ×12○	5,850
Ether	1,500
Fresh Water ×48	9,600
Full Heal ×36◆	16,200
Guard Spec. ×12●	6,300
Honey ×12	3,600
HP Up ×12●▲	99,960
Hyper Potion ×36◆	32,400
Iron ×12●▲	99,960
Lava Cookie ▲	1,000
Max Repel ×36◆	18,900
Moomoo Milk ×48	24,000
Old Gateau △	1,000
Protein ×12●▲	99,960
RageCandyBar ●○	2,000
Revive ×36◆	40,500
X Accuracy ×12○	8,550
X Attack ×12▲	4,500
X Defend ×12△	4,950
X Sp. Def ×12△	3,150
X Special ×12▲	3,150
X Speed ×12●	3,150
Zinc ×12○△	99,960

Items at Rank 9	Price
Calcium ×12○△	99,960
Carbos ×12○△	99,960
Dire Hit ×12○	5,850
Ether	1,500
Fresh Water ×48	9,600
Full Heal ×36◆	16,200
Guard Spec. ×12●	6,300
Honey ×12	3,600
HP Up ×12●▲	99,960
Hyper Potion ×36◆	32,400
Iron ×12●▲	99,960
Lava Cookie ▲	1,000
Max Repel ×36◆	18,900
Moomoo Milk ×48	24,000
Old Gateau △	1,000
PP Up	12,500
Protein ×12●▲	99,960
RageCandyBar ●○	2,000
Revive ×36◆	40,500
X Accuracy ×12○	8,550
X Attack ×12▲	4,500
X Defend ×12△	4,950
X Sp. Def ×12△	3,150
X Special ×12▲	3,150
X Speed ×12●	3,150
Zinc ×12○△	99,960

Items at Rank 10	Price
Calcium ×12○△	99,960
Carbos ×12○△	99,960
Dire Hit ×12○	5,850
Ether	1,500
Fresh Water ×48	9,600
Full Heal ×48◆	21,600
Guard Spec. ×12●	6,300
Honey ×12	3,600
HP Up ×12●▲	99,960
Hyper Potion ×48◆	43,200
Iron ×12●▲	99,960
Lava Cookie ▲	1,000
Max Repel ×48◆	25,200
Max Revive	5,000
Moomoo Milk ×48	24,000
Old Gateau △	1,000
PP Up	12,500
Protein ×12●▲	99,960
RageCandyBar ●○	2,000
Revive ×48◆	54,000
X Accuracy ×12○	8,550
X Attack ×12▲	4,500
X Defend ×12△	4,950
X Sp. Def ×12△	3,150
X Special ×12▲	3,150
X Speed ×12●	3,150
Zinc ×12○△	99,960

● Available when the shop owner came from *Pokémon Black* ○ Available when the shop owner came from *Pokémon White* ▲ Available when the shop owner came from *Pokémon Black 2* △ Available when the shop owner came from *Pokémon White 2* ◆ Added when the avenue's rank is 15 or higher and after you enter the Hall of Fame

Flower Shop

Shop's Name	● Rank 1 to 3	● Rank 4 to 7	● Rank 8 and up
	Florist [Shop owner name]	[Shop owner name]'s Flowers	[Shop owner name]'s Garden

A Flower Shop sells Berries and Mulch. The selection of items are different depending on which version the shop owner came from. If you have Flower Shops run by shop owners from each of these versions (*Pokémon Black Version 2*, *Pokémon White Version 2*, *Pokémon Black Version*, and *Pokémon White Version*), you can buy 40 kinds of Berries and four kinds of Mulch.

▶ Buy
How are you?
Give the person a different job
See you!

Arpo's Garden:
Berries are the blessings of nature!

Items at a Flower Shop
(When the shop owner came from *Pokémon Black*)

Items	Shop's Rank	Price
Cheri Berry ×4	Rank 1 and up	600
Rawst Berry ×4	Rank 1 and up	600
Stable Mulch	Rank 1 to 2	400
Oran Berry × 4	Rank 2 and up	600
Stable Mulch ×2	Rank 3 to 5	800
Lum Berry ×4	Rank 3 and up	800
Persim Berry ×4	Rank 3 and up	600
Chilan Berry ×4	Rank 4 and up	2,000
Leppa Berry	Rank 4 and up	1,500
Kasib Berry ×4	Rank 5 and up	2,000
Coba Berry ×4	Rank 6 and up	2,000
Stable Mulch ×4	Rank 6 and up	1,600
Yache Berry ×4	Rank 7 and up	2,000
Occa Berry ×4	Rank 8 and up	2,000
Petaya Berry ×4	Rank 8 and up	2,000
Tamato Berry ×4	Rank 9 and up	3,000
Grepa Berry ×4	Rank 10	3,000
Hondew Berry ×4	Rank 10	3,000

Items at a Flower Shop
(When the shop owner came from *Pokémon White*)

Items	Shop's Rank	Price
Chesto Berry ×4	Rank 1 and up	600
Pecha Berry ×4	Rank 1 and up	600
Gooey Mulch	Rank 1 to 2	400
Aspear Berry ×4	Rank 2 and up	600
Gooey Mulch ×2	Rank 3 to 5	800
Lum Berry ×4	Rank 3 and up	800
Sitrus Berry × 4	Rank 3 and up	800
Haban Berry ×4	Rank 4 and up	2,000
Leppa Berry	Rank 4 and up	1,500
Payapa Berry ×4	Rank 5 and up	2,000
Chople Berry ×4	Rank 6 and up	2,000
Gooey Mulch ×4	Rank 6 and up	1,600
Passho Berry ×4	Rank 7 and up	2,000
Apicot Berry ×4	Rank 8 and up	2,000
Liechi Berry ×4	Rank 8 and up	2,000
Qualot Berry ×4	Rank 9 and up	3,000
Kelpsy Berry ×4	Rank 10	3,000
Pomeg Berry ×4	Rank 10	3,000

Items at a Flower Shop
(When the shop owner came from *Pokémon Black 2*)

Items	Shop's Rank	Price
Cheri Berry ×4	Rank 1 and up	600
Rawst Berry ×4	Rank 1 and up	600
Growth Mulch	Rank 1 to 2	400
Oran Berry × 4	Rank 2 and up	600
Growth Mulch ×2	Rank 3 to 5	800
Lum Berry ×4	Rank 3 and up	800
Persim Berry ×4	Rank 3 and up	600
Leppa Berry	Rank 4 and up	1,500
Razz Berry ×4	Rank 4 and up	600
Colbur Berry ×4	Rank 5 and up	2,000
Growth Mulch ×4	Rank 6 and up	1,600
Tanga Berry ×4	Rank 6 and up	2,000
Kebia Berry ×4	Rank 7 and up	2,000
Ganlon Berry ×4	Rank 8 and up	2,000
Wacan Berry ×4	Rank 8 and up	2,000
Tamato Berry ×4	Rank 9 and up	3,000
Grepa Berry ×4	Rank 10	3,000
Hondew Berry ×4	Rank 10	3,000

Items at a Flower Shop
(When the shop owner came from *Pokémon White 2*)

Items	Shop's Rank	Price
Chesto Berry ×4	Rank 1 and up	600
Pecha Berry ×4	Rank 1 and up	600
Damp Mulch	Rank 1 to 2	400
Aspear Berry ×4	Rank 2 and up	600
Damp Mulch ×2	Rank 3 to 5	800
Lum Berry ×4	Rank 3 and up	800
Sitrus Berry × 4	Rank 3 and up	800
Bluk Berry ×4	Rank 4 and up	600
Leppa Berry	Rank 4 and up	1,500
Babiri Berry ×4	Rank 5 and up	2,000
Charti Berry ×4	Rank 6 and up	2,000
Damp Mulch ×4	Rank 6 and up	1,600
Shuca Berry ×4	Rank 7 and up	2,000
Rindo Berry ×4	Rank 8 and up	2,000
Salac Berry ×4	Rank 8 and up	2,000
Qualot Berry ×4	Rank 9 and up	3,000
Kelpsy Berry ×4	Rank 10	3,000
Pomeg Berry ×4	Rank 10	3,000

Raffle Shop

Shop's Name	● Rank 1 to 3	● Rank 4 to 7	● Rank 8 and up
	Dream ★ [Shop owner name]	Lucky ★ [Shop owner name]	Happy ★ [Shop owner name]

You can draw one raffle at a raffle shop every day. You can get one of 10 prizes. When the shop's rank goes up, you will have a better chance to get a better item.

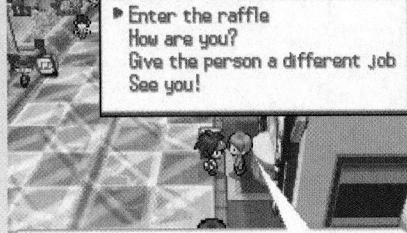

▶ Enter the raffle
How are you?
Give the person a different job
See you!

Happy ★ Jephew:
The grand prize is a Master Ball!

Prizes at a Raffle Shop

Grade	Prize	Grade	Prize
1st Prize	Master Ball	6th Prize	Max Elixir
2nd Prize	Rare Candy	7th Prize	Max Ether
3rd Prize	PP Max	8th Prize	Ultra Ball
4th Prize	PP Up	9th Prize	Full Heal
5th Prize	Max Revive	10th Prize	Berry Juice

405

Beauty Salon

Shop's Name	● Rank 1 to 3	● Rank 4 to 7	● Rank 8 and up
	Barber (Shop owner name)	Salon (Shop owner name)	Studio (Shop owner name)

A Beauty Salon is a place where you can make Pokémon more friendly and lower Pokémon's base stats. Use it when you want to make Pokémon friendly to evolve them or retrain your strong Pokémon.

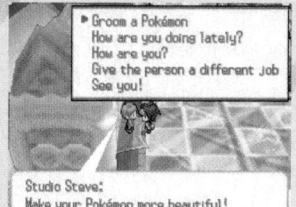

Studio Steve:
Make your Pokémon more beautiful!

The effects of the Beauty Salon menu

Menu	Effect
Brushing	It helps the Pokémon grow friendly.
Shampoo	It helps the Pokémon grow pretty friendly.
Smile Cut	It helps the Pokémon grow very friendly.
Beauty Cut	It helps the Pokémon grow significantly friendly.
Royal Cut	It helps the Pokémon grow immensely friendly.
Slender Makeup	It helps the Pokémon grow friendly and lowers the base HP.
Calm Makeup	It helps the Pokémon grow friendly and lowers the base Attack stat.
Gentle Makeup	It helps the Pokémon grow friendly and lowers the base Defense stat.
Mellow Makeup	It helps the Pokémon grow friendly and lowers the base Sp. Atk stat.
Warm Makeup	It helps the Pokémon grow friendly and lowers the base Sp. Def stat.
Slow Makeup	It helps the Pokémon grow friendly and lowers the base Speed stat.

The menu of a Beauty Salon
(When the shop owner came from *Pokémon Black 2*)

Menu	Rank	Price
Slender Makeup	Rank 1 and up	4,000
Brushing	Rank 1 and up	1,000
Shampoo	Rank 1 and up	1,500
Smile Cut	Rank 1 and up	2,000
Beauty Cut	Rank 2 and up	2,500
Calm Makeup	Rank 3 and up	4,000
Gentle Makeup	Rank 4 and up	4,000
Mellow Makeup	Rank 5 and up	4,000
Warm Makeup	Rank 6 and up	4,000
Slow Makeup	Rank 7 and up	4,000
Warm Makeup 2	Rank 8 and up	8,000
Slow Makeup 2	Rank 8 and up	8,000
Mellow Makeup 2	Rank 9 and up	8,000
Slender Makeup 3	Rank 10	20,000
Calm Makeup 3	Rank 10	20,000
Gentle Makeup 3	Rank 10	20,000

The menu of a Beauty Salon
(When the shop owner came from *Pokémon White 2*)

Menu	Rank	Price
Slow Makeup	Rank 1 and up	4,000
Brushing	Rank 1 and up	1,000
Shampoo	Rank 1 and up	1,500
Smile Cut	Rank 1 and up	2,000
Royal Cut	Rank 2 and up	3,000
Warm Makeup	Rank 3 and up	4,000
Mellow Makeup	Rank 4 and up	4,000
Gentle Makeup	Rank 5 and up	4,000
Calm Makeup	Rank 6 and up	4,000
Slender Makeup	Rank 7 and up	4,000
Calm Makeup 2	Rank 8 and up	8,000
Gentle Makeup 2	Rank 8 and up	8,000
Slender Makeup 2	Rank 9 and up	8,000
Mellow Makeup 3	Rank 10	20,000
Warm Makeup 3	Rank 10	20,000
Slow Makeup 3	Rank 10	20,000

Antique Shop

Shop's Name	● Rank 1 to 3	● Rank 4 to 7	● Rank 8 and up
	(Shop owner name)'s Antiques	Gallery (Shop owner name)	(Shop owner name) Museum

At an Antique Shop, you can have goods you bought, such as chunks, stones, and rocks, appraised on the spot.

Janus Museum:
Find a rare treasure!

Rare treasures at an Antique Shop

Rare Treasures	Rank	Price
Chunk C Rank	Rank 1 and up	500
Super Big Box	Rank 1 and up	350
Dirty Stone	Rank 2 and up	200
Chunk B Rank	Rank 3 and up	750
Jagged Rock	Rank 3 and up	300
Big Box	Rank 4 and up	450
Black Stone	Rank 5 and up	300
Chunk A Rank	Rank 6 and up	1,500
Rugged Rock	Rank 7 and up	400
Ordinary Box	Rank 7 and up	650
Rough Rock	Rank 8 and up	500
Dingy Stone	Rank 8 and up	400
Chunk S Rank	Rank 9 and up	2,000
Polished Rock	Rank 10	600
Small Box	Rank 10	750
Dusty Stone	Rank 10	500

Appraisal results of rare treasures

Rare Treasures	Game Card that the shop owner came from	Item you can get after appraisal
Chunk	Pokémon Black, Pokémon White, Pokémon Black 2, or Pokémon White 2	Big Nugget, Nugget, Ultra Ball, Great Ball, Poké Ball, Red Shard, or Blue Shard Yellow Shard, Green Shard, or Hard Stone
Stone	Pokémon Black or Pokémon Black 2	Water Stone, Thunderstone, Moon Stone, Dusk Stone, Dawn Stone, Float Stone, Everstone, or Hard Stone
	Pokémon White or Pokémon White 2	Leaf Stone, Fire Stone, Sun Stone, Shiny Stone, Odd Keystone, Float Stone, Everstone, or Hard Stone
Rock	Pokémon Black or Pokémon Black 2	Helix Fossil, Old Amber, Root Fossil, Armor Fossil, Rock Gem, Rare Bone, or Float Stone Everstone or Hard Stone
	Pokémon White or Pokémon White 2	Dome Fossil, Claw Fossil, Skull Fossil, Cover Fossil, Plume Fossil, Rare Bone, Float Stone, Everstone, or Hard Stone
Box	Pokémon Black	Sacred Ash, Big Pearl, Pearl, King's Rock, DeepSeaTooth, DeepSeaScale, or Big Mushroom TinyMushroom, Heart Scale, or Hard Stone
	Pokémon White	Sacred Ash, Big Pearl, Pearl, Metal Coat, Dragon Scale, Up-Grade, or Big Mushroom TinyMushroom, Heart Scale, or Hard Stone
	Pokémon Black 2	Sacred Ash, Big Pearl, Pearl, Protector, Magmarizer, Reaper Cloth, or Big Mushroom TinyMushroom, Heart Scale, or Hard Stone
	Pokémon White 2	Sacred Ash, Big Pearl, Pearl, Dubious Disc, Electirizer, Prism Scale, or Big Mushroom TinyMushroom, Heart Scale, or Hard Stone

Café

Shop's Name	● Rank 1 to 3	● Rank 4 to 7	● Rank 8 and up
	Deli (Shop owner name)	(Shop owner name)'s Kitchen	Bistro (Shop owner name)

A Café is a place where you can make Pokémon more friendly and raise Pokémon's base stats. Select a menu item and select a Pokémon you want to feed from your party. The menus are different depending on which version the shop owner came from.

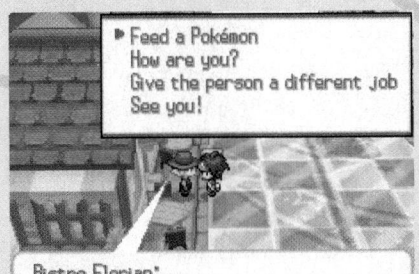

Bistro Florian:
Always offering five-star tastes!

The effects of the Café menu

Menu	Effect
Friendly Drink	It helps a Pokémon who had it grow slightly friendly.
Friendly Lunch	It helps a Pokémon who had it grow friendly.
Friendly Combo	It helps a Pokémon who had it grow pretty friendly.
Wonder Brunch	It raises a Pokémon's level by one.
Wonder Dessert	It raises a Pokémon's level by three.
Wonder Dinner	It raises a Pokémon's level by eight.
Power Lunch A	It raises the base HP a lot when a Pokémon eats it.
Power Lunch B	It raises the base Attack stat a lot when a Pokémon eats it.
Power Lunch C	It raises the base Defense stat a lot when a Pokémon eats it.
Power Lunch D	It raises the base Sp. Atk stat a lot when a Pokémon eats it.
Power Lunch E	It raises the base Sp. Def stat a lot when a Pokémon eats it.
Power Lunch F	It raises the base Speed stat a lot when a Pokémon eats it.
Loyalty Meal	It raises a Pokémon's level by one.
Secret Dish A	It raises the base HP significantly when a Pokémon eats it.
Secret Dish B	It raises the base Attack stat significantly when a Pokémon eats it.
Secret Dish C	It raises the base Defense stat significantly when a Pokémon eats it.
Secret Dish D	It raises the base Sp. Atk stat significantly when a Pokémon eats it.
Secret Dish E	It raises the base Sp. Def stat significantly when a Pokémon eats it.
Secret Dish F	It raises the base Speed stat significantly when a Pokémon eats it.

The Café menu
(When the shop owner came from *Pokémon Black 2*)

Menu	Rank	Price
Power Lunch A	Rank 1 and up	36,000
Friendly Drink	Rank 1 and up	500
Friendly Lunch	Rank 1 and up	1,000
Wonder Brunch	Rank 2 and up	15,000
Loyalty Meal	Rank 3 and up	14,000
Power Lunch B	Rank 4 and up	36,000
Friendly Combo	Rank 4 and up	2,000
Power Lunch C	Rank 5 and up	36,000
Power Lunch D	Rank 6 and up	36,000
Power Lunch E	Rank 7 and up	36,000
Wonder Dessert	Rank 8 and up	45,000
Secret Dish F	Rank 8 and up	72,000
Power Lunch F	Rank 8 and up	36,000
Secret Dish E	Rank 9 and up	72,000
Wonder Dinner	Rank 10	96,000
Secret Dish D	Rank 10	72,000

The Café menu
(When the shop owner came from *Pokémon White 2*)

Menu	Rank	Price
Power Lunch F	Rank 1 and up	36,000
Friendly Drink	Rank 1 and up	500
Friendly Lunch	Rank 1 and up	1,000
Wonder Brunch	Rank 2 and up	15,000
Loyalty Meal	Rank 3 and up	14,000
Power Lunch E	Rank 4 and up	36,000
Friendly Combo	Rank 4 and up	2,000
Power Lunch D	Rank 5 and up	36,000
Power Lunch C	Rank 6 and up	36,000
Power Lunch B	Rank 7 and up	36,000
Wonder Dessert	Rank 8 and up	45,000
Secret Dish C	Rank 8 and up	72,000
Power Lunch A	Rank 8 and up	36,000
Secret Dish B	Rank 9 and up	72,000
Wonder Dinner	Rank 10	96,000
Secret Dish A	Rank 10	72,000

Nursery

Shop's Name	● Rank 1 to 3	● Rank 4 to 7	● Rank 8 and up
	(Shop owner name)'s Place	(Shop owner name)'s Corner	(Shop owner name) Land

A Nursery is a place where you can hatch Pokémon Eggs fast. There are two conditions to build a Nursery: raise the avenue's rank to 15 or higher and enter the Hall of Fame.

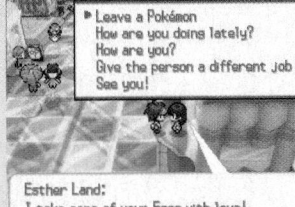

Esther Land:
I take care of your Eggs with love!

The menu at a Nursery

Menu	Rank	Price
Warm Lv. 1	Rank 1 and up	600
Warm Lv. 2	Rank 2 and up	1,200
Warm Lv. 3	Rank 4 and up	1,800
Warm Lv. 4	Rank 7 and up	2,200
Warm Lv. 5	Rank 8 and up	2,500

 **Tip**

The appearance changes when the shop's rank goes up

Shops will be remodeled when the rank goes up, and they will have new products. When a shop reaches Rank 4 and Rank 8, a special remodel will be done and the appearance of the shop will change dramatically.

When a Nursery's rank goes up

Rank 1 to 3

Rank 4 to 7

Rank 8 and up

Have Fun with Entralink Funfest Missions

Play Funfest Missions by yourself or with a hundred people

A Funfest Mission is a minigame that sets a goal for you to achieve. New Funfest Missions are added when you reach a new place in your adventure, when you speak to a certain person, and so on.

How to start a Funfest Mission

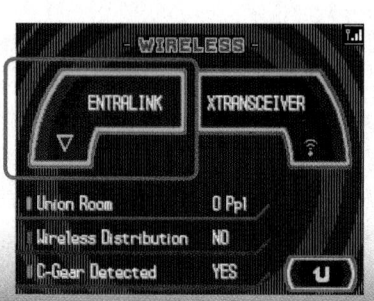

1 Tap "ENTRALINK" on your C-Gear

Tap "WIRELESS" and then "ENTRALINK" to go to the Entralink.

2 Check the Entree in the center of the Entralink

When you arrive at the Entralink, head north, and press the A Button in front of the Entree in the center.

3 Tap "ACCEPT A FUNFEST MISSION"

Tap "ACCEPT A FUNFEST MISSION," and choose the Funfest Mission you want to play.

To clear a Funfest Mission, you'll have a goal to achieve

When you visit the Entralink for the first time, try the Funfest Mission "The First Berry Search!" Once you've cleared this Funfest Mission, you can attempt others. Each Funfest Mission has a time limit. To clear a mission, you need to collect items, battle Pokémon Trainers, or achieve other goals within the time limit. During a mission, the progress status will be displayed and updated on the Touch Screen.

Funfest Mission info

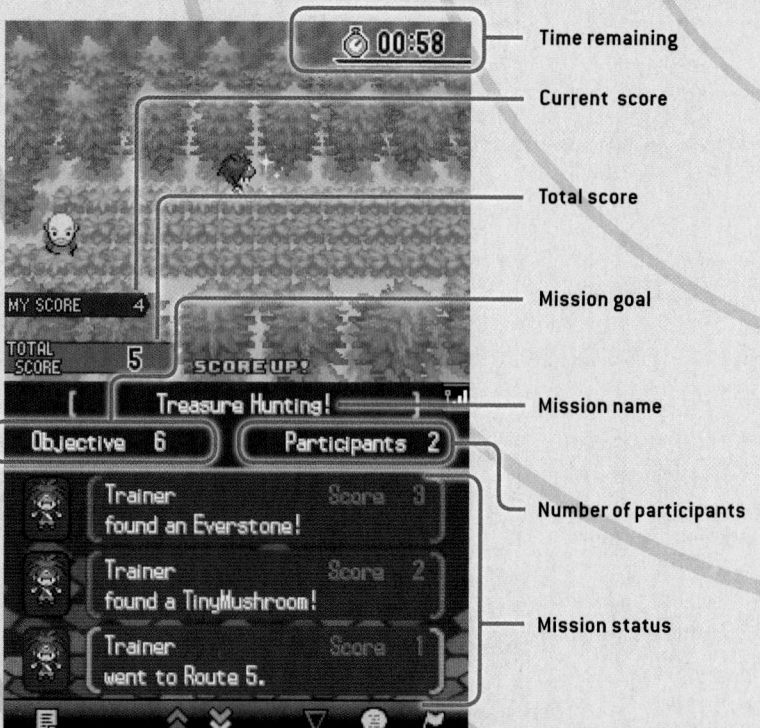

- Time remaining
- Current score
- Total score
- Mission goal
- Mission name
- Number of participants
- Mission status

You can participate in the Funfest Missions of players nearby

What's most exciting about Funfest Missions is that you can play with other players via wireless communications. When someone is playing a Funfest Mission, nearby players will receive a notice. When you receive this notice, you can participate in that Funfest Mission. High-level Funfest Missions are difficult to clear. Cooperating with a lot of people will improve your chances of clearing these missions.

How to join a Funfest Mission

1 Receive a notice on your Tag Log

When a person nearby is playing a Funfest Mission, "FUNFEST MISSION!" will appear on your Tag Log.

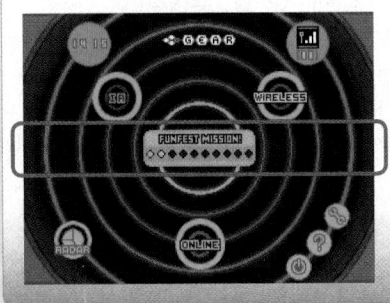

2 Participate in a Funfest Mission

Tap the Tag Log to open it. Choose "YES" if you want to join the Funfest Mission.

3 Play another person's Funfest Mission

Play the Funfest Mission. Depending on your progress in your adventure, you might not be able to join a particular mission.

Clearing more missions levels up your Entree and gives you more Pass Powers

Clear a Funfest Mission, and you'll receive Pass Orbs or other rewards, and your Entree levels up. Your Black Level goes up when the person who started the Funfest Mission is playing *Pokémon Black 2*, and your White Level goes up if the person is playing *Pokémon White 2*. As the level of the Entree goes up, you can use more Pass Powers.

Raising the Entree's levels

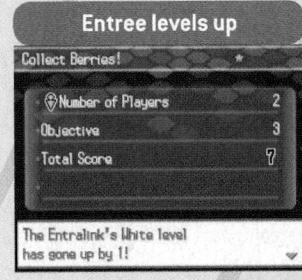

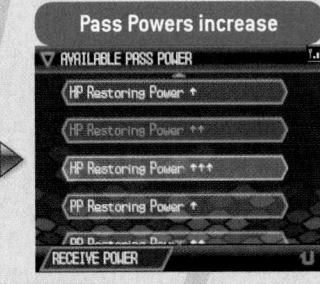

See p. 413 for Pass Powers.

Play Funfest Missions and collect Medals

Clear all the Funfest Missions, and you can receive a total of 11 different Medals. Join others' Funfest Missions as well as starting your own missions, and collect all the Medals!

 10 People Funfest
 30 People Funfest
 Scored 100
 Scored 1,000
 Mission Host Lv. 1
 Mission Host Lv. 2

 Participant Lv. 1
 Participant Lv. 2
 Achiever Lv. 1
 Achiever Lv. 2
Funfest Complete

Check p. 531 for the Medal list.

Try all the Funfest Missions!

There are 44 Funfest Missions for you to play. The higher the mission level or your score in clearing it, the more rewards you can get. If you scored twice as high as the goal in Lv. 3 or in a special Funfest Mission, you can receive a double-score reward.

How to start and complete Funfest Missions

Funfest Mission	Game	Funfest Mission Lv. 1		Funfest Mission Lv. 2		Funfest Mission Lv. 3		Special Funfest Mission	
		Target	Time limit	Target	Time limit	Target	Time limit	Target	Time limit
The First Berry Search! ◆	Both *Pokémon Black 2* and *Pokémon White 2*	Collect 5 Berries	3 min.	—	—	—	—	—	—
Collect Berries!	Both *Pokémon Black 2* and *Pokémon White 2*	Collect 3 Berries	3 min.	Collect 6 Berries	3 min.	Collect 12 Berries	3 min.	Collect 25 Berries	3 min.
Find Lost Items!	Both *Pokémon Black 2* and *Pokémon White 2*	Collect 10 lost items	5 min.	Collect 15 lost items	5 min.	Collect 20 lost items	5 min.	Collect 40 lost items	5 min.
Find Lost Boys!	Both *Pokémon Black 2* and *Pokémon White 2*	Find 4 boys	3 min.	Find 8 boys	3 min.	Find 16 boys	3 min.	Find 50 boys	3 min.
Enjoy Shopping!	Both *Pokémon Black 2* and *Pokémon White 2*	Shop 3 times	3 min.	Shop 6 times	3 min.	Shop 12 times	3 min.	Shop 25 times	3 min.
Find Audino!	Both *Pokémon Black 2* and *Pokémon White 2*	Defeat or catch 1 Audino	5 min.	Defeat or catch 5 Audino	5 min.	Defeat or catch 10 Audino	5 min.	Defeat or catch 50 Audino	5 min.
Search for ? Pokémon! ◆	Both *Pokémon Black 2* and *Pokémon White 2*	Defeat or catch 3 Pokémon	3 min.	Defeat or catch 5 Pokémon	3 min.	Defeat or catch 10 Pokémon	3 min.	Defeat or catch 50 Pokémon	5 min.
Train with Martial Artists!	Both *Pokémon Black 2* and *Pokémon White 2*	Defeat 2 martial artists	5 min.	Defeat 4 martial artists	5 min.	Defeat 8 martial artists	5 min.	Defeat 100 martial artists	5 min.
Sparring with ? Trainers! ◆	Both *Pokémon Black 2* and *Pokémon White 2*	Defeat 10 martial artists	3 min.	Defeat 30 martial artists	3 min.	Defeat 50 martial artists	3 min.	Defeat 100 martial artists	5 min.
Get Rich Quick!	*Pokémon Black 2* only	Find 3 treasures	3 min.	Find 6 treasures	3 min.	Find 12 treasures	3 min.	Find 25 treasures	3 min.
Treasure Hunting!	*Pokémon White 2* only	Find 6 items	3 min.	Find 12 items	3 min.	Find 24 items	3 min.	Find 50 items	3 min.
Exciting Trading!	*Pokémon Black 2* only	Talk to 2 people	5 min.	Talk to 4 people	5 min.	Talk to 8 people	5 min.	Talk to 50 people	5 min.
Exhilarating Trading!	*Pokémon White 2* only	Talk to 2 people	5 min.	Talk to 4 people	5 min.	Talk to 8 people	5 min.	Talk to 50 people	5 min.
Find Emolga!	Both *Pokémon Black 2* and *Pokémon White 2*	Defeat or catch 1 Emolga	5 min.	Defeat or catch 5 Emolga	5 min.	Defeat or catch 10 Emolga	5 min.	Defeat or catch 30 Emolga	5 min.
Wings Falling on the Drawbridge	Both *Pokémon Black 2* and *Pokémon White 2*	Collect 5 wings	3 min.	Collect 10 wings	3 min.	Collect 40 wings	3 min.	Collect 100 wings	3 min.
Find Treasures!	Both *Pokémon Black 2* and *Pokémon White 2*	Collect 5 treasures	3 min.	Collect 10 treasures	3 min.	Collect 40 treasures	3 min.	Collect 100 treasures	3 min.
Mushrooms' Hide-and-Seek!	Both *Pokémon Black 2* and *Pokémon White 2*	Defeat or catch 3 Foongus	5 min.	Defeat or catch 10 Foongus	5 min.	Defeat or catch 30 Foongus	5 min.	Defeat or catch 5 Foongus	3 min.
Find Mysterious Ores!	*Pokémon Black 2* only	Collect 10 ores	5 min.	Collect 20 ores	5 min.	Collect 30 ores	5 min.	Collect 30 ores	3 min.
Find Shining Ores!	*Pokémon White 2* only	Collect 10 ores	5 min.	Collect 20 ores	5 min.	Collect 30 ores	5 min.	Collect 30 ores	3 min.
The ? Lost Treasures ◆	Both *Pokémon Black 2* and *Pokémon White 2*	Collect 2 treasures	5 min.	Collect 4 treasures	5 min.	Collect 10 treasures	5 min.	Collect 30 treasures	5 min.
Big Harvest of Berries!	Both *Pokémon Black 2* and *Pokémon White 2*	Collect 6 Berries	3 min.	Collect 12 Berries	3 min.	Collect 24 Berries	3 min.	Collect 100 Berries	3 min.
Ring the Bell...	Both *Pokémon Black 2* and *Pokémon White 2*	Ring the bell once	3 min.	Ring the bell twice	3 min.	Ring the bell 8 times	3 min.	Ring the bell 10 times	3 min.
The Bell That Rings ? Times ◆	Both *Pokémon Black 2* and *Pokémon White 2*	Ring the bell 3 times	3 min.	Ring the bell 5 times	3 min.	Ring the bell 7 times	3 min.	Ring the bell 10 times	3 min.
Path to an Ace!	Both *Pokémon Black 2* and *Pokémon White 2*	Defeat 3 Ace Trainers	5 min.	Defeat 6 Ace Trainers	5 min.	Defeat 12 Ace Trainers	5 min.	Defeat 50 Ace Trainers	5 min.
Shocking Shopping!	Both *Pokémon Black 2* and *Pokémon White 2*	Shop 4 times	3 min.	Shop 8 times	3 min.	Shop 32 times	3 min.	Shop 100 times	3 min.
Memory Training! ◆	Both *Pokémon Black 2* and *Pokémon White 2*	Answer 6 quizzes correctly	3 min.	Answer 10 quizzes correctly	3 min.	Answer 12 quizzes correctly	3 min.	Answer 50 quizzes correctly	5 min.
Push the Limit of Your Memory...	Both *Pokémon Black 2* and *Pokémon White 2*	Answer 5 quizzes correctly	5 min.	Answer 10 quizzes correctly	5 min.	Answer 40 quizzes correctly	5 min.	Answer 50 quizzes correctly	3 min.
Find Rustling Grass!	Both *Pokémon Black 2* and *Pokémon White 2*	Defeat or catch 5 Pokémon	10 min.	Defeat or catch 10 Pokémon	10 min.	Defeat or catch 20 Pokémon	10 min.	Defeat or catch 100 Pokémon	10 min.
Find Shards!	Both *Pokémon Black 2* and *Pokémon White 2*	Collect 3 shards	3 min.	Collect 16 shards	3 min.	Collect 32 shards	3 min.	Collect 100 shards	3 min.
Forgotten Lost Items	*Pokémon Black 2* only	Collect 5 lost items	2 min.	Collect 10 lost items	2 min.	Collect 50 lost items	2 min.	Collect 100 lost items	2 min.
Not-Found Lost Items	*Pokémon White 2* only	Collect 5 lost items	2 min.	Collect 10 lost items	2 min.	Collect 50 lost items	2 min.	Collect 100 lost items	2 min.
What Is the Best Price?	*Pokémon Black 2* only	Shop 6 times	3 min.	Shop 12 times	3 min.	Shop 40 times	3 min.	Shop 50 times	3 min.
What Is the Real Price?	*Pokémon White 2* only	Shop 6 times	3 min.	Shop 12 times	3 min.	Shop 40 times	3 min.	Shop 50 times	3 min.
Give Me the Item!	Both *Pokémon Black 2* and *Pokémon White 2*	Help 10 people	5 min.	Help 15 people	5 min.	Help 20 people	5 min.	Help 40 people	5 min.
Do a Great Trade-Up!	Both *Pokémon Black 2* and *Pokémon White 2*	Help 3 people	3 min.	Help 6 people	3 min.	Help 80 people	3 min.	Help 10 people	3 min.
Search Hidden Grottoes!	Both *Pokémon Black 2* and *Pokémon White 2*	Defeat or catch 1 Pokémon	10 min.	Defeat or catch 3 Pokémon	10 min.	Defeat or catch 10 Pokémon	10 min.	Defeat or catch 3 Pokémon	5 min.
Noisy Hidden Grottoes!	*Pokémon Black 2* only	Defeat or catch 3 Pokémon	10 min.	Defeat or catch 5 Pokémon	10 min.	Defeat or catch 10 Pokémon	10 min.	Defeat or catch 30 Pokémon	10 min.
Quiet Hidden Grottoes!	*Pokémon White 2* only	Defeat or catch 3 Pokémon	10 min.	Defeat or catch 5 Pokémon	10 min.	Defeat or catch 10 Pokémon	10 min.	Defeat or catch 30 Pokémon	10 min.
Fishing Competition!	Both *Pokémon Black 2* and *Pokémon White 2*	Catch 5 Pokémon	3 min.	Catch 10 Pokémon	3 min.	Catch 20 Pokémon	3 min.	Catch 30 Pokémon	3 min.
Mulch Collector!	Both *Pokémon Black 2* and *Pokémon White 2*	Collect 6 Mulches	3 min.	Collect 12 Mulches	3 min.	Collect 24 Mulches	3 min.	Collect 9 Mulches	1 min. 30 sec.
Where Are Fluttering Hearts?	Both *Pokémon Black 2* and *Pokémon White 2*	Collect 10 items	5 min.	Collect 20 items	5 min.	Collect 40 items	5 min.	Collect 100 items	5 min.
Rock-Paper-Scissors Competition!	Both *Pokémon Black 2* and *Pokémon White 2*	Defeat 5 Preschoolers	3 min.	Defeat 10 Preschoolers	3 min.	Defeat 50 Preschoolers	3 min.	Defeat 100 Preschoolers	3 min.
Take a Walk with Eggs!	Both *Pokémon Black 2* and *Pokémon White 2*	Hatch 3 Eggs	10 min.	Hatch 12 Eggs	10 min.	Hatch 50 Eggs	10 min.	Hatch 100 Eggs	10 min.
Find Steelix!	Both *Pokémon Black 2* and *Pokémon White 2*	Defeat or catch 1 Steelix	5 min.	Defeat or catch 5 Steelix	5 min.	Defeat or catch 10 Steelix	5 min.	Defeat or catch 30 Steelix	5 min.

◆ Funfest Missions that end when you reach the goal don't have double-score rewards.

 **Tip** # Learn how to get special Funfest Missions

On the screen where you choose a Funfest Mission, enter the hidden command shown on the right. A special mission for each Funfest Mission will be available.

The hidden command that makes special Funfest Missions available

| SELECT | ↓↓↓↑↑↑↑ | SELECT |

◆ Control your Nintendo DS system as shown above. Press +Control Pad for ↑↓.

Time limit	When available	To participate	Reward	Double-score reward
(no extension on time limit)	Available from the start	Obtain the C-Gear	Pass Orb	—
(no extension on time limit)	Clear "The First Berry Search!"	Obtain the C-Gear	Pass Orb	Premier Ball
(no extension on time limit)	Clear "Collect Berries!"	Obtain the C-Gear	Pass Orb	Premier Ball
(no extension on time limit)	Clear "The First Berry Search!"	Obtain the C-Gear	Pass Orb	Moomoo Milk ×12
(no extension on time limit)	Clear "Find Lost Boys!"	Obtain the C-Gear	Pass Orb	Nugget
(no extension on time limit)	Clear "The First Berry Search!"	Obtain the C-Gear	Pass Orb	Max Repel ×10
Finding a Pokémon in rustling grass or dust clouds adds 30 seconds to the time limit.	Clear "Find Audino!"	Obtain the C-Gear	Pass Orb	
(no extension on time limit)	Speak to the old man in the Central Area in Castelia City	Obtain the Bicycle	Pass Orb	Max Revive
Defeating one martial artist adds 60 seconds to the time limit.	Clear "Train with Martial Artists!"	Obtain the Bicycle	Pass Orb	—
(no extension on time limit)	Talk to the Pokémon Ranger in the Desert Resort	Obtain the C-Gear	Pass Orb	Star Piece ×5
(no extension on time limit)	Talk to the Pokémon Ranger in the Desert Resort	Obtain the C-Gear	Pass Orb	Star Piece ×5
(no extension on time limit)	Trade items for the first time in Anville Town	Obtain the C-Gear	Pass Orb	Nugget
(no extension on time limit)	Trade items for the first time in Anville Town	Obtain the C-Gear	Pass Orb	Nugget
(no extension on time limit)	Enter Route 5	Enter Route 5	Pass Orb	Max Repel ×10
(no extension on time limit)	Talk to the man on the Driftveil Drawbridge	Walk on the Driftveil Drawbridge	Pass Orb	Rare Candy
(no extension on time limit)	Speak to the Worker in the Relic Passage	Enter Driftveil City	Pass Orb	Comet Shard
(no extension on time limit)	Battle a Foongus that pretends to be a Poké Ball (Either win, run away from, or catch it.)	Enter Route 6	Big Mushroom	BalmMushroom
(no extension on time limit)	Talk to the Lady in Chargestone Cave	Obtain the C-Gear	Pass Orb	Max Revive ×5
(no extension on time limit)	Talk to the Lady in Chargestone Cave	Obtain the C-Gear	Pass Orb	Max Revive ×5
Finding a treasure adds 30 seconds to the time limit.	Clear "Find Mysterious Ores!"	Obtain the C-Gear	Pass Orb	—
(no extension on time limit)	Talk to the Backpacker in Mistralton City	Obtain the C-Gear	Pass Orb	Lum Berry ×10
(no extension on time limit)	Enter Celestial Tower	Enter Mistralton City	Pass Orb	Stardust ×5
Ringing the bell adds 60 seconds to the time limit.	Clear "Ring the Bell..."	Enter Mistralton City	Pass Orb	
(no extension on time limit)	Enter Opelucid City	Speak with Iris in Opelucid City	Pass Orb	Rare Candy
(no extension on time limit)	Talk to the man wearing sunglasses in the Pokémon Center in Undella Town	Obtain the C-Gear	Pass Orb	Rare Candy
Answering a Harlequin's quiz adds 30 seconds to the time limit.	Talk to the old man in Humilau City	Obtain the C-Gear	Heart Scale	—
(no extension on time limit)	Clear "Memory Training!"	Obtain the C-Gear	Pass Orb	Heart Scale ×5
(no extension on time limit)	Enter the Hall of Fame	Obtain the C-Gear	Pass Orb	Max Repel ×10
(no extension on time limit)	Enter the Hall of Fame	Obtain the C-Gear	Pass Orb	Star Piece ×5
(no extension on time limit)	Enter the Hall of Fame	Enter the Hall of Fame	Pass Orb	Premier Ball ×5
(no extension on time limit)	Enter the Hall of Fame	Enter the Hall of Fame	Pass Orb	Premier Ball ×5
(no extension on time limit)	Enter the Hall of Fame	Enter the Hall of Fame	Pass Orb	Heart Scale ×1
(no extension on time limit)	Enter the Hall of Fame	Enter the Hall of Fame	Pass Orb	Heart Scale ×1
(no extension on time limit)	Enter the Hall of Fame	Enter the Hall of Fame	Max Repel	PP Max
(no extension on time limit)	Clear "Give Me the Item!"	Enter the Hall of Fame	Pass Orb	Nugget
(no extension on time limit)	Enter the Hall of Fame	Enter the Hall of Fame	Pass Orb	Big Mushroom ×10
(no extension on time limit)	Clear "Search Hidden Grottoes!"	Enter the Hall of Fame	Pass Orb	Premier Ball ×5
(no extension on time limit)	Clear "Search Hidden Grottoes!"	Enter the Hall of Fame	Pass Orb	Premier Ball ×5
(no extension on time limit)	Receive a Super Rod from Cedric Juniper in Nuvema Town	Obtain a Super Rod	Pass Orb	Dive Ball ×10
(no extension on time limit)	Talk to the Pokémon Breeder in the Abundant Shrine area	Obtain the C-Gear	Pass Orb	Pearl String
(no extension on time limit)	Talk to the man in front of the Pokémon Center in Humilau City after entering the Hall of Fame	Obtain the C-Gear	Pass Orb	Heart Scale ×10
(no extension on time limit)	Talk to the Preschooler in a house in Striaton City	Obtain the C-Gear	Pass Orb	Lucky Punch ×5
(no extension on time limit)	Speak to the old woman in the Pokémon Day Care on Route 3	Speak to the old woman in the Pokémon Day Care	Pass Orb	Rare Candy
(no extension on time limit)	Enter the Hall of Fame	Enter the Hall of Fame	Pass Orb	Max Repel ×10

Communications **3**

Use Tag Mode with Other Pokémon Fans

Tag Mode ## Exchange info as you pass by

Tag Mode enables you to exchange information with other *Pokémon Black 2*, *Pokémon White 2*, *Pokémon Black*, and *Pokémon White* players. Open the Tag Log, and you can check detailed information and gameplay status of passersby. As long as the Nintendo DS system is on, even if it's closed, data is exchanged automatically.

Tag Log

Tap →

- Statistician rank (p. 414)
- **Favorite Medal and number of Medals**
- **Thank others**
- **Send message**
  Tap to enter a message of up to 8 characters

Tap

Pass Power screen

- **Set Pass Powers**
  You can set up to three kinds of Pass Powers at the Entree in the Entralink
- **Warp to the Entralink**

Information about nearby people

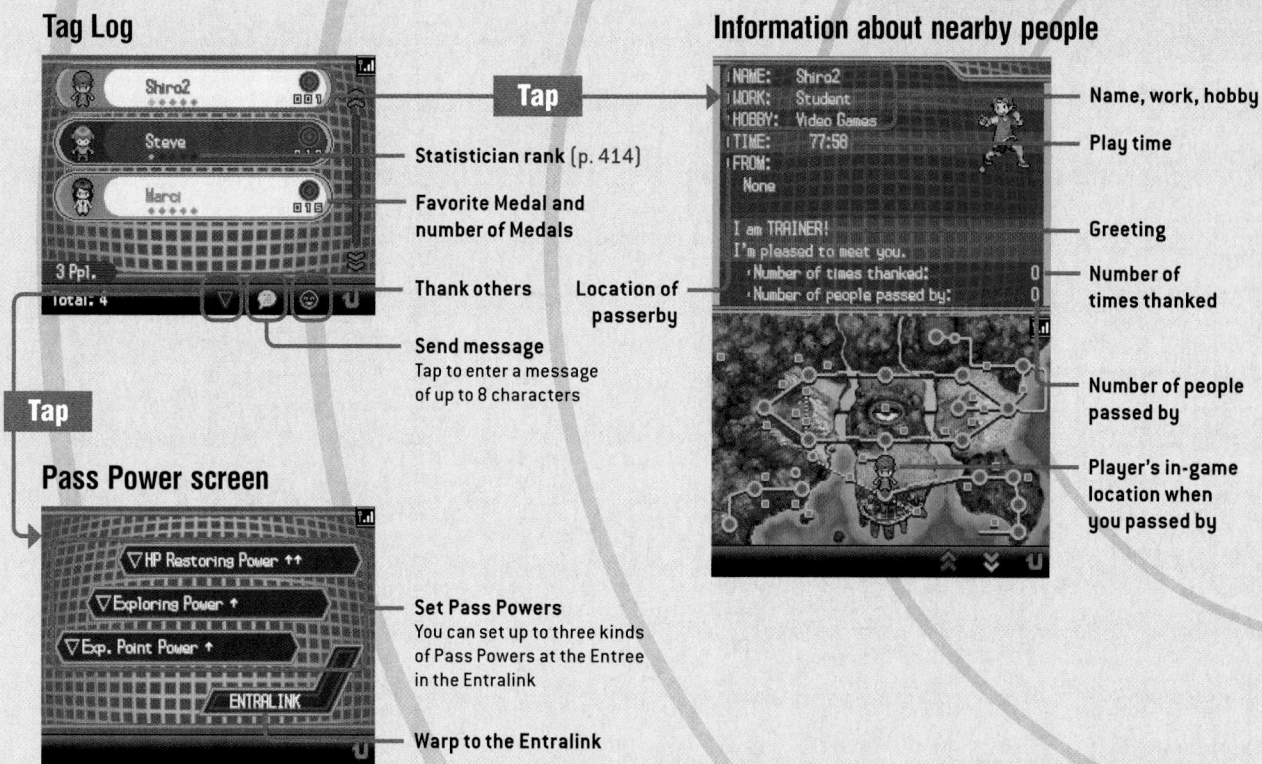

- Name, work, hobby
- Play time
- Greeting
- Number of times thanked
- **Location of passerby**
- Number of people passed by
- Player's in-game location when you passed by

Pass near many people and collect Medals

You can receive a total of eight different Medals for Tag Mode. You can get the Heavy Traffic Medal for passing 1,000 people or more. You can get the Pass Power MAX Medal for using Pass Powers 100 times or more. Pokémon events are a great opportunity to pass near a lot of people!

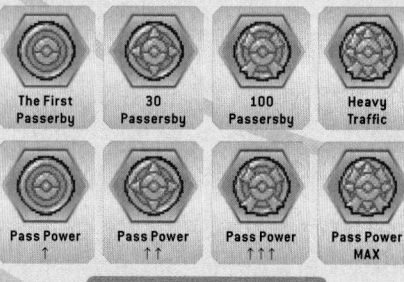

Check p. 531 for the Medal list.

Pass Powers — Pass Powers you gain from the Entree

Clear Funfest Missions, level up your Entree, and activate up to three Pass Powers. You can have up to three Pass Powers in effect, and you and passersby can use them.

Effects of Pass Powers

Pass Power	Necessary Pass Orbs	How long it lasts	Effect	Minimum Entree level Black Lv.	Minimum Entree level White Lv.
Encounter Power ↑	2	3 min.	Increases the chance of encountering wild Pokémon a little	Lv. 9	Lv. 3
Encounter Power ↑↑	3	3 min.	Increases the chance of encountering wild Pokémon	Lv. 12	Lv. 8
Encounter Power ↑↑↑	4	3 min.	Increases the chance of encountering wild Pokémon a lot	Lv. 19	Lv. 14
Encounter Power ↓	2	3 min.	Decreases the chance of encountering wild Pokémon a little	Lv. 0	Lv. 5
Encounter Power ↓↓	3	3 min.	Decreases the chance of encountering wild Pokémon	Lv. 0	Lv. 10
Encounter Power ↓↓↓	4	3 min.	Decreases the chance of encountering wild Pokémon a lot	Lv. 0	Lv. 26
Hatching Power ↑	3	3 min.	Helps Eggs hatch a little faster	Lv. 0	Lv. 13
Hatching Power ↑↑	4	3 min.	Helps Eggs hatch faster	Lv. 0	Lv. 22
Hatching Power ↑↑↑	5	3 min.	Helps Eggs hatch much faster	Lv. 0	Lv. 30
Befriending Power ↑	2	3 min.	Helps Pokémon grow friendly a little faster	Lv. 0	Lv. 7
Befriending Power ↑↑	3	3 min.	Helps Pokémon grow friendly faster	Lv. 0	Lv. 19
Befriending Power ↑↑↑	4	3 min.	Helps Pokémon grow friendly much faster	Lv. 0	Lv. 25
Bargain Power ↑	3	3 min.	Poké Mart gives a 10% discount	Lv. 13	Lv. 0
Bargain Power ↑↑	4	3 min.	Poké Mart gives a 25% discount	Lv. 22	Lv. 0
Bargain Power ↑↑↑	5	3 min.	Poké Mart gives a 50% discount	Lv. 30	Lv. 0
HP Restoring Power ↑	2	—	Restores the HP of the lead Pokémon by 20	Lv. 0	Lv. 0
HP Restoring Power ↑↑	3	—	Restores the HP of the lead Pokémon by 50	Lv. 0	Lv. 2
HP Restoring Power ↑↑↑	4	—	Restores the HP of the lead Pokémon by 200	Lv. 0	Lv. 16
PP Restoring Power ↑	2	—	Restores the PP of 4 moves of the lead Pokémon by 5	Lv. 7	Lv. 0
PP Restoring Power ↑↑	3	—	Restores the PP of 4 moves of the lead Pokémon by 10	Lv. 19	Lv. 0
PP Restoring Power ↑↑↑	4	—	Restores all PP of 4 moves of the lead Pokémon	Lv. 25	Lv. 0
Exp. Point Power ↑	2	3 min.	Increases the Exp. Points from a battle a little	Lv. 0	Lv. 0
Exp. Point Power ↑↑	3	3 min.	Increases the Exp. Points from a battle	Lv. 2	Lv. 0
Exp. Point Power ↑↑↑	4	3 min.	Increases the Exp. Points from a battle very much	Lv. 16	Lv. 0
Exp. Point Power ↓	2	3 min.	Decreases the Exp. Points from a battle a little	Lv. 3	Lv. 9
Exp. Point Power ↓↓	3	3 min.	Decreases the Exp. Points from a battle	Lv. 8	Lv. 12
Exp. Point Power ↓↓↓	4	3 min.	Decreases the Exp. Points from a battle very much	Lv. 14	Lv. 19
Prize Money Power ↑	2	3 min.	The prize money from a battle becomes 150% the usual amount	Lv. 5	Lv. 0
Prize Money Power ↑↑	3	3 min.	The prize money from a battle becomes 200% the usual amount	Lv. 10	Lv. 0
Prize Money Power ↑↑↑	4	3 min.	The prize money from a battle becomes 300% the usual amount	Lv. 26	Lv. 0
Capture Power ↑	4	3 min.	Increases the chance to catch Pokémon a little	Lv. 5	Lv. 5
Capture Power ↑↑	5	3 min.	Increases the chance to catch Pokémon	Lv. 11	Lv. 11
Capture Power ↑↑↑	6	3 min.	Increases the chance to catch Pokémon a lot	Lv. 30	Lv. 30
Exploring Power ↑	5	3 min.	Increases the chance of finding rustling grass and dust clouds a little	Lv. 0	Lv. 0
Exploring Power ↑↑	10	3 min.	Increases the chance of finding rustling grass and dust clouds	Lv. 5	Lv. 5
Exploring Power ↑↑↑	15	3 min.	Increases the chance of finding rustling grass and dust clouds a lot	Lv. 15	Lv. 15
Grotto Power ↑	5	3 min.	Increases the chance of encountering Pokémon in Hidden Grottoes a little	Lv. 10	Lv. 10
Grotto Power ↑↑	10	3 min.	Increases the chance of encountering Pokémon in Hidden Grottoes	Lv. 20	Lv. 20
Grotto Power ↑↑↑	15	3 min.	Increases the chance of encountering Pokémon in Hidden Grottoes a lot	Lv. 30	Lv. 30
Lucky Power ↑	10	3 min.	Increases the chance of encountering uncommon Pokémon a little	Lv. 7	Lv. 7
Lucky Power ↑↑	20	3 min.	Increases the chance of encountering uncommon Pokémon	Lv. 21	Lv. 21
Lucky Power ↑↑↑	30	3 min.	Increases the chance of encountering uncommon Pokémon. Increases the chance of encountering Shiny Pokémon	Lv. 49	Lv. 49
Exploring Power S	50	10 min.	Increases the chance of finding rustling grass and dust clouds a lot for a long time	Lv. 0	Lv. 100
Grotto Power S	50	20 min.	Increases the chance of encountering Pokémon in Hidden Grottoes a lot for a long time	Lv. 50	Lv. 50
Lucky Power S	50	10 min.	Increases the chance of encountering uncommon Pokémon for a long time. Increases the chance of encountering Shiny Pokémon	Lv. 100	Lv. 0

Tip — Special conditions can activate some Pass Powers

Some Pass Powers are activated under special conditions. The effects are the same as those of "↑↑↑," but they last for 30 minutes. Meet the conditions to activate them and use them for your adventure.

How to activate special Pass Powers

Special Pass Power	How to activate the Pass Power
Hatching Power S	Pass by a player who plays a foreign version of *Pokémon Black 2*, *Pokémon White 2*, *Pokémon Black*, or *Pokémon White*.
Bargain Power S	The total number of people in your Tag Log becomes a multiple of 100.
Befriending Power S	Tag Log reaches a count of 20 for game versions different from yours.
Exp. Point Power S	Tag Log reaches a count of 30 people.
Prize Money Power S	Tag Log reaches a count of 20 for characters of the opposite gender.
Capture Power S	Tag Log reaches a total number of people that's a good turning point number (11–99,999).

Passerby Analytics | # Join Passerby Analytics and complete requests

Passerby Analytics HQ is located in Castelia City. Accept requests from the leader and collect Tag Mode data using your C-Gear Survey Radar. When you complete a request, you'll receive an item as a reward. As you complete more requests, your statistician rank goes up and you'll receive more requests.

Trainer was appointed as a statistician!

Passerby Analytics HQ

Pie chart
Check your statistician rank, number of people passed by, number of times thanked, etc.

Answer questionnaires
Answer all questionnaires, and more surveys become available for you to conduct.

Enter something you say when you're happy

Leader of Passerby Analytics HQ
When you speak to him for the first time, you can join Passersby Analytics. After that, you can accept survey requests and report the results.

Enter thank-you messages for Tag Mode

Enter your greetings for Tag Mode

How to complete a Passerby Survey

1 Speak to the leader and pick a survey to conduct

Talk to the leader and accept a request. Choose the type of survey, either timed or head-count, and which survey you want to conduct.

Will you accept this survey request?

2 Let your C-Gear Survey Radar conduct a requested survey

Open your C-Gear Survey Radar and tap "SELECT A SURVEY." Once you select a survey, pass by people and collect data.

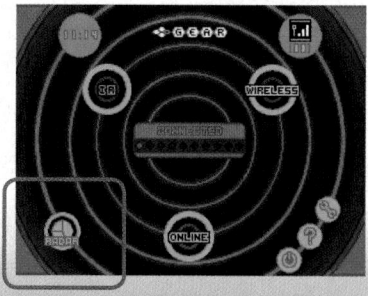

3 Speak to the leader to receive a reward

When you complete the survey using the Survey Radar, go to Passerby Analytics HQ and talk to the leader. He'll give you a reward.

Trainer obtained a Great Ball!

Passerby Analytics | # Complete a lot of requests and raise your statistician rank

Your statistician rank will go up as you complete requests. As your rank goes up, you'll get more requests. When you complete all the requests, you'll receive a Rare Candy.

You'll become a "B-rank statistician" if you complete a requested survey

Statistician Rank

Rank	How to reach this rank	Number of ● to be displayed
C	Default, just joined	
B	Complete 4 surveys	●●●●●
A	Complete 10 surveys	●●●●● ●●
S	Complete 16 surveys	●●●●● ●●●
S+	Complete 21 surveys	●●●●● ●●●●●

Passerby Analytics — Complete all 46 requests

You can receive 23 surveys at Passerby Analytics HQ, and each one can be done as a head-count survey and a timed survey. Pass by many people and complete all the requests.

Surveys requested by Passerby Analytics HQ

Request No.	Survey	Request	Available When	Request Type	To Complete the Survey	Reward
1	How Do You Play the Game	Which version is more popular?	Available from the start	Timed survey	Collect Tag Mode data for 2 hours or more	Great Ball
				Head-count survey	Collect Tag Mode data from 5 passersby or more	
2		The first Pokémon you picked?	Available from the start	Timed survey	Collect Tag Mode data for 2 hours or more	Net Ball
				Head-count survey	Collect Tag Mode data from 5 passersby or more	
3		How long have you been playing?	Available from the start	Timed survey	Collect Tag Mode data for 4 hours or more	Timer Ball
				Head-count survey	Collect Tag Mode data from 10 passersby or more	
4	Details about People	More men or more women?	Available from the start	Timed survey	Collect Tag Mode data for 4 hours or more	Dusk Ball
				Head-count survey	Collect Tag Mode data from 10 passersby or more	
5		The most common job?	When your statistician rank reaches B	Timed survey	Collect Tag Mode data for 4 hours or more	Heal Ball
				Head-count survey	Collect Tag Mode data from 10 passersby or more	
6		The most common hobby?	When your statistician rank reaches B	Timed survey	Collect Tag Mode data for 4 hours or more	Quick Ball
				Head-count survey	Collect Tag Mode data from 10 passersby or more	
7	Pokémon Favorites	More popular, battles or trades?	When your statistician rank reaches B	Timed survey	Collect Tag Mode data for 8 hours or more	Hyper Potion
				Head-count survey	Collect Tag Mode data from 20 passersby or more	
8		Favorite kind of Pokémon?	When your statistician rank reaches B	Timed survey	Collect Tag Mode data for 8 hours or more	Revive
				Head-count survey	Collect Tag Mode data from 20 passersby or more	
9		Favorite Pokémon type?	When your statistician rank reaches B	Timed survey	Collect Tag Mode data for 8 hours or more	Pearl
				Head-count survey	Collect Tag Mode data from 20 passersby or more	
10	Ideals and Values	Where do people prefer to live?	When your statistician rank reaches B	Timed survey	Collect Tag Mode data for 8 hours or more	Stardust
				Head-count survey	Collect Tag Mode data from 20 passersby or more	
11		About what's most important	When your statistician rank reaches A	Timed survey	Collect Tag Mode data for 12 hours or more	Heart Scale
				Head-count survey	Collect Tag Mode data from 30 passersby or more	
12	Likable People	Favorite kinds of people?	When your statistician rank reaches A	Timed survey	Collect Tag Mode data for 12 hours or more	Big Mushroom
				Head-count survey	Collect Tag Mode data from 30 passersby or more	
13	Future Goals	About the future	When your statistician rank reaches A	Timed survey	Collect Tag Mode data for 12 hours or more	Big Pearl
				Head-count survey	Collect Tag Mode data from 30 passersby or more	
14	Entertainment	Which songs can you relate to?	When your statistician rank reaches A	Timed survey	Collect Tag Mode data for 12 hours or more	Star Piece
				Head-count survey	Collect Tag Mode data from 30 passersby or more	
15		Favorite music?	When your statistician rank reaches A	Timed survey	Collect Tag Mode data for 16 hours or more	PP Up
				Head-count survey	Collect Tag Mode data from 40 passersby or more	
16		About TV and movies	When your statistician rank reaches A	Timed survey	Collect Tag Mode data for 16 hours or more	HP Up
				Head-count survey	Collect Tag Mode data from 40 passersby or more	
17	What If...	Where would you go with a time machine?	When your statistician rank reaches S	Timed survey	Collect Tag Mode data for 16 hours or more	Carbos
				Head-count survey	Collect Tag Mode data from 40 passersby or more	
18		What if...?	When your statistician rank reaches S	Timed survey	Collect Tag Mode data for 16 hours or more	Iron
				Head-count survey	Collect Tag Mode data from 40 passersby or more	
19	Sports and Pastimes	Most popular kind of game?	When your statistician rank reaches S	Timed survey	Collect Tag Mode data for 20 hours or more	Protein
				Head-count survey	Collect Tag Mode data from 50 passersby or more	
20		About a holiday	When your statistician rank reaches S	Timed survey	Collect Tag Mode data for 20 hours or more	Zinc
				Head-count survey	Collect Tag Mode data from 50 passersby or more	
21	More about Pokémon	How many years playing Pokémon?	When your statistician rank reaches S	Timed survey	Collect Tag Mode data for 20 hours or more	Calcium
				Head-count survey	Collect Tag Mode data from 50 passersby or more	
22		Most popular Gym Leader?	When your statistician rank reaches S+	Timed survey	Collect Tag Mode data for 24 hours or more	Rare Bone
				Head-count survey	Collect Tag Mode data from 100 passersby or more	
23		Most fun part of Pokémon?	When your statistician rank reaches S+	Timed survey	Collect Tag Mode data for 24 hours or more	Nugget
				Head-count survey	Collect Tag Mode data from 100 passersby or more	

Tip — Two survey types

Each survey has a head-count survey and a timed survey. A head-count survey is a survey to collect information from a fixed number of people. When you go to a place where a lot of people gather, choose this type of survey. A timed survey is a survey to collect information for a fixed period of time. If you have time to spend, you may be able to complete it more easily.

Head-count survey

This is a survey to collect data for a specified number of people.

Timed survey

This is a survey to collect data for a specified time.

The C-Gear's Three Communication Modes

Communications 4

IR, Wireless, and Online Features

The C-Gear is a device for using the communication functions in *Pokémon Black 2* and *Pokémon White 2*. Just tap buttons displayed on the Touch Screen, and you can use different communication features. Learn how to use your C-Gear—the basics of communication.

How to use the C-Gear

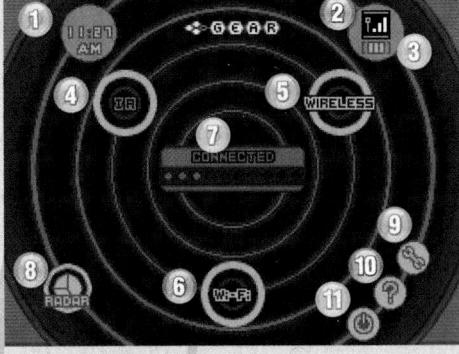

 Current time

 Reception
The more antennas are shown, the better the reception is.

 Battery charge

 Trade, battle, and more using IR (Infrared Connection)

 Use wireless communications to warp to the Entralink or activate the Xtransceiver

 Use Game Sync via Nintendo Wi-Fi Connection

 Open the Tag Log (Image when you haven't passed by anyone.)

 Open the Tag Log (Image when you have passed by other players.)

 Open the Tag Log
(Image when there are other players in Funfest Missions nearby).

 Open the Survey Radar

 Change the arrangement of the "IR," "WIRELESS," and "ONLINE" buttons

 Open Help for detailed information about the C-Gear

 Turn the C-Gear off or on

What the colors on your C-Gear mean

IR	Status
Blinks slowly in red	Normal

Wireless	Status
Blinks slowly in yellow	Normal
Blinks fast in yellow	Someone is calling you on the Xtransceiver
Blinks slowly in red	Wireless Pokémon distribution etc. have been detected
Blinks slowly in blue	Someone is in the Union Room
Blinks slowly in pink	Tag Mode and Survey Radar have been detected, or you can join a Funfest Mission that someone has started

Online	Status
Blinks slowly in green	Nintendo Wi-Fi Connection available at home, etc.
Blinks gently in blue	Normal
Blinks slowly in blue	Connected to Nintendo Zone or a wireless public network
Blinks slowly in red	Free access point available, or Nintendo Wi-Fi Connection settings haven't been completed on your Nintendo DS system

Communicate Easily Using Infrared Connection

Communications **5**

Connecting with IR is quick and easy

IR is a communication method that allows you to battle and trade with your friends and family members by just facing your Nintendo DS systems toward each other. Tap "IR" on the C-Gear to battle, trade, or use Feeling Check.

Game features using IR

◎ Battle

Any Pokémon can participate in IR battles. They are all set to Lv. 50 during battles. Trainers can also use the Wonder Launcher during the battle (p. 438).

◎ Trade

Each person offers one Pokémon in a trade using IR. Talk with your friend and trade for the Pokémon you both want.

◎ Feeling Check

The Feeling Check is a game to check your compatibility with your friend. The result is shown as a number. The number of Sweet Hearts you can receive depends on the score.

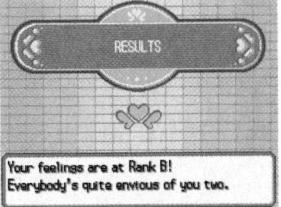

Scores and the number of Sweet Hearts you receive

Score	Sweet Hears you receive
0 to 79	1
80 to 99	2
100	3

◎ Exchange Friend Codes

Just tap "IR" on your C-Gear and then "FRIEND CODE," and you can exchange Friend Codes with your friend.

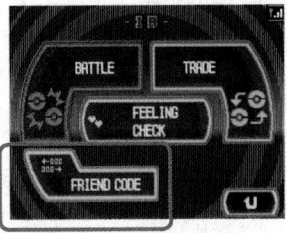

What you can do after exchanging Friend Codes

Use the Xtransceiver to call each other

Use the Wi-Fi Club in Pokémon Center 2F

Communicate using IR and collect Medals

You can receive a total of 16 different Medals when you battle, trade, exchange Friend Codes, and use the Feeling Check.

 Link Battle Amateur
 Link Battle Pioneer
 Link Battle Expert
 Born to Battle
 Beginning Trader
 Occasional Trader
 Frequent Trader
 Great Trade-Up

 Opposite Trader
 Pen Pal
 First Friend
 Extensive Friendship
 Broad Friendship
 Global Connection
 Feeling Master
 Ace of Hearts

Check p. 532 for the Medal list.

Have Fun with Friends Using Wireless Communications

Play games with friends nearby

Wireless communications allow you to link up with your good friends and other players within about 30 feet. You need to exchange Friend Codes to use the Xtransceiver.

Game features using wireless communications

Xtransceiver

Up to four people can talk to each other face-to-face with the Xtransceiver if you use your Nintendo DSi, Nintendo DSi XL, Nintendo 3DS, or Nintendo 3DS XL. You can also play two minigames.

Chat (up to 4 people)

Balloon Catch

Balloon Ka-boom

Entralink

Try Funfest Missions in the Entralink (p. 408). You can play with up to 100 people!

Union Room

Enter the Union Room in Pokémon Center 2F to enjoy various game features, such as battle, trade, drawing, and Spin Trade, with the people there.

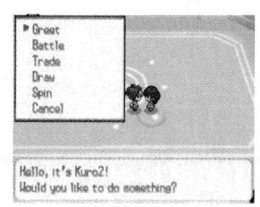

What you can do in the Union Room

Show your Trainer Card to the person you talked to

Trade Pokémon with the person you talked to

Battle with the person you talked to

Draw with up to five people

Spin Trade Eggs with two to five people

Chat with all people in the room using easy chat

Use Wireless and Online and collect Medals

You can receive a total of 19 different Medals related to Wireless and Online communications. Enjoy battle, trade, Spin Trade in the Union Room, and minigames on the Xtransceiver to collect Medals.

 Link Battle Amateur

Link Battle Pioneer

Link Battle Expert

Born to Battle

Beginning Trader

Occasional Trader

Frequent Trader

Great Trade-Up

Opposite Trader

Pen Pal

 Spin Trade Whiz

 Minigame Fan

 Minigame Buff

Minigame Expert

 Best Minigamer

 Balloon Rookie

 Balloon Technician

 Balloon Expert

Balloon Conqueror

Check p. 532 for the Medal list.

Play with People From Far Away with Nintendo Wi-Fi Connection

Play with distant friends and players abroad

Set up your DS system for Nintendo WFC, and you can have fun with your friends no matter where they are. To use the Wi-Fi Club, you need to exchange Friend Codes. For Random Matchup and GTS, you don't need to exchange Friend Codes. You can even communicate with players in other countries.

Game features using Nintendo Wi-Fi Connection

Wi-Fi Club

Go to the Wi-Fi Club in Pokémon Center 2F. Gather with people you have exchanged Friend Codes with and enjoy battle, trade, and Xtransceiver communication.

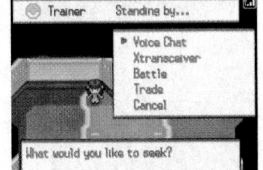

What you can do in the Wi-Fi Club

Use the Xtransceiver with the person you talked to

Trade Pokémon with the person you talked to

Battle with the person you talked to

Voice chat even during battle or trade

Random Matchup

You can have a Random Matchup on Pokémon Center 2F. Connect to Nintendo Wi-Fi Connection and you'll automatically be matched up with another player for a Pokémon battle.

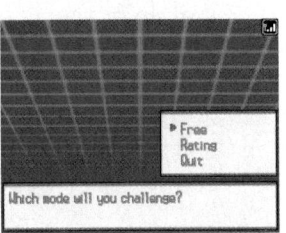

GTS (Global Trade Station)

Enjoy global trade on Pokémon Center 2F. You can trade Pokémon with people all across the globe. There are two ways to trade: GTS and GTS Negotiations.

Battle Videos

Check Battle Videos on Pokémon Center 2F. You can watch Battle Videos collected from all over the world and register your Battle Video.

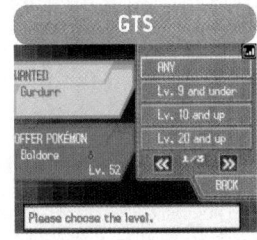

Xtransceiver

Chat with your friends using the Xtransceiver. You can draw graffiti on each other!

Musical Photo

Check and register a picture you took during a Musical.

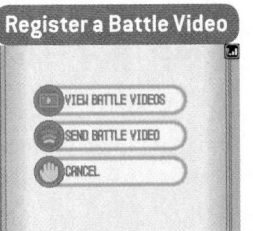

See p. 421 for Game Sync, another feature of the C-Gear.

The Pokémon Global Link

http://www.pokemon-gl.com/

Visit the PGL every day for many fun features

The Pokémon Global Link is a website that expands your play experience for *Pokémon Black 2*, *Pokémon White 2*, *Pokémon Black*, and *Pokémon White*. Enhance your Pokémon lifestyle by registering your *Pokémon Black 2* and *Pokémon White 2*

at the PGL. The latest version includes new features in the Pokémon Dream World and the ability to see Global Trade Station and Global Battle Union info both in one place.

Home page (after you log in)

Your info
On My Page, you can add or switch your Game Cards.

E-Z Mail
Send mail using fixed phrases to Friends, Trade Pals, and Dream Pals.

Game Card in Use
"Switch Game Cards" to switch your Game Card to another registered Game Card.

Tucked-in Pokémon
A tucked-in Pokémon is displayed when tucked in using Game Sync.

Pokémon Dream World NEW!
(p. 422)

Promotions
See the current list of promotions.

Support
Illustrated manuals and guides full of easy instructions for beginners.

Reports NEW!

Wi-Fi Competitions
Enter a Pokémon battle competition using Nintendo Wi-Fi Connection.

Customize
Receive C-Gear skins, Pokédex skins, and Pokémon Musical shows (p. 424).

● Get a special Gothorita with the Hidden Ability Shadow Tag

Enter this special password at the PGL to get a Gothorita with the Hidden Ability Shadow Tag. Shadow Tag prevents opponents from fleeing battle. You can stop the opponent in its tracks and attack it with powerful moves like Psyshock and Future Sight.

Password: PGLPK15G

 **Tip** — **No access for 100 days or more turns Berries into Dream Points**

If you haven't logged in for 100 days or more, the Berries in your Treasure Chest in the Pokémon Dream World are converted to Dream Points (except for one of each type of Berry). You gain 10 Dream Points for each Berry converted this way.

Register Game Sync IDs of *Pokémon Black 2* and *Pokémon White 2*

If you've already registered Game Sync IDs of the previous *Pokémon Black Version* and *Pokémon White Version*, add Game Sync IDs of *Pokémon Black Version 2* and *Pokémon White* Version 2. Once you register them, you can switch Game Cards any time after you log in.

How to add Game Sync IDs

◉ Nintendo DS/Nintendo 3DS Steps

Set up your DS system for Nintendo WFC. Tap "ONLINE" on the C-Gear and then "GAME SYNC." The Game Sync ID for the Game Card you're playing will be issued. Then, choose a Pokémon from your PC Boxes to tuck in. Once the Pokémon falls asleep, the steps on your system are done.

Tap "GAME SYNC" on the C-Gear

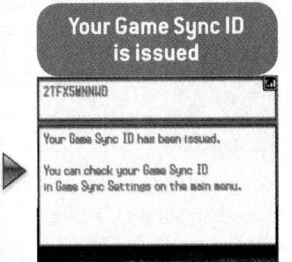
Your Game Sync ID is issued

◉ PC Steps

After logging in to the Pokémon Global Link, click "Add Game Card" under the logo of the Game Card you're playing. Enter the Game Sync ID issued in *Pokémon Black Version 2* or *Pokémon White Version 2*, and click "Register." The Game Card will be added.

Click "Add Game Card"

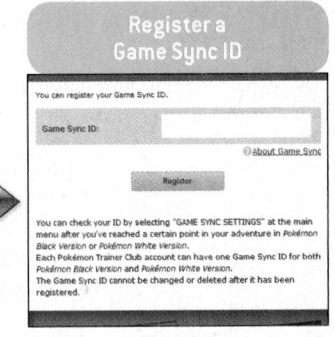
Register a Game Sync ID

See p. 420 when you access the Pokémon Global Link for the first time.

Tip

Bonuses for those who have registered *Pokémon Black* and *Pokémon White*

Ongoing promotions give two bonuses to everyone who has already registered *Pokémon Black Version* or *Pokémon White Version* and added *Pokémon Black Version 2* or *Pokémon White Version 2*. Through these promotions, you can receive three C-Gear skins and three Pokémon Dolls. Access the Pokémon Global Link to see how to get the presents.

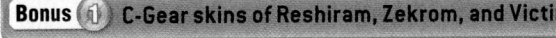
Bonus ① C-Gear skins of Reshiram, Zekrom, and Victini

Bonus ② Pokémon Dolls of Snivy, Tepig, and Oshawott

◆ The registration period for these promotions is October 4, 2012, through January 17, 2013.

Enjoy the new features in the Pokémon Dream World

The Pokémon Dream World is a dream world that unfolds in the Pokémon Global Link. Use Game Sync to tuck in a Pokémon and send it to this world. The Pokémon Dream World has also been upgraded in the relaunch of the Pokémon Global Link. These are the newly added features.

New features in the Pokémon Dream World

The Icy Cave opens on the Island of Dreams

Now you can visit the new area called the Icy Cave from the Island of Dreams. Three minigames, which you can enjoy with Pokémon you meet, have also been added (p. 389).

Pokémon you can meet on the Island of Dreams have dramatically changed

Log in with *Pokémon Black Version 2* or *Pokémon White Version 2*, and you'll meet different Pokémon than before on the Island of Dreams.

See p. 390 for Pokémon you can meet in the Pokémon Dream World.

Tucked-in Pokémon determine which area is easy to go

You can visit six areas on the Island of Dreams. The area you see is determined randomly, but depending on your tucked-in Pokémon, you can go to a certain area more easily.

See p. 388 for Pokémon types that affect the area you visit.

Example of Pokémon's types and easy areas to go

Water -type Pokémon	▷	◉ Sparkling Sea
Grass -type Pokémon	▷	◉ Pleasant Forest
Ice -type Pokémon	▷	◉ Icy Cave
Ghost -type Pokémon	▷	◉ Spooky Manor

More Décor items to decorate your home

Many Décor items to decorate your home have been added. Check the Dream Catalogue in your home.

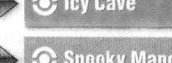

The waiting time has been shortened to 20 hours

You can play the Pokémon Dream World for one hour a day. In the past, you needed to wait for 24 hours to access it again. Now the waiting time has been shortened by four hours, and you can play again 20 hours later.

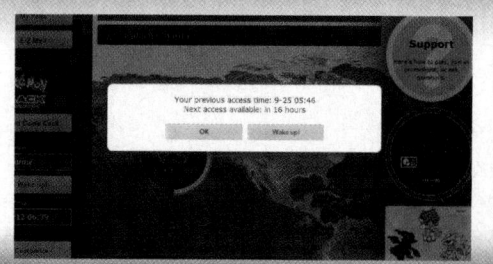

Check information in Reports

Reports show Pokémon trade and battle results from all over the world. Four types of data are gathered here: GTS (Global Trade Station), GBU (Global Battle Union), Wi-Fi Competitions, and Game Sync World Records. These great features tell you how popular or strong particular Pokémon are in the world.

Contents of Reports

● GTS (Global Trade Station)

The GTS is a system that helps you trade Pokémon with players all over the world using Nintendo Wi-Fi Connection (p. 419). Reports show detailed information about the GTS, such as rankings of most traded Pokémon and most deposited Pokémon. This information is updated weekly.

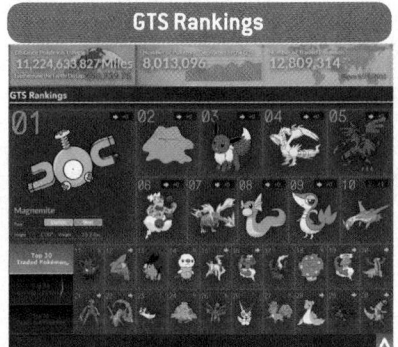

GTS Rankings

Top 30 most traded Pokémon, most desirable Pokémon, etc. are displayed.

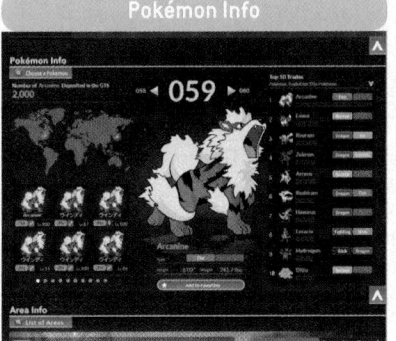

Pokémon Info

You can check detailed information such as the number of a certain Pokémon deposited.

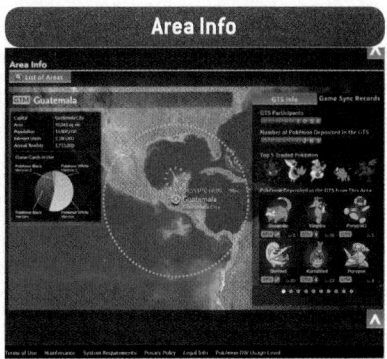

Area Info

You can check the number of GTS participants and popular Pokémon in a selected area.

● GBU (Global Battle Union)

The GBU gathers and stores battle records of Random Matchups (Rating Mode) using Nintendo Wi-Fi Connection. New seasons kick off every three months, and the Rankings for each season are displayed. You can also check out which Pokémon are most frequently chosen for battle. This information is updated weekly.

GBU Rankings

Check top-rated players in the Rankings. Rankings are also displayed by battle format.

Pokémon Info

Check the top 10 Pokémon most frequently chosen as party Pokémon. Also, check Pokémon frequently chosen with a selected Pokémon.

Wi-Fi Competitions

Wi-Fi Competitions are battle competitions that you enter from the Pokémon Global Link. Reports show past competitions, the rankings of participants, and information about Pokémon used by strong players. If you participated in a competition, click "My Ranking" to see your Ranking.

Wi-Fi Competitions

Review a list of past Wi-Fi Competitions. Select a competition to see the detailed information.

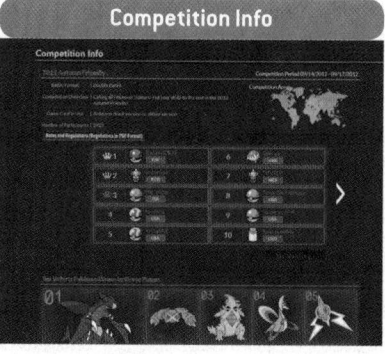

Competition Info

Check the Rankings of participants of the selected competition.

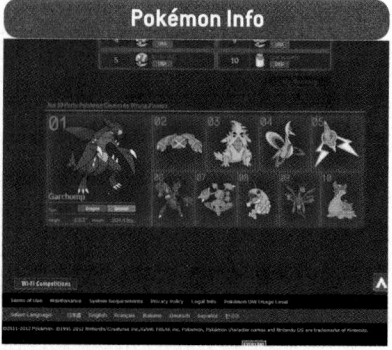

Pokémon Info

Check top 10 party Pokémon chosen by strong players.

Game Sync World Records

Game Sync World Records show various data gathered from save data of players all over the world. This information is updated weekly.

Game Sync World Records

Examples of Game Sync World Records

1. Top Healing Locations
2. Top Hatching Locations
3. Top Nickname Locations
4. Top Fishing Locations
5. Top Heal-at-Home Locations

Customize and make your *Pokémon Black 2* and *Pokémon White 2* cooler

The "Customize" button on the home page allows you to download C-Gear skins, Pokédex skins, and Musical shows. Change the look of your game and make it even cooler!

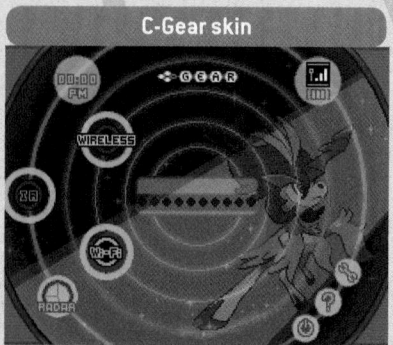

C-Gear skin

Download a C-Gear skin, and you can change the design significantly.

Pokédex skin

You can change the screen you see when you choose "POKÉDEX" on your game menu.

Musical show

Enjoy a new show in the Pokémon Musical in Nimbasa City.

◆ Some C-Gear skins, Pokédex skins, and Musical shows are available for a limited time only through the Pokémon Global Link.

Pokémon Battle Primer

Train Pokémon and Battle

The strategy of Pokémon battles is deep and engaging. See if you can become a Pokémon battle master!

In *Pokémon Black Version 2* and *Pokémon White Version 2*, you can battle against your nearby friends and family, as well as against other players from around the world. Training your Pokémon to be strong and having a deep knowledge of Pokémon are the keys to victory in battles against other players. Learn all there is to know about training and battling Pokémon to become a battle master.

The fun of battling — Battling against other players is a ton of fun!

1 The Pokémon you carefully train will be great in battle

Spend time carefully training your Pokémon and they will grow strong. Use the Pokémon you trained to seize victory in battles against other players.

2 Use certain techniques to dramatically increase a Pokémon's strength

Just by teaching a Pokémon certain moves, or having it hold certain items, it can become dramatically stronger. With certain techniques, you can totally change your battling style.

3 There's always a chance to make a comeback

Even if you find yourself in a pinch in a battle, there's always a chance to turn the tables on your opponent if you carefully choose your Pokémon's moves, Abilities, and held items. The battle's not over until it's over, so don't give up.

4 Predict your opponent's moves for a great victory

Try to think ahead of your opponent and predict what moves he or she will make multiple turns in advance. If your predictions turn out to be correct and you win the battle as a result, you'll feel on top of the world.

5 Play with people from far away

By connecting to Nintendo Wi-Fi Connection, you can battle against other players who are far away from you. You'll encounter new and often unpredictable strategies in battles against players you've never met.

6 Record your wins and losses on your Trainer Card

As you play more and more Link Battles, your wins and losses will be recorded on the back of your Trainer Card. Show your win record off to your friends!

Against Other Players

The fun of training

Carefully train your Pokémon and not only will you grow attached to them, but they'll do great in battles, too!

1 Show off the powerful Pokémon you trained from a low level

If you train a Pokémon up from a low level, it will grow strong. Surprise everyone by showing off the powerful Pokémon you trained.

2 Use the best training method for each Pokémon

Pokémon have different stats, so learn about each individual Pokémon's strengths and weaknesses. Then decide whether you want to further develop those strengths or supplement for the weaknesses. Figure out the best training method for each Pokémon.

3 You can learn a lot about battling, too

Even if you have a strong Pokémon, you won't be able to defeat your opponents in battle without sound strategies. To avoid losing, study up on winning strategies and tactics.

4 Find the perfect combo for each of your Pokémon

A combo is the right combination of a Pokémon's moves and its Ability to produce a desired effect that helps you win the battle. As you become more knowledgeable about Pokémon, always be thinking about what kind of combos you can create.

5 Learn all about Pokémon types and Abilities

In order to come up with effective battling styles and combos, you'll need to have a deep knowledge about Pokémon. Learn all about the Ability, moves, and held items of the Pokémon you trained while enjoying the game.

6 You'll love Pokémon even more

Simply by carefully considering how you want to train your Pokémon, you will begin to learn a lot about them. By doing so, you'll grow even more fond of your Pokémon.

Pokémon Battles Introduction **1**

Master All the Battle Formats to Win

Get to know the battle formats so you can win in every one

The battle formats in *Pokémon Black Version 2* and *Pokémon White Version 2* can be split into four types. Learn about the rules and characteristics of each format so you can win in every one.

Single Battle

Each side battles with one Pokémon at a time

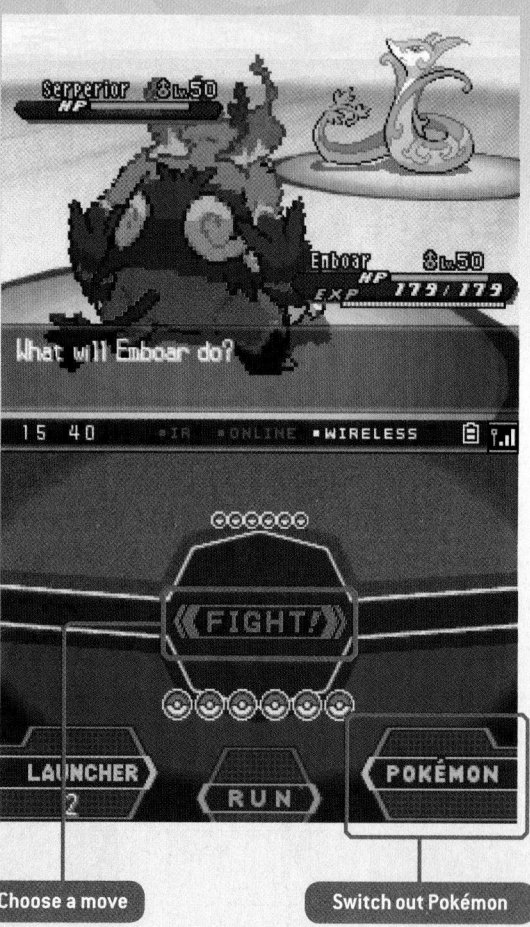

Choose a move

Switch out Pokémon

Each Pokémon Trainer sends out one Pokémon to battle. On each turn, you and your opponent can take one action each. In general, the Pokémon with the higher Speed stat gets to take its action first. Tap the Pokémon icon on the Touch Screen to swap out for another Pokémon in your party. It takes one turn to switch, though.

Double Battle

Each side battles with two Pokémon at a time

Choose a move

Switch out Pokémon

Each Pokémon Trainer sends out two Pokémon to battle. In Double Battles, the range of an attack is important, and attacks that can hit both of your opponent's Pokémon become very useful. Double Battles will require you to learn even more about moves and their effects than in Single Battles. It's important to come up with effective ways to combine Pokémon moves, held items, and Abilities in Double Battles.

Triple Battle

Each side battles with three Pokémon at a time

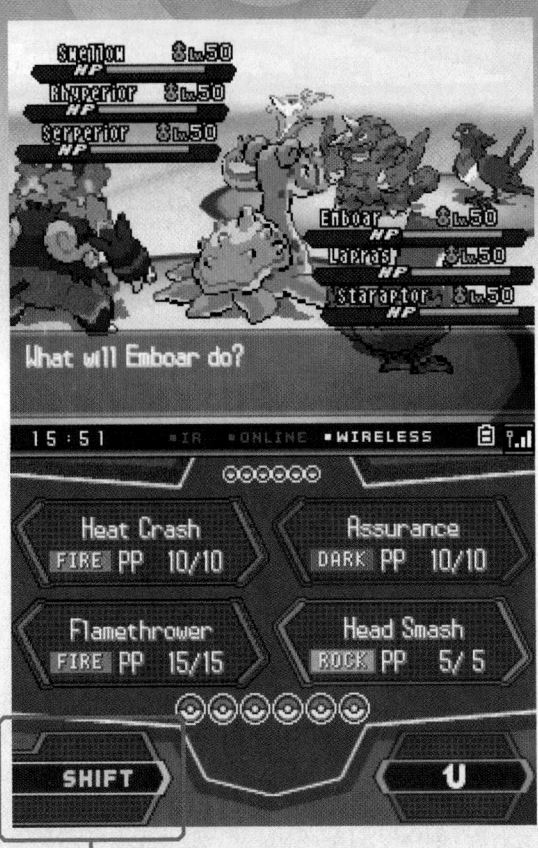

Swap the Pokémon in the middle with the Pokémon on the left or right side

Each Pokémon Trainer sends out three Pokémon to battle. The Pokémon in the middle can target any of the opposing Trainer's three Pokémon. The Pokémon on the left and right can target only the Pokémon directly in front of itself and the Pokémon in the middle. Triple Battles can be very demanding, as they require you to battle while shifting around your Pokémon.

Rotation Battle

In this evolved form of the Single Battle format, each side battles with three Pokémon at a time

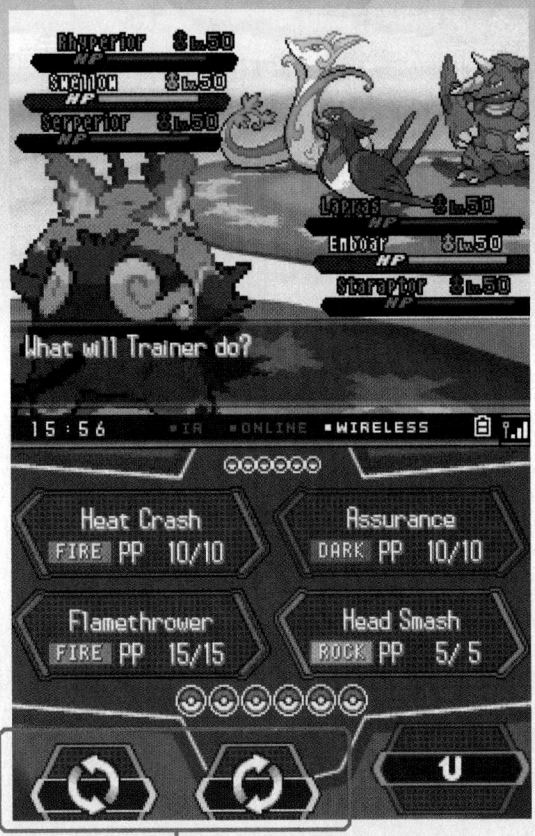

Rotate in one of the Pokémon from the back and use its attack that same turn

Each Pokémon Trainer sends out three Pokémon to battle. Unlike Triple Battles, you and your opponent can take only one action per turn in Rotation Battles. It's up to you which of your Pokémon will take an action on any given turn. What makes Rotation Battles unique is that Pokémon can move and attack on the same turn. Even a Pokémon in the back can move to the front and attack on the same turn.

Single Battles are basic one-on-one battles

Single Battles are the simplest battle format. Since both you and your opponent have only one Pokémon each on the field, you generally only have to worry about what move you will use next. The most basic tactic is to attack your opponent with moves that can exploit its weaknesses. There are many strategic elements in Single Battles, such as how you train your Pokémon, what moves you teach them, what items you give them to hold, etc. You'll need to understand each of these elements and learn how to utilize a variety of tactics if you want to be successful in Single Battles. One such tactic you'll need to learn is how to unleash powerful combos with a single Pokémon.

About the front position

When attacking

EXAMPLE ● The Force Palm move

A Pokémon attacks the opposing Trainer's one Pokémon. Remember, there's a chance the Pokémon could be switched with a waiting party Pokémon.

When a Pokémon uses a status move on itself

EXAMPLE ● The Reflect move

With no allies in the field, status moves that normally affect your entire party affect only the user.

When the opponent switches out his or her Pokémon

EXAMPLE ● The Force Palm move

If the opposing Trainer switches out his or her Pokémon, the attack you chose will hit the newly switched in Pokémon.

When using moves that affect the entire field

EXAMPLE ● The Sunny Day move

When a move affects the entire field, both your Pokémon and your opponent's Pokémon equally receive the effects.

Tip — Other things to know about Single Battles

Combos are generally performed with just one Pokémon

A combo is a battle tactic that combines the effects of moves, Abilities, and items. A combo can be performed even with just a single Pokémon.

Attacks affect only one Pokémon

Even if a move could affect more than one opposing Pokémon at a time, in Single Battles it affects only the one opposing Pokémon you face.

Format **2** **Double Battle** **More strategic options open up in two-on-two battles**

In Double Battle, you and the opposing Trainer send out two Pokémon each, making a total of four Pokémon on the field. The Pokémon at the head of your party stands on the left, and the second Pokémon stands on the right. Compared with Single Battles, the number of strategic options and possible actions you need to be aware of increases dramatically. With certain attacks, one of your Pokémon may be able to hit both of the opposing Trainer's Pokémon, and one of his or her Pokémon may be able to attack both of your Pokémon. You'll need to think ahead carefully and choose your next move from a variety of possibilities. Learn how to take advantage of many different tactics and combos.

Basic ranges of move effects in Double Battles

When the Pokémon on the left attacks

The Pokémon on the left can attack either of the opposing Trainer's Pokémon.

When the Pokémon on the right attacks

The Pokémon on the right can attack either of the opposing Trainer's Pokémon.

When the range is adjacent

EXAMPLE ● The Discharge move

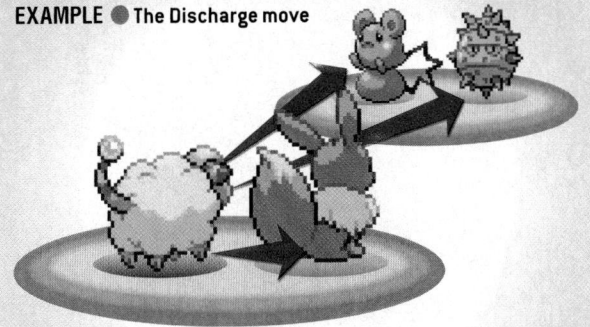

Depending on a move's range, it might affect not only the opposing Trainer's two Pokémon, but also your ally Pokémon.

When a Pokémon uses a status move on itself

EXAMPLE ● The Helping Hand move

Effect of a status move

When you have an ally on the battlefield, a status move can affect the user or the ally.

Tip ## Other things to know about Double Battles

Combos make use of the moves and Abilities of two Pokémon

In Double Battles, you can make your turn really count by combining the moves, Abilities, and items of both your Pokémon. Certain powerful moves inflict damage on your ally Pokémon as well as the opponent's Pokémon. By using the right Pokémon, however, you can ensure that such moves inflict damage only on your opponents.

Format 3 | Triple Battle | **Position matters in three-on-three Triple Battles**

In Triple Battles, you and the opposing Trainer send out three Pokémon each, making six Pokémon in the field. The Pokémon at the head of your party is placed on the left, the second Pokémon in the middle, and the third Pokémon on the right. Be sure to remember that the Pokémon at the head of your party is not placed in the center at the start of a battle.

The Pokémon in the middle can target any of the opposing Trainer's three Pokémon. The Pokémon on the left and right have a limited range. Each can target only the Pokémon right in front of itself and the Pokémon in the middle, not the Pokémon on the far side of its position. Any of your Pokémon can also use status moves on its allies.

Basic ranges of move effects in Triple Battles

When the Pokémon on the left attacks

The Pokémon on the left in Triple Battles can reach the Pokémon directly across from it and the Pokémon in the middle.

When the Pokémon on the right attacks

The Pokémon on the right in Triple Battles can reach the Pokémon directly across from it and the Pokémon in the middle.

When the Pokémon in the middle attacks

The Pokémon in the middle can use a move on any of the opposing Trainer's three Pokémon.

When a move has a long effect range

EXAMPLE ● The Wing Attack move

Long-range moves can reach the Pokémon on the far side even if the user isn't in the middle position.

Tip | **Predict the order in which Pokémon will make their moves**

Imagine a situation where you are one attack away from defeating one of your opponent's Pokémon. In such a situation, it's important to attack with a Pokémon that has a high enough Speed stat that will allow it to land the finishing blow before the opponent's Pokémon gets a chance to make its move. By attacking first, you can prevent your opponent from making a move at all. In Triple Battles, where there are six Pokémon on the field, it's especially important to consider the move order.

Weavile

Whimsicott

⊙ STATS
HP
Attack
Defense
Sp. Atk
Sp. Def
Speed

⊙ STATS
HP
Attack
Defense
Sp. Atk
Sp. Def
Speed

Triple Battle Characteristics 1 — Train Pokémon for Triple Battles

Moves that were unremarkable in Single Battles and Double Battles can be strikingly effective in Triple Battles. One such example is the Ally Switch move, which switches the user's place with one of its allies. This move can be especially useful when the user is on the far left or far right side. To be a star in Triple Battles, you'll need to train Pokémon that have the potential to shine in this format. It's up to you how you develop strategies for Triple Battles. Find the Pokémon to fill the roles in your strategies, and train each Pokémon with care.

Examples of Pokémon that perform well in Triple Battles

The Wide Guard move protects allies from attacks

Mantine

| Move | Wide Guard | Rock |

This move protects from multiple-targeting moves for one turn. If used on more than one turn in a row, its chance of failing increases.

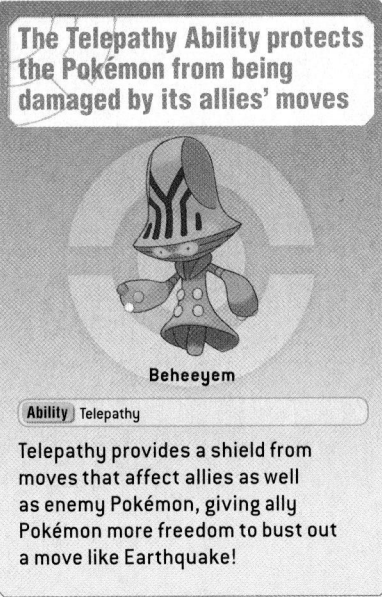

The Telepathy Ability protects the Pokémon from being damaged by its allies' moves

Beheeyem

| Ability | Telepathy |

Telepathy provides a shield from moves that affect allies as well as enemy Pokémon, giving ally Pokémon more freedom to bust out a move like Earthquake!

The Healer Ability heals allies' status conditions

Audino

| Ability | Healer |

Every turn, it tries to heal its allies (but not itself) of status conditions. It succeeds one-third of the time.

Triple Battle Characteristics 2 — Develop a Triple Battle formation

In Triple Battles, a Pokémon's position is a critical factor you need to know to sort out attacks. The Pokémon in the middle can target any of the opposing Trainer's three Pokémon, and it is vulnerable to attacks from all three opposing Pokémon. That central position means that the Pokémon in the middle has a different role to play than those on the right and left. It's a good idea to set up the central position with a Pokémon that has high Defense and Sp. Def stats. Get the most out of the far left and right positions by placing Pokémon that know long-range moves such as Acrobatics and Aura Sphere. You'll need to think carefully about placement if you want to exploit each of your Pokémon's unique characteristics to the fullest.

Good positioning in Triple Battles

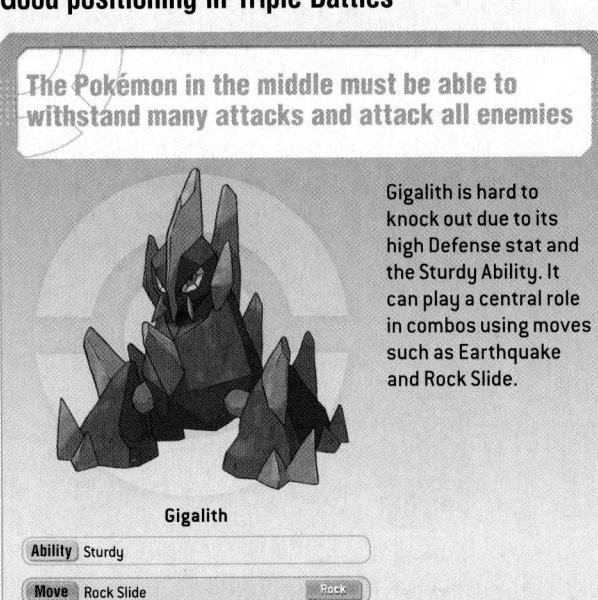

The Pokémon in the middle must be able to withstand many attacks and attack all enemies

Gigalith is hard to knock out due to its high Defense stat and the Sturdy Ability. It can play a central role in combos using moves such as Earthquake and Rock Slide.

Gigalith

| Ability | Sturdy |
| Move | Rock Slide | Rock |

Place Pokémon with long-range moves on the right and left

Pokémon that know long-range moves can really help out when placed on the left or right side. The opposing Trainer may think the Pokémon farthest away can't reach their Pokémon, but you'll soon dispel that illusion!

Pelipper

| Move | Water Pulse | Water |
| Move | Hurricane | Flying |

Format **4** **Rotation Battle** **A Rotation Battle is an evolved form of Single Battle**

In Rotation Battles, you and the opposing Trainer send out three Pokémon each, for a total of six Pokémon in the field. The Pokémon at the head of your party is placed in front, and the remaining two in back. You can choose to use a move from any of your Pokémon, front or back. If you choose a move from one of the Pokémon in back, that Pokémon will rotate to the front. Only the Pokémon in front can be attacked.

About the front position

When attacking

Your front Pokémon can attack only the Pokémon that your opponent rotates to his or her front position.

When being attacked

Your front Pokémon can be attacked only by the Pokémon that your opponent rotates to his or her front position.

About the back positions

When you choose a move from a Pokémon in the back

To use a move, a Pokémon rotates to the front.

If you choose a move of a Pokémon in back, that Pokémon rotates to the front and uses the move.

Rotating a Pokémon to the back won't remove its Confused status condition

When it returns to the back, it remains Confused.

For example, a Pokémon affected by the Confused condition will stay Confused even if it's rotated to the back. If it's withdrawn from the field, however, its status condition will go away.

 **Tip** **Confuse the opposing Pokémon to make it difficult for them to use moves**

In a Rotation Battle, each player can choose moves from any of their three Pokémon, making a total of 12 selectable moves at any time. Try to inflict status conditions such as Sleep, Paralysis, and Confusion on as many of your opponent's Pokémon as possible to make it more difficult for them to execute moves. Doing so could also limit your opponent's possible range of moves, allowing you to more easily predict what move he or she will use, and bringing you one step closer to victory.

Gengar

Move Confuse Ray | Ghost

Jolteon

Move Thunder Wave | Electric

Rotation Battle Characteristics **1** Use moves effective against all opposing Pokémon

In Rotation Battles, not only your Pokémon but also the opposing Trainer's Pokémon can rotate freely. You don't know which of his or her Pokémon will be affected by the move your Pokémon uses. Your best bet is to pick moves that are effective against all three Pokémon, so you benefit no matter which of the opposing Trainer's Pokémon winds up in front.

Example of choosing a move based on the foe's Pokémon types

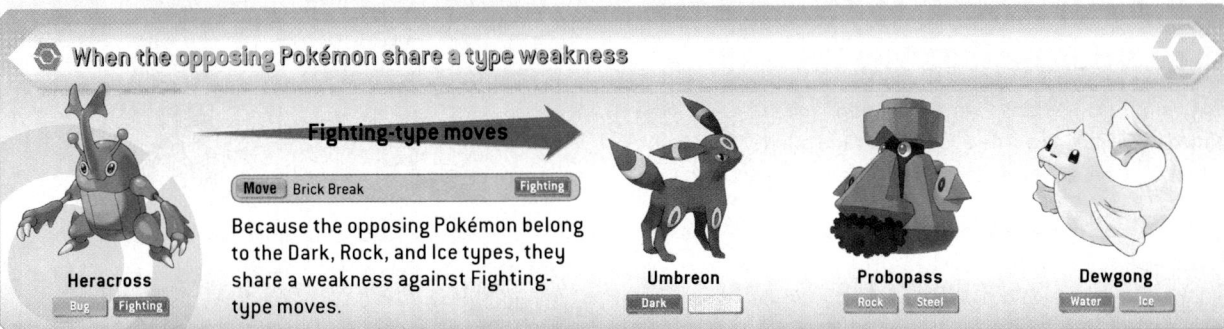

When the opposing Pokémon share a type weakness

Fighting-type moves →

Move Brick Break — Fighting

Because the opposing Pokémon belong to the Dark, Rock, and Ice types, they share a weakness against Fighting-type moves.

Heracross — Bug / Fighting

Umbreon — Dark

Probopass — Rock / Steel

Dewgong — Water / Ice

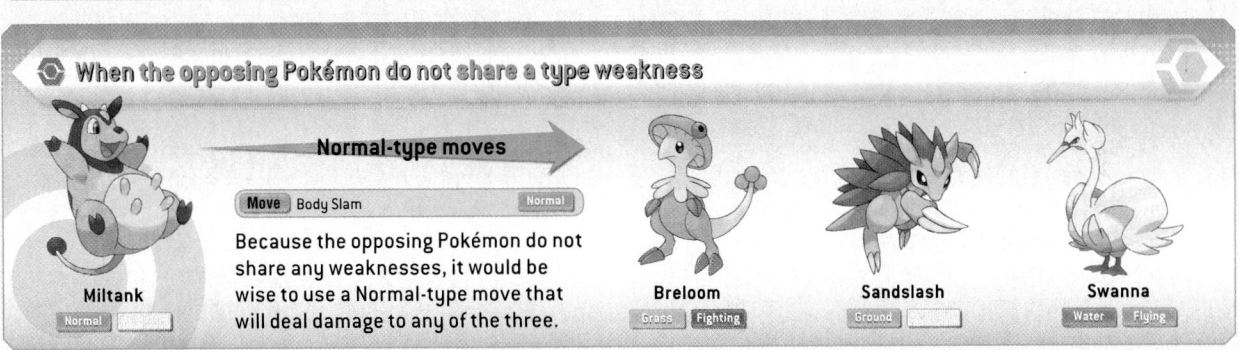

When the opposing Pokémon do not share a type weakness

Normal-type moves →

Move Body Slam — Normal

Because the opposing Pokémon do not share any weaknesses, it would be wise to use a Normal-type move that will deal damage to any of the three.

Miltank — Normal

Breloom — Grass / Fighting

Sandslash — Ground

Swanna — Water / Flying

Rotation Battle Characteristics **2** Compose your team with a creative eye

Some Abilities block all damage from moves of a certain type. For example, Water Absorb and Storm Drain provide complete damage protection from Water-type moves. If you place a Pokémon that might have a protective Ability in back, you'll make the opposing Trainer think twice. Will he or she dare to use a move that might be completely wasted?

Abilities that provide protection from damage by certain types

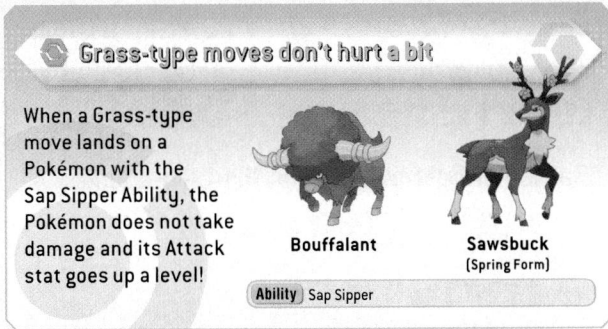

Grass-type moves don't hurt a bit

When a Grass-type move lands on a Pokémon with the Sap Sipper Ability, the Pokémon does not take damage and its Attack stat goes up a level!

Bouffalant

Sawsbuck (Spring Form)

Ability Sap Sipper

Fire-type moves provide welcome warmth

Fire-type moves used against a Pokémon with the Flash Fire Ability won't damage it, but will increase the power of its Fire-type moves by 50%.

Ninetales

Flareon

Ability Flash Fire

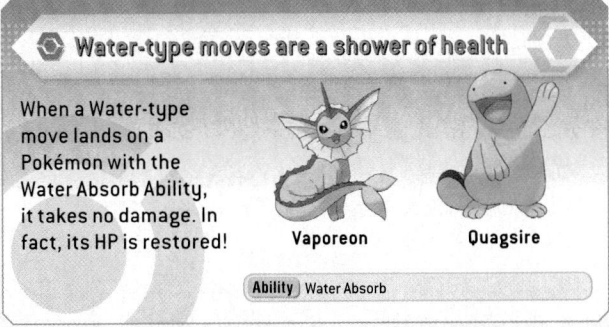

Water-type moves are a shower of health

When a Water-type move lands on a Pokémon with the Water Absorb Ability, it takes no damage. In fact, its HP is restored!

Vaporeon

Quagsire

Ability Water Absorb

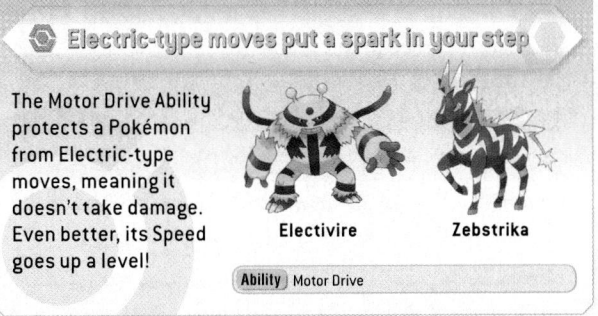

Electric-type moves put a spark in your step

The Motor Drive Ability protects a Pokémon from Electric-type moves, meaning it doesn't take damage. Even better, its Speed goes up a level!

Electivire

Zebstrika

Ability Motor Drive

Pokémon Battles Introduction 2

Connect with Link Battle and Battle Anyone

Choose your Battle Format based on how you want to battle and what connection method you will use

Pokémon Black Version 2 and *Pokémon White Version 2* are loaded with ways to battle your friends and others. Choose the right way to battle for any connection and every occasion.

IR — Battle using the C-Gear

With IR (Infrared Connection), you can easily battle your friends and family simply by positioning your Nintendo DS systems so they face each other. It's easy to get started. From the C-Gear on the Touch Screen, tap the IR icon and then tap Battle. The rules for IR battles are decided in advance. Any Pokémon can participate, and each Pokémon's level will automatically be set to Lv. 50 for the duration of the battle. You'll also always be able to use the Wonder Launcher with this type of battle (p. 438). When there are four participants, the leader of each team should first connect with his or her partner and then the two leaders of each team should connect to each other to begin the battle.

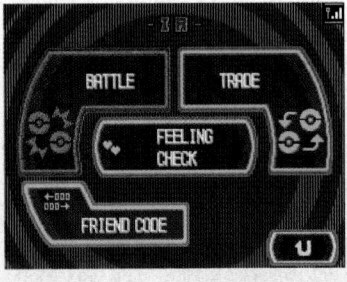

Always keep some Pokémon in your Battle Box so you are ready to accept challenges.

Wireless Communications — Union Room battles

In the Union Room on the second floor of the Pokémon Center, you can enjoy battles against friends and family. Talk to another player in the room and select "Battle" from the list to challenge him or her to a battle. If they accept, you will enter the battle. If you are challenged to a battle by another player, select "Yes" to enter the battle. You can configure the rules for battles in the Union Room before the battle begins. After choosing the Battle Format, decide whether or not to restrict the level of Pokémon that can participate. If you choose Flat Battle, any Pokémon above Lv. 50 will be set to Lv. 50 for the duration of the battle. Pokémon below Lv. 50 will remain the same level. Finally, decide whether or not to enable the Wonder Launcher.

▶ Greet
Battle
Trade
Draw
Spin
Cancel

Hello, it's Kuro2!
Would you like to do something?

In the Union Room, you can battle people you don't know. Be brave and challenge them.

Battle Formats available with the C-Gear

- Single Battle
- Double Battle
- Triple Battle
- Rotation Battle
- Multi Battle
- Launcher Battle

Battle Formats available in the Union Room

- Single Battle
- Double Battle
- Triple Battle
- Rotation Battle
- Multi Battle
- Launcher Battle

Online ▶ Battles at the Wi-Fi Club

Using Nintendo Wi-Fi Connection, you can battle distant friends at the Wi-Fi Club located on the second floor of the Pokémon Center. Once inside the room, examine the monitor in the back of the room to find an opponent. Alternatively, you can directly speak to one of the players who is seeking an opponent. A battle icon will appear above the head of players who are seeking a battle opponent. You can configure the rules for battles in the Wi-Fi Club. After choosing the Battle Format, decide whether or not to restrict the level of Pokémon that can participate. If you choose Flat Battle, any Pokémon above Lv. 50 will be set to Lv. 50 for the duration of the battle. Pokémon below Lv. 50 will remain the same level. Finally, decide whether or not to enable the Wonder Launcher.

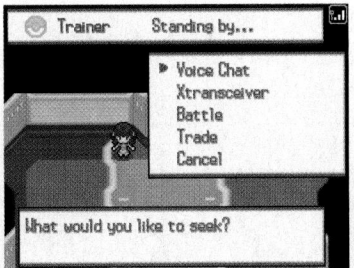

To enjoy the Wi-Fi Club, you'll need to have exchanged Friend Codes with your friends.

Online ▶ Random Matchups at the Global Terminal

You can test your skills in Random Matchups in the Global Terminal on the second floor of the Pokémon Center. In a Random Matchup, you are automatically paired up with a random opponent to battle. You can choose either the Free mode or Rating mode. In Free mode, there are no restrictions for the opponent you will be matched up against. In Rating mode, you will be matched up with opponents based on your performance in battles. In order to participate in Rating mode, you first need to register on the Pokémon Global Link (p. 420). Once you've completed registration you can participate in Rating mode. For each battle you complete in Rating Mode, your Rating will go up or down depending on whether you won or not. This ensures that you are always being matched up with opponents of a similar skill level.

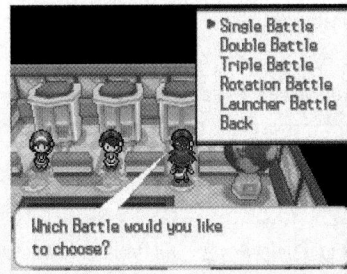

The overall battle, as well as each turn, both have time limits. This means you need to be able to make quick decisions in Random Matchup battles.

Battle Formats available at the Wi-Fi Club

◉ **Single Battle**

◉ **Double Battle**

◉ **Triple Battle**

◉ **Rotation Battle**

◉ Multi Battle

◉ Launcher Battle

Battle Formats available in Random Matchup

◉ **Single Battle**

◉ **Double Battle**

◉ **Triple Battle**

◉ **Rotation Battle**

◉ Multi Battle

◉ **Launcher Battle**

WONDER LAUNCHER — Use items during Link Battles

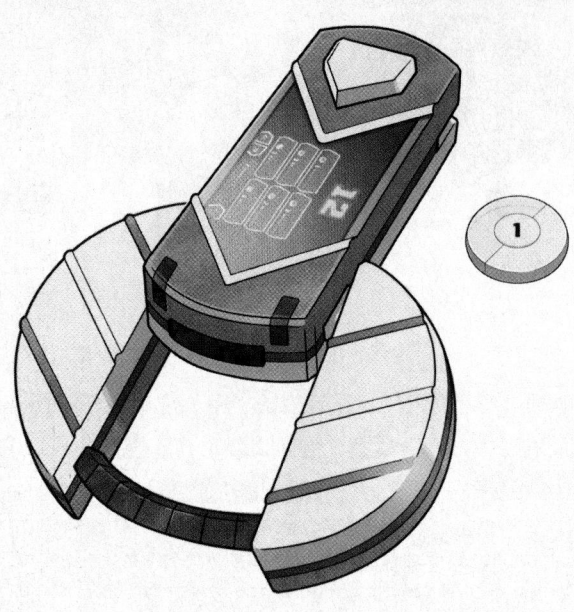

The Wonder Launcher is a device that charges energy with each turn and enables Trainers to use items on their Pokémon during battles. Items used via the Wonder Launcher boost a Pokémon's stats, increase the accuracy of a move, restore a Pokémon's HP, or cure status conditions. The more energy that charges up, the more effective items you can use. For example, if you let 14 energy points charge up, you can use Max Revive, which revives a fainted Pokémon and fully restores its HP.

How to use the Wonder Launcher

1 Energy will be charged each turn

Your launcher gains one energy point at the beginning of a turn. Determine in advance which item you want to use, and then save up enough energy points.

2 Use the Wonder Launcher

When you have enough energy to use the item you want, choose "LAUNCHER" to use it.

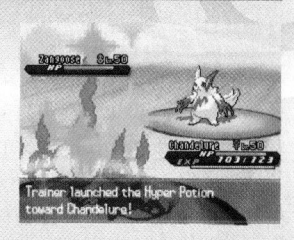

How charging energy works

1 One energy point will be charged at the beginning of your turn.

2 When you use an item, the energy decreases by the amount you use. Even if it fails and no effects results, that energy is still spent.

3 In a Triple Battle, if you have fewer than three Pokémon on your team, more energy will be charged.

4 In a Multi Battle, each player has his or her own pool of energy points.

 **Tip** — ## Where the Wonder Launcher can be used

In battles using IR, the Wonder Launcher is always enabled. By selecting "Wonder Launcher On," the Wonder Launcher can be enabled in battles using wireless communications or Nintendo Wi-Fi Connection. Select "Launcher Battle" from the Global Terminal to play Random Matchups with the Wonder Launcher enabled. Launcher Battles are Triple Battles where the Wonder Launcher has been enabled.

Wonder Launcher items and energy requirements

Energy	Item	Effect
1	Item Urge	Makes an ally Pokémon use its held item
2	Potion	Restores the HP of a Pokémon by 20 points
3	Ability Urge	Activates an Ability that normally has an effect when a Pokémon joins a battle
	Dire Hit	Raises the critical-hit ratio of a target Pokémon significantly, but only once
	Guard Spec.	Prevents stat reduction among the Trainer's party Pokémon for five turns
	X Accuracy	Raises the accuracy of a target Pokémon by one level
	X Attack	Raises the Attack stat of a target Pokémon by one level
	X Defend	Raises the Defense stat of a target Pokémon by one level
	X Sp. Def	Raises the Sp. Def stat of a target Pokémon by one level
	X Special	Raises the Sp. Attack stat of a target Pokémon by one level
	X Speed	Raises the Speed stat of a target Pokémon by one level
4	Antidote	Lifts the effect of Poison from a Pokémon
	Awakening	Awakens a Pokémon from Sleep
	Burn Heal	Heals a Pokémon that is Burned
	Ice Heal	Defrosts a Pokémon that has been Frozen
	Parlyz Heal	Eliminates Paralysis from a Pokémon
	Super Potion	Restores the HP of one Pokémon by 50 points
5	Dire Hit 2	Raises the critical-hit ratio of a target Pokémon (with the effect increasing every time it's used)
	Item Drop	Makes an ally Pokémon drop a held item
	X Accuracy 2	Raises the accuracy of a target Pokémon by two levels
	X Attack 2	Raises the Attack stat of a target Pokémon by two levels
	X Defend 2	Raises the Defense stat of a target Pokémon by two levels
	X Sp. Def 2	Raises the Sp. Def stat of a target Pokémon by two levels
	X Special 2	Raises the Sp. Atk stat of a target Pokémon by two levels
	X Speed 2	Raises the Speed stat of a target Pokémon by two levels
6	Full Heal	Cures all status conditions
7	Dire Hit 3	Greatly raises the critical-hit ratio of a target Pokémon (with the effect increasing every time it's used)
	X Accuracy 3	Raises the accuracy of a target Pokémon by three levels
	X Attack 3	Raises the Attack stat of a target Pokémon by three levels
	X Defend 3	Raises the Defense stat of a target Pokémon by three levels
	X Sp. Def 3	Raises the Sp. Def stat of a target Pokémon by three levels
	X Special 3	Raises the Sp. Atk stat of a target Pokémon by three levels
	X Speed 3	Raises the Speed stat of a target Pokémon by three levels
8	Hyper Potion	Restores the HP of one Pokémon by 200 points
9	Reset Urge	Restores any stat changes of an ally Pokémon
10	Max Potion	Completely restores the HP of a single Pokémon
11	Revive	Revives a fainted Pokémon and restores half its HP
12	Ether	Restores the PP of a Pokémon's move by 10 points
	X Accuracy 6	Raises the accuracy of a target Pokémon by six levels
	X Attack 6	Raises the Attack stat of a target Pokémon by six levels
	X Defend 6	Raises the Defense stat of a target Pokémon by six levels
	X Sp. Def 6	Raises the Sp. Def stat of a target Pokémon by six levels
	X Special 6	Raises the Sp. Atk stat of a target Pokémon by six levels
	X Speed 6	Raises the Speed stat of a target Pokémon by six levels
13	Full Restore	Fully restores the HP and heals any status conditions of a single Pokémon
14	Max Revive	Revives a fainted Pokémon and fully restores its HP

◆ Item Urge has no effect on Pokémon with the Klutz Ability. If you use Item Urge on a Pokémon holding a Berry that has no effect in battle, or use it when a Pokémon with the Unnerve Ability is in the battle, you will fail in using the item, but the energy will still be spent.

 **Tip**

Some Wonder Launcher items have exclusive effects

Reset Urge restores any stat changes of an ally Pokémon. It's a Wonder Launcher-exclusive item. You'll also find items like X Speed 6, which provides six times the effect of its normal counterpart.

Master Type Matchups

Master how Pokémon and move types interact and you'll enjoy Pokémon battles even more

Let's review the relationship between Pokémon types and move types. When you know the other Pokémon's type, you should be able to use the right move to defeat it even if it seemed too strong to beat before.

Type Technique 1   Know both the Pokémon types and move types

There are two things to consider when thinking of types: Pokémon types and move types. When a Pokémon uses a move of its own type, the move inflicts more damage. Depending on the type of move used and the type of the Pokémon receiving it, damage can increase or decrease.

Pokémon types and move types

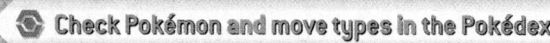

Check Pokémon and move types in the Pokédex

Dex No.	534
Name	Conkeldurr
Type	FIGHT
OT	Trainer
ID No.	24056
Exp. Points	344960
To Next Lv.	15870

The Pokémon's type

There are 17 Pokémon types in total. Some Pokémon have two types.

FIGHT Hammer Arm PP 10/10
ROCK Stone Edge PP 5/5
FIGHT Focus Punch PP 20/20
FIGHT Superpower PP 5/5

The move's type

Every move has its own type. Pokémon can learn moves that are of different types from their own.

Both move type and the defending Pokémon's type determine effectiveness

1   The attacker's move type and the defending Pokémon's type determine the matchup

Electric-type moves deal normal damage to Bug-type Pokémon. Use Fire-type moves against a Bug-type Pokémon to exploit its weakness and inflict double damage.

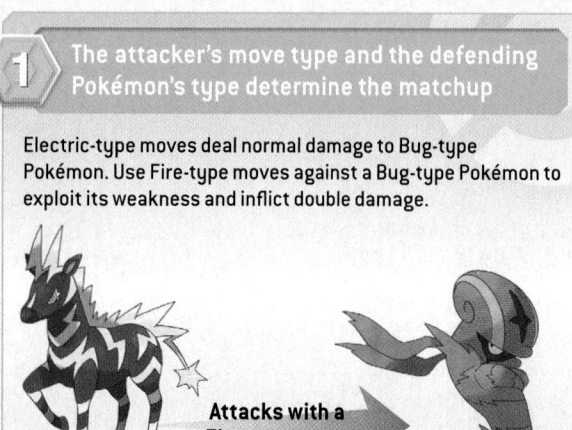

Attacks with a Fire-type move

Zebstrika   Electric

Accelgor   Bug

2   Depending on the matchup, moves can inflict normal damage

Grass-type moves will only deal half damage when used against a Fire-type Pokémon. Use Normal-type moves to inflict standard damage.

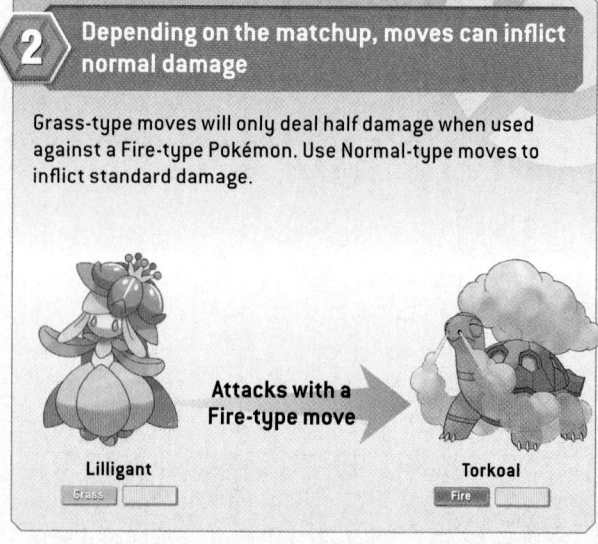

Attacks with a Fire-type move

Lilligant   Grass

Torkoal   Fire

Type Technique 2 — Know both the Pokémon types and move types

One of the most basic battle techniques is to increase the damage your Pokémon deal. You can increase damage by using moves that have a good type matchup against the opposing Pokémon. Deal as much damage as you can in as few turns as possible to quickly defeat your opponent.

Basic methods to increasing damage

1 A move does double damage when used on a Pokémon who's weak against that move's type

A move does double damage when used on a Pokémon who's weak against that move's type. Try to remember which move types are effective against which Pokémon types.

Makuhita
`Fighting`

Attacks with a
Rock-type move

Rapidash
`Fire`

Damage
200%

Rock-type moves are a good matchup against Fire-type Pokémon, so they deal twice as much damage as normal.

2 When a Pokémon uses moves of its own type, those moves do 50% more damage

Give your Pokémon moves a power boost by matching the type with the Pokémon. Those moves do 50% more damage. Even if your Pokémon don't know any moves of a type that the opponent is weak to, you can expect more damage if your Pokémon use moves of its own type.

Makuhita
`Fighting`

Attacks with a
Fighting-type move

Rapidash
`Fire`

Damage
150%

Both the Pokémon type and the move type are Fighting, so the move inflicts 50% more damage.

Basic methods of damaging opponents with two types

1 A move that is super effective against both types does four times the usual damage

When a defending Pokémon has two types, you can sometimes do much more damage than usual. When your Pokémon's move is super effective against both its types, it does four times the normal damage.

Mismagius
`Ghost`

Attacks with a
Rock-type move

Volcarona
`Bug` `Fire`

Damage
400%

Rock-type moves are super effective against both Bug type and Fire type, so the move does four times the normal damage.

2 A move that is not very effective against both types does 1/4 the usual damage

In certain situations where the opposing Pokémon has two types, some of your moves may end up doing very little damage. When one of your moves is not very effective against both types, it will do only 1/4 the usual damage.

Mismagius
`Ghost`

Attacks with a
Grass-type move

Volcarona
`Bug` `Fire`

Damage
25%

Grass-type moves are not very effective against both Bug type and Fire type, so they only do 1/4 the usual damage.

See the Pokémon Weakness Chart on p. 578 ▶

Teamwork is the key to Pokémon battles. One way to form a strong team is to figure out the right mix of Pokémon types to tackle any challenge. As the example below shows, having a team from a variety of types allows you to exploit your opponent's weaknesses no matter what Pokémon they have.

An example of how to form a good team around your main Pokémon

◎ When your main Pokémon is Garchomp

As a Pokémon that belongs to both the Dragon and Ground types, Garchomp is weak against Ice-type moves. That's why you want Tyranitar to add its Rock-type moves to the team. These moves are especially good against Ice-type Pokémon. Tyranitar is weak against Fighting-type moves. That's why you want to have Charizard with its Flying-type moves, which are strong against Fighting-type Pokémon. Charizard is weak against Electric-type moves. For those Electric-type Pokémon, you have Garchomp with its Ground-type moves.

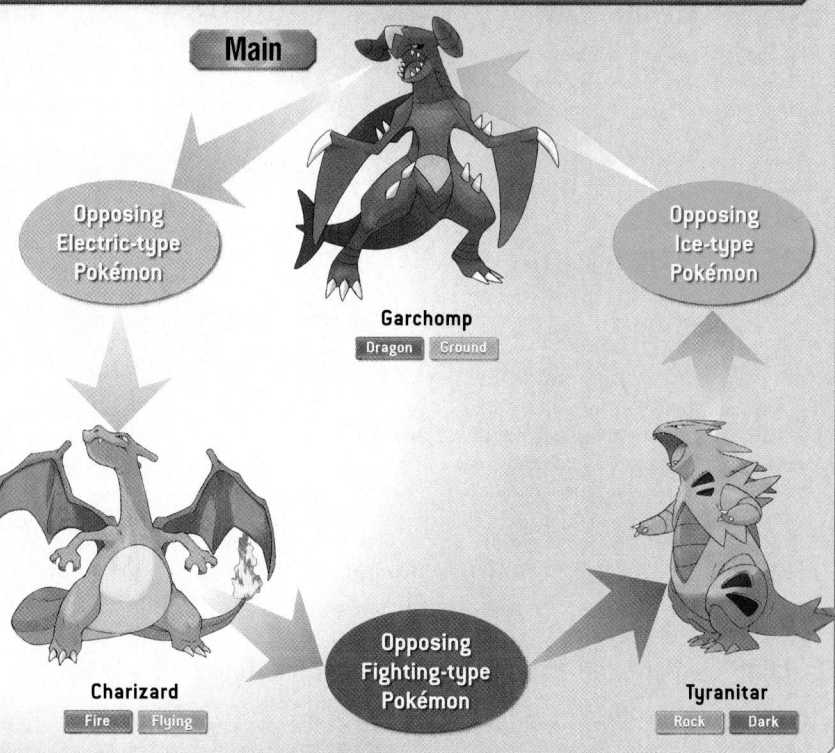

Main

Garchomp
Dragon Ground

Opposing Electric-type Pokémon

Opposing Ice-type Pokémon

Charizard
Fire Flying

Opposing Fighting-type Pokémon

Tyranitar
Rock Dark

◎ When your main Pokémon is Metagross

As a Steel-type Pokémon, Metagross is weak against Fire-type moves. That's why you want Swampert on your team with its Water-type moves, which are good against Fire-type Pokémon. Swampert is weak against Grass-type moves. So you want Vanilluxe with its Ice-type moves against Grass-type Pokémon. Vanilluxe is weak against Fighting-type moves. For those Fighting-type Pokémon, you have Metagross with its Psychic-type moves.

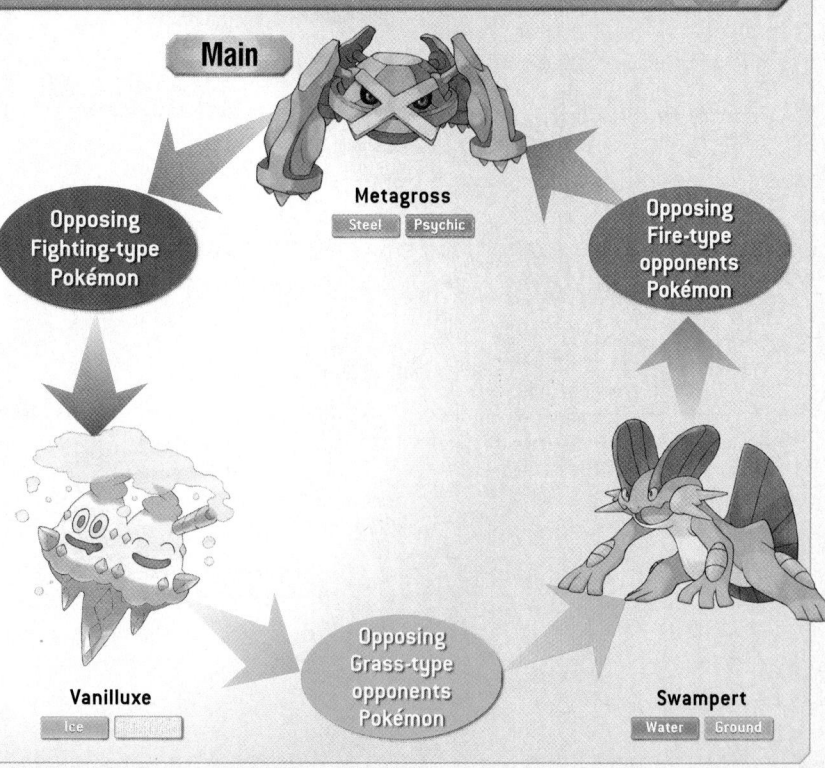

Main

Metagross
Steel Psychic

Opposing Fighting-type Pokémon

Opposing Fire-type opponents Pokémon

Vanilluxe
Ice

Opposing Grass-type opponents Pokémon

Swampert
Water Ground

Type Technique **4** Send out Pokémon that are immune to moves of a certain type

Some Pokémon types are not affected by moves of certain types. For example, Ghost-type Pokémon are not affected at all by Normal- or Fighting-type moves, and Flying-type Pokémon are not affected by Ground-type moves. Also, some Pokémon types prevent certain status conditions. For instance, Fire-type Pokémon cannot be Burned and Ice-type Pokémon cannot be Frozen. With this knowledge, you can nullify the effects of some moves and stay a step ahead in battle.

Pokémon immunities to move types and status conditions

Type	Description
Normal	• Immune to all Ghost-type moves
Fire	• Does not become Burned
Grass	• Immune to Leech Seed
Ice	• Does not become Frozen • Immune to damage from the Hail weather condition
Poison	• Immune to the Poison and Badly Poisoned conditions • Nullifies the effect of Toxic Spikes as it gets sent out (Poison-type Pokémon with the Levitate Ability, and Pokémon that are both Poison type and Flying type, will not nullify the effect of Toxic Spikes)
Ground	• Immune to all Electric-type moves • Immune to Thunder Wave (status moves are not usually not affected by types, but the exception is Thunder Wave, which has no effect on Ground-type Pokémon) • Immune to damage from the Sandstorm weather condition
Flying	• Immune to all Ground-type moves • Not affected by Spikes or Toxic Spikes
Rock	• Immune to damage from the Sandstorm weather condition (instead its Sp. Def stat is increased by 50%)
Ghost	• Immune to all Normal- and Fighting-type moves
Dark	• Immune to all Psychic-type moves
Steel	• Immune to all Poison-type moves • Immune to the Poison and Badly Poisoned conditions • Immune to damage from the Sandstorm weather condition

---

 **Tip** ## Ways to use moves on Pokémon that are otherwise immune to them

In some cases, the opponent's Pokémon may be immune to all of your Pokémon's moves. You should be prepared to deal with such cases. There are certain moves and Abilities that will let you cause damage to those Pokémon who are otherwise immune to your moves. Utilize such moves and Abilities to really catch your opponent off guard.

Use the effects of certain moves to inflict damage with otherwise ineffective moves

Using the following moves will allow you to hit Pokémon with types of moves against which they are otherwise immune.

Move	Odor Sleuth	Normal
Move	Foresight	Normal
Move	Gravity	Psychic
Move	Miracle Eye	Psychic

Use the effects of certain Abilities to inflict damage with otherwise ineffective moves

A Pokémon with the Scrappy Ability can hit Ghost-type Pokémon with Normal- and Fighting-type moves.

Ability	Scrappy

Know Stats for Battling and Raising Pokémon

Understand your Pokémon's stats to help it shine in battles

Each Pokémon has stats. There are six stats, and the higher the number, the better. Understanding stats helps you train and battle with Pokémon.

Stats Technique **1** Overall strength depends on six stats

Your Pokémon's stats determine crucial battle elements, such as the damage when hit or the order of Pokémon moves within a turn in battle. When a Pokémon levels up, its stats also go up.

Overall strength depends on six stats

HP

The Pokémon's health. If attacks reduce its HP to 0, the Pokémon faints.

Speed

How fast the Pokémon moves. The higher this number, the better your chance to use moves before other Pokémon.

 Stats affecting physical moves

Attack

The Pokémon's attack power. The higher this number, the more damage the Pokémon does with physical moves.

Defense

The Pokémon's defensive ability. The higher this number, the less damage the Pokémon takes from physical moves.

 Stats affecting special moves

Sp. Atk

The Pokémon's attack power. The higher this number, the more damage the Pokémon does with special moves.

Sp. Def

The Pokémon's defensive ability. The higher this number, the less damage the Pokémon takes from special moves.

Stats that affect physical and special moves

Stats that affect physical moves

The Attack stat of the attacking Pokémon and the Defense stat of the defending Pokémon affect the result.

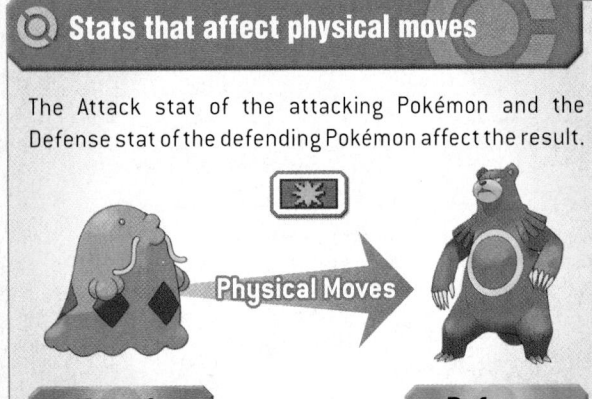

Attack → Physical Moves → Defense

Stats that affect special moves

The Sp. Atk stat of the attacking Pokémon and the Sp. Def stat of the defending Pokémon affect the result.

Sp. Atk → Special Moves → Sp. Def

Stats Technique **2** Put these high-stat Pokémon in your battle party

The Pokémon below will be a great addition to your battle party. This section shows off some particularly impressive Pokémon that can be found in *Pokémon Black 2* and *Pokémon White 2*. For each of the stats, three Pokémon that excel [in that] stat are shown. Consider how to train them, battle with [them,] and battle against them.

High-stat Pokémon

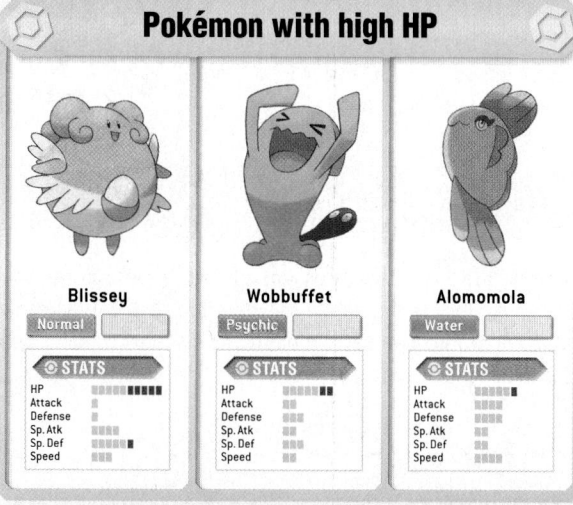

Pokémon with high HP

Blissey — Normal
STATS — HP, Attack, Defense, Sp. Atk, Sp. Def, Speed

Wobbuffet — Psychic
STATS — HP, Attack, Defense, Sp. Atk, Sp. Def, Speed

Alomomola — Water
STATS — HP, Attack, Defense, Sp. Atk, Sp. Def, Speed

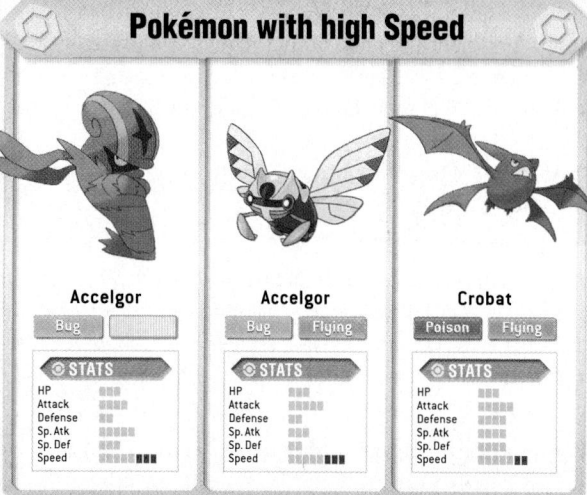

Pokémon with high Speed

Accelgor — Bug
STATS — HP, Attack, Defense, Sp. Atk, Sp. Def, Speed

Accelgor — Bug / Flying
STATS — HP, Attack, Defense, Sp. Atk, Sp. Def, Speed

Crobat — Poison / Flying
STATS — HP, Attack, Defense, Sp. Atk, Sp. Def, Speed

Pokémon with high Attack

Kyurem (Black Kyurem) — Dragon / Ice
STATS — HP, Attack, Defense, Sp. Atk, Sp. Def, Speed

Rampardos — Rock
STATS — HP, Attack, Defense, Sp. Atk, Sp. Def, Speed

Zekrom — Dragon / Electric
STATS — HP, Attack, Defense, Sp. Atk, Sp. Def, Speed

Pokemon with high Sp. Atk

Kyurem (White Kyurem) — Dragon / Ice
STATS — HP, Attack, Defense, Sp. Atk, Sp. Def, Speed

Chandelure — Ghost / Fire
STATS — HP, Attack, Defense, Sp. Atk, Sp. Def, Speed

Reshiram — Dragon / Fire
STATS — HP, Attack, Defense, Sp. Atk, Sp. Def, Speed

Pokémon with high Defense

Shuckle — Bug / Rock
STATS — HP, Attack, Defense, Sp. Atk, Sp. Def, Speed

Steelix — Steel / Ground
STATS — HP, Attack, Defense, Sp. Atk, Sp. Def, Speed

Aggron — Steel / Rock
STATS — HP, Attack, Defense, Sp. Atk, Sp. Def, Speed

Pokemon with high Sp. Def

Shuckle — Bug / Rock
STATS — HP, Attack, Defense, Sp. Atk, Sp. Def, Speed

Regice — Ice
STATS — HP, Attack, Defense, Sp. Atk, Sp. Def, Speed

Umbreon — Dark
STATS — HP, Attack, Defense, Sp. Atk, Sp. Def, Speed

Inflict Status Conditions to Get an Edge

Inflicting status conditions brings you one step closer to victory

Status conditions are unfavorable in general and include Poison, which reduces the affected Pokémon's HP a little every turn, and Paralysis, which lowers the affected Pokémon's Speed stat. Keep your Pokémon healthy and inflict them on the opposing Pokémon to increase your chance of victory.

Status Condition Technique 1 — Basic status conditions

When Pokémon have status conditions, they will not be able to perform to their full potential—failing to use moves or losing HP every turn. It's a lot easier to face Pokémon with status conditions rather than healthy ones. On the other hand, if your Pokémon are hit with status conditions, your opponent will have an easier time in battle, putting you at a disadvantage. Status conditions can determine the flow of battle, so it's good to learn all you can about them.

Paralysis = 25%   confused = ?
Status conditions at a glance   *Flinch = 30%   Attract = 50% = 18.75€*

Sleep	Poison	Paralysis

● The affected Pokémon closes its eyes.	● The affected Pokémon turns purple.	● The affected Pokémon turns yellow.
Excluding the use of specific moves, the target becomes unable to attack. This condition can wear off during battle.	The target's HP decreases each turn. Does not wear off on its own.	There's a 25% chance that the Pokémon can't attack. The target's Speed is also lowered. Does not wear off on its own.
Pros The affected Pokémon is unable to use moves.	**Pros** Reduces the affected Pokémon's HP gradually.	**Pros** Lowers the affected Pokémon's Speed.

Burned	Frozen	Confused

● The affected Pokémon turns red.	● The affected Pokémon turns blue.	● The affected Pokémon's color doesn't change, but an animation will appear above its head.
HP decreases each turn. Attack is also lowered. Does not wear off on its own.	Excluding the use of specific moves, the target becomes unable to attack. This condition can wear off during battle.	The affected Pokémon will sometimes attack itself. This condition can wear off during battle.
Pros Lowers Attack.	**Pros** The affected Pokémon is unable to use moves.	**Pros** The affected Pokémon may attack itself.

Status Condition Technique **2** Inflict status conditions on opposing Pokémon to get closer to victory

Use moves and Abilities to inflict status conditions. There are two types of moves that can inflict status conditions. Some moves are purely support moves that only inflict status conditions, and others are attack moves that have additional effects that inflict status conditions. Certain Abilities can inflict status conditions on opponents when the user is hit by an attack, so put these to good use. Having status condition inflicting moves and Abilities in your strategy will give you an edge in battle.

Moves and Abilities that cause status conditions

◎ Sample move that inflicts Sleep status

Move	Hypnosis	Psychic

The Hypnosis move has a low accuracy rating at 60, but it inflicts Sleep on the opponent if it hits. Pokémon such as Watchog and Yanma are able to learn it.

Watchog

◎ Sample move that inflicts Burned status

Move	Will-O-Wisp	Fire

Will-O-Wisp is a move that inflicts the Burned status condition if it hits the opponent. Use TM61 and you can teach the move to most Ghost- and Fire-type Pokémon.

Banette

◎ Sample Ability that inflicts the Poison status condition

Ability	Poison Point

If a Pokémon with the Poison Point Ability is directly hit by an attack, it has a 30% chance to inflict the Poison status condition on the opponent. Pokémon such as Roserade and Whirlipede have this Ability.

Roserade

◎ Sample Ability that inflicts the Paralysis status condition

Ability	Static

If a Pokémon with the Static Ability is directly hit by an attack, it has a 30% chance to inflict the Paralysis status condition on the opponent. Pokémon such as Ampharos and Stunfisk have this Ability.

Ampharos

Status Condition Technique **3** Your Pokémon will be hard to defeat if you can prevent status conditions

Just as you try to inflict status conditions, the opposing Trainer is thinking how to inflict status conditions on your Pokémon. Some moves and Abilities can prevent or heal those status conditions. If your Pokémon are affected by status conditions, stay cool and be ready to use such moves and Abilities. Once the opposing Trainer has found out you have ways to prevent or heal status conditions, he or she will have to consider a new strategy.

Moves and Abilities can prevent or help Pokémon recover from status conditions

◎ Sample move that prevents status conditions

Move	Safeguard	Normal

Safeguard is a move that prevents your side from being affected by status conditions for five turns. The effect remains even if the user switches out.

Lumineon

◎ Sample Ability that helps allies recover from status conditions

Ability	Healer

Healer is an Ability that gives an ally a one-third chance of recovering from status conditions. It's useful in Double and Triple Battles.

Alomomola

Pokémon Battles Introduction **6**

Become a Pokémon Move Master

Knowing the features and effects of moves is the key to victory

While landing big damage with powerful attack moves is crucial, moves that inflict status conditions are also essential to tipping the battle in your favor. Understand each move's effects, and you'll know what to do when the situation calls for just the right move.

Move Technique **1** Teach your Pokémon moves

Pokémon can learn moves in six different ways. Learning moves by leveling up is the most common way, but some moves can be learned through more unusual methods.

Teach such rare moves to your Pokémon to really catch your opponent off guard, giving you an advantage in battle.

Ways to teach moves to Pokémon

◎ Learn by leveling up

Safeguard is a move that prevents your side from being affected by status conditions for five turns. The effect remains even if the user switches out.

◎ Use TMs and HMs

Use TMs and HMs to teach Pokémon moves that they cannot learn by leveling up.

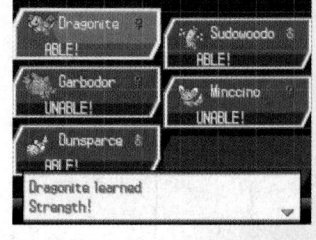

◎ Have people teach moves to your Pokémon

The starter Pokémon and Dragon-type Pokémon can learn moves from other people.

◎ Give Shards to learn moves

Give a certain amount of Shards to the master Move Tutor to be taught moves. There are four master Move Tutors.

◎ Remember a move

The PWT's reminder girl will help your Pokémon remember a move that it previously forgot in exchange for one Heart Scale.

◎ Egg Moves

Find Pokémon Eggs at the Pokémon Day Care and the Pokémon that hatches from it may know Egg Moves (p. 485).

Move Technique 2 — Master moves by understanding their elements

Moves have many elements other than their types. Each move has fixed elements such as power, range, and accuracy. Use a move with a high power rating and you will inflict a large amount of damage on your opponent. Accuracy becomes important when battling opposing Pokémon with high evasion. Also, in Double and Triple Battles, range really matters. Learn the various elements of moves, and teach your Pokémon moves that fit your battle style.

Elements of a move

◎ Power

Attack moves have a numeric value called power. It's a crucial element for determining how much damage is done to the target. The larger this number is, the more damage your Pokémon does.

About power

1. Each attack move has a power value
2. The more power the move has, the more damage it will do
3. Other elements besides power determine the amount of damage

◎ Range

The range of opponents that will be affected by the move is displayed. Some moves affect only one Pokémon, some affect two Pokémon at once, while others affect the user of the move.

About range

1. Range is the area the move's effects reach
2. Each move has a fixed range
3. Some moves even affect your allies

◎ Accuracy

Accuracy indicates how easily a move will land. The max value is 100. If a move has an accuracy of 50, it will land only half of the time.

About accuracy

1. Use items to raise accuracy
2. You can lower the accuracy of opposing Pokémon with moves
3. Some moves always land regardless of accuracy

◎ PP (Power Points)

The number of times a move can be used is called PP. Every time you use a move, its PP decrease by one. When no PP are left, your Pokémon can't use that move. The more powerful moves have fewer PP.

About PP

1. Use a Leppa Berry to restore PP
2. Increase the maximum PP with PP Up
3. When the PP for every move is exhausted, your Pokémon use Struggle

◎ Physical moves and special moves

Attack moves are divided into two types: physical and special moves. Physical moves are related to a Pokémon's Attack stat, and special moves are related to the Sp. Atk stat.

About physical moves and special moves

1. Physical moves are related to the Attack and Defense stats
2. Special moves are related to the Sp. Atk and Sp. Def stats
3. Some items and Abilities are related to kinds of attacks

◎ Direct attacks

Direct attacks make direct contact with the target Pokémon. Many direct attacks are physical moves. Abilities have effects on many of the direct attacks.

About direct attacks

1. Most direct attacks are physical moves
2. A few direct attacks are special moves
3. Direct attacks can trigger items and Abilities

Move Technique 3 Use moves to inflict status conditions

Some moves inflict status conditions on the target. Status condition moves might not do much damage at first, but they can give you the opening you need. They can seal off the opposing Pokémon's moves, lower its stats, or slowly erode its HP to give you an advantage.

Advantage of status-condition-inflicting moves

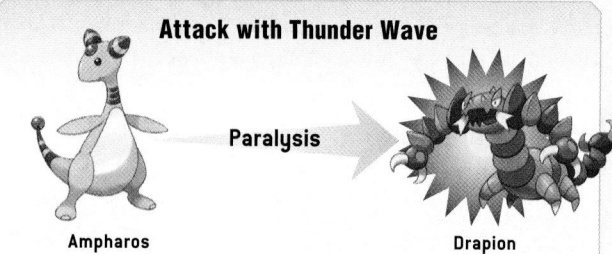

Attack with Thunder Wave

Ampharos → Paralysis → Drapion

Inflicting the Paralysis status condition lowers the target's Speed and reduces the chance you'll be hit by an attack.

Examples of status-condition-inflicting moves

Move	Type	Power	Accuracy	Effect	Some Pokémon that can learn it
Confuse Ray	Haunter	—	100	Inflicts the Confused status condition on the target	Vulpix, Golbat, and others
Glare	Normal	—	90	Inflicts Paralysis	Dunsparce, Seviper, and others
Hypnosis	Psychic	—	60	Inflicts the Sleep status condition on the target	Yanma, Lunatone, and others
Poison Gas	Poison	—	80	Poisons the target	Muk, Garbodor, and others
Spore	Grass	—	100	Inflicts the Sleep status condition on the target	Parasect, Foongus, and others
Stun Spore	Grass	—	75	Inflicts Paralysis	Tangela, Roselia, and others
Supersonic	Normal	—	55	Inflicts the Confused status condition on the target	Magneton, Pelipper, and others
Thunder Wave	Electric	—	100	Inflicts Paralysis	Ampharos, Probopass, and others
Toxic	Poison	—	90	Badly Poisons the target	Roselia, Scolipede, and others
Will-O-Wisp	Fire	—	75	Burns the target	Banette, Yamask, and others

Move Technique 4 Alter your Pokémon's stats with support moves

Moves can be used to raise and lower stats of your battling Pokémon. For example, if you raise Attack or Sp. Atk, you can do more damage to your target. Also, if you lower your opponent's Speed, you can move before your opponent. Put yourself in an advantageous position by altering stats.

Advantages of stat-raising moves

Use the move Work Up

Attack and Sp. Atk both rise

Stoutland

Raises Attack and Sp. Atk, so you can do massive damage with both physical and special moves.

Some moves that raise your stats

Move	Type	Power	Accuracy	Effect	Examples of Pokémon that can learn it
Coil	Poison	—	—	Raises the user's Attack, Defense, and accuracy by 1	Dunsparce, Seviper, and others
Cotton Guard	Grass	—	—	Raises the user's Defense by 3	Ampharos, Altaria, and others
Hone Claws	Dark	—	—	Raises the user's Attack and accuracy by 1	Sneasel, Skorupi, and others
Quiver Dance	Bug	—	—	Raises the user's Sp. Atk, Sp. Defense, and Speed by 1	Butterfree, Lilligant, and others
Work Up	Normal	—	—	Raises the user's Attack and Sp. Attack by 1	Stoutland, Hydreigon, and others

Some moves that lower the target's stats

Move	Type	Power	Accuracy	Effect	Examples of Pokémon that can learn it
Cotton Spore	Grass	—	100	Lowers the target's Speed by 2	Ampharos, Cottonee, and others
Fake Tears	Dark	—	100	Lowers the target's Sp. Defense by 2	Zorua, Gothitelle, and others
FeatherDance	Flying	—	100	Lowers the target's Attack by 2	Unfezant, Swanna, and others
Scary Face	Normal	—	100	Lowers the target's Speed by 2	Raticate, Metang, and others
Tickle	Normal	—	100	Lowers the target's Attack and Defense by 1	Tangela, Minccino, and others

◆ Pokémon that learn a move as an Egg Move or by TM are listed when there aren't any Pokémon that learn the move

Move Technique 5 — Frustrate the opposing Trainer with moves that have additional effects

Some attack moves deliver additional effects that let them do more than just damage the target. Get an advantage in battle with these additional effects! They can as lower your target's stats, raise your own stats, or inflict status conditions on the target. You can put your opponent at a serious disadvantage by using moves that have a guaranteed chance to trigger additional effects.

Advantage of moves with additional effects

Attack with Electroweb

Galvantula → Damage + Additional Effect → Speed Decreases — Xatu

The target's Speed is lowered at the same time as the attack. This makes it easier to use moves before the opposing Pokémon.

Some moves with a stat-related additional effect

Move	Type	Power	Accuracy	Effect	Examples of Pokémon that can learn it
Acid Spray	Poison	40	100	100% chance of lowering the target's Sp. Def by 2	Garbodor, Eelektrik, and others
Electroweb	Electric	55	95	100% chance of lowering the target's Speed by 1	Joltik, Galvantula, and others
Razor Shell	Water	75	95	50% chance of lowering the target's Defense by 1	Shellder, Samurott, and others
Bulldoze	Ground	60	100	100% chance of lowering the target's Speed by 1	Rhydon, Flygon, and others
Flame Charge	Fire	50	100	100% chance of raising the user's Speed by 1	Emboar, Zebstrika, and others
Struggle Bug	Bug	30	100	100% chance of lowering the target's Sp. Atk by 1	Shuckle, Leavanny, and others
Low Sweep	Fighting	60	100	100% chance of lowering the target's Speed by 1	Machamp, Sawk, and others

Some moves that deliver status conditions

Move	Type	Power	Accuracy	Effect	Examples of Pokémon that can learn it
DragonBreath	Dragon	60	100	30% chance of inflicting Paralysis on the target	Onix, Altaria, and others
Inferno	Fire	100	50	100% chance of burning the target	Vulpix, Heatmor, and others
Poison Jab	Poison	80	100	30% chance of poisoning the target	Qwilfish, Toxicroak, and others
Powder Snow	Ice	40	100	10% chance of leaving the target Frozen	Piloswine, Beartic, and others
Scald	Water	80	100	30% chance of burning the target	Golduck, Panpour, and others

Move Technique 6 — Strike before opposing Pokémon

Speed determines which Pokémon attacks first in battle. But that doesn't mean a Pokémon with low Speed is always stuck playing catch-up. Moves like Quick Attack or Aqua Jet can hit first regardless of Speed. With moves like these, you can get the drop on an opposing Pokémon with very high Speed.

Advantages to attacking first

Attack with Mach Punch

Ledian — Always strikes first → Swellow

Always strikes first. However, if the opposing Pokémon also uses a move that strikes first, the Pokémon with the highest Speed will attack first.

Some moves that always attack first

Move	Type	Power	Accuracy	Effect	Examples of Pokémon that can learn it
Aqua Jet	Water	40	100	Always strikes first	Dewgong, Sharpedo, and others
ExtremeSpeed	Normal	80	100	Always strikes first (faster than others moves that strike first except for Fake Out)	Arcanine, Lucario, and others
Fake Out	Normal	40	100	Always strikes first (faster than other moves that strike first, but only works on the first turn it is used)	Nuzleaf, Liepard, and others
Ice Shard	Ice	40	100	Always strikes first	Shellder, Glaceon, and others
Mach Punch	Fighting	40	100	Always strikes first	Ledian, Breloom, and others
Quick Attack	Normal	40	100	Always strikes first	Jolteon, Yanma, and others

◆ When the opposing Pokémon uses a similar move on the same turn, the Speed stat determines which attack goes

Move Technique 7 — Strike accurately with sure-hit moves

A move's accuracy determines its chances of hitting a target, but the opposing Pokémon can raise their evasion with moves or even lower your Pokémon's accuracy, which makes it hard to land moves. In such a situation, attack with sure-hit moves.

Advantage of sure-hit moves

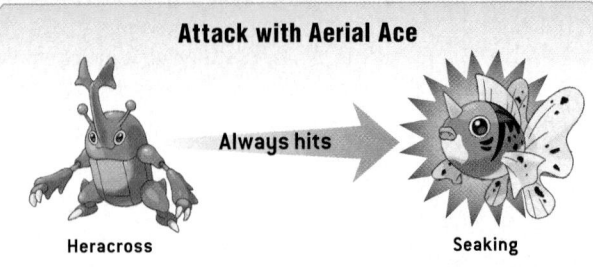

Attack with Aerial Ace

Heracross → Always hits → Seaking

Aerial Ace always hits the opponent regardless of the user's accuracy or the target's evasion.

Examples of sure-hit moves

Move	Type	Power	Accuracy	Effect	Examples of Pokémon that can learn it
Aerial Ace	Flying	60	—	Sure hit	Heracross, Braviary, and others
Aura Sphere	Fighting	90	—	Sure hit	Lucario, Mienshao, and others
Faint Attack	Dark	60	—	Sure hit	Flygon, Crustle, and others
Magical Leaf	Grass	60	—	Sure hit	Roselia, Leafeon, and others
Shadow Punch	Haunter	60	—	Sure hit	Gengar, Golurk, and others
Shock Wave	Electric	60	—	Sure hit	Zebstrika, Emolga, and others
Swift	Normal	60	—	Sure hit	Sandslash, Skarmory, and others
Trump Card	Normal	—	—	Sure hit and the move's power increases as its PP decreases	Eevee, Slowking, and others
Vital Throw	Fighting	70	—	Always strikes later than normal, but has perfect accuracy	Pinsir, Throh, and others

Moves that make the next move a sure-hit move

Move	Type	Power	Accuracy	Effect	Examples of Pokémon that can learn it
Lock-On	Normal	—	—	The user's next move is a sure hit during the next turn	Magnezone, Klinklang, and others
Mind Reader	Normal	—	—	The user's next move is a sure hit during the next turn	Poliwrath, Breloom, and others
Telekinesis	Psychic	—	—	For three turns, most moves will hit the target	Munna, Gothitelle, and others

Move Technique 8 — Accuracy changes the tides of battle

A move's accuracy determines its chances of hitting a target. The higher the target's evasion, the easier it is for the target to dodge the move. You can create an ideal situation by lowering the opposing Pokémon's accuracy and raising your Pokémon's evasion to attack without getting hit.

Advantages of lowering accuracy

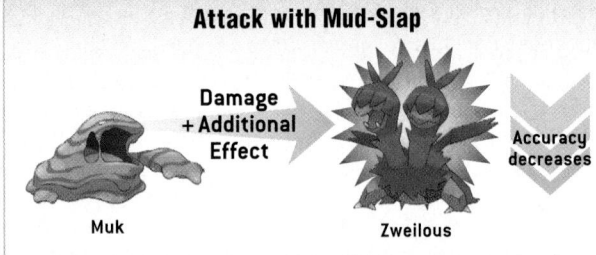

Attack with Mud-Slap

Muk → Damage + Additional Effect → Zweilous → Accuracy decreases

Mud-Slap has a power of just 20, but if it hits, it is guaranteed to lower the target's accuracy by 1.

Some accuracy-related moves

Move	Type	Power	Accuracy	Effect	Examples of Pokémon that can learn it
Hone Claws	Dark	—	—	Raises the user's Attack and accuracy by 1	Liepard, Zoroark, and others
Mud-Slap	Ground	20	100	100% chance of lowering the target's accuracy by 1	Muk, Krookodile, and others
Sand-Attack	Ground	—	100	Lowers the target's accuracy by 1	Gliscor, Gigalith, and others
SmokeScreen	Normal	—	100	Lowers the target's accuracy by 1	Weezing, Skuntank, and others

Some evasion-related moves

Move	Type	Power	Accuracy	Effect	Examples of Pokémon that can learn it
Minimize	Normal	—	—	Raises the user's evasiveness by 2.	Drifblim, Lampent, and others
Miracle Eye	Psychic	—	—	Attacks land easily regardless of the target's evasion	Metagross, Beheeyem, and others
Odor Sleuth	Normal	—	—	Attacks land easily regardless of the target's evasion	Growlithe, Grumpig, and others
Sweet Scent	Normal	—	100	Lowers the target's evasion by 1	Tropius, Carnivine, and others

Move Technique 9 — Recovery moves get you out of trouble

Once a Pokémon's HP drops to 0, it faints and can no longer battle. So it's a good idea to have a Pokémon who knows HP-restoring moves. There also exist moves that can cure status conditions. As long as you have some healing power on your team, you'll be ready for long battles.

Advantage of status-recovery moves

Use Recover

Recovers half of max HP

Starmie

Recover restores the HP of the user by half of its max HP. It can't be used on ally Pokémon.

Some HP-recovery moves

Move	Type	Power	Accuracy	Effect	Some Pokémon that can learn it
Aqua Ring	Water	—	—	Restores some HP each turn	Seaking, Azumarill, and others
Drain Punch	Fighting	75	100	Restores HP by half of the damage dealt to the target	Seismitoad, Mienshao, and others
Giga Drain	Grass	75	100	Restores HP by half of the damage dealt to the target	Tangrowth, Amoonguss, and others
Heal Pulse	Psychic	—	—	Restores the target's HP by up to half of its max HP	Lucario, Alomomola, and others
Pain Split	Normal	—	—	The user and target's HP is added, then equally shared	Reuniclus, Lampent, and others
Recover	Normal	—	—	Restores HP by up to half of the user's max HP	Starmie, Accelgor, and others
Rest	Psychic	—	—	Fully restores HP, but makes the user sleep for two turns	Shuckle, Wailord, and others

Some status-recovery moves

Move	Type	Power	Accuracy	Effect	Some Pokémon that can learn it
Heal Bell	Normal	—	—	Heals status conditions of all your party Pokémon	Skitty, Chimecho, and others
Healing Wish	Psychic	—	—	User faints, but fully heals the next Pokémon's HP and status conditions	Clefairy, Chimecho, Lopunny, Alomomola, and others
Psycho Shift	Psychic	—	90	Shifts the user's Poisoned, Badly Poisoned, Sleep, Paralyzed, or Burned condition to the target and heals the user	Noctowl, Latias, Latios, Cresselia, and others
Refresh	Normal	—	—	Heals Poisoned, Paralyzed, and Burned conditions	Lickitung, Altaria, and others

Move Technique 10 — Prevent damage with protective moves

Some moves protect your Pokémon from opposing Pokémon's moves that turn. Well-timed use of moves like Protect and Detect can stop a move—no matter how high its power. Moves such as Wide Guard can protect all of your allies in Double Battles and Triple Battles.

Advantages of protective moves

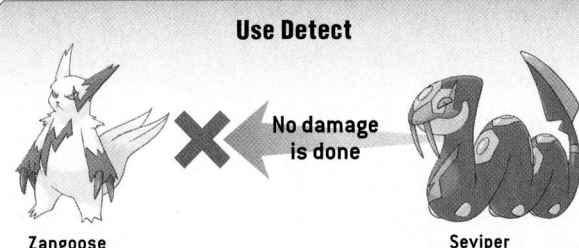

Use Detect

No damage is done

Zangoose   Seviper

Detect protects your Pokémon from the opposing Pokémon's moves that turn. It doesn't have any effect on moves that the opponent uses which target itself.

Some protective moves

Move	Type	Power	Accuracy	Effect	Some Pokémon that can learn it
Detect	Fighting	—	—	Protects the user from moves of opposing Pokémon on that turn	Zangoose, Yanmega, and others
Protect	Normal	—	—	Protects the user from moves of opposing Pokémon on that turn	Aggron, Crawdaunt, and others
Quick Guard	Fighting	—	—	Protects the user and all allies from first-strike moves	Sawk, Escavalier, and others
Wide Guard	Rock	—	—	Protects the user and allies from physical and special moves that target multiple Pokémon	Mantine, Carracosta, and others

◆ Using protective moves consecutively makes them more likely to fail.

Some moves that remove protecting effects

Move	Type	Power	Accuracy	Effect	Some Pokémon that can learn it
Feint	Normal	30	100	Hits even targets that used Protect, Detect, Quick Guard, and Wide Guard on that turn, and removes their effects	Farfetch'd, Heracross, Skarmory, Trapinch, and others

Move Technique 11 — Manipulate the weather to power up moves

Some moves can be used to change the weather, and other moves have effects that change depending on the weather. For example, the move Blizzard always hits when the weather condition is Hail. When the weather condition is Sunny, the amount of HP healed by Synthesis increases. Try building a team that uses the weather as an ally.

Advantage of weather moves

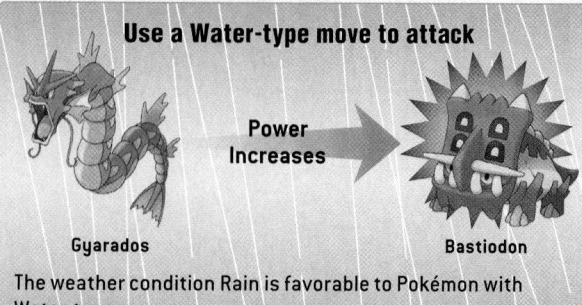

Use a Water-type move to attack

Gyarados → Power Increases → Bastiodon

The weather condition Rain is favorable to Pokémon with Water-type moves.

Examples of weather-changing moves

Move	Type	Power	Accuracy	Effect	Examples of Pokémon that can learn it
Hail	Ice	—	—	Changes the weather condition to Hail for five turns All Pokémon other than Ice-type Pokémon take damage each turn	Dewgong, Castform, Walrein, Glaceon, and others
Rain Dance	Water	—	—	Changes the weather condition to Rain for five turns	Castform, Jellicent, and others
Sandstorm	Rock	—	—	Changes the weather condition to Sandstorm for five turns Sp. Def of Rock-type Pokémon goes up by 50% All Pokémon other than Rock-, Steel-, and Ground-type Pokémon take damage each turn	Steelix, Tyranitar, Flygon, Excadrill, and others
Sunny Day	Fire	—	—	Changes the weather condition to Sunny for five turns	Castform, Leafeon, and others

Examples of moves affected by weather

Move	Type	Power	Accuracy	Effect	Examples of Pokémon that can learn it
Blizzard	Ice	120	70	Always hits when the weather condition is Hail	Piloswine, Castform, and others
Growth	Normal	—	—	Raises the user's Attack and Sp. Atk by 1 Raises by 2 when the weather condition is Sunny	Tangela, Nuzleaf, Cottonee, Petilil, and others
Hurricane	Flying	120	70	Always hits when the weather condition is Rain Accuracy is halved when the weather condition is Sunny	Dragonite, Pelipper, Swanna, Volcarona, and others
SolarBeam	Grass	120	100	Usually requires one turn to charge, but goes off right away when the weather condition is Sunny	Sunflora, Sawsbuck, and others
Synthesis	Grass	—	—	Recovers HP. Effect changes depending on the weather	Leafeon, Amoonguss, and others
Thunder	Electric	120	70	Always hits when the weather condition is Rain Accuracy is halved when the weather condition is Sunny	Jolteon, Ampharos, Electivire, Zekrom, and others

Move Technique 12 — Limit the opposing Pokémon's actions

You can disrupt your opponent's plans by limiting the moves his or her Pokémon can use. Using moves that prevent your opponent from choosing moves freely can turn the tide of battle in your favor. For example, Encore forces the target to keep using the same move. If you use this when the opposing Pokémon uses a support move, it won't be able to use any damaging moves.

Advantage to moves that limit the target's moves

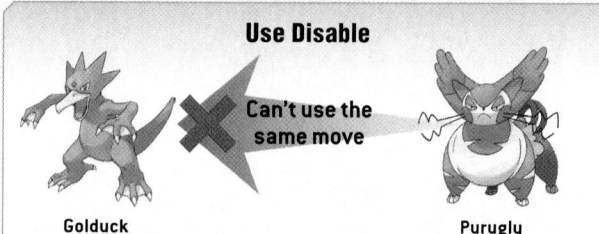

Use Disable

Golduck — Can't use the same move — Purugly

Disable prevents the target from using the move it used before it was hit by Disable for four turns.

Examples of moves that limit your opponent's moves

Move	Type	Power	Accuracy	Effect	Examples of Pokémon that can learn it
Disable	Normal	—	100	Target cannot use the move it just used for four turns	Golduck, Cofagrigus, and others
Embargo	Dark	—	100	Target cannot use items for five turns	Banette, Mandibuzz, and others
Encore	Normal	—	100	Target must use the move it used last for three turns	Slaking, Emolga, and others
Heal Block	Psychic	—	100	Target cannot restore HP with moves for five turns	Claydol, Bronzong, and others
Taunt	Dark	—	100	Target can use only attack moves for three turns	Sharpedo, Vanilluxe, and others
Torment	Dark	—	100	Target cannot use the same move twice in a row	Liepard, Bisharp, and others

Move Technique 13 — Use switching moves to take control of the battle

Switching out Pokémon is an important tactic. Normally, it takes a turn to switch Pokémon, but moves with switching effects can help you switch our your Pokémon without wasting a turn. Also, some moves force the opposing Trainer to switch his or her Pokémon. Use moves like these when you are facing an unfavorable matchup.

Advantage of switching moves

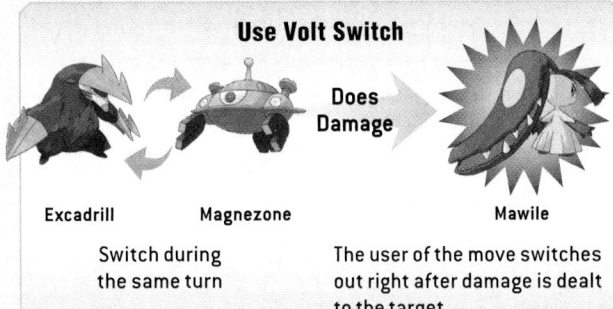

Use Volt Switch

Does Damage

Excadrill   Magnezone   Mawile

Switch during the same turn

The user of the move switches out right after damage is dealt to the target.

Some moves that let you switch Pokémon

Move	Type	Power	Accuracy	Effect	Examples of Pokémon that can learn it
Ally Switch	Psychic	—	—	User switches places with an ally but fails if user is in the center position in a Triple Battle	Alakazam, Xatu, Claydol, Beheeyem, and others
Baton Pass	Normal	—	—	User switches with a party Pokémon and passes stat changes to it	Lopunny, Watchog, and others
U-turn	Bug	70	100	User switches with a party Pokémon after attacking	Yanmega, Mienshao, and others
Volt Switch	Electric	70	100	User switches with a party Pokémon after attacking	Magnezone, Emolga, and others

Some moves that make the opposing Trainer switch Pokémon

Move	Type	Power	Accuracy	Effect	Examples of Pokémon that can learn it
Circle Throw	Fighting	60	90	Forces the opposing Trainer to switch Pokémon after the attack lands	Poliwrath, Throh, and others
Dragon Tail	Dragon	60	90	Forces the opposing Trainer to switch Pokémon after the attack lands	Dragonite, Druddigon, and others
Roar	Normal	—	100	Forces the opposing Trainer to switch Pokémon	Aggron, Stoutland, and others
Whirlwind	Normal	—	100	Forces the opposing Trainer to switch Pokémon	Tropius, Sigilyph, and others

Some moves to prevent Pokémon switching

Move	Type	Power	Accuracy	Effect	Examples of Pokémon that can learn it
Block	Normal	—	—	Prevents the target from being able to switch	Tangrowth, Probopass, and others
Mean Look	Normal	—	—	Prevents the target from being able to switch	Crobat, Umbreon, and others
Spider Web	Bug	—	—	Prevents the target from being able to switch	Ariados, Galvantula, and others

◆ Moves that switch Pokémon, or force switching of opposing Pokémon, won't switch them if no Pokémon are available to switch into battle.

Move Technique 14 — Affect items with moves

Having a Pokémon hold an item gives it an advantage in battle. Your opponent's strategy will often make use of held items. Disrupting your opponent's tactics with moves that make his or her Pokémon's held items unusable—or steal them instantly—makes it easier to fight.

Advantage of moves that affect items

Attack with Thief

Do damage and steal an item

Raticate   Cinccino

Thief lets you deal damage to your target and steal its held item.

Some moves related to items

Move	Type	Power	Accuracy	Effect	Examples of Pokémon that can learn it
Acrobatics	Flying	55	100	If the user isn't holding an item, attack does double damage	Gligar, Archeops, and others
Bestow	Normal	—	—	If the target isn't holding an item, the user's held item is transferred to the target	Clefairy, Tropius, and others
Fling	Dark	—	100	The user throws its held item to attack the target	Muk, Weavile, and others
Incinerate	Fire	30	100	Burns the Berry being held by the target, making it unusable	Pansear, Darmanitan, and others
Recycle	Normal	—	—	A previously used held item can be used again	Pansage, Garbodor, and others
Switcheroo	Dark	—	100	Swaps items between the user and the target	Hypno, Linoone, and others
Thief	Dark	40	100	When the target is holding an item and the user is not, the user can steal the target's item	Raticate, Kecleon, and others

Move Technique **15** Change your opponent's Abilities with moves

Each Pokémon has its own Ability. One of the basics of Pokémon battles is using Abilities that prevent status conditions or reduce the damage done by moves to turn the battle in your favor. Your opponent will surely use Pokémon Abilities as part of his or her strategy, so use moves to change those Abilities and disrupt your opponent.

Advantage of Ability-changing moves

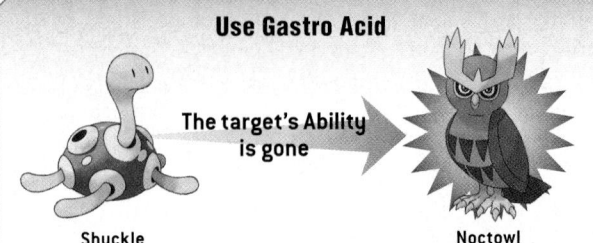

Use Gastro Acid

The target's Ability is gone

Shuckle → Noctowl

Gastro Acid removes the effects of the target's Ability as long as it is in battle. Use it to nullify any strategy that depends on Abilities.

Some Ability-changing moves

Move	Type	Power	Accuracy	Effect	Examples of Pokémon that can learn it
Entrainment	Normal	—	100	Makes the target's Ability the same as the user's	Lopunny, Durant, and others
Gastro Acid	Poison	—	100	Disables the target's Ability	Shuckle, Cradily, and others
Role Play	Psychic	—	—	Copies the target's Ability	Mr. Mime, Stantler, and others
Simple Beam	Normal	—	100	Changes the target's Ability to Simple	Audino, Beheeyem, and others
Skill Swap	Psychic	—	—	Swap Abilities with the target	Butterfree, Reuniclus, and others
Worry Seed	Grass	—	100	Changes the target's Ability to Insomnia	Sunflora, Budew, and others

◆ Targets with certain Abilities are immune to these kinds of moves.

Move Technique **16** Come from behind with a one-hit knockout

Even if your opponent has a lot of HP left, certain moves can make it faint in just one blow. Their accuracy is a low 30, but if these moves hit, they can get you out of a dangerous situation. Also, some moves—such as Explosion—will make the user faint in exchange for doing big damage. When your Pokémon's HP is dwindling, such a move may turn the battle around.

Advantages to one-hit KO moves

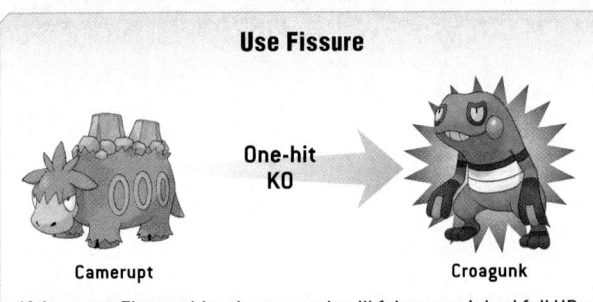

Use Fissure

One-hit KO

Camerupt → Croagunk

If the move Fissure hits the target, it will faint even it had full HP.

One-hit KO moves

Move	Type	Power	Accuracy	Effect	Examples of Pokémon that can learn it
Fissure	Ground	—	30	The target faints with one hit	Camerupt, Whiscash, and others
Guillotine	Normal	—	30	The target faints with one hit	Kingler, Haxorus, and others
Horn Drill	Normal	—	30	The target faints with one hit	Seaking, Excadrill, and others
Sheer Cold	Ice	—	30	The target faints with one hit	Vanilluxe, Beartic, and others

◆ If the target's level is higher than the user's, these moves will not hit.

Moves that make the user faint

Move	Type	Power	Accuracy	Effect	Examples of Pokémon that can learn it
Explosion	Normal	250	100	The user faints after using it	Drifblim, Ferrothorn, and others
Final Gambit	Fighting	—	100	Does damage to the target equal to the user's remaining HP Causes the user to faint after using the move	Primeape, Staraptor, Riolu, Accelgor, and others
Healing Wish	Psychic	—	—	The user faints, but the next Pokémon's HP and status are fully healed	Clefairy, Chimecho, Lopunny, Alomomola, and others
Memento	Dark	—	100	The user faints and lowers the target's Attack and Sp. Atk by 2	Muk, Weezing, Skuntank, Lampent, and others
Selfdestruct	Normal	200	100	The user faints after using it	Forretress, Claydol, and others

Move Technique 17 Use moves that can hit multiple Pokémon at once to gain an advantage

Moves with a range of "Many Others" can hit multiple opponent Pokémon at the same time in Double Battles and Triple Battles. The power of damaging attack moves goes down when they hit multiple opponents, but the benefit of attacking multiple opponents at once with a single attack is huge. Moves with a range of "Adjacent" hit both your opponents and your allies at the same time, so be sure to come up with a way to protect your allies from the attack.

Advantages of moves that can hit multiple targets

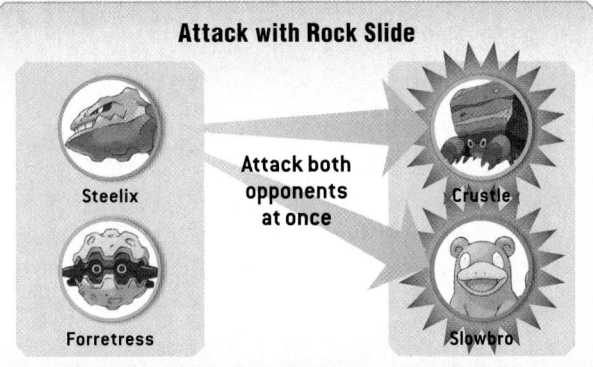

Attack with Rock Slide

Steelix

Forretress

Attack both opponents at once

Crustle

Slowbro

The range of Rock Slide is "Many Others," so it can inflict damage on multiple opponents at once.

Some moves that can hit multiple targets at once

Move	Type	Power	Accuracy	Effect	Some Pokémon that can learn it
Blizzard	Ice	120	70	10% chance of leaving the target frozen	Piloswine, Castform, and others
Heat Wave	Fire	100	90	10% chance of burning the target	Growlithe, Volcarona, and others
Razor Wind	Normal	80	100	Builds power on the first turn and attacks on the second and critical hits land more easily	Gligar, Zangoose, and others
Rock Slide	Rock	75	90	30% chance to cause the target to flinch	Steelix, Shuckle, and others
Swift	Normal	60	—	A sure hit	Sandslash, Golbat, and others

Some moves that also hit allies

Move	Type	Power	Accuracy	Effect	Some Pokémon that can learn it
Discharge	Electric	80	100	30% chance of inflicting Paralysis on the target	Magneton, Jolteon, and others
Earthquake	Ground	100	100	Standard attack	Tyranitar, Krookodile, and others
Sludge Wave	Poison	95	100	10% chance of poisoning the target	Tentacruel, Muk, and others
Surf	Water	95	100	Standard attack	Golduck, Dewgong, and others

Move Technique 18 Long-range attacks are the secret to Triple Battle success

In Triple Battles, you and the opposing Trainer both put three Pokémon into battle. Normally, the Pokémon on the far left can't hit the Pokémon on the far right, and the Pokémon on the far right can't hit the Pokémon on the far left. So most of the time, any one of your Pokémon can attack only two of your opponent's three Pokémon. However, if you use a long-range move, you can hit the opposing Pokémon on the opposite side from the user. These attacks are very useful when you want to focus your attacks on one of the opposing Pokémon and knock it out as quickly as possible. Place Pokémon with long-range moves on the left and right sides of your team in Triple Battles.

Advantages of moves that can hit multiple targets

Attack with Acrobatics

Gliscor

Dusknoir

Dustox

The Pokémon on the opposite far end can be attacked

Seismitoad

Sudowoodo

Beautifly

Acrobatics is a long-range move, so it can reach the opposing Pokémon on the far end.

Some long-range moves

Move	Types	Powers	Accuracy	Effect	Some Pokémon that can learn it
Acrobatics	Flying	55	100	If the user isn't holding an item, attack does double damage	Gliscor, Emolga, and others
Aura Sphere	Fighting	90	—	A sure hit	Togekiss, Mienshao, and others
Dark Pulse	Dark	80	100	20% chance of making target flinch	Tyranitar, Mandibuzz, and others
Dragon Pulse	Dragon	90	100	Standard attack	Kingdra, Hydreigon, and others
Heal Pulse	Psychic	—	—	Restores the target's HP by up to half of its max HP	Lucario, Audino, and others
Water Pulse	Water	60	100	20% chance of inflicting the Confused status condition	Wailord, Jellicent, and others

Pokémon Battles Introduction 7

Use Pokémon Abilities to Their Fullest

Know your opponent's Abilities and get the edge in battle

Pokémon Abilities have a variety of effects, such as increasing the damage done to opposing Pokémon by an attack or inflicting status conditions on the attacker when receiving an attack. If you can master Abilities, you will always have the edge over others in battle.

Ability Techniques **1 A Pokémon's Ability is determined by its species**

Every Pokémon has an Ability, which is determined by that Pokémon's species. Even if the species has two or more possible Abilities, each individual Pokémon will have only one of those Abilities. Abilities will also affect which moves will be most useful for battle. Look for ways to take advantage of a Pokemon's Ability when battling.

Abilities change based on Pokémon species

Scrafty's Abilities

Ability Shed Skin

When afflicted with a status condition during battle, the Pokémon has a 1 in 3 chance of naturally recovering each turn.

Ability Moxie

Raises the Pokémon's Attack by 1 when an opposing Pokémon is defeated in battle by one of its moves.

Shiftry's Abilities

Ability Chlorophyll

When the weather condition is Sunny during battle, the Pokémon's Speed is doubled.

Ability Early Bird

Allows the Pokémon to wake more quickly when an opposing Pokémon gives it the Sleep status condition.

Tip **Some Pokémon have Hidden Abilities**

Some Pokémon have Hidden Abilities. These Abilities are normally never found in Pokémon that appear in the wild, but Pokémon found in Hidden Grottoes or received from ingame events may possess them. Pokémon you find in the Pokémon Dream World may also have such Hidden Abilities (p. 390).

Pachirisu's Abilities

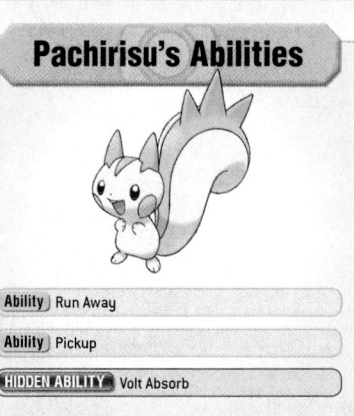

Ability Run Away

Ability Pickup

HIDDEN ABILITY Volt Absorb

Cubone's Abilities

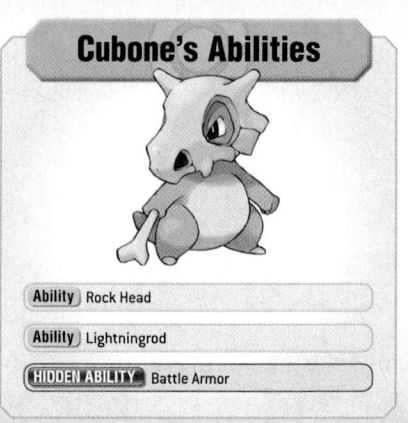

Ability Rock Head

Ability Lightningrod

HIDDEN ABILITY Battle Armor

Ability Techniques 2 — Abilities that activate on entering battle

Some Abilities activate as soon as the Pokémon enters a battle. For example, when a Pokémon with the Sand Stream Ability comes into battle, the weather condition immediately changes to Sandstorm. Such Abilities activate when the battle starts or when the Pokémon with this type of Ability is switched into battle. Consider this factor when choosing a Pokémon to put at the head of your party or making tactics that include switching.

Advantages of Abilities that activate on entering battle

Intimidate Ability is activated

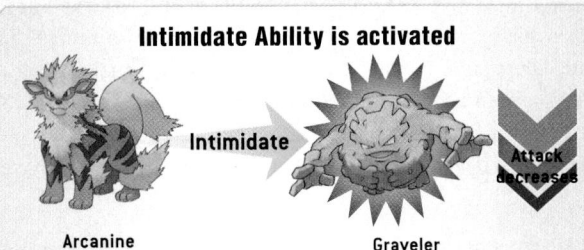

Arcanine → Intimidate → Graveler (Attack decreases)

Put a Pokémon with the Intimidate Ability in battle to lower the opposing Pokémon's Attack by one level.

Some Abilities that activate when a Pokémon enters a battle

Ability	Effect	Pokémon with this Ability
Forewarn	Identifies one of the opposing Pokémon's moves when the Pokémon enters battle. Damaging moves with high power are prioritized	Jynx, Musharna, and others
Frisk	Checks an opposing Pokémon's held item when the Pokémon enters battle	Banette, Gothitelle, and others
Intimidate	Lowers opposing Pokémon's Attack by 1 when the Pokémon enters battle	Growlithe, Stoutland, and others
Sand Stream	Changes the weather condition to Sandstorm when the Pokémon enters battle	Tyranitar, Hippowdon, and others

Ability Techniques 3 — Take advantage of Abilities that power up particular move types

Some Abilities raise the power of moves if certain conditions are met. For example, Torrent increases the power of Water-type moves when HP is low. The lower your Pokémon's HP, the more damage it can do. Knowing about Abilities like this can help you when you're in trouble.

Advantage of Abilities that raise moves' power

Swarm Ability is activated

Use Bug-type moves aggressively when your Pokémon has little HP remaining. Power will be higher than normal.

Bug-type moves' Power goes up — Escavalier

Some Abilities that power-up particular move types

Ability	Effect	Pokémon with this Ability
Adaptability	Increases the power boost received by using a move of same type as the Pokémon	Eevee, Porygon-Z, and others
Blaze	Raises the power of Fire-type moves by 50% when the Pokemon's HP drops to 1/3 or less	Pignite, Emboar, and others
Overgrow	Raises the power of Grass-type moves by 50% when the Pokemon's HP drops to 1/3 or less	Servine, Serperior, and others
Sand Force	When the weather condition is Sandstorm, the power of Ground-, Rock-, and Steel-type moves increases by 30%. Sandstorm does not damage the Pokémon	Drilbur, Excadrill, Landorus Incarnate Forme, and others
Swarm	Raises the power of Bug-type moves by 50% when the Pokemon's HP drops to 1/3 or less	Escavalier, Durant, and others
Torrent	Raises the power of Water-type moves by 50% when the Pokemon's HP drops to 1/3 or less	Dewott, Samurott, and others

 **Tip** — Make opposing Trainers hesitate with Pokémon that have three Abilities

Even if a species has three possible Abilities, each individual Pokémon will have only one of them. Usually, however, the opposing Trainer won't know which one it is. For example, Bronzong could have the Levitate Ability, which would completely protect it from the Ground-type moves it is usually weakest against. Or it could have the Heatproof Ability, which would halve the damage it takes from its other weakness: Fire types. The opposing Trainer will have no idea which weakness to target.

Bronzong's baffling Abilities confound opposing Trainers

Ability	Levitate
Ability	Heatproof
HIDDEN ABILITY	Heavy Metal

Bronzong

Ability Techniques 4 | **Use Abilities that activate when attacking**

Some Abilities activate when the Pokémon with that Ability uses a move. For example, when a Pokémon with the Super Luck Ability damages an opposing Pokémon, its critical-hit ratio increases. In the same way, the Mold Breaker Ability helps a Pokémon hit a target that is normally protected by its own Ability. Combine Abilities with moves that take advantage of them for devastating attacks.

Advantages of offensive Abilities

Sheer Force Ability is activated

Power raised in place of any additional effects

Darmanitan   Lunatone

When the Pokémon uses a move with an additional effect that effect does not materialize, but instead the move's power goes up by 30%.

Some Abilities that activate on using a move

Ability	Effect	Pokémon with this Ability
Compoundeyes	Raises accuracy by 30%	Butterfree, Galvantula, and others
Guts	Attack stat rises by 50% when the Pokémon is affected by a status condition	Raticate, Conkeldurr, and others
Hustle	Raises Attack by 50%, but lowers the accuracy of physical moves by 20%	Remoraid, Zweilous, and others
Infiltrator	Moves can hit even if the target used Reflect, Light Screen, Safeguard, or Mist	Cottonee, Whimsicott, and others
Iron Fist	Increases the power of punching moves	Golett, Golurk, and others
Mold Breaker	Use moves on targets regardless of their Abilities	Pinsir, Rampardos, and others
Poison Touch	30% chance of inflicting the Poison status condition when the Pokémon uses a direct attack	Seismitoad and others
Prankster	Gives priority to status moves	Cottonee, Whimsicott, and others
Reckless	Raises the power of moves with recoil damage	Hitmonlee, Bouffalant, and others
Rivalry	If the target is the same gender, the power of the Pokemon's move goes up Against the opposite gender, the move's power goes down and if the target's gender is unknown, the move's power doesn't change	Axew, Fraxure, Haxorus, and others
Sheer Force	When a move with an additional effect is used, the power increases by 30%, but the additional effect is lost	Darmanitan, Druddigon, and others
Stench	10% chance the target flinches when the Pokémon damages the target with a move	Muk, Garbodor, and others
Super Luck	Heightens the critical-hit ratio of the Pokémon's moves	Absol, Unfezant, and others
Technician	If the move's power is 60 or below, its power will increase by 50%	Ambipom, Cinccino, and others

Ability Techniques 5 | **Use damage-preventing Abilities to get an edge**

Some Abilities prevent damage from particular move types. For example, Pokémon with the Sap Sipper Ability don't receive damage from Grass-type attacks. When switching Pokémon or using combos in Double and Triple Battles, knowing these Abilities is essential.

Advantages of damage-preventing Abilities

Levitate Ability is activated

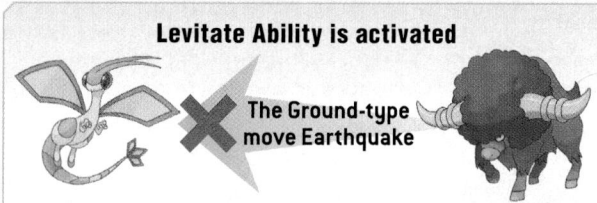

The Ground-type move Earthquake

Flygon   Bouffalant

Pokémon with the Levitate Ability are not damaged by Ground-type attacks.

Some Abilities that power up particular move types

Ability	Effect	Pokémon with this Ability
Flash Fire	When the Pokémon is hit by a Fire-type move, it doesn't take damage and the power of its Fire-type moves increase by 50%	Ninetales, Growlithe, Chandelure, Heatmor, and others
Levitate	Gives full immunity to all Ground-type moves	Flygon, Carnivine, and others
Lightningrod	Draws all Electric-type moves to the Pokémon. When the Pokémon is hit by an Electric-type move, it doesn't take damage and its Sp. Atk goes up by 1	Marowak, Manectric, Rhydon, Zebstrika, and others
Motor Drive	When the Pokémon is hit by an Electric-type move, it doesn't take damage and its Speed goes up by 1	Electivire, Zebstrika, and others
Sap Sipper	When the Pokémon is hit by a Grass-type move, it doesn't take damage and its Attack goes up by 1	Sawsbuck, Bouffalant, and others
Volt Absorb	When the Pokémon is hit by an Electric-type move, it doesn't take damage and its HP is restored	Jolteon, Lanturn, and others
Water Absorb	When the Pokémon is hit by a Water-type move, it doesn't take damage and its HP is restored	Poliwrath, Jellicent, and others

Ability Techniques 6 — Confound your opponent with Abilities that activate when a Pokémon is hit

Some Pokémon's Abilities activate when a move hits them. For example, Rough Skin and Iron Barbs both lower the opposing Pokémon's HP when a Pokémon with one of these Abilities is hit by a direct attack. The Pressure Ability removes an extra PP when the opposing Pokémon uses a move against your Pokémon. These Abilities make it harder for your opponent to use the moves he or she wants to use and give you a clear advantage.

Advantages of hit-activated Abilities

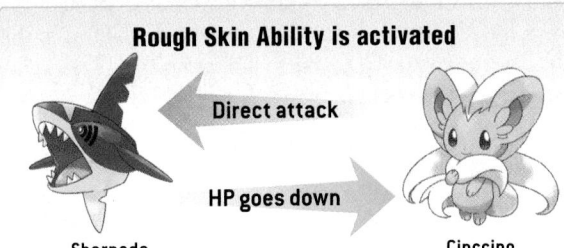

Rough Skin Ability is activated

Direct attack

HP goes down

Sharpedo — Cinccino

The Rough Skin Ability reduces the HP of opposing Pokémon that hit the Pokémon with a direct attack

Some Abilities that activate when hit

Ability	Effect	Pokémon with this Ability
Cursed Body	30% chance of disabling the move used to hit the Pokémon	Frillish, Jellicent, and others
Cute Charm	30% chance of making the attacker infatuated when hit by a direct attack.	Clefairy, Delcatty, and others
Effect Spore	30% chance of inflicting the Poison, Paralysis, or Sleep status condition on an attacker when hit with a direct attack.	Breloom, Amoonguss, and others
Flame Body	30% chance of inflicting the Burned status condition on the attacker when hit by a direct attack	Chandelure, Volcarona, and others
Iron Barbs	Slightly reduces the HP of an opponent that hits the Pokémon with a direct attack	Ferroseed, Ferrothorn
Justified	When the Pokémon is hit by a Dark-type move, Attack goes up by 1	Cobalion, Terrakion, and others
Mummy	Changes the attacker's Ability to Mummy when hit by a direct attack	Yamask, Cofagrigus
Poison Point	30% chance of inflicting the Poison status condition on an attacker when hit by a direct attack	Seadra, Scolipede, and others
Pressure	When the Pokémon is hit by an opposing Pokémon's move, depletes 1 additional PP from that move	Absol, Vespiquen, and others
Rough Skin	Slightly reduces the HP of an opponent that hits the Pokémon with a direct attack	Sharpedo, Druddigon, and others
Shell Armor	Opposing Pokémon's moves will not land a critical hit	Cloyster, Crawdaunt, and others
Solid Rock	Minimizes the damage from supereffective moves	Camerupt, Carracosta, and others
Static	30% chance of inflicting the Paralysis status condition on an attacker when hit by a direct attack	Ampharos, Emolga, and others
Sturdy	One-hit knockout moves like Horn Drill and Sheer Cold don't work. Leaves the Pokémon with 1 HP if hit by a move that would knock it out when its HP is full	Shuckle, Aggron, Gigalith, Crustle, and others
Weak Armor	When the Pokémon is hit by a physical attack, Defense goes down 1, but Speed goes up 1	Garbodor and others

Ability Techniques 7 — Use Abilities that activate when attacking

Abilities can prevent certain status conditions or heal them after they are inflicted. For example, the Insomnia Ability will protect a Pokémon from the Sleep status condition. Meanwhile, Pokémon with the Shed Skin Ability can recover from status conditions. These Abilities can save your bacon when you are facing a foe trying to inflict status conditions.

Advantages of status-condition preventing Abilities

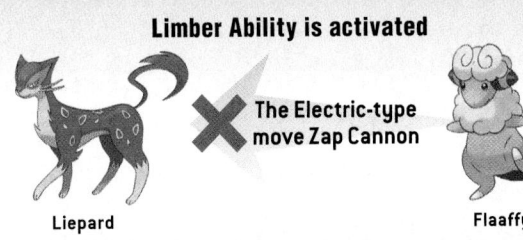

Limber Ability is activated

The Electric-type move Zap Cannon

Liepard — Flaaffy

Pokémon with the Limber Ability are immune to Paralysis.

Some status condition-related Abilities

Ability	Effect	Pokémon with this Ability
Guts	Attack stat rises by 50% when the Pokémon is affected by a status condition	Heracross, Conkeldurr, and others
Insomnia	Protects against the Sleep status condition	Ariados, Banette, and others
Limber	Protects against the Paralysis status condition	Liepard, Stunfisk, and others
Magma Armor	Prevents the Frozen status condition	Magcargo, Camerupt, and others
Own Tempo	Protects against the Confused condition	Grumpig, Lickilicky, and others
Shed Skin	33% chance every turn that a status condition will be healed	Dragonair, Seviper, and others
Synchronize	When the Pokémon receives the Poison, Paralysis, or Burned status condition, this inflicts the same condition on the attacker	Eevee, Umbreon, and others

8 # Pokémon with stat-changing Abilities thrive

Abilities can raise a Pokémon's stats, lower an opposing Pokémon's stats, and even protect a Pokémon from having its stats lowered. One great advantage of these Abilities is that they work automatically. Unlike stat-altering moves, you don't have to spend a turn to use them.

Advantage of Abilities that raise stats

Moxie Ability is activated

Attack increases — The opponent is knocked out

Krookodile   Magnezone

When the Pokémon knocks out an opposing Pokémon with a move, its Attack goes up by 1. This gives the Pokémon an advantage over the next Pokémon it faces in battle.

Examples of stat-related Abilities

Ability	Effect	Pokémon with this Ability
Anger Point	Raises Attack to the maximum when the Pokémon is hit by a critical hit	Primeape, Tauros, and others
Big Pecks	Prevents Defense from being lowered	Unfezant, Swanna, and others
Clear Body	Protects against stat-lowering moves and Abilities	Tentacruel, Metagross, and others
Defiant	When an opponent's move or Ability lowers the Pokémon's stats, its Attack goes up 2	Pawniard, Bisharp, and others
Download	Raises Attack or Sp. Atk by 1, depending on whether the opposing Pokémon's Defense or Sp. Def is lower	Porygon, Porygon2, Porygon-Z, and others
Hustle	Raises Attack by 50%, but lowers the accuracy of the Pokémon's physical moves by 20%	Corsola, Zweilous, and others
Hyper Cutter	Prevents Attack from being lowered	Pinsir, Gliscor, and others
Minus	Raises Sp. Atk by 50% if an ally Pokémon has the Plus or Minus Ability	Minun, Klinklang, and others
Moxie	When the Pokémon knocks out an opposing Pokémon with a move, its Attack goes up 1	Krookodile, Scrafty, and others
Plus	Raises Sp. Atk by 50% if an ally Pokémon has the Plus or Minus Ability	Plusle, Klinklang, and others
Steadfast	Raises Speed by 1 every time the Pokémon flinches	Lucario, Gallade, and others
Unaware	Ignores the stat changes of the opposing Pokémon	Bibarel, Swoobat, and others
Unburden	Doubles Speed if the Pokémon loses or consumes its held item. Its Speed returns to normal if the Pokémon holds another item. No effect if the Pokémon starts battle with no held item	Drifloon, Drifblim, Purrloin, Liepard, and others

9 # Be a rainmaker with weather-related Abilities

Abilities can be affected by weather conditions just as moves can be. For example, the Swift Swim Ability doubles a Pokémon's Speed when the weather condition is Rain. You can combine Abilities and weather conditions to create a situation that strongly favors your team.

Examples of weather-related Abilities

Sand Rush Ability is activated

Speed increases

Herdier

The Sand Rush Ability doubles Speed when the weather condition is Sandstorm.

Examples of weather-related Abilities

Ability	Effect	Pokémon with this Ability
Chlorophyll	Doubles Speed in the Sunny weather condition	Shiftry, Leavanny, etc.
Hydration	Cures status conditions at the end of the turn in the Rain weather condition	Dewgong, Palpitoad, and others
Ice Body	Gradually restores HP in the Hail weather condition. Hail does not damage the Pokémon	Walrein, Vanilluxe, and others
Leaf Guard	Protects the Pokémon from status conditions in the Sunny weather condition	Leafeon, Swadloon, and others
Overcoat	Prevents damage from the Sandstorm and Hail weather conditions	Vullaby, Mandibuzz, and others
Rain Dish	Gradually restores HP in the Rain weather condition	Lombre, Ludicolo, and others
Sand Rush	Doubles Speed in the Sandstorm weather condition. Sandstorm does not damage the Pokémon	Herdier, Stoutland, Drilbur, Excadrill, and others
Snow Cloak	Raises evasion in the Hail weather condition. Hail does not damage the Pokémon	Glaceon, Beartic, and others
Solar Power	Sp. Atk is increased by 50% when the weather condition is Sunny, but some HP is lost every turn	Sunkern, Sunflora, Tropius, and others
Swift Swim	Doubles Speed in the Rain weather condition	Seaking, Seismitoad, and others

Pokémon Battles Introduction 8

Use Items to Develop New Strategies

Held items make your Pokémon even stronger

A Pokémon can only hold one item. Many items are useful in battle. The effects vary by each type of item, so look for items that fit your battle style.

Item Techniques 1 — Many different types of items can be held by Pokémon

You'll find many different items in the game, all with different uses and characteristics. Some items are triggered only when your Pokémon attacks, while others come in handy when your Pokémon takes an attack or heal your Pokémon's HP. Some items will help play up your Pokémon's strong points, while others help to compensate for its weaknesses. Many species of Pokémon can excel in battle when they are given an item to hold.

Examples of items for battles

Silk Scarf	A Pokémon holding it has boosts the power of Normal-type moves
King's Rock	A Pokémon holding it has a 30% chance of making the target flinch when the Pokémon attacks
Quick Claw	Sometimes the holder strikes first
BrightPowder	When held by a Pokémon, it lowers the opposing Pokémon's accuracy
Leftovers	A Pokémon holding it regains 1/16 of its total HP each turn
Life Orb	When held by a Pokémon, that Pokémon will lose 1/10 of its HP every time that it attacks, but the power of its moves will be increased by 30%

Further characteristics of items for battles

1. Some items can hurt the holder.

2. Some moves and Abilities help the Pokémon can fight more effectively if it doesn't hold an item.

3. Items used up in battles with friends or on the Battle Subway will return after the battle.

Tip — Some items will take effect only once during battle

Among the many kinds of items, some will grant their effects constantly while others can be used just once before they disappear. For example, a Fire Gem will increase the power of Fire-type moves by 50% just once. This makes it ill suited for long, drawn-out battles, but it is incredibly useful when you are feeling the burn and want to bring a battle to a quick end. Consider your battle style and the moves and Abilities of your Pokémon when it comes to using items.

Examples of single-use items

Red Card	A Pokémon holding this item forces the opposing Pokémon to switch out if it uses an attack
Focus Sash	When held by a Pokémon, it will prevent the Pokémon from fainting from a single-hit knockout move and the Pokémon will retain 1 HP
White Herb	When held by a Pokémon, this item can restore a stat that has been lowered
Fire Gem	When held by a Pokémon, it lowers the opposing Pokémon's accuracy

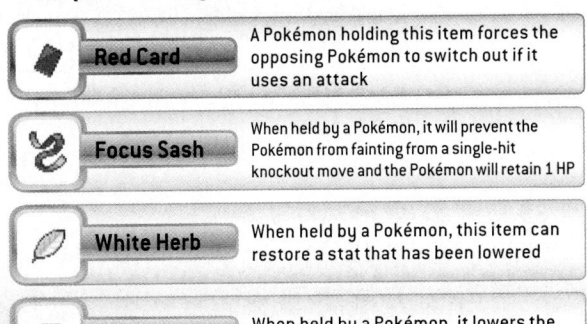

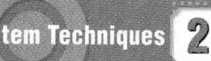

Item Techniques **2** Held items can power up attacks

Some items will boost the power of your Pokémon's attacks when held. For example, the Muscle Band is an item that ups the power of any physical moves for the Pokémon holding it. Since this helps you deal greater damage to the opposing Pokémon, you can defeat your opponent in less turns. Learn the effects of items to do massive damage to opposing Pokémon.

Advantages of damage-increasing items

How the Expert Belt works

Increases damage taken from opponent's weakness: Rock-type moves

Omastar | Accelgor

When a Pokémon holding an Expert Belt uses a supereffective move, the move's power increases.

Examples of items for attacking

Item	Effect
Big Root	Increases the HP restored by the holder's HP-draining moves, such as Giga Drain or Horn Leech
Binding Band	Doubles the damage done every turn by moves like Bind or Wrap
Black Belt	Raises the power of Fighting-type moves
BlackGlasses	Raises the power of Dark-type moves
Draco Plate	Raises the power of Dragon-type moves
Expert Belt	Raises the power of supereffective moves by 20%
Magnet	Raises the power of Electric-type moves
Metal Coat	Raises the power of Steel-type moves
Metronome	Raises the power of a move used in consecutive turns
Miracle Seed	Raises the power of Grass-type moves
Muscle Band	Raises the power of physical moves
Mystic Water	Raises the power of Water-type moves
Razor Claw	Raises the critical-hit ratio of the holder's attacks
Razor Fang	Attacks have a 10% chance of making the target flinch
Rock Incense	Raises the power of Rock-type moves
Scope Lens	Raises the critical-hit ratio of the holder's attacks
Sharp Beak	Raises the power of Flying-type moves
Silk Scarf	Raises the power of Normal-type moves
Soft Sand	Raises the power of Ground-type moves
Spell Tag	Raises the power of Ghost-type moves
TwistedSpoon	Raises the power of Psychic-type moves
Wave Incense	Raises the power of Water-type moves
Wide Lens	Raises the accuracy of the holder's moves by 10%
Wise Glasses	Raises the power of special moves
Zoom Lens	Raises the holder's accuracy by 20% when it moves after the opposing Pokémon

Item Techniques **3** Use items to get the jump on opposing Pokémon

In battle, striking before your opponent will allow you to shape the battle to your advantage. Normally your Speed stat determines whether your Pokémon or the opposing Pokémon get to go first. However, some items—like the Quick Claw—allow your Pokémon to go first regardless of its Speed.

Advantages of Berries that help you move first

How the Quick Claw item works

Strike first regardless of Speed

Vespiquen | Crobat

Giving your Pokémon a Quick Claw gives it the chance to move first, regardless of how high the opposing Pokémon's Speed stat is.

Advantages of Berries that help you move first

Item	Effect
Choice Scarf	The holder can only use one move, but Speed increases by 50%
Quick Claw	Allows the holder to attack first
Salac Berry	Raises the holder's Speed stat by 1 when its HP becomes low

Item Techniques **4** Held items can help with defense

Items can also prevent your Pokémon from being knocked out or can reduce the amount of damage done by types of moves the holder is weak against. Have your Pokémon hold items that help when they are hit to keep your team out of trouble.

Advantages of damage-reducing items

How the Coba Berry works

Decreases damage taken from your Pokémon's weakness: Flying-type moves

Conkeldurr

Yanmega

A Pokémon holding a Coba Berry takes less damage from a supereffective Flying-type move.

Examples of items for defending

Item	Effect
Absorb Bulb	When the holder is hit by a Water-type move, its Sp. Atk goes up by 1
Air Balloon	The holder floats in the air, protecting it from Ground-type moves, but the balloon will pop when the holder is hit by an attack
BrightPowder	Lowers the opposing Pokémon's accuracy
Cell Battery	When the holder is hit by an Electric-type move, its Attack goes up by 1
Eviolite	Raises Defense and Sp. Def by 50% when held by a Pokémon that can still evolve
Focus Band	The holder has a 1/10 chance of surviving with 1 HP when it receives damage that would KO it
Focus Sash	Leaves the holder with 1 HP when hit by a move that would KO it, but only when its HP is full
Rocky Helmet	Does damage to the Pokémon that hit the holder with a direct attack

Examples of Berries that reduce damage from attacks

Item	Effect
Charti Berry	Halves damage taken from supereffective Rock-type moves
Coba Berry	Halves damage taken from supereffective Flying-type moves
Colbur Berry	Halves damage taken from supereffective Dark-type moves
Occa Berry	Halves damage taken from supereffective Fire-type moves
Passho Berry	Halves damage taken from supereffective Water-type moves
Rindo Berry	Halves damage taken from supereffective Grass-type moves
Shuca Berry	Halves damage taken from supereffective Ground-type moves
Wacan Berry	Halves damage taken from supereffective Electric-type moves
Yache Berry	Halves damage taken from supereffective Ice-type moves

Item Techniques **5** Berries can turn a crisis into an opportunity

Some Berries work when the Pokémon holding them have just a little HP left, or they restore PP when it is gone. The Sitrus Berry, for example, restores HP by up to 1/4 of the holder's max HP when its HP falls to half or lower. Items that work in a bad situation can give your team a chance for a come-from-behind victory!

Advantages of Berries that work in a pinch

How the Leppa Berry works

PP are restored

Lopunny

Lopunny regains 10 PP thanks to the Leppa Berry, which gives it a chance to strike back.

Examples of Berries that activate when HP or PP is low

Item	Effect
Lansat Berry	Raises the holder's critical-hit ratio when its HP is low
Leppa Berry	Restores PP by 10 when the PP of a holder's move is 0
Oran Berry	Restores HP by 10 when the holder's HP falls to half or lower
Sitrus Berry	Restores HP by 1/4 of the holder's max HP when its HP falls to half or lower
Starf Berry	Raises a stat 2 levels when the holder's HP is low

Item Techniques 6 Heal HP and status conditions with items

Some items can heal HP and status conditions. Leftovers, for example, restores a little HP every turn. If you use such items, you can get out of a bad situation or stand tough with Pokémon that are hard to knock out.

Advantages of status condition-healing items

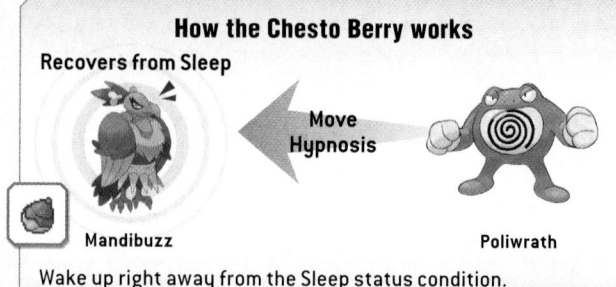

How the Chesto Berry works

Recovers from Sleep

Move
Hypnosis

Mandibuzz   Poliwrath

Wake up right away from the Sleep status condition.

Some items related to HP and status conditions

Item	Effect
Leftovers	Restores a little HP every turn
White Herb	Restores lowered stats (goes away after use)

Some Berries that heal status conditions

Item	Effect
Aspear Berry	The holder is cured when given the Frozen status condition (goes away after use)
Cheri Berry	The holder is cured when given the Paralyzed status condition (goes away after use)
Chesto Berry	The holder is cured when given the Sleep status condition (goes away after use)
Lum Berry	The holder is cured of all status conditions (goes away after use)
Pecha Berry	The holder is cured when given the Poison status condition (goes away after use)
Persim Berry	The holder is cured when given the Confused status condition (goes away after use)
Rawst Berry	The holder is cured when given the Burned status condition (goes away after use)

Item Techniques 7 Master items with negative effects

Some items don't seem to help your Pokémon when held. For example, Lagging Tail makes the Pokémon holding it always attack last, regardless of Speed stats. You can put the opposing Trainer at a disadvantage by using the Bestow move to stick an opposing Pokémon with one of these items.

Advantages of items with harmful effects

How Life Orb works

Life Orb's effects add more damage

Jellicent   Octillery

Life Orb reduces the holder's HP, but also gives it the power to do massive damage.

Examples of harmful held items

Item	Effect
Choice Band	The holder can only use one move, but Attack increases by 50%
Choice Scarf	The holder can only use one move, but Speed increases by 50%
Choice Specs	The holder can only use one move, but Sp. Atk increases by 50%
Flame Orb	Inflicts Burn on the holder during battle.
Full Incense	The holder strikes last
Iron Ball	Lowers Speed and if the holder has the Levitate Ability or is a Flying-type Pokémon, Ground-type moves will now hit it
Lagging Tail	The holder strikes last
Life Orb	Lowers the holder's HP by 1/10 each time it attacks, but raises the power of moves by 30%
Toxic Orb	Inflicts Badly Poisoned status on the holder during battle

Berries that restore HP but inflict Confused status condition

Item	Effect
Aguav Berry	Restores HP but inflicts the Confused condition if the Pokémon dislikes Bitter flavors (goes away after use)
Figy Berry	Restores HP but inflicts the Confused condition if the Pokémon dislikes Spicy flavors (goes away after use)
Iapapa Berry	Restores HP but inflicts the Confused condition if the Pokémon dislikes Sour flavors (goes away after use)
Mago Berry	Restores HP but inflicts the Confused condition if the Pokémon dislikes Sweet flavors (goes away after use)
Wiki Berry	Restores HP but inflicts the Confused condition if the Pokémon dislikes Dry flavors (goes away after use)

Item Techniques 8 — Use items to extend the duration of moves

A few items extend the duration of a move's effect. These items extend the effects of weather-changing moves or extend moves that halve the damage your Pokémon takes, like Reflect or Light Screen. Extend these favorable situations even a little longer to put victory in your grasp.

Advantages of items that affect move duration

How Icy Rock works

Hail lasts longer

Castform

When a Pokémon holding Icy Rock uses Hail, the weather condition Hail continues longer

Some items that affect move duration

Item	Effect
Damp Rock	Extends the duration of the Rain weather condition from the move Rain Dance
Grip Claw	Extends the duration of moves like Bind and Wrap
Heat Rock	Extends the duration of the Sunny weather condition from the move Sunny Day
Icy Rock	Extends the duration of the Hail weather condition from the move Hail
Light Clay	Extends the duration of moves like Reflect and Light Screen
Smooth Rock	Extends the duration of the Sandstorm weather condition from the move Sandstorm

Item Techniques 9 — Escape from danger with switching-related items

Pokémon can also take advantage of held items related to switching. The Shed Shell lets the holder switch out even when a move that prevents switching, like Mean Look, was used on it. Items can help you swap in a different party member—or force an opposing Pokémon to switch out—and create a favorable situation.

Advantages of switching-enabling items

Eject Button item is activated

Receive attack

Houndoom   Vanilluxe   Grumpig

Swaps out that turn

A Pokémon holding the Eject Button can be swapped out with a Pokémon waiting in your party.

Switching-related Items

Item	Effect
Eject Button	If the holder is hit by an attack, its action is canceled and it switches with a party Pokémon (goes away after use)
Red Card	If the holder is hit by an attack, the opposing Trainer must switch Pokémon (goes away after use)
Shed Shell	The holder can always be switched out

 **Tip** — Find some more unique items!

Many items have unique effects. The Float Stone halves a Pokémon's weight. Sticky Barb sticks to an attacker and reduces its HP every turn, while Ring Target makes moves hit even if they should be neutralized by type matchups. Figuring out how they all work best may be difficult, but it's worth it to give them all a try.

Item that changes a Pokémon's weight

 Float Stone

Halves the weight of the Pokémon holding it. This can change the effects of weight-influenced moves such as Grass Knot and Low Kick.

Item that affects type matchups

 Ring Target

If you pass it to a Ghost-type, for example, Normal- and Fighting-type moves will damage it.

Item related to direct attacks

 Sticky Barb

If a Pokémon holds a Sticky Barb and is directly attacked, the Sticky Barb attaches itself to the attacker. If it sticks, the opponent will receive a little damage every turn.

Adapt Your Strategy to Win Battles

Defeat opponents quickly and prevent damage to your Pokémon

Battles are tough. Nobody wants to lose, least of all your opponent. So when it's all on the line, what strategy works best to conserve your team's HP while taking out your opponent's Pokémon? Study the tips below and experiment to find your own best techniques.

Battle Strategy **1** Take these actions in Pokémon battles

While teaching moves and raising Pokémon are important, those things alone aren't enough to win battles. Your actions in battle are very important. Even a single bad decision can cost you the battle. Making the right decision at the right time many times in a battle will raise your win-loss ratio. Strong Trainers choose actions that will keep them from losing, no matter what the situation.

Basic actions for winning Pokémon battles

Action **1** Do as much damage as possible

Knocking out all of your foe's Pokémon is the condition for winning a battle. When you understand which moves do the most damage to your opponent, battles become much more fun.

Action **2** Reduce damage taken as much as possible

While you want to damage your opponents, your foe will choose moves that deliver big damage to your Pokémon as well. That's why you need to think up ways to reduce damage.

Action **3** Anticipate your foes' actions

When you try thinking from your opponent's perspective, sometimes you can guess what he or she will try next. Imagine the types of moves your opponent could use, or if they are likely to switch Pokémon. Then you'll know what to do.

Action **4** Disrupt your foe's tactics

Defeating even one of the Pokémon at the center of your foe's strategy gives you a huge advantage. You can disrupt combos by preventing an opponent from using a single move. Bring victory your way by disrupting your opponent's tactics.

Battle Strategy **2** Switch Pokémon to gain a type advantage

Sometimes, the Pokémon you have in battle won't know any moves that take advantage of the opponent's weaknesses. At times like these, you can often defeat an opponent more quickly by switching in another Pokémon from your party. You have to use up a turn to switch your Pokémon, but you have a better chance to defeat the opponent in fewer turns. Also, you're better off switching in a different Pokémon if the opponent is likely to use a move that is super effective against your Pokémon.

Switch Pokémon to gain a type advantage

Your Pokémon

Magnezone
`Rock`

No type advantage

Switch immediately

Claydol
`Ground` `Psychic`

Foe's Pokémon

Type advantage

Garbodor
`Poison`

Use the Ground-type moves Claydol learns to attack Garbodor's weakness.

Battle Strategy **3** Switch in Pokémon immune to your opponent's attacks

So now you know to switch out your Pokémon if your opponent has a type advantage in order to reduce the amount of damage your Pokémon take. But you should also try to predict what moves your opponent will use, and send out a Pokémon who's strong against—or even completely immune to—those moves. If you successfully switch in a Pokémon whose type isn't affected by the opponent's moves, you'll be in great shape.

Switch in Pokémon that are immune to your opponent's attacks

Your Pokémon

Simipour
`Water`

Switch out

Pupitar
`Rock` `Ground`

Foe's Pokémon

Type advantage

Does no damage

Jolteon
`Electric`

Electric-type moves are Simipour's weakness, so switch in Pupitar, which is not affected by Electric-type moves.

 **Tip** ## Learn your opponent's moves before you switch out

If the opponent has moves that are strong against your Pokémon, they're bound to get used. You can stick around and use Protect or Detect to negate your opponent's attacks. If your foe uses a move with a type advantage, you'll know which Pokémon to switch in.

469

Battle Strategy 4 — Predict your opponent's next move

The turn when a opponent switches Pokémon can be used any way you want. That's why it's important to pay attention to when an opponent may switch out. Put yourself in your opponent's shoes and try to predict the next move. For example, if the opponent thinks his or her Pokémon might get hit by a move it's weak against, he or she is probably thinking about switching that Pokémon out. Anticipate when your foe will switch and make most of your "free" turn!

When a foe will likely switch Pokémon

1 When your Pokémon might target the opponent's weakness

You put a Grass-type Pokémon in battle, and your foe chose a Water- and Ground-type Pokémon. Your foe's Pokémon will take four times the normal amount of damage from a Grass-type attack. If your foe doesn't have any other tricks in store, it's very likely he or she will switch Pokémon.

2 When a Pokémon is taking damage each turn from Leech Seed or similar moves

Leech Seed damages the target every turn and restores your Pokémon's HP. However, if the Pokémon affected by Leech Seed is swapped out, the move's effects go away. In a situation like this, your foe will probably be thinking about switching Pokémon.

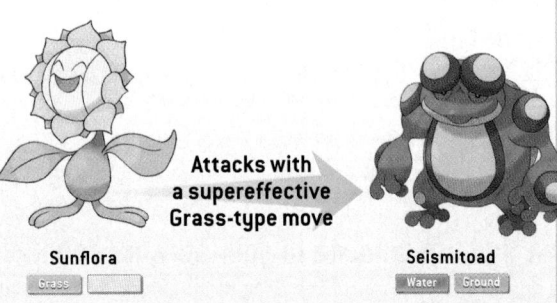

Attacks with a supereffective Grass-type move

Sunflora — Grass

Seismitoad — Water Ground

Roselia — Grass Poison

Attacks with Leech Seed

Magneton — Electric Steel

Battle Strategy 5 — What to do when you think the opposing Trainer is switching Pokémon

Don't let your guard down—even when you can strike your opponent's weakness. If your foe switches Pokémon to a type that your Pokémon's move has no effect on, you may find yourself in big trouble. When you think a switch is coming up, try to predict what Pokémon will be used next. Choose a move that can deal damage to the Pokémon you expect your opponent to switch in!

Anticipate switching and attack

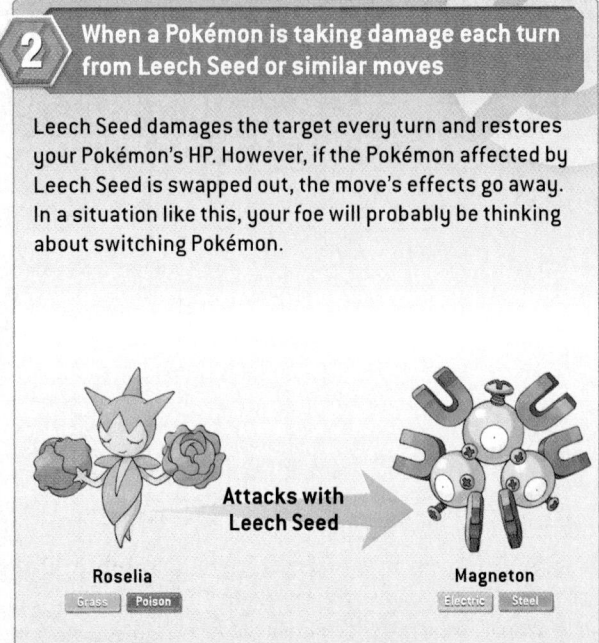

Your Pokémon

Normal-type attack

Quagsire — Water Ground

Attack with a Normal-type move, which can damage most opponents

Foe's Pokémon

Luxray — Electric

Switch out

Altaria — Dragon Flying

Battle Strategy 6 — Snatch victory at the last minute

Don't give up if your Pokémon's HP gets low. The moment when it looks like your Pokémon will be knocked out is the time to step up actions to defeat your opponent. If you teach your Pokémon moves that get stronger when it's in trouble, you will always have a chance to come back from behind.

Examples of moves that work better when the user's HP is low

◎ Come from behind with big damage

Move Flail — Normal

The lower the user's HP, the more damage Flail does. Its power is maximized when the user has 1 HP and is just about to be defeated.

◎ Restore HP at the last second

Move Pain Split — Normal

Pain Split adds the user's HP and the target's, then splits the total between them. When the target still has lots of HP, your Pokémon can recover quickly.

Battle Strategy 7 — Change the weather to turn the tides of battle

Weather influences some Pokémon moves and Abilities. If you choose moves that change the weather, you can create a favorable situation for yourself while putting your opponent at a disadvantage, and send victory your way. Create teams that take advantage of the weather!

Main features of special weather conditions

Sunny

1. Raises the power of Fire-type moves by 50%
2. Lowers the power of Water-type moves by 50%
3. Prevents the Frozen condition
4. SolarBeam can be used on the first turn
5. Doubles the effect of the move Growth
6. Increases the amount of HP recovered with Synthesis etc.
7. Doubles the Speed of Pokémon with the Chlorophyll Ability
8. Makes Pokémon with Leaf Guard Ability immune to status conditions

Rain

1. Raises the power of Water-type moves by 50%
2. Lowers the power of Fire-type moves by 50%
3. The move Thunder always hits
4. The move Hurricane always hits
5. Doubles the Speed of Pokémon with the Swift Swim Ability
6. Heals status conditions of Pokémon with the Hydration Ability

Sandstorm

1. Damages all Pokémon except for Ground, Rock, and Steel types
2. Raises Rock-type Pokémon's Sp. Def by 50%
3. Pokémon with the Magic Guard Ability are not damaged
4. Pokémon with the Overcoat Ability are not damaged
5. Increases Speed of Pokémon with the Sand Rush Ability
6. Increases Speed of Pokémon with the Sand Rush Ability

Hail

1. Damages all Pokémon except for Ice types
2. Pokémon with the Magic Guard Ability are not damaged
3. Pokémon with the Overcoat Ability are not damaged
4. Raises evasion of Pokémon with the Snow Cloak Ability
5. Restores HP of Pokémon with the Ice Body Ability
6. The move Blizzard always hits

2 Master the Art of the Combo

Take what you know about moves, Abilities, and items, and put it all together in a winning strategy

A combo is a combination of Pokémon moves, Abilities, or held items. When you use them together in just the right way, it makes a big difference in battle.

Combine different elements to create clever combos

Combos are a tactic for winning the battle that exhibit even more powerful effects than normal moves by combining many different elements, such as moves and Abilities. So many different combos exist that surely some of them are still unknown. Try creating combos by putting together moves, Abilities, and items that seem like they might work. Then, give them a try in battle.

The elements of combos

1. Move
2. Ability
3. Item
4. Type

The elements of combos

Move + Move Combo

One move can make another move more powerful or compensate for another move's weakness.

Move + Item Combo

Giving the Pokémon an item to hold makes moves powerful or compensates for the weakness of those moves.

Ability + Move Combo

An Ability can increase the power of a move or compensate for the weakness of a move.

Type + Move Combo

When a Pokémon's move will hit its ally, pair it up with a Pokémon of a type that won't take damage from that move.

Main advantages of combos

1. Pull off bigger effects by combining different elements such as moves, Abilities, and items.
2. Sometimes Pokémon can avoid damage from attacks that should have hit them.
3. Sometimes the negative effects of moves, Abilities, or items can be neutralized.

Combo 1

Ability	+	Move	+	Item
Scrappy		Last Resort		Normal Gem

The Scrappy Ability lets the Pokémon hit Ghost-type Pokémon with Normal- and Fighting-type moves. Last Resort is a powerful Normal-type move. Let the Pokémon hold a Normal Gem, which boosts the power of a Normal-type move one time, to make the attack even more powerful.

Herdier
Normal
ABILITIES
● Intimidate
● Sand Rush
● Scrappy

Combo 2

Ability	+	Move
Mold Breaker		Earthquake

With the Mold Breaker Ability, a Pokémon can hit a target that is normally protected by its Ability. So Earthquake, a Ground-type move with a power of 100, would hit Pokémon with the Levitate Ability. Use this combo to shake up any Trainers who thought their Pokémon were safe. Get momentum and win!

Pinsir
Bug
ABILITIES
● Hyper Cutter
● Mold Breaker
● Moxie

Combo 3

Ability	+	Move
Skill Link		Tail Slap

The move Tail Slap hits two to five times in a single turn. If a Pokémon with the Skill Link Ability uses it, it can always hit the target five times. The power of each hit is small, but it can deal damage five times every turn, so the target can take huge damage unexpectedly.

Cinccino
Normal
ABILITIES
● Cute Charm
● Technician
● Skill Link

Combo 4

Ability	+	Move	+	Item
Sheer Force		Rock Slide		Life Orb

The move Rock Slide has an additional effect of causing the target to flinch. If a Pokémon with the Sheer Force Ability uses the move, the additional effect doesn't happen, but the power increases by 30%. Additionally, if you let the Pokémon hold a Life Orb, the power will be almost doubled. Rock Slide has a starting power of 75, so this combo has a huge amount of power!

Hariyama
Fighting
ABILITIES
● Thick Fat
● Guts
● Sheer Force

Combo 5

Ability	+	Move	+	Item
Reckless		Hi Jump Kick		Wide Lens

A Pokémon with the Reckless Ability can increase the power of moves that can also hurt the user, such as Hi Jump Kick and Double-Edge. Hi Jump Kick is a move with a power of 130. Let the Pokémon hold a Wide Lens, which boosts the accuracy of moves, and it has a better chance to do huge damage to the target.

Mienshao
Fighting
ABILITIES
● Inner Focus
● Regenerator
● Reckless

Combo 6

Ability	+	Item	+	Move
Toxic Boost		Toxic Orb		Facade

When a Pokémon with the Toxic Boost Ability has the status condition Poison or Badly Poisoned, the power of its physical moves increases by 50%. Give it a Toxic Orb, which will make it Badly Poisoned, and use the move Facade—its power is doubled when the user has a status condition. The effects of the Ability and the move are combined, and Facade can deal triple the normal amount of damage!

Zangoose
Normal
ABILITIES
● Immunity
● Toxic Boost

◆ Pokémon's Abilities shown in red are Hidden Abilities.

Combo 7

Ability	+	Item
Flare Boost		Flame Orb

When a Pokémon with the Flare Boost Ability is Burned, the power of special moves increases by 50%. Have your Pokémon hold a Flame Orb, and it will be Burned. If you teach the Pokémon powerful moves such as Shadow Ball and Psychic, it can attack the target with 50% more power.

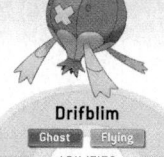
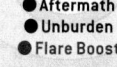

Drifblim
Ghost / Flying
ABILITIES
● Aftermath
● Unburden
● Flare Boost

Combo 8

Ability	+	Move	+	Move
Simple		Calm Mind		Stored Power

For a Pokémon with the Simple Ability, the effects of stat changes and evasion become more powerful. Teach the Pokémon the move Calm Mind to raise its Sp. Atk and Sp. Def. Then, use the move Stored Power. The more the user's stats are raised, the greater the damage the Pokémon can deal.

Swoobat
Psychic / Flying
ABILITIES
● Unawares
● Klutz
● Simple

Combo 9

Ability	+	Move
Prankster		Quash

Prankster is an Ability that gives priority to status moves. Use the move Quash on a target with the higher Speed stat. Quash suppresses the target and makes its move go last. If your foe is taking advantage of the high Speed stat of his or her team, you can disrupt the strategy.

Murkrow
Dark / Flying
ABILITIES
● Insomnia
● Super Luck
● Prankster

Combo Technique 2 — Combos that overcome the weakness of a move or Ability

Combo 1

Move	+	Item
Rest		Chesto Berry

Rest completely restores HP, but the user is afflicted with the Sleep status condition. Have the user hold a Chesto Berry so it wakes up right away. Since it wakes up immediately, it can move during the next turn.

Whiscash
Water / Ground
ABILITIES
● Oblivious
● Anticipation
● Hydration

Combo 2

Move	+	Item
Outrage		Persim Berry

Outrage has a power of 120 and hits two to three turns in a row, but it has a nasty habit of inflicting the Confused status on its user. Having it hold a Persim Berry will undo the Confused status as soon as it occurs.

Krookodile
Ground / Dark
ABILITIES
● Intimidate
● Moxie
● Anger Point

Combo 3

Move	+	Item
Sky Attack		Power Herb

The Sky Attack move has an amazing power of 140, but it requires one turn to charge before it is unleashed on the second. Have a Pokémon hold a Power Herb and it can use Sky Attack on the first turn. However, a Power Herb goes away after one use, so use this combo in a critical moment.

Skarmory
Steel / Flying
ABILITIES
● Keen Eye
● Sturdy
● Weak Armor

◆ Pokémon's Abilities shown in red are Hidden Abilities.

Combo 4

Item — Choice Scarf **+** **Move** — Trick

A Choice Scarf boosts the Speed of the holder by 50%, but restricts the holder to a single move. Use the move Trick to switch items with the target and force it to hold the Choice Scarf. Because the target is forced to keep using the same move, you can restrict the actions of the target.

Sableye
Dark / Ghost
ABILITIES
● Keen Eye
● Stall
● Prankster

Combo 5

Move — After You **+** **Move** — Focus Punch **+** **Move** — Focus Punch

Focus Punch is a move with a power of 150, but it will fail if the user is attacked before it is used. In a Double Battle, have your other Pokémon use the move After You on the Pokémon that knows Focus Punch, and it will be guaranteed to attack next and before it can take damage.

Lopunny
Normal
ABILITIES
● Cute Charm
● Klutz
● Limber

Golurk
Ground / Ghost
ABILITIES
● Iron Fist
● Klutz
● No Guard

Combo 6

Ability — Own Tempo **+** **Move** — Flatter

The move Flatter raises the target's Sp. Atk, but also leaves it Confused. However, a Pokémon with the Own Tempo Ability is immune to being Confused. Use Flatter on the ally with the Own Tempo Ability, and its Sp. Atk will be raised with no downside.

Ludicolo
Water / Grass
ABILITIES
● Swift Swim
● Rain Dish
● Own Tempo

Illumise
Bug
ABILITIES
● Oblivious
● Tinted Lens
● Prankster

Combo 7

Move — Surf **+** **Move** — Wide Guard

The move Wide Guard blocks wide-ranging attacks. It also protects the user's allies. If your other Pokémon uses a move like Surf, which also hits allies, your side will be protected by the effect of Wide Guard.

Seismitoad
Water / Ground
ABILITIES
● Swift Swim
● Poison Touch
● Water Absorb

Hitmonlee
Fighting
ABILITIES
● Limber
● Reckless
● Unburden

Combo 8

Move — Discharge **+** **Ability** — Volt Absorb **+** **Move** — Helping Hand

Discharge is a move with a power of 80, but it hits allies, too. Use a Pokémon with the Volt Absorb Ability as an ally so it won't take damage from Discharge. Even better, have the ally use the move Helping Hand, which will raise the power of Discharge by 50%.

Magnezone
Electric / Steel
ABILITIES
● Magnet Pull
● Sturdy
● Analytic

Pachirisu
Electric
ABILITIES
● Run Away
● Pickup
● Volt Absorb

Combo 9

Ability — Slow Start **+** **Move** — Worry Seed

The Slow Start Ability halves Attack and Speed for five turns after the Pokémon enters battle. Let an ally Pokémon use the move Worry Seed and change the Ability to Insomnia. That way, the Pokémon can exert its true strength from the second turn.

Regigigas
Normal
ABILITY
● Slow Start

Jumpluff
Grass / Flying
ABILITIES
● Chlorophyll
● Leaf Guard
● Infiltrator

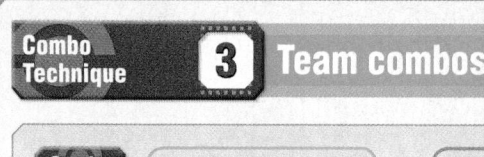

Combo Technique 3 — Team combos

Combo 1

Ability Drought	+	**Move** Lava Plume	+	**Ability** Flash Fire

For a Pokémon with the Simple Ability, the effects of stat changes and evasion become more powerful. Teach the Pokémon the move Calm Mind to raise its Sp. Atk and Sp. Def. Then, use the move Stored Power. The more the user's stats are raised, the greater the damage the Pokémon can deal.

Ninetales
Fire
ABILITIES
● Flash Fire
● Drought

Camerupt
Fire | Ground
ABILITIES
● Magma Armor
● Solid Rock
● Anger Point

Heatran
Fire | Steel
ABILITY
● Flash Fire

Combo 2

Ability Drizzle	+	**Ability** Swift Swim	+	**Ability** Rain Dish

When a Pokémon with the Drizzle Ability enters battle, it starts to rain. In Rain, if an ally's Ability is Swift Swim, its Speed doubles. If an ally's Ability is Rain Dish, the Pokémon restores HP in every turn. Get the weather on your side!

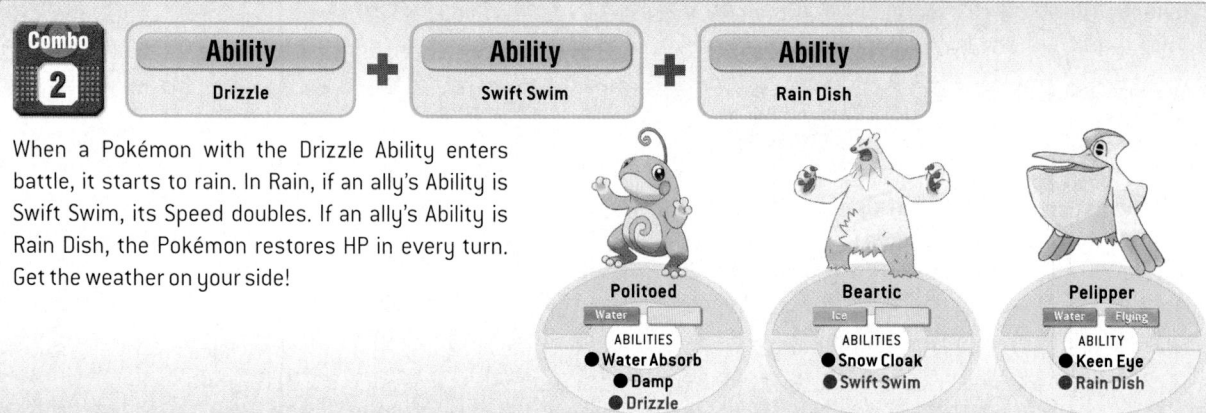

Politoed
Water
ABILITIES
● Water Absorb
● Damp
● Drizzle

Beartic
Ice
ABILITIES
● Snow Cloak
● Swift Swim

Pelipper
Water | Flying
ABILITY
● Keen Eye
● Rain Dish

Combo 3

Ability Snow Warning	+	**Ability** Overcoat	+	**Ability** Snow Cloak

When a Pokémon with the Snow Warning Ability enters battle, it starts hailing. In Hail, if an ally's Ability is Overcoat, the Pokémon is protected from damage. If an ally's Ability is Snow Cloak, evasion is raised and the Pokémon is less likely to be attacked.

Abomasnow
Grass | Ice
ABILITIES
● Snow Warning
● Soundproof

Leavanny
Bug | Grass
ABILITIES
● Swarm
● Chlorophyll
● Overcoat

Mamoswine
Ice | Ground
ABILITY
● Oblivious
● Snow Cloak
● Thick Fat

Combo 4

Ability Sand Stream	+	**Ability** Sand Force	+	**Ability** Sand Rush

When a Pokémon with the Sand Stream Ability enters battle, a Sandstorm kicks up. If an ally's Ability is Sand Force, the power of its Ground-, Rock-, and Steel-type moves increases by 30%. If an ally's Ability is Sand Rush, its Speed goes up, and the Pokémon won't take damage from Sandstorm.

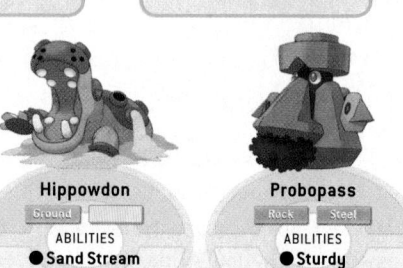

Hippowdon
Ground
ABILITIES
● Sand Stream
● Sand Force

Probopass
Rock | Steel
ABILITIES
● Sturdy
● Magnet Pull
● Sand Force

Stoutland
Normal
ABILITY
● Intimidate
● Sand Rush
● Scrappy

◆ Pokémon's Abilities shown in red are Hidden Abilities.

Tip — Protect yourself from your foe's combos

An opponent who is used to battling will probably have several combos at the ready. You should have some ways to protect yourself when your opponent starts to use a combo. Many methods are effective when disrupting combos. For example, you could make the opponent's Pokémon unable to use moves, prevent them from using items, or force them to switch out. Choose the optimal means, depending on your opponent.

Ways to counter combos

Overcome item-based combos

If an opponent is using an item-based combo, keep your opponent's Pokémon from using items. Some options are the move Thief, which steals the target's item, or the moves Embargo and Magic Room, which suppress the effect of items. Either way, you can disrupt the combo.

Move	Thief	Dark
Move	Embargo	Dark
Move	Magic Room	Psychic

Banette

Prevent two-Pokémon combos

Forcing your opponent to switch a Pokémon is one trick for disrupting combos that require two Pokémon. The moves Roar and Dragon Tail can force a switch, and your opponent's two-Pokémon combo won't work anymore.

| Move | Dragon Tail | Dragon |
| Move | Roar | Normal |

Tyranitar

Prevent foes from using moves freely

Another effective method of dealing with combos is creating a situation in which the foe can't use moves freely. Torment keeps an opponent from using the same move twice in a row, and Taunt prevents a target from using status moves. This will disrupt your opponent's tactics.

| Move | Torment | Dark |
| Move | Taunt | Dark |

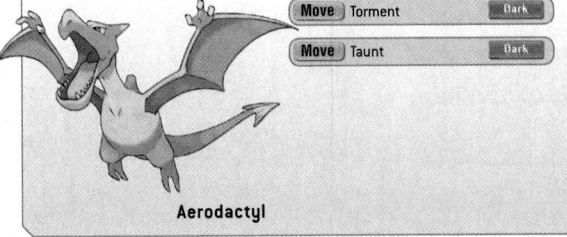

Aerodactyl

Dodge moves you sense are coming

When the opponent has set up a combo, and you suspect an attack is coming during the next turn, use a move that protects your Pokémon from damage. A carefully timed Protect or Detect can prevent damage and give you a chance to counterattack.

Move	Detect	Fighting
Move	Protect	Normal
Move	Wide Guard	Rock
Move	Quick Guard	Fighting

Hitmontop

Use Imprison as a countermeasure

Imprison prevents the target from using three other moves that the user knows. If you can keep a move that is part of your opponent's combo from being used, it will give you an advantage.

| Move | Imprison | Psychic |

Zoroark

Disrupt combos that use Abilities

Use the move Simple Beam, which changes the target's Ability to Simple, or Entrainment, which makes the target's Ability the same as the user's. By doing this, you can block the opposing Trainer from setting up a combo that uses an Ability.

| Move | Simple Beam | Normal |
| Move | Entrainment | Normal |

Audino

When a Battle Is Lost, Consider These Three Points

Always believe you can win and never give up

You will do your best, but the opposing Trainer will be coming at you with everything he or she's got as well—so there's no such thing as an easy victory, no matter what kind of battle it is. Try and try again until victory is in your grasp. When you just can't win, you might want to rethink your strategy.

Point to Reconsider **1** **Try changing your Pokémon's moves**

Try changing the combination of the four moves you can teach a Pokémon. Teaching a Pokémon an unusual move can allow you to get the drop on opposing Trainers. When you test moves, sometimes you think of new ways to battle. In addition to TMs, consider some moves that can be remembered or taught by Move Tutors. When you want to forget an HM, visit the Move Deleter in the Pokémon World Tournament area.

Examples of ways to teach new moves

Use TMs to teach new moves

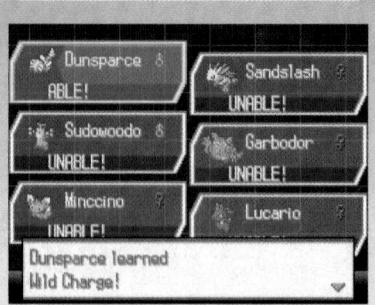

TMs are useful items that let you teach a move as often as you like. Teach moves to many Pokémon and test the move's effects in actual battles.

Trade Heart Scales to remember moves

> The user intimidates the target with the pattern on its belly to cause paralysis.
>
> | | POWER | — | ACCURACY | 90 |
> |---|---|---|---|---|
> | NORMAL Take Down | | PP | 20/20 | |
> | FLYING Roost | | PP | 10/10 | |
> | NORMAL Glare | | PP | 30/30 | |
>
> Dunsparce remembered the move Glare.

The reminder girl at the PWT will help your Pokémon remember a move in exchange for one Heart Scale.

Give a master Move Tutor Shards to learn moves

Learn moves from master Move Tutors in Driftveil City, Lentimas Town, Humilau City, and Nacrene City.

Examples of useful attack moves

1 Moves that target weakness of the opposing Pokémon you have trouble with.

2 Moves that target weakness of the same type as your Pokémon.

3 Moves that always hit or that strike first.

4 Moves that inflict status conditions.

Point to Reconsider **2** Change your Pokémon's held item

Your Pokémon's held items can easily sway the outcome of a battle. Depending on the item's effect, it can strengthen your Pokémon's strong points or compensate for its weaknesses. Change items to bring out your Pokémon's untapped potential.

Examples of rethinking items

If you lost because a status condition left you unable to act

When afflicted by a status condition, you can't always take the action you want to take. Have your Pokémon hold a Lum Berry to heal status conditions.

If you lost because your Pokémon are too slow

If you are losing because you can't strike first, try having your Pokémon hold a Quick Claw, which sometimes lets you strike first.

If you lost because you took a lot of damage from a big move

If you lose because the opposing Pokémon's moves are just too strong, try the Focus Sash, which leaves the holder with 1 HP.

Point to Reconsider **3** Change the lead Pokémon

Sometimes the Pokémon at the front of your party can make it easier to battle. It's ideal if it can hit the opposing Pokémon with a supereffective move or use a move that inflicts a status condition. If the opposing Trainer feels pressured to swap Pokémon on the first turn, you have an immediate advantage. Lead with your best!

Examples of the difference the lead Pokémon makes

Have a Pokémon that knows multiple move types lead your party

Teach it moves of different types, and you can use supereffective moves against many Pokémon types.

Drapion

Move	Thunder Fang	Electric
Move	Ice Fang	Ice
Move	Fire Fang	Fire

Have a Pokémon that has high Speed lead your party

Put a Pokémon with high Speed at the front of your party. You can strike first if the Pokémon has a high Speed stat.

Electrode

⊘ STATS	
HP	▮▮▮
Attack	▮▮▮
Defense	▮▮▮
Sp. Atk	▮▮▮▮
Sp. Def	▮▮▮▮
Speed	▮▮▮▮▮▮▮▮

Have a Pokémon that knows a switching move lead your party

It's often useful to use moves that let you attack and switch at the same time, or those that force the opposing Trainer to switch Pokémon.

Eelektrik

| Move | Volt Switch | Electric |
| Move | U-turn | Bug |

🎖 Tip Use PP Up to increase PP

Each move has a fixed number of PP. Powerful moves generally have fewer PP, so you might use them up quickly in battle. Use PP Up or PP Max to raise the maximum PP of your best moves.

Find the Right Pokémon to Train

You have many Pokémon to choose from, but not all of them have the qualities you're looking for

Each Pokémon is unique. Even among Pokémon of the same species, no two have the same stats and Nature. Out of all of the Pokémon in the world, search out the one that is best for your strategy.

Selection Tip 1 — Look for Pokémon with high stats

Stats differ significantly depending on the species of Pokémon involved. If you want to use strong moves one after another, you should catch Pokémon with high Attack and Sp. Atk stats. If you want to move first, the Speed stat is important. The Pokémon that will perform best will depend on your battle strategy. Choose Pokémon that fit your strategy and form your own team.

Stats differ depending on the species of Pokémon

Slaking have a high Attack stat

STATS
HP
Attack
Defense
Sp. Atk
Sp. Def
Speed

Slaking

A Pokémon with a high Attack stat like Slaking inflicts great damage on its target with physical moves such as Giga Impact and Hammer Arm.

Chandelure have a high Sp. Atk stat

STATS
HP
Attack
Defense
Sp. Atk
Sp. Def
Speed

Chandelure

A Pokémon with a high Sp. Atk stat like Chandelure inflicts great damage on its target with special moves such as Shadow Ball and Overheat.

Crobat have a high Speed stat

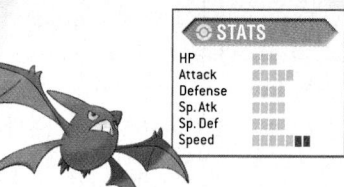

STATS
HP
Attack
Defense
Sp. Atk
Sp. Def
Speed

Crobat

A Pokémon with a high Speed stat like Crobat has a better chance to get the first attack. It can take the lead using moves with status effects like Toxic and Confuse Ray.

Tip — Remember the elements relevant to stats

When choosing a Pokémon to raise, pay attention to the elements that will be relevant to their stats. The Pokémon's species, as well as its Characteristic and its inherent strengths, are all important elements. Its gender, Ability, and friendliness will not have any affect on its stats.

Elements relevant to stats

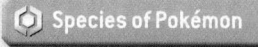 Species of Pokémon    Nature

 Characteristic    Inherent strength

 Base stats    Level

---

For each Pokémon's stats, see the National Pokédex beginning on p. 14

Selection Tip **2** Catch multiples of the same Pokémon and compare them

Even within the same species, stats differ from one Pokémon to another because each Pokémon has inherent strengths for each stat. Catch many Pokémon and compare them. If two Pokémon are at the same level, the Pokémon with higher stats has higher inherent strength. If a Pokémon has higher inherent strength, its stats grow faster when it levels up.

Inherent strength is different even among Pokémon of the same species

⚙ Comparison of stats among Growlithe

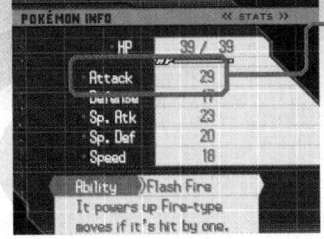

High Attack

When this Growlithe uses a physical move such as Flare Blitz or Crunch, it inflicts major damage on the opposing Pokémon.

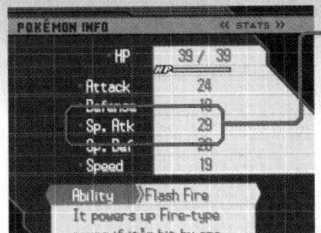

High Sp. Atk

This Growlithe can inflict more damage with special moves such as Flamethrower and Heat Wave.

Selection Tip **3** Check the strengths of your Pokémon

After finishing the main story, a person called the Judge will show up in the Battle Subway in Nimbasa City. The Judge can tell you the inherent strengths of individual Pokémon. He will tell you his impression of the overall potential your Pokémon inherently has and what particular stats will grow the strongest.

The Judge shows up after the main story

You'll find the Judge near the bottom of the stairs in the Gear Station.

What the Judge tells you

1 **Overall evaluation of stats**

I see, I see... This Pokémon's potential is [This Pokémon has] ●●●. That's my determination, and it's final.

Words that fill ●●●

outstanding potential overall	⬆ High
relatively superior potential overall	
above average overall	
decent all around	⬇ Low

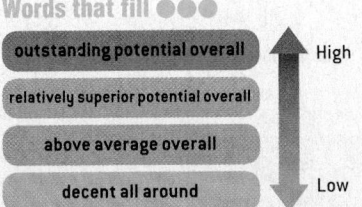

2 **The most outstanding stat(s)**

Incidentally, I would say the best potential lies in its ●●●. And its ●●● is also good.

◆ When your Pokémon has two stats which are equally high, the Judge will tell you about both.

Words that fill ●●●

HP	Sp. Atk
Attack	Sp. Def
Defense	Speed

3 **Lastly, whether ② is high or low**

●●● in that regard. That's how I judged it.

Words that fill ●●●

It can't be better	⬆ High
It's fantastic	
It's very good	
It's rather decent	⬇ Low

Selection Tip **4** Check Pokémon's Characteristics and Natures

The Summary screen in your Pokédex or in the PC Box will show you your Pokémon's Characteristic and Nature. The Pokémon's Characteristic tells you which stat is inherently high. Its Nature tells you which stat grows faster when it levels up.

Use Characteristics to guess the inherent strength of Pokémon

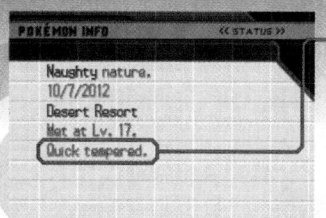

◎ Comparison of Sandile's Characteristics

POKÉMON INFO   《 STATUS 》

Naughty nature.
10/7/2012
Desert Resort
Met at Lv. 17.
Quick tempered.

Characteristic for a superior Attack stat

"Quick tempered" indicates that the Pokémon's inherent strength lies in its Attack.

POKÉMON INFO   《 STATUS 》

Brave nature.
10/7/2012
Desert Resort
Met at Lv. 15.
Impetuous and silly.

Characteristic for a superior Speed stat

"Impetuous and silly" indicates that the Pokémon's inherent strength lies in its Speed.

Natures affect Pokémon's stat growth

"Brave" boosts the growth of the Attack stat

Elekid

A Brave Pokémon's Attack stat grows faster.

● **Nature Brave**

Attack grows quickly

Speed grows slowly

"Mild" boosts the growth of the Sp. Atk stat

Magby

A Mild Pokémon's Sp. Atk stat grows faster.

● **Nature Mild**

Sp. Atk grows quickly

Defense grows slowly

"Timid" boosts the growth of the Speed stat

Lillipup

A Timid Pokémon's Speed stat grows faster.

● **Nature Timid**

Speed grows quickly

Attack grows slowly

See p. 520 for more on Natures and Characteristics.

Tip Make use of Abilities to help you find the Pokémon you are looking for

Pokémon with certain attributes can help you find wild Pokémon. If you put one of these Pokémon at the head of your party, it will be easier to find the specific Pokémon you are looking for. For example, if you have a Pokémon with the Synchronize Ability at the head of your party, you will find more Pokémon with the same Nature as that Pokémon.

Main attributes to help you meet certain Pokémon

Pokémon with the same Nature

Ability Synchronize

Espeon

A lead Pokémon with this Ability increases the likelihood of encountering Pokémon with the same Nature.

Pokémon of a high level

Ability Keen Eye

Rufflet

A lead Pokémon with this Ability decreases the likelihood of encountering low-level Pokémon.

Pokémon of the opposite gender

Ability Cute Charm

Jigglypuff

A lead Pokémon with this Ability increases the likelihood of encountering Pokémon of the opposite gender.

Raise Pokémon from Eggs

Pokémon can learn unusual moves depending on the combination of Pokémon you leave at the Pokémon Day Care

You can get Eggs from the Pokémon Day Care. Pokémon hatched from Eggs may already know moves that wild Pokémon usually won't learn, and they can inherit high stats. So if you raise them, they can perform very well in battles.

Tip to Raise Pokémon from Eggs **Leave Pokémon at the Pokémon Day Care and find Eggs**

Leave one ♂ (male) and one ♀ (female) Pokémon at the Pokémon Day Care. If the two belong to the same Egg Group, an Egg will be found after some time. If you ask the old man in front of the Day Care, he will tell you how well the two Pokémon get along. The more they like each other, the sooner you might find an Egg!

> **OT's Name and Trainer ID**
>
> These fields on the Summary screen will indicate whether you received the Pokémon in a trade.

Improve your chances for finding an Egg

1 **Leave Pokémon of the same species**

♂ **Male Pokémon**   ♀ **Female Pokémon**

If you leave male and female Pokémon from the same Egg Group at the Pokémon Day Care, you will have a chance of finding an Egg. If you leave male and female Pokémon of the same species at the Day Care, the chance of finding an Egg will be even higher.

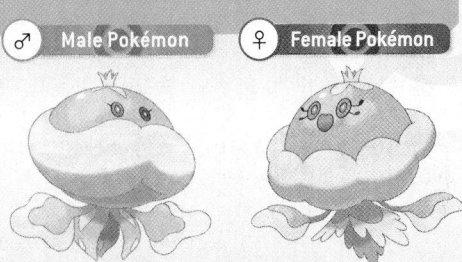

2 **Leave a Pokémon you got in a trade**

If either one of the two Pokémon you leave at the Pokémon Day Care was obtained from a trade, you will have a better chance to find an Egg. Try leaving two Pokémon with different OT names and ID numbers.

3 **Get the Oval Charm**

After you complete the Unova Pokédex, go speak with Professor Juniper in Nuvema Town and receive an Oval Charm. With this item, it's easier to find Eggs at the Pokémon Day Care.

Trainer obtained the Oval Charm!

For more information on Eggs, see p. 365.

Tip to Raise Pokémon from Eggs **2** ## Have a Pokémon inherit traits

A Pokémon hatched from an Egg may have traits that wild Pokémon wouldn't have because it can inherit moves, Nature, and inherent strength from the Pokémon left at the Pokémon Day Care. Drop off some of your favorite Pokémon at the Pokémon Day Care, and you may be able to hatch a Pokémon that has inherited some of their traits.

Traits that a hatched Pokémon can inherit

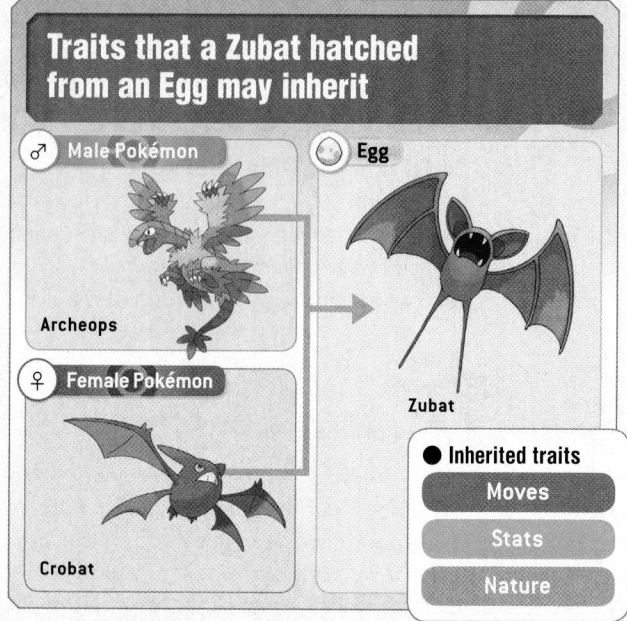

Traits that a Zubat hatched from an Egg may inherit

♂ Male Pokémon
Archeops

♀ Female Pokémon
Crobat

◉ Egg

Zubat

● Inherited traits
Moves
Stats
Nature

Tip to Raise Pokémon from Eggs **3** ## Have a Pokémon inherit moves

You can pass on a move from the two Pokémon you leave at the Pokémon Day Care to the Pokémon that will be hatched from the Egg. Usually, newly hatched Pokémon only know the moves that their species can learn at Lv. 1. However, depending on which two Pokémon you leave at the Pokémon Day Care, the moves known by your newly hatched Pokémon may differ. For example, hatched Pokémon sometimes already know a move that they usually learn by leveling up. This happens when both of the two Pokémon you left at the Pokémon Day Care have learned the move. Pokémon may also hatch knowing a move that is usually learned by using a TM. This can happen when the male Pokémon that you leave at the Pokémon Day Care knows such a move.

Rules of inherited moves

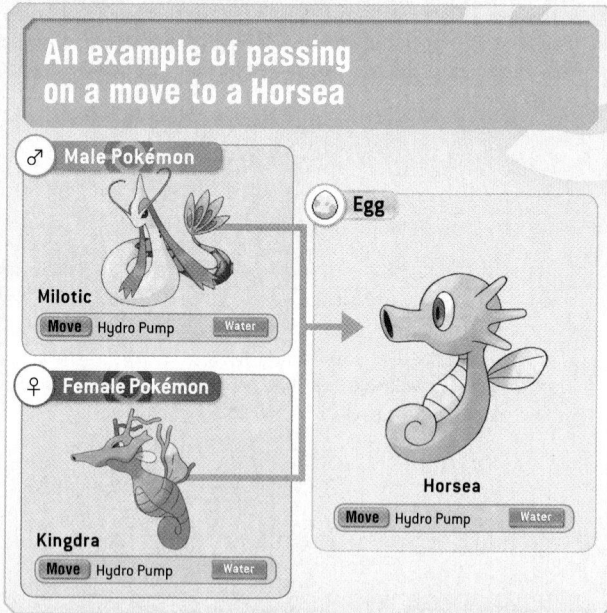

An example of passing on a move to a Horsea

♂ Male Pokémon
Milotic
Move Hydro Pump Water

♀ Female Pokémon
Kingdra
Move Hydro Pump Water

◉ Egg

Horsea
Move Hydro Pump Water

Moves that the hatched Pokémon can know

1. A hatched Pokémon may know a move that the Pokémon species learns at Lv. 1

2. If both Pokémon at the Pokémon Day Care have the same level-up move, the hatched Pokémon may have that level-up move

3. The hatched Pokémon may know a move that the ♂ (male) Pokémon knows and that it could learn from a TM

For the Egg Groups of Pokémon, see p. 369. ▶

Tip to Raise Pokémon from Eggs **4** Teach Your Pokémon Egg Moves

Pokémon may hatch from Eggs already knowing moves that they usually wouldn't learn. These moves are called Egg Moves. For example, Doduo doesn't learn Mirror Move by leveling up. However, if a male Pokémon left at the Pokémon Day Care knows Mirror Move, a Pokémon hatched from the Egg that is found may inherit the move. Because there are many unexpected Egg Moves, you can surprise the opposing Trainer in battle and take the lead.

Egg Moves are:

An Egg Move for Doduo

♂ **Male Pokémon**

Swablu
Move Mirror Move **Flying**

♀ **Female Pokémon**

Dodrio

Egg

Doduo
Move Mirror Move **Flying**

A rule of Egg Moves

1 Moves that a male Pokémon knows and that the hatched Pokémon can learn as an Egg Move

Tip to Raise Pokémon from Eggs **5** You can't control the hatched Pokémon's Ability

If a Pokémon species has more than one possible Ability, you can't predict in advance which Ability a Pokémon hatched from an Egg will have. For example, if you drop off a Conkeldurr with the Guts Ability at the Pokémon Day Care and you find an Egg, it will often hatch into a Timburr with the Guts Ability, but it could also hatch into a Timburr with the Sheer Force Ability. Here are the basics when a Pokémon hatched from an Egg comes from a species with more than one Ability.

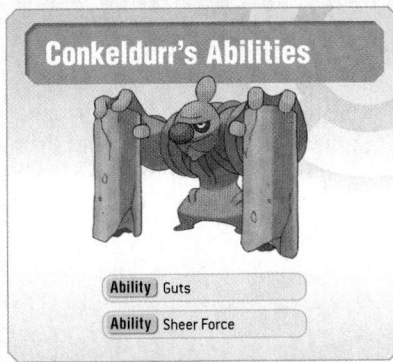

Conkeldurr's Abilities

Ability Guts

Ability Sheer Force

A hatched Pokémon could have any of its species' Abilities

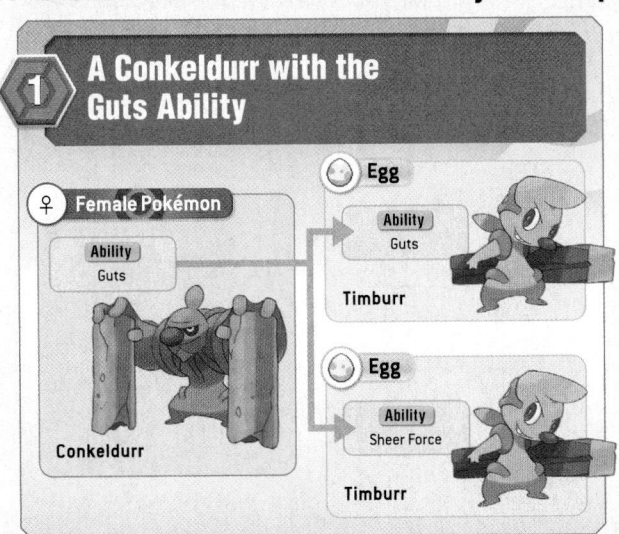

1 **A Conkeldurr with the Guts Ability**

♀ **Female Pokémon**

Ability Guts

Conkeldurr

Egg
Ability Guts
Timburr

Egg
Ability Sheer Force
Timburr

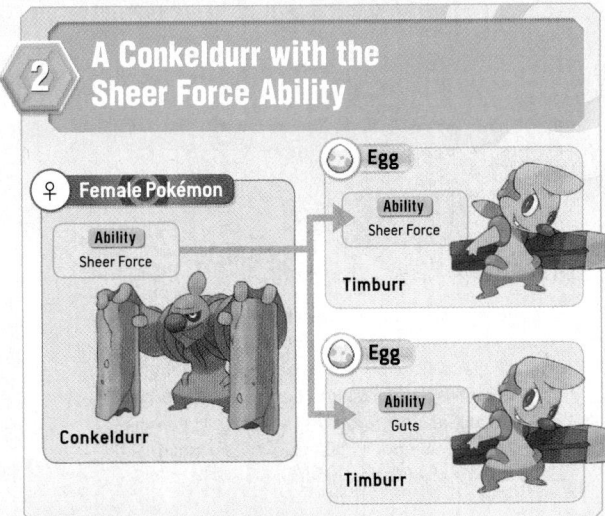

2 **A Conkeldurr with the Sheer Force Ability**

♀ **Female Pokémon**

Ability Sheer Force

Conkeldurr

Egg
Ability Sheer Force
Timburr

Egg
Ability Guts
Timburr

◆ The Ability of a Pokémon hatched from an Egg is more likely to be the Ability of the female Pokémon left at the Day Care.

Tip to Raise Pokémon from Eggs **6** **Hidden Abilities can be inherited**

The Pokémon that you find in Hidden Grottoes around the Unova region and those that you befriend in the Pokémon Dream World using the Pokémon Global Link may have Hidden Abilities. If you leave a female Pokémon with a Hidden Ability at the Pokémon Day Care, the Pokémon that hatches from the Egg you find may have inherited that Hidden Ability. However, Hidden Abilities cannot be passed on from male Pokémon.

Granbull's Abilities
Ability Intimidate
Ability Quick Feet
HIDDEN ABILITY Rattled

Rules for inheriting Abilities

1 **Example of Snubbull inheriting the Intimidate Ability**

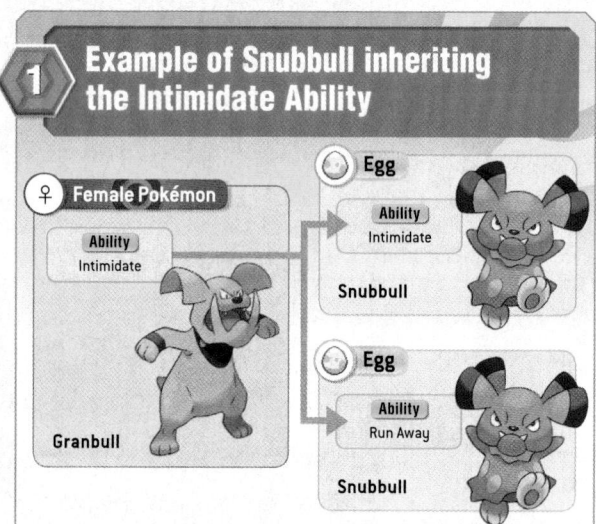

Drop off a female Granbull with the Intimidate Ability with a male Pokémon from the same Egg group. The Egg that will be found will hatch into a Snubbull with either the Run Away or the Intimidate Ability. A Snubbull with the Intimidate Ability will evolve into a Granbull with the Intimidate Ability.

1 **Example of Snubbull eventually inheriting the Quick Feet Ability**

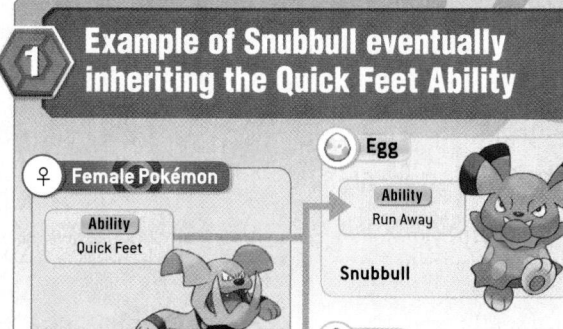

Drop off a female Granbull with the Quick Feet Ability with a male Pokémon from the same Egg group. The Egg that will be found will hatch into a Snubbull with either the Run Away or the Intimidate Ability. A Snubbull with the Run Away Ability will evolve into a Granbull with the Quick Feet Ability.

3 **Example of Snubbull inheriting the Rattled Ability**

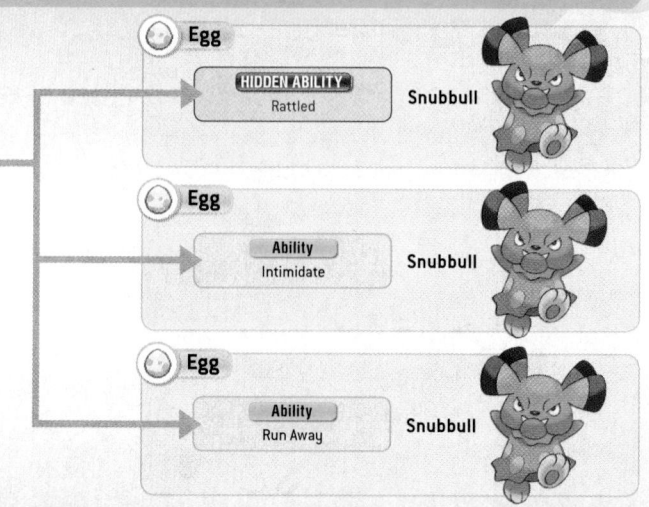

Drop off a female Granbull with the Rattled Hidden Ability with a male Pokémon from the same Egg Group. The Egg that will be found will hatch into a Snubbull with either the Hidden Ability Rattled, or one of the regular Abilities, Run Away or Intimidate. A Snubbull with the Rattled Hidden Ability will evolve into a Granbull with the Rattled Hidden Ability.

◆ The Ability of a Pokémon hatched from an Egg is more likely to be the Ability of the female Pokémon left at the Day Care.
◆ If the male Pokémon has a Hidden Ability, even if you leave it with a Ditto, the Hidden Ability will not be passed on. A Hidden Ability must be inherited from the female.

Tip to Raise Pokémon from Eggs **7** Have a Pokémon inherit a high stat

There are ways to pass inherent strength on to a Pokémon that hatches from an Egg. For example, when you leave a Pokémon that has a high inherent strength in Attack at the Pokémon Day Care, have it hold a Power Bracer. It passes the holder's inherent strength in Attack on to the Pokémon that will hatch from the Egg. When you are raising Pokémon for battles, try to find many Eggs using this method, then hatch them and pick a newly hatched Pokémon with overall high stats.

Basics of inheriting stats

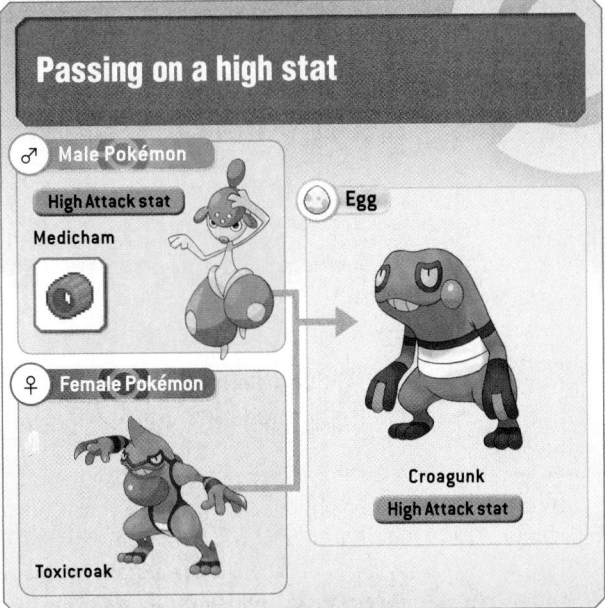

Passing on a high stat

♂ Male Pokémon

High Attack stat

Medicham

Egg

♀ Female Pokémon

Toxicroak

Croagunk

High Attack stat

Items that pass on inherent strengths

 Power Weight
Passes the holder's inherent strength in HP on to the Pokémon that hatches from the Egg

 Power Bracer
Passes the holder's inherent strength in Attack on to the Pokémon that hatches from the Egg

 Power Belt
Passes the holder's inherent strength in Defense on to the Pokémon that hatches from the Egg

 Power Lens
Passes the holder's inherent strength in Sp. Atk on to the Pokémon that hatches from the Egg

 Power Band
Passes the holder's inherent strength in Sp. Def on to the Pokémon that hatches from the Egg

 Power Anklet
Passes the holder's inherent strength in Speed on to the Pokémon that hatches from the Egg

Tip to Raise Pokémon from Eggs **8** A hatched Pokémon can inherit a Nature

Nature is essential to raising a Pokémon with high stats. Which stat increases quickly when the Pokémon levels up is determined by its Nature. So if you want to pass on the Jolly Nature of the Pokémon you left at the Pokémon Day Care to a hatched Pokémon, let the Pokémon hold an Everstone. The hatched Pokémon will always have the same Jolly Nature.

Rules to inherit a Nature

Passing on a high stat

♂ Male Pokémon

Zangoose

Nature | Jolly

Egg

♀ Female Pokémon

Flareon

Eevee

Nature | Jolly

Items that pass on a Nature

 Everstone
The Nature of the Pokémon holding it is unfailingly passed on to the Egg

◆ Either the male or the female Pokémon can hold the Everstone for this effect.

Master the Art of Strengthening Pokémon

Battling a lot of wild Pokémon is vital for raising strong Pokémon

With some patience and dedication, your Pokémon can grow up tougher than you ever expected. Use the following training tips to raise strong Pokémon, capable of challenging your friends and family, the Battle Subway, and even the Pokémon World Tournament!

 Training Tip **1** **Max out base stats to maximize Pokémon stats**

The higher a Pokémon's stats, the more effectively it will be able to battle. To raise a Pokémon with high stats, you'll have to increase each of its six base stats, which determine its stat growth. If you properly raise these base stats ahead of time, then each time your Pokémon levels up, its stats will grow higher and higher.

An example of the effect of raising base stats

Stats grow even quicker when leveling up

Raise the base HP stat a lot

HP increases greatly upon leveling up

Wobbuffet

Rules of base stats

1 There's no in-game way to see base stats.

2 Every Pokémon has six stats, and each stat has its own base stat number.

3 A high base stat will have a greater increase when the Pokémon levels up.

4 You can only max out two of your Pokémon's six base stats.

How to raise base stats

1 Use items to raise base stats

Using nutritious drinks like HP Up or Calcium, as well as Wings like the Health Wing or Genius Wing, can raise your Pokémon's base stats.

2 Use the Pokémon in battles or have it hold an Exp. Share

Pokémon's base stats can be raised by taking part in battles. A Pokémon can also have its base stats increased by holding an Exp. Share, even if it doesn't participate in a battle.

3 Use Macho Brace, Pokérus, etc.

Having a Pokémon hold a Macho Brace will make its base stats increase more than usual. It can also increase its base stats greatly by being infected with the mysterious virus known as the Pokérus (p. 491).

Training Tip **2** # Give Pokémon items to raise their base stats

Items can raise Pokémon's base stats. There are items for each of the six stat categories, such as HP Up to raise base HP or Protein to raise the base Attack stat. They are most effective when you use them on Pokémon that you have just caught.

Effect of raising base stats

Higher base stats mean higher stat gain

Level up a Pokémon after giving it Calcium and Carbos

Sp. Atk and Speed stats go up

Kabutops

An example of increased base stats

Combine nutritious drinks and other methods to raise base stats

You can use up to 10 nutritious drinks on one Pokémon for each stat category. The improvements don't stop there, however. With many battles and the use of Wings like the Muscle Wing, you can raise your Pokémon's base stats all the way to their limit.

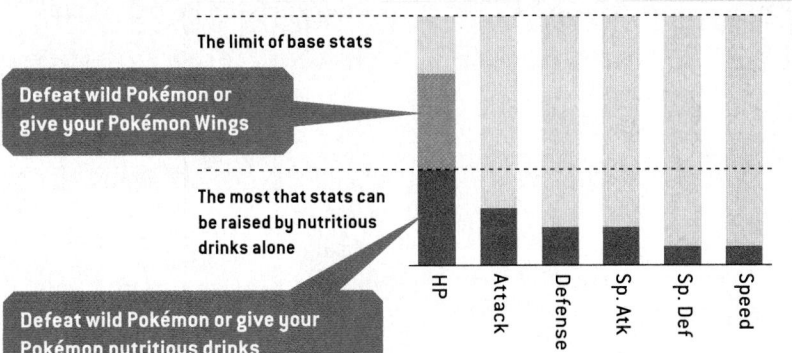

The limit of base stats

Defeat wild Pokémon or give your Pokémon Wings

The most that stats can be raised by nutritious drinks alone

Defeat wild Pokémon or give your Pokémon nutritious drinks

HP / Attack / Defense / Sp. Atk / Sp. Def / Speed

Nutritious drinks that raise base stats

HP Up
Raises the base HP stat of a Pokémon. It can be used up to the limit for nutritious drinks.

Protein
Raises the base Attack stat of a Pokémon. It can be used up to the limit for nutritious drinks.

Iron
Raises the base Defense stat of a Pokémon. It can be used up to the limit for nutritious drinks.

Calcium
It raises the base Sp. Atk stat. It can be used up to the limit for nutritious drinks.

Zinc
Raises the base Sp. Def stat. It can be used up to the limit for nutritious drinks.

Carbos
Raises the base Speed stat of a Pokémon. It can be used up to the limit for nutritious drinks.

Wings that raise base stats

HP Up
It slightly increases the base HP. It can be used up to the limit for the base stat.

Muscle Wing
It slightly increases the base Attack stat. It can be used up to the limit for the base stat.

Resist Wing
It slightly increases the base Defense stat. It can be used up to the limit for the base stat.

Genius Wing
It slightly increases the base Sp. Atk stat. It can be used up to the limit for the base stat.

Clever Wing
It slightly increases the base Sp. Def stat. It can be used up to the limit for the base stat.

Swift Wing
It slightly increases the base Speed stat. It can be used up to the limit for the base stat.

Training Tip 3 Pick your battles based on the stats you want to maximize

A Pokémon raises its base stats when it defeats opponents. Which base stat gets raised depends on which Pokémon your Pokémon defeats. Examples of Pokémon that raise each base stat are shown below. Defeat many of the Pokémon that will raise the base stat you want to improve.

Examples of Pokémon that raise specific base stats

Pokémon that raise Defense

Ducklett
Best location
Driftveil Drawbridge (Pokémon Shadows)

Azurill
Best location
Route 20 (water surface)

Pokémon that raise Attack

Sandile
Best location
Route 4

Darumaka
Best location
Route 4

Pokémon that raise Defense

Yamask
Best location
Relic Castle 1F

Sandshrew
Best location
Relic Castle 1F

Pokémon that raise Sp. Atk

Litwick
Best location
Celestial Tower 2F

Elgyem
Best location
Celestial Tower 5F

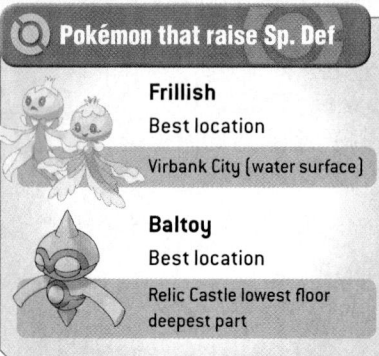

Pokémon that raise Sp. Def

Frillish
Best location
Virbank City (water surface)

Baltoy
Best location
Relic Castle lowest floor deepest part

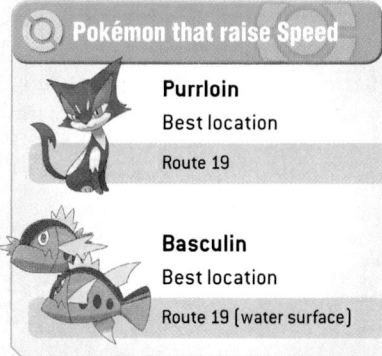

Pokémon that raise Speed

Purrloin
Best location
Route 19

Basculin
Best location
Route 19 (water surface)

◆ Base points will be raised the same amount regardless which of Frillish or Basculin's forms you defeat.

Hold items to raise a certain base stat in battles

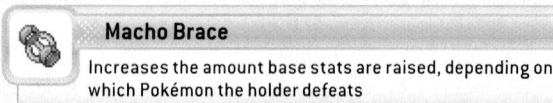

Macho Brace
Increases the amount base stats are raised, depending on which Pokémon the holder defeats

Training Tip 4 Use items to get the base stat you want

Some held items will boost the amount base stats are raised in battles. Take the Power Bracer, for example. It reduces the Speed stat, but it promotes Attack gain. The holder can also get the standard base stat increases for the Pokémon it defeats.

Items that raise a certain base stat when held in battles

Power Weight
Promotes HP gain

Power Lens
Promotes Sp. Atk gain

Power Bracer
Promotes Attack gain

Power Band
Promotes Sp. Def gain

Power Belt
Promotes Defense gain

Power Anklet
Promotes Speed gain

| Training Tip | 5 | Take advantage of the mysterious power of Pokérus |

The mysterious Pokérus very infrequently infects Pokémon in your party when they battle wild Pokémon. Pokémon with Pokérus will have their base stats raised even more than usual when they gain experience in battle. If you're lucky enough to have Pokérus in your party, use it to raise your Pokémon!

Keep Pokérus in your PC

Keep a Pokémon infected with Pokérus in your PC, and the Pokérus will stick around.

Pokérus rules

1 Infrequently infects your Pokémon when they battle wild Pokémon.

2 Increases the amount base stats go up in battle.

3 Battling can cause it to spread to adjacent party Pokémon.

4 Disappears after one to four days, but infected Pokémon's base stats will continue to increase at an accelerated rate.

5 Doesn't disappear while the Pokémon is stored in a PC Box.

| Training Tip | 6 | Once you've maxed out base stats, go level up |

You can only get the base stats so high. There is a limit for each base stat, and there is also a limit for the total of all six base stats. After you've entered the Hall of Fame, call Bianca on the Xtransceiver and select "Please look at effort." If Bianca says your Pokémon has worked really hard, then that means your Pokémon has raised its base stats to their limits. All you need to do then is earn Experience Points and level them up!

Ask Bianca on the Xtransceiver

Have Bianca judge your party Pokémon's effort. She will tell you how far your Pokémon's base stats have been raised.

Items related to Experience Points

	Lucky Egg
	Earns extra Experience Points (1.5 times the amount of Experience Points it normally would)

	Exp. Share
	Get some of the Experience Points even if the holder is not in battle

Effective ways to earn Experience Points

1 Challenge the Elite Four and the Champion in the Pokémon League again, and battle against high-level wild Pokémon.

2 After entering the Hall of Fame, revisit Big Stadium and Small Court in Nimbasa City to challenge Trainers who have gotten stronger.

3 Challenge the Black Tower in Black City or the White Treehollow in White Forest.

4 Leave a Pokémon at the Pokémon Day Care.

5 Trade Pokémon with your friends and raise each other's Pokémon.

A single Pokémon cannot have all six of its base stats raised to their maximum levels. You can only max out two stats at most. So when you train, focus on just two or three stats, building up your Pokémon's strengths. Even if your Pokémon have reached the limit for certain stats, there is still room for adjustment. Giving your Pokémon certain Berries will allow you to decrease their different base stats. By reducing a base stat that previously had reached its limit, you will be able to raise a different base stat instead. Use these Berries when your Pokémon accidentally maxes out some base stats during your adventure and help mold them to have a different strength for battle.

Effect of items to lower base stats

You can raise Pokémon suitable for your strategy by lowering base stats

Give a Hondew Berry to your oft-used Pokémon

Deliberately lower your Pokémon's Sp. Atk. stat

Liepard

Now you can raise its Speed as much as its Sp. Atk went down

Give it Carbos

Berries that lower base stats

 Pomeg Berry
It lowers the base HP stat. It makes the Pokémon more friendly.

 Kelpsy Berry
It lowers the base Attack stat. It makes the Pokémon more friendly.

 Qualot Berry
It lowers the base Defense stat. It makes the Pokémon more friendly.

 Hondew Berry
It lowers the base Sp. Atk stat. It makes the Pokémon more friendly.

 Grepa Berry
It lowers the base Sp. Def stat. It makes the Pokémon more friendly.

 Tamato Berry
It lowers the base Speed stat. It makes the Pokémon more friendly.

 **Tip** ## Lower base stats at the Beauty Salon in Join Avenue

Beauty Salons in Join Avenue have special treatments that can lower your Pokémon's base stats: Slender Makeup, Calm Makeup, Gentle Makeup, Mellow Makeup, Warm Makeup, and Slow Makeup (p. 406). As the rank of a Beauty Salon goes up, further treatments that can decrease your base stats a great deal at once will also appear. Develop Join Avenue and help your Beauty Salon improve in rank, and it will come in handy when you want to adjust one of your Pokémon's base stats.

Money		
₽ 484320	Gentle Makeup 3	₽ 10200
	Mellow Makeup 2	₽ 6480
	Warm Makeup 2	₽ 6480
	Slow Makeup 2	₽ 6480
	Slow Makeup	₽ 3240
	Warm Makeup	₽ 3240
	Mellow Makeup	₽ 3240
	Gentle Makeup	₽ 3240
	Calm Makeup	₽ 3240

The makeup helps the Pokémon grow friendly. It lowers the base Speed stat significantly.

The stats you should raise will differ wildly depending on how you prefer to battle. Since you cannot raise all of a Pokémon's base stats to their limits, you will need to choose which base stats you will abandon. If you raise an originally high stat even more, you can enhance traits that will be different from other Pokémon, and make the best use of your Pokémon's strengths.

Examples of building up Pokémon's strengths in base stats

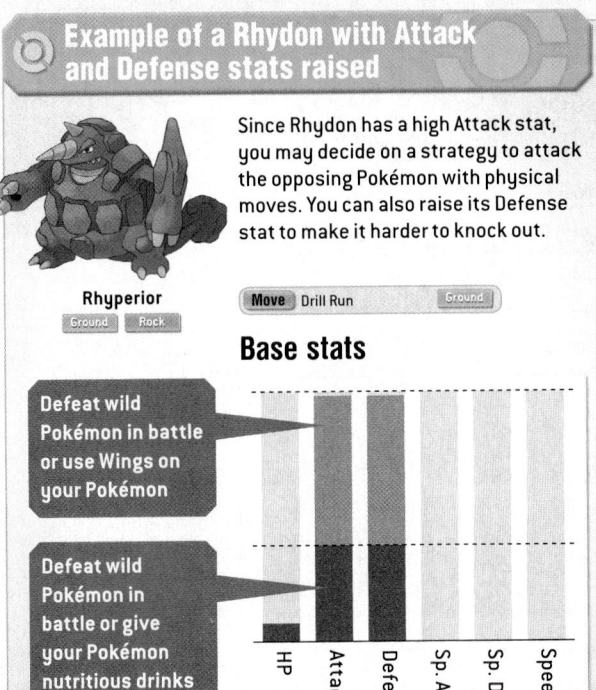

Example of a Rhydon with Attack and Defense stats raised

Since Rhydon has a high Attack stat, you may decide on a strategy to attack the opposing Pokémon with physical moves. You can also raise its Defense stat to make it harder to knock out.

Rhyperior
Ground Rock

Move | Drill Run | Ground

Base stats

Defeat wild Pokémon in battle or use Wings on your Pokémon

Defeat wild Pokémon in battle or give your Pokémon nutritious drinks

HP | Attack | Defense | Sp. Atk | Sp. Def | Speed

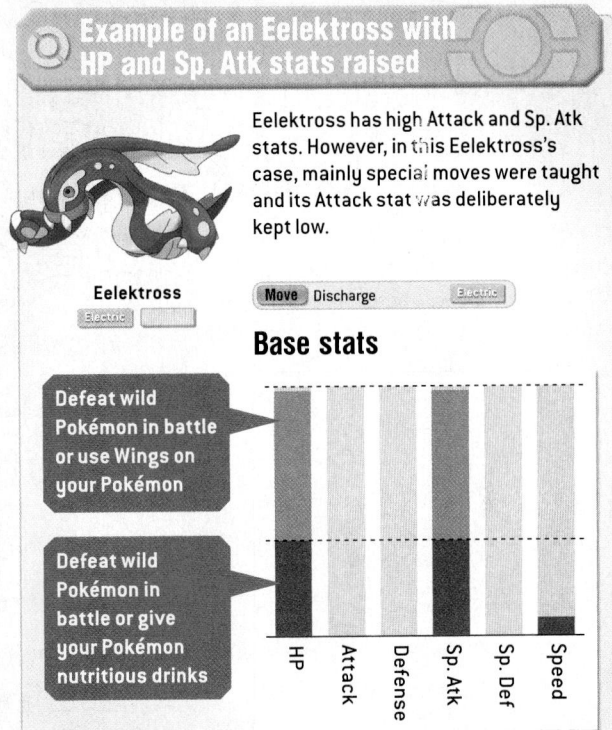

Example of an Eelektross with HP and Sp. Atk stats raised

Eelektross has high Attack and Sp. Atk stats. However, in this Eelektross's case, mainly special moves were taught and its Attack stat was deliberately kept low.

Eelektross
Electric

Move | Discharge | Electric

Base stats

Defeat wild Pokémon in battle or use Wings on your Pokémon

Defeat wild Pokémon in battle or give your Pokémon nutritious drinks

HP | Attack | Defense | Sp. Atk | Sp. Def | Speed

 **Tip** ### Pokémon can still do well with low stats

You don't have to raise every single stat of your Pokémon. For example, if a Pokémon battles with only special moves and doesn't use physical moves, it cannot make use of its Attack stat, no matter how high it is. Raise your Pokémon so they can make full use of their strengths.

① Moves to make use of high stats

If your Pokémon battles only with physical moves, you don't have to raise its Sp. Atk, which influences special moves. Instead, raise its Attack stat.

② Moves that inflict fixed damage

The stats of a Pokémon do not affect a move that inflicts fixed damage on its opponent, such as Dragon Rage.

③ Moves that share stats with the opponent

The higher the opposing Pokémon's stats are than the user's, the more effective moves like Guard Split and Power Split become.

④ Moves that get stronger when the Pokémon is slow

The slower the user is compared to its target, the more damage it can inflict with the move Gyro Ball.

 **Tip**

Develop Join Avenue to raise your Pokémon

Join Avenue is a large shopping district that you will become manager of. You will have to develop it by encouraging guests to visit shops and open stores of their own. There are eight different kinds of stores that will help you with your adventure and with raising your Pokémon. This section will focus on introducing the stores that can raise or lower your Pokémon's base stats. Help Join Avenue grow and use its amenities to make your Pokémon stronger (p. 400).

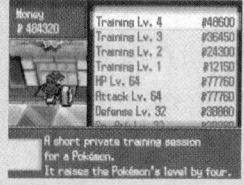

 Dojo

You can raise Pokémon's levels and base stats at Dojos. Raising the Dojo's rank will add more services that can increase your Pokémon's stats even more.

The Dojo's main offerings

Service	Effect	Price
Training Lv. 1	Raises a Pokémon's level by 1	15,000
HP Lv. 4	Raises the base HP stat of a Pokémon by a little	6,000
Attack Lv. 4	Raises the base Attack stat of a Pokémon by a little	6,000
Defense Lv. 4	Raises the base Defense stat of a Pokémon by a little	6,000
Sp. Atk Lv. 4	Raises the base Sp. Atk stat of a Pokémon by a little	6,000
Sp. Def Lv. 4	Raises the base Sp. Def stat of a Pokémon by a little	6,000
Speed Lv. 4	Raises the base Speed stat of a Pokémon by a little	6,000

 Beauty Salon

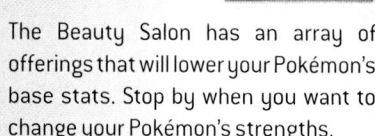

The Beauty Salon has an array of offerings that will lower your Pokémon's base stats. Stop by when you want to change your Pokémon's strengths.

The Beauty Salon's main offerings

Service	Effect	Price
Slender Makeup	Lowers the base HP stat of a Pokémon by a little	4,000
Calm Makeup	Lowers the base Attack stat of a Pokémon by a little	4,000
Gentle Makeup	Lowers the base Defense stat of a Pokémon by a little	4,000
Mellow Makeup	Lowers the base Sp. Atk stat of a Pokémon by a little	4,000
Warm Makeup	Lowers the base Sp. Def stat of a Pokémon by a little	4,000
Slow Makeup	Lowers the base Speed stat of a Pokémon by a little	4,000

 Café

You can raise Pokémon's levels and base stats at Cafés. The menu will vary depending on whether the owner of the Café has come from *Pokémon Black Version 2* or *Pokémon White Version 2*, or *Pokémon Black Version* or *Pokémon White Version*. If you get both varieties of Café, you'll be able to raise all of your Pokémon's base stats.

The Café's main offerings

Service	Effect	Price
Wonder Brunch	Raises a Pokémon's level by 1	15,000
Power Lunch A	Raises the base HP stat of a Pokémon quite a bit	36,000
Power Lunch B	Raises the base Attack stat of a Pokémon quite a bit	36,000
Power Lunch C	Raises the base Defense stat of a Pokémon quite a bit	36,000
Power Lunch D	Raises the base Sp. Atk stat of a Pokémon quite a bit	36,000
Power Lunch E	Raises the base Sp. Def stat of a Pokémon quite a bit	36,000
Power Lunch F	Raises the base Speed stat of a Pokémon quite a bit	36,000
Loyalty Meal	Raises a Pokémon's level by 1	14,000
Secret Dish A	Raises the base HP stat of a Pokémon by a lot	72,000
Secret Dish B	Raises the base Attack stat of a Pokémon by a lot	72,000
Secret Dish C	Raises the base Defense stat of a Pokémon by a lot	72,000
Secret Dish D	Raises the base St. Atk stat of a Pokémon by a lot	72,000
Secret Dish E	Raises the base St. Def stat of a Pokémon by a lot	72,000
Secret Dish F	Raises the base Speed stat of a Pokémon by a lot	72,000

See p. 400 for more on Join Avenue.

Plan Ahead to Raise Pokémon That Fit Your Strategy

Plan carefully and raise your Pokémon thoroughly, and they will do even better

Depending on the strategy you want to develop, which Pokémon you use and how you raise them will differ. Raise your Pokémon while keeping in mind how you wish to battle. The more thoughtfully you raise your Pokémon, the better they will do in battles.

Making Plans 1 Determine your goal first, then choose Pokémon to raise

Select Pokémon species based on moves you want to use, or pick Pokémon with Abilities suitable for your strategy. It's easier to create a plan if you visualize your ideal battle strategy.

What moves do you want?

If you want to use Head Charge

Head Charge is a move that only Bouffalant can learn. Bouffalant has a high Attack stat. Raise it in a way that will give it an even higher Attack stat.

Bouffalant

If you want to use Head Charge

Ally Switch is a move that causes your allies to switch sides in a Triple Battle. It can be taught to Pokémon like Gallade and Claydol using TM51 Ally Switch.

Gallade

If you want to use Horn Leech

Only Sawsbuck can learn Horn Leech. It allows Sawsbuck to attack and restore HP at the same time, making it difficult to knock out. Raise your Sawsbuck with high Attack and this move will be even more effective.

Sawsbuck
Spring Form

If you want to use Soak

You may want to use the move Soak to change an opposing Pokémon's type and throw a wrench in the plans of those who build their strategy on type. You could have Octillery learn it to use in battle.

Octillery

Examples of selecting Abilities of Pokémon you raise

Choosing an Ability for Arbok

If you select the Intimidation Ability, the opposing Pokémon's Attack stats will be lowered. If you choose the Shed Skin Ability, however, your Pokémon will have a 1/3 chance of recovering from status conditions each turn.

Arbok

Choosing an Ability for Golurk

Iron Fist is an Ability that raises the strength of punching moves. You should choose the Iron Fist Ability if you plan to teach Golurk moves like Hammer Arm and Focus Punch.

Golurk

Making Plans **2** Determine your advantages when attacking

Pokémon with high Attack stats will deal great damage when attacking with physical moves. Pokémon with high Sp. Atk stats will deal great damage when attacking with special moves.

Whether a Pokémon is good at physical moves or special moves depends on the Pokémon's stats.

Types of moves change how you raise your Pokémon's stats

Raise the Attack stat for Pokémon that mainly use physical moves

Honchkrow have a high Attack stat. They learn powerful physical moves, so take advantage of that by focusing on raising their base Attack stat.

Honchkrow

⦿ STATS	
HP	
Attack	
Defense	
Sp. Atk	
Sp. Def	
Speed	

Move	Night Slash	Dark
Move	Sky Attack	Flying
Move	Tailwind	Flying
Move	Snatch	Dark

Raise the Sp. Atk stat for Pokémon that mainly use special moves

Volcarona have a high Sp. Atk stat. They learn powerful special moves, so take advantage of that by focusing on raising their base Sp. Atk stat.

Volcarona

⦿ STATS	
HP	
Attack	
Defense	
Sp. Atk	
Sp. Def	
Speed	

Move	Bug Buzz	Bug
Move	Flamethrower	Fire
Move	Quiver Dance	Bug
Move	Sunny Day	Fire

Making Plans **3** Change learned moves depending on your strategy

Deciding the right combination of moves to teach to your Pokémon can be fun and challenging. Keeping the basics in mind, however, will help you make these decisions.

Important points for combining moves

1. Strategies and learned moves differ depending on the Pokémon's stats and Abilities.

2. Single Battles, Double Battles, and Triple Battles all require different strategies and learned moves.

3. Teaching both attack moves and support moves provides a good balance.

4. If your Pokémon have multiple types of attack moves, they can face various types of opponents.

An example of learned moves

A Gliscor for Single Battles

Gliscor can give opposing Pokémon the Badly Poisoned status condition with the Toxic move. A good strategy is to use Toxic, then have it guard itself with Protect while waiting for the opponent's HP to decrease. In a battle against a Steel-type Pokémon (which are immune to Poison-type attacks), use the Ground-type move Earthquake.

Gliscor

Move	Sky Uppercut	Fighting
Move	Earthquake	Ground
Move	Toxic	Poison
Move	Protect	Normal

Use the Strongest Pokémon in the Region!

Have Pokémon with high stats perform well in battle

Now to introduce some powerful Pokémon that can achieve great feats in battle! The following chart offers two powerful Pokémon of each type: one that excels at physical moves, and one that is better at special moves. Use this reference when trying to decide which Pokémon to raise and how.

Normal-Type Elites

The only weakness of Normal-type Pokémon is Fighting-type moves

✳ Physical

Slaking

Normal

ABILITY
● Truant

Slaking is among the top class of all Pokémon when it comes to Attack. Because of its Truant Ability, it can only move every other turn, but this means it can use Giga Impact without any drawbacks.

◎ STATS

HP	▰▰▰▱▱
Attack	▰▰▰▰▰▰
Defense	▰▰▰▱▱
Sp. Atk	▰▰▱▱▱
Sp. Def	▰▰▱▱▱
Speed	▰▰▰▱▱

● Representative Move

Move Giga Impact — Normal

Its power is 150, and when Slaking uses it, it can devastate opposing Pokémon.

◎ Special

Porygon-Z

Normal

ABILITIES
● Adaptability
● Download
● Analytic

Teach it special moves like Tri Attack to make use of its high Sp. Atk stat. Because Porygon-Z is a Normal type, any Normal-type moves it uses get a power boost.

◎ STATS

HP	▰▰▱▱▱
Attack	▰▰▱▱▱
Defense	▰▰▱▱▱
Sp. Atk	▰▰▰▰▱
Sp. Def	▰▰▱▱▱
Speed	▰▰▰▱▱

● Representative Move

Move Tri Attack — Normal

A 20% chance of inflicting the Paralysis, Burned, or Frozen status condition on the target.

Fire-Type Elites

Fire-type moves are super effective against Grass- and Steel-type Pokémon

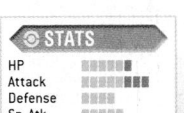

✳ Physical

Darmanitan (Standard Mode)

Fire

ABILITIES
● Sheer Force
● Zen Mode

Because its Attack is high, it will be effective to focus your strategy on physical moves. The Flare Blitz move does some damage to Darmanitan, but mostly deals a huge amount of damage to the opposing Pokémon.

◎ STATS

HP	▰▰▰▱▱
Attack	▰▰▰▰▰▱
Defense	▰▰▱▱▱
Sp. Atk	▰▱▱▱▱
Sp. Def	▰▱▱▱▱
Speed	▰▰▰▱▱

● Representative Move

Move Flare Blitz — Fire

This move's power is 120, but the user also takes 1/3 of the damage dealt.

◎ Special

Arcanine

Fire

ABILITIES
● Intimidate
● Flash Fire
● Justified

Arcanine has a high Attack stat, but strategies based on its Sp. Atk are by no means a bad alternative. If you have it learn the high-powered Overheat and Heat Wave moves, it will knock out opponents without breaking a sweat.

◎ STATS

HP	▰▰▰▱▱
Attack	▰▰▰▰▱
Defense	▰▰▱▱▱
Sp. Atk	▰▰▰▱▱
Sp. Def	▰▰▱▱▱
Speed	▰▰▰▰▱

● Representative Move

Move Overheat — Fire

This move's power is 140, but after using it, the user's Sp. Atk drops by 2.

Water-Type Elites

Water-type moves blast into Rock and Ground types' weak points

Physical

Gyarados

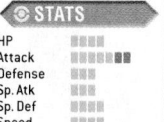

Water | Flying

ABILITIES
- Intimidate
- Moxie

With its high Attack, Gyarados pins down opposing Pokémon with its powerful physical moves. If you raise its Attack and Speed with the Dragon Dance move, the damage it can do to opponents with physical moves will be even greater.

STATS

HP ▪▪▪▪
Attack ▪▪▪▪▪▪▫
Defense ▪▪▪
Sp. Atk ▪▪▪
Sp. Def ▪▪▪
Speed ▪▪▪▪

● Representative Move

Move | Aqua Tail | Water

With a power of 90, this move is one of the best Water-type moves.

Special

Jellicent

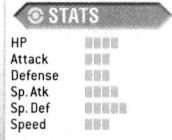

Water | Ghost

ABILITIES
- Water Absorb
- Cursed Body
- Damp

Jellicent's Sp. Def is even higher than its Sp. Atk. If you use the special move Recover, which restores Jellicent's own HP while attacking the opposing Pokémon, you will be able to hold out in even the longest battles.

STATS

HP ▪▪▪▪
Attack ▪▪▪
Defense ▪▪▪
Sp. Atk ▪▪▪▪
Sp. Def ▪▪▪▪▪
Speed ▪▪▪

● Representative Move

Move | Water Spout | Water

When the user's HP is full, this move has a power of 150.

Grass-Type Elites

Grass-type Pokémon have many weaknesses, but they can devastate Water types

Physical

Ferrothorn

Grass | Steel

ABILITY
- Iron Barbs

Ferrothorn has a high Attack, but you can also strategize around its high Defense and Sp. Def stats. Its Ingrain move will restore its own HP, while its Power Whip move deals huge damage to the opposing Pokémon.

STATS

HP ▪▪▪
Attack ▪▪▪▪▪
Defense ▪▪▪▪▪▫
Sp. Atk ▪▪▪
Sp. Def ▪▪▪▪▪
Speed ▪

● Representative Move

Move | Power Whip | Grass

Has a lower accuracy at only 85, but this physical move has a power of 120.

Special

Lilligant

Grass

ABILITIES
- Chlorophyll
- Own Tempo
- Leaf Guard

With its high Sp. Atk, you will want to focus your battle strategy on special moves. Petal Dance is a move that inflicts the Confused status condition on the user after several turns, but a Lilligant with the Own Tempo Ability won't become Confused.

STATS

HP ▪▪▪
Attack ▪▪▪
Defense ▪▪▪
Sp. Atk ▪▪▪▪▪▪
Sp. Def ▪▪▪
Speed ▪▪▪▪▪

● Representative Move

Move | Petal Dance | Grass

Attacks powerfully for 2–3 turns, but then the user becomes Confused.

Electric-Type Elites

The only weakness of Electric types is Ground-type moves

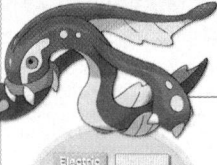

Physical

Eelektross

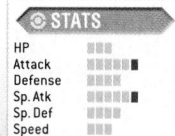

Electric

ABILITY
- Levitate

Eelektross has high Attack and Sp. Atk stats. If you raise yours with an emphasis on its Attack, it will be able to pull off strong physical moves. And because its Levitate Ability, it can escape Ground attacks!

STATS

HP ▪▪▪
Attack ▪▪▪▪▪▪
Defense ▪▪▪▪▪
Sp. Atk ▪▪▪▪▪▪
Sp. Def ▪▪▪▪
Speed ▪▪▪

● Representative Move

Move | Wild Charge | Electric

This move's power is 90, but the user also takes 1/4 of the damage given

Special

Magnezone

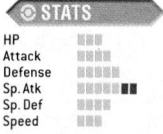

Electric | Steel

ABILITIES
- Magnet Pull
- Sturdy
- Analytic

Magnezone has incredibly high Sp Atk. It can learn moves like Thunderbolt and the 120-power Zap Cannon. That move's accuracy is low, so it's best to use it along with the Lock-On move.

STATS

HP ▪▪▪
Attack ▪▪▪▪
Defense ▪▪▪▪▪
Sp. Atk ▪▪▪▪▪▪▫▫
Sp. Def ▪▪▪▪
Speed ▪▪▪

● Representative Move

Move | Zap Cannon | Electric

This move's power is 120, and it unfailingly inflicts the Paralysis status condition on the target.

Ice-Type Elites

Ice-type moves petrify Dragon types in their path

✦ Physical

Mamoswine

You will want to use the physical move Icicle Crash to optimize Mamoswine's high Attack stat. Have Swinub learn it as an Egg Move and then evolve it into Mamoswine.

| Ice | Ground |

ABILITIES
- Oblivious
- Snow Cloak
- Thick Fat

◎ STATS

HP	■■■■
Attack	■■■■■■
Defense	■■■■
Sp. Atk	■■■■
Sp. Def	■■■■
Speed	■■■■

● Representative Move

| Move | Icicle Crash | Ice |

A move with a power of 85. It has a 30% chance of making the target flinch.

◎ Special

Vanilluxe

Since it has a high Sp. Atk stat, attack with special moves like Ice Beam and Blizzard. Blizzard will never miss when the weather is hail.

| Ice | |

ABILITIES
- Ice Body
- Weak Armor

◎ STATS

HP	■■■
Attack	■■■■
Defense	■■■■
Sp. Atk	■■■■■■
Sp. Def	■■■■
Speed	■■■■

● Representative Move

| Move | Ice Beam | Ice |

This attack has a power of 95 and a 10% chance of inflicting the Frozen status condition.

Fighting-Type Elites

Fighting-type moves blast right through the defenses of Rock- and Steel-type Pokémon

✦ Physical

Conkeldurr

A Conkeldurr with the Guts Ability will have its already-high Attack multiplied by 1.5 when it is afflicted with a status condition. Have it hold a Flame Orb or Toxic Orb, and it can unleash powerful physical moves.

| Fighting | |

ABILITIES
- Guts
- Sheer Force

◎ STATS

HP	■■■■
Attack	■■■■■■■
Defense	■■■■
Sp. Atk	■■■
Sp. Def	■■■
Speed	■■■

● Representative Move

| Move | Hammer Arm | Fighting |

This move has 100 power, but it also lowers the user's Speed by 1 after use.

◎ Special

Lucario

Lucario has high Attack and Sp. Atk stats. For a Lucario that excels in special moves, some good options are Aura Sphere, learned at Lv. 51, and Dragon Pulse, learned at Lv. 60.

| Fighting | Steel |

ABILITIES
- Steadfast
- Inner Focus
- Justified

◎ STATS

HP	■■■
Attack	■■■■■■
Defense	■■■
Sp. Atk	■■■■■
Sp. Def	■■■
Speed	■■■■■

● Representative Move

| Move | Aura Sphere | Fighting |

With 90 power, Aura Sphere is the strongest of the moves that hit without fail.

Poison-Type Elites

Aim for victory with smart strategy and strong poison

✦ Physical

Crobat

Crobat has one of the highest Speed stats among all Pokémon. Have it learn physical moves like Cross Poison and Poison Fang to quickly snag victory in battle.

| Poison | Flying |

ABILITIES
- Inner Focus
- Infiltrator

◎ STATS

HP	■■■
Attack	■■■■
Defense	■■■
Sp. Atk	■■■
Sp. Def	■■■
Speed	■■■■■■

● Representative Move

| Move | Cross Poison | Poison |

Critical hits land more easily with this move. It also has a 10% chance of inflicting the Poison status condition on the target.

◎ Special

Toxicroak

Toxicroak has high Attack and Sp. Atk stats. When it comes to special moves, the high-power Sludge Bomb and Venoshock, which does double damage to poisoned opponents, are both effective.

| Poison | Fighting |

ABILITIES
- Anticipation
- Dry Skin
- Poison Touch

◎ STATS

HP	■■■
Attack	■■■■■
Defense	■■■
Sp. Atk	■■■■
Sp. Def	■■■
Speed	■■■■■

● Representative Move

| Move | Sludge Bomb | Poison |

This move has a power of 90 and a 30% chance of inflicting the Poison status condition on the target.

Ground-Type Elites

Ground-type Pokémon are immune to Electric-type moves

⚡ Physical

Excadrill

| Ground | Steel |

ABILITIES
- ● Sand Rush
- ● Sand Force
- ● Mold Breaker

Excadrill has an incredibly high Attack. Have it learn the most powerful of the Ground-type physical moves: Earthquake. The Drill Run move, which often deals critical hits, is also good to have in your roster.

⚙ STATS

HP	▪▪▪▪
Attack	▪▪▪▪▪▪▪
Defense	▪▪▪
Sp. Atk	▪▪▪
Sp. Def	▪▪▪
Speed	▪▪▪▪▪

● Representative Move

Move Earthquake　　　　　　Ground

This move has a power of 100. Strikes allies as well as opposing Pokémon.

◎ Special

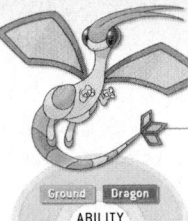

Flygon

| Ground | Dragon |

ABILITY
- ● Levitate

Flygon's stats are quite high overall and it maintains a good balance. If you wish to have it learn the powerful Earth Power and DragonBreath moves, work on increasing its Sp. Atk stat.

⚙ STATS

HP	▪▪▪
Attack	▪▪▪▪▪
Defense	▪▪▪▪
Sp. Atk	▪▪▪▪
Sp. Def	▪▪▪▪
Speed	▪▪▪▪▪

● Representative Move

Move Earth Power　　　　　　Ground

With a power of 90, this is one of the most powerful of Ground-type special moves.

Flying-Type Elites

Ground-type moves don't even touch Flying-type Pokémon

⚡ Physical

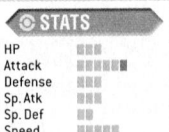

Staraptor

| Normal | Flying |

ABILITIES
- ● Intimidate
- ● Reckless

Use Staraptor's high Attack well and strike with powerful physical moves. The Close Combat move, learned at Lv. 34, and the Brave Bird move, learned at Lv. 49 are particularly recommended.

⚙ STATS

HP	▪▪▪
Attack	▪▪▪▪▪
Defense	▪▪▪
Sp. Atk	▪▪▪
Sp. Def	▪▪
Speed	▪▪▪▪▪

● Representative Move

Move Brave Bird　　　　　　Flying

This move's power is 120, but the user also takes 1/3 of the damage given.

◎ Special

Togekiss

| Normal | Flying |

ABILITIES
- ● Hustle
- ● Serene Grace
- ● Super Luck

Togekiss has a high Sp. Atk stat. Use the special moves Air Slash and Aura Sphere in battle. Both can be learned by giving a Heart Scale to the reminder girl at the Pokémon World Tournament.

⚙ STATS

HP	▪▪▪
Attack	▪▪▪
Defense	▪▪▪▪
Sp. Atk	▪▪▪▪▪▪
Sp. Def	▪▪▪▪▪
Speed	▪▪▪▪

● Representative Move

Move Air Slash　　　　　　Flying

This special move has a power of 75 and a 30% chance of making the target flinch.

Psychic-Type Elites

Psychic types are resistant to Fighting- and Poison-type moves

⚡ Physical

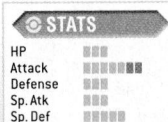

Gallade

| Psychic | Fighting |

ABILITIES
- ● Steadfast
- ● Justified

Gallade has a high Attack stat. Use Psycho Cut, one of the few Psychic-type physical moves, and the Fighting-type physical move Close Combat to deal massive damage to targets.

⚙ STATS

HP	▪▪▪
Attack	▪▪▪▪▪▪▪
Defense	▪▪▪
Sp. Atk	▪▪▪
Sp. Def	▪▪▪▪
Speed	▪▪▪▪

● Representative Move

Move Psycho Cut　　　　　　Psychic

Its power is only 70, but this move often lands critical hits for great damage.

◎ Special

Reuniclus

| Psychic | |

ABILITIES
- ● Overcoat
- ● Magic Guard
- ● Regenerator

Use Reuniclus's high Sp. Atk to fight with special moves. Use Calm Mind, learned with TM04, to raise its Sp. Atk and then release the move Psychic for an effective combo.

⚙ STATS

HP	▪▪▪▪
Attack	▪▪▪
Defense	▪▪▪
Sp. Atk	▪▪▪▪▪▪▪
Sp. Def	▪▪▪▪
Speed	▪▪

● Representative Move

Move Psychic　　　　　　Psychic

This move has 90 power and a 10% chance of lowering the target's Sp. Def by 1.

Bug-Type Elites

Bug-type moves can strike down Psychic and Dark types easily

☀ Physical

Heracross

ABILITIES
- ● Swarm
- ● Guts
- ● Moxie

Heracross, with its high Attack stat, has plenty of moves to learn, including physical moves. Have it learn the Bug-type move Megahorn and the Fighting-type move Close Combat for effective battling.

● Representative Move

Move	Megahorn	Bug

Has a lower accuracy at only 85, but this physical move has a power of 120.

STATS
HP	▪▪▪
Attack	▪▪▪▪▪▪▪▫
Defense	▪▪▪
Sp. Atk	▪▪▪
Sp. Def	▪▪▪▪
Speed	▪▪▪▪▪

◎ Special

Volcarona

ABILITY
- ● Flame Body

Raise Volcarona to Lv. 100 and it will learn Fiery Dance. Use the Bug Buzz move, learned at Lv. 70, to utilize its high Sp. Atk and press your advantage against opposing Pokémon.

● Representative Move

Move	Bug Buzz	Bug

A move with a power of 90. It has a 10% chance of lowering the target's Sp. Def by 1.

STATS
HP	▪▪▪
Attack	▪▪▪
Defense	▪▪▪
Sp. Atk	▪▪▪▪▪▪▫
Sp. Def	▪▪▪▪
Speed	▪▪▪▪▪

Rock-Type Elites

Rock-type moves make Flying- and Ice-type Pokémon crumble

☀ Physical

Gigalith

ABILITIES
- ● Sturdy
- ● Sand Force

Gigalith has high Attack and Defense stats. It can withstand attacks from others while dealing great damage in return with powerful physical moves like Stone Edge and Rock Slide.

● Representative Move

Move	Stone Edge	Rock

This move's power is 100, and it is more likely than most to land a critical hit.

STATS
HP	▪▪▪▪
Attack	▪▪▪▪▪▪▫
Defense	▪▪▪▪▪▪
Sp. Atk	▪▪▪
Sp. Def	▪▪▪
Speed	▪▪

◎ Special

Tyranitar

ABILITIES
- ● Sand Stream
- ● Unnerve

Tyranitar has high Attack, but developing it around its special moves will allow you to take opponents by surprise. Hatch a Larvitar that knows AncientPower as an Egg Move and then evolve it into Tyranitar.

● Representative Move

Move	AncientPower	Rock

This move has a 10% chance of raising the user's stats by 1.

STATS
HP	▪▪▪▪
Attack	▪▪▪▪▪▪▫
Defense	▪▪▪▪▪
Sp. Atk	▪▪▪▪
Sp. Def	▪▪▪▪
Speed	▪▪▪

Ghost-Type Elites

Ghost-type Pokémon feel no pain from Normal- or Fighting-type moves

☀ Physical

Dusknoir

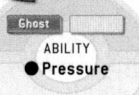

ABILITY
- ● Pressure

Dusknoir has high Defense and Sp. Def, so it is well suited to long, drawn-out battles. It can withstand attacks while dealing out damage with physical moves like Shadow Sneak and Shadow Punch.

● Representative Move

Move	Shadow Sneak	Ghost

This move strikes before others, so it can knock out a Pokémon before it can hit back.

STATS
HP	▪▪
Attack	▪▪▪▪
Defense	▪▪▪▪▪▪
Sp. Atk	▪▪▪
Sp. Def	▪▪▪▪▪▪
Speed	▪▪

◎ Special

Chandelure

ABILITIES
- ● Flash Fire
- ● Flame Body

Chandelure has an extremely high Sp. Atk stat. Once it evolves, it does not learn moves by leveling up, so have it learn moves as Lampent or use TMs to get strong special moves for battle.

● Representative Move

Move	Shadow Ball	Ghost

This move has a 20% chance of lowering the target's Sp. Def by 1.

STATS
HP	▪▪▪
Attack	▪▪▪
Defense	▪▪▪
Sp. Atk	▪▪▪▪▪▪▪
Sp. Def	▪▪▪▪
Speed	▪▪▪▪

Dragon-Type Elites

Dragon-type Pokémon's stats are in a class of their own

Physical

Haxorus

Because of its extremely high Attack stat, focus your fighting strategy on high-powered physical moves. If you raise its Attack with the Swords Dance move, the damage it can do to opponents with physical moves will be even greater.

Dragon

ABILITIES
● Rivalry
● Mold Breaker
● Unnerve

STATS

HP
Attack
Defense
Sp. Atk
Sp. Def
Speed

● Representative Move

Move Outrage **Dragon**

This move attacks 2–3 times in a row, then leaves the user Confused.

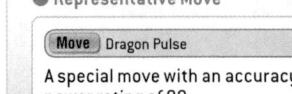

Special

Salamence

Salamence has high Attack and Sp. Atk stats. If you are training one to focus on special moves, don't miss Dragon Pulse. You can get this special move by giving 10 Blue Shards to the master Move Tutor in Lentimas Town.

Dragon **Flying**

ABILITIES
● Intimidate
● Moxie

STATS

HP
Attack
Defense
Sp. Atk
Sp. Def
Speed

● Representative Move

Move Dragon Pulse **Dragon**

A special move with an accuracy of 100 and a power rating of 90.

Dark-Type Elites

Dark-type Pokémon can brush off Psychic-type moves

Physical

Zoroark

Zoroark has high Attack, Sp. Atk, and Speed stats. Have it learn physical moves. The Night Slash move lands plenty of critical hits and makes it easy to deal opposing Pokémon a good amount of damage.

Dark

ABILITY
● Illusion

STATS

HP
Attack
Defense
Sp. Atk
Sp. Def
Speed

● Representative Move

Move Night Slash **Dark**

Its power is only 70, but this move often lands critical hits for great damage.

Special

Hydreigon

Utilize Hydreigon's high Sp. Atk and have it learn mostly special moves. Using the powerful Dark Pulse and Dragon Pulse moves will allow you to do great damage to opposing Pokémon.

Dark **Dragon**

ABILITY
● Levitate

STATS

HP
Attack
Defense
Sp. Atk
Sp. Def
Speed

● Representative Move

Move Dark Pulse **Dark**

A move with a power of 80. It has a 20% chance of making the target flinch, as well.

Steel-Type Elites

Steel-type Pokémon halve the damage taken from 11 types of moves

Physical

Metagross

Metagross can learn plenty of high-powered moves, like the Steel-type Meteor Mash and the Psychic-type Zen Headbutt. When a Pokémon with such high Attack uses these moves, battle should quickly turn in your favor.

Steel **Psychic**

ABILITY
● Clear Body
● Light Metal

STATS

HP
Attack
Defense
Sp. Atk
Sp. Def
Speed

● Representative Move

Move Meteor Mash **Steel**

This move has a power of 100 and a 20% chance of lowering the user's Attack by 1.

Special

Klinklang

Klinklang's stats are quite high overall and it has a good balance. If you will be raising it to focus on special moves, use TM91 to teach it the powerful Flash Cannon move.

Steel

ABILITY
● Plus
● Minus
● Clear Body

STATS

HP
Attack
Defense
Sp. Atk
Sp. Def
Speed

● Representative Move

Move Flash Cannon **Steel**

This move has a 10% chance of lowering the target's Sp. Def by 1.

Pokémon Black Version 2 & Pokémon White Version 2: The Official National Pokédex & Guide

Adventure Data

Pokémon Moves

Explanations of the Move List

Move............ The move's name
Type............ The move's type
Kind............ Physical moves deal more damage when a Pokémon's Attack is high. Special moves deal more damage when a Pokémon's Sp. Atk is high. Status moves cause effects, such as status conditions.
Pow.............. The move's attack power
Acc............... The move's accuracy
PP .... How many times the move can be used
Range .... The number and types of targets the move affects
Long .... Moves that can target the Pokémon on the other side during Triple Battles
DA .... Moves that require direct contact with the target

Range Guide

■ Normal: The move affects the selected target.

■ Self: The move affects only the user.

■ 1 Ally: The move affects an adjacent ally in Double, Triple, and Multi Battles.

■ Self/Ally: The move affects the user or one of its allies at random.

■ Your Party: The move affects your entire party, including party Pokémon who are still in their Poké Balls.

■ 1 Random: The move affects one of the opposing Pokémon at random.

■ Many Others: The move affects multiple Pokémon at the same time.

■ Adjacent: The move affects the surrounding Pokémon at the same time.

■ Your Side: The move affects the side of the field where your Pokémon are.

■ Other Side: The move affects the opponent's side of the field.

■ Both Sides: The move affects the entire playing field without regard to opposing and ally Pokémon.

■ Varies: The move is influenced by things like the opposing Pokemon's move or the user's type, so the effect and range are not fixed.

A

Move	Type	Kind	Pow.	Acc.	PP	Range	Long	DA	Effect
Absorb	Grass	Special	20	100	25	Normal	—	—	Restores HP by up to half of the damage dealt to the target.
Acid	Poison	Special	40	100	30	Many Others	—	—	A 10% chance of lowering the targets' Sp. Def by 1. Its power is weaker when it hits multiple Pokémon.
Acid Armor	Poison	Status	—	—	40	Self	—	—	Raises the user's Defense by 2.
Acid Spray	Poison	Special	40	100	20	Normal	—	—	Lowers the target's Sp. Def by 2.
Acrobatics	Flying	Physical	55	100	15	Normal	○	○	Attack's power is doubled if the user isn't holding an item.
Acupressure	Normal	Status	—	—	30	Self/Ally	—	—	Raises a random stat by 2.
Aerial Ace	Flying	Physical	60	—	20	Normal	○	○	A sure hit.
Aeroblast	Flying	Special	100	95	5	Normal	○	—	Critical hits land more easily.
After You	Normal	Status	—	—	15	Normal	—	—	The user helps the target and makes it use its move right after the user, regardless of its Speed. It fails if the target was going to use its move right after anyway, or if the target has already used its move this turn.
Agility	Psychic	Status	—	—	30	Self	—	—	Raises the user's Speed by 2.
Air Cutter	Flying	Special	55	95	25	Many Others	—	—	Critical hits land more easily. Its power is weaker when it hits multiple Pokémon.
Air Slash	Flying	Special	75	95	20	Normal	○	—	A 30% chance of making the target flinch (unable to use moves on that turn).
Ally Switch	Psychic	Status	—	—	15	Self	—	—	The user switches places with an ally. It fails if the user or target is in the middle (works only when the target is on the other end).
Amnesia	Psychic	Status	—	—	20	Self	—	—	Raises the user's Sp. Def by 2.
AncientPower	Rock	Special	60	100	5	Normal	—	—	A 10% chance of raising the user's Attack, Defense, Speed, Sp. Atk, and Sp. Def stats by 1.
Aqua Jet	Water	Physical	40	100	20	Normal	—	○	Always strikes first. The user with the higher Speed goes first if similar moves are used.
Aqua Ring	Water	Status	—	—	20	Self	—	—	Restores a little HP every turn.
Aqua Tail	Water	Physical	90	90	10	Normal	—	○	A regular attack.
Arm Thrust	Fighting	Physical	15	100	20	Normal	—	○	Attacks 2–5 times in a row in a single turn.
Aromatherapy	Grass	Status	—	—	5	Your Party	—	—	Heals status conditions of all your Pokémon, including those in your party.
Assist	Normal	Status	—	—	20	Self	—	—	Uses a random move from one of the Pokémon in your party that is not in battle.
Assurance	Dark	Physical	50	100	10	Normal	—	○	Attack's power is doubled if the target has already taken some damage in the same turn.
Astonish	Ghost	Physical	30	100	15	Normal	—	○	A 30% chance of making the target flinch (unable to use moves on that turn).
Attack Order	Bug	Physical	90	100	15	Normal	—	—	Critical hits land more easily.
Attract	Normal	Status	—	100	15	Normal	—	—	Leaves the target unable to attack 50% of the time. Only works if the user and the target are of different genders.
Aura Sphere	Fighting	Special	90	—	20	Normal	○	—	A sure hit.
Aurora Beam	Ice	Special	65	100	20	Normal	—	—	A 10% chance of lowering the target's Attack by 1.
Autotomize	Steel	Status	—	—	15	Self	—	—	Raises the user's Speed by 2 and lowers its weight by 220 lbs.
Avalanche	Ice	Physical	60	100	10	Normal	—	○	Attack's power is doubled if the user has taken damage from the target that turn.

B

Move	Type	Kind	Pow.	Acc.	PP	Range	Long	DA	Effect
Barrage	Normal	Physical	15	85	20	Normal	—	—	Attacks 2–5 times in a row in a single turn.
Barrier	Psychic	Status	—	—	30	Self	—	—	Raises the user's Defense by 2.
Baton Pass	Normal	Status	—	—	40	Self	—	—	User swaps out with an ally Pokémon and passes along any stat changes.
Beat Up	Dark	Physical	—	100	10	Normal	—	—	Attacks once for each Pokémon in your party, including the user. Does not count Pokémon that have fainted or have status conditions.
Belly Drum	Normal	Status	—	—	10	Self	—	—	The target loses half of its maximum HP but raises its Attack to the maximum.
Bestow	Normal	Status	—	—	15	Normal	—	—	If the target is not holding an item and the user is, the user can give that item to the target. Fails if the user is not holding an item or the target is holding an item.
Bide	Normal	Physical	—	—	10	Self	—	○	Inflicts twice the damage received during the next 2 turns. Cannot choose moves during those 2 turns.
Bind	Normal	Physical	15	85	20	Normal	—	○	Inflicts damage over 4–5 turns. The target cannot flee during that time.
Bite	Dark	Physical	60	100	25	Normal	—	○	A 30% chance of making the target flinch (unable to use moves on that turn).
Blast Burn	Fire	Special	150	90	5	Normal	—	—	The user can't move during the next turn. If the target is Frozen, it will be thawed.
Blaze Kick	Fire	Physical	85	90	10	Normal	—	○	A 10% chance of inflicting the Burned status condition on the target. If the target is Frozen, it will be thawed. Critical hits land more easily.
Blizzard	Ice	Special	120	70	5	Many Others	—	—	A 10% chance of inflicting the Frozen status condition on the targets. Is 100% accurate in the Hail weather condition. Its power is weaker when it hits multiple Pokémon.
Block	Normal	Status	—	—	5	Normal	—	—	The target can't escape. If used in a Trainer battle, it prevents the opposing Trainer from switching out a Pokémon.
Blue Flare	Fire	Special	130	85	5	Normal	—	—	A 20% chance of inflicting the Burned status condition on the target. If the target is Frozen, it will be thawed.
Body Slam	Normal	Physical	85	100	15	Normal	—	○	A 30% chance of inflicting the Paralysis status condition on the target.
Bolt Strike	Electric	Physical	130	85	5	Normal	—	○	A 20% chance of inflicting the Paralysis status condition on the target.
Bone Club	Ground	Physical	65	85	20	Normal	—	—	A 10% chance of making the target flinch (unable to use moves on that turn).
Bone Rush	Ground	Physical	25	90	10	Normal	—	—	Attacks 2–5 times in a row in a single turn.
Bonemerang	Ground	Physical	50	90	10	Normal	—	—	Attacks twice in a row in a single turn.
Bounce	Flying	Physical	85	85	5	Normal	○	○	The user flies into the air on the first turn and attacks on the second. A 30% chance of inflicting the Paralysis status condition on the target.

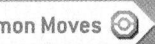
Move	Type	Kind	Pow.	Acc.	PP	Range	Long	DA	Effect
Brave Bird	Flying	Physical	120	100	15	Normal	○	○	The user takes 1/3 of the damage inflicted.
Brick Break	Fighting	Physical	75	100	15	Normal	—	○	This move is not affected by Reflect. It removes the effect of Reflect and Light Screen.
Brine	Water	Special	65	100	10	Normal	—	—	Attack's power is doubled if the target's HP is at half or below.
Bubble	Water	Special	20	100	30	Many Others	—	—	A 10% chance of lowering the targets' Speed by 1. Its power is weaker when it hits multiple Pokémon.
BubbleBeam	Water	Special	65	100	20	Normal	—	—	A 10% chance of lowering the target's Speed by 1.
Bug Bite	Bug	Physical	60	100	20	Normal	—	○	If the target is holding a Berry with a battle effect, the user eats that Berry and uses its effect.
Bug Buzz	Bug	Special	90	100	10	Normal	—	—	A 10% chance of lowering the target's Sp. Def by 1.
Bulk Up	Fighting	Status	—	—	20	Self	—	—	Raises the user's Attack and Defense by 1.
Bulldoze	Ground	Physical	60	100	20	Adjacent	—	—	Lowers the targets' Speed by 1. Its power is weaker when it hits multiple Pokémon.
Bullet Punch	Steel	Physical	40	100	30	Normal	—	○	Always strikes first. The user with the higher Speed goes first if similar moves are used.
Bullet Seed	Grass	Physical	25	100	30	Normal	—	—	Attacks 2–5 times in a row in a single turn.

C

Move	Type	Kind	Pow.	Acc.	PP	Range	Long	DA	Effect
Calm Mind	Psychic	Status	—	—	20	Self	—	—	Raises the user's Sp. Atk and Sp. Def by 1.
Camouflage	Normal	Status	—	—	20	Self	—	—	Changes the user's type to match the environment. Tall grass/Lawn: Grass type. Path/Sand/Entralink/Swamp: Ground type. Cave: Rock type. Water surface/Puddle/Shoal: Water type. Snow/Ice: Ice type. Indoors: Normal type.
Captivate	Normal	Status	—	100	20	Many Others	—	—	Raises the user's Sp. Atk by 2. Only works if the user and the target are of different genders.
Charge	Electric	Status	—	—	20	Self	—	—	Doubles the attack power of an Electric-type move used the next turn. Raises the user's Sp. Def by 1.
Charge Beam	Electric	Special	50	90	10	Normal	—	—	A 70% chance of raising the user's Sp. Atk by 1.
Charm	Normal	Status	—	100	20	Normal	—	—	Lowers the target's Attack by 2.
Chatter	Flying	Special	60	100	20	Normal	○	—	May inflict the Confused status condition on the target. Chance depends on the volume of the sound you recorded (Chatot only).
Chip Away	Normal	Physical	70	100	20	Normal	—	○	The target's stat changes don't affect this move.
Circle Throw	Fighting	Physical	60	90	10	Normal	—	—	Ends wild Pokémon battles after attacking. In a Double Battle with wild Pokémon or if the wild Pokémon's level is higher than the users, no additional effect takes place. In a battle with a Trainer, this move forces another Pokémon to switch in. If there is no Pokémon to switch in, no additional effect takes place.
Clamp	Water	Physical	35	85	15	Normal	—	○	Inflicts damage over 4–5 turns. The target cannot flee during that time.
Clear Smog	Poison	Special	50	—	15	Normal	—	—	Eliminates every stat change of the target.
Close Combat	Fighting	Physical	120	100	5	Normal	—	○	Lowers the user's Defense and Sp. Def by 1.
Coil	Poison	Status	—	—	20	Self	—	—	Raises the user's Attack, Defense, and accuracy by 1.
Comet Punch	Normal	Physical	18	85	15	Normal	—	○	Attacks 2–5 times in a row in a single turn.
Confuse Ray	Ghost	Status	—	100	10	Normal	—	—	Inflicts the Confused status condition on the target.
Confusion	Psychic	Special	50	100	25	Normal	—	—	A 10% chance of inflicting the Confused status condition on the target.
Constrict	Normal	Physical	10	100	35	Normal	—	—	A 10% chance of lowering the target's Speed by 1.
Conversion	Normal	Status	—	—	30	Self	—	—	Changes the user's type to that of one of its moves.
Conversion 2	Normal	Status	—	—	30	Normal	—	—	Changes the user's type to one that is strong against the last move the target used.
Copycat	Normal	Status	—	—	20	Self	—	—	Uses the last move used.
Cosmic Power	Psychic	Status	—	—	20	Self	—	—	Raises the user's Defense and Sp. Def by 1.
Cotton Guard	Grass	Status	—	—	10	Self	—	—	Raises the user's Defense by 3.
Cotton Spore	Grass	Status	—	100	40	Normal	—	—	Lowers the target's Speed by 2.
Counter	Fighting	Physical	—	100	20	Varies	—	○	If the user is attacked physically, this move inflicts twice the damage done to the user. Always strikes last.
Covet	Normal	Physical	60	100	40	Normal	—	○	When the target is holding an item and the user is not, the user can steal that item. A regular attack if the target is not holding an item.
Crabhammer	Water	Physical	90	90	10	Normal	—	○	Critical hits land more easily.
Cross Chop	Fighting	Physical	100	80	5	Normal	—	○	Critical hits land more easily.
Cross Poison	Poison	Physical	70	100	20	Normal	—	○	Critical hits land more easily. A 10% chance of inflicting the Poison status condition on the target.
Crunch	Dark	Physical	80	100	15	Normal	—	○	A 20% chance of lowering the target's Defense by 1.
Crush Claw	Normal	Physical	75	95	10	Normal	—	○	A 50% chance of lowering the target's Defense by 1.
Crush Grip	Normal	Physical	—	100	5	Normal	—	○	The more HP the target has left, the greater the attack's power (max 120).
Curse	Ghost	Status	—	—	10	Varies	—	—	Lowers the user's Speed by 1 and raises its Attack and Defense 1. If used by a Ghost-type Pokémon, the user loses half of its maximum HP, but the move lowers the target's HP by 1/4 of its maximum every turn.
Cut	Normal	Physical	50	95	30	Normal	—	○	A regular attack.

D

Move	Type	Kind	Pow.	Acc.	PP	Range	Long	DA	Effect
Dark Pulse	Dark	Special	80	100	15	Normal	○	—	A 20% chance of making the target flinch (unable to use moves on that turn).
Dark Void	Dark	Status	—	80	10	Many Others	—	—	Inflicts the Sleep status condition on the targets.
Defend Order	Bug	Status	—	—	10	Self	—	—	Raises the user's Defense and Sp. Def by 1.
Defense Curl	Normal	Status	—	—	40	Self	—	—	Raises the user's Defense by 1.
Defog	Flying	Status	—	—	15	Normal	—	—	Lowers the target's evasion by 1. Nullifies the effects of Light Screen, Reflect, Safeguard, Mist, Spikes, Toxic Spikes, and Stealth Rock on the target's side.
Destiny Bond	Ghost	Status	—	—	5	Self	—	—	If the user faints due to damage from a Pokémon, that Pokémon faints as well.
Detect	Fighting	Status	—	—	5	Self	—	—	The user evades all attacks that turn. If used in succession, its chance of failing rises.
Dig	Ground	Physical	80	100	10	Normal	—	○	The user burrows underground on the first turn and attacks on the second.
Disable	Normal	Status	—	100	20	Normal	—	—	The target can't use the move it just used for 4 turns.
Discharge	Electric	Special	80	100	15	Adjacent	—	—	A 30% chance of inflicting the Paralysis status condition on the targets. Its power is weaker when it hits multiple Pokémon.
Dive	Water	Physical	80	100	10	Normal	—	○	The user dives deep on the first turn and attacks on the second.
Dizzy Punch	Normal	Physical	70	100	10	Normal	—	○	A 20% chance of inflicting the Confused status condition on the target.
Doom Desire	Steel	Special	140	100	5	Normal	—	—	Attacks the target after 2 turns. This move is affected by the target's type.
Double Hit	Normal	Physical	35	90	10	Normal	—	○	Attacks twice in a row in a single turn.
Double Kick	Fighting	Physical	30	100	30	Normal	—	○	Attacks twice in a row in a single turn.
Double Team	Normal	Status	—	—	15	Self	—	—	Raises the user's evasion by 1.
Double-Edge	Normal	Physical	120	100	15	Normal	—	○	The user takes 1/3 of the damage inflicted.
DoubleSlap	Normal	Physical	15	85	10	Normal	—	○	Attacks 2–5 times in a row in a single turn.
Draco Meteor	Dragon	Special	140	90	5	Normal	—	—	Lowers the user's Sp. Atk by 2.
Dragon Claw	Dragon	Physical	80	100	15	Normal	—	○	A regular attack.

Pokémon Moves

D

Move	Type	Kind	Pow.	Acc.	PP	Range	Long	DA	Effect
Dragon Dance	Dragon	Status	—	—	20	Self	—	—	Raises the user's Attack and Speed by 1.
Dragon Pulse	Dragon	Special	90	100	10	Normal	○	—	A regular attack.
Dragon Rage	Dragon	Special	—	100	10	Normal	○	—	Deals a fixed 40 points of damage.
Dragon Rush	Dragon	Physical	100	75	10	Normal	—	○	A 20% chance of making the target flinch (unable to use moves on that turn).
Dragon Tail	Dragon	Physical	60	90	10	Normal	—	—	After attacking, it ends wild Pokémon battles. In a Double Battle with wild Pokémon or if the wild Pokémon's level is higher than the user's, no additional effect takes place. In a battle with a Trainer, this move forces another Pokémon to switch in. If there is no Pokémon to switch in, no additional effect takes place.
DragonBreath	Dragon	Special	60	100	20	Normal	—	—	A 30% chance of inflicting the Paralysis status condition on the target.
Drain Punch	Fighting	Physical	75	100	10	Normal	—	○	Restores HP by up to half of the damage dealt to the target.
Dream Eater	Psychic	Special	100	100	15	Normal	—	—	Only works when the target is asleep. Restores HP by up to half of the damage dealt to the target.
Drill Peck	Flying	Physical	80	100	20	Normal	○	○	A regular attack.
Drill Run	Ground	Physical	80	95	10	Normal	—	○	Critical hits land more easily.
Dual Chop	Dragon	Physical	40	90	15	Normal	—	○	Attacks twice in a row in a single turn.
DynamicPunch	Fighting	Physical	100	50	5	Normal	—	○	Inflicts the Confused status condition on the target.

E

Move	Type	Kind	Pow.	Acc.	PP	Range	Long	DA	Effect
Earth Power	Ground	Special	90	100	10	Normal	—	—	A 10% chance of lowering the target's Sp. Def by 1.
Earthquake	Ground	Physical	100	100	10	Adjacent	—	—	Does twice the damage if targets are underground due to using Dig. Its power is weaker when it hits multiple Pokémon.
Echoed Voice	Normal	Special	40	100	15	Normal	—	—	If this move is used every turn, no matter which Pokémon uses it, its power increases (max 200). If no Pokémon uses it in a turn, the power returns to normal.
Egg Bomb	Normal	Physical	100	75	10	Normal	—	—	A regular attack.
Electro Ball	Electric	Special	—	100	10	Normal	—	—	The faster the user is than the target, the greater the attack's power (max 150).
Electroweb	Electric	Special	55	95	15	Many Others	—	—	Lowers the targets' Speed by 1. Its power is weaker when it hits multiple Pokémon.
Embargo	Dark	Status	—	100	15	Normal	—	—	The target can't use items for 5 turns. The Trainer also can't use items on that Pokémon.
Ember	Fire	Special	40	100	25	Normal	—	—	A 10% chance of inflicting the Burned status condition on the target. If the target is Frozen, it will be thawed.
Encore	Normal	Status	—	100	5	Normal	—	—	The target is forced to keep using the last move it used. This effect lasts 3 turns.
Endeavor	Normal	Physical	—	100	5	Normal	—	○	Inflicts damage equal to the target's HP minus the user's HP.
Endure	Normal	Status	—	—	10	Self	—	—	Leaves the user with 1 HP when hit by a move that would KO it. If used in succession, its chance of failing rises.
Energy Ball	Grass	Special	80	100	10	Normal	—	—	A 10% chance of lowering the target's Sp. Def by 1.
Entrainment	Normal	Status	—	100	15	Normal	—	—	Makes the target's Ability the same as the user's. Fails with certain Abilities, however.
Eruption	Fire	Special	150	100	5	Many Others	—	—	If the user's HP is low, this move has lower attack power. If the targets are Frozen, they will be thawed. Its power is weaker when it hits multiple Pokémon.
Explosion	Normal	Physical	250	100	5	Adjacent	—	—	The user faints after using it. Its power is weaker when it hits multiple Pokémon.
Extrasensory	Psychic	Special	80	100	30	Normal	—	—	A 10% chance of making the target flinch (unable to use moves on that turn).
ExtremeSpeed	Normal	Physical	80	100	5	Normal	—	○	Always strikes first. Faster than other moves that strike first, except Fake Out. (If two Pokémon use this move, the one with the higher Speed goes first.)

F

Move	Type	Kind	Pow.	Acc.	PP	Range	Long	DA	Effect
Facade	Normal	Physical	70	100	20	Normal	—	○	Attack's power is doubled if the user has a Paralysis, Poison, or Burned status condition.
Faint Attack	Dark	Physical	60	—	20	Normal	—	○	A sure hit.
Fake Out	Normal	Physical	40	100	10	Normal	—	○	Always strikes first and makes the target flinch (unable to use moves on that turn). Only works on the first turn after the user is sent out. Faster than other moves that strike first.
Fake Tears	Dark	Status	—	100	20	Normal	—	—	Lowers the target's Sp. Def by 2.
False Swipe	Normal	Physical	40	100	40	Normal	—	○	Always leaves 1 HP, even if the damage would have made the target faint.
FeatherDance	Flying	Status	—	100	15	Normal	—	—	Lowers the target's Attack by 2.
Feint	Normal	Physical	30	100	10	Normal	—	—	Always strikes first. Faster than other moves that strike first, except Fake Out. If two Pokémon use this move, or the other Pokémon uses the ExtremeSpeed move, the one with the higher Speed goes first. Can hit targets using Protect, Detect, Quick Guard, or Wide Guard, and eliminates the effects of those moves.
Fiery Dance	Fire	Special	80	100	10	Normal	—	—	A 50% chance of raising the user's Sp. Atk by 1. If the target is Frozen, it will be thawed.
Final Gambit	Fighting	Special	—	100	5	Normal	—	○	Does damage to the target equal to the user's remaining HP. If the move lands, the user faints.
Fire Blast	Fire	Special	120	85	5	Normal	—	—	A 10% chance of inflicting the Burned status condition on the target. If the target is Frozen, it will be thawed.
Fire Fang	Fire	Physical	65	95	15	Normal	—	○	A 10% chance of inflicting the Burned status condition or making the target flinch (unable to use moves on that turn). If the target is Frozen, it will be thawed.
Fire Pledge	Fire	Special	50	100	10	Normal	—	—	When combined with Water Pledge or Grass Pledge, the power and effect change. If combined with Water Pledge, the power is 150 and it becomes a Water-type move. It will create a rainbow that turn which will last for the next 3 turns, making it more likely that your team's moves will have additional effects. If combined with Grass Pledge, the power is 150 and it remains a Fire-type move. The surrounding area becomes a sea of fire, which damages opposing Pokémon, except Fire types, that turn and the next 3 turns. If the target is Frozen, it will be thawed.
Fire Punch	Fire	Physical	75	100	15	Normal	—	○	A 10% chance of inflicting the Burned status condition on the target. If the target is Frozen, it will be thawed.
Fire Spin	Fire	Special	35	85	15	Normal	—	—	Inflicts damage over 4–5 turns. The target cannot flee during that time. If the target is Frozen, it will be thawed.
Fissure	Ground	Physical	—	30	5	Normal	—	—	The target faints with one hit if the user's level is equal to or greater than the target's level. The higher the user's level is compared to the target's, the more accurate the move is.
Flail	Normal	Physical	—	100	15	Normal	—	—	The lower the user's HP is, the more damage this move does to the target.
Flame Burst	Fire	Special	70	100	15	Normal	—	—	In Double and Triple Battles, it damages the Pokémon next to the target as well.
Flame Charge	Fire	Physical	50	100	20	Normal	—	○	Raises the user's Speed by 1. If the target is Frozen, it will be thawed.
Flame Wheel	Fire	Physical	60	100	25	Normal	—	○	A 10% chance of inflicting the Burned status condition on the target. If the target is Frozen, it will be thawed. This move can be used even if the user is Frozen. If the user is Frozen, this also thaws the user.
Flamethrower	Fire	Special	95	100	15	Normal	—	—	A 10% chance of inflicting the Burned status condition on the target. If the target is Frozen, it will be thawed.
Flare Blitz	Fire	Physical	120	100	15	Normal	—	○	The user takes 1/3 of the damage inflicted. A 10% chance of inflicting the Burned status condition. If the target is Frozen, it will be thawed. This move can be used even if the user is Frozen. If the user is Frozen, this also thaws the user.
Flash	Normal	Status	—	100	20	Normal	—	—	Lowers the target's accuracy by 1.
Flash Cannon	Steel	Special	80	100	10	Normal	—	—	A 10% chance of lowering the target's Sp. Def by 1.
Flatter	Dark	Status	—	100	15	Normal	—	—	Inflicts the Confused status condition on the target, but also raises its Sp. Atk by 1.
Fling	Dark	Physical	—	100	10	Normal	—	—	The user attacks by throwing its held item at the target. Power and effect vary depending on the item.
Fly	Flying	Physical	90	95	15	Normal	○	○	The user flies into the air on the first turn and attacks on the second.

Move	Type	Kind	Pow.	Acc.	PP	Range	Long	DA	Effect
Focus Blast	Fighting	Special	120	70	5	Normal	—	—	A 10% chance of lowering the target's Sp. Def by 1.
Focus Energy	Normal	Status	—	—	30	Self	—	—	Heightens the critical-hit ratio of the user's subsequent moves.
Focus Punch	Fighting	Physical	150	100	20	Normal	—	○	Always strikes last. The move misses if the user is hit before this move lands.
Follow Me	Normal	Status	—	—	20	Self	—	—	This move is given priority. Opposing Pokémon aim only at the user.
Force Palm	Fighting	Physical	60	100	10	Normal	—	○	A 30% chance of inflicting the Paralysis status condition on the target.
Foresight	Normal	Status	—	—	40	Normal	—	—	Attacks land easily regardless of the target's evasion. Makes Ghost-type Pokémon vulnerable to Normal- and Fighting-type moves.
Foul Play	Dark	Physical	95	100	15	Normal	—	○	The user turns the target's power against it. Damage varies depending on the target's Attack and Defense.
Freeze Shock	Ice	Physical	140	90	5	Normal	—	—	Builds power on the first turn and attacks on the second. A 30% chance of inflicting the Paralysis status condition on the target.
Frenzy Plant	Grass	Special	150	90	5	Normal	—	—	The user can't move during the next turn.
Frost Breath	Ice	Special	40	90	10	Normal	—	—	Always delivers a critical hit.
Frustration	Normal	Physical	—	100	20	Normal	—	○	The lower the user's friendship, the greater the attack's power.
Fury Attack	Normal	Physical	15	85	20	Normal	—	○	Attacks 2–5 times in a row in a single turn.
Fury Cutter	Bug	Physical	20	95	20	Normal	—	○	This move doubles in power with every successful hit (up to 5 hits). Power returns to normal once it misses.
Fury Swipes	Normal	Physical	18	80	15	Normal	—	○	Attacks 2–5 times in a row in a single turn.
Fusion Bolt	Electric	Physical	100	100	5	Normal	—	—	Attack's power is doubled if used immediately after Fusion Flare.
Fusion Flare	Fire	Special	100	100	5	Normal	—	—	Attack's power is doubled if used immediately after Fusion Bolt. If the target is Frozen, it will be thawed. This move can be used even if the user is Frozen. If the user is Frozen, this also thaws the user.
Future Sight	Psychic	Special	100	100	10	Normal	—	—	Attacks the target after 2 turns. This move is affected by the target's type.

G

Move	Type	Kind	Pow.	Acc.	PP	Range	Long	DA	Effect
Gastro Acid	Poison	Status	—	100	10	Normal	—	—	Disables the target's Ability.
Gear Grind	Steel	Physical	50	85	15	Normal	—	○	Attacks twice in a row in a single turn.
Giga Drain	Grass	Special	75	100	10	Normal	—	—	Restores HP by up to half of the damage dealt to the target.
Giga Impact	Normal	Physical	150	90	5	Normal	—	○	The user can't move during the next turn.
Glaciate	Ice	Special	65	95	10	Many Others	—	—	Lowers the targets' Speed by 1. Its power is weaker when it hits multiple Pokémon.
Glare	Normal	Status	—	90	30	Normal	—	—	Inflicts the Paralysis status condition on the target.
Grass Knot	Grass	Special	—	100	20	Normal	—	○	The heavier the target, the greater the attack's power.
Grass Pledge	Grass	Special	50	100	10	Normal	—	—	When combined with Water Pledge or Fire Pledge, the power and effect change. If combined with Water Pledge, the power is 150 and it remains a Grass-type move. The surrounding area will become a swamp, which lowers the Speed of opposing Pokémon that turn and the next 3 turns. If combined with Fire Pledge, the power is 150 and it becomes a Fire-type move. The surrounding area becomes a sea of fire, which damages opposing Pokémon, except Fire types, that turn and the next 3 turns. If the target is Frozen, it will be thawed.
GrassWhistle	Grass	Status	—	55	15	Normal	—	—	Inflicts the Sleep status condition on the target.
Gravity	Psychic	Status	—	—	5	Both Sides	—	—	Raises the accuracy of all Pokémon in battle for 5 turns. Ground-type moves will now hit a Pokémon with the Levitate Ability or a Flying-type Pokémon. Prevents the use of Bounce, Fly, Hi Jump Kick, Jump Kick, Magnet Rise, Splash, Sky Drop, and Telekinesis. Pulls any airborne Pokémon to the ground.
Growl	Normal	Status	—	100	40	Many Others	—	—	Lowers the targets' Attack by 1.
Growth	Normal	Status	—	—	40	Self	—	—	Raises the user's Attack and Sp. Atk by 1. Raises them by 2 when the weather condition is Sunny.
Grudge	Ghost	Status	—	—	5	Self	—	—	If the user faints because of a move, that move's PP drops to 0.
Guard Split	Psychic	Status	—	—	10	Normal	—	—	The user and the target's Defense and Sp. Def are added, then divided equally between them.
Guard Swap	Psychic	Status	—	—	10	Normal	—	—	Swaps Defense and Sp. Def changes between the user and the target.
Guillotine	Normal	Physical	—	30	5	Normal	—	○	The target faints with one hit if the user's level is equal to or greater than the target's level. The higher the user's level is compared to the target's, the more accurate the move is.
Gunk Shot	Poison	Physical	120	70	5	Normal	—	—	A 30% chance of inflicting the Poison status condition on the target.
Gust	Flying	Special	40	100	35	Normal	○	—	Does twice the damage if the target is in the sky due to using moves such as Fly or Bounce.
Gyro Ball	Steel	Physical	—	100	5	Normal	—	○	The faster the user is than the target, the greater the attack's power (max 150).

H

Move	Type	Kind	Pow.	Acc.	PP	Range	Long	DA	Effect
Hail	Ice	Status	—	—	10	Both Sides	—	—	Changes the weather condition to Hail for 5 turns, damaging all Pokémon except Ice types every turn.
Hammer Arm	Fighting	Physical	100	90	10	Normal	—	○	Lowers the user's Speed by 1.
Harden	Normal	Status	—	—	30	Self	—	—	Raises the user's Defense by 1.
Haze	Ice	Status	—	—	30	Both Sides	—	—	Eliminates every stat change of the targets.
Head Charge	Normal	Physical	120	100	15	Normal	—	○	The user takes 1/4 of the damage inflicted.
Head Smash	Rock	Physical	150	80	5	Normal	—	○	The user takes 1/2 of the damage inflicted.
Headbutt	Normal	Physical	70	100	15	Normal	—	○	A 30% chance of making the target flinch (unable to use moves on that turn).
Heal Bell	Normal	Status	—	—	5	Your Party	—	—	Heals status conditions of all your Pokémon, including those in your party.
Heal Block	Psychic	Status	—	100	15	Many Others	—	—	Targets cannot have HP restored by moves, etc. for 5 turns.
Heal Order	Bug	Status	—	—	10	Self	—	—	Restores HP by up to half of the user's maximum HP.
Heal Pulse	Psychic	Status	—	—	10	Normal	○	—	Restores the target's HP by up to half of its maximum HP.
Healing Wish	Psychic	Status	—	—	10	Self	—	—	The user faints, but fully heals the next Pokémon's HP and status conditions.
Heart Stamp	Psychic	Physical	60	100	25	Normal	—	○	A 30% chance of making the target flinch (unable to use moves on that turn).
Heart Swap	Psychic	Status	—	—	10	Normal	—	—	Swaps all stat changes between the user and the target.
Heat Crash	Fire	Physical	—	100	10	Normal	—	○	The heavier the user is than the target, the greater the attack's power (max 120).
Heat Wave	Fire	Special	100	90	10	Many Others	—	—	A 10% chance of inflicting the Burned status condition on the targets. If the targets are Frozen, they will be thawed. Its power is weaker when it hits multiple Pokémon.
Heavy Slam	Steel	Physical	—	100	10	Normal	—	○	The heavier the user is than the target, the greater the attack's power (max 120).
Helping Hand	Normal	Status	—	—	20	1 Ally	—	—	Strengthens the attack power of one ally's moves by 50%.
Hex	Ghost	Special	50	100	10	Normal	—	—	Deals twice the usual damage to a target affected by status conditions.
Hi Jump Kick	Fighting	Physical	130	90	10	Normal	—	○	If this move misses, the user loses half of its maximum HP.
Hidden Power	Normal	Special	—	100	15	Normal	—	—	Type and attack power change depending on the user.
Hone Claws	Dark	Status	—	—	15	Self	—	—	Raises Attack and accuracy by 1.
Horn Attack	Normal	Physical	65	100	25	Normal	—	○	A regular attack.

Pokémon Moves

H

Move	Type	Kind	Pow.	Acc.	PP	Range	Long	DA	Effect
Horn Drill	Normal	Physical	—	30	5	Normal	—	○	The target faints with one hit if the user's level is equal to or greater than the target's level. The higher the user's level is compared to the target's, the more accurate the move is.
Horn Leech	Grass	Physical	75	100	10	Normal	—	○	Restores HP by up to half of the damage dealt to the target.
Howl	Normal	Status	—	—	40	Self	—	—	Raises the user's Attack by 1.
Hurricane	Flying	Special	120	70	10	Normal	○	—	A 30% chance of inflicting the Confused status condition on the target. Is 100% accurate in the Rain weather condition and 50% accurate in the Sunny weather condition. It hits even Pokémon that are in the sky due to using moves such as Fly and Bounce.
Hydro Cannon	Water	Special	150	90	5	Normal	—	—	The user can't move during the next turn.
Hydro Pump	Water	Special	120	80	5	Normal	—	—	A regular attack.
Hyper Beam	Normal	Special	150	90	5	Normal	—	—	The user can't move during the next turn.
Hyper Fang	Normal	Physical	80	90	15	Normal	—	○	A 10% chance of making the target flinch (unable to use moves on that turn).
Hyper Voice	Normal	Special	90	100	10	Many Others	—	—	Its power is weaker when it hits multiple Pokémon.
Hypnosis	Psychic	Status	—	60	20	Normal	—	—	Inflicts the Sleep status condition on the target.

I

Move	Type	Kind	Pow.	Acc.	PP	Range	Long	DA	Effect
Ice Ball	Ice	Physical	30	90	20	Normal	—	○	Attacks consecutively over 5 turns or until it misses. Cannot choose other moves during this time. Inflicts greater damage with every successful hit. Does twice the damage if used after Defense Curl.
Ice Beam	Ice	Special	95	100	10	Normal	—	—	A 10% chance of inflicting the Frozen status condition on the target.
Ice Burn	Ice	Special	140	90	5	Normal	—	—	Builds power on the first turn and attacks on the second. A 30% chance of inflicting the Burned status condition on the target.
Ice Fang	Ice	Physical	65	95	15	Normal	—	○	A 10% chance of inflicting the Frozen status condition or making the target flinch (unable to use moves on that turn).
Ice Punch	Ice	Physical	75	100	15	Normal	—	○	A 10% chance of inflicting the Frozen status condition on the target.
Ice Shard	Ice	Physical	40	100	30	Normal	—	—	Always strikes first. The user with the higher Speed goes first if similar moves are used.
Icicle Crash	Ice	Physical	85	90	10	Normal	—	—	A 30% chance of making the target flinch (unable to use moves on that turn).
Icicle Spear	Ice	Physical	25	100	30	Normal	—	—	Attacks 2–5 times in a row in a single turn.
Icy Wind	Ice	Special	55	95	15	Many Others	—	—	Lowers the targets' Speed by 1. Its power is weaker when it hits multiple Pokémon.
Imprison	Psychic	Status	—	—	10	Self	—	—	Opposing Pokémon cannot use a move if the user knows that move as well.
Incinerate	Fire	Special	30	100	15	Many Others	—	—	Burns up the Berry being held by each of the targets, which makes the Berries unusable. If the targets are Frozen, they will be thawed. Its power is weaker when it hits multiple Pokémon.
Inferno	Fire	Special	100	50	5	Normal	—	—	Inflicts the Burned status condition on the target. If the target is Frozen, it will be thawed.
Ingrain	Grass	Status	—	—	20	Self	—	—	Restores a little HP every turn. The user cannot be switched out after using this move. Ground-type moves will now hit the user even if it is a Flying-type Pokémon or has the Levitate Ability.
Iron Defense	Steel	Status	—	—	15	Self	—	—	Raises the user's Defense by 2.
Iron Head	Steel	Physical	80	100	15	Normal	—	○	A 30% chance of making the target flinch (unable to use moves on that turn).
Iron Tail	Steel	Physical	100	75	15	Normal	—	○	A 30% chance of lowering the target's Defense by 1.

J

Move	Type	Kind	Pow.	Acc.	PP	Range	Long	DA	Effect
Judgment	Normal	Special	100	100	10	Normal	—	—	A regular attack. This move's type changes according to the Plate that Arceus is holding.
Jump Kick	Fighting	Physical	100	95	10	Normal	—	○	If this move misses, the user loses half of its maximum HP.

K

Move	Type	Kind	Pow.	Acc.	PP	Range	Long	DA	Effect
Karate Chop	Fighting	Physical	50	100	25	Normal	—	○	Critical hits land more easily.
Kinesis	Psychic	Status	—	80	15	Normal	—	—	Lowers the target's accuracy by 1.
Knock Off	Dark	Physical	20	100	20	Normal	—	○	The target drops its held item. It gets the item back after the battle.

L

Move	Type	Kind	Pow.	Acc.	PP	Range	Long	DA	Effect
Last Resort	Normal	Physical	140	100	5	Normal	—	○	Fails unless the user has used each of its other moves at least once.
Lava Plume	Fire	Special	80	100	15	Adjacent	—	—	A 30% chance of inflicting the Burned status condition on the targets. If the targets are Frozen, they will be thawed. Its power is weaker when it hits multiple Pokémon.
Leaf Blade	Grass	Physical	90	100	15	Normal	—	○	Critical hits land more easily.
Leaf Storm	Grass	Special	140	90	5	Normal	—	—	Lowers the user's Sp. Atk by 2.
Leaf Tornado	Grass	Special	65	90	10	Normal	—	—	A 50% chance of lowering the target's accuracy by 1.
Leech Life	Bug	Physical	20	100	15	Normal	—	○	Restores HP by up to half of the damage dealt to the target.
Leech Seed	Grass	Status	—	90	10	Normal	—	—	Steals HP from the target every turn. Keeps working after the user switches out. Does not work on Grass types.
Leer	Normal	Status	—	100	30	Many Others	—	—	Lowers the targets' Defense by 1.
Lick	Ghost	Physical	20	100	30	Normal	—	—	A 30% chance of inflicting the Paralysis status condition on the target.
Light Screen	Psychic	Status	—	—	30	Your Side	—	—	Halves the damage to the Pokémon on your side from special moves. Effect lasts 5 turns even if the user is switched out. Effect is weaker in Double and Triple Battles.
Lock-On	Normal	Status	—	—	5	Normal	—	—	The user's next move will be a sure hit.
Lovely Kiss	Normal	Status	—	75	10	Normal	—	—	Inflicts the Sleep status condition on the target.
Low Kick	Fighting	Physical	—	100	20	Normal	—	○	The heavier the target, the greater the attack's power.
Low Sweep	Fighting	Physical	60	100	20	Normal	—	○	Lowers the target's Speed by 1.
Lucky Chant	Normal	Status	—	—	30	Your Side	—	—	The Pokémon on your side take no critical hits for 5 turns.
Lunar Dance	Psychic	Status	—	—	10	Self	—	—	The user faints, but fully heals the next Pokémon's HP, PP, and status conditions.
Luster Purge	Psychic	Special	70	100	5	Normal	—	—	A 50% chance of lowering the target's Sp. Def by 1.

M

Move	Type	Kind	Pow.	Acc.	PP	Range	Long	DA	Effect
Mach Punch	Fighting	Physical	40	100	30	Normal	—	○	Always strikes first. The user with the higher Speed goes first if similar moves are used.
Magic Coat	Psychic	Status	—	—	15	Self	—	—	Reflects moves with effects like Leech Seed or those that inflict the Sleep, Poison, Paralysis, or Confused status conditions.
Magic Room	Psychic	Status	—	—	10	Both Sides	—	—	No held items will have any effect for 5 turns. Fling cannot be used to throw items while Magic Room is in effect.

Move	Type	Kind	Pow.	Acc.	PP	Range	Long	DA	Effect
Magical Leaf	Grass	Special	60	—	20	Normal	—	—	A sure hit.
Magma Storm	Fire	Special	120	75	5	Normal	—	—	Inflicts damage over 4–5 turns. The target cannot flee during that time. If the target is Frozen, it will be thawed.
Magnet Bomb	Steel	Physical	60	—	20	Normal	—	—	A sure hit.
Magnet Rise	Electric	Status	—	—	10	Self	—	—	Nullifies Ground-type moves for 5 turns.
Magnitude	Ground	Physical	—	100	30	Adjacent	—	—	Attack power shifts between 10, 30, 50, 70, 90, 110, and 150. Does twice the damage to targets using Dig. Its power is weaker when it hits multiple Pokémon.
Me First	Normal	Status	—	—	20	Varies	—	—	Copies the target's chosen move and uses it with increased power. Fails if it does not strike first.
Mean Look	Normal	Status	—	—	5	Normal	—	—	The target can't escape. If used in a Trainer battle, it prevents the opposing Trainer from switching out a Pokémon.
Meditate	Psychic	Status	—	—	40	Self	—	—	Raises the user's Attack by 1.
Mega Drain	Grass	Special	40	100	15	Normal	—	—	Restores HP by up to half of the damage dealt to the target.
Mega Kick	Normal	Physical	120	75	5	Normal	—	○	A regular attack.
Mega Punch	Normal	Physical	80	85	20	Normal	—	○	A regular attack.
Megahorn	Bug	Physical	120	85	10	Normal	—	○	A regular attack.
Memento	Dark	Status	—	100	10	Normal	—	—	The user faints, but the target's Attack and Sp. Atk are lowered by 2.
Metal Burst	Steel	Physical	—	100	10	Varies	—	—	Targets the Pokémon that most recently damaged the user with a move. Inflicts 1.5 times the damage taken.
Metal Claw	Steel	Physical	50	95	35	Normal	—	○	A 10% chance of raising the user's Attack by 1.
Metal Sound	Steel	Status	—	85	40	Normal	—	—	Lowers the target's Sp. Def by 2.
Meteor Mash	Steel	Physical	100	85	10	Normal	—	○	A 20% chance of raising the user's Attack by 1.
Metronome	Normal	Status	—	—	10	Self	—	—	Uses one move randomly chosen from all possible moves.
Milk Drink	Normal	Status	—	—	10	Self	—	—	Restores HP by up to half of the user's maximum HP.
Mimic	Normal	Status	—	—	10	Normal	—	—	Copies the target's last-used move (copied move has a PP of 5). Fails if used before the opposing Pokémon uses a move.
Mind Reader	Normal	Status	—	—	5	Normal	—	—	The user's next move will be a sure hit.
Minimize	Normal	Status	—	—	20	Self	—	—	Raises the user's evasion by 2.
Miracle Eye	Psychic	Status	—	—	40	Normal	—	—	Attacks land easily regardless of the target's evasion. Makes Dark-type Pokémon vulnerable to Psychic-type moves.
Mirror Coat	Psychic	Special	—	100	20	Varies	—	—	If the user is attacked with a special move, this move inflicts twice the damage done to the user. Always strikes last.
Mirror Move	Flying	Status	—	—	20	Normal	—	—	Uses the last move that the target used.
Mirror Shot	Steel	Special	65	85	10	Normal	—	—	A 30% chance of lowering the target's accuracy by 1.
Mist	Ice	Status	—	—	30	Your Side	—	—	Protects against stat-lowering moves and additional effects for 5 turns.
Mist Ball	Psychic	Special	70	100	5	Normal	—	—	A 50% chance of lowering the target's Sp. Atk by 1.
Moonlight	Normal	Status	—	—	5	Self	—	—	Recovers HP. Recovers 1/2 of the user's maximum HP. In Sunny weather conditions, recovers 2/3 of the user's maximum HP. In Rain/Sandstorm/Hail weather, recovers 1/4 of the user's maximum HP.
Morning Sun	Normal	Status	—	—	5	Self	—	—	Recovers HP. Recovers 1/2 of the user's maximum HP. In Sunny weather conditions, recovers 2/3 of the user's maximum HP. In Rain/Sandstorm/Hail weather, recovers 1/4 of the user's maximum HP.
Mud Bomb	Ground	Special	65	85	10	Normal	—	—	A 30% chance of lowering the target's accuracy by 1.
Mud Shot	Ground	Special	55	95	15	Normal	—	—	Lowers the target's Speed by 1.
Mud Sport	Ground	Status	—	—	15	Both Sides	—	—	The power of Electric-type moves drops to 1/3 of normal as long as the user is in battle.
Muddy Water	Water	Special	95	85	10	Many Others	—	—	A 30% chance of lowering the targets' accuracy by 1. Its power is weaker when it hits multiple Pokémon.
Mud-Slap	Ground	Special	20	100	10	Normal	—	—	Lowers the target's accuracy by 1.

N

Move	Type	Kind	Pow.	Acc.	PP	Range	Long	DA	Effect
Nasty Plot	Dark	Status	—	—	20	Self	—	—	Raises the user's Sp. Atk by 2.
Natural Gift	Normal	Physical	—	100	15	Normal	—	—	Type and attack power change according to the Berry held by the user. The Berry is consumed when this move is used. This move fails if the user is not holding a Berry.
Nature Power	Normal	Status	—	—	20	Varies	—	—	Move varies depending on the environment. Tall grass/Lawn: Seed Bomb. Path/Sand/Entralink: Earthquake. Cave: Rock Slide. Swamp: Mud Bomb. Water surface/Puddle/Shoal: Hydro Pump. Snow: Blizzard. Ice: Ice Beam. Indoors: Tri Attack.
Needle Arm	Grass	Physical	60	100	15	Normal	—	○	A 30% chance of making the target flinch (unable to use moves on that turn).
Night Daze	Dark	Special	85	95	10	Normal	—	—	A 40% chance of lowering the target's accuracy by 1.
Night Shade	Ghost	Special	—	100	15	Normal	—	—	Deals a fixed amount of damage equal to the user's level.
Night Slash	Dark	Physical	70	100	15	Normal	—	○	Critical hits land more easily.
Nightmare	Ghost	Status	—	100	15	Normal	—	—	Lowers the target's HP by 1/4 of maximum every turn. Fails if the target is not asleep.

O

Move	Type	Kind	Pow.	Acc.	PP	Range	Long	DA	Effect
Octazooka	Water	Special	65	85	10	Normal	—	—	A 50% chance of lowering the target's accuracy by 1.
Odor Sleuth	Normal	Status	—	—	40	Normal	—	—	Attacks land easily regardless of the target's evasion. Makes Ghost-type Pokémon vulnerable to Normal- and Fighting-type moves.
Ominous Wind	Ghost	Special	60	100	5	Normal	—	—	A 10% chance of raising the user's Attack, Defense, Speed, Sp. Atk, and Sp. Def stats by 1.
Outrage	Dragon	Physical	120	100	10	1 Random	—	○	Attacks consecutively over 2–3 turns. Cannot choose other moves during this time. The user becomes Confused after using this move.
Overheat	Fire	Special	140	90	5	Normal	—	—	Lowers the user's Sp. Atk by 2. If the target is Frozen, it will be thawed.

P

Move	Type	Kind	Pow.	Acc.	PP	Range	Long	DA	Effect
Pain Split	Normal	Status	—	—	20	Normal	—	—	The user and target's HP are added, then divided equally between them.
Pay Day	Normal	Physical	40	100	20	Normal	—	—	Increases the amount of prize money received after battle (the user's level, multiplied by the number of attacks, multiplied by 5).
Payback	Dark	Physical	50	100	10	Normal	—	○	Attack's power is doubled if the user strikes after the target.
Peck	Flying	Physical	35	100	35	Normal	○	○	A regular attack.
Perish Song	Normal	Status	—	—	5	Adjacent	○	—	All adjacent Pokémon in battle will faint after 3 turns, unless switched out.
Petal Dance	Grass	Special	120	100	10	1 Random	—	○	Attacks consecutively over 2–3 turns. Cannot choose other moves during this time. The user becomes Confused after using this move.
Pin Missile	Bug	Physical	14	85	20	Normal	—	—	Attacks 2–5 times in a row in a single turn.
Pluck	Flying	Physical	60	100	20	Normal	○	—	If the target is holding a Berry with a battle effect, the user eats that Berry and uses its effect.
Poison Fang	Poison	Physical	50	100	15	Normal	—	○	A 30% chance of inflicting the Badly Poisoned status condition on the target. Damage from being Badly Poisoned increases with every turn.
Poison Gas	Poison	Status	—	80	40	Many Others	—	—	Inflicts the Poison status condition on the targets.
Poison Jab	Poison	Physical	80	100	20	Normal	—	○	A 30% chance of inflicting the Poison status condition on the target.

509

Pokémon Moves

P

Move	Type	Kind	Pow.	Acc.	PP	Range	Long	DA	Effect
Poison Sting	Poison	Physical	15	100	35	Normal	—	—	A 30% chance of inflicting the Poison status condition on the target.
Poison Tail	Poison	Physical	50	100	25	Normal	—	○	A 10% chance of inflicting the Poison status condition on the target. Critical hits land more easily.
PoisonPowder	Poison	Status	—	75	35	Normal	—	—	Inflicts the Poison status condition on the target.
Pound	Normal	Physical	40	100	35	Normal	—	○	A regular attack.
Powder Snow	Ice	Special	40	100	25	Many Others	—	—	A 10% chance of inflicting the Frozen status condition on the targets. Its power is weaker when it hits multiple Pokémon.
Power Gem	Rock	Special	70	100	20	Normal	—	—	A regular attack.
Power Split	Psychic	Status	—	—	10	Normal	—	—	The user and the target's Attack and Sp. Atk are added, then divided equally between them.
Power Swap	Psychic	Status	—	—	10	Normal	—	—	Swaps Attack and Sp. Atk changes between the user and the target.
Power Trick	Psychic	Status	—	—	10	Self	—	—	Swaps original Attack and Defense stats (does not swap stat changes).
Power Whip	Grass	Physical	120	85	10	Normal	—	○	A regular attack.
Present	Normal	Physical	—	90	15	Normal	—	—	Attack power varies: 40 (40% chance), 80 (30% chance), or 120 (10% chance). A 20% chance of healing the target by 1/4 of its maximum HP.
Protect	Normal	Status	—	—	10	Self	—	—	The user evades all attacks that turn. If used in succession, its chance of failing rises.
Psybeam	Psychic	Special	65	100	20	Normal	—	—	A 10% chance of inflicting the Confused status condition on the target.
Psych Up	Normal	Status	—	—	10	Normal	—	—	Copies the target's stat changes to the user.
Psychic	Psychic	Special	90	100	10	Normal	—	—	A 10% chance of lowering the target's Sp. Def by 1.
Psycho Boost	Psychic	Special	140	90	5	Normal	—	—	Lowers the user's Sp. Atk by 2.
Psycho Cut	Psychic	Physical	70	100	20	Normal	—	—	Critical hits land more easily.
Psycho Shift	Psychic	Status	—	90	10	Normal	—	—	Shifts the user's Paralysis, Poison, Badly Poisoned, Burned, or Sleep status conditions to the target and heals the user.
Psyshock	Psychic	Special	80	100	10	Normal	—	—	Damage depends on the user's Sp. Atk and the target's Defense.
Psystrike	Psychic	Special	100	100	10	Normal	—	—	Damage depends on the user's Sp. Atk and the target's Defense.
Psywave	Psychic	Special	—	80	15	Normal	—	—	Inflicts damage equal to the user's level multiplied by a random value between 0.5 and 1.5.
Punishment	Dark	Physical	—	100	5	Normal	—	○	The higher the target's stat changes, the greater the attack's power.
Pursuit	Dark	Physical	40	100	20	Normal	—	○	Does twice the usual damage if the target is switching out.

Q

Move	Type	Kind	Pow.	Acc.	PP	Range	Long	DA	Effect
Quash	Dark	Status	—	100	15	Normal	—	—	The user suppresses the target and makes it move last that turn. Fails if the target has already used its move that turn.
Quick Attack	Normal	Physical	40	100	30	Normal	—	○	Always strikes first. The user with the higher Speed goes first if similar moves are used.
Quick Guard	Fighting	Status	—	—	15	Your Side	—	—	The user protects itself and its allies from first-strike moves. If used in succession, its chance of failing rises.
Quiver Dance	Bug	Status	—	—	20	Self	—	—	Raises the user's Sp. Atk, Sp. Def, and Speed by 1.

R

Move	Type	Kind	Pow.	Acc.	PP	Range	Long	DA	Effect
Rage	Normal	Physical	20	100	20	Normal	—	○	Attack rises by 1 with each hit the user takes.
Rage Powder	Bug	Status	—	—	20	Self	—	—	This move goes first. Opposing Pokémon aim only at the user.
Rain Dance	Water	Status	—	—	5	Both Sides	—	—	Changes the weather condition to Rain for 5 turns, strengthening Water-type moves.
Rapid Spin	Normal	Physical	20	100	40	Normal	—	○	Releases the user from moves such as Bind, Wrap, Leech Seed, and Spikes.
Razor Leaf	Grass	Physical	55	95	25	Many Others	—	—	Critical hits land more easily. Its power is weaker when it hits multiple Pokémon.
Razor Shell	Water	Physical	75	95	10	Normal	—	○	A 50% chance of lowering the target's Defense by 1.
Razor Wind	Normal	Special	80	100	10	Many Others	—	—	Builds power on the first turn and attacks on the second. Critical hits land more easily. Its power is weaker when it hits multiple Pokémon.
Recover	Normal	Status	—	—	10	Self	—	—	Restores HP by up to half of the user's maximum HP.
Recycle	Normal	Status	—	—	10	Self	—	—	A held item that has been used can be used again.
Reflect	Psychic	Status	—	—	20	Your Side	—	—	Halves the damage to the Pokémon on your side from physical moves. Effect lasts 5 turns even if the user is switched out. Effect is weaker in Double and Triple Battles.
Reflect Type	Normal	Status	—	—	15	Normal	—	—	The user becomes the same type as the target.
Refresh	Normal	Status	—	—	20	Self	—	—	Heals Poison, Paralysis, and Burned conditions.
Rest	Psychic	Status	—	—	10	Self	—	—	Fully restores HP, but makes the user Sleep for 2 turns.
Retaliate	Normal	Physical	70	100	5	Normal	—	○	Attack's power is doubled if an ally fainted in the previous turn.
Return	Normal	Physical	—	100	20	Normal	—	○	The higher the user's friendship, the greater the attack's power.
Revenge	Fighting	Physical	60	100	10	Normal	—	○	Attack's power is doubled if the user has taken damage from the target that turn.
Reversal	Fighting	Physical	—	100	15	Normal	—	○	The lower the user's HP is, the more damage this move does to the target.
Roar	Normal	Status	—	100	20	Normal	—	—	Ends wild Pokémon battles. If the opposing Pokémon's level is higher than the user's, this move fails. In a Double Battle with wild Pokémon, this move fails. In a battle with a Trainer, this move forces the opposing Trainer to switch Pokémon. When there is no Pokémon to switch in, this move fails.
Roar of Time	Dragon	Special	150	90	5	Normal	—	—	The user can't move during the next turn.
Rock Blast	Rock	Physical	25	90	10	Normal	—	—	Attacks 2–5 times in a row in a single turn.
Rock Climb	Normal	Physical	90	85	20	Normal	—	○	A 20% chance of inflicting the Confused status condition on the target.
Rock Polish	Rock	Status	—	—	20	Self	—	—	Raises the user's Speed by 2.
Rock Slide	Rock	Physical	75	90	10	Many Others	—	—	A 30% chance of making the targets flinch (unable to use moves on that turn). Its power is weaker when it hits multiple Pokémon.
Rock Smash	Fighting	Physical	40	100	15	Normal	—	○	A 50% chance of lowering the target's Defense by 1.
Rock Throw	Rock	Physical	50	90	15	Normal	—	—	A regular attack.
Rock Tomb	Rock	Physical	50	80	10	Normal	—	—	Lowers the target's Speed by 1.
Rock Wrecker	Rock	Physical	150	90	5	Normal	—	—	The user can't move during the next turn.
Role Play	Psychic	Status	—	—	10	Normal	—	—	Copies the target's Ability. Fails with certain Abilities, however.
Rolling Kick	Fighting	Physical	60	85	15	Normal	—	○	A 30% chance of making the target flinch (unable to use moves on that turn).
Rollout	Rock	Physical	30	90	20	Normal	—	○	Attacks consecutively over 5 turns or until it misses. Cannot choose other moves during this time. Inflicts greater damage with every successful hit. Does twice the damage if used after Defense Curl.
Roost	Flying	Status	—	—	10	Self	—	—	Restores HP by up to half of the user's maximum HP, but brings Flying-type Pokémon to the ground for that turn.
Round	Normal	Special	60	100	15	Normal	—	—	When multiple Pokémon use this move in a turn, the first one to use it is followed immediately by the others. Attack's power is doubled when following another Pokémon using the same move.

Move	Type	Kind	Pow.	Acc.	PP	Range	Long	DA	Effect
Sacred Fire	Fire	Physical	100	95	5	Normal	—	—	A 50% chance of inflicting the Burned status condition on the target. If the target is Frozen, it will be thawed. This move can be used even if the user is Frozen. If the user is Frozen, this also thaws the user.
Sacred Sword	Fighting	Physical	90	100	20	Normal	—	○	The target's stat changes don't affect this move.
Safeguard	Normal	Status	—	—	25	Your Side	—	—	Protects the Pokémon on your side from status conditions for 5 turns. Effects last even if the user switches out.
Sand Tomb	Ground	Physical	35	85	15	Normal	—	—	Inflicts damage over 4–5 turns. The target cannot flee during that time.
Sand-Attack	Ground	Status	—	100	15	Normal	—	—	Lowers the target's accuracy by 1.
Sandstorm	Rock	Status	—	—	10	Both Sides	—	—	Changes the weather condition to Sandstorm for 5 turns. The Sp. Def of Rock-type Pokémon increases. All Pokémon other than Rock, Steel, and Ground types take damage each turn.
Scald	Water	Special	80	100	15	Normal	—	—	A 30% chance of inflicting the Burned status condition on the target. This move can be used even if the user is Frozen. If the user is Frozen, this also thaws the user.
Scary Face	Normal	Status	—	100	10	Normal	—	—	Lowers the target's Speed by 2.
Scratch	Normal	Physical	40	100	35	Normal	—	○	A regular attack.
Screech	Normal	Status	—	85	40	Normal	—	—	Lowers the target's Defense by 2.
Searing Shot	Fire	Special	100	100	5	Adjacent	—	—	A 30% chance of inflicting the Burned status condition on the targets. If the targets are Frozen, they will be thawed. Its power is weaker when it hits multiple Pokémon.
Secret Power	Normal	Physical	70	100	20	Normal	—	—	A 30% chance of one of the following additional effects, depending on the environment. Tall grass/Lawn: Sleep status condition. Path/Sand/Entralink: lowers accuracy by 1. Cave: the target flinches. Water surface/Puddle/Shoal: lowers Attack by 1. Swamp: lowers Speed by 1. Snow/Ice: Frozen status condition. Indoors: Paralysis status condition.
Secret Sword	Fighting	Special	85	100	10	Normal	—	—	Damage depends on the user's Sp. Atk and the target's Defense.
Seed Bomb	Grass	Physical	80	100	15	Normal	—	—	A regular attack.
Seed Flare	Grass	Special	120	85	5	Normal	—	—	A 40% chance of lowering the target's Sp. Def by 2.
Seismic Toss	Fighting	Physical	—	100	20	Normal	—	○	Deals a fixed amount of damage equal to the user's level.
Selfdestruct	Normal	Physical	200	100	5	Adjacent	—	—	The user faints after using it. Its power is weaker when it hits multiple Pokémon.
Shadow Ball	Ghost	Special	80	100	15	Normal	—	—	A 20% chance of lowering the target's Sp. Def by 1.
Shadow Claw	Ghost	Physical	70	100	15	Normal	—	○	Critical hits land more easily.
Shadow Force	Ghost	Physical	120	100	5	Normal	—	○	Makes the user invisible on the first turn and attacks on the second. Strikes the target even if it is using Protect or Detect.
Shadow Punch	Ghost	Physical	60	—	20	Normal	—	○	A sure hit.
Shadow Sneak	Ghost	Physical	40	100	30	Normal	—	○	Always strikes first. The user with the higher Speed goes first if similar moves are used.
Sharpen	Normal	Status	—	—	30	Self	—	—	Raises the user's Attack by 1.
Sheer Cold	Ice	Special	—	30	5	Normal	—	—	The target faints with one hit if the user's level is equal to or greater than the target's level. The higher the user's level is compared to the target's, the more accurate the move is.
Shell Smash	Normal	Status	—	—	15	Self	—	—	Lowers the user's Defense and Sp. Def by 1 and raises the user's Attack, Sp. Atk, and Speed by 2.
Shift Gear	Steel	Status	—	—	10	Self	—	—	Raises the user's Speed by 2 and Attack by 1.
Shock Wave	Electric	Special	60	—	20	Normal	—	—	A sure hit.
Signal Beam	Bug	Special	75	100	15	Normal	—	—	A 10% chance of inflicting the Confused status condition on the target.
Silver Wind	Bug	Special	60	100	5	Normal	—	—	A 10% chance of raising the user's Attack, Defense, Speed, Sp. Atk, and Sp. Def stats by 1.
Simple Beam	Normal	Status	—	100	15	Normal	—	—	Changes the target's Ability to Simple. Fails with certain Abilities, however.
Sing	Normal	Status	—	55	15	Normal	—	—	Inflicts the Sleep status condition on the target.
Sketch	Normal	Status	—	—	1	Normal	—	—	Copies the last move used by the target. The user then forgets Sketch and learns the new move.
Skill Swap	Psychic	Status	—	—	10	Normal	—	—	Swaps Abilities between the user and target. Fails with certain Abilities, however.
Skull Bash	Normal	Physical	100	100	15	Normal	—	○	Builds power on the first turn and attacks on the second. It raises the user's Defense stat by 1 on the first turn.
Sky Attack	Flying	Physical	140	90	5	Normal	○	—	Builds power on the first turn and attacks on the second. Critical hits land more easily. A 30% chance of making the target flinch (unable to use moves on that turn).
Sky Drop	Flying	Physical	60	100	10	Normal	○	○	The user takes the target into the sky, then damages it by dropping it during the next turn. Does not damage Flying-type Pokémon.
Sky Uppercut	Fighting	Physical	85	90	15	Normal	—	○	It hits even Pokémon that are in the sky due to using moves such as Fly and Bounce.
Slack Off	Normal	Status	—	—	10	Self	—	—	Restores HP by up to half of the user's maximum HP.
Slam	Normal	Physical	80	75	20	Normal	—	—	A regular attack.
Slash	Normal	Physical	70	100	20	Normal	—	○	Critical hits land more easily.
Sleep Powder	Grass	Status	—	75	15	Normal	—	—	Inflicts the Sleep status condition on the target.
Sleep Talk	Normal	Status	—	—	10	Self	—	—	Only works when the user is asleep. Randomly uses one of the user's moves.
Sludge	Poison	Special	65	100	20	Normal	—	—	A 30% chance of inflicting the Poison status condition on the target.
Sludge Bomb	Poison	Special	90	100	10	Normal	—	—	A 30% chance of inflicting the Poison status condition on the target.
Sludge Wave	Poison	Special	95	100	10	Adjacent	—	—	A 10% chance of inflicting the Poison status condition on the targets. Its power is weaker when it hits multiple Pokémon.
Smack Down	Rock	Physical	50	100	15	Normal	—	—	Ground-type moves will now hit a Pokémon with the Levitate Ability or a Flying-type Pokémon. They will also hit Pokémon that are in the sky due to using moves such as Fly and Bounce.
SmellingSalt	Normal	Physical	60	100	10	Normal	—	○	Does twice the usual damage to targets with Paralysis, but heals that status condition.
Smog	Poison	Special	20	70	20	Normal	—	—	A 40% chance of inflicting the Poison status condition on the target.
SmokeScreen	Normal	Status	—	100	20	Normal	—	—	Lowers the target's accuracy by 1.
Snarl	Dark	Special	55	95	15	Many Others	—	—	Lowers the targets' Sp. Atk by 1. Its power is weaker when it hits multiple Pokémon.
Snatch	Dark	Status	—	—	10	Self	—	—	Steals the effects of recovery or stat-changing moves used by the target on that turn.
Snore	Normal	Special	40	100	15	Normal	—	—	Only works when the user is asleep. A 30% chance of making the target flinch (unable to use moves on that turn).
Soak	Water	Status	—	100	20	Normal	—	—	Changes the target's type to Water.
Softboiled	Normal	Status	—	—	10	Self	—	—	Restores HP by up to half of the user's maximum HP.
SolarBeam	Grass	Special	120	100	10	Normal	—	—	Builds power on the first turn and attacks on the second. In Sunny weather conditions, attacks on first turn. In Rain/Sandstorm/Hail weather conditions, the power is halved.
SonicBoom	Normal	Special	—	90	20	Normal	—	—	Deals a fixed 20 points of damage.
Spacial Rend	Dragon	Special	100	95	5	Normal	—	—	Critical hits land more easily.
Spark	Electric	Physical	65	100	20	Normal	—	○	A 30% chance of inflicting the Paralysis status condition on the target.
Spider Web	Bug	Status	—	—	10	Normal	—	—	The target can't escape. If used in a Trainer battle, it prevents the opposing Trainer from switching out a Pokémon.
Spike Cannon	Normal	Physical	20	100	15	Normal	—	—	Attacks 2–5 times in a row in a single turn.
Spikes	Ground	Status	—	—	20	Other Side	—	—	Damages Pokémon as they are sent out to the opposing side. Power rises with each use, up to 3 times. Ineffective against Flying-type Pokémon and Pokémon with the Levitate Ability.
Spit Up	Normal	Special	—	100	10	Normal	—	—	Deals damage determined by how many times the user has used Stockpile. Fails if the user has not used Stockpile first. Nullifies Defense and Sp. Def stat increases caused by Stockpile.
Spite	Ghost	Status	—	100	10	Normal	—	—	Takes 4 points from the PP of the target's last used move.
Splash	Normal	Status	—	—	40	Self	—	—	No effect.

Pokémon Moves

S

Move	Type	Kind	Pow.	Acc.	PP	Range	Long	DA	Effect
Spore	Grass	Status	—	100	15	Normal	—	—	Inflicts the Sleep status condition on the target.
Stealth Rock	Rock	Status	—	—	20	Other Side	—	—	Damages Pokémon as they are sent out to the opposing side. Damage is subject to type matchups.
Steamroller	Bug	Physical	65	100	20	Normal	—	○	A 30% chance of making the targets flinch (unable to use moves on that turn). Does twice the damage to a target using Minimize when it hits.
Steel Wing	Steel	Physical	70	90	25	Normal	—	○	A 10% chance of raising the user's Defense by 1.
Stockpile	Normal	Status	—	—	20	Self	—	—	Raises the user's Defense and Sp. Def by 1. Can be used up to 3 times.
Stomp	Normal	Physical	65	100	20	Normal	—	○	A 30% chance of making the target flinch (unable to use moves on that turn). Does twice the damage to a target using Minimize when it hits.
Stone Edge	Rock	Physical	100	80	5	Normal	—	—	Critical hits land more easily.
Stored Power	Psychic	Special	20	100	10	Normal	—	—	The higher the user's stat changes, the greater the attack's power.
Storm Throw	Fighting	Physical	40	100	10	Normal	—	○	Always delivers a critical hit.
Strength	Normal	Physical	80	100	15	Normal	—	○	A regular attack.
String Shot	Bug	Status	—	95	40	Many Others	—	—	Lowers the targets' Speed by 1.
Struggle	Normal	Physical	50	—	1	Normal	—	○	This move becomes available when all other moves are out of PP. The user takes damage equal to 1/4 of its maximum HP. Inflicts damage regardless of type matchup.
Struggle Bug	Bug	Special	30	100	20	Many Others	—	—	Lowers the targets' Sp. Atk by 1. Its power is weaker when it hits multiple Pokémon.
Stun Spore	Grass	Status	—	75	30	Normal	—	—	Inflicts the Paralysis status condition on the target.
Submission	Fighting	Physical	80	80	25	Normal	—	○	The user takes 1/4 of the damage inflicted.
Substitute	Normal	Status	—	—	10	Self	—	—	Uses 1/4 of maximum HP to create a copy of the user.
Sucker Punch	Dark	Physical	80	100	5	Normal	—	○	This move attacks first and deals damage only if the target's chosen move is an attack move.
Sunny Day	Fire	Status	—	—	5	Both Sides	—	—	Changes the weather condition to Sunny for 5 turns, strengthening Fire-type moves.
Super Fang	Normal	Physical	—	90	10	Normal	—	○	Halves the target's HP.
Superpower	Fighting	Physical	120	100	5	Normal	—	○	Lowers the user's Attack and Defense by 1.
Supersonic	Normal	Status	—	55	20	Normal	—	—	Inflicts the Confused status condition on the target.
Surf	Water	Special	95	100	15	Adjacent	—	—	Does twice the damage if the target is using Dive when attacked. Its power is weaker when it hits multiple Pokémon.
Swagger	Normal	Status	—	90	15	Normal	—	—	Inflicts the Confused status condition on the target, but also raises its Attack by 2.
Swallow	Normal	Status	—	—	10	Self	—	—	Restores HP, the amount of which is determined by how many times the user has used Stockpile. Fails if the user has not used Stockpile first. Nullifies Defense and Sp. Def stat increases caused by Stockpile.
Sweet Kiss	Normal	Status	—	75	10	Normal	—	—	Inflicts the Confused status condition on the target.
Sweet Scent	Normal	Status	—	100	20	Many Others	—	—	Lowers the targets' evasion by 1.
Swift	Normal	Special	60	—	20	Many Others	—	—	A sure hit. Its power is weaker when it hits multiple Pokémon.
Switcheroo	Dark	Status	—	100	10	Normal	—	—	Swaps items between the user and the target.
Swords Dance	Normal	Status	—	—	30	Self	—	—	Raises the user's Attack by 2.
Synchronoise	Psychic	Special	70	100	15	Adjacent	—	—	Inflicts damage on any Pokémon of the same type as the user. Its power is weaker when it hits multiple Pokémon.
Synthesis	Grass	Status	—	—	5	Self	—	—	Recovers HP. Recovers 1/2 of the user's maximum HP. In Sunny weather conditions, recovers 2/3 of the user's maximum HP. In Rain/Sandstorm/Hail weather, recovers 1/4 of the user's maximum HP.

T

Move	Type	Kind	Pow.	Acc.	PP	Range	Long	DA	Effect
Tackle	Normal	Physical	50	100	35	Normal	—	○	A regular attack.
Tail Glow	Bug	Status	—	—	20	Self	—	—	Raises the user's Sp. Atk by 3.
Tail Slap	Normal	Physical	25	85	10	Normal	—	○	Attacks 2–5 times in a row in a single turn.
Tail Whip	Normal	Status	—	100	30	Many Others	—	—	Lowers the targets' Defense by 1.
Tailwind	Flying	Status	—	—	30	Your Side	—	—	Doubles the Speed of the Pokémon on your side for 4 turns.
Take Down	Normal	Physical	90	85	20	Normal	—	○	The user takes 1/4 of the damage inflicted.
Taunt	Dark	Status	—	100	20	Normal	—	—	Prevents the target from using anything other than attack moves for 3 turns.
Teeter Dance	Normal	Status	—	100	20	Adjacent	—	—	Inflicts the Confused status condition on the targets.
Telekinesis	Psychic	Status	—	—	15	Normal	—	—	Makes the target float for 3 turns. All moves land regardless of their accuracy except for Ground-type moves and one-hit KO moves such as Sheer Cold and Horn Drill.
Teleport	Psychic	Status	—	—	20	Self	—	—	Ends wild Pokémon battles.
Thief	Dark	Physical	40	100	10	Normal	—	○	When the target is holding an item and the user is not, the user can steal that item.
Thrash	Normal	Physical	120	100	10	1 Random	—	○	Attacks consecutively over 2–3 turns. Cannot choose other moves during this time. The user becomes Confused after using this move.
Thunder	Electric	Special	120	70	10	Normal	—	—	A 30% chance of inflicting the Paralysis status condition on the target. Is 100% accurate in the Rain weather condition and 50% accurate in the Sunny weather condition. It hits even Pokémon that are in the sky due to using moves such as Fly and Bounce.
Thunder Fang	Electric	Physical	65	95	15	Normal	—	○	A 10% chance of making the target flinch (unable to use moves on that turn).
Thunder Wave	Electric	Status	—	100	20	Normal	—	—	Inflicts the Paralysis status condition on the target. Does not work on Ground types.
Thunderbolt	Electric	Special	95	100	15	Normal	—	—	A 10% chance of inflicting the Paralysis status condition on the target.
ThunderPunch	Electric	Physical	75	100	15	Normal	—	○	A 10% chance of inflicting the Paralysis status condition on the target.
ThunderShock	Electric	Special	40	100	30	Normal	—	—	A 10% chance of inflicting the Paralysis status condition on the target.
Tickle	Normal	Status	—	100	20	Normal	—	—	Lowers the target's Attack and Defense by 1.
Torment	Dark	Status	—	100	15	Normal	—	—	Makes the target unable to use the same move twice in a row.
Toxic	Poison	Status	—	90	10	Normal	—	—	Inflicts the Badly Poisoned status condition on the target. Damage from being Badly Poisoned increases with every turn.
Toxic Spikes	Poison	Status	—	—	20	Other Side	—	—	Lays a trap of poison spikes on the opposing side that inflict the Poison status condition on Pokémon that switch into battle. Using Toxic Spikes twice inflicts the Badly Poisoned condition. Toxic Spikes' effects end when a Poison-type Pokémon switches into battle. Ineffective against Flying-type Pokémon and Pokémon with the Levitate Ability.
Transform	Normal	Status	—	—	10	Normal	—	—	The user transforms into the target. The user has the same moves and Ability as the target (all moves have 5 PP).
Tri Attack	Normal	Special	80	100	10	Normal	—	—	A 20% chance of inflicting the Paralysis, Burned, or Frozen status condition on the target.
Trick	Psychic	Status	—	100	10	Normal	—	—	Swaps items between the user and the target.
Trick Room	Psychic	Status	—	—	5	Both Sides	—	—	For 5 turns, Pokémon with lower Speed go first. First-strike moves still go first. Self-canceling if used again while Trick Room is still in effect.
Triple Kick	Fighting	Physical	10	90	10	Normal	—	○	Attacks 3 times in a row in a single turn. Power raises from 10 to 20 to 30 as long as it continues to hit.
Trump Card	Normal	Special	—	—	5	Normal	—	○	A sure hit. The move's power increases as its PP decreases.
Twineedle	Bug	Physical	25	100	20	Normal	—	—	Attacks twice in a row in a single turn. A 20% chance of inflicting the Poison status condition on the target.
Twister	Dragon	Special	40	100	20	Many Others	—	—	A 20% chance of making the targets flinch (unable to use moves on that turn). Does twice the damage if the targets are in the sky due to using moves such as Fly or Bounce. Its power is weaker when it hits multiple Pokémon.

Move	Type	Kind	Pow.	Acc.	PP	Range	Long	DA	Effect
Uproar	Normal	Special	90	100	10	1 Random	—	—	The user makes an uproar for 3 turns. During that time, no Pokémon can fall asleep.
U-turn	Bug	Physical	70	100	20	Normal	—	○	After attacking, the user switches out with another Pokémon in the party.

V

Move	Type	Kind	Pow.	Acc.	PP	Range	Long	DA	Effect
Vacuum Wave	Fighting	Special	40	100	30	Normal	—	—	Always strikes first. The user with the higher Speed goes first if similar moves are used.
V-create	Fire	Physical	180	95	5	Normal	—	○	Lowers the user's Defense, Sp. Def, and Speed by 1. If the target is Frozen, it will be thawed.
Venoshock	Poison	Special	65	100	10	Normal	—	—	Does twice the damage to a target that has the Poison or Badly Poisoned status condition.
ViceGrip	Normal	Physical	55	100	30	Normal	—	○	A regular attack.
Vine Whip	Grass	Physical	35	100	15	Normal	—	○	A regular attack.
Vital Throw	Fighting	Physical	70	—	10	Normal	—	○	Always strikes later than normal, but has perfect accuracy.
Volt Switch	Electric	Special	70	100	20	Normal	—	—	After attacking, the user switches out with another Pokémon in the party.
Volt Tackle	Electric	Physical	120	100	15	Normal	—	○	The user takes 1/3 of the damage inflicted. A 10% chance of inflicting the Paralysis status condition on the target.

W

Move	Type	Kind	Pow.	Acc.	PP	Range	Long	DA	Effect
Wake-Up Slap	Fighting	Physical	60	100	10	Normal	—	○	Does twice the usual damage to a sleeping target, but heals that status condition.
Water Gun	Water	Special	40	100	25	Normal	—	—	A regular attack.
Water Pledge	Water	Special	50	100	10	Normal	—	—	When combined with Fire Pledge or Grass Pledge, the power and effect change. If combined with Fire Pledge, the power is 150 and it remains a Water-type move. It will create a rainbow that turn which will last for the next 3 turns, making it more likely that your team's moves will have additional effects. If combined with Grass Pledge, the power is 150 and it becomes a Grass-type move. The surrounding area will become a swamp, which lowers the Speed of opposing Pokémon that turn and the next 3 turns.
Water Pulse	Water	Special	60	100	20	Normal	○	—	A 20% chance of inflicting the Confused status condition on the target.
Water Sport	Water	Status	—	—	15	Both Sides	—	—	The power of Fire-type moves drops to 1/3 of normal as long as the user is in battle.
Water Spout	Water	Special	150	100	5	Many Others	—	—	If the user's HP is low, this move has lower attack power. Its power is weaker when it hits multiple Pokémon.
Waterfall	Water	Physical	80	100	15	Normal	—	○	A 20% chance of making the target flinch (unable to use moves on that turn).
Weather Ball	Normal	Special	50	100	10	Normal	—	—	In special weather conditions, this move's type changes and its attack power doubles. Sunny weather condition: Fire type. Rain weather condition: Water type. Hail weather condition: Ice type. Sandstorm weather condition: Rock type.
Whirlpool	Water	Special	35	85	15	Normal	—	—	Inflicts damage over 4–5 turns. The target cannot flee during that time. Does twice the damage if the target is using Dive when attacked.
Whirlwind	Normal	Status	—	100	20	Normal	—	—	Ends wild Pokémon battles. If the opposing Pokémon's level is higher than the user's, this move fails. In a Double Battle with wild Pokémon, this move fails. In a battle with a Trainer, this move forces the opposing Trainer to switch Pokémon. When there is no Pokémon to switch in, this move fails.
Wide Guard	Rock	Status	—	—	10	Your Side	—	—	Protects from special and physical moves that target multiple Pokémon. If used in succession, its chance of failing rises.
Wild Charge	Electric	Physical	90	100	15	Normal	—	○	The user takes 1/4 of the damage inflicted.
Will-O-Wisp	Fire	Status	—	75	15	Normal	—	—	Inflicts the Burned status condition on the target.
Wing Attack	Flying	Physical	60	100	35	Normal	○	○	A regular attack.
Wish	Normal	Status	—	—	10	Self	—	—	Restores 1/2 of maximum HP at the end of the next turn. Works even if the user has switched out.
Withdraw	Water	Status	—	—	40	Self	—	—	Raises the user's Defense by 1.
Wonder Room	Psychic	Status	—	—	10	Both Sides	—	—	Each Pokémon's Defense and Sp. Def stats are swapped for 5 turns.
Wood Hammer	Grass	Physical	120	100	15	Normal	—	○	The user takes 1/3 of the damage inflicted.
Work Up	Normal	Status	—	—	30	Self	—	—	Raises the user's Attack and Sp. Atk by 1.
Worry Seed	Grass	Status	—	100	10	Normal	—	—	Changes the target's Ability to Insomnia. Fails with certain Abilities, however.
Wrap	Normal	Physical	15	90	20	Normal	—	—	Inflicts damage over 4–5 turns. The target cannot flee during that time.
Wring Out	Normal	Special	—	100	5	Normal	—	○	The more HP the target has left, the greater the attack's power (max 120).

XYZ

Move	Type	Kind	Pow.	Acc.	PP	Range	Long	DA	Effect
X-Scissor	Bug	Physical	80	100	15	Normal	—	○	A regular attack.
Yawn	Normal	Status	—	—	10	Normal	—	—	Inflicts the Sleep status condition on the target at the end of the next turn unless the target switches out.
Zap Cannon	Electric	Special	120	50	5	Normal	—	—	Inflicts the Paralysis status condition on the target.
Zen Headbutt	Psychic	Physical	80	90	15	Normal	—	○	A 20% chance of making the target flinch (unable to use moves on that turn).

Field Moves

Move	Field Moves
Chatter	You can record your voice. It's played in battle.
Cut	Cuts down small trees so your party may pass.
Dig	Pulls you out of spaces like caves, returning you to the last entrance you went through.
Dive	In patches of darker water, you can dive to the bottom to explore the seafloor.
Flash	Illuminates dark caves.
Fly	Whisks you instantly to a town or city you've visited before.
Milk Drink	Distributes part of the user's own HP among teammates.
Softboiled	Distributes part of the user's own HP among teammates.
Strength	Moves large rocks and pushes them into holes to create a new path.
Surf	Allows you to move across water.
Sweet Scent	Attracts wild Pokémon and makes them appear.
Teleport	Transports you to the last Pokémon Center you used (cannot be used in caves or similar places).
Waterfall	Allows you to climb up and down waterfalls.

Pokémon Moves

Where to find TMs and HMs and learn other moves

How to obtain TMs

No.	Move	How to obtain	Price
1	Hone Claws	Victory Road	—
2	Dragon Claw	Dragonspiral Tower	—
3	Psyshock	Giant Chasm Crater Forest	—
4	Calm Mind	Striaton City Poké Mart	80,000
5	Roar	Route 23	—
6	Toxic	Seaside Cave	—
7	Hail	Mistralton City Poké Mart	50,000
8	Bulk Up	Striaton City Poké Mart	80,000
9	Venoshock	Defeat Roxie at the Virbank City Pokémon Gym	—
10	Hidden Power	Receive for 18 BP at the Battle Subway or the Pokémon World Tournament	—
11	Sunny Day	Mistralton City Poké Mart	50,000
12	Taunt	Route 23	—
13	Ice Beam	Giant Chasm	—
14	Blizzard	Mistralton City Poké Mart	70,000
15	Hyper Beam	Shopping Mall 2F on Route 9	90,000
16	Light Screen	Nimbasa City Poké Mart	30,000
17	Protect	Receive for 6 BP at the Battle Subway or the Pokémon World Tournament	—
18	Rain Dance	Mistralton City Poké Mart	50,000
19	Telekinesis	Route 18	—
20	Safeguard	Receive for 6 BP at the Battle Subway or the Pokémon World Tournament	—
21	Frustration	From a Team Plasma Grunt at Floccesy Ranch	—
22	SolarBeam	Pinwheel Forest	—
23	Smack Down	Receive for 18 BP at the Battle Subway or the Pokémon World Tournament	—
24	Thunderbolt	From your rival on Victory Road (after you defeat him for the fifth time)	—
25	Thunder	Lacunosa Town Poké Mart	70,000
26	Earthquake	Route 15	—
27	Return	From Bianca in Aspertia City (after obtaining the Aspertia City Gym Badge)	—
28	Dig	Route 4	—
29	Psychic	Route 13	—
30	Shadow Ball	Reversal Mountain	—
31	Brick Break	Receive for 12 BP at the Battle Subway or the Pokémon World Tournament	—
32	Double Team	Receive for 6 BP at the Battle Subway or the Pokémon World Tournament	—
33	Reflect	Nimbasa City Poké Mart	30,000
34	Sludge Wave	Receive for 24 BP at the Battle Subway or the Pokémon World Tournament	—
35	Flamethrower	From an old man in a house on Route 23	—
36	Sludge Bomb	Route 8	—
37	Sandstorm	Mistralton City Poké Mart	50,000
38	Fire Blast	Lacunosa Town Poké Mart	70,000
39	Rock Tomb	Relic Castle	—
40	Aerial Ace	Talk to a boy in a house in Mistralton City and you'll find it in the field to the south of the runway (after obtaining the Mistralton City Gym Badge)	—
41	Torment	Castelia Sewers (spring and summer only)	—
42	Facade	From a Parasol Lady in the gate between the Marine Tube and Humilau City	—
43	Flame Charge	From a Battle Girl on the Tubeline Bridge	—
44	Rest	From a Guitarist in Castelia City	—
45	Attract	From a girl in Castelia City	—
46	Thief	Virbank Complex	—
47	Low Sweep	Wellspring Cave	—
48	Round	Receive for 18 BP at the Battle Subway or the Pokémon World Tournament	—
49	Echoed Voice	From a woman in the Musical Theater in Nimbasa City	—
50	Overheat	N's Castle	—
51	Ally Switch	Receive for 24 BP at the Battle Subway or the Pokémon World Tournament	—
52	Focus Blast	Wellspring Cave	—
53	Energy Ball	Aspertia City	—
54	False Swipe	From a man in Reversal Mountain (after completing the Reversal Mountain Habitat List)	—
55	Scald	Defeat Marlon at the Humilau City Pokémon Gym	—
56	Fling	Route 6	—
57	Charge Beam	From a Battle Girl in a house in Lentimas Town	—
58	Sky Drop	Mistralton City	—
59	Incinerate	Receive for 6 BP at the Battle Subway or the Pokémon World Tournament	—
60	Quash	Receive for 24 BP at the Battle Subway or the Pokémon World Tournament	—
61	Will-O-Wisp	Celestial Tower	—
62	Acrobatics	Defeat Skyla at the Mistralton City Pokémon Gym	—
63	Embargo	Driftveil City	—
64	Explosion	Receive for 24 BP at the Battle Subway or the Pokémon World Tournament	—
65	Shadow Claw	Celestial Tower	—
66	Payback	Route 16	—
67	Retaliate	Plasma Frigate	—
68	Giga Impact	Shopping Mall 2F on Route 9	90,000
69	Rock Polish	Reversal Mountain	—
70	Flash	From a man with sunglasses in Castelia City	—
71	Stone Edge	Twist Mountain	—
72	Volt Switch	Defeat Elesa at the Nimbasa City Pokémon Gym	—
73	Thunder Wave	Nimbasa City Poké Mart	10,000
74	Gyro Ball	Nimbasa City Poké Mart	10,000
75	Swords Dance	Receive for 18 BP at the Battle Subway or the Pokémon World Tournament	—
76	Struggle Bug	Defeat Burgh at the Castelia City Pokémon Gym	—
77	Psych Up	Receive for 24 BP at the Battle Subway or the Pokémon World Tournament	—
78	Bulldoze	Defeat Clay at the Driftveil City Pokémon Gym	—
79	Frost Breath	Receive for 12 BP at the Battle Subway or the Pokémon World Tournament	—
80	Rock Slide	Mistralton Cave	—
81	X-Scissor	Route 7	—
82	Dragon Tail	Defeat Drayden at the Opelucid City Pokémon Gym	—
83	Work Up	Defeat Cheren at the Aspertia City Pokémon Gym	—
84	Poison Jab	Moor of Icirrus	—
85	Dream Eater	Dreamyard	—
86	Grass Knot	Pinwheel Forest	—
87	Swagger	Receive for 18 BP at the Battle Subway or the Pokémon World Tournament	—
88	Pluck	Receive for 18 BP at the Battle Subway or the Pokémon World Tournament	—
89	U-turn	Receive for 12 BP at the Battle Subway or the Pokémon World Tournament	—
90	Substitute	Twist Mountain	—
91	Flash Cannon	Twist Mountain Outside	—
92	Trick Room	Abundant Shrine	—
93	Wild Charge	Victory Road	—
94	Rock Smash	From a man in Virbank Complex (after defeating three Workers)	—
95	Snarl	From a Backpacker in Lostlorn Forest	—

How to obtain HMs

No.	Move	How to obtain	Price
1	Cut	From Roxie in Virbank City (after defeating Team Plasma Grunts)	—
2	Fly	From Bianca on Route 5	—
3	Surf	From Cheren on Route 6	—
4	Strength	From your rival in the Castelia Sewers (after defeating Team Plasma Grunts)	—
5	Waterfall	From N on Victory Road	—
6	Dive	From your rival in Undella Town (after the Hall of Fame)	—

Moves taught in exchange for Shards

■ Moves taught by the master Move Tutor in Driftveil City in exchange for Red Shards

Move	No. of Red Shards needed
Bounce	4
Bug Bite	2
Covet	2
Drill Run	4
Dual Chop	6
Fire Punch	10
Gunk Shot	8
Ice Punch	10
Iron Head	4
Low Kick	8
Seed Bomb	6
Signal Beam	4
Super Fang	6
ThunderPunch	10
Uproar	6

■ Moves taught by the master Move Tutor in Lentimas Town in exchange for Blue Shards

Move	No. of Blue Shards needed
Aqua Tail	8
Block	6
Dark Pulse	10
Dragon Pulse	10
Earth Power	8
Electroweb	6
Foul Play	8
Gravity	10
Hyper Voice	6
Icy Wind	6
Iron Defense	2
Iron Tail	6
Last Resort	2
Magic Coat	4
Magnet Rise	4
Superpower	10
Zen Headbutt	8

■ Moves taught by the master Move Tutor in Humilau City in exchange for Yellow Shards

Move	No. of Yellow Shards needed
Bind	2
Drain Punch	10
Giga Drain	10
Heal Bell	4
Heat Wave	10
Knock Off	4
Pain Split	10
Role Play	8
Roost	6
Sky Attack	8
Snore	2
Synthesis	6
Tailwind	10
ThunderPunch	10

■ Moves taught by the master Move Tutor in Nacrene City in exchange for Green Shards

Move	No. of Green Shards needed
After You	8
Endeavor	12
Gastro Acid	6
Helping Hand	8
Magic Room	8
Outrage	10
Recycle	10
Skill Swap	12
Sleep Talk	12
Snatch	12
Spite	8
Stealth Rock	10
Trick	10
Wonder Room	8
Worry Seed	6

Moves taught by other people

Move	How to obtain
Blast Burn	Pokémon World Tournament (PWT)
Draco Meteor	Drayden's house in Opelucid City (talk to Drayden after the Hall of Fame)
Fire Pledge	Pokémon World Tournament (PWT)
Frenzy Plant	Pokémon World Tournament (PWT)
Grass Pledge	Pokémon World Tournament (PWT)
Hydro Cannon	Pokémon World Tournament (PWT)
Water Pledge	Pokémon World Tournament (PWT)

Pokémon Abilities

Ability	Effect in battle	Effect when the Pokémon is the lead in your party
Adaptability	Increases the power boost received by using a move of same type as the Pokémon.	—
Aftermath	Knocks off 1/4 of the attacking Pokémon's HP when a direct attack causes the Pokémon to faint.	—
Air Lock	Eliminates effects of weather on Pokémon.	—
Analytic	The power of its move is increased by 30% when the Pokémon moves last.	—
Anger Point	Raises the Pokémon's Attack to the maximum when hit by a critical hit.	—
Anticipation	Warns if your foe's Pokémon has supereffective moves or one-hit KO moves.	—
Arena Trap	Prevents the foe's Pokémon from fleeing or switching out. Ineffective against Flying-type Pokémon and Pokémon with the Levitate Ability.	It makes it easier to encounter wild Pokémon.

Ability	Effect in battle	Effect when the Pokémon is the lead in your party
Bad Dreams	Slightly lowers the HP of sleeping Pokémon every turn.	—
Battle Armor	Opposing Pokémon's moves will not hit critically.	—
Big Pecks	Prevents Defense from being lowered.	—
Blaze	Raises the power of Fire-type moves by 50% when the Pokémon's HP drops to 1/3 or less.	—

Ability	Effect in battle	Effect when the Pokémon is the lead in your party
Chlorophyll	Double Speed in the Sunny weather condition.	—
Clear Body	Protects against stat-lowering moves and Abilities.	—
Cloud Nine	Eliminates effects of weather on Pokémon.	—
Color Change	Changes the Pokémon's type into the type of the move that just hit it.	—
Compoundeyes	Raises accuracy by 30%.	Raises encounter rate with wild Pokémon holding items.
Contrary	Makes stat changes have an opposite effect (increase instead of decrease and vice versa).	—
Cursed Body	A 30% chance of inflicting Disable on the move the opponent used to hit the Pokémon.	—
Cute Charm	A 30% chance of inflicting the Infatuated condition when hit with a direct attack.	Raises encounter rate of wild Pokémon of the opposite gender.

Ability	Effect in battle	Effect when the Pokémon is the lead in your party
Damp	Pokémon on neither side can use Selfdestruct and Explosion. Nullifies the Aftermath Ability.	—
Defeatist	The Pokémon's Attack and Sp. Atk gets halved when HP becomes half or less.	—
Defiant	When an opponent's move or Ability lowers the Pokémon's stats, the Pokémon's Attack rises by 2.	—
Download	When the Pokémon enters battle, this Ability raises its Attack by 1 if the foe's Pokémon's Defense is lower than its Sp. Def, and raises it's Sp. Atk by 1 if the foe's Pokémon's Sp. Def is lower than its Defense.	—
Drizzle	Makes the weather Rain when the Pokémon enters battle.	—
Drought	Makes the weather Sunny when the Pokémon enters battle.	—
Dry Skin	Restores HP when the Pokémon is hit by a Water-type move. Restores HP in the Rain weather condition. However, the Pokémon receives increased damage from Fire-type moves. Takes damage every turn when in the Sunny weather condition.	—

Ability	Effect in battle	Effect when the Pokémon is the lead in your party
Early Bird	The Pokémon wakes quickly from the Sleep status condition.	—
Effect Spore	A 30% chance of inflicting the Poison, Paralysis, or Sleep status conditions when hit with a direct attack.	—

Ability	Effect in battle	Effect when the Pokémon is the lead in your party
Filter	Minimizes the damage received from supereffective moves.	—
Flame Body	A 30% chance of inflicting the Burned status condition when hit with a direct attack.	Facilitates hatching Eggs in your party.
Flare Boost	Increases the power of special moves by 50% when Burned.	—
Flash Fire	When the Pokémon is hit by a Fire-type move, its Fire-type moves increase Power by 50% rather than taking damage.	—
Flower Gift	Raises Attack and Sp. Def of the Pokémon in the Sunny weather condition.	—
Forecast	Changes Castform's form and type. Sunny weather condition: changes to Fire type. Rain weather condition: changes to Water type. Hail weather condition: changes to Ice type.	—
Forewarn	Reveals a move an opponent knows when the Pokémon enters battle. Damaging moves with high power are prioritized.	—
Friend Guard	Reduces damage done to allies by 25%.	—
Frisk	Checks an opponent's held item when the Pokémon enters battle.	—

Ability	Effect in battle	Effect when the Pokémon is the lead in your party
Gluttony	Allows the Pokémon to use its held Berry sooner when it has low HP.	—
Guts	Attack stat rises by 50% when the Pokémon is affected by a status condition.	—

Ability	Effect in battle	Effect when the Pokémon is the lead in your party
Harvest	A 50% chance of restoring the Berry the Pokémon used at turn end and 100% chance when the weather condition is Sunny.	—
Healer	A 33% chance every turn that an ally Pokémon's status condition will be healed.	—
Heatproof	Halves damage from Fire-type moves and from the Burned status condition.	—
Heavy Metal	Doubles the Pokémon's weight.	—
Honey Gather	If the Pokémon isn't holding an item, it will sometimes be left holding Honey after a battle (even if it didn't participate). Its chance of finding Honey increases with its level.	—
Huge Power	Doubles the Pokémon's Attack.	—
Hustle	Raises Attack by 50%, but lowers the accuracy of the Pokémon's physical moves by 20%.	Lowers encounter rate with high-level wild Pokémon.
Hydration	Cures status conditions at the end of the turn in the Rain weather condition.	—
Hyper Cutter	Prevents Attack from being lowered.	—

Ability	Effect in battle	Effect when the Pokémon is the lead in your party
Ice Body	Gradually restores HP in the Hail weather condition instead of taking damage.	—
Illuminate	No effect.	It makes it easier to encounter wild Pokémon.
Illusion	Appears in battle disguised as the last Pokémon in the party.	—
Immunity	Protects against the Poison status condition.	—
Imposter	Transforms itself into the Pokémon it is facing as it enters battle.	—
Infiltrator	Moves can hit even if the target used Reflect, Light Screen, Safeguard, or Mist.	—
Inner Focus	The Pokémon doesn't flinch by additional effect of a move.	—
Insomnia	Protects against the Sleep status condition.	—
Intimidate	Lowers opponents' Attack by 1 when the Pokémon enters battle.	Lowers encounter rate with low-level wild Pokémon.
Iron Barbs	Slightly reduces the HP of an opponent that hits the Pokémon with a direct attack.	—
Iron Fist	Increases the power of Ice Punch, Fire Punch, ThunderPunch, Mach Punch, Mega Punch, Comet Punch, Bullet Punch, Sky Uppercut, Drain Punch, Focus Punch, Dizzy Punch, DynamicPunch, Hammer Arm, Meteor Mash, and Shadow Punch.	—

Ability	Effect in battle	Effect when the Pokémon is the lead in your party
Justified	When the Pokémon is hit by a Dark-type move, Attack goes up by 1.	—

Ability	Effect in battle	Effect when the Pokémon is the lead in your party
Keen Eye	Prevents accuracy from being lowered.	Lowers encounter rate with low-level wild Pokémon.
Klutz	The Pokémon's held items have no effect.	—

Ability	Effect in battle	Effect when the Pokémon is the lead in your party
Leaf Guard	Protects the Pokémon from status conditions when in the Sunny weather condition.	—
Levitate	Gives full immunity to all Ground-type moves.	—
Light Metal	Halves the Pokémon's weight.	—
Lightningrod	Draws all Electric-type moves to the Pokémon. When the Pokémon is hit by an Electric-type move, Sp. Atk goes up by 1 rather than taking damage.	—
Limber	Protects against the Paralysis status condition.	—
Liquid Ooze	When an opposing Pokémon uses an HP-draining move, it damages the user instead.	—

Ability	Effect in battle	Effect when the Pokémon is the lead in your party
Magic Bounce	Reflects status moves.	—
Magic Guard	The Pokémon will not take damage from anything other than a direct attack. Nullifies the Liquid Ooze, Aftermath, Rough Skin, and Iron Barbs Abilities, the Sandstorm and Hail weather conditions, as well as status conditions such as Poison, Badly Poisoned, Burned, Nightmare, Curse, Leech Seed, Bind, Sand Tomb, Fire Spin, Clamp, and Magma Storm. The effects of Stealth Rock, Spikes, Wrap, Flame Burst, and Fire Pledge are negated as are the item effects from Black Sludge, Sticky Barb, Life Orb, and Rocky Helmet. The Pokémon also receives no recoil or move-failure damage from attacks.	—
Magma Armor	Prevents the Frozen status condition.	Facilitates hatching Eggs in your party.
Magnet Pull	Prevents Steel-type Pokémon from fleeing or switching out.	Raises encounter rate with wild Steel-type Pokémon.
Marvel Scale	Defense stat increases by 50% when the Pokémon is affected by a status condition.	—
Minus	Raises Sp. Atk by 50% when another ally has the Ability Plus or Minus.	—
Mold Breaker	Use moves on targets regardless of their Abilities. Does not nullify Abilities that have effects after an attack. For example, the Pokémon can score a critical hit against the target with Battle Armor, but it will still take damage from Rough Skin.	—
Moody	Raises one stat by 2 and lowers another by 1 at turn end.	—
Motor Drive	When the Pokémon is hit by an Electric-type move, Speed goes up by 1 rather than taking damage.	—
Moxie	When the Pokémon knocks out an opponent with a move, Attack goes up 1.	—
Multiscale	Halves damage when HP is full.	—
Multitype	Type changes according to the Plate Arceus is holding.	—
Mummy	Changes the Ability of the opponent that hits the Pokémon with a direct attack to Mummy.	—

Ability	Effect in battle	Effect when the Pokémon is the lead in your party
Natural Cure	Cures the Pokémon's status conditions when it switches out.	—
No Guard	Moves used by or against the Pokémon always strike their targets.	It makes it easier to encounter wild Pokémon.
Normalize	All of the Pokémon's moves become Normal-type moves.	—

Ability	Effect in battle	Effect when the Pokémon is the lead in your party
Oblivious	Protects against the Infatuated status condition.	—
Overcoat	Protects the Pokémon from weather damage, such as Sandstorm and Hail.	—
Overgrow	Raises the power of Grass-type moves by 50% when the Pokémon's HP drops to 1/3 or less.	—
Own Tempo	Protects against the Confused status condition.	—

Ability	Effect in battle	Effect when the Pokémon is the lead in your party
Pickpocket	Steals an item when hit with a direct attack. It fails if the user is already holding an item.	—
Pickup	Picks up the item the foe's Pokémon used that turn at the end of the turn. Fails if the user is already holding an item.	If the Pokémon has no held item, it sometimes picks one up after battle (even if it didn't participate). It picks up different items depending on its level.
Plus	Raises Sp. Atk by 50% when another ally has the Ability Plus or Minus.	—
Poison Heal	Restores HP every turn if the Pokémon has the Poison status condition.	—

Pokémon Abilities

 P

Ability	Effect in battle	Effect when the Pokémon is the lead in your party
Poison Point	A 30% chance of inflicting the Poison status condition when hit with a direct attack.	—
Poison Touch	A 30% chance of inflicting the Poison status condition when the Pokémon uses a direct attack.	—
Prankster	Gives priority to status moves.	—
Pressure	When the Pokémon is hit by an opponent's move, it depletes 1 additional PP from that move.	Lowers encounter rate with high-level wild Pokémon.
Pure Power	Doubles the Pokémon's Attack.	—

Q

Ability	Effect in battle	Effect when the Pokémon is the lead in your party
Quick Feet	Increases Speed by 50% when the Pokémon is affected with status conditions.	Lowers wild Pokémon encounter rate.

R

Ability	Effect in battle	Effect when the Pokémon is the lead in your party
Rain Dish	Gradually restores HP in the Rain weather condition.	—
Rattled	When the Pokémon is hit by a Ghost-, Dark-, or Bug-type move, Speed goes up by 1.	—
Reckless	Raises the power of moves with recoil damage.	—
Regenerator	Restores 1/3 its HP when withdrawn from battle.	—
Rivalry	If the target is the same gender, the Pokémon's Attack goes up. If the target is of the opposite gender, its Attack goes down. No effect when the gender is unknown.	—
Rock Head	No recoil damage from moves like Take Down and Double-Edge.	—
Rough Skin	Slightly reduces the HP of an opponent that hits the Pokémon with a direct attack.	—
Run Away	The Pokémon can always escape from a battle with a wild Pokémon .	—

S

Ability	Effect in battle	Effect when the Pokémon is the lead in your party
Sand Force	Raises the power of Ground-, Rock-, and Steel-type moves by 30% in the Sandstorm weather condition. Sandstorm does not damage the Pokémon.	—
Sand Rush	Doubles Speed in the Sandstorm weather condition. Sandstorm does not damage the Pokémon.	—
Sand Stream	Makes the weather Sandstorm when the Pokémon enters battle.	Lowers encounter rate with wild Pokémon in the Sandstorm weather condition.
Sand Veil	Raises evasion in the Sandstorm weather condition. Sandstorm does not damage the Pokémon.	
Sap Sipper	When the Pokémon is hit by a Grass-type move, Attack goes up by 1 rather than taking damage.	—
Scrappy	Allows the Pokémon to hit Ghost-type Pokémon with Normal- and Fighting-type moves.	—
Serene Grace	Doubles chances of moves inflicting additional effects.	—
Shadow Tag	Prevents the opposing Pokémon from fleeing or switching out. If both your and the opposing Pokémon have this Ability, the effect is cancelled.	—
Shed Skin	A 33% chance every turn of curing the Pokémon's status conditions.	—
Sheer Force	When moves with an additional effect are used, power increases by 30%, but the additional effect is lost.	—
Shell Armor	Opposing Pokémon's moves will not hit critically.	—
Shield Dust	Protects the Pokémon from additional effects of moves.	—
Simple	The effects of stat changes become more powerful.	—
Skill Link	Moves that strike successively strike the maximum number of times (2–5 times means it always strikes 5 times).	—
Slow Start	Halves Attack and Speed for 5 turns after the Pokémon enters battle.	—
Sniper	Moves that deliver a critical hit deal a great amount of damage.	—
Snow Cloak	Raises evasion in the Hail weather condition. Hail does not damage the Pokémon.	Lowers encounter rate with wild Pokémon in the Hail weather condition.
Snow Warning	Makes the weather Hail when the Pokémon enters battle.	—
Solar Power	Raises Sp. Atk by 50%, but takes damage every turn in the Sunny weather condition.	—
Solid Rock	Minimizes the damage received from supereffective moves.	—
Soundproof	Protects the Pokémon from sound-based moves: Snore, Heal Bell, Screech, Sing, Chatter, Metal Sound, GrassWhistle, Uproar, Supersonic, Growl, Hyper Voice, Roar, Perish Song, Bug Buzz, Round, and Echoed Voice.	—
Speed Boost	Raises Speed by 1 every turn.	—
Stall	The Pokémon's moves are used last in the turn.	—
Static	A 30% chance of inflicting the Paralysis status condition when hit with a direct attack.	Raises encounter rate with wild Electric-type Pokémon.
Steadfast	Raises Speed by 1 every time the Pokémon flinches.	—
Stench	A 10% chance of making the target flinch when the Pokémon uses a move to deal damage.	Lowers wild Pokémon encounter rate.
Sticky Hold	The Pokémon's held item cannot be stolen.	Makes Pokémon bite more often when fishing.
Storm Drain	Draws all Water-type moves to the Pokémon. When the Pokémon is hit by an Water-type move, Sp. Atk goes up by 1 rather than taking damage.	—
Sturdy	Protects the Pokémon against one-hit KO moves like Horn Drill and Sheer Cold. Leaves the Pokémon with 1 HP if hit by a move that would knock it out when its HP is full.	—
Suction Cups	Nullifies moves like Whirlwind, Roar, and Dragon Tail, which would force Pokémon to switch out.	Makes Pokémon bite more often when fishing.
Super Luck	Heightens the critical-hit ratio of the Pokémon's moves.	—
Swarm	Raises the power of Bug-type moves by 50% when the Pokémon's HP drops to 1/3 or less.	—
Swift Swim	Doubles Speed in the Rain weather condition.	—
Synchronize	When the Pokémon receives the Poison, Paralysis, or Burned status condition, this inflicts the same condition.	Raises encounter rate with wild Pokémon with the same Nature.

T

Ability	Effect in battle	Effect when the Pokémon is the lead in your party
Tangled Feet	Raises evasion when the Pokémon has the Confused status condition.	—
Technician	If the move's power is 60 or less, its power will increase by 50%. Also takes effect if a move's power is altered by itself or by another move.	—
Telepathy	Prevents damage from allies.	—
Teravolt	Use moves on targets regardless of their Abilities. Does not nullify Abilities that have effects after an attack. For example, the Pokémon can score a critical hit against the target with Battle Armor, but it will still take damage from Rough Skin.	—
Thick Fat	Halves damage from Fire- and Ice-type moves.	—
Tinted Lens	Nullifies the type disadvantage of the Pokémon's not-very-effective moves: 1/2 damage turns into regular damage, 1/4 damage turns into 1/2 damage.	—

518

T

Ability	Effect in battle	Effect when the Pokémon is the lead in your party
Torrent	Raises the power of Water-type moves by 50% when the Pokémon's HP drops to 1/3 or less.	—
Toxic Boost	Increases the power of physical moves by 50% when it has the Poison status condition.	—
Trace	Makes the Pokémon's Ability the same as the opponent's, except for certain Abilities like Forecast and Trace.	—
Truant	The Pokémon can use a move only once every other turn.	—
Turboblaze	Use moves on targets regardless of their Abilities. Does not nullify Abilities that have effects after an attack. For example, the Pokémon can score a critical hit against the target with Battle Armor, but it will still take damage from Rough Skin.	—

U

Ability	Effect in battle	Effect when the Pokémon is the lead in your party
Unaware	Ignores the stat changes of the opposing Pokémon, except Speed.	—
Unburden	Doubles Speed if the Pokémon loses or consumes a held item. Its Speed returns to normal if the Pokémon holds another item. No effect if the Pokémon starts out with no held item.	—
Unnerve	Prevent the opposing Pokémon from eating Berries.	—

V

Ability	Effect in battle	Effect when the Pokémon is the lead in your party
Victory Star	The accuracy of its allies and itself is 10% higher.	—
Vital Spirit	Protects against the Sleep status condition.	Lowers encounter rate with high-level wild Pokémon.
Volt Absorb	When the Pokémon is hit by an Electric-type move, HP is restored rather than taking damage.	—

W

Ability	Effect in battle	Effect when the Pokémon is the lead in your party
Water Absorb	When the Pokémon is hit by a Water-type move, HP is restored rather than taking damage.	—
Water Veil	Prevents the Burned status condition.	—
Weak Armor	When the Pokémon is hit by a physical attack, Defense goes down 1, but Speed goes up 1.	—
White Smoke	Protects against stat-lowering moves and Abilities.	Lowers wild Pokémon encounter rate.
Wonder Guard	Protects the Pokémon against all moves except supereffective ones.	—
Wonder Skin	Makes status moves more likely to miss.	—

Z

Ability	Effect in battle	Effect when the Pokémon is the lead in your party
Zen Mode	When over half its HP is lost, it changes form.	—

Items picked up with the Pickup Ability

Item	Low									Lv. 100
Potion	◎									
Antidote	○	◎								
Super Potion	○	○	◎							
Great Ball	○	○	○	◎						
Repel	○	○	○	○	◎					
Escape Rope	○	○	○	○	○	◎				
Full Heal	○	○	○	○	○	○	◎			
Hyper Potion	○	○	○	○	○	○	○	◎		
Ultra Ball	△	△	○	○	○	○	○	○	◎	
Revive		△	△	○	○	○	○	○	○	◎
Rare Candy			△	△	○	○	○	○	○	○
Sun Stone				△	△	○	○	○	○	○
Moon Stone					△	△	○	○	○	○
Heart Scale						△	△	○	○	○
Full Restore			▲	▲			△	△	○	○
Max Revive								△	△	○
PP Up									△	△
Max Elixir										△
Nugget	▲	▲								
King's Rock		▲	▲							
Ether					▲	▲				
Iron Ball						▲	▲			
Prism Scale							▲	▲	▲	▲
Elixir								▲	▲	
Leftovers									▲	▲

◎ Often found ○ Sometimes found △ Rarely found ▲ Almost never found

Pokémon Natures and Characteristics

Pokémon's Natures

Each individual Pokémon has a Nature, which affects how its stats grow when it levels up.

Pokémon's stats	ATTACK	DEFENSE	SPEED	SP. ATK	SP. DEF
Adamant	○			▲	
Bashful					
Bold	▲	○			
Brave	○		▲		
Calm	▲				○
Careful				▲	○
Docile					
Gentle		▲			○
Hardy					
Hasty		▲	○		
Impish		○		▲	
Jolly			○	▲	
Lax		○			▲
Lonely	○	▲			
Mild		▲		○	
Modest	▲			○	
Naive			○		▲
Naughty	○				▲
Quiet			▲	○	
Quirky					
Rash				○	▲
Relaxed		○	▲		
Sassy			▲		○
Serious					
Timid	▲		○		

○ Gains more upon leveling up
▲ Gains less upon leveling up

Pokémon's Characteristics

On top of having a Nature, each individual Pokémon has a Characteristic. This also affects how the Pokémon's stats grow when it levels up.

Stat that grows easily	Characteristic
HP	Loves to eat.
	Often dozes off.
	Often scatters things.
	Scatters things often.
	Likes to relax.

Stat that grows easily	Characteristic
ATTACK	Proud of its power.
	Likes to thrash about.
	A little quick tempered.
	Likes to fight.
	Quick tempered.

Stat that grows easily	Characteristic
DEFENSE	Sturdy body.
	Capable of taking hits.
	Highly persistent.
	Good endurance.
	Good perseverance.

Stat that grows easily	Characteristic
SPEED	Likes to run.
	Alert to sounds.
	Impetuous and silly.
	Somewhat of a clown.
	Quick to flee.

Stat that grows easily	Characteristic
SP. ATK	Highly curious.
	Mischievous.
	Thoroughly cunning.
	Often lost in thought.
	Very finicky.

Stat that grows easily	Characteristic
SP. DEF	Strong willed.
	Somewhat vain.
	Strongly defiant.
	Hates to lose.
	Somewhat stubborn.

Items

A

Item	Explanation	Main Ways to Obtain	Price
Absorb Bulb	Raises the holder's Sp. Atk by 1 when it is hit by a Water-type move. Goes away after use.	Exchange for 16 BP at the PWT or Battle Subway / Very rarely held by wild Roselia	—
Adamant Orb	When held by Dialga, it raises the power of Dragon- and Steel-type moves.	Dragonspiral Tower	—
Air Balloon	The holder floats and Ground-type moves will no longer hit the holder. The balloon pops when the holder is hit by an attack.	From the old man on 25F in Driftveil City's Driftveil Chateau Hotel / Exchange for 12 BP at the PWT or Battle Subway	—
Amulet Coin	Doubles prize money from a battle if the holding Pokémon joins in.	From a man on the first floor of a building in Castelia City	—
Antidote	Cures the Poison status condition.	Poké Mart (after obtaining one Gym Badge) / Route 9 Shopping Mall 1F	100
Armor Fossil	A Pokémon Fossil. When restored, it becomes Shieldon.	Receive from the Worker in Twist Mountain / Join Avenue Antique Shop (when the owner is from Pokémon Black Version or Pokémon Black Version 2)	300
Awakening	Cures the Sleep status condition.	Poké Mart (after obtaining one Gym Badge) / Route 9 Shopping Mall 1F	250

B

Item	Explanation	Main Ways to Obtain	Price
BalmMushroom	A fragrant mushroom. Can be sold to the Maid on Route 5 for 25,000.	Very rarely held by wild Foongus and Amoonguss / From a man in a house in Accumula Town	—
Berry Juice	Restores the HP of one Pokémon by 20 points.	Undella Town / Held by wild Shuckle / Battle all three Trainers on the Royal Unova (Tuesday)	—
Big Mushroom	A big mushroom. Can be sold to the Poké Mart for 2,500. Can be sold to the Maid on Route 5 for 5,000.	Sometimes held by wild Foongus and Amoonguss / Prize for the correct answer in the Pansage, Pansear, or Panpour Show in Striaton City / Join Avenue Antique Shop	350
Big Nugget	A big nugget of pure gold. Can be sold to the old gentleman in Icirrus City for 30,000.	From the man in Chargestone Cave / Twist Mountain (winter) / Route 3 / Nature Preserve / Very rarely held by wild Garbodor	500 ◆
Big Pearl	A big pearl. Can be sold to the Poké Mart for 3,750. Can be sold to the old gentleman in Icirrus City for 7,500.	Relic Passage / Route 14 / Village Bridge / Sometimes held by wild Shellder and Cloyster	350 ◆
Big Root	Increases the amount of HP recovered when the holder uses an HP-draining move by 30%.	From the man on 25F of Driftveil City's Driftveil Continental Hotel	—
Binding Band	Doubles the damage done every turn by moves like Bind or Wrap when held.	Exchange for 8 BP at the PWT or Battle Subway	—
Black Belt	When held by a Pokémon, it boosts the power of Fighting-type moves.	From the woman in Icirrus City's Pokémon Center / Sometimes held by wild Throh and Sawk	—
Black Flute	A glass flute. Can be sold to the billionaire in Undella Town for 8,000.	From the sunglasses-wearing man on Route 13	—
Black Sludge	If the holder is a Poison-type Pokémon, it restores HP during battle. If the holder is any other type, it reduces HP during battle instead.	Castelia Sewers (spring, summer) / Sometimes held by wild Grimer and Trubbish, often held by Muk and Garbodor	—
BlackGlasses	When held by a Pokémon, it boosts the power of Dark-type moves.	Castelia City Back Street (spring, summer)	—
Blue Flute	A glass flute. Can be sold to the billionaire in Undella Town for 7,000.	From the sunglasses-wearing man on Route 13	—
Blue Shard	Give to the master Move Tutor in Lentimas Town to have him teach your Pokémon moves.	Desert Resort / Mistralton Cave / Village Bridge / Route 13 / Route 17	500 ◆
BrightPowder	Lowers the accuracy of the holder's opponents.	Route 4 (Pokémon White Version 2) / From the girl in Anville Town (when you talk to her after finding her lost Pansage in Nimbasa City)	—
Bug Gem	When held by a Pokémon, it boosts the power of a Bug-type move by 50% one time. Goes away after use.	Found in dust clouds inside caves	—
Burn Drive	A cassette to be held by Genesect. It changes Techno Blast to a Fire-type move.	Visit P2 Laboratory with Genesect in your party and defeat a Scientist in a Pokémon battle (Pokémon Black Version 2).	—
Burn Heal	Cures the Burned status condition.	Poké Mart (after obtaining one Gym Badge) / Route 9 Shopping Mall 1F	250

C

Item	Explanation	Main Ways to Obtain	Price
Calcium	Raises the base Sp. Atk stat of a Pokémon.	Route 9 Shopping Mall 3F / Exchange for 1 BP at the PWT or Battle Subway	9,800
Carbos	Raises the base Speed stat of a Pokémon.	Route 9 Shopping Mall 3F / Exchange for 1 BP at the PWT or Battle Subway	9,800
Casteliacone	Castelia City's famous ice cream. Cures all status conditions.	Castelia City's Casteliacone shop	100
Cell Battery	When the holder is hit by an Electric-type move, Attack goes up by 1. Goes away after use.	Exchange for 16 BP at the PWT or Battle Subway	—
Charcoal	When held by a Pokémon, it boosts the power of Fire-type moves.	Castelia City / From the woman on 1F of Castelia City's Battle Company	—
Chill Drive	A cassette to be held by Genesect. It changes Techno Blast to an Ice-type move.	Visit P2 Laboratory with Genesect in your party and defeat a Scientist in a Pokémon battle (Pokémon White Version 2).	—
Choice Band	The holder can use only one of its moves, but Attack increases by 50%.	Exchange for 24 BP at the PWT or Battle Subway	—
Choice Scarf	The holder can use only one of its moves, but Speed increases by 50%.	Exchange for 24 BP at the PWT or Battle Subway	—
Choice Specs	The holder can use only one of its moves, but Sp. Atk increases by 50%.	Exchange for 24 BP at the PWT or Battle Subway	—
Claw Fossil	A Pokémon Fossil. When restored, it becomes Anorith.	Receive from the Worker in Twist Mountain / Join Avenue Antique Shop (when the owner is from Pokémon White Version or Pokémon White Version 2)	300
Cleanse Tag	Helps keep wild Pokémon away if the holder is the first one in the party.	From the chairman of Icirrus City's Pokémon Fan Club (when you show him a Pokémon you've raised 50 to 98 levels)	—
Clever Wing	Raises the base Sp. Def stat of a Pokémon by a little. Can be used until the stat reaches its maximum value.	Step on the shadows of flying Pokémon (Driftveil Drawbridge / Marvelous Bridge) / Reward for clearing Areas 6 through 9 in Black Tower (White Treehollow)	—
Comet Shard	A shard that fell to the ground when a comet approached. Can be sold to the old gentleman in Icirrus City for 60,000.	Dragonspiral Tower / Very rarely held by wild Clefairy, Lunatone and Solrock	—
Cover Fossil	A Pokémon Fossil. When restored, it becomes Tirtouga.	Receive from Lenora in Nacrene City / Join Avenue Antique Shop (when the owner is from Pokémon White Version or Pokémon White Version 2)	300

◆Cheapest price the item can be purchased for at a Join Avenue Antique Shop. ●Price when purchased at a Join Avenue Market. ■Price when purchased at Black City (White Forest).

Items

D

Item	Explanation	Main Ways to Obtain	Price
Damp Mulch	A fertilizer to be spread on soft soil in regions where Berries are grown. The Pokémon Breeder in Mistralton City will buy it for 1,000.	Hidden Grottoes / Join Avenue Flower Shop (when the owner is from *Pokémon White Version 2*)	400
Damp Rock	Extends the duration of the move Rain Dance when held.	From the woman on Route 8 (talk to her during the morning)	—
Dark Gem	When held by a Pokémon, it boosts the power of a Dark-type move by 50% one time. Goes away after use.	Found in dust clouds inside caves	—
Dawn Stone	Evolves certain Pokémon.	Dreamyard / From the woman on Route 2 (show her a Pokémon with the Solid Rock Ability) / Found in dust clouds inside caves	60,000 ■
DeepSeaScale	When held by Clamperl, it doubles Sp. Def. Link Trade Clamperl while it holds the DeepSeaScale to evolve it into Gorebyss.	Sometimes held by wild Chinchou, Lanturn, and Gorebyss / White Forest (Saturdays and Sundays after clearing Area 5 of the White Treehollow)	2,000
DeepSeaTooth	When held by Clamperl, it doubles Sp. Atk. Link Trade Clamperl while it holds the DeepSeaScale to evolve it into Huntail.	Sometimes held by wild Carvanha, Sharpedo, and Huntail / White Forest (Saturdays and Sundays after clearing Area 2 of the White Treehollow)	1,000
Destiny Knot	When held, it shares the Infatuation status condition when it is afflicted by it.	From a woman in Castelia City	—
Dire Hit	Significantly raises the critical-hit ratio of the Pokémon on which it is used (can be used only once).	Route 9 Shopping Mall 3F / Nacrene City's store	650
Dome Fossil	A Pokémon Fossil. When restored, it becomes a Kabuto.	Receive from the Worker in Twist Mountain / Join Avenue Antique Shop (when the owner is from Pokémon White Version or *Pokémon White Version 2*)	300
Douse Drive	A cassette to be held by Genesect. It changes Techno Blast to a Water-type move.	Visit P2 Laboratory with Genesect in your party and defeat a Scientist in a Pokémon battle (*Pokémon White Version 2*).	—
Draco Plate	When held by a Pokémon, it boosts the power of Dragon-type moves. (When held by Arceus, it shifts Arceus's type to Dragon type.)	Undella Bay	—
Dragon Fang	When held by a Pokémon, it boosts the power of Dragon-type moves.	Victory Road / Sometimes held by wild Bagon and Druddigon	—
Dragon Gem	When held by a Pokémon, it boosts the power of a Dragon-type move by 50% one time. Goes away after use.	Found in dust clouds inside caves	—
Dragon Scale	Link Trade Seadra while it holds the Dragon Scale to evolve it into Kingdra.	Victory Road / Sometimes held by wild Horsea and Seadra / White Forest (Saturdays and Sundays after clearing Area 8 of the White Treehollow)	4,000
Dread Plate	When held by a Pokémon, it boosts the power of Dark-type moves. (When held by Arceus, it shifts Arceus's type to Dark type.)	Abyssal Ruins 1F	—
Dubious Disc	Link Trade Porygon2 while it holds the Dubious Disc to evolve it into Porygon-Z.	P2 Laboratory / Black City (Saturdays, Sundays after clearing Area 10 in Black Tower)	60,000
Dusk Stone	Evolves certain Pokémon.	Strange House / Twist Mountain / Found in dust clouds inside caves / Black City (Monday through Friday after clearing Area 8 in Black Tower)	40,000

E

Item	Explanation	Main Ways to Obtain	Price
Earth Plate	When held by a Pokémon, it boosts the power of Ground-type moves. (When held by Arceus, it shifts Arceus's type to Ground type.)	Abyssal Ruins 1F	—
Eject Button	If the holder is hit by an attack, it switches places with a party Pokémon. Goes away after use.	Twist Mountain (winter) / Exchange for 16 BP at the PWT or Battle Subway	—
Electirizer	Link Trade Electabuzz while it holds the Electirizer to evolve it into Electivire.	Plasma Frigate (*Pokémon White Version 2*) / Join Avenue Antique Shop (when the owner comes from *Pokémon White Version 2*)	350
Electric Gem	When held by a Pokémon, it boosts the power of an Electric-type move by 50% one time. Goes away after use.	Found in dust clouds inside caves	—
Elixir	Restores the PP of all of a Pokémon's moves by 10 points.	Route 6 / Route 7 / Route 9 / Dragonspiral Tower	—
Energy Root	Restores the HP of one Pokémon by 200 points. Very bitter (lowers a Pokémon's friendship).	Driftveil City Market / From a fan at Pokéstar Studios	800
EnergyPowder	Restores the HP of one Pokémon by 50 points. Very bitter (lowers a Pokémon's friendship).	Driftveil City Market / From the man at the gate on the east side of Route 8 / From a fan at Pokéstar Studios	500
Escape Rope	Use it to escape instantly from a cave or a dungeon.	Poké Mart (after obtaining one Gym Badge) / Route 9 Shopping Mall 1F	550
Ether	Restores the PP of a Pokémon's move by 10 points.	Talk to the man in Virbank Complex three times / Castelia City's Battle Company / Join Avenue Market	1,500
Everstone	Prevents Pokémon evolution when held.	From the man on 23F of Driftveil City's Driftveil Luxury Suites / Often held by wild Roggenrola and Boldore	200 ◆
Eviolite	Raises Defense and Sp. Def by 50% when held by a Pokémon that can still evolve.	From the man on 1F of a building in Castelia City (when the number of Seen Pokémon in the Pokédex is 40 or more)	—
Exp. Share	The holder earns Experience Points without even going into battle.	From the Janitor in Castelia City's Battle Company / From the chairman of Icirrus City's Pokémon Fan Club (show him a Pokémon you raised 25 to 49 levels)	—
Expert Belt	Raises the power of supereffective moves by 20%.	From the man in Driftveil City's Market (when you have a Pokémon of Lv. 30 or higher in your party) / Very rarely held by wild Throh and Sawk	—

F

Item	Explanation	Main Ways to Obtain	Price
Fighting Gem	When held by a Pokémon, it boosts the power of a Fighting-type move by 50% one time. Goes away after use.	Found in dust clouds inside caves	—
Fire Gem	When held by a Pokémon, it boosts the power of a Fire-type move by 50% one time. Goes away after use.	Found in dust clouds inside caves	—
Fire Stone	Evolves certain Pokémon.	Lentimas Town / Exchange for 3 BP at the PWT or Battle Subway / Found in dust clouds inside caves	20,000 ■
Fist Plate	When held by a Pokémon, it boosts the power of Fighting-type moves. (When held by Arceus, it shifts Arceus's type to Fighting type.)	Abyssal Ruins 1F	—
Flame Orb	Inflicts Burned status condition on the holder during battle.	Reversal Mountain (*Pokémon White Version 2*) / Exchange for 16 BP at the PWT or Battle Subway	—
Flame Plate	When held by a Pokémon, it boosts the power of Fire-type moves. (When held by Arceus, it shifts Arceus's type to Fire type.)	Abyssal Ruins 1F	—
Float Stone	Halves the holder's weight.	From the Linebacker on 2F of Drayden's house (Opelucid City) / Twist Mountain Outside / Join Avenue Antique Shop	200
Fluffy Tail	Allows the holder to always run away from a wild Pokémon encounter.	Show the woman in Accumula Town a Pokémon with a height of 17 feet or more	—

522

◆Cheapest price the item can be purchased for at a Join Avenue Antique Shop. ●Price when purchased at a Join Avenue Market. ■Price when purchased at Black City (White Forest).

Item	Explanation	Main Ways to Obtain	Price
Flying Gem	When held by a Pokémon, it boosts the power of a Flying-type move by 50% one time. Goes away after use.	Found in dust clouds inside caves	—
Focus Band	10% chance of leaving the holder with 1 HP when it receives damage that would KO it.	Exchange for 12 BP at the PWT or Battle Subway	—
Focus Sash	Leaves the holder with 1 HP when hit by a move that would KO it when its HP is full. Goes away after use.	Exchange for 24 BP at the PWT or Battle Subway	—
Fresh Water	Restores the HP of one Pokémon by 50 points.	Vending machines / Receive from Clyde at Pokémon Gyms	200
Full Heal	Cures all status conditions.	Poké Mart (after obtaining five Gym Badges) / Route 9 Shopping Mall 1F	600
Full Incense	When held by a Pokémon, it makes it move later.	Driftveil Market	9,600
Full Restore	Fully restores the HP and heals any status conditions of a single Pokémon.	Poké Mart (after obtaining eight Gym Badges)	3,000

Item	Explanation	Main Ways to Obtain	Price
Genius Wing	Raises the base Sp. Atk stat of a Pokémon by a little. Can be used until the stat reaches its maximum value.	Step on the shadows of flying Pokémon (Driftveil Drawbridge / Marvelous Bridge) / Reward for clearing Areas 6 through 9 in Black Tower (White Treehollow)	—
Ghost Gem	When held by a Pokémon, it boosts the power of a Ghost-type move by 50% one time. Goes away after use.	Found in dust clouds inside caves	—
Gooey Mulch	A fertilizer to be spread on soft soil in regions where Berries are grown. The Pokémon Breeder in Mistralton City will buy it for 1,000.	Hidden Grottoes / Join Avenue Flower Shop (when the owner is from Pokémon White Version)	400
Grass Gem	When held by a Pokémon, it boosts the power of a Grass-type move by 50% one time. Goes away after use.	Found in dust clouds inside caves	—
Green Shard	Give to the master Move Tutor in Nacrene City to have him teach your Pokémon moves.	Desert Resort / Route 12 / Route 23 / Clay Tunnel / Moor of Icirrus / Join Avenue Antique Shop	500
Grip Claw	Extends the duration of moves like Bind and Wrap.	Route 4 (Pokémon Black Version 2) / Sometimes held by wild Sneasel	—
Griseous Orb	When held by Giratina, it changes it into its Origin Forme, and boosts the power of Dragon- and Ghost-type moves.	Dragonspiral Tower	—
Ground Gem	When held by a Pokémon, it boosts the power of a Ground-type move by 50% one time. Goes away after use.	Found in dust clouds inside caves	—
Growth Mulch	A fertilizer to be spread on soft soil in regions where Berries are grown. The Pokémon Breeder in Mistralton City will buy it for 1,000.	Hidden Grottoes / Join Avenue Flower Shop (when the owner is from Pokémon Black Version 2)	400
Guard Spec.	Prevents stat reduction among the Trainer's party Pokémon for five turns.	Route 9 Shopping Mall 3F / Nacrene City's store	700

Item	Explanation	Main Ways to Obtain	Price
Hard Stone	When held by a Pokémon, it boosts the power of Rock-type moves.	Relic Passage / sometimes held by wild Corsola and Nosepass / Join Avenue Antique Shop	200
Heal Powder	Cures all status conditions. Very bitter (lowers a Pokémon's friendship).	Driftveil City Market / From a boy on Driftveil Drawbridge (talk to him when Charizard is in your party)	450
Health Wing	Raises the base HP stat of a Pokémon by a little. Can be used until the stat reaches its maximum value.	Step on the shadows of flying Pokémon (Driftveil Drawbridge / Marvelous Bridge) / Reward for clearing Areas 6 through 9 in Black Tower (White Treehollow)	—
Heart Scale	Give one to the reminder girl at the PWT, and she will have your Pokémon remember a move it has forgotten.	Desert Resort / Castelia City / Castelia Sewers (spring, summer) / By showing the woman in Driftveil City the Pokémon she wants to see / Route 6 / Route 14	350 ◆
Heat Rock	Extends the duration of the move Sunny Day when held.	From the woman on Route 8 (talk to her during the afternoon)	—
Helix Fossil	A Pokémon Fossil. When restored, it becomes an Omanyte.	Receive from the Worker in Twist Mountain / Join Avenue Antique Shop (when the owner is from Pokémon Black Version or Pokémon Black Version 2)	300
Honey	Use in tall grass or in a cave to make wild Pokémon appear.	Sometimes held by wild Combee / Join Avenue Market	3,600 (for 12)
HP Up	Raises the base HP stat of a Pokémon.	Route 9 Shopping Mall 3F / Exchange for 1 BP at the PWT or Battle Subway	9,800
Hyper Potion	Restores the HP of one Pokémon by 200 points.	Poké Mart (after obtaining three Gym Badges) / Route 9 Shopping Mall 1F	1,200

Item	Explanation	Main Ways to Obtain	Price
Ice Gem	When held by a Pokémon, it boosts the power of an Ice-type move by 50% one time. Goes away after use.	Found in dust clouds inside caves	—
Ice Heal	Cures the Frozen status condition.	Poké Mart (after obtaining one Gym Badge) / Route 9 Shopping Mall 1F	250
Icicle Plate	When held by a Pokémon, it boosts the power of Ice-type moves. (When held by Arceus, it shifts Arceus's type to Ice type.)	Abyssal Ruins 1F	—
Icy Rock	Extends the duration of the move Hail when held.	From the woman on Route 8 (talk to her during the night / late night)	—
Insect Plate	When held by a Pokémon, it boosts the power of Bug-type moves. (When held by Arceus, it shifts Arceus's type to Bug type.)	Abyssal Ruins 1F	—
Iron	Raises the base Defense stat of a Pokémon.	Route 9 Shopping Mall 3F / Exchange for 1 BP at the PWT or Battle Subway	9,800
Iron Ball	Lowers the holder's Speed. If the holder has the Levitate Ability or is a Flying-type Pokémon, Ground-type moves now hit it.	Exchange for 12 BP at the PWT or Battle Subway	—
Iron Plate	When held by a Pokémon, it boosts the power of Steel-type moves. (When held by Arceus, it shifts Arceus's type to Steel type.)	Abyssal Ruins 1F	—

K

Item	Explanation	Main Ways to Obtain	Price
King's Rock	When the holder hits a target with an attack, the is a 10% chance the target will flinch. Certain Pokémon evolve when Link Traded while holding this item.	Home of the main character of the last game in Nuvema Town / Sometimes held by wild Poliwhirl and Poliwrath / Join Avenue Antique Shop (when the owner is from Pokémon Black Version)	350

L

Item	Explanation	Main Ways to Obtain	Price
Lagging Tail	When held by a Pokémon, it makes it move later.	Sometimes held by wild Slowpoke, Lickitung, and Lickilicky	—
Lava Cookie	Lavaridge Town's famous specialty. Cures all status conditions.	Battle all four Trainers on the Royal Unova (Monday, Wednesday, Friday) / From a fan at Pokéstar Studios	1,000 ●
Lax Incense	Lowers the accuracy of the holder's opponents.	Driftveil Market	9,600
Leaf Stone	Evolves certain Pokémon.	Route 7 / Exchange for 3 BP at the PWT or Battle Subway / Found in dust clouds inside caves	1,000 ■
Leftovers	Restores the holder's HP by 1/16th of its maximum HP every turn.	Castelia Sewers	—
Lemonade	Restores the HP of one Pokémon by 80 points.	Vending machines / From the Waitress at Nacrene City's Café Warehouse (Saturdays)	350
Life Orb	Lowers the holder's HP by 10% of its max HP each time it attacks, but raises the power of moves by 30%.	Exchange for 24 BP at the PWT or Battle Subway	—
Light Clay	Extends the duration of moves like Reflect and Light Screen.	Route 4 (Pokémon White Version 2) / Sometimes held by wild Golurk	—
Luck Incense	Doubles prize money from a battle if the holding Pokémon joins in.	Driftveil Market	9,600
Lucky Egg	Increases the number of Experience Points received from battle by 50%.	From Professor Juniper in the Celestial Tower	—
Lucky Punch	When held by Chansey, it raises the critical-hit ratio of its moves.	Successfully complete the Entralink Funfest Mission Rock-Paper-Scissors Competition with a double score.	—
Lustrous Orb	When held by Palkia, it raises the power of Dragon- and Water-type moves.	Dragonspiral Tower	—

M

Item	Explanation	Main Ways to Obtain	Price
Macho Brace	When held, it halves Speed, but makes it easier to raise base stats.	From the Infielder in the Nimbasa City gate	—
Magmarizer	Link Trade Magmar while it holds the Magmarizer to evolve it into Magmortar.	Plasma Frigate (Pokémon Black Version 2) / Join Avenue Antique Shop (when the owner comes from Pokémon Black Version 2)	350
Magnet	When held by a Pokémon, it boosts the power of Electric-type moves.	Chargestone Cave	—
Max Elixir	Restores the PP of all of a Pokémon's moves completely.	Plasma Frigate / Victory Road / Icirrus City (winter) / Striaton City / Join Avenue Raffle Shop (6th prize)	—
Max Ether	Restores the PP of a Pokémon's move completely.	Desert Resort / Route 13 / Join Avenue Raffle Shop (7th prize)	—
Max Potion	Completely restores the HP of a single Pokémon.	Poké Mart (after obtaining seven Gym Badges) / Route 9 Shopping Mall 1F	2,500
Max Repel	Prevents weak wild Pokémon from appearing for 250 steps after its use.	Poké Mart (after obtaining five Gym Badges) / Route 9 Shopping Mall 1F	700
Max Revive	Revives a fainted Pokémon and fully restores its HP.	Route 20 (autumn) / Plasma Frigate / From Rood in Giant Chasm / Victory Road / From your mom after you enter the Hall of Fame	5,000 ●
Meadow Plate	When held by a Pokémon, it boosts the power of Grass-type moves. (When held by Arceus, it shifts Arceus's type to Grass type.)	Abyssal Ruins 1F	—
Mental Herb	The holder cures itself when moves like Taunt, Encore, Disable, Heal Block, or Attract make it unable to use moves freely. Goes away after use.	Sometimes held by wild Sewaddle, Swadloon, and Leavanny	—
Metal Coat	When held by a Pokémon, boosts the power of Steel-type moves. Link Trade certain Pokémon while they hold the Metal Coat to evolve them.	Chargestone Cave / Clay Tunnel / Sometimes held by wild Magnemite, Steelix, and Metang	350 ◆
Metal Powder	When held by Ditto, Defense doubles.	Sometimes held by wild Ditto	—
Metronome	Raises the power of a move used consecutively when held.	Lacunosa Town / From the woman in the house in Accumula Town (show her a Kricketot and then a Whismur)	—
Mind Plate	When held by a Pokémon, it boosts the power of Psychic-type moves. (When held by Arceus, it shifts Arceus's type to Psychic type.)	Abyssal Ruins 1F	—
Miracle Seed	When held by a Pokémon, it boosts the power of Grass-type moves.	Castelia City Empty Lot / From the woman on 1F of Castelia City's Battle Company (when you answer Snivy) / Sometimes held by wild Maractus	—
Moomoo Milk	Restores the HP of one Pokémon by 100 points.	Driftveil City Market / From a fan at Pokéstar Studios / Join Avenue Market	500
Moon Stone	Evolves certain Pokémon.	Route 6 / Giant Chasm Crater Forest / Dreamyard / Found in dust clouds inside caves	200 ◆
Muscle Band	When held by a Pokémon, it boosts the power of physical moves.	Exchange for 8 BP at the PWT or Battle Subway	—
Muscle Wing	Raises the base Attack stat of a Pokémon by a little. Can be used until the stat reaches its maximum value.	Step on the shadows of flying Pokémon (Driftveil Drawbridge / Marvelous Bridge) / Reward for clearing Areas 6 through 9 in Black Tower (White Treehollow)	—
Mystic Water	When held by a Pokémon, it boosts the power of Water-type moves.	Route 4 / From the woman on 1F of Castelia City's Battle Company (when you answer Oshawott) / Sometimes held by wild Castform	—

N

Item	Explanation	Main Ways to Obtain	Price
NeverMeltIce	When held by a Pokémon, it boosts the power of Ice-type moves.	Dragonspiral Tower entrance (winter) / Sometimes held by wild Cryogonal	—
Normal Gem	When held by a Pokémon, it boosts the power of a Normal-type move by 50% one time. Goes away after use.	Found in dust clouds inside caves	—
Nugget	A nugget of pure gold. Can be sold to the Poké Mart for 5,000. Can be sold to the old gentleman in Icirrus City for 10,000.	Desert Resort / From the man in Chargestone Cave / Reversal Mountain / Route 9 / Route 14	500 ◆

◆ Cheapest price the item can be purchased for at a Join Avenue Antique Shop. ● Price when purchased at a Join Avenue Market. ■ Price when purchased at Black City (White Forest)

 O

Item	Explanation	Main Ways to Obtain	Price
Odd Incense	When held by a Pokémon, it boosts the power of Psychic-type moves.	Driftveil Market	9,600
Odd Keystone	A vital item that is needed to keep a stone tower from collapsing. Voices can be heard from it occasionally.	Join Avenue Antique Shop (when the owner comes from Pokémon White Version or Pokémon White Version 2)	200
Old Amber	A piece of amber that contains genetic material. When restored, it becomes Aerodactyl.	Receive from the Worker in Twist Mountain / Join Avenue Antique Shop (when the owner is from Pokémon Black Version or Pokémon Black Version 2)	300
Old Gateau	Old Chateau's hidden specialty. Cures all status conditions.	Battle all five Trainers on the Royal Unova (Thursday) / From Cedric Juniper in Dragonspiral Tower	1,000 ●
Oval Stone	Level up Happiny while it holds the Oval Stone in the morning, afternoon, or evening to evolve it into Chansey.	Found in dust clouds inside caves / White Forest (Monday through Friday after clearing Area 10 of the White Treehollow)	6,000

P

Item	Explanation	Main Ways to Obtain	Price
Parlyz Heal	Cures the Paralysis status condition.	Poké Mart (after obtaining one Gym Badge) / Route 9 Shopping Mall 1F	200
Pass Orb	A mysterious orb that generates Pass Powers.	Successfully complete Entralink Funfest Missions	—
Pearl	A pretty pearl. Can be sold to the Poké Mart for 700. Can be sold to the old gentleman in Icirrus City for 1,400.	Castelia Sewers / Walk Mienfoo in Humilau City / Join Avenue Antique Shop	350
Pearl String	Very large pearls that sparkle in a pretty silver color. Can be sold to the old gentleman in Icirrus City for 25,000.	Route 17 / As a gift from Join Avenue guests	—
Plume Fossil	A Pokémon Fossil. When restored, it becomes Archen.	Receive from Lenora in Nacrene City / Join Avenue Antique Shop (when the owner is from Pokémon White Version or Pokémon White Version 2)	300
Poison Barb	When held by a Pokémon, it boosts the power of Poison-type moves.	Route 22 / Sometimes held by wild Beedrill, Qwilfish, and Roselia	—
Poison Gem	When held by a Pokémon, it boosts the power of a Poison-type move by 50% one time. Goes away after use.	Found in dust clouds inside caves	—
Poké Doll	Allows the holder to always run away from a wild Pokémon encounter.	Route 9 Shopping Mall / Show the boy in Accumula Town a Pokémon with a height of eight inches or less	—
Poké Toy	Allows the holder to always run away from a wild Pokémon encounter.	Virbank City / Route 4 (guess the Pokémon cry imitation correctly) / Route 9 Shopping Mall 1F	1,000
Potion	Restores the HP of one Pokémon by 20 points.	Poké Mart (from the start) / Route 9 Shopping Mall 1F	300
Power Anklet	Halves the holder's Speed, but makes the Speed base stat easier to raise.	Exchange for 16 BP at the PWT or Battle Subway	—
Power Band	Halves the holder's Speed, but makes the Sp. Def base stat easier to raise.	Plasma Frigate (Pokémon Black Version 2) / From the girl in the house on Route 13 (Pokémon White Version 2) / Exchange for 16 BP at the PWT or Battle Subway	—
Power Belt	Halves the holder's Speed, but makes the Defense base stat easier to raise.	Plasma Frigate (Pokémon White Version 2) / Exchange for 16 BP at the PWT or Battle Subway	—
Power Bracer	Halves the holder's Speed, but makes the Attack base stat easier to raise.	Exchange for 16 BP at the PWT or Battle Subway	—
Power Herb	The holder can immediately use a move that requires a one-turn charge. Goes away after use.	Exchange for 16 BP at the PWT or Battle Subway	—
Power Lens	Halves the holder's Speed, but makes the Sp. Atk base stat easier to raise.	From the girl in the house on Route 13 (Pokémon Black Version 2) / Exchange for 16 BP at the PWT or Battle Subway	—
Power Weight	Halves the holder's Speed, but makes the HP base stat easier to raise.	Exchange for 16 BP at the PWT or Battle Subway	—
PP Max	Increases the max number of PP as high as it will go.	Victory Road / Pinwheel Forest / Dragonspiral Tower / Route 18 / Join Avenue Raffle Shop (3rd prize)	—
PP Up	Increases the max number of PP by 1 level.	PWT / Route 6 / Celestial Tower / Reversal Mountain / Route 12 / Route 21 / Route 22 / Giant Chasm	12,500 ●
Pretty Wing	A pretty wing. Sell to the Poké Mart for 100.	Step on the shadows of flying Pokémon (Driftveil Drawbridge / Marvelous Bridge) / From a fan at Pokéstar Studios	—
Prism Scale	Link Trade Feebas while it holds the Prism Scale to evolve it into Milotic.	From the man in Undella Town's Pokémon Center / Route 1 / Join Avenue Antique Shop (when the owner is from Pokémon White Version 2)	350
Protector	Link Trade Rhydon while it holds the Protector to evolve it into Rhyperior.	Wellspring Cave / Black City (Saturdays, Sundays after clearing Area 2 of Black Tower)	10,000
Protein	Raises the base Attack stat of a Pokémon.	Route 9 Shopping Mall 3F / Exchange for 1 BP at the PWT or Battle Subway	9,800
Psychic Gem	When held by a Pokémon, it boosts the power of a Psychic-type move by 50% one time. Goes away after use.	Found in dust clouds inside caves	—
Pure Incense	Helps keep wild Pokémon away if the holder is the first one in the party.	Driftveil Market	9,600

Q

Item	Explanation	Main Ways to Obtain	Price
Quick Claw	Allows the holder to strike first sometimes.	From the woman in the east gate in Castelia City / Sometimes held by wild Sandshrew, Sandslash, and Sneasel	—
Quick Powder	When held by Ditto, Speed doubles.	Often held by wild Ditto	—

R

Item	Explanation	Main Ways to Obtain	Price
RageCandyBar	Mahogany Town's famous snack. Restores the HP of one Pokémon by 20.	Battle all six Trainers on the Royal Unova (Saturday) / From a fan at Pokestar Studios	2,000 ●
Rare Bone	A rare bone. Can be sold to the sunglasses-wearing man on Route 18 for 10,000.	Castelia Sewers (spring, summer) / Clay Tunnel / Twist Mountain / Very rarely held by wild Crustle	300 ◆
Rare Candy	Raises a Pokémon's level by 1.	Route 20 (autumn) / Virbank City / Relic Passage / Lostlorn Forest / Route 22 / Seaside Cave	—
Razor Claw	Boosts the holder's critical-hit ratio. Level up Sneasel while it holds the Razor Claw at night or late night to evolve it into Weavile.	Giant Chasm Crater Forest / Exchange for 8 BP at the PWT or Battle Subway	—

R

Item	Explanation	Main Ways to Obtain	Price
Razor Fang	When the holder hits a target with an attack, the is a 10% chance the target will flinch. Level up Gligar while it holds the Razor Fang in the evening or at night to evolve it into Gliscor.	Route 11 / Exchange for 8 BP at the PWT or Battle Subway	—
Reaper Cloth	Link Trade Dusclops while it holds the Reaper Cloth to evolve it into Dusknoir.	Dreamyard / Join Avenue Antique Shop (when the owner is from Pokémon Black Version 2)	350
Red Card	If the holder is hit by an attack, the opposing Trainer is forced to switch out the attacking Pokémon. Goes away after use.	Exchange for 16 BP at the PWT or Battle Subway	—
Red Flute	A glass flute. Can be sold to the billionaire in Undella Town for 7,500.	From the sunglasses-wearing man on Route 13	—
Red Shard	Give to the master Move Tutor in Driftveil City to have him teach your Pokémon moves.	From the old man in Nimbasa City's Pokémon Center / Desert Resort / Route 13 / Route 22 / Clay Tunnel	500 ◆
Relic Band	A bracelet made by a civilization about 3,000 years ago. The billionaire in Undella Town will buy it for 100,000.	Abyssal Ruins 2F, 3F	—
Relic Copper	A copper coin made by a civilization about 3,000 years ago. The billionaire in Undella Town will buy it for 1,000.	Abyssal Ruins 1F, 2F	—
Relic Crown	A crown made by a civilization about 3,000 years ago. The billionaire in Undella Town will buy it for 300,000.	Abyssal Ruins Top Floor	—
Relic Gold	A gold coin made by a civilization about 3,000 years ago. The billionaire in Undella Town will buy it for 100,000.	Abyssal Ruins 1F, 2F, 3F	—
Relic Silver	A silver coin made by a civilization about 3,000 years ago. The billionaire in Undella Town will buy it for 5,000.	Abyssal Ruins 1F, 2F, 3F	—
Relic Statue	A stone figure made by a civilization about 3,000 years ago. The billionaire in Undella Town will buy it for 200,000.	Abyssal Ruins 1F, 2F, 3F	—
Relic Vase	A vase made by a civilization about 3,000 years ago. The billionaire in Undella Town will buy it for 50,000.	Abyssal Ruins 1F, 2F, 3F	—
Repel	Prevents weak wild Pokémon from appearing for 100 steps after its use.	Poké Mart (after obtaining one Gym Badge) / Route 9 Shopping Mall 1F	350
Resist Wing	Raises the base Defense stat of a Pokémon by a little. Can be used until the stat reaches its maximum value.	Step on the shadows of flying Pokémon (Driftveil Drawbridge / Marvelous Bridge) / Reward for clearing Areas 6 through 9 in Black Tower (White Treehollow)	—
Revival Herb	Revives a fainted Pokémon. Very bitter (lowers a Pokémon's friendship).	Driftveil Market	2,800
Revive	Revives a fainted Pokémon and restores half of its HP.	Poké Mart (after obtaining three Gym Badges) / Route 9 Shopping Mall 1F	1,500
Ring Target	Moves that would otherwise have no effect will hit the holder.	From the woman on 2F of Drayden's House in Opelucid City	—
Rock Gem	When held by a Pokémon, it boosts the power of a Rock-type move by 50% one time. Goes away after use.	Found in dust clouds inside caves	—
Rock Incense	When held by a Pokémon, it boosts the power of Rock-type moves.	Driftveil Market	9,600
Rocky Helmet	Does damage to the Pokémon that hit the holder with a direct attack.	From a man at PWT / Relic Passage	—
Root Fossil	A Pokémon Fossil. When restored, it becomes Lileep.	Receive from the Worker in Twist Mountain / Join Avenue Antique Shop (when the owner is from Pokémon Black Version or Pokémon Black Version 2)	300
Rose Incense	When held by a Pokémon, it boosts the power of Grass-type moves.	Driftveil Market	9,600

S

Item	Explanation	Main Ways to Obtain	Price
Sacred Ash	Revives all fainted Pokémon in your party and fully restores their HP.	Join Avenue Antique Shop	350
Scope Lens	Boosts the holder's critical-hit ratio.	From the man in Castelia City's Battle Company / Exchange for 8 BP at the PWT or Battle Subway	—
Sea Incense	When held by a Pokémon, it boosts the power of Water-type moves.	Driftveil Market	9,600
Sharp Beak	When held by a Pokémon, it boosts the power of Flying-type moves.	From the woman in Mistralton City's Cargo Service / Sometimes held by wild Fearow and Doduo	—
Shed Shell	The holder can always be switched out.	Sometimes held by wild Scraggy and Scrafty	—
Shell Bell	Restores the holder's HP by up to 1/8th of the damage dealt to the target.	From an old man on 1F of Driftveil City's Driftveil Grand Hotel (when the number of Seen Pokémon in the Pokédex is 70 or more) / Humilau City	—
Shiny Stone	Evolves certain Pokémon.	Abundant Shrine / Dragonspiral Tower / Found in dust clouds inside caves / White Forest (Monday through Friday after clearing Area 8 of the White Treehollow)	4,000
Shoal Salt	Salt found in the Shoal Cave. Can be sold to the Maid on Route 5 for 7,000.	Route 17 (use the Dowsing MCHN)	—
Shoal Shell	A seashell found in the Shoal Cave. Can be sold to the old gentleman in Icirrus City for 7,000.	Route 17 (use the Dowsing MCHN)	—
Shock Drive	A cassette to be held by Genesect. It changes Techno Blast to an Electric-type move.	Visit P2 Laboratory with Genesect in your party and defeat a Scientist in a Pokémon battle (Pokémon Black Version 2).	—
Silk Scarf	When held by a Pokémon, it boosts the power of Normal-type moves.	Virbank Complex	—
SilverPowder	When held by a Pokémon, it boosts the power of Bug-type moves.	Sometimes held by wild Butterfree and Masquerain / Held by wild Volcarona	—
Skull Fossil	A Pokémon Fossil. When restored, it becomes Cranidos.	Receive from the Worker in Twist Mountain / Join Avenue Antique Shop (when the owner is from Pokémon White Version or Pokémon White Version 2)	300
Sky Plate	When held by a Pokémon, it boosts the power of Flying-type moves. (When held by Arceus, it shifts Arceus's type to Flying type.)	Abyssal Ruins 1F	—
Smoke Ball	Allows the holder to always run away from wild Pokémon.	Reversal Mountain Outside / From the woman in a house in Opelucid City / Sometimes held by wild Koffing and Weezing	—
Smooth Rock	Extends the duration of the move Sandstorm when held.	From the woman on Route 8 (talk to her during the evening)	—
Soda Pop	Restores the HP of one Pokémon by 60 points.	Vending machines / From the Waitress at Nacrene City's Café Warehouse (Wednesdays)	300
Soft Sand	When held by a Pokémon, it boosts the power of Ground-type moves.	From the sunglasses-wearing man in Desert Resort / Sometimes held by wild Trapinch and Stunfisk	—

◆Cheapest price the item can be purchased for at a Join Avenue Antique Shop. ●Price when purchased at a Join Avenue Market. ■Price when purchased at Black City (White Forest)

S

	Item	Explanation	Main Ways to Obtain	Price
	Soothe Bell	The holder's friendship improves more quickly.	From the old lady in the house in Nimbasa City (when the lead Pokémon in your party has high friendship)	—
	Soul Dew	When held by Latios or Latias, it raises both the Sp. Atk and Sp. Def stats.	Dreamyard (after catching Latias or Latios)	—
	Spell Tag	When held by a Pokémon, it boosts the power of Ghost-type moves.	From the old woman in Lentimas Town's Pokémon Center / Strange House / Sometimes held by wild Banette and Yamask	—
	Splash Plate	When held by a Pokémon, it boosts the power of Water-type moves. (When held by Arceus, it shifts Arceus's type to Water type.)	Undella Bay	—
	Spooky Plate	When held by a Pokémon, it boosts the power of Ghost-type moves. (When held by Arceus, it shifts Arceus's type to Ghost type.)	Abyssal Ruins 1F	—
	Stable Mulch	A fertilizer to be spread on soft soil in regions where Berries are grown. The Pokémon Breeder in Mistralton City will buy it for 1,000.	Hidden Grottoes / Join Avenue Flower Shop (when the owner is from Pokémon Black Version)	400
	Star Piece	A shard of a pretty gem that sparkles in a red color. Can be sold to the Poké Mart for 4,900. Can be sold to the old gentleman in Icirrus City for 9,800.	Route 13 / Giant Chasm / Route 23 / Sometimes held by wild Staryu and Starmie	—
	Stardust	Lovely, red-colored sand. Can be sold to the Poké Mart for 1,000. Can be sold to the old gentleman in Icirrus City for 2,000.	Desert Resort / Route 4 / Smash the challenge rock in Pinwheel Forest (when you have a Fighting-type in your party)	—
	Steel Gem	When held by a Pokémon, it boosts the power of a Steel-type move by 50% one time. Goes away after use.	Found in dust clouds inside caves	—
	Stick	When held by Farfetch'd, it raises the critical-hit ratio of its moves.	Sometimes held by wild Farfetch'd	—
	Sticky Barb	Damages the holder every turn. It can stick to an opponent that touches the holder with a direct attack.	Route 20 (autumn) / Sometimes held by wild Cacturne and Ferroseed	—
	Stone Plate	When held by a Pokémon, it boosts the power of Rock-type moves. (When held by Arceus, it shifts Arceus's type to Rock type.)	Abyssal Ruins 1F	—
	Sun Stone	Evolves certain Pokémon.	Giant Chasm Crater Forest / Pinwheel Forest / Found in dust clouds inside caves	200 ◆
	Super Potion	Restores the HP of one Pokémon by 50 points.	Poké Mart (after obtaining one Gym Badge) / Route 9 Shopping Mall 1F	700
	Super Repel	Prevents weak wild Pokémon from appearing for 200 steps after its use.	Poké Mart (after obtaining three Gym Badges) / Route 9 Shopping Mall 1F	500
	Sweet Heart	Restores the HP of one Pokémon by 20 points.	Use the Feeling Check feature with Infrared Connection / From a fan in Pokéstar Studios	—
	Swift Wing	Raises the base Speed stat of a Pokémon by a little. Can be used until the stat reaches its maximum value.	Step on the shadows of flying Pokémon (Driftveil Drawbridge / Marvelous Bridge) / Reward for clearing Areas 6 through 9 in Black Tower (White Treehollow)	—

T

	Item	Explanation	Main Ways to Obtain	Price
	Thick Club	When held by Cubone or Marowak, Attack is doubled.	Entralink Funfest Mission Great Trade-Up	—
	Thunderstone	Evolves certain Pokémon.	Chargestone Cave / Exchange for 3 BP at the PWT or Battle Subway / Found in dust clouds inside caves	10,000 ■
	TinyMushroom	A tiny mushroom. Can be sold to the Poké Mart for 250. Can be sold to the Maid on Route 5 for 500.	Often held by wild Foongus and Amoonguss / Hidden Grottoes / Join Avenue Antique Shop	350
	Toxic Orb	Inflicts the Badly Poisoned status condition on the holder during battle.	Reversal Mountain (Pokémon Black Version 2) / Exchange for 16 BP at the PWT or Battle Subway	—
	Toxic Plate	When held by a Pokémon, it boosts the power of Poison-type moves. (When held by Arceus, it shifts Arceus's type to Poison type.)	Abyssal Ruins 1F	—
	TwistedSpoon	When held by a Pokémon, it boosts the power of Psychic-type moves.	Castelia Sewers	—

U

	Item	Explanation	Main Ways to Obtain	Price
	Up-Grade	Link Trade Porygon while it holds the Up-Grade to evolve it into Porygon2.	From Cheren in Pinwheel Forest / Striaton City / Black City (Saturdays, Sundays after clearing Area 8 in Black Tower)	40,000

W

	Item	Explanation	Main Ways to Obtain	Price
	Water Gem	When held by a Pokémon, it boosts the power of a Water-type move by 50% one time. Goes away after use.	Found in dust clouds inside caves	—
	Water Stone	Evolves certain Pokémon.	Route 19 / Exchange for 3 BP at the PWT or Battle Subway / Found in dust clouds inside caves	2,000 ■
	Wave Incense	When held by a Pokémon, it boosts the power of Water-type moves.	Driftveil Market	9,600
	White Flute	A glass flute. Can be sold to the billionaire in Undella Town for 8,000.	From the sunglasses-wearing man on Route 13	—
	White Herb	Restores lowered stats. Goes away after use.	Exchange for 16 BP at the PWT or Battle Subway	—
	Wide Lens	Raises the holder's accuracy by 10%.	Route 4 (Pokémon Black Version 2) / Exchange for 8 BP at the PWT or Battle Subway / Sometimes held by wild Yanma and Yanmega	—
	Wise Glasses	When held by a Pokémon, it boosts the power of special moves.	Exchange for 8 BP at the PWT or Battle Subway	—

XYZ

	Item	Explanation	Main Ways to Obtain	Price
	X Accuracy	Raises the accuracy of a Pokémon on which it is used.	Route 9 Shopping Mall 3F / Nacrene City's store	950
	X Attack	Raises the Attack stat of a Pokémon on which it is used by one level.	Route 9 Shopping Mall 3F / Nacrene City's store	500
	X Defend	Raises the Defense stat of a Pokémon on which it is used by one level.	Route 9 Shopping Mall 3F / Nacrene City's store	550

Items

XYZ

Item	Explanation	Main Ways to Obtain	Price
X Sp. Def	Raises the Sp. Def stat of a Pokémon on which it is used by one level.	Route 9 Shopping Mall 3F / Nacrene City's store	350
X Special	Raises the Sp. Atk of a Pokémon on which it is used by one level.	Route 9 Shopping Mall 3F / Nacrene City's store	350
X Speed	Raises the Speed of a Pokémon on which it is used by one level.	Route 9 Shopping Mall 3F / Nacrene City's store	350
Yellow Flute	A glass flute. Can be sold to the billionaire in Undella Town for 7,500.	From the sunglasses-wearing man on Route 13	—
Yellow Shard	Give to the master Move Tutor in Humilau City to have him teach your Pokémon moves.	Desert Resort / Mistralton Cave / Route 12 / Striaton City / Join Avenue Antique Shop	500
Zap Plate	When held by a Pokémon, it boosts the power of Electric-type moves. (When held by Arceus, it shifts Arceus's type to Electric type.)	Abyssal Ruins 1F	—
Zinc	Raises the base Sp. Def stat of a Pokémon.	Route 9 Shopping Mall 3F / Exchange for 1 BP at the PWT or Battle Subway	9,800
Zoom Lens	Raises the holder's accuracy by 20% when it moves after the opposing Pokémon.	Exchange for 12 BP at the PWT or Battle Subway	—

◆Cheapest price the item can be purchased for at a Join Avenue Antique Shop.●Price when purchased at a Join Avenue Market.■Price when purchased at Black City (White Forest).

Key items

Move	Explanation	Main Ways to Obtain	Price
Bicycle	A folding Bicycle that lets you travel faster than running.	Receive from the Harlequin in Castelia City	—
Colress MCHN	A special device that brings out the potential of Pokémon. Use it on Crustle in Seaside Cave.	Receive from Colress on Route 22	—
Dark Stone	Zekrom's body was destroyed and changed into this stone. It waits for a hero to appear.	From N in N's Castle (Pokémon Black Version 2) after you defeat him	—
DNA Splicers	Use them once to fuse Kyurem with Zekrom (Reshiram). Use them again to separate the Pokémon.	Giant Chasm (after catching Kyurem)	—
Dowsing MCHN	A cutting-edge device that alerts you to hidden items.	Receive from Bianca in Castelia City	—
Dropped Item	When you find the Dropped Item in the amusement park in Nimbasa City, the Trainer who dropped it will give you a call.	Get in Nimbasa City	—
Gracidea	Shaymin can change Forme when holding this item (except at night).	Receive from the woman in Lacunosa Town's Pokémon Center (when Shaymin is in your party and you don't have the Gracidea)	—
Grubby Hanky	A handkerchief dropped by a regular customer at Café Warehouse in Nacrene City.	From the Waitress at Nacrene City's Café Warehouse (Sunday)	—
Light Stone	Reshiram's body was destroyed and changed into this stone. It waits for a hero to appear.	From N in N's Castle (Pokémon White Version 2) after you defeat him	—
Lunar Wing	Allows Cresselia to appear on Marvelous Bridge.	Strange House	—
Magma Stone	Allows Heatran to appear in Reversal Mountain.	Route 18	—
Medal Box	Holds the Medals you've obtained and records information about Medals.	Receive from Mr. Medal in Floccesy Town	—
Oval Charm	Eggs are discovered more easily at the Pokémon Day Care.	Receive from Professor Juniper when the number of Caught Pokémon in the Unova Pokédex reaches 297	—
Pal Pad	A useful pad that records friends and good times.	In the Bag from the start	—
Permit	A permit that grants access to the Nature Preserve from Mistralton City's Cargo Service.	Receive from Professor Juniper when the number of Seen Pokémon in the Unova Pokédex reaches 297	—
Plasma Card	A card key needed to enter the password in the Plasma Frigate.	Receive from a Team Plasma Grunt in the Plasma Frigate	—
Prop Case	A lovely case to store Props for your Pokémon to wear in the Musical.	Receive from the owner at the Musical Theater in Nimbasa City	—
Reveal Glass	Changes Tornadus, Thundurus, and Landorus's Formes.	Obtained when you go to the Abundant Shrine with the Landorus caught in Pokémon Dream Radar in your party	—
Shiny Charm	Raises encounter rate with Shiny Pokémon.	Receive from Professor Juniper in Nuvema Town when you catch every Pokémon in the National Pokédex	—
Super Rod	The best fishing rod. Use it to catch Pokémon from the waterside.	Receive from Cedric Juniper in Nuvema Town	—
Town Map	A very convenient map that can be viewed anytime.	Receive from Hugh's sister in Aspertia City	—
Vs. Recorder	Records your battles with friends and in battle facilities.	Get from the person you team up with in Nimbasa City (after defeating Ingo and Emmet)	—
Xtransceiver	A cutting-edge transceiver with a camera that lets you chat with up to three other people.	Get right away	—

Poké Balls

Move	Explanation	Main Ways to Obtain	Price
Poké Ball	An item for capturing wild Pokémon.	Poké Mart (from the start)/Route 9 Shopping Mall 2F	200
Dive Ball	A Poké Ball that makes it easier to catch Pokémon that live in the water.	Poké Marts in Undella Town and Humilau City	1,000
Dream Ball	A Poké Ball that magically appears in your Bag in the Entree Forest.	Only appears in your Bag when you are catching Pokémon in the Entree Forest	—
Dusk Ball	A Poké Ball that does better at night and in caves.	Poké Marts in Driftveil City, Lentimas Town, and Opelucid City/Route 9 Shopping Mall 2F	1,000
Great Ball	A Poké Ball that provides a higher Pokémon catch rate than a standard Poké Ball.	Poké Mart (after obtaining one Gym Badge)/Route 9 Shopping Mall 2F	600

Poké Balls

	Move	Explanation	Main Ways to Obtain	Price
	Heal Ball	A gentle Poké Ball that heals the caught Pokémon's HP and status.	Poké Marts in Virbank City, Castelia City, Lentimas Town, and Victory Road/Route 9 Shopping Mall 2F	300
	Luxury Ball	A Poké Ball that endears you to caught Pokémon.	Poké Marts in Undella Town, Humilau City, Victory Road, and the Pokémon League	1,000
	Master Ball	It is the ultimate ball that will surely catch any wild Pokémon.	From Professor Juniper in Mistralton City/From Colress in the Plasma Frigate when it's by P2 Laboratory (after defeating him)	—
	Nest Ball	A Poké Ball with a higher capture rate against weaker Pokémon.	Poké Marts in Castelia City, Driftveil City, and Lentimas Town/Route 9 Shopping Mall 2F	1,000
	Net Ball	A Poké Ball with a high success rate against Bug- and Water-type Pokémon.	Poké Marts in Virbank City, Castelia City, and Driftveil City/Route 9 Shopping Mall 2F	1,000
	Premier Ball	A rare Poké Ball made in commemoration of an event.	Buy 10 or more Poké Balls at once	—
	Quick Ball	A Poké Ball with a good capture rate when thrown right at the start of battle.	Poké Marts in Opelucid City, Victory Road, and the Pokémon League/Route 9 Shopping Mall 2F	1,000
	Repeat Ball	A Poké Ball that excels at catching Pokémon you've caught before.	Poké Marts in Victory Road, the Pokémon League, and Accumula Town	1,000
	Timer Ball	A Poké Ball that does better after more turns have elapsed in battle.	Poké Marts in Opelucid City, Victory Road, and the Pokémon League/Route 9 Shopping Mall 2F	1,000
	Ultra Ball	A Poké Ball that provides a higher Pokémon catch rate than a Great Ball.	Poké Mart (after obtaining five Gym Badges)/Route 9 Shopping Mall 2F	1,200

Berries

	Move	Explanation	Main Ways to Obtain	Price
	Aguav Berry	Holder restores some of its own HP when its HP falls to half or less, but if the holder dislikes Bitter flavors, it gains the Confused status condition.	Prize for Spin Trades in the Union Room	—
	Apicot Berry	Holder's Sp. Def goes up 1 when its HP falls to half or less.	Join Avenue Flower Shop (when the owner is from *Pokémon White Version*)	2,000 (for 4)
	Aspear Berry	Holder can heal itself of the Frozen status condition.	Show the Harlequin in Castelia City's Studio Castelia the Pokémon he wants to see/Route 11 (after defeating Pokémon Ranger Crofton or Thalia)	600 ▲ (for 4)
	Babiri Berry	Halves damage the holder takes from supereffective Steel-type moves.	Join Avenue Flower Shop (when the owner is from *Pokémon White Version 2*)	2,000 (for 4)
	Belue Berry	—	Not obtainable in these versions	—
	Bluk Berry	—	From the man in Lacunosa Town's Pokémon Center (night/late night)/Join Avenue Flower Shop (when the owner is from *Pokémon White Version 2*)	600 (for 4)
	Charti Berry	Halves damage the holder takes from supereffective Rock-type moves.	Sometimes held by wild Swellow/Join Avenue Flower Shop (when the owner is from *Pokémon White Version 2*)	2,000 (for 4)
	Cheri Berry	Holder can heal itself of the Paralysis status condition.	Show the Harlequin in Castelia City's Studio Castelia the Pokémon he wants to see/Route 5 (after defeating Pokémon Ranger Lois)	600 ▲ (for 4)
	Chesto Berry	Holder can heal itself of the Sleep status condition.	Show the Harlequin in Castelia City's Studio Castelia the Pokémon he wants to see/Chargestone Cave (after defeating Pokémon Ranger Louis or Briana)	600 ▲ (for 4)
	Chilan Berry	Halves damage the holder takes from Normal-type moves.	Join Avenue Flower Shop (when the owner is from *Pokémon Black Version*)	2,000 (for 4)
	Chople Berry	Halves damage the holder takes from supereffective Fighting-type moves.	Join Avenue Flower Shop (when the owner is from *Pokémon White Version*)	2,000 (for 4)
	Coba Berry	Halves damage the holder takes from supereffective Flying-type moves.	Join Avenue Flower Shop (when the owner is from *Pokémon Black Version*)	2,000 (for 4)
	Colbur Berry	Halves damage the holder takes from supereffective Dark-type moves.	Join Avenue Flower Shop (when the owner is from *Pokémon Black Version 2*)	2,000 (for 4)
	Cornn Berry	—	Not obtainable in these versions	—
	Custap Berry	The holder's move is more likely to strike first during the next turn when its HP becomes low.	Not obtainable in these versions	—
	Durin Berry	—	Not obtainable in these versions	—
	Enigma Berry	When the holder is damaged by a supereffective attack, some HP is restored.	Not obtainable in these versions	—
	Figy Berry	Holder restores its own HP when its HP falls to half or less, but if the holder dislikes Spicy flavors, it gains the Confused status condition.	Prize for Spin Trades in the Union Room	—
	Ganlon Berry	Holder raises its Defense stat by 1 when its HP becomes low.	Join Avenue Flower Shop (when the owner is from *Pokémon Black Version 2*)	2,000 (for 4)
	Grepa Berry	Slightly raises the Pokémon's friendship, but lowers its base Sp. Def stat.	Buy from the woman on Route 5/Prize for Spin Trades in the Union Room	200 (for 5)
	Haban Berry	Halves damage the holder takes from supereffective Dragon-type moves.	From Axew on 19F of the Grand Hotel Driftveil/Join Avenue Flower Shop (when the owner is from *Pokémon White Version*)	2,000 (for 4)
	Hondew Berry	Slightly raises the Pokémon's friendship, but lowers its base Sp. Atk stat.	Buy from the woman on Route 5/Prize for Spin Trades in the Union Room	200 (for 5)
	Iapapa Berry	Holder restores some of its own HP when its HP falls to half or less, but if the holder dislikes Sour flavors, it gains the Confused status condition.	Prize for Spin Trades in the Union Room	—
	Jaboca Berry	When the holder takes damage from a physical attack, the Pokémon that landed the attack is also damaged.	Not obtainable in these versions	—
	Kasib Berry	Halves damage the holder takes from supereffective Ghost-type moves.	Join Avenue Flower Shop (when the owner is from *Pokémon Black Version*)	2,000 (for 4)
	Kebia Berry	Halves damage the holder takes from supereffective Poison-type moves.	Join Avenue Flower Shop (when the owner is from *Pokémon Black Version 2*)	2,000 (for 4)
	Kelpsy Berry	Slightly raises the Pokémon's friendship, but lowers its base Attack stat.	Buy from the woman on Route 5/Prize for Spin Trades in the Union Room	200 (for 5)
	Lansat Berry	Raises the critical-hit ratio of the holder's attacks when its HP falls to half or less.	From a Trainer on the 15th platform stop during a Battle Subway win streak	—
	Leppa Berry	Holder restores 10 PP to a move when that move's PP reaches 0.	From a man in Lacunosa Town (night, late night)/Route 20 (after defeating Pokémon Ranger Bret or Malory in the autumn)	1,500 ▲

Berries

	Move	Explanation	Main Ways to Obtain	Price
	Liechi Berry	Holder raises its Attack stat by 1 when its HP becomes low.	Join Avenue Flower Shop (when the owner is from *Pokémon White Version*)	2,000 (for 4)
	Lum Berry	Holder can heal itself of any status condition.	From the man in Lacunosa Town (night, late night)/From the Baker at Village Bridge (show her a Pokémon with the Honey Gather Ability)	800 ▲ (for 4)
	Mago Berry	Holder restores some of its own HP when its HP falls to half or less, but if the holder dislikes Sweet flavors, it gains the Confused status condition.	Prize for Spin Trades in the Union Room	—
	Magost Berry	—	Not obtainable in these versions	—
	Micle Berry	Raises the accuracy of the holder's moves by 20% one time when its HP becomes low.	Not obtainable in these versions	—
	Nanab Berry	—	Not obtainable in these versions	—
	Nomel Berry	—	Not obtainable in these versions	—
	Occa Berry	Halves damage the holder takes from supereffective Fire-type moves.	Join Avenue Flower Shop (when the owner is from *Pokémon Black Version*)/Sometimes held by wild Pansage	2,000 (for 4)
	Oran Berry	Holder restores its own HP by 10 when its HP falls to half or less.	From Alder on Route 19/Often held by wild Furret, Bibarel, Pansage, Pansear, and Panpour	600 ▲ (for 4)
	Pamtre Berry	—	Not obtainable in these versions	—
	Passho Berry	Halves damage the holder takes from supereffective Water-type moves.	Join Avenue Flower Shop (when the owner is from *Pokémon White Version*)/Sometimes held by wild Pansear	2,000 for 4
	Payapa Berry	Halves damage the holder takes from supereffective Psychic-type moves.	Join Avenue Flower Shop (when the owner is from *Pokémon White Version*)	2,000 (for 4)
	Pecha Berry	Holder can heal itself of the Poison status condition.	Show the Harlequin in Castelia City's Studio Castelia the Pokémon he wants to see/From the man in Lacunosa Town (night, late night)	600 ▲ (for 4)
	Persim Berry	Holder can heal itself of the Confused status condition.	Seaside Cave (after defeating Pokémon Ranger Mikiko or Johan)/Often held by wild Spoink, Gothita, and Solosis	600 ▲ (for 4)
	Petaya Berry	Raises the holder's Sp. Atk stat by 1 when its HP becomes low.	Join Avenue Flower Shop (when the owner is from *Pokémon Black Version*)	2,000 (for 4)
	Pinap Berry	—	Not obtainable in these versions	—
	Pomeg Berry	Slightly raises the Pokémon's friendship, but lowers its base HP stat.	Buy from the woman on Route 5/Prize for Spin Trades in the Union Room	200 (for 5)
	Qualot Berry	Slightly raises the Pokémon's friendship, but lowers its base Defense stat.	Buy from the woman on Route 5/Prize for Spin Trades in the Union Room	200 (for 5)
	Rabuta Berry	—	Not obtainable in these versions	—
	Rawst Berry	Holder can heal itself of the Burned status condition.	Show the Harlequin in Castelia City's Studio Castelia the Pokémon he wants to see/Desert Resort (after defeating Pokémon Ranger Anja or Jaden)	600 ▲ (for 4)
	Razz Berry	—	Join Avenue Flower Shop (when the owner is from *Pokémon Black Version 2*)	600 (for 4)
	Rindo Berry	Halves damage the holder takes from supereffective Grass-type moves.	Sometimes held by wild Finneon, Lumineon, and Panpour/Join Avenue Flower Shop (when the owner is from *Pokémon White Version 2*)	2,000 (for 4)
	Rowap Berry	When the holder takes damage from a special attack, the Pokémon that landed the attack is also damaged.	Not obtainable in these versions	—
	Salac Berry	Holder raises its Speed stat by 1 when its HP becomes low.	Join Avenue Flower Shop (when the owner is from *Pokémon White Version 2*)	2,000 (for 4)
	Shuca Berry	Halves damage the holder takes from supereffective Ground-type moves.	Join Avenue Flower Shop (when the owner is from *Pokémon White Version 2*)	2,000 (for 4)
	Sitrus Berry	Holder restores its own HP by 1/4 of its max HP when its HP falls to half or less.	Route 13 (after defeating Pokémon Ranger Dianne or Daryl)/From the woman on Village Bridge	800 ▲ (for 4)
	Spelon Berry	—	Not obtainable in these versions	—
	Starf Berry	Raises one of the holder's stats by 2 when its HP falls to half or less.	From a Trainer on the 29th platform stop during a Battle Subway win streak	—
	Tamato Berry	Slightly raises the Pokémon's friendship, but lowers its base Speed stat.	Buy from the woman on Route 5/Prize for Spin Trades in the Union Room	200 (for 5)
	Tanga Berry	Halves damage the holder takes from supereffective Bug-type moves.	Join Avenue Flower Shop (when the owner is from *Pokémon Black Version 2*)	2,000 (for 4)
	Wacan Berry	Halves damage the holder takes from supereffective Electric-type moves.	Join Avenue Flower Shop (when the owner is from *Pokémon Black Version 2*)	2,000 (for 4)
	Watmel Berry	—	Not obtainable in these versions	—
	Wepear Berry	—	Not obtainable in these versions	—
	Wiki Berry	Holder restores some of its own HP when its HP falls to half or less, but if the holder dislikes Dry flavors, it gains the Confused status condition.	Prize for Spin Trades in the Union Room	—
	Yache Berry	Halves damage the holder takes from supereffective Ice-type moves.	Join Avenue Flower Shop (when the owner is from *Pokémon Black Version*)	2,000 (for 4)

▲ Price when purchased at a Join Avenue Flower Shop.

Mail

Greet Mail
Price 50

Sold in
Aspertia City, Virbank City, Floccesy Town, Castelia City

Favored Mail
Price 50

Sold in
Aspertia City, Virbank City, Floccesy Town, Castelia City

RSVP Mail
Price 50

Sold in
Aspertia City, Virbank City, Floccesy Town, Castelia City

Thanks Mail
Price 50

Sold in
Aspertia City, Virbank City, Floccesy Town, Castelia City

Inquiry Mail
Price 50

Sold in
Aspertia City, Virbank City, Floccesy Town, Castelia City

Like Mail
Price 50

Sold in
Aspertia City, Virbank City, Floccesy Town, Castelia City

Reply Mail
Price 50

Sold in
Aspertia City, Virbank City, Floccesy Town, Castelia City

BridgeMail S
Price 50
Sold in
Nacrene City

BridgeMail D
Price 50

Sold in
Driftveil City

BridgeMail T
Price 50
Sold in
Icirrus City

BridgeMail V
Price 50

Sold in
Opelucid City

BridgeMail M
Price 50

Sold in
Black City, White Forest

Medals

Special Medals

Name	How to Obtain
First Step	Participate in the Medal Rally (Receive it with the Medal Box)
Participation Prize	Go to the Medal Office in Castelia City after collecting 50 Medals
Rookie Medalist	Collect 50 Medals and advance to the Rookie Rank
Elite Medalist	Collect 100 Medals and advance to the Elite Rank
Master Medalist	Collect 150 Medals and advance to the Master Rank
Legend Medalist	Collect 200 Medals and advance to the Legend Rank
Top Medalist	Obtain all Medals

Adventure Medals

Name	How to Obtain
Light Walker	Take 5,000 steps
Middle Walker	Take 10,000 steps
Heavy Walker	Take 20,000 steps
Honored Footprints	Take 100,000 steps

Name	How to Obtain
Step-by-Step Saver	Save 10 times or more
Busy Saver	Save 20 times or more
Experienced Saver	Save 50 times or more
Wonder Writer	Save 100 times or more
Pokémon Center Fan	Have Pokémon's health restored in Pokémon Centers a certain number of times
Signboard Starter	Read five Trainer Tips signs
Signboard Savvy	Read 15 Trainer Tips signs
Graffiti Gazer	Notice graffiti behind a sign
Starter Cycling	Ride a Bicycle for the first time
Easy Cycling	Ride a Bicycle 30 times or more
Hard Cycling	Ride a Bicycle 100 times or more
Pedaling Legend	Ride a Bicycle 500 times or more
Old Rod Fisherman	Reel in a Pokémon for the first time
Good Rod Fisherman	Reel in 10 or more Pokémon

◉ Medals

◆ Adventure Medals

	Name	How to Obtain
	Super Rod Fisherman	Reel in 50 or more Pokémon
	Mighty Fisher	Reel in 100 or more Pokémon
	Normal-type Catcher	Catch all the Normal-type Pokémon in the Unova Pokédex
	Fire-type Catcher	Catch all the Fire-type Pokémon in the Unova Pokédex
	Water-type Catcher	Catch all the Water-type Pokémon in the Unova Pokédex
	Electric-type Catcher	Catch all the Electric-type Pokémon in the Unova Pokédex
	Grass-type Catcher	Catch all the Grass-type Pokémon in the Unova Pokédex
	Ice-type Catcher	Catch all the Ice-type Pokémon in the Unova Pokédex
	Fighting-type Catcher	Catch all the Fighting-type Pokémon in the Unova Pokédex
	Poison-type Catcher	Catch all the Poison-type Pokémon in the Unova Pokédex
	Ground-type Catcher	Catch all the Ground-type Pokémon in the Unova Pokédex
	Flying-type Catcher	Catch all the Flying-type Pokémon in the Unova Pokédex
	Psychic-type Catcher	Catch all the Psychic-type Pokémon in the Unova Pokédex
	Bug-type Catcher	Catch all the Bug-type Pokémon in the Unova Pokédex
	Rock-type Catcher	Catch all the Rock-type Pokémon in the Unova Pokédex
	Ghost-type Catcher	Catch all the Ghost-type Pokémon in the Unova Pokédex
	Dragon-type Catcher	Catch all the Dragon-type Pokémon in the Unova Pokédex
	Dark-type Catcher	Catch all the Dark-type Pokémon in the Unova Pokédex
	Steel-type Catcher	Catch all the Steel-type Pokémon in the Unova Pokédex
	Unova Catcher	Complete the Unova Pokédex and receive an award certificate from the Game Director in Castelia City
	National Catcher	Complete the National Pokédex and receive an award certificate from the Game Director in Castelia City
	30 Boxed	Deposit 30 or more Pokémon in the PC Boxes
	120 Boxed	Deposit 120 or more Pokémon in the PC Boxes
	360 Boxed	Deposit 360 or more Pokémon in the PC Boxes
	Boxes Max	Deposit 720 Pokémon in the PC Boxes
	Capturing Spree	Catch 50 or more Pokémon in a day
	Vending Virtuoso	Buy 10 or more drinks at vending machines
	Lucky Drink	Get a bonus at a vending machine
	Evolution Hopeful	Evolve a Pokémon for the first time
	Evolution Tech	Evolve Pokémon 10 times or more
	Evolution Expert	Evolve Pokémon 50 times or more
	Evolution Authority	Evolve Pokémon 100 times or more
	Ace Pilot	Travel using Fly a certain number of times
	Hustle Muscle	Drop a boulder using Strength a certain number of times
	Trash Master	Check trash cans a certain number of times
	Dowsing Beginner	Find a hidden item for the first time using the Dowsing MCHN
	Dowsing Specialist	Find 10 or more hidden items using the Dowsing MCHN
	Dowsing Collector	Find 50 or more hidden items using the Dowsing MCHN
	Dowsing Wizard	Find 150 or more hidden items using the Dowsing MCHN
	Naming Champ	Give Pokémon nicknames a certain number of times
	Television Kid	Watch TV a certain number of times
	Regular Customer	Shop a certain number of times

	Name	How to Obtain
	Moderate Customer	Spend 10,000 or more at shops
	Great Customer	Spend 100,000 or more at shops
	Indulgent Customer	Spend 1,000,000 or more at shops
	Super Rich	Spend 10,000,000 or more at shops
	Smart Shopper	Buy 10 Poké Balls at once and receive a Premier Ball
	Sweet Home	Have your mom restore your Pokémon's HP at your home in Aspertia City
	The First Passerby	Pass by a person for the first time with Tag Mode
	30 Passersby	Pass by 30 or more people with Tag Mode
	100 Passersby	Pass by 100 or more people with Tag Mode
	Heavy Traffic	Pass by 1,000 or more people with Tag Mode
	Pass Power ↑	Use a Pass Power for the first time
	Pass Power ↑↑	Use 10 or more Pass Powers
	Pass Power ↑↑↑	Use 50 or more Pass Powers
	Pass Power MAX	Use 100 or more Pass Powers
	Dozing Capture	Catch a Pokémon in the Entree Forest for the first time
	Sleeping Capture	Catch 10 or more Pokémon in the Entree Forest
	Deep Sleep Capture	Catch 50 or more Pokémon in the Entree Forest
	Sweet Dreamer	Catch 100 or more Pokémon in the Entree Forest
	Hidden Grotto Adept	Find all the Hidden Grottoes
	Egg Beginner	Hatch a Pokémon Egg for the first time
	Egg Breeder	Hatch 10 or more Pokémon Eggs
	Egg Elite	Hatch 50 or more Pokémon Eggs
	Hatching Aficionado	Hatch 100 or more Pokémon Eggs
	Day-Care Faithful	Leave many Pokémon at the Pokémon Day Care on Route 3
	Archeology Lover	Have a Pokémon Fossil restored in the Nacrene Museum in Nacrene City
	Pure Youth	Catch N's Pokémon
	Lucky Color	Catch a Shiny Pokémon
	Pokérus Discoverer	Catch a Pokémon infected with the Pokérus
	Castelia Boss	Defeat the three Trainers on the Back Street in Castelia City
	Rail Enthusiast	Hear information on all the trains in Anville Town
	Wailord Watcher	See a Wailord at the Marine Tube
	Face Board Memorial	Take a photo at the face board in Humilau City
	Heavy Machinery Pro	Give correct answers to five questions the Heavy Machinery Pro in Twist Mountain gives you
	Ruins Raider	Reach the deepest part of the Abyssal Ruins in Undella Bay
	Diamond Dust	See the Diamond Dust
	Bridge Enthusiast	Visit all the bridges in the Unova region
	Around Unova	Visit every city and town in the Unova region
	Great Adventurer	Obtain all 97 Adventure Medals except this Medal

Battle Medals

Name	How to Obtain
Battle Learner	Go through 100 or more battles
Battle Teacher	Go through 200 or more battles
Battle Veteran	Go through 400 or more battles
Battle Virtuoso	Go through 2,000 or more battles
Link Battle Amateur	Have a Link Battle for the first time
Link Battle Pioneer	Have 10 or more Link Battles
Link Battle Expert	Have 50 or more Link Battles
Born to Battle	Have 100 or more Link Battles
Magikarp Award	Use the move Splash in a battle
Never Give Up	Use the move Struggle in a battle
Noneffective Artist	Use moves that aren't very effective because of a bad matchup
Supereffective Savant	Use supereffective moves a certain number of times
Subway Low Gear	Try the Battle Subway for the first time
Subway Accelerator	Try the Battle Subway 10 times or more
Subway Top Gear	Try the Battle Subway 50 times or more
Runaway Express	Try the Battle Subway 100 times or more
Single Express	Beat the Subway Boss in a Single Train in the Battle Subway
Double Express	Beat the Subway Boss in a Double Train in the Battle Subway
Multi Express	Beat the Subway Boss in a Multi Train in the Battle Subway
Test Novice	Take the first Battle Test in the Battle Institute in Nimbasa City
Test Fan	Take 10 Battle Tests in the Battle Institute in Nimbasa City
Test Enthusiast	Take 30 Battle Tests in the Battle Institute in Nimbasa City
Exam Genius	Take 50 Battle Tests in the Battle Institute in Nimbasa City
Exp. Millionaire	Earn 1,000,000 Exp. Points in a day
BP Wealthy	Earn 100 BP
Superb Locator	Meet a certain number of Pokémon who appear in special conditions such as rustling grass and dust clouds
Battle Repeater	Battle with 30 or more Trainers in Big Stadium and Small Court in Nimbasa City
Cruise Connoisseur	Take 10 or more cruises on the *Royal Unova* in Castelia City
Driftveil Mightiest	Win the Driftveil Tournament in the PWT
Rental Champ	Win the Rental Tournament in the PWT
Mix Champ	Win the Mix Tournament in the PWT
Unova Mightiest	Win the Unova Leaders Tournament in the PWT
Kanto Mightiest	Win the Kanto Leaders Tournament in the PWT
Johto Mightiest	Win the Johto Leaders Tournament in the PWT
Hoenn Mightiest	Win the Hoenn Leaders Tournament in the PWT
Sinnoh Mightiest	Win the Sinnoh Leaders Tournament in the PWT
Mightiest Leader	Win the World Leaders Tournament in the PWT
World's Mightiest	Win the Champions Tournament in the PWT
Rental Master	Win the Rental Master Tournament in the PWT
Mix Master	Win the Mix Master Tournament in the PWT
All Types Champ	Win all the Type Expert Tournaments in the PWT

Name	How to Obtain
Tower Junior	Explore up to Area 5 in the Black Tower in Black City
Tower Master	Explore up to Area 10 in the Black Tower in Black City
Treehollow Junior	Explore up to Area 5 in the White Treehollow in White Forest
Treehollow Master	Explore up to Area 10 in the White Treehollow in White Forest
20 Victories	Beat 20 Trainers in the Black Tower or the White Treehollow
50 Victories	Beat 50 Trainers in the Black Tower or the White Treehollow
100 Victories	Beat 100 Trainers in the Black Tower or the White Treehollow
1,000 Wins	Beat 1,000 Trainers in the Black Tower or the White Treehollow
Undefeated: Easy	Defeat all Trainers in Area 2, 3, 4 or 5 in the Black Tower or the White Treehollow
Undefeated: Hard	Defeat all Trainers in Area 6,7, 8, 9, or 10 in the Black Tower or the White Treehollow
Pinpoint: Easy	Clear Area 2, 3, 4 or 5 within four battles in the Black Tower or the White Treehollow
Pinpoint: Hard	Clear Area 6,7, 8, 9, or 10 within six battles in the Black Tower or the White Treehollow
Quick Clear: Easy	Clear Area 2, 3, 4 or 5 within 100 steps in the Black Tower or the White Treehollow
Quick Clear: Hard	Clear Area 6,7, 8, 9, or 10 within 1,000 steps in the Black Tower or the White Treehollow
Battle Guru	Obtain all 55 Battle Medals except this Medal

Entertainment Medals

Name	How to Obtain
Beginning Trader	Trade a Pokémon by Link Trade for the first time
Occasional Trader	Trade Pokémon 10 times or more by Link Trade
Frequent Trader	Trade Pokémon 50 times or more by Link Trade
Great Trade-Up	Trade Pokémon 100 times or more by Link Trade
Opposite Trader	Link Trade between *Pokémon Black 2* and *Pokémon White* or *Pokémon White 2*; or between *Pokémon White 2* and *Pokémon Black* or *Pokémon Black 2*
Pen Pal	Write Mail and have a Pokémon hold it
Talented Cast Member	Participate in Pokémon Musicals a certain number of times
Rising Star	Receive a good review for the first time in a Pokémon Musical
Big Star	Receive five good reviews in Pokémon Musicals
Superstar	Receive 10 good reviews in Pokémon Musicals
Musical Star	Receive 30 good reviews in Pokémon Musicals
Trendsetter	Collect all the Props used in Pokémon Musicals
10 Followers	Ten fans gather at the reception after a Pokémon Musical
First Friend	Register a Friend Code in your Pal Pad for the first time
Extensive Friendship	Register five or more Friend Codes in your Pal Pad
Broad Friendship	Register 10 or more Friend Codes in your Pal Pad
Global Connection	Register the maximum number of Friend Codes in your Pal Pad
Spin Trade Whiz	Play Spin Trade in the Union Room a certain number of times
Feeling Master	Play Feeling Check via Infrared Connection (IR) a certain number of times
Ace of Hearts	Score 80 points or more in Feeling Check via Infrared Connection (IR)
Ferris Wheel Fan	Meet a lot of people at the Ferris wheel in Nimbasa City
New Guide	Guide 10 or more customers in Join Avenue
Elite Guide	Guide 20 or more customers in Join Avenue
Veteran Guide	Guide 50 or more customers in Join Avenue
Guiding Champ	Guide 100 or more customers in Join Avenue

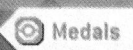 Medals

Entertainment Medals

Name	How to Obtain
Shop Starter	Create five shops in Join Avenue
Shop Builder	Create 10 shops in Join Avenue
Shop Constructor	Create 20 shops in Join Avenue
Extreme Developer	Create 50 shops in Join Avenue
OK Souvenir Getter	Receive 10 or more souvenirs from visitors in Join Avenue
Good Souvenir Getter	Receive 30 or more souvenirs from visitors in Join Avenue
Great Souvenir Getter	Receive 50 or more souvenirs from visitors in Join Avenue
Tycoon of Souvenirs	Receive 100 or more souvenirs from visitors in Join Avenue
Avenue of Fame	Develop Join Avenue and earn the right to give it an original name
Minigame Fan	Play minigames on the Xtransceiver 10 times or more
Minigame Buff	Play minigames on the Xtransceiver 30 times or more
Minigame Expert	Play minigames on the Xtransceiver 50 times or more
Best Minigamer	Play minigames on the Xtransceiver 100 times or more
Balloon Rookie	Reach a total of 50 points in minigames on the Xtransceiver
Balloon Technician	Reach a total of 200 points in minigames on the Xtransceiver
Balloon Expert	Reach a total of 500 points in minigames on the Xtransceiver
Balloon Conqueror	Reach a total of 1,000 points in minigames on the Xtransceiver
New Face Hero	Release a starring movie for the first time in Pokéstar Studios
Hero Movie Star	Release the full series of *Brycen-Man Strikes Back* in Pokéstar Studios
Cop Movie Master	Release the full series of *Full Metal Cop* in Pokéstar Studios
UFO Movie Master	Release the full series of *Invaders* in Pokéstar Studios
Monster Movie Master	Release the full series of *Big Monster* in Pokéstar Studios
Sci-Fi Movie Master	Release the full series of *Timegate Traveler* in Pokéstar Studios
Romantic Movie Star	Release the full series of *Love and Battles* in Pokéstar Studios
Fantasy Movie Master	Release the full series of *Mystery Doors of the Magical Land* in Pokéstar Studios
Comedic Movie Star	Release the full series of *The Giant Woman* in Pokéstar Studios
Horror Movie Star	Release the full series of *Red Fog of Terror* in Pokéstar Studios
Robot Movie Master	Release the full series of *Everlasting Memories* in Pokéstar Studios
Ghost Movie Master	Release the full series of *Ghost Eraser* in Pokéstar Studios
Hero Ending	Release *Brycen-Man Strikes Back Harder* in Pokéstar Studios
Popular Movie Star	Release all movies in Pokéstar Studios
Masterpiece Star	Release all movies with happy endings in Pokéstar Studios
Blockbuster Star	Reach 100 billion box sales in Pokéstar Studios
First Cult Classic	Release a movie with a weird ending in Pokéstar Studios for the first time
Cult Classic Star	Release all movies with weird endings in Pokéstar Studios
10 People Funfest	Play an Entralink Funfest Mission with 10 people or more
30 People Funfest	Play an Entralink Funfest Mission with 30 people or more
Scored 100	Score 100 or more points in an Entralink Funfest Mission
Scored 1,000	Score 1,000 or more points in an Entralink Funfest Mission
Mission Host Lv. 1	Host 10 or more Entralink Funfest Missions
Mission Host Lv. 2	Host 50 or more Entralink Funfest Missions

Name	How to Obtain
Participant Lv. 1	Participate in an Entralink Funfest Mission for the first time
Participant Lv. 2	Participate in 10 or more Entralink Funfest Missions
Achiever Lv. 1	Clear 30 or more Entralink Funfest Missions
Achiever Lv. 2	Clear 100 or more Entralink Funfest Missions
Funfest Complete	Clear all Entralink Funfest Missions
Good Night	Use Game Sync to wake up a tucked-in Pokémon
Beginning of Memory	Use Memory Link and see a link event for the first time
Memory Master	Use Memory Link and see all the link events
Entertainment Master	Obtain the other 74 Entertainment Medals

Challenge Medals

Name	How to Obtain
Normal-type Champ	Win the Pokémon League and enter the Hall of Fame with only Normal-type Pokémon
Fire-type Champ	Win the Pokémon League and enter the Hall of Fame with only Fire-type Pokémon
Water-type Champ	Win the Pokémon League and enter the Hall of Fame with only Water-type Pokémon
Electric-type Champ	Win the Pokémon League and enter the Hall of Fame with only Electric-type Pokémon
Grass-type Champ	Win the Pokémon League and enter the Hall of Fame with only Grass-type Pokémon
Ice-type Champ	Win the Pokémon League and enter the Hall of Fame with only Ice-type Pokémon
Fighting-type Champ	Win the Pokémon League and enter the Hall of Fame with only Fighting-type Pokémon
Poison-type Champ	Win the Pokémon League and enter the Hall of Fame with only Poison-type Pokémon
Ground-type Champ	Win the Pokémon League and enter the Hall of Fame with only Ground-type Pokémon
Flying-type Champ	Win the Pokémon League and enter the Hall of Fame with only Flying-type Pokémon
Psychic-type Champ	Win the Pokémon League and enter the Hall of Fame with only Psychic-type Pokémon
Bug-type Champ	Win the Pokémon League and enter the Hall of Fame with only Bug-type Pokémon
Rock-type Champ	Win the Pokémon League and enter the Hall of Fame with only Rock-type Pokémon
Ghost-type Champ	Win the Pokémon League and enter the Hall of Fame with only Ghost-type Pokémon
Dragon-type Champ	Win the Pokémon League and enter the Hall of Fame with only Dragon-type Pokémon
Dark-type Champ	Win the Pokémon League and enter the Hall of Fame with only Dark-type Pokémon
Steel-type Champ	Win the Pokémon League and enter the Hall of Fame with only Steel-type Pokémon
One and Only	Win the Pokémon League and enter the Hall of Fame with only one Pokémon in your party
Supreme Challenger	Obtain the other 18 Challenge Medals

Items held by wild Pokémon

Sometimes Pokémon that appear in the wild hold items. When you catch a Pokémon that's holding an item, you get that item. Some items, such as SilverPowder, Shed Shell, and Mental Herb, can't be obtained in any other way.

National No.	Pokémon	Always holding	Often holding	Sometimes holding	Rarely holding
012	Butterfree	—	—	SilverPowder	—
015	Beedrill	—	—	Poison Barb	—
022	Fearow	—	—	Sharp Beak	—
027	Sandshrew	—	—	Quick Claw	—
028	Sandslash	—	—	Quick Claw	—
035	Clefairy	—	Leppa Berry	Moon Stone	Comet Shard
036	Clefable	—	Leppa Berry	Moon Stone	—
037	Vulpix	Rawst Berry	—	—	—
038	Ninetales	Rawst Berry	—	—	—
058	Growlithe	—	Rawst Berry	—	—
061	Poliwhirl	—	—	King's Rock	—
062	Poliwrath	—	—	King's Rock	—
079	Slowpoke	—	—	Lagging Tail	—
081	Magnemite	—	—	Metal Coat	—
082	Magneton	—	—	Metal Coat	—
083	Farfetch'd	—	—	Stick	—
084	Doduo	—	—	Sharp Beak	—
088	Grimer	—	—	Black Sludge	—
089	Muk	—	Black Sludge	—	Toxic Orb
090	Shellder	—	Pearl	Big Pearl	—
091	Cloyster	—	Pearl	Big Pearl	—
108	Lickitung	—	—	Lagging Tail	—
109	Koffing	—	—	Smoke Ball	—
110	Weezing	—	—	Smoke Ball	—
116	Horsea	—	—	Dragon Scale	—
117	Seadra	—	—	Dragon Scale	—
120	Staryu	—	Stardust	Star Piece	—
121	Starmie	—	Stardust	Star Piece	—
132	Ditto	—	Quick Powder	Metal Powder	—
147	Dratini	—	—	Dragon Scale	—
148	Dragonair	—	—	Dragon Scale	—
149	Dragonite	—	—	Dragon Scale	—
162	Furret	—	Oran Berry	Sitrus Berry	—
170	Chinchou	—	—	DeepSeaScale	—
171	Lanturn	—	—	DeepSeaScale	—
186	Politoed	—	—	King's Rock	—
193	Yanma	—	—	Wide Lens	—
203	Girafarig	—	—	Persim Berry	—
208	Steelix	—	—	Metal Coat	—
211	Qwilfish	—	—	Poison Barb	—
213	Shuckle	Berry Juice	—	—	—
215	Sneasel	—	Grip Claw	Quick Claw	—
222	Corsola	—	—	Hard Stone	—
230	Kingdra	—	—	Dragon Scale	—
277	Swellow	—	—	Charti Berry	—
284	Masquerain	—	—	SilverPowder	—
286	Breloom	—	—	Kebia Berry	—
297	Hariyama	—	—	King's Rock	—
299	Nosepass	—	—	Hard Stone	—
300	Skitty	—	Pecha Berry	—	—
301	Delcatty	—	Pecha Berry	—	—
304	Aron	—	—	Hard Stone	—
305	Lairon	—	—	Hard Stone	—
315	Roselia	—	—	Poison Barb	Absorb Bulb
317	Swalot	—	—	Big Pearl	—
318	Carvanha	—	—	DeepSeaTooth	—
319	Sharpedo	—	—	DeepSeaTooth	—
322	Numel	Rawst Berry	—	—	—
323	Camerupt	Rawst Berry	—	—	—
325	Spoink	—	Persim Berry	—	—
326	Grumpig	—	Persim Berry	—	—
328	Trapinch	—	—	Soft Sand	—
332	Cacturne	—	—	Sticky Barb	—
335	Zangoose	—	—	Quick Claw	—
337	Lunatone	—	—	Moon Stone	Comet Shard
338	Solrock	—	—	Sun Stone	Comet Shard
351	Castform	Mystic Water	—	—	—
352	Kecleon	—	—	Persim Berry	—
354	Banette	—	—	Spell Tag	—
366	Clamperl	—	—	Big Pearl	—

◆ Items in the "Rarely holding" column can only be found by catching Pokémon in the dark grass.

National No.	Pokémon	Always holding	Often holding	Sometimes holding	Rarely holding
367	Huntail	—	—	DeepSeaTooth	—
368	Gorebyss	—	—	DeepSeaScale	—
369	Relicanth	—	—	DeepSeaScale	—
370	Luvdisc	—	Heart Scale	—	—
371	Bagon	—	—	Dragon Fang	—
375	Metang	—	—	Metal Coat	—
376	Metagross	—	—	Metal Coat	—
400	Bibarel	—	Oran Berry	Sitrus Berry	—
407	Roserade	—	—	Poison Barb	—
415	Combee	—	—	Honey	—
416	Vespiquen	—	—	Poison Barb	—
426	Drifblim	—	—	—	Air Balloon
427	Buneary	—	Pecha Berry	—	—
428	Lopunny	—	Pecha Berry	—	—
436	Bronzor	—	—	Metal Coat	—
441	Chatot	—	—	Metronome	—
451	Skorupi	—	—	Poison Barb	—
453	Croagunk	—	—	Black Sludge	—
454	Toxicroak	—	—	Black Sludge	—
456	Finneon	—	—	Rindo Berry	—
457	Lumineon	—	—	Rindo Berry	—
462	Magnezone	—	—	Metal Coat	—
463	Lickilicky	—	—	Lagging Tail	—
469	Yanmega	—	—	Wide Lens	—
511	Pansage	—	Oran Berry	Occa Berry	—
513	Pansear	—	Oran Berry	Passho Berry	—
515	Panpour	—	Oran Berry	Rindo Berry	—
523	Zebstrika	—	Cheri Berry	—	—
524	Roggenrola	—	Everstone	Hard Stone	—
525	Boldore	—	Everstone	Hard Stone	—
531	Audino	—	Oran Berry	Sitrus Berry	—
536	Palpitoad	—	Pecha Berry	—	—
537	Seismitoad	—	Pecha Berry	—	—
538	Throh	—	—	Black Belt	Expert Belt
539	Sawk	—	—	Black Belt	Expert Belt
540	Sewaddle	—	—	Mental Herb	—
541	Swadloon	—	—	Mental Herb	—
542	Leavanny	—	—	Mental Herb	—
543	Venipede	—	—	Poison Barb	—
544	Whirlipede	—	—	Poison Barb	—
545	Scolipede	—	—	Poison Barb	—
554	Darumaka	—	Rawst Berry	—	—
556	Maractus	—	—	Miracle Seed	—
557	Dwebble	—	—	Hard Stone	—
558	Crustle	—	—	Hard Stone	Rare Bone
559	Scraggy	—	—	Shed Shell	—
560	Scrafty	—	—	Shed Shell	—
562	Yamask	—	—	Spell Tag	—
568	Trubbish	—	—	Black Sludge	Nugget
569	Garbodor	—	Black Sludge	Nugget	Big Nugget
572	Minccino	—	Chesto Berry	—	—
573	Cinccino	—	Chesto Berry	—	—
574	Gothita	—	Persim Berry	—	—
575	Gothorita	—	Persim Berry	—	—
576	Gothitelle	—	Persim Berry	—	—
577	Solosis	—	Persim Berry	—	—
578	Duosion	—	Persim Berry	—	—
579	Reuniclus	—	Persim Berry	—	—
587	Emolga	Cheri Berry	—	—	—
590	Foongus	—	TinyMushroom	Big Mushroom	BalmMushroom
591	Amoonguss	—	TinyMushroom	Big Mushroom	BalmMushroom
597	Ferroseed	—	—	Sticky Barb	—
613	Cubchoo	—	Aspear Berry	—	—
614	Beartic	—	Aspear Berry	—	—
615	Cryogonal	—	—	NeverMeltIce	—
618	Stunfisk	—	—	Soft Sand	—
621	Druddigon	—	—	Dragon Fang	—
623	Golurk	—	—	Light Clay	—
637	Volcarona	SilverPowder	—	—	—

Items that certain people will buy from you

There are people in the Unova region who will buy certain items, and they will pay handsomely for them. If you sell items to these people, they will pay twice what the Poké Mart will buy the item for. Some items, such as BalmMushroom, Pearl String, and some of the items found in the Abyssal Ruins, are only purchased by these people.

■ Items the Maid in the trailer on Route 5 buys

Item	Price	Item	Price	Item	Price	Item	Price
Shoal Salt	7,000	Cheri Berry	20	Stick	200	Chilan Berry	20
Honey	500	Magost Berry	500	Enigma Berry	30,000	Mago Berry	20
Iapapa Berry	20	Soda Pop	300	Aspear Berry	20	Tamato Berry	20
RageCandyBar	6,000	Pomeg Berry	20	Nanab Berry	500	Micle Berry	30,000
Passho Berry	20	Lansat Berry	30,000	Colbur Berry	20	Lemonade	350
Custap Berry	30,000	Lucky Egg	200	Kelpsy Berry	20	Moomoo Milk	500
Wiki Berry	20	Pamtre Berry	500	Nomel Berry	500	Cornn Berry	500
Payapa Berry	20	Jaboca Berry	30,000	Spelon Berry	500	Pecha Berry	20
Grepa Berry	20	Shuca Berry	20	Sweet Heart	100	Old Gateau	4,000
Fresh Water	200	Apicot Berry	20	Pinap Berry	500	Petaya Berry	20
Big Mushroom	5,000	Starf Berry	30,000	Coba Berry	20	Yache Berry	20
Occa Berry	20	Razz Berry	500	Haban Berry	20	Chople Berry	20
Sitrus Berry	20	Wepear Berry	500	Aguav Berry	20	Charti Berry	20
Oran Berry	20	Wacan Berry	20	Kebia Berry	20	Rabuta Berry	500
Watmel Berry	500	Leftovers	200	Casteliacone	2,000	Lum Berry	20
BalmMushroom	25,000	Qualot Berry	20	Leppa Berry	20	Ganlon Berry	20
Chesto Berry	20	Tanga Berry	20	Figy Berry	20	Babiri Berry	20
Kasib Berry	20	Rawst Berry	20	Lava Cookie	4000	Rindo Berry	20
Salac Berry	20	TinyMushroom	500	Rare Candy	10,000	Rowap Berry	30,000
Persim Berry	20	Liechi Berry	20	Bluk Berry	500	Hondew Berry	20
Berry Juice	1,500	Durin Berry	500	Belue Berry	500		

■ Items the Pokémon Breeder on the runway in Mistralton City buys

Item	Price
Damp Mulch	1,000
Growth Mulch	1,000
Stable Mulch	1,000
Gooey Mulch	1,000

■ Items the billionaire in a house in Undella Town buys

Item	Price	Item	Price
Blue Flute	7,000	Relic Crown	300,000
Red Flute	7,500	Relic Gold	10,000
Yellow Flute	7,500	Relic Silver	5,000
Black Flute	8,000	Relic Statue	200,000
White Flute	8,000	Relic Vase	50,000
Relic Band	100,000	Relic Copper	1,000

■ Items the Gentleman in Icirrus City's Pokémon Center buys

Item	Price	Item	Price	Item	Price	Item	Price
Blue Shard	200	Thunderstone	3,000	Comet Shard	60,000	Star Piece	9,800
Red Shard	200	Float Stone	1,000	Sun Stone	3,000	Stardust	2,000
Dark Gem	200	Everstone	1,000	Moon Stone	3,000	Fire Stone	3,000
Shoal Shell	7,000	Yellow Shard	200	Icy Rock	1,000	Fire Gem	200
Heat Rock	1,000	Nugget	10,000	Big Nugget	30,000	Oval Stone	1,500
Rock Gem	200	Grass Gem	200	Electric Gem	200	Water Stone	3,000
Psychic Gem	200	Ghost Gem	200	Poison Gem	200	Water Gem	200
Big Pearl	7,500	Ice Gem	200	Dragon Gem	200	Green Shard	200
Pearl String	25,000	Smooth Rock	1,000	Normal Gem	200	Bug Gem	200
Fighting Gem	200	Damp Rock	1,000	Steel Gem	200	Dawn Stone	3,000
Hard Stone	500	Ground Gem	200	Shiny Stone	3,000	Dusk Stone	3,000
Odd Keystone	3,000	Pearl	1,400	Flying Gem	200	Leaf Stone	3,000

■ Items the sunglasses-wearing man in the prefab house on Route 18 buys

Item	Price
Rare Bone	10,000

Pokémon Moves Reverse Lookup

The number in the brackets is the level at which the Pokémon leans the move. [E] indicates an Egg Move. Form(e) names of Pokémon such as Giratina, Shaymin, Basculin, Tornadus, Thundurus, Landorus, Kyurem, etc. are abbreviated in parentheses.

A

Move	Pokémon that can learn it				
Absorb	043 Oddish [1]	044 Gloom [1]	114 Tangela [10]	140 Kabuto [6]	141 Kabutops [1, 6]	191 Sunkern [1]
	192 Sunflora [1]	252 Treecko [6]	253 Grovyle [1, 6]	254 Sceptile [1, 6]	267 Beautifly [1, 10]	270 Lotad [5]
	271 Lombre [5]	285 Shroomish [1]	286 Breloom [1]	315 Roselia [1]	331 Cacnea [1, 5]	332 Cacturne [1, 5]
	387 Turtwig [9]	388 Grotle [9]	389 Torterra [1, 9]	406 Budew [1]	465 Tangrowth [10]	546 Cottonee [1]
	548 Petilil [1]	556 Maractus [1]	590 Foongus [1]	591 Amoonguss [1]	592 Frillish [5]	593 Jellicent [1, 5]
Acid	023 Ekans [20]	024 Arbok [20]	043 Oddish [9]	044 Gloom [1,9]	069 Bellsprout [23]	070 Weepinbell [23]
	072 Tentacool [12]	073 Tentacruel [12]	213 Shuckle [E]	331 Cacnea [E]	345 Lileep [8]	346 Cradily [1,8]
	537 Seismitoad [36]	603 Eelektrik [19]	604 Eelektross [1]	607 Litwick [E]	616 Shelmet [4]	
Acid Armor	088 Grimer [40]	089 Muk [43]	134 Vaporeon [29]	218 Slugma [E]	316 Gulpin [E]	489 Phione [31]
	490 Manaphy [31]	577 Solosis [E]	582 Vanillite [31]	583 Vanillish [31]	584 Vanilluxe [31]	592 Frillish [E]
	607 Litwick [E]	615 Cryogonal [29]	616 Shelmet [32]			
Acid Spray	023 Ekans [28]	024 Arbok [32]	072 Tentacool [26]	073 Tentacruel [26]	088 Grimer [E]	194 Wooper [E]
	211 Qwilfish [E]	223 Remoraid [E]	316 Gulpin [34]	317 Swalot [38]	434 Stunky [32]	435 Skuntank [32]
	568 Trubbish [12]	569 Garbodor [12]	603 Eelektrik [49]	617 Accelgor [1, 4]		
Acrobatics	TM62	041 Zubat [30]	042 Golbat [33]	083 Farfetch'd [37]	169 Crobat [33]	187 Hoppip [28]
	188 Skiploom [32]	189 Jumpluff [34]	207 Gligar [22]	390 Chimchar [39]	391 Monferno [46]	392 Infernape [52]
	472 Gliscor [22]	511 Pansage [31]	513 Pansear [31]	515 Panpour [31]	566 Archen [28]	567 Archeops [28]
	587 Emolga [30]					
Acupressure	072 Tentacool [E]	084 Doduo [28]	085 Dodrio [28]	213 Shuckle [E]	307 Meditite [39]	308 Medicham [42]
	451 Skorupi [13]	452 Drapion [13]	453 Croagunk [E]	556 Maractus [29]		
Aerial Ace	TM40	021 Spearow [17]	022 Fearow [17]	083 Farfetch'd [13]	214 Heracross [10]	276 Taillow [34]
	277 Swellow [38]	278 Wingull [42]	396 Starly [25]	397 Staravia [28]	398 Staraptor [28]	580 Ducklett [15]
	581 Swanna [15]	627 Rufflet [23]	628 Braviary [23]			
Aeroblast	249 Lugia [43]					
After You	Taught by someone	035 Clefairy [58]	043 Oddish [E]	143 Snorlax [E]	175 Togepi [53]	176 Togetic [53]
	179 Mareep [E]	194 Wooper [E]	287 Slakoth [E]	427 Buneary [43]	428 Lopunny [43]	446 Munchlax [E]
	504 Patrat [23]	505 Watchog [25]	531 Audino [40]	548 Petilil [44]	556 Maractus [57]	572 Minccino [49]
Agility	015 Beedrill [31]	016 Pidgey [29]	017 Pidgeotto [32]	018 Pidgeot [32]	021 Spearow [25]	022 Fearow [29]
	025 Pikachu [37]	046 Paras [E]	048 Venonat [E]	058 Growlithe [30]	077 Ponyta [37]	078 Rapidash [37]
	083 Farfetch'd [31]	084 Doduo [E]	085 Dodrio [41]	098 Krabby [E]	107 Hitmonchan [6]	116 Horsea [23]
	117 Seadra [23]	118 Goldeen [47]	119 Seaking [56]	123 Scyther [17]	135 Jolteon [29]	137 Porygon [12]
	142 Aerodactyl [17]	144 Articuno [36]	145 Zapdos [43]	146 Moltres [15]	147 Dratini [25]	148 Dragonair [25]
	149 Dragonite [25]	160 Feraligatr [30]	163 Hoothoot [E]	165 Ledyba [30]	166 Ledian [36]	167 Spinarak [33]
	168 Ariados [37]	170 Chinchou [E]	179 Mareep [E]	190 Aipom [29, E]	203 Girafarig [14]	206 Dunsparce [E]
	207 Gligar [E]	212 Scizor [17]	215 Sneasel [20]	226 Mantine [32]	227 Skarmory [12]	230 Kingdra [23]
	233 Porygon2 [12]	237 Hitmontop [37]	252 Treecko [31]	253 Grovyle [35]	254 Sceptile [35]	255 Torchic [E]
	276 Taillow [43]	277 Swellow [49]	278 Wingull [38, E]	283 Surskit [31]	291 Ninjask [38]	311 Plusle [38]
	312 Minun [48]	318 Carvanha [36]	319 Sharpedo [45]	333 Swablu [E]	368 Gorebyss [10]	370 Luvdisc [9]
	375 Metang [38]	376 Metagross [38]	386 Deoxys (Spd) [73]	393 Piplup [E]	396 Starly [33]	397 Staravia [38]
	398 Staraptor [41]	418 Buizel [41]	419 Floatzel [51]	424 Ambipom [29]	427 Buneary [33]	428 Lopunny [33]
	441 Chatot [E]	447 Riolu [E]	451 Skorupi [E]	456 Finneon [E]	458 Mantyke [32]	474 Porygon-Z [12]
	522 Blitzle [36]	523 Zebstrika [42]	540 Sewaddle [E]	543 Venipede [29]	544 Whirlipede [32]	545 Scolipede [33]
	550 Basculin [E]	566 Archen [21]	567 Archeops [21]	570 Zorua [37]	571 Zoroark [39]	585 Deerling [E]
	587 Emolga [46]	595 Joltik [37]	596 Galvantula [40]	617 Accelgor [32]	632 Durant [16]	641 Tornadus [37]
	642 Thundurus [37]					
Air Cutter	016 Pidgey [E]	041 Zubat [26]	042 Golbat [28]	083 Farfetch'd [21]	169 Crobat [28]	227 Skarmory [23]
	278 Wingull [33]	441 Chatot [E]	519 Pidove [15]	520 Tranquill [15]	521 Unfezant [15]	527 Woobat [21]
	528 Swoobat [21]	561 Sigilyph [21]	580 Ducklett [E]	641 Tornadus [25]		
Air Slash	006 Charizard [1]	016 Pidgey [49, E]	017 Pidgeotto [57]	018 Pidgeot [62]	041 Zubat [45]	042 Golbat [52]
	083 Farfetch'd [49]	123 Scyther [53]	146 Moltres [50]	163 Hoothoot [33]	164 Noctowl [37]	169 Crobat [52]
	193 Yanma [54]	226 Mantine [36]	227 Skarmory [42]	276 Taillow [53]	277 Swellow [61]	278 Wingull [46]
	284 Masquerain [47]	357 Tropius [51]	384 Rayquaza [35]	414 Mothim [41]	416 Vespiquen [37]	458 Mantyke [36]
	468 Togekiss [1]	469 Yanmega [54]	479 Rotom (Fan) ◆	492 Shaymin (Sky) [64]	501 Oshawott [E]	519 Pidove [29]
	520 Tranquill [32]	521 Unfezant [33]	527 Woobat [32]	528 Swoobat [32]	540 Sewaddle [E]	561 Sigilyph [41]
	580 Ducklett [27]	581 Swanna [27]	587 Emolga [E]	627 Rufflet [41]	628 Braviary [41]	629 Vullaby [41]
	630 Mandibuzz [41]	641 Tornadus [43]				
Ally Switch	TM51	064 Kadabra [24]	065 Alakazam [24]			
Amnesia	001 Bulbasaur [E]	032 Nidoran ♂ [E]	052 Meowth [E]	054 Psyduck [43]	055 Golduck [49]	079 Slowpoke [41]
	080 Slowbro [43]	098 Krabby [E]	108 Lickitung [E]	114 Tangela [E]	143 Snorlax [9]	150 Mewtwo [50]
	151 Mew [60]	161 Sentret [36]	162 Furret [42]	170 Chinchou [E]	173 Cleffa [E]	183 Marill [E]
	187 Hoppip [E]	194 Wooper [23]	195 Quagsire [24]	203 Girafarig [E]	218 Slugma [32]	219 Magcargo [32]
	220 Swinub [48]	221 Piloswine [58]	222 Corsola [E]	226 Mantine [E]	273 Seedot [E]	287 Slakoth [25]
	289 Slaking [25]	316 Gulpin [17]	317 Swalot [17]	320 Wailmer [37]	321 Wailord [37]	322 Numel [19]
	323 Camerupt [19]	324 Torkoal [49]	325 Spoink [E]	339 Barboach [18]	340 Whiscash [18]	345 Lileep [E]
	346 Cradily [29]	351 Castform [E]	368 Gorebyss [19]	369 Relicanth [18]	378 Regice [41]	379 Registeel [41]
	386 Deoxys (Def) [73]	387 Turtwig [E]	399 Bidoof [29]	400 Bibarel [33]	422 Shellos [E]	425 Drifloon [40]
	426 Drifblim [46]	446 Munchlax [9]	458 Mantyke [E]	480 Uxie [46]	513 Pansear [25]	527 Woobat [29]
	528 Swoobat [29]	531 Audino [E]	559 Scraggy [E]	568 Trubbish [40]	569 Garbodor [46]	626 Bouffalant [E]
	631 Heatmor [46]	636 Larvesta [80]				
AncientPower	004 Charmander [E]	050 Diglett [E]	098 Krabby [E]	102 Exeggcute [E]	104 Cubone [E]	114 Tangela [40]
	131 Lapras [E]	138 Omanyte [37]	139 Omastar [37]	140 Kabuto [46]	141 Kabutops [54]	142 Aerodactyl [25]

Move	Pokémon that can learn it					
AncientPower (continued)	144 Articuno [29]	145 Zapdos [29]	146 Moltres [29]	151 Mew [50]	152 Chikorita [E]	158 Totodile [E]
	175 Togepi [33]	176 Togetic [33]	193 Yanma [33]	194 Wooper [E]	206 Dunsparce [19, E]	218 Slugma [28]
	219 Magcargo [28]	220 Swinub [E]	221 Piloswine [1]	222 Corsola [20]	231 Phanpy [E]	246 Larvitar [E]
	249 Lugia [57]	250 Ho-Oh [57]	251 Celebi [28]	258 Mudkip [E]	303 Mawile [E]	318 Carvanha [E]
	322 Numel [E]	341 Corphish [E]	343 Baltoy [21]	344 Claydol [21]	345 Lileep [43]	346 Cradily [36]
	347 Anorith [31]	348 Armaldo [31]	352 Kecleon [55]	369 Relicanth [43]	377 Regirock [33]	378 Regice [33]
	379 Registeel [33]	382 Kyogre [45]	383 Groudon [45]	384 Rayquaza [45]	408 Cranidos [33]	409 Rampardos [36]
	410 Shieldon [28]	411 Bastiodon [28]	465 Tangrowth [40]	469 Yanmega [33]	473 Mamoswine [1]	483 Dialga [10]
	484 Palkia [10]	485 Heatran [1]	487 Giratina (Alt) [10]	487 Giratina (Ori) [10]	561 Sigilyph [E]	564 Tirtouga [18]
	565 Carracosta [18]	566 Archen [18]	567 Archeops [18]	643 Reshiram [15]	644 Zekrom [15]	646 Kyurem [15]
	646 Kyurem (Blk) [15]	646 Kyurem (Wht) [15]				
Aqua Jet	007 Squirtle [E]	055 Golduck [1]	086 Seel [31]	087 Dewgong [31]	140 Kabuto [31]	141 Kabutops [31]
	147 Dratini [E]	158 Totodile [E]	183 Marill [E]	211 Qwilfish [E]	283 Surskit [E]	318 Carvanha [31]
	319 Sharpedo [34]	370 Luvdisc [E]	395 Empoleon [36]	418 Buizel [24]	419 Floatzel [24]	501 Oshawott [29]
	502 Dewott [33]	503 Samurott [33]	550 Basculin [13]	564 Tirtouga [15]	565 Carracosta [15]	594 Alomomola [9]
	614 Beartic [1]	647 Keldeo [1]				
Aqua Ring	007 Squirtle [E]	072 Tentacool [E]	086 Seel [23]	087 Dewgong [23]	090 Shellder [E]	118 Goldeen [27]
	119 Seaking [27]	134 Vaporeon [25]	170 Chinchou [42]	171 Lanturn [52]	183 Marill [28]	184 Azumarill [31]
	222 Corsola [38, E]	226 Mantine [39]	278 Wingull [E]	320 Wailmer [E]	350 Milotic [49]	363 Spheal [E]
	366 Clamperl [E]	368 Gorebyss [24]	370 Luvdisc [46, E]	382 Kyogre [30]	393 Piplup [E]	418 Buizel [E]
	456 Finneon [33]	457 Lumineon [35]	458 Mantyke [39]	489 Phione [54]	490 Manaphy [54]	515 Panpour [E]
	535 Tympole [20]	536 Palpitoad [20]	537 Seismitoad [20]	580 Ducklett [24]	581 Swanna [24]	594 Alomomola [5]
Aqua Tail	Taught by someone	007 Squirtle [E]	008 Wartortle [32]	009 Blastoise [32]	054 Psyduck [32]	055 Golduck [32]
	086 Seel [43]	087 Dewgong [49]	118 Goldeen [32]	130 Gyarados [35]	147 Dratini [35]	148 Dragonair [39]
	149 Dragonite [39]	158 Totodile [43]	159 Croconaw [51]	160 Feraligatr [63]	183 Marill [20]	184 Azumarill [21]
	211 Qwilfish [45]	339 Barboach [35]	340 Whiscash [39]	350 Milotic [29]	367 Huntail [46]	368 Gorebyss [46]
	369 Relicanth [E]	382 Kyogre [65]	399 Bidoof [E]	418 Buizel [38, E]	419 Floatzel [46]	456 Finneon [E]
	484 Palkia [24, 42]	501 Oshawott [35]	502 Dewott [41]	503 Samurott [45]	515 Panpour [E]	550 Basculin [28]
	564 Tirtouga [41]	565 Carracosta [45]	572 Minccino [E]	647 Keldeo [37]		
Arm Thrust	296 Makuhita [7]	297 Hariyama [1, 7]	499 Pignite [17]	500 Emboar [17]		
Aromatherapy	045 Vileplume [1]	046 Paras [43]	047 Parasect [51]	113 Chansey [E]	152 Chikorita [42, E]	153 Bayleef [50]
	154 Meganium [60]	173 Cleffa [E]	187 Hoppip [43]	315 Roselia [43]	420 Cherubi [E]	440 Happiny [E]
	492 Shaymin (Land) [64]	548 Petilil [28]	585 Deerling [28]	586 Sawsbuck [28]		
Assist	052 Meowth [E]	096 Drowzee [E]	161 Sentret [E]	215 Sneasel [E]	300 Skitty [22]	327 Spinda [E]
	390 Chimchar [E]	431 Glameow [29]	432 Purugly [29]	509 Purrloin [6]	510 Liepard [1,6]	
Assurance	015 Beedrill [34]	019 Rattata [25]	020 Raticate [29]	021 Spearow [29]	022 Fearow [35]	052 Meowth [41]
	053 Persian [49]	056 Mankey [25]	057 Primeape [25]	084 Doduo [E]	109 Koffing [12]	110 Weezing [12]
	142 Aerodactyl [E]	197 Umbreon [25]	198 Murkrow [25, E]	203 Girafarig [28]	227 Skarmory [E]	232 Donphan [31]
	246 Larvitar [E]	261 Poochyena [29]	262 Mightyena [32]	318 Carvanha [26]	319 Sharpedo [26]	336 Seviper [E]
	359 Absol [E]	408 Cranidos [24]	409 Rampardos [24]	431 Glameow [E]	461 Weavile [1]	498 Tepig [31]
	499 Pignite [36]	500 Emboar [38]	501 Oshawott [E]	504 Patrat [31]	509 Purrloin [28]	510 Liepard [31]
	527 Woobat [12]	528 Swoobat [1, 12]	551 Sandile [16]	552 Krokorok [16]	553 Krookodile [16]	610 Axew [7]
	611 Fraxure [1, 7]	612 Haxorus [1, 7]	613 Cubchoo [E]	624 Pawniard [33]	625 Bisharp [33]	633 Deino [E]
Astonish	021 Spearow [E]	041 Zubat [8]	042 Golbat [1, 8]	050 Diglett [7, E]	051 Dugtrio [7]	092 Gastly [E]
	169 Crobat [1, 8]	190 Aipom [8]	198 Murkrow [1]	200 Misdreavus [10]	203 Girafarig [1]	206 Dunsparce [E]
	211 Qwilfish [E]	234 Stantler [7]	261 Poochyena [E]	270 Lotad [1]	271 Lombre [1]	272 Ludicolo [1]
	293 Whismur [11]	294 Loudred [1, 11]	295 Exploud [1, 11]	302 Sableye [11]	303 Mawile [1]	320 Wailmer [17]
	321 Wailord [17]	333 Swablu [4]	334 Altaria [1, 4]	345 Lileep [1]	346 Cradily [1]	352 Kecleon [1]
	353 Shuppet [1]	355 Duskull [14]	356 Dusclops [14]	358 Chimecho [9]	396 Starly [E]	424 Ambipom [1, 8]
	425 Drifloon [4]	426 Drifblim [1, 4]	429 Mismagius [1]	430 Honchkrow [1]	433 Chingling [9]	434 Stunky [E]
	453 Croagunk [1]	454 Toxicroak [1]	477 Dusknoir [14]	478 Froslass [1, 10]	479 Rotom [1]	479 Rotom (Heat) [1]
	479 Rotom (Wash) [1]	479 Rotom (Frst) [1]	479 Rotom (Fan) [1]	479 Rotom (Mow) [1]	511 Pansage [E]	513 Pansear [E]
	515 Panpour [E]	562 Yamask [1]	563 Cofagrigus [1]	577 Solosis [E]	582 Vanillite [7]	583 Vanillish [1, 7]
	584 Vanilluxe [1, 7]	587 Emolga [E]	590 Foongus [8]	591 Amoonguss [1, 8]	605 Elgyem [E]	607 Litwick [1]
	608 Lampent [1]	618 Stunfisk [E]	622 Golett [1]	623 Golurk [1]	633 Deino [E]	641 Tornadus [1]
	642 Thundurus [1]					
Attack Order	416 Vespiquen [45]					
Attract	TM45	267 Beautifly [31]	300 Skitty [8]	301 Delcatty [1]	350 Milotic [41]	370 Luvdisc [27]
	413 Wormadam (Plnt) [41]	413 Wormadam (Sand) [41]	413 Wormadam (Trsh) [41]	431 Glameow [44]	432 Purugly [52]	456 Finneon [10]
	457 Lumineon [1,10]	527 Woobat [25]	528 Swoobat [25]	531 Audino [15]		
Aura Sphere	150 Mewtwo [93]	151 Mew [100]	448 Lucario [51]	468 Togekiss [1]	483 Dialga [37]	484 Palkia [37]
	487 Giratina (Alt) [37]	487 Giratina (Ori) [37]	619 Mienfoo [61]	620 Mienshao [70]		
Aurora Beam	072 Tentacool [E]	086 Seel [27]	087 Dewgong [27]	090 Shellder [37]	091 Cloyster [1]	116 Horsea [E]
	134 Vaporeon [21]	138 Omanyte [E]	140 Kabuto [E]	223 Remoraid [14, E]	224 Octillery [1, 14]	225 Delibird [E]
	245 Suicune [29]	363 Spheal [25]	364 Sealeo [25]	365 Walrein [25]	456 Finneon [E]	488 Cresselia [29]
	615 Cryogonal [25]					
Autotomize	074 Geodude [E]	205 Forretress [32]	208 Steelix [19]	227 Skarmory [39]	304 Aron [39]	305 Lairon [45]
	306 Aggron [48]	524 Roggenrola [E]	582 Vanillite [E]	599 Klink [31]	600 Klang [31]	601 Klinklang [31]
Avalanche	090 Shellder [E]	124 Jynx [39]	131 Lapras [E]	215 Sneasel [E]	220 Swinub [E]	238 Smoochum [35]
	258 Mudkip [E]	361 Snorunt [E]	459 Snover [E]	582 Vanillite [19]	583 Vanillish [19]	584 Vanilluxe [19]
	613 Cubchoo [E]					

Pokémon Moves Reverse Lookup

B

Move	Pokémon that can learn it				
Barrage	102 Exeggcute [1]	103 Exeggutor [1]			
Barrier	063 Abra [E]	072 Tentacool [29]	073 Tentacruel [29]	090 Shellder [E]	096 Drowzee [E]	122 Mr. Mime [1]
	150 Mewtwo [1]	151 Mew [40]	222 Corsola [1]	239 Elekid [E]	240 Magby [E]	345 Lileep [E]
	366 Clamperl [E]	439 Mime Jr. [1]	462 Magnezone [1]	471 Glaceon [29]	517 Munna [E]	605 Elgyem [E]
Baton Pass	048 Venonat [E]	122 Mr. Mime [46]	123 Scyther [E]	133 Eevee [33]	151 Mew [80]	161 Sentret [39]
	162 Furret [46]	165 Ledyba [22]	166 Ledian [24]	167 Spinarak [E]	175 Togepi [41]	176 Togetic [41]
	190 Aipom [11]	203 Girafarig [23]	207 Gligar [E]	251 Celebi [37]	255 Torchic [E]	283 Surskit [43]
	291 Ninjask [45]	300 Skitty [E]	303 Mawile [31]	307 Meditite [E]	311 Plusle [44]	312 Minun [44]
	313 Volbeat [E]	314 Illumise [E]	327 Spinda [E]	359 Absol [E]	367 Huntail [33]	368 Gorebyss [33]
	418 Buizel [E]	424 Ambipom [11]	425 Drifloon [44]	426 Drifblim [52]	427 Buneary [26]	428 Lopunny [26]
	439 Mime Jr. [46]	504 Patrat [33]	505 Watchog [39]	517 Munna [E]	540 Sewaddle [E]	545 Scolipede [30]
	585 Deerling [E]	587 Emolga [E]	616 Shelmet [E]	619 Mienfoo [E]	632 Durant [E]	
Beat Up	004 Charmander [E]	023 Ekans [E]	029 Nidoran ♀ [E]	032 Nidoran ♂ [E]	050 Diglett [E]	056 Mankey [E]
	190 Aipom [E]	203 Girafarig [E]	215 Sneasel [28]	228 Houndour [25, E]	229 Houndoom [26]	273 Seedot [E]
	546 Cottonee [E]	551 Sandile [E]				
Belly Drum	004 Charmander [E]	060 Poliwag [31]	061 Poliwhirl [37]	079 Slowpoke [E]	104 Cubone [E]	108 Lickitung [E]
	143 Snorlax [17]	173 Cleffa [E]	183 Marill [E]	216 Teddiursa [E]	240 Magby [E]	263 Zigzagoon [45]
	264 Linoone [59]	296 Makuhita [25]	297 Hariyama [27]	554 Darumaka [30]	555 Darmanitan [30]	
Bestow	035 Clefairy [19]	102 Exeggcute [53]	113 Chansey [20]	172 Pichu [E]	175 Togepi [25]	176 Togetic [25]
	225 Delibird [20]	242 Blissey [20]	263 Zigzagoon [33]	264 Linoone [41]	357 Tropius [57]	417 Pachirisu [E]
	519 Pidove [E]	531 Audino [E]				
Bide	098 Krabby [E]	138 Omanyte [E]	165 Ledyba [E]	172 Pichu [E]	191 Sunkern [E]	204 Pineco [20]
	205 Forretress [20]	206 Dunsparce [E]	213 Shuckle [1]	214 Heracross [E]	222 Corsola [1]	241 Miltank [15]
	258 Mudkip [15]	259 Marshtomp [15]	260 Swampert [15]	273 Seedot [1]	307 Meditite [1]	308 Medicham [1]
	328 Trapinch [17]	329 Vibrava [17]	330 Flygon [17]	361 Snorunt [1]	393 Piplup [22, E]	394 Prinplup [24]
	401 Kricketot [1]	402 Kricketune [1]	417 Pachirisu [1]	504 Patrat [8]	505 Watchog [8]	532 Timburr [8]
	533 Gurdurr [1, 8]	534 Conkeldurr [1, 8]	538 Throh [5]	539 Sawk [5]	548 Petilil [E]	564 Tirtouga [1, E]
	565 Carracosta [1]	590 Foongus [12]	591 Amoonguss [1, 12]	613 Cubchoo [9]	614 Beartic [1, 9]	616 Shelmet [8]
	618 Stunfisk [5]					
Bind	Taught by someone	095 Onix [1]	114 Tangela [17]	127 Pinsir [4]	208 Steelix [1]	352 Kecleon [4]
	356 Dusclops [1]	455 Carnivine [1]	465 Tangrowth [17]	477 Dusknoir [1]	538 Throh [1]	599 Klink [21]
	600 Klang [21]	601 Klinklang [21]	603 Eelektrik [9]	615 Cryogonal [1]	631 Heatmor [1]	
Bite	004 Charmander [E]	007 Squirtle [16]	008 Wartortle [16]	009 Blastoise [16]	019 Rattata [10, E]	020 Raticate [10]
	023 Ekans [9]	024 Arbok [1, 9]	029 Nidoran ♀ [21]	030 Nidorina [23]	041 Zubat [12]	042 Golbat [12]
	052 Meowth [6]	053 Persian [1, 6]	058 Growlithe [1]	059 Arcanine [1]	115 Kangaskhan [13]	130 Gyarados [20]
	133 Eevee [17]	136 Flareon [17]	138 Omanyte [7]	139 Omastar [1, 7]	142 Aerodactyl [1]	158 Totodile [13]
	159 Croconaw [13]	160 Feraligatr [13]	169 Crobat [12]	206 Dunsparce [E]	209 Snubbull [7]	210 Granbull [7]
	215 Sneasel [E]	220 Swinub [E]	228 Houndour [16]	229 Houndoom [16]	234 Stantler [E]	243 Raikou [1]
	244 Entei [1]	245 Suicune [1]	246 Larvitar [1]	247 Pupitar [1]	248 Tyranitar [1]	258 Mudkip [E]
	261 Poochyena [13]	262 Mightyena [1, 13]	294 Loudred [20]	295 Exploud [20]	303 Mawile [11]	309 Electrike [28]
	310 Manectric [30]	318 Carvanha [1]	319 Sharpedo [1]	328 Trapinch [1]	336 Seviper [5]	359 Absol [20]
	361 Snorunt [10]	362 Glalie [1, 10]	367 Huntail [6]	371 Bagon [5]	372 Shelgon [1, 5]	373 Salamence [1, 5]
	387 Turtwig [21]	388 Grotle [22]	389 Torterra [22]	403 Shinx [17]	404 Luxio [18]	405 Luxray [18]
	417 Pachirisu [E]	431 Glameow [E]	447 Riolu [E]	449 Hippopotas [7]	450 Hippowdon [1, 7]	451 Skorupi [1]
	452 Drapion [1]	455 Carnivine [7]	471 Glaceon [17]	504 Patrat [6]	505 Watchog [1, 6]	506 Lillipup [8]
	507 Herdier [1, 8]	508 Stoutland [1, 8]	511 Pansage [19]	513 Pansear [19]	515 Panpour [19]	550 Basculin [10]
	551 Sandile [4]	552 Krokorok [1, 4]	553 Krookodile [1, 4]	564 Tirtouga [8]	565 Carracosta [8]	566 Archen [E]
	621 Druddigon [9]	632 Durant [11]	633 Deino [9]	634 Zweilous [1, 9]	635 Hydreigon [1, 9]	641 Tornadus [13]
	642 Thundurus [13]					
Blast Burn	Taught by someone					
Blaze Kick	106 Hitmonlee [45]	257 Blaziken [36]	390 Chimchar [E]	447 Riolu [E]		
Blizzard	TM14	124 Jynx [60]	144 Articuno [71]	220 Swinub [44]	221 Piloswine [52]	238 Smoochum [48]
	245 Suicune [85]	351 Castform [40]	361 Snorunt [46]	362 Glalie [51]	363 Spheal [43]	364 Sealeo [47]
	365 Walrein [52]	459 Snover [41]	460 Abomasnow [47]	471 Glaceon [45]	473 Mamoswine [52]	478 Froslass [51]
	479 Rotom (Frst) ◆	582 Vanillite [49]	583 Vanillish [53]	584 Vanilluxe [59]	613 Cubchoo [45]	614 Beartic [45]
	646 Kyurem [78]	646 Kyurem (Blk) [78]	646 Kyurem (Wht) [78]			
Block	Taught by someone	074 Geodude [E]	079 Slowpoke [E]	095 Onix [E]	102 Exeggcute [E]	143 Snorlax [41]
	158 Totodile [E]	185 Sudowoodo [26]	299 Nosepass [8, E]	331 Cacnea [E]	361 Snorunt [E]	411 Bastiodon [30]
	437 Bronzong [33]	438 Bonsly [26]	465 Tangrowth [56]	476 Probopass [1, 8]	557 Dwebble [E]	645 Landorus [1]
Blue Flare	643 Reshiram [100]					
Body Slam	031 Nidoqueen [35]	035 Clefairy [40]	039 Jigglypuff [33]	058 Growlithe [E]	060 Poliwag [21]	061 Poliwhirl [21]
	108 Lickitung [E]	118 Goldeen [E]	124 Jynx [44]	131 Lapras [18]	143 Snorlax [36]	152 Chikorita [34, E]
	153 Bayleef [40]	154 Meganium [46]	179 Mareep [E]	183 Marill [E]	194 Wooper [E]	218 Slugma [46]
	219 Magcargo [52]	220 Swinub [E]	231 Phanpy [E]	241 Miltank [24]	287 Slakoth [E]	298 Azurill [E]
	304 Aron [E]	317 Swalot [26]	320 Wailmer [E]	322 Numel [E]	324 Torkoal [33]	336 Seviper [E]
	341 Corphish [E]	357 Tropius [37]	363 Spheal [19]	364 Sealeo [19]	365 Walrein [19]	366 Clamperl [E]
	382 Kyogre [15]	387 Turtwig [E]	410 Shieldon [E]	422 Shellos [29]	423 Gastrodon [29]	425 Drifloon [E]
	432 Purugly [45]	443 Gible [E]	446 Munchlax [36]	449 Hippopotas [E]	498 Tepig [E]	538 Throh [29]
	564 Tirtouga [E]	569 Garbodor [25]	590 Foongus [E]	616 Shelmet [40]	631 Heatmor [E]	633 Deino [48]
	634 Zweilous [48]	635 Hydreigon [48]				
Bolt Strike	644 Zekrom [100]					
Bone Club	104 Cubone [7]	105 Marowak [1,7]				
Bone Rush	104 Cubone [37]	105 Marowak [43]	448 Lucario [29]	630 Mandibuzz [51]		
Bonemerang	104 Cubone [21]	105 Marowak [21]				

◆ When Rotom becomes Frost Rotom, it learns the move Blizzard. When it changes back to Rotom, it forgets the move.

Move	Pokémon that can learn it				
Bounce	Taught by someone	077 Ponyta [45]	078 Rapidash [45]	186 Politoed [37]	187 Hoppip [46]	188 Skiploom [56]
	189 Jumpluff [64]	190 Aipom [E]	226 Mantine [46]	298 Azurill [23]	320 Wailmer [44]	321 Wailord [54]
	325 Spoink [50]	326 Grumpig [60]	427 Buneary [56]	428 Lopunny [56]	456 Finneon [45]	457 Lumineon [53]
	458 Mantyke [46]	556 Maractus [E]	618 Stunfisk [35]	619 Mienfoo [49]	620 Mienshao [49]	
Brave Bird	016 Pidgey [E]	041 Zubat [E]	083 Farfetch'd [55]	084 Doduo [E]	198 Murkrow [49]	227 Skarmory [E]
	250 Ho-Oh [15]	257 Blaziken [49]	276 Taillow [E]	396 Starly [37]	397 Staravia [43]	398 Staraptor [49]
	580 Ducklett [41]	581 Swanna [47]	627 Rufflet [59]	628 Braviary [63]	629 Vullaby [59]	630 Mandibuzz [63]
Brick Break	TM31	106 Hitmonlee [17]	127 Pinsir [18]	214 Heracross [25]	539 Sawk [29]	559 Scraggy [20]
	560 Scrafty [20]					
Brine	007 Squirtle [E]	086 Seel [33]	087 Dewgong [33]	090 Shellder [44]	098 Krabby [39]	099 Kingler [51]
	116 Horsea [30]	117 Seadra [30]	120 Staryu [36]	131 Lapras [37]	138 Omanyte [28]	139 Omastar [28]
	170 Chinchou [E]	211 Qwilfish [33, E]	230 Kingdra [30]	278 Wingull [E]	279 Pelipper [34]	297 Hariyama [1]
	318 Carvanha [E]	320 Wailmer [31]	321 Wailord [31]	349 Feebas [E]	366 Clamperl [E]	367 Huntail [28]
	369 Relicanth [E]	370 Luvdisc [E]	393 Piplup [29]	394 Prinplup [33]	395 Empoleon [33]	422 Shellos [E]
	456 Finneon [E]	501 Oshawott [E]	515 Panpour [34]	550 Basculin [E]	564 Tirtouga [28]	565 Carracosta [28]
	580 Ducklett [E]	592 Frillish [32]	593 Jellicent [32]	594 Alomomola [41]	613 Cubchoo [21]	614 Beartic [21]
Bubble	007 Squirtle [7]	008 Wartortle [1, 7]	009 Blastoise [1, 7]	060 Poliwag [5]	061 Poliwhirl [1, 5]	072 Tentacool [E]
	098 Krabby [1]	099 Kingler [1]	116 Horsea [1]	117 Seadra [1]	170 Chinchou [1]	171 Lanturn [1]
	183 Marill [1]	184 Azumarill [1]	222 Corsola [8]	226 Mantine [1]	230 Kingdra [1]	283 Surskit [1]
	284 Masquerain [1]	298 Azurill [1]	341 Corphish [1]	342 Crawdaunt [1]	393 Piplup [8]	394 Prinplup [8]
	395 Empoleon [1, 8]	458 Mantyke [1]	489 Phione [1]	490 Manaphy [1]	535 Tympole [1]	536 Palpitoad [1]
	537 Seismitoad [1]	592 Frillish [1]	593 Jellicent [1]			
BubbleBeam	060 Poliwag [25, E]	061 Poliwhirl [27]	062 Poliwrath [1]	072 Tentacool [19]	073 Tentacruel [19]	090 Shellder [E]
	098 Krabby [15]	099 Kingler [15]	116 Horsea [18]	117 Seadra [18]	120 Staryu [22]	138 Omanyte [E]
	140 Kabuto [E]	170 Chinchou [31]	171 Lanturn [35]	183 Marill [13]	184 Azumarill [13]	186 Politoed [1]
	211 Qwilfish [E]	222 Corsola [17]	223 Remoraid [18]	224 Octillery [18]	226 Mantine [1,7]	230 Kingdra [18]
	245 Suicune [8]	270 Lotad [25]	271 Lombre [25]	283 Surskit [25]	298 Azurill [13]	341 Corphish [20]
	342 Crawdaunt [20]	393 Piplup [18]	394 Prinplup [19]	395 Empoleon [19]	458 Mantyke [7]	489 Phione [24]
	490 Manaphy [24]	535 Tympole [12]	536 Palpitoad [12]	537 Seismitoad [12]	550 Basculin [E]	580 Ducklett [19]
	581 Swanna [19]	592 Frillish [13]	593 Jellicent [13]	647 Keldeo [13]		
Bug Bite	Taught by someone	010 Caterpie [15]	013 Weedle [15]	046 Paras [E]	048 Venonat [E]	127 Pinsir [E]
	165 Ledyba [E]	168 Ariados [1]	204 Pineco [9]	205 Forretress [1,9]	213 Shuckle [42]	265 Wurmple [15]
	283 Surskit [E]	290 Nincada [E]	291 Ninjask [1]	328 Trapinch [E]	401 Kricketot [16]	412 Burmy [15]
	413 Wormadam (Plnt) [15]	413 Wormadam (Sand) [15]	413 Wormadam (Trsh) [15]	414 Mothim [15]	415 Combee [13]	451 Skorupi [20]
	452 Drapion [20]	469 Yanmega [E]	540 Sewaddle [8]	541 Swadloon [1,8]	542 Leavanny [1,8]	543 Venipede [22]
	544 Whirlipede [23]	545 Scolipede [23]	557 Dwebble [23]	558 Crustle [23]	588 Karrablast [E]	595 Joltik [18]
	596 Galvantula [18]	631 Heatmor [36]	632 Durant [26]	636 Larvesta [40]		
Bug Buzz	012 Butterfree [42]	049 Venomoth [59]	123 Scyther [E]	165 Ledyba [41, E]	166 Ledian [53]	193 Yanma [57]
	267 Beautifly [41]	269 Dustox [41]	284 Masquerain [61]	290 Nincada [E]	313 Volbeat [41, E]	314 Illumise [41, E]
	402 Kricketune [46]	414 Mothim [47]	415 Combee [29]	469 Yanmega [57]	540 Sewaddle [36]	588 Karrablast [28]
	589 Escavalier [28]	595 Joltik [48]	596 Galvantula [60]	616 Shelmet [44]	617 Accelgor [44]	636 Larvesta [70]
	637 Volcarona [70]	649 Genesect [55]				
Bulk Up	TM08	256 Combusken [28]	257 Blaziken [28]	383 Groudon [60]	532 Timburr [28]	533 Gurdurr [29]
	534 Conkeldurr [29]	538 Throh [33]	539 Sawk [33]			
Bulldoze	TM78	050 Diglett [18]	051 Dugtrio [18]	074 Geodude [32]	075 Graveler [36]	076 Golem [36]
	111 Rhyhorn [30]	112 Rhydon [30]	232 Donphan [1]	328 Trapinch [21]	329 Vibrava [21]	330 Flygon [21]
	645 Landorus [19]					
Bullet Punch	066 Machop [E]	107 Hitmonchan [16]	212 Scizor [1]	236 Tyrogue [E]	296 Makuhita [E]	307 Meditite [E]
	375 Metang [32]	376 Metagross [32]	447 Riolu [E]	453 Croagunk [E]		
Bullet Seed	069 Bellsprout [E]	102 Exeggcute [17]	187 Hoppip [19]	188 Skiploom [20]	189 Jumpluff [20]	192 Sunflora [25]
	223 Remoraid [38]	224 Octillery [46]	226 Mantine [1]	252 Treecko [E]	273 Seedot [E]	285 Shroomish [E]
	357 Tropius [E]	459 Snover [E]	511 Pansage [E]	556 Maractus [E]	573 Cinccino [1]	597 Ferroseed [E]

Move	Pokémon that can learn it				
Calm Mind	TM04	065 Alakazam [42]	234 Stantler [27]	243 Raikou [78]	244 Entei [78]	245 Suicune [78]
	249 Lugia [93]	250 Ho-Oh [93]	280 Ralts [28]	281 Kirlia [31]	282 Gardevoir [33]	307 Meditite [25]
	308 Medicham [25]	382 Kyogre [60]	392 Infernape [58]	448 Lucario [47]	517 Munna [35]	527 Woobat [29]
	528 Swoobat [29]	605 Elgyem [43]	606 Beheeyem [45]	619 Mienfoo [25]	620 Mienshao [25]	
Camouflage	120 Staryu [15]	414 Mothim [35]	540 Sewaddle [E]	585 Deerling [1]	586 Sawsbuck [1]	618 Stunfisk [17]
Captivate	012 Butterfree [40]	029 Nidoran ♀ [43]	030 Nidorina [50]	032 Nidoran ♂ [43]	033 Nidorino [50]	037 Vulpix [47]
	052 Meowth [46]	053 Persian [56]	077 Ponyta [E]	174 Igglybuff [E]	234 Stantler [53]	238 Smoochum [E]
	241 Miltank [35]	282 Gardevoir [60]	300 Skitty [46, E]	302 Sableye [E]	303 Mawile [E]	314 Illumise [E]
	349 Feebas [E]	350 Milotic [25]	368 Gorebyss [28]	370 Luvdisc [51, E]	413 Wormadam (Plnt) [35]	413 Wormadam (Sand) [35]
	413 Wormadam (Trsh) [35]	416 Vespiquen [41]	431 Glameow [32]	432 Purugly [32]	442 Spiritomb [E]	456 Finneon [26]
	457 Lumineon [26]	478 Froslass [31]	495 Snivy [E]	509 Purrloin [33]	570 Zorua [E]	572 Minccino [39]
	574 Gothita [E]	607 Litwick [E]				
Charge	100 Voltorb [1]	101 Electrode [1]	145 Zapdos [36]	170 Chinchou [50]	171 Lanturn [64]	172 Pichu [E]
	179 Mareep [15, E]	180 Flaaffy [16]	181 Ampharos [16]	309 Electrike [44]	310 Manectric [54]	311 Plusle [38]
	312 Minun [38]	403 Shinx [34]	404 Luxio [39]	405 Luxray [44]	417 Pachirisu [E]	479 Rotom [57]
	479 Rotom (Heat) [57]	479 Rotom (Wash) [57]	479 Rotom (Frst) [57]	479 Rotom (Fan) [57]	479 Rotom (Mow) [57]	522 Blitzle [8]
	523 Zebstrika [1, 8]	587 Emolga [10]	599 Klink [6]	600 Klang [1, 6]	601 Klinklang [1, 6]	642 Thundurus [55]
Charge Beam	TM57	100 Voltorb [22]	101 Electrode [22]	377 Regirock [49]	378 Regice [49]	379 Registeel [49]
	599 Klink [26]	600 Klang [26]	601 Klinklang [25]	602 Tynamo [1]	603 Eelektrik [1]	

C

Move	Pokémon that can learn it					
Charm	001 Bulbasaur [E]	029 Nidoran ♀ [E]	043 Oddish [E]	052 Meowth [E]	077 Ponyta [E]	133 Eevee [29, E]
	143 Snorlax [E]	161 Sentret [E]	172 Pichu [1]	173 Cleffa [1]	174 Igglybuff [1]	175 Togepi [1]
	176 Togetic [1]	209 Snubbull [1]	210 Granbull [1]	216 Teddiursa [36]	231 Phanpy [33]	263 Zigzagoon [E]
	280 Ralts [43]	281 Kirlia [50]	285 Shroomish [E]	298 Azurill [10]	300 Skitty [25]	312 Minun [21]
	314 Illumise [9]	360 Wynaut [1]	370 Luvdisc [4]	380 Latias [55]	417 Pachirisu [9]	427 Buneary [46]
	428 Lopunny [46]	431 Glameow [25]	432 Purugly [25]	439 Mime Jr. [1]	440 Happiny [1]	446 Munchlax [1]
	456 Finneon [E]	481 Mesprit [46]	489 Phione [9]	490 Manaphy [9]	506 Lillipup [E]	509 Purrloin [E]
	527 Woobat [E]	546 Cottonee [28]	548 Petilil [E]	572 Minccino [27]	574 Gothita [46]	575 Gothorita [50]
	576 Gothitelle [54]	577 Solosis [19]	578 Duosion [19]	579 Reuniclus [19]	585 Deerling [36]	586 Sawsbuck [36]
	587 Emolga [E]	613 Cubchoo [29]				
Chatter	441 Chatot [21]					
Chip Away	027 Sandshrew [E]	029 Nidoran ♀ [E]	031 Nidoqueen [23]	032 Nidoran ♂ [E]	034 Nidoking [23]	098 Krabby [E]
	104 Cubone [E]	108 Lickitung [37]	111 Rhyhorn [34]	112 Rhydon [34]	115 Kangaskhan [31]	143 Snorlax [25]
	158 Totodile [29]	159 Croconaw [33]	160 Feraligatr [37]	214 Heracross [16]	216 Teddiursa [E]	246 Larvitar [14]
	247 Pupitar [14]	248 Tyranitar [14]	287 Slakoth [37]	288 Vigoroth [43]	289 Slaking [37]	296 Makuhita [E]
	341 Corphish [E]	408 Cranidos [28]	409 Rampardos [28]	446 Munchlax [25]	463 Lickilicky [37]	464 Rhyperior [30]
	532 Timburr [24]	533 Gurdurr [24]	534 Conkeldurr [24]	550 Basculin [16]	559 Scraggy [27]	560 Scrafty [27]
	621 Druddigon [31]					
Circle Throw	062 Poliwrath [53]	115 Kangaskhan [E]	293 Whismur [E]	427 Buneary [E]	447 Riolu [E]	538 Throh [37]
Clamp	090 Shellder [25]	366 Clamperl [1]				
Clear Smog	069 Bellsprout [E]	092 Gastly [E]	109 Koffing [15]	110 Weezing [15]	116 Horsea [E]	126 Magmar [19]
	240 Magby [19]	324 Torkoal [E]	351 Castform [E]	422 Shellos [E]	425 Drifloon [E]	467 Magmortar [19]
	568 Trubbish [34]	569 Garbodor [34]	590 Foongus [39]	591 Amoonguss [43]	607 Litwick [E]	
Close Combat	056 Mankey [49, E]	057 Primeape [59]	058 Growlithe [E]	066 Machop [E]	106 Hitmonlee [57]	107 Hitmonchan [66]
	127 Pinsir [E]	209 Snubbull [E]	214 Heracross [34]	216 Teddiursa [E]	237 Hitmontop [55]	296 Makuhita [40]
	297 Hariyama [52]	335 Zangoose [47]	391 Monferno [36]	392 Infernape [36]	398 Staraptor [34]	448 Lucario [55]
	475 Gallade [59]	539 Sawk [49]	638 Cobalion [73]	639 Terrakion [73]	640 Virizion [73]	647 Keldeo [73]
Coil	023 Ekans [44]	024 Arbok [56]	206 Dunsparce [37]	336 Seviper [49]	495 Snivy [31]	496 Servine [36]
	497 Serperior [38]	603 Eelektrik [54]				
Comet Punch	107 Hitmonchan [1]	115 Kangaskhan [1]	165 Ledyba [9]	166 Ledian [1,9]	532 Timburr [E]	
Confuse Ray	037 Vulpix [15]	038 Ninetales [1]	041 Zubat [19]	042 Golbat [19]	054 Psyduck [E]	072 Tentacool [E]
	092 Gastly [19]	093 Haunter [19]	094 Gengar [19]	121 Starmie [22]	122 Mr. Mime [21]	126 Magmar [26]
	131 Lapras [7]	140 Kabuto [E]	169 Crobat [19]	170 Chinchou [12]	171 Lanturn [17]	177 Natu [23]
	178 Xatu [23]	179 Mareep [25]	180 Flaaffy [29]	181 Ampharos [29]	197 Umbreon [17]	198 Murkrow [E]
	200 Misdreavus [14]	222 Corsola [E]	226 Mantine [11]	234 Stantler [23]	240 Magby [26]	280 Ralts [E]
	292 Shedinja [31]	302 Sableye [46]	313 Volbeat [E]	314 Illumise [E]	325 Spoink [18]	326 Grumpig [18]
	345 Lileep [22]	346 Cradily [22]	349 Feebas [E]	353 Shuppet [E]	355 Duskull [17]	356 Dusclops [17]
	366 Clamperl [E]	416 Vespiquen [1]	436 Bronzor [11]	437 Bronzong [E]	439 Mime Jr. [E]	442 Spiritomb [1]
	451 Skorupi [E]	458 Mantyke [11]	467 Magmortar [26]	477 Dusknoir [17]	478 Froslass [19]	479 Rotom [1]
	479 Rotom (Heat) [1]	479 Rotom (Wash) [1]	479 Rotom (Frst) [1]	479 Rotom (Fan) [1]	479 Rotom (Mow) [1]	486 Regigigas [1]
	505 Watchog [20]	577 Solosis [E]	592 Frillish [E]	607 Litwick [10]	608 Lampent [10]	609 Chandelure [1]
	615 Cryogonal [45]					
Confusion	012 Butterfree [1,10]	032 Nidoran ♂ [E]	048 Venonat [11]	049 Venomoth [11]	054 Psyduck [15]	055 Golduck [15]
	064 Kadabra [1,16]	065 Alakazam [1,16]	079 Slowpoke [14]	080 Slowbro [14]	096 Drowzee [9]	097 Hypno [1,9]
	102 Exeggcute [1]	103 Exeggutor [1]	114 Tangela [1]	122 Mr. Mime [1]	150 Mewtwo [1]	163 Hoothoot [21]
	164 Noctowl [22]	187 Hoppip [E]	196 Espeon [9]	199 Slowking [14]	203 Girafarig [1]	238 Smoochum [15]
	251 Celebi [1]	269 Dustox [1,10]	280 Ralts [6]	281 Kirlia [1,6]	282 Gardevoir [1,6]	307 Meditite [8]
	308 Medicham [1,8]	337 Lunatone [1]	338 Solrock [1]	343 Baltoy [1]	344 Claydol [1]	358 Chimecho [14]
	368 Gorebyss [6]	375 Metang [1,20]	376 Metagross [1,20]	385 Jirachi [1]	413 Wormadam (Plnt) [23]	413 Wormadam (Sand) [23]
	413 Wormadam (Trsh) [23]	414 Mothim [23]	433 Chingling [14]	436 Bronzor [1]	437 Bronzong [1]	439 Mime Jr. [1]
	475 Gallade [1,6]	480 Uxie [1]	481 Mesprit [1]	482 Azelf [1]	488 Cresselia [1]	494 Victini [1]
	527 Woobat [1]	528 Swoobat [1]	574 Gothita [3]	575 Gothorita [1,3]	576 Gothitelle [1,3]	605 Elgyem [1]
	606 Beheeyem [1]					
Constrict	072 Tentacool [8]	073 Tentacruel [1, 8]	114 Tangela [1]	138 Omanyte [1]	139 Omastar [1]	167 Spinarak [8]
	168 Ariados [1, 8]	213 Shuckle [1]	224 Octillery [1, 6]	345 Lileep [1]	346 Cradily [1]	425 Drifloon [1]
	426 Drifblim [1]	465 Tangrowth [1]	592 Frillish [E]			
Conversion	137 Porygon [1]	233 Porygon2 [1]	474 Porygon-Z [1]			
Conversion 2	137 Porygon [1]	233 Porygon2 [1]	474 Porygon-Z [1]			
Copycat	122 Mr. Mime [4]	173 Cleffa [13]	174 Igglybuff [17]	185 Sudowoodo [1]	238 Smoochum [41]	300 Skitty [18]
	311 Plusle [24]	312 Minun [24]	327 Spinda [10]	427 Buneary [E]	438 Bonsly [1]	439 Mime Jr. [4]
	440 Happiny [5]	447 Riolu [19]	481 Mesprit [61]	501 Oshawott [E]		
Cosmic Power	035 Clefairy [34]	120 Staryu [48]	337 Lunatone [29]	338 Solrock [29]	343 Baltoy [31]	344 Claydol [31]
	385 Jirachi [60]	386 Deoxys (Nor) [73]	386 Deoxys (Atk) [73]	493 Arceus [1]	561 Sigilyph [48]	
Cotton Guard	179 Mareep [36]	180 Flaaffy [43]	181 Ampharos [46]	187 Hoppip [E]	333 Swablu [39]	334 Altaria [42]
	546 Cottonee [37]	556 Maractus [55]				
Cotton Spore	179 Mareep [11]	180 Flaaffy [11]	181 Ampharos [11]	187 Hoppip [34]	188 Skiploom [40]	189 Jumpluff [44]
	315 Roselia [E]	331 Cacnea [49]	332 Cacturne [59]	406 Budew [E]	546 Cottonee [17]	547 Whimsicott [1]
	556 Maractus [18]					
Counter	004 Charmander [E]	019 Rattata [E]	027 Sandshrew [E]	029 Nidoran ♀ [E]	032 Nidoran ♂ [E]	046 Paras [E]
	056 Mankey [E]	066 Machop [E]	107 Hitmonchan [61]	111 Rhyhorn [E]	113 Chansey [E]	115 Kangaskhan [E]
	123 Scyther [E]	143 Snorlax [E]	152 Chikorita [E]	185 Sudowoodo [33]	190 Aipom [E]	194 Wooper [E]
	202 Wobbuffet [1]	204 Pineco [E]	207 Gligar [E]	214 Heracross [19]	215 Sneasel [E]	216 Teddiursa [E]
	228 Houndour [E]	231 Phanpy [E]	236 Tyrogue [E]	237 Hitmontop [28]	255 Torchic [E]	258 Mudkip [E]

Move	Pokémon that can learn it					
Counter (continued)	270 Lotad [E]	286 Breloom [25]	287 Slakoth [43]	288 Vigoroth [37]	289 Slaking [43]	296 Makuhita [E]
	331 Cacnea [E]	335 Zangoose [E]	360 Wynaut [15]	386 Deoxys (Def) [97]	390 Chimchar [E]	410 Shieldon [E]
	422 Shellos [E]	440 Happiny [E]	446 Munchlax [E]	447 Riolu [6]	448 Lucario [6]	453 Croagunk [E]
	532 Timburr [E]	539 Sawk [21]	551 Sandile [E]	557 Dwebble [E]	559 Scraggy [E]	570 Zorua [E]
	588 Karrablast [E]	610 Axew [E]				
Covet	Taught by someone	056 Mankey [1]	058 Growlithe [E]	083 Farfetch'd [E]	133 Eevee [21, E]	155 Cyndaquil [E]
	161 Sentret [E]	173 Cleffa [E]	174 Igglybuff [E]	190 Aipom [E]	216 Teddiursa [1]	217 Ursaring [1]
	261 Poochyena [E]	263 Zigzagoon [29]	264 Linoone [35]	287 Slakoth [31]	289 Slaking [31]	300 Skitty [36]
	314 Illumise [45]	417 Pachirisu [E]	498 Tepig [E]	509 Purrloin [E]	511 Pansage [E]	513 Pansear [E]
	515 Panpour [E]	587 Emolga [E]				
Crabhammer	098 Krabby [41]	099 Kingler [56]	341 Corphish [38]	342 Crawdaunt [44]		
Cross Chop	054 Psyduck [E]	056 Mankey [37]	057 Primeape [41]	066 Machop [43]	067 Machoke [44]	068 Machamp [44]
	216 Teddiursa [E]	239 Elekid [E]	240 Magby [E]	296 Makuhita [E]	447 Riolu [E]	453 Croagunk [E]
Cross Poison	046 Paras [E]	047 Parasect [1]	167 Spinarak [47]	168 Ariados [55]	169 Crobat [1]	207 Gligar [E]
	347 Anorith [E]	451 Skorupi [49]	452 Drapion [49]	595 Joltik [E]		
Crunch	004 Charmander [E]	019 Rattata [22]	020 Raticate [24]	024 Arbok [22]	029 Nidoran♀ [37]	030 Nidorina [43]
	058 Growlithe [39, E]	111 Rhyhorn [E]	115 Kangaskhan [37]	142 Aerodactyl [33]	143 Snorlax [49]	158 Totodile [27, E]
	159 Croconaw [30]	160 Feraligatr [32]	203 Girafarig [46]	208 Steelix [37]	209 Snubbull [49, E]	210 Granbull [59]
	216 Teddiursa [E]	228 Houndour [49]	229 Houndoom [56]	243 Raikou [43]	246 Larvitar [41]	247 Pupitar [47]
	248 Tyranitar [47]	252 Treecko [52]	261 Poochyena [53]	295 Exploud [40]	303 Mawile [36]	309 Electrike [E]
	318 Carvanha [28]	319 Sharpedo [28]	328 Trapinch [34]	336 Seviper [45]	341 Corphish [47]	342 Crawdaunt [57]
	361 Snorunt [31]	362 Glalie [31]	365 Walrein [1]	367 Huntail [42]	371 Bagon [46]	372 Shelgon [50]
	373 Salamence [53]	384 Rayquaza [15]	387 Turtwig [37]	388 Grotle [42]	389 Torterra [45]	403 Shinx [33]
	404 Luxio [38]	405 Luxray [42]	408 Cranidos [E]	419 Floatzel [1]	434 Stunky [E]	445 Garchomp [48]
	447 Riolu [E]	449 Hippopotas [31]	450 Hippowdon [31]	451 Skorupi [45]	452 Drapion [49]	455 Carnivine [41]
	485 Heatran [33]	504 Patrat [16]	505 Watchog [16]	506 Lillipup [22]	507 Herdier [24]	508 Stoutland [24]
	511 Pansage [43]	513 Pansear [43]	515 Panpour [43]	550 Basculin [24]	551 Sandile [28]	552 Krokorok [28]
	553 Krookodile [28]	559 Scraggy [38]	560 Scrafty [38]	564 Tirtouga [21]	565 Carracosta [21]	566 Archen [35]
	567 Archeops [35]	603 Eelektrik [39]	604 Eelektross [1]	621 Druddigon [25]	632 Durant [31]	633 Deino [25]
	634 Zweilous [25]	635 Hydreigon [25]	641 Tornadus [49]	642 Thundurus [49]	643 Reshiram [71]	644 Zekrom [71]
Crush Claw	027 Sandshrew [E]	028 Sandslash [22]	111 Rhyhorn [E]	115 Kangaskhan [E]	155 Cyndaquil [E]	215 Sneasel [E]
	252 Treecko [E]	255 Torchic [E]	287 Slakoth [E]	335 Zangoose [22]	347 Anorith [55]	348 Armaldo [67]
	529 Drilbur [E]	604 Eelektross [1]	621 Druddigon [E]	627 Rufflet [46]	628 Braviary [46]	
Crush Grip	486 Regigigas [75]					
Curse	001 Bulbasaur [E]	041 Zubat [E]	074 Geodude [E]	079 Slowpoke [1]	080 Slowbro [1]	083 Farfetch'd [E]
	088 Grimer [E]	092 Gastly [E]	093 Haunter [12]	094 Gengar [12]	095 Onix [4]	102 Exeggcute [E]
	108 Lickitung [E]	109 Koffing [E]	111 Rhyhorn [E]	131 Lapras [E]	133 Eevee [E]	142 Aerodactyl [E]
	143 Snorlax [E]	185 Sudowoodo [E]	191 Sunkern [E]	194 Wooper [E]	199 Slowking [1]	200 Misdreavus [E]
	206 Dunsparce [E]	208 Steelix [4]	218 Slugma [E]	220 Swinub [E]	222 Corsola [E]	227 Skarmory [E]
	241 Miltank [E]	246 Larvitar [E]	255 Torchic [E]	258 Mudkip [E]	287 Slakoth [E]	304 Aron [E]
	309 Electrike [E]	316 Gulpin [E]	320 Wailmer [E]	322 Numel [29]	323 Camerupt [29]	324 Torkoal [12]
	335 Zangoose [E]	345 Lileep [E]	347 Anorith [E]	353 Shuppet [19]	354 Banette [1,19]	355 Duskull [30]
	356 Dusclops [30]	357 Tropius [E]	358 Chimecho [E]	359 Absol [E]	363 Spheal [E]	377 Regirock [17]
	378 Regice [17]	379 Registeel [17]	387 Turtwig [17]	388 Grotle [17]	389 Torterra [17]	399 Bidoof [45]
	400 Bibarel [53]	408 Cranidos [E]	410 Shieldon [E]	422 Shellos [E]	433 Chingling [E]	438 Bonsly [E]
	442 Spiritomb [1]	446 Munchlax [E]	449 Hippopotas [E]	477 Dusknoir [30]	498 Tepig [E]	517 Munna [E]
	524 Roggenrola [E]	557 Dwebble [E]	562 Yamask [29]	563 Cofagrigus [29]	564 Tirtouga [35]	565 Carracosta [35]
	568 Trubbish [E]	597 Ferroseed [9]	598 Ferrothorn [1,9]	607 Litwick [43]	608 Lampent [45]	616 Shelmet [13]
	618 Stunfisk [E]	622 Golett [40]	623 Golurk [40]	631 Heatmor [E]		
Cut	HM01					

▶ D

Move	Pokémon that can learn it					
Dark Pulse	Taught by someone	092 Gastly [36]	093 Haunter [44]	094 Gengar [44]	246 Larvitar [32]	247 Pupitar [34]
	248 Tyranitar [34]	355 Duskull [E]	430 Honchkrow [75]	442 Spiritomb [49]	448 Lucario [1]	461 Weavile [47]
	491 Darkrai [93]	570 Zorua [E]	574 Gothita [E]	629 Vullaby [46]	630 Mandibuzz [46]	633 Deino [E]
	641 Tornadus [73]	642 Thundurus [73]				
Dark Void	491 Darkrai [66]					
Defend Order	416 Vespiquen [17]					
Defense Curl	027 Sandshrew [1]	028 Sandslash [1]	035 Clefairy [13]	039 Jigglypuff [5]	040 Wigglytuff [1]	074 Geodude [1]
	075 Graveler [1]	076 Golem [1]	095 Onix [E]	108 Lickitung [9]	113 Chansey [1]	143 Snorlax [4]
	155 Cyndaquil [22]	156 Quilava [24]	157 Typhlosion [24]	161 Sentret [4]	162 Furret [1,4]	174 Igglybuff [5]
	183 Marill [10]	184 Azumarill [10]	185 Sudowoodo [E]	206 Dunsparce [1]	231 Phanpy [1]	232 Donphan [1]
	233 Porygon2 [1]	241 Miltank [5]	242 Blissey [1]	320 Wailmer [E]	322 Numel [E]	363 Spheal [1]
	371 Bagon [E]	399 Bidoof [9, E]	400 Bibarel [1]	417 Pachirisu [E]	420 Cherubi [E]	427 Buneary [1]
	428 Lopunny [1]	438 Bonsly [1]	446 Munchlax [4]	463 Lickilicky [9]	498 Tepig [13]	499 Pignite [13]
	500 Emboar [13]	517 Munna [1]	518 Musharna [1]	543 Venipede [1]	544 Whirlipede [1]	545 Scolipede [1]
	590 Foongus [E]	622 Golett [1]	623 Golurk [1]			
Defog	016 Pidgey [E]	041 Zubat [E]	123 Scyther [E]	163 Hoothoot [E]	273 Seedot [E]	276 Taillow [E]
	425 Drifloon [E]	441 Chatot [E]	566 Archen [E]	580 Ducklett [6]	581 Swanna [1, 6]	627 Rufflet [32]
	628 Braviary [32]	629 Vullaby [32]	630 Mandibuzz [32]			
Destiny Bond	092 Gastly [40]	093 Haunter [50]	094 Gengar [50]	109 Koffing [40, E]	110 Weezing [46]	200 Misdreavus [E]
	202 Wobbuffet [1]	211 Qwilfish [53]	280 Ralts [E]	316 Gulpin [E]	331 Cacnea [57]	332 Cacturne [71]
	353 Shuppet [E]	355 Duskull [E]	360 Wynaut [15]	416 Vespiquen [53]	425 Drifloon [E]	442 Spiritomb [E]
	478 Froslass [59]	487 Giratina (Alt) [24]	487 Giratina (Ori) [24]	562 Yamask [49]	563 Cofagrigus [57]	

Pokémon Moves Reverse Lookup

D

Move	Pokémon that can learn it				
Detect	104 Cubone [E]	107 Hitmonchan [51]	133 Eevee [E]	145 Zapdos [15]	193 Yanma [17]	237 Hitmontop [51]
	252 Treecko [41]	253 Grovyle [47]	254 Sceptile [51]	296 Makuhita [E]	302 Sableye [22]	307 Meditite [11]
	308 Medicham [1,11]	335 Zangoose [33]	359 Absol [44]	396 Starly [E]	447 Riolu [E]	448 Lucario [1]
	469 Yanmega [17]	482 Azelf [16]	501 Oshawott [E]	504 Patrat [11]	505 Watchog [11]	519 Pidove [22]
	520 Tranquill [23]	521 Unfezant [23]	532 Timburr [E]	559 Scraggy [E]	570 Zorua [E]	619 Mienfoo [9]
	620 Mienshao [1,9]					
Dig	TM28	027 Sandshrew [30]	028 Sandslash [30]	050 Diglett [34]	051 Dugtrio [40]	095 Onix [43]
	206 Dunsparce [31]	208 Steelix [43]	290 Nincada [45]	328 Trapinch [29]	443 Gible [31]	444 Gabite [40]
	445 Garchomp [40]	449 Hippopotas [19]	450 Hippowdon [19]	529 Drilbur [19]	530 Excadrill [19]	551 Sandile [31]
	552 Krokorok [32]	553 Krookodile [32]	632 Durant [41]			
Disable	023 Ekans [E]	029 Nidoran ♀ [E]	032 Nidoran ♂ [E]	037 Vulpix [E]	039 Jigglypuff [13]	040 Wigglytuff [1]
	048 Venonat [1]	049 Venomoth [1]	054 Psyduck [11]	055 Golduck [11]	064 Kadabra [18]	065 Alakazam [18]
	079 Slowpoke [19]	080 Slowbro [19]	086 Seel [E]	088 Grimer [12]	089 Muk [12]	092 Gastly [E]
	096 Drowzee [5]	097 Hypno [1, 5]	108 Lickitung [25]	115 Kangaskhan [E]	116 Horsea [E]	150 Mewtwo [1]
	167 Spinarak [E]	199 Slowking [19]	234 Stantler [E]	280 Ralts [E]	327 Spinda [E]	331 Cacnea [E]
	335 Zangoose [E]	351 Castform [E]	352 Kecleon [E]	353 Shuppet [E]	355 Duskull [6]	356 Dusclops [1, 6]
	358 Chimecho [E]	361 Snorunt [E]	425 Drifloon [E]	433 Chingling [E]	463 Lickilicky [25]	477 Dusknoir [1, 6]
	491 Darkrai [1]	562 Yamask [5, E]	563 Cofagrigus [1, 5]	595 Joltik [E]	605 Elgyem [E]	
Discharge	025 Pikachu [42]	081 Magnemite [43]	082 Magneton [51]	125 Electabuzz [36]	135 Jolteon [37]	137 Porygon [40]
	145 Zapdos [50]	170 Chinchou [39]	171 Lanturn [47]	179 Mareep [32]	180 Flaaffy [38]	181 Ampharos [40]
	233 Porygon2 [40]	239 Elekid [33]	243 Raikou [57]	299 Nosepass [39]	309 Electrike [41, E]	310 Manectric [49]
	311 Plusle [E]	312 Minun [E]	403 Shinx [41]	404 Luxio [48]	405 Luxray [56]	417 Pachirisu [41]
	462 Magnezone [51]	466 Electivire [36]	474 Porygon-Z [40]	476 Probopass [39]	479 Rotom [64]	479 Rotom (Heat) [64]
	479 Rotom (Wash) [64]	479 Rotom (Frst) [64]	479 Rotom (Fan) [64]	479 Rotom (Mow) [64]	522 Blitzle [32]	523 Zebstrika [36]
	587 Emolga [50]	595 Joltik [35]	596 Galvantula [48]	599 Klink [42]	600 Klang [44]	601 Klinklang [44]
	603 Eelektrik [29]	604 Eelektross [1]	618 Stunfisk [25]	642 Thundurus [43]		
Dive	HM06	086 Seel [41]	087 Dewgong [45]	320 Wailmer [41]	321 Wailord [46]	367 Huntail [37]
	368 Gorebyss [37]	369 Relicanth [57]	489 Phione [61]	490 Manaphy [61]		
Dizzy Punch	115 Kangaskhan [34]	165 Ledyba [E]	241 Miltank [E]	313 Volbeat [E]	327 Spinda [28]	352 Kecleon [E]
	427 Buneary [36]	428 Lopunny [36]	486 Regigigas [1]	579 Reuniclus [41]		
Doom Desire	385 Jirachi [70]					
Double Hit	084 Doduo [32]	110 Weezing [29]	115 Kangaskhan [19]	123 Scyther [49]	190 Aipom [32]	203 Girafarig [32]
	212 Scizor [49]	215 Sneasel [E]	335 Zangoose [E]	393 Piplup [E]	418 Buizel [27]	419 Floatzel [29]
	424 Ambipom [32]	427 Buneary [E]	473 Mamoswine [33]	633 Deino [E]	634 Zweilous [1]	
Double Kick	029 Nidoran ♀ [9]	030 Nidorina [9]	031 Nidoqueen [1]	032 Nidoran ♂ [9]	033 Nidorino [9]	034 Nidoking [1]
	058 Growlithe [E]	077 Ponyta [E]	104 Cubone [E]	106 Hitmonlee [1]	135 Jolteon [17]	155 Cyndaquil [E]
	194 Wooper [E]	203 Girafarig [E]	234 Stantler [E]	252 Treecko [E]	256 Combusken [16]	257 Blaziken [16]
	335 Zangoose [E]	390 Chimchar [E]	403 Shinx [E]	522 Blitzle [E]	539 Sawk [13]	585 Deerling [10]
	586 Sawsbuck [10]	638 Cobalion [?]	639 Terrakion [?]	640 Virizion [?]	647 Keldeo [?]	
Double Team	TM32	025 Pikachu [21]	123 Scyther [37]	193 Yanma [11]	276 Taillow [19]	277 Swellow [19]
	280 Ralts [10]	281 Kirlia [1, 10]	282 Gardevoir [1, 10]	291 Ninjask [20]	313 Volbeat [5]	359 Absol [25]
	361 Snorunt [4]	362 Glalie [1, 4]	386 Deoxys (Spd) [17]	396 Starly [13]	397 Staravia [13]	398 Staraptor [13]
	469 Yanmega [1, 11]	475 Gallade [1, 10]	478 Froslass [1, 4]	479 Rotom [15]	479 Rotom (Heat) [15]	479 Rotom (Wash) [15]
	479 Rotom (Frst) [15]	479 Rotom (Fan) [15]	479 Rotom (Mow) [15]	488 Cresselia [1]	491 Darkrai [47]	566 Archen [8]
	567 Archeops [8]	587 Emolga [E]	617 Accelgor [1, 8]			
Double-Edge	001 Bulbasaur [27]	002 Ivysaur [31]	003 Venusaur [31]	019 Rattata [31]	020 Raticate [39]	039 Jigglypuff [53]
	058 Growlithe [E]	074 Geodude [46]	075 Graveler [58]	076 Golem [58]	077 Ponyta [E]	095 Onix [49]
	104 Cubone [43]	105 Marowak [53]	113 Chansey [54]	115 Kangaskhan [E]	133 Eevee [37]	143 Snorlax [54]
	155 Cyndaquil [55, E]	156 Quilava [64]	157 Typhlosion [69]	161 Sentret [E]	165 Ledyba [38]	166 Ledian [48]
	175 Togepi [45]	176 Togetic [45]	183 Marill [23]	184 Azumarill [25]	185 Sudowoodo [40]	187 Hoppip [E]
	191 Sunkern [37]	192 Sunflora [37]	193 Yanma [45, E]	204 Pineco [56]	205 Forretress [56]	206 Dunsparce [34]
	207 Gligar [E]	208 Steelix [49]	209 Snubbull [E]	214 Heracross [E]	216 Teddiursa [E]	220 Swinub [E]
	231 Phanpy [42]	241 Miltank [E]	242 Blissey [54]	258 Mudkip [E]	299 Nosepass [E]	300 Skitty [42]
	304 Aron [46]	305 Lairon [56]	306 Aggron [65]	313 Volbeat [45]	318 Carvanha [E]	320 Wailmer [E]
	322 Numel [47]	327 Spinda [46]	341 Corphish [E]	358 Chimecho [33]	359 Absol [E]	369 Relicanth [50]
	371 Bagon [55]	372 Shelgon [61]	373 Salamence [70]	382 Kyogre [80]	385 Jirachi [40]	387 Turtwig [E]
	396 Starly [E]	399 Bidoof [E]	408 Cranidos [E]	410 Shieldon [E]	434 Stunky [E]	438 Bonsly [40]
	443 Gible [E]	446 Munchlax [E]	449 Hippopotas [44]	450 Hippowdon [50]	459 Snover [E]	494 Victini [65]
	522 Blitzle [E]	531 Audino [50]	543 Venipede [43]	544 Whirlipede [50]	545 Scolipede [55]	550 Basculin [36]
	551 Sandile [E]	585 Deerling [46]	586 Sawsbuck [52]	588 Karrablast [56]	616 Shelmet [E]	636 Larvesta [50]
DoubleSlap	035 Clefairy [10]	036 Clefable [1]	039 Jigglypuff [25]	040 Wigglytuff [1]	060 Poliwag [15]	061 Poliwhirl [15]
	062 Poliwrath [1]	113 Chansey [12]	122 Mr. Mime [11]	124 Jynx [15]	172 Pichu [E]	186 Politoed [1]
	190 Aipom [E]	242 Blissey [12]	300 Skitty [15]	301 Delcatty [1]	418 Buizel [E]	439 Mime Jr. [11]
	531 Audino [10]	568 Trubbish [14]	569 Garbodor [14]	572 Minccino [13]	574 Gothita [14]	575 Gothorita [14]
	576 Gothitelle [14]	594 Alomomola [13]	619 Mienfoo [17]	620 Mienshao [17]		
Draco Meteor	Taught by someone					
	TM02	006 Charizard [1]	330 Flygon [55]	371 Bagon [50]	372 Shelgon [55]	373 Salamence [61]
	443 Gible [27]	444 Gabite [33]	445 Garchomp [33]	483 Dialga [28]	484 Palkia [28]	487 Giratina (Alt) [28]
	487 Giratina (Ori) [28]	566 Archen [48]	567 Archeops [56]	610 Axew [28]	611 Fraxure [28]	612 Haxorus [28]
	621 Druddigon [27]	644 Zekrom [54]				
Dragon Dance	004 Charmander [E]	116 Horsea [38]	117 Seadra [48]	130 Gyarados [44]	131 Lapras [E]	147 Dratini [51, E]
	148 Dragonair [61]	149 Dragonite [61]	158 Totodile [E]	230 Kingdra [48]	246 Larvitar [E]	334 Altaria [34]
	339 Barboach [E]	341 Corphish [E]	357 Tropius [E]	371 Bagon [E]	381 Latios [55]	384 Rayquaza [60]
	559 Scraggy [E]	610 Axew [32]	611 Fraxure [32]	612 Haxorus [32]		

Move	Pokémon that can learn it				
Dragon Pulse	Taught by someone	004 Charmander [E]	116 Horsea [42]	117 Seadra [57]	131 Lapras [E]	147 Dratini [E]
	230 Kingdra [57]	333 Swablu [42]	334 Altaria [48]	349 Feebas [E]	371 Bagon [E]	380 Latias [80]
	381 Latios [80]	384 Rayquaza [90]	448 Lucario [60]	566 Archen [E]	610 Axew [41, E]	611 Fraxure [42]
	612 Haxorus [42]	633 Deino [32]	634 Zweilous [32]	635 Hydreigon [32]	643 Reshiram [54]	646 Kyurem [57]
	646 Kyurem (Blk) [57]	646 Kyurem (Wht) [57]				
Dragon Rage	004 Charmander [16]	005 Charmeleon [17]	006 Charizard [17]	116 Horsea [E]	130 Gyarados [23]	147 Dratini [15]
	148 Dragonair [15]	149 Dragonite [15]	371 Bagon [E]	443 Gible [7]	444 Gabite [7]	445 Garchomp [1,7]
	610 Axew [10]	611 Fraxure [1,10]	612 Haxorus [1,10]	621 Druddigon [18]	633 Deino [1]	634 Zweilous [1]
	635 Hydreigon [1]	643 Reshiram [1]	644 Zekrom [1]	646 Kyurem [1]	646 Kyurem (Blk) [1]	646 Kyurem (Wht) [1]
Dragon Rush	004 Charmander [E]	111 Rhyhorn [47]	147 Dratini [41, E]	148 Dragonair [47]	149 Dragonite [47]	249 Lugia [15]
	304 Aron [E]	333 Swablu [E]	371 Bagon [E]	443 Gible [37]	444 Gabite [49]	445 Garchomp [55]
	633 Deino [42]	634 Zweilous [42]	635 Hydreigon [42]			
Dragon Tail	TM82	147 Dratini [31]	148 Dragonair [33]	149 Dragonite [33]	330 Flygon [45]	373 Salamence [80]
	621 Druddigon [45]					
DragonBreath	095 Onix [25]	116 Horsea [E]	142 Aerodactyl [E]	147 Dratini [E]	208 Steelix [25]	252 Treecko [E]
	329 Vibrava [35]	330 Flygon [35]	334 Altaria [35]	349 Feebas [E]	371 Bagon [E]	372 Shelgon [32]
	373 Salamence [32]	380 Latias [20]	381 Latios [20]	443 Gible [E]	483 Dialga [1]	484 Palkia [1]
	487 Giratina (Alt) [1]	487 Giratina (Ori) [1]	566 Archen [31]	567 Archeops [31]	633 Deino [17]	634 Zweilous [17]
	635 Hydreigon [17]	643 Reshiram [29]	644 Zekrom [29]	646 Kyurem [29]	646 Kyurem (Blk) [29]	646 Kyurem (Wht) [29]
Drain Punch	Taught by someone	165 Ledyba [E]	285 Shroomish [E]	307 Meditite [E]	453 Croagunk [E]	532 Timburr [E]
	537 Seismitoad [44]	559 Scraggy [E]	619 Mienfoo [33]	620 Mienshao [33]		
Dream Eater	TM85	092 Gastly [33]	093 Haunter [39]	094 Gengar [39]	163 Hoothoot [57]	164 Noctowl [67]
	280 Ralts [50]	281 Kirlia [59]	282 Gardevoir [73]	442 Spiritomb [19]	491 Darkrai [84]	517 Munna [41]
Drill Peck	021 Spearow [37]	022 Fearow [47]	084 Doduo [41]	085 Dodrio [47]	145 Zapdos [71]	177 Natu [E]
	198 Murkrow [E]	227 Skarmory [E]	393 Piplup [39]	394 Prinplup [46]	395 Empoleon [52]	
Drill Run	Taught by someone	022 Fearow [53]	111 Rhyhorn [45]	112 Rhydon [47]	206 Dunsparce [43]	464 Rhyperior [47]
	529 Drilbur [43]	530 Excadrill [55]				
Dual Chop	Taught by someone	444 Gabite [24]	445 Garchomp [24]	610 Axew [13]	611 Fraxure [13]	612 Haxorus [13]
DynamicPunch	062 Poliwrath [32]	066 Machop [49]	067 Machoke [55]	068 Machamp [55]	239 Elekid [E]	240 Magby [E]
	286 Breloom [45]	296 Makuhita [E]	307 Meditite [E]	331 Cacnea [E]	453 Croagunk [E]	532 Timburr [E]
	533 Gurdurr [37]	534 Conkeldurr [37]	622 Golett [30]	623 Golurk [30]		

E

Move	Pokémon that can learn it				
Earth Power	Taught by someone	031 Nidoqueen [43]	034 Nidoking [43]	050 Diglett [29]	051 Dugtrio [33]	218 Slugma [55, E]
	219 Magcargo [67]	222 Corsola [47]	299 Nosepass [43]	322 Numel [26]	323 Camerupt [26]	328 Trapinch [39, E]
	329 Vibrava [39]	330 Flygon [39]	339 Barboach [E]	343 Baltoy [37]	344 Claydol [40]	383 Groudon [65]
	387 Turtwig [E]	476 Probopass [43]	483 Dialga [33]	484 Palkia [33]	485 Heatran [73]	487 Giratina (Alt) [33]
	487 Giratina (Ori) [33]	493 Arceus [20]	529 Drilbur [E]	535 Tympole [E]	566 Archen [E]	618 Stunfisk [E]
	633 Deino [E]	645 Landorus [43]				
Earthquake	TM26	027 Sandshrew [46]	028 Sandslash [46]	050 Diglett [40]	051 Dugtrio [50]	074 Geodude [39]
	075 Graveler [47]	076 Golem [47]	111 Rhyhorn [56]	112 Rhydon [62]	194 Wooper [33]	195 Quagsire [36]
	220 Swinub [37]	221 Piloswine [46]	232 Donphan [46]	246 Larvitar [46]	247 Pupitar [54]	248 Tyranitar [54]
	259 Marshtomp [46]	260 Swampert [52]	322 Numel [40]	323 Camerupt [46]	328 Trapinch [55]	339 Barboach [39]
	340 Whiscash [45]	383 Groudon [35]	389 Torterra [32]	449 Hippopotas [37]	450 Hippowdon [40]	464 Rhyperior [62]
	473 Mamoswine [46]	529 Drilbur [33]	530 Excadrill [36]	551 Sandile [43]	552 Krokorok [48]	553 Krookodile [54]
	622 Golett [45]	623 Golurk [50]	645 Landorus [55]			
Echoed Voice	TM49	163 Hoothoot [25]	164 Noctowl [27]	441 Chatot [37]	535 Tympole [38]	536 Palpitoad [42]
	537 Seismitoad [49]	572 Minccino [33]				
Egg Bomb	103 Exeggutor [27]	113 Chansey [42]	242 Blissey [42]			
Electro Ball	025 Pikachu [18]	081 Magnemite [32]	082 Magneton [34]	100 Voltorb [29]	101 Electrode [29]	125 Electabuzz [22]
	170 Chinchou [28]	171 Lanturn [30]	179 Mareep [22]	180 Flaaffy [25]	181 Ampharos [25]	239 Elekid [22]
	309 Electrike [E]	311 Plusle [29]	312 Minun [29]	417 Pachirisu [25]	462 Magnezone [34]	466 Electivire [22]
	479 Rotom [43]	479 Rotom (Heat) [43]	479 Rotom (Wash) [43]	479 Rotom (Frst) [43]	479 Rotom (Fan) [43]	479 Rotom (Mow) [43]
	587 Emolga [26]	595 Joltik [29]	596 Galvantula [29]			
Electroweb	Taught by someone	167 Spinarak [E]	595 Joltik [15]	596 Galvantula [15]		
Embargo	TM63	228 Houndour [37]	229 Houndoom [41]	261 Poochyena [41]	262 Mightyena [47]	335 Zangoose [19]
	337 Lunatone [21]	338 Solrock [21]	353 Shuppet [38]	354 Banette [40]	461 Weavile [1]	474 Porygon-Z [34]
	551 Sandile [22]	552 Krokorok [22]	553 Krookodile [22]	570 Zorua [41]	571 Zoroark [44]	574 Gothita [19]
	575 Gothorita [19]	576 Gothitelle [19]	624 Pawniard [41]	625 Bisharp [41]	629 Vullaby [50]	630 Mandibuzz [50]
Ember	004 Charmander [7]	005 Charmeleon [1,7]	006 Charizard [1,7]	037 Vulpix [1]	038 Ninetales [1]	058 Growlithe [6]
	077 Ponyta [9]	078 Rapidash [1,9]	126 Magmar [1,5]	136 Flareon [9]	146 Moltres [1]	155 Cyndaquil [10]
	156 Quilava [10]	157 Typhlosion [1,10]	218 Slugma [1,5]	219 Magcargo [1,5]	228 Houndour [1]	229 Houndoom [1]
	240 Magby [8]	244 Entei [1]	255 Torchic [10]	256 Combusken [1,13]	257 Blaziken [1,13]	322 Numel [5]
	323 Camerupt [1,5]	324 Torkoal [1]	351 Castform [10]	371 Bagon [25]	372 Shelgon [25]	373 Salamence [25]
	390 Chimchar [7]	391 Monferno [1,7]	392 Infernape [1,7]	467 Magmortar [1,5]	498 Tepig [7]	499 Pignite [1,7]
Ember	500 Emboar [1,7]	607 Litwick [1]	608 Lampent [1]	636 Larvesta [1]	637 Volcarona [1]	035 Clefairy [4]
	054 Psyduck [E]	056 Mankey [E]	060 Poliwag [E]	063 Abra [E]	066 Machop [E]	069 Bellsprout [E]
	086 Seel [13, E]	087 Dewgong [13]	122 Mr. Mime [18]	165 Ledyba [E]	172 Pichu [E]	173 Cleffa [4]
	175 Togepi [17]	176 Togetic [17]	187 Hoppip [E]	191 Sunkern [E]	194 Wooper [E]	213 Shuckle [5]
	280 Ralts [E]	287 Slakoth [E]	288 Vigoroth [1, 7]	289 Slaking [1, 7]	298 Azurill [E]	311 Plusle [17]
	312 Minun [17]	313 Volbeat [E]	314 Illumise [25, E]	316 Gulpin [23]	317 Swalot [23]	327 Spinda [E]
	360 Wynaut [1]	363 Spheal [7]	364 Sealeo [1, 7]	365 Walrein [1, 7]	390 Chimchar [E]	427 Buneary [E]
	439 Mime Jr. [18]	441 Chatot [E]	501 Oshawott [31]	502 Dewott [36]	503 Samurott [38]	

Pokémon Moves Reverse Lookup

E

Move	Pokémon that can learn it				
Ember (continued)	509 Purrloin [E]	531 Audino [E]	546 Cottonee [E]	554 Darumaka [E]	572 Minccino [15]	587 Emolga [38]
	613 Cubchoo [E]	616 Shelmet [E]				
Endeavor	Taught by someone	015 Beedrill [40]	019 Rattata [34]	020 Raticate [44]	060 Poliwag [E]	084 Doduo [46, E]
	085 Dodrio [54]	104 Cubone [41]	105 Marowak [49]	114 Tangela [E]	115 Kangaskhan [E]	191 Sunkern [25]
	206 Dunsparce [46]	231 Phanpy [E]	237 Hitmontop [60]	252 Treecko [E]	258 Mudkip [46]	259 Marshtomp [53]
	260 Swampert [61]	276 Taillow [E]	277 Swellow [28]	293 Whismur [E]	304 Aron [E]	341 Corphish [E]
	396 Starly [17]	397 Staravia [18]	398 Staraptor [18]	409 Rampardos [30]	498 Tepig [E]	527 Woobat [47]
	528 Swoobat [47]	546 Cottonee [44]	566 Archen [38]	567 Archeops [40]	577 Solosis [28]	578 Duosion [28]
	579 Reuniclus [28]	610 Axew [E]	646 Kyurem [71]	646 Kyurem (Blk) [71]	646 Kyurem (Wht) [71]	
Endure	001 Bulbasaur [E]	027 Sandshrew [E]	029 Nidoran ♀ [E]	032 Nidoran ♂ [E]	046 Paras [E]	050 Diglett [E]
	060 Poliwag [E]	074 Geodude [E]	098 Krabby [E]	104 Cubone [E]	106 Hitmonlee [49]	113 Chansey [E]
	115 Kangaskhan [43]	123 Scyther [E]	133 Eevee [E]	140 Kabuto [26]	141 Kabutops [26]	146 Moltres [22]
	172 Pichu [E]	185 Sudowoodo [E]	187 Hoppip [E]	191 Sunkern [E]	204 Pineco [E]	206 Dunsparce [40]
	214 Heracross [1]	220 Swinub [14]	221 Piloswine [14]	222 Corsola [35]	227 Skarmory [E]	231 Phanpy [28]
	236 Tyrogue [E]	241 Miltank [E]	255 Torchic [E]	283 Surskit [E]	288 Vigoroth [25]	290 Nincada [E]
	296 Makuhita [37]	297 Hariyama [47]	299 Nosepass [E]	322 Numel [E]	324 Torkoal [E]	325 Spoink [E]
	328 Trapinch [E]	345 Lileep [E]	366 Clamperl [E]	371 Bagon [E]	399 Bidoof [E]	410 Shieldon [33]
	411 Bastiodon [36]	417 Pachirisu [17]	427 Buneary [6]	428 Lopunny [6]	438 Bonsly [E]	440 Happiny [E]
	447 Riolu [1]	473 Mamoswine [14]	480 Uxie [16]	494 Victini [9]	506 Lillipup [E]	522 Blitzle [E]
	532 Timburr [E]	538 Throh [41]	539 Sawk [41]	540 Sewaddle [29]	548 Petilil [E]	554 Darumaka [E]
	557 Dwebble [E]	562 Yamask [E]	572 Minccino [E]	588 Karrablast [8]	590 Foongus [E]	594 Alomomola [E]
	607 Litwick [E]	610 Axew [E]	613 Cubchoo [25]	614 Beartic [25]	616 Shelmet [E]	618 Stunfisk [30]
	619 Mienfoo [E]	632 Durant [E]	636 Larvesta [E]			
Energy Ball	TM53	252 Treecko [51]	270 Lotad [45]	345 Lileep [50]	346 Cradily [56]	492 Shaymin (Land) [73]
	492 Shaymin (Sky) [73]	546 Cottonee [35]	548 Petilil [35]	585 Deerling [32]	586 Sawsbuck [32]	
Entrainment	311 Plusle [63]	312 Minun [63]	427 Buneary [53]	428 Lopunny [53]	433 Chingling [25]	531 Audino [25]
	542 Leavanny [43]	548 Petilil [37]	632 Durant [46]			
Eruption	155 Cyndaquil [58]	156 Quilava [68]	157 Typhlosion [74]	244 Entei [85]	323 Camerupt [52]	324 Torkoal [E]
	383 Groudon [50]					
Explosion	TM64	074 Geodude [43]	075 Graveler [53]	076 Golem [53]	100 Voltorb [47]	101 Electrode [57]
	109 Koffing [37]	110 Weezing [40]	204 Pineco [34]	205 Forretress [42]	273 Seedot [43]	337 Lunatone [49]
	338 Solrock [49]	343 Baltoy [49]	344 Claydol [61]	377 Regirock [1]	378 Regice [1]	379 Registeel [1]
	425 Drifloon [50]	426 Drifblim [60]	434 Stunky [49]	435 Skuntank [61]	482 Azelf [76]	524 Roggenrola [40]
	525 Boldore [55]	526 Gigalith [55]	568 Trubbish [47]	569 Garbodor [59]	597 Ferroseed [55]	598 Ferrothorn [67]
Extrasensory	037 Vulpix [39, E]	102 Exeggcute [47]	155 Cyndaquil [E]	163 Hoothoot [45]	164 Noctowl [52]	175 Togepi [E]
	234 Stantler [49]	243 Raikou [64]	244 Entei [64]	245 Suicune [64]	249 Lugia [23]	250 Ho-Oh [23]
	274 Nuzleaf [49]	293 Whismur [E]	325 Spoink [E]	343 Baltoy [28]	344 Claydol [28]	358 Chimecho [46]
	406 Budew [E]	436 Bronzor [39]	437 Bronzong [42]	480 Uxie [51]	481 Mesprit [51]	482 Azelf [51]
	570 Zorua [E]	641 Tornadus [31]	643 Reshiram [43]	645 Landorus [31]		
	059 Arcanine [34]	147 Dratini [E]	384 Rayquaza [75]	386 Deoxys (Spd) [97]	448 Lucario [65]	468 Togekiss [1]
	493 Arceus [40]					

F

Move	Pokémon that can learn it				
Facade	TM42	390 Chimchar [31]	519 Pidove [43]	520 Tranquill [50]	521 Unfezant [55]	554 Darumaka [19]
	555 Darmanitan [19]	559 Scraggy [42]	560 Scrafty [45]			
Faint Attack	016 Pidgey [E]	021 Spearow [E]	037 Vulpix [20, E]	041 Zubat [E]	050 Diglett [E]	052 Meowth [22]
	053 Persian [22]	084 Doduo [E]	126 Magmar [12]	127 Pinsir [E]	163 Hoothoot [E]	174 Igglybuff [E]
	177 Natu [E]	185 Sudowoodo [19]	193 Yanma [E]	197 Umbreon [21]	198 Murkrow [35, E]	207 Gligar [19]
	209 Snubbull [E]	215 Sneasel [10]	216 Teddiursa [15]	217 Ursaring [15]	228 Houndour [32]	229 Houndoom [35]
	240 Magby [12]	274 Nuzleaf [31]	275 Shiftry [1]	287 Slakoth [19]	289 Slaking [19]	290 Nincada [E]
	296 Makuhita [E]	300 Skitty [29]	302 Sableye [32]	303 Mawile [26]	327 Spinda [14]	328 Trapinch [7]
	329 Vibrava [1, 7]	330 Flygon [1, 7]	331 Cacnea [29]	332 Cacturne [29]	352 Kecleon [7]	353 Shuppet [22]
	354 Banette [22]	355 Duskull [E]	359 Absol [E]	431 Glameow [17]	432 Purugly [17]	436 Bronzor [21]
	437 Bronzong [21]	438 Bonsly [19]	442 Spiritomb [E]	451 Skorupi [17]	453 Croagunk [17]	454 Toxicroak [17]
	455 Carnivine [27]	461 Weavile [10]	467 Magmortar [12]	472 Gliscor [19]	491 Darkrai [29]	509 Purrloin [E]
	557 Dwebble [13]	558 Crustle [13]	559 Scraggy [9, E]	560 Scrafty [1, 9]	570 Zorua [17]	571 Zoroark [17]
	574 Gothita [24]	575 Gothorita [24]	576 Gothitelle [24]	585 Deerling [16]	586 Sawsbuck [16]	588 Karrablast [E]
	590 Foongus [20]	591 Amoonguss [20]	595 Joltik [E]	621 Druddigon [E]	624 Pawniard [17]	625 Bisharp [17]
	629 Vullaby [23]	630 Mandibuzz [23]	631 Heatmor [E]	632 Durant [E]		
Fake Out	007 Squirtle [E]	052 Meowth [9]	053 Persian [1,9]	086 Seel [E]	115 Kangaskhan [7]	122 Mr. Mime [E]
	172 Pichu [E]	190 Aipom [E]	215 Sneasel [E]	225 Delibird [E]	236 Tyrogue [1]	238 Smoochum [E]
	271 Lombre [11]	274 Nuzleaf [19]	296 Makuhita [13]	297 Hariyama [13]	300 Skitty [1, E]	301 Delcatty [1]
	302 Sableye [18]	307 Meditite [E]	327 Spinda [E]	352 Kecleon [E]	390 Chimchar [E]	427 Buneary [E]
	431 Glameow [1]	432 Purugly [1]	439 Mime Jr. [E]	453 Croagunk [E]	509 Purrloin [21]	510 Liepard [22]
	559 Scraggy [E]	619 Mienfoo [13]	620 Mienshao [1,13]			
Fake Tears	124 Jynx [28]	133 Eevee [E]	158 Totodile [E]	173 Cleffa [E]	174 Igglybuff [E]	216 Teddiursa [1, E]
	217 Ursaring [1]	238 Smoochum [28]	285 Shroomish [E]	293 Whismur [E]	298 Azurill [E]	300 Skitty [E]
	303 Mawile [6]	311 Plusle [21, 35]	312 Minun [35]	314 Illumise [E]	327 Spinda [E]	361 Snorunt [E]
	417 Pachirisu [E]	427 Buneary [E]	431 Glameow [E]	438 Bonsly [1]	509 Purrloin [E]	527 Woobat [E]
	546 Cottonee [E]	562 Yamask [E]	570 Zorua [9]	572 Minccino [E]	574 Gothita [10]	575 Gothorita [1, 10]
	576 Gothitelle [1, 10]	585 Deerling [E]	629 Vullaby [E]			

Move	Pokémon that can learn it					
False Swipe	TM54	083 Farfetch'd [45]	104 Cubone [27]	105 Marowak [27]	123 Scyther [13]	212 Scizor [13]
	253 Grovyle [53]	254 Sceptile [59]	290 Nincada [25]	335 Zangoose [29]	475 Gallade [50]	542 Leavanny [1]
	588 Karrablast [25]	589 Escavalier [25]	610 Axew [24]	611 Fraxure [24]	612 Haxorus [24]	
FeatherDance	016 Pidgey [25]	017 Pidgeotto [27]	018 Pidgeot [27]	021 Spearow [E]	083 Farfetch'd [E]	163 Hoothoot [E]
	177 Natu [E]	198 Murkrow [E]	255 Torchic [E]	333 Swablu [E]	393 Piplup [E]	396 Starly [E]
	441 Chatot [53]	519 Pidove [36]	520 Tranquill [41]	521 Unfezant [44]	580 Ducklett [21]	581 Swanna [21]
Feint	025 Pikachu [34]	052 Meowth [54]	053 Persian [68]	083 Farfetch'd [43]	106 Hitmonlee [25]	107 Hitmonchan [21]
	123 Scyther [61]	127 Pinsir [E]	141 Kabutops [1]	193 Yanma [E]	207 Gligar [E]	212 Scizor [61]
	214 Heracross [37]	215 Sneasel [E]	227 Skarmory [20]	228 Houndour [E]	236 Tyrogue [E]	237 Hitmontop [33]
	239 Elekid [E]	255 Torchic [E]	296 Makuhita [E]	302 Sableye [E]	307 Meditite [22]	308 Medicham [22]
	319 Sharpedo [1]	328 Trapinch [61]	335 Zangoose [E]	352 Kecleon [14]	359 Absol [1]	391 Monferno [26]
	392 Infernape [26]	434 Stunky [18]	435 Skuntank [18]	447 Riolu [11]	448 Lucario [11]	453 Croagunk [E]
	469 Yanmega [38]	475 Gallade [45]	616 Shelmet [E]	619 Mienfoo [E]		
Fiery Dance	637 Volcarona [100]					
Final Gambit	019 Rattata [E]	050 Diglett [E]	056 Mankey [53]	057 Primeape [63]	213 Shuckle [E]	290 Nincada [E]
	335 Zangoose [E]	336 Seviper [E]	396 Starly [41]	397 Staravia [48]	398 Staraptor [57]	447 Riolu [55]
	494 Victini [81]	550 Basculin [51]	616 Shelmet [56]	617 Accelgor [56]		
Fire Blast	TM38	037 Vulpix [42]	077 Ponyta [41]	078 Rapidash [41]	126 Magmar [55]	136 Flareon [45]
	240 Magby [43]	244 Entei [71]	250 Ho-Oh [37]	351 Castform [40]	383 Groudon [90]	467 Magmortar [55]
	513 Pansear [34]	643 Reshiram [78]				
Fire Fang	004 Charmander [25]	005 Charmeleon [28]	006 Charizard [28]	024 Arbok [1]	058 Growlithe [21]	059 Arcanine [1]
	111 Rhyhorn [E]	136 Flareon [21]	142 Aerodactyl [1]	208 Steelix [1]	209 Snubbull [1, E]	210 Granbull [1]
	228 Houndour [28, E]	229 Houndoom [30]	232 Donphan [1]	244 Entei [50]	248 Tyranitar [1]	261 Poochyena [E]
	295 Exploud [1]	303 Mawile [E]	309 Electrike [E]	310 Manectric [1]	371 Bagon [E]	373 Salamence [1]
	403 Shinx [E]	445 Garchomp [1]	450 Hippowdon [1]	452 Drapion [1]	472 Gliscor [1]	485 Heatran [17]
	506 Lillipup [E]	508 Stoutland [1]	551 Sandile [E]	554 Darumaka [11]	555 Darmanitan [11]	621 Druddigon [E]
	633 Deino [E]	643 Reshiram [1]				
Fire Pledge	Taught by someone					
Fire Punch	Taught by someone	063 Abra [E]	066 Machop [E]	092 Gastly [E]	096 Drowzee [E]	107 Hitmonchan [36]
	126 Magmar [29]	149 Dragonite [1]	181 Ampharos [1]	239 Elekid [E]	240 Magby [29]	257 Blaziken [1]
	307 Meditite [E]	308 Medicham [1]	356 Dusclops [1]	390 Chimchar [E]	427 Buneary [E]	466 Electivire [1]
	467 Magmortar [29]	477 Dusknoir [1]	486 Regigigas [1]	513 Pansear [E]	554 Darumaka [22]	555 Darmanitan [22]
	559 Scraggy [E]					
Fire Spin	004 Charmander [43]	005 Charmeleon [50]	006 Charizard [56]	037 Vulpix [12]	058 Growlithe [E]	077 Ponyta [25]
	078 Rapidash [25]	126 Magmar [15]	136 Flareon [25]	146 Moltres [8]	228 Houndour [E]	240 Magby [15]
	244 Entei [22]	255 Torchic [25]	324 Torkoal [17]	338 Solrock [9]	390 Chimchar [33]	391 Monferno [39]
	392 Infernape [42]	467 Magmortar [15]	485 Heatran [57]	513 Pansear [E]	607 Litwick [7]	608 Lampent [7]
	631 Heatmor [16]	637 Volcarona [30]				
Fissure	050 Diglett [45]	051 Dugtrio [57]	131 Lapras [E]	143 Snorlax [E]	220 Swinub [E]	231 Phanpy [E]
	320 Wailmer [E]	323 Camerupt [59]	324 Torkoal [E]	328 Trapinch [73]	339 Barboach [47]	340 Whiscash [57]
	363 Spheal [E]	383 Groudon [75]	410 Shieldon [E]	413 Wormadam (Sand) [47]	422 Shellos [E]	449 Hippopotas [50]
	450 Hippowdon [60]	529 Drilbur [47]	530 Excadrill [62]	618 Stunfisk [61]	645 Landorus [67]	
Flail	007 Squirtle [E]	027 Sandshrew [E]	037 Vulpix [E]	043 Oddish [E]	046 Paras [E]	052 Meowth [E]
	074 Geodude [E]	083 Farfetch'd [E]	084 Doduo [E]	095 Onix [E]	098 Krabby [45, E]	099 Kingler [63]
	114 Tangela [E]	116 Horsea [E]	118 Goldeen [21]	119 Seaking [21]	127 Pinsir [E]	129 Magikarp [30]
	133 Eevee [E]	140 Kabuto [E]	152 Chikorita [E]	158 Totodile [22]	159 Croconaw [24]	160 Feraligatr [24]
	170 Chinchou [9, E]	171 Lanturn [9]	172 Pichu [E]	185 Sudowoodo [1, 5]	204 Pineco [E]	206 Dunsparce [49]
	211 Qwilfish [E]	214 Heracross [E]	220 Swinub [40]	222 Corsola [52]	223 Remoraid [E]	231 Phanpy [6]
	263 Zigzagoon [37]	270 Lotad [E]	287 Slakoth [49]	289 Slaking [49]	324 Torkoal [42]	327 Spinda [50]
	328 Trapinch [E]	335 Zangoose [E]	339 Barboach [E]	349 Feebas [30]	370 Luvdisc [31]	393 Piplup [E]
	413 Wormadam (Plnt) [38]	413 Wormadam (Sand) [38]	413 Wormadam (Trsh) [38]	417 Pachirisu [E]	427 Buneary [E]	431 Glameow [E]
	438 Bonsly [5]	456 Finneon [E]	480 Uxie [61]	504 Patrat [E]	535 Tympole [34]	536 Palpitoad [37]
	537 Seismitoad [39]	540 Sewaddle [43]	550 Basculin [46]	557 Dwebble [41]	558 Crustle [50]	564 Tirtouga [E]
	572 Minccino [E]	588 Karrablast [49]	613 Cubchoo [36]	614 Beartic [36]	618 Stunfisk [55]	
Flame Burst	004 Charmander [28]	005 Charmeleon [32]	006 Charizard [32]	037 Vulpix [23]	058 Growlithe [28]	126 Magmar [22]
	155 Cyndaquil [E]	218 Slugma [23]	219 Magcargo [23]	240 Magby [22]	255 Torchic [22]	309 Electrike [E]
	322 Numel [15]	323 Camerupt [15]	324 Torkoal [E]	434 Stunky [22]	467 Magmortar [22]	494 Victini [41]
	513 Pansear [22]	514 Simisear [1]	607 Litwick [20]	608 Lampent [20]	609 Chandelure [1]	631 Heatmor [31]
Flame Charge	TM43	077 Ponyta [21]	078 Rapidash [21]	155 Cyndaquil [28]	156 Quilava [35]	157 Typhlosion [35]
	494 Victini [25]	498 Tepig [15]	499 Pignite [15]	500 Emboar [15]	522 Blitzle [18]	523 Zebstrika [18]
	636 Larvesta [30]	649 Genesect [18]				
Flame Wheel	019 Rattata [E]	058 Growlithe [17]	077 Ponyta [13, E]	078 Rapidash [13]	155 Cyndaquil [19]	156 Quilava [20]
	157 Typhlosion [20]	390 Chimchar [17]	391 Monferno [19]	392 Infernape [19]	554 Darumaka [E]	636 Larvesta [60]
Flamethrower	TM35	004 Charmander [37]	005 Charmeleon [43]	006 Charizard [47]	037 Vulpix [34]	058 Growlithe [34]
	126 Magmar [49]	146 Moltres [36]	155 Cyndaquil [40]	156 Quilava [46]	157 Typhlosion [48]	218 Slugma [50]
	219 Magcargo [59]	228 Houndour [44]	229 Houndoom [50]	240 Magby [40]	244 Entei [36]	255 Torchic [43]
	322 Numel [43]	324 Torkoal [28]	390 Chimchar [47]	435 Skuntank [34]	467 Magmortar [49]	498 Tepig [33]
	499 Pignite [39]	500 Emboar [43]	631 Heatmor [51]	643 Reshiram [22]		
Flare Blitz	004 Charmander [E]	006 Charizard [77]	037 Vulpix [E]	058 Growlithe [45, E]	077 Ponyta [49]	078 Rapidash [49]
	155 Cyndaquil [E]	240 Magby [E]	256 Combusken [54]	257 Blaziken [66]	391 Monferno [56]	392 Infernape [68]
	494 Victini [73]	498 Tepig [43]	499 Pignite [52]	500 Emboar [62]	554 Darumaka [33]	555 Darmanitan [33]
	636 Larvesta [100]					
Flash	TM70	313 Volbeat [1]				

547

Pokémon Moves Reverse Lookup

F

Move	Pokémon that can learn it				
Flash Cannon	TM91	009 Blastoise [1]	081 Magnemite [35]	082 Magneton [39]	379 Registeel [73]	462 Magnezone [39]
	483 Dialga [50]	597 Ferroseed [52]	598 Ferrothorn [61]			
Flatter	029 Nidoran ♀ [33]	030 Nidorina [38]	032 Nidoran ♂ [33]	033 Nidorino [38]	096 Drowzee [E]	179 Mareep [E]
	302 Sableye [E]	314 Illumise [29]	417 Pachirisu [E]	453 Croagunk [50]	454 Toxicroak [62]	527 Woobat [E]
	574 Gothita [28]	575 Gothorita [28]	576 Gothitelle [28]	629 Vullaby [E]	630 Mandibuzz [19]	
Fling	TM56	057 Primeape [1]	088 Grimer [29]	089 Muk [29]	104 Cubone [33]	105 Marowak [37]
	113 Chansey [34]	190 Aipom [36]	216 Teddiursa [57]	242 Blissey [34]	263 Zigzagoon [49]	264 Linoone [65]
	279 Pelipper [46]	289 Slaking [55]	424 Ambipom [36]	446 Munchlax [41]	461 Weavile [28]	511 Pansage [28]
	513 Pansear [28]	515 Panpour [28]				
Fly	HM02	373 Salamence [50]	384 Rayquaza [65]			
Focus Blast	TM52					
Focus Energy	015 Beedrill [13]	019 Rattata [7]	020 Raticate [1, 7]	029 Nidoran ♀ [E]	032 Nidoran ♂ [7]	033 Nidorino [7]
	034 Nidoking [1]	056 Mankey [1]	057 Primeape [1]	066 Machop [7]	067 Machoke [1, 7]	068 Machamp [1, 7]
	104 Cubone [17]	105 Marowak [17]	106 Hitmonlee [21]	115 Kangaskhan [E]	116 Horsea [14]	117 Seadra [14]
	123 Scyther [5]	127 Pinsir [1]	161 Sentret [E]	212 Scizor [5]	223 Remoraid [22]	224 Octillery [22]
	230 Kingdra [14]	231 Phanpy [E]	237 Hitmontop [6]	240 Magby [E]	246 Larvitar [E]	255 Torchic [7]
	256 Combusken [1, 7]	257 Blaziken [1, 7]	276 Taillow [4]	277 Swellow [1, 4]	288 Vigoroth [1]	296 Makuhita [1]
	297 Hariyama [8]	318 Carvanha [8]	319 Sharpedo [1, 8]	322 Numel [E]	323 Camerupt [12]	328 Trapinch [E]
	371 Bagon [20]	372 Shelgon [20]	373 Salamence [E]	390 Chimchar [E]	402 Kricketune [22]	408 Cranidos [6]
	409 Rampardos [6]	410 Shieldon [E]	425 Drifloon [13]	426 Drifblim [13]	434 Stunky [1]	435 Skuntank [1]
	494 Victini [1]	501 Oshawott [13]	502 Dewott [13]	503 Samurott [13]	532 Timburr [4]	533 Gurdurr [1, 4]
	534 Conkeldurr [1, 4]	538 Throh [9]	539 Sawk [9]	551 Sandile [E]	554 Darumaka [E]	610 Axew [E]
	626 Bouffalant [36]	633 Deino [4]	634 Zweilous [1, 4]	635 Hydreigon [1, 4]		
Focus Punch	004 Charmander [E]	056 Mankey [E]	074 Geodude [E]	107 Hitmonchan [56]	115 Kangaskhan [E]	165 Ledyba [E]
	209 Snubbull [E]	214 Heracross [E]	239 Elekid [E]	285 Shroomish [E]	288 Vigoroth [49]	296 Makuhita [E]
	390 Chimchar [E]	427 Buneary [E]	532 Timburr [46]	533 Gurdurr [53]	534 Conkeldurr [53]	554 Darumaka [E]
	559 Scraggy [49]	560 Scrafty [58]	613 Cubchoo [E]	622 Golett [55]	623 Golurk [70]	
Follow Me	035 Clefairy [16]	161 Sentret [19]	162 Furret [21]	175 Togepi [21]	176 Togetic [21]	417 Pachirisu [E]
	447 Riolu [E]					
Force Palm	286 Breloom [29]	296 Makuhita [28]	297 Hariyama [32]	307 Meditite [29]	308 Medicham [29]	447 Riolu [15]
	448 Lucario [15]	532 Timburr [E]	619 Mienfoo [29]	620 Mienshao [29]		
Foresight	007 Squirtle [E]	016 Pidgey [E]	048 Venonat [1]	049 Venomoth [1]	054 Psyduck [E]	056 Mankey [E]
	066 Machop [19]	067 Machoke [19]	068 Machamp [19]	083 Farfetch'd [E]	106 Hitmonlee [37]	115 Kangaskhan [E]
	131 Lapras [E]	140 Kabuto [E]	142 Aerodactyl [E]	155 Cyndaquil [E]	161 Sentret [1]	162 Furret [1]
	163 Hoothoot [1]	164 Noctowl [1]	175 Togepi [E]	193 Yanma [1]	203 Girafarig [E]	215 Sneasel [E]
	236 Tyrogue [1]	258 Mudkip [19]	259 Marshtomp [20]	260 Swampert [20]	283 Surskit [E]	296 Makuhita [E]
	300 Skitty [4]	302 Sableye [4]	307 Meditite [E]	353 Shuppet [E]	355 Duskull [9]	356 Dusclops [9]
	396 Starly [E]	427 Buneary [1]	428 Lopunny [1]	447 Riolu [E]	448 Lucario [E]	469 Yanmega [1]
	477 Dusknoir [9]	486 Regigigas [1]	504 Patrat [1]	532 Timburr [E]	636 Larvesta [E]	
Foul Play	Taught by someone	052 Meowth [E]	198 Murkrow [45]	228 Houndour [40]	229 Houndoom [45]	273 Seedot [E]
	302 Sableye [50]	352 Kecleon [E]	430 Honchkrow [45]	434 Stunky [E]	509 Purrloin [E]	551 Sandile [37]
	552 Krokorok [40]	553 Krookodile [42]	570 Zorua [29]	571 Zoroark [29]		
Freeze Shock	646 Kyurem (Blk) [50]					
Frenzy Plant	Taught by someone					
Frost Breath	TM79					
Frustration	TM21	427 Buneary [13]				
Fury Attack	015 Beedrill [1,10]	021 Spearow [9]	022 Fearow [1,9]	032 Nidoran ♂ [19]	033 Nidorino [20]	078 Rapidash [40]
	083 Farfetch'd [7]	084 Doduo [14]	085 Dodrio [14]	111 Rhyhorn [12]	112 Rhydon [1,12]	118 Goldeen [31]
	119 Seaking [31]	127 Pinsir [E]	214 Heracross [7]	221 Piloswine [33]	227 Skarmory [17]	232 Donphan [25]
	333 Swablu [10]	334 Altaria [10]	393 Piplup [25]	394 Prinplup [28]	395 Empoleon [28]	396 Starly [E]
	441 Chatot [17]	464 Rhyperior [1,19]	588 Karrablast [16]	589 Escavalier [16]	626 Bouffalant [11]	627 Rufflet [5]
	628 Braviary [1,5]	629 Vullaby [5]	630 Mandibuzz [1,5]			
Fury Cutter	027 Sandshrew [14]	028 Sandslash [14]	046 Paras [17]	047 Parasect [17]	083 Farfetch'd [1]	123 Scyther [25]
	207 Gligar [16]	212 Scizor [25]	253 Grovyle [16]	291 Ninjask [20]	328 Trapinch [E]	335 Zangoose [8]
	347 Anorith [37]	348 Armaldo [37]	402 Kricketune [10]	416 Vespiquen [5]	418 Buizel [E]	472 Gliscor [16]
	475 Gallade [17]	501 Oshawott [19]	502 Dewott [20]	503 Samurott [20]	557 Dwebble [1]	588 Karrablast [13]
	595 Joltik [12]	596 Galvantula [12]	624 Pawniard [9]	625 Bisharp [1,9]	632 Durant [6]	649 Genesect [7]
Fury Swipes	019 Rattata [20]	027 Sandshrew [20]	028 Sandslash [20]	029 Nidoran ♀ [19]	030 Nidorina [20]	052 Meowth [14]
	053 Persian [14]	054 Psyduck [22]	055 Golduck [22]	056 Mankey [9]	057 Primeape [9]	155 Cyndaquil [E]
	161 Sentret [13]	162 Furret [13]	167 Spinarak [22]	168 Ariados [23]	190 Aipom [18]	215 Sneasel [16]
	216 Teddiursa [8]	217 Ursaring [8]	264 Linoone [29]	271 Lombre [15]	288 Vigoroth [19]	290 Nincada [14]
	291 Ninjask [14]	292 Shedinja [14]	302 Sableye [15]	335 Zangoose [E]	352 Kecleon [10]	390 Chimchar [15]
	391 Monferno [16]	392 Infernape [16]	399 Bidoof [E]	416 Vespiquen [13]	418 Buizel [E]	424 Ambipom [18]
	431 Glameow [20]	432 Purugly [20]	434 Stunky [10]	435 Skuntank [10]	461 Weavile [16]	509 Purrloin [12]
	510 Liepard [12]	511 Pansage [13]	512 Simisage [1]	513 Pansear [13]	514 Simisear [1]	515 Panpour [13]
	516 Simipour [1]	529 Drilbur [12]	530 Excadrill [12]	570 Zorua [13]	571 Zoroark [13]	613 Cubchoo [17]
	614 Beartic [17]	631 Heatmor [21]				
Fusion Bolt	644 Zekrom [50]	646 Kyurem (Blk) [43]				
Fusion Flare	643 Reshiram [50]	646 Kyurem (Wht) [43]				
Future Sight	054 Psyduck [E]	064 Kadabra [48]	065 Alakazam [48]	079 Slowpoke [E]	096 Drowzee [61]	097 Hypno [61]
	122 Mr. Mime [E]	131 Lapras [E]	150 Mewtwo [15]	175 Togepi [E]	177 Natu [36]	178 Xatu [42]
	183 Marill [E]	196 Espeon [25]	203 Girafarig [E]	225 Delibird [E]	249 Lugia [79]	250 Ho-Oh [79]
	251 Celebi [64]	280 Ralts [39]	281 Kirlia [45]	282 Gardevoir [53]	325 Spoink [E]	337 Lunatone [45]
	339 Barboach [43]	340 Whiscash [51]	351 Castform [E]	355 Duskull [49]	356 Dusclops [61]	358 Chimecho [E]

Move	Pokémon that can learn it					
Future Sight (continued)	359 Absol [36]	385 Jirachi [55]	433 Chingling [E]	436 Bronzor [29]	437 Bronzong [29]	439 Mime Jr. [E]
	477 Dusknoir [61]	480 Uxie [36]	481 Mesprit [36]	482 Azelf [36]	488 Cresselia [38]	493 Arceus [60]
	517 Munna [31]	527 Woobat [36]	528 Swoobat [36]	574 Gothita [31]	575 Gothorita [31]	576 Gothitelle [31]
	577 Solosis [31]	578 Duosion [31]	579 Reuniclus [31]			

G

Move	Pokémon that can learn it					
Gastro Acid	Taught by someone	023 Ekans [36]	024 Arbok [44]	069 Bellsprout [35]	070 Weepinbell [35]	213 Shuckle [27]
	316 Gulpin [49]	317 Swalot [59]	336 Seviper [34]	345 Lileep [36]	346 Cradily [46]	495 Snivy [40]
	496 Servine [48]	497 Serperior [56]	590 Foongus [E]	595 Joltik [23]	596 Galvantula [23]	603 Eelektrik [64]
Gear Grind	599 Klink [16]	600 Klang [1, 16]	601 Klinklang [1, 16]			
Giga Drain	Taught by someone	001 Bulbasaur [E]	041 Zubat [E]	043 Oddish [37]	044 Gloom [47]	046 Paras [38]
	047 Parasect [44]	048 Venonat [E]	069 Bellsprout [E]	102 Exeggcute [E]	114 Tangela [36, E]	140 Kabuto [E]
	187 Hoppip [43]	188 Skiploom [52]	189 Jumpluff [59]	191 Sunkern [22]	192 Sunflora [22]	252 Treecko [46]
	267 Beautifly [38]	270 Lotad [E]	285 Shroomish [37]	315 Roselia [25, E]	387 Turtwig [41]	388 Grotle [47]
	389 Torterra [51]	406 Budew [E]	455 Carnivine [E]	465 Tangrowth [36]	470 Leafeon [25]	495 Snivy [34]
	496 Servine [40]	497 Serperior [44]	546 Cottonee [26]	548 Petilil [26]	556 Maractus [26]	590 Foongus [28]
	591 Amoonguss [28]	616 Shelmet [37]	617 Accelgor [37]	640 Virizion [37]		
Giga Impact	TM68	128 Tauros [63]	142 Aerodactyl [81]	143 Snorlax [57]	232 Donphan [54]	248 Tyranitar [82]
	466 Electivire [62]	486 Regigigas [100]	506 Lillipup [40]	507 Herdier [61]	508 Stoutland [59]	589 Escavalier [56]
	610 Axew [61]	611 Fraxure [66]	612 Haxorus [74]	626 Bouffalant [61]		
Glaciate	646 Kyurem [50]					
Glare	023 Ekans [12]	024 Arbok [12]	206 Dunsparce [28]	336 Seviper [23]	495 Snivy [E]	621 Druddigon [E]
Grass Knot	TM86	511 Pansage [34]				
Grass Pledge	Taught by someone					
GrassWhistle	001 Bulbasaur [E]	152 Chikorita [E]	191 Sunkern [7, E]	192 Sunflora [7]	252 Treecko [E]	315 Roselia [22, E]
	331 Cacnea [E]	406 Budew [E]	420 Cherubi [E]	455 Carnivine [E]	459 Snover [13]	460 Abomasnow [13]
	470 Leafeon [17]	511 Pansage [E]	541 Swadloon [1]	546 Cottonee [E]	548 Petilil [E]	556 Maractus [E]
	585 Deerling [E]					
Gravity	Taught by someone	035 Clefairy [49]	113 Chansey [E]	174 Igglybuff [E]	356 Dusclops [1]	385 Jirachi [45]
	440 Happiny [E]	476 Probopass [1]	477 Dusknoir [1]	493 Arceus [10]	524 Roggenrola [E]	561 Sigilyph [38]
	597 Ferroseed [E]					
Growl	001 Bulbasaur [3]	002 Ivysaur [1,3]	003 Venusaur [1,3]	004 Charmander [1]	005 Charmeleon [1]	006 Charizard [1]
	021 Spearow [1]	022 Fearow [1]	025 Pikachu [1]	029 Nidoran ♀ [1]	030 Nidorina [1]	035 Clefairy [1]
	050 Diglett [4]	051 Dugtrio [1,4]	052 Meowth [1]	053 Persian [1]	077 Ponyta [1]	078 Rapidash [1]
	079 Slowpoke [5]	080 Slowbro [1,5]	084 Doduo [1]	085 Dodrio [1]	086 Seel [3]	087 Dewgong [1,3]
	104 Cubone [1]	105 Marowak [1]	113 Chansey [1]	131 Lapras [1]	133 Eevee [9]	152 Chikorita [1]
	153 Bayleef [1]	154 Meganium [1]	163 Hoothoot [1]	164 Noctowl [1]	175 Togepi [1]	176 Togetic [1]
	179 Mareep [1]	180 Flaaffy [1]	181 Ampharos [1]	199 Slowking [5]	200 Misdreavus [1]	203 Girafarig [1]
	231 Phanpy [1]	232 Donphan [1]	241 Miltank [3]	242 Blissey [1]	255 Torchic [1]	256 Combusken [1]
	257 Blaziken [1]	258 Mudkip [1]	259 Marshtomp [1]	260 Swampert [1]	263 Zigzagoon [1]	264 Linoone [1]
	270 Lotad [3]	271 Lombre [3]	272 Ludicolo [1]	276 Taillow [1]	277 Swellow [1]	278 Wingull [1]
	279 Pelipper [1]	280 Ralts [1]	281 Kirlia [1]	282 Gardevoir [1]	300 Skitty [1]	311 Plusle [1]
	312 Minun [1]	320 Wailmer [4]	321 Wailord [1,4]	322 Numel [1]	323 Camerupt [1]	333 Swablu [1]
	334 Altaria [1]	358 Chimecho [6]	363 Spheal [1]	364 Sealeo [1]	365 Walrein [1]	393 Piplup [1]
	394 Prinplup [1,4]	395 Empoleon [1,4]	396 Starly [1]	397 Staravia [1]	398 Staraptor [1]	399 Bidoof [5]
	400 Bibarel [1,5]	401 Kricketot [1]	402 Kricketune [1]	417 Pachirisu [1]	418 Buizel [4]	419 Floatzel [1,4]
	429 Mismagius [1]	431 Glameow [8]	432 Purugly [1,8]	433 Chingling [6]	441 Chatot [5]	509 Purrloin [3]
	510 Liepard [1,3]	519 Pidove [4]	520 Tranquill [1,4]	521 Unfezant [1,4]	531 Audino [1]	535 Tympole [1]
	536 Palpitoad [1]	537 Seismitoad [1]	572 Minccino [3]	585 Deerling [4]	586 Sawsbuck [1,4]	605 Elgyem [4]
	606 Beheeyem [1,4]	613 Cubchoo [5]	614 Beartic [1,5]			
Growth	001 Bulbasaur [25]	002 Ivysaur [28]	003 Venusaur [28]	046 Paras [33]	047 Parasect [37]	069 Bellsprout [7]
	070 Weepinbell [1, 7]	114 Tangela [20]	191 Sunkern [1]	192 Sunflora [1]	273 Seedot [7]	274 Nuzleaf [7]
	285 Shroomish [33]	314 Illumise [E]	315 Roselia [4]	331 Cacnea [9]	332 Cacturne [1, 9]	357 Tropius [1]
	387 Turtwig [E]	406 Budew [4]	413 Wormadam (Plnt) [29]	420 Cherubi [7]	421 Cherrim [1, 7]	455 Carnivine [1]
	459 Snover [E]	465 Tangrowth [20]	492 Shaymin (Land) [1]	492 Shaymin (Sky) [1]	495 Snivy [13]	496 Servine [13]
	497 Serperior [13]	546 Cottonee [4]	547 Whimsicott [1]	548 Petilil [4]	549 Lilligant [1]	556 Maractus [6]
	590 Foongus [6, E]	591 Amoonguss [1, 6]				
Grudge	037 Vulpix [44]	092 Gastly [1]	109 Koffing [E]	200 Misdreavus [50]	280 Ralts [E]	292 Shedinja [45]
	353 Shuppet [46]	354 Banette [52]	355 Duskull [E]	442 Spiritomb [E]	562 Yamask [41]	563 Cofagrigus [45]
Guard Split	063 Abra [E]	213 Shuckle [45]	343 Baltoy [34]	344 Claydol [34]	380 Latias [75]	562 Yamask [33]
	563 Cofagrigus [33]	605 Elgyem [50]	606 Beheeyem [56]	616 Shelmet [E]		
Guard Swap	063 Abra [E]	096 Drowzee [E]	122 Mr. Mime [1]	150 Mewtwo [57]	177 Natu [47]	178 Xatu [59]
	197 Umbreon [45]	203 Girafarig [1]	227 Skarmory [E]	303 Mawile [E]	307 Meditite [E]	605 Elgyem [E]
	616 Shelmet [52]					
Guillotine	098 Krabby [31]	099 Kingler [37]	127 Pinsir [47]	207 Gligar [55]	341 Corphish [53]	342 Crawdaunt [65]
	472 Gliscor [55]	610 Axew [51]	611 Fraxure [54]	612 Haxorus [58]	624 Pawniard [62]	625 Bisharp [71]
	632 Durant [61]					
Gunk Shot	Taught by someone	023 Ekans [49]	024 Arbok [63]	088 Grimer [43]	089 Muk [49]	224 Octillery [1]
	316 Gulpin [59, E]	317 Swalot [73]	353 Shuppet [E]	568 Trubbish [45]	569 Garbodor [54]	
Gust	012 Butterfree [16]	016 Pidgey [9]	017 Pidgeotto [1, 9]	018 Pidgeot [1, 9]	041 Zubat [E]	049 Venomoth [31]
	083 Farfetch'd [E]	144 Articuno [1]	245 Suicune [22]	249 Lugia [9]	250 Ho-Oh [9]	267 Beautifly [13]
	269 Dustox [13]	278 Wingull [E]	284 Masquerain [22]	290 Nincada [E]	328 Trapinch [E]	357 Tropius [1]
	414 Mothim [26]	415 Combee [1]	416 Vespiquen [1]	425 Drifloon [8]	426 Drifblim [1, 8]	456 Finneon [17]

Pokémon Moves Reverse Lookup

G

Move	Pokémon that can learn it				
Gust (continued)	457 Lumineon [17]	519 Pidove [1]	520 Tranquill [1]	521 Unfezant [1]	527 Woobat [8]	528 Swoobat [1, 8]
	547 Whimsicott [10]	561 Sigilyph [1]	580 Ducklett [E]	629 Vullaby [1]	630 Mandibuzz [1]	637 Volcarona [1, 20]
	641 Tornadus [1]					
Gyro Ball	TM74	027 Sandshrew [34]	028 Sandslash [34]	039 Jigglypuff [37]	081 Magnemite [53]	082 Magneton [67]
	100 Voltorb [43]	101 Electrode [51]	109 Koffing [29]	120 Staryu [30]	157 Typhlosion [1]	204 Pineco [42]
	205 Forretress [50]	237 Hitmontop [42]	241 Miltank [41]	436 Bronzor [35]	437 Bronzong [36]	462 Magnezone [67]
	463 Lickilicky [61]	597 Ferroseed [21]	598 Ferrothorn [21]			

H

Move	Pokémon that can learn it				
Hail	TM07	086 Seel [53]	087 Dewgong [65]	144 Articuno [85]	351 Castform [20]	361 Snorunt [40]
	362 Glalie [40]	363 Spheal [31]	364 Sealeo [31]	365 Walrein [31]	471 Glaceon [37]	473 Mamoswine [40]
	478 Froslass [40]	582 Vanillite [40]	583 Vanillish [42]	584 Vanilluxe [42]	613 Cubchoo [49]	614 Beartic [53]
Hammer Arm	074 Geodude [E]	108 Lickitung [E]	112 Rhydon [42]	115 Kangaskhan [E]	185 Sudowoodo [47]	217 Ursaring [67]
	239 Elekid [E]	241 Miltank [E]	260 Swampert [69]	287 Slakoth [E]	289 Slaking [67]	293 Whismur [E]
	376 Metagross [45]	377 Regirock [81]	378 Regice [81]	379 Registeel [81]	383 Groudon [20]	408 Cranidos [E]
	464 Rhyperior [42]	500 Emboar [1]	532 Timburr [40]	533 Gurdurr [45]	534 Conkeldurr [45]	554 Darumaka [E]
	555 Darmanitan [35]	622 Golett [50]	623 Golurk [60]	641 Tornadus [79]	642 Thundurus [79]	645 Landorus [79]
Harden	011 Metapod [1, 7]	014 Kakuna [1, 7]	088 Grimer [4]	089 Muk [1, 4]	095 Onix [1]	098 Krabby [11]
	099 Kingler [11]	120 Staryu [1]	127 Pinsir [11]	140 Kabuto [1]	141 Kabutops [1]	185 Sudowoodo [E]
	207 Gligar [7]	208 Steelix [1]	211 Qwilfish [9]	214 Heracross [E]	218 Slugma [14]	219 Magcargo [14]
	222 Corsola [4]	266 Silcoon [1, 7]	268 Cascoon [1, 7]	273 Seedot [3]	274 Nuzleaf [3]	290 Nincada [1]
	291 Ninjask [1]	292 Shedinja [1]	299 Nosepass [4]	304 Aron [1]	305 Lairon [1]	306 Aggron [1]
	337 Lunatone [1]	338 Solrock [1]	341 Corphish [7]	342 Crawdaunt [1, 7]	343 Baltoy [1]	344 Claydol [1]
	347 Anorith [1]	348 Armaldo [1]	369 Relicanth [1]	413 Wormadam (Sand) [29]	422 Shellos [4]	423 Gastrodon [1, 4]
	438 Bonsly [E]	472 Gliscor [1, 7]	524 Roggenrola [4]	525 Boldore [1, 4]	526 Gigalith [1, 4]	582 Vanillite [4]
	583 Vanillish [1, 4]	584 Vanilluxe [1, 4]	597 Ferroseed [1]	598 Ferrothorn [1]	610 Axew [E]	636 Larvesta [E]
Haze	007 Squirtle [E]	023 Ekans [41]	024 Arbok [51]	041 Zubat [41]	042 Golbat [47]	060 Poliwag [E]
	072 Tentacool [E]	084 Doduo [E]	088 Grimer [E]	092 Gastly [E]	098 Krabby [E]	109 Koffing [26]
	110 Weezing [26]	118 Goldeen [E]	134 Vaporeon [33]	138 Omanyte [E]	147 Dratini [E]	169 Crobat [47]
	177 Natu [E]	194 Wooper [43]	195 Quagsire [48]	198 Murkrow [11]	211 Qwilfish [E]	223 Remoraid [E]
	226 Mantine [E]	283 Surskit [37]	333 Swablu [E]	336 Seviper [38]	349 Feebas [E]	425 Drifloon [E]
	430 Honchkrow [1]	434 Stunky [E]	458 Mantyke [E]	491 Darkrai [57]	562 Yamask [9]	563 Cofagrigus [1, 9]
	568 Trubbish [E]	607 Litwick [E]	615 Cryogonal [21]			
Head Charge	626 Bouffalant [31]					
Head Smash	032 Nidoran♂ [E]	222 Corsola [E]	231 Phanpy [E]	304 Aron [E]	369 Relicanth [78]	408 Cranidos [46]
	409 Rampardos [58]	498 Tepig [37]	499 Pignite [44]	500 Emboar [50]	559 Scraggy [53]	560 Scrafty [65]
	566 Archen [E]	633 Deino [E]				
Headbutt	050 Diglett [E]	079 Slowpoke [23]	080 Slowbro [23]	086 Seel [1]	087 Dewgong [1]	096 Drowzee [13, 29]
	097 Hypno [13, 29]	104 Cubone [11]	105 Marowak [1, 11]	185 Sudowoodo [E]	199 Slowking [23]	206 Dunsparce [E]
	209 Snubbull [19]	210 Granbull [19]	226 Mantine [16]	263 Zigzagoon [9]	264 Linoone [1, 9]	285 Shroomish [21]
	286 Breloom [21]	304 Aron [8]	305 Lairon [1, 8]	306 Aggron [1, 8]	309 Electrike [E]	351 Castform [15]
	357 Tropius [1]	361 Snorunt [19]	362 Glalie [19]	371 Bagon [16]	372 Shelgon [1, 16]	373 Salamence [1, 16]
	399 Bidoof [17]	400 Bibarel [18]	408 Cranidos [1]	409 Rampardos [1]	410 Shieldon [E]	418 Buizel [E]
	438 Bonsly [E]	453 Croagunk [E]	458 Mantyke [16]	494 Victini [17]	524 Roggenrola [10]	525 Boldore [1, 10]
	526 Gigalith [1, 10]	550 Basculin [7]	554 Darumaka [14]	555 Darmanitan [14]	559 Scraggy [12]	560 Scrafty [12]
	588 Karrablast [20]	589 Escavalier [20]	603 Eelektrik [1]	604 Eelektross [1]	605 Elgyem [18]	606 Beheeyem [18]
	624 Pawniard [E]	626 Bouffalant [E]	633 Deino [12]	634 Zweilous [12]	635 Hydreigon [12]	
Heal Bell	Taught by someone	113 Chansey [E]	209 Snubbull [1]	241 Miltank [48]	251 Celebi [1]	300 Skitty [39]
	358 Chimecho [38]	440 Happiny [E]	531 Audino [E]			
Heal Block	251 Celebi [55]	292 Shedinja [52]	337 Lunatone [37]	338 Solrock [37]	343 Baltoy [45]	344 Claydol [54]
	381 Latios [5]	436 Bronzor [45]	437 Bronzong [52]	562 Yamask [E]	574 Gothita [33]	575 Gothorita [34]
	576 Gothitelle [34]	577 Solosis [46]	578 Duosion [50]	579 Reuniclus [54]	605 Elgyem [8]	606 Beheeyem [1, 8]
	642 Thundurus [31]					
Heal Order	416 Vespiquen [29]					
Heal Pulse	079 Slowpoke [58]	080 Slowbro [68]	113 Chansey [38]	152 Chikorita [E]	199 Slowking [58]	242 Blissey [38]
	280 Ralts [23]	281 Kirlia [25]	282 Gardevoir [25]	358 Chimecho [49]	370 Luvdisc [E]	380 Latias [65]
	381 Latios [65]	420 Cherubi [E]	448 Lucario [42]	475 Gallade [25]	531 Audino [35]	594 Alomomola [17]
Healing Wish	035 Clefairy [55]	113 Chansey [50]	242 Blissey [50]	251 Celebi [73]	282 Gardevoir [1]	358 Chimecho [57]
	380 Latias [85]	385 Jirachi [50]	420 Cherubi [E]	427 Buneary [63]	428 Lopunny [63]	439 Mime Jr. [E]
	481 Mesprit [76]	492 Shaymin (Land) [91]	531 Audino [E]	548 Petilil [E]	594 Alomomola [57]	
Heart Stamp	124 Jynx [21]	238 Smoochum [21]	241 Miltank [E]	527 Woobat [15]	528 Swoobat [15]	
Heart Swap	490 Manaphy [76]					
Heat Crash	498 Tepig [27]	499 Pignite [31]	500 Emboar [31]			
Heat Wave	Taught by someone	006 Charizard [71]	037 Vulpix [E]	058 Growlithe [41, E]	146 Moltres [64]	218 Slugma [E]
	322 Numel [E]	324 Torkoal [55]	390 Chimchar [E]	485 Heatran [81]	513 Pansear [E]	607 Litwick [E]
	631 Heatmor [E]	637 Volcarona [50]				
Heavy Slam	066 Machop [E]	076 Golem [69]	095 Onix [E]	143 Snorlax [52]	205 Forretress [70]	231 Phanpy [E]
	296 Makuhita [46]	297 Hariyama [62]	304 Aron [43]	305 Lairon [51]	306 Aggron [57]	320 Wailmer [50]
	321 Wailord [70]	410 Shieldon [46]	411 Bastiodon [58]	436 Bronzor [49]	437 Bronzong [58]	486 Regigigas [90]
	498 Tepig [E]	524 Roggenrola [E]	623 Golurk [43]			
Helping Hand	Taught by someone	029 Nidoran♀ [25]	030 Nidorina [28]	032 Nidoran♂ [25]	033 Nidorino [28]	058 Growlithe [12]
	113 Chansey [E]	133 Eevee [1]	134 Vaporeon [1]	135 Jolteon [1]	136 Flareon [1]	161 Sentret [16]
	162 Furret [17]	183 Marill [16]	184 Azumarill [16]	187 Hoppip [1]	191 Sunkern [E]	196 Espeon [1]
	197 Umbreon [1]	213 Shuckle [E]	236 Tyrogue [1, E]	241 Miltank [E]	263 Zigzagoon [E]	285 Shroomish [E]

Move	Pokémon that can learn it					
Helping Hand (continued)	296 Makuhita [E]	298 Azurill [16]	300 Skitty [E]	311 Plusle [10]	312 Minun [10]	313 Volbeat [33]
	314 Illumise [33]	380 Latias [10]	381 Latios [10]	385 Jirachi [15]	390 Chimchar [E]	403 Shinx [E]
	420 Cherubi [13]	421 Cherrim [13]	440 Happiny [E]	470 Leafeon [1]	471 Glaceon [1]	475 Gallade [39]
	506 Lillipup [12]	507 Herdier [12]	508 Stoutland [12]	517 Munna [E]	527 Woobat [E]	531 Audino [1]
	542 Leavanny [32]	546 Cottonee [31]	548 Petilil [31]	572 Minccino [7]	573 Cinccino [1]	594 Alomomola [49]
	638 Cobalion [25]	639 Terrakion [25]	640 Virizion [25]	647 Keldeo [25]		
Hex	037 Vulpix [28, E]	072 Tentacool [43]	073 Tentacruel [47]	092 Gastly [43]	093 Haunter [55]	094 Gengar [55]
	200 Misdreavus [23]	206 Dunsparce [E]	351 Castform [E]	353 Shuppet [26]	354 Banette [26]	355 Duskull [38]
	356 Dusclops [42]	359 Absol [E]	361 Snorunt [E]	425 Drifloon [27]	426 Drifblim [27]	477 Dusknoir [42]
	479 Rotom [50]	479 Rotom (Heat) [50]	479 Rotom (Wash) [50]	479 Rotom (Frst) [50]	479 Rotom (Fan) [50]	479 Rotom (Mow) [50]
	487 Giratina (Alt) [50]	487 Giratina (Ori) [50]	562 Yamask [17]	563 Cofagrigus [17]	592 Frillish [43]	593 Jellicent [45]
	607 Litwick [28]	608 Lampent [28]	609 Chandelure [1]			
Hi Jump Kick	106 Hitmonlee [29]	236 Tyrogue [E]	257 Blaziken [1]	307 Meditite [32]	308 Medicham [32]	447 Riolu [E]
	559 Scraggy [31]	560 Scrafty [31]	619 Mienfoo [53]	620 Mienshao [56]		
Hidden Power	TM10	199 Slowking [1]	201 Unown [1]	307 Meditite [15]	308 Medicham [15]	412 Burmy [20]
	413 Wormadam (Plnt) [20]	413 Wormadam (Sand) [20]	413 Wormadam (Trsh) [20]	414 Mothim [20]	422 Shellos [16]	423 Gastrodon [16]
	577 Solosis [14]	578 Duosion [14]	579 Reuniclus [14]	605 Elgyem [22]	606 Beheeyem [22]	
Hone Claws	TM01	215 Sneasel [25]	431 Glameow [48]	432 Purugly [30]	451 Skorupi [30]	452 Drapion [30]
	461 Weavile [25]	509 Purrloin [24]	510 Liepard [26]	529 Drilbur [22]	530 Excadrill [22]	571 Zoroark [1, 9]
	621 Druddigon [5]	627 Rufflet [14]	628 Braviary [14]			
Horn Attack	032 Nidoran♂ [21]	033 Nidorino [23]	111 Rhyhorn [1]	112 Rhydon [1]	118 Goldeen [11]	119 Seaking [11]
	128 Tauros [8]	214 Heracross [1]	232 Donphan [1]	464 Rhyperior [1]	588 Karrablast [E]	626 Bouffalant [16]
Horn Drill	032 Nidoran♂ [45]	033 Nidorino [58]	077 Ponyta [E]	086 Seel [E]	111 Rhyhorn [63]	112 Rhydon [71]
	118 Goldeen [41]	119 Seaking [47]	131 Lapras [E]	464 Rhyperior [71]	530 Excadrill [31]	
Horn Leech	586 Sawsbuck [37]					
Howl	037 Vulpix [E]	058 Growlithe [E]	155 Cyndaquil [E]	228 Houndour [4]	229 Houndoom [1, 4]	261 Poochyena [5]
	262 Mightyena [1, 5]	293 Whismur [15]	294 Loudred [1, 15]	295 Exploud [1, 15]	309 Electrike [12]	310 Manectric [1, 12]
	322 Numel [E]	403 Shinx [E]	506 Lillipup [E]			
Hurricane	016 Pidgey [53]	017 Pidgeotto [62]	018 Pidgeot [68]	144 Articuno [92]	146 Moltres [92]	149 Dragonite [81]
	278 Wingull [49]	279 Pelipper [63]	547 Whimsicott [46]	580 Ducklett [46]	581 Swanna [55]	637 Volcarona [90]
	641 Tornadus [67]					
Hydro Cannon	Taught by someone					
Hydro Pump	007 Squirtle [40]	008 Wartortle [48]	009 Blastoise [60]	054 Psyduck [46]	055 Golduck [54]	060 Poliwag [38]
	061 Poliwhirl [48]	072 Tentacool [47]	073 Tentacruel [52]	090 Shellder [61]	116 Horsea [35]	117 Seadra [40]
	118 Goldeen [E]	120 Staryu [52]	130 Gyarados [41]	131 Lapras [49]	134 Vaporeon [45]	138 Omanyte [55]
	139 Omastar [75]	158 Totodile [50, E]	159 Croconaw [60]	160 Feraligatr [76]	170 Chinchou [57]	171 Lanturn [57]
	183 Marill [40]	184 Azumarill [46]	211 Qwilfish [57]	223 Remoraid [42]	224 Octillery [52]	226 Mantine [49, E]
	230 Kingdra [40]	245 Suicune [71]	249 Lugia [37]	258 Mudkip [42]	271 Lombre [45]	279 Pelipper [58]
	283 Surskit [E]	318 Carvanha [E]	320 Wailmer [47]	321 Wailord [62]	339 Barboach [E]	350 Milotic [37]
	351 Castform [40]	367 Huntail [51]	368 Gorebyss [51]	369 Relicanth [71]	370 Luvdisc [40]	371 Bagon [E]
	382 Kyogre [90]	393 Piplup [43, E]	394 Prinplup [51]	395 Empoleon [59]	418 Buizel [45]	419 Floatzel [57]
	458 Mantyke [49, E]	479 Rotom (Wash) [◆]	484 Palkia [50]	501 Oshawott [43]	502 Dewott [52]	503 Samurott [62]
	515 Panpour [E]	535 Tympole [42]	536 Palpitoad [47]	537 Seismitoad [53]	564 Tirtouga [51]	565 Carracosta [61]
	592 Frillish [49]	593 Jellicent [53]	594 Alomomola [61]	647 Keldeo [67]		
Hyper Beam	TM15	130 Gyarados [47]	142 Aerodactyl [65]	147 Dratini [61]	148 Dragonair [75]	149 Dragonite [75]
	223 Remoraid [46]	224 Octillery [58]	233 Porygon2 [67]	246 Larvitar [55]	247 Pupitar [67]	248 Tyranitar [73]
	295 Exploud [79]	328 Trapinch [49]	329 Vibrava [49]	330 Flygon [49]	344 Claydol [36]	375 Metang [50]
	376 Metagross [62]	377 Regirock [89]	378 Regice [89]	379 Registeel [89]	384 Rayquaza [80]	386 Deoxys (Nor) [97]
	386 Deoxys (Atk) [97]	467 Magmortar [67]	474 Porygon-Z [67]	493 Arceus [80]	599 Klink [57]	600 Klang [64]
	601 Klinklang [72]	649 Genesect [73]				
Hyper Fang	019 Rattata [16]	020 Raticate [16]	399 Bidoof [21]	400 Bibarel [23]	417 Pachirisu [49]	504 Patrat [28]
	505 Watchog [32]					
Hyper Voice	Taught by someone	039 Jigglypuff [49]	161 Sentret [47]	162 Furret [56]	186 Politoed [48]	293 Whismur [51]
	294 Loudred [65]	295 Exploud [71]	333 Swablu [E]	384 Rayquaza [20]	441 Chatot [57]	493 Arceus [30]
	535 Tympole [45]	536 Palpitoad [51]	537 Seismitoad [59]	572 Minccino [43]	633 Deino [58]	634 Zweilous [64]
	635 Hydreigon [68]	643 Reshiram [92]	644 Zekrom [92]	646 Kyurem [92]	646 Kyurem (Blk) [92]	646 Kyurem (Wht) [92]
Hypnosis	037 Vulpix [E]	041 Zubat [E]	052 Meowth [E]	054 Psyduck [E]	060 Poliwag [8]	061 Poliwhirl [1, 8]
	062 Poliwrath [1]	077 Ponyta [E]	092 Gastly [1]	093 Haunter [1]	094 Gengar [1]	096 Drowzee [1]
	097 Hypno [1]	102 Exeggcute [1]	103 Exeggutor [1]	122 Mr. Mime [E]	163 Hoothoot [5]	164 Noctowl [1, 5]
	186 Politoed [1]	193 Yanma [38]	234 Stantler [10]	280 Ralts [45]	281 Kirlia [53]	282 Gardevoir [65]
	327 Spinda [23]	337 Lunatone [9]	349 Feebas [E]	358 Chimecho [1]	425 Drifloon [E]	431 Glameow [13]
	432 Purugly [13]	433 Chingling [1]	436 Bronzor [5]	437 Bronzong [1, 5]	439 Mime Jr. [E]	442 Spiritomb [13]
	491 Darkrai [20]	504 Patrat [18]	505 Watchog [18]	517 Munna [19]	518 Musharna [1]	519 Pidove [E]
	561 Sigilyph [4]					

Move	Pokémon that can learn it					
Ice Ball	060 Poliwag [E]	225 Delibird [E]	258 Mudkip [E]	363 Spheal [13]	364 Sealeo [13]	365 Walrein [13]
Ice Beam	TM13	086 Seel [47]	087 Dewgong [55]	090 Shellder [52]	131 Lapras [32]	144 Articuno [43]
	223 Remoraid [34]	224 Octillery [40]	362 Glalie [37]	378 Regice [73]	382 Kyogre [35]	582 Vanillite [35]
	583 Vanillish [36]	584 Vanilluxe [36]	615 Cryogonal [33]	646 Kyurem [22]	646 Kyurem (Blk) [22]	646 Kyurem (Wht) [22]
Ice Burn	646 Kyurem (Wht) [50]					
Ice Fang	024 Arbok [1]	111 Rhyhorn [E]	130 Gyarados [32]	142 Aerodactyl [1]	158 Totodile [20]	159 Croconaw [21]
	160 Feraligatr [21]	208 Steelix [1]	209 Snubbull [1, E]	210 Granbull [1]	221 Piloswine [24]	245 Suicune [50]

◆ When Rotom becomes Wash Rotom, it learns the move Hydro Pump. When it changes back to Rotom, it forgets the move.

Pokémon Moves Reverse Lookup

I

Move	Pokémon that can learn it					
	248 Tyranitar [1]	261 Poochyena [E]	295 Exploud [1]	303 Mawile [E]	309 Electrike [E]	318 Carvanha [16]
	319 Sharpedo [16]	361 Snorunt [28]	362 Glalie [28]	365 Walrein [44]	367 Huntail [24]	403 Shinx [E]
	419 Floatzel [1]	450 Hippowdon [1]	452 Drapion [1]	471 Glaceon [21]	472 Gliscor [1]	473 Mamoswine [24]
	506 Lillipup [E]	508 Stoutland [1]	633 Deino [E]			
Ice Punch	Taught by someone	063 Abra [E]	066 Machop [E]	092 Gastly [E]	096 Drowzee [E]	107 Hitmonchan [36]
	124 Jynx [18]	158 Totodile [E]	215 Sneasel [E]	225 Delibird [E]	238 Smoochum [E]	239 Elekid [E]
	307 Meditite [E]	308 Medicham [1]	356 Dusclops [1]	427 Buneary [E]	460 Abomasnow [1]	477 Dusknoir [1]
	486 Regigigas [1]	559 Scraggy [E]	613 Cubchoo [E]			
Ice Shard	086 Seel [17]	087 Dewgong [17]	090 Shellder [28]	131 Lapras [10]	144 Articuno [15]	215 Sneasel [47, E]
	220 Swinub [24]	225 Delibird [E]	231 Phanpy [E]	361 Snorunt [37]	459 Snover [26]	460 Abomasnow [26]
	471 Glaceon [25]	478 Froslass [37]	582 Vanillite [E]	615 Cryogonal [5]		
Icicle Crash	091 Cloyster [52]	220 Swinub [E]	614 Beartic [37]			
Icicle Spear	086 Seel [E]	090 Shellder [13, E]	220 Swinub [E]	222 Corsola [E]	582 Vanillite [1]	583 Vanillish [1]
	584 Vanilluxe [1]					
Icy Wind	Taught by someone	086 Seel [11]	087 Dewgong [1, 11]	122 Mr. Mime [E]	140 Kabuto [E]	215 Sneasel [14]
	220 Swinub [21]	221 Piloswine [21]	225 Delibird [E]	327 Spinda [E]	361 Snorunt [13]	362 Glalie [13]
	378 Regice [9]	393 Piplup [E]	439 Mime Jr. [E]	459 Snover [9]	460 Abomasnow [1, 9]	461 Weavile [14]
	471 Glaceon [9]	478 Froslass [13]	582 Vanillite [13]	583 Vanillish [13]	584 Vanilluxe [13]	613 Cubchoo [13]
	614 Beartic [1, 13]	615 Cryogonal [17]	646 Kyurem [1]	646 Kyurem (Blk) [1]	646 Kyurem (Wht) [1]	
Imprison	037 Vulpix [18]	088 Grimer [E]	200 Misdreavus [E]	234 Stantler [49]	280 Ralts [34]	281 Kirlia [39]
	282 Gardevoir [45]	353 Shuppet [E]	355 Duskull [E]	436 Bronzor [9]	437 Bronzong [1,9]	442 Spiritomb [E]
	480 Uxie [6]	481 Mesprit [6]	482 Azelf [6]	517 Munna [13]	527 Woobat [19]	528 Swoobat [19]
	562 Yamask [E]	570 Zorua [53]	571 Zoroark [59]	577 Solosis [E]	582 Vanillite [E]	605 Elgyem [25]
	606 Beheeyem [25]	607 Litwick [24]	608 Lampent [24]	643 Reshiram [8,64]	644 Zekrom [8,64]	645 Landorus [7]
	646 Kyurem [8,64]	646 Kyurem (Blk) [8,64]	646 Kyurem (Wht) [8,64]			
Incinerate	TM59	494 Victini [1]	513 Pansear [10]	554 Darumaka [6]	555 Darmanitan [1,6]	631 Heatmor [1]
Inferno	004 Charmander [46]	005 Charmeleon [54]	006 Charizard [62]	037 Vulpix [50]	077 Ponyta [33]	078 Rapidash [33]
	155 Cyndaquil [46]	156 Quilava [53]	157 Typhlosion [56]	218 Slugma [E]	228 Houndour [56]	229 Houndoom [65]
	324 Torkoal [60]	494 Victini [57]	607 Litwick [38]	608 Lampent [38]	631 Heatmor [61]	
Ingrain	001 Bulbasaur [E]	043 Oddish [E]	069 Bellsprout [E]	102 Exeggcute [E]	114 Tangela [1]	152 Chikorita [E]
	191 Sunkern [4, E]	192 Sunflora [4]	222 Corsola [E]	315 Roselia [34]	331 Cacnea [25]	332 Cacturne [25]
	345 Lileep [15]	346 Cradily [1,15]	455 Carnivine [21]	459 Snover [31]	460 Abomasnow [31]	465 Tangrowth [1]
	548 Petilil [E]	556 Maractus [33]	590 Foongus [18]	591 Amoonguss [18]	597 Ferroseed [35]	598 Ferrothorn [35]
	Taught by someone	007 Squirtle [34]	008 Wartortle [40]	009 Blastoise [46]	090 Shellder [E]	204 Pineco [39]
	205 Forretress [46]	212 Scizor [37]	222 Corsola [29]	246 Larvitar [E]	303 Mawile [41]	304 Aron [15]
	305 Lairon [15]	306 Aggron [15]	324 Torkoal [44]	347 Anorith [E]	366 Clamperl [1]	375 Metang [47]
	376 Metagross [53]	377 Regirock [41]	379 Registeel [41]	386 Deoxys (Def) [73]	410 Shieldon [19]	411 Bastiodon [19]
	436 Bronzor [19]	437 Bronzong [19]	447 Riolu [E]	476 Probopass [1, 4]	524 Roggenrola [20]	525 Boldore [20]
	526 Gigalith [20]	529 Drilbur [E]	544 Whirlipede [22]	557 Dwebble [E]	564 Tirtouga [E]	582 Vanillite [E]
	589 Escavalier [40]	597 Ferroseed [26]	598 Ferrothorn [26]	622 Golett [17]	623 Golurk [17]	624 Pawniard [46]
	625 Bisharp [46]	632 Durant [56]				
Iron Head	Taught by someone	104 Cubone [E]	142 Aerodactyl [57]	212 Scizor [53]	246 Larvitar [E]	303 Mawile [56]
	304 Aron [25, E]	305 Lairon [25]	306 Aggron [25]	322 Numel [E]	379 Registeel [73]	408 Cranidos [E]
	410 Shieldon [42]	411 Bastiodon [51]	413 Wormadam (Trsh) [47]	443 Gible [E]	485 Heatran [65]	589 Escavalier [37]
	597 Ferroseed [43]	598 Ferrothorn [46]	624 Pawniard [54]	625 Bisharp [57]	626 Bouffalant [E]	632 Durant [36]
	638 Cobalion [37]					
Iron Tail	Taught by someone	023 Ekans [E]	029 Nidoran ♀ [E]	032 Nidoran ♂ [E]	052 Meowth [E]	058 Growlithe [E]
	086 Seel [E]	095 Onix [40]	111 Rhyhorn [E]	147 Dratini [E]	161 Sentret [E]	179 Mareep [E]
	208 Steelix [40]	240 Magby [E]	246 Larvitar [E]	304 Aron [36]	305 Lairon [40]	306 Aggron [40]
	335 Zangoose [E]	336 Seviper [E]	349 Feebas [E]	408 Cranidos [E]	417 Pachirisu [E]	434 Stunky [E]
	443 Gible [E]	451 Skorupi [E]	483 Dialga [42]	495 Snivy [E]	504 Patrat [E]	572 Minccino [E]
	587 Emolga [E]	610 Axew [E]	621 Druddigon [E]			

J

Move	Pokémon that can learn it					
Judgment	493 Arceus [100]					
Jump Kick	106 Hitmonlee [13]	234 Stantler [43]	427 Buneary [23]	428 Lopunny [23]	585 Deerling [24]	586 Sawsbuck [24]
	619 Mienfoo [37]	620 Mienshao [37]				

K

Move	Pokémon that can learn it					
Karate Chop	056 Mankey [13]	057 Primeape [13]	066 Machop [10]	067 Machoke [1, 10]	068 Machamp [1, 10]	239 Elekid [E]
	240 Magby [E]	539 Sawk [25]				
Kinesis	064 Kadabra [1]	065 Alakazam [1]				
Knock Off	Taught by someone	063 Abra [E]	066 Machop [E]	069 Bellsprout [27]	070 Weepinbell [27]	072 Tentacool [E]
	083 Farfetch'd [9]	098 Krabby [E]	108 Lickitung [13]	114 Tangela [27]	138 Omanyte [E]	140 Kabuto [E]
	165 Ledyba [E]	207 Gligar [10]	213 Shuckle [E]	232 Donphan [10]	278 Wingull [E]	296 Makuhita [19]
	297 Hariyama [19]	302 Sableye [29]	341 Corphish [26, E]	342 Crawdaunt [26]	347 Anorith [E]	353 Shuppet [1]
	354 Banette [Nor]	386 Deoxys (Def) [25]	386 Deoxys (Spd) [25]	451 Skorupi [5]	452 Drapion [1,5]	
	463 Lickilicky [13]	465 Tangrowth [27]	472 Gliscor [1,10]	486 Regigigas [1]	527 Woobat [E]	564 Tirtouga [E]
	566 Archen [E]	572 Minccino [E]	588 Karrablast [E]	619 Mienfoo [E]	629 Vullaby [E]	

L

Move	Pokémon that can learn it					
Last Resort	Taught by someone	019 Rattata [E]	052 Meowth [E]	133 Eevee [41]	134 Vaporeon [41]	135 Jolteon [41]
	136 Flareon [41]	161 Sentret [E]	174 Igglybuff [E]	175 Togepi [49]	176 Togetic [49]	190 Aipom [43]
	196 Espeon [41]	197 Umbreon [41]	231 Phanpy [37]	255 Torchic [E]	300 Skitty [E]	311 Plusle [51]
	385 Jirachi [65]	417 Pachirisu [45]	424 Ambipom [43]	431 Glameow [E]	433 Chingling [22]	440 Happiny [E]
	446 Munchlax [57]	470 Leafeon [41]	471 Glaceon [41]	482 Azelf [61]	506 Lillipup [36]	507 Herdier [42]
	508 Stoutland [51]	531 Audino [55]	572 Minccino [45]			
Lava Plume	126 Magmar [36]	136 Flareon [37]	155 Cyndaquil [37]	156 Quilava [42]	157 Typhlosion [43]	218 Slugma [37]
	219 Magcargo [37]	240 Magby [33]	244 Entei [57]	322 Numel [22]	323 Camerupt [22]	324 Torkoal [39]
	383 Groudon [15]	467 Magmortar [36]	485 Heatran [49]			
Leaf Blade	071 Victreebel [47]	083 Farfetch'd [E]	182 Bellossom [1]	253 Grovyle [29]	254 Sceptile [29]	357 Tropius [E]
	470 Leafeon [45]	475 Gallade [1]	495 Snivy [28]	496 Servine [32]	497 Serperior [32]	542 Leavanny [36]
	640 Virizion [67]					
Leaf Storm	001 Bulbasaur [E]	071 Victreebel [47]	102 Exeggcute [E]	103 Exeggutor [47]	114 Tangela [E]	152 Chikorita [E]
	182 Bellossom [53]	192 Sunflora [43]	251 Celebi [82]	252 Treecko [E]	253 Grovyle [59]	254 Sceptile [67]
	275 Shiftry [49]	315 Roselia [E]	357 Tropius [71, E]	387 Turtwig [45]	388 Grotle [52]	389 Torterra [57]
	406 Budew [E]	413 Wormadam (Plnt) [47]	479 Rotom (Mow) ◆	492 Shaymin (Sky) [91]	495 Snivy [43]	496 Servine [52]
	497 Serperior [62]	511 Pansage [E]	542 Leavanny [50]	548 Petilil [46]		
Leaf Tornado	071 Victreebel [27]	275 Shiftry [19]	357 Tropius [47]	455 Carnivine [31]	495 Snivy [16]	496 Servine [16]
	497 Serperior [16]					
Leech Life	041 Zubat [1]	042 Golbat [1]	046 Paras [11]	047 Parasect [1, 11]	048 Venonat [17]	049 Venomoth [17]
	069 Bellsprout [E]	167 Spinarak [12]	168 Ariados [12]	169 Crobat [1]	193 Yanma [E]	290 Nincada [5]
	291 Ninjask [1, 5]	292 Shedinja [5]	402 Kricketune [14]	595 Joltik [1]	596 Galvantula [1]	616 Shelmet [1]
	617 Accelgor [1]	636 Larvesta [10]	637 Volcarona [1, 10]			
Leech Seed	001 Bulbasaur [7]	002 Ivysaur [1,7]	003 Venusaur [1,7]	046 Paras [E]	102 Exeggcute [11]	114 Tangela [E]
	152 Chikorita [E]	187 Hoppip [22]	188 Skiploom [24]	189 Jumpluff [24]	191 Sunkern [13, E]	192 Sunflora [13]
	251 Celebi [1]	252 Treecko [E]	270 Lotad [E]	273 Seedot [E]	285 Shroomish [13]	286 Breloom [1,13]
	315 Roselia [16]	331 Cacnea [13]	332 Cacturne [13]	357 Tropius [E]	387 Turtwig [29]	388 Grotle [32]
	389 Torterra [33]	420 Cherubi [10]	421 Cherrim [10]	455 Carnivine [E]	459 Snover [E]	492 Shaymin (Land) [19]
	492 Shaymin (Sky) [19]	495 Snivy [19]	496 Servine [20]	497 Serperior [20]	511 Pansage [16]	546 Cottonee [8]
	547 Whimsicott [1]	548 Petilil [8]	549 Lilligant [1]	556 Maractus [E]	585 Deerling [13]	586 Sawsbuck [13]
	597 Ferroseed [E]					
Leer	021 Spearow [5]	022 Fearow [1,5]	023 Ekans [1]	024 Arbok [1]	032 Nidoran♂ [1]	033 Nidorino [1]
	056 Mankey [1]	057 Primeape [1]	058 Growlithe [8]	066 Machop [1]	067 Machoke [1]	068 Machamp [1]
	083 Farfetch'd [1]	090 Shellder [20]	098 Krabby [9]	099 Kingler [1,9]	104 Cubone [13]	105 Marowak [13]
	115 Kangaskhan [1]	116 Horsea [8]	117 Seadra [1,8]	123 Scyther [1]	125 Electabuzz [1]	126 Magmar [1]
	130 Gyarados [26]	138 Omanyte [19]	139 Omastar [19]	140 Kabuto [11]	141 Kabutops [1,11]	147 Dratini [1]
	148 Dragonair [1]	149 Dragonite [1]	155 Cyndaquil [1]	156 Quilava [1]	157 Typhlosion [1]	158 Totodile [1]
	159 Croconaw [1]	160 Feraligatr [1]	177 Natu [1]	178 Xatu [1]	212 Scizor [1]	214 Heracross [1]
	215 Sneasel [1]	216 Teddiursa [1]	217 Ursaring [1]	227 Skarmory [1]	228 Houndour [1]	229 Houndoom [1]
	230 Kingdra [1,8]	234 Stantler [3]	239 Elekid [1]	240 Magby [1]	243 Raikou [1]	244 Entei [1]
	245 Suicune [1]	246 Larvitar [1]	247 Pupitar [1]	248 Tyranitar [1]	252 Treecko [1]	253 Grovyle [1]
	254 Sceptile [1]	261 Poochyena [E]	302 Sableye [1]	309 Electrike [9]	310 Manectric [1,9]	318 Carvanha [1]
	319 Sharpedo [1]	331 Cacnea [1]	332 Cacturne [1]	335 Zangoose [1]	341 Corphish [13]	342 Crawdaunt [1,13]
	355 Duskull [1]	356 Dusclops [1]	357 Tropius [1]	359 Absol [4]	361 Snorunt [1]	362 Glalie [1]
	371 Bagon [10]	372 Shelgon [1,10]	373 Salamence [1,10]	386 Deoxys (Nor) [1]	386 Deoxys (Atk) [1]	386 Deoxys (Def) [1]
	386 Deoxys (Spd) [1]	390 Chimchar [1]	391 Monferno [1]	392 Infernape [1]	403 Shinx [5]	404 Luxio [1,5]
	405 Luxray [1,5]	408 Cranidos [1, E]	409 Rampardos [1]	434 Stunky [E]	451 Skorupi [1]	452 Drapion [1]
	459 Snover [1]	460 Abomasnow [1]	461 Weavile [1]	466 Electivire [1]	467 Magmortar [1]	475 Gallade [1]
	477 Dusknoir [1]	478 Froslass [1]	485 Heatran [9]	495 Snivy [4]	496 Servine [1,4]	497 Serperior [1,4]
	504 Patrat [3]	505 Watchog [1,3]	506 Lillipup [1]	507 Herdier [1]	508 Stoutland [1]	511 Pansage [4]
	512 Simisage [4]	513 Pansear [4]	514 Simisear [1]	515 Panpour [4]	516 Simipour [1]	519 Pidove [8]
	520 Tranquill [1,8]	521 Unfezant [1,8]	532 Timburr [1]	533 Gurdurr [1]	534 Conkeldurr [1]	538 Throh [1]
	539 Sawk [1]	551 Sandile [1]	552 Krokorok [1]	553 Krookodile [1]	559 Scraggy [1]	560 Scrafty [1]
	566 Archen [1]	567 Archeops [1]	570 Zorua [1]	571 Zoroark [1]	588 Karrablast [4]	589 Escavalier [1,4]
	610 Axew [4]	611 Fraxure [1,4]	612 Haxorus [1,4]	621 Druddigon [1]	624 Pawniard [6]	625 Bisharp [1,6]
	626 Bouffalant [1]	627 Rufflet [1]	628 Braviary [1]	629 Vullaby [1]	630 Mandibuzz [1]	638 Cobalion [1]
	639 Terrakion [1]	640 Virizion [1]	647 Keldeo [1]			
Lick	086 Seel [E]	088 Grimer [1]	092 Gastly [1]	093 Haunter [1]	094 Gengar [1]	108 Lickitung [1]
	124 Jynx [1, 5]	143 Snorlax [12, E]	209 Snubbull [13]	210 Granbull [13]	216 Teddiursa [1]	217 Ursaring [1]
	238 Smoochum [5]	336 Seviper [1]	352 Kecleon [1]	446 Munchlax [12, E]	463 Lickilicky [1]	506 Lillipup [E]
	511 Pansage [7]	512 Simisage [1]	513 Pansear [7]	514 Simisear [1]	515 Panpour [7]	516 Simipour [1]
	631 Heatmor [1]					
Light Screen	TM16	025 Pikachu [45]	035 Clefairy [46]	100 Voltorb [26]	101 Electrode [26]	113 Chansey [46]
	120 Staryu [33]	122 Mr. Mime [22]	125 Electabuzz [26]	145 Zapdos [64]	152 Chikorita [31]	153 Bayleef [36]
	154 Meganium [40]	165 Ledyba [14]	166 Ledian [14]	179 Mareep [43]	180 Flaaffy [52]	181 Ampharos [57]
	239 Elekid [26]	242 Blissey [46]	269 Dustox [31]	439 Mime Jr. [22]	466 Electivire [26]	561 Sigilyph [24]
	577 Solosis [16]	578 Duosion [16]	579 Reuniclus [16]	587 Emolga [34]	615 Cryogonal [37]	
Lock-On	081 Magnemite [46]	082 Magneton [56]	137 Porygon [45]	223 Remoraid [6]	233 Porygon2 [45]	299 Nosepass [50]
	377 Regirock [57]	378 Regice [57]	379 Registeel [57]	462 Magnezone [56]	474 Porygon-Z [45]	476 Probopass [50]
	524 Roggenrola [E]	599 Klink [51]	600 Klang [56]	601 Klinklang [60]	649 Genesect [11]	
Lovely Kiss	124 Jynx [1, 8]					
Low Kick	Taught by someone	056 Mankey [1]	057 Primeape [1]	066 Machop [1]	067 Machoke [1]	068 Machamp [1]
	077 Ponyta [E]	125 Electabuzz [8]	185 Sudowoodo [1, 8]	239 Elekid [8]	255 Torchic [E]	331 Cacnea [E]
	427 Buneary [E]	438 Bonsly [8]	447 Riolu [E]	466 Electivire [1, 8]	505 Watchog [1]	511 Pansage [E]

◆ When Rotom becomes Mow Rotom, it learns the move Leaf Storm. When it changes back to Rotom, it forgets the move.

Pokémon Moves Reverse Lookup

L

Move	Pokémon that can learn it					
Low Kick (continued)	513 Pansear [E]	515 Panpour [E]	532 Timburr [12]	533 Gurdurr [12]	534 Conkeldurr [12]	559 Scraggy [1]
	560 Scrafty [1]	619 Mienfoo [E]				
Low Sweep	TM47	066 Machop [13]	067 Machoke [13]	068 Machamp [13]	539 Sawk [17]	
Lucky Chant	035 Clefairy [37]	043 Oddish [25]	044 Gloom [29]	102 Exeggcute [E]	172 Pichu [E]	175 Togepi [E]
	177 Natu [12]	178 Xatu [12]	222 Corsola [23]	238 Smoochum [31]	280 Ralts [17]	281 Kirlia [17]
	311 Plusle [E]	312 Minun [E]	325 Spoink [E]	351 Castform [E]	370 Luvdisc [17]	420 Cherubi [40]
	421 Cherrim [48]	429 Mismagius [1]	481 Mesprit [31]	517 Munna [5]	518 Musharna [1]	519 Pidove [E]
	531 Audino [E]	580 Ducklett [E]				
Lunar Dance	488 Cresselia [84]					
Luster Purge	381 Latios [35]					

M

Move	Pokémon that can learn it					
Mach Punch	107 Hitmonchan [16]	165 Ledyba [17]	166 Ledian [17]	236 Tyrogue [E]	240 Magby [E]	286 Breloom [23]
	391 Monferno [14]	392 Infernape [14]	532 Timburr [E]			
Magic Coat	Taught by someone	137 Porygon [56]	203 Girafarig [E]	206 Dunsparce [E]	233 Porygon2 [56]	325 Spoink [21]
	326 Grumpig [21]	352 Kecleon [E]	359 Absol [E]	428 Lopunny [1]	474 Porygon-Z [56]	517 Munna [E]
Magic Room	Taught by someone	122 Mr. Mime [E]	337 Lunatone [53]	439 Mime Jr. [E]	574 Gothita [48]	575 Gothorita [53]
	576 Gothitelle [59]					
Magical Leaf	001 Bulbasaur [E]	069 Bellsprout [E]	122 Mr. Mime [1]	152 Chikorita [20]	153 Bayleef [22]	154 Meganium [22]
	173 Cleffa [16]	176 Togetic [1]	182 Bellossom [23]	251 Celebi [19]	252 Treecko [E]	280 Ralts [21]
	281 Kirlia [22]	282 Gardevoir [22]	315 Roselia [19]	331 Cacnea [E]	357 Tropius [31]	407 Roserade [1]
	420 Cherubi [19]	421 Cherrim [19]	429 Mismagius [1]	455 Carnivine [E]	459 Snover [E]	470 Leafeon [21]
	492 Shaymin (Land) [10]	492 Shaymin (Sky) [10]	495 Snivy [E]	511 Pansage [E]	548 Petilil [19]	640 Virizion [13]
Magma Storm	485 Heatran [96]					
Magnet Bomb	081 Magnemite [18]	082 Magneton [18]	462 Magnezone [18]	476 Probopass [1,11]	649 Genesect [22]	
Magnet Rise	Taught by someone	081 Magnemite [49]	082 Magneton [62]	100 Voltorb [40]	101 Electrode [46]	137 Porygon [23]
	205 Forretress [60]	233 Porygon2 [23]	375 Metang [1]	376 Metagross [1]	462 Magnezone [62]	474 Porygon-Z [23]
	476 Probopass [1]	582 Vanillite [E]	636 Larvesta [E]	649 Genesect [1]		
Magnitude	027 Sandshrew [17]	028 Sandslash [17]	050 Diglett [15]	051 Dugtrio [15]	074 Geodude [15]	075 Graveler [15]
	076 Golem [15]	108 Lickitung [E]	111 Rhyhorn [E]	232 Donphan [19]	299 Nosepass [E]	322 Numel [8]
	323 Camerupt [1,8]	339 Barboach [26]	340 Whiscash [26]	369 Relicanth [E]	498 Tepig [E]	524 Roggenrola [E]
	622 Golett [25]	623 Golurk [25]				
Me First	019 Rattata [E]	079 Slowpoke [E]	108 Lickitung [41]	127 Pinsir [E]	150 Mewtwo [71]	151 Mew [70]
	161 Sentret [42]	162 Furret [50]	177 Natu [20]	178 Xatu [20]	234 Stantler [55, E]	261 Poochyena [E]
	359 Absol [60, E]	418 Buizel [E]	448 Lucario [19]	453 Croagunk [E]	463 Lickilicky [41]	522 Blitzle [E]
	540 Sewaddle [E]	580 Ducklett [E]	617 Accelgor [28]	619 Mienfoo [E]		
Mean Look	041 Zubat [34]	042 Golbat [38]	088 Grimer [E]	092 Gastly [8]	093 Haunter [8]	094 Gengar [8]
	124 Jynx [25]	169 Crobat [38]	197 Umbreon [37]	198 Murkrow [41]	200 Misdreavus [19]	203 Girafarig [E]
	238 Smoochum [25]	280 Ralts [E]	302 Sableye [60, E]	355 Duskull [41]	356 Dusclops [49]	359 Absol [E]
	477 Dusknoir [49]	495 Snivy [E]	504 Patrat [31]	505 Watchog [36]	551 Sandile [E]	562 Yamask [45]
	563 Cofagrigus [51]	574 Gothita [E]	624 Pawniard [E]	629 Vullaby [E]		
Meditate	056 Mankey [E]	066 Machop [E]	096 Drowzee [21]	097 Hypno [21]	106 Hitmonlee [5]	122 Mr. Mime [8]
	238 Smoochum [E]	239 Elekid [E]	307 Meditite [4]	308 Medicham [1,4]	439 Mime Jr. [8]	453 Croagunk [E]
	619 Mienfoo [5]	620 Mienshao [1,5]				
Mega Drain	043 Oddish [21]	044 Gloom [23]	045 Vileplume [1]	114 Tangela [23, E]	140 Kabuto [36]	141 Kabutops [36]
	182 Bellossom [1]	187 Hoppip [25]	188 Skiploom [28]	189 Jumpluff [29]	191 Sunkern [10]	192 Sunflora [10]
	252 Treecko [26]	267 Beautifly [24]	270 Lotad [19]	272 Ludicolo [1]	285 Shroomish [17]	286 Breloom [17]
	315 Roselia [13]	345 Lileep [E]	387 Turtwig [24]	388 Grotle [27]	389 Torterra [27]	406 Budew [13]
	407 Roserade [1]	465 Tangrowth [23]	495 Snivy [22]	496 Servine [24]	497 Serperior [24]	546 Cottonee [13]
	547 Whimsicott [1]	548 Petilil [13]	549 Lilligant [1]	556 Maractus [13]	590 Foongus [15]	591 Amoonguss [15]
	616 Shelmet [20]	617 Accelgor [20]				
Mega Kick	106 Hitmonlee [53]					
Mega Punch	074 Geodude [E]	107 Hitmonchan [46]	115 Kangaskhan [25]	151 Mew [10]	240 Magby [E]	622 Golett [21]
	623 Golurk [21]					
Megahorn	034 Nidoking [58]	078 Rapidash [1]	111 Rhyhorn [67]	112 Rhydon [77]	118 Goldeen [57]	119 Seaking [72]
	214 Heracross [46, E]	234 Stantler [E]	359 Absol [E]	464 Rhyperior [77]	503 Samurott [1]	545 Scolipede [1]
	586 Sawsbuck [1]	588 Karrablast [E]	626 Bouffalant [41]			
Memento	050 Diglett [E]	088 Grimer [48]	089 Muk [57]	109 Koffing [45]	110 Weezing [54]	187 Hoppip [49]
	188 Skiploom [60]	189 Jumpluff [69]	200 Misdreavus [E]	218 Slugma [E]	280 Ralts [E]	355 Duskull [E]
	381 Latios [85]	422 Shellos [E]	425 Drifloon [E]	434 Stunky [43]	435 Skuntank [51]	442 Spiritomb [43]
	480 Uxie [76]	546 Cottonee [E]	562 Yamask [E]	570 Zorua [E]	607 Litwick [33]	608 Lampent [33]
Metal Burst	302 Sableye [E]	303 Mawile [E]	304 Aron [50]	305 Lairon [62]	306 Aggron [74]	410 Shieldon [37]
	411 Bastiodon [43]	483 Dialga [24]	625 Bisharp [1]	638 Cobalion [67]		
Metal Claw	004 Charmander [E]	027 Sandshrew [E]	046 Paras [E]	098 Krabby [21]	099 Kingler [21]	158 Totodile [E]
	207 Gligar [E]	212 Scizor [21]	215 Sneasel [22]	216 Teddiursa [E]	290 Nincada [38]	304 Aron [11]
	305 Lairon [11]	306 Aggron [11]	335 Zangoose [E]	341 Corphish [19]	347 Anorith [19]	348 Armaldo [19]
	375 Metang [1,20]	376 Metagross [1,20]	379 Registeel [9]	394 Prinplup [16]	395 Empoleon [16]	443 Gible [E]
	448 Lucario [1]	461 Weavile [22]	483 Dialga [6]	529 Drilbur [15]	530 Excadrill [15]	597 Ferroseed [14]
	598 Ferrothorn [14]	621 Druddigon [E]	624 Pawniard [25]	625 Bisharp [25]	632 Durant [21]	638 Cobalion [13]
	649 Genesect [1]					
Metal Sound	081 Magnemite [29]	082 Magneton [29]	140 Kabuto [41]	141 Kabutops [45]	227 Skarmory [31]	304 Aron [32]
	305 Lairon [34]	306 Aggron [34]	410 Shieldon [10]	411 Bastiodon [1, 10]	413 Wormadam (Trsh) [29]	436 Bronzor [31]
	437 Bronzong [31]	448 Lucario [24]	462 Magnezone [29]	485 Heatran [25]	529 Drilbur [E]	599 Klink [45]
	600 Klang [48]	601 Klinklang [48]	624 Pawniard [38]	625 Bisharp [38]	632 Durant [66]	649 Genesect [33]

Move	Pokémon that can learn it					
Meteor Mash	035 Clefairy [52]	375 Metang [44]	376 Metagross [44]			
Metronome	035 Clefairy [31]	036 Clefable [1]	113 Chansey [E]	151 Mew [20]	173 Cleffa [E]	175 Togepi [5]
	176 Togetic [1,5]	209 Snubbull [E]	440 Happiny [E]	446 Munchlax [1]		
Milk Drink	241 Miltank [11]					
Mimic	039 Jigglypuff [45]	122 Mr. Mime [15, E]	173 Cleffa [E]	185 Sudowoodo [15]	209 Snubbull [E]	438 Bonsly [33]
	439 Mime Jr. [15, E]	441 Chatot [33]				
Mind Reader	060 Poliwag [E]	062 Poliwrath [43]	106 Hitmonlee [33]	144 Articuno [22]	236 Tyrogue [E]	283 Surskit [E]
	286 Breloom [37]	290 Nincada [19]	291 Ninjask [19]	292 Shedinja [19]	307 Meditite [18]	308 Medicham [18]
	315 Roselia [E]	406 Budew [E]	447 Riolu [E]	540 Sewaddle [E]	616 Shelmet [E]	
Minimize	035 Clefairy [25]	036 Clefable [1]	088 Grimer [18]	089 Muk [18]	113 Chansey [23]	120 Staryu [25]
	211 Qwilfish [9]	242 Blissey [23]	425 Drifloon [E]	426 Drifblim [1]	607 Litwick [3]	608 Lampent [1, 3]
Miracle Eye	064 Kadabra [22]	065 Alakazam [22]	150 Mewtwo [29]	177 Natu [17]	178 Xatu [17]	238 Smoochum [E]
	375 Metang [26]	376 Metagross [26]	561 Sigilyph [1]	574 Gothita [E]	605 Elgyem [11]	606 Beheeyem [1,11]
Mirror Coat	007 Squirtle [E]	072 Tentacool [E]	100 Voltorb [50]	101 Electrode [62]	202 Wobbuffet [1]	203 Girafarig [E]
	222 Corsola [45]	226 Mantine [E]	245 Suicune [43]	258 Mudkip [E]	325 Spoink [E]	345 Lileep [E]
	349 Feebas [45]	360 Wynaut [15]	386 Deoxys (Def) [97]	422 Shellos [E]	428 Lopunny [1]	458 Mantyke [E]
	462 Magnezone [1]	471 Glaceon [33]	495 Snivy [E]	574 Gothita [E]	582 Vanillite [44]	583 Vanillish [47]
	584 Vanilluxe [50]	594 Alomomola [E]				
Mirror Move	016 Pidgey [45]	017 Pidgeotto [52]	018 Pidgeot [56]	021 Spearow [21]	022 Fearow [23]	083 Farfetch'd [E]
	084 Doduo [E]	163 Hoothoot [E]	175 Togepi [E]	198 Murkrow [E]	255 Torchic [37]	256 Combusken [43]
	276 Taillow [E]	333 Swablu [34]	441 Chatot [9]	561 Sigilyph [34]	580 Ducklett [E]	629 Vullaby [64]
	630 Mandibuzz [70]					
Mirror Shot	081 Magnemite [25]	082 Magneton [25]	205 Forretress [31]	413 Wormadam (Trsh) [26]	462 Magnezone [25]	582 Vanillite [26]
	583 Vanillish [26]	584 Vanilluxe [26]	597 Ferroseed [30]	598 Ferrothorn [30]	599 Klink [36]	600 Klang [36]
	601 Klinklang [36]					
Mist	007 Squirtle [E]	060 Poliwag [E]	131 Lapras [4]	144 Articuno [8]	147 Dratini [E]	150 Mewtwo [36]
	170 Chinchou [E]	194 Wooper [43]	195 Quagsire [48]	220 Swinub [35]	221 Piloswine [37]	222 Corsola [E]
	245 Suicune [36]	270 Lotad [11]	278 Wingull [14, E]	279 Pelipper [14]	283 Surskit [37]	320 Wailmer [24]
	321 Wailord [24]	333 Swablu [15]	334 Altaria [15]	349 Feebas [E]	393 Piplup [36]	394 Prinplup [42]
	395 Empoleon [46]	422 Shellos [E]	459 Snover [21, E]	460 Abomasnow [21]	473 Mamoswine [37]	488 Cresselia [20]
	535 Tympole [E]	582 Vanillite [16]	583 Vanillish [16]	584 Vanilluxe [16]	592 Frillish [E]	594 Alomomola [E]
	615 Cryogonal [21]					
Mist Ball	380 Latias [35]					
Moonlight	035 Clefairy [43]	043 Oddish [33]	044 Gloom [41]	102 Exeggcute [E]	197 Umbreon [33]	269 Dustox [20]
	302 Sableye [E]	313 Volbeat [13]	314 Illumise [13]	488 Cresselia [57]	517 Munna [17]	
Morning Sun	048 Venonat [E]	058 Growlithe [E]	077 Ponyta [E]	175 Togepi [E]	191 Sunkern [E]	196 Espeon [33]
	267 Beautifly [20]	420 Cherubi [E]	421 Cherrim [1]	519 Pidove [E]	636 Larvesta [E]	
Mud Bomb	023 Ekans [33]	024 Arbok [39]	050 Diglett [26, E]	051 Dugtrio [28]	054 Psyduck [E]	060 Poliwag [41]
	061 Poliwhirl [53]	088 Grimer [21]	089 Muk [21]	113 Chansey [E]	194 Wooper [19]	195 Quagsire [19]
	220 Swinub [18]	221 Piloswine [18]	258 Mudkip [E]	259 Marshtomp [25]	260 Swampert [25]	300 Skitty [E]
	322 Numel [E]	339 Barboach [14]	340 Whiscash [14]	422 Shellos [11]	423 Gastrodon [11]	440 Happiny [E]
	453 Croagunk [29]	454 Toxicroak [29]	473 Mamoswine [18]	535 Tympole [E]	618 Stunfisk [21]	
Mud Shot	027 Sandshrew [E]	060 Poliwag [28, E]	061 Poliwhirl [32]	090 Krabby [19]	098 Shellder [E]	099 Kingler [19]
	118 Goldeen [E]	138 Omanyte [25]	139 Omastar [25]	140 Kabuto [16, E]	141 Kabutops [16]	194 Wooper [9]
	195 Quagsire [9]	220 Swinub [E]	223 Remoraid [E]	259 Marshtomp [16]	260 Swampert [16]	283 Surskit [E]
	328 Trapinch [E]	339 Barboach [E]	369 Relicanth [E]	383 Groudon [1]	443 Gible [E]	535 Tympole [16]
	536 Palpitoad [16]	537 Seismitoad [16]	550 Basculin [16]	618 Stunfisk [13]	626 Bouffalant [E]	645 Landorus [1]
Mud Sport	007 Squirtle [E]	074 Geodude [4]	075 Graveler [1,4]	076 Golem [1,4]	079 Slowpoke [E]	095 Onix [1]
	098 Krabby [1]	099 Kingler [1]	118 Goldeen [E]	158 Totodile [E]	194 Wooper [5, E]	195 Quagsire [1,5]
	208 Steelix [1]	220 Swinub [5]	221 Piloswine [1,5]	226 Mantine [E]	234 Stantler [E]	252 Treecko [E]
	258 Mudkip [24]	263 Zigzagoon [21]	264 Linoone [23]	339 Barboach [6]	340 Whiscash [1,6]	341 Corphish [E]
	347 Anorith [7]	348 Armaldo [1,7]	349 Feebas [E]	366 Clamperl [E]	369 Relicanth [36]	370 Luvdisc [E]
	393 Piplup [E]	422 Shellos [2]	423 Gastrodon [1,2]	458 Mantyke [E]	473 Mamoswine [1,5]	515 Panpour [E]
	529 Drilbur [1]	530 Excadrill [1]	535 Tympole [E]	568 Trubbish [E]	618 Stunfisk [1]	
Muddy Water	007 Squirtle [E]	072 Tentacool [E]	108 Lickitung [E]	116 Horsea [E]	134 Vaporeon [37]	138 Omanyte [E]
	183 Marill [E]	194 Wooper [47]	195 Quagsire [53]	259 Marshtomp [37]	260 Swampert [39]	298 Azurill [E]
	339 Barboach [E]	366 Clamperl [E]	369 Relicanth [E]	382 Kyogre [20]	422 Shellos [37]	423 Gastrodon [41]
	535 Tympole [27]	536 Palpitoad [28]	537 Seismitoad [28]	550 Basculin [E]	618 Stunfisk [40]	
Mud-Slap	050 Diglett [12]	051 Dugtrio [12]	083 Farfetch'd [E]	088 Grimer [7]	089 Muk [1,7]	118 Goldeen [E]
	213 Shuckle [E]	220 Swinub [11]	221 Piloswine [11]	231 Phanpy [E]	258 Mudkip [6]	259 Marshtomp [1,6]
	260 Swampert [1,6]	263 Zigzagoon [E]	290 Nincada [31]	304 Aron [4]	305 Lairon [1,4]	306 Aggron [1,4]
	316 Gulpin [E]	328 Trapinch [13]	329 Vibrava [13]	330 Flygon [13]	339 Barboach [1]	340 Whiscash [1]
	343 Baltoy [7]	344 Claydol [7]	369 Relicanth [E]	393 Piplup [E]	418 Buizel [E]	422 Shellos [1]
	423 Gastrodon [1]	453 Croagunk [E]	454 Toxicroak [1,3]	473 Mamoswine [11]	506 Lillipup [E]	524 Roggenrola [17]
	525 Boldore [17]	526 Gigalith [17]	529 Drilbur [8]	530 Excadrill [1,8]	551 Sandile [19]	552 Krokorok [19]
	553 Krookodile [19]	572 Minccino [E]	616 Shelmet [E]	618 Stunfisk [1]	622 Golett [5]	623 Golurk [1,5]
	626 Bouffalant [E]					

N

Move	Pokémon that can learn it					
Nasty Plot	038 Ninetales [1]	041 Zubat [E]	052 Meowth [38]	053 Persian [44]	096 Drowzee [53, E]	097 Hypno [53]
	122 Mr. Mime [E]	151 Mew [90]	172 Pichu [18]	175 Togepi [E]	190 Aipom [39]	199 Slowking [36]
	200 Misdreavus [E]	228 Houndour [52, E]	229 Houndoom [60]	238 Smoochum [E]	273 Seedot [E]	275 Shiftry [1]
	302 Sableye [E]	311 Plusle [56]	312 Minun [56]	331 Cacnea [E]	352 Kecleon [E]	390 Chimchar [23]

Pokémon Moves Reverse Lookup

Move	Pokémon that can learn it					
Nasty Plot (continued)	424 Ambipom [39]	430 Honchkrow [35]	439 Mime Jr. [E]	441 Chatot [E]	442 Spiritomb [37]	447 Riolu [47]
	453 Croagunk [38]	454 Toxicroak [41]	461 Weavile [20]	474 Porygon-Z [1]	482 Azelf [46]	491 Darkrai [75]
	509 Purrloin [42]	510 Liepard [50]	511 Pansage [E]	513 Pansear [E]	515 Panpour [E]	562 Yamask [E]
	570 Zorua [49]	571 Zoroark [54]	605 Elgyem [E]	629 Vullaby [14]	630 Mandibuzz [14]	642 Thundurus [61]
Natural Gift	043 Gloom [29]	044 Vileplume [E]	046 Paras [1]	069 Bellsprout [E]	084 Doduo [E]	102 Exeggcute [37, E]
	113 Chansey [E]	114 Tangela [33, E]	133 Eevee [E]	143 Snorlax [E]	152 Chikorita [23]	153 Bayleef [26]
	154 Meganium [26]	161 Sentret [E]	191 Sunkern [31, E]	192 Sunflora [31]	204 Pineco [23]	205 Forretress [23]
	231 Phanpy [19]	241 Miltank [E]	249 Lugia [85]	250 Ho-Oh [85]	251 Celebi [46]	252 Treecko [E]
	270 Lotad [15]	285 Shroomish [E]	315 Roselia [E]	333 Swablu [21]	334 Altaria [21]	357 Tropius [67, E]
	406 Budew [E]	420 Cherubi [E]	440 Happiny [E]	446 Munchlax [49, E]	459 Snover [E]	465 Tangrowth [33]
	480 Uxie [66]	481 Mesprit [66]	482 Azelf [66]	492 Shaymin (Land) [46]	492 Shaymin (Sky) [46]	493 Arceus [1]
	495 Snivy [E]	511 Pansage [40]	513 Pansear [40]	515 Panpour [40]	546 Cottonee [E]	548 Petilil [E]
	582 Vanillite [E]	585 Deerling [E]				
Nature Power	001 Bulbasaur [E]	043 Oddish [E]	102 Exeggcute [E]	114 Tangela [E]	152 Chikorita [E]	155 Cyndaquil [E]
	191 Sunkern [E]	222 Corsola [E]	270 Lotad [7]	271 Lombre [7]	272 Ludicolo [1]	273 Seedot [13]
	274 Nuzleaf [13]	357 Tropius [E]	420 Cherubi [E]	585 Deerling [41]	586 Sawsbuck [44]	
Needle Arm	331 Cacnea [45]	332 Cacturne [53]	556 Maractus [22]			
Night Daze	570 Zorua [57]	571 Zoroark [64]				
Night Shade	092 Gastly [15]	093 Haunter [15]	094 Gengar [15]	163 Hoothoot [E]	167 Spinarak [15]	168 Ariados [15]
	177 Natu [6]	178 Xatu [6]	198 Murkrow [21]	302 Sableye [8]	353 Shuppet [7]	354 Banette [1,7]
	355 Duskull [1]	356 Dusclops [1]	386 Deoxys (Nor) [9]	386 Deoxys (Atk) [9]	386 Deoxys (Def) [9]	386 Deoxys (Spd) [9]
	441 Chatot [E]	477 Dusknoir [1]	562 Yamask [13]	563 Cofagrigus [13]	577 Solosis [E]	592 Frillish [9]
	593 Jellicent [1,9]	607 Litwick [13]	608 Lampent [13]	622 Golett [35]	623 Golurk [35]	
Night Slash	027 Sandshrew [E]	051 Dugtrio [1]	052 Meowth [49]	053 Persian [61]	083 Farfetch'd [33, E]	123 Scyther [45, E]
	141 Kabutops [72]	167 Spinarak [E]	207 Gligar [E]	212 Scizor [45]	214 Heracross [1]	216 Teddiursa [E]
	227 Skarmory [50]	254 Sceptile [1]	255 Torchic [E]	287 Slakoth [E]	290 Nincada [E]	319 Sharpedo [56]
	335 Zangoose [E]	336 Seviper [31, E]	341 Corphish [35]	342 Crawdaunt [39]	359 Absol [41]	402 Kricketune [42]
	403 Shinx [E]	430 Honchkrow [55]	434 Stunky [37]	435 Skuntank [41]	451 Skorupi [38, E]	452 Drapion [38]
	461 Weavile [35]	469 Yanmega [1]	472 Gliscor [27]	475 Gallade [1]	501 Oshawott [E]	509 Purrloin [37]
	510 Liepard [43]	557 Dwebble [E]	571 Zoroark [30]	610 Axew [E]	613 Cubchoo [E]	615 Cryogonal [57]
	621 Druddigon [40]	624 Pawniard [49]	625 Bisharp [49]	631 Heatmor [E]		
Nightmare	092 Gastly [47]	093 Haunter [61]	094 Gengar [61]	097 Hypno [1]	442 Spiritomb [E]	491 Darkrai [38]
	517 Munna [29]	562 Yamask [E]				

Move	Pokémon that can learn it					
Octazooka	116 Horsea [E]	223 Remoraid [E]	224 Octillery [25]			
Odor Sleuth	052 Meowth [E]	058 Growlithe [10]	059 Arcanine [1]	179 Mareep [E]	203 Girafarig [5]	220 Swinub [1]
	221 Piloswine [1]	228 Houndour [20]	229 Houndoom [20]	231 Phanpy [1]	261 Poochyena [17]	262 Mightyena [17]
	263 Zigzagoon [17]	264 Linoone [17]	309 Electrike [25]	310 Manectric [25]	325 Spoink [10]	326 Grumpig [1, 10]
	399 Bidoof [E]	418 Buizel [E]	446 Munchlax [1]	473 Mamoswine [1]	498 Tepig [9]	499 Pignite [1, 9]
	500 Emboar [1, 9]	506 Lillipup [5]	507 Herdier [1, 5]	508 Stoutland [1, 5]	527 Woobat [4]	528 Swoobat [1, 4]
	585 Deerling [E]	631 Heatmor [6]				
Ominous Wind	177 Natu [44]	178 Xatu [54]	200 Misdreavus [E]	284 Masquerain [1]	351 Castform [E]	353 Shuppet [E]
	355 Duskull [E]	425 Drifloon [20]	426 Drifblim [20]	442 Spiritomb [25]	478 Froslass [22]	479 Rotom [29]
	479 Rotom (Heat) [29]	479 Rotom (Wash) [29]	479 Rotom (Frst) [29]	479 Rotom (Fan) [29]	479 Rotom (Mow) [29]	487 Giratina (Alt) [6]
	487 Giratina (Ori) [6]	491 Darkrai [1]	562 Yamask [25]	563 Cofagrigus [25]	592 Frillish [27]	593 Jellicent [27]
Outrage	Taught by someone	004 Charmander [E]	058 Growlithe [43]	115 Kangaskhan [46]	116 Horsea [E]	147 Dratini [55]
	148 Dragonair [67]	149 Dragonite [67]	210 Granbull [67]	246 Larvitar [E]	384 Rayquaza [50]	443 Gible [E]
	553 Krookodile [60]	610 Axew [56]	611 Fraxure [60]	612 Haxorus [66]	621 Druddigon [62]	633 Deino [62]
	634 Zweilous [71]	635 Hydreigon [79]	643 Reshiram [85]	644 Zekrom [85]	645 Landorus [85]	646 Kyurem [85]
	646 Kyurem (Blk) [85]	646 Kyurem (Wht) [85]				
Overheat	TM50	479 Rotom (Heat) ◆	494 Victini [97]	554 Darumaka [42]	555 Darmanitan [54]	607 Litwick [61]
	608 Lampent [69]					

Move	Pokémon that can learn it					
Pain Split	Taught by someone	109 Koffing [E]	200 Misdreavus [32]	316 Gulpin [E]	355 Duskull [E]	442 Spiritomb [E]
	577 Solosis [33]	578 Duosion [34]	579 Reuniclus [34]	592 Frillish [E]	594 Alomomola [E]	607 Litwick [55]
	608 Lampent [61]	618 Stunfisk [E]				
Pay Day	052 Meowth [30]	509 Purrloin [E]				
Payback	TM66	037 Vulpix [31]	092 Gastly [26]	093 Haunter [28]	094 Gengar [28]	128 Tauros [24]
	200 Misdreavus [37]	204 Pineco [31]	205 Forretress [36]	209 Snubbull [43]	210 Granbull [51]	246 Larvitar [37]
	247 Pupitar [41]	248 Tyranitar [41]	279 Pelipper [22]	325 Spoink [40]	326 Grumpig [46]	331 Cacnea [41]
	332 Cacturne [47]	355 Duskull [46]	356 Dusclops [58]	425 Drifloon [16]	426 Drifblim [16]	436 Bronzor [41]
	437 Bronzong [46]	477 Dusknoir [58]	486 Regigigas [65]	559 Scraggy [23]	560 Scrafty [23]	597 Ferroseed [47]
	598 Ferrothorn [53]					
Peck	021 Spearow [1]	022 Fearow [1]	032 Nidoran♂ [1]	033 Nidorino [1]	034 Nidoking [1]	083 Farfetch'd [1]
	084 Doduo [1]	085 Dodrio [1]	118 Goldeen [1]	119 Seaking [1]	145 Zapdos [1]	163 Hoothoot [1]
	164 Noctowl [9]	175 Togepi [E]	177 Natu [1]	178 Xatu [1]	198 Murkrow [1]	221 Piloswine [1]
	227 Skarmory [1]	255 Torchic [16]	256 Combusken [17]	257 Blaziken [17]	276 Taillow [1]	277 Swellow [1]
	333 Swablu [1]	334 Altaria [1]	393 Piplup [15]	394 Prinplup [15]	395 Empoleon [15]	441 Chatot [1]
	473 Mamoswine [1]	556 Maractus [1]	588 Karrablast [1]	589 Escavalier [1]	627 Rufflet [1]	628 Braviary [1]

Move	Pokémon that can learn it					
Perish Song	086 Seel [E]	092 Gastly [E]	104 Cubone [E]	124 Jynx [55]	131 Lapras [27]	174 Igglybuff [E]
	183 Marill [E]	186 Politoed [1]	198 Murkrow [E]	200 Misdreavus [46]	238 Smoochum [45]	251 Celebi [91]
	333 Swablu [48]	334 Altaria [57]	359 Absol [65, E]	402 Kricketune [50]	493 Arceus [90]	
Petal Dance	001 Bulbasaur [E]	003 Venusaur [32]	043 Oddish [41]	044 Gloom [53]	045 Vileplume [53]	154 Meganium [32]
	192 Sunflora [28]	315 Roselia [37]	421 Cherrim [25]	549 Lilligant [46]	556 Maractus [38]	
Pin Missile	015 Beedrill [28]	135 Jolteon [25]	167 Spinarak [36]	168 Ariados [41]	204 Pineco [E]	211 Qwilfish [37]
	263 Zigzagoon [25]	315 Roselia [E]	331 Cacnea [21]	332 Cacturne [21]	406 Budew [E]	451 Skorupi [9]
	452 Drapion [9]	543 Venipede [E]	556 Maractus [10]	595 Joltik [E]	597 Ferroseed [18]	598 Ferrothorn [18]
Pluck	TM88	022 Fearow [1]	085 Dodrio [1]	145 Zapdos [22]	277 Swellow [1]	334 Altaria [1]
	566 Archen [15]	567 Archeops [15]	629 Vullaby [10]	630 Mandibuzz [1, 10]		
Poison Fang	023 Ekans [E]	029 Nidoran ♀ [45]	030 Nidorina [58]	041 Zubat [37]	042 Golbat [42]	048 Venonat [41]
	049 Venomoth [47]	169 Crobat [42]	261 Poochyena [E]	303 Mawile [E]	336 Seviper [27]	451 Skorupi [23]
	452 Drapion [23]					
Poison Gas	088 Grimer [1]	089 Muk [1]	096 Drowzee [17]	097 Hypno [17]	109 Koffing [1]	110 Weezing [1]
	316 Gulpin [9]	317 Swalot [1, 9]	434 Stunky [4]	435 Skuntank [1, 4]	568 Trubbish [1]	569 Garbodor [1]
Poison Jab	TM84	015 Beedrill [37]	032 Nidoran ♂ [37]	033 Nidorino [43]	072 Tentacool [36]	073 Tentacruel [38]
	078 Rapidash [1]	083 Farfetch'd [1]	119 Seaking [1]	167 Spinarak [43]	168 Ariados [50]	211 Qwilfish [49]
	336 Seviper [42]	453 Croagunk [43]	454 Toxicroak [49]	464 Rhyperior [1]	472 Gliscor [1]	
Poison Sting	013 Weedle [1]	023 Ekans [4]	024 Arbok [1]	027 Sandshrew [5]	028 Sandslash [1, 5]	029 Nidoran ♀ [13]
	030 Nidorina [13]	031 Nidoqueen [1]	032 Nidoran ♂ [13]	033 Nidorino [13]	034 Nidoking [1]	072 Tentacool [1]
	073 Tentacruel [1]	167 Spinarak [1]	168 Ariados [1]	207 Gligar [1]	211 Qwilfish [1]	265 Wurmple [5]
	315 Roselia [7]	331 Cacnea [1]	332 Cacturne [1]	407 Roserade [1]	416 Vespiquen [1]	451 Skorupi [1]
	452 Drapion [1]	453 Croagunk [8]	454 Toxicroak [1, 8]	543 Venipede [5]	544 Whirlipede [1, 5]	545 Scolipede [1, 5]
	595 Joltik [E]					
Poison Tail	023 Ekans [E]	029 Nidoran ♀ [E]	032 Nidoran ♂ [E]	207 Gligar [E]	336 Seviper [12]	451 Skorupi [E]
	543 Venipede [19]	544 Whirlipede [19]	545 Scolipede [19]	621 Druddigon [E]		
PoisonPowder	001 Bulbasaur [13]	002 Ivysaur [13]	003 Venusaur [13]	012 Butterfree [12]	043 Oddish [13]	044 Gloom [13]
	045 Vileplume [1]	046 Paras [6]	047 Parasect [1, 6]	048 Venonat [13]	049 Venomoth [13]	069 Bellsprout [15]
	070 Weepinbell [15]	102 Exeggcute [21]	114 Tangela [14]	152 Chikorita [9]	153 Bayleef [1, 9]	154 Meganium [1, 9]
	187 Hoppip [12]	188 Skiploom [12]	189 Jumpluff [12]	285 Shroomish [25]	414 Mothim [29]	465 Tangrowth [14]
	546 Cottonee [22]	590 Foongus [E]				
Pound	035 Clefairy [1]	039 Jigglypuff [9]	088 Grimer [1]	089 Muk [1]	096 Drowzee [1]	097 Hypno [1]
	113 Chansey [1]	124 Jynx [1]	151 Mew [1]	173 Cleffa [1]	174 Igglybuff [9]	192 Sunflora [1]
	238 Blissey [1]	242 Blissey [1]	252 Treecko [1]	253 Grovyle [1]	254 Sceptile [1]	274 Nuzleaf [1]
	293 Whismur [1]	294 Loudred [1]	295 Exploud [1]	316 Gulpin [1]	317 Swalot [1]	393 Piplup [1]
	427 Buneary [1]	428 Lopunny [1]	440 Happiny [1]	456 Finneon [1]	457 Lumineon [1]	531 Audino [1]
	532 Timburr [1]	533 Gurdurr [1]	534 Conkeldurr [1]	568 Trubbish [1]	569 Garbodor [1]	572 Minccino [1]
	574 Gothita [1]	575 Gothorita [1]	576 Gothitelle [1]	594 Alomomola [1]	619 Mienfoo [1]	620 Mienshao [1]
	622 Golett [1]	623 Golurk [1]				
Powder Snow	124 Jynx [1, 11]	144 Articuno [1]	220 Swinub [8]	221 Piloswine [1, 8]	238 Smoochum [11]	351 Castform [10]
	361 Snorunt [1]	362 Glalie [1]	363 Spheal [1]	364 Sealeo [1]	365 Walrein [1]	459 Snover [1]
	460 Abomasnow [1]	473 Mamoswine [1, 8]	478 Froslass [1]	582 Vanillite [E]	613 Cubchoo [1]	614 Beartic [1]
Power Gem	053 Persian [32]	120 Staryu [43]	179 Mareep [29]	180 Flaaffy [34]	181 Ampharos [35]	199 Slowking [1]
	200 Misdreavus [55]	222 Corsola [41]	299 Nosepass [32]	302 Sableye [43]	325 Spoink [33]	326 Grumpig [35]
	416 Vespiquen [25]	476 Probopass [32]	483 Dialga [19]	484 Palkia [19]	525 Boldore [25]	526 Gigalith [25]
Power Split	122 Mr. Mime [E]	213 Shuckle [45]	343 Baltoy [34]	344 Claydol [34]	381 Latios [75]	439 Mime Jr. [E]
	562 Yamask [33]	563 Cofagrigus [33]	605 Elgyem [50]	606 Beheeyem [58]		
Power Swap	037 Vulpix [E]	102 Exeggcute [E]	114 Tangela [E]	122 Mr. Mime [1]	150 Mewtwo [57]	177 Natu [47]
	178 Xatu [54]	196 Espeon [45]	203 Girafarig [1]	273 Seedot [E]	307 Meditite [E]	333 Swablu [E]
	605 Elgyem [E]	617 Accelgor [52]				
Power Trick	063 Abra [E]	066 Machop [E]	204 Pineco [E]	207 Gligar [E]	213 Shuckle [31]	307 Meditite [43]
	308 Medicham [49]	343 Baltoy [17]	344 Claydol [17]			
Power Whip	001 Bulbasaur [E]	069 Bellsprout [E]	108 Lickitung [53]	114 Tangela [53]	455 Carnivine [51]	463 Lickilicky [53]
	465 Tangrowth [53]	598 Ferrothorn [40]				
Present	113 Chansey [E]	172 Pichu [E]	173 Cleffa [E]	174 Igglybuff [E]	175 Togepi [E]	183 Marill [E]
	209 Snubbull [E]	225 Delibird [1]	241 Miltank [E]	440 Happiny [E]		
Protect	TM17	007 Squirtle [22]	008 Wartortle [24]	009 Blastoise [24]	090 Shellder [16]	091 Cloyster [1]
	098 Krabby [29]	099 Kingler [32]	138 Omanyte [34]	139 Omastar [34]	204 Pineco [1]	205 Forretress [1]
	258 Mudkip [37]	259 Marshtomp [42]	260 Swampert [46]	269 Dustox [17]	279 Pelipper [25]	304 Aron [29]
	305 Lairon [29]	306 Aggron [29]	313 Volbeat [29]	324 Torkoal [36]	341 Corphish [23]	342 Crawdaunt [23]
	347 Anorith [25]	348 Armaldo [25]	361 Snorunt [22]	362 Glalie [22]	372 Shelgon [30]	373 Salamence [30]
	381 Latios [25]	410 Shieldon [1]	411 Bastiodon [1]	412 Burmy [1]	413 Wormadam (Plnt) [10]	413 Wormadam (Sand) [10]
	413 Wormadam (Trsh) [10]	414 Mothim [1]	475 Gallade [53]	481 Mesprit [16]	541 Swadloon [20]	543 Venipede [15]
	544 Whirlipede [15]	545 Scolipede [15]	562 Yamask [1]	563 Cofagrigus [1]	564 Tirtouga [11]	565 Carracosta [11]
	594 Alomomola [21]	616 Shelmet [28]				
Psybeam	012 Butterfree [24]	046 Paras [E]	048 Venonat [25]	049 Venomoth [25]	054 Psyduck [E]	064 Kadabra [28]
	065 Alakazam [28]	096 Drowzee [25]	097 Hypno [25]	109 Koffing [E]	118 Goldeen [E]	122 Mr. Mime [25]
	137 Porygon [?]	165 Ledyba [E]	167 Spinarak [E]	170 Chinchou [E]	196 Espeon [21]	200 Misdreavus [28]
	203 Girafarig [19]	223 Remoraid [10]	224 Octillery [1, 10]	226 Mantine [1]	233 Porygon2 [?]	269 Dustox [24]
	283 Surskit [14]	325 Spoink [14]	326 Grumpig [1, 14]	327 Spinda [1]	343 Baltoy [17]	344 Claydol [17]
	352 Kecleon [18]	413 Wormadam (Plnt) [32]	413 Wormadam (Sand) [32]	413 Wormadam (Trsh) [32]	414 Mothim [32]	439 Mime Jr. [25]
	456 Finneon [E]	474 Porygon-Z [?]	517 Munna [11]	518 Musharna [1]	561 Sigilyph [18]	574 Gothita [16]
	575 Gothorita [16]	576 Gothitelle [16]	605 Elgyem [15]	606 Beheeyem [15]		

Pokémon Moves Reverse Lookup

P

Move	Pokémon that can learn it				
Psych Up	TM77	054 Psyduck [39]	055 Golduck [43]	079 Slowpoke [54]	080 Slowbro [62]	096 Drowzee [33]
	097 Hypno [33]	150 Mewtwo [22]	196 Espeon [29]	199 Slowking [54]	307 Meditite [36]	308 Medicham [36]
	325 Spoink [15]	326 Grumpig [15]	327 Spinda [41]	505 Watchog [29]	605 Elgyem [36]	606 Beheeyem [36]
Psychic	TM29	048 Venonat [47]	049 Venomoth [55]	064 Kadabra [46]	065 Alakazam [46]	079 Slowpoke [45]
	080 Slowbro [49]	096 Drowzee [49]	097 Hypno [49]	122 Mr. Mime [39]	150 Mewtwo [64]	151 Mew [30]
	167 Spinarak [40]	168 Ariados [46]	177 Natu [66]	178 Xatu [66]	196 Espeon [37]	199 Slowking [45]
	203 Girafarig [37]	238 Smoochum [38]	280 Ralts [32]	281 Kirlia [36]	282 Gardevoir [40]	325 Spoink [44]
	326 Grumpig [52]	337 Lunatone [33]	338 Solrock [33]	368 Gorebyss [42]	375 Metang [41]	376 Metagross [41]
	380 Latias [60]	381 Latios [60]	385 Jirachi [20]	386 Deoxys (Nor) [41]	386 Deoxys (Atk) [41]	386 Deoxys (Def) [41]
	386 Deoxys (Spd) [41]	413 Wormadam (Plnt) [44]	413 Wormadam (Sand) [44]	413 Wormadam (Trsh) [44]	414 Mothim [44]	439 Mime Jr. [39]
	488 Cresselia [93]	517 Munna [37]	527 Woobat [41]	528 Swoobat [41]	561 Sigilyph [44]	574 Gothita [37]
	575 Gothorita [39]	576 Gothitelle [39]	577 Solosis [37]	578 Duosion [39]	579 Reuniclus [39]	605 Elgyem [39]
	606 Beheeyem [39]					
Psycho Boost	386 Deoxys (Nor) [89]	386 Deoxys (Atk) [89]	386 Deoxys (Def) [89]	386 Deoxys (Spd) [89]		
Psycho Cut	064 Kadabra [40]	065 Alakazam [40]	096 Drowzee [E]	150 Mewtwo [43]	307 Meditite [E]	327 Spinda [E]
	359 Absol [49]	475 Gallade [36]	488 Cresselia [66]	624 Pawniard [E]		
Psycho Shift	163 Hoothoot [49]	164 Noctowl [57]	175 Togepi [E]	177 Natu [33]	178 Xatu [37]	198 Murkrow [E]
	380 Latias [50]	381 Latios [50]	386 Deoxys (Nor) [57]	386 Deoxys (Atk) [57]	386 Deoxys (Def) [57]	386 Deoxys (Spd) [57]
	488 Cresselia [75]	561 Sigilyph [E]				
Psyshock	TM03	096 Drowzee [57]	097 Hypno [57]	103 Exeggutor [17]	325 Spoink [38]	326 Grumpig [42]
	574 Gothita [25]	575 Gothorita [25]	576 Gothitelle [25]	577 Solosis [25]	578 Duosion [25]	579 Reuniclus [25]
Psystrike	150 Mewtwo [100]					
	092 Gastly [E]	109 Koffing [E]	122 Mr. Mime [15]	200 Misdreavus [1]	325 Spoink [7]	326 Grumpig [1, 7]
	337 Lunatone [17]	338 Solrock [17]	358 Chimecho [30]	380 Latias [1]	381 Latios [1]	429 Mismagius [1]
	436 Bronzor [15]	437 Bronzong [15]	517 Munna [1]	561 Sigilyph [8]	577 Solosis [1]	578 Duosion [1]
	579 Reuniclus [1]					
Punishment	052 Meowth [E]	056 Mankey [45]	057 Primeape [53]	174 Igglybuff [E]	215 Sneasel [44, E]	228 Houndour [E]
	241 Miltank [E]	249 Lugia [50]	250 Ho-Oh [50]	289 Slaking [61]	302 Sableye [36]	303 Mawile [E]
	336 Seviper [E]	359 Absol [E]	392 Infernape [29]	434 Stunky [E]	461 Weavile [44]	493 Arceus [1]
	570 Zorua [45]	571 Zoroark [49]	629 Vullaby [28]	630 Mandibuzz [28]	645 Landorus [13]	
Pursuit	015 Beedrill [22]	016 Pidgey [E]	019 Rattata [13]	020 Raticate [13]	021 Spearow [13]	022 Fearow [13]
	023 Ekans [E]	029 Nidoran ♀ [E]	041 Zubat [E]	046 Paras [E]	050 Diglett [E]	084 Doduo [19]
	085 Dodrio [19]	107 Hitmonchan [11]	123 Scyther [9]	128 Tauros [15]	142 Aerodactyl [E]	143 Snorlax [E]
	161 Sentret [E]	167 Spinarak [E]	190 Aipom [E]	193 Yanma [30, E]	197 Umbreon [9]	198 Murkrow [5]
	206 Dunsparce [10]	212 Scizor [9]	214 Heracross [E]	215 Sneasel [E]	227 Skarmory [E]	228 Houndour [E]
	236 Tyrogue [E]	237 Hitmontop [10]	246 Larvitar [E]	252 Treecko [16]	253 Grovyle [17]	254 Sceptile [17]
	263 Zigzagoon [E]	276 Taillow [30]	278 Wingull [30]	287 Slakoth [E]	333 Swablu [E]	335 Zangoose [12]
	353 Shuppet [E]	355 Duskull [25]	356 Dusclops [25]	359 Absol [12]	375 Metang [23]	376 Metagross [23]
	386 Deoxys (Nor) [33]	386 Deoxys (Atk) [33]	386 Deoxys (Spd) [33]	396 Starly [E]	408 Cranidos [10]	409 Rampardos [10]
	416 Vespiquen [9]	418 Buizel [18]	419 Floatzel [18]	430 Honchkrow [1]	434 Stunky [E]	442 Spiritomb [1]
	446 Munchlax [E]	451 Skorupi [16, E]	452 Drapion [16]	453 Croagunk [15]	454 Toxicroak [15]	469 Yanmega [30]
	477 Dusknoir [25]	495 Snivy [E]	504 Patrat [E]	506 Lillipup [E]	509 Purrloin [15]	510 Liepard [15]
	522 Blitzle [22]	523 Zebstrika [22]	543 Venipede [12]	544 Whirlipede [12]	545 Scolipede [12]	551 Sandile [E]
	570 Zorua [5]	571 Zoroark [1, 5]	587 Emolga [16]	588 Karrablast [E]	595 Joltik [E]	616 Shelmet [E]
	621 Druddigon [E]	624 Pawniard [E]	626 Bouffalant [1]	631 Heatmor [E]		

Q

Move	Pokémon that can learn it				
Quash	TM60	198 Murkrow [65]	430 Honchkrow [65]			
Quick Attack	016 Pidgey [13]	017 Pidgeotto [13]	018 Pidgeot [1, 13]	019 Rattata [4]	020 Raticate [1, 4]	021 Spearow [E]
	025 Pikachu [13]	026 Raichu [1]	037 Vulpix [10]	038 Ninetales [1]	041 Zubat [E]	078 Rapidash [1]
	083 Farfetch'd [E]	084 Doduo [5, E]	085 Dodrio [1, 5]	123 Scyther [1]	125 Electabuzz [1]	127 Pinsir [E]
	133 Eevee [13]	134 Vaporeon [13]	135 Jolteon [13]	136 Flareon [13]	155 Cyndaquil [13, E]	156 Quilava [13]
	157 Typhlosion [13]	161 Sentret [7]	162 Furret [1, 7]	177 Natu [E]	193 Yanma [6]	196 Espeon [13]
	197 Umbreon [13]	207 Gligar [13]	212 Scizor [1]	215 Sneasel [8]	225 Delibird [E]	237 Hitmontop [15]
	239 Elekid [1]	243 Raikou [22]	252 Treecko [11]	253 Grovyle [1, 11]	254 Sceptile [1, 11]	255 Torchic [28]
	256 Combusken [32]	257 Blaziken [32]	273 Seedot [E]	276 Swellow [8]	277 Swellow [1, 8]	278 Wingull [22]
	283 Surskit [7]	284 Masquerain [1, 7]	309 Electrike [17]	310 Manectric [17]	311 Plusle [1]	312 Minun [7]
	313 Volbeat [17]	314 Illumise [17]	328 Trapinch [E]	335 Zangoose [5]	359 Absol [9]	396 Starly [5]
	397 Staravia [1, 5]	398 Staraptor [1, 5]	399 Bidoof [E]	403 Shinx [E]	417 Pachirisu [5]	418 Buizel [11]
	419 Floatzel [1, 11]	427 Buneary [16]	428 Lopunny [16]	431 Glameow [E]	447 Riolu [1]	448 Lucario [1]
	461 Weavile [1, 8]	466 Electivire [1]	469 Yanmega [1, 6]	470 Leafeon [13]	471 Glaceon [13]	472 Gliscor [13]
	491 Darkrai [11]	492 Shaymin (Sky) [28]	494 Victini [1]	519 Pidove [11]	520 Tranquill [1, 11]	521 Unfezant [1, 11]
	522 Blitzle [1]	523 Zebstrika [1]	566 Archen [1]	567 Archeops [1]	587 Emolga [4]	617 Accelgor [1, 13]
	638 Cobalion [1]	639 Terrakion [1]	640 Virizion [1]	649 Genesect [1]		
Quick Guard	107 Hitmonchan [31]	122 Mr. Mime [46]	237 Hitmontop [46]	390 Chimchar [1]	448 Lucario [33]	539 Sawk [45]
	566 Archen [25]	567 Archeops [25]	589 Escavalier [1,8]	619 Mienfoo [45]	638 Cobalion [55]	639 Terrakion [55]
	640 Virizion [55]	647 Keldeo [55]				
Quiver Dance	012 Butterfree [46]	049 Venomoth [63]	267 Beautifly [45]	269 Dustox [45]	284 Masquerain [68]	414 Mothim [50]
	549 Lilligant [28]	637 Volcarona [59]				

R

Move	Pokémon that can learn it					
Rage	015 Beedrill [19]	057 Primeape [28]	084 Doduo [10]	085 Dodrio [1, 10]	095 Onix [10]	104 Cubone [23]
	105 Marowak [23]	115 Kangaskhan [22]	128 Tauros [5]	158 Totodile [8]	159 Croconaw [8]	160 Feraligatr [1, 8]
	206 Dunsparce [1]	208 Steelix [10]	209 Snubbull [31]	210 Granbull [35]	228 Houndour [E]	234 Stantler [E]
	276 Taillow [6]	318 Carvanha [6]	319 Sharpedo [1, 6]	333 Swablu [E]	371 Bagon [1]	372 Shelgon [1]
	373 Salamence [1]	522 Blitzle [E]	550 Basculin [E]	551 Sandile [E]	552 Krokorok [1]	553 Krookodile [1]
	554 Darumaka [9]	555 Darmanitan [1, 9]	626 Bouffalant [6]			
Rage Powder	012 Butterfree [34]	046 Paras [49]	047 Parasect [59]	048 Venonat [E]	114 Tangela [E]	167 Spinarak [E]
	187 Hoppip [31]	188 Skiploom [36]	189 Jumpluff [39]	455 Carnivine [E]	590 Foongus [45]	591 Amoonguss [54]
	637 Volcarona [80]					
Rain Dance	TM18	007 Squirtle [37]	008 Wartortle [44]	009 Blastoise [53]	060 Poliwag [18]	061 Poliwhirl [18]
	079 Slowpoke [49]	080 Slowbro [55]	130 Gyarados [38]	131 Lapras [22]	145 Zapdos [85]	183 Marill [31]
	184 Azumarill [35]	194 Wooper [37]	195 Quagsire [41]	243 Raikou [71]	245 Suicune [15]	249 Lugia [29]
	270 Lotad [37]	350 Milotic [33]	351 Castform [20]	422 Shellos [22]	423 Gastrodon [22]	437 Bronzong [1]
	456 Finneon [13]	457 Lumineon [13]	489 Phione [69]	490 Manaphy [69]	535 Tympole [31]	536 Palpitoad [33]
	537 Seismitoad [33]	564 Tirtouga [48]	565 Carracosta [56]	580 Ducklett [34]	581 Swanna [34]	592 Frillish [37]
	593 Jellicent [37]	641 Tornadus [61]				
Rapid Spin	007 Squirtle [19]	008 Wartortle [20]	009 Blastoise [20]	027 Sandshrew [9, E]	028 Sandslash [9]	072 Tentacool [E]
	090 Shellder [E]	120 Staryu [10]	121 Starmie [1]	140 Kabuto [E]	204 Pineco [17]	205 Forretress [17]
	225 Delibird [E]	232 Donphan [6]	236 Tyrogue [E]	237 Hitmontop [24]	324 Torkoal [23]	327 Spinda [E]
	343 Baltoy [4]	344 Claydol [1, 4]	347 Anorith [E]	529 Drilbur [5, E]	530 Excadrill [1, 5]	615 Cryogonal [13]
Razor Leaf	001 Bulbasaur [19]	002 Ivysaur [20]	003 Venusaur [20]	043 Oddish [E]	069 Bellsprout [39]	070 Weepinbell [39]
	071 Victreebel [1]	152 Chikorita [6]	153 Bayleef [1,6]	154 Meganium [1,6]	191 Sunkern [16]	192 Sunflora [16]
	270 Lotad [37]	274 Nuzleaf [1]	275 Shiftry [1]	315 Roselia [11]	357 Tropius [11]	387 Turtwig [13]
	388 Grotle [13]	389 Torterra [1,13]	406 Budew [E]	413 Wormadam (Plnt) [26]	420 Cherubi [E]	455 Carnivine [E]
	459 Snover [5]	460 Abomasnow [1,5]	470 Leafeon [9]	540 Sewaddle [15]	541 Swadloon [1]	542 Leavanny [1,15]
	546 Cottonee [19]					
Razor Shell	090 Shellder [32]	501 Oshawott [17]	502 Dewott [17]	503 Samurott [17]		
Razor Wind	021 Spearow [E]	116 Horsea [E]	123 Scyther [33, E]	203 Girafarig [E]	207 Gligar [E]	212 Scizor [33]
	252 Treecko [E]	273 Seedot [E]	274 Nuzleaf [37]	335 Zangoose [E]	357 Tropius [E]	359 Absol [57]
	418 Buizel [35]	419 Floatzel [41]	519 Pidove [32]	520 Tranquill [36]	521 Unfezant [38]	540 Sewaddle [E]
	610 Axew [E]					
Recover	064 Kadabra [36]	065 Alakazam [36]	120 Staryu [12]	121 Starmie [1]	137 Porygon [18]	150 Mewtwo [79]
	194 Wooper [E]	218 Slugma [19]	219 Magcargo [19]	222 Corsola [10]	233 Porygon2 [18]	249 Lugia [71]
	250 Ho-Oh [71]	251 Celebi [1]	302 Sableye [50]	307 Meditite [50]	308 Medicham [62]	345 Lileep [E]
	350 Milotic [E]	352 Kecleon [1]	380 Latias [45]	381 Latios [45]	386 Deoxys (Nor) [81]	386 Deoxys (Def) [81]
	386 Deoxys (Spd) [81]	422 Shellos [46]	423 Gastrodon [54]	433 Chingling [E]	474 Porygon-Z [18]	493 Arceus [70]
	577 Solosis [24]	578 Duosion [24]	579 Reuniclus [24]	592 Frillish [17, E]	593 Jellicent [17]	605 Elgyem [46]
	606 Beheeyem [50]	615 Cryogonal [49]	616 Shelmet [49]	617 Accelgor [49]		
Recycle	Taught by someone	122 Mr. Mime [32]	137 Porygon [34]	233 Porygon2 [34]	439 Mime Jr. [32]	446 Munchlax [17]
	511 Pansage [37]	513 Pansear [37]	515 Panpour [37]	568 Trubbish [3]	569 Garbodor [1,3]	
Reflect	TM33	064 Kadabra [30]	065 Alakazam [30]	102 Exeggcute [7]	122 Mr. Mime [7]	144 Articuno [50]
	152 Chikorita [17]	153 Bayleef [18]	154 Meganium [18]	163 Hoothoot [17]	164 Noctowl [17]	165 Ledyba [14]
	166 Ledian [14]	243 Raikou [36]	439 Mime Jr. [22]	561 Sigilyph [28]	577 Solosis [3]	578 Duosion [1,3]
	579 Reuniclus [1,3]	615 Cryogonal [37]				
Reflect Type	120 Staryu [40]	151 Mew [1]	380 Latias [70]			
Refresh	007 Squirtle [E]	054 Psyduck [E]	060 Poliwag [E]	108 Lickitung [45]	113 Chansey [9]	131 Lapras [E]
	152 Chikorita [E]	177 Natu [E]	183 Marill [E]	222 Corsola [13]	242 Blissey [9]	258 Mudkip [E]
	276 Taillow [E]	298 Azurill [E]	333 Swablu [29]	334 Altaria [29]	350 Milotic [9]	366 Clamperl [E]
	380 Latias [30]	381 Latios [30]	385 Jirachi [25]	440 Happiny [9]	463 Lickilicky [45]	493 Arceus [50]
	531 Audino [5]	535 Tympole [E]	594 Alomomola [E]			
Rest	TM44	039 Jigglypuff [29]	086 Seel [21]	087 Dewgong [21]	128 Tauros [19]	143 Snorlax [28]
	161 Sentret [28]	162 Furret [32]	213 Shuckle [20]	216 Teddiursa [43]	217 Ursaring [47]	263 Zigzagoon [41]
	264 Linoone [53]	293 Whismur [45]	294 Loudred [57]	295 Exploud [57]	299 Nosepass [22]	320 Wailmer [27]
	321 Wailord [27]	325 Spoink [29]	326 Grumpig [29]	339 Barboach [31]	340 Whiscash [33]	363 Spheal [37]
	364 Sealeo [39]	365 Walrein [39]	369 Relicanth [64]	383 Groudon [30]	384 Rayquaza [30]	385 Jirachi [5,30]
	476 Probopass [22]	480 Uxie [1]	481 Mesprit [1]	482 Azelf [1]	613 Cubchoo [41]	614 Beartic [41]
Retaliate	TM67	058 Growlithe [32]	104 Cubone [47]	105 Marowak [59]	501 Oshawott [37]	502 Dewott [44]
	503 Samurott [50]	506 Lillipup [29]	507 Herdier [33]	508 Stoutland [36]	539 Sawk [37]	638 Cobalion [31]
	639 Terrakion [31]	640 Virizion [31]	647 Keldeo [31]			
Return	TM27	428 Lopunny [13]				
Revenge	019 Rattata [E]	056 Mankey [E]	066 Machop [25]	067 Machoke [25]	068 Machamp [25]	083 Farfetch'd [E]
	106 Hitmonlee [1]	107 Hitmonchan [1]	127 Pinsir [15]	190 Aipom [E]	204 Pineco [E]	211 Qwilfish [29]
	214 Heracross [E]	237 Hitmontop [1]	296 Makuhita [E]	332 Cacturne [1]	335 Zangoose [26]	396 Starly [E]
	449 Hippopotas [E]	453 Croagunk [22]	454 Toxicroak [22]	461 Weavile [1]	486 Regigigas [25]	501 Oshawott [25]
	502 Dewott [28]	503 Samurott [28]	504 Patrat [E]	538 Throh [21]	550 Basculin [E]	618 Stunfisk [50]
	621 Druddigon [35]	624 Pawniard [E]	626 Bouffalant [26]	641 Tornadus [19]	642 Thundurus [19]	
Reversal	019 Rattata [E]	050 Diglett [E]	056 Mankey [E]	058 Growlithe [19]	106 Hitmonlee [61]	111 Rhyhorn [E]
	115 Kangaskhan [55]	123 Scyther [E]	155 Cyndaquil [E]	161 Sentret [E]	172 Pichu [E]	193 Yanma [E]
	214 Heracross [43]	228 Houndour [E]	241 Miltank [E]	255 Torchic [E]	288 Vigoroth [55]	296 Makuhita [43]
	297 Hariyama [57]	307 Meditite [46]	308 Medicham [55]	447 Riolu [29]	494 Victini [33]	506 Lillipup [33]
	507 Herdier [38]	508 Stoutland [42]	532 Timburr [E]	538 Throh [53]	539 Sawk [53]	589 Escavalier [49]
	610 Axew [E]	619 Mienfoo [57]	620 Mienshao [63]	626 Bouffalant [E]		
Roar	TM05	037 Vulpix [7]	058 Growlithe [1]	059 Arcanine [1]	142 Aerodactyl [9]	209 Snubbull [25]
	210 Granbull [27]	228 Houndour [13]	229 Houndoom [13]	243 Raikou [15]	244 Entei [15]	261 Poochyena [21]

Pokémon Moves Reverse Lookup

R

Move	Pokémon that can learn it				
Roar (continued)	262 Mightyena [22]	293 Whismur [35]	294 Loudred [43]	295 Exploud [45]	304 Aron [18]	305 Lairon [18]
	306 Aggron [18]	309 Electrike [36]	310 Manectric [42]	403 Shinx [21]	404 Luxio [23]	405 Luxray [23]
	498 Tepig [39]	499 Pignite [47]	500 Emboar [55]	506 Lillipup [26]	507 Herdier [29]	508 Stoutland [29]
	633 Deino [20]	634 Zweilous [20]	635 Hydreigon [20]			
Roar of Time	483 Dialga [46]					
Rock Blast	074 Geodude [22]	075 Graveler [22]	076 Golem [22]	090 Shellder [E]	095 Onix [E]	111 Rhyhorn [23]
	112 Rhydon [23]	138 Omanyte [46]	139 Omastar [56]	213 Shuckle [E]	222 Corsola [31]	223 Remoraid [E]
	224 Octillery [1]	299 Nosepass [18]	347 Anorith [49]	348 Armaldo [55]	410 Shieldon [18]	413 Wormadam (Sand) [26]
	464 Rhyperior [23]	476 Probopass [18]	524 Roggenrola [14]	525 Boldore [14]	526 Gigalith [14]	557 Dwebble [5]
	558 Crustle [1,5]	568 Trubbish [E]	573 Cinccino [1]			
Rock Climb	027 Sandshrew [E]	074 Geodude [E]	095 Onix [E]	111 Rhyhorn [E]	207 Gligar [E]	263 Zigzagoon [E]
	399 Bidoof [E]	443 Gible [E]	529 Drilbur [E]	543 Venipede [40, E]	544 Whirlipede [46]	545 Scolipede [50]
	551 Sandile [E]	559 Scraggy [45]	560 Scrafty [51]	595 Joltik [E]	597 Ferroseed [E]	598 Ferrothorn [1]
	621 Druddigon [49]	626 Bouffalant [E]	632 Durant [E]			
Rock Polish	TM69	074 Geodude [8]	075 Graveler [1,8]	076 Golem [1,8]	095 Onix [19]	337 Lunatone [13]
	338 Solrock [13]	557 Dwebble [19]	558 Crustle [19]			
Rock Slide	TM80	095 Onix [34]	142 Aerodactyl [73]	185 Sudowoodo [29]	208 Steelix [34]	213 Shuckle [38]
	218 Slugma [41]	219 Magcargo [44]	246 Larvitar [19]	247 Pupitar [19]	248 Tyranitar [19]	299 Nosepass [29]
	323 Camerupt [33]	328 Trapinch [25]	329 Vibrava [25]	330 Flygon [25]	337 Lunatone [25]	338 Solrock [25]
	438 Bonsly [29]	476 Probopass [29]	524 Roggenrola [27]	525 Boldore [30]	526 Gigalith [30]	529 Drilbur [29]
	530 Excadrill [29]	532 Timburr [31]	533 Gurdurr [33]	534 Conkeldurr [33]	557 Dwebble [29]	558 Crustle [29]
	564 Tirtouga [45]	565 Carracosta [51]	566 Archen [45]	567 Archeops [51]	639 Terrakion [37]	645 Landorus [49]
Rock Smash	TM94	539 Sawk [1]				
Rock Throw	074 Geodude [11]	075 Graveler [11]	076 Golem [11]	095 Onix [7]	185 Sudowoodo [1, 12]	208 Steelix [7]
	213 Shuckle [23]	218 Slugma [10]	219 Magcargo [1, 10]	299 Nosepass [11]	337 Lunatone [5]	338 Solrock [5]
	377 Regirock [9]	438 Bonsly [12]	532 Timburr [16]	533 Gurdurr [16]	534 Conkeldurr [16]	564 Tirtouga [E]
	566 Archen [5]	567 Archeops [1, 5]	645 Landorus [25]			
Rock Tomb	TM39	095 Onix [13]	185 Sudowoodo [22]	208 Steelix [13]	343 Baltoy [10]	344 Claydol [10]
	369 Relicanth [15]	438 Bonsly [22]	524 Roggenrola [14]	645 Landorus [1]		
Rock Wrecker	464 Rhyperior [86]	557 Dwebble [43]	558 Crustle [55]			
Role Play	Taught by someone	064 Kadabra [42]	096 Drowzee [E]	122 Mr. Mime [43]	234 Stantler [33]	327 Spinda [E]
	439 Mime Jr. [43]	511 Pansage [E]	513 Pansear [E]	515 Panpour [E]		
Rolling Kick	066 Machop [E]	106 Hitmonlee [9]	237 Hitmontop [1]	239 Elekid [E]		
Rollout	027 Sandshrew [7]	028 Sandslash [7]	039 Jigglypuff [21]	074 Geodude [18]	075 Graveler [18]	095 Onix [E]
	100 Voltorb [15]	101 Electrode [15]	108 Lickitung [33]	138 Omanyte [16]	139 Omastar [16]	143 Snorlax [44]
	155 Cyndaquil [49]	156 Quilava [57]	157 Typhlosion [61]	183 Marill [10]	184 Azumarill [10]	185 Sudowoodo [E]
	206 Dunsparce [4]	211 Qwilfish [17]	213 Shuckle [1]	218 Slugma [E]	231 Phanpy [15]	232 Donphan [15]
	241 Miltank [19]	299 Nosepass [E]	320 Wailmer [11]	321 Wailord [1, 11]	322 Numel [E]	361 Snorunt [E]
	363 Spheal [E]	399 Bidoof [13, E]	400 Bibarel [13]	417 Pachirisu [E]	420 Cherubi [E]	438 Bonsly [E]
	446 Munchlax [44]	463 Lickilicky [33]	498 Tepig [21]	499 Pignite [23]	500 Emboar [23]	543 Venipede [1]
	544 Whirlipede [1]	545 Scolipede [E]	554 Darumaka [3]	555 Darmanitan [1, 3]	564 Tirtouga [5]	565 Carracosta [1, 5]
	568 Trubbish [E]	577 Solosis [7]	578 Duosion [1, 7]	579 Reuniclus [1, 7]	590 Foongus [E]	597 Ferroseed [6]
	598 Ferrothorn [1, 6]	622 Golett [9]	623 Golurk [9]			
Roost	Taught by someone	016 Pidgey [37]	017 Pidgeotto [42]	018 Pidgeot [44]	021 Spearow [33]	022 Fearow [41]
	083 Farfetch'd [E]	142 Aerodactyl [E]	144 Articuno [57]	145 Zapdos [57]	146 Moltres [57]	149 Dragonite [1]
	163 Hoothoot [53]	164 Noctowl [62]	177 Natu [E]	198 Murkrow [E]	206 Dunsparce [25]	276 Taillow [E]
	278 Wingull [26, E]	279 Pelipper [28]	333 Swablu [E]	396 Starly [E]	441 Chatot [41]	519 Pidove [18]
	520 Tranquill [18]	521 Unfezant [18]	527 Woobat [E]	561 Sigilyph [E]	580 Ducklett [30]	581 Swanna [30]
	587 Emolga [E]	629 Vullaby [E]				
Round	TM48	039 Jigglypuff [17]	333 Swablu [18]	334 Altaria [18]	441 Chatot [29]	535 Tympole [9]
	536 Palpitoad [1,9]	537 Seismitoad [1,9]				

S

Move	Pokémon that can learn it				
Sacred Fire	250 Ho-Oh [43]					
Sacred Sword	638 Cobalion [42]	639 Terrakion [42]	640 Virizion [42]	647 Keldeo [43]		
Safeguard	TM20	012 Butterfree [36]	037 Vulpix [36]	038 Ninetales [1]	086 Seel [51]	087 Dewgong [61]
	122 Mr. Mime [50]	131 Lapras [43]	146 Moltres [43]	147 Dratini [45]	148 Dragonair [53]	149 Dragonite [53]
	150 Mewtwo [86]	152 Chikorita [39]	153 Bayleef [46]	154 Meganium [54]	165 Ledyba [14]	166 Ledian [14]
	175 Togepi [37]	176 Togetic [37]	202 Wobbuffet [1]	213 Shuckle [16]	249 Lugia [65]	250 Ho-Oh [65]
	251 Celebi [10]	333 Swablu [13]	334 Altaria [13]	350 Milotic [45]	358 Chimecho [41]	360 Wynaut [15]
	370 Luvdisc [55]	380 Latias [15]	381 Latios [15]	436 Bronzor [25]	437 Bronzong [25]	439 Mime Jr. [50]
	456 Finneon [29]	457 Lumineon [29]	488 Cresselia [11]	594 Alomomola [45]		
Sand Tomb	027 Sandshrew [23]	028 Sandslash [23]	051 Dugtrio [26]	095 Onix [37]	185 Sudowoodo [E]	204 Pineco [E]
	207 Gligar [E]	213 Shuckle [E]	328 Trapinch [10]	329 Vibrava [1, 10]	330 Flygon [1, 10]	387 Turtwig [E]
	438 Bonsly [E]	443 Gible [19, E]	444 Gabite [19]	445 Garchomp [19]	449 Hippopotas [25, E]	450 Hippowdon [25]
	551 Sandile [13]	552 Krokorok [13]	553 Krookodile [13]	557 Dwebble [E]		
Sand-Attack	016 Pidgey [5]	017 Pidgeotto [1, 5]	018 Pidgeot [1, 5]	027 Sandshrew [3]	028 Sandslash [1, 3]	050 Diglett [1]
	051 Dugtrio [1]	083 Farfetch'd [1]	133 Eevee [5]	134 Vaporeon [5]	135 Jolteon [5]	136 Flareon [5]
	140 Kabuto [21]	141 Kabutops [21]	179 Mareep [E]	190 Aipom [4]	196 Espeon [5]	197 Umbreon [5]
	207 Gligar [4]	227 Skarmory [6]	234 Stantler [15]	255 Torchic [19]	256 Combusken [21]	257 Blaziken [21]
	261 Poochyena [9]	262 Mightyena [1, 9]	263 Zigzagoon [13]	264 Linoone [13]	290 Nincada [9]	291 Ninjask [1, 9]
	292 Shedinja [9]	296 Makuhita [4]	297 Hariyama [1, 4]	328 Trapinch [4]	329 Vibrava [1, 4]	330 Flygon [1, 4]
	331 Cacnea [17]	332 Cacturne [17]	347 Anorith [E]	396 Starly [E]	424 Ambipom [1, 4]	431 Glameow [E]
	443 Gible [3]	444 Gabite [1, 3]	445 Garchomp [1, 3]	449 Hippopotas [1]	450 Hippowdon [1]	451 Skorupi [E]

Move	Pokémon that can learn it					
Sand-Attack (continued)	470 Leafeon [5]	471 Glaceon [5]	472 Gliscor [1, 4]	504 Patrat [13]	505 Watchog [13]	506 Lillipup [E]
	509 Purrloin [10]	510 Liepard [1, 10]	522 Blitzle [E]	524 Roggenrola [7]	525 Boldore [1, 7]	526 Gigalith [1, 7]
	551 Sandile [7]	552 Krokorok [1, 7]	553 Krookodile [1, 7]	557 Dwebble [11]	558 Crustle [1, 11]	559 Scraggy [5]
	560 Scrafty [1, 5]	568 Trubbish [E]	585 Deerling [7]	586 Sawsbuck [1, 7]	632 Durant [1]	
Sandstorm	TM37	027 Sandshrew [42]	028 Sandslash [42]	095 Onix [52]	208 Steelix [52]	246 Larvitar [5]
	247 Pupitar [1, 5]	248 Tyranitar [1, 5]	299 Nosepass [36]	328 Trapinch [44]	329 Vibrava [44]	330 Flygon [44]
	331 Cacnea [53]	332 Cacturne [65]	343 Baltoy [41]	344 Claydol [47]	443 Gible [13]	444 Gabite [13]
	445 Garchomp [1, 13]	476 Probopass [36]	524 Roggenrola [33]	525 Boldore [42]	526 Gigalith [42]	529 Drilbur [40]
	530 Excadrill [49]	551 Sandile [40]	552 Krokorok [44]	553 Krookodile [48]	645 Landorus [61]	
Scald	TM55	515 Panpour [22]	516 Simipour [1]			
Scary Face	004 Charmander [19]	005 Charmeleon [21]	006 Charizard [21]	020 Raticate [20]	021 Spearow [19]	023 Ekans [E]
	066 Machop [46]	067 Machoke [51]	068 Machamp [51]	088 Grimer [E]	092 Gastly [E]	111 Rhyhorn [19]
	112 Rhydon [19]	128 Tauros [11]	136 Flareon [29]	142 Aerodactyl [1]	158 Totodile [15]	159 Croconaw [15]
	160 Feraligatr [15]	167 Spinarak [5]	168 Ariados [1, 5]	209 Snubbull [1]	210 Granbull [1]	217 Ursaring [38]
	232 Donphan [39]	246 Larvitar [23]	247 Pupitar [23]	248 Tyranitar [23]	261 Poochyena [33]	262 Mightyena [37]
	284 Masquerain [26]	318 Carvanha [11]	319 Sharpedo [11]	322 Numel [E]	336 Seviper [E]	367 Huntail [19]
	371 Bagon [40]	372 Shelgon [43]	373 Salamence [43]	375 Metang [35]	376 Metagross [35]	382 Kyogre [5]
	383 Groudon [5]	384 Rayquaza [5]	403 Shinx [37]	404 Luxio [49]	405 Luxray [49]	408 Cranidos [19]
	409 Rampardos [19]	410 Shieldon [E]	434 Stunky [E]	443 Gible [E]	451 Skorupi [41]	452 Drapion [43]
	464 Rhyperior [19]	473 Mamoswine [58]	483 Dialga [1]	484 Palkia [1]	485 Heatran [41]	487 Giratina (Alt) [1]
	487 Giratina (Ori) [1]	532 Timburr [37]	533 Gurdurr [41]	534 Conkeldurr [41]	550 Basculin [41]	551 Sandile [34]
	552 Krokorok [36]	553 Krookodile [36]	559 Scraggy [34]	560 Scrafty [34]	563 Cofagrigus [34]	566 Archen [11]
	567 Archeops [11]	570 Zorua [21]	571 Zoroark [21]	588 Karrablast [40]	610 Axew [16]	611 Fraxure [16]
	612 Haxorus [16]	621 Druddigon [13]	624 Pawniard [22]	625 Bisharp [22]	626 Bouffalant [E]	627 Rufflet [19]
	628 Braviary [19]	629 Vullaby [E]	633 Deino [52]	634 Zweilous [55]	635 Hydreigon [55]	646 Kyurem [43]
Scratch	004 Charmander [1]	005 Charmeleon [1]	006 Charizard [1]	027 Sandshrew [1]	028 Sandslash [1]	029 Nidoran ♀ [1]
	030 Nidorina [1]	031 Nidoqueen [1]	046 Paras [1]	047 Parasect [1]	050 Diglett [1]	051 Dugtrio [1]
	052 Meowth [1]	053 Persian [1]	054 Psyduck [1]	055 Golduck [1]	056 Mankey [1]	057 Primeape [1]
	140 Kabuto [1]	141 Kabutops [1]	158 Totodile [1]	159 Croconaw [1]	160 Feraligatr [1]	161 Sentret [1]
	162 Furret [1]	190 Aipom [1]	215 Sneasel [1]	216 Teddiursa [1]	217 Ursaring [1]	255 Torchic [1]
	256 Combusken [1]	257 Blaziken [1]	287 Slakoth [1]	288 Vigoroth [1]	289 Slaking [1]	290 Nincada [1]
	291 Ninjask [1]	292 Shedinja [1]	302 Sableye [1]	335 Zangoose [1]	347 Anorith [1]	348 Armaldo [1]
	352 Kecleon [1]	359 Absol [1]	390 Chimchar [1]	391 Monferno [1]	392 Infernape [1]	424 Ambipom [1]
	431 Glameow [5]	432 Purugly [1,5]	434 Stunky [1]	435 Skuntank [1]	461 Weavile [1]	509 Purrloin [1]
	510 Liepard [1]	511 Pansage [1]	513 Pansear [1]	515 Panpour [1]	529 Drilbur [1]	530 Excadrill [1]
	570 Zorua [1]	571 Zoroark [1]	610 Axew [1]	611 Fraxure [1]	612 Haxorus [1]	621 Druddigon [1]
	624 Pawniard [1]	625 Bisharp [1]				
Screech	019 Rattata [E]	023 Ekans [17]	024 Arbok [17]	042 Golbat [1]	046 Paras [E]	048 Venonat [E]
	050 Diglett [E]	052 Meowth [17]	053 Persian [17]	054 Psyduck [25]	055 Golduck [25]	056 Mankey [21]
	057 Primeape [21]	072 Tentacool [40]	073 Tentacruel [43]	081 Magnemite [39]	082 Magneton [45]	088 Grimer [32]
	089 Muk [32]	090 Shellder [E]	095 Onix [31]	100 Voltorb [19]	101 Electrode [19]	104 Cubone [E]
	108 Lickitung [49]	109 Koffing [E]	125 Electabuzz [42]	140 Kabuto [E]	158 Totodile [36]	159 Croconaw [42]
	160 Feraligatr [50]	165 Ledyba [E]	169 Crobat [1]	170 Chinchou [E]	179 Mareep [E]	190 Aipom [25, E]
	193 Yanma [46]	197 Umbreon [29]	198 Murkrow [E]	200 Misdreavus [E]	206 Dunsparce [1]	207 Gligar [35]
	208 Steelix [31]	215 Sneasel [32]	222 Corsola [E]	223 Remoraid [1]	239 Elekid [36]	240 Magby [E]
	246 Larvitar [10]	247 Pupitar [1, 10]	248 Tyranitar [1, 10]	252 Treecko [21]	253 Grovyle [23]	254 Sceptile [23]
	291 Ninjask [20]	293 Whismur [31]	294 Loudred [37]	295 Exploud [37]	304 Aron [E]	318 Carvanha [18]
	319 Sharpedo [18]	329 Vibrava [34]	330 Flygon [34]	336 Seviper [16]	347 Anorith [E]	352 Kecleon [32]
	353 Shuppet [4]	354 Banette [1, 4]	367 Huntail [10]	402 Kricketune [34]	408 Cranidos [42]	409 Rampardos [51]
	410 Shieldon [E]	424 Ambipom [25]	434 Stunky [7]	435 Skuntank [7]	446 Munchlax [20]	447 Riolu [24]
	451 Skorupi [E]	461 Weavile [32]	462 Magnezone [45]	463 Lickilicky [49]	466 Electivire [42]	469 Yanmega [46]
	472 Gliscor [35]	501 Oshawott [E]	504 Patrat [E]	522 Blitzle [E]	540 Sewaddle [E]	543 Venipede [8]
	544 Whirlipede [1, 8]	545 Scolipede [1, 8]	588 Karrablast [E]	595 Joltik [7]	596 Galvantula [7]	599 Klink [39]
	600 Klang [40]	601 Klinklang [40]	632 Durant [E]	633 Deino [E]	649 Genesect [1]	
Searing Shot	494 Victini [1]					
Secret Power	037 Vulpix [E]	043 Oddish [E]	048 Venonat [E]	054 Psyduck [E]	096 Drowzee [E]	175 Togepi [E]
	193 Yanma [E]	203 Girafarig [E]	206 Dunsparce [E]	307 Meditite [E]	517 Munna [E]	531 Audino [20]
	577 Solosis [E]					
Secret Sword	647 Keldeo ◆					
Seed Bomb	Taught by someone	001 Bulbasaur [37]	103 Exeggutor [1]	187 Hoppip [E]	191 Sunkern [43]	285 Shroomish [41, E]
	286 Breloom [41]	315 Roselia [E]	331 Cacnea [E]	387 Turtwig [E]	406 Budew [E]	420 Cherubi [E]
	459 Snover [E]	511 Pansage [22]	512 Simisage [1]	556 Maractus [E]	597 Ferroseed [E]	
Seed Flare	492 Shaymin (Land) [100]	492 Shaymin (Sky) [100]				
Seismic Toss	056 Mankey [17]	057 Primeape [17]	066 Machop [22]	067 Machoke [22]	068 Machamp [22]	127 Pinsir [8]
	214 Heracross [E]	216 Teddiursa [E]	241 Miltank [E]	296 Makuhita [31]	297 Hariyama [37]	313 Volbeat [E]
	493 Arceus [1]	538 Throh [13]				
Selfdestruct	074 Geodude [29]	075 Graveler [31]	076 Golem [31]	100 Voltorb [33]	101 Electrode [35]	109 Koffing [23]
	110 Weezing [23]	185 Sudowoodo [E]	204 Pineco [6]	205 Forretress [1, 6]	343 Baltoy [25]	344 Claydol [25]
	438 Bonsly [E]	446 Munchlax [E]	568 Trubbish [E]	597 Ferroseed [38]	598 Ferrothorn [38]	649 Genesect [77]
Shadow Ball	TM30	092 Gastly [29]	093 Haunter [33]	094 Gengar [33]	200 Misdreavus [41]	292 Shedinja [59]
	302 Sableye [57]	353 Shuppet [30]	354 Banette [30]	425 Drifloon [36]	426 Drifblim [40]	562 Yamask [37]
	563 Cofagrigus [39]	607 Litwick [49]	608 Lampent [53]			
Shadow Claw	TM65	006 Charizard [1]	302 Sableye [39]	352 Kecleon [49]	487 Giratina (Alt) [42]	487 Giratina (Ori) [42]
Shadow Force	487 Giratina (Alt) [46]	487 Giratina (Ori) [46]				

Pokémon Moves Reverse Lookup

S

Move	Pokémon that can learn it					
Shadow Punch	088 Grimer [E]	093 Haunter [25]	094 Gengar [25]	356 Dusclops [37]	477 Dusknoir [37]	622 Golett [13]
	623 Golurk [13]					
Shadow Sneak	088 Grimer [E]	167 Spinarak [19]	168 Ariados [19]	200 Misdreavus [E]	280 Ralts [E]	292 Shedinja [38]
	302 Sableye [25]	352 Kecleon [22]	353 Shuppet [16, E]	354 Banette [16]	355 Duskull [22]	356 Dusclops [22]
	442 Spiritomb [1, E]	477 Dusknoir [22]	487 Giratina (Alt) [19]	487 Giratina (Ori) [19]		
Sharpen	137 Porygon [1]	615 Cryogonal [9]				
Sheer Cold	087 Dewgong [34]	131 Lapras [55]	144 Articuno [78]	362 Glalie [59]	363 Spheal [49]	364 Sealeo [55]
	365 Walrein [65]	382 Kyogre [75]	459 Snover [46]	460 Abomasnow [58]	582 Vanillite [53]	583 Vanillish [58]
	584 Vanilluxe [67]	613 Cubchoo [57]	614 Beartic [66]	615 Cryogonal [61]		
Shell Smash	090 Shellder [56]	138 Omanyte [52]	139 Omastar [67]	213 Shuckle [34]	219 Magcargo [38]	324 Torkoal [65]
	366 Clamperl [51]	557 Dwebble [37]	558 Crustle [1, 43]	564 Tirtouga [38]	565 Carracosta [40]	
Shift Gear	599 Klink [48]	600 Klang [52]	601 Klinklang [54]			
Shock Wave	125 Electabuzz [15]	170 Chinchou [E]	239 Elekid [15]	309 Electrike [E]	403 Shinx [E]	466 Electivire [15]
	479 Rotom [22]	479 Rotom (Heat) [22]	479 Rotom (Wash) [22]	479 Rotom (Frst) [22]	479 Rotom (Fan) [22]	479 Rotom (Mow) [22]
	522 Blitzle [11, E]	523 Zebstrika [11]	587 Emolga [22, E]	618 Stunfisk [E]	642 Thundurus [25]	
Signal Beam	Taught by someone	048 Venonat [35, E]	049 Venomoth [37]	086 Seel [E]	087 Dewgong [1, 7]	116 Horsea [E]
	118 Goldeen [E]	137 Porygon [29]	167 Spinarak [34]	171 Lanturn [40]	179 Mareep [39]	
	180 Flaaffy [47]	181 Ampharos [51]	193 Yanma [E]	211 Qwilfish [34]	223 Remoraid [30]	224 Octillery [34]
	226 Mantine [1]	233 Porygon2 [29]	283 Surskit [E]	313 Volbeat [25]	328 Trapinch [E]	363 Spheal [E]
	403 Shinx [E]	456 Finneon [E]	458 Mantyke [E]	474 Porygon-Z [29]	595 Joltik [34]	596 Galvantula [34]
	649 Genesect [40]					
Silver Wind	012 Butterfree [28]	049 Venomoth [1]	123 Scyther [E]	165 Ledyba [25, E]	166 Ledian [29]	193 Yanma [E]
	267 Beautifly [34]	269 Dustox [34]	284 Masquerain [40]	290 Nincada [E]	313 Volbeat [34]	314 Illumise [E]
	414 Mothim [38]	456 Finneon [49]	457 Lumineon [59]	540 Sewaddle [E]	637 Volcarona [50]	
Simple Beam	263 Zigzagoon [E]	300 Skitty [E]	531 Audino [45]	605 Elgyem [29]	606 Beheeyem [29]	649 Genesect [62]
Sing	035 Clefairy [7]	036 Clefable [1]	039 Jigglypuff [1]	040 Wigglytuff [1]	113 Chansey [31]	131 Lapras [1]
	173 Cleffa [7]	174 Igglybuff [1]	238 Smoochum [18]	242 Blissey [31]	298 Azurill [E]	300 Skitty [11]
	301 Delcatty [1]	311 Plusle [E]	312 Minun [E]	333 Swablu [8]	334 Altaria [1, 8]	402 Kricketune [18]
	441 Chatot [13]	572 Minccino [21]	573 Cinccino [1]			
Sketch	235 Smeargle [1, 11, 21, 31, 41, 51, 61, 71, 81, 91]					
Skill Swap	Taught by someone	048 Venonat [E]	063 Abra [E]	096 Drowzee [E]	102 Exeggcute [E]	177 Natu [E]
	200 Misdreavus [E]	203 Girafarig [E]	280 Ralts [E]	325 Spoink [E]	352 Kecleon [E]	355 Duskull [E]
	358 Chimecho [E]	433 Chingling [E]	561 Sigilyph [E]	577 Solosis [40]	578 Duosion [43]	579 Reuniclus [45]
	605 Elgyem [E]					
Skull Bash	001 Bulbasaur [E]	007 Squirtle [31]	008 Wartortle [36]	009 Blastoise [39]	029 Nidoran ♀ [E]	104 Cubone [E]
	111 Rhyhorn [E]	118 Goldeen [E]	319 Sharpedo [50]	324 Torkoal [E]	369 Relicanth [E]	399 Bidoof [E]
	459 Snover [E]	529 Drilbur [E]	626 Bouffalant [E]			
Sky Attack	Taught by someone	021 Spearow [E]	146 Moltres [78]	163 Hoothoot [E]	164 Noctowl [1]	198 Murkrow [E]
	227 Skarmory [E]	249 Lugia [99]	250 Ho-Oh [99]	276 Taillow [E]	334 Altaria [64]	468 Togekiss [1]
	519 Pidove [50]	520 Tranquill [50]	521 Unfezant [66]	561 Sigilyph [51]		
Sky Drop	TM58	142 Aerodactyl [49]	627 Rufflet [50]	628 Braviary [50]		
Sky Uppercut	107 Hitmonchan [41]	207 Gligar [45]	256 Combusken [50]	257 Blaziken [59]	286 Breloom [33]	427 Buneary [E]
	447 Riolu [E]	472 Gliscor [45]				
Slack Off	079 Slowpoke [36]	080 Slowbro [36]	287 Slakoth [13]	289 Slaking [1,13]	390 Chimchar [41]	391 Monferno [49]
	449 Hippopotas [E]					
Slam	023 Ekans [26]	025 Pikachu [26]	069 Bellsprout [41]	070 Weepinbell [41]	086 Seel [E]	095 Onix [28]
	098 Krabby [35, E]	099 Kingler [44]	108 Lickitung [29]	114 Tangela [43]	138 Omanyte [28]	147 Dratini [21]
	148 Dragonair [21]	149 Dragonite [21]	161 Sentret [25]	162 Furret [28]	185 Sudowoodo [15]	190 Aipom [E]
	194 Wooper [15]	195 Quagsire [15]	208 Steelix [28]	226 Mantine [E]	231 Phanpy [24]	232 Donphan [24]
	252 Treecko [36]	253 Grovyle [41]	254 Sceptile [43]	298 Azurill [20, E]	303 Mawile [E]	357 Tropius [E]
	408 Cranidos [E]	438 Bonsly [15]	455 Carnivine [E]	458 Mantyke [E]	463 Lickilicky [29]	465 Tangrowth [43]
	495 Snivy [25]	496 Servine [28]	497 Serperior [28]	504 Patrat [36]	505 Watchog [43]	564 Tirtouga [E]
	572 Minccino [37]	633 Deino [28]	634 Zweilous [28]	635 Hydreigon [28]		
Slash	004 Charmander [34]	005 Charmeleon [39]	006 Charizard [41]	027 Sandshrew [26]	028 Sandslash [26]	046 Paras [27]
	047 Parasect [29]	050 Diglett [37]	051 Dugtrio [45]	052 Meowth [33]	053 Persian [37]	083 Farfetch'd [19]
	123 Scyther [29]	141 Kabutops [40]	158 Totodile [34]	159 Croconaw [39]	160 Feraligatr [45]	161 Sentret [E]
	207 Gligar [27]	212 Scizor [29]	215 Sneasel [35]	216 Teddiursa [29]	217 Ursaring [29]	227 Skarmory [45]
	255 Torchic [34]	256 Combusken [39]	257 Blaziken [42]	264 Linoone [47]	287 Slakoth [E]	288 Vigoroth [31]
	291 Ninjask [31]	319 Sharpedo [30]	335 Zangoose [15]	347 Anorith [43]	348 Armaldo [46]	352 Kecleon [27]
	359 Absol [28]	402 Kricketune [26]	416 Vespiquen [21]	418 Buizel [E]	431 Glameow [37]	432 Purugly [37]
	434 Stunky [22]	435 Skuntank [22]	443 Gible [25]	444 Gabite [28]	445 Garchomp [28]	451 Skorupi [E]
	469 Yanmega [43]	475 Gallade [22]	483 Dialga [15]	484 Palkia [15]	487 Giratina (Alt) [15]	487 Giratina (Ori) [15]
	488 Cresselia [47]	503 Samurott [36]	509 Purrloin [30]	510 Liepard [34]	529 Drilbur [26]	530 Excadrill [26]
	542 Leavanny [29]	557 Dwebble [31]	558 Crustle [31]	588 Karrablast [32]	589 Escavalier [32]	595 Joltik [26]
	596 Galvantula [26]	610 Axew [20]	611 Fraxure [20]	612 Haxorus [20]	613 Cubchoo [33]	614 Beartic [33]
	615 Cryogonal [41]	621 Druddigon [21]	624 Pawniard [30]	625 Bisharp [30]	627 Rufflet [28]	628 Braviary [28]
	631 Heatmor [41]	643 Reshiram [36]	644 Zekrom [36]	646 Kyurem [36]	646 Kyurem (Blk) [36]	646 Kyurem (Wht) [36]
Slash	649 Genesect [29]					
Sleep Powder	001 Bulbasaur [13]	002 Ivysaur [13]	003 Venusaur [13]	012 Butterfree [12]	043 Oddish [17]	044 Gloom [17]
	048 Venonat [29]	049 Venomoth [29]	069 Bellsprout [13]	070 Weepinbell [13]	071 Victreebel [1]	102 Exeggcute [23]
	114 Tangela [4]	187 Hoppip [16]	188 Skiploom [16]	189 Jumpluff [16]	315 Roselia [E]	406 Budew [E]
	455 Carnivine [4]	465 Tangrowth [4]	548 Petilil [10]			
Sleep Talk	Taught by someone	054 Psyduck [E]	056 Mankey [E]	079 Slowpoke [E]	086 Seel [E]	108 Lickitung [E]
	118 Goldeen [E]	131 Lapras [E]	143 Snorlax [33]	174 Igglybuff [E]	194 Wooper [E]	206 Dunsparce [E]

Move	Pokémon that can learn it					
Sleep Talk (continued)	216 Teddiursa [E]	241 Miltank [E]	261 Poochyena [E]	263 Zigzagoon [E]	287 Slakoth [E]	293 Whismur [45]
	294 Loudred [57]	295 Exploud [63]	320 Wailmer [E]	324 Torkoal [E]	363 Spheal [E]	369 Relicanth [E]
	399 Bidoof [E]	441 Chatot [E]	449 Hippopotas [E]	498 Tepig [E]	513 Pansear [E]	517 Munna [E]
	531 Audino [E]	535 Tympole [E]	554 Darumaka [E]	572 Minccino [E]	585 Deerling [E]	613 Cubchoo [E]
	618 Stunfisk [E]	631 Heatmor [E]				
Sludge	001 Bulbasaur [E]	088 Grimer [15]	089 Muk [15]	109 Koffing [18]	110 Weezing [18]	258 Mudkip [E]
	316 Gulpin [14]	317 Swalot [1,14]	422 Shellos [E]	568 Trubbish [18]	569 Garbodor [18]	
Sludge Bomb	TM36	088 Grimer [26]	089 Muk [26]	109 Koffing [34]	110 Weezing [34]	316 Gulpin [44]
	317 Swalot [52]	453 Croagunk [45]	454 Toxicroak [54]	568 Trubbish [29]	569 Garbodor [29]	
Sludge Wave	TM34	072 Tentacool [50]	073 Tentacruel [56]	088 Grimer [37]	089 Muk [37]	
Smack Down	TM23	074 Geodude [25]	075 Graveler [27]	076 Golem [27]	095 Onix [22]	208 Steelix [22]
	524 Roggenrola [23]	525 Boldore [23]	526 Gigalith [23]	557 Dwebble [17]	558 Crustle [17]	564 Tirtouga [31]
	565 Carracosta [31]	639 Terrakion [13]				
SmellingSalt	056 Mankey [E]	066 Machop [E]	108 Lickitung [E]	209 Snubbull [E]	255 Torchic [E]	293 Whismur [E]
	296 Makuhita [22]	297 Hariyama [22]	304 Aron [E]	327 Spinda [E]	331 Cacnea [E]	453 Croagunk [E]
	532 Timburr [E]	619 Mienfoo [E]				
Smog	092 Gastly [E]	109 Koffing [4]	110 Weezing [1, 4]	126 Magmar [1]	136 Flareon [33]	218 Slugma [1]
	219 Magcargo [1]	228 Houndour [8]	229 Houndoom [1, 8]	240 Magby [1]	316 Gulpin [E]	324 Torkoal [4]
	434 Stunky [E]	467 Magmortar [1]	498 Tepig [19]	499 Pignite [20]	500 Emboar [20]	607 Litwick [5]
	608 Lampent [1, 5]	609 Chandelure [1]				
SmokeScreen	004 Charmander [10]	005 Charmeleon [10]	006 Charizard [1, 10]	109 Koffing [7]	110 Weezing [1, 7]	116 Horsea [4]
	117 Seadra [1, 4]	126 Magmar [8]	155 Cyndaquil [6]	156 Quilava [1, 6]	157 Typhlosion [1, 6]	218 Slugma [E]
	230 Kingdra [1, 4]	240 Magby [8]	293 Whismur [E]	324 Torkoal [20]	434 Stunky [14]	435 Skuntank [14]
	442 Spiritomb [E]	467 Magmortar [1, 8]				
Snarl	TM95					
Snatch	Taught by someone	023 Ekans [E]	052 Meowth [E]	215 Sneasel [40]	261 Poochyena [E]	352 Kecleon [E]
	353 Shuppet [42]	354 Banette [46]	386 Deoxys (Nor) [49]	386 Deoxys (Def) [49]	431 Glameow [E]	446 Munchlax [52]
	461 Weavile [40]	509 Purrloin [39]	510 Liepard [47]	570 Zorua [E]	577 Solosis [10]	578 Duosion [1,10]
	579 Reuniclus [1,10]	621 Druddigon [E]	631 Heatmor [26]			
Snore	Taught by someone	079 Slowpoke [E]	108 Lickitung [E]	143 Snorlax [28]	206 Dunsparce [E]	209 Snubbull [E]
	216 Teddiursa [43]	217 Ursaring [49]	223 Remoraid [E]	231 Phanpy [E]	287 Slakoth [E]	293 Whismur [E]
	320 Wailmer [E]	325 Spoink [29]	326 Grumpig [29]	339 Barboach [31]	340 Whiscash [33]	363 Spheal [37]
	364 Sealeo [39]	365 Walrein [39]	369 Relicanth [E]	393 Piplup [E]	535 Tympole [E]	
Soak	054 Psyduck [36]	055 Golduck [38]	118 Goldeen [51]	119 Seaking [63]	223 Remoraid [50]	224 Octillery [64]
	279 Pelipper [1]	298 Azurill [E]	320 Wailmer [E]	456 Finneon [54]	457 Lumineon [66]	550 Basculin [32]
	594 Alomomola [33]					
Softboiled	113 Chansey [16]	242 Blissey [16]				
SolarBeam	TM22	002 Ivysaur [44]	003 Venusaur [53]	045 Vileplume [65]	102 Exeggcute [43]	146 Moltres [71]
	152 Chikorita [45]	153 Bayleef [54]	154 Meganium [66]	191 Sunkern [34]	192 Sunflora [34]	338 Solrock [45]
	357 Tropius [61]	383 Groudon [80]	420 Cherubi [37]	421 Cherrim [43]	546 Cottonee [46]	556 Maractus [50]
	585 Deerling [51]	586 Sawsbuck [60]	590 Foongus [43]	591 Amoonguss [49]	615 Cryogonal [53]	
SonicBoom	081 Magnemite [11]	082 Magneton [1, 11]	100 Voltorb [8]	101 Electrode [1, 8]	167 Spinarak [E]	193 Yanma [14]
	329 Vibrava [1]	330 Flygon [1]	418 Buizel [1]	419 Floatzel [1]	462 Magnezone [1, 11]	469 Yanmega [14]
	517 Munna [1]					
Spacial Rend	484 Palkia [46]					
Spark	081 Magnemite [21]	082 Magneton [21]	100 Voltorb [12]	101 Electrode [1, 12]	170 Chinchou [20]	171 Lanturn [20]
	243 Raikou [29]	299 Nosepass [25]	309 Electrike [20]	310 Manectric [20]	311 Plusle [15]	312 Minun [15]
	339 Barboach [E]	403 Shinx [13]	404 Luxio [13]	405 Luxray [13]	417 Pachirisu [13]	462 Magnezone [21]
	476 Probopass [25]	522 Blitzle [25]	523 Zebstrika [25]	587 Emolga [13]	602 Tynamo [1]	603 Eelektrik [1]
	618 Stunfisk [E]					
Spider Web	167 Spinarak [29]	168 Ariados [32]	595 Joltik [1]	596 Galvantula [1]		
Spike Cannon	091 Cloyster [13]	139 Omastar [40]	222 Corsola [27]			
Spikes	091 Cloyster [28]	138 Omanyte [E]	204 Pineco [28]	205 Forretress [28]	211 Qwilfish [1]	227 Skarmory [28]
	315 Roselia [E]	331 Cacnea [33]	332 Cacturne [35]	361 Snorunt [E]	386 Deoxys (Def) [33]	406 Budew [E]
	543 Venipede [E]	556 Maractus [E]	557 Dwebble [E]	568 Trubbish [E]	597 Ferroseed [E]	616 Shelmet [E]
Spit Up	023 Ekans [25]	024 Arbok [27]	071 Victreebel [1]	086 Seel [E]	088 Grimer [E]	109 Koffing [E]
	171 Lanturn [27]	194 Wooper [E]	211 Qwilfish [25]	218 Slugma [E]	279 Pelipper [39]	303 Mawile [51]
	316 Gulpin [39]	317 Swalot [45]	322 Numel [E]	336 Seviper [E]	345 Lileep [57]	346 Cradily [66]
	363 Spheal [E]	387 Turtwig [E]	422 Shellos [E]	425 Drifloon [32]	426 Drifblim [34]	449 Hippopotas [E]
	455 Carnivine [37]	631 Heatmor [56]				
Spite	Taught by someone	023 Ekans [E]	037 Vulpix [E]	052 Meowth [E]	092 Gastly [5]	093 Haunter [1, 5]
	094 Gengar [1, 5]	109 Koffing [E]	190 Aipom [E]	200 Misdreavus [5, E]	206 Dunsparce [7]	215 Sneasel [E]
	228 Houndour [E]	234 Stantler [E]	292 Shedinja [25]	353 Shuppet [10]	354 Banette [10]	429 Mismagius [1]
	442 Spiritomb [1]	618 Stunfisk [E]				
Splash	060 Poliwag [E]	116 Horsea [E]	129 Magikarp [1]	173 Cleffa [E]	187 Hoppip [1]	188 Skiploom [1]
	189 Jumpluff [1]	225 Delibird [E]	226 Mantine [E]	298 Azurill [1]	320 Wailmer [1]	321 Wailord [1]
	325 Spoink [1]	326 Grumpig [1]	349 Feebas [1]	360 Wynaut [1]	370 Luvdisc [1]	427 Buneary [1]
	428 Lopunny [1]	456 Finneon [E]	458 Mantyke [E]			
Spore	046 Paras [22]	047 Parasect [22]	285 Shroomish [45]	590 Foongus [50]	591 Amoonguss [62]	
Stealth Rock	Taught by someone	074 Geodude [E]	075 Graveler [42]	076 Golem [42]	095 Onix [16, E]	185 Sudowoodo [E]
	204 Pineco [E]	208 Steelix [16]	220 Swinub [E]	227 Skarmory [E]	246 Larvitar [E]	299 Nosepass [E]
	304 Aron [E]	345 Lileep [E]	410 Shieldon [E]	438 Bonsly [E]	524 Roggenrola [30]	525 Boldore [36]
	526 Gigalith [36]	557 Dwebble [24]	558 Crustle [24]	597 Ferroseed [E]	624 Pawniard [E]	
Steamroller	076 Golem [18]	543 Venipede [33]	544 Whirlipede [37]	545 Scolipede [39]		

Pokémon Moves Reverse Lookup

S

Move	Pokémon that can learn it					
Steel Wing	016 Pidgey [E]	021 Spearow [E]	041 Zubat [E]	083 Farfetch'd [E]	123 Scyther [E]	142 Aerodactyl [E]
	177 Natu [E]	227 Skarmory [34]	276 Taillow [E]	333 Swablu [E]	396 Starly [E]	441 Chatot [E]
	519 Pidove [E]	561 Sigilyph [E]	566 Archen [E]	580 Ducklett [E]	629 Vullaby [E]	
Stockpile	023 Ekans [25]	024 Arbok [27]	071 Victreebel [1]	086 Seel [E]	088 Grimer [E]	109 Koffing [E]
	171 Lanturn [27]	194 Wooper [E]	211 Qwilfish [25]	218 Slugma [E]	279 Pelipper [39]	303 Mawile [51]
	316 Gulpin [39]	317 Swalot [45]	322 Numel [E]	336 Seviper [E]	345 Lileep [57]	346 Cradily [66]
	363 Spheal [E]	387 Turtwig [E]	422 Shellos [E]	425 Drifloon [25]	426 Drifblim [25]	446 Munchlax [28]
	449 Hippopotas [E]	455 Carnivine [37]	568 Trubbish [23]	569 Garbodor [23]	631 Heatmor [56]	
Stomp	077 Ponyta [17]	078 Rapidash [17]	079 Slowpoke [E]	098 Krabby [25]	099 Kingler [25]	103 Exeggutor [1]
	108 Lickitung [21]	111 Rhyhorn [8]	112 Rhydon [1,9]	115 Kangaskhan [E]	203 Girafarig [10]	234 Stantler [13]
	241 Miltank [8]	244 Entei [E]	246 Larvitar [E]	258 Mudkip [E]	293 Whismur [E]	294 Loudred [29]
	295 Exploud [29]	304 Aron [E]	322 Numel [E]	357 Tropius [17]	377 Regirock [1]	378 Regice [1]
	379 Registeel [1]	408 Cranidos [E]	459 Snover [E]	463 Lickilicky [21]	464 Rhyperior [1,9]	522 Blitzle [29]
	523 Zebstrika [31]	626 Bouffalant [E]				
Stone Edge	TM71	074 Geodude [50]	075 Graveler [64]	076 Golem [64]	095 Onix [46]	111 Rhyhorn [52]
	112 Rhydon [56]	185 Sudowoodo [43]	208 Steelix [46]	213 Shuckle [49]	246 Larvitar [50]	247 Pupitar [60]
	248 Tyranitar [63]	299 Nosepass [46]	337 Lunatone [41]	338 Solrock [41]	377 Regirock [73]	464 Rhyperior [56]
	476 Probopass [46]	485 Heatran [88]	524 Roggenrola [36]	525 Boldore [48]	526 Gigalith [48]	532 Timburr [43]
	533 Gurdurr [49]	534 Conkeldurr [49]	639 Terrakion [67]	645 Landorus [73]		
Stored Power	035 Clefairy [28]	133 Eevee [E]	173 Cleffa [E]	175 Togepi [E]	177 Natu [39]	178 Xatu [47]
	280 Ralts [54]	281 Kirlia [64]	282 Gardevoir [80]	358 Chimecho [E]	433 Chingling [E]	475 Gallade [64]
	494 Victini [89]	517 Munna [47]	527 Woobat [E]	561 Sigilyph [E]		
Storm Throw	127 Pinsir [33]	538 Throh [25]				
Strength	HM04					
String Shot	010 Caterpie [1]	013 Weedle [1]	167 Spinarak [1]	168 Ariados [1]	265 Wurmple [1]	540 Sewaddle [1]
	541 Swadloon [1]	542 Leavanny [1]	595 Joltik [1]	596 Galvantula [1]	636 Larvesta [1, E]	637 Volcarona [1]
Struggle	—					
Struggle Bug	TM76	213 Shuckle [12]	401 Kricketot [6]	540 Sewaddle [22]	542 Leavanny [22]	616 Shelmet [16]
	617 Accelgor [16]					
Stun Spore	012 Butterfree [12]	043 Oddish [15]	044 Gloom [15]	045 Vileplume [1]	046 Paras [6]	047 Parasect [1, 6]
	048 Venonat [23]	049 Venomoth [23]	069 Weepinbell [17]	070 Victreebel [1]	102 Exeggcute [19]	114 Tangela [30]
	182 Bellossom [1]	187 Hoppip [14]	188 Skiploom [14]	189 Jumpluff [14]	267 Beautifly [17]	284 Masquerain [33]
	285 Shroomish [9]	286 Breloom [1, 9]	315 Roselia [10]	406 Budew [10]	455 Carnivine [E]	465 Tangrowth [30]
	546 Cottonee [10]	548 Petilil [22]	590 Foongus [E]			
Submission	062 Poliwrath [1]	066 Machop [34]	067 Machoke [36]	068 Machamp [36]	127 Pinsir [26]	390 Chimchar [E]
	529 Drilbur [E]					
Substitute	TM90	122 Mr. Mime [29]	352 Kecleon [37]	439 Mime Jr. [29]	479 Rotom [36]	479 Rotom (Heat) [36]
	479 Rotom (Wash) [36]	479 Rotom (Frst) [36]	479 Rotom (Fan) [36]	479 Rotom (Mow) [36]		
Sucker Punch	019 Rattata [19]	020 Raticate [19]	023 Ekans [E]	032 Nidoran♂ [E]	050 Diglett [23]	051 Dugtrio [23]
	092 Gastly [22]	093 Haunter [22]	094 Gengar [22]	115 Kangaskhan [49]	161 Sentret [31]	162 Furret [36]
	167 Spinarak [26]	168 Ariados [28]	177 Natu [E]	185 Sudowoodo [36]	198 Murkrow [55]	200 Misdreavus [E]
	228 Houndour [E]	261 Poochyena [49, E]	262 Mightyena [62]	300 Skitty [E]	302 Sableye [E]	303 Mawile [46, E]
	327 Spinda [32]	331 Cacnea [37]	332 Cacturne [41]	352 Kecleon [43]	353 Shuppet [34]	354 Banette [34]
	359 Absol [52, E]	431 Glameow [41]	438 Bonsly [36]	442 Spiritomb [31]	453 Croagunk [31]	454 Toxicroak [31]
	509 Purrloin [46]	510 Liepard [55]	556 Maractus [42]	570 Zorua [E]	595 Joltik [40]	596 Galvantula [46]
	621 Druddigon [E]	624 Pawniard [E]	631 Heatmor [E]			
Sunny Day	TM11	126 Magmar [42]	146 Moltres [85]	182 Bellossom [1]	191 Sunkern [40]	192 Sunflora [40]
	240 Magby [36]	250 Ho-Oh [29]	273 Seedot [31]	351 Castform [20]	420 Cherubi [22]	421 Cherrim [22]
	437 Bronzong [1]	467 Magmortar [42]	470 Leafeon [37]	546 Cottonee [40]	548 Petilil [40]	556 Maractus [45]
Super Fang	Taught by someone	019 Rattata [28]	020 Raticate [34]	399 Bidoof [37]	400 Bibarel [43]	417 Pachirisu [37]
	504 Patrat [21]	505 Watchog [22]				
Superpower	Taught by someone	031 Nidoqueen [58]	127 Pinsir [43, E]	158 Totodile [48]	159 Croconaw [57]	160 Feraligatr [71]
	183 Marill [37, E]	184 Azumarill [42]	304 Aron [E]	328 Trapinch [67]	341 Corphish [E]	377 Regirock [25]
	378 Regice [25]	379 Registeel [25]	386 Deoxys (Atk) [49]	387 Turtwig [E]	399 Bidoof [41]	400 Bibarel [48]
	498 Tepig [E]	532 Timburr [49]	533 Gurdurr [57]	534 Conkeldurr [57]	538 Throh [49]	554 Darumaka [39]
	555 Darmanitan [47]	614 Beartic [1]	621 Druddigon [55]	628 Braviary [51]		
Supersonic	012 Butterfree [1]	029 Nidoran♀ [E]	032 Nidoran♂ [E]	041 Zubat [4]	042 Golbat [1, 4]	048 Venonat [5]
	049 Venomoth [1, 5]	072 Tentacool [5]	073 Tentacruel [1, 5]	081 Magnemite [4]	082 Magneton [1, 4]	084 Doduo [E]
	090 Shellder [8]	091 Cloyster [1]	108 Lickitung [5]	118 Goldeen [7]	119 Seaking [1, 7]	138 Omanyte [E]
	142 Aerodactyl [1]	147 Dratini [E]	163 Hoothoot [E]	165 Ledyba [6]	166 Ledian [1, 6]	169 Crobat [1, 4]
	170 Chinchou [1]	171 Lanturn [1]	183 Marill [E]	193 Yanma [22]	211 Qwilfish [E]	223 Remoraid [E]
	226 Mantine [1, 3]	276 Taillow [E]	278 Wingull [6]	279 Pelipper [6]	293 Whismur [21]	294 Loudred [23]
	295 Exploud [23]	329 Vibrava [29]	330 Flygon [29]	366 Clamperl [E]	370 Luvdisc [E]	393 Piplup [E]
	441 Chatot [E]	458 Mantyke [3]	462 Magnezone [1, 4]	463 Lickilicky [5]	469 Yanmega [22]	489 Phione [16]
	490 Manaphy [16]	527 Woobat [E]	535 Tympole [5]	536 Palpitoad [1, 5]	537 Seismitoad [1, 5]	
Surf	HM03					
Swagger	TM87	056 Mankey [33]	057 Primeape [35]	096 Drowzee [45]	097 Hypno [45]	128 Tauros [48]
	186 Politoed [27]	199 Slowking [41]	244 Entei [43]	261 Poochyena [25]	262 Mightyena [27]	274 Nuzleaf [43]
	289 Slaking [36]	318 Carvanha [21]	319 Sharpedo [21]	336 Seviper [9]	364 Sealeo [32]	365 Walrein [32]
	395 Empoleon [24]	403 Shinx [25]	404 Luxio [28]	405 Luxray [28]	410 Shieldon [24]	411 Bastiodon [24]
	416 Vespiquen [49]	430 Honchkrow [E]	432 Purugly [38]	453 Croagunk [24]	454 Toxicroak [24]	459 Snover [17]
	460 Abomasnow [17]	519 Pidove [39]	520 Tranquill [45]	521 Unfezant [49]	551 Sandile [25]	552 Krokorok [25]
	553 Krookodile [25]	555 Darmanitan [17]	559 Scraggy [16]	560 Scrafty [16]	614 Beartic [29]	641 Tornadus [7]
	642 Thundurus [7]					

Move	Pokémon that can learn it					
Swallow	023 Ekans [25]	024 Arbok [27]	071 Victreebel [1]	086 Seel [E]	088 Grimer [E]	109 Koffing [E]
	171 Lanturn [27]	194 Wooper [E]	218 Slugma [E]	279 Pelipper [39]	303 Mawile [51]	316 Gulpin [39]
	317 Swalot [45]	322 Numel [E]	336 Seviper [E]	345 Lileep [57]	346 Cradily [66]	363 Spheal [E]
	387 Turtwig [E]	422 Shellos [E]	425 Drifloon [32]	426 Drifblim [34]	446 Munchlax [33]	449 Hippopotas [E]
	455 Carnivine [37]	568 Trubbish [23]	569 Garbodor [23]	631 Heatmor [56]		
Sweet Kiss	172 Pichu [13]	173 Cleffa [10]	174 Igglybuff [13]	175 Togepi [9]	176 Togetic [1, 9]	238 Smoochum [8]
	311 Plusle [E]	312 Minun [E]	370 Luvdisc [37]	417 Pachirisu [29]	427 Buneary [E]	440 Happiny [12]
	456 Finneon [E]	492 Shaymin (Land) [82]	492 Shaymin (Sky) [82]	531 Audino [E]		
Sweet Scent	001 Bulbasaur [21]	002 Ivysaur [23]	003 Venusaur [23]	043 Oddish [5]	044 Gloom [1, 5]	046 Paras [E]
	069 Bellsprout [29]	070 Weepinbell [29]	071 Victreebel [1]	152 Chikorita [28]	153 Bayleef [32]	154 Meganium [34]
	182 Bellossom [1]	191 Sunkern [E]	213 Shuckle [22]	216 Teddiursa [22]	217 Ursaring [22]	270 Lotad [E]
	283 Surskit [13]	284 Masquerain [1, 13]	303 Mawile [16]	314 Illumise [5]	315 Roselia [31]	357 Tropius [21]
	407 Roserade [1]	415 Combee [1]	416 Vespiquen [1]	420 Cherubi [E]	455 Carnivine [17]	492 Shaymin (Land) [37]
	492 Shaymin (Sky) [37]	495 Snivy [E]	548 Petilil [E]	556 Maractus [3]	590 Foongus [24]	591 Amoonguss [24]
Swift	027 Sandshrew [11]	028 Sandslash [11]	041 Zubat [23]	042 Golbat [24]	053 Persian [28]	100 Voltorb [36]
	101 Electrode [40]	120 Staryu [18]	121 Starmie [1]	125 Electabuzz [12]	150 Mewtwo [8]	155 Cyndaquil [31]
	156 Quilava [31]	157 Typhlosion [31]	165 Ledyba [33]	166 Ledian [41]	169 Crobat [24]	190 Aipom [22]
	196 Espeon [17]	204 Pineco [E]	223 Remoraid [E]	227 Skarmory [9]	239 Elekid [E]	309 Electrike [E]
	311 Plusle [31]	312 Minun [31]	318 Carvanha [E]	342 Crawdaunt [30]	385 Jirachi [10]	386 Deoxys (Spd) [49]
	403 Shinx [E]	417 Pachirisu [21]	418 Buizel [21]	419 Floatzel [21]	424 Ambipom [22]	466 Electivire [12]
	480 Uxie [21]	481 Mesprit [21]	482 Azelf [21]	517 Munna [E]	550 Basculin [1]	572 Minccino [19]
	617 Accelgor [25]	619 Mienfoo [21]	620 Mienshao [21]			
Switcheroo	023 Ekans [E]	053 Persian [1]	097 Hypno [1]	190 Aipom [E]	264 Linoone [1]	309 Electrike [E]
	331 Cacnea [E]	336 Seviper [E]	418 Buizel [E]	427 Buneary [E]	546 Cottonee [E]	
Swords Dance	TM75	020 Raticate [1]	027 Sandshrew [38]	028 Sandslash [38]	083 Farfetch'd [25]	123 Scyther [57]
	127 Pinsir [40]	207 Gligar [50]	212 Scizor [57]	291 Ninjask [25]	335 Zangoose [43]	341 Corphish [44]
	342 Crawdaunt [52]	359 Absol [33]	395 Empoleon [11]	448 Lucario [37]	470 Leafeon [29]	472 Gliscor [50]
	475 Gallade [31]	501 Oshawott [41]	502 Dewott [49]	503 Samurott [57]	529 Drilbur [36]	530 Excadrill [42]
	542 Leavanny [46]	588 Karrablast [52]	589 Escavalier [52]	610 Axew [46]	611 Fraxure [48]	612 Haxorus [50]
	624 Pawniard [57]	625 Bisharp [63]	626 Bouffalant [56]	638 Cobalion [49]	639 Terrakion [49]	640 Virizion [49]
	645 Landorus [37]	647 Keldeo [49]				
Synchronoise	054 Psyduck [E]	096 Drowzee [37]	097 Hypno [37]	133 Eevee [E]	163 Hoothoot [41]	164 Noctowl [47]
	177 Natu [E]	280 Ralts [E]	293 Whismur [41]	294 Loudred [51]	295 Exploud [55]	352 Kecleon [58]
	358 Chimecho [54]	441 Chatot [49]	517 Munna [25]	527 Woobat [E]	561 Sigilyph [31]	605 Elgyem [53]
	606 Beheeyem [63]					
Synthesis	Taught by someone	001 Bulbasaur [33]	002 Ivysaur [39]	003 Venusaur [45]	043 Oddish [E]	069 Bellsprout [E]
	102 Exeggcute [E]	152 Chikorita [12]	153 Bayleef [12]	154 Meganium [12]	187 Hoppip [4]	188 Skiploom [1, 4]
	189 Jumpluff [1, 4]	191 Sunkern [28]	252 Treecko [E]	270 Lotad [E]	273 Seedot [21]	315 Roselia [46, E]
	357 Tropius [41, E]	387 Turtwig [33]	388 Grotle [37]	389 Torterra [39]	406 Budew [E]	455 Carnivine [E]
	470 Leafeon [33]	492 Shaymin (Land) [28]	548 Petilil [17]	549 Lilligant [1]	556 Maractus [15]	585 Deerling [E]
	590 Foongus [35]	591 Amoonguss [35]				

Move	Pokémon that can learn it					
Tackle	001 Bulbasaur [1]	002 Ivysaur [1]	003 Venusaur [1]	007 Squirtle [1]	008 Wartortle [1]	009 Blastoise [1]
	010 Caterpie [1]	016 Pidgey [1]	017 Pidgeotto [1]	018 Pidgeot [1]	019 Rattata [1]	020 Raticate [1]
	048 Venonat [1]	049 Venomoth [1]	074 Geodude [1]	075 Graveler [1]	076 Golem [1]	077 Ponyta [1]
	079 Slowpoke [1]	080 Slowbro [1]	081 Magnemite [1]	082 Magneton [1]	090 Shellder [1]	095 Onix [1]
	100 Voltorb [5]	101 Electrode [1, 5]	109 Koffing [1]	110 Weezing [1]	120 Staryu [1]	128 Tauros [1]
	129 Magikarp [15]	133 Eevee [1]	134 Vaporeon [1]	135 Jolteon [1]	136 Flareon [1]	137 Porygon [1]
	143 Snorlax [1]	152 Chikorita [1]	153 Bayleef [1]	154 Meganium [1]	155 Cyndaquil [1]	156 Quilava [1]
	157 Typhlosion [1]	163 Hoothoot [1]	164 Noctowl [1]	165 Ledyba [1]	166 Ledian [1]	179 Mareep [1]
	180 Flaaffy [1]	181 Ampharos [1]	183 Marill [1]	184 Azumarill [1]	187 Hoppip [10]	188 Skiploom [1, 10]
	189 Jumpluff [1, 10]	193 Yanma [1]	196 Espeon [1]	197 Umbreon [1]	199 Slowking [1]	203 Girafarig [1]
	204 Pineco [1]	205 Forretress [1]	208 Steelix [1]	209 Snubbull [1]	210 Granbull [1]	211 Qwilfish [1]
	214 Heracross [1]	220 Swinub [1]	222 Corsola [1]	226 Mantine [1]	231 Phanpy [1]	233 Porygon2 [1]
	234 Stantler [1]	236 Tyrogue [1]	241 Miltank [1]	258 Mudkip [1]	259 Marshtomp [1]	260 Swampert [1]
	261 Poochyena [1]	262 Mightyena [1]	263 Zigzagoon [1]	264 Linoone [1]	265 Wurmple [1]	285 Shroomish [5]
	286 Breloom [1, 5]	296 Makuhita [1]	297 Hariyama [1]	299 Nosepass [1]	300 Skitty [1]	304 Aron [1]
	305 Lairon [1]	306 Aggron [1]	309 Electrike [1]	310 Manectric [1]	313 Volbeat [1]	314 Illumise [1]
	322 Numel [1]	323 Camerupt [1]	327 Spinda [1]	337 Lunatone [1]	338 Solrock [1]	349 Feebas [15]
	351 Castform [1]	369 Relicanth [1]	370 Luvdisc [1]	387 Turtwig [1]	388 Grotle [1]	389 Torterra [1]
	394 Prinplup [1]	395 Empoleon [1]	396 Starly [1]	397 Staravia [1]	398 Staraptor [1]	399 Bidoof [1]
	400 Bibarel [1]	403 Shinx [1]	404 Luxio [1]	405 Luxray [1]	410 Shieldon [1]	411 Bastiodon [1]
	412 Burmy [10]	413 Wormadam (Plnt) [1]	413 Wormadam (Sand) [1]	413 Wormadam (Trsh) [1]	414 Mothim [1]	420 Cherubi [1]
	421 Cherrim [1]	436 Bronzor [1]	437 Bronzong [1]	443 Gible [1]	444 Gabite [1]	445 Garchomp [1]
	446 Munchlax [1]	449 Hippopotas [1]	450 Hippowdon [1]	458 Mantyke [1]	462 Magnezone [1]	469 Yanmega [1]
	470 Leafeon [1]	471 Glaceon [1]	474 Porygon-Z [1]	476 Probopass [1]	495 Snivy [1]	496 Servine [1]
	497 Serperior [1]	498 Tepig [1]	499 Pignite [1]	500 Emboar [1]	501 Oshawott [1]	502 Dewott [1]
	503 Samurott [1]	504 Patrat [1]	505 Watchog [1]	506 Lillipup [1]	507 Herdier [1]	508 Stoutland [1]
	524 Roggenrola [1]	525 Boldore [1]	526 Gigalith [1]	540 Sewaddle [1]	541 Swadloon [1]	542 Leavanny [1]
	550 Basculin [1]	554 Darumaka [1]	555 Darmanitan [1]	585 Deerling [1]	586 Sawsbuck [1]	597 Ferroseed [1]
	598 Ferrothorn [1]	602 Tynamo [1]	633 Deino [1]			
Tail Glow	313 Volbeat [21]	490 Manaphy [1]				

Pokémon Moves Reverse Lookup

Move	Pokémon that can learn it				
Tail Slap	037 Vulpix [E]	418 Buizel [E]	572 Minccino [25]	573 Cinccino [1]		
Tail Whip	007 Squirtle [4]	008 Wartortle [1, 4]	009 Blastoise [1, 4]	019 Rattata [1]	020 Raticate [1]	025 Pikachu [5]
	026 Raichu [1]	029 Nidoran ♀ [7]	030 Nidorina [7]	031 Nidoqueen [1]	037 Vulpix [4]	052 Meowth [E]
	054 Psyduck [4]	055 Golduck [1, 4]	077 Ponyta [4]	078 Rapidash [1, 4]	104 Cubone [3]	105 Marowak [1, 3]
	111 Rhyhorn [1]	112 Rhydon [1]	113 Chansey [5]	115 Kangaskhan [10]	118 Goldeen [1]	119 Seaking [1]
	128 Tauros [3]	133 Eevee [1]	134 Vaporeon [1]	135 Jolteon [1]	136 Flareon [1]	172 Pichu [5]
	183 Marill [2]	184 Azumarill [1, 2]	187 Hoppip [7]	188 Skiploom [1, 7]	189 Jumpluff [1, 7]	190 Aipom [1]
	194 Wooper [1]	195 Quagsire [1]	196 Espeon [1]	197 Umbreon [1]	209 Snubbull [1]	210 Granbull [1]
	242 Blissey [5]	263 Zigzagoon [5]	264 Linoone [1, 5]	298 Azurill [2]	300 Skitty [1]	352 Kecleon [1]
	417 Pachirisu [E]	424 Ambipom [1]	431 Glameow [E]	464 Rhyperior [1]	470 Leafeon [1]	471 Glaceon [1]
	498 Tepig [3]	499 Pignite [1, 3]	500 Emboar [1, 3]	501 Oshawott [5]	502 Dewott [1, 5]	503 Samurott [1, 5]
	522 Blitzle [4]	523 Zebstrika [1, 4]	572 Minccino [2]	587 Emolga [7]		
Tailwind	Taught by someone	012 Butterfree [30]	016 Pidgey [41]	017 Pidgeotto [47]	018 Pidgeot [50]	142 Aerodactyl [E]
	144 Articuno [64]	178 Xatu [27]	198 Murkrow [51]	245 Suicune [57]	279 Pelipper [52]	519 Pidove [46]
	520 Tranquill [54]	521 Unfezant [60]	547 Whimsicott [28]	561 Sigilyph [11]	580 Ducklett [37]	581 Swanna [40]
	627 Rufflet [37]	628 Braviary [37]	629 Vullaby [37]	630 Mandibuzz [37]	641 Tornadus [55]	
Take Down	001 Bulbasaur [15]	002 Ivysaur [15]	003 Venusaur [15]	029 Nidoran ♀ [E]	032 Nidoran ♂ [E]	058 Growlithe [23]
	077 Ponyta [29]	078 Rapidash [29]	086 Seel [37]	087 Dewgong [39]	090 Shellder [1]	111 Rhyhorn [41]
	112 Rhydon [1]	113 Chansey [21]	128 Tauros [41]	133 Eevee [41]	142 Aerodactyl [41]	163 Hoothoot [29]
	164 Noctowl [32]	170 Chinchou [23]	171 Lanturn [23]	179 Mareep [18, E]	180 Flaaffy [20]	181 Ampharos [20]
	203 Girafarig [E]	204 Pineco [12]	205 Forretress [12]	206 Dunsparce [22]	209 Snubbull [37]	210 Granbull [43]
	211 Qwilfish [41]	214 Heracross [28]	216 Teddiursa [E]	220 Swinub [28, E]	221 Piloswine [28]	226 Mantine [27]
	231 Phanpy [10]	234 Stantler [21]	242 Blissey [27]	258 Mudkip [28]	259 Marshtomp [31]	260 Swampert [31]
	261 Poochyena [45]	262 Mightyena [52]	273 Seedot [E]	293 Whismur [E]	304 Aron [22]	305 Lairon [22]
	306 Aggron [22]	318 Carvanha [38]	322 Numel [31]	323 Camerupt [31]	333 Swablu [25]	334 Altaria [25]
	339 Barboach [E]	358 Chimecho [22]	369 Relicanth [29]	370 Luvdisc [14]	374 Beldum [1]	375 Metang [1]
	376 Metagross [1]	396 Starly [29]	397 Staravia [33]	398 Staraptor [33]	399 Bidoof [33]	400 Bibarel [38]
	403 Shinx [E]	408 Cranidos [15]	409 Rampardos [15]	410 Shieldon [15]	411 Bastiodon [15]	420 Cherubi [31]
	421 Cherrim [35]	443 Gible [15]	444 Gabite [15]	445 Garchomp [15]	449 Hippopotas [19]	450 Hippowdon [19]
	458 Mantyke [27]	464 Rhyperior [41]	473 Mamoswine [28]	498 Tepig [25]	499 Pignite [28]	500 Emboar [28]
	506 Lillipup [15]	507 Herdier [15]	508 Stoutland [15]	522 Blitzle [25]	524 Roggenrola [E]	531 Audino [30]
	543 Venipede [E]	550 Basculin [20]	554 Darumaka [E]	568 Trubbish [25]	585 Deerling [20]	586 Sawsbuck [20]
	588 Karrablast [37]	636 Larvesta [20]	638 Cobalion [19]	639 Terrakion [19]	640 Virizion [19]	647 Keldeo [19]
Taunt	TM12	052 Meowth [25]	053 Persian [25]	198 Murkrow [31]	215 Sneasel [1]	261 Poochyena [37]
	262 Mightyena [42]	319 Sharpedo [40]	335 Zangoose [40]	341 Corphish [32]	342 Crawdaunt [34]	359 Absol [17]
	386 Deoxys (Atk) [25]	390 Chimchar [9]	391 Monferno [9]	392 Infernape [1, 9]	402 Kricketune [38]	410 Shieldon [6]
	411 Bastiodon [1, 6]	441 Chatot [25]	453 Croagunk [10]	454 Toxicroak [10]	461 Weavile [1]	510 Liepard [38]
	515 Panpour [25]	519 Pidove [25]	520 Tranquill [27]	521 Unfezant [27]	554 Darumaka [35]	555 Darmanitan [39]
	570 Zorua [25]	571 Zoroark [25]	582 Vanillite [22]	583 Vanillish [22]	584 Vanilluxe [22]	610 Axew [36]
	611 Fraxure [36]	612 Haxorus [36]				
Techno Blast	649 Genesect [1]					
Teeter Dance	043 Oddish [E]	122 Mr. Mime [E]	270 Lotad [E]	327 Spinda [37]	331 Cacnea [E]	439 Mime Jr. [E]
	549 Lilligant [10]					
Telekinesis	TM19	064 Kadabra [34]	065 Alakazam [34]	381 Latios [70]	517 Munna [43]	574 Gothita [40]
	575 Gothorita [43]	576 Gothitelle [45]				
Teleport	063 Abra [1]	064 Kadabra [1]	065 Alakazam [1]	177 Natu [9]	178 Xatu [9]	280 Ralts [12]
	281 Kirlia [1, 12]	282 Gardevoir [1, 12]	344 Claydol [1]	386 Deoxys (Nor) [17]	386 Deoxys (Atk) [17]	386 Deoxys (Def) [17]
	475 Gallade [1, 12]	605 Elgyem [E]				
Thief	TM46	262 Mightyena [57]	352 Kecleon [1]			
Thrash	034 Nidoking [35]	056 Mankey [41]	057 Primeape [47]	058 Growlithe [E]	077 Ponyta [E]	084 Doduo [50]
	085 Dodrio [60]	104 Cubone [31]	105 Marowak [33]	127 Pinsir [36]	128 Tauros [55]	130 Gyarados [1]
	155 Cyndaquil [E]	158 Totodile [41, E]	159 Croconaw [48]	160 Feraligatr [58]	216 Teddiursa [50]	217 Ursaring [58]
	221 Piloswine [41]	234 Stantler [E]	246 Larvitar [28]	247 Pupitar [28]	248 Tyranitar [28]	318 Carvanha [E]
	320 Wailmer [E]	327 Spinda [55]	339 Barboach [E]	371 Bagon [E]	387 Turtwig [E]	408 Cranidos [E]
	443 Gible [E]	473 Mamoswine [41]	498 Tepig [E]	522 Blitzle [43]	523 Zebstrika [53]	550 Basculin [56]
	551 Sandile [46]	552 Krokorok [52]	554 Darumaka [27]	555 Darmanitan [27]	566 Archen [51]	567 Archeops [61]
	603 Eelektrik [74]	613 Cubchoo [53]	614 Beartic [59]	626 Bouffalant [51]	627 Rufflet [64]	628 Braviary [70]
	636 Larvesta [90]	641 Tornadus [85]	642 Thundurus [85]			
Thunder	TM25	025 Pikachu [50]	125 Electabuzz [55]	135 Jolteon [45]	145 Zapdos [78]	179 Mareep [46]
	180 Flaaffy [56]	181 Ampharos [62]	239 Elekid [43]	243 Raikou [85]	309 Electrike [52]	310 Manectric [66]
	311 Plusle [42]	312 Minun [42]	466 Electivire [55]	642 Thundurus [67]	644 Zekrom [78]	
Thunder Fang	024 Arbok [1]	059 Arcanine [1]	111 Rhyhorn [E]	135 Jolteon [21]	142 Aerodactyl [1]	208 Steelix [1]
	209 Snubbull [1, E]	210 Granbull [1]	228 Houndour [E]	229 Houndoom [1]	232 Donphan [1]	243 Raikou [50]
	248 Tyranitar [1]	261 Poochyena [E]	295 Exploud [1]	303 Mawile [E]	309 Electrike [33, E]	310 Manectric [37]
	373 Salamence [1]	403 Shinx [29, E]	404 Luxio [33]	405 Luxray [35]	450 Hippowdon [1]	452 Drapion [1]
	472 Gliscor [E]	506 Lillipup [1]	508 Stoutland [1]	551 Sandile [E]	621 Druddigon [E]	632 Durant [E]
	633 Deino [E]	644 Zekrom [1]				
Thunder Wave	TM73	025 Pikachu [10]	081 Magnemite [15]	082 Magneton [15]	125 Electabuzz [19]	135 Jolteon [33]
	145 Zapdos [8]	147 Dratini [5]	148 Dragonair [1, 5]	149 Dragonite [1, 5]	170 Chinchou [6]	171 Lanturn [1, 6]
	172 Pichu [10]	179 Mareep [4]	180 Flaaffy [1, 4]	181 Ampharos [1, 4]	239 Elekid [19]	299 Nosepass [15]
	309 Electrike [4]	310 Manectric [1, 4]	311 Plusle [3]	312 Minun [3]	417 Pachirisu [33]	462 Magnezone [15]
	466 Electivire [19]	476 Probopass [15]	479 Rotom [1]	479 Rotom (Heat) [1]	479 Rotom (Wash) [1]	479 Rotom (Frst) [1]
	479 Rotom (Fan) [1]	479 Rotom (Mow) [1]	522 Blitzle [15]	523 Zebstrika [1, 15]	595 Joltik [4]	596 Galvantula [1, 4]
	602 Tynamo [1]	603 Eelektrik [1]				

Move	Pokémon that can learn it					
Thunderbolt	TM24	025 Pikachu [29]	026 Raichu [1]	125 Electabuzz [49]	239 Elekid [40]	466 Electivire [49]
	603 Eelektrik [44]	618 Stunfisk [45]	644 Zekrom [22]			
ThunderPunch	Taught by someone	063 Abra [E]	066 Machop [E]	092 Gastly [E]	096 Drowzee [E]	107 Hitmonchan [36]
	125 Electabuzz [29]	149 Dragonite [1]	172 Pichu [E]	181 Ampharos [30]	239 Elekid [29]	240 Magby [E]
	307 Meditite [E]	308 Medicham [1]	356 Dusclops [E]	390 Chimchar [E]	427 Buneary [E]	466 Electivire [29]
	467 Magmortar [1]	477 Dusknoir [1]	486 Regigigas [1]	559 Scraggy [E]		
ThunderShock	025 Pikachu [1]	026 Raichu [1]	081 Magnemite [7]	082 Magneton [1, 7]	125 Electabuzz [1, 5]	135 Jolteon [9]
	145 Zapdos [1]	172 Pichu [1]	179 Mareep [8]	180 Flaaffy [1, 8]	181 Ampharos [1, 8]	239 Elekid [5]
	243 Raikou [8]	462 Magnezone [1, 7]	466 Electivire [1, 5]	479 Rotom [1]	479 Rotom (Heat) [1]	479 Rotom (Wash) [1]
	479 Rotom (Frst) [1]	479 Rotom (Fan) [1]	479 Rotom (Mow) [1]	587 Emolga [1]	599 Klink [11]	600 Klang [1, 11]
	601 Klinklang [1, 11]	618 Stunfisk [9]	642 Thundurus [1]			
Tickle	043 Oddish [E]	066 Machop [E]	069 Bellsprout [E]	072 Tentacool [E]	098 Krabby [E]	114 Tangela [46]
	131 Lapras [E]	133 Eevee [E]	138 Omanyte [43]	139 Omastar [48]	172 Pichu [E]	173 Cleffa [E]
	190 Aipom [15]	263 Zigzagoon [E]	270 Lotad [E]	287 Slakoth [E]	298 Azurill [E]	300 Skitty [E]
	303 Mawile [E]	320 Wailmer [E]	340 Whiscash [1]	345 Lileep [E]	349 Feebas [E]	387 Turtwig [E]
	420 Cherubi [E]	424 Ambipom [15]	439 Mime Jr. [1]	456 Finneon [E]	465 Tangrowth [46]	511 Pansage [E]
	513 Pansear [E]	515 Panpour [E]	546 Cottonee [E]	572 Minccino [9]	573 Cinccino [1]	574 Gothita [7]
	575 Gothorita [1, 7]	576 Gothitelle [1, 7]	587 Emolga [E]	594 Alomomola [E]	631 Heatmor [E]	
Torment	TM41	198 Murkrow [61]	274 Nuzleaf [25]	390 Chimchar [25]	391 Monferno [29]	509 Purrloin [19]
	510 Liepard [19]	511 Pansage [25]	551 Sandile [10]	552 Krokorok [10]	553 Krookodile [10]	570 Zorua [33]
	571 Zoroark [34]	624 Pawniard [14]	625 Bisharp [1, 14]			
Toxic	TM06	269 Dustox [38]	315 Roselia [40]	316 Gulpin [28]	317 Swalot [30]	416 Vespiquen [33]
	434 Stunky [27]	435 Skuntank [27]	543 Venipede [36]	544 Whirlipede [41]	545 Scolipede [44]	568 Trubbish [36]
	569 Garbodor [39]	590 Foongus [32]	591 Amoonguss [32]			
Toxic Spikes	015 Beedrill [25]	029 Nidoran ♀ [31]	030 Nidorina [35]	032 Nidoran ♂ [31]	033 Nidorino [35]	048 Venonat [E]
	072 Tentacool [15]	073 Tentacruel [15]	091 Cloyster [1]	138 Omanyte [E]	167 Spinarak [E]	204 Pineco [E]
	205 Forretress [1]	211 Qwilfish [1]	315 Roselia [28]	451 Skorupi [34]	452 Drapion [34]	543 Venipede [E]
	568 Trubbish [7]	569 Garbodor [1, 7]				
Transform	132 Ditto [1]	151 Mew [1]				
Tri Attack	021 Spearow [E]	051 Dugtrio [1]	082 Magneton [1]	085 Dodrio [34]	137 Porygon [51]	233 Porygon2 [51]
	474 Porygon-Z [51]	635 Hydreigon [1]	649 Genesect [44]			
Trick	Taught by someone	064 Kadabra [52]	065 Alakazam [52]	122 Mr. Mime [36, E]	161 Sentret [E]	263 Zigzagoon [E]
	302 Sableye [E]	313 Volbeat [E]	325 Spoink [E]	327 Spinda [E]	352 Kecleon [E]	353 Shuppet [50]
	354 Banette [58]	439 Mime Jr. [36, E]	479 Rotom [1]	479 Rotom (Heat) [1]	479 Rotom (Wash) [1]	479 Rotom (Frst) [1]
	479 Rotom (Fan) [1]	479 Rotom (Mow) [1]	577 Solosis [E]			
Trick Room	TM92	474 Porygon-Z [1]				
Triple Kick	237 Hitmontop [19]					
Trump Card	083 Farfetch'd [E]	115 Kangaskhan [E]	133 Eevee [45]	199 Slowking [49]	206 Dunsparce [E]	312 Minun [51]
	341 Corphish [E]	422 Shellos [E]	501 Oshawott [E]			
Twineedle	015 Beedrill [16]	090 Shellder [E]	167 Spinarak [E]	451 Skorupi [E]	543 Venipede [E]	589 Escavalier [1, 13]
Twister	016 Pidgey [E]	017 Pidgeotto [22]	018 Pidgeot [22]	116 Horsea [26]	117 Seadra [26]	130 Gyarados [29]
	147 Dratini [11]	148 Dragonair [1, 11]	149 Dragonite [1, 11]	226 Mantine [E]	230 Kingdra [26]	278 Wingull [E]
	350 Milotic [17]	371 Bagon [E]	384 Rayquaza [1]	443 Gible [E]	458 Mantyke [E]	495 Snivy [E]

Move	Pokémon that can learn it					
Uproar	Taught by someone	016 Pidgey [E]	019 Rattata [E]	021 Spearow [E]	050 Diglett [E]	084 Doduo [23]
	085 Dodrio [23]	102 Exeggcute [1]	115 Kangaskhan [E]	163 Hoothoot [13]	164 Noctowl [13]	193 Yanma [27]
	258 Mudkip [E]	271 Lombre [37]	288 Vigoroth [1, 13]	293 Whismur [5]	294 Loudred [1, 5]	295 Exploud [1, 5]
	300 Skitty [E]	309 Electrike [E]	327 Spinda [E]	358 Chimecho [17]	396 Starly [E]	433 Chingling [17]
	441 Chatot [45]	469 Yanmega [27]	479 Rotom [8]	479 Rotom (Heat) [8]	479 Rotom (Wash) [8]	479 Rotom (Frst) [8]
	479 Rotom (Fan) [8]	479 Rotom (Mow) [8]	482 Azelf [31]	519 Pidove [E]	535 Tympole [23]	536 Palpitoad [23]
	537 Seismitoad [23]	550 Basculin [4]	551 Sandile [E]	554 Darumaka [17]	574 Gothita [E]	582 Vanillite [10]
	583 Vanillish [1, 10]	584 Vanilluxe [1, 10]	641 Tornadus [1]	642 Thundurus [1]		
U-turn	TM89	187 Hoppip [37]	188 Skiploom [44]	189 Jumpluff [49]	193 Yanma [49]	207 Gligar [30]
	456 Finneon [42]	457 Lumineon [48]	469 Yanmega [49]	472 Gliscor [30]	566 Archen [41]	567 Archeops [45]
	571 Zoroark [1]	617 Accelgor [40]	619 Mienfoo [41]	620 Mienshao [41]		

Move	Pokémon that can learn it					
V-create	—					
Vacuum Wave	107 Hitmonchan [26]	123 Scyther [1]	236 Tyrogue [E]	447 Riolu [E]	453 Croagunk [E]	
Venoshock	TM09	336 Seviper [20]	451 Skorupi [27]	452 Drapion [27]	453 Croagunk [36]	454 Toxicroak [36]
	543 Venipede [26]	544 Whirlipede [28]	545 Scolipede [28]			
ViceGrip	098 Krabby [5]	099 Kingler [1,5]	127 Pinsir [1]	303 Mawile [21]	341 Corphish [10]	342 Crawdaunt [1,10]
	599 Klink [1]	600 Klang [1]	601 Klinklang [1]	632 Durant [1]		
Vine Whip	001 Bulbasaur [9]	002 Ivysaur [9]	003 Venusaur [1, 9]	069 Bellsprout [1]	070 Weepinbell [1]	071 Victreebel [1]
	114 Tangela [7]	152 Chikorita [E]	455 Carnivine [11]	465 Tangrowth [7]	495 Snivy [7]	496 Servine [1, 7]
	497 Serperior [1, 7]	511 Pansage [10]				
Vital Throw	066 Machop [31]	067 Machoke [32]	068 Machamp [32]	127 Pinsir [22]	296 Makuhita [10]	297 Hariyama [10]
	538 Throh [17]	619 Mienfoo [E]				
Volt Switch	TM72	587 Emolga [42]				
Volt Tackle	—					

Pokémon Moves Reverse Lookup

W

Move	Pokémon that can learn it					
Wake-Up Slap	035 Clefairy [22]	039 Jigglypuff [41]	060 Poliwag [35]	061 Poliwhirl [43]	066 Machop [37]	067 Machoke [40]
	068 Machamp [40]	122 Mr. Mime [E]	124 Jynx [33]	238 Smoochum [E]	241 Miltank [55]	285 Shroomish [E]
	296 Makuhita [34, E]	297 Hariyama [42]	300 Skitty [32]	431 Glameow [E]	439 Mime Jr. [E]	453 Croagunk [E]
	478 Froslass [28]	532 Timburr [20]	533 Gurdurr [20]	534 Conkeldurr [20]	572 Minccino [31]	594 Alomomola [29]
Water Gun	007 Squirtle [13]	008 Wartortle [13]	009 Blastoise [13]	054 Psyduck [8]	055 Golduck [1,8]	060 Poliwag [11]
	061 Poliwhirl [11]	079 Slowpoke [11]	080 Slowbro [11]	116 Horsea [11]	117 Seadra [1,11]	120 Staryu [6]
	121 Starmie [1]	131 Lapras [1]	134 Vaporeon [9]	138 Omanyte [10]	139 Omastar [10]	158 Totodile [6]
	159 Croconaw [1,6]	160 Feraligatr [1,6]	170 Chinchou [17]	171 Lanturn [12]	183 Marill [7]	184 Azumarill [7]
	194 Wooper [1]	195 Quagsire [1]	199 Slowking [9]	211 Qwilfish [13]	223 Remoraid [1]	224 Octillery [1]
	230 Kingdra [1,11]	258 Mudkip [10]	259 Marshtomp [1,10]	260 Swampert [1,10]	270 Lotad [E]	278 Wingull [1]
	279 Pelipper [1]	298 Azurill [7]	320 Wailmer [7]	321 Wailord [1,7]	339 Barboach [10]	340 Whiscash [10]
	347 Anorith [13]	348 Armaldo [1,13]	350 Milotic [1]	351 Castform [1]	363 Spheal [1]	364 Sealeo [1]
	365 Walrein [1]	366 Clamperl [1]	369 Relicanth [8]	370 Luvdisc [7]	400 Bibarel [15]	418 Buizel [15]
	419 Floatzel [15]	456 Finneon [6]	457 Lumineon [1,6]	501 Oshawott [7]	502 Dewott [1,7]	503 Samurott [1,7]
	515 Panpour [10]	550 Basculin [1]	564 Tirtouga [1]	565 Carracosta [1]	580 Ducklett [1]	581 Swanna [1]
Water Pledge	Taught by someone					
Water Pulse	007 Squirtle [25]	008 Wartortle [28]	009 Blastoise [28]	054 Psyduck [18]	055 Golduck [18]	060 Poliwag [E]
	072 Tentacool [33]	073 Tentacruel [34]	079 Slowpoke [28]	080 Slowbro [28]	086 Seel [E]	090 Shellder [E]
	116 Horsea [E]	118 Goldeen [17]	119 Seaking [17]	131 Lapras [14]	134 Vaporeon [17]	138 Omanyte [17]
	147 Dratini [E]	158 Totodile [E]	170 Chinchou [E]	199 Slowking [28]	211 Qwilfish [E]	222 Corsola [E]
	223 Remoraid [26, E]	226 Mantine [19]	278 Wingull [17]	279 Pelipper [17]	320 Wailmer [21]	321 Wailord [21]
	327 Spinda [E]	339 Barboach [22]	340 Whiscash [22]	347 Anorith [E]	350 Milotic [13]	363 Spheal [E]
	366 Clamperl [E]	367 Huntail [15]	368 Gorebyss [15]	370 Luvdisc [22]	382 Kyogre [1]	422 Shellos [7]
	423 Gastrodon [1,7]	456 Finneon [22]	457 Lumineon [22]	458 Mantyke [19]	484 Palkia [6]	489 Phione [46]
	490 Manaphy [46]	501 Oshawott [25]	502 Dewott [25]	503 Samurott [25]	535 Tympole [E]	564 Tirtouga [E]
	580 Ducklett [13]	581 Swanna [13]	582 Vanillite [E]	592 Frillish [22]	593 Jellicent [22]	594 Alomomola [25]
Water Sport	054 Psyduck [1]	055 Golduck [1]	060 Poliwag [1, E]	061 Poliwhirl [1]	086 Seel [7]	118 Goldeen [1]
	119 Seaking [1]	158 Totodile [E]	183 Marill [5, E]	184 Azumarill [1,5]	226 Mantine [E]	271 Lombre [19]
	278 Wingull [E]	279 Pelipper [1]	283 Surskit [19]	284 Masquerain [1,19]	298 Azurill [5, E]	339 Barboach [6]
	340 Whiscash [1,6]	350 Milotic [5]	363 Spheal [E]	369 Relicanth [E]	370 Luvdisc [E]	380 Latias [25]
	393 Piplup [11]	394 Prinplup [E]	399 Bidoof [E]	406 Budew [7]	418 Buizel [7]	419 Floatzel [1,7]
	458 Mantyke [E]	489 Phione [1]	490 Manaphy [1]	501 Oshawott [11]	502 Dewott [1,11]	503 Samurott [1,11]
	515 Panpour [16]	580 Ducklett [3]	581 Swanna [1,3]	592 Frillish [1]	593 Jellicent [1]	594 Alomomola [1]
	007 Squirtle [E]	223 Remoraid [E]	320 Wailmer [34]	321 Wailord [34]	382 Kyogre [50]	592 Frillish [61]
	593 Jellicent [69]					
Waterfall	HM05	118 Goldeen [37]	119 Seaking [40]			
Weather Ball	069 Bellsprout [E]	249 Lugia [1]	250 Ho-Oh [1]	351 Castform [30]	361 Snorunt [E]	407 Roserade [1]
	420 Cherubi [E]	425 Drifloon [E]	584 Vanilluxe [1]			
Whirlpool	090 Shellder [40]	131 Lapras [E]	138 Omanyte [E]	170 Chinchou [E]	258 Mudkip [33, E]	320 Wailmer [14]
	321 Wailord [14]	339 Barboach [E]	366 Clamperl [E]	367 Huntail [1]	368 Gorebyss [1]	393 Piplup [32]
	394 Prinplup [37]	395 Empoleon [39]	418 Buizel [31]	419 Floatzel [35]	456 Finneon [38]	457 Lumineon [42]
	489 Phione [39]	490 Manaphy [39]	550 Basculin [1]	564 Tirtouga [1]		
Whirlwind	012 Butterfree [22]	016 Pidgey [17]	017 Pidgeotto [17]	018 Pidgeot [17]	021 Spearow [E]	041 Zubat [E]
	142 Aerodactyl [E]	143 Snorlax [E]	163 Hoothoot [E]	193 Yanma [E]	198 Murkrow [E]	227 Skarmory [E]
	249 Lugia [1]	250 Ho-Oh [1]	267 Beautifly [27]	269 Dustox [27]	275 Shiftry [1]	276 Taillow [E]
	284 Masquerain [54]	296 Makuhita [16]	297 Hariyama [16]	325 Spoink [E]	357 Tropius [27]	396 Starly [21]
	397 Staravia [23]	398 Staraptor [23]	408 Cranidos [E]	446 Munchlax [E]	449 Hippopotas [E]	451 Skorupi [E]
	561 Sigilyph [14]	627 Rufflet [55]	628 Braviary [57]	629 Vullaby [55]	630 Mandibuzz [57]	637 Volcarona [40]
Wide Guard	068 Machamp [1]	099 Kingler [1]	106 Hitmonlee [41]	122 Mr. Mime [1]	226 Mantine [23, E]	237 Hitmontop [1]
	258 Mudkip [E]	296 Makuhita [E]	387 Turtwig [E]	410 Shieldon [E]	458 Mantyke [23, E]	486 Regigigas [40]
	532 Timburr [E]	538 Throh [45]	564 Tirtouga [25]	565 Carracosta [25]	594 Alomomola [53]	620 Mienshao [45]
Wild Charge	TM93	309 Electrike [49]	310 Manectric [61]	403 Shinx [45]	404 Luxio [53]	405 Luxray [63]
	522 Blitzle [39]	523 Zebstrika [47]	603 Eelektrik [59]			
Will-O-Wisp	TM61	037 Vulpix [26]	353 Shuppet [13]	354 Banette [13]	355 Duskull [33]	356 Dusclops [33]
	477 Dusknoir [33]	562 Yamask [21]	563 Cofagrigus [21]	607 Litwick [16]	608 Lampent [16]	
Wing Attack	006 Charizard [36]	016 Pidgey [33]	017 Pidgeotto [37]	018 Pidgeot [38]	041 Zubat [15]	042 Golbat [15]
	123 Scyther [21]	142 Aerodactyl [1]	146 Moltres [1]	149 Dragonite [55]	163 Hoothoot [E]	169 Crobat [15]
	193 Yanma [43]	198 Murkrow [15, E]	207 Gligar [E]	226 Mantine [14]	276 Taillow [13]	277 Swellow [13]
	278 Wingull [9]	279 Pelipper [1, 9]	396 Starly [9]	397 Staravia [9]	398 Staraptor [1, 9]	430 Honchkrow [1]
	458 Mantyke [14]	566 Archen [1]	567 Archeops [1]	580 Ducklett [9]	581 Swanna [1, 9]	627 Rufflet [10]
	628 Braviary [1, 10]					
Wish	133 Eevee [E]	172 Pichu [E]	173 Cleffa [E]	174 Igglybuff [E]	175 Togepi [29]	176 Togetic [29]
	177 Natu [28]	178 Xatu [30]	203 Girafarig [E]	238 Smoochum [E]	282 Gardevoir [17]	300 Skitty [E]
	311 Plusle [E]	312 Minun [E]	314 Illumise [21]	327 Spinda [E]	358 Chimecho [E]	380 Latias [5]
	385 Jirachi [1]	433 Chingling [E]	519 Pidove [E]	531 Audino [E]	594 Alomomola [37]	
Withdraw	007 Squirtle [10]	008 Wartortle [10]	009 Blastoise [1, 10]	080 Slowbro [37]	090 Shellder [4]	091 Cloyster [1]
	138 Omanyte [1]	139 Omastar [1]	213 Shuckle [1]	324 Torkoal [7]	387 Turtwig [5]	388 Grotle [1, 5]
	389 Torterra [1, 5]	557 Dwebble [7]	558 Crustle [1, 7]	564 Tirtouga [1]	565 Carracosta [1]	
Wonder Room	Taught by someone	054 Psyduck [50]	055 Golduck [60]	079 Slowpoke [E]	200 Misdreavus [E]	338 Solrock [53]
	577 Solosis [48]	578 Duosion [53]	579 Reuniclus [59]	605 Elgyem [56]	606 Beheeyem [68]	
Wood Hammer	103 Exeggutor [37]	185 Sudowoodo [1]	389 Torterra [1]	459 Snover [36]	460 Abomasnow [36]	556 Maractus [E]
Work Up	TM83	128 Tauros [29]	504 Patrat [26]	506 Lillipup [19]	507 Herdier [20]	508 Stoutland [20]
	554 Darumaka [25]	555 Darmanitan [25]	633 Deino [38]	634 Zweilous [38]	635 Hydreigon [38]	638 Cobalion [61]
	639 Terrakion [61]	640 Virizion [61]	647 Keldeo [61]			

Move	Pokémon that can learn it					
Worry Seed	Taught by someone	001 Bulbasaur [31]	002 Ivysaur [36]	003 Venusaur [39]	069 Bellsprout [E]	102 Exeggcute [33]
	187 Hoppip [40, E]	188 Skiploom [48]	189 Jumpluff [54]	191 Sunkern [19]	192 Sunflora [19]	252 Treecko [E]
	273 Seedot [E]	285 Shroomish [29, E]	331 Cacnea [E]	387 Turtwig [E]	406 Budew [16]	420 Cherubi [28]
	421 Cherrim [30]	455 Carnivine [E]	492 Shaymin (Land) [55]	492 Shaymin (Sky) [55]	546 Cottonee [E]	548 Petilil [E]
	556 Maractus [E]	585 Deerling [E]	597 Ferroseed [E]			
Wrap	023 Ekans [1]	024 Arbok [1]	069 Bellsprout [11]	070 Weepinbell [1,11]	072 Tentacool [22]	073 Tentacruel [22]
	108 Lickitung [17]	147 Dratini [1]	148 Dragonair [1]	149 Dragonite [1]	213 Shuckle [9]	336 Seviper [1]
	350 Milotic [1]	358 Chimecho [1]	386 Deoxys (Nor) [1]	386 Deoxys (Atk) [1]	386 Deoxys (Def) [1]	386 Deoxys (Spd) [1]
	433 Chingling [1]	463 Lickilicky [17]	495 Snivy [10]	496 Servine [1,10]	497 Serperior [1,10]	631 Heatmor [E]
Wring Out	069 Bellsprout [47]	070 Weepinbell [47]	072 Tentacool [54]	073 Tentacruel [61]	108 Lickitung [57]	114 Tangela [49]
	124 Jynx [49]	138 Omanyte [51]	140 Kabuto [51]	141 Kabutops [63]	152 Chikorita [E]	224 Octillery [28]
	316 Gulpin [54]	317 Swalot [66]	336 Seviper [53, E]	345 Lileep [64, E]	346 Cradily [76]	455 Carnivine [47]
	463 Lickilicky [57]	465 Tangrowth [49]	495 Snivy [37]	496 Servine [44]	497 Serperior [50]	592 Frillish [55]
	593 Jellicent [61]					

Move	Pokémon that can learn it					
X-Scissor	TM81	046 Paras [54]	047 Parasect [66]	123 Scyther [41]	127 Pinsir [29]	207 Gligar [40]
	212 Scizor [41]	254 Sceptile [16]	291 Ninjask [52]	335 Zangoose [36]	347 Anorith [61]	348 Armaldo [73]
	402 Kricketune [30]	472 Gliscor [40]	542 Leavanny [39]	557 Dwebble [35]	558 Crustle [38]	588 Karrablast [44]
	589 Escavalier [44]	632 Durant [51]	649 Genesect [51]			

Move	Pokémon that can learn it					
Yawn	007 Squirtle [E]	054 Psyduck [E]	079 Slowpoke [1]	080 Slowbro [1]	133 Eevee [E]	143 Snorlax [20]
	175 Togepi [13]	176 Togetic [13]	194 Wooper [29]	195 Quagsire [31]	199 Slowking [1]	206 Dunsparce [16]
	216 Teddiursa [E]	218 Slugma [1]	219 Magcargo [1]	230 Kingdra [1]	258 Mudkip [E]	261 Poochyena [E]
	287 Slakoth [1]	289 Slaking [1]	316 Gulpin [6]	317 Swalot [1, 6]	322 Numel [36, E]	323 Camerupt [39]
	324 Torkoal [E]	358 Chimecho [25]	363 Spheal [E]	369 Relicanth [22]	393 Piplup [E]	399 Bidoof [25]
	400 Bibarel [28]	422 Shellos [E]	449 Hippopotas [13]	450 Hippowdon [1, 13]	480 Uxie [31]	498 Tepig [E]
	506 Lillipup [E]	509 Purrloin [E]	513 Pansear [16]	517 Munna [7]	531 Audino [E]	554 Darumaka [E]
	613 Cubchoo [E]	616 Shelmet [25]	618 Stunfisk [E]			

Move	Pokémon that can learn it					
Zap Cannon	081 Magnemite [57]	082 Magneton [73]	137 Porygon [62]	145 Zapdos [92]	205 Forretress [64]	233 Porygon2 [62]
	299 Nosepass [50]	377 Regirock [65]	378 Regice [65]	379 Registeel [65]	386 Deoxys (Atk) [81]	462 Magnezone [73]
	474 Porygon-Z [62]	476 Probopass [50]	599 Klink [54]	600 Klang [60]	601 Klinklang [66]	603 Eelektrik [69]
	649 Genesect [66]					
Zen Headbutt	Taught by someone	041 Zubat [E]	048 Venonat [37]	049 Venomoth [41]	054 Psyduck [29]	055 Golduck [29]
	079 Slowpoke [32, E]	080 Slowbro [32]	096 Drowzee [41]	097 Hypno [41]	108 Lickitung [E]	128 Tauros [35]
	163 Hoothoot [37]	164 Noctowl [42]	177 Natu [E]	199 Slowking [32]	203 Girafarig [41]	234 Stantler [38, E]
	241 Miltank [29]	270 Lotad [31]	271 Lombre [31]	300 Skitty [E]	302 Sableye [53]	313 Volbeat [37]
	314 Illumise [37]	320 Wailmer [E]	325 Spoink [26, E]	326 Grumpig [26]	340 Whiscash [1]	359 Absol [E]
	369 Relicanth [E]	371 Bagon [35]	372 Shelgon [37]	373 Salamence [37]	375 Metang [29]	376 Metagross [29]
	380 Latias [40]	381 Latios [40]	385 Jirachi [35]	386 Deoxys (Nor) [65]	386 Deoxys (Atk) [65]	386 Deoxys (Def) [65]
	386 Deoxys (Spd) [65]	408 Cranidos [37]	409 Rampardos [43]	446 Munchlax [E]	486 Regigigas [50]	494 Victini [49]
	517 Munna [23]	559 Scraggy [E]	605 Elgyem [32]	606 Beheeyem [32]	636 Larvesta [E]	644 Zekrom [43]

Pokémon Abilities Reverse Lookup

Hidden Abilities are listed as well. Form(e) names of Pokémon such as Giratina, Shaymin, Basculin, Tornadus, Thundurus, Landorus, Kyurem, etc. are abbreviated in parentheses.

A

Ability	Pokémon that have this Ability					
Adaptability	133 Eevee	341 Corphish	342 Crawdaunt	349 Feebas	474 Porygon-Z	550 Basculin (Red)
	550 Basculin (Blue)					
Aftermath	100 Voltorb	101 Electrode	425 Drifloon	426 Drifblim	434 Stunky	435 Skuntank
	568 Trubbish	569 Garbodor				
Air Lock	384 Rayquaza					
Analytic	081 Magnemite	082 Magneton	120 Staryu	121 Starmie	137 Porygon	233 Porygon2
	462 Magnezone	474 Porygon-Z	504 Patrat	505 Watchog	605 Elgyem	606 Beheeyem
Anger Point	056 Mankey	057 Primeape	128 Tauros	323 Camerupt	551 Sandile	552 Krokorok
	553 Krookodile					
Anticipation	133 Eevee	339 Barboach	340 Whiscash	413 Wormadam	453 Croagunk	454 Toxicroak
Arena Trap	050 Diglett	051 Dugtrio	328 Trapinch			

B

Ability	Pokémon that have this Ability					
Bad Dreams	491 Darkrai					
Battle Armor	104 Cubone	105 Marowak	140 Kabuto	141 Kabutops	347 Anorith	348 Armaldo
	451 Skorupi	452 Drapion				
Big Pecks	016 Pidgey	017 Pidgeotto	018 Pidgeot	441 Chatot	519 Pidove	520 Tranquill
	521 Unfezant	580 Ducklett	581 Swanna	629 Vullaby	630 Mandibuzz	
Blaze	004 Charmander	005 Charmeleon	006 Charizard	155 Cyndaquil	156 Quilava	157 Typhlosion
	255 Torchic	256 Combusken	257 Blaziken	390 Chimchar	391 Monferno	392 Infernape
	498 Tepig	499 Pignite	500 Emboar			

C

Ability	Pokémon that have this Ability					
Chlorophyll	001 Bulbasaur	002 Ivysaur	003 Venusaur	043 Oddish	044 Gloom	045 Vileplume
	069 Bellsprout	070 Weepinbell	071 Victreebel	102 Exeggcute	103 Exeggutor	114 Tangela
	182 Bellossom	187 Hoppip	188 Skiploom	189 Jumpluff	191 Sunkern	192 Sunflora
	273 Seedot	274 Nuzleaf	275 Shiftry	357 Tropius	420 Cherubi	465 Tangrowth
	470 Leafeon	540 Sewaddle	541 Swadloon	542 Leavanny	546 Cottonee	547 Whimsicott
	548 Petilil	549 Lilligant	556 Maractus	585 Deerling	586 Sawsbuck	
Clear Body	072 Tentacool	073 Tentacruel	374 Beldum	375 Metang	376 Metagross	377 Regirock
	378 Regice	379 Registeel	600 Klang	601 Klinklang		
Cloud Nine	054 Psyduck	055 Golduck	108 Lickitung	333 Swablu	334 Altaria	463 Lickilicky
Color Change	352 Kecleon					
Compoundeyes	012 Butterfree	048 Venonat	193 Yanma	290 Nincada	595 Joltik	596 Galvantula
Contrary	213 Shuckle	327 Spinda				
Cursed Body	353 Shuppet	354 Banette	478 Froslass	592 Frillish	593 Jellicent	
Cute Charm	035 Clefairy	036 Clefable	039 Jigglypuff	040 Wigglytuff	173 Cleffa	174 Igglybuff
	300 Skitty	301 Delcatty	350 Milotic	428 Lopunny	572 Minccino	573 Cinccino

D

Ability	Pokémon that have this Ability					
Damp	054 Psyduck	055 Golduck	060 Poliwag	061 Poliwhirl	062 Poliwrath	116 Horsea
	117 Seadra	186 Politoed	194 Wooper	195 Quagsire	230 Kingdra	258 Mudkip
	259 Marshtomp	260 Swampert	592 Frillish	593 Jellicent		
Defeatist	566 Archen	567 Archeops				
Defiant	056 Mankey	057 Primeape	083 Farfetch'd	393 Piplup	394 Prinplup	395 Empoleon
	432 Purugly	624 Pawniard	625 Bisharp	628 Braviary	641 Tornadus (Incr)	642 Thundurus (Incr)
Download	137 Porygon	233 Porygon2	474 Porygon-Z	649 Genesect		
Drizzle	186 Politoed	382 Kyogre				
Drought	037 Vulpix	038 Ninetales	383 Groudon			
Dry Skin	046 Paras	047 Parasect	124 Jynx	453 Croagunk	454 Toxicroak	

E

Ability	Pokémon that have this Ability					
Early Bird	084 Doduo	085 Dodrio	115 Kangaskhan	165 Ledyba	166 Ledian	177 Natu
	178 Xatu	191 Sunkern	192 Sunflora	203 Girafarig	228 Houndour	229 Houndoom
	273 Seedot	274 Nuzleaf	275 Shiftry			
Effect Spore	045 Vileplume	046 Paras	047 Parasect	285 Shroomish	286 Breloom	590 Foongus
	591 Amoonguss					

Ability	Pokémon that have this Ability					
Filter	122 Mr. Mime	439 Mime Jr.				
Flame Body	077 Ponyta	078 Rapidash	126 Magmar	218 Slugma	219 Magcargo	240 Magby
	467 Magmortar	607 Litwick	608 Lampent	609 Chandelure	636 Larvesta	637 Volcarona
Flare Boost	425 Drifloon	426 Drifblim				
Flash Fire	037 Vulpix	038 Ninetales	058 Growlithe	059 Arcanine	077 Ponyta	078 Rapidash
	136 Flareon	228 Houndour	229 Houndoom	485 Heatran	607 Litwick	608 Lampent
	609 Chandelure	631 Heatmor				
Flower Gift	421 Cherrim					
Forecast	351 Castform					
Forewarn	096 Drowzee	097 Hypno	124 Jynx	238 Smoochum	517 Munna	518 Musharna
Friend Guard	035 Clefairy	039 Jigglypuff	173 Cleffa	174 Igglybuff	440 Happiny	
Frisk	040 Wigglytuff	161 Sentret	162 Furret	193 Yanma	234 Stantler	353 Shuppet
	354 Banette	469 Yanmega	574 Gothita	575 Gothorita	576 Gothitelle	

Ability	Pokémon that have this Ability					
Gluttony	069 Bellsprout	070 Weepinbell	071 Victreebel	143 Snorlax	213 Shuckle	263 Zigzagoon
	264 Linoone	325 Spoink	326 Grumpig	446 Munchlax	511 Pansage	512 Simisage
	513 Pansear	514 Simisear	515 Panpour	516 Simipour	631 Heatmor	
Guts	019 Rattata	020 Raticate	066 Machop	067 Machoke	068 Machamp	136 Flareon
	214 Heracross	217 Ursaring	236 Tyrogue	246 Larvitar	276 Taillow	277 Swellow
	296 Makuhita	297 Hariyama	403 Shinx	404 Luxio	405 Luxray	532 Timburr
	533 Gurdurr	534 Conkeldurr	538 Throh			

Ability	Pokémon that have this Ability					
Harvest	102 Exeggcute	103 Exeggutor	357 Tropius			
Healer	113 Chansey	182 Bellossom	242 Blissey	531 Audino	594 Alomomola	
Heatproof	436 Bronzor	437 Bronzong				
Heavy Metal	304 Aron	305 Lairon	306 Aggron	436 Bronzor	437 Bronzong	
Honey Gather	216 Teddiursa	415 Combee				
Huge Power	183 Marill	184 Azumarill	298 Azurill			
Hustle	019 Rattata	020 Raticate	029 Nidoran ♀	030 Nidorina	032 Nidoran ♂	033 Nidorino
	175 Togepi	176 Togetic	222 Corsola	223 Remoraid	225 Delibird	415 Combee
	468 Togekiss	554 Darumaka	632 Durant	633 Deino	634 Zweilous	
Hydration	086 Seel	087 Dewgong	131 Lapras	134 Vaporeon	238 Smoochum	339 Barboach
	340 Whiscash	368 Gorebyss	370 Luvdisc	489 Phione	490 Manaphy	535 Tympole
	536 Palpitoad	580 Ducklett	581 Swanna	594 Alomomola	616 Shelmet	617 Accelgor
Hyper Cutter	098 Krabby	099 Kingler	127 Pinsir	207 Gligar	303 Mawile	328 Trapinch
	341 Corphish	342 Crawdaunt	472 Gliscor			

Ability	Pokémon that have this Ability					
Ice Body	086 Seel	087 Dewgong	361 Snorunt	362 Glalie	363 Spheal	364 Sealeo
	365 Walrein	471 Glaceon	582 Vanillite	583 Vanillish	584 Vanilluxe	
Illuminate	120 Staryu	121 Starmie	170 Chinchou	171 Lanturn	313 Volbeat	505 Watchog
Illusion	570 Zorua	571 Zoroark				
Immunity	143 Snorlax	207 Gligar	335 Zangoose			
Imposter	132 Ditto					
Infiltrator	041 Zubat	042 Golbat	169 Crobat	187 Hoppip	188 Skiploom	189 Jumpluff
	336 Seviper	442 Spiritomb	546 Cottonee	547 Whimsicott		
Inner Focus	041 Zubat	042 Golbat	063 Abra	064 Kadabra	065 Alakazam	083 Farfetch'd
	096 Drowzee	097 Hypno	107 Hitmonchan	115 Kangaskhan	149 Dragonite	169 Crobat
	197 Umbreon	203 Girafarig	215 Sneasel	361 Snorunt	362 Glalie	447 Riolu
	448 Lucario	538 Throh	539 Sawk	554 Darumaka	619 Mienfoo	620 Mienshao
	624 Pawniard	625 Bisharp				
Insomnia	096 Drowzee	097 Hypno	163 Hoothoot	164 Noctowl	167 Spinarak	168 Ariados
	198 Murkrow	225 Delibird	353 Shuppet	354 Banette	430 Honchkrow	
Intimidate	023 Ekans	024 Arbok	058 Growlithe	059 Arcanine	128 Tauros	130 Gyarados
	209 Snubbull	210 Granbull	211 Qwilfish	234 Stantler	237 Hitmontop	262 Mightyena
	284 Masquerain	303 Mawile	373 Salamence	397 Staravia	398 Staraptor	403 Shinx
	404 Luxio	405 Luxray	507 Herdier	508 Stoutland	551 Sandile	552 Krokorok
	553 Krookodile	645 Landorus (Ther)				
Iron Barbs	597 Ferroseed	598 Ferrothorn				
Iron Fist	107 Hitmonchan	166 Ledian	390 Chimchar	391 Monferno	392 Infernape	622 Golett
	623 Golurk					

Pokémon Abilities Reverse Lookup

J

Ability	Pokémon that have this Ability					
Justified	058 Growlithe	059 Arcanine	359 Absol	448 Lucario	475 Gallade	638 Cobalion
	639 Terrakion	640 Virizion	647 Keldeo			

K

Ability	Pokémon that have this Ability					
Keen Eye	016 Pidgey	017 Pidgeotto	018 Pidgeot	021 Spearow	022 Fearow	083 Farfetch'd
	107 Hitmonchan	161 Sentret	162 Furret	163 Hoothoot	164 Noctowl	215 Sneasel
	227 Skarmory	278 Wingull	279 Pelipper	302 Sableye	396 Starly	431 Glameow
	434 Stunky	435 Skuntank	441 Chatot	451 Skorupi	452 Drapion	504 Patrat
	505 Watchog	580 Ducklett	581 Swanna	627 Rufflet	628 Braviary	
Klutz	427 Buneary	428 Lopunny	527 Woobat	528 Swoobat	622 Golett	623 Golurk

L

Ability	Pokémon that have this Ability					
Leaf Guard	114 Tangela	187 Hoppip	188 Skiploom	189 Jumpluff	465 Tangrowth	470 Leafeon
	541 Swadloon	548 Petilil	549 Lilligant			
Levitate	092 Gastly	093 Haunter	094 Gengar	109 Koffing	110 Weezing	200 Misdreavus
	201 Unown	329 Vibrava	330 Flygon	337 Lunatone	338 Solrock	343 Baltoy
	344 Claydol	355 Duskull	358 Chimecho	380 Latias	381 Latios	429 Mismagius
	433 Chingling	436 Bronzor	437 Bronzong	455 Carnivine	479 Rotom	480 Uxie
	481 Mesprit	482 Azelf	487 Giratina (Ori)	488 Cresselia	602 Tynamo	603 Eelektrik
	604 Eelektross	615 Cryogonal	635 Hydreigon			
Light Metal	212 Scizor	374 Beldum	375 Metang	376 Metagross		
Lightningrod	025 Pikachu	026 Raichu	104 Cubone	105 Marowak	111 Rhyhorn	112 Rhydon
	118 Goldeen	119 Seaking	172 Pichu	309 Electrike	310 Manectric	464 Rhyperior
	522 Blitzle	523 Zebstrika				
Limber	053 Persian	106 Hitmonlee	132 Ditto	427 Buneary	428 Lopunny	431 Glameow
	509 Purrloin	510 Liepard	618 Stunfisk			
Liquid Ooze	072 Tentacool	073 Tentacruel	316 Gulpin	317 Swalot		

M

Ability	Pokémon that have this Ability					
Magic Bounce	177 Natu	178 Xatu	196 Espeon			
Magic Guard	035 Clefairy	036 Clefable	063 Abra	064 Kadabra	065 Alakazam	173 Cleffa
	561 Sigilyph	577 Solosis	578 Duosion	579 Reuniclus		
Magma Armor	218 Slugma	219 Magcargo	323 Camerupt			
Magnet Pull	081 Magnemite	082 Magneton	299 Nosepass	462 Magnezone	476 Probopass	
Marvel Scale	147 Dratini	148 Dragonair	350 Milotic			
Minus	309 Electrike	310 Manectric	312 Minun	599 Klink	600 Klang	601 Klinklang
Mold Breaker	127 Pinsir	408 Cranidos	409 Rampardos	529 Drilbur	530 Excadrill	550 Basculin (Red)
	550 Basculin (Blue)	610 Axew	611 Fraxure	612 Haxorus	621 Druddigon	
Moody	223 Remoraid	224 Octillery	235 Smeargle	361 Snorunt	362 Glalie	399 Bidoof
	400 Bibarel					
Motor Drive	466 Electivire	522 Blitzle	523 Zebstrika	587 Emolga		
Moxie	127 Pinsir	130 Gyarados	214 Heracross	262 Mightyena	373 Salamence	430 Honchkrow
	551 Sandile	552 Krokorok	553 Krookodile	559 Scraggy	560 Scrafty	
Multiscale	149 Dragonite	249 Lugia				
Multitype	493 Arceus					
Mummy	562 Yamask	563 Cofagrigus				

N

Ability	Pokémon that have this Ability					
Natural Cure	113 Chansey	120 Staryu	121 Starmie	222 Corsola	242 Blissey	251 Celebi
	315 Roselia	333 Swablu	334 Altaria	406 Budew	407 Roserade	440 Happiny
	492 Shaymin (Land)					
No Guard	066 Machop	067 Machoke	068 Machamp	588 Karrablast	622 Golett	623 Golurk
Normalize	300 Skitty	301 Delcatty				

O

Ability	Pokémon that have this Ability					
Oblivious	079 Slowpoke	080 Slowbro	108 Lickitung	124 Jynx	199 Slowking	220 Swinub
	221 Piloswine	238 Smoochum	314 Illumise	320 Wailmer	321 Wailord	322 Numel
	339 Barboach	340 Whiscash	363 Spheal	364 Sealeo	365 Walrein	463 Lickilicky
	473 Mamoswine					
Overcoat	090 Shellder	091 Cloyster	372 Shelgon	412 Burmy	413 Wormadam	540 Sewaddle
	541 Swadloon	542 Leavanny	577 Solosis	578 Duosion	579 Reuniclus	589 Escavalier
	616 Shelmet	629 Vullaby	630 Mandibuzz			

Ability	Pokémon that have this Ability					
Overgrow	001 Bulbasaur	002 Ivysaur	003 Venusaur	152 Chikorita	153 Bayleef	154 Meganium
	252 Treecko	253 Grovyle	254 Sceptile	387 Turtwig	388 Grotle	389 Torterra
	495 Snivy	496 Servine	497 Serperior			
Own Tempo	079 Slowpoke	080 Slowbro	108 Lickitung	199 Slowking	235 Smeargle	270 Lotad
	271 Lombre	272 Ludicolo	322 Numel	325 Spoink	326 Grumpig	327 Spinda
	431 Glameow	432 Purugly	463 Lickilicky	548 Petilil	549 Lilligant	

Ability	Pokémon that have this Ability					
Pickpocket	215 Sneasel	461 Weavile				
Pickup	052 Meowth	190 Aipom	216 Teddiursa	231 Phanpy	263 Zigzagoon	264 Linoone
	417 Pachirisu	424 Ambipom	446 Munchlax	506 Lillipup		
Plus	179 Mareep	180 Flaaffy	181 Ampharos	311 Plusle	599 Klink	600 Klang
	601 Klinklang					
Poison Heal	285 Shroomish	286 Breloom	472 Gliscor			
Poison Point	029 Nidoran ♀	030 Nidorina	031 Nidoqueen	032 Nidoran ♂	033 Nidorino	034 Nidoking
	117 Seadra	211 Qwilfish	315 Roselia	406 Budew	407 Roserade	543 Venipede
	544 Whirlipede	545 Scolipede				
Poison Touch	088 Grimer	089 Muk	453 Croagunk	454 Toxicroak	537 Seismitoad	
Prankster	198 Murkrow	302 Sableye	313 Volbeat	314 Illumise	447 Riolu	509 Purrloin
	510 Liepard	546 Cottonee	547 Whimsicott	641 Tornadus (Incr)	642 Thundurus (Incr)	
Pressure	142 Aerodactyl	144 Articuno	145 Zapdos	146 Moltres	150 Mewtwo	243 Raikou
	244 Entei	245 Suicune	249 Lugia	250 Ho-Oh	320 Wailmer	321 Wailord
	356 Dusclops	359 Absol	386 Deoxys	416 Vespiquen	442 Spiritomb	461 Weavile
	477 Dusknoir	483 Dialga	484 Palkia	487 Giratina (Alt)	624 Pawniard	625 Bisharp
	646 Kyurem					
Pure Power	307 Meditite	308 Medicham				

Ability	Pokémon that have this Ability					
Quick Feet	135 Jolteon	210 Granbull	216 Teddiursa	217 Ursaring	261 Poochyena	262 Mightyena
	263 Zigzagoon	264 Linoone	285 Shroomish	543 Venipede	544 Whirlipede	545 Scolipede

Ability	Pokémon that have this Ability					
Rain Dish	007 Squirtle	008 Wartortle	009 Blastoise	072 Tentacool	073 Tentacruel	270 Lotad
	271 Lombre	272 Ludicolo	278 Wingull	279 Pelipper	283 Surskit	
Rattled	129 Magikarp	165 Ledyba	185 Sudowoodo	206 Dunsparce	209 Snubbull	210 Granbull
	261 Poochyena	293 Whismur	366 Clamperl	438 Bonsly	613 Cubchoo	
Reckless	106 Hitmonlee	111 Rhyhorn	112 Rhydon	397 Staravia	398 Staraptor	464 Rhyperior
	550 Basculin (Red)	619 Mienfoo	620 Mienshao	626 Bouffalant		
Regenerator	079 Slowpoke	080 Slowbro	114 Tangela	199 Slowking	222 Corsola	250 Ho-Oh
	465 Tangrowth	531 Audino	577 Solosis	578 Duosion	579 Reuniclus	590 Foongus
	591 Amoonguss	594 Alomomola	619 Mienfoo	620 Mienshao	641 Tornadus (Theri)	
Rivalry	029 Nidoran ♀	030 Nidorina	031 Nidoqueen	032 Nidoran ♂	033 Nidorino	034 Nidoking
	403 Shinx	404 Luxio	405 Luxray	519 Pidove	520 Tranquill	521 Unfezant
	610 Axew	611 Fraxure	612 Haxorus			
Rock Head	074 Geodude	075 Graveler	076 Golem	095 Onix	104 Cubone	105 Marowak
	111 Rhyhorn	112 Rhydon	142 Aerodactyl	185 Sudowoodo	208 Steelix	304 Aron
	305 Lairon	306 Aggron	369 Relicanth	371 Bagon	372 Shelgon	438 Bonsly
	550 Basculin (Blue)					
Rough Skin	318 Carvanha	319 Sharpedo	443 Gible	444 Gabite	445 Garchomp	621 Druddigon
Run Away	010 Caterpie	013 Weedle	019 Rattata	020 Raticate	043 Oddish	048 Venonat
	077 Ponyta	078 Rapidash	084 Doduo	085 Dodrio	133 Eevee	161 Sentret
	162 Furret	190 Aipom	206 Dunsparce	209 Snubbull	261 Poochyena	417 Pachirisu
	427 Buneary	504 Patrat	506 Lillipup			

Ability	Pokémon that have this Ability					
Sand Force	050 Diglett	051 Dugtrio	299 Nosepass	422 Shellos	423 Gastrodon	449 Hippopotas
	450 Hippowdon	476 Probopass	524 Roggenrola	525 Boldore	526 Gigalith	529 Drilbur
	530 Excadrill	645 Landorus (Incr)				
Sand Rush	027 Sandshrew	028 Sandslash	507 Herdier	508 Stoutland	529 Drilbur	530 Excadrill
Sand Stream	248 Tyranitar	449 Hippopotas	450 Hippowdon			
Sand Veil	027 Sandshrew	028 Sandslash	050 Diglett	051 Dugtrio	074 Geodude	075 Graveler
	076 Golem	207 Gligar	231 Phanpy	232 Donphan	246 Larvitar	331 Cacnea
	332 Cacturne	443 Gible	444 Gabite	445 Garchomp	472 Gliscor	618 Stunfisk

Pokémon Abilities Reverse Lookup

Ability	Pokémon that have this Ability					
Sap Sipper	183 Marill	184 Azumarill	203 Girafarig	234 Stantler	241 Miltank	298 Azurill
	522 Blitzle	523 Zebstrika	585 Deerling	586 Sawsbuck	626 Bouffalant	
Scrappy	115 Kangaskhan	241 Miltank	276 Taillow	277 Swellow	294 Loudred	295 Exploud
	507 Herdier	508 Stoutland				
Serene Grace	113 Chansey	175 Togepi	176 Togetic	206 Dunsparce	242 Blissey	385 Jirachi
	440 Happiny	468 Togekiss	492 Shaymin (Sky)	585 Deerling	586 Sawsbuck	648 Meloetta
Shadow Tag	202 Wobbuffet	360 Wynaut	575 Gothorita	576 Gothitelle		
Shed Skin	011 Metapod	014 Kakuna	023 Ekans	024 Arbok	147 Dratini	148 Dragonair
	247 Pupitar	266 Silcoon	268 Cascoon	336 Seviper	401 Kricketot	412 Burmy
	559 Scraggy	560 Scrafty	588 Karrablast			
Sheer Force	031 Nidoqueen	034 Nidoking	098 Krabby	099 Kingler	128 Tauros	208 Steelix
	296 Makuhita	297 Hariyama	303 Mawile	328 Trapinch	371 Bagon	408 Cranidos
	409 Rampardos	532 Timburr	533 Gurdurr	534 Conkeldurr	555 Darmanitan	621 Druddigon
	627 Rufflet	628 Braviary	645 Landorus (Incr)			
Shell Armor	090 Shellder	091 Cloyster	098 Krabby	099 Kingler	131 Lapras	138 Omanyte
	139 Omastar	324 Torkoal	341 Corphish	342 Crawdaunt	366 Clamperl	387 Turtwig
	388 Grotle	389 Torterra	557 Dwebble	558 Crustle	589 Escavalier	616 Shelmet
Shield Dust	010 Caterpie	013 Weedle	049 Venomoth	265 Wurmple	269 Dustox	
Simple	322 Numel	399 Bidoof	400 Bibarel	527 Woobat	528 Swoobat	
Skill Link	090 Shellder	091 Cloyster	572 Minccino	573 Cinccino		
Slow Start	486 Regigigas					
Sniper	015 Beedrill	021 Spearow	022 Fearow	116 Horsea	117 Seadra	167 Spinarak
	168 Ariados	223 Remoraid	224 Octillery	230 Kingdra	451 Skorupi	452 Drapion
Snow Cloak	220 Swinub	221 Piloswine	471 Glaceon	473 Mamoswine	478 Froslass	613 Cubchoo
	614 Beartic					
Snow Warning	459 Snover	460 Abomasnow				
Solar Power	004 Charmander	005 Charmeleon	006 Charizard	191 Sunkern	192 Sunflora	357 Tropius
Solid Rock	323 Camerupt	464 Rhyperior	564 Tirtouga	565 Carracosta		
Soundproof	100 Voltorb	101 Electrode	122 Mr. Mime	293 Whismur	294 Loudred	295 Exploud
	410 Shieldon	411 Bastiodon	439 Mime Jr.	459 Snover	460 Abomasnow	626 Bouffalant
Speed Boost	193 Yanma	255 Torchic	256 Combusken	257 Blaziken	291 Ninjask	318 Carvanha
	319 Sharpedo	469 Yanmega				
Stall	302 Sableye					
Static	025 Pikachu	026 Raichu	100 Voltorb	101 Electrode	125 Electabuzz	172 Pichu
	179 Mareep	180 Flaaffy	181 Ampharos	239 Elekid	309 Electrike	310 Manectric
	587 Emolga	618 Stunfisk				
Steadfast	066 Machop	067 Machoke	068 Machamp	123 Scyther	236 Tyrogue	237 Hitmontop
	447 Riolu	448 Lucario	475 Gallade			
Stench	044 Gloom	088 Grimer	089 Muk	434 Stunky	435 Skuntank	568 Trubbish
	569 Garbodor					
Sticky Hold	088 Grimer	089 Muk	316 Gulpin	317 Swalot	422 Shellos	423 Gastrodon
	568 Trubbish	617 Accelgor				
Storm Drain	345 Lileep	346 Cradily	422 Shellos	423 Gastrodon	456 Finneon	457 Lumineon
	556 Maractus					
Sturdy	074 Geodude	075 Graveler	076 Golem	081 Magnemite	082 Magneton	095 Onix
	185 Sudowoodo	204 Pineco	205 Forretress	208 Steelix	213 Shuckle	227 Skarmory
	232 Donphan	299 Nosepass	304 Aron	305 Lairon	306 Aggron	369 Relicanth
	410 Shieldon	411 Bastiodon	438 Bonsly	462 Magnezone	476 Probopass	524 Roggenrola
	525 Boldore	526 Gigalith	539 Sawk	557 Dwebble	558 Crustle	564 Tirtouga
	565 Carracosta					
Suction Cups	224 Octillery	345 Lileep	346 Cradily			
Super Luck	175 Togepi	176 Togetic	198 Murkrow	359 Absol	430 Honchkrow	468 Togekiss
	519 Pidove	520 Tranquill	521 Unfezant			
Swarm	015 Beedrill	123 Scyther	165 Ledyba	166 Ledian	167 Spinarak	168 Ariados
	212 Scizor	214 Heracross	267 Beautifly	313 Volbeat	402 Kricketune	414 Mothim
	540 Sewaddle	542 Leavanny	543 Venipede	544 Whirlipede	545 Scolipede	588 Karrablast
	589 Escavalier	595 Joltik	596 Galvantula	632 Durant		
Swift Swim	054 Psyduck	055 Golduck	060 Poliwag	061 Poliwhirl	062 Poliwrath	116 Horsea
	118 Goldeen	119 Seaking	129 Magikarp	138 Omanyte	139 Omastar	140 Kabuto
	141 Kabutops	211 Qwilfish	226 Mantine	230 Kingdra	270 Lotad	271 Lombre
	272 Ludicolo	283 Surskit	347 Anorith	348 Armaldo	349 Feebas	367 Huntail
	368 Gorebyss	369 Relicanth	370 Luvdisc	418 Buizel	419 Floatzel	456 Finneon
	457 Lumineon	458 Mantyke	535 Tympole	536 Palpitoad	537 Seismitoad	564 Tirtouga
	565 Carracosta	614 Beartic				
Synchronize	063 Abra	064 Kadabra	065 Alakazam	151 Mew	177 Natu	178 Xatu
	196 Espeon	197 Umbreon	280 Ralts	281 Kirlia	282 Gardevoir	517 Munna
	518 Musharna	605 Elgyem	606 Beheeyem			

Ability	Pokémon that have this Ability					
Tangled Feet	016 Pidgey	017 Pidgeotto	018 Pidgeot	084 Doduo	085 Dodrio	327 Spinda
	441 Chatot					
Technician	052 Meowth	053 Persian	122 Mr. Mime	123 Scyther	212 Scizor	235 Smeargle
	237 Hitmontop	286 Breloom	424 Ambipom	439 Mime Jr.	572 Minccino	573 Cinccino
Telepathy	202 Wobbuffet	280 Ralts	281 Kirlia	282 Gardevoir	307 Meditite	308 Medicham
	360 Wynaut	483 Dialga	484 Palkia	487 Giratina (Alt)	517 Munna	518 Musharna
	605 Elgyem	606 Beheeyem				
Teravolt	644 Zekrom	646 Kyurem (Blk)				
Thick Fat	086 Seel	087 Dewgong	143 Snorlax	183 Marill	184 Azumarill	220 Swinub
	221 Piloswine	241 Miltank	296 Makuhita	297 Hariyama	298 Azurill	325 Spoink
	326 Grumpig	363 Spheal	364 Sealeo	365 Walrein	432 Purugly	446 Munchlax
	473 Mamoswine					
Tinted Lens	012 Butterfree	048 Venonat	049 Venomoth	163 Hoothoot	164 Noctowl	314 Illumise
	414 Mothim	469 Yanmega	561 Sigilyph			
Torrent	007 Squirtle	008 Wartortle	009 Blastoise	158 Totodile	159 Croconaw	160 Feraligatr
	258 Mudkip	259 Marshtomp	260 Swampert	393 Piplup	394 Prinplup	395 Empoleon
	501 Oshawott	502 Dewott	503 Samurott			
Toxic Boost	335 Zangoose					
Trace	137 Porygon	233 Porygon2	280 Ralts	281 Kirlia	282 Gardevoir	
Truant	287 Slakoth	289 Slaking	632 Durant			
Turboblaze	643 Reshiram	646 Kyurem (Wht)				

Ability	Pokémon that have this Ability					
Unaware	036 Clefable	194 Wooper	195 Quagsire	399 Bidoof	400 Bibarel	527 Woobat
	528 Swoobat					
Unburden	106 Hitmonlee	252 Treecko	253 Grovyle	254 Sceptile	425 Drifloon	426 Drifblim
	509 Purrloin	510 Liepard	617 Accelgor			
Unnerve	052 Meowth	053 Persian	142 Aerodactyl	217 Ursaring	228 Houndour	229 Houndoom
	248 Tyranitar	284 Masquerain	416 Vespiquen	595 Joltik	596 Galvantula	610 Axew
	611 Fraxure	612 Haxorus				

Ability	Pokémon that have this Ability					
Victory Star	494 Victini					
Vital Spirit	056 Mankey	057 Primeape	125 Electabuzz	126 Magmar	225 Delibird	236 Tyrogue
	239 Elekid	240 Magby	288 Vigoroth	466 Electivire	467 Magmortar	506 Lillipup
Volt Absorb	135 Jolteon	170 Chinchou	171 Lanturn	417 Pachirisu	642 Thundurus (Theri)	

Ability	Pokémon that have this Ability					
Water Absorb	060 Poliwag	061 Poliwhirl	062 Poliwrath	131 Lapras	134 Vaporeon	170 Chinchou
	171 Lanturn	186 Politoed	194 Wooper	195 Quagsire	226 Mantine	331 Cacnea
	332 Cacturne	458 Mantyke	535 Tympole	536 Palpitoad	537 Seismitoad	556 Maractus
	592 Frillish	593 Jellicent				
Water Veil	118 Goldeen	119 Seaking	226 Mantine	320 Wailmer	321 Wailord	367 Huntail
	418 Buizel	419 Floatzel	456 Finneon	457 Lumineon	458 Mantyke	
Weak Armor	095 Onix	138 Omanyte	139 Omastar	140 Kabuto	141 Kabutops	218 Slugma
	219 Magcargo	227 Skarmory	557 Dwebble	558 Crustle	569 Garbodor	582 Vanillite
	583 Vanillish	584 Vanilluxe	629 Vullaby	630 Mandibuzz		
White Smoke	324 Torkoal	631 Heatmor				
Wonder Guard	292 Shedinja					
Wonder Skin	049 Venomoth	300 Skitty	301 Delcatty	561 Sigilyph		

Ability	Pokémon that have this Ability					
Zen Mode	555 Darmanitan					

How and Where to Meet Special Pokémon

National Pokédex No.	Pokémon		Level	Location	Item Needed	Conditions to Appear	
377	Regirock		65	Clay Tunnel Rock Peak Chamber	—	—	
378	Regice		65	Clay Tunnel Iceberg Chamber	—	Change the Key System setting to Iceberg Chamber with Unova Link's Key System.	
379	Registeel		65	Clay Tunnel Iron Chamber	—	Change the Key System setting to Iron Chamber with Unova Link's Key System.	
380	Latias		68	Dreamyard (Pokémon White Version 2)	—	—	
381	Latios		68	Dreamyard (Pokémon Black Version 2)	—	—	
480	Uxie		65	Nacrene City	—	After meeting it in the Cave of Being	
481	Mesprit		65	Celestial Tower	—	After meeting it in the Cave of Being	
482	Azelf		65	Route 23	—	After meeting it in the Cave of Being	
485	Heatran		68	Reversal Mountain	Magma Stone	—	
486	Regigigas		68	Twist Mountain	—	Put Regirock, Regice, and Registeel in your party	
488	Cresselia		68	Marvelous Bridge	Lunar Wing	—	
593	Jellicent ♂ (Hidden Ability)		40	Undella Bay (Pokémon Black Version 2)	—	Every Monday	
593	Jellicent ♀ (Hidden Ability)		40	Undella Bay (Pokémon White Version 2)	—	Every Thursday	
612	Haxorus (Shiny)		60	Nature Preserve	—	—	
628	Braviary (Hidden Ability)		25	Route 4 (Pokémon White Version 2)	—	Every Monday	
630	Mandibuzz (Hidden Ability)		25	Route 4 (Pokémon Black Version 2)	—	Every Thursday	
637	Volcarona		35 (65)	Relic Castle Lowest floor, deepest room	—	—	
638	Cobalion		45 (65)	Route 13	—	—	
639	Terrakion		45 (65)	Route 22	—	—	
640	Virizion		45 (65)	Route 11	—	—	
643	Reshiram		70	Dragonspiral Tower Seventh Floor (Pokémon White Version 2)	—	—	
644	Zekrom		70	Dragonspiral Tower Seventh Floor (Pokémon Black Version 2)	—	—	
646	Kyurem		70	Giant Chasm Cave's Deepest Part	—	—	

How to meet it again if you defeat it in battle	How to meet it again if you run from battle	How to meet it again if you lose the battle
Defeat the Elite Four and the Champion at the Pokémon League (comes back until you catch it)	Defeat the Elite Four and the Champion at the Pokémon League (comes back until you catch it)	Return for a rematch after being returned to the Pokémon Center
Defeat the Elite Four and the Champion at the Pokémon League (comes back until you catch it)	Defeat the Elite Four and the Champion at the Pokémon League (comes back until you catch it)	Return for a rematch after being returned to the Pokémon Center
Defeat the Elite Four and the Champion at the Pokémon League (comes back until you catch it)	Defeat the Elite Four and the Champion at the Pokémon League (comes back until you catch it)	Return for a rematch after being returned to the Pokémon Center
Defeat the Elite Four and the Champion at the Pokémon League (comes back until you catch it)	Defeat the Elite Four and the Champion at the Pokémon League (comes back until you catch it)	Return for a rematch after being returned to the Pokémon Center
Defeat the Elite Four and the Champion at the Pokémon League (comes back until you catch it)	Defeat the Elite Four and the Champion at the Pokémon League (comes back until you catch it)	Return for a rematch after being returned to the Pokémon Center
Defeat the Elite Four and the Champion at the Pokémon League (comes back until you catch it)	Defeat the Elite Four and the Champion at the Pokémon League (comes back until you catch it)	Return for a rematch after being returned to the Pokémon Center
Defeat the Elite Four and the Champion at the Pokémon League (comes back until you catch it)	Defeat the Elite Four and the Champion at the Pokémon League (comes back until you catch it)	Return for a rematch after being returned to the Pokémon Center
Defeat the Elite Four and the Champion at the Pokémon League (comes back until you catch it)	Defeat the Elite Four and the Champion at the Pokémon League (comes back until you catch it)	Return for a rematch after being returned to the Pokémon Center
Defeat the Elite Four and the Champion at the Pokémon League (comes back until you catch it)	Defeat the Elite Four and the Champion at the Pokémon League (comes back until you catch it)	Return for a rematch after being returned to the Pokémon Center
Defeat the Elite Four and the Champion at the Pokémon League (comes back until you catch it)	Defeat the Elite Four and the Champion at the Pokémon League (comes back until you catch it)	Return for a rematch after being returned to the Pokémon Center
Defeat the Elite Four and the Champion at the Pokémon League (comes back until you catch it)	Defeat the Elite Four and the Champion at the Pokémon League (comes back until you catch it)	Return for a rematch after being returned to the Pokémon Center
Go to Undella Bay on the next Monday	Go to Undella Bay on the next Monday	Return for a rematch after being returned to the Pokémon Center
Go to Undella Bay on the next Thursday	Go to Undella Bay on the next Thursday	Return for a rematch after being returned to the Pokémon Center
Defeat the Elite Four and the Champion at the Pokémon League (comes back until you catch it)	Defeat the Elite Four and the Champion at the Pokémon League (comes back until you catch it)	Return for a rematch after being returned to the Pokémon Center
Go to Route 4 on the next Monday	Go to Route 4 on the next Monday	Return for a rematch after being returned to the Pokémon Center
Go to Route 4 on the next Thursday	Go to Route 4 on the next Thursday	Return for a rematch after being returned to the Pokémon Center
Defeat the Elite Four and the Champion at the Pokémon League (comes back until you catch it) When it comes back, its level goes up to Lv. 65.	Defeat the Elite Four and the Champion at the Pokémon League (comes back until you catch it) When it comes back, its level goes up to Lv. 65.	Return for a rematch after being returned to the Pokémon Center
Defeat the Elite Four and the Champion at the Pokémon League (comes back until you catch it) When it comes back, its level goes up to Lv. 65.	Defeat the Elite Four and the Champion at the Pokémon League (comes back until you catch it) When it comes back, its level goes up to Lv. 65.	Return for a rematch after being returned to the Pokémon Center
Defeat the Elite Four and the Champion at the Pokémon League (comes back until you catch it) When it comes back, its level goes up to Lv. 65.	Defeat the Elite Four and the Champion at the Pokémon League (comes back until you catch it) When it comes back, its level goes up to Lv. 65.	Return for a rematch after being returned to the Pokémon Center
Defeat the Elite Four and the Champion at the Pokémon League (comes back until you catch it) When it comes back, its level goes up to Lv. 65.	Defeat the Elite Four and the Champion at the Pokémon League (comes back until you catch it) When it comes back, its level goes up to Lv. 65.	Return for a rematch after being returned to the Pokémon Center
Defeat the Elite Four and the Champion at the Pokémon League (comes back until you catch it)	Defeat the Elite Four and the Champion at the Pokémon League (comes back until you catch it)	Return for a rematch after being returned to the Pokémon Center
Defeat the Elite Four and the Champion at the Pokémon League (comes back until you catch it)	Defeat the Elite Four and the Champion at the Pokémon League (comes back until you catch it)	Return for a rematch after being returned to the Pokémon Center
Defeat the Elite Four and the Champion at the Pokémon League (comes back until you catch it)	Defeat the Elite Four and the Champion at the Pokémon League (comes back until you catch it)	Return for a rematch after being returned to the Pokémon Center

Pokémon Weakness Chart—National Pokédex

A

Pokémon	Type		Ability		Hidden Ability	Weak against these move types						X Immune to these move types	
Abomasnow	Grass	Ice	Snow Warning		Soundproof	★Fire	Fighting	Poison	Flying	Bug	Rock	Steel	
Abra	Psychic		Synchronize	Inner Focus	Magic Guard	Bug	Ghost	Dark					
Absol	Dark		Pressure	Super Luck	Justified	Fighting	Bug					Psychic	
Accelgor	Bug		Hydration	Sticky Hold	Unburden	Fire	Flying	Rock					
Aerodactyl	Rock	Flying	Rock Head	Pressure	Unnerve	Water	Electric	Ice	Rock	Steel		Ground	
Aggron	Steel	Rock	Sturdy	Rock Head	Heavy Metal	★Fighting	★Ground	Water				Poison	
Aipom	Normal		Run Away	Pickup		Fighting						Ghost	
Alakazam	Psychic		Synchronize	Inner Focus	Magic Guard	Bug	Ghost	Dark					
Alomomola	Water		Healer	Hydration	Regenerator	Grass	Electric						
Altaria	Dragon	Flying	Natural Cure		Cloud Nine	★Ice	Rock	Dragon				Ground	
Ambipom	Normal		Technician	Pickup		Fighting						Ghost	
Amoonguss	Grass	Poison	Effect Spore		Regenerator	Fire	Ice	Flying	Psychic				
Ampharos	Electric		Static		Plus	Ground							
Anorith	Rock	Bug	Battle Armor		Swift Swim	Water	Rock	Steel					
Arbok	Poison		Intimidate	Shed Skin		Ground	Psychic						
Arcanine	Fire		Intimidate	Flash Fire	Justified	Water	Ground	Rock				Fire ◆2	
Arceus	Bug		Multitype			Fire	Flying	Rock					
Arceus	Dark		Multitype			Fighting	Bug					Psychic	
Arceus	Dragon		Multitype			Ice	Dragon						
Arceus	Electric		Multitype			Ground							
Arceus	Fighting		Multitype			Flying	Psychic						
Arceus	Fire		Multitype			Water	Ground	Rock					
Arceus	Flying		Multitype			Electric	Ice	Rock				Ground	
Arceus	Ghost		Multitype			Ghost	Dark					Normal	Fighting
Arceus	Grass		Multitype			Fire	Ice	Poison	Flying	Bug			
Arceus	Ground		Multitype			Water	Grass	Ice				Electric	
Arceus	Ice		Multitype			Fire	Fighting	Rock	Steel				
Arceus	Normal		Multitype			Fighting						Ghost	
Arceus	Poison		Multitype			Ground	Psychic						
Arceus	Psychic		Multitype			Bug	Ghost	Dark					
Arceus	Rock		Multitype			Water	Grass	Fighting	Ground	Steel			
Arceus	Steel		Multitype			Fire	Fighting	Ground				Poison	
Arceus	Water		Multitype			Grass	Electric						
Archeops	Rock	Flying	Defeatist			Water	Electric	Ice	Rock	Steel		Ground	
Ariados	Bug	Poison	Swarm	Insomnia	Sniper	Fire	Flying	Psychic	Rock				
Armaldo	Rock	Bug	Battle Armor		Swift Swim	Water	Rock	Steel					
Aron	Steel	Rock	Sturdy	Rock Head	Heavy Metal	★Fighting	★Ground	Water				Poison	
Articuno	Ice	Flying	Pressure			★Rock	Fire	Electric	Steel			Ground	
Audino	Normal		Healer	Regenerator		Fighting						Ghost	
Axew	Dragon		Rivalry	Mold Breaker	Unnerve	Ice	Dragon						
Azelf	Psychic		Levitate			Bug	Ghost	Dark				Ground ◆1	
Azumarill	Water		Thick Fat	Huge Power	Sap Sipper	Grass	Electric					Grass ◆4	
Azurill	Normal		Thick Fat	Huge Power	Sap Sipper	Fighting						Ghost	Grass ◆4

B

Pokémon	Type		Ability		Hidden Ability	Weak against these move types						X Immune to these move types	
Bagon	Dragon		Rock Head		Sheer Force	Ice	Dragon					Electric	
Baltoy	Ground	Psychic	Levitate			Water	Grass	Ice	Bug	Ghost	Dark	Electric	Ground ◆1
Banette	Ghost		Insomnia	Frisk	Cursed Body	Ghost	Dark					Normal	Fighting
Barboach	Water	Ground	Oblivious	Anticipation	Hydration	★Grass						Electric	
Basculin (Blue-Striped Form)	Water		Rock Head	Adaptability	Mold Breaker	Grass	Electric						
Basculin (Red-Striped Form)	Water		Reckless	Adaptability	Mold Breaker	Grass	Electric						
Bastiodon	Rock	Steel	Sturdy		Soundproof	★Fighting	★Ground	Water				Poison	
Bayleef	Grass		Overgrow			Fire	Ice	Poison	Flying	Bug			
Beartic	Ice		Snow Cloak		Swift Swim	Fire	Fighting	Rock	Steel				
Beautifly	Bug	Flying	Swarm			★Rock	Fire	Electric	Ice	Flying		Ground	
Beedrill	Bug	Poison	Swarm		Sniper	Fire	Flying	Psychic	Rock				
Beheeyem	Psychic		Telepathy	Synchronize	Analytic	Bug	Ghost	Dark					
Beldum	Steel	Psychic	Clear Body		Light Metal	Fire	Ground					Poison	
Bellossom	Grass		Chlorophyll		Healer	Fire	Ice	Poison	Flying	Bug			
Bellsprout	Grass	Poison	Chlorophyll		Gluttony	Fire	Ice	Flying	Psychic				
Bibarel	Normal	Water	Simple	Unaware	Moody	Grass	Electric	Fighting				Ghost	
Bidoof	Normal		Simple	Unaware	Moody	Fighting						Ghost	
Bisharp	Dark	Steel	Defiant	Inner Focus	Pressure	★Fighting	Fire	Ground				Poison	Psychic
Blastoise	Water		Torrent		Rain Dish	Grass	Electric						
Blaziken	Fire	Fighting	Blaze		Speed Boost	Water	Ground	Flying	Psychic				
Blissey	Normal		Natural Cure	Serene Grace	Healer	Fighting						Ghost	

★ Deals 4 times damage. ◆1 Ability prevents damage. ◆2 May deal damage depending on the Pokémon's Ability. ◆3 Damage may be prevented depending on the Pokémon's Ability. ◆4 Hidden Ability prevents damage.

Pokémon	Type		Ability	Hidden Ability	Weak against these move types						X Immune to these move types		
Blitzle	Electric		Lightningrod	Motor Drive	Sap Sipper	Ground						Electric ◆1	Grass ◆4	
Boldore	Rock		Sturdy		Sand Force	Water	Grass	Fighting	Ground	Steel				
Bonsly	Rock		Sturdy	Rock Head	Rattled	Water	Grass	Fighting	Ground	Steel				
Bouffalant	Normal		Reckless	Sap Sipper	Soundproof	Fighting						Ghost	Grass ◆2	
Braviary	Normal	Flying	Keen Eye	Sheer Force	Defiant	Electric	Ice	Rock				Ground	Ghost	
Breloom	Grass	Fighting	Effect Spore	Poison Heal	Technician	★Flying	Fire	Ice	Poison	Psychic				
Bronzong	Steel	Psychic	Levitate	Heatproof	Heavy Metal	Fire	Ground ◆3					Poison		
Bronzor	Steel	Psychic	Levitate	Heatproof	Heavy Metal	Fire	Ground ◆3					Poison		
Budew	Grass	Poison	Natural Cure	Poison Point		Fire	Ice	Flying	Psychic					
Buizel	Water		Swift Swim		Water Veil	Grass	Electric							
Bulbasaur	Grass	Poison	Overgrow		Chlorophyll	Fire	Ice	Flying	Psychic					
Buneary	Normal		Run Away	Klutz	Limber	Fighting						Ghost		
Burmy	Bug		Shed Skin		Overcoat	Fire	Flying	Rock						
Butterfree	Bug	Flying	Compoundeyes		Tinted Lens	★Rock	Fire	Electric	Ice	Flying		Ground		

C

Pokémon	Type		Ability	Hidden Ability	Weak against these move types						X Immune to these move types		
Cacnea	Grass		Sand Veil		Water Absorb	Fire	Ice	Poison	Flying	Bug		Water ◆4		
Cacturne	Grass	Dark	Sand Veil		Water Absorb	★Bug	Fire	Ice	Fighting	Poison	Flying	Psychic	Water ◆4	
Camerupt	Fire	Ground	Magma Armor	Solid Rock	Anger Point	★Water	Ground					Electric		
Carnivine	Grass		Levitate			Fire	Ice	Poison	Flying	Bug		Ground ◆1		
Carracosta	Water	Rock	Solid Rock	Sturdy	Swift Swim	★Grass	Electric	Fighting	Ground					
Carvanha	Water	Dark	Rough Skin		Speed Boost	Grass	Electric	Fighting	Bug			Psychic		
Cascoon	Bug		Shed Skin			Fire	Flying	Rock						
Castform (Normal)	Normal		Forecast			Fighting						Ghost		
Castform (Rainy Form)	Water		Forecast			Grass	Electric							
Castform (Snowy Form)	Ice		Forecast			Fighting	Rock	Steel						
Castform (Sunny Form)	Fire		Forecast			Water	Ground	Rock						
Caterpie	Bug		Shield Dust		Run Away	Fire	Flying	Rock						
Celebi	Psychic	Grass	Natural Cure			★Bug	Fire	Ice	Poison	Flying	Ghost	Dark		
Chandelure	Ghost	Fire	Flash Fire	Flame Body		Water	Ground	Rock	Ghost	Dark		Normal	Fighting	Fire ◆2
Chansey	Normal		Natural Cure	Serene Grace	Healer	Fighting						Ghost		
Charizard	Fire	Flying	Blaze		Solar Power	★Rock	Water	Electric				Ground		
Charmander	Fire		Blaze		Solar Power	Water	Ground	Rock						
Charmeleon	Fire		Blaze		Solar Power	Water	Ground	Rock						
Chatot	Normal	Flying	Keen Eye	Tangled Feet	Big Pecks	Electric	Ice	Rock				Ground	Ghost	
Cherrim	Grass		Flower Gift			Fire	Ice	Poison	Flying	Bug				
Cherubi	Grass		Chlorophyll			Fire	Ice	Poison	Flying	Bug				
Chikorita	Grass		Overgrow			Fire	Ice	Poison	Flying	Bug				
Chimchar	Fire		Blaze		Iron Fist	Water	Ground	Rock						
Chimecho	Psychic		Levitate			Bug	Ghost	Dark				Ground ◆1		
Chinchou	Water	Electric	Volt Absorb	Illuminate	Water Absorb	Grass	Ground					Electric ◆2	Water ◆4	
Chingling	Psychic		Levitate			Bug	Ghost	Dark				Ground ◆1		
Cinccino	Normal		Cute Charm	Technician	Skill Link	Fighting						Ghost		
Clamperl	Water		Shell Armor		Rattled	Grass	Electric							
Claydol	Ground	Psychic	Levitate			Water	Grass	Ice	Bug	Ghost	Dark	Electric	Ground ◆1	
Clefable	Normal		Cute Charm	Magic Guard	Unaware	Fighting						Ghost		
Clefairy	Normal		Cute Charm	Magic Guard	Friend Guard	Fighting						Ghost		
Cleffa	Normal		Cute Charm	Magic Guard	Friend Guard	Fighting						Ghost		
Cloyster	Water	Ice	Shell Armor	Skill Link	Overcoat	Grass	Electric	Fighting	Rock					
Cobalion	Steel	Fighting	Justified			Fire	Fighting	Ground				Poison		
Cofagrigus	Ghost		Mummy			Ghost	Dark					Normal	Fighting	
Combee	Bug	Flying	Honey Gather		Hustle	★Rock	Fire	Electric	Ice	Flying		Ground		
Combusken	Fire	Fighting	Blaze		Speed Boost	Water	Ground	Flying	Psychic					
Conkeldurr	Fighting		Guts	Sheer Force		Flying	Psychic							
Corphish	Water		Hyper Cutter	Shell Armor	Adaptability	Grass	Electric							
Corsola	Water	Rock	Hustle	Natural Cure	Regenerator	★Grass	Electric	Fighting	Ground					
Cottonee	Grass		Prankster	Infiltrator	Chlorophyll	Fire	Ice	Poison	Flying	Bug				
Cradily	Rock	Grass	Suction Cups		Storm Drain	Ice	Fighting	Bug	Steel			Water ◆4		
Cranidos	Rock		Mold Breaker		Sheer Force	Water	Grass	Fighting	Ground	Steel				
Crawdaunt	Water	Dark	Hyper Cutter	Shell Armor	Adaptability	Grass	Electric	Fighting	Bug			Psychic		
Cresselia	Psychic		Levitate			Bug	Ghost	Dark				Ground ◆1		
Croagunk	Poison	Fighting	Anticipation	Dry Skin	Poison Touch	★Psychic	Ground	Flying				Water ◆2		
Crobat	Poison	Flying	Inner Focus		Infiltrator	Electric	Ice	Psychic	Rock			Ground		
Croconaw	Water		Torrent			Grass	Electric							
Crustle	Bug	Rock	Sturdy	Shell Armor	Weak Armor	Water	Rock	Steel						
Cryogonal	Ice		Levitate			Fire	Fighting	Rock	Steel			Ground ◆1		
Cubchoo	Ice		Snow Cloak		Rattled	Fire	Fighting	Rock	Steel					
Cubone	Ground		Rock Head	Lightningrod	Battle Armor	Water	Grass	Ice				Electric		
Cyndaquil	Fire		Blaze			Water	Ground	Rock						

◉ Pokémon Weakness Chart—National Pokédex

D

Pokémon	Type		Ability		Hidden Ability	Weak against these move types						X Immune to these move types		
Darkrai	Dark		Bad Dreams			Fighting	Bug					Psychic		
Darmanitan (Standard Mode)	Fire		Sheer Force		Zen Mode	Water	Ground	Rock						
Darmanitan (Zen Mode)	Fire	Psychic			Zen Mode	Water	Ground	Rock	Ghost	Dark				
Darumaka	Fire		Hustle		Inner Focus	Water	Ground	Rock						
Deerling	Normal	Grass	Chlorophyll	Sap Sipper	Serene Grace	Fire	Ice	Fighting	Poison	Flying	Bug	Ghost	Grass ◆2	
Deino	Dark	Dragon	Hustle			Ice	Fighting	Bug	Dragon			Psychic		
Delcatty	Normal		Cute Charm	Normalize	Wonder Skin	Fighting						Ghost		
Delibird	Ice	Flying	Vital Spirit	Hustle	Insomnia	★Rock	Fire	Electric	Steel			Ground		
Deoxys	Psychic		Pressure			Bug	Ghost	Dark						
Dewgong	Water	Ice	Thick Fat	Hydration	Ice Body	Grass	Electric	Fighting	Rock					
Dewott	Water		Torrent			Grass	Electric							
Dialga	Steel	Dragon	Pressure		Telepathy	Fighting	Ground					Poison		
Diglett	Ground		Sand Veil	Arena Trap	Sand Force	Water	Grass	Ice				Electric		
Ditto	Normal		Limber		Imposter	Fighting						Ghost		
Dodrio	Normal	Flying	Run Away	Early Bird	Tangled Feet	Electric	Ice	Rock				Ground	Ghost	
Doduo	Normal	Flying	Run Away	Early Bird	Tangled Feet	Electric	Ice	Rock				Ground	Ghost	
Donphan	Ground		Sturdy		Sand Veil	Water	Grass	Ice				Electric		
Dragonair	Dragon		Shed Skin		Marvel Scale	Ice	Dragon							
Dragonite	Dragon	Flying	Inner Focus		Multiscale	★Ice	Rock	Dragon				Ground		
Drapion	Poison	Dark	Battle Armor	Sniper	Keen Eye	Ground						Psychic		
Dratini	Dragon		Shed Skin		Marvel Scale	Ice	Dragon							
Drifblim	Ghost	Flying	Aftermath	Unburden	Flare Boost	Electric	Ice	Rock	Ghost	Dark		Normal	Fighting	Ground
Drifloon	Ghost	Flying	Aftermath	Unburden	Flare Boost	Electric	Ice	Rock	Ghost	Dark		Normal	Fighting	Ground
Drilbur	Ground		Sand Rush	Sand Force	Mold Breaker	Water	Grass	Ice				Electric		
Drowzee	Psychic		Insomnia	Forewarn	Inner Focus	Bug	Ghost	Dark						
Druddigon	Dragon		Rough Skin	Sheer Force	Mold Breaker	Ice	Dragon							
Ducklett	Water	Flying	Keen Eye	Big Pecks	Hydration	★Electric	Rock					Ground		
Dugtrio	Ground		Sand Veil	Arena Trap	Sand Force	Water	Grass	Ice				Electric		
Dunsparce	Normal		Serene Grace	Run Away	Rattled	Fighting						Ghost		
Duosion	Psychic		Overcoat	Magic Guard	Regenerator	Bug	Ghost	Dark						
Durant	Bug	Steel	Swarm	Hustle	Truant	★Fire						Poison		
Dusclops	Ghost		Pressure			Ghost	Dark					Normal	Fighting	
Dusknoir	Ghost		Pressure			Ghost	Dark					Normal	Fighting	
Duskull	Ghost		Levitate			Ghost	Dark					Normal	Fighting	Ground ◆1
Dustox	Bug	Poison	Shield Dust			Fire	Flying	Psychic	Rock					
Dwebble	Bug	Rock	Sturdy	Shell Armor	Weak Armor	Water	Rock	Steel						

E

Pokémon	Type		Ability		Hidden Ability	Weak against these move types						X Immune to these move types		
Eelektrik	Electric		Levitate									Ground ◆1		
Eelektross	Electric		Levitate									Ground ◆1		
Eevee	Normal		Run Away	Adaptability	Anticipation	Fighting						Ghost		
Ekans	Poison		Intimidate	Shed Skin		Ground	Psychic							
Electabuzz	Electric		Static		Vital Spirit	Ground								
Electivire	Electric		Motor Drive		Vital Spirit	Ground						Electric ◆1		
Electrike	Electric		Static	Lightningrod	Minus	Ground						Electric ◆2		
Electrode	Electric		Soundproof	Static	Aftermath	Ground								
Elekid	Electric		Static		Vital Spirit	Ground								
Elgyem	Psychic		Telepathy	Synchronize	Analytic	Bug	Ghost	Dark						
Emboar	Fire	Fighting	Blaze			Water	Ground	Flying	Psychic					
Emolga	Electric	Flying	Static		Motor Drive	Ice	Rock					Ground	Electric ◆4	
Empoleon	Water	Steel	Torrent		Defiant	Electric	Fighting	Ground				Poison		
Entei	Fire		Pressure			Water	Ground	Rock						
Escavalier	Bug	Steel	Swarm	Shell Armor	Overcoat	★Fire						Poison		
Espeon	Psychic		Synchronize		Magic Bounce	Bug	Ghost	Dark						
Excadrill	Ground	Steel	Sand Rush	Sand Force	Mold Breaker	Fire	Water	Fighting	Ground			Electric	Poison	
Exeggcute	Grass	Psychic	Chlorophyll		Harvest	★Bug	Fire	Ice	Poison	Flying	Ghost	Dark		
Exeggutor	Grass	Psychic	Chlorophyll		Harvest	★Bug	Fire	Ice	Poison	Flying	Ghost	Dark		
Exploud	Normal		Soundproof		Scrappy	Fighting						Ghost		

F

Pokémon	Type		Ability		Hidden Ability	Weak against these move types						X Immune to these move types		
Farfetch'd	Normal	Flying	Keen Eye	Inner Focus	Defiant	Electric	Ice	Rock				Ground	Ghost	
Fearow	Normal	Flying	Keen Eye		Sniper	Electric	Ice	Rock				Ground	Ghost	
Feebas	Water		Swift Swim		Adaptability	Grass	Electric							
Feraligatr	Water		Torrent			Grass	Electric							
Ferroseed	Grass	Steel	Iron Barbs			★Fire	Fighting					Poison		

580

★ Deals 4 times damage.　◆1 Ability prevents damage.　◆2 May deal damage depending on the Pokémon's Ability.　◆3 Damage may be prevented depending on the Pokémon's Ability.　◆4 Hidden Ability prevents damage.

Pokémon	Type		Ability		Hidden Ability	Weak against these move types						X Immune to these move types		
Ferrothorn	Grass	Steel	Iron Barbs			★Fire	Fighting					Poison		
Finneon	Water		Swift Swim	Storm Drain	Water Veil	Grass	Electric					Water ◆2		
Flaaffy	Electric		Static		Plus	Ground								
Flareon	Fire		Flash Fire		Guts	Water	Ground	Rock				Fire ◆1		
Floatzel	Water		Swift Swim		Water Veil	Grass	Electric							
Flygon	Ground	Dragon	Levitate			★Ice	Dragon					Electric	Ground ◆1	
Foongus	Grass	Poison	Effect Spore		Regenerator	Fire	Ice	Flying	Psychic					
Forretress	Bug	Steel	Sturdy			★Fire						Poison		
Fraxure	Dragon		Rivalry	Mold Breaker	Unnerve	Ice	Dragon							
Frillish	Water	Ghost	Water Absorb	Cursed Body	Damp	Grass	Electric	Ghost	Dark			Normal	Fighting	Water ◆2
Froslass	Ice	Ghost	Snow Cloak		Cursed Body	Fire	Rock	Ghost	Dark	Steel		Normal	Fighting	
Furret	Normal		Run Away	Keen Eye	Frisk	Fighting						Ghost		

G

Pokémon	Type		Ability		Hidden Ability	Weak against these move types						X Immune to these move types		
Gabite	Dragon	Ground	Sand Veil		Rough Skin	★Ice	Dragon					Electric		
Gallade	Psychic	Fighting	Steadfast		Justified	Flying	Ghost							
Galvantula	Bug	Electric	Compoundeyes	Unnerve	Swarm	Fire	Rock							
Garbodor	Poison		Stench	Weak Armor	Aftermath	Ground	Psychic							
Garchomp	Dragon	Ground	Sand Veil		Rough Skin	★Ice	Dragon					Electric		
Gardevoir	Psychic		Synchronize	Trace	Telepathy	Bug	Ghost	Dark						
Gastly	Ghost	Poison	Levitate			Psychic	Ghost	Dark				Normal	Fighting	Ground ◆1
Gastrodon	Water	Ground	Sticky Hold	Storm Drain	Sand Force	★Grass						Electric	Water ◆2	
Genesect	Bug	Steel	Download			★Fire						Poison		
Gengar	Ghost	Poison	Levitate			Psychic	Ghost	Dark				Normal	Fighting	Ground ◆1
Geodude	Rock	Ground	Rock Head	Sturdy	Sand Veil	★Water	★Grass	Ice	Fighting	Ground	Steel	Electric		
Gible	Dragon	Ground	Sand Veil		Rough Skin	★Ice	Dragon					Electric		
Gigalith	Rock		Sturdy		Sand Force	Water	Grass	Fighting	Ground	Steel				
Girafarig	Normal	Psychic	Inner Focus	Early Bird	Sap Sipper	Bug	Dark					Ghost	Grass ◆4	
Giratina (Altered Forme)	Ghost	Dragon	Pressure		Telepathy	Ice	Ghost	Dragon	Dark			Normal	Fighting	
Giratina (Origin Forme)	Ghost	Dragon	Levitate			Ice	Ghost	Dragon	Dark			Normal	Fighting	Ground ◆1
Glaceon	Ice		Snow Cloak		Ice Body	Fire	Fighting	Rock	Steel					
Glalie	Ice		Inner Focus	Ice Body	Moody	Fire	Fighting	Rock	Steel					
Glameow	Normal		Limber	Own Tempo	Keen Eye	Fighting						Ghost		
Gligar	Ground	Flying	Hyper Cutter	Sand Veil	Immunity	★Ice	Water					Electric	Ground	
Gliscor	Ground	Flying	Hyper Cutter	Sand Veil	Poison Heal	★Ice	Water					Electric	Ground	
Gloom	Grass	Poison	Chlorophyll		Stench	Fire	Ice	Flying	Psychic					
Golbat	Poison	Flying	Inner Focus		Infiltrator	Electric	Ice	Psychic	Rock			Ground		
Goldeen	Water		Swift Swim	Water Veil	Lightningrod	Grass	Electric					Electric ◆4		
Golduck	Water		Damp	Cloud Nine	Swift Swim	Grass	Electric							
Golem	Rock	Ground	Rock Head	Sturdy	Sand Veil	★Water	★Grass	Ice	Fighting	Ground	Steel	Electric		
Golett	Ground	Ghost	Iron Fist	Klutz	No Guard	Water	Grass	Ice	Ghost	Dark		Normal	Electric	Fighting
Golurk	Ground	Ghost	Iron Fist	Klutz	No Guard	Water	Grass	Ice	Ghost	Dark		Normal	Electric	Fighting
Gorebyss	Water		Swift Swim		Hydration	Grass	Electric							
Gothita	Psychic		Frisk			Bug	Ghost	Dark						
Gothitelle	Psychic		Frisk		Shadow Tag	Bug	Ghost	Dark						
Gothorita	Psychic		Frisk		Shadow Tag	Bug	Ghost	Dark						
Granbull	Normal		Intimidate	Quick Feet	Rattled	Fighting						Ghost		
Graveler	Rock	Ground	Rock Head	Sturdy	Sand Veil	★Water	★Grass	Ice	Fighting	Ground	Steel	Electric		
Grimer	Poison		Stench	Sticky Hold	Poison Touch	Ground	Psychic							
Grotle	Grass		Overgrow		Shell Armor	Fire	Ice	Poison	Flying	Bug				
Groudon	Ground		Drought			Water	Grass	Ice				Electric		
Grovyle	Grass		Overgrow		Unburden	Fire	Ice	Poison	Flying	Bug				
Growlithe	Fire		Intimidate	Flash Fire	Justified	Water	Ground	Rock				Fire ◆2		
Grumpig	Psychic		Thick Fat	Own Tempo	Gluttony	Bug	Ghost	Dark						
Gulpin	Poison		Liquid Ooze	Sticky Hold	Gluttony	Ground	Psychic							
Gurdurr	Fighting		Guts	Sheer Force		Flying	Psychic							
Gyarados	Water	Flying	Intimidate		Moxie	★Electric	Rock					Ground		

H

Pokémon	Type		Ability		Hidden Ability	Weak against these move types						X Immune to these move types		
Happiny	Normal		Natural Cure	Serene Grace	Friend Guard	Fighting						Ghost		
Hariyama	Fighting		Thick Fat	Guts	Sheer Force	Flying	Psychic							
Haunter	Ghost	Poison	Levitate			Psychic	Ghost	Dark				Normal	Fighting	Ground ◆1
Haxorus	Dragon		Rivalry	Mold Breaker	Unnerve	Ice	Dragon							
Heatmor	Fire		Gluttony	Flash Fire	White Smoke	Water	Ground	Rock				Fire ◆2		
Heatran	Fire	Steel	Flash Fire			★Ground	Water	Fighting				Poison	Fire ◆1	
Heracross	Bug	Fighting	Swarm	Guts	Moxie	★Flying	Fire	Psychic						

Pokémon Weakness Chart—National Pokédex

H

Pokémon	Type		Ability		Hidden Ability	Weak against these move types						X Immune to these move types		
Herdier	Normal		Intimidate	Sand Rush	Scrappy	Fighting						Ghost		
Hippopotas	Ground		Sand Stream		Sand Force	Water	Grass	Ice				Electric		
Hippowdon	Ground		Sand Stream		Sand Force	Water	Grass	Ice				Electric		
Hitmonchan	Fighting		Keen Eye	Iron Fist	Inner Focus	Flying	Psychic							
Hitmonlee	Fighting		Limber	Reckless	Unburden	Flying	Psychic							
Hitmontop	Fighting		Intimidate	Technician	Steadfast	Flying	Psychic							
Ho-Oh	Fire	Flying	Pressure		Regenerator	★Rock	Water	Electric				Ground		
Honchkrow	Dark	Flying	Insomnia	Super Luck	Moxie	Electric	Ice	Rock				Ground	Psychic	
Hoothoot	Normal	Flying	Insomnia	Keen Eye	Tinted Lens	Electric	Ice	Rock				Ground	Ghost	
Hoppip	Grass	Flying	Chlorophyll	Leaf Guard	Infiltrator	★Ice	Fire	Poison	Flying	Rock		Ground		
Horsea	Water		Swift Swim	Sniper	Damp	Grass	Electric							
Houndoom	Dark	Fire	Early Bird	Flash Fire	Unnerve	Water	Fighting	Ground	Rock			Psychic	Fire ◆2	
Houndour	Dark	Fire	Early Bird	Flash Fire	Unnerve	Water	Fighting	Ground	Rock			Psychic	Fire ◆2	
Huntail	Water		Swift Swim		Water Veil	Grass	Electric							
Hydreigon	Dark	Dragon	Levitate			Ice	Fighting	Bug	Dragon			Psychic	Ground ◆1	
Hypno	Psychic		Insomnia	Forewarn	Inner Focus	Bug	Ghost	Dark						

I

Pokémon	Type		Ability		Hidden Ability	Weak against these move types						X Immune to these move types		
Igglybuff	Normal		Cute Charm		Friend Guard	Fighting						Ghost		
Illumise	Bug		Oblivious	Tinted Lens	Prankster	Fire	Flying	Rock						
Infernape	Fire	Fighting	Blaze		Iron Fist	Water	Ground	Flying	Psychic					
Ivysaur	Grass	Poison	Overgrow		Chlorophyll	Fire	Ice	Flying	Psychic					

J

Pokémon	Type		Ability		Hidden Ability	Weak against these move types						X Immune to these move types		
Jellicent	Water	Ghost	Water Absorb	Cursed Body	Damp	Grass	Electric	Ghost	Dark			Normal	Fighting	Water ◆2
Jigglypuff	Normal		Cute Charm		Friend Guard	Fighting						Ghost		
Jirachi	Steel	Psychic	Serene Grace			Fire	Ground					Poison		
Jolteon	Electric		Volt Absorb		Quick Feet	Ground						Electric ◆1		
Joltik	Bug	Electric	Compoundeyes	Unnerve	Swarm	Fire	Rock					Ground		
Jumpluff	Grass	Flying	Chlorophyll	Leaf Guard	Infiltrator	★Ice	Fire	Poison	Flying	Rock		Ground		
Jynx	Ice	Psychic	Oblivious	Forewarn	Dry Skin	Fire	Bug	Rock	Ghost	Dark	Steel	Water ◆4		

K

Pokémon	Type		Ability		Hidden Ability	Weak against these move types						X Immune to these move types		
Kabuto	Rock	Water	Swift Swim	Battle Armor	Weak Armor	★Grass	Electric	Fighting	Ground					
Kabutops	Rock	Water	Swift Swim	Battle Armor	Weak Armor	★Grass	Electric	Fighting	Ground					
Kadabra	Psychic		Synchronize	Inner Focus	Magic Guard	Bug	Ghost	Dark						
Kakuna	Bug	Poison	Shed Skin			Fire	Flying	Psychic	Rock					
Kangaskhan	Normal		Early Bird	Scrappy	Inner Focus	Fighting						Ghost		
Karrablast	Bug		Swarm	Shed Skin	No Guard	Fire	Flying	Rock						
Kecleon	Normal		Color Change			Fighting						Ghost		
Keldeo (Ordinary Form)	Water	Fighting	Justified			Grass	Electric	Flying	Psychic					
Keldeo (Resolute Form)	Water	Fighting	Justified			Grass	Electric	Flying	Psychic					
Kingdra	Water	Dragon	Swift Swim	Sniper	Damp	Dragon								
Kingler	Water		Hyper Cutter	Shell Armor	Sheer Force	Grass	Electric							
Kirlia	Psychic		Synchronize	Trace	Telepathy	Bug	Ghost	Dark						
Klang	Steel		Plus	Minus	Clear Body	Fire	Fighting	Ground				Poison		
Klink	Steel		Plus	Minus		Fire	Fighting	Ground				Poison		
Klinklang	Steel		Plus	Minus	Clear Body	Fire	Fighting	Ground				Poison		
Koffing	Poison		Levitate			Psychic						Ground ◆1		
Krabby	Water		Hyper Cutter	Shell Armor	Sheer Force	Grass	Electric							
Kricketot	Bug		Shed Skin			Fire	Flying	Rock						
Kricketune	Bug		Swarm			Fire	Flying	Rock						
Krokorok	Ground	Dark	Intimidate	Moxie	Anger Point	Water	Grass	Ice	Fighting	Bug		Electric	Psychic	
Krookodile	Ground	Dark	Intimidate	Moxie	Anger Point	Water	Grass	Ice	Fighting	Bug		Electric	Psychic	
Kyogre	Water		Drizzle			Grass	Electric							
Kyurem	Dragon	Ice	Pressure			Fighting	Rock	Dragon	Steel					
Kyurem (Black Kyurem)	Dragon	Ice	Teravolt			Fighting	Rock	Dragon	Steel					
Kyurem (White Kyurem)	Dragon	Ice	Turboblaze			Fighting	Rock	Dragon	Steel					

★ Deals 4 times damage. ◆1 Ability prevents damage. ◆2 May deal damage depending on the Pokémon's Ability. ◆3 Damage may be prevented depending on the Pokémon's Ability. ◆4 Hidden Ability prevents damage.

I

Pokémon	Type		Ability		Hidden Ability	Weak against these move types						✗ Immune to these move types		
Lairon	Steel	Rock	Sturdy	Rock Head	Heavy Metal	★Fighting	★Ground	Water				Poison		
Lampent	Ghost	Fire	Flash Fire	Flame Body		Water	Ground	Rock	Ghost	Dark		Normal	Fighting	Fire ♦2
Landorus (Incarnate Forme)	Ground	Flying	Sand Force		Sheer Force	★Ice	Water					Electric	Ground	
Landorus (Therian Forme)	Ground	Flying	Intimidate			★Ice	Water					Electric	Ground	
Lanturn	Water	Electric	Volt Absorb	Illuminate	Water Absorb	Grass	Ground					Electric ♦2	Water ♦4	
Lapras	Water	Ice	Water Absorb	Shell Armor	Hydration	Grass	Electric	Fighting	Rock			Water ♦2		
Larvesta	Bug	Fire	Flame Body			★Rock	Water	Flying						
Larvitar	Rock	Ground	Guts		Sand Veil	★Water	★Grass	Ice	Fighting	Ground	Steel	Electric		
Latias	Dragon	Psychic	Levitate			Ice	Bug	Ghost	Dragon	Dark		Ground ♦1		
Latios	Dragon	Psychic	Levitate			Ice	Bug	Ghost	Dragon	Dark		Ground ♦1		
Leafeon	Grass		Leaf Guard		Chlorophyll	Fire	Ice	Poison	Flying	Bug				
Leavanny	Bug	Grass	Swarm	Chlorophyll	Overcoat	★Fire	★Flying	Ice	Poison	Bug	Rock			
Ledian	Bug	Flying	Swarm	Early Bird	Iron Fist	★Rock	Fire	Electric	Ice	Flying		Ground		
Ledyba	Bug	Flying	Swarm	Early Bird	Rattled	★Rock	Fire	Electric	Ice	Flying		Ground		
Lickilicky	Normal		Own Tempo	Oblivious	Cloud Nine	Fighting						Ghost		
Lickitung	Normal		Own Tempo	Oblivious	Cloud Nine	Fighting						Ghost		
Liepard	Dark		Limber	Unburden	Prankster	Fighting	Bug					Psychic		
Lileep	Rock	Grass	Suction Cups		Storm Drain	Ice	Fighting	Bug	Steel			Water ♦4		
Lilligant	Grass		Chlorophyll	Own Tempo	Leaf Guard	Fire	Ice	Poison	Flying	Bug				
Lillipup	Normal		Vital Spirit	Pickup	Run Away	Fighting						Ghost		
Linoone	Normal		Pickup	Gluttony	Quick Feet	Fighting						Ghost		
Litwick	Ghost	Fire	Flash Fire	Flame Body		Water	Ground	Rock	Ghost	Dark		Normal	Fighting	Fire ♦2
Lombre	Water	Grass	Swift Swim	Rain Dish	Own Tempo	Poison	Flying	Bug						
Lopunny	Normal		Cute Charm	Klutz	Limber	Fighting						Ghost		
Lotad	Water	Grass	Swift Swim	Rain Dish	Own Tempo	Poison	Flying	Bug						
Loudred	Normal		Soundproof		Scrappy	Fighting						Ghost		
Lucario	Fighting	Steel	Steadfast	Inner Focus	Justified	Fire	Fighting	Ground				Poison		
Ludicolo	Water	Grass	Swift Swim	Rain Dish	Own Tempo	Poison	Flying	Bug						
Lugia	Psychic	Flying	Pressure		Multiscale	Electric	Ice	Rock	Ghost	Dark		Ground		
Lumineon	Water		Swift Swim	Storm Drain	Water Veil	Grass	Electric					Water ♦2		
Lunatone	Rock	Psychic	Levitate			Water	Grass	Bug	Ghost	Dark	Steel	Ground ♦1		
Luvdisc	Water		Swift Swim		Hydration	Grass	Electric							
Luxio	Electric		Rivalry	Intimidate	Guts	Ground								
Luxray	Electric		Rivalry	Intimidate	Guts	Ground								

M

Pokémon	Type		Ability		Hidden Ability	Weak against these move types						✗ Immune to these move types		
Machamp	Fighting		Guts	No Guard	Steadfast	Flying	Psychic							
Machoke	Fighting		Guts	No Guard	Steadfast	Flying	Psychic							
Machop	Fighting		Guts	No Guard	Steadfast	Flying	Psychic							
Magby	Fire		Flame Body		Vital Spirit	Water	Ground	Rock						
Magcargo	Fire	Rock	Magma Armor	Flame Body	Weak Armor	★Water	★Ground	Fighting	Rock					
Magikarp	Water		Swift Swim		Rattled	Grass	Electric							
Magmar	Fire		Flame Body		Vital Spirit	Water	Ground	Rock						
Magmortar	Fire		Flame Body		Vital Spirit	Water	Ground	Rock						
Magnemite	Electric	Steel	Magnet Pull	Sturdy	Analytic	★Ground	Fire	Fighting				Poison		
Magneton	Electric	Steel	Magnet Pull	Sturdy	Analytic	★Ground	Fire	Fighting				Poison		
Magnezone	Electric	Steel	Magnet Pull	Sturdy	Analytic	★Ground	Fire	Fighting				Poison		
Makuhita	Fighting		Thick Fat	Guts	Sheer Force	Flying	Psychic							
Mamoswine	Ice	Ground	Oblivious	Snow Cloak	Thick Fat	Fire	Water	Grass	Fighting	Steel		Electric		
Manaphy	Water		Hydration			Grass	Electric							
Mandibuzz	Dark	Flying	Big Pecks	Overcoat	Weak Armor	Electric	Ice	Rock				Ground	Psychic	
Manectric	Electric		Static	Lightningrod	Minus	Ground						Electric ♦2		
Mankey	Fighting		Vital Spirit	Anger Point	Defiant	Flying	Psychic							
Mantine	Water	Flying	Swift Swim	Water Absorb	Water Veil	★Electric	Rock					Ground	Water ♦2	
Mantyke	Water	Flying	Swift Swim	Water Absorb	Water Veil	★Electric	Rock					Ground	Water ♦2	
Maractus	Grass		Water Absorb	Chlorophyll	Storm Drain	Fire	Ice	Poison	Flying	Bug		Water ♦2,4		
Mareep	Electric		Static		Plus	Ground								
Marill	Water		Thick Fat	Huge Power	Sap Sipper	Grass	Electric					Grass ♦4		
Marowak	Ground		Rock Head	Lightningrod	Battle Armor	Water	Grass	Ice				Electric		
Marshtomp	Water	Ground	Torrent		Damp	★Grass						Electric		
Masquerain	Bug	Flying	Intimidate		Unnerve	★Rock	Fire	Electric	Ice	Flying		Ground		
Mawile	Steel		Hyper Cutter	Intimidate	Sheer Force	Fire	Fighting	Ground				Poison		
Medicham	Fighting	Psychic	Pure Power		Telepathy	Flying	Ghost							
Meditite	Fighting	Psychic	Pure Power		Telepathy	Flying	Ghost							
Meganium	Grass		Overgrow			Fire	Ice	Poison	Flying	Bug				
Meloetta (Aria Forme)	Normal	Psychic	Serene Grace			Bug	Dark					Ghost		

M

Pokémon	Type		Ability		Hidden Ability	Weak against these move types						✕ Immune to these move types		
Meowth	Normal		Pickup	Technician	Unnerve	Fighting						Ghost		
Mesprit	Psychic		Levitate			Bug	Ghost	Dark				Ground ◆1		
Metagross	Steel	Psychic	Clear Body		Light Metal	Fire	Ground					Poison		
Metang	Steel	Psychic	Clear Body		Light Metal	Fire	Ground					Poison		
Metapod	Bug		Shed Skin			Fire	Flying	Rock						
Mew	Psychic		Synchronize			Bug	Ghost	Dark						
Mewtwo	Psychic		Pressure			Bug	Ghost	Dark						
Mienfoo	Fighting		Inner Focus	Regenerator	Reckless	Flying	Psychic							
Mienshao	Fighting		Inner Focus	Regenerator	Reckless	Flying	Psychic							
Mightyena	Dark		Intimidate	Quick Feet	Moxie	Fighting	Bug					Psychic		
Milotic	Water		Marvel Scale		Cute Charm	Grass	Electric							
Miltank	Normal		Thick Fat	Scrappy	Sap Sipper	Fighting						Ghost	Grass ◆4	
Mime Jr.	Psychic		Soundproof	Filter	Technician	Bug	Ghost	Dark						
Minccino	Normal		Cute Charm	Technician	Skill Link	Fighting						Ghost		
Minun	Electric		Minus			Ground								
Misdreavus	Ghost		Levitate			Ghost	Dark					Normal	Fighting	Ground ◆1
Mismagius	Ghost		Levitate			Ghost	Dark					Normal	Fighting	Ground ◆1
Moltres	Fire	Flying	Pressure			★Rock	Water	Electric				Ground		
Monferno	Fire	Fighting	Blaze		Iron Fist	Water	Ground	Flying	Psychic					
Mothim	Bug	Flying	Swarm		Tinted Lens	★Rock	Fire	Electric	Ice	Flying		Ground		
Mr. Mime	Psychic		Soundproof	Filter	Technician	Bug	Ghost	Dark						
Mudkip	Water		Torrent		Damp	Grass	Electric							
Muk	Poison		Stench	Sticky Hold	Poison Touch	Ground	Psychic							
Munchlax	Normal		Pickup	Thick Fat	Gluttony	Fighting						Ghost		
Munna	Psychic		Forewarn	Synchronize	Telepathy	Bug	Ghost	Dark						
Murkrow	Dark	Flying	Insomnia	Super Luck	Prankster	Electric	Ice	Rock				Ground	Psychic	
Musharna	Psychic		Forewarn	Synchronize	Telepathy	Bug	Ghost	Dark						

N

Pokémon	Type		Ability		Hidden Ability	Weak against these move types						✕ Immune to these move types		
Natu	Psychic	Flying	Synchronize	Early Bird	Magic Bounce	Electric	Ice	Rock	Ghost	Dark		Ground		
Nidoking	Poison	Ground	Poison Point	Rivalry	Sheer Force	Water	Ice	Ground	Psychic			Electric		
Nidoqueen	Poison	Ground	Poison Point	Rivalry	Sheer Force	Water	Ice	Ground	Psychic			Electric		
Nidoran ♀	Poison		Poison Point	Rivalry	Hustle	Ground	Psychic							
Nidoran ♂	Poison		Poison Point	Rivalry	Hustle	Ground	Psychic							
Nidorina	Poison		Poison Point	Rivalry	Hustle	Ground	Psychic							
Nidorino	Poison		Poison Point	Rivalry	Hustle	Ground	Psychic							
Nincada	Bug	Ground	Compoundeyes			Fire	Water	Ice	Flying			Electric		
Ninetales	Fire		Flash Fire		Drought	Water	Ground	Rock				Fire ◆1		
Ninjask	Bug	Flying	Speed Boost			★Rock	Fire	Electric	Ice	Flying		Ground		
Noctowl	Normal	Flying	Insomnia	Keen Eye	Tinted Lens	Electric	Ice	Rock				Ground	Ghost	
Nosepass	Rock		Sturdy	Magnet Pull	Sand Force	Water	Grass	Fighting	Ground	Steel				
Numel	Fire	Ground	Oblivious	Simple	Own Tempo	★Water	Ground					Electric		
Nuzleaf	Grass	Dark	Chlorophyll	Early Bird		★Bug	Fire	Ice	Fighting	Poison	Flying	Psychic		

O

Pokémon	Type		Ability		Hidden Ability	Weak against these move types						✕ Immune to these move types		
Octillery	Water		Suction Cups	Sniper	Moody	Grass	Electric							
Oddish	Grass	Poison	Chlorophyll		Run Away	Fire	Ice	Flying	Psychic					
Omanyte	Rock	Water	Swift Swim	Shell Armor	Weak Armor	★Grass	Electric	Fighting	Ground					
Omastar	Rock	Water	Swift Swim	Shell Armor	Weak Armor	★Grass	Electric	Fighting	Ground					
Onix	Rock	Ground	Rock Head	Sturdy	Weak Armor	★Water	★Grass	Ice	Fighting	Ground	Steel	Electric		
Oshawott	Water		Torrent			Grass	Electric							

P

Pokémon	Type		Ability		Hidden Ability	Weak against these move types						✕ Immune to these move types		
Pachirisu	Electric		Run Away	Pickup	Volt Absorb	Ground						Electric ◆4		
Palkia	Water	Dragon	Pressure		Telepathy	Dragon								
Palpitoad	Water	Ground	Swift Swim	Hydration	Water Absorb	★Grass						Electric		
Panpour	Water		Gluttony			Grass	Electric							
Pansage	Grass		Gluttony			Fire	Ice	Poison	Flying	Bug				
Pansear	Fire		Gluttony			Water	Ground	Rock						
Paras	Bug	Grass	Effect Spore	Dry Skin		★Fire	★Flying	Ice	Poison	Bug	Rock	Water ◆2		
Parasect	Bug	Grass	Effect Spore	Dry Skin		★Fire	★Flying	Ice	Poison	Bug	Rock	Water ◆2		
Patrat	Normal		Run Away	Keen Eye	Analytic	Fighting						Ghost		
Pawniard	Dark	Steel	Defiant	Inner Focus	Pressure	★Fighting	Fire	Ground				Poison	Psychic	
Pelipper	Water	Flying	Keen Eye		Rain Dish	★Electric	Rock					Ground		
Persian	Normal		Limber	Technician	Unnerve	Fighting						Ghost		

584

★ Deals 4 times damage. ◆1 Ability prevents damage. ◆2 May deal damage depending on the Pokémon's Ability. ◆3 Damage may be prevented depending on the Pokémon's Ability. ◆4 Hidden Ability prevents damage.

Pokémon	Type		Ability		Hidden Ability	Weak against these move types						X Immune to these move types		
Petilil	Grass		Chlorophyll	Own Tempo	Leaf Guard	Fire	Ice	Poison	Flying	Bug				
Phanpy	Ground		Pickup		Sand Veil	Water	Grass	Ice				Electric		
Phione	Water		Hydration			Grass	Electric							
Pichu	Electric		Static		Lightningrod	Ground						Electric ♦ 4		
Pidgeot	Normal	Flying	Keen Eye	Tangled Feet	Big Pecks	Electric	Ice	Rock				Ground	Ghost	
Pidgeotto	Normal	Flying	Keen Eye	Tangled Feet	Big Pecks	Electric	Ice	Rock				Ground	Ghost	
Pidgey	Normal	Flying	Keen Eye	Tangled Feet	Big Pecks	Electric	Ice	Rock				Ground	Ghost	
Pidove	Normal	Flying	Big Pecks	Super Luck	Rivalry	Electric	Ice	Rock				Ground	Ghost	
Pignite	Fire	Fighting	Blaze			Water	Ground	Flying	Psychic					
Pikachu	Electric		Static		Lightningrod	Ground						Electric ♦ 4		
Piloswine	Ice	Ground	Oblivious	Snow Cloak	Thick Fat	Fire	Water	Grass	Fighting	Steel		Electric		
Pineco	Bug		Sturdy			Fire	Flying	Rock						
Pinsir	Bug		Hyper Cutter	Mold Breaker	Moxie	Fire	Flying	Rock						
Piplup	Water		Torrent		Defiant	Grass	Electric							
Plusle	Electric		Plus			Ground								
Politoed	Water		Water Absorb	Damp	Drizzle	Grass	Electric					Water ♦ 2		
Poliwag	Water		Water Absorb	Damp	Swift Swim	Grass	Electric					Water ♦ 2		
Poliwhirl	Water		Water Absorb	Damp	Swift Swim	Grass	Electric					Water ♦ 2		
Poliwrath	Water	Fighting	Water Absorb	Damp	Swift Swim	Grass	Electric	Flying	Psychic			Water ♦ 2		
Ponyta	Fire		Run Away	Flash Fire	Flame Body	Water	Ground	Rock				Fire ♦ 2		
Poochyena	Dark		Run Away	Quick Feet	Rattled	Fighting	Bug					Psychic		
Porygon	Normal		Trace	Download	Analytic	Fighting						Ghost		
Porygon-Z	Normal		Adaptability	Download	Analytic	Fighting						Ghost		
Porygon2	Normal		Trace	Download	Analytic	Fighting						Ghost		
Primeape	Fighting		Vital Spirit	Anger Point	Defiant	Flying	Psychic							
Prinplup	Water		Torrent		Defiant	Grass	Electric							
Probopass	Rock	Steel	Sturdy	Magnet Pull	Sand Force	★Fighting	★Ground	Water				Poison		
Psyduck	Water		Damp	Cloud Nine	Swift Swim	Grass	Electric							
Pupitar	Rock	Ground	Shed Skin			★Water	★Grass	Ice	Fighting	Ground	Steel	Electric		
Purrloin	Dark		Limber	Unburden	Prankster	Fighting	Bug					Psychic		
Purugly	Normal		Thick Fat	Own Tempo	Defiant	Fighting						Ghost		

Q

Pokémon	Type		Ability		Hidden Ability	Weak against these move types						X Immune to these move types		
Quagsire	Water	Ground	Damp	Water Absorb	Unaware	★Grass						Electric	Water ♦ 2	
Quilava	Fire		Blaze			Water	Ground	Rock						
Qwilfish	Water	Poison	Poison Point	Swift Swim	Intimidate	Electric	Ground	Psychic						

R

Pokémon	Type		Ability		Hidden Ability	Weak against these move types						X Immune to these move types		
Raichu	Electric		Static		Lightningrod	Ground						Electric ♦ 4		
Raikou	Electric		Pressure			Ground								
Ralts	Psychic		Synchronize	Trace	Telepathy	Bug	Ghost	Dark						
Rampardos	Rock		Mold Breaker		Sheer Force	Water	Grass	Fighting	Ground	Steel				
Rapidash	Fire		Run Away	Flash Fire	Flame Body	Water	Ground	Rock				Fire ♦ 2		
Raticate	Normal		Run Away	Guts	Hustle	Fighting						Ghost		
Rattata	Normal		Run Away	Guts	Hustle	Fighting						Ghost		
Rayquaza	Dragon	Flying	Air Lock			★Ice	Rock	Dragon				Ground		
Regice	Ice		Clear Body			Fire	Fighting	Rock	Steel					
Regigigas	Normal		Slow Start			Fighting						Ghost		
Regirock	Rock		Clear Body			Water	Grass	Fighting	Ground	Steel				
Registeel	Steel		Clear Body			Fire	Fighting	Ground				Poison		
Relicanth	Water	Rock	Swift Swim	Rock Head	Sturdy	★Grass	Electric	Fighting	Ground					
Remoraid	Water		Hustle	Sniper	Moody	Grass	Electric							
Reshiram	Dragon	Fire	Turboblaze			Ground	Rock	Dragon						
Reuniclus	Psychic		Overcoat	Magic Guard	Regenerator	Bug	Ghost	Dark						
Rhydon	Ground	Rock	Lightningrod	Rock Head	Reckless	★Water	★Grass	Ice	Fighting	Ground	Steel	Electric		
Rhyhorn	Ground	Rock	Lightningrod	Rock Head	Reckless	★Water	★Grass	Ice	Fighting	Ground	Steel	Electric		
Rhyperior	Ground	Rock	Lightningrod	Solid Rock	Reckless	★Water	★Grass	Ice	Fighting	Ground	Steel	Electric		
Riolu	Fighting		Steadfast	Inner Focus	Prankster	Flying	Psychic							
Roggenrola	Rock		Sturdy		Sand Force	Water	Grass	Fighting	Ground	Steel				
Roselia	Grass	Poison	Natural Cure	Poison Point		Fire	Ice	Flying	Psychic					
Roserade	Grass	Poison	Natural Cure	Poison Point		Fire	Ice	Flying	Psychic					
Rotom	Electric	Grass	Levitate			Fire	Ice	Poison	Bug			Ground ♦ 1		
Rotom (Fan Rotom)	Electric	Ghost	Levitate			Ghost	Dark					Normal	Fighting	Ground ♦ 1
Rotom (Frost Rotom)	Electric	Ice	Levitate			Fire	Fighting	Rock				Ground ♦ 1		
Rotom (Heat Rotom)	Electric	Fire	Levitate			Water	Rock					Ground ♦ 1		
Rotom (Mow Rotom)	Electric	Water	Levitate			Grass						Ground ♦ 1		
Rotom (Wash Rotom)	Electric	Flying	Levitate			Ice	Rock					Ground		
Rufflet	Normal	Flying	Keen Eye	Sheer Force		Electric	Ice	Rock				Ground	Ghost	

585

◉ Pokémon Weakness Chart—National Pokédex

S

Pokémon	Type		Ability		Hidden Ability	Weak against these move types						X Immune to these move types		
Sableye	Dark	Ghost	Keen Eye	Stall	Prankster							Normal	Fighting	Psychic
Salamence	Dragon	Flying	Intimidate		Moxie	★Ice	Rock	Dragon				Ground		
Samurott	Water		Torrent			Grass	Electric							
Sandile	Ground	Dark	Intimidate	Moxie	Anger Point	Water	Grass	Ice	Fighting	Bug		Electric	Psychic	
Sandshrew	Ground		Sand Veil		Sand Rush	Water	Grass	Ice				Electric		
Sandslash	Ground		Sand Veil		Sand Rush	Water	Grass	Ice				Electric		
Sawk	Fighting		Sturdy	Inner Focus		Flying	Psychic							
Sawsbuck	Normal	Grass	Chlorophyll	Sap Sipper	Serene Grace	Fire	Ice	Fighting	Poison	Flying	Bug	Ghost	Grass ◆2	
Sceptile	Grass		Overgrow		Unburden	Fire	Ice	Poison	Flying	Bug				
Scizor	Bug	Steel	Swarm	Technician	Light Metal	★Fire						Poison		
Scolipede	Bug	Poison	Poison Point	Swarm	Quick Feet	Fire	Flying	Psychic	Rock					
Scrafty	Dark	Fighting	Shed Skin	Moxie		Fighting	Flying					Psychic		
Scraggy	Dark	Fighting	Shed Skin	Moxie		Fighting	Flying					Psychic		
Scyther	Bug	Flying	Swarm	Technician	Steadfast	★Rock	Fire	Electric	Ice	Flying		Ground		
Seadra	Water		Poison Point	Sniper	Damp	Grass	Electric							
Seaking	Water		Swift Swim	Water Veil	Lightningrod	Grass	Electric					Electric ◆4		
Sealeo	Ice	Water	Thick Fat	Ice Body	Oblivious	Grass	Electric	Fighting	Rock					
Seedot	Grass		Chlorophyll	Early Bird		Fire	Ice	Poison	Flying	Bug				
Seel	Water		Thick Fat	Hydration	Ice Body	Grass	Electric							
Seismitoad	Water	Ground	Swift Swim	Poison Touch	Water Absorb	★Grass						Electric		
Sentret	Normal		Run Away	Keen Eye	Frisk	Fighting						Ghost		
Serperior	Grass		Overgrow			Fire	Ice	Poison	Flying	Bug				
Servine	Grass		Overgrow			Fire	Ice	Poison	Flying	Bug				
Seviper	Poison		Shed Skin		Infiltrator	Ground	Psychic							
Sewaddle	Bug	Grass	Swarm	Chlorophyll	Overcoat	★Fire	★Flying	Ice	Poison	Bug	Rock			
Sharpedo	Water	Dark	Rough Skin		Speed Boost	Grass	Electric	Fighting	Bug			Psychic		
Shaymin (Land Forme)	Grass		Natural Cure			Fire	Ice	Poison	Flying	Bug				
Shaymin (Sky Forme)	Grass	Flying	Serene Grace			★Ice	Fire	Poison	Flying	Rock		Ground		
Shedinja	Bug	Ghost	Wonder Guard			Fire	Flying	Rock	Ghost	Dark		Type *1 outside of the five to the left		
Shelgon	Dragon		Rock Head		Overcoat	Ice	Dragon							
Shellder	Water		Shell Armor	Skill Link	Overcoat	Grass	Electric							
Shellos	Water		Sticky Hold	Storm Drain	Sand Force	Grass	Electric					Water ◆2		
Shelmet	Bug		Hydration	Shell Armor	Overcoat	Fire	Flying	Rock						
Shieldon	Rock	Steel	Sturdy		Soundproof	★Fighting	★Ground	Water				Poison		
Shiftry	Grass	Dark	Chlorophyll	Early Bird		★Bug	Fire	Ice	Fighting	Poison	Flying	Psychic		
Shinx	Electric		Rivalry	Intimidate	Guts	Ground								
Shroomish	Grass		Effect Spore	Poison Heal	Quick Feet	Fire	Ice	Poison	Flying	Bug				
Shuckle	Bug	Rock	Sturdy	Gluttony	Contrary	Water	Rock	Steel						
Shuppet	Ghost		Insomnia	Frisk	Cursed Body	Ghost	Dark					Normal		
Sigilyph	Psychic	Flying	Wonder Skin	Magic Guard	Tinted Lens	Electric	Ice	Rock	Ghost	Dark		Ground		
Silcoon	Bug		Shed Skin			Fire	Flying	Rock						
Simipour	Water		Gluttony			Grass	Electric							
Simisage	Grass		Gluttony			Fire	Ice	Poison	Flying	Bug				
Simisear	Fire		Gluttony			Water	Ground	Rock						
Skarmory	Steel	Flying	Keen Eye	Sturdy	Weak Armor	Fire	Electric					Poison	Ground	
Skiploom	Grass	Flying	Chlorophyll	Leaf Guard	Infiltrator	★Ice	Fire	Poison	Flying	Rock		Ground		
Skitty	Normal		Cute Charm	Normalize	Wonder Skin	Fighting						Ghost		
Skorupi	Poison	Bug	Battle Armor	Sniper	Keen Eye	Fire	Flying	Psychic	Rock					
Skuntank	Poison	Dark	Stench	Aftermath	Keen Eye	Ground						Psychic		
Slaking	Normal		Truant			Fighting						Ghost		
Slakoth	Normal		Truant			Fighting						Ghost		
Slowbro	Water	Psychic	Oblivious	Own Tempo	Regenerator	Grass	Electric	Bug	Ghost	Dark				
Slowking	Water	Psychic	Oblivious	Own Tempo	Regenerator	Grass	Electric	Bug	Ghost	Dark				
Slowpoke	Water	Psychic	Oblivious	Own Tempo	Regenerator	Grass	Electric	Bug	Ghost	Dark				
Slugma	Fire		Magma Armor	Flame Body	Weak Armor	Water	Ground	Rock						
Smeargle	Normal		Own Tempo	Technician	Moody	Fighting						Ghost		
Smoochum	Ice	Psychic	Oblivious	Forewarn	Hydration	Fire	Bug	Rock	Ghost	Dark	Steel			
Sneasel	Dark	Ice	Inner Focus	Keen Eye	Pickpocket	★Fighting	Fire	Bug	Rock	Steel		Psychic		
Snivy	Grass		Overgrow			Fire	Ice	Poison	Flying	Bug				
Snorlax	Normal		Immunity	Thick Fat	Gluttony	Fighting						Ghost		
Snorunt	Ice		Inner Focus	Ice Body	Moody	Fire	Fighting	Rock	Steel					
Snover	Grass	Ice	Snow Warning		Soundproof	★Fire	Fighting	Poison	Flying	Bug	Rock	Steel		
Snubbull	Normal		Intimidate	Run Away	Rattled	Fighting						Ghost		
Solosis	Psychic		Overcoat	Magic Guard	Regenerator	Bug	Ghost	Dark						

586

★ Deals 4 times damage.　◆ 1 Ability prevents damage.　◆ 2 May deal damage depending on the Pokémon's Ability.　◆ 3 Damage may be prevented depending on the Pokémon's Ability.　◆ 4 Hidden Ability prevents damage.

Pokémon	Type		Ability		Hidden Ability	Weak against these move types						X immune to these move types		
Solrock	Rock	Psychic	Levitate			Water	Grass	Bug	Ghost	Dark	Steel	Ground ♦1		
Spearow	Normal	Flying	Keen Eye		Sniper	Electric	Ice	Rock				Ground	Ghost	
Spheal	Ice	Water	Thick Fat	Ice Body	Oblivious	Grass	Electric	Fighting	Rock					
Spinarak	Bug	Poison	Swarm	Insomnia	Sniper	Fire	Flying	Psychic	Rock					
Spinda	Normal		Own Tempo	Tangled Feet	Contrary	Fighting						Ghost		
Spiritomb	Ghost	Dark	Pressure		Infiltrator							Normal	Fighting	Psychic
Spoink	Psychic		Thick Fat	Own Tempo	Gluttony	Bug	Ghost	Dark						
Squirtle	Water		Torrent		Rain Dish	Grass	Electric							
Stantler	Normal		Intimidate	Frisk	Sap Sipper	Fighting						Ghost	Grass ♦4	
Staraptor	Normal	Flying	Intimidate		Reckless	Electric	Ice	Rock				Ground	Ghost	
Staravia	Normal	Flying	Intimidate		Reckless	Electric	Ice	Rock				Ground	Ghost	
Starly	Normal	Flying	Keen Eye			Electric	Ice	Rock				Ground	Ghost	
Starmie	Water	Psychic	Illuminate	Natural Cure	Analytic	Grass	Electric	Bug	Ghost	Dark				
Staryu	Water		Illuminate	Natural Cure	Analytic	Grass	Electric							
Steelix	Steel	Ground	Rock Head	Sturdy	Sheer Force	Fire	Water	Fighting	Ground			Electric	Poison	
Stoutland	Normal		Intimidate	Sand Rush	Scrappy	Fighting						Ghost		
Stunfisk	Ground	Electric	Static	Limber	Sand Veil	Water	Grass	Ice	Ground			Electric		
Stunky	Poison	Dark	Stench	Aftermath	Keen Eye	Ground						Psychic		
Sudowoodo	Rock		Sturdy	Rock Head	Rattled	Water	Grass	Fighting	Ground	Steel				
Suicune	Water		Pressure			Grass	Electric							
Sunflora	Grass		Chlorophyll	Solar Power	Early Bird	Fire	Ice	Poison	Flying	Bug				
Sunkern	Grass		Chlorophyll	Solar Power	Early Bird	Fire	Ice	Poison	Flying	Bug				
Surskit	Bug	Water	Swift Swim		Rain Dish	Electric	Flying	Rock						
Swablu	Normal	Flying	Natural Cure		Cloud Nine	Electric	Ice	Rock				Ground	Ghost	
Swadloon	Bug	Grass	Leaf Guard	Chlorophyll	Overcoat	★Fire	★Flying	Ice	Poison	Bug	Rock			
Swalot	Poison		Liquid Ooze	Sticky Hold		Ground	Psychic							
Swampert	Water	Ground	Torrent		Damp	★Grass						Electric		
Swanna	Water	Flying	Keen Eye	Big Pecks	Hydration	★Electric	Rock					Ground		
Swellow	Normal	Flying	Guts		Scrappy	Electric	Ice	Rock				Ground	Ghost	
Swinub	Ice	Ground	Oblivious	Snow Cloak	Thick Fat	Fire	Water	Grass	Fighting	Steel		Electric		
Swoobat	Psychic	Flying	Unaware	Klutz	Simple	Electric	Ice	Rock	Ghost	Dark		Ground		

T

Pokémon	Type		Ability		Hidden Ability	Weak against these move types						X immune to these move types		
Taillow	Normal	Flying	Guts		Scrappy	Electric	Ice	Rock				Ground	Ghost	
Tangela	Grass		Chlorophyll	Leaf Guard	Regenerator	Fire	Ice	Poison	Flying	Bug				
Tangrowth	Grass		Chlorophyll	Leaf Guard	Regenerator	Fire	Ice	Poison	Flying	Bug				
Tauros	Normal		Intimidate	Anger Point	Sheer Force	Fighting						Ghost		
Teddiursa	Normal		Pickup	Quick Feet	Honey Gather	Fighting						Ghost		
Tentacool	Water	Poison	Clear Body	Liquid Ooze	Rain Dish	Electric	Ground	Psychic						
Tentacruel	Water	Poison	Clear Body	Liquid Ooze	Rain Dish	Electric	Ground	Psychic						
Tepig	Fire		Blaze			Water	Ground	Rock						
Terrakion	Rock	Fighting	Justified			Water	Grass	Fighting	Ground	Psychic	Steel			
Throh	Fighting		Guts	Inner Focus		Flying	Psychic							
Thundurus (Incarnate Forme)	Electric	Flying	Prankster		Defiant	Ice	Rock					Ground		
Thundurus (Therian Forme)	Electric	Flying	Volt Absorb			Ice	Rock					Ground	Electric ♦1	
Timburr	Fighting		Guts	Sheer Force		Flying	Psychic							
Tirtouga	Water	Rock	Solid Rock	Sturdy	Swift Swim	★Grass	Electric	Fighting	Ground					
Togekiss	Normal	Flying	Hustle	Serene Grace	Super Luck	Electric	Ice	Rock				Ground	Ghost	
Togepi	Normal		Hustle	Serene Grace	Super Luck	Fighting						Ghost		
Togetic	Normal	Flying	Hustle	Serene Grace	Super Luck	Electric	Ice	Rock				Ground	Ghost	
Torchic	Fire		Blaze		Speed Boost	Water	Ground	Rock						
Torkoal	Fire		White Smoke		Shell Armor	Water	Ground	Rock						
Tornadus (Incarnate Forme)	Flying		Prankster		Defiant	Electric	Ice	Rock				Ground		
Tornadus (Therian Forme)	Flying		Regenerator			Electric	Ice	Rock				Ground		
Torterra	Grass	Ground	Overgrow		Shell Armor	★Ice	Fire	Flying	Bug			Electric		
Totodile	Water		Torrent			Grass	Electric							
Toxicroak	Poison	Fighting	Anticipation	Dry Skin	Poison Touch	★Psychic	Ground	Flying				Water ♦2		
Tranquill	Normal	Flying	Big Pecks	Super Luck	Rivalry	Electric	Ice	Rock				Ground	Ghost	
Trapinch	Ground		Hyper Cutter	Arena Trap	Sheer Force	Water	Grass	Ice				Electric		
Treecko	Grass		Overgrow		Unburden	Fire	Ice	Poison	Flying	Bug				
Tropius	Grass	Flying	Chlorophyll	Solar Power	Harvest	★Ice	Fire	Poison	Flying	Rock		Ground		
Trubbish	Poison		Stench	Sticky Hold	Aftermath	Ground	Psychic							
Turtwig	Grass		Overgrow		Shell Armor	Fire	Ice	Poison	Flying	Bug				
Tympole	Water		Swift Swim	Hydration	Water Absorb	Grass	Electric					Water ♦4		
Tynamo	Electric		Levitate									Ground ♦1		

T

Pokémon	Type		Ability		Hidden Ability	Weak against these move types						X Immune to these move types	
Typhlosion	Fire		Blaze			Water	Ground	Rock					
Tyranitar	Rock	Dark	Sand Stream		Unnerve	★Fighting	Water	Grass	Ground	Bug	Steel	Psychic	
Tyrogue	Fighting		Guts	Steadfast	Vital Spirit	Flying	Psychic						

U

Pokémon	Type		Ability		Hidden Ability	Weak against these move types						X Immune to these move types	
Umbreon	Dark		Synchronize		Inner Focus	Fighting	Bug					Psychic	
Unfezant	Normal	Flying	Big Pecks	Super Luck	Rivalry	Electric	Ice	Rock				Ground	Ghost
Unown	Psychic		Levitate			Bug	Ghost	Dark				Ground ◆1	
Ursaring	Normal		Guts	Quick Feet	Unnerve	Fighting						Ghost	
Uxie	Psychic		Levitate			Bug	Ghost	Dark				Ground ◆1	

V

Pokémon	Type		Ability		Hidden Ability	Weak against these move types						X Immune to these move types	
Vanillish	Ice		Ice Body		Weak Armor	Fire	Fighting	Rock	Steel				
Vanillite	Ice		Ice Body		Weak Armor	Fire	Fighting	Rock	Steel				
Vanilluxe	Ice		Ice Body		Weak Armor	Fire	Fighting	Rock	Steel				
Vaporeon	Water		Water Absorb		Hydration	Grass	Electric					Water ◆1	
Venipede	Bug	Poison	Poison Point	Swarm	Quick Feet	Fire	Flying	Psychic	Rock				
Venomoth	Bug	Poison	Shield Dust	Tinted Lens	Wonder Skin	Fire	Flying	Psychic	Rock				
Venonat	Bug	Poison	Compoundeyes	Tinted Lens	Run Away	Fire	Flying	Psychic	Rock				
Venusaur	Grass	Poison	Overgrow		Chlorophyll	Fire	Ice	Flying	Psychic				
Vespiquen	Bug	Flying	Pressure		Unnerve	★Rock	Fire	Electric	Ice	Flying		Ground	
Vibrava	Ground	Dragon	Levitate			★Ice	Dragon					Electric	Ground ◆1
Victini	Psychic	Fire	Victory Star			Water	Ground	Rock	Ghost	Dark			
Victreebel	Grass	Poison	Chlorophyll		Gluttony	Fire	Ice	Flying	Psychic				
Vigoroth	Normal		Vital Spirit			Fighting						Ghost	
Vileplume	Grass	Poison	Chlorophyll		Effect Spore	Fire	Ice	Flying	Psychic				
Virizion	Grass	Fighting	Justified			★Flying	Fire	Ice	Poison	Psychic			
Volbeat	Bug		Illuminate	Swarm	Prankster	Fire	Flying	Rock					
Volcarona	Bug	Fire	Flame Body			★Rock	Water	Flying					
Voltorb	Electric		Soundproof	Static	Aftermath	Ground							
Vullaby	Dark	Flying	Big Pecks	Overcoat	Weak Armor	Electric	Ice	Rock				Ground	Psychic
Vulpix	Fire		Flash Fire		Drought	Water	Ground	Rock				Fire ◆1	

W

Pokémon	Type		Ability		Hidden Ability	Weak against these move types						X Immune to these move types	
Wailmer	Water		Water Veil	Oblivious	Pressure	Grass	Electric						
Wailord	Water		Water Veil	Oblivious	Pressure	Grass	Electric						
Walrein	Ice	Water	Thick Fat	Ice Body	Oblivious	Grass	Electric	Fighting	Rock				
Wartortle	Water		Torrent		Rain Dish	Grass	Electric						
Watchog	Normal		Illuminate	Keen Eye	Analytic	Fighting						Ghost	
Weavile	Dark	Ice	Pressure		Pickpocket	★Fighting	Fire	Bug	Rock	Steel		Psychic	
Weedle	Bug	Poison	Shield Dust		Run Away	Fire	Flying	Psychic	Rock				
Weepinbell	Grass	Poison	Chlorophyll		Gluttony	Fire	Ice	Flying	Psychic				
Weezing	Poison		Levitate			Psychic						Ground ◆1	
Whimsicott	Grass		Prankster	Infiltrator	Chlorophyll	Fire	Ice	Poison	Flying	Bug			
Whirlipede	Bug	Poison	Poison Point	Swarm	Quick Feet	Fire	Flying	Psychic	Rock				
Whiscash	Water	Ground	Oblivious	Anticipation	Hydration	★Grass						Electric	
Whismur	Normal		Soundproof		Rattled	Fighting						Ghost	
Wigglytuff	Normal		Cute Charm		Frisk	Fighting						Ghost	
Wingull	Water	Flying	Keen Eye		Rain Dish	★Electric	Rock					Ground	
Wobbuffet	Psychic		Shadow Tag		Telepathy	Bug	Ghost	Dark					
Woobat	Psychic	Flying	Unaware	Klutz	Simple	Electric	Ice	Rock	Ghost	Dark		Ground	
Wooper	Water	Ground	Damp	Water Absorb	Unaware	★Grass						Electric	Water ◆2
Wormadam (Plant Cloak)	Bug	Grass	Anticipation		Overcoat	★Fire	★Flying	Ice	Poison	Bug	Rock		
Wormadam (Sandy Cloak)	Bug	Ground	Anticipation		Overcoat	Fire	Water	Ice	Flying			Electric	
Wormadam (Trash Cloak)	Bug	Steel	Anticipation		Overcoat	★Fire						Poison	
Wurmple	Bug		Shield Dust			Fire	Flying	Rock					
Wynaut	Psychic		Shadow Tag		Telepathy	Bug	Ghost	Dark					

N F W G E L F P G F A B R G O D S

★ Deals 4 times damage.　◆ 1 Ability prevents damage.　◆ 2 May deal damage depending on the Pokémon's Ability.　◆ 3 Damage may be prevented depending on the Pokémon's Ability.　◆ 4 Hidden Ability prevents damage.

XYZ

Pokémon	Type		Ability		Hidden Ability	Weak against these move types					X Immune to these move types	
Xatu	Psychic	Flying	Synchronize	Early Bird	Magic Bounce	Electric	Ice	Rock	Ghost	Dark	Ground	
Yamask	Ghost		Mummy			Ghost	Dark				Normal	Fighting
Yanma	Bug	Flying	Speed Boost	Compoundeyes	Frisk	★Rock	Fire	Electric	Ice	Flying	Ground	
Yanmega	Bug	Flying	Speed Boost	Tinted Lens	Frisk	★Rock	Fire	Electric	Ice	Flying	Ground	
Zangoose	Normal		Immunity		Toxic Boost	Fighting					Ghost	
Zapdos	Electric	Flying	Pressure			Ice	Rock				Ground	
Zebstrika	Electric		Lightningrod	Motor Drive	Sap Sipper	Ground					Electric ◆1	Grass ◆4
Zekrom	Dragon	Electric	Teravolt			Ice	Ground	Dragon				
Zigzagoon	Normal		Pickup	Gluttony	Quick Feet	Fighting					Ghost	
Zoroark	Dark		Illusion			Fighting	Bug				Psychic	
Zorua	Dark		Illusion			Fighting	Bug				Psychic	
Zubat	Poison	Flying	Inner Focus		Infiltrator	Electric	Ice	Psychic	Rock		Ground	
Zweilous	Dark	Dragon	Hustle			Ice	Fighting	Bug	Dragon		Psychic	

Type Matchup Chart

Defending Pokémon's Type

Types are assigned both to moves and to the Pokémon themselves. These types can greatly affect the amount of damage dealt or received in battle, so learn how they line up against one another and give yourself the edge in battle.

(handwritten notes: Dragon → Ice, Fire →)

Attacking Pokémon's Move Type / Defending Pokémon's Type

Attacking \ Defending	Normal	Fire	Water	Grass	Electric	Ice	Fighting	Poison	Ground	Flying	Psychic	Bug	Rock	Ghost	Dragon	Dark	Steel
Normal													▲	×			▲
Fire		▲	▲	◉		◉						◉	▲		▲		◉
Water		◉	▲	▲					◉				◉		▲		
Grass		▲	◉	▲				▲	◉	▲		▲	◉		▲		▲
Electric			◉	▲	▲				×	◉					▲		
Ice		▲	▲	◉		▲			◉	◉					◉		▲
Fighting	◉					◉		▲		▲	▲	▲	◉	×		◉	◉
Poison				◉				▲					▲	▲			×
Ground		◉		▲	◉			◉		×		▲	◉				◉
Flying				◉	▲		◉					◉	▲				▲
Psychic							◉	◉			▲					×	▲
Bug		▲		◉			▲	▲		▲	◉			▲		◉	▲
Rock		◉				◉	▲		▲	◉		◉					▲
Ghost	×										◉			◉	▲	▲	▲
Dragon															◉		▲
Dark							▲				◉			◉	▲	▲	▲
Steel		▲	▲		▲	◉							◉				▲

Legend

- ◉ Very effective "It's super effective!" ×2
- (No icon) Normal damage ×1
- ▲ Not too effective "It's not very effective" ×0.5
- × No effect "It doesn't affect..." ×0

- ● Fire-type Pokémon cannot be afflicted with the Burned condition.
- ● Grass-type Pokémon are immune to Leech Seed.
- ● Ice-type Pokémon are immune to the Frozen condition and take no damage from hail.
- ● Poison-type Pokémon are immune to the Poison and Badly Poisoned conditions, even when switching in with Toxic Spikes in play. Poison-type Pokémon nullify Toxic Spikes (unless these Pokémon are also Flying type or have the Levitate Ability).
- ● Ground-type Pokémon are immune to Thunder Wave and take no damage from a sandstorm.
- ● Flying-type Pokémon cannot be damaged by Spikes when switching in, or become afflicted with a Poison or Badly Poisoned condition due to switching in with Toxic Spikes in play.
- ● Rock-type Pokémon take no damage from a sandstorm. Their Sp. Def also goes up in a sandstorm.
- ● Steel-type Pokémon take no damage from a sandstorm. They are also immune to the Poison and Badly Poisoned conditions. Even if switched in with Toxic Spikes in play, they will not be afflicted by the Poison or Badly Poisoned condition.

Pokémon Dream Radar

Catch the Pokémon found in a place called the Interdream Zone in this virtual shooting game. Fire at the Dream Clouds that float around in this space to find hiding Pokémon or discover items. Insert *Pokémon Black 2* or *Pokémon White 2* into your Nintendo 3DS system, and when you receive the research data that was sent, the Pokémon you caught will be transfered.

● How *Pokémon Dream Radar* works

Search Phase	Battle Phase	Upgrade Phase
In this phase, you shoot a Beam at Dream Clouds. Then you collect the Pokémon, items, or balls of energy called Dream Orbs that come out of the clouds by shooting the Beam at them.	You catch Pokémon in this phase. Hit the Pokémon with the Beam as it moves around. Fill up the gauge in the upper left of the screen to catch it.	In this phase, you upgrade your device. Power up your Beam and Visoscope, and make it easier to catch Pokémon.

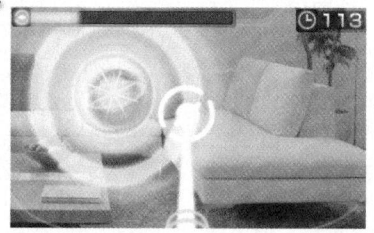

Catch these Pokémon

Many of the Pokémon found in *Pokémon Dream Radar* can't be caught in *Pokémon Black Version 2* or *Pokémon White Version 2*. With a few exceptions, these Pokémon have a Hidden Ability.

Tornadus	Thundurus	Landorus
Therian Forme	Therian Forme	Therian Forme

Smoochum Porygon Spiritomb Togepi Rotom Ralts

Game Information

Pokémon Dream Radar
- Publisher: The Pokémon Company
- Distributor: Nintendo
- Developer: Creatures Inc./
  GAME FREAK inc.
- Platform: Nintendo 3DS
- Genre: Action
- Players: 1
- Connectivity: None
- Release Date:
  October 7, 2012 (Sunday)
- Rating: E

Pokédex 3D Pro

Pokédex 3D Pro is an upgraded version of the Nintendo 3DS application *Pokédex 3D*. It's packed with information about every known Pokémon. See Pokémon from a variety of different angles by rotating and zooming in on them. Watch Pokémon move and even hear their cries. This Pokédex is also equipped with a function that lets you hear how the names of Pokémon are pronounced in six different languages.

It's an electronic Pokédex packed with Pokémon information

Pokédex 3D Pro is download software, so you can start it up even while *Pokémon Black 2* or *Pokémon White 2* is inserted in your Nintendo 3DS system. You can also use it to look up strategic information, like what Pokémon would be strong against the Pokémon of a Gym Leader you just can't beat.

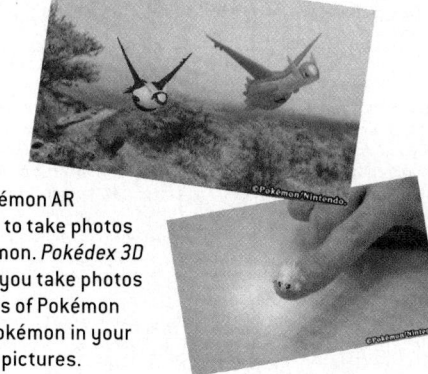

Use Pokémon AR Markers to take photos of Pokémon. *Pokédex 3D Pro* lets you take photos of groups of Pokémon or put Pokémon in your favorite pictures.

Game Information

Pokédex 3D Pro
- Publisher: The Pokémon Company
- Distributor: Nintendo
- Developer: Creatures Inc.
- Platform: Nintendo 3DS
- Genre: Application
- Players: 1
- Connectivity: None
- Release Date:
  November 8, 2012 (Thursday)
- Rating: E

How to purchase this download software at the Nintendo eShop

Pokémon Dream Radar and *Pokédex 3D Pro* are only available as download software. They can be purchased in the Nintendo eShop, which you access from the Nintendo 3DS system.

On the Nintendo 3DS HOME Menu, select Nintendo eShop

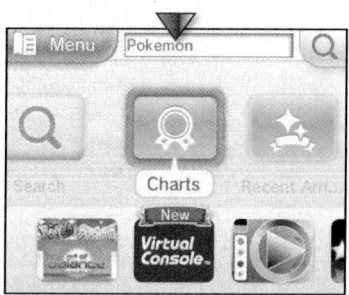

You can search for this software by entering the keyword "Pokemon" into the search field. Tap "Purchase" on the purchase confirmation screen to buy the software.

When the download is complete, the software will be added to the HOME Menu.

CREDITS
The Pokémon Company
INTERNATIONAL

Pokémon Black Version 2 & *Pokémon White Version 2*
The Official National Pokédex & Guide: Volume 2

EDITOR-IN-CHIEF
Michael G. Ryan

PROJECT MANAGER
Emily Luty (Bridge Consulting Group)

TRANSLATORS
Hisato Yamamori
Tim Hove
David Numrich
Sayuri Munday
Jillian Nonaka

EDITORS
Kellyn Ballard
Blaise Selby
Hollie Beg
Wolfgang Baur

COVER DESIGNERS
Eric Medalle
Bridget O'Neill

ACKNOWLEDGEMENTS
Kenji Okubo
Heather Dalgleish
Amy Levenson
Yasuhiro Usui
Mikiko Ryu
Rey Perez
Antoin Johnson
Misty Thomas
Hiromi Kimura (The Creative Group)
Sachiko Kimura

DESIGN & PRODUCTION
Prima Games
Donato Tica
Mark Hughes
Jamie Knight
Melissa Smith
Shaida Boroumand

99 Lives Design, LLC
Adam Crowell
Emily Crowell
Oliver Crowell
Sonja Morris

ISBN: 978-0-307-89560-8

Published in the United States by The Pokémon Company International.
333 108th Ave NE, Suite 1900, Bellevue, WA 98004 U.S.A.
1st Floor Building 4, Chiswick Park, 566 Chiswick High Road
London, W5 4YE United Kingdom

Printed in the United States of America using materials from the *Pokémon Black
Version 2* & *Pokémon White Version 2*: Complete National Pokédex. Original
Japanese Pokédex and Strategy Guide published in Japan by OVERLAP, Inc.

ORIGINAL JAPANESE POKÉDEX AND STRATEGY GUIDE:
Planning, Page Layout, Writing & Map Development:
Shusuke Motomiya and ONEUP, Inc.
Art Direction, Design & Layout: RAGTIME CO., LTD., and SUZUKIKOUBOU, Inc.